Here's what readers are saying about Randy Alcorn's novels:

"I have just finished reading Randy Alcorn's new novel. *Deception* is the same high quality as Randy's related novels *Deadline* and *Dominion*. All three are page-turners.... Randy is a gifted writer. I strongly recommend that you read his books."
CHUCK NORRIS, SIX-TIME WORLD KARATE CHAMPION, INTERNATIONAL FILM AND TELEVISION STAR, AND CREATOR OF THE WORLD COMBAT LEAGUE AND THE KICKSTART FOUNDATION

"Randy Alcorn's *Deception* is a fiction thriller that delivers. It was as engaging to me as books by Crichton or Clancy. I really resonated with the main character, Ollie Chandler. He tells it like it is, with sarcasm and humor. I'm sure glad Randy can't paint, or I'd be in big trouble!"
RON DICIANNI, AWARD-WINNING ARTIST AND AUTHOR OF *BEYOND WORDS*

"Randy Alcorn is amazing. He's one of my all-time favorite authors."
KAREN KINGSBURY, BESTSELLING AUTHOR OF THE REDEMPTION SERIES AND THE FIRSTBORN SERIES

"With humor, verve, and his usual attention to detail, Randy Alcorn has crafted a detective story that grips on page one and doesn't let go. Ollie Chandler won my admiration and Mike Hammer, aka "Mulch," won my heart as *Deception* explored the nature of man, the deceit of evil, and the breadth of eternity. Not to be missed."
ANGELA HUNT, AUTHOR OF *UNCHARTED*

"Alcorn has written a novel that combines the suspense of John Grisham and the theological pondering of C. S. Lewis."
NEW MAN MAGAZINE FOR *DEADLINE*

"[*Deadline*] is for clear thinkers who enjoy a good argument. There can be no mistaking—and there should be no ignoring—the vital message of this book."
FRANK PERETTI, BESTSELLING AUTHOR OF *THIS PRESENT DARKNESS*

"Randy Alcorn has hit it out of the park. *Deadline* is riveting. Motivating. Intriguing. Provocative. And it's for the mystery lovers too. Many books feed the mind. Some feed the heart. *Deadline* nourishes both."
STU WEBER, AUTHOR OF *TENDER WARRIOR*

"My hat is off to Randy Alcorn for his novel *Dominion*. Wow, what a book. It was a great read, and entertaining, fascinating, and educational as well. I enjoyed it immensely and learned from it too, and what could be better than that? We need more of such books."

DOUGLAS GRESHAM, AUTHOR OF *LENTEN LANDS: MY CHILDHOOD WITH JOY DAVIDMAN AND C. S. LEWIS* AND *JACK'S LIFE: THE LIFE STORY OF C. S. LEWI*; CO-PRODUCER, *THE LION, THE WITCH AND THE WARDROBE*

"Alcorn's writing remains top-notch, and he fills the pages with enough tension to cause ulcers."

BOOKSTORE JOURNAL FOR *DOMINION*

"Astonishing book."

THE LAMPLIGHTER FOR *DOMINION*

"*Dominion* is a murder mystery in the best tradition of the genre—but it is written with a steely-edged factualness that is nothing short of haunting."

WORLD MAGAZINE

"This is one of those rare books that I (a woman) enthusiastically recommend to men but am confident women will enjoy as well... Alcorn takes the reader on a suspense-filled journey between heaven and earth, into the depths of darkness itself."

THE RIVENDELL REPORT FOR *DEADLINE*

DECEPTION

a novel

RANDY ALCORN

MULTNOMAH
BOOKS

DECEPTION
PUBLISHED BY MULTNOMAH BOOKS
12265 Oracle Boulevard, Suite 200
Colorado Springs, Colorado 80921
A division of Random House Inc.

ISBN 978-1-60142-099-2

The Library of Congress has cataloged the original hardcover edition as follows:
Alcorn, Randy C.
    Deception : a novel / Randy Alcorn.
       p. cm.
    I. Title.
PS3551.L292D45 2007
813'.54—dc22

                           2006039133

Printed in the United States of America
2008—First Trade Paperback Edition

10 9 8 7 6 5 4 3 2 1

ACKNOWLEDGMENTS

My heartfelt thanks to Doreen Button, who looked over the manuscript in detail and made suggestions at critical points, all the way through proofreading.

Thanks to my friend and skilled editor Rod Morris for our partnership on yet another project. Thanks also to Julee Schwarzburg for her graciousness, attention to detail, and editorial input, as well as to Jennifer Barrow, for her outstanding copyediting. And to Rebekah Nafziger and Adrienne Spain for proofreading, and Pamela McGrew for typesetting.

Thanks to Kevin Marks and Doug Gabbert, for your encouragement and patience with this project. And to Sharon Znachko, for all your work and your kind words…thanks, sis.

I'm grateful to all those who have been part of the Multnomah family—including my friend Jay Echternach—and to my dedicated partners at WaterBrook who will help get this book into people's hands. And to the booksellers, without whom it wouldn't matter that I write books.

Thanks to the DesignWorks Group and especially to Tim Green for his great work on the *Deception* cover, as well as the new covers for *Deadline* and *Dominion*. (And thanks to Lawrence and Robin Green, who get some credit for Tim.)

Thanks to the staff of Eternal Perspective Ministries, who do so much for me and who put up with a lot while I was buried in this project. Specifically, thanks to my assistants, Kathy Norquist and Linda Jeffries; my secretary, Bonnie Hiestand; and our bookkeeper and diligent proofreader, Janet Albers. Bonnie in particular spent many hours deciphering my handwritten changes when I was reading the book aloud.

Thanks to Diane Meyer for her interest in a spin-off book from *Deadline* and *Dominion* and her encouragement after reading an early draft. Also for her great job on the study questions. And to all the readers who've written me about those books, published in 1994 and 1996, who asked me to write another, not expecting to wait this long.

Thanks to our dear friend Sue Keels, for coming up with the title *Deception* while we were brainstorming during a glorious vacation. Thanks also to my buddy Steve Keels, Sue's husband, who regularly made helpful comments, such as "Aren't you done with that book yet?"

Special thanks to Detective Sergeant Tom Nelson, who helped me years ago with *Deadline* and *Dominion* and who cheerfully answered many questions over many months concerning *Deception*. Thanks also to my friends Jim Seymour, police officer, and Darrell MacKay, arson investigator, for your helpful insights.

Thanks to Sarah Ballenger for her research on various questions. And to Amy Campbell for entering my manuscript changes on short notice, while trying not to let it spoil the book for her.

Thanks to Tony and Martha Cimmarrusti, Carlos and Gena Norris, Stu Weber, Carol Hardin, Ken and Joni Tada, Sarah Thebarge, and our Sunday night football group, for comments they made that contributed to this book though they didn't know it. Thanks to Dave Stout for introducing me years ago to one of Ollie's mottoes.

Thank you, Frank and Myrna Eisenzimmer and Randy and Sue Monnes, for offering me places to write that proved to be great sanctuaries. And to our EPM Prayer Partners, whose prayers as I wrote this book may prove to be the single greatest human contribution to it.

Heartfelt thanks to my wife and best friend, Nanci, whose encouraging comments on the manuscript kept me going in rough times and who thoughtfully gave me permission to go back to work many times when neither of us wanted me to.

Thanks to my precious daughters, Karina and Angela, who made valuable comments on the prologue, and to my wonderful sons, Dan Franklin and Dan Stump, whose lives and interactions contributed to portions of the book. Thanks to Angie also for the medical insights. Thanks to our grandsons, Jake, Ty, and Matt, endless sources of delight when I came in from my office needing a joy transfusion.

I also want to acknowledge Rex Stout, creator of the Nero Wolfe mysteries, written in the 1930s to 1960s. Ollie, my viewpoint character, admires Nero Wolfe and Archie Goodwin. Now and then I've put into Ollie's mouth some of Stout's expressions, a tribute to him. I couldn't give Stout credit each time, nor can I remember all I've absorbed from many pleasant hours reading his books. So I credit him here for what are probably several dozen of his phrases or ideas scattered throughout this book.

Finally and most importantly, thank You, my Lord Jesus, for sustaining me through this project, which was delayed by innumerable unanticipated events in order to conform to Your perfect timing. I pray above all that You are pleased by it and will use it as You see fit.

*"Those who seek my life set their traps,
those who would harm me talk of my ruin;
all day long they plot deception."*
PSALM 38:12

"Messin' with me's like wearin' cheese underwear down rat alley."
OLLIE CHANDLER

Prologue

"I fear that if the matter is beyond humanity it is certainly beyond me."
SHERLOCK HOLMES,
THE ADVENTURES OF THE DEVIL'S FOOT

IN A DARK ROOM punctured by a bare hundred-watt bulb, two newspaper clippings on the card table appeared whitish gray, four others dim and yellow. Agile fingers arranged them chronologically so the handiwork could be better displayed.

Should they be placed in a scrapbook? What if they were found? Of all places, surely no one would try to break into this one. The world's full of stupid people, but not that stupid.

Most of the people in the clippings had been stupid. But over the years, one by one, they'd been abruptly liberated of their stupidity. And the world had been liberated of them.

A penciled list of names dropped to the table, by the playing cards, next to the clippings.

It was time for another stupid person to go away.

But which one?

The liberator brooded thirty minutes, forearm bulging, squeezing hard a small object.

Finally, one name rose to the top.

The mastermind wrote the name down, then covered it with the ace of spades.

1

WEDNESDAY, NOVEMBER 6

MY CHEST POUNDING like a dryer load of army boots, I knocked the noisemaker off its cradle, then groped for it in the darkness. Three enormous red digits—2:59—assaulted my eyes.

"Hello?" The voice on the phone was deep and croaky. "Detective Ollie Chandler?"

I nodded my head, admitting it.

"Chandler?"

"Yeah."

"You didn't answer your cell." His voice was a hacksaw cutting a rain gutter. "You awake?"

"No. But…you may as well finish the job."

"In bed?"

"Mowin' the lawn. Who died?"

I've been waiting all my life for good news from a 3:00 a.m. phone call. It's been a wait of Chicago Cubs proportions.

Many imagine that middle-of-the-night phone calls mean someone's been killed. I don't imagine it. It's true.

Jake Woods tells me there's a God in charge of the universe. I'm not convinced. But if there is, I'd appreciate it if He'd schedule murders during day shift.

"Victim's Jimmy Ross," Sergeant Jim Seymour said. I pictured him sitting home in his underwear. Not a pretty picture.

"Drug dealer."

I didn't shed a tear. They say cops are cynical. To me drug dealers are a waste of protoplasm. They should be shot, injected, then put on the electric chair at a low setting.

"Officer Sayson's the patrol," Sergeant Seymour said. "1760 Southeast Clinton, apartment 34." I scratched it down in the dark, postponing those first daggers of light.

As I hung up, I sensed a presence in the dark room and reached toward the nightstand for my Smith and Wesson 340 revolver. I saw the whites of two eyes three feet away. My hand clenched the revolver. Suddenly I recognized the sympathetic eyes of Mike Hammer, my bullmastiff, who spends his nights getting in and out of my bed, licking my toes to reassure me he's back.

Slowly I withdrew my hand from the gun, not wanting to send the wrong message to my bullie.

What was wrong with me? How could I forget Mike Hammer, my roommate and best friend? I shuddered, remembering five years ago, when I drew the gun on Sharon when she came back to bed after taking Advil.

The problem with morning is that it comes before my first cup of coffee. I stumbled toward the kitchen, fingertips on the hallway wall, stubbing my toe on the exercise bike Sharon bought me. I've used it twice in four years. I keep it around to maintain the illusion that it's making me healthy. Since this helps me justify the next cheeseburger, it's worth every penny she paid.

I keep water in my top-of-the-line Mr. Coffee, poured to the ten-cup mark, with Starbucks French roast always waiting. In my quest for maximum darkness, I load the filter to the top. Whether it's 7:00 a.m. or 3:00 a.m., I can throw the switch and, even though the world's going to hell in a handbasket, coffee's brewing...so there's hope.

I leaned against the fridge and pulled the pot off the burner every few ounces to get what was there. I'd mainline it if I could. Sharon told me maybe I should drink less coffee now that Juan Valdez named his donkey after me.

Trying to remember whether I'd had three hours of sleep or two, I put Mike Hammer—I call him Mulch for short—out the back door to do his business. Every morning he acts like it's his first time, a privilege he's been waiting for all his life. After two minutes outside for him and six more ounces of coffee for me, Mulch blew open the door to get his biscuit.

I abandoned Mr. Coffee and headed for the bathroom. I put my face two inches from the showerhead and let the water pummel me.

Presumably I dressed, poured the last of the coffee into my thirty-ounce mug, and said good-bye to two of my favorite people—Mulch and Mr. Coffee. Mulch licked my face. I wiped off Mulch-slobber and tossed the paper towel at the sink, coming up short. I slowly shut the front door, watching Mulch shred the paper towel—his reward whenever I miss.

"You're in charge while I'm gone."

Mulch loves it when I say that.

It was early November but felt like late December. Like a polar bear on ice, I negotiated the slick walk to my white Ford Taurus. I dropped into the driver's seat and kicked aside a Big Gulp cup and a Burger King bag, which expelled the scent of French fries like a perfume spray bottle. I must have been on a stakeout the night before. Maybe two nights before. Eventually I'd remember.

You shouldn't assume I was conscious during all this. A detective establishes his routine so he can do it in his sleep. You wake up on the way, more at each stoplight. By the time you really need consciousness, it's usually there. You just hope it doesn't arrive at the scene after you do.

It was dripping cold. I drew the window half down to double-team with the coffee. Every few blocks I stuck my face out—I learned this from Mulch—and gulped a quick fix of wet oxygen. Then I pulled in my frozen face and warmed it with the coffee. It's a ritual, like those Scandahoovean men who go back and forth from ice baths to saunas.

The Portland night, nearly uninhabited, smelled of frosty rain on asphalt. It reminded me of working the beat, night shift. One year I saw no daylight between November and February. From what I heard, I didn't miss much.

When you're on the "up team"—on call for the next murder—getting yanked from the netherworld in the middle of the night comes with the territory. It's the only thing easier now since Sharon died: I don't have to worry about her worrying about me.

I turned onto Burnside, next to Max, the light-rail tracks, where there's only one lane. Occasionally people don't understand that what I'm doing is more important than what they're doing. The moron in front of me—only the fourth car I'd seen—just sat there in his lowrider Acura Integra, figuring that since it's 3:23 a.m., he can chat with someone on the curb, even after the light's turned green.

My Taurus is a slicktop—unmarked. Cop on the inside, civilian on the outside. Usually that's handy. Not this time. I honked. Nothing.

I honked again. Then I reached to my right and typed in the license number on my mobile data computer. I honked a third time.

The bozo charged out of his car, yelling and swearing. When he was two feet from my window, I pulled my Glock 19 and pointed it at his face.

"Get out of my way. *Now.*"

He froze, with the fixated expression of a man wetting his pants. He scuttled back to his car sideways, like a crab, and hopped in, banging his head on the door frame. He turned his key with a garbage-disposal grind, forgetting he'd left the car running. He screeched through the now-red light.

I flipped on my flashing red and blue grill-mounted strobes. He edged to the right, and I passed with an inch clearance. My computer screen flashed. I lowered my passenger window and shouted, "Have a nice day, Nathan Roberts!"

Okay, maybe when he approached my car I should have identified myself as a cop. But many people assume that if you're a cop you won't shoot them. I didn't want Nathan to labor under this assumption.

Having been a cop for thirty years, I find that you can get most of what you want with a kind word. But sometimes, as Al Capone put it, you can get more of what you want with a kind word and a gun.

"Sayson?" I spoke into the car phone. "Chandler. Homicide. On my way. 1760 Southeast Clinton? Apartments?"

"Greenbridge Arms. Third floor, four doors left off the elevator. Apartment 34's sealed. My partner's checking on neighbors. Dozen people heard the shots. One possible witness."

"Be there in five."

When I'm on the up team, anybody who kills somebody does it on my watch. That means they're messin' with me. And messin' with me's like wearin' cheese underwear down rat alley.

I pulled up to the Greenbridge Arms, studying the four-story brick building. I settled next to one of three patrol cars in a no parking zone, beside a van labeled KAGN.

Four criminals rushed me, armed with notepads, pens, electronic gadgets, and cameras. Crips and Bloods have a name. So do these—journalists.

"What can you tell us, Detective Chandler?" The *Oregon Tribune* reporter brandished her notepad, poison pen ready to scribble.

"Nothing. If you check your notes, you'll see I just arrived."

"They're denying us entrance to the apartments."

"Good for them." This was standard procedure, but reporters—thinking they're royalty—are outraged when they aren't allowed to trample a crime scene.

"Victim's name's Jimmy Ross, apartment 34. Right?"

Apparently someone on police radio had slipped up and said the victim's name. "There's a victim?"

"We called neighbors, and they confirmed it was Jimmy Ross. True?"

"Why would I tell you?"

"What's the harm? We heard it on the radio. We just want you to confirm it."

"Don't hold your breath."

"We're just doing our job."

"You're getting in the way of me doing *my* job. Monitor your own calls."

"Cops don't own the airwaves. The public deserves to know what's going on."

I turned away as her photographer took a photo. He grabbed the sleeve of my trench coat. I yanked it back. I turned toward him. His camera flash did that dagger thing in my eyes.

"Out of my face!"

I saw the red light of a television news camera right behind him. Images of my anger management class assaulted me. I'd sworn I'd never subject myself to that again.

I smiled and waved to the camera. "Just kidding! Actually, I want to thank you folks for coming. I wish I had time for tea and crumpets, but we have a crime to solve and people's lives to protect, so if it doesn't inconvenience you, I'll be going up to the crime scene now. Enjoy."

The *Tribune* and TV reporters and their cameramen followed me to the front door of the apartments, where Officer Brandon Gentry opened the door for me. He and I nodded at each other, two professionals trying to beat off the vultures. I wondered if he was an anger management alumnus. They should give us a secret hand signal. I signed his log sheet and wrote down the time: 3:39 a.m.

The TV cameraman pushed open the front door and did a quick sweep with his video. As I stepped in the elevator, I said, "Officer Gentry, there's a van illegally parked. I think it has the letters KAGN on it. Would you please write a parking citation?"

The door closed and I tried not to ponder how the media, especially the *Tribune*, had been my judge, jury, and nearly my executioner fifteen years before. I needed to switch gears to the job at hand. At least I was awake.

The elevator was old, with a bad case of asthma. As I got out on the third floor, I popped in a stick of Black Jack gum—my crime scene entrance ritual.

I headed up the hall to the left and saw a cop, midtwenties, poised like a jackal guarding pharaoh's tomb.

"Sayson?"

He nodded, too eagerly. Academy written all over him, Officer Sayson exuded a Secret Service alertness. If he lives long enough, eventually it'll give way to the fear of dying on duty and leaving behind kids and the wife he's promised not to forsake. Eagerness to jump into the middle of a dangerous situation is inversely proportionate to age. Twenty years ago I was chasing armed fugitives down back alleys, by myself. Now my first thought is to call for SWAT teams, armored cars, helicopters, guided missiles, or stealth bombers—whatever's available.

I'm a Vietnam vet. Someone watching my back means everything. Officer Sayson was protecting my crime scene; he was my new best friend.

Entering apartment 34, I stepped from hallway to crime scene. There, sprawled in a death pose, was Jimmy Ross, two shots to the head. Physical evidence all over the place, with a bonus: a sealed Ziploc bag of Ecstasy and a half-spilled sack of meth. No need for a lab report to tell me what was what.

Sayson introduced me to the apartment manager, who assured me Ross lived alone. No wife, live-in girlfriend, brother, cousin, friend, or roommate. Sayson consulted two neighbors who'd noticed lots of coming and going. The manager appeared shocked, as if he'd never suspected one of his renters was a drug dealer. Go figure.

Since most murders are done by family members, that's where you look first. Domestic arguments normally begin in the living room, where weapons are limited. They migrate to the kitchen, where weapons abound, or the bedroom, where there's a gun, which has a way of ending fights. This argument had stayed in the living room. No sign the killer had been anywhere else—only between the door and body. Didn't fit the domestic murder profile.

Sayson told me the paramedic who'd come twenty minutes ago had pronounced Jimmy Ross dead. I looked at what used to be the man. He was dead all right.

The medical examiner, Carlton Hatch—I'd seen him at a dozen other homicides—showed up ten minutes after I did. Most MEs ask you to call them when you want the body removed, after the crime scene's clean and detailed. Unless time of death is unknown, the ME may not arrive until three or four hours later. Not Hatch. Every time I've worked with him, he's come immediately, like an autograph hound to an NFL team hotel.

Hatch is a number two pencil, head pink and bald like an eraser. He carries a man-purse and wears a nicely fitted suit beneath a poorly fitted face. His pointy chin isn't a good match for his pale, bloated cheeks. Too much chlorine in his gene pool.

I gazed down at my Wal-Mart jacket over my flannel shirt spotted with yesterday's bacon and cheese omelet. I considered my rumpled slacks, pockets holding Tuesday's Taco Bell receipt and a packet of hot sauce. Then I looked again at the ME's tailored suit.

"Tuxedo at the dry cleaners?" I asked him.

His smile came quick and left quicker. This guy should be home watching *Quincy* reruns. I wanted to be home sleeping it off or watching Jack Bauer interrogate a terrorist.

"Blood spattered here." Hatch pointed to the wall. "Isn't that interesting?"

I nodded, though it wasn't. I prefer the CSI techs, who quietly collect evidence, report to me, and let me interpret it. The ME's specialty is the state of the body: cause and time of death. I like it when people stick to their specialties.

"Probable cause of death gunshots to the head," he said slowly, as if he had drawn on years of training to come up with this. Any kindergartner could have told me the same.

"Another splatter here. Don't you find that interesting?"

"Isn't that what you'd expect with two head shots at close range?" I asked.

"Still, it's interesting."

"As interesting as last month's cricket scores," I said.

Two CSIs in forensic bunny suits arrived. One vacuumed; the other photographed. They collected blood samples, carpet fibers, and anything possibly containing DNA fragments. I sketched the scene on a yellow pad. I supplemented with dozens of photos on my Olympus digital camera. Nice change from the Polaroids we used to take.

"Chandler?" The loud voice startled everybody. Barging in the door was my partner, Manny Domast, wiry, short, and high-strung, like one of those yippy dogs who starts the day with five cappuccinos.

"You look terrible," he said.

Manny's grumpy at 10:00 a.m. At 3:48 a.m. the difference isn't noticeable.

"What we got?" he asked.

"It's interesting," I said, eyeing the ME, who chose that moment to formally declare that Ross had died one to two hours ago. Good estimate, since the gunshots eighty minutes ago woke up all tenants except the hard rock fans.

After CSI went over Ross's cell phone, I checked its directory, jotted down the numbers of the last five incoming and outgoing calls. Manny listened to messages. He contacted two of the callers, a middle-of-the-night fishing expedition. Meanwhile, I talked with the wide-eyed ponytailed witness in apartment 36.

She'd been walking up and down the hallway at 2:30 a.m.

"Why?" I asked.

"I had rats in my legs." She gave a detailed description of a tall black guy with lots of hair and red sweatpants who'd been in the hallway five minutes before she heard the shots. He'd scared her. She pretended not to look at him.

Within twenty minutes, Manny and I determined it was a case of a drug dealer blown away by his competitor. A turf dispute. We found one bullet embedded in the floor, probably the second shot. Apparently the other bullet hadn't exited. Fingerprints with slight blood traces were on the doorknob. But there was no indication that the killer had touched the victim, so it seemed likely the blood was the killer's, though what made him bleed wasn't obvious. Perhaps a small pre-existing wound that reopened without him knowing it? DNA tests wouldn't be back for months, but I called headquarters to see if we could get the lab to do a rush on the three good fingerprints collected.

Murder is never convenient, but solving a murder can be routine. This one had routine written all over it. The only thing missing was the killer's name, Social Security card, and a confession written in lipstick on the bathroom mirror.

While Manny canvassed the apartments, I went to the hallway's end and stepped outside onto a rickety fire escape. I opened my mouth wide, gulping life.

It seemed so easy. A good description and fingerprints and DNA.

That's when I should have suspected something was wrong.

Napoleon said—I heard this on the History Channel while eating Cheetos with Mulch—that every campaign has ten minutes in which the battle's won or lost. Sometimes investigations are that way. Looking back, the ten minutes in which I botched that investigation were right when everything fell together perfectly.

I got a call from precinct saying an anonymous tipster had heard Lincoln Caldwell boast of offing another drug dealer. By 6:00 a.m., we found tall, big-haired Lincoln Caldwell, asleep in his room, red sweatpants hanging on his bedpost. His gun, in the top dresser drawer, had been recently fired. As I looked at the four rounds left in it, I didn't need ballistics to convince me that the gun would prove a perfect match for the rounds that killed Ross. His cell phone confirmed he'd called Ross six hours earlier.

He denied it all, naturally. They always do. We arrested him and hauled him in.

I felt like a crossword puzzle champion holding a puzzle any kid could solve. I'm a Sherlock Holmes fan. I like to follow bread crumbs, not six baguettes leading me to someone standing twelve feet away who hands me a business card saying "Lincoln Caldwell, Murderer."

Still, I couldn't argue with the bottom line. Two drug dealers for the price of one. One dead, the other off the streets for however long the court decides. Never long enough for me.

Sometimes the bad guys help out the good guys by doing what we can't—blowing each other away. Kill a killer and you may save a half dozen lives. Kill a drug dealer and you may save a couple dozen. That's what cops say to each other off the record. And cop-to-cop is always off the record.

I once cracked a case based on my discovery that one Monday morning a woman had broken her routine by ordering a grande white chocolate mocha. Remarkable for one reason: Every weekday for five years she'd gone to the same coffee shop and ordered a tall skinny latte. Something had to account for her cel-ebratory mood. I checked on her because her husband had died of "natural causes" on Saturday. The white mocha tipped me off that she might have contributed to those natural causes.

It took me a whole baseball season to prove it, but by the time the Yankees took the field for the first game of the World Series, I'd got her. No prize. No bonus. No street named after me. No letters of gratitude from husbands whose wives were on the verge of ordering their first white chocolate mochas. But that's okay. I don't do it for the thanks. I do it because justice is my job, my one contribution to a world that is truly—and I mean big time—a mess.

I'm saying this because the devil's in the details. Jimmy Ross's murder didn't require turning over rocks. Everything that mattered fell into place. Even if we never identified the tipster, when they processed the fingerprints and the weapon and the blood DNA, it would be a trifecta, a perfect triangle of independent evidence. Together they were irrefutable. The case was open and shut. Lincoln Caldwell was our man.

I spent more time on the paperwork than investigating. When two and two make four, you don't try to refigure it six different ways to see if it comes out three or five. You tie a bow around it, give it to the district attorney, and move on. You hoist a beer or two and watch a football game and tell yourself that even though you're no Mother Teresa, you've done something that mattered. Case closed.

Of my 204 murder cases, I've solved 177. That's 87 percent. The rest, cold cases, still burn deep in my gut. Every year or two, sometimes on vacation, I solve one of those oldies in my quest to raise my batting average to .900. Of course, if I ever make that, I'll want more.

I sent a man to jail for a double murder he didn't commit. Bradford Downs. I know his face well. Two credible witnesses offered convincing testimony to back up compelling physical evidence. He claimed innocence, but his record made that hard to believe. After ten years of appeals, he was executed by lethal injection.

Turns out the witnesses were the real killers. We'd never have known if the one dying hadn't confessed and offered proof...three years after an innocent man was put to death.

Maybe there is something as bad as murder and getting away with it—being murdered for a murder you didn't commit. Since I put him away, that makes me an accessory to murder.

Bradford Downs's face wouldn't be my first choice to fill the back of my eyelids when the lights go out, but some nights there he is.

So why am I telling you this? Because I didn't realize that morning at Jimmy Ross's apartment that nothing was as it appeared. That case was open and shut all right...open and shut on a dead-wrong conclusion. And I fell for the setup. That makes me mad. It makes me even madder that it was only fate or circumstances or luck or providence—whichever you believe in doesn't matter to me—that made me realize it.

Portland homicide has five teams, so Manny and I get every fifth murder. It was our next murder, the one fourteen days later, that pulled the rug out from under me. Eventually it woke me to a shocking truth that forever revised the story of Jimmy Ross and Lincoln Caldwell.

That second murder turned me, my job, and my friendships upside down. It shook all the change out of my pockets. It threatened to bring down a police department, end my career, and place me inside a white chalk outline, with some other homicide detective trying to figure out who murdered me.

Not one of those 204 cases prepared me for that next murder, where sinister eyes, hidden in the shadows of a violated house, gazed out at me through a broken window. It was the most unconventional and baffling case I've ever worked.

If that's not enough, my investigation threatened to end the lives of people I cared about.

And, ultimately, that's exactly what it did.

2

*"Watson here will tell you that I never can resist
a touch of the dramatic."*
SHERLOCK HOLMES, *THE NAVAL TREATY*

MONDAY, NOVEMBER 18

IN THE MORNINGS I go fishing.

By the side of my bed.

For clean clothes.

I seldom catch much.

This morning, though, I made a great find. Buried under Tuesday's blue shirt was my favorite flannel, also blue. It was a good omen.

On mornings when I don't have to rush, I flip on the coffee, grab two oat-nut English muffins, and follow Mulch onto the back porch, where my toaster is. I toast those suckers until they're carbon-based life forms. Then I smother them with butter and a thin slice of Limburger cheese. Years ago Sharon banned the toaster to the back porch, far from smoke detectors.

My next ritual, on lazy mornings, is to quick-fry a couple of eggs and three bacons for Mulch. If I don't have time to stop at Lou's Diner, I join Mulch with three eggs and four bacons of my own, splitting the fourth with him. The highlight for Mulch and me is when we get a double yolk.

I stabbed an egg covered with Tabasco sauce. If there's a God, thinking up food was one of His best moves. So were dogs. Some of the best friends I've ever had were dogs. If I manage not to die soon, I may be good for a couple more. I'm considering Nero, for Nero Wolfe, my favorite detective. Or Archie, for Archie Goodwin, Nero Wolfe's legman.

The more people I've met, the more I've come to appreciate my dog. After Sharon died, Mulch was developing male pattern baldness. I was afraid he'd contracted some fatal dog disease, so I stopped giving him beer and bacon for a couple of weeks. That just made him grouchy. Then one day, running my hand over his head, I noticed a wad of fur between my fingers. I realized I'd been petting him within an inch of his life.

And you know what? He would gladly have become a bald bullie for me. That's more love than I've known from anybody. Beside Jake Woods, my best human friend. And Sharon, of course. Without Sharon I don't hang out or play cards or see movies with couples anymore. When I'm with them, I can't stop think-ing about her. It's like the hole your tongue keeps going to when you've lost a tooth.

One fall day four years ago I was walking Mulch at Laurelhurst Park, where you can let your dog off-leash in a designated area. I unhooked him early. He went after a squirrel. I chased him. Rounding a big fir, I saw Mulch, who'd forgotten the squirrel, beeline to a park bench. He trotted right up to a guy in a business suit, whose back was to me, and hiked his leg on him. For a moment the guy didn't notice, then he looked down and swore at my dog, kicking his rear.

Then I saw the man's face. It was Edward Lennox, the brand new chief of police, talking with Portland's mayor, the distinguished Garrison Branch. I stayed behind the tree and whistled. Mulch ran around it, passing me. I chased him through some rhodies, and we both slipped down into a thick grassy area piled with old leaves, where he licked my face mercilessly. That's when I nicknamed him Mulch.

We walked back to our car the long way. I took Mulch to Burgerville and bought him a Tillamook cheeseburger. Got one for myself to keep him company and gave him the last gulp of my blackberry shake.

In the years since, as Chief Lennox has led our police force, I've come to real-ize that Mulch, from the beginning, was an extraordinary judge of character. Lennox has been chief of police five years. In dog years, that's thirty-five, but it feels like more. For most Portland cops, his reign has been a long, cold winter.

By the time I read the paper and took Mulch for a walk and changed the oil in my Taurus, it was lunchtime. Mulch's stomach growled. I checked the cupboard. Hiding behind the Ovaltine were the cans of Dinty Moore beef stew and SpaghettiOs. Sharon was wine, shrimp salad, Perrier, and asparagus. I'm beer, pizza, cream soda, and SpaghettiOs.

Not a day goes by when I don't wish she were here to give me a hard time about SpaghettiOs.

An hour later I crossed the Hawthorne Bridge, turned left on First, and pulled into the parking garage on my right, opening the gate with my precinct key card. I parked, then walked to the northwest corner, crossed Madison to the north, then Second Street to the west and entered the Justice Center, home of the Portland Police Bureau. I veered to the elevators. The uniformed officer nodded. Since most of this building is a jail, with a 676-inmate capacity, his job's more important than it appears.

The elevator gives only five options for the sixteen floors. Floors 2 and 3 are courtrooms, 4 to 11 jail floors, accessible only by authorized personnel.

Twelfth floor's intelligence, identification, juvenile, and narcotics. Thirteenth floor's the DA's office and Internal Affairs, where for six months I spent more time than I care to remember. They'd gotten bad information from the *Tribune* and went after my scalp.

I pushed fourteen for detective division. It has only one place the general public can go—the reception desk, with a thick bulletproof window and no door that opens from the outside. All the detectives hang their hats here, everyone from robbery and pawnshop details to homicide.

I hadn't even made it through security before Mitzie called, "Chief needs to see you."

"Let me get settled first."

"His assistant said it's urgent."

"Does that mean I'll have to wait one hour instead of two?"

I went to my workstation and looked out the huge windows, soaking in the panoramic view of Portland. It all seemed so tranquil from up there. So ordered and peaceful. Years ago it was just a bunch of buildings to me. Now it's more than that. Feels like nothing should escape your sight up here. Ironic that such a grand view is from homicide. My job takes me lower to the ground, where things aren't so lofty and inspiring.

I retraced my steps to the elevator and pushed floor 15, home of the chief of police's office and the media room. If any chief ever wanted to be near media, it was Lennox.

After passing through security, I was escorted into the waiting area outside the chief's office. It brought back memories of when a cop could walk right through the chief's open door. Now who'd want to?

I saw on the walls three paintings, two of which were classical, with people centuries old wearing funny hats and looking serene. The other was vague and surreal, the type I saw in a gallery that Sharon made me go to in retaliation for pretending I had the flu so I could watch a play-off game and miss her family gathering. They were paintings you had to develop a taste for. I was still at the gag reflex stage.

The chief's assistant, Mona, fifty-five trying to look thirty-five, marched toward me. Her perfume arrived three seconds before she did. Her aide, twenty-five trying to look thirty-five, walked eighteen inches behind her, leaning forward to hear every word.

"Sit," Mona said. "Chief Lennox will be with you soon. He's on an important phone call."

I started to sit in a chair facing away from the chief's office.

"No," Mona said, waving her hand, propelling the perfume toward me like nerve gas. "There, on the couch. Chief Lennox prefers people to sit on the couch. But you *must* take off that raincoat."

"It's a trench coat. Columbo wore a raincoat. Sam Spade wore a trench coat…and a fedora." I waved my hat at her.

Her assistant looked curious, but Mona Estée Lauder, lip curled, looked at me like I was an idiot.

"Humphrey Bogart in *The Maltese Falcon*? Raincoats are to trench coats what a minivan is to a sports car." I posed dramatically, like a fashion model on the runway. "Notice the ten buttons, epaulets, shoulder straps, and D rings. In the inside pocket we have—"

"It's wet and it stinks. Keep it off the couch." Mona marched off, her assistant smiling back at me. The younger woman was too new to realize she didn't need to be cordial with working stiffs who put away bad guys. She could save her smiles for journalists and the public.

I sat down, still wearing the coat. I gazed across the corridor into the inner sanctum—throne room of the King of Police.

A long man with a big jaw threw his voice at the speaker phone on his desk, leaning toward it, bawling it out. He was gangly and mechanical. Yet his voice was smooth and commanding, a radio voice, the kind that comes in handy for banana republic dictators and Eastern European tyrants.

"That's not going to cut it," Lennox said. "Those dogs won't bark." A few minutes later I heard, "He's dumb as a post."

The chief's king of clichés. *What next,* I wondered? *Soft as a baby's bottom?*

His office, I knew from prior visits, was the size of a tennis court, his private bathroom big enough for Ping-Pong.

On the coffee table in front of me were a number of magazines, including the *New Yorker*, with its stupid highbrow comics, and *Architectural Digest*. No cop, gun, or sports magazines. Four news and two home decor periodicals.

Next to me was a lamp stand with an eight-by-ten photo of the chief, his wife, and presumably his teenage daughter. What it was doing out here I didn't know, but maybe it was a statement: "All this is my turf."

I studied the photo of the Lennox family. The chief looked noble, refined, confident—right down to the perfect triangle of the handkerchief folded in his suit coat pocket. He looked far better in the picture than in real life. Maybe somebody had altered his face in Photoshop. Or maybe it was his makeup.

His wife, prim as her husband, had the smile of a woman who's looked at more cameras than books. The teenager had too many rings in her face. Beneath the hardware she was pretty but looked miserable. Her face screamed, "Let me out of this picture!" If I had that much metal in my skin, I'd feel lousy too.

If this is the picture they chose, I'd hate to see the rejects.

It made me think of Kendra, my younger daughter. When she was a little girl, she couldn't get enough of me. That all stopped as a teenager. She's thirty now and lives in Beaverton, on Portland's west side. Fourteen miles away. Might as well be Neptune, which as far as I know is still a planet.

When she turned fourteen, Kendra became an explosive compound of hormones and acne, replete with habitual eye-rolling and a terminal case of protruding lip. At fifteen, she was a walking melodrama. She lived in two modes: despondency and rampage. Whichever she was currently in, I always longed for the other. I lost her at sixteen. I was told it was just a phase, that she'd come back. She never did.

This couch had known a thousand posteriors, and so far it had spent forty minutes getting to know mine. This was Lennox World, and I was but a bit player in it. He strutted around his office, in front of the framed awards, trophies, and VIP photographs visible from the hall. One with Clinton, one with Bush. He had his bases covered.

Why the open door? He had to have an audience. People kept passing by, glancing into the inner sanctum. They could remark at the dinner table, "I saw the chief of police today. He smiled at me."

I crossed and uncrossed my legs, trying to invent a new way of doing it. Why was I here? Students get called to the principal for two reasons. One I've seen in a Hallmark commercial but never experienced: The boss wants to congratulate you. The second reason: You're in trouble. That one I know. I felt like a fly called to meet with the spider.

Ten feet away, Lennox's voice rose, dripping with disdain. Apparently some minion was daring to question him. "There's no way that's going to happen. Learn to live with it. No pain, no gain. Am I clear on that point?"

He had little hair but plenty of jaw, which is more important in police work. I'm talking Jay Leno jaw. And teeth that had more man-hours invested in them than the Hoover Dam. Why not? Teeth are a politician's greatest asset, and the chief was a PR man. He'd grinned his way to the top.

Our police department doesn't exist merely as an arm of law and justice. We exist to further the chief's reputation, make him look good, and allow Portland to be a stepping-stone toward his lifelong dream of being Chicago chief of police.

At that moment, two cameramen and a television reporter walked by. They slowed outside the chief's office. He smiled broadly and waved to them. One of the cameramen gave him an "okay if I shoot?" look. The chief nodded and smiled warmly, oblivious to the poor sap on the other end of the phone.

"He's really a fun guy," the reporter said.

There isn't a cop I know who'd call him a fun guy.

While peering in at Lennox, I caught sight of his full-length mirror. A cop with a full-length mirror? I wondered how many hours he'd watched himself, practicing looking natural.

I saw my face in the lower corner of the mirror. I stuck out my tongue. Then I held up my hand, moving thumb and fingers together in a yakety-yak. The chief turned and looked at me. I went seamlessly into a wave, smiling at him.

Anyway I hoped it was seamless.

The chief emphatically hung up and walked toward his door.

I looked at my watch. I'd been sitting fifty-three minutes.

"Sorry for the wait," he said, not sounding sorry. "It was important."

"So I was told."

He didn't offer his hand, which was fine with me since shaking it would have required touching him.

"Time gets away from you in a job like this."

"No problem. I'm just working a murder investigation. No need to hurry on my account."

The chief looked me over like you do a bad piece of fruit. "I'm the chief of police. I have many important responsibilities."

We stared at each other to see who would blink. I stared at his mostly bald head. Despite his Mexico vacations and tanning booth visits, it had a gray pall. The slight sheen reminded me of a steelhead fresh out of the river. I saw slight streaks of makeup, a big joke among the cops. The chief lived for his photo ops.

I looked at his eyes, the color of last week's barbecue coals. Like a propane stove, they could be turned off and on. Right now they were off. "You're still wearing that raincoat."

"Trench coat."

"You wear it to defy me, don't you?"

"I wear it because the classic detectives wore it. It helps create the mood, the mindset."

"You look like an oddball."

"Maybe Sam Spade and Philip Marlowe looked like oddballs, but they did their job. I do mine."

"This isn't a novel. This is the real world."

"We're all inspired by different things." I gestured at his artwork, none of which inspired me.

"All right, Chandler…I know we have some history. We need to get on the same team, lock arms." He invited me into his office with a sweeping gesture, like I was entering the home of the pope, Vince Lombardi, or Chuck Norris.

"Sit down," he said, shutting the door. "I'm going to tell you the unvarnished truth. These are challenging times. We need to set aside our differences for the greater good."

I knew whose greater good he meant. Still, I sensed a conciliatory tone. *What's up with that?*

"I have an idea I want to bounce off you."

Lennox didn't bounce ideas off you; he dumped them on you. Something was up.

"I told you to sit down," he said.

"I've got a back spasm. Been sitting too long."

"Sit down."

I'm three inches taller than the chief, and he doesn't like looking up at me. I stretched myself on tiptoes for about five seconds, then sat.

"What's that smell?" He leaned down, two feet from my face.

I ran through the options: coffee, beer, smoke from Rosie O'Grady's pub, Limburger cheese on my morning muffin, Jade East, English Leather Lime. Since I hadn't worn the last two since I was a junior higher, I finally said, "My gum? Black Jack?"

"It smells terrible. And it leaves a black film on your teeth."

"That's licorice."

"I've been looking through your file," he said. "Before I took over, you were cited for 'inappropriate levity.' Do you recall why?"

"It would be hard to pinpoint."

"During Christmas season you answered your phone, 'Ho, ho, ho…homicide.'"

"Oh yeah."

"And what is the public supposed to think? We take our work seriously here, Detective."

"I thought it was an internal line. Another cop."

"That doesn't make it right. We need to set examples for each other. And don't you agree we need to give the public a good impression?"

"I agree that we need to do our jobs."

"And you don't consider leaving a good impression part of your job?"

The sweat on his forehead was building.

"Sometimes we're pulling double shifts, haven't slept for a day and a half. What we do is serious. A little humor helps."

"Appropriate humor."

"Yes, sir." I don't know if my voice conveyed respect. If it did, it was lying.

"You're a rule bender, Chandler," he said, saying the word like Jack Bauer would say *terrorist*.

"I'm a risk taker. I do what it takes to get my job done."

"Policies govern how you can do your job."

"Some policies keep me from doing my job."

"So you ignore them?"

"I try to figure out how I can fulfill them and still catch the bad guys."

"That has to change."

"If it does, fewer bad guys will get caught."

His face turned cherry. I knew he was about to explode into a lecture I'd heard before. But he didn't. That unnerved me.

"Why are you telling me this now, sir? What's going on?"

He took a file folder and scanned neatly typed notes. He took a deep breath. "The *Oregon Tribune* and the police department have a long history of tense relations."

"You mean we hate each other's guts?"

"You'll be glad to know, Detective Chandler, that you have the opportunity to help mend fences."

"I do?"

"You know Raylon Berkley?"

"The *Tribune* publisher? Sure. He's an idiot."

"He's brilliant. And a potential ally to our cause."

"What cause would that be?"

"The cause of…this police department. What we stand for. Justice."

"What did I miss? What happened to make an enemy an ally?"

"Raylon has never been our enemy. The media's job is to press hard, ask the difficult questions, hold us accountable."

"And lie about us?"

"You're talking about your situation fifteen years ago?"

"Berkley was there then. He never struck me as an ally."

"He doesn't write the stories."

"No, but he pays to have them written, then makes the bucks when they're sold."

"Actually, the *Tribune* has lost money the last two years."

"That's what I hear. You have no idea how many sleepless nights it's caused me."

He lifted still another file folder that showed rubber band marks. "You feel the *Tribune* accused you of police brutality."

"It's more than a feeling."

"The investigation cleared you."

"Sure. But our neighbors, my wife's coworkers, and my kids' friends will always think I beat up that guy unnecessarily, and I did it because of his skin color. I used force against him because he was acting violently and putting people at risk."

"So you said."

"So I said because it's true."

"You're going to have to get beyond your stereotype of Raylon Berkley."

"Why? Is he a new homicide sergeant?"

"Look, Chandler, the last two years haven't just been bad for the *Tribune*. They've been bad for the Portland Police."

I agreed, though I would have taken it back five years, to the day he became chief, not long before Mulch introduced himself to his pant leg.

He picked up a clipboard that held what looked like a dozen pages of hand-written notes. "We've had a series of shootings, two where officers were found liable for the deaths of innocent citizens."

"The *Tribune* found them liable."

"In one case they were right."

"Okay. Blalock was a jerk and deserved to be busted. I'm all for that. I hate dirty cops. But what about Collins? Sure, he's back on the streets, but nobody trusts him. You can't do your job when everybody thinks you strong-armed a store owner and destroyed his shop."

"It looked bad."

"And who made it look bad, before all the facts came in, before the two witnesses came forward who saw the store owner pull his gun on the cop? The *Tribune* and the news stations. Collins's life will never be the same. Trust me. People still think I'm a racist and brutalized some helpless guy."

"My point is, our problems with police behavior and the fund-raiser and the embezzlement…it's hurt our image."

"So? Where are we going here?" I squirmed, feeling like I was wearing a wool sweater with no undershirt.

"Raylon Berkley and I have had lunch a half dozen times the last two months. We've come up with a plan we believe can be good for both of us. Something that will bolster the public's understanding of our department and at the same time increase sales of the *Tribune*. Raylon has taken it to their directors, and I've taken it to our advisory council. Everybody's on board."

"What board are they on?"

"You have to remember that PR is everything."

"Everything? What about justice?"

"Well, yes, justice, naturally. But you can't have justice without good public relations. Anyway, in order to be on the same team with the *Tribune*, in order for them to see us as we are, we need to spend time together, see each other at work, get to know each other."

"Like…dating?"

"A crude analogy," he said. "But there's truth in it."

"Look, I've got murders to solve. Are you going to tell me what's going on here?"

He shook like a volcano about to erupt.

Instead, he calmly said, "We have a plan. A *Tribune* reporter will cover a murder case, working alongside one of our homicide detective teams, start to finish. They'll be there from crime scene to lab, interviews, every aspect of the investigation. The reporter will write it up for the public—" he raised his hand when he saw my face—"leaving out anything that could compromise the investigation. Two days a week an article will be written, allowing the readers of the *Trib* to follow the investigation."

"Tell me you're kidding."

"Look at the success of *COPS*. It shows people what we really do. People love it. Just like they love *CSI*."

"Right, and they expect cases to be solved like they are on *CSI*. And juries now demand *CSI*-type evidence to prove guilt when it normally doesn't work that way. And people who watch *COPS* figure out ways to outsmart the system."

"But people have gained a much greater understanding of our work. It's helped our image. We need it here in Portland. I had a few conditions, of course, and so did Raylon. All but one of his conditions were reasonable."

"I think it's a big mistake. But you don't need my permission."

"I certainly don't."

"So again I ask, why am I here?"

The barbecue coals in his eye sockets flamed on. Lenox slammed down his clipboard on his desk, three inches from my fingers. "Because Raylon Berkley's condition is that his reporter has to work with *you*."

"I'M NOT ASKING YOU," the chief said, wagging his finger at me. "This isn't a democracy."

"There's no way I can do my job with a journalist in my pocket. Ridiculous!"

"It's not your call, Detective."

"What about Jack Glissan or Brandon Phillips? They're perfect. Veterans. Punctual. Look good in suits. They're fit. Hair's nice, everything the public likes."

"For once we agree," Lennox said. "That's what I told Raylon. But no, he said, 'I want Ollie Chandler.'"

"Had he been drinking?"

"I couldn't believe it either," the chief said. "Why choose a velvet Elvis when you can have a Monet?"

"I have a velvet Elvis hanging in my garage. Who's Mohnay?"

He nodded, as if proving a point.

"So why does Berkley want me?"

"He said it's because you're colorful and interesting and you have a history."

"I'm good-looking and brilliant too, but Glissan or Phillips are still better choices."

He stood, face red, waving his hands like a conductor. "I think the real reason was stated—the exact words were, 'Chandler can act like a moron.' I think he hopes you will."

"I'll bet you stuck up for me when he said that."

"He didn't say it. *I* did. You're a fish out of water. And your career direction…you're up a creek without a paddle."

"One day my ship will come in. You can't judge a book by its cover."

"Raylon thinks the handwriting's on the wall. When you mess up, readership increases. After all, idiots can be interesting."

You're an idiot and you're not interesting, I said.

Okay, I didn't *say* it, but I thought it. And that's why I'm putting it in italics. (I'm hoping eventually to turn this into a detective novel. I figure any idiot can write one of those.)

"Well, if *you* don't want me to do it, and *I* don't want to do it, why are we even talking about it?"

"Because…we're that desperate." He sighed and plopped into his chair.

"We?"

"Our future's at stake."

"Do you mean your future?" Chicago was on his mind.

"The future of the police department!"

"Are they considering dismantling the department and having the city run by gangs and vigilantes? Because I'm thinking that may not work too well. Didn't work in Chicago."

"It's signed, sealed, and delivered. You're going to do it. Unless you want to turn in your badge and find a job in mall security."

With three hours' sleep and eight cups of coffee, I had one nerve left and the chief was getting on it. I stood and walked to the door.

"Malls have their upsides. There's a pet store. Caramel corn. Starbucks. Hot Dog on a Stick. Beats the lousy vending machines in detective division."

I walked out the door, right past Mona and her cute little lapdog, who pretended they weren't eavesdropping. The chief followed me. I turned and said, "Chicago winters are rough anyway. As we speak, it's probably raining cats and dogs."

I rarely leave the Justice Center until after rush hour. But I had to escape.

I went out of my way to gaze on the cornerstone inscribed with Martin Luther King's words: "Injustice anywhere is a threat to justice everywhere." Ironic that he spoke those words while locked up in a place like this. It burned me that injustice still worms its way inside the building that bears those words.

I crossed the Morrison Bridge, got on I-84 east, then exited early and pulled into a 7-Eleven on Halsey. Bought a six-pack of Bud, then drove to a Minit Mart two miles down Stark Street and bought another six-pack. When you're a cop, you have to be careful. Somebody might think you have a drinking problem.

My last stop was Taco Bell, where I ordered a bean burrito, two chicken chalupas, and a steak gordita. I turned on the car radio and in forty seconds heard about a kidnapping, arson, and an escaped child molester. I punched it off.

I walked in my front door, and Mulch did the doggy dance of joy. I let him out onto my splintery back deck, catching the faint smell of burnt English muffins, gazing at my measly yellowish lawn and its unspread pile of moldy bark dust, by the rotting elm tree.

I grabbed two beers and poured one into Mulch's bowl. He lapped it up. Then

I popped in a *24* DVD and settled onto the couch. I handed Mulch a chalupa. He inhaled it in three seconds.

When Nero Wolfe, master detective, wants a beer, he presses a button and Fritz comes in with a tray. I don't have a Fritz. Or a Theodore to tend the orchids. Or an Archie to do my legwork. All I've got is Mulch. But I wouldn't trade him even for Fritz, Theodore, and Archie.

I love Nero Wolfe and Jack Bauer and Chuck Norris. They're my escape from a world that doesn't make sense, a world I find myself liking less every day.

I pressed the remote and watched Jack Bauer save the country despite the bureaucrats. Justice prevails. It's a nice thought. After the fifth beer it's almost believable.

If there is a God, I wonder if He gets as tired of this world as I do.

TUESDAY, NOVEMBER 19, 6:30 A.M.

My shaky, headache-riddled memories of the night before included *Walker, Texas Ranger* roundhouse kicking a gang of thugs into tomorrow and Jack Bauer chopping a bad guy's hand off to save the city from a nuclear bomb. Or something.

They say that when the boogeyman goes to sleep, he checks his closet for Chuck Norris. Superman wears Chuck Norris pajamas. Chuck Norris doesn't sleep; he waits.

That's why I like Chuck Norris and Jack Bauer. They do what the rest of us can't. Hey, they can get McDonald's breakfast after ten thirty. They scare the crud out of bad guys, and they give us hope that maybe in the end good will beat out evil.

I also remembered my conversation with the chief, reason enough to drink myself into unconsciousness. At least I'd made it all the way to bed this time.

I sipped coffee to pull myself back into the world I'd checked out of twelve hours ago. Beer pulls me out; coffee pulls me back. A bungee cord effect.

I pulled three case files out of my briefcase. The Jimmy Ross murder was on top. It had been so easy, but a few things about it niggled at me, like a carpenter ant munching wood siding.

Let it go. Why was that case still bugging me?

I stood on Justice Center floor 14, the detective floor, at the watercooler, watching bubbles rise. The sun coming through the windows of Portland Homicide was suddenly eclipsed. I looked up. Hovering over me was a human planetoid.

"Clarence Abernathy," I said. I stepped back so as not to be sucked in by his gravity. "Big as life. Bigger."

"Hello, Detective."

I suppose we both felt awkward, like guys who should be friends by now but aren't. We see each other once a week, at Lou's, for lunch with Jake. Never anywhere else. Clarence and I get along only if Jake's there. Without him, our chemistry goes bad.

He wore a meticulous black suit, maroon tie, and dress shoes, looking like a CEO or corporate attorney. His clothes appear permanently ironed. He's a columnist for the *Oregon Tribune*, where most of the reporters dress like war protestors. But Abernathy always looks like he's come from the tailor.

His back's half an acre. There's so much of the man you're tempted to stare. He's no more than thirty pounds overweight—not bad for a guy who maybe hit three hundred pounds at fifteen.

"I haven't been here since…since Dani…" He peered out the huge windows overlooking Portland, his voice sounding like distant thunder. I remembered that night we'd met, at his sister's house, forty minutes after she'd been murdered.

"You're wondering why I'm here." His words were clean and precise, like a Shakespearean actor. He gave me a half smile.

"Being a detective, I think I just figured it out. Are you the chosen one?"

"When I heard Berkley cut a deal with your chief and wanted someone assigned to you, I volunteered. I figured I'd rescue you from my colleagues."

"Am I supposed to feel relieved that I'm ending up with you rather than one of those arrogant journalists who thinks he knows everything?"

"It could be worse. I could be one of those arrogant cops who thinks he knows everything. Besides, I figured I was the only one who could get past your…idiosyncrasies."

"Never underestimate a reporter's ability to overestimate his ability."

"They call us journalists now."

"Yeah, and they call drug addicts chemically dependent. Doesn't Berkley know we're friends? I mean, as much as a cop and a *journalist* can be friends."

"Berkley knows your reputation. So he wanted to assign you a woman or a minority."

"Are you the woman or the minority?"

"You're a pain, Chandler. What was I thinking?"

Clarence sounded like a disgruntled bull. I like that sound, so I make a point of pushing his buttons. Jake is our buffer, managing to keep us civil. It'd been years since I'd gone one-on-one with Clarence.

"C'mon, sit down," I said. "Give the sun a chance to shine. So you think we're going to be partners?"

"Not partners. Two guys doing their jobs. I'll be happy if we don't kill each other."

"Can we lower our sights to something more realistic? Like, we'll kill each other, but quickly and with minimal suffering?"

"I assume your chief made the decision without you?"

"Quit calling him *my* chief. I've been sideswiped. Berkley and Lennox are a couple of big egos. And they're using us."

"Your chief isn't keen on you either. Berkley said he called you King of the Idiots."

"He actually said King of the Idiots?"

"Don't take it personally."

"Like his opinion matters to me. King's not bad. Beats Queen. Or Jack. Actually, you're lucky, Abernathy. Not many journalists get to see a mastermind at work. Watson wrote up Sherlock Holmes. Every Holmes needs a Watson."

"I'm not your Watson. Anyway, here's the deal. The moment you get notified of a murder, you're to call me. Immediately. You give me the address, and you're not supposed to do anything until I get there. I need to see everything as the case unfolds."

"You're already taking charge?"

"My job is to observe and communicate how you do your work, start to finish."

"Just you, right, and just day-shift hours?"

"You haven't seen the agreement? Check your e-mail. You know how to open an attachment, right? It says you must include me in any actions taken on the case. If it intrudes too much into my private life, I make that call, but most of the time I'll join you. Nights too."

"What if having a journalist around intrudes into my *professional* life?"

"That would be a problem...if your opinion mattered."

"It'll just be you? Not one of those nitwits like Kost or Button?"

"Kost's no nitwit. No comment on Button. Anyway, when it comes to the murder, Carp will be on call too. You remember Lynn Carpenter?"

"The photographer who helped us on your sister's case?"

"You liked her didn't you?"

"She was okay. Considering she's...one of you. But at the *crime scene*? We've got professionals taking pictures."

"Carp's a professional."

"I meant a *real* professional. Police department. I can't let a newspaper—"

"Read your e-mail. The agreement says pictures can be taken, but before anything's published you'll see it. You'll be asked to approve. If we disagree, we say so and your chief makes the call."

Clarence pulled out one of those miniature computer doohickeys and poked at it with a magic wand.

"So," he said, "how long before we'll be working a case?"

"We try not to put murders on the calendar anymore. It was nice for planning vacations, but it looked suspicious."

"Approximately."

"Do I appear to be all-knowing?"

"Not remotely."

I sighed. "Manny and I get every fifth murder. There've been, let's see, three murders since Jimmy Ross, you know, the dude Lincoln Caldwell blew away? Doyle and Suda are working on the guy who went over the bridge last night. Glissan and Barrows are next. Murder rate's been unusual. We're already on deck."

"So what's your best guess? Based on averages."

"Block out everything from now until next month, and you should have it covered. Or if you want things to move quicker, kill somebody yourself."

"I'm considering it," he said.

I didn't like the way he looked at me. He scribbled something and handed me a business card. It was neat and professional. "That's my cell number."

"Got it already." I waved my phone at him.

"Now you have it in your wallet. If your cell dies, you can still find a phone and call me. Don't forget. I need to be there from the beginning."

Apparently I told my face I was unhappy.

"It could be worse," Clarence said. "We could be television. Cameras and bright lights."

"That's next. After that, they'll film the murders live." I shook my head. "I'm telling you, Abernathy, the detectives are going to think this is a sellout. That *I'm* a sellout."

"Berkley said your chief's the one who suggested it."

"You're saying '*your* chief' on purpose, aren't you?"

I walked away. This is usually a good move when you feel like decking somebody.

THURSDAY, NOVEMBER 21

There was a time in my life when I would have been sound asleep at 3:07 a.m. without assistance. That time passed when lightning struck two years ago, and somebody yanked Sharon from my life.

Since then I've had to use sleeping pills, or my preferred pharmaceutical, Budweiser. I'd been on a bender at Rosie O'Grady's pub the night before, so when the phone rang at 3:07, I wasn't sure if I'd gone to bed three hours or twenty minutes ago.

"Chandler?" the raspy voice said. "It's me."

Why do people say "It's me"? What's the alternative—demon possession?

"Who's you?"

"Lieutenant Mike Petersen."

I saw his image rising from the ashes of my torched mind: built like an oak, but with rougher bark, mosslike hair coming out his ears.

"Hang on a second." He was whispering, which meant he was trying not to wake his wife. "Okay. There's been an incident." If you drive a bus, an incident is a fender bender or two passengers squabbling over a seat. If you're a cop, incidents involve bombs, attacks, crashes, and mayhem. When you're a homicide detective, incidents are murders.

"One body. 2230 Southeast Oak. House is green with—"

"Yellow tape and cop cars out front?" I said, legs heavy as sandbags. Wading through the darkness and feeling cold kitchen tile against my bare feet, I flipped Mr. Coffee. "Who's patrol?"

"Officers Dorsey…and Guerino."

"Do I know them?"

"If I were you, I could answer that."

"Grumpy, Lieutenant?"

"You know what time it is?"

"3:11?"

"My grandkids are spending the night. I'm in the hallway." He gave me Dorsey's number.

"Got it. Go back to bed."

"Don't forget to call your shadow."

"Huh?"

"The *Tribune* reporter. What's his name? The big black guy who used to do sports."

My gut squirmed like a fish tossed on the bank. "Abernathy."

"Chief said to make sure you call Abernathy. I'll call Manny. Longer trip for him. Wait for Abernathy before you go in. That's what the chief said. You're calling him?"

"Got it."

I hung up and started to call Abernathy. I stopped. I emptied into my giant Seahawks mug the first eight ounces from the coffeepot. Nice and black. I go through bags of coffee like they're paper towels.

What was that? Something in my driveway. Sounded like a car door latching. I reached for the nearest gun, the Ruger P-97 in the cupboard, behind two coffee mugs.

I went to the front window and looked at the driveway. Nothing. I snuck out into the garage, opened the door, and followed my Ruger. I studied my car. Okay. Came around to the front porch. Okay. I realized only then how cold it was, especially on my legs. I wasn't wearing pants.

In case someone was watching, I posed like Dirty Harry, lacking only a .44 Magnum, shoes, and pants. I backed into the garage and shut the door.

I replaced the P-97 in the cupboard, took the Browning in the Seahorse waterproof case out of the medicine cabinet, set it in the soap dish, and took my shower. I threw on the least offensive clothes lying by the bed and tucked a tie in my jacket pocket. I pulled on a dark blue stocking cap and put my black Sam Spade fedora over it. I grabbed my cell phone and headed to the car. As I pulled out, I punched numbers.

"Dorsey."

"Ollie Chandler, homicide. On my way. What we got?"

"Scene's pretty clean, but the vic's a mess. Something went sideways here, Detective. He—"

"All I need to know. Be there in ten. Keep everybody out, okay?"

I prefer not to hear crime scene descriptions over the phone. I like to rely on my own eyes. I want to see what I see, not what somebody else says I should see. I'd get patrol's report after my own wheels were turning.

As I drove, I noticed something in the passenger seat. A box. It said Wally's Donuts. In it was a single glazed donut, with telltale signs that it'd recently had five companions.

There were three reasons I didn't eat it. One, I didn't remember buying those donuts. Two, I didn't remember going to Wally's Donuts. Three, I didn't remember ever *hearing* of Wally's Donuts.

The last six months, when I come home late from Rosie O'Grady's, there's a lot I don't remember. But donuts from a place I'd never heard of? It wasn't like me to have eaten five donuts. If I'd bought these, I would've eaten all six. Or given the last one to Mulch. Could I have been drunk enough to leave a donut in the car?

What's going on? The donut wasn't my only issue. Why did they call me? Manny and I aren't the up team. We're on deck. *Aren't we?* But then, if I couldn't remember buying a box of donuts…

My plan was to call Abernathy once I arrived at the scene. I'd still be in the car, so I could tell him I hadn't entered yet. That would give me a head start. I'd be holding the cards when he got there.

At the scene were a dozen people, two in bathrobes covered by coats. Crime scenes are magnets. Fortunately, at 3:30 a.m. not as many gawkers are available, and most journalists are sleeping in their crypts, or doing whatever vampires do when they're not sucking blood.

My biggest concern was the swarm of uniforms. It looked like the Policemen's Ball. That always makes me nervous. The greater the numbers, the greater the potential for contaminated evidence. Cops, firemen, paramedics, all kinds of trained and helpful people can trample a scene and destroy or bury evidence.

I saw two EMTs smoking cigarettes outside the ambulance across the street. That always means somebody's dead.

Two civilian cars in the driveway, patrol car at the curb. On the porch, two cops were having an animated exchange with somebody.

I reached into my trench coat's inner pocket for my Black Jack gum. Nothing. I patted it down. No Black Jack? Bad luck. I dialed Abernathy's cell number. One ring.

"Yeah?"

"It's Chandler. Sorry to get you up."

"I *am* up."

"Just got a call, Eeyore. There's been a murder."

"No kidding."

I stepped out of the car. "The address is—"

"2230 Southeast Oak."

On the porch, one officer was looking at me, the other was eyeing the big guy in suit and tie, who was pointing at the house numbers with his cell phone, glaring at me.

"Oh, boy."

I approached, identified myself to the uniforms, then looked up at the shall-we-say tense face of Clarence Abernathy.

"So you 'just' got a call?"

"It was at 3:07. Only twenty minutes ago."

He looked at his watch. "Twenty-six minutes ago. Twenty-two minutes ago *I* got a call."

"The lieutenant?"

"He said you'd call me, but just in case…"

Light shone on our faces from the video camera of a bozo named Jordan who comes to murder scenes and sells footage to two of the TV stations.

"Hey, Jordan, we're having a private conversation here. Mind turning that off?" Jordan didn't say anything. He kept filming.

"Shaq here wanted us to let him in," Dorsey said. "Can you believe that?"

"Yeah," I said. "It's just like him."

It was a cold night. Abernathy had steam rising from his forehead, like it was the fourth quarter in a long, icy drive up Lambeau Field.

"We had an agreement," Clarence said.

"I kept it. I didn't enter the crime scene before calling you. I still haven't entered the crime scene."

"That's why people don't trust cops. You're liars."

I saw Guerino's hand lower a few millimeters toward his pistol. It was a flinch, but I notice things.

Jordan stepped over the yellow tape onto the lawn. I wanted to put a couple of Glock holes through his camera, but I figured that might win me a return trip to anger management.

Officer Guerino shouldered up by Dorsey and gave Abernathy a hard stare, which he apparently thought was intimidating. But staring a man in the Adam's apple, or craning your neck so he's looking down your nostrils, does not intimidate.

"You need coffee," I said to Clarence. "Here's my thermos. Leave some for me."

He eyed the thermos like it harbored an Ebola culture.

"Look," I said, "you want to stand here and fight while the body gets cold? We could sit on the lawn and play pinochle. You and Guerino can be partners."

Abernathy stared at Guerino. Finally the cop blinked.

"Or how 'bout I go in the door and do my job?"

"Your job was to call me."

"I called you. Want to watch me work? Fine. Otherwise, quit whining and go back to bed."

"You crossed me and you lied," Abernathy said. "I won't forget it."

"Does this mean," I said, tapping my fingers on the yellow crime scene tape, "that the honeymoon's over?"

4

"My mind rebels at stagnation. Give me problems, give me work, give me the most abstruse cryptogram, or the most intricate analysis, and I am in my own proper atmosphere."
SHERLOCK HOLMES, *THE SIGN OF FOUR*

THURSDAY, NOVEMBER 21, 3:45 A.M.

I PULLED ON LATEX GLOVES and foot covers, then handed a pair of each to Abernathy.

"Never take these off. Got it? Take them off for one second, and you're on the other side of the yellow tape."

His hands didn't fit the one-size-fits-all. He grumbled but wrestled them on, short of his wrists.

"Crime scene contamination's our worst enemy. Somebody visits her cousin and discovers he's been murdered. She picks up the phone and calls 911. She's handled the phone, the doorknob, possibly the victim. All contamination."

He was taking notes now, so I figured I was forgiven. This was my chance to shine in the newspaper I hated.

"The 911 operator tells her don't touch anything else; wait outside for the cops. She might still use the toilet, wash her hands, get a glass of water, pick up her cousin's picture, and make three more phone calls."

Clarence tried to read his handwriting and glared at the gloves.

"Here's where I take my first mental photograph of the crime scene. Ready?"

I turned the corner into the living room. After hundreds of homicides, I've learned that what I first see is the image that stays with me. What struck me this time was a smell—the coppery scent of blood that hadn't dried.

As I looked at the face of the victim, something crawled across the nape of my neck—it felt like a big spider with wet feet.

I recognized the man on the floor. He was a professor at Portland State University. I'd sat in on one of his classes years ago—I was trying to remember exactly when and why since I never attended there. I hadn't seen him since...or had I? Actually, it felt like I'd seen him more recently. But where?

His face was a color it shouldn't have been. I don't mean he looked dead. I mean he didn't look like a dead person is supposed to look. His skin had a hint of blue, but not the shade of asphyxiation.

And yet...around his neck was a rope, bright blue with red flecks in it. The rope was three feet long, and the excess beyond the noose was too short to hang from anything. The end was cut smooth, barely fraying. I stared at the knot, which raised a host of knot-making memories from my childhood. Though it was tied snugly, his neck and throat showed no signs it had been tighter, no signs he'd been hung. I looked above me at an undisturbed ceiling.

The source of the smell was a wound in his chest. Given the shirt fabric, it appeared to be two shots, close together, over the heart. His shirt was soaked.

Multiple causes of death on one body?

I'd never been in this house. *Why did it seem familiar?* It was as if I'd been here in a dream. A recent dream. I tried to shake off the déjà vu.

The victim's clothes swallowed him. I remembered him as bigger in that class-room. Death had shrunk him 20 percent. I studied his dark eyes, open and vacant. They looked like manholes over hell.

I used to stare at stiffs without taking death personally. Lately it's been differ-ent. I've been pondering that the death rate is 100 percent, and I'm not going to be the exception. I wonder…does everyone slip into a dreamless sleep? Part of me hopes so. Hell scares me. Heaven scares me almost as much.

Suddenly I realized I was holding hands with a dead man. I dropped it. I looked up, hoping Abernathy wasn't watching. He was.

The victim's wallet was stuffed in his right front pocket. I examined his driver's license and another picture ID.

"Professor William Palatine," I said. A tech informed me Palatine had taught at PSU for many years.

"What do you call those outfits?" Clarence asked, pointing at two criminalists.

"Bunny suits. The technical name is biohazard coveralls. Protects them from contact with body fluids. And protects the evidence from them."

Already one criminalist was on his hands and knees fussing with carpet fiber.

"Why's he that color?" I asked.

"What color?" the criminalist said, reluctantly turning from fiber, his first love, to flesh.

"Bluish."

He shrugged. "You're the detective."

"I'm the detective who's asking the criminalist why he's that color."

He looked around the room as if, having no opinion of his own, he wanted to borrow one. "ME'll run a tox."

I pointed to the computer. "Check the keyboard for prints?"

He looked at me as if the question didn't deserve an answer. One thing I've learned in decades of detective work: I'd rather get dirty looks now than find out later that somebody messed up.

"We'll get the bullets first," he said.

"How many?"

"Two through his chest. Presumably in the floor."

"He was on the floor like this when shot?"

"Looks like it."

"Seen the bedroom?" It was Officer Guerino.

I followed his pointing finger to the hallway leading to the back left of the house. The bedroom was mostly neat and tidy, bed made, drawers shut, light lemon smell. But the outside window had been broken.

I looked it over. Entry point? Break-in? No. Not a big enough hole in the glass. And too jagged. No blood evident. Anyone coming in this way would have taken a couple more whacks at it and cleared the jagged glass before entering. They probably knocked it in, then decided on another entry.

I stared out the fractured window into the darkness. A single streetlight was blocked by a tall maple still holding a third of its leaves. Then I realized what wasn't lying at my feet: broken glass.

"What are you seeing?" Abernathy sounded like Darth Vader with a head cold.

"The glass didn't fall inside." I shone my flashlight on the carpet to make sure I wasn't contaminating evidence.

"So?"

"So it has to be outside." I stepped forward carefully and looked out the window, following the beam.

"There." I pointed outside to broken glass on the ground.

"This wasn't an attempted break-in. It was an attempted break-*out*."

"Who?"

"Palatine? Hard to imagine the killer breaking the window from the inside. Why risk waking the neighbors?"

"Why wouldn't he unlock the window and pull it up? There's room to crawl out. Not for you or me, but he's not that big."

"Maybe he was running and panicked, threw himself at the window. If so, fibers from his clothes may show up on the glass." I knelt down. "There's a shoe impression here in the carpet. And a slight mud residue. And there's a little glass too. I see five shards. Sometimes there's a bounce-back when glass bends out and comes back before breaking.

I went to the closet and took out a right dress shoe, then brought it over and put it by the mark. I looked inside. "Professor wore a size 8. This print is about size 10. It's pointed toward the window. Why would a killer look out a broken window visible from the front of the house? It's like he stood right here, peering into the darkness."

I stepped back and took a couple dozen pictures with my Olympus Stylus 500. First of the shoe impression, then the rest of the room.

"Why so many pictures?" Clarence asked.

"No downside. It has a one-gig memory card, so I can take over five hundred high-resolution photos. These are the only shots we'll get of an undisturbed crime scene."

I pulled a yellow pad from my trench coat and started sketching the room, the window, everything.

"Pictures aren't enough?"

"I make my own record. Photographs are no substitute for what you see in real time. Plus it impresses the scene on your memory. Later, when you view the pictures, they stimulate a three-dimensional image in your mind. If I don't sketch, it's not as clear."

I walked back into the living room, confirming that CSI would record the shoe print and collect the shards on the bedroom carpet. They assured me they would. I leaned over the body and manipulated the ankles. Pressed on the stomach. Tried to turn the head. Locked. Stomach was tying up, but extremities moved well.

"Medical examiner's going to say time of death was four hours ago."

"Oh, is he now?" a new voice asked. I turned to see the number two pencil in a suit, carrying his man-purse.

"Carlton Hatch—the Johnny-on-the-spot medical examiner. Two cases in a row!"

"Interesting," he said, nodding at the body.

I said to Clarence, "Dr. Hatch will be your only competition for best dressed at a murder scene."

I've never met a criminalist, medical examiner, or coroner like the ones on TV, who appear to have given up careers in modeling to pursue a love of dead bodies. Most of the real ones look like Hatch but dress like street people.

"Interesting," Hatch said. "I'm sure you noticed the skin. Something's in the bloodstream."

"Poison?"

Clarence's phone rang. He stepped away.

"We may have a couple different causes of death to choose from," Hatch said. "What's primary and what's secondary? The rope has nothing to do with it." He carefully pulled back the unbuttoned shirt and pointed to Palatine's shoulder. "Needle marks."

"Drugs?"

"Insulin, probably. He's diabetic according to his chain."

I reached for the silver metallic tag and fingered it in my gloved hand. Framed by red medical symbols, including snakes, it said, "Medical Warning: Insulin Dependent Diabetic."

"Interesting," Hatch said. "No needle marks in his stomach."

I went to the refrigerator and poked around, finding an insulin bottle next to the orange juice.

"Clarence, you're diabetic, aren't you?"

He nodded as he shut his phone.

"Wear one of these medical IDs?"

"For the first year. Now it's sitting in a drawer."

"The professor was diabetic. Dr. Hatch thinks he injected something. Or somebody did. Maybe a poison. Help me lift him."

Clarence looked like he was ready to put in for a new assignment. We lifted the right side, Hatch supervising and warning caution. Nothing underneath. We lifted the left and found a needle underneath. I picked it up.

"Like your insulin syringes?" I asked Clarence.

"No. It looks like the older style I used ten or fifteen years ago."

Hatch studied it. "The residue's blue, while insulin is either clear or milky. It's 100 ccs."

Clarence reached in his coat pocket and pulled out a little black packet. He unzipped it and produced a small white plastic syringe with an orange cap.

"That's 50 ccs," Hatch said, like a mechanic looking at a spark plug.

I resumed sketching the floor plan, drawing in body location, furniture, telephone, computer. I took out a measuring tape and stretched it from body to walls, three directions.

I heard commotion at the front door. Clarence's cell phone rang again.

"Carp's at the front door," he said. "They won't let her in."

"They won't let a newspaper photographer into a *crime scene*? What's wrong with those cops?"

I walked to the front door. Lynn Carpenter stood there, camera in hand, *Tribune* ID hanging from her neck, like it said FBI or CTU or something. Guerino's arm stretched out in front of her.

"Can you believe this?" Dorsey asked.

"A newspaper photographer!" Guerino said.

"I hate to be the one to say it, boys. Let her in."

"A *reporter* and a *photographer* inside a crime scene?"

"Next year they'll be selling Cracker Jacks and letting in the general public," I said. "Ten dollars a head. Box seats for forty bucks. Touch the corpse for a hundred. Then they'll be auctioning crime scene memorabilia on eBay."

"This is wrong," Guerino moaned.

"Tell me about it." I handed gloves and foot covers to Carp. "Keep 'em on."

"Nice to see you too, Detective," she said.

I felt slightly bad considering she'd been a big help on Clarence's sister's case ten years ago.

"I'm Ollie, your tour guide."

I extended my hand, glove touching glove. Her face melted into a smile. I can be a real charmer with the ladies. Carp had changed since I'd last seen her. She'd been a quiet tomboy; now she was warmer and more feminine. Age had softened her. I liked it.

With most of the team staring at her, I cleared my throat and said, "I got an e-mail from Chief Lennox." I looked at Clarence. "It even had an attachment. The deal is that the *Oregon Tribune*—our beloved newspaper, so cherished by this police department—can take pictures of this crime scene. They can't print any photo without department clearance. Can't divulge sensitive information. They won't jeopardize our investigation. Anyway, that's what they tell me. If they get in your way, respectfully Taser them or beat them senseless with a nightstick."

There were a number of chuckles, including Carp's. None from Abernathy.

Carp's camera started flashing. Clarence was looking over my shoulder like a three-hundred-pound gargoyle. I walked to the professor's desk, turning my best side to the camera.

"Walk me through procedure," Clarence said.

"Yes, sir," I said. "I've written Ollie's Rules of Investigation. I'll give you a copy. Ninety-two of them. The first ten are never touch anything. Number 11 is protect the scene. Number 12 is write everything down. Number 13 is don't trust what anybody else writes down. Number 14 is don't trust anyone who says they didn't touch anything, especially if they keep insisting on it."

"What were you doing with the measuring tape?"

"Triangulating body location. An inch here and there can make all the difference."

I went to the front door and asked Dorsey, "Witnesses?"

"Nobody. The people we've talked to came when they saw the patrol cars or got a wake-up call from the media. Some are from those apartments."

He pointed at a two-story building the next street over, where most of the blinds were closed. I saw one television on, and in the next apartment, barely visible, someone with elbows pointed outward, which made me think they might be holding binoculars.

"Nobody we've talked with on this street saw anything—except somebody noticed two vagrants who often wander over here from their settlement three streets down."

"Who made the 911 call?"

He shrugged. "Want me to check?"

"Manny'll handle it. Talk to the rubbernecks?" I pointed to the dozen people on the other side of a police tape, including three kids who should've been in bed.

"We've focused on protecting the scene."

"Good choice." I turned back to Clarence. "Once I finish here, we'll canvass for witnesses, take written statements."

"These guys collecting stuff in the bags—are they called CSIs? Or criminologists?"

"Criminologists aren't evidence collectors, they're experts in why criminals commit crimes. What you know as CSIs are what we call criminalists. They're crime scene techs, evidence collectors. They make sketches, usually a detailed drawing later. They're more artistic than detectives."

He peered at my sketch on the yellow pad. "I hope so. Keisha drew better than that in first grade. Where do they take the bags?"

"Evidence locker. They maintain a chain of custody. If we have a particular lab request, we ask. Otherwise, they check for fingerprints, DNA traces, et cetera. Then they search for a match." I looked up at him. "Can I do my job now?"

"Part of your job is helping me do mine."

"Yeah. The attachment."

Carlton Hatch loudly pronounced death. Everybody else stifled their smirks.

"What's the medical examiner's role?" Clarence asked.

"He's the ranking official at the crime scene, even over the lead detective. Which is why I don't like him showing up early. Generally, they estimate cause of death and time of death, then go over the results of the autopsy. Then revise as needed. They usually show up on the scene later. Not Carlton Hatch."

"Chandler!"

Manny Domast exploded into the room. There are advantages to having a thirty-six-year-old partner who's a former gangbanger. He's street savvy, shrewd, bold. A pit bull.

He's also sixty-grit sandpaper.

"What took you so long?" I asked.

"We weren't the up team, man. What happened?"

"Not sure. Maybe a sick detective or two deaths in one night? Somehow we got bumped up to the top."

"That's crazy, man. Maria's pulling a shift at the hospital. I had to get the kids dressed and into the car. Who wants to take three kids under five in the middle of the night?"

"Detective Domast," said James Earl Jones, or someone borrowing his voice. "It's been a long time."

Manny twirled to look straight into the knot in Clarence Abernathy's tie.

"It's just gettin' worse," Manny said.

"You read your e-mail, right?" I asked. "And the attachment?"

"Where'd you find him this time of night?" Manny said. "Jazzy's Barbecue?"

"We've been investigating," Clarence said, "while you were fighting chickens behind Taco Bell."

"Whoa, hold it," I said. "Look, you guys don't like each other, and I don't like either of you. But we've got a job to do. Manny, meet Lynn Carpenter, *Tribune* photographer."

Carp extended her hand. Manny didn't.

"*Photographer?*"

"I thought the same. Before I realized how the public good would be served with crime scene photos."

"But that'll compromise—"

"Supposedly that's not going to happen."

"It's all in the attachment," Clarence said. Not sweetly.

I asked a criminalist, "Those chairs clean? The table?" I looked at Clarence and Manny. "Sit down, both of you."

Neither budged.

"Sit!"

Clarence sat. Manny pulled up a chair on the opposite side.

"Let's get you up to speed, Manny." We did.

Manny and Clarence and I once drove to a baseball game in Seattle, with Obadiah, Clarence's dad, the best man I've ever known. Obadiah's presence had made them civil. It was a long time ago. Obadiah Abernathy's magic was gone.

Manny gave Clarence one last hundred-yard stare, from two feet away, then went to the bedroom to examine the broken window.

"Manny's got an attitude," I said to Carp. "In time, he grows on you." *Like mildew.*

I stood beside the professor's desk looking at two piles of papers, one with a red C on the top, the other unmarked.

"Philosophy 102," I read. "Ethics."

"May I touch them?" Clarence asked.

"As long as your gloves are on. Careful."

Clarence shuffled through them. "Mostly Cs and Bs. A few Ds. Not a single A. Either he's a tough grader or he was in a bad mood."

"Or his students are dunderheads," Carp said.

Dunderheads? I liked it. She was winning me over.

"Interesting," Dr. Hatch said, pointing at the computer monitor.

"One thing at a time." I flipped through the stacks. "Fifteen graded. Five to go."

Next to the papers were seven piles of playing cards, faceup, with other cards staggered below them.

"Solitaire?" Abernathy asked.

"I've seen murders over poker, never solitaire. But it gives us the victim's frame of mind, doesn't it?"

"What do you mean?"

"He'd stopped grading papers. If he was playing solitaire, he was bored, wanting to kill time."

"Or taking a break from the papers," Manny said, reappearing. "Rewarding himself."

"Or he might have been distracted from his work," I said. "Knew something was looming. Nervous. Expecting someone? Check out the last card facing up, by the main deck. What do you see, Abernathy?"

"The ace of spades."

"Anything strike you as strange?"

"No."

"It hasn't been played."

"So?"

"Look, he's got two aces played above, diamonds and clubs, with a two and a three on it. With this kind of solitaire, when you flip an ace you play it then build on it. It's a no-brainer. You don't leave it sitting there like that. You make your play. Unless you're interrupted."

"Meaning what?"

"He stopped midstream. When someone came to the door, if that's what happened, he was playing solitaire, not grading papers."

I noticed a criminalist poised over the professor's body, shining a flashlight.

"What you seeing?" I asked.

"A strand of hair," he said. "Not the professor's."

"Perfect," I said. "Bag it."

"Mind if I move that lamp?" Carp asked.

"Don't touch anything," I said. "I'll do it."

"About three inches back from the screen," Carp said.

"Hey, I'm here to serve you *Trib* folks. Can I order you a pizza?"

"Double pepperoni, double cheese," Carp said, smiling.

I froze. "Who told you that?"

"Told me what?"

"My favorite pizza. Double pepperoni, double cheese."

"That's my favorite pizza," Carp said. "Always has been."

It was one of those magical moments. If it had been a movie, the music would have changed. Lynn Carpenter was speaking my love language.

"I'll search the desk," I said, eyeing Carp. "Manny, you want to grill the rubbernecks?"

"Nobody's done that?" He was out the door, pulling out pad and pen, a warrior looking for a war.

In the professor's oak desk, I discovered paper clips, rubber bands, a roll of peppermint BreathSavers, an unopened Snickers bar, reading glasses, three blue and four black Pilot G2 gel pens, three phone numbers without names, a Matt Hasselbeck rookie card, and a Shaun Alexander MVP card. Plus a nearly empty 8.45-ounce bottle of Pelikan fountain pen ink, royal blue.

I showed the ink bottle to Clarence.

"They still make fountain pens?" he asked.

"I just realized," Carp said, pointing to a corkboard covered with pictures, including a newspaper clipping. "I know this man. I took that picture. He was receiving the Rotary Club community service award." She scanned the article. "For his 'investment in the lives of young people.' It goes to one college professor each year."

"When was it taken?" I asked.

"June, I think." She stepped closer. "Yeah. The June 13 edition. So I took it June 12."

"What was he like?"

"Seemed a bit...taken with himself."

"Yeah," I said, stepping in close beside her to view the picture. "Some men can be real jerks. Not every man's humble and sensitive like me."

She nodded knowingly.

"What've you found, Chandler?" Another familiar voice. I turned.

"*Suda*? What are you doing here?"

Kim Suda's one of our two female homicide detectives. She's all female and all detective, petite but powerful, with a fifth degree black belt in Tae Kwon Do. She was wearing a stylish maroon coat.

"I live six blocks from here. I couldn't sleep, so I took a drive. Heard about it on the monitor and figured I'd check it out."

"You don't get enough murders?"

"Professional hazard. Architects look at buildings; I check out murders. You've never dropped by someone else's crime scene?"

Truth was, I had. Three times.

"It's getting to be a rock concert in here," I said. "Make yourself useful...get that patrol out; then tell me if you see something helpful."

"You got it, boss." Within ten seconds she had her hand on the arm of a uniformed officer. Smiling sweetly, she led him out the door.

"Who's she?" Clarence asked.

"Kim Suda. Homicide detective. Been in the department five years. Chris Doyle's her partner."

"Strange time to drop by."

"We detectives are strange people."

Clarence nodded, more vigorously than necessary.

I saw Suda and Carpenter watching each other. No smiles. Two attractive females suspicious of each other? Both wanting to impress me?

Once upon a time I thought I understood women.

What an idiot.

Clarence and Carp drifted from me, walking around the room talking and picture-taking.

I munched on the Snickers bar. It had been checked for prints. No sense letting it rot in the evidence room.

"Carp's going outside to take pictures of the neighborhood," Abernathy announced. "Eventually we'll want to use one or two for a feature. Will they let her back in?"

"Got your ticket stub?" I asked her.

"Thought maybe you'd stamp my hand."

"Once we start doing general admissions we'll have to do that. Tell Guerino and Dorsey I said they should let you back in. Let me know if they give you problems."

She smiled again. I'm not used to all these smiles at murder scenes. I looked at her, heart aflutter. She'd had me at double cheese.

I walked over to the far end of the couch, against the wall. I noticed crumbs on the ground. Big crumbs.

"What's this?" I asked the criminalist.

"Figured you'd want to see it as is before we vacuumed."

"What do you make of it?"

"Crumbs," he said.

"What kind?"

"Graham cracker?"

I looked closely. Someone had sat on the couch eating.

On my hands and knees, I looked over every inch of the coffee table. It was clean except for two identical circular stains two feet apart. They looked recent, slight moisture still evident. I took close-up photos of both stains, jotting down which picture corresponded to which stain. Then I took a wide-angle of the coffee table in relation to the couch, noting the location of the crumbs.

"You can bag the crumbs," I told the tech. "Need them all?"

"Nope. Maybe a third."

I reached down and picked up three big crumbs. I went to my briefcase and took out a water bottle to get the taste of Snickers off my palate. I put the yellow-brownish crumbs in my mouth.

"Not graham cracker," I said. "Granola bar. The crunchy type, not chewy. With a nut component. Maybe almond. Or hazelnut."

"They could use your mouth in the crime lab."

I went to the kitchen sink and found what I was looking for: two glasses, one with a residue of white wine.

"Test this," I said to the criminalist. "Fingerprints and DNA."

I searched for a wine bottle. Nothing in the fridge, garbage, or on the counter.

"I want to know what kind of wine."

Two empty bottles of Budweiser sat on the counter to the left of the sink. "At least he drank a good beer," I said.

"Bag them?"

"Why not?"

Ten minutes later I was back on the floor, hunting more crumbs (being a specialist in food particles), when I noticed something by the corner of the right front leg of the couch, six inches from the north wall. It was blue and black. I scooted over, stared at it in disbelief, then picked it up.

"What are you doing?" Kim Suda's voice sounded accusing, but her voice usually does.

I snapped my neck around. "Nothing." I heard the nerves in my voice. Had she seen what I picked up? I hid it in my hand and stood.

"What are *you* doing, Suda? It's my crime scene."

"You sound like you did it."

"If I'd done it, it would've been between nine and five."

"What's in your hand?"

"Nothing. What's in your brain?"

"Find something?" the tech asked.

"Nada," I said, putting my hand in my coat pocket while my body ran interference. "Just a shadow. Bathroom done?"

"Good to go. Nothing big. Hair samples with his brush. Follicles, presumably his. I left the toothbrushes for you to see. Two of them. We'll take them for saliva."

I walked to the bathroom. One Sonicare electric toothbrush, plugged into the charger. The other was a Colgate, old and frayed. Clarence joined me.

"Excuse me," I said to Clarence. "I have some business."

I locked the bathroom door. I heard my heart pound as I took out the piece of paper. I stared at it. It was a gum wrapper.

Black Jack.

I left the bathroom, preoccupied with my discovery, but determined to finish my job undistracted and figure out the gum wrapper later.

I examined the professor's closet, filled with shirts, Dockers, sport coats and ties, and a dozen pairs of shoes. Men shouldn't have that many shoes. On the left side of the closet was a red plastic storage box turned catawampus and with a crack in it, like something heavy had been on it. Everything else was neat and tidy, remarkably unlike my closet.

I checked the spare bedroom, mainly used for storage. Nothing stood out. But I took pictures anyway in hopes that eventually the house would yield its secrets to me. Clarence and Carpenter periodically crowded me, nearly stepping on my heels. I was winsomely gracious, especially to the double cheese pizza girl.

When I returned to the living room, the professor was still dead.

I began to systematically examine the photographs on the wall. Vacations in Hawaii and Mexico and the Caribbean, judging by the locals. In one he was speaking behind the lectern in an academic environment. In several he was wearing robes and regalia.

"The peacock displays his feathers," I said. "Graduation?"

Clarence nodded and pointed. "That one's a formal lectureship."

I looked at a couple of hanging frames that displayed academic degrees. Doctorate from Princeton.

I was about to examine the photos on the mantel when Dr. Hatch spoke.

"Interesting," he said, staring again at the computer screen. It reminded me I'd been distracted from the desk twenty minutes ago when Suda appeared. I hadn't made my way back.

"Mouse is on the left side," Clarence said. "He was lefthanded?"

Hatch was leaning over the desk, staring at the screen, his hand to the left of the monitor, inches from the mouse.

"Don't touch it," I said.

"Relax," the criminalist chimed in from the dining room table. "It was wiped clean."

"Then somebody used it."

"Besides the professor?" Clarence asked. "How do you know?"

"Do you wipe prints off your mouse?"

I picked up the reading glasses sitting on the desk and read aloud the words on the screen. "I, Dr. William Palatine, do not deserve to live. I've crossed boundaries and forfeited my life. I admit my arrogance. I deserve judgement. I should be cast into a deep sea with a millstone around my neck."

"A suicide note?" Clarence asked.

"Ever hear a suicide note that sounds like that? What's the millstone mean?"

Everybody looked at each other and shrugged.

"It's from the Bible," Clarence said. "Millstones were large rocks used to grind grain. They might weigh a couple hundred pounds. Jesus said if anyone hurt one of His children, he'd be better off cast into the sea with a millstone around his neck."

"The professor probably didn't type it, but if he did, it's a forced confession," Manny said. "I say the guy threatened to kill him if he didn't type it. Or the killer typed it himself. Either way, the words are the killer's."

"What's your next move," Clarence whispered, "now that you ate the victim's candy bar?"

"That won't show up in an article, will it?"

"Depends on whether you start keeping your word."

"Excuse me while I play solitaire. Okay if I handle the cards?" I asked the criminalist.

"Carefully. Gloves can smudge prints."

I picked up the ace of spades by the edges.

There were seven columns of cards. A deck was facedown, and next to it, faceup, was a small stack. Knowing I had a dozen photos, I took the ace of spades and played it. I started flipping up every third card carefully, by the edges.

"You're finishing a dead man's game of solitaire?" Clarence asked.

"Not only was the ace up, he had two good plays after that. Game definitely wasn't over. Like I said, he was interrupted."

Hatch cleared his throat.

"Time of death?" I asked.

"That's going to be tough," Hatch said. "May depend on what was injected and how it would likely affect rigor mortis."

"Your best guess?"

"Ten thirty to midnight."

I wanted a smaller window than ninety minutes. Hopefully someone heard the shots. I pressed the phone's message button. "No messages."

"It's digital, so it has a magnetized erase," Manny said. "No recovery."

I pressed Play Greeting.

A tenor voice spoke, as if from another world: *"This is Dr. William Palatine.*

Nietzsche said, 'All things are subject to interpretation; whichever interpretation prevails at a given time is a function of power and not truth.' Leave a message."

After a moment of silence and profound meditation, Manny mumbled, "What a jerk."

"He was a philosophy professor," I said. "Apparently he wanted everyone to know it."

"A student might be impressed," Suda said. "Anybody else would be annoyed."

"An answering machine greeting is self-expression," I said. "Like bumper stickers. They say something about the man."

"Right," Manny said. "They say he's an arrogant son of a—"

I held up my hand. "With the press here, we might want to guard our observations about the deceased."

"Let's find out who the professor called last."

"The philosophy hotline?" Manny said. Manny's not an Ivy Leaguer.

I pressed redial and waited. A voice started speaking. The words were clear enough but the voice sounded like someone gargling gravel.

"After the tone, leave your name, number, and the location of the money. I'll get back to you as soon as it's safe for you to come out of hiding."

I stared at the phone. Then at the redial button.

"Voice mail? Answering machine?" Manny asked.

I nodded.

"And?"

I disconnected, then pressed redial, hoping I'd heard wrong. I listened again, then hung up.

"What was the message?" Clarence asked. "Whose number is it?"

"It's...mine."

"*Scotland Yard feels lonely without me,
and it causes an unhealthy excitement among
the criminal classes.*"
SHERLOCK HOLMES, *THE DISAPPEARANCE OF LADY
FRANCES CARFAX*

"YOU DIDN'T DIAL your number by habit?" Manny asked.

"I couldn't have."

"Why not?"

"For one thing, it's not my habit. I never call myself. If I want to talk to myself, I just start talking. I'm always right there. Besides, I'd know I wasn't home."

"You sure you pressed redial?"

"Positive."

"But...you didn't know the professor, right?" Clarence asked.

"No."

"Never met him?" Suda asked.

"Not exactly. I sat in the back, visiting one of his classes years ago."

"Why?" Manny asked.

"I don't remember."

"Why would you be his last call?" Clarence asked.

I was on the wrong side of the questions. It didn't feel good.

"Maybe it was about a murder," Suda said. "Like thinking he was going to be the victim?"

"He'd just call the police. Not me."

"Unless he had a personal reason," Abernathy said.

"Like what?"

"Did the professor leave you a message?" Suda asked.

"Not sure if I checked my messages last night."

The truth was, I didn't even remember coming home last night. I'd been at Rosie O'Grady's, but after that...it was like a dream of a dream.

"So," Clarence said, "retrieve your messages and find out."

"I will when I get home."

"You don't know how to retrieve your messages remotely?" Clarence asked.

"Just call your number, put in your code, and listen to your messages," Manny said. His tone suggested I had the IQ of a split-leaf philodendron.

"I don't know any code."

Manny phoned my number and pressed buttons. "Usually a preset code." He disconnected and tried three combinations. "Nothin'," he said, looking disgusted.

"Anyone I want to hear from calls me on my cell." No one seemed to buy it.

"Take over," I told Manny. "Make sure the place is sealed. Goin' home to check messages."

"I'll follow you," Clarence said.

"No."

"It's part of the investigation."

"Manny needs you here." I didn't look up, but I felt their glares hitting me from both sides.

"Go through the professor's speed dial options," I told Manny. "Contact those he called most. See what they know."

"I'll get phone company records," Manny said. As I left the room he called, "And read the stupid manual about retrieving messages."

Clarence and I walked out the door right into the hands of the media standing in front of the crowd of neighbors.

"Clarence? What're you doing here?" one reporter said. "This is my assignment."

"Guess nobody told night beat I'd be handling the case," Clarence said. "Sorry. It's a couple of features a week. Guess you still need to report the news."

"Why were you inside? They never let us inside."

I started my car. The whiny reporter stood right there, a foot from the car, even though he could see I couldn't back up. Occasionally journalists block your car like they're that protester in Tiananmen Square who stopped the tanks. I edged the car, just touching him. He backed off a few inches until I bumped him again. Then I popped the car in neutral and gunned it, motor screaming. He jumped to the side, falling into bushes.

That dude in Tiananmen Square never flinched.

I unlocked the front door. Mulch was all over me. When he saw Clarence, his lip twitched.

"Big guy's with me," I reassured him.

Clarence put out his hand. Mulch sniffed it, licked it, then started investigating his pant leg and constructing a mental image of Clarence's dog.

"Okay, Mulch, we're here to check messages. Looks like we've got two." I punched the button.

"*11:17 p.m. Ollie, it's Brandon Phillips. Saw you forty minutes ago, pulling out of Rosie O'Grady's. You were headed west, away from home. You looked kind of…well, your driving was a little…anyway, thought I should check up on you. Hoped you'd turned around and made it home by now. Later.*"

"Who's Brandon Phillips?" Clarence asked.

"One of the homicide detectives."

"Who's Rosie?"

"Let's hear the other message."

This time I played my voice first. It sounded like the guy in an old Western who'd had been cut down after the lynching started and was hoarse the rest of his life. I've never smoked, but when restaurants had smoking sections, on hearing my voice they took me straight there. My voice didn't get this way because a thug smashed my Adam's apple with a crowbar (though that did happen once). It's been this way since the summer between sixth and seventh grade. Some guys wake up with a golden bass voice; I woke up with a cement truck in my throat.

After my voice, we waited for the professor's. "*11:37 p.m.*" Five seconds of nothing. No sound, except faint breathing, as if waiting for me to pick up. I played it again, turning out the lights to focus on the sound. Yeah. Breathing.

"You weren't home at 11:37?"

"Maybe not. Or I'd gone to bed. Or I was home but didn't check messages."

"That's pretty vague."

"You accusing me of something?"

"Why would I accuse you?" Clarence asked. "Just wondering why you don't remember. You answered the phone when the lieutenant called about the murder, right?"

I held up my cell. "Everything comes through this. Unless they can't get me; then they call the home number."

"Apparently the professor didn't have your cell number."

"I'd like to know how he had my home number. It's unlisted."

"What do we do now?"

"You do whatever reporters do," I said. "I'm going to sit down, have coffee, and Mulch and I are going to think this through."

"You want to cancel lunch with Jake?"

"We have to eat anyway. And it's Jake's turn to buy. Lunch isn't for six hours. I'm not canceling yet."

Clarence took off, eager to start writing, even though I warned him he couldn't say much.

Manny would make sure the crime scene was preserved. Before returning, I wanted to look over my notes. With sugarless gum in his drawer, the professor didn't strike me as a Black Jack kind of guy. His toothy grin in the photos on the mantel and the walls suggested he got his teeth polished. People who speak in public for a living don't film up their teeth with Black Jack. We Black Jack chewers are an elite group, and if we took a vote, based on his teeth, we'd kick the professor off

Black Jack Island. I bump into a Black Jack chewer once in a blue moon. There's instant camaraderie, partly because it defies all reason, like being a Raiders fan.

So what was a Black Jack wrapper doing at the professor's? And why couldn't I remember coming home? And what was with Wally's Donuts?

I plugged in my camera and downloaded my photos into my notebook computer. I went through them one by one, enlarging some. Whenever I found myself wanting a better angle, I jotted a note for when I returned.

I sat in my old brown recliner, the one Sharon special ordered and we picked up at Clemmer's Furniture, east of Gresham. I reached out and touched the horizontal eight-by-ten photo on the table next to the chair, taken ten months before Sharon died. It was of all the Portland homicide detectives and their spouses, so there were about seventeen of us in the picture, including three unmarried. It happened to be the best picture of Sharon and me anywhere. I should ask a computer nerd to do one of those Photoshop things so the picture would just be me and Sharon, maybe on a beach in Hawaii, though that wouldn't work since I was in coat and tie and she was wearing her favorite black dress. I still have that dress in the closet. Sometimes I take it out to remember her scent.

My mind went back to the crime scene. I was searching it, comparing sketch with pictures, romancing it, asking it to whisper secrets in my ear.

I heard the ring tone of the phone at CTU headquarters, where Jack Bauer works. It was my cell. "Manny" showed in the display.

"Jack Bauer," I answered.

"I sealed the crime scene. Body's been taken away."

"Where you standing?"

"By the front door, about to lock up."

"Look into the room, turn immediately to your left, and walk five feet. See that miniature bookshelf that's maybe three feet high?"

"Yeah?"

"There's a greenish book, hardcover, on top."

"How do you know—?"

"I have a photographic memory for crime scenes."

"You're in Photoshop."

"What's the book called?"

"It's by…some honcho named Bertrand Russell. Title's *Why I Am Not a Christian*."

"No kidding? Okay, leave it right there. Going fishing for witnesses?"

"Yeah. Those second-floor apartments on the next street have a clear view of the house. You?"

"Studying the scene."

"It's right here."

"You know my methods, Watson."

"Watson was a gringo."

I studied the pictures and read my notes. I printed out six photos. Next thing I knew, it was 9:15. I called Clarence and told him I was returning to the scene. I gave White's Market beef to Mulch, with a dab of Sweet Baby Ray's barbecue sauce. Then I was out the door.

I scanned titles on Palatine's bookshelves, ignoring those by German men with long last names. My eyes landed on Sherlock Holmes. I opened it up. The spine cracked, and its first few pages stuck together. Didn't take a skilled detective to figure out it was a gift Professor Smart Guy never opened. Too bad, since it beat to blazes everything else on his shelves.

When Abernathy arrived, I pointed to the Holmes book. "Watson showed Holmes to the world. Your words will immortalize me—until the afternoon, when people put the *Tribune* on the bottom of the birdcage."

"If you end up looking good, which is unlikely, you'll frame the article. If you look bad, you'll blame me and trash it. I was a sports columnist, remember? The guys who whined about my criticisms loved my praise."

"When you feature my brilliance, I'll tack it on my wall."

"You'll have to show your brilliance first."

"I have."

"I must have blinked. You didn't even know how to retrieve phone messages. And you ate a dead man's Snickers bar."

"Not going to let it drop, are you?" I leaned against the bookcase. "You want brilliance? I'll show you something I learned from Nero Wolfe and Archie Goodwin."

"You haven't told me who they are, and I'm not going to look it up."

"Nero Wolfe was the last of the great detectives. Always stayed in his old brownstone on West Thirty-fifth Street in New York. He weighed a seventh of a ton—like you only a lot shorter. He was a gourmet. Kept ten thousand orchids. Sent Archie Goodwin out to do his investigating, bringing back the facts so Wolfe could apply his brain and solve the crime."

"He wasn't real?"

"It's fiction, okay, but to me he's real. As real as you and me and Mulch and Lou's onion ring platter. Forty-seven books, written by Rex Stout. Classics. Stout was the best. Hemingway was a hack."

"So what did you learn from them that can help us?"

"Archie Goodwin once paged through every book on a shelf."

"*All* of them?" He looked at the professor's books.

"There're just a couple hundred. People can stick something important between the pages. Notes. Letters. Business cards. Then they forget them, and eventually they're back on the shelves. Hidden evidence."

"Needle in a haystack."

"We can do it in an hour or two. The point is to flip pages, not read."

After some intellectual yawners, I came to The Adventures of Huckleberry Finn. I fingered it and inhaled the smell of old pages. My grandfather used to do that, when books were few enough to instill reverence. I'd picked up the book-sniffing habit and never lost it, though it seems wasted on the slick mass-produced stuff.

Clarence and I paged through Plato. René Descartes. John Locke. Some woman named René with a mustache. Voltaire. Rousseau. Adam Smith. Kant. Nietzsche. Francis Bacon (Mulch's favorite philosopher).

"Here's a phone number inside the back cover of Karl Marx," Clarence said.

"Think it's Marx's home number?" I asked.

No response.

"Who was your favorite Marx brother? Mine was Harpo."

Still no response. I jotted down the number.

Five minutes later, Clarence said, "Here's a travel book for Maui. Same thing— phone number inside the back cover."

"We've got a pattern now. Look for it."

I remembered the green book. I went over to the small bookcase and picked up *Why I Am Not a Christian*. I slipped it in my briefcase.

We found a few more phone numbers in the backs of books—strangely, not one of them with a name.

I turned and looked around at all the mementos and photos taped, pinned, and hung on the wall. "There's lots of visual evidence in this room. It's cluttered…hard to see what's really here. I'm going to call in some eyes." I punched 2 on my cell phone, for the department.

"Mitzie? Ollie. I'm going to drop by some case notes before lunch. If you can type them this afternoon, I'd appreciate it. Hey, who's hanging around the donuts? Cimmatoni? No thanks. Anyone else? Yeah, Phillips is fine."

When Phillips came to the phone, I said, "You busy?"

"Always."

"I'm in the first twenty-four hours of this case. Could use your eyes. 2230 Southeast Oak."

"Want me to bring Cimma?"

"Uh, no…this is more up your alley. Just need one pair of eyes. Yours."

"Okay. Give me fifteen."

I sat in front of the computer. They'd removed the hard drive and taken the keyboard for computer forensics, but the monitor was still there.

"Something's wrong. Didn't think about it last night. The professor was just a couple inches shorter than me, wasn't he? This chair's way too high. If they want to use the keyboard, tall people lower the seat and short people raise it, right? Sit in this chair."

Clarence looked ridiculous, the keyboard way too low.

"How tall would someone be who'd put a chair at this setting?" I asked.

"Five foot? A woman?"

"Or a fourth grader? A jockey?" I knelt, looking at the metal rod on the chair adjustment. "See the marks? That's the normal position, the professor's setting. What does that tell you?"

"Someone else used it."

"Palatine was grading. Played solitaire. Then someone adjusted the chair. You don't do that unless you're sitting a while. If it's just a minute, why bother? I say they did it to type the confession."

"Then wouldn't their prints show up on the keyboard?"

"We'll see when tests come back." I walked toward the fireplace.

"Look at the photos on the mantel," I said. "What do you see?"

Clarence moved in for a closer look. "Mediocre quality pictures in cheap stand-up frames."

"How many?"

"Nine."

"Four on one side and five on the other," I said. "Now, look at all the picture groupings on the wall. Everything's balanced, symmetrical. So why the imbalance on the mantel?"

I stepped up onto the hearth to get a closer look. "Yeah. The dust tells the tale."

"What tale?" Clarence got on his tiptoes and could see the top without climbing.

"The four pictures on this side...they've been moved to equal spacing. But there were five pictures, just like on the other side. One picture's been taken. Someone didn't want us to notice, so he filled in the spaces."

"Why?"

"Because he thought if we noticed a photo was missing, it might incriminate him."

"How?"

"Don't know. But if it wouldn't, why cover it up? Why not just snatch the picture and forget it? He took that photo for a reason—it was important to him. But it was also important to him that we didn't notice."

"So far you've got him carrying away a wine bottle and a five-by-seven picture frame."

"There's a reason for every action. This brings us one step closer to the killer."

"Anybody home?"

Brandon Phillips is that ageless sort who looked old in his twenties when I met him and now in his forties looks young. He was a Golden Gloves boxer, rugged, leathery face like a mountain climber. Broad shoulders, big chest. And fit? I could see him offering his water to Sherpas climbing Everest as he passed them.

I introduced Phillips to Clarence and said, "I humbly request your observations on my crime scene. And thanks for not dropping by uninvited, like Suda did last night."

Phillips cleared his throat. Though we were standing right in front of the mantel, with me leaning against the brick, he walked immediately to the other end of the room. "Lots of books. Computer's nice. Wide-screen. Flat. He buys over the Internet."

"How do you know?"

"It's a Dell. I've seen that model on the website. You can only get it online. It's not available in stores…not in Portland anyway."

"See?" I said to Clarence. "You never know what you'll get from a detective."

Phillips walked around making other observations. Nothing particularly helpful.

"What about at this end? What do you see?" I pointed toward the mantel and the photos.

"Lots of pictures." Phillips coughed. He cleared his throat and rubbed his face.

"You okay?"

"I need the bathroom." He walked quickly around the corner and I heard the door shut.

"What's with him?" Clarence asked.

I shrugged. He came back five minutes later.

"Anything wrong?" I asked.

"Allergies. I'm fine."

"So, what do you see on this mantel?"

"He's no photographer."

"Yeah, but proud of his work. Nine photos up there, huh?" I pointed to the mantel.

"Hang on. I have to call Cimma." Phillips stepped into the other room, and I heard his muffled voice. A minute later he reappeared. "Cimma needs me."

"I didn't think Cimma needed anybody."

"One more witness on our case. Cimma wants me to see if I can catch him before lunch. Sorry."

Fifteen seconds later Phillips was gone. I looked at Clarence and shrugged.

I swung by detective division at eleven to drop off case notes for Mitzie to type. I was fortunate to find one of the precious few police only parking spaces on Second Street, just south of Madison, a stone's throw from the Justice Center. I was back in my car ten minutes later because though Lou's Diner is only five blocks away, the midday sky was dark, threatening rain. It looked like it had been rubbed hard with gray finger paint. It made me thirsty.

I got to Lou's early enough to think through the case before Jake and Clarence arrived. And have a couple of beers. Lou's is "The Diner Time Forgot." The jukebox was playing "Surfin' USA." Archie, Betty, and Veronica could have been sitting in the next booth. I'd be Jughead, since I play his part, downing the cheeseburgers.

I love old diners, but nothing compares to this one. Lou's son Rory keeps the place sparkling, unlike Ralph's Diner on Ankeny, where you need a crowbar to remove syrup bottles from the lazy Susan.

Three years ago, Jake, Clarence, and I started meeting at Lou's on Thursdays for lunch. We all work downtown, so we rarely miss, and work in a second lunch during the week whenever we can. We shoot the breeze about lots of things, but sometimes Jake gets us talking about…well, spiritual stuff. Once they tried to get me to read something called *The Purpose-Driven Life*. I told them I already had a purpose-driven life. Justice—hunting down criminals in a Clint Eastwood, Chuck Norris, Jack Bauer sort of way. I don't see religion as a solution, but a problem. My job is to hunt down the bad guys God lets get away. Jake said maybe I'm serving God's ends and He's using me to get the bad guys. Whatever.

We can hardly have lunch without the afterlife intruding into the conversation. But I don't want to die trusting that God will make things okay. I want to make them okay right here, right now. Is that so much to ask? If I can make things right, I do. So if God can make things right, why doesn't He?

These are not popular questions to ask Christians. Jake and Clarence listen and nod and say they understand my questions, that they too once struggled with such things. But I must have faith, I must trust, I must believe, and all will be better. Well, sorry, but I just *don't*. And most of the time, frankly, I don't want to.

Sometimes these guys are stubborn and opinionated. I feel like they're taking the moral high ground, like the rest of us aren't good enough for them. I guess I'm saying ours is a complicated friendship.

I looked at my watch. 11:52. I waved to Rory and pulled out my wallet. "This is for my beers."

"I can just put it on your bill," he said.

"Jake's turn to buy. And take my bottles and the glass, would you?"

"I brewed your dark Italian roast extra bold. You'll love it."

"You're a good man, Rory. If you ever get murdered, I'll go after the guy. That's a promise."

"*Grazie*, Mr. Ollie."

Okay, I feel guilty for what I said about Jake and Clarence. Because there's another side, and I guess it's why I keep meeting them for lunch. The conversations sometimes bug me, but they make me think. Occasionally they're downright interesting. And yes, Jake asked my permission, and I've agreed to talk about the Bible now and then. These guys aren't total morons, and they have hope. I admit that it seems a naive and baseless hope. And yet…there's a certain comfort in being around people who really believe—deep in their gut—that one day things will be better than they are now.

It seems like if you become a Christian, everything's supposed to be great, right? You live happily ever after because you go to heaven, and that makes up for life's miseries. Never mind that people—like my Sharon—suffer and die, and murderers get away. After all, there's pie in the sky by and by.

Sorry, but I'd rather have my pie here and now. Speaking of which, I'd noticed that huckleberry was Lou's pie of the day.

My phone rang. Manny again.

"You need to listen to the 911 call about the professor."

"Who called? A neighbor?"

"Didn't identify himself. Came from a cell phone, but wasn't traceable. It was an old one without GPS. Dispatch sent us an audio file."

"I'm going back to the scene after lunch. Then I'll swing by the office and listen to the call."

Jake appeared that moment, smiled broadly, shook my hand with a vise grip, and sat down. We traded small talk, exchanging theories on the Seahawks. Pretty soon we were laughing.

Clarence arrived and sat next to Jake. It's a big booth, but their side was suddenly full.

Nobody had to look at the menu. Rory came over and asked, "The usual?" Everyone nodded. Lou's serves a mean cheeseburger.

"Okay," Jake said. "Last week we said we'd read the first eight chapters of the book of John. How'd we do?"

"I had a busy week," I said. "Couldn't squeeze it in."

"Five minutes a day or one reading of half an hour? Come on. That's just a sitcom."

"I like sitcoms better."

"John 8 relates to your work as a detective."

"How's that?"

Jake opened his Bible, full of underlines. "Jesus says, 'If you hold to my teaching, you are really my disciples. Then you will know the truth, and the truth will set you free.' He says the truth will set us free from lies."

"Whose truth we talkin' about?"

"*The* truth. He says we're slaves, but 'if the Son sets you free, you will be free indeed.' He's talking about freedom from deception."

"Every day I sift through the lies people tell," I said. "I dig for the truth all the time."

"I'm grateful you do, Ollie. We all benefit from your work. Now check out what Jesus says about Satan in the next verse: 'He was a murderer from the beginning, not holding to the truth, for there is no truth in him. When he lies, he speaks his native language, for he is a liar and the father of lies.' So Satan is a murderer, and he lies to cover up his murders. That should interest a homicide detective."

"The devil must be a good liar," I said.

"The best," Jake said. "Lying is his native language."

"The truth challenges our assumptions," Clarence said. "It's more comfortable just to believe the lies. We fall for lies because we're wired that way."

"In my work, deception is fatal."

"Jesus said the truth sets us free," Jake said. "In an investigation, once you see through the lies, when you discover the truth, don't you feel free?"

"It's an adrenaline rush. Nothing like it."

"Well, then, we'll pray that God will help you see the truth. To see through the lies."

"What do you mean?"

"In your investigation. The Palatine case."

"Okay. I guess your prayers can't hurt."

"Who knows?" Jake said with a cocky smile. "Since it's the God of all truth and the Enemy of all deception that we're praying to, our prayers may even help."

"Fine," I said. "Fine" is what Jack Bauer and Chloe say whenever they don't like a situation, such as having to cooperate with terrorists.

I escaped by going over to the jukebox, a vintage Rock-Ola straight from the sixties boasting "Stereo" in ostentatious letters, like they'd split the atom. Three songs for a quarter, just like the old days. Rory told me he'd added new selections. I spotted one and selected C3: "Bridge over Troubled Water."

"Wow," Jake said. "Takes me back to Nam."

I nodded. As we listened, Jake and I relived memories half a world away and almost a lifetime ago. Clarence was probably thinking of his brother who died in Nam. I found myself sitting in the Mekong Delta with Neal Crane, a Mississippi farm boy, and listening to Simon and Garfunkel in the evening, when it cooled down to the midnineties.

I heard Neal's twang as he said, "What's up, bro?" and backslapped me with his big right arm. Neal and I would talk about friendlies and hostiles, about Old Miss football, about our dreams after the war, maybe living near each other and raising our families. Two months later Neal stepped on a land mine. He was gone.

Rory waded into our sea of Garfunkel-induced melancholy to bring us burgers and onion rings. That quickly we were back at Lou's, jibing and laughing again.

Jake and Clarence turned down dessert, but it didn't keep them from hefty bites of my huckleberry pie with French vanilla ice cream. Clarence took some extra insulin. I sipped my coffee. The pot Rory brewed for me was nice and dark, which is why I always go over the top and give him a 10 percent tip.

"Okay if I talk about the investigation?" I asked, noting the closest people were sitting three booths away. "Off the record?"

They nodded. I got up and put quarters in the jukebox to get cover from the Four Seasons, Turtles, and Monkees. There's a speaker over our booth that projects into the room but allows us to hear each other.

I told Jake about the solitaire game and the ace of spades.

"At first I thought it proved he was interrupted. He was about to play the ace, but something happened—phone rang, somebody came to the door, he heard a noise outside, whatever. But now I don't buy it. Interrupted before you turn it over? Sure. But after you see the ace? Nah. Phone rings, teakettle whistles, someone comes to the door, maybe you stop turning cards. But once you turn up an ace, you play it instantly, before anything else."

"You make it sound like a science," Clarence said.

"I was testing it last night. You see an ace, you play it, in a heartbeat."

"Yet there it sat," Clarence said. "So what's your point?"

"Somebody else placed it, not Palatine. Probably the murderer. Pulled it out of the deck after he killed the professor."

"You're sure?"

"Somebody sat down in front of the cards and messed with them...and maybe turned to type that stuff on the computer too. And why the ace of spades? Random? I don't think so."

"Isn't it the death card?" Jake asked.

"Exactly. Symbolism."

"But who kills someone, then sits around fiddling with cards?" Jake said. "Why risk being caught?"

"Maybe he was relishing what he'd done," I said. "But he was unusually comfortable at a murder scene. Why wasn't he more afraid of being caught? Consider the time involved with the rope, typing, messing with playing cards."

"It's like he was waiting for something," Jake said.

"Waiting for him to die?" Clarence asked.

"And when he'd waited long enough, he put the bullets in his chest. Then there's the wineglasses."

"Wineglasses?" Clarence asked.

"In the sink. You were off with Carp when I found them. Two wineglasses with a white wine residue. Couldn't see fingerprints."

"What do you think it means?"

"Maybe the professor had a guest earlier, came and went before the murder. But why wipe prints off the glasses? Could be the murderer was his guest. If they're drinking together, he knows him."

"Then he'd have good reason to wipe the glasses," Jake said. "His anyway."

"But where's the wine bottle? Not in the house. Not in the trash. Nowhere. Manny searched, and he's good. Looks like the killer took it. Why? Why take the risk of carrying a wine bottle from a murder scene if you don't want to be noticed and might need to run?"

We sat there quietly. No takers.

"I've got questions too," Clarence said. "Like, why didn't the neighbors hear the gunshots?"

"Could've had a silencer," I said. "Then the shots aren't much louder than a cough. Not enough to wake someone. If it was an apartment in the still of the night maybe, but not in a house next door or across the street."

Sherlock Holmes smoked while contemplating evidence and occasionally listened to himself play the violin. We sipped Rory's dark Italian coffee. And listened to the Rock-Ola spin a 45, "It Ain't Me, Babe."

"Ollie Chandler doesn't understand, does he?"

"Even Jake and Clarence don't fully understand."

"Yes, but they know the One who knows all. And therefore they have a framework to understand what Ollie can't."

"And yet he seeks the truth, doesn't he?"

"He seeks one kind of truth. The kind that leads to the incrimination and capture of others. He seeks truth that will expose them and justify himself. But does he seek truth that would expose himself?"

"Does any man seek such truth unless the King empowers him?"

"There's always much to be learned from watching them, isn't there?"

"Yes. Just as there was much to be learned from watching us when we walked that world."

I drove toward the professor's house, preoccupied. Suddenly I realized I'd gone three blocks too far. It was an unfamiliar part of town. I turned around at the next driveway, circling quickly by a little hole-in-the-wall with an old beat-up sign. It said "Wally's Donuts." I braked and swung back into the parking lot, popping the car into park before it stopped, lurching. I looked at the donut box still sitting in the passenger seat.

Wally's Donuts.

The guy didn't speak English, but after I showed him my badge, he got me on the phone with Big Wally himself, who said he'd closed the place up at ten thirty last night, but they have a Wednesday night special on donuts in the dozen and half dozen boxes, and they probably sold six hundred donuts to eighty different people, and he's bad with faces, and it's all cash, no credit or debit cards, so no records.

Back in my car, I stared at a donut and a box. I closed my eyes and walked through the scattered events of the night before, moving the jigsaw pieces around, trying to make them fall into place.

They wouldn't.

THURSDAY, NOVEMBER 21, 1:30 P.M.

TAPED TO MY DASHBOARD are the words of Detective Hercule Poirot: "It is the brain, the little gray cells, on which one must rely. One must seek the truth within—not without."

I was searching inside myself, looking for the truth. I was pondering the professor but also thinking, inexplicably, of Jimmy Ross and Lincoln Caldwell. That irritated me.

As a detective, sometimes you sense something's wrong, but you don't know what. Something was wrong on my old case, and plenty was wrong on my new one. My little gray cells were telling me that.

When I arrived back at the crime scene, I decided to call in more eyes to help me see what I was missing.

"Jack? You're in Lloyd Center area, right? How's your case going?"

"All done but the paperwork. Guy shot his wife's boyfriend. He confessed. Open and shut. I hear we both got called to murders the same night. Yours as easy as ours?"

"I don't think so. We're back at the house of the professor who lost his tenure last night. I need a second opinion."

"Noel's with me."

"Bring him."

After I gave Jack the address, Clarence—pen and pad in hand—asked, "More detectives? Is it normal to do all this consulting?"

"Never did it in the old days. But they've changed policy. We've had too many cases where something important was missed that other guys would've noticed. Someone who knows electrical work, plumbing, music, or art will pick up on things another detective misses. Phillips knows his Dell computers. Probably makes no difference, but it could. So we help each other out. It's fun to get called to a scene where you don't have to do the grunt work. You can just look around and throw out your ideas like you're a character in a murder mystery."

↔

I heard the sound of heavy shoes. Next thing I knew, one of those shoes stepped on my foot.

"That's inappropriate behavior," I told Noel Barrows.

Noel's a good golfer, but it's all in his arms and wrists. His feet are klutzy.

"Sorry." Noel smiled like a schoolboy.

Okay, he's a likable klutz. Especially likable at a poker game, where he's as excited by a good hand as a little girl at her birthday party. He doesn't know the meaning of a poker face. Which is why we always invite him back.

Jack shook my hand, then saw Clarence, who you don't have to be a detective to notice. "Clarence Abernathy, right?"

He nodded.

"Jack Glissan. My partner's Noel Barrows. I used to love your column."

"Used to?" I heard the smile in my voice.

"You're still a great writer. I just read you more when you did sports."

"Jack started as a detective back when they solved crimes the old-fashioned way," I said. "Killing a chicken and examining its entrails."

"Twenty years ago this month, on November 4," Jack said, "Ollie and I started our three-year partnership as detectives." He paused. "It was the worst three years of my life."

I laughed. "He's joking," I said to Clarence. "He loved me as a partner."

Jack shook his head, deadpan.

"They assigned you to Ollie, Clarence?" Jack asked. "What'd you do to deserve that kind of punishment?"

"That's what I've been asking myself."

"Jack's got lots of candles on his cake," I said, "but the frosting's still moist. And they say Abernathy's okay too, once you get used to him. I haven't gotten used to him. Okay, guys, look around the room. Tell me what you see."

"Guy was playing cards with somebody?" Jack walked over to the table by the computer. "No, looks like solitaire. They're running prints on the cards, obviously. Was the computer on?"

"Yeah. Interesting message typed in." I handed him a printout of the supposed confession.

"Sound like something he'd write?"

"No," I said.

"The killer wrote it?"

"Maybe."

Jack pointed to the two piles of student papers. "Gonna read 'em?"

"Think it's worth it?"

"Probably not. But you never know."

I looked at Clarence. "You have to sift through lots of rocks and mud to find the gold."

He jotted it down. Maybe I'd have to read the *Tribune* after all.

I played the professor's message machine, with the Nietzsche quote. Jack raised his eyebrows and Noel grinned.

"What a piece of work," Jack said. "Guess I shouldn't speak ill of the dead, but…"

"Pretentious, wasn't he?" I said. "Any advice?"

"Check students' grades," Jack said. "Who'd the professor fail last semester that kept him from graduating or made him lose a scholarship or go on drugs or take up shoplifting? Anybody with an ax to grind."

"It's all about motive," I said to Clarence. I pointed the guys toward the mantel. "Check out the pictures."

Jack looked them over. "He's in half of these himself, mostly with students. Look, he's ten years younger in this picture. Maybe five years in this one. And that one looks recent, judging by the gray hairs. It's like he never took his pictures down. He only added. Check out that bulletin board. He's got pictures tacked on pictures. There must be a hundred of them."

"One hundred nineteen," I said. "Lots of them are group photos, so there's got to be five hundred people in these, mostly students. Guess he hadn't heard about photo albums. The place is neat and tidy, except for these pictures. Looks like a third of them were taken right here. Apparently he handed off his camera so he could be in them. Wanted to remind himself how handsome he was."

"And how young and attractive his students are," Clarence said.

Jack studied the pictures closely. "Did he have family?"

"Father's deceased, mother's in a rest home. Brother's a doctor. Manny checked into him. They fight a lot."

"Brothers do that," Clarence said.

Jack and Noel nodded. So did I. I haven't talked with my brother for two years.

Noel kept staring at the mantel. "Something's fishy," he finally said. He paused, looking side to side like we were under FBI surveillance. He whispered, as if a high-powered eavesdropping device were pointed at us. "Something's really fishy."

"Am I supposed to ask, 'What's fishy?' Noel, or are you going to tap it out on my foot in Morse code?"

"I'm telling you, it's fishy."

"You're telling me nothing. Telling is when you get to the part after 'it's fishy.'"

Noel turned and said, "Okay, I'll tell you."

"Good," I said. "I was just about to do a Jack Bauer and hook you up to battery cables."

"Don't you love that show? Remember the one where Tony shoots the—"

"Shut up and tell me what's fishy!"

"Somebody removed a picture," Noel said. "See, there's four on this side and five on that side." He climbed on the hearth and pointed to the top of the mantel. "Look at the dust. They've been moved recently. I don't think the dead guy did it, because everything else is...arranged just right."

"Symmetrical," I said.

"Couldn't there have been an odd number of pictures to start with?" Clarence asked.

"He'd have put one in the middle," Jack said.

Jack put his arm around Noel, twenty-five years his junior. "Good catch. Let him focus and he earns his paycheck."

"If we find that picture," I said, "I bet we'll solve this crime."

"There's a possible witness here at those apartments with the view of Oak Street," Manny told me on the phone. "She saw something, but she's a case. Maybe you can charm her. She's your type. Second floor. 205. Name's Rebecca Butler."

Twenty minutes later Clarence and I were standing outside apartment 205. Painted lime green, the hallway was a fake clean with the smell of heavy chemicals that sterilize dirt without removing it. Four decades of cumulative neglect.

I knocked.

"Who's it?" a woman's voice shouted.

"Detective Ollie Chandler. Police."

"That spic send you?" Still shouting.

"Officer Domast? He's my partner."

"Too bad for you," she said, now peering through the fish-eye. "Don't look like a cop. Why should I believe you're a cop? Show me a donut."

"Crack the door, and I'll show you my badge."

"After you tie me up and rob me. Hold it up to the peephole."

I held up my badge.

"Move it to the right. No the other way. No, not that close. You're dumb enough to be a cop."

Finally the dead bolt snapped back, but the door didn't open.

I waited.

"You didn't open the door," I called, not letting my voice in on my attitude.

"You can't open a door yourself? It's not much harder than pickin' up a donut."
Two donut cracks and we weren't even in the door.

"We can come in?"

"It's unlocked," she called. "I'm watching my soaps."

We walked into a living room that looked like it had thrown up on itself.

She was sitting, curled up in a seventies recliner, wearing sweatpants and a mustard-stained undersized T-shirt that showed way more than I wanted to see. She was surrounded by a bag of Lay's potato chips and a jumbo bag of Cheetos, a liter of Pepsi plus two empties, and stained paper plates.

Her eyes were close-set, squinty and molelike, as if she hadn't seen the sun for a year. Her age was a difficult call. Forty-five? People don't age as much when they don't see the sun. Cheetos and Lay's probably help the skin too with all that oil. Like her apartment building, she was showing forty years of cumulative neglect. If she'd been painted lime green, it would have been a perfect match.

She didn't look up until the commercial, ten seconds after we entered.

"I'm Ollie. This is—"

"Who's the black guy?"

"Clarence. He's studying to be a cop when he grows up. Pretend he's not here. He's used to it."

"Can you dunk it?" she asked him.

"I used to be able to," Clarence said.

"Too fat now, huh?"

He said nothing, but his eyes spoke volumes. Forgoing handwritten notes, he flipped open his PDA, stylus in hand.

"I thought you people could dunk it even when you're old and fat. Hey, do you know Stevie Wonder?"

"Not personally."

"I like his music. Tell him for me, would you? 'Tutti Frutti's my favorite."

"That was Little Richard," Clarence said.

"And 'Hit the Road Jack.'"

"Ray Charles."

"You know them, too?"

"Yeah. Stevie, Richard, Ray, and I meet for chitlins and cornbread every Friday night."

Not bad, I nodded to Clarence. "Mrs. Butler, could you—"

"I'm not a Mrs. My no-good husband left me."

"Ms. Butler, could—"

"I'm not one of those either."

"Miss Butler—"

"Do I look like I'm nineteen?"

"No," I said. "You certainly don't."

"What's that supposed to mean?"

"Only that you are a youthful yet mature woman. May I call you Rebecca?"

"Friends call me Becky."

"All right, Becky, did you—"

"We're not friends."

"Okay…did you see a man come out of the professor's house last night?"

"Who's the professor?"

"The man who lives in the house where you told my partner—"

"The spic?"

"We prefer to call him Hispanic. You told my partner you saw a man come out of the professor's house."

"Whatever."

"What did he look like?"

"The spic? Short and wiry. Burr under his saddle."

"No. I mean the man coming out the professor's door…the man you saw. What did he look like?"

"Like Abraham Lincoln," she said.

Now we were getting somewhere. Abe Lincoln wouldn't blend into a crowd. "Tall?" I asked.

"No. Medium. About my brother's size."

"How tall's your brother?"

"I'm not on trial here. Neither's my brother."

"You mentioned your brother. I've not had the privilege of meeting him."

"It's no privilege."

"Is he six feet tall?"

"Who?"

"Your brother."

"You're still on my brother?"

"I'll get off your brother as soon as you answer my question. Is he six feet tall?"

"My brother? You crazy?"

"Look, ma'am, I've never seen your brother. I can't begin to guess how tall he is. I'm assuming you *have* seen him. Could you just take a guess?"

"Six inches taller than me."

"How tall are you?" She was still sitting, like she'd been poured into the recliner.

"You going to ask me how much I weigh, too?"

"Only if you tell me your brother weighs forty pounds more than you."

She glared at me.

"Could you stand, please?"

"I've been up and down all day, answering the phone and the door and trying to fix the antenna for my soaps, and now you're asking me to stand?"

My face, if it was following orders, looked earnest and sympathetic. "I've got all day, but I don't want you to miss your soaps. How about you stand just for a second then answer a few more questions, and we'll leave you alone?"

She stood slowly, but it didn't take long for her to get straight.

Five-foot-one, at most.

"Then your brother's about five seven?"

"You tell me."

"If he were my brother, I would."

"Don't get smart with me, Kojak."

She aimed a frown at me, and when I wouldn't let it land, she aimed it at Clarence. It landed.

"I'm not getting smart," I said. "You'll know when I get smart. So was he thin?"

"He used to be, but he's been laid off and watches lots of TV. Loves the soaps and *Oprah* and *Dr. Phil*. He's put on fifty pounds."

"Who are you talking about?"

"My brother!" She looked at me like I was a finalist on *American Idiot*.

"Let's forget about your brother, okay?"

"It's about time. I told you he has nothing to do with this. He's written bad checks and spent time in the pokey, but he's no killer. And for sure he doesn't know any professors."

"I'll bet he doesn't. How about the man who was at the professor's door? Was he thin?"

"Nope. Pudgy. Like you."

Clarence looked up from his PDA. He folded the lid.

I paused, putting my tongue between my teeth to keep them from locking. "Did I miss an episode?"

"Whatcha mean?" she asked.

"I mean…in what way did this man remind you of Abraham Lincoln?"

"He had a beard!" she said, with a look that confirmed I wasn't merely a finalist for *American Idiot*, but had been crowned.

"Lots of hair?"

"He was bald."

I stared at her, giving the words time to go through my universal translator. It wasn't working. "Bald…like Abraham Lincoln?"

"Don't know if Lincoln was bald. He always wore a hat."

"Not when he bathed."

"What are you, a pervert?"

"No, ma'am. So, you're saying he was short, mostly bald, pudgy, and looked like Abraham Lincoln? I'm glad to hear he had a beard."

"*Of course* he had a beard. How could he look like Lincoln and not have a beard?"

"Black?"

"Nope. I told you, he was a white guy."

"Do you think he could dunk it?" I couldn't resist. It was worth it to see Abernathy. "What I meant is was his *beard* black?"

"Not many blacks in this building," she said.

"How fortunate for them," Clarence muttered.

"I repeat—was his beard black?"

"No way. This guy was…maybe Swedish. A pale face. What's that other country that's part of Sweden?"

"Norway?"

"Yeah, he looked sort of like one of those cow milkers with their red barns. Yellow hair. Funny accents. Go out naked in the freezing water."

"You heard his voice?"

"How could I hear his voice? He was across the street, and *Law & Order* was on. It was during the last commercial."

I jotted it down. That put it around 10:50.

"You said he was bald, but he had yellow hair?"

"Yeah. The part that wasn't bald was blond. You know, like what's-his-name, the football announcer…Terry Bradshaw? The guy that played for the Cowboys?"

"Steelers. He played for the Pittsburgh Steelers."

"Did not."

"Did too. So the beard was blond?"

"Grayish. Salt-and-pepper. But more salt than pepper. More like Lawry's seasoned salt. You know, sort of orangish."

"An orange beard?"

"Just a tint of orange, that's all I'm saying."

"What was he wearing?"

"Jeans. Coat. Shoes. I dunno. Plus the stocking cap."

"Stocking cap?"

"Yeah. It was black. Or green. Could've been blue. Hard to tell it was so dark out."

I paused, sorting it through. "If he had on a stocking cap, how do you know he was bald…and blond?"

"Look, don't try to make this my problem. I didn't kill Dr. Einstein."

Sometimes you keep fishing; sometimes you just cut bait and walk.

"We'll be going now," I said. "We have business elsewhere."

She waved her hand, grabbed the remote, and turned up the volume.

"Where's our business?" Clarence asked as we shut the door behind us.

"On planet earth."

He scrunched his face. "Maybe you cops earn your pay after all."

"I may be King of the Idiots," I said, "but my kingdom is vast, and my subjects are everywhere."

*"Is there any point to which you would
wish to draw my attention?"*
"To the curious incident of the dog in the night-time."
"The dog did nothing in the night-time."
"That was the curious incident."
SHERLOCK HOLMES, *SILVER BLAZE*

THURSDAY, NOVEMBER 21, 6:30 P.M.

WE HAD THREE more interviews after Rebecca Butler, but hers turned out to be the most productive. At least we got a time, 10:50 p.m., when a man, the Abraham Lincoln clone, came to the front door. Maybe. If it was the right night. And right program. And right commercial break. And right house...Dr. Einstein's.

I headed home in thick traffic on a stormy afternoon, dark clouds pressing on the car tops. Driving was slow, and radio didn't interest me. When I'm caught in traffic on a rainy day, sometimes my car becomes a cocoon, and I'm transferred back to childhood. Thoughts from long ago resurfaced. Those led me into a series of reflections, somewhat random, but related at their core.

My grandmother was a Baptist, and she took it out on the rest of us. She told me God was watching. He was out to get me when I did something bad. This meant He was out to get me seventy times a day. Grandma's favorite phrase was "the day of reckoning." Since she believed that most of what I wanted was sinful, I knew I'd be toast on the day of reckoning. It scared me. That was her point. Drive the fear of God into me.

It had a side effect she didn't intend.

God reading my mind and spying on me and wanting to skewer me made Him seem petty. Like He had nothing better to do than wait until I thought or did something wrong...which, trust me, would never be a long wait.

My options were to disbelieve in Him. Or give up trying to please Him. Or live with constant guilt because I wasn't the kind of person He—and my grandmother—wanted me to be. I've never been a big fan of helpless, self-flagellating guilt, so I turned away from "spiritual things" to "worldly things." I liked cars, sports, girls, and everything else that sends a guy to hell.

Jake Woods assures me that not all Baptists are like my grandmother. I have no plans to find out.

I'm not religious, but that doesn't mean I don't care about whether things are right. I care about that more than anything.

If I told you "Justice is my middle name," it might surprise you that I mean it literally. My given name is Oliver Justice Chandler. My middle name came from my mother's grandfather, Justice Elwin Carlson, a bricklayer. His father had lived in Justice, Illinois. He was named after a town, not a virtue. But the name Justice shaped me.

As a kid, I wasn't wild about Oliver, but I was proud of my middle name. My favorite comic book? *The Brave and the Bold*, featuring the Justice League of America. My favorite Justice Leaguer? Green Lantern, test pilot Hal Jordan, given the ring of power by a dying alien. I dreamed about the Justice League, about flying in with my green cape and rescuing people and making things right. I wore a green ring to bed every night for five years. I'd take my flashlight under my covers and read comics way past midnight, waking up with my face on the pages.

At age ten, I recited Green Lantern's words a bazillion times a day. Fifty years later, as Mulch would testify if he could, the words still roll off my tongue: "In brightest day, in darkest night, no evil shall escape my sight. Let those who worship evil's might, beware my power…Green Lantern's light!"

Hal Jordan's closest friend was Green Arrow, real name Oliver Queen, so my first name made the big time too. But Green Arrow's powers weren't great enough for me—I wanted to protect the solar system, Green Lantern style. As far back as I can remember, this passion for justice fueled me.

I didn't feel like waiting until some far-off day of reckoning. When guys ganged up on somebody, I went after them. I figured, if you can do the reckoning today, why wait? Green Lantern wouldn't.

As the years went on, my little boy's naïveté gave way to the cruel facts of life. I sort of believed in God when I was a kid, but it didn't hold up. When you once had faith and no longer do, I suppose it's like a woman carrying a dead baby. The sight of live babies becomes painful. Maybe that's why Jake and Clarence bother me sometimes. But I guess I never had a faith of my own. It was my grandmother's, foisted upon me like a backpack loaded with stones, strapped to me till I was big enough to cast it off.

In the months before she died, Sharon ended up believing like the Christians. I saw the peace it gave her, but you know what—people find peace believing in Krishna or the Dalai Lama or Oprah or chocolate or multilevel marketing.

I don't doubt Geneva Abernathy's or Janet Woods's sincerity—I'll always be grateful for the care they gave Sharon when she was dying. But I sort of think they took advantage of my wife. She needed encouragement. But Christianity? I thought we were doing okay without it. I was there for her. I felt like they were saying, and she was saying, she needed someone else.

Before I lost her to death, I'd already lost her to Jesus.

↔

The dark was already two hours old when I turned up the street to the old brownstone, 151st and Yamhill. It's actually a single-story ranch house, built in 1968. But I call it "the old brownstone" because that's what Archie Goodwin named the three-level house in New York City where he lived with Nero Wolfe, detective genius.

The moment I turned the corner onto Yamhill, I slowed to a crawl. The living room light of the old brownstone was on, as it should have been. But the light in my office, which I keep on through the dark winter, wasn't.

Any normal person would assume the bulb had burned out. But I'm a cop. I parked roadside, sixty feet from my house. I approached the house like a black cat. A cat with Daddy Glock in one paw and Baby Glock strapped to his ankle.

I ducked under the bedroom window and moved across the front porch, then slowly turned the front doorknob. Locked, as I'd left it. I inserted the key and quietly opened the door. A loud noise followed, then a jumping movement, straight at me.

"Hello, boy," I whispered. "You don't have company, do you?"

Something in Mulch's eyes kept my guard up. When your dog greets you the same way every day, you know when something's different. I walked back to my office, which years ago had been Kendra's bedroom. The door was shut. But I never shut that door. The office has a western exposure, and Mulch likes to bask in the afternoon sunlight, which is why I leave the blinds open…and the door.

I entered and looked at the office window, seeing the back side of my security sticker that warns you a SWAT team, two Black Hawks, Vin Diesel, and Force 10 from Navarone will appear if you even think about intruding. I'm too cheap to actually pay for the service, but the stickers were three for a buck, and there's no monthly charge.

Window was unlocked. I'd opened it yesterday for fresh air, but surely I'd relocked it. I always do.

I examined the floor for footprints. Nothing.

I poked the barrel of my Glock into the mirrored sliding closet door and pushed it open slowly. I got it open a foot, then yanked. It slammed against the far side. Mulch barked up a storm, then jumped and grabbed a coat sleeve, pulling it to the ground.

It was an old army surplus coat I'd used for hunting a few times. Mulch taught it a lesson it won't soon forget.

I checked the rest of the house systematically. Everything appeared secure. My Browning was in the middle cabinet. I reached below the bathroom sink, behind the Lysol, and checked my Kimber Gold Math .45. Since kids never visit the old brownstone, I'd hidden it there, figuring if under fire I'd be on the ground, so it was a good place for it. I breathed easier, knowing all my babies were sleeping peacefully.

I went back to the office to see if the desk lamp bulb was burned out. I turned the switch. Light.

Had I forgotten to leave it on? Maybe. But turning it on was as routine as making coffee. And the door closed? I turned on the hallway light. Scratch marks all over the door. Fresh? I could see grooved varnish. I put a sheet of printer paper under Mulch's front right paw. I ran my hand over the paw and several brown flecks dropped to the paper. Perfect match. He'd been trying to get in the door.

Was he going after an intruder?

I looked at his worried eyes. "Talk to me, boy. Tell me what happened here."

I don't know where instinct comes from. I've heard about whale language and saw a film about how bees convey information to each other. And read a book about a gorilla named Sema who used sign language to communicate abstract concepts. I'm telling you, animals are smart. Generally you can trust them more than people. But when it comes to extracting detailed information from dogs, it's not easy.

Mulch looked at me with such earnestness that for a split second I thought he was going to spill it. If there's a world where dogs talk, I'd like to live there. But tonight Mulch's lips were sealed.

I grabbed a bag of carrots. I don't eat them, but Mulch does. Once he finishes his meat, I've seen him go for carrots and corn before apple pie. He even likes broccoli and cauliflower, especially with a dab of gravy. This came in handy when Sharon was on a crusade to feed me vegetables. I'd shovel them under the table to Mulch. In biology this is called a symbiotic relationship. It means everybody's happy.

We had Dinty Moore beef stew with Jiffy cornbread muffins, which always soothes him. I made a fire and pulled my recliner toward it, then turned on Rex Stout's *Over My Dead Body*. I lined up my Budweisers while Nero Wolfe and Archie Goodwin came into my living room, read by Michael Pritchard, who seems like an old friend now. Mulch usually lies on the right side of my recliner, where I reach down to stroke him. This time he crawled up on my lap. He's a lot of dog. But then, I've got a lot of lap.

With my left hand, I reached to the inside back flap of the recliner and felt for the duct tape, and under it the 9 mm SIG-Sauer P226. I looked at the coffee table, two feet from my elevated slippers, at the three-year-old Family Circle magazine. It was Sharon's. I could never bring myself to throw it out. Next to Sharon's magazine lay one of my best old friends besides Mulch, Jake Woods, and Mr. Coffee…Daddy Glock.

Nothing like a cozy Oregon night in the old brownstone.

Manny and I sat at our adjoining workstations, forty feet into homicide detail, to the right of the aisle. Conference rooms and offices are to the left. My desk reaches to the windows. Manny's desktop has pictures of his wife and kids and is otherwise squeaky clean. I have a few snapshots of Sharon, oases in the midst of a hopeless desert of papers, some from cases closed three months ago. It only takes me ten minutes to clear off my desk, but requires an empty drawer to stuff it all into. No drawers were currently empty.

Manny and I had been discussing the case for over an hour, disagreeing in our interpretations of the evidence whenever possible. When Clarence showed up, Manny disappeared.

"It's confirmed," I told Clarence. "The killer used the professor's keyboard."

"Fingerprints?"

"Nope."

"Then how do you know?"

"Because no prints. They were wiped clean."

Out of the blue, Clarence asked, "How's Kendra?"

He'd taken me by surprise. He nodded at the picture where she and Sharon were hugging.

"Your daughter."

"I know who she is."

"I haven't seen her for years," Clarence said. "Not since…Sharon's funeral."

"Haven't seen much of her myself. She's…I don't know. Something's wrong with our chemistry. One of us needs our fuse box rewired. Kendra's granola. Hates anything you have to plug in, unless it's a computer, a microwave, or a hair dryer. She says the advancements of civilization have ruined the environment. She used to tell me how air conditioners are killing us. Then we had that hot summer, and she got an air conditioner at Costco. I made the mistake of mentioning it."

"Do you call her?"

"I saw her every few months after Sharon died. Then it was only on Thanksgiving and Christmas. Then Thanksgiving was so awkward she started making excuses about Christmas. Everything I say irritates her."

"You? Irritating?"

"Once when she came over she had a bumper sticker on her car that said, 'Meat is murder.' So I said, 'If meat is murder, I'm a serial killer.' That's how our night started."

"Still no word from Andrea?"

Just hearing her name felt like a punch in the gut. I told Clarence I needed to take a walk. I took the elevator to ground level and walked the streets around the Justice Center. The clean rain fell lightly on my eyelashes, an occasional drop hanging on for dear life before plunging to the pavement. Just when I thought I'd adjusted to the cold, a gust of wind rushed up Madison to quick-freeze my lashes, winter reminding me that it had a lot more to dish out and it would do it in its own sweet time.

The good thing about winters is they're always followed by spring. You remember what it was two months ago, and you reassure yourself with what it will be like two months from now.

Andrea's my older daughter. Always troubled. Only her mom could keep her stable. And after Sharon died, Andrea floundered. Six months later she disappeared. No forwarding address. I've made a hundred calls. Friends say she's never contacted them. She ran away as a kid, and she's run away as an adult. I keep thinking she'll come back, that one day I'll get a call. Hasn't happened.

I walked the concrete maze, taking Madison to Second, then to Jefferson, around the Federal Building. I stared into cracks only to periodically look up into drips of rain. As I walked, I pondered fatherhood.

Children are terrorists. They work you over with sleep deprivation. They make you say and do things you're not responsible for, like promising that if they'll go back to sleep you'll buy them a yacht when they turn six.

I feel like I no longer have children. All that links us is genetic material and the hole in my heart. Andrea's out of reach. Maybe I could take a few months off and hunt her down. But then what? She didn't want anything to do with me. Obviously that hasn't changed.

As for Kendra, it's even harder. I call her periodically, but I've learned to have a stiff drink first. It's brutal.

Kendra lives twenty minutes away, but there's a thousand light-years between us.

I went into fatherhood an ignoramus, and I emerged twenty-five years later not knowing how to go back and unscramble the eggs. I'd been determined to be Ward Cleaver. Instead I became my father—there, but barely. My daughters have never forgiven my absence.

Neither have I.

I remember the spring, summer, and fall with my daughters, before the cold hardness of winter settled in. But the winter had been so long now, so many years I'd nearly given up hope that spring would ever come, that our relationships might someday thaw.

The last night we'd had a discussion, the night I was telling Clarence about, Kendra told me I was modern and she was postmodern. I said I knew Post Toasties, but please explain postmodern. She said modern meant I believed in truth, absolute rights and wrongs. She explained that enlightened postmoderns, such as herself, realize there's no such thing as truth or moral absolutes. I said, "So criminals are postmodern, right?" She said I was a dinosaur. I thought about how much money I'd spent to send her to Portland State, where she could learn to be a moron, whereas she could have skipped college entirely and become a moron for nothing.

I might have even said something to that effect. If I did, it was not well-received.

That night Kendra slammed the door and didn't look back. I watched her drive off in her meat-is-murder-mobile and knew the cold war was on. That same night I said good-bye to five months of sobriety. I haven't come back yet. Haven't even been to a meeting.

Life makes outrageous promises. It seldom delivers. Just thinking about it, walking downtown in the eye-numbing Oregon air, made me thirsty again.

An hour later Clarence and I drove to the professor's house to meet Manny and walk the neighborhood. We got out at the corner of 22nd and Oak. Manny saw us as he approached from Pine, following his scowl.

"Tell us where to go," I said, though I wouldn't recommend putting it that way to Manny.

"What took you? We're way behind. Here's a list of apartments I've covered in the big complex," he said, pointing. "I'm canvassing all houses within a two-block perimeter. If I find a Dumpster or anyplace good for a toss, I'll cover it."

"Want company?"

"We'll cover more ground working alone."

"Clarence comes with me," I said. It saves time to let Manny do what he wants. As long as he's still on the waiting list for that personality transplant, it's easier for everyone that he works alone.

Manny was halfway across the street when he called back, "Listened to the 911 yet?"

I shook my head.

"Check it out!"

We walked in the door of the Franklin Terrace apartments. No sign of a manager. We climbed to the second floor, starting a couple doors down from Rebecca Butler, where I knew other apartments had a view of the professor's house. When we came to the first number not on Manny's list, I knocked.

"We just knock on doors?" Clarence whispered.

"Unless you have a better idea," I said. "If you do, send a memo to the whole department. Include an attachment."

A tall pale guy with frazzled hair and a greasy ponytail opened the door, looking out suspiciously.

"Police," I said. "Mind if we come in?"

The guy mumbled something that wasn't "stay out," so we entered. The smell of burned cocaine and aged meat was in the air. Drug paraphernalia lay on the table. He wasn't bothering to cover up.

I walked to the window. "See that house across Oak, the gray one?"

He looked, but I wasn't sure he saw. His eyes said, "Nobody's home."

I pointed at the weather-beaten Colt on the table.

"That yours?"

He hesitated, apparently trying to think of the best answer as opposed to the true one. Nothing came out.

I picked up the gun with a paper towel and smelled it. Not fired recently. I opened the chamber. Not loaded. I don't like loaded weapons nearby when I'm with someone I don't know—or my sister-in-law.

"Did you see or hear anything over there last night?"

No head motion detectable.

"Gunshot?"

He shook his head, barely.

"What's your name?"

Nothing. I'd have to avoid the hard questions.

"That your wallet sitting there?"

Slight nod, or maybe it was the breeze and his head was loose.

"Can you show me your ID?"

His head bobbed, but his body didn't move.

"Open it please," I said.

"Go ahead."

"Only because you're telling me to," I said, looking at Clarence like he might have to testify. I checked. "Nice meeting you, Ryan Moffat." I handed his driver's license to Clarence.

"Take down the info, Watson. Tell you what, Mr. Moffat, we'll come back later. Meanwhile, get some sleep. Just say no to drugs a couple of days. Have some coffee when you get up. You drink coffee? It's a legal drug. You should try it. We'll talk more when your brain returns, if you still have one. Okay?"

He nodded. Clarence finished scribbling. I backed out the door, something I learned to do years ago after I got a surprise steak knife between my shoulder blades, courtesy of a guy I'd thought was comatose.

After the door closed, Clarence asked, "Why didn't you take his gun?"

"Second amendment."

"You think it's his?"

"Maybe not, but no time for the paperwork. Wasn't the right caliber for our murder."

"Drugs were sitting right there."

"And did you notice the three DVD players and half dozen car stereos in original boxes? No? How about the dozen Fleetwood Mac: Greatest Hits CDs still in their wrappers? When he's not breaking into cars and houses, he's shoplifting. It all supports his habit."

"And...you're letting him get away with it?"

"Let's set aside the issue of whether he really invited us in so I could confiscate illegal items in plain sight without a warrant. Do you know how many hours it would take to arrest him? How many depositions and court appearances and answering his lawyer's insinuations that I planted it to set up his model-citizen client, who, if we keep him out of jail, will probably discover the cure for Hodgkin's disease? I'm telling you, it's not worth it."

"But you can't just turn the other way."

"I saw three people jaywalking earlier."

"It's not the same."

"You live in an idealistic world."

"This is Mr. Justice-Is-My-Middle-Name talking?"

"If I started arresting people for the little stuff, I'd never solve a murder. I'm looking for murderers, not addicts and burglars. I'd enforce the laws against small crimes if the system didn't punish me for it. And if criminals got more than a judge's stern look."

We walked to the next door. I lifted my hand to knock.

"I'm not carrying a gun," Clarence said, eyeing a creepy-looking resident staring at us.

"Relax. If you need one, most of these apartments have a couple of guns stashed. Statistically you have a much greater chance of being killed by a family member or friend than a stranger."

"That's comforting. I'll have to remember to have strangers over for Christmas and not turn my back on Geneva and the kids."

"You're really nervous, aren't you?"

"These tenants are mostly white. They see a big black guy at the door, and it's scary. People can get nervous, and nervous people can be violent."

"You're right. You could get killed. But that's a chance I'm willing to take."

"Very funny."

"I thought you were a Christian...aren't you ready for heaven? Isn't that what you're always talking about?"

"I may be ready for heaven, but that doesn't mean I have a death wish!"

"You could always explain in your article that you were afraid to interview witnesses."

"I wouldn't be if I were a white guy wearing a badge and carrying a gun."

"Yeah, yeah," I said. "Chicken," I whispered.

"What did you say?"

"I said I'm thinking of a chicken sandwich for lunch. Getting tired of Whoppers."

The interviews were going nowhere when Manny called.

"I found a gun."

"Where?"

"In a Dumpster by Lone Fir Cemetery, Twenty-third and Stark. Across from Central Catholic High School. No serial number."

"Wine bottle?"

"No. And I sifted everything."

"Glad it was you. Clarence couldn't fit in a Dumpster. Sure it's our gun?"

"It's a Taurus Millennium Pro, 9 mm, recently fired. Two or three blocks from Palatine's. Nobody would ditch a decent piece like this unless it was hot. You could get a couple hundred bucks for it easy. Lucky a Dumpster-diver didn't see it."

"It's been wiped clean?"

"I think I see a couple of prints, but hard to say."

"Tell forensics to put a rush on it."

"Like always."

After seven short interviews that yielded nothing, Clarence and I settled at Burger King for a late lunch. I wanted something else, but I'd inadvertently committed myself to a chicken sandwich.

"We haven't come up with much today," Clarence said.

"Remember how I said it's like panning for gold?"

"And you don't know in advance what's mud and rocks and what's gold."

"Exactly. The more you see and hear, the more questions you ask, the wider you throw your net, the better your chances. It's like casting a line when you're not catching anything. It seems pointless—but you can't catch a fish without doing it. Any cast has better chances than no cast. Eventually you get a bite. Other apartments have a good view of Palatine's house. There's another guy Manny wants us to follow up on. Beats scraping stuff off the bottom of Dumpsters. Let's go back and pan for gold."

We visited apartments; then I phoned the lab, called people who knew the professor, and tracked down a half dozen items on the Internet. I got home at 7:00 p.m., let out Mulch, and gave him a couple of Purina Beggin' Strips, bacon and cheese. Took a little bite myself. Not that bad, but too salty. Mulch and I wrestled.

My couch is so clean you could eat off it—in fact, I often do. While I cooked a DiGiorno pizza, I put on my extra-large gray hooded Barlow Bruins sweatshirt—a gift from Sharon's niece five years ago—stepped into my Emu slippers, tossed a pillow on the couch and put my feet on the coffee table, then grabbed the remote.

When you live by yourself long enough, you begin to think the world's a stage. You're the lead, and the people around you are actors in supporting roles. Sometimes, like when they deliver mail or fry you a steak, they make your life more convenient. Sometimes, like when they cut into your lane or foist a journalist on your investigation—or tell you that someone looked like Abraham Lincoln except that he was short, pudgy, blond, bald, and wearing a stocking cap—they don't.

If the stuff about me being the lead sounds insightful, it's because it came from Sharon. If my calling is to take down the bad guys, hers was to remind me it wasn't all about me. I needed that reminder. I wish she could come back and remind me again. I wish she could come back for any reason.

I've turned her into a saint: Saint Sharon of Calcuttafornia and her sisters of charity. I never liked Saint Sharon's sisters, but that's another story. (I never saw their endearing qualities, hidden beneath their bitter exteriors, because, being a man, I just didn't get it. Men never do.) Sharon was from Venus and I was from Mars, and her sisters were from somewhere on the dark side of Pluto, no offense to the dog. (And I don't care if people say it's no longer a planet. For all I know, scientists on Pluto took a vote and decided Earth's no longer a planet.)

Sharon wasn't perfect, but I don't remember the specifics of her imperfection. I would have taken a bullet for her any day. What I took instead was a nuclear blast in my face the day she died. Or maybe it was the next morning when I woke up without her beside me, when I got up to go visit her in the hospital, trying to shake that bad dream about her dying, then realized it hadn't been a dream.

The fallout continues, like the ash that dropped on us from Mount St. Helens for weeks back in 1980. My throat's ash dry.

Occasionally I see the sun, but mostly I live under the mushroom cloud.

A homicide detective is something between an atheist and a monk. Since Sharon died, I've been closer to atheist. Yet sometimes when I least expect it, a flash of light, a face in a crowd, the feel of a breeze, the smell of the air, make me suddenly feel like she's alive. That's when for fleeting moments I feel like that medieval monk detective I watch on PBS, Brother Cadfael. Sometimes he drinks wine, and I wonder, after the show's over, if he doesn't drink a lot more.

I went to the fridge and this time bypassed the Bud and reached for the

Gewürztraminer, which I like but can't pronounce. I raised a toast to Sharon, and then to Brother Cadfael, and then to Mulch and his predecessor, Philip Marlowe, two of history's greatest dogs. Thirty minutes later the wine was gone. I hoped I'd soon follow.

The darkness felt thick enough to lean on. I leaned, but it didn't hold me up. The next thing I knew it was midnight, three hours since Mulch had stolen the last pizza bone from my plate. I dragged myself to bed.

"Give him peace, Lord," she said.

"I offer him peace," the One beside her said. "So far he hasn't chosen to receive it. I don't force My peace on anyone."

"It's hard for Ollie," she said.

"I know. I made him." He smiled.

"You didn't make him so stubborn. He got that way on his own."

"With the help of a world that isn't what it was meant to be…and forces that deceive him."

"Will he accept Your offer? You know the answer."

"Yes, I know. But I wouldn't impose upon you such weighty knowledge. You're too small for it, little one." He put His arm around her. "He calls you Saint Sharon."

She smiled. "I wasn't as great as he remembers me."

"No. But much that he remembers is truer than he realizes. You did become a saint there. You had moments, even days, of greatness, especially as you lay in that bed, walking with Me when you could no longer walk on your legs."

"You were so faithful to me, Lord. Every day. Sometimes I doubted it. Now that I'm here with You, I wonder why I doubted."

"It's not an easy world to live in. I lived there too, you know. It's not the Eden I made, nor is it the new earth I will make. It's the in-between world, the isthmus between heaven and hell."

"For most of my life, I never saw that."

"But you came to see it. And now you see it much more. Ollie's right. You are Saint Sharon. And one day you will be Queen Sharon. You shall rule a city."

"I can hardly believe that."

"If you, being here and looking into My eyes, can hardly believe what I tell you, then is it surprising that Ollie, being there and without Me, finds it impossible to believe?"

"It is impossible to believe without You, isn't it?"

"That doesn't mean exactly what you think it means. But the words are true enough."

"Please draw him to Yourself, would You, Lord?"

"I will do what I will do. But it may prove more difficult than you imagine."

"Nothing's too hard for You."

"I mean that it will be hard for him. But some things were hard for Me too."

Sharon saw the terrible scars on His hands. She bowed her head and whispered, "Thank You."

I woke at 6:00 a.m., realizing I still hadn't listened to that 911. I went to my home computer to access precinct e-mail.

The e-mail accompanying the recording, from dispatch, said, "Unusually short call. From cell phone, no GPS. Somebody was driving. You can hear traffic."

I opened the audio file and watched the colorful sound wave depictions on my screen. The voice sounded muffled, like someone had wrapped a washcloth around the phone.

"You better send somebody to the professor's house at 2230 Southeast Oak Street. Something fishy's going on."

I played it three times.

Something *fishy?*

"Each fact is suggestive in itself. Together they have a cumulative force."

SHERLOCK HOLMES, *THE ADVENTURE OF THE BRUCE-PARTINGTON PLANS*

SATURDAY, NOVEMBER 23

I STOPPED AT LOU'S for breakfast and my fourth and fifth cups of coffee. I did something I never do—I actually bought a *Tribune*, which killed me, but it was too early to get somebody's castoff. Knowing this was the day, I eagerly searched for Clarence's article. Found it on B1 just as Bill Haley and the Comets promised they'd rock around the clock till broad daylight.

After some opening remarks about the nature of his investigative articles and the ground rules, he wrote this:

> Detective Ollie Chandler is a brilliant and quick-witted homicide detective with exceptional deductive skills and street smarts. He's a police department legend for his offbeat methods that solve crimes and coax confessions.
>
> But, sources tell me, Chandler's a risk taker and rule bender who drives his procedure-conscious superiors crazy. If not for his success rate, he'd have been squeezed out of the department years ago, wisecracking his way as a security guard at Clackamas Town Center, raiding cheese and sausage samples at Hickory Farms.
>
> Ollie Chandler is unorthodox and pit-bull determined. He's also cynical, like most homicide detectives, and at times can be hard-boiled. He hates the *Tribune* and says he doesn't read it, but why do I believe he's going to be reading this column?

I put the paper down and looked around Lou's to see if anybody was watching. The coast was clear. I started reading again.

> My assignment is to tell it like it is. This won't be a PR job for the Portland Police, but it won't be an attack piece either. Truth is, Chandler and I got off to a rocky start when he failed to honor our agreement to call me the moment he was assigned to a murder. I told him he reinforced the image of cops who don't keep their commitments. People like me have as hard a time trusting cops as he has trusting journalists.

Chandler appears to be a competent and thorough investigator, once you put on your wise-guy filter to get past his mask—I think it's a mask—of Columbo-type incompetence. He lacks the skills to remotely retrieve a message from his own answering machine, and I can only deduce that his VCR is flashing 12:00 as I write. But he isn't paid to be high-tech.

Time will tell whether he's on the right track to solving this murder. Detective Chandler assures me he'll live up to his reputation for brilliance. If I don't see it myself, I'm sure he'll point it out to me so I can inform my readers…you folks with poor enough taste to read the *Oregon Tribune*.

I parked my car on Jackson Street in North Portland, where Clarence lives in his sister's old house. I knocked on the front door. When he answered, I held up the newspaper.

"This was out of bounds."

"The part about you being competent and thorough?"

"The answering machine part. And the VCR. And me not keeping a commitment. Cheap shots."

Clarence stepped out on the front porch, a place that held bad memories for us both. I could still see the placement of the shells from the automatic weapon that had killed his sister ten feet from where we stood.

"The cheap shot," Clarence said, "was you not following through on a commitment, *not* my pointing out that you didn't. I'm going to tell the truth. You do good, you'll look good. Act like a jerk, you'll look like a jerk in print. It's up to you. I'm not going to coddle you."

"Watson didn't make Sherlock Holmes look bad."

"He showed he was a drug addict, for crying out loud!" Clarence raised his left arm, and his oven-mitt hand nearly hit the porch ceiling. "You need thicker skin."

"The part about the answering machine could compromise my investigation."

"No one knows what I'm talking about. No one's asked. If they do, I'll just say I left you a message, which I did. And you didn't know how to retrieve it, which you didn't."

"The murderer will know."

"So? You trying to impress him?"

"You compromise this investigation, we're tearing up that e-mail attachment. I'll resign before I let the *Tribune* help a killer slip away."

"If a killer slips away, it won't be because of me. You're capable of bungling your own case."

We traded stares. I exchanged hellos with Geneva. Clarence and I didn't exchange good-byes.

Three hours later, Manny and I stood again in the professor's living room. Unfortunately, Clarence felt like he had to be there too.

"Can you absolutely eliminate suicide?" Clarence asked.

"Yeah," Manny said. "You can put a noose around your neck, inject yourself with poison, and even shoot yourself in the chest. But only once. The second shot's tough. But he was nearly dead before the shots anyway. Which makes both shots a problem."

"So he could have injected himself before someone else shot him," Clarence said. "If he were going to kill himself, did he maybe *want* to suffer?"

"Penance?" I asked. "Doesn't fit Palatine's profile. Neither does suicide." I waved my hand at all the pictures. "He was too infatuated with himself."

"He'd been grading papers," Manny said. "Who grades papers as his final act on earth?"

"I've seen lots of suicides," I said. "This is murder. We have to assume that everything means something. So why the noose? Why bother with suggestions of suicide when it's so obvious it wasn't? Either our perp's an idiot or he thinks I'm an idiot."

"Could be both," Manny said. "And could be right in both cases. He's playin' with us."

"Or trying to send a message."

SATURDAY, NOVEMBER 23, 1:00 P.M.

The greasy, unshaven man peeked out his door, past the chain, at Clarence and me.

"Paul Frederick?" I showed him my badge. He studied it, moving his reading glasses up and down.

"I'm with homicide. My partner's Manny Domast. Stopped by earlier. Asked me to follow up."

Frederick unlatched the chain and put a butcher knife on the kitchen counter. Clarence ogled it.

Midfifties, Frederick had a crossword puzzle smile like a hockey player who couldn't afford dental work. His eyes were droopy, disinterested. His hair went everywhere—Einstein with a perm in a wind tunnel. This was where the similarity to Einstein ended. He wore what may have been pajamas and looked like he'd been dragged through a hedge by a mule team.

"He's a jerk."

"Who?"

"Your partner."

"Yes. However, being a jerk is not a prosecutable crime." I walked to the window and pointed down to the professor's house. "Good view. What'd you see and hear? If you answer, I won't send my partner back to ask you."

"You wouldn't…would you?"

"Answer me and maybe I won't." Manny makes good cop/bad cop easy.

Frederick moved to a sagging card table with a cage on it. Inside was a golden teddy bear hamster poised by his wheel, stroking his whiskers and appearing to have an IQ twenty points higher than his caregiver.

"I'm not answering."

"Too bad," I said. "See my other partner here? I could leave the two of you alone. He'll eat your hamster like it was a tater tot."

Clarence covered his face. I couldn't look at him.

Frederick stepped between me and his hamster. Voice squeaking, he asked, "You threatening us?"

"I wouldn't put it that way."

"You better not hurt Brent," he said to Clarence.

"Your hamster's named Brent?" I asked.

He nodded.

"If you love Brent, you'll answer my questions."

He looked at me long and hard, then took a comb out of his pocket and ran it over Brent, who squealed with delight. Finally he said, "A guy knocked on the door. I could see the professor inside look through the peephole."

"How'd you know he was a professor?"

"Read the newspaper."

I pointed at Palatine's house. "You saw him through the living room window? Blinds were up?"

"Down but open. You know, so I could see the professor—there's a bright light over his computer. I saw the guy on the other side of the door, under the porch light, same time."

I walked out onto his paint-peeled deck. He followed me, keeping an eye on Clarence and Brent. "Quite a view."

"Professor was sitting by his computer, reading or something."

I noticed binoculars hanging from a lawn chair.

"Then what?"

"The guy at the door gave him something. Then the professor let him in. They stood and talked."

"What happened next? Don't leave out the details."

He wrinkled his nose. "I don't have time for this."

He walked to the sink and reached underneath. As I pulled my Glock from its shoulder holster, he pulled out a handful of hamster food. Brent had the munchies.

I pointed at the binoculars. "I see your days are busy. You can take a little time now or a lot later...at the police station...with my partner Manny. We can bring in a subpoena, all kinds of court orders. Clarence can be Brent's sitter. But he has to be fed every couple hours. Clarence, I mean. Your choice."

He lowered his eyes, such as they were, to keep me from looking into his brain, such as it was.

"What you want to know?"

"How long between the time this visitor went in and the time he left?"

"Forty minutes? An hour?"

"I don't know. That's why I'm asking you."

"Forty minutes."

"What else did you see?"

"Nothin'."

"There a reason you seem reluctant to offer information?"

"You accusing me of something?"

"I don't know. You guilty of something?"

"I didn't do anything." Suddenly his face softened, and his voice went limp. "You have to believe me."

"Actually, I *don't* have to believe you. Look, Mr. Frederick, both of us want this to be over. I'm sure Clarence and Brent want it to be over. You have your binoculars. Earlier you said the guy at the door gave him something. What?"

Frederick stared at us, like we were conspirators. "How should I know what he gave him?"

"Because you're the witness. Witnesses witness things. How big was it?"

"I was clear up here."

"The binoculars bring you seven times closer. Just take a guess at the size and shape."

"Maybe it was a picture."

"A picture?"

"He unfolded it. Maybe someone lost his dog."

"His dog?"

"Somebody came to my door with a picture of their dog."

"That same day?"

"No. Months ago."

"What did he look like?"

"Just a little black dog. A mutt, maybe some terrier in him."

"I mean the person holding up the...picture or whatever."

"She was maybe forty years old."

"The person at the professor's door?"

"No. The woman showing me the picture of her dog."

"I'm talking about the guy across the street, at the professor's house, Wednesday night. The one you said was holding something up for the professor. What did he look like? White? Black? Hispanic? Asian?"

He nodded.

"Which you nodding at?"

"White maybe."

"Size?"

"Looked sort of big. Maybe heavy."

"Hair color?"

"Couldn't see it. Maybe a gray sweatshirt, with the hood up. Or...wearing a stocking cap, I think."

"What color was the cap?"

"Dark blue."

Finally two points of agreement. I was tempted to ask if he looked like Abraham Lincoln. I also thought if we have a lineup, it would be great to have a Lincoln look-alike to see the expression on Rebecca "my friends call me Becky" Butler's face.

"If we end up with a suspect, we'll get back to you to identify him."

Suddenly his eyes lit up and his shoulders straightened. "One of those police lineups where you pick out the guy?"

"Would you like that?"

"Yeah. That's cool."

"We're all about cool. What happened next, after he gave him the little poster or showed it to him, and he let him in the door?"

"Don't know."

"You must've kept watching."

"Not when he closed the blinds."

"The professor closed the blinds?"

"The other guy."

"Didn't you get a clear look at him then?"

"I was watching the professor."

"How'd he look?"

"Surprised. I was looking at his surprised face when he disappeared."

"Disappeared?"

"Behind the blinds. One second he was there, the next he vanished. Poof."

"You call 911?"

"Why? People shut the blinds so people don't spy on them. I shut my blinds. You never know, a pervert might be spying on you."

"Yeah," Clarence said.

"It's not like I saw a murder or something."

"You may not have seen it, but it happened."

We went over details, trying to fasten down the times.

"All right, Mr. Frederick, we'll be in touch. Think of anything else, here's my cell number."

As we walked to his door, he stood between Brent and Clarence. He pulled out a piece of newspaper lining the bottom of the hamster cage and replaced it with a page from today's *Tribune*. I'm not kidding—it was page B-1.

"Enjoy, Brent," I said, as we went out the door. "Brent's about to bury your byline," I said to Clarence.

"Don't use me to threaten people."

"I'll use anything and anybody to get the job done. You don't like it, shadow the paperboy. You see Brent quiver when he looked at you?"

"At least you got something from this Frederick character."

"He didn't want to help until we came to the lineup. Suddenly he sees himself on TV. Now he's civic-minded." I shook my head. "Whatever it takes."

"He acted guilty, didn't he?"

"Ask somebody a question and if they're guilty, they always assume you're accusing them. Ask a guilty woman, 'How well did you know Bob Smith?' and she hears, 'I know all about your affair with Bob Smith.' Frederick's guilty all right. But of what? Voyeurism? Tax evasion? Welfare fraud? Claiming Brent as a dependent? Everybody's guilty of something. It's probably not the professor's murder. But once we feed him some suspect photos, who knows? He might hand us the killer."

Clarence and I picked up drinks to go at a Seattle's Best. I treated myself to the special, a Butterfinger mocha. He had a skinny latte. No wonder he's such a grouch.

We were back downtown in homicide detail, at the Justice Center, reports laid out in front of us.

"Lab confirms bedroom window was broken from the inside," I said. "Most of the glass was on the outside. But, like I pointed out, some thin shards fell inside. CSI vacuumed the carpet and found more. No blood, skin fragments, or DNA. No fingerprints. But when they tried to put together all the fragments, the ones from the floor and the ones outside, some were missing. That could mean they're stuck in the bottom of someone's shoes."

"The killer's?"

"Hopefully. But here's the zinger. You know what I said about crime scene contamination? Well, remember that long strand of hair with that nice root on the professor's body? We got a rush job on it. Guess whose hair?"

"No clue."

"Kim Suda's! Can you believe it? Hairnets should be mandatory. She crashes my scene, and then she's careless enough to drop hair on the dead guy!"

"I've got a general question about murder investigations," Clarence said. "For my articles. Once you come up with suspects, how do you choose the most likely?"

"Study them. Find out their background and habits, patterns and prejudices. People are predictable. A certain kind of personality exposed to a certain kind of circumstances responds with a certain attitude and behavior…including murder."

"Sounds deterministic, doesn't it?"

"I'll look it up and let you know."

"Not everything's easily explained. Sometimes we deceive ourselves. Sometimes people deceive us."

"I'm a professional observer. A student of human nature. Everybody can be explained."

"You got to know my daddy pretty well, didn't you?"

"In such a short time, yeah, I did."

"You remember his background, the shame and humiliation, that he couldn't take his family to eat in most restaurants, that he had to use a different restroom and drinking fountain. You remember how the cops tortured him in that Mississippi jail?"

"Wish I could forget."

"So, given your philosophy of human behavior, how do you explain my daddy? How do you explain the man that he was?"

I sat there pondering the question and fighting the lump in my throat. "Your daddy was the finest man I ever met. And…to tell you the truth, I can't explain the way he was."

I sat there waiting for him to tell me it was God who touched his heart, Jesus who gave him the power to forgive.

But he didn't say it. He just sat there. All the responses I was ready to give were stuck in my ammo box. And the longer they stayed there, the weaker they looked. I thought about that old man, who played in the Negro Leagues. He knew Satchel Paige, can you imagine that? Jackie Robinson, Hank Aaron, Willie Mays—he knew them all.

The corners of my eyes got hot and wet when I thought about that sheriff and his deputy and how they beat and tortured Obadiah Abernathy. I'd dreamed of getting my hands on them. I wouldn't use a baseball bat or a fork on them like they used on him. I'd want to feel my fingers around their throats. I wouldn't kill them maybe, but I'd make them wish they were dead.

Obadiah Abernathy—I never detected an ounce of bitterness. He'd been dead years now. Other than that day to and from Seattle for a Mariners game and a couple of fishing trips, I never spent more than three hours with him. Yet he became more of a daddy to me than my father had in fifty years.

But Mr. Abernathy's gone now. He left a big space.

"Ollie?" The voice was out of place.

"Jake? What are you doing here?" I looked around to confirm that I was still in homicide.

"When we were at Lou's, I forgot to give you something from Carly."

As he put the white envelope in my hand, I cleared my throat. "I meant to ask you…how is Carly?"

"Not so good. Her immune system's getting weaker, and she keeps catching stuff. Pneumonia twice. Infections all the time."

"I'm sorry," I said.

"She's in good spirits though. She's an amazing girl."

"Yeah."

"She asks me about her Uncle Ollie."

"I've been thinking of dropping by."

"It would mean a lot to her."

Quick 'as that, Jake was gone. I opened the card. It was a white dog wearing four red sneakers, camera close to his snout. I laughed. Inside it said, "Saw this and thought of you, Uncle Ollie. I love you and miss you. Carly."

I drew my sleeve across my face and stood up. Not sure why I stood up, except that I wanted to do something.

I see dead people. A lot. But I can't stand to see a young woman like Carly waste away. The last few months, my coward's way of not seeing her die has been not to see her at all.

How do you find hope in a world where men like Obadiah Abernathy and girls like Carly Woods suffer and die?

Clarence ran off to his daughter's volleyball game. I dropped by a stop 'n' rob to get two corn dogs and a thirty-two-ouncer. I sat in the parking lot guessing which customers were criminals and what crimes they'd committed. This is how cops while away time. But mainly, I thought about the Palatine case. I didn't like what I was thinking.

I went back to the Justice Center, to the evidence room, and put in a request to check out something that had been processed. The clerk documented this in the chain of custody records. I walked out with a blue rope, still in its evidence bag, inside a plain plastic WinCo sack.

I drove to George's Marine Supply, between downtown and my home, one of two big nautical stores I know of. George was in. I showed him my credentials and handed him the three feet of rope, which CSI had cut through the noose while leaving the knot intact, since knots can be valuable evidence.

George examined the rope like Tiger Woods examines a driver.

"Bowline knot," he said.

I nodded.

After a long pause, George said, "Polyester, three-millimeter fiber. A Marlow. Comes in four colors, all obnoxiously bright. There's a fluorescent pink, a purple, and a greenish yellow. Then this here blue, with the red woven into it. It has a low-stretch polyester core with high-tenacity, good for tie-downs and control lines. It's smooth to minimize friction through blocks and leads."

"You carry it?"

"Used to but stopped three years ago. People want white and brown and con-servative colors. I think David Strickland still carries it, over at Strickland's Sail Shop on Eighty-second. I've got a Marlow catalog. Want me to look it up?"

Within two minutes he produced a page with the four rope colors he'd described. He had an extra catalog, so he tore out the page and gave it to me.

"Tell David Strickland hi from George."

I waved my thanks and sat in the driver's seat for ten minutes, picking up a few scraps of corn dog with my fingertips and thinking. I swore, louder than I meant to.

I wasn't going to Strickland's Sail Shop.

A pessimist has many pleasant surprises, an optimist many disappointments. Pessimism is safer. After years of optimism that didn't pan out, I find life less diffi-cult when I keep my expectations low.

But some days things go just right—beautifully, perfectly, to the point that I'm tempted to revert to optimism. You want to bottle those days and just break out into a big grin.

This wasn't one of those days.

Jake Woods and Clarence Abernathy were probably winding down their after-noons with their families, looking forward to sitting around a campfire singing

"Kum Bay Yah" and counting their blessings.

Me, I counted roadblocks, annoyances, and uncertainties. I contemplated the meaning of the gnawing suspicion that had come over me at George's Marine Supply. A suspicion I didn't dare verbalize to anyone.

So I made my way to Rosie O'Grady's Irish pub, where they water the drinks like geraniums, but if you buy them by the bottle you can still get the real stuff. I was there by four thirty, several hours earlier than usual.

My pessimism had nothing to do with my nagging suspicions and certainly nothing to do with not knowing where my older daughter is or even if she's alive and not seeing my other daughter for nearly a year. Nothing to do with Kendra changing her plans and not showing up last Christmas and not inviting me over on my birthday, or hers. Nothing to do with the fact that I'd left two messages inviting her to come with me to Thanksgiving at Jake's place, which was five days away and counting down. I hadn't heard from her and didn't expect to.

Rosie's was heavy with the smell of tap beer and fried grease.

"Hey, here comes the man. He's early today. Must've gotten his quota of jay-walkers."

Not wearing a uniform saves me from these lines where I'm not known, but not at Rosie's.

"Hide your pipe bomb. It's the fuzz."

This is a guy from the sixties who never stopped smoking pot long enough to realize we're no longer called the fuzz.

Some NASCAR wannabe named Mikey, dressed in a Jimmie Johnson T-shirt and hat and wearing a Lowe's team jacket, stood up putting his hands in the air. "I didn't do it!" he called, breaking into uproarious laughter.

Sometimes even sober people do that when cops walk into a room. They think it's original and hugely funny.

In the years I was on patrol, no one ever said anything brilliant when I pulled them over. But in their memories, people are dazzlingly clever.

Mikey isn't done yet: "So I says to the cop, 'I can't reach my license unless you hold my beer and my cell phone.'"

Another goofball chimes in: "Thank you, sir. The last officer only gave me a warning, too!" It falls flat. No laughter. He's banished to the audience. Mikey is now king of Comedy Central, on stage by himself, a legend in his own mind.

"So this cop says to me, 'Sir, your eyes look red. Have you been drinking?' So I says, 'Officer, your eyes look glazed. Have you been eating donuts?'"

Pretty soon everybody's putting in their two cents, shelling out their cop stories.

I picked up my beer and moved to the far end of the bar, resisting the temptation to head-butt somebody onto the pool table.

Billy the bartender approached, supposing I must need a new beer after the long walk. He was right. His face was a doughy pool of flesh in the eerie light of the Michelob neon. There were shreds of red peanut skins between his teeth.

To some guys, a bartender's like a priest or therapist. To me, he's just a pharmacist with a limited inventory. Sometimes I talk with Billy. Not tonight.

The guys three stools away suddenly got louder. They're funny drunks. I'm a quiet drunk. Funny drunks think everything's hilarious. They're Seinfeld, only he got the breaks and they didn't. Being such accomplished humorists apparently makes them feel better about the affair their wife's having or that their kids are doing drugs while they pour their miserable lives away at Rosie's.

I ask for another beer and point to where I'm about to vanish, then walk into the cool darkness to a small table where no one will be tempted to sit by me. In the safety of the darkness I pull out what I keep stashed in my trench coat's inner pocket: orange foam earplugs. I put on my black fedora to make me feel Bogart-like, sitting in the shadows.

Sometimes I just sit there and think about Sharon. I drink to stop thinking about her, but as I drink I think about her more. Sometimes, just for a second, I fall under a spell that she's home waiting for me. And Kendra's a little girl who adores her daddy. What am I doing here with these drunken bums and the bartender with peanut skins on his teeth when they're waiting for me at home?

So I stand, stagger a little, and remember Sharon's dead. And Kendra's lost. Then I sit down again. Next thing I know it's half-past Cinderella, and somehow I'm home, falling into bed. Most times I don't recall hitting the mattress. I wake up and wonder where I am. These days I seem to lose two or three hours routinely.

It's now 5:15, morning after my latest binge. I wake up to the cranial jackhammer. Seeing me bonding with Mr. Coffee, Mulch already has bacon fantasies, but my thoughts are limited to French roast, my drug of choice.

As the little gray cells start to wake up, I contemplate the jerks in the bar, trying to remember what they really said and what I really said and rehearsing what I should have said and indulging my fantasy of taking them all out with a series of head butts.

Wouldn't have been worth the paperwork. And then there's anger management...

After two eighteen-ounce cups of French roast, the sun still wasn't threatening to rise. I lacked sufficient fuel for takeoff, so I cooked a round of bacon and eggs, with blackened English muffins. I decided to do what I'd been dreading since leaving George's Marine Supply yesterday afternoon. I knew what I'd find when I looked in my garage, but I still hoped I was wrong.

I stepped onto the back porch, Mulch at my feet, but I felt dizzy and needed to sit. I thought about sitting on my grandfather's back porch and him teaching me to tie knots, including the bowline. I didn't know Grandpa well, but those knots he taught me were more than I ever got from my father. Dad threw me a ball once. He got mad when I threw it back too low. Said he wasn't going to waste his time with a kid who couldn't even toss a baseball.

I pulled myself up, leaning on Mulch, and opened the door to a pitch-black garage. I turned on the wimpy overhead light. The hundred-watt bulb was fifteen feet up, nearly worthless, barely enough to illuminate the velvet Elvis I bought roadside in Arizona twenty years ago as an anniversary gift for Sharon. I grabbed a flashlight and looked on the shelves, past toolboxes, hoses, and transmission fluid. I pointed the light up to the storage platform behind me, built to take advantage of the dead space. It was full of boxes of junk Sharon had asked me to toss. Miscellaneous sailing paraphernalia reminded me how, after Sharon died, I bought that used sailboat. I'd been out in it three lousy times in two years. Finally sold it.

I stopped rummaging and shone the flashlight around the garage. I passed Elvis and held the beam on an old blue plastic box by two studded snow tires. I stood over it, hands shaking.

I opened the box, pushed aside a block and tackle, some lures and line, and found a couple of ropes.

I pulled one of them out, laid it on the cement floor, pushed back Mulch, and aimed the flashlight. The rope's end had been cut neatly by something sharp. Stretching it out, I guessed that three feet had been cut off, recently, since even in a dusty garage the cut fiber was still sparkling clean.

The rope was bright blue, with a red weave. Polyester with three-millimeter fibers. A Marlow.

I'd bought it three years ago at Strickland's Sail Shop.

"I do not think there are any insuperable difficulties. Still, it is an error to argue in front of your data. You find yourself insensibly twisting them round to fit your theories."
SHERLOCK HOLMES, *THE ADVENTURE OF WISTERIA LODGE*

SUNDAY, NOVEMBER 24

MY IDEA OF FUN is not discovering that the rope around the neck of a murder victim is mine. I sipped coffee at my kitchen table, pondering it.

Finally, I picked up that thought and set it on a shelf, making room on my mind's tabletop to spread out Professor William Palatine. Who was he? And what made me think I was supposed to already know?

By all accounts, Palatine was brilliant, accomplished, and occasionally charming. He was popular among the students—especially intellectuals and females. Female intellectuals? They were crazy about him. Even so, I wouldn't want to trade places with William Palatine. Not sure how much Teacher of the Year and a Princeton diploma means when you're alive, but I'm pretty sure I know how much they matter when you're dead.

In the absence of determinative evidence, you have to know the victim to figure out the most likely person to have killed him. That's why I had to get to know Professor Palatine. Especially since the last phone call he ever made was to me.

Had I been home that night, maybe Palatine and I would have chatted. Or maybe he would've said, "There's a man with a gun; he's 5' 10", carrying a box and wearing a Pizza Hut jacket. The name on the jacket is Reggie."

Jake tells me death's not a hole, but a doorway—that dead people are now alive on the other side. He said that about Sharon. I hope he's right. For her sake anyway. I don't know what I hope about me. Or the professor.

I'm a trained observer of the real world. I know nothing about what lies beyond the senses. This much I do know…when a man is lying on his living room floor with a few gallons of his blood soaked into a blue carpet that's now dark purple, he is not mostly dead, but as Miracle Max said in *The Princess Bride*, "he's all dead."

Solving a murder is a final gift to the deceased. Whether they know about this gift, or whether they can ever know anything again, is a matter of debate, a debate Jake and Clarence love to engage me in.

If Palatine has a soul and there's a God, then it's God's job to judge his soul. Even though I have the distinct feeling I wouldn't have liked him, when it comes to the crimes against his body, if anyone's going to get him justice, it's me.

That's what I do. I get justice for the dead.

After moving from the kitchen to my office, down the hall past the bathroom, I opened up files of photocopied letters Palatine had sent. Many of them appeared to be love letters, saying how his heart was pierced and he felt a fire within and how he hated to be separated from her, blah, blah, blah. Yet not one of the letters addressed a woman by name. If I'd written love letters to Sharon, I'd have put her name on them.

And why make the photocopies? What was his future use for them?

The professor's signature was there on other documents in his files. It was fancy and borderline illegible. Only the *W* and the *P* were clear—except the *Dr.*, which was prominent and unmistakable.

I spent the next hour reading various things written by him in school papers, as well as two introductions online from when he was a visiting lecturer in the ivied halls of academia.

I read again the printout of his supposed "I deserve to die" confession on the computer screen.

I went to the shelf and got down my *Webster's* dictionary. I looked up the word *judgement*.

I stayed home all afternoon, making phone calls, trying to reconstruct Palatine.

Manny and I are both on T-Mobile, for the free minutes, since we can exchange a dozen calls a day. In the last three hours this was call six.

"You know his stupid habit of not putting a name with the number?" Manny asked. "I've been calling all the numbers on papers in his desk. A real estate agent, plumber, and computer tech. A student named Brandy who said she had no idea why he had her phone number. He'd never called. But there was another number. A private detective."

"No kidding? Who?"

"Ray Eagle."

"Wait…the guy who helped us with Abernathy's sister's case? Why would the professor have his number?"

"Ray Eagle," Manny said, clearly irritated, "says to give you this message: 'If Ollie Chandler wants to know why the professor called me, I'll meet him at the precinct tomorrow morning.' He said he read Abernathy's article on the investigation, so he's invited too."

I heard the slow burn in Manny's voice.

"Can you join us?"

"No. I've got work to do. Trying to solve a murder."

Mulch got restless and talked me into a 9:00 p.m. walk. As we headed toward a nearby greenway, a light, cool rain blew into my face, and a thought hit me like a bolt out of nowhere.

What if that call to me from the professor's house wasn't made by him? What if it was made by the last person there after he died?

Before leaving for work, I saw Saturday's newspaper on the recycle pile. It inspired me to pull out the VCR manual. I put on my reading glasses and found the page about setting the clock. I didn't manage to set the correct time, but at least I stopped it from flashing. I raised a Budweiser in victory when it turned to 12:01.

You never know when some smart-aleck journalist might drop by.

Ray Eagle, short and athletic looking, wearing wire-rimmed glasses, Levis, and an OSU baseball cap, met Clarence and me at the Justice Center. I refreshed my memory before he came. He'd been a Detroit cop fifteen years, five as a detective before moving back to Portland.

After we took five minutes to catch up, I asked, "So what was the professor doing with your number?"

"Palatine called me twice. He wouldn't identify himself. Caller ID gave me nothing. I had the next call traced."

"How?" I asked.

"Friends in the right places," he said. "I used to be a cop, remember? Anyway, he called from his home, not the college. He said he'd gotten some threats, but they were oblique."

"He used the word *oblique*?"

"Yeah. I checked it online five seconds after he said it to make sure I knew what it meant."

"It's a college professor word," I said. "They throw it out there to impress you. Journalists do the same."

"People like you are why we write at a sixth-grade level," Clarence said.

"If I were one of your readers, I'd be insulted."

"If you were one of our readers, you'd be informed."

"You guys need a counselor," Ray said, raising his hands.

"What was the threat about?" I asked.

"He'd been getting phone calls every week, near midnight. The caller implied that Palatine was going to be held accountable for how he'd wronged someone. I think he knew what it was about but didn't tell me."

"Why'd he call you?"

Ray took off his glasses and cleaned them on his shirt. "Somebody recommended me. I told him if he thought his life was being threatened he should call the police. He didn't want to. His second call was Tuesday morning, thirty-six hours before he was killed. When I heard about the murder, I wished I'd done more. Maybe I should've called the cops."

"Why didn't you call us after the murder?"

"Cops don't like PIs sticking their noses in. I figured you'd be calling me. Sure enough, you did."

After Ray Eagle left, I drove the five minutes to the PSU library, by the Park Blocks. It would have been a fresh but drippy half mile walk. Showing my badge to a wide-eyed librarian, I requested the videos of the professor's lectures, which I'd learned existed from a previous call. He carried three videos and escorted me to a private viewing room with an uncomfortable metal chair.

I'd asked computer forensics to send me all Palatine's lecture notes. With a keyword search, I'd located the notes corresponding to these exact lectures and had them with me. Two were the same presentation from his Philosophy 102: Ethics class, given in back-to-back sessions. I watched both sessions to see what I could learn about him. What struck me was how he would roll his eyes up, as if searching for a word. Then suddenly he'd come up with it, when it was right there in front of him in his notes and he'd said the same thing in the previous class, also rolling back his eyes and searching for that same perfect phrase.

In other words, Palatine was the south end of a northbound horse.

He spoke about the dominance in literature and philosophy of dead white males. Never mind that he was a white male. And dead to boot.

He talked about the naïveté of believing in moral absolutes. Listening to the professor, and the student comments that mirrored him, reminded me that many educated people believe there's no such thing as right and wrong. And that many educated people, therefore, are stupid.

Why would I be a cop if there wasn't right and wrong? Steal their skateboard, stereo, or spouse, and suddenly they believe in moral absolutes.

I'm no church boy, but the Christians have it right on this one. When you deal every day with crimes against people, you can't stomach all this waffling on right and wrong. As I listened to the lectures, it struck me as odd how much money people are willing to pay to be taught ethics by people who don't believe in ethics.

It ticks me off that all of us are paying the price for raising a generation that doesn't know the difference between right and wrong

But what would I know? I'm no college graduate. I'm just a working stiff, trying to keep the next person from being mugged or raped or murdered by people who—guess what—don't believe in moral absolutes.

Jake called me about football at my place that night. He assured me that many philosophy teachers these days believe in moral absolutes, and Palatine was a throwback to moral relativism. Well, okay, but do universities offer students their money back when the philosophies they learned there ruin their lives…and other people's?

The professor's lectures were as heavy on ego as they were light on morals. After the fourth video, I was surprised someone hadn't killed him years ago. And dumped him and his smart-aleck philosophy-quoting answering machine into the Willamette River.

For the third and final time I absolutely ruled out suicide. Could a gun, in a recoil back on the finger, fire a second time? Maybe. Could a man put a noose around his neck and put a gun to his chest? Sure. But after watching Palatine's lectures, I decided I'd never seen a man with less self-loathing. If he killed himself, he'd have done it the easiest way, mourning humanity's loss of himself.

After leaving the PSU library and entering the real world, I pulled up the collar of my trench coat, pulled down my wool fedora, and leaned into the icy rain to my car eighty feet away. I thought of my cousin Harvey in San Diego. Maybe I should move there. If I did, I'd stay away from Harvey. But the weather sounded great.

I went to the old brownstone for lunch and worked through the afternoon. Sarge knows I work well at home, so he gives me a long leash. I changed into sweatpants and sweatshirt, sat down at the kitchen table, threw away the mail, heated Nalley chili, smothered it in cheddar cheese and chopped onion, and sat back with a box of Ritz crackers, thinking step by step through the crime.

After getting a second glass of milk, I found myself staring at the message on my fridge: "Examine the evidence. Then follow wherever it leads."

Monday night football, usually at Jake's, was at the brownstone tonight. I scanned the house, put in some elbow grease, and ten minutes later the place was spotless.

Clarence came at five thirty to show me a draft of his next article. I told him to strike a couple of sentences that said too much.

"You'll notice my VCR clock isn't blinking," I said nonchalantly.

"It's three hours fast," he said.

"It was made on the East Coast."

Jake joined us, the pizza arrived, and one of those great kickers named Jason set a football on the tee.

During halftime my cell rang.

"No kidding? You're sure?" I hung up, staring at nothing.

"What?" Jake asked.

"The Franklin Terrace apartments."

"What happened?" Clarence asked.

"Our binocular-gazing hamster-loving Mr. Paul Frederick...the guy who told us the man at the professor's door might've been wearing a stocking cap and looking for his lost dog?"

"How could I forget him?"

"They say he had an accident thirty minutes ago. He fell off his second-story deck. He's dead."

10

"I must take the view that when a man embarks upon a crime, he is morally guilty of any other crime which may spring from it."
SHERLOCK HOLMES, *THE ADVENTURE OF THE PRIORY SCHOOL*

WE TURNED OFF FOOTBALL. Sitting there in my living room, Clarence and I told Jake about Frederick and what he saw at the professor's through his binoculars.

"Are you going to Frederick's to check it out?" Clarence asked.

"It's Karl and Tommi's case. I have to let them sort things out first."

"Frederick actually fell?"

"Yeah," I said. "After he was pushed. Gravity'll do that."

"Why would somebody kill him?" Jake asked.

"Because they knew he saw something."

"But how would they know?"

"My question exactly. Did someone tail us to the apartments to see who we were interviewing? I keep thinking about those narrow apartment hallways with their creaky steps and floorboards. How could somebody follow us without us seeing him?"

"But we talked with maybe ten people," Clarence said. "Manny talked with more, didn't he? They haven't been killed. Why single out Frederick?"

"He'd seen the guy at the professor's from a distance. Did the killer have eagle eyes? Did he spot him up there with the binoculars? Or was it something Frederick told us that made him worth killing? Or something he *might* tell us but hadn't yet? But how could anyone know?"

Clarence shook his head, saying something about how short life is.

"Frederick left a handwritten will," I said.

"He did?"

"Yeah. He designated you as Brent's legal guardian."

"Who's Brent?" Jake asked.

"Forget it," Clarence said.

"This guy Frederick getting killed," I said. "It's another example of why I don't believe in God."

"You believe in free choice?" Jake asked.

"Yeah."

"Doesn't free choice demand the freedom to choose evil?"

"Not if it causes this much suffering."

"How much suffering is acceptable? Can you have real choices without consequences, both good and bad?"

I shrugged.

"Isn't it inconsistent," Clarence piped in, "to say it's good for God to give us free choice, but then say He shouldn't allow evil consequences from evil choices?"

"You can't have it both ways," Jake said.

These guys were a regular tag team.

"I've made some bad choices," I said. "If I had it to do over again, I'd have been there for my daughters. But if God's all-powerful, couldn't He have made me do it right in the first place?"

"*Made* you do it right?" Jake asked. "What do you want, for God to make us all into Stepford wives?"

"I always thought the Stepford wives were kinda cute."

"If I were to offer to make things okay in your life, but to do it I had to take away your ability to choose, would you take me up on it? Ask me to make all your decisions for you?"

"Then it would be your life, not mine," I said.

"Exactly. So how can you expect God to give us free choice, then fault Him because He did? What could He do to make you happy?"

"Give me Sharon back."

Jake nodded. "He went so far as to give His life on the cross and conquer death in His resurrection so that you and Sharon and everybody who accepts His gift could be together forever."

"So you say. I've looked at Christianity, and I don't like what I see."

"You don't like love, grace, forgiveness, justice, feeding the hungry and caring for the sick? You know where hospitals came from? Christians. Atheists and agnostics aren't behind prison reform. They're not the ones who got slavery outlawed. It was Christians."

"Don't forget the Crusades and inquisitions and all the killjoys, like my grandmother. If I were to judge Christ by some Christians I know, He'd look pretty bad."

"I agree," Jake said. (I hate it when he says that. It throws me off.) "So why don't you judge Christ by Himself instead of by others?"

"Christians are just into rules and dos and don'ts."

"Some are," Jake said. "But I can't think of anything more pointless than Christianity without Christ. And nothing more exciting than knowing Jesus and following Him."

"Pardon me for not agreeing."

"You don't need my pardon," Jake said. "But you're my friend, and friends tell each other the truth. I'm asking you, Ollie, take your focus off the church and off Christians you've known, and just look at Jesus. Read the Gospel of John, and judge Him by what He said and did, not by everybody who claims His name. Who did He claim to be? Investigate. Then make up your own mind about Him. And stop assuming things are as they appear."

"In other words," Clarence said, "practice what you preach."

It was time to change the subject. I pulled out my yellow notepad. "Here's my verse for the day. It's from Dashiell Hammett's *The Continental Op*. He says, 'In the case of a murder it is possible sometimes to take a shortcut to the end of the trail, by first finding the motive.'"

"How do you find that shortcut?" Jake asked.

"By figuring out who benefits from Palatine's death. Someone's trying to come out ahead. Possible motives? Money. Power. Romance. Business. Revenge. Self-preservation. Justice. Somebody thinks the murder makes perfect sense. They think they'll sleep better knowing he's dead. It's 99 percent motive. Remember that *Purpose Driven Life* study you guys tried to con me into?"

"Yeah," Jake said. "We were hoping to bilk you out of your mansion in the Caribbean."

"Well, let me tell you about the purpose driven murder. There's always a purpose, always a motive. Find it and you have the killer. But to find the killer you must know the victim. That's why I listened to the professor's lectures and why I'm becoming a student of philosophy. That's why I'm reading Bertrand Russell." Okay, I'd read eight pages. "Which reminds me, has somebody written *Nietzsche for Dummies?*"

"So what are the possible motives?" Clarence asked.

"Nothing unusual about the professor's finances. Doesn't appear to have been a big gambler. Manny called his attorney about the will. Has no kids. Divorced. Looks like it goes to his brother, a wealthy doctor."

"Romance?" Jake asked.

"Possibly. Hell knows no fury like a woman scorned. Isn't that in the Bible?"

"Nice try," Jake said.

"What about a student?" Clarence asked.

"Maybe a student was humiliated by the professor. Manny says last term three students were caught plagiarizing papers from the Internet. Palatine flunked them. Manny'll pay them a visit."

Clarence was taking notes.

"The question with murder," I said, "is always this—*who's better off* because this person is dead? Better off in body, mind, or bank account? A victim's abused wife is better off. A victim's girlfriend's husband is better off because he's eliminated the competition and gotten revenge. Whose life's easier because Palatine's gone? Or rather, who might imagine his life would be easier? Because murder complicates his life in ways he never imagined."

"Your sins will find you out," Jake said.

"A man reaps what he sows," Clarence said.

After a pause, I cleared my throat and said, "A rolling stone gathers no moss?"

11:00 Monday night, Mulch and I kicked back on the couch. I was still pondering Frederick's murder. Suddenly, I thought of something he'd said to us. A mental picture formed. Why hadn't it dawned on me before?

If I was right, it would explain how the killer might have known what Frederick said to us. And why, knowing that, he might kill him. The two fit, like gun and holster.

I thought it through backward and forward. Usually I fear that I won't discover the truth. This was one of the few times I'd been afraid I *had* discovered it.

My nerves were like worms on a fishhook.

The one thing that keeps me from drinking at night is the need to stay sharp to figure out a case. But this time, if my mind was catching the right scent, the last thing I wanted to do was stay sharp. I didn't want to go where the evidence was leading me.

I had to say yes either to the train of thought or to the six-pack.

It was an easy choice.

*"Let us get a firm grip of the very little which
we do know, so that when fresh facts arise
we may be ready to fit them into their places."*
SHERLOCK HOLMES, *THE ADVENTURE OF THE DEVIL'S
FOOT*

TUESDAY, NOVEMBER 26, 8:00 A.M.

I WOKE UP with a hippopotamus sitting on my head. The fact that it was invisible unnerved me.

By the time I got to the office the hippo was the size of a rock badger—not overwhelming, just annoying. At nine, crime lab said the toxicology report was ready. Clarence joined me.

"It's bizarre," the tech said, handing me his report. "Somebody injected this guy with over twelve ounces of ink. Pelikan ink, royal blue, same stuff in the bottle, only more. Maybe he found extra bottles. Or brought his own. He used that syringe you found at the scene."

"Injection was where we saw the marks in his shoulder?"

"Yeah."

"Why so many?"

"You know how many injections from a 100-cc needle it takes to make twelve ounces?" he asked. "Do the math."

Clarence closed his eyes, mumbling something about thirty cubic centimeters in an ounce. "Even with that big syringe, at least four shots. Could've been a half dozen."

"That's a break for us. The killer wouldn't do that without a specific reason. You don't just notice a couple of ink bottles in a drawer and say, 'Hey, I'll kill him with fountain pen ink.' It's too bizarre and time-consuming."

"Maybe a sadist wanted him to die slowly."

"In the killer's mind it made perfect sense. It wasn't random."

The first seventy-two hours after a murder are critical. Unfortunately, it had been six days. Clarence couldn't make lunch, so it was Jake and me at Lou's.

I took the six steps to the Rock-Ola, which reminds me of the robot in *Lost in Space*, and pressed B9, "Mr. Tambourine Man."

As we waited for burger baskets, I said, "Okay, it's not suicide. Not the work of a serial killer. I mean, we aren't finding other people injected with ink with nooses around their necks. And it's not a hired killer."

"Why not?" Jake asked.

"Too messy. All those unnecessary garnishes. Somebody's trying to make a statement. To mock us or to tell us something. A professional killer would be in and out in two minutes. This guy hung around, maybe forty minutes. It wasn't business. It was personal."

"I don't understand why the killer would leave all that evidence," Jake said. "The insulin, the syringe, the ink, the injections, the rope, the gun. Why bother?"

"Right. And don't forget the crumbs and the wineglasses," I said. "Why not just whack the guy and leave? My theory is, he's trying to overwhelm us with evidence. It's brilliant. There's enough evidence that we can't tell what's real and what's phony."

"What do you mean?" Jake asked, squeezing a lemon slice in his Diet Coke.

"The chair, for instance. Normally you'd say this was a short person. But maybe it's a tall person making it appear that a short person adjusted the chair."

"Or maybe it really *is* a short person."

"Exactly. That's the problem. Suppose the killer tripped up and left some real evidence. How would we distinguish that from the contrived evidence? At first I thought somebody wanted to be caught. Now I think they're smart enough to know there're always some bread crumbs. So they've crumbled a whole loaf and spread it out. How do you find the real bread crumbs—or know when you've found them?"

"Whoever your killer is," Jake said, "he seems to know enough about investigations to realize how to mess one up."

"Yeah." Jake didn't know how close to home he was hitting.

My phone gave me its "missed a call" ring. The message was Manny saying, "Ballistics confirmed murder weapon's the Taurus."

"Good news," I told Jake. "The Dumpster gun's the murder weapon. Now we wait to see about fingerprints."

I took a celebratory bite of cheeseburger. I'm telling you, Rory's a master. Emeril's got nothing on him but a TV show.

"There's something else," I said, wiping my mouth. "I don't think the professor called me that night."

"But…I thought you said he did."

"His phone was used to call my number. That doesn't mean he was the caller."

"You're thinking it was…?"

"The killer," I said.

"How would the killer know your number?"

"Same way as the professor. There are ways to get unlisted numbers."

"But why call you? The killer wouldn't know you'd be investigating the case. Even *you* didn't know, right?"

"And if he was going to call me, why linger at the murder scene to do it?" I picked up a printout. "I've been going over the confession. Listen: 'I, Dr. William Palatine, do not deserve to live. I've crossed boundaries and forfeited my life. I admit my arrogance. I deserve judgement. I should be cast into a deep sea with a millstone around my neck.'"

"First time I've heard that," Jake said. "Weird."

"The prints were wiped off the keyboard, so Palatine didn't write it. Probably the killer. But here's the best part. Up to now, I've had to deal with a ninety-minute window for time of death. Computer forensics told me this afternoon that the file wasn't saved by the user, but it was autosaved."

"So?"

"The automatic file recovery was set to save every five minutes, whenever a change had been made. It backed up last at 11:40. That means the killer was still there, typing, after 11:35. And I got my phone message at 11:37. I say he was wrapping things up. He'd just finished off Palatine or was about to. Once he fires those two shots, he's got to get out of the house. Time of death was probably 11:30 to 11:40. Given the multiple injections and everything else, I don't see how it could have been before, say, 11:20. A ten- or twenty-minute spread's worlds better than ninety."

"What time did that woman say she saw the professor let the guy in?"

"Becky Butler pinpointed the commercial break that put it about 10:50 p.m. So the guy was in the house with him at least forty-five minutes."

"Isn't that an awfully long time?" Jake asked.

"Yeah. The killer wasn't in a hurry. And I want to know why."

It was twenty minutes out of my way, but after leaving Lou's I decided to swing by Dea's In and Out in Gresham for an orange malt. I listened to a Nero Wolfe audio, *Murder by the Book*. Sometimes I hear something I can use in my investigation.

But I was distracted, mulling over the case. I was looking for a crumb, a trace, a scrap of a hint. Anything. I was trying to discredit my unsettling hunch, unsuccessfully.

I'd attempted five times to contact the professor's brother, the doctor. I turned off Nero Wolfe and pulled to the side of the road as we finally connected.

"You've heard my messages?" I asked. "I need to meet with you as soon as possible."

"The next three days are impossible," Dr. Warner Palatine said. "I've got a few minutes now while they transport a patient. Then I scrub in for an emergency surgery."

"Let's get started." The orange malt could wait. "I have the impression you and your brother weren't real close."

"We saw each other Thanksgiving, Christmas, birthdays. Two years ago we spent a week together at Sunriver. It wasn't fun. What? Thirty ccs? No way. I told you twenty." I heard muffled voices.

"Doctor?"

"Sorry. I'm back."

"So did you talk to your brother on the phone?"

"I used to, but I got tired of his stupid answering machine. Did you know every week he'd have a quote from a different philosopher? Even when we were kids, he was a show-off."

"How old was he when he became a diabetic?"

"Who?"

"Your brother."

"What are you talking about? Bill wasn't a diabetic."

"But…he was insulin-dependent."

"No way…unless it happened in the last month, and that's impossible. Too old for type 1."

"But he was wearing one of those ID tags on a chain. Plus, a needle and insulin in the fridge."

"Speaking of chains, somebody's yanking yours, detective. The one thing Bill talked to me about was his medical condition, enlarged prostate and all. He'd call me to double-check his doctor's advice. He was taking Diovan for high blood pressure."

"Yeah, we found it in the medicine cabinet."

"I've been his free medical consultant for twenty years. No co-pay. Type 1, insulin-dependent? No way. I'd know about it. Look, I've got to get to surgery."

I pulled the file from my beat-up briefcase and searched my crime scene notes. Then I called the evidence room.

"I need information right now on a piece of bagged evidence. It's on the Palatine murder, November 20. Last Wednesday. It's the medical ID chain that was around his neck. I need to know exactly what it says."

I sat there feeling dumb for not checking his medical records. But what's the point of faking a medical condition on a dead man?

"Okay," said the tech. "On the back side it says 'MedIDs.' On the front side, in a red imprint, it says 'Insulin-Dependent Diabetic.' And under that it says 'See wallet card.'"

"Is his wallet still bagged?"

"It's here."

"Can you check for a wallet card?"

"Isn't this your job? You want me to interview witnesses, too?"

"Just check, would you?"

"He's got his health insurance card. The rest is credit cards, a coffee card, and a few pictures. That's it. There's no medical card."

I contacted Palatine's primary physician, assured him of my credentials, and he confirmed that Palatine wasn't diabetic.

I left a message for Manny and called Clarence to fill him in.

"So if the professor wasn't a diabetic," I said, "where'd the insulin bottle come from? And whose chain was hanging around his neck?"

"A man's brain originally is like a little empty attic. A fool takes in all the lumber he comes across, so that the knowledge which might be useful to him gets crowded out. For every addition of knowledge you forget something that you knew before. It is of the highest importance, therefore, not to have useless facts elbowing out the useful ones."
SHERLOCK HOLMES, *A STUDY IN SCARLET*

TUESDAY, NOVEMBER 26, 3:00 P.M.

I VISITED Paul Frederick's apartment, with Detectives Karl Baylor and Tommi Elam as my tour guides but found nothing helpful. The neighbors testified that Frederick would hang over the edge of his deck, spying on people with his binoculars. He'd often do it at night. This time he'd leaned too far.

Yeah, right.

As I waited for the elevator on the ground floor of the Justice Center, Clarence walked in the front door. I held the elevator for him and prepared him for our appointment by saying, "You can learn a lot about someone by studying their computer." We exited on floor 14, entered detective division, and this time turned right, away from my workstation, to computer forensics. There we met Detective Julia Stager.

"The professor visited plenty of raunchy websites," Stager said. "He thought he'd erased them, but we can pull up everything. Keep that in mind, gentlemen. There's no such thing as a private moment."

She handed me the list.

"Palatine searched for the kinds of things you'd expect a philosophy teacher to search for. And he also entered lots of names to search for phone numbers. Ninety percent of them were women's. Sometimes he reverse searched, entering phone numbers to try to identify the name."

"Someone he contacted might've had a motive," I said. "Or a boyfriend."

"Or husband or brother," Clarence said. "Or father."

"Given his indiscretions, he made some enemies."

"The sites marked were in his favorites folder," Stager said. "Here's an unlikely one."

"Bill's Fountain Pen Page?" I asked.

"Yeah, and two sites about collecting fountain pens."

Manny had told me he'd found a dozen fountain pens in Palatine's office at the college and even more at his home, in a shoe box. Plus those three I'd found in his desk.

"Not many people use fountain pens anymore, do they?" Clarence asked.

"The professor did. Which means I've developed a keen interest in fountain pens."

WEDNESDAY, NOVEMBER 27

The next morning I asked Clarence to meet me at Lou's at 7:30 a.m. before sitting in on his first detectives' meeting at nine.

Before the pancakes and western omelets were served, and after Clarence had rolled his eyes at "Puff the Magic Dragon" and put in a request for the Supremes, I said, "There's something you need to hear before you come to the meeting. I've been thinking about Paul Frederick. You know how he said the man at the door gave the professor something or was holding something up for him to look at, like a little poster?"

"Yeah?"

"I think he was showing him ID."

"What kind of ID?"

"Well, who shows ID to gain entrance?"

"Cops?"

"Or FBI. Arson investigators. Someone associated with law enforcement. Not that long of a list."

"Are you saying…the killer could be a cop?"

"Killers can be anybody with a motive, and cops have motives just like everybody else. If the guy was holding up ID and it persuaded the professor to let him in the door, it could've been a cop. Let's go back to our original question of why someone would kill Frederick," I said, as "Puff" gave way to "My World Is Empty Without You."

"If he thought Frederick told us something incriminating. Or that he could?"

"Right. But what puzzled us is how would he know what he said to us?"

"He wouldn't. It was just you, me, and him. Unless…a bugging device?"

"I considered that. But how would he know to plant one in the first place? How else could he find out?"

Clarence shrugged.

"Didn't you take notes?"

"Sure, but nobody saw them. You playing 'blame the journalist' again?"

"You're certain your editor didn't see them? Carp? A custodian looking on your desk?"

"I keep them in my briefcase. It's with me at all times." Clarence pointed to his black leather case, which looked like it had come off the assembly line that morning.

"Do you take it with you when go to the bathroom?"

"Of course not."

"Does it have a lock?"

"Yes. But—"

"You don't use it, do you?"

"No reason to."

"Unless you're carrying eyewitness testimony in a murder case."

"You think someone at the *Trib* is the murderer?"

"No reason they couldn't be. I'll grant you it's unlikely. Unfortunately, there's another possibility."

"What?"

"I took notes too."

"What did you do with them?"

"What I always do. Gave them to Mitzie in the secretarial pool so she could type them for me."

"You think the typist is a killer?"

"This typist is sixty-four years old and weighs a hundred pounds. But someone could see it on her desk when she steps away. People pass by her desk all the time."

"Not people off the street," Clarence said. "It's pretty high security."

"I've thought about it. We've got custodians. Maintenance staff. Secretaries. And of course...cops."

"You think...?"

"Mitzie types it into the system. She saves the file on the server. She e-mails it to me. And to top it off she gives me a hard copy. That's how I like it. My notes of the Frederick interview might have sat for hours on Mitzie's desk. But even if she typed them right away, one of the detectives could've accessed the file or hard copy."

"But...one of the detectives?"

"Why not? Someone knows Frederick saw some things. They kill him to shut him up or keep him from remembering something critical. Dead men don't pick you out in a lineup."

"That's a serious accusation," Clarence said, leaning forward.

I got up and pressed a few more rose-colored buttons, invoking the artistry of Herman's Hermits and the Dave Clark Five.

We no longer had to whisper once we were under the melodious strains of "I'm 'Enery the Eighth, I yam, 'Enery the Eighth, I yam, I yam."

"It's a hypothesis. Unfortunately, it's holding up. Think about how much time this guy spent at the crime scene. Who would take that risk? But if a guy had his police monitor on, he'd know exactly when dispatch called for patrol. He could be out of the house in a heartbeat. Hey, even if he was found at the scene, he could tell patrol he heard it on his monitor and was nearby, so he came to check it out. If you're a cop, you can do that."

"But—"

"Consider the phone call to my house from the professor's. My home phone's unlisted, but all the homicide detectives have it. He uses official ID to get Palatine's door open. He has access to the information Frederick gave us and knows he might ID him. He can enter Frederick's apartment the same way we did—by showing his badge. Only a handful of people could've read my notes and learned what Frederick told us. And most of them are homicide detectives."

"You really believe one of the detectives killed Professor Palatine?"

Hearing Clarence say it made it seem more real. More frightening.

"You have no clue how badly I want to be wrong."

Clarence and I walked single file through detective division, since no aisle is wide enough to accommodate us side by side.

"Team meeting's once a week," I said. "We update each other on our cases. Compare notes. Helps to have a fresh perspective."

"We do that at the *Trib* sometimes. Call in other reporters and pick each other's brains."

"That must be slim pickin's."

When we walked into the conference room, Detectives Brandon Phillips, Kim Suda, and Chris Doyle were already there. They were huddled, but the moment we entered, Doyle stood and headed for the coffee.

Tommi Elam walked in behind us, smacking her bubble gum louder than any forty-two-year-old should. Tommi's chin and nose don't quite match, but it's a good chin and a good nose. She's not beautiful, but she's cute. A little sister type. She's big sister to her partner, Karl, who's ten years younger. Her gum cracking reminds me of a gangster's girlfriend in a B movie. But she's the most likable person in homicide.

Tommi walked toward Clarence. Heavy makeup surrounded her left eye, which was puffy and bloodshot. The lower eyelid showed underlying red and purple. I'd noticed this late last week. If it was still this bad, I'd hate to have seen it when it happened.

"I'm Tommi Elam," she said to Clarence, sticking out her hand like she was chairperson of the homicide Welcome Wagon.

"Clarence Abernathy."

"The columnist. That's what I thought! That piece you wrote on volunteerism in the inner city?"

"Yes?"

"It was excellent."

"Thanks. I appreciate that."

"It's great to have you here, Clarence. Let me know if I can do anything for you." Tommi sat in front.

"She's a compulsive liar," I whispered to Clarence. "She's in therapy."

He gave me his look.

"Here comes Karl Baylor, Tommi's partner," I said. "I'm sure he'll introduce himself to you. He's a Christian, so you two might understand each other."

"Clarence Abernathy, right?" Baylor said, smiling broadly. Ten seconds into the conversation he was calling Clarence "brother," in the Christian sense I suppose, since Baylor's white as I am. This guy pushes my buttons. He should either have something done to his teeth or stop smiling so much. He always has to let people know he's a Christian.

"Don't we have the greatest view of the city from up here?" Baylor gushed like a tour guide.

His voice irritates me. It's like his diaphragm needs a larger outlet than his throat affords. It's always spurting out words in loud, spasmodic bursts of dogmatism.

"Welcome to the inner sanctum, Clarence." It was Jack Glissan, offering his hand. He waved to Noel, his partner, over by the concessions. "I'll have a Sprite."

"Sure," Noel said, then looked at Clarence and me. "Get you guys a soda?"

"I'm good," Clarence said.

"Coke," I said.

"Coca-Cola?"

I nodded, smiling at the blend of personalities that make up our homicide department. I felt guilty for suspecting them.

Manny walked through the doorway, looking for a seat by himself. He took the second seat from Bryce Cimmatoni, which guaranteed the seat between them wouldn't get taken. Who sits between two megagrouches?

Sergeant Jim Seymour stood behind the flimsy wooden podium. Things started to quiet.

"What's he doing here?" Doyle asked, pointing at Clarence.

"You've probably heard," Sarge said, "Clarence Abernathy is observing the William Palatine murder investigation. Part of the arrangement Chief Lennox made with the *Tribune* is for Abernathy to attend this meeting, but only while it's pertinent to that case."

"Great," said Suda, with a fake good-natured tone.

"Yippee," said Phillips, not bothering to fake the tone.

Tommi grinned and rolled her eyes at Clarence, like "this is the sort of stuff we have to put up with every day." Her makeup under her tender left eye was wearing off.

"No offense," I whispered to Clarence, "but cops are as fond of the media as a Frenchman is fond of deodorant."

"So we'll start with the Palatine case. Chandler?"

I handed out notes, summarized what we'd found, the limited lab results, witness interviews, the options we were considering. Naturally, I didn't say what I was *really* thinking about the killer's identity.

"Manny and I are open," I said. "Suggestions?"

"It's obvious," said a face grooved by time and trouble. Cimmatoni's jaw is so solid it doesn't move when he talks. He looks as if he could bite off a steel rod like a pepperoni stick. His voice is huge, the sort ancient orators must have used to speak on hillsides to a thousand people. Too bad Cimmatoni usually says nothing worth listening to.

"What's obvious?" I asked.

"It was a transient. A street person."

"We know what a transient is," I said. "Didn't you say the same thing when the priest was murdered by that CEO?" That got two chortles, a guffaw, and a giggle.

"Transients are your default murderers, aren't they, Cimma?" Doyle asked.

"Half our unsolved crimes are probably transients. Could be a gang member, but they're too obvious. Probably four dozen transients with digs within a quarter-mile of that house. I'll lay two to one on a transient."

"I'll put down twenty bucks," I said.

He looked like he didn't believe me, but I didn't take it personally. He hadn't believed anybody for a couple of decades.

Phillips was looking over the notes I'd handed out. "Why'd he turn blue?"

"The killer injected him repeatedly with ink," I said. There was a low whistle and some grimaces. "Summary of the toxicology report's on page three. Blue fountain pen ink."

"Traceable?"

"We're working on it."

"The noose?" Sarge asked.

"A special rope sold in nautical supply stores, used mostly for tying boats. But unless it's a recent purchase, or he used a credit card or made a cash purchase in a store where there's a security camera…"

"Once you get a suspect," Doyle said, "take his picture to boating stores."

"A suspect would be nice," I said.

"Transient," Cimmatoni muttered.

"Rope important or just a diversion?" Suda asked.

"You tell me," I said. "And here's one. Talked to his brother, who's a doctor. Palatine wore a medical chain identifying him as an insulin-dependent diabetic. Insulin bottle in the fridge. Needles in the drawer. But the professor wasn't a diabetic."

"Plus the only needle marks were in his shoulder," Clarence said. "Diabetics don't take injections there."

The silence was deafening. Outsiders never came to these meetings. That an outsider would speak was unthinkable. That the speaking outsider was a journalist was strike three.

"Why don't you take over the investigation?" Manny mumbled. "We'll write your useless columns."

"I didn't know you could write," Clarence said.

Manny's usual scowl cranked up a notch.

"People leave evidence because they're hurried," I said, "or careless, or want to be caught. Doesn't seem like he was in a hurry. But why the noose? Injection? Fountain pen ink? Insulin bottle? Needle? What does it all mean?"

"The noose suggests suicide," Karl Baylor said.

"Or execution," Cimmatoni said.

Until then, that thought hadn't crossed my mind. Two miles to the north of us, in Washington, they still hang people. Only by the condemned prisoner's request, so it's rare, but it happens. This fit the note on the computer screen and other indications that the professor had been brought to justice. But what had he done to warrant execution? If we knew, it would point to the killer.

"It doesn't have to make sense," Cimmatoni said. "Killers aren't brainiacs."

"Even when it doesn't appear to make sense, it does," I said, "if you're in the head of the killer."

"Yeah, and to be in his head it helps if you *are* the killer."

I stared at Cimmatoni. Why had he said that?

"Okay," Sarge said, "we've had more murders in the last four weeks than in the previous three months. Everybody has an open case, so we've got lots of ground to cover. Suda and Doyle, you're next. Mr. Abernathy, you're excused."

Clarence put his notepad in his briefcase and snuck out. I waved bye-bye to him, kissing the air, feeling a little smug that at least we weren't letting the *Trib* in on everything.

It seemed a long wait between breakfast with Clarence at Lou's and lunch at New York Burrito by the Federal Building, across from the Justice Center.

The only downside was that Manny was with me, and he's not a happy eater.

He made a face at his burrito. I don't mean he showed displeasure by raising his eyebrow. I mean he made an actual face. Manny's eating skills are remarkably similar to his people skills.

My partner doesn't just have a lot of issues; he's got the whole subscription.

Personality aside, however, in most respects Manny's a good partner. He's efficient, hard-nosed, and lock-jawed determined. If he catches a scent, that dog'll hunt. And he knows how to turn the thumbscrews, especially with the young and cocky. He'd make Jack Bauer proud. The world's full of personality—I don't need that in a partner.

Right now I was contemplating how to tell Manny what I was thinking about the killer being a detective.

"I don't like Abernathy coming to our meeting," he said, turning his displeasure from the burrito to me. "And I don't like him working on our case."

"Neither do I. But he's a decent guy. Almost a friend."

Manny stopped chewing and stared me down.

"Speaking loosely. In the broadest sense of *friend*. But he's a journalist. Now, if he were his father, it'd be a pleasure to have him around."

"His father was his only good feature," Manny said. "Too bad he's gone for good."

"Gone for good?"

"Yeah. Dead. You know what dead means, right?"

"It comes up now and then in this business."

"Dead is dead."

"Some say people still live after they die," I said. "That they just go somewhere else."

"Yeah, and some say we were made by aliens and at night they take us up on their ships and perform experiments."

"And that proves there's no life after death?"

"You turning religious on me?"

"No." I said it too quickly, hearing my defensiveness and wondering how I'd suddenly fallen on the other side of the argument. "You sound like Nietzsche."

"You looked up Nietzsche, didn't you?" Manny asked. "You didn't know jack about Nietzsche, and you looked him up."

"Nietzsche schmietzsche," I said, as Manny swallowed his last bite, leaving half a dead burrito, and headed out the door.

This was the deepest philosophical discussion Manny and I've ever had. It bothered me to hear him say what I'd thought myself, that Obadiah Abernathy no longer existed. Something inside, buried deep, told me this couldn't be true. And if it were, the universe was just a cruel joke.

I consoled myself with the remnants of Manny's burrito.

↔

I'd left my notebook in the office, but I jotted down my thoughts on a New York Burrito sack. It wasn't the Gettysburg Address, but it was a piece of work:

1. The killer planned the murder methodically, including the bizarre elements with the noose and the ink injections. He may have stayed forty-five minutes at the crime scene.
2. The killer knew how long it would take the cops to get there. He might have had a police monitor.
3. The killer took unnecessary measures that might make him vulnerable, like he was daring a detective to catch him. He took the time and trouble to put on the noose, inject the ink, and remove items, at least a photo and a wine bottle.
4. The killer—almost certainly—knew the private number of a homicide detective and called him from the scene.
5. The killer believes he knows investigative procedures well enough to get around them. He may take pride in his ability to outwit homicide detectives.

Seeing it in black and white was disturbing. I wanted to add a sixth point, but I wasn't sure I could. "The killer—possibly—planted incriminating evidence at the scene, including a Black Jack wrapper and a rope belonging to me. And he may have planted a donut in my car."

But if he used my rope and planted my wrapper and Wally's donut and called me from the scene, he was setting me up. Did he believe I was going to investigate the case? Or was he expecting it to be someone else, knowing that whoever did would find the evidence against me and I might be tagged with a homicide?

But something bothered me more. I couldn't remember the night of the murder. It was just…not there in my mind. Had I come home from Rosie's? Or had I gone to the professor's house?

Strange how anxiety over a blackout due to drinking can make you want to drink more.

"The plot thickens."
SHERLOCK HOLMES, *A STUDY IN SCARLET*

A JOURNEY OF A THOUSAND MILES begins with a single step.

Falling down a flight of stairs begins the same way.

The step my little gray cells had taken—that the murderer was one of our own detectives—was that kind of step.

As I walked slowly back to the Justice Center, under a thick cloud cover, I marveled at how that awful thought, on its face inconceivable, had walked right in the back door of my mind, taken off its shoes, and thrown itself on my cerebral couch. And like my cousin from South Carolina who showed up twenty years ago with a backpack and a pet boa, it showed no signs of leaving.

We're the fraternity of detectives. It's a brotherhood, including Tommi and Kim, who are brothers with different shapes and higher voices. Comrades in arms, for crying out loud. Even Cimma.

Like my platoon in Nam. We didn't all like each other, but we'd die for each other. We watched each others' backs. That's what cops do. That's what the brotherhood does.

And I was going after one of them?

"I wish you were here, Sharon," I said aloud, looking up but seeing no crack in the clouds. "I need you. I need to talk with you."

"I know, Ollie. I know. But there's someone you need a lot more than me. He can do for you far more than I ever could. Talk to Him. Turn to Him. I love you. More importantly, He loves you."

In the conference room near our work area, I walked Manny through my written points on the burrito sack.

"That's ridiculous. Your prime suspect is one of *us*?"

"Why is it ridiculous? Because you know them? Killers are always known by people. They always work with somebody. Everybody goes on TV when it all comes out and says he was a nice guy and washed their car and made them cookies and they had no clue."

"There's no way."

"Okay," I said. "If you were going to kill somebody, how would you do it?"

"I have to fight for time to go to my son's T-ball games," Manny said. "I don't have time to stage a murder."

"But if you *did* stage a murder, you'd be successful, wouldn't you?"

"You tryin' to say somethin' to me?" He stood, fists clenched tight, as if he were a gang member again and I was calling him out.

"My point is, if anybody's going to know how to pull off a murder and not get caught, it's a homicide detective, right? Any of us could do it."

He went to the door. "I'm going back to the professor's hood. I say somebody saw something. And about your theory?"

"Yeah?"

"You're losin' it."

Was I?

A homicide detective would know what *not* to do—all the things we catch people on. If I were going to kill somebody, I'd plan it so nobody would catch me.

If I was sober, that is.

I headed to Sergeant Jim Seymour's office. I took a breath and walked in. His office is well-organized, and he must have a dozen pictures of his wife and four kids, in everything from baseball to band.

"What's with that?" he asked, pointing at the sack in my hand.

I read him the burrito bag. After I'd made my case for the murderer being a detective, Sarge kept blinking at me like maybe I'd disappear after one more blink.

"I don't know what else to think," I said. "It's a hunch, but it's based on evidence. I have to consider it."

"We've got ten homicide detectives. You going to check their alibis? Let's say five of them were home alone or with their wives, then what? You'll suspect that their wives, or Tommi's husband, may be lying. Where's this going to take us? Who're you going to eliminate? Manny?"

"How can I?"

"Did you say that to his face?"

"No."

"I wouldn't recommend it. What about Jack? You going after him?"

"Sure. Everybody. Jack'll understand."

"Right. I'm sure the whole team will be dripping with sympathy."

"Look, means and opportunity come easily for us, don't they? It's all about motive. So can't homicide detectives have a motive to kill someone?"

"Sure, but…not this crew. Don't you know them better than that, Ollie? You still read your murder mysteries, don't you?"

"Yeah."

"Me too. What if you read that the prime suspects in a murder mystery were a bunch of homicide detectives?"

"Well, in a book I might think it was…lame."

"That's what I think."

"Okay, in a novel I'd never make ten homicide detectives the murder suspects. The author would be an idiot to even try it. But this is the real world."

"You said ten suspects. You mean *nine*, right? Unless you're suspecting yourself."

"Hey, it could be eleven. You have access to everything. If the evidence leads me to you, what should I do?"

"Investigate me," Sarge said. "Clear me or keep me on the suspect list."

"Then that's what I have to do with everybody."

I took the elevator down two floors to criminalist detail. The receptionist confirmed Phil Oref was there. I signed in, and she buzzed me through the security door.

As I went down the hall I saw a technician making tool marks on wood to see what they looked like, then glanced into ballistics, where they were testing guns. While the state crime lab has lots of scientists, criminalists are sworn officers, so you get to know them cop-to-cop. Sometimes you can ask a favor.

I shook Phil's hand, and we talked about the case for a few minutes.

"Know when we'll get the fingerprints on the Dumpster gun, the murder weapon? We need them pronto."

"You need everything pronto. Bates is on those. He's way behind."

"It's urgent!"

"Like always. Something else on your mind, Detective?"

"I have a confession to make," I said. "Keep it confidential?"

"Long as it's not murder."

"Last week, at the professor's house, the murder scene…you remember?"

"Be a while before I forget that one."

"Anyway, I got this terrible itch on my palm."

Phil held up his hands like stopping traffic. "You're not going to tell me you took off a glove?"

"Just for a second. Right then I saw something on the floor, by the couch, and instinct kicked in…I picked it up."

He whistled. "You contaminated evidence."

I produced the sealed bag.

"Gum wrapper? *Black Jack?* I didn't know they still made this stuff."

"They didn't for a long time."

"What was that other one, you know, um…?"

"Beemans?"

"No."

"Clove?"

"Yeah. They still make Clove?"

"You're talking to an expert. Every three years they produce Clove and Black Jack and Beemans too. I stock up on Black Jack."

"You're chewing it right now, aren't you? I can smell it. You sure it didn't just fall out of your pocket at the professor's?"

"That's what I've been wondering."

The truth is, I knew I had no gum that night. No way it fell out of my pocket. But this isn't something you tell the criminalist.

"What you want?"

"I know these wrappers can hold a print." I nodded toward the bag.

"Usually inside the wrapper, the white part. You want me to run it for you outside the system, that it? Don't want it officially entered as evidence?"

"As long as it just shows my print, either I contaminated it or just dropped it. But if someone else's print comes up…"

"Okay, Detective, I won't tell on you. We all make mistakes. Even Mr. Have-you-checked-the-keyboard-for-prints? I probably won't even tell anyone you ate the corpse's Snickers bar."

"You said you checked it for prints. It was unopened, so no saliva. Why waste it?"

"There've got to be rules against eating evidence. I should ask the chief. You not only contaminated evidence; you removed it from the crime scene. You're a piece of work, Chandler."

"You remember that journalist, Abernathy? If I'd told people what happened, it'd be in the paper, and we'd all look bad."

"You'd look bad."

"Not just me. CSI team had been all over the part of the room where I found the wrapper. I shouldn't have picked it up, but that never would've been an issue if you guys had done your job."

"I don't believe you."

"If I dropped it, okay, you're clear. But if it was already there, you guys should have seen it. While we're at it, I could mention how on the Danny Stump case you forgot to take prints from the orange juice glass, and on the Eric Wood case you knocked the houseplant on the bloodstained carpet."

"It was 3:00 a.m. I was tired!"

"It's *always* 3:00 a.m., Phil. We're always tired. Anyway, check out the gum wrapper for me. And get it back to me directly. ASAP."

"You guys always want it yesterday."

"Today would be fine."

"Tomorrow's Thanksgiving. After that, we'll see."

"Remember, this is just between us, okay?"

When I returned at three, Clarence was at my workstation, looking over the crime scene notes and lab reports.

"Insulin bottles have an expiration date on them," he said without saying hello. "What's the date on that bottle you found in the professor's fridge?"

I called the evidence room, and five minutes later Wanda had the bag and said, "Let's see, expiration date is…wow."

"What?"

"It expired in June…nine and a half years ago."

When I told Clarence he said, "You can use it a few months after expiration. A year's pushing it. Nearly ten years? Nobody'd keep it that long."

"Nice catch, Abernathy. There has to be a reason somebody held on to it. Could've been found in a drawer that hadn't been cleared out for years. But once you find it, why keep it? Why not toss it?"

"You know how I said that big syringe reminded me of the ones I used to have? I'll bet it's as old as the insulin."

"We figure out where that insulin and needle came from," I said, "and why someone held on to them ten years…and why they'd bring them to the murder scene and leave them there…we're in business!"

"Guess what," Sergeant Seymour said, leaning down over my desk, where I could see the hairs climbing out his ears. "The chief wants to meet with you, me, the lieutenant, and the captain."

"I talked to you, what, two hours ago? Word travels quickly."

"You know the drill. If it affects the larger police force, I have to take it to the lieutenant. He took it to the captain, and you know who he took it to. Now the four of us get to have a meeting. Thanks for messing up everybody's day before Thanksgiving!"

"Chief's office?"

"He's coming here. Fifteen minutes."

"But I was supposed to—"

"Doesn't matter. Drop it. You think the rest of us were doing crossword puzzles?"

Fifteen minutes later, Sarge called me into a conference room. Immediately in front of me sat Lieutenant Taylor Nicks, a bead of sweat on his forehead, which gravity was toying with. To my right was Captain Justin Swiridoff, expressionless. To my left was Chief Edward Lennox, in a suit worth more than the combined value of all clothing I'd bought in the last five years.

"What do you think you're doing?" Lennox asked.

Sergeant Seymour gestured for me to sit. I examined the chair. It didn't have straps and electrical wiring, so I sat.

"I'm doing what I always do. I'm going where the evidence points. I don't know how to do detective work any other way."

"You'd better learn another way," Lennox said. "You realize what you'd do to this department if you send the message that *one of our own* killed a popular college professor?"

"What difference would it make if he was a college professor or a plumber or a homeless guy? And why does it matter if he was popular?"

"You're trying to goad me. My point is you can't just go off, head over heels, like a chicken with its head cut off. We just can't afford more bad publicity. And the worst publicity I can imagine is acting as if one of our own murdered someone!"

"Nobody's *acting as if*. It's a working hypothesis. If it turns out to be wrong, I'll be thrilled. I'm just saying that's where the evidence seems to point." I stood up, stretched my torso, then sat back down when I saw the looks. "Doctors, lawyers, accountants, teachers, and grocery clerks have all killed people. Why not a homicide detective? Who'd be better at it? The more murders you've worked on, the more you know about murder. And how you can get away with it."

"Inconceivable," Lennox said. Captain Swiridoff nodded vigorously. Lieutenant Nicks nodded moderately. Sarge nodded slightly. The higher in the chain of command, the greater the head movement.

"Why is it inconceivable?"

"How can you even ask that question?" Lennox rubbed his moist gray forehead, swirling his makeup. "Captain? Lieutenant? Sergeant? Can you tell this man why it's just *unthinkable*?"

"We have good people here," Swiridoff said. "Our detectives solve murders; they don't commit them. Chief's right. The public would eat us alive if we tagged a detective."

"Wouldn't they eat us alive," I asked, "if we looked the other way because we knew he was one of us?"

"Lieutenant?" Lennox's voice sounded whiny.

"The evidence can be interpreted different ways," Nicks said. "There's no proof it's one of the detectives. We should operate on the assumption it's *not*. Trace down all the other leads first. Naturally, everything's complicated by your friend Abernathy working with you."

"It wasn't my idea." I stared at Lennox, whose lower teeth were moving out and back against his upper lip.

"If the newspaper gets an inkling of what you're thinking," Swiridoff said, "it could tear apart the department."

"You...haven't said anything to Abernathy, have you?" Lennox asked, his face drained of blood.

I thought of how I'd unveiled my suspicions to Abernathy, shocking him with the prospect that a detective could be the murderer. I hoped no one noticed my slight hesitation.

"Like I'd drop so much as a *hint* to a *Tribune* reporter that I suspected a cop? What kind of a dimwit do you think I am?"

I was holding a hand of nothing, seven high. Folding wasn't an option. Bluffing was my only chance.

"You're an idiot," Lennox said. "But I'll grant you, nobody's *that* big an idiot."

Apparently he'd forgotten I was King of the Idiots.

"Sergeant," Lennox said, "you haven't said anything to talk sense into this man."

Seymour looked at the chief, captain, and lieutenant, in that order. He'd been a cop most of his life.

"If he's making a rush to judgment, I'd try to talk him out of it," Sarge said. "Chandler cuts corners, and I've had to pick up the pieces. Still, he's one of the best detectives I've ever seen."

The sweet talk made me blush and grin.

"But I wouldn't underestimate how big a dimwit he could be. He may just be warming up."

I stopped grinning.

"Still," Sarge said, "the evidence suggests we may have an internal problem. I don't see how we can overlook it. Our job is to follow the evidence and solve the crime. How it makes us look doesn't matter."

"You've been a police officer how long, Sergeant?" Lennox asked.

"Thirty-five years, sir."

"And you were last promoted when?"

"Fifteen years ago. I like my job. It's what I—"

"Yes. No doubt. But perhaps you aren't qualified to assess how important our public image is. We work for the people. They pay our salary. What they think of us *does* matter."

"But it's secondary, not primary. And I believe they'll think more highly of us when we catch killers—whoever they are."

I could have kissed Sergeant Seymour. And if you saw his mug, you'd understand what that means.

"No one's saying to look the other way," Swiridoff said. "We're just saying, use discretion."

"It's essential that Abernathy doesn't catch wind of this possibility," Lennox said. "I'm going to tell Raylon Berkley the deal's off. I don't want Abernathy on this case."

"Won't that look suspicious?" Nicks asked.

"I'll give him a good reason and offer alternatives. Meanwhile, I'm counting on you three men to make sure Detective Chandler stays within his limits and does *not* damage our image. When it comes to your future in this department—all of you—there are other fish in the sea. Am I clear on that point?"

The captain and lieutenant nodded. Sarge's neck went rigid.

"Am I clear on that, Sergeant?"

"Very clear."

"As for you, Chandler, if you mishandle this case, it'll be your last. These men are my witnesses. If your career goes down in flames, you won't be alone. I'll hold any or all of your superiors accountable. Do you hear what I'm saying? All of you?"

Everybody nodded. Even me.

I drove home in the darkness. I didn't turn on the radio, or Michael Pritchard reading Nero Wolfe. I even turned off my cell phone. My body was behind the wheel, but my mind was elsewhere. My meeting with the brass was bugging me; so were nagging thoughts about the gum wrapper and rope. My mind landed on the discussions with Jake and Clarence. They'd raised again the two events I can never escape…Sharon's death being one of them.

Maybe it was the looming shadow of Thanksgiving. Holidays can do that to you when you have great memories of a past but no hope for a future. Maybe it's the holiday's name. You know you're far better off than most people who've ever lived, but you're still not happy. And part of you refuses to give thanks because you've lost so much and you feel like you deserve better than what you've gotten.

Then I felt guilty, because I hate entitlement, whining, and ingratitude—three things ruining our country. Yet when I look inside myself, I see the things I hate. Sometimes I think maybe what's wrong with this world is that it's made up of people like me.

During my first years as a detective, I never discussed my work with Sharon. I figured it would depress her. What depressed her was that I shut her out. I kept it inside, but it ate at me.

"Let me in," she'd say.

"You don't want in," I'd say.

"Some wives can live with their husband's silence. I can't. If you don't trust me enough to let me in, it's going to destroy our marriage."

I started doing what my superiors wouldn't approve. I'd fill her in on a case. It made me feel better. We could talk about it for hours. When I said, "You've got to be sick of this," she'd say, "I'd rather have us talk about a murder case than talk about nothing." Then magically, once we talked it out, we could move on to other things. And I was no longer shutting her out.

Sharon was my closest friend and I was hers. Until her last days, that is, when she spent more and more time with Janet Woods, Geneva Abernathy, and Sue Keels. "I love those ladies," she said. "That Geneva—her smile seems lit from the inside, like a big candle flame coming through a carved pumpkin."

My wife said things like that.

"When I'm with them, I feel encouraged," she said. "I feel hope."

"And when you're with me?"

"I feel your love. It seems like the love was late in coming. But now that it's here, I'm so grateful. But…"

"But?"

"But when I'm with you, I don't feel much hope. Long-term hope, I mean. You're always trying to give me hope that I'm going to beat this cancer. But I don't know if I *can* beat it."

"Don't say that."

"You mean well, Ollie. You've become my cheerleader, and I love you for it. But I *am* going to die."

"Stop it!" Hot blood flooded my brain.

"Okay, let's say I *do* beat this cancer. Then what? Does that mean I won't die? Of course not. I'll die at a different time, maybe in a different way. You'll die too. I just want to be ready. Geneva and Janet and Sue are helping me get ready."

"They're helping you give up, that's what they're doing! They're throwing dirt on your grave!"

"No, they're not. They're showing me God loves me and—"

"God loves you? Then why's He doing this to you?"

"I don't know, Ollie. There's a lot I don't know. But I want to spend the time I have left—whether it's weeks or years—learning more about Him."

"Fine. Whatever."

"Following Jesus is like a fresh start. I feel like I've been wasting my life."

"On me? And Kendra and Andrea? We're a waste?"

"What a terrible thing to say. You know I don't think that."

Her tears started flowing, and my stupid heart broke.

"Sorry."

"Even my death is about you, isn't it, Ollie?"

"What's that supposed to mean?"

"You're the detective. Why don't you figure it out?"

My job is figuring out why people died. But I'll never figure out why Sharon died.

When she was near the end, Jake said to me, "God loves you and Sharon."

If God loved us, why didn't He help us? Why isn't Sharon still alive? If He's in control of everything…then He's the one who killed Sharon. So why would I trust my wife's killer?

Thanksgiving? For what?

"They say that genius is an infinite capacity for taking pains. It's a very bad definition, but it does apply to detective work."
SHERLOCK HOLMES, *A STUDY IN SCARLET*

THURSDAY, NOVEMBER 28

THANKSGIVING DAY.

My daughter Kendra hadn't returned my call—she usually doesn't—so I drove toward Jake's house to join his family and the family of Finney Keels, Jake's old buddy who died years ago.

I pulled up across the street from Jake's and tried to find motivation to get out of the car and face another holiday with a group that didn't include Sharon. After ten minutes, I walked to the front door.

The first person to greet me was Little Finn, Finney Keels's Down syndrome boy. He wasn't so little anymore, but his face was still that of a child.

"Hi dere, Unca Ollie!" He put his arms around me.

"Still working at the health club, Finn?"

"Yeah, Mr. Eisenzimmer says I'm his best 'ployee!"

"I'll bet you're one fine 'ployee."

"No, it's 'ployee," he said.

I nodded and smiled.

"Uncle Ollie!"

I turned and looked at the familiar smile of the young woman in the wheelchair. I came close to her, bending down. Carly Woods, brown-haired with a hint of red, reached out and hugged me. She was so thin now it was like being hugged by dried-up branches. She felt brittle, and I was afraid to squeeze lest she crack.

Carly seems to like me. I'm grateful for her naïveté, but I can't stand what she's going through. It isn't right. Her son Finney, named after Little Finn's dad, Finney Keels, shook my hand politely and firmly. I liked that. He looks like his grandfather Jake.

Jake gave me his muscular Vietnam vet handshake. Janet fawned over me, taking my coat and offering me malted milk balls, which she knows I love. When you come to gatherings alone, it helps to have something to do with your hands…and your mouth.

"Ollie!" Sue Keels, still blond and petite, threw her arms around me. "I've really missed you."

Funny how you know when people mean what they say.

I see Sue only a couple of times a year when I pick up Little Finn and take him to a ball game or a movie, usually with Jake. I got to know her while investigating her husband's murder. She's dated a few guys since then, one or two I've met at our Thanksgiving gatherings, but she's never remarried. She's a sweetheart, and she'd be a great catch for any guy with a high tolerance for talk about Jesus. But with her it's more than talk. She gives me hope that her beliefs aren't empty, and that, in the end, maybe Sharon's weren't either.

Sue's daughter Angela and granddaughter Karina were there, with Sue's grandsons Ty, Matthew, and Jake. (People get named after each other in these families). The three boys are an entertaining little trio—binky-sucker, stair-climber, and fridge-raider.

It wasn't long before we'd grabbed hands, Carly on one side and Little Finn on the other. I knew what was coming. Different people pray before meals, but usually Little Finn steals the show.

"God in heaven," Finn said, much louder than necessary, "tank You dat You are dere and here and everywhere else, even under da bed and in da closet and on da roof, and in dat scary corner in da garage by da paint cans. Tank You for takin' care of me and my mom and sister and niece and nephews, and everybody else's nieces and nephews and cousins and children and parents and grandmothers and grandfathers and great-grandmothers, and da people they don't know very well too."

There were amens and nods and smiles. I know because I was looking around the table, not being much of a prayer guy. One time I closed my eyes in a group setting and opened them to see a gun pointed at a hostage. Since then I've made it a habit not to close my eyes in public.

Little Finn was going right on, as if he were talking to a real person.

"Tank You, Jesus, dat my dad's dere with You and he's lookin' forward to seein' me again just like I want to see him. Please make dat happen soon, Lord. Say hi to him for me, and hi to Unca Clarence's daddy, Mr. Abernathy, and his sister and niece and say hi to Unca Ollie's wife, Sharon, who also died. And Carly is going to be joining them soon too, so please tell everybody she's coming, okay?"

I looked at Jake and Janet and saw tears come to their eyes, and when I looked at Carly, right beside me, I saw a huge smile on her face. She nodded and said a soft "Yes, Lord."

"And Jesus," Finn wasn't done, "tank You for this Thanksgiving dinner and for Aunt Janet and my mom, Mrs. Susan Keels, and for everybody who came with food, including da pie somebody bought at Safeway. And God, we also pray for

Unca Ollie dat he repent and come to Jesus and admit that he's a big sinner."

Little Finn squeezed my left hand and Carly squeezed my right, and she looked up at me and laughed hysterically. It was contagious, and others started laughing. I laughed too.

Little Finn went right on, "And God please forgive everybody for laughin' in da midda of my prayer, but we do wanna laugh tonight, just not during da prayer, so help me to finish this prayer so it will be 'kay to laugh. In Jesus' name..."

"Amen!" Five people said at once, and Little Finn was done. Now he was laughing too.

I looked at him and marveled that he could be in his twenties now and still a child. He reminded me of Obadiah Abernathy, a man I'd known in his eighties, who even then was childlike. It made me long for the childhood I'd left behind too soon. One that my father or Nam or job or the realities of life and death had taken from me.

The meal was wonderful—turkey and dressing and gravy and corn and the most wonderful biscuits drenched in butter and strawberry jam. I had three tall glasses of milk, plus sparkling cider that Finn told me I just had to drink.

Afterward we sat around the living room telling stories. Jake and I talked about our tours in Vietnam. They asked me to tell them detective stories. I obliged, and they seemed interested. The children made everybody laugh, and Champ, Jake's old springer spaniel, sat at my side, where I scratched him nonstop. Mulch would demand an explanation.

Dogs know the people who love them, and they know enough not to walk away from a good thing. If only we were that smart.

As it got dark, I looked around for Carly but couldn't find her. The conversation had broken into groups of threes and fours, and I stood and stretched and inched my way toward the hall closet and my trench coat. Jake caught me.

"Carly wants you to say good-bye before you leave. She's in her room."

I knocked on the partly open door.

"Come in."

Carly was lying in her bed, all tucked in, with her right arm outside the covers. Her son Finney's head was on a pillow next to her. Her smile lit up the room. I know that's a cliché worthy of the chief, but I don't care. It did.

"Uncle Ollie, I'm so glad you came."

"Wouldn't leave without saying good-bye," I said.

She whispered to Finney. He jumped off the bed and walked out of the room telling me, "I'm going to have blackberry pie." I smiled my approval.

"How you feeling?" I asked Carly.

"Not great. I get so tired. But I'm grateful. It could be a lot worse."

I stood there and stared, like an idiot.

"It may not be much longer," she said.

"What do you mean?"

"Maybe you missed that part of Little Finn's prayer," she said, grinning. "In case you haven't heard, I'm supposed to die pretty soon."

"No, you're not." I knew it was stupid the moment I said it. Sometimes I need a filter between my brain and my tongue.

"Sounds like you've got inside information. Maybe you could fill me in. And the doctors, too!" She laughed.

How could she laugh?

"Don't feel bad for me. I know where I'm going."

"Good," I said, which seemed better than saying, "How could you *possibly* know that?"

"Jesus promised He was preparing a place for His followers so we could live with Him forever." Her voice was light and airy.

"So I've been told."

"Do you believe it?"

"Sometimes I want to."

"And sometimes you don't?"

I nodded.

"Aunt Sharon believed in Jesus."

"Yeah. She changed her thinking a lot before…" I trailed off.

"She died."

"Before I lost her."

"When you know where someone's gone, you haven't lost them," she said, sticking her thin, shivering arm under the covers.

"I'm just not as sure as you are."

"If you knew Jesus, you'd feel differently."

"I'm not a religious man, Carly."

"Neither am I. I mean I'm obviously not a man, but I'm not religious either."

"You sure sound religious to me."

"Because I believe Jesus and love Him? That's not religion. It's just love and trust. Trust in what I've seen."

"You mean what you *haven't* seen."

"No. First, all those years ago I saw what Jesus did to my dad. How He changed him through and through. You've known my dad a long time. You've seen it, haven't you?"

I nodded.

"Then I saw what He did in my mom's life. And finally I experienced Him myself. He changed me from the inside out. I believe Him. I believe His promises. I believe in the resurrection and the new earth. I believe that He's going to take away all the pain and wipe away all the tears. Those are His promises. I'm taking them to the bank."

"Good for you," I said. I didn't hear conviction in my voice. I suspect she didn't either.

"It's only good for me if God keeps His promises. But I believe He does."

She pulled out that arm again and beckoned me to come close. I could hear her breathing now in little puffs.

"Can I pray for you, Uncle Ollie?"

I nodded numbly. I can't tell you what she said except, like Little Finn, she sounded like she was talking to a real person. I can't explain it. It was really...well, not religious. She said the names Andrea and Kendra. Not hearing what she said about them, even their names stabbed my heart.

An "Amen" yanked me out of my fog.

"I may not see you again here," Carly said. "But I hope I'll see you again there. And if I do, let's make a date to walk the new earth together, okay? Maybe visit the New Grand Canyon or the New Mount Everest or the New Lake Victoria. Maybe even the New Portland. Without any crime or suffering or death."

"What would I do for a living?"

She laughed. "You'd be living all right...and you'd find plenty to do. You'd love every minute of it. I know you would."

I looked at the floor. I couldn't bear to look at her. She was so much more alive than I was.

She stretched her arms out to me, like an angel but better, and I felt her thin fingers on the back of my neck and something light on my cheek. I heard her say, "I love you."

I stumbled out of her room and out the front door. Somebody said something to me. I don't know who or what.

I pushed my way into the cold east wind, weak in my stomach and my legs, feeling something sticking to my face. I barely made it to the car, fumbled with the keys, and dropped them. I swore. I sat in the car a long time before I realized I was shaking. I turned the key and continued to sit. It might have been ten minutes later when I noticed a curtain move and saw Janet looking at me. Afraid Jake would come out, I pulled away.

I went home, thinking of Jake and Janet and Carly and Finney and Sue and Little Finn—and Sharon too. I felt a lingering warmth inside, harpooned by sharp cold.

How could I explain what I'd seen?

How could Carly Woods believe in a God who was letting her just shrivel up and die?

"I'm so happy Carly's coming soon."

"So am I."

"It's going to be hard on Jake and Janet to lose her."

"Did you not hear My daughter's words, Finney?"

"Right. They're not going to lose her because they'll know she's here with You. But they don't know what it's like here. I sure didn't. It's so much better than I imagined."

"I've told them about this place and much more about the new earth, but somehow they don't grasp it."

"Wherever You are, it's heaven."

"So it is, Finney. But the best is yet to come. I will relocate all of this, all of us, to a new realm. There you and your people will at last reign over the earth, exercising dominion as I intended from the beginning when I made your planet and the morning stars shouted for joy."

Finney Keels entered into the Carpenter's joy, He who was the maker and repairer of people and worlds. Finney felt his companion's arm rest on his shoulder, an arm that felt extraordinarily light considering it had created the universe.

FRIDAY, NOVEMBER 29, 9:00 A.M.

"Chandler? Phil Oref, criminalist detail."

"You finally got that fingerprints report?"

"On the gun in the Dumpster? Not my assignment. I'm calling about your gum wrapper."

"You can get me results in two days when you've already taken a week on the gun?"

"I'll say it again. I have nothing to do with the gun. We're understaffed, Detective."

"What you got on the gum wrapper?"

"One thumbprint, 60 percent of a whole, and a partial finger, both yours."

"Mine?"

"Yeah. That's what you were expecting, right?"

"Right. Nothing else though?"

"Just yours. Must have dropped from your pocket. You want me to put this into the evidence room with the rest of the stuff?"

"No," I said a little too emphatically. "I better get it back. I was a dope to touch it with my glove off."

"Yeah, you were."

"At least I didn't contaminate a blood sample."

"It was 3:00 a.m., okay? I'll have it here in an evidence bag, inside a manila envelope with your name on it, for you to pick up. Won't have a case number since it's outside the system. I could get in trouble for this. So could you. You owe me, Detective."

"Actually, we're even now."

I drove ten minutes to the Property Evidence Warehouse at Seventeenth and Jefferson, by Lincoln High School. It's an old cement building with ramps that looks like it was a giant auto repair shop in a previous life. Once you get past sign-in and back to the evidence viewing room, the tables and chairs are bare and uninviting. But rather than go through the hoops of checking out evidence and having to bring it back, I decided to set up camp and tackle four evidence boxes we seized from Palatine's file cabinet the night of the murder. With help, I found the boxes stacked in P-8, on rack shelving like Costco or Home Depot.

It took me two hours to go through three boxes of papers. Talk about panning mud and rocks. I nearly gave up, partly because the evidence viewing room is within smelling range of the two vaults in the back of the warehouse, which contain guns and drugs. I couldn't smell the guns but caught periodic whiffs of marijuana. The primary offender, though, was crank, or meth, which smells like cat urine with a touch of fingernail polish. A couple of hours is all I can take.

In the back of the final box, which had the contents of the lowest file drawer, was a thick folder labeled "Special papers." On top was a student's five-year-old paper with a red grade on it: A+. Under it was a paper two years old, another seven years old, and fifteen more student papers, all marked A or A+, with dates ranging from fifteen years to three months ago.

I started reading these papers one by one. I'm no philosopher, but I've read great writers—including Rex Stout, Mickey Spillane, Dashiell Hammett, and Ross Macdonald. I'm talking the giants. So I know good writing and bad writing when I see it. Most of these papers were not good writing. No one would accuse these students of plagiarism.

Some papers had numbers penciled after the grade. The highest was a ten, the lowest was a one, and most were in between.

It was then I realized that not one of the papers was written by a guy.

I picked one paper I'd read, a treatise on a dude named Hobbes, with a red smiling face next to the A+, and a penciled number 3 next to that. The paper was written by a Cassandra Fields. I barely stayed awake while reading and decided to track her down to find out why the professor gave her an A+ and a smiley face for such mediocre writing.

I drove back to the Justice Center. If you want to find out about somebody quickly, it helps to be a cop. Within fifteen minutes I had a fax of Cassandra's college transcript, knew where she lived and with whom and that she worked in the Multnomah County library, just a few minutes away. After another call, I found she'd be at work for three more hours. She agreed to meet me in a library conference room during her break, as long as I had proper ID.

Cassandra was attractive, though she'd put on weight since college. I knew this because I recognized her flaming red hair. She was one of dozens of young girls in the professor's pictures.

She led me to a conference room with an ancient Greece theme, including a model of the Parthenon.

"As I said, I'm investigating the murder of Professor William Palatine. We're talking to former students. You remember him?"

"Yes."

"You remember what grade you got in his class?"

"I had him for two classes. I think I…got As."

"Did you usually get As in your classes?"

Her face flushed, and she looked down. "Sometimes."

"Well," I said, looking at the top paper in my file, "in four years at the university, you got a total of three As. Two were from Professor Palatine. The other was a PE class."

"You have my transcript?"

"Yes."

"Why?" She was wringing her hands.

"Were you close to the professor?"

"I haven't seen him since I graduated."

"Were you seeing him before you graduated?"

"Yes, of course…I mean, I always saw him in class."

"Only in class?"

"Mainly in class."

"Ever go to his home?"

The best lie detector is experience. I've learned that some people spout lies too quickly, like a counterpunch. Some weigh and measure their lies to get the words right. For others, like Cassandra, the delay comes from a crisis of conscience in which they try to decide whether to lie or tell the truth. Her face and her hands told her story.

"I have a picture of you taken in his home."

Her eyes widened and face whitened. "He took pictures?"

I nodded.

"I was never that kind of girl," she said. "He was the first…" She started crying. "I've always regretted it. It makes me feel cheap. At first I thought I was special. He was never mean, really, but when he was finished with me, I knew it."

"Did he write you poetry?"

She snapped backward as if I'd slapped her. "How did you know that?"

"Still have it?"

"I burned it years ago."

"You remember what it looked like? Was the ink sort of thick?"

She nodded.

"What color was it?"

"Blue."

"Did it look like this?" I handed her a card, the one from Palatine's file drawer, with the three quotes about love.

"How did…? I burned it!"

"This one wasn't to you."

The redness came back to her face, which got wetter. She was using her sleeve. I wished I had Kleenex.

"Can I get you anything? A glass of water?"

She shook her head. "What are you going to do with the photos? Do people have to see them?"

"I only know of one."

I handed it to her. She was standing in the picture with four other girls, two of them between her and the professor.

"That's it?" she asked.

"Yes."

"But I thought you said…"

"I just said I had a photo of you taken in his house."

"Okay. Well…that's good."

"Thank you, Miss Fields. I'll call you if I have more questions."

I stood and moved to the door. She sat motionless.

"Are you coming out?"

She shook her head, no eye contact. "I'll just stay here for now."

"I'm…sorry."

Her face rested on her hands, which were palm down on the table. I saw a box of Kleenex at the front desk, grabbed a handful, and took them back to Cassandra Fields. Still looking down, she sobbed when she clutched them. I put my hand lightly on her shoulder, then left her to her demons.

I grabbed a late lunch at the Pizza Schmizza three blocks south of the library, but it didn't settle, so I left some, which shows how hard Cassandra's story hit me. I returned to the central precinct at the Justice Center and made phone calls. There's no point in telling you details about the other contacts I made, following up on A+ papers in Palatine's file. Five of the nine I was able to reach on the telephone admitted that they'd had a relationship with Palatine. He hadn't kept these papers for their literary value, but as reminders of something else.

But when the afternoon had finished, it was Cassandra Fields who haunted me, because hers was the only face I'd seen. I couldn't shake her vulnerability, hurt, and shame. Had I been her father or brother I might have considered killing Palatine myself.

I'm no Victorian. I don't much care what people do in their private lives. But a professor is in a power position, and if he abuses his power and seduces his students, and especially if he does it repeatedly, I think something should be done to him. Maybe not death, but something permanent.

Short of that, I'd volunteer to beat him within a millimeter of his life, because though I don't use the metric system, I know a millimeter is a lot less than an inch.

I sat down in front of Billy the Bartender at Rosie O'Grady's, munching on pretzels and peanuts. "What time did I leave here a week ago Wednesday night?"

"Like I should remember if *you* don't?" Billy squinted at me. "Haven't seen you since you was here Saturday."

"I'm talking the Wednesday before that. When I came in the door, you were ragging on Mayor Branch's "Beautify Portland" plan and how much it was going to cost Rosie's. Remember when I left?"

"Checking out your own alibi?"

"Just answer my question."

"Little after ten, I reckon. Ten thirty outside. Early for you. I asked if you wanted a cab, but you wasn't in a mood to listen."

"What mood was I in?"

"Ticked off."

"About what?"

"Government. Religion. Education. The mayor. That newspaper guy. The police chief. You name it."

"I mentioned the chief?"

"You called him names. Want I should repeat them?"

"What did I say about education?"

"You was groanin' about liberal communist college professors who act like cops are the criminals."

"I said that?"

"And a hundred other things. You pushed a customer who made a crack about donuts."

"I didn't push anybody."

"Yeah you did. People were backing off. I heard one guy say you're a lot tougher than you look…said he'd seen you knock somebody cold with a head butt. That true?"

"You're sure I was gone by ten thirty?"

"Pretty sure," he said, wiping the bar with a wet towel. "Get a memory, will you? Then you won't have to use mine."

I've had plenty of firsts. My first kiss, Heidi Holstrom, third grade. My first transistor radio—high-tech, costing me a twenty-dollar fortune—on which I listened to Elvis and Buddy Holly. My first date with Sharon at the original Spaghetti Factory in downtown Portland, back when spumoni ice cream had those little candied fruit doohickeys in it. My first NFL game, in Seattle at the old Kingdome, watching Jim Zorn and Steve Largent. My first World Series, in New York, Yankees versus Braves. My first arrest. My first solved homicide.

Most of the firsts, with the exception of my inauguration to the oven of Vietnam, when I melted into a puddle, I remember fondly. But today was another first.

I considered my inability to remember what I'd done after leaving Rosie's. I thought about Wally's Donuts, three lousy blocks from the professor's. I thought about the Black Jack gum wrapper I'd removed from the crime scene. I weighed Billy's testimony that I was mad enough to push people around.

It was another first for me when I wrote a new name on my suspect list.

Mine.

"Nothing clears up a case so much as stating it to another person."
SHERLOCK HOLMES, *SILVER BLAZE*

SATURDAY, NOVEMBER 30

I HAD MEANS. I had opportunity. I didn't have an alibi, and while it seemed that the alcohol in my system would have prevented me from the crime, it also might have emboldened me. Tangible evidence—both the gum wrapper and the rope—placed me at the scene.

But what could have been my motive? Did it lay in the gaps of my existence, the blackouts that had increased in frequency and duration?

One of the sore points in comics history is that Hal Jordan, Green Lantern, failed to save Coast City, his childhood home, from destruction. That failure turned him mad. Unable to prevent this terrible injustice, he tried to right all wrongs, but resorted to wrongdoing to do it. The great champion of good turned evil.

My meals with Jake and Clarence at Lou's Diner were up to two a week—a bonus for working with Clarence, since it was natural to include Jake, who we trust and who we're both more comfortable around than each other. This time we were meeting on a Saturday, after which Clarence and I would be working on the case. I sat at our booth, getting in a few beers before my buddies arrived, admiring the orange flower Rory called a gerbera daisy.

A dilemma is a problem for which you can see no solution.

When you work with a bunch of guys you'd die for in a heartbeat—even if you don't like them all—and you follow the evidence, which tells you the murder was committed by one of them…and will cause mega-resentment from the other detectives…and make a community that's already suspicious of cops believe they've been proven right…and when you're working every day not just with cops you can't trust, but a journalist…this is a dilemma. It weighed on me enough that it threatened my appetite, though the threat proved hollow.

Jake entered, said hi, then went right to the Rock-Ola, pressing C3. The haunting lyrics of "Bridge over Troubled Water" transported us again, and we were both thinking of Vietnam.

Clarence walked in halfway through, and my companions looked as melancholic as I felt. But eventually Rory came to the rescue, burgers dripping with Tillamook cheese and Lou's special sauce, a doctored Thousand Island dressing. A mouthwatering feast that cures your ailments...or masks them, and I'll settle for that.

"*Buonissimo?*" Rory asked, after we took our first bites.

"Buonissimo," we said in unison, wiping our mouths.

Over lunch, Clarence talked about the hordes of boys interested in his teenage daughter, Keisha. Clarence asked, "What did you guys do when boys paid attention to your daughters?"

Jake deferred to me, which was odd, since he's the good dad and I'm not. Still, it was nice to give an opinion on something besides murder or the problem of evil.

"I remember once we were at Dea's, enjoying a father-daughter time, with extra fry sauce. In the middle of my Long Burger, I notice a guy, maybe seventeen, giving Kendra the eye. While she was looking at him, I unsnapped my SIG-Sauer P226, lifted it halfway out of the holster, and stared him down like he was a stray dog rummaging my flower garden. His eyes turned saucerlike, he left the remnants of his burger, and hit the pavement."

Clarence was smiling, which he should do more often since it makes him look like his father.

"Anyway," I continued, "Kendra was oblivious to what I'd done, which came in handy because these situations started happening a couple times a week. Approximately two dozen teenage boys, seeing me handle my pistol, decided there were other girls to look at besides Kendra. Finally she started noticing. 'It makes me want to totally die when he does that,' she told Sharon. Once upon a time she thought it was cool I was a detective, but eventually it became a great deal lower on the food chain than if I'd been a guitarist or assistant manager at Gap."

"She went off to college, right?" Clarence said, as the Rock-Ola told us our answers were "Blowin' in the Wind."

"When she went to Portland State, she moved downtown, and I saw her a lot less. But I felt just as protective. Even after college, she was dating some loser, and I found out he'd knocked her down and slapped her around. She tried to keep Sharon from telling me, but I found out when I bumped into her girlfriend at Starbucks. Kendra was shuffling around like a bag lady, in a daze, waiting for the jerk to come back and beat her up again. When I saw her at Christmas a month later, she'd heard her ex-boyfriend was limping. Apparently he'd been beaten up in an alley by a guy wearing a ski mask."

"No kidding?" Clarence said.

"Yeah. Her boyfriend bragged that he got in some good punches, even though the guy was 6'5" and used a bat on him. So he wasn't only a woman-beater; he was a liar."

"How do you know he was lying?"

"Because I'm only 6'1", he didn't land a single punch, and I didn't use a bat. It was just Fist One and Fist Two." I held them up.

Clarence started to laugh but looked at Jake and said, "Is he serious?"

Jake nodded.

For once, neither of them knew what to say.

At one thirty, Clarence and I set up camp at the Justice Center, where there's extra elbow room on Saturdays. That's good, because my workstation is too small for the two of us. Anything is. As Clarence sat writing on his notebook computer, I finished the final paperwork on the Lincoln Caldwell case.

Given Chief Lennox's threats, I'd half expected Clarence to be yanked from the case by now. Apparently Raylon Berkley wasn't willing to pull his fox out of the henhouse and was holding Lennox to his commitment.

"Look, Ollie...you found my sister's killer," Clarence said. "I owe you for that. I'm concerned what's going to happen if you pursue this theory that the killer's a detective."

"You want me to back off too?"

"Don't cops make it hard on other cops who...?"

"Who turn them in? Squeal like a pig? Guys believe the golden rule is *cops don't tell on cops.* Since nobody looks after cops—it's not like the *Tribune's* watching our back—it becomes 'we take care of our own.' If you don't, you're a traitor."

"Can't you explore other options first?"

"You think I want this? Nothing's worse than a dirty cop. And since when are you looking out for me?"

"My daddy liked you, Ollie. And he was a good judge of character."

"Still am, son. Still am." The man watching the unfolding events on earth smiled broadly and laughed loudly, reaching up to slap the back of the huge warrior beside him.

It suddenly clicked, seeming to come out of nowhere. I snapped my fingers at Clarence.

"My daughter took a class from Palatine. That's when I visited his classroom. With Kendra!"

"That just came to you?"

"It was one of my sporadic attempts to be involved in my daughter's life. I went to a couple of her classes. She made me promise not to show my gun or arrest anybody for smoking pot. It wasn't a warm and fuzzy day. Maybe that's why I'd pushed it to the back burner. It must have been…maybe ten years ago."

"Call her. Talk to her about the professor."

"There're hundreds of students who took his class recently."

"None of them would be your daughter."

"It's not that easy."

"You've got a reason to meet with your daughter. Take advantage of it."

"No way."

"If you found out where Andrea is, would you call her?"

"Of course."

"Well, you know where Kendra is. Call her."

I shook my head. Clarence grabbed my cell phone from the desk. "I'll call her. What's her number?"

"Forget it."

"You don't know her number, do you?"

"I don't know anybody's number. I speed dial."

"What's her speed dial number?"

When I didn't answer, Clarence pressed 1. "This retrieves messages? Oops. 911." He cancelled.

"If you don't give that back, you'll need 911." I reached for it, but he turned his back, which is roughly the size of Fenway's Green Monster.

"Who's 2? Homicide." Clarence was pressing each number and waiting to see the ID pop up before he stopped the call. "3 is…Lou's Diner. 4 is…Flying Pie Pizza? 5 is…Jake. I'll let him know he got beat by pizza. 6 is…Ollie, I'm touched. I made your top six."

"Only because the video store closed. You got bumped up. I plan to replace you with Krispy Kreme."

"Number 7 is…Kendra! How's that for detective work?"

"Give me my phone or I'll pistol-whip you."

"Is this Kendra?" Clarence asked.

I froze.

"Hi, this is Clarence Abernathy. You know, your dad's friend? From the *Trib*?" Clarence paused. "No, that's Jake Woods. I'm the other columnist. Yes, the big guy. There's something else about me you may have noticed. No? Really? I'm black. Yeah. Most people pick up on that." He laughed. "Anyway, can I ask you a question? Do you remember your philosophy prof from PSU?" He paused. "Dr. Palatine, right. You do? Good."

With a lightning move I snatched the phone out of his ham-bone mitt.

"Hi, sweetie, this is Dad. I apologize for Mr. Abernathy. He can be irritating."

"He sounds nice," she said.

"He's not."

"What do you want?"

"You had Philosophy with Dr. Palatine?"

"I took him for 101, then Ethics and another class. Uh…Logic, I think."

"Do you remember that day, maybe ten years ago, when I went with you to a couple classes?"

"I've tried to forget. Mom was going to come because it was a family visit day, but she got sick. She begged you to take her place. You didn't want to."

"It wasn't that I didn't want to, I just—"

"No, you didn't want to. More important things to do. Like always. You left my other class early."

"Wasn't that the all-women class?"

"Feminist Literature. There were two boys in the class. Anyway, you didn't like it. What's new? So, I hear Professor Palatine died."

"I'm investigating his case."

"Why am I not surprised? What do you want from me?"

"It's been a while since we talked."

"You didn't call me. Your friend Clarence called. About the investigation?"

"Well…sort of." I scowled at Clarence, who gave me a smug look. "Listen, since you had Palatine for three classes, would you mind talking to me about him? Telling me what you remember?"

"I'm busy. My job keeps me going."

"How about tonight?"

"You think I'm not doing something on a Saturday night?"

"Tomorrow?"

"Lots of people knew Dr. Palatine better than me. I was only at his house once."

"You were at his house?"

"He had groups of students over. There were maybe eight of us one night."

"Well…it's been a while since we've gotten together. Could I meet you at Lou's Diner?"

"Do they serve vegetarian meals?"

"Uh, I don't know. I don't think I've seen…Lou's has salads, right Clarence?"

"Their steak salad's great."

"Yeah, right," I said to Kendra. "There's a steak salad with bacon and—"

"Do you know what vegetarian means? I don't eat meat."

"Look, you could order the steak salad without the steak and the bacon, just with…you know, whatever's left. What about tomorrow night at seven?"

"It would have to be Monday night. Eight would be better."

"That's pretty late for dinner, isn't it?"

"No, it's not."

"Okay. Lou's is on Yamhill, near Fourth, halfway between Pizza Schmizza and Chipotle Mexican Grill, you know where—"

"I've seen it. It's near Pioneer Place, Saks Fifth Avenue, Gap, all the great shops."

"Right. There's those too."

"That diner looks…out of it."

"Lou's is cutting-edge retro. Nonsmoking. Has flowers and everything. You'll love it. See you Monday at eight?"

She hung up.

I looked at Clarence and his stupid smile.

"What?" I said. "You've never seen a guy ask his daughter to dinner? No Monday night football for me."

I pressed 3.

"Lou's Diner."

"Rory? Ollie. Listen, do you guys have vegetarian food?"

He chuckled. "This is a funny joke, Mr. Ollie."

"This isn't a joke. My daughter's a vegetarian."

"I am so sorry to hear that."

"Yeah, stuff happens. Anyway I'm meeting her there for dinner Monday night. Could you make her a steak salad without the steak and bacon? And with lots of extra tomatoes and green stuff?"

"Lettuce?"

"Yeah. Lettuce is good. How about cheese? Cheese isn't meat, is it?"

"I do not think so. I am Italian. I never run out of cheese. But some vegetarians don't eat dairy products, no?"

"That's scary. Anyway, be sure you don't run out of lettuce, okay?"

"We have many salads in a part of the menu you perhaps have never seen. All right, Mr. Ollie. I will reserve your booth and have some special flowers, *bellissimo*."

"*Grazie*," I said, hoping I didn't mispronounce it.

I was going to have dinner alone with my vegetarian daughter.

Why did it feel like I was walking the Green Mile?

SUNDAY, DECEMBER 1, 8:15 A.M.

While waiting for Mr. Coffee, I looked across the street at Kyle Hanson's. He'd told me he'd be gone this weekend—he always tells me when he's leaving town, figuring why not have a cop keep his eye on the place. I decided he wouldn't mind me bor-rowing his Sunday edition of the *Tribune*.

I searched for Abernathy's column. There it was: "Follow the Evidence." Sipping French roast, I read it:

Today December begins. Thanksgiving's behind us, Christmas ahead.

For many people the holidays are lonely. For those whose loved ones have been killed, the loneliness is magnified. I know that firsthand.

Every day I have an unusual opportunity—to observe the investigation of the murder of Professor William Palatine. Detective Ollie Chandler tells me I still can't divulge many specifics since they could compromise the investigation. Some of what's already been uncovered is fascinating. Soon I'll be able to tell you more. It'll be worth your wait.

Meanwhile, let me tell you what I've learned. First, investigative jour-nalists and police detectives have a lot in common. It's their job to suspect people. And to catch those who've done wrong. We are, at our best, seek-ers of the truth.

Detective Chandler's motto is, "Examine the evidence. Then follow it wherever it leads." He takes nothing for granted. He looks at crumbs on a carpet that seem insignificant. He assumes the opposite. Until proven irrel-evant, he treats everything as vital.

Detective Chandler knows that sometimes the evidence takes you where you don't want to go. He told me of a homicide detective who fol-lowed evidence that led to the conviction of the detective's little sister, now in her thirties. You can't let your preferences or wishful thinking blind you to the truth, Chandler says.

Since I can't yet release case details, today I want to relate this "follow the evidence" thread to Friday's CBS special, "Investigating the Life and Death of Jesus." Christmas and Easter season are the two times columnists are allowed to raise questions related to the Christian faith. You've read thoughts from *Tribune* writers who are Muslims and Jews. This reflects part of our commitment to multiculturalism and religious tolerance. In light of this, I'm sure readers will be tolerant of this column, even if they disagree with my conclusions.

Here's my thought: Each of us is called to act as a homicide detective to answer the question "Who killed Jesus and why?" There was a murder and a corpse—for three days anyway. Since the apostles died for believing Christ rose from the grave, it raises the question: Would they have died for what they knew to be false when they could save their lives simply by telling the truth? Would that make any sense at all?

Jesus said, "The truth will set you free." He also said, "I am the way, the truth and the life; no man comes to the Father but by me." Not a popular statement. One that helped get Him crucified. But then, Jesus wasn't a popularity-seeker. He was a truth-teller.

The homicide detective has much to teach us. Follow the truth wherever it leads you. Even if you don't like where it leads.

If the evidence suggests that Jesus wasn't who He claimed to be and that He didn't rise from the grave, then we should have the courage to follow the evidence, even if it means walking away from our churches.

On the other hand, it may lead to something even more radical. Perhaps you'll have to abandon your skepticism and accept the claims of Jesus. And—dare I say it—maybe you'll need to give church a chance.

In the wake of Thanksgiving, you may be wondering who you should be thanking and why. Think of Thanksgiving as a signpost pointing to Christmas, and you'll find the answer.

In the four weeks of this Christmas season, as we ponder the person whose birth splits history into BC and AD, let's examine the intriguing evidence concerning Jesus Christ—his birth, life, death, resurrection, and ascension. If we take the time to carefully examine the evidence, then—and only then—we can "follow it wherever it leads."

I put the paper down. My name was mentioned. My motto was the theme. Nothing bad was said about me. Shouldn't I feel flattered?

So why was that knot in my stomach?

Sunday afternoon Jake Woods invited me to go shooting with him in the Mount Hood forest near Zigzag, a fifty-minute drive from Portland. I felt like shooting something—anything that I could pretend was a professor who'd exploited girls.

I sat by Jake in his black Chevy Tahoe, which has approximately enough room for a rugby team.

I figured Jake would ambush me with something spiritual. So far it was just small talk: sports, weather, work, and guns. It was only a matter of time before he'd bring up Clarence's column.

Tired of waiting, I beat him to it. "Clarence thinks we should all take a closer look at Christianity. Okay, if this God of yours is really good and He's really in control, why does all this bad stuff happen? Murders and rapes and starvation and professors taking advantage of girls and child abuse in churches and all that?"

"That's the oldest and most common argument people use for not believing in God."

"You admit it?"

"I don't think it's a valid argument, but it's certainly understandable."

"How do you answer it?"

"Well, first I'd say it's God who gave us a moral compass. It's that sense of justice He put in you that causes you to raise this question in the first place."

"You're giving Him credit for my doubts?"

"In a way, yeah. God isn't afraid of us and our questions any more than a lion's afraid of a gerbil. Read the Bible—it raises the problem of evil again and again. You haven't come up with something new, Ollie. Prophets and psalmists ask why good people suffer and why evil people appear to get away with their crimes. Take Psalm 10. It starts off by asking, 'Why, O LORD, do you stand far off? Why do you hide yourself in times of trouble?' Then it talks about the evil man and how he prospers and imagines he's going to get away with it. But he won't."

Jake pointed to his glove box. "Grab the Bible in there and turn to Psalm 10. I want you to read a few verses."

I took it out. He told me to open to the middle, and sure enough I was in the Psalms. I found Psalm 10, and he told me to jump in and read a particular verse.

"'His mouth is full of curses and lies and threats; trouble and evil are under his tongue.' I've seen plenty of that," I said. "Next it says, 'He lies in wait near the villages; from ambush he murders the innocent, watching in secret for his victims.' Whoa. This guy's a killer."

"You'd be surprised what's in that book," Jake said. "Keep reading."

"'He lies in wait like a lion in cover; he lies in wait to catch the helpless; he catches the helpless and drags them off in his net. His victims are crushed, they collapse; they fall under his strength. He says to himself, "God has forgotten; he covers his face and never sees."'"

"Yeah, exactly," I said. "That's what bugs me. God doesn't seem to be paying attention to what's going on down here."

"Keep reading."

"'Arise, LORD! Lift up your hand, O God. Do not forget the helpless. Why does the wicked man revile God? Why does he say to himself, "He won't call me to account"?'"

I put Jake's Bible down on the floor, still open. It's a little creepy to have a Bible on your lap.

"People appear to get away with evil for a while," Jake said. "But one day it'll be different."

"What day would that be?"

"When they die and face God. And when Christ returns to set up His kingdom. When the final judgment comes."

"If there's a God, why doesn't He just bring that final judgment now?"

"Is that really what you want? God says He holds off judgment because He's merciful to us. He gives us time to repent. Are you ready to face judgment?"

I picked up the Bible and read again. "'But you, O God, do see trouble and grief; you consider it to take it in hand. The victim commits himself to you; you are the helper of the fatherless. Break the arm of the wicked and evil man; call him to account for his wickedness that would not be found out.' Wow, it actually says 'break his arm.' Now we're talking."

We turned left onto the old dirt road headed to our firing range. It was suddenly bumpy.

"There's one last verse, isn't there?" Jake asked. "Read it."

"It's bumpy," I said.

"Don't be a wimp."

"'The LORD is King for ever and ever; the nations will perish from his land. You hear, O LORD, the desire of the afflicted; you encourage them, and you listen to their cry, defending the fatherless and the oppressed, in order that man, who is of the earth, may terrify no more.'"

"Did you catch that?" Jake asked as I closed the Bible and put it back in the glove box, where it couldn't bite me. "God's saying He's going to make it all right one day. I heard Clarence's daddy say once, 'God doesn't settle all His accounts in October.' The judgment is coming—and if you're eager to see it come, you'd better remember that once it comes, it'll be final."

"I'm not going to sit on my hands waiting for God's justice to come."

"Who said anything about sitting on our hands? We're supposed to do what we can to bring justice now. But God's the ultimate judge. Justice doesn't always come here and now, but God promises it'll come there and then."

"There's a cop saying that goes, 'There's no *justice*. There's *just us*.' If we don't make things right, they won't be right. Get it? There's just us."

Jake pulled over by a fallen tree. He turned to me.

"I get it, but you're dead wrong. There's not just us. There's God."

"You really think God's doing His part?"

"Not as fast as you'd like or in the same way maybe, but, yes, I do. Absolutely. Would you be willing to wait an hour or a day or a week for a criminal to come to justice? Well, if God's willing to wait fifty years, your wait to you may be longer than God's wait to Him."

We stepped out of the Tahoe.

"What am I supposed to do, turn and look the other way while people are murdered? Pretend it's all right?"

"Of course it's not all right," Jake said, as we pulled out our guns. "The question is whether it's God's fault or ours."

"That's a lot of blame to lay on people."

"So you blame God instead? Brings us right back to where we started. Where do you get your sense of justice that makes you believe crime and suffering are so wrong?"

"I guess I was born with it."

We took out a dozen pop cans and placed them on stumps and low limbs.

As we loaded, Jake said, "You were born with a sense of justice? Well, then it didn't come from you, did it? It came from the One who made you. You believe evil is wrong because God knows it's wrong and made you to know it too. Ironic, isn't it?"

I lined up the first shot, calling the Mountain Dew can seventy feet away. I squeezed gently. *Boom.* I saw bark fly off a tree ten feet behind. I was two inches high and to the right.

"What's ironic?" I asked.

"You're using standards of justice that could only come from God in order to argue that there is no God."

Jake eyed the same target, then squeezed the trigger gently. The can went flying.

On our way home, after two hours serial-killing pop cans, the CTU headquarters phone rang, and since *24* wasn't on I checked my cell. Incoming call from Criminalist Detail.

"It's Phil Oref. You know Bates was assigned to process prints on the gun ballistics ID'd as the murder weapon? I volunteered to take it off his hands. Went ahead and ran the prints."

"No kidding? What'd you find?"

"Two index fingerprints. From angle and placement on the gun, I'm guessing they're both the left index finger."

"You ran the prints?"

"Naturally."

"Any match?"

"You won't believe it."

"Try me."

"The fingerprints on the gun belong to a Portland cop."

"Which one?" I asked, holding my breath.

"Detective Noel Barrows."

16

"It's every man's business to see justice done."
SHERLOCK HOLMES, *THE CROOKED MAN*

MONDAY, DECEMBER 2, 7:00 A.M.

I'D HAD A ROUGH time sleeping Sunday night. As I sat at my homicide desk, floating above the Portland gray, my usually iron stomach felt like I was deep-sea fishing in a typhoon. I was dreading two confrontations: first with Noel Barrows, accusing him of murder; second, having dinner with Kendra.

Why did Kendra terrify me more than Noel? Part of me desperately wanted to see her. Part of me didn't—the same part that in Nam didn't relish walking through a field of claymore mines.

As for Noel, how would I approach him? And what would I tell his partner, Jack, my old friend, who's like a father to him?

Sometimes when your theory is confirmed, it makes you go back and question your theory. Noel Barrows? I'm not saying Noel's a Boy Scout but...*murder?* Not only Palatine, but Frederick?

When I'm worried, I putter. I pulled open my file drawer and looked at the murder mystery I started writing four years ago, *The Bacon and Cheese Murders*. It isn't Ross Macdonald. It isn't even Ronald McDonald. But at least I wrote it myself, as declared by the header with my name on every one of its 280 pages. Maybe eventually I'd finish it. Meanwhile, I have my real life murder mystery to solve.

I'd asked Manny and Clarence to meet me at 8:00 a.m. in the Justice Center. We claimed a small conference room. Manny and Clarence chose opposite corners of the ring, me in the referee position.

I told them about Noel's prints on the gun.

"You're saying Barrows killed Palatine?" Clarence asked.

"I'm withholding judgment."

"Let me get this straight," Manny said. "First, without any clear evidence, you conclude it's a homicide detective. Now, when you actually have hard evidence, you're backing off? His fingerprints are on a gun I found in a Dumpster two blocks from the murder, which ballistics says was the murder weapon?"

"I'm just keeping an open mind. I'll grant you Noel's not the sharpest knife in the drawer. As Cimma would say, he's no brainiac. But is he stupid enough to dump the gun in a nearby Dumpster?"

"What now?" Clarence asked. "Do you arrest Noel?"

"No. I want to squeeze out anything I can before he hears what we've got and gets his defenses up."

"You're still considering other suspects?" Clarence asked.

"I learned years ago never to decide a case is over until I'm certain of holes in alibis and solid grounds for arrest and conviction. We're not there yet."

"Did you check out those half dozen phone numbers written in the backs of the professor's books?" Clarence asked.

I shook my head. More important things on my mind. "I've got a job for Carp. Think she'd do it?"

"Maybe, if she'd get a photo exclusive if something comes of it."

"You journalists always have an angle."

"Yeah…and you detectives don't?"

An hour later, Noel entered homicide. I poured him coffee and we chatted.

"Heard you had a golf tournament this weekend." You know when you've pushed a man's passion button. He went on for five minutes about what a great tournament it was and how he shaved four strokes off last year and finished in the top ten.

"How's your investigation going?" Noel asked.

I shrugged. "The usual. Panning for gold. You've looked at the reports, haven't you?"

"A little. Pretty busy with our own cases."

"The professor was arrogant, don't you think?"

"Yeah," Noel said, grinning. "A phone message quoting the philosopher of the week? Gimme a break."

I leaned against the wall. "Hey, remember when you came to the professor's house the day after the murder? When you pointed to the pictures on the mantel and noticed something was wrong?"

"Yeah."

"Well, that missing picture idea was really helpful. What exactly was it you kept saying? Was it 'something's funny'?"

"Something's fishy."

"Yeah. Something's fishy." I slapped him on the shoulder. "Thanks again, Noel."

"Okay…you're welcome."

I walked back to my workstation, where I reached in my pocket and turned off the recorder.

↔

"I need you to run a voice analysis," I said to Criminalist Mike Bates, handing him an envelope marked "Voice Needing Identification," 911 recording inside. "But this time I want results pronto."

"You have to give me a voice to compare it to. That's how the sound spectrograph works."

I handed him a second envelope marked "Suspect's Voice."

"Preferably using some of the same words."

"Done," I said.

"Whose voice is the one I'm comparing?"

"I'd rather not say. Just tell me if it's a match."

"I can tell you if it's a positive or probable identification, or if it's a positive or probable elimination. But we're really backed up."

"You're *always* backed up. It's important."

"It's *always* important."

"Look, I waited a week for prints on that Taurus 9 mil before Phil got me results. I can't wait a week for this. I need it tomorrow."

After a drive in pounding rain, Clarence and I ran through the parking lot at Lou's. We hung his overcoat and my trench coat and fedora to drip dry beside our booth, next to the jukebox. I put in a quarter and pressed "I Get Around," "Eve of Destruction," and "A World Without Love." Clarence put in his own quarter and made his selections more carefully.

Jake arrived two minutes after Clarence and I were both seated. "Weren't we just here a few days ago?" he asked. "I love you guys and I love Lou's, but this is going to stretch my waistline."

Rory walked eagerly to our table. "Welcome to my friends. Mr. Ollie, you return tonight? Dinner with your daughter?"

"Yeah. Eight o'clock. You'll have vegetables, right?"

"Many vegetables. Abundant lettuce. And fine pastas, without meat."

My body was at that booth, but my mind was on Noel.

"So, guys, did we do our reading?" Jake referred to *Mere Christianity*, a book by C. S. Lewis that he's been trying to get me to read for years. He'd assigned a portion to read, but I don't take well to assignments.

"Been a little busy," I said. "Solving murders and all that."

"*Mere Christianity*'s opened my eyes."

"So you've said…again and again."

"You could shut me up by reading it."

"If I thought it would work, I'd do it."

"You read detective novels. It's shorter than most of them."

"But there's a big difference," I said. "I *want* to read those novels. I'm a believer in free choice. The right to read what I want."

"Glad to hear you believe in free choice. I hope that means you're no longer blaming God for giving it to us."

"You're becoming a nag, Jake."

"Can't friends try to influence each other when they think it's in their best interests?"

"Say what you want, I'm not reading that book."

"Why? Afraid it might make sense? As a detective, I'd think you'd want to examine the evidence. Didn't you read Clarence's article?"

"Oh, yeah," I said, looking at Abernathy. "Quoting me to encourage people to investigate Jesus? You weren't trying to send me a message, were you?"

"No different than the message I've been trying to send you for years."

"Hey, I've read books. I read *The Da Vinci Code*."

They both laughed.

"I know you didn't like it, but why laugh?"

"Because," Clarence said, "it's full of historical errors and false claims that any junior high kid could refute after spending twenty minutes checking facts on Google."

"Heard of G. K. Chesterton?" Jake asked. "He said that when people stop believing in God, they'll believe in anything."

"Heard of W. C. Fields?" I asked. "He said, 'Everyone must believe in something; I believe I'll have another beer.'"

"Chesterton's point was that when you reject the truth, you become gullible. You lose your common sense. Somebody writes a book like *The Da Vinci Code*, and since people don't know history or the Bible and haven't bothered to investigate the facts, they end up believing stuff that's so ridiculous it's embarrassing."

"You guys think you know it all." I pushed back my empty cup.

"I'm well aware of how little I know," Jake said. "That's why I choose to trust what God has said in the Bible rather than trust myself."

"Does it occur to you how judgmental it is to think you're going to heaven and other people are going to hell?"

"I'm just telling you what Jesus said. He talked about hell more than anyone else, and I think He knew what He was talking about. He doesn't want us to go there. He died and rose so we wouldn't have to go there."

Soon we were munching on cheeseburgers. Clarence's selections were playing, including Chuck Berry wailing, "No Particular Place to Go."

"Okay, guys, this time I've got something for you to read." I pulled it out of my coat pocket. "It's by Bertrand Russell. It's called *Why I Am Not a Christian.*"

"You got that from the professor's," Clarence said, like I'd firebombed a church.

"I'm borrowing it," I said. "The professor won't be needing it."

"I'm afraid by now he realizes the flaws in that book," Jake said.

"It's just one essay by that title," I said, holding it up. "But there's lots of stuff in the other essays you wouldn't like either. So here's my deal. You read this; then I'll read your *Mere Christianity.*"

"Great," Jake said. "I'll pick up copies for me and Clarence; then we can all discuss it." Clarence nodded. Jake reached his right hand across the table and shook mine. "After we're done, you'll read *Mere Christianity* and we'll talk about it. It's a deal."

"You're really going to read this?" My voice cracked, like a fifteen-year-old's.

"I look forward to it."

"But it's not…"

"Not what?"

"Not…Christian."

"No kidding?" Jake said. "A book called *Why I Am Not a Christian* that's not Christian? Man, I feel blindsided. You should have warned me."

"I didn't think you'd want to read it."

"This book doesn't scare me a bit. The Bible always holds up to attacks. Besides, I promised to read it. And if a man's word and his handshake can't be depended on, well…"

"Speaking of the Bible," I said around a mouthful of burger, looking at Clarence, "remember that confession on the professor's computer screen said something about millstones? You said it was from Jesus."

"But you decided Palatine didn't write it," Clarence said.

"He was dying or dead when it was typed. But here's my point: Isn't that the sort of thing *you* guys would say? I mean, you're always quoting Bible verses."

"You think we killed the professor?" Jake asked, smiling.

"No, but it seems obvious the killer wrote it. And if he did, that means the killer was a Bible quoter. What do you think about that?"

I liked the bewildered expressions on their faces. I was grinning when I swallowed a large gulp of my blackberry shake. It gave me a brain freeze, but it was worth it.

When Jack Glissan left homicide at 1:40 p.m., I went to Noel Barrows's workstation and said, "We need to talk—now." I escorted Noel into the conference room, where Manny and Clarence were already waiting in uncomfortable silence.

"Hi, guys," Noel said. "What's up?"

I started on the Seahawks and Rams. He said he was pumped about the big Hurricanes and Gators matchup next Saturday.

I groped for more small talk. "I saw you coming out of the Starbucks by Pioneer Square Saturday morning, didn't I? I was at Lou's Diner. Must have been heading off for your tournament, huh?"

He shrugged. "Are you accusing me of something?"

"Why would I accuse you? It's not a crime to go to Starbucks."

"Why am I here?"

"Okay," I said. "There's no easy way to ask this. Where were you between ten thirty and midnight Wednesday, November 20?"

He studied my face, then Manny's and Clarence's. "Is this a joke? Did Jack put you up to this?"

"It's no joke. Where were you?"

"That was like…two weeks ago."

"Twelve days."

"Night before Thanksgiving?"

"Seven nights before."

He looked down and started mumbling and moving his fingers, apparently trying to sort out what he'd done the last twelve days and what fell on what night.

"That Monday night I was at Jack's for football—same every week. Going over there tonight. Most nights I watch the golf channel pretty late. I guess that Wednesday could have been one of them."

"Anybody see you?"

"I have an apartment. People walk the hallways, but I don't think I came out, so they wouldn't have seen me. No roommate."

"Too bad." I reached into my briefcase and pulled out the gun in its evidence bag. "Ever seen this?"

He looked it over. "Sure, I've seen them. Looks like this one's been around the block."

"It's a Taurus Millennium Pro, 9 mm," I said. "Have you seen this *particular* gun?"

"I don't think so. Why?"

"Because it's got your fingerprints on it."

A long awkward silence. "I've taken guns away from lots of people. I guess they could have my prints on them."

"This gun's special. It was used to kill Professor Palatine."

"And my prints are on it?"

"Yeah."

"How's that possible?"

"We were hoping you could tell us, Noel."

Suddenly the conference room door flew open. I stood, looking at the red face of Jack Glissan.

"What's going on here?"

"I'm having a private interview with Noel."

"Private? With Domast? And Abernathy?"

"You read the memo. I have to include him."

"What's going on, Ollie?" Jack asked. "I heard the murder weapon has prints."

"Word gets around."

"You're not accusing Noel?"

"His fingerprints are on the gun. It was found in a Dump—"

"I don't care if it was found under his pillow. He didn't do it!"

"Were you with him between, say, 10:45 and 11:45 November 20?"

"No, but I saw him at 2:00 a.m. at our murder scene that same night."

"Two and a half hours after Palatine's murder? That doesn't help." I turned to Noel, whose usually tan face was two shades lighter. "Where were you?"

"I told you. Home. Alone. We were on call, right? I must have gone to bed early."

"I'll ask you again: Can anyone confirm your alibi?"

Noel shook his head.

"Hold on," Jack said. "A week ago Wednesday night? I went out that night and dropped your golf DVD by your place. Around 11:15."

Noel stared at him blankly.

"Don't try it, Jack," I said.

"You'd gone to bed early. Remember, Noel?"

Noel's chin dropped. He looked at Jack for his next move.

"I dropped by because you're usually up till midnight. I figured you were gone. So before I got the key from…you know, where you hide it…I rang the bell. And you came to the door. Said I was sorry for waking you up. That's how it happened."

"Stop it," I said. "You're just going to make it worse. Noel said no one saw him home. No alibi."

"Don't you remember, Noel?" Jack pleaded.

Noel raised his hand. "Jack's telling the truth. That's how it happened."

Jack smiled. I looked back and forth between them.

"Except it was on Tuesday night," Noel said. "I'd been at Jack and Linda's. I really did leave Jack the golf DVD. I went to bed early, and he dropped it by and rang the bell, just like he said. Except it wasn't Wednesday night, it was Tuesday."

Jack's and my jaw dropped in unison.

"Jack was telling the truth." Noel turned to Jack, with eyes that said "let it go." "You just got the night wrong."

Jack started to argue. But neither Noel nor I was going to let him win.

MONDAY, DECEMBER 2, 8:14 P.M.

I rushed in the door at Lou's Diner, fourteen minutes late. Kendra was in our booth. On the table sat a beautiful arrangement of a dozen red roses, baby's breath and all.

"Sorry I'm late," I told her. "The traffic was—"

She waved her hand, giving me that look that said she'd heard it all before.

"You look nice," I said. She'd put on weight, but so had I. Pointing to her silver chain necklace, I said, "I like that."

"Mom gave it to me for my high school graduation," she said, in a way that sounded like I'd never given her anything. "I wouldn't expect you to remember."

I settled in on my side of the booth. "Been waiting long?"

"Yes," she said. "The man says they have a vegetable plate."

"Good. Vegetable plates are always good."

Silence.

"I'd hoped you'd join me for Thanksgiving," I said, not mentioning that she'd never responded to my messages.

"With all those people? I don't think so."

"We could have eaten at my place. Just you and me and Mulch."

She didn't look up from the menu.

Rory came to take our order. "It is so nice to meet your daughter, Mr. Ollie. She told me she'd like the vegetable plate. Will you have the usual?"

"The usual" means three different things at Lou's, depending on time of day. My breakfast usual is a western omelet and hash browns with a giant buttermilk pancake. My lunch usual is a cheeseburger and fries or onion rings. My dinner usual is New York steak with a baked potato and all the trimmings. I pictured large hunks of medium rare meat in clear view of the vegetable plate. It didn't seem wise.

"I've been having so many vegetable plates, I'm thinking tonight I'll go with a steak *salad*," I said. "With Thousand Island."

Rory looked at me with big sympathetic eyes, but he nodded, took the menus, and left.

The next fifteen minutes were like pulling teeth. I couldn't get more than a sentence at a time from Kendra. She didn't ask me anything. The silence between my questions kept getting longer.

"How about those Seahawks?" I asked.

Nothing.

I pulled out a quarter and asked her if she had any favorite oldies. "Nope." So I chose a few of Sharon's: "I Got You Babe," "Never My Love," and "Cherish." I saw "Honey" by Bobby Goldsboro, but I knew where to draw the line. Still, Kendra didn't appear impressed.

Finally, Rory came with the meal. Kendra looked at her vegetable plate and seemed to reluctantly approve. Then she looked at my steak salad.

"How can you eat that?" she asked.

"What? Thousand Island?"

"Animal flesh."

"I'm having a steak salad because it's the closest I can get to a compromise between what I'd like to eat and what you'd like me to eat. I thought you'd appreciate the lettuce and tomatoes. Look, cucumbers and olives and these little…jobbers. They're vegetables, aren't they? I thought you'd approve."

"It's not just what we eat. It's what we *don't* eat. You wouldn't eat your dog, would you?"

"*Mulch*?" I dropped my fork. I couldn't believe the words had come out of my daughter's mouth.

"Some societies eat dogs," she said. "That doesn't make it right, does it?"

"No."

"Then why do you think it's okay to eat cows?"

"Well, for one thing…they're a lot bigger."

"So it's okay to eat big dogs?"

"Could we stop talking about eating dogs?"

"What's the difference?"

"Dogs are like people. Cows are like…pheasants, except not so gamy. And they don't fly. I mean the aerodynamics…just getting airborne would—"

"I don't think it's right to eat animals."

"Sweetheart, look, you can eat whatever you want. But—and this is just me, okay—I didn't fight my way to the top of the food chain just to become a vegetarian."

She scowled. "You need to get more exercise too."

"I run around all day."

"Don't they have mandatory fitness programs for cops? They should. If you don't watch it, you're going to cut ten or twenty years off your life."

Why would that matter to you?

We ate in silence. She finished her vegetables. I polished off my cow.

Since all attempts at bonding had failed, I took a deep breath and said, "About my investigation—can I ask you a question?"

"You and your investigations."

"If I were Ichiro, would you say, 'You and your baseball'?"

"You're no Ichiro."

"But what I do isn't worthless. It saves lives, you know. I mean human lives. Not cows."

"You didn't talk with me when I was growing up," she said.

"We talked more than you remember."

"There were things I'd ask you about, and you'd never tell me. Personal things, family things. I had to go to Mom to find out. You'd always change the subject. I'd ask you about Grandpa. Nothing. I'd ask you about my br—"

"You were in Professor Palatine's class?"

"Yes."

"Did he ever make a move on you?"

"A *move?*"

"Did he get fresh with you?"

"Dad, you're so out of it."

"Just pretend I'm retro. Retro's cool, right?"

She shook her head at me, but I saw a slight smile.

"So…did Dr. Palatine ever show a romantic interest in you?"

"Well, *this* is certainly awkward."

"You said we never talked about personal things. I'm making up for it."

"Well, it's personal, I'll give you that." Her smile evaporated. "No. He only went after the pretty girls."

"You're a pretty girl."

"I mean the *really* pretty girls."

I would have hated Palatine for coming on to my daughter. Now I hated him for not considering her pretty enough. The truth is, my daughter's history with men is…not so good. Her relationships have been many, and with the shelf life of yogurt.

"I didn't mean to imply you were that kind of girl," I said, then bit my lip.

"I need to be going."

"Okay."

She sat still. Finally I stood. I stepped toward her and put my hand on her shoulder, not close enough for her to bite it.

"Go home," she said, voice strained. "I'll be leaving in a few minutes. I just feel a little dizzy."

"Need help?"

"Just leave, would you?"

"I'll take you to your car. No, I'll drive you home."

"You're so stubborn."

"Your mom used to say we were the two most stubborn people she knew."

Finally, Kendra eased herself out of the booth, standing awkwardly. That's when I realized my daughter was pregnant.

"Of all the facts presented to us, we had to pick just those which we deemed to be essential, and then piece them together in their order, so as to reconstruct this very remarkable chain of events."
SHERLOCK HOLMES, *THE NAVAL TREATY*

TUESDAY, DECEMBER 3, 8:00 A.M.

"**DID YOU SEE THIS?**" Kim Suda pushed the newspaper in front of my face, at my desk.

I was staring at a photograph of Professor William Palatine, on his back, on the floor, noose around his neck. I checked the paper's date. December 3: today.

"This is a joke, right? Somebody printed one of those dummies. This can't be the real *Tribune*."

"I bought it off a newsstand."

I read the article, written by Mike Button. Among other things, he said, "An anonymous source inside the Portland Police revealed that the leading suspect in the Palatine murder investigation is a street person. He'll likely be arrested within the week."

I punched 6 for Abernathy. No answer. I declined leaving a message lest it be used against me at my murder trial.

I stewed in my juices fifteen minutes, skulking back and forth in homicide, eyes on the glass entrance. Finally, I saw Abernathy. I locked my laser stare on him when he was still twenty feet away.

"You're off this case, Abernathy. It's over!"

A half dozen heads turned our way, secretaries to detectives.

"First I knew of this is when Geneva showed me the paper this morning."

"You expect me to believe that?"

"It's the truth." He raised his right catcher's mitt.

"Your friend Carpenter gave those photos to someone."

"They belong to the *Trib*, not Carp. She's a pro, our best photojournalist. She's turned down offers from the *LA Times* and *Chicago Tribune*. She'd never pull a stunt like this. She says the photos were on file, ready to go in case we got clearance."

"Never happened."

"I know that. Carp's as mad as you and I are. Somebody got hold of them and took it to print."

"Who?"

"Button refuses to identify his source." Clarence's face looked as hot as mine felt. "He's willing to be a first amendment martyr. I think he wants to go to jail. Winston doesn't understand how it got through editorial without coming to him. I told Button he'd be fired. Winston says they're discussing it on the upper levels. Berkley's involved."

"Too late for that, isn't it?"

"I know it's false about the street person, but it's better than spilling the truth, isn't it? Does it really compromise the investigation?"

"Confidential crime scene information in public hands? Of course it compromises the investigation. Until now, if we interview suspects and they make an unguarded comment about the noose around the neck or the skin color or body position, it'd be enough to finger them. Now their only mistake—and I'll grant you it's a big one—is reading the *Tribune*."

"Look, I'm sorry. But I didn't do it. And it wasn't just photos either. It was information, some accurate, some false, like the street person part. It wasn't from you, me, or Carp. Could it have come from Manny?"

Clarence didn't notice Manny had just come up behind him, newspaper in hand.

"From me? I don't work for the *Tribune*, hotshot."

"You didn't leak anything?" I asked Manny.

He gave me his thousand-yard stare, the one that would make Clint Eastwood melt like a salted slug. Manny redirected his stare to Clarence, then threw the newspaper on the floor in front of him. He stepped on it, grinding his heel into it.

My sentiments exactly.

"I heard the scuttlebutt about Noel Barrows," Officer Taylor Burchatz said over the phone at my workstation. "For what it's worth, I saw him the night of the Palatine murder."

"Where?"

"At the Do Drop Inn, 59th and Foster."

"You're sure it was Barrows?"

"Absolutely. It's not like we're friends, but I know him well enough to recognize him."

"What time did you see him?"

"I came at nine thirty. Left late, close to midnight. He was there the whole time."

"You're sure it was Wednesday—week before last?"

"Yeah."

"Nice try. Everybody wants to give Noel an alibi."

"You calling me a liar?"

"Look, Noel says he was home alone that night. What kind of a half-wit would withhold his alibi for murder?"

"All I know is, I saw him."

"Who else was there?"

"Bartender's Barry. He might remember. There were probably a half dozen guys hanging around him. I know a few first names—Stu, Steve, Alan."

"Exactly when did you leave?"

"After sports. I saw highlights of the Blazer game."

"Sports is over about 11:25. You're saying Noel was still there?"

"Yeah."

"This isn't a put-on? If you've talked to Barry and got him to go along with this, we're talking perjury, obstruction of justice, and—"

"I don't know what your deal is, Chandler. I'm calling because I thought maybe you wouldn't want to go after an innocent man. An innocent cop. Figured I should speak up. Maybe you want him to go down? That it? Maybe I should call a lieutenant or captain or somebody who wants to hear the truth?"

"Calm down," I said. "I'll call Barry now and check it out. If it's true, I owe you an apology."

Ninety minutes later, Manny, Clarence, and I sat at the conference table, door closed. Noel and Jack walked in together.

"Why are you here?" I asked Jack.

"Because I'm Noel's partner. And friend."

"But you're not his lawyer. Let him talk, okay? Don't put words in his mouth. Not like last time. Got it?"

Jack's face flushed, but he nodded.

"I've been doing this many years," I said to Noel. "I've told countless suspects that they're lying about their alibi, and that's what I'm going to tell you."

"Hold on, Ollie," Jack said. "You can't just—"

"Shut up and let me finish, Jack." I looked at Noel. "But until now I've never once sat down with a murder suspect and accused him of lying about *not* having an alibi."

"What are you talking about?" Jack said.

I stepped between Jack and Noel to get Noel's full attention. "I got a call from an Officer Burchatz. He saw you that night at the Do Drop Inn."

Noel's face twitched. His hands shook.

"He said you were still there when he left, near midnight."

"Maybe he's got the wrong night," Noel said.

"No. I talked with Barry, the bartender. He says it must have been midnight when you left. You were there with a half dozen guys. He gave me names. I already called Stu, Steve, and Alan. These guys aren't Phi Beta Brilliant, but all three confirm you were there."

Jack looked at Noel. "Is it true?"

Noel looked like a junior high boy who'd been caught red-handed.

"Did I miss something," I said, "or was your bacon just saved? Why in the ever-lovin' world would you deny a murder alibi?"

Noel stood, face flushed, hands darting. "Look, we were the up team, for crying out loud. You know department policy. You're not supposed to be drinking when you're on call!"

"It's not just department policy," Jack said. "It's my policy. No exceptions. Ever."

"I know," Noel said. "But we'd been on call for a week. I figured, what are the chances of somebody getting murdered that night? So I just…went to the Do Drop."

"Let me get this straight," I said. "You have this alibi, with multiple witnesses, proving you couldn't have committed a murder for which there's evidence against you. And you wouldn't tell us this because…Jack would be disappointed you'd had a few drinks?"

"He always tells me to stay off the drinks and go to bed early," Noel said. "I…didn't want to admit it."

"So now you're 'admitting' that you were at the Do Drop Inn between 10:45 and 11:45?"

"No," he said.

"You weren't?"

"It was more like between 9:00 and 12:15. I guess I got home around twelve thirty."

"Actually, Noel, between 9:00 and 12:15 *includes* between 10:45 and 11:45. Jack will explain it to you." I've spent days trying to wring the truth out of people, but this was ridiculous. "Write down the names of guys there that night." I handed him my pad and a pen.

He jotted down five names, two of which were new. Blushing, he handed it back to me.

Jack threw his arms around Noel. "Congratulations, bud. You've got yourself an alibi!"

Noel smiled sheepishly.

"But," Jack said, "if you ever go to a bar again when we're on call, I'll kill you myself!"

I left the conference room, head aching and thinking about that other little item. Noel's fingerprints were still on the murder weapon.

I called Phil, asking how a man with an ironclad alibi could have his fingerprints on the murder weapon, even though he swears he didn't touch it. He couldn't explain it but said he'd get back to me.

For an hour at my desk, I examined with a magnifying glass a hundred of the professor's photos we'd bagged from his house, looking for a particular camera angle. I couldn't find what I was looking for.

I called Manny, who rarely hangs around precinct. "I want you to go over our list of the professor's family and friends and colleagues. Call and ask if they have pictures taken at the professor's house, anytime in the last three years. If they do, I want to borrow them. We'll make copies and return them."

One thing I like about Manny is that he seldom asks why. Within an hour, he called back. He'd already talked with three people who had pictures taken at the professor's. The professor's sister-in-law, easier to get hold of than her doctor husband, said she had a couple dozen.

There were a number of things I needed to do, but I lacked manpower. I needed to recruit some.

I called Paul Anderson, ex-skater and beat cop and now larceny detective. He knows the streets better than anybody. He said he and his partner were on surveillance, but I was welcome to join them. I got his location, grabbed Clarence, and headed for my car.

When Clarence and I approached, Paul was sitting in an unmarked car with his partner, Gerald Griffin. I knocked on their passenger-side back door. After Griffin lowered his hardware, we crawled into the backseat, and I gave them a peace offering...a box of Krispy Kremes.

As Anderson smacked his lips on a warm glazed, I said, "You wouldn't have a half day to spare for an old friend who's an underresourced homicide detective?"

"Wish I did, Ollie. If there were a moratorium on theft, I'd be glad to help."

"Who you watching?"

"Clancy Baines, the guy in the navy blue sweatshirt." He pointed. "Word is he robbed the liquor store on Twelfth and made away with a sackful of bills. Fifteen hundred dollars—way more than they should've had in the till. We're sure the money's in his room. Positive he's behind a dozen other robberies. We take this dude and crime plummets."

"Insufficient grounds for a search warrant?"

"And he knows it," Griffin said.

"He's a drug dealer too," Paul said. "We're hoping to see him sell so we can get a warrant. But he's not going to deal in front of us. He just steps around a corner. He's got his soldiers keeping their eyes out. They know exactly where we are." He nodded toward two teenage boys leaning against the wall ten feet away, pretending not to look at us.

"So," Griffin said, "he's not only robbing the community; he's robbing our time."

"If I get him for you in the next twenty minutes," I said, "would you give me four hours each?"

"You kidding? We'd give you a whole day each. But how—"

"Two entrances to the apartments, front and back?"

"Yeah, but—"

"Okay, after we step out of the car, give us five minutes. Then you get out and stretch. I'll call your cell. Answer, sound excited, say you'll be there right away, and lay rubber when you take off. Then circle the block and wait out of sight. In ten minutes or so, Clancy Baines will be running out the front door, carrying the money."

"What are you talking about?" Griffin asked. "Why would—?"

"When you see the bag or box or whatever, you'll have grounds for believing it's the money and you can look at it. Then you take him in. I'll call you later about your indentured servitude."

"Come on, Ollie, you can't possibly—"

"Just do it," I said.

Clarence and I went to the back of the apartments. He wanted an explanation, but I told him, "Just follow my taillights, okay? I need you right here at the back door. You got a good look at Clancy Baines? He'll be carrying something in his hand. Make a threatening move toward him."

"What do you mean?"

"Just plant your body in front of him, that's all. One look at you will probably be enough. Make it so his only other option is the front door."

"But why—"

"Just do it, okay?"

He sighed and nodded.

I peeked around the corner and saw Anderson outside his car, the two street soldiers within earshot. I punched his number and watched him answer. I said, "There's a bank robbery, kidnapping, assault, rioting, terrorist activity, pipe bombs, and a hijacking at the county courthouse! We need you here now! Pronto! Get going, you lazy no-good cop! Peel rubber! And don't stop for donuts!"

I disconnected and heard his excited voice from the street. He might have over-acted, but when the tires screeched, everybody noticed. He was gone.

I waited, giving Anderson and Griffin time to park and sneak back on foot. I called to make sure they were in position. Anderson said they were lurking in the shadows, with a clear view.

"Ready?" I asked Clarence.

I grabbed handfuls of newspaper that had blown up against the apartment, stepped in the back door, found a metal garbage can in the hallway, then pushed it into a tiled alcove. I put in about half the day's *Tribune*, flicked a BIC lighter I keep in my trench coat, and watched the smoke rise. No one was in the hall, so I let the smoke build. The alarm didn't trigger, so I pulled the alarm on the wall.

This alarm was...well, alarming. Really loud. I yelled, "Fire!" and the manager yelled, "Fire!" and pretty soon a dozen people were yelling, "Fire!" Within ten sec-onds residents were rushing out their doors. Some took longer, getting kids, pets, pictures, and iPods. Several ran *into* the building, past the manager who was wav-ing everyone out. Clancy Baines rushed in, turned the corner, right through the smoke, and ran up the stairs, three at a time.

Within a minute, Baines was back down the stairs, a bulging Nike gym bag in hand. He ran pell-mell toward the back of the building, where he was met by the hulking frame of Clarence Abernathy. Baines pivoted and ran out the front door, clutching that gym bag like it held ten grand.

I stepped to the front door and watched Baines run into the street, where Anderson and Griffin grabbed him. I watched Anderson zip open the bag and smile broadly. Griffin was talking to Baines while he handcuffed him.

I went to the manager and identified myself as a cop. "The fire's in that garbage can," I said, pointing. Fifteen seconds later he had a fire extinguisher on it, and within a few minutes the smoke was clearing.

I walked out the back to Clarence. "Who says the *Tribune* is worthless? It makes first-class smoke. A man's brought to justice, and we've got a day's work each from two grateful cops."

We walked to my car. Clarence turned back to gaze at the smoky apartment and then at me. We heard the sirens of the approaching fire truck, and when it flashed past, I pulled out and headed to Baja Fresh for lunch. A Steak Burrito Ultimo, with four containers of those chopped tomatoes, was callin' my name.

As I drove, Abernathy looked back at the scene and a couple of times opened his mouth like a goldfish. In a way unusual for journalists, he didn't know what to say.

"It is fortunate for this community that I am not a criminal."
SHERLOCK HOLMES, *THE ADVENTURE OF THE BRUCE-PARTINGTON PLANS*

TUESDAY, DECEMBER 3, 1:45 P.M.

ON OUR WAY BACK to the Justice Center from the fire and Baja Fresh, Phil Oref called.

"You're not going to believe this. First, those *are* the fingerprints of Noel Barrows on the murder weapon."

"So what am I not going to believe?"

"I studied the prints with a close-up lens. I found traces of plastic."

"So?"

"Somebody took the detective's fingerprint, made a plastic mold, then pressed it down to leave Barrows's prints. In other words, the prints are his, but he never touched the gun. The prints were planted."

"You're certain?"

"I found definite traces of the kind of moldable plastic you can duplicate a print from. It's exactly what I'd use if I were framing somebody."

"I've heard that could be done. But it's rare, isn't it?"

"Extremely. I've never seen it. I've played with doing it myself, to see how hard it would be. But I never would've looked for it if you hadn't told me about the alibi. You have to look for it to see it. And you'd really need to know what you're doing to plant it."

"Who would know how to do that kind of thing?"

"People like me. Or you, if you did your homework."

"Can you show me how it's done?"

"Sure. I'll have to pick up a couple of things. Meet me in my office at four."

I set up a five o'clock appointment with Noel Barrows, who wanted to know why. I told him I might have good news for him, but we'd have to see.

At 2:40 I got a call from the security desk. "Someone from the *Tribune* is asking to see you."

"If his name's Mike Button, have him shot and handcuffed; then dump him on my desk."

"It's a she. Name's Lynn Carpenter."

"I'm on my way." I sucked in my gut and greeted her at the door. "Sit down," I gestured to the empty table by the coffee and donuts, twelve feet from the entrance. Everybody was busy, and it offered more privacy than my workstation.

"What a view," she said, gazing down at the city below.

"Only the best for my special guests," I said, charmer that I am. "To what do I owe the pleasure of your company?" They say stuff like that in the movies.

"I'm really bugged by that photo in the *Trib*." She pulled out an eight-by-ten enlargement of the infamous picture.

"I was slightly bugged by that myself."

"Somebody got hold of a digital photo file and gave it to Button. He won't tell who. To tell you the truth, I figured they knew my password and got into my computer files at the *Trib*. But they didn't."

"How do you know?"

"Because I went through every single picture I took. There's no match. Same subject matter, naturally, but always the angle's slightly off or the flash shadows next to the corpse aren't quite long enough. There's even something on the ground in the picture that wasn't there when I took mine." She pointed to a rectangular object near Palatine's right leg. "Looks like one of those bags the criminalists carry."

"Yeah. An evidence bag."

"But my point is, I didn't take this picture."

"You're certain?" I asked.

"Positive. But you and I and the ME were the only ones taking pictures, right?"

"I wonder who has access to Carlton Hatch's photos?"

"Look," Carp said, "why not get me all your photo files, and the ME's? I'll go through them one by one and make the match. I'll be able to tell you exactly which photo and who took it."

"You'd do that?"

"I can't have the *Trib* pay me for it, but I'll do it on my own time."

"I'll call Hatch and get his photos. I'll give you mine on a thumb drive right now—they're on my laptop. But I took a few hundred. That's tons of work...are you sure?"

"It's really bugging me," she said. "Besides, I figure I'll get a pizza or two out of it."

"Or three," I said. "Double pepperoni, double cheese."

She smiled at me with her eyes.

Man. Things were rollin'.

↔

At four o'clock, an animated Phil Oref welcomed us into an evidence lab. He was happy to see Clarence, who might make him famous once he got cleared to tell the story in the *Trib*. I'd invited Carp to join us, so Phil might see his picture in the paper too.

"Faking a fingerprint 101. Here's how it works." Phil rubbed his hands together. "First you need an original. Latent fingerprints are just body sweat and fat, oil left on items you touch—glasses, doorknobs, ceramic coffee mugs." He pointed to a glass of water. "Hand me that."

Clarence grabbed the glass and passed it to Phil, who wore gloves, and held it up to the overhead light.

"You've just given me your thumbprint, index finger, and a partial of your middle. Let's use the index finger. I sprinkle it with colored powder, which sticks to the oil, and there you see a clear print."

Sure enough, there it was.

"You can spread the powder with a thin brush, but not necessary in this case. You can also use cyanoacrylate, the main ingredient in superglue. It reacts with the fat residue; then it forms this solid white substance. See?

"You can use black tape to grab the substance. You scan it or photograph it with a digital camera."

He demonstrated, then took a few close-ups and downloaded them.

"Once it's digitized, you can do graphic refurbishment to brush up the print's image." He pointed at an enlargement of the fingerprint on the wide-screen monitor. He cleaned up a smeared print line. "The goal is to get an exact image of the fingerprint. Then you can use a standard laser printer to print it out on a transparency slide."

He made the print, pointed, and said, "The printer toner forms a relief." He took us through two more steps involving wood glue, glycerin, and the creation of the dummy print. Then he said, "Now, you pull it off the foil and cut it to finger size. And use this theatrical glue to attach the dummy to your finger."

As Carp took pictures, Phil held up his right hand with the dummy fingerprint on his index finger, rubbed it on his left palm, then picked up a coffee mug from the desk. "And now, with the help of a little body oil, everything I touch leaves the fingerprint of Clarence Abernathy."

"You make it look easy," Clarence said.

"Actually, it's tough. Little mistakes can distort the print. Whoever did this knew what he was doing. Probably practiced."

"But you didn't figure that out when you first saw it?" Clarence asked.

"Nobody would. It was only when I thought to look for trace chemicals that I hit the jackpot. I found traces of glycerin and a little cyanoacrylate."

"You normally don't test for those?" I asked.

"Why would I? This is a one in a million. When you called and told me he had a solid alibi, that's when I checked."

"Eventually Noel would have come forward and admitted where he was, assuming he wasn't willing to endure capital punishment rather than admit to Jack he'd had some drinks. But suppose he'd been home alone that night. The scary thing is, if he didn't have the alibi, Noel could have been prosecuted."

"Any expert would've testified these were his prints on the murder weapon," Phil said. "It could've been enough to put him away."

Clarence, Carp, and I were walking out of Criminalist Detail when Mike Bates poked his head out a door. "Chandler? Just got the results on that voice comparison you gave me. The one where they both use the word *fishy*."

"Yeah?"

"There's a probable elimination. It's not the same voice."

"You're sure?"

"No. Probable means not sure. But I'm 98 percent sure it's not the same guy."

Double elimination for Noel, in the space of twenty minutes.

True, there was a one in fifty chance Noel was the caller. More likely, though, the caller knew Noel and his quirky use of *fishy*. Who would know better than one of the detectives? And if they went to the trouble to plant his fingerprints, why not put another nail in his coffin with the 911 tape?

And if Noel was being framed...why not somebody else?

Clarence went back to homicide, where he'd be joining me for my five o'clock appointment with Noel. Carp lingered at the elevator. She said the magic words "double cheese" as we parted. On the way back, I stopped to scope out the donut situation. As usual, the one with colored sprinkles was the only one left. Why do they even make them?

While contemplating this mystery at 4:45, I noticed my workstation fifteen feet away. I happened to be in a position to see something under it. Specifically, a pair of legs. And whoever they belonged to was wearing panty hose. Tentatively, I eliminated Cimma, Manny, and Clarence.

The top of the divider panel above my desk has thin cracks. I sometimes look through them from the desk side to see who's stalking the donuts, but I'd never looked through from this side.

The head was definitely female, bent over, searching my file drawers. My instinct was to say "Gotcha," but I decided to watch. If you stop people then ask them what they were doing, they lie to you. The best way to find out what they're doing is to watch them do it.

Apparently she wasn't finding what she was looking for. She stood up and went through the papers on my desk—notes and messages, business cards and mail. I had the feeling she'd done this already, and this was a retry.

She looked up at the crack and seemed to stare right at me. I froze. She glanced back down and quickly shuffled papers again.

Was she looking for my case notes? I had them. This was a wake-up call never to leave them at my desk, not even for a bathroom break. She walked to the aisle, turned and looked toward the security entrance, and returned to her desk, which fortunately is on the far side of where I was hunched over.

Now I had another question to deal with.

Why was Kim Suda snooping in my files?

At 5:00 p.m., Noel, Jack, Clarence, and I met in the conference room. I'd baked the crow, now I had to eat it. I explained Phil's demonstration of how Noel's fingerprints had been faked. I said that since Clarence had been there when I accused Noel, it was only right that he witness my apology. So…I apologized.

Noel took it pretty well. Jack? Not so well.

"They said it was one in a million," I told Jack, my oldest friend on the force. "The fingerprints seemed definitive. I was just following the evidence. What would you have done?"

"I'd try knowing the people I work with," he said. "And maybe trusting them."

I extended my hand to Noel, and he shook it.

"No hard feelings?" I asked.

"No." He blushed.

"Jack?"

I stuck out my hand. He shook it unenthusiastically. I saw the hard feelings in his eyes. He walked out the door behind Noel.

"I may have just lost a friend," I said to Clarence.

"You were doing your job."

"Things are not as they appear. Another of my mottoes, but I was blindsided. What bugs me is I didn't think to ask the forensic guys to look for a fake print. I'd read it could be done, but it never occurred to me."

"You can't think of everything," Clarence said.

"When it's this important, I have to. Whoever did this isn't dumb enough to leave their prints on a gun. And if they do, they're not going to dump it two blocks from the scene. Why not dump it in the river three miles away? They knew we'd check Dumpsters. That's standard procedure."

I flipped to my list of five observations that pointed to a detective. I wrote down two more beneath.

6. The killer knew how to fake fingerprints and place them on the gun.
7. The killer knew it would be SOP to search all Dumpsters within four blocks of the scene. He knew where to put the murder weapon so it would be found, while appearing that he didn't want it to be found.

So far the killer had planted evidence against at least two of us, Noel and me. Was this his joke, trying to send the department into confusion, give us bad PR? Or was he really trying to put me or Noel away?

Why Noel? And why me? What did we have in common? Were we arbitrary choices? Or did the killer have an ax to grind? And if so, was he planning to grind it again?

19

WEDNESDAY, DECEMBER 4, 2:00 A.M.

THE FOLLOWING HAPPENED between 1:00 a.m. and 2:00 a.m.: no sleep.

I was watching *24* on a portable DVD player in my car. I know I really shouldn't do that, but it keeps me awake in the wee hours of noncritical surveillance.

Critical surveillance requires unswerving attention. This didn't. I was scoping out a house one hundred feet away. I looked up every three seconds, and a second later I looked down. A world-class sprinter couldn't move to or from the house out of my line of sight.

Jack Bauer and I are alike. We take down the bad guys. We're tough as nails, yet tenderhearted. We're misunderstood, Jack and I, tragic and heroic. We're both always in trouble with our superiors. We've both lost our wives and have complicated relationships with our daughters. We're both handsome. The ladies love us. But the biggest similarity is this: Neither of us gets any sleep.

I sat there nursing my Big Gulp, neck aching from turning to the right. If I didn't reposition the car soon to equalize my neck twists, I'd have a chiropractor on my back.

I turned my flashlight to my shirt, recognizing a spot from yesterday morning's Egg McMuffin. The second stain was coffee, probably last night's venti latte.

It was the third spot that intrigued me. Using my detective skills, I pulled the fabric up close and put my tongue on the reddish-brown spot. Of course. The steak Burrito Ultimo, Baja Fresh.

I wondered if the department would cover charges for a cleaner's bill for food stains. I pictured Sarah Ballenger in accounting rolling her eyes.

In novels, detectives on surveillance see and hear all kinds of things. Suspects raise their voices and say, "Okay, now that we stole his diamonds, let's go dump Harvey's body in the lake." They may even say "in the lake, eh?" so you know the killer's a Canadian.

Unfortunately, in real life people don't say things they already know for the benefit of the eavesdropper. And if you're sitting outside someone's house for the night, chances are they'll do nothing more exciting than go to bed. They sleep soundly; you don't.

But Kim Suda was a light sleeper, I'd heard her say, and seeing her rifle through my papers got under my skin. It would probably be a wasted night, but I was willing to chance it.

I have nothing against time. Time is what keeps everything from happening at once. But on a stakeout, time can get on your nerves.

Good thing I had a companion.

"Want another Cheeto?" I stuck back my hand, and Mulch gratefully closed his lips, taking care not to bite me.

Clarence called. "Still on your stakeout?" he asked. "Geneva's asleep."

"I'd hope so. It's 2:10 a.m.!"

"Thought I'd come join you."

"Suda's light's still on, but she's probably reading and won't emerge from the cave until daylight. This cul-de-sac's dead."

"I want to write up a stakeout."

"Imagine sitting in a car doing nothing for eight hours. That's pretty much it. Just go out in your garage right now and sit there all night. You'll get the idea. Besides, I don't want somebody seeing Goliath get in my car."

"You said nobody's around."

"Okay. Park around the corner. No lights. Then walk to my car nonchalantly. Knock twice on the passenger window, or I might have to shoot you."

Fifteen minutes later the double knock came. I unlocked the door, and the offensive line of the New England Patriots sat beside me.

Mulch growled as Clarence got in, but I gave him another Cheeto, and soon he was licking Clarence's face.

"You bring a dog on a stakeout?"

"Only when I can pull him away from his poker game."

No response.

"You ever seen that art with the dogs playing poker? I got mine with my velvet Elvis."

No response.

There's nothing like stakeout conversation. Sports, politics, how to reach out to your pregnant thirty-year-old unmarried daughter, guns, movies—you bounce in and out of stuff. The next hour was a panoply of randomness. (Sharon used *panoply* once in Scrabble, and I liked it.)

"Your eyes'll get used to the dark."

He picked up a corn dog wrapper and mustard packet at his feet. "I'm not sure I want them to."

Clarence stared behind the driver's seat at the archaeological dig. He excavated a berry pie wrapper from the Neolithic era.

"You are what you eat," he said.

"That makes me an Izzy's pizza," I replied. "There's one piece left." I opened the glove box and pulled it out. "Want it?"

Clarence refused. I put it back, and pretty soon we were talking about family.

"I stopped going to my family reunions after my sister's second marriage," I said. "She showed up with this guy at a family gathering, called him Bob, but never introduced him. No explanation. It was like *Bewitched*, with the two Darrins—like if they don't say anything, we won't notice *this isn't the same guy*! You know what I'm saying?"

"Who's Darrin?"

"*Bewitched*."

"I never saw *Bewitched*."

"It's on cable. Wouldn't take you long to catch up." This was another reminder that Clarence and I grew up on different planets.

"Daddy wasn't much for TV. He wanted us to read."

"Wish your daddy were here right now. With him, a stakeout would be a pleasure. I could listen to his stories forever."

"I'm sure he'll be telling them forever," Clarence said. "And there'll be lots of fresh stories to tell on the new earth. He always said it would be the great adventure. If you're with us, you'll get to listen to his stories…and they'll be better than ever."

"You managed to work it in, didn't you?"

"What?"

"The Christian stuff. Heaven. The whole nine yards."

"Hey, you pitched the ball to me. I just took a swing." He tried to stretch, unsuccessfully.

"For future reference, on stakeouts you need to be shorter than six five," I said, "or bring your own car. It also helps to have the bladder capacity of five people."

After five minutes of silence I said, "Ever notice that stakeout rhymes with takeout? If you get a Bonzer Steak from Outback, like I do sometimes, then it's a STEAK-out. Get it? I mean, spelled S–T–E–A–K–O—"

"I get it!"

"I've got a surprise for you." I pushed the seat back, reached past my coat, and pulled a box from the sealed plastic container I use to keep Mulch out of the food.

Clarence looked at the box. "Krispy Kreme donuts?"

He said it like they were bad. "You Christians got something against donuts?"

"Per capita, Christians eat more donuts than anybody. You should come to our men's meetings."

"How much are the donuts?"

"Voluntary donations. For you, free."

"Do you have to stay for the Bible study, or can you just pick up the donuts and leave?"

"You have to stay ten minutes for each donut you eat. That'll keep you there for the whole hour."

I opened the box and handed it to him. "I have a buddy who writes murder mysteries, and he's always calling me for advice. This guy mentions Krispy Kreme in his books, like three times on a single page, hoping somebody who works with the company will give him a gift certificate or a year's supply or something."

"That doesn't sound professional."

"Yeah, people can be so pathetic. Pass me a Krispy Kreme, will you?"

Clarence reached for the glazed raspberry.

"No, give me the New York cheesecake. No, that's a chocolate iced glazed cruller, Mulch's favorite. Pass it over to him, would you? Sorry, that's key lime pie." He closed the box and dropped it on my lap.

I pointed at the house. "Look, Suda's moving. Light went on in the front room."

I saw blinds open slightly and a face peeking out the bay window, looking the other direction, straight out, then at us.

"Don't move," I said. "Stay exactly where you are."

Ten minutes later it was boredom as usual. Hopes rise and fall on stakeouts.

"So, tell me about your world," I said. "Berkley's concerned about subscribers?"

"Revenues are down. Too many competing news sources—TV, radio, the Internet."

"Plus people finally realizing the *Tribune*'s garbage."

"You say you don't read the paper, so you don't know what you're criticizing, do you?"

"You walk the beat with our street cops? Didn't think so. You don't know who you're criticizing."

"Where I come from 'beat cop' has another meaning. When you've been beaten just for being black, you don't overflow with trust."

"Don't judge us all by the bad ones."

"My point exactly," Clarence said. "And if you think you could write better than what you read in the *Trib*, submit me a column. If it's good enough, I'll see that it's printed."

"No kidding?"

"No kidding. Tell your own story. First person, detective talking to the people about investigating murders. Go for it. Turn it in when you're ready."

"I will."

"Pardon me if I don't hold my breath. Anyway, tell me about this police morale problem."

"You think I'm going to say something you can use against us?"

"Off the record."

"Morale? Well, there's the budget cuts, not to mention all the bad publicity the *Trib*'s given us."

"The *Trib* didn't shoot an unarmed law-abiding citizen."

"That was one in a million, okay? People don't appreciate cops. Truth is, we risk our lives every day for whiners and gripers. And cops are getting laid off. Guys come to work, check for blood on their office doorposts, and hope the angel of death passes them over."

"Sounds like you've been reading the Bible."

"Just a figure of speech." I hesitated, not knowing how to say it. "Listen, I know there are racist cops. And I know what they did to your daddy. I want you to know I'd have been proud to have him as my father."

"You would've gotten funny looks if he were your father. Still, I appreciate what you're saying. Daddy really enjoyed the time he spent with you. He liked you. I never thought I'd tell you this, but Geneva says I should…"

"What?"

"Before he died, Daddy asked me to keep an eye on you."

"Why?"

"Well, since you asked…he wanted you to know Jesus."

"He said that?"

Kim Suda's front door opened. She walked briskly to her car, got in, and pulled out of the driveway. We ducked low, though she probably wouldn't have seen us anyway since I'd parked past her place behind another car.

I waited until she turned right off Patty Court onto Woodard, then started the car and followed her to the next turn, right again on 78th, then left on Jackson. Eventually we were on Stark. I had to stay way behind her because of the light traffic. She drove Stark to 162nd, turned right, and took a quick left into the parking lot of a 7-Eleven. I pulled into a real estate building lot across the street. I turned off my lights and backed around so I had a clear view of the store Suda entered. I grabbed my binoculars from under the front seat.

"There's a small pair in the glove box," I said to Clarence. "Just toss the pizza to Mulch."

He handed the pizza back, where an invisible entity dismembered it. Clarence held up his binoculars. "We're going to watch what she buys? Seems a little…intrusive."

"That's surveillance," I said.

She'd veered left and gone to the far end of the store by a glass cooler filled with milk. She slowed down near a man whose back was to us. He was flipping through a magazine. I got out of the car and found the best place in the shadows, which put me right next to a rhododendron bush. I had to keep moving to keep her in view, but fortunately the front of the store was glass.

Suda turned up an aisle where she appeared to be looking at medications. Sominex? I could see her face once in a while, but a slight move one way or the other obscured her. I saw her face and realized her lips were moving.

"She's talking," I said to Clarence, who'd exited the car and was now mostly behind the rhody, eclipsing the moon and looking over my shoulder.

"Talking to herself?"

"No, to that guy in the black coat standing a couple of feet from her on the other side of the aisle. See him?"

"Why don't they stand closer if they're talking?"

"Because they don't want to *look* like they're talking. Suda and this guy didn't come together, and they won't leave together."

They talked for five minutes. I could see only the guy's back. He was wearing a navy blue stocking cap. I looked away only to take an occasional glance at Mulch, who was exploring the inside of the car without supervision. I could see Suda's lips moving periodically. I wished I'd studied lipreading. The man handed her something.

"What's that?" I asked.

"A brown envelope."

"Evidence? A payoff? Bet it's not a birthday card."

Suda stepped to the cooler, opened the door, and grabbed a bottled water. Walking up a different aisle, away from the guy she'd been talking to, she made her purchase, got in her car, and headed back onto Stark.

"Why aren't we following her?" Clarence asked.

"Because we know who she is and where she lives."

The man continued to gaze at his magazine. A minute after Suda pulled away, he took it to the front desk. Paid cash. With his stocking cap pulled down and various things blocking my view, it was hard to get a good look at his face. But just as he pointed his remote to unlock his car, he looked up. The streetlight caught his face.

"I don't believe it," I said.

"It looks like…"

We both slunk back to the car. I turned the key, but kept the lights off. "Stay low."

After he was a hundred feet down the road, I followed. No traffic, either to fight or cover me. He went all the way down to Foster, turned left, then turned right exactly where I knew he would. Still a hundred feet back, I saw him slow down, turn into a driveway, and stop. I couldn't see it, but I knew he was punching a code and a gate was swinging open.

We sat there, car idling.

"Was it really him?" Clarence asked.

"Yeah. If I had the slightest doubt, I don't now because that's his driveway he just went up, security entrance and all. I don't know what it means, but we just found a gold nugget in the rocks and mud. Kim Suda had a clandestine meeting and a handoff at 3:15 a.m....with Edward Lennox, chief of police!"

"There is nothing more deceptive than an obvious fact."
SHERLOCK HOLMES, *THE HOUND OF THE BASKERVILLES*

WEDNESDAY, DECEMBER 4, 10:00 A.M.

I DIED IN 2003, when Sharon died. I went on breathing, but it was a technicality.

Since then I've felt alive only at key points in an investigation when the adrenaline flows, or in isolated moments with close friends, like Mulch or Jake.

These thoughts came over me at 10:00 a.m., which is late to sleep in, unless you've gone to bed at 5:00 a.m. I sat up in my bed, sipping French roast and feeling Mulch's hot breath on my toes. He seemed to have a stomachache; he'd been emitting fumes reminiscent of a paper mill.

My old brownstone is a sanctuary from human beings, which is why I usually don't answer the door and seldom answer the phone. When Sharon was around, I enjoyed people more.

She was kind, but honest. Once she told me, "You dance like a guy tilting a pinball machine. Relax." So I learned to relax, becoming suave and debonair. At least I stopped tilting her.

We danced the jitterbug. The slow jitterbug, not the fast one. Neither of us ever wanted it to end.

But it did.

The coffee was cold now. Not much reason to get out of bed. But even less to stay there.

As I drove to downtown Portland, I phoned Officer Paul Anderson, calling in the hours he and Griffin owed me for flushing their holdup man out of his apartment. Tomorrow was Kim Suda's day off. Could one of them follow her to lunch, to her martial arts class, to anywhere and everywhere? Maybe take pictures?

I walked into Grayson's Fine Pens, a store for fountain pen connoisseurs. I'd never been in such a store and didn't know they existed until seeing it on a website. The fountain pen specialist had a contemplative look on an expansive face, with cheeks so fleshy they could use support. There were two sets of shoulders, his and the suit's. His tie had been loosened, and his white dress shirt was a mass of wrinkles.

"Rupert Bolin at your service," he said.

When he leaned over, a ridge of white flesh emerged above his low-slung belt. I thought of taking his picture and posting it on my refrigerator as a warning. Relatively speaking, I'm still a fine specimen. Rupert was about nine hundred Krispy Kremes ahead of me.

I showed him a half dozen of the professor's fountain pens. He looked them over, called them by name, nodded appreciatively at two of them, and dismissed the other four as pens for lowlifes. He spoke rapturously of the joy of fountain pens. Here I'd wasted my life bringing killers to justice when I could have been a pen collector.

"What do people do with fountain pens?" I asked.

He looked at me as if I'd asked, "What do people do with a porterhouse steak?"

"Humor me," I said. "Pretend I know nothing about fountain pens."

He sighed, looking upward. I followed his gaze. Ceiling tiles.

"Where do I begin? A fountain pen is a fine instrument in the hands of a master artist. Artisans use fountain pens for special occasions. For important documents. For poetry and love letters. And sketch art, the type you might frame."

I nodded earnestly.

"It's a hobby you should consider. We had our first Portland fountain pen show in 2004, at the Embassy Suites. It was a big success. You must have heard about it."

"I'm sure I must have. Was it on ESPN?"

"It was thrilling."

"I can only imagine. Who wants to watch the Packers play the Bears when you can go to a fountain pen show?"

"My sentiments exactly. We have a strong presence on the Internet, you know."

"Do we?"

"There are over fifty websites of fountain pen dealers, hobbyists, and enthusiasts."

"Fifty? I wouldn't have thought there'd be more than thirty-five."

"You've no doubt visited the sites."

"No doubt." I'd visited one. "I found you on Bill's Fountain Pen website."

He beamed.

"Look," I said, "I adore fountain pens, but I'm having a hard time explaining my devotion to…the uninitiated. Novices. You know what I'm saying?"

He nodded sympathetically. "In an age of e-mails and BICs—" he nearly spat the word—"and cookie-cutter mass production, fountain pens are elegant. They tie us to the past. They are handheld history. In an age of encroaching illiteracy, they make us more cultured, more refined, more literary."

"More literary?"

"They make us better wordsmiths. They stimulate thought and reflection. They are tools of articulation and civility."

"Okeydokey," I said. "And...how does that all work?"

"When you put the nib of the pen in the ink, you can write perhaps eight words. Maybe a short sentence. Then you have to dip the pen again."

"Seems inconvenient."

He looked like I'd called his mother a name. "The best things in life take time. A love letter takes time. People are so used to keyboards and e-mails that they've lost the love of thoughtful language. They don't stop to think. They just spew out words. No wonder the writing is so thoughtless, so careless, so urbane, so..."

"Quick?"

"Quick is not always good."

I thought of a few instances when it isn't and nodded.

He insisted that I drop my business card in the drawing for a set of three fancy fountain pens on display. The sign said the set was worth two hundred dollars, which was about $198 more than I would have paid for it. He also insisted that I sign up for his monthly fountain pen newsletter. I pulled out my BIC pen, saw his shocked stare, assured him I'd found it on the sidewalk, then took the green Paradise fountain pen he handed me and started to write the address of Clarence Abernathy. But I wasn't sure on the house number, so I wrote my address instead.

For a change of pace, I met my cronies at Powell's City of Books. Occupying a whole city block, with over a million new and used books, it's a book lover's paradise. They display a framed article from the *Washington Post* calling it "the best bookstore in the world." Powell's probably thinks the *Washington Post* is the best newspaper in the world, but that's another issue. I don't go to Powell's for the politics.

I came an hour early to find a space at the world's largest bookstore, with the world's smallest parking garage. Six thousand in-store customers a day, and they have forty lousy spaces. I wedged into an imaginary space, and when an attendant scowled, I showed him my badge and he backed away so I wouldn't smell the marijuana.

No matter what you believe, you can find a section in Powell's to make you feel better about it and another section to make you question it or get mad at somebody. I go there when I want to feel literary and absorb wisdom. Looking at the bestseller tables near the entrance, I wonder about the wisdom part. But I love that old-book smell, and they've got the great detective novels buried amidst the not-so-great.

I entered at Tenth and Burnside determined to book my way to World Cup Coffee and Tea, passing by new arrivals, literature, classics, and reference works to get to sci-fi, thrillers, and mysteries. With seven thousand mysteries to sort through, there's lots of rocks and mud but plenty of gold awaiting discovery. Everybody's a detective at Powell's. Right when I got to the section I wanted, I had to stop. One minute of Powell's time is one hour of real time.

I put on imaginary blinders to beeline to Clarence and Jake at the World Cup, by the humor and audio books, where some come for free Wi-Fi and I come for the walnut sticky buns and chocolate croissants. They trust you with five books, so I've spent lots of time here with Ross Macdonald and Raymond Chandler—no relation—occasionally getting goo on their pages. That's part of the character of used books.

Joining Clarence and Jake in the cafe, I chose a grilled chicken and Gouda cheese sandwich, while Clarence took the egg salad and Jake a corn and black bean salad with chicken tortilla soup.

Two minutes after ordering we were talking about issues raised in Russell's *Why I Am Not a Christian* and Lewis's *Mere Christianity*. Though I didn't bring the books, it took Jake and Clarence only five minutes to find both on the shelves while I worked over my sandwich.

"God's existence is wishful thinking," I said after ten minutes of discussion. "It makes people feel better to think there's a supreme being."

"For me it was the opposite," Jake said. "The last thing I wanted was to believe in God. It required changes I didn't want to make. God has a way of interfering with your life. Big time. It was only later that I realized the changes were in my best interest."

"So," Clarence said, "your wishful thinking wasn't that God existed, but that He didn't?"

"Exactly. That's what C. S. Lewis experienced. Ultimately, he bowed to the God he desperately didn't want to believe in. When he became a theist, before he became a Christian, he called himself the most reluctant convert in all of England. Lewis went from atheism to agnosticism to belief in God. Later he came to believe in Christ. And that's when he really found joy."

I'd left room for a walnut sticky bun with extra butter. (I may die a few years sooner, but I'll die happy.)

"But what if I don't *want* to become a Christian?"

"Isn't that where the wishful thinking comes in?" Jake asked. "Shouldn't you just want to believe whatever's true? I mean, if Jesus isn't who He claimed to be, then *don't* believe in Him. If He is, then do. It's not about what you want to believe, but what's really true."

"You don't want to believe the murderer's a detective," Clarence said. "But you do believe it, right?"

"I go where the evidence leads."

"So ask yourself where the evidence leads when it comes to Jesus," Jake said. "It's not about your preference, like choosing between a walnut sticky bun and a chocolate croissant."

"Don't mock me. It was a tough call."

"My point is, faith shouldn't be about what suits our tastes, but about the truth the evidence points to."

"So if you disagree with what we believe," Clarence said, "then try to talk us out of it—take your best shot. We don't want to believe what's false."

"You guys will get talked out of your faith when hell freezes over."

"What is it that holds you back?" Jake said. "Not only from Christ, but from the idea that there's a God?"

"The Holocaust. Stalin. The Killing Fields. Idi Amin. Rwanda. Jeffrey Dahmer. What I saw in Vietnam. A couple hundred murder cases. How's that for starters? People get away with murder. Where's the justice?"

"Daddy used to say, 'Nobody gets away wid nothin'," Clarence said.

"How could he say that? After what those dirty cops did to him?"

"It used to bother me how Daddy would forgive people. It made me think he was weak." Somebody with green hair, waiting for coffee, heard Clarence's voice and stared. If I had green hair, I wouldn't stare at anybody.

"I couldn't have been more wrong," Clarence continued. "He knew God would bring justice, but he was willing to wait. He said to me, 'They still has time to repent. If they doesn't, yo' daddy would sooner be the mule they whip than stand in their shoes before almighty God and be burnt to ashes by the fire of His holiness.'"

"He really said that?"

"I've never forgotten it. My point is, what makes you think God will let people get away with all this stuff? The Bible teaches that He won't. There's going to be a judgment for everything that's been done, good and bad. God promises that repeatedly."

"But why wait? I've seen parents kill their children, children kill their parents, a teenage boy torture his little brother. Why didn't God just throw lightning bolts and fry these lowlifes?"

"I've seen evil too, you know," Jake said. "I was in Nam. I saw Finney and Doc die. They were my best friends. My Carly's dying as we speak."

"My sister and niece were murdered," Clarence said. "Daddy saw a lot more evil than I ever have, probably more than you. He believed God has reasons for allowing these things that we can't understand."

"I don't buy it. Sometimes I just want to go out there and save hundreds of people by performing a few executions. You know how many people die because of drug dealers?"

"So if you were in charge," Clarence said, "there'd be no mercy, no opportunity to repent? Bad people would all die. But…maybe you deserve to die too. Maybe we're all worse than you think. That's what the Bible says."

"Don't try to put me in the same box with murderers and rapists. That's one of the things that frosts me about you Christians," I said, standing up. "One of the many things."

When I returned to detective division, two attractive women were standing near my workstation. One was dressed in fashion magazine clothes. Her outfit screamed money. The other was Linda Glissan, Jack's wife. Linda always looks nice, but she and Sharon used to shop for bargains at Nordstrom Rack. Even that can strain a detective's salary.

"Hi, Ollie." Linda hugged me. I don't get hugged often. "You've met Sheila Phillips, Brandon's wife, haven't you?"

"I don't believe I've had the pleasure," she said, stretching out her hand, which momentarily unnerved me, since her fingernails looked like red-polished Ginsu knives. So this was Phillips's wife. He'd married her a year ago, eighteen months after his divorce. I'd heard about Sheila. She lived up to it.

"I brought you some of those chocolate pecan muffins you like," Linda said, handing me a bag.

"Thanks."

"Jack and I miss you."

"Look, Linda, I'm sorry. I…"

"It's okay. I miss Sharon too. She was one of my best friends."

I nodded, aware of Sheila, who seemed to be studying us.

"We've stopped asking you over because we don't want to bug you. But when you're ready, let us know. Or just drop by, okay? You're always welcome at our house."

Her invitation reminded me that it was approaching twenty-four hours before my second dinner with Kendra, this time at her home. I was shocked when she'd asked. I wanted to see her again, but if they made body armor for the heart, I'd be bidding for it on eBay.

I said good-bye to Linda, pretending I had to make a phone call. As I called to check my messages I watched Sheila Phillips out of the corner of my eye.

Why was she staring at me?

↔

Clarence and I planted ourselves in an empty conference room, where the boxy wooden chairs weren't comfortable but we could talk more freely than at my workstation.

"When you have a limited number of suspects," I said, "you start by eliminating people, one by one. Suppose it's one of the detectives. Who do we eliminate?"

"You?" Clarence asked.

"I hope so," I said, followed by a laugh I hoped didn't sound forced. This wasn't the time to bring up that I couldn't remember anything between my first half hour at Rosie O'Grady's and getting the phone call at 3:07 a.m.

"Manny?"

"I can't see a motive. His alibi's as good as you could expect—home with wife and kids. But I'll call Maria and worm it out of her, just to make sure."

"You're going to check up on your own partner?"

"He'd understand. Well, maybe he wouldn't. But he'd check up on me."

"Who else is off the list? Jack?"

"Why?"

"For one thing, when you called him to the crime scene, he didn't seem nervous."

"Jack's an old friend. But for now he stays on the list. But do I think he'd do it? No way."

Clarence looked at his list. "Tell me about Brandon Phillips."

"Efficient, smart, observant. Heck of a poker player. Cleans out guys in the Friday night games. I was losing too much money, so I don't go anymore. Brandon's a good detective."

"He's nervous," Clarence said.

"Why do you say that?"

"Remember at the professor's house? Said he had allergies, but it seemed like an excuse. He was twitching and seemed anxious to leave. He wasn't responsive to your questions."

"He knew that Dell computer was a mail-order only model. Like I said, he's observant."

"You and Noel both noticed the missing picture on the mantel. Phillips didn't."

"Did you?"

"No, but I'm not a detective." Clarence looked at his list. "How tall is Suda?"

"Five one?"

"You've thought about—"

"The desk chair adjusted for a short person? Suda can be a pain, and she's up to her eyeballs in something. But...a killer?"

"How about Tommi?"

"She's a mom—five kids, ranging three years old to high school."

"Moms never kill people?"

"If the professor told her kids not to wear seat belts or breathed on them when he had the flu, maybe."

We talked until Clarence had gone through the whole list. "Congratulations, detective," he said. "You've eliminated everybody. Since none of your suspects killed the professor, he must still be alive. Somebody better dig him up."

Smart guy.

I headed home to the old brownstone in the dark. I turned onto 150th, eighty feet from my house, then threw on the brakes. A shadow moved, then disappeared behind my garage. I pulled my car over the curb onto my lawn, headlights pointed where I saw the shadow. I jammed it into park, grabbed a flashlight out of the glove box, and popped out, gun pulled.

"Police officer! Don't move!"

Somebody pulled himself over the wood fence on my side yard. I ran through my neighbor's side yard, flashlight in one hand, Glock in the other.

"Stop or I'll shoot!"

As I passed the window on my right, I saw Donna, the neighbor lady, horrified. When I got past the back edge of their house, I heard a crack and felt an explosion on the right side of my skull. I felt warm blood before I hit the ground.

Someone wearing a ski mask was on top of me. He had both his hands on my gun. I hit the left side of his face with my flashlight. He stood, staggering, and threw my gun over the fence.

I tried to stand, then fell back to the ground. I saw him disappear into the hedge at the back of my neighbors' yard. That's the last thing I remember until hearing somebody yell, "Donna, call 911!"

"Did you see him?" I asked.

"The guy in the magazine?" someone said. "I saw his grump. He was over the fence in a frimbo. I came out when I heard the yardarm. He threw something over the brumbello."

"What?" I tried to say.

"You're the car, right? My mother the car."

That's what it sounded like. In retrospect, I think he must have said, "My neighbor the cop."

Patrol arrived, then the EMTs in an ambulance. Despite the objections of the good-hearted Obrists, who'd brought me into their house, I staggered out the back door to point out things for the officers to look for. I told them they needed to find footprints and fetch my gun and make sure nobody contaminated the crime scene. They seemed to think they didn't need my advice.

Next thing I knew, the uniforms were escorting me back into the house and telling the Obrists not to let me move. Donna had just fixed me tea, Earl Grey, which is what Jean-Luc Picard, my favorite captain, drinks on *Star Trek: The Next Generation*. I'd never tried it. It was awful. But she was so attentive that I kept thanking her for it.

The EMTs thought I had a concussion and insisted on taking me in. I insisted otherwise, telling them I didn't need a doctor—it was only a little crack in the skull and I get a couple a week. No brain fluid leaking out my ears, so no big deal.

Manny showed up and seemed almost concerned. I should get cracked in the head more often. I told him I wanted to check out signs of entry at the old brownstone. We went to my back porch. I was more light-headed than I let on, grabbing on to a tree limb and a fence post to keep me up. Mulch looked out the sliding glass door at Manny, showed his teeth, and barked like crazy until he saw me and began his doggy dance of joy.

I unlocked the back door, and next thing I knew Mulch was licking my head wounds.

"Give me a minute," I said to Manny, going into the bathroom. Mrs. Obrist had wiped off most of the blood before the EMTs got there, which made it easier to call them off. But there was still wet blood in my hair. Red puffiness was working its way over the right side of my face.

I put my head in the sink. After the water drained, the sink had a reddish stain. I dried my hair with a bath towel, then walked out when I heard Mulch's growling and a string of Hispanic swear words. Between Manny and Mulch I wasn't sure who was doing more growling, but when I thought I heard Mulch swear at Manny in Spanish, I decided it was time to sit down, take it easy, and avoid Earl Grey.

When you're a detective and also the victim, you want to question yourself, put the pieces together, and solve the crime. But I wasn't thinking clearly. Manny, apparently, was doing the thinking for me. He had me sitting on my recliner and even took off my shoes and brought me my slippers.

An hour later, my face was experimenting with new and different colors. Having abandoned a pinkish brown, it had settled on a puffy purple.

I heard Mulch barking again. Next thing I know, Jake and Clarence are in my living room. Sue Keels showed up and tried to talk me into going to the emergency room. She said a concussion was possible, that my eyes didn't look right. I was a

Klingon warrior who'd been assimilated by the Borg, and she was worried about me going to sleep. Being a man and a cop, naturally I refused. Bart Starr, who was feeding pineapples to my kangaroo, agreed with me. Since Sue's an emergency room nurse, I figured she could take care of me even without all those machines. She messed with my head and did stuff that made it feel worse at first and better later.

Finally Sue said, "Looks like you guys are ready for a men's night," and took off. Jake and Clarence and I hung out for a couple more hours. They made popcorn and dug out the cookie dough ice cream I'd bought the day before at WinCo. I try to eat ice cream within two days; no point risking freezer burn.

Sergeant Seymour called and ordered me to stay home the next day. He said that if he found out I'd conducted interviews or done surveillance, he'd suspend me. He also said something about the Nebraska Cornhuskers taking the Space Shuttle into Lake Michigan to find the lost city of Atlantis, but after that he stopped making sense.

Jake and Clarence and I talked and laughed. There were lots of stories, the best ones about Clarence's daddy. It reminded me of Vietnam, how hard you laugh when you've lived through an attack.

Occasionally I nearly forgot my head was about to explode.

"There is nothing more stimulating than a case where everything goes against you."
SHERLOCK HOLMES, *THE HOUND OF THE BASKERVILLES*

THURSDAY, DECEMBER 5, 10:00 A.M.

I WOKE UP with a jackhammer beating on the little gray cells.

Sometimes you're the dog; sometimes you're the fire hydrant. I wasn't fond of being the hydrant. I couldn't have managed three eggs, five strips of bacon, and two English muffins without Mulch's help.

Later Manny dropped by my house and left me forty-one pictures of the professor's living room, which he'd collected from Palatine's family and friends. I quickly eliminated thirty-eight of them, then looked under the magnifying glass at the other three, examining the professor's mantel. One photo showed nine pictures on the mantel, with one dead center, four on each side, evenly spaced. I focused in on the second picture from the right. I could tell only that there were a few people in it, like most of the other pictures. I assumed one was the professor.

I picked up the phone and called Lynn Carpenter at the *Tribune*.

"Lynn?" I asked. "Can I call you Lynn?"

"Give it a try and see what happens. I'm calling you Ollie. Clarence said you had an eventful evening. I've been worried about you. You okay?"

"No permanent damage. Can I ask you a favor?"

"Name it."

An hour later a courier picked up a pile of photos. I'd taken photos of the photos with my Olympus, for fear they could be sucked into the *Tribune*'s black hole, never to see the light of day unless it was on the front page. Carp assured me no one else would even see them. But I've heard too many assurances from journalists to believe it. Even if they like double cheese and they're worried about me.

Jake and Clarence had promised to help me get through an entire day away from investigating. A little late for that, but they said they'd bring over lunch from Lou's, and who was I to argue?

By the time they arrived at the old brownstone at twelve thirty, the jackhammer had mellowed to a bass drum, and I had an appetite.

"Rory insisted lunch was on him," Jake said. "He threw in onion rings, extra fries, extra sauce, and—you're not going to believe this—an orange malt." He pulled it out and held it up for me.

"But Lou's doesn't make orange malts."

"They do now. Rory went out and got the mix. When he found out you'd been two-timing him at Dea's, it lit a fire under him. He said, 'Only the best for Mr. Ollie.'"

I grabbed the metal container—Rory had gone all out—and pressed the cold against the right side of my face.

"Food from Lou's again…almost makes the assault worthwhile."

What followed was a feast that food critics—who prefer French meals consisting of small, wet animals you try to exterminate in your garden—would raise their noses at, but that real people love.

"Did you know I'm having dinner with my daughter tonight?"

"Terrific," Jake said. "At Lou's again?"

"No. Her place. She invited me. Probably regretted it the second she did it, but I said yes. I think we're both bracing ourselves. The gloves always seem to come off when we talk privately."

"Just getting together is progress," Clarence said.

"Between the two of us, we'll find a way to ruin it."

My cell rang just as I was polishing off the onion rings, dipping them into the last bit of horseradish. It was the professor's brother, returning my calls. Finally.

"I'm scheduled for surgery, so let's make it quick."

"I haven't been doing squat myself. Just eating burgers with my homeys. You know how it is—the cop's life. Okay, here's my question. Did you ever drink with your brother?"

"What makes that your business?"

"Was he a wine drinker?"

"Wine was all he drank."

"What kind?"

"Mostly merlot and cabernet sauvignon. The merlot was Beringer Brothers. Not sure about the cabernet."

"Are those…red wines or white?"

He laughed. "Red."

"I'm a beer drinker."

"Obviously."

"Okay," I said. "Name three beers made by Anheuser-Busch, besides Budweiser."

"Uh…I'm not sure."

"Obviously." Wine snob. "Okay, what white wine did your brother drink?"

"None. He didn't like white wine."

"But…there was residue of white wine in two glasses in his house. The lab hasn't confirmed it officially, but one tech said it smelled like a Riesling."

"I can guarantee you Bill wasn't drinking it. Unless he was out of reds."

"There were two bottles in the rack and more in the garage. All red."

"They're waiting for me in surgery."

"Knock 'em dead." I sucker punched the red key to hang up before he could.

"You already knew somebody took the bottle of white wine," Clarence said.

"But now it looks like they brought it too. Why would the killer bring wine to the murder scene? Did he offer it to the professor? Did the professor drink it or turn it down? And if he turned it down, maybe the killer drank from both glasses. That's why he wiped them both."

"Your sergeant told you not to work on the case," Jake said. He and Clarence cleaned up after the meal like a couple of housemaids.

"I should have you ladies come more often."

Clarence looked around. "Yeah, you really should."

Jake picked up *Why I Am Not a Christian* from the coffee table, where it sat on top of *Mere Christianity*.

"Been doing your reading?" I asked him before he could ask me.

Jake smiled and pulled his own copy of *Why I Am Not a Christian* out of his briefcase. He turned pages, then read aloud.

"Russell says, 'I think that you must have a certain amount of definite belief before you have a right to call yourself a Christian. The word does not have quite such a full-blooded meaning now as it had in the times of Saint Augustine and Saint Thomas Aquinas. In those days, if a man said that he was a Christian it was known what he meant.' He's right on target," Jake said.

"I didn't think you'd agree with *anything* this guy says."

"Why not?"

"Well, he's no friend of Christians."

"No, but that doesn't mean he's always wrong. I'm not afraid of the truth. I read lots of people I disagree with. How about you?"

I shrugged, which is what I do instead of answering when I don't like my answer.

"Obviously," Jake said, "I disagree with Russell's view of Jesus as being just a good man and a decent teacher."

"You fault him for saying Jesus was a good man?"

"No. For saying Jesus was *just* a good man. That He wasn't God. When I first read *Mere Christianity*, Lewis got through to me when he argued that people can't logically say that."

"Why not?"

"Because Jesus claimed to be God and to forgive sins. So He was either deceived or lying. The only other possibility is that He was telling the truth. When I considered the possibilities and weighed His words, I decided He wasn't a liar and He wasn't deceived. He was really who He claimed to be."

"At least look at the evidence," Clarence said.

"Look guys, I'm tired, and I'm expected at Kendra's tonight. I'll need my strength. I'd better take a nap."

Jake stood and put his hand on my shoulder. "Give our love to Kendra. Tell her we miss seeing her. Anything we can get you before we leave?"

"Warm milk, maybe, and you can read me a bedtime story, from C. S. Lewis no doubt. Then you can warm up my jammies in the microwave and tuck me in for my nap."

Right then the doorbell rang. Clarence opened the door, and Mrs. Obrist marched in holding a tray with delicate china on it.

"Feeling better?" she said to me. "Since you liked it so much, I brewed you another pot of Earl Grey."

The phone jarred me awake, and I saw 3:00 on the clock. Why was I not surprised? But the room wasn't dark enough. That's when I realized it was p.m., not a.m.

"Sarge here. Chief Lennox wants to see you right away. I told him I'd ordered you to stay home after last night's incident, but he was adamant."

"I'm right here if he wants to drop by."

"I'm afraid he meets everybody at his office."

Everybody but Kim Suda, whom he meets in the middle of the night at a convenience store.

"He says he needs you here by four. Sorry."

It was 4:48, and I'd been waiting outside the chief's office fifty-one minutes. This time his door was closed. I'd just squished chewed-up Black Jack gum between two pages of *Architectural Digest* when he appeared, shaking the hand of someone in an expensive suit.

In public the chief kisses not only babies but a particular part of the human anatomy, mentioned by cops two hundred times a day, which I will not name in case my grandchildren—if I could be so lucky—one day read this.

In private, when dealing with those under him—which is everyone wearing a badge—the chief acts like the animal with the same anatomical name.

The chief walked the suit down the hall, then reappeared, all smiled out. Eyeing my trench coat, he beckoned me inside like snobs summon a waiter.

"Don't bother sitting—you won't be here long."

I sat. "I'm feeling dizzy after being attacked last night. Thanks for sending the flowers."

He did a double take. I saw him make a mental note to tell his assistant not to send me flowers next time. That's when he'd find out she hadn't.

"I've been looking over your paperwork," Lennox said. "Despite our warning, you're insisting that one of our own is guilty."

"I'm not insisting. I'm just concluding it, based on the evidence."

"And now you have a supposed assault?"

"*Supposed* assault?" I said, pointing at my face, sporting all the colors of the rainbow and—I might add—not covered by makeup.

"Are you going to say next that one of your fellow detectives was skulking around the back of your house, lying in wait for you?"

"I don't know who it was. But detectives can skulk. We're professional skulkers. Cimmatoni skulks. Why couldn't he do his skulking in my backyard? And furthermore—"

"If you don't resolve this case in a satisfactory manner, it'll cost you your job. If you do it right, I'll offer you a transfer anywhere, a promotion, a pay raise—you name it."

"You're offering to pay me to ignore evidence pointing to a cop? If that's what you're saying, tell me directly."

The chief sat there uncomfortably, as one does when his head is in that location. He knew enough not to answer my question with a yes. But neither did he say no. He waved the back of his hand at me.

"I think we know where we stand, Detective. Close the door behind you."

As I walked out of the chief's office and shut the door, my eyes fell on that photo of him, his wife, and his daughter. The moment I saw it, lightning struck. I pulled my Olympus from my trench coat pocket and took a picture of the picture.

I fought traffic and returned home at 5:50. Hours of time to experience eight minutes of being threatened and bribed.

I opened my laptop to the crime scene pictures, then to the photos of the photos on the mantel. I scrolled through them until I landed on one in particular. There, in the third frame on the left side, was a picture with the professor's arm around a girl on his left and another on his right, with two boys to the outside. I didn't need to look at the picture I'd taken an hour ago to recognize that one of the girls was Chief Lennox's daughter.

↔

I fell asleep, this time in the recliner, and woke up at seven. I showered and found a clean shirt and was heading toward Kendra's house when I got stuck behind a fender bender. I considered calling her, but I knew whatever I said would sound like an excuse. I had such a track record of excuses that legitimate reasons don't count. I'm the dad who cried wolf.

I rolled down the window. The smell of brakes and wet asphalt didn't help my head. I thought about flipping on the siren, but I didn't want to get another reprimand, like the time I used sirens to get home in time to watch the season finale of *24*.

I pulled up to Kendra's apartment; she'd been here eighteen months. It was only my second visit, though I'd driven by a dozen times hoping to catch a glimpse of her. As I walked to her door, I noticed the bushes, the bad lighting, and figured out six hiding places and three escape routes for an assailant. I'd talked to the manager about it when I was here the first time. I'd do it again, but this time I wouldn't make the mistake of mentioning it to Kendra.

The number on her door was hanging loose, so I reached for my Swiss Army knife that hangs from a thin metal wire on the inside of my belt. It was the only gift my father ever gave me. He'd thought it clever that it wasn't kept in the pocket but hidden under the belt. As far as I knew this was the full extent of my heritage from my father. I wondered what my daughters would say I'd passed on to them.

I straightened the number, then tightened the screw. I breathed deeply and knocked. I heard her on the other side, looking through the fish-eye lens.

"What were you doing?" she asked, before the door completely opened. She stepped out and looked at the door. "I should've known. Like I'm not capable of fixing a crooked number."

"I know you're capable. I just—"

"I didn't open the door before looking through the peephole."

"Good. Did you have the Mace in your hand just in case?"

"No. But when I saw it was you, I wished I did."

I laughed. It would have been one of those perfect father-daughter moments…if she'd laughed too.

Not that it was a full-fledged scowl. It was more a look of moderate disapproval. But I learned many years ago that the mildest disapproval from a daughter is a twisted knife in her father's heart. In my visits to Kendra over the years, I'd walked away with bloodstained shirts. Andrea was a long-term hemorrhage. Kendra was a recurrent stabbing.

In all fairness, I've fired off my share of rounds at her too. I always found myself looking back and rewording things. But it was too late. It's always too late.

She'd invited me to dinner, yet I was sure an hour later she'd regret it. I looked at her knowing that whatever I said or didn't say would be wrong. Just then I remembered I had something in my hand. I held them out to her.

"What are those?"

"Gerbera daisies," I said.

She didn't take them. I set them on a magazine on the coffee table. Apparently this wasn't right, since she quickly scooped them up, rescuing the magazine.

"Kendra, is there any chance we could…you know…have a good relationship?"

"It's a little late for that."

"Could you just…give it a try?"

"Am I supposed to feel guilty? Like it was my fault?"

"I didn't mean that. It was my fault, not yours. Really. But I was hoping maybe the judgment would expire."

"*I'm* being judgmental?"

"No. A judgment's a legal decision against somebody. It expires after ten years. I just meant—"

"You think I don't know what a judgment is? You've always thought I'm stupid."

I'd never thought that. But I was beginning to wonder.

"Remember Stephen, the guy I was in love with?"

"Short guy with the goatee?"

"That was Sedgwick. He loved me too. Stephen was the guy you harassed."

"Remind me."

"We see you at a restaurant, and I make the mistake of going to the restroom. You tell him if he ever hurts me, you'll kill him and make it look like an accident."

"Okay, the guy with all the piercings. I said it good-naturedly."

"Right, which is why you gave him three examples of how you might kill him."

"It was two examples. I'd just started the third when you got back. I never even finished."

"It's funny to you, but he was terrified. And it's my life you messed up."

"You think Stephen was the right guy for you? Because if you do, I'll get a metal detector and go find him tomorrow and apologize. I mean it."

"You'd do that?"

"In a heartbeat. Just say the word."

"No. He wasn't the right guy for me."

"Is he the…" I paused as if I'd stepped on a land mine, and any attempt to lift the foot would blow off a leg.

"Father of my child? No." Long pause. "You wouldn't like him."

"Do you?"

"I thought I did, but he's gone. Didn't want the responsibility. Anybody who'd leave me because I'm having his baby would leave me for a dozen other reasons."

"Or a hundred. I meant what I said, sweetheart. I'll help you financially. Or any other way."

"Abortion? That was the father's solution."

"I'd never want you to hurt yourself like that."

"Thank you."

"I'll do anything, and on your terms. I love you. I want to help you."

She stared at me, as if trying to figure out a Rubik's Cube.

"The side of your face is bruised," she said. "What happened?"

I told her the story. As I did, her face softened. She got me a cold pack and medications, natural ones, the kind that didn't require the killing of ducks or armadillos. She asked me to put on some orange ointment made out of kumquats or something. It smelled funny but felt good. Mulch could lick it off when I got home.

Over dinner we talked civilly. I asked her about her work as a real estate agent. We stayed away from the hundred subjects that would divide us and talked about the dozen we had in common. Especially Sharon. This was the first time since her mother died that Kendra and I had gone thirty minutes without fighting.

It was the best meal of vegetables, fruits, nuts, and carrot juice I've ever had. To be there with my little girl, no darts flying for the last two hours, was…a taste of heaven.

As I left, she thanked me for the flowers. I wouldn't have traded that moment for all the cheeseburgers and orange malts in the world.

"Data! Data! Data! I can make no bricks without clay!"
SHERLOCK HOLMES, *THE ADVENTURE OF THE COPPER BEECHES*

FRIDAY, DECEMBER 6, 10:30 A.M.

MY REGRET IN NOT REPORTING to work the day before was that I hadn't seen the other homicide detectives and couldn't study their faces. Whoever had attacked me Wednesday night would likely have a bruise, where I struck him with the flashlight. But only four others were in Friday, and by then a bruise could have been covered. Cimmatoni was gimpy, probably his rheumatism. No bruises were obvious. Everyone kept their distance but Tommi. And she hadn't been my assailant. He'd been too strong. It must have been a man.

I left headquarters to meet Carp in her home office in Northwest Portland, near Wallace Park, twelve minutes from downtown. Her furniture was modern. No clutter, yet the house seemed comfortable and fit her. I admired her wall hangings—award-winning photos she'd taken of bridges, buildings, forests, mountains, lakes, animals, and people. I've done enough crime scene photography to appreciate good stuff. I vaguely sensed that something was missing. Then it came to me—no photos of dead bodies.

She took me into her photo lab and sat me down next to her in front of a twenty-one-inch monitor displaying a wallpaper of multicolored flowers in a meadow with breathtaking clarity.

"That's beautiful," I said.

"Thanks." I was slow to figure out she'd taken the picture.

"I've superenlarged the mantel and the photos on it in five of the pictures taken in the last year before the murder." Then she took my own photos of Palatine's mantel, and my close-ups of each picture. "Each of these pictures shows nine photos, but there were eight after the murder. The ninth is missing. Just like you figured."

I nodded.

She called up another image on the monitor. "Here's my best resolution of that missing photo, using a computer enhanced sharpening feature. It shows the professor and two females, a blonde and a brunette. Based on his height you can judge theirs. Obviously their faces are blurred. Even eye color's questionable with this degree of enlargement and enhancement. Sorry."

"Considering they were just tiny spots in the background on the originals, I'm amazed you got this much." I pointed to something shiny. "Jewelry?"

"Earrings on this girl and part of a chain necklace on this one. If not for reflection from the original flash, we wouldn't see them. You're positive you don't have anything taken with a digital camera?"

"These were from Palatine's camera, a Canon SLR," I said.

"Good camera, but it's all film, not digital. For magnification this extreme, I need a digital file."

She pushed her chair back from the computer. "So who swiped the photo from the mantel?"

"My money's on the murderer. The question is why."

"Because of the identity of the girls in the picture, right?"

"One of them anyway."

"You think the professor had a compromising relationship?"

"He seemed to have a pattern of compromising relationships. But the killer must have thought the girls would point a finger at him."

"Or maybe the girls' jewelry?" Carp said.

"I never thought of that."

She smiled. "Find me another picture, taken with a digital camera, even if it's just the mantel in the background again. Maybe I'll get you faces you can recognize."

"Thanks."

"Don't mention it. I'm one of those helpful journalists."

"Lunchtime," I said. "Thinking what I'm thinking?"

She raised her eyebrows. "Double cheese, double pepperoni? I know just the place. I'll drive."

She took my arm, pulling me to her front door. Once you know their love language, everything falls into place.

Two hours later I took Abernathy with me to meet Jenn Lennox, who insisted we meet at a Starbucks in Gresham, on Division, next to Red Robin.

"Interviewing the chief's daughter is strictly under the lid," I said.

"Won't she tell her father?"

"Let's hope they don't have that kind of relationship."

"What kind?"

"The talking kind."

"Why are we at Starbucks?"

"She didn't think a donut shop was cool. I had to guarantee she could have a venti Frappaccino. Told her the sky was the limit."

We sat in the most private corner, not wanting to bump elbows with the Wi-Fiers or buoyant caffeine-happy greeters or be seen by passersby. Truth is, I used to spend lots of time at Starbucks. I was named employee of the month twice without ever working there. But one-third the price plus unlimited refills at Lou's lured me away.

The girl appeared, dressed like she'd raided the giveaway table at Salvation Army. If she didn't live up to *my* apparel standards, you can imagine what a sight she was.

She had a face that could have set off a thousand metal detectors. Rings everywhere—lips, cheek, eyebrows, half a dozen on the ears. She was a walking jewelry store. It was the same unhappy face from the family portrait, but it weighed a few pounds more, both in flesh and metal. Her hair was purple and orange.

"Jenn Lennox?"

"Mr. Detective?" she asked through her chewing gum. Her voice was baby talk, and her eyelashes batted like a butterfly. I don't know if her flirtatiousness was conscious. Maybe it was her way of fishing for Frappaccinos.

I ordered the drinks from a friendly young guy named Matt, plus the double chocolate brownie she informed me she couldn't live without. She marched over to a stack of coffee mugs near a CD rack displaying a young male musician. She took out her cell phone and held it up to take a picture. She squealed, thrilled she'd gotten this photo. While we waited, she popped her gum, then picked it off her lip rings. Her hair was making its way to her left eye. She pulled it back, but it kept obeying the law of gravity. She kept pulling down her skirt. It obeyed a different law.

She was a little girl trying to look grown-up. It wasn't working. No coffee or chocolate yet, and she was already so jittery she could jump-start a car. She kept chewing her fingernails, but there was nothing left. I was afraid she was going to start on mine.

After sitting with her five minutes, we learned that she knew everything and hated everyone. Kids have always been know-it-alls. I was, I guess. But I don't recall the cynicism going so deep. The chief's daughter reminded me of my Andrea at that age.

"How did you know Professor Palatine?"

"That's what this is about? You said you wanted information." Her voice was no longer baby talk, but nasal and whiny. Made me miss the baby talk.

"You said you wanted a Frappaccino. You got what you came for, and a brownie too. How about the information? If it's good, I'll give you a Frap to go. Tell me about the professor."

She leaned forward. "I'm a senior, and they said we could take a course at Portland State. Figured I'd do it to meet guys. Philosophy was one option. It sounded cool."

"Why were you at the professor's house?"

"He invited new students over."

"Do you remember who took this picture?" I handed it to her.

"Gross," she said. "I don't know who took it."

"Who else was there?"

"The four of us in the picture and the professor."

"Plus whoever took the picture."

"The professor mainly talked with the other two girls. Cheerleader types."

She said it with a secretive voice—the type that makes you want to ask questions to find out what she's hiding. So I asked for a while before I figured out she had nothing to hide. Any secrets were an inch below the surface, eager to get out...and absolutely useless.

"I have to pee," she said. In a moment she was gone.

I saw the look on Clarence's face. He appeared unsympathetic both to her and her bladder. I had the feeling she'd used a word his children don't.

She returned, talkative, caffeine sinking in, along with the promise of imminent sugar from the Starbucks chocolate-hazelnut biscotti and the package of chocolate-covered coffee beans she'd wrangled from me in exchange for renewed interest in our conversation. I looked at the drinks and minidesserts and considered that I'd already paid for three full lunches at Burgerville. *This better be worth it.*

High on the list of things cops don't like are: wandering, and inability to answer a question without interjecting irrelevant self-disclosure. (Relevant self-disclosure: I killed the guy; I saw the guy who killed the guy. Irrelevant self-disclosure: I was finishing up my skinny vanilla latte when I saw this dress at the Gap, and I thought Brandy would be so jealous if she saw me in it, and I...")

"How'd you like the philosophy class?"

"I hated it."

"What'd you think of the professor?"'

"I hated him."

"The boy with you in the picture?"

"I hated him."

"What'd you think of the cheerleader girls?"

"I despised them."

Good. There *was* a thesaurus in her brain.

She looked at Clarence, then me, then said, "Boring."

Two boys walked in the door, and in an instant she was up greeting them. She took out her cell phone and took pictures of them. Then she posed with one of the boys and coerced the other into taking a picture of the two of them, Starbucks counter behind them. She said her friend Tasha "just won't *believe* I saw you here." She punched buttons on her phone and sent the photo to Tasha apparently and said she'd have to download it when she got home and post it on MySpace.

I took note that caffeine helps people say and do stupid things with more energy and enthusiasm. I beckoned her over and asked if we could wrap it up.

"Do you think I'm silly, Detective?" It was one of the first nonsilly things she'd said.

"The thought occurred to me," I said. "But if you have evidence to the contrary, now would be a good time to present it."

"My parents think I'm no good."

"Are they right?"

"What?"

"*Are* you no good?"

She thought about it. "My father thinks he knows everything. He's always telling me what to do. And he's never happy with my choices."

It struck me—that's how I felt about God. A killjoy who never liked what I did, so why try? And if He didn't like me, okay, I didn't like Him either.

"It's not easy being a dad," I said.

"Sometimes he's just mean."

"My guess is—" I couldn't resist—"his bark is worse than his bite."

"You sound like him."

"Listen, if you remember something about the professor, or about someone who hated him, I mean way more than you did, call me, would you?"

I handed her my card.

"Will my dad find out?"

"Not if you call this number. Your dad doesn't answer the phone in detective division."

An hour later, weather cooperating, I decided not to take on city traffic and instead walk the half mile to Portland State University. I passed Seattle's Best, a caffeine oasis located in the middle of a three-hundred-foot desert between two Starbucks. Had I not just been at a Starbucks with Jenn Lennox, I would have stopped. Suddenly, realizing I could justify it on the basis that I needed to warm my hands, I turned around and ordered a large coffee.

I walked to Broadway, then headed south to the Park Blocks and Portland State

University. The artsy attractions along the way made it more interesting than two laps around a track. I've never actually entered the Portland Art Museum, but I feel cultured walking by it. Besides, there's a Polish sausage vendor on that sidewalk who's made meat into an art form.

At the University Station Post Office, I asked a vacant-looking underclassman where I'd find the academic dean. He scrunched his face, mumbled about a provost, then pointed, as far as I could tell, to the second building, Cramer Hall. The directory led me to the third floor.

A secretary assured me they didn't call them deans, but provosts. The academic provost was Dr. Hedstrom. He'd been a highly reputed sociology professor before that, she explained. I nodded, like I cared. She told me to wait in an undersized chair while she fetched him. I paced. The hallowed halls of academia are not my home.

Two minutes later, the secretary returned to the reception area, followed by a provost-looking individual. He was a thick-throated, chinless man who could have shaved from cheek to Adam's apple without angling the blade. There's a lot of gravity in this world, and Hedstrom was carrying more than his share. I'm no lightweight, but if I'm a moon, he's Jupiter. Shoulders stooped, head tipped forward like it needed something to prop it, he made eye contact with the floor tiles. He beckoned with his fingers. I followed, shifting to my lowest gear not to rearend him.

We entered his office, which smelled of polished wood. His redwood bookcases were masterpieces. A picture on the wall showed him standing straight and slim forty years ago with a college basketball team. He'd probably shrunk three inches since then. It's a tough world that makes a man shrink. One day, like all of us I thought, he's going to just disappear. And then what? What's on the other side? Nothing? Something? What?

Hey, he'd been a highly reputed professor. Maybe I should ask him.

Nah.

"I am Dr. Elwin Hedstrom," he said, as if I should be impressed.

"Nice to meet you," I said, lying.

He laced his fingers at the Greenwich median of his equator and plunged into what I'd told him I wanted to discuss.

"I had my issues with Dr. Palatine."

"Did you?"

"He assumed that humans are social beings by their nature and subscribed to the position of Francisco de Vitoria that statally organized peoples were in need of a legal order to govern their mutual relations."

It's hard to know what to say to such a statement.

"A rather Thomistic assumption, don't you think?" Hedstrom said. "He was too eclectic and in many respects Hegelian."

"I know that name. Pro bowler or NASCAR driver?"

He produced an unfriendly chuckle. "How quickly we make light of what we don't understand."

"That was a Wolfian assumption," I said.

"Thomas Wolf?"

"Nero Wolfe."

The professor grinned, but the grin started at his teeth. My inner child, wishing to correct this, considered whether to raise his lower teeth or drop his lower lip. I chose to resist the instinct to give him, as the old philosophers might have put it, a knuckle sandwich.

The verbal sparring continued: He tested me by using bigger words and more abstract concepts, citing names of sociologists and philosophers. I tested him by dropping the names Sam Spade, Philip Marlowe, Lew Archer, and Jack Bauer. Before long we each knew the other was a moron.

"Anything unusual you can tell me about Professor Palatine?"

"Unusual?"

"I didn't make the word up. It means different or remarkable."

His head shook slowly, as if someone else were doing it for him. It was then that I noticed a little wooden mount on his desk, which contained a small ink bottle and a dark blue fountain pen.

"As the academic dean, sorry provost, you've probably heard your share of gripes about teachers, right? I'm looking for people who disliked Dr. Palatine. Any complaints lodged against him?"

I learned years ago never to take my eyes off someone's face when I ask a question or when they're answering. At the sound of one particular word, maybe a name or place, there's a facial twitch, smile, frown, smirk, a flash of anger in the eyes, a look of fear or discomfort. That look may disappear in a heartbeat. Miss it, you miss everything. I'd just seen something in Hedstrom.

It took him time to find his tongue. Soon after he did, I wished he hadn't. He jabbered ten minutes without saying anything. He spoke Sominex, wrapping it up with: "One would, indeed, have to have had a long history in academics to appreciate the high standards we have rigorously met over the decades. We are absolutely aware, if I may put it that way, of our responsibility to maintain the highest standards of academic achievement and with that to provide an example of personal and contextual fidelity to certain established ethical norms, as recognized by and indeed fostered by the larger university. We must operate consistently within our own consensus of mutually acceptable norms. Inevitably certain concerns are raised, but we cannot assume these to be authentic. We have a responsibility to our faculty, our students, and, yes, to our constituency. We make no pretense of perfection, but we maintain the highest standards of humanistic ideals, as it were. Do you follow my meaning?"

"Indeed," I said. "Actually, I may possibly, to put it that way, have missed your meaning, so to speak. If there was one, as it were."

He stared impassively, but I saw fire in his eyes, and I was glad to have lit it.

"This university," Hedstrom continued, "must operate by our own consistent standards which may be beyond your grasp. I am not certain you comprehend either the intricacies or, shall we say, the delicacies incumbent upon one entrusted with the position that the stewards of this academic community have seen fit to bestow upon myself."

"That sounds like a Plutonian approach."

"Do you mean Platonic?"

"No. Plato was a philosopher. Pluto was a dog in the Disney cartoons. Smaller than Mickey Mouse, but he's a dog…go figure. You may be more familiar with Goofy, who reminds me of some of your statements."

He looked at me through half-closed eyes, trying to appear above it all. He wasn't. The fire in his eyes was raging now. All the better, as I hoped it would cause him to say whatever he was holding back.

"Where were you the night of November 20, between the hours of 10:00 p.m. and midnight?"

"See here. I have been academic provost of this university for fifteen years, am a graduate of Dartmouth, and have been honored by the American Society of College Professors."

"You must be proud of yourself. Where were you the night of November 20?"

"I wouldn't know. That was last month."

"Sixteen days ago. Care to guess?"

His head shook again, the same way, as if pulled by strings.

"In the Ivy League you had to use the little gray cells occasionally, didn't you? Summon up that genius that got you through Dartmouth. Check a calendar; then tell me what you were doing two weeks ago Wednesday night."

For the next fifteen minutes I tried to shake him empty, like a bag of peanuts. But he was a lot to shake, and I had little to show for it. He wasn't telling me what I needed to hear. Feeling I'd lost a battle, I decided to leave him with something to ponder.

"Our discussion raises a question, something you can ask your students. If Goofy and Pluto are both dogs, and the world of Disney should operate by its own consistent standards, then how come Goofy stands on two legs and Pluto on all four? And why is Pluto's nose on the ground, while yours is up your—" I pointed to his doctoral certificate in its golden frame. "A doctoral thesis has probably already been written on the Pluto/Goofy conundrum, but if not, you should tackle it."

"What did you say your name was, Detective?" Hedstrom picked up his fountain pen, dipped it, then rested its point on fancy stationery.

"Cimmatoni, two *m*'s. Bryce Cimmatoni."

He wrote it down.

It was getting dark, so I boarded a TriMet bus to get me back to the parking garage. As I drove home, I kept rolling Hedstrom over my investigative tongue. I didn't like the aftertaste.

I considered changing my policy and conducting interviews unarmed. One of these times I was going to lose it. Pistol-whipping a professor does not look good on one's résumé when you're trying to get your next job as security cop at Toys "R" Us.

Maybe you wonder if I regret not having punched the academic provost in his piehole. The truth is, I *do* regret it. I wish now I would have.

Because if I had, he might not have stayed late at his office. And if he'd gone home early and his wife had nursed his aching jaw, fixed him chicken soup, and fed him Rocky Road ice cream, maybe he wouldn't have taken Polo, his Yorkshire terrier, out for a 9:30 p.m. walk in Montavilla Park.

And if he hadn't done that, maybe at 9:46 p.m. he wouldn't have been shot to death.

23

"She is the daintiest thing under a bonnet on this planet."
SHERLOCK HOLMES, *A SCANDAL IN BOHEMIA*

"WHY WOULD SOMEONE KILL Dr. Hedstrom?" Clarence asked.

"His wallet was stolen. Looks like a mugging."

"You believe that?"

"Not for a second," I said. "The killer thought Hedstrom knew something. You attended university. What would an academic dean know about professors?"

"He'd know the complaints filed against them."

"I need to see those complaints."

Hedstrom's murder investigation fell to Chris Doyle and Kim Suda. Obviously, they'd be consulting me since I was one of the last to see him alive. I left them a message that I'd be spending most of my Saturday at the precinct. They dropped in around 11:00 a.m. Doyle's lazy eyelids reminded me of a frog.

"Okay, that's it," he said, after five minutes.

"That's what? You asked me three questions."

"Lots of people to talk with."

"You'll be getting back to me?"

"We know where you work."

"I'll give you my notes from the Hedstrom interview."

"If we want them, we'll ask." Doyle smirked at Suda. They seemed to be enjoying an inside joke.

"I need to search Hedstrom's files to see what he had on Palatine."

"Don't think you can do that," Doyle said, setting his meaty chin.

"Why not?"

"His records are part of our case. You handle yours, we'll handle ours."

"The cases are related."

"You don't know that. You're the one who's been saying the killer's a detective. People are wondering if it's you."

"Who's wondering that?"

"It's our case. We don't want any tampering."

"And nothing picked up and removed from the crime scene," Suda said. "Like gum wrappers, for instance." She eyeballed me.

Pretending to ignore her comment and wondering who'd talked to her, I said, "Find out what complaints are on file against William Palatine. It's vital to my case."

"You're on a fishing expedition," Doyle said. "Outrageous speculations are your style."

"Is it just me, Chris, or did you have a second bowl of stupid for breakfast?" He glared.

"Really, what's your theory?" I asked. "Why'd Hedstrom get killed?"

"Robbery that went south. Doubt they meant to kill him."

"A shot to the head wasn't meant to kill? Somebody could've watched and studied, then laid in wait. Is taking his dog out for a late walk a habit? After a nine o'clock program's over?"

"Oh, is that how detectives do it? We talked with Hedstrom's secretary. She said you picked a fight with him. The guy who picks a fight shortly before someone's murdered is a suspect."

"Hedstrom was arrogant and irritating, but I can handle that. I haven't killed you yet, have I?"

"One other question, Chandler," Doyle said. "Where were you between 9:30 and 10:00 last night?"

"You're wearin' cheese underwear, Doyle."

"What's that supposed to mean, goofball?"

I turned my back on him. I needed to create distance between my fists and his face.

I came home early and found the television on. I pulled my gun, but I wasn't that concerned since when I leave the remote on the couch Mulch sometimes sits on the power button. Sure enough, he was watching the Fighting Irish at Nebraska.

Mulch had raided the garbage can under the kitchen sink. I'd forgotten to stretch the little bungee cord across the knobs. I gave him a stern look and threatened to reduce his bacon ration, but when I saw his face pucker up, I took it back.

I hadn't fixed Mulch a home-cooked meal for a while, so I took out the George Foreman grill and treated us to Hillshire Farm sausages. I had Koch's horseradish and Sweet Baby Ray's barbecue sauce and a pan of Brussels sprouts for Mulch. He loves those puppies when the butter's meltin' all over them. It's one of the few health foods Sharon introduced us to that stuck.

The kitchen phone rang. While I was looking at the phone waiting for the message, Mulch, seeing I was distracted, went for the plate. Sausages fell to the ground. I quickly crouched to put my body between Mulch and the sausages. Just then the room exploded.

Glass flew everywhere, and I didn't know what hit my left shoulder, buckshot or window pieces. It sounded like a shotgun at close range. I wasn't aware of feeling anything until I looked at my gray Mariners sweatshirt, with three holes in it, inches apart. My right hand reached above me to the King Cobra revolver, duct-taped beneath the kitchen table. I yanked it off, slowly opened the back door, and peeked out. Mulch rushed out, growled ferociously, and raced the intruder to the swinging gate. I heard him yelp when it slammed into his face.

Our neighbor, Mr. Obrist, looked over his fence.

"What's going on now? A bomb?"

"Uh, no, it was just an…incident. Somebody paid me a visit."

"Who?"

"My wife's sister, maybe? Not much damage. Some glass to sweep up."

"You're bleeding."

"No big deal…I just…" I looked at my sweatshirt. I could swear it had been gray. I didn't remember having a red sweatshirt. It's the last thing I recall, except my gun slipping from my fingers.

This time no wrangling with the EMTs about whether to go to the hospital. Unconscious men who've lost a quart of blood aren't in a position to wrangle.

Next thing I knew I was hearing electronic noises and looking up at Jake and Clarence. Jake handed me a cup of ice.

"You guys keep showing up when I have an incident."

"Incident?" Clarence said. "You were nearly killed."

"Mulch okay?"

"He wasn't hit," Jake said, "but he's concerned about you. Janet's with him."

"Mulch saved my life."

"How's that?"

"My left shoulder was where my chest had been a quarter of a second earlier. If Mulch hadn't gone for the sausage right then, I wouldn't have ducked."

"Sounds like the providence of God," Clarence said.

"I'm thinking it was Mulch liking sausage."

"They're not mutually exclusive," Jake said. "You think God couldn't use the instincts He put in Mulch to save you?"

"That phone call? I wonder if I wasn't supposed to stand and answer it to give the shooter a clearer look."

"This is getting way too dangerous," Clarence said.

I nodded. "Good thing I've usually got a bodyguard the size of a buffalo to take a bullet for me."

SUNDAY, DECEMBER 8

I escaped the hospital the next day, leaving the other inmates behind. After being face-licked by my bullie, I entered the old brownstone and found my big Glock still on the coffee table in the living room, where I'd left him before heading to the kitchen and almost getting my head blown off while eating sausage. I held Daddy Glock close because it'd been years since we'd spent a night apart. He seemed okay.

Thanks to Jake, my kitchen now featured a four-by-five-foot piece of plywood where a window had been. I walked the house, checking my other guns. At the back of the closet was my original pellet gun, the one I shot out streetlights with forty-five years ago. Mom had threatened to confiscate it, even though I warned her that if she wanted to take my gun, she'd have to pry it from my cold dead fingers. She said she was glad to oblige and cracked me over the head with a broom handle, then hid my gun for thirty days. That was the last time I messed with Mom.

I like my guns spread around the house, like drink coasters. But I'd rather have to put all of them away someplace safe because grandchildren are visiting. Would Kendra let her kid come over? Did I dare hope? She'd visited me in the hospital, and though she'd scolded me for not being more careful, it was a Sharon sort of scolding.

Mr. Obrist had retrieved the King Cobra from the deck after I fell. I duct taped it back under the kitchen table, a three-foot portion of which was battle-scarred by buckshot. I considered replacing it, but now it was wartime memorabilia. Better than anything I could buy on eBay. Maybe someday my grandchild could point to it and say, "Tell me that story, Gramps!"

You can't blame a guy for hoping.

The table would also remind me that life is short…and I'd once more teetered on its edge.

I thought about all those close calls, the times in Vietnam and on the streets as a patrol cop and a couple of car accidents and the situations I'd faced hunting down killers. The more I thought about it, the more I came to a realization.

I was one lucky guy.

"How blind we were to Your presence there," Finney said to the Carpenter, shaking his head. "Looking back, with my memory so clear now, I've begun to see how You were with us, guiding, protecting, providing, hundreds of times each day."

"Ten thousand times a day," Obadiah Abernathy said. "We couldna got single breath widout You, my sweet Lord. Every heartbeat was a gift. Yet we was fools enough to wonder if You cared. We was so impatient. And ungrateful."

"But you know better now, My friends," the Carpenter said, smiling. "And even there, you'd begun to realize and to say thanks. For that I commend you both. Well done."

"It was so cloudy then," Finney said. "Now it's so clear."

"It will become clearer still," the Carpenter said, stretching out His right arm. "You have much more to learn. When you look back at your lives on earth, you'll see much I was doing that you never guessed. What you called luck was My providence. I was there even in what you considered disaster. In the new world you'll experience new joys daily. But you'll also discover, as I peel back the layers, what I did for you in the old world. This is what My Father promised you: that in the coming ages He might show you the incomparable riches of His grace, expressed in His kindness to you…the kindness He demonstrated in Me."

SUNDAY EVENING, DECEMBER 8

That night my tender shoulder, which was in far better shape than it could have been, was talking to me. Other aches and pains joined in. I sat back in the recliner and sipped a cream soda while Mulch chewed a soup bone.

When you make a living related to dying, it puts a curious spin on your life. I suppose morticians feel it and medical examiners and oncologists. I know homicide detectives do. On the one hand you feel sorry for the victim and his family. On the other hand, you're excited, because there's a problem to be solved. Mathematicians and scientists and accountants enjoy solving problems. I doubt they feel any guilt about it.

You'd think anyone who deals constantly with death would be forced to come to grips with his own mortality. But it's possible to see your death as inevitable, as I do, yet never as imminent. Sure, I'll die, but not this minute or hour or day or week or month or year. Always death seems decades away, years at least.

But when you take metal and glass in your flesh and realize how close it came to your head, it makes you stop and think. And yet, I found myself denying it even then. I've cheated death before, and I'll do it again. Will I tell myself that until the moment I die?

I looked at my left hand and imagined it was the hand of a corpse, then a skeleton. The destruction of the flesh, accelerated in the *Indiana Jones* movies, seems fiction. Yet what is more certain than death?

When Sharon was dying, I wished her doctors were as good at finding out reasons for death as I am. I wished the problem could be solved with one more night's work. And I wished that her Christian friends would just shut up. When I heard several of them say, "I know God's going to heal her," I almost believed it. When He didn't, I wanted to hunt them down and smack 'em.

I'm not sure how I went from pondering my mortality to being ticked off at Christians, but it happened. See, in my thinking, Christians tend to be either idiots or hypocrites. I'm not fond of either. I'm not saying there aren't good Christians— Jake and Clarence are, and Obadiah Abernathy certainly was. What I'm saying is that, to me, looking for honest Christians is like searching to find clams in a bowl of cheap chowder.

These people who think they can beat the devil with a big toothy smile ought to work homicide or vice or sex crimes for a week. Reality will put a sag on the corners of your mouth.

I hear this stuff about Jesus taking away people's sickness and financial woes. Yet Christians are poor and get sick and die like everybody else, don't they? I mean, do you know any two-hundred-year-old Christians? Sharon prayed to be healed. Her Christian friends prayed for her healing. Didn't happen.

All that health-and-wealth mumbo jumbo on the Big-Hair Channel? It's just pretense, isn't it? And all those "Jesus wants you well" televangelists that collect offerings from people trying to buy their way out of suffering and death—don't those preachers just quietly grow old and die of cancer and strokes like everybody else?

I can't stand these holier-than-thous, with their swaggering self-righteousness, their spiritual one-upmanship.

Buddy Darson was my partner for two years when I wore a uniform. Buddy's a deacon or a trustee or a grand pooh-bah in some church. But he lied on his reports, cheated the clock, stole supplies from the department, and looked down the barmaids' blouses.

Some of the most racist cops I've ever known say they're Christians. If that's what it means to be a Christian, I'm better off a pagan. At least I'm not a hypocrite. That counts for something.

I hope.

I don't live in the sweet by-and-by. I live in the nasty here and now. And if I can take down perps and save kids' lives and keep women from being raped, it may not make me Saint Francis of Assisi, but hey, it's better than turning my cheek while scumbags rule the city.

These are thoughts that go through my mind when it dawns on me that at any moment someone in the shadows could put a bullet through my head.

MONDAY, DECEMBER 9

Jake told me it doesn't make sense to be at work two days after you're shot through your back window, but I wanted to make a statement to someone who likely would see me at work: "You missed me, bozo." Well, not missed, but the damage wasn't that serious. I practiced not wincing in front of the mirror, but sometimes, after a quick movement, I felt the tears in my eyes. Since my doctor wasn't watching, I doubled my pain meds.

When Manny came to my desk and asked me if I was okay, I assured him it was nothing. I no longer point to my extra chair because neither of us wants him there. Apparently I convinced him not to feel sorry for me, since within five minutes he was waving a handful of papers in my face.

"I got to the professor's house late, remember?" Manny said. "So this morning I asked for their report."

"Whose report?"

"Patrol's. Dorsey and Guerino. Obviously you didn't read it."

"Why should I? They filled me in when I got there."

"They tell you they left the scene?"

"They what?"

"It's right there." He tossed the report on my desk. "A guy across the street grabs another guy, takes something and runs. So they run after him."

"Dorsey and Guerino? Both of them?"

I looked over the report. I felt the heat rising off my forehead.

I called patrol. "Sergeant Parfitt? Did you know Dorsey and Guerino abandoned the Palatine crime scene?"

"I knew. There was good reason. Didn't you read the report?"

"Just did. But there's no such thing as a good reason. I need to meet with those guys pronto. The scene may have been compromised."

"Day off for both. You really need me to call them in?"

"Absolutely."

Time passes slowly when I'm mad. An hour later Dorsey and Guerino, in plainclothes, walked in. I know the look of two guys trying to get their stories straight.

"What's he doing here?" Guerino asked, pointing at Clarence.

"He's my bodyguard. And he's been assigned to this case."

"I'm not talking in front of him."

"Chief says he stays. This meeting's off the record, right Clarence?"

He nodded.

I held up their report. "You left the crime scene."

"We were only gone three minutes," Dorsey said. "Five at most."

"Your job was to protect the scene."

"The professor was dead," Dorsey said. "Somebody pulled a knife on a living person."

"One of you should have stayed."

"Pursue a criminal without backup? The same manual that says we stay at the crime scene also says we can't ignore a crime against a person. And we shouldn't pursue without backup if a partner's available."

"He wasn't available. He was confined to the scene." I sighed. "Tell me exactly what happened."

"The guy with the knife yelled at the other guy to give him his wallet," Dorsey said.

I turned to Guerino. "Describe the men," I said, holding up my hand to silence Dorsey.

"I can't."

"Why not?"

"They were wearing ski masks."

"You mean the assailant was wearing a ski mask?"

"Both were."

Words escaped me.

"Look, one of them pulled a knife on the other one," Dorsey said, through my hand.

"You're saying the victim was wearing a ski mask?"

"It was cold," Guerino said.

"Yeah, all kinds of innocent citizens wear ski masks in Portland."

"We didn't dress him," Dorsey said.

"Victims don't wear ski masks. People who don't want to be identified wear ski masks. Criminals wear ski masks. Who else wears a ski mask?"

"Skiers?" Guerino said.

"Was there snow on the ground?" I asked. "Did they have skis and poles and goggles and an SUV and mugs of hot chocolate? Was there a Saint Bernard?"

"You're a jerk," Dorsey said.

"Why didn't you tell me you'd left the scene?"

"We knew you'd be mad, and—" Guerino stopped when he saw Dorsey's eyes.

"You and Abernathy here were having a tizzy fit," Dorsey said. "You never asked us for a report, and we had no chance to tell you. You wanted us to stay out of your precious crime scene. We put it all in our report. Not our fault if you didn't read it. Speaking of which, if we hadn't gone after a guy running around threatening people with a knife, you realize the liability?"

"But two guys in ski masks?"

"Okay, looking back at it…but at the time we saw a knife pulled and somebody accosted. We can't ignore that. Maybe it looks different from behind a desk, but that's how it works on the streets."

"Don't tell me how it works on the streets. I wore a uniform for ten years."

"Bet you couldn't fit into it now," Guerino said.

"Bet your brain could fit in a walnut shell." I started pacing. "Once you chased them, did you keep them in sight?"

"The guy on the ground said, 'I'm okay—get him.'"

"So you took orders from a man wearing a ski mask?"

"Stop with the ski mask, would you? We chased the guy. He went over a fence, into a backyard. Guerino went over after him, and I ran on the sidewalk hoping to head him off."

"And?"

"He disappeared."

"Like you disappeared from the crime scene?"

Dorsey stood, leaning forward on the table. "Look, as soon as we lost the guy, we ran back to the scene."

"Let me guess. The victim was gone."

"Yeah."

"No way anybody bothered the scene," Guerino said. "It was just a few minutes."

"You think they would have left you a note saying they'd been there? You know what can be taken from or left at a crime scene in three to five minutes? They say intelligence skips a generation. The good news is, your kids will be brilliant."

"Word is," Dorsey said, "you're blaming detectives for the murder. So—now you can blame patrol for something else. That seems to be your way. Blame cops. Me, I blame criminals."

"My way is to do my job. I expect you to do yours."

Guerino started to talk. Dorsey tugged him out the door.

"You were hard on them," Clarence said.

I'd forgotten he was in the room. "Now you're defending cops? Make up your mind."

"They were trying to protect someone."

"Someone wearing a ski mask." I felt my fist hit the table. "Compromised crime scenes drive me crazy. Gawkers come through, neighbors, passersby. Footprints and fingerprints and dirt falling off pant legs and fibers from uniforms…you know what that does?"

"It irritates you."

"You still don't get it. Why would two men in a fight, right in front of police officers, both be wearing ski masks? Nobody pulls a knife when cops are standing across the street. The ski mask guys were putting on an act."

He pondered it a moment before the light turned on. "To distract the cops and pull them from the crime scene?"

"Exactly. And then what happened?"

"The cops chased one guy."

"And what did the so-called victim do?"

Clarence whistled softly. "Walk across the street and enter Palatine's house?" He opened his notebook computer and started typing.

"So," I said, "do we have *two* killers or one? Was the second guy his accomplice for the murder, too? Had the killer left something at the crime scene? Or did he go back to plant something? Either way the scene was contaminated. He had to evacuate when patrol arrived, but he got back in long enough to do what he wanted. Whatever that was."

I threw down my pen and stretched back in the chair, moaning when a sharp pain went through my shoulder. While Clarence eyed me, I checked the bandage. The blood stain wasn't too bad, and I didn't feel like changing it again.

"I need more manpower. Too much to check out."

"You could set another fire in an apartment," Clarence said.

"Don't think it hasn't occurred to me."

"What would you think about using Ray Eagle?"

"Ray's great," I said. "Best private detective I've worked with. But the department's not going to pay him."

"He'll do it for free."

"Why would he do that?"

"I called this morning. He said business has been light. I told him if he volunteered, his name would make it into my articles, several times. It's an opportunity to make a name for himself."

"Free advertising?"

"Not exactly free. Like you said, he won't get paid for his work. But it'll buy him advertising."

I found Ray's number in my Rolodex.

"Ray? Ollie Chandler. How soon can you start?"

He said he was ready to go.

"How will the chief feel," Clarence asked, "when he hears you've brought in a private investigator to do police work?"

I shrugged. "I'll jump off that bridge when I come to it."

24

TUESDAY, DECEMBER 10

BEFORE OUR MORNING WALK, Mulch emptied his half-gallon water bowl. Fully loaded, he was ready to reclaim the city. Mulch's life consists of eating, playing, and sleeping. And while sleeping, he dreams of eating and playing.

Not a bad life. I've considered trading straight across. Right now, with my aching shoulder, it seemed particularly appealing, though I'd never do that to Mike Hammer.

Ever walked into a room and forgot what you came for? This is how dogs operate, except they aren't frustrated by it. They just find something interesting in the room they've entered for reasons now forgotten. Considering all that's happened in my life, a case could be made for a dog's memory.

Speaking of dogs, I spent most of the day like a dog chasing a parked car. I had nothing to show for it but a flat nose.

"I wish we had the DNA results," I told Abernathy as we sat in the Paradise Bakery in Pioneer Place, at Fifth and Morrison. "Palatine's blood could be mixed with the murderer's for all we know. The killer's saliva could be on the beer bottles. We might have collected all the proof that first night."

"What's the holdup on those tests?" Clarence asked. "It's been three weeks."

"Three weeks? That would be a record for DNA evidence. We could only wish."

"I've got another article due tomorrow. You won't let me say much more about the case—talk to me about DNA evidence."

"If we get a DNA match, it's definitive," I said, sounding brilliant. "There's a one in ten billion chance of one person's DNA matching another's. Chances of winning a fifty-million-dollar lottery are way better. Takes a lot more than chemicals and plastic impressions to fake DNA."

"So the rate of solved cases has gone way up, right?"

"That should be happening, but we didn't even start our DNA database until 1992. There's a bunch of criminals we have no DNA for. They can't get flagged because they're not in the database. Then there's this ridiculous wait for results."

"How long?"

"Guess."

"More than three weeks, obviously. A month?"

"Try three to four months."

"You can't be serious."

"While waiting, we're supposed to keep building our case. Fine, unless we're building it against the wrong guy! I spent three months building my case against a woman. Then the DNA samples we'd collected two hours after the murder ended up proving it was a guy who wasn't even on our radar screen. The temptation is to wait and see so you're not wasting your time. But if there's no match, it's a cold case. Lieutenant says 20 percent of the findings absolve the primary suspects, whether it's homicides or burglaries or gas station holdups. You wait three months to discover you've focused on the wrong people."

"And if not for the DNA you might have put them away?"

"If a jury thought the evidence was persuasive."

"So you're telling me those blood samples from Palatine's house are just sitting at the crime lab?"

"Blood, saliva, you name it, sitting there waiting. And that's not the only back-log. Since 2001 they've required DNA samples of all convicted felons to be entered into the database. Over seventy thousand have been entered, but last I heard we had more than twenty thousand DNA sample cards waiting to be processed."

"What's stopping it?"

"Funny you should ask. The *Oregon Tribune*."

"What are you talking about?"

"Remember how the *Trib* advocated police budget cuts? Back in 2003 we cut the state's forensic staff from 135 to 50 people. Far more samples, far more work to do, and fewer and fewer workers to do it."

"I didn't know that."

"It's your job to know. Why haven't you investigated it? Every time cops do something wrong, you tell everybody the juicy details, including false ones."

"The concern is citizen safety. The police department has had its problems."

"Wouldn't citizens be safer if we didn't have to wait three months to get violent criminals off the streets?"

"Can I quote you on that?"

"You can quote me as saying that, by defending police budget cuts, the *Tribune* is responsible for deaths, rapes, and robberies that wouldn't have happened if we'd had data entered sooner."

"I don't agree."

"You don't have to agree. Just quote me."

"It's…unnecessarily accusatory."

"In other words, the *Trib* can dish it out, but you can't take it."

"Look, I'm just trying to inform people. People love this investigation stuff. We can capitalize on the popularity of *CSI*."

"*CSI* is television magic," I said, downing my milk, which I'd rationed perfectly to cover my last bite of an apple fritter. (If you don't gauge it right, you have to get more milk or another fritter.) "They take in a sample and ten minutes later, or an hour, or a day, they have results. In the real world, we wait a hundred days. With enough people, everything could be processed in two days. Go over to Clackamas crime lab headquarters and check out the high-tech gear. They can turn molecular evidence into digital data, then put it into a database. But staff's so limited, it takes forever."

"You're saying it could get done in two days instead of a hundred?"

"And you know what burns me? If the killer's a detective, he knows how long this takes. He probably didn't leave DNA evidence at the scene, but even if he did, it drives me bonkers that he knows he's safe for another two months!"

At three thirty Clarence and I needed to surface for air, so we met Jake in Terry Schrunk Plaza, a block from the Justice Center and three from the *Tribune*. It was sunny but chilly, so we talked as we walked.

A man had been beaten up yesterday and was in critical condition. I pointed to chalk marks on the pavement and blood residue. "I still say there's no way a good God allows this kind of evil and suffering." I wasn't going to let them worm out of it.

"What are your favorite movies?" Jake said.

"What's that got to do with anything?"

"Humor me."

"*Braveheart. Gladiator. Saving Private Ryan. Schindler's List. Amistad. Air Force One.* Stallone and Norris movies in Vietnam. *Twelve O'Clock High. The Shootist* and everything else with John Wayne. *Star Wars. Lord of the Rings.*"

"Okay, good. Now think about the qualities of the characters you admire in each of those movies. What are they?"

Cold wind made me catch my breath. "Courage. Heroism. Sacrifice. Justice."

"And compassion, mercy, love?"

"Those are good too."

"These are the same things you admire in people in real life, right?"

"So?"

"So think about it. Would you ever have been able to see courage without danger? Or heroism without desperate situations? Compassion without suffering? Justice without injustice? Sacrifice without a need?"

I shrugged.

"The virtues of good people inspire us. And in the movies you named, just like in real life, we wouldn't see those virtues if not for evil or suffering."

"I guess that's one way to look at it, but it's a terrible price to pay, isn't it?" I pointed back to the crime scene.

"So, if you could snap your fingers and remove all evil and suffering that's ever existed, would you?"

"Wouldn't you?"

"Well, if we did, there'd be no Helen Keller, Frederick Douglass, Sojourner Truth, Abraham Lincoln, Harriet Tubman, Corrie ten Boom, Dietrich Bonhoeffer, Martin Luther King, or William Wilberforce."

"Who's Sojourner Truth? Or Harriet Tubman?"

Clarence turned and gave me a look. Suddenly I had a good idea.

"And think about Jesus," Jake said. "How would we know the extent of His love and grace if there'd never been evil and suffering?" He put his hand on my shoulder as we walked. "Don't you think it's inconsistent to say on the one hand that all these virtues that surface in the face of evil and suffering are good, then claim there's no way a good God could allow evil and suffering?"

I shook my head. "When people maim and kill each other, it throws a switch inside me. I do what I can to bring justice now. God seems to wait around a lot."

"He says He waits and withholds judgment to give us time to repent and get our lives right with Him," Jake said. "Justice has been restrained. What you're mad at God about—that He's been withholding judgment—is what's kept us all alive, giving us opportunity to repent and accept His grace."

"Isaiah says," Clarence added, "that God will bring justice 'like a pent-up flood.' He's not going to wait forever."

"That time should have come by now," I said.

Jake stopped in the middle of the plaza, so I stopped too. He looked at me and said, "And if it would have, where would you be?"

I sat at my desk, reading the *Tribune* again. It was getting to be a habit. Pretty soon I'd need a support group.

I have to give Clarence credit for his article. Not only did he write about the backup at the crime lab; he called on citizens to raise funds to help us catch up. He proposed fund-raising dinners and car washes. He even suggested a bumper sticker: "Support your police crime lab," and he said he'd put one on his own car.

I called a novelty shop to get one made for him.

My neck tensed when I saw Karl Baylor coming my way.

"Hi, Ollie. How are you?" His thick fingers looked like pork sausages, pressed together. When I shook his protruding hand it was a pliable lump.

"I need to talk to you about the moider."

Detective Baylor grew up in New York before moving to Oregon when he was in high school. I don't know the difference between Brooklyn, Queens, and the Bronx. All I know is that Baylor never says "murder"; he says "moider." This wouldn't be annoying if he were an accountant. But when you're a homicide detective, you use the word, what, three times a minute? Hearing "moider" 180 times an hour can drive you bonkers. Which I believe is also near Brooklyn.

"I've heard you think it's one of us," he said.

"That committed the moider?"

He nodded. Baylor has a reddish face that's big and broad, with insufficient features to fill it. I keep thinking something's missing, but when I count eyes, ears, nose, and mouth, they're all there.

He smiled broadly. It irritated me. Baylor lives under the curse of self-imposed merriment. Unfortunately, the rest of us have to put up with it.

"Isn't it a beautiful day?" he said in an auctioneer's voice, pointing out through the windows to the blue sky overlooking Portland. "Doesn't it just make you want to thank God for His goodness?"

"No."

Someone needs to tell Baylor it's not smart to talk like this to people who are strung tight at three hours of sleep, drink eight cups of coffee a day, and carry loaded weapons.

"You don't like me, do you?" Baylor asked.

The truth is, I disliked him from the first time I saw him, with that toothy televangelist smile and Christian paraphernalia in his cubicle. I feel guilty enough. I don't need large-print Bible verses screaming at me every time I walk by his workstation.

"Look, Detective, I'm all for jolliness. I manage a respectable amount myself. But when someone acts jolly because they think they're supposed to, it bugs me. I know you want to spread your happiness. But it would make some of us happier if you'd keep it to yourself."

He stepped toward me, leaning forward. Baylor's a personal space invader and has the kind of breath no mint can cure. He carries a tin of jiggling Altoids; thousands have perished in vain.

"I'm sorry I bother you," Baylor said.

"Look, nobody from New York is supposed to be happy. LA, okay. It may be drug-induced happy. It may be fake happy, but at least it's...conceivable. But New Yorkers are supposed to be rude and sullen." I paused. "Is Cimmatoni from New York?"

"Pittsburgh. You want me to act like Cimmatoni?"

"It's a start."

He smiled ear to ear. I wanted to deck him.

"What are you after, Detective?" I asked.

"I just wanted to let you know that people are getting concerned. They're...wondering if it's true you think one of *us* was involved in the Palatine moider."

"Tell them to come talk to me, would you?"

"Good idea," Baylor said. "God bless you."

"And you too, Tiny Tim. God bless us, every one."

WEDNESDAY, DECEMBER 11, 9:00 A.M.

Homicide was decorated for Christmas, tree and all. An elf had been busy last night. But thanks to the killer and me, the prevalent spirit wasn't the spirit of Christmas.

I arrived ten minutes early for the detective meeting and sat at a far corner of the conference room thinking of Kendra's visit the night before. I was sure I'd done everything right. I'd hidden the meat at the back of the freezer behind extra-large Costco-size bags of carrots, peas, and string beans, enough to feed a vegetarian army.

For an hour straight we'd been getting along without noticing it. But the moment I did notice, it all fell apart. In my relationship with my daughter, I am Wile E. Coyote, who can blissfully run ten feet beyond the cliff's edge...but only until he notices.

It was 10:15 when, out of the blue, Kendra declared that condoms should be distributed in schools to prevent diseases and pregnancies. So I said yeah, and how about we use the same strategy to solve the problem of battered women by handing out boxing gloves to abusive men.

At 10:23 Kendra marched out the door, slamming it. Mulch hid under Sharon's old hutch. My Wile E. Coyote face, succumbing to gravity, was plastered at the bottom of Father-Daughter Canyon. Somewhere in the distance I heard Road Runner's *beep-beep* mocking me. Every fatherly device I've ever tried was made by Acme.

↔

"Settle in," Sergeant Seymour said. I looked up to see a full room. The closest person was six feet from me.

"First, we're glad Ollie's still with us." Light applause followed—very light. Tommi and Karl. "We're hoping it was a freak incident and it won't happen again, but we're encouraging him to be cautious. Meanwhile, everybody's overworked and we've got to prioritize. I've asked Jack and Noel to help Karl and Tommi on the Frederick case. We've got more to work on there than with Dr. Hedstrom, which seems to have quickly dead-ended. I've got to keep Ollie and Manny on Palatine, so they're out of the rotation for now. This is triage. It's not ideal, but we've got to pull together and make it work."

"So why were we told to block off ninety minutes for a meeting?" Cimmatoni asked.

"It relates to the Palatine case. Detective Chandler's going to carry the ball."

"Great," Suda said.

Tommi gave her a disapproving look. I noticed dark swollen bags under Tommi's eyes.

Sarge didn't know I'd come at 5:00 a.m. to place Ray Eagle's miniature camcorder, looking like a nondescript plastic container, sitting on a front shelf surrounded by manuals. It was pointing at the detectives.

It's easier to get forgiveness than permission, and if no one finds out, you don't have to get forgiveness either. I pressed the record button on the remote in my coat pocket.

"Sarge asked me to read my conclusions about the Palatine case." One look at Sarge's face caused a revision. "He didn't ask me. He gave me permission." Here's what Manny and I are thinking." I saw Manny's expression. "All right, Manny's not so sure. Here's what *I'm* thinking."

"Can we move this along?" Doyle asked.

"Tonight it'll be three weeks since Palatine was murdered. Since then two others have been murdered because of what they knew or saw."

"Speculation," Doyle said. "And those aren't your cases."

"I'm going to read this," I said, holding up a paper. "Please withhold comments till I finish."

"First, the killer planned this meticulously, including the bizarre elements with the noose and ink injections.

"Second, the killer stayed dangerously long at the site. Apparently he knew nobody heard anything, even the broken window, and nobody called 911. Why would he stay unless he knew cops wouldn't come sooner, and he wouldn't be caught? Maybe he had access to a police monitor or experience with police procedure.

"Third, the killer took unnecessary measures that could make him vulnerable, as if he were daring detectives to catch him. He knew enough to avoid being caught, yet he took the time to inject the ink and remove items from the scene."

"What items?" Phillips asked.

"At least one framed photograph and a wine bottle."

"How do you know that?" Doyle asked.

"It's in his report," Tommi said.

"Fourth," I said, "the killer probably came back to the scene after patrol got there and before the detectives arrived. That's in my notes too."

"Fifth, the killer knew how to fake fingerprints and where to place them on the gun."

"We're sure those were fake?" Cimmatoni said, looking at Noel.

"Positive," Sarge said. "Internal Affairs had three lab experts examine it to make sure. They all agreed. Noel's in the clear."

"Leave it to IA," Suda said. "Bet they were disappointed not to hammer one of us."

"Sixth, the killer—I think—knew it was department SOP to search Dumpsters within four blocks of the scene. So he knew where to put the murder weapon—the one with the planted fingerprints."

I got several nods on this one.

"Seventh, the killer—most likely—knew the private phone number of a homicide detective, my number, and called me from the scene."

"Anybody can get a phone number," Cimmatoni said.

"I thought the professor made the call," Kim said.

"We think it was the killer," I said. "Anyway, the killer seemed to know homicide investigative procedures well enough to get around them. And because he took chances and left unnecessary evidence, this may be a game for him."

"That about it?" Sarge asked.

"Any…tentative conclusions based on what I've said?" I asked the group.

I saw the dissatisfied faces.

"Are you thinking…" Karl Baylor stopped and thought how to rephrase it. "The killer's a cop?"

Brandon Phillips looked around the room. "He's thinking more than that. He's thinking the killer was a homicide detective. He's thinking the guy's right in this room."

"Guy or gal," I said, nodding at Tommi and Kim.

"Nice to be included," Tommi said, laughing unnaturally. Suda wasn't smiling.

There's an old theory about announcing something shocking to a group and watching each person's expression to see who's least shocked. Old theories don't always work. And when your pool of suspects is homicide detectives, they're even less viable. We're used to studying people's faces. We know what we'd be looking for—and therefore how to avoid looking ourselves.

But I also knew that gradually faces would become less guarded. That's why I had the video running. It would be my game film.

"Since Noel was framed, does that eliminate him?" Tommi asked.

"Not necessarily," I said, trying to be inclusive. "He has access to his own fingerprints. He could have done it."

"Yeah," Noel said. "I've always wanted to frame myself for murder."

"What about you, Chandler?" Doyle asked. "Eliminated yourself as a suspect?"

"I didn't do it, if that's what you're asking."

"Right," Cimmatoni said. "Why don't we just take a poll and find out which of us *did* do it. That would save time."

"I know this is awkward," I said.

"It's not just awkward," Suda said. "It's ridiculous. I can't believe you're doing this, Chandler. Did Internal Affairs put you up to this?"

"The evidence put me up to it."

I pulled out of my coat pocket a handful of scrap papers. "Everybody gets a paper. Write your name on it, fold it, and pass it in." One minute of corporate whining later, Tommi picked them up.

I held up the scrap papers. "The person whose name is drawn will be the first to say where they were between 10:45 and 11:45 November 20."

"I don't believe this," Phillips said.

"Chandler's a horse's rear end," Cimmatoni said, or something to that effect.

"Okay," I said, pulling scraps out of my pocket and setting them on the table in front of Tommi. "Draw."

Tommi picked out of the middle, unfolded it, and read, "Kim Suda."

So began an hour of alibis.

"Professor Moriarty is not a man who lets the grass grow under his feet. You will not wonder that my first act on entering your rooms was to close your shutters, and that I have been compelled to ask your permission to leave the house by some less conspicuous exit than the front door."
SHERLOCK HOLMES, *THE FINAL PROBLEM*

THREE HOURS LATER, Clarence and I sat in Ray Eagle's living room, in Vancouver, Washington, across the I-205 bridge from Portland. His furniture was brown, red, and gray, with American Indian paintings on the wall. The chair I was sitting in disproved my theory that attractive furniture is uncomfortable. I rested my feet on a soft bulgy thing Clarence called an ottoman.

Ray connected his camcorder to his TV. He said to me, "So, you see Suda rifling your files, tail her, see her secret meeting with the chief, and her name gets drawn first? A one out of ten chance."

I reached in my right coat pocket and pulled out a bunch of folded paper scraps. I handed them to Clarence.

He looked through them.

"But…they all say Kim Suda."

Ray laughed.

"The trench coat has a pocket divider," I said. "I took the papers they wrote on and stuck them in back. The ones I wrote on were in front."

"You did this in front of a group of professional detectives?" Ray laughed again.

"I didn't want to give Suda more time to think. I wasn't going to take Clarence's approach and leave it up to providence."

"But…Tommi drew other names, right?" Clarence said.

"I replaced my scraps with theirs while everyone watched Suda."

Ray turned on the video and handed me the remote control, making me king.

"Wait," Clarence said. "Did they know they were being videotaped?"

I tried not to laugh.

"Isn't that illegal? Or unethical?"

"Go check with a lawyer or a priest, and get back to us," I said. "Me, I'm just looking to solve a murder. If it helps, pretend I have a photographic memory and we've hired professional actors to re-create the scene as I recall it. That would be just as unfair as this is. We're here to evaluate their body language, responses, anything that could indicate innocence or guilt."

I passed out that photo of the detectives and spouses, taken before Sharon died. Carp had made a dozen copies for me since I needed to flash detective faces around.

"Before Suda answers, let me fill you in. She's short, maybe five one. Fit. Strong but feminine. Great conditioning. She chased a twenty-year-old gangbanger ten blocks before taking him in. Her partner, Chris Doyle, was her backup, four blocks behind. They say he was lying in a heap hyperventilating while Kim handcuffed the perp. Suda moves to her own beat, music playing in her head."

"What about Doyle?" Ray asked.

"A Hercule Poirot when it comes to his soft mannerisms, but the similarity ends there. Reminds me of Jessica Fletcher because people around him have a way of dying. Smokes himself to death, and nobody's eager for him to stop. Anyway, here we go."

I pressed play and was back in the room where all this had happened four hours ago. Except this time I had two more sets of eyes, could see faces at will, and had the freedom to pause and rewind.

"I was at a friend's house pretty late," Suda said.

"What friend?" I heard myself ask.

"Someone who doesn't want to be identified."

Long pause, then Chris Doyle said, "She dropped by my house."

The room was one collective smirk.

"It wasn't what you think," Chris said.

"What would be wrong with what they think?" Suda asked him, ignoring the tittering.

"We were together until you got that text message from your mother about 11:20."

"Your mother sends text messages?" Cimmatoni asked.

"She's high-tech. Was spending the weekend with me and wasn't feeling well. I needed to get home."

"We were together until 11:20," Doyle said. "That's close to time of death, right? And wasn't the killer supposedly there forty minutes earlier? Then you called me when you got home, say 11:40."

"Proves nothin'," Cimma said.

"Yeah," Suda said. "I always make calls while I'm murdering someone. It calms my nerves."

"Clears me though, right?" Doyle said. "I mean, I was home at 11:15 and 11:45 when you called, right, Kimmy? I mean Suda." His chubby face glowed like a Christmas light.

"Kimmy?" Noel said.

"*Kimmy*," Tommi said, putting her hand over her smile.

Suda glared.

"Why didn't you stay home with your mother?" I asked. "What brought you back out at four in the morning when you dropped by our murder scene?"

"None of your business."

"Hiding something?"

"I'm a light sleeper. Occasionally I get up and drive. I had the monitor on and heard about the murder. It was close to my place, so I stopped in."

"Anyway," Chris said. "Back to Kim's phone call at 11:45. That covers me, right?"

"It would," Suda said, "if I'd called your home phone. But I called your cell."

"Way to take him, Kimmy," Cimma said. "You could've been anywhere, Doyle. You're what, ten minutes from the dead guy's? You could have been standing over his body when she called…if she called."

Doyle froze, dragging me back to the present, where we were sitting in Ray's living room. Ray had grabbed the remote and paused.

"Look at his face," Ray said.

Chris's face had gone from red to stark white. It's as if a plug had been pulled, and all the blood drained out. His Adam's apple was moving, but he was swallowing nothing. I didn't need a polygraph to measure his nerves, not when I'd heard him live, and not now that I watched him again.

Clarence typed furiously on his notebook computer.

"You're going to keep that to yourself, right?" I asked him.

"For now."

"Maybe forever. You can't tell anybody I taped this."

He pretended to ignore me.

"He looks guilty," Ray said.

"Doyle or Abernathy?"

"Tell us more about Chris Doyle," Ray said.

"He worked a couple of cases with me when Manny was out and Suda had a family emergency. Doyle's…like a duck on the lake. He's calm on the surface, looks like he's doing nothing, but underneath those legs are paddling. If the perps leave their fingerprints on everything, or they look into surveillance cameras and hand notes written on the back of their phone bills to bank tellers, saying 'Give me all the money,' Doyle will nab them. But he's no creative genius. This crime seems too intricate for him."

"Somebody told me, 'Things aren't always as they seem,'" Clarence said.

Ray walked behind me. "He just looks like your average red-faced guy drinking beer and watching his Buffalo Bills play in December."

"Except Doyle would be more likely to watch ballet," I said. "I think he has sugarplums dancing in his head.

"Okay." I pointed to the screen. "This next guy's Noel."

"The guy who was framed? Plus he's got a solid alibi? Six guys in a bar plus the bartender?" Ray asked. "Are they all close to him…and each other?"

"Just bar buddies. Acquaintances."

"Hard to believe six guys and a bartender would be in on a conspiracy to protect him," Ray said. "What's Noel like?"

"He's a good old boy, nice golfing tan. Smart enough to be an average detective. Doesn't have to be brilliant. He works with Jack."

I stepped toward the screen and pointed out Jack Glissan. "Jack can tell you the names and dates of crimes committed twenty years ago. He's the brains."

We heard Noel's alibi then listened to Manny's. Home with Maria until she left at 10:45 to work night shift at the hospital. Manny was at the house with three kids, who were sleeping until the 3:00 a.m. murder call. He dropped the kids at his sister's. He seemed agitated just talking about it, saying "We weren't the up team" and complaining about journalists coming to a murder scene.

"Okay, Brandon Phillips is next," I said. "His name's about to be drawn."

Ray zoomed in.

"He's looking at his BlackBerry," Clarence said, getting up to point at the object in his hand. "Checking e-mail?"

"Or rehearsing his alibi?" Ray asked.

"Phillips is a detail man," I said. "Precise. Methodical. We did a couple of cases together. Nice guy, but he drove me nuts. He was like a fussy little maid looking for dust in every corner."

"The scars on his face," Ray said. "Acne?"

"Golden Gloves boxer. He reminded us, maybe to make excuses for his face. He's okay, but when you press him, he can get a steel rod up his back. Last year I happened to be driving down his street to avoid traffic. He was shoveling snow in his driveway, and it was like a Wayne Gretzky slap shot."

I pointed to the screen. "The next part's interesting."

After I asked his alibi, Phillips seemed to be thinking for five seconds, then finally looked at Jack and said, "Was that the night we were at your place talking about that cold case at Lloyd Center?"

Jack nodded.

"It was a couple of hours," Brandon said. "Maybe I got there at ten? I had a couple beers, but you were on call, so you couldn't drink. So I left when? Midnight?"

"Closer to twelve thirty," Jack said, a little red-faced when he caught my eye. After all, he'd claimed to drop by Noel's at eleven thirty that night—back when Noel needed an alibi. "Linda came downstairs and reminded me I needed sleep."

"She'll confirm that?" I asked Jack, instantly regretting it when I saw his face.

I paused the tape, then rewound. "So when I ask Phillips for his alibi, what do you see?"

"He's…trying to remember," Clarence said. "Then suddenly he does."

"Which makes you think what?" I asked.

"He hadn't given it much thought?"

"Hold it," Ray said. "The guy's been sitting there twenty minutes. He *had* to be thinking about how he'd answer the question."

"Exactly," I said. "This isn't a man trying to remember. This is a man pretending to try to remember."

"What's the difference?" Clarence said.

"The difference between innocence and guilt?" Ray asked.

"Would Jack and his wife lie for him?" Clarence added.

I've tried not to like Phillips—maybe because he's strong and good-looking and fifteen years younger and the consummate detective. But he isn't an easy guy to dislike. There're those little things. Like him calling me after he'd seen me at Rosie's, wondering if I was okay.

Besides, Cimmatoni was his partner. If he was going to murder somebody, wouldn't he have taken out Cimma years ago?

I froze the frame, and we studied Bryce Cimmatoni. He's a specimen—looks like he was born to conduct mysterious business in nightclub back rooms with guys named Giuseppe and Bruno. You could see him breaking a piano player's fingers for being delinquent on his loan or putting a horse head in somebody's bed. Cimma doesn't give an inch, a cent, or a rip.

But I'd still take a bullet for him. That's how it works.

As I looked at Cimma on film, he was pale with four or five splotches of red. His face had no insulation between lumber and Sheetrock. His hair was gray and receding. His jaw—pit-bull solid—looked like it had been clamping down on people for decades.

His face seemed incurably unhappy and therefore unreadable since it always looked the same—disgusted.

"Is he as tough as he looks?" Ray asked.

"Tougher. He gets no points for personality, but he's a decent detective. His wife Martha was drop-dead gorgeous in her day and at sixty is still striking. She's an oncology nurse. Sweetest person you'll ever meet. She rivals Tommi. How she ended up with Cimma, I don't have a clue."

Come to think of it, I don't know how Sharon ended up with me. When Tommi drew Cimmatoni's name, he set his jaw and said, "I'm not answering."

"Why not?" Sarge asked.

"I have my reasons."

"If you have an answer that clears you," I asked, "how will it be helped by aging?"

"I need to think about it."

"When people need to think about it, it's to get their lies straight."

Cimmatoni might not have killed Palatine, but if looks could kill, I'd have keeled over on the spot.

"He doesn't look happy," Ray said, which was like saying water looks wet. "He never answered?"

"Nope. If he has an alibi, he's not talking."

"What do you think?" Ray asked. "Could Cimmatoni kill Palatine? And Frederick? And the academic dean?"

"He could kill a man in a heartbeat," I said, "if he thought he had good reason to and could get away with it. He worked vice and sex crimes for years. Transferred to homicide four years ago."

"Do you know why?"

"Because he likes to see dead people?"

"What exactly are we looking for?" Clarence asked.

"It's like studying game film," I said. "There's a lot to see. Isolate it. What do you notice about their sitting positions and eye contact and body language? A murderer's always interested in discussions of a murder, just like a home run hitter's interested in discussions of his home run. Even more, since his life could be on the line."

Ray pointed at the screen. "Tommi and Noel look casual. Jack and Cimmatoni interested. But I'd say there's extreme interest by Kim Suda, Chris Doyle, and Brandon Phillips. Look where Phillips is seated. Freeze that frame."

"He's on the front of his chair," I said. "The front eight inches. Why? Nervousness, uncertainty, fear? He's extremely absorbed."

We did this for two hours, starting and stopping, rewinding and commenting, each of us, especially Clarence, jotting down notes. We were only halfway through and it was three o'clock.

"Snack break," Ray said, reading my mind. He threw stuff in the oven while Clarence and I made phone calls. Minutes later we were at Ray's kitchen table, eating Hot Pockets sausage and pepperoni pizza snacks.

"We've got a ways to go," I said. "Let's watch while we eat."

Thirty seconds later I pushed pause again.

"You can enlarge this?" I asked Ray.

"Who you interested in?"

"Noel. He keeps looking down. Why?"

Ray fast-forwarded until Cimmatoni got up for a drink. Suddenly there was a clear view of Noel. Ray zoomed in.

"He's reading something. A magazine I think," Clarence said.

Ray enlarged it as far as he could. "The picture has lots of green and blue above it. Something yellow there and a little white object and a—"

"It's a golf green," I said. "He's reading a golf magazine. Figures. In Noel's mind, work's for people who don't know how to golf."

"What about that guy?" Clarence asked, grabbing the remote and freezing the frame on one man.

"Brilliant, athletic, witty, uncommonly handsome," I said. "Oliver Justice Chandler. Look at that kisser. What does it say?"

"That you need more sleep," Clarence said.

"Question," Ray said. "Has Tommi ever had a romantic relationship with any of these guys?"

"Ten years ago she had something with Phillips," I said. "He's on his second marriage since then. Anyway, Tommi's no whiner, but she got hurt. Felt like Phillips used her, I think."

"She reliable?"

"Tommi? Cal Ripken reliable."

"Married?"

"Yeah. Her husband Peter's a veterinarian."

Tommi offered her alibi in the video. "Peter and I were home alone. Went to bed probably by 10:30. We talked and read."

"Talked and read?" Cimmatoni grunted.

"We love to talk—we're soul mates."

She took ribbing for this.

"Well, we are," she said. "On our five-year anniversary, I put on my wedding dress and Peter rented a tux, and we stood in the same spot we were married."

In the secretarial pool they would have said, "How sweet." Homicide is not the secretarial pool.

Tommi's alibi was simple, straightforward, and the next worst alibi to "I was home alone." It meant that only one other person needed to lie besides her. And that person happened to be her soul mate.

When I asked his alibi, Karl Baylor said, "Tiffany and I were on a marriage retreat. At the Gresham Holiday Inn."

"Just that night?"

"Tuesday and Wednesday nights. Wednesday we visited friends from church, in their room."

"Write down their names, would you?" I felt the ice, not as much from Karl as from Tommi.

"What time did you go back to your room?"

"10:30? 10:45?"

"And you just…went to bed?"

"Lights out at eleven or so, I guess."

"That was it?"

"One final session after breakfast the next morning. I didn't see the paper. When we were driving home Thursday, we heard about the moider on the radio."

Tommi drew Jack Glissan's name.

"Jack's like the coach every guy loves, the one who brings out the best in them. Mind like a steel trap. Last month he took me out to dinner for the twentieth anniversary of the first day we worked together as partners. Not perfect, but I'd trust my life to him. I have. Heck, we were in a bowling league together."

"That settles it," Clarence said. "Killers don't bowl."

"Could Jack be a killer?" I asked. "Anybody could be. Ray could be the killer. His phone number was in the professor's desk. I could be the killer."

"Could you?" Clarence said.

"I don't mean in this case." I hoped my face didn't look like my gut felt. "But with a strong motive, like if somebody pilfered my Fritos…" I eyed my plate, then Ray.

"I only took two."

"It starts with two, then it's a bag, then it's my car, and next my retirement funds."

"I bought that bag of Fritos," Ray said.

"Once they landed on my plate they became mine. That's the law."

"Can we get back to Jack Glissan?" Clarence asked.

"Jack's retiring in the next year or two. Loves to golf, travel with Linda. I don't think he'd do that to her—run the risk of leaving her alone if he was caught."

On the video, Jack told the same story Phillips had, sitting in his living room and Linda coming downstairs and seeing them after eleven.

All in all, some detectives had convincing alibis and some weak ones. But what alibi can you expect for ten thirty until midnight? Playing poker with a half dozen federal judges?

Sitting on Ray's couch I was lost in this thought, then realized one last question remained on the video. I groped for the remote, which had slipped behind a cushion.

"What's your alibi, Chandler?" Doyle spouted off.

I almost pressed fast-forward but knew how it would look.

"At Rosie O'Grady's pub."

"Figures," Cimmatoni said. "How late?"

"Got there at nine, then drove straight home." As I said it, Wally's Donuts, one of them in particular, filled my brain. For all I knew, I'd been abducted by aliens. The hours were missing.

"Then what?"

"Went to bed, slept until I got the call about the moider." I eyed Baylor and pulled a chuckle from Jack.

"So you don't have an alibi?"

"Just my dog, Mulch."

"I called you from Jack's just after eleven," Phillips said. "You didn't answer your cell or your home phone. I'd seen you leaving Rosie's before I went to Jack's, and you didn't look—"

"I didn't feel like answering," I said. Never mind that I didn't remember the phone ringing…or being home to hear it ring.

Clarence and Ray both looked at me silently. The tape finished five minutes later. I turned it off when Sarge dismissed the group. Ray restarted it to watch people's reactions after the meeting. I could feel the same chill in the air as I had that morning. Not one person talked to me—except Tommi, who doesn't count since she would tell Charles Manson to have a nice day.

"Wish we had tapes of their private conversations afterward," Ray said.

"This hasn't made you popular," Clarence said.

I shook my head. "Law enforcement's most sacred credo, on a par with don't shoot innocent bystanders, is *don't tell on another cop*. Nobody seems willing to take care of cops. People take cheap shots at us. The *Tribune* comes to mind. So, as they say, 'we take care of our own.' You're not supposed to violate that. I've crossed the line. And there's no going back."

"One way or the other," Ray said, "somebody's going to make you pay."

"It is one of the curses of a mind with a turn like mine that I must look at everything with reference to my own special subject. You look at these scattered houses, and you are impressed by their beauty. I look at them, and the only thought which comes to me is a feeling of their isolation and of the impunity with which crime may be committed there."
SHERLOCK HOLMES, *THE ADVENTURE OF THE COPPER BEECHES*

THURSDAY, DECEMBER 12

WHEN IT COMES TO RELATIONSHIPS, I'm like a battery-operated screwdriver that has to be recharged for twenty-four hours to be useful for ten minutes.

For twenty years, whole weeks of my family life went by without my family. All things considered, it's amazing our marriage lasted. Sharon gets the credit. I didn't deserve my wife. And she didn't deserve me. She deserved a lot better. I'm ashamed to say I love her more now than I did when she was alive. I'd like to tell her I'm sorry.

Part of me says there's no way I'll ever see my wife again. One, there may be no heaven. Two, if there is a heaven, I won't be there.

As for Kendra, there's a hint of progress. I keep calling her. She doesn't seem to resent me as much. I'm holding my breath because one wrong move and I may not see her for another two years. I told her again I'd do what I could to help with the baby. Kendra may be there to choose my nursing home. But I wonder how much I'll see her between now and then.

We met at the parking garage. Jake would drive us out in the country, past Sandy to Calamity Jane's, a great burger place. We figured we'd take a break from Lou's and use the extra drive time to discuss the case.

Before Jake got us across the Morrison Bridge, I decided to stir things up.

"Why would anyone want to go to heaven? When my grandmother spoke about heaven, it was the last place I wanted to go. Who wants to be a ghost anyway? My idea of utopia was a place like earth, where you could have fun and ride bikes and play baseball and go deep into the forest and dive into lakes and eat good food."

"Sounds to me like the new earth," Clarence chimed in from the backseat.

"Exactly," Jake said. "The Bible says the heaven we'll live in forever will be a new earth, this same earth without the bad stuff. God doesn't give up on His original creation. He redeems it. And we'll have these same bodies made better. The Bible teaches the exact opposite of what you're saying—we won't be ghosts. We'll eat and drink and be active on a redeemed earth."

"So you'll still be Jake Woods?" I asked.

"Yeah—without the bad parts. We'll be able to enjoy creation's beauty and rule the world the way God intended us to. Baseball and riding bikes? Why not?"

Clarence leaned forward. "The thing you want is exactly what God promises. Earth with all the good and none of the bad. Heaven on earth."

"Wish I could believe that."

"What's stopping you?" Jake asked.

"Same song, different verse. A world of injustice and suffering is part of it. Another part is hypocrite Christians."

"Okay," Jake said, "suppose there is a God and Jesus really died on the cross for people's sins. Suppose He rose from the grave and offers eternal life to everybody who trusts Him."

"That's a lot to suppose."

"And suppose there really is a devil. Now, if you were the devil, what would you do to keep people from believing in Christ?"

"Never thought about it."

"I know what I'd do. I'd get people to claim they're Christians when they aren't. I'd get them to do terrible things in Christ's name. Then I'd try to persuade un-believers to focus on those terrible things done by so-called Christians, instead of on the wonderful things done by Jesus. Then I'd try to get Christians to be self-righteous hypocrites who don't care about the needy, but only themselves."

"You're blaming the devil for what Christians do? Like the Crusades?"

"I'm saying the devil's behind lots of evil, yeah, but so are people. And I'm say-ing people can claim to be Christians even though they aren't. And sure, people can be real Christians and mess up, big time. But true, humble followers of Jesus are everywhere, and if you knew them, Ollie, you'd be drawn to Christ. If not for Clarence's sister being murdered, you'd never have met Obadiah Abernathy. You wouldn't have been touched by him because you wouldn't even know he existed."

"He was one of a kind," I said.

"Actually," Clarence said, "there are plenty of good-hearted, humble, and lov-able Christians like my daddy. All the attention falls on false Christians or loudmouths or hypocrites. But the gospel's about Jesus."

"The fact remains: Some Christians are mean and hateful. I've met them."

"So have I," Clarence said. "Read some of those Christian blogs, and look at how they love to gang up on people, kicking them with their words when half the time they don't know what they're talking about."

"Christians can be jerks," Jake said. "We're unanimous on that one. Sometimes they're just nominal Christians. Other times they may be real Christians full of flaws. I have plenty myself."

"At least you admit it," I said.

"But it makes no sense," Jake said, "to reject Jesus because some of His followers are hypocrites. The Bible never says that to be saved you have to believe in Christians. It says you have to believe in Jesus."

"I still don't want to be associated with judgmental hypocrites."

"It's pretty judgmental to call all of us Christians hypocrites, isn't it?" Clarence asked. "Speaking of which, if you discovered other detectives were withholding evidence because they thought it had been planted against them, wouldn't you say they were wrong for covering it up?"

"Yes, but—"

"By your own standards you—Oliver Justice Chandler—have been unjust. That's hypocrisy, isn't it?"

"Well, I don't claim to be godly."

"You claim to love justice, don't you? Yet you violate standards of justice. Lots of people, including you, don't live consistently with what they profess to believe. Christians don't have a monopoly on hypocrisy. The justice you believe in is good, even when you violate it, right? Well, the Jesus that Christians believe in is good, even when we violate His teachings. Even when we're hypocrites."

It's scary when Jake and Clarence make sense.

"Mind if I change the subject?" I said. "I've been thinking about our murderer. This guy doesn't kill as a last resort. It's become a habit."

"Which puts you in danger," Clarence said. "You could have been killed."

I shrugged it off. "I'm still kicking, aren't I?" We pulled into the Calamity Jane's parking lot. I could taste the County Fair Burger, smothered in grilled onions. I jumped out of the car, eager to get moving. As we walked to Jane's door, I said, "To catch a killer, you have to think like a killer. If the killer's a bricklayer, you have to think like a bricklayer, know how he'd kill someone. In this case, you have to think like a homicide detective. The bad news is, any homicide detective is going to be tough to catch because he knows the ropes. The good news is, I'm a homicide detective, so I know how they think. But we've had three deaths and a shotgun blast through my window. I've got to do something to get ahead of this guy."

THURSDAY, DECEMBER 12, 6:00 P.M.

Clad in an extra-large A&E Nero Wolfe T-shirt and my blue plaid boxers, I sprawled back on my faded brown recliner. With a plate of Ritz crackers on my lap, a jar of Skippy peanut butter between my saggy white knees, and a tall glass of milk in my right hand, I was unlikely to make the cover of *Gentleman's Quarterly*.

I plunged into my Wolfe book, *Over My Dead Body*, enjoying the artistry of

Rex Stout, who as far as I'm concerned is twice the writer Faulkner ever was (not that I've ever read Faulkner).

After finishing a chapter, I rewarded myself by spreading Skippy on Ritz. I wasn't sure there was a heaven, or the heaven on earth Jake and Clarence said was coming, but this might be a foretaste.

Mulch was working peanut butter off the roof of his mouth. Suddenly he froze, his tail rigid. He stared out the dining room window looking out on my backyard. I heard a slight growl, then the first of dozens of loud barks. He ran to the back door and scratched. I looked outside the window. Nothing.

Mulch has conned me into checking the backyard for intruders countless times, and I wasn't about to fall for it again. I finally managed to calm him down.

Sitting back in my recliner, I thought I heard a creak on the back porch, the sort of creak that bothers women, like Sharon, who thought that every noise required an explanation. Being a man, I ignored it.

I leaned the Nero Wolfe book against my chest, dabbed my knife into the peanut butter, lifted the cracker to my lips, then bit slowly. Oh, yeah.

Thump. No denying the noise, but it sounded more distant and higher. Mouth full, I set down the jar and moved the recliner forward as Mulch attacked the back door.

I reached underneath the recliner on the left side and pulled out my SIG-Sauer, removing the duct tape. With my right hand I grabbed my Glock out of its shoulder holster, lying on the coffee table. People occasionally have good reasons to be on my front porch. Never the back. Like young Kevin Costner in *Silverado*, I was going out a two-fisted gunman, covering both sides. And for good measure, I put on my Baby Glock ankle holster, which may have looked a little funny considering I was in my boxers.

I walked to the kitchen, mouth dry with peanut butter. I moved past Mulch, peering out the new, clean window. Nothing. Same thing I'd seen before a shotgun blast nearly answered my questions about the afterlife.

I opened the door slowly and stepped out, nudging it shut with the Glock's barrel. I heard a shuffling noise in the garage, six feet to my right. If these were mice, they must be fifty-pounders.

I pivoted, pointing both guns at the roof. I stepped backward to the edge of the porch. Nothing above. Nothing in the yard. I turned toward the garage. Due to a gap at the bottom of the garage door, I'd had a cat in the garage, an occasional bird, even a possum. But when a shotgun has been recently fired at you from your back porch, you have no assurances concerning noises in your garage.

I turned the handle to the garage door and pushed it open, hugging the side of the frame. I pointed inward, SIG in my left hand, waiting to see if it would draw fire. Nothing.

I stepped into the garage, flipped on that wimpy overhead light, and treaded

slowly by boxes, looking backward and forward. I hadn't been out here since finding the nautical rope.

The garage was still. I heard nothing. Elvis, framed in the corner shadows,
looked like he wanted to warn me. Just then I realized I'd looked forward, backward, and down. I looked up just as something dropped around my neck.

I was choking, unable to breathe, spitting out chunks of Ritz crackers and
peanut butter. My legs were flailing wildly, as if detached from my body. I was dangling a foot above the concrete floor. I heard my gun bounce beneath me.
Something was pulling me up. A noose. I was suffocating.

I heard a noise above me, quick movement, and the sense of someone coming
down a ladder ten feet away in the shadows, then rushing by under me. I thought
I saw a ski mask, but wasn't sure. Whoever it was exited out the door I'd entered.

Hanging there in my boxer shorts, time seemed to slow as I contemplated what
a humiliating way to die this would be. I pictured my detective colleagues taking
my photograph, Kim Suda laughing at my underwear and Cimmatoni shaking his
head in disgust. I even saw Carlton Hatch looking at my body—a still, blue
corpse—then in a moment of drama declaring my death. I hoped Carp wouldn't
see me this way and, above all, Kendra.

I tried to scream as I dangled. What came upon me next was a profound fear:
that Jake and Clarence were right. And I was too late to do anything about it. Sharon
had sensed light and comfort shortly before she died. I felt only darkness and dread.

The more I fought the rope, the quicker my life eked away. The garage light
dimmed completely. I lost all hope. Suddenly, a voice spoke inside my head.

Your gun.

I sensed something in my right hand. It seemed impossible I hadn't dropped it.
The SIG had fallen from my left hand, but my grip on the Glock had tightened.
It felt like part of my hand. Somehow I managed to pull it upward. I put the barrel an inch from the rope above my head. Despite the dimness, I saw an old wasp's
nest and a spiderweb.

I tried to find my trigger finger and move it, then heard an explosion. The
recoil nearly knocked the gun from my weakened hand. I pointed it at the rope
again and fired, hanging on. Nothing. My feet were still a foot above the garage
floor. Finally, darkness enveloping me, in what I knew was my last chance I lifted
the gun again, put the barrel near the rope, and pulled the trigger.

Still hearing the explosion, I felt my feet touch ground and my dead weight
crumble onto concrete. Simultaneously, I felt relief on my throat and severe pain
in my lower body. I felt and heard, in the same awful moment, my head hit the
concrete. In the split second before unconsciousness, I knew I was slipping into a
pool of darkness, either sleep or death.

"It is cocaine, a seven-per-cent solution.
Would you care to try it?"
SHERLOCK HOLMES, *THE SIGN OF FOUR*

SOMETIMES IN THE NIGHT wind I hear the world groaning like it knows it was made for something better. I see it in Mulch's eyes. He knows something's wrong. When I flip past those lame reality shows with pathetic people unveiling their emptiness for everyone to see, it's like they're crying out, "Something's wrong, and I don't know how to make it better; will somebody help me?"

These vague notions swirling in my brain suddenly gave way to the blurred image of Jake Woods.

"What happened?"

I was talking, but what I heard wasn't me. I sounded like one of those cowboys in the movies that survived a hanging and never got his voice back. My normal voice wasn't much different, come to think of it.

Seeing Jake above me, I wondered if he'd died too.

"You're going to be okay," Jake said. "It was a close one."

"How…?"

"Your neighbor, Mr. Obrist, heard the shots. He found you in your garage. He loosened the rope around your neck and called 911."

"Where?"

"Emmanuel Hospital. They just moved you from Emergency."

"Throat…sore."

"Yeah," Clarence said, obscuring the ceiling light. "That comes with being hung."

"Making fun of me?"

"No," Clarence said. "If we were making fun of you, we'd be mentioning your boxer shorts."

"We've been praying for you," Jake said. "We didn't want to lose you."

It was a tender moment of male bonding, so I said, "Get me a beer?"

"Can't do that," Jake said. "But I think I can manage water."

"Ice chips," a kind voice said.

I looked up and it was a young brown-haired nurse whose name tag said

"Emily Arnold." She tipped the ice chips to my mouth. I took them in and they felt good, until water made its way down to my throat. I flinched.

"I'll get the doctor," she said.

The doctor was apparently playing the back nine, so it was just me and Clarence and Jake. I told them the part of the story they didn't know; they told me the rest. Nurse Emily came back and checked on me a few more times. She seemed smarter and more helpful than a doctor anyway. When I asked when I could eat onion rings again, she thought it would be within a few days. That's my kind of nurse.

When she left, Jake said, "I'm so thankful."

"That somebody lynched me in my own garage?"

"That you weren't killed."

"And here I was wondering why God thought He needed to hang me."

"So instead of thanking God, you're blaming Him?" Clarence said.

"It was a miracle," Jake said. "God saved your life."

"Didn't I save my own life by shooting the rope?"

"That's one way of looking at it," Jake said.

"Yeah. The wrong way," Clarence said. "The doctor told us it's nearly impossible for you to have held on to the gun in the first place—and then to have fired it right through the rope?"

"I'm a man who does the impossible," I whispered. "What can I say?"

"You can say, 'Thank You, God,'" Jake said. "Because if He hadn't kept that gun in your hand and steadied it in front of that rope and given you strength to pull the trigger, you'd be dead."

"God's given you another chance," Clarence said.

"Another chance to get this killer."

"Another chance," Jake said, "to prepare for the death you narrowly escaped."

Two hours later Manny and Sergeant Seymour came to my room. Despite getting the evil eye from the new nurse on shift, they explained how someone had screwed my own block and tackle unit into the upper storage platform of my garage. This jury-rigged gallows had taken a half hour's work anyway, so when I heard the noise, it was exactly when he wanted me to hear it, to lure me out to the garage. He had every intention of hanging me. That I was in my underwear was an unanticipated bonus.

"Let me get this straight," Manny said. "You had a gun in your hand, and you saw the person who hung you running out the door—and you didn't fire at him?"

I explained that I didn't know I had the gun, but it sounded lame. Finally I said,

"Wait until you get hung, then you'll understand."

Manny had talked with all my neighbors, including the Obrists, and no one had seen the guy. Naturally.

"We're considering posting a guard at your house," Sarge said.

"What? I can take care of myself."

"You got assaulted by a guy in your backyard, someone unloaded a shotgun at you, and now you were hung in your garage? I'm thinking maybe you can't take care of yourself."

I pleaded with him not to do it. I'm the type of guy who protects people, not who's protected by them. I mean, did Green Lantern have a bodyguard?

"You're just lucky you're alive," Sarge said.

After they left, I lay there in that empty room, wondering if it was more than luck. I thought about what Jake and Clarence had said. And in case anyone was listening, as I slipped into a semidrugged sleep, I whispered, "Thank You."

SATURDAY, DECEMBER 14

When the Friday afternoon examination showed no damage beyond a raw neck and a bruised trachea, a six-inch melon bruise on the right side of my head, a gash in my knee, and a general sense that I'd been pushed through a cheese shredder, the doctor reluctantly gave in to my pleas to go home to Mulch, provided I wear the protective collar around my neck and stay home for three days.

I solemnly agreed.

I kept my promise for one evening, but Saturday morning I couldn't sleep, so I was first on the detective floor at five thirty. Not many show up on Saturdays, so it's a good day to work. I'll grant that I was making another statement. Even if few people saw me working Saturday, word would spread. "Missed me again." I sat down at the snack table, looking out the window at Portland drizzle.

A hungry dog hunts best. Being the target of a second assassination attempt increased my hunger to capture this guy; third strike and I felt sure I'd be out.

At six thirty a voice behind me said, "Hey, man. You don't look so great." It was Jack Glissan. He sat across from me, drinking something that smelled suspiciously like Earl Grey. He said, "It's a ghost town this time of day."

I nodded.

"I heard you had to wear one of those collars," he said.

"I gave it to Mulch. He loves foam rubber. I'll clean up the shreds tonight."

"You haven't changed," Jack said, smiling but showing his age.

This episode had strained our relationship, I knew. It had strained my relationship with everybody.

"Sorry about what happened," Jack said. "And sorry I didn't visit. So somebody really wants to take you down?"

Suddenly I was saying, "You know when Linda and Sharon used to go to AA?"

"Yeah. Every Tuesday night."

"Linda still go?"

"Sometimes. Not often. Drinking's not as big for her anymore. I've learned to keep the stuff out of the house. Except small quantities of beer, which she doesn't like, so it's no threat. Have to keep her away from wine."

"Any problem with it yourself?"

"A drinking problem? No. But no reason for me to bring it home when it could trip her up. We have to look out for each other, you know?"

"Yeah." I poured more coffee and stirred in French vanilla Coffee-Mate. "Has Linda ever...blacked out?"

"Couple of times, when it was really bad. Why?"

"Because...I've blacked out. More than a couple of times. And I can't remember what happened. I drink because I don't want to remember. You know, Sharon and...all that."

"I know. I'm sorry. She was a good woman."

"The best. I've had times when I've been out places, and I can't remember what I was doing. Especially between when I leave the bar and get home. It's like a big gap. Sometimes not just the fifteen-minute drive. An hour or two. Then I wonder, what was I doing all that time?"

"Still going to AA?"

I shook my head, pouring in more creamer.

"You should."

"It's not my thing."

"That's what everybody says till they realize how much of their lives they've been missing."

"Yeah," I said. "But sometimes missing part of your life is the whole point, isn't it?"

"Ain't it strange what these folks think?" Obadiah Abernathy asked.

"And what they don't think," said Ruby Abernathy.

The Carpenter nodded. "They cling to youth and health with a white-knuckled grip. But they don't take time to prepare themselves for what awaits them on the other side."

"Looking back," Ruby said, "I wonder why I was so afraid to grow old. Every day brought me one day closer to being here with You."

"So many of them store their treasures there," He said. "So every day they move toward their deaths, they're moving away from their treasures. But if they store their treasures here, every day they're moving toward their treasures."

Obadiah nodded. "The one who spends his life movin' away from his treasures is goin' to despair. But the one who spends his life movin' toward his treasures is goin' to rejoice!"

The Carpenter smiled and nodded.

"Ollie Chandler's lost hope, hasn't he?" Obadiah asked.

"He once looked forward to the future," the Carpenter said, "yet it didn't materialize as he'd hoped. Even when it did, it failed to satisfy. Now he no longer dares to hope. It saves him disappointment. He doesn't yet realize that I am the One he longs for."

"And You never disappoints," Obadiah said. "I can testifies to that. Elyon's Word tells us to look forward to a new heaven and a new earth, the home of righteousness. Yet how often they seems content only to look forward to a new car. Or business deal. Or the next round of golf." He shook his head in wonder. "Rarely do they look forward to that glorious world You promised."

"As they age, they imagine they pass their peaks," the Carpenter said. "But Elyon's children never pass their peaks. The best is never behind God's children. The best is always ahead."

"I wish sometimes we could talk to our Clarence," Obadiah said. "And Harley. And our grandchillens. And Ollie Chandler. I could tell 'em that the last of their lives before they dies is *not* the last of their lives. When they dies they go on a-livin'. They just moves to another place. Clarence believes it in his head, but maybe not his heart. Ollie doesn't believe it at all."

"Our lives here are so rich, better by far than our lives ever were there," Ruby said.

"Yet even here we awaits resurrection mornin'," Obadiah said, smiling broadly. "And the meantime's as sweet as lickin' the spoon of Mama's beef stew on the stove. We long for Elyon to bring His kingdom to earth, where we gonna live again on that world *You* made for us," he said to the Carpenter. Obadiah bowed his knee before Him, Ruby bowing by his side.

"What I have planned is far beyond what even you imagine," He said to Obadiah, placing His hands on their heads. "Together, as My kings and queens, you will reign with Me over a new universe. And billions of years from now, you will still be young."

Though I told myself I didn't want attention, I was disappointed at how few people came by my desk to give me their sympathy so I could brush them off and be the tough guy, saying something like, "Hanging, what hanging?" But after Jack left, only Cimma had come in, and he only said, "You okay?" without breaking his gimpy stride. Paul Anderson and a couple of larceny detectives came by and asked for my story, but that was it.

So I sat and read the *Tribune*. Then I decided to read one last time an article not yet printed in the *Trib*, but which was about to be submitted. It was a guest column written by a cop:

Call me Ollie.

The full name's Oliver Justice Chandler.

I am a detective.

The detective must set aside assumptions that blind him to the truth. He must follow the evidence wherever it leads.

Beneath every mystery, every unsolved crime, is an unseen world of habits, attitudes and motives. It's a world detectives must explore. That's why I walk our city's asphalt jungle.

Detectives must familiarize ourselves with what lies in the shadows. We must learn to see the unseen. Optimists believe the human heart is good. They're surprised by evil and quick to deny it, in themselves and others. Many murderers show regret at being caught. But they believe their crime was justified.

There's good in the unseen realm, but there's also evil. There's a malice that drives men's hearts toward unspeakable crimes. The detective is a truth hunter. He must pursue truth relentlessly.

I've known model sons who've given their frail mothers love and care. "He's a wonderful boy," everyone says. But probing deep, I have broken the skin and exposed the pus underneath. A homicidal pus. It surfaces in an over-heard conversation, a scrawled note, subtle signs of resentment and blame.

After discovering these threads of evidence, I sew them together to prove that a model son was his mother's murderer.

Right now at least one murderer is reading this column. He thinks he'll get away with three murders and attempts on my own life. He's wrong. I'm going to catch him.

Like Green Lantern of old, I am a relentless seeker of truth and upholder of justice. I make my pledge to this city as Green Lantern did: "In brightest day, in darkest night, no evil shall escape my sight. Let those who worship evil's might, beware my power…Green Lantern's light!"

Crime must be punished. Justice must be done. The boil must be lanced, the pus removed.

The name's Chandler. Ollie Chandler. I am a detective.

Justice is my middle name.

↔

Crossing the Morrison Bridge heading east, I decided to drop off my masterpiece at Clarence's house in North Portland.

Clarence's house is immaculate, lawn edged and alive even in winter, and picket fence a perfect glossy white. It doesn't remind me of my place. Geneva hugged me, and a couple of teenagers—Clarence's daughter Keisha and her cousin Celeste—extended their hands, made eye contact, and distinctly said "Hello." No mumbling. Respect is big in the Abernathy family. Clarence's daddy would be proud.

"Here's my guest article," I announced to Clarence, handing it to him, neatly printed out in a cool font called Franklin Gothic Medium, which I picked out after trying a couple dozen.

"I'll read it and let you know."

"Why not read it now?"

He sat down at the kitchen table while Geneva offered coffee. Earl Grey was mercifully absent. She took me in the family room and showed me another Negro League team picture they'd located, the 1949 Birmingham Black Barons. There was Obadiah Abernathy, smile bigger than life.

After fifteen minutes lost in memorabilia and telling Geneva how much I missed her father-in-law, I came back to Clarence, now sitting in the living room. My eye caught a furry little creature in a cage, spinning on a wheel.

"Didn't know you had a hamster," I said.

"Clarence brought him home last week," Geneva said. "He's adorable. The kids love him."

"What's his name?"

"Brent," she said.

Clarence pretended to read, ignoring my grin.

"What do you think of my article?" I asked.

"Well," Clarence said, "I hardly know what to say."

"That good?"

"It needs…a little editing."

"What do you mean *editing*?"

Clarence pointed toward an *American Heritage* dictionary on the shelf. "Look it up."

"What's wrong with it?"

"It's a bit…melodramatic. 'Call me Ollie'? 'The name's Chandler. Ollie Chandler. I am a detective'?"

"You make it sound silly."

"It sounds silly on its own. Reminds me of *Dragnet*."

"I like Joe Friday."

"It shows."

"What else?"

"'Justice is my middle name'?"

"Justice *is* my middle name."

"I know, but… Anyway, who's Green Lantern?"

I looked at him. "Charter member, Justice League of America. Dell Comics. Hal Jordan, test pilot. What college did you go to?"

"Oregon State University."

"What'd they teach you anyway?"

He pointed at my article. "Asphalt jungle? And the pus thing's got to go."

"Why?"

"People read the paper over breakfast. We don't want them puking on the *Trib*."

"Isn't that redundant?"

"And yet you want to write for it, don't you?"

"You said I could."

"No pus. I'll ratchet down the melodrama so nobody laughs at you."

"I want to see your edit before it goes to press."

"I've got to get Celeste to volleyball."

"Go ahead. But you and your loved ones sleep peacefully tonight because of the work I do. You and Geneva and the kids and Brent."

He straightened his back and saluted me. "Go, walk our city's asphalt jungle, Green Lantern. For your middle name is Justice. And you are Ollie Chandler, detective…lancer of boils and relentless foe of pus."

I suspect he wasn't entirely sincere.

28

"When Gregson, or Lestrade, or Athelney Jones are out of their depths—which, by the way, is their normal state—the matter is laid before me."
SHERLOCK HOLMES, *THE SIGN OF FOUR*

MONDAY, DECEMBER 16, 12:15 P.M.

IT WAS A COLD DAY but sunny; time for lunch at Lou's again. On our table was one big light blue bloom. Rory called it a hydrangea. I took his word for it.

"You used to come only on Thursdays," Rory said. "I am happy to see you more often."

"We've got more to talk about right now," I said.

"It is always a pleasure to serve the three of you." I found myself wishing more people were like Rory Santelli. It would be a better world.

I asked the guys if this time we could put a hold on the Christian stuff. I wasn't in the mood.

They asked me what was next on the Palatine case. I said hang on and pulled out the only quarter I had. I looked for "MacArthur Park," history's longest song, with the quality of lyrics—sung by an actor, not a singer—that makes it seem even longer. I pressed C5 three times. If we needed it, that should cover us a couple of days.

"I'm going to check out a few alibis myself," I said as I sat down. "Karl Baylor first."

"Why Karl?" Clarence asked.

"I don't like the way he struts around showing off his gun."

"You're criticizing a man for being attached to his gun?" Jake asked.

"He's a Jesus freak. Isn't he supposed to be a pacifist?"

"If he were a pacifist, you'd berate him for that too," Jake said. "You're not judging him because he's a Christian, are you?"

"He can kiss the Blarney stone or worship the dung beetle for all I care."

"Listen to yourself."

"You try listening to me first, and let me know how it is."

"I *have* been listening—and trust me, you're not missing much. Seriously, Ollie, what have you got against Baylor?"

"I just don't like him."

"I detect a history, Detective. You going to deny that?"

"Okay." I gestured too dramatically, then put my hands around the coffee cup to keep them down. "After Sharon died, I came back to the office. It was…weird."

"Like people didn't know what to say."

"Yeah. Exactly."

"Same thing happened when Finney and Doc were killed."

"Same with Dani and Felicia," Clarence said. "People say nothing, or sometimes they say the wrong thing."

"Anyway," I said, "most guys looked the other way or said 'Sorry' when they passed by. Jack and Noel took me out for a beer. We talked about sports. Tommi was the only one who hugged me, which was fine. I don't want to be hugged by Cimmatoni. Kim Suda got me a Hallmark card. Point is, I didn't have to say anything back."

"What did Baylor do?"

My hands started moving, and I restrained them again. "He comes up to me by the snack table and says, 'I'm sorry.' Okay. Thought he was done. But no, he's a *Christian*. He has to say something more. So he says, 'She's with Jesus; she's better off.' She's better off? She's dead, for crying out loud. And if there's a Jesus, He's got plenty of other people with Him. Why did He need my wife? But Baylor still wouldn't stop. He says, 'Somehow it'll all work out for the best.'"

"He really said that?" Clarence asked.

"I'll never forget it. Then he quoted from the Bible, saying her death was really a good thing."

"I'll bet it was Romans 8:28," Clarence said. "'All things work together for good to those who love God.'"

"That was it. He was saying my wife's better off without me."

"That's not what he meant," Jake said.

"You're as big a know-it-all as he is, aren't you?"

"I'm just saying that—"

"Jesus has Sharon, but I don't. I'm supposed to be happy about that?"

"MacArthur Park" started over. They both looked at the Rock-Ola, then at me.

"Not again," Clarence mumbled.

"Hey, I only had a quarter. You wanna limbo with Chubby Checker, cough up your own two bits!"

"Okay," Jake said, "Baylor shouldn't have said it that way. I think he was trying to comfort, but he used the wrong words. The passage he quoted is true, but there's a right place and time and way to say it. That was the wrong one. I've done the same thing…we Christians can be dopes, just like everybody else."

"*More* than everybody else. Give me an atheist any day. Give me Bertrand Russell. He'd never say something stupid like that."

"Don't set up atheists as your role models. Professor Palatine was a Bertrand Russell fan. You don't idolize him, do you?"

"I don't even think God exists," I said.

"If He doesn't," Jake said, "then why are you so mad at Him?"

I stared at him, but he didn't melt. "At least an atheist wouldn't tell me God had a reason for killing Sharon. What it comes down to is if there's a God and He's all-powerful, then He chose for her to die. Am I right or am I wrong?"

"There's truth in it, but I wouldn't put it that way exactly," Jake said.

"Right. Because your job is to be God's PR guy, to run interference, bolster His public image."

"He doesn't need me for PR."

"Yeah? Well, He's not doing so well on His own."

"He doesn't look at His approval ratings. And we don't get a vote." Jake cocked his head. "Did you tell Baylor how you felt when he said that?"

"No, Dr. Phil. I didn't."

As I walked out the door Richard Harris was singing "Someone left a cake out in the rain."

Right, I thought. *Exactly.*

MONDAY, DECEMBER 16, 3:30 P.M.

Two hours later I sat in the Gresham WinCo parking lot, wearing a Mariners baseball cap and an old camo jacket, faded green and brown. No trench coat, no fedora. I don't wear glasses except for reading, but I have a pair of thick ones with uncorrected lenses for special occasions. I'd never met Karl Baylor's wife, but if I ever saw her again, I didn't want to be recognized.

I'd followed her from her house. I watched her get out of her navy blue Toyota. She was short and energetic, walking briskly, two kids in tow.

After studying her movements in WinCo, I positioned myself at the end of the next aisle. As she was slowly moving her cart, looking at a display of Nalley bread and butter pickles, I backed into her, assuming the posture of someone who'd established position. It's an art form, like Allen Iverson drawing the charge.

Her cart hit me.

"I'm so sorry," she said. "I should have been watching."

"No problem." I looked at her, like she was familiar. "Didn't I see you at that church... Um, Good Shepherd, was that it?"

"Yes. Good Shepherd Community Church. You go there?"

"Not often." As in, not ever.

"I'm Tiffany Baylor," she said, reaching out her little hand. "My husband's Karl.

These are our children, Matthew and Kivren."

I smiled at the cute kids. "When I was at your church, seems like they were talking about a couples conference. In Gresham, right?"

"The Holiday Inn on Hogan. Karl and I went. It was great."

"Nice you could get the time off."

"Usually they're on weekends but this was a Tuesday and Wednesday night. Karl's schedule's weird. He's a police officer."

I raised my hands. "I didn't do it."

She laughed. "People always say stuff like that. He's a detective. Anyway, he works weird hours. Sometimes in the middle of the night."

"You were lucky to make it through the conference without him getting called out."

"Actually he did get called out on police business after we'd gone to bed. But by the time I woke up, he was back. He was tired, but he can get by on a few hours' sleep."

"Too bad he got called away your first night."

"Second night. Tuesday we were together every minute. It was glorious."

"I have a buddy who's a police detective in LA. He and his wife go to bed at ten, but she says he gets 3:00 a.m. calls."

She nodded. "Same with Karl. That night he got called after 10:30, but I was asleep, barely heard the phone. He gets up, kisses me good night. Next thing I know it's morning, and he's there beside me. Said he was gone just a few hours. I sleep like a log when we're away from the kids." She giggled like a schoolgirl, taking a jar of red hot salsa from Matthew and putting it back on the shelf.

"What do you do?" she asked.

"Self-employed," I said. "Management consulting. Pays the bills while I write a novel."

"I lead a women's Bible study at church on Wednesday mornings. Your wife might enjoy it."

"Oh. My wife isn't...she died."

"Oh, I'm sorry." At least she didn't quote the Bible to tell me it was okay. "I shouldn't have assumed you... Sometimes I talk before I think. I'm really sorry. I hope we see you in church again. I'd love for you to meet Karl. I know you'd like him. What did you say your name is?"

"Uh, Joe. Joe Greenley. Pleasure to meet you, Tiffany."

"What'd you learn about Karl Baylor?" Clarence asked as we sat at my workstation.

"I like his wife better than I like him. Also, he's a liar. His alibi doesn't hold."

"No kidding?"

"That Wednesday night he left around 10:30. Supposedly he was called away on police business. His wife didn't see him until morning. He could've been gone five hours, and she wouldn't have known."

"He wouldn't have needed five hours," Clarence said.

"Two would have been plenty. Hotel's maybe twenty minutes from Palatine's."

"Who called him?"

"Couldn't have been homicide. There were just two cases that night, ours and Jack and Noel's. But he told his wife it was police work. He lied to her. And to us."

"You got all that out of her?"

I nodded.

"Think Baylor will be mad at you for interviewing his wife?"

"She didn't know she was being interviewed."

"How could she not know?"

"You'd be surprised what people don't know. Things aren't always as they appear, remember? That can work in the detective's favor too. It's a game, really. We have to outplay other people in order to outplay the killer."

"You make it sound like chess."

"I play chess. Most criminals play checkers. Take my murder before last. Lincoln Caldwell blows away Jimmy Ross. He lets himself be seen in the hallway, in his red sweatpants, of all things. Then he leaves fingerprints at the scene. And manages to cut himself and leave blood! Stupid is as stupid does. Caldwell holds a patent on stupid."

"Stupid." Clarence said, pointing pen at pad. "Got it."

"The smart ones have a plan. They wear gloves. Disguises. Even a ski mask works. If they know police procedure, they know if they're not holding a gun they won't be shot, even if they're running away, not without multiple warnings. Even then it's a last resort."

"And he'd know they'd have to get back to the crime scene quick," Clarence said.

"Right. He knows they'd have to break off pursuit and hightail it back to Palatine's."

Clarence scratched more notes. "A homicide detective would make a smart killer."

"Sure. Take your friend Karl Baylor, who told one lie to his wife and another to us to give him an alibi."

"He's not my friend. I met him two weeks ago."

"Suppose the killer's disguise isn't a ski mask. Suppose it's being a church-attending guy. Going to church places him above suspicion."

"Sounds to me like that's what makes you suspect him."

"I've tagged killers who go to church every Sunday."

"You've probably tagged killers who help the poor. That doesn't mean people who help the poor should be your primary suspects."

"A homicide detective would think it through, do his homework, draw up a plan. Wouldn't use a credit card to buy fertilizer for an explosive. Doesn't ask, 'Anybody know how much cyanide it takes to kill someone?' People remember those questions. He doesn't Google 'how to kill your boss' so his hard drive has a history of murder tips. If he does, he uses someone else's computer or knows how to erase his seven times so computer forensics can't recover it. If he prints hard copy, he burns it, doesn't put it out in his trash. Doesn't stand in front of surveillance cameras at the department store where he buys a pickax."

"He knows how you think as well as you know how he'd think, right?"

"Detectives peel away layers of lies to find the truth buried beneath. A smart killer creates the illusion he didn't do it. He makes sure no evidence points to him and some evidence points elsewhere."

"Like the fingerprints?"

"Nearly worked. But he also raises suspicions. This investigation's like walking through a circus fun house. You see a lot, but it's distorted. We have to get past the deception to see things as they really are."

"You're a truth seeker," Clarence said. "And truth seekers have open minds?"

"Sure. It's not enough to know somebody's lying. Many people lie. We need to know why they're lying. Sherlock Holmes said people lie for three reasons: to gain, to cover, or to protect. So what's your friend Karl Baylor hoping to gain by his lies? Who's he covering? Who's he protecting? My guess? Just himself."

WEDNESDAY, DECEMBER 18, 7:00 P.M.

The homicide detail gathered for a reception at the Heathman Hotel in downtown Portland. Sergeant Seymour kicked it off by saying, "Things have been tense lately. We got permission from the captain to use some budgeted funds for this party. No offense intended in not inviting spouses, but we thought we needed some positive time just for the team. We've got crab cakes, deli cheeses, baked breads, Greek salad, cheesecakes, and blackberry pie. You're off duty, and we've got your favorite drinks. Karl and Tommi are the up team, so there's water and coffee and pop for them. Everybody else, drink up!"

While Bing Crosby sang "White Christmas" in the background, Chris and Kim huddled, giving me dirty looks.

I'd suggested to Sarge that we have this party. I'd done my homework and made sure everybody's favorite alcohol was present, from Chris's Coors Light, to Cimmatoni's Scotch, to Phillips's wine coolers, to Tommi's Chablis, to the Budweisers that covered the rest of us.

It was then that Phillips dragged out of his pocket a compact surveillance device detector and started sweeping the room with it.

Jack teased him as he walked around the edges of the room, moving it up and down the walls, sweeping it under the tables, and even into the Christmas tree.

"Who'd be bugging us?" Tommi asked when he was half done.

Phillips said nothing but looked straight at me. It had come to that.

Ten minutes later, after the room passed the test, I said with all the indignation I could muster, "You actually think I'd rig something up at a Christmas party and treat you like you're a bunch of lowlifes?"

"Sorry," Phillips said. "I had to check."

I walked away, shaking my head in disgust. I leaned against the wall by myself, next to a tall decorative plant. Tommi came over and put her hand on my arm. "Everybody's under pressure, and things have been tense. Brandon didn't mean anything by it."

"I may not seem like a sensitive guy," I said. "But I gotta tell you, that really hurt."

Tommi talked to me another five minutes, trying to cheer me up. When she walked back toward her table, I turned away, looked into the camera I'd rigged up inside the thick plant, and grinned.

An audience of three was watching me in the small room next door, requested from the Heathman for "police business." Officer Paul Anderson still owed me three hours, and I promised to bring him some refreshments. Ray Eagle was taping through the surveillance device that he told me had an 80 percent chance of not being seen even if someone brought a bug sweeper. I told him nobody'd do that. I don't know what made Phillips suspicious, but I could've kissed Ray.

I couldn't see the camera lens peeking out of its green and brown casing, but I knew it was there. I looked that direction and mouthed, "Ray, I owe you a donut." Then I said in a hoarse whisper, "Hi, Paul. Hey, Clarence...how's Brent? Can you dunk it?"

It was Clarence's job to record everybody's drink intake. I'd explained my theory: "The murderer has to stay alert. That means if he's smart—and this guy's smart—he'll drink less. He knows he needs his wits. He knows it's important not to let something slip. If you're innocent, you're not worried. You can drink all you want."

Clarence had been there an hour early to see exactly where each drink was. The camera had a wide-angle lens, but he wouldn't be able to read labels. Cimmatoni was drinking Scotch like a fish. Jack and Noel downed beers at a fair pace. Tommi had Diet Coke but worked in half a Chablis before someone reminded her she was on the up team. Karl Baylor had Dr. Pepper. Kim Suda, V8. Manny seemed under par with the drinking. I felt guilty keeping him out of the loop on the surveillance but had to treat him as a suspect.

Chris Doyle opened a beer, but I never saw him drink it. That's way under par—not just a birdie, but an eagle, maybe a hole in one. Though the Coors Light was right beside him, he resorted to water. I had water in a dark cup so it wasn't obvious I wasn't drinking booze.

People ate at one of three tables. Lots of hushed tones and private conversations. By 8:30 desserts had been eaten. The room grew quiet.

"Still chasing one of us, Chandler?" Chris Doyle boomed.

After an uncomfortable silence I said, "There've been three murders, and they're all linked to Palatine. Anybody can see the evidence suggests it could be one of us. They're threatening to turn it over to Internal Affairs or bring in an outside agency. Then we'll all be guilty until proven innocent. That what you want?"

"So instead you're going to be our judge?" Suda asked. "I'd take my chances with the outside agency."

"State police?" I asked.

"Or Department of Justice?" Sarge said. "Attorney General's office?"

A hotel staffer walked in, but when eleven known cops turned and stared at her, she said, "Let me know if you need anything," then pivoted on her heel and disappeared.

"Ninety percent of us are innocent," I said. "But the only way to establish our innocence is to establish someone else's guilt. If the killer isn't in this room, I'll be relieved. But if he is...then don't all the rest of us want him caught?"

"Easy for you to say," Chris Doyle said.

"Easy for me?" I opened my shirt collar, showing the rope burns.

"Not to mention the shotgun blast through his kitchen window," Tommi said.

I was hoping Ray could zoom in and get a reading on faces.

I pride myself on my ability to expect the unexpected. But what happened next confirmed that truth really is stranger than fiction.

Bryce Cimmatoni, who'd been downing Scotch for an hour and a half without saying a word, cleared his throat. "I have something to say."

Everyone was riveted, because Cimmatoni has a history of making his normally rude remarks without asking for the floor.

"I planned the murder," he said. "I scoped out his house. I knew what I had to do. I knew I could get away. I hated the man. He didn't deserve to live. I thought through every step, every detail. I remember the night I decided to kill him."

"There is an appalling directness about your questions, Watson. They come at me like bullets."
SHERLOCK HOLMES, *THE VALLEY OF FEAR*

I'VE NEVER SEEN a group of cops more stunned. The room was completely silent. Everyone froze, including me.

When Cimmatoni talked, he kept his chin low, against the crown of his chest, then looked through the tops of his eyes like a boxer in a crouch. His head tilted forward, and he gazed up from under his brows. Even in a confession, I felt like an uppercut was coming.

"What'd you do?" I asked.

"Went to his house. I'd picked the murder weapon. Untraceable."

"Did he come to the door?"

"Yeah."

"Let you in?"

"Yeah."

"Then what?"

"I pulled my gun."

Tommi did something no one else would have considered. She went and sat down next to Cimmatoni. "Why, Bryce? What did he do to you?"

"Sold drugs to my nephew, my sister's only kid. Kenny overdosed, went into a coma. Year later they pulled the plug."

"The professor sold drugs to your nephew?" I asked.

He looked up, dazed, trying to think his way through the Scotch. He scrunched his forehead.

"Professor?...No. He was a drug dealer, on Fourth and Alameda."

"You killed him?"

He gazed long and hard. "Threatened him. Waved my gun in his face, stuck the barrel up his mouth till I couldn't push it any farther. Sometimes I wish I'd pulled the trigger. They let him out of prison six months ago. He's selling drugs again. I drive by and look at him once a week. Sometimes I pull my gun and just sit there, thinking about it."

"What's stopped you from killing him?" I asked.

"I knew I could do it. I knew I could get away with it. I knew he deserved it. But...I'm a cop."

"So, Bryce, you didn't really kill anybody?" Phillips asked.

"Came so close I could taste it. Felt the pressure on my trigger finger. Close enough to see it in my mind, to see the blood splatter."

"But you didn't really do it," Tommi said. "Right?"

Cimmatoni nodded.

Never was a party as over as that one.

While everyone collected their things and headed for the door, I stood and stared at Bryce Cimmatoni. I wondered how many skeletons were in his closet, and how many things didn't come out of his lips that could've. I've seen a lot of drunks, including the one who looks back at me from the mirror. But never have I seen a better argument for not getting drunk around people you know.

I knocked on the room next door, one light, one heavy, one light. Paul Anderson peeked out and let me in. Clarence handed me his list:

Cimmatoni—Six Scotch and waters

Phillips—one wine cooler

Jack—two Budweisers

Noel—three Budweisers

Manny—one Irish Cream, one beer

Tommi—one glass of wine, half-finished, one Diet Coke

Karl Baylor—two Dr. Peppers, one decaf coffee, no alcohol

Kim Suda—one V8, one diet Sprite, no alcohol

Chris—one Coors Light (unfinished), two waters, two cups decaf

Ollie—water

"We'll talk about it tomorrow," I said. "We're done for the day."

They nodded. I drove home, but stopped for two hours at Rosie O'Grady's, where I didn't drink water.

I don't have many dreams I can remember. And I've found that the wonder and terror of a dream dissipates in telling it.

My dream that Wednesday night doesn't remember like a dream. It remembers like reality, which is why I'm still shaking from it.

It began in a fantastically beautiful place, with trees, flowers, gardens, rivers, lakes, and animals, including dogs of every breed. It was a huge city with stunning architecture, massive gates, and colorfully dressed people coming in and out. The people smiled and laughed—not the forced smiles and guarded laughter of someone trying to be happy. It was the irreplaceable joy of a person who *is* happy, with no thought of trying. The people there reminded me of Little Finn and Obadiah Abernathy.

I saw a writer and two artists contemplating boats going down the great river. People on the boats waved and occasionally jumped into the water, laughing. Those beside the river picked fruit off trees, smiling broadly at unprecedented tastes. They offered fruit to each other, freely taking bites and comparing. And the fragrances—I can still smell them, like the gardenias at Lou's but far more fresh and potent. A hundred different fragrances, each distinct. And a spectrum of colors, thousands of colors, including ones I remember but can't describe.

Some people ran, some played basketball and tennis, some chased and wrestled on the ground with animals—including lions, cheetahs, and panthers. Others rested. Everyone did what they wanted. I saw no scars, limps, disabilities, no one dragged down by age or disease or bad memories or emotional baggage. No one appeared cynical, suspicious, or threatening. No one taped guns under tables. A city with all the beauty of the country and with no hint of fear.

People's nods to each other seemed to say, "We're passing each other now, but one day we'll be introduced, and we'll eat or walk or play together and enjoy each others' stories."

It dawned on me that while there was much to do and the place called out for me to explore it, I was out of a job. The last thing this place needed was a homicide detective. It was like a brand-new earth, a planet that couldn't be bad any more than water can be dry. I knew that everything in me, every skill and gift and passion, every thirst for knowledge, could be invested forever in the endless pursuits of this fascinating world.

I was immersed in sweetness, in joy itself. I saw two great warriors standing at the gate of the city, admitting some while turning away others, according to whether their names were written in a huge open book on a great wooden stand just inside the gate.

A realization suddenly hit me like a spear thrown hard at my chest. I wasn't really inside this world. I'd been outside looking in.

Right then there appeared an old-fashioned train, vintage 1920, bound for the city gates only a hundred feet away. It pulled up next to me. From inside the train an arm reached down to me. A hand rested on my shoulder, a strong, coal-black hand, white under the fingernails.

I looked up through the train window into those big moist eyes. He said something to me. Though the dream itself began to fade after I wrote it down, that voice and these words are as clear now as when they'd just been spoken: "Son, it's gettin' late now. Soon be time to go home. Can't get on board widout yo' ticket. You has yo' ticket yet?"

Suddenly the train pulled away. Obadiah Abernathy never took his eyes off me until he was at the gate. Then he turned to enter that glorious world. In a moment the train had entered the city and disappeared into its wonders. I'd been left on the outside, standing under the forbidding glare of the guardians at the gate.

I awoke shivering, T-shirt soaking wet. I had no instinct to reach for my gun. I knew this was a danger no gun could save me from.

THURSDAY, DECEMBER 19

"It's all about perspective," I said to Ray and Clarence at Lou's, admiring the yellow flower I didn't recognize but that smelled like honey. Ray had pressed "Hey, Jude" and was timing it, betting me a milkshake it was longer than "MacArthur Park."

"You have to see things not as you assume they'd be, but as they truly are. In the face of the truth, your assumptions are often proved wrong."

"So sometimes you have to let go of your assumptions to see the truth?" Clarence asked.

"Exactly."

"And some people are too stubborn to let go and take a fresh look at the situation?"

"Yeah. But you'll never be a great detective if you can't reexamine your assumptions."

"Assumptions," Clarence said, "like…a good God can't allow suffering? And because some Christians are jerks, Jesus isn't worth believing in?"

"Those are more like conclusions than assumptions," I said. "But that's not our topic, is it? Any thoughts on last night's drama at the Heathman?"

"Quite a performance by Cimmatoni," Ray said.

"Crazy as it was, I sympathize with Cimma," I said. "I've committed hundreds of murders."

"This a confession?" Ray asked.

"I've committed murders in my mind. In detail. It's my job. If I hadn't, I wouldn't be such a great detective."

"And the other detectives, they do the same, right?" Ray said. "Play out murders in their minds?"

"Like a manager plays out a baseball game. To catch a thief, you have to think like one."

"Hey, Jude" ended. "Seven minutes four seconds," I said. "'MacArthur Park' beats it by seventeen seconds." Ray coughed up for an orange malt. "'American Pie' is eight minutes, but it came on two sides of a 45, so it doesn't count," I said. Ray took off, knowing he'd been schooled. After my malt, Clarence and I stood by my car discussing the case.

"Chandler!" It was Manny, face strung tight, eyes on fire. He came uncomfortably close to me and Clarence. "You homeboys cookin' it up?"

"Settle down, Manny," I said. "What's up?"

"What's up is that you called Maria to check my alibi."

"Well, you said you were with the kids. Who else was I supposed to call? Your kids?"

"Ever do that and I'll take you down myself," he said, index finger thumping my chest. "Hear me?"

"Threatening murder isn't the best way to get your name off a suspect list."

"Why am I even on the suspect list?"

"Because *everybody's* on it."

"You suspect me of something, you come to me first. Got it?"

"Well, that's a great relational principle there, and I'm sure Oprah would approve, but when it comes to suspect lists, you don't check out alibis by asking people if they're telling the truth. It's too easy for the killer to say yes, don't you think?"

"And what's *your* alibi?" Manny spat.

"Rosie O'Grady's pub."

"So if I was to talk to the bartender, he'd say you were there?"

"Yeah."

"What if he says you left before 10:00?"

"I'd say you checked up on me."

"Yeah. How does it feel?"

"I thought you were there until midnight," Clarence said.

"That what he told you?" Manny asked. "Then he's a liar. Maybe there's a job for him at the *Tribune*! You could always use another liar."

"The truth is…I don't know when I left Rosie's."

"You do know because the bartender told you, like he did me."

"My partner, who was checking my alibi."

"After I found out you were checking mine."

"So we're even."

"We're not even. You threw the first punch."

"And you punched him back," Clarence said. "Sounds even to me."

"You don't know nothin' about street fighting, do you, Mr. Suit and Tie suburb boy?"

"Don't call me boy."

"I'll call you boy if I want to, boy." He pivoted, standing ten inches from my face. "And what about the Black Jack you stole from the crime scene, Detective?"

"A blackjack at the crime scene?" Clarence asked.

"Not the weapon, the gum, goofball," Manny said.

"The weapon's a lot more dangerous than the gum," I said. "You could slap a guy with the gum, and it wouldn't even draw blood."

"This wise guy here found a Black Jack wrapper at the crime scene and picked it up, hid the evidence."

"Is that true?" Clarence asked.

I nodded.

"Why didn't you tell me?"

"It had his fingerprints on it," Manny said. "He knew it would. Didn't you, Chandler?"

Somebody'd been spilling my secrets.

"Your fingerprints were on something found at the crime scene?" Clarence asked.

"Finally sinking in, boy?" Manny turned back toward me. "You don't know where you were at the time of the murder, do you?"

"No."

"Instead of withholding evidence and treating us like we're killers, you should be turning yourself in." Manny thumped me on the chest again with the knuckles of his closed fist. Hard.

"You need to calm down." Clarence stepped between us.

"Stay out of this, *boy*," Manny said.

Before I knew what was happening, Clarence bear-hugged Manny and squeezed him like a bagpipe. Manny's wiry, athletic, and quick. But Abernathy had him in a death grip. Manny kicked and grunted, but his feet were eighteen inches off the ground, and all he was getting was Clarence's shins. He was a Jack Russell wrestling a Rottweiler.

"Let him go," I said.

Then I saw something in Clarence's eyes that scared me. I heard a sickening crunch. I pulled my Glock and pointed it at Clarence's forehead.

"I mean it, Abernathy. Let him go."

Clarence's eyes were wild one moment and tame the next. He dropped Manny to the parking lot like a rag doll.

Gun still in my right hand, I knelt by Manny. He was catching his breath and drenched with sweat. "You okay?"

"Rib's...broken."

"I'm...sorry," Clarence said to me, from above.

"You might want to tell Manny," I said. "My ribs are still attached."

"Sorry," Clarence said.

Manny stood up, more quickly than he should have. I was trying to support him when he threw a hard punch that landed short of Abernathy's chin, right on his left pectoral. Apparently the rib wouldn't let him extend the punch, because it's the first time I've ever seen Manny miss a punch.

Clarence made no effort to retaliate. His usually straight neck was bent.

"We're not even yet," Manny said. "But we're gonna be, *boy.*"

"I'm sorry," Clarence said, dazed. "I shouldn't have…"

"Let's get you to the hospital," I said.

"I'm fine," Manny said, wheezing.

"Either I drive you or I'm calling 911."

I tried to support Manny on one side with Clarence on the other, but it wasn't working. His eyes were drooping now. I was trying to ease him to the ground when Clarence picked him up in his arms. Manny offered no resistance.

I put my gun away and held my 1 button for 911.

THURSDAY, DECEMBER 19, 3:00 P.M.

On the bright side, the fight between Clarence and Manny took the focus off my belonging on the suspect list. And lying about my alibi. And blacking out. And withholding self-incriminating evidence from the crime scene.

If I wasn't sure I was innocent, why should anyone else believe I was?

Clarence and I sat in another emergency room, this one at Adventist Medical Center. It was my third trip to emergency in two weeks. Nice not being the patient for once.

"I'm sorry," Clarence said.

"You've mentioned that," I said. "Repeatedly. Manny had it coming. He always has it coming. But if we were to give everybody what they had coming, we'd all be in jail, wouldn't we?"

"I won't blame him if he presses charges."

"Manny? An old street fighter like him? He won't press charges. He handles things himself. How's your insurance?"

"Insurance?"

"Health? Disability? Life? You might want to check it out. But the good news is, Manny hated your guts already. I doubt this is going to make it much worse."

"I'm a Christian. I shouldn't have done that."

"Yeah, well, I've seen lots of Christians do what they shouldn't." I looked at him. "On the other hand, I've rarely heard them admit they were wrong. It's refreshing."

"Daddy'd be ashamed of me."

"I got to know your daddy pretty well. He's the main reason I'm willing to put up with you. But he was awfully proud of you. I think he'd be proud of you for admitting you're wrong."

Something inside me, like a voice, suggested I should admit I'd been wrong about some things too. Fortunately, I could ignore it.

A nurse came out. Her name tag said Angela Stiz. "You're police officers, right? Manuel's your friend?"

I nodded, letting Clarence become an honorary police officer and honorary friend of Manny.

"Dr. Nakamura sent me. He's with another patient, but he'll be out when he can. Your friend, Manuel…he's got a broken rib with a contusion. Bruised lung but not punctured. He's lucky. He says some wild man squeezed him. Probably a meth addict. When people are on meth, they do crazy things."

"We deal with lots of crazies," I said.

"We get our share in here too," Angela confirmed.

"Somebody's got to protect the decent folk from the crazies," I said. "Right, Officer Abernathy?"

Clarence didn't give me the satisfaction of looking my way.

"The guy's in jail, right?" Angela asked. "Off the streets?"

"Well, he's not on the streets," I said. "Probably having a pleasant conversation with someone who doesn't have a clue that he broke a cop's rib while suffocating him. But he'll be out on the streets again. I pity the people who'll have to deal with him."

"Me too," Angela said. "I wish there weren't so many nutcases out there."

"He's really going to be okay?" Clarence asked.

"I think so. He's a little cranky, but anybody would be after what he went through."

"Yeah," I said. "Usually Manny's a sweetheart, but when you're attacked so viciously, it can change you."

"Listen," Nurse Angela said, "why don't you go visit him, one at a time? Seeing his friends will cheer him up. You want to go first, Officer?" she said to Abernathy.

"Yeah, you go first, Clarence," I said. "That'll make him feel better. You've always had a calming effect on Manny."

"Follow me," she said.

"Come on, Clarence. It'll do him good. Do you have your Bible with you?" I looked at Nurse Angela. "He's sort of a police chaplain. He can quote Scriptures about turning the other cheek and things like that. He's like a big brother to Manny. Extremely big."

"If you don't have your Bible, I can get you one," she said, cheerfully.

"No. Thanks."

"Tell you what," I said. "We'll give Manny a little more time before we see him. We'll just be out here…praying for him."

"That's nice," she said. "He's fortunate to have friends like you."

I sat there, feeling a warm smugness. After a minute of silence it still felt good.

"What about you?" Clarence said.

"What about me?"

"You said it was refreshing to hear me admit I was wrong. What about you? You lied about your alibi? And the Black Jack wrapper had your prints on it? And you removed incriminating evidence from a crime scene?"

"Okay, I lied, but it wasn't a big lie. In Washington DC it would pass for the unvarnished truth. Senators would swear by it on their mothers' graves."

"The great defender of justice rationalizes his injustice," Clarence said. "Guess I'm not the only hypocrite, am I? You were really so drunk you don't remember where you were?"

"I don't."

"That's a serious problem," Clarence said.

"Yeah."

"So you're not only a hypocrite, but you're on the suspect list, aren't you?"

I no longer felt smug.

"While the individual man is an insoluble puzzle, in the aggregate he becomes a mathematical certainty. You can, for example, never foretell what any one man will do, but you can say with precision what an average number will be up to. Individuals vary, but percentages remain constant."
SHERLOCK HOLMES, *THE SIGN OF FOUR*

FRIDAY, DECEMBER 20

CLARENCE AND I walked the streets on a beautiful Portland morning, sunny, crisp, and chilly. Christmas was on the signs, in the shops, on the trees, and in the air. A blue-jeaned, red-jacketed guitarist played "Silent Night." I dropped a buck in his open guitar case. Call me a philanthropist. Me and Bill Gates. I don't tire of Christmas.

What I do tire of are the things that keep me from enjoying Christmas. Unsolved murders are among them. We were walking toward the parking garage to Clarence's SUV, which had two bicycles in the back since I'd given in to Clarence's badgering and agreed to go for a ride.

Clarence drove across the Hawthorne Bridge and southeast to Johnson Creek, where we parked and got on the Springwater Corridor Trail.

"Motive is everything," I told Clarence between huffs and puffs as we rode our bikes toward Gresham. "If we find the motive, we have him...or her. And to find the motive, we have to learn what we can, not just about the professor but about each detective. That's how we find out where they crossed paths, how the circles of their lives overlapped—where they came from, where they've traveled, common interests. And why a homicide detective would murder this guy."

I raised my hand, signaling him to slow down. My face was freezing even though I was dressed like the Stay Puft Marshmallow Man. Sharon wouldn't have let me out of the house.

"You work with these detectives," Clarence said. "Don't you know them well enough?"

"Everybody has things they don't want other people to know. But I have a theory that's proven pretty reliable. My theory is that most murderers can be understood by the kind of person they were in high school. Stop pedaling faster when I'm talking! Why are we doing this anyway?"

"To get you in shape," Clarence said, looking obnoxiously snazzy in his black Adidas sweat suit. "So far we've worked off maybe half a donut. Keep talking. I'm slowing down."

"Anyway," I said, "when you look at a murderer and his type of murder, 90 percent of the time you see the seeds scattered back in high school. If somebody was killed with a cello, and you find out one of the suspects was a high school cellist…well, there you go."

"A cello?"

"Just an example. Not a great one. Anyway, I'm going to be asking the detectives some questions, and I'll ask Ray to compare their answers with what he digs up. If something doesn't jibe, or they leave out something important, we'll ask why."

"Sounds like you're fishing."

"Yeah," I said, turning off the trail at 181st when I saw a McDonalds. "And a good fisherman knows where to cast his line."

The detective floor conference room was chilly in more ways than one.

"You're going to interrogate us as a group…again?" Chris Doyle asked.

"It's not an interrogation," I said.

"Who you think you're kidding?" Brandon Phillips said. "We do this for a living."

"I'm going to ask you questions about growing up, family, and school."

"I'm not going to waste my time with this," Bryce Cimmatoni said, standing.

"Cimma, sit," Sergeant Seymour said as he would to a Doberman. "I don't like this any more than you, but we're on the verge of losing control. If Internal Affairs takes over, it'll get ugly. If an outside agency comes in…it'll be a nightmare. We're going to do this with everyone present, because we're accountable to each other. If someone's lying, someone else may know. If you do, challenge them on it, here and now. Or come to me or Chandler afterward. Time's running out."

"You don't have to confess this time, Cimma," Kim Suda said, followed by a ripple of laughter and whispers. Cimmatoni didn't smile.

"This time I'm starting," I said. "I grew up in Milwaukee, Wisconsin. Moved to Portland when I was fifteen. Went to Franklin High. Have one brother, one sister. My dad was a tavern owner. He also had an amusement machine business: pinballs, jukeboxes, pool tables, shuffleboards. My house was full of the stuff. Everybody came over for parties."

I looked out at the blank faces, all except Tommi Elam's. She seemed fascinated.

"I bet most of you didn't know that," I said. "See what a bonding thing this can be?"

"It would help if we even slightly cared," Doyle said.

"In high school I played football and did track and field, shot put and discus."

"Don't care," Doyle muttered.

"Tommi? Tell us about family and high school."

"Born and raised in Portland. Dad owned a marina. We were always boating. I was into waterskiing. Went to Grant High School. Go Generals! Two sisters and a brother. In high school I was shy. Enlisted in the army after graduating. At my reunions, no one can believe I became a cop."

"What kind of school activities?"

"Volleyball. National Honor Society. That was about it."

"What about you, Cimma? What'd your dad do?"

"Steel mill."

"You must have been into sports, big strapping guy like you. Football?"

"Linebacker. Three years varsity."

"Clubs or social groups?"

"No."

"School dances?"

"No."

"Anything you liked to do? Hobbies?"

"No."

"Macramé? Decoupage? Scrapbooking?"

He glared.

"Well, that was helpful. How about you, Kim?"

"Born in Santa Clarita, California. Just a regular high school kid. But I did go to dances." She smiled at Bryce, not warmly. "My friends and I hung around Magic Mountain. Had annual passes."

"Cheerleader?"

"No way. I played basketball and softball. First base. Batted third. Won the state championship my senior year. We were up by one, and their best hitter tried to stretch a right field triple into a homer. I was the cut off. Threw her out at home." She acted it out, winding up her left arm and emulating the throw.

"How's this going to help catch a killer?" Doyle asked in a whining nasal tone that made me want to Glock-whip him on the spot.

"Just go with it, okay?"

"None of this is okay," Phillips said. "It's irrelevant. A total waste!"

"Manny?" I asked.

He winced from his rib injury, which defanged his glare. "I dropped out of high school."

"Family?"

"Three brothers and a sister."

"Activities?"

"Gangs and drugs. Reformed, then became a cop." Manny's concise. "This is stupid," he added.

When you're doing something awkward, such as accusing coworkers of murder and trying to accumulate incriminating information, it's always nice to have your partner behind you.

"Karl?" Baylor's face wasn't as sour as the others. It was worth a try.

"One brother. Raised in Brooklyn, then moved sixteen miles from here. Went to Barlow High School. Graduated 1996. I was the starting point guard on the basketball team. Tennis, second doubles."

"Favorite teachers?"

"Tom Johnson, Gene Saling, Linda Saling, Tom Starr, Andrew Pate."

Wow. He knew his favorites. I looked at Jack Glissan. "I know all about you, Jack."

"So since you're old friends," Doyle said, "he's not a suspect, but we are?"

"Didn't mean it that way."

"Look, who cares?" Jack said. "Raised in Bellingham. Played football, basketball, and baseball. Came down here to Linfield in McMinnville, then moved to Portland. Never left."

"Noel?"

"Grew up in Liberty Lake, a suburb of Spokane. Only child. Dad was a mail carrier. Took up golf after high school. I was visiting Portland, checking into law enforcement, and somebody introduced me to Jack. He talked me into police academy."

"Anything else?"

"Well, high school four years. Anything in particular you're looking for?"

Three people checked their watches at once. One of them was Sarge.

"Chris?"

Doyle looked up from his watch. "Grew up in Indianapolis. My father was a teacher."

"High school?"

"College."

"What subject?"

"History mainly."

"Mother?"

"She was born and raised in Stratford, England. Graduated from Oxford, King's College. Taught literature there before marrying my father. She tutored my sister and me in the queen's English."

"I never knew that, Chris," Tommi said.

"Sports?" I asked.

"Wasn't into sports then."

"Not a stud like you are now?" Cimmatoni asked.

"Other activities?"

"Not really."

"Chris," Suda said, "didn't you tell me you were on the chess team?"

In a room starved for laughs, the effect was immediate.

"He went out with an injury his senior year," Noel said, "or he would've nabbed a scholarship."

More laughter. Chris steamed. I play chess and respect it. Chess is difficult and challenging and a lot saner than rugby. But cops generally don't wear their chess club sweaters to work.

"Five more minutes, Chandler," Sarge said, pointing at his watch.

"We're down to you, Phillips," I said, realizing that without an outright confession of guilt, this session had been an unqualified disaster.

"Where'd you grow up, Brandon?"

"Texas."

"Where in Texas?"

"Dallas area."

"Remember the name of the town?"

He glared. "Irving."

"Sports?"

"Cross-country. Baseball."

"What school?"

He shook his head like it didn't matter.

"That's it." Sarge dismissed us.

"Well, that was productive," Doyle said, looking at me like I was as dumb as I felt.

"Genius, Chandler," Cimmatoni said, his shoulder bumping me hard as he pushed past me.

"Wasn't a total loss," Noel said. "We found out Chris was on the chess team."

After I'd spent an hour being ragged on one at a time by a half dozen of the detectives about my stupid little meeting about family and schools, Lieutenant Taylor Nicks called me in. My favorite part of his office is the sign saying, "Complaints? Take a number." The number's attached to the pin of a hand grenade.

"I'll get right to it," Nicks said. "You need to back off from your—" he looked down at a piece of paper—"wild accusations."

"Are you saying this on your own?"

"You've…" he looked at the paper again, "gotten completely out of hand. You're a bull in a China shop. You're not a team player. You need to toe the line or you'll…" he looked down again, "be sent packing."

"That doesn't sound like you, Lieutenant. But it does sound familiar."

"It's my job to tell you this. I'm following orders."

"Like I'm following the evidence."

"I understand," he said. "But if you keep it up, you may be asked to resign. If you don't resign, you may be dismissed."

"Fired? You'd do that?"

"I wouldn't. But I don't know how I could stop it. Anything you want me to tell someone who thinks the department would be better off without you?"

"Only that I think the killer would agree."

"Anything else?"

"Remember when you came by my house when Sharon was sick? You met my bullmastiff, Mike Hammer."

"Sure. Nice dog."

"Mike Hammer likes to sink his teeth into tennis balls, sticks, stuffed animals, you name it. Now when he's ready to, he'll drop those things at your feet. But try to take them away, and he'll latch on to them with the teeth-clamp of death."

Long pause.

"You're like your dog. That what you're saying?"

"We both like red meat—and we don't like it when somebody tries to take it away."

"That all?"

"No. If I were fired, I think Clarence Abernathy would just tell the world why, without regard for our precinct's image. You know how journalists can be. Everybody'd know I was fired because I was going after a guilty cop."

"I can say that to…whoever might be interested?" Nicks asked. He jotted a note.

"And you can say I won't go down easily. You can tell him he's bit off more than he can chew. And I smell a rat. And no snake in the grass is going to keep me from doing my job."

"Good. You're dismissed."

I stood. "And something's rotten in Denmark. You can say that too."

He nodded.

"And all's fair in love and war."

"Get out of here." He seemed to be biting his lip. "And shut the door."

I did.

Parting is such sweet sorrow.

↔

The Chief, even when he has somebody else do his dirty work, makes you feel like a rat being shaken by a Rottweiler.

Truth is, I don't want to lose my job. It's a little late to start over as a professional hockey player or home decorating consultant or Cinnabon employee, though the fringe benefits are tempting. Nobody hires guys to wear capes and come to their parties as Green Lantern.

I retreated to my cave, the old brownstone, guarded by my trusty sentinel. I sat on the couch because I still smell Sharon there. She didn't wear much perfume. It's actually her I smell.

I went to the closet and pulled out a Seahawks blanket I got her for our anniversary, on April 3. You may think it was a lousy gift, but she loved it. She was that kind of woman—a football-loving woman, a pizza-loving woman. A Hall of Fame woman. She bundled up in that Seahawks blanket all the time and still thanked me for it five years later. I'll never wash it because her scent's stronger there than anywhere else.

I can't smell Sharon as much as I used to. I'm afraid one of these days I won't smell her at all. And then the last living trace of her will be gone forever.

I have thousands of pictures of dead bodies and less than a dozen of my own wife. If I were a contortionist, I'd kick my rear end for this.

Will she just disappear as my memories fade? When I'm gone, will Saint Sharon be no longer?

"Open his eyes, Lord," she said. "Help him see the unseen—to behold Your kindnesses to him."

"I grant him hundreds of graces each day, from the air he breathes to the food he eats to the roof over his head. He sees none of them, so it's no surprise that he doesn't see the greatest gift I offer him. I've been patient, not wishing him to perish."

"But the clock's ticking."

"Yes, Saint Sharon," He said with a smile, placing His arm around her. "But I am bigger than the clock."

I left home for Rosie O'Grady's, returning three hours later. I'd managed to sip a few beers slowly and was proud of not being drunk. I turned the corner and saw a flashlight on in my dark house.

Not again. My head instinctively ached.

I drove past the house and pulled to the curb sixty feet away. I waited two minutes before the flashlight came on again.

I called Jake's cell. "Where are you?"

"Home," he said.

"Can you drive to the old brownstone right now? Just pull in the driveway and sit there. That's all I'm asking."

"Do I bring my service revolver, Sherlock?"

"Good idea."

"You're serious?"

I hung up and worked my way into the backyard behind the elm tree, next to the moldy pile of bark dust.

Five minutes later I saw the front of the house light up and knew Jake had arrived. The inside flashlight went off. Within five seconds the back door opened.

Fear kicked in when I realized Mulch wasn't barking.

I followed the guy over the fence, through the Atkins' backyard. I was grateful for that much, since as far as I know the Atkins don't drink Earl Grey tea. He ran to a parked car, opened the door, and as he did, I saw he wasn't a he.

He was a she.

He was Kim Suda.

I couldn't follow her. I decided it was in my best interest to know it was her without her knowing I knew. I was also worried about Mulch. As Suda drove away, I ran back to the house, legs sore from my bike ride.

I ran to the front yard and raised my hands until Jake lowered his Walther from its bead on the center of my chest.

"What's going on?" he asked.

"Intruder. I followed him. Her."

"Her?"

"Tell you later. I think Mulch's down."

My keys rattled, but still I heard nothing. Truth is, I prayed Mulch was okay. There are no atheists when your dog's in a foxhole. Or something like that.

I opened the door, where Mulch is positioned 100 percent of the time when I enter. Nothing.

"Mulch! Mike Hammer?"

I tripped over something big and baggy on the floor. Mulch. No movement.

"No. No."

The light flipped on and I was looking at Jake six feet behind me.

"He isn't moving," I said. I smelled something, then saw it. A half pound of raw hamburger six inches from his mouth.

"It's like he's asleep," Jake said.

"Is there a 911 for dogs?" I asked.

"There's a vet named Megan at our church. I'll call her."

I lifted Mulch onto the couch. I shook him. One eye opened just enough to show his inner eyelid.

Five minutes later Dr. Megan Wood showed up. She put her hands on Mulch's chest and by his snout. I pointed out the hamburger.

"We hide pills in hamburger. I think someone gave him a sedative."

"They slipped Mulch a mickey?"

"Hamburger's the best way."

"It'd work for me," I said. "What should I do? Make him coffee? Coke? There's a hangover recipe with Tabasco sauce and black pepper."

"Sounds like you've had some experience. His breathing's normal. I don't think it's an overdose, just a deep sleep that he'll come out of eventually. No sense taking him to my office. He'll be more comfortable here."

She wrote down her cell number and handed it to me. I told her I'd never forget her, and if she needed a homicide detective, I was her man.

Jake was checking out the whole house, pointing his father's Walther P38, taken from a Nazi soldier, into every nook and cranny. I put Sharon's Seahawks blanket over Mulch and sat beside him. Jake's one of the few people I trust with a gun as much as I'd trust myself. He was a Green Beret in Nam.

Half an hour later I talked Jake into leaving. For the rest of the evening I thought about Kim Suda, trying to connect the dots. I never left Mulch for more than a few minutes, but I noticed a few things in my office that seemed out of place. The phone on my desk was positioned perfectly, at a right angle to the front edge of the desk. Too perfect.

I disconnected it from the wall. Then I opened the mouthpiece quietly. In it I found a tiny device.

Kim Suda had bugged my phone.

I heard a gurgle eight feet away. I rushed back to see two tired eyes peering at me. I stretched out my hand, and he licked it. I hugged him and fried him some bacon, unleashing its magical healing properties. He ate it slowly but gratefully.

Mike Hammer was back.

And I vowed to make the dog drugger pay.

"Come, Watson, come! The game is afoot.
Not a word! Into your clothes and come!"
SHERLOCK HOLMES, *THE ADVENTURE OF THE ABBEY*
GRANGE

MULCH SLEPT NEXT TO ME. For breakfast, I made him waffles and threw an extra egg into the mix. He likes them fluffy. I usually toss him waffle portions, and he jumps to catch them. Never misses. But this time I hand-fed him, in bed. He seemed to appreciate the extra butter.

When Ray arrived two hours later, we stood on my front lawn, Mulch on his leash, breathing deeply. Some places you want to close your mouth and keep the air out. Not Oregon. The air's so incredibly good, you want to keep breathing just to remind yourself.

"Suda's toast," I said. "She invaded my home, planted a bug, and drugged my dog. That's as low as it gets. *Kim Suda.* Even her name sounds dark and slippery. Just try it on your tongue—*Kim Suda*. Close your eyes. Whisper it in the dark a few times. It'll give you the willies."

Ray closed his eyes and whispered, which is more than I could've gotten Abernathy to do.

Then he pulled out his bug detector, a TD-53, to sweep my house. He told me he'd test it on the phone I already knew was bugged. He said I should just do what I usually did, talk to Mulch but not to him. He suggested I turn on music too. Johnny Cash, the only country singer I ever liked, sang in the background to cover for us.

When we got two feet into my office, three feet from the phone, the audible tone on the TD-53 clicked faster and faster, like a Geiger counter. Ray turned it low enough not to be heard by whoever was listening in. The signal was strong.

Ray found two other bugging devices, one by the kitchen phone, perfectly hidden in the seam of a pen holder. The other was inside the lamp shade by my recliner.

We stepped outside to discuss it. I wanted the two we'd just found deactivated, but we'd leave active the one in my office phone.

We went to the front of the house, and he turned on the bug sweeper to check my car. Nothing. Still, he beckoned to his car and we got in to talk.

"A phone bug and two others?" Ray said. "Wow. I'm pretty sure I found everything, but some bugs can be turned on and off remotely, and when they're off they can be missed."

"They're department issue, aren't they?" I asked.

"Technically a private party can get them, but given these brands and considering the cheaper equipment you can buy publicly, I'm sure it's police department hardware. Which means she's in big trouble."

"Can you access e-mail without someone knowing?" I asked.

"Private? On a secure system?"

"Her computer's thirty feet from my desk, but she's usually carting around her laptop."

"Wireless?"

"I guess. Is that good?"

"I'll let you know."

Ray called me at 11:00 a.m.

"Suda's home and her computer's running, but she's not on it. I'm parked curbside at her neighbor's, inside her wireless range. She's got a good firewall. Can't get in without an alphanumeric password. You're going to have to check her desktop. Computer stays on at the precinct, right?"

"Unless there's a power outage."

"That means some people will leave their e-mail open," he said. "It's Saturday, so she probably won't be in, right? If Outlook's open, just watch the screen and make sure there's no movement. Otherwise if she's accessing remotely you'll bump her off."

I went to detective detail and moseyed over to Kim Suda's desk. Outlook was open. I did an MSN desktop search for "Ollie" and "Chandler." It turned up some old e-mails to and from me, as well as a few recent derogatory comments about me exchanged by my fellow detectives, referring to me by a variety of anatomical terms. I opened her sent file and looked at the last ten e-mails.

Found an e-mail sent at 11:45 last night. It was the shortest I'd come across. All it said was, "Job done. Everything set."

She'd done a job on me and Mulch, and I wondered if that's what she meant. The e-mail went to an address without a name: wearp@verizon.net.

I Googled "wearp" at my desk and tried searching for listed e-mail addresses. I found only forty-six people in America with the last name Wearp. Glad it wasn't Jones. Finally I called Ray Eagle and briefed him.

I sat there thinking about dinner for me and Mulch. It was Saturday night, so my thoughts went to one place. One of the greatest natural resources of the Pacific Northwest—found nowhere else—is Burgerville USA, where hot beef under Tillamook cheddar cheese with the works can be bought alongside an unforgettable blackberry shake.

Sharon worked in a Burgerville on Eighty-second and Glisan, before we had kids. She'd give me extra fries and sometimes another slice of cheddar. In our last ten years together, besides Lou's and Dea's, it was my next favorite place to take her for special occasions. We used to kick up our heels and go there on Saturday nights. Sharon would call me a romantic fool.

Hugh Mulhaney, a cynical cop who's been divorced three times, told me, "Being single's really great. You make up the rules. You don't call anyone to say you'll be late. Don't have to justify yourself to anyone. No one pokes you when you snore. No one suggests you clean out the rain gutters when the Cowboys are playing the Giants."

Sharon would never make me miss a game over gutters, but if she were here, I'd do it for her in a heartbeat.

Ray called. "Name's not Wearp. It's W. Earp, as in Wyatt Earp."

"Shootout at the OK Corral?"

"Got a billing address for the account."

"So who's Wyatt Earp?"

"Would you believe…Edward Lennox?"

Two things I've learned. First, never stand between Mulch and a bush he's sniffing. Second, never trust Chief Lennox.

Ray, Clarence, Manny, and I sat in Ray's living room. Manny, moving stiffly due to his broken rib, eyed Abernathy repeatedly, despite the big guy's continual apologies and offers to help. Manny didn't want to be there with us, but then Manny doesn't want to be anywhere. He went on and on about the miserable failure it had been when I quizzed the detectives about their backgrounds.

Finally I stopped him. "We've got to know motives, and to do it we've got to find out people's backgrounds, families, interests, habits. Their secrets. Since it didn't work in our group setting—"

"Disaster," Manny muttered.

"I asked Ray to do his own checking." I looked at him. "You're on."

He glanced at an old brown clipboard, like a coach would use. "Truth is, I started on this a week ago. It represents lots of phone calls, Internet research, and beating the bushes."

"We supposed to be impressed?" Manny asked, bringing Christmas cheer. "You haven't told us anything."

"Tommi Elam first," Ray said. "Her father was a writer. He grew up in England—like Chris Doyle's mother. Her dad met her mom while she was vacationing in England. He moved here to marry her. He's successful enough to pay the bills. And he was involved in the kids' education. Taught them to read and write."

"No kidding?" I asked. "Never heard her say that."

"He was a collector. Music, coins, stamps, baseball cards, pens, rare books, even a dozen typewriters from various eras."

"How'd you find this out?"

"Somebody who admired his work made a website about him. Tommi's divorced. Her first husband was a radical activist. Environmental stuff—chained himself to a tree. And animal rights. She got a restraining order against him. Said he was abusive and that he cheated on her."

"She ever get violent with him?"

"No record of it. There were custody disputes. Two kids by that marriage. Now they're in high school."

"Where's the ex-husband?"

"Passed away at age forty-four, two years ago, five years after their divorce. Surprise heart attack while jogging. No prior condition. Here's something. Tommi went to Grant, same high school as Palatine. But he was older so they weren't there at the same time."

"She have brothers or sisters?" I asked. "One of them might have known him."

Ray jotted a note, then continued. "Bryce Cimmatoni grew up in Pittsburgh. He's a congenital Steelers fan, but we can't blame him for that. His father worked in a steel mill. Most people of that profile resent those above and below them on the social ladder."

"You're a psychologist, too?" I asked.

"Does it describe Cimmatoni?"

"Yeah, except he also resents those who are level with him on the social ladder. I don't think he's ever met anyone, on or off a ladder, he doesn't resent. Except his wife."

"About his upbringing—his records are sketchy. Doesn't look like he was popular."

"Surprise," Manny said.

I looked at him. "Not everybody can be Mr. Sunshine like you."

"Not many social activities," Ray said. "Won a chemistry award. First two years in college he was premed."

"Cimmatoni?" I said.

"Yeah. He was accepted into med school. His sister was murdered, and next thing you know he became a cop."

"No kidding?"

"Shot in the head."

"He's never mentioned his sister's murder," I said.

"You hang out with him?"

"No. But cops are like old ladies. There's always gossip. How come I've never heard that story? You heard it?" Manny shook his head.

"Some people don't like to talk about stuff like that," Clarence said. "I don't talk about my sister's murder."

"How'd you find this out about his sister?"

"Cimmatoni's other sister has a blog. I did a search on Bryce Cimmatoni, and three minutes later I'm reading the inside story of the family, including the sister's murder. She's the one who said her brother decided to be a cop instead of a doctor."

"A blog?"

"Yeah, I forgot—you don't know how to use your answering machine either. I was able to access Cimmatoni's Internet history—don't ask me how."

"Let's leave it there unless it's relevant," I said.

Ray flipped a couple of pages. It's odd to be a detective for a living and find yourself scared to hear what a detective can find out about you.

"Kim Suda," Ray said. "There's some interesting things she didn't mention. In high school she got in big trouble for fighting three times. Twice with girls."

"Catfights?"

"She was the Queen Cat. In one case she broke two teeth of the cheerleader who was homecoming queen."

"Ouch."

"Suda was suspended and the other girl wasn't."

"What about the third time?"

"She decked a male teacher."

"You're kidding."

"She claimed he made a lewd comment to her. He went to the hospital. There were rumblings of a lawsuit, but he didn't pursue it. I checked court records."

"Sue a teenage girl for decking you? No thanks."

"Suda has an old boyfriend, Skeets, some brainiac at Microsoft. He supplies her software. Still has a crush on her, I think."

"Where do you come up with this stuff?" Clarence asked.

"Karl Baylor." Ray flipped another page and smiled as he ignored Clarence's question. "Single-parent home. Dad wasn't around. Close to his mom. No great student, but he didn't get in trouble."

"Figures," I said.

"Transcript said he was a journalism student. In Barlow High School's library I got a copy of a school newspaper editorial he wrote. Baylor was a Christian."

"Still is," I said, restraining myself.

"Good article. You should read it."

"This stealth evangelism, Ray?"

"No. If it were stealth, you wouldn't have seen it coming. Baylor has a petite wife, two kids, and two hamsters."

"Hamsters? Don't let Clarence near them. He'd dunk 'em in a heartbeat."

Abernathy's eyes threw darts at me.

"How's Brent doing, anyway? Remember that Boys Town emblem? You and Brent could do one, with Brent on your shoulder: 'He ain't heavy, he's my hamster.'"

All three of them stared. I can't help myself.

"Jack's records are harder to get to," Ray said to me. "He's even older than you."

"Funny."

"Everything checks out. Wrestling. Student body president. Model citizen. Did you know his daughter died when she was at Linfield College?"

"Yeah," I said. "She was friends with my daughter. Kendra was at Portland State while Melissa was at Linfield."

"How'd she die?" Clarence said.

"Suicide. She got on drugs. Coke and meth. Grades dropped. Became despondent."

"Jack's wife's an alcoholic," Ray said.

I felt my neck tighten. "What's that got to do with anything?"

"You're looking for information. Secrets. Problems, you said. Doesn't that qualify?"

"She's been sober for years."

"Glad to hear it," Ray said.

"It's private information."

"So's everything else I'm giving you. I didn't know some of the detectives had immunity."

"They don't."

Everybody was looking at me. Ray went on.

"Noel Barrows grew up in Liberty Lake, Washington. Dad was a postal worker."

"So he said."

"Found a couple of job references from back in the day. They were good. No rocket scientist, but competent, dependable. In high school, average grades. Got into trouble once. Caught smoking dope. Played baseball two years."

"Not golf?"

"He took up golf after high school," Clarence reminded me.

"He's good," Ray said. "Two years ago, he placed fifth in a big club tournament."

"Dirt on Noel?" I asked.

"No, but something sad. His senior year, two weeks before graduation, his parents went to Idaho for the weekend. When they were coming back, fifty miles from home, a drunk driver hit them head-on. Killed both parents."

"Amazing what you don't know about people you work with," I said.

"Clarence's report says Chris Doyle was on the chess team," Ray said. "Turns out he was also into drama big time. Four years. Six plays. Three starring roles."

"Doyle?" I said. "You gotta be kidding."

"But get this. His dad taught at the University of Pennsylvania. According to Clarence's notes, Doyle said his dad taught history."

"Yeah?"

"He did. Two years. But his main subject, for twenty years, wasn't history. It was philosophy."

"Doyle's father was a college philosophy prof?"

"Yep. Like he said, his mother was from England and was hands-on with the kids' education."

"A cop with a white collar background," I said.

"Something else. He declared bankruptcy five years ago. Had a gambling problem. Impulsive buyer. Turns out he's a rich kid who squandered his inheritance, mostly from his mother's side. This was interesting: When he was twenty, he lied on his résumé to get a job at a retail stationery store. Didn't get fired, but his employer put it on record. Also, he's been in therapy."

"You mean counseling?"

"It's in department records, but it's confidential."

"How does a private eye get into police records?"

"I've done some favors for cops. Including one in records."

"They must've been big favors."

Manny's phone rang. He nodded a couple of times and said, "Okay, be there in fifteen." He hung up. "Gotta go," he said and was gone. No tears at his parting.

"What about Brandon Phillips?" I asked Ray.

"Got some police personnel stuff. You know the competency tests?"

"Yeah?"

"He scored second highest in the department. Near genius."

"I was highest?"

He laughed. "Not quite. But among the detectives, you were third out of ten. Phillips scored one of the highest in the physical fitness tests too, the ones with aerobics, weight lifting, and flexibility."

"He outscored me there, too?"

"Slightly."

"Years ago Phillips and I played together on the precinct fast-pitch softball team. He could knock a home run from either side of the plate."

"Something else," Ray said, putting a check mark in his notes. "Phillips has lots of money...and unlike Doyle, he hasn't run out of it."

"I've seen his Audi," I said.

"And his wife drives a six-month-old Porsche. But here's something odd. She doesn't work outside the home. And have you seen their house?"

"No. Heard it's nice."

"Ninety-eighth percentile nice. CEO type nice. I drove to it. So where does the money come from? Not a detective's salary. Not an inheritance—parents alive on both sides. He's a heck of a card player, I hear, but that's a lot of lifestyle to buy with poker winnings."

"Check it out, will you?"

"I've got his date of birth, but I can't find a Brandon Phillips who was in high school near Irving, Texas, during those years. Okay, the other person with a history of violence was your partner, who just left us."

"Fortunate for you," I said. "Manny was a gangbanger. Took down some rival gang members."

"Always a fighter. Expelled his sophomore year."

"Then went back and got his GED. I know."

"Did you know he was convicted of assault and battery twice, and assault with a deadly weapon as a sixteen-year-old?"

"I knew it was serious and he did time as a juvie. Don't know details. Manny's not the type to open up over a latte."

"He might get mad enough for his violent instincts to be triggered," Ray said.

"Manny has a go-nuts button. I try not to push it. I'm not one to pick a fight." I looked at Clarence, who didn't look back.

"Four years ago," Ray said, "Manny's wife went down in a hit-and-run."

"She nearly died," I said. "Still limps. Lots of rehab."

"Never found who did it, right?" Ray asked.

"Two witnesses, but neither got the license. Drove him crazy that it was a hit-and-run."

I stood and extended my hand to Ray Eagle. "That's the whole gang. I gotta say, you're good, Ray. Not the kind of incompetence I expected from a private eye. You ever want to be a real detective again, I'll give you a reference for Portland Police."

"No thanks. Left that behind me in Detroit. I like my freedom. Call my own shots. I figure out the best way to do it, then I just do it. No bureaucracy. Don't have to raise my hand and ask to go to the bathroom. Don't get called into the chief's office. Plus, I can go to my kids' games. And usually my wife isn't wondering whether I'll be shot today."

"On second thought, keep me in mind if you ever want to hire somebody."

He laughed. "I'll do that. Listen, I wasn't sure if I should mention it, but I did check out somebody else."

"Who?"

"Detective Ollie Chandler."

"You checked on me?"

"Are you a Portland homicide detective?"

"I didn't ask you to check on me."

"So…you're off limits? You don't want to hear it?"

"I'm guessing I already know it."

"In your case I didn't go back to high school. They didn't keep records in those days, or they were all on papyrus and it's crumbled."

"You should be on TV."

"I did get access to some department records. You've got a history of insubordination. And anger management issues."

"That's your best shot?"

"According to a couple of records you've got a serious drinking problem. In at least one case, you blacked out."

"I…where did you get that information?"

"That same somebody who owed me a favor."

"That somebody could lose their job."

"They could but they won't. Since your file says you're known for taking shortcuts, I figured you'd understand. Then there was the investigation into the police brutality charge."

"I was cleared of all charges. The guy was on drugs and was threatening innocent people. I was doing my job."

"I figured you were, but—"

"You don't have to figure anything."

"The last thing was about some difficult things in your own family history. Especially your wife and your—"

"Stop right now! That's enough!" I was standing, my finger pointing at him.

"Oookay then," Ray said. "Sorry. I thought…" He looked at Clarence.

"Anything else you want me to do?" Ray asked.

"No."

"I could check everybody's alibis."

"I've got that covered."

"I could double-check, and we could compare notes."

"It's covered. Your job's done."

I was out the door in ten seconds, stalking game in the asphalt jungle, looking for a jaywalker I could take down and handcuff.

After my forehead sweat was cooled by the wind, I started to wonder what Ray and Clarence were discussing right now. I suspected there might be mention of drinking and anger management.

And I resented it.

32

SUNDAY, DECEMBER 22

ALL YOUR LIFE you're a wannabe, until you wake up one morning, and you're a has-been.

And you think, where was that part in the middle when you arrived, when you were living the dream?

Did I miss it?

This is why days off aren't the draw they once were. With time on my hands I find myself asking these kinds of questions. In lieu of answers I consult the bottle, which disappoints, but I know that, so my expectations are low. Anesthetics don't have to offer anything great—pain relief, though temporary, is often the best offer on the table.

I told myself I wouldn't start drinking until after lunch. Since I hate violating my commitments, I adjusted that to not taking my third drink until after lunch.

I opened up the Palatine file, now three folders. Unlike 90 percent of us Oregonians, Clarence and Ray go to church Sunday mornings, like Jake does. They look to the Bible for inspiration. Others look to the newspaper. I look to my case notes.

Seven thirty that evening, Ray Eagle called, waking me from a postpizza nap.

"Turns out Tommi's brother and the professor were the same year. On the same water polo team. Looks like he's a dentist in Portland—names and ages match anyway. Don't know if they hung out besides that. I'd have to call people in their class. I've got some names. Worth my time?"

"Low priority."

"Also, did you know Tommi has a medical condition?"

"No."

"Severe migraines. She takes Imitrex. Comes in pills and injections—she uses the injections."

"Never seen her do it. Or heard her mention it."

"She's had it for years."

"Can you really afford to contribute all this work, Ray?" I was being extra nice after walking out on him the day before.

"Even though Clarence can't put into print all I'm doing, he gave me a favorable mention in his last article."

"I noticed."

"I've already gotten four phone calls. Two of them are new jobs. It's paying off. And even if it wasn't, I'm glad to help."

Every police detective should have a Ray Eagle.

MONDAY, DECEMBER 23, 10:15 A.M.

The chief left a message that he wanted me at his office by 9:30. I took files and phone and set up for business in his waiting area. I brought in a Coke, an apple, dry-roasted peanuts, a Swiss Miss Pudding cup, and a plastic spoon.

Okay, maybe I was making a point. It wasn't lost on Mona, who repeatedly insisted I clean up. I cheerfully ignored her. I overheard her explain to someone around the corner that her duties now included working with the chief periodically at his home office, and, yes, it was perfectly fine with the chief's wife, who was always home anyway.

I file information, never knowing when it'll come in handy.

Lennox finally emerged and stared at everything I'd spread out on the table. "Pick up your mess."

"Yes, sir. Didn't know the wait would only be forty-five minutes this time."

He talked at me, not to me, for ten minutes. "You've been living off the fat of the land around here. You better wake up and smell the coffee. Keep your fingers crossed, mister, because I have the power to take you down. And don't think I won't."

"Yes, sir. You are a mover and shaker. A force to be reckoned with."

"You'd better believe it!"

"It's always darkest before the dawn," I said. "When the going gets tough, the tough get going."

"Are you mocking me?"

"When in Rome, do as the Romans do."

"Who do you think you are?"

My plan to anger him was working. We were at war.

"To be or not to be."

"Get out!"

I turned, and as I did something fell out of my hand.

"Pick up that garbage."

I pretended not to hear him. As I looked back I saw him pick up the wrapper and put it in his wastebasket.

I joined Clarence and Manny in a small conference room. Clarence had stopped returning Manny's glares since breaking his ribs, but Manny was his typical cheery self, with all the charm of a DMV employee.

"Been checking on family members," Manny said. "Brandon Phillips's wife and Linda Glissan took a class with the professor last year."

"How could so many people have been in that guy's classes?" Clarence asked.

"The department has an arrangement with Portland State," I said. "Spouses of officers can take classes at reduced rates, something like fifty bucks a class. Dozens of PPD wives have done it. Some are working on degrees. Sharon took a couple of classes with Linda. Palatine's taught twenty-five years. He was popular. Maybe it's not as odd as it seems."

"Brandon's wife's a looker," Manny said.

"I noticed. The professor would've definitely noticed. Phillips never mentioned his wife was in Palatine's class. You worked with Phillips while Cimmatoni and I were away, right? I think Cimma's knee went out, and I was…"

"Sharon had just died."

"Anyway, what were his habits?"

Manny turned up his palms. "We were on two stakeouts."

"You must have missed my stakeout wit and charm."

"Phillips keeps his mouth shut. I like that."

Manny and Clarence looked at each other, Clarence nodding. Glad to give them this bonding moment.

"He must have drunk a gallon of coffee," Manny said. "And he ate a half dozen granola bars."

"Granola bars? Soft or crunchy?"

"Who cares?"

"I'll bet they're crunchy."

I walked out the door to Phillips's desk. He was out. I looked at his keyboard closely, with the light on my keychain. Down between the keys I saw yellowish-brown particles. I looked both ways, then opened two of his desk drawers. At the back of the second, I found his stash—six Nature Valley pecan crunch granola bars. I took one and shut the drawer.

I showed Manny and Clarence my discovery. They weren't impressed. I decided not to explain. Nero Wolfe holds things back from Archie, like Sherlock Holmes did from Watson, so at the unveiling of a crime's solution, his deductions seem more brilliant.

Manny took off, and Clarence and I settled down at my workstation. I pulled open a file drawer between us. Clarence spotted a file in the front. He pulled it out.

"*The Bacon and Cheese Murders*?" he asked. "Wait…it says Ollie Chandler. You wrote this?"

"It's my first fiction."

"You've written nonfiction?"

"Just that article I gave you the other day."

He flipped through it, then read aloud: "Frankie the Knife tried to shake me, but I stuck to him like a mustard plaster. Frankie was hog ugly, face like a bucket of mud. Walking down Broadway, he was as inconspicuous as a tarantula on a slice of angel food cake. When I jumped him on Alder, the streetlight showed the vein in his forehead beating like a ragtime drummer on bathtub gin. Next thing he knew I was slapping him around like a pinball machine with body English."

"What do you think?" I asked.

"I'm speechless," Clarence said. "A pinball machine with body English?"

"Pretty cool, huh? Raymond Chandler was the greatest writer of hard-boiled detective stories. Lots of people ask if we're related, but I've never found a link between my Chandlers and his."

"You think about crime, you read about crime, apparently you even write about crime." Clarence stopped, appearing to weigh his words. "Off the record, could you have killed the professor?"

"I'm capable of it, if that's what you mean."

"Really?"

"So are you. Suppose somebody murdered Geneva and got away with it. He was cleared, but you know for a fact he did it. And suppose you know he'll kill someone else, even your own kids. He's threatened to do it. So tell me, would you just turn the other cheek? I'm not saying I'd kill him. But if no justice was coming and more people were in danger? I'd consider it."

"I'd take him out in a heartbeat." It was Manny, who'd suddenly reappeared at his desk. Manny has no future in politics.

"I'd like to believe I'd leave justice to God," Clarence said, "not take it into my own hands."

Manny groaned, putting his hand on his rib.

"With your family's lives on the line?" I said. "The first question about these homicide detectives is, are they smart enough to kill and have a good chance of getting away with it? In each case, given their experience and knowledge of murder investigations, the answer's yes. Second, are they bold enough to do it? And third, are they motivated enough? You can't answer the last question until you figure out what that motivation could be. If it's revenge for something horrific or prevention of future crimes, that might be enough."

"What if two detectives were in on it together?" Clarence asked.

"What are the chances of two homicide detectives working together who are both cold-blooded murderers? Okay, they might rough somebody up. But plan a murder?"

"Have you talked about how to kill someone?" Clarence asked.

"Sure." I looked at Manny. He nodded. "But pharmacists probably discuss what drug they'd use to kill someone. And mechanics probably say if they were going to sabotage a car, that's how they'd do it. But few of them actually do it. Especially not together. If I were going to murder someone, I wouldn't let anybody in on it. Nobody would see me do it."

"Nobody but God."

Clarence has this way of ending conversations.

MONDAY, DECEMBER 23, 6:20 P.M.

I talked with McKay Kunz, the night shift's head custodian at the Justice Center, about timetables and procedures for dumping garbage. Then I headed for the parking garage to bail out my car.

"I finally got around to checking out the six phone numbers from the backs of the professor's books," Ray Eagle said as I crossed the bridge and negotiated the ramp onto I-84 in a rainy rush hour. "Two are nonworking numbers, two belong to someone else now, and two to the original owners. But I linked up the old ones to past owners. In four cases I confirmed numbers belonging to women who at one time knew the professor. Two had been in his class; two others had dated him. One remembered him fondly; two sounded pretty cold. One ice-cold."

"Why didn't he put names next to the numbers?" I asked.

"For fear someone would see it? Maybe he didn't want to have to explain why he had their numbers. But how could he remember who the numbers belonged to?"

"Probably thinking one at a time," I said. "The girl was on his mind, and he figured he wouldn't forget. Years later he wouldn't care. He always had a book with him, so books were his scratch pads. Fountain pens and love letters aside, to the professor women weren't much more than numbers anyway."

By 7:30 Mulch was walking me through his day. I usually don't grasp the details, but his general points come through. He'd had a good day, barked at a number of joggers, but missed me. And was thinking about bacon.

I did this interacting with Mulch in my office so whoever was listening to the recording on the chief's behalf would know their bug was still working. When Mulch had gotten everything off his chest, including his guilt in the confiscation and mangling of a Zero candy bar I'd left on my desk, I opened my Picasa photo program, called up the Palatine murder scene pictures, and turned on the slide program. As hundreds of slides appeared for three seconds each, I looked, hoping to see something new.

I'd taken six pictures of the hallway, and the last of those showed Kim Suda, at the far end, coming out of the professor's bedroom, talking with a criminalist. I hit the space bar, pausing it, studying the picture. Something seemed peculiar, but I wasn't sure what.

I hit the escape key, called up the picture for editing, and enlarged Suda's face about six times. She looked different. In particular, her hair was mussed. Usually it's perfect. Yeah, she'd come in from the cold, but Suda's the type to find a mirror. But there was more. Suda seemed…something about her face. She looked…nervous.

In the darkness of December 23, I gave in to Mulch's begging, forgave him for the Zero bar, and took him for a walk. A light snow fell, swirling in the streetlights. I opened my mouth and caught snowflakes on my tongue. Mulch barked and jumped up, mouth open, and caught some flakes himself. I laughed and Mulch strutted happily beside me. He's fascinated by the outdoors each time, like he's never seen it before. I was that way as a kid. Snow was magic back then. Usually magic has no hold on me anymore. But the snow drew me out of myself and into something beyond me, an enchanting greatness.

There's something about fresh Oregon air. It gives me an electric charge to the little gray cells. That's what happened at 8:23 as we walked by the yellow house with the yappy dog who's always on his fourth espresso. When lightning struck inside my head, I stood still ten seconds, then turned and ran toward the old brownstone, dragging Mulch on his leash. He thought it was a grand romp.

I charged in the front door, went to my office, and pulled out one of the three thick files from my briefcase. I flipped through papers.

Finally I found what I was looking for: my copy of the crime scene log sheet, signed off by officers Dorsey and Guerino. I examined it to see exactly who had been granted entry to Palatine's house that night.

Nowhere in the log was the name Kim Suda.

"You will remember, Watson, how the dreadful business of the Abernetty family was first brought to my notice by the depth which the parsley had sunk into the butter upon a hot day."
SHERLOCK HOLMES, *THE ADVENTURE OF THE SIX NAPOLEONS*

TUESDAY, DECEMBER 24, 8:00 A.M.

YESTERDAY HAD BEEN A LONG ONE. After my discovery that Kim Suda wasn't in the crime scene log, Mulch and I had driven back to the Justice Center to meet with McKay Kunz, head custodian. I told him I needed something a suspicious character had tossed in the fifteenth-floor lobby garbage can.

Unfortunately, Kunz said, and he thought he'd made this clear to me when I called earlier, all the trash from the floor had been dumped into two giant bags at 8:00, so now I'd have to sort through everything from that floor to find what was in the lobby trash.

Wearing plastic gloves, I found what I was looking for after thirty minutes, put it in a plastic bag, joined Mulch in the car, and headed home.

This morning I called the patrol sergeant at 8:00 a.m., hoping to meet again with Dorsey and Guerino. He said they couldn't be accessed until 1:00 p.m., and then only if it was absolutely necessary since this was Christmas Eve day, for criminy's sake. I assured him it was absolutely necessary.

I was going to have to wait five hours to hear their story about Suda. I called Jake and Clarence and told them I'd have to leave by 12:30, so we met for lunch at 11:30. In honor of Christmas, Rory had six long-stemmed red roses and six white lilies at our table. Only one problem with this festive setting: Rory was wearing an elf hat. I'm all for civil liberties, but I draw the line at grown men wearing elf hats. He offered us complimentary hats, but we declined, though Jake and I tried to get Clarence to try one on.

We were deep in discussion when I heard a familiar voice behind me.

"Ollie! Merry Christmas!"

I cringed. What was Karl Baylor doing at my restaurant? I looked up at him. He was wearing an elf hat.

"I've heard you talk about this place," he said. "Thought we'd try it today since we start fixing Christmas breakfast tonight."

"Noting the 'we,'" I turned further to see a smiling young woman.

"Ever met my wife, Tiffany?"

I paused a moment too long. "No."

"Sweetheart, this is Ollie Chandler. I've mentioned him."

I saw the glimmer of recognition. "I think we've met."

"Maybe at the detective dinner last spring," I said, knowing I'd skipped those dinners since Sharon died.

"Seems like recently."

"I was working undercover as your mailman."

She laughed. "That was it. Nice to meet you."

Karl removed his elf hat and held it in his hands while he talked with Clarence and called him "brother" and introduced him to Tiffany. She seemed impressed to meet Jake, another columnist she enjoyed. I was glad to have her occupied with anyone besides me.

Rory pointed the Baylors to a booth fifteen feet away. They sat down across from each other. Fortunately, Tiffany faced the other direction.

"The Baylors seem nice," Jake said. "I was expecting a couple of terrorists."

"I'll take a rain check on laughing."

After a few minutes, the Baylors stood and switched sides. Tiffany stared at me. She looked away only when I glanced at her. Every time this happened, I scooted a few more inches into the booth. Soon I was out of her line of sight.

I needed to get back for Dorsey and Guerino, and Jake was taking off early for Christmas Eve, so we parted, wishing each other Merry Christmas. They invited me to join their families, and I said no. Kendra and I were going it alone.

"See you at the *Tribune* at 3:00?" I asked Clarence.

"Need to be home by 4:00. Sure it can't wait?"

"Positive. Doesn't anybody put in full days anymore? Carp's expecting me. You can leave by 3:30."

Afterward I sat in the parking lot, finding in my briefcase the typed notes of my interview with Rupert Bolin, fountain pen aficionado. I glanced at his business card and called him as I drove back to the Justice Center.

"Remember telling me about the different reasons people use fountain pens? You mentioned love letters."

"Oh, yes, it's so romantic. Women love the old-fashioned ways. It's not like scratching out something with an ordinary pen. Or, heaven forbid, sending an e-mail. Every letter written with a fountain pen is an original. Sometimes I write a saucy one to my wife, with the finest pen and ink money can buy."

"I'm sure she's overcome with excitement," I said.

"Yes, indeed," he replied. "We have several special pens and superior stationery that I highly recommend for you to write exquisite letters to that special woman who has captured your heart."

"I don't have…"

I stopped. I wondered how the phrase "double cheese, double pepperoni" written in fine fountain pen ink on a superior stationery, might move the heart of Lynn Carpenter.

I opened the official crime scene log from Records, so it'd be ready for Dorsey and Guerino. They arrived at 1:05 p.m.

"What'd we do this time?" Guerino asked.

"You guys know Kim Suda, right? She's standing by the watercooler, but don't stare, okay?"

They both stared, then nodded.

"Do either of you remember her coming into the professor's house that night?"

"She was there," Guerino said.

"I know she was there. I'm asking if you remember her arrival."

Dorsey shrugged. "Must have been when I was talking to the gawkers." He looked at Guerino. "You signed her in, right?"

"I don't remember her coming to the door. But I went inside a couple of times to point stuff out to the criminalists. You must've been there when she came."

"Nope."

"Here's the logbook," I said. "Check it out. Neither of you signed her in. Her name's not there."

"But…one of us was at the door at all times," Dorsey said. "That's SOP."

"Not leaving the scene's SOP too."

"You say the words *ski mask* once," Dorsey said, "and we're going to duke it out right here."

"Forget that. Now think, guys." I looked at the log and pointed name by name. "Remember the ambulance, the two paramedics coming in? Two criminalists? Then me and Clarence? Hatch, the medical examiner? Lynn Carpenter, *Trib* photographer? Then Manny, the grouch. And three uniforms named Nick Goin, Chris Warren, and Alex Helm, who you let in for reasons I don't understand."

"It was because—"

"I don't care. I only care whether you remember them."

"Sure," Dorsey said. "I told Guerino you'd have a cow if we let them in."

"It was a pretty big cow," I said. "Okay, then there were two more criminalists they called for, after I left the scene. They were the last two you signed in. Remember them?"

"A wiry guy." Dorsey looked at the log. "Carlo Failla. And a young gal, red hair…Kristin Wennerlind."

"Okay," I said. "So you're telling me you remember every single one of these people who logged in? Now, I'll ask you again. Do you remember Kim Suda arriving?"

They both shook their heads.

"But we know she was there," Guerino said.

Their faces showed they didn't understand what it meant.

I did.

34

*"My body has remained in this armchair and has,
I regret to observe, consumed in my absence two
large pots of coffee and an incredible amount of tobacco."*
SHERLOCK HOLMES, *THE HOUND OF THE BASKERVILLES*

TUESDAY, DECEMBER 24, 1:50 P.M.

I HAVE FOND MEMORIES of Christmas Eve day as a kid. My brother and my buddies Gary Swan and Wayne and Lynn Kim and I, and my black lab Ranger, would gather at the Kims' house, sleds and saucers in tow. I had a hot pink saucer that, on the snow, could be seen from Mars.

We'd spend the day sliding down any slope within walking distance and make it back, fingers frozen, to Mom. She thawed us out with Ovaltine while Bing Crosby sang "White Christmas" on the big old 33 album platter, back when our RCA record player let us choose between speeds—33 or 45 or 78. We loved to switch them to the wrong speed so Bing sounded like Alvin and the Chipmunks.

I could still taste the chocolate malt of the Ovaltine and remember looking longingly at all the presents under the Christmas tree, a bunch with my name on them. Before the night was over, I'd unwrap those treasures.

Now, forty-five years later, this was Christmas Eve day too. But my life was no longer spent dreaming dreams. My job was unraveling nightmares. Still, truth is, since my childhood dreams of being an astronaut or a pro-wrestler or Green Lantern hadn't materialized, I couldn't think of any way I'd rather spend the day than solving a murder.

I phoned the chief's daughter. "Jenn Lennox?"

"Yeah?"

"Detective Chandler."

"What do *you* want?"

"When you were at the professor's house…that was just two and a half months ago?"

"I don't know. Couple of weeks after the first class."

"According to records, your class started in late September. That would put the get-together mid-October?"

"I guess."

"When you were at Palatine's that night, did you have your cell phone?"

"Always."

"You didn't take any pictures with your phone did you?"

"Probably. Wait, yeah, I did. Pictures of the professor and other students."

"In front of the fireplace?"

"I think so."

"Still have them?"

"Probably not."

"Don't you save any pictures?"

"Only ones I want. I don't keep pictures of people I hate. Not like Tasha. She keeps everything on her computer. She's a geek."

"You're sure you don't have those pictures? Can you check?"

"Why?"

"If you find them I'll give you a Starbucks card."

"How much?"

"Ten dollars."

She laughed. "Not worth it."

"Twenty-five dollars?"

"Thirty."

"Okay. You find me some pictures taken in the professor's living room that night—but they have to be where the fireplace mantel is visible—then I'll give you a thirty-dollar Starbucks card."

And they say we don't negotiate with terrorists.

At 2:00 p.m. Suda entered the conference room. To soften her, I'd brought in a cup of coffee and a white frosted donut with those colored sprinkles that irritate me.

"Coffee and donut?" I asked.

She shook her head and sat down. "I have twenty minutes, that's it."

"What time did you come to the professor's house November 20?"

"Near four, I think."

"I guess if I needed to know, I could just check the log."

"I guess." No twitch.

"You did sign the log, didn't you?"

"Probably."

"Could you point out your signature?" I handed her the log. "We've got paramedics, criminalists, Clarence and me, Hatch, Lynn Carpenter, Manny, and the uniforms you ushered out. You must have come in somewhere between me and the uniforms. So...why didn't you sign in?"

"They know me."

"They know me. And Hatch. And Manny. They signed us in."

"It was a zoo when I got there."

"Guerino and Dorsey remember talking with you inside and when you left. They don't remember you arriving."

"What's your point?"

"Where'd you park?"

"Around the corner."

"What corner?"

"The street next to the professor's. 22nd?"

"I left before you did, to check my messages at home. I took 22nd down to Stark. I didn't see your car. And it wasn't on Oak either."

"There were lots of cars."

"I notice cars. Was it your red Toyota Camry?"

"I guess."

"Why would you have to guess?"

"Yeah, it was my car. It's a Camry. It's red."

"How many feet from Oak were you parked?"

"Forty?"

"East side of 22nd?"

"West. Look," she said, "you showed up at one of my investigations, remember? Did I harass you about it?"

"I'm not harassing you."

She got up, teeth clenched, and stormed out of the room in a cold front. If she'd had a broom, she could have flown.

Have I mentioned I have a way with women?

I removed a few of the sprinkles and ate her donut.

I was going to meet Clarence at the *Trib*, but I had an extra fifteen minutes, so I stopped by to see Phil in crime lab. He wished me Merry Christmas. At least he wasn't wearing an elf hat. I handed him a clear evidence bag.

"Look," I said, "here's that gum wrapper, still sealed in your bag. I realize it was careless of me to drop it at the crime scene, but I shouldn't have picked it up. And I shouldn't have asked you to give it back to me. It puts us both at risk. I don't feel right holding on to it."

"Conscience?"

"You don't need to mention this. You'd be in as much trouble as I would."

"Okay. I'll just put it with the other evidence. I'll just change the date and leave it unmarked. Doubt if anyone'll notice. Nobody needs to know. As long as nobody needs to know about that contaminated blood sample."

"Merry Christmas," I said.

Clarence had been routinely invading my workspace. I returned the favor that afternoon. It was dry, so I decided to cut through Terry Schrunk Plaza south to Jefferson and head four blocks west to Broadway, where I turned left and entered the front door of the *Oregon Tribune*.

When the two gals at the front desk of the *Trib* asked for my ID, I showed them. When that didn't appear good enough, I showed them my Glock in my shoulder holster. I showed it to the security guard, along with my ID. He told me I might have to surrender my weapon. I told him that my Glock and I are conjoined twins and it would require a delicate surgery. I wondered if he felt up to it. He got on the phone. They let me through, then said, "Mr. Abernathy will come down."

"No thanks," I said. "I'm going up." Not that I knew exactly where I was going. I'd visited the *Tribune* about as often as I'd visited the Kremlin. No offense to the Kremlin.

Journalists are nervous about people with guns. This is understandable since they do so much to aggravate gun-owners. They write columns about how regular people shouldn't be allowed to have guns. Of course, I don't think journalists should be allowed to write words, which have destroyed more lives than guns. These thoughts contributed to my self-righteous swagger as I walked through the state capitol of self-righteousness.

I bumped into Clarence as I was about to get in the elevator. Clarence is a lot to bump into.

"I told them I'd come down to meet you," he said.

"What a coincidence. I told them I'd come up to meet you. Apparently we were both right. I'm tired of you occupying my world. I feel like occupying yours for a change."

"It's my job to be part of your world. It's not your job to be here."

"Here I am. Loaded firearm and all." I said the words loud, drunk loud, though I hadn't had a drink since yesterday. I patted my jacket and watched people look at us nervously.

"Homicide," I said loudly.

One woman in dress and high heels and fancy scarf, who I recognized as a columnist, turned pale.

"Don't worry," I told her. "I don't commit them. I investigate them. There've been threats about vigilantes going after journalists because of slander. I'm here to guard your life."

"He's joking," Clarence said.

It was fun, a Christmas present to myself, turning the tables and making people nervous who make their living making others nervous.

Clarence's editor Winston blew in like a hurricane. "Who do you think you are, barging in here?" he bellowed, Louis Armstrong-like, with cheeks to match.

"I think I am Police Detective Ollie Chandler. Wait, hold on." I pulled out my ID card, read it, and said, "I *am* Detective Ollie Chandler, and I'm paid to barge into places. Excuse me if my presence is inconvenient and uncomfortable. You journalists have always been sensitive to my convenience and comfort, and I certainly want to reciprocate."

Winston, his mammoth cheeks red, scowled. I scowled back. His natural face gave him a big advantage. He was the Grinch who stole Christmas. If an elf hat had been nearby, I would have crammed it over his head.

"Okay, enough holiday cheer," I said to Clarence. "Where's Carp?"

Clarence led me through the giant maze, explaining that most photojournalists just had workstations but Carp had her own office.

She greeted us warmly. I presented her with three Papa Murphy's coupons. "Clipped them myself." She gave me an endearing look.

I sat down and showed Carp the crime scene log. "You signed in at 3:51, but they didn't sign you out when you left to take the pictures on the street. When was that?"

"That'll be easy," she said. "The pictures all have a date and time stamp." She maximized her photo program and looked at the slides on her screen, then checked Properties. "Looks like I took all those pictures in eight minutes, between 4:46 and 4:54."

"That was quick."

"It was spooky out there. I don't hang around murders like you do."

I flipped through the neighborhood pictures on her computer screen three times. "No red Camry. Suda's car wasn't where she said it was."

"Why would she lie?" Clarence said.

"And why would she park away from the scene? Above all, why didn't she sign in? And why don't Dorsey and Guerino remember her arriving?"

"Is it really that important that she didn't sign in?" Clarence asked. "I mean, obviously she was there. We all saw her."

"Suppose the officers were right and she didn't slip by them," I said.

"But she had to slip by," Clarence said. "What other explanation is there?"

I looked at them both, preparing to say what I'd been thinking: "When Dorsey and Guerino arrived at Palatine's, Kim Suda was already in the house."

35

"That hurts my pride, Watson. It is a petty feeling, no doubt, but it hurts my pride."
SHERLOCK HOLMES, *THE FIVE ORANGE PIPS*

TUESDAY, DECEMBER 24, 7:30 P.M.

KENDRA ARRIVED at the old brownstone for Christmas Eve dinner, bringing a vegetable stew, a fruit salad with watermelon and grapes and pineapple, and a festive display of raw vegetables, including minicarrots and those little jobbers that look like corn on the cob. I pulled out some Thousand Island dressing for dip, so it wasn't a total loss.

Bing Crosby was dreaming of a White Christmas, and Nat King Cole sang about chestnuts roasting on an open fire. Kendra pretended that wasn't cool, but eventually sang along. And when the snow started falling, we stood on my deck and enjoyed it together. Kendra insisted we hear from Bing again. It was just my little girl and me and Mulch and the snow and the music. It was Christmas, and I didn't want it to end and tried to stop reminding myself it would.

We sat on the couch, her under her mom's blue Seahawks blanket, me covered with Mulch. We reminisced about Christmases past and how her mom always loved watching *It's a Wonderful Life* with Jimmy Stewart. Kendra opened a Target gift card from me and a scarf she'd never wear. I opened up a Best Buy gift card from her and a tie I'll never wear. Our hearts overflowed with yuletide thanks.

Kendra also gave me *It's a Wonderful Life* on DVD, beaming in light of our remembrances, and one other gift. At first I thought it was a big red handkerchief. Then I saw it had a point and "Merry Christmas" embroidered on it in green letters.

"Put it on, Dad."

"Yes, ma'am."

We watched Jimmy Stewart and laughed and cried and ate popcorn and talked about the movie and her job and her pregnancy and how she missed her mother and sister, all with a tray of rabbit food in front of us, Mulch wondering when the baby back ribs were coming, and me wearing an elf hat.

WEDNESDAY, DECEMBER 25, 7:30 A.M.

I sat in my UCLA Bruins sweatshirt in Carly Woods's room at Adventist Medical Center. Her face was pale, eyes red. After their Christmas Eve celebration, at 3:00 a.m., when most bad things happen, she'd had a seizure.

Janet and Jake insisted on stepping out of the room to grab something to eat. They took Carly's boy, Finney. An empty Christmas stocking hung from the tray, which had a cup of ice water on it, surrounded by some wrapping paper and candy.

"Want a Whitman's Sampler?" Carly asked. I declined. "Milk Duds?" Shook my head. "You're looking at my Whoppers, aren't you?"

"Okay," I said, holding out my hand. She filled it.

"What'd you get for Christmas?" I asked.

"Some CDs and clothes, but best of all, books." She pointed at the stack. They included a slipcased set of the Chronicles of Narnia and *Perelandra*, *The Problem of Pain*, and *Mere Christianity*.

"A C. S. Lewis theme," I said. I noticed there were no books by Bertrand Russell and decided he wasn't a popular writer for people in hospitals.

"Two were presents. I asked Dad to bring the rest. I wanted to reread them. *The Problem of Pain* is pretty relevant right now." She smiled like she had no reason not to. "Have you read the Narnia stories?"

"I saw the first movie."

"What'd you think of Aslan?"

"What about him?"

"Wouldn't you like to meet him?"

"Yeah, I guess so."

"He's Jesus, you know."

"I was thinking of him as a lion. King, protector, defender of justice."

"He's all that and more. Have you thought about the self-restraint and love it took for Aslan to let the witch and the evil creatures beat him up and shave him and kill him so he could take the punishment Edmund deserved?"

I nodded.

"The real King didn't just die for Edmund. He died for me. And you."

"I never argue with young women in hospitals."

"I can take it. Argue with me."

"I'm glad you find comfort in it. But to me, it's just a story."

"Some stories aren't true. Some are. This one is."

I looked at her, wanting both to agree and to argue.

"Let me read you something." She picked up her copy of *The Lion, the Witch, and the Wardrobe* and flipped back a few pages from the dog-ear.

"When the Beavers first tell the children about Aslan, Susan asks this question:

"Is he—quite safe? I shall feel rather nervous about meeting a lion."

"That you will, dearie, and no mistake," said Mrs. Beaver; "if there's anyone who can appear before Aslan without their knees knocking, they're either braver than most or else just silly."

"Then he isn't safe?" said Lucy.

"Safe?" said Mr. Beaver; "don't you hear what Mrs. Beaver tells you? Who said anything about safe? 'Course he isn't safe. But he's good. He's the King, I tell you."

"What does it mean that he's not safe?" I asked.

"For one thing," Carly said, "I love Him, and I'm dying." She laughed without a hint of cynicism. "He's faithful, but not predictable. I know He loves me; I know I'll go to heaven. I know the best is yet to come. But I also know that meanwhile, life here under the curse isn't real easy."

"I've noticed."

"We can ask Him to take away pain and suffering and death, but for now it's part of our lives. But He's going to get rid of it, once and for all. I was reading this morning in Isaiah 25...pass me my Bible, would you?"

She took it with both hands, so frail I cringed. "I'll read you three verses, where He's talking about the new earth:

> On this mountain the LORD Almighty will prepare a feast of rich food for all peoples, a banquet of aged wine—the best of meats and the finest of wines. On this mountain he will destroy the shroud that enfolds all peoples, the sheet that covers all nations; he will swallow up death forever. The Sovereign LORD will wipe away the tears from all faces; he will remove the disgrace of his people from all the earth. The LORD has spoken. In that day they will say, "Surely this is our God; we trusted in him, and he saved us. This is the LORD, we trusted in him; let us rejoice and be glad in his salvation."

"A banquet?" I asked. "Best meats? Finest wines?"

"I thought that might get your attention."

"My grandmother, who was a church warden or something, never talked about feasts and wine. She just warned against gluttony and drunkenness."

"Right now I don't have an appetite," Carly said, "so I'm thinking about God swallowing up death forever and wiping away the tears. I can't tell you what that means to me."

She reached her hand out. I held it, so delicate and fragile.

She said, "I asked Mom and Dad to leave when you got here because I wanted to make you an offer."

"An offer?"

"You probably don't think I have much to offer right now, but really I do."

"I'm listening."

"If you want me to...I could say hi to Aunt Sharon for you."

"Carly, stop it."

"I could give her a hug for you."

"But...I mean..." I put my face in my right hand, still holding hers with my left. "Yeah. Hug Sharon for me."

"You know, you can go to heaven some day, Uncle Ollie. Then you can hug her yourself."

I couldn't think of anything to say.

"The clock's not ticking just for me," she said. "You spend your life around dying people. You should know."

"You never give up on me, do you, Carly?"

"Nope. Neither does Little Finn. Or Dad. I know I'm going to see Mom and Dad and Finney and Uncle Clarence there some day. I'm going to see Uncle Finney real soon, I think. And I really want to see you again too." A little tear fell from one of her Bambi eyes. "I want to see you in heaven."

She squeezed my hand. There was no strength in me. But in that weak little hand I felt a superhuman strength.

"You know what you need to do, don't you?" she asked.

"Trust. Believe. Accept. Confess. Repent." I recited the checklist.

"Wow." She grinned. "Not bad."

"I can repeat what your dad's been telling me for years. Doing it's the problem."

"Why?"

"Okay, if there's a God and He loves you, then why are you...like this?"

"Dying? It's okay, you can say it."

"I don't want to say it."

"I'll say it. I'm dying. Can't say it's fun. I mean, I'd rather be playing tennis or at the mall. But then if I was, I wouldn't be talking with you like this, would I? And I wouldn't be spending hours with my parents every day. And I wouldn't be seeing Mom and Dad care for Finney. Sad as I am about leaving my son behind, I know that soon I'll be happier than I've ever been in my life."

"You really believe that."

"I really do."

"Wish I could."

"You can."

"It's not that easy."

"I didn't say it was easy. It's your choice. Make it while you still can." She smiled. "You like being the rogue, the unbeliever, the black sheep. Kind of your identity, isn't it? I know you get tired of people saying they're praying for you. So I won't say it."

"Thanks for restraining yourself."

She laughed. "You're funny. You're just a teddy bear. You're this big skeptic with all your tough questions and smart remarks. I love you."

In a flash I saw Kendra as a four-year-old saying she loved me. When I heard Carly say it, I felt like she was my daughter. I didn't want to lose her. I could barely see her now. Something was in my eyes. Carly leaned forward. I felt her arms around me. She couldn't squeeze me, but I squeezed her, gently.

"It's okay," she said. "Don't worry. I'm going to be fine. I really am. And I'm going to give Sharon a really big hug for you."

I stumbled out the door. Carly was on the inside of something, and I was on the outside. And I knew, without doubt, she was in a far better place. Part of me wanted to join her there, and part of me just wanted to run to the elevator. Instead I walked briskly. When I got to the parking lot, snow pelting me, washing my face, I ran to the car.

I sat there, head against the steering wheel, smelling wet upholstery, and wondering why that dying girl was so much happier than I was…so much happier than I've ever been.

"Stand at the window here. Was there ever such a dreary, dismal, unprofitable world? See how the yellow fog swirls down the street and drifts across the duncoloured houses. What could be more hopelessly prosaic and material?...Crime is commonplace, existence is commonplace, and no qualities save those which are commonplace have any function upon earth."

SHERLOCK HOLMES, *THE SIGN OF FOUR*

THURSDAY, DECEMBER 26, 9:30 A.M.

CHRISTMAS DAY had been a disappointment. Kendra, long ago, had planned to be with a friend's family. I was grateful we'd had Christmas Eve together, but Christmas was an anticlimax. Mulch and I lounged around the brownstone after my visit to Carly. Bing and Nat weren't enough to pick us up. Not even Alvin and the Chipmunks singing "Christmas, Don't Be Late." Mulch loves those Chipmunks, but the merriment was fleeting. The snow stopped falling. As the day spent itself, the gray morphed into darkness.

In those hours of melancholy I decided that Sharon was Christmas, and Christmas died with her. Mulch's eyes were pitiful, like he was remembering bygone days as a Russian refugee. Dogs can't be happy when their people are sad.

I turned on the radio to the all-Christmas-all-the-time station and heard Andy Williams croon, "It's the most wonderful time of the year." I turned it off. I agree with the sentiment, when Christmas is still ahead. But when it actually comes, I ask myself, *Is this all?* Why is it so much better in the anticipating than in the reality? Or is there a reality that's supposed to last beyond the day itself?

I understand why the suicide rate's higher on holidays. Ironically, so's the murder rate. People alone kill themselves. People together kill each other. What a messed up world. We could use a new one.

I read Sherlock Holmes's *The Red-Headed League* for the sixth time. (I put a checkmark on the stories every time I read them.) Sometimes they pull me up. But not on a lonely Christmas. If Christmas can be lonely, what hope is there for other days?

The more I drank the darker it felt, until I stopped feeling. The bottle never brings happiness, but it can cover misery for a while.

Thursday morning I dragged myself to the office, bleary-eyed. Forty ounces of coffee hadn't facilitated a resurrection. I drank the last twelve ounces without looking at the mug any more than I'd look at a needle when the nurse gives me a shot. If there were a caffeine IV, I'd have plugged in.

I sat there alone, I don't know how long, the Christmas blues and the hangover keeping me from focusing on the case.

I remembered my grandmother talking to me about heaven once. We'd no longer have these corrupt bodies, she said. We'd no longer be doing earthly things like eating or drinking or going to carnivals or pizza joints.

I asked her if we'd be able to swim, run, and play baseball. She said we'd no longer want to do worldly things like that. All we'd want to do is sing and play zithers and go to church. That sealed it for me. I didn't want to go to heaven.

Strange how Grandma talked about heaven but made me not want to go there. Obadiah Abernathy, on the other hand, was one of the few who made me want to go there. Most people I'd never want to spend a day with. It takes a rare person to make me think I'd enjoy spending forever with them.

When Clarence showed up, it was obvious his Christmas had been better than mine. He nearly bordered on being cheerful. Trying to cure that, I said, "Mark Twain claimed it was heaven for atmosphere but hell for company."

"Meaning what?" Clarence asked, in a voice that makes Darth Vader sound like he's in the Vienna Boys Choir.

"Meaning that heaven might keep your feet from the fire, but you'll have more fun with your buddies in hell."

"You think anyone will have fun in hell? It's God who made fun. He invented laughter. God has a sense of humor. The devil doesn't."

I kept thinking about that dream. And hearing the voice of Obadiah Abernathy: "Can't get on board widout yo' ticket."

I didn't tell Clarence about the dream, for the same reason I wouldn't hand ammo to someone pointing his gun at me.

Obadiah Abernathy shook his head. "I loves that man, but he gots it all wrong. It's You he should be thinkin' 'bout. With You, any place is heaven. Widout You, any place is hell. And hell's got nothin' to offer nobody, that's fo' sure."

"You're a loyal servant, Obadiah." The Carpenter laughed and put His arm around him. "Ollie Chandler's mostly wrong, yet…he's closer to being right than you think."

"What do you mean?"

"He saw something in you. He saw *Me* in you."

"He did?"

The Carpenter smiled. "Those most like Me never seem to realize it. They're more aware of their failings."

"That's somethin' I knowed plenty 'bout."

"Yes. And I love you for it. Ollie Chandler's far from Me, yet not so far. For in

Me he moves and breathes and has his being. He loves what he does because I'm in it. He loves logic and deductions and the exhilaration of search and discovery, all from Me. What he hates about life is the part that's not from Me. Even what he loves in food and football is a reflection of the way I made him and the earth itself."

"I saw You in baseball, Lord, all those years. I played it for You, You know I did. It drew me closer to You, my sweet Jesus. Some of us ball players been talkin', You know."

"Yes, I know." His smile broke out again.

"We're thinkin' on the new earth there'll maybe be baseball again."

"Can you think of a single reason why there wouldn't be?"

"Before I got here, I could have thought of some. Now I can't."

"Ollie's love for sports is a love for being connected, being part of a team with a common goal. I made your bodies and minds to reach upward, to improve, excel, have dominion, find joy and pleasure in the small and large. To see and draw close to Me."

"I don' think I really knowed that."

"You sensed it. And you lived it. Ollie saw Me in you. So you see, it's not only you he wants to be with. It's Me."

"But he doesn't know that."

"No. Clarence and Jake and Carly and the others must help him understand. I've put them there for him. It's their job to point him to Me, just as you did."

"What a wondrous job that is," Obadiah said, smiling remarkably like the One he spoke to. "What a truly wondrous job."

An e-mail appeared from Carp. It said "Photos attached." Manny had collected the originals, all taken in Palatine's living room, from various people, including Palatine's sister-in-law. I'd asked Carp to enlarge them, hoping to find what was in the "missing picture." I clicked open Photoshop.

Doyle stood with a cup in his hand and pretended he wasn't staring at my screen. I turned the screen away from him.

The first three pictures were terrible, but Carp had ordered them worst to best. The fifth picture was clear enough to make out a blonde and a brunette by the professor, but the facial features were indiscernible.

I felt a presence behind me and turned to see Tommi.

"Pictures?" she asked. "Family?"

"This is private, Tommi. Sorry." She walked away, pretending her feelings weren't hurt.

I called up the last picture, which was slightly better overall. The jewelry was a little clearer, including the chain necklace. Still, these could be any of a million girls. Whoever they were, the killer had wanted this picture—and not wanted the homicide detectives to see it.

What I'd give for clarity. I was so close I could taste it.

I decided to print it anyway, on the color printer by the copy machine. When I went to get it, Chris Doyle bumped shoulders with me.

"Sorry," I said.

"Watch where you're going." That's when I realized he'd done it deliberately.

"Got a problem with me, Chris?"

"Everybody's got a problem with you."

"Just doing my job."

"You're doing a lousy job. And we're sick and tired of you."

I thought of eight different ways I could take him. But I had other things on my mind.

Chris Doyle, the Pillsbury Doughboy, was wearin' cheese underwear and walkin' down rat alley.

He was beggin' for a whuppin'.

37

"It was a straight left against a slogging ruffian. I emerged as you see me. Mr. Woodley went home in a cart."
SHERLOCK HOLMES, *THE ADVENTURE OF THE SOLITARY CYCLIST*

THURSDAY, DECEMBER 26, 11:00 A.M.

I STEPPED OUT for a brisk walk in the asphalt jungle.

Walking to the west side of the Justice Center, I looked across Third Street to Chapman Square, with its shade trees now skeletal and even its resilient evergreens flinching in the cold wind. I considered crossing to Terry Schrunk Plaza but instead turned around and headed east down Madison, toward the Hawthorne Bridge.

Despite the teaser on Christmas eve, the dream of a white Christmas hadn't materialized. It seldom does in Portland. Now the day after Christmas, a heavy twenty-five-degree air pressed on my eyes, which watered, threatening to freeze. Tough as it can feel, winter has its own mystique, one of the reasons I like living in Oregon, where the seasons are well defined. Going out in the cold is an escape for me.

And perhaps a metaphor of my life.

I crossed Madison, then walked by two homeless guys, hands out. I ignored them. Then, on the corner of First Street, I came to a woman in bulky layers of old clothes under what looked like a Russian soldier's survival coat. She stood, leaning on a rusted shopping cart, exposed to cold and wind, unprotected by buildings.

She didn't look at me, didn't ask me for anything. Turning to make sure no one saw me, I removed my wallet and gave her a five. "Get some hot coffee," I said, pointing to Kaffee Bistro. She said a quiet "thank you," but didn't go for coffee. Maybe it was free somewhere in her world, at a rescue mission or something. I don't usually give cash to street people, but on a cold day after Christmas, I couldn't stand that she was out on the streets, with all she had to show for fifty years stuffed in a lousy Safeway cart.

I walked toward the southwest edge of the Hawthorne Bridge, knowing it would offer an arctic wake-up, especially with the twenty-mile-an-hour wind. In my four-block walk thus far, in one moment I'd inhaled absolute freshness, with all its promise, then the next exhaust fumes, then garbage, then urine, then a poor woman who hadn't bathed in months.

It reminded me that this world has survived two thousand Christmases, but somehow the promise of Christmas hasn't yet been kept.

I walked on to the bridge's pedestrian path, where the wet air over the Willamette River, splitting Portland in half, assaulted my face. I looked east hoping to catch a glimpse of Mount Hood. Nothing. I looked north at Tom McCall Waterfront Park, so alive in summer, so dead now. I looked west at the Justice Center and KOIN Tower, then southeast, across the river, toward the Oregon Museum of Science and Industry. I contemplated all the creativity, the ingenious design and countless man-hours invested in this great city.

I considered the paradox of its stunning outward beauty coupled with its stinking underbelly, two worlds impossibly coexistent. I thought about how great Portland could be if only things were different. If *we* were different. I thought it's the same with every city, every town. And I thought about how every day our leaders, local and national, keep spouting off promises that never come true.

I still vote because I couldn't sleep if I didn't. But I don't read the literature anymore, the latest blueprints for utopia. I refuse to listen to the campaign commercials that no longer stop in November. I can't change the channel fast enough.

There must be sincere leaders concerned about justice and helping people who need help and stopping crime. There must be leaders who know what to do besides point fingers and make promises. But I can't find them.

The political parties and talking heads serve up words that are shelled husks. I'm sick of them. I wished the cold east wind on my face would blow away empty words forever, or bury them beneath the icy river I peered down upon.

I wondered how many people had jumped off this bridge, how many finally gave up on a life that offers dreams only to kill them. I wondered how many jumpers had once believed that this world offers solutions to the problems of evil, suffering, and death.

I used to try sifting through the political rocks and mud, but I never found the gold. I can't stand the wonks and opinion polls and PR automatons who conduct their stupid studies and put their finger in the wind to find out what they should say next. The world will never be rescued by opinion polls. And from where I stand, rescue is what we need.

For ten years I listened to Rush Limbaugh and Bill Maher and others on every side. I'd agree with one, then the other, but I couldn't stomach the arrogance and word-wrangling and oversimplification and disdain. I didn't need help getting angry. I couldn't see conservative rage or liberal rage doing anything more than propagating themselves into sanctified smugness, which smells no better on one side of the political aisle than the other.

So now I just say no to news. I try to catch killers by day, then retreat by night to Nero Wolfe and *24* and *Star Trek* reruns, leaving the universe to self-destruction or Borg invasion or spontaneous utopia, not putting my money on the latter.

I would never jump off a bridge, I thought as I stood there. I recalled two occasions in the last year when I'd sat on my bed, Glock loaded, once having felt its muzzle on my right temple. That's how I'd do it if I ever did.

I gazed east one last time, still hoping to catch a glimpse of Mount Hood, outrageously beautiful, a giant snow cone this time of year. But what is to me the world's most beautiful mountain remained hopelessly hidden in the clouds.

A hundred feet onto the Hawthorne Bridge, I leaned over the south side, raised my arms, and clenched my fists. I screamed into the cold wind, knowing nobody could hear me.

My scream lasted five seconds. When it was done, I put my hand to my raw throat, then walked back past other cold people, homeless and hopeless, to the Justice Center.

When I returned to detective division, I wasn't the only one with a red face. Chris Doyle was on the prowl, face sweaty, a pale crimson, looking for someone to bump into.

Not just anyone. Me.

"You're pathetic, Chandler," Doyle shouted, posturing like a peacock without the goods.

Eight pairs of eyes locked on us. Apparently he'd let it be known that he was going to teach me a lesson. He could have let me thaw first.

"We don't want you here anymore," Doyle said.

"Does this mean you're going to stop paying my salary, Chris?"

"We don't deserve to be treated like criminals."

"Suspects. Criminals are the ones we arrest. Nearly everybody here is innocent. Are you?"

"You think I did it?"

"I don't know. Did you?"

His fists were clenched so tight his knuckles were white.

"I think you're a disgrace," he said.

"I don't give a rat's patootie what you think, chess boy."

He took a step forward. I held my ground.

"That's your opening move?" I said. "If the professor had been bored to death, you'd be my prime suspect."

His fist connected with my jaw half a second later. I staggered backward.

"Over here," Phillips yelled. "Chris and Ollie. Hog fight!"

It was like high school, everybody running to the end of the courtyard to see the fight.

I stood there fingering my lip and opening and closing my jaw, testing the hinges. I sized up the Pillsbury Doughboy.

"It's smackdown!" Noel said, grinning like a moron.

"Take him, Doyle!" Cimmatoni called.

"Twenty bucks on Ollie," Jack said. He pulled a Jackson out of his wallet and waved it. Jack had seen me head butt guys into tomorrow, so he figured it was easy money.

Doyle was waiting for me to make the next move while he caught his breath. I was waiting for the crowd to settle in at ringside.

"Chandler couldn't take my grandmother," Suda said.

"He's not fighting your grandmother," Jack said. "He's fighting Doyle."

"They should sumo wrestle," Cimmatoni said.

"That's not a pretty picture," Phillips said.

"Nobody tell Tommi or she'll call Sarge," Suda said.

"Sarge is over there," Barrows said, pointing, "pretending he's not watching."

I wiped blood with the Taco Bell napkin from my trench coat pocket. "Just a flesh wound," I said, ditching the coat.

"He's taking off the Sam Spade coat," Phillips said. "He means business."

Doyle ran four steps to me and took another swing. I smelled tobacco as it whiffed by. I ducked then punched him twice, first with a left, then with a right, both in his doughy center. With another right, I plastered the pack of Marlboros in his shirt pocket, sitting him on the back of his lap. But the Doughboy rose again, asking to be popped back in the oven. Doyle surprised me with one more solid crack on my chin. I saw fog and stepped backward. Then I came back with two more stomach punches. I've learned from Jack Bauer not to leave a mark.

"Chess players are slow movers, aren't they?"

He lunged forward, and I swung a haymaker with my right and dropped him like a manhole cover.

I was ready to finish him with my killer head butt, but your opponent needs to be standing to head butt him right. Doyle was rolling on the floor holding his jaw, then stomach, then jaw, then stomach. I wished I'd got him somewhere lower to give him a third choice.

I stood over him and leaned down. "Checkmate, bozo."

Suda tended to Doyle and glared up at me like I'd jumped him with a two-by-four and stolen his lunch money.

I pointed both index fingers at her and bounced on my toes: "Your grand-mother's next, Suda."

"My grandmother has a fourth degree black belt in Tae Kwon Do."

"Dog drugger," I said without thinking. She looked surprised.

Chris Doyle's what Nero Wolfe calls a nincompoop. But I gained some respect for him that day. He wasn't the pushover I expected. The Pillsbury Doyleboy showed some game.

Things aren't always what they appear.

THURSDAY, DECEMBER 26, 12:30 P.M.

Jake and Clarence and I planned to meet again at Powell's City of Books, where an hour's browsing gets me through about one percent of one of the nine color coded rooms with something like seventy thousand square feet. They boast 122 major subject areas and thirty-five hundred different subsections, about a hundred of which interest me. But that hundred contain tens of thousands of books. Powell's buys three thousand used books a day over the counter, so if you can't find it today, you'll have twenty thousand new titles to choose from next week.

I spent my "hour early" in the Gold Room, where aisles 313–319 are myster-ies, maybe ten thousand of them. On the other side of the Gold Room I spied a man reading *Green Eggs and Ham* to a five-year-old Sam-I-am sitting in a tiny wooden chair beside him. I froze, wondering if I would ever have the chance to read books to grandchildren and wondering why I hadn't taken time to read to my own kids. Was reading to my grandchildren another dream that wouldn't come true?

Next thing I knew, the hour had flown by and I'd moved through maybe five feet of books, which at Powell's is like a quarter lap in the Indianapolis 500.

There were too many ears in World Cup Coffee and Tea, so after some chitchat over sandwiches and fabulous Sumatra Mandheling coffee (according to the sign) and a walnut sticky bun to go, Clarence and Jake and I searched the endless nooks and crannies for the right place to talk. We settled, appropriately, near religion in the Red Room, in view of philosophy and journalism in the Purple Room.

I'd caught him staring, but when we finally settled down in our place, Jake asked for a full explanation of the bruises on my face. I walked them through the brawl with Doyle, blow by blow, like it was Frazier versus Ali.

There in the City of Books, Jake handed me one he'd brought with him: Bertrand Russell's *Why I am Not a Christian.*

I pointed to the philosophy stacks. "There's twenty more of those over there. You didn't have to bring your own."

"It's not mine," Jake said. "Last time we talked about this, I accidentally took your book. I finished the final essay last night, and guess what I found on the back page."

He opened it up to show a phone number: 555-570-6089.

"That's the seventh number," I said, halt in my voice.

"Something wrong?"

"It seems...vaguely familiar. Ray'll check it out."

"I had an interesting conversation with Raylon Berkley," Clarence said. "He told me Lennox wants to pull you from the Palatine case."

I wasn't surprised to hear this secondhand, considering the source. "Why'd Berkley tell you?" I asked Clarence.

"He wanted to see how I'd take it."

"I'm working on how I'm taking it. How did you take it?"

"I said you were smart-mouthed, opinionated, stubborn, outrageous, difficult to deal with. That you're always stepping over the line. I didn't mention that you confiscated from a crime scene self-incriminating evidence, lied about your alibi, and set a fire in an apartment complex."

"Nobody's perfect," I said. "I also threatened a hamster, but when you tuck Brent in tonight, tell him I didn't mean it."

"I informed Berkley that if Lennox pulled you from the case I'd tell the public why."

"He try to talk you out of it?"

"He told me he wouldn't let the *Trib* print those kinds of accusations against Lennox. I said I thought the *Trib* was committed to print the truth."

"What planet you been living on?"

"That's the smart-mouthed part of you I mentioned. Anyway, we went toe-to-toe. I told him if the *Trib* wouldn't let me write the truth, there's an alternative paper that would. An alternative paper that's already offered me a job twice. I told him my first article for my new employer would be about the chief's sabotage of the Palatine investigation and Berkley and the *Trib's* complicity in it."

"You really said that?"

"I told him I wondered what that would do for the spiraling sales of the *Trib*." Clarence looked me straight in the eyes. "You're not the only one who cares about justice."

"Them boys is gettin' themselves in trouble, ain't they?" Obadiah said. "But I has to say, I'm proud of 'em for it."

"So am I." He nodded thoughtfully. "So am I."

↔

Lack of sleep and frustration at not having my hands around the killer's throat were bringing me to a boil. What began as a discussion among friends had degenerated into something else. Still sitting in our nook at Powell's, I raised my hands, knocking three paperbacks out of alignment. "You want me to just blindly believe without asking questions?"

"No," Jake said. "Ask your questions. I just think you need to listen to God's answers. He's in charge of the universe. His fingerprints are on everything."

"That's a bad analogy to use with a homicide detective, bucko. If God's fingerprints are on everything, doesn't that mean they're on every weapon used to kill the innocent? Is He behind my daughter's disappearance too? If good people aren't rewarded and bad people aren't punished, the universe isn't fair. Injustice drives me nuts. If I could take it all away, I would. If He can, why doesn't He?"

"What makes you think He doesn't…or won't?" Jake said. "Is justice ever done in this life? Sometimes. But those times it's not done here and now, it will be done on the other side of death."

"How can you know that?"

"Because God promises it in the Bible." Clarence pointed to a long line of them forty feet away. "It says, 'Man is destined to die once, and after that to face judgment.'"

"I get tired of you quoting these verses when the fact remains that people who don't deserve to die do. All the time. Every day. And where's God when they die?"

"He's right there offering love and forgiveness," Jake said.

"Stop kidding yourself. God doesn't give a rip."

"You're drawing conclusions about God without knowing Him," Jake said.

"I know He killed my wife!" I'd raised my voice. "And that isn't all He did."

"What else?" Jake asked.

"None of your business."

"You need to give God a chance."

"Why give him a chance? He killed Sharon." I shouted it, jumping to my feet. "And He killed our son!"

38

"It is quite a three-pipe problem."
SHERLOCK HOLMES, *THE RED-HEADED LEAGUE*

I'D YELLED "He killed our son" before I knew what I was saying. Dozens of people at Powell's turned like I'd dumped kerosene on the New Age section and torched it. The place fell stony silent.

"Your *son*?" Clarence whispered, standing next to me. "But…you don't have a son."

"Not since your God killed him."

Jake said, "Ollie, I'm so sorry about Chad."

"You know about Chad?"

"Sharon told Janet."

"Why didn't you say something?"

"Sharon said you didn't want us to know. I was hoping eventually you'd bring him up."

"You had a son?" Clarence asked.

I blew out air and sat down, trying to ignore the stares.

"Chad was born three years after Kendra. When he was two years old, some bozo rear-ended us. Chad was strapped in, but it jarred him. Apparently he had some…condition. I've forgotten the name. They say if it wouldn't have been the car, it would have been something else."

Clarence's eyes watered.

"I don't want your pity," I said. "But I'm never going to forgive God for taking away my son. What does He know about how we suffer? I wouldn't take wives from their husbands and sons from their fathers. I'll never see my son again. Trust a God who looked the other way? No, I won't do it."

I was down the stairs and headed to the garage before either of them could answer. I didn't want to hear answers when there were none. In the face of what happened to Chad and Sharon, words were an insult.

I drove west on Burnside, not knowing where I was going, under the gloom of dark clouds that buried the sun. Appropriate, because when Chad died, thick clouds surrounded me, and I couldn't see or hear or breathe. I didn't console myself with Sharon; I consoled myself with booze. Like someone said at an AA meeting, first I took a drink, then the drink took a drink, then the drink took me. It was ten years before I sobered up and saw the sun again. Then, when Sharon died, the stars dropped out of the sky. Since then I haven't found much reason to stay sober.

Randomly, now deep on the west side, toward Beaverton, I drove by an abandoned graveyard, where the headstones seemed arbitrarily placed, many of them bleached, crooked, and sinking. Part of me welcomed the day when my name would be on such a stone. Part of me dreaded it, with a fear that tore up my insides so much my hands shook on the steering wheel.

"He doesn't understand."

"No."

"He doesn't realize that though he's tortured by his memories of me, my life's gone right on in a better place. And he doesn't have a clue that sometimes I'm allowed to see and hear him."

"They don't believe the Scriptures," Sharon said, "that there's rejoicing here in the presence of the angels over the work God's doing in their lives on earth. They think of this place as disinterested in what's happening there. They don't realize their planet is center stage in His unfolding drama of redemption. They're on the playing field. Those in the grandstands are watching."

"Here with my Father, I've gotten to know my earthly father too."

"You know him far better than he ever knew you," Sharon said.

"Will I be with him again?" Chad asked. "Will Elyon answer that prayer?"

"He says we must wait and see. But we don't need to wait to know that He's always good. Your father doesn't understand Elyon's purposes. What's now clear to us makes no sense to him. Yet even we don't understand it all, do we?"

"His ways are above our ways, and His thoughts above our thoughts," Chad said smiling. "But to me, that's beautiful. Whatever we don't yet grasp leaves us more to learn about Him."

Chad grasped his mother's hand. "I hope to walk beside my earthly father again—this time on an earth no longer cursed."

"His relationships with us, though interrupted, need never end. But he must come to trust the One he blames—and that will not be easy."

"Let's pray for him again, Mother."

Arms around each other, mother and son talked to Elyon about a man driving aimlessly on back roads, a man so far away he had no idea they were there, yet so close they could almost reach out and touch him.

A night-after-Christmas party had been scheduled at Chief Lennox's house. I'd never been in the chief's house, only by it. Most recently in the middle of the night, when we'd followed him from the 7-Eleven where he met Kim Suda.

This time the gate was open, and an officer was letting people pass because he recognized them or they showed ID. Turned out the mailbox was in a different zip code than the house.

I'd heard a lot about that house. What I'd heard didn't do it justice.

I'll probably never marry again, because if I did, my wife would want to buy this house, and if I took my retirement savings and held up a couple of banks, I still wouldn't be able to afford the down payment, and then she'd dream about it and show me pictures of it, and then she'd cry and I'd feel like a loser for letting her down, and my daughter would end up siding with her, and pretty soon our formerly romantic evenings of blackberry shakes at Burgerville and bowling at Mt. Hood Lanes would have a cloud cast over them. So it's better all around for me never to marry again.

About forty people showed up, but only three other homicide detectives—Suda, Chris Doyle, and Brandon Phillips, without his wife. There were fancy hors d'oeuvres. I searched for Cheez Whiz and cocktail wienies on a toothpick but finally settled for what was there, though I couldn't tell what it was. I wrapped up items in a napkin and stuffed them in my trench coat pocket for Mulch. When he smells it on me and I don't come through with the goods, he sulks.

The chief's wife was the perfect hostess. Thirty minutes into the party I told her, red-faced, that I was having some…personal problems and I needed to be in the bathroom for a while, but I didn't want to keep anybody out of the main bathroom.

She looked at me sympathetically. "Go all the way to the end of the hall and turn left. There's a bathroom on your right just past Ed's office."

"I'm embarrassed," I said.

"Happens to all of us. I won't say anything."

I thanked her profusely, then followed her directions. I came to the chief's office, looked both ways, and disappeared inside.

Twelve minutes later, I reappeared, looking for something to drink to calm my shakes and hoping the wienies and Cheez Whiz appetizers had shown up.

No such luck.

"The pressure of public opinion can do in the town what the law cannot accomplish."
SHERLOCK HOLMES, *THE ADVENTURE OF THE COPPER BEECHES*

FRIDAY, DECEMBER 27, 2:15 P.M.

"THE OPEN HOUSE was a big hit," Mona said.

"I expected more men would attend," Chief Lennox said.

He sounded like he was sulking. I couldn't see him, since he and his secretary were in his home office and I was in mine, sipping A&W root beer. The remote unit was picking up a clear signal, thanks to Ray's high-tech booster.

"I was surprised to see Chandler here," she said.

"Maybe he's seen the light and realizes he needs to get on my good side."

I'd just swallowed some root beer, and suddenly it was spurting out my nose.

"Did you hear something?" the chief asked.

I grabbed a paper towel to clean up. Though I was in the far corner of my office, I'd been heard. I'd turned my monitor low so their voices wouldn't be picked up by their own bug. But I'd assumed my office audio was being recorded and monitored at the precinct, not in the chief's home office. With bugs going both directions, I'd need to be careful.

Great thing about that bug on the chief's phone, one of the two spares Suda planted at my house, was that it not only picked up calls but also any voice within five feet.

"Chandler's at home today?"

"Our friend in detective detail says he's working at home today. I've heard him off and on," Mona said. "It's all recorded, but most of it's wasted. Thirty minutes ago I checked, and he was singing to his dog. Something about bacon and eggs and cats."

"Pathetic," the chief said.

"You'd think we'd hear something interesting. Occasionally he's on the phone, but he never says anything significant. He calls out on his cell phone from another room, for better reception I think, but then I can't hear him. We've had a week of voice-activated recording, but it hasn't amounted to much. And the bugs in the other parts of the house still aren't working."

"Maybe I should send Suda back. If he'd just talk with Abernathy or that PI in his office, we'd know what's going on. And maybe be able to head him off."

"You could get in trouble for this, Ed." I heard Mona's voice tremble. "Is it worth it?"

"If we're caught, I'll say it's because I had substantial reason to suspect him of murder. Including that gum wrapper he stole from the scene."

How'd he know about that?

"We need to find out what he's up to. Maybe we should bug that Ray Eagle character too."

"Could you justify that?"

"You know how I feel about this, Mona. That's one reason we need to have these conversations away from the precinct. As chief I have to make difficult judgment calls. I feel more freedom here in my home office."

"Has that *Tribune* reporter come through?"

"Button promised me he'd deliver Abernathy's notes on the investigation, but nothing so far. I told him no more leads if he doesn't."

I double-checked my recording device. Lights on.

Mona said, "The last inside tip the public got related to the vagrant."

"Right. Let's get the names of all the bums in that area then run background checks. Find the toughest record. We can provide some evidence, get a positive ID, and at least bring him in as a suspect."

"But..."

"What?"

"If he's innocent..."

"You aren't listening. I don't want you to find someone innocent, I want you to find someone guilty. That's the point of the background check."

A cynical laugh came out of my mouth. Covered it too late.

"What was that?" Lennox asked.

"Sounds like Chandler laughed. Wonder what he's laughing at?"

"He doesn't need a reason. The man's a clown. An idiot."

King of the Idiots. But Lennox was in danger of dethroning me.

Obadiah Abernathy. Why do I keep thinking about that old man? Was it because I wished I'd had a real father? Mr. Abernathy's gone. I attended his funeral. And yet...his faith was so real, his life so...right. I just can't believe it ended when he died.

Clarence told me what his daddy said on his deathbed, about the people he was supposedly greeting in heaven. Was he delusional? Or was he seeing things I'll never see?

That old man haunts me, comforts me, gives me hope. But he also unnerves me. Because if he was right about heaven, maybe he was right about hell. And that scares the bejeebers out of me.

Especially when I think about him asking me if I have my ticket because the train's about to leave.

"Lord, put Yo' gracious hand on Mr. Chandler." Obadiah's eyes shone bright.

The great guardians standing around the small but powerful man bowed their heads in respect for the One he addressed.

"Do what it takes to make him not so full of himself. Show him who he really is. And who You really are. Would You do that? For me? And for him? And for Your glory? Would You do that, my sweet Jesus?"

I sat at my detective division workstation making phone calls, looking around and turning my head, my voice low. I alerted Clarence to keep his notes under lock and key because the chief wanted them. And to keep his eyes on Mike Button. I warned Ray to look out for somebody bugging him, even though it was hard to believe the chief would go that far. Ray told me the number Jake found in the back of the professor's *Why I Am Not a Christian* was a convenience store's. Dead end.

I sat down, trying to clear my mind, attempting again to think like the killer. It isn't easy for me to think like a drug dealer, a lawyer, a con artist, or a Pistons fan. But thinking like a homicide detective? That should come naturally. What would I do if I were…what I am?

Frame somebody for my murder? Only if they were guilty of a crime just as bad or worse. I hated to admit it, but I understood the chief's logic about framing someone if I knew that person was guilty of something else.

Would I leave conflicting evidence to confuse investigators and delay resolution with rabbit trails? This could force the detectives to move on to the next case, making it likely they'd never solve this one.

Like the first glimpse of sunrise, another possibility hit me. If I were a Portland homicide detective planning a murder and wanted to be sure I wouldn't be found out, what would I do?

Of course. There it was. So simple. So obvious.

Why hadn't I thought of it before?

"I think that you know me well enough to understand that I am by no means a nervous man. At the same time, it is stupidity rather than courage to refuse to recognize danger when it is close upon you."
SHERLOCK HOLMES, *THE FINAL PROBLEM*

FRIDAY, DECEMBER 27, 3:40 P.M.

I SAT AT MY WORKSTATION, but my mind kept going back to Chad. Saying his name aloud to Jake and Clarence had unlocked the closet I'd hidden him in.

I was thinking if Chad hadn't died, maybe I'd have been a better father to Kendra and Andrea. Maybe everything would have been different. When the girls brought him up, I'd refused to talk about him. We'd all paid a price for that.

"How's the investigation going?" Karl Baylor asked.

Startled, I looked up at him. My instinct was to go on offense. "What if I told you that one of the detectives who says they were alone with their spouse at the time of the murder was lying?"

"That's a serious charge."

"As a Christian, you have convictions against lying, don't you?"

He hesitated too long. "Of course."

"Lying to a police investigator, and to your wife, is pretty serious, isn't it?"

I packed up my stuff from the table and headed off the floor, leaving him squirming.

SATURDAY, DECEMBER 28

By bringing up Chad, I'd opened Pandora's box. When I got the Saturday lunch invitation from Jake and Clarence, I knew what we'd be talking about.

I walked in and they were both sitting there, with "MacArthur Park" playing. "It's still going from the last time," Jake said, grinning.

"No better way to stretch a quarter," I said. But after it finally ended I was relieved to hear subsequent songs with more sophisticated lyrics, such as "Go granny, go granny, go granny, go."

We'd been seated at Lou's Diner only five minutes when Jake brought up Chad, like I knew he would. Before he could rationalize or minimize, I jumped on it.

"You can't understand what it was like to lose my only son," I said. "Or Sharon."

"No," Jake said, "but I understand what it's like to have my two best friends killed and to have my only child dying."

"And I understand," Clarence said, "what it was like to have my sister murdered. And my niece. And to lose my mama and daddy. And I know something about injustice too. I have a forty-year-old memory of his screams when those cops tortured him in that Mississippi jail. Just a month ago I woke up hearing his screams."

"So maybe," Jake said, "we understand more than you think."

"You believe God has hidden purposes," I said. "Well, I'm not one for hidden purposes. I say, lay them out on the table. I don't like being kept in the dark."

"But you're not God," Jake said. "If we were running the universe, everything would be a mess. Our minds just aren't big enough to wrap around God's purposes. That's where trust comes in."

"Right," I said. "You trust Him. I don't."

"You said you don't believe in hidden purposes?" Clarence asked. "And you don't want to be kept in the dark. Aren't you being hypocritical?"

"How?"

"In the Palatine case you've withheld self-incriminating evidence, placed hidden cameras, and now you've bugged the chief of police. I'll bet you had good reasons for all those, didn't you?"

"Yeah," I said. "Just like I had a good reason for setting the fire at the apartments."

"So you've done outrageous things and kept people in the dark, but you had hidden purposes. And you thought you were accomplishing something good. But do you think other people would understand and appreciate you for it?"

"No, probably not."

"Well, then, don't you think God might have some hidden reasons for doing what He does and allowing what He allows and even for keeping you in the dark? Some of your reasons probably aren't as good as you think, but is it possible God's hidden reasons might all be good, even though we can't understand them?"

I squirmed. "My son, my wife, your friends, your sister. Your God sits off in a corner of the universe, nice and safe. And we get stuck with the injustice and heartache."

"You couldn't be more wrong," Jake said. "God never sat off in a corner of the universe, nice and safe. He did the opposite. To save us, He became one of us. He faced all the hardships. Nobody ever suffered like Jesus did. He took on all our sins and sufferings. He endured the Holocaust and the Killing Fields and the sufferings of the slaves and everything else—including Chad's and Sharon's deaths—on that cross."

"You really believe that?"

"With all my heart. The Bible says that God's Spirit groans for us, awaiting our redemption. You think God doesn't care? His Son was innocent. After they beat Him mercilessly, they sent Him to a shameful and excruciating death."

"You'd think if He was God, He could've stopped them," I said.

"He could have. But He restrained Himself because it was the only way to rescue us. God had to forsake His only Son on that cross, causing Jesus to cry out in agony, asking God why. You feel like you're in the dark? He was in the dark, literally, as He hung on that cross. The Father buried His only Son in a foreign land. Talk about heartbreak. That was the biggest heartbreak the universe has ever known. Or ever will."

After a long silence, Clarence said, "Daddy used to say to me, 'Son, never waste your suffering—God has a purpose for it.' He doesn't want us to suffer alone, Ollie. He's there for us. And we're here for you."

"We'd do anything for you, old buddy." Jake put his hand on my shoulder. "But don't ever forget: God's no stranger to suffering. He knows exactly what it's like to lose His only Son."

"However, wretch as he was, he was still living under the shield of British law, and I have no doubt, Inspector, that you will see that, though that shield may fail to guard, the sword of justice is still there to avenge."
SHERLOCK HOLMES, *THE RESIDENT PATIENT*

MONDAY, DECEMBER 30

UNDER THREAT of being prosecuted for aiding and abetting a murderer, Mike Button, esteemed *Tribune* reporter, kissed good-bye journalism's bill of rights, singing like a bird. Unfortunately, what he sang wasn't helpful. He claimed an anonymous source mailed the crime scene photo that the *Trib* had published. An anonymous source would have lacked credibility. An "unnamed source" sounded better. He'd withheld the name not on principle, but because he knew no name.

Button produced the mailing envelope. The lab was examining it for possible prints and saliva on envelope and stamp. I figured each would prove a dead end. I knew Chief Lennox had fed a false lead to Button, but I still didn't believe he'd supplied the photograph.

Carp and I discussed these developments in her office, perfectly neat except for two rows of empty Diet Coke cans on her windowsill.

"Remember that evidence kit by the professor's leg in that photo in the paper?" she asked. "Take a look at this enlargement." She pointed to the screen and lightened the picture. "Watch what happens when I sharpen it."

She sharpened it twice. The second time it came to life. I saw perforation marks, six clamps evenly spaced near the edges, and what appeared to be a flap, raised from the object and pointing to the five o'clock position.

"That's no evidence kit," I said.

"If I superimpose this ruler, it shows you true size. Look at its depth."

"Less than an inch! It must be six inches across and eight inches tall."

"Pretty close. It's the back side of a five-by-seven photo frame."

TUESDAY, DECEMBER 31, NOON

I'd asked Jake to meet me alone at Lou's. I'd had a few beers when some misguided stranger selected a song Rory had apparently just added: "Achy Breaky Heart." I had to call Rory over and explain to him why this song didn't belong at Lou's Diner and why, if it wasn't removed within ten minutes, I would have to empty my Glock into the Rock-Ola, which I didn't want to do because I always liked that robot in *Lost in Space*.

Rory was extracting "Achy Breaky Heart," looking at me nervously, and Jake arrived, while the beer bottles were still on the table.

I asked him about Carly. She wasn't doing well.

"Sorry to bug you today," I said. "You must be exhausted."

"You're not bugging me. Carly's sleeping, and Geneva's at the hospital with Janet. What's up?"

"I need to...tell you something," I said. "I don't know why, but I do. Clarence knows some of this but not all. Promise not to tell him?"

"I guess."

I cleared my throat to shift the gravel.

"I don't know where I was when Palatine was killed."

"What do you mean?"

"I came home from Rosie's bar, but I lost at least two hours."

"You...lost it?"

"It's a blank. And it's not the first time."

"Blackouts?"

I nodded. "I'm on my own suspect list."

"You think you might have killed him?"

"Not really, but...I'm sure that Black Jack wrapper was already there. And when I drove to the murder scene there was a box in my car from Wally's Donuts, which is just three blocks from the professor's house. I don't remember going there. But...I've done other things I don't remember. I don't know why I'd kill the professor, but...something doesn't feel right."

Rory came to our table with another beer. When I lifted it, Jake grabbed my wrist.

"You've had four," Jake said.

I shook his hand off. Rory retreated.

"Now you're counting my beers? Counting my calories too?"

"I can't count that high. But I can count to four. Or five."

"What's your point?"

"You've been drinking more. It shows."

"Who made you my judge?"

"I'm not judging you. I want to help you."

"I don't need your help. It's New Year's Eve." I lifted the bottle. "Beauty's in the eye of the beer holder."

He yanked it out of my hand, and it spilled over my right arm and onto the table.

"It's not funny, Ollie."

"I'm not laughing." I stared him down while wiping my sleeve on my pants.

"I needed your help once, remember?" Jake asked. "I came to you about Doc and Finney after...what happened. I asked you to stand with me when Janet and I remarried. And I hope I've been there for you a few times."

I nodded. "When the *Trib* smeared me, you stood up for me. And when Sharon was dying..."

"Ollie, I'm going to say something you won't like."

"You already have."

"Think you know what it is?"

"You're going to tell me I need help."

"Yeah, but maybe not the help you're thinking."

"You're going to go Christian on me."

"I'm not *going* Christian; I am a Christian. Beneath your drinking problem there's a thirst for something more. Someone more."

"Yeah, yeah, I know this script."

"Just listen. One time Jesus stood before a crowd and said, 'If anyone is thirsty, let him come to me and drink.' He's the only one who can quench your thirst."

"I'll stick with beer, thanks."

"Beer isn't what you're thirsty for. Jesus went on to say, 'Whoever believes in me...streams of living water will flow from within him.' If you ask Him, God will give you peace and a perspective you've never had."

"I'm not looking for peace and perspective."

"Yes, you are. You've just been looking in the wrong places. Maybe you haven't been looking that hard, but don't kid yourself. You're looking. Everybody is."

"You seem pretty sure of yourself."

"I've been where you are, without Christ. Even when I didn't know it, I was searching for Him. He invites you to believe in Him and accept the gift He bought for you when He died."

"You sound like an evangelist."

"I'm just quoting Jesus, okay? I'm telling you how He changed my life."

"You want me as a notch on your Christian gun."

"You know me better than that. I'll love you and be your friend if you never come to Christ. Sure, it'll break my heart because I love Him and I love you. And I know how much you need Him."

"What's this got to do with me having a beer?"

"When you're reaching for your fifth beer, you're looking for something the beer can't give you."

"You know how many times I've said good-bye to the bottle?" I said. "It's like 'just say no to drugs.' Nice thought. Well, some people just say no to drugs, but the drugs don't listen. I was sober for years. But after Chad and then Sharon, and Andrea dropping off the face of the planet, and my problems with Kendra, and some of the cases I've worked…"

"It's been tough for you."

"You going to tell Clarence about this conversation?"

"Not if you don't want me to."

"I don't."

"Fine. But Clarence is in your corner too. He's rooting for you. So's Carly." When he said her name, he choked and his eyes misted. "She loves you, Ollie. Janet does too. Anyway, I wanted to tell you that at my church we have recovery groups."

"For alcoholics?"

"Yeah, for alcoholics and for other issues too. One group is called grief recovery."

"No thanks. I can take care of myself."

He looked at me long and hard. "Actually, Ollie, you can't."

The chief was working at home again. After fifteen minutes I fell asleep listening to the chief's fatally boring conversation with a city councilman. Mulch licked my face awake.

"Paul Hines, crime lab. Calling back about that Black Jack gum wrapper in the evidence bag, from the Palatine case."

"Yes, it took you long enough to get back to me," Lennox said. "I'd have thought the chief of police wouldn't have to wait for a return call. Were you able to confirm that it has the detective's prints?"

"Detective?"

"Yes, Detective Ollie Chandler. That's whose prints are on the wrapper, right?"

"No."

"You're sure? No prints?"

"No. I mean, prints, yeah, but…"

"Speak up, man. Whose prints did you find?"

"Well, sir, they're…*yours*."

The pause was so long I thought he'd detected the bug. Finally he said, "Hines, this is a setup. Don't breathe a word to anyone. Understand? I need you to take home those results and keep them until we meet… Tomorrow's New Year's…all right, you come in Thursday, day after tomorrow, 9:00 a.m. No. Forget that. Bring it to me right now. Come straight to my home office. You know how to get there?"

"Yes, but, sir…"

"Listen to me. Bring the evidence bag with the wrapper inside. Understand?"

"But sir, I can't remove an evidence bag—"

"Yes. Yes, you can. I'm the chief of police. You answer to me. Put it in something inconspicuous, and leave as soon as you can. Press the button at my gate, identify yourself, and I'll let you in. I'll expect you within the hour. Cross me on this, and you'll be sorry. Cooperate and you've got a bright future. Follow me?"

"Yes, sir."

I looked at the recording device, saw the numbers moving, and grinned. I fixed Mulch and me some Ovaltine, mine hot, his lukewarm. We might not have much of a New Year's Eve party, but this was cause to celebrate.

Mulch listened attentively as I nuzzled him and whispered in his ear, "Getting the chief's print on that gum wrapper, sorting through the trash, and making the switch in the evidence bag paid off, fella. You were the first to wet on the chief's pant leg. But you won't be the last."

42

"You have been in Afghanistan, I perceive."
SHERLOCK HOLMES, *A STUDY IN SCARLET*

WEDNESDAY, JANUARY 1, 8:15 A.M.

IT HAD BEEN A TAME New Year's Eve. After Mulch and I celebrated with the Ovaltine, I met Kendra at Starbucks. She had a triple-shot macchiato because she wanted to stay up past midnight at a party with her friends. It felt wrong that I didn't know her friends anymore. And I forced myself not to ask how her baby would feel about three shots of coffee. It was part of my new strategy of avoiding fights with my daughter.

Jake's New Year's party, my original plan, had been cancelled because Carly was still in the hospital. I'm not a Times Square fan. Watching the events prior to the ball drop is as entertaining as C-SPAN. Mulch and I welcomed the new year reading Nero Wolfe by firelight.

Groucho Marx said, "Outside a dog, a book is man's best friend. Inside a dog, it's too dark to read." At midnight I gave Mulch a second Budweiser.

As the fireworks went off, I contemplated another year of my existence, wondering if this would be my last and trying to figure out how much it would matter.

Now, the day after, sleeping fitfully and getting up at eight, I'd gone to Mr. Coffee to plug myself into French roast.

Last night images and voices had haunted my dreams. Obadiah Abernathy and Sharon and a young man I didn't recognize were talking. Then something happened. I wasn't sure what. I woke up, heart racing, at 3:14. But I fell back asleep ten minutes later and resumed my dream, where a girl had joined Obadiah, Sharon, and the young man. I thought at first she was Kendra. Then I realized it was Carly Woods. The four of them and some other people hugged and laughed. They all seemed so alive, so happy.

And, once more, I stood outside the circle of their happiness.

Jake called at 9:45.

"I have bad news," he said. "It's Carly."

I froze.

"She's gone."

My tongue stuck.

"You don't have to say anything, Ollie. But…pray for us, would you?"

"Pray?"

"I'm sorry. I forgot."

"It's okay," I said. "Is there…anything I can do?"

"No. Thanks."

"When…did she die?" I asked.

"A little after three."

"Is Janet…okay?"

"No. But we gave Carly to God years ago. Really, she was just on loan to us. She belongs to God, and now He's taken her back. Not easy to let go. God's been preparing us for this…except I guess you're never really prepared. You know how it was with Sharon."

"Need anybody there?"

"Clarence and Geneva are here. Friends from church are coming, already bringing meals. We'd love to see you if you want to come sometime."

"I don't have much to offer."

"You're our friend. That's enough."

"Okay…hang in there."

That was stupid. I've been around death more than my share. But I've never known what to say beyond "I'm sorry" or "I'll fry the guy who did it."

It's harder when you can't go after the killer.

I didn't want to go to Jake and Janet's and hang around with Christians. It bugs me that they think they know something about death the rest of us don't. On the other hand, who had more to offer Jake and Janet now—them or me? Not me. They'd be reading the Bible. What would I read? Nero Wolfe? Bertrand Russell? *The Wizard of Id*?

I shut my blinds, made sure the door was locked, and got on my knees. Mulch climbed on the couch and put his nose up to mine. His eyes looked sad. Dogs know.

"God, I guess You heard Jake ask me to do this. I've only done it once before, when I asked You to spare Sharon. You didn't. I don't know if You're there. Probably not. But if You are, please help my friend Jake. And Janet. And if Carly…I mean if people still live after they die…well, I hope she's okay."

I was embarrassed. I told myself, if there's no God, there's no one to be embarrassed in front of. Somehow it didn't make me feel better.

Once again, somebody wonderful had died. Somebody who didn't deserve to die. Meanwhile a million people who deserved to die went right on living.

Why?

I had no words of wisdom or comfort. I had nothing to offer my friends.

Maybe that's what really bothered me. Others could offer them the one thing I don't have—hope.

Funny though. Now I had a third reason to want to go to heaven. Sharon Chandler, Obadiah Abernathy, and Carly Woods. The Christians would tell me I should only want to be with Jesus. But I don't know Jesus. I did know them.

For a moment I wondered, did what I loved about Sharon, Obadiah, and Carly come from Jesus? Then my thoughts went to someone else, someone I'd tried to put out of my mind for twenty-five years. Chad.

I felt wetness on my face. Mulch, sad-eyed, licked the tears. I hugged him.

Mulch kept me from feeling alone in the universe.

One moment Carly Woods was awake in a world of pain. The next moment she felt herself falling to sleep. A rush of sound and light awakened her.

At first she thought she was walking through a glowing passageway. Then she realized she was being carried, effortlessly, in mighty arms.

Behind her was a ruined paradise, a wasteland waiting to be reclaimed. Ahead of her was a world of substance and light, overflowing with color. The place beckoned her to come dive into it, to lose herself and find herself in something greater than she'd ever known. In one moment, Carly Woods had moved from midnight to sunrise.

"Awesome!" she said.

"Yes," said a deep, resonant voice above her. She turned and looked up at the rock-chiseled face of a great creature, a shining warrior, looking like a man, yet different. She'd never seen anything like him. Yet somehow she thought she'd known him for years. She sensed he was rescuing her, that his job was to carry the wounded to where they'd be made well.

"I am Tor-el, servant of Elyon, God Most High. I have served Him by watching over you each day of your life in the Shadowlands."

"I never knew."

"Elyon knew," he said, the edges of his lips turning barely upward. "That is all that matters."

She turned to look where she was going. With every step the warrior took, she saw more color, detail, and activity. She could taste and smell life. The place reached out to her, pulling her in, as a magnet pulls iron filings.

"I'm getting stronger," Carly said, recognizing her voice, but realizing it was much fuller. She'd never liked the sound of her voice. Now she did.

"I thought my life was over. It feels like it's just begun."

The voice above her spoke again. "The end is behind you, little one. This is the beginning that has no end."

People crowded against a beautiful white fence, reaching their arms toward her. She heard their applause and an enchanting laughter. The warrior put her down.

She turned and said, "Thank you, Tor-el. For everything. I…I'd like to talk more."

"We will. There is much for you to discover in the new world and much to learn about what happened in that world. It will be my honor to guide you. But now is the time for celebration and greeting. Your welcoming committee awaits you."

She ran toward the joy and leapt carelessly into it. The years of sickness had been but labor pains. Now she was being born into heaven.

Uncle Clarence's father, smiling broadly, waved to her, beckoning her to come in. Standing next to him was a woman she'd seen only in pictures…Ruby Abernathy, Clarence's mother.

"Carly!"

It was Uncle Finney, a voice she hadn't heard in many years. She ran toward him and threw herself into his arms. They laughed. He whispered to her. Then they danced. And as they danced, Carly caught a glimpse of a young man she didn't know but thought she should and next to him a woman so beautiful and vibrant that she felt unworthy to speak her name.

"Aunt Sharon?"

"We've been waiting for you, Carly," she said. They hugged hard. And then Carly hugged her a second time, even tighter.

"That was from—"

"Ollie," Sharon said. "I know, sweetheart. Thank you. But there's someone else waiting to greet you."

Sharon bowed her knees to the ground, and bright light shone on her face. All who were around her bowed too, eyes fixed behind Carly, who turned to behold the most beautiful sight she'd ever seen.

She saw the brightness of a billion galaxies, contained in one person. She beheld a man who was God, Creator of the Universe. His face was as young as a child's, yet His eyes had seen all that had ever been and all that ever would be. This was God Himself. He put His hands upon her shoulders. She thrilled at His touch.

"Welcome, Carly, daughter of God!" He smiled broadly, the smile of a Galilean carpenter. "Well done, my good and faithful servant. Enter into your Master's joy!"

He hugged her and she hugged Him back, realizing she'd felt this embrace before. She'd been sad not to marry a man on earth. But she knew now that this was her Bridegroom, the object of all her longing, the fulfillment of all her dreams.

"My Jesus," she whispered.

"My Carly," He whispered back.

When the embrace ended, it continued, even as they stepped back to gaze upon each other.

He put out His hand to her face, and she saw on it a terrible scar. She stared at His other hand and at His feet. She fell to her knees, overcome.

He knelt beside her and looked into her eyes. She saw in Him an ancient pain that was the doorway to eternal pleasures.

"It was worth it, Carly," He said. "For you, I would do it all again."

43

"On the contrary, Watson, you can see everything. You fail, however, to reason from what you see. You are too timid in drawing your inferences."
SHERLOCK HOLMES, *THE ADVENTURE OF THE BLUE CARBUNCLE*

THURSDAY, JANUARY 2

I'D ASKED CARP to provide me a copy of the photo mysteriously given to Mike Button at the *Trib*. She'd made the comparison to all the photos taken; no match. Nothing with the photo frame we'd mistaken for an evidence kit.

"So…" I said, "you didn't take the picture. I didn't. Carlton Hatch didn't."

"Who's left?" Carp asked.

"The criminalists. The paramedics. The patrol cops on guard, Dorsey and Guerino. It's SOP to have a camera accessible."

"What about that other detective who showed up?"

"Kim Suda—of course! Detectives always have a camera."

"And she sent it to Button?"

"Why not? She was working with the chief when she bugged my place. Maybe she was working for him when she gave the photo to the *Trib*."

I must have scowled when I said *Trib*, because Carp asked, "To one of those dirty rotten journalists, huh?"

"Yeah," I said. "I mean…*Trib* photographers are great. It's the writers I don't trust." I searched her face to see if I'd closed the door on future pizzas.

"That's okay," she said. "I don't trust half of 'em myself. From what you've told me about police detectives, I trust them even less."

Our booth at Lou's is secluded, in the far right-hand corner, at the back. It allows us to see every direction. We know when we're being approached. The speakers connected to the jukebox that keep it relatively quiet in our corner but send out a layer of filtering sound. You don't discuss a murder investigation where someone can eavesdrop.

I'd invited Ray Eagle, but Clarence and I arrived fifteen minutes early. Jake was out of the loop until after tomorrow's funeral. Clarence pulled out four quarters, apparently motivated by fear of "MacArthur Park." We listened to Ray Charles, "The Night Time (Is the Right Time)," and the Drifters, "Under the Boardwalk," then Mahalia Jackson, "He's Got the Whole World in His Hands," singing like she believed it. Okay, the lyrics weren't as notable as "someone left a cake out in the rain," but it was mood music, one of the reasons I go to Lou's Diner.

"I'm going to tell you something I never thought I would," Clarence said, seeming nervous. "You know how I said my daddy liked you and asked me to look out for you?"

"Yeah. Made me feel pretty good."

"Well, he said something else. He said, 'Son, won't be easy for you, but you need to be full of grace and truth so Mr. Chandler can see Jesus in you.' He said, 'Truth comes hard for some, Antsy, but for you truth comes easy. It's grace that comes hard.'"

I laughed, partly at how Clarence's voice was a bigger version of his father's and partly at how perfectly he captured his daddy's inflections.

He went on: "'Ollie Chandler needs to sees grace in you. You hear me, boy? And when he does, he'll know he's seein' a miracle.'"

We both laughed.

"Daddy's eyes sparkled when he said it. You know, he could rebuke me, and somehow I still felt loved. Anyway, Ollie, I've done better praying for you than looking out for you. And I'm not sure you've seen much grace in me."

"More than you realize," I said. "Now Manny maybe hasn't been overwhelmed by your grace, but…"

"Don't remind me," Clarence said, shaking his head.

"One of the biggest regrets of my sorry life is that I knew your daddy for such a short time."

"You know what I'd say to that, don't you?"

"Yeah. That if I want to know your daddy longer, I could choose to live where he's going to live forever."

"See, I didn't even have to say it, did I?"

By the time Ray arrived, I'd moved the gardenias to make room for an album Carp had put together for me, with photos of each homicide detective.

"Helps to visualize suspects," I explained. "But it's weird that I've known all the suspects for years."

After Rory took our orders, we ran out of water. I brought the pitcher over to the counter for a refill.

"*Scusi*, Mr. Ollie. I noticed your pictures on the table," Rory said. "I know you talk about important things, so I stay away. And if I see or hear something, I never tell anyone."

"I trust you, Rory. You know that."

"It is probably not important, but I have a good memory for faces. I recognized two of the people in these pictures. They have come here before."

I took the water pitcher to the table and exchanged it for the pictures. I brought them back to Rory.

He pointed first to the picture of Karl Baylor. "This man was in last week, Christmas Eve day. You were here and greeted him."

"Sure. I know him."

"He and his wife seemed nice. They left a generous tip. But a woman in one of your pictures came at 6:00, when I opened."

I showed him Tommi Elam.

"Not her."

I turned two pages. The moment he saw Kim Suda's picture he said, "That is the woman."

"You're positive?"

"She was by herself. Acting strangely. I would look over, and she seemed busy doing something; then she would see me looking and would talk into her cell phone. She would turn and twist in the booth as if she was trying to get better reception. She even moved to the other side."

"Interesting."

"But something else very odd. Because she was alone, I offered her to sit at a table or small booth. But she wanted the big booth." He pointed.

"*Our* booth?"

"Yes. I told her up to six people can sit there. Naturally, if it is you and Mr. Clarence, then not so many—"

"Yeah, I know."

"She is a small person, and it seemed strange for her to sit in that big booth by herself."

"When was this?"

"A Wednesday morning—she had the special, my vegetable omelet, with the sautéed red peppers. A week ago yesterday. I am certain."

"Thanks, Rory. You have a sharp eye. Don't mention this at our booth, all right?"

He put his finger in front of his lips.

I went to the booth and promptly knocked the water pitcher onto the table, requiring a mass exodus. I apologized for being a clumsy fool. Rory came to clean up, but I said we should move. When we'd relocated to another booth at the opposite side of the diner, I asked Ray Eagle if he had the bug sweeper in his van.

While Clarence watched from twenty feet away, Ray ran the TD-53 over our booth. It activated. I turned on my miniflashlight, opened my pocketknife, and pointed with the blade at a bug, skillfully planted in the woodwork. I went to the other side, guided by his detector, and pointed to a matching bug. They were barely noticeable even under the light.

Ray went to our new booth and ran the sweeper. Nothing. He walked around to all the other booths. Nothing. Only one booth made the TD-53 excited—the one I'd been spending three hours a week in, discussing a murder case.

"Killing people's bad," I said, as my fingers became fists. "Shooting at me's irritating. Hanging in my garage? Unpleasant. Placing a bug in my house? Annoying. Drugging my dog? Let's not even go there. But now...planting bugs in our booth at *Lou's Diner*? This time they've gone too far."

44

*"You must play your cards as best you can when such
a stake is on the table."*
SHERLOCK HOLMES, "THE ADVENTURE OF CHARLES
AUGUSTUS MILVERTON"

SUNDAY, JANUARY 5, 3:00 P.M.

THE GRAVESIDE SERVICE for Carly Woods, for family and close friends only,
was excruciating. People cried, laughed, and sang. I didn't sing and I didn't laugh.

After we drove to the church for her memorial service, I looked at the people
sitting around me. I picked out likely wife beaters, child molesters, drug users, a
woman who'd poisoned her first husband, and a teenager who would eventually
kill a classmate.

The decent ones seemed gullible, unaware that sitting in a church service
doesn't make someone a saint. Their minds are at ease, right up to the moment
the smiling usher pulls a knife and shoves it through their heart.

Cynical? I suspect people who refuse to cooperate. I suspect people too eager
to cooperate. I suspect people who aren't friendly and people who are. When our
new neighbor moved in and he was friendly, I ran a criminal background check
on him. I just like to keep my head out of the sand. It's a good way to stay alive.
I mean, only if that's important to you.

There's something ironic about a skeptic sitting in church. It's like a vegetarian at a steak house. The people around you have tastes that you just don't
have...and frankly don't want.

It's especially ironic to be pondering this as you sit in the front row, guest of
the bereaved family...a church family. Don't get me wrong. I was honored. But
boy, was I a fish out of water.

The one consolation was Kendra coming with me. She'd met Carly and liked
her, but they weren't close. She knew it meant a lot to me, so she came.

As music played and somebody sang about "The Far Country," a slide show
of Carly's life played on the big screen. The little girl pictures were adorable, the
troubled adolescence evident, but in the last number of years Carly's face was different. A grown woman whose face had reverted to childhood. She'd become
innocent again. I remembered how she called me "Uncle Ollie." I knew she loved
me. I loved her too but wasn't good at showing it. Story of my life.

Soon my face was hot and wet. I wondered why they didn't open a window or something. I felt Kendra's hand on my arm, but I couldn't look at her.

Jake stood. I've heard him preach a few dozen sermons at me, but I wasn't prepared for this. He tried to speak three times. The words started but stopped. He grabbed the sides of the podium and tried again.

"I'm not a preacher. I'm just…a father." I felt it in my throat. "And the only reason I'm up here is that I was asked to do this by someone I couldn't say no to. Carly. I told her I'd probably break down. She said, 'If you do, it's okay. They'll understand, Daddy.'"

"I said—" Jake's voice broke. "Well, I'll leave that between us. The last few months, the last years, Carly and Janet and I have found encouragement in God's Word. I want to read from 2 Timothy 4:6–8. Paul says, 'The time has come for my departure. I have fought the good fight, I have finished the race, I have kept the faith. Now there is in store for me the crown of righteousness, which the Lord, the righteous Judge, will award to me on that day.'

"Paul calls his death a departure. A relocation. It's not ceasing to exist; it's just moving from one place to another. Paul knew that the moment he died he'd be with Jesus. He wrote, 'To depart and be with Christ, which is better by far.'"

Jake gripped the podium, knuckles white.

"It's hard on us, but Carly's more alive and happier this moment than she's ever been. Death isn't a hole; it's a doorway. It's not the end of life; it's a transition to new life. The best isn't behind us if we know Jesus. The best is still ahead."

How can you say that, Jake? How can you know?

Jake glanced at his notes, then looked up. "One day Carly said to me, 'We're homesick for Eden, aren't we, Daddy?' I liked that—homesick for Eden, for its beauties and pleasures and health and relationships. The Bible says heaven's our home. It's paradoxical, isn't it? Our home's a place we've never been. We're not at home in this world because we were made for a better world. The Bible calls it the new earth."

Jake looked at people all over the congregation, then at his family members sitting next to me in the front row. But he wasn't looking at me. He didn't want me to think he was talking to me. Naturally, he was.

"God wants us to have joy…yet we end up searching for joy in all the wrong places, and instead we find addictions and hollowness and misery."

Yep.

"Janet and I and Carly have clung to God's promises in Revelation 21 and 22: 'Then I saw a new heaven and a new earth…. I saw the Holy City, the new Jerusalem, coming down out of heaven from God…. And I heard a loud voice from the throne saying, "Now the dwelling of God is with men, and he will live with them. They will be his people, and God himself will be with them and be their God.'" It says, '[God] will wipe every tear from their eyes. There will be no more death or mourning or crying or pain, for the old order of things has passed away.' And then in the next chapter it says, 'No longer will there be any curse.'

"Second Peter 3:13 says, 'In keeping with his promise we are looking forward to a new heaven and a new earth, the home of righteousness.' Well, that's what our family's been looking forward to. We know there's a reunion ahead. And we know that someday we're going to walk the new earth together.

"Maybe you're thinking this is a memorial service, so I should be talking just about Carly, not about Jesus."

You got it, Jake.

"Well, Jesus was and is the most important person in Carly's life, and she made me promise I'd tell you about Him. For all I know she may be listening right now. I'm not going to let her down. One day I'll join her...I'll see my little girl again."

He stopped. The pause was long and gut-wrenching.

"God is so holy that He can't allow sin into His presence. Romans 3:23 says, '*All* have sinned and fall short of the glory of God.' Because we're sinners, we can't enter heaven as we are. God loves us just the way we are, but He loves us too much to let us stay this way. That's why Christ came, to change us.

"So heaven is *not* our default destination. Unless our sin problem is dealt with, the only place we can go is where God isn't...and that's hell. Judging by what's said at most funerals, you'd think everyone's going to heaven. But Jesus said otherwise. The Bible says we're not good enough to go to heaven on our own."

I squirmed. Jake had a captive audience, and he knew it. Unless a murder was discovered in the next few minutes, I couldn't escape.

"How much does God love us?" Jake asked. "He went to hell for us on the cross so that we wouldn't have to. God took on our worst suffering so we could go to heaven. What more would you ask God to do than what He's done for you?

"Like any gift, forgiveness can be offered, but it isn't ours until we receive it—and we can only do that through repenting and confessing our sins and saying yes to God's offer. If you haven't done that, you can do it quietly now."

Jake the evangelist. He wasn't this way when I first met him. He's a far better man in most ways, but this part irritates me.

"I began the message by reading from Revelation 21. I'll finish with reading a few more verses: '"It is done. I am the Alpha and the Omega, the Beginning and the End. To him who is thirsty I will give to drink without cost from the spring of the water of life."'"

Weird. Right when he said those words I was thinking how thirsty I was.

↔

Afterward we had a huge dinner at Jake's church. When I was finishing my second dessert, pecan pie, Jake asked, "How was your dinner?"

"Well, I didn't drink the Kool-Aid."

He stared blankly.

"Jim Jones. Guyana. Religious cult. Poisoned Kool-Aid. Get it?"

"So, what did you think?"

"The coffee was a little weak. Great pie though."

"What did you think of the service?"

"Didn't know any of the songs except 'Amazing Grace.' You guys don't sing familiar stuff, do you?"

"What did you want, the Beach Boys? Anyway, thanks for coming, Ollie."

"I...wouldn't have missed it. I mean...it was Carly."

Jake's face collapsed, and he put his arms around me. I felt him shaking. We hugged a long time, longer than I've ever hugged a man, though I don't keep a book on that sort of thing.

When we let go, I saw Kendra looking at us. Tears were streaming down her face. I put my arm around my little girl. Now she was hugging me.

"I'm glad you have each other," Jake said to us. "Be grateful. Don't let go of each other, okay? Fathers and daughters shouldn't have regrets. Carly and I didn't have any."

Janet came up beside Jake. Now they were hugging.

Kendra and I walked out, my arm around her shoulder.

I wasn't sure how a man could feel so incredibly empty and full at the same time.

"Beyond the obvious facts that he has at some time done manual labor, that he takes snuff, that he is a Freemason, that he has been in China, and that he has done a considerable amount of writing lately, I can deduce nothing else."
SHERLOCK HOLMES, *THE RED-HEADED LEAGUE*

MONDAY, JANUARY 6, 9:30 A.M.

JANUARY 6 WAS MY BIRTHDAY. Like the crabby uncle in the retirement home in that Hallmark commercial, I had no intention of letting others in on it. I always put in a full day's work on my birthday, proving to myself I'm not a little girl.

On Mulch's birthday I drove east on Burnside to buy him a Dea's longburger, fries, and an orange malt—which usually gives him a brain freeze. If Mulch could drive or handle money, I knew he'd do the same for me.

Tired of looking over my shoulder at people who might have shot and hung me, I deserted my post in detective division and turned the corner for the elevator. There stood Kim Suda. I joined her for a forty-second wait, in complete silence.

There are times in detective work when you need to be subtle, and other times you need to be confrontational. But in both cases the goal is the same—to try to catch people off guard and put doubts in their minds, and to read their responses like a polygraph. I'd been subtle with Suda. This seemed like the time to go on offense.

When we got in the elevator, she pressed the ground floor button before I could.

"What would you say," I started, "if I told you that the chief claims you were the one who bugged my house? And that he told me you were covering your tracks by setting me up for Palatine's murder?"

"You're lying," Suda said.

"What if he told me you might have planted Noel's fingerprints on the gun? How easy would it be for you to have Noel's fingerprints? Your desk is eight feet from his. You could get a Black Jack wrapper out of my trash any day. What if I told you that the chief said, confidentially, you should be at the top of my suspect list?"

She stared at me, trying to keep a poker face. It wasn't working. I saw doubt in her eyes. I'd tipped her off when I'd called her a dog drugger. But now it didn't sound like a guess. Suddenly her face hardened.

"You don't scare me, Chandler. I didn't break into your house. You don't have proof, or you'd be showing your cards. You're bluffing."

"You wore your gloves, but there's something that proves you were at my house," I said. "It's going to come back to haunt you."

"Dream on," she said.

"You always have your camera with you, don't you? You think I don't know you took a picture of the professor after he was murdered? And got it to Mike Button at the *Trib*?"

"You're so lame," Suda said.

"If I'm lying, how did I know it was you? If the chief didn't tell me, who else could have?"

Right on cue, the elevator opened, and ten seconds later Kim Suda was outside the Justice Center, walking rapidly, as if she were escaping.

After a brisk two-block walk to Waterfront Park, I returned to bad news: I'd been ordered again to Shelob's Lair, the chief's office. This was my fifth summons in nine weeks. I went to the bathroom with a bag, took off my shirt, and got myself ready, just in case our conversation proved interesting.

As usual, I sat and waited. This time I brought two ESPN magazines. I read one and hid the other under a couch cushion for my next visit.

Lennox was born seventy years too late and in the wrong country. He was doing his best to compensate for having missed his chance to be commandant of a slave labor camp.

Finally he stepped out and said to Mona, "Any calls?"

"Yeah," I said under my breath. "Your proctologist called. They found your head in your—"

"Chandler!" Though he couldn't have heard me, he beckoned, and before I was through the door he asked, "Situation changed with the professor?"

"No. He's still dead."

"They did a routine security sweep of my home office this morning. Guess what they found."

"Jimmy Hoffa? D. B. Cooper? Elvis?"

"They found a bug."

"A cockroach? I know an exterminator named Jim Bob—"

"An electronic bug."

"No kidding. Did you run a check to see whose it was?"

He squeezed the shiny fountain pen in his hand. "It was issued by this department."

"You don't say."

"Don't play games with me, Chandler. I know what you did."

"Are you suggesting I planted a bug in your house?"

"Yes! My wife said she sent you to the bathroom by my office. You had opportunity."

"But you said it was issued by this department, right? If I'd requisitioned it, there'd be paperwork. They would've entered the serial number in records. They could tell you exactly who checked it out. In fact, why don't I call them right now and ask."

I reached toward the phone on his desk. The chief let loose with a string of words rivaling Nixon's Watergate tapes.

"I have good news," I said. "That bugging device didn't cost the department anything. I found it right in my living room. Somebody here at Police Headquarters tried to bug me. Can you imagine?"

"You think you know who it was?" Lennox asked, pretending ice water ran through his veins while sweat was dripping down his forehead, smearing his makeup.

"Oh yeah. We both know."

"You can't prove anything."

"Even if the detective who planted it confessed?"

"Detective?"

"What if I told you she admitted the whole thing?"

When I said "she," his face froze.

"Suppose we've got her on tape, including her middle-of-the-night meeting with you at a 7-Eleven?"

He sucked a breath and coughed.

"What would you say if I told you she left a partial print on one of the bugs? And there's a match? What would Kim Suda do?"

He sat back in his chair, considering his hand. "It looks like we have each other here, Detective."

"Actually, I have more of you than you have of me."

"I had legitimate grounds for placing a bug. You didn't."

"There's a legal process for placing a bug, cop or not. All I did was find department equipment someone placed at my house. Then I returned it to the home office of the chief of police, the one who checked it out in the first place. Okay, maybe I forgot to mention I'd returned it. And maybe I forgot to turn it off."

"You won't get away with this."

"And you won't get away with setting up some vagrant as the murderer. Tell Mona to back off on that. It's recorded. Speaking of which, if I wake up dead, Clarence and Jake and two others get a copy of the recording and documentation. I've got backups and copies. You better hope I don't die even of natural causes, because if I do, you're toast."

"You mean, you think the *chief of police* would harm you?"

"You've already broken the law. For all I know you killed the professor. I narrowed it down to the detectives—but couldn't the chief of police get his hands on everything a detective could…and more?"

I pulled from my pocket the picture of his daughter and the professor.

He snatched it.

"Got more," I said.

He stared at the picture as I stood and walked out.

I took the elevator, hoping I'd set him and Suda at odds with each other. If one didn't trust the other, somebody might sell out. Though he'd be frustrated about what I had on him, he had every reason to believe I had no knowledge of the other bugging devices in my home office or at our booth at Lou's.

Once I got in my car, I unbuttoned my shirt and checked the mini-digital recorder with the cord that ran up to my tie. I played it back.

"Jimmy Hoffa? D. B. Cooper? Elvis?"

My voice was clear.

"They found a bug."

His voice was clear.

I listened to the beginning of the profanity.

I needed to make a copy.

Sitting in my car, preferring to work out of sight from a murderer, I marked three points on a Portland map.

I made a conference call to Clarence and Ray.

"Manny's wife," I said. "That hit-and-run that nearly killed her? It happened on a direct line between the professor's home and Portland State."

"Coincidence?" Clarence asked.

"Hundreds of people, thousands, live near that line. But what if Manny learned something and he confronted Palatine about the hit-and-run?"

"You're not saying that happened?"

"I don't know what I'm saying." I told them about my meeting with the chief.

"You really told Lennox you gave us documentation in case you die?" Clarence said.

"You've watched too many movies," Ray said, laughing.

"I was winging it, okay? Somebody's made a couple of attempts on me. Figured I may as well cover my...bases."

"You mentioned us by name?" Clarence said. "Couldn't somebody come after us too?"

"No more than a one in four chance."

"I didn't know you'd found Kim Suda's fingerprints on the bug," Clarence said. "I didn't."

"You said you did."

"No. I said, 'What if I were to tell you that I found Kim Suda's fingerprints on the bug?' You made the same assumption the chief did. You both need to listen better."

After I complimented Rory on the hot pink gerbera daisies floating in a clear bowl, I explained to Jake and Clarence I'd have to cut lunch short because I had to do something back at the Justice Center, then pick up Mulch, who was going to work for me. They asked me to elaborate, but I wanted to keep it a surprise.

"Remember that article Clarence wrote," Jake said, "about investigating a murder mystery—who killed Jesus?"

"Yeah. I remember."

"I really think you should do it. Investigate who killed Jesus and why. What happened to the body? Why were His disciples willing to die for declaring that Jesus rose from the dead? Think you could handle that case?"

"I'm a homicide detective, not a priest."

"It's not a job for a priest. It's a job for a homicide detective. Apply your professional skills, your honed instincts, to the murder of Jesus."

"It'll be tough interviewing two-thousand-year-old witnesses. Might have to repeat my questions. Or do you propose time travel?"

"The historical documents are still available," Jake said. "Including extensive eye-witness testimony."

"Yeah," Clarence said. He pushed his Bible across the table.

"That's a Bible," I said.

"The historical evidence is there," Jake said. "Read it. Then make up your own mind."

"Tell you what," I said. "I'll make you a deal. If I solve the Palatine case and catch the killer, I'll pursue that investigation."

"Deal," Jake said, reaching out his hand to seal it. "But try not to die before you've investigated what's waiting for you after death."

"I'll do my best," I said.

"Seriously," Clarence said, "you don't know how much time you've got left. You've nearly been killed twice. You need to be ready, Ollie. If Daddy were here, he'd tell you, 'Can't get on board widout yo' ticket.'"

I felt like I'd been punched in the gut. "What'd you say?"

"You can't get on board without your ticket. When we were kids, Daddy was always reminding us to get on the train to heaven and that Jesus was the only ticket." He stared at me. "Something wrong?"

"You sure your daddy said that?"

"Said it all the time when I was growing up. You ever hear him say it?"

I shook my head slowly.

The lie seemed preferable to the explanation.

Clarence met me twenty minutes later at the Justice Center.

"Cover me," I told him as I started toward the opposite side of Kim Suda's workstation, behind the divider.

"What do I say if someone's coming?" he whispered.

"You'll figure it out."

"What are you doing? What's in that bag?"

"The less you know the better."

"Are you putting a bug under her desk? Are you crazy?"

I looked both ways.

"She's sitting right there," he whispered. "Wait until she leaves!"

"It's got to be now. If somebody comes, clear your throat. Loud."

While Clarence pretended to admire the map of Old Portland on the wall, I got on my knees on the back side of Suda's cubicle. I crawled underneath and looked at her shoes, no more than twelve inches from my hands. I heard her voice on the phone. I got the goods out of my bag and went to work.

Two minutes later her feet pulled back. She stood and called, "Abernathy! What are you doing? Where's Chandler?"

I froze, most of me under her cubicle, but a prominent part of me sticking out.

Clarence walked over to her quickly, cutting her off. They were standing face-to-face (actually Suda's face to Abernathy's second shirt button). This was my guess since all I could see was their feet.

"He's working on a project," Clarence said. "I was just looking at this map."

I didn't know how long this was going to last, so I crawled past their feet and over to Tommi Elam's chair. I slunk up into her chair, and just a moment later, Chris Doyle said, "What are you doing with Tommi's stuff?"

"Just leaving her a note," I said.

"I thought you said he was working on a project," Suda said to Clarence.

"I was. You'd think I was a terrorist or something." I wrote, "Tommi, give me a call. Ollie."

"You're worse than a terrorist," Doyle said. "You're a traitor."

"You going to teach me another lesson, like last time? Sarge says we've got a meeting in two hours," I said, standing up. "See you there. And next time you want to brawl, Doyle, don't bring a pawn to do a king's job."

I showed up for the special 3:00 p.m. detectives meeting five minutes late. When I walked in, every eye fell on me.

Mulch led the way, excitedly looking for some place to pee. I yanked his leash.

"What's going on?" Doyle yelled, jumping to his feet.

"I gave him permission," Sarge said.

"Somebody broke into my house and planted two police department bugs," I said. "Mulch was there. They knocked him out with a sedative. They also managed to get their scent on this towel." I held up the kitchen towel. "Mulch has been smelling it, and now he's going to see if someone in the room matches the scent."

There were howls of protest mixed with laughter from Jack Glissan and Tommi Elam, both of whom know Mulch.

I gave Mulch a whiff of the towel, then unleashed him. He ran to the center of the room, sliding on the tile. Nose in the air, he turned a sharp left toward Kim Suda. He went right for her legs, sniffing her unmercifully. She kicked him in the chops, which couldn't have felt good considering her martial arts skills. He barked at her.

"Back!" she screamed.

"He won't hurt you," Tommi said, but Suda wasn't hearing it.

"It was you, Suda," I said. "Mulch doesn't like people breaking in and giving him hamburger mickeys."

"You can't do this," Suda yelled, heading for the door. "Get him off me!"

Mulch chased her, nosing his snout into her pant leg and shoes and latching on. She gave him one last kick, and she was gone.

The detectives were all on their feet. Doyle was steaming.

"She really broke into your house and planted a bug?" Phillips asked.

"Mulch just gave her a positive ID," I said.

"You made your point," Sarge said. "Now get that mutt outta here!"

↔

"I never knew Mulch was a trained police dog," Clarence said to me fifteen minutes later in the basement of the police parking structure. He looked admiringly at Mike Hammer, who was sitting proudly in the backseat of my car.

"He isn't."

"I wrote a story on police dogs. Not every dog can isolate one human scent like that, not in a room with all those people."

I reached under my seat and pulled out the kitchen towel, then pushed it up to Clarence's face.

"It smells like...bacon."

"Yeah. When you were standing guard and I was down on my hands and knees on the other side of Suda's cubicle? I was smearing bacon grease on her shoes and pant legs."

"You mean...?"

"Mulch goes crazy at the smell of bacon. And all without special training."

I opened my stakeout Tupperware and took out four strips of cooked bacon. Three seconds later, they'd gone on to the afterlife.

"It is murder, refined, cold-blooded, deliberate murder. My nets are closing upon him. There is but one danger which can threaten us. It is that he should strike before we are ready to do so. Another day—two at the most—and I have my case complete, but until then guard your charge as closely as ever a fond mother watched her ailing child."
SHERLOCK HOLMES, *THE HOUND OF THE BASKERVILLES*

MONDAY, JANUARY 6, 4:00 P.M.

AFTER MULCH'S DETECTIVE DEBUT, I dropped him at Lynn Carpenter's. It was her day off and she'd agreed to dog-sit so I could get back downtown to face Kim Suda. Chris Doyle insisted on being there. Sergeant Seymour agreed, despite my objections.

"Tell us your story," Sarge said to Suda.

"I already told you—"

"Repeat yourself. Why'd you come to the professor's house that night? And why'd you lie about where you parked your car?"

"I didn't lie."

Sarge threw down Carp's photos. "This is both sides of Oak and 22nd Street, taken by the *Trib* photographer while you were still at the crime scene. Do you see your car anywhere?"

Suda chewed her lips, but inside she was chewing her brain. Finally she said, "No."

"Is your car invisible, or are you lying?" Sarge asked.

"I was on foot. I don't live that far away."

"Yeah," Doyle said, "she lives just down—"

"Shut up, Chris." Sarge's voice was a fist. He turned to Suda. "You suddenly remember you were on foot once we prove your car wasn't there? Start giving it straight—now!"

Suda looked down, then at Sarge, then Doyle. Not me.

"Here's another question not to answer," I said. "Why didn't you sign the log?"

"I told you."

"You lied. I say you didn't sign the log because you were already in the house."

She shifted, crossing and uncrossing her arms, trying to manage her body language but failing.

"When did you show up at the crime scene?" I asked. "In time to kill the professor?"

She wasn't budging. I had another card to play.

"You know that strand of hair on the professor, the one that turned out to be yours? I talked to Phil and the CSI techs. They claim that strand was bagged within fifteen minutes of when they arrived at the scene."

"So?"

"So that was thirty minutes before anybody remembers seeing you there. There's only one explanation. You were at the crime scene before any of us."

"Spill it now, or you're going to regret it," Sarge said.

"Okay, okay!" Eyes flashing, she put up her hands and pushed back her chair. "Six weeks ago, early November, somebody sent me an e-mail. Couldn't trace the source. They warned me that the professor was…a ladies' man, but worse. They said he exploited young women. Sarge, you know I worked three years as a decoy."

"If you're telling the truth," Sarge said, "whoever sent the e-mail knew this would push your button."

"It did. I hate those kinds of men. So…I followed him and bumped into him at a Starbucks. That's how we met. We went out a few times. The last one was the same night he…"

"Died?" I said.

"You *dated* him?" Chris asked.

"Well, *he* thought it was a date. To me it was a sting. I was ready for him to try something; then I was going to take him down. Teach him a lesson."

"On what legal basis?" Sarge asked.

"I was off duty. As a private citizen I have a right to defend myself against a man who's pressuring me, don't I?"

I nodded. For once, I was liking Kim Suda.

"You *dated* him?" Chris repeated.

"I met Bill—Palatine—for dinner at Salty's. He behaved okay, for a jerk."

"Bill?" Chris said.

"Yes, Bill!" Kim said. "Anyway, I followed him to his house."

"His house?" Chris said.

"One more echo, Doyle, and you're outta here," Sarge said. "Got that?"

"Soon as we're at his house, he gets a phone call. Suddenly he's upset, tells me I need to go. Says he'll call me back later that evening. He didn't."

"Maybe he just wasn't attracted to you," Doyle said.

"Thanks, Chris."

"I mean, I work with you and I wasn't attracted to you for a long time."

"Yeah, well, that was tough on me because I was always so crazy about you," Suda said. "Anyway, fast-forward to 11:20. I'm at Chris's house and I get a text message on my phone, from Bill. He says, 'I need to see you right away. Come to my house. Urgent.'"

"Those were the exact words?" I asked.

"Close enough."

"You told me you needed to get home," Chris said. "You lied to me."

"Anyway, I show up and see a broken window. Lights out. Didn't feel like a burglary. Dark and heavy. I peeked in a window and saw his right arm. No movement. I drove off, thinking I'd call 911 anonymously. But then it hit me. He'd rushed me out of there, and I'd left my coat. No ID in it, but odds and ends in the pocket. And of all things, whoever was investigating this crime would be somebody I work with, who'd recognize my maroon coat. Even men might figure that out."

"We might," I said. Or not.

"So I decided to go back for the coat. But I had to get rid of the car—couldn't let anybody see it at a murder scene. I drove to my house, then ran back and entered a gate to the backyard. Door's unlocked. I go in with a flashlight and find the body. First time I've seen a murder victim I was dating ninety minutes earlier."

"Dating," Doyle muttered. Sarge stared him down like he was squashing a bug.

"I find my coat and suddenly see lights in the driveway. I'm peeking out the broken window at patrol. I don't think I've been seen, but there's no way out. So I get in Bill's closet and push back through the clothes and stand on a plastic storage box while they search the house. They're at the far side of the place, so I call Chris on the cell, ready to cut it off if they come my direction."

"That's why you were whispering," Chris said. "You said you were with your mother. That she was sleeping."

"I lied again, okay?"

"You're the one she called to lie to," I pointed out to Doyle. "That makes you special."

"You said you called because you were sorry you had to run off," Doyle said.

"I was sorry. But also…I was trying to…well…"

"Establish an alibi," Sarge said.

"Right," I said. "Why else would you risk being heard?"

"I was scared. I needed to talk with you, Chris. Really. Anyway, I disconnect when one of the officers comes down the hallway. He enters the bedroom, turns on the lights, and looks around. He opens the closet door, bends over, sees nothing. He didn't pull back the clothes to see if someone was standing on that plastic box."

"I'll send a memo," Sarge said.

"So I stay there for what seems like an hour. At first I just hear the patrol guys. Then there's some commotion, and I hear one of them yelling out front. Then I hear someone else in the house, in the kitchen, I think. I hear a clank, like a glass or a bottle. Then someone walks in the bedroom but doesn't turn on the light.

He…or she…I don't know, stands by the window, then shines a flashlight, like he's looking for something, on the floor, the bed, everywhere."

"What did he look like?" I asked.

"No clue. I was looking through clothes, then through a door crack, into a dark room. Who was it? Do you know?"

I shook my head. I thought it was the killer, but I didn't have a name, and I wasn't going to let Suda think I didn't consider her the killer.

"What next?" Sarge asked.

"I'm wondering where the patrol guys are and why they let this other person in. I think maybe they're just standing outside, but no, I hear them again, arguing. Then people start arriving one or two at a time. Now the lights are on and they're coming in and out of Palatine's bedroom. Including you, Chandler. You were talking with Abernathy, by the window, then down on your hands and knees and taking pictures. I'm peeking at you through the crack. I shift my feet just a little, and next thing I know the plastic box under me cracks. Thought I was toast."

"I remember the noise."

"Fortunately," she said, "you checked the right side of the closet and just pointed the flashlight to my side."

Sarge glared at me. "Memo."

"Hey," I said, "there couldn't have been more than four feet between what I could see at the bottom and top of the closet."

"I scrunched down," she said. "That shrunk me a foot. It's all I needed."

"So if criminals are short enough," Sarge said to me, "you'll miss 'em?"

"You were stupid not to check," Suda said.

"You, on the other hand, were brilliant, so here we sit."

"Keep talking, Suda," Sarge said.

"So I wait and make sure no one's in the room. I back out of the closet, looking like I'd just stepped in, and start examining the floor. Phil, the criminalist, walks in and gives me a funny look. We start talking; then I work my way out to where you were."

"I was right. You didn't sign in because you were already there."

"But I didn't kill the professor."

"Sure."

"He was already dead. It's the truth."

"As opposed to the lies you told us before?"

"Give her a break," Chris said.

"I'll give Kimmy a break after I hear her next story. The one where she broke into my house, drugged my dog, and planted illegal bugs."

"I'm sure," Sarge said, "you had good reasons for doing that too?"

"I don't know what I'm supposed to tell you," Suda said.

"The truth?" Sarge said.

"Now seems like a good time to mention that when you ran from my house after planting the bug, I followed you to your car. You were parked on Albers, north side of the road facing east. You hopped in the car, did a U-turn, and headed west."

"But...if you saw me, why that drama with your dog going after me?"

"Because I couldn't prove I saw you. And Mulch deserved some payback."

"I didn't hurt him."

"You hurt his pride. He's sensitive."

"He liked the hamburger."

"He likes it better when it doesn't knock him cold."

"Suda, you've really dug a hole for yourself," Sarge said. "What made you decide to go to Chandler's?"

"Before you tell another lie," I said, "I should point out that we saw you go to the 7-Eleven on 162nd and Stark at 2:40 a.m. on December 4. And we saw the man you met."

Suda's stormy eyes looked frostbitten. Her face fell in surrender. She turned to Sarge. "I don't think I should say this in front of everybody."

"Doyle, get out," Sarge said. "Shut the door behind you."

Chris moved to the door, slothlike.

"Gives you time to make the chess team reunion," I said.

"We're not finished, Chandler," Doyle said, pointing his finger at me.

"You going to gang up on me with three other pawns?" I looked at him sympathetically. "If it makes you feel any better, Kimmy's meeting with the guy in the 7-Eleven wasn't a date."

He slammed the door. The window shook.

"Maybe I need a lawyer," Suda said, "but here it is. Lennox asked me into his office a couple of weeks ago. He said he'd been examining the Palatine case. He had me scared. I thought I'd been found out—about being at the murder scene. Anyway, he said Chandler had become the investigation's focal point, the main suspect."

"He said that?" Sarge said.

"He mentioned there was evidence, you had no alibi, and you'd been drinking and angry that night. He asked how good I was at getting into a house and planting a surveillance device. I told him I was good. I asked if it was legal. He claimed he had a court order."

"Ask to see it?" Sarge said.

"I'm supposed to ask the chief of police to prove he's not lying?"

"What you did was a felony."

"When I'm ordered to do it, in the line of duty, as part of an investigation...by the chief of police?"

"Anything else you've done I should know about?" Sarge asked.

She shook her head.

"What about photographing the dead professor and giving the picture to the *Trib*?" I asked.

"You still on that?" she said. "I didn't have my camera. And if I had, I certainly wouldn't have used it. A flash in a dark house at night? With a body on the floor?"

"Then who took that picture?"

"How should I know?"

I nearly mentioned the bugs she planted at Lou's Diner but restrained myself. That was my hole card.

"You're dismissed," Sarge said to me.

Suda stood up.

"Have plans this evening?" he asked her.

She nodded.

"Cancel them. I'm not done with you."

It was a long day, but I've seldom had a birthday present better than Mulch going after Kim Suda's pant legs.

I left downtown for the second time and picked up Mulch from Carp's house, where she'd baked him pizza snack muffins. His eyes begged me to marry her.

"Any developments on the professor's picture in the *Trib*?" Carp asked.

"Kim Suda swears she didn't take the picture and didn't give it to Mike Button. At first I assumed she was lying, but she admitted other things. Why deny that one? But if it wasn't Suda or me or you or Hatch or the patrol guys or the criminalists..."

"There's one person you're forgetting," Carp said.

"Who?"

"The killer. The killer took the picture."

"Yeah, he took the picture from the mantel. I'm talking about the photograph of the professor's body."

"So am I," Carp said. "I mean the killer was holding the camera—he removed the photograph from the mantel, laid it on the floor, then snapped that photo of the professor's body. And he's the anonymous source who got the photo to Mike Button."

I started to argue. I stopped. A minute of silence later I said, "Pizza's on me. Ice cream too."

She said she was teaching a class at Portland Community College but took a rain check. I hoped she wouldn't forget.

We stopped at WinCo. Mulch stayed in the car. Generally he's banned from public places where there's food. Once I brought him into the Fred Meyer grocery section wearing a green jacket, undercover as an in-training guide for the blind. But it was samples day. After a few incidents, one involving a roasted chicken, they asked us to leave.

I picked up a tub of Breyers cookie dough ice cream. We were going to celebrate.

I pulled up to the old brownstone and thought I saw a window blind move. Not again. I pulled my Glock and quietly moved to the front door. Mulch picked up on my mood and slunk along next to me, growling softly.

I turned the handle. When I realized it was unlocked, I whispered in Mulch's ear, "Get 'em," and pushed the door open. Mulch bounded in, growling ferociously.

As the door opened I heard a loud noise and pointed the Glock toward it. I heard screaming and flipped on the light to see the faces of two men and one woman, and someone else on the floor with Mulch on top of him. It was then I realized what I'd heard. It had been the word *surprise*.

Jake pulled Mulch off Mr. Obrist, gave him a cookie, and immediately he calmed down. (Mulch, not Mr. Obrist, who needed more than a cookie to calm him.)

As I holstered my gun, Clarence showed me the Flyin' Pie pizza and an ice cream cake from Baskin-Robbins: Jamoca Almond Fudge. I grabbed my sack from the porch and quickly buried the cookie dough in the back of the freezer, where it would remain hidden for at least a day.

Mrs. Obrist led her husband home, saying something about cardiorespiratory issues. Jake explained that when he and Clarence got in, Mr. Obrist came over, thinking the house was being invaded. So Jake and Clarence had invited them to the surprise. In retrospect, they realized it hadn't been a good plan.

Jake and Clarence sang "Happy Birthday" to me and didn't sound too bad. Maybe it's all the singing they do at church.

At nine I thanked them and told them to get home to their families. After they left, Mulch and I finished off the ice cream cake. It was my birthday, and I was determined to leave no evidence.

Fifteen minutes later I heard something on the porch. I opened the door with my right hand, holding the Glock in my left.

"Happy birthday, Daddy," Kendra said.

She held out a box that said TCBY. "It's a yogurt pie, mocha almond. It has only half the calories of ice cream."

"Yeah, ice cream'll kill you," I said. "Hey, say hi to Mulch while I take this into the kitchen. Be right back." I ran in, grabbed the Baskin-Robbins box, stuffed it in the garbage, and ran water over the four bowls.

Kendra and Mulch and I had a great time in the living room over mocha almond yogurt, which was surprisingly good.

"Since it's only half the calories," I said to Kendra, "I guess I can eat twice as much."

It was smooth sailing the whole evening. I didn't ask anything about how cows feel about yogurt. Kendra gave Mulch his own bowl. Afterward he curled up at her feet. It was my happiest birthday since Sharon died.

TUESDAY, JANUARY 7, 12:45 P.M.

It's hard to work on the detective floor when you figure the killer's within sixty feet of you and can walk by anytime and see what's on your computer screen or listen to your conversations. That's why Lou's Diner had become my honorary office. I'd had several meetings in other booths, in light of the bugs, but for today's meeting with Ray Eagle I deliberately chose our booth. I had prepped him ahead of time so we shared the same script.

"I think I'm being followed," I said to Ray.

"I've been looking over my shoulder too," Ray said. "If somebody planted a bug in your living room, there's no telling what else they're doing."

"I didn't want Clarence and Jake here. I'm going to give you some sensitive information. Once you see what it is, you'll know what to do with it."

"How sensitive?"

"It includes thirty pages of police department records."

"No joke? Where is it?"

"Couldn't bring it here. Somebody may realize the records were copied. If I was caught giving them to you, we'd be dead meat. If we're being followed, they could apprehend us on suspicion of a felony—divulging classified information. Internal Affairs would crucify me."

"So how am I going to get the papers? You come to my house? I go to yours?"

"Not with possible tails. And either of our houses could be bugged—in my case rebugged. Here's how the pros do it. We meet somewhere we've never been. We both make sure we're not tailed, or that we shake the tail. That's a lot easier after dark. Let's meet tonight, 1:30 a.m."

"Could we make it a little earlier?"

"Midnight's as early as I'll go. You know that big white building on 55th and Hawthorne, on the hill? The mansion?"

"The one they made into a seminary?"

"Yeah, that's it. Western Seminary." I pulled out my Thomas Guide and pointed. "There's a back parking lot right here on the corner of 57th and Madison. You can get in from either street. Nice hedge for privacy. Easy access but inconspicuous. Nobody's there at night. I've scoped it out. Just drive in and I'll be waiting. Shouldn't be chained, but if it is, park on 57th in front of the chain. I'll get out and hand you the documents."

"Isn't this a bit cloak-and-dagger?"

"Look, I've got lab reports, department e-mails, evidence incriminating Brandon Phillips and Kim Suda. This is hot stuff. If I was caught giving you police info, I'd lose my job in a heartbeat. And you'd lose your license."

"It's worth the risk?"

"I've done night exchanges before. Just can't let anyone know where and when. We'll be okay. Don't make copies of what I give you. After you've gone over it, burn it. Shredder's not good enough. They know you're helping me and might be sorting your trash."

"I feel like we're in a movie," Ray said with a sly smile.

"Can't use our cars. I'm borrowing a friend's black Cadillac STS, four door. You got somebody's you can use?"

"Going fancy? Well, my brother's got a silver BMW 530i, four door."

"Perfect. Midnight tonight. Whoever gets there first, stay in the car until the other arrives. I'll get out and hand you the papers; then we're gone."

"We really have to do it like this? Not a quick transfer at a public place?"

"Trust me." I winked at Ray. "I know what I'm doing."

47

"Bear in mind one of the phrases in that queer old legend and avoid the moor in those hours of darkness when the powers of evil are exalted."
SHERLOCK HOLMES, *THE HOUND OF THE BASKERVILLES*

TUESDAY, JANUARY 7, 2:00 P.M.

SERGEANT SEYMOUR told me he'd given Kim Suda a stern warning. There'd be an investigation.

"You believe her?" he asked me. "The part about the chief?"

"I saw them together. And I saw an e-mail she sent to him confirming that she'd done a job for him. That same night she planted the bugs at my place and messed with Mulch."

I handed Sarge the e-mail printout.

After rereading it a few times and bawling me out for holding it back, he said, "Why would Lennox risk his career?"

"Maybe he thinks his career is over if a police detective's guilty of murder. What's more important to him than anything else?"

"His image." Sarge scowled.

"So if the evidence makes the chief look really bad, that might explain his obsession with a cover-up. I think he's desperate to come out of this thing intact. And he's arrogant enough to think he can get away with it."

"I don't care if he's not available," I said, in the privacy of Sarge's office, which he loaned me for a half hour. "Tell him it's a call from the police department. You have caller ID? Check where I'm calling from. Portland Police."

"I'd need to give him your name," she said.

"Tell him I'm an informant. Anonymous. I've got incriminating information he'll want to have. Tell him if he doesn't get it from me tonight, I'm giving it to the newspaper. And it's not going to make him look good."

Amazing how placing an anonymous phone call from the police department can make a political VIP who was "absolutely unavailable" instantly available.

I finished the call by telling him, "I'll be driving a silver BMW 530i, four door. You come to me. I'll roll down the window. Now listen, I want you to hand me twenty sheets of blank eight-and-a-half-by-eleven paper in a plain brown envelope."

"But why—?"

"Never mind why. In exchange, I'll give you a file of information that'll show you what they've been doing under your nose. Got it?"

Five minutes later, I made a second call, finally talking my way through to the man I wanted. "Never mind who this is. I'm a police insider, and I've got a major story. Involves mishandling of the Palatine murder investigation. Ollie Chandler's a jerk, and this'll take him down."

"Why are you calling me? I can give you the names and numbers of—"

"It's you or it's nobody. You know that mansion on 55th and Hawthorne, on the hill, the one they turned into a seminary? There's a back parking lot, quiet and inconspicuous, off 57th and Madison. I'll meet you there at midnight. Come by yourself."

"Many people work for me. I'll send one of them."

"You do and he'll get nothing. If it's not important enough to show your face, I'll give it to a TV station. You can watch it on the news. I'll spread the word you turned the story down. I'll be driving a black Cadillac STS, four door. Dim your lights. Don't want faces visible."

After a long pause he said, "All right. I'll be there at midnight."

The man once known as William Palatine thought he was having a nightmare. After the disturbing phone call that had changed his evening plans, he'd been at his desk, alternating between correcting papers and playing solitaire, when he heard the knock. He shouldn't have trusted him.

He remembered the agony of his death. But why was he still conscious? He was a materialist. Nothing exists but natural phenomena. The mind was merely the brain. Man was but an animal. God was a myth. There was no life after death.

It hit him like a sledgehammer: "Nietzsche was wrong. God's not dead. He's alive, and I must answer to Him."

He saw the deceptions he'd told. He saw the faces of girls he'd seduced. He saw their shame. He saw their tears, their violated trust, their regrets. In one case, he saw her death.

He felt the full weight of guilt he'd guarded himself from. His only prayer had been answered: He didn't want God, and God wasn't here. Palatine had chosen this misery.

It turned a screw into his aching head. The hell he'd laughed at was now his residence. He knew, intuitively, that it always would be. The era of choice was past. This was the era of consequence.

Where were Hobbes and Sartre and Heidegger now? Where were Hume, Schopenhauer, and Camus? Where was Bertrand Russell? Their thoughts had been magnificent, captivating, compelling.

And, in the most important respects, wrong.

William Palatine's identity as the brilliant philosophy professor meant nothing here. The oppressive terror of utter aloneness descended on him like sharp talons.

The torment was in knowing it could have been avoided. There'd been a lifetime of opportunity to seek and knock and ask, to examine the evidence, to find the truth. But that life was over, and with it, opportunity. What he faced now was not life but mere existence, in torment.

He'd made his living speaking great ideas to students. Some of the ideas were true. Many weren't. Had he suspected it before? He'd been part of a grand scheme of deception, orchestrated by powers who'd first deceived him then used him to deceive others.

He wanted the opportunity to talk his way out of hell. He'd always been good with words. But eloquence meant nothing in a place where truth was known and unchallengeable.

In philosophy classes he had ignored or mocked—depending on his mood—the claims of Jesus. One thing he'd never done was to teach those claims, letting students investigate and draw their own conclusions. No, he'd stood between them and the truth, dealing them his prepackaged suite of conclusions. They wouldn't have to think. He'd done their thinking for them.

William Palatine had argued persuasively that God did not exist.

Bible? Myth.

Creation? Legend.

Incarnation? Fiction.

Resurrection? Invention.

Heaven and hell? Nonexistent.

The adoring looks of students, once ego-fuel, haunted him.

The judgment awaited him, he knew, but his sentence was certain. He saw a great and terrible face, twisted and hideous. The Father of Deception. Palatine cringed in fear at the thought that someone so incalculably evil had used him. He'd served a malevolent being he'd never believed in. He saw other twisted beings now. He'd been deceived by forces beyond his imagination, forces whose existence he'd denied. He caught a terrifying glimpse of hordes of these evil beings with gruesome faces. They'd hated him every moment they'd used him. Now they found pleasure in his misery.

Countless millions of poor followers of Jesus, whom he'd disdained as ignoramuses, had been right. They'd faithfully followed their Master, living lives of grace, truth, and quiet dignity. None of them were here.

How many students who'd been raised to worship Jesus had he led away from the truth? How many, under his teaching, had forever deserted their churches or felt superior to their pathetic parents who'd paid their tuition but were stupid enough to believe the Bible?

"I am Dr. William Palatine." He spoke the words but could not hear them. They evaporated into the nothingness.

He had been William Palatine. Now he was nobody.

On earth he'd rejected God while enjoying His provisions. But it was clear that God's absence meant the absence of all God gives. No God, no good. Forever.

A wave came across him. Some extension of God's presence, like a wind blowing through hell's desert. Was this the same presence that in heaven caused men to be filled with joy and awe and love? Here it was unbearable. God's love felt like wrath, His joy like torture. The consuming fire of God that was purity and goodness and comfort to those who loved the light was searing punishment to those who loved darkness. Including the once-William Palatine.

"Get away from me! Get away!"

The tedium crushed him already, though he'd been here a short time. What would a million years of this do to him? No sleep. No escape. An end without end.

"I had a choice!" he screamed in rage and horror. His scream sounded like a crazed animal, caught in a trap. The terror of hearing his own scream was exceeded only by the horror of his realization:

No one else would hear his cry.

No one would ever rescue him.

Having taken down Suda, I was on a roll. It was time to face off with Karl Baylor.

One-on-one in the conference room, I raked Baylor over the coals about his phony alibi. He refused to explain. Finally, right when I was thinking of how Jack Bauer would find some electrical wires or inject him with truth serum, Tommi Elam walked in the conference room door.

"This is private," I said.

"If it's about Karl's alibi, I have something to say."

"In that case, sit down."

"Don't do it," Karl said, standing up.

"I have no choice," Tommi said.

"If you know something about that night and why your Christian partner would lie to his wife and to me, you can speak up. Or you can be charged with obstructing justice, maybe as an accomplice to murder."

"Karl wasn't the only one who lied," Tommi said. "I did too."

"But...you said you were in bed with Peter that night. You remember Peter...your soul mate?"

"After eleven I wasn't with Peter."

"Tommi, don't—"

"Shut up, Karl," I said. "Okay, Tommi, if you weren't with Peter, where were you?"

She put her face in her hands. "I was with Karl."

48

"My correspondence is a varied one and I am somewhat upon my guard against any packages which reach me."
SHERLOCK HOLMES, *THE ADVENTURE OF THE DYING DETECTIVE*

TUESDAY, JANUARY 7, 4:00 P.M.

I'D SEEN PLENTY of affairs among cops. But I hadn't seen this one coming.

"I look forward to hearing what your wife thinks about this," I told Baylor. "And Tommi's husband."

"Peter knows all about it," Tommi said.

"He does?"

"I left the house around 10:30. He called me about midnight to see where I was."

"You answered?"

"I told him I was with Karl."

"Well, that was...honest."

"He said he was sorry."

"*He* was sorry?" I asked. "I'd have thought you'd be sorry."

She raised both arms, and her face contorted. "I didn't hit him, you idiot. He hit me!"

I'd never heard Tommi Elam call anyone names. I was her first idiot.

"But...weren't you two having an affair?"

"I'm married to him!"

"Not Peter. Karl."

"An affair? With *Karl*?" Tommi said. "You *are* an idiot. I called Karl because Peter and I had a fight. For the first and only time, he hit me. He'd been fired that day and was drinking and...anyway, I was so upset I ran out of the house and started driving. I didn't know who to turn to. I was sitting in Shari's in a corner booth with a wet washcloth and ice some poor waiter gave me. Karl and Tiffany know Peter and me, and they're always telling me God loves us. I was desperate for help, so I called him."

"Why didn't you tell your wife you went to meet Tommi?" I asked Karl.

"What makes you think I didn't?"

"Well, I..." This didn't seem the time to mention our conversation at WinCo.

"Tiffany doesn't like wakingup when I get called out or come back. As soon as we got up in the morning I told her exactly what happened. We agreed that if anyone saw me leave the hotel, we'd say I got called out on 'police business,' which it was. It was one cop calling another cop, her partner, for help. We wanted to protect Tommi's privacy."

"But," I said to Tommi, "when you gave your alibi, you said—"

"You think I'm going to tell a roomful of detectives my husband hit me?"

"Yeah, it would be a little awkward to say, 'I was sucker punched by my soul mate.'"

Tommi started bawling, and Karl said, "Was that really necessary? You trying to be cruel?"

One moment I'm certain the guy's the world's biggest jerk. Now he's suggesting I'm a bigger one.

He was right.

At 11:30 p.m. I parked my car on Salmon, off 60th, four blocks from the seminary parking lot. I'd told Ray Eagle he didn't need to come, but after the part he'd played in the setup, he couldn't stay away. He approached my passenger door window.

"I just drove by the spot," Ray said, voice sounding like a junior high boy pulling a prank. "I can't believe it's so dark. Two streetlights out, the two closest to the parking lot—who'd have thought it? And there's a chain, but it isn't across the driveway. Perfect."

"Yeah," I said, tossing a recently cut chain link in the backseat, next to my eighteen-inch bolt cutter and pellet gun.

Ray gave me a look. It reminded me of Clarence. And my mother.

The cold night worked in my favor because it was natural to have my coat collar turned up. No trench coat or fedora tonight. I had my old green ski jacket and my blue stocking cap. Ray probably wouldn't have been recognized anyway, but he wore a heavy scarf up to his mouth. We walked on opposite sides of the street, staggered so no one would think we knew each other.

Ray turned south on 58th. I walked Salmon to 57th and headed the block to Madison, leaning on a garage sale cane. I ambled, trying to time it right, looking as nonthreatening as possible, knowing there were observers. I saw three of them spread out at different locations, looking everywhere but at the corner of 57th and Madison, which meant that's what they were interested in. One young woman was talking on a cell, and a harmless looking man carried a bottle in a sack.

At 11:59, just as I hobbled twenty feet north of Madison, a black Cadillac STS rounded the corner, barely visible because two streetlights had inexplicably gone out. The car slowly turned right, then took another right into the unchained drive-way.

I crossed the street and continued south on the sidewalk across from the parking lot, where I could just make out the Cadillac, lights out.

Just then another car arrived from the east, turning south, then into the seminary parking lot. The silver BMW pulled in, rolling up close to the Cadillac, dimming his lights.

They sat for a minute while I continued to shuffle, peeking back over my shoulder as a curious bystander might. Who'd make the first move? My bet was on the Cadillac's driver. He opened his door and stepped out, too quickly to let the inside light show his face. He walked to the BMW's window, carrying a large envelope. The BMW window went down.

Suddenly the place exploded. Strobe lights came from both entries to the drive-way and from the back of the seminary bookstore. Eight well-armed bodies rushed the cars.

"Police! Get out…now!" a huge voice demanded through a megaphone. "You…drop what's in your hand. On the ground!"

The man from the Cadillac dropped the envelope, then dropped to the ground, saying something. No one was listening. The man in the BMW hadn't moved quickly enough. Someone yanked his door open. I heard the stress on the hinge.

"What's going on?" the man asked. "Don't you know who—?"

An officer turned the short older man and pushed him against the BMW. "Hands behind your back." I thought I recognized the cop's voice. Paul Anderson.

Someone handcuffed the tall man facedown on the ground. Neither resisted, so things started to calm down. It was then that Anderson turned around the smaller man and someone said, "Hang on, isn't that…?"

Paul Anderson, a foot from his face, finished the sentence.

"Raylon Berkley? From the *Tribune*?" His voice cracked.

"Let me up!" the man on the ground yelled. "Now!"

When he stood the light fell on his face. They didn't have to ask for his ID.

Fifty feet away, I had the perfect view of a magical moment. So did the award-winning pizza-loving *Tribune* photographer, who'd received an anonymous tip that something momentous would happen at this corner around midnight.

While cops tried to wave her off, she took a dozen photos of Garrison Branch.

The mayor of Portland.

In handcuffs.

49

"Results without causes are much more impressive."
SHERLOCK HOLMES, *THE ADVENTURE OF THE SPECKLED BAND*

FORTY PEOPLE IN PAJAMAS and bathrobes were on their front porches within thirty seconds. It was the Fourth of July six months early.

After some phone calls from the arresting officers, both Raylon Berkley and Mayor Branch were released, with profuse apologies. By the time the situation was resolved, I'd walked around on the other side of the hedge, where I heard the soundtrack. The mayor promised there'd be an investigation. "Whoever was behind this will be held accountable!" Berkley promised that the *Tribune* would expose the blunders of this "so-called police department." Both men swore a lot, which I guess is a way of reclaiming your manhood when you've been emasculated.

There's plenty of injustice in their city, but these two men were not accustomed to being on the receiving end of it.

I had no ax to grind with Mayor Branch. But he and Berkley were the leverage I needed on Chief Lennox. If they were in his pocket before, they weren't now. If push came to shove, somebody might listen if Lennox transferred me to the badlands of Dakota or suspended me or tried to pull a cover-up. After this episode, Lennox's wielding of power would be under close scrutiny. He'd have to think twice before any questionable move, including pulling me off the Palatine case. That's what I wanted. Revenge for Mulch and Lou's Diner was a nice bonus.

Ray and I went to Shari's for a piece of pie. He seemed too jumpy to enjoy it. He'd hung back far enough that he didn't see all the juicy stuff but said even from a block away the lights and sound were spectacular. After Ray and I went our separate ways, about 1:15 a.m., I thought I should head home to Mulch, but I was driving right past Rosie O'Grady's. Halfway through my third beer it was time to visit the restroom, where celebrated Irish sports heroes, most of them rugby players, are featured on the walls. I made it back to my table and resumed my beer. My phone rang.

"What's up, Phillips?"

"Sorry to bug you so late, but I know you're usually up. Hear about the arrest? Raylon Berkley and the mayor. Somebody set them up."

"Bummer. Who ordered the arrest?"

"I hear it was Chief Lennox. But that's not why I called. We need to talk."

"Okeydokey."

"Not at the precinct."

"Okeydokey."

"Are you all right?"

"I'm...okeydokey."

"You're at Rosie O'Grady's, aren't you?"

"How'd you know? Tailin' me?"

"You're drunk."

"Not yet. But I'm workin' on it."

"I'll come by your house in the morning. 8:00?"

"That early?" I looked at my watch. 1:52.

"It's important. Go home and get some sleep."

"I'll finish this one. Then I'm out the door."

"You shouldn't be driving."

"Just had three drinks. Or five."

"See you in the morning. I still don't think you should drive."

"Bye, Mom."

I tried to polish off the beer, but I tipped it onto the table, drenching the left arm of my trench coat. I stood to leave. I don't lose my balance easily, but I stumbled. Needed to get out to fresh air. I walked toward my car, but wasn't seeing right.

I tried my keys in two cars that weren't mine. Needed to sit. Tried another car. It worked. Opened the door and put one arm on the hood, one on the door. All I could do to stand. Made my way into the front seat. Before driving, seemed like I should lay my head on the passenger seat.

"Hey!" Felt something on my shoulder. "I asked if you're all right. Want me to call 911?"

Bright light in my eyes. Beard and mustache, security uniform.

"You need to get out of this here parking lot, mister. Bar's closed. Somebody could mug you and steal your car. You need to go home. I'll get some coffee. Hang on."

I fell back asleep. Next thing I knew I smelled something strange, vaguely familiar. I was aware of my shirt feeling wet. Apparently I'd slopped that beer everywhere. I opened my eyes, and the guard was standing over me with a Styrofoam cup of coffee.

"You need this to drive. Drink it, then head home, okay?"

"Okeydokey."

He walked away, disappearing around the Dumpster behind Rosie O'Grady's. No other cars in the parking lot. Had to get home.

WEDNESDAY, JANUARY 8, 3:00 A.M.

Phone rang at 3:19. Close enough to call it 3:00. I knew what that meant.

"Chandler? Sergeant Seymour. Don't hang up. This is the third time I've called."

"Huh?"

"I have to tell you something."

"Tell me?"

"I need you to understand me."

"Understand?"

"You must have been on a bender, Chandler. Listen, get up now and throw cold water on your face. Hear me? I'll wait for you. That's an order!"

"Yes, sir," I said to Captain Weber of the third armored division in Da Nang. Not sure he heard me since I hadn't seen him for thirty-seven years.

I lowered my throbbing head over the sink and repeatedly slapped my face with cold water. Didn't reach for a towel. Didn't think of that until I got back to my bed and discovered my soaked T-shirt.

"Okay, Captain."

"It's Sergeant Seymour."

"Manny and I aren't the up team again…are we?" Okay, I'm not sure that's what I actually said, but that question was attempting to make it to my tongue.

"It's one of the guys."

"Platoon?"

"Listen to me, Ollie. It's one of the detectives. It's Brandon Phillips."

"Phillips?"

"He's dead."

Sarge went on, talking gibberish. Finally I put down the phone.

I wanted to drop to the bed, but I dragged myself toward the kitchen. Somehow I shuffled to Mr. Coffee.

When I came back, I saw last night's T-shirt, lying beside the bed. It looked strange. I picked it up.

The shirt had a dark four-inch circle on the front. I pulled it to my face and smelled. I choked, pulling it back. I'd first smelled that on clothes in Vietnam. And I'd smelled it on clothes at many murders. But never on my own shirt.

I put on plastic gloves, laid my shirt on the kitchen floor and stared, trying to remember. Finally, three cups later, I went to the utility drawer, took out scissors, and started cutting.

"We balance probabilities and choose the most likely. It is the scientific use of the imagination."
SHERLOCK HOLMES, *THE HOUND OF THE BASKERVILLES*

I SHOWED UP at the home of Brandon Phillips two hours after he'd been found.

Cimmatoni and Phillips should have been the up team. But with Phillips the victim, Sergeant Seymour had examined the workload. Manny and I were on Palatine and refused for obvious reasons to turn to detectives for assistance. Ray, Clarence, Paul Anderson, and his partner had been help I could trust. Jack and Noel were still assisting Karl and Tommi on the Frederick case, so Sarge gave the Phillips case to Kim Suda and Chris Doyle. Their last, the Hedstrom murder, was recent but had already dead-ended. I'd never seen a backup like this. And we'd just lost one of our five teams.

"Look what the cat dragged in," Suda said. "What are you doing here?"

"I was in the neighborhood. I think that's what you said when you came out of the closet at my last murder, wasn't it, Kimmy? Of course, I wasn't hiding here when you arrived."

"Where are your gloves?" she asked. "Wouldn't want you to contaminate the scene."

"What time was the murder?" I asked.

"Gunshot heard at 2:36," Doyle said, looking at Phillips. "No murder though. Offed himself."

Dr. Marsh was the ME on duty. Carlton Hatch treats the body like it's the shroud of Turin. Marsh has the deft touch of an airport baggage handler. He flipped Phillips's arms around like a rag doll.

"Apparent suicide," Marsh said.

"Based on what?" I asked.

"Gun in his hand and brains on the floor."

"Made to look like suicide," I said.

"Hence the word *apparent.*"

"Where's Sheila?"

"Staying at her sister's," Doyle said. "Apparently she and Phillips had been having problems. If she needs an alibi, she's got one. It's a three-hour drive, and she was with her sister's family all evening."

"I talked with Sheila," Suda said. "She's a mess. Who wouldn't be? Wait. What's this?" Suda pointed at a dark scrap of cloth four feet from the body, two feet to my right.

Doyle bent over it. "Fabric," he said. "Blood soaked. It's been cut."

Suda gestured to one of the CSIs. "You drop this?"

"No," he said, staring at the cloth. "It wasn't there."

"Had to be," Doyle said.

"We've been here two hours," the criminalist said. "We have thirteen evidence bags, marked and ready for the lab. We picked up everything. You telling me we all missed this—including you?"

Suda gave me the evil eye. She wrote on her pad, then took three pictures of the scrap. "Bag it," she said. The criminalist picked it up with tweezers and put it in a plastic bag.

I met Sarge outside his office when he arrived at 7:00 a.m.

"I'm going to need the lab results from the Phillips investigation," I said. "We have to assume he was killed because of what he knew about Palatine. It was no suicide."

"That's a lot to assume."

"You think it's a coincidence he had something to tell me, then suddenly he was killed?"

Sarge shrugged.

"I don't trust Suda and Doyle on this investigation," I said.

"That's funny. They don't trust you on the Palatine investigation."

"Come on. Can you trust a woman hiding in a closet at a murder scene? She breaks into my house and plants illegal bugs. Abuses my dog. Now a detective dies, and she's in charge of the investigation?"

"Look, Suda's in big trouble. After the investigation she'll be suspended, at least. But that doesn't make her the killer. And right now, we're buried in murder cases. We need her. Anyway, remember, she planted the bugs under orders from the chief."

"Even he doesn't have the authority to do that."

"My point is, she wasn't winging it." Sarge shook his head. "What's happening to this department? One of our best has just died, and one of us might have killed him? It's a nightmare."

"I need those lab results as soon as they're done."

Sarge nodded. "I'll give Doyle the lab results on the Palatine case. And I'll tell him you're getting the results on this one."

"But I don't want—"

"The universe isn't about what you want, Chandler. Get used to it."

Phillips's death was too late to make the morning paper, but the arrest at the seminary dominated the front page. Oddly, pictures at the scene didn't include the faces of Berkley and Branch. If anyone else had been in the pictures, their mugs would be right there on page one, no matter how humiliating.

I called Carp's cell, which two days ago replaced Flyin' Pie on my autodial.

"I saw your pictures. Nice. But what happened to the ones with your publisher and the mayor?"

"Don't get me started," she said. "I've been yelling at people all morning, and I've left two voice mails with Berkley. I chose two great photos with Branch and Berkley. They were going in, until Berkley called and nixed them."

"Sounds like censorship," I said. "Funny how journalists don't play by their own rules."

"Stop taking shots at journalists. I'm a journalist. Berkley's an aristocrat."

"Sorry. I heard Berkley yell at you to stop taking pictures. I thought it was pretty cool you didn't stop."

"Of course I didn't stop. I do my job no matter who tells me not to."

"That's my girl."

"Got to go. Couple of heads here I haven't bitten off yet."

I looked at the newspaper again.

The front page featured two pictures of police officers, one of them with a big old guy leaning on a cane in the background. The article quoted Police Chief Lennox, who said a full investigation was being conducted to get to the bottom of the false intelligence that had been given to the police, who had acted in good faith, having every reason to believe a felony was in process in the seminary parking lot. He apologized to his "dear friend," seventy-three-year-old Raylon Berkley, and to his "close friend" Mayor Branch, and vowed that such a thing would never happen again in our great city…blah blah blah.

The article said it was a private meeting between the two. "When asked why they would meet in a seminary parking lot at midnight, both men declined to answer."

It would have been a perfect morning.

If only Brandon Phillips wasn't dead.

And my T-shirt wasn't bloodstained.

They got a thirty-hour rush on the bloodstains in the Phillips case because the victim was a detective. By crime lab standards this was a jet on afterburners.

"Evidence is in," Sarge said. "I told the lab you'd be there along with Suda."

The criminalist, Kathy Strade, handed Suda and me identical pages at the same time. It gave the results of fourteen pieces of evidence. Suda scanned them one at a time, but I turned immediately to number fourteen, then went back to the top.

"That last little scrap we found on the floor?" Suda asked the criminalist.

"It was a freshly cut swatch of white fabric. Soaked with Phillips's blood, like everything else," said the criminalist.

"How do you suppose it got there, Chandler?"

I shrugged.

"Looked like a part of somebody's T-shirt," Strade said. "It's like it was cut out and left there deliberately. But that'd be crazy."

"Unless somebody found evidence elsewhere they didn't want to turn in," Suda said. "By dropping it at the crime scene they'd get the state to test and see whose blood was on it."

"Who'd do such a thing?" I asked.

"Maybe the person who arrived on the crime scene when there were only thirteen pieces of evidence and suddenly there were fourteen." Considering she'd bugged my house and drugged my Mulch, her morally superior look wasn't convincing.

I assumed that classic "I'm just a man, so I'm stupid" pose, which usually works. Kathy Strade seemed to buy it.

I walked out thinking that either somebody was going all-out to frame me, or I'd done something so unthinkable I'd blocked it out. I'd need to burn my bloodstained T-shirt, with the hole in it, when I got home.

I was knocked out in that car, I told myself. Obviously I hadn't killed Phillips. If someone was trying to frame me, they'd have left something from me at the scene. The evidence report showed they hadn't. They were playing with me, showing me they had control.

By the time Clarence and I arrived at the morgue, on Knott Street, the forensic pathologist, Dr. Robert Jones, had finished undressing, weighing, photographing, and fingerprinting Brandon Phillips...or what was once Brandon Phillips. The body had been pulled from the cooler.

I reassured Jones that Clarence was there under authority of the chief, and there was an e-mail attachment, for heaven's sake. Once Clarence asked him to spell his name and he sensed his fifteen minutes of fame, all was well. I nodded my approval to Clarence, who'd asked a man named Robert Jones how he spelled it.

Homicide autopsies are done in a special room, designed to limit access and protect evidence. Organs are removed and weighed, injuries photographed, measured, probed, and numbered. I figured this would be a long one, two hours, because when the victim's one of our own, we have to get it right. And when the killer's one of our own, well…

The doctor's phone rang. He pushed his Bluetooth earpiece and chatted with his son in Boston while cutting up a dead man in Portland.

Dr. Jones hit a point of disagreement with his son and paced twenty feet away. Clarence was looking green and miserable. I examined Phillips's right hand, gently moving each finger. I stopped with the index finger. The trigger finger. I wiggled it as Clarence watched.

"Please," Dr. Jones said, abandoning his son in Boston. "Hands off."

"Any suggestion this wasn't a suicide?" I asked.

"Not that I can see."

"Take a close look at that right index finger."

"It seems…unusually angled."

"Like it was broken?" I asked.

"Yes. But…it couldn't be."

"Why not?" Clarence asked.

"Because there's no swelling," I said. I asked the doctor, "But what if it was broken after he was already dead?"

"Then…" Robert Jones, spelled J-o-n-e-s, looked at me, then at Clarence, and said, "there wouldn't be any swelling."

Clarence wrote it down.

"Nice catch," I said to Jones. "Most guys would've missed that."

Jones wrapped it up in Boston, then turned to the microphone suspended over the body. He started speaking, looking at Clarence out of the corner of his eye.

"White male measuring 71 inches in length, weighing 189 pounds. Overall appearance consistent with stated age of 49, though unusually fit. Body cold with complete rigor mortis. No lacerations. All physical damage is to skull and brain. Appears to have been penetrated by a single high-velocity bullet shot from a handgun at close range. Though the bullet passed through and wasn't recovered, the wound is consistent with that of a 9 mm revolver of the sort recovered on the scene next to the body. No other abnormalities…with the exception of—" he looked at Clarence sideways "—an apparently broken index finger." He flipped a switch, shutting off the recorder.

"*Apparently* broken?" I asked.

He reversed the recorder and played "exception of" then stopped and said, "a broken index finger. I surmise, due to lack of swelling, the finger may have been broken postmortem."

"May have been?"

He rewound again and said, "The finger was probably broken postmortem." He stopped it.

"Probably? Why not certainly? Any other explanation?"

He wasn't going to change his report again, not while I was there.

Heading out the door, I turned and said, "Dr. Jones, if you find a case where a freshly broken finger of a live person doesn't swell, would you send it to me? Put it in an e-mail attachment. I'd love to see it."

Clarence and I walked around Lawndale and Chapman parks, beautiful even in winter, especially in the light snowfall. We stopped for coffee near the steps of the Multnomah County Courthouse. We walked an extra thirty feet to escape the pocket of air that smelled of wet cigarette fumes, where jury duty candidates had surfaced to smoke.

"I've been asking myself again what I would do if I were a homicide detective planning a murder in Portland to minimize the chances of me being caught. The answer came to me. Know what it is?"

He didn't.

"Think about it," I said. "The answer has the potential of landing this investigation on the runway."

"I'm still on Brandon Phillips," Clarence said. "If what you said is true, how could his finger break after he was dead?"

"If he were alone, it couldn't. But suppose somebody was trying to wrap his finger around the trigger, and it kept popping out. So he squeezed it in there real tight. Still popped out. So he squeezed it harder. If he was strong and angry or scared enough, adrenaline flowing, he could've snapped the finger. By the way, guns don't normally stay in the hand in a suicide. They drop to the floor, a couple of feet from the body."

I hated myself for not meeting with Phillips in the middle of the night. If I hadn't been drinking my life away at Rosie's, maybe he'd still be alive.

Clarence and I drove the I-205 bridge to Vancouver, Washington, and arrived at Ray Eagle's at 4:00 p.m. I found that red chair that didn't look comfortable but was, and my legs reacquainted themselves with his ottoman.

"I never heard your answer to something you asked me earlier," Clarence said, sinking into Ray's couch. "If you were a homicide detective and were going to kill somebody, how would you make sure you'd get away with it?"

"You answer first," I said to Ray.

"I'd take into account every procedure followed by the other detectives and myself and make sure I didn't do a single thing to give myself away. Obviously, I'd wear gloves and cover my face. I'd have a backup plan in which I could justify my presence even if found at the scene."

"Good answer," I said. "But I've got an even better one. It hit me the other day. If I were going to kill someone in Portland, I'd just wait until my partner and I were the up team. Then I'd commit the murder."

"So you'd be called to the scene," Ray said. "To investigate the same murder you just committed?"

"Right. So now, even if I left a strand of hair or a fingerprint at the murder scene, it's okay, because everybody knows I was there—legitimately. I could even confiscate evidence."

"Like you confiscated the Black Jack wrapper," Clarence said.

"Right. Except I didn't leave that, because I didn't kill the guy. It was planted."

"But if your theory's correct," Clarence said, "doesn't that mean that either you or Manny are the murderers? You were the up team."

"We were on call when the professor was found. But murders aren't investigated in the order they're committed."

"They're not?"

"They're investigated in the order they're discovered. By a fluke, another murder was discovered just before the professor's, the one near Lloyd Center, where the guy shot his wife's boyfriend. The up team got called to that murder instead."

"Jack and Noel," Clarence said. He clenched both my shoulders in his big mitts. "You're saying Jack or Noel killed the professor?"

"There is a master hand here. It is no case of sawed-off shotguns and clumsy six-shooters. You can tell an old master by the sweep of his brush. I can tell a Moriarty when I see one. This crime is from London, not from America."
SHERLOCK HOLMES, *THE VALLEY OF FEAR*

FRIDAY, JANUARY 10, 11:30 A.M.

AS I STOOD JAWING with a Fourth Street vendor who cooks the best hot dogs in Portland, Ray Eagle called.

"You know that seventh phone number I told you was a convenience store?"

"The one in the back of the Bertrand Russell book?" I said. "What about it?"

"Turns out that number's been the store's for nine years. Before that it was out of commission for a year. But for a fifteen-year period ending ten years ago, guess whose home number it was."

"Too tired to guess."

"Jack and Linda Glissan's."

No wonder that number rang a bell. Working on the assumption that the professor didn't consider Jack a great dating prospect, that narrowed the field to his wife, Linda, and his daughter, Melissa, who'd been alive when the Glissans still had that number.

I hoofed it back to the precinct and entered Sergeant Seymour's office, closing the door. I told him about the phone number in the professor's book.

"We need to take a closer look at Jack," I said.

He nodded reluctantly.

"He's my friend," I said. "But I have to check him out."

Two hours later I was summoned to Chief Lennox's office.

I hadn't seen the chief since he'd set up the sting that took down those two notorious felons, Raylon Berkley and Mayor Branch. He'd probably avoided me so I wouldn't be able to gloat. I had, however, done a great deal of private gloating.

The chief couldn't accuse me of anything without revealing that he'd ordered illegal bugs in a public establishment. I'd removed them the day after the sting. Till then, who knows how many private conversations had been recorded at Lou's. He couldn't expose me without incriminating himself. So he found something else to jump on me about.

"I'm told you're going after Jack Glissan now."

Two hours and word had already reached him? Sheesh.

"First, Glissan's innocent," he said. "Second, if we had concerns about him, we could retire him early. Or if absolutely necessary, demote him. Put him back on the street."

"Yeah, that would encourage the community," I said. "Assign killers to drive our streets and protect our people."

"We wouldn't tell them. Jack would volunteer. But he's not guilty. Remember innocent until proven guilty? Doesn't that include cops? Jack is supposed to be your friend. If you had evidence, it'd be different."

"There's evidence. I'm continuing to gather it."

"Captain Swiridoff tells me you suspect Palatine was involved with Jack's daughter."

"Possibly. Plus there's the—"

"How could that account for a murder ten years later?"

"Revenge is a dish best served cold."

"That's a cliché," the chief said.

"Now that's the pot calling the kettle black."

"That's a cliché too. You're embarrassing yourself. All you're doing in this investigation is making the department look bad."

"All I'm doing is trying to keep the department from *being* bad. How it looks isn't my concern."

"You admit it!"

Like I'd confessed a murder.

"Your job's on the line, Chandler. Embarrass Jack, and I'll make sure you pay for it."

"You're still threatening me? Don't you get it? You laid the trap at the seminary parking lot based on what Ray Eagle and I said in a booth at Lou's Diner. What other conversations between my buddies and me did you listen in on? And how many other citizens sat in that booth? Can you imagine the scandal? Private citizens illegally recorded at a public establishment. And two of those recorded work for the *Tribune*! I grant you, they were probably evangelizing me—they usually are—but the point is, they're journalists, first amendment junkies, civil liberties freaks, covered under the Bill of Rights, along with car thieves and hit men. They tell the world that cops were eavesdropping…talk about a PR problem. There'd be a media feeding frenzy. After the lawsuit against this department, Lou's could be a 10-million-dollar restaurant."

"You wouldn't."

"One of them saw the bugs. He's eager to know who did it." It seemed better leverage not to mention that Clarence and Jake already knew. "They'll fill pages with this story. Can you imagine someone at Police Headquarters doing this? Zero political savvy. He'd be ruined. The man would have to be an idiot. King of the Idiots."

I went out the door, ticked not just because of his dirty tricks, but because he'd accused me of using clichés.

As I walked out I saw his daughter Jenn's sullen face in that family photo, and I found myself wishing she was more like her friend Tasha, who kept…all her stupid phone photos.

Why hadn't I thought of that before?

"Ever find those pictures with the professor?" I asked Jenn Lennox on the phone.

"Told you I didn't keep them."

"Did you ask your friend Tasha?"

"Why?"

"Because you said Tasha keeps everything. And aren't you always sending photos to her?"

"Oh." Long pause. "So if Tasha has it, do I get the Starbucks card or does she?"

"Both of you get one."

"I'll call you back."

Ten minutes later she called. "Tasha has some pictures at Palatine's. She'll send them to you, once we get the Starbucks cards. Forty dollars each."

"We agreed on thirty, just for you." Finally we settled on twenty-five each. I said, "No cards until I see the pictures."

"No pictures until I see the cards."

I swore an oath as a police officer to surrender the Starbucks cards once I got the pictures. Were it possible to strangle someone over phone lines, I'd be on death row.

Ten minutes later my phone buzzed. I went online to access pictures sent to my account. Surprisingly, the images weren't bad. In two, Palatine's mantel was visible. I sent them on to Carp. She called me back and said I should pay her a visit at the *Trib*.

I was there in twenty minutes.

"These are low resolution pictures, but the photo you're interested in is visible. I've made as many sharpness and contrast corrections as I could. The lighting's not bad. The faces aren't sharp, but not nearly as blurry as they were in those other photos I enlarged."

I looked at the first picture. It was much better. I had the sense that I recognized one of the faces. Then I looked at the silver chain around her neck…a high school graduation present from her mother.

I looked at the last picture. No doubt now who the girl was.

Kendra Chandler. My daughter.

I drove directly to Kendra's real estate office, near Parkrose High. She seemed surprised. I'd pulled into the parking lot before, to watch her through the window and make sure she was all right. One day I took out my compressor and put air in one of her tires. But this was the first time I'd shown my face inside.

"Got a few minutes?" I asked.

"I've got a break coming. We can sit in the staff room."

She introduced me, awkwardly, to a few of her coworkers. I took a good look at the three men, comparing their faces to wanted posters. I asked Kendra a few questions about her Christmas with the other family, pretending I wasn't jealous, then jumped in.

"This picture was on Dr. Palatine's mantel." I handed it to her.

"No way," she said, studying it. "Dad, I'm thirty. This would've been, what, ten years ago?"

"I was surprised to see him with you."

"Well, I happened to be in the picture, but it wasn't me he was interested in."

"The other girl?"

"You do know who that is, don't you?"

"Should I?"

"It's Melissa. Melissa Glissan. You used to work with her dad, remember?"

"I still work with him. I guess I forgot what Melissa looked like."

"Well, she'd bleached her hair blond. Maybe that threw you."

"You didn't tell me you and Melissa were in the professor's class together."

"Why should I? I didn't even remember until I saw this picture. Brings back memories."

"So Melissa knew Palatine."

"She knew him all right."

"Why'd you say it that way?"

"Well…they were just…" Her face turned red. "You know what I said. He liked the pretty girls."

I had two main memories of Melissa. One, a sunny day when she was eight years old, laughing hysterically with Kendra on our Slip 'N Slide. Two, the night I got the phone call, around 3:00 a.m. as I recall, that she'd taken her life.

It made me wonder about my Andrea, and whether she was still alive. It's hard when a man to feels powerless to take care of those he loves.

I asked myself...*Who would remove a photograph of Palatine, Kendra, and Melissa?*

I went back to the precinct and reopened Melissa Glissan's case file. I zeroed in on her roommate at Linfield College, Cherianne Takalo. I put Ray on it, and thirty minutes later he'd traced her down under her married name, in Grosse Point, Michigan. He had her home phone, work, and cell numbers.

"Ray, you scare me," I said.

I put Manny on some background research on Melissa. Anything that might be relevant. He said I was wasting his time. I told him he was paid to waste his time.

I called Cherianne. She hadn't heard the professor was dead.

"Just that name, Dr. Palatine, brings back memories," she said.

"Good ones?"

"No."

"Did you know Melissa was involved with him?"

"She talked about him all the time. He complimented her writing. She really fell for him."

"A crush?"

"She loved him. She'd read his little love notes and his sappy poetry. She showed me some. He never signed them. I wondered if he was covering his tracks so he could deny he sent them. I never met the guy, but I thought it was a big mistake getting involved with a professor."

"You knew about the drugs?"

"She only had two classes at PSU, the rest were at Linfield. She was back in our room every night. She was devastated when the professor told her not to call him anymore. She started smoking pot. I asked her not to do it in our room. I warned her it was messing her up. But that didn't help her, so she started snorting coke. She got more depressed and was sleeping more and more. Stopped doing her homework. Stopped caring."

"This was all a backlash to the professor rejecting her?"

"Melissa thought he was going to marry her. He turned out to be a jerk. I told her to just walk away. I mean, she had a decent boyfriend her own age."

"Melissa had a boyfriend?"

"She broke up with him for the professor. But he still loved her."

"What was his name?'

"It's been a long time. Ten years. Um…David? No, wait. Donald. I don't remember his last name. I only saw him twice. I think he stayed at her parents' house when he was in town."

"In town? Where did he live?"

"In the South, maybe? I remember he'd had a long flight. Wait…I remember now. It was weird. He wouldn't say where he was from. And when I asked Melissa, she wouldn't tell me. Said something about him having family problems and maybe he was going to make a break from them and start a new life."

"What was he like?"

"Nice. Maybe insecure."

"You said you saw him twice. When was the second time?"

"A few days before Melissa died."

"He was in Portland?"

"Yeah. Melissa had broken it off with him over the phone, I think. He flew in to talk her out of it. He didn't want to lose her."

"He knew there was another guy?"

"She tried not to tell him. I'm afraid I was the one who let it out."

"He knew it was the professor?"

"Melissa had told him. I felt terrible."

"How long were Donald and Melissa together?"

"They were on and off a couple of years. They got serious the summer before our junior year. When we came back to the dorm in September, she talked a lot about him. He came for a few weeks that summer and stayed at Melissa's parents' house."

"What's Donald doing now?"

"No clue. I knew Melissa's parents, and I really liked them. We kept in touch the first year after Melissa died, but I transferred to Michigan State. Just couldn't come back after my roommate died, you know? Could you do me a favor, Mr. Chandler? Do you have a photo of Melissa's parents?"

"Probably."

"Would you mind sending me one? I do scrapbooks, and I've got pictures of Melissa. But I'd like a picture of her parents. They were always nice to me."

"I could probably find something."

Cherianne gave me her address. I gave her my number. If Sharon were around, she'd know right where to look in our albums for a photo of Jack and Linda. I'd probably send her a copy of the detectives and spouses group photo, but at least she'd have Melissa's parents. Not to mention the best photo of Sharon and me. Carp would make me a copy.

Meanwhile, I shifted gears to Donald.

Where was he? And why hadn't the police reports or anyone else—especially Jack and Linda—mentioned him?

Manny chose that moment to call. "Doing the background check you wanted on Melissa Glissan."

"You got something?"

"Most of it's irrelevant, like I told you it'd be."

"But you got something, didn't you, or you wouldn't have called."

"Turns out she was an insulin-dependent diabetic."

I looked over Melissa's death report again. Toxicology reported drug use—methamphetamine and some indications she'd also snorted coke. The hanging had been the cause of death. But without the drugs would she have hung herself? Naturally her parents didn't think so. They'd said she'd never been on drugs until she'd recently become depressed.

I checked statistics. There's a much higher rate of suicide by hanging among men than women. Still, it happens.

I was just about to close Melissa's file when my eyes fell on a red scribble. It was probably just the slip of a pen, but it was enough to draw my attention to something else: the date. The report had been filed on November 21. Melissa's date of death was November 20.

I looked again at the estimated time of death. A neighbor had heard a noise, which in retrospect was probably when she hung herself. She'd died just after 11:35 p.m.

Melissa Glissan died exactly ten years before the professor.

Not just ten years to the day, but to the hour.

Likely, to the minute.

*"There are limits, you see, to our friend's intelligence.
It would have been a coup-mattre had he deduced
what I would deduce and acted accordingly."*
SHERLOCK HOLMES, *THE FINAL PROBLEM*

FRIDAY, JANUARY 10, 3:00 P.M.

I DROPPED BY JACK'S DESK, and we small talked. He mentioned Linda would be out all night at a get-together with old college roommates in Corvallis, ninety minutes away. He and Noel were going to a Winterhawks game after dinner.

Jack left at 4:30. I called Carp and asked if I could borrow her car. When I came by, I also asked if she could doctor up a couple photos for me. When I showed her what I wanted, she smiled. But didn't ask questions. I like that.

At 6:25 p.m. I sat in Carp's silver Subaru Impreza, across the street from the Nine Daggers Tavern near 39th and Belmont. My Taurus slicktop wouldn't stick out to most people, but cops notice cars. Carp's car was cleaner than most operating rooms, and since she'd seen the archaeological dig in my car, she asked me not to eat in it. Where are you supposed to eat dinner if not in a car? But I promised.

With the help of my ProStaff binoculars, I watched Jack and Noel eat dinner, looking like father and son. It took me back to when Jack was my partner, and we'd come weekly to the Nine Daggers. We had a ritual. After arresting a killer, one month later we'd down a bottle of wine, our toast to taking out the bad guy. In a few cases we celebrated annually. I still remembered Harvey Blanda, April 11, and Theda Pranke, July 27.

Jack always made it interesting. He made it seem like we were doing something that mattered. If Sharon were still alive, we'd be with Jack and Linda every week, like the old days.

I felt like a louse tailing Jack. I didn't know what I was looking for.

After dinner they got in Jack's car and drove away, I assumed to the hockey game. I headed the other direction.

When I broke into Jack Glissan's house that night, it felt creepy. I'd remembered that Jack and Linda had left Melissa's room as it was. Some visit a gravesite. Some bring the ashes into their home. They kept the room as it was. A shrine. Every day it reminded them of Melissa's life…and death.

Sharon kept Chad's favorite little gray sweatpants and white muscle shirt. Every time I saw it, it cut my heart. It also made me think about the guy who rear-ended us. If Jack and Linda blamed anyone for Melissa's death, her room might have kept that anger alive.

I shone my flashlight, close range, around Melissa's room. I recalled Jack and I coming in there with her and Kendra when they were grade-schoolers. The only time I remembered being in Melissa's room after her death was with Sharon. Linda showed us around, like a curator, making speeches about various items in the room. I thought there had been a journal or a diary and maybe a photo album.

In Melissa's top dresser drawer, I found her scrapbook. What interested me most were the last three months of her junior year of college, preceding her suicide. Three photos had been removed. Why?

I snuck into Jack's office. I went through his desk drawers, checking files with the flashlight. In the lower right drawer I found one called "Melissa's Case."

I opened it, disappointed to see only two photos, glossies that reflected too much of the flashlight. I went into the bathroom, closed the door, and turned on the light. One picture was of a man holding a hardbound book, appearing to read from it. The book was red. On the cover I saw several words, one of them "Poems."

The man was Professor William Palatine.

The other picture was of the professor with two young women. I knew instantly I'd seen it, or rather a low-quality replica of it, in Carp's office. This photo had been visible on the fireplace mantel, in the photo that cost me fifty Starbucks.

It was a clear photograph of Melissa Glissan and Kendra Chandler, but the left third of the photo had been cut off. The professor was gone.

I heard a noise. In a microsecond I switched off the light.

I stood still in the darkness, hoping no one had seen the light in the door crack. I thought of crawling into the bathtub and hiding behind the shower curtain, but I didn't want to risk the noise. Suddenly the door flew open and the light streamed on.

I was looking down the barrel of a gun.

"Who are you?" he asked.

"Detective Ollie Chandler," I said. "Jack's friend. Who are you?"

"Jack's brother."

"Warren?"

We'd met two or three times, but it had been years.

"What are you doing here?" he asked, voice edgy.

"Want to see my ID?" I said. Never reach for your pocket without permission when a nervous man is pointing a gun at your face.

"I remember," he said. "You're the dopey one."

It's good to be remembered.

"That's me."

If I was Dopey, he was Grumpy. I was hoping the other dwarves weren't with him.

"Could you lower the gun, please?"

"I asked what you're doing here."

"I have a good reason," I said. "I'll explain. What are *you* doing here?"

"Visiting from Redding. Linda's gone, and Jack's at a hockey game. I hate hockey. Had dinner with an old friend; now I'm back. What's your story?"

"We're planning a party to honor Jack for forty years on the detective force," I said, holding up three pictures.

"You stealing from Jack?"

"Not stealing. Planting." I handed him the pictures. "It's a prank. Fake photos of him arresting celebrities. Look here—he's with Lucille Ball. This one's with Frank Sinatra. See we're rubbing it in that he's been around long enough to have dealt with those people. Funny, huh? We're all going to come back to his office, and I'll pull out this stack that I was just going to hide up there in his closet. I'm a prankster. You know, the dopey one. I was just planting them when I heard a noise. Afraid it was Jack, so I hid in the bathroom. You can't let Jack know, okay? It's a surprise."

"When's the party?"

"Soon. Real soon. I'd love to invite you, but it's just the detectives. After the party's over, he'll tell you all about it. I'm not sure even Linda knows. One of the wives is pulling it off, maybe."

He put down his gun, looking at the photos. He smiled. "Where'd you get these made?"

"My friend's a professional photographer. She does miracles with Photoshop."

"There had to be a better way to do this than breaking in," Grumpy said.

"I figured if anybody caught me, it'd be Jack. We'd get a good laugh out of it."

"If he didn't shoot you first," Warren said. "You're lucky I know how to handle a gun."

We moved down the hall. "Just let me put the pictures up here." I slid them under an old Kodak slide tray on the upper closet shelf. "All right, I'm going now. Good thing I'm a cop and you know I'm his friend, huh? Don't say anything until after his party, okay?"

He nodded like an insider. "Can you get me a copy of the one with Jack and Frank Sinatra?"

"Sure," I said.

As we walked to the front door, I pointed to a family photo, Jack and Linda and Melissa. "Must be tough to lose a child like that."

"Yeah," he said, as he opened the door and stepped out behind me.

His voice was ice-cold. Under the porch light, what I saw on his face wasn't grief or hurt. It was rage.

When I got to the car, I pulled out of my coat pocket the photograph of Melissa and Kendra and put it under the flashlight.

I put myself in Jack's place. If Kendra had committed suicide and I had a few miscellaneous pictures, what would I do with them? Why put it in a file? And if I did, I wouldn't call it "Kendra's Case." Because "case" is a murder I'm investigating.

Was that what "Melissa's Case" meant to Jack? If so, why did he have this picture of Melissa and Kendra? And why was the professor cut out? Was this a huge coincidence—or was this the actual photo taken from the crime scene and now defaced? If so, did that mean Jack was the murderer?

On my way home I called Carp. "Thanks for the pictures of Jack and the celebrities. Thought it wouldn't be necessary, but they saved my bacon."

"Speaking of bacon," she said, "there's a new place on Third and Ash called McGraw's Outlaw Barbecue. Supposedly they have killer ribs wrapped in bacon. Meet me there for lunch tomorrow, 11:45?"

"Sure," I said.

What a woman.

I called Tommi and asked if she might put together a party for Jack for his years of service. I suggested she talk to Linda and see if it could be at Jack's so we could see his memorabilia.

"You're kidding me, right?" Tommi said. "Didn't you read the e-mails?"

"I'm not always good with e-mails. Especially attachments."

She laughed. "Sarge felt bad about not having a detectives New Year's party with everything that's happened. Only a few of us were at the chief's. With Brandon's death, they decided to honor him. It's not exactly a party, obviously, but it's a get-together. And it's at Jack and Linda's tomorrow night! You knew that, right? You're just kidding me. Anyway, I'm sure we could honor Jack too. That's a great idea."

"Should have read my e-mail. Could have helped in a conversation I had twenty minutes ago."

"Hey, Ollie? I think it's sweet that you're being so sensitive to Jack. How many men would be thoughtful enough to suggest we all get together and honor him like that?"

"Sometimes you women underestimate us men. We're a lot more sensitive than you give us credit for."

"You're right," Tommi said. "I really owe you an apology."

"It is a question of cubic capacity. A man with so large a brain must have something in it."
SHERLOCK HOLMES, *THE ADVENTURE OF THE BLUE CARBUNCLE*

IN LIGHT OF BRANDON'S DEATH and Jack being honored, Chief Lennox came to the get-together.

Well, whoop-de-do.

Lennox invited Clarence, hoping he'd put a good spin on the camaraderie of the detectives in this tragic time. The chief came prepared, makeup and all.

We all dressed up, rare for this group. I wore my old blue sport coat. Sharon hated that coat, which was perfect because she never nagged me to wear it.

I wasn't going to ruin Jack's party. He'd served honorably forty years. Until he'd murdered a man. Apparently more than one. Including Phillips.

"As you know," Sarge said, "this gathering hasn't been on the calendar long. With Brandon's death, we considered canceling it. But it seemed like we needed another chance to connect. Brandon's funeral's Monday, and we'll honor him there, but we could…think about him now.

"Brandon was a fine cop. An outstanding detective. And a good man. We already miss him. Let's bow our heads in silence a minute, in tribute to our comrade—and to our commitment to find his killer."

That minute of silence felt like five. After some told stories about Phillips, we switched gears to honor the living, Jack Glissan, for forty years of service.

Captain Swiridoff said, "Brandon Phillips would have been the first to join us in tribute to a man he deeply respected, Jack Glissan."

Those words hit me like a harpoon through a lung.

He presented a trophy, a pretty cool-looking one. It was a pewter Sherlock Holmes, with a deerstalker cap and a drop-stem pipe.

Lieutenant Nicks said, "Jack Glissan's the finest detective I've ever known." After a long pause he added, "present company excepted." There were a few laughs.

I noticed Chief Lennox looking down through his reading glasses at notes, mouthing words.

Sarge said, "Anybody got some stories about Jack?"

Tommi told a funny stakeout story about working with Jack as a first-year detective. They even got Cimma to tell a story where Jack rescued him out of a sewer.

"Jack's been a partner and a friend, like family to me," Noel said.

Tommi teared up and Noel teared up and a couple of us made fun of him, as we men like to do to help get us through tender moments.

Abruptly, the chief strode across the front of the room and turned to address us, like he was Patton and we were his army.

"In the toughest of times, Jack Glissan has been a model Portland detective. He's a man of integrity. A champion of justice. He's a role model. He's the face not only of this department, but of our Portland Police."

Clarence was writing down every word. I wondered if the words were forming themselves into a noose, since Lennox would be quoted on the front page when Jack Glissan went down.

"When he retires, his loss will be deeply felt. I hope we'll have him several more years at least." The chief hit stride saying, "Jack Glissan is as good as gold. He does his job rain or shine. He pulls out the stops in his defense of justice. He's fit as a fiddle…"

"Hard as nails," Suda whispered.

"A force to be reckoned with," I muttered.

"White as a ghost," Clarence said.

"Up a creek without a paddle," I said, my double meaning unknown.

"He whispers sweet nothings in my ear."

I turned. It was Linda Glissan, two drinks in hand, headed back to Jack.

"Sorry," I said.

"We're on the same page," Linda said, smiling. "Jack and I are going to get some laughs out of this."

The chief droned on. "These have been the times that try men's souls. The eye of accusation has been turned upon this detective department. This is the price we pay for working on the front lines. I'm confident the reputation of this detective department, and of the Portland Police, will come out unscathed. And we can salute Jack Glissan as a man we're all proud to have represent us."

He spoke as if to thousands, as in a capitol rotunda, way too loud and emphatic for a living room. Applause was polite but restrained.

Sarge stood. "Before we eat, any more tributes to Jack?"

Eyes fell on me.

"Jack's been a great detective," I said. "I consider myself privileged to have been his friend."

"There's plenty to eat," Linda said, saving me. "The department paid for the food and drinks, so make yourselves at home. And fill your pockets when you leave."

While Jack was pumping hands, I took my drink and sat in the back hallway, leaning against the wall. I looked at the doorway to Jack's office. He used to have foosball in there. We'd spent hours battling while Linda and Sharon talked in the living room.

I considered whether to pull out those pictures of him arresting Lucille Ball and Frank Sinatra. No. It was pointless now.

A familiar voice said, "I noticed your wording. Jack's *been* a great detective. I consider myself privileged to *have been* his friend."

"I do," I said, looking up at Jack.

"But you didn't say 'I consider myself privileged to *be* his friend.'"

He had a wineglass in his hand.

"Special occasion," he said. "I told them to take every ounce of it out of the house when the party's over so Linda doesn't have to look at it." He took a gulp. "How's the investigation?"

"Now's not the time. It's a party. We're honoring you."

"May as well just say it, old buddy."

"Okay. I know the truth."

"What truth?"

"About Melissa. And Palatine. And what you did."

I pulled a replica of the sliced picture of Melissa and Kendra from my sport coat pocket and showed it to Jack. He stared at it, nodding. His face turned stormy for a moment. Then his eyes got wet.

"Know what it's like to lose your child? Sorry. I know you do. But Melissa was my only child. My little girl. At least you still have Kendra. And Andrea maybe. Every day I see Melissa's face, the color of eggplant, hanging there. I see the rope around her neck. Knowing what I knew about the professor, what would you have done?"

"I understand why it bothered you to see your daughter's picture on his mantel," I said. "I can see why you'd want to remove it. But why didn't you destroy it? You knew I was looking for it."

"Ever try to destroy your daughter's picture?"

"No."

"I didn't expect you to break into my house and steal it. Not even a warrant? We used to be friends."

"Weren't you the one who always said, 'Follow the evidence'?"

"My mistake," he said, mustering a faint smile.

"It looks like a few different fingerprints on the photo. I turned it in. Yeah, even without a warrant. This is a copy. I'm guessing we've got your prints and some of the professor's. Not like you to slip up."

He shrugged. "You do things differently when it's your daughter. Maybe part of you knows you're wrong, and you need to give fate a fair chance of catching you."

"You believe in fate?"

"I don't believe in anything. Not since Melissa died. There's no justice. There's just us."

It sounded chilling when Jack said it.

I turned to him. "Do I have to build the case, or will you admit you killed him?"

He looked like a three-legged rat in a gallon of motor oil.

"What about your alibi?" I asked. "I can see Linda lying to protect you. But Phillips? Why?"

"Phillips didn't lie for me. I lied for him."

"You lost me."

"Phillips begged me to give him an alibi."

"You're saying…he killed the professor?"

"He asked me what I'd been doing that night. I told him I was home with Linda. He was with another woman. Cheating on Sheila. He'd told her he was out working on a case. His alibi for the Palatine murder was the other woman. But he couldn't say that or Sheila would find him out. He asked if I'd say he was with me and Linda."

"So Phillips thought you were lying to give him an alibi…when he was providing one for you."

"I had Linda. He thought I was doing him this big favor." Jack shook his head and sighed.

"And then…Phillips grew a conscience? You knew he was going to tell me he'd lied? Which meant you'd lied. That's why you killed him?"

"You've got it all figured out, don't you?" he said lifelessly. "Don't be hard on Linda. She didn't know what I'd done. She goes to bed at ten, out like a light. I stay up till one. She lied about coming downstairs at 11:30 because I asked her to protect Phillips. I never told her why. Sheila's her friend."

I nodded, not feeling the usual adrenaline rush at cornering a killer.

"Have you thought about the irony that Kendra's in that picture with Melissa?" Jack asked. "We were friends then. They were friends. It could've been your daughter. What if the professor had seduced Kendra? What if she'd taken her life?"

"Then I'd have beaten the livin' tar out of him. And if I killed him, you'd be coming after me."

"Maybe I would," Jack said.

"But killing Phillips? I thought I knew you better than that."

"It's been a long time since you knew me, Ollie. When a man takes your daughter away, you can't get past it. Some sins can't be forgiven."

"It's been ten years."

"It's been simmering ten years. Finally it boiled over."

"But he didn't actually kill her."

"Sure he did. He seduced her; then he moved on and rejected her. She couldn't get over him, couldn't deal with the shame. She started taking drugs to numb the pain. Can you imagine that?"

"Yeah. I can."

"Finally she shut everybody out and killed herself. Her roommate knew about Palatine. I called around at the college assuming we could at least get him fired. I filed a complaint. They looked into it, said he denied it. No proof. No justice."

"Frederick, Hedstrom, and Phillips didn't hurt Melissa."

Jack stared into the hallway's dark shadows.

"Why play games at the crime scene?"

He slid down beside me, sitting on the floor. Our shoulders touched.

"It all meant something. The ink—love letters he wrote her. The noose—the way she killed herself. The insulin—her condition that gave her mood swings, made her more susceptible to depression."

"What triggered it? The ten-year anniversary of her death?

"It was the *Tribune*."

"What do you mean?"

"Five or six months ago, there's this article about the professor getting an award—Teacher of the Year. There's a picture with two starry-eyed girls, students. One of them was looking at him, and I just got the feeling she was about to be another conquest, like Melissa. I couldn't handle it. Something snapped. I thought, *This guy deserves the death penalty for what he did to my daughter. And he's messing with other guys' daughters?* And he's not just getting away with it. He's getting awards. But what put me over is that this article came out on Melissa's birthday."

"June 12," I said, remembering the conversation with Carp.

"It was that picture in the *Trib* that made me want to go after him. If not for him, she'd still be alive. If not for the *Trib*, he'd still be alive. I realized the tenth anniversary of her death was only five months away. I decided to wait."

"But if the date was preset, that means you only had a one in five chance of investigating the case yourself."

"I figured if we got the case, it was destiny saying I'd get away with it. If one of the other four teams got it, I'd see what happened. I'd make it a fair fight. You got the call instead of us. Ironic since the professor died first. If someone had called 911 within an hour, or the second victim had been stabbed instead of shot and not discovered until later, Palatine would have been found first, and I'd have investigated the case. Piece of cake."

I stared at my old friend. Something he'd said kept going through my mind. *Some sins can't be forgiven.*

"I need to talk to Linda," Jack said.

"Did Noel know about it?"

"Noel? I'd never drag that boy into it. I made sure he knew nothing. This was between me and the professor. Noel's young. He's got a life in front of him. I talk to Noel about nearly everything, but never Melissa. That was private. Between me and Linda. Between me and…Palatine."

Jack picked up a drink he'd set aside. He extended his arm as if to make a toast to someone invisible.

"You're going to arrest me," he said.

"Yeah."

"Can we wait until after the party?"

I nodded. "I'm sorry, Jack."

"I know." He put his hand on my knee.

We leaned against the wall next to each other, me and my old buddy, like two little boys figuring out what to do on a rainy day. The best partner I'd ever had. Why couldn't it have been Cimmatoni or Baylor or Suda…any of them? Why did it have to be Jack?

"Tell Noel I'm sorry," Jack said. "He'll feel…left out. He'd follow me to Mars. But I didn't want him to."

"What are you guys doing on the floor?" Linda leaned down and kissed Jack.

"We need to talk," Jack said, standing.

"Slip away during the party? Sounds romantic."

"In my office."

"But…we have guests."

He took Linda's hand and led her into his office. For twenty-seven minutes I watched the door, warding off people who periodically came asking, "Where's the man of honor? Where's Linda? We're low on hors d'oeuvres."

Finally Linda walked alone out of Jack's office. She looked at me, eyes pleading. "Is it true?"

I nodded.

Just that moment Tommi came around the corner and said, "Linda, I hope you don't mind. I got out some more drinks and deli rolls and chips. You okay?"

Linda nodded, wiping her eyes. They rejoined the party.

I didn't see Jack, but the door to his office closed. I walked out and got another drink. I sat in the far corner of the living room, by myself. I turned off the lamp next to me. Karl Baylor came over to cheer me up, saying something about what a great day God had made.

Three minutes later came the explosion. The sound of a high-velocity handgun.

Ten pistols were drawn simultaneously. Mine wasn't one of them.

Six cops rushed down the hallway, a raging flood of law-enforcement adrenaline, into Jack's office.

I stayed seated in the dark, near the grand piano, where I turned my eyes away from the motionless profile of Linda Glissan, hanging on to a plate of vegetables and dip. Before a word came from the bedroom, while there was still only the silence of disbelief, the plate slipped out of her hands and crashed on the kitchen floor, shrapnel flying everywhere.

54

"I put myself in the man's place, and, having first gauged his intelligence, I try to imagine how I should myself have proceeded under the same circumstances."
SHERLOCK HOLMES, *THE ADVENTURE OF THE MUSGRAVE RITUAL*

WEDNESDAY, JANUARY 15, 2:00 P.M.

I STOOD AWKWARDLY at Jack Glissan's wake, at his sister's house, eating but tasting nothing.

The four days since Jack's suicide had been a blur of trauma, shock, and remembrance. Brandon Phillips had died Wednesday, Jack Saturday. Brandon's service had been Monday, Jack's two days later. Counting Carly's, it had been my third funeral in two weeks. The Grim Reaper was getting more than his share of people I knew. I wondered if I'd be next.

I stepped out on the back porch, wishing I smoked.

Linda walked up next to me. "He was a good man."

"I know," I said, mostly believing it.

"After I left his office, did you think he might take his life?"

"No," I lied.

"I can't believe he did this to me. Not after Melissa's suicide. He didn't just kill himself. He killed me. I'm almost as angry as I'm sad."

I'd walked away from Jack's office thinking of him, not her. I knew now I'd done her wrong. Jake and Clarence would say Jack should have faced the consequences of his sin, repented, turned to God. Maybe that would have happened to him in prison.

"He loved you," I said. "He probably thought he'd save you the agony of newspapers, trial, imprisonment."

"You think I'd rather be spared that than have him alive?"

"No."

"He wasn't thinking of me."

"He loved you."

"Would you have done that to Sharon?"

"I don't know. In the same situation? Maybe."

"Then you're as selfish as Jack was."

"I'd try to figure out how to spare Sharon the most grief. Maybe I'd make the wrong choice."

"Who else knows Jack killed that professor?"

"We felt like we could sit on it till the funeral, to do more fact-checking. We didn't want anything to cast a shadow on Jack's memory. For now. Sarge sat down with the lieutenant and captain. I'm sure the chief knows."

"You could have let Jack go."

"If things were reversed, you think Jack would have let me go?"

"No."

"Would you have advised him to?"

"Maybe not. But I can still hate you for it."

"I hate me for it. Why shouldn't you?"

I'm not a hugger, but Linda is. I felt I should take a step toward her. I did. She turned and walked away, like a robot, where the parts work but it's all stiff, as if there's no flesh, nothing human.

Some sins can't be forgiven, Jack said.

If that was true, I'd committed at least one of them.

I stayed on the wake's fringes. I was in a hallway without a bathroom, so it was low traffic. I wanted to leave but was putting in my time.

Someone stopped and looked up the hallway at me. Noel. I'd managed to stay away from him that night at Jack's. We hadn't been alone since.

He approached, his eyes red and tired. "What did you say to him?"

"I'm sorry, Noel."

He pushed me, then came at me and landed one fist on my chest, then another and another. I stood there, taking it, hoping it counted for penance. But his blows weren't that heavy. He quietly ran out of steam, then put his arms around me. He sobbed. His hug lasted five seconds. I was not born to be a man-hugger.

"I don't believe it," Noel said. "Jack wouldn't kill himself. And he would never kill anybody else."

"He admitted he did."

"But…how could he keep it from me?"

It was unthinkable to Noel that Jack could murder somebody. But it was even more unthinkable that he could leave Noel out of it if he did. I wondered what he would have done had Jack asked him. Kill the professor along with him?

"Phillips was his alibi," Noel said. "Why would Phillips lie? I don't get it."

"Wouldn't you lie if Jack asked you to?"

"Probably. But…why did he ask Phillips instead of me?"

"Because he cared more about you than Phillips," I said, choosing not to correct the details. "He told me he wouldn't do anything to hurt you."

"He could've told me."

"He didn't want you to be an accessory to murder." I sipped more Irish whiskey, which I don't even like.

"Why didn't he talk to me before he killed himself?"

"Maybe he didn't want to face you after what he did. He told me to let you know how sorry he was."

"He said that?"

"Yeah."

"Jack was no killer."

"He confessed it."

"Why should I believe you?"

"Remember when you and Jack came to the professor's house? You noticed a picture missing from the mantel?"

He nodded. "It looked fishy."

"I found it at Jack's house. It was a photo of the professor and Jack's daughter. We enlarged a picture in which that same photo was visible on the mantle."

"But…maybe Jack had his own print of the same picture."

"Got a rush on the fingerprints. The professor's prints are on the one at Jack's. Perfect wear marks on the photo matching Palatine's frame. No doubt."

"Theft isn't the same as murder."

"Come on, Noel. It places Jack at the crime scene."

"We were at the scene the next morning. *You* called Jack and asked us to come."

"You're saying he could have stolen the picture then?"

"Why not? He sees his daughter's picture and grabs it, then takes it home and cuts out the professor."

"He *admitted* to me he killed Palatine."

"You have a signed confession? Maybe you want to cover up for somebody. And Jack killed a *cop* too? No!"

"Then why did he take his life, Noel?"

He swallowed hard. "That's what I keep asking myself."

"He'd go to prison for the rest of his life. Two homicides. Three if he pushed Frederick at the apartment. Four if he killed Hedstrom."

"You believe Jack was a homicidal maniac?"

"Well…when a guy confesses and then offs himself, it's pretty convincing."

He glared at me. I raised my hands. "Sorry."

Suddenly I had Gumby legs. I slunk to the floor, back against the wall, just as I'd done at Jack's. Noel paced.

"Did he talk to you much about his daughter?" I asked.

"Melissa? One day, last summer I think, he was quiet and moody all day. He yelled at me. Then apologized. Turns out it was his daughter's birthday. Jack was ripped up about it."

I looked down the hall and caught a glimpse of Suda and Doyle. My instinct kicked in.

"Jack ever say anything about Kim Suda?"

"Why?"

"Did he?"

Noel blew out air. "Six months ago Tommi kept saying I should ask Suda out. This was before she and Chris were dating...or whatever. Anyway, I mention it to Jack and he says, 'Stay away from Kim Suda.' I ask him why. Jack says he didn't trust her, and I should just stay away. Wouldn't tell me why."

"Any guesses?"

Noel shook his head, eyes dazed, looking like one of Peter Pan's lost boys.

FRIDAY, JANUARY 17, 10:00 A.M.

Two days after Jack's funeral, I was trying to tie up loose ends. They weren't tying. Jack had killed the professor. But three innocent people, including Phillips? I couldn't buy it any more than Noel could.

I went over it again and again. Had Phillips killed the others, and Jack executed him for his crimes? But why would Phillips do it?

A thought surfaced in the gray cells. Had Jack given Phillips an alibi for a murder Phillips really committed? He'd confessed to an affair and wanted an alibi. But Jack wouldn't have asked for proof he'd been with a woman that night, would he?

Or could Phillips have been with Jack, not in the Glissan home, but at the professor's? Could they have committed the murder together?

I didn't want to face Linda Glissan again. But I had to.

The woman answering the door at Linda's looked like her skinny cousin, ten years older. But it was Linda. She'd shrunk. In just two days, she looked hollow, like a discount liposuctionist had vacuumed away her flesh, especially in her face and shoulders.

She said nothing. I sat on the couch. She didn't offer me coffee. This was Linda's ghost.

"How much did you know, Linda? About Jack and the professor?"

"Before it happened?"

I nodded.

"Jack told me I shouldn't talk about that."

She looked like she might crumble if I pressed her. I couldn't. Not now.

"Did Noel know anything?"

"Jack was protective. He would've kept Noel out of it. Don't know what Noel's going to do without him. Don't know what I'm going to do."

"I know you feel I didn't handle things well with Jack. You're probably right. But if Jack didn't kill Phillips and the others, we need to know who did. If you think of anything, would you call me?"

She said nothing. Maybe this time she'd hug me. When it was clear she wouldn't, I considered putting my arm around her. I've invested many hours at the firing range. But nobody taught me how to comfort. Skeptics aren't built to comfort.

I said an awkward good-bye, leaving Linda to her tears.

"There's so much confusion and deception there," Carly said. "Why can't they see things as they really are?"

"For the same reason that so often, when you lived there, you didn't," the Carpenter said. "There's a veil of blindness over that dark world. It goes far deeper than you realized."

"It's insanity," she said.

"They long for light, but hate it because it hurts their eyes. They prefer the comfort of darkness to the pain of sight."

Carly walked beside the Carpenter till they came to the portals, where both humans and angels stood looking at the Shadowlands.

"They complain about evil and suffering," the Carpenter said, "yet commit acts of evil and inflict suffering on others and on themselves. They ignore My warnings, then wonder why I permit what they choose."

"I'm amazed at Your patience, Lord."

"Earth under the curse is about to end. The day of judgment, and of deliverance, draws near. Justice comes as surely as sunrise—the question is which of them will be ready for it."

FRIDAY, JANUARY 17, 2:00 P.M.

As I stepped out of the car by the Nine Darts Tavern, my *24* control room phone rang.

"It's Linda. We need to talk."

"Thought we just did."

"Can you come by tonight? Around seven?"

"I can. But the last person who said they needed to talk to me was Brandon

Phillips. He died before we talked. It would have been nice if he'd told me what was on his mind when he called. Can you give me a hint?"

"Be here at seven."

"Between now and then, don't answer the door, okay?"

I sauntered up to the Nine Darts, walked to the bar for the first time in fifteen years, and showed my badge to the extra-large guy in the medium T-shirt. I figured him for the owner because no employee could get away with looking so sloppy. He seemed unimpressed by my badge.

"I'm here to ask you about two cops, regulars. Jack Glissan and Noel Barrows." I described them. "Sometimes they sit in that booth." I pointed. "You may have heard. Jack's dead."

"Offed himself," the guy said, a hint of regret at lost revenues. "What you want?"

"I need to see their receipts."

"Not without a court order. Lots of coppers come here. I don't give information."

I took out my badge again. "Take a closer look. I'm a copper too."

"I don't care if you're the Sultan of Bahrain. You get a court order, I'll talk. Otherwise, you can walk."

"You're not their attorney or their priest. There's no bartender-client privilege. Show me their receipts."

"Why should I?"

I looked around the room. "So I won't have to turn you over to my buddies at the fire department."

"Whadda ya mean?"

I looked at the ceiling then hit my fist on the wall. "You're up to code for Afghanistan, maybe. USA, you're subcode everywhere. Exposed wiring there in the corner. See those cracks outside the bathroom? Where that hairy insect just disappeared? I'm seeing half a dozen violations, and I'm not even trying. This place is a firetrap. Nothing you can't fix. With twenty thousand dollars in repairs."

"I don't have a thousand dollars."

"Then you better cough up receipts. Pronto."

"We just keep 'em six weeks, till the credit charges clear."

"I'll take what you've got."

"Don't have time to sort them out."

"I do."

"You can't take them outta here."

"Sit me down at a table with a light, and keep the roaches away."

↔

Three hours later, at 6:30, I pulled up across the street from Linda Glissan's. Since we needed dinner anyway, I decided to keep an eye on Linda's place while we ate. Mulch and I shared three Burgerville Tillamook cheeseburgers, a blackberry shake, and a large fry. I told him I was headed for the house and he should stay out of the glove box, which still smelled like Izzy's pizza. He gave me that look dogs give you, then put his snout up to the glove box.

Linda let me in. She asked why I wasn't wearing my trench coat. I told her I had my reasons. But I was relieved to see her alive and hoped she'd talk quickly. She did.

"I don't know what Jack would want me to tell you. But he left me alone, so he can't blame me for doing what I think's right. Late one night last July or August, I came to the kitchen to make tea. Jack and Noel were just around the corner, here in the living room. I heard them talking. Jack said, 'I could do it and I wouldn't get caught.'

"Naturally, I listened. Noel said something like, 'Jack, you can't. You've been a model cop.' Jack said, 'He killed our daughter, just as if he put that noose around her neck. He deserves to die.' Noel insisted Jack couldn't do it. Then Jack asked Noel if he'd turn him in if he did."

"What did Noel say?"

"He said he wouldn't turn him in, but Noel begged him not to put him in that situation. Noel refused to give him an alibi. He said he couldn't live with himself if he did that. Then Jack said he had to figure out a way to do it that didn't put himself at risk. He said he loved me too much to put me through that."

"Why didn't you tell me this before? Why that other story?"

"Because I didn't want to admit I knew about him killing the professor. I was afraid you'd consider me an accomplice. But now…I feel like I have to tell you or you'll think Noel was involved."

"So…what happened when you heard all this?"

"I scared them both to death. I stood right there, just out of sight, and said, 'I couldn't sleep that night; Jack and I stayed up after midnight watching *Air Force One*.' Then I stepped out from the kitchen and said, 'Will that alibi work?'"

"What'd they do?"

"Jack jumped up. He said, 'This is a private conversation.' I laughed at him, asking if he was actually bawling me out for eavesdropping while he was planning a murder! Then I told him I'd reread Melissa's journal. I knew how smitten she was with…that professor. Her journal documented the slide, page by page, until she was so depressed and drugged she stopped writing. I told Jack I'd thought for years the man deserved to die."

"You said that?"

"That's why I took that class with Sheila Phillips. I wanted to watch him up close, see what attracted Melissa to him. After three weeks I couldn't stomach it. The last night of class I saw him talking to one of the students. I watched the professor and the girl in the parking lot. She followed his car, and Sheila and I followed hers. He went into his house. She parked around the corner, then went through a fence to his back door. I got out and watched, in the shadows. He let her in. I saw him kiss her. That was it for me. I wanted him dead."

"You hadn't told Jack that?"

"Not till then. I didn't want him to think I was a terrible person. Truth is, when I heard him talking to Noel, I was relieved. Isn't that weird? I was relieved Jack wanted to kill him too."

"What happened next?"

"Jack asked Noel to leave, which Noel was happy to do. He kept telling Jack not to do it. He warned me not to be part of it. I suppose he thought we'd come to our senses. Jack said later he told Noel not to worry, that we'd given up on the idea."

"You're positive Noel wasn't involved?"

"Absolutely. You know that, right? Noel was in a bar with a bunch of people when the murder happened. Jack was mad at him for drinking when they were the up team. But he was relieved that Noel was off the hook. Jack said it was an airtight alibi. Isn't that true?"

"Yeah," I said. "I just need to know what Noel knew about Jack. And the murder."

"Well, Noel must have put it together once Palatine was killed, since he knew Jack had talked about it. Even I didn't know when Jack was going to do it. He kept me in the dark, to protect me I guess. He said I was never to tell anybody about anything. I'm violating that now."

"Apparently he decided he wanted Phillips for an alibi too," I said, testing her.

"No. Phillips came to Jack. He needed an alibi."

"Why?"

"Jack wouldn't tell me. But since we both knew Phillips didn't do it and it established Jack's alibi, why not?"

"You're certain Noel wasn't in on the murder?"

"Noel wanted nothing to do with it."

We talked another twenty minutes. I thanked her for her honesty. I went to the door, and this time she hugged me.

It felt good.

"I have been beaten four times—three times by men, and once by a woman."
SHERLOCK HOLMES, *THE FIVE ORANGE PIPS*

SATURDAY, JANUARY 18, 8:30 A.M.

I SAT AT LOU'S, in our bug-free booth. Clarence would be joining me later but said to eat without him since he'd have breakfast with Geneva.

I enjoyed my country omelet, hash browns, and the big buttermilk pancake Rory offers as a toast alternative. Admiring the yellow calla lilies, I flipped through Chris Doyle's report on Brandon Phillips. At a poignant musical moment on the Rock-Ola—"My folks were always putting him down (down, down)"—my eyes landed on two lines.

"Phillips had one outstanding financial judgement against him, but it was only for $1200… It's my judgement that Phillips could have taken his life, or could have been murdered."

It wasn't his conclusion that interested me. It was his spelling.

Clarence walked in to "…sorry I hurt you, leader of the pack." I didn't notice any tears.

"How do you spell the word *judgment*?" I asked him.

"How do Americans spell it?"

"No, how do Kuwaitis spell it?"

"The American spelling is j-u-d-g-m-e-n-t."

"Wouldn't you expect a highly educated cop to spell it right?"

"Who do you mean?"

"Chris Doyle, son of college professors."

"I'd expect Doyle to spell it with an *e* after the *g*."

"Why?"

"His mom taught him the Queen's English, remember? Judgement, with an *e* after the *g*, is the British spelling."

"How did you know that?"

"I'm a journalist. We read. We spell. We're educated."

"You've never read Nero Wolfe," I said, taking the wind out of his "I'm an intellectual" sails.

↔

I asked Ray who could do a chemical analysis on short notice. He said he knew just the man: Darrell MacKay, who formerly worked crime lab but now is a private investigator with his own lab. Ray drove us forty minutes to his place, near Battleground, northeast of Vancouver, Washington.

We parked next to an RV and entered a large split entry home, me wearing a Seahawks jacket and carrying a black garbage bag. A dark-haired guy with a winter tan, early forties, came out to meet us.

"Darrell, this is Ollie Chandler," Ray said. "And Clarence Abernathy." MacKay wore a Vikings cap, but otherwise seemed normal.

We went down a hallway past the master bedroom. He opened the door to the last room on the left. A Bunsen burner's flame licked the underside of a glass beaker. Vapor rose out of it into a tube. No kidding. I felt like I'd walked into 221b Baker Street, residence of Sherlock Holmes.

The most impressive piece, for a home lab, was the centrifuge.

"What does it do?" Clarence asked MacKay, which was akin to asking Rupert Bolin what a fountain pen does.

"The motor puts any substance in rotation around a fixed axis, so centrifugal force separates lighter and heavier components."

"I flunked chemistry," I said. "Apparently you didn't."

"Forensic toxicology is my passion. Solving crimes with science and technology. I love it. Don't spread it around, but the DA's office comes to me when they can't afford to wait for test results. They came last month because they didn't trust the chain of custody. There've been cases where detectives try to test evidence without officially turning it in."

"That's reprehensible," I said, avoiding eye contact with Ray as I swallowed my Black Jack.

"Define forensics—and toxicology," Clarence said, pen poised. "I want to get it straight so nobody whines about journalistic inaccuracies." He gave me the eye.

"Forensics is the use of science and technology to investigate and establish facts in criminal court. Toxicology is the science of adverse effects of chemicals on living organisms."

"In this case I was the living organism," I said.

"So you think someone put something in your beer?" MacKay asked.

I took my trench coat out of the garbage bag and showed him the arm that had gotten drenched in the beer that night at Rosie O'Grady's when Brandon Phillips called me. The same night he turned up dead.

MacKay put his nose to it. "Smells like beer. You sure you didn't just have a few too many?"

"I know what a few too many is. There's a firecracker; then there's a bomb. This was a bomb. That's why I didn't wash the coat. And haven't been wearing it."

MacKay took the sleeve and looked at it with a magnifying glass. "Most of it's still water repellant, but it's worn enough that the beer soaked into spots and left a residue.

He clamped something viselike on it. He collected a few flakes into a miniature test tube. Next he put in a drop of some long-named chemical. No reaction. He cleaned the test tube and started over with a few more residue flakes in the tube. This time the chemical turned the flakes green.

"I've narrowed it down," MacKay said.

"That quick? I'm used to waiting days."

"It's not just beer. There's a toxin. Specifically, an aldehyde or a ketone. Which narrows it down to six or seven substances."

"What substances?' Clarence asked, pen ready.

He named three of them, each at least a dozen letters, before Clarence raised his hand. "I'll pass."

MacKay said to me, "Considering the greenish stain and its effects on you and that there isn't a smell, I've got a hunch." He picked out two more bottles and put a sterile eyedropper in each. "I'm using benzidine dihydrochloride to see if there's a reaction."

Apparently there was, because he said, "Bingo."

We waited for him to redo and confirm the results.

"Yeah. Chloralhydrate. It's used as a sedative and sleep aid or as a dental anesthetic for children. And in bigger doses, as an anesthetic for large animals." He grabbed a thick brown book off the wall.

"Why'd somebody use it on me?"

"Because you're a large animal?" Ray asked.

"It mixes easily into alcohol. Can't taste it. Induces sleep. Deep sleep."

"You got that right," I said.

He started reading aloud portions of a study of chloralhydrate done on two-year-old male mice. He read, "Russo and Levis, 1992, found chloralhydrate to be capable of inducing aneuploidy in mouse spermatocytes."

"That's more than I want to know," I said.

"If you hadn't been awakened," MacKay said, "you might have been out six hours. Even if you'd gotten a blood test, chloralhydrate decomposes internally so quickly that it's undetectable beyond four hours. Never shows up in an autopsy."

"Autopsy?"

"Yeah. It can be fatal. Finish your beer?"

"Mostly."

"We'd never have been able to prove what it was without the beer soaked into your trench coat. It paid off being a sloppy drinker."

MONDAY, JANUARY 20, 7:00 P.M.

It was two months to the day since the professor's murder. But the string included Frederick, Hedstrom, and Phillips, not to mention four unrelated deaths. Because of the high profile of the Palatine case and its apparent connection with three others, Manny and I had been given a bye when our number next came up. But Sergeant Seymour told me that next time, especially with Phillips gone, we'd have to take it. No problem now since the Palatine murder had been solved, right?

Then why did it feel wrong? Why couldn't I let it go?

It was Monday Night Football again, at Jake's. I called to say I'd be there by halftime. I thought I wanted to be alone and went to dinner at the Old Spaghetti Factory.

Sometimes I get a craving for the pasta smothered in Mizithra Cheese, which I discovered in 1969, the first year the original Old Spaghetti Factory opened on Second Street downtown. I took Sharon, and we watched the silent movies while we waited an hour to be seated, which you always did back then. When we could, we'd eat in the streetcar. It was cheap, and we went twice a month. We loved it.

The problem with the Old Spaghetti Factory in Clackamas, fifteen minutes from my house, isn't that it looks so different than the original. There's still brass headboards and wrought iron chandeliers and a streetcar. No more silent movies, not so long a wait, but the food hasn't changed much. The Mizithra's still fabulous. The menu still says of Mizithra what it's always said: "A toothsome treat for cheese lovers; legend has it that Homer lived on this while composing the *Iliad*." Still the best Thousand Island dressing in Portland. Couples still sit across from each other, lost in conversation.

What's changed is that Sharon isn't with me anymore.

Despite the toothsome treat, I walked out realizing that I craved more than Mizithra. Some places you should never eat at by yourself. I'd just been at one of them.

Twenty minutes later I was at Jake's. Early in the fourth quarter, he opened Carly's old dorm room fridge, stocked with drinks.

"Get you a pop?" Jake asked.

"Coke," I said.

Jake handed it to me. My eyes were aimed at the television, but my little gray cells were working, triggered by the word *pop*.

The sounds of cheering, announcers and Jake's voice woke me to the outside world.

"Sherlock Holmes," I said, "solved a case based on the depth parsley had sunk into the butter on a hot day."

"Did he now?" Jake said. "I've got some trivia for you—there's 3:32 left in the fourth quarter, it's tied, and the Seahawks are deep in Eagles territory."

"Why would somebody born and raised in the Pacific Northwest, never having lived elsewhere, ask, 'You want a soda?'"

Jake shrugged, looking at me like I was losing it. "I don't know."

"The answer is, he wouldn't."

"I suspect myself. Of coming to conclusions too rapidly."
SHERLOCK HOLMES, *THE NAVAL TREATY*

CLARENCE AND I sat in Ray Eagle's living room. I claimed the red chair and ottoman for my tired legs, and Ray sat beside me in a low-back armchair. I handed him the page from my yellow pad on which I'd written three lines of dialogue.

Noel: "Get you a soda?"

Ollie: "Sure. I'll take a Coke."

Noel: "Coca-Cola?"

"Okay, but what does it mean?" Ray asked, handing the pad back to me.

"It means Noel didn't grow up in Washington."

"Yes, he did. I checked it out, remember?"

"I say he didn't."

"Why?"

"It's right here." I held up the page. "He asked me if I wanted a soda. You're from this area, right?"

"Born in southeast Portland. Moved to Detroit at twenty-one, stayed there fifteen years, and moved back here about twenty years."

"What do you call a soft drink?"

"Pop. Called it pop here and called it pop in Detroit."

"I grew up in Milwaukee, and we said soda. My cousin Lance in Madison said pop. When I was in LA, it was soda. When I moved up here to Portland thirty years ago, I thought people sounded stupid when they said pop. Swore I'd never give in. But after ten years, one day Sharon pointed out I was saying pop, just like the locals. The point is, a lifelong Northwesterner calls it pop, not soda."

"I grew up in Mississippi, before we moved to Chicago." Clarence said. "To us any soft drink was a Coke. That's what you call it. If you're drinking 7-Up, it's still a Coke."

"That's the second tip-off," I said. "When I told him I wanted a Coke, Noel asked, 'Coca-Cola?' A Northwesterner would never ask that. Of course a Coke is Coca-Cola. It couldn't be anything else."

"But I'm telling you," Ray said, "Noel grew up in Liberty Lake, Washington. I ran the background check."

"Double-check it. Find out where his parents came from. A kid could learn his words for soft drinks from parents, but his friends would be calling it pop. I don't believe he'd call it anything else if he really grew up there. Anyway, check it out."

I gave them photocopies of Jack and Noel's receipts from the Nine Darts Tavern. I explained that Linda had a class Wednesday nights, so Jack and Noel normally ate there. They usually had the same thing week to week: Jack fried chicken and Noel a burger and fries. Both would usually have two beers. The tab was the same every week, one beer more or less. But one night, the night of November 27, their tab was twenty-five dollars more than usual. Did Linda skip class and join them that night? Nope—hamburger and fried chicken, as usual. But no beers. Instead, a bottle of wine and nearly double their usual tip.

"So tell me," I said to Clarence and Ray, "why do two beer drinkers order wine?"

"Special occasion?" Clarence said. "To make a toast?"

"To celebrate," Ray said. "Graduation. Engagement. Birth of a child. Promotion. Your team wins the World Series."

"And that's when you leave a big tip, because you're happy, feeling generous," I said. "But none of those things happened November 27. Okay, it was the day before Thanksgiving, but they'd be together for Thanksgiving the next day. So what else do homicide detectives celebrate?"

"Solving a murder," Ray said.

"When I was his partner, Jack liked to celebrate one week after nailing the bad guy. Look at that date again."

"November 27," Ray said.

"What was one week earlier?"

"November 20," Clarence said. "The night of Palatine's murder. But…Jack and Noel had a murder case that same night. They were celebrating that one, right? Didn't they solve it?"

"Jack said it was easy, a no-brainer. The guy confessed within hours. Not worth celebrating. Plus, that murder was actually early morning November 21. But anyway, it's not the date of a murder you celebrate, it's the date you solve it or the killer's arrested, or brought to justice."

"What's your point?" Clarence asked.

"Well, who was brought to justice one week earlier, on November 20? Palatine. Maybe this time they were celebrating not an arrest, but an execution."

They pondered it quietly.

"There's more," I said. "Flip back a couple pages, and check the receipt. They weren't just at the Nine Darts one week after the murder. They were there the night of the murder. They didn't have beer, but they were the up team so that makes sense. But there's a second sales receipt, after the dinner, next page. They bought something for $24.99."

"A bottle of Riesling," Clarence said, reading the receipt.

"White wine. Since it's a separate transaction, not part of the dinner, the bottle of wine was to go. The Nine Darts owner confirmed that. Jack paid for it, and they took it with them."

Ray stared at me. "And that same night, two people drank white wine at Palatine's. And took the bottle with them when they left."

I came home for lunch and found the answering machine blinking.

"Who called?" I asked Mulch. When he didn't answer, I pushed New Messages.

"Detective Chandler? This is Cherianne Takalo in Michigan. I got the photo you sent. Thank you! That's just how I remember Melissa's parents. Thanks for the note saying which ones are you and your wife. But...something I don't understand. You were asking me about Donald, like you didn't know him. Anyway...call me back if you want to."

I called back. "Cherianne? Ollie Chandler. I didn't understand your message...your comment about Donald."

"I just thought it was odd that you asked me about Donald like you didn't know him."

"I don't."

"But he's standing right next to you in the picture."

"What...? Hang on." I walked over to the table by the recliner and lifted the framed picture of Portland's homicide detectives and wives. "I'm looking at it. Who are you talking about?"

"Okay, the guy on your left side, with the brown hair and silly grin, standing right next to Melissa's dad and mom."

"That's Noel Barrows, Jack's partner."

Long pause. "Are you sure?"

"Of course I'm sure."

"Wow. He looks just like Melissa's boyfriend, Donald."

Sarge let me use the phone in his office again that afternoon.

"Noel Barrows grew up in Liberty Lake," Ray Eagle insisted, "and I've got the records, transcripts, and pictures to prove it. Grade school, high school. Cub

Scouts. His parents died in a car wreck his senior year. After graduating he got a summer job in Helena, Montana, then stayed there. That's the last anyone in Liberty Lake saw him. Ended up calling a realtor and selling his parents' house without even coming back to town. Signed papers through the mail."

"You have pictures?"

"Yearbook."

"They're a perfect match to Noel?"

"I wouldn't call it perfect. He was heavy in high school. He's lost maybe thirty pounds. Hair's thinned some. I guess he looks as close to his high school picture as I do to mine—which isn't all that close. People change. But I do have something interesting. I think you should call the guy in Helena who rented him the room."

"Why?"

"I won't spoil it. Told him you'd probably call. Name's Joey Netelesky. Ask him about Noel."

"Don't recall every tenant from ten years ago," Netelesky told me ten minutes later, "but I'll never forget that boy. One day he just pulls up stakes. Leaves a buncha stuff behind. No forwarding address. Didn't say so much as 'See ya later, alligator.'"

Without warning, he violently spit some chaw. I pushed away the apple fritter in front of me.

"But he wasn't in trouble with the law. Didn't make sense. And somethin' else, by cracky. He left full payment for his rent. Cash money. Fact is, he left more than he owed."

"That's got to be unusual."

"I've rented houses and apartments twenty years, partner, had lotsa skip-outs, but this youngster's the only one ever paid more than he owed. Left the place so clean you could lick mashed banana off the floor. But he forgets some spendy stuff, like his stereo, which he listened to all the time, so why would he leave it? And he never even picks up his cleaning deposit! All told, cost hisself four hundred dollars, I reckon, plus the stuff he leaves behind. Why would a body do that?"

After hanging up, I considered it.

A body'd do that because he didn't want a blemish on his record. He didn't want police involved. He didn't want someone trying to trace him. And he might not have known the rental amount, so he leaves more than enough. Refundable cleaning deposit? He didn't know—or didn't want to show his face. Leaving a place so clean you could lick mashed banana off it? Not just to make mashed-banana-lickers happy. Maybe to eliminate forensic evidence.

Four hundred dollars and somebody else's stereo is a cheap price for a new identity, especially if you take possession of a guy's parents' assets. Then sell the house, with an easily forged signature, without ever showing your face where people might notice your face had changed.

A chill went over me. I sat there at Sarge's desk, looking out the windows to Homicide, seeing the man I knew as Noel Barrows reading a golf magazine while munching on a sandwich.

All I could think about was one thing: What happened to the body of the real Noel Barrows?

"There are some trees, Watson, which grow to a certain height, and then suddenly develop some unsightly eccentricity. You will see it often in humans."
SHERLOCK HOLMES, *THE ADVENTURE OF THE EMPTY HOUSE*

ONCE A PARADIGM SHIFT OCCURS, you see everything differently. In Palatine's living room, Clarence had commented how brothers sometimes fight. Looking back, I could see in my mind's eye how Noel had chuckled and nodded his head, like someone who'd experienced it. Yet he claimed to be an only child.

Was it really true that the Noel Barrows I knew was not the boy who grew up in Liberty Lake, Washington? And if he wasn't, then who was he?

But no, I told myself. What about Linda Glissan's testimony that Noel refused to cooperate with the murder? And what about his airtight alibi?

TUESDAY, JANUARY 21, 3:00 P.M.

I sat in Linda's living room, me in Jack's chair, her on the leather couch nearby. This time she offered coffee, and I took it. Nice and dark. Jack and I both liked it that way. Sometimes I add cream, but Jack always took it black, no compromise.

"I was looking through Melissa's case file," I said.

"Why?"

"I'm digging. If Jack didn't kill those other men, somebody did. Who had a motive? I interviewed Melissa's old roommate, Cherianne Takalo."

"Cherianne? I haven't thought about her for years. Where is she?"

"Outside Detroit. She told me about the professor. And she claims Melissa had a boyfriend named Donald, who came and stayed with you and Jack. Then when she broke up with him, he came back to talk her out of it."

"No," Linda said. "He only came out once, when he stayed with us. Next time he came to Portland was for the funeral."

"Where'd he live?"

"I don't remember exactly. We didn't have much of a chance to know him. I picked him up at the airport the night before the funeral."

"What time did Noel arrive?"

"I don't know. It's been ten years. I just remember picking him up... Wait. You called him Noel."

"Donald changed his name to Noel Barrows, didn't he?"

"How did you know?"

"Why were you hiding it?"

She stood, wringing her hands, pivoted, then fell back on the couch. "Noel…Donald, was crushed by Melissa's death. He'd stayed with us three weeks that summer. No one out here knew him. After the funeral, he didn't want to go home. He had an abusive mother and some troubles. He needed a fresh start and wanted to change his name. He even asked if he could take our name, but that seemed a little…premature." She smiled. "Jack helped him out. Noel got his name changed and entered the police academy."

"He assumed the name of a dead kid from Liberty Lake, Washington."

"He was about his age and didn't have family. Donald wasn't hurting anybody."

"Look, Linda, I've read Melissa's investigation files. There isn't anything about a boyfriend named Donald. They interviewed you and Jack. Why didn't you tell them?"

"Why? Noel had nothing to do with her being on drugs. Or the suicide. That was the professor's fault. Melissa and Noel had broken up. We were sorry because we really liked him. They were good for each other. I think sometimes how Melissa could have stayed with Noel and married him. We'd probably have grandchildren now and…" She kept swallowing but appeared to be out of tears.

"You really thought Noel wasn't in Portland until the funeral?"

"He wasn't. He stayed with us three weeks that summer. That's when we got to know him. Jack was on vacation two weeks. They played golf all the time. But like I said, he didn't come back until just before the funeral, maybe four days after Melissa died. I'm the one who called Noel to tell him. He was in…well, he wasn't in Portland."

"Cherianne Takalo says he was here before Melissa died."

"That's ridiculous."

"Why would she lie?"

"Ask Noel. He'll tell you he just came for the funeral."

"How about you call him and invite him over right now?"

Forty minutes later Noel showed up at Linda's. They hugged. She offered him a pop. Not a soda. Not a Coke.

"What are you doing here?" Noel asked me.

"When you came for Melissa's funeral, you flew to Portland straight from Pennsylvania, right?"

"Pennsylvania?" Noel looked at Linda.

"He's fishing," Linda said. "I wouldn't tell him where you're from."

"I'm from Liberty Lake, Washington," Noel said.

"No, you're not, but we'll get back to that," I said. "Melissa's funeral was Saturday, November 26, two days after Thanksgiving. When did you fly in?"

He looked at Linda. "What's going on?"

"What's going on, Noel," I said, "is that your real name is Donald."

"That's a lie." His sideglance at Linda showed he thought she'd betrayed him.

"He already knew," Linda said to him, putting her hand on his arm. "He called you Donald."

Noel paused. "It's not illegal to change your name."

"It's illegal to assume an identity."

"I had my reasons."

"Yeah, your previous girlfriend had died too." It was a shot in the dark. I watched both their faces.

"It was an accident," he said, making my bluff pay off.

"One girlfriend dies in an accident, next girlfriend commits suicide. What a coincidence."

Linda gave Noel a vacant, eerie stare.

"But you called me…back home," Noel said to her. "To tell me Melissa had died."

"That's right," Linda said, her voice lifting.

"Think back," I said. "I'll bet you got his answering machine, didn't you?"

"It's been ten years. I can't remember some things ten days ago. But it's like that terrible time is engraved in my brain. I do remember—when I left the message, I decided I couldn't say she'd died. But," she looked at Noel, "you called me back just a few hours later. I broke the news to you. You were devastated."

"I returned your call as soon as I got home from work."

"You called from Portland and checked your messages back home," I said. "It isn't hard." Okay, it was hard for *me*, but I figured it wasn't for him.

"No way."

"How could you know where he called from?" I asked Linda. "You didn't have caller ID back then, did you?"

She shook her head. She turned to Noel. "You told me you'd fly in for the funeral. You called me back and gave me details. I picked you up at the airport."

"Not where you could see him coming from the gate," I said.

"Outside baggage claim," she said to Noel. "Curbside. That's where you asked me to come."

"Right," he said. "I was there with my bags. You remember."

"Probably took a taxi to the airport," I said. "Just stood curbside with your bags, as if you'd just flown in. Piece of cake."

"You stayed with us, at our place," Linda said. "But…you were already in Portland?"

He coughed, from his waist. "I flew in Friday night, like I said. Just before you picked me up."

"Well, Donald, I have a sworn statement from Melissa's roommate that you were in Portland a few days before she died."

"My name's Noel." He looked at Linda. I saw his wheels turning, wondering if now was the time to give up part of the lie. He sighed. "Okay, I flew in early to talk with Melissa. It was private, so we didn't announce it to you and Jack. I'm sorry."

Linda's eyes sank. She didn't move, but she'd been leaning toward Noel and now leaned away.

"If your point was to visit Melissa," I said, "why wouldn't you want her parents to know? Why wouldn't you stay here like you did before, have a good time, play some golf?"

"Melissa was upset. She told me about the professor. I tried to talk her out of suicide."

"She told you she was suicidal?" Linda jumped off the couch.

"Palatine had messed up her mind."

"No one told me she was suicidal. I'm her mother. I might have been able to stop her."

"Linda…" He reached out to her, and she backed away. "Jack knew I was here. He just thought it might look awkward if…"

"*Jack* knew you were here? I don't believe you. You're lying. And *awkward*? Melissa died that night. You acted shocked when I told you on the phone. You were in Portland? You knew she was dead?"

"I heard it on the news that morning. I *was* shocked."

"You pretended you were hearing it from me."

"I thought you should be the one to tell me. I owed you that."

"You owed me that? You owed me the truth!" She slapped him. "Get out of my house!"

He looked at her sadly, apologetically. As he walked to the door, his gaze fell on me. What I saw took my breath away.

It wasn't irritation. It was murder.

"Improbable as it is, all other explanations are more improbable still."
SHERLOCK HOLMES, *SILVER BLAZE*

AFTER NOEL, OR DONALD, WALKED OUT, I stood in Linda Glissan's living room, in air too thick to breathe.

"Why didn't he contact Jack and me?" Linda asked, hands on her face. "Why didn't he stay with us? Why did he pretend?"

I walked around the living room, stepped into the kitchen and back out.

"What are you doing?"

"Walk me through it, Linda. That night you overheard Jack and Noel, when Jack was talking about killing the professor. You came to the kitchen to make tea?"

"Yes."

"Was that unusual?"

"I do it every night. I turn off the TV at ten and make my chamomile tea to help me sleep. I take it to the bedroom."

"So Jack would know you'd be coming to the kitchen a little after ten."

"I suppose."

"Boil water on the stove?"

"Microwave." She pointed to it at the end of the kitchen, close to the living room.

"Do me a favor and make your tea like always, okay?"

"I don't want tea."

"I'll drink it. Humor me."

She went to the cupboard, took out a mug, opened the fridge and poured water from a Brita pitcher, then put the mug in the microwave. She pressed three buttons, making three loud beeps. While the microwave heated the water, she opened the cupboard and grabbed a tea bag. I hoped chamomile wasn't like Earl Grey.

"Come here," I said, turning the corner from the kitchen to the living room.

I pointed to the recliner ten feet away, couch on one side, glider on the other. "That's Jack's favorite chair, the recliner?"

She nodded.

"Wouldn't they have to be raising their voices for you to hear them in the kitchen? I mean, knowing you were in the house, wouldn't it be strange to discuss murder in anything above a whisper?"

"They weren't raising their voices," Linda said. "They were sitting right here." She pointed to the floral patterned love seat just around the corner from the kitchen, ten feet closer than the recliner.

I sat on the love seat. The microwave sounded. I followed her the five feet into the kitchen where she put in the tea bag, dipped it and stirred, and handed me the cup. I took one sip and decided that all those years I'd gone without chamomile tea were well spent. Just give me coffee, then at bedtime knock me over the head with a mallet.

I stepped back to the living room and put the tea down on the coffee table in front of the love seat.

"These two men, cops, were sitting together here in this flowered love seat instead of over there on Jack's favorite recliner and that comfortable couch?"

"What's your point?"

"That they sat over here for one reason—so you'd overhear them."

"But...*why?*"

"Maybe Jack wanted to test you, to see how you'd feel about his plan to kill the professor."

"But...why involve Noel?"

"What if they scripted their conversation so if it came to it, you'd testify that Noel had nothing to do with the murder?"

"You think Jack would deceive me like that?"

"When a man's planning murder, is one more deception that big? He wanted to protect you and Noel both. When we were conducting interviews as partners, Jack would sometimes pretend he was angry, confused, or distracted. We'd rehearse which of us would say what and exactly when. I used to tell him he'd be a great con artist."

"He wouldn't con me."

"Unless he thought it wouldn't hurt you, maybe even help you. He knew when you came to the kitchen. He heard the beeps when you set the microwave. He knew you'd be standing there five feet from a love seat where two self-respecting men would never sit. It was rehearsed. If you stepped in and said what you did, fine. If you said nothing, fine. To Jack, your silence would be permission. If you opposed the plan, Jack could change his mind if he wanted to. No downside."

"You really think...?"

"I need to know Donald's last name."

"I can't tell you. I promised Jack I never would."

"Police academy runs a background check."

"He had a perfect background. He assumed the identity of that kid who died years ago."

"That's what he told you? Here's the truth—he assumed the identity of a guy who'd disappeared a few weeks before, and his body's never been found."

"How could he do that? People would know."

"Donald did his homework. He found someone who looked like him, whose parents had died, who wasn't close to relatives, had moved where no one knew him. No friends or neighbors or relatives to say, 'That's not him.' Who'd know it wasn't the real Noel Barrows? He could probably show up at a class reunion today and fake his way through it."

She shook her head.

"Linda, at least tell me where he came from."

"He shouldn't have lied to me, but Noel's a decent person, lovable and kind. I keep my promises. Lots of Donalds around. Good luck finding his last name."

Linda ushered me out the door, and I drove home to Mulch. My dog beside me, looking up at the computer screen, I spent the evening searching the web. After testing the number of Donalds in America and randomly reading a hundred last names to Cherianne Takalo over the phone, none of which were familiar to her, I saw this was going nowhere.

On a whim I Googled the words *soda*, *pop*, and *Coke*. My first hit was www.popvssoda.com. Within ten minutes, I was grateful to Al Gore for inventing the Internet, and for the geeks who waste their lives stocking it with generally useless—but in this case invaluable—information.

WEDNESDAY, JANUARY 22, 9:20 A.M.

I called Clarence and Ray to my house and, trying to appear casual, sat them on both sides of me in front of my computer.

I went to the website and clicked to the county breakdowns at www.popvssoda.com/countystats/total-county.html.

"Okay, green and yellow are where people say soda. If you ask for a soda, you're from California, Arizona, or the Northeast—New York, Jersey, or New England. Or maybe, Missouri or Nebraska. Pop's what you call your dad."

"What's all the blue?" Clarence asked.

"That's where people call soft drinks pop. Ohio, Michigan, Minnesota, most of the Midwest says pop. Everybody in Oregon and Washington calls it pop, except two small Oregon counties on the California border. But there's not a county in Washington that favors soda over pop. Soda's a cake ingredient. You grow up in Liberty Lake, you just say pop. Period."

"Okay, that confirms your theory," Ray said. "But how does it help us find which of a gazillion Donalds assumed the identity of Noel Barrows?"

"That's where it gets good. Check this out." I pointed to the red dots on the map. "Many Southerners, like Clarence when he was in Mississippi, call any soft drink a Coke. Now look at this—the map shows places where there's an even split between those who call it soda and those who call it Coke." I clicked to another page. "In Florida, 45 percent say soda, 46 percent say Coke, and less than 4 percent say pop. You've got a population that's split dead-even between soda and Coke."

"So what?" Ray asked.

"So yesterday I think back to Noel telling me how excited he was about the Miami Hurricanes playing the Florida Gators. Who gets excited about Oregon playing Oregon State? Not people in Florida, right? So I started wondering about a Northwest guy having such a passionate interest in two Florida teams. Yesterday morning, guided by this Internet map, I called a half dozen Florida police stations in areas where it's an even split between soda and Coke."

"I'm impressed with your research," Ray said.

"That's high praise coming from you. Anyway, I'm talking to Detective Gary Hunt, formerly of Tampa, now Miami-Dade County, which includes Miami and surrounding areas. Gary says he grew up calling it soda, but half the people there call every pop a Coke. Once in a while it gets confusing. If he's at the fridge and somebody requests a Coke, sometimes he clarifies by asking "Coca-cola?"

"Like Noel did," Clarence said.

"I figured maybe it wasn't a needle in a haystack now, but a needle in a bale of hay. I asked him if he knew of any cases involving a young man named Donald who may have disappeared ten years ago. I said he might have been in trouble, from a rough home, and his girlfriend died in an accident. He said it didn't ring a bell, but he'd ask around and check the records. Figured I'd never hear back from him. But last night after I came home from Linda Glissan's, as Mulch and I were eating Polish sausages and sauerkraut, guess who calls."

"Detective Hunt," Clarence said.

"Turns out there was a young man named Donald Meyer. Twelve years ago he'd been a suspect in the murder of his girlfriend. He'd been cleared, but some thought he was guilty. One day he disappears. Even his own mother claimed she didn't know where he'd gone. Since he was twenty-one and no longer a suspect, nobody searched for him."

"So you think Donald Meyer became Noel Barrows," Ray said. "But Noel doesn't have a Florida accent, does he?"

"Accents can be unlearned," I said. "Radio people and actors do it all the time. If you assume the identity of a Northwesterner, you retrain your voice."

"But if Noel changed his name, Jack must have known."

"He did. But he trusted Noel enough not to check him out. Or maybe he checked, but there was no arrest, no charge, no record. Just an investigation. He was cleared."

"Why would Jack agree to this identity change?"

"Wanted to get him into the police academy, save him the hassle of the question marks from Florida. He believed his tale of abuse."

"Was Noel's family abusive?" Clarence asked.

"I'll let you know. I fly this afternoon to Miami, to call on Donald Meyer's mother."

"I have frequently gained my first real insight into the character of parents by studying their children. This child's disposition is abnormally cruel, merely for cruelty's sake, and whether he derives this from his smiling father, as I should suspect, or from his mother, it bodes evil of the poor girl who is in their power."
SHERLOCK HOLMES, *THE ADVENTURE OF THE COPPER BEECHES*

THURSDAY, JANUARY 23, 10:30 A.M.

MIAMI WAS WARM and humid even in January. Gary Hunt had picked me up at the airport Wednesday night and actually had me spend the night at his house, in a room with his two mastiffs, who together outweigh even me and who when we wrestled proved to be a formidable tag team. Gary's bubbly wife, who made me muffins and a killer breakfast, was very nice, but the dogs were a blast.

Considering Detective Hunt has plenty of crime of his own to deal with, I was blown away by this degree of cop cooperation, which included hospitality. I scanned their bookshelves, and wouldn't you know it, there were several Bibles and a bunch of books by C. S. Lewis. And nothing by Bertrand Russell.

Next morning Gary took me to Miami-Dade County Police Headquarters, gave me keys to the car he'd arranged for me, and handed me a MapQuest print-out pointing me to the doorstep of Brenda Meyer, 13.7 miles away.

The closer I got to the Meyer house, the more my stomach flip-flopped. I finally turned onto the designated street in a run-down neighborhood and drove the exact distance indicated on the map. Seeing no number on a weather-beaten gray house, I parked by the weed-choked yard. A half dozen side boards hung at all angles by single nails. Several were on the ground. The topsy-turvy roof needed redoing years ago.

No sign there'd been flowers, just dead grass. Front door had been white in a former life, but most of the white had peeled. What remained was a brownish gray. The house was beyond dingy—as if color had chosen to keep its distance.

The moment Donald Meyer's mother opened the front door, I smelled the house's inside. The smell pushed its way out like fresh-baked bread, but it was any-thing but fresh. Gagged me. I couldn't identify the smell and didn't want to.

The room was somehow misshapen and grotesque. I'm talking about the smell and the room because I don't want to speak about the woman. But I have to.

She was all teeth, bones, and gristle. I can't tell you the color of her eyes, only that they were cold and flinty. I always notice eye color, just as I notice the color of hair roots and whether a man's sideburns are equal length. But the hardness of her eyes kept their color from registering.

When she stuck out her hand, it was all rings and knuckles. She was so skeletal she appeared to have died, yet there she was, moving around. It seemed unnatural, indecent. I wanted to leave, to get fresh air. I took care not to turn my back or let down my guard, watching her as she sat on a recliner, stained with who knows what. When she reached for something under a pile of old junk mail, I reached for my Glock. She pulled out a cough drop, used, sticking to newspaper. She put it in her mouth, paper bits and all.

In the thirty-five years I've been a cop, I've been deeply afraid maybe just a few dozen times. This was one of them.

"You came about Donald."

Her voice was unnaturally deep, the raspiness suggesting she'd been smoking a few hundred years. I smelled sulfur. No sign of cigarettes or ashtrays. It smelled like garbage had been slow burning for eons.

"I wondered if he was dead," she said.

"Why?"

"Never found the body. Not that they tried." She didn't look sad. She didn't look happy. "What'd you say he calls himself?"

"Noel."

"Last name?"

"Sorry, I can't give that now. I promise to tell you later."

She shrugged. "Don't care."

Donald's mother spoke like someone who had to remind herself how to do it, as if she hadn't talked to a live human being for years. Or hadn't *been* a live human being for years.

As she spoke, I noticed a spider web connecting the left arm of her chair to the seat. A spider in the center was wrapping up an insect. The smell of the room wasn't cigarette smoke. It was death.

Speaking of spiders, when she said "they never found the body," I'd felt those spiders with wet feet again, crawling on the nape of my neck. I had the unnerving feeling that she hadn't spent much of her existence in one of these tricky little human bodies and had yet to get the hang of it.

"I was in labor thirty-five hours," she said. "Donald didn't want to come out."

Looking at her, I couldn't blame him.

"He and his brother were no good. Never should have had them."

She said it matter-of-factly.

"Donald had a brother?"

"Don't know where he is either."

"Younger or older?"

She shrugged, as if it didn't matter. "Younger."

On the walls there were no family pictures, only drab random images, including pictures from magazines that had no place in a home, one with a girl pointing a gun to her head.

"Donald was never the same after his girlfriend died."

"You knew her?"

"She came over a couple times. That was too many. Never liked her."

"What was her name?"

"Carrie." She smiled wickedly.

"He knew her in high school?"

She nodded.

"How did she die?"

"Car accident. Drove herself right off the road, hundred feet down to the rocks." She grinned. "Stupid girl."

"Did you know about a girlfriend Donald had in Oregon?"

"Don't know nothin' 'bout Oregon."

I waited, finding it hard to talk. Finally she spoke again.

"Wasn't good with girls. Couldn't keep 'em in line. Couldn't do much of anything except that stupid golf. Won a few tournaments. I never saw any money. He may as well be dead. What does it matter to me?"

"He became a cop."

"Donald?" She shook her head, in wonder or disgust. For her, the two seemed interchangeable.

"What was Carrie's last name?"

The corners of her mouth lifted slightly. "Graves."

"You said Donald had a brother. Never heard him mention a brother."

"Bet he never mentioned me neither."

He'd mentioned she was dead. Sitting there, I wasn't sure he'd lied.

"Did he mention his girlfriends?" She spit the word *girl*.

I shook my head.

"Always had bad luck with girls. Tramps."

"Did he have many girlfriends?"

"Not enough for him. Too many for me."

"You said Donald's brother was younger. How much younger?"

"Seventeen months."

"That's close."

"Too close. Shouldn't have let them be born. They was always partners in crime."

"What do you mean?"

"When they was little, it was harmless. Rodney would distract a store owner while Donald filled his pockets with candy or a radio or something. No big deal."

"Sure, no big deal," I said. Unless you're the store owner.

"Later they was always breakin' in to places. Stole a couple of cars together. Two peas in a pod." She glanced at a far wall, too dark to see.

I stood, walked to the wall, and found a small picture. I blew dust off it, took it to a window, and held it to the light. Two teenage boys. Both of them looked like Noel might have fifteen years ago.

"They could be twins."

"People couldn't tell 'em apart. Sometimes they even tricked me. Thought it was funny fooling their mother. Ungrateful punks. Their daddy beat 'em hard. Shoulda beat 'em harder. Maybe it woulda worked." She laughed.

"Mind if I borrow this picture to make a copy?"

"Keep it."

"I'll send it back. I just want—"

"Take it. Never want to see 'em again."

They peered at the tortured planet through the portal. "There's so much evil there," the young man said. "When they sense a supernatural evil, you'd think they'd turn to a supernatural good. My father is burdened not only by injustice but by malevolence. And the disappointment of his unfulfilled dreams."

The young man's mother nodded. "I wish I could have helped your father grasp the truth that one day the wicked will be judged. And one day the paralyzed will know the joy of running in a meadow and the pleasure of swimming. And many of those murdered will stand tall, never knowing dread or suffering again. And His children who seemed robbed of a childhood will know the wonders of eternal adventures on a new earth."

"My father longs for exactly what our Father promises. But above all, he longs for Elyon Himself."

"We won't give up on him, will we?" Sharon Chandler asked, putting her arm around him and pulling him to herself.

"No, Mother," Chad said, smiling. "We won't."

In the Miami airport that night, I thought I was calling Clarence, but Kendra answered the phone. I'd pressed the wrong button. "Hey," I said. "I'm in Miami."

"Miami? What're you doing there?"

"This is crazy for me to ask, and I'm sure it won't work but...I'm flying back to Portland. I'll be in at eight o'clock tonight. Any chance you could pick me up at the airport?"

"Yeah. I could do that."

"Outside Delta's baggage claim?"

"Sure."

After contemplating Donald's family during a long plane ride, when I got into Kendra's car, I told her how good it was to see her. And how grateful I was for her and her mother and her sister, wherever she is…and her little brother.

When I mentioned her mom and Andrea and Chad, Kendra cried. So did I.

It was a wet ride home.

THURSDAY, JANUARY 23, 9:45 P.M.

"You know your open-door policy?" I asked Captain Swiridoff, as I stood on his front porch.

"That's in my office. This is my house." He looked at me as if I were homeless and holding a sign: *Will solve murders for food.*

"I guess I should invite you in. What's going on, Detective?"

"I need a search warrant."

He frowned. "Can you be more specific?"

"I want to go into the home of one of our detectives and examine his shoe."

"Which one?"

"The right shoe. Maybe the left one too."

"No, I mean which detective?"

"Noel Barrows."

"I'm listening."

After telling him about the photo ID by Melissa's roommate, Cherianne, and my research into pop, soda, and Coke, he said, "I thought Barrows had a solid alibi for the professor's murder."

"He does. Better than solid."

"He couldn't have been there, right? Jack killed the professor. By himself. Jack admitted it. Jack's wife vouches for it. Jack killed himself over it. I don't see what you're going for."

I tried to explain how Jack and Noel, two grown men, sat in that love seat, how I thought they'd scripted it for Linda and Jack was protecting Noel. The captain's hand wasn't reaching toward the phone to call a judge for a search warrant.

I went back to my pop and soda angle, told him about Gary Hunt in Dade County and Noel's mother, and how Donald aka Noel had been a suspect in the murder of his girlfriend and that he was in Portland when his next girlfriend, Jack's daughter, died.

"You're certain?"

"Positive." I told him about Cherianne Takalo.

He'd been taking notes and flipped back and forth, left hand on his chin. Finally he said, "I'll get the list of judges."

The captain returned with a file and read off several names. We both kept shaking our heads until he got to Ann Sugrue.

"She's our woman," I said.

Judge Sugrue had granted search warrants when threads of evidence raised significant questions. She didn't require proof as a condition for attempting to find proof.

The captain called her. Sugrue told him she'd be in bed at eleven and wouldn't answer the door after that and said something about her Dobermans and that her husband had been a military sniper. Forty minutes later, at 10:50, we presented the judge with the search warrant draft in which we specified Noel's shoes and possible glass shards. Because I was also fishing—a term you never use with a judge—we included lots of generalities, including carpet fibers from the crime scene and "documents or photographs demonstrating the suspect's possible involvement in the murder of William Palatine." This could include notes, phone numbers, journals, handwritten letters, word processing files, e-mails, and the ever-popular e-mail attachment.

I wasn't sure Judge Sugrue would approve it, but her husband and Dobermans and she'd had a long day, so she signed quickly, which is what we look for in a judge unless it's *our* personal liberties at stake. I didn't agonize over this, since the Bill of Rights wasn't written to ensure murderers' access to more victims.

At 11:20, Manny and I and Dan Ekstrom, a uniformed officer, showed up at Noel's apartment. I couldn't bring Clarence, in case Noel went ballistic.

Noel wasn't home. The apartment manager, upon examining our IDs and getting his reading glasses to go over the warrant, finally unlocked the apartment door and asked us to lock up because he had *Sleepless in Seattle* on pause and his wife would be getting ticked.

We entered Noel's apartment and saw a card table in the middle of the living room, with playing cards faceup in multiple stacks. A completed game of solitaire. The ace of spades sat by itself, in the center.

Sitting on the table was a black plastic tray with pens, paper clips, a small notepad, and a golf ball. This was directly under a desk lamp with no shade, just a bare hundred-watt light bulb. I turned on the lamp. The light was blinding.

After wondering about the function of the golf ball, I went into the bedroom for Noel's shoes. He had eight pairs on his rack. We bagged seven, leaving his slippers and flip-flops.

Against the far wall of the bedroom was a small desk. In one of the drawers I found a love letter, undated and faded. It contained poetry about misty eyes and yellow hair and tender shoulders. I read it to Manny, which made him uncomfortable. The letter was written in a distinctive blue ink, from a fountain pen. I didn't need Rupert the Penmeister to tell me that.

"Color's royal blue," I said. "Just like what was injected into the professor. And Palatine wrote this love letter."

"The professor was in love with Noel?"

"The letter's not to Noel, smart guy. I'm betting it was to Melissa Glissan, which would make it over ten years old. It's not signed, naturally. The professor's love letters never were."

How had Noel gotten the letter? When Cherianne told Noel about the professor, had he searched Melissa's things and found it? Had he confronted her with this letter?

Had Noel gone through police academy and been groomed for detective work by Jack, anticipating that some day he'd avenge himself on William Palatine?

In the bottom desk drawer, I found several disguises, including a beard and mustache. I have a few of these myself that I've used at stakeouts and tails.

In the medicine cabinet I found an Advil bottle with a clear liquid inside. I opened it and smelled. Nothing. This needed to go to the lab.

We confiscated these and a few other items, hoping they'd stand up in court. But even if they didn't, they might convince the homicide detectives. Noel needed to be convicted by that jury of his peers.

We left the required copy of the warrant and a receipt of all items taken, a total of thirty-six, next to the lamp on the card table.

Looking over the place one last time before leaving, I noticed the edge of a file folder barely protruding under an ink blotter on the card table. I pulled it out. It was full of neatly cut newspaper clippings, all from the *Tribune*. There were a couple of cases I knew Jack and Noel had solved. But there were other cases, notably Professor Palatine, Paul Frederick, and Dr. Hedstrom. And the picture of Palatine's body and the article by Mike Button.

Though it confirmed my hypothesis, it stunned me to see them together like this. At the back of the file was one more clipping. Before pulling it out, I held my breath, expecting it to feature the story of Detective Brandon Phillips.

It didn't. Seeing it put a lump in my throat, only partly because my name was in the article.

It concerned the murder of Jimmy Ross and the arrest of Lincoln Caldwell.

60

"There's the scarlet thread of murder running through the colorless skein of life, and our duty is to unravel it, and isolate it, and expose every inch of it."
SHERLOCK HOLMES, *A STUDY IN SCARLET*

WHAT WOULD NOEL'S REACTION be when he saw the warrant and the receipt for all the items we'd removed from his apartment? He'd be angry and scared. Maybe he'd make a drastic move. Incriminate himself.

I thought through step by step what a man might do who'd killed Palatine and perhaps three others. There was no turning back. If someone proved a serious threat to him, what would he do?

What would I do if I were a murderer like him?

I'd kill Ollie Chandler.

He'd already tried twice.

If he set his mind to it this time, what would keep him from succeeding?

FRIDAY, JANUARY 24, 10:00 A.M.

Once again I sat at the Glissans' in Jack's favorite chair.

"I can't bear to think that the only two people I've ever really loved took their lives," Linda said. "You know how that makes me feel? Death's hard enough. Suicide's unbearable."

I weighed my words. "Linda, I need to tell you some things. First, I know Donald's last name was Meyer."

"Who told you?"

"I flew to Dade County and met his mother."

"Really? What's she like?"

"There's nothing I can say to do her justice." My skin crawled. "I'll tell you about her later. Right now I need you to tell me about Noel and the relationship you and Jack had with him."

She sighed and looked at her hands, clasped together on her lap. "Jack was the father figure, but Noel usually came up with the ideas. Even when Jack didn't feel like it, Noel would talk him into golfing or fishing or a ball game...or going out to dinner, even when it messed up Jack's plans."

"I thought Jack called the shots."

"Sometimes. But when Noel wants something, which is often, he knows how to get it. He could make Jack think it was his own idea. Noel was our bridge back to Melissa since they were so close. He became our Melissa substitute. We'd lost our daughter, but now we had an adopted son. We felt we owed him something for all the grief he'd been through, and his terrible family background. It was therapy for us to take care of him."

"I have some things to say that won't be easy to hear," I said.

I told her more about Noel's girlfriend dying in Florida, how he was a major suspect. She turned so pale I came over to sit close, lest she fall off the couch.

"You brought up Melissa's suicide," I said. "I've been thinking maybe it wasn't suicide."

Her eyes pleaded, one part wanting me to be wrong, another right. "You mean you think it was Noel?"

Her eyes told me she'd been wondering the same thing.

"May I ask you something?"

He put His hand on her shoulder. "Always, Carly."

"Uncle Ollie has all these questions. He thinks You don't care, that You look the other way from evil, that You could do more to deal with suffering."

"I hear that daily. Hourly. From people scattered across the Shadowlands."

"May I ask...what's Your answer?"

"Think, my child. Did My Father look the other way and abandon His creation? Did we ignore evil and let it forever reign victorious? Did I stay off in some far corner of the universe and keep My distance? Or did I come to the dark planet to face it head on?"

She looked into His eyes, nodding.

"This is My answer—you have seen it before." He stretched out His hands, and she studied the scars and put her fingers on them. "Tell Me, My beloved. Do these look like the hands of a God who does not care?"

Innocent people don't labor to avert suspicion. It rarely occurs to the innocent that they'll look guilty. It's the guilty who think about whether they'll look guilty.

Why wouldn't Noel want Jack and Linda to know he was in town before Melissa died? Only one reason made sense to me—because he thought she was going to die. And if she did, he didn't want them to connect it to him.

Noel was covering his tracks even before he killed her.

But if Noel was the killer, why did he point out the missing picture that could ultimately incriminate him? And why plant his fingerprints on the gun? But above all, what about his ironclad alibi?

Something was still wrong.

It was time to visit the Do Drop Inn.

FRIDAY, JANUARY 24, 2:00 P.M.

I sat on an uncomfortable stool at the Do Drop, legs dangling awkwardly. The bartender reminded me of Billy at Rosie's, except more amiable. This was Barry, who called seven weeks ago to confirm Noel's alibi, and who I'd bought a drink for twenty minutes ago, and since then two more. He'd already told me about his childhood growing up on the Yukon River, son of missionaries, hunting and fishing and not having to use indoor bathrooms and living the good life. If Barry the Bartender were getting married tomorrow, I was a lock for best man.

Kendra had been changing my habits, so I tried Diet Coke. For me, booze was out of the question. Not only was I on duty, but the most important meeting of my life with all the detectives was scheduled for 3:30, ninety minutes away. I had to be sharp. Barry would have to drink for the both of us. So far he was doing his job.

"Was Noel acting strange that night?" I asked.

"Sure. He'd had too much to drink. Or he was mixing booze with speed or something."

"But he wasn't supposed to be drinking at all. He was on call. You saw him drinking?"

"Well…I was just passing out pitchers. They were pouring their own. I guess I assumed he was drinking, like everybody. He's sort of an odd guy."

"How's that?"

"Like, I remember the night he first comes to the bar. He introduces himself to me. Real friendly. Tells me his name, that he's a homicide detective. Like he's trying to impress me, you know? Usually I learn about guys as time goes on, but he wanted me to know who he was right away. I figured, maybe that's just him. But from then on, he didn't talk so much. I'd just say, 'Hi, Noel,' and he'd nod and hang out on the fringes, like…" Barry's voice trailed off.

"Like what?"

"Like he was putting in time. The guys ask him about being a detective, and he tells a few good stories, but then clams up. Mostly keeps to himself."

"Where was he sitting that night of November 20?"

"If I hadn't been asked so many times back in November, I wouldn't have a clue, but now that night's carved in my brain. He was sitting right down there on the end, wearing his Dolphins jacket. Don't see many of those around here."

Dolphins jacket? A gold nugget among the mud and rocks, and Ray and Manny and I hadn't dug it up.

"Anything unusual happen that night?"

"One thing weird. Vicki, the barmaid, makes a comment to him about being careful not to trip her. He gives her a blank look."

"Why is that weird?"

"Because two weeks earlier Noel accidentally swings his leg out, and Vicki spills a pitcher of beer on him. Not something you forget. So she reminds him, and he says, 'Yeah, I forgot,' or something. I think, *How could you forget, man?* His pants got soaked with beer. Everybody has a good laugh, including him. It was just two weeks before. I figured he's so drunk he can't remember. He says he has a bad headache. Maybe that's it."

"You just noticed the strange behavior that night?"

"That's the thing. He'd been acting weird the night before too. He wasn't himself. Looked, I don't know…different. I'm here six nights a week, and he's been maybe a two- or three-nights-a-week guy since he first started. Noel's okay. Not in trouble, is he? Hope he doesn't have a brain tumor or something."

Barry the bartender had said, "He wasn't himself." Maybe literally.

Was it possible Noel had a look-alike stand in for him? Someone with the sense to say he was tired and had a headache, excusing himself for seeming out of it? They all knew Noel, but not really. No one knew him well enough to realize it wasn't him. Drinking dulls the senses. From what I'd seen of Noel's brother, Rodney, it wouldn't be easy to tell them apart.

I'd said Noel wasn't the sharpest knife in the drawer.

I'd been dead wrong.

At three I met Clarence at a bench in the plaza, to rehearse my 3:30 meeting with the detectives. I needed the fresh air. It was cold but dry and sunny.

"What will you tell them?" Clarence asked.

"What I have is persuasive cumulatively, but none of the evidence on its own is enough. No proof. I've gone over it with Sarge and Lieutenant Nicks. We can't arrest Noel. The lab tests aren't back. Anybody can clip things from newspapers. An anonymous love letter? What does that prove? Sure, ten years ago Noel assumed the name of some dead guy who disappeared. Maybe he ripped off his inheritance, but Ray's been working on it, and it's not clear. There's no proof he killed the real Noel Barrows or that he's even dead. One girlfriend died in a car crash. Another committed suicide after breaking up with him. Those aren't crimes. He even has a great alibi, the best of the whole lot, the night the professor was killed."

"But you think that was his brother at the bar."

"How can I prove it? It sounds weak, like I'm grasping at straws."

"Are you?"

"I've put together a file to draw from." I held it up on my clipboard. "He doesn't know I've met his mother."

"But remember how Noel pointed out that a picture was missing from the mantel? You said it yourself—that was a key piece of evidence. Why would he hand it to you?"

"Because he knew that's what we'd think. The murderer would never point that out—and therefore, by pointing it out, we'd know he wasn't the murderer."

"But it was important evidence."

"That bothered me until this morning. I talked to Mitzie, who types my notes from crime scenes. I dropped my notes in her inbox by 11:00 a.m. the day after the murder. I didn't get them back until late that afternoon. But guess what—her records show that Noel came to her office that day at 11:15, asking her to retrieve something from the files. He had to sign for it, so it's documented. She was in the file room at least a minute, she said. That gives him time to look through her inbox and grab my notes. Record shows he came back ten minutes later to return what he'd borrowed from the file. She walks out to refile it, and he puts my notes back in her inbox. Meanwhile he's made a photocopy. Has a detailed report. He knows my conclusion about the pictures on the mantel before he ever shows up at the scene."

"So he just mentioned out to you what he knew you'd already figured out?"

"Right. It does him no harm. In fact does him good, because how could we suspect someone who hands us critical information?"

"And you really think he planted his own fingerprints on the murder weapon?"

"When there's proof someone framed you, how could anybody believe you're guilty? It worked like a charm."

"But remember the films we watched with Ray? The detectives' meeting? When Noel was reading a golf magazine?"

"Yeah," I said. "A nervous person looks at his PDA. A bored or disinterested person looks at a golf magazine. Isn't that what I said?"

"Right. Change your mind?"

"He's sitting in a meeting of detectives being told, 'One of you is a killer.' No way you casually look through a magazine. It was a pretense. He wanted to look disinterested. I underestimated this guy. Things aren't what they appear."

"People aren't what they appear," Clarence said. "You trusted Noel more than you did Karl Baylor."

"Can't argue with you there." I latched the top button on my trench coat, sealing out the cold wind. "Let's head back."

As the Justice Center loomed in front of us, I glanced at my watch. "In ten minutes, I've got to make my case against Noel."

"Don't you think you need God's help?" Clarence asked.

"Maybe," I said.

There on Second Street, ten feet outside the entrance to the Justice Center, Clarence prayed aloud for me and the detectives and the meeting. He asked for wisdom and justice.

My stomach was so tied in knots I hardly minded it.

61

"Do you feel a creeping, shrinking sensation, Watson, when you stand before the serpents in the Zoo, and see the slithery, gliding, venomous creatures, with their deadly eyes and wicked, flattened faces? Well, that's how Milverton impresses me. And yet I can't get out of doing business with him."
SHERLOCK HOLMES, *THE ADVENTURE OF CHARLES AUGUSTUS MILVERTON*

FRIDAY, JANUARY 24, 3:30 P.M.

SERGEANT SEYMOUR STOOD UP in the large conference room in front of eight detectives. No Clarence, no smuggled surveillance equipment. I felt like a junior lawyer about to argue his first case before the Supreme Court.

"Look," Sarge said as the room quieted, "it's been crazy, with the plumbing problems and everything else. Backed up toilets don't make for good morale. I know it's late in the day, but there's something we've got to do if we're going to get these murders off our backs. So I'm handing the meeting over to Chandler."

I stood up, feeling like a left-wing commie addressing the John Birch Society. I'd made my plan to present the evidence and bring the charges, modeled after Nero Wolfe's practice of pulling suspects together and unveiling his deductions. Now it seemed like a whopping mistake, promising to bomb like the now legendary "where'd you grow up" meeting. But there was no turning back.

"All right," I said. "Sit back and relax. This could take an hour." Moans and groans ran their course. "But by then, I hope you'll agree we may have solved a murder...maybe four murders."

That got their attention.

"I'm going to lay it out. I'll tell you my conclusions. Some I can prove; some are educated guesses. You're the jury."

"You're a joke, Chandler," Cimmatoni said.

"I recommend this be a monologue, not a dialogue." I looked at Cimmatoni. "That means, I talk, you listen. You challenge me early, we'll be here late. Hear me out."

As I spoke, I felt the tension ratchet up.

"Is it hot in here?" I asked.

Tommi and Karl shook their heads. I wiped sweat and took off my trench coat.

"We all know Jack Glissan was a decent man. He loved his daughter Melissa, his only child. Some of you didn't know her. Melissa went to college at Linfield, but her philosophy teacher became ill midsemester, and they couldn't find a replacement. She had to have the credit, so Portland State allowed her to pick up classes there. Eventually she got depressed, turned to drugs. On November 20, she died—ruled a suicide by hanging."

Chris Doyle slapped his hand on his doughboy thigh. "What's that got to do with—"

"Shut up!" Sarge barked.

"Talking to her roommate and ex-boyfriend, Jack discovers that her philosophy professor seduced her. Within a few months he dumped her. While she fell apart, Palatine went on to his next conquest. Jack filed a complaint at the university, but since there wasn't proof, nothing happened. Ten years go by and the anger simmers on the back burner. Jack hates Palatine. Then seven months ago, on June 12 he sees this picture and article in the *Tribune*."

I held up the newspaper, compliments of Carp. "There's the heading: 'PSU philosophy prof named Teacher of the Year.' Jack sees Palatine in this picture next to a young female student, and he can't stand it any longer. Something snaps. He decides to kill the professor."

"You know this?" Karl asked.

"Eighty percent of it's straight from Jack. He confessed to me."

"So you say." Kim Suda scowled.

"Anniversaries were big with Jack. On November 4, he took me to dinner. Why? It was twenty-five years to the day after we started working as partners. Several of you have had toasts with Jack on anniversaries of solving crimes, haven't you?"

At least three heads nodded.

"You're not nodding, Noel. Why? You know it better than anyone. You know the tenth anniversary of Jack's daughter's death was huge. Did the rest of you know that Palatine was murdered, to the hour, likely to the minute, ten years after Melissa Glissan died? Of course, *you* knew that, Noel."

"Why would I?"

"Because you helped him do it."

"You're accusing *Noel* of murdering Palatine?" Tommi asked.

"And Brandon Phillips."

Cimmatoni locked his eyes, laserlike, on Noel.

"Accusing Jack is a low blow," Noel said. "I resent that more than accusing me. Okay, Jack had some issues, and he took his life. That's hard for me to accept. But kill somebody? You say he confessed to you—I say you're lying. Jack Glissan was no killer."

Doyle, Suda, and Cimmatoni all nodded their agreement.

"You going to tell us," Noel asked, "about the Black Jack wrapper you found at Palatine's and didn't turn in because it had your fingerprints on it?"

"Is that true?" Baylor asked.

"Yes, but—"

"Is it also true," Noel said, "that you'd been drunk and had a blackout the night the professor was killed? And another blackout when Phillips was killed?"

"Well, I've had a few—"

"And that you had Brandon's blood on you?" Doyle asked.

"You dropped that blood-soaked clothing fragment at our crime scene," Suda said. "Admit it."

"True?" Sarge asked.

"Not...exactly," I said. "Okay, some of it's true, but—"

"There's going to be a full investigation," Sarge said. "You're in big trouble, Chandler."

"He's fingering me to cover his guilt," I said, pointing at Noel.

"He planted his own fingerprints?" Cimmatoni asked.

I stood there with my mouth open. I skimmed the papers in my file and held up three faxed sheets.

"These are flight manifests confirming Noel made a trip from Miami to Portland. They're dated ten years ago November 18, two days before Melissa Glissan was murdered."

"You're saying Noel also murdered Jack's daughter?" Tommi asked.

"Let me see those," Cimmatoni grabbed the papers from me. "These are alphabetized by last name. Where's Barrows?"

"You see Donald Meyer?" I asked. "I circled it."

"So? Who's Donald Meyer?" Cimmatoni asked. "What're you trying to pull, Chandler? You stand there waving these papers, pretending you have Noel's name on a ten-year-old flight manifest, which could be fake anyway. Then when I call your bluff, you pick a passenger name we've never heard of as proof that *Barrows* was on board?"

"Noel's heard of Donald Meyer, haven't you?"

"Who is he?" Noel asked.

"He's you. He's from Florida. And he has a brother."

"I'm from Washington," Noel said. "Liberty Lake. And I'm an only child." He spoke calmly, like a psychologist to a confused patient.

"A boy named Noel Barrows was from Liberty Lake. But your name was Donald Meyer, and you grew up in Dade County, Florida, outside Miami."

"I grew up in Liberty Lake. Ask my friends, Mike Clark, Bill Moon, Amy Mishima, Nancy Moore. I went to grade school and high school with them. Ask my next-door neighbors, Kevin and Alan and Jeannine Sturdy, and their mom, Carrie. Ask my teachers, Mrs. Johnson and Mr. Barber and Mr. Gradin and Mr. Holevas."

"None of them have seen Noel Barrows for thirteen years," I said, addressing the jury. "Sure, he did his homework. He knows their names. They'll all say they had Noel Barrows in class, or lived next door to him. And yeah, his age, height, and hair color generally fit. But he's not the same person."

"This is ridiculous," Doyle said, moving toward the door. "Brandon was murdered, Jack took his life, and now Chandler's trying to lynch Noel…all based on unsubstantiated accusations. I'm done."

"Sit," Sarge said. "That's not a request. All of you, calm down. Chandler's going to present some evidence…aren't you?"

"But why would this Donald assume the identity of Noel Barrows?" Baylor asked.

"Okay," I said, sighing louder than I intended. "Donald Meyer met Melissa one summer, apparently at a golf camp in California." I looked at Noel. I saw the flash in his eyes. "They exchanged numbers, talked on the phone over several months. Eventually he came out to Portland to meet Melissa's parents, Jack and Linda. He stayed with them three weeks. Hit it off with them. But later Melissa broke up with him. She didn't explain why. Enraged, Noel flew out here from Miami to reclaim his stolen property or to punish her. He didn't tell her or her parents he was coming. He found out from her roommate that Melissa was in love with her philosophy professor at PSU. He was livid. He confronted Melissa. A day or two later she was hanging from a rope."

"But if the Glissans knew him as Donald," Tommi said, "they'd know about the name change."

"After Melissa died, Jack and Linda welcomed Donald. They golfed together; he stayed with them, grieved with them supposedly. He expressed an interest in law enforcement. Jack took him under his wing. Donald had family troubles in Florida and wanted a fresh start. Maybe Jack's grief blinded him, but he went along with the name change. He gave Noel Barrows a written endorsement for the police academy. Later Jack recommended you," I was looking at Noel, "for a patrol job with Portland Police. When you made detective, Jack requested you as his partner. He mentored you. Cops talk a lot. So do golfing buddies. So what did you two talk about?"

Noel shrugged.

"Sometimes you talked about Melissa. Both of you blamed the professor for her death."

"Why not?" Suda asked. "He should've been shot."

"He was," I said, then looked at Noel. "On some of those long nights on stakeouts, I say you talked about the professor. Then when the *Tribune* published the article praising him, Jack, or maybe it was you, said, 'I wish we could get him.' And the other said, 'Why don't we?' And you figured, who better to get away with it than a couple of homicide detectives?"

"That's insane," Doyle said. "Jack's wife's positive Noel wasn't involved. Plus, he has an airtight alibi. Weren't there a half dozen guys at a tavern who say he was with them? You saying they were all that drunk, or they're all lying?"

"They believed they were with Noel. But it was somebody else."

"A clone or a shape-shifter?" Doyle asked.

"Donald Meyer's brother."

"He has a twin?" Tommi asked.

"Brother seventeen months younger. I met their mother in Dade County yesterday morning." Noel stared bullets at me. "They looked enough alike that when they were in high school they could fool their teachers. They made alibis for each other even then. Check out this picture she gave me." I handed it to Baylor.

"Which one's you?" he asked Noel. Tommi, Suda, and Cimma crowded close to see it.

"You and your photographer girlfriend do that in Photoshop?" Noel asked. "That's a phony picture. I don't have a brother and my mother's dead."

"So you believe Noel's brother sat in for him at the bar to establish his alibi?" Baylor said.

I reached in my briefcase and pulled out a yearbook. "I requisitioned this from Dr. Michael M. Krop Senior High School in Dade County. It's a genuine yearbook. No Photoshop."

"I was an only child."

"Noel Barrows was an only child. Donald Meyer had a brother named Rodney." I held up the yearbook. "I've marked a few pages. Anybody want a look?"

Cimmatoni grabbed it and flipped to the first page marked with a sticky note. Baylor and Suda hovered close for a good look.

"Donald Meyer sure looks like you." Cimmatoni flipped to the next marked page. "Rodney Meyer looks like you too."

"Check out page 84," I said. Cimmatoni flipped to the next sticky note.

"What is it?" Tommi asked.

"Golf team," Cimmatoni said.

"You're in the picture, Noel," Suda said. "Only the name underneath says Donald Meyer."

"This is just another frame. Can't you see that?"

Knowing it was time for my hole card, I flipped the lid on my laptop and said, "You want proof? Take a look at the fingerprints of Donald Meyer, in trouble with Dade County three times. On the left is Donald's fingerprint; on the right is Noel's print, on file with our department. Tell me what you see."

A crowd gathered close around the laptop, everyone but Noel and Doyle.

"Perfect match," Cimmatoni growled.

"So it's true." Tommi looked at Noel. "Donald Meyer and Noel Barrows are the same person."

62

*"In a modest way I have combated evil, but to take
on the Father of Evil himself would, perhaps,
be too ambitious a task."*
SHERLOCK HOLMES, *THE HOUND OF THE BASKERVILLES*

"STILL DENY YOU'RE DONALD MEYER?" I asked, pointing at the matching fingerprints.

Noel Barrows stood up and addressed the group. "Look, I admit I had my problems as a kid. But I got my life together. I wanted to be a cop. I was afraid they'd screen me out. Jack didn't think that was fair. He encouraged me to change my name."

"You didn't just change your name," I said. "You adopted a dead man's identity."

"It gave me a fresh start. That doesn't make me a murderer!"

"I know about overcoming legal problems to become a cop," Manny said. "But I didn't have to change my name."

"When was the last time you saw your brother?" I asked Noel.

"Haven't seen him for years. Don't even know where he lives."

"You claimed you grew up in Washington," Manny said.

"If you knew my family, you'd understand why I had to leave and start over. When you take a new identity, you can't just announce it."

"What happened to the real Noel Barrows?" Manny asked.

"I was checking grave stones and death notices," Noel said. "Then I heard this guy had disappeared. That's why I chose him. He was gone, but not dead apparently, so there wasn't a death certificate. It was easier to take his name as long as I stayed at a distance."

"Missing people usually reappear," I said. "If he did, you'd be in big trouble."

"I took a chance."

"I don't think so."

"What are you suggesting?" Tommi asked.

"The real Noel Barrows was the perfect choice," I said to Donald. "He looks enough like you that somebody who hadn't seen him for five years could think you're him. Appearances change, memories aren't reliable. But no way you could fool family and close friends."

"Exactly," Noel said. "I chose him because he'd moved away, didn't stay in touch."

"I say you chose him *before* he disappeared. You shopped for the right age and appearance, someone without family. You knew he wouldn't reappear for one simple reason—you killed him and hid his body."

"You're crazy," Noel said.

"Is there anyone you're not accusing Noel of killing?" Chris Doyle said. "He's not old enough to have shot JFK, is he?"

I looked at Noel. "What would you say if I told you I could place you in Helena, Montana, ten years ago, where the real Noel Barrows had been living since he left Liberty Lake? What if I said I could put you there the same weekend he disappeared without a trace?"

"I'd say you're lying."

No, just bluffing. But I saw his lip tremble. That moment I realized I'd overlooked something.

Noel, like every detective in the room, was armed.

When you're gouging somebody with a hot poker, you generally don't want his hand twelve inches from a deadly weapon. But I hadn't won over all the detectives, so trying to take his weapon might galvanize support for him.

"I believe Jack killed Palatine," I said to Noel. "But you killed him too. And I think you—not Jack—pushed Frederick off his deck and murdered Dr. Hedstrom and Phillips. Jack wouldn't kill them. Maybe he killed himself out of guilt, thinking he led you down this path of murders, not knowing you'd killed others before the professor. Including his own daughter."

Noel shook his head emphatically.

"Was killing Palatine your idea and Jack went along?" I asked.

"That's a lie. Ask Linda Glissan. She'll tell you. Okay, maybe I should have turned Jack in when he talked about killing Palatine. But I thought I'd convinced him not to. He told me he wouldn't. My mistake was believing him. He must have lost it to kill the others. I had no reason to kill them."

"Frederick saw you at the professor's door," I said. "Hedstrom? You knew I'd interviewed him. You saw the report Mitzie typed up, didn't you? You knew that as academic dean, Hedstrom had on file every complaint about Palatine."

"I never heard of Hedstrom till he was dead."

"Jack and Linda both said that Jack went to the academic dean after Melissa died, to lodge his complaint. I requisitioned Hedstrom's files like I suggested Doyle and Suda do, but they didn't think it was worth it," I said, eyeing them. "Manny found Jack's accusation, his original letter. You knew Hedstrom, if pressed, could surrender that information. So you killed him. You knew if Jack was incriminated, you could be next."

"You're full of yourself, Chandler," Noel said, laughing.

I wondered if anyone else noticed his right hand settle unnaturally on his chest, inches from his shoulder holster. I put my hand on my heart too and saw Manny do the same. It looked like we were preparing for the Pledge of Allegiance.

"What about Phillips?" Cimmatoni asked.

I stepped just two feet from Noel. "You knew Brandon Phillips had figured something out. You knew he was about to tell me. Maybe he'd confronted you, or confronted Jack and said he was going to admit he'd lied about his alibi, which would pull the rug out from under Jack, and in turn, maybe from under you. Anyway, you killed him before he could talk."

"You're a liar and a drunk," Noel said. "And you have no proof of anything."

"You're right about me being a drunk. But I'm sober now. I don't know if there's a hell or whether you'd go there for killing Palatine. But I'm pretty sure killing the others is enough to get you there. For all I know, if he was about to talk, you'd have killed Jack too."

That pushed Noel's rage button, which I was hoping for.

"Who talked to Jack right before he took his life?" he yelled as he stood. "Who threatened him? You did. Not me!"

"I'm not the one who had two girlfriends die violently after breaking up with me."

"I admit I changed my name. The rest is a pack of lies. It's all speculation. There's no proof."

I saw a few nods. Even those who believed what I'd said knew there's a difference between belief and proof. Proving he was Donald Meyer hadn't proven he was a killer. If I had a rabbit, I'd have to pull it out of the hat.

I looked at Noel again. "The impressions on the carpet in Palatine's bedroom, by the window—your shoes match them."

"What shoes?"

"Your black size 10 Rockport World Town Classics that we confiscated with a search warrant."

"A search warrant on a fellow detective." Noel looked around the room. "How's that for teamwork and loyalty?"

"The sole of your shoes matches the impressions and dirt marks on Palatine's carpet."

"It's a common shoe," Noel said. "Or maybe somebody was framing me again. Remember those fake fingerprints?"

"Yeah. What about that, Chandler?" Cimmatoni asked.

"Ingenious. Only the innocent have evidence planted against them, right? So Noel put himself inside the circle of the innocent. Who made that 911 call, using your term *fishy*? I'm betting on your brother Rodney. You planted evidence against me and half the rest of us. We were innocent, so you joined the innocents by being framed."

Noel smiled as an artist smiles at his masterpiece. "Somebody tried to frame me from the beginning, and I think it was you, Chandler. I was cleared of the fingerprints and the 911 call, remember? I was at the Do Drop Inn. All kinds of people will testify to it."

"You were smart. But know where you messed up?"

I looked to see if he would flinch. He didn't.

"Those black Rockports we confiscated? Guess what they found just yesterday in the bottom of your right shoe?"

Noel's face held steady.

"A shard of glass the lab identified as belonging to the professor's broken window. It's all the proof we need."

Noel smiled. "You're lying. There's no glass in the bottom of those shoes."

I let the words hang ut there, and looked around the room. "Cimmatoni, do you know whether you have a tiny glass shard imbedded on the bottom of your shoe? Karl, do you? Manny? Tommi? I don't. Is there anyone here who knows for sure that any particular shoe sitting in your closet at home doesn't have a piece of glass in it?"

Tommi and Karl shook their heads. The others pondered it.

"No? Then I have a question, Donald. How can you possibly know you don't have a glass shard in the bottom of your Rockports?"

He folded, then unfolded his arms.

"The only way you could know is if you went over them inch by inch to make sure there's no glass. And no one would do that in the first place…except the killer."

There were twenty seconds of eerie quiet. Then his right hand, resting on his chest, moved left. Manny and I jumped the same moment. I grabbed Noel's right hand.

"Disarm him," I said.

Cimmatoni held him, and Baylor checked his ankles. Baylor produced the gun from Noel's ankle strap two seconds after Cimmatoni held up his Smith and Wesson from the shoulder holster.

"Get off him!" Doyle yelled.

"He was going for his gun," I said.

"Let go of my hand," Noel said. I let go and he opened his fist to show a stick of gum. "I just got gum out of my shirt pocket. That's a crime too? At least it's not Black Jack."

Noel got a sympathetic look from Tommi. I got dirty looks from Suda and Doyle.

"I have to use the restroom," Noel said.

"Not without an escort," I said. "Anybody join me?"

"I'll go," Cimma said.

"Don't let him out of your sight," Sarge said. "I want him back here in five minutes. Everybody else, stay put."

As we walked out the door, I positioned myself behind and to Noel's left, Cimma walked beside him on the right. I put my hand on Noel's shoulder, and he shook it off. I put it back and clenched it.

We headed toward the detective division men's room, only to see a sign on the door: Out of Order. A pool of water had accumulated under the door crack.

"Waiting area restroom," Cimma said.

We walked through the security door into the empty waiting room, elevator on our right, restrooms on our left.

"Watch him," I said to Cimma.

I walked into the restroom, checked the garbage, pulled a paper towel, and looked under the sink. I even looked inside the toilet tank. All clear. Hey, if I can duct tape a gun under the kitchen table, somebody else can do it in a public restroom.

"All clear," I said. "Let's frisk him again."

"He's clean," Cimma said, but frisked him anyway.

Noel, trying to maintain some dignity, walked toward the restroom.

"Don't lock it," I said, "or we kick the door down, got it?"

When he closed the door, Noel's shoulders were sagging, like a man who knew he'd been beat. After he'd been in less than a minute, though the toilet hadn't flushed, he opened the door. His left arm pushed the door forward and his right arm swung up.

I was looking down the barrel of a 9 mm Beretta PXR Storm, with a magazine capacity of seventeen rounds. I knew this because it was on my wish list.

"Drop your gun," he said to Cimma, "or I blow his head off." Cimma dropped it. "Inside," he said.

When we were both inside, I saw something out of the corner of my eye, a white bottle. I heard the sound of an aerosol spray. My last memory was pain on the right side of my skull and feeling something wet on my nose and mouth, then seeing the restroom disappear.

The next voice I heard was Sarge's. "What happened?"

The left side of my head felt like it had been teed up for a Tiger Woods driver.

Sarge pulled me to my knees. I saw Cimmatoni strung out beside me, face flat, tasting the restroom floor. Karl Baylor stepped past me and knelt to check Cimma.

"Smells like knockout spray," Sarge said. "Chloroform or ether. But where'd he get it?"

"Same place he got the gun," I mumbled.

"He's got a *gun?*"

Sarge stepped out and yelled at the gal by the entry window. "Call for a lock-down! Detective Noel Barrows is a fugitive, armed and dangerous. Tell the guards at the Second and Third Street entrances not to let him out!"

He ran toward her, took the phone, and gave his own message.

"Get me the Second Street door guard!" Sarge barked. "No, don't pull him away! Post two other guards pronto. Then put him on."

Sarge roared at me. "How long were you out here before he escaped?"

"Just a few minutes. I think."

"Then he's got a five-minute head start!" Sarge said. He talked into the phone. "You saw him go out the front door? Three minutes ago? You see which way he turned?" He put down the phone and yelled, "He's on the streets! Maybe to his car. Somebody call the parking garage, and get some officers there. Now!"

People scrambled to make the call.

Ten seconds later Sarge looked at me and a dazed, flat-faced Cimmatoni, supported by Karl Baylor. He confirmed that Noel hadn't stolen guns from either of us. His Beretta was enough.

They led us back to the conference room and sat us down. Three phone calls later, Sarge turned to the seven remaining homicide detectives and said, "Noel's disappeared."

FRIDAY, JANUARY 24, 4:10 P.M.

MY BRAIN WAS STILL FUZZY. All I could think was, *Where did he get the gun and the knockout spray?*

Someone said they'd seen his car parked in the primo spot at the corner of Second and Madison, twenty seconds from the Justice Center's east entrance. That meant he didn't have to walk to the basement parking garage and deal with steps or elevators. He'd been prepared for a quick exit. He could have turned right and crossed the Hawthorne Bridge in a heartbeat, or headed north to the Morrison Bridge and from there could take I-5 to Seattle or Salem or wherever he wanted.

"His car," Sergeant Seymour said. "What is it? Silver...?" He snapped his fingers.

"Chrysler Sebring," Baylor said. "Two years old."

"Four door?"

"Two door," Cimmatoni said, reentering the land of the living.

"Get out the license number. APB. Top priority."

I smiled to myself. Noel wasn't the only one thinking ahead. Yesterday I'd planted a bird dog under his left rear fender. Wherever he was headed, we'd be able to trace him.

Lenny the maintenance man arrived to fix the toilets. Sarge bawled him out because if he'd come earlier, a cop-killer wouldn't have escaped. Ten minutes later Lenny emerged from the restroom.

"What was the problem?" Sarge asked.

Lenny held up a soaking wet wad of paper. "Some jerk flushed like fifty pages of paper down each of the toilets."

"Paper?"

He offered two pages to Sarge, who pulled plastic gloves from his pocket before handling the wet paper. He held it up to the light and read the smeared words.

"'I felt the heat rise off the gritty pavement. The smog was so thick you could slice it up and serve it like day-old bread.'" He looked further down the page at the next sentence he could read. "I grabbed Alfredo by the throat and said, 'You're nothin' but a two-bit pawnshop palooka.'"

"What kind of nonsense is this?" Sarge asked. "Wait, there's something at the top. It says... *The Bacon and Cheese Murders*. By... Ollie Chandler?"

An hour later, thanks to the bird dog, four patrol cars were following Noel's car up I-84 East. Three state police cars and six more officers had gathered down the interstate in Hood River, ready to take him.

Meanwhile, I needed a shower and change of clothes. Just aftr sunset I drove home to the old brownstone. Kids were shooting baskets under the streetlights as I opened the garage door to bring in the trash can. Inside, I pulled down the door and was greeted by the barrel of a pistol, a Beretta, which had grown a silencer since I'd seen it nearly two hours ago.

"Hands behind your back," said the detective formerly known as Noel Barrows. "Nose against the wall."

I felt cold metal closing on my wrists. I heard the snap and felt the ache.

"Where'd you get the Beretta?" I asked.

"Hid it in the paper towel dispenser."

"You thought ahead. Even got yourself out of a secure area by flushing my novel down the toilet."

"If it ever gets published, it won't be the last time it sees a toilet. I figured your meeting was to hammer me in front of the detectives. Getting a search warrant and confiscating my stuff was a clue."

"I left you your bedroom slippers. No hard feelings?"

"I'm taking all your pieces. Move and I blow your head off."

He reached inside my coat to the shoulder holster and got my Glock. He raided my coat pocket and took my Smith and Wesson 340 revolver.

"How many pockets in this stupid raincoat?"

"Actually, it's a trench—"

"Shut up. Sit down. Jack told me you always carry a third piece strapped to your ankle. Flail your leg, you'll never walk again."

He pulled up my right pant leg, exposing my shin.

"You need a tanning booth."

Gun pointed at my kneecap, he loosened the strap of my ankle holster and took it off, Baby Glock and all.

"Not much of a gun," he said.

I hoped for a chance to prove him wrong. Between guns and keys, he stuffed my hardware into every pocket he had.

"Why are you here?" I asked.

"Where'd you expect me to be? My apartment, with the cops? Or driving up the interstate with your bird dog?"

"I'm impressed you found it. Hope you didn't take personally anything I said at our meeting."

"We won't be staying here," Noel said, looking out the garage door window. He nodded toward the neighborhood kids still shooting baskets under the eerie glow of the streetlights. "But we'll wait till the crowd thins. Be dark in thirty minutes."

"So until then…we'll just chat in my garage?"

"We're going in your back door."

Gun pressed into my lower spine, I stepped out of the garage onto the back deck.

"Familiar territory for you, isn't it?" I said. "You and your noose and shotgun."

"Think I couldn't have gotten you with the shotgun? I was just playing with you."

"If Mulch hadn't made me duck, it would've been playing rough."

"I'm taking off your cuffs so you can grab his collar. I won't hesitate to shoot you both. This is a quality silencer. Your neighbors won't hear it."

There's only one smartest dog in the world, and every little boy has him. I love Mulch, and he's got great street smarts, but instead of something clever like waiting under the kitchen table to attack Noel, he just stood with his paws stretched up on the kitchen window and barked like crazy.

Noel handed me my keys. Beretta in his right hand, he carried a gym bag in his left. "Open the door slowly, grab his collar, and stay six feet in front of me. Lure him into a room, and close the door. Don't go in yourself, or I'll shoot you both. Dog comes at me, I kill him. Got it?"

I opened the door. Mulch was snarling now, showing his teeth, his eyes riveted on Noel behind me. I took his collar. Mulch is a great judge of character. I'd have let him go in a heartbeat if Noel didn't have the gun trained on him. I got him to my bedroom door, opened it, and pushed him in, then tried to close the door.

Mulch put it in reverse, wormed his way back out, made a quick turn, and chased Noel into the kitchen. He got his teeth on Noel's leg, and I was sure I'd hear the gun.

What happened next showed that Noel didn't trust his silencer like he claimed. I heard a thud then a yelp from Mulch as he fell to the floor. I ran to him. Noel held his gun gingerly in his hand. I cradled Mulch in my arms, wiping blood flowing out of his right ear. His teeth were showing, including a broken one, but he was as still as a piece of wood.

"He's a goner," Noel said.

I felt metal clamp on my right wrist again. He pulled it behind my back to my other wrist and snapped it in place. Both hands behind me, I put my head against Mulch's chest. I heard a heart beating. Mine.

Donald Meyer had pistol-whipped my dog. I no longer wanted to take him in. I wanted to take him down. I wanted to kill him. But I'd need to bide my time. I'd get justice for Brandon Phillips and Melissa Glissan and Paul Frederick and too many to count on one hand. Including Mulch.

Meyer pushed me down in the recliner and strapped me with duct tape he'd found in my garage.

"Don't they know how dark it is?" he asked, looking out the front window blinds at the ball players.

Though all I wanted was to get my hands on his throat, I had to calm myself. I should get any information I could, in case I survived this. I breathed deeply, and spoke calmly.

"Was it you or Jack at Palatine's front door, showing the ID?"

I was hoping he'd be proud of his work and would talk.

He opened his bag and pulled out a metal detector, then ran it over my coat. It activated. He ransacked my coat pockets until he found a metallic dot. He held it up and smiled.

"A GPS, so they can find you. Well, the problem is, you're home, recovering from your wounds, so you're not missing. We'll just leave it right here in your living room." He set it on the TV.

Next he pulled from his gym bag a TD-53 bug detector, like Ray Eagle's, then ran it over my chest. The Geiger counter effect kicked in faster and faster as he moved it toward my chest. He waved his wand over my shirt and it started beeping. Pulling back some of the duct tape holding me in the chair, he opened my shirt.

"You wired yourself." He laughed.

"In case you came after me."

He put his fingers under the white surgical tape that made an X on my chest, holding the bug in place. He ripped one of the tapes off and I winced, eyes watering. Then he ripped off the other. Next time Jack Bauer wants terrorists to give him information, I recommend pulling their chest hairs.

Donald took out the miniature recording device and looked it over. "Just a recorder, no live transmission. Good." He dropped it on my kitchen floor and ground it flat.

"You know what you could've gotten for that on eBay? I meant to say this earlier, but I'll say it now: 'I'm recording you.' Oops. Should I have mentioned it sooner?"

"You thought I wouldn't check whether you're wired. What an idiot."

It wasn't the first time I'd been called an idiot, but when the guy calling you that has a big gun with a silencer and a recent track record of at least four murders, you don't sass him. And you certainly don't make cracks about his mother.

"Like mother, like son," I said.

He slapped me with the back of his hand. Harder than the Pillsbury Doyleboy can hit, I'll tell you that.

"I hate her."

"What'd your mother do to you, Donald?"

"None of your business."

"I met her. She's something. She said your father beat you up."

"My father wasn't the problem. He left my mother because he was afraid of her."

"What'd she do?"

"Things I'd never do to anyone."

Considering what he'd done, that said it all.

"Should be dark in fifteen minutes," he said, peeking out the blinds at the ball players.

"So now you can answer my question—was it Jack or you who showed the ID at Palatine's front door?"

"Me. I'd called him in advance, told him we were conducting an investigation into a student complaint concerning him. Said we just wanted to hear his side of it and I'd be over in ten minutes. He saw my ID and let me in. I closed the blinds, then let Jack in the back door."

"You saw Frederick over at the apartments?"

"I saw somebody standing there on his deck. Since I couldn't describe him, I figured he couldn't describe me. But when I read your interview notes and found out about the binoculars, I knew he could be trouble."

"So you killed him?"

"If he identified me, I'd be dead. It was self-defense."

"Interesting definition of self-defense."

I was taped, hands behind me, in my recliner, knowing that my SIG-Sauer P226 was ten inches out of reach, taped under the chair bottom.

Donald moved Sharon's old rocking chair by the window. My wrists were on fire.

"The noose symbolized Melissa's hanging?"

"Jack's idea. He explained it to the professor as he tightened it around his neck. Said his daughter hung herself, but that as far as Jack was concerned, Palatine tied the rope. I didn't mention to Jack where I got the rope." He smiled.

"Were you really trying to frame me? Or distract me?"

"Having fun with you. When he found out later where I'd gotten the rope, and about the Black Jack wrapper, he bawled me out. I wanted people to question you, give you some serious headaches. I've never liked you."

"I'm crushed, Donald. I'll have to call my therapist."

The corners of his lips barely raised, like his mother's. The rotten apple hadn't fallen far from that tree.

"Your plan," I said, "was that you'd be investigating the murder you'd committed. The second murder that night spoiled things for you, didn't it? What were the chances that you'd be assigned to another murder before Palatine's was called in?"

"We shouldn't have counted on neighbors to call. We should've called sooner. One of those twists of fate."

"November 20 was the anniversary of Melissa's death. But you only had a one in five chance of being the up team that night, right?"

Have you ever asked a question you didn't know the answer to, and just before the last syllable comes out of your mouth you suddenly know? I said it: "You bumped yourself up the list, didn't you? By murdering people."

"Just a homeless guy and a drug dealer. No big deal."

"You killed Jimmy Ross, didn't you? And framed Lincoln Caldwell?"

"You're not as stupid as you look, Chandler. Come to think of it, nobody's as stupid as you look. Yeah, I tested my fake fingerprint skills with Lincoln Caldwell's prints. Blood sample from Lincoln's apartment to leave on Jimmy's doorknob? Easy. Needles everywhere. Getting someone with outstandings to come over in the red sweatpants? Piece of cake. Heard that guy died of an overdose a week later. Shame."

"How many people have you killed, Noel?" I deliberately addressed Noel the cop rather than Donald the serial killer in the unlikely hope they were separate personalities and the cop still had a conscience.

"None that deserved to live. You know the riffraff we deal with. They get the kids on dope. They're responsible for half the crime in this city. These lousy judges won't put them away. Even if they do, they get retirement at the state prison, compliments of the taxpayers. You know what they say—there's no justice...just us."

64

"I go into a case to help the ends of justice.... I claim the right to work in my own way and give my results at my own time—complete rather than in stages."
SHERLOCK HOLMES, *THE VALLEY OF FEAR*

FRIDAY, JANUARY 24, 6:30 P.M.

I DIDN'T KNOW where he was planning to take me. I wanted to get as much information as I could, in the unlikely hope that I'd be alive to deliver it. I twisted myself in the chair to try to look at his eyes.

"You must have been squirming that night when you got the call to the other crime scene. You couldn't turn it down."

"Right after Rodney called 911 from his old cell phone, before patrol got to Palatine's, Sarge sent us to the other murder, where the guy murdered his wife's boyfriend. After all that planning. That's when we realized you'd get our case."

"Which changed everything," I said. "Since you were sure you'd be investigating your own crime scene, you didn't have to be as careful, did you? If your prints were somewhere, it just meant you'd been careless, left your gloves off. Hair follicle on the victim? Hey, you examined him. Your shoe print by the window? You'd say, 'Sorry, my shoe covering came off.' But once you realized you wouldn't investigate your case, you must've wondered whether you left evidence. That's why you came back to the scene wasn't it? That whole episode with the ski masks."

Noel smiled. "Jack and I were a couple of blocks away. We figured we'd just sit and wait until patrol got there and called in the murder. Then we'd get our call and step in to solve the crime. When Sarge sent us to the other murder, Jack panicked."

"Why?"

Noel laughed. "That old man prided himself on how careful he was. Even after he sent me back to the scene to double-check—when I'd already gone over everything and taken the wine bottle—an hour later, at the other murder scene, he realizes he left his reading glasses right on the professor's desk!"

"Those were Jack's glasses?"

I remembered using those glasses to read the confession on the computer screen. I, and the criminalists, had assumed they were the professor's. No checks run for a stray hair or partial print? Donald was right—I *was* an idiot!

"Was it Jack or Rodney wearing the other ski mask?"

"Rodney. We had fun with it. He loved being chased. I told him they'd have to break off pursuit and get back to Palatine's. But it gave me time to get the bottle."

"Where was Jack?"

"By then, at the other crime scene. I met him there twenty minutes later. Rodney dropped me off a few blocks away."

Donald stood again, gazing through the blinds. I pictured him peering out Palatine's broken window. "When they going to stop the basketball? Maybe I should just shoot them."

"Did you plant Brandon's granola bar?"

"You ID'd that? I was hoping you would."

"The 100 cc needle—was I supposed to suspect Tommi for that, since she uses a syringe for a medical condition?"

"She does? No kidding. That's great." He laughed. "That was one of Melissa's old needles. Sentimental value. Symbolism. I kept a little collection."

"Keep a collection for the other girlfriends you murdered?"

He stared at me, looking so much like his mother that I changed the subject.

"Whose idea was the wine?"

"We always drank a glass of Riesling to celebrate bringing killers to justice. We figured, let's bring our own bottle and do it on the spot."

"Jack and I used to make a toast when we brought someone to justice," I said. "But we didn't kill them."

"Saves time. In case you haven't noticed, the other way isn't working. The professor wasn't in jail. Didn't even lose his teaching job. Got awards instead."

"Did Palatine run for his bedroom and break the window trying to get out?"

"He didn't have the guts to do anything. I dragged him in there because I knew he and Melissa had been…intimate in that room. I wanted him to know why he was going to die. He took what belonged to me."

"How did Jack feel about it?"

"He didn't like me taking the pictures. But we thought we'd be back in an hour investigating, so he wasn't that worried."

"You supplied the picture to Mike Button?"

"They printed everything I wanted them to. My own picture in the *Trib*! I saved that clipping."

"Did you know Melissa's picture was in that photo?"

"Of course. Facedown. Didn't think you'd figure that out, but congratulations. Too bad nobody'll mention it at your funeral."

The funeral reference reinforced my need to buy extra time. Fortunately Noel enjoyed talking. He'd put a lot of work into this murder and wanted some credit.

He gazed, face tense, at the basketball players.

"What about Rosie O'Grady's? While I was in the bathroom, you put chloral-hydrate in my beer?"

He grinned. "That was Rodney. He was sitting in a corner and knew you'd have to make a pit stop. So when you did, he walked by and dumped it in your beer. Easy. But it shouldn't have lasted in your system. How'd they identify it as chloralhydrate?"

"I took a sample." Okay, I spilled it on my sleeve. "Got it tested."

"You were heads up enough to take a sample? How…maybe you're not a complete moron. Not that it matters. They can't trace it back to us anyway. Rodney had a gallon container of the stuff. Always buys in bulk. He poured it into the Columbia River and said five minutes later fish were floating." He laughed loudly.

"The security guard who woke me in Rosie's parking lot…your brother?"

"Yeah. He loves disguises. I collected some blood from the scene, to incriminate somebody, and when I called Rodney, he said you were passed out in your car. So we figured, perfect, why not put Phillips's blood on your shirt? So I dropped by and gave it to him, and he poured it on you before he woke you up."

"Why'd he wake me and give me coffee?"

"We didn't want anybody finding you and giving you an alibi, swearing you were too far from the scene or too drunk to have done it."

"But why kill Phillips?"

"I overheard him talking with Jack by our workstation. He said he was going to admit to you that he'd lied about his alibi. Jack said it was okay. Well, it wasn't okay with me. You'd be asking why Jack was so willing to lie and maybe figure he wanted more alibi than Linda could give him. But then you'd ask, Why would Jack need it? Pretty soon you'd be thinking about me. I couldn't let that happen."

He peered out the window again. "Come on, goofballs, give it up. We gotta go."

"Where you so eager to take me?"

"I could kill you right here. Maybe I want to keep you alive. But remember, as we go to the car, I've got this gun with a silencer in my coat pocket and this knife." He held it up, sharp and shiny. "You try anything, I won't hesitate to kill you where you stand. If you cooperate, you may live. Choice is yours."

I didn't think he was bluffing. I twisted my head around, trying to see Mulch.

"Can I look at my dog?"

"Say please."

"Please."

"No, you can't."

If the recliner were half its weight, I could jump to my feet and swing the chair around and sideswipe him. I wanted to stomp him. After a minute's silence, I composed myself.

"I still don't understand how Palatine's window broke."

"We thought somebody'd call 911 when they heard the shots. But we were listening to police radio. Nothing. Jack said the insulation was too good. Maybe people just thought it was a backfire. He suggested I break the bedroom window. Soon as I did, lights go on in the neighborhood. But a few minutes later they go out. I'm standing there, lights out in the room so no one could see me, and I'm looking out this broken window at these witnesses. Left my shoe impression, huh? Thought of that later and removed a little glass, like you figured out. Think you're pretty smart, don't you? Anyway, I was assuming somebody'd call 911. Nobody did! It's sad. Two gunshots and a broken window? It's like people don't watch out for their neighbors anymore."

"That must really bother a community-minded guy like you."

"We left through the back door. Jack's car was three blocks away, by Wally's Donuts." He smiled.

"We sat and listened to the scanner. Nobody was calling. Finally Jack said to have Rodney make the anonymous 911 call. When he used the word *fishy*, that wasn't planned. Just a word we grew up using."

It had been so dark so long I couldn't believe they were still shooting baskets.

"Five minutes, boys, and I swear I'm going to start shootin'."

Just when I feared Donald's fuse was going to break, he smirked and said, "How'd you like my spelling of *judgement*?"

"You did that to point us to Doyle?"

"Yeah. Adjusted the chair to point to Suda. Put the mouse on the left side since she's left-handed. And Phillips is ambidextrous. Did you know that? And the Bible verse about the millstone? Made you think of Karl Baylor, didn't I?"

"Not really," I lied, thinking he was too proud of himself. "But you don't strike me as a Bible scholar."

"I went to Sunday school when my father was around. Hated it. Hated him. Sunday school never took for me."

"No kidding?"

We'd been there thirty-five minutes. Twice he made calls on his cell phone, whispering.

Donald had dumped the bird dog by now, probably smashed it. Presumably, he'd parked close enough to get to the old brownstone on foot. My cell phone had rung three times without an answer, Donald looking at it each time. Maybe somebody'd put two and two together and realize he'd come after me.

Just then my cell rang again. Donald leaned to look at it. "Kendra? Your daughter? Maybe she'll be the one to find your body."

An assault team could be in position outside. If so, they'd wait for the ball players to stop. If there was a shoot-out, they couldn't risk innocents in the line of fire. But the delay had been in my favor. They'd had time to set up.

Finally, the game stopped. A minute later it was completely quiet.

Donald uncuffed me. I was tempted to try something, but I felt the muzzle pushing on the center of my back, heart level.

"Put on your stupid raincoat. We're going in your car."

I walked in front of him out the front door, ready to hit the ground to give the snipers a clean shot. I looked for signs of an assault team. As it should be, I couldn't see them.

He led me to the passenger seat and helped me in, looking at the vacant street. I was in the car. They'd get him as he walked to the driver's side.

Donald got in and pulled out of my driveway. Nothing.

As we turned off 150th, he said, "Thought they'd jump me, didn't you? You don't know beans, Chandler. After I left the precinct, I took off your bird dog, went to a truck stop, and planted it on an eighteen-wheeler headed to Idaho. Talked to the driver myself. They're tracing the bird dog, but they're looking for my car, so they'll think somehow I snuck by them in traffic. By the time they realize it's on a truck, I figure it'll be a couple more hours. They just think you're home napping after a tough day. Too bad for you."

I thought now would be a good time for a dying alien to show up and offer me a chance to be Green Lantern.

If no one was coming to the rescue, I'd have to wing it. If I waited too long, I'd be dead. But if I moved too soon, at the wrong time, I'd be dead too. I had to either create a distraction or wait for one. My options were limited. I needed at least one second of uncertainty.

Donald put on a Bluetooth earpiece and punched a number on his cell phone, on his lap. His gun stayed in his left hand, butt sidled against his stomach, pointing at my left side.

"On my way," he said to someone. "You took care of him? Perfect. He's checking in? Okay. Be there in ten."

"I was forced to confess that I had at last met an antagonist who was my intellectual equal. My horror at his crimes was lost in my admiration of his skill."
SHERLOCK HOLMES, *THE FINAL PROBLEM*

FRIDAY, JANUARY 24, 7:45 P.M.

I SAT THERE IN THE FRONT SEAT of my own car, wrists bent like pretzels, contemplating my Baby Glock under the Kleenex in the glove box. I've got three Baby Glocks, the triplets, and I love them all. Now I wished I'd hidden one in the crack in the passenger side seat upholstery, the one place my hands could access. A guy could be handcuffed behind his back, in the passenger seat of his car. Why hadn't I anticipated that?

If only Baby was within reach, I could grab it, turn sideways toward the window, point it behind my back at Donald, and spray him with slugs. Preferably at a stoplight.

Donald pulled into Dr. Alexander's podiatry clinic, adjacent to his apartment complex. He didn't know I'd put a bird dog on my car too. Just in case. Sergeant Seymour had rolled his eyes at me when I'd told him. Given that I was out of contact and my car was moving now, would it get their attention? If they traced it here, I hoped they'd realize we'd gone to Donald's apartment.

But why were we here? Donald was a fugitive. A cop or two would be posted at his apartment despite the decoy moving up the highway. He had to know that.

"I'm going to uncuff you again. We'll walk naturally to the apartments. There's an inside hallway. We'll pass people. Act like we're old friends. Hey, we *are* old friends. Don't forget I've got the gun and the knife if I need to keep it quiet. You say or do anything fishy, I won't just kill you, I'll kill them. Got it?"

I was willing to risk my life, already up for grabs. But was I willing to risk the lives of bystanders? In conflicts like these, men without consciences have certain advantages.

One step behind me, Donald talked cheerily when someone appeared in the hallway. "Hi, Jessica. How's Stuart doing in school?"

We walked toward his apartment, third on the right.

Where were the cops? Who'd been on the other end of that phone call?

If he hadn't been a cop, I would have tried something right as we went through his door. But he was too focused, too alert. Maybe if I behaved, he wouldn't put the cuffs back on. Maybe I'd get a chance.

Donald shoved a chair in the center of his studio apartment. He told me to sit by the card table. I looked at the ace of spades lying there. I felt compelled to nudge it with my finger. Underneath it was a piece of scratch paper with one name: Ollie Chandler.

I'd been compliant for the last half hour at my house and for the car ride and the walk into the apartment. Now that we were here, on his turf, Donald's comfort level was instinctively higher. If I could maintain my low threat level, that would work to my advantage. The fact that he hadn't handcuffed me was promising. I asked myself what Jack Bauer would do. I wished I had Chloe out there helping me with a notebook computer and a satellite.

Donald produced two big duffel bags. One appeared already packed. He started packing the other. He spoke aloud as he went from closet to drawers. "Heavy jacket. Light jacket. Ammo. Candles. Matches. Scissors."

He must have further use for me. Not for ransom. The chief wouldn't trade a bar of hotel soap for me. But as a hostage, I might have value. Or, and this seemed more likely, he had just the right burial place planned for me and wanted me to get there on my own two feet, making it a lot easier for him. Likely it was a favorite spot, where others were already buried, including the real Noel Barrows.

I felt those wet-footed spiders on my neck.

I'd been close to death before. This time I could taste it. My conversations with Jake and Clarence came back to me. Whatever they had that I didn't, it made them ready to die in a way I wasn't. This was no time for soul-searching...but maybe it was the only time left.

Donald opened every drawer, then looked around the room. He'd stuffed the duffel bag with warm waterproof clothes, a sleeping bag, even a small propane stove. He took a gigantic black trash bag from the closet and crammed it in the duffel. I hoped its function wasn't what I thought it might be. He also had a white trash bag stuffed with something light. He opened the first duffel and stuffed it in.

Donald spoke now, excitedly. "I've scoped out a half dozen places in the mountains where I could live for a year without being found. Once I grow a beard and put on glasses, when I come out for groceries nobody'll notice. I worked in vice. I've seen a hundred fake IDs, and I've made three different ones, two for fallback."

He couldn't stand not bragging about it.

"Eventually I'll come out of the woods and watch myself on *America's Most Wanted*. By then my hair'll be red. I'll either be lean or bulked up, maybe as fat as you. Haven't decided. Fat sounds more fun."

"What will you do, run Ferris wheels at carnivals?"

Okay, it was random, but when you're buying minutes of life, you take what little the gray cells give you.

"I have a plan for that too. I've got this bag of cash, taken here and there on the street." He pointed at the white bag. "Twenty-three thousand dollars, from drug dealers, pimps, and lowlifes. That'll tide me over. Maybe someday I'll set up an office, hang a shingle: Private Investigator."

"Why'd you call my house from Palatine's?"

"A little joke while waiting for the professor to die. I witnessed Melissa's death. I didn't want to miss his death. It was ten years to the minute. Not almost. Exactly."

He opened his fridge and began pulling stuff out.

"Oh, yeah, the Budweiser bottles at Palatine's. If they ever run the DNA tests, guess whose saliva's on the bottles?"

"Whose?"

"Yours. Took them right from your garage. Got 'em when I got the rope."

"But it's your saliva on the wineglasses."

"Jack's. Not mine. While Jack looked the place over, I said I'd wash the glasses. I washed mine with soap and water, and I wiped off Jack's prints, but didn't touch the rim of his glass and left wine residue in it. I'm sure his saliva traces are there. It'll look like Jack celebrated with wine and you with Budweiser. True to form. Surprised they haven't found your prints on the bottles yet. They will."

He looked at the food in front of him, doing inventory. "Beef, mustard, onion, bread, butter, soda."

"For the record, people from the Pacific Northwest don't say soda. We say pop."

"Thanks for pointing that out. It could trip me up."

"It already did."

"Yeah, and here we are, me with the gun and you looking up its barrel." He pointed it at my face. "Who was it that tripped up?"

Donald's cell rang. He listened, then said, "Good. See you then."

He moved quickly now.

It's a strange thing to be in a situation where your adrenaline is flowing like water through a fire hose but you have to appear relaxed.

Why hadn't he killed me yet? Did he still think there was reasonable doubt on the other murders? I had to admit that the circumstantial evidence against him wasn't absolute. He hadn't confessed to the detectives. Sure, he bolted from the precinct, but innocent people have run when they believed they were being framed. His attorney could argue that in court. The planted fingerprints and 911 call made to sound like him could lead to reasonable doubt. Not to mention that I'd held out evidence against myself, which contaminated all evidence I'd presented against him. He hadn't harmed me or Cimmatoni, though he could have. He didn't even take our weapons. Girlfriends dying? It happens. Taking the identity of Noel Barrows would get him a hand slap, but it wasn't that serious given his subsequent service to society.

Think like he's thinking, I told myself. He wants it to be like the other murders. No proof that he did it. He just needs me to disappear. To get me to where he'll dispose of my body. Then, in his worst-case scenario, if they find him someday, there'd be no proof he'd killed me or anyone else. He ran because he was framed. Yeah, that's what he must be thinking. Which meant once we got in the car again, away from civilization, every mile would mean less hope of survival.

I turned slightly so he couldn't see my left hand. I reached to my belt, where my pocketknife hung on the inside from its thin metal wire.

My cooperation had relaxed Donald's guard. If I talked, maybe he wouldn't realize I was doing something else.

"I remember when I first met Jack. He taught me how to…"

While I talked, I took the knife in my right hand and cut my left palm, deep. I cupped my hand to contain the pool of blood so it wasn't dripping on the carpet yet. I walked toward the couch. A few drops landed on the carpet, but he didn't notice. I sat on the couch, talking about Jack, my left hand still blocked from his view. I let the blood flow behind the cushion. I hung my hand over the side of the couch and wiped it into the fabric, then let it spill freely onto the carpet. Blood flowed to the end of my index finger and thumb, and I flicked it onto wall and curtain. All this time I droned on and on, keeping my body between him and my left hand.

While that hundred-watt bulb was blinding, it left the corners of the room shadowed, allowing me to make DNA deposits all over without being noticed.

While Noel finished packing food into plastic bags, I continued to talk about Jack. I walked toward the window.

"The blinds are down, Chandler. Nobody's seeing you."

I talked about a particular stakeout on a case that involved an orangutan. By now my blood had marked a chair, a bookcase, and several CD covers.

"They're going to find your brother," I said.

"He stuck around too long. When you said you saw me at Starbucks, I realized he had to get out of town, or we'd get tripped up. Fortunately you're too stupid to figure out that it wasn't me you saw."

He stared, and I stood still. "You still don't know why there's no cop here, do you, Chandler? I called Rodney back to town when you searched my apartment. Ten minutes before we got here, he posed as the assistant manager and visited the officer right at my door." Noel smiled. "He took the officer for a ride. He's checking in with his sergeant regularly and saying everything's okay."

"And if he stops cooperating?"

"He'll die."

"Your brother's a killer too?"

Noel laughed. "I'm the nice brother."

Left hand behind me, smearing the wall by the stereo, I said, "Ask yourself what Jack would want you to do. Don't you think you should turn yourself in?"

Picking up the two duffel bags, he froze. "What are you doing?"

He turned on a second light, then a third. He looked around the room at the bloodstains.

"Show me your hand. Your left hand!"

I squeezed it tight, then held it up, letting a nice bloody dribble fall on his cream-colored carpet. He grabbed a kitchen towel and threw it at me. "Wrap it up."

"You can kill me, but they still have the case I built against you. And now my blood's all over. You'll never get it clean. It's a killer's worst nightmare—physical evidence everywhere, in your own home."

He stared at the carpet, not seeing my right hand, which I raised at that moment and swiped across his left arm with my knife. It was a clean cut, good and bloody, though I missed the inside of his wrist, which I was going for. His blood hit the floor within seconds.

As he stepped back and grabbed his arm, clutching the gun awkwardly, I threw the knife at his face. It hit his cheek, the blade piercing his skin before it fell. I reached in my pocket then threw his golf ball at him. It bounced off his forehead with a loud thud. These things all happened with a couple of seconds, and now I charged him. But he backed up, his gun's muzzle pointed at me, then suddenly stepped forward and I knew he would shoot. The gun was now six inches from the bridge of my nose.

"That's two blood sources in the carpet, yours and mine," I said. "Your house is going to scream, 'Killer.' And your face is going to have a nice scar. And a big bruise on your forehead."

Granted, if he made it to the woods, it might just be squirrels and deer taking a second look at him. But it was a long way to the woods.

He pushed the gun to my forehead, pressing muzzle against thin flesh. As I stepped back, he kept coming, pushing it harder.

"I'll kill you right here, right now."

My cell phone, in his pocket, rang. He pulled it out, dropped it on the ground, and stomped on it.

"You make a good point, Chandler. Now that I know I'd have to face murder charges if I'm ever discovered—which I don't plan to be—why should I risk taking you somewhere else to kill you? Who cares where your body ends up? Why not leave it right here? You just took away my only reason for not killing you here and now."

It was a good point.

One I maybe should have thought of sooner.

66

"Yes, the setting is a worthy one.
If the devil did desire to have a hand in
the affairs of men..."
SHERLOCK HOLMES, *THE HOUND OF THE BASKERVILLES*

HE PUSHED THE MUZZLE into my right temple. "Say your prayers."

I started to, wishing I had more time.

Five seconds later he pulled the gun back, pushed me to the bathroom, and ordered me to clean up. Waving his Beretta at the medicine cabinet, he told me to wrap a bandage and athletic tape around my hand.

"I've decided I'm not done with you," he said in a voice like his mother's. "I've got a place all picked out for you. Others are waiting for you to join them, and I don't want to disappoint them."

He stood in the bathroom doorway and never took his eye off me. After ordering me out, he gave one last sweeping gaze of the apartment. I stood six feet from the front door, and he was two feet behind me. He gestured for me to move to the door.

I walked wide to the right, pretending not to notice a stereo wire, and tripped on it, landing on my face in front of the door. It was hard not to take an athletic roll, but it had to look like an accident.

"Get up, idiot."

I positioned myself with my bandaged left hand pushing up on the floor. I pulled up my left pant leg with my right hand and grabbed the Baby Glock, then shot Donald Meyer in the right shoulder. He screamed. His Beretta dropped to the floor.

I punched his wounded shoulder twice with my bandaged left hand and backed him against the wall. I took the knife out of his pocket and searched him for other weapons while he moaned and groaned like a sissy.

"I took that gun from your ankle holster," he said, like I'd treated him unfairly.

"I have *two* ankles, dunderhead. You only saw one of my white shins, remember? Speaking of which, in prison they don't tan much. And the golfing's seriously limited."

"You were carrying *four* guns? Nobody carries four guns." He was writhing, but he wouldn't let it go. "Who could possibly need four guns?"

"Me. Today."

He grasped his shoulder moaning, tears coming to his eyes.

"Baby Glock's not much of a gun, huh? Enough to make you into a crybaby, you little sissy. Messin' with me's like wearin' cheese underwear down rat alley."

I punched his right shoulder. "Don't forget it, numskull." I punched it again. "That one's for pistol-whipping my dog."

I cuffed Donald extra tight, and we headed down the hallway. "Get ready to walk the Green Mile, scumbag." One of the neighbors came out her door, and I nodded and smiled.

"Help me," Donald said to her. "This man assaulted me."

I flipped open my badge. "I'm a police officer, ma'am. He's under arrest."

"I'm the police officer," Donald said. "You know me."

"He is a police officer," she said to me, pointing at Donald. "I know he is." She pulled out her cell phone.

"Yes, ma'am, but he's the police officer in handcuffs, and I'm the police officer with the big gun." I pulled Donald's Beretta from my pocket.

She nodded and started to put away her cell phone.

"May I use that, ma'am?" I'd confiscated Donald's phone and his earpiece, but didn't want to contaminate evidence by using it.

I reached out my bloody left hand and took it, then called Jake and asked him to go immediately to my house. I told him to call Megan Wood, the vet who'd come to Mulch's rescue earlier.

I called 911, then Sergeant Seymour. Before I could say anything he said, "You been napping? They're still tracing Noel's car up I-84. Set up two roadblocks, but somehow he got away."

"Actually, Sarge, Donald's right here with me. Want to talk to the little whiner?"

Sarge insisted I not leave the building until backup arrived. While I was waiting by the front door, I was deliberately a little lax, hoping Donald would try something. He decided to kick me where it hurts in the hopes that he could make a run for it. After he took his best shot, a little high, I pocketed the Beretta, stepped toward him, grabbed his jacket with both hands, and yanked his head toward mine. My head met him halfway. It sounded like two coconuts fired from cannons, colliding with each other. My coconut is harder, so he was unconscious before hitting the floor.

When Sarge showed up with backup, he hugged me This was uncomfortable enough, but then I had to explain Donald's condition. Sarge said Donald's attorney would accuse me of brutality, but I didn't care. It was worth it.

The EMTs focused on Donald, who finally regained consciousness. Despite everyone's urging, I insisted I didn't need another hospital visit. I told the paramedics I was on a first name basis with a nurse named Angela at Adventist Medical Center, and she would vouch for me. They settled for bandaging my hand and treating my forehead, which had been a skin donor to Donald's forehead. The rest was bumps and bruises, the worst from falling on my face as part of my act of clumsiness. At least it was the opposite side of my face from when I'd fallen from the knockout spray. I like to spread out the damage.

I insisted on going home to see Mulch. If I wouldn't go to the hospital, Sarge insisted I go to precinct. I called home and Jake answered.

"I've got somebody here who wants to talk to you," he said.

I heard a grunt, a nuzzle, a sneeze, and a familiar little growl.

"Hi, Clarence," I said.

"It's Mulch," Jake said. "He's got a headache. Megan says it's a concussion, and she's taking him in to the clinic. But she's optimistic. She knows him pretty well by now."

"To the right of the microwave, the upper cupboard has five pounds of the best beef jerky money can buy. The sky's the limit for Mulch. Have some yourself. Take a handful home for Champ. Tell Megan to fill her pockets."

"She'll be thrilled."

I entered the Justice Center, carrying a box from my car. Clarence was waiting in detective division when I arrived. He came straight to me, put his arm around me, and asked if I was okay. Every detective was there, seven of us now, without Brandon Phillips, Jack Glissan, and Noel Barrows, aka Donald Meyer. Sergeant Seymour joined us minutes later.

They wanted to hear my story and led me into the conference room. We'd all been in this same room just six hours ago. They kept interrupting with questions, which was okay because Karl brought in three boxes of Krispy Kremes and Tommi two gallons of milk. I felt like royalty.

As I told the story there were lots of smart comments, but I felt part of the team for the first time in two months.

"Okay, I believe you about Noel," Chris Doyle said. "But where's evidence that's beyond reasonable doubt?"

"In fact," Kim Suda said to me, "for Palatine's murder, and Brandon's too, there's more physical evidence against you than against him, right?"

I nodded.

"What's to keep Noel from saying he ran from us because you framed him?" Sarge said. "He wanted to escape to prove he was innocent. He's still got the alibi in the tavern, unless you can produce his brother."

"I can't," I said.

"So it sounds like a wild guess," Suda said. "But that's not all. Noel's attorney calls a criminalist to the stand, maybe Phil Oref, and he has to testify that you tampered with evidence, right? Chris and I have to testify that bloody fabric appeared at the scene after you showed up. Put that with Noel's fake fingerprints and the Black Jack gum and if your DNA's really on the beer bottle…that's plenty of reasonable doubt."

"But look at what just happened," Clarence said. "This guy assaulted Ollie at his house, knocked out Mulch, handcuffed Ollie and abducted him to his place, where Ollie's blood's everywhere."

"But he could reverse everything," Cimmatoni said, looking at me. "He could claim you caught him, took him to your place, and brained your dog yourself."

"That wouldn't hold up with a jury of dog owners," Tommi said.

"It was your car that went to his place," Sarge said. "It looks like you drove him there."

"And cutting your palm, your blood all over his apartment?" Doyle said. "They could see that as you trying to corroborate your made-up story. You admit you cut your own hand. What actual harm did he inflict on you, some bruises? You're the one who shot him. You tried to frame him with fake prints, he'll say. You tried to frame him again by cutting your hand with your own knife."

"It's not like you'd be convicted of anything," Baylor said. "We all know now he's guilty. But sometimes you can't prove what you know. This is way more than enough reasonable doubt to get him acquitted."

"We've got plenty of dead people," Sarge said, sighing. "I say he walks unless we find irrefutable evidence, something that couldn't have been falsified, that's not just our gut feelings or your word against his."

After another big gulp of milk, washing down the last bite of a glazed raspberry-filled Krispy Kreme, I said, "Would a recording of Noel's confession help?"

They all stared at me. If he'd been there, the chief would have said you could hear a pin drop.

"But…you don't have that," Suda said. "You told us he found the wire and pulled it."

"When people suspect you're wired, what do they do?" I asked.

"Search for it," Suda said.

"When do they stop searching?"

"After they look and don't find it."

"Or?"

"After they do find it," Tommi said.

"Right. When they find a wire, they stop looking for a wire. Just like when they find the gun on your right ankle, they don't look for a gun on your left ankle."

"What are you saying, Chandler?" Cimmatoni asked.

"You're all making the same assumption Donald did. That there was only one wire."

I stood, asked the ladies to excuse me, reached back under my boxer shorts, and pulled out the tiny device taped there, with a thin wire that came out by my belt buckle, where the miniature microphone was. I held the device, retrieved from my boxers, in my palm.

"Gross," Suda said.

"I turned on this little gadget with my index finger since my hands were conveniently cuffed right there. It sent a signal to a device in the trunk of my car, with a six-hour recording capacity. Since Donald commandeered my car, it was in signal range at his apartment." I picked up the box I'd carried in and showed them the recorder from my car.

They insisted we play it right then. I'd tell them when to fast-forward, to find the relevant parts. They ordered pizza delivery, and somebody brought in pop (not soda). It was like the Waltons settling into the living room to listen to FDR on the radio. They listened intently for a couple of hours, until Sarge's voice came on the recording, and Donald was in custody.

"Well, it's good enough for me, but it won't hold up in court," Cimmatoni said.

"Might depend on the judge," I said. "I did inform Donald he was being taped, remember? He destroyed the other device, but I was referring to this one. And I used the present tense—I said 'I'm recording you.' Present tense, not past. It's all right there. I can't help it if he didn't understand plain English. If I were a judge, I'd equate that with informing Donald he was being recorded."

"If you were a judge," Sarge said, "you'd equate saying, 'Talk or I'll shoot you,' with reading someone their Miranda rights."

FRIDAY, JANUARY 24, 9:40 P.M.

After hearing the recording, Manny, Sarge, and Lieutenant Nicks interrogated Donald Meyer. Captain Swiridoff was already in touch with the DA about reopening the Melissa Glissan case as a possible murder by her boyfriend, Donald Meyer.

Precinct electronics experts would be working all night on duplicating and gleaning highlights from the recordings of my adventures with Donald.

The captain told me to go home and get a good night's sleep because there'd be a 10:00 a.m. press conference, and we'd have to be coached by Chief Lennox's press secretary about what to say and what not to say. Swiridoff instructed me to find something to wear that looked respectable, "even if you have to borrow it."

Clarence was having a ball, in a Clarence sort of way, which shows itself in a look of sober intensity as he scratches down notes.

↔

I took off to join Mulch at home. He was back from the vet and being babysat by Jake and Janet. She was caressing Mulch's ears and feeding him snacks. Mike Hammer was milking it. When he saw me, he jumped and nearly knocked me over. We wrestled carefully since he had tape and bandages between his ear and jaw.

Before Jake and Janet left, Jake said to me, "Okay if I tell God thanks for protecting you like He did?"

I nodded.

"Thank You, Father, for answering our prayers and keeping Ollie safe."

That was all.

"You want to thank Him, Ollie?" Jake asked.

I shut my eyes tight, like praying people do. "God…if You're there, I guess I owe You one. And…especially, thanks that Mulch made it."

Janet hugged me, and it felt good. Jake hugged me, and I didn't hurl. It had been a record day for man-hugs, including Sarge's. I hoped I wouldn't get used to it.

Mulch and I stayed up late. After watching Jack Bauer and Chuck Norris, I picked up Sharon's old Bible, which Janet had not-very-inconspicuously left on my recliner. I started reading parts she'd underlined.

The phone rang at 11:30.

"Daddy? It's Kendra."

"Hi, honey."

"Jake called me a few hours ago, but I just got his message. Are you okay? I'm coming over now!"

"It's late. You need your sleep."

It was nearly midnight when she got here and 2:45 when she left. The three hours seemed like thirty minutes. She played on the floor with Mulch and let him lick her face, and not once did she mention salads, meat, wetlands, or gun control. She even said she was grateful I was carrying that fourth gun. I introduced her to each of my Baby Glocks, the triplets. She said they were cute. When she was leaving, while we stood at the door, she wrapped her arms around me and hugged me.

My little girl hugging me. It doesn't get any better than that.

I'm not going to tell you much of what we said to each other, not because it would embarrass me, but because the telling couldn't capture the magic, and it would leave you thinking it was less than it was.

But we did talk about the woman we loved more than anyone, who we'd lost, the boy we never had much opportunity to know, and the girl we missed so much. And when Kendra told me how angry she was that her mom had been taken, I said I understood and felt the same way. But maybe, I said, we couldn't own her any more than you can own a comet or a sunset or fresh rain on a dry dusty day. You're glad to experience them, they make you happy, but when they're gone, instead of being mad, maybe you should just be grateful they were there for you in the first place.

Okay, I maybe didn't say it that poetically, but that's how I wrote it down later.

I said that if Jake and Clarence were right, maybe one day we could actually see Sharon again and be with her. Maybe Chad too, who knows? Kendra asked me if I really believed that. I said I didn't know, but I was beginning to think it's possible.

Instead of arguing, Kendra hugged me. I hugged her back, on this Guinness day of hugs. We held on to each other. And for the first time I could remember, I felt hope.

That night I was grateful for the sand in the top half of my hourglass. Still, I knew much less remained on top than had already fallen. And it seemed like the more gravity drained the top half, the faster the sand was falling.

67

SATURDAY, JANUARY 25, 10:00 A.M.

AN ARMY OF REPORTERS marched past Chief Lennox's office, its door wide open, with the chief's honors displayed like bowling trophies.

Detectives rarely talk with the press. Jack Glissan and Brandon Phillips were our golden boys, but now they're gone. As Obadiah Abernathy said, "We's here, then we's gone, like a warm breath on a cold day."

Sixty of us crammed in a media room made for thirty. I was surprised to see Jake.

"This is big stuff," he said. "I'll get a few columns out of it myself. Couldn't miss your moment of glory."

Lennox's press secretary introduced the chief like he was a rock star, saying he'd been *magna cum something* at some university back east with a lousy football team, which probably hadn't produced many good cops either. If Mulch hadn't had a toothache and a migraine, I'd have wished he were there to reacquaint himself with Lennox's pant leg.

"We have news this morning that is both good and bad," Lennox said, riding the room's aura of excitement. "For our police force and our city stand or fall together. The bad news is that Detective Noel Barrows has been arrested for the murder of William Palatine. He's a suspect in another case being investigated as I speak."

Try five other cases, I thought.

"The good news is that this man has been arrested, charged, and if found guilty, will be punished. From the beginning I told our people, we must chase down the killer, no matter who he is, no matter what the consequences. When we first suspected it could be one of our own, I insisted we do our jobs no matter how bad it might look for us. We pulled out the stops, chased down every lead. We left no stone unturned."

We came out like gangbusters.

"I'm proud of our detective department. And I assure you that one bad apple has *not* spoiled the barrel."

Lennox droned on, alluding to his critical behind-the-scenes role in this case. Someone interrupted, "What about the suicide of Jack Glissan, Barrows's partner? Was he involved in any of the murders?"

"We're investigating the extent to which Detective Glissan might have become aware of his partner's crimes."

No reason to sully the reputation of an exemplary cop and hurt his widow, and the department, and the chief. Damage control. Deception. All for a good cause.

Though Clarence was in the second row, raising his hand continually, somehow the chief managed not to notice him, the equivalent of not noticing a Humvee in your dining room.

"I will personally oversee the investigation of Noel Barrows," the chief said, "making sure every *t* is crossed and every *i* is dotted. Time for just one more question."

Clarence stood and started talking even though the chief was pointing to a reporter three rows back on the other side, a reporter known for throwing softballs at the chief and playing poker with him Saturday nights.

"As you know," Clarence said in his 'Luke, I am your father' voice, "I was assigned to cover this case."

"Yes, since our police department has nothing to hide," Lennox said, "I invited a *Tribune* reporter to cover this investigation from the beginning."

"I worked daily alongside Detective Ollie Chandler, observing his handling of this case," Clarence said. "In my opinion, he did an outstanding job. Do you have any comments on Detective Chandler's performance?"

"Yes, I have commended him for his comportment."

I don't know what comportment means, but I'd have thought commending someone would include some actual communication with that person—some nice words, a greeting card, a box of chocolates, or tickets to a Seahawks game. Apparently not.

Clarence wasn't satisfied. "Ollie Chandler put his life on the line and was in mortal danger three times. Without his tireless efforts, Noel Barrows wouldn't have been caught. Do you agree, Chief Lennox?"

"Well…he had a significant role, as did our entire team. As general of this army, I'm proud of all my soldiers."

"You sound as if you played some role in solving this crime."

"As chief of police, I play a role in everything this department does."

Clarence's face hardened. "While I was involved in this case, I was never aware of you doing anything to help solve it."

"You're here to ask questions, not to make statements," Lennox said, squeezing the podium, makeup running. "But I assure you that my role in this, while behind the scenes, was substantial. I supervised the detectives involved. Nothing happens in this department without my being part of it."

"Including multiple murders?"

Man, I *love* that Clarence Abernathy. Score one for the journalists.

The chief halted, stumbled, and explained something about the best-laid plans of mice and men and when the going gets tough, the tough get going.

When the chief thanked everyone for coming and stepped away, waving like a candidate, one of the television reporters asked, "Clarence, would you answer some questions?"

Abernathy nodded. For the next twenty minutes he repeatedly gave me credit, using words like *brilliant*, *brave*, and *pit-bull determination*. He only mentioned my "idiosyncrasies" a couple of times and Krispy Kremes once. Clarence also gave high praise to Manny, who sat quietly but took notice. He paid tribute to Ray Eagle, doing everything short of passing out his business phone number.

I made a mental note to commend him for his comportment.

After three more questions Clarence pointed to me and said, "The man you really should talk to is Detective Ollie Chandler."

The smiling Lynn Carpenter winked as she turned her camera toward me, in my blue sport coat. A dozen other cameras, still and video, followed. The questions came, none hostile. For the first time I could remember, it was fun to look into the faces of the media.

I answered questions for forty minutes. Afterward, several journalists introduced themselves to me and shook my hand. Two actually thanked me for doing my job. They seemed almost human. But, I reminded myself, things often aren't what they appear.

When the others had left, Carp took a few more pictures, then kissed her finger and put it on one of my half dozen facial owies. She said she was glad I was okay. As she went out the door, she mouthed words that touched me in ways hard for a man to express: "double cheese, double pepperoni."

SATURDAY, JANUARY 25, 12:20 P.M.

It was noon when the press conference finally ended, sixty minutes after the chief stepped out, meaning three-fourths of it took place without him. Jake said he was buying at Lou's. Rory knocked himself out with a display of yellow pansies, which despite the name were pretty cool.

Jake said the tunes were on him, and a minute later Jan and Dean joined us in the booth, singing "Little Deuce Coupe." They were followed by Buddy Holly and the Crickets performing "Peggy Sue." I nodded at Rory, who looked up at the picture of him and his dad with Buddy and the gang.

"Did you see Lennox peeking in the door?" Jake asked, laughing. "He couldn't stand it that the press conference was still going after he left."

"There's still a lot I don't get," Clarence said. "Why would Glissan and Barrows take those chances? Why leave the wineglasses, use the noose, the insulin bottles, and leave Melissa's chain on the professor?"

"For Jack, maybe it was trying to play fair, give us a chance to catch him if somehow he didn't work the case. For Noel, it was arrogance. Criminal master-minds think they're invincible. Jack often consulted me on cases, and it might look suspicious if he didn't on this one. Noel figured from the beginning I'd probably visit the scene, see some evidence, maybe recognize the rope, learn about the Black Jack and the phone call. He wanted to play with me, unnerve me. It backfired."

"I understand Jack never suspected that Noel killed Melissa," Jake said. "But he had to figure out Noel had killed those other people, right?"

"Once Frederick and Hedstrom died, Jack had to know," I said. "But he had a blind loyalty to Noel. If Jack confronted him, we'll probably never know what was said."

"What's going to happen in court?" Clarence asked. "If they don't allow your recording, is there enough evidence to convict him?"

"Noel's a master of deception. He'll convince his attorney he's innocent. Maybe a jury too. Jack wouldn't betray Noel, but Noel made sure evidence pointed to Jack. Melissa's chain, the insulin bottles, the unwashed wineglass with Jack's DNA, if the lab ever comes up with it. I can hear Noel suggesting to Jack it would honor Melissa to use her needle, insulin, and chain. But those could point to Jack, not Noel. Nobody but Jack and Linda would realize Noel's connection to Melissa. He never thought he'd be exposed as Donald Meyer."

"Noel really took Jack in, didn't he?" Jake asked.

"Talk about irony," I said. "They bonded by their grief at Melissa's death, but the guy the Glissans bonded with, the one they wish had fathered their grandchildren, was their daughter's killer. Jack befriends him, does stakeouts with him, golfs with him, drinks a toast to him in honor of Melissa, never suspecting this guy murdered his little girl."

Jake shook his head. "And what jury would believe a man would plant his own fingerprints at the scene of a crime? He eliminated himself as a suspect by making himself a suspect, then proving he'd been framed. Wow."

"By planting evidence against you," Clarence asked.

"The gun wasn't found until seven hours after the murder. He probably put it there after he knew we were investigating. Noel had practice producing fake prints—from what Phil told us, he could probably do it in two hours. In this case, he wouldn't even have to find someone's print. He plants his own prints, then puts the gun in the Dumpster. Manny finds it. It's that simple."

"Talk about things not being as they seem," Clarence said. "His alibi. I know he looks like his brother, but wouldn't you think one of those guys could tell the difference?"

"That bugged me too until I found out Noel had been going to the Do Drop Inn two or three times a week for just five weeks and always when they were watching a ball game. Eyes were on the television. He has the same build, same hair as his brother, voice almost identical. Maybe women sit around and study each other's faces. These guys were staring at TV, beer, peanuts, lotto results, or pool balls, not at each other. He was hanging out with men who'd only seen him in a bar, say four times each, and always when they were drinking. He'd been there just enough for them to know his name and general appearance. Perfect alibi. They'd swear it was him, but a close facsimile would be good enough to fool them."

"Speaking of Rodney Meyer, do you think they'll find him?" Clarence asked.

"Who knows? I'm just grateful he let the officer go. Maybe he's waiting for Noel in his hideout in the woods."

"You said Noel had duplicated fingerprints before," Jake said. "When was that?"

"Remember the Jimmy Ross murder? Killed by Lincoln Caldwell? You'll read about this in the next few days when it's official. Heck, maybe you'll write about it. I called Phil and asked him to take a closer look at Lincoln Caldwell's fingerprints. He said sure enough, same thing. Definite traces of glycerin. Fake prints."

"You're saying Noel killed Jimmy Ross?"

"And framed Lincoln Caldwell. Two for the price of one."

"Where's Caldwell?"

"In jail awaiting trial. So he thinks. Soon as the paperwork's done—Manny's on it now—Caldwell will be released. I'm going over to see him myself. Bringing him a box of chocolates."

"Chocolates?"

"Flowers seemed inappropriate. I got those See's chocolates. Classy. I had a couple to make sure they're okay. Caldwell won't notice."

Rory brought three hot fudge sundaes. Clarence said he couldn't, but after hearing us groan with ecstasy, he shot some insulin and dug in.

"I keep thinking about Rodney," I said. "Donald claimed his brother's the mean one. If that's true, one of these days I might wake up dead."

"One of these days we'll each wake up dead," Jake said. "The question is what we'll wake up to. And whether we'll be ready for it."

"You know my favorite part?" Clarence asked. "What linked the professor to Melissa Glissan, before you saw her in the picture, was the phone number in the back of a book called *Why I Am Not a Christian*. The Lord sovereignly used that book, written as an argument against Him, to accomplish His purposes. In fact, if Jake hadn't read through that book to the final page, you might not have solved this murder. So how about you follow through with your commitment and read *Mere Christianity*—or, better yet, the Bible?"

"Maybe I will," I said. "But right now, I want to present you two with a gift."

I pulled out a classy little bag, with two identical gifts in fancy wrapping paper. Clarence opened the perfectly tied ribbon while Jake ripped into his.

At the same time they said, "A fountain pen?"

"Rupert Bolin called this morning and had these sent over. I won a drawing." I pulled another fountain pen from my pocket, same design and different color from theirs. "He reminded me that in an age of encroaching illiteracy, fountain pens are tools of articulation and civility. And since you write for a living, and I'm a budding novelist, I figure we can be the three literary amigos. Plus, Rupert says you can use them to write saucy letters to your wives."

"I have something for you too, Ollie," Clarence said.

He handed me an envelope. I opened it. My heart nearly stopped.

"A fifty-dollar gift certificate to Krispy Kreme?"

"The manager of the Krispy Kreme on 82nd sent it as thanks for mentioning them three times in my articles."

I stood up and threw my arms around Abernathy. "It's like winning the lottery. I think I'm gonna cry."

Jake laughed. Clarence wasn't so sure.

See, Clarence has an agenda for me—to find Jesus. And I've got one for him. If he's so happy about Jesus, I think he should let his face know about it. Like his daddy did.

Sure enough, next moment a big smile spread across Clarence's kisser. I was looking at Obadiah Abernathy.

"Any final thoughts, gentlemen," I said, "before we lay this case to rest?"

"Noel didn't look like a murderer," Clarence said.

"Murderers seldom do."

"To quote a brilliant detective, things often aren't as they appear," Clarence said. "You'd made up your mind about Jack, Noel, Karl, and Lincoln Caldwell. But you were dead wrong about all of them. You had to follow the evidence before you could uncover the deception."

I nodded. "Jake?"

"Well, you've told us that you don't believe God will bring justice. Or that Jesus is who He claimed to be—the only way to God. So if you were wrong about Noel, Jack, Karl, and Caldwell, could you be wrong about God too? Could you be wrong about Jesus?"

"I suppose."

"Is Jesus important enough to justify you conducting an investigation?" Clarence asked.

"Follow the evidence wherever it leads," Jake said. "That's all we're asking you to do."

Clarence nodded.

Apparently, it was unanimous.

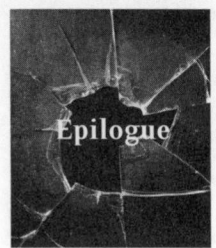

Epilogue

FRIDAY, APRIL 25

IT'S BEEN THREE MONTHS since I solved the Palatine murder and Donald Meyer was taken into custody. Rodney Meyer hasn't been found.

I've been hanging out a lot with Kendra. We've been to the Old Spaghetti Factory three times. We went April 3, Sharon's and my anniversary. I told her stories about her mother and me in the original Spaghetti Factory thirty-five years ago. Kendra said she remembers us taking her there as a little kid and sitting in the streetcar. So on April 3 we waited for seating in the streetcar. I talked her into trying the Mizithra since no cows are killed to make it. She loved it. It was one of the best nights of my life.

I'm back to one day a week with Jake and Clarence at Lou's. We're reading together—I forget what. Jake talked me into going with him to a recovery group thingie at his church. It wasn't as lame as I expected.

Lynn Carpenter and I made a list of fifteen pizza places in the greater Portland area. Last night we hit number seven, DiCianni's, a new place in Gresham, with outdoor seating by a stand of honeysuckles, beautiful in the unusually warm spring weather.

This morning the phone rang at 3:00 a.m. on the dot, according to those big red digits. I groped for the phone in the darkness.

"Who died?" I groaned.

"Daddy? It's me."

"Kendra? Sweetheart? You okay?"

"I went into a quick labor four hours ago."

"What? Need a police escort?"

"Relax, make some coffee. I'm in the hospital, safe and sound. Things went superfast, one in a hundred the doctor said. Anyway, the bottom line—you have a grandson."

"The baby's born?"

"Yeah. And he's adorable. He's right here with me."

"He's born?"

"Yeah. Otherwise he wouldn't be in my arms."

"No kidding?"

"No kidding. Drink that coffee and it'll all make sense."

"Wow. I'll be there soon."

"And Daddy?"

"Yeah."

"Guess what I named the baby."

"Baby Glock?" I thought that was pretty good for 3:00 a.m.

She giggled. "No. Justice Oliver Chandler."

"No kidding?"

"I can see Mom in him. You too."

I jumped up, switched on the French roast, hugged Mulch, gave him a Tender Tbonz Sizzlin' Steak snack, and told him he had a nephew. Then I looked at my smiling mug in the bathroom mirror.

Justice Oliver? Wow. That beat Jack Bauer or Nero Wolfe. It even beat Baby Glock. And I liked the initials: My grandson was a JOC.

I'm driving to the hospital right now. Tonight I'll round up my guns, unload them, and store them high, out of my grandson's reach. And then I'll get him a Seahawks jacket and pick out a couple dozen children's books I can read to the little Sam-I-am.

I've been waiting all my life to get good news from a 3:00 a.m. phone call. Well, this morning it finally happened.

Maybe there's a God after all.

And maybe there really is a two thousand-year-old murder mystery worth investigating.

Justice Oliver Chandler?

No kidding.

"And will not God bring about justice for his chosen ones,
who cry out to him day and night?
Will he keep putting them off?
I tell you, he will see that they get justice, and quickly."
JESUS
LUKE 18:7-8

"Stop judging by mere appearances, and make a right judgment."
JESUS
JOHN 7:24

"Who are you?" they asked.
"Just what I have been claiming all along," Jesus replied.
JOHN 8:25-26

Man is destined to die once, and after that to face judgment.
HEBREWS 9:27

DISCUSSION QUESTIONS

Warning: Contains spoilers. Read only after you finish the book!

1. Can you relate to Ollie Chandler? If so, in what ways? (Besides a fondness for pastry.) How are you different than Ollie? What do you like and dislike about him?

2. What are some of your favorite scenes in *Deception* and why? Who are some of your favorite characters? (If you read the prequels *Deadline* or *Dominion*, in what ways is this book similar, and in what ways is it different?)

3. What are your overall impressions of the book, positive or negative? What did you take away from it that might stick with you awhile?

4. Why do you think Randy Alcorn named the book *Deception*? What forms did deception take in this book? What forms has it taken in your life or someone close to you?

5. Ollie often feels like he's on the outside looking in when he views the hope and faith in Jake, Clarence, Little Finn, and others. Has there been a time in your life when you experienced this feeling? Explain.

6. Ollie hesitates to believe in a good God because he sees injustice all around him. Read Matthew 5:6 and Luke 18:7–8. What does Jesus tell us about those who long for justice, like Ollie, and the God who loves them?

7. Ollie had a number of difficult questions for God such as, why do people suffer, why did He let Sharon die, and if He can make things right quickly, why doesn't He? There are no easy answers, but what would you say to Ollie—or the Ollies you know? What hidden purposes might God have for the heartbreaking troubles people often face? (See an article by the author, "How Could a Good God Allow Evil and Suffering?" at www.epm.org/articles/allowevil.html.)

8. Ollie drinks excessively to try to relieve the pain caused by his wife's death and his struggling relationships with his daughters. What things do you find yourself doing to avoid feeling pain in your life? What other pain-relieving activities are common in our culture?

9. When you read about Carly entering heaven, what touched you the most? How does your view of heaven compare with this scene in *Deception*? What do you think about the allusions to a future New Earth? Have you been taught to look forward to a New Earth, as 2 Peter 3:13 says we should be doing? (See the author's book *Heaven* for more information on the New Earth.)

10. Does reading about Professor Palatine's after-death experience affect your views about hell? What struck you about it?

11. When Sharon was sick and later died, well-meaning Christians made some unintentionally hurtful remarks to Ollie. Why do you think this sometimes happens? What do you say or do when someone you are close to is really hurting like Ollie was? What do you say to people who are without faith in Christ? Do you believe Romans 8:28 is true? Why or why not? Is there a right time and a right way to share what's true, and a wrong time and a wrong way to do it?

12. Jake and Clarence are loyal friends to Ollie. They're usually sensitive to Ollie's skepticism, yet they seem unapologetic for talking about Christ. What does this teach you about friendships with unbelievers? Also, Jake told Ollie the hard truth when he needed to. Do you think this was right? How do your friendships compare to Ollie's with Jake and Clarence?

13. If you're not a Christian, what did you learn about Christians in *Deception*? If you are a believer, what did you learn about non-Christians, including how they view Christians? What misperceptions do Christians and non-Christians sometimes have about each other? How can we improve our relationships with each other? (What do you learn from Ollie's respect for Obadiah Abernathy, whom he met in *Dominion*? Why was Ollie so touched by this old man?)

14. Do you relate to Ollie's heartache and struggles related to his children—one whom he lost, one who has chosen to cut off contact with him, and one,

Kendra, with whom he doesn't get along? Admitting that he wasn't the best father, Ollie finally started working hard at his relationship with Kendra. Is it possible for difficult relationships with family members to improve over time? Why or why not?

15. How do the following verses describe God? Deuteronomy 1:31, Psalm 68:5, Isaiah 49:15–16, Matthew 6:8–9, and Luke 13:34. How do they change or enhance your view of God as our Father or parent?

16. In a scene with Sharon, the Lord tells her that we humans long for the light, but hate it because it hurts our eyes; that we sometimes prefer the comfort of darkness to the pain of sight. Are there situations in the world around you, or in your own life, that this describes? Explain.

17. Jake told Ollie that death is not a hole but a doorway, but Ollie doesn't know what to think. Read John 5:24. What are your own beliefs about life after death? On what do you base these beliefs? What do people in our society commonly believe about the afterlife, and on what do they base their beliefs?

18. Seeing Jake's and Clarence's hope and faith, something in Ollie wants to believe, but his deeply ingrained belief system is that you can only put faith in what you can see. Whether you're a Christian or not, what holds you back from fully believing the claims of Jesus Christ?

19. A theme running throughout *Deception* is that many things are not as they first appear. What situations or people in the book ended up not being what they first seemed to be?

20. "Examine the evidence. Then follow wherever it leads." This quote was taped to Ollie's fridge. At the end of *Deception*, Ollie decided to examine the two-thousand-year-old murder of Jesus mystery. Where do you think his investigation might lead? Have you undertaken that investigation? If so, where has it led you? If not, what's keeping you from it?

ABOUT THE AUTHOR

Randy Alcorn is the founder and director of Eternal Perspective Ministries (EPM), www.epm.org. Prior to 1990, when he started EPM, he served as a pastor for fourteen years. He has spoken around the world and has taught on the adjunct faculties of Multnomah Bible College and Western Seminary in Portland, Oregon.

Randy is the bestselling author of twenty-five books (over 3 million in print), including the novels *Deadline* and *Dominion* (prequels to *Deception*), *Lord Foulgrin's Letters*, *The Ishbane Conspiracy*, *Edge of Eternity*, the Gold Medallion winner *Safely Home*, and his 2007 children's picture book *Wait Until Then*.

His nonfiction works include *Money, Possessions, and Eternity*; *Pro-Life Answers to Pro-Choice Arguments*; *In Light of Eternity*; *The Treasure Principle*; *The Grace and Truth Paradox*; *The Purity Principle*; *The Law of Rewards*; *Why Pro-Life?*; *Heaven*; *50 Days of Heaven*; and *Heaven for Kids*.

Randy has written for many magazines and produces the popular complimentary periodical Eternal Perspectives. He's been a guest on over six hundred radio and television programs, including *Focus on the Family, Family Life Today, The Bible Answer Man, Revive Our Hearts, Truths That Transform,* and *Faith Under Fire*.

The father of Karina (married to Dan Franklin) and Angela (married to Dan Stump), Randy lives in Gresham, Oregon, with Nanci, his wife and best friend. They have four delightful grandsons, Jake, Matt, Ty, and Jack. Randy enjoys hanging out with his family, playing tennis, biking, conducting research, and reading.

RANDY ALCORN
FICTION

DEADLINE

When tragedy strikes those closest to him, award-winning journalist Jake Woods must draw upon all his resources to uncover the truth about their suspicious accident. Soon he finds himself swept up in a murder investigation that is both complex and dangerous. Unaware of the threat to his own life, Jake is drawn in deeper and deeper as he desperately searches for the answers to the immediate mystery at hand and—ultimately—the deeper meaning of his own existence.

DOMINION

When two senseless killings hit close to home, columnist Clarence Abernathy seeks revenge for the murders—and, ultimately, answers to his own struggles regarding race and faith. After being dragged into the world of inner-city gangs and racial conflict, Clarence is encouraged by fellow columnist Jake Woods (from the bestseller *Deadline*) to forge an unlikely partnership with a redneck homicide detective. Soon the two find themselves facing the powers of darkness that threaten the dominion of earth, while unseen eyes watch from above.

RANDY ALCORN
MORE GREAT FICTION

LORD FOULGRIN'S LETTERS

Foulgrin, a high-ranking demon, instructs his subordinate on how to deceive and destroy Jordan Fletcher and his family. It's like placing a bugging device in hell's war room, where we overhear our enemies assessing our weaknesses and strategizing attacks. *Lord Foulgrin's Letters* is a *Screwtape Letters* for our day, equally fascinating yet distinctly different—a dramatic story with earthly characters, setting, and plot. A creative, insightful, and biblical depiction of spiritual warfare, this book will guide readers to Christ-honoring counterstrategies for putting on the full armor of God and resisting the devil.

THE ISHBANE CONSPIRACY

Jillian is picture perfect on the outside, but terrified of getting hurt on the inside. Brittany is a tough girl who trusts almost no one. Ian is a successful athlete who dabbles in the occult. And Rob is a former gangbanger who struggles with guilt, pain, and a newfound faith in God. These four college students will face the ultimate battle between good and evil in a single year. As spiritual warfare rages around them, a dramatic demonic correspondence takes place. Readers can eavesdrop on the enemy, and learn to stave off their own defeat, by reading *The Ishbane Conspiracy*.

Nonfiction titles from
RANDY ALCORN

THE TREASURE PRINCIPLE:
Unlocking the Secret of Joyful Giving

Bestselling author Randy Alcorn uncovers the revolutionary key to spiritual transformation: joyful giving! Jesus gave his followers this life-changing formula that guarantees not only kingdom impact, but immediate pleasure and eternal rewards.

THE PURITY PRINCIPLE:
God's Safeguards for Life's Dangerous Trails

God has placed warning signs and guardrails to keep us from plunging off the cliff. Find straight talk about sexual purity in Randy Alcorn's one-stop handbook for you, your family, and your church.

THE GRACE AND TRUTH PARADOX:
Responding with Christlike Balance

Living like Christ is a lot to ask! Discover Randy Alcorn's two-point checklist of Christlikeness—and begin to measure everything by the simple test of grace and truth.

PROLIFE ANSWERS TO PROCHOICE ARGUMENTS

This revised and updated guide offers timely information and inspiration from a "sanctity of life" perspective. Real answers to real questions appear in logical and concise form.

FREQUENTLY USED SYMBOLS

β	beta coefficient, a measure of an asset's riskiness.
b	the fraction of a firm's earnings retained rather than paid out. It is equal to $(1-D/E)$, where D/E is the ratio of dividends (D) to earnings (E).
CAPM	capital asset pricing model.
CAR	cumulative average residuals.
CF	cash flow; CF_t is cash flow in period t.
CML	capital market line.
COV_{ij}	the covariance of the returns between assets i and j.
D	dividend per share of stock; D_t is dividend per share during period t.
DM	deutschemark (West German currency).
EBIT	earnings before interest and taxes.
EPS	earnings per share.
E(R)	the expected return; $E(R_t)$ is the expected return during period t.
FV	future value.
FVIF	future value interest factor for a lump sum.
FVIFA	future value interest factor for an annuity.
g	growth rate in earnings, dividends, or stock prices.
I	rate of inflation.
k	required rate of return.
£	pound (United Kingdom currency).
P	price of a share of stock; P_o is price of a share of stock today.
p/e	the price/earnings ratio.
PPP	purchasing power parity.
PV	the present value.
PVIF	the present value interest factor for a lump sum.
PVIFA	the present value interest factor for an annuity.
r_{ij}	the correlation coefficient between assets i and j.
RFR	the rate of return on a risk-free asset.
ROA	return on assets.
ROE	return on equity.
SML	security market line.
Σ	summation sign (capital sigma).
σ	standard deviation (lowercase sigma).
t	tax rate. time when used as a subscript (e.g., D_t—the dividend in year t).
V	the value of an asset; V_j is the value of asset j.
¥	yen (Japanese currency).
YTM	yield to maturity.

INVESTMENT ANALYSIS AND PORTFOLIO MANAGEMENT

THIRD EDITION

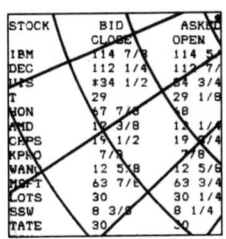

INVESTMENT ANALYSIS AND PORTFOLIO MANAGEMENT

THIRD EDITION

FRANK K. REILLY
BERNARD J. HANK PROFESSOR
UNIVERSITY OF NOTRE DAME

THE DRYDEN PRESS
CHICAGO FORT WORTH SAN FRANCISCO
PHILADELPHIA MONTREAL TORONTO
LONDON SYDNEY TOKYO

Acquisitions Editor: Ann Heath
Developmental Editor: Jan Richardson
Project Editor: Teresa Chartos
Design Supervisor: Rebecca Lemna
Production Manager: Barb Bahnsen
Permissions Editor: Cindy Lombardo
Director of Editing, Design, and Production: Jane Perkins
Text Designer: Lucy Lesiak Design
Copy Editor and Indexer: Maggie Jarpey
Compositor: Impressions, Inc.
Text Type: 10/12 ITC Cheltenham

Library of Congress Cataloging-in-Publication Data

Reilly, Frank K.

   Investment analysis and portfolio management / Frank K. Reilly. —
3rd ed.
      p.   cm.
      Includes bibliographies and indexes.
      ISBN 0-03-025498-1
      1. Investments. 2. Investment analysis. 3. Portfolio management.
I. Title.
HG4521.R396   1989
332.6--dc19   88-36709
                                                                  CIP

Printed in the United States of America
901-016-98765432
Copyright © 1989, 1985, 1979 by The Dryden Press, a division of Holt, Rinehart and
Winston, Inc.

Address orders:
The Dryden Press
Orlando, Florida 32887

Address editorial correspondence:
The Dryden Press
908 N. Elm St.
Hinsdale, IL 60521

The Dryden Press
Holt, Rinehart and Winston
Saunders College Publishing

CFA Examinations used throughout text are reprinted with permission from The Institute
of Chartered Financial Analysts, Charlottesville, Virginia.

Cover
Globe image source: Harlan Wallach, Phil Gagliano/AVALON STUDIOS, CHICAGO
London Stock Exchange photo: © Ted Horowitz/The Stock Market.
New York Stock Exchange photo: © Robert Essel/The Stock Market.
Tokyo Stock Exchange photo: © Ken Straiton/The Stock Market.

TO
MY BEST FRIEND AND WIFE,
THERESE,
AND OUR GREATEST GIFTS AND
SOURCES OF HAPPINESS,
FRANK K. III,
CLARENCE R. II, AND WHITNEY
THERESE B.
EDGAR B.

The Dryden Press Series in Finance

PREFACE

Preparing this third edition has been challenging for two reasons. First, many changes have occurred in our securities markets during the last four years in terms of theory, new financial instruments, and trading practices. Second, and even more significant, capital markets have become global. Consequently, almost every chapter in this edition includes a discussion of how the investment practice or theory is influenced by the globalization of investments. This treatment is a departure from the traditional approach of discussing international investing in one chapter.

This text is addressed to both graduate and advanced undergraduate students who are looking for an in-depth discussion of investments and portfolio management. The presentation of the material is intended to be rigorous and empirical, without being overly quantitative. A proper discussion of the modern developments in investments and portfolio theory must be rigorous. The detailed discussion of numerous empirical studies reflects my personal belief that it is essential for our theories to be exposed to the real world and to be judged on the basis of how well they help us understand and explain reality. To make room for the most recent studies and results in this edition, I have condensed some of the older studies and have deleted a few.

The text has been thoroughly updated. In addition to chapter revisions, we have also greatly enhanced the problem sets. This edition includes approximately 70 new problems and 25 new CFA exam questions.

**MAJOR
CHANGES
AND ADDITIONS
IN THE THIRD
EDITION**

Chapter 1　Consideration of the impact of exchange rate risk on the risk premium.

Chapter 2　Discussion of the world bond market and equity market, along with a description of bonds and equity in the United States and the world. Includes discussion of returns on art and antiques and a new appendix on tax considerations.

Chapter 3　Combination of Chapters 3 and 4 of the second edition. The new appendix includes detailed discussion of the October 1987 market crash from the Brady Commission Report. The chapter also includes detailed discussion of the operation of equity markets in Japan and London.

Chapter 4　Consideration of major U.S. bond series and a number of the non-U.S. equity and bond series in addition to the well-known U.S. equity market indicator series. More than 25 market indicator series are described.

Chapter 6　Discussion of evidence on the efficient market hypothesis (EMH) expanded to consider recent evidence on the January effect, the day-of-the-week effect, the Value Line Enigma, and the small-firm anomaly.

Chapter 10　Consideration of the world bond market, along with detailed analysis of the operation of bond markets in Japan, the United Kingdom, and Germany and fixed-income securities available in these countries. The two bond chapters (10 and 11) have been moved forward in the book because bonds are often easier to understand than equity securities.

Chapter 11　Detailed discussion of not only duration but also convexity.

Chapter 12　Use of a new example throughout the chapter based on Quaker Oats. Includes a three-way component breakdown of the return on equity consistent with the Du-Pont analysis, a discussion of cash flows relative to long-term debt and total debt, and a composite summary analysis that includes Quaker Oats, the food industry, and the S&P 400 Index. All debt ratios have been computed with and without deferred taxes.

Chapter 13　Analysis of the aggregate U.S. economy and market, plus an example of an analysis of non-U.S. economies and security markets. The estimates indicate the differences among economies and security markets and the difficulty of this global analysis.

Chapter 15　Combination of the company analysis and growth company analysis.

Chapter 16　Discussion of technical analysis includes new techniques, such as the CBOE put-call ratio, speculators' bullish stock index futures, stocks above 200-day moving average, and block uptick-downtick ratio. Also shows how technical analysis is applied to non-equity markets, interest rates, and international analysis (non-U.S. equity markets and exchange rates).

Chapter 17 Discussion on testing the asset-pricing model considers recent evidence on the CAPM and the continuing controversy on tests and evidence related to the APT.

Chapter 18 Discussion of bond portfolio strategy considers new developments in active bond portfolio management (e.g., the analysis of junk bonds), dedication, immunization, and contingent immunization, along with an example of a world bond portfolio allocation strategy.

Chapter 21 Extensive discussion of international and global investment funds and a new appendix listing these funds.

Chapter 22 New, separate chapter on options, including a detailed discussion of options on various stock market and industry indexes. Also includes a discussion of options on foreign currencies and how these can be used to hedge the purchase or sale of non–U.S. stocks and bonds.

Chapter 23 Expanded discussion of warrants and convertibles, along with consideration of Americus Trusts and foreign currency warrants.

Chapters 24 Consideration of the use of futures contracts in proand 25 gram trading, portfolio insurance, and the hedging of global portfolios for exchange rate risk.

Appendix B The CFA Code of Ethics

ANCILLARIES

The *Instructor's Manual and Test Bank*, by Frank K. Reilly and Stan Jacobs, Central Washington University, contains more than 500 new multiple-choice questions and problems, with solutions, as well as chapter outlines and notes, answers to the end-of-chapter questions, a discussion of how to use the new stock market simulation disk, and suggestions for using the excerpt from the 1988 Brady Commission report.

The *Stock Market Simulation*, prepared by Peter Bobko, Guilford College, allows students to select a portfolio of securities, track the performance of the selected portfolio, mutual funds, bonds, and the stock market over a period of time, and then observe the effects of diversification. The disk is packaged free with each new copy of *Investment Analysis and Portfolio Management*, third edition.

Available for purchase:

Security Analysis for Portfolio Construction and Management, by Wayne E. Boyet, Nicholls State University, is a software package and workbook that allows students to input and manipulate data using sophisticated models and statistical programs used in investment analysis. An accompanying manual contains complete instructions for using the disks, with textual discussions of each program. The package is an ideal supplement to this text and also suitable for use with any investments text.

Managing Investments: A Case Approach, by Michael A. Berry, The Darden School of the University of Virginia, and S. David Young, Tulane University, contains 36 Harvard-style cases and 10 technical notes. It is appropriate for use either as the core text or as a supplement for investments courses. Based on real-world problems, the book gives students hands-on experience in applying theoretical principles and models to decisions faced by individual investors and portfolio managers. A comprehensive *Instructor's Manual,* which includes detailed teaching notes for the cases, and a Lotus template disk with data and models to enhance the case analysis process are available upon adoption of *Managing Investments.*

ACKNOWLEDGMENTS So many people have helped me in a myriad of ways that I almost hesitate to list them since I may miss someone. I must begin with the University of Notre Dame because of its direct support and the understanding of my associates. Also, I want to thank the Bernard J. Hank family, who have endowed the Chair that helped bring me back to this beautiful place called Notre Dame and provided support for my work. Several of my colleagues at Notre Dame have been extremely helpful. Jim Wittenbach did a great job of updating the tax appendix, which made the "simplified" new tax laws comprehensible. Shanta Hegde helped a lot on the commodity futures chapter (Chapter 24) and was almost wholly responsible for the financial futures chapter (Chapter 25). Kevin Scanlon was my "super" reviewer who provided rapid turnaround and very insightful suggestions.

Other reviewers for this edition were:

George Aragon, *Boston College*

Carol Billingham, *Central Michigan University*

Robert Brown, *University of Colorado at Boulder*

Thomas Eyssell, *University of Missouri at St. Louis*

Eurico Ferreira, *Clemson University*

Stan Jacobs, *Central Washington University*

Christopher Ma, *Texas Tech University*

Steven Mann, *University of South Carolina*

Lalatendu Misra, *University of Texas, San Antonio*

John Peavy, *Southern Methodist University*

I was fortunate to have the following excellent reviewers for earlier editions:

Robert Angell, *East Carolina University*

Brian Belt, *University of Missouri at Kansas City*

Arand Bhattacharya, *University of Cincinnati*

Gerald A. Blum, *Babson College*

Dosoung Choi, *University of Tennessee*

Eugene F. Drzycimski, *University of Wisconsin at Oshkosh*

Eric Emory, *Sacred Heart University*

James Feller, *Middle Tennessee State University*

Eurico Ferreira, *Clemson University*

Michael Ferri, *John Carroll University*

Joseph E. Finnerty, *University of Illinois*

Harry Friedman, *New York University*

R. H. Gilmer, *University of Mississippi*

Stephen Goldstein, *University of South Carolina*

Steven Goldstein, *Robinson-Humphrey/American Express*

Keshav Gupta, *Oklahoma State University*

Ronald Hoffmeister, *Arizona State University*

Ron Hutchins, *Eastern Michigan University*

A. James Ifflander, *Arizona State University*

Kwang Jun, *Michigan State University*

Jaroslaw Komarynsky, *Northern Illinois University*

Danny Litt, *Century Software Systems/UCLA*

Miles Livingston, *University of Florida*

John Mathys, *DePaul University*

Dennis McConnell, *University of Maine*

Jacob Michaelsen, *University of California, Santa Cruz*

Nicholas Michas, *Northern Illinois University*

Lalatendu Misra, *University of Texas, San Antonio*

George Philippatos, *University of Tennessee*

George Pinches, *University of Kansas*

Rose Prasad, *Central Michigan University*

George A. Racette, *University of Oregon*

Bruce Robin, *Old Dominion University*

James Rosenfeld, *Emory University*

Stanley D. Ryals, *Investment Counsel, Inc.*

Frederic Shipley, *DePaul University*

Douglas Southard, *Virginia Polytechnic Institute*

Harold Stevenson, *Arizona State University*

David E. Upton, *Virginia Commonwealth University*

E. Theodore Veit, *University of Central Florida*

Bruce Wardrep, *East Carolina University*

Rolf Wubbels, *New York University*

Valuable comments and suggestions have come from my former graduate students at the University of Illinois: Paul Fellows, University of Iowa; Wenchi Wong, DePaul University; and David Wright, University of Notre Dame. Once more I was blessed with a bright, dedicated research assistant when I needed it most. Rahul Correa was prompt and careful but also showed creativity and good analytical skills.

Current and former colleagues have been very helpful: Patricia Bick (Library), Yu Chi Chang, Bill Nichols, Juan Rivera, and Norlin Rueschhoff, at the University of Notre Dame; C. F. Lee, University of Illinois; Donald Tuttle, Indiana University; and John M. Wachowicz, University of Tennessee. As always, some of the best insights and most stimulating comments came during the too infrequent runs with my very good friend, Jim Gentry of the University of Illinois.

I am convinced that professors who want to write a book that is academically respectable but also relevant and realistic require help from "the real world." I have been very fortunate to develop relationships with a number of individuals (including some former students) whom I consider my "contacts with reality."

I especially want to thank Robert Conway, who was the managing director of the London office of Goldman Sachs & Co., for suggesting in 1986 that it was essential to globalize all facets of the new edition because of the rapidly evolving global market. This was some of the most important advice I have ever received, and it has had a profound effect on this book.

The following individuals graciously provided important insights and material:

Sharon Athey, *Alex Brown & Co.*

Lowell Benson, *Robert A. Murray Partners*

David G. Booth, *Dimensional Fund Advisors, Inc.*

Leon C. Brand, *Merrill Lynch Pierce Fenner & Smith*

Roy D. Burry, *Kidder, Peabody & Co.*

Richard Caccione, *Fitch Investors Service, Inc.*

Thomas Coleman, *Adler, Coleman and Co. (NYSE)*

Robert Conway, *Goldman Sachs & Co.*

William Cornish, *Duff & Phelps*

Robert J. Davis, *Davpat, Inc.*

Robert J. Davis, Jr., *Paine, Webber*

Philip Delaney, Jr., *Northern Trust Bank*

Peter O. Dietz, *Frank Russell Japan*

William Dwyer, *Moody's Investors Service, Inc.*

Steven G. Einhorn, *Goldman Sachs & Co.*

Sam Eisenstadt, *Value Line*

Kenneth Fisher, *Forbes*

John J. Flanagan, Jr., *Stokes, Hoyt and Co. (NYSE)*

Martin S. Fridson, *Morgan Stanley & Co.*

Patricia A. Genley, *United Mutual Fund Selector*

Sir Nicholas Goodison, *London Stock Exchange*

Eduardo Haim, *Shearson Lehman Hutton Inc.*

William J. Hank, *Moore Financial Corporation*

Jim Johnson, *Options Clearing Corporation*

John W. Jordan II, *The Jordan Company*

Andrew Kalotay, *Salomon Brothers*

C. Prewitt Lane, *Todd Investment Advisors*

Martin Leibowitz, *Salomon Brothers*

Douglas R. Lempereur, *Templeton Investment Counsel, Inc.*

Robert Levine, *Kidder, Peabody & Co.*

John Maginn, *Mutual of Omaha*

Richard McCabe, *Merrill Lynch Pierce Fenner & Smith*

Michael McCowin, *Harris Trust & Savings Bank*

Terrence J. McGlinn, *McGlinn Capital Markets*

Robert Milne, *Duff & Phelps*

Robert G. Murray, *First Interstate Bank of Oregon*

Reed Parker, *Duff & Phelps*

John J. Phelan, Jr., *New York Stock Exchange*

Philip J. Purcell III, *Dean Witter Financial Services Group*

Jack Pycik, *First Interstate Bank of Northern Indiana*

Robert Quinn, *Salomon Brothers*

Robert L. Raclin, *Merrill Lynch Pierce Fenner & Smith*

Chet Ragavan, *Merrill Lynch Pierce Fenner & Smith*

John C. Rudolf, *Oppenheimer & Co., Inc.*

Stanley Ryals, *Investment Counsel, Inc.*

Ron Ryan, *Ryan Labs, Inc.*

Barry Schnepel, *Merrill Lynch Pierce Fenner & Smith*

Jun Shimizu, *Tokyo Stock Exchange*

Mark H. Sladkus, *Morgan Stanley & Co.*

Jim Stork, *Duff & Phelps*

Richard H. Tierney, *The Bond Buyer*

Anthony Vignola, *Kidder, Peabody & Co.*

Jeffrey M. Weingarten, *Goldman Sachs & Co.*

Thomas V. Williams, *Kemper Financial Services*

Robert Wilmouth, *National Futures Association*

Richard S. Wilson, *Merrill Lynch Pierce Fenner & Smith.*

I continue to benefit from the help and consideration of the dedicated people at the Institute of Chartered Financial Analysts: Darwin Bayston, Tom Bowman, Whit Broome, Hap Butler, Pete Morley, and everybody's favorite, Peggy Slaughter.

Thankfully, Phyllis Sandfort forgets the pain between editions, so she agreed to type this third edition. Her patience, understanding, and willingness to type late at night and provide rapid and accurate turnaround (with some help from her daughter Cindy) made it possible for this to be a 1989 edition rather than 1990. My secretary, Donna Smith, kept the rest of my life in some sort of order; and, believe me, that is not a trivial task.

The crew at Dryden did their usual great job of "gentle prodding" that is so difficult with an author who tends to be over-committed. Ann Heath was the acquisitions editor; Jan Richardson was the developmental editor with the difficult task of chief "prodder." Teresa Chartos was the project editor who brought it from messy manuscript and sloppy exhibits to a bound volume.

As always, my greatest gratitude is to my family—past, present, and future. My parents gave me life and helped me understand love and how to give it. My in-laws created my greatest gift and continuously give through their daughter. Most important is my wife, who provides love, understanding, and support at early morning breakfast and throughout the day and night. We thank God for our children, who make it all worthwhile and ensure that our lives are full of love, fun, and excitement.

Frank K. Reilly
Notre Dame, Indiana
March 1989

ABOUT THE AUTHOR

Frank K. Reilly is the Bernard J. Hank Professor of Business Administration, and former dean of the College of Business Administration at the University of Notre Dame. Holding degrees from the University of Notre Dame (B.B.A.), Northwestern University (M.B.A.), and the University of Chicago (Ph.D.), Professor Reilly has taught at the University of Illinois, the University of Kansas, and the University of Wyoming in addition to the University of Notre Dame. He has several years of experience as a senior securities analyst as well as experience in stock and bond trading. A Chartered Financial Analyst (CFA) and a member of the Council of Examiners, the Council on Education and Research, and the grading committee of the Institute of Chartered Financial Analysts, Professor Reilly has been president of the Financial Management Association, the Midwest Business Administration Association, and the Eastern Finance Association. He is also on the board of directors of the First Interstate Bank of Northern Indiana, the Investment Analysts Society of Chicago, and the Academy of Financial Services. As the author of more than one hundred articles, monographs, and papers, his work has appeared in numerous publications, including *Journal of Finance, Journal of Financial and Quantitative Analysis, Financial Management, Financial Analysts Journal, Financial Review*, and *Journal of Portfolio Management*. In addition to *Investment Analysis and Portfolio Management*, Third Edition, Professor Reilly is the author of another textbook, *Investments*, Second Edition (The Dryden Press, 1986).

Professor Reilly was named on the list of *Outstanding Educators in America* and has received both the University of Illinois Alumni Association Graduate Teaching Award and the Outstanding Educator Award from the M.B.A. class at the University of Illinois. He is editor of *Readings and Issues in Investments* and has been a member of the editorial boards of *Financial Management, The Financial Review, Journal of Financial Education*, and *Quarterly Review of Economics and Business*. He is included in *Who's Who in Finance and Industry, Who's Who in America*, and *Who's Who in the World*.

CONTENTS

THE INVESTMENT
PART I BACKGROUND

CHAPTERS

The chapters in this section will provide a background for the study of investments by addressing the following questions:

- Why do people invest?
- What investments are available?
- How do securities markets function?
- How and why are our securities markets changing?
- How can you determine the market behavior of common stocks and/or bonds?
- What relevant information can be found concerning potential investments?

In the first chapter we consider why individuals invest and what factors determine an investor's required rate of return on an investment. The latter point will be very important in subsequent analyses. Because one of the important tenets of investment theory is the need to diversify, we discuss several alternative investment instruments, along with their historical rates of return and risk, in the second chapter. In Chapter 3, we examine the function of markets in general, and securities markets specifically, concentrating on the markets for bonds and common stocks. Significant changes have occurred recently in the operation of the securities market, including a trend toward a global market. We will discuss these changes and probable future changes as well.

The behavior of securities markets is often measured in terms of changes in various stock market and bond market series. Because these series are used in a number of ways, we examine them in depth and compare several of them in Chapter 4. The final chapter in this section covers sources of information on various aspects of investments.

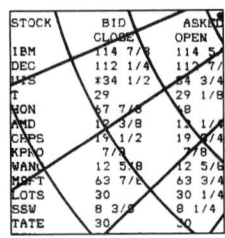

CHAPTER 1

THE INVESTMENT SETTING

THE CONCEPT OF INVESTMENT[1]

For most of our lives, we will be earning and spending money. Rarely, though, will our current money income exactly balance our consumption desires. At some point we may have more money than we want to spend; at others we may want to purchase more than we can afford. These imbalances will usually lead us to either negative or positive saving (*negative saving* meaning *borrowing funds*) in order to maximize the benefits (*utility*) from our income.

When current money income exceeds current consumption desires, people tend to save the excess. They might put the savings under a mattress or bury it in the backyard until some future time when consumption desires exceed current income. Or they may believe it is worthwhile to give up the immediate possession of these savings for a future larger amount of money that will be used for consumption. This trade-off of *present* consumption for a higher level of *future* consumption is the essence of saving and investment.

In contrast, when current money income is less than current consumption desires, people may attempt to trade part of their *future* money income stream for a higher level of *current* consumption. This is the practice of *borrowing*, described earlier as *negative saving*. Sometimes, however, funds are not borrowed for consumption but rather for investment at rates of return above the cost of borrowing.

[1] The discussion in this section draws heavily on Irving Fisher, *The Theory of Interest* (New York: Macmillan, 1930; reprinted Augustus M. Kelley, 1961); J. Hirshleifer, "Investment Decision under Uncertainty: Choice-Theoretic Approaches," *Quarterly Journal of Economics* 79 no. 4 (November 1965): 509–536; and Eugene F. Fama and Merton H. Miller, *The Theory of Finance* (New York: Holt, Rinehart and Winston, 1972), Chapter 1.

Obviously, those who defer current consumption expect to receive a greater amount in the future than was foregone. Conversely, those who consume or invest more than current income must be willing to pay back a greater amount in the future. The rate of exchange between *certain future consumption* (future dollars) and *certain current consumption* (current dollars) is the *pure rate of interest* or the *pure time value of money*. The rate of exchange between current and future consumption is established in the capital market as a result of the supply of excess income available to be invested at a given point in time and the demand for excess consumption (borrowing). If the cost of exchanging $100 of certain income today is $104 of certain income one year from today, the pure rate of exchange on a risk-free investment is said to be 4 percent (104/100 − 1).

The pure time value of money is a "real" rate since it indicates the increase in "real" goods and services desired. The investor is giving up $100 of consumption today in order to subsequently consume $104 of goods and services *at today's prices*. If investors expect a change in prices, they will adjust their required rate of return to compensate for it. Thus, if they expect prices to increase (i.e., they expect inflation) at the rate of 2 percent during the period of investment, they will increase their rate of exchange by 2 percent. In our example, the investor would require $106 in the future to compensate for giving up the $100 of consumption now (a 6 percent rate of exchange instead of 4 percent).

Finally, if future payment is not certain, investors will require a rate of return that exceeds the pure time value of money plus the inflation rate. This excess amount is called a *risk premium*. In our previous example, the investor would require some amount in excess of $106 one year from today, possibly $110, representing a $4, or 4 percent, risk premium.

INVESTMENT DEFINED

An investment can be defined as *the current commitment of funds for a period of time in order to derive a future flow of funds that will compensate the investing unit (1) for the time the funds are committed, (2) for the expected rate of inflation, and (3) also for the uncertainty involved in the future flow of funds.*[2] This encompasses all types of investments, whether they be corporate investments in machinery, plant, and equipment, government investments in flood control, or investments by individuals in stocks, bonds, commodities, or real estate. In all cases the investor is trading a *known* dollar amount today for some *expected* future stream of payments or benefits that will exceed the current outlay. The alternative investments that are considered by various investing units (corporations, governments, and individuals) differ only with regard to the institutional characteristics of the investment and some unique factors that must be considered in the analysis (e.g., differential taxes).

---

[2] It is recognized that the uncertainty involved is a function of the asset's unique uncertainty and also its relationship with all other assets in the portfolio. The exact nature of this uncertainty is considered in a later chapter. At this point it is necessary to recognize only that the investor requires that the expected cash flows compensate for this uncertainty, however defined.

MEASURES OF RETURN AND RISK

As already mentioned, the return on an investment is influenced by the uncertainty, or risk, involved (in addition to other factors). Let us briefly discuss how the return and the risk are measured before examining the factors that determine the required rate of return.

MEASURE OF RETURN

The purpose of investing is to defer current consumption and thereby add to our wealth so that it will be possible to consume more in the future. Therefore, when we talk about a return on an investment, we are concerned with the *increase in wealth resulting from this investment*. As an example, if you commit $100 to an investment at the beginning of a year and you get back $110 at the end of the year, your return on the investment (i.e., your increase in wealth) was $10. Because the actual dollar amount committed to alternative investments differs, it is typical to express it as a *rate of return* that indicates a relationship between the amount invested and the amount returned:

$$\text{Percentage Rate of Return} = \frac{\text{Ending Wealth} - \text{Beginning Wealth}}{\text{Beginning Wealth}} \times 100$$

$$= \frac{\$110 - \$100}{\$100} = \frac{\$10}{\$100} = .10 \times 100 = 10\%.$$

This 10 percent represents the rate of increase in wealth. Many investments provide you with a flow of cash in addition to changing value while the funds are invested. These cash flows must also be considered when computing the addition to your wealth. Because a particular investment may be only a portion of your wealth, it is appropriate to consider the rate of return on each investment. Therefore, a more general specification of rate of return is

$$\text{Percentage Rate of Return} = \frac{\text{Ending Value} - \text{Beginning Value} + \text{Cash Flows}}{\text{Beginning Value}} \times 100.$$

If we consider the prior example and add a $3 dividend cash flow to it, the rate of return would be

$$\text{Percentage Rate of Return} = \frac{\$110 - \$100 + \$3}{\$100}$$

$$= \frac{\$10 + \$3}{\$100} = \frac{\$13}{\$100} = .13 \times 100 = 13\%.$$

[handwritten margin note: total rr = capital appreciation + cash flow]

The rate of increase in wealth for this portion of your portfolio would therefore be 13 percent. This *total* rate of return of 13 percent can be broken down into capital appreciation (the change in price), which was 10 percent, and cash flow (i.e., dividend income), which was 3 percent.

RISK AND UNCERTAINTY

Although in a formal sense, there is a difference between risk and uncertainty, our discussion will not make such a distinction since the terms are often used interchangeably or to explain each other. Risk is thought of as *uncertainty regarding the expected rate of return from an investment.* When an investor is considering an investment, he "expects" a certain rate of return. If you were to ask, the investor might say 10 percent, which is really a *point estimate* of his *total* expectation. If you were to press further, he might acknowledge that he is not certain of this return, that under certain conditions the rate of return might go as low as negative 10 percent or as high as 25 percent. The point is, the larger the range of possible returns, the more uncertain the investor is regarding the actual return, and, therefore, the greater the risk is.

It is possible to determine how certain an investor is regarding the expected rate of return on an investment by analyzing his subjective probability distribution of expected returns. Here all *possible* returns are assigned probabilities ranging from zero (no chance of this return) to one (complete certainty). The probabilities are usually subjective estimates by the investor or analyst or can be based upon past frequencies (e.g., about 30 percent of the time the rate of return on this particular investment was 10 percent). Let us begin with an example of perfect certainty; i.e., the investor is supposedly certain of a return of 5 percent. This can be envisioned as follows:

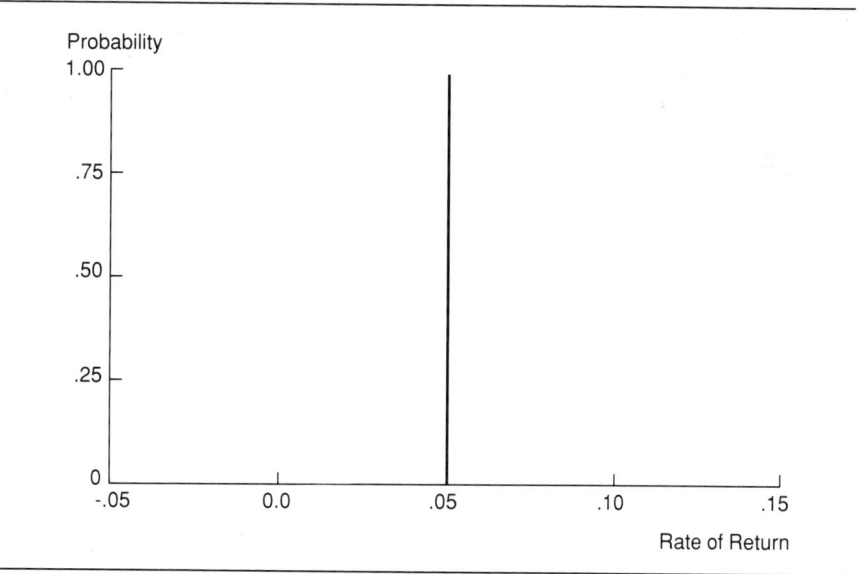

In the case of uncertainty there is only one possible return, and the probability of receiving that return is 1.0. The *expected* return from an investment is defined as:

Expected Return = Σ (Probability of Return) (Possible Return)
$$E(R_i) = \Sigma \ (P_i)(R_i).$$

In this case it would be

$$E(R_i) = (1.0)(.05) = .05.$$

An alternative example would be a case in which an investor believed several rates of return were possible under different conditions. If there were a strong economic environment with high corporate profits and little or no inflation, the rate of return on common stock could be as high as 20 percent. If there were an economic decline and a higher than average rate of inflation, similar to what happened during 1981–1982, it could be a negative 20 percent. Finally, if there were no major change in the economic environment, it would probably approach the long-run average of 10 percent. The investor's estimated probabilities for each of these potential states based upon past experience might be as follows.

STATE OF NATURE	PROBABILITY	RATE OF RETURN
Strong economy—no inflation	.15	.20
Weak economy—above average inflation	.15	−.20
No major change in the economy	.70	.10

This set of potential outcomes can be visualized as follows:

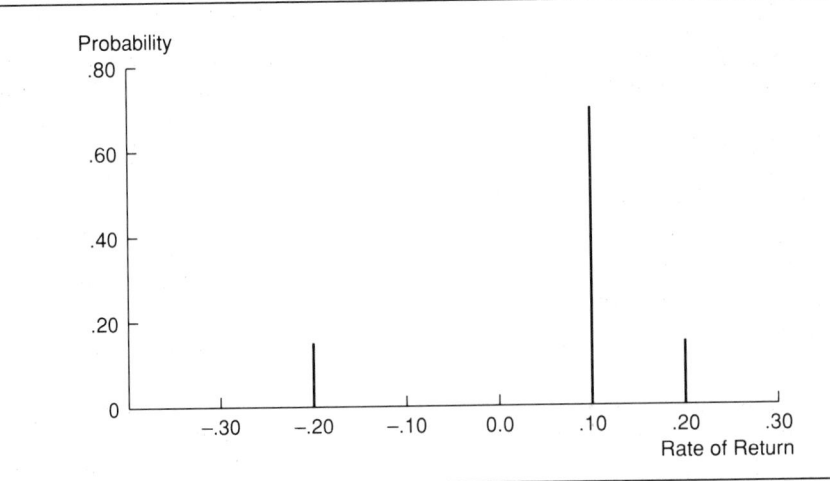

The computation of the expected rate of return $[E(R_i)]$ is as follows:

$$E(R_i) = (.15)(.20) + (.15)(-.20) + (.70)(.10)$$
$$= .07.$$

Obviously, the investor is more uncertain regarding this investment than the prior investment with its single possible return. An investment with ten possible outcomes ranging from negative 40 percent to 50 percent, with equal probabilities for each rate of return, would be graphed like this:

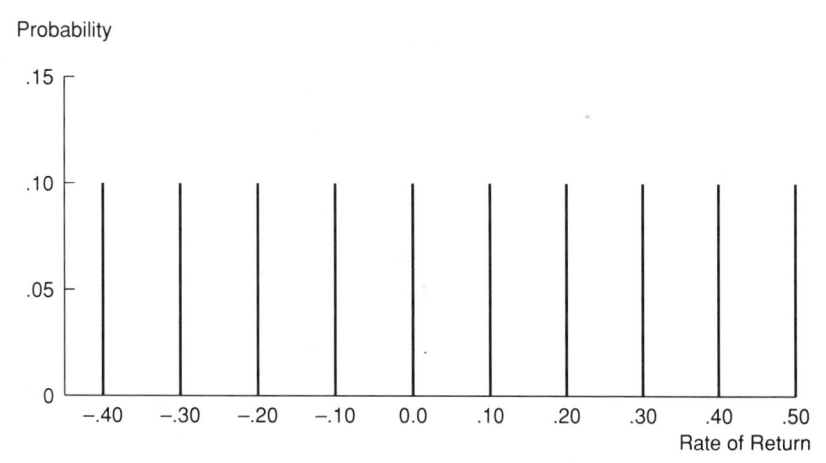

In this case there are numerous outcomes from a wide range of possibilities. The expected rate of return $[E(R_i)]$ would be

$$E(R_i) = (.10)(-.40) + (.10)(-.30) + (.10)(-.20) + (.10)(-.10) + (.10)(0.0)$$
$$+ (.10)(.10) + (.10)(.20) + (.10)(.30) + (.10)(.40)$$
$$+ (.10)(.50) = .05.$$

Note that the *expected* rate of return is the same as it was in the certainty case, but the investor is highly uncertain about what the *actual* rate of return will be. This would be considered a high-risk investment because of that uncertainty.

MEASURE OF RISK

We have shown that the uncertainty, or risk, of an investment can be determined by the range of possible outcomes and the probability of each one occurring. What is needed now is a *measure* of the dispersion of returns. The range of the distribution is one measure. Another possible measure that has received support in some theoretical work on portfolio theory is the *variance* of the estimated distribution of expected returns or the square root of the variance, i.e., the *standard deviation* of the distribution. These statistics are meant as indicators of deviations of possible rates of return from the expected rate of return and are computed as follows:

$$\text{Variance } (\sigma^2) = \Sigma(\text{Probability})(\text{Possible Return} - \text{Expected Return})^2$$
$$= \Sigma(P_i) [R_i - E(R_i)]^2.$$

The larger the variance is, everything else remaining constant, the greater the dispersion of expectations and the greater the uncertainty, or risk, of the investment.

The variance for the perfect-certainty example would be as follows:

$$(\sigma^2) = \Sigma\, P_i[R_i - E(R_i)]^2$$
$$= 1.0(.05 - .05)^2 = 1.0(0.0) = 0.$$

Note that in the case of perfect certainty there is *no variance of return* because there is *no deviation from expectations* and therefore *no risk or uncertainty*. The variance for the second example would be

$$\sigma^2 = \Sigma\, P_i[R_i - E(R_i)]^2$$
$$= [(.15)(-.20 - .07)^2 + (.15)(.20 - .07)^2 + (.70)(.10 - .07)^2]$$
$$= .0141.$$

As noted, the standard deviation is the square root of the variance and so is equal to

$$\text{Standard Deviation} = \sqrt{\Sigma\, P_i[R_i - E(R_i)]^2}.$$

For the second example, the standard deviation (σ) would be

$$\sigma = \sqrt{.0141}$$
$$= .11874.$$

In some cases, an unadjusted variance or standard deviation can be misleading if all else is not held constant, that is, if there are major differences in the expected rate of return. In such cases, a popular measure of *relative variability* —risk per unit of return—is the coefficient of variation:

Coefficient of Variation = Standard Deviation of Returns/Expected Rate of Return

$$CV = \frac{\sigma_i}{E(R_i)}.$$

The *CV* for the preceding example would be

$$CV = \frac{.11874}{.07000}$$
$$= 1.696.$$

It is generally assumed that investors are *risk averse.* Given a choice between two investments that have the same expected rate of return, they will choose the one with the smaller standard deviation and thus smaller relative risk.

DETERMINANTS OF REQUIRED RATES OF RETURN

There are two important points to consider regarding required rates of return. First, *the overall level of required rates of return for all investments changes dramatically over time.* An example of such changes can be seen from what happened to the promised yield on Moody's Aaa corporate bonds (the highest-grade corporate bonds). Yields were over 5 percent

TABLE 1.1
Promised Yields on Alternative Bonds

TYPE OF BOND	1981	1982	1983	1984	1985	1986	1987	1988
U.S. government: 3-month treasury bills	14.03	10.61	8.61	9.52	7.48	5.97	5.78	6.67
U.S. government: long-term	12.87	12.23	10.84	11.99	10.75	8.14	8.64	8.98
Aaa corporate	14.17	12.79	12.04	12.71	11.37	9.02	9.38	9.71
Baa corporate	16.04	16.11	13.55	14.19	12.72	10.39	10.58	10.83

Source: *Federal Reserve Bulletin,* various issues.

during the 1930s, declined to about 3 percent in the 1940s, rose to over 14 percent in the early 1980s, and then declined to about 9 percent during the late 1980s. Obviously, it is important to understand why the required rate on a security changes over time.

The second point regarding required returns is that *there is a wide range of required rates of return for alternative investments.* As an example, Table 1.1 contains a list of promised yields on alternative bonds. The point is, all of these are bonds, and yet the yields differ significantly. One could detect even greater differences among promised yields on common stock, real estate, and so forth. Because the required returns on all investments change over time, and because of the large differences among them, investors should be aware of the following components that determine the required rate of return.

THE RISK-FREE RATE[3]

The risk-free rate (RFR) is the basic exchange rate, assuming no uncertainty about future flows; that is, the investor knows with certainty what cash flows he will receive and when he will receive them. There is no probability of default on the investment. Earlier this was referred to as the *pure time value of money,* because the only sacrifice the lender made was deferring use of the money (consumption) for a period of time. This rate of interest is the price charged for the exchange between current goods (consumption) and future goods. Two factors, one psychological, or subjective, and one objective, influence this price. The subjective factor is the *time preference of individuals for the consumption of income.* When individuals give up $100 of consumption this year, how much consumption do they want a year from now to compensate for that sacrifice? The degree of this human desire for consumption influences the rate of compensation required. The time preference will vary among individuals, and a composite rate will be determined by the market. While this composite rate will change over time, it should do so gradually.

The objective factor that influences the risk-free rate is the *set of investment opportunities available in the economy.* The investment opportun-

---

[3] This subsection draws heavily from Irving Fisher, *The Theory of Interest* (New York: Macmillan, 1930; reprinted Augustus M. Kelley, 1961) Chapters 4, 7, and 16.

ities are a function of the *long-run real growth rate of the economy*. There-fore, a change in the economy's long-run growth rate causes a change in *all* investment opportunities and a change in the required rates of return on all investments. Three factors influence the real growth rate of the economy: (1) the long-run growth rate of the labor force, (2) the long-run growth rate of the average number of hours worked by the labor force, and (3) the long-run growth rate of the productivity of the labor force (measured by the output per hour of employees). When examining these variables, you should emphasize *long-run* trends and not be misled by short-run changes caused by cyclical fluctuations. The overall performance of these factors has generally suggested a real growth rate of about 2.5 percent as follows:

Long-run growth rate of labor force	1.5 to 2.0 percent
Long-run growth rate of average number of hours worked	−0.5 to 0.0 percent
Long-run growth rate of labor productivity	1.0 to 3.0 percent

Unfortunately, the growth rate of productivity declined to about 1.0 percent during the 1970s and the 1980s and was even negative for several years. As a result, the real growth rate of the U.S. economy was about 3.0 percent during the 1960s but only about 2.0 to 2.5 percent during the 1970s and 1980s.[4]

As the investment opportunities in an economy increase or decrease due to changes in the long-run real growth rate, the risk-free rate of return should likewise increase or decrease. Thus, there is a *positive* relationship between the investment opportunities in an economy and the RFR. Again, while investment opportunities, and therefore the RFR, can change over time, these changes are likely to be gradual.

FACTORS INFLUENCING THE NOMINAL (MONEY) RATE ON RISK-FREE INVESTMENTS

Because the factors that determine the level of the risk-free rate are long-term variables that change only gradually, one might expect the required rate on a risk-free investment to be quite stable over time. As noted previously, however, long-term corporate bonds were not stable over the period from 1930 through 1988. A more specific example is presented by the average yield on U.S. government Treasury bills (T-bills) for the period of 1967 to 1987 (see Table 1.2). This example is quite relevant, since government T-bills are a prime example of a default-free investment due to the government's unlimited ability to derive income from taxes or the creation of money. Especially notable is the steady increase in 1968 and 1969, a sharp decline in 1971, and a mammoth increase (close to 75 percent) in 1973. Again, following a decline to below 5 percent in 1976, rates increased to over 14 percent in 1981 before declining to less than 6 percent in 1986 and 1987. To summarize, rates almost tripled in a period of five

---

[4] For a discussion of the components and changes over time, see *Economic Report of the President* (Washington, D.C.: U.S. Government Printing Office, 1987).

TABLE 1.2
Average Yields on U.S. Government Three-Month Treasury Bills

1967	4.29
1968	5.34
1969	6.67
1970	6.39
1971	4.33
1972	4.07
1973	7.03
1974	7.84
1975	5.80
1976	4.98
1977	5.27
1978	7.19
1979	10.07
1980	11.43
1981	14.03
1982	10.61
1983	8.61
1984	9.52
1985	7.47
1986	5.97
1987	5.78
1988	6.67

Source: *Federal Reserve Bulletin*, various issues.

years and then declined by almost 60 percent in five years, proving that the *nominal* (money) rate of interest on a default-free investment is definitely not stable in the long run or the short run, even though the underlying determinants of the RFR are quite stable. Therefore, the other factors that influence the *nominal* risk-free rate, also referred to as *money rates* or *market rates*, must be considered. Two such factors are (1) the relative ease or tightness in the capital market and (2) the expected rate of inflation.

RELATIVE EASE OR TIGHTNESS. A change in the relative ease or tightness is a short-run phenomenon caused by a temporary disequilibrium in the supply and demand of future income streams or capital. As an example, it could be caused by an unexpected change in monetary policy or the federal deficit. The market rate on risk-free investments might change due to temporary ease or tightness in the capital market but the effect is only short term, because in the long run the higher or lower interest rates would affect supply and demand.

EXPECTED INFLATION.[5] Up to this point the discussion has been in "real" terms unaffected by changes in the price level. In discussing the rate of

---

[5] This section draws heavily on Irving Fisher, *The Theory of Interest* (New York: Macmillan, 1930; reprinted Augustus M. Kelley, 1961) Chapter 2.

exchange between current and future consumption, it was assumed that a 4 percent required rate of return meant that an investor was willing to give up $1 of consumption today in order to consume $1.04 worth of goods and services one year from now. Because the exchange rate assumed *no change in prices*, a 4 percent increase in money wealth would mean a 4 percent increase in potential consumption of goods and services. If, however, the price level is going to increase during the period of investment, the required rate of return would be increased by the rate of inflation to compensate. Assume that you want a 4 percent rate of return on a risk-free investment; this is a "real" required rate of return. Assume you expect prices to increase by 3 percent during the investment period. You should increase your required rate of return by approximately this amount to about 7 percent $[(1.04 \times 1.03) - 1]$.[6] If you do not increase your required return, the $104 you receive at the end of the year will represent a "real" return of only 1 percent, not 4 percent. Since prices have increased by 3 percent during the year, what previously cost $100 now costs $103, so you can only consume about 1 percent more at the end of the year ($104/103) − 1). If you had required a 7 percent nominal return (in current dollars), your real consumption would have increased by 4 percent ($107/103) − 1. Therefore, an investor's *nominal* required rate of return (in current dollars) on a risk-free investment should be

Nominal RFR = (1 + "Real" RFR)(1 + Expected Rate of Inflation) − 1.

Given the formulation, you can calculate the real risk-free rate of return on an investment as follows:

$$\text{Real RFR} = \frac{[(1 + \text{Nominal Risk-Free Rate of Return})]}{(1 + \text{Rate of Inflation})} - 1.$$

As an example, assume that the nominal return on U.S. government T-bills was 9 percent during a given year, and the rate of inflation during the same period was 5 percent. In this instance, the "real" rate of return on these T-bills was 3.8 percent as follows:

$$\text{Real RFR} = [(1 + .09)/(1 + .05)] - 1$$
$$= 1.038 - 1$$
$$= .038.$$

The nominal (market) rate of interest on a risk-free investment is therefore not a good estimate of the real RFR, because it can be changed dramatically in the short run by temporary ease or tightness in the capital market—and in the long run by changes in the expected rate of inflation. Clearly, the significant changes in the average yield on T-bills shown in Table 1.2 were due to the large changes in the expected rate of inflation during this period.

[6] While the actual relationship is multiplicative, it is often approximated by adding the two rates. In the current example, the result from multiplying is 7.12 percent versus the approximation of 7.0 percent.

TABLE **1.3**
Annual Rates of Inflation: 1967–1988

(Based upon changes in the Consumer Price Index, 1967 = 100)

1967	2.9
1968	4.2
1969	5.4
1970	5.9
1971	4.3
1972	3.3
1973	6.2
1974	11.0
1975	9.1
1976	5.8
1977	6.5
1978	7.7
1979	11.3
1980	13.5
1981	10.4
1982	6.1
1983	3.2
1984	4.0
1985	3.8
1986	1.1
1987	4.4
1988	4.4

Source: *Federal Reserve Bulletin*, various issues; *Economic Report of the President* (Washington, D.C.: U.S. Government Printing Office, 1989).

An indication of the impact and the volatility of inflation can be derived from the annual rates of inflation contained in Table 1.3.[7]

THE COMMON EFFECT. Note that all the factors discussed thus far regarding the required rate of return *affect all investments equally.* Irrespective of whether the concern is with stocks, bonds, real estate, or machine tools, if the expected rate of inflation increases from 2 percent to 6 percent, the required return on *all* investments should increase by 4 percent. On the other hand, if there is a general easing in the capital market that causes a decline in the market RFR of 1 percent, then the required return on *all* investments will decline by 1 percent.

RISK PREMIUM   A risk-free investment was defined as one for which the investor is certain of the amount and timing of the expected income stream. In contrast, an investor in the real world is typically not certain of the income he will receive, when he will receive it, or if he will receive it. Not only is there uncertainty involved in most investments, but there is a wide spectrum of

[7] For an analysis of short-term interest rates and inflation, see Albert E. Burger, "An Explanation of Movements in Short-Term Interest Rates," St. Louis Federal Reserve *Review* 58 no. 7 (July 1976): 10–22; Eugene F. Fama, "Short-Term Interest Rates as Predictors of Inflation," *American Economic Review* 65 no. 3 (June 1975): 513–518.

uncertainty running from basically risk-free items, such as government T-bills, to highly uncertain items, such as the common stock of small companies engaged in speculative operations like oil exploration. Most investors will require an incremental rate of return on an investment to compensate for uncertainty. This additional required rate of return is the *risk premium* that is added to the nominal RFR. While the risk premium represents a composite of all uncertainty, it is possible to consider several major sources of uncertainty, namely, business risk, financial risk (leverage), liquidity risk, and exchange rate risk.

Business risk is the uncertainty of income flows caused by the nature of the firm's business. When a firm or an individual borrows money, the ability to repay the loan and pay interest on it is a function of the certainty of the income flows to the firm or individual. As the income flows of the borrower become more uncertain, the uncertainty of the flows to the lender increases. Therefore, the lender will consider the distribution of income flows that the borrower receives and assign a risk premium on the basis of this distribution. An example of a borrower with no uncertainty of income flows is the U.S. government, because of its power to tax and print money. In contrast, a small oil-drilling firm has a potential set of returns that ranges from a large probability of no income to a small probability of a very large income. This uncertainty of income caused by the basic business of the firm is typically measured by the distribution of the firm's operating income (defined as earnings before interest and taxes, EBIT) over time. Thus, the more volatile the firm's operating income is over time relative to its mean income, the greater the business risk.[8]

In turn, the firm's operating income volatility is a function of its sales volatility and its operating leverage. Assuming a constant profit margin, if sales fluctuate over time, operating income will fluctuate. Hence, one can consider sales volatility the prime determinant of operating earnings volatility (business risk). One must also consider the production function of the firm. If all production costs are variable costs, then operating income will vary according to sales variability. In contrast, if some costs are fixed, (e.g., depreciation, administration, research), then operating income will be more volatile than sales. Depending upon where the firm is operating relative to its breakeven point, its earnings can increase by more than sales during good times and decline by more than sales during bad times. This effect of fixed operating costs on the volatility of operating earnings is referred to as *operating leverage*.[9] Therefore, a firm's business risk is measured in terms of the coefficient of variation of operating earnings, which is a function (f) of sales volatility and operating leverage.

$$\text{Business Risk} = f(\text{Volatility of Operating Earnings})$$
$$\text{Operating Earnings Volatility} = f(\text{Sales Volatility, Operating Leverage})$$

---

[8] For a more detailed discussion of the measure, see J. Fred Weston and Thomas E. Copeland, *Managerial Finance,* 8th ed. (Hinsdale, Ill.: The Dryden Press, 1986), 17, 554.

[9] For a general discussion of operating leverage, see Eugene Brigham, *Financial Management,* 5th ed. (Hinsdale, Ill.: The Dryden Press, 1988), 598–602.

Financial risk is the uncertainty introduced by the method of financing an investment. If a firm uses only equity to finance a project, only business risk is involved. In such a case, the variability of income to the ultimate owner is the same as the variability of operating income (assuming a constant tax rate). If, in addition to using equity, a firm borrows money to help finance an investment, it introduces fixed financing charges (interest) that must be paid prior to paying the owners (the equity holders). As a result, the uncertainty (variability) of returns to the investor increases because of the method of financing the investment. This increase in uncertainty due to fixed-cost financing is referred to as *financial risk or leverage* and causes investors to increase their risk premium.[10]

Liquidity risk is the uncertainty introduced by the secondary market for an investment. When an investor gives up current consumption (commits funds) by investing, there is an expectation that at some future time the investment will mature (as with a bond) or that the investor will be able to sell it to someone else (convert it into cash) and use the proceeds for current consumption or other investments. Given a desire to liquidate an investment (convert it into the most liquid of all assets—cash), the investor is faced with two uncertainties: (1) How long will it take to make the conversion? (2) What price will be received? There is similar uncertainty for a buyer: How long will it take to acquire the asset and what will be the price? The ability to buy or sell an investment quickly without a substantial price concession is known as *liquidity*.[11] The greater the uncertainty regarding when the investment can be bought or sold, or the greater the price concession required to buy or sell it, the greater the liquidity risk is.[12]

An asset with almost no liquidity risk is a U.S. government Treasury bill that can be bought or sold in minutes at a price almost identical to the quoted price. An example of an *illiquid asset* would be a specialized machine or a parcel of real estate in a remote area, because it might take a long time to find a buyer, and the selling price could vary substantially from expectations.

Exchange rate risk is the uncertainty of returns on securities acquired in a different currency. This particular risk is a major consideration for investors who buy and sell assets around the world. For example, a U.S. investor who buys Japanese stock denominated in yen must not only consider the uncertainty of the return in yen (i.e., the firm's business risk and financial risk), but also uncertainty regarding the exchange value of the yen. Assume that you bought 100 shares of Mitsubishi Electric at 1,050 yen per share when the exchange rate was 135 yen to the dollar, so your dollar cost was about $7.78 per share (1,050/135). A year later you sell

---

[10] For a discussion of financial leverage, see O. Maurice Joy, *Introduction to Financial Management,* 3d ed. (Homewood, Ill.: Richard D. Irwin, 1983), 478–493.

[11] For an analysis of the impact, see William L. Fouse, "Risk and Liquidity: The Keys to Stock Price Behavior," *Financial Analysts Journal* 32 no. 3 (May–June 1976): 35–45.

[12] There is also an explicit transaction cost for the purchase or sale that is beyond this uncertainty. In the case of stocks this would be the broker's commission *after* you have determined the price to be paid or received for the asset.

the 100 shares at 1,200 yen, when the exchange rate is 150 yen to the dollar. In terms of local currency (the yen), the stock has increased in value by about 14 percent (1,200/1,050), so this would be the return for a Japanese investor. For a U.S. investor the return is much less because during this time period, the yen has weakened relative to the dollar by about 11 percent (i.e., it requires more yen to buy a dollar—150 versus 135). At the new exchange rate, the stock is worth $8 per share (1,200 yen/150). Therefore, the return to the U.S. investor would be about 3 percent versus 14 percent for the Japanese investor. The difference is the decline in the value of the yen relative to the dollar. Clearly, the exchange rate could have gone in the other direction (the dollar could have weakened against the yen), and the U.S. investor would have experienced a local currency return as well as a gain from the exchange rate change.

The point is, when investing globally (which will be emphasized throughout this book) you must consider the additional uncertainty of exchange rate changes. This exchange rate risk will differ according to the uncertainty of a given country's exchange rate with the United States (assuming a U.S. investor). A good measure of this uncertainty would be the absolute variability of the exchange rate or its beta with a composite exchange rate. These alternative measures of exchange rate risk are discussed in Chapter 19 when we discuss international diversification.

The risk premium on an investment is, therefore, determined by the basic uncertainty of expected returns to the investor, and this is influenced by (1) sales volatility and operating leverage (business risk), (2) any added uncertainty of returns caused by how the investment is financed (financial risk), (3) the uncertainty involved in buying or selling the investment (liquidity risk), and (4) the uncertainty due to changing exchange rates when you invest outside your own country (exchange rate risk).

$$\text{Risk Premium} = f(\text{Business Risk, Financial Risk,}$$
$$\text{Liquidity Risk, Exchange Rate Risk})$$

RISK PREMIUM AND PORTFOLIO THEORY

An alternative view of risk has been derived from extensive work in portfolio theory and capital market theory by Markowitz, Sharpe, and others. These theories are dealt with in greater detail in Chapters 7 and 8, but their impact on the risk premium should be mentioned briefly. This prior work indicated that investors should use an *external market* measure of risk. It has been shown that all rational, profit-maximizing investors want to hold a completely diversified *market portfolio* of risky assets, and they borrow or lend to arrive at the desired risk level. Consequently, the relevant risk measure for an individual asset is its *co-movement (covariance) with the market portfolio*. This covariance is referred to as an asset's *systematic risk*. It is that portion of an individual asset's total variance attributable to the variability of the total market portfolio. In addition, individual assets have variance that is due to unique features, called *unsystematic variance*, or risk. Such risk is generally considered unimportant because it is eliminated in a large, diversified portfolio. Therefore, under these assumptions *the risk premium for an individual earning asset is a function of the asset's systematic risk with the aggregate market portfolio of risky assets.*

$$\text{Risk Premium} = f\,(\text{Systematic Market Risk})$$

Some might expect a conflict between these two alternative measures of risk, the market measure of risk (systematic risk) and the fundamental determinants of risk (business risk, financial risk, liquidity risk, and exchange rate risk). The fact is, a number of studies that have examined the relationship between systematic risk and accounting variables used to measure these fundamental risk variables have generally concluded that *there is a significant relationship between the risk measures.*[13] Therefore, the two definitions of risk are not contradictory but instead are parallel and complementary. This consistency seems logical because, in a properly functioning capital market, the market measure of the risk should reflect the fundamental risk characteristics of the asset. Therefore, one can specify

$$\text{Risk Premium} = f\,(\text{Business Risk, Financial Risk,}$$
$$\text{Liquidity Risk, Exchange Rate Risk})$$

or

$$\text{Risk Premium} = f\,(\text{Systematic Market Risk})\,.$$

SUMMARY OF REQUIRED RATE OF RETURN

The overall required rate of return on alternative investments is determined by three variables: (1) The economy's real RFR, which is influenced by the investment opportunities in the economy (i.e., the long-run real growth rate); (2) variables that influence the nominal RFR, which include short-run ease or tightness in the capital market and expected inflation (*the first two sets of variables are the same for all investments)*; and (3) variables that influence the risk premium on investments, such as business risk, financial risk, liquidity risk, and exchange rate risk, or systematic market risk.

RELATIONSHIP BETWEEN RISK AND RETURN

To better illustrate the foregoing material, Figure 1.1 graphs the relationship between risk and return with an emphasis on what causes changes in required rates of return over time. The graph shows that investors increase their required return as perceived uncertainty increases. The slope of the market line indicates the return per unit of risk required by all investors. Highly risk-averse investors would have a steeper line, and vice versa.

Given the composite market line prevailing at a point in time, investors would select investments that are consistent with their risk preferences.

---

[13] This will be discussed more fully in later chapters. A brief review of several of these studies is contained in Donald J. Thompson II, "Sources of Systematic Risk in Common Stocks," *Journal of Business* 49 no. 2 (April 1976): 173–188.

FIGURE 1.1
Relationship between Risk and Return

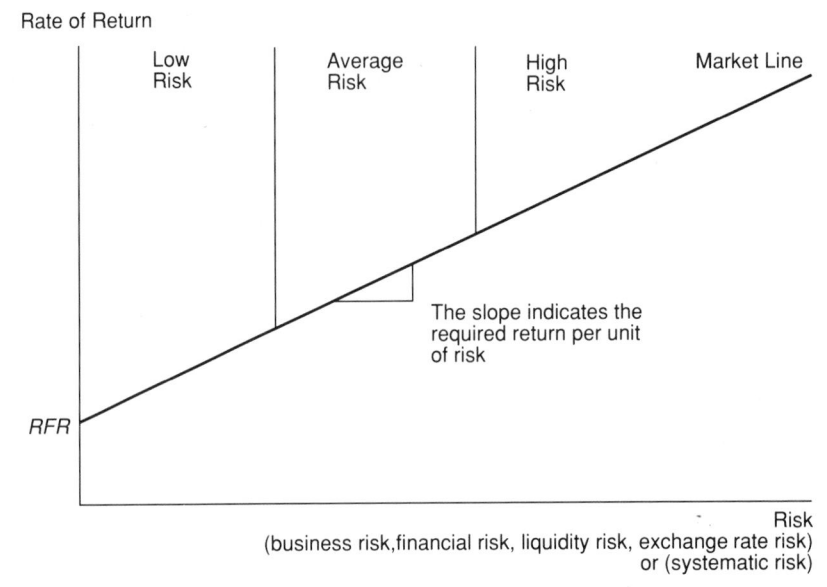

Some will consider only low-risk investments, while others welcome high-risk investments.

The graph in Figure 1.2 shows what happens to the market line when capital market conditions or expected inflation is considered. The dashed line indicates a parallel *shift* in the market line caused by either temporary tightness in the capital market or an increase in the expected rate of inflation. The parallel shift in the line reflects the fact that these changes affect *all* investments irrespective of their level of risk.

SUMMARY

Expected income streams and patterns of desired consumption rarely match. Certain economic units have more income than they want to consume (savings) and are willing to trade current consumption for a larger amount of future consumption. In contrast, others have more current consumption desires than income and want to *dissave* (borrow future income). The rate of exchange between current and future consumption, assuming no risk, is the time value of money. Because the required rate of return differs substantially among alternative investments, and because the required return on specific investments changes over time, the factors that influence the required rate of return must be considered. The three major variables are the "real" RFR, factors that influence the (nominal) market rate on risk-free investments (most notably inflation), and the risk premium. The required rate of return on all investments is affected by changes

FIGURE 1.2
Effect of Capital Market Conditions on Market Line

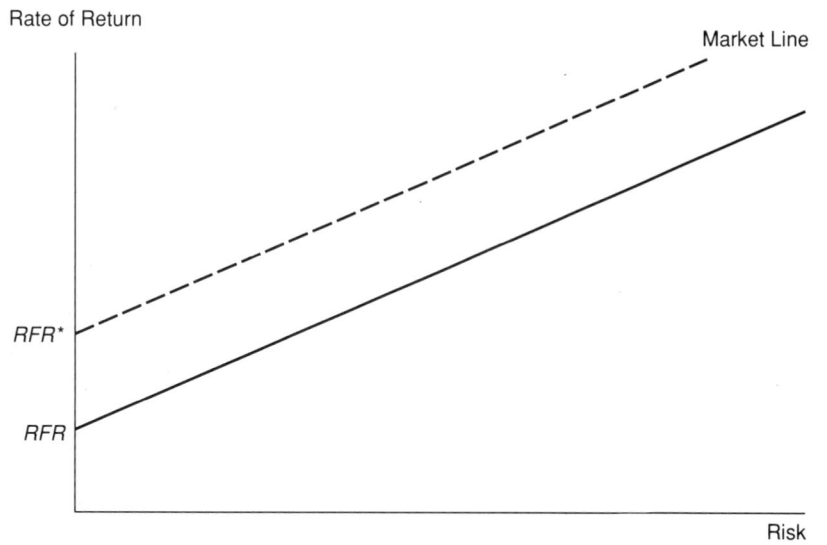

RFR* = nominal risk-free rate

in the nominal RFR, so the factor causing all differences *among* investments at a point in time is the risk premium.

QUESTIONS

1. Why do people invest? Be specific regarding when they are willing to invest and what they expect to receive in the future.

2. Define an investment.

3. Why do people engage in negative saving or dissaving? Be specific.

4. As a student are you saving or dissaving? What do you expect to derive from this activity?

5. Divide a person's life from ages 20 to 70 into ten-year segments and discuss what the saving or dissaving patterns during each of these periods are likely to be and why.

6. Would you expect the saving-dissaving pattern to differ by occupation (e.g., for a doctor versus a plumber)? Why or why not?

7. *The Wall Street Journal* reported that the yield on common stocks is about 4 percent, while a study at the University of Chicago contends that the rate of return on common stocks has averaged about 9 percent. Reconcile these statements.

8. The variance of the distribution of expected rates of return has been suggested as a good measure of uncertainty. Discuss the reasoning behind this measure and its purpose.

9. What are the three major determinants of an investor's required rate of return on an investment? Discuss each of these briefly.

10. Discuss the two major factors that determine the market nominal risk-free rate (RFR). Discuss which of these factors would be more volatile over the business cycle. Why?

11. Discuss the four factors that contribute to the risk premium of an investment.

12. You own stock in the Edgar Company, and you notice that after a recent bond offering the firm's debt/equity ratio has gone from 30 percent to 45 percent. Discuss the effect this change will have on the variability of the net income stream, other factors being constant. Would you change your required rate of return on the common stock of the Edgar Company? Discuss.

13. Draw a properly labeled graph of the market line and indicate where you would expect the following investments to plot along that line. Discuss your reasoning.

13a. Common stock of large firms

13b. U.S. government bonds

13c. Low-grade corporate bonds

13d. Common stock of a new, small firm

14. Discuss in nontechnical terms why you would change your nominal required rate of return if you expected the rate of inflation to go from zero (no inflation) to 7 percent. Give an example of what would happen if you did not change your required rate of return under these conditions.

15. Assume the long-run growth rate of the economy increased by 1 percent and the expected rate of inflation increased by 4 percent. What would happen to the required rate of return on government bonds, common stocks, and real estate? How would the effect differ? Show this graphically.

16. Discuss an example of a liquid investment asset and an illiquid asset. Indicate specifically why they are liquid or illiquid.

17. *CFA Examination III* (*June 1981*) As part of your portfolio planning process, it is suggested that you estimate the "real" long-run growth potential of the economy.

17a. Identify and explain three major determinants of the economy's real long-run growth. [15 minutes]

17b. Briefly discuss the outlook for each of these three determinants of long-term growth. Present approximate estimates for each of these components and calculate the composite real growth potential for the next five years. (While you should provide a calculation, the emphasis should be on the process rather than on specific numbers.) [10 minutes]

PROBLEMS

1. At the beginning of last year you invested $2,000 in 50 shares of the Shepard Corporation. During the year Shepard paid dividends of $3 per share. At the end of the year you sold the 50 shares for $48 a share. Compute your total rate of return on these shares, and indicate how much was a capital gain and what was the dividend yield.

2. The rate of return computed in Problem 1 is a *nominal* rate of return. Assuming that the rate of inflation during the year was 4 percent, compute the *real* rate of return on this investment. What would be the real rate of return if the rate of inflation were 8 percent?

3. A stockbroker calls you and suggests that you invest in the May Computer Company. After analyzing the annual report and other material, you feel that the distribution of rates of return is as follows:

POSSIBLE RATE OF RETURN	PROBABILITY
−.50	0.05
−.20	0.15
−.10	0.10
.25	0.30
.45	0.20
.60	0.20

3a. Compute the expected return $[E(R_i)]$ on this stock.

3b. Compute the standard deviation of the expected return for this one year.

4. You have studied the recent past history of both the U.S. economy and your portfolio and concluded that next year the following relationships are possible:

ECONOMIC STATUS	PROBABILITY	RATE OF RETURN
Weak economy	.20	−10%
Static economy	.75	10%
Strong economy	.05	15%

Fred Smithton, you next-door neighbor, has studied the recent past history of both the Japanese economy and his portfolio of Japanese stocks and concluded that next year the following relationships are possible:

ECONOMIC STATUS	PROBABILITY	RATE OF RETURN
Weak economy	.30	−15%
Static economy	.50	12%
Strong economy	.20	25%

4a. What is your expected rate of return $[E(R_i)]$ for next year?

4b. For your portfolio, compute the standard deviation of rates of return for the one-year period.

4c. What is Fred's expected rate of return $[E(R_i)]$ for next year?

4d. For Fred's portfolio, compute the standard deviation of rates of return for the one-year period.

4e. What conclusions, if any, can be drawn from the comparison of the two portfolios?

5. Based on your calculations for the problem immediately preceding,

5a. Compute the coefficient of variation for your portfolio.

5b. Compute the coefficient of variation for Fred's portfolio.

5c. Which portfolio contains the greatest amount of risk? Explain.

5d. With the addition of these computations, do you wish to revise your answer to Problem 4, part e? Why or why not?

5e. Under what circumstances is it unnecessary to compute the coefficient of variation?

6. During the past year you had a portfolio that contained U.S. government T-bills, government long-term bonds, and common stocks. The rates of return on each of them were as follows:

	PERCENT
U.S. government T-bills	8.50
U.S. government long-term bonds	10.75
Common stocks	13.10

During the year, the Consumer Price Index (1967 = 100) went from 340 to 364. Compute the rate of inflation during this year, and then compute the real rates of return on each of the assets in your portfolio by using the inflation rate.

7a. You are informed that the long-run real growth rate of the economy over the next five-year period will average 4 percent. In addition, you see in a bank newsletter that the average annual rate of inflation during this five-year period is expected to be about 5 percent. What would you expect the nominal rate of return to be on U.S. government T-bills during this period?

7b. Given what you know from part (a) and the fact that you want a 4 percent risk premium to own common stocks, what would your required rate of return be on common stocks?

8. Assume that during the past year the Consumer Price Index increased by 5 percent. Real rates of return were as follows for three types of securities:

	PERCENT
U.S. government T-bills	3.00
U.S. long-term bonds	3.75
Common stocks	6.50

8a. What are the nominal rates of return for each of these securities?

8b. If next year the nominal rates all rise by 25 percent, while inflation climbs from 5 percent to 6 percent, what will be the real rate of return on each security?

REFERENCES

Fama, Eugene F., and Miller, Merton H. *The Theory of Finance*. New York: Holt, Rinehart and Winston, 1972.

Fisher, Irving. *The Theory of Interest*. New York: Macmillan, 1930; reprinted Augustus M. Kelley, 1961.

Hirshleifer, J. "Investment Decisions under Uncertainty: Choice-Theoretic Approaches," *Quarterly Journal of Economics* 79 no. 4 (November 1965).

COMPUTATION OF VARIANCE AND STANDARD DEVIATION

APPENDIX 1A

The variance and standard deviation are measures of how the actual values (rates of return) differ from the expected value (mean) of a given series of values. As noted, it is possible to conceive of other measures of dispersion, but the variance and standard deviation are the best known because of their uses in statistics and probability theory. Variance is defined as follows:

$$\text{Variance } (\sigma^2) = \Sigma(\text{Probability})(\text{Possible Return} - \text{Expected Return})^2$$
$$= \Sigma(P_i)[R_i - E(R_i)]^2 .$$

Consider the following example discussed in the chapter:

PROBABILITY OF POSSIBLE RETURN (P_i)	POSSIBLE RETURN (R_i)	$P_i R_i$
.15	.20	.03
.15	−.20	−.03
.70	.10	.07
		$\Sigma = .07$

Therefore, the expected return $[E(R_i)]$ is 7 percent. The dispersion of this distribution in terms of the variance is as follows:

PROBABILITY (P_i)	RETURN (R_i)	$R_i - E(R_i)$	$[R_i - E(R_i)]^2$	$P_i[R_i - E(R_i)]^2$
.15	.20	.13	.0169	.002535
.15	−.20	−.27	.0729	.010935
.70	.10	.03	.0009	.000630
				$\Sigma = .014100$

Thus, the variance (σ^2) is equal to .014100. The standard deviation is equal to the square root of the variance as follows:

$$\text{Standard Deviation } (\sigma) = \sqrt{\Sigma P_i[R_i - E(R_i)]^2} .$$

Consequently, the standard deviation for the preceding example above would be

$$\sigma_i = \sqrt{.0141} = .11874.$$

This would indicate a standard deviation of approximately 11.87 percent. Therefore, one could describe this distribution as having a mean (expected value) of 7 percent and a standard deviation of 11.87 percent.

In many instances an investor might want to compute the variance or standard deviation for a historical series. Assume that you are given the following information on annual rates of return for common stocks listed on the New York Stock Exchange (NYSE):

YEAR	ANNUAL RATE OF RETURN
19–1	.07
19–2	.11
19–3	−.04
19–4	.12
19–5	−.06

In this case, we are not dealing with expected rates of return, but actual returns. Therefore, we can assume equal probabilities, and the expected value (i.e., the mean value, $\overline{R}$) of the series is simply the sum of the series divided by the number of observations. In this example it is .04 (.20/5). The variance and standard deviation would be as follows:

YEAR	R_i	$R_i - \overline{R}$	$(R_i - \overline{R})^2$	
19–1	.07	.03	.0009	$\sigma^2 = .0286/5$
19–2	.11	.07	.0049	$= .00572$
19–3	−.04	−.08	.0064	
19–4	.12	.08	.0064	$\sigma = \sqrt{.00572}$
19–5	−.06	−.10	.0110	$= .0756$
			$\Sigma = .0286$	

Accordingly, regarding the performance of stocks during this period of time, one would say that the average rate of return was 4 percent and the standard deviation of annual rates of return was 7.56 percent.

COEFFICIENT OF VARIATION

In some instances one might want to compare the dispersion of two different series. A problem with the variance or the standard deviation is that they are *absolute* measures of dispersion; therefore, they can be influenced by the magnitude of the original numbers. When it is necessary to compare series with very different values, it is desirable to have a *relative* measure of dispersion. A potential measure that indicates this relative dispersion is the coefficient of variation, which is defined as follows:

$$\text{Coefficient of Variation } (CV) = \frac{\text{Standard Deviation}}{\text{Expected Return}}.$$

The larger this value is, the greater the dispersion *relative* to the expected return. For the previous example, the *CV* would be:

$$CV = \frac{.0756}{.0400} = 1.89 \,.$$

It would be possible to compare this value to a comparable figure for a very different distribution. Assume you wanted to compare this to another investment alternative that had a mean return of 10 percent and a standard deviation of 9 percent. On the basis of the standard deviations alone, the second series has greater dispersion and might be considered higher risk (i.e., 9 percent versus 7.56 percent). In fact, the relative dispersion is much less.

$$CV_1 = \frac{.0756}{.0400} = 1.89$$

$$CV_2 = \frac{.0900}{.1000} = 0.90.$$

Considering the relative dispersion and the total distribution, most investors would probably prefer the second series.

PROBLEMS

1. Your expectations from a one-year investment in Wang Computers are as follows:

PROBABILITY	RATE OF RETURN
.15	−.25
.25	−.10
.30	.00
.25	.10
.05	.25

1a. For this investment, compute the
   1) expected return
   2) variance
   3) standard deviation
   4) coefficient of variation.

1b. Under what conditions can the standard deviation alone be used to measure the relative risk of two investments?

1c. Under what conditions must the coefficient of variation be used to measure the relative risk of two investments?

2. You have just purchased 100 shares of Grace Munitions Company at $50 per share. Having second thoughts about your investment, you wish to reevaluate the return potential and record the following estimates:

PROBABILITY	POTENTIAL PRICE	POTENTIAL DIVIDEND
.2	52	.25
.1	52	.50
.3	55	.25
.1	55	.50
.2	60	.25
.1	60	.50

2a. What is the expected rate of return on your investment?

2b. What are the variance and standard deviation of the return?

3. On the basis of the following annual rates of return, compute the mean rate of return and standard deviation of return for government T-bills and common stocks.

YEAR	T-BILLS	COMMON STOCK
19–4	.073	.180
19–5	.084	−.063
19–6	.081	.300
19–7	.087	.236
19–8	.080	−.094

Discuss these two alternative investments in terms of the average return, the absolute risk involved, and the relative risk of each.

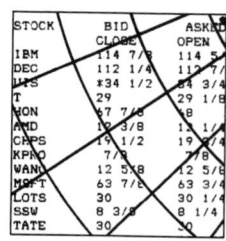

CHAPTER 2

ALTERNATIVE INVESTMENTS IN A GLOBAL CAPITAL MARKET

Like any book on investments, this one emphasizes common stocks. However, you should remember that numerous investment instruments are available in the United States and throughout the world, offering a broad range of alternatives. Indeed, there has been a two-stage explosion of investment alternatives during the past 15 years. First, numerous new instruments were created and are being created in the domestic market with the introduction of organized exchanges for trading options and futures. Second, the evolving globalization of the capital markets has produced still more alternatives, across international boundaries.[1] The principles of valuation and portfolio management discussed in this book are applicable to a variety of investments, although in some cases there may be problems in deriving inputs for the valuation models.

One of the main reasons for considering numerous different investments is the benefit derived from *diversification*, which can be defined as owning alternative investments with different return patterns over time with the intent that when one investment is yielding a low or negative rate of return, another will enjoy above normal returns. The overall result should be relatively stable earnings for the collection of investments (also referred to as the *portfolio*). While subsequent chapters contain a detailed discussion of diversification, at this point you should recognize that *proper diversification results in less variability in the rates of return for a portfolio over time and, therefore, helps reduce the uncertainty, or risk, of the portfolio.*

TYPES OF INVESTMENTS

The purpose of this chapter is to briefly discuss some of the major, worldwide investment alternatives that you should consider for your portfolio. It will become apparent that some alternatives are not appropriate for

---

[1] In this regard, see Scott E. Pardee, "Internationalization of Financial Markets," *Federal Reserve Bank of Kansas City Economic Review* (February 1987): 3–7.

TABLE 2.1
Total Debt Outstanding of the Eighteen Major Actively Traded Bond Markets
(U.S. dollar terms–millions)

	1983		1985		1987	
	$	%	$	%	$	%
U.S. dollar	2,074	50.2	2,830	49.8	3,717	41.7
Japanese yen	756	18.3	1,070	18.8	2,033	22.8
Deutschemark	312	7.6	417	7.3	783	8.8
Italian lira	175	4.2	278	4.9	554	6.2
U.K. sterling	174	4.2	207	3.6	310	3.5
French franc	104	2.5	174	3.1	334	3.7
Canadian dollar	149	3.6	171	3.1	228	2.6
Swedish krona	68	1.6	88	1.5	146	1.6
Danish krone	69	1.6	103	1.8	171	1.9
Swiss franc	59	1.4	77	1.4	142	1.6
Dutch guilder	47	1.1	70	1.2	130	1.5
Belgian franc	34	0.8	51	0.9	96	1.1
Australian dollar	52	1.3	60	1.1	91	1.0
Spanish peseta	21	0.5	34	0.6	76	0.8
Norwegian krone	17	0.4	22	0.4	36	0.4
ECU	3	0.1	10	0.2	37	0.4
Irish punt	7	0.2	11	0.2	22	0.2
New Zealand dollar	6	0.2	8	0.1	15	0.2
Total	$4,129	100.0	$5,681	100.0	$8,920	100.0

Source: "Size of the World Bond Markets: Year-End 1987" (July 1988). Merrill Lynch Capital Markets, International Fixed Income Research Department.

investors with certain risk or liquidity preferences. However, in addition to the obvious alternatives of bonds and stocks, some rather unusual possibilities exist that should be considered. We conclude the chapter with an analysis of the risk and return experience for several investment instruments and consider the relationship among the returns for these various investments.

MAKEUP OF THE WORLD BOND MARKET

Before we describe the various individual fixed-income instruments that are available, it is interesting to consider the overall size and structure of the world bond market as shown by the data in Table 2.1. Note that although the U.S. bond market is still the dominant sector of the world market, it constitutes less than one-half of the $8.9 trillion total and it has steadily declined in relative size since 1983. In contrast, the Japanese yen, deutschemark, and Italian lira segments have grown in absolute and relative size and currently make up an additional 38 percent of the world bond market. Therefore, the largest four segments account for about 80 percent of the total, with additional significant segments in British sterling, French francs, and the Canadian dollar.

An analysis of the overall market by segments within individual countries is done in Chapter 10. This subsequent analysis will show that in terms of government bonds, municipal, corporate and Eurobonds, the aggregate government borrowing typically constitutes about one-third of the total, with some differences among countries.

Again, the important point is that there is a very substantial fixed-income market outside the United States of which investors should be aware.

FIXED-INCOME INVESTMENTS

Fixed-income investments have a fixed payment schedule wherein the investor is promised specific payments at predetermined times, although the legal force behind the promise varies. At one extreme, if the contractual payment is not made at the appointed time, the issuing firm can be declared bankrupt. In other cases, the payments must be made only if they are earned (an income bond); while in some instances, the payment does not have to be made unless the board of directors votes for it (preferred stock).

SAVINGS ACCOUNTS. It is probably not necessary to describe savings accounts except to indicate that they are an example of a fixed-income investment. An individual who deposits funds in a savings account at a bank or savings and loan association (S&Ls) is really lending money to the institution and so derives a fixed payment. Because these investments are considered very low-risk (almost all are insured), convenient, and (normally) liquid, the rate of return on them is generally low compared to other alternatives. Banks and savings and loan associations have created several new savings account instruments that should also be considered.

The *passbook savings account* has no minimum balance, and funds can be withdrawn at any time with very little loss of interest. Due to its flexibility, the promised interest on passbook accounts is relatively low. For investors with larger amounts of funds who are willing to give up liquidity, banks and S&Ls developed *certificates of deposits (CDs)*, which involve minimum amounts (typically $500) and specified time periods (e.g., three months, six months, one year, two and one-half years). The promised rates on these CDs are higher than those for passbook savings, and the rate increases with the length of deposit. If the investor wants to cash in a CD prior to its stated expiration date, there is a heavy penalty in terms of the interest received on the money.

For investors with large sums of money (a minimum of $10,000), it has always been possible to invest in *Treasury bills (T-bills)*, which are short-term obligations (three to twelve months) of the U.S. government. To compete against T-bills, banks and S&Ls developed *money market certificates,* which involve a minimum investment of $10,000 and a minimum maturity of six months. The promised rate on these certificates fluctuates at some premium over the weekly rate on six-month T-bills. These certificates can be redeemed only at the bank of issue, and there is a penalty for early withdrawal of funds.

Capital market instruments are lending obligations that trade in the open market—that is, you can buy and sell them to other individuals or institutions. These include the following categories:

- U.S. Treasury securities
- U.S. agency securities
- Municipal bonds
- Corporate bonds

U.S. TREASURY SECURITIES.[2] All government (U.S. Treasury) securities are fixed-income instruments that generally differ in terms of *time to maturity* when they are initially issued. Specifically, bills are for less than a year, notes are from one to ten years, and bonds are for over ten years. Obviously, the maturities change over time, and securities that were initially 20-year bonds become 8-year bonds and act like 8-year notes. U.S. government obligations are riskless in terms of default and are very liquid (i.e., you can buy or sell them quickly at a known price through government security dealers).

very liquid

U.S. AGENCY SECURITIES. Agency securities are not direct obligations of the Treasury but rather are sold by various agencies of the government to support specific programs. Examples include the Federal National Mortgage Association (FNMA), which sells bonds and uses the proceeds to purchase mortgages from insurance companies or savings and loans, and the Federal Home Loan Bank (FHLB), which sells bonds and loans the money to its 12 banks, which in turn provide credit to savings and loans and other mortgage-granting institutions. Other agencies include the Government National Mortgage Association (GNMA), Banks for Cooperatives, Federal Land Banks (FLB), and the Federal Housing Administration (FHA).

While the securities issued are not direct obligations of the government, they are virtually default-free, generally are fairly liquid (especially the shorter-term issues), and typically sell at a slight yield premium to Treasury issues.

MUNICIPAL BONDS. Municipal bonds are issued by municipalities (states, cities, towns, etc.) and can be either *general obligation bonds*, wherein the full taxing power of the municipality is used to pay for them, or *revenue bonds*, wherein the interest is paid from revenue generated by a particular project (e.g., the revenue for interest on sewer bonds comes from water taxes).

A major feature distinguishing municipal bonds is that they are *tax-exempt*, meaning the interest earned from them is exempt from taxation by the federal government and by the state that issued the bond, provided the investor is a resident of that state. This feature is important to investors in high-tax brackets. A marginal tax rate of 30 percent means that a regular bond with an interest rate of 8 percent yields a net return after taxes of only 5.60 percent [$.08 \times (1 - .30)$]. A tax-free bond with a 6 percent yield would be preferable. For this reason, yields on municipal bonds are lower

---

[2] Chapter 15 contains a detailed discussion of marketable bonds, including government securities, municipal bonds, and corporate bonds.

(generally by about 70 to 80 percent) than the yields on comparable taxable bonds.

CORPORATE BONDS. Corporate bonds can be broken down in terms of issuer (industrial corporations, public utility corporations, or railroads), in terms of quality (the rating assigned by an agency on the basis of probability of default), in terms of maturity (short term, intermediate term, or long term), or based upon the contractual promise to the investor (whether a bond is a debenture, a mortgage bond, an income bond, or a convertible bond as described later).

All bonds include an *indenture*, which is the legal document that sets forth the obligation of the issuer with regard to payment, restrictions, and such features as call provisions and sinking funds.[3] *Call provisions* indicate when a firm may call the bonds for redemption (prior to maturity) and at what price. The *sinking fund* specifies what payments the issuer must make to redeem a given percent of the outstanding issue prior to maturity. These features are important during periods of high and changing interest rates.

DEBENTURES. Debentures are promises to pay interest and principal without collateral, which means the lender is dependent upon the success of the borrower to receive the promised payment. Debenture owners usually have first call on the earnings and uncollateralized assets of a firm. If an interest payment is not made, the debenture owners can declare the firm bankrupt and claim its assets to pay off the bonds.

MORTGAGE BONDS. Mortgage bonds are similar to debentures, but in case of bankruptcy, there are specific assets pledged as backing for them. Examples include bonds backed by specific liens on land, buildings, or equipment.

INCOME BONDS. Income bonds have a stipulated coupon and interest payment schedule, but the interest is due and payable only if the company earns the interest payment by a stipulated date. If the required amount is not earned, the interest payment does not have to be made and the firm cannot be declared bankrupt. Instead, the interest payment is considered in arrears and, if subsequently earned, must be paid off. Given the lack of legal guarantees related to these payments, an income bond is not considered as safe as a debenture or a mortgage bond.

CONVERTIBLE BONDS. Covertible bonds have all the characteristics of other bonds with the added feature that they can be converted into the

---

[3] The importance of indenture provisions increased during 1987 and 1988 when numerous bond issues experienced major downgradings in their ratings because of debt issued in connection with leveraged buyouts (LBOs) or restructurings. For an early discussion of this phenomenon, see Richard S. Wilson, "Corporate Restructurings and Rating Changes," Merrill Lynch Capital Markets (January 1986). More recent discussions include, James Grant and T. I. Forstmann, "Corporate Finance: Leveraged to the Hilt," *The Wall Street Journal* (October 25, 1988), p. A22; and Matthew Winkler and Tom Herman, "Corporate Market Remains in Disarray," *The Wall Street Journal* (October 25, 1988), p. C1, C21.

common stock of the company that issued the bond. As an example, a firm could issue a $1,000 face-value bond and stipulate that owners of the bond could, at their discretion, turn the bond in to the issuing corporation and convert it into 40 shares of the firm's common stock. These bonds are very attractive because they combine a fixed-income feature with the ability to be converted into the common stock of the firm should the firm do well. Because of their desirability, convertible bonds generally have lower interest rates than comparable straight debentures of the firm, and the yield differential increases with the growth potential of the company because the conversion potential is of greater value.[4] A negative feature is that these bonds are almost always subordinated to the straight debt of the firm, so during reorganizations or buyouts that entail heavy fixed-income financing, they are rated lower.

A similar feature is the sale of bonds with *warrants* attached that allow the bondholder to purchase the firm's common stock from the firm at a specified price for a given time period. The purchase price for the stock set in the warrant is typically above the price of the stock at the time the bond is issued, but below the expected future price. The warrant makes the straight bond more desirable, which lowers the yield on the bonds and also provides the firm with *future equity capital* when the holder exercises the warrant and buys the stock from the firm (assuming the stock price rises above the price stipulated in the warrant).

ZERO COUPON BONDS. Unlike the typical bond, a zero coupon bond promises no interest payments during the life of the bond, but only the payment of the principal at maturity. Therefore, the value of the bond is the discounted value of the principal payment at the required rate of return. As an example, the value of a bond that promises to pay $10,000 in five years is $6,806, if you require 8 percent on this bond—that is, the present value factor for five years at 8 percent, assuming annual compounding is .6806. These instruments have some unique advantages for corporations issuing them and for tax-free investors (e.g., pension funds or IRA investments by individuals). They will be discussed further in Chapter 17.

INTERNATIONAL BOND INVESTING. As noted earlier, more than one-half of all fixed-income securities are from countries outside the United States. The description of these securities is complicated because they can be differentiated by the location of the issuer (e.g., United States, United Kingdom, Japan), the location of the primary trading market (e.g., the United States, London), the domicile of the primary buyers, and the currency denominations (e.g., dollars, yen, pound sterling). The following discussion considers examples of each of these characteristics.

THE EUROBOND MARKET. A Eurobond is an international bond denominated in a currency other than that of the country of the issuer. This would

---

[4] For a further discussion of convertible bonds and warrants, see Chapter 23.

include Eurodollar bonds, Euro-yen bonds, Euro-deutschemark bonds, and Euro-sterling bonds. As a specific example, a Eurodollar bond would be one that is denominated in U.S. dollars but underwritten by an international syndicate, and sold at issue to non–U.S. investors. An example would be a U.S. dollar bond issue by General Motors sold in London. Because these securities are issued in Europe, they are not approved by the SEC and, therefore, cannot be sold to U.S. citizens at the original issue. They are typically issued in Europe, with the major concentration in London.

It is possible to issue similar bonds denominated in yen or deutschemarks. As an example, the issuer of Euro-yen bonds that are sold in London may be a sovereign government, a corporation, or a supranational agency. After these Eurobonds have been seasoned for three to nine months, they can be bought and sold by U.S. citizens.[5]

YANKEE BONDS. Yankee bonds are sold in the United States, denominated in U.S. dollars, but issued by a borrower of different nationality (e.g., a German or French corporation). This allows a U.S. citizen to buy a bond of a foreign firm but receive all payments in U.S. dollars, eliminating exchange rate risk. Similar bonds from other countries would include the "Bulldog Market," which involves British sterling-denominated bonds issued by non-British firms, or the "Samurai Market," which involves yen-denominated bonds issued by non-Japanese issuers.

INTERNATIONAL DOMESTIC BONDS. The third major sector would be bonds sold by an issuer within the country of issue in that country's currency—such as a bond sold by a Japanese corporation in Japan, denominated in yen. A U.S. investor acquiring such a bond would receive maximum diversification from such a purchase, but would become exposed to exchange rate risk between the yen and the U.S. dollar.

PREFERRED STOCK. Preferred stock is a fixed-income security because a yearly payment is stipulated that is either a coupon (e.g., 5 percent of the face value) or a stated dollar amount (e.g., $5 preferred). Preferred stock differs from bonds in that its payment (which is a dividend) is not legally binding and, for each period, must be voted on by the firm's board of directors, as is a common stock dividend. Even if the firm earned enough money to pay the preferred stock dividend, the board of directors could vote to withhold it; and, because most preferred stock is cumulative, the unpaid dividends would accumulate.

Although preferred dividends are not legally binding, they are considered binding in a practical sense because of the credit implications of a missed dividend. Because, unlike the interest on bonds, preferred stock dividend payments cannot be deducted from the taxes of the issuing firm, this source of financing has not been popular, except among utilities. Ex-

---

[5] Because of the growth of the Eurodollar market there are separate bond indicator series for these bonds that will be described and discussed in Chapter 4.

cluding utilities, preferred stocks constitute less than 3 percent of all new corporate financing. However, due to the fact that corporations can legally exclude 80 percent of intercompany dividends from taxable income, preferred stocks have become attractive investments for at least some financial corporations. Their demand has led to the unusual situation of the yield on high-grade preferred stock typically being lower than that of high-grade bonds.

EQUITY INSTRUMENTS

COMMON STOCK. Common stock, a popular choice for investing, represents *ownership* of a firm. Thus, holders of common stock share in the company's successes and problems. If, like IBM or Xerox, the company does very well, the investor can become very wealthy. In contrast, the investor can lose money if the firm goes bankrupt, as the once formidable Penn Central, W. T. Grant, and Interstate Department Stores did, and is forced to liquidate its assets. The point is, common stock entails all the advantages and disadvantages of ownership and is a relatively risky investment compared to most fixed-income securities.

MAKEUP OF THE WORLD EQUITY MARKET

Similar to the world bond market, the equity market is widely dispersed geographically. As shown in Figure 2.1, as of the end of 1987, 31 percent of total value was in the United States and 42 percent in Japan. The third largest segment, about 9 percent, was in the United Kingdom, followed by West Germany with almost 3 percent. Thus, the top four countries constituted about 85 percent of the total. Because the great majority of the equity market is outside the United States, investors should become familiar with non–U.S. opportunities and determine the impact of adding such securities to a portfolio of U.S. stocks. As indicated by Table 2.2, the result of such international equity diversification should be a higher rate of return. Returns in the U.S. market were the highest during only one of the 15 years shown in the table, and the average return in the United States was the lowest of the six countries. Also, as will be discussed later in the chapter, correlations among returns imply that international diversification also reduces risk.

COMMON STOCK CLASSIFICATIONS

It is possible to classify equity investments according to (1) the nature of the firm, (2) its type of business, or (3) its earnings potential.

CLASSIFICATION BY BUSINESS LINE. Common stocks can be categorized by function or general business line (industrial firms, utilities, transportation, or financial institutions).

CLASSIFICATION BY OPERATING PERFORMANCE. Another technique for classifying companies is in terms of their internal operating performance (growth companies, cyclical companies, and defensive companies). This breakdown is discussed in Chapter 13.

FIGURE 2.1

Breakdown of World Equity Markets (Total Valuation = $7.15 Trillion, December 31, 1987)

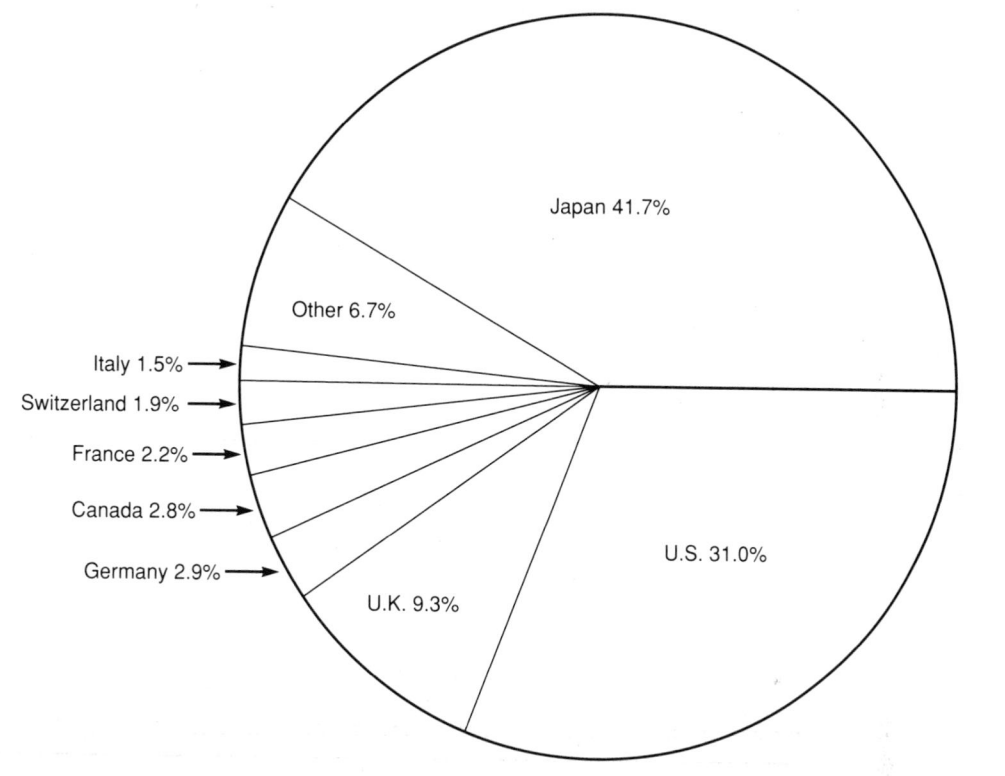

Source: Morgan Stanley, *Capital International Perspective,* New York (January 1988).

INVESTMENT COMPANIES

Up to this point we have been discussing individual securities that can be acquired from the government, a state or municipality, or a corporation. However, rather than buying an individual stock or bond issued by one of these sources, you may choose to acquire shares in an investment company that owns a number of individual stocks, bonds, or a combination of the two. Specifically, an investment company sells shares in itself and uses the proceeds (the money invested in the investment company) to acquire bonds, stocks, or other investment instruments. As a result, an investor who acquires shares in an investment company is a partial owner of the investment company, which in turn owns the stock or bonds. Therefore, the investor owns part of the *portfolio* of stocks or other investment instruments. Investment companies are usually identified by the types of investment instruments they acquire. Some of the major types are as follows:[6]

---

[6] See Chapter 24 for a detailed discussion of investment companies.

TABLE 2.2
Annual Rates of Return on Equity for Six Major Countries, 1973–1987

YEAR	JAPAN	US	UK	GERMANY	FRANCE	CANADA
1973	−24.2	−15.9	−23.1	−23.3	− 7.1	− **4.4**
1974	− 9.2	−29.7	−32.3	− **1.7**	−30.8	−29.3
1975	16.2	31.5	**138.2**	37.5	30.7	12.9
1976	18.7	**19.2**	− 3.8	− 6.5	−17.0	6.1
1977	− 5.2	−11.5	**41.1**	8.6	− 6.4	4.8
1978	23.5	1.1	2.7	3.8	**46.6**	23.5
1979	2.2	12.3	4.4	−12.4	17.0	**38.5**
1980	6.9	25.9	**27.1**	− 4.6	9.1	25.1
1981	**16.1**	− 9.7	7.2	− 0.6	−17.6	−13.9
1982	4.1	14.7	**22.1**	12.5	8.6	1.6
1983	23.3	17.3	23.1	36.5	**56.4**	28.6
1984	24.8	1.4	**26.0**	6.4	15.8	− 5.9
1985	14.6	26.4	15.2	**74.8**	46.5	20.8
1986	49.2	14.6	22.3	5.5	**49.7**	5.7
1987	**10.4**	2.0	4.2	−36.4	−29.4	3.1
Average	11.4	6.6	**18.3**	6.7	11.5	7.8

Note: Best-performing market each year is indicated in bold type.
Source: "World Investment Strategy Highlights" (London: Goldman, Sachs International Corp., March 1988). Reprinted with permission from Goldman, Sachs & Co.

MONEY MARKET FUNDS. Money market funds are companies that generally invest in high-quality money market instruments like T-bills, high-grade commercial paper (public short-term loans) from various corporations and large CDs from the major money center banks. The yields on the money market portfolios are always above those on normal bank CDs, because the investment by the money market fund is larger and the fund can commit to a longer maturity than the typical individual. In addition, the returns on the commercial paper the fund acquires are above the prime rate. The typical minimum initial investment is $1,000. There is no sales commission, and minimum additions are $250 to $500. Notably, you can always withdraw funds from your money market fund without penalty, and you receive interest to the day of withdrawal. Because of the high yields available and the extreme flexibility and liquidity, these funds have grown to over $200 billion in 1988.

BOND FUNDS. Bond funds generally invest in various long-term government, corporate, or municipal bonds. They differ in terms of the bond quality ratings assigned to bonds in the fund by various rating services. Specifically, the funds range from those that invest only in risk-free government bonds to those that concentrate in lower-rated corporate or municipal bonds, also referred to as *high-yield* or *junk bonds.*

COMMON STOCK FUNDS. Common stock funds invest in a variety of common stocks depending upon the stated investment objective, which can range from income stocks to growth stocks to gold-mining stocks. Recently numerous *sector funds* have been created that concentrate in one industry or narrow sector of the economy, such as chemicals, electric utilities, health, housing, and technology. These funds are diversified within a sector but forego broad diversification across the total market, so an investor in one of these funds can do much better or worse than the aggregate market.

BALANCED FUNDS. Balanced funds invest in a combination of bonds and stocks of various sorts depending on the stated objective of the fund.

SPECIAL EQUITY INSTRUMENTS

In addition to straight common stock investments, it is also possible to invest in *options* to acquire common stock at a specified price. The two major option instruments available are *warrants* and *puts and calls*.

WARRANTS. As indicated earlier in the discussion of fixed-income investments, a warrant is an option issued by a corporation that gives the holder the right to acquire a firm's common stock from the company at a specified price within a designated time period. The warrant does not constitute ownership of the stock, only the option to buy the stock.

OPTIONS. A call option is similar to a warrant since it is an option to buy the common stock of a company at a specified price (referred to as the *striking price*) within a certain period. The call option differs from a warrant because it is not issued by the company but by another investor willing to "write" such an option, and also it is typically for a much shorter period (less than a year versus over five years for warrants).

A put option allows the holder to sell a given stock at a specified price during a designated time period. It is used by investors who expect the stock price to decline during that period or by investors who own the stock and want *downside* protection (i.e., protection from a price decline).

In addition to options on individual stocks, options are also available on major stock market indicator series such as Standard & Poor's 500 Index, the NYSE Composite series, and the Value Line Composite Average. (These market indicator series are discussed in Chapter 4, and options are considered in Chapter 22.)

FOREIGN EQUITIES. American citizens think nothing of buying TV sets and automobiles produced by companies in Japan, Germany, and France, but they seldom consider the common stock of these firms. This is a mistake, because the earnings of many foreign firms have grown substantially as a result of increasing sales to the U.S. market. In addition, foreign equities are attractive because of the diversification possibilities they offer due to the different sales and earnings patterns of foreign companies compared to U.S. firms.[7] The correlation between the rates of return on foreign stocks and U.S. stocks is much lower than it is among alternative U.S. stocks.

---

[7] Chapter 19 contains a detailed analysis of international diversification, including a discussion of prior empirical studies of this topic.

There are several ways to acquire foreign common stocks:

- Direct purchase or sale of foreign shares in the United States, at a foreign stock exchange or at the stock exchange in the country where the firm is located
- Purchase or sale of "American shares"
- Purchase or sale of American Depository Receipts (ADRs)
- Purchase or sale of international mutual funds

The most difficult and complicated transaction takes place in the country where the firm is located, because it must be carried out in the foreign currency and the shares then transferred to the United States. This routine can be cumbersome, especially if it is not done very often. A second alternative, the transaction in a foreign exchange outside the country (such as buying shares of a French firm on the London Exchange), is easier. In this example, the shares would be denominated in pounds and the transfer process should be swift, assuming the broker has a membership or connection on the London Exchange. Finally, one could purchase a select number of foreign stocks that are listed on the New York or American Stock Exchange, which is similar to buying a U.S. stock. While only a limited number of foreign firms qualify for listing and are willing to accept the cost of it, the number is growing (as of the end of 1987, there were 67 foreign firms listed on the NYSE).[8] A somewhat similar alternative is the purchase of so-called American shares, which is the purchase of securities issued in the United States by a transfer agent acting on behalf of the foreign firm. Again, because of the added effort and expense incurred by the foreign firm, there is a limited number of American shares available.

Clearly, the best way to acquire foreign shares directly is through *American Depository Receipts (ADRs)*—certificates of ownership issued by a U.S. bank that holds the shares in safekeeping as a convenience to a potential investor. These ADRs can be issued at the discretion of the bank, based upon the potential demand for the stock. The shareholder absorbs the additional handling costs through higher transfer expenses that are deducted from dividend payments.[9]

The final alternative for participation is the purchase or sale of *international mutual funds* that invest all or a portion of their funds in stocks of firms outside the United States. The alternatives range from *global funds* that invest in the U.S. stocks but also in foreign stocks to *international funds* that invest almost wholly outside the United States. In turn, international funds can (1) diversify across many countries, (2) concentrate in a segment of the world (e.g., the Pacific basin), or (3) concentrate in a specific country (e.g., the Japan Fund, the Korea Fund). Clearly a mutual fund is the easiest path to global investing, since the purchase or sale of

[8] The listing requirements for the major exchanges are discussed in Chapter 3.

[9] A detailed discussion of the ADR process and the numerous stocks that are available is considered in Chapter 19. Many of the stocks listed on the exchanges are in the form of ADRs.

one of these funds is no different from a transaction for a comparable U.S. mutual fund.

In summary, non–U.S. equities constitute almost 70 percent of the world market, and they offer excellent opportunities to experience superior rates of return and reduce the risk of your total portfolio. Therefore, it is worth the effort to become familiar with these opportunities.

COMMODITIES TRADING

Most individuals with excess funds to invest will consider buying stocks or bonds, but very few investors ever consider trading commodities. While some characteristics of commodities trading probably justify caution, many aspects of this trading are very similar to buying and selling stock.[10] As an investor you should be aware of the similarities between stocks and commodities and not be intimidated by some of the unique characteristics of commodity trading.

SPOT CONTRACTS. In one sense, the commodity exchanges function like any other market, simply dealing in the purchase and sale of commodities (corn, wheat, etc.) for current delivery and consumption. This necessary function brings together those who produce commodities (farmers) and those who consume them (food processors). Anyone who wants to buy a commodity for current delivery goes to a *spot market* and acquires the available supply. There is a spot market for each commodity and prices fluctuate depending upon current supply and demand.

FUTURE CONTRACTS. The bulk of trading on the commodity exchanges is in *future contracts,* which are contracts for the delivery of a commodity at some future date, usually within nine months. The price reflects what the participants believe the future will be for the commodity. In July of a given year one could speculate on the future prices for wheat on the Chicago Board of Trade in September and December and in March and May of the next year. If investors expected the price to rise, they could buy contracts now and sell them later; if they expected the prices to fall, they could sell contracts now and buy similar contracts later to cover the sale when the price declines. The number of commodities available for trading is quite large and increasing over time, as shown by the quotations in *The Wall Street Journal.*

Several factors distinguish investing in commodities from investing in stocks. One of these is the greater use of leverage, which increases the volatility of returns. Specifically, because an investor puts up only a small proportion of the value of the contract (10 to 15 percent), when the price of the commodity changes, the change in the *total* value of the contract is large compared to the amount invested. Another unique aspect is the term of the investment. While stocks can have an infinite maturity, commodity contracts are almost never for more than a year.

---

[10] Similarities and differences are considered in Chapter 24, where commodities are discussed in detail.

FINANCIAL FUTURES. In addition to futures contracts on commodities, a recent innovation has been the introduction of futures contracts on financial instruments such as T-bills and Treasury bonds. These futures contracts allow bond portfolio managers and financial managers to hedge against volatile interest rates. There are also currency futures that can be used to speculate on or hedge against changes in exchange rates. These are discussed in detail in Chapter 25, along with futures on stock market series such as the S&P (Standard and Poor's) 500, and the Value Line Index.

REAL ESTATE

Real estate investments are somewhat like commodities in that most investors consider this area interesting and probably profitable but believe that it is limited to a select group of experts with large capital bases. The fact is, there are feasible real estate investments that do not require large capital commitments. We will begin our discussion by considering low-capital alternatives.

REAL ESTATE INVESTMENT TRUSTS (REIT). An REIT is basically a closed-end mutual fund (these terms are defined in Chapter 21) designed to invest in various real estate properties. The idea is similar to a common stock mutual fund except that the funds are used to invest in property and buildings rather than in stocks and bonds. There are several types of REITs.

Construction and development trusts lend the money required during the initial construction of a building or shopping center. *Mortgage trusts* are involved in long-term financing of various properties, acquiring the long-term mortgage once the construction is completed.

Equity trusts own various income-producing properties such as office buildings, shopping centers, or apartment houses, so an investor who buys an equity trust is buying a portfolio of income-producing properties. REITs have experienced periods of great popularity and significant depression in line with changes in the aggregate economy and the money market. While they are subject to unique cyclical risks, it appears that the concept is viable for investors interested in real estate investments.[11]

DIRECT REAL ESTATE INVESTMENTS. The most common type of direct real estate investment is the purchase of a home, the largest investment most people ever make. Today a single-family house usually costs over $95,000.[12] The purchase of a home is considered an investment because, as the buyer, you are committing a sum of money for a number of years that you hope to get back along with some excess return when the house is sold. The financial commitment includes a down payment (typically 10 to 20 percent

---

[11] Mary Greenbaum, "The Return of the REITs," *Fortune,* (May 18, 1981): 111–112; Diane Harris, "Prime REITs for Would-Be Moguls," *Money* (April 1984): 93–96.

[12] The average price of a new home in early 1988 was in excess of $100,000 according to the Federal Home Loan Bank.

of the purchase price) and specific payments made over a 20- to 30-year period.

RAW LAND. Another form of direct real estate investment is the purchase of raw land with the intent of selling it in the future at a profit. Since it is necessary to make mortgage payments and pay all taxes until you sell the lot, an obvious risk is the general lack of liquidity of such an asset compared to most stocks and bonds.

APARTMENT BUILDINGS. It is possible to acquire an apartment building with a low down payment, then derive enough from the rents to pay the expenses of the building, including the mortgage payments. For the first few years following the purchase, there is generally no reported income from the building because of deductible expenses, including depreciation. Subsequently, there is a cash flow and an opportunity to profit from the sale of the building.[13]

LAND DEVELOPMENT. The idea of buying raw land, dividing it into individual lots, and building houses on it is a feasible form of investment, but such an undertaking requires a substantial commitment of capital, time, and expertise. Clearly, the rates of return from a successful housing development can be significant.[14]

LOW-LIQUIDITY INVESTMENTS

Most of the investment alternatives mentioned thus far are generally traded on national markets and have good liquidity. While the investments discussed in this section are viable alternatives for individual investors, they are typically not considered by financial institutions, because they are fairly illiquid and have high transaction costs. Many of these assets are sold at auctions, and there is substantial uncertainty regarding the expected price under such conditions. Further, as mentioned, the transaction cost on these investments is usually very high compared to that on bonds and stocks. The reason is that there is no national market for these investments, so local dealers must be compensated for the added carrying costs and the cost of searching for buyers or sellers. Given these disadvantages, low-liquidity investments are viewed by many observers as being more in the nature of hobbies, even though the rates of return can be substantial.

ANTIQUES. The obvious antique investors are dealers who acquire them in order to refurbish and sell them at a profit. Based upon the value of antiques established at large public auctions, it appears that returns to serious collectors may be substantial, but there can be liquidity problems for the normal antiques owned by individuals. The subsequent discussion of rates of return on various assets will provide some evidence on returns.

---

[13] For a discussion of this alternative, see Diane Harris, "An Investment for Rent." *Money* (April 1984): 87–90.

[14] For a review of studies that have examined returns on real estate, see G. Stacy Sirmans and C. F. Sirmans, "The Historical Perspective of Real Estate Returns," *Journal of Portfolio Management* 13, no. 3 (Spring 1987): 22–31. What these returns and risk measures imply for portfolio management is discussed in James R. Webb and Jack A. Rubens, "How Much in Real Estate? A Surprising Answer," *Journal of Portfolio Management* 13, no. 3 (Spring 1987): 10–14.

ART. Some paintings have experienced significant increases in value and thereby generated large rates of return for the owner/investor.[15] However, using art as an investment vehicle typically requires substantial knowledge, a large capital base to acquire the work of well-known artists, and an ability to absorb high transaction costs.

COINS AND STAMPS. The market for coins and stamps is fragmented compared to the stock market, but it is more liquid than the market for art and antiques. Indeed, the volume of coins and stamps traded has prompted the publication of weekly and monthly price lists.[16] An investor can get a widely recognized grading specification on a coin or stamp and, once graded, a coin or stamp can usually be sold quite quickly through a dealer. Again, it is important to recognize that the *spread* between the price the dealer will pay to buy the stamp or coin (the *bid*) and the selling price from the dealer (the *ask*) is going to be fairly large compared to the spread on stocks and bonds.

DIAMONDS. While diamonds can be and have been good investments during many periods, it is important to recognize that (1) they can be very illiquid, (2) the grading process is generally quite subjective, (3) most investment-grade gems require substantial investments, and (4) there is no positive cash flow during the holding period until the stone is sold. In addition, during the holding period there are costs related to insurance and storage, and subsequently there are appraisal costs before selling.[17]

HISTORICAL RETURNS ON ALTERNATIVE INVESTMENTS

Numerous studies have considered the rates of return available on common stocks. Now a growing interest in bonds has prompted several studies on their performance as well. In deference to the impact of inflation, some studies have examined the *nominal* versus *real* rates of return on investments. A few have examined the performance of other assets such as real estate, foreign stocks, art, antiques, and commodities. This section contains a review of some of the major studies.

STOCKS, BONDS, AND T-BILLS

A set of studies by Ibbotson and Sinquefield examined historical nominal and real rates of return for six major classes of assets in the United States: (1) common stocks, (2) small capitalization stocks, (3) long-term U.S. government bonds, (4) long-term corporate bonds, (5) U.S. Treasury bills,

---

[15] Two recent popular examples were the sale of two paintings by Van Gogh: "Irises" for $53.9 million and "The Sunflowers" for $36 million. For a full listing and discussion of art sold at auction, see Jerry E. Patterson, "A Dazzling Year," *Institutional Investor*, International Edition (September 1987): 324–339.

[16] A weekly publication for coins is *Coin World* by Amos Press Inc., 911 Vandemark Rd., Sidney, Oh. 45367. There are several monthly coin magazines, including *Coinage* (Encino, Calif.: Behn-Miller Publications, Inc.). Amos Press also publishes several stamp magazines, including *Linn's Stamp News* and *Scott Stamp Monthly*. These magazines provide current prices for coins and stamps and articles on investing in these assets.

[17] For a discussion of problems and opportunities, see "When to Put Your Money into Gems," *Business Week*, March 16, 1981, 158–161.

and (6) consumer goods (a measure of inflation).[18] For each asset, the authors calculated total rates of return reflecting dividend or interest income as well as capital gains or losses (there was no adjustment for taxes or transaction costs).

Given the monthly and annual rates of return, the authors computed geometric and arithmetic mean returns as well as nine monthly returns series derived from the basic series. Four of these were net returns reflecting different premiums. The first was a *risk premium*—the net return from investing in common stocks rather than in risk-free U.S. Treasury bills. There was also a *small stock premium*—the return on small capitalization stocks minus the return on total stocks (the S&P 500). The third was a *maturity premium*—the net return derived from investing in long-term government bonds rather than short-term U.S. Treasury bills. Finally was the *default premium*—the difference in net returns between long-term risky corporate bonds and long-term risk-free government bonds. The authors also derived five inflation-adjusted returns for the initial five series—"real" returns for common stocks, small capitalization stocks, Treasury bills, long-term government bonds, and long-term corporate bonds.

A summary of the results for the basic and derived series is contained in Table 2.3. The geometric mean returns are always lower than the arithmetic returns, and the difference increases with the standard deviation of returns.[19]

Over the period of 1926 to 1987, all common stocks returned 9.9 percent a year compounded annually and experienced a risk premium of 6.2 percent and inflation-adjusted real returns of 6.6 percent per year. Small capitalization stocks (i.e., the smallest 20 percent of stocks measured by market value listed on the NYSE) experienced a geometric mean return of 12.1 percent and an arithmetic return of 17.7 percent. The geometric mean premium return for these small firms compared to the broad cross section of stocks was 2.0 percent; the arithmetic mean premium was 3.7 percent.

Although common stocks experienced higher rates of return than the other asset groups, their returns were also more volatile as measured by the standard deviation of annual returns. These results for the small capitalization stocks should be kept in mind when reading Chapter 6 on efficient markets, since a number of studies have examined this relative performance in detail.

Over the period of 1926 to 1987 long-term U.S. government bonds experienced a 4.3 percent annual return, a real return of 1.2 percent, and a maturity premium (compared to Treasury Bills) of 0.8 percent. The returns on these bonds were far less volatile than the annual returns on common stocks.

---

[18] The original study was Roger G. Ibbotson and Rex A. Sinquefield, "Stocks, Bonds, Bills and Inflation: Year-by-Year Historical Returns (1926–1974)," *Journal of Business* 49, no. 1 (January 1976): 11–47. While it was updated in several monographs, the current update is contained in *Stocks, Bonds, Bills, and Inflation: 1988 Yearbook* (Chicago: Ibbotson Associates).

[19] The difference between the arithmetic and geometric mean is discussed in the appendix to this chapter. Readers not familiar with the difference should read this before proceeding further.

TABLE 2.3
Basic and Derived Series: Historical Highlights (1926–1987)

SERIES	ANNUAL GEOMETRIC MEAN RATE OF RETURN	ARITHMETIC MEAN OF ANNUAL RETURNS	STANDARD DEVIATION OF ANNUAL RETURNS
Common stocks	9.9%	12.0%	21.1%
Small capitalization stocks	12.1	17.7	35.9
Long-term corporate bonds	4.9	5.2	8.5
Long-term government bonds	4.3	4.6	8.5
U.S. Treasury bills	3.5	3.5	3.4
Consumer Price Index	3.0	3.2	4.8
Equity risk premium	6.2	8.3	21.1
Small stock premium	2.0	3.7	19.0
Default premium	0.6	0.7	3.0
Maturity premium	0.8	1.1	8.0
Common stock—inflation adjusted	6.6	8.8	21.2
Small capitalization stocks—inflation adjusted	8.8	14.2	35.2
Long-term corporate bonds—inflation adjusted	1.8	2.3	10.0
Long-term government bonds—inflation adjusted	1.2	1.7	10.2
U.S. Treasury bills—inflation adjusted	0.4	0.5	4.4

Source: Ibbotson, Roger G., and Rex A. Sinquefield, Stocks, Bonds, Bills, and Inflation (SBBI), 1982, updated in *SBBI 1987 Yearbook*, Ibbotson Associates Inc., Chicago. Reprinted with permission.

Over the total period the annual compound rate of return on long-term corporate bonds was 4.9 percent, the default premium was only 0.6 percent, and the inflation-adjusted return was 1.8 percent. The volatility of corporate and government bonds was equal.

During the entire period, the nominal return on U.S. Treasury bills was 3.5 percent a year, while the inflation-adjusted return was 0.4 percent. The standard deviation of nominal returns was the lowest of all of the series examined, although the inflation-adjusted T-bill series was more volatile.

This study indicated that the rates of returns on various asset groups were generally consistent with the uncertainty of annual returns as measured by the standard deviation of annual returns.

WORLD PORTFOLIO ANALYSIS

Ibbotson, Siegel, and Love examined the performance of numerous assets, not only in the United States, but in the world.[20] Specifically, for the period of 1960 to 1984 they constructed a value-weighted portfolio of equities, bonds, cash, real estate, and monetary metal from the United States, Northern and Western Europe, Japan, Hong Kong, Singapore, Canada, and Australia. The analysis considered annual returns and risk measures, as well as cross correlations. Table 2.4 contains a summary of the average annual

[20] Roger G. Ibbotson, Laurence B. Siegel, and Kathryn S. Love, "World Wealth: Market Values and Returns," *Journal of Portfolio Management* 12, no. 1 (Fall 1985): 4–23.

TABLE 2.4
World Capital Market Total Annual Returns 1960–1984

	COMPOUND RETURN[a]	ARITHMETIC MEAN	STANDARD DEVIATION[b]	COEFF. VAR.[c]
Equities				
United States	8.81%	10.20%	16.89%	1.66
Foreign				
Europe	7.83	8.94	15.58	1.74
Asia	15.14	18.42	30.74	1.67
Other	8.14	10.21	20.88	2.04
Equities total	9.08	10.21	15.28	1.46
Bonds				
United States				
Corporate[d]	5.35	5.75	9.63	1.67
Government	5.91	6.10	6.43	1.05
United States total	5.70	5.93	7.16	1.21
Foreign				
Corporate domestic	8.35	8.58	7.26	0.85
Government domestic	5.79	6.04	7.41	1.23
Crossborder	7.51	7.66	5.76	0.75
Foreign total	6.80	7.01	6.88	0.98
Bonds total	6.36	6.50	5.56	0.86

	COMPOUND RETURN[a]	ARITHMETIC MEAN	STANDARD DEVIATION[b]	COEFF. VAR.[c]
Cash equivalents				
United States	6.49	6.54	3.22	0.49
Foreign	6.00	6.23	7.10	1.14
Cash total	6.38	6.42	2.92	0.45
Real Estate[e]				
Business	8.49	8.57	4.16	0.49
Residential	8.86	8.93	3.77	0.42
Farms	11.86	12.13	7.88	0.65
Real Estate total	9.44	9.49	3.45	0.36
Metals				
Silver	9.14	20.51	75.34	3.67
Gold	9.08	12.62	29.87	2.37
Metals total	9.11	12.63	29.69	2.35
U.S. market wealth portfolio	8.63	8.74	5.06	0.58
Foreign market wealth portfolio	7.76	8.09	8.48	1.05
World market wealth portfolios				
Excluding metals	8.34	8.47	5.24	0.62
Including metals	8.39	8.54	5.80	0.68
U.S. inflation rate	5.24	5.30	3.60	0.68

[a]Equal to geometric mean.

[b]Standard deviation from arithmetic mean.

[c]Coefficient of variation equals standard deviation/arithmetic mean.

[d]Including preferred stock.

[e]United States only.

Source: Roger G. Ibbotson, Laurence B. Siegel, and Kathryn S. Love, "World Wealth: Market Values and Returns," *The Journal of Portfolio Management* 12, no. 1 (Fall 1985): 4–23. Reprinted with permission.

TABLE 2.5
Correlation Matrix of World Capital Market Security Returns

	U.S. EQUITIES	U.S. CORPORATE BONDS	U.S. GOVT. BONDS	TOTAL U.S. BONDS	U.S. CASH	BUS. REAL ESTATE
U.S. equities	1.000	0.323	−0.006	−0.166	−0.079	0.164
Europe equities	0.640	0.117	−0.201	−0.045	−0.178	0.286
Asia equities	0.237	0.033	0.067	−0.007	−0.159	0.218
Other equities	0.807	0.019	−0.296	−0.160	−0.112	0.243
Foreign total equities	0.672	0.075	−0.226	−0.074	−0.162	0.332
World total equities	0.964	0.243	−0.105	0.075	0.125	0.233
U.S. corporate bonds and perferred stock	0.323	1.000	0.863	0.962	0.136	0.152
U.S. government bonds	−0.006	0.863	1.000	0.967	0.332	0.206
U.S. total bonds	0.166	0.962	0.967	1.000	−0.247	0.192
Foreign domestic corporate bonds	0.050	0.264	0.085	0.180	−0.265	0.165
Foreign domestic government bonds	−0.024	0.265	0.117	0.192	−0.217	0.249
Crossborder bonds	0.255	0.807	0.607	0.721	−0.054	0.203
Foreign total bonds (incl. Crossborders)	0.052	0.323	0.153	0.242	−0.234	0.228
World total bonds	0.124	0.692	0.561	0.646	−0.085	0.256
U.S. cash	0.079	0.136	0.332	−0.247	1.000	0.681
Foreign cash	−0.386	−0.225	0.143	−0.192	0.010	0.231
World total cash	−0.238	−0.029	0.236	−0.141	0.891	0.705
Business real estate	0.164	0.152	0.206	0.192	0.681	1.000
Residential real estate	0.125	−0.030	0.066	0.017	0.497	0.493
Farm real estate	0.171	0.273	0.267	−0.274	−0.046	0.016
U.S. total real estate	0.054	−0.123	0.040	−0.082	0.405	0.318
Gold	−0.088	−0.323	−0.206	−0.280	0.210	0.586
Silver	0.116	−0.187	−0.109	−0.153	0.123	0.188
World total metals	−0.086	−0.326	−0.207	−0.282	0.207	0.220
U.S. market wealth portfolio	0.917	0.393	0.152	0.284	0.130	0.394
Foreign market wealth portfolio	0.510	0.236	−0.083	0.080	−0.258	0.329
World market wealth portfolio (excl. metals)	0.861	0.377	0.066	0.231	−0.037	0.407
World market wealth portfolio (incl. metals)	0.757	0.207	−0.023	0.093	−0.004	0.390

Source: Adapted from Roger G. Ibbotson, Laurence B. Siegel, and Kathryn S. Love, "World Wealth: Market Values and Return," *The Journal of Portfolio Management* 12, no. 1 (Fall 1985): 4–23. Reprinted with permission.

rates of return (both geometric and arithmetic), the standard deviation of returns, and the coefficient of variation for the period of 1960 to 1984.

INDIVIDUAL ASSET RETURN AND RISK. The results in Table 2.4 are generally consistent with expectations in terms of the annual rates of return and the risk related to these returns as measured by the standard deviation. For example, silver had the highest arithmetic rate of return (20.51 percent), but also the largest standard deviation (75.34) while U.S. cash equivalents had fairly low returns (6.29 percent) and the smallest standard deviation (3.10).

RESIDENTIAL STRUCTURES	FARM LAND	TOTAL REAL ESTATE	GOLD	SILVER	U.S. MARKET PORT.	WORLD MARKET INC. METALS
0.125	−0.171	0.054	0.088	0.116	0.917	0.757
0.202	−0.097	0.156	0.032	0.052	0.605	0.706
−0.080	−0.003	−0.033	0.046	−0.181	0.209	0.351
0.356	−0.063	0.288	0.140	0.410	0.754	0.753
0.141	−0.065	0.129	0.044	−0.020	0.626	0.732
0.133	−0.139	0.083	−0.058	−0.070	0.886	0.805
−0.030	−0.273	−0.123	−0.323	−0.187	0.393	0.207
0.055	−0.267	−0.040	−0.206	0.109	0.152	−0.023
0.107	0.274	−0.082	−0.280	−0.153	0.284	0.093
0.091	0.176	0.164	0.001	0.286	0.153	0.380
0.293	0.103	0.303	0.107	−0.054	0.171	0.426
0.108	0.049	0.123	−0.046	−0.076	0.395	0.404
0.225	0.125	0.256	0.062	−0.136	0.191	0.429
0.191	−0.013	0.172	−0.079	−0.177	0.288	0.389
0.447	−0.046	0.405	0.210	0.123	0.130	−0.004
0.317	0.306	0.399	0.419	−0.203	−0.233	0.105
0.528	0.096	0.529	0.366	−0.014	0.103	0.046
0.493	0.016	0.518	0.219	0.188	0.394	0.390
1.000	0.214	0.916	0.586	0.532	0.442	0.552
0.214	1.000	0.570	0.517	0.351	−0.019	0.133
0.916	0.570	1.000	0.684	0.580	0.371	0.531
0.586	0.517	0.684	1.000	0.438	0.104	0.427
0.532	0.351	0.580	0.438	1.000	0.291	0.283
0.596	0.526	0.696	0.999	0.477	0.111	0.427
0.422	−0.019	0.371	0.104	0.291	1.000	0.873
0.174	−0.008	0.177	0.025	−0.110	0.533	0.727
0.365	−0.014	0.332	0.075	0.142	0.925	0.924
0.552	0.133	0.531	0.427	0.283	0.873	1.000

INDIVIDUAL ASSET RELATIVE RISK. The coefficients of variation (CV), which indicate *relative* variability, displayed a wide range of values. The lowest CVs were experienced by the cash equivalents and the various real estate investments. Silver had the highest CV value because of its very large standard deviation, and corporate bonds the next highest because of a relatively small mean return. The equity CVs ranged from 1.46 to 2.04, with the U.S. equity market about in the middle (1.66). Finally, the world market portfolios had rather low CVs (0.62 and 0.68), evidencing the benefits of international diversification as related to risk.

TABLE 2.6
Annual Rates of Return for Sotheby's Indexes, The S&P 500 Stock, Bond Market Series, One-Year Government Bonds, and Inflation 1976–1987 (September Year End)

	OLD MAST.	19C EURO.	IMPR. PT.-IM.	MOD. PAINT.	AMER. PAINT.	CONT. CERAM.	CHIN. CERAM.	ENGL. SILVER	CONT. SILVER
1976	5.00	− 1.00	7.00	5.00	29.00	21.00	59.00	−11.00	−11.00
1977	24.76	19.19	6.54	2.86	32.56	27.27	13.84	6.74	3.37
1978	32.06	35.59	16.67	22.22	49.12	38.31	33.15	30.53	22.83
1979	29.48	34.37	31.58	34.85	23.53	22.54	46.47	33.07	29.20
1980	13.83	4.65	17.71	14.61	11.11	28.74	30.88	24.24	22.60
1981	−21.96	−21.78	16.02	13.73	21.14	−11.01	− 0.65	−21.95	−20.11
1982	0.00	3.98	6.69	5.60	8.26	−11.04	0.22	14.38	− 6.29
1983	9.04	7.65	16.86	12.24	9.15	2.26	− 3.26	19.67	16.42
1984	15.62	11.67	6.38	9.45	17.57	4.41	8.32	8.22	3.21
1985	15.13	13.18	17.03	13.62	7.81	0.00	0.82	25.74	10.56
1986	4.84	0.40	16.44	25.44	8.19	2.11	0.00	13.42	7.87
1987	15.18	21.20	53.01	55.24	14.85	10.35	13.17	3.25	4.69
Means:									
Arith.	11.92	10.76	17.66	17.91	19.36	11.24	16.83	12.19	6.94
Geom.	10.98	9.68	17.04	17.12	18.78	10.18	15.26	10.98	5.99
Std. dev.	14.50	15.84	13.26	14.93	12.62	16.09	20.76	16.49	14.64
Coeff. var.	1.22	1.47	0.75	0.83	0.65	1.43	1.23	1.35	2.11

Source: Frank K. Reilly, "Risk and Returns on Art and Antiques: The Sotheby's Indexes," Eastern Finance Association Meeting, April 1987. (Updated June 1988.)

CORRELATIONS AMONG ASSET RETURNS. Table 2.5 presents a correlation matrix of major U.S. and world assets. The first column indicates that U.S. equities have reasonably high correlation with European equities (0.640) and other foreign equities (0.807) but rather low correlation with Asian equities (0.237). Also, U.S. equities have a negative correlation with U.S. government bonds (-0.006), farm real estate (-0.171), and gold (-0.088). High positive correlations indicate investments that should be avoided if you wish to diversify. Low positive or negative correlations indicate assets that you should consider seriously for diversification purposes. Beyond these suggestions, the correlations in Table 2.5 can help you select other investments that would provide good diversification alternatives for your portfolio.

ART AND ANTIQUES

There is not much known about the rates of return and risk on art and antiques because the markets are very fragmented, and there is very little reporting of transaction prices. The best-known indexes of art and antiques were developed by Sotheby Parke Bernet, better known as Sotheby's, one of the major art auction firms in the world. This index covers 12 areas of art and antiques plus a weighted aggregate series. Reilly examined these series for the period of 1975 to 1987 in terms of rates of return, measures

AMER. FURN.	FR. CONT. FURN.	ENGL. FURN.	FIXED WT. INDEX	UNWTD. INDEX	VALUE WT. INDEX	ONE-YR. T BOND	SLHGC BD. -IND.	S&P 500	CPI
9.00	4.00	25.00	11.09	11.75	11.75	5.35	16.66	30.45	5.48
10.10	16.35	24.80	15.17	15.70	16.41	4.83	8.65	− 4.15	6.60
11.67	22.31	25.00	28.01	28.29	29.47	6.45	2.76	11.94	8.23
11.94	33.11	25.13	32.31	29.61	29.79	9.67	3.81	12.45	12.19
14.67	17.77	4.92	16.82	17.14	17.50	10.80	− 1.55	21.14	12.67
21.51	− 6.04	5.47	− 3.47	− 2.14	− 1.75	14.77	− 1.26	− 2.73	10.97
1.91	7.34	− 2.59	2.71	2.37	2.18	11.93	33.51	9.97	5.02
12.21	8.55	17.49	9.45	10.69	9.31	8.48	15.26	44.25	2.89
0.84	6.30	16.51	9.89	9.04	9.79	9.65	8.61	4.79	4.22
34.44	1.11	6.11	11.16	12.13	10.72	8.22	21.17	14.77	3.18
17.28	4.40	17.02	10.04	9.78	9.93	6.77	20.67	31.70	1.75
18.95	11.93	32.89	28.52	21.23	22.88	5.48	− 0.38	43.36	4.29
13.71	10.59	16.48	14.31	13.80	14.00	8.53	10.66	18.16	6.46
13.40	10.15	16.01	13.86	13.45	13.62	8.50	10.18	17.15	6.40
8.95	10.50	10.81	10.67	9.39	9.75	3.00	10.96	16.30	3.73
0.65	0.99	0.66	0.75	0.68	0.70	0.35	1.03	0.90	0.58

of risk, and the correlation among the series.[21] Table 2.6 shows these data plus returns for one-year Treasury bonds, the Shearson Lehman Hutton Government/Corporate Bond Index, the Standard & Poor's 500 Stock Index, and the annual inflation rate as indicated by the Consumer Price Index.[22]

These results indicate that you cannot generalize about the performance of art and antiques. As shown, the average annual compound rates of return (i.e., the geometric means) ranged from about 19 percent (American paintings) to about 6 percent (continental silver). Similarly, the standard deviations varied from 21 percent (Chinese ceramics) to about 9 percent (American furniture) while the coefficients of variation varied from about 0.65 (American paintings, American furniture, and English furniture) to 2.11 (continental silver). The ranking on a year-to-year basis likewise changed dramatically over time. The art and antique results compared to the bond and stock indexes indicate that the financial assets provide results about midway among these series.

---

[21] Frank K. Reilly, "Risks and Returns on Art and Antiques: The Sotheby's Indexes," Eastern Finance Association meeting, April 1987. The results reported have been updated through September 1987.

[22] These bond and stock series are described in detail in Chapter 4.

TABLE 2.7
Correlation Coefficients among Annual Rates of Return for Art, Antiques, Stocks, and Bonds (1976–1987)

	OLD MAST.	19C EURO	IMPR. PT. -IM.	MOD PAINT.	AMER. PAINT.	CONT. CERAM.	CHIN. CERAM.
Old Masters	—	—	—	—	—	—	—
19C Euro paint.	0.951	—	—	—	—	—	—
Impr.-pt. imp paint.	0.200	0.361	—	—	—	—	—
Mod. paint.	0.253	0.417	0.960	—	—	—	—
Amer. paint.	0.438	0.443	−0.116	−0.047	—	—	—
Cont. ceramics	0.764	0.645	0.085	0.115	0.699	—	—
Chin. ceramics	0.428	0.368	0.068	0.087	0.564	0.740	—
English silver	0.741	0.730	0.135	0.184	−0.020	0.392	0.097
Cont. silver	0.792	0.752	0.312	0.350	0.090	0.584	0.258
Amer. furn.	−0.135	−0.120	0.382	0.297	−0.233	−0.153	−0.231
Fr. & cont. furn.	0.821	0.834	0.315	0.353	0.414	0.741	0.558
Eng. furn.	0.558	0.574	0.469	0.519	0.532	0.575	0.467
Fixed wt. index	0.843	0.887	0.630	0.672	0.417	0.736	0.559
Unwtd. index	0.887	0.898	0.498	0.543	0.494	0.817	0.606
Value wtd. index	0.875	0.891	0.513	0.565	0.524	0.826	0.610
One-yr. T-bond	−0.604	−0.520	−0.166	−0.210	−0.352	−0.553	−0.321
SLHGC bd. index	−0.190	−0.182	−0.470	−0.433	−0.417	−0.490	−0.315
S&P 500	0.025	0.041	0.494	0.469	−0.364	−0.008	0.049
CPI	0.065	0.068	0.101	0.050	0.352	0.416	0.493

Source: Frank K. Reilly, "Risk and Returns on Art and Antiques: The Sotheby's Indexes," Eastern Finance Association Meeting, April 1987. (Updated June 1988)

The correlation matrix of these assets in Table 2.7 indicates, first, that the correlations between art/antiques and bonds are generally negative while the correlations with stocks are typically quite low. This would suggest that this mix of financial and real assets might provide good diversification. Second, the correlations of some of these assets with the rate of inflation are fairly high, which means that they might be good inflation hedges.[23]

SUMMARY

You should be aware of all investment alternatives—including those in the world capital market[24]—for two reasons. First, until you know the variety of risk and return choices available, you cannot decide on the ones that suit you. For example, one reader, after becoming familiar with commodities trading, may decide that it is much too speculative to be considered, while another may find it very exciting and decide to commit a large share of resources to it. Second, assuming that the rates of return for alternative investments are not highly correlated, the variance of returns for an investor's total portfolio can be substantially reduced through proper diversi-

[23] This concept of an inflation hedge will be discussed in the appendix to Chapter 13.

[24] There are obviously many investment alternatives we are not able to cover. For a collection of articles on alternative investments by various authors, see Leo Barnes and Stephen Feldman, eds., *Handbook of Wealth Management* (New York: McGraw-Hill, 1977).

ENGL. SILVER	CONT. SILVER	AMER. FURN.	FR. CONT. FURN.	ENGL. FURN.	FIXED WT. INDEX	UNWTD. INDEX	VALUE WTD. INDEX	ONE-YR. T BOND	SLHGC BD. -IND.	S&P 500	CPI
—	—	—	—	—	—	—	—	—	—	—	—
—	—	—	—	—	—	—	—	—	—	—	—
—	—	—	—	—	—	—	—	—	—	—	—
—	—	—	—	—	—	—	—	—	—	—	—
—	—	—	—	—	—	—	—	—	—	—	—
—	—	—	—	—	—	—	—	—	—	—	—
—	—	—	—	—	—	—	—	—	—	—	—
—	—	—	—	—	—	—	—	—	—	—	—
0.915	—	—	—	—	—	—	—	—	—	—	—
0.032	0.060	—	—	—	—	—	—	—	—	—	—
0.686	0.795	−0.282	—	—	—	—	—	—	—	—	—
0.005	0.259	−0.098	0.451	—	—	—	—	—	—	—	—
0.576	0.739	0.010	0.850	0.708	—	—	—	—	—	—	—
0.642	0.799	0.016	0.880	0.669	0.979	—	—	—	—	—	—
0.599	0.766	−0.013	0.877	0.690	0.984	0.996	—	—	—	—	—
−0.152	−0.241	−0.005	−0.267	−0.767	−0.526	−0.528	−0.528	—	—	—	—
0.095	−0.242	−0.141	−0.347	−0.411	−0.453	−0.438	−0.477	−0.048	—	—	—
0.111	0.226	0.140	−0.016	0.336	0.246	0.184	0.162	−0.405	0.103	—	—
0.064	0.217	−0.037	0.477	−0.099	0.251	0.296	0.312	0.458	−0.648	−0.438	—

fication that considers the correlations among the returns for various assets.

Studies on the historical rates of return for common stocks and other investment alternatives (including bonds, commodities, real estate, foreign securities, art, and antiques) point toward two generalizations:

1. There is typically a positive relationship between the rate of return earned on an asset and the variability of its historical rate of return. This is expected in a world of risk-averse investors who require a higher rate of return to compensate for more uncertainty.
2. The correlation among rates of return for selected alternative investments is typically quite low—especially for U.S and foreign common stocks and financial assets and real assets as represented by art and antiques. This confirms the advantage of diversification among investments.

QUESTIONS

1. What are the major advantages to investing in the common stock rather than the corporate bonds of the same company? What are the major disadvantages?
2. If you wanted to invest in bonds and limited yourself to only U.S. bonds, what proportion of the world bond market would you be ignoring? Does it seem reasonable to limit yourself in this manner?

3. When you invest in Japanese or German bonds, what is the major risk you must consider besides yield changes within the country? Briefly discuss this risk.

4. Discuss briefly why an investor might prefer utility common stocks to industrial common stocks.

5. If the returns from transportation stocks are not correlated with the returns from financial stocks, discuss whether this will benefit an investor who has both types of stock in his portfolio. Why or why not?

6. How does a bond differ from a common stock in terms of the certainty of returns over time? Draw a simple time-series graph to demonstrate the pattern of returns you envision.

7. You are a wealthy individual in a high tax bracket. Discuss why you would consider investing in a municipal bond rather than a straight corporate bond even though the promised yield on the municipal bond is lower.

8. You can acquire convertible bonds from a growth company or from a utility. Both firms have straight debentures that yield 9 percent. Given the conversion feature, discuss which convertible bond would have the lower yield, and indicate the reason for the difference.

9. Define a spot commodity contract and a future commodities contract.

10. Define an REIT and briefly discuss the alternative types.

11. Discuss the difference in liquidity between an investment in raw land and an investment in common stock. Be specific as to why and how they differ. (Hint: Begin by defining liquidity.)

12. Define a stock warrant and a call option. Discuss how they differ.

13. Why would you expect the returns on foreign stocks to have low correlation with the returns on U.S. stocks? Which results in Table 2.5 do not confirm this expectation; which results support it?

14. Why is it contended that antiques and art are generally illiquid investments? Why are coins and stamps considered to be more liquid than antiques and art? Consider what is required in selling the various assets.

15. You have a fairly large portfolio of U.S. stocks and bonds. You meet a financial planner at a social gathering who suggests that you should consider adding some gold to your portfolio for purposes of diversification. Discuss whether the correlation results in Table 2.5 tend to support this suggestion.

16. You are an avid collector/investor of American paintings. Based upon the results in Table 2.6, how would you probably feel about your results during the period of 1976–1987? You are considering going into another field of art, and you are conscious of the importance of diversification. Based upon the results in Table 2.7, which areas should you avoid and which ones should you consider?

PROBLEMS

1. A contract involves 5,000 bushels of wheat. Since wheat is selling for $3.80 a bushel, the total value of the contract is $19,000, and given a margin of 15 percent, an investor would have to put up $2,850 to purchase it. Ignoring

commissions, if the price of wheat increases to $4.05 a bushel, what is the percentage of change in the value of the contract, and what is the investor's return on the investment? Assuming a decline in price to $3.50 a bushel, what is the rate of return? Show all calculations.

2. Each week in *Barron's* there is a set of stock indexes for foreign countries entitled, "World Stock Markets Indexes." For a recent week, determine the percent change in the index for Japan, Germany, and Australia, and compare this to the percent change in the Dow-Jones Industrial Average for the same period. Do the results indicate any benefits to diversification among securities from these countries? Why or why not?

3. *CFA Examination 1 (June 1980):* The following information is available concerning the historical risk and return relationships in the U.S. capital markets:

U.S. Capital Markets Total Annual Returns, 1947–1978

Investment Category	Arithmetic Mean	Geometric Mean	Standard Deviation of Return[a]
Common stocks	11.80%	10.30%	18.0%
Preferred stocks	3.30	2.90	9.2
Treasury bills	3.53	3.51	2.1
Long government bonds	2.60	2.40	6.2
Long corporate bonds	2.40	2.20	6.7
Real estate	8.19	8.14	3.5

[a] Based upon arithmetic mean.
Source: Adapted from R. G. Ibbotson and C. L. Fall, "The U.S. Market Wealth Portfolio," *The Journal of Portfolio Management.*

3a. Explain why the geometric and arithmetic mean returns are not equal and whether one or the other may be more useful for investment decision making. [5 minutes]

3b. For the time period indicated, rank these investments on a risk-adjusted basis from most to least desirable. Explain your rationale. [6 minutes]

3c. Assume the returns in these series are normally distributed.
   (1) Calculate the range of returns that an investor would expect to achieve 95 percent of the time from holding common stocks. [4 minutes]
   (2) Suppose an investor holds real estate for this time period. Determine the probability of at least breaking even on this investment. [5 minutes]

3d. Assume you are holding a portfolio composed entirely of real estate. Give the justification, if any, for adopting a mixed-asset portfolio by adding long-term government bonds. [5 minutes]

4. The following are average annual rates of return for alternative investment instruments:

U. S. government T-bills	7.50
Common stock	12.25
Long-term corporate bonds	11.50
Long-term government bonds	10.25
Small-capitalization common stock	15.30

On the basis of these returns, compute the following:

4a. The common stock risk premium

4b. The small-firm stock risk premium

4c. The maturity premium

4d. The default premium

5. The annual rate of inflation during the period specified in Problem 4 was 7 percent. Compute the real rate of return on these alternative investment instruments.

REFERENCES

Altman, Edward I., and Scott A. Nammacher. *Investing in Junk Bonds.* New York: John Wiley and Sons, 1987.

Barnes, Leo, and Stephen Feldman, eds. *Handbook of Wealth Management.* New York: McGraw-Hill, 1977.

Brick, John R., H. Kent Baker, and John A. Haslem, eds. *Financial Markets Instruments and Concepts.* 2d ed. Reston, Va.: Reston Publishing Co., Inc., 1986.

Cabeem, Richard. *Standard Handbook of Stamp Collecting.* New York: Thomas Y. Crowell Company, 1957.

Darst, David M. *The Handbook of the Bond and Money Markets.* New York: McGraw-Hill, 1981.

Fabozzi, Frank, and Irving M. Pollack, eds. *The Handbook of Fixed Income Securities.* 2d ed. Homewood, Ill., Dow Jones-Irwin, 1987.

Fisher, Lawrence, and James H. Lorie. *A Half Century of Returns on Stocks and Bonds.* Chicago: University of Chicago Graduate School of Business, 1977.

Ibbotson, Roger G., Laurence B. Siegel, and Kathryn S. Love. "World Wealth: Market Values and Returns." *Journal of Portfolio Management.* 12, no. 1 (Fall 1985).

Reilly, Frank K. "Risks and Returns on Art and Antiques: The Sotheby's Indexes." Eastern Finance Association Meeting, April 1987.

Rush, Richard H. *Antiques as an Investment.* New York: Bonanza Books, 1968.

Rush, Richard H. *Art as an Investment.* Englewood Cliffs, N.J.: Prentice-Hall, 1961.

Stigum, Marcia. *The Money Market: Myth, Reality and Practice.* Homewood, Ill.: Dow Jones-Irwin, 1978.

Teweles, Richard J., Charles V. Harlow, and Herbert L. Stone. *The Commodity Futures Trading Guide.* New York: McGraw-Hill, 1969.

Wilson, Richard S. *Corporate Senior Securities.* Chicago: Probus Publishing Co., 1987.

APPENDIX 2A   GEOMETRIC MEAN RETURNS

To examine the average returns on an investment over an extended period of time, the typical measure used is the *arithmetic average* of annual rates of return. As will be shown, the arithmetic average return can be biased upward if there is substantial variability in the returns over time. An alternative measure of the central tendency is the *geometric mean* of the annual returns. This measure is considered superior by some investigators because it is the same formulation that is used to derive compound interest and so provides a proper measure of the true ending-wealth position for the investment involved.

ARITHMETIC MEAN BIAS

As is known, the arithmetic mean (designated here by $\bar{X}$) is the sum of each value in a distribution divided by the total number of observations.

$$\bar{X} = \Sigma X/n.$$

A problem occurs if there are large changes in the annual returns over time. Consider the example in which a nondividend-paying stock goes from $50 to $100 during Year 1 and back to $50 during Year 2. The annual returns would be

- Year 1: 100%
- Year 2: −50%

Obviously, during the two years there was no return on the investment. Yet, the arithmetic mean return would be

$$[(+100) + (-50)]/2 = 50/2 = 25\%.$$

In this case, although there was no change in wealth, and therefore no return, the arithmetic mean rate of return is computed at 25 percent.

GEOMETRIC MEAN

The geometric mean (designated by G) is the nth root of the product arrived at by multiplying the values in the distribution by each other. Specifically, it is

$$G = \Pi X^{1/n},$$

where Π stands for product. When calculating the geometric mean returns, it is customary to use holding-period returns, which are the yields plus 1.0 (e.g., a positive 10 percent return is designated 1.10 and a negative 15 percent return as 0.85). This is done because a negative yield makes the geometric mean calculation meaningless. As an example of the geometric mean, consider the extreme example used in the previous discussion of the arithmetic mean:

	YIELD (PERCENT)	HOLDING-PERIOD RETURN
Year 1:	100	2.00
Year 2:	-50	0.50

$$G = (2.00 \times 0.50)^{1/2} = (1.00)^{1/2} = 1.00 - 1.00 = 0\%.$$

To get the yield, 1.00 is subtracted from the geometric holding-period return. As can be seen, this answer of a zero rate of return is consistent with the ending-wealth position of the investor. The investor ended where he began and therefore had a 0 percent annual rate of return during the period.

EXTENDED EXAMPLE. Consider the following example using rounded percentage of price changes for a stock market series during a recent ten-year period.

YEAR	PERCENTAGE OF PRICE CHANGE	HOLDING-PERIOD CHANGE
1	15.00	1.15
2	-17.00	0.83
3	-28.00	0.72
4	38.00	1.38
5	18.00	1.18
6	-17.00	0.83
7	$- 3.00$	0.97
8	4.00	1.04
9	12.00	1.12
10	8.00	1.08

$$\bar{X} = \Sigma X/n = 30/10 = 3.0\%$$
$$G = \Pi X^{1/n}$$
$$= 1.1334^{1/10} = 1.012604 - 1.00 = 1.3\%.$$

As shown, the arithmetic mean price change is more than two times as large as the geometric mean price change. Because of the upward bias in the arithmetic mean, it will always be larger (except where all returns are equal), and *the discrepancy will be wider with a more volatile series.* If there is a large difference between the arithmetic mean and the geometric mean, it can be inferred that the returns were very volatile.

PROBLEMS   1. For the following percentage price changes,

YEAR	PERCENTAGE OF PRICE CHANGE
1984	15
1985	−12
1986	18
1987	−02
1988	15

1a. What is the arithmetic mean rate of return?

1b. What is the geometric mean rate of return?

2. As a junior analyst for Hutton, Button and Sutton, you obtain the following data:

YEAR	DIVIDENDS
1981	$ .97
1982	.94
1983	.90
1984	.87
1985	.80
1986	.70
1987	1.65
1988	1.68

2a. What is the 1981 to 1988 growth rate? (Hint: use your compound interest or present value table, with $.97 treated as the original value and $1.68 treated as the ending value.)

2b. What is the growth rate if the first two years are averaged and used as a starting point, and the last two years are averaged and used as the ending point? (Note: 1981.5 is now treated as the starting point and 1987.5 as the ending point.)

2c. What is the geometric mean of the annual percent change of dividends?

2d. Why do the answers in parts a, b, and c differ? Which is the most accurate? Why?

APPENDIX 2B # COVARIANCE AND CORRELATION

COVARIANCE

Since most students have been exposed to the concept of covariance, the following discussion is set forth in intuitive terms with an example to help recall the concept.[1]

Covariance is an absolute measure of the extent to which two sets of numbers move together over time, that is, move up or down together. In this regard "move together" means they are generally above their means or below their means at the same time. Covariance between i and j is defined as

$$Cov_{ij} = \frac{\Sigma(i - \bar{i})(j - \bar{j})}{N}.$$

If we define $(i - \bar{i})$ as i' and $(j - \bar{j})$ as j', then

$$Cov_{ij} = \frac{\Sigma i'j'}{N}.$$

Obviously, if both numbers are consistently above or below their individual means at the same time, their products will be positive, and the average will be a large positive value. In contrast, if the i value is below its mean when the j value is above its mean, or vice versa, their products will be large negative values, and you would find negative covariance. Table 2B.1 should make this clear. In this example the two series generally moved together, so there was positive covariance. As noted, this is an *absolute* measure of their relationship and, therefore, can range from $+\infty$ to $-\infty$. Note that the covariance of a variable with itself is its variance.

CORRELATION

To obtain a relative measure of a given relationship, we use the correlation coefficient (r_{ij}), which is a normalized measure of the relationship:

$$r_{ij} = \frac{Cov_{ij}}{\sigma_i \sigma_j}.$$

You will recall from your introductory statistics course that

$$\sigma_i = \sqrt{\frac{\Sigma(i - \bar{i})^2}{N}}$$

---

[1] A more detailed, rigorous treatment of the subject can be found in any standard statistics text including Ya-lun Chou, *Statistical Analysis* (New York: Holt, Rinehart and Winston, 1975), 152–156.

TABLE 2B.1
Calculation of Covariance

OBSERVATION	i	j	$i - \bar{i}$	$j - \bar{j}$	$i'j'$
1	3	8	-4	-4	16
2	6	10	-1	-2	2
3	8	14	$+1$	$+2$	2
4	5	12	-2	0	0
5	9	13	$+2$	$+1$	2
6	11	15	$+4$	$+3$	12
Σ	42	72			34
Mean	7	12			
Cov_{ij}	$=\dfrac{34}{6}=+5.67$				

so, if two series move completely together, then the covariance would equal $\sigma_i\sigma_j$ and

$$\frac{Cov_{ij}}{\sigma_i\sigma_j} = 1.0.$$

The correlation coefficient would equal unity in this case, and we would say the two series are perfectly correlated. Because we know that

$$r_{ij} = \frac{Cov_{ij}}{\sigma_i\sigma_j},$$

we also know that $Cov_{ij} = r_{ij}\sigma_i\sigma_j$, which is a relationship that may be useful when computing the standard deviation of a portfolio, because, in many instances, the relationship between two securities is stated in terms of the correlation coefficient rather than the covariance.

Continuing the example given in Table 2B.1, the standard deviations are computed in Table 2B.2, as is the correlation between i and j. As shown, the two standard deviations are rather large and similar but not exactly the same. Finally, when the positive covariance is normalized by the product of the two standard deviations, the results indicate a correlation coefficient of .898, which is obviously quite large and close to 1.00. Apparently, these two series are highly related.

PROBLEMS

1. As an analyst for Lerill Mynch, you have calculated the following annual returns for both Alpha-Omega Corporation and Beta-Tau Industries.

YEAR	ALPHA-OMEGA'S RATE OF RETURN	BETA-TAU'S RATE OF RETURN
1984	5	5
1985	12	15
1986	-11	5
1987	10	7
1988	12	-10

TABLE 2B.2
Calculation of Correlation Coefficient

OBSERVATION	$i - \bar{i}$ [a]	$(i - \bar{i})^2$	$j - \bar{j}$ [a]	$(j - \bar{j})^2$
1	-4	16	-4	16
2	-1	1	-2	4
3	$+1$	1	$+2$	4
4	-2	4	0	0
5	$+2$	4	$+1$	1
6	$+4$	$\underline{16}$	$+3$	$\underline{9}$
		42		34

$$\sigma_i^2 = 42/6 = 7.00 \qquad \sigma_j^2 = 34/6 = 5.67$$
$$\sigma_i = \sqrt{7.00} = 2.65 \qquad \sigma_j = \sqrt{5.67} = 2.38$$
$$r_{ij} = Cov_{ij}/\sigma_i\sigma_j = \frac{5.67}{(2.65)(2.38)} = \frac{5.67}{6.31} = .898.$$

[a] from Table 2B.1

Your manager suggests that since these companies produce similar products, he is interested in your calculation of covariance. Derive the covariance number requested and show all calculations.

2. In order to impress your manager, you decide to go the extra step and calculate the coefficient of correlation using the data provided in Problem A1. Prepare a table showing your calculations and include a brief discussion of how to interpret the results.

APPENDIX 2C TAX CONSIDERATIONS

INTRODUCTION

This appendix provides an overview of the tax laws that pertain to investments in stocks, bonds, options, and futures contracts. Consideration is also given to individual retirement accounts and Keogh plans for the self-employed. The information provided should help investors maximize their after-tax rate of return on security transactions as well as augment their retirement income.

DIVIDENDS

Distribution of all or part of a corporation's current or accumulated earnings and profits to its shareholders is called a *dividend*. Any payment in excess of a corporation's current and accumulated earnings and profits is not a dividend but rather a distribution of capital. Capital distributions are usually not taxable to the shareholder, since they reduce the basis of the shareholder's stock. When they exceed the shareholder's basis, *capital gain* results. Dividends are taxable and includable in full in each shareholder's gross income. The dividend exclusion of $100 ($200 on a joint return) available to individual taxpayers prior to 1987 has been repealed by the Tax Reform Act (TRA) of 1986.

CAPITAL GAINS AND LOSSES

Under prior law, individuals preferred to have income classified as a capital gain rather than ordinary income because the capital gain was taxed more favorably. However, the TRA of 1986 repealed the 60 percent capital gains exclusion, and now both long-term and short-term capital gains are taxed like ordinary income. Nevertheless, taxpayers are still required to classify gains and losses as capital versus ordinary. Therefore, it is very important to understand which types of property qualify for capital asset treatment. Section 1221 of the Internal Revenue Code (IRC) explains that investment and personal-use property (stocks, bonds, patents, personal automobiles, personal residences, jewelry, and other personal effects of an individual) are so classified.

Items that specifically do not qualify for capital asset treatment include (1) inventory or stock in trade; (2) copyrights, literary compositions, letters or memorandums, and similar property created by the taxpayer; (3) accounts receivable and notes receivable acquired in the ordinary course of business; (4) depreciable or real property used in a trade or business; and (5) certain U.S. government publications. These items, as a general rule, generate ordinary income or loss when sold or exchanged.

Unrealized gain or loss cannot be included in an individual's computation of capital gains or losses. To be included the property must be disposed of in some manner, usually sold or exchanged.

The TRA of 1986 also requires taxpayers to continue the holding-period rules that differentiate long-term gains and losses. If an asset acquired after December 31, 1987, is held for more than one year (more than six months for property acquired before January 1, 1988), the resulting gain or loss will be classified long. An asset held for one year or less (six months or less for property acquired before January 1, 1988) will generate short-term gain or loss. The computation is based on calendar months, with the day the property is acquired not being included and the day of disposal being included in the holding period. Thus, the starting date for determining the holding period is the day after the property's acquisition. Property purchased on January 15, 1988 and disposed of on January 15, 1989 would generate short-term gain or loss, since the asset was held for exactly one year. If the property had been disposed of on January 16, 1989, the resulting gain or loss would have been long term.

COMBINING CAPITAL GAINS AND LOSSES. A *net long-term capital gain (NLTCG)* results if gains exceed losses. A *net long-term capital loss (NLTCL)* results if losses exceed gains. Short-term capital gains and short-term capital losses combine to generate either a *net short-term capital gain (NSTCG)* or a *net short-term capital loss (NSTCL)*.

If the above netting process creates either a NSTCG and a NLTCL or a NSTCL and a NLTCG, it is necessary to offset the positive and negative numbers. The Internal Revenue Code defines the excess of NLTCG over NSTCL as a net capital gain (NCG). If a net capital loss (NCL) occurs, the taxpayer will be permitted to offset a portion of ordinary income (explained later). An NCG will be reported as follows.

TAX TREATMENT OF NET CAPITAL GAIN (NCG). The treatment of NCG prior to 1987 was to include it fully in gross income. Then the taxpayer was allowed to deduct 60 percent of the NLTCG in excess of NSTCL as a deduction toward *adjusted gross income (AGI)*. For example, a taxpayer reporting a NLTCG of $36,000 and an NSTCL of $6,000 would increase gross income by $30,000 and be permitted to deduct $18,000 toward AGI because of the 60 percent deduction. As previously noted, the 60 percent exclusion is no longer available; therefore, an NCG is now treated as ordinary income and is taxable in full. As a result, beginning in 1988, an NCG could be taxed (for some individuals) at a maximum marginal rate of 33 percent.

Example: Mr. Jones determines the following information when reviewing transactions for the current year:

Long-term capital gain	$4,600
Long-term capital loss	($4,000)
Short-term capital gain	$ 100
Short-term capital loss	($ 600)

Mr. Jones's net capital gain (NCG) is computed as follows:

LTCG	$4,600	
LTCL	(4,000)	
NLTCG		$ 600
STCG	$ 100	
STCL	(600)	
NSTCL		(500)
NCG		$ 100

The entire NCG of $100 must be taken into income and will be taxed as ordinary income to Mr. Jones.

NET CAPITAL LOSS AS AN OFFSET AGAINST ORDINARY INCOME. As mentioned previously, if a net capital loss (NCL) occurs, the individual taxpayer is allowed to deduct all or a portion of this loss as a deduction toward AGI. The deduction (referred to as the net capital loss deduction) cannot exceed $3,000. A taxpayer is permitted to deduct both short-term and long-term losses on a dollar-for-dollar basis. The two-for-one restriction applicable to long-term losses prior to 1987 was eliminated by the TRA of

1986. When offsetting ordinary income, the NSTCL is utilized first and then the NLTCL (on a two-for-one basis) is used.

Example: Assume that Jo Ann Johnson has an STCL of $2,700 and a NLTCL of $5,400 generated by 1988 activities. Her NCL for 1988 is computed as follows:

STCG	$ 0	
STCL	(2,700)	
NSTCL		($2,700)
LTCG	$ 0	
LTCL	(5,400)	
NLTCL		($5,400)
NCL		($8,100)

Jo Ann's net capital loss deduction for 1988 would be $3,000, consisting of $2,700 of short-term losses and $300 of long-term losses. She would be eligible for a capital loss carryover as follows.

CAPITAL LOSS CARRYOVER. Because of the ceiling imposed on the net capital loss deduction, it is possible that all of the loss will not be used in the year in which it is generated. In these instances, the individual taxpayer is permitted to carry the loss forward.

Net short-term capital losses that are not fully used up are carried forward indefinitely to subsequent tax years. The NSTCL carryover is treated as an STCL in the carryover periods, and it combines with other short-term items to determine NSTCL or NSTCG for the carryover period.

Net long-term capital losses that are not fully used up are likewise carried forward indefinitely to subsequent tax years. The NLTCL carryover will be treated as a LTCL and will combine with the long-term capital gains and losses of the carryover period to generate NLTCG or NLTCL.

Example: In the preceding example for Jo Ann Johnson, the amount of short-term capital loss carryover that will enter into the computation of 1989 NSTCL or NSTCG will be $0. Since the short-term losses are applied first, the full $2,700 was used. The amount of long-term capital loss carryover that will move into the 1989 computation of NLTCL, or NLTCG, will be $5,100 ($5,400 less $300).

BONDS

Interest income from bonds may be fully included in gross income or totally excluded, depending upon the nature of the obligation. For example, interest on corporate bonds and obligations of the United States represents taxable income. However, interest on obligations of possessions of the United States (i.e., Puerto Rico) is exempt. The increment in the value of U.S. savings bonds (Series E before 1980 and Series EE after 1979) purchased at a discount is taxable as interest income. The period in which this increment is recognized will vary, depending upon whether the taxpayer is on a cash basis or an accrual basis. An *accrual-basis taxpayer* must include annually each year's increment as interest income. On the other hand, a *cash-basis taxpayer* may elect to include annually each year's increment as interest income or defer recognition of the increment until the bonds either mature or are surrendered. As a general rule, most individuals elect the latter approach. When a taxpayer elects to report interest income annually, the election is applicable to all bonds owned as well as those acquired in the future.

Example: Karen Brooks, a cash-basis taxpayer, purchased a Series EE bond at a local bank during the current year for $500. When the bond matures in ten years she will receive $1,000. At the end of the first year the redemption value of the bond is $528. Karen may elect to recognize the increment in value of $28 as interest income currently. Alternatively, she may defer recognition of any income until the bond matures in ten years, at which time she will report $500 of interest income ($1,000 proceeds minus $500 cost).

Interest income on obligations of states or any political subdivision (cities, towns, villages, and counties) is exempt. State and local government bonds (referred to as *municipal bonds*) are therefore very attractive to wealthy taxpayers, because the after-tax rate of return can be greater when compared to taxable bonds.

In determining whether to invest in a tax-exempt bond, an investor should compute the equivalent yield of a taxable bond. This can be done by subtracting the taxpayer's marginal tax bracket from 1.0 and dividing the result into the yield of a tax-exempt bond. Assume a taxpayer in the 33 percent marginal tax bracket is considering purchasing State of Michigan bonds yielding 7.9 percent. Dividing .67 (i.e., 100 − .33) into 7.9 percent results in a taxable equivalent yield of 11.8 percent.

AMORTIZATION OF BOND PREMIUM. The amount paid in excess of a bond's face value is called a *premium.* Investors in tax-exempt bonds are required to *amortize* (i.e., write off) the bond premium whereas those who acquire taxable bonds may elect to amortize the bond premium over the remaining life of the bond. In the case of a tax-exempt bond, the amortized premium allowed each year reduces the cost basis of the bond. However, because the interest income on municipal bonds is exempt from taxes, no interest deduction is allowed. With respect to a taxable bond, the amortized premium for the year not only reduces the bond's cost basis, but also results in an interest expense deduction.

Example: On January 1 of the current year, Ed Smith purchased taxable bonds from the XYZ Corporation with a face value of $80,000 for $86,000. The bonds pay an annual interest rate of 9 percent and mature in ten years. Ed elects to amortize the premium of $6,000 over the life of the bonds. Each year until the bonds mature he will report $7,200 of interest income ($80,000 × .09) and $600 of amortized premium ($6,000/10) will be treated as an interest deduction. (He will report income of $6,600 each year: $7,200 − $600.) Further, Ed will reduce his basis in the XYZ Corporation bonds by $600 each year. Consequently, at the end of the first year, Ed's basis for the XYZ Corporation bonds will be $85,400 ($86,000 − $600).

Example: Assume in the previous example that Ed Smith purchased tax-exempt municipal bonds rather than taxable bonds. In this case, he would be required to amortize the bond premium, thereby reducing his cost basis for the bonds by $600 each year. This adjustment of the bond's basis by $600 each year is required so that Mr. Smith will not realize a loss when the face value of the bonds is paid at maturity. However, no interest deduction would be allowed.

AMORTIZATION OF ORIGINAL ISSUE DISCOUNT. If an investor pays less than face value for a bond, the difference is called a *discount.* For example, if a cash-basis taxpayer acquired a $10,000 corporate bond paying 8 percent interest and maturing in 20 years for $9,000, the discount, which is referred to as the *original issue discount (OID),* would amount to $1,000. Assuming the taxpayer was not required to amortize the discount over the life of the bond, he or she would be able to recognize a capital gain of $1,000 when the bond matured in 20 years. The gain of $1,000 represents the difference between the bond's face value at maturity ($10,000) and the taxpayer's basis in the bond ($9,000). In other words, the investor would be able to convert ordinary income into favorable capital gain treatment.

Unfortunately, this strategy will not work, because the Internal Revenue Code requires taxpayers to *amortize the original issue discount over the life of the bond.* The portion of the discount amortized each year represents ordinary income to the investor and also increases the holder's tax basis in the bonds. The method used to amortize the discount is rather complex and beyond the scope of this appendix. Suffice it to say that the amortization method now required is similar to the results produced by use of the effective interest method.

The IRC contains an important exception in that a discount that does not qualify as an original issue discount need not be amortized. This exception applies when the discount is less than one-fourth of 1 percent of the redemption price of the bond at maturity, multiplied by the number of years to maturity. Consequently, even with small discounts it is possible to convert ordinary interest income into a capital gain.

Example: Paula White acquired $60,000 of ABC Corporation bonds for $58,600 during the current year. The bonds pay an annual interest rate of 8 percent and mature in ten years. The discount of $1,400 does not represent original issue discount because $1,400 is less than $1,500 (i.e., .0025 × $60,000 × 10 = $1,500). Therefore, Paula will not be required to amortize the discount. As a result, rather than reporting a portion of the discount as interest income each year over the life of the bonds, she will report $1,400 of capital gain when the bond is redeemed at maturity in ten years. Note that the original issue discount rules are not applicable to state and local bonds or to U.S. savings bonds discussed previously.

RETIREMENT OF BONDS. As explained earlier, one of the key elements of a capital gain or loss is the occurrence of a sale or exchange. Although the retirement of a bond does not, under the general rule, represent a sale or exchange, the IRC contains an exception whereby such retirements qualify for sale or exchange treatment. Consequently, a taxpayer will receive capital gain or loss treatment equal to the difference between the bond's tax basis and its redemption value.

OPTIONS

A gain or loss attributable to the sale or exchange of a *purchased option* to buy or sell property, or a loss that results from failure to exercise an option, is considered to have the same character as the property to which the option relates. When a loss results from the failure to exercise an option, the option is deemed to have been sold or exchanged on the date it expired.

Example: Jack Carpenter purchased an option to acquire 100 shares of Appleton Inc. stock. When the value of the Appleton stock appreciated in value, Jack elected to sell the option for more than its cost rather than exercise the option and receive the stock. As a result, he will recognize a capital gain equal to the excess of the sale price of the option minus the cost of the option. This is because the stock (if acquired) would have been a capital asset in Jack's hands. Had Jack sold the option for less than its cost, the resulting loss would be treated as a capital loss.

The tax treatment to an individual who *grants an option* on stocks, securities, commodities, or commodity futures depends upon whether the option is exercised. If the option is not exercised, the amount received for the option is treated as a short-term capital gain upon expiration of the option. On the other hand, if the option is exercised, the amount received for the option is added to the sales proceeds of the option property. In this case, the nature of the gain or loss (i.e., ordinary or capital) depends upon the type of property which is sold. The grantee (option holder) adds the cost of the option to the purchase price of the option property.

Example: Gary Underwood purchased 200 shares of ABC Incorporated stock on January 1, 1984, for $2,500. On March 1, 1988, he wrote a call option on the ABC stock giving Alice Black (the option holder) the right to acquire the 200 shares for $3,500 within the following 150 days. For writing the call option Gary received a call premium of $400.

If Alice Black elects not to exercise the option, Gary will be required to recognize a $400 short-term capital gain on the date the option expires. However, should Alice exercise the option by paying Gary $3,500 for the stock on July 1, 1988, he will have a long-term capital gain of $1,400 ($3,500 + $400 − $2,500). Alice's basis in the ABC stock will amount to $3,900 ($3,500 + $400).

FUTURES CONTRACTS

A *commodity future* is a contract for the sale or purchase of a specified amount of a commodity at a future date for a fixed price. It is considered to be a capital asset, so a capital gain or loss results from its purchase and sale—unless it is used in *hedging transactions*. When a taxpayer in the ordinary course of a trade or business deals in commodity futures as a form of price insurance, he or she is involved in hedging. An example would be a corn farmer trading in corn futures as discussed in Chapter 18. Such hedging transactions generate ordinary gains and losses.

INDIVIDUAL RETIREMENT ACCOUNTS

Individual retirement accounts (IRAs) have become very popular in the United States since they were introduced in the middle 1970s. There are two reasons for their popularity: (1) contributions to an IRA are deductible on the taxpayer's federal income tax return and (2) the income earned on the assets placed in an IRA is compounded tax-free. Consequently, an individual who makes annual contributions to an IRA over a period of 20 or more years is able to accumulate a significant nest egg for his or her retirement years.

The TRA of 1986 modified the rules pertaining to IRAs, but left certain provisions unchanged. Basically, a taxpayer is eligible to make a deductible contribution to an IRA if he or she (1) has earned compensation from employment such as wages, salaries, tips, commissions, and bonuses or earnings from self-employment and (2) has not reached age $70\frac{1}{2}$ by the end of the taxable year. Starting in 1985 all taxable alimony received by a divorced spouse is treated as compensation for IRA purposes.

An eligible individual may deduct up to the lesser of $2,000 or 100 percent of compensation. If both spouses have earned compensation and make contributions to their own individual IRA, the deduction for each spouse is figured separately. A taxpayer whose spouse has no compensation may establish a *spousal IRA* and contribute up to the lesser of $2,250 or 100 percent of compensation. The contribution may be split in any manner between the working and nonworking spouse, provided no more than $2,000 is placed in either IRA in a given year. Under a special provision included in the TRA of 1986, a nonworking spouse with a small amount of compensation may elect to be treated as having no earned income for the year in order to utilize a spousal IRA. For example, under prior law, if a nonworking spouse received $75 for jury duty, the couple's total IRA contribution for the year was limited to $2,075. The election to ignore the jury-duty fee enables the couple to contribute $2,250 through a spousal IRA.

Example: John Adams is 66 years old and single. During the current year he received $2,800 in wages from part-time work as a maintenance man at his church. He also earned $19,000 in interest on corporate bonds. The maximum amount John can contribute to an IRA and deduct for the current taxable year is $2,000 (i.e., the lesser of $2,000, or 100 percent of his compensation of $2,800).

Example: Assume that John Adams in the previous example is married and that Mrs. Adams, who is also 66 years of age, received $3,000 in wages from part-time employment. Since each spouse has compensation during the current year, both may contribute $2,000 to their own IRA for a total deduction of $4,000 on a joint return. If Mrs. Adams had no earnings, Mr. Adams could establish a spousal IRA and make a deductible contribution, split between the two spouses, of $2,250.

Beginning in 1987, the rules modified by the TRA of 1986 permit individuals to continue (as under prior law) to make fully deductible contributions to an IRA under one or the other following conditions:

1. Neither the individual nor the individual's spouse is an active participant in a qualified retirement plan.
2. The individual is an active participant in a qualified retirement plan and has adjusted gross income below the "applicable dollar amount."

The term "applicable dollar amount" varies depending upon the individual's filing status as follows: (1) $25,000 for an unmarried individual, (2) $40,000 for a married couple filing jointly, and (3) zero for a married couple filing separate returns. On a joint return, if one spouse belongs to a qualified retirement plan, both spouses are deemed to belong. On the other hand, married taxpayers filing separate returns need not take into consideration whether the other spouse is a participant in a qualified plan.

A taxpayer whose adjusted gross income exceeds the levels outlined here must reduce his or her annual IRA deduction by 20 percent of the excess. Consequently, the following individuals who are participants in qualified plans would be unable to make a deductible contribution to an IRA: single taxpayers with AGI of $35,000 or more, married taxpayers filing a joint return with AGI of $50,000 or more, and married taxpayers filing separate returns with AGI of $10,000 or more. These individuals can, however, still make a nondeductible contribution to an IRA up to the lesser of $2,000 or 100 percent of compensation ($2,250 for a spousal IRA). The earnings on nondeductible contributions will accumulate on a tax-deferred basis. That is, they will not be subject to tax until withdrawn.

Example: John Adams is 45 years old and single. During the current year his compensation amounted to $56,000. Because his employer does not have a pension program, he is allowed to make a deductible contribution of $2,000 to his IRA for 1988.

Example: Ed and Linda Witt received compensation of $25,000 and $13,000, respectively, during 1988. Ed is an active participant in his employer's qualified retirement plan. Because their combined adjusted gross income on a joint return is under $40,000, each is entitled to contribute and deduct $2,000 (i.e., for a total of $4,000) to an IRA for 1988.

Example: Assume in the previous example that Linda's compensation for the year amounts to $21,000 or a combined adjusted gross income on a joint return for 1988 of $46,000. Again, Ed and Linda may each contribute $2,000 to an IRA. However, the deduction for each contribution will be reduced by $1,200 (i.e., $46,000 − $40,000 = $6,000 × 20% = $1,200) to $800. If Ed and Linda elected to file separately, Ed's 1988 contribution of $2,000 to his IRA would be nondeductible. This is because his AGI exceeds $10,000. Linda's $2,000 contribution to her IRA would be fully deductible for 1988 because she is not a participant in a qualified plan.

A taxpayer is deemed to have made a contribution to an IRA on the last day of the preceding taxable year if the contribution is made no later than the due date for filing the individual's return (not including extensions). In other words, a contribution made on April 15, 1988, by a calendar-year individual would be deductible on the taxpayer's 1987 return. Moreover, to receive a deduction for the preceding taxable year, the IRA need not be set up until the due date for filing the income tax return.

An IRA can be established with, for example, a bank, credit union, savings and loan association, brokerage firm, or mutual fund. In addition, insurance companies issue individual retirement annuities.

An individual is entitled to withdraw funds from an IRA once he or she attains the age of $59\frac{1}{2}$. However, to avoid penalties, a taxpayer must begin making withdrawals by April 1 of the year following the year in which he or she reaches age $70\frac{1}{2}$. Payments must be made over the participant's expected lifetime or over the life expectancies of the participant and his or her named beneficiary. Alternatively, payments may be made in a lump sum. Distributions from an IRA, other than nondeductible contributions, which may be recovered tax-free, are taxed in full as ordinary income in the year received.

KEOGH (H.R. 10) PLANS

A taxpayer who is self-employed is allowed to establish a *Keogh plan* (sometimes referred to as an *H.R. 10 plan*). Self-employed individuals include, among others, sole proprietors, partners in a partnership, independent contractors, consultants, and corporate directors. The maximum contribution to a Keogh plan will vary depending upon whether a defined-benefit plan or a defined-contribution plan has been established.

A *defined-benefit Keogh plan* provides a formula that pre-establishes the annual retirement benefit an individual will receive. A pension actuary computes the amount that must be contributed to the plan each year in order to accumulate the funds needed to pay the retirement benefits. The maximum annual retirement benefit that an individual can receive under a defined-benefit plan is limited to the lesser of $90,000 or 100 percent of average compensation for the three highest years of employment.

A *defined-contribution Keogh plan* defines the amount to be contributed to the plan each year. An individual's retirement income is not known in advance. Rather, the amount available at retirement depends upon how well contributions to the plan have been invested over the years. The amount contributed each year to a defined-contribution plan is limited to the lesser of 25 percent of net earnings from self-employment or $30,000. However, beginning in 1984, earned income is calculated net of contributions made to the qualified plan.

Example: Dr. C. N. Dubble is a partner in an optometry practice. During 1988 Dr. Dubble had earned income of $150,000. He contributed $30,000 to a defined-contribution Keogh plan during the year. The 25 percent limit would be applied as follows:

Dr. Dubble's earned income before contribution	$150,000
Less: contribution to the H.R. 10 plan	(30,000)
Earned income after contribution	$120,000
25 percent of reduced amount	$ 30,000

Because of the way you must determine the earned income after the contribution, the maximum amount effectively becomes 20 percent of earned income before contribution.

Unlike an IRA, a taxpayer must begin a *new* Keogh plan no later than the last day of the taxable year in order to obtain a deduction for that year. However, subsequent contributions made prior to the due date for filing the return (including extensions) are deductible in the prior year. Thus, for a plan to be eligible for 1988, it must be established by December 31, 1988. Once it is established, subsequent contributions within the limit made up to April 15, 1989, are also deductible for 1988.

SUMMARY

Certain tax laws affect an individual's investment and retirement strategies, and a wide variety of tax-planning opportunities are currently available to taxpayers for reducing their federal income tax liability. Having an appreciation of these opportunities is very important for those who wish to maximize their net worth.

REFERENCES

Prentice-Hall 1988 Federal Tax Handbook. Englewood Cliffs, N.J.: Prentice-Hall, Inc., 1988.

Your Federal Income Tax for Individuals (Publication 17). Washington, D.C.: Department of the Treasury, Internal Revenue Service, 1987.

Hoffman, William H., Eugene Willis, and James E. Smith. *1989 Annual Edition West's Federal Taxation: Individual Income Taxes.* St. Paul, Minn.: West Publishing Co., 1988.

Planning for Your Retirement: IRA & Keogh Plans. Chicago, Ill.: Commerce Clearing House, Inc., 1987.

Pratt, James W., Jane O. Burns, and William N. Kulsrud. *1989 Annual Edition Individual Taxation.* Homewood, Ill.: Richard D. Irwin, Inc., 1988.

Individual Retirement Plans after Tax Reform. Chicago, Ill.: Commerce Clearing House, Inc., 1987.

Tax-Saving Plans for Self-Employed after Tax Reform. Chicago, Ill.: Commerce Clearing House, Inc., 1987.

PROBLEMS

1. Assume that Fred Langston's investment results for 1989 turn out as follows:

Long-term capital gain	$3,750
Long-term capital loss	($1,250)
Short-term capital gain	$ 200
Short-term capital loss	($ 300)

1a. Determine Mr. Langston's net capital gain (NCG) for 1989.

1b. If Mr. Langston's marginal tax rate is 33 percent, what is the tax liability as the result of these investments?

2. Assume that Jane Renton's investment results for 1989 turn out as follows:

Long-term capital gain	$ 750
Long-term capital loss	($1,450)
Short-term capital gain	$ 200
Short-term capital loss	($3,600)

2a. Determine Ms. Renton's net capital loss (NCL) for 1989.

2b. If Ms. Renton's marginal tax rate is 33 percent, what is the 1989 tax savings as the result of these investments?

2c. What is the capital loss carryover?

3. On January 1 of the current year, Sam Cool purchases 75 of Amazon International's $1,000 par bonds for $82,500. These bonds will mature in 15 years and have an annual coupon interest rate of 8 percent. If Sam chooses to amortize the premium,

3a. What interest income will he report for the first year?

3b. What interest income will he report for the third year?

3c. What will be Sam's basis after Year 3?

3d. How would these answers differ if the bonds purchased had been municipal bonds?

4. Grace Trent purchased 100 shares of Larchmont Technological Industries for $18 per share. One year later she wrote an option giving Rob Rather a three-month option to purchase these shares at $21.50 per share, and she received a premium of $350.

4a. What are the tax consequences for Grace Trent if
    (1) Rob does not exercise the option.
    (2) Rob exercises the option at the end of three months when the shares are selling at $30 per share.

4b. What are the tax consequences for Rob Rather if
    (1) He does not exercise the option.
    (2) He exercises the option at the end of three months when the shares are selling at $30 per share and then immediately sells the shares.

5. In 1988 Tom Piccard had $127,000 of earned income and has contributed $17,000 to a defined-contribution Keogh pension plan. What is Tom's allowed additional contribution on the last day to add to the plan?

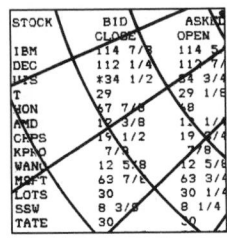

CHAPTER 3

ORGANIZATION AND FUNCTIONING OF SECURITIES MARKETS

FINANCIAL MARKETS

The stock market, Wall Street, and the Dow Jones Industrials are part and parcel of our everyday experience. Each evening we find out how they fared on the television news broadcasts; each morning we read about their prospects for a rally or decline in the pages of our daily newspaper. Yet how the domestic and world markets actually function is imperfectly understood by most. It is the purpose of this chapter to describe the global securities markets, both primary and secondary, indicate how they have evolved and have changed, and identify those involved in them.

WHAT IS A MARKET?

A *market* is the means through which buyers and sellers are brought together to aid in the transfer of goods and/or services. Several aspects of this general definition seem worthy of emphasis. First, it is not necessary for a market to have a physical location. It is only necessary that the buyers and sellers can communicate regarding the relevant aspects of the purchase or sale.

Second, the market does not necessarily own the goods or services involved. When we discuss what is required for a "good" market, you will note that ownership is not involved; the basic criterion is the smooth, cheap transfer of goods and services. In the case of most financial markets, those who establish and administer the market do not own the assets; they simply provide a physical location or electronic system that allows potential buyers and sellers to interact, and they help the market to function by providing information and transfer facilities.

Finally, a market can deal in any variety of goods and services. For any commodity with a diverse clientele, a market should evolve to aid in the transfer of that commodity. Both buyers and sellers will benefit from its existence. Though, basically, we take markets for granted, they are vital to our economy.

FACTORS THAT DETERMINE A "GOOD" MARKET

One enters a market in order to buy or sell a commodity quickly at a price justified by the prevailing supply and demand. To determine this price, one must have timely and accurate information on past transactions in terms of volume and price and on all currently outstanding bids and offers. Therefore, one attribute of a good market is *availability of information.*

Another prime requirement is *liquidity,* meaning the ability to buy or sell an asset (1) quickly and (2) at a known price, that is, a price not substantially different from the prior price, assuming no new information is available. Both aspects are necessary for a liquid market. An asset's ability to be sold quickly—sometimes referred to as its *marketability*—is a necessary, but not a sufficient, condition for liquidity. The price must be certain as well. A factor that contributes to liquidity is *price continuity,* meaning prices do not change much from one transaction to the next unless substantial new information becomes available.

Suppose new information is not forthcoming, and the last transaction was at a price of $20. If the next trade is at 20 1/8, the market would be considered reasonably continuous.[1] Obviously, it is necessary to have a continuous market without large price changes between trades in order to have a liquid market. A continuous market also requires *depth.* Numerous potential buyers and sellers must be willing to trade at prices above and below the current market price. These buyers and sellers enter the market when there are changes in supply and/or demand and thereby ensure that there are no drastic price changes.

Another factor contributing to a good market is the *transaction cost.* The lower the cost (in terms of the percentage of the value of the trade), the more efficient the market is. Thus, if the cost of a transaction is 2 percent of the value of the trade on one market and 5 percent on another market, the 2 percent market is the one to trade in. Most microeconomic textbooks define an *efficient market* as one in which the cost of the transaction is minimized. This attribute is referred to as *internal efficiency.*[2]

Finally, a buyer or seller wants the prevailing market price to adequately reflect all the available supply and demand factors in the market. If such conditions change as a result of new information, the price should change accordingly. Therefore, prices adjust quickly to new information regarding supply or demand. This attribute is referred to as *external efficiency.*

In summary, a good market for goods and services has the following characteristics:

---

[1] The reader should be aware that common stocks are sold in increments of eighths that are equal to $0.125. Therefore, 20 1/8 means the stock sold at $20.125 per share.

[2] Richard R. West, "On the Difference between Internal and External Market Efficiency," *Financial Analysts Journal* 31, no. 6 (November–December 1975): 30–34.

1. Timely and accurate information on the price and volume of past transactions and on prevailing supply and demand.
2. Liquidity, meaning an asset can be bought or sold quickly (marketability) at a price close to the price of previous transactions, assuming no new information has been received (price continuity). Price continuity requires depth, meaning a number of buyers and sellers are willing and able to enter the market at prices above and below current prices.
3. Low transaction cost (internal efficiency), meaning that all aspects of the transaction entail low costs, including the cost of reaching the market, the actual brokerage cost involved in the transaction, as well as the cost of transferring the asset.
4. Rapid adjustment of prices to new information (external efficiency), meaning that the prevailing price reflects all available information regarding the asset.

ORGANIZATION OF THE SECURITIES MARKET

Before discussing the specific operation of the securities market, it is important that we understand its overall organization. The principal distinction is between *primary markets,* where new securities are sold, and *secondary markets,* where outstanding securities are bought and sold. Within each of these markets there is a further division based upon the economic unit that issued the security (the government, states or municipalities, or corporations). In the following discussion, we will consider each of these major segments of the securities market with an emphasis on the individuals involved and the functions they perform.

PRIMARY MARKETS

The primary market is the one in which new issues of bonds, preferred stock or common stock, are sold by government units, municipalities, or companies to acquire new capital.[3] The proceeds go to the issuing unit as new capital.

GOVERNMENT ISSUES[4]

All government issues are fixed-income securities subdivided into three segments based upon the original maturity of the security. *Treasury bills* are negotiable, noninterest-bearing securities with an original maturity of one year or less. They are currently issued for three months, six months, or one year. *Treasury notes* have an original maturity of two to ten years, and they have generally been issued as 2-, 3-, 4-, 5-, 7- and ten-year notes. Finally, *Treasury bonds* have an original maturity of more than ten years.

To sell bills, notes, and bonds, the Treasury relies upon the Federal Reserve System's *auctions.* Treasury bills are pure discount bonds since

---

[3] For an excellent set of studies related to the primary market, see Michael C. Jensen and Clifford W. Smith, Jr., eds. "Symposium on Investment Banking and the Capital Acquisition Process," *Journal of Financial Economics* 15, no. 1–2 (January–February 1986). The lead article reviews the theory and practice of capital raising: Clifford W. Smith, Jr., "Investment Banking and the Capital Acquisition Process," 3–29.

[4] This subsection benefited from Marcia Stigum and Frank J. Fabozzi, "U.S Treasury Notes and Bonds," in *Handbook of Fixed Income Securities,* 2d ed. edited by Frank J. Fabozzi and Irving Pollack (Homewood, Ill.: Dow Jones-Irwin, 1986).

they do not involve any interest payments (as discussed in Chapter 2, they are zero coupon securities). In an auction held each week, institutions and some individuals submit price bids below par that imply a specific yield (the bidding process and pricing is discussed in detail in Chapter 20).

Treasury notes and bonds are likewise sold at auction by the Federal Reserve, but the bids are yields rather than prices—that is, the Treasury specifies how much it wants and when the notes or bonds will mature. After receiving the competitive bid yields, the Treasury determines the *stop-out bid* (the highest yield it will accept) based upon the bids received and how much it wants to borrow. It then sets the coupon on the security to the nearest one-eighth of 1 percent necessary to make the *average* price charged to the successful bidders equal to 100 or less. Once the coupon is set, all other prices are determined based upon the yield bid (all investors get the yield they bid assuming they were below the stop-out yield). There are also many *noncompetitive bids* where the bidders are willing to pay the average price of the accepted competitive tenders.

MUNICIPAL ISSUES[5]   New municipal bond issues are sold by one of three methods: competitive bid, negotiations, or private placement. *Competitive bid* sales typically involve a sealed bid in which the bond issue is sold to the bidding syndicate of underwriters that submits the lowest-interest cost bid in accordance with the stipulations set forth by the issuer. *Negotiated sales* are contractual arrangements between an underwriter and the issuer wherein the underwriter helps the issuer prepare the bond issue with the understanding that they have the exclusive right to sell the issue. *Private placements* involve the sale of a bond issue by the issuer directly to an investor or group of investors (usually institutions).

Note that in two of the three methods there is an *underwriting* function involved, which is the intermediating service between the issuer and investors. Specifically, in the case of competitive bids or negotiated bids, the underwriter will typically purchase the entire issue from the issuer, relieving the issuer from the risk and responsibility of selling and distributing the bonds. Subsequently, the underwriter sells the issue to the investing public. In the case of municipal bonds this function is performed by both investment banking firms and commercial banks.

The underwriting function can involve three services: origination, distribution, and risk-bearing. *Origination* involves the design of the bond issue and initial planning. *Risk-bearing* takes place when the underwriter acquires the total issue and accepts the responsibility and risk of reselling it for more than the purchase price paid to the issuer. *Distribution* is the art of selling it, typically with the help of a selling syndicate that includes other investment banking firms. In the case of a negotiated bid, the underwriter will carry out all three services, while in the instance of a competitive bid, the issuer specifies the characteristics of the issue in terms

---

[5] This section draws heavily from David S. Kidwell and Eric H. Sorensen, "Investment Banking and the Underwriting of New Municipal Issues" in *The Municipal Bond Handbook* edited by F. J. Fabozzi, S. G. Feldstein, I. M. Pollack and F. G. Zard (Homewood, Ill.: Dow Jones-Irwin, 1983).

of amount, maturities, and call features prior to the bidding related to coupons. The issuer may have received advice on the characteristics, but this would have been on a fee basis, not involving the underwriter. Finally, in the case of a private placement, there is no risk-bearing involved, but an investment banker could assist in locating potential buyers and negotiating the characteristics of the issue.

You will recall from Chapter 2 that municipal bonds are either general obligation bonds (GOs) or revenue bonds. Commercial banks dominate in the management of GO bond sales and investment banking firms in revenue bond sales. The Glass-Steagall Act of 1933 prohibits commercial banks from underwriting most revenue bonds. There is significant pressure to change this regulation, which would have a major impact on this market as well as the underwriting of corporate debt.

The municipal bond market has experienced two major trends during the past ten years. The first has been the shift toward negotiated bond issues versus competitive bids. In 1976 about 42 percent of the issues were negotiated compared to almost 75 percent in 1986. The second trend is the shift toward a preponderance of revenue bond issues. In 1976 the GO-revenue bond division was almost exactly 50–50, while almost 75 percent were revenue issues in 1985 and about 62 percent in 1986. These two trends are related, since there is a tendency for revenue issues to be negotiated. Whereas many states require that GO bond issues be sold through competitive bidding, there is seldom such a requirement for revenue issues.

CORPORATE ISSUES

Corporate issues include both fixed-income and equity issues (common stock). Corporate bond issues are almost always sold through a negotiated arrangement with an investment banking firm that has an ongoing relationship with the issuing firm. With an emerging global capital market and an explosion of new instruments, the origination function is becoming more important, because the corporate financial officer will probably not be completely familiar with the several markets around the world and the new instruments. The fact is, one of the ways investment banking firms compete is through creating new instruments that appeal to existing investors or finding a new set of investors for an issue the firm is selling. In either case, the cost of new capital to the issuer will be lower because of the expertise of the investment banker.

Once the issue is specified, the bond underwriter will put together a syndicate of other major underwriters and a selling group for the distribution. In the case of common stock, *new issues* are typically divided into two groups. The first and largest group is that of *seasoned* new issues offered by companies with existing public markets for their securities. An example would be General Motors selling a new issue of common stock. There is an existing public market for General Motors common stock, and the company is increasing the number of outstanding shares in order to acquire new equity capital.

The second major category in the new issues market is generally referred to as *initial public offerings (IPOs)*. An example would be a small company selling common stock to the public for the first time. In this case, there is no existing public market for the stock, that is, the company has been *closely held*.[6]

New issues (seasoned or initial) are typically underwritten by investment bankers who acquire the total issue from the company and, in turn, sell the issue to interested investors. The underwriter gives advice to the corporation on the general characteristics of the issues, its pricing, and the timing of the offering. He also accepts the risk of selling the new issue after acquiring it from the corporation.[7]

ALTERNATIVE RELATIONSHIPS WITH INVESTMENT BANKER

Arrangements made by the company and the underwriter typically take one of three forms: negotiation, competitive bid, or *best efforts*. The negotiated arrangement, which is the most common, has already been discussed in connection with municipal issues.[8]

A corporation may also specify the type of securities to be offered (common stock, preferred stock, or bonds) and then may solicit competitive bids from investment banking firms. This is typically done by utilities, which, in many cases, are *required* to submit their issues for competitive bids. While the cost of the issue is reduced in this arrangement, there is also a reduction in the services provided by the investment banker—the banker will give less advice but will still underwrite the issue.[9]

Alternatively, an investment banker can agree to become involved with an issue and sell it on a *best-efforts* basis. This is usually done with speculative new issues. The point is, the investment banker does not really underwrite the issue since he does not buy it. The stock is owned by the company, and the investment banker acts as a broker to sell whatever is possible at a stipulated price. The investment banker's commission on such an issue is less than on an issue he underwrites. With either a negotiated relationship or a best-efforts arrangement, the lead investment banker typically will form an *underwriting syndicate* of other investment bankers to spread the risk and also help in the sales. In addition, if the issue is very large, the lead underwriter and underwriting syndicate will form a *selling group* of smaller firms to help in the distribution.

---

[6] For an analysis of the effect of a new outstanding equity issue, see Richard H. Pettway and Robert C. Radcliffe, "Impacts of New Equity Sales Upon Electric Utility Share Prices," *Financial Management* 14, no. 1 (Spring 1985): 16–25. An example of an IPO was by Genentech in 1982, which had been a very successful privately held firm prior to this offering. A study that examines the price performance for IPOs and discusses prior studies is Robert E. Miller and Frank K. Reilly, "An Examination of Mispricing, Returns, and Uncertainty for Initial Public Offerings," *Financial Management,* 16, no. 2 (Summer 1987): 28–42.

[7] For a more detailed discussion and analysis of the investment banking industry, see Dennis E. Logue and John R. Lindvall, "The Behavior of Investment Bankers: An Econometric Investigation," *Journal of Finance* 29, no. 1 (March 1974): 203–215; and Gershon Mandelker and Arthur Ravic, "Investment Banking: An Economic Analysis of Optimal Underwriting Contracts," *Journal of Finance* 32, no. 3 (June 1977): 683–694.

[8] For a discussion of the underwriting process, see Richard A. Brealey and Stewart C. Myers, *Principles of Corporate Finance,* 3d ed. (New York: McGraw-Hill, 1988), Chapter 15.

[9] A study that considers the relative merits of negotiated versus competitive bid underwritings is S. Bhagat and P. A. Frost, "Issuing Costs to Existing Shareholders in Competitive and Negotiated Underwritten Public Utility Equity Offerings," *Journal of Financial Economics,* 15, no. 1 (January–February 1986): 213–232.

This typical practice of negotiated arrangements and numerous investment banking firms in the syndicate and selling group has changed with the introduction of *Rule 415*. This rule was introduced by the SEC during 1982 on an experimental basis and subsequently approved on a permanent basis. It basically stipulates that large firms are allowed to register security issues and sell the issues piecemeal during the two years following the initial registration (these are referred to as *shelf registrations* because the issues are on the shelf and can be taken down and sold on short notice whenever it suits the issuing firm). As an example, IBM could register an issue of 5 million shares of common stock during 1989 and sell a million shares in early 1989, another million late in 1989, 2 million shares in early 1990, and the rest in late 1990. Each of these offerings can be made with little notice or paperwork by one underwriter or several. In fact, in many instances the lead underwriter will handle the whole deal without a syndicate or may use only one or two other firms. This arrangement has been supported by large corporations because it provides great flexibility for them, involves lower registration fees and expenses, and allows the firms issuing the securities to request competitive bids from several investment banking firms. On the other hand, concern has been expressed that these shelf registrations do not allow investors enough time to examine the firm issuing the securities and it reduces the ability of small underwriters to participate (i.e., the syndicates are smaller, and selling groups are almost nonexistent). Notably, shelf registrations have typically been used for the sale of straight debentures rather than common stock or convertible issues.[10]

Finally, primary offerings can be placed *privately* rather than being sold publicly. In such an arrangement, referred to as a *private placement,* the firm, with the assistance of an investment banker, designs an issue and finds a small group of institutions willing to acquire a significant position in the firm involved. The firm enjoys lower costs, since it is not necessary to prepare the extensive registration statement for a public offering. On the other side, the institution typically benefits, because the issuing firm provides a higher return due to the cost savings. Note that the buyer (e.g., institution) should *require* a higher return because of the lower liquidity of the security (there is generally no secondary market for these issues after the original sale).[11]

SECONDARY MARKETS

Secondary markets permit trading in outstanding issues. In this case, a stock or bond issue has already been sold to the public, and it is traded between current and potential owners. The proceeds from a sale in the

---

[10] For further discussion of this rule, see A. F. Ehbar, "Upheaval in Investment Banking," *Fortune,* August 23, 1982, 90ff.; Beth McGoldrick, "Life with Rule 415," *Institutional Investor* 17, no. 2 (February 1983): 129–133; and Robert J. Rogowski and Eric H. Sorensen, "Deregulation in Investment Banking: Shelf Registrations, Structure and Performance," *Financial Management,* 14, no. 1 (Spring 1985): 5–15.

[11] For further discussion of these issues, see Patrick A. Hays, Michael Joehnk, and Ronald W. Melicher, "Differential Determinants of Risk Premiums in the Public and Private Corporate Bond Markets," *Journal of Financial Research* 2, no. 2 (Fall 1979): 143–152.

secondary market do not go to the issuing unit (i.e., the government, municipality, or company) but rather to the current owner of the security.

IMPORTANCE OF SECONDARY MARKETS

Before discussing the various segments of the secondary market, we must consider its overall importance. Because the secondary market involves the trading of securities initially sold in the primary market it is providing *liquidity* to the individuals who acquired these securities. After acquiring securities in the primary market, you will want to be able to sell them again (in order to acquire other securities, buy a house, go on a vacation, or whatever). The primary market would be seriously hampered without the liquidity provided by the secondary market, because investors would hesitate to acquire securities in the primary market if they felt they could not subsequently sell them in the secondary market.

Secondary markets are also important to the issuing unit because the prevailing market price of the security is determined by action there. Therefore, any new issues of outstanding stocks or bonds sold in the primary market are necessarily priced in the secondary market. As a result, capital costs for the government, municipalities, and corporations are determined in the secondary market.

SECONDARY BOND MARKETS

The secondary markets for bonds distinguish among the bonds issued by the government, municipalities, or corporations.

SECONDARY GOVERNMENT AND MUNICIPAL BOND MARKETS. Government bonds are traded by bond dealers distinguished by the type of government bonds they handle, Treasury bonds or agency bonds. For the Treasury issues there is a set of 35 primary dealers, including large banks in major cities like New York, Chicago, and Tokyo and some of the large investment banking firms (e.g., Merrill Lynch, Morgan Stanley, Nomura Securities). These institutions and/or other firms also make markets for government agency issues, but there is no formal set of dealers for agency securities.[12]

Banks are active in municipal bond trading because a large part of their investment portfolios is committed to them. Also, many large investment banking firms have municipal bond departments because they are active in underwriting these issues. Notably, the primary and secondary markets for municipal bonds experienced a major slowdown during 1987. The primary market was affected by two factors: first, the Tax Reform Act of 1986 that restricted the purposes of municipal bonds, and second, there were fewer refundings in 1987 when interest rates increased. As a result, the volume of new municipal issues peaked in 1985, declined in 1986, and declined again in 1987 to a level below 1984. The volume of trading in the secondary market declined due to lower primary market

---

[12] For a detailed discussion of the government dealer market, see Kenneth D. Garbade, *Securities Markets* (New York: McGraw-Hill, 1982), Chapter 21, and Chapter 10 of this book.

volume, but also because of an increase in yield volatility that discouraged many investors.[13]

SECONDARY CORPORATE BOND MARKET. The secondary market for corporate bonds has two major segments, the exchanges and the over-the-counter market. The major *exchange* for bonds is the New York Stock Exchange (NYSE). As of the end of 1987 there were almost 2,500 corporate bond issues listed on the NYSE with a par value of about $305 billion and a market value of approximately $253 billion.[14] On a typical day there are about 2,600 trades, and the volume of trading is about $38 million. In addition, there are about 340 issues listed on the American Stock Exchange (AMEX), with a market value of almost $20 billion and a typical daily volume of over $3 million. All corporate bonds not listed on one of the exchanges are traded over-the-counter by dealers who buy and sell for their own account.

FINANCIAL FUTURES MARKET. In addition to the market for the bonds, recently a market has developed for *futures contracts* for these bonds—that is, contracts that allow the holder to buy or sell a specified amount of a given bond issue at a stipulated price. These futures contracts and the futures market are discussed in detail in Chapter 25.

SECONDARY EQUITY MARKETS

Secondary equity markets are usually broken down into three major groups: the major *national exchanges,* including the New York Stock Exchange, the American Stock Exchange, the Tokyo Stock Exchange, and the London Exchange; *regional exchanges* in cities like Chicago, San Francisco, Boston, Osaka (Japan), Nagoya (Japan), and Dublin; and the *over-the-counter market* for trading in securities not listed on an organized exchange.

The first two groups, referred to as *listed* securities exchanges, are similar, differing only in terms of size and geographic emphasis. They are both formal organizations that have a specified group of members that may use the facilities of the exchange and a specified group of securities (stocks or bonds) that have qualified for *listing.* In addition, the prices of securities listed on these exchanges are determined via an *auction process,* whereby interested buyers and sellers submit bids and asks for a given stock to a central location for that stock. The bids and asks are recorded by a *specialist* assigned to that stock. Shares of stock are then sold to the highest bidder and bought from the individual or institution with the lowest asking price (the lowest offering price).

NATIONAL SECURITIES EXCHANGE. Two securities exchanges in the United States are generally thought of as being national in scope: the New York

---

[13] Alexander Peers, "Municipal Bond Market's New Volatility Leaves Many Traditional Investors Cold," *The Wall Street Journal,* July 20, 1987, 19; Randall Smith, "Municipal Bond Business Hits a Slump," *The Wall Street Journal,* August 7, 1987, 28; and Alexander Peers, "How Municipal Bonds Went from Cash Cow to a White Elephant," *The Wall Street Journal,* December 4, 1987, 1, 12.

[14] *Fact Book* (New York: New York Stock Exchange, 1988), 41. If you include U.S. government issues and non-U.S. issues of companies, banks, and governments, you will find there are more than 3,300 issues with a par value and market value of more than $1,600 billion.

TABLE 3.1
Listing Requirements for Stocks on the NYSE and AMEX

	NYSE	AMEX
Pre-tax income last year	$ 2,500,000	$ 750,000
Pre-tax income last 2 years	$ 2,000,000	$ 400,000[b]
Net tangible assets	$16,000,000	$4,000,000
Shares publicly held	1,100,000	500,000
Market value of publicly held shares: maximum	$18,000,000[a]	$3,000,000
minimum	$ 9,000,000[a]	—
Number of round-lot holders (100 shares or more)	2,000	800

[a]This minimum required market value varies over time, depending upon the value of the NYSE Common Stock Index. For specifics, see the *1985 NYSE Fact Book*, 34–36.
[b]For AMEX, this is "net income last year."
[c]This is the only minimum for AMEX.
Source: *NYSE Fact Book* (New York: New York Stock Exchange, 1988); and *AMEX Fact Book* (New York: American Stock Exchange, 1987).

Stock Exchange (NYSE) and the American Stock Exchange (AMEX). Outside the United States each country typically has one national exchange, such as the Tokyo Stock Exchange (TSE), the London Exchange, the Frankfurt Stock Exchange, and the Paris Bourse. They are considered national because of the large number of securities they list, the wide geographic dispersion of the firms listed, and their diverse clientele of buyers and sellers.

THE NEW YORK STOCK EXCHANGE (NYSE). The New York Stock Exchange (NYSE), which is the largest organized securities market in the United States, was established in 1817 as the New York Stock and Exchange Board. The name was changed to the New York Stock Exchange in 1863.

At the end of 1987, there were 1,647 companies with stock listed on the NYSE, and 2,244 stock issues (common and preferred), with a total market value of over $2,200 billion. The specific listing requirements for the NYSE as of 1988 are contained in Table 3.1. The average number of shares traded daily on the exchange has increased steadily and substantially, as shown in Table 3.2. Notably, prior to the 1960s the average daily volume was less than 3 million shares, compared to current average volume in excess of 188 million shares and record volume of over 600 million shares.

The NYSE has dominated the other listed exchanges in the United States. An analysis of the percentage breakdown of share volume on U.S. exchanges indicates that during the past decade the NYSE has consistently accounted for about 80 percent of all shares traded on listed exchanges, as compared with about 10 percent for the AMEX and about 10 percent for all regional exchanges combined. Because the price of shares on the NYSE tends to be higher than that of shares on the AMEX, the percentage of value of trading on the NYSE has averaged about 85 percent, compared

TABLE 3.2
Average Daily Reported Share Volume Traded on Selected National Stock Exchanges (Thousands)

YEAR	NYSE	AMEX	TOKYO
1940	751	171	NA
1945	1,422	435	NA
1950	1,980	583	NA
1955	2,578	912	NA
1960	3,042	1,113	90,000
1965	6,176	2,120	116,000
1970	11,564	3,319	144,000
1975	18,551	2,138	183,000
1980	44,871	6,427	359,000
1981	46,853	5,310	377,000
1982	65,052	5,287	275,000
1983	85,334	8,225	365,000
1984	91,190	6,107	361,000
1985	109,169	8,337	428,000
1986	141,028	11,773	709,000
1987	188,938	13,858	962,000

Source: *NYSE Fact Book* (New York: New York Stock Exchange), various issues; *AMEX Fact Book* (New York: American Stock Exchange), various issues; *Tokyo Stock Exchange Fact Book* (Tokyo: Tokyo Stock Exchange, 1988).

with less than 5 percent for the AMEX and a little over 10 percent for the regional exchanges.[15]

The volume of trading and dominant position are reflected in the price of membership on the Exchange (referred to as a *seat*). As shown in Table 3.3, the price of membership has fluctuated in line with trading volume and other factors that influence the profitability of membership.

THE AMERICAN STOCK EXCHANGE (AMEX). The American Stock Exchange (AMEX) was begun by a group of persons who traded unlisted shares at the corner of Wall and Hanover Streets in New York and was referred to as the Outdoor Curb Market. In 1910 formal trading rules were established and the name was changed to the New York Curb Market Association. The members moved inside a building in 1921 and continued to trade mainly in unlisted stocks (i.e., stocks not listed on one of the registered exchanges) until 1946, when listed stocks finally outnumbered unlisted stocks. The current name was adopted in 1953.[16]

The AMEX is a national exchange in the United States distinct from the NYSE, mostly because except for a fairly short period in the late 1970s,

[15] For a breakdown of shares traded and value of shares traded, see Securities and Exchange Commission, *Annual Report* (Washington, D.C.: U.S. Government Printing Office); and New York Stock Exchange, *Fact Book* (New York: New York Stock Exchange).

[16] For a further discussion of the development of the AMEX, see Robert Sobel, *The Curbstone Brokers: The Origins of the American Stock Exchange* (New York: Macmillan, 1970).

TABLE **3.3**
Membership Prices on the NYSE and the AMEX (Thousands of Dollars)

	NYSE		AMEX			NYSE		AMEX	
	HIGH	LOW	HIGH	LOW		HIGH	LOW	HIGH	LOW
1925	150	99	38	9	1980	275	175	252	95
1935	140	65	33	12	1981	285	220	274	200
1945	95	49	32	12	1982	340	190	285	180
1955	90	49	22	12	1983	425	310	325	261
1960	162	135	60	51	1984	400	290	255	160
1965	250	250	80	55	1985	480	310	160	115
1970	320	130	185	70	1986	600	455	285	145
1975	138	55	72	34	1987	1,150	605	420	265

Source: *NYSE Fact Book* (New York: New York Stock Exchange), various issues and *AMEX Fact Book* (New York: American Stock Exchange), various issues.

no stocks are listed on the NYSE and AMEX at the same time. The AMEX has been quite innovative in listing foreign securities over the years. There were about 40 foreign issues listed in 1987, and trading in these issues constituted about 10 percent of total volume.[17] Further, there were warrants listed on the AMEX for a number of years before the NYSE would list them. Also, the AMEX has become a major options exchange since January 1975, when it began with options on six NYSE-listed securities. In 1982 the AMEX expanded into options on debt instruments (10-year Treasury notes and 13-week Treasury bills) and in 1983 listed options on market indices and industry-based indices. Finally, in 1985 trading began in options on gold bullion. Therefore, currently there is trading in 136 individual stock options (115 NYSE stocks and 21 OTC stocks), two broad-based index options, two industry-based options, two interest-rate options, and a commodities option.

At the end of 1987 there were approximately 950 stock issues listed on the AMEX.[18] As shown in Table 3.2, average daily trading volume has fluctuated substantially over time but overall has grown from below 500,000 shares to almost 14 million shares a day in 1987.

The American Stock Exchange is national in scope and, although also located in New York, is distinct from the NYSE in terms of listing requirements, specific companies listed, and instruments traded (i.e., a large options exchange). Because of the differences, most large brokerage firms are members of both exchanges.

TOKYO STOCK EXCHANGE **(TSE).** There are eight stock exchanges in Japan, of which Tokyo, Osaka, and Nagoya are the largest. In terms of dominance of its country's market, the TSE is similar to the NYSE. Specifically, about 83 percent of shares and value of shares are traded on the TSE. Notably,

---

[17] *AMEX Fact Book* (New York: American Stock Exchange, 1987).

[18] The requirements for listing on the AMEX are contained in Table 3.1.

TABLE 3.4
Volume and Value of Foreign Stocks Listed on the Tokyo Stock Exchange

YEAR	NUMBER OF LISTED COMPANIES AT YEAR-END	VOLUME (THOUSANDS OF SHARES)		VALUE (MILLIONS OF YEN)	
		TOTAL	DAILY AVERAGE	DAILY TOTAL	AVERAGE
1982	12	1,271	4.5	18,257	64.1
1983	11	4,974	17.4	126,858	443.6
1984	11	4,522	15.8	93,118	324.5
1985	21	131,424	461.1	853,336	2,994.2
1986	52	309,701	1,110.0	1,151,863	4,128.5
1987	88	755,203	2,756.2	3,469,228	12,661.4

Source: Tokyo Stock Exchange *Fact Book* (Tokyo: Tokyo Stock Exchange), various issues.

the value of equity trading there has grown to the point where the TSE surpassed the NYSE during 1987 and became the largest single exchange in the world.

The Tokyo Stock Exchange Co. Ltd. was established in 1878 and was replaced in 1943 by the Japan Securities Exchange, a quasi-governmental organization that involved a merger of all existing exchanges in Japan. The Japan Securities Exchange was dissolved in 1947, and the Tokyo Stock Exchange in its present form was established in 1949. Currently there are about 1,640 companies listed on the exchange with a total market value of 428,000 billion yen (about $3.3 trillion). As shown in Table 3.2 average daily share volume has increased by more than ten times, from 90 million shares per day in 1960 to over 960 million shares in 1987. Growth in the *value of shares traded* has increased much faster, because the value figure is also affected by the rising price of the shares that will be discussed in Chapter 4. From 1960 to 1987, it grew by more than 30 times.

Both domestic and foreign stocks are listed on the Tokyo Exchange. The domestic stocks are further divided between the First and Second Section stocks. The 250 most active stocks on the First Section and all foreign stocks are traded on the stock trading floor. Trading in all other stocks (about 1,350) is conducted by computer. Member firms have on-line terminals in their offices where they enter buy and sell orders that are received at the exchange. The *Saitori* member clerks in the computer-assisted trading room at the TSE match buying and selling orders on the electronic "book" display screen and send back confirmations to the parties to the trade. The same information is also recorded on the trade-report printer and displayed on all stock-quote screens on the trading floor.

Besides domestic stocks, there are foreign company stocks listed on the exchange and specifically traded on the TSE foreign stock market opened in December 1973. As shown in Table 3.4, a limited number of foreign companies was listed until a major increase began in 1985. As shown, the value of daily average trading increased to over 12 billion yen in 1987, reflecting the sharp increase in the number of listed foreign corporations and the growing interest in foreign stocks among Japanese investors.

LONDON STOCK EXCHANGE (LSE). The largest established securities market in the United Kingdom, generally referred to as "The Stock Exchange," is the London Stock Exchange. Since 1973 it has served as the Stock Exchange of Great Britain and Ireland, with operating units in London, Dublin, and six other cities. Both listed securities (bonds and equities) and unlisted securities are traded on the LSE. The listed equity segment involves over 2,600 companies (4,900 security issues) with a market value in excess of 1,175.987 million pounds (approximately 1,900 million dollars). Of the 2,600 companies listed on the exchange, about 600 are foreign firms, which is the largest number on any exchange.

The stocks listed on the exchange are divided into three groups: Alpha, Beta, and Gamma. The Alpha stocks are the 65 most actively traded stocks, and the Betas are the next 500 most active stocks. In Alpha and Beta stocks, market-makers are required to provide firm bid-ask quotes that are available to all members of the exchange. The rest of the stocks are Gamma stocks, for which market quotations are only indicative and must be confirmed before a trade. All equity trades must be reported to the Stock Exchange Automated Quotations (SEAQ) within five minutes, although only trades in Alpha stocks are reported in full on the screen.

UNLISTED SECURITIES MARKET (USM). Started by the LSE in 1980, the Unlisted Securities Market (USM) handles smaller companies that have too short a trading record for full listing on the exchange. As of 1986 there were 368 companies on the USM with a total market value of 5,000 million pounds.

OTHER NATIONAL EXCHANGES. Other national exchanges are located in Frankfurt, Toronto, and Paris. In addition, there is the *International Federation of Stock Exchanges,* established in 1961. Members include 33 exchanges or national associations of stock exchanges in 28 countries. Located in Paris, the Federation's 28 full members and 5 associate members meet every autumn to promote a closer collaboration among its members and contribute to the development of securities markets.[19]

Probably the newest national stock exchange is in Beijing, China, established in 1986 in response to the opening up of the Chinese economy. As of 1987 only three stocks were listed, and there was almost no trading taking place, although the members of the exchange met daily.

THE GLOBAL 24-HOUR MARKET. Throughout our discussion of the global securities market we will tend to emphasize the three markets in New York, London, and Tokyo because of their relative size and importance but also because they represent the major segments of a worldwide 24-

---

[19] For an excellent discussion of equity markets around the world, see Bryan deCaires, ed. *The GT Guide to World Equity Markets, 1987* (London: Euromoney Publications Plc, 1987); Thomas J. Carroll, ed. *International Guide to Security Exchanges* (New York: Peat, Marwick, Mitchell & Co., 1986); and David Smyth, *Worldly Wise Investor* (New York: Franklin Watts, 1988).

hour market. Specifically, you will often hear about a continuous market where investment firms "pass the book" around the world. This means that the major active market in securities moves around the globe during the trading hours for these three markets. Consider the individual trading hours for each of the three exchanges translated into a 24-hour Eastern Standard clock:

	Local Time (24 hr.)	24-Hr. EST Clock
New York Stock Exchange	9:30–16:00	0930–1600
Tokyo Stock Exchange	9:00–11:00	2300–0100
	13:00–15:00	0300–0500
London Stock Exchange	8:15–16:15	0215–1015

Therefore, you can conceive of trading starting in New York and going until 1600 in the afternoon, being picked up by Tokyo late in the evening, and going until 0500 in the morning (with some overlap with London), and continuing in London until it begins in New York again (with some overlap) at 9:30. Alternatively, you can envision that the trading begins in Tokyo at 2300 hours and goes until 0500, then moves to London and ends the day in New York. One gets this sense of the flow since the first question a London trader asks in the morning is, "What happened in Tokyo?" and the U.S. trader asks, "What happened in Tokyo and what is happening in London?" The point is, the markets are *almost continuous in time* and certainly *related in economic events.* You are not dealing with three separate and distinct exchanges but one interrelated world market.[20]

REGIONAL SECURITIES EXCHANGES

Regional exchanges have basically the same operating procedures as the NYSE and AMEX but differ in terms of their listing requirements and the geographic distribution of the firms listed. There are two main reasons for the existence of regional stock exchanges. First, they provide trading facilities for local companies that are not large enough to qualify for listing on one of the national exchanges. Their listing requirements are typically less stringent than are those of the national exchanges presented in Table 3.1. Second, they list firms that are also listed on one of the national exchanges for local brokers who are not members of a national exchange. As an example, American Telephone and Telegraph and General Motors are both listed on the NYSE, but they are also listed on several regional exchanges. This dual listing allows a local brokerage firm that is not large enough to purchase a membership on the NYSE (for $200,000 or more) to buy and sell shares of a dual-listed stock (e.g., General Motors) using its membership on a regional exchange. As a result, the broker will not have to go through the NYSE and give up part of his commission. Currently, between 65 and 90 percent of the volume on regional exchanges is attrib-

---

[20] For an example of global trading, see "How Merrill Lynch Moves Its Stock Deals All Around the World," *The Wall Street Journal,* November 9, 1987, 1, 19; and "Opportunity and Risk in the 24-Hour Global Marketplace," (New York: Coopers and Lybrand, 1987).

utable to trading in dual-listed issues. The regional exchanges in the United States are

- Midwest Stock Exchange (Chicago)
- Pacific Stock Exchange (San Francisco–Los Angeles)
- PBW Exchange (Philadelphia–Baltimore–Washington)
- Boston Stock Exchange (Boston)
- Spokane Stock Exchange (Spokane, Washington)
- Honolulu Stock Exchange (Honolulu, Hawaii)
- Intermountain Stock Exchange (Salt Lake City)

The first three exchanges (Midwest, Pacific, PBW) account for about 90 percent of all regional exchange volume. In turn, total regional volume is about 9 to 10 percent of total exchange volume.

In Japan there are eight stock exchanges, with the Tokyo Stock Exchange being the national exchange that accounts for about 83 percent of total volume in the country. The exchange in Osaka accounts for about 12 percent and in Nagoya for about 4.5 percent of the total volume. The remaining exchanges in Kyoto, Hiroshima, Fukuoto, Niigata, and Sapporo account for less than 1 percent of volume.

The United Kingdom has one stock exchange in London with operating units in seven cities, including Dublin, Belfast, Birmingham, Manchester, Bristol, Liverpool, and Glasgow. West Germany has eight stock exchanges, with its national exchange in Frankfurt where about 50 percent of the trading occurs. There are regional exchanges in Dusseldorf, Munich, Hamburg, Berlin, Stuttgart, Hanover, and Bremen.

Without belaboring the point, each country typically has one national exchange that accounts for the majority of trading and several regional exchanges with less stringent listing requirements to allow trading in smaller firms. Recently, several of the national exchanges have created a second-tier market that is a division of the national exchange and allows some of the smaller firms to be traded as part of the national exchange. In general, the fortunes of the regional exchanges have fluctuated substantially over time, based upon interest in small, young firms and/or institutional interest in stocks dually listed on national and regional exchanges.

THE OVER-THE-COUNTER (OTC) MARKET

The over-the-counter market (OTC) includes trading in all stocks not listed on one of the exchanges but can also include trading in stocks that are listed. This latter arrangement, referred to as the *third market,* is discussed in the following section. The OTC market is composed of three segments: (1) NASDAQ/NMS, which are stocks that not only qualify to be on the NASDAQ system but also have a large market value, trading activity, and a minimum number of market-makers,[21] (2) NASDAQ, which are stocks that qualify for inclusion on NASDAQ but are not large enough for the NMS, and (3) a large group of OTC stocks that do not qualify for NASDAQ

---

[21] NASDAQ is an acronym for National Association of Securities Dealers Automated Quotations. The system is discussed in detail in a subsequent subsection. NMS is the acronym for the National Market System.

TABLE 3.5
Number of Companies and Issues and Average Daily Volume of Trading on NASDAQ, 1974–1987

YEAR	NUMBER OF COMPANIES	NUMBER OF ISSUES	AVERAGE DAILY VOLUME (THOUSANDS)
1974	2,463	2,564	4,660
1975	2,467	2,579	5,500
1976	2,495	2,627	6,660
1977	2,456	2,575	7,640
1978	2,475	2,582	10,960
1979	2,543	2,670	14,430
1980	2,894	3,050	26,450
1981	3,353	3,687	30,920
1982	3,264	3,664	33,330
1983	3,901	4,467	62,880
1984	4,097	4,723	59,920
1985	4,136	4,784	82,139
1986	4,417	5,189	113,583
1987	4,706	5,537	149,262

Source: *NASDAQ Fact Book* (Washington, D.C.: National Association of Securities Dealers, Inc., 1988): 5
Reprinted with permission.

but are quoted in the "pink sheets" published by the National Quotation Bureau (NQB). The requirements for inclusion on NASDAQ and the NAS-DAQ/NMS are listed in Table 3.6.

SIZE. There are 2,900 issues included on the NASDAQ, National Market System (NMS). In addition, another 2,400 stocks are traded on the NASDAQ system but are not a part of the NMS. Finally, there are about 11,000 OTC stocks that are regularly quoted in the NQB pink sheets. Table 3.5 sets forth the growth in the number of companies, issues, and volume of trading on NASDAQ. As of April 1988 over 300 issues on NASDAQ were foreign stocks that trade in the United States just as U.S. stocks do. About 200 of these issues trade on NASDAQ and a foreign exchange—for example, Toronto. Many of the large NASDAQ stocks are among the 97 issues traded as American Depository Receipts (ADRs). Also in March 1988 NASDAQ developed a link with the Singapore Stock Exchange that specifically allows 24-hour trading going from NASDAQ in New York to Singapore to a NAS-DAQ/London link and back to New York.

While the OTC is dominant in terms of the number of issues, the TSE and the NYSE are still dominant in terms of the total value of trading. In 1987 the approximate value of equity trading was as follows: TSE ($1,750 billion), NYSE ($1,550 billion), and NASDAQ ($1,200 billion).

There is tremendous diversity in the OTC because there are no minimum requirements for a stock to be traded. Therefore, stocks can range from those of small, unprofitable companies to large, very profitable firms.

On the upper end, all U.S. government bonds are traded on the OTC market, and the majority of bank and insurance stocks. Finally, there are about 100 listed stocks that are also traded on the OTC (the third market)—for example, AT&T, General Motors, IBM, and Xerox.

OPERATION OF THE OTC. As noted, any stock can be traded on the OTC as long as someone indicates a willingness to "make a market" (take a position) in the stock, that is, buy or sell for his or her own account (which means acting as a dealer).[22] This is in contrast to the situation on the listed exchanges, where the specialist keeps the book and attempts to match others' buy and sell orders. Therefore, the OTC market is referred to as a *negotiated market,* in which investors directly negotiate with dealers. Exchanges are *auction markets,* with the specialist acting as the intermediary (auctioneer).

THE **NASDAQ** SYSTEM. NASDAQ is an automated electronic quotation system that serves the vast OTC market. Because any number of dealers can elect to make a market in an OTC stock, it is possible to have ten or more market-makers for a given stock, and it is common to have three to five. Historically, a major problem for a broker trying to buy or sell an OTC stock for a customer has been determining the current quotations by specific market-makers. With NASDAQ, all dealer quotes are available immediately, and the broker can check the quotation machine and call the dealer with the best market, verify that the quote has not changed, and make the sale or purchase. The NASD has specified three levels for the NASDAQ system to serve firms with different needs and interests.[23]

Level 1 provides a single median *representative quote* for firms that want a current quote on OTC stocks but do not consistently buy or sell OTC stocks for their customers and are not market-makers. This composite quote is changed constantly to adjust for any changes by individual market-makers.

Level 2 provides *instantaneous current quotations* by all market-makers in a stock for firms that consistently trade OTC stocks. Given an order to buy or sell, brokers check the quotation machine and call the market-makers with the best market for their purposes (highest bid if they are selling, lowest offer if buying) and consummate the deal.

Level 3 is for OTC market-makers. Such firms want Level 2, but they also need the capability to enter and change their own quotations, which is what Level 3 provides.

LISTING REQUIREMENTS FOR **NASDAQ.** The reporting of quotes and volume of trading for the OTC is contained in two lists: a National Market System (NMS) list and a regular NASDAQ list. As of 1988, there were four sets of listing requirements. The first is for initial listing on any NASDAQ system and is the least stringent. The second is for automatic (mandatory) inclu-

---

[22] *Dealer* and *market-maker* are synonymous.

[23] An analysis of the impact of NASDAQ is contained in Hans R. Stoll, "Dealer Inventory Behavior: An Empirical Investigation of NASDAQ," *Journal of Financial and Quantitative Analysis* 11, no. 3 (September 1976): 359–380.

TABLE 3.6
Qualification Standards for Inclusion in NASDAQ and NASDAQ/NMS

STANDARD	FOR INITIAL NASDAQ INCLUSION (DOMESTIC COMMON STOCKS)	CRITERIA FOR VOLUNTARY NASDAQ/NMS INCLUSION	
		ALTERNATIVE 1	ALTERNATIVE 2
Registration under Section 12(g) of the Securities Exchange Act of 1934 or equivalent	Yes	Yes	Yes
Total assets	$2 million	$2 million	$8 million
Tangible assets	—	—	—
Capital and surplus	$1 million	$1 million	$8 million
Net income	—	$300,00 in Latest or 2 or 3 last fiscal years	—
Operating history	—	—	4 years
Public float (shares)	100,000	350,000	800,000
Market value of float	—	$2 million	$8 million
Minimum bid	—	$3	—
Trading volume	—	—	—
Shareholders of record	300	300	300
Number of market-makers	2	2	2

Note: On August 5, 1988 the NASD filed with the SEC for substantially higher NMS qualification standards but this filing was not yet approved at the time of publication of this book.

Source: *NASDAQ Fact Book,* (Washington, D.C.: National Association of Securities Dealers, Inc., 1987): 16. Reprinted with permission.

sion on the NASDAQ/NMS system, which provides up-to-the-minute volume and last-sale information for the competing market-makers, as well as end-of-the-day information on total volume, high, low, and closing prices for these stocks. In addition, there are two sets of criteria for voluntary participation on the NMS by companies with different characteristics. Voluntary Alternative 1 is for companies that are not as large in assets or net worth but have substantial earnings, while Alternative 2 is for large companies that are not necessarily as profitable. These four sets of criteria are set forth in Table 3.6.

A SAMPLE TRADE.   Assume you are considering the purchase of 100 shares of Apple Computer. Although Apple is large enough and profitable enough to be eligible for listing on a national exchange, the company has never applied for listing because it enjoys a very active market on the OTC. (It is one of the volume leaders with daily volume typically above 500,000 shares and often in excess of 1,000,000 shares.) Therefore, when you contact your broker, he or she will consult the NASDAQ electronic quotation machine to determine the current markets for AAPL, the trading symbol for Apple Computer.[24] He would see that about 15 dealers are making a market in AAPL. An example of differing quotes might be as follows:

[24] Trading symbols are one- to four-letter codes used to designate stocks. Whenever a trade is reported on a stock ticker the trading symbol is used. Many are obvious, like GM (General Motors), F (Ford Motors), GE (General Electric), T (American Telephone and Telegraph).

DEALER	BID	ASK
1	44 1/2	44 3/4
2	44 3/8	44 5/8
3	44 1/4	44 5/8
4	44 3/8	44 3/4

Assuming that these are the best markets available from the total group, your broker would call either Dealer 2 or 3, the two with the lowest offering prices. After verifying the quote, your broker would tell one of these dealers that he wants to buy 100 shares of AAPL at 44 5/8 ($44.625 a share). Because your firm was not a market-maker in the stock, the firm would act as a broker for you and charge $4,462.50 plus a commission for the trade. If the broker had been a market-maker in AAPL and had the asking price of 44 5/8, then he would have sold the stock to you at 44 5/8 *net* (without commission). If you had been interested in selling 100 shares of Apple Computer instead of buying, the broker would have contacted Dealer 1, who made the highest bid.

CHANGING DEALER INVENTORY.   At this point let us consider the quotation an OTC dealer would give to change inventory on a given stock. For example, assume Dealer 4, with a current quote of 44 3/8 bid–44 3/4 ask, decides to increase his holdings of AAPL. The quotes on the NASDAQ quote machine indicate that the highest bid is currently 44 1/2. The dealer can increase the bid to 44 1/2 and get some of the business currently going to Dealer 1 or take a more aggressive action of raising the bid to 44 5/8 and buy all the stock that is offered—including some from Dealers 2 or 3, who are offering it at 44 5/8. In this example, the dealer raises his bid but does not change his asking price, which was above that of Dealers 2 or 3. Thus, this dealer is going to buy stock but probably will not sell any. If the dealer had excess stock, he or she would keep the bid below the market (lower than 44 1/2) and reduce the asking price to 44 5/8 or less. Dealers are constantly changing their bid and/or their ask price, depending upon their current inventory or the outlook for the stock.[25]

THE THIRD MARKET.   The term *third market* is used to describe over-the-counter trading of shares listed on an exchange. While most transactions in listed stocks take place on an exchange, an investment firm that is not a member of an exchange can make a market in a listed stock. Most of the activity on this market is conducted by large financial institutions trading in well-known stocks like AT&T, IBM, and Xerox. Success or failure depends upon whether the OTC market in these stocks is as good as the exchange market and what is the relative cost of the transaction compared to the cost on the exchange. While current volume is below that experienced in 1975 prior to negotiated commissions, the third market continues to serve a very important function during rare periods when trading is not

---

[25] A number of studies have examined the determinants of the dealers bid-ask spread. For a review article, see Kalman J. Cohen, Stephen F. Maier, Robert A. Schwartz, and David K. Whitcomb, "Market Makers and the Market Spread: A Review of Recent Literature," *Journal of Financial and Quantitative Analysis* 14, no. 4 (November 1979): 813–836.

available on the NYSE either because trading is suspended or the exchange is closed.[26]

THE FOURTH MARKET. The term *fourth market* is used to describe the direct trading of securities between two parties with no broker intermediary. In almost all cases, both parties involved are institutions. When you think about it, a direct transaction is really not that unusual. If you own 100 shares of AT&T and decide to sell them, there is nothing wrong with simply asking your friends or associates if any of them would be interested in buying the stock at a mutually agreeable price and making the transaction directly. Investors typically buy or sell stock through a broker because it is faster and easier. Also, you may get better execution because there is a good chance of finding the "best" buyer through a broker. You are willing to pay a fee (i.e., a commission) for these liquidity services. The fourth market evolved because of the substantial brokerage fee charged institutions with large orders. At some point it becomes worthwhile for institutions to attempt to deal directly with each other and save the brokerage fee. Assume an institution decides to sell 100,000 shares of AT&T, which is selling for about $30 a share (total value of $3 million). The average commission on such a transaction prior to negotiated rates in 1975 was about 1 percent of the value of the trade, or about $30,000. Because of this cost, it became attractive for a selling institution to spend some time and effort finding another institution interested in increasing its holding of AT&T and negotiating a direct sale. Currently, such transactions cost about 5 cents a share, which implies a cost of $5,000—lower, but still not trivial. Because of the diverse nature of the fourth market and the lack of reporting requirements, there are no data available regarding its specific size or growth. Apparently, it still exists but is smaller than it was prior to negotiated commissions.

DETAILED ANALYSIS OF THE EXCHANGE MARKET

Because of the importance of the listed exchange market, it must be dealt with at some length. In this section we discuss the several types of membership on the exchanges, the major types of orders used, and finally the function of the specialist, or equivalent central market-maker in non-U.S. markets. These individuals are a critical component of a "good" exchange market.

EXCHANGE MEMBERSHIP

Listed securities exchanges in the United States typically have four major categories of membership: (1) specialist, (2) commission broker, (3) floor-broker, and (4) registered trader. Specialists, who constitute about 25 percent of the total membership on exchanges, will be discussed after a description of alternative orders on the exchange.

Commission brokers are employees of a member firm who buy or sell for the customers of the firm. When an investor places an order to buy or

---

[26] Rhonda L. Rundle, "Jefferies 'Third Market' Trading Often Steals Show from Exchanges," *The Wall Street Journal*, July 12, 1984, 29.

sell stock through a registered representative of a brokerage firm that is a member of the exchange, it will contact its commission broker on the floor of the exchange. That broker will go to the appropriate post on the floor and buy or sell the stock as instructed.

Floor brokers are members of an exchange who act as brokers on the floor for other members. They are typically not connected with a member firm and own their own seat. As an example, when commission brokers for Merrill Lynch become too busy to handle all of their orders, they will ask one of the floor brokers to help them. At one time they were referred to as "$2 brokers" because that is what they received for each order. Currently they receive about $4 per 100-share order.

Registered traders are allowed to use their membership to buy and sell for their own account. They therefore save the commission on their own trading, and observers believe they have an advantage because they are on the floor. The exchanges and others believe they should be allowed these advantages because they provide the market with added liquidity, but there are regulations regarding how they trade and how many registered traders can be in a trading crowd around a specialists' booth at a point in time. Registered traders in recent years have become *registered competitive market-makers (RCMM),* who have specific trading obligations set by the exchange. Their activity is reported as part of the specialist group.[27]

TYPES OF ORDERS   It is important to understand the different types of orders used by individual investors and the specialist in his dealer function.

MARKET ORDERS. The most frequent type of order, *market order,* is an order to buy or sell a stock at the best price currently prevailing. An investor who wants to sell some stock using a market order indicates a willingness to sell immediately at the highest bid available at the time the order reaches the specialist on the exchange. A *market buy order* indicates the investor is willing to pay the lowest offering price available at the time the order reaches the floor of the exchange. Market orders are used when an individual wants to effect a transaction quickly (wants immediate liquidity) and is willing to accept the prevailing market price. Assume you are interested in General Electric (GE), and you called your broker to find out the current "market" on the stock. The quotation machine indicates that the prevailing market is 65 bid–65 1/4 ask. This means that currently the highest bid on the books of the specialist is 65; that is, $65 is the most that anyone has offered to pay for GE. The lowest offer is 65 1/4, the lowest price anyone is willing to accept for selling the stock. If you placed a market buy order for 100 shares, you would buy 100 shares at $65.25 a share (the lowest ask price) for a total cost of $6,525 plus commission. If you sub-

---

[27] Prior to the late 1970s, there were also odd-lot dealers who bought and sold to individuals with orders for less than a round lot (usually 100 shares). Recently, this function is either handled by the specialist or by some large brokerage firms.

mitted a *market sell order* for 100 shares, you would sell the shares at $65 each and receive $6,500, less commission.

LIMIT ORDERS. With a *limit order,* the individual placing the order specifies the buy or sell price. You might submit a bid to purchase 100 shares of Coca-Cola stock at $50 a share when the current market is 55 bid–55 1/4 ask, with the expectation that the stock will decline to $50 in the near future. You must also indicate how long the limit order will be outstanding. The alternatives, in terms of time, are basically without bounds—they can be instantaneous ("fill or kill," meaning fill instantly or cancel it), for part of a day, for a full day, for several days, a week, a month, or open-ended, which means the order is *good until canceled (GTC).* Rather than wait for a given price on a stock, your broker will give the limit order to the specialist, who will put it in his book and act as the broker's representative. When and if the market reaches the limit order price, the specialist will execute the order and inform your broker. The specialist receives a small part of the commission for rendering this service.

SHORT SALES. Most investors purchase stock (i.e., go *long*) with the expectation that they will derive their return from an increase in value. If you believe that a stock is overpriced, however, and want to take advantage of an expected decline in the price, you sell the stock *short.* A *short sale* is the sale of stock that is not owned with the intent of purchasing it later at a lower price. Specifically, you would borrow the stock from another investor through your broker, sell it in the market, and subsequently purchase it again at a price lower (you hope) than the price at which you sold it, thereby replacing it. The investor who lent the stock has the proceeds of the sale as collateral. In turn, this investor can invest these funds in short-term risk-free securities. While there is no time limit on a short sale, the lender can indicate a desire to sell the shares, in which case your broker must find another investor to make the loan.[28]

Two technical points in connection with short sales are important. First, a short sale can be made only on an *uptick trade,* meaning the price of the sale must be higher than the last trade price. The reason for this restriction is that the exchanges do not want traders to be able to *force* a profit on a short sale by pushing the price down through continually selling short. Therefore, the transaction price for a short sale must be an uptick or, if there is no change in price, the previous price must have been higher than its previous price (a *zero uptick*). An example of a zero uptick is the following set of transaction prices: 42, 42 1/4, 42 1/4. You could sell short at 42 1/4 even though it is no change from the previous trade at 42 1/4. Second, the short seller is responsible for the dividends to the investor who lent the stock. The purchaser of the short-sale stock receives the

---

[28] For a discussion of short-selling strategies, see Brett Duval Fromson, "Shortseller in the Bull Market," *Fortune,* August 31, 1987, 52, 53, 54, 56. For a discussion of profitable results, see Gary Putka, "Fortune Smiles on Short Side of Market," *The Wall Street Journal,* October 27, 1987, 5.

dividend from the corporation, so the short seller must pay a similar dividend to the lender.

SPECIAL ORDERS. In addition to these general orders, there are several special types of orders. One is a *stop loss order,* which is a conditional market order whereby the investor indicates a willingness to sell a stock if the stock drops to a given price. Assume you buy a stock at 50 and expect it to go up. Still, if you are wrong, you want to minimize or limit your losses, so you could put in a stop loss order at 45, in which case, if the stock dropped to 45, your stop loss order would become a *market sell order,* and the stock would be sold at the prevailing market price. The order does not guarantee that you will get the $45; you can get a little bit more or a little bit less. Because of the possibility of market disruption caused by a large number of stop loss orders, exchanges, on occasion, have canceled all such orders on certain stocks and have not allowed brokers to accept further stop loss orders on the issues involved. Another type of stop loss, but on the other side, is a *stop buy order.* This is used by an investor who has sold stock short and wants to minimize any loss in case the stock begins to increase in value. This is a conditional buy order at a price above the price at which the investor sold the stock short. Assume you sold a stock short at 50, expecting it to decline to 40. To protect yourself from an increase, you could put in a stop buy order to purchase the stock if it reached a price of 55. This conditional buy order would hopefully limit any loss on the short sale to approximately $5 a share.

MARGIN TRANSACTIONS. Given any type of order, an investor can pay for the stock with cash or can borrow part of the cost, that is, can *leverage* the transaction. Leverage is accomplished by buying or selling *on margin,* which means that the investor pays some cash and borrows the rest through his broker, putting up the stock for collateral. As shown in Figure 3.1, the dollar amount of margin credit extended by brokers and dealers increased substantially between early 1985 and late 1987. The rate charged on the loan by the broker is typically 1 percent above the rate charged by the bank making the loan. In turn, the bank rate is referred to as the *call money rate,* which is generally about 1 percent below the prime rate. For example, in August 1988 the prime rate was 9 1/2 percent, and the call money rate was 8 3/4–9 percent. The determination of the maximum proportion that can be borrowed is set by the Federal Reserve Board under Regulations T and U, enacted during the 1930s because it was contended that the excessive credit extended for stock acquisition contributed to the stock market collapse of 1929. Since the enactment of the regulations, the *margin requirement* (the proportion of total value that must be paid for in cash) has varied from 40 percent (you could borrow 60 percent of the value) to 100 percent (no borrowing allowed). As of August 1988, the specified *initial margin requirement* by the Federal Reserve was 50 percent, although individual investment firms can require a higher rate. After the initial pur-

FIGURE **3.1**
Borrowing against Stocks
Amount of Margin Credit Extended by Brokers and Dealers at End of Month
(in Billions of Dollars)

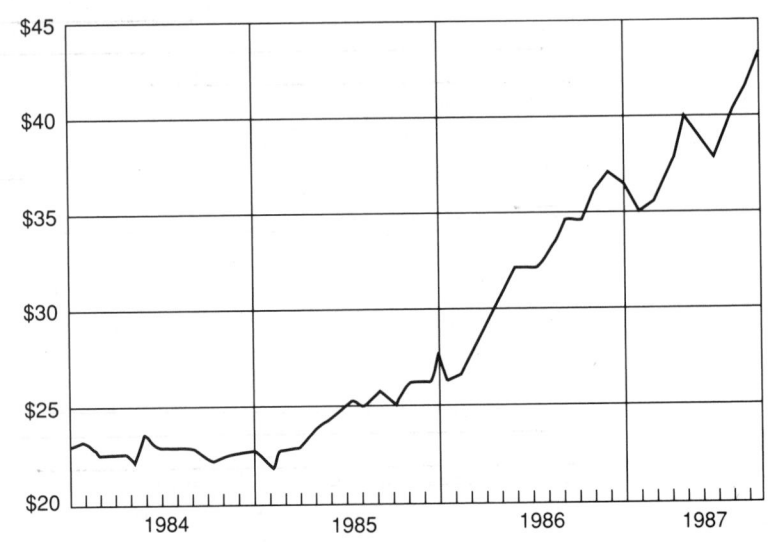

Source: Federal Reserve Board, Washington, D.C., 1988.

chase, changes in the market price of the stock will cause changes in the proportion of *equity* (equity equals the market value of the collateral stock minus the amount borrowed). Obviously, if the stock price increases, the investor's equity *as a proportion of the total market value of the stock* will increase (that is, the investor's margin will exceed the initial margin requirement).

Assume that you acquired 200 shares of a $50 stock (total cost is $10,000). Given a 50 percent initial margin, you borrowed $5,000, making your initial equity $5,000. If the stock price increases to $70 a share, the total market value is $14,000, and your equity is now $9,000, or 64 percent ($9,000/$14,000). In contrast, if the stock price declined to $40 a share, the total market value would be $8,000, and your equity would be $3,000 or 37.5 percent ($3,000/$8,000). At this point, the relevant criterion is the *maintenance margin,* the required proportion of equity to the total value of the stock. At present, the minimum maintenance margin specified by the Federal Reserve is 25 percent, but, again, individual firms can dictate a higher margin for their customers. If the stock price declines to the point where your equity drops below 25 percent of the total value of the stock position, the account is considered *undermargined,* and you must provide more equity. (You will receive a *margin call* so informing you.) If you do not respond with the required funds in the time allotted, the stock will be sold to pay off the loan (the time allowed to meet the call varies between investment firms and market conditions—that is, under volatile conditions the time allowed can be shortened drastically). To continue the example, if the stock declines to $30 a share, the total market value of the stock would be $6,000, and your equity would be $1,000, which is only about 17 percent of the total value ($1,000/$6,000). Thus, you would receive a margin call for approximately $667, which would give you equity of $1,667, or 25 percent of the total value of the account ($1,667/$6,667).[29]

You should recognize that buying on margin provides all the advantages and disadvantages of leverage; the lower the margin, the more you can borrow, and the greater the percentage gain or loss on your investment when the stock price increases or decreases. The leverage factor is equal to 1/percent margin. Thus, if the margin is 50 percent, the leverage factor is 2, that is, 1/50. This means that if the rate of return on the stock is plus or minus 10 percent, the return on the equity for an investor who borrowed 50 percent of the purchase price would be plus or minus 20 percent. If the margin declines to 33 percent, you can borrow more (67 percent), and the leverage factor is 3, that is, 1/.33. Therefore, when you acquire stock or other investments using margin, you are increasing the financial risk of the investment beyond that inherent in the security itself, and you should increase your required rate of return accordingly.[30]

1/.5

THE SPECIALIST

With justification, the stock exchange specialist, or his equivalent on other exchanges, has been referred to as the center of the auction market. As noted, a major requirement for a "good" market is liquidity, which is heavily dependent upon how the specialist or counterpart does his job.

Our initial discussion will center on the specialist in U.S. markets, followed by a consideration of comparable individuals on exchanges in other countries. The specialist is a member of the exchange who applies to the exchange for stocks to be assigned to him.[31] The typical specialist will handle about 15 stocks. The capital required is either $500,000 or enough to purchase 5,000 shares of each stock assigned, whichever is greater. There was substantial pressure to increase the capital requirement following the October 1987 crash, since the Brady Commission Report indicated that the lack of capital was a contributing factor to the price volatility (a chapter from the Brady Report that discusses the market crash is included as an appendix to this chapter).

FUNCTIONS OF THE SPECIALIST. Specialists have two major functions. First, they serve as *brokers* who handle the limit orders or special orders placed with member brokers. An individual broker who receives a limit order to

[29] For a discussion of heavy margin calls following the market decline in October 1987, see Karen Slater, "Margin Calls Create Dilemma for Investors," *The Wall Street Journal,* October 23, 1987, 21.

[30] For a discussion on the tax implications, see Jill Bettner, "Brokers Begin Pushing Margin Loans—But Critics Say Borrowers Should Beware," *The Wall Street Journal,* August 26, 1987, 17.

[31] Most specialists are part of a *specialist unit* that can be a formal organization of specialists (a specialist firm) or a set of independent specialists who join together to spread the workload and the risk of the stocks assigned to the unit.

purchase a stock at $5 below the current market does not have the time or inclination to constantly watch the stock to see when and if the decline takes place. Therefore, the broker leaves the limit order (or a stop loss or stop buy order) with the specialist, who enters it in his book and executes it when appropriate. For this service the specialist receives a portion of the broker's commission on the trade.

The second major function of specialists is to act as *dealers* in the stocks assigned to them in order to maintain a "fair and orderly market." They are expected to buy and sell for their own account when there is insufficient public supply or demand to provide a continuous, liquid market. In this function they act like dealers on the OTC market. If a stock is currently selling for about $40 per share, the current bid and ask in an auction market (without the intervention of the specialist) might be a 40 bid–41 ask. If market buy and sell orders arrive in a random fashion, the price of the stock would fluctuate between 40 and 41 constantly—a movement of 2.5 percent between trades. Most investors would probably consider such a price pattern too volatile; the market would not be considered continuous. The specialist is expected to provide an alternative bid and/or ask that will narrow the spread and thereby provide greater price continuity over time. In this example, the specialist would either enter a bid of 40 1/2 or 40 3/4 or an ask of 40 1/2 or 40 1/4 to narrow the spread to one-half or one-quarter point. The specialist can enter either side of the market, depending upon several factors. The trend of the market is one factor. Since specialists are committed to being a stabilizing force in the market, they are expected to buy or sell against the market when prices are clearly moving in one direction (buying stock for their own inventory when there is an excess of sell orders and the market is definitely declining and selling stock from their inventory or selling short when there is an excess of buy orders and the market is rising). Note, they are not expected to prevent the prices from rising or declining, but only to ensure that the prices change in an orderly fashion.

Another factor affecting what side of the market the specialist enters is his current inventory position in the stock. If a specialist has a large inventory position in a given stock, all other factors being equal, he would probably enter on the ask (sell) side in order to reduce his heavy inventory. In contrast, if previous market action had prompted heavy selling from his inventory, or short sales, the specialist would tend toward the bid (buy) side to rebuild his inventory or close out his short positions. Finally, the position of his book (i.e., the specialist's information on all limit orders for a stock) will influence his actions. If the specialist notes numerous limit buy orders (bids) close to the current market and very few limit sell orders (asks), he might surmise that the most likely future move for the stock, in the absence of any new information, is toward a higher price (because there is apparently heavy demand and limited supply). Under such conditions, the specialist would probably be on the bid side of the quote to accumulate stock in anticipation of an increase.

INCOME OF THE SPECIALIST. The specialist derives income from both major functions. The actual breakdown between the two will depend upon the specific stock. In the case of a very actively traded stock (e.g., IBM), there is not much need for the specialist to act as a dealer, because substantial public interest in the issue creates a tight market. In this case his major concern (and main source of income for this stock) is maintaining the limit orders for the stock. In contrast, for a stock with low trading volume and substantial price volatility, the specialist would have to be an active dealer and his income from that stock will depend upon his ability to trade in it profitably. A major advantage for specialists when trading the stock is their book, which contains all the limit orders for the stock. Only specialists are supposed to see the book, giving them a monopoly source of very important information. A full set of limit orders, representing the current supply and demand curve for a stock, provides the specialist with a good idea of the probable future direction of that stock. This information should allow them to profit on their dealer transactions despite being forced to buy or sell against the market for short periods of time.[32] In addition, the income derived from acting as a broker can be substantial and is basically without risk. Most specialists attempt to balance their portfolio between some strong broker stocks that provide a steady riskless source of income and some stocks that require an active dealer role.

Given the capital committed to the specialist function and the risk involved in acting as a dealer, one might wonder about the rate of return that specialists receive on their capital. An SEC study indicated substantial variation in the monthly income of specialist units, with the greatest variability experienced by units that have high inventory activity, that is, are most active in market-making. An analysis of gross income per month relative to the average dollar of investment indicated that the annual rate of return for high-activity units was over 80 percent and the return for the medium activity group was about 110 percent, while the low-activity group had an average rate of return of almost 190 percent.[33] Four points regarding these results are important. First, it appears that the returns are clearly above normal. Second, the least active specialist units receive the greatest return, which is disturbing since it is inconsistent with the purpose of the position. Third, these rates of return are for the period prior to negotiated rates; therefore, it is almost certain that current returns are not as large, but specific data are not available. Finally, following the October crash,

---

[32] For evidence that the specialists do not fare too badly even when they are forced to trade against the market, see Frank K. Reilly and Eugene F. Drzycimski, "The Stock Exchange Specialist and the Market Impact of Major World Events," *Financial Analysts Journal* 31, no. 4 (July–August 1975): 27–32. Also, if there is a major imbalance in trading due to new information, the specialist can request a temporary suspension of trading. For an analysis of what occurs during the period surrounding these suspensions, see Michael H. Hopewell and Arthur L. Schwartz, Jr., "Temporary Trading Suspensions in Individual NYSE Securities," *Journal of Finance* 33, no. 5 (December 1978): 1355–1373; and Frank J. Fabozzi and Christopher K. Ma, "The Over-the-Counter Market and New York Stock Exchange Trading Halts," *The Financial Review* 23, no. 4 (November 1988): 427–437.

[33] United States House Committee on Interstate and Foreign Commerce, subcommittee on Commerce and Finance. Securities Industry Study: Report and Hearings. 92nd Congress, 1st and 2nd sessions, 1972, Chapter 12.

there is substantial pressure for the specialists to increase their capital positions, which would probably cause a reduction in the rate of return on them.[34]

MARKET-MAKERS OUTSIDE THE UNITED STATES

TOKYO STOCK EXCHANGE. The TSE has a total of 97 "regular members" and *Saitori* members. Similar to the United States, a membership requires the purchase of a seat, which currently costs about 1.15 billion yen (about $8 million). For each membership, the firm is allowed several people on the floor of the exchange depending upon its trading volume and capital position (the average number is 20 per firm for a regular member and almost 90 per *Saitori* member). The employee of a regular member is called a *trading clerk,* while the employees of a *Saitori* member are called *intermediary clerks.* Regular members buy and sell securities on the TSE either as agent or principal (i.e., broker or dealer). *Saitori* members specialize in acting as intermediaries (brokers) for securities transactions among regular members, and they also maintain the book for regular limit orders (stop loss and stop buy orders as well as short selling are not allowed). They are similar to the U.S. exchange specialist in that they match buy and sell orders for customers, handle limit orders, and are not allowed to deal with public customers. They differ from the U.S. exchange specialist since they do not act as a dealer to maintain an orderly market—this function is left to the regular member, who, unlike the *Saitori* member, is allowed to buy and sell for his own account.

TSE membership is available to companies (corporations) licensed by the minister of finance. Member applicants may request any of four licenses: (1) to trade securities as a dealer, (2) to trade as a broker, (3) to underwrite new securities on secondary offerings, or (4) to handle retail distribution of new or outstanding securities. While a firm may have more than one license, it is prohibited from acting as principal and agent in the same transaction. The minimum capital required varies from 200 million to 3 billion yen ($1 million to $15 million) depending upon the type of license(s) held.

Although Japan's securities laws state that foreign securities firms may obtain membership on the exchanges, the individual exchanges determine whether membership will be granted. Currently there are 23 foreign members on the TSE. Six were admitted in February 1986 and an additional 17 were granted membership in late 1987. The enrollment fee was 1.15 billion yen (about $8 million).[35]

LONDON STOCK EXCHANGE (LSE). Historically, members on the LSE were either *brokers,* who could only act as an agent trading shares on behalf of

---

[34] For a proposed means of evaluating specialists, see Amir Barnea, "Performance Evaluation of NYSE Specialists," *Journal of Financial and Quantitative Analysis* 9, no. 4 (September 1974): 511–535.

[35] Some observers have questioned the pure economics of these memberships, but the firms have defended them as a means of becoming a part of the very lucrative Japanese financial community. In this regard, see Kathryn Graven, "Tokyo Stock Exchange's Broker-Fees Cut Is Seen Trimming Foreign Firms' Profits," *The Wall Street Journal,* October 2, 1987, 17.

customers, or *jobbers,* who could act as a market-maker buying and selling shares as a principal. The exchange went through a major change to a deregulated environment on October 27, 1986 (referred to as the "Big Bang"). Currently brokers are allowed to make markets in various equities and gilts (British government bonds), and conversely, jobbers are allowed to deal with non-stock exchange members (the public and institutions). A further discussion of changes after the "Big Bang" is contained in the following section on changes in the capital markets.

Membership is granted based upon experience and competency, and there are no citizenship or residency requirements. As of July 1986, 5,191 individual memberships were held by 214 broker firms and 22 jobbers. While membership is acquired on an individual basis, the operational unit is a firm. It pays a membership fee based upon the number of exchange-approved members employed during its first year of membership. Subsequently each member firm pays an annual charge equal to 1 percent of its gross revenues.

CHANGES IN THE SECURITIES MARKETS

WHY THE MARKET IS CHANGING

Prior to 1965 the operations of the securities markets were fairly stable, but subsequent changes have been significant and are sure to affect the future. Almost all the changes over the past 25 years were prompted by the significant growth of trading by large financial institutions like banks, insurance companies, pension funds, and investment companies. The trading patterns and requirements of institutions are different from those of individual investors, for whom the market mechanism was originally developed.

EVIDENCE OF INSTITUTIONALIZATION. The growing impact of large financial institutions is evidenced by data on *block* trades (transactions involving at least 10,000 shares) and size of trades (Table 3.7). Financial institutions are the main source of large block trades; and the number of block trades has grown steadily, from an average of 9 per day in 1965 to over 3,600 a day in 1987. On average, such trades constitute one-half of all the volume on the exchange. Institutional involvement is also reflected in the average size of trades, which has grown consistently, from about 200 shares in 1965 to over 2,100 shares in 1987 (Table 3.7).

EFFECTS OF INSTITUTIONAL INVESTORS ON THE SECURITIES MARKETS

One can conceive of the following five major effects of an institutional market:

1. The imposition of negotiated (competitive) commission rates
2. The influence of block trades
3. The creation of a tiered trading market
4. The impact of institutions on stock price volatility
5. The development of a national market system (NMS)

TABLE 3.7
Block Transactions[a] and Average Shares per Sale on the NYSE

YEAR	TOTAL NUMBER OF BLOCK TRANSACTIONS	TOTAL NUMBER OF SHARES IN BLOCK TRADES (000)	PERCENTAGE OF REPORTED VOLUME	AVERAGE NUMBER OF BLOCK TRANSACTIONS PER DAY	AVERAGE SHARES PER TRADE
1965	2,171	48,262	3.1	9	224
1966	3,642	85,298	4.5	14	240
1967	6,685	169,365	6.7	27	257
1968	11,254	292,680	10.0	50	302
1969	15,132	402,063	14.1	61	357
1970	17,217	450,908	15.4	68	388
1971	26,941	692,536	17.8	106	428
1972	31,207	766,406	18.5	124	443
1973	29,233	721,356	17.8	116	449
1974	23,200	549,387	15.6	92	438
1975	34,420	778,540	16.6	136	495
1976	47,632	1,001,254	18.7	188	559
1977	54,275	1,183,924	22.4	215	641
1978	75,036	1,646,905	22.9	298	717
1979	97,509	2,164,726	26.5	305	787
1980	133,597	3,311,132	29.2	528	872
1981	145,564	3,771,442	31.8	575	1,013
1982	254,707	6,742,481	41.0	1,007	1,305
1983	363,415	9,842,080	45.6	1,436	1,434
1984	433,427	11,492,091	49.8	1,713	1,781
1985	539,039	14,222,272	51.7	2,139	1,878
1986	665,587	17,811,335	49.9	2,631	1,881
1987	920,679	24,497,241	51.2	3,639	2,112

[a]10,000 shares or more.

Source: *NYSE Fact Book* (New York: New York Stock Exchange, various issues).

NEGOTIATED COMMISSIONS

BACKGROUND. When the NYSE was formally established in 1792 by the signing of the Buttonwood Agreement, it was agreed that the members would carry out all trades in designated stocks on the exchange, and that they would charge nonmembers on the basis of a *minimum commission schedule,* which meant that nobody could engage in price cutting. Because the market was designed for individual investors, the pricing of trading services (i.e., the minimum commission schedule) was developed to compensate for the handling of small orders and made no allowance for the substantial economies of scale involved in trading large orders for institutions. As a result, when institutions became more active in the mid-1960s, they were paying substantially more in commissions than the cost of the transaction.

The initial reaction to the excess commissions was the use of *give-ups* wherein brokers agreed to pay part of their commissions (sometimes as much as 80 percent) to other brokerage houses or research firms (who were providing services to the institution) designated by the institution making the trade. (These commission dollars were referred to as *soft dollars.*)

Another response was the increased use of the *third market,* where commissions were not fixed as they were on the NYSE. As a result, from 1965 to 1972, third-market volume grew steadily in absolute terms and as a percentage of volume on the NYSE. There was a decline after 1972 because of the change in commission structure, as will be discussed in the following section.

The fixed commission structure also fostered the development and use of the *fourth market,* where two institutions deal directly with one another and therefore save the full commission. Finally, some institutions attempted to become members of one of the exchanges. The NYSE and AMEX would not allow institutional members, but some of the regional exchanges admitted the institutions to increase trading volume.

IMPOSITION OF NEGOTIATED COMMISSIONS. Beginning in 1970, the SEC considered implementing negotiated commissions, wherein the fixed commission structure did not hold, and the broker and customer could negotiate the commission involved. Although there was opposition by the NYSE and its member firms, the SEC began a program of negotiated commissions on large transactions and finally allowed negotiated commissions on all transactions on May 1, 1975 (May Day).

The effect on commissions charged has been dramatic. Initially, the negotiated commissions were stated in terms of discounts from pre–May Day fixed rates. The discounts started at 30 percent and increased to over 50 percent on *no-brainers* (relatively small trades on liquid stocks, such as 2,000 shares of AT&T). Currently, commissions for institutions are stated in cents per share (e.g., 5 to 10 cents per share) irrespective of the price of the stock, which implies a very large discount on high-priced shares. Although initially there was little discounting for trades by individuals, eventually discount brokers appeared who charged for only straight transactions (no research advice, no safekeeping, etc.).[36] Notably, the discounts vary depending on the size of the trade. The discount firms advertise extensively in *The Wall Street Journal* and *Barron's.*

There were numerous mergers and liquidations by smaller investment firms after May Day, suggesting that there will be fewer, but larger and stronger, full-service firms in the industry.[37]

During the period of fixed minimum commissions, it was cheaper for most institutions to buy research using soft dollars than to establish extensive in-house research staffs. With competitive rates, there were no excess commissions available, and the institutions used large brokerage

---

[36] See Tim Carrington, "Discounters Are Taking Ever-Wider Slice of Broker Commissions, SIA Study Finds," *The Wall Street Journal,* March 7, 1983, 7.

[37] Carol J. Loomis, "The Fight for Financial Turf," *Fortune,* December 28, 1981, 54–65; and Carol J. Loomis, "Where Does Wall Street's Shakeout Leave Its Customers?" *Fortune,* June 19, 1978, 140–144.

firms that had good trading capability plus well-staffed research departments. As a result, most independent research firms either disbanded or merged with full-service brokerage firms.

Regional stock exchanges flourished during the early 1970s because they helped institutions distribute soft dollars, allowed institutions to become members, and were a conduit for trading large blocks. With negotiated rates, there were few excess commission dollars and little incentive for the institutions to maintain memberships. Hence, some observers expected regional exchanges to be adversely affected. Apparently, the unique trading capability developed by these exchanges and their ability to implement block trades were somewhat effective because relative trading on these exchanges as a group has been maintained.

The third market expanded rapidly from 1965 to 1972 because of low commission trading by institutions. In contrast, when the commissions on the exchanges declined after May Day, relative trading volume on the third market also declined. While it still exists in 1988, third-market trading is currently only about 1 percent of NYSE volume, compared to about 7 percent pre-1972.

SUMMARY OF EFFECTS.   There has been a significant decline in total commissions paid and a consequent change in the size and structure of the industry. While independent research firms and the third market have contracted, regional stock exchanges have felt little impact.[38]

EFFECTS OF BLOCK TRADES AND SPECIALISTS

The increase in block trading by institutions has been a major test of the market's liquidity. The specialist system had three problems with regard to block trading: *capital, commitment,* and *contacts* (the "three Cs."). First, specialists were undercapitalized when it came to dealing in large blocks. It had become more difficult for the specialist to come up with the capital needed to acquire 10,000 or 20,000 shares. Second, even when specialists had the capital, they may have been unwilling to commit themselves because of the risk involved. Finally, specialists are not allowed to deal directly with non-brokers (Rule 113 of the NYSE). Because they cannot contact institutions to determine interest in a "block" brought by another institution, they are cut off from the major source of demand for blocks and are reluctant to take a position in a "thinly" traded stock.

BLOCK HOUSES.   This lack of capital, commitment, and contacts by specialists created a vacuum in block trading and resulted in the development of *block houses.* Block houses help institutions locate other institutions with an interest in buying or selling given stocks. They are brokerage firms (members and nonmembers of an exchange) that stand ready to help buy or sell blocks for institutions. A good block house has the requisites mentioned before: (1) the capital required to position a large block, (2) willingness to commit this capital to a block transaction, and (3) contacts among institutions.

---

[38] An article that discusses some of these factors is, Seha M. Tinic and Richard R. West, "The Securities Industry under Negotiated Brokerage Commissions: Changes in the Structure and Performance of New York Stock Exchange Member Firms," *Bell Journal of Economics* 11, no. 1 (Spring 1980): 29–41.

EXAMPLE OF A BLOCK TRADE. Assume a mutual fund owns 250,000 shares of Ford Motors and decides to sell 50,000 shares of this position through Goldman Sachs & Company (GS&Co.), a large active block house that is a lead underwriter for Ford and knows institutions with an interest in the stock. The trader for the mutual fund would contact a block trader at Goldman Sachs, tell him that he wants to sell the 50,000 share block, and ask what GS&Co. can do about it. Traders at Goldman Sachs would contact several institutions that own Ford to see if any of them would like to add to their position and determine the institution's bid. Assume that GS&Co. receives commitments from four different institutions for a total of 40,000 shares at an average price of 49 5/8 (the last sale of Ford on the NYSE was 49 3/4). At this point, Goldman Sachs might go back to the mutual fund and bid 49 1/2 minus a negotiated commission for the total 50,000 shares. Assuming the fund accepts the bid, Goldman Sachs now owns the block and will immediately sell 40,000 shares to the four institutions that made prior commitments and also "position" 10,000 shares. (This means that they own the 10,000 shares and must eventually sell them at the best price possible.) Because GS&Co. is a member of the NYSE, the block will be processed (*crossed*) on the exchange as one transaction of 50,000 shares at 49 1/2. In the process, the specialist on the NYSE may take some of the stock to fill limit orders on his book at prices between 49 1/2 and 49 3/4. For working on this trade, GS&Co. has received a negotiated commission, but it has committed almost $500,000 to position the 10,000 shares. The major risk to GS&Co. is the possibility of a subsequent price change on the 10,000 shares. If it can sell the 10,000 shares for 49 1/2 or more, it will just about break even on the position and have the commission as income. If the price weakens, it may have to sell the position at 49 1/4 and take a loss on it. This loss of about $2,500 will offset the income from the commission.

This example indicates the importance of having the *contacts* to quickly find institutions with an interest, the *capital* to position a portion of the block, and the willingness to *commit* that capital to the block trade. Without all three, the transaction would not have taken place.

DEVELOPMENT OF TIERED TRADING MARKETS

The dominance of trading by institutions has resulted in a distinction among individual stocks based upon their appeal to institutions. The result is a *tiered market,* which occurs when investors are willing to pay different price-earnings ratios for alternative stocks with basically the same risk and growth characteristics. The prevailing tiered market is concentrated on large-capitalization firms. Institutions will shift between industries and types of companies (growth, cyclical, etc.), but the overriding criterion is size; they will generally not acquire a small firm. This preference for large-capitalization firms is a logical consequence of institutional portfolio managers who want to maximize return for a given level of risk. As discussed in Chapter 2, a major tool for minimizing risk is diversification. Unfortunately, there is a cost to diversification, because it requires owning numerous stocks, and there are also costs of administration and research on these stocks, all of which reduce the rate of return. Therefore, a portfolio manager should not overdiversify. Several studies that we will discuss in Chapter 7 have shown that it is possible to derive most of the benefits of diversification with a portfolio of 30 to 40 stocks. Although most large institutions would probably need more than 40 stocks to properly diversify, a number much over 100 is probably excessive. The point is, if you have a portfolio with a large dollar value and a self-imposed limit on the number of stocks that you want to include, *the value of each holding must be substantial.* As an example, if you assume a $1 billion institutional portfolio that contains 50 stocks, each holding must have an average value of $20 million; if the portfolio contains 100 stocks, each holding must have an average value of $10 million.

To ensure liquidity, institutions typically limit their ownership of an issue to a maximum of 5 percent of the outstanding issue. (This is a legal limit for mutual funds, but most managers impose a lower limit.) Assuming a limit of 5 percent and an average value of each holding of $10 million, the market value of each firm's total outstanding stock must be $200 million ($10 million ÷ .05). If each holding averages $20 million, and the limit is 5 percent, the average total market value of each company must be $400 million.

Therefore, when institutions become interested in companies for performance reasons, they also require that these companies be large. Because of this size constraint, the large institutions concentrate their attention on a universe of less than 700 stocks.[39] Many observers contend that they concentrate on a substantially smaller number (300 to 400). This means that large institutions, who dominate trading in the secondary market, are concentrating on a relatively small proportion of available public firms. Specifically, most institutions will consider only about 700 firms at most, compared to about 9,000 public stocks (you will recall that there are about 2,000 issues on the NYSE, 1,000 on the AMEX, and a total of 6,000 on the OTC). The result is that the majority of trading is concentrated in about 8 percent of the available stocks.

EFFECT OF A TIERED SECONDARY MARKET

Because institutions are looking at a relatively small number of companies, the secondary markets for the remaining stocks traded by individuals will deteriorate. Therefore, while the secondary markets for the large institutional stocks will improve substantially, the one for small firms will deteriorate, seriously affecting the primary market for these companies. A study of common stocks in three market tiers indicated that the lower-tier firms experienced a decline in relative market liquidity and dividend payout and an increase in stock price volatility and financial leverage.[40]

---

[39] Frank K. Reilly, "A Three-Tier Stock Market and Corporate Financing," *Financial Management* 4, no. 3 (Autumn 1975): 7–15.

[40] Frank K. Reilly and Eugene F. Drzycimski, "An Analysis of the Effects of a Multi-Tiered Stock Market," *Journal of Financial and Quantitative Analysis,* 16, no. 4 (November 1981): 559–575.

INSTITUTIONS AND STOCK PRICE VOLATILITY

Some observers have contended that there should be a strong positive relationship between institutional trading and stock price volatility, because institutions trade in large blocks and/or they tend to trade together (i.e., trade in parallel). While these contentions are based on intuitive arguments or very ad hoc evidence, empirical studies that have examined the relationship between trading by large financial institutions and stock price volatility have never supported the folklore.[41] In a capital market where trading has become dominated by institutions, the best environment is one where all institutions are actively involved, since *they provide liquidity for one another and for noninstitutional investors.*

The final change caused by the increase in institutional trading is the development of a National Market System (NMS), which is intended to provide greater efficiency and competition.

A NATIONAL MARKET SYSTEM (NMS)

Although there is no one generally accepted definition of a national market, four major characteristics are generally expected:

1. Centralized reporting of all transactions
2. A centralized quotation system
3. A centralized limit-order book (CLOB)
4. Free and open competition among all qualified market-makers.

CENTRALIZED REPORTING

Centralized reporting requires a composite tape on which all transactions in a stock would be reported regardless of where the transactions took place. As one watched the tape, you might see a trade in GM on the NYSE, another trade on the Midwest, and a third on the OTC. The intent is to report all completed trades on the tape and thereby provide full information on all securities traded.

As of June 1975, the NYSE began operating a central tape that includes all NYSE stocks traded on other exchanges and on the OTC.[42] There has been significant growth in the volume of shares reported on the consolidated tape as shown in Table 3.8. The breakdown among the seven exchanges and two OTC markets is contained in Table 3.9. These data indicate that this aspect of a National Market System (NMS) has already been introduced for stocks listed on the NYSE.

CENTRALIZED QUOTATION SYSTEM

A centralized quotation system would contain the quotes for a given stock from all market-makers on the national exchanges, the regional exchanges, and the OTC. A broker who requested the market for GM would be given the prevailing quotes on the NYSE, any regional exchanges on which GM is listed, and those by several OTC market-makers. The broker should complete the trade on the market with the best quote for his client.

---

[41] In this regard, see Frank K. Reilly and John M. Wachowicz, "How Institutional Trading Reduces Market Volatility," *Journal of Portfolio Management* 5, no. 2 (Winter 1979): 11–17; Neil Berkman, "Institutional Investors and the Stock Market," *New England Economic Review* (November–December 1977): 60–77; and Frank K. Reilly and David J. Wright, "Block Trades and Aggregate Stock Price Volatility," *Financial Analysts Journal* 40, no. 2 (March–April 1984): 54–60.

[42] *New York Stock Exchange Fact Book* (New York: New York Stock Exchange, 1987), 7.

TABLE 3.8
Consolidated Tape Volume (Thousands of Shares)

1976	6,281,008	1981	13,679,194	1986	42,478,164
1977	6,153,173	1982	19,203,590	1987	55,472,855
1978	8,147,569	1983	25,362,458		
1979	9,254,044	1984	27,455,178		
1980	12,935,607	1985	32,988,595		

Source: *NYSE Fact Book* (New York: New York Stock Exchange, 1988): 18.

INTERMARKET TRADING SYSTEM

Currently there is a centralized quotation system available—the *Intermarket Trading System (ITS)*, developed by the American, Boston, Midwest, New York, Pacific, and Philadelphia Stock Exchanges and the NASD. ITS consists of a central computer facility with interconnected terminals in the participating market centers. As shown in Table 3.10, the number of issues included, the volume of trading, and the size of trades have all experienced substantial growth. Of the 1,537 issues included on the system in 1987, 1,335 were stocks listed on the NYSE and 202 were on the AMEX.

Brokers and market-makers in each market center can indicate specific buying and selling commitments through a composite quotation display, showing the current quote for each eligible stock in all participating market centers. Using current quotes a broker or market-maker in any market center can thus determine where to execute a customer's orders. If a better price is available in another market, he sends a message to that market center, committing himself to buy or sell at the price quoted. When his commitment is accepted, he receives a message telling him that the transaction has taken place. The following example illustrates how ITS works.

A broker on the NYSE has a market order to sell 100 shares of IBM stock. The quotation display on the floor of the NYSE shows that the best current bid for IBM has been entered on the Pacific Stock Exchange (PSE), and he decides to take advantage of that bid. He enters a firm commitment on the NYSE terminal to sell 100 shares at the bid on the PSE. Within seconds, the commitment is flashed on the CRT screen and is also printed

TABLE 3.9
Exchanges and Markets Involved in the Consolidated Tape with Percentage of Volume during 1987

	PERCENTAGE		PERCENTAGE
ASE	0.00	NASD	1.90
Boston	1.29	NYSE	86.17
Cincinnati	0.42	Pacific	3.02
Instinet	0.09	Philadelphia	1.40
Midwest	5.71		

Source: *NYSE Fact Book* (New York: New York Stock Exchange, 1988): 18.

TABLE 3.10
Intermarket Trading System Activity

| | | DAILY AVERAGE | | |
YEAR	ISSUES ELIGIBLE	SHARE VOLUME	EXECUTED TRADES	AVERAGE SIZE OF TRADE
1978 (April)	300	235,000	377	623
1979	687	827,600	1,402	590
1980	884	1,565,900	2,868	546
1981	947	2,144,700	3,659	586
1982	1,039	3,264,100	4,697	695
1983	1,120	4,104,000	5,645	727
1984	1,160	4,692,200	5,404	868
1985	1,288	5,669,400	5,867	966
1986	1,278	7,222,100	7,712	987
1987	1,537	8,608,559	8,573	1,004

Source: *NYSE Fact Book* (New York: New York Stock Exchange, 1988): 20.

out at the PSE specialists' post, where it is executed against the PSE bid. After the commitment is accepted, a short message reports an execution back to New York, and the trade is reported on the consolidated tape. Brokers on both sides of the transaction receive an immediate confirmation, and a journal of all transactions is transmitted to the appropriate market centers at the end of the day. Thereafter, each broker completes his own clearance and settlement procedure.

The ITS system currently provides centralized quotations for stocks listed on the NYSE, and on the NYSE screen it specifies whether a bid or ask away from the NYSE market is superior to that on the New York market. Note that there are several characteristics the system lacks. It does not have the capability for automatic execution at the best market. Instead you must contact the market-maker and indicate that you want to buy or sell. Possibly, when a NYSE broker goes to "hit" another market, the bid or ask will be withdrawn. Also, it is not mandatory that a broker go to the best market. Although the best price is at another market center, a broker might consider it inconvenient to transact on that exchange if the price difference is not substantial. It is almost impossible to audit such actions. Still, even with these shortcomings, there has been substantial technical and operational progress made related to a central quotation system.

CENTRAL LIMIT-ORDER BOOK (CLOB)

Substantial controversy surrounds the idea of a central limit-order book (CLOB) that would contain all limit orders from all exchanges. Ideally, the CLOB would be visible to everyone, and all market-makers and traders could fill orders on the CLOB. Currently most limit orders are placed with the specialist on the NYSE and, when a transaction *on the NYSE* reaches the stipulated price, the order is filled by the NYSE specialist, who receives some part of the commission for rendering this service. The NYSE has opposed a CLOB because the NYSE specialists do not want to share this very lucrative business. While the technology for a CLOB is available, it is difficult to estimate when it will become a reality.

COMPETITION BETWEEN MARKET-MAKERS (RULE 390)

Competing market-makers have always prevailed on the OTC market, but competition has been opposed by the NYSE. The argument in favor of competition among market-makers is that it forces dealers to make better markets in terms of their bids and asks, or they will not do any business. If competition improves the market for the stock (i.e., reduces the bid-ask spread), this improvement should be reflected in market data. Several studies have indicated that the more competition (i.e., the more dealers), the smaller the spread is.[43]

In contrast, the NYSE argues that a *central auction market* provides the best market, because it forces all orders to the one central location, which ensures the best auction market. To create a concentrated market the NYSE has Rule 390, stating that, unless specifically exempted by the exchange, members must obtain the permission of the exchange before carrying out a transaction in a listed stock off the exchange. This rule is intended to ensure that all volume comes to the NYSE, so that the exchange can provide the most complete auction market. The exchange contends that Rule 390 is necessary to protect the auction market, arguing that if the rule is eliminated, members will be tempted to trade on or off the exchange, and many orders will be *internalized* (i.e., brokers will match orders from the holdings of their own customers, and the orders will not come to the exchange for exposure to the full auction market). In general, a "fragmented" dealer market is envisioned, which the exchange contends is not as good as the central auction. In contrast, Hamilton contends that the adverse effects of fragmentation are more than offset by the benefits of competition.[44]

Competing arguments aside, the SEC contends that its mandate from Congress under the Investment Act of 1975 is to help establish an open, competitive market without restrictions like Rule 390. The remaining question is when and how Rule 390 will be eliminated. Progress in achieving this final phase of the NMS has been slow because of strong opposition by members of the investment community and caution by the SEC.[45]

---

[43] Seha M. Tinic and Richard R. West, "Competition and the Pricing of Dealer Service in the Over-the-Counter Stock Market," *Journal of Financial and Quantitative Analysis* 7, no. 3 (June 1972): 1707–1727; and George J. Benston and Robert L. Hagerman, "Determinants of Bid-Asked Spreads in the Over-the-Counter Market," *Journal of Financial Economics* 1, no. 4 (December 1974): 353–364.

[44] James L. Hamilton, "Marketplace Fragmentation Competition and the Efficiency of the Stock Exchange," *Journal of Finance* 34, no. 1 (March 1979): 171–187; and James L. Hamilton, "Marketplace Organization and Marketability: NASDAQ, the Stock Exchange and the National Market System," *Journal of Finance* 33, no. 2 (May 1978): 487–503.

[45] Stan Crock and Richard E. Rustin, "Work on a National Stock-Trading System Lags Badly: Some Blame Brokers and SEC," *The Wall Street Journal*, February 2, 1979, 32; "SEC Hit by House Unit for Slow Progress in Creation of National Securities Market," *The Wall Street Journal*, September 12, 1980, 3; and Stan Crock, "SEC's Aim to Start National Stock Market Triggers Partisan Crossfire in Congress," *The Wall Street Journal*, February 26, 1981, 9.

NEW TRADING SYSTEMS

As daily trading volume has gone from 5 or 10 million shares to over 170 million shares, it has become necessary to introduce new technology into the trading process. Currently, the NYSE is capable of handling daily volume of over 500 million shares as shown in October 1987. The following are some recent technological innovations that assist in the trading process.

SUPER DOT. Super Dot is an electronic order-routing system through which member firms transmit market and limit orders in NYSE-listed securities directly to the post where the securities are traded or to the member firm's booth. After the order has been executed, a report of execution is returned directly to the member firm office over the same electronic circuit that brought the order to the floor, and the execution is submitted directly to the comparison systems. Member firms can enter market orders up to 2,099 shares and limit orders in round or odd lots up to 30,099 shares. At the end of 1987 there were 183 participating member firm subscribers and an average of 154,000 orders moved through the system on an average day.

OPENING AUTOMATED REPORT SERVICE (OARS). OARS, the opening feature of the Super Dot system, is designed to accept member firm's pre-opening market orders up to 5,099 shares and provides rapid, systematic execution and immediate reporting. OARS automatically and continuously pairs buy and sell orders and presents the imbalance to the specialist prior to the opening of a stock, which helps the specialist determine the opening price. It is now operational for all issues.

MARKET ORDER SYSTEM. Super Dot's post-opening market order system is designed to accept member firm's post-opening market orders up to 2,099 shares. The system guarantees that all execution reports will be delivered within three minutes. In fact, during 1987, 92 percent were reported within two minutes.

LIMIT ORDER SYSTEM. The limit order system electronically files orders that are to be executed when and if a specific price is reached. The system accepts limit orders up to 99,999 shares, appends a turnaround number, and delivers printed orders to the trading post or the member firm's booth for storage. *Good-'til* cancelled orders that are not executed on the day of submission are automatically stored until executed or cancelled.

ELECTRONIC DISPLAY BOOK SYSTEM. This system replaces the specialist's handwritten limit order book with electronically generated display screens. It facilitates the recording, execution, and reporting of limit and market orders and helps eliminate processing errors. At the end of 1987, there were over 100 electronic display books in operation involving more than 600 stocks on the exchange floor.

GLOBAL MARKET CHANGES

LONDON STOCK EXCHANGE. Beyond the changes in the U.S. markets, the London Stock Exchange initiated several major changes on October 27, 1986. The changes were so numerous and significant that the event was referred to as the "Big Bang."

Prior to the "Big Bang" brokers could act only as an agent trading for customers, while a jobber could act as a market-maker. Currently, brokers can act as market-makers, and jobbers can deal with the public and institutions. Also all commissions have become fully negotiated.

Previously the stock exchange was self-regulated. A bill established recognition for a new body known as the Securities and Investments Board (SIB), which has power delegated to it by the secretary of state for trade and industry. The SIB is similar to the SEC in the United States and has the power to delegate its power to a *self-regulated organization (SRO)*. It is speculated that such an arrangement will be approved for the exchange.

The gilts market has been restructured to resemble the U.S. government securities market. The Bank of England has approved a system whereby 27 primary dealers make markets in U.K. government securities, and a limited number of interdealer brokers transact with the primary dealers. This new arrangement has created a much more competitive environment.

Among several changes related to the reporting of trades is a system called Stock Exchange Automated Quotations (SEAQ) International, which is an electronic market-price information system similar to NASDAQ that supports off-floor trading and provides price quotations to stock exchange members and institutional investors. In addition, real-time prices are being shared with the NYSE while the NASD is providing certain U.S OTC prices to the London market. Also, as discussed earlier, there are 35 U.S. OTC stocks available for 24-hour trading between New York, Singapore, and London.[46] An important change has been the increased access to membership on the exchange. Foreign firms are now being admitted to membership, and member firms can be wholly owned by organizations outside the country. As a result, some U.S. banks have acquired British stockbrokers, and several major U.S. firms are now members of the exchange.

SOME EFFECTS OF THE "BIG BANG." Clearly an overriding effect of the "Big Bang" has been increased competition at all levels from the brokers on the floor to the LSE member firms and firms trading gilts. Probably one of the most visually striking changes is what has happened to the trading floor of the LSE. Prior to October 1986 the activity on the floor of the LSE was similar to what happened on the NYSE and the TSE—a large number of people gathered around trading posts and moved between the phones and the posts. Currently, the exchange floor is completely deserted except for some trading in stock options. With the advent of competitive market-makers on the floor of the exchange, it became apparent that it would be

---

[46] Priscilla Ann Smith, "Shares Snap Out of Three-Day Slump as Biggest Gainers are Foreign Issues," *The Wall Street Journal,* March 30, 1988, 28.

just as easy to conduct business from a location away from the exchange using the SEAQ system—that is, buy and sell listed stocks using competitive quotes on SEAQ. As indicated, the SEAQ system is similar to the NASDAQ system in the United States that helped the LSE develop it.

The rest of the effects can be summarized by the phrase "more business, less profit." Specifically, there is more activity throughout the system (stock-trading volume quadrupled from October 1986 to October 1987), but the profit margins are much smaller or nonexistent due to the intense competition. In the process, many firms have merged or been acquired by new firms from the United States, Japan, or Germany. These new firms are very aggressive and willing to accept lower returns during this initial period in order to establish a market presence. In addition, in the process of developing an organization, they have increased their staffs and general overhead. As indicated, the result is small or negative profits. Notably, these difficult conditions were present before the October crash that affected markets around the world.[47]

TOKYO STOCK EXCHANGE (TSE). Thus far, the changes on the TSE have been minimal, because the exchange has resisted competitive pressures through regulation. Notably, trading commissions are based upon fixed-scale rates that vary by the type and value of the transactions. For most transactions it is a fixed charge plus a percent of the value of the trade.

As indicated earlier, as of early 1988 there were only 23 foreign members of the TSE after the membership change in December 1987. Probably the biggest change related to the Japanese is the impact that Japanese firms have had on the rest of the global market. Specifically, four Japanese investment firms dominate the Japanese financial market: Nomura, Daiwa, Nikko, and Yamaichi. The equity base and market value of these firms exceed all U.S. firms and all firms from other countries. They have become major players in both London and the United States. The result has been increased competition and lower rates, especially for fixed-income securities, but also for equities.[48]

PARIS BOURSE. As an indication of the awareness of changes taking place, the Paris Bourse, while relatively small, has initiated changes in January 1988 that were similar to the "Big Bang" in London. Specifically, the big brokerage houses had a monopoly on stock trading, which is being opened up gradually to French and foreign banks. Also some of these firms will merge with banks to acquire the capital needed to trade in a world market. They will also begin moving to a continuous auction market rather than

---

[47] Craig Forman, "Britain's Deregulation Leaves a Casualty Trail in Securities Industry," *The Wall Street Journal,* October 14, 1987, 1, 18; Craig Forman, "Banged Up by Big Bang, Stock Exchange in London Is Facing Its Biggest Challenge," *The Wall Street Journal,* November 8, 1988, C10.

[48] For a further discussion of the impact of the Japanese on the world capital market, see Daniel Burstein, "Rising Sun on Wall Street," *New York,* March 2, 1987; Howard Rudnitsky, Allan Sloan and Peter Fuhrman, "Land of the Rising Stocks," *Forbes,* May 18, 1987, 139–143; "Japan on Wall Street," *Business Week,* September 7, 1987, 82–90; and "The Evolution of the Tokyo Capital Market and Nomura Securities," a sponsored section in, *Institutional Investor* 22, no. 4 (April 1988): 157–168.

the call market that currently operates for two hours a day. Interestingly, as of mid-1988 they do not plan to introduce competitive commissions.[49]

FUTURE DEVELOPMENTS

Besides the expected effects of the specific factors discussed (the NMS, a global capital market, etc.), some overall changes are expected in capital markets. Once aware of potential changes, you can concentrate on understanding why they are happening and contemplate the effect of them.

While there has been an increase in the number of individuals owning stocks and bonds, there has also been a preference for this ownership to be through financial institutions (i.e., investment companies), because most individuals feel that it is too difficult and time-consuming to do their own analysis. With this increase in fund sales has come a proliferation of new funds that provide numerous opportunities to diversify. This includes foreign (international) stock and bond funds, *sector funds* that are limited to an industry or economic segment, and alternative fixed-income funds (government, municipal, and corporate). As an example, Fidelity Management has over 25 common stock sector funds that range from aircraft and bioengineering to telephone and utilities. This trend toward new specialized funds will continue and could expand to possibly include other investment alternatives such as stamps, coins, and art.

Further, it is likely that there will be a major change in the makeup and type of firms in the financial services industry. Prior to 1960 the securities industry was composed of specialty firms that concentrated in one segment of investments such as stocks, bonds, commodities, real estate, or insurance. A major trend is toward *financial supermarkets* that consider all of these investment alternatives around the world. Prime examples would be Sears Financial Corporation and Merrill Lynch, who have acquired insurance and real estate subsidiaries and would like to move into banking if allowed.[50] At the other end of the spectrum are large banks such as Citicorp who want to become involved in investment banking and all phases of the investment business.[51]

In contrast to supermarkets, some firms will decide they do not want to be all things to all people and will go the specialty "boutique" route and attempt to provide a unique financial product that is superior to what is available at a supermarket. Examples would include discount brokers or special research firms (e.g., firms that concentrate their research efforts in one industry or one type of investment).

---

[49] Fiona Gleizes, "Paris Bourse Begins Its Own 'Big Bang' In Effort to Rival London's Exchange," *The Wall Street Journal*, January 4, 1988, 15. For a discussion of changes in Germany, see Terence Roth, "Frankfurt's Bourse Makes Its Mark, and Then Some," *The Wall Street Journal*, October 26, 1988, C1, 15.

[50] Richard E. Rustin, "Wall Street Mergers May Basically Change U.S. Financial System," *The Wall Street Journal*, April 22, 1981, 1.

[51] Richard L. Hudson, "SEC Seeks Tighter Rules for Most Banks that Offer Full-Line Brokerage Services," *The Wall Street Journal*, October 28, 1983, 5; and Daniel Hertzberg and Tim Carrington, "Controversy Engulfs Banking Industry In Wake of Fed's Latest Nonbank Ruling," *The Wall Street Journal*, December 16, 1983, 6.

SUMMARY

The securities market is divided into primary and secondary markets. Secondary markets are important for primary markets. The major segments of the secondary markets include listed exchanges (the NYSE, the AMEX, TSE, LSE, and regional exchanges), the over-the-counter market, the third market, and the fourth market.

There have been many changes in our securities markets since 1965, many of them due to an increase in institutional trading, and the rapidly evolving global markets. This discussion is important because numerous changes have occurred and many more changes are yet to come.

QUESTIONS

1. Define a market, and briefly discuss the characteristics of a "good" market.

2. You own 100 shares of General Motors stock, and you want to sell it because you need the money to make a down payment on a car. Assume there is absolutely no secondary market system in common stocks. How would you go about selling the stock? Discuss what you would have to do to find a buyer, how long it might take, and the price you might receive.

3. Define liquidity, and discuss the factors that contribute to it. Give an example of a liquid asset and an illiquid asset, and discuss why they are considered liquid and illiquid.

4. Define a primary and secondary market for securities, and discuss how they differ. How is the primary market dependent on the secondary market?

5. Give an example of an initial public offering (IPO) in the primary market. Give an example of a seasoned equity issue in the primary market. Discuss which would involve greater risk to the buyer.

6. Find an advertisement for a recent primary offering by a corporation in *The Wall Street Journal.* Based upon the information in the ad, indicate the characteristics of the security sold and the major underwriters. How much new capital did the firm derive from the offering before commissions were paid?

7. Briefly explain the difference between a competitive bid and a negotiated underwriting.

8a. How do the two U.S. national stock exchanges differ from each other?

8b. Briefly describe how the TSE differs from the NYSE in size and operation.

9. Based upon the figures in Table 3.3, there is typically a major difference in the price paid for a seat on the NYSE compared to the AMEX. How would you explain this difference?

10. What are the major reasons for the existence of regional stock exchanges? How do they differ from the national exchanges?

11. How does the OTC market differ from the listed exchanges?

12. Which segment of the secondary market (listed or OTC) is larger in terms of the number of issues? In terms of the value of the issues traded? Discuss which has more diversity in terms of the size of the companies and the quality of the issues.

13. What is the NASDAQ system? Discuss the three levels of NASDAQ in terms of what they provide and who would subscribe to each.

14a. Define the third market. Give an example of a third market stock.

14b. Define the fourth market. Discuss why a financial institution would use the fourth market.

15. Briefly define each of the following terms and give an example:
    a. Market order
    b. Limit order
    c. Short sale
    d. Stop loss order.

16. Briefly discuss the two major functions and sources of income for the specialist.

17. What is the high-risk segment of the specialists' dealer function? Why is it high-risk? What aspect of the specialist position reduces the risk involved and also increases potential return? Be specific.

18. Describe the duties of the *Saitori* member on the TSE and discuss how his duties differ from the NYSE specialist.

19. Discuss the overall reason why the secondary equity market has experienced major changes since 1965.

20. Discuss the empirical evidence that attests to the growth in institutional trading.

21. What were give-ups? Why did they exist in the fixed commission world?

22. What is meant by the term *negotiated commissions?* When was May Day? When was the "Big Bang"?

23. In the discussion of block trades and the specialist, it was noted that the specialist is hampered by the three Cs. Discuss each of the three Cs as it relates to block trading.

24. Describe block houses, and explain why they evolved. Describe what is meant by *positioning* part of a block.

25. Define a tiered trading market. It is contended that the tiered market of the 1970s and 1980s is heavily concerned with the size of the companies involved. Discuss why size is important to an institutional portfolio manager.

26. Discuss the intuitive argument for the expectation that there will be a positive relationship between institutional trading and stock price volatility. Did the empirical results support the intuitive expectations? What do these results imply regarding the desirability of institutional trading?

27a. Describe the major attributes of the national market system (NMS).

27b. Briefly describe the ITS and what it contributes to NMS. Discuss the growth of the ITS.

PROBLEMS

1. In the section of *The Wall Street Journal* on government bonds, entitled "Treasury Bonds, Notes and Bills," what is the current bid and yield on the 8 1/2 of 1997?

2. The initial margin requirement is 60 percent. You have $30,000 to invest in a stock selling for $75 a share. Ignoring taxes and commissions, show the impact on the rate of return if the stock rises to $100 a share and also if it

declines to $40 a share, assuming (a) you pay cash for the stock, and then (b) you buy it using the maximum amount of leverage available.

3. Tom has a margin account and deposits $30,000. Assuming that the prevailing margin requirement is 45 percent, commissions are ignored, and Amalgamated Pickle Corporation is selling at $27 per share,

3a. How many shares can be purchased using the maximum allowable margin?

3b. What is Tom's profit (loss) if Amalgamated's price
    (1) Rises to $35?
    (2) Falls to $20?

3c. If the maintenance margin is 30 percent, to what price can Amalgamated Pickle fall before Tom receives a margin call?

4. Suppose you buy a round lot of Redfern Industries stock on 55 percent margin when it is selling at $25 a share. The broker charges a 10 percent annual interest rate, and commissions are 3 percent of the total stock value on both the purchase and sale. If at year-end you receive a $0.90 per share dividend and sell the stock for 32 5/8, what is your rate of return on the investment?

5. You decide to sell 100 shares of Bluefin Fisheries short when it is selling at its yearly high of 52 1/4. Your broker tells you that your margin requirement is 55 percent and that the commission on the purchase is $155. While you are short, Bluefin pays a $1.50 per share dividend. At the end of one year you buy 100 shares of Bluefin at 42 3/8 to close out your position and are charged a commission of $145 and an 8 percent interest rate on the money borrowed. What is your rate of return on the investment?

REFERENCES

Amex Fact Book. New York: American Stock Exchange, published annually.

Baumol, William J. *The Stock Market and Economic Efficiency*. New York: Fordham University Press, 1965.

Beidleman, Carl, ed. *The Handbook of International Investing*. Chicago: Probus Publishing Company, 1987.

Cohen, Kalman J., Stephen F. Maier, Robert A. Schwartz, and David K. Whitcomb. "Market Makers and the Market Spread: A Review of Recent Literature." *Journal of Financial and Quantitative Analysis* 14, no. 4 (November 1979).

de Caines, Bryan, ed. *The GT Guide to World Equity Markets, 1987*. London: Euromoney Publications Plc, 1987.

Fabozzi, Frank J., and Frank G. Zarb, eds. *Handbook of Financial Markets*. 2d ed. Homewood, Ill.: Dow Jones-Irwin, 1986.

Garbade, Kenneth D. *Securities Markets*. New York: McGraw-Hill, 1982.

Grabbe, J. Orlin. *International Financial Markets*. New York: Elsevier, 1986.

Jensen, Michael C., and Clifford W. Smith, eds. "Symposium on Investment Banking and the Capital Acquisition Process." *Journal of Financial Economics* 15, no. 1–2 (January–February 1986).

Loll, Leo M., and Julian G. Buckley. *The Over-the-Counter Securities Markets*. 4th ed. Englewood Cliffs, N.J.: Prentice-Hall, 1981.

Lorie, James H., Peter Dodd, and Mary Hamilton Kimpton. *The Stock Market: Theories and Evidence*. 2d ed. Homewood, Ill.: Richrd D. Irwin, 1985.

Melton, William C. "Corporate Equities and the National Market System." Federal Reserve Bank of New York, *Quarterly Review.* (Winter 1978–1979).

NASDAQ Fact Book. (Washington, D.C.: National Association of Securities Dealers, Inc.) Published monthly.

NYSE Fact Book. New York: New York Stock Exchange. Published annually.

Peake, Junius W. "The National Market System." *Financial Analysts Journal* 34, no. 4 (July–August 1978).

Reilly, Frank K., and John Wachowicz. "How Institutional Trading Reduces Market Volatility." *Journal of Portfolio Management* 5, no. 2 (Winter 1979).

Reilly, Frank K., and David J. Wright. "Block Trades and Stock Price Volatility." *Financial Analysts Journal* 11, no. 2 (March–April 1984).

Scholes, Myron S. "The Market for Securities: Substitution Versus Price-Pressure and the Effects of Information on Share Prices" *Journal of Business.* 45, no. 2 (April 1972).

Schwartz, Robert A. *Equity Markets: Structure, Trading, and Performance.* New York: Harper and Row, 1988.

Smyth, David. *Worldly Wise Investor.* New York: Franklin Watts, 1988.

Sobel, Robert. *The Big Board.* New York: The Free Press, 1965.

Sobel, Robert. *The Curbstone Brokers: The Origins of the American Stock Exchange.* New York: Macmillan, 1970.

Sobel, Robert. *NYSE: A History of the New York Stock Exchange, 1935–1975.* New York: Weybright and Talley, 1975.

Solnik, Bruno. *International Investments.* Reading, Mass.: Addison-Wesley Publishing Co., 1988.

Tinic, Seha M., and Richard R. West. "The Securities Industry under Negotiated Brokerage Commissions: Changes in the Structure and Performance of New York Stock Exchange Member Firms." *The Bell Journal of Economics* 11, no. 1 (Spring 1980).

Tokyo Stock Exchange Fact Book. (Tokyo: Tokyo Stock Exchange). Published annually.

Viner, Aron. *Inside Japanese Financial Markets.* Homewood, Ill.: Dow Jones-Irwin, 1988.

West, Richard R., and Seha M. Tinic. *The Economics of the Stock Market.* New York: Praeger Publishers, 1971.

APPENDIX 3A # THE OCTOBER 1987 CRASH

This appendix includes Chapter Four from the "Report of the Presidential Task Force on Market Mechanisms," also referred to as "The Brady Report" since the Chairman of the Task Force was Nicholas F. Brady. This chapter from the report provides an excellent description of what transpired during the critical period of October 14, 1988, through October 20, 1988. The point is, while "The Crash" actually occurred on Monday, October 19th, there was a major buildup to it during the prior week; and then the day following the crash, on October 20, there was almost a complete collapse of the market. Therefore, to really understand what happened on October 19, it is necessary to understand the entire week of the crash.

In addition, you will quickly recognize that this crash was not limited to common stocks on the U.S. equity market, but also involved futures markets in the United States, as well as equity markets around the world, most notably the markets in Tokyo and London. Two concepts are integral to understanding the interaction of the equity and futures markets of today and tomorrow: *portfolio insurance* and *program trading*. The following is a brief introduction to these concepts that will assist you in understanding Chapter Four from the report. A more detailed consideration of these concepts, including examples, is contained in Chapter 25 of this text.

PORTFOLIO INSURANCE

Investments in risky assets such as stocks are characterized by relatively high upside potential but are also, unfortunately, associated with high downside risk as well, whereas a safe asset such as Treasury bills guarantees a minimum return (i.e., low downside risk). *Portfolio insurance* is an investment strategy that seeks to combine in a portfolio the favorable features of both the risky and safe assets. Through dynamic allocation of funds between the risky and safe assets, portfolio insurance programs attempt to guarantee a minimum return on the portfolio in a bear market while retaining a substantial portion of the upside potential in a bull market. A simple example of portfolio insurance is a protective put option, that is, an insured portfolio consisting of a long position in a common stock (or portfolio) and a long position in the associated European put option, with an exercise price equal to the minimum desired value of the common stock at the option expiration date. At expiration, the holder of the protective put is guaranteed the exercise price of the option at the minimum; and if the stock price exceeds the exercise price, he stands to benefit substantially from the stock's upside potential. The proportions of investment in the risky and riskless assets (T-bills) are determined by a put option pricing model, and the makeup of the portfolio is constantly revised to ensure that it replicates the payoffs to a put option at expiration. The critical point related to the aggregate market is that as stock prices rise, some T-bills are sold, and the proceeds are used to buy back some shares. In contrast, as stock prices fall, the rebalancing involves selling additional shares short and investing the proceeds in T-bills.

PROGRAM TRADING

The prices of so-called *derivative* assets, such as futures and options contracts, should bear a systematic relationship to the underlying asset prices in order to preclude arbitrage opportunities. For instance, the price of a futures contract should be approximately equal to the price of the underlying asset plus the net cost of carrying that asset to the delivery day. If the market price of the futures contract were higher than the underlying asset price plus the cost of carry, one could earn nearly risk-free profits by selling the overpriced futures contract and simultaneously borrowing and buying the underlying asset. *Program trading* refers to computer-aided investment strategies designed to profit from temporary discrepancies between the prices of the derivative securities and their underlying assets.

The following report refers to a number of instances when the prices of the futures contracts were substantially below the value of the underlying stocks, thereby triggering program trading wherein there was buying in the futures market and simultaneous selling of stocks on the exchanges, which caused significant stock price declines.

THE MARKET BREAK*

On Wednesday morning, October 14, 1987, the U.S. equity market began the most severe one-week decline in its history. The Dow stood at over 2,500 on Wednesday morning. By noon on Tuesday of the next week, it was just above 1,700, a decline of almost one third. Worse still, at the same time on Tuesday, the S&P 500 futures contract would imply a Dow level near 1,400.

INTRODUCTION

This precipitous decline began with several "triggers," which ignited mechanical, price-insensitive selling by a number of institutions following portfolio insurance strategies and a small number of mutual fund groups. The selling by these investors, and the prospect of further selling by them, encouraged a number of aggressive trading-oriented institutions to sell in anticipation of further declines. These aggressive trading-oriented institutions included, in addition to hedge funds, a small number of pension and endowment funds, money management firms and investment banking houses. This selling in turn stimulated further reactive selling by portfolio insurers and mutual funds. Selling pressure in the futures market was transmitted to the stock market by the mechanism of index arbitrage. Throughout the period, trading volume and price volatility increased dramatically. This may suggest that a broad range of investors all decided to reduce their positions in equities. In reality, a limited number of investors played the dominant role during this tumultuous period.

THE DAYS BEFORE THE BREAK (OCTOBER 14 TO 16)

WEDNESDAY, OCTOBER 14. The stock market's break began with two events which contributed to a revaluation of stock prices and triggered the reactive selling which would exacerbate the decline the following week. At 8:30 a.m., Eastern Time,[1] the government announced that the merchandise trade deficit for August was $15.7 billion, approximately $1.5 billion above the figure expected by the financial markets. Within seconds, traders in the foreign exchange markets sold dollars in the belief that the value of the dollar would have to fall further before the deficit could narrow. The German Deutschemark and the Japanese yen rose dramatically in value. Treasury bond traders, fearing that a weakening dollar could both discourage international investment in U.S. securities and stimulate domestic inflation, sold on the London market and on the U.S. bond market, when

---

* Submitted to the President of the United States, the Secretary of the Treasury, and the Chairman of the Federal Reserve Board, January 1988.
[1] Throughout the Report, all times are Eastern Time.

FIGURE 3A.1

Takeover Stock Index vs. S&P 500 Index Normalized Price Series: December 1986 to October 21, 1987

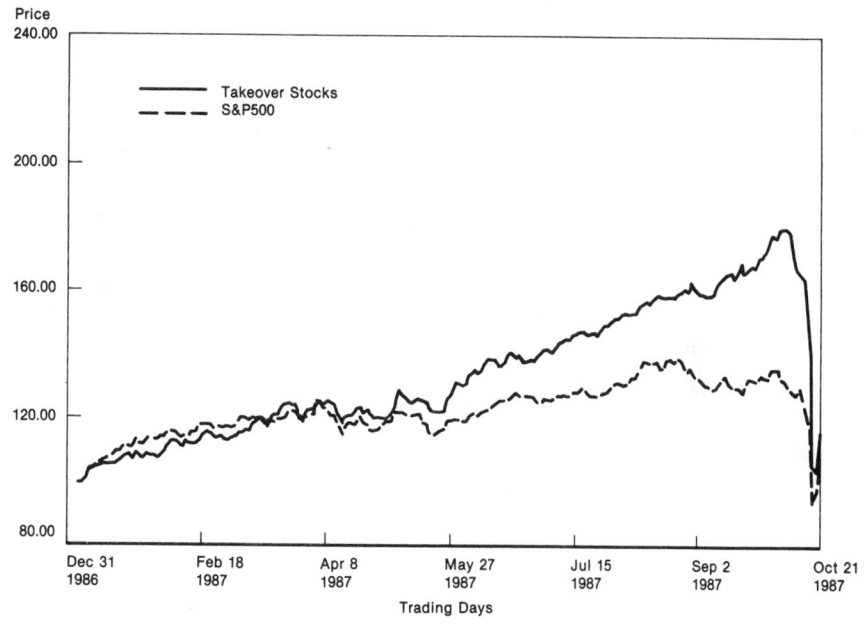

Takeover Stock Index:

Allegis, USG Corp., Tenneco, Gillette, Newmont Mining, GAF Corp., Irving Bank, Kansas City Southern Industries, Telex, Sante Fe Southern Pacific, Dayton Hudson

it opened. The Treasury's bellwether 30-year bond began to trade above a 10 percent yield for the first time in two years. Equity returns at current levels became even less attractive compared to returns on bonds.

The second event was the announcement early Wednesday that members of the House Ways and Means Committee were filing legislation to eliminate tax benefits associated with the financing of corporate takeovers. While rumors of the legislation had been circulating on Wall Street for several weeks, its actual announcement had a galvanizing effect on investors, particularly risk arbitrageurs, who specialize in buying shares of takeover candidates. Figures 3A.1 and 3A.2 show the performance of a small number of takeover candidates compared to that of the S&P 500 index. As risk arbitrageurs came to appreciate the seriousness of the legislative initiative, they began to liquidate their positions, collapsing the prices of takeover shares. These stocks had led the bull market up and now, during the week of October 14 to October 20, they would begin to lead it back down again.

In response to these events, the equity market declined immediately on Wednesday's opening. The S&P 500 futures contract fell sharply as

FIGURE 3A.2
Takeover Stock Index vs. S&P 500 Index Normalized Price Series: October 9, 1987 to October 23, 1987

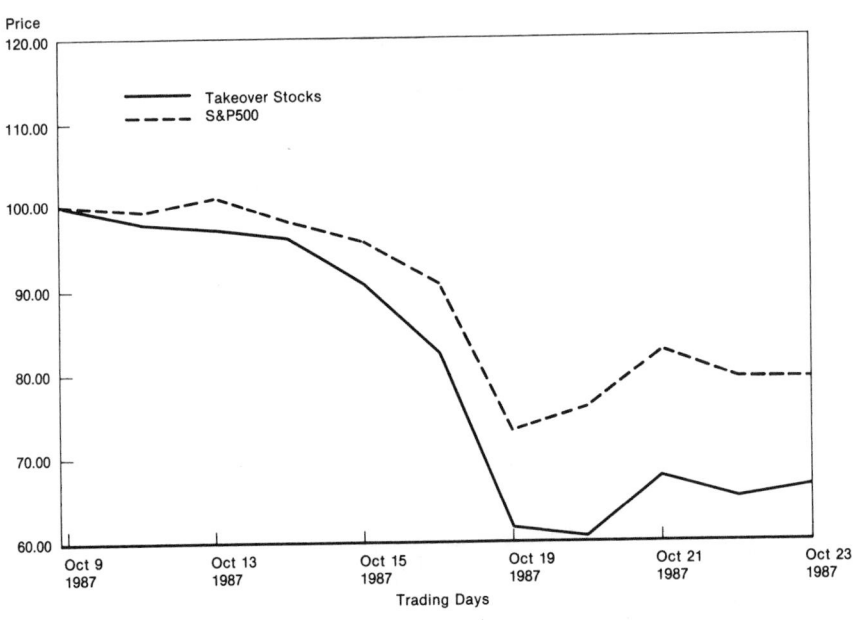

Takeover Stock Index:
Allegis, USG Corp., Tenneco, Gillette, Newmont Mining, GAF Corp., Irving Bank, Kansas City Southern Industries, Telex, Sante Fe Southern Pacific, Dayton Hudson.

trading-oriented investors sold. This was followed by large block sales of individual stocks on the NYSE as institutions joined the selling. The Dow dropped 44 points in the first half hour. During this period, index arbitrage program sales through the NYSE's Designated Order Turnaround ("DOT") automated execution system, totaled almost $200 million, which was 18 percent of volume, double the normal level.[2]

Index arbitrageurs attempt to profit from price differences in futures and stocks either by simultaneously buying futures and selling baskets of stock or vice versa. This arbitrage activity usually has the effect of elim-

---

[2] The data, on which the analysis contained in the Report and Studies is based, are taken primarily from databases containing individual transactions on the NYSE, CME (for stock index futures), and the Amex and CBOE (for stock index options). For NYSE stocks, the staff of the Task Force assembled databases showing transactions for broker-dealers, for all large institutions clearing trades through the Depository Trust Company, and for all trades done through the DOT system. For the CME, Amex and CBOE, the staff assembled databases containing all transactions by customer and end-of-day positions of all large traders. As a basis for verifying and elaborating on the information contained in these databases, the staff had access to information on a sample of transactions supplied to the SEC and CFTC by large institutional investors, broker-dealers, and the various exchanges and supplied to the Task Force by certain large institutional investors. In addition, the Task Force spoke in person with many market participants and representatives of the exchanges and regulatory bodies.

FIGURE 3A.3
S&P Index and Futures Contract: Wednesday, October 14, 1987

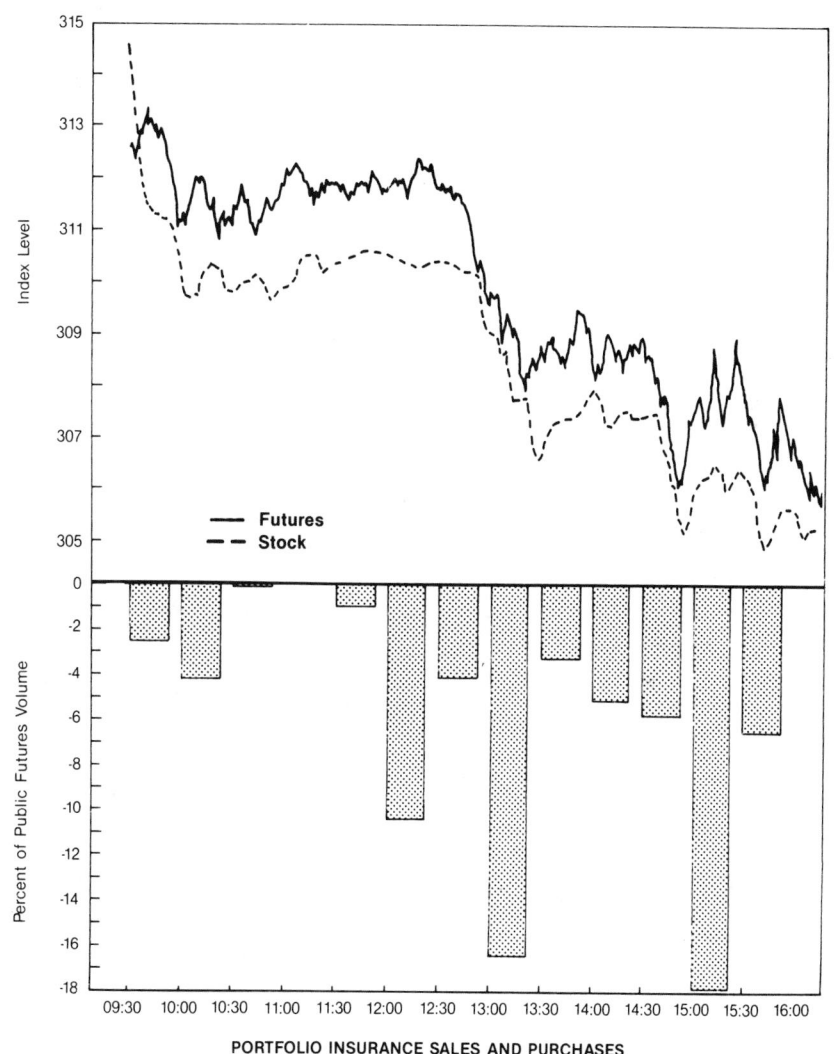

PORTFOLIO INSURANCE SALES AND PURCHASES

inating the price differences. It also transfers buying or selling pressure between the futures market and the stock market.

The morning decline was followed by another 45 point decline between 12:15 p.m. and 1:15 p.m. This midday decline was the result mainly of selling in the futures market by portfolio insurers (see Figure 3A.3) and, then, the transmission of this selling activity back into the stock market by the actions of index arbitrageurs who bought futures and sold stocks

FIGURE 3A.4
Dow Jones Industrial One Minute Chart: Wednesday, October 14, 1987

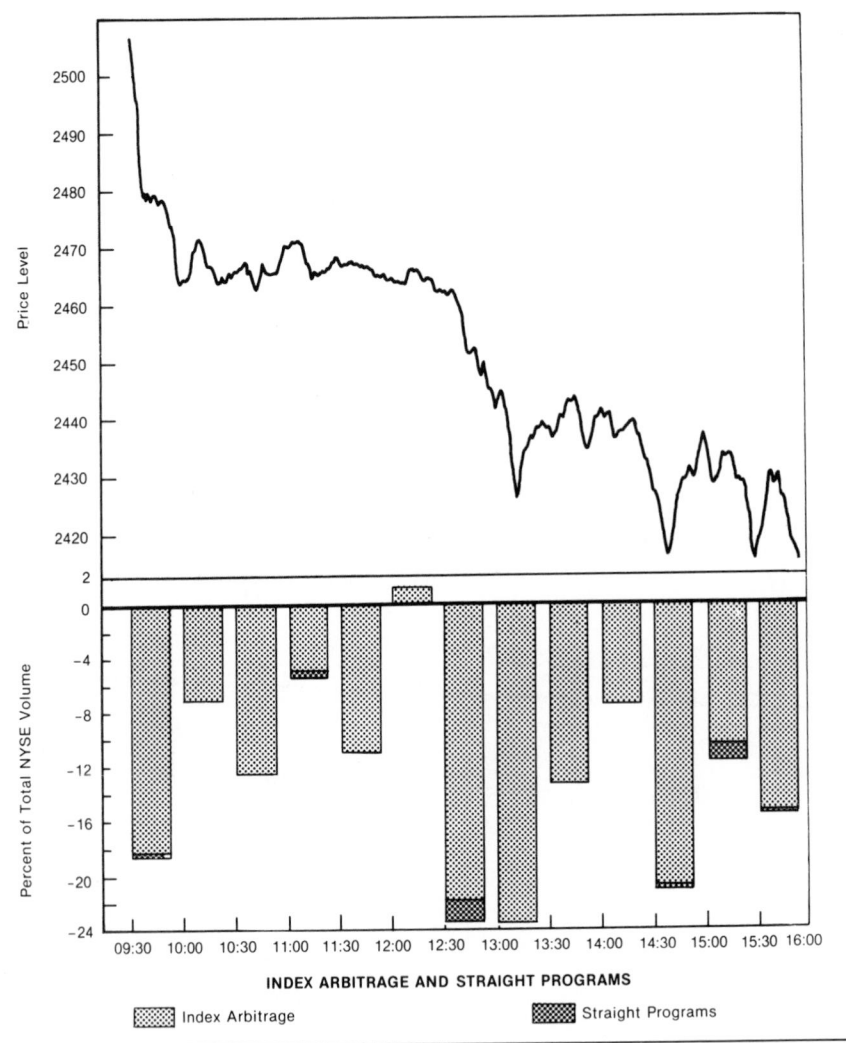

INDEX ARBITRAGE AND STRAIGHT PROGRAMS

Index Arbitrage   Straight Programs

(see Figures 3A.4 and 3A.5). Index arbitrage activity during this hour was $300 million, almost 25 percent of volume.

Portfolio insurance, a strategy using computer-based models, computes optimal stock-cash ratios at various market price levels. Rather than buying and selling stocks as the market moves, most portfolio insurers adjust the stock-cash ratio within their clients' investment portfolios by trading index futures. Indeed, several major portfolio insurance vendors are authorized to trade only futures, and have no access to their clients' stock portfolios.

FIGURE 3A.5

S&P Index and Futures Contract Spread: Wednesday, October 14, 1987

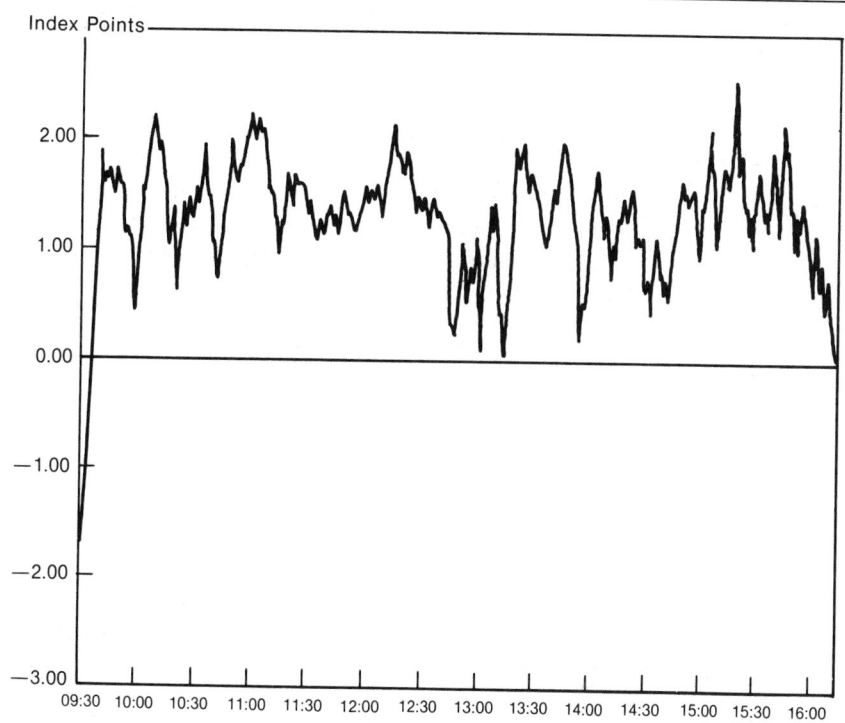

At the end of Wednesday there was a sell-off by trading-oriented institutions. Institutional sellers moved large blocks in the stock market and sold futures as well. In the last half hour, the Dow fell 17 points. Index arbitrage sales were $140 million, 15 percent of volume.

For the day, the Dow was down an historic 95 points on volume of 207 million shares. Of this volume, index arbitrage sales through DOT were $1.4 billion, 17 percent of volume or twice the normal level. The 20 largest NYSE member firms sold as principal $689 million of stock. Trading-oriented investors in the futures market were net sellers of about $500 million. Portfolio insurance selling was heavy, particularly in early and mid-afternoon.

THURSDAY, OCTOBER 15. Selling in Tokyo and London overnight continued the pattern seen in New York and Chicago on Wednesday. When the U.S. markets opened, they were greeted by heavy selling from portfolio insurers. During the first half hour, this group sold approximately 2,500 futures contracts ($380 million), more than 26 percent of public volume. The Dow opened 20 points down on heavy volume of 48 million shares in the first half hour, with approximately 60 percent of the trading in large blocks of 10,000 shares or more. Even with the opening drop in the Dow, the futures went to a discount.

Despite the opening, the Dow recovered during the day and was down only four points at 3:30 p.m. In the last 30 minutes of trading, however, it fell another 53 points to close down 57 points for the day. This sharp decline on heavy volume so late in the day bewildered investors. Broad-based selling by futures market participants, including portfolio insurers, led the fall, and index arbitrage activity quickly followed to bring the stock market into line (see Figures 3A.6–3A.8). Index arbitrage amounted to almost $175 million in stock sales on the NYSE, and straight selling of stock baskets amounted to another $100 million; together the two trading strategies accounted for approximately one quarter of the last half hour's volume on the NYSE. Throughout the day, a concentration of trading activity was evident. Seven aggressive trading institutions sold a total of just over $800 million of stocks, about 9 percent of NYSE volume.

FRIDAY, OCTOBER 16. Despite the sell-off at the close on Thursday in the U.S., trading in Tokyo on Friday was quiet. London was closed because of a freak hurricane.

Trading in the U.S. markets Friday was affected strongly by the expiration of options on several stock indices. A few firms noted for trading heavily in options were major participants on both sides of the futures market. Because the marked decline in stock prices had made it difficult for options traders to hedge effectively in the options market, much of their activity spilled into the futures market, where they sold futures as a hedge. In so doing, they responded in a manner similar to the reactive decisions of portfolio insurers. All told, options traders accounted for 7 percent of gross selling and 6 percent of gross buying in the futures market.

The stock market was relatively quiet until 11:00 a.m., with the Dow down only seven points, when futures selling by portfolio insurers picked up significantly, running over 2,000 contracts, or $300 million of stock, an hour (see Figures 3A.9–3A.11). Index arbitrageurs quickly transmitted this pressure to the stock market, selling $183 million of stock, 18 percent of NYSE volume. The Dow fell 30 points.

The stock market rallied briefly but then plummeted 70 points between noon and 2:00 p.m. Index arbitrage selling was active, accounting for about 16 percent of NYSE volume between 1:00 p.m. and 2:00 p.m. Large block transactions accounted for about half the volume in the 30 stocks making up the Dow. After a technical trading rally fizzled at about 2:30 p.m., the decline quickened in the last half hour of trading. Between 3:30 p.m. and 3:50 p.m., the Dow fell 50 points, then recovered 22 points in the last 10 minutes of trading. During this last half hour, index arbitrageurs had gross sales of $620 million of stock, and institutions sold $151 million of stock baskets. Together, this $771 million of stock sales through the DOT system made up 45 percent of NYSE sales volume during this period.[3]

---

[3] These gross sales exceed the numbers shown in Figure 3A.20, which are net. All volume numbers in the daily graphs represent net sales or purchases for the period.

FIGURE 3A.6
S&P Index and Futures Contract: Thursday, October 15, 1987

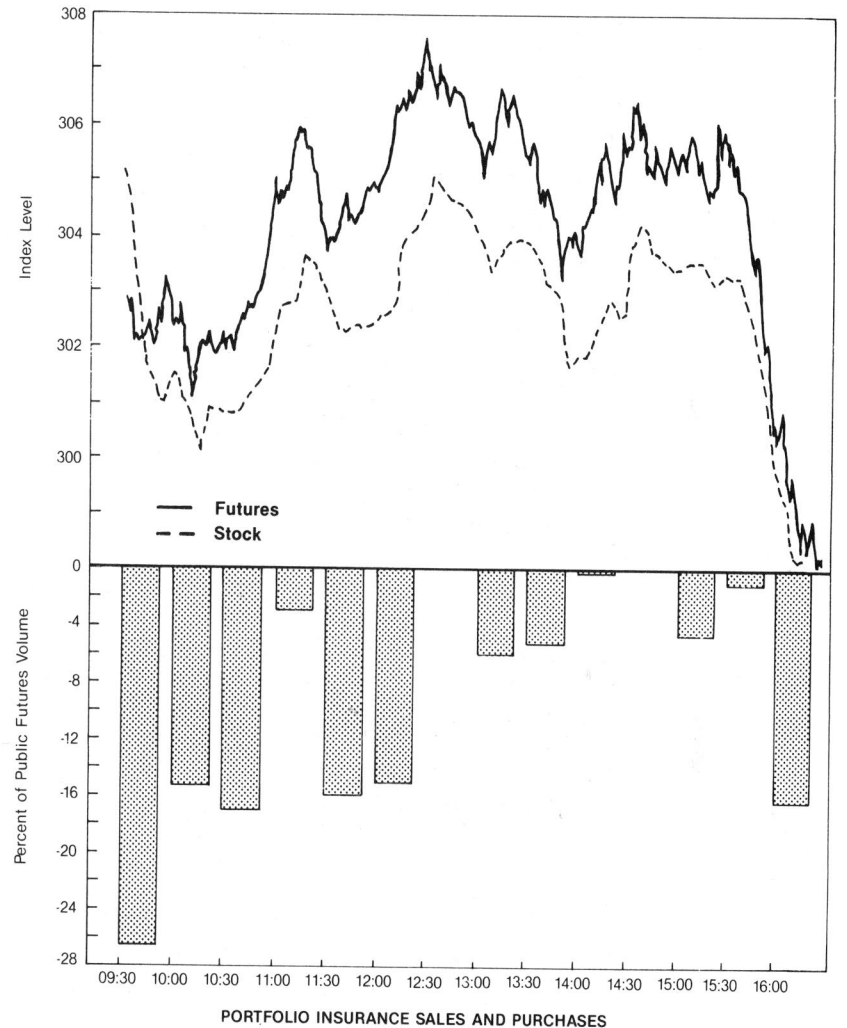

The Dow was off 108 points, the largest one day drop ever, on volume of 338 million shares. Sales by aggressive trading institutions were especially heavy and concentrated. Four of them sold over $600 million of stock in total. To put this in perspective, an investor transacting $10 million on a normal day would be considered an active trader.

Portfolio insurers and index arbitrageurs were also active. Five of the top seven net sellers in futures were portfolio insurers. As a group they accounted for sales equivalent to $2.1 billion of stock, 17 percent of the

FIGURE **3A.7**
Dow Jones Industrial One Minute Chart: Thursday, October 15, 1987

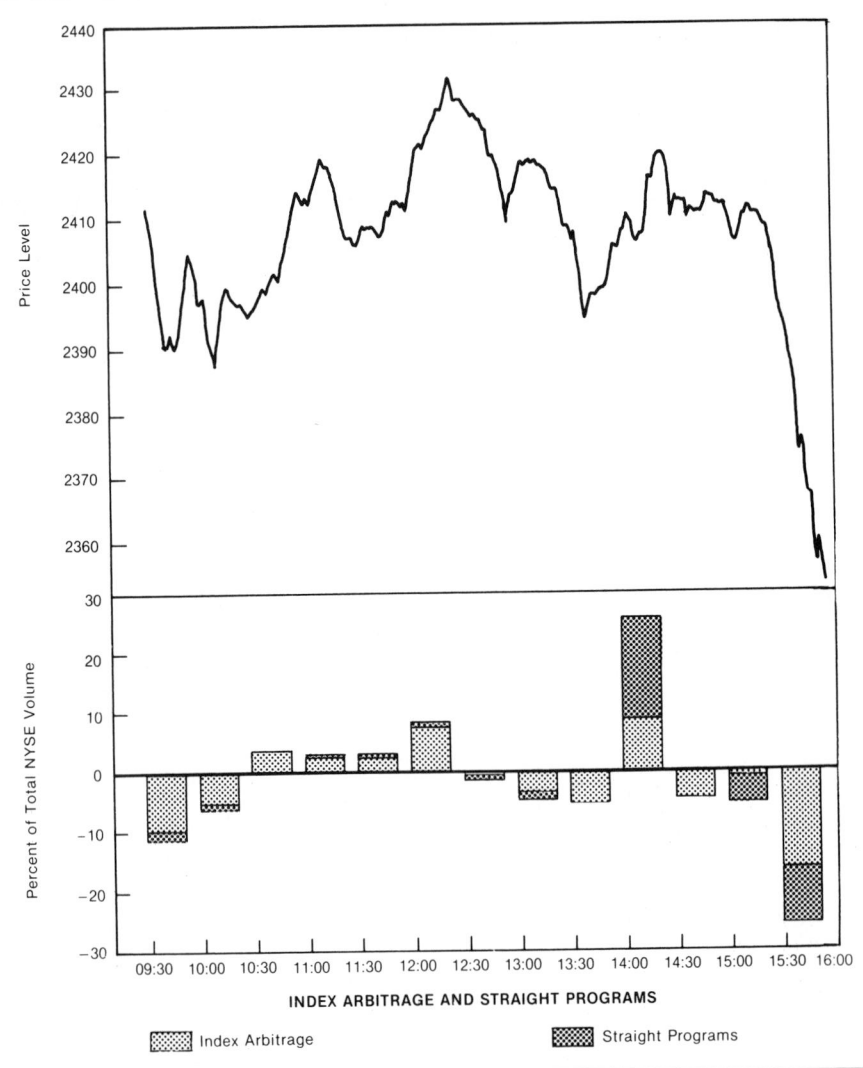

non-market maker future sales. Index arbitrageurs transmitted $1.7 billion of selling pressure to the stock market.

THE THREE DAYS IN PERSPECTIVE. During October 14 to 16, the Dow fell by over 250 points. The selling was triggered primarily by two proximate causes: disappointingly poor merchandise trade figures, which put downward pressure on the dollar in currency markets and upward pressure on long term interest rates; and the filing of anti-takeover tax legislation, which

FIGURE 3A.8
S&P Index and Futures Contract Spread: Thursday, October 15, 1987

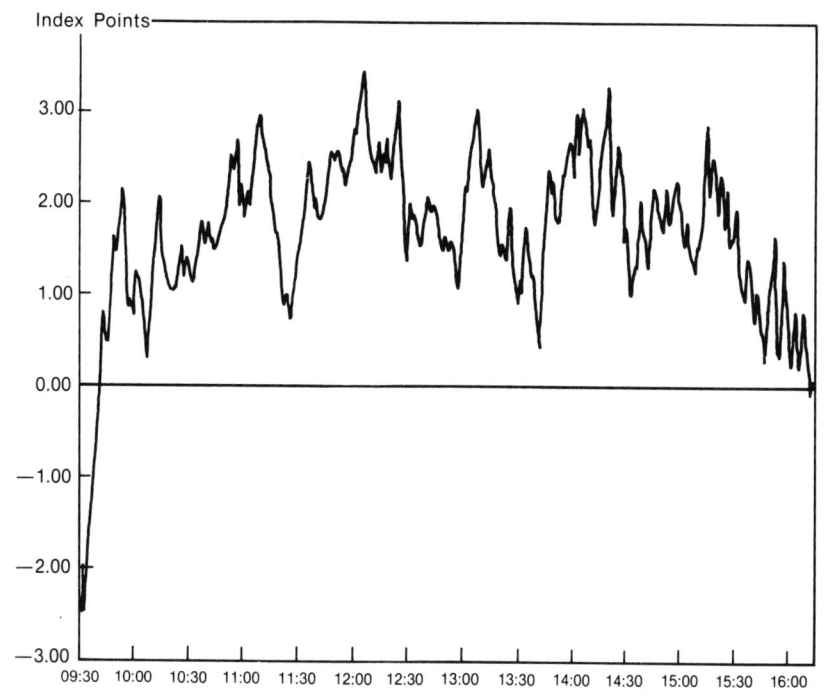

caused risk arbitrageurs to sell stocks of takeover candidates resulting in their precipitate decline and a general ripple effect throughout the market. The market's decline created a huge overhang of selling pressure—enough to crush the equity markets in the following week. This overhang was concentrated within two categories of reactive sellers, portfolio insurers and a few mutual fund groups, and exacerbated by the actions of a number of aggressive trading-oriented institutions selling in anticipation of further declines.

An example may help illustrate the extent of the portfolio insurance overhang by Friday's close. One portfolio insurance client had followed exactly the instructions of its advisor during the Wednesday to Friday period. Over the weekend, the advisor informed the client that, based on Friday's market close, it should sell on Monday 70 percent of its remaining equities in order to conform to the parameters of the insurance model. This is, of course, an extreme example. But the typical portfolio insurance model calls for stock sales in excess of 20 percent of a portfolio in response to a 10 percent decline in the market.

Various sources indicate that $60 to $90 billion of equity assets were under portfolio insurance administration at the time of the market break.[4]

---

[4] Assets under portfolio insurance administration increased more than fourfold during 1987.

FIGURE 3A.9
S&P Index and Futures Contract: Friday, October 16, 1987

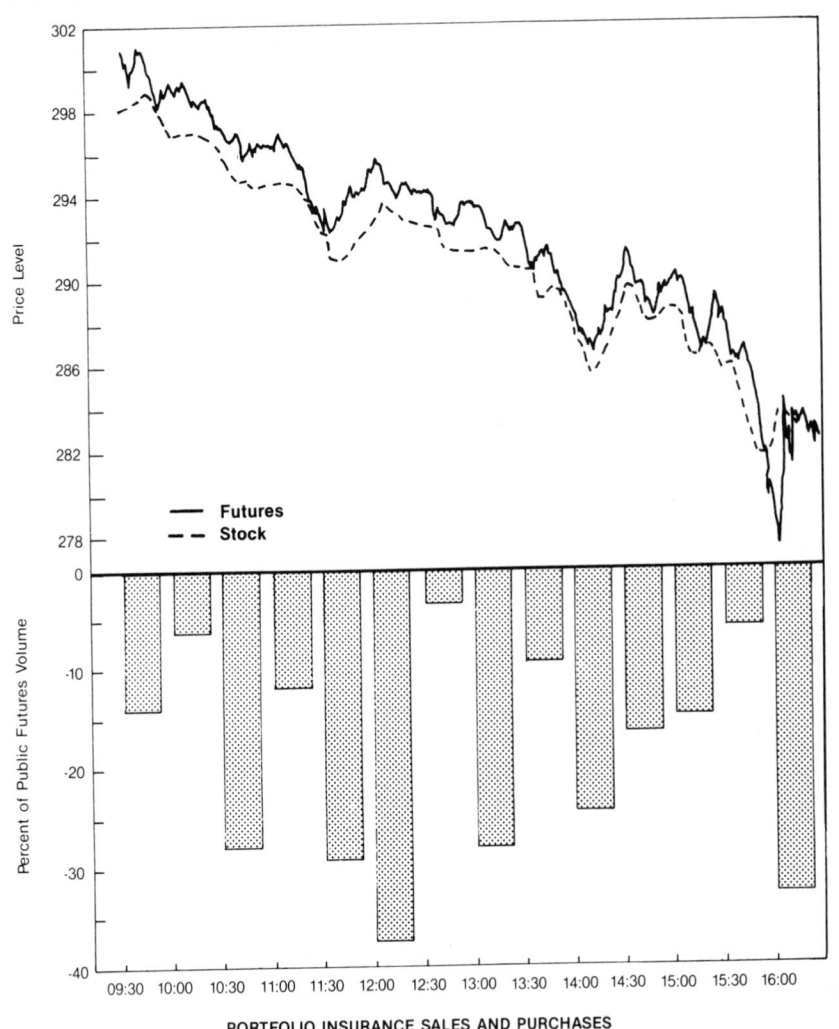

PORTFOLIO INSURANCE SALES AND PURCHASES

Two consequences were evident. First, portfolio insurers were very active sellers during the Wednesday to Friday period. In the futures market, where they concentrated their activity during this week, they sold the equivalent in stocks of approximately $530 million on Wednesday, $965 million on Thursday and $2.1 billion on Friday. Second, they approached Monday with a huge amount of selling already dictated by their models. With the market already down 10 percent, their models dictated that, at a minimum, $12 billion (20 percent of $60 billion) of equities should already have been sold. Less than $4 billion had in fact been sold.

FIGURE 3A.10
Dow Jones Industrial One Minute Chart: Friday, October 16, 1987

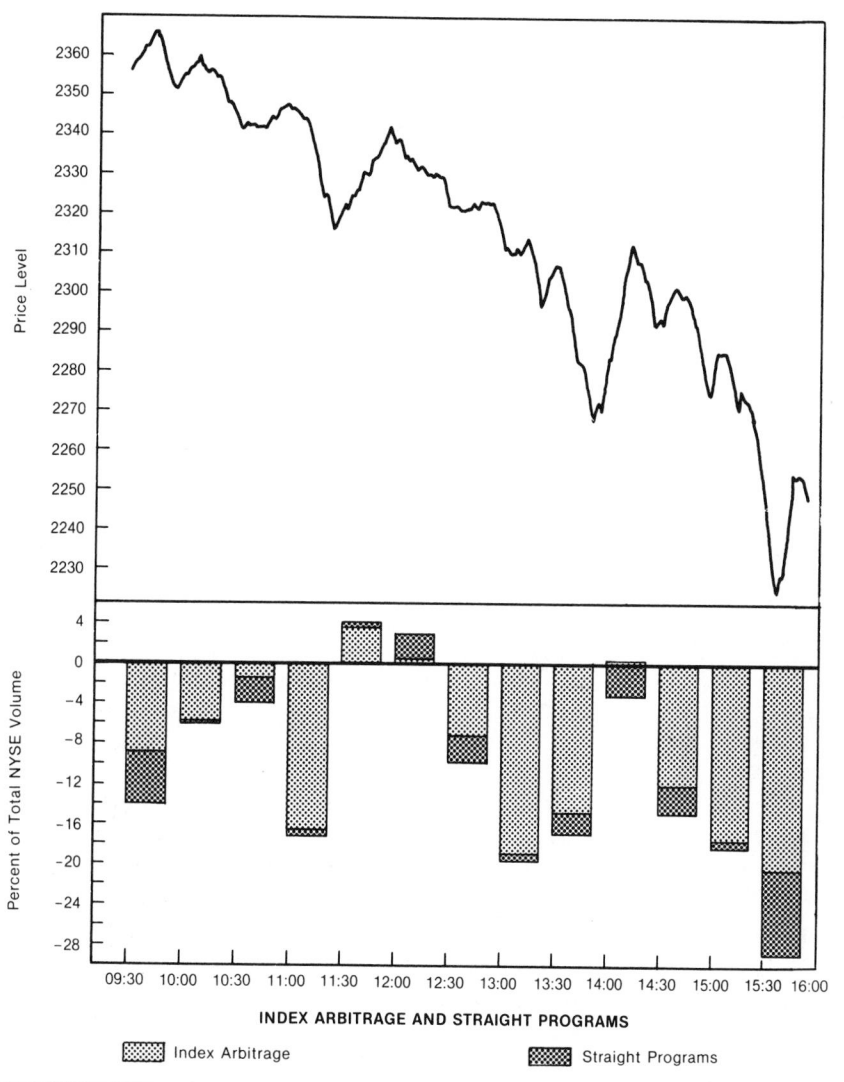

A small number of mutual fund groups were also confronted with an overhang. These funds had designed strategies which made it easy for customers to redeem mutual fund shares. On Friday alone, customer redemptions at these funds exceeded fund sales of stock by $750 million. These customers were entitled to repayment based on market prices at the close on Friday. These funds also received substantial redemption requests over the weekend.

FIGURE 3A.11
S&P Index and Futures Contract Spread: Friday, October 16, 1987

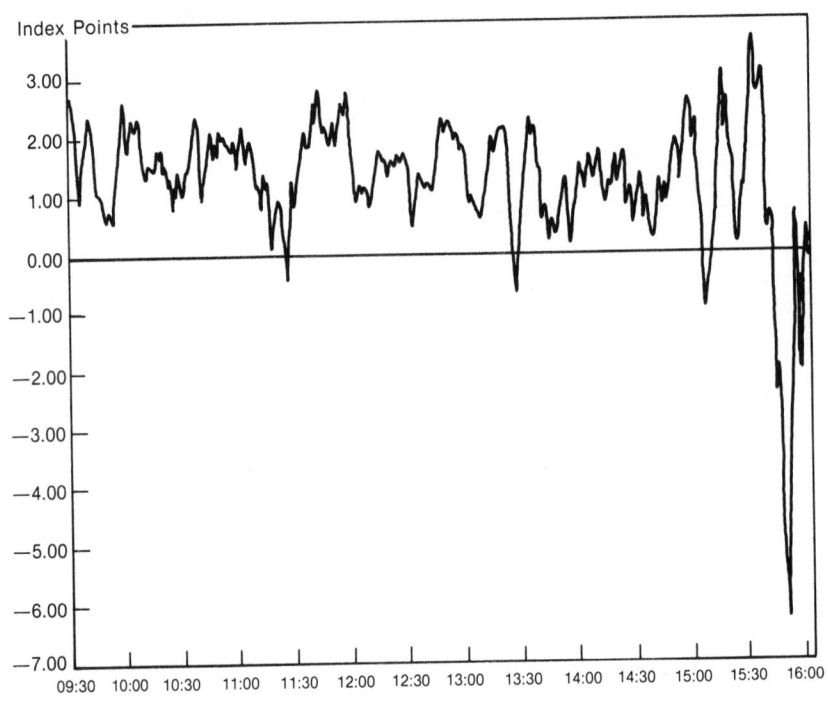

The activities of a small number of aggressive trading-oriented institutions both contributed to the decline during this week and posed the prospect of further selling pressure on Monday. These traders could well understand the strategies of the portfolio insurers and mutual funds. They could anticipate the selling those institutions would have to do in reaction to the market's decline. They could also see those institutions falling behind in their selling programs. The situation presented an opportunity for these traders to sell in anticipation of the forced selling by portfolio insurers and mutual funds, with the prospect of repurchasing at lower prices.

During this period, these trading-oriented institutions were active, typically on both sides of the market and often on the same day. On Thursday, seven of these trading-oriented institutions sold a total of just over $800 million of stocks, 9 percent of NYSE volume. The same institution was the fourth largest seller of stocks and the second largest buyer. This institution also ranked third and fourth, respectively, in futures sales and purchases and was active in options trading. On Friday, seven aggressive trading-oriented institutions sold more than $100 million each; four of the seven also bought more than $100 million. That day traders as a group sold $1.4 billion of stocks and bought $1.1 billion. Their activities on these days were a prelude to Monday's sell-off.

Index arbitrage was active throughout the three day period to transmit selling pressure from the futures market to the stock market. But as several charts make apparent (see Figures 3A.4, 3A.7, and 3A.10), it was the timing of arbitrage activities, rather than the aggregate daily level, which had a specific impact on the stock market. Heavy index arbitrage activity was most often coincident with substantial intraday stock market moves.

MONDAY, OCTOBER 19

In Tokyo, the Nikkei Index, Japan's equivalent of the Dow, fell 2.5 percent. Investors in London sold shares heavily, and by midday the market index there was down 10 percent. Selling of U.S. stocks on the London market was stoked by some U.S. mutual fund managers who tried to beat the expected selling on the NYSE by lightening up in London. One mutual fund group sold just under $90 million of stocks in London.

Selling activity shifted to the U.S. when the equity markets opened. At 9:15 a.m., the MMI futures opened down 2.5 percent from an already weak close on Friday. Fifteen minutes later the S&P 500 futures also opened down under heavy selling pressure by portfolio insurers. During the first half hour of trading, a few portfolio insurers sold futures equivalent to just under $400 million of stocks, 28 percent of the public volume.

By the scheduled 9:30 a.m. opening on the NYSE, specialists faced large order imbalances. In the DOT system alone, almost $500 million of market sell orders were loaded before the market opened. Of this total, $250 million were sales by index arbitrageurs responding to an apparent record futures discount. The remaining $250 million included straight sell programs by a few portfolio insurers permitted by their clients to sell stocks as well as futures; this group would sell more or less consistently from the opening to the closing bell. There were also large sell orders on the floor for blocks of individual stocks by a small number of mutual funds.

Faced with this massive order imbalance, many specialists did not open trading in their stocks during the first hour. Nevertheless, volume was impressive; in the first half hour alone about $2 billion crossed the tape. Of this total, about $500 million, roughly 25 percent of volume in this period, came from one mutual fund group. Slightly less came from the execution of orders in the DOT system for index arbitrageurs and portfolio insurers. In addition, even as these trades were being executed through DOT, another $500 million of sell orders were being loaded into the system backlog. Thus, sell orders from a few institutional traders overwhelmed the stock market at the opening (see Figures 3A.12–3A.14).

During the first hour, the reported levels of the S&P and Dow indices reflected out-of-date Friday closing prices for the large number of stocks which had not yet been opened for trading. The result was an apparent record discount for the futures relative to stocks. Based on this apparent discount, index arbitrageurs entered sell-at-market orders through DOT, planning to cover by later purchases of futures at lower prices. However, specialists ultimately opened their stocks at sharply lower levels, in line with the prices at which futures had opened earlier. As this fact became evident, index arbitrageurs realized they had sold stock at prices lower

FIGURE 3A.12
S&P Index and Futures Contract: Monday, October 19, 1987

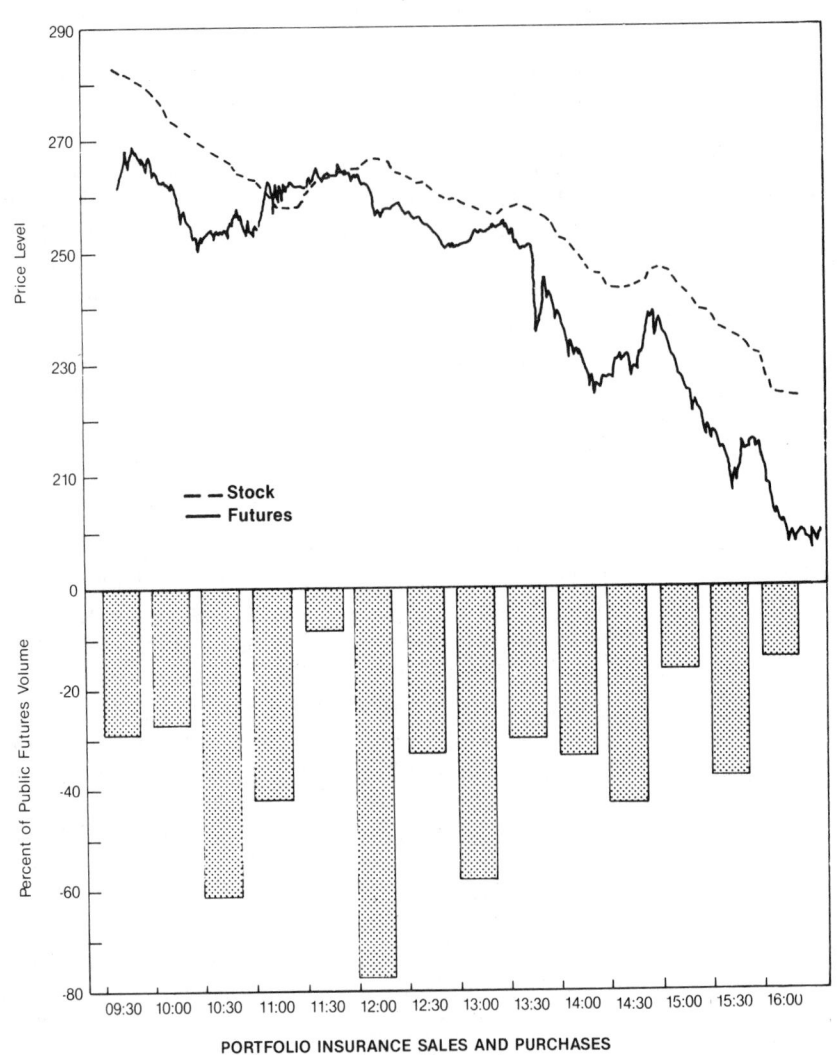

PORTFOLIO INSURANCE SALES AND PURCHASES

than expected. By 10:30 a.m., when most stocks had opened, the Dow was around 2,150 compared with the Friday close of near 2,250.

Starting around 10:50 a.m., these arbitrageurs rushed to cover their positions through purchases of futures. The result was an immediate rise in the futures market. By 11:00 a.m., futures were at a premium, and the stock market in turn began an hour-long rally.

Even as the futures and then the stock markets rallied, one portfolio insurance client began to modify its selling strategy in response to the anticipated volume of sales. On previous days and during the first hour

FIGURE **3A.13**
Dow Jones Industrial One Minute Chart: Monday, October 19, 1987

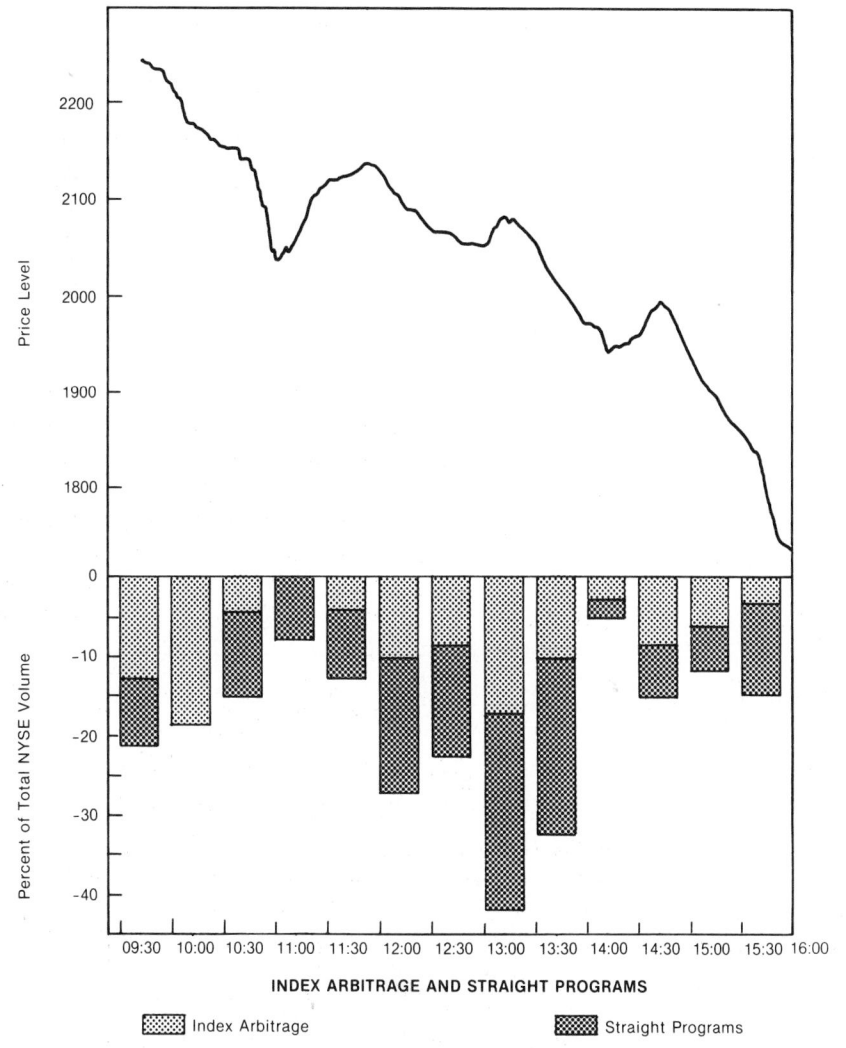

of Monday, this institutional investor had relied on futures sales as the method to increase its cash position. Around 10:30 a.m., this institution augmented futures sales with straight stock sell programs through DOT. These sales of stock baskets by this institution would ultimately continue in 13 waves of almost $100 million each until about 2:00 p.m. and total just under $1.1 billion.

Thus, one hour into the trading day, two mechanisms were operating at high volume through DOT to transmit futures selling pressure to the stock market: index arbitrage and the diversion of portfolio insurance sales from the futures market into straight stock sell programs.

Figure **3A.14**
S&P Index and Futures Contract Spread: Monday, October 19, 1987

Trading on the NYSE and CME is shown schematically in Figure 3A.15. In New York, the stock exchange traded about $21 billion of stock. In Chicago, the CME traded futures equivalent to almost $20 billion, of which about 50 percent was trading by public customers. Including trading by specialists and market makers, almost $41 billion of stock or equivalent futures was traded on these exchanges.

The selling pressure in futures led to discounts of historic size. In response to these huge discounts, three mechanisms came into play to transmit selling pressure from futures to stocks. First, index arbitrage executed $1.7 billion of program sales through DOT, matched by equivalent futures purchases. Second, there were additional straight program sales of stock equal to $2.3 billion. Most of this was portfolio insurance selling diverted from the futures market to the stock market by the large discount. Taken together, arbitrage programs and straight sell programs totaled $4 billion, almost 20 percent of the sales on the first 600 million share day in the NYSE's history. These program sales would no doubt have been even higher if the DOT system had functioned more effectively after 2:00 p.m. Third, some indeterminant portion of the $41 billion of purchases was diverted from more expensive stocks to cheaper futures.

FIGURE 3A.15
Schematic of Sales and Purchases NYSE Stocks and CME Futures: Monday, October 19, 1987

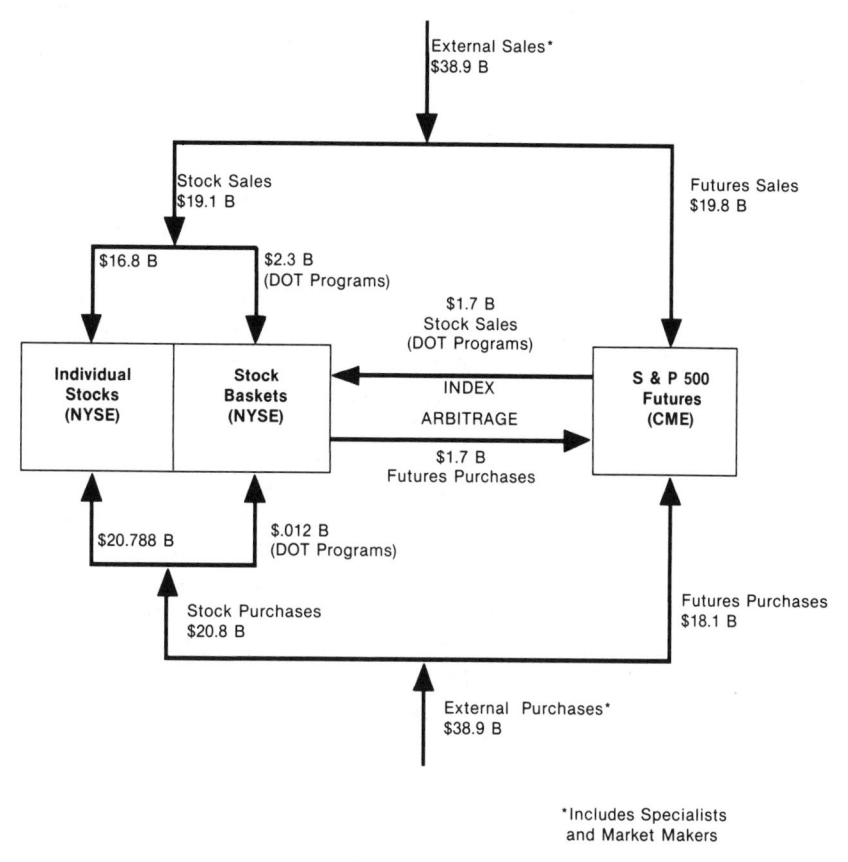

Starting around 11:40 a.m., portfolio insurance sales overwhelmed the rally. Between then and 2:00 p.m., the Dow fell from 2,140 to 1,950, a decline of just under 9 percent. The last 100 points of this decline occurred after reports began circulating that the NYSE might close. The break below 2,000 was the first time this level had been penetrated since January 7, 1987. Over these two hours, the futures index fell 14.5 percent. Portfolio insurance activity intensified. Between 11:40 a.m. and 2:00 p.m., in the futures market portfolio insurers sold approximately 10,000 contracts, equivalent to about $1.3 billion and representing about 41 percent of futures volume exclusive of market makers (i.e. locals). In addition, portfolio insurers authorized to sell stock directly sold approximately $900 million in stocks on the NYSE during this period. In the stock and futures markets combined, portfolio insurers contributed over $3.7 billion in selling pressure by early afternoon.

Throughout most of this period, index arbitrage had succeeded in transmitting futures selling pressure back to the stock market. After about 2:00 p.m., exchange sales slowed because of concerns about delays in DOT and the consequent ineffective execution of basket sales. Another source of sales through DOT stopped at around 2:00 p.m. when the one institution which had already sold 13 baskets of stock, each worth just under $100 million, discontinued its sell program. Up until this hour, index arbitrage and straight program selling totaled $3.2 billion. Relieved of these selling pressures, the stock market enjoyed a brief respite. The Dow rallied back to the psychologically important 2,000 level by 2:45 p.m.

The result of the withdrawal of some index arbitrage and diverted portfolio insurer sales from the DOT system was that neither mechanism was sufficient to keep the stock and futures markets from disconnecting. Enormous discounts of futures relative to stocks were free to develop as the futures market plummeted, disconnected from the stock market.

The rest of Monday afternoon was disastrous. Heavy futures selling continued by a few portfolio insurers. In the last hour and one half of futures trading, these institutions sold 6,000 contracts, the equivalent of $660 million of stock. With some index arbitrageurs unwilling to sell stock through DOT, they also withdrew from the futures side of their trading, denying buying support to the futures market, allowing it to fall to a discount of 20 index points. In addition, the appearance of this dysfunctionally large discount inhibited buyers in the stock market. With these stock buyers gone, the Dow sank almost 300 points in the last hour and one quarter of stock trading, to close at 1,738. Portfolio insurance futures selling continued even after stocks closed.

All told, Monday, October 19 was perhaps the worst day in the history of U.S. equity markets. By the close of trading, the Dow index had fallen 508 points, almost 23 percent, on volume of 604 million shares worth just under $21 billion. Even worse, the S&P 500 futures had fallen 29 percent on total volume of 162,000 contracts, valued at almost $20 billion.

This record volume was concentrated among relatively few institutions. In the stock market, the top four sellers alone accounted for $2.85 billion, or 14 percent of total sales. The top 15 sellers as a group accounted for $4.1 billion, or about 20 percent of total sales. The top 15 buyers purchased $2.2 billion, almost 11 percent of total volume.[5] In the futures market the top 10 sellers accounted for sales equivalent to $5 billion, roughly 50 percent of the non-market maker total volume.

The contribution of a small number of portfolio insurers and mutual funds to the Monday selling pressure is even more striking. Out of total NYSE sales of just under $21 billion, sell programs by three portfolio insurers made up just under $2 billion. Block sales of individual stocks by a few mutual funds accounted for another $900 million. About 90 percent of these sales were executed by one mutual fund group. In the futures

---

[5] This compares with specialist buying power estimated to be no more than $3 billion at the start of Monday.

market, portfolio insurer sales amounted to the equivalent of $4 billion of stocks, or 34,500 contracts, equal to over 40 percent of futures volume, exclusive of locals' transactions; $2.8 billion was done by only three insurers. In the stock and futures markets together, one portfolio insurer sold stock and futures with underlying values totaling $1.7 billion. Huge as this selling pressure from portfolio insurers was, it was a small fraction of the sales dictated by the formulas of their models.

TUESDAY, OCTOBER 20

Overnight the Tokyo and London stock markets declined dramatically, falling just under 15 percent. In the U.S., the Federal Reserve issued a statement just before the equity market's opening that it would provide needed liquidity to the financial system. On U.S. equity markets, the start of trading Tuesday stood in marked contrast to Monday. Both stock and futures markets opened with dramatic rises. On the NYSE, many stocks could not open due to "buyside" order imbalances. The majority of these imbalances were made up of "market orders," primarily from value-oriented investors and traders with short stock or futures positions. The NYSE specialists, burdened with more than $1 billion in stock inventories at Monday's close, opened stocks at higher levels and reduced their inventories. In the first hour, the Dow index rose just under 200 points (see Figures 3A.16–3A.18).

In the futures market, the S&P 500 contract opened up 10 percent at 223. Buying pressure came from aggressive trading-oriented institutions who wanted to buy the market but were unsure how quickly they could get execution on the NYSE. Buying pressure also came from traders wanting to close out short positions after hearing rumors about the financial viability of the CME's clearinghouse. These rumors were unfounded, although two New York investment banks had to wait until late in the afternoon before receiving variation margin payments totaling about $1.5 billion from the CME clearinghouse. The rumors did affect Tuesday's trading, with futures volume dropping 22 percent below Monday's level.

The morning rally in the futures market ended abruptly at 10:00 a.m., as heavy selling by portfolio insurers and traders overwhelmed buying. Portfolio insurance selling in the first hour totaled the equivalent of almost $900 million of stock. The futures contract quickly moved to an enormous discount (as large as 40 index points) as the market went into freefall, plummeting 27 percent between 10:00 a.m. and 12:15 p.m. By the end of this period, portfolio insurance sales for the day totaled the equivalent of $1.75 billion of stock; by the end of the day it added up to 40 percent of futures activity of public sellers. At its low, the S&P 500 futures contract price implied a Dow level of about 1,400. Contributing greatly to this freefall was the lack of index arbitrage buying which would normally have been stimulated by the huge discount of futures to stock. At its opening, the NYSE had prohibited broker-dealers from using the DOT system to execute index arbitrage orders for their own accounts. As on Monday afternoon, the primary linkage between the two markets had been disconnected.

FIGURE **3A.16**
S&P Index and Futures Contract: Tuesday, October 20, 1987

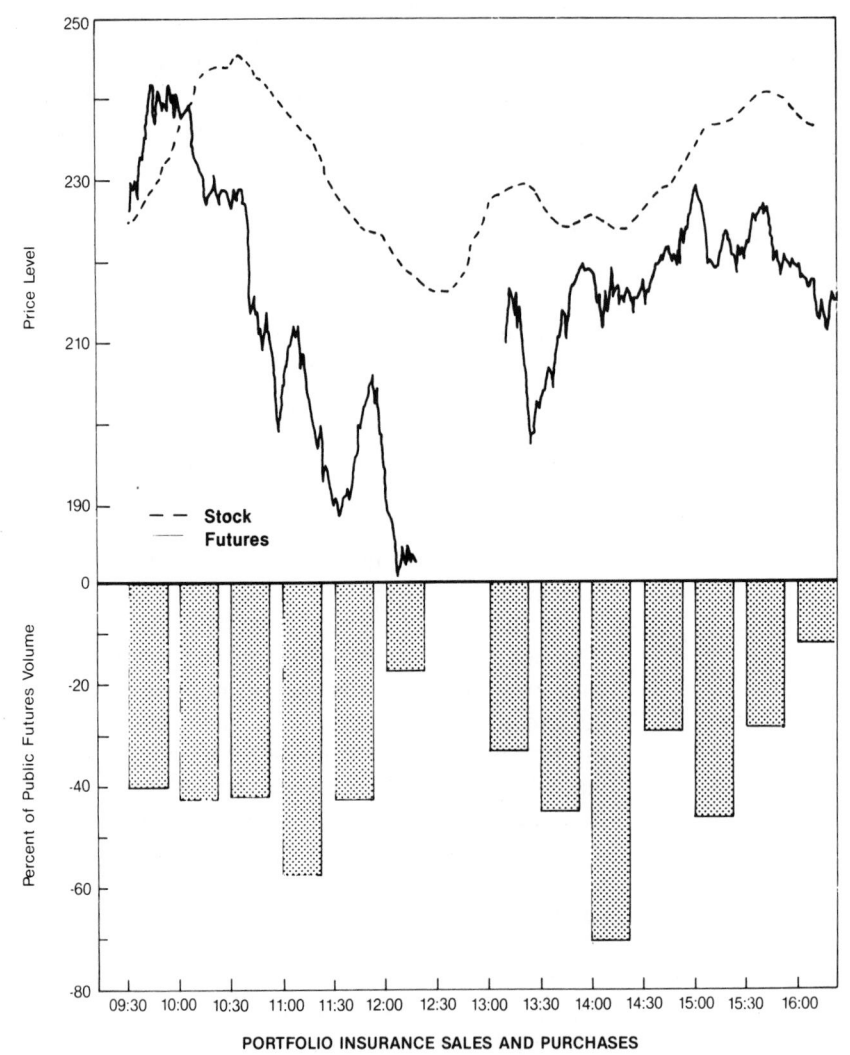

PORTFOLIO INSURANCE SALES AND PURCHASES

The stock market also ran out of buying support by midmorning and began to follow the futures market down. Although individual stocks were opening and closing again at various times all morning and early afternoon, record or near-record volume was executed in every half hour period. During the first two hours, 259 million shares were traded. Selling pressure was widespread, much of it from mutual funds who were dealing with expected redemptions, portfolio insurers who were switching from selling futures to selling stocks, and some index arbitrageurs. In addition, the

FIGURE 3A.17
Dow Jones Industrial One Minute Chart: Tuesday, October 20, 1987

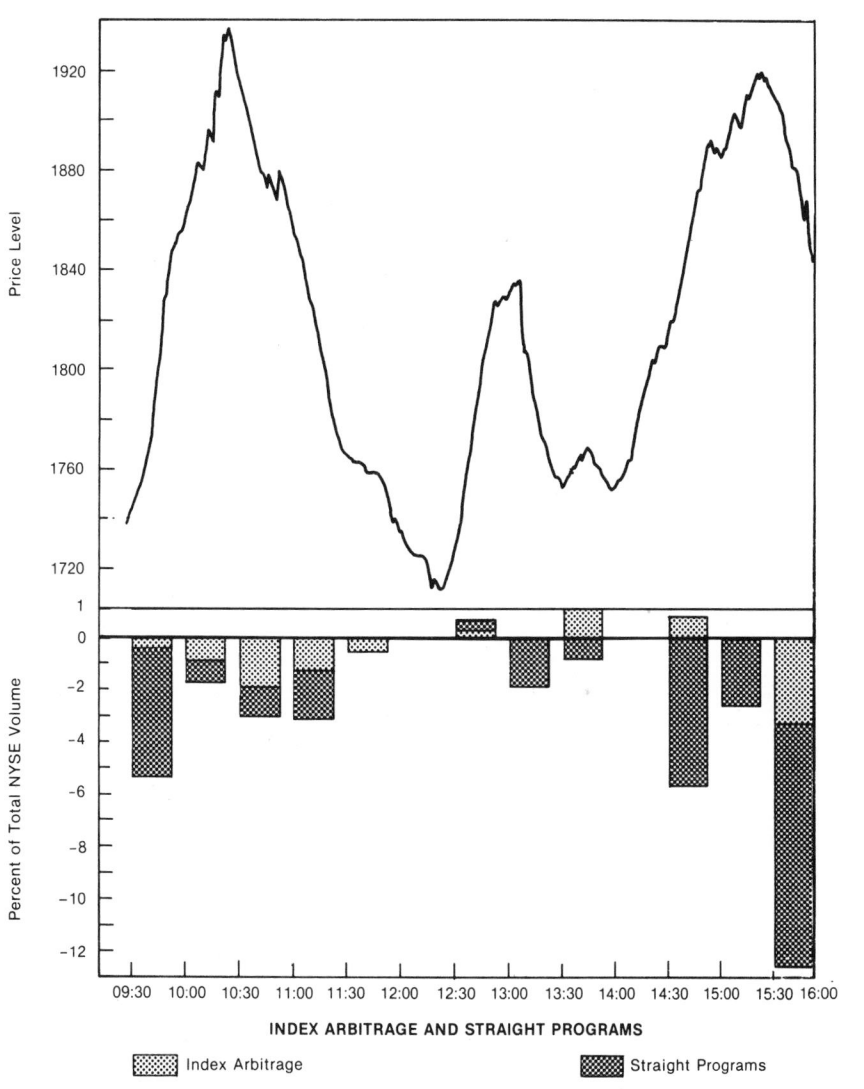

INDEX ARBITRAGE AND STRAIGHT PROGRAMS

Index Arbitrage   Straight Programs

large discount between futures and stocks acted as a "billboard," worrying many investors that further declines were imminent. By 12:30 p.m., the Dow had fallen to just above 1,700.

At this point a number of exchanges closed trading temporarily. The CBOE suspended trading at 11:45 a.m., based on its rule that trading on the NYSE must be open in at least 80 percent of the stocks which constitute the options index it trades. At 12:15 p.m., the CME announced a trading

Figure 3A.18
S&P Index and Futures Contract Spread: Tuesday, October 20, 1987

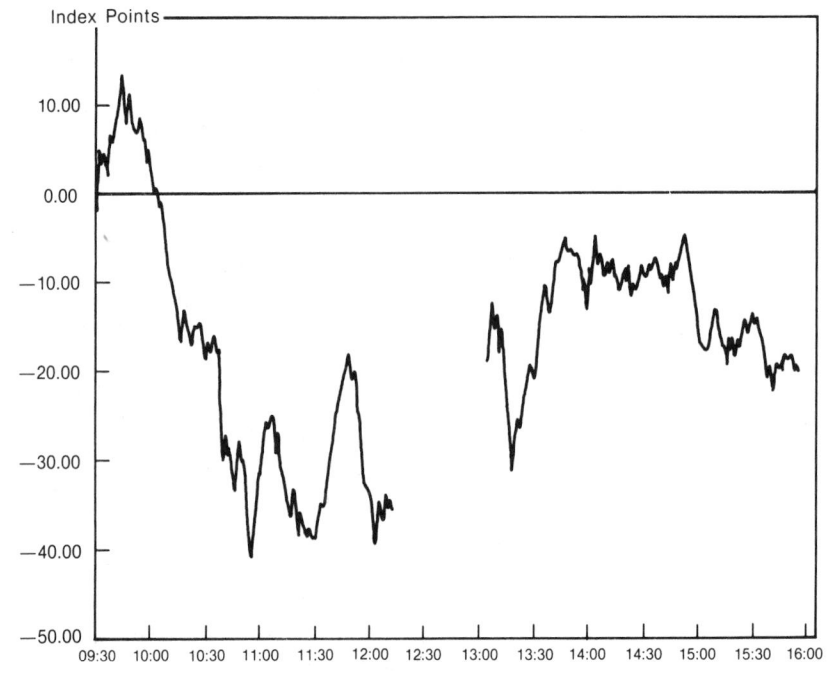

suspension in reaction to individual stock closings on the NYSE and the rumor of the imminent closing of the NYSE itself.

During Tuesday morning, the dynamics of trading in stocks and futures had become dysfunctional. The futures market was falling under selling pressure from portfolio insurers. Normally, the large discount would have attracted buyers; under the current circumstances, however, some potential buyers were afraid of the credit risk perceived to exist in futures and many stock investors were simply not authorized to buy futures. In addition, index arbitrage activity was limited because DOT was no longer available to some market participants. Because of the futures discount, those market professionals who could sell stocks did so. At the same time, the huge discount at which futures were selling made stocks look "expensive" and stifled buying demand in the stock market. The stock market "drafted" down in the wake of the futures market. The result was sell-side order imbalances in both markets, leading to the near disintegration of market pricing.

Closing the futures market had a number of marked effects on the equity market. On the sell side, it disconnected most of the portfolio insurers from the market. On the buy side, there was no longer a "cheap" futures alternative to buying stocks. Finally, the negative psychology of the "billboard" effect was eliminated. The reaction of the stock market was dramatic: the Dow rallied 125 points in the next 45 minutes.

When the futures market reopened just after 1:00 p.m., it was still at a substantial 17 point discount to stocks. Many of the effects which had rallied the stock market were reversed. Portfolio insurers resumed selling futures and the stock market began drafting down again. The Dow lost almost 100 points in the next half hour.

By early Tuesday afternoon, the equity market was again in freefall and needed reassurance. This came from a series of announced stock buyback programs by major corporations. By committing to these programs, the corporations provided needed support for the future level of their stocks. The buying power represented by these announced programs would ultimately total over $6 billion by Tuesday evening.[6] Around 2:00 p.m., the combined effect of buybacks already announced and those expected turned the equity market around. The Dow rallied 170 points between 2:00 p.m. and 3:30 p.m. After a decline in the last 30 minutes induced by program sales, the Dow closed with a net gain for the day of over 100 points, the largest gain on record.

Although Monday was the day of the dramatic stock market decline, it was midday Tuesday that the securities markets and the financial system approached breakdown. First, the ability of securities markets to price equities was in question. The futures and stock markets were disconnected. There were few buyers in either market and individual stocks ceased to trade. Investors began to question the value of equity assets.

Second, and more serious, a widespread credit breakdown seemed for a period of time quite possible. Amid rumors, subsequently revealed to be unfounded, of financial failures by some clearinghouses and several major market participants, and exacerbated by the fragmentation and complexity of the clearing process, the financial system came close to gridlock. Intermarket transactions required funds transfers and made demands for bank credit almost beyond the capacity of the system to provide.

SUMMARY

Although the equity market's behavior during this week was complex and rich in detail, several important themes emerge. First, reactive selling by institutions, which followed portfolio insurance strategies and sought to liquidate large fractions of their stock holdings regardless of price, played a prominent role in the market break. By reasonable estimates, the formulas used by portfolio insurers dictated the sale of $20 to $30 billion of equities over this short time span. Under such pressure, prices must fall dramatically. Transaction systems, such as DOT, or market stabilizing mechanisms, such as the NYSE specialists, are bound to be crushed by such selling pressure, however they are designed or capitalized.

Second, a few mutual funds sold stock in reaction to redemptions. To the market their behavior looked much like that of the portfolio insurers,

---

[6] A number of companies made buyback announcements during Monday afternoon and Tuesday morning. Those made early Tuesday afternoon, however, came from many "blue chip" companies and seemed sufficient to turn the tide of investor sentiment.

that is, selling without primary regard to price. Third, some aggressive trading-oriented investors, seizing the profit opportunity presented by the predictable forced selling by other institutions, contributed to the market break. Fourth, much of the selling pressure was concentrated in the hands of surprisingly few institutions. A handful of large investors provided the impetus for the sharpness of the decline.

Fifth, as the Figures showing intraday trading patterns make clear, futures and stock market movements were inextricably related. Portfolio insurers sold in the futures market, forcing prices down. The downward price pressure in the futures market was then transmitted to the stock market by index arbitrage and diverted portfolio insurance sales. While index arbitrageurs may not have accounted for a substantial part of total daily volume, they were particularly active during the day at times of substantial price movements. They were not, however, the primary cause of the movements; rather, they were the transmission mechanism for the pressures initiated by other institutions.

Finally, there were periods when the linkage between stock and futures markets became completely disconnected, leading to a freefall in both markets.

The juxtaposition of a record 508 point decline on Monday and a record 102 point bounceback on Tuesday suggests that these trading forces outstripped the capacity of market infrastructures.

The over-the-counter market and foreign stock markets experienced concurrent declines. The dominant position of NYSE stocks made such a sympathetic reaction predictable.

Figure 3A.19
NYSE Large Institutional Dollar Volume—Sales[1] (In Millions of Dollars)

	October 15	October 16	October 19	October 20
Sell				
Portfolio insurers	$257	$566	$1,748	$698
Other pension	190	794	875	334
Trading-oriented investors	1,156	1,446	1,751	1,740
Mutual funds	1,419	1,339	2,168	1,726
Other financial	−516	959	1,416	1,579
Total	3,538	5,104	7,598	6,077
Index arbitrage (included in above)	717	1,592	1,774	128

[1]Sample does not include: (1) individual investors, (2) institutional accounts with purchases and sales less than $10 million per day and (3) certain sizeable broker/dealer trades.

FIGURE **3A.20**
NYSE Large Institutional Dollar Volume—Purchases[1] (In Millions of Dollars)

	OCTOBER 15	OCTOBER 16	OCTOBER 19	OCTOBER 20
Buy				
Portfolio insurers	$201	$161	$449	$863
Other pension	368	773	1,481	920
Trading-oriented investors	1,026	1,081	1,316	1,495
Mutual funds	998	1,485	1,947	1,858
Other financial	798	1,221	2,691	2,154
Total	3,391	4,721	7,884	7,290
Index arbitrage (included in above)	407	394	110	32

[1]Sample does not include: (1) individual investors, (2) institutional accounts with purchases and sales less than $10 million per day and (3) certain sizeable broker/dealer trades.

FIGURE **3A.21**
CME Large Trader Sales (Dollar Amounts in Millions)

	OCTOBER 14	OCTOBER 15	OCTOBER 16	OCTOBER 19	OCTOBER 20
Sell					
Portfolio insurers	$ 534	$ 969	$ 2,123	$ 4,037	$ 2,818
Arbitrageurs	$ 108	$ 407	$ 392	$ 129	$ 31
Options	$ 554	$ 998	$ 1,399	$ 898	$ 635
Locals	$ 7,325	$ 7,509	$ 7,088	$ 5,479	$ 2,718
Other pension	$ 37	$ 169	$ 234	$ 631	$ 514
Trading-oriented investors	$ 1,993	$ 2,050	$ 3,373	$ 2,590	$ 2,765
Foreign	$ 398	$ 442	$ 479	$ 494	$ 329
Mutual funds	$ 46	$ 3	$ 11	$ 19	$ 40
Other financial	$ 49	$ 109	$ 247	$ 525	$ 303
Published total	$16,949	$18,830	$19,640	$18,987	$13,641
Volume accounted for	$11,045	$12,655	$15,347	$14,801	$10,152
Percent accounted for	65.2	67.2	78.1	78.0	74.4
Portfolio insurance: Percent of publicly accounted for volume	14.37	18.80	25.70	43.30	37.91

FIGURE 3A.22
CME Large Trader Purchases (Dollar Amounts in Millions)

	OCTOBER 14	OCTOBER 15	OCTOBER 16	OCTOBER 19	OCTOBER 20
Buy					
Portfolio insurers	$ 71	$ 171	$ 109	$ 112	$ 505
Arbitrageurs	$ 1,313	$ 717	$ 1,705	$ 1,582	$ 119
Options	$ 594	$ 864	$ 1,254	$ 915	$ 554
Locals	$ 7,301	$ 7,530	$ 7,125	$ 5,682	$ 2,689
Other pensions	$ 90	−$ 76	$ 294	$ 447	$ 1,070
Trading-oriented investors	$ 1,494	$ 2,236	$ 3,634	$ 4,510	$ 4,004
Foreign	$ 240	$ 298	$ 443	$ 609	$ 418
Mutual funds	$ 0	$ 27	$ 73	$ 143	$ 51
Other financial	$ 155	$ 57	$ 126	$ 320	$ 517
Published total	$16,949	$18,830	$19,640	$18,987	$13,641
Volume accounted for	$11,259	$11,976	$14,763	$14,320	$ 9,915
Percent accounted for	66.4	63.6	75.2	75.4	72.7
Portfolio insurance: Percent of publicly accounted for volume	1.80	3.86	1.43	1.31	6.98

FIGURE 3A.23
CME Large Trader Contract Volume—Sales (In Number of Contracts)

	OCTOBER 14	OCTOBER 15	OCTOBER 16	OCTOBER 19	OCTOBER 20
Sell					
Portfolio insurers	3,460	6.413	14,627	34,446	26,146
Arbitrageurs	700	2,700	2,700	1,100	285
Options	3,589	6,618	9,643	7,667	5,890
Locals	47,426	49,773	48,847	46,753	25,214
Other pension	238	1,122	1,615	5,387	4,770
Trading-oriented investors	12,906	13,587	23,246	22,098	25,651
Foreign	2,575	2,927	3,301	4,212	3,050
Mutual funds	300	19	77	160	375
Other financial	317	720	1,705	4,478	2,808
Published total	109,740	124,810	135,344	162,022	126,562
Contracts accounted for	71,511	83,879	105,761	126,301	94,189
Percent accounted for	65	67	78	78	74

Figure 3A.24
CME Large Trader Contract Volume—Purchases (In Number of Contracts)

	OCTOBER 14	OCTOBER 15	OCTOBER 16	OCTOBER 19	OCTOBER 20
Buy					
Portfolio insurers	461	1,136	751	964	4,682
Arbitrageurs	8,500	4,750	11,750	13,500	1,100
Options	3,848	5,725	8,639	7,804	5,049
Locals	47,272	49,911	49,098	48,487	24,945
Other pension	582	504	2,029	3,816	9,931
Trading-oriented investors	9,673	14,823	25,043	38,482	37,149
Foreign	1,553	1,972	3,051	5,199	3,874
Mutual funds	0	179	505	1,217	473
Other financial	1,006	378	867	2,727	4,793
Published total	109,740	124,810	135,344	162,022	126,562
Contracts accounted for	72,895	79,378	101,733	122,196	91,996
Percent accounted for	66	64	75	75	73

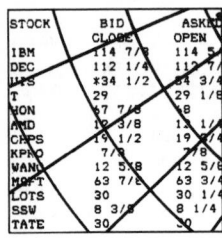

CHAPTER 4

SECURITY MARKET INDICATOR SERIES

A fair statement regarding security market indicator series—especially those outside the United States—is that everybody talks about them, but few people understand them. Even those investors familiar with widely publicized stock market series such as the Dow Jones Industrial Average usually know very little about indicator series for the U.S. bond market or series for non–U.S. stock markets such as Tokyo or London.

Although portfolios are obviously composed of many different individual stocks, investors typically ask, "What happened to the market today?" The reason for this question is that if an investor owns more than a few stocks or bonds, it is cumbersome to follow each stock or bond individually in order to determine the composite performance of the portfolio. Also there is an intuitive notion that most individual stocks or bonds move with the aggregate market. Therefore, if the overall market rose, an individual's portfolio probably also increased in value. To supply investors with a composite report on market performance, some financial publications or investment firms have developed stock market and bond market indicator series.

In this chapter we will consider some specific uses of U.S. and non–U.S. stock market and bond market indicator series and examine the major indicator series in detail, including long- and short-run price movements for some of them.

USES OF MARKET INDICATOR SERIES

There are at least four specific uses for security market indicator series. A primary application is to examine total market returns over a specified time period and use derived returns as a benchmark to judge the performance of individual portfolios. A basic assumption is that any investor should be able to derive a rate of return comparable to the "market" return by randomly selecting a large number of stocks or bonds from the total market; hence, a superior portfolio manager should consistently do better than the market. An indicator series for the aggregate stock or bond markets can therefore be used to judge the performance of professional money managers. However, one should be sure to analyze the differential risk for the portfolios being judged as compared to the market indicator series as well.

A somewhat related use is the employment of the indicator series to develop an index portfolio. If it is difficult for the majority of money managers to consistently outperform some specified market indicator series on a risk-adjusted basis over time, an obvious alternative is to invest in a portfolio that will emulate this portfolio. This notion led to the creation of *index funds* whose purpose is simply to track the changes in the specified market series over time—that is, derive similar rates of return.[1] While the original concept was related to common stocks, the development of comprehensive, well-specified bond market indicator series has replicated the phenomenon in the fixed-income area.[2]

Securities analysts, portfolio managers, and others use the series to examine the factors that influence aggregate security price movements, since the series provide a way to measure such movements. A subset of this use is to analyze the relationship among stock and bond returns of different countries such as the relationship between U.S., Japanese, and German stock price movements.

Another group interested in an aggregate market series are "technicians," who believe past price changes can be used to predict future price movements.

Finally, work in portfolio theory has shown that the relevant risk for an individual risky asset is its *systematic risk,* determined by the relationship between the rates of return for the security and the rates of return for a market portfolio of risky assets.[3] Therefore, it is necessary when computing the systematic risk for an individual risky asset (security) to relate its returns to the returns for an aggregate market indicator series that is used as a proxy for the risky asset portfolio.

DIFFEREN-TIATING FACTORS IN CONSTRUCTING MARKET INDICATOR SERIES

Because indicator series are intended to reflect the overall movements of a group of securities, it is necessary to consider which factors are important in computing any average intended to represent a total population.

SAMPLES

The size of the sample, the breadth of the sample, and the source of the sample used to construct a series are all important. A small percent of the total population will provide valid indications of the behavior of the total population if the sample is properly selected. In fact, at some point the

---

[1] For a discussion of this concept, see A. F. Ehber, "Index Funds—An Idea whose Time is Coming," *Fortune* (June 1976): 145–148.

[2] See Fran Hawthorne, "The Battle of the Bond Indexes," *Institutional Investor* 20, no. 4 (April 1986).

[3] This concept and its justification are discussed in Chapter 8.

costs of taking a larger sample will almost certainly outweigh any benefits of increased size. The sample should be *representative* of the total population, of course, or its size will be meaningless; a large biased sample is no better than a small biased sample. The sample can be generated by completely random selection or by a nonrandom one designed to incorporate the characteristics desired. Finally, the source of the sample becomes important if there are any differences between alternative segments of the population, in which case samples from each segment are required.

WEIGHTING

Our second concern is with the weight given to each member in the sample. Three principal weighting schemes are used: (1) a price-weighted series, (2) a value-weighted series, and (3) an unweighted series, or what would be described as an equally weighted series.

COMPUTATIONAL PROCEDURE

Our final consideration is with the computational procedure used. One alternative is to take a simple arithmetic average of the various members in the series. Another is to compute an index and have all changes, whether of price or value, reported in terms of the basic index. Finally, some prefer using a geometric average of the components.

ALTERNATIVE STOCK MARKET INDICATOR SERIES

PRICE-WEIGHTED SERIES

A price-weighted series is an arithmetic average of current prices, which means that, in fact, movements are influenced by differential prices.

DOW-JONES INDUSTRIAL AVERAGE. The best-known price series is also the oldest and certainly the most popular, the Dow-Jones Industrial Average (DJIA). This is a price-weighted average of 30 large, well-known industrial stocks that are generally the leaders in their industry (blue chips) and are listed on the NYSE. It is derived by totaling the current prices of the 30 stocks and dividing the sum by a divisor that has been adjusted to take account of stock splits and changes in the sample over time.[4] The adjustment of the divisor is demonstrated in Table 4.1.

$$DJIA_t = \sum_{i=1}^{30} P_{it}/D_{adj},$$

where

$$DJIA_t = \text{the value of the DJIA on day } t$$

$$P_{it} = \text{the closing price of stock } i \text{ on day } t$$

$$D_{adj} = \text{the adjusted divisor on day } t.$$

In Table 4.1 three stocks are employed to demonstrate the procedure used

---

[4] A complete list of all events that have caused a change in the divisor since the DJIA went to 30 stocks on October 1, 1928, is contained in Phyllis S. Pierce, ed., *The Dow-Jones Investor's Handbook* (Homewood, Ill.: Dow-Jones Books, 1987).

TABLE 4.1
Example of Change in DJIA Divisor When a Sample Stock Splits

	BEFORE SPLIT	AFTER THREE-FOR-ONE SPLIT BY STOCK A	
	Prices	Prices	
A	30	10	
B	20	20	
C	10	10	
	60 ÷ 3 = 20	40 ÷ X = 20	X = 2 (New Divisor)

to derive a new divisor for the DJIA when a stock splits. When stocks split, the divisor becomes smaller. An idea of the cumulative effect of splits can be derived from the fact that the divisor as of November 1988 was 0.703.

The new divisor ensures that the new value for the series is the same as it would have been without the split. In this case, the pre-split index value was 20. Therefore, after the split, given the new sum of prices, the divisor is adjusted downward to maintain this value of 20. The divisor is also changed if there is a change in the sample makeup of the series, which does not happen very often.

Because the series is price weighted, a high-priced stock carries more weight than a low-priced stock, so, as shown in Table 4.2, a 10 percent change in a $100 stock ($10) will cause a larger change in the series than a 10 percent change in a $30 stock ($3). In Case A, the $100 stock increases by 10 percent, which causes a 5.5 percent increase in the average; in Case B, the $30 stock increases by 10 percent, and the average only rises by 1.7 percent.

The DJIA has been criticized over time on several counts. First, the sample used for the series is limited. It is difficult to conceive that 30 nonrandomly selected blue-chip stocks can be representative of the 1,800 stocks listed on the NYSE. Beyond the limited number, the stocks included

TABLE 4.2
Demonstration of the Impact of Differently Priced Shares on a Price-weighted Indicator Series

	PERIOD T	PERIOD T + 1	
		CASE A	CASE B
A	100	110	100
B	50	50	50
C	30	30	33
Sum	180	190	183
Divisor	3	3	3
Average	60	63.3	61
Percentage change		5.5	1.7

are, by definition, offerings of the largest and most prestigious companies in various industries. Therefore, the DJIA probably reflects price movements for large, mature blue-chip firms rather than for the typical company listed on the NYSE. Several studies have pointed out that price movements of the DJIA have not been as volatile as they have been for other market indicator series and that the long-run returns on the DJIA are not comparable to the other NYSE stock indicator series.

In addition, because the DJIA is price weighted, when companies have a stock split, their prices decline, and therefore their weight in the DJIA is reduced—even though they may be large and important. Therefore, the weighting scheme causes a downward bias in the DJIA, because the stocks that have higher growth rates will have higher prices; and since such stocks tend to split, they will consistently lose weight within the index.[5] Regardless of the several criticisms made of the DJIA, there is a fairly close relationship between the daily percentages of its price changes and comparable price changes for other NYSE indicators. Dow-Jones also publishes an average of 20 stocks in the transportation industry and an average of 15 stocks for utilities. Detailed reports of the averages are contained in *The Wall Street Journal* and *Barron's,* including hourly figures.

NIKKEI-DOW JONES AVERAGE. Also referred to as the Nikkei Stock Average Index, the Nikkei-Dow Jones Average is an arithmetic average of prices for 225 stocks on the First Section of the Tokyo Stock Exchange (TSE). This is the most well-known series in Japan since it has been used to show stock price trends since the reopening of the TSE. Notably, it was formulated by Dow Jones and Company, and, similar to the DJIA, it is a price-weighted series rather than value-weighted, so a large dollar change for a small company will have the same impact of a similar price change of a large firm. It is also criticized because the 225 stocks included only comprise about 20 percent of all stocks on the First Section.

The results for this index are reported daily in *The Wall Street Journal* and the *Financial Times* and weekly in *Barron's.*

VALUE-WEIGHTED SERIES

A value-weighted index is generated by deriving the initial total market value of all stocks used in the series (Market Value = Number of Shares Outstanding × Current Market Price). This figure is typically established as the base and assigned an index value of 100. Subsequently, a new market value is computed for all securities in the index, and the current market

---

[5] For discussions of these problems, see H. L. Butler, Jr., and J. D. Allen, "The Dow-Jones Industrial Average Reexamined," *Financial Analysts Journal* 35, no. 6 (November–December 1979): 37–45; and E. E. Carter and K. J. Cohen, "Stock Averages, Stock Splits, and Bias," *Financial Analysts Journal* 23, no.3 (May–June 1967): 77–81.

TABLE 4.3
Example of Computation of a Value-Weighted Index

STOCK	SHARE PRICE	NUMBER OF SHARES	MARKET VALUE
December 31, 1989			
A	$10.00	1,000,000	$ 10,000,000
B	15.00	6,000,000	90,000,000
C	20.00	5,000,000	100,000,000
Total			$200,000,000
			Base Value Equal to an Index of 100
December 31, 1990			
A	$12.00	1,000,000	$ 12,000,000
B	10.00	12,000,000[a]	120,000,000
C	20.00	5,500,000[b]	110,000,000
Total			$242,000,000

$$\text{New Index Value} = \frac{\text{Current Market Value}}{\text{Base Value}} \times \text{Beginning Index Value}$$

$$= \frac{\$242,000,000}{\$200,000,000} \times 100$$

$$= 1.21 \times 100$$

$$= 121$$

[a]Stock split two-for-one during year.
[b]Company paid a 10 percent stock dividend during the year.

value is compared to the initial "base" value to determine the percentage of change, which in turn is applied to the beginning index value of 100.

$$\text{Index}_t = \frac{\Sigma P_t Q_t}{\Sigma P_b Q_b} \times \text{Beginning Index Value},$$

where

Index_t = index value on day t

P_t = ending prices for stocks on day t

Q_t = number of outstanding shares on day t

P_b = ending prices for stocks on base day

Q_b = number of outstanding shares on base day.

A simple example for a three-stock index is shown in Table 4.3. As can be seen, there is an *automatic adjustment* for stock splits and other capital changes in a value-weighted index because the decrease in the stock price is offset by an increase in the number of shares outstanding. In a value-weighted index, the importance of individual stocks in the sample is dependent on the market value of the stocks. Therefore, a percentage change in the value of a large company has a greater impact than a comparable percentage change for a small company. As shown in Table 4.3, if we begin with a base value of $200 million, and the only change is a 20 percent increase in the value of Stock A, which has a beginning value of $10 million, the ending index value will be $202 million, or an index of 101. In contrast, if only Stock C increases by 20 percent from $100 million, the ending value will be $220 million, or an index value of 110.

STANDARD & POOR'S INDEXES. The first company to widely employ a market value index was Standard & Poor's Corporation (S&P). Using 1935–1937 as a base period, the firm computed the index for 425 industrial stocks, 50 utilities, and 25 transportation firms. In addition there was a 500-stock composite index. The base period was subsequently changed to 1941–1943 and the base value to 10. All the S&P series were again changed significantly on July 1, 1976, when the stocks considered were changed to 400 industrials, 40 utilities, 20 transportation, and 40 financial. A number of OTC stocks were added because, as noted in Chapter 3, most of the major banks and insurance companies have been traded on the OTC market. Therefore, to construct a relevant financial index, it was necessary to break the tradition of including only NYSE-listed stocks.[6] S&P has also constructed over 90 individual industry series. Daily figures for the major S&P indexes are carried in *The Wall Street Journal, The Financial Times,* and other newspapers, and weekly data are contained in *Barron's.* S&P has a weekly publication titled *The Outlook* that contains weekly values for all the industry groups. Extensive historical data on all these indexes and other financial series are contained in S&P's annual publication, *Trade and Securities Statistics.*

NEW YORK STOCK EXCHANGE INDEX. In 1966 the NYSE derived five market value indexes (industrial, utility, transportation, financial, and a composite index, which contains the other four) with figures available back to 1940. (The December 31, 1965, figures are equal to 50.) In contrast to other indexes, the various NYSE series are not based upon a sample of stocks but include all stocks listed on the exchange. Therefore, questions about the number of stocks in the sample or the breadth of the sample do not arise as long as it is recognized that these indexes are limited to stocks listed on the NYSE. However, because the index is value-weighted, the stocks of large companies still control major movements in the index. For example, the 500 stocks in the Standard & Poor's Composite Index represent 74 percent of the market value of all stocks on the NYSE although they are only about 28 percent of exchange listings in terms of numbers.[7]

---

[6] For a further discussion of the specific changes, see *S&P 500 Stock Index Adds Financial, Transportation Groups* (New York: Standard & Poor's Corp., 1976). For a detailed discussion of the computation and potential adjustment of all the series, see *Trade and Securities Statistics* (New York: Standard & Poor's Corp., annual).

[7] For a detailed discussion of the index, see Stan West and Norman Miller, "Why the New NYSE Common Stock Indexes?" *Financial Analysts Journal* 23, no. 3 (May–June 1967): 49–54. For a listing of daily values for each year and a matrix of growth rates in the NYSE Index for the period 1972 to the present, see the annual *NYSE Fact Book* (New York: New York Stock Exchange).

NASDAQ SERIES. A comprehensive set of price indicator series for the OTC market was developed by the National Association of Securities Dealers (NASD). These NASDAQ-OTC Price Indicator Series were released to the public on May 17, 1971, with figures available from February 5, 1971. (The index value was 100 as of February 5.) Through NASDAQ, the NASD provides daily, weekly, and monthly sets of stock price indicators for OTC securities in different industry categories. All domestic OTC common stocks listed on NASDAQ are included in the indexes, and new stocks are included when they are added to the system. The 4,219 issues contained in the NASDAQ-OTC Price Indexes have been divided into seven categories:[8]

1. Composite (4,219 issues)
2. Industrials (2,932 issues)
3. Banks (189 issues)
4. Insurance (135 issues)
5. Other finance (745 issues)
6. Transportation (88 issues)
7. Utilities (100 issues).

Because the indexes are value-weighted, they are heavily influenced by the largest 100 stocks on the NASDAQ system. Most of the NASDAQ series are reported daily in *The Wall Street Journal,* and weekly in *Barron's.* Annual high, low, and close figures for all years since 1974 are contained in the *NASDAQ Fact Book,* which has been published annually since 1983 by the NASD.

AMERICAN STOCK EXCHANGE. The AMEX developed a Price Change Index in 1966 but subsequently commissioned the creation of a value-weighted series referred to as the Market Value Index. This new series was released in September 1973 with a base level of 100 as of August 31, 1973, and figures available back to 1969. On July 5, 1983, the Market Value Index was adjusted to one-half its previous level, so now it has a base level of 50. The index includes common shares, ADRs, and warrants but does not include rights, preferred stock, or "when-issued" stock. Daily figures for the index are available in *The Wall Street Journal,* weekly data are in *Barron's,* and monthly closing values from 1969 are contained in the *AMEX Fact Book.*

WILSHIRE 5000 EQUITY INDEX. The Wilshire 5000 Equity Index is a value-weighted index published by Wilshire Associates (Santa Monica, California) that derives the dollar value of 5,000 common stocks, including all NYSE and AMEX issues, plus the most active stocks on the OTC market. The specific weighting is about 82 percent NYSE, 4 percent AMEX, and 14 percent OTC, which means that the NYSE has the greatest influence because of its higher market value. The index was created in 1974 with month-

[8] Securities on the NASDAQ system not included in any of the indexes are warrants, preferred stocks, foreign stocks, and common stocks that are listed on an exchange but traded OTC (i.e., third-market stocks).

end values computed back to December 1970. Beginning December 1979, it was calculated daily. The Wilshire 5000 base is its December 31, 1980, capitalization of $1,404,596 billion. The index currently appears daily in *The Wall Street Journal* and several other major daily papers and has been published weekly in *Barron's* since January 1975.

THE RUSSELL INDEXES. Three separate but overlapping indexes are the Russell 3000, the Russell 1000, and the Russell 2000. The Russell 3000 consists of the 3,000 largest U.S. stocks by market capitalization and represents 97 percent of the U.S. equity market in terms of market value. The Russell 1000 consists of the 1,000 largest capitalization U.S. stocks. The smallest stock in this index has a market value of $350 million. In terms of the discussion in Chapter 3, this index would include the top-tier stocks in which most money managers invest. The Russell 2000 is an index of small stocks and consists of the smallest 2,000 stocks in the Russell 3000 index. The firms in the 2,000 series range in size from approximately $350 million to $30 million, and the total value of all the stocks in the Russell 2000 represents about 10 percent of the total capitalization.

The creators of these indexes contend that they are pure because they include only U.S. stocks. Also, the first is more comprehensive with 3,000 stocks, while the size separation between the 1,000 and 2,000 series allows for analysis of the institutional segment as well as the small-firm segment, which has become a popular sector based upon efficient-market studies (discussed in Chapter 6). These indexes are reported weekly in *Barron's*.

FINANCIAL TIMES *ACTUARIES SHARE INDEXES*. *The Financial Times* Actuaries Share indexes are for stocks listed on the London Stock Exchange (LSE). They relate current market capitalizations of each index to the market capitalization at the base date (April 10, 1962), adjusted for intervening capital changes. The following is the breakdown of LSE stocks as of late 1987:

Industrial group index	483
Oils	17
	500 Index
Financial group index	113
Others	124
	737 All-Share Index

The sample is broken down into 34 subsections. The advantage of this index is that it is very broad and therefore reflects the movements of the total London market. Also, because it is a market value–weighted series, it can be used to measure long-term market movements and to evaluate portfolio performance. The All-Share Index and all of its components are reported daily in *The Financial Times*.

TOKYO STOCK EXCHANGE PRICE INDEX. The price index of the Tokyo Stock Exchange was devised in July 1969 to take account of various defects noted in the TSE-Dow Jones Stock Price Average (the NIKKEI Stock Average), namely, limited sample and price-weighting. It is a composite index of all common stocks listed on the First Section of the Tokyo Stock Exchange. The index is basically a measure of the changes in aggregate market value of TSE common stocks. The base of 100 for the index is the market value at the close on January 4, 1968. In similar fashion to the S&P indexes, the base market value is adjusted to reflect nonprice changes such as new listings, delistings, and mergers.

The composite index is supplemented by subgroup indexes for each of 28 industry groups and three size groups: large (over 200 million shares listed), medium (between 60 and 200 million shares listed), and small (less than 60 million shares listed). The index results are published daily in *The Financial Times*.

UNWEIGHTED PRICE INDICATOR SERIES

In an unweighted index, all stocks carry equal weight regardless of their price and/or their value. A $20 stock is as important as a $40 stock, and the total market value of the company is not important. Such an index can be used by an individual who randomly selects stocks for his portfolio. One way to visualize an unweighted series is to assume that equal dollar amounts are invested in each stock in the portfolio. Thus, an equal $1,000 investment in each stock would work out to 50 shares of a $20 stock, 100 shares of a $10 stock, and 10 shares of a $100 stock.

UNIVERSITY OF CHICAGO SERIES. The best known unweighted (or equal-weighted) stock market series are those constructed by Lawrence Fisher while at the University of Chicago.[9] These series were used in a series of studies conducted by Fisher and James Lorie that examined the performance of stocks on the NYSE.[10] They have been used extensively in subsequent empirical studies.

VALUE LINE AVERAGES. The *Value Line Composite Average* is an index based on an equally weighted geometric average of the percent changes for the approximately 1,700 stocks included with June 30, 1961, set at 100. The average consists of all stocks regularly reviewed in *The Value Line Investment Survey* and broken down into the following major categories and 146 subgroups.

[9] Lawrence Fisher, "Some New Stock Market Indexes," *Journal of Business* 39, no. 1, Part II (January 1966 supplement): 191–225.

[10] Lawrence Fisher and James H. Lorie, "Rates of Return on Investments in Common Stock," *Journal of Business* 37, no. 1 (January 1964): 1–21; L. Fisher and J. H. Lorie, "Rates of Return on Investments in Common Stock: The Year-By-Year Record, 1926–1965," *Journal of Business* 41, no. 3 (July 1968): 291–316; and Lawrence Fisher, "Outcomes for 'Random' Investments in Common Stock Listed on the New York Stock Exchange," *Journal of Business* 38, no. 2 (April 1965): 149–161.

TABLE 4.4
Example of a Computation of Value Line Index

STOCK	SHARE PRICE		INDEX OF CHANGE
	T	T+1	
X	10	12	1.20
Y	22	20	.91
Z	44	47	1.07

$\Pi = 1.20 \times .91 \times 1.07$
$\quad = 1.168$
$\quad\quad 1.168^{1/3} = 1.0531$

Index Value (T) $\times$ 1.0531 = Index Value (T+1)

	NUMBER OF STOCKS
Industrials	1499
Utilities	177
Rails	19
Composite	1695

More than 80 percent of the stocks comprising the Value Line Averages are listed on the NYSE. The average is computed as follows:

Each market day the closing price of each stock is divided by the preceding day's close, with the preceding day set at an index of 100. The resulting indexes of change for that day are geometrically averaged for the 1,695 stocks. You will recall from the appendix to Chapter 2 that a *geometric average* is defined as the *n*th root of the product of *N* items. In other words, it is the square root of two items, the cube root of three items, and so on. In the case of the *Value Line Average,* it is the 1,695th root of the product of the 1,695 ratios. The geometric average of change for each day is then multiplied by the value of the average on the preceding day to get the latest value. Table 4.4 contains an example of a computation involving three stocks. Note that there is no consideration of the market value, and the price level does not have an impact because you are dealing with percentage changes. Finally, it is a geometric average of the percentage changes rather than an arithmetic average.

When stock splits or dividends occur, the preceding day is adjusted accordingly, and the index of change computed thereafter. As stocks are added to *The Value Line Investment Survey,* the average is enlarged. Additions and deletions of stocks present no problem to the average because of its large base and method of construction. Daily figures for the Value Line (VL) composite average are contained in *The Wall Street Journal,* and weekly data are in *Barron's.*

INDICATOR DIGEST *INDEX.* All stocks on the NYSE are included in the *Indicator Digest* Index. Compared to value-weighted series that are heavily influenced by large firms, the series is intended to be more representative of all stocks on the exchange. In several instances, it reached a trough earlier than other indicator series and continued to be depressed after some of the "popular" market indicator series resumed rising during a bull market. Such a difference would indicate that the market increase was heavily influenced by the large, popular stocks contained in the DJIA or the Standard & Poor's market indicator series.

FINANCIAL TIMES *ORDINARY SHARE INDEX*. Sometimes known as the 30-Share Index because it includes 30 heavily traded blue-chip stocks listed on the LSE, the *Financial Times* Ordinary Share Index is similar to the DJIA because it includes a limited number of blue-chip stocks, but it differs because it is an unweighted index (i.e., similar to the Value Line indexes it is a geometric average of the rates of return for the 30 stocks). The index has an unbroken history back to 1935 with a limited number of changes in the sample over time. While about half the constituents are unchanged from the beginning, the index includes oils and financial firms, so it is not only an industrial index.

The creators of the index recognize that using a geometric average of the rates of return during a period of time biases the series downward compared to other series (see the discussion in Appendix 2A). Therefore, it is pointed out that the series is sensitive to the short-term movements ("mood") of the market, but it should not be used as a long-term measure of market returns for evaluating portfolio performance. *The Financial Times All-Share Index* described earlier is considered more appropriate for long-term portfolio performance analysis. Daily figures for this 30-share index are contained in *The Financial Times* and *The Wall Street Journal*, with weekly data in *Barron's*.

ALTERNATIVE BOND MARKET INDICATOR SERIES[11]

While investors may not know a lot about the various stock market indicator series, they know almost nothing about the several bond market series, because these fixed-income series are relatively new and not widely published. Knowledge regarding these bond series is becoming more important because of the growth of fixed-income mutual funds and the consequent need to have a reliable set of benchmarks to use in evaluating performance.[12] Also, because the performance of many fixed-income money managers has not been able to match that of the aggregate bond market,

---

[11] The discussion in this section draws heavily from Frank K. Reilly, Wenchi Wong, and David J. Wright, "An Analysis of Alternative Bond Market Indicator Series," Financial Management Association Meeting, New York, October 1986 (revised August 1988).

[12] For a discussion of what is involved in the evaluation of bond portfolios, see Peter D. Dietz, Russell Fogler, and Donald J. Hardy, "The Challenge of Analyzing Bond Portfolio Returns," *Journal of Portfolio Management* 6, no. 3 (Spring 1980); Peter D. Dietz, Russell Fogler, and Anthony U. Rivers, "Duration, Nonlinearity, and Bond Portfolio Performance," *Journal of Portfolio Management* 7, no. 3 (Spring 1981); Gifford Fong, Charles Pearson, and Oldrick Vasicek, "Bond Performance: Analyzing Sources of Return," *Journal of Portfolio Management* 9, no. 3 (Spring 1983).

there has been a growing interest in bond index funds, prompting the development of an index to emulate.[13]

Notably, the creation and computation of a bond market indicator series is both more diverse and more difficult than a stock market series for several reasons. First, the universe of bonds is much broader than that of stocks, ranging from U.S. Treasury securities to bonds in default. Also, the universe of bonds is changing constantly, because bond maturities change over time. Further, the volatility of bond prices is affected by duration, which is likewise changing constantly because of changes in maturity, coupon, and market yield (see Chapter 11). Finally, there can be significant problems in correctly pricing the individual bond issues in an indicator series.

MERRILL LYNCH TAXABLE BOND INDEXES (TBIs). The Merrill Lynch Taxable Bond Indexes (TBIs) track more than 5,000 issues and consist of several corporate and U.S. government master indexes supplemented by more than 150 subindexes segmenting the market by coupon, quality, industry, and maturity. The Merrill Lynch TBIs include U.S. Treasury and agency issues, investment-grade corporates, Yankee and Canadian instruments (including World Bank debt issues in the United States and securities of international agencies), mortgage securities, Eurodollar securities, zero coupon TIGRS, as well as high-yield corporate bonds. The performance indicators capture all rating changes, new issues, and early retirement of debt.

To qualify for inclusion in the Merrill Lynch universe of taxable bonds, securities must have the following characteristics: be non-convertible, have a maturity of at least one year, a minimum par value of $10 million, and be rated by Standard and Poor's or Moody's. Prices for U.S. Treasury and agency securities come directly from the Merrill Lynch Government Securities trading floor. These issues make up approximately 73 percent of the entire TBI bond universe. Prices of corporate bonds are obtained from a series of trader-supervised pricing matrices provided by the Merrill Lynch Bond Pricing Service.

The calculated rates of return are total returns, including price change, accrued interest, and coupon income reinvested in the specific bond. All components of returns are market value–weighted using the current prices and amounts publicly held. The index value is set to 100 at the inception date, which varies by index—it is 1976 for the major government and corporate indexes and 1984 for the High Yield Master.

RYAN INDEX. The Ryan Index is a daily total return series derived by computing the equal-weighted average of the daily returns of seven recently issued Treasury auction issues with the following maturities: 2-, 3-, 4-, 5-, 7-, 10-, and 30-years. The index level is calculated each day by

---

[13] For a discussion of this phenomenon, see Fran Hawthorne, "The Battle of the Bond Indexes," *Institutional Investor* 20, no. 4 (April 1986).

compounding the previous day's index by the current day's total return. Only Treasury auction issues are used because it is contended that all bonds are priced off the government yield curve. Further, it is felt that this set of bonds is a good reflection of the prevailing risk-reward environment for the bond market, because maturity and the shape of the yield curve determine most of the return of a bond.

SALOMON BROTHERS (SB) BROAD INVESTMENT-GRADE BOND INDEXES. The monthly total rate-of-return Salomon Brothers (SB) indexes were introduced in October 1985, with data available back to 1980. These investment-grade bond indexes currently include about 3,800 individually priced Treasury/agency, corporate, and mortgage securities with the following criteria: maturity of one year or longer; a minimum of $25 million outstanding; all Treasury/agencies except flower bonds; corporate bonds rated BBB or better; and mortgage bonds including conventional pass-throughs.

Every issue in the SB Broad Index (which is a composite of a number of subindexes) is priced on the bid side by the trader responsible for making a market in that security. The Broad Index return is the market-weighted total return of all securities included in the index. Total returns include price change, principal payments, coupon payments, accrued interest, and reinvestment income on intramonth cash flows using the rate on one-month T-bills.

THE SHEARSON LEHMAN HUTTON (SLH) INDEXES. Over 4,000 issues are included in the Shearson Lehman Hutton (SLH) indexes, based upon the following criteria for inclusion: minimum outstanding principal of $25 million; minimum maturity of one year; issues in the mortgage index must have a minimum of $15 million outstanding. All total returns are market value–weighted. The pricing of issues is a combination of trader pricing and a proprietary algorithm. For the Government Bond Index, the GNMA Pass-Through Index and the Yankee Bond Index, all the issues are priced by traders. Approximately 60 percent of the corporate issues are trader-priced, but because these are the large issues, they constitute 84 percent of their market value. The smaller corporate issues are priced using a proprietary algorithm that considers coupon, maturity, industry group, rating, sinking fund, call features, and credit data. The computerized pricing is verified against actual market quotations.

MERRILL LYNCH CONVERTIBLE SECURITIES INDEXES. In March 1988 Merrill Lynch introduced a set of indexes related to convertible securities with data beginning in January 1987. The convertible master index that contains 550 to 600 issues consists of three major subgroups: U.S. domestic convertible bonds, Eurodollar convertible bonds issued by U.S. corporations, and U.S. domestic convertible preferred stocks. Within each group there are further breakdowns based upon maturity and quality. The criteria for inclusion are that the issues must be publicly held issues of U.S. corporations with minimum par value of issue of $25 million and minimum

Table 4.5
Merrill Lynch International Bond Performance Indexes

	No. of Issues	Amt. (Local)	Amt. (U.S.$)	Pct. of Master	Maturity Date	Adj. for Call Duration	Yield
Eurobond master index	3,039	—	$334.8	100.0	1993/07/26	4.1	7.3
Non-dollar Eurobond master index	2,190	—	$190.0	—	1994/02/21	4.3	6.8
Eurobond Indexes							
Eurodollar	849	144.8	144.8	43.8	1992/10/30	3.8	7.78
Euro-Canadian dollar	180	14.1	10.2	3.1	1992/11/04	4.0	9.65
Euro-yen	131	4,355.9	27.5	8.1	1993/10/05	4.9	5.87
Euro-sterling	118	7.2	10.7	3.1	1993/08/08	4.3	11.03
Euro-deutschemark	562	106.9	55.6	16.4	1993/04/03	4.2	6.01
Euro-Swiss franc	666	78.9	48.9	14.5	1996/10/05	4.5	4.92
Euro-French franc	45	24.4	3.8	1.1	1993/05/31	4.7	9.17
Euro-guilder	78	9.9	4.6	1.3	1991/11/22	3.8	6.16
ECU	223	20.3	21.8	6.4	1993/01/07	4.1	8.32
Euro-Australian dollar	138	8.0	5.3	1.6	1990/09/26	2.8	13.89
Euro-New Zealand dollar	49	2.9	1.6	0.5	1989/10/26	2.3	15.56
			$334.8	100.0			
Foreign Bond Markets							
Samurai	41	5,169.5	32.7	—	1994/02/28	3.5	6.16
Bulldog	27	3.1	4.6	—	2009/12/21	8.2	11.93
Foreign guilder	85	16.5	7.6	—	1995/01/11	5.8	7.35
			44.9				

Note: The sum of the Eurobond indexes ($334.8 billion) uses end-of-month exchange rates, while the U.S. dollar amount of the Euro-bond Master Index ($330.6 billion) uses beginning-of-month exchange rates. The shares of the Eurobond Master Index shown in Column 4 are the actual shares used to calculate the December Master Index values.

maturity of one year. All bankrupt issues are excluded and also issues that are convertible into cash, bonds, or preferred stocks as a result of mergers.

MERRILL LYNCH INTERNATIONAL BOND INDEXES. In addition to the numerous indexes related to the U.S. bond market, Merrill Lynch has developed a set of indexes that are intended to measure the total return performances of the major Eurobond and foreign bond markets. Specifically, there are indexes for eleven Eurobond markets plus a Eurobond Master Index and also indexes for three foreign bond markets as shown in Table 4.5.

These Merrill Lynch International Bond Performance Indexes measure the total returns of these markets in both local currency and U.S. dollar terms on a monthly basis from December 1985. The Eurodollar Index is available since December 1982. The universe for these indexes is all straight bonds in each of the major Eurobond and foreign bond markets with the following criteria: minimum one year maturity; ten million or more in local currency outstanding, nonconvertible or without warrants (as long as they trade actively, it is not necessary that they be rated). From this universe, a sample is selected. The criteria for the sample is the same as the universe with the additional criteria that the issue be publicly traded and have a rating of BBB (Baa) or better if it is rated. The bonds in the universe determine the weights used to calculate the weighted average returns. The weights represent the par value outstanding at the beginning of each month using current exchange rates.

Each of the Eurobond and foreign bond markets are broken down into appropriate subindexes based upon the issues and maturity categories. These indexes are comparable with the Merrill Lynch U.S. Domestic Taxable Bond Indexes except for the weighting scheme used. As noted, although the returns are calculated based upon a sample from the universe, the weights are based upon the relative value of the bonds *in the universe.* This ensures that the index reflects the characteristics of the entire universe of bonds and not only the specific bonds for which prices are available. Also the maturity categories are based on the term to maturity even if the bonds are trading on the yield to call. Duration is calculated to maturity, but also to call date if the bond is trading on the yield to call.

SALOMON BROTHERS INTERNATIONAL BOND AND MONEY MARKET PERFORMANCE INDEXES. These indexes are intended to provide a comprehensive measure of the total return performance of high-quality securities in major international sectors of the bond and money markets. The indexes were introduced in September 1981 with historical information dating back to January 1, 1978, when the indexes equaled 100 (Eurodollar zeros were added in March 1982, and Australian Government bonds were added in October 1984). For each of eight major countries, there is typically a domestic government bond series, a Eurocurrency bond, and a domestic money market security in local currency terms and in U.S. dollar terms. There is also a market value–weighted and unweighted composite world bond index and money market index. The results for these indexes are reported monthly in *Global Investor.*

COMPOSITE SECURITY MARKET SERIES

Beyond the numerous series that are intended to measure the performance of equity and fixed-income markets in individual countries, several firms have developed composite series that reflect the performance of all securities in a given country. These composite series attest to the importance of diversifying, not only among various segments of the equity market, but also between equities and bonds. In addition, as noted throughout this book, investors must recognize the fact that world capital markets are becoming integrated. This has led to the construction of world capital market indexes.

MERRILL LYNCH–WILSHIRE CAPITAL MARKETS INDEX (MLWCMI). A market value–weighted index called Merrill Lynch–Wilshire Capital Markets Index (MLWCMI) was created to measure the total return performance of the combined U.S. taxable fixed-income and equity markets. It is basically a combination of the Merrill Lynch fixed-income indexes and the Wilshire 5,000 common stock index. As such, it tracks more than 10,000 stocks and bonds.

Because of its makeup it is useful as a total portfolio performance benchmark and can form the basis both for passive portfolio management and for decisions to actively manage and specifically deviate from the following market mix (as of June 30, 1987):

SECURITY	$ IN BILLIONS	PERCENT OF TOTAL
Treasury bonds	$1,085	20.94
Agency bonds	166	3.19
Mortgage bonds	467	8.81
Corporate bonds	453	8.74
OTC stocks	331	8.74
AMEX stocks	105	6.38
NYSE stocks	2,586	49.92
	$5,193	100.00

FT-ACTUARIES WORLD INDICES. The FT-Actuaries World Indices are jointly compiled by The Financial Times Limited, Goldman, Sachs & Co., and County NatWest/Wood Mackenzie in conjunction with the Institute of Actuaries and the Faculty of Actuaries. Approximately 2,500 equity securities in 24 countries are measured, covering at least 70 percent of the total value of all domestic exchange–listed companies in each country. Medium and small capitalization stocks with proven investor interest are included along with major international equities. An independent committee oversees the calculation of the indices and ensures adherence to World Index Policy Committee rules. A major requirement of the committee is that all securities allow direct holdings of shares by foreign nationals.

The indexes are market value–weighted arithmetic averages of the *price relatives* of the constituents, The base date is December 31, 1986 = 100. The index results are reported in U.S. dollars, U.K. pounds sterling, and the local currency of the country. Index levels and related performance figures are calculated daily after the New York markets close, and they are published the following day in *The Financial Times*. The 24 countries and the proportion of market capitalization attributable to the country index in U.S. dollars is as follows (as of September 1988):[14]

Australia	1.46	Hong Kong	0.72	Norway	0.05
Austria	0.06	Ireland	0.12	Singapore	0.13
Belgium	0.62	Italy	1.42	South Africa	0.52
Canada	2.06	Japan	41.83	Spain	0.91
Denmark	0.21	Malaysia	0.07	Sweden	0.28
Finland	0.06	Mexico	0.05	Switzerland	0.92
France	2.13	Netherlands	1.17	United Kingdom	9.08
West Germany	2.98	New Zealand	0.15	United States	32.99

[14] The proportion of market capitalizations indicated here differ from those shown in Chapter 3 as of December 31, 1987. The major differences are for the United States and Japan—i.e., in March 1987 the U.S. proportion is larger than Japan, while in December 1987 the Japanese proportion is the largest. The fact is, during this interval (in April 1987) the Japanese market surpassed the United States in size on the basis of market value. In this regard, see Peter Gumbel, "Japan Stock Market Overtakes the U.S. as World's Largest," *The Wall Street Journal* (April 13, 1987): 27. Also, the more recent data in Table 4.7 reflects the change.

In addition to the individual countries and the World Index, there are several geographic subgroups as shown in Table 4.6.

MORGAN STANLEY CAPITAL INTERNATIONAL INDEXES. These indices are designed to measure the performance of the stock markets of the United States, Europe, Canada, Mexico, Australia, and the Far East as well as that of international industry groups. The Morgan Stanley Capital International Indexes consist of 3 international, 19 national, and 38 international industry indexes. They are based on the share prices of some 1,375 companies listed on stock exchanges in 19 countries. The combined market capitalization of these companies represents approximately 60 percent of the aggregate market value of the stock exchanges of these countries.

All the indexes are arithmetic averages weighted by the market value of the stocks included. The countries included, the number of stocks, and market values for stocks in the various countries and groups is contained in Table 4.7.

In addition to reporting the indexes in U.S. dollars and the country's local currency, the following valuation information is available: (1) price-to-book-value ratio (P/BV), (2) price-to-cash-earnings (earnings plus depreciation) ratio (P/CE), (3) price-to-earnings ratio (P/E), and (4) dividend yield (YLD). These ratios help in analyzing different valuation levels among countries and over time for specific countries. Also, they are available for each of the International Industry Indexes, which will be considered in more detail in the industry analysis chapter.

Computed daily and monthly, the indexes are reported in Morgan Stanley monthly and quarterly publications, specifically the *Morgan Stanley Capital International Perspective.* Monthly issues focus on recent stock-market performance and on comparisons of market valuation factors within countries and international industry groups. Quarterly issues include graphs on 2,000 of the largest companies in the world. Absolute and relative performance to the world index is shown for the latest 22 years, together with operating data for the last five years.

Notably, the Morgan Stanley group index for Europe, Australia, and the Far East (EAFE) is being used as the basis for futures and options contracts on the Chicago Mercantile Exchange and the Chicago Board Options Exchange.

EUROMONEY–FIRST BOSTON GLOBAL STOCK INDEX. The Euromoney–First Boston Global Stock Index is a market value–weighted set of indexes for 17 individual countries and a composite world index. The series was initiated in 1986, with December 31, 1985 at 100. The results are reported in local currency and also in U.S. dollar terms. Monthly results for the individual countries are reported in *Global Investor*.

SALOMON-RUSSELL WORLD EQUITY INDEX. A series of indexes for 22 individual countries and a world index called the Salomon-Russell World Equity Index were initiated in 1988. This index combines the Russell 1000

TABLE 4.6
FT-Actuaries World Indices. Jointly compiled by The Financial Times Limited, Goldman, Sachs & Co., and County NatWest/Wood Mackenzie in conjunction with the Institute of Actuaries and the Faculty of Actuaries.

NATIONAL AND REGIONAL MARKETS FIGURES IN PARENTHESES SHOW NUMBER OF STOCKS PER GROUPING	THURSDAY OCTOBER 13, 1988				
	U.S. DOLLAR INDEX	DAY'S CHANGE %	POUND STERLING INDEX	LOCAL CURRENCY INDEX	GROSS DIV. YIELD
Australia (91)	142.85	+0.6	121.44	117.10	4.20
Austria (17)	91.32	+1.2	77.63	86.23	2.46
Belgium (63)	125.92	+1.0	107.04	119.71	4.23
Canada (126)	122.92	+0.3	104.50	107.57	3.14
Denmark (39)	136.65	+0.4	116.16	130.47	2.30
Finland (26)	117.33	+3.3	99.74	105.58	1.67
France (130)	101.65	+1.9	86.41	98.97	3.28
West Germany (102)	82.42	+1.2	70.06	78.01	2.38
Hong Kong (46)	104.69	+0.3	89.00	105.02	4.79
Ireland (18)	138.74	+0.3	117.95	132.85	3.79
Italy (100)	79.42	+1.6	67.51	80.42	2.50
Japan (456)	165.79	+0.4	140.94	134.19	0.55
Malaysia (36)	133.55	−0.4	113.53	137.56	3.09
Mexico (13)	150.76	+0.0	128.16	377.14	1.44
Netherland (38)	106.24	+1.6	90.31	99.52	4.89
New Zealand (26)	72.55	+0.7	61.67	61.11	6.43
Norway (25)	114.03	−1.7	96.94	104.09	2.76
Singapore (26)	116.83	+0.1	99.32	108.81	2.50
South Africa (60)	109.12	+0.6	92.76	96.37	4.46
Spain (42)	145.29	+0.8	123.51	132.47	3.02
Sweden (35)	126.33	+0.0	107.39	116.93	2.44
Switzerland (56)	80.42	+0.6	68.37	76.76	2.20
United Kingdom (322)	133.36	+1.5	113.37	113.37	4.63
USA (582)	112.38	+0.4	95.53	112.38	3.55
Europe (1,013)	109.61	+1.4	93.18	99.29	3.73
Pacific Basin (681)	162.38	+0.4	138.03	132.20	0.77
Euro-Pacific (1,694)	141.29	+0.7	120.11	118.97	1.70
North America (708)	112.93	+0.4	96.00	112.10	3.53
Europe Ex. UK (691)	94.74	+1.3	80.54	90.69	2.99
Pacific Ex. Japan (225)	121.25	+0.5	103.07	107.18	4.38
World Ex. US (1,893)	140.35	+0.7	119.31	118.48	1.77
World Ex. UK (2,153)	129.13	+0.5	109.77	116.66	2.12
World Ex. So. Af. (2,415)	129.61	+0.6	110.18	116.47	2.33
World Ex. Japan (2,019)	112.11	+0.8	95.30	107.46	3.64
The World Index (2,475)	129.49	+0.6	110.08	116.34	2.35

Base values: Dec. 31, 1986 = 100; Finland: Dec. 31, 1987 = 115.037 (U.S. $ Index), 90.791 (Pound Sterling) and 94.94 (Local).

Copyright, The Financial Times Limited, Goldman, Sachs & Co., County Nat West Securities Ltd. 1987.

Mexican market closed Oct. 12.

Source: Courtesy of Goldman, Sachs & Co.

WEDNESDAY OCTOBER 12, 1988			DOLLAR INDEX		
U.S. DOLLAR INDEX	POUND STERLING INDEX	LOCAL CURRENCY INDEX	1988 HIGH	1988 LOW	YEAR AGO (APPROX.)
141.94	121.46	117.30	152.31	91.16	165.39
90.22	77.21	86.11	98.18	83.72	101.76
124.73	106.74	119.65	139.89	99.14	120.75
122.51	104.83	107.34	128.91	107.06	129.00
136.08	116.45	131.09	136.65	111.42	121.29
113.54	97.16	103.47	139.53	106.78	—
99.73	85.34	97.85	101.65	72.77	99.08
81.42	69.68	77.70	82.42	67.78	99.03
104.41	89.35	104.76	111.86	84.90	152.46
138.27	118.33	133.49	144.25	104.60	156.26
78.19	66.91	79.83	81.74	62.99	96.70
165.12	141.30	134.54	177.27	133.61	151.51
134.11	114.76	138.52	154.17	107.83	176.38
150.76	129.01	377.14	180.07	90.07	364.35
104.60	89.51	98.78	110.66	95.23	118.79
72.07	61.68	61.38	84.05	64.42	129.33
116.06	99.31	107.00	132.23	98.55	179.32
116.74	99.90	109.32	135.89	97.99	169.65
108.44	92.79	95.77	139.07	98.26	187.79
144.09	123.31	132.47	164.47	130.73	163.56
126.32	108.10	117.72	126.33	96.92	134.67
79.92	68.39	76.80	86.75	74.13	110.14
131.38	112.43	112.43	141.18	120.66	158.41
111.89	95.75	111.89	113.64	99.19	121.96
108.12	92.52	98.66	110.82	97.01	127.21
161.71	138.38	132.52	172.26	130.81	151.95
140.29	120.06	118.94	147.53	120.36	142.11
112.45	96.23	111.63	114.16	99.78	122.34
93.55	80.06	90.27	94.74	80.27	107.80
120.67	103.26	107.28	128.27	87.51	157.63
139.37	119.27	118.44	146.49	120.26	142.27
128.45	109.92	116.54	131.77	111.77	132.04
128.82	110.24	116.28	132.39	113.26	134.04
111.26	95.21	106.95	112.43	100.00	126.20
128.70	110.13	116.14	132.28	113.37	134.39

with the Salomon-Russell PMI 600. In turn, the PMI stands for Primary Market Index, which is a capitalization weighted index of 600 non–U.S. stocks covering about 65 percent of the market capitalization in each of the 22 markets. Stocks were selected on the basis of their adjusted capitalizations (that considered crossownership) and liquidity (trading volume).

TABLE 4.7
Market Coverage of Morgan Stanley Capital International (MSCI) Indexes

AT 31 MARCH 1988	COMPANIES INCLUDED IN PERSPECTIVE NUMBER	COMPANIES INCLUDED IN INDEXES NUMBER	WEIGHT IN MSCI WORLD INDEX %	MARKET VALUE OF COMPANIES INCLUDED IN INDEXES $ BILLION	TOTAL MARKET VALUE OF COUNTRIES INCLUDED $ BILLION	MARKET COVERAGE OF INDEXES %
Austria	15	10	0.1	3.6	6.3	56.9
Belgium	32	20	0.6	27.1	53.7	50.4
Denmark	30	26	0.2	10.3	20.4	50.4
Finland	31	21	0.2	11.3	21.3	53.2
France	114	86	2.0	89.6	151.4	59.2
Germany	105	57	2.8	126.4	205.7	61.5
Italy	115	67	1.4	69.1	119.7	57.7
Netherlands	38	21	1.4	61.7	77.6	79.6
Norway	19	15	0.2	7.2	13.0	55.4
Spain	47	32	1.0	46.6	85.9	54.2
Sweden	57	38	0.9	38.9	59.1	65.8
Switzerland	97	50	1.6	72.6	132.8	54.6
U.K.	203	131	8.6	394.2	692.5	56.9
Europe	903	574	21.0	958.6	1,639.4	58.5
Australia	93	64	1.3	59.1	116.7	50.6
Hong Kong	46	32	0.7	35.0	60.8	57.6
Japan	381	239	43.0	1,961.9	3,540.0	55.4
New Zealand	23	15	0.2	7.8	16.5	47.6
Singapore/Malaysia	61	55	0.5	21.8	36.6	59.5
EAFE	1,507	979	66.7	3,044.2	5,410.0	56.3
Canada	110	83	2.5	114.0	219.5	51.9
South African Gold Mines	30	21	0.3	12.8	21.4	59.6
USA	482	328	30.5	1,390.4	2,349.8	59.2
World	2,129	1,411	100.0	4,561.4	8,000.7	57.0

Note: These are estimates (market value of investment companies and of foreign-domiciled companies are excluded to avoid double-counting).
Source: Morgan Stanley Capital International (New York: Morgan Stanley & Co.).

COMPARISON OF INDICATOR SERIES CHANGES OVER TIME

The individual series and the world index are all presented in local currency and U.S. dollar terms. Again, monthly results are reported in *Global Investor*.

This section contains a discussion of price movements in the different series for various daily, monthly, or annual intervals, depending on availability.

CORRELATIONS AMONG DAILY EQUITY PRICE CHANGES

Table 4.8 contains a matrix of the correlation coefficients of the daily percentage of price changes for a set of U.S. and non–U.S. equity-market indicator series during the period of January 4, 1972 through December 31, 1987 (4,013 observations). This recent 16-year period was selected because data were available for most of the major equity series.

Most of the differences in the correlations of daily percentages of price changes are apparently attributable to differences in the sample of stocks, that is, differences in the firms listed on the alternative stock exchanges. Most of the major series except the DJIA, the NIKKEI Stock Average, the Value Line (VL) series, and the FT Ordinary Share Index, are market value–weighted indexes that include a large number of stocks (the DJIA and NIKKEI are price-weighted, and the VL and FT Ordinary Share series are unweighted). Therefore, the computational procedure is generally similar, the sample sizes are large (except for the DJIA and the FT-30 Share Index), and the samples represent either a large segment of the total population in terms of value or all members of the population. Thus, the major difference among several of the series lies in the members of the population; the stocks are from different segments of the stock market or from different countries.

Very high positive correlation (0.88 to 0.94) is shown among the alternative series that include almost all NYSE stocks (the DJIA, S&P 400, S&P 500, and the NYSE composite). This indicates that, on a short-run basis, even the DJIA, which has been criticized, is a very adequate indicator of price movements on the NYSE.

In contrast, there is significantly lower correlation between each of these NYSE series and the AMEX series and also these NYSE series with the NASDAQ indexes. These significant differences in stock price movements suggest the possibility that the U.S. market is segmented.[15] Further, the relationship between the Value Line Index that contains stocks from all exchanges and the other U.S. series is likewise about .74 to .80. Besides some difference in sample, recall that the VL Index is also an unweighted series.

The importance of recognizing the global investment environment can be seen from the correlations among the U.S. series and those from London and Tokyo. The relationships among the three London series varied from .88 to .96 and the two Tokyo series were correlated about .91, even though the sample sizes and the computations differ, which attests to the importance of the basic sample.

The relative strength of the U.S.–London relationship (it ranged from .16 to .34) compared to the U.S.–Tokyo relationship (which ranged from .08 to .22) is not unexpected and confirms the suggestion that one of the benefits of global investing is the opportunity for diversification that reduces the variance of returns for a total portfolio. These results for this time period not only indicate the benefits of non-U.S. investments, but also point toward a preference for the Japanese market. Because of the growing economic interdependencies between the two countries, these correlations will probably increase over time.

CORRELATIONS AMONG MONTHLY BOND SERIES   The correlations among the alternative monthly bond return series contained in Table 4.9 are all exceptionally strong (they range from .91 to .99), confirming that although the level of interest rates differs due to the

---

[15] For a study that considers this notion, see Frank K. Reilly, "Evidence Regarding a Segmented Stock Market," *Journal of Finance* 27, no. 3 (June 1972): 607–625.

TABLE 4.8
Correlation Coefficients among Daily Percentage of Price Changes for Alternative Equity Market Indicator Series: January 4, 1972 to December 31, 1987 (4,013 Observations)

	DJIA	S&P 400	S&P 500	NYSE COMP.	AMEX VALUE INDEX
DJIA	—				
S&P 400	0.958	—			
S&P 500	0.951	0.977	—		
NYSE composite	0.933	0.961	0.954	—	
AMEX value index	0.705	0.747	0.747	0.765	—
NASDAQ industrials	0.746	0.778	0.773	0.798	0.821
NASDAQ composite	0.753	0.783	0.780	0.809	0.823
VL composite	0.837	0.858	0.855	0.878	0.846
Wilshire 5000	0.907	0.939	0.933	0.918	0.777
FT. 30-Share	0.165	0.172	0.173	0.183	0.217
FT. 500	0.198	0.207	0.209	0.217	0.261
FT. all-share	0.198	0.207	0.207	0.217	0.262
NIKKEI	0.080	0.081	0.077	0.099	0.168
TSE index	0.104	0.101	0.107	0.120	0.185

risk premium, the overriding factors in changes in interest rates over time (that affect the rates of return) are the risk-free rate and changes in inflation expectations.

ANNUAL STOCK PRICE CHANGES

The annual percentage of price changes for the major stock price indicator series are contained in Table 4.10. One would expect some definite differences among the price changes and measures of risk for the various series (due to the different sources of the samples). For example, the NYSE series should have lower rates of return and risk measures than the AMEX and OTC series. The overall results generally confirm these expectations, although in recent years the AMEX and OTC results were much lower than expected, given a rising market. This reflects the popularity of large blue-chip stocks, especially the demand by Japanese investors. The low rate of return for the Value Line Series is due to the use of a geometric average in calculating daily changes (recall the discussion in Chapter 2).

The LSE had higher rates of change but also much greater variability than the U.S. series. The TSE likewise had higher average price changes, but its measures of variability were not much greater. This would imply that on a risk adjusted basis, the Japanese market provided the best results. Note that it was also the Japanese market that had very low correlation with alternative U.S. stock market series, which indicates that this market is a prime source of diversification benefits.

NASDAQ INDEX	NASDAQ COMP.	VL	WILSHIRE 5000	FT. 30-SH.	FT. ALL-SHARE	FT. 500	NIKKEI	TSE INDEX
— 0.947	—							
0.881	0.899	—						
0.806	0.804	0.862	—					
0.242	0.257	0.242	0.290	—				
0.274	0.292	0.282	0.341	0.885	—			
0.274	0.293	0.288	0.240	0.882	0.962	—		
0.186	0.209	0.179	0.146	0.122	0.155	0.162	—	
0.193	0.216	0.193	0.163	0.115	0.162	0.163	0.906	—

ANNUAL BOND RATES OF RETURN

Table 4.11 contains the annual total rates of return for the various bond-market indicator series. You cannot directly compare the bond and stock results, because the bond results are *total* rates of return versus annual percentage price change results for stocks (some of the stock series do not report dividend data).

Within the bond series, the major comparison should be among the average rate of return and the risk measures, because although the monthly rates of return are correlated, we would expect a difference in the level of return that would reflect the differential risk premiums. The results generally confirm our expectations, as shown by the lower returns and risk measures for the government series followed by higher returns and risk for corporates and the highest returns and risk for the mortgage series. Note that there is consistency among the sector results for alternative series, e.g., the results for the government bond series are similar regardless of the firm (Merrill, Ryan, Salomon, or Shearson).

SUMMARY

Given the several uses of security market indicator series, it is important to know how they are constructed and the differences among them. The following list contains the numerous series available for stocks and bonds in the United States and the world (PW = price-weighted; MVW = market value–weighted; UW = unweighted or equal-weighted; PVW = par value–weighted):

TABLE 4.9
Correlation Coefficients among Monthly Bond Rate-of-Return Series: January 1980 to December 1987 (96 Observations)

	MLGC	MLG	MLC	MLD	MLM	SLHGC	SLHG	SLHC	SLHM	SLHY	SLHA	SBB	SBG	SBC	SBM	RYAN
MLGC	—															
MLG	.993	—														
MLC	.983	.956	—													
MLD	.998	.990	.984	—												
MLM	.939	.920	.945	.956	—											
SLHGC	.997	.991	.978	.997	.944	—										
SLHG	.991	.997	.956	.988	.921	.994	—									
SLHC	.981	.957	.992	.985	.959	.984	.960	—								
SLHM	.939	.922	.943	.954	.980	.946	.925	.957	—							
SLHY	.981	.964	.982	.983	.936	.982	.966	.985	.935	—						
SLHA	.995	.986	.981	.997	.959	.998	.989	.988	.963	.984	—					
SBB	.995	.988	.978	.997	.953	.997	.989	.985	.954	.985	.997	—				
SBG	.985	.994	.943	.981	.907	.987	.995	.948	.908	.960	.980	.985	—			
SBC	.977	.951	.992	.980	.946	.987	.951	.993	.942	.983	.980	.980	.939	—		
SBM	.952	.937	.950	.965	.985	.955	.936	.962	.992	.949	.970	.967	.924	.952	—	
RYAN	.986	.988	.955	.985	.928	.987	.990	.960	.929	.963	.984	.986	.988	.952	.942	—

Source: Frank K. Reilly, Wenchi Wong, and David Wright, "An Analysis of Alternative Bond Market Indicator Series," Financial Management Association Meeting, October 1986 (Revised August 1988).

SECURITY MARKET INDICATOR SERIES

STOCK MARKET SERIES

U.S. Series

    Dow Jones Industrial Average (PW)
    S&P 400 (MVW)
    S&P 500 (MVW)
    NYSE Composite and subindexes (MVW)
    AMEX Value Index (MVW)
    NASDAQ OTC Composite and subindexes (MVW)
    Wilshire 5000 (MVW)
    Value Line Composite (UW)
    Russell 3000 (MVW)
    Russell 1000 (MVW)
    Russell 2000 (MVW)

Non–U.S. Series

    Financial Times Ordinary Share Index (UW)
    Financial Times 500 Stocks (MVW)
    Financial Times All-Share (MVW)
    NIKKEI Stock Average (PW)
    Tokyo Stock Exchange Index (MVW)

World Equity Series

    FT-Actuaries World Indexes (MVW)
    Morgan Stanley Capital International Indexes (MVW)
    Euromoney-First Boston Global Stock Indexes (MVW)
    Salomon-Russell World Equity Indexes (MVW)

BOND MARKET SERIES

U.S. Series

    Merrill Lynch (MVW)
    Ryan Financial Group (UW)
    Salomon Brothers (MVW)
    Shearson Lehman Hutton (MVW)
    Merrill Lynch Convertible Securities Indexes (MVW)

Non–U.S. Bond Market Series

    Merrill Lynch International Bond Indexes (PVW)←
    Salomon Brothers International Bond Performance Indexes (MVW)

COMPOSITE STOCK-BOND SERIES

U.S. Series

    Merrill Lynch–Wilshire Capital Markets Index (MVW)

A comparison of short-run and long-run price changes for the alternative series indicates that the computational differences are not nearly as important as the differences in the sample of securities included. Finally, the results for the various securities were generally consistent with expectations of risk and return.

QUESTIONS

1. Discuss briefly several uses of security market indicator series.
2. What major factors must be considered when constructing a market indicator series? Put another way, what characteristics differentiate indicator series?

TABLE 4.10
Percentage Price Changes in Stock Price Indicator Series: 1972–1987

	DJIA	S&P 400	S&P 500	NYSE COMP.	AMEX VALUE INDEX	NASDAQ INDUST.
1972	14.58	16.10	15.63	14.27	10.33	13.63
1973	−16.58	−17.38	−17.37	−19.63	−30.00	−36.88
1974	−27.57	−29.93	−29.72	−30.28	−33.22	−32.44
1975	38.44	31.92	31.55	31.86	38.40	43.38
1976	17.86	18.42	19.15	21.50	31.58	23.68
1977	−17.27	−12.35	−11.50	− 9.30	16.43	9.30
1978	− 3.15	2.39	1.06	2.13	17.73	15.92
1979	4.19	12.88	12.31	15.54	64.10	38.10
1980	14.93	27.62	25.77	25.68	41.25	49.19
1981	− 9.23	−11.22	− 9.73	− 8.67	− 8.13	−12.27
1982	19.60	14.95	14.76	13.95	6.23	19.32
1983	20.27	18.16	17.27	17.46	30.95	18.31
1984	− 4.33	− 0.40	0.81	0.75	− 9.07	−20.00
1985	27.66	25.86	26.33	26.15	20.50	23.78
1986	22.58	17.30	16.87	12.98	7.30	6.06
1987	2.26	3.90	12.21	− 0.25	− 1.42	− 3.21

Average of Annual Changes (Arithmetic Mean)

1972–1987	6.52	7.39	7.84	7.20	12.68	9.74

Standard Deviation of Annual Changes

1972–1987	17.84	17.12	16.76	16.96	25.03	24.50

Average Annual Compound Rate of Change (Geometric Mean)

1972–1987	4.95	5.90	6.40	5.73	9.73	6.70

3. Explain how a market indicator series is price-weighted. In such a case, would you expect a $100 stock to be more important than a $25 stock? Why?

4. What are the major criticisms of the Dow-Jones Industrial Average?

5. Explain how to compute a value-weighted series.

6. How does a price-weighted series adjust for stock splits? A value-weighted series?

7. Describe an unweighted price-indicator series and describe how you would construct such a series. Assume a 10 percent price change in IBM ($120/ share; 30 million shares outstanding) and Coors Brewing ($30/share and 10 million shares outstanding). Which change will have the greater impact on such an indicator series? Why?

8. If you correlated percentage changes in the Wilshire 5,000 equity index with percentage changes in the NYSE composite, the AMEX index, and the NASDAQ composite index, would you expect a difference in the results? Why or why not?

9. Substantial correlation exists among the daily percentage of price changes for the alternative NYSE price indicator series. Discuss what is responsible

NASDAQ COMP.	VL COMP.	WILSH. 5000	FT. 30-SH.	FT. 500 INDEX	FT. ALL-SHARE	NIKKEI AVE.	TSE INDEX
17.18	0.78	14.86	5.38	9.72	12.11	91.91	101.40
−31.06	−35.46	−20.96	−31.94	30.84	−31.36	−17.30	−23.71
−35.11	−33.47	−31.49	−53.02	−54.39	−55.34	−11.37	− 9.01
29.76	44.35	32.83	132.78	141.35	136.33	19.18	15.99
26.10	32.23	21.69	− 5.59	− 1.01	− 3.87	14.51	18.69
7.33	0.48	− 6.98	36.85	41.45	41.18	− 2.51	− 5.16
12.31	4.31	3.96	− 2.99	2.92	2.70	23.33	23.48
28.11	24.44	19.28	−12.04	2.54	4.30	9.46	2.24
33.88	18.28	27.61	14.56	24.57	27.07	3.33	7.50
− 3.21	− 4.43	− 8.43	11.78	7.88	7.24	7.95	15.42
18.67	15.32	12.86	12.50	27.44	22.07	4.36	4.10
19.87	22.28	18.74	30.00	19.27	23.10	23.42	23.26
−11.67	− 8.97	− 1.25	22.84	29.29	26.02	16.66	24.81
31.86	20.72	27.18	18.73	15.20	15.18	13.61	14.89
7.51	5.01	12.48	16.13	22.18	22.34	42.61	48.31
− 5.40	−10.69	1.49	4.52	4.59	4.16	21.35	10.89
9.10	5.95	7.74	12.53	16.45	15.83	16.28	17.07
20.67	21.16	17.55	37.99	39.36	38.52	23.88	26.92
6.84	3.64	6.16	6.80	10.36	9.81	14.19	14.44

for this similarity: size of sample, source of sample, or method of computation?

10. How did the historical annual price movements for the various NYSE price indicator series differ in terms of average annual price changes and variability of annual price changes? Were the differences generally consistent with economic theory? Discuss.

11. Compare stock price indicator series for the three U.S. equity-market segments (NYSE, AMEX, OTC) for the period 1972–1987. Discuss whether the results in terms of average annual price change and risk (variability of price changes) were consistent with economic theory.

12. What are the major differences between the three *Financial Times* indexes? Discuss which series is similar to the S&P 500 Index.

13. The NIKKEI Stock Average is similar to which U.S. stock price series? How is it similar?

14. Discuss the relationship between the two stock price indicator series for the Tokyo Stock Exchange (TSE) and the three indicator series for the London

TABLE 4.11
Bond Market Series: Arithmetic and Geometric Mean Annual Rates of Return and Standard Deviation of Monthly Rates of Return: 1976–1987

| | SHEARSON LEHMAN HUTTON | | | | | |
	GOVT./ CORP.	GOVT.	CORP.	MORTGAGE- BACKED	YANKEE BOND	AGGREGATE BOND
1976	15.59	12.35	19.34	16.31	15.08	15.60
1977	2.98	2.81	3.16	1.90	5.23	3.03
1978	1.19	1.80	0.35	2.41	2.91	1.40
1979	2.30	5.40	− 2.11	0.13	− 0.43	1.93
1980	3.06	5.19	− 0.29	0.65	1.91	2.70
1981	7.26	9.36	2.95	0.07	3.48	6.25
1982	31.09	27.74	39.21	43.04	35.82	32.62
1983	8.00	7.39	9.27	10.13	9.43	8.35
1984	15.02	14.50	16.63	15.79	16.38	15.15
1985	21.30	20.43	24.06	25.21	25.99	22.10
1986	15.62	15.31	16.53	13.43	16.27	15.26
1987	2.29	2.20	2.56	4.28	1.89	2.76
Arithmetic Mean						
1976–1987	10.48	10.37	10.97	11.11	11.16	10.55
1980–1987	12.96	12.77	13.87	14.08	13.90	13.15
Geometric Mean						
1976–1987	10.13	10.12	10.36	10.48	10.68	10.18
1980–1987	12.59	12.49	13.22	13.33	13.34	12.75
Standard Deviation (Monthly Returns)						
1976–1987	2.21	1.94	2.81	3.03	2.69	2.30
1980–1987	2.50	2.22	3.17	3.52	3.10	2.62

Source: Frank K. Reilly, Wenchi Wong, and David J. Wright, "An Analysis of Alternative Bond Market Indicator Series," Financial Management Association Meeting, October 1986 (Revised August 1988).

Stock Exchange. Do the same for the TSE series and two NYSE series. Explain why these relationships differ.

15. You are informed that the Wilshire 5000 market value–weighted series increased by 16 percent during a specified period, while a Wilshire 5000 equal-weighted series increased by 23 percent during the same period. Discuss what this difference in results implies.

16. Briefly discuss the uses for bond market indicator series.

17. Why is it contended that bond market series are more difficult to construct and maintain than stock market series? Discuss five alternative subindexes you could construct from a composite corporate bond series.

18. The Wilshire 5000 market value–weighted index increased by 20 percent while the Merrill Lynch–Wilshire Capital Markets Index increased by 12 percent during the same period. What does this difference in results imply?

19. The Russell 1000 declined by 12 percent during the past year while the Russell 2000 declined by only 4 percent. Discuss what this implies regarding

	MERRILL LYNCH				SALOMON BROTHERS				RYAN INDEX
GOVT./ CORP.	GOVT.	CORP.	DOMESTIC	MORTGAGE	BROAD	TREASURY AGENCY	CORP.	MORTGAGE PASS-THROUGH	
14.76	11.90	18.81	14.80	15.22					
3.10	2.59	3.81	3.02	1.87					
1.24	1.83	0.34	1.30	2.00					
2.27	5.34	− 2.21	2.10	0.54					
3.49	5.06	0.54	2.99	0.47	2.90	5.37	− 0.32	0.50	2.65
7.00	9.55	2.30	6.43	2.34	6.53	9.74	2.75	1.18	6.93
29.83	26.90	35.53	30.91	40.15	31.51	26.91	37.12	41.34	32.50
7.78	8.84	9.32	8.03	9.51	8.26	7.18	8.05	10.83	5.27
15.12	14.83	16.21	15.20	15.83	14.93	14.33	16.04	15.77	15.11
21.82	20.64	25.36	22.40	25.45	22.30	20.45	24.93	25.68	24.24
15.63	15.39	16.30	15.22	13.14	15.44	15.48	17.03	13.44	17.19
2.10	2.17	1.84	2.40	3.53	2.59	2.13	2.06	4.06	0.48
10.35	10.25	10.88	10.40	10.84					
12.83	12.67	13.43	12.95	13.80	13.06	12.70	13.57	14.10	13.05
10.01	10.00	10.13	10.05	10.27					
12.50	12.40	12.84	12.57	13.15	12.68	12.44	12.95	13.41	12.57
2.21	1.98	2.71	2.27	2.97					
2.52	2.26	3.10	2.60	3.45	2.55	2.19	3.09	3.43	2.84

differential segments of the market. Also discuss whether this difference in performance is what you would expect based on what you know about these two series.

PROBLEMS

1. You are given the following information regarding prices for a sample of stocks:

STOCK	NUMBER OF SHARES	PRICE	
		T	$T + 1$
A	1,000,000	80	100
B	10,000,000	30	35
C	30,000,000	15	20

1a. Construct a *price-weighted* series for these three stocks, and compute the percentage change in the series for the period from T to $T + 1$.

1b. Construct a *value-weighted* series for these three stocks, and compute the percentage change in the series for the period from *T* to *T* + 1.

1c. Briefly discuss the difference in the results for the two series.

2a. Given the data in Problem 1, construct an equal-weighted series by assuming $1,000 is invested in each stock. What is the percentage change in wealth for this portfolio?

2b. Compute the percentage of price change for each of the stocks in Problem 1. Compute the arithmetic average of these changes. Discuss how this answer compares to the answer in part a.

2c. Compute the geometric average of the percentage changes in part b. Discuss how this result compares to the answer in part b.

3. For the last five trading days, on the basis of figures in *The Wall Street Journal,* compute the daily percentage price changes for the following price indicator series:

3a. DJIA

3b. S&P 400

3c. AMEX Market Value Series

3d. NASDAQ Industrial Index

3e. FT-30 share Index

3f. NIKKEI Stock Price Average
Discuss the difference in results for a and b, a and c, a and d, a and e, a and f, and e and f. What do these differences imply regarding diversifying within the United States versus diversifying between countries?

4.

	PRICE			SHARES		
COMPANY	A	B	C	A	B	C
Day 1	12	23	52	500	350	250
Day 2	10	22	55	500	350	250
Day 3	14	46	52	500	175[a]	250
Day 4	13	47	25	500	175	500[b]
Day 5	12	45	26	500	175	500

[a] Split at close of Day 2
[b] Split at close of Day 3

4a. Calculate a Dow-Jones Industrial Index for Days 1 through 5.

4b. What effects have the splits had in determining the next day's index? (Hint: think of the relative weighting of each stock.)

4c. From a copy of a recent *Wall Street Journal* find the divisor that is currently being used in calculating the DJIA. (Normally this value can be found on the inside back pages.)

5. Utilizing the price and volume data in the preceding problem, (a) calculate a Standard & Poor's Index for Days 1 through 5 using a beginning index value of 10, and (b) identify what effects the splits have had in determining the next day's index. (Hint: think of the relative weighting of each stock.)

6. Using Table 4.10 on page 176 of your text, calculate the average annual rate

of change in each of the indexes for the period 1978 to 1987, using (a) the arithmetic mean and (b) the geometric mean.

REFERENCES

Butler, H. L., Jr., and J. D. Allen. "The Dow-Jones Industrial Average Re-Reexamined." *Financial Analysts Journal* 35, no. 6 (November–December 1979).

Eubank, Arthur A., Jr. "Risk-Return Contrasts: NYSE, AMEX, and OTC." *Journal of Portfolio Management* 3, no. 4 (Summer 1977).

Fisher, Lawrence. "Some New Stock Market Indexes." *Journal of Business* 39, no. 1, Part II (January 1966 Supplement).

Hawthorne, Fran. "The Battle of the Bond Indexes." *Institutional Investor* 20, no. 4 (April 1986).

Lorie, James H., Peter Dodd, and Mary Hamilton Kimpton. *The Stock Market: Theories and Evidence.* 2d ed. (Homewood, Ill.: Richard D. Irwin, 1985).

Reilly, Frank K. "Price Changes in NYSE, AMEX and OTC Stocks Compared." *Financial Analysts Journal* 27, no. 2 (March–April 1971).

Reilly, Frank K., Wenchi Wong, and David J. Wright. "An Analysis of Alternative Bond Market Indicator Series." Financial Management Association Meeting, New York, October 1986.

Williams, Arthur III, and Noreen N. Conwell. "Fixed Income Indices" in *Handbook of Fixed Income Securities.* 2d. ed. edited by Frank J. Fabozzi and Irving M. Pollack (Homewood, Ill.: Dow-Jones Irwin, 1987).

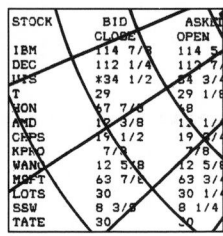

CHAPTER 5

SOURCES OF INFORMATION ON INVESTMENTS

In the chapters that follow, we will discuss the factors that influence aggregate security prices, the prices for securities issued by various industries, and the unique factors that influence the returns on individual securities. In this chapter we will describe some of the major sources of information needed for these analyses. Relevant information is both important and difficult to obtain, especially in the current global capital market. The outline of the presentation follows:

- Aggregate economic analysis
    Government sources
    Bank publications
- Aggregate stock market analysis
    Government publications
    Commercial publications
    Brokerage firm reports
- Industry analysis
    S&P Industry Survey
    Trade associations
    Industry magazines
- Individual stock analysis
    Company-generated information
    Commercial publications
    Brokerage firm reports
    Investment magazines
    Academic journals
    Computerized data sources.

SOURCES FOR AGGREGATE ECONOMIC ANALYSIS

This section is concerned with data used in estimating overall economic changes for the United States and other major countries as contrasted to data regarding the aggregate securities markets (stocks, bonds, etc.).

U.S. GOVERNMENT SOURCES

It should come as no surprise that the main source of information on the U.S. economy is the federal government, which issues a variety of publications on the topic.

Federal Reserve Bulletin is a monthly publication issued by the Board of Governors of the Federal Reserve System. It is the primary source for almost all monetary data, including monetary aggregates, factors affecting member bank reserves, member bank reserve requirements, Federal Reserve open market transactions, and loans and investments of all commercial banks. In addition, it contains figures on financial markets, including interest rates and some stock market statistics; data for corporate finance, including profits, assets, and liabilities of corporations; extensive nonfinancial statistics on output, the labor force, and the GNP; and an extensive section on international finance.

Survey of Current Business is a monthly publication issued by the U.S. Department of Commerce that gives details on national income and production figures. It is probably the best source for current, detailed information on all segments of the gross national product and national income. It also contains a listing of industrial production for numerous segments of the economy. The survey is an excellent secondary source for labor statistics (employment and wages), interest rates, and statistics on foreign economic development.

Economic Indicators is a monthly publication prepared for the Joint Economic Committee by the Council of Economic Advisers. It contains monthly and annual data on output, income, spending, employment, production, prices, money and credit, federal finance, and the international economic situation.

Business Conditions Digest (BCD) is a monthly publication issued by the Department of Commerce's Census Bureau, containing data and charts relating to economic indicators derived by the National Bureau of Economic Research (NBER). The NBER has developed a set of economic timing series. The series, called *leading indicators,* consistently indicate future trends in the economy. *Coincident indicators* are a series that turn with the general economy, and are used to define business cycles. A set of series that tends to turn up or down after the general economy does is called *lagging indicators.*[1] Basic data for the major series and analytical charts are provided in the *BCD.* In addition, it contains composite and analytical measures such as diffusion indexes and rate of change series.

Quarterly Financial Report (QFR) is prepared by the Federal Trade Commission and contains aggregate statistics on the financial position of U.S. corporations. Based upon an extensive quarterly sample survey, the

---

[1] These series are discussed more extensively in Chapter 12 where they are related to stock market movements.

QFR presents estimated statements of income and retained earnings, balance sheets, and related financial and operating ratios for all manufacturing corporations. The publication also includes data on mining and trade corporations. The statistical data are classified by industry and, within the manufacturing group, by size.

Business Statistics is a biennial supplement to the *Survey of Current Business* that contains extensive historical data for about 2,500 series contained in the survey. The historical data contains monthly data for the past four or five years, quarterly data for the previous ten years, and annual data back to 1947 if available. A notable feature is a section of explanatory notes for each series that describes the series and indicates the original source for the data.

Historical Chart Book is an annual supplement to the *Federal Reserve Bulletin* that contains long-range financial and business series. There is an excellent section on the various series that indicates the source of the data.

Each January, the president of the United States prepares the *Economic Report of the President,* which he transmits to Congress. The report indicates what has transpired during the past year, discusses the current environment, and considers the current major economic problems facing the country. This publication also contains an extensive document entitled, "The Annual Report of the Council of Economic Advisers," which generally runs over 150 pages and contains a detailed discussion of developments in the domestic and international economies gathered by the council (the group that advises the president on economic policy). An appendix contains statistical tables relating to income, employment, and production. The tables typically provide annual data from the 1940s and in some instances from 1929.

Statistical Abstract of the United States, published annually since 1878, is the standard summary of statistics on the social, political, and economic organization of the United States. Prepared by the Bureau of the Census, it is designed to serve as a convenient statistical reference and as a guide to other statistical publications and sources. This volume, which currently runs over 900 pages, includes a selection of data from many statistical publications, both government and private.

BANK PUBLICATIONS

In addition to the government material, there are data and comments on the economy published by various banks. These generally appear monthly and are free of charge. They can be categorized as publications of the Federal Reserve Banks or of commercial banks.

PUBLICATIONS OF FEDERAL RESERVE BANKS. The Federal Reserve System is divided into 12 Federal Reserve districts with a major Federal Reserve bank in each location as follows:[2]

---

[2] Specific addresses for each of the district banks and names of major personnel are contained in the *Federal Reserve Bulletin,* published monthly by the Federal Reserve Board.

1. Boston   *Federal Reserve Bank Locations*
2. New York
3. Philadelphia
4. Cleveland
5. Richmond
6. Atlanta
7. Chicago
8. St. Louis
9. Minneapolis
10. Denver
11. Dallas
12. San Francisco.

Each of the Federal Reserve district banks has a research department that issues periodic reports. While the various bank publications differ, monthly reviews, which are available to interested parties, are published by all district banks. These reviews typically contain one or several articles of interest and regional statistics. A major exception is the St. Louis Federal Reserve Bank, which publishes statistical releases weekly, monthly, and quarterly containing extensive national and international data in addition to its monthly review.[3]

PUBLICATIONS OF COMMERCIAL BANKS. A number of large banks prepare monthly letters available to interested individuals. These letters generally contain a comment on the current and future outlook of the economy and specific industries or segments of the economy.

NON–U.S. ECONOMIC DATA

In addition to data on the U.S. economy, it is important to gather data on other countries where you might consider investing. Some of the available sources follow:[4]

The *Economic Intelligence Unit (EIU)* publishes 83 separate quarterly reviews and an annual supplement covering the economic and business conditions and outlook for 160 countries. The reviews consider the economy, trade and finance, and trends in investment and consumer spending along with discussions of the political environment. Tables contain data on economic activity and foreign trade.

The *EIU* also publishes *European Trends,* which contains a discussion of the aggregate economic environment for the overall European community and the world.

The *Organization for Economic Cooperation and Development (OECD)* publishes semiannual surveys showing recent trends and policies and assesses short-term prospects for each country. An annual volume (*Historical*

---

[3] An individual can request to be put on the mailing list for any of these publications (free) by writing to Federal Reserve Bank of St. Louis, P.O. Box 442, St. Louis, MO 63166.

[4] This discussion draws heavily from Daniells, *Business Information Sources,* rev. ed. (Berkeley, Calif.: University of California Press, 1986).

Statistics) contains annual percent change data for the most recent 20 years.

The Business International Corp. publishes an annual book entitled *Worldwide Economic Indicators* that contains data for 131 countries on population, gross domestic product (GDP), wages and prices, foreign trade, and a number of specific items for the most recent four years.

Demographic Yearbook, published by the United Nations, contains statistics on population, births, deaths, life expectancy, marriages, and divorces for about 240 countries.

International Marketing Data and Statistics, published by Euromonitor Publications Inc. of London, is an annual guide that contains data for 132 non-European countries covering population, employment, production, trade, the economy, and other economic data.

United Nations Statistical Yearbook is a basic reference book of extensive economic statistics on all UN countries (population, construction, industrial production, etc.).

Eurostatistics, a monthly publication by the Statistical Office of the European Communities (Luxembourg), contains statistics for short-term economic analysis in 10 European community countries and the United States. There are generally data for six years covering industrial production, employment and unemployment, external trade, prices, wages, and finance.

U.S. International Trade Administration, International Economic Indicators is a quarterly publication of the U.S. Government Printing Office that contains comparative economic indicators and trends in the United States and its seven principal industrial competitors: France, Germany, Italy, Netherlands, United Kingdom, Japan, and Canada. The data is organized in five parts: general indicators, trade indicators, price indicators, finance indicators, and labor indicators. Notably, the sources for the data are contained at the back of the booklet.

International Financial Statistics, a monthly publication (with a yearbook issue) of the International Monetary Fund, is an essential source of current financial statistics such as exchange rates, fund position, international liquidity, money and banking statistics, interest rates (including LIBOR), prices, and production.[5]

International Monetary Fund, Balance of Payments Yearbook is a two-part publication. The first part contains detailed balance-of-payments figures for over 110 countries, while the second part contains world totals for balance-of-payments components and aggregates.

United Nations Yearbook of International Trade Statistics is an annual report on import statistics over a four-year period for each of 166 countries. The commodity figures for each country are given by commodity code.

United Nations Yearbook of National Account Statistics is a comprehensive source of national account data that contains detailed statistics for 155 countries on domestic product and consumption expenditures, national income, and disposable income for a 12-year period.

---

[5] LIBOR is an acronym for London Interbank Borrowing Rate. It is used as a base rate for many international financial transactions.

Also, some individual countries publish national income studies with detailed breakdowns as well as annual statistical reports that contain the more important statistics and include bibliographical sources for the tables. Examples would include Brazil, Great Britain, Japan, and Switzerland.

Similar to the United States, major banks in various countries publish bulletins or letters that contain statistical reviews for the individual countries. Examples include:

- *Bank of Canada Review* (monthly)
- *Bank of England* (quarterly)
- *Bank of Japan* (monthly)
- *National Bank of Belgium* (monthly)
- *Deutsche Bundesbank* (monthly)

In addition to these several specific sources of data, you should be aware of the following bibliographies:

G. R. Dicks, ed. *Sources of World Financial and Banking Information.* Westport, Conn.: Greenwood Press, 1981. A descriptive list of nearly 5,000 financial and banking sources arranged by country.

David Hoopes, ed. *Global Guide to International Business.* New York: File Publications, 1983. A descriptive list by country of source information about that country.

Index of International Statistics. Washington, D.C.: Congressional Information Service. A monthly descriptive guide and index to statistical publications by the world's major international government organizations.

AGGREGATE STOCK MARKET ANALYSIS

Several government publications provide useful data on the stock market, but the bulk of detailed information is provided by private firms. Some of the government publications discussed earlier (e.g., *Federal Reserve Bulletin* and *Survey of Current Business)* contain financial market data such as interest rates and stock prices.

GOVERNMENT PUBLICATIONS

The main source of data in this area is the Securities and Exchange Commission (SEC), which is the federal agency responsible for regulating the operation of the securities markets and collecting data in this regard. The *Annual Report of the SEC* is published for the fiscal year ending in June. It contains a detailed discussion of important developments during the year and comments on the SEC's disclosure system and regulation of the securities markets. Finally, it includes a statistics section containing historical data on many security market series.

COMMERCIAL PUBLICATIONS

Considering the numerous advisory services in existence, a section dealing with their publications could become voluminous. Therefore, our intent is to list and discuss only the major services and allow you to develop your own list of other available sources. An excellent source of advertisements for these services is *Barron's*.

New York Stock Exchange Fact Book is an annual publication of the NYSE. The book is an outstanding source of current and historical data on activity on the NYSE, as well as comparative data on the AMEX, the OTC, and institutional trading.

Amex Fact Book is a comparable data book for the American Stock Exchange. The first book (entitled *Amex Databook*) was published in 1969 with subsequent editions in 1971, 1973, and 1976. The title was changed to *Amex Statistical Review* in 1981 and to *Amex Fact Book* in 1983. It is now published annually and contains pertinent information on the exchange, its membership, administration, and trading activities.

NASDAQ Fact Book is a data book for the OTC market. First published in 1983 and now issued annually, it contains extensive data on trading volume and information related to the stocks on the NASDAQ system. It also discusses past growth and future plans for the NASDAQ market system.

Tokyo Stock Exchange Fact Book is an annual publication published by and containing information on the TSE. It is similar to the fact books prepared by U.S. institutions and contains extensive data related to stocks trading on the exchange, members of the exchange, and the price action of stocks traded on the TSE and other Japanese exchanges.

American Banker Yearbook is an annual publication by the publisher of *American Banker,* a daily newspaper serving the financial services industry (this newspaper is described later in this section). The *Yearbook* contains a review of the events of the year plus an extensive statistical section that includes operating and size data on commercial banks, finance companies, mortgage banking, thrifts, and also international banking (the top 100 banks in the world).

The Bond Buyer Yearbook is an annual publication by the publisher of *The Bond Buyer,* a daily newspaper related to the fixed-income market (this newspaper is described later in this section). In addition to a review of the major events of the year, there are extensive statistics related to the municipal bond market such as the volume of long-term and short-term issues in total by purpose and by states, the interest rates on alternative issues, the top underwriters, and the top counseling firms. Needless to say, this is the major source of data related to the tax-exempt bond market.

The Wall Street Journal, published by Dow-Jones and Company, is a daily national business newspaper published five days a week. It contains complete listings for the NYSE, the AMEX, the NASDAQ-OTC market, U.S. bond markets, options markets, and commodities quotations. There are also quotes for foreign stocks and bonds and non–U.S. stock market indicator series. It is recognized worldwide as a prime source of financial and business information for the United States.[6]

Investor Daily, billed as "America's Business Newspaper," was initiated in 1984 as competition to *The Wall Street Journal.* It provides much of the same information but also attempts to provide added information related

---

[6] A booklet that includes a discussion of many of the features of *The Wall Street Journal* is "A Future Manager's Guide to *The Wall Street Journal.*" Copies are available from *The Wall Street Journal,* Educational Service Bureau, P.O. Box 300, Princeton, NJ 08540.

to stock prices, earnings, and trading volume. An extensive set of U.S. general market indexes, including several unique to it, are included. It contains little, however, on non–U.S. markets.

The Financial Times is published five times a week in London with issues printed in New York and Los Angeles. While it could be considered a British version of *The Wall Street Journal,* it is actually much more, because it has a true *world* perspective on the financial news. While it does an outstanding job of reporting financial news related to England, it also does very well on U.S. data (stock and bond quotes and security market indicator series) and also contains news and data for Japan and other countries. Most important, however, is its global perspective in discussing and interpreting the news. Such a perspective is critical in the rapidly evolving global securities market environment.

The Bond Buyer is a daily newspaper (five days a week) that concentrates on news and quotes related to the overall bond market, with special emphasis on the municipal bond market—indeed, its caption reads, "The Authority on Municipal Bonds Since 1891." Besides news stories on events that affect bonds, there are extensive listings of new and forthcoming bond sales, bond calls and redemptions, and information on bond ratings. There are also numerous market indicator series reported with the emphasis on fixed-income series.

The American Banker is referred to as "The Daily Financial Services Newspaper." It contains articles on topics of interest to bankers and others involved in the financial services industry—such as legislation and general news of the industry and major banks. There is also a brief summary of the financial markets related to Treasuries, financial futures, and mortgage securities.

Barron's is a weekly publication of Dow-Jones and Company that typically contains about six articles on topics of interest to investors and the most complete weekly listing of prices and quotes for all U.S. financial markets. It provides weekly data on individual stocks and the latest information on earnings and dividends as well as quotes on commodities, stock options, and financial futures. Finally, toward the back (typically the last four pages), there is an extensive statistical section with detailed information on the U.S. securities market for the past week.[7] There is also a list of values for a fairly extensive set of world security market indicator series and an "International Trader" section that discusses price movements in the major global stock markets.

The Asian Wall Street Journal is a weekly publication of *The Wall Street Journal* that concentrates on the Asian region. It includes detailed economic news and stock and bond quotes related to this area of the global market.

Credit Markets is a weekly newspaper by the publishers of *The Bond Buyer.* It provides a longer-term overview of the major news items that

---

[7] A booklet that discusses many of the features in *Barron's* and how the series are used by technicians is Martin E. Zweig, *Understanding Technical Forecasting.* It is likewise available, free of charge, from *The Wall Street Journal,* Educational Service Bureau, P.O. Box 300, Princeton, NJ 08540.

affect Treasury, corporate, and individual fixed-income securities. There is also an extensive statistical section listing bond calls, redemptions, and the long-term calendar of upcoming issues along with several security market series.

Banking World is a concise weekly newspaper from the publishers of *American Banker*. It contains a summary of all the major news stories from Washington, the Federal Reserve, and all sectors of the financial services industry. There is news on marketing, technology, federal and state regulations, and specific financial firms.

Financial Services Week is a weekly publication from Fairchild Publications that is billed as "The Financial Planner's Newspaper." It contains articles on the overall stock and bond market, but also considers insurance and special features such as "Planning for Dentists," and "Baby-Boomers and Financial Services." It also gives information on tax changes and other legislation of importance to financial planners.

International Financing Review is a weekly magazine that contains stories and data regarding international investment banking firms and the international securities markets, with an emphasis on fixed-income securities and global economies and politics. It is published by IFR Publishing Ltd. (97 Middlesex St., London EL 7EZ).

Equities International, a weekly magazine that, like the preceding one, is also produced by IFR Publishing, deals with global markets but concentrates on equity instruments such as common stock, warrants, convertibles, options, and futures. The emphasis is on major trends and events in countries around the world. There is a complete listing of stock market indicator series for major global markets.

Euro Week, billed as "The Euromarket's First Newspaper," contains discussions related to notes, bonds, and stocks throughout Europe as well as longer articles on major news items in individual countries. A capital markets guide provides information on major securities issues forthcoming. Finally, there is a brief summary of the market indicator series for various countries and a listing of the top investment banking firms in various categories (Eurobonds; Euro-equities) based upon the value of the issues underwritten.

The Dow-Jones Investor's Handbook contains the complete DJIA results for each year along with earnings and dividends for the series since 1939. Individual reports on common and preferred stocks and bonds listed on the NYSE and AMEX, including high and low prices, volume, dividends, and the year's most active stocks, are also included.[8]

Business and Investment Almanac, published annually by Dow Jones-Irwin and edited by Sumner N. Levine, contains a wide range of information on the economy, various industries, U.S. and foreign securities markets, and individual investments (stocks, bonds, options, futures, real estate, diamonds, and other collectibles). It concludes with a very helpful business and information directory.

---

[8] Prior to 1980 the firm published handbooks on several other topics, including *Barron's Market Laboratory*, *The Dow-Jones Commodities Handbook*, and *The Dow-Jones Stock Options Handbook*.

The Wall Street Waltz is a book that contains 90 charts dealing with financial cycles and trends of historical interest put together by Kenneth Fisher. Examples include "Price-to-Book Value Ratios" from 1921; "Stock Prices Abroad" (stock prices for seven foreign countries); and charts of the South Seas Bubble from 1719 to 1720. It provides excellent historical and current perspective.

Trade and Securities Statistics is a service of Standard & Poor's that includes historical data on various economic and security price series and a monthly supplement that updates the series for the recent period. There are two major sets of data: (1) business and financial and (2) security price index record. Within the business and finance section are long-term statistics on trade, banking, industry, prices, agriculture, and financial trends.

The security price index record contains historical data for all of the Standard & Poor's indexes. This includes the 500 stocks broken down into 88 individual groups. The four main groups are industrials, rails, utilities, and financial firms. There are also four supplementary group series: capital goods companies, consumer goods, high-grade common stocks, and low-priced common stocks. In addition to the stock price series, Standard & Poor's has derived a quarterly series of earnings and dividends for each of the four main groups. The earnings series includes data from 1946 to the present.

The booklet also contains data on daily stock sales on the NYSE from 1918 on and historical yields for a number of corporate and government bond series.

BROKERAGE FIRM REPORTS

As a means of competing for investor's business, brokerage firms provide, among other services, information and recommendations on the outlook for securities markets (bonds and stocks). These reports are typically prepared monthly and distributed to customers (or potential customers) of the firm free of charge. In the competition for institutional business, investment firms have generated reports that are quite extensive and sophisticated. Among the brokerage firms issuing these reports are Goldman Sachs & Company; Kidder Peabody & Co.; Merrill Lynch, Pierce, Fenner & Smith; Morgan Stanley; and Salomon Bros.

Beyond these reports on the U.S. security markets, several investment banking firms have begun to publish extensive reviews of the world markets. The economic outlook for the major countries is discussed along with import/export and exchange rate considerations that culminate in evaluations of the outlook for the specific industries specified as *global industries* and also recommendations related to world bond and stock markets. Examples of such publications include the following:

- Goldman Sachs International Corp.'s monthly publication, *World Investment Strategy Highlights,* begins with world investment factors such as economic activity, monetary conditions, and interest rates and moves to individual country reports for about 12 individual countries and groups. The culmination is a recommended world portfolio strategy that considers individual country expectations and exchange rate forecasts.

- Morgan Stanley Capital International has a monthly publication that provides up-to-date pricing and valuation data on individual stocks and world industries. As an example, it is assumed that an analyst or a portfolio manager would evaluate U.S. chemical firms as part of the global chemical industry, not just the U.S. chemical industry. This set of world data allows the analyst or portfolio manager to examine stocks across industries and countries.

  The firm also has a quarterly publication that provides over 20 years of share price information (adjusted for capital changes) for 1,700 of the largest companies in the world, representing over 75 percent of the world's market capitalization. The most recent balance sheet is provided, along with five years of operating data.

- The Fixed Income Group of Kidder Peabody & Co. publishes *The International Report,* a monthly publication that suggests a global investment strategy for the fixed-income market based on world markets. Specifically, the Group considers global fixed-income returns, yields, and exchange rates, including specific country analysis for the United States, Japan, West Germany, the United Kingdom, and other countries of current interest. It also publishes a monthly *Capital Markets Chartbook* that contains numerous charts on output, demand (consumer spending, personal income), inflation, Federal Reserve data, domestic interest rates, international interest rates, and other international economic statistics.

- The Merrill Lynch Capital Markets Group publishes *World Bond Monitor,* a biweekly analysis of international bond yields, spreads, and yield curves that specifically considers the U.S. dollar bond market, the floating rate note market, U.K. sterling bond market, Japanese yen bond market, Deutschemark bond market, Dutch guilder bond market, world inflation, and yields in currency hedged instruments. It also publishes monthly the *International Fixed Income Strategy* that considers the global perspective for the dollar, the world climate for bonds, and specific market perspectives for the Japanese yen, sterling bond market, and DM-block market. The report concludes with an international fixed-income strategy for the coming six months.

- Salomon Brothers Inc., has three interlocking monthly reports: *Global Fixed-Income Investment Strategy, Global Equity Investment Strategy,* and *Global Economic Outlook and Asset Allocation.* The reports give recommendations on the basis of the outlook for the U.S. and world economies and markets for a total world portfolio, including a global fixed-income-equity allocation that considers the exchange rate outlook.

- Nomura Research Institute (NRI) publishes *Nomura Investment Review,* a monthly publication that analyzes and projects the general investment climate in Japan and the rest of the world. While the emphasis is on the Japanese economy and its securities markets, there is also an extensive discussion of the world stock markets as well as various sectors (industries). The result is a world portfolio structure recommendation and also suggestions for specific stocks in the portfolio.

Nomura Research Institute is an independently managed research company affiliated with the Nomura Securities Co., Ltd.

• Daiwa Securities Co. Ltd. has a quarterly publication, *Tokyo Stock Market Quarterly Review,* that includes an in-depth analysis of the Japanese economy and securities market and also contains an extensive discussion of numerous markets around the world.

INDUSTRY ANALYSIS

There are only a few publications with extensive information on a wide range of industries. The major sources of data on various industries are industry publications and magazines and trade associations.

INDUSTRY PUBLICATIONS

Standard & Poor's Industry Survey is a two-volume reference work divided into 34 segments dealing with 69 major domestic industries. Coverage in each area is divided into a basic analysis and a current analysis. The basic analysis examines the prospects for that particular industry, then analyzes trends and problems presented in historical perspective. Major segments of the industry are spotlighted, and a comparative analysis of the principal companies in the industry is included. The current analysis provides information on the latest developments in the industry and available industry, market, and company statistics, along with appraisals of the investment outlook for the industry.

Standard & Poor's Analysts Handbook contains selected income account and balance sheet items along with related financial ratios for the Standard & Poor's industry groups. It is typically not available until about seven months after year-end. With these fundamental income and balance sheet series, it is possible to compare the major factors bearing on group stock price movements (e.g., sales, profit margins, earnings). These data are used extensively in the industry analysis chapter. Figure 5.1 is a sample page.

Other journals of various industries are an excellent source of data and general information. Depending upon the industry, there can be several publications—the computer industry has spawned at least five such magazines. Examples of industry publications include the following:

• *Computers*
• *Real Estate Today*
• *Chemical Week*
• *Modern Plastics*
• *Paper Trade Journal*
• *Automotive News.*

FIGURE 5.1
Sample Page from Standard & Poor's Analysts Handbook

CHEMICALS

Per Share Data—Adjusted to stock price index level. Average of stock price indexes, 1941-1943=10

	Sales	Oper. Profit	Profit Margin %	Depr.	Income Taxes	Earnings Per Share	Earnings % of Sales	Dividends Per Share	Dividends % of Earn.	Price 1941-1943=10 High	Price Low	Price/Earn. Ratio High	Price/Earn. Ratio Low	Div. Yields % High	Div. Yields % Low	Book Value Per Share	Book Value % Return	Working Capital	Capital Expenditures
1957	17.38	4.44	25.55	1.28	1.59	1.95	11.22	1.43	73.33	47.21	37.97	24.21	19.47	3.77	3.03	13.11	14.87	5.18	2.36
1958	16.89	4.01	23.74	1.36	1.25	1.69	10.01	1.36	80.47	49.76	38.27	29.44	22.64	3.55	2.73	13.81	12.24	5.14	1.79
1959	19.34	5.16	26.68	1.40	1.90	2.23	11.53	1.47	65.92	61.60	48.57	27.62	21.78	3.03	2.39	14.75	15.12	5.76	1.62
1960	19.97	4.82	24.14	1.50	1.65	2.08	10.42	1.46	70.19	60.80	44.15	29.23	21.23	3.31	2.40	15.79	13.17	5.67	2.29
1961	20.67	4.96	24.00	1.66	1.64	2.08	10.06	1.55	74.52	56.69	47.55	27.25	22.86	3.26	2.73	16.66	12.48	5.68	2.17
1962	23.55	5.92	25.14	1.88	2.01	2.42	10.28	1.67	69.01	54.31	39.16	22.44	16.18	4.26	3.07	17.34	13.96	6.75	2.33
1963	26.69	6.60	24.73	2.10	2.22	2.75	10.30	1.83	66.55	62.36	52.50	22.68	19.09	3.49	2.93	18.61	14.78	7.77	2.71
1964	31.88	7.99	25.06	2.41	2.58	3.34	10.48	1.99	59.58	72.87	62.96	21.82	18.85	3.16	2.73	20.09	16.63	8.99	3.85
1965	34.52	8.59	24.88	2.64	2.55	3.41	9.88	1.89	55.43	76.78	68.78	22.52	20.17	2.75	2.46	21.94	15.54	9.90	4.88
1966	38.18	8.97	23.49	2.88	2.58	3.50	9.17	1.94	55.43	75.38	49.82	21.54	14.23	3.89	2.57	23.51	14.89	9.93	5.41
1967	38.63	8.12	21.02	3.15	1.99	2.84	7.35	1.87	65.85	60.53	50.87	21.31	17.91	3.68	3.09	24.40	11.64	10.21	5.07
1968	43.96	9.37	21.31	3.51	2.56	3.16	7.19	2.00	63.29	61.43	50.20	19.44	15.89	3.98	3.26	26.25	12.04	11.21	4.59
1969	47.18	9.55	20.24	3.70	2.52	3.17	6.72	1.94	61.20	57.95	40.08	18.28	12.64	4.84	3.35	27.17	11.67	11.79	5.40
1970	47.51	8.89	18.71	3.90	1.95	2.70	5.68	1.90	70.37	47.11	36.93	17.45	13.68	5.14	4.03	27.77	9.72	11.75	5.95
1971	49.55	9.36	18.89	3.99	2.07	2.93	5.91	1.90	64.85	58.71	47.56	20.04	16.23	3.99	3.24	29.48	9.94	12.97	5.25
1972	54.18	10.77	19.88	4.15	2.66	3.61	6.66	1.97	54.57	67.13	56.40	18.60	15.62	3.49	2.93	30.64	11.78	14.51	5.00
1973	64.00	13.54	21.16	4.23	3.91	5.10	7.97	2.08	40.78	72.95	55.46	14.30	10.87	3.75	2.85	33.84	15.07	16.39	6.39
1974	85.47	17.01	19.90	4.76	5.10	6.79	7.94	2.21	32.55	68.80	47.20	10.13	6.95	4.68	3.21	38.34	17.71	18.71	10.26
1975	80.33	15.24	18.97	4.92	4.18	5.51	6.86	2.18	39.56	74.63	48.76	13.54	8.85	4.47	2.92	39.26	14.03	17.59	11.95
1976	91.16	17.47	19.17	5.49	4.52	6.59	7.23	2.48	37.63	89.70	67.27	13.61	10.21	3.69	2.76	43.27	15.23	18.93	12.97
1977	101.01	18.44	18.26	6.37	4.31	6.16	6.10	2.78	45.13	72.45	52.70	11.76	8.56	5.28	3.84	46.55	13.23	19.77	12.10
1978	112.76	20.82	18.46	7.21	5.07	7.16	6.35	3.10	43.30	59.62	46.05	8.33	6.43	6.73	5.20	50.65	14.14	22.27	12.13
1979	129.30	22.59	17.47	7.51	5.13	9.17	7.09	3.38	36.86	61.04	51.75	6.66	5.64	6.53	5.54	54.58	16.80	24.87	12.48
1980	140.37	20.86	14.86	7.73	4.03	8.07	5.75	3.56	44.11	64.88	49.70	8.04	6.16	7.16	5.49	60.53	13.33	25.83	15.11
1981	143.65	21.09	14.68	7.72	4.79	7.71	5.37	3.37	43.71	73.84	52.81	9.58	6.85	6.38	4.56	65.84	11.71	29.45	15.26
1982	159.01	21.85	13.74	9.56	5.52	5.21	3.28	3.57	68.52	63.30	45.44	12.15	8.72	7.86	5.64	65.63	7.94	26.03	15.89
1983	161.68	23.41	14.48	10.18	6.66	4.98	3.08	3.66	73.49	81.75	57.95	16.41	11.64	6.32	4.48	66.32	7.51	22.60	12.06
1984	168.26	26.85	15.96	9.84	7.97	7.39	4.39	4.00	54.13	75.82	61.58	10.26	8.33	6.50	5.28	68.72	10.75	21.35	13.35
1985	151.04	24.21	16.03	10.47	3.84	2.34	1.55	3.91	167.09	91.58	63.14	39.14	26.98	6.19	4.27	60.10	3.89	18.64	13.90
R1986	142.01	27.14	19.11	11.64	5.92	7.95	5.60	6.04	75.97	132.68	87.43	16.69	11.00	6.91	4.55	58.74	13.53	20.02	13.63
1987	171.62	33.40	19.46	12.25	10.21	12.75	7.43	4.72	37.02	185.85	118.65	14.58	9.31	3.98	2.54	68.96	18.49	25.94	15.02

Stock Price Indexes for this group extend back to 1926.
*Air Products & Chemicals (4-10-85)
*Dow Chemical (7-30-47)
*du Pont de Nemours (1-2-18)
*Ethyl Corp. (2-25-87)
*Goodrich (B.F.) (transferred from Tire and Rubber) (7-22-87)
*Hercules Inc. (formerly Hercules Powder) (9-17-30)
*Monsanto Co. (1-16-35)
*Quantum Chemicals (formerly National Distillers & Chemicals) (transferred from Beverages (Distillers)) (7-22-87)

*Rohm & Haas (transferred from Chemicals Div.) (4-10-85)
*Union Carbide Co. (12-31-25)
Airco Inc. (formerly Air Reduction) (1-2-18 to 2-5-75)
Allied Chemical Corp. (1-2-18 to 7-25-79) (transferred to Chemicals Div.)
American Cyanamid (9-17-30 to 7-25-79)
American Potash & Chem. (2-14-62 to 1-3-68)
Atlas Powder (1-16-35 to 7-23-47)
Celanese Corp. (4-10-85 to 2-25-87) (transferred from Chemicals Div.)
Chemetron Corp. (formerly Nat'l Cylinder Gas) (4-16-58 to 2-5-75)

Columbian Carbon (12-31-25 to 2-7-62)
Commercial Solvents (12-31-25 to 6-16-65)
GAF Corp. (formerly General Aniline & Film) (6-16-65 to 2-5-75)
Hooker Chemical (1-3-68 to 7-30-68)
Olin Corp. (formerly Olin-Mathieson Chemical) (1-2-18 to 2-5-75)
Stauffer Chemical Co. (7-25-79 to 4-10-85)
United Carbon (1-16-35 to 7-23-47)
U.S. Industrial Chemicals (5-11-38 to 8-1-51)

Source: Standard & Poor's Analysts Handbook (New York: Standard & Poor's Corp., 1988) Reprinted with permission.

TRADE ASSOCIATIONS

Trade associations are organizations set up by those involved in an industry or a general area of business to provide information for such topics as education, advertising, lobbying for legislation, and problem solving. Trade associations gather extensive statistics for the industry. Examples of such organizations follow:[9]

- Iron and Steel Institute
- American Railroad Association
- National Consumer Finance Association
- Institute of Life Insurance
- American Bankers Association
- Machine Tool Association.

INDIVIDUAL STOCKS

An obvious source of information about a company is the company itself. Indeed, in the case of some small firms, it may be the only source of information because there is not enough trading activity in the firm's stock to justify its inclusion in studies issued by commercial services.

COMPANY-GENERATED INFORMATION

ANNUAL REPORTS. All firms with publicly traded stock are required to prepare and distribute to their stockholders an annual report of financial operations and current financial position. In addition to basic information, most reports contain a discussion of what happened during the year and some consideration of future prospects. Most firms also publish *quarterly financial reports* that include a brief income statement for the interim period and, sometimes, a balance sheet. These reports can be obtained directly from the company. To find an address for a company you should consult Volume 1 of *Standard & Poor's Register of Corporations, Directors, and Executives,* which contains an alphabetical listing, by business name, of approximately 37,000 corporations.

SECURITY PROSPECTUS. When a firm wants to sell some securities (bonds, preferred stock, or common stock) in the primary market to raise new capital, the Securities and Exchange Commission (SEC) requires that it file a registration statement describing the securities being offered and offering financial information on the company (more extensive information than that required in an annual report) as well as nonfinancial information on the firm's operations and personnel. A condensed version of the registration statement, referred to as a *prospectus,* is published by the underwriting firm and contains most of the relevant information. Copies of a prospectus for a current offering can be obtained from the underwriter or from the company. The investment banking firms will often advertise the offerings in publications like *The Wall Street Journal, Barron's,* or the *Financial Times.*

REQUIRED SEC REPORTS. In addition to registration statements, the SEC requires three *periodic statements* from publicly held firms. First, the 8-K

---

[9] For a more extensive list, see *Encyclopedia of Associations* (Detroit: Gale Research Company, 1977).

form is filed each month, reporting any action that affects the debt, equity, amount of capital assets, voting right, or other changes that might have a significant impact on the stock.

Second, the 9-K form is an unaudited report filed every six months, containing revenues, expenses, gross sales, and special items. It typically contains more extensive information than the quarterly statement.

Finally, the 10-K form is an annual version of the 9-K but is even more complete. The SEC requires that firms indicate in their annual reports that a copy of their 10-K is available from the company upon request without charge.

COMMERCIAL PUBLICATIONS

Numerous advisory services supply information on the aggregate market and individual stocks. A partial list follows:

Standard & Poor's Corporation Records is a set of seven volumes. The first six contain basic information on all types of corporations (industrial, financial) arranged alphabetically. The volumes are in binders and are updated throughout the year. The seventh volume is a daily news volume that contains recent data on all companies listed in all the volumes.

Standard & Poor's Stock Reports are comprehensive two-page reports on numerous companies with stocks listed on the NYSE, AMEX, and traded OTC. They include the near term sales and earnings outlook, recent developments, key income statement and balance sheet items, and a chart of stock price movements. They are in bound volumes by exchange and are revised every three to four months. A sample page is shown in Figure 5.2.

Standard & Poor's Stock Guide is a monthly publication that contains, in compact form, pertinent financial data on more than 5,000 common and preferred stocks. A separate section covers over 400 mutual fund issues. For each stock, the guide contains information on price ranges (historical and recent), dividends, earnings, financial position, institutional holdings, and a ranking for earning and dividend stability. It is a very useful quick reference for almost all actively traded stocks, as is shown by the example in Figure 5.3.

Standard & Poor's Bond Guide is a monthly publication that contains the most pertinent comparative financial and statistical information on a broad list of bonds including domestic and foreign bonds (about 3,900 issues), 200 foreign government bonds, and about 650 convertible bonds.

The Outlook is a weekly publication of Standard & Poor's Corporation that contains advice regarding the general market environment and on specific groups of stocks or industries (e.g., high-dividend stocks, stocks with low price-to-earnings ratios, high-yielding bonds, stocks likely to increase their dividends). Weekly stock index figures for 88 industry groups and other market statistics are included.

Moody's Industrial Manual is similar to the Standard & Poor's Corporation Records service with the difference that this service is organized by type of corporation (i.e., industrial, utility, etc.). The two-volume service is published once a year and covers industrial companies listed on the

FIGURE 5.2
Sample Page from Standard & Poor's Stock Reports

Int'l Business Machines 1210

NYSE Symbol IBM Options on CBOE (Jan-Apr-Jul-Oct) In S&P 500

Price	Range	P-E Ratio	Dividend	Yield	S&P Ranking	Beta
Jul. 25'88	1988					
122⅜	129½-104¼	14	4.40	3.6%	A+	0.79

Summary

IBM is the world's largest manufacturer of computers and information processing equipment and systems, ranging from microcomputers to large-scale mainframes. Profits in 1988 and 1989 should continue the modest uptrend begun in 1987, aided by new product introductions and continuing cost containment efforts.

Current Outlook

Earnings for 1989 should advance to $11.20 a share from the $9.50 estimated for 1988 which is before a $0.53 gain from a change in accounting.

The $1.10 quarterly dividend is the minimum expectation.

Gross income should rise approximately 7% in both 1988 and 1989, aided by higher capital spending for computers in the U.S. and new product introductions, including the A/400 minicomputer designed to replace the popular 3X workstation line, additions to the PS/2 PC line, and enhancements to larger mainframe systems. Margins should benefit from a continuing cost reduction program.

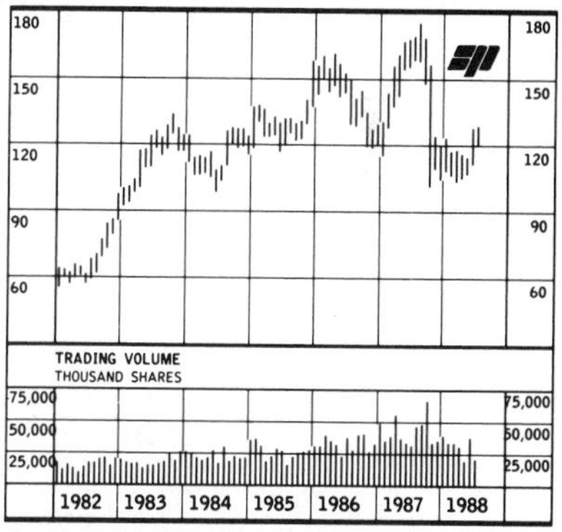

Gross Income (Billion $)

Quarter:	1988	1987	1986	1985
Mar.	11.75	10.68	10.13	9.77
Jun.	13.60	12.80	12.27	11.43
Sep.	---	12.73	11.91	11.70
Dec.	---	18.01	16.95	17.16
	---	54.22	51.25	50.06

Gross income for the first half of 1988 rose 8.0%, year to year, primarily due to reporting gains provided by a weaker dollar. After a $0.61 a share charge for operating consolidations, net income fell 3.4%, to $3.20 a share (before a $0.53 special credit) from $3.25.

Capital Share Earnings ($)

Quarter:	1988	1987	1986	1985
Mar.	1.57	1.30	1.65	1.61
Jun.	1.63	1.95	2.12	2.30
Sep.	E2.10	2.00	1.76	2.40
Dec.	E4.20	3.47	2.28	4.36
	E9.50	8.72	7.81	10.67

Important Developments

Jul. '88—Significant enhancements to the top end Sierra mainframe line providing up to 56% more throughput were announced for autumn delivery. In June the AS/400 minicomputer line was introduced to replace the workhorse System 36 and 38 machines; it is expected to be available in quantity by late August. Separately, a number of production, marketing and sales force consolidations were announced to further reduce the employee head count.

Nov. '87—Management reported that it expected the computer industry to grow at a 6% to 9% annual rate before inflation over the next few years and remained hopeful that IBM's revenues would grow at the same pace. Due to recent cost cutting efforts, earnings were projected to expand at a faster rate than sales.

Next earnings report expected in mid-Oct.

Per Share Data ($)

Yr. End Dec. 31	1987	1986	1985	1984	1983	1982	1981	1980	1979	1978
Book Value	**62.81**	55.40	50.60	41.79	38.02	33.13	30.66	28.18	25.64	23.14
Earnings	**8.72**	7.81	10.67	10.77	9.04	7.39	5.63	6.10	5.16	5.32
Dividends	**4.40**	4.40	4.40	4.10	3.71	3.44	3.44	3.44	3.44	2.88
Payout Ratio	**50%**	56%	41%	38%	41%	47%	62%	56%	67%	54%
Prices—High	**175⅞**	161⅞	158¾	128½	134¼	98	71½	72¾	80½	77½
Low	**102**	119¼	117⅜	99	92¼	55⅝	48⅜	50⅜	61⅛	58¾
P/E Ratio—	**20-12**	21-15	15-11	12-9	15-10	13-8	13-9	12-8	16-12	15-11

Data as orig. reptd. Adj. for stk. div(s). of 300% Jun. 1979. E-Estimated.

Standard NYSE Stock Reports
Vol. 55/No. 148/Sec. 12

August 2, 1988

Standard & Poor's Corp.
25 Broadway, NY, NY 10004

continued

Source: *Standard & Poor's Stock Reports* (New York: Standard & Poor's Corp., 1988). Reprinted with permission.

FIGURE 5.2 *continued*

1210   International Business Machines Corporation

Income Data (Million $)

Year Ended Dec. 31	Revs.	Oper. Inc.	% Oper. Inc. of Revs.	Cap. Exp.	Depr.	Int. Exp.	Net Bef. Taxes	Eff. Tax Rate	Net Inc.	% Net Inc. of Revs.
1987	54,217	11,269	20.8%	4,304	3,527	619	² 8,609	38.9%	5,258	9.7%
1986	51,250	11,175	21.8%	4,620	3,316	604	² 8,389	42.9%	4,789	9.3%
1985	50,056	14,281	28.5%	6,430	3,051	443	²11,619	43.6%	6,555	13.1%
1984	45,937	14,446	31.4%	5,473	3,215	408	²11,623	43.4%	6,582	14.3%
1983	40,180	13,216	32.9%	4,930	3,627	390	² 9,940	44.8%	5,485	13.7%
1982	34,364	11,618	33.8%	6,685	3,562	514	² 7,930	44.4%	¹4,409	12.8%
1981	29,070	9,356	32.2%	6,845	3,329	480	² 5,988	44.8%	3,308	11.4%
1980	26,213	8,499	32.4%	6,592	2,759	¹325	² 5,897	39.6%	3,562	13.6%
1979	22,863	7,566	33.1%	5,991	2,321	140	5,553	45.8%	3,011	13.2%
1978	21,076	7,511	35.6%	4,046	2,070	55	5,798	46.3%	3,111	14.8%

Balance Sheet Data (Million $)

Dec. 31	Cash	Current Assets	Current Liab.	Ratio	Total Assets	Ret. on Assets	Long Term Debt	Common Equity	Total Cap.	% LT Debt of Cap.	Ret. on Equity
1987	6,967	31,020	13,377	2.3	63,688	8.7%	3,858	38,263	47,271	8.2%	14.6%
1986	7,257	27,749	12,743	2.2	57,814	8.7%	4,169	34,374	43,067	9.7%	14.5%
1985	5,622	26,070	11,433	2.3	52,634	13.7%	3,955	31,990	39,595	10.0%	22.4%
1984	4,362	20,375	9,640	2.1	42,808	16.4%	3,269	26,489	31,815	10.3%	26.4%
1983	5,536	17,270	9,507	1.8	37,243	15.6%	2,674	23,219	26,606	10.1%	25.2%
1982	3,300	13,014	8,209	1.6	32,541	14.1%	2,851	19,960	23,134	12.3%	22.9%
1981	2,029	10,303	7,320	1.4	29,586	11.7%	2,669	18,161	21,082	12.7%	19.0%
1980	2,112	9,925	6,526	1.5	26,703	13.9%	2,099	16,453	18,734	11.2%	22.7%
1979	3,771	10,851	6,445	1.7	24,530	13.3%	1,589	14,961	16,690	9.5%	21.2%
1978	4,031	10,321	5,810	1.8	20,771	15.7%	286	13,494	13,889	2.1%	24.0%

Data as orig. reptd. **1.** Reflects accounting change. **2.** Incl. equity in earns. of nonconsol. subs.

Business Summary

IBM is the largest manufacturer of data processing equipment and systems. Industry segment contributions in recent years:

Gross revenues	1987	1986
Processors/peripherals	46%	48%
Workstations	19%	18%
Programs/maint./other	31%	30%
Federal systems	4%	4%

Sales provided 67% of revenues in 1987, software and services 27%, and rentals 6%. Foreign operations contributed 54% of revenues in 1987 and 63% of profits.

Processors manipulate data through the operation of a stored program. Peripherals include printers, copiers, storage and telecommunication devices. Office products include small business computers, intelligent workstations and typewriters. Program products include applications and systems software. Other revenues are derived from supplies and unit record equipment, and education and testing materials. The Federal systems group serves the U.S. government.

Dividend Data

Dividends have been paid since 1916. A dividend reinvestment plan is available.

Amt. of Divd. $	Date Decl.	Ex-divd. Date	Stock of Record	Payment Date
1.10	Oct. 27	Nov. 5	Nov. 12	Dec. 10'87
1.10	Jan. 26	Feb. 4	Feb. 10	Mar. 10'88
1.10	Apr. 25	May 5	May 11	Jun. 10'88
1.10	Jul. 26	Aug. 4	Aug. 10	Sep. 10'88

Next dividend meeting: late Oct. '88.

Finances

Research, development and engineering expense totaled $5.4 billion (10.0% of gross income) in 1987, versus $5.2 billion (10.2%) in 1986.

Capitalization

Long Term Debt: About 4,267,000,000 incl. $1.25 billion of 7⅞% debs. conv. into com. at $153.66 a share.

Capital Stock: 591,550,765 shs. ($1.25 par). Institutions hold approximately 48%. Shareholders of record: 787,988.

Office—Armonk, New York 10504. **Tel**—(914) 765-1900. **Stockholder Relations Dept**—590 Madison Ave., NYC 10022. **Tel**—(212) 735-7000. **Chrmn**—J. F. Akers. **Treas**—D. A. Finley. **Investor Contact**—J. C. Clippard. **Dirs**—J. F. Akers, S. D. Bechtel, Jr., H. Brown, J. E. Burke, F. T. Cary, W. T. Coleman, Jr., T. F. Frist, Jr., C. A. Hills, N. deB. Katzenbach, N. O. Keohane, A. J. Krowe, J. D. Kuehler, R. W. Lyman, J. R. Munro, T. S. Murphy, J. R. Opel, P. J. Rizzo, W. W. Scranton. **Transfer Agents**—Company's NYC & Chicago offices. **Registrars**—Morgan Guaranty Trust Co., NYC; First National Bank, Chicago. **Incorporated** in New York in 1911.

Information has been obtained from sources believed to be reliable, but its accuracy and completeness are not guaranteed.   Robert S. Natale, CFA

FIGURE 5.3
Example from Standard & Poor's Stock Guide

64 Con-CPC — Standard & Poor's Corporation

¶S&P 500 •Options

Index	Ticker Symbol	Name of Issue (Call Price of Pfd. Stocks)	Market	Com. Rank. & Pfd. Rating	Par Val.	Inst.Hold Cos	Inst.Hold Shs. (000)	Principal Business
1	CFMI	**Convenient Food Mart**	OTC	B+	10¢	10	377	Licensor of retail food strs
2•[1]	CVGT	**Convergent Inc**	OTC	NR	No	99	19386	Mfr & markets computer sys
3	CSOL	**Convergent Solutions**	OTC	NR	1¢	1	30	Converg't tech compat softw
4	CNV	**Convertible Hldgs**	NY,M	NR	10¢	7	261	Dual purpose investment co
5	Pr	**Cm income shares(9.30'97)**	NY	NR	10¢	3	32	Com-cap gain:Pfd-yield
6	CVST	**Convest Energy**	OTC	NR	1¢	5	642	Oil & gas explor,dev,prod'n
7	CEP	**ConVest Energy Ptnrs**[52]	AS	NR	No	1	4	Oil & gas explor,dev,prod'n
8	CNVX	**Convex Computer**	OTC	NR	1¢	50	5644	Mfrs minisupercomputers
9•[2]	COO	**Cooper Cos**	NY	NR	10¢	72	5436	Mfrs eye care products
10	COOLV	**Cooper Development Corp**[55]	OTC	NR	10¢	13	168	Research in biotechnology
¶11•[3]	CBE	**Cooper Indus**	NY,B,M,P	A—	5	378	29506	Worldwide mfr electronic prod
12	ZAPS	**Cooper LaserSonics**[57]	OTC	NR	10¢	15	1584	Medical devices/dental prod
13	CTB	**Cooper Tire & Rubber**	NY,M	↑A	1	71	4880	Mfr auto & truck tires
¶14	ACCOB	**Coors (Adolph)**[58]	OTC	B	No	101	9915	Western brewer:ceramic,food
15	CFG	**Copelco Fin'l Svcs**	AS	NR	10¢	9	1175	Leasing hi tech medical eqp
16	COP	**Copley Properties**	AS	NR	1	13	560	Real estate investment trust
17	COS	**Copperweld Corp**	NY,B,M,Ph	C	83 1/3¢	24	1209	Mfrs alloy steel, specialty
18	Pr	**$2.48cm Cv[61]Exch Pfd([62]26.488)**	NY	B+	1	6	267	tub'g:bimetallic rod & wire
19	COPY	**CopyTele Inc**	OTC	NR	1¢	8	488	Dev flat panel data display
20	CORC	**Corcom, Inc**	OTC	B—	No	17	1445	Digital circuitry filters
21	CORD	**Cordis Corp**	OTC	C	1	74	9130	Specialized medical devices
22	CRI	**Core Indus**	NY,M	B+	1	46	4256	Electr,agric,veh,constr prod
23	CSFN	**CoreStates Financial**	OTC	A	1	209	19504	Bank hldg:Phila Nat'l Bank
¶24•[4]	GLW	**Corning Glass Works**	NY,B,M,P,Ph	B+	5	332	25610	Mfrs specialty glass prod
25	CCRS	**Corporate Capital Res**	OTC	NR	2½¢	1	62	Inv in start-up/dev stage cos
26	CCAX	**Corrections Corp Amer**	OTC	NR	1	15	1493	Supplies prison mgmt svcs
27	CBL	**Corroon & Black**	NY,B,M,P	A—	25¢	103	10568	Insurance brokerage
28	CRVS	**Corvus Systems**	OTC	NR	No	15	1491	Disk drives & micro computers
29	CSMO	**Cosmo Communications**	OTC	NR	1¢	13	719	Mfrs consumer electronic prod
30	CCA	**Cosmopolitan Care**	AS	NR	1¢	5	247	Temporary personnel svcs
31	CSTR	**Costar Corp**	OTC	B—	10¢	2	17	Mfrs,mkts laboratory prod
32	COST	**Costco Wholesale**	OTC	NR	1¢	28	3694	Wholesale membership wrhse
33	CSLH	**Cotton Sts Lf & Hlth**	OTC	B	1	3	34	Insurance: life,health
34	CTF	**Counsellors Tandem**	NY,M	NR	1¢	4	833	Closed-end investment co
35	Pr	**7¼%cm Pfd([63]51.50)**	NY	A	1¢	3	276	invest in utility cos
36	CWTS	**Country Wide Transport**	OTC	NR	1¢	24	868	Irregular-route truck'g svc
37	CCR	**Countrywide Credit Ind**	NY,B,M,P	B+	5¢	44	4171	Services mtge loans
38	CWM	**Countrywide Mtge Inv**	NY,M	NR	1¢	19	1285	Invest in single-family mtgs
39	CSBA	**County Savings Bank**	OTC	NR	1	4	638	Savings bank, California
40	CRRC	**Courier Corp**	OTC	B+	1	19	645	Commercial printer
41	COU	**Courtaulds, plc ADR**	AS,B	NR	p25	4	708	Rayon yarn, British Isles
42	CUZZ	**Cousins Home Furnish'g**	OTC	NR	1¢	5	299	Sells furniture/appliances
43	COUS	**Cousins Properties**	OTC	NR	1	27	3038	Real estate develop: jt vent
44	COVT	**Covington Technol**[71]	OTC	NR	12½¢	3	100	Home builder, California
45	CPN	**CP National**	NY,B,M,P	A+	2½	53	2029	Electric, gas, tel utility
¶46•[1]	CPC	**CPC Int'l**	NY,B,C,M,P,Ph	A	25¢	419	47218	Grocery pr:corn wet milling

Index	Price Range 1971-86 High	1971-86 Low	1987 High	1987 Low	1988 High	1988 Low	Feb. Sales in 100s	February, 1988 Last Sale Or Bid High	Low	Last	%Div. Yield	P-E Ratio
1	16	2⅛	20⅝	8	14¾	11⅞	220	14¾	13½	14¾B	...	11
2	40¾	4⅛	11⅞	2⅞	4⅞	2¾	50251	3¾	2¾	3½B	...	d
3	....	....	3⅜	1½	2½	2	1180	2¼	2⅛	2¼B	...	5
4	9¾	6½	8¾	3⅜	5	3⅞	5500	5	4¼	5	...	..
5	14⅛	10½	14⅛	8⅝	11½	10½	3130	11½	10⅞	11⅜	9.5	..
6	2⅜	¼	¼	⅛	⅛	⅛	240	⅛	⅛	⅛B	...	d
7	14⅝	1⅝	5⅜	1⅛	1¾	1⅜	132	1¾	1⅜	1⅜	...	d
8	10½	7½	22	6⅜	9⅜	6¼	37459	8⅞	6¼	8⅝B	...	28
9	28¾	11⅞	20	5¾	12¼	8½	23412	12⅛	9¾	11⅞	3.4	4
10	112½	9⅜	20	6	14¾	7	2409	13½	11¾	12B	...	1
11	62	4½	74½	39	61	51⅜	22078	61	52⅞	58¼	3.1	17
12	6⅛	2⅛	2⅝	½	1¾	¾	19909	1⅝	1⅜	1½B	...	d
13	28¾	1¼	39¾	22¼	34⅞	28¼	2822	34⅞	30¼	33⅜	1.6	11
14	35½	9½	30	16¼	20⅛	16⅞	12136	20⅛	19¼	20B	2.5	15
15	....	....	10⅜	3⅜	5⅝	4⅛	372	5⅝	4⅝	5¼	...	6
16	20	16	22⅞	14⅝	19⅜	16¾	744	19⅜	18¼	18⅝	9.0	19
17	31¾	3⅞	12⅝	5⅜	9⅞	7⅞	578	9⅞	8¼	9⅝	...	11
18	29½	15⅞	25½	17¾	23¾	22¼	801	23¾	22¼	22⅝	11.0	..
19	16	2⅞	16⅞	3⅜	8⅛	6¼	10301	8⅛	6¼	7¾B	...	d
20	16½	4⅜	6½	2¾	4⅞	3¼	1544	4⅞	3½	4½B	...	30
21	30⅝	1 7/16	21¼	8⅝	17⅛	10⅝	40461	17⅛	12⅜	17B	...	d
22	18¾	1¼	17⅞	9	13½	10⅞	799	13½	11⅝	13¼	5.1	15
23	44⅛	4⅞	42¾	29⅛	40¾	33⅜	27367	40¾	37⅝	39⅝B	3.8	10
24	81½	12½	77	34¾	58⅜	44¾	23347	58⅜	51⅛	58	2.6	14
25	3⅝	¼	2⅝	¼	¾	¼	7008	¾	¼	⅝B	...	..
26	9½	7½	13¾	3	5¾	4	1140	4½	4	4B	...	d
27	43½	2⅞	37½	22	34¼	28	8124	34¼	28⅞	32¾	2.6	16
28	22⅝	½	1⅛	⅛	⅝	¼	6318	½	⅜	½B	...	d
29	35	2¾	5⅝	2⅜	2⅞	2⅜	358	2¾	2½	2⅝B	...	d
30	6½	2⅜	4¾	1⅛	2⅞	1⅜	794	2⅞	2¼	2¼	...	d
31	12¼	½	12¼	9	12	9¾	234	12	10¼	11¼B	...	15
32	19½	8½	15¼	5⅝	12⅜	8⅜	19087	12⅜	9½	12B	...	67
33	9¾	1¾	7¾	5	5¾	4¾	87	5¾	5⅛	5⅛B	4.7	9
34	10½	9¾	10⅛	3⅜	6	4¼	2247	6	5⅜	5¾	4.2	..
35	50¼	49⅛	50¾	44	46⅛	45⅜	452	46⅛	45⅜	46¼B	7.8	..
36	....	....	15¼	3⅜	6	3¾	5125	5	3¾	5B	...	8
37	14¼	1/16	17¼	4¾	9⅝	5⅝	15253	9⅝	7	9⅛	s2.2	8
38	19⅛	9½	19½	5¼	8	6⅜	4197	8	6⅝	6⅞	14.0	5
39	9	5¾	9⅛	4⅛	5¼	4¼	698	5¼	4¾	5¼B	...	4
40	20¾	1	27½	14½	16½	14¼	824	16½	14¼	15¾B	2.5	19
41	4¾	⅞	8½	4½	6¾	5½	48	6	5⅝	5½B	3.1	8
42	18	2	3⅞	1⅛	2⅞	1⅛	3965	2⅞	2⅜	2¾B	...	d
43	14½	⅛	17¼	10½	13	11½	2718	12½	11½	12B	5.0	14
44	8⅝	⅛	1⅞	½	¾	½	2303	⅝	½	⅝B	...	..
45	39½	6 5/16	34½	22⅜	29⅞	23⅞	2677	29⅞	27⅛	28½	5.9	12
46	42⅞	5⅞	58½	26	47⅝	39½	46952	47⅝	42	47⅝	3.0	11

Uniform Footnote Explanations—See Page 1. Other: [1]P:Cycle 1. [2]ASE:Cycle 2. [3]ASE:Cycle 1. [4]CBOE:Cycle 2. [51]Yr Dec'85. [52]L.P. Dep Units. [53]▲$2.17,'86. [54]®$2.85,'87. [55]Plan dstr of 0.2 shr Cooper Co Pfd. [56]®$3.46,'87. [57]Vote Apr 13,name chge to Cooper Life Sciences. [58]Cl'B', non-vtg. [59]5 Mo Dec'85. [60]Stk dstr of CSC Indus Inc. [61]Co may exch for $25 amt,9.92% Cv Deb'08. [62]Thru 8-31-88,scale to $25 in '93. [63]11 Mo Dec'83. [64]®$2.05,'87. [65]Fr 10-30-89,scale to $50 in'93. [66]®$1.10,'86. [67]Excl subsid pfd. [68]23 Wk Dec,'85. [69]□$0.25,'84. [70]Inc cap gains,'87. [71]Approve hldg co,Covington Development Gr. [72]®$2.20,'87.

continued

Source: *Standard & Poor's Stock Guide* (New York: Standard & Poor's Corp., 1988). Reprinted with permission.

FIGURE 5.3 continued

Common and Preferred Stocks

Con-CPC 65

Index	◆ Splits	Cash Divs. Ea.Yr. Since	Latest Payment Per$	Latest Payment Date	Ex. Div.	Total $ So Far 1988	Ind. Rate	Paid 1987	Cash& Equiv. Mil-$	Curr. Assets	Curr. Liab.	Balance Sheet Date	Lg Trm Debt Mil-$	Shs.000 Pfd.	Shs.000 Com.	Earnings Years End	1983	1984	1985	1986	1987	Last 12 Mos.	Interim Period	1986	1987	Index
1*			0.043	4-22-85	3-26	....	Nil	....	8.26	26.5	12.0	9-30-87	20.2		3066	Dc	0.32	0.66	0.62	0.74	P0.68	1.35	9 Mo Sep	0.43	1.04	1
2*			None	Since Public		....	Nil	....	4.56	200.1	73.8	9-30-87	20.0		4377	Dc	0.40	d0.38	0.32	0.73	0.45	d0.68	3 Mo Dec	0.05	0.04	2
3			None	Since 3-30-88		....	Nil	....	4.56	6.40	1.12	9-30-87	0.03		4368	Je	0.06	d0.31	d0.08	d0.06	0.44	d0.44				3
4			None	Since Public		....	Nil	....				2-26-88		13605	13605	Je			34.34	99.63	99.64					4
5		1985	0.27	1-13-88	12-23	0.27	1.08	1.28	Net Asset Val $9.48			2-5-88			13605	Dc			99.64	99.64	99.38					5
6			None	Since Public		....	Nil	....	Net Asset Val $9.50				0.81		13119	Dc	d0.13	d0.01	0.21	d0.24	P*0.31	d0.13	9 Mo Sep	d0.12	d0.01	6
7			0.10	5-23-86	5-5	....	Nil	....	0.12	1.55	2.86	9-30-87			5307	Dc			d2.50	d2.50	d2.75	d2.75	9 Mo Sep	d1.73	d0.10	7
8			None	Since Public		....	Nil	....	0.04	1.64	11.7	9-30-87	68.7		17048	Dc	d0.36	d0.56	d0.44	d0.15	*d0.31	d3.01				8
9*		1984	None	Since Public		....	Nil	0.10	82.0	121.	15.8	9-30-87	371.		20074	Oc	3.00	0.80	d1.60	d4.60	P*3.00	3.00				9
10*			Q0.10	1-15-88	12-28	0.10	0.40	0.40	5.3	137.	11.4	10-31-87	1.37		3239	Sp	3.00	0.80	.c6.80	.c6.80	.17.69	17.69				10
11		1947	Q0.45	4-1-88	12-21	0.87	1.80	1.66	7.85	1520	809.	9-30-87	70.5	19	49089	Dc	1.29	2.13	2.79	3.04	P*3.47	3.47	9 Mo Sep	0.22	0.21	11
12*		1950	None	Since Public		....	Nil	....	0.58	349.	38.4	9-30-87	7.03		21985	Dc		2.46	1.84	2.28	P*0.52	3.02					12
13			None	Since 3-31		.13	0.50	0.46	53.3	465.	48.4	9-30-87	3.1		3458	Dc	2.15	1.28	1.65	P1.32	3.02					13
14*		1970	Q0.12½	2-16-88	1-25	0.12½	0.50	0.50	131.	207.	20.7	10-4-87			36583	Dc	2.55	0.40	0.55	0.92	P1.32	1.32				14
15			None	Since Public		....	Nil	....	Equity per sh $5.08			9-30-87	177.		5600	Sp	0.33		0.55	0.92	0.92	0.91					15
16		1985	Q0.42	1-11-88	12-21	0.42	1.68	1.67½	Equity per sh $17.81	25.7	91.5	9-30-87	8.84	1000	4008	Dc	d2.64	b0.26	0.62	1.36	P0.87	0.96	9 Mo Sep	1.05	0.65	16
17			Nil		2-23	....	Nil	....	Cv into 1.1196 com $22.33		35.1	9-30-87	59.6	1000	8649	Dc	bd1.42	b0.80	d2.90	d1.01		0.87					17
18		1983	Q0.62	3-1-88	2-8	0.62	2.48	2.48	0.65	.070	0.69	7-31-87	1.33		10809	Dc	0.13	0.14	0.04	d0.04		0.15	9 Mo Jul	d0.12	d0.10	18
19*			None	Since Public		....	Nil	....	5.30	17.8	2.65	9-26-87			3467	Sp	0.61	0.83	d1.14	d0.12	P0.15	0.15				19
20*			None	Since Public		....	Nil	....								Dc										20
21*		1943	None Paid		3-1	.33	Nil	0.63	1.20	74.0	38.1	12-31-87	27.1		13370	Je	*0.35	1.44	0.60	d0.42	P0.64	d4.01	6 Mo Dec	d0.08	*0.13	21
22*			Q0.17	3-28-88	3-29	.75	1.50	1.36	0.48	99.8	32.4	11-30-87	20.8		9737	Au	0.74	1.08	c6.05	0.82	P4.22	0.82	3 Mo Nov	d0.20	0.25	22
23*		1844	Q0.37½	4-1-88	3-8	.74	1.48	1.40	89.8 Book Value $25.18		42.8	10-4-87	*627	2793	39000	Dc	*2.19	2.11	*2.53	▲*3.70	P*4.10	4.10				23
24*		1881	None Paid			....	Nil	....	5.08			9-30-87	436.		10277	Sp		0.41	*0.09.07	P0.07	P0.20	3.81					24
25*																										25
26		1948	None Since Public		1-29	....	Nil	....	1.32	4.07	7.50	9-30-87	4.22		8769	Nv	*d0.30	d0.46	d0.39	d0.35	P0.22	d0.22	6 Mo Nov	d0.17	*0.06	26
27			None Since Public			....	Nil	....	2.74	166.	5.71	9-30-87	29.8		18441	My	0.80	d0.31	1.57	2.25	P*2.11	d0.67	9 Mo Nov	d0.08	0.16	27
28			None Since Public			....	Nil	....	2.96	11.3	12.2	11-30-87	1.18		29660	My	0.45	pd0.48	pd0.64	d1.15	d0.67	0.44	9 Mo Oct	0.29	0.01	28
29			None Since Public			....	Nil	0.21	1.84	45.8	24.4	11-30-87	0.68		5060	Dc	0.55	0.48	d2.16	d0.01	d0.67	0.09					29
30			None Since Public			....	Nil	....	0.82	25.1	12.0	10-31-87	6.13		5289	Ja	0.14	0.25	0.10	88.50	d0.14	0.14					30
31		1974	None Paid			....	Nil	....	2.37	10.2	3.94	8-29-87	1.79		1702	Nv	0.54	0.67	0.94	d0.25	P*0.74	0.74	12 Wk Nov	d0.02	*0.02	31
32			Q0.06	3-31-88	3-11	.12	0.24	0.24	13.8	231.	203.	11-22-87	129.		24378	Au		d0.28	0.51	d0.15	*0.14	0.18					32
33		1985	Q0.06	3-31-88	3-11	.12	0.24	0.24	Equity per shr $8.43		18.5	10-31-87			2748	Au	0.50	1.34	d0.58	88.50	P*0.54	0.54					33
34			Q0.90½	1-29-88	12-24	.90½	3.62	3.66½	Equity per shr $4.85		244.	2-1-87		800	4452	Dc							Mand red 10-30-96 $50			34
35		1987	Q0.90½	1-29-88	12-24	.90½	3.62	3.66½	Net Asset Val $50.00																	35
36		1978	None Since Public		12-21	.05	Nil	.287	15.9	7.79	9-30-87	15.3		4400	Dc	0.17	*0.30	0.45	0.45		0.62	9 Mo Sep	0.31	0.48	36
37		1985	0.25	2-11-88	12-21	.06	0.06	.285	Equity per shr $9.49		13.0	9-30-87	391.7		15951	Dc	0.44	0.29	*0.45	2.27		1.29	9 Mo Nov	0.82	0.69	37
38*			0.24	4-10-87	4-2	.24	Nil	5%	Equity per shr $6.74			9-30-87	84.6	1024	7745	Dc		0.61	1.11	1.62	P1.29	1.35	9 Mo Sep	1.32	1.05	38
39*			5% Stk	3-3-88			Nil	5% Stk	Book Value $6.74			9-30-87	10.2		5915	Dc	0.82		1.17	1.82	1.99	1.99	3 Mo Sep	1.38	1.20	39
40*		1919	Q0.10	1-15-88	12-24	0.10	0.40	0.40	0.01	28.5	23.2	12-26-87			1802	Sp							3 Mo Dec			40
41*		1913	0.048	1-27-88	12-9	0.048		0.157	247.	1020	614.	3-31-87	187.	3500	379400	Mr	*0.31	d0.30	0.44	0.61	d1.61	0.70	6 Mo Dec	0.23	0.38	41
42					2-16				0.37	17.4	15.1	12-31-87	15.2		10965	Dc	0.23	d0.85	1.83	d0.62	d1.61	d1.08	6 Mo Dec	d0.61	0.08	42
43*		1980	Q0.15	3-7-88		0.30	0.60	0.37	Equity per shr $6.45			1-31-87	13.4		17165	Dc	0.41	1.79	0.59	.173	d1.61	0.87	6 Mo Dec	0.28	d0.02	43
44		1943	None Paid			....	Nil	....	Equity per shr $0.53			9-30-87	12.5	72	13902	Dc	2.03	0.37	d0.99	d2.09	P*2.31	2.31	6 Mo Dec	0.28	d0.41	44
45*		1920	Q0.36	3-18-88	12-28	0.36	1.44	1.24	232.	1337	1178	9-30-87	556.		81918	Dc	1.40	1.99	1.46	2.36	P4.34	4.34	9 Mo Sep	d0.09	d0.01	45
46																										46

◆ Stock Splits & Divs By Line Reference Index ¹5-for-4,'85.10%,'86.10%,'86,twice'87. ²5-for-4,'87. ³3-for-4,'83. ⁴4-for-1,'83. ⁵2-for-1,'85. ⁶*10%'83 ⁷*10%'83 ⁸·¹⁰¹1-for-10 REVERSE,'87 ¹¹Vote Apr 13 on 1-for-10 REVERSE,'87 ¹²2-for-1,'83.
¹²²5-for-4,'85.5-for-4,'87. ²⁰²Vote Apr 13. ²¹4-for-1,'83. ²³2-for-1,'83,'85. ²⁴2-for-1,'85. ²⁴²2-for-1,'86. ²⁴³2-for-1,'86. ³¹2-for-1,'86,'87. ³²*Adj for 5%,'87. ³⁹³Adj for 5% & divs,ex Mar 9. ⁴⁰³3-for-2,'86.
⁴⁵⁵5-for-4,'83,84.3-for-2,'86,'87. ⁴²2-for-1,'83 ⁴²2-for-1,'87. ⁴⁴3-for-1,'83. ⁴⁴²2-for-1,'85. ⁴⁵Adj for 10% stk div,ex Mar 9. ⁴⁵³3-for-2,'85,'86

NYSE, the AMEX, and regional exchanges. Notably, there is also a section on international industrial firms. Also, an industrial news report section covers events that occurred after publication of the basic manual.

Moody's OTC Industrial Manual is similar to the *Moody's Industrial Manual* of listed firms but is limited to stocks traded on the OTC market. Supplementary volumes contain information on recent developments.

Moody's Public Utility Manual provides information on public utilities, including electric and gas, gas transmission, telephone, and water companies. It also contains a news report section.

Moody's Transportation Manual covers the transportation industry, including railroads, airlines, steamship companies, electric railway, bus and truck lines, oil pipe lines, bridge companies, and automobile and truck leasing companies. A supplementary transportation news report is also published.

Moody's Bank and Finance Manual is published in two volumes and covers the field of financial services represented by banks, savings and loan associations, credit agencies of the U.S. government, all phases of the insurance industry, investment companies, real estate firms, real estate investment trusts, and miscellaneous financial enterprises.

Moody's Municipal and Government Manual is published in two volumes and contains data on the U.S. government, all the states, state agencies, and over 13,500 municipalities. There is also some excellent information and data on foreign governments and international organizations.

Moody's International Manual provides financial information on about 3,000 major foreign corporations.

The Value Line Investment Survey is published in two parts. Volume 1 contains basic historic information on about 1,700 companies as well as a number of analytical measures of earnings stability, growth rates, a common stock safety factor, and a timing factor rating. A number of studies have examined the usefulness of the ratings for investment purposes and the overall impact of the ratings on rates of return. The results of these studies have implications for the efficient markets hypothesis and will be discussed in the efficient markets chapter. It also includes extensive two-year *projections* for the given firms and three-year *estimates* of performance. As an example, in early 1990 it will include an earnings projection for 1990, 1991, and 1992–1994. The second volume includes a weekly service that provides general investment advice and also recommends individual stocks for purchase or sale. An example of a company report is shown in Figure 5.4.

The Value Line OTC Special Situations Service is published 24 times a year for the experienced investor who is willing to accept high risk in the hope of realizing exceptional capital gains. In each issue, past recommendations are discussed and eight to ten new stocks are presented for consideration.

Daily Stock Price Records, published quarterly by Standard & Poor's, has individual volumes for the NYSE, the AMEX, and the OTC market. Each quarterly book is divided into two parts. Part 1, "Major Technical

FIGURE 5.4
Sample Listing from Value Line

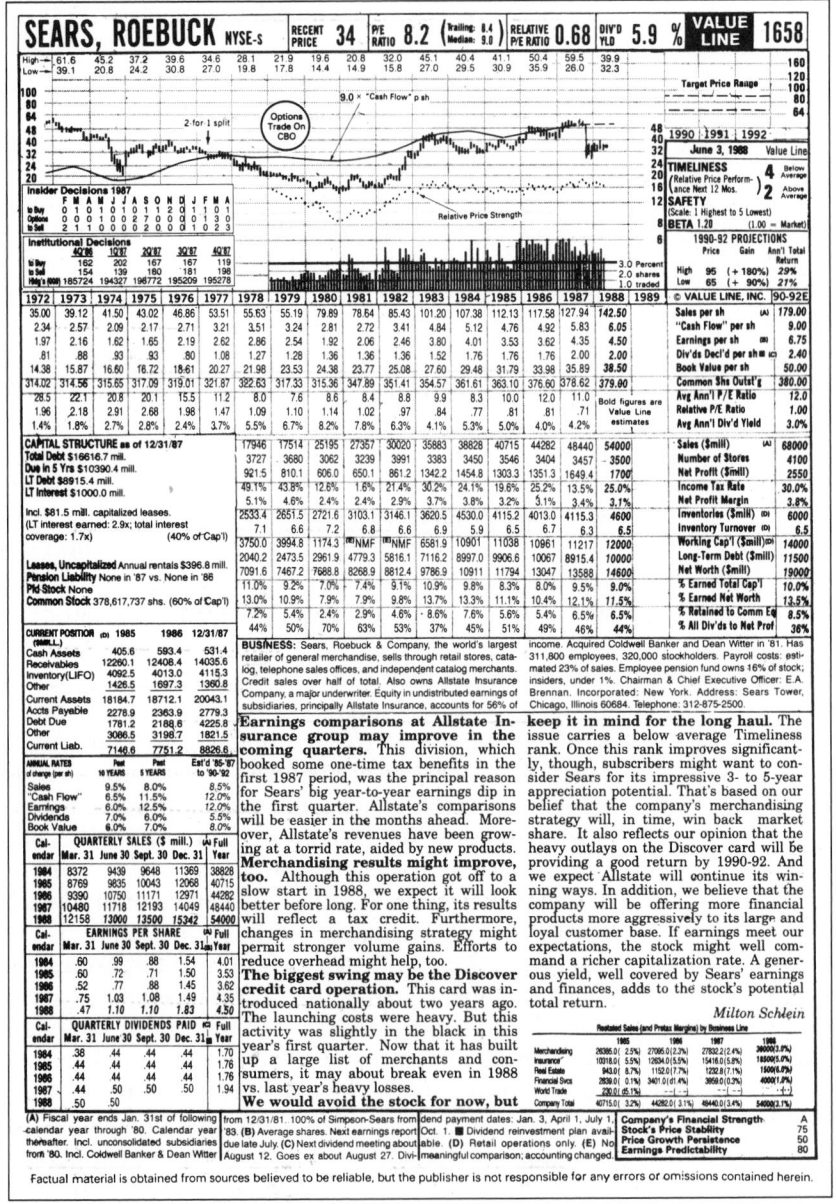

Source: Copyright © 1988 by Value Line, Inc.; Used by permission.

Indicators of the Stock Market," is devoted to market indicators widely followed as technical guides to the stock market and includes price indicator series, volume series, and data on odd lots and short sales. Part 2, "Daily and Weekly Stock Action," gives daily high, low, close, and volume information and data on short interest for the stock, insider trading information, a 200-day moving average of prices, and a weekly relative strength series. The books for the NYSE and AMEX are available from 1962 on; the OTC books begin in 1968.

Many brokerage firms prepare reports on individual firms. In some cases, these are rather objective and contain only basic information, but others contain specific recommendations.

INVESTMENT MAGAZINES

Forbes is published twice monthly and contains 12 to 14 articles on individual companies and industries. Several regular columnists discuss the economy, the aggregate money and stock markets, and the commodity markets.

Financial World is likewise published twice a month and generally contains about six articles on companies, industries, and the overall market and a large number of regular features on taxes and options. It also has a section containing market data.

The Wall Street Transcript is published weekly as a composite of sources of information other than market quotations. It contains texts of speeches made at analysts' meetings, copies of brokerage house reports on companies and industries, and interviews with corporate officials. It also includes discussions of forthcoming new stock issues.

The Media General Financial Weekly is published every Monday and contains a series of feature articles and columns. Of primary interest is a comprehensive set of financial and statistical information on 3,400 common stocks, including every common stock listed on the NYSE and the AMEX and over 700 OTC issues. There are also charts on 60 major industry groups.

OTC Review is a monthly publication devoted to the analysis and discussion of stocks traded on the OTC market. It usually contains an analysis of an industry that is dominated by OTC companies and a discussion of three or four individual firms. In addition, there are extended earnings reports on OTC firms, name changes, stock exchange listings, and statistics on OTC trading (price and volume).

Fortune, published bi-weekly by Time Inc., contains extensive articles on the economy, politics, individual companies, securities markets, and personal investing. The magazine is well-known for its special annual report on the *Fortune 500* and also the *Fortune 1000* largest industrial firms in the country. Several financial items concerning these firms are discussed. There is also a listing of large nonindustrial firms and, finally, a listing of major foreign companies.

Money, published monthly by Time Inc., deals specifically with topics of interest to individual investors, including articles on individual companies and general investment suggestions (e.g., "How to Determine Your

Net Worth"; "The Why and How of Investing in Foreign Securities"). Also, each issue presents an actual financial planning discussion with an individual or couple.

Pension and Investment Age is a newspaper of corporate and institutional investing, published every other Monday. It is intended for those who are involved in pension investing, either as a corporate manager or as a money manager of pension funds assets. The emphasis is on stories and interviews related to pension fund management. There is substantial consideration of personnel changes.

Institutional Investor is published monthly by Institutional Investors Systems and written by a professional staff. It is aimed at professional investors and portfolio managers with emphasis on what is happening to the investment industry.

Financial Planning, a monthly publication billed as "The Magazine for Financial Service Professionals," is specifically intended for individuals involved in financial planning and published by the Financial Services Information Company (Two Concourse Parkway, Atlanta, GA 30328). It contains a number of feature articles on alternative investment products and procedures, important regulatory information affecting financial planning (e.g., tax legislation), industry discussions, and specific investments (e.g., mutual funds, real estate, equipment leasing).

Global Finance is a monthly magazine published by Global Information, Inc. (55 John Street, New York, NY 10038). It contains a number of general articles on trends around the world. It is probably best described as an international version of *Institutional Investor* since it is written for the practicing money manager or investment professional. It also contains regular columns on topics like venture capital, hedging, and investment strategies.

Global Investor is published monthly except July/August and December/January by Euromoney Publications PLC (Nestor House, Playhouse Yard, London ECUV 5EX). Similar to *Global Finance,* it contains articles on various markets, international instruments, and specific money management firms. There are also regular columns on the overall bond and stock markets and an extensive section on international bond and stock indicator series—for example, FT-Actuaries World Index and Morgan Stanley Capital International Stock Market Indexes. The address for North American subscriptions is Reed Business Publishing, 205 East 42nd Street, New York, NY 10017.

ACADEMIC JOURNALS

The material in academic journals differs from that in investment magazines in timeliness and general orientation. Investment magazines are concerned with the *current* investment environment and with providing advice for current action. The material is generally nonquantitative. In contrast, the articles in academic journals are longer, more theoretical and quantitative in approach, and typically not intended to be immediately applicable. They deal with long-run implications for investments.

Journal of Finance is a quarterly published by the American Finance Association. The articles are almost all by academicians and are rather theoretical and empirical. The typical issue includes 15 articles, notes and comments, and book reviews.

Journal of Financial and Quantitative Analysis is a quarterly published by the University of Washington. It is very similar to the *Journal of Finance* in that almost all articles are by academicians. It differs in that it contains fewer articles in the area of monetary economics.

Journal of Financial Economics is published quarterly by North Holland Publishing Company in collaboration with the Simon Graduate School of Management of the University of Rochester. The intent of the quarterly is to publish academic research in the areas of consumption and investment decisions under uncertainty, portfolio analysis, efficient markets, and the normative theory of financial management.

Financial Analysts Journal is published six times a year by the Financial Analysts Federation. An issue contains six or seven articles of interest to practicing financial analysts and/or portfolio managers, a regular feature on securities regulation, and book reviews. The articles are authored by a combination of academicians and practitioners.

Journal of Portfolio Management, published quarterly by Institutional Investors Systems, is intended to be a forum for academic research of interest to the practicing portfolio manager. Over half the articles are written by academicians but are written to be read by the practitioner. In many instances it will contain less technical and mathematical versions of studies previously published in heavily academic journals.

Financial Management, published quarterly by the Financial Management Association, is intended for executives and academicians interested in the financial management of a firm. It also contains investment-related articles on such topics as stock splits, dividend policy, mergers, initial public offerings, and stock listings when it is shown that such events are important to the financing decisions of a firm.

The Financial Review is a quarterly journal jointly sponsored by the Eastern Finance Association and the Midwest Finance Association. It is a general finance journal directed at the academic community. About half of its articles are concerned with capital markets, investments, and portfolio management.

Journal of Financial Research is a joint quarterly publication of the Southern Finance Association and the Southwestern Finance Association. It contains articles on financial management, investments, financial institutions, capital market theory, and portfolio theory.

The C.F.A. Digest is published quarterly by the Institute of Chartered Financial Analysts. Its purpose is to provide, as a service to members of the investment community, abstracts of published articles from a wide variety of academic and nonacademic journals of interest to financial analysts and portfolio managers.

There are a number of general business and economics journals that include articles on finance and some specifically on investments. One of the foremost is the *Journal of Business,* published by the University of Chicago, which has contained some outstanding articles in the area of investments. Other journals to consider include *Quarterly Review of Economics and Business* (University of Illinois), *Review of Business and Economic Research* (University of New Orleans), *Journal of Business Research* (North Holland Publishing Co.), *American Economic Review* (American Economic Association), *Journal of Political Economy* (University of Chicago), *Rand Journal of Economics* (American Telephone and Telegraph), and *Journal of Applied Corporate Finance* (The Continental Bank).

COMPUTERIZED DATA SOURCES

In addition to the numerous published sources of data, some of the financial service firms have developed computerized data sources. Again, owing to space limitations, only the major sources will be discussed.

Compustat is a computerized data bank of financial data developed by Standard & Poor's and currently handled by a subsidiary, Investors Management Services (P.O. Box 239, Denver, CO 80201). The Compustat tapes contain 20 years of data for approximately 2,220 listed industrial companies, 1,000 OTC companies, 175 utilities, 120 banks, and 500 Canadian firms. There are also quarterly tapes that contain 20 years of quarterly financial data for over 2,000 industrial firms and 12 years of quarterly data for banks and utilities. The specific financial data on the annual tapes includes almost every possible item from a firm's balance sheet and income statement as well as stock market data (stock prices and trading volume).

Value Line Data Base contains historical annual and quarterly financial and market data for 1,600 industrial and finance companies. The annual data begins in 1954, and quarterly data starts in 1963. In addition to historical data, there is an estimate of dividend and earnings for the coming year and the services' opinion regarding stability and timing.

Compact Disclosure is a data base contained on a compact disk that includes corporate information on over 4,000 public companies filing with the SEC. It is provided by Disclosure Information Group, 5161 River Road, Bethesda, MD 20816.

The Center for Research in Security Prices (CRSP) at the University of Chicago (Graduate School of Business, Chicago, IL 60637) has developed the *University of Chicago Stock Price Tapes*, a set of monthly stock price tapes and daily stock prices. The monthly tapes contain month-end prices from January 1926 to the present (updated annually) for every stock listed on the NYSE. Stock prices are adjusted for all stock splits, dividends, and any other capital changes. There is also a daily stock price tape that contains the daily high, low, and close since July 1962 for every stock listed on the NYSE. CRSP has recently been developing similar tapes for stocks on the AMEX and the OTC.

Media General Data Bank is provided by Media General Financial Services, Inc. (P.O. Box 26991, Richmond, VA 23261). The data bank includes current price and volume data plus major corporate financial data on 2,000 major companies. In addition, ten years of daily price and volume information is provided on over 8,000 issues of approximately 4,000 firms on the NYSE, AMEX, and the OTC. Finally, there are price and volume data on several major market indicator series.

ISL Daily Stock Price Tapes are prepared by Interactive Data Corporation (122 E. 42nd St., New York, NY 10017) and are issued quarterly. They contain the same information contained in the *Daily Stock Price Records,* published by Standard & Poor's and discussed earlier in this chapter.

SUMMARY

Investors must be aware of the major sources of information on the U.S. and world economy, the aggregate securities markets around the globe, alternative industries, and individual firms. You should use the information in this chapter as a *starting* point and attempt to spend time in a university library examining these and the many other sources available. Four books that would help in this regard are

Paul Wasserman, ed. *Encyclopedia of Business Information Sources.* 3d ed. Detroit: Gale Research Co., 1976.

P. M. Daniells. *Business Information Sources.* 2d ed. Berkeley, Calif.: University of California Press, 1986.

Michanie Sylvia. *Course Syllabus for Information Sources of Business and Economics.* Brooklyn, NY: Pratt Institute School of Library and Information Science, 1977.

Fortune Investment Information Directory. Guilford, Conn.: The Dushkin Publishing Group, Inc. 1986. This booklet contains a listing and brief description of numerous newspapers, magazines, investment letters, and books. There is also an excellent listing of software and databases of interest to investors in stocks, bonds, futures, and options.

QUESTIONS

1. Name at least three sources of information on the gross national product for the past ten years.

2. Name two sources of information on rates of exchange with major foreign countries.

3. Assume you are interested in the steel and auto industries and want to compare production for these two industries to industrial production for the economy. Discuss how you would you do it, what data you would use, and where you would get the data.

4. You are told that there is a relationship between the growth rate of the money supply and stock price movements. Where would you obtain the data to verify this relationship?

5. You are an analyst for Hot Stock Investment Company, and the head of research tells you he just got a tip on an OTC firm, the Baron Corporation. He wants data on the company's sales, earnings, and recent stock price movements. Discuss several sources for this information (one source is insufficient because the company may not be big enough to be included in some of them).

6. The head of your research department indicates that the investment committee has decided to become involved in global investing. To get started, they want you to recommend two sources of macroeconomic data for

various countries: two sources of industry information and two sources of company data. Discuss your recommendations.

7. As an individual investor, discuss four publications you believe you should subscribe to (besides *The Wall Street Journal*). In your discussion indicate what is contained in each publication and why it is appropriate for you as an individual investor. Be sure that at least two of these relate to the international securities market.

8. As the director of a newly established investment research department, discuss the first four investment services that you will subscribe to, and justify each selection.

9. Select one company from the NYSE, the AMEX, and the OTC, and look up the name and address of the financial officer you would contact to obtain recent financial reports.

SOURCES OF INVESTMENT INFORMATION

- American Banker-Bond Buyer, A division of International Thomson Publishing Corporation, One State Street Plaza, New York, NY 10004.
- American Stock Exchange, 86 Trinity Place, New York, NY 10006.
- *Business Statistics,* obtained from Superintendent of Documents, U.S. Government Printing Office, Washington, DC 20402. Approximate price, $9.
- *The Wall Street Journal* and *Barron's,* available from Dow-Jones & Co., 200 Burnett Rd., Chicopee, MA 01021.
- *Dow-Jones Handbook* (published annually), available from Dow-Jones Books, P.O. Box 455, Chicopee, MA 01021. Approximate price, $7.
- *Economic Indicators,* available from Superintendent of Documents, U.S. Government Printing Office, Washington, DC 20402. Approximate price, $15/year.
- *Economic Report of the President,* available from Superintendent of Documents, U.S. Government Printing Office, Washington, DC 20402. Approximate price, $10.
- *Federal Reserve Bulletin,* available from the Division of Administrative Services, Board of Governors of the Federal Reserve System, Washington, DC 20551. Approximate cost, $20/year.
- *Financial Times,* available from Bracken House, Cannon Street, London EC4P 4BY England. There is a U.S. office: 44 East 60th Street, New York, NY 10022.
- *Institutional Investor, Inc.,* available from 488 Madison Avenue, New York, NY 10022.
- London Stock Exchange, Trogmorton Street, London EG2N 1HP, England.
- Moody's Investor's Services, Inc., 99 Church Street, New York, NY 10007.
- National Association of Securities Dealers, Inc., 1735 K Street, N.W., Washington, DC 20006.
- New York Stock Exchange, 11 Wall Street, New York, NY 10005.

- *Quarterly Financial Report,* available from Superintendent of Documents, U.S. Government Printing Office, Washington, DC 20402. Approximate price, $15/year.
- Standard & Poor's Corporation, 345 Hudson Street, New York, NY 10014.
- *Statistical Abstract of the United States,* available from the Superintendent of Documents, U.S. Government Printing Office, Washington, DC 20402. Approximate price, $14 (cloth), $4 (paper).
- *Statistical Bulletin,* available from the Superintendent of Documents, U.S. Government Printing Office, Washington, DC 20402. Approximate price, $20/year.
- *Survey of Current Business,* available from Superintendent of Documents, U.S. Government Printing Office, Washington, DC 20402. Approximate price, $25/year.
- Tokyo Stock Exchange. The Exchange has an office in New York: TSE, New York Research Office, 100 Wall Street, New York, NY 10005.
- *Value Line Services,* available from Arnold Bernhard and Company, Inc., 5 East 44th Street, New York, NY 10017.

PART II — MODERN DEVELOPMENTS IN INVESTMENT THEORY

CHAPTERS

As with any analytical study, the analysis of investments requires that a theoretical framework first be established. Part II therefore covers several major theories of the last 30 years.

In the late 1950s the *random walk hypothesis* was developed, postulating that stock price changes over time were similar to a random series. This early work eventually became part of a much larger theory known as the *efficient market hypothesis* (EMH) that considered how these stock price changes related to different sets of information. Studies related to EMH are important because of what they can tell us about our financial markets. Therefore, in Chapter 6 we will examine the hypothesis along with numerous studies supporting it, as well as some not supporting it—that is, anomalies. We will also consider the implications of these findings for various segments of the investment industry. These implications tend to be misunderstood, so you should read the section carefully and keep an open mind.

Another major development in investment theory, developed by Harry Markowitz in 1954, is a *basic portfolio model* based on the idea of diversifying to reduce the overall risk of the portfolio. Markowitz also derived a risk measure for individual securities. This basic portfolio model is presented in detail in Chapter 7.

In 1964 William Sharpe and several other authors extended the basic portfolio model into a *general equilibrium model* that included an alternative risk measure for all risky assets. Chapter 8 contains a fairly detailed discussion of these developments and an explanation of the relevant risk measure implied by this asset valuation model, generally referred to as the *capital asset pricing model* (CAPM). We have introduced the CAPM at this early stage because the risk measure implied is used in the subsequent analysis chapters.

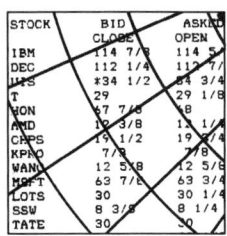

CHAPTER 6

EFFICIENT CAPITAL MARKETS

Several very important implications for security valuation and portfolio management are derived from the theories of efficient capital markets. Some of these implications are not very pleasant to accept, so it is crucial for you to become aware of them early and avoid "future shock." Also, this knowledge is useful in the subsequent chapters on analysis.

There are four major sections in this chapter. First is a discussion of why capital markets should be efficient. Next, we consider the alternative *efficient market hypotheses* (EMH) and the tests of these hypotheses. The results for a number of the studies on this topic are presented and discussed in the third section. The final section deals with the implications of the results for technicians, fundamental security analysts, and portfolio managers.

RATIONALE OF THE EFFICIENT CAPITAL MARKETS THEORY

An initial, and very important, premise of an efficient market is that a large number of profit-maximizing participants are concerned with the analysis and valuation of securities, and that these participants operate independently of each other. A second assumption is that new information regarding securities comes to the market in a random fashion, and the announcements over time are generally independent from one another. A third assumption, especially crucial, is that *investors adjust security prices rapidly to reflect the effect of new information*. While the price adjustment made is not always perfect, it is unbiased. (That is, sometimes there is an overadjustment or an underadjustment, but one cannot predict which it will be.) The attempt to adjust the security price takes place rapidly because of the large number of profit-maximizing investors. The combined effect of (1) information coming in a random, independent fashion, and (2) numerous investors who adjust stock prices rapidly to reflect this new information is that *price changes are independent and random.* A crucial point is that the adjustment process requires a large number of investors who follow the movements of the security, analyze the impact of new information on it, and buy or sell the security in a way that causes the price to adjust to reflect the new information. This implies that efficient markets require some minimum amount of trading and that *more trading by more investors should cause faster price adjustment*—that is, more efficiency. We will return to this concept when we discuss some anomalies regarding the EMH.

Finally, because security prices adjust to all new information and, therefore, supposedly reflect all public information at any point in time, the security prices that prevail at any point in time should be an unbiased reflection of all currently available information—including the risk involved. Therefore, *the expected returns implicit in the current price reflect the risk involved.*

ALTERNATIVE EFFICIENT MARKET HYPOTHESES

Most of the early work on efficient market theory was done under the random walk hypothesis and contained extensive empirical analysis without much theory behind it. The first real synthesis of the theory and an analysis of the empirical evidence was made by Eugene Fama in a 1970 *Journal of Finance* article,[1] which was the initial presentation of the efficient market theory in terms of the so-called *fair game model.*

EXPECTED RETURN OR FAIR GAME MODEL[2]

Unlike work done under the random walk hypothesis, which dealt with price movement over time, the fair game model deals with price at a specified period. It assumes that the price of a security fully reflects all available information at that point in time. The model requires that the price-formation process be specified in enough detail so that it is possible to indicate what is meant by "fully reflect." Most of the available models of equilibrium prices formulate prices in terms of rates of return that are dependent on alternative definitions of risk. All such expected return theories of price formation can be described notationally as follows:

$$E(\tilde{P}_{j,t+1} \mid \phi_t) = [1 + E(\tilde{r}_{j,t+1} \mid \phi_t)]P_{j,t}, \qquad 6.1$$

where

E = expected value operator

$p_{j,t}$ = price of security j at time t

$p_{j,t+1}$ = price of security j at time $t + 1$

$r_{j,t+1}$ = the one period percent rate of return for security j during period $t + 1$

[1] Eugene F. Fama, "Efficient Capital Markets: A Review of Theory and Empirical Work," *Journal of Finance* 25, no. 2 (May 1970): 383–417.

[2] This section is drawn heavily from Fama, ibid.

ϕ_t = the set of information that is assumed to be "fully reflected" in the security price at time t.

Equation 6.1 indicates that the expected price of security j, given the full set of information available at time t (ϕ_t), is equal to the current price times 1 plus the expected return on security j, given the set of available information. This expected future return should reflect the set of information available at t, which includes the state of the world at time t, including all current and past values of any relevant variables such as earnings, the GNP, and so forth. In addition, it is assumed that this information set includes knowledge of all the relevant relationships among variables—that is, how alternative economic series relate to each other and how they relate to security prices.

If equilibrium market prices can be stated in terms of expected returns that "fully reflect" the information set ϕ_t, this implies that it is not possible to derive trading systems or investment strategies based on this current information set and experience returns beyond what should be expected on the basis of risk. Thus, let us define $x_{j,t+1}$ as the difference between the actual price in $t + 1$ and the expected price in $t + 1$:

$$x_{j,t+1} = p_{j,t+1} - E(p_{j,t+1}|\phi_t).\qquad 6.2$$

Equation 6.2 can be described as a definition of *excess market value* for security j, because it is the difference between the actual price and the expected price projected at t on the basis of the information set ϕ_t. In an efficient market,

in efficient market, expected diff = 0

$$E(\tilde{x}_{j,t+1}|\phi_t) = 0.\qquad 6.3$$

This equation indicates that the market reflects a "fair game" with respect to the information set ϕ, meaning that investors can be confident that current prices fully reflect all available information and are consistent with the risk involved.

Fama divided the overall efficient market hypothesis (EMH) and the empirical tests into three categories depending upon the information set involved: (1) weak-form EMH, (2) semistrong-form EMH, and (3) strong-form EMH.

WEAK-FORM EFFICIENT MARKET HYPOTHESIS

The weak-form EMH assumes that current stock prices fully reflect all *stock-market* information, including the historical sequence of prices, price changes, trading volume, and any other market information such as odd lot transactions. It consequently implies that there should be no relationship between past price changes and future price changes—that price changes are independent. Therefore, any *trading rule* (the conditions under which an investor will buy or sell stock) that depends upon past price changes or any past market data to predict future price changes should be of little value.

SEMISTRONG-FORM EFFICIENT MARKET HYPOTHESIS

The semistrong-form EMH asserts that *security prices adjust rapidly to the release of all new public information;* therefore, stock prices fully reflect all public information. The semistrong hypothesis encompasses the weak-form hypothesis, because all market information is public (stock prices, trading volume, etc.). Public information also includes all nonmarket information, such as earnings, stock splits, economic news, and political news. Thus, investors who act on important new information after it is public should not be able to derive above-average profits from the transaction, considering the cost of trading, because the security price already reflects the effect of the new public information.

STRONG-FORM EFFICIENT MARKET HYPOTHESIS

The strong-form EMH contends that stock prices fully reflect *all* information (public and otherwise); hence, no group of investors has a monopolistic access to information relevant to the formation of prices. Therefore, no group of investors should be able to consistently derive above-average profits. The strong-form hypothesis encompasses both the weak and semistrong forms. Further, it requires the assumption not only of efficient markets (where prices adjust rapidly to the release of new public information), but also of *perfect markets,* in which all information is available to everyone at the same time.

TESTS AND RESULTS OF EFFICIENT MARKET HYPOTHESES

There have been two groups of tests for the weak-form efficient market hypothesis. The first involves statistical tests of independence between stock price changes. The second entails specific testing of trading rules that attempt to generate investment decisions on the basis of past market information as opposed to a simple buy-and-hold policy (i.e., simply buying stock at the beginning of a test period and holding it to the end).

TESTS OF WEAK-FORM HYPOTHESIS

STATISTICAL TESTS OF INDEPENDENCE. As discussed earlier, in an efficient capital market, stock price changes should be independent and random, because new information comes to the market in a random, independent fashion, and stock prices adjust rapidly to this new information. Two major statistical tests have been employed to verify this. First, autocorrelation tests check for independence. That is, is there significant positive or negative correlation in price changes over time? Does the percentage price change on day t correlate with the percentage price change on day $t - 1$, $t - 2$, or $t - 3$?[3] Those who support the theory of efficient capital markets would expect insignificant correlations for all such combinations.

Analysis of the serial correlations between stock price changes has been done by various authors for several different intervals, including one day, four days, nine days, and sixteen days.[4] The results have consistently

---

[3] For a discussion of tests of independence, see S. Christian Albright, *Statistics for Business and Economics* (New York: Macmillan Publishing Co., 1987): 515–517.

[4] Sidney S. Alexander, "Price Movements in Speculative Markets: Trends or Random Walks," *Industrial Management Review* 2, no. 2 (May 1961): 7–26; Eugene F. Fama, "The Behavior of Stock Market Prices," *Journal of Business* 38, no. 1 (January 1965): 34–105; and Eugene Fama and James MacBeth, "Risk, Return and Equilibrium: Empirical Tests," *Journal of Political Economy* 81, no. 3 (May–June 1973): 607–636.

revealed insignificant correlation in stock price changes over time. The typical range of correlation coefficients is from $+0.10$ to -0.10, but the degrees of correlations are typically not statistically significant. Individual stocks have a slight negative correlation in stock price changes, whereas price changes for aggregate market indicator series have a slight positive correlation. However, Lawrence Fisher has shown that this difference in correlation is probably caused by the fact that the numerous stocks in the market indicator series close at different points in time during a day. Therefore, stocks that close early have some lag in price adjustment to late news that is picked up the following day. In any case, the empirical evidence from serial correlation tests has consistently indicated that stock price changes over time are in general statistically independent. Consequently, past price changes are not sufficient to project future price changes.

The second statistical test of independence involves *runs,* which occur when there is no difference between two changes; two or three consecutive positive or consecutive negative price changes is one run. When the price change is to a different sign (e.g., a negative price change followed by a positive price change), the run is ended, and a new run begins.[5] If there are too many or too few runs for a given series, it is probably not a random series, because there is too much correlation in the signs.

Tests of stock price runs have confirmed the independence of stock price changes over time in that the actual number of runs consistently falls into the range expected for a random series. Both statistical tests mentioned here have likewise supported the EMH when repeated on the OTC market.[6]

While daily, weekly, and monthly data consistently support the weak-form EMH, individual transaction price changes do not. A study by Niederhoffer and Osborn that examined price changes for individual transactions on the NYSE found significant serial correlation,[7] as did a study by Ken Carey.[8] However, the authors did not attempt to show that the dependence in price movements could be used to derive above-average risk-adjusted returns. It is unlikely that you could use this small correlation due to the market-making activities of the specialist to derive excess profits, considering the high transaction costs required by this trading strategy.

TESTS OF TRADING RULES. The second group of tests of the weak-form hypothesis was prompted by the assertion that the prior statistical tests were too rigid to pinpoint the very intricate price patterns examined by technical analysts.[9] Therefore, investigators attempted to examine specific technical trading rules through simulation. Advocates of an efficient market

---

[5] For the details of a runs test, see Albright, *Statistics for Business and Economics,* pp. 695–699.

[6] Robert L. Hagerman and Richard D. Richmond, "Random Walks, Martingales and the OTC," *Journal of Finance* 28, no. 4 (September 1973): 897–909.

[7] Victor Neiderhoffer and M. F. Osborn, "Market-Making and Reversal on the Stock Exchange," *Journal of American Statistical Association* 61, no. 316 (December 1966): 897–916.

[8] Kenneth Carey, "A Model of Individual Transactions Stock Prices," (Ph.D. dissertation, University of Kansas, 1971).

[9] Many of these trading techniques are discussed in Chapter 16.

hypothesized that investors using any technical trading rule could not derive rates of return greater than returns from a buy-and-hold policy if the trading rule depended solely on past market information (i.e., price data, volume data).

The trading rule studies compared the investment results derived from such a simulation, including commission costs, to the results from a simple buy-and-hold policy. Three major pitfalls awaited the investigators: (1) they had to use only data that were publicly available in the decision rule (e.g., the earnings for a firm as of December 31 may not be publicly available until April 1); (2) they had to include all transaction costs involved in implementing the trading strategy, because most trading rules involve many more transactions than a simple buy-and-hold policy does; and (3) they had to make sure that the final results are risk-adjusted, because the trading rule might simply select high-risk securities that should experience higher returns.

Two operational problems have been encountered in these tests. First, most trading rules require substantial subjective interpretation, so it is not possible to test some technical rules. Second, because there is an almost infinite number of potential trading rules, it is not possible to test all of them. As a result, only the better known rules have been examined.

Also, the tests that have been conducted may be somewhat biased. Specifically, studies have concentrated on the simpler trading rules that many technicians contend are rather naive. In addition, these studies typically employ readily available data from the NYSE that are biased toward well-known, heavily traded stocks that certainly should enjoy efficient markets. Recall that markets are more likely to be efficient if there are a large number of aggressive, profit-maximizing investors who attempt to adjust stock prices to reflect new information. This implies that efficiency is dependent on trading in that the more trading there is in a security, the more efficient the market should be. Alternatively, limited trading activity may not be sufficient to move the security to the new equilibrium price that reflects the new information.

The most popular trading technique has been to use *filter rules,* in which a stock is traded when its price change exceeds the filter set for it. As an example, assuming a 5 percent filter, when the stock price has risen 5 percent from some base, the technical analyst contends that this movement indicates a *breakout,* meaning that stock prices will continue to rise (so technical traders would acquire the stock to take advantage of the continued rise). A 5 percent decline from some peak price would identify a breakout on the downside, meaning the prices will continue to decline (so traders would sell the stock acquired previously and possibly even sell it short).

Studies of this trading rule have used a range of filters from 1/2 percent to 50 percent. The results have indicated that by using small filters and not taking account of trading commission, one can derive above-average profits. Such results are consistent with the small correlation in price changes discussed earlier. Notably, the use of small filters results in numerous trades and substantial commissions, and when these trading commissions are considered, all the apparent trading profits turned to losses. These conclusions were true for the Alexander studies and also for the Fama and Blume studies.[10]

Trading techniques have been simulated that used odd lot figures, advanced-decline ratios, and short sales or short positions. In a few cases there were slight profits, but generally these simulations failed to outperform a buy-and-hold policy after taking account of commissions. Pinches reviewed a number of these studies and concluded that, beyond a few exceptions, the studies of mechanical trading rules do not indicate that profits can be generated by these rules.[11]

In summary, it appears that the great bulk of the evidence generated by simulating mechanical trading rules supports the weak form of the EMH.

TESTS OF SEMISTRONG-FORM HYPOTHESIS

Recall that the semistrong EMH asserts that security prices adjust rapidly to the release of all new public information; that is, stock prices fully reflect all public information. Studies of the semistrong EMH have involved one or both of the following:

1. Examination of price movements around the time of an important announcement to see when the expected price adjustment took place: Did security prices adjust before, during, or after the announcement was made? The EMH would imply that prices adjust either before the announcement, because of news leaks or some such phenomenon, or during the period of announcement.

2. Examination of the potential for above-average risk-adjusted rates of return assuming an investor acquired some set of securities after an announcement was made public. The question is, would such an investor have enjoyed above-average risk-adjusted profits compared to those from a buy-and-hold policy after transaction costs?

ADJUSTMENT FOR MARKET EFFECTS. Irrespective of the test, it is necessary to adjust the individual stock price movements (or the security returns) for aggregate price movements (or market returns) during the period considered. The point is, a 5 percent price change in a stock during the period surrounding an announcement is not meaningful until you know what the aggregate stock market did during the same period and how this stock normally acts under such conditions; e.g., if the market experienced

---

[10] Sidney S. Alexander, "Price Movements in Speculative Markets: Trends or Random Walks, Number 2," *Industrial Management Review* 5 (Spring 1964): 25–46; and Eugene F. Fama and Marshall Blume, "Filter Rules and Stock Market Trading Profits," *Journal of Business* 39, no. 1 (January 1966 Supplement): 226–241.

[11] George Pinches, "The Random Walk Hypothesis and Technical Analysis," *Financial Analysts Journal* 26, no. 2 (March–April 1970): 104–110. Two recent studies provide support for some technical trading rules that use a three-part filter or adjust relative strength for the January effect. In this regard, see John S. Brush, "Eight Relative Strength Models Compared," *Journal of Portfolio Management* 13, no. 1 (Fall 1986): 21–28; and Stephen W. Pruitt and Richard E. White, "Who Says Technical Analysts Can't Beat the Market?" *Journal of Portfolio Management* 14, no. 3 (Spring 1988): 55–58.

a 10 percent change, the 5 percent change may be lower than expected. Authors recognized the need for such adjustments and typically assumed (pre-1970) that the individual stocks should experience returns equal to those of the aggregate market. Therefore, the adjustment process entailed subtracting the market return from the actual return to derive so-called *abnormal* returns as follows:

$$AR_{it} = R_{it} - R_{mt}, \qquad\qquad 6.4$$

where

> AR_{it} = the abnormal rate of return on security *i* during period *t*
>
> R_{it} = the rate of return on security *i* during period *t*
>
> R_{mt} = the rate of return on a market index during period *t*.

Using the previous example in which the stock experienced a 5 percent price increase and the market increased 10 percent, the abnormal price change would be minus 5 percent.

FAMA, FISHER, JENSEN, AND ROLL STUDY. An alternative adjustment technique was suggested by Fama, Fisher, Jensen, and Roll (FFJR) in a study that examined the impact of stock splits.[12] Based upon work in capital market theory, the study contended that the market adjustment procedure should recognize that individual securities have a unique relationship with the market. A given stock will tend to rise or decline more or less than the market.[13] This unique relationship can be derived by computing a regression of stock returns and market returns for a period prior to and subsequent to a significant economic event as follows:

$$R_{it} = a_i + \beta_i R_{mt} + e, \qquad\qquad 6.5$$

where

> R_{it} = the rate of return on security *i* during period *t*
>
> a_i = the intercept or constant for security *i* in the regression
>
> β_i = the regression slope coefficient for security *i* equal to $cov_{im/\sigma m^2}$
>
> R_{mt} = the rate of return on a market index during period *t*
>
> e = a random error that sums to zero.

Given that the deviations from the regression line are random, one would expect them to sum to zero over long periods of time. Given the parameters of this model, the expected return for a stock can be derived for a specified

---

[12] E. F. Fama, L. Fisher, M. Jensen, and R. Roll, "The Adjustment of Stock Prices to New Information," *International Economic Review* 10, no. 1 (February 1969): 1–21.

[13] We will explore this model in detail in the following two chapters.

market rate of return. As an example, assume the following values for a sample firm:

$$a_i = -.01$$

$$\beta_i = 1.3.$$

In this instance, if the market return (R_{mt}) during a specified period was 8 percent, the expected return for stock i would be as follows:

$$E(R_{it}) = -.01 + 1.3\,(.08)$$
$$= .094.$$

In turn, the abnormal return (AR_{it}) would be equal to the actual return minus the expected return:

$$AR_{it} = R_{it} - E(R_{it}) \,. \qquad\qquad 6.6$$

In this example, if the actual return for the stock during this period were 12 percent, the abnormal return would be

$$AR_{it} = .12 - .094$$
$$= .026 \,.$$

During this period, the stock experienced a rate of return that was 2.6 percent more than expected where expectations were based upon what the aggregate market did and the stock's relationship with the market. The main point of this adjustment technique is that over a long period, these abnormal returns *should cancel out;* that is, they should sum to zero. Alternatively, if there is significant new information that is positive or negative, it should be reflected in these abnormal returns. Therefore, it is possible to examine the impact of an announcement or an event *and its timing* by examining what happens to these abnormal returns surrounding the announcement or event.[14]

Thus, if a firm announced a significant increase in earnings, it would not only be possible to determine the impact of this announcement on the security returns (i.e., were the abnormal returns positive), but also to determine when the impact took place. The typical procedure is to examine the abnormal returns during individual periods surrounding an event and to derive a series of *cumulative abnormal returns (CAR)* to determine the total impact of the event.

$$CAR_i = \sum_{t=1}^{N} AR_{it} \qquad\qquad 6.7$$

To summarize, various tests of the semistrong EMH either examine ab-

---

[14] You should keep in mind that this adjustment technique is based upon the capital asset pricing model (CAPM) that will be discussed in the next two chapters. This dependence on the CAPM means that many of the tests of the EMH are really *joint* tests of the EMH and CAPM. That is, if tests don't work out, it can be either because the markets are not efficient *or* the CAPM is misspecified. This notion will be discussed as we progress through the tests.

normal price changes surrounding the announcements of new information to see when the price adjustment took place, or they examine abnormal rates of return for a period immediately after an announcement to determine whether it would have been possible for an investor to derive above-average risk-adjusted rates of return (i.e., significant abnormal returns) by investing on the basis of public information. The numerous studies in this area are best organized in terms of specific events such as announcements of stock splits, exchange listings, and accounting changes.

STOCK SPLIT STUDIES. One of the more popular kinds of information to examine is stock splits. Some believe that the prices of stocks that split increase in value because the shares are priced lower, which increases demand for them. In contrast, advocates of efficient markets would not expect a change in value, reasoning that the firm has simply issued additional stock and nothing fundamentally affecting value has occurred.

An early test of the semistrong hypothesis is the well-known FFJR study, which hypothesized that stock splits alone do not cause higher rates of return because they add nothing to the value of a firm.[15] Therefore, there should be no significant price change following a split because, in an efficient market, investors would adjust for the forthcoming stock split prior to the announcement. Any relevant information (e.g., earnings growth) that caused the split would have already been discounted.[16]

One reason for expecting a price increase is that companies typically raise their dividends when they split their stock. The dividend change has an information effect because it indicates that management is confident that it will have a new, higher level of earnings in the future, which will justify a higher level of dividends. Therefore, the price increase that accompanies a dividend increase is not caused by the dividend itself but by the expected earnings information it transmits.

To determine the effect on the stocks, FFJR derived unique parameters for each stock relative to the market and computed abnormal returns for the period 20 months before and after the stock split. It was hypothesized that any abnormal information derived from the split would show up in the abnormal price changes. Consistent positive residuals surrounding splits would indicate the presence of good information, and vice versa. The analysis was intended to determine whether the positive effects took place before or after the split. The total sample was divided into two groups: stocks that split and increased their dividend rate, and those that split but did not increase their dividend rate.

While both groups experienced positive abnormal price changes prior to the split, stocks that split but did not increase their dividend experienced abnormal price declines following the split. In fact, within 12 months

---

[15] E. F. Fama, L. Fisher, M. Jensen, and R. Roll, "The Adjustment of Stock Prices to New Information," *International Economic Review* 10, no. 1 (February 1969): 1–21.

[16] For a detailed analysis of why firms split their stock, see Josef Lakonishok and Baruch Lev, "Stock Splits and Stock Dividends: Why, Who and When," *Journal of Finance* 42, no. 4 (September 1987): 913–932.

the no-dividend-increase stocks lost all their accumulated abnormal gains. In contrast, stocks that split and also increased their dividend experienced no abnormal returns after the split.

These results indicated that stock splits alone do not result in higher rates of return for stockholders. They also support the semistrong EMH because they indicate that the price adjustment occurs prior to a split. The authors concluded that investors cannot gain from the information on a split after the public announcement. Hausman, West, and Largay confirmed that conclusion when they examined monthly data.[17] Reilly and Drzycimski also found strong support for the EMH using daily price and volume data for the period surrounding the announcement of stock splits.[18] In contrast, though, positive results on the day of the announcement and subsequent days were reported in a study by Grinblatt, Masulis, and Titman.[19]

In summary, most studies attribute no short-run or long-run positive impact on security returns to a stock split, although a recent study yielded results that indicate the need for further research.[20]

NEW ISSUE STUDIES. During the 1960s a number of closely held companies decided to go public by selling some of their common stock. Determining the appropriate price for an *initial public offer (IPO)* is a difficult task. Because of uncertainty about the price and the risk involved in underwriting such issues, it was hypothesized that the underwriters would tend to underprice the new issues so that investors who acquired them *at the offering price* would tend to receive abnormal profits.[21] Another question concerned how fast the market would adjust to the underpricing. The typical test of market efficiency considered the returns to an investor who acquired the IPO *in the after market* (the public price after the offering) and held it for various periods.[22] The results on the two questions of interest (underpricing and market efficiency) were quite consistent. Without exception, all the studies indicated that, on average, new issues yield abnormally positive short-run returns, assuming a purchase at the offering price. Most authors attribute these excess returns to underpricing by the

---

[17] W. H. Hausman, R. R. West, and J. A. Largay, "Stock Splits, Price Changes, and Trading Profits: A Synthesis," *Journal of Business* 44, no. 1 (January 1971): 69–77.

[18] Frank K. Reilly and Eugene F. Drzycimski, "Short-Run Profits from Stock Splits," *Financial Management* 10, no. 3 (Summer 1981): 64–74.

[19] Mark S. Grinblatt, Ronald W. Masulis, and Sheridan Titman, "The Valuation Effects of Stock Splits and Stock Dividends," *Journal of Financial Economics* 13, no. 4 (December 1984): 461–490.

[20] Another question of interest related to stock splits is the impact on the liquidity and volatility of the stocks involved. For a study on this question, see Ohlson and Penman, "Volatility Increases Subsequent to Stock Splits," *Journal of Financial Economics* 14, no. 2 (June 1985): 251–266.

[21] For a discussion of these reasons, see Frank K. Reilly and Kenneth Hatfield, "Investor Experience with New Stock Issues," *Financial Analysts Journal* 25, no. 5 (September–October 1969): 73–80.

[22] Other studies that consider these questions include Roger G. Ibbotson, "Price Performance of Common Stock New Issues," *Journal of Financial Economics* 2, no. 3 (September 1975): 235–272; Dennis E. Logue, "On the Pricing of Unseasoned New Issues, 1965–1969," *Journal of Financial and Quantitative Analysis* 8, no. 1 (January 1973): 91–103; Frank K. Reilly, "Further Evidence on Short-Run Results for New Issue Investors," *Journal of Financial and Quantitative Analysis* 8, no. 1 (January 1973): 83–90; Frank K. Reilly, "New Issues Revisited," *Financial Management* 6, no. 4 (Winter 1977): 28–42; and B. M. Neuberger and C. A. LaChapelle, "Unseasoned New Issue Price Performance on Three Tiers: 1975–1980," *Financial Management* 12, no. 3 (Autumn 1983): 23–28.

underwriters for various reasons. The results also support the semistrong EMH, because it appears the market adjusted the prices almost immediately for the underpricing. The returns from acquiring IPOs after the offering and holding them for various periods generally yielded returns consistent with the added risk involved in these new issues. Rapid price adjustment is most evident in the recent studies, which showed that prices adjust by the day following the offering.[23] A more recent line of research has taken for granted the strong empirical evidence on underpricing and concentrates on the theoretical arguments that explain the extent of underpricing in terms of information asymmetry among traders.[24]

EXCHANGE LISTING.   Another economic event that is expected to have a significant impact on a firm and its stock is the decision to become listed on a national exchange or, specifically, to become listed on the NYSE, because it is the largest and most prestigious exchange. It is hypothesized that such a listing will increase the market liquidity of the stock and possibly add to the prestige of the firm. There are two questions of interest. First, does listing on a major exchange permanently increase the value of the firm? Second, given the change in expectations or perceptions surrounding the listing, is it possible to derive abnormal returns from investing in the stock when the listing is announced or at the time of the actual listing?

In addressing these questions, Van Horne found positive abnormal price changes for newly listed stocks during the period before listing; but after considering transaction costs and certain biases, he concluded that it was not possible to derive abnormal profits from the event.[25] Goulet, in addition to considering price changes, also examined the effect on shares outstanding, sales of stock, and the number of stockholders.[26] Typically, there was an increase in shares outstanding and stockholders but a decrease in stock price after the listing. It is not clear whether an investor could profit from this price change.

While these earlier studies tended to support the EMH, several subsequent studies provide contrary evidence. Specifically, Ying, Lewellen, Schlarbaum, and Lease (YLSL) found positive (risk-adjusted) abnormal

---

[23] In this regard, see Robert E. Miller and Frank K. Reilly, "An Examination of Mispricing, Returns, and Uncertainty for Initial Public Offerings," *Financial Management* 16, no. 2 (January 1987): 33–38; and Andrew J. Chalk and John W. Peavy, III, "Initial Public Offerings: Daily Returns, Offering Types and the Price Effect," *Financial Analysts Journal* 43, no. 5 (September–October 1987): 65–69. Chalk and Peavy find long-run abnormal returns, but they do not adjust for the substantially higher risk of IPOs and the higher transaction costs of low-priced issues.

[24] See Randolph Beatty and Jay Ritter, "Investment Banking, Reputation, and the Underpricing of Initial Public Offerings," *Journal of Financial Economics* 15, no. 1 (March 1986): 213–232; J. R. Ritter, "The 'Hot' Issue Market of 1980," *Journal of Business* 57, no. 2 (April 1984): 215–240; and K. Rock, "Why New Issues are Underpriced," *Journal of Financial Economics* 15, no. 1 (March 1986): 187–212.

[25] James C. Van Horne, "New Listings and Their Price Behavior," *Journal of Finance* 25, no. 4 (September 1970): 783–794.

[26] Waldemar M. Goulet, "Price Changes, Managerial Actions, and Insider Trading at the Time of Listing," *Financial Management* 3, no. 1 (Spring 1974): 30–36.

returns prior to listing but negative abnormal returns during most months after listing.[27]

Notably, the public information related to a listing comes with the announcement to apply, because almost all firms receive a confidential review prior to applying, so virtually all applications are approved. YLSL found a significant positive abnormal return of 7.54 percent during the application announcement month and a 5.00 percent abnormal return (without commission) during the subsequent month. This would be evidence against the semistrong EMH, since it implies that an investor could experience an abnormal risk-adjusted return based upon public information. Even with a reasonable commission, this abnormal return should persist. Apparently, the negative abnormal returns after the listing were not large enough for profitable short sales.

Sanger and McConnell used weekly data for a sample of stocks that listed over the period 1966–1977 to examine the impact of the NASDAQ system on the benefits of listing.[28] Because the NASDAQ system improved the market-making ability on the OTC by reducing cost and risk, it was theorized that it might reduce the relative liquidity benefits of listing on the NYSE.

Similar to prior studies, almost all stocks performed very well during the year prior to the first announcement of the potential listing in the *NYSE Weekly Bulletin*. Also, the listing stocks experienced significant positive abnormal returns during the week of the application announcement and the following week. These positive returns occurred before and after NAS-DAQ, but the degree of the abnormal returns was much lower after NAS-DAQ, and some were insignificant. Consistent with prior studies, the stocks experienced significant negative abnormal returns immediately following the actual listing and this persisted before and after NASDAQ (the average abnormal loss is about 3 percent during the first two weeks).

The results indicate statistically significant positive abnormal returns between the announcement and actual listing and significant negative abnormal returns after listing, which is evidence against the semistrong EMH. Still, are these statistically significant returns large enough to provide substantial rates of return for an investor using a trading rule and considering transaction costs? McConnell and Sanger assumed that an investor acquired the stocks after the announcement, sold them the week after they were actually listed, and also sold them short at this time, finally offsetting the short sales six weeks after listing.[29] While both sets (pre- and post-NASDAQ) provided positive returns after commissions, the pre-NASDAQ sample had larger positive excess returns between the announcement and listing dates and smaller negative excess returns after listing. Implementing

+ abnormal hi returns prior & during listing, neg. abnormal after [handwritten margin note]

---

[27] Louis K. W. Ying, W. G. Lewellen, G. G. Schlarbaum, and R. C. Lease, "Stock Exchange Listings and Securities Returns," *Journal of Financial and Quantitative Analysis* 12, no. 4 (September 1977): 415–432.

[28] Gary C. Sanger and John J. McConnell, "Stock Exchange Listings, Firm Value, and Security Market Efficiency: The Impact of NASDAQ," *Journal of Financial and Quantitative Analysis* 21, no. 1 (March 1986): 1–25.

[29] John J. McConnell and Gary C. Sanger, "A Trading Strategy for New Listings on the NYSE," *Financial Analysts Journal* 40, no. 1 (January/February 1984): 34–38.

the trading rule with commissions, the pre-NASDAQ sample experienced a 3.31 percent excess return during a 14-week period, or a 12.83 percent annualized return, while the post-NASDAQ sample had a 1.37 percent return during a 13-week period for an annualized excess return of 5.75 percent. Although these results indicate evidence against the semistrong EMH, because these returns are market-adjusted by the S&P 500, they are not completely risk-adjusted. Specifically, the total risk (standard deviation) or systematic risk (beta) for the sample stocks did not change significantly after listing (this has been confirmed in several other studies).[30] Notably, the level of systematic risk was above 1.0 before and after listing—that is, it was approximately 1.10, which means that these stocks had risk above the market level.

Howe and Kelm considered the effect of a U.S firm listing on a non–U.S. exchange in addition to a U.S. listing.[31] The three exchanges considered were Basel, Frankfurt, and Paris.[32] Their results indicated that the first overseas listing was harmful, based upon cumulative abnormal returns, while the impact of second and third listings was insignificant.[33]

In summary, the results regarding new listings indicate no long-run effects on value or risk but provide some evidence of short-run profit opportunities. Such profit opportunities based on public information would not support the semistrong EMH.

STOCK PRICES AND WORLD EVENTS. Reilly and Dryzcimski examined the adjustment of stock prices to the announcement of seven unexpected world events.[34] The results consistently indicated that stock prices adjusted during the time interval between the close before the announcement and *before the market opened* after the announcement (supporting the EMH). There were some large stock price changes after the opening but the direction of these changes was not consistent.

Pierce and Roley examined the daily response of stock prices to announcements about money supply, inflation, real economic activity, and the discount rate.[35] In all instances they examined the unexpected component of the announcement and found that there was an impact from

---

[30] Frank Fabozzi and R. A. Hershkoff, "The Effect of the Decision to List on a Stock's Systematic Risk," *Review of Business and Economic Research* 14, no. 2 (Spring 1979): 77–82; William Reints and Peter Vanderberg, "The Impact of Changes in Trading Location on a Security's Systematic Risk," *Journal of Financial and Quantitative Analysis* 10, no. 5 (December 1975): 881–890; and Kent Baker and James Spitzfaden, "The Impact of Exchange Listing on the Cost of Equity Capital," *The Financial Review* 17, no. 3 (September 1982): 128–141.

[31] John S. Howe and Kathryn Kelm, "The Stock Price Impacts of Overseas Listings," *Financial Management* 16, no. 3 (Autumn 1987): 51–56.

[32] Unfortunately, they were not able to analyze listings on the London Exchange because the exchange did not provide the necessary data, and the Tokyo Stock Exchange was not included because there were only seven listings during the sample period.

[33] The listings of bonds on the NYSE was not of value to the stockholders according to C. Boardman, F. Dark, and R. Lease, "On the Listing of Corporate Debt: A Note," *Journal of Financial and Quantitative Analysis* 21, no. 1 (March 1986): 107–114.

[34] Frank K. Reilly and Eugene F. Drzycimski, "Tests of Stock Market Efficiency Following Major World Events," *Journal of Business Research* 1, no. 1 (Summer 1973): 57–72.

[35] Douglas K. Pierce and V. Vance Roley, "Stock Prices and Economic News," *Journal of Business* 59, no. 1 (January 1985): 49–67.

monetary policy announcements, a limited impact from inflation, and no discernible effect from the other variables. It appears that most of the response does not persist beyond the announcement day, which is consistent with the EMH.

Jain examined the hourly stock returns and trading volume response to surprise announcements about money supply, consumer prices, producer prices, industrial production, and the unemployment rate.[36] The only variables that affected stock prices were money supply and the CPI, and none of the announcements affected trading volume. The results provided strong support for the EMH, since the effect of the information on stock prices was reflected in about one hour.

ANNOUNCEMENTS OF ACCOUNTING CHANGES. Numerous studies have analyzed the impact of announcements of accounting changes on stock prices. These studies implicitly contend that the capital markets are relatively efficient, so that if accounting changes are important, the stock prices will react to the announcement of them—especially if the accounting change will affect the economic value of the firm. If an accounting change affects only *reported* earnings but has no economic significance, its announcement should have no impact on stock prices.

IMPACT OF ANNUAL EARNINGS REPORTS. Brown and Ball examined the differential stock price movements during the year prior to announcements for companies that had experienced good and poor earnings reports.[37] While companies with abnormally good earnings reports experienced positive abnormal stock price performance, about 85 percent of the stock price adjustment occurred prior to release of the annual report. This indicated that stock prices adjust before the new information regarding annual earnings, probably because of prior quarterly reports.

Haugen, Ortiz, and Arjona found that the earnings announcements had a more significant impact on Mexican stocks than on U.S. stocks.[38] Also, there was evidence of a significant lag (approximately six months) in the response of stock prices to earnings reports in Mexico. They concluded that the U.S market is relatively more efficient, while the Mexican market provides greater opportunities for aggressive management.

EFFECT OF DEPRECIATION CHANGES. Archibald examined how the market reacted to a change from accelerated depreciation to straight-line depreciation for financial statement purposes.[39] All the sample firms experienced an increase in their reported profits. However, since this change has no real economic impact, an efficient market advocate would hypothesize no abnormal price changes, while those who assume that investors are naive

---

[36] Prom C. Jain, "Response of Hourly Stock Prices and Trading Volume to Economic News," *Journal of Business* 61, no. 2 (April 1988): 219–231.

[37] Philip Brown and Ray Ball, "An Empirical Evaluation of Accounting Income Numbers," *Journal of Accounting Research* 6, no. 2 (Autumn 1963): 159–178.

[38] Robert A. Haugen, Edgar Ortiz, and Enrique Arjona, "Market Efficiency: Mexico versus the U.S." *Journal of Portfolio Management* 12, no. 1 (Fall 1985): 28–33.

[39] T. Ross Archibald, "Stock Market Reaction to the Depreciation Switch-Back," *Accounting Review* 47, no. 1 (January 1972): 22–30.

would expect positive abnormal stock price changes because of higher reported earnings. The majority of abnormal returns before the accounting change were negative, as were the abnormal price changes during the subsequent five months. These results supported the EMH, because stock prices appeared to be reacting to poor earnings performance by these firms.

Kaplan and Roll examined investor reaction to two accounting changes that affected only financial statements: (1) the switch in 1964 to the flow-through method of reporting investment credit, and (2) the switch back from reporting accelerated depreciation to reporting straight-line depreciation.[40] The abnormal price movements were generally negative except during the few weeks surrounding the announcements, which indicates that firms making accounting changes are typically performing poorly. There was some temporary benefit from the accounting change and the resulting higher reported earnings, but the average negative price changes resumed and continued to the end of the test period. Consistent with an efficient market, such practices are unsuccessful in permanently affecting stock prices.

EFFECT OF INVENTORY CHANGES.   Two studies have examined the effect of changes in inventory valuation methods from *FIFO (first-in, first-out)* to *LIFO (last-in, first-out),* or vice versa, during periods of significant inflation. Two alternative hypotheses were suggested by Sunder regarding stock price changes in the period surrounding the announcement of the changes.[41] If naive investors rely on reported earnings, a change to LIFO will result in a decrease in earnings and stock prices should decline. In contrast, if investors rely on the economic value of the firm, stock prices should increase after the accounting change because this change causes an increase in cash flow (lower reported earnings and taxes payable means higher cash flow). The consistently positive abnormal price changes supported the hypotheses that changes in stock prices are associated with changes in the economic value of the firms. Reilly, Smith, and Hurt, testing the same hypotheses, found positive abnormal price changes during the announcement month and the two subsequent months, which likewise supported the EMH.[42]

SOME ANOMALIES   While a lot of evidence supports the semistrong EMH, a growing number of studies have provided contrary evidence. In this section we discuss a number of these studies and also consider a pattern that might explain some of the results.

QUARTERLY EARNINGS REPORTS.   Numerous studies by Latané and associates on the usefulness of quarterly reports consistently have failed to

---

[40] Robert S. Kaplan and Richard Roll, "Investor Evaluation of Accounting Information: Some Empirical Evidence," *Journal of Business* 45, no. 2 (April 1972): 225–257.

[41] Shyam Sunder, "Stock Price and Risk Related to Accounting Changes in Inventory Valuation," *The Accounting Review* 50, no. 2 (April 1975): 305–315.

[42] Frank K. Reilly, Ralph E. Smith, and Ron Hurt, "Stock Market Reaction to Changes in Inventory Valuation Methods," Financial Management Association Meeting, Kansas City, Mo., October 1975.

support the semistrong EMH.[43] A study by Joy, Litzenberger, and McEnally (JLM) examined firms that experienced unanticipated changes in quarterly earnings using three categories based on the deviation from expectations: (1) any deviation from expectations, (2) a deviation of plus or minus 20 percent, and (3) a deviation of at least 40 percent.[44] They examined abnormal price changes from 13 weeks prior to the announcement to 26 weeks following it. The abnormal price movements for the "any deviation" category for companies with good earnings was about 1 to 2 percent during the period, compared to transaction costs of 2 to 3 percent, indicating a lack of profit opportunities. For the 20-percent-above-expectations category, the post-announcement gain was about 4 percent, compared to 5 to 6 percent gains for the 40-percent-above-expectations sample. These abnormal returns exceeded transaction costs. The price adjustment to unfavorable earnings performance was more rapid, and there were no abnormal returns for any category.

These results suggest that favorable information contained in quarterly earnings reports is not instantaneously reflected in stock prices. Also, the authors found a significant relationship between the size of the unexpected earnings performance and the post-announcement stock price change.

In reviewing many of these studies, Joy and Jones noted problems in several of the earlier studies that they believed were remedied in the more recent ones.[45] While acknowledging some possibility of debate on minor points, they stated,

> We conclude from the array of studies we have reviewed that market inefficiencies exist with respect to earnings reports.[46]

Ball reviewed 20 studies of price reaction to earnings announcements and found that the post-announcement risk-adjusted abnormal returns are consistently positive, which is inconsistent with market efficiency.[47] In contrast to Joy and Jones, he contended that the abnormal returns are due to problems with the two-parameter asset pricing model (the CAPM) used to derive expected returns, not market inefficiences. Watts found significant abnormal returns even after making all the adjustments suggested by Ball.[48] He explicitly showed that the abnormal returns were due to market inefficiencies rather than the CAPM, but noted the abnormal returns were small and not completely consistent over time.

[43] Representative studies in the area are H. A. Latané, O. Maurice Joy, and Charles P. Jones, "Quarterly Data, Sort-Rank Routines, and Security Evaluation," *Journal of Business* 43, no. 4 (October 1970): 427–438; and C. Jones and R. Litzenberger, "Quarterly Earnings Reports and Intermediate Stock Price Trends," *Journal of Finance* 25, no. 1 (March 1970): 143–148.

[44] O. Maurice Joy, Robert H. Litzenberger, and Richard W. McEnally, "The Adjustment of Stock Prices to Announcements of Unanticipated Changes in Quarterly Earnings," *Journal of Accounting Research* 15, no. 2 (Autumn 1977): 207–225.

[45] O. Maurice Joy and Charles P. Jones, "Earnings Reports and Market Efficiencies: An Analysis of Contrary Evidence," *Journal of Financial Research* 2, no. 1 (Spring 1979): 51–63.

[46] Ibid., 62.

[47] Ray Ball, "Anomalies in Relationships between Securities' Yields and Yield-Surrogates," *Journal of Financial Economics* 6, no. 2/3 (June–September 1978): 103–126.

[48] Ross L. Watts, "Systematic 'Abnormal' Returns after Quarterly Earnings Announcements," *Journal of Financial Economics* 6, no. 2/3 (June–September 1978): 127–150.

The more recent earnings announcement studies have employed the concept of _standardized unexpected earnings (SUE)_.[49] Rather than examine the percentage differences between actual and expected, the idea has been to normalize the difference between actual and expected earnings for the quarter by the standard error of estimate from the regression used to derive the expected earnings figure. Therefore, the SUE is

$$\frac{\text{Reported } EPS_t - \text{Predicted } EPS_t}{\begin{array}{c}\text{Standard Error of Estimate for the}\\ \text{Estimating Regression Equation}\end{array}}.$$

The predicted earnings are estimated by a time series model that considers the earnings during the prior 20 quarters and includes quarterly dummy variables that adjust for any seasonal factors. Therefore, the SUE indicates how many standard errors the reported EPS figure is above or below the predicted EPS figure. The typical categories are greater than 4.0, between 4.0 and 3.0, between 3.0 and 2.0, and so on, all the way to less than −4.0.

An extensive analysis by Rendleman, Jones, and Latané (RJL) using a very large sample and daily returns provided evidence that large SUEs were accompanied by significant abnormal stock price changes.[50] These results contrasted with the earlier findings by Reinganum that the abnormal returns between high and low SUE portfolios were not statistically different from zero.[51] The RJL results were confirmed for the time period examined by Reinganum (1975–1977) but also for the longer period of 1971–1980. RJL also examined the impact of different risk adjustments or no risk adjustment (implicitly assuming the various SUE portfolios have comparable risk levels) and concluded that the results were not sensitive to the risk adjustments. The analysis of daily data from 20 days before the announcement to 90 days after the announcement indicated that 31 percent of the total response in stock returns came before the announcement, 18 percent on the day of the announcement, and 51 percent afterwards.

Foster, Olsen, and Sherlin examined several reasons for the earnings drift following earnings announcements and confirmed the prior results using different earnings expectations models.[52] The unexpected earnings explained over 80 percent of the subsequent stock price drift for the total time period and several subperiods.

---

[49] These include Henry A. Latané and Charles P. Jones, "Standardized Unexpected Earnings—A Progress Report," _Journal of Finance_ 32, no. 5 (December 1977): 1457–1465; and Henry A. Latané and Charles Jones, "Standardized Unexpected Earnings: 1971–1977," _Journal of Finance_ 34, no. 3 (June 1979): 717–724.

[50] Richard J. Rendlemen, Jr., Charles P. Jones, and Henry A. Latané, "Empirical Anomalies Based on Unexpected Earnings and the Importance of Risk Adjustments," _Journal of Financial Economics_ 10, no. 3 (November 1982): 269–287; and C. P. Jones, R. J. Rendlemen, Jr., and H. A. Latané, "Earnings Announcements: Pre- and Post-Responses," _Journal of Portfolio Management_ 11, no. 3 (Spring 1985): 28–32.

[51] M. Reinganum, "Misspecification of Capital Asset Pricing," _Journal of Financial Economics_ 9, no. 1 (March 1981): 19–46.

[52] George Foster, Chris Olsen, and Terry Shevlin, "Earnings Releases, Anomalies, and the Behavior of Security Returns," _Accounting Review_ 59, no. 4 (October 1984): 574–603.

In summary, <u>the evidence from studies on unexpected quarterly earn-ings announcements generally are not consistent with semistrong market efficiency</u>.

PRICE-EARNINGS RATIOS AND RETURNS. Basu tested the EMH by exam-ining the relationship between the historical price-earnings (p/e) ratios for stocks and the returns on the stocks.[53] It is contended that low p/e stocks will outperform high p/e stocks because growth companies enjoy high p/e ratios, but the market tends to overestimate the growth potential and thus overvalues these growth companies while undervaluing low-growth firms with low p/e ratios. A relationship between the historical p/e ratios and subsequent market performance would constitute evidence against the semistrong EMH, because investors could use historical p/e ratios to generate abnormal returns.

Basu divided the stocks into five p/e classes and determined the risk and return for portfolios of high and low p/e ratio stocks. The average annual rates of return ranged from 9 percent for high p/e ratio stocks to 16 percent for the low p/e ratio group. An unexpected result was that the low p/e ratio group also had lower risk. Performance measures that con-sider return and risk indicated that low p/e ratio stocks experienced su-perior results relative to the market, while high p/e ratio stocks had sig-nificantly inferior results.[54] While subsequent analysis indicated some impact of taxes and transaction costs, <u>it was concluded that publicly avail-able p/e ratios possess valuable information</u>. Obviously, these results are <u>not consistent with semistrong efficiency</u>.

THE SIZE EFFECT. Two authors examined the impact of size (measured by total market value) on the risk-adjusted rates of return.[55] All stocks on the NYSE (Banz) or on the NYSE and the AMEX (Reinganum) were ranked on the basis of market value and divided into ten equally weighted port-folios. The risk-adjusted abnormal returns for extended periods (10–15 years) indicated that the small firms consistently experienced significantly larger risk-adjusted returns than the larger firms. They contended that the Basu p/e ratio results were really small-firm effects, and that it is size, not p/e ratio, that caused the Basu results. Subsequently, Basu reexamined Reinganum's results using a different sample period and different portfolio creation techniques.[56] Although the results differed from Reinganum's, the

---

[53] S. Basu, "Investment Performance of Common Stocks in Relation to Their Price-Earnings Ratios: A Test of the Efficient Market Hypothesis," *Journal of Finance* 32, no. 3 (June 1977): 663–682; and S. Basu, "The Information Content of Price-Earnings Ratios," *Financial Management* 4, no. 2 (Summer 1975): 53–64.

[54] Composite performance measures are discussed in Chapter 20.

[55] R. W. Banz, "The Relationship between Return and Market Value of Common Stocks," *Journal of Financial Economics* 9, no. 1 (March 1981): 3–18; and Marc R. Reinganum, "Misspecification of Capital Asset Pricing: Empirical Anomalies Based on Earnings Yield and Market Values," *Journal of Financial Economics* 9, no. 1 (March 1981): 19–46.

[56] S. Basu, "The Relationship between Earnings Yield, Market Value, and Return for NYSE Common Stocks," *Journal of Financial Economics* 12, no. 1 (June 1983): 129–156.

highest risk-adjusted returns were in portfolios with both small firms and low p/e ratios.

Recall that these studies on market efficiency are dual tests of the EMH and the CAPM. Abnormal returns may occur because the markets are not efficient, or because the market model is not properly specified and therefore does not provide correct estimates of expected returns. Reinganum contended that the abnormal returns were because the simple one-period CAPM is an inadequate description of the real-world capital markets.[57]

Roll suggested that the riskiness of the small firms was improperly measured.[58] He believed that because small firms are traded less frequently, the risk measures obtained using daily returns data seriously understate the actual small-firm portfolio risk. The infrequent trading of small firms causes an increase in serial correlation of prices over time and a decrease in the variance of returns. If this is correct, gross measures of risk (the standard deviation of returns) are reduced, and the covariance of returns for the stock with the market portfolio is reduced, so the stock's beta is lower. Earlier, Dimson suggested adding lagged and leading market returns to the market model and summing the coefficients to arrive at the beta for infrequently traded stocks.[59] Reinganum computed betas for the alternative market value portfolios using the standard *ordinary least-squares (OLS) model* and using Dimson's *aggregated coefficients model* and found a substantial difference in the betas estimated by the alternative methods; e.g., the smallest firm portfolio beta was 0.75 using OLS and 1.69 using the aggregated coefficients method.[60] The difference between betas narrowed with size until the largest firm portfolio beta was 0.98 with OLS and 0.97 with aggregated coefficients. The results supported Dimson and Roll regarding the underestimation of risk for small firms. To test whether these new betas could explain the large differences in rates of return, Reinganum related the returns to the betas and firm size and likewise found that risk for small firms is underestimated, but the difference in beta still did not account for the very large difference in rates of return.

Chan, Chen, and Hsieh employed a multi-factor pricing model with several risk variables and found the difference in returns between the top and bottom groups was only about 1 or 2 percent, compared to about 12 percent before the multi-factor adjustment for risk.[61] This implies that most of the difference in returns can be explained by *complete measures of risk.*

Stoll and Whaley confirmed that total market value varies inversely with risk-adjusted returns but also found a strong positive correlation be-

[57] Marc R. Reinganum, "Abnormal Returns in Small Firm Portfolios," *Financial Analysts Journal* 37, no. 2 (March–April 1981): 52–57.

[58] Richard Roll, "A Possible Explanation of the Small Firm Effect," *Journal of Finance* 36, no. 4 (September 1981): 879–888.

[59] Elroy Dimson, "Risk Measurement When Shares Are Subject to Infrequent Trading," *Journal of Financial Economics* 7, no. 2 (June 1979): 197–226.

[60] Marc R. Reinganum, "A Direct Test of Roll's Conjecture on the Firm Size Effect," *Journal of Finance* 37, no. 1 (March 1982): 27–35.

[61] K. C. Chan, Nai-fu Chen, and David A. Hsieh, "An Exploratory Investigation of the Firm Size Effect," *Journal of Financial Economics* 14, no. 3 (September 1985): 451–471.

tween average price per share and market value; firms with small market value have low stock prices.[62] Because transaction costs vary inversely with price per share, they must be considered when examining the small-firm effect. Transaction costs include both the dealer's bid-ask spread and the broker's commission. Specifically, when using a market order, you would buy at the ask price and sell at the bid price and also have a broker's commission on the transaction. Both of these components vary with price—that is, the proportional bid-ask spread varies inversely with price,[63] and the commission is a decreasing function of price per share. Specifically, the proportional bid-ask spread varies from 2.93 percent for small-value stocks to 0.69 percent for large-value stocks, while the broker's commission was 3.84 percent for small firms and 2.02 percent for large firms. This indicates a total difference in transaction cost of 4.06 percent between large and small firms, a combined cost of 2.93 plus 3.84 (6.77 percent) for small firms and 0.69 plus 2.02 (2.71 percent) for large firms. This differential in transaction cost, with frequent trading, can have a significant impact on the results. Assuming daily transactions, the original small-firm effects are reversed, while with less trading, the original abnormal returns recur. The point is, subsequent studies on the small-firm effect should consider transaction costs and specify realistic holding period assumptions.

IMPACT OF ANNUAL REBALANCING. Reinganum investigated whether strategies that buy and hold securities for longer periods of time yield results similar to a daily trading strategy.[64] As before, the rates of return differed systematically, depending on market capitalizations. The smallest-firm portfolio experienced a 32.77 percent return, compared to 9.47 percent for the largest-firm portfolio. The Dimson risk measure varied from 1.58 for the smallest firm portfolio to 0.96 for the largest firm portfolio. Reinganum contended that the differential rates of return would require a market risk premium of over 37 percent, which is clearly excessive.

Two holding period strategies were considered: a one-year holding period, with rebalancing every year, and a buy-and-hold strategy, which assumed holding the original portfolios from 1963 through 1980. With annual rebalancing the small-firm portfolio grew from $1 in 1963 to over $46 without commissions, while $1 in the largest-firm portfolio grew to about $4. The results were monotonic across portfolios with one exception, and typically consistent over time. Most of the very small firms came from the AMEX. The results with no rebalancing likewise indicated the superiority of small firms. A dollar in the small-firm portfolio grew to about $11, while $1 in the large-firm portfolio grew to over $4 (about the same as annual

[62] Hans R. Stoll and Robert E. Whaley, "Transactions Costs and the Small Firm Effect," *Journal of Financial Economics* 12, no. 1 (June 1983): 57–80.

[63] Seha M. Tinic, "The Economics of Liquidity Service," *Quarterly Journal of Economics* 86, no. 1 (February 1972): 79–93; and George Benston and R. Hagerman, "Determinants of Bid-Ask Spreads in the Over-the-Counter Market," *Journal of Financial Economics* 1, no. 4. (December 1974): 353–364.

[64] Marc R. Reinganum, "Portfolio Strategies Based on Market Capitalization," *Journal of Portfolio Management* 9, no. 2 (Winter 1983): 29–36.

rebalancing). There was no explicit consideration of transaction costs with annual rebalancing, because the differential returns were so large that any reasonable difference in transaction costs could not overcome this return superiority. The author concluded,

> Over time, the returns of the big winners more than offset the losses within the small-firm portfolio, and these extremely large returns apparently account for the superior performance of the small-capitalization companies over the large ones.[65]

In summary, the small firms outperformed the large firms even after considering risk and transaction costs, assuming annual rebalancing.

Most studies on size effect employed large data bases and long time periods (30 to 50 years) to show that this phenomenon has existed for many years. In contrast, Brown, Kleidon, and Marsh examined the performance over various intervals of time and concluded that the effect is not stable.[66] During some periods they found the negative relationship derived by others, but during others (e.g., 1967–1975), they found a positive relationship where large firms outperformed the small firms. Incidentally, some casual evidence indicates that this positive relationship also held during the recent four-year period of 1984–1987.

IMPACT OF TRADING ACTIVITY. Arbel and Strebel considered an additional influence beyond size—attention or neglect.[67] They measured attention in terms of the number of analysts who regularly follow a stock and divided the stocks into three groups: (1) highly followed, (2) moderately followed, and (3) neglected. They confirmed the small-firm effect but also found a neglected-firm effect caused by the lack of information and limited institutional interest. The neglected-firm concept applied across size classes, suggesting that institutions might be wise to invest in medium-sized neglected firms and individuals in small neglected firms.

Peavy and Goodman examined the p/e ratio question with adjustments for firm size, industry effects, and infrequent trading.[68] They attempted to eliminate the size problem by considering only firms with a market value above $100 million and to control the industry effect by examining only firms within three industries (electronics, paper/container, and food). To overcome the infrequent trading problem, they used quarterly intervals and considered only stocks with an average monthly trading volume exceeding 25,000 shares. Given these adjustments, they found that the risk-adjusted returns for stocks in the lowest p/e ratio quintile for all three industries were superior to those in the highest p/e ratio quintile.

---

[65] Ibid., 36.

[66] Philip Brown, Allen W. Kleidon, and Terry A. Marsh, "New Evidence on the Nature of Size-Related Anomalies in Stock Prices," *Journal of Financial Economics* 12, no. 1 (June 1983): 33–56.

[67] Avner Arbel and Paul Strebel, "Pay Attention to Neglected Firms!" *Journal of Portfolio Management* 9, no. 2 (Winter 1983): 37–42.

[68] John W. Peavy, III, and David A. Goodman, "The Significance of P/Es for Portfolio Returns," *Journal of Portfolio Management* 9, no. 2 (Winter 1983): 43–47.

James and Edmister examined the impact of trading volume by considering the relationship between returns, market volume, and trading activity.[69] They confirmed the relationship between size and rates of return and then considered the impact of trading volume as an alternative explanation for these results, since there is a strong positive correlation between size and trading activity. This is an appealing relationship because it would justify the excess return for small stocks on the basis of poor market liquidity (i.e., a liquidity premium). The results indicated no significant difference between the mean returns of the highest and lowest trading activity portfolios nor an inverse relationship between trading activity and mean daily returns. A test on firms with roughly equivalent trading activity confirmed the existence of a size effect. In summary, the size anomaly could not be explained by differential trading activity (i.e., market liquidity).

The differential information hypothesis of Barry and Brown contends that firms with less information require higher returns.[70] Using the period of listing as a proxy for information, they found a negative relationship between returns and the period of listing adjusting for firm size and the January effect.

In summary, the firm size effect on rates of return has emerged as a major anomaly in the efficient markets literature. Numerous attempts to explain the anomaly—in terms of superior risk measurements, transaction costs, analysts' attention, trading activity, and differential information—have failed. Apparently, the two strongest explanations are the risk measurements that consider the significant impact of infrequent trading or other risk factors (changes in the risk premium) and the differential in transaction costs. Depending on the frequency of trading (i.e., the investment horizon), the combination of these two factors may account for most of the differential. Given these results, it is not surprising that Dimson and Marsh warn that the size effect must be considered in any event study that contains sample firms with significantly different market values and that uses long intervals.[71]

THE JANUARY ANOMALY. Several years ago Branch proposed a unique trading rule for those interested in taking advantage of tax selling.[72] Investors tend to engage in tax selling toward the end of the year to establish losses on stocks that have declined during the current year or prior years. After the new year, there is a tendency to reacquire these stocks or reinvest the proceeds from the prior tax sale. This scenario implies downward pressure on stock prices in late November and December and a positive impact in early January. Efficient market advocates would not expect such

[69] Christopher James and Robert Edmister, "The Relation between Common Stock Returns, Trading Activity, and Market Value," *Journal of Finance* 38, no. 4 (September 1983): 1075–1086.

[70] Christopher B. Barry and Stephen J. Brown, "Differential Information and the Small Firm Effect," *Journal of Financial Economics* 13, no. 2 (June 1984): 283–294.

[71] Elroy Dimson and Paul Marsh, "Event Study Methodologies and the Size Effect: The Case of UK Press Recommendations," *Journal of Financial Economics* 17, no. 1 (September 1986): 113–142.

[72] Ben Branch, "A Tax Loss Trading Rule," *Journal of Business* 50, no. 2 (April 1977): 198–207.

a seasonal pattern to persist; it should be eliminated by arbitrageurs who would buy in December and subsequently sell in early January.

Dyl supported the tax selling hypothesis when he found that trading volume was abnormally high during December for stocks that had experienced large losses during the previous year, and volume was abnormally low for stocks that had experienced large gains.[73] There were significant positive abnormal returns during January for stocks that had experienced losses during the prior year.

Roll confirmed the price pattern on the last day of December and the first four days of January, finding that stocks with negative returns over the entire preceding year had higher returns around January 1.[74] On the question of whether the entire year-end return is caused by tax selling or size, the results indicated that smallness had an effect beyond volatility and tax selling. To examine the impact of transaction costs, Roll assumed a purchase on the second-to-last day of the year and a sale on the fourth day of the new year that generated returns of 6.89 percent for the NYSE and 14.2 percent for the AMEX. Applying the 6.77 percent commissions estimated by Stoll and Whaley for small firms, they still had excess returns of 3.94 percent for the NYSE and 10.3 percent for the AMEX. Assuming a purchase at the high price for the second-to-last trading day and sales at the low price on the fourth day of the new year, and also adding commissions, there was no profit on the NYSE, but there was still an excess return on the AMEX. Roll concluded that because of transaction costs, arbitrageurs must not be eliminating the January tax selling anomaly.

Keim, in analyzing the relation between abnormal returns and market value during each month of the year, found a negative relationship between size and abnormal returns, but the strongest relationship was always in January, where nearly 50 percent of the overall size effect occurred.[75] In fact, more than 50 percent of the January effect was concentrated in the first week of trading, particularly on the first day of the year.

Following the earlier work by Rozeff and Kinney,[76] Reinganum found large abnormal returns at the beginning of January, consistent with tax-loss selling.[77] Still, small firms that did very well the prior year also experienced large abnormal returns in early January, which is not consistent with tax selling.

Brown, Keim, Kleidon, and Marsh examined the January effect using Australian data, because the year-end for tax purposes in Australia is June 30, making the seasonal tax effect occur in July.[78] The results indicated

---

[73] Edward A. Dyl, "Capital Gains Taxation and Year-End Stock Market Behavior," *Journal of Finance* 32, no. 1 (March 1977): 165–175.

[74] Richard Roll, "Vas Ist Das?" *Journal of Portfolio Management* 9, no. 2 (Winter 1983): 18–28.

[75] Donald B. Keim, "Size-Related Anomalies and Stock Return Seasonality," *Journal of Financial Economics* 12, no. 1 (June 1983): 13–32.

[76] Michael S. Rozeff and William R. Kinney, Jr., "Capital Market Seasonality: The Case of Stock Returns," *Journal of Financial Economics* 3, no. 4 (December 1976): 379–402.

[77] Marc R. Reinganum, "The Anomalous Stock Market Behavior of Small Firms in January: Empirical Tests for Tax-Loss Selling Effects," *Journal of Financial Economics* 12, no. 1 (January 1983): 89–104.

[78] Philip Brown, Donald B. Keim, Allan W. Kleidon, and Terry A. Marsh, "Stock Return Seasonalities and the Tax-Loss Selling Hypothesis," *Journal of Financial Economics* 12, no. 1 (June 1983): 105–127.

pronounced seasonals in December, January, July, and August, with the largest impacts in January and July. While the results for July support the tax selling hypothesis, the January impact cannot be thus explained, which led the authors to conclude that the January seasonal impact and the tax year may be more a case of correlation than causation.

Berges, McConnell, and Schlarbaum document the January effect using Canadian data for the period 1951–1980, but Canada did not introduce the capital gains tax until 1973.[79] Therefore, the tax-loss selling pressure hypothesis cannot be the entire explanation for the January effect, nor did their study find a concentration of the small-firm effect in January.

Chang and Pinegar indicate support for the tax-loss selling hypothesis based upon an analysis of long-term government and corporate bonds, with most of the support coming from lower-rated bonds (BB and B), especially those offering greatest incentives for year-end tax-loss sales and subsequent large gains in January.[80] Since they also derived January gains that cannot be explained by tax selling, they acknowledge tax-loss selling is probably not the only cause of January gains.

Tinic and West highlighted the January effect by examining the seasonality of the relationship between expected return and risk.[81] Consistent with prior studies, the risk-return relationship for the total period was fairly weak but there was a very strong seasonal in the relationship. Specifically, there was no significant relationship in any single month except January, nor during the other eleven months combined.

Keim analyzed dividend yields and stock returns overall and found a nonlinear relationship in January.[82] Specifically, the zero dividend securities had the largest return, and for the rest of the groups there was a positive relationship between the dividend yield and the stock returns. He likewise found a strong seasonal pattern, because except for January, there was no relationship between these two variables—that is, the dividend yield–stock return relationship was concentrated in January.

Lakonishok and Smidt found a year-end effect in trading volume for small firms, the most active day being the last day of the year and above-normal trading activity continuing in January.[83]

In summary, the January anomaly is intriguing because it is so pervasive. Its relationship with the small-firm effect is fascinating because of the apparent speed of the impact. This seasonal impact also influences

[79] Angel Berges, John J. McConnell, and Gary G. Schlarbaum, "The Turn-of-the-Year in Canada," *Journal of Finance* 39, no. 1 (March 1984): 185–192.

[80] Eric C. Chang and J. Michael Pinegar, "Return Seasonality and Tax-Loss Selling in the Market for Long-Term Government and Corporate Bonds," *Journal of Financial Economics* 17, no. 2 (December 1986): 391–415.

[81] Seha M. Tinic and Richard R. West, "Risk and Return: January vs. the Rest of the Year," *Journal of Financial Economics* 13, no. 4 (December 1984): 561–574.

[82] Donald B. Keim, "Dividend Yields and Stock Returns: Implications of Abnormal January Returns," *Journal of Financial Economics* 14, no. 3 (September 1985): 473–489; Donald B. Keim "Dividend Yields and the January Effect," *Journal of Portfolio Management* 12, no. 2 (Winter 1986): 54–60.

[83] Josef Lakonishok and Seymour Smidt, "Volume and Turn-of-the-Year Behavior," *Journal of Financial Economics* 13, no. 3 (September 1984): 435–455; and Josef Lakonishok and Seymour Smidt, "Trading Bargains in Small Firms at Year-End," *Journal of Portfolio Management* 12, no. 3 (Spring 1986): 24–29.

the dividend yield effect and trading volume, and a tax-loss explanation of this anomaly has received partial or full support in several studies. Despite a plethora of studies, the January anomaly persists in posing as many questions as it answers.[84]

OTHER CALENDAR EFFECTS. While not as significant as the January anomaly, there are several other "calendar" effects, including a monthly effect, a weekend/day-of-the-week effect, and an intraday effect. Ariel examined 19 years of data and found a significant monthly effect in stock returns wherein all the market's cumulative advance occurred during the first half of trading months.[85]

The weekend effect has been documented by French and also by Gibbons and Hess.[86] French examined daily returns for the Standard & Poor's Composite Index from 1953 to 1977 and found the mean return for Monday was significantly negative in each of the five five-year subperiods and during the full period. In contrast, the average return for the other four days was positive. Gibbons and Hess found similar results for the period of July 1962 to December 1968 and several subperiods. (Their research included returns for the Center for Research in Security Prices (CRSP) as well as the S&P 500.) They also found that the negative returns on Monday applied to individual stocks and to Treasury bills.

Keim and Stambaugh confirmed the negative Monday results using a longer time period (back to 1928 for the S&P 500) and additional individual stocks from stock exchanges and also active OTC stocks.[87] In the process they documented that the effect is similar for different sized firms and for exchange-traded or OTC stocks. Rogalski decomposed the Monday effect that is typically measured from Friday close to Monday close into (1) a pure weekend effect from Friday close to Monday open and (2) a Monday trading effect from the Monday open to the Monday close.[88] He found that all of the negative Monday effect in prior studies was contained in the average Friday close to Monday open return, referred to as the *weekend effect,* and otherwise the Monday trading effect was positive. Further, by segmenting day-of-the-week returns into January and the rest of the year, he found that the Monday effect and the nontrading weekend effect were on average positive in January and negative for all other months. Also the size effect appeared only in January.

---

[84] An article that reviews these studies and others is Donald B. Keim, "The CAPM and Equity Return Regularities," *Financial Analysts Journal* 42, no. 3 (May–June 1986): 19–34.

[85] Robert A. Ariel, "A Monthly Effect in Stock Returns," *Journal of Financial Economics* 18, no. 1 (March 1987): 161–174.

[86] Kenneth R. French, "Stock Returns and the Weekend Effect," *Journal of Financial Economics* 8, no. 1 (March 1980): 55–70; and Michael R. Gibbons and Patrick Hess, "Day of the Week Effects and Asset Returns," *Journal of Business* 54, no. 4 (October 1981): 579–596. For an earlier study, see F. Cross, "The Behavior of Stock Prices on Fridays and Mondays," *Financial Analysts Journal* 29, no. 6 (November–December 1973): 67–69; and a subsequent note, see Josef Lakonishok and Maurice Levi, "Weekend Effects on Stock Returns: A Note," *Journal of Finance* 37, no. 2 (June 1982): 883–889.

[87] Donald B. Keim and Robert F. Stambaugh, "A Further Investigation of the Weekend Effect in Stock Returns," *Journal of Finance* 39, no. 3 (July 1984): 819–835.

[88] Richard J. Rogalski, "New Findings Regarding Day-of-the-Week Returns over Trading and Non-Trading Periods: A Note," *Journal of Finance* 39, no. 5 (December 1984): 1603–1614.

Using even shorter-term observations, Smirlok and Stacks examined hourly observations for the DJIA for each trading day between January 1, 1963, through December 31, 1983, including three subperiods.[89] They found a change in the pattern of returns before and after 1974. The results for the recent period 1974–1983 were consistent with Rogalski's finding that the Monday effect is concentrated in the weekend effect. Before 1974, however, the Monday effect was concentrated in the Monday trading period. Hourly results indicated that the effect has tended to move up. Specifically, recently the effect is during the weekend while the Monday trading effect has turned positive because the negative Monday morning effect is swamped by positive Monday afternoon returns.

Harris examined transactions data from the NYSE for 14 months between December 1, 1981, and January 31, 1983.[90] This breakdown of the data allowed an analysis across firms and over time. For large firms, the negative Monday effect occurred before the market opened (it was a weekend effect), while for smaller firms most of it occurred during the day on Monday (it was a Monday trading effect). When the author examined 15 minute intervals during the day, he found that the only differences occurred during the first 45 minutes of the day—on Monday morning prices tended to drop, while on other weekday mornings they increased. Otherwise, price patterns during the day were similar. He also found a strong tendency for prices to rise on the last trade of the day.

THE VALUE LINE ENIGMA. Value Line (VL) is a large well-known advisory service that publishes financial information on approximately 1,700 stocks (see Chapter 5 for an example of a Value Line company report). One of the items included in its report is a *timing rank,* which indicates Value Line's expectation regarding a firm's common stock performance over the coming 12 months. A rank of 1 is the most favorable performance and 5 the worst. This ranking system, initiated in April 1965, is based upon a filter rule that assigns numbers based upon four factors:

1. An earnings and price rank of each security relative to all others
2. A price momentum factor
3. Year-to-year relative changes in quarterly earnings
4. A quarterly earnings "surprise" factor that compares actual quarterly earnings to VL estimated earnings.

The firms are ranked based upon a composite score for each firm. The top and bottom 100 are ranked 1 and 5 respectively, the next 300 from the top and bottom are ranked 2 and 4, and the rest (approximately 900) are ranked 3. Rankings are assigned every week based upon the latest data. Given the factors considered, the major changes each week are due

---

[89] Michael Smirlock and Laura Stacks, "Day-of-the-Week and Intraday Effects in Stock Returns" *Journal of Financial Economics* 17, no. 1 (September 1986): 197–210.

[90] Lawrence Harris, "A Transaction Data Study of Weekly and Intradaily Patterns in Stock Returns," *Journal of Financial Economics* 16, no. 1 (May 1986): 99–117.

to stock price changes that affect the price momentum variable and the earnings-price relationship. Notably, all of the data used to derive the four factors is public information.

The preliminary ranking is made every Wednesday, and the final ranking is sent to the printer on Friday (there are typically about five or six changes between Wednesday and Friday due to unusual new information). The publication with the new rankings is ready to be distributed on the following Wednesday, and Value Line attempts a staggered mailing so that everyone will receive the service with the rankings on Friday.

Several years after the ranking was started, Value Line indicated that the performance of the stocks in the various classes differed substantially. Specifically, the stocks rated 1 substantially outperformed the market, and the stocks rated 5 seriously underperformed the market (the performance figures did not include dividend income but also did not charge commissions). The first major academic study of the ability of the Value Line system by Black constructed portfolios of firms grouped by rank and revised the portfolios monthly.[91] He concluded that rank-1 firms outperformed rank-5 firms by 20 percent per year on a risk-adjusted basis over the 1965–1970 period. He contended that even with round-trip transaction costs of 2 percent, the net rate of return for a long position in rank-1 stocks would have been positive.

Holloway examined the top 100 stocks in rank and concluded that if you consistently owned these stocks by adjusting your portfolio weekly, the returns would be superior only before transaction costs, not after.[92] Finally, a buy-and-hold policy that assumed annual portfolio revisions to maintain a portfolio of rank-1 stocks generated abnormal returns after transaction costs.

Copeland and Mayers examined the performance of the VL recommendations between 1965 and 1978 using a future benchmark technique that avoids some of the biases of historical returns data as the benchmark (because historical stock price performance is a criteria in the VL system).[93] The abnormal returns were consistent with the rankings but only the returns for rank 5 were significantly negative and continued for 13 weeks, implying that VL has the ability to select underperformers. An analysis of a strategy of buying stocks that moved up in rank and selling short those that moved down indicated significant abnormal (negative) returns for the portfolio of down-ranked stock, while the returns for the higher ranked stocks were significant only in limited cases. Finally, while some of the abnormal returns for the rank-5 portfolios were *statistically* significant, the absolute size of the abnormal returns did not indicate gross inefficiency, because after transaction costs, the trading rules would not have been profitable.

---

[91] Fischer Black, "Yes, Virginia, There Is Hope: Tests of the Value Line Ranking System," *Financial Analysts Journal* 29, no. 5 (September–October 1973): 10–14.

[92] Clark Holloway, "A Note on Testing an Aggressive Investment Strategy Using Value Line Ranks," *Journal of Finance* 36, no. 3 (June 1981): 711–719.

[93] Thomas E. Copeland and David Mayers, "The Value Line Enigma (1965–1978): A Case Study of Performance Evaluation Issues," *Journal of Financial Economics* 10, no. 3 (November 1982): 289–321.

Stickel found that while all rank changes effect stock prices, the most significant impact occurs when stocks go from rank 2 to 1.[94] Although changes from 1 to 2, 2 to 3, and 3 to 2 are followed by statistically significant changes, the size is much less than for a move from 2 to 1. Stickel contends that the price movements require three days, but he counts Thursday as Day 0 because some people might receive the *Value Line Survey* on Thursday. Clearly, after Monday, there is no significant impact. He also found that smaller firms have a larger reaction to changes in rank (especially from 2 to 1, 3 to 2, and 2 to 3), and the change requires several days. However, acting upon the rank change from 2 to 1 for the smallest firms would not be profitable due to the large transaction costs of small firms. Therefore, while there is evidence of information content in VL rank changes, and the price adjustment is not instantaneous, the absolute price change is not large enough to generate excess returns after the cost of transacting.

Huberman and Kandel concentrate on the relationship between the VL recommendation and firm size to see if the VL record is because of the firm size phenomenon.[95] When VL rankings were divided by firm size, the VL-based portfolios clearly outperformed the size-based portfolios. When only January returns are considered, all the size-based excess returns were positive, while the VL-based returns were not. Also, the VL-based excess returns declined as size increased, consistent with Stickel's results. Overall, these results imply no relationship between the VL rankings and size, because the VL record does not diminish when you control for size. Also, while the VL service favors large firms, it is better at predicting the relative returns on small-firm stocks.

Peterson examined the daily price changes around the release of initial reviews of common stock by VL to determine the information effect of these new rankings and the speed of adjustment.[96] The market model is derived from a period after the initial review and inclusion, and the analysis considers the day before official release, the release day, and the following day (typically Thursday, Friday, and Monday). The returns for rank-1 portfolios were significant on Days −1, 0, and +1, individually and combined. The results for Day −1 are due to leakage or early arrival of the *Value Line Survey*. The results for Day 0 and +1 could be due to the late arrival of the survey or the time required to adjust the price to the new information. On Day 0, there were significant returns only for rank-2 portfolios and on Day −1 for rank-4 portfolios. The lack of significant abnormal returns implies that these other rankings contain very little information. Interestingly, there were no significant price changes on Day +2 or subsequent days. It is concluded that there is information in some of the

[94] Scott E. Stickel, "The Effect of Value Line Investment Survey Changes on Common Stock Prices," *Journal of Financial Economics* 14, no. 1 (March 1985): 121–143.

[95] Gur Huberman and Shmuel Kandel, "Value Line Rank and Firm Size," *Journal of Business* 60, no. 4 (October 1987): 577–589.

[96] David R. Peterson, "Security Price Reactions to Initial Reviews of Common Stock by the Value Line Investment Survey," *Journal of Financial and Quantitative Analysis* 22, no. 4 (December 1987): 483–494.

rankings (mainly rank 1), but the market is fairly efficient in adjusting to them.

In summary, the several studies on the Value Line enigma appear to indicate that there is information in the VL rankings (especially either rank 1 or 5) and in changes in the rankings (especially going from 2 to 1). While these changes in rank have a larger effect on smaller firms, there is no direct relationship between the VL rankings and the size anomaly. Further, most of the recent evidence indicates that the market is fairly efficient, since the abnormal adjustments appear to be complete by Day +2. An analysis over time indicates a faster adjustment during recent years. Also, while there is evidence of statistically significant price changes, there is also mounting evidence that it is not possible to derive abnormal returns after considering realistic transaction costs.

SUMMARY REGARDING SEMISTRONG EMH. The evidence regarding the semistrong EMH is mixed. Numerous studies dealing with specific events (e.g., stock splits, world events, accounting changes) consistently support the semistrong hypothesis in that they indicate a swift reaction of security prices to new information and suggest investors generally cannot derive abnormal returns by acting after the announcement of the event. At the same time, during the past several years a number of anomalies have been derived and tested. Specifically, evidence regarding the reporting of unexpected quarterly earnings and the performance by low p/e stocks and stocks of small firms does not support the hypothesis. Several studies have attempted to explain these small-firm results in terms of the measures of risk, trading volume, and transaction costs. Further, there appears to be a January anomaly that supposedly was due entirely to tax selling, but subsequent work has indicated that there must be other explanations as well. Also, the January effect has been a factor in numerous other areas (size, risk-return relationship, dividend yield). Finally, the Value Line enigma contends that the VL rankings have information content and may be used to derive excess returns. The results indicate that only certain rankings or rank changes have valuable information (as indicated by price changes), although according to the most recent evidence, it is probably not possible to derive excess returns after transaction costs.

TESTS OF STRONG-FORM HYPOTHESIS

The strong-form efficient market hypothesis contends that stock prices fully reflect all information (public and private). Therefore, no investors possess information that would allow them to consistently generate above-average profits. This hypothesis is extremely rigid, requiring that stock prices adjust rapidly to new public information but also that no group have monopolistic access to specific information. Thus, it implies that all information is readily available to all investors at the same time.

The tests of this hypothesis have examined the performance of alternative groups of investors to determine whether any identifiable group has consistently experienced above-average risk-adjusted returns. Such results would indicate that either they had monopolistic access to important information or they consistently had the ability to act on public information before other investors could, which would imply that the market was not adjusting stock prices to *all* new information rapidly. Three major groups have been examined in this regard: (1) corporate insiders, (2) stock exchange specialists, and (3) professional money managers.

CORPORATE INSIDER TRADING. Securities laws require that individuals defined as *corporate insiders* report their transactions (purchases or sales) in the stock of the firm for which they are insiders to the SEC each month. Insiders are typically defined as major corporate officers, members of the board of directors, and owners of 10 percent or more of any equity class of securities. About six weeks after the reporting period, this insider trading information is made public by the SEC. Investigators have used it to identify how corporate insiders have traded and whether their transactions were generally profitable; that is, did they buy, on balance, before abnormally good price movements and sell, on balance, before poor market periods for their stock?[97] These studies have generally indicated that corporate insiders consistently enjoyed profits that were significantly above average. The results do not support the strong-form EMH, which requires that all investors have equal access to information.

A study by Pratt and DeVere indicated that public investors who consistently traded with the insiders based upon announced insider transactions would have enjoyed excess risk-adjusted returns (after commissions).[98] Kerr tested whether this was still true using 1976 data and concluded that the market had eliminated this inefficiency.[99] Trivoli contends that you can substantially increase the returns from using insider trading information by combining it with key financial ratios.[100] Nunn, Madden, and Gombola contend that you should consider what group of insiders is doing the buying and selling.[101] Seyhun confirmed the basic notion that insiders can predict abnormal stock prices when he found that they purchase stock prior to abnormal price increases and sell before abnormal declines.[102] He confirmed the Nunn, Madden, Gombola findings that more knowledgeable insiders such as board chairmen or officer-directors are

---

[97] The major studies on this topic are James H. Lorie and Victor Niederhoffer, "Predictive and Statistical Properties of Insider Trading," *Journal of Law and Economics* 11, (April 1968): 35–53; Shannon P. Pratt and Charles W. DeVere, "Relationship between Insider Trading and Rates of Return for NYSE Common Stocks, 1960–1966," in *Modern Developments in Investment Management*, 2d ed., ed. James Lorie and Richard Brealey (New York: Praeger Publishers, 1978): 259–272; Joseph E. Finnerty, "Insiders and Market Efficiency," *Journal of Finance* 31, no. 4 (September 1976): 1141–1148; and Joseph E. Finnerty, "Insiders Activity and Inside Information: A Multivariate Analysis," *Journal of Financial and Quantitative Analysis* 11, no. 2 (June 1976): 205–215. An indication of the popularity of this information is that *The Wall Street Journal* started a weekly column regarding this data during 1988.

[98] Pratt and DeVere, "Relationship between Insider Trading and Rates of Return."

[99] Halbert Kerr, "The Battle of Insider Trading and Market Efficiency," *Journal of Portfolio Management* 6, no. 4 (Summer 1980): 47–50.

[100] George W. Trivoli, "How to Profit from Insider Trading Information," *Journal of Portfolio Management* 6, no. 4 (Summer 1980): 51–56.

[101] Kenneth P. Nunn, Jr., Gerald P. Madden, and Michael J. Gombola, "Are Some Insiders More 'Inside' Than Others?" *Journal of Portfolio Management* 9, no. 3 (Spring 1982): 18–22.

[102] H. Nejat Seyhun, "Insiders' Profits, Costs of Trading, and Market Efficiency," *Journal of Financial Economics* 16, no. 2 (June 1986): 189–212.

better at predicting prices than other insiders. His results also agreed with Kerr since the realizable return to outsiders who attempted to act on the basis of insider reports was non-positive (after considering the appropriate trading costs that included the bid-ask spread plus the commission fee, as suggested by Stoll and Whaley). These results, which support the EMH, held even with the assumption of selective trading rules based on types of insiders or volume of trading. Alternatively, Lee and Solt found it is not possible to use *aggregate* insider trading activity as a guide to market timing.[103]

STOCK EXCHANGE SPECIALISTS. As discussed in Chapter 3, the stock exchange specialist has monopolistic access to information about unfilled limit orders. Therefore, one would expect specialists to derive above-average returns. An SEC study found that the specialist sells above his last purchase on 83 percent of all his sales and buys below his last sale on 81 percent of all his purchases.[104] One would expect such activity to provide above-average returns, as was confirmed in the *Institutional Investor Study (IIS)*, which indicated that the average return on capital exceeded 100 percent.[105] Reilly and Drzycimski found that, following major unexpected world announcements, the typical stock exchange specialist, acting *as he is directed,* would have consistently made profits on the trades following such announcements.[106]

PERFORMANCE OF PROFESSIONAL MONEY MANAGERS. The studies of professional money managers are more realistic and widely applicable than the analysis of insiders and specialists, because money managers typically do not have monopolistic access to important new information. Because they are highly trained professionals who work full time at investment management, if any "normal" set of investors should be able to derive above-average profits, it should be this group. Also, if any noninsider should be able to derive inside information, professional money managers should, because they conduct extensive management interviews.

Most studies have examined mutual funds, because performance data is readily available on them. Only recently have data been available for bank trust departments, insurance companies, and investment advisers. Several mutual fund studies have indicated that most funds have not been able to match the performance of a buy-and-hold policy.[107] When risk-

---

[103] Wayne Y. Lee and Michael E. Solt, "Insider Trading: A Poor Guide to Market Timing," *Journal of Portfolio Management* 12, no. 4 (Summer 1986): 65–71.

[104] *Report of the Special Study of the Security Markets* (Washington, D.C.: Securities and Exchange Commission, 1963): Part 2, 54.

[105] U.S. Securities and Exchange Commission, *Institutional Investor Study Report,* 92nd Congress, 1st Session, House Document No. 92–64 (Washington, D.C.: U.S. Government Printing Office, 1971).

[106] Frank K. Reilly and Eugene F. Drzycimski, "The Stock Exchange Specialist and the Market Impact of Major World Events," *Financial Analysts Journal* 31, no. 4 (July–August 1975): 27–32.

[107] Notable studies include William F. Sharpe, "Mutual Fund Performance," *Journal of Business* 39, no. 1 (January 1966 Supplement): 119–139; Michael Jensen, "The Performance of Mutual Funds in the Period 1945–1964," *Journal of Finance* 23, no. 2 (May 1968): 389–416; and Jack L. Treynor, "How to Rate Management of Investment Funds," *Harvard Business Review* 43, no. 1 (January–February 1965): 63–75. These studies and others on this topic are reviewed in Chapter 20.

Table 6.1
Annual Rates of Return during Alternative Periods Ending December 31, 1987

	1 Year	2 Years	4 Years	6 Years	8 Years	10 Years
U.S. Equity Broad Universes						
Equity accounts	3.5	10.5	13.7	17.9	17.3	17.1
Equity pooled accounts	4.2	10.2	12.8	15.7	15.1	14.6
Equity-oriented separate accounts	4.2	10.4	13.9	17.7	17.3	16.8
Special equity pooled accounts	−3.1	3.2	5.9	12.1	13.6	15.6
Mutual Fund Universes						
Balanced and income mutual funds	2.0	9.1	12.6	15.9	14.7	14.3
Growth mutual funds	3.8	9.3	9.7	13.9	14.3	16.2
U.S. Equity Style Universes						
Earnings growth accounts	6.8	12.7	14.1	17.4	18.2	18.1
Small capitalization accounts	−1.3	3.9	7.7	15.8	17.0	17.6
Price-driven accounts	2.3	9.2	13.8	18.8	17.4	16.8
Market-oriented accounts	5.2	11.4	15.2	17.8	17.4	16.4
S&P 500 Index	5.2	11.7	15.0	17.3	16.0	15.3
Number of Universes with Returns above the S&P 500	1	1	1	5	6	8

Source: Frank Russell Analytical Services, Tacoma, WA.

adjusted returns were examined without considering commission costs, slightly more than half of the money managers did better than the overall market. When commission costs, load fees, and management costs were considered, approximately two-thirds of the mutual funds generally failed to match aggregate market performance. Also, funds were inconsistent in their performance.[108] These results supported the strong-form EMH, because most mutual fund managers, using publicly available information (and anything else available), could not consistently outperform a buy-and-hold policy.

Some recent performance figures for other institutional investors have generally been consistent with the mutual fund results, though not directly comparable to them, because the multi-institution figures generally report only annualized rates of return. Frank Russell Co. collects and reports these data as part of its performance evaluation service. Table 6.1 contains the mean rates of return for several investment groups compared to the Standard & Poor's 500 Index.[109]

The first set of universes are banks that generally never experienced returns above the Standard & Poor's 500 during the last four years, but the equity-oriented separate accounts did better in terms of rates of return for the six-, eight-, and ten-year comparisons. The mutual funds never had

[108] Robert C. Klemkosky, "How Consistently Do Managers Manage?" *Journal of Portfolio Management* 3, no. 2 (Winter 1977): 11–15.
[109] The results for these individual accounts have an upward bias because they consider only accounts retained—i.e., if a firm or bank does a poor job on an account and the client leaves, those results would not be included.

superior results except for the growth mutual funds that did better for the ten-year period. Finally, some of the equity-style universes did better for the six-, eight-, and ten-year periods, although these results were not adjusted for risk. As stated, these results are generally consistent with the mutual fund results and would support the EMH.

While tests of the strong-form EMH generated mixed results, most relevant evidence supported it. Results for corporate insiders and stock exchange specialists did not support the hypothesis, because it appears that they have monopolistic access to important information and they use it to derive abnormal returns. In contrast, numerous studies of performance by professional money managers indicated that they could not consistently outperform a buy-and-hold policy. Because this last group is similar to most investors who do not have access to inside information, their results are considered most relevant, which implies support for the strong-form hypothesis.

IMPLICATIONS OF EFFICIENT CAPITAL MARKETS

Overall evidence implies that the equity market is generally efficient for most investors, but there are also some well-documented anomalies. Let us consider the implication of these results for investment analysts and portfolio managers.

EFFICIENT MARKETS AND TECHNICAL ANALYSIS

It is widely recognized that a belief in technical analysis and the notion of efficient markets are directly opposed. Technical analysts contend that stock prices move in trends that persist. They believe that when new information comes to the market, it is not immediately available to everyone; it is typically disseminated from the informed professional to the aggressive investing public and then to the great bulk of investors. The belief in such a pattern of events is in direct contrast to the EMH, which contends that the adjustment of security prices to new information is very rapid.

If the capital market is efficient and prices fully reflect all relevant information, any technical trading system that depends only upon past trading data cannot be of any value, because by the time the information is public, the price adjustment has taken place. Therefore, a purchase or sale using a technical trading rule should not generate abnormal returns after taking account of commissions.

EFFICIENT MARKETS AND FUNDAMENTAL ANALYSIS

Advocates of *fundamental analysis* believe that the intrinsic value for a security is determined by underlying economic variables such as current and future earnings and risk variables, together with the current market price. Fundamental analysts believe that occasionally the market price and intrinsic value differ, but eventually the market will recognize the discrepancy and correct it. Therefore, if an analyst can do a superior job of *estimating* intrinsic value, he can consistently acquire undervalued securities and derive above-average returns. The following discussion considers the implications of efficient markets on aggregate market analysis, industry analysis, company analysis, and portfolio management.

While several studies that will be discussed in Chapter 13 indicate that market analysis can be very rewarding, the EMH indicates that a market projection cannot depend only upon past data; there must be an *accurate estimate* of the variables that influence the overall economy and the aggregate stock market. An investment based upon a model using only historical economic data should not do better than a buy-and-hold policy.

Likewise, the discussions in Chapters 14 and 15 indicate that industry and stock analysis should be of value, but the EMH implies that it is necessary to understand the variables that determine stock prices and to project movements in these valuation variables. As an example, Niederhoffer and Regan showed that the crucial difference between the stocks that enjoyed the best and worst price performance during a given year was the relationship between estimated earnings and actual earnings—that is, unexpected earnings.[110] Therefore, if you can do a superior job of consistently projecting earnings that are significantly different from general expectations, it is possible to achieve a superior stock selection record.

Theory and evidence agree that it is not impossible, though it is very difficult, to be a consistently superior analyst. A superior analyst must understand what variables are relevant for changes in valuation and must be able to consistently estimate future values for these variables. To determine who the superior analysts are, the following relatively simple evaluation system has been suggested. Examine the performance of numerous buy and sell recommendations made by an analyst over time relative to the performance of randomly selected stocks of the same risk class. If the analyst produces results that are consistently better than random selection, he is a superior analyst. The consistency requirement is crucial, because one would expect randomly selected securities to outperform the market about half the time.

A text on security valuation can indicate the relevant variables and point out the important techniques to consider, but the actual estimate is as much an art as it is a science. If the estimates were mechanical, you could program a computer to do them, and there would be no need for analysts. Therefore, the superior analyst must understand what is important and have the ability to *estimate* these variables.

EFFICIENT MARKETS AND PORTFOLIO ANALYSIS

Prior studies have indicated that professional money managers cannot beat a simple buy-and-hold policy on a risk-adjusted basis. One explanation is that there are no superior analysts and the cost of research is what causes these inferior results. Another explanation (favored by the author, with no empirical support) is that institutions employ both superior and inferior analysts, and recommendations by the few superior analysts are offset by the costs and recommendations of the inferior analysts.

---

[110] Victor Niederhoffer and Patrick J. Regan, "Earnings Changes, Analysts Forecast, and Stock Prices," *Financial Analysts Journal* 28, no. 3 (May–June 1972): 65–71.

The point is, there are ways of increasing returns for a given portfolio without superior analysts. Sharpe and Cooper found a good relationship between the returns for a portfolio of stocks in period *t,* and risk measures in the prior period. This means it is possible to build a portfolio of stocks that will conform to a client's risk preferences, *using historical risk information,* and receive a rate of return consistent with the risk level specified.[111] Lorie, Dodd, and Kimpton set forth how the portfolio should be managed in a world with efficient capital markets to provide maximum risk-adjusted returns for the client.[112] First, the portfolio manager should determine and measure the client's risk preferences, recognizing that the client's other investments may influence his portfolio preference. After quantifying the client's risk preferences, the manager should derive a given risk portfolio by investing a certain proportion of the wealth available into a completely diversified portfolio of risky assets and the rest into a risk-free asset.[113]

Assuming that the portfolio manager is not capable of predicting future market movements, the third task is to maintain the specified risk level rather than attempting to change the risk posture of the portfolio based upon market expectations. Because of changing market values, the composite risk of a portfolio can change without overt action, so it may become necessary to trade to rebalance the portfolio. Finally, it is important to minimize transaction costs by considering the following three factors. One is minimizing taxes for the client. How this is accomplished will vary, but it should be given prime consideration when carrying out transactions. Second, reduce trading turnover to the level necessitated by liquidity needs and risk control (trades needed to maintain a given risk level). Finally, attempt to minimize the liquidity costs of trades by using stocks that have low trading costs, and are relatively liquid. To accomplish this, orders to buy or to sell several stocks should be submitted at net prices that approximate the specialist's quote (i.e., submit a limit order to buy stock at the bid price or sell it at the ask price). The stock that is bought or sold first is the one that meets your criteria, and all other orders are withdrawn.

In summary, a portfolio manager without superior analysts should do the following:

1. Determine and quantify the risk preferences of the client.
2. Construct the appropriate portfolio by dividing the total portfolio between risk-free assets and a completely diversified risky-asset portfolio.
3. Maintain the specified risk level.
4. Minimize total transaction costs.

---

[111] William F. Sharpe and Guy M. Cooper, "Risk-Return Classes of New York Stock Exchange Common Stocks, 1931–1967," *Financial Analysts Journal* 28, no. 2 (March–April 1972): 46–54, 81.

[112] James H. Lorie, Peter Dodd, and Mary Hamilton Kimpton, *The Stock Market: Theories and Evidence,* 2d ed. (Homewood, Ill.: Richard D. Irwin, 1985), 84–86.

[113] There is a detailed discussion of this in Chapters 7 and 8.

INDEX FUNDS. The prior discussion indicates that, assuming efficient capital markets and few truly superior analysts, a large amount of money should be managed so that the performance matches the aggregate market and costs are minimized. In response, three institutions have instigated *market funds,* also referred to as *index funds.* Index funds are security portfolios specially designed to duplicate the performance of the overall security market as represented by some specified market index series. Three major funds were started in the early 1970s: (1) American National Bank and Trust Company of Chicago, (2) Batterymarch Financial Management Corporation of Boston, and (3) Wells Fargo Investment Advisors.[114] All these equity portfolios were designed to match the performance of the S&P 500 Index. The ability of the three major index funds to match the market has been documented by the author. The correlation of quarterly rates of return for the index funds and the S&P 500 for the period 1975–1987 generally exceeded 0.98, which indicates the funds clearly fulfill their stated goal of matching market performance.

PORTFOLIO MANAGEMENT WITH SUPERIOR ANALYSTS. Security analysts with superior insights and analytical ability should obviously be utilized. The problem is recognizing them while avoiding using inferior analysts. The evaluation system suggested earlier should help reveal the truly superior analysts and should be consistently updated to determine continued superiority. The superior analysts should make investment recommendations for a certain proportion of the portfolio, ensuring that the risk preferences of the client are maintained. Also, superior analysts should be encouraged to *concentrate their efforts in the second tier of stocks.* Recall that in Chapter 3 we discussed the three-tier market created by the need of institutions for liquid securities. The middle tier consists of companies large enough to be acquired by most institutions, although probably not the largest 25 to 30 institutions.[115] Middle-tier firms possess the required liquidity, but they do not receive the attention of top-tier stocks, so the markets may not be as efficient. Thus, you should concentrate analytical skills on these stocks for which the probabilities of finding a temporarily undervalued security are greater. As discussed earlier in the chapter, Arbel and Strebel found superior returns for stocks followed by fewer analysts.

EFFICIENCY IN EUROPEAN EQUITY MARKETS

With rare exception, the discussion in this chapter has been concerned with the EMH as applied to the U.S. equity market. Because of the growing importance of world markets, a natural question would be how efficient are securities markets outside the United States. While there have been numerous studies dealing with this set of questions, a reasonably thorough presentation of the studies would substantially lengthen the chapter. For-

---

[114] A. F. Ehrbar, "Index Funds—An Idea Whose Time Is Coming," *Fortune* (June 1976): 145–148; John H. Langbein and Richard A. Posner, "Market Funds and Trust-Investment Law," *American Bar Foundation Research Journal* 1976, no. 1: 1–34; and John H. Langbein and Richard A. Posner, "Market Funds and Trust Investment Law II," *American Bar Foundation Research Journal* 1977, no. 1: 1–27.

[115] Frank K. Reilly, "A Three-Tier Stock Market and Corporate Finance," *Financial Management* 4, no. 3 (Autumn 1975): 7–15.

tunately, Gabriel Hawawini has authored a monograph that specifically reviews over 200 studies examining the behavior of European stock prices and evaluating the efficiency of European equity markets.[116] Table 1 of the monograph contains a list of over 280 references of studies covering 14 Western European countries from Austria to the United Kingdom. All the studies are classified by country and also for each country into one of five categories:

1. Market model, beta estimation, and diversification
2. Capital asset pricing model and arbitrage pricing model
3. Weak-form tests of market efficiency
4. Semistrong-form tests of market efficiency
5. Strong-form tests of market efficiency.

The author offers the following overall conclusion after acknowledging that European markets are smaller and less active than U.S. markets.

> Our review of the literature indicates that despite the peculiarities of European equity markets, the behavior of European stock prices is, with few exceptions, surprisingly similar to that of U.S. common stocks. That is true even for countries with extremely narrow equity markets such as Finland. The view that most European equity markets, particulary those of smaller countries, are informationally inefficient does not seem to be borne out by the data. We will see that most of the results of empirical tests performed on European common stock prices are generally in line with those reported by researchers who used U.S. data.

This implies that when one considers securities outside the United States, it is appropriate to assume a level of efficiency similar to that of the U.S. markets.

SUMMARY

It is necessary to consider efficient capital markets at this point because there are implications of such markets for security analysis and portfolio management. Capital markets should be efficient, because there are numerous rational, profit-maximizing investors who react quickly to the release of new information. Assuming prices reflect new information, they are unbiased estimates of the securities' true, intrinsic value, and there should be a consistent relationship between the return on an investment and its risk.

The voluminous research on the EMH has been divided into three segments, and each has been tested separately. The weak-form EMH states that stock prices fully reflect all market information, so any trading rule that uses past market data to predict future returns should not be of value. Test results consistently support the weak-form EMH.

---

[116] Gabriel Hawawini, *European Equity Markets: Price Behavior and Efficiency*, Monograph 1984–4/5, Monograph Series in Finance and Economics, Salomon Brothers Center for the Study of Financial Institutions, Graduate School of Business, New York University, 1984.

The semistrong EMH asserts that security prices adjust rapidly to the release of all public information. The tests of this hypothesis either examine abnormal price movements surrounding the announcement of important new information or analyze whether investors could derive above-average returns from trading on the basis of public information. The test results have been mixed. On the one hand, the results for numerous studies related to economic events such as stock splits and accounting changes consistently support the semistrong hypothesis. In contrast, some recent studies that examined exchange listings, unexpected quarterly earning announcements, low p/e stocks, small firms, neglected stocks, and stocks ranked by Value Line, as well as the January effect, do not support the hypothesis.

The strong-form EMH states that security prices reflect all information. This implies that nobody has monopolistic access to important information, so no group should be able to derive above-average returns consistently. The results for corporate insiders and stock exchange specialists do not support the strong-form hypothesis. In contrast, the results for professional money managers do support the hypothesis because their performance was typically inferior to results achieved with buy-and-hold policies.

The EMH indicates that technical analysis should be of no value. All forms of fundamental analysis are useful, but they are difficult to implement, because they require the ability to *estimate future values* for relevant economic variables. It is possible to be a superior analyst, but it is very difficult because it requires superior projections. Portfolio managers should constantly evaluate analysts to determine whether their performance is superior. Without superior analysts, the portfolio should be run like an index fund. In contrast, superior analysts should be allowed to make decisions, but they should concentrate on middle-tier firms, where there is a higher probability of discovering misvalued stocks.

There is some good news and some bad news. The good news is that the practice of security analysis and portfolio management is not an art that has been lost to the great computer in the sky. These are still viable professions for those willing to extend the effort and able to accept the pressures. The bad news is that, because of many bright, hard-working people with extensive resources, the game is not easy. In fact, the aforementioned competitors have created a very efficient capital market in which it is extremely difficult for most analysts and portfolio managers to be superior.

QUESTIONS

1. Discuss the rationale for expecting the existence of an efficient capital market.

2. Based upon the factors that contribute to an efficient market, what would you look for if you were trying to identify an efficient market versus a less efficient or inefficient market for a stock?

3. Define and discuss the weak-form EMH.

4. Describe the two sets of tests used to examine the weak-form EMH.

5. Define and discuss the semistrong EMH.

6. Describe the two general tests used to examine the semistrong EMH. Discuss whether you expect the results from the two different tests to be consistent.

7. Using the standard one-factor CAPM, describe how you would derive abnormal risk-adjusted returns for a stock during a period surrounding a significant economic event. Give an example.

8. It is contended that many tests of the semistrong EMH are actually a joint test of the CAPM and the EMH. Explain this contention, and discuss its impact on the small-firm studies.

9. When the EMH is tested using alternative trading rules versus a buy-and-hold policy, three common mistakes can bias the results against the EMH. Discuss each individually, and explain why it would cause a bias.

10. Describe the results of a study that supported the semistrong EMH. Discuss why the results supported the hypothesis.

11. Describe the results of a study that did not support the semistrong EMH. Discuss why the results did not support the hypothesis.

12. Define and discuss the strong-form EMH. Discuss why some observers contend that the strong-form hypothesis really requires a *perfect market* in addition to efficient markets.

13. Discuss in general terms how one would go about testing the strong-form EMH. Consider why these tests are relevant, and give a brief example.

14. Describe the results of a study that does not support the strong-form EMH. Discuss specifically why these results do not support the hypothesis.

15. Describe the results of a study that indicates support for the strong-form EMH. Discuss specifically why these results support the hypothesis.

16. What are the implications of the EMH for the use of technical analysis?

17. What are the implications of the EMH for fundamental analysis? Be specific, and discuss what the EMH does and does not imply.

18. In a world with efficient capital markets, what is required to be a superior analyst? Be specific.

19. Discuss in detail how you would test whether an analyst is truly superior.

20. What are the implications of an efficient market for a portfolio manager without any superior analysts? Specifically, how should he run his portfolio?

21. Describe an index fund. What are its purposes? How is such a fund run?

22. Discuss some observers' contention that index funds are the ultimate answer in a world with efficient capital markets.

23. At a social gathering you meet the portfolio manager for the trust department of a local bank. He confides to you that he has been following the recommendations of his six analysts for an extended period and has found that two are superior, two are average, and two are clearly inferior. What would you recommend that he do in terms of running his portfolio? Be specific.

24. Do you think the development of a tiered market has any implications for the discussion of efficient capital markets? If so, what are they?

25. Are you surprised by the findings related to the EMH described by Hawawini for the European equity markets? Why or why not?

26. Describe a test of the weak-form EMH for the Japanese stock market, and indicate where you would get the required data.

PROBLEMS

1. Compute the abnormal rates of return for the following stocks during period t (ignore differential systematic risk):

Stock	R_{it}	R_{mt}
C	10.5	11.0
E	8.5	7.0
F	14.7	10.0
T	12.0	10.0
W	13.2	12.1

R_{it}—return for stock i during period t.
R_{mt}—return for the aggregate market during period t.

2. Compute the abnormal rates of return for the five stocks in Problem 1 assuming the following systematic risk measures (betas):

Stock	i
C	0.80
E	1.30
F	1.10
T	1.15
W	1.20

3. Compare the abnormal returns in Problems 1 and 2 and discuss the reason for the difference in each case.

4. An analyst gives you the following data regarding the performance of a group of stock recommendations and a matched set of stocks (matched in terms of beta). Would you judge this individual to be a superior analyst? Discuss your reasoning.

Stock	Beginning Price	Ending Price	Dividend
W	43	47	1.50
W-match	22	24	1.00
M	75	73	2.00
M-match	42	38	1.00
R	28	34	1.25
R-match	18	16	1.00
L	52	57	2.00
L-match	38	44	1.50
C	63	68	1.75
C-match	32	34	1.00

REFERENCES

Ball, Ray. "Anomalies in Relationships between Securities' Yields and Yield-Surrogates." *Journal of Financial Economics* 6, no. 2/3 (June–September 1978).

Ball, Ray. "Changes in Accounting Techniques and Stock Prices." *Empirical Research in Accounting.* Supplement to *Journal of Accounting Research* 10 (1972).

Ball, Ray. "Risk, Return, and Disequilibrium—An Application to Changes in Accounting Techniques." *Journal of Finance* 27, no. 2 (May 1972).

Banz, R. W. "The Relationship between Return and Market Value of Common Stocks." *Journal of Financial Economics* 9, no. 1 (March 1981).

Barry, Christopher B., and Stephen J. Brown. "Differential Information and the Small Firm Effect." *Journal of Financial Economics* 13, no. 2 (June 1984).

Basu, S. "Investment Performance of Common Stocks in Relation to Their Price-Earnings Ratios: A Test of the Efficient Market Hypothesis." *Journal of Finance* 32, no. 3 (June 1977).

Basu, Senjoy. "The Relationship between Earnings Yield, Market Value and Return for NYSE Common Stocks." *Journal of Financial Economics* 12, no. 1 (June 1983).

Beatty, Randolph, and Jay Ritter. "Investments Banking, Reputation, and the Underpricing of Initial Public Offerings." *Journal of Financial Economics* 15, no. 1 (March 1986).

Black, Fischer. "Yes, Virginia, There Is Hope: Tests of the Value Line Ranking System." *Financial Analysts Journal* 29, no. 5 (September–October 1973).

Brown, Phillip, and Ray Ball. "An Empirical Evaluation of Accounting Income Numbers." *Journal of Accounting Research* 6, no. 2. (Autumn 1963).

Brown, Philip, Donald B. Keim, Allan W. Kleidon, and Terry A. Marsh. "Stock Return Seasonalities and the Tax-Loss Selling Hypothesis." *Journal of Financial Economics* 12, no. 1 (June 1983).

Copeland, Thomas E., and David Mayers. "The Value Line Enigma (1965–1978): A Case Study of Performance Evaluation Issues." *Journal of Financial Economics* 10, no. 3 (November 1982).

Dimson, Elroy. "Risk Measurement When Shares Are Subject to Infrequent Trading." *Journal of Financial Economics* 7, no. 2 (June 1979).

Fama, Eugene F. "The Behavior of Stock Prices." *Journal of Business* 38, no. 1 (January 1965).

Fama, Eugene F. "Efficient Capital Markets: A Review of Theory and Empirical Work." *Journal of Finance* 25, no. 2 (May 1970).

Fama, Eugene F., L. Fisher, M. Jensen, and R. Roll. "The Adjustment of Stock Prices to New Information." *International Economic Review* 10, no. 1 (February 1969).

Fama, Eugene F., and J. MacBeth. "Risk Return and Equilibrium, Some Empirical Results." *Journal of Political Economy* 81, no. 2 (May 1977).

Finnerty, Joseph E. "Insiders and Market Efficiency." *Journal of Finance* 31, no. 4 (September 1976).

Foster, George, Chris Olsen, and Terry Shevlin. "Earnings Releases, Anomalies, and the Behavior of Security Returns." *Accounting Review* 59, no. 4 (October 1984).

Grinblatt, Mark S., Ronald W. Masulis, and Sheridan Titman. "The Valuation Effects of Stock Splits and Stock Dividends." *Journal of Financial Economics* 13, no. 4 (December 1984).

Hawawini, Gabriel. *European Equity Markets: Price Behavior and Efficiency,* Monograph 1984-4/5. Monograph Series in Finance and Economics, Salomon Brothers Center for the Study of Financial Institutions, Graduate School of Business, New York University, 1984.

Huberman, Gur, and Shmuel Kandel. "Value Line Rank and Firm Size." *Journal of Business* 60, no. 4 (October 1987).

Joy, O. Maurice, Robert H. Litzenberger, and Richard W. McEnally. "The Adjustment of Stock Prices to the Announcements of Unanticipated Changes in Quarterly Earnings." *Journal of Accounting Research* 15, no. 2 (Autumn 1977).

Keim, Donald B. "Dividend Yields and Stock Returns: Implications of Abnormal January Returns." *Journal of Financial Economics* 14, no. 3 (September 1985).

Keim, Donald B. "Size-Related Anomalies and Stock Return Seasonality." *Journal of Financial Economics* 12, no. 1 (June 1983).

Lakonishok, Josef, and Seymour Smidt. "Volume and Turn-of-the-Year Behavior." *Journal of Financial Economics* 13, no. 3 (September 1984).

Langbein, John H., and Richard A. Posner. "Market Funds and Trust-Investment Law." *American Bar Foundation Research Journal* 1976 no. 1.

Latané, H. A., and Charles Jones. "Standardized Unexpected Earnings: 1971–1977." *Journal of Finance* 34, no. 3 (June 1979).

Lorie, James H., and Victor Niederhoffer. "Predictive and Statistical Properties of Insider Trading." *Journal of Law and Economics* 11 (April 1968).

Miller, Robert E., and Frank K. Reilly. "An Examination of Mispricing, Returns, and Uncertainty for Initial Public Offerings." *Financial Management* 16, no. 2 (January 1987).

Peterson, David R. "Security Price Reactions to Initial Reviews of Common Stock by the Value Line Investment Survey." *Journal of Financial and Quantitative Analysis* 22, no. 4 (December 1987).

Reilly, Frank K., and Eugene F. Drzycimski. "Short-Run Profits from Stock Splits." *Financial Management* 10, no. 3 (Summer 1981).

Reilly, Frank K., and Kenneth Hatfield. "Investor Experience with New Stock Issues." *Financial Analysts Journal* 25, no. 5 (September–October 1969).

Reinganum, Marc R. "Misspecification of Capital Asset Pricing: Empirical Anomalies Based on Earnings Yield and Market Values." *Journal of Financial Economics* 9, no. 1 (March 1981).

Reinganum, Marc R. "The Anomalous Stock Market Behavior of Small Firms in January: Empirical Tests for Tax-Loss Selling Effect." *Journal of Financial Economics* 12, no. 1 (January 1983).

Rendlemen, Jr., Charles P. Jones, and Henry A. Latané. "Empirical Anomalies Based on Unexpected Earnings and the Importance of Risk Adjustments." *Journal of Financial Economics* 10, no. 3 (November 1982).

Rock, K. "Why New Issues are Underpriced." *Journal of Financial Economics* 15, no. 1 (March 1986).

Roll, Richard. "A Possible Explanation of the Small Firm Effect." *Journal of Finance* 36, no. 4 (September 1981).

Sanger, Gary C., and John J. McConnell. "Stock Exchange Listings, Firm Value, and Security Market Efficiency: The Impact of NASDAQ." *Journal of Financial and Quantitative Analysis* 21, no. 1 (March 1986).

Seyhun, H. Nejat. "Insiders' Profits, Costs of Trading, and Market Efficiency." *Journal of Financial Economics* 16, no. 2 (June 1986).

Stoll, Hans R., and Robert E. Whaley. "Transactions Costs and the Small Firm Effect." *Journal of Financial Economics* 12, no. 1 (June 1983).

Tinic, Seha M., and Richard R. West. "Risk and Return: January vs. the Rest of the Year." *Journal of Financial Economics* 13, no. 4 (December 1984).

Watts, Ross L. "Systematic 'Abnormal' Returns After Quarterly Earnings Announcements." *Journal of Financial Economics* 6, no. 2/3 (June–September 1978).

Ying, Louis K. W., W. G. Lewellen, G. G. Schlarbaum, and R. C. Lease. "Stock Exchange Listings and Securities Returns." *Journal of Financial and Quantitative Analysis* 12, no. 4 (September 1977).

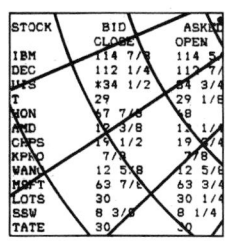

CHAPTER 7

AN INTRODUCTION TO PORTFOLIO MANAGEMENT

The study of portfolio theory and capital market theory is generally placed near the end of a text on investments because it is considered necessary to deal with the analysis of individual securities first. However, there is a general principle of risk derived from portfolio theory that must be understood prior to analyzing individual securities. Therefore, this chapter explains portfolio theory step by step, introducing the basic portfolio risk formula that is so important to understand when you combine different assets. The following chapter introduces capital market theory with an emphasis on the risk measure for individual assets.

AN OPTIMUM PORTFOLIO

One basic assumption of portfolio theory is that any investor wishes to maximize the returns from his investments. In order to adequately deal with such an assumption, certain ground rules must be laid. First, the portfolio being considered by an individual should include all of his assets and liabilities, not only stocks or even only marketable securities, but also such items as the investor's car, house, and less marketable assets like coins, stamps, antiques, furniture, and so forth. The full spectrum of assets must be considered, because the returns from all of these assets interact, and this interaction is important. Hence, a good portfolio is not simply a collection of individually good assets.

RISK AVERSION

A second assumption is that investors are basically *risk averse,* meaning that, given a choice between two assets with equal rates of return, they will select the asset with the lower level of risk. Evidence that most investors are risk averse is their purchase of various types of insurance, including life insurance, car insurance, and health insurance. Insurance is basically a current certain outlay of a given amount to guard against an uncertain, possibly larger outlay in the future. People who purchase in-

255

surance are willing to pay to avoid the risk of a potentially large future loss. Further evidence of risk aversion is the difference in *promised yield* (the required rate of return) for different grades of bonds that supposedly have different degrees of risk. It increases as you go from AAA (the lowest risk class) to AA to A, and so on. This means that investors require a higher rate of return in order to accept higher risk.

The foregoing does not imply that everybody is risk averse, or that investors are completely risk averse regarding all financial commitments. Not everybody buys insurance for everything. Some people have no insurance against anything, either by choice or because they cannot afford it. In addition, some individuals buy insurance and also gamble at race tracks or in Las Vegas, where it is known that the expected returns are negative, which means that participants are willing to pay for the excitement of the risk involved. This combination of risk preference and risk aversion can be explained by a utility function that is not completely concave or convex but is a combination of the two that depends upon the amount of money involved. Friedman and Savage speculate that such is the case for people who like to gamble for small amounts (in lotteries or nickel slot machines) but insure themselves against large losses like fire or accidents.[1] However, most investors committing large sums of money to developing a portfolio of earning assets are risk averse, so there should be a positive relationship between expected return and expected risk.

DEFINITION OF RISK

While there is a difference in the specific definitions of *risk* and *uncertainty,* for our purposes and in most financial literature the two terms are used interchangeably. In fact, one way to define *risk* is as the uncertainty of future outcomes. An alternative definition might be the probability of an adverse outcome.

MARKOWITZ PORTFOLIO THEORY

In the 1950s and early 1960s a large segment of the investment community talked about risk, but there was no measurable specification for the term. The portfolio model, however, required investors to quantify their risk variable. The basic portfolio model, developed by Harry Markowitz, derived the expected rate of return for a portfolio of assets and an expected risk measure.[2] Markowitz showed that the variance of the rate of return was a meaningful measure of risk under a reasonable set of assumptions and derived the formulas for computing the variance of the portfolio. This formula not only indicated the importance of diversifying to reduce risk, but also showed how to effectively diversify. The Markowitz model is based on several assumptions regarding investor behavior:

---

[1] Milton Friedman and Leonard J. Savage, "The Utility Analysis of Choices Involving Risk," *Journal of Political Economy* 56, no. 3 (August 1948): 279–304.

[2] Harry Markowitz, "Portfolio Selection,"*Journal of Finance* 7, no. 1 (March 1952): 77–91; and Harry Markowitz, *Portfolio Selection—Efficient Diversification of Investments* (New Haven, Conn.: Yale University Press, 1959).

*Markowitz
Assumptions :*

1. Investors consider each investment alternative as being represented by a probability distribution of expected returns over some holding period.
2. Investors maximize one-period expected utility, and their utility curves demonstrate diminishing marginal utility of wealth.
3. Investors estimate risk on the basis of the variability of expected returns.
4. Investors base decisions solely on expected return and risk, so their utility curves are a function of expected return and variance (or standard deviation) of returns only.
5. For a given risk level, investors prefer higher returns to lower returns. Similarly, for a given level of expected return, investors prefer less risk to more risk.

Under these assumptions, a single asset or portfolio of assets is considered to be *efficient* if no other asset or portfolio of assets offers a higher expected return with the same (or lower) risk, or lower risk with the same (or higher) expected return.

One of the best-known measures of risk is the *variance,* or *standard deviation of expected returns*. It is a statistical measure of the dispersion of returns around the expected value. A larger value indicates greater dispersion, all other factors being equal. The idea is that the more dispersed the returns, the greater the uncertainty of those returns in any future period. Another measure of risk is the *range of returns* based upon the assumption that a larger range of returns, from the lowest to the highest, means greater uncertainty regarding future expected returns.

Instead of using measures that analyze any deviation from expectations, some believe that the investor should be concerned only with returns below expectations—deviations below the mean value. A measure for this is the *semivariance,* and an extension of that measure would be deviations below zero, or negative returns. Both measures implicitly assume that investors want to minimize the damage from below-average returns. Obviously, they would welcome positive returns or returns above expectations, so these are not considered when measuring risk. Although there are numerous potential measures of risk, we will use the variance, or standard deviation of returns, because (1) this measure is somewhat intuitive, (2) it is a correct risk measure, and (3) it has been used in most of the theoretical asset pricing models.

**EXPECTED RATES
OF RETURN**

The expected rate of return for a portfolio of assets is simply the weighted average of the expected rates of return for the individual assets in the portfolio. The weights are the proportion of total value for the asset. The expected return for a hypothetical individual asset is computed as shown in Table 7.1, where we assume that we have estimated equal probabilities for all the potential returns.

The expected return for an individual asset with the set of potential returns and probabilities used in the example would be 11 percent. The

TABLE 7.1
Computation of the Expected Return for an Individual Risky Asset

PROBABILITY	POTENTIAL RETURN (%)	EXPECTED RETURN (%)
.25	.08	.0200
.25	.10	.0250
.25	.12	.0300
.25	.14	.0350
		$E(R) = .1100$

expected return for a hypothetical four-asset portfolio is shown in Table 7.2. The expected return for the total portfolio would be 11.5 percent. The effect of adding or dropping any security from the portfolio would be easy to determine, given the new weights based on value and the expected returns for each of the assets. This computation of the expected return for the portfolio [$E(R_{port})$] can be generalized as follows:

$$E(R_{port}) = \sum_{i=1}^{n} W_i R_i ,$$

where

W_i = the percent of the portfolio in asset i

R_i = the expected rate of return for asset i.

VARIANCE (STANDARD DEVIATION) OF RETURNS

It was mentioned earlier that we would be using the variance, or the standard deviation of returns, as the measure of risk. (You will recall that the standard deviation is the square root of the variance.) Therefore, at this point we will demonstrate the computation of the standard deviation of returns for an individual asset. Subsequently, after discussing some other statistical concepts, we will consider the determination of the standard deviation for a portfolio of assets.

TABLE 7.2
Computation of the Expected Return for a Portfolio of Risky Assets

WEIGHT (W_i) (% OF PORTFOLIO)	EXPECTED SECURITY RETURN (R_i)	EXPECTED PORTFOLIO RETURN ($W_i \times R_i$)
.20	.10	.0200
.30	.11	.0330
.30	.12	.0360
.20	.13	.0260
		$E(R_{port}) = .1150$

TABLE 7.3
Computation of the Variance for an Individual Risky Asset

POTENTIAL RETURN (R_i)	EXPECTED RETURN $E(R_i)$	$R_i - E(R_i)$	$[R_i - E(R_i)]^2$	P_i	$(R_i - E(R_i))^2 P_i$
.08	.11	−.03	.0009	.25	.000225
.10	.11	−.01	.0001	.25	.000025
.12	.11	.01	.0001	.25	.000025
.14	.11	.03	.0009	.25	.000225
					.000500

Variance (σ^2) = .00050
Standard Deviation (σ) = .02236

The variance, or standard deviation, is a measure of the variation of possible rates of return, R_i, from the expected rate of return, $E(R_i)$, as follows:

$$\text{Variance } (\sigma^2) = \sum_{i=1}^{n} [R_i - E(R_i)]^2 P_i,$$

where P_i is the probability of the possible rate of return, R_i.

$$\text{Standard Deviation } (\sigma) = \sqrt{\sum_{i=1}^{n} [R_i - E(R_i)]^2 P_i}.$$

The computation of the variance and standard deviation for the individual risky asset in Table 7.1 is set forth in Table 7.3.

Two basic concepts in statistics, covariance and correlation, must be understood before considering the derivation of the risk of the portfolio.

COVARIANCE OF RETURNS—DISCUSSION AND EXAMPLE. *Covariance* is a measure of the degree to which two variables "move together" over time. In portfolio analysis, we usually are concerned with the covariance of rates of return rather than prices or some other variable.[3] A positive covariance means the returns tend to move in the same direction at the same time, and a negative covariance indicates the opposite. The *magnitude* of the covariance depends upon the variances of the individual return series, as well as on the relationship between the series.

Table 7.4 contains the monthly closing prices and dividends for Avon and IBM. Given this data, it is possible to compute monthly rates of return for these two stocks during 1987. Figures 7.1 and 7.2 contain a time series plot of the monthly rates of return for the two stocks. While the two return

---

[3] Returns, of course, can be measured in a variety of ways, depending upon the type of asset being considered. The reader will recall that we defined returns (R_i) in Chapter 1 as:

$$R_i = \frac{EV - BV + CF}{BV}$$

where *EV* is ending value, *BV* is beginning value, and *CF* is the cash flow during the period.

TABLE 7.4
Computation of Monthly Rates of Return

	AVON			IBM		
DATE	CLOSING PRICE	DIVIDEND	RATE OF RETURN (%)	CLOSING PRICE	DIVIDEND	RATE OF RETURN (%)
12/86	27.000			120.000		
1/87	30.125	0	11.57	128.750	0	7.29
2/87	30.000	0	−0.41	139.500	0	8.35
3/87	31.125	0.5	5.42	150.125	1.1	8.41
4/87	31.000	0	−0.40	160.125	0	6.66
5/87	29.875	0	−3.63	160.000	0	−0.08
6/87	33.750	0.5	14.64	162.500	1.1	2.25
7/87	37.000	0	9.63	161.000	0	−0.92
8/87	37.750	0	2.03	168.375	0	4.58
9/87	35.125	0.5	−5.63	150.750	1.1	−9.81
10/87	24.125	0	−31.32	122.500	0	−18.74
11/87	22.250	0	−7.77	110.750	0	−9.59
12/87	25.750	0.5	17.98	115.500	1.1	5.28
			$\overline{R}_{AVON} = 1.01$			$\overline{R}_{IBM} = 0.31$

FIGURE 7.1
Time Series of Returns for Avon: 1987

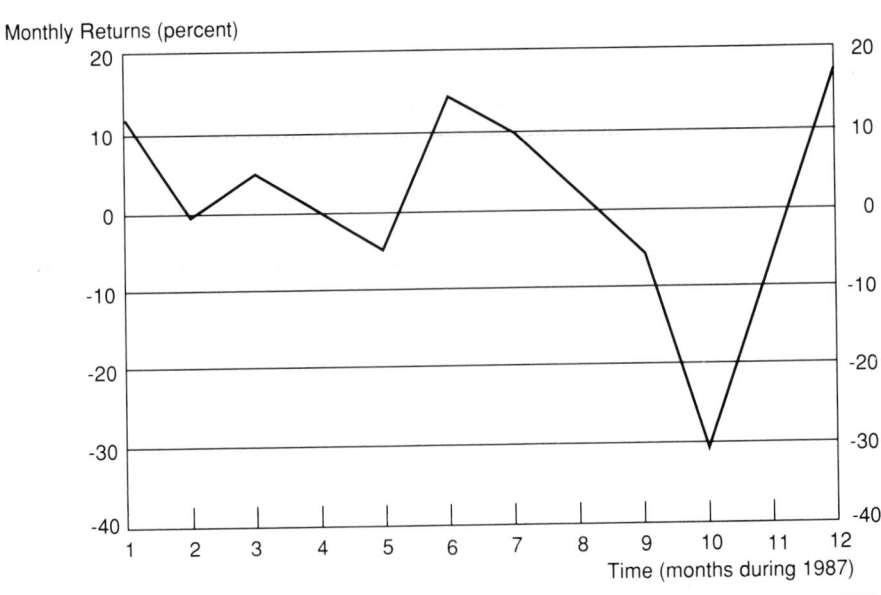

Monthly Returns (percent)

Time (months during 1987)

FIGURE 7.2
Time Series of Returns for IBM: 1987

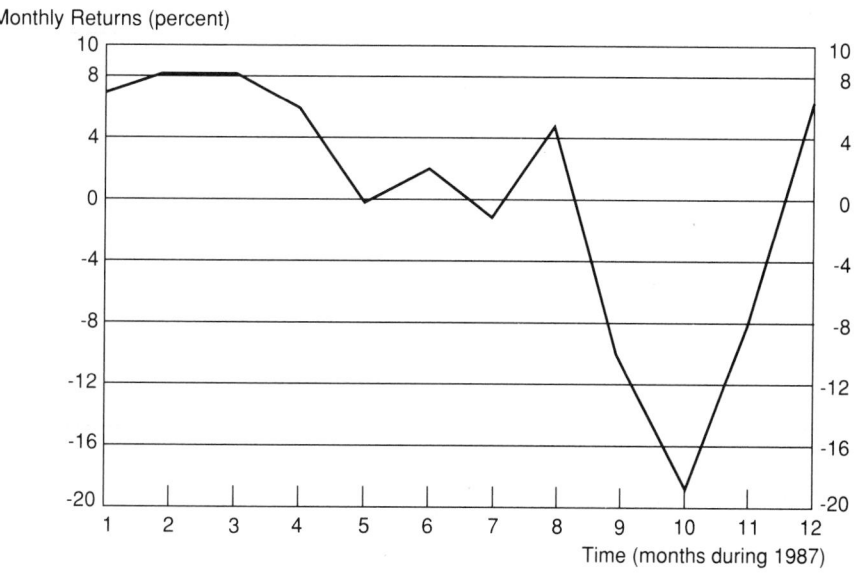

Monthly Returns (percent)

Time (months during 1987)

series moved together during some months, in other months they moved in opposite directions. The purpose of the covariance measure is to provide an *absolute* measure of their movement together over time.

For two assets, *i* and *j*, the covariance of rates of return is defined as

$$Cov_{ij} = E\{[R_i - E(R_i)][R_j - E(R_j)]\} .$$

The application of this formula to the monthly rates of return for Avon and IBM during 1987 is defined as

$$\frac{1}{12} \sum_{i=1}^{12} [R_i - E(R_i)][R_j - E(R_j)] .$$

As can be seen, if the rates of return for one stock are above its mean rate of return during a given period, and the returns for the other stock are likewise above its mean during this same period, then the product of these deviations from the mean is positive (i.e., the covariance will be some large positive value). If, however, the returns on one stock are above its mean return while the returns on the other are below its mean return, the product is negative. If this contrary movement happened consistently, the covariance between the two rates of return series would be a large negative value.

As an example, Table 7.5 contains the monthly rates of return during 1987 for Avon and IBM as computed in Table 7.4. One might expect the

TABLE 7.5
Computation of Covariance of Returns for Avon and IBM: 1987

| | MONTHLY RETURN (%) | | AVON | IBM | |
MM/YY	AVON (R_i)	IBM (R_j)	$R_i - E(R_i)$	$R_j - E(R_j)$	$(R_i - E(R_i)) \times (R_j - E(R_j))$
1/87	11.57	7.29	10.57	6.99	73.804
2/87	−0.41	8.35	−1.42	8.04	−11.452
3/87	5.42	8.41	4.41	8.10	35.699
4/87	−0.40	6.66	−1.41	6.36	− 8.963
5/87	−3.63	−0.08	−4.64	−0.38	1.782
6/87	14.64	2.25	13.64	1.94	26.506
7/87	9.63	−0.92	8.62	−1.23	−10.597
8/87	2.03	4.58	1.02	4.27	4.352
9/87	−5.63	−9.81	−6.64	−10.12	67.179
10/87	−31.32	−18.74	−32.33	−19.05	615.664
11/87	−7.77	−9.59	−8.78	−9.90	86.912
12/87	17.98	5.28	16.97	4.98	84.437
					$\Sigma = 965.325$
					$\text{Cov}_{ij} = \dfrac{1}{12} \times 965.325 = 80.44$

returns for the two stocks to have reasonably low covariance because of the differences in the products these firms produce (cosmetics and computers). The expected returns $E(R)$ were the arithmetic mean of the monthly returns:

$$E(R_i) = 1/12 \sum_{i=1}^{12} R_{it}$$

and

$$E(R_j) = 1/12 \sum_{i=1}^{12} R_{jt} .$$

All figures (except those in the last column) were rounded to the nearest hundreth of 1 percent. As shown, the average monthly return was 1.01 percent on Avon and 0.31 percent on IBM stock. From the results of the last column, we can derive the covariance between these two stocks as follows:

$$\text{Cov}_{ij} = \frac{1}{12} \times 965.325$$
$$= 80.44 .$$

Interpretation of a number like 80.44 is difficult; is it high or low for covariance? We know the relationship is generally positive, but it is not possible to be more specific. Figure 7.3 shows a scatter diagram with paired values of R_{it} and R_{jt} plotted against each other. This plot demonstrates the linear nature and strength of the relationship.

COVARIANCE AND CORRELATION. Covariance is affected by the variability of the two individual return series. Therefore, a number such as the 80.44

FIGURE 7.3
Scatter Plot of Monthly Returns for Avon and IBM: 1987

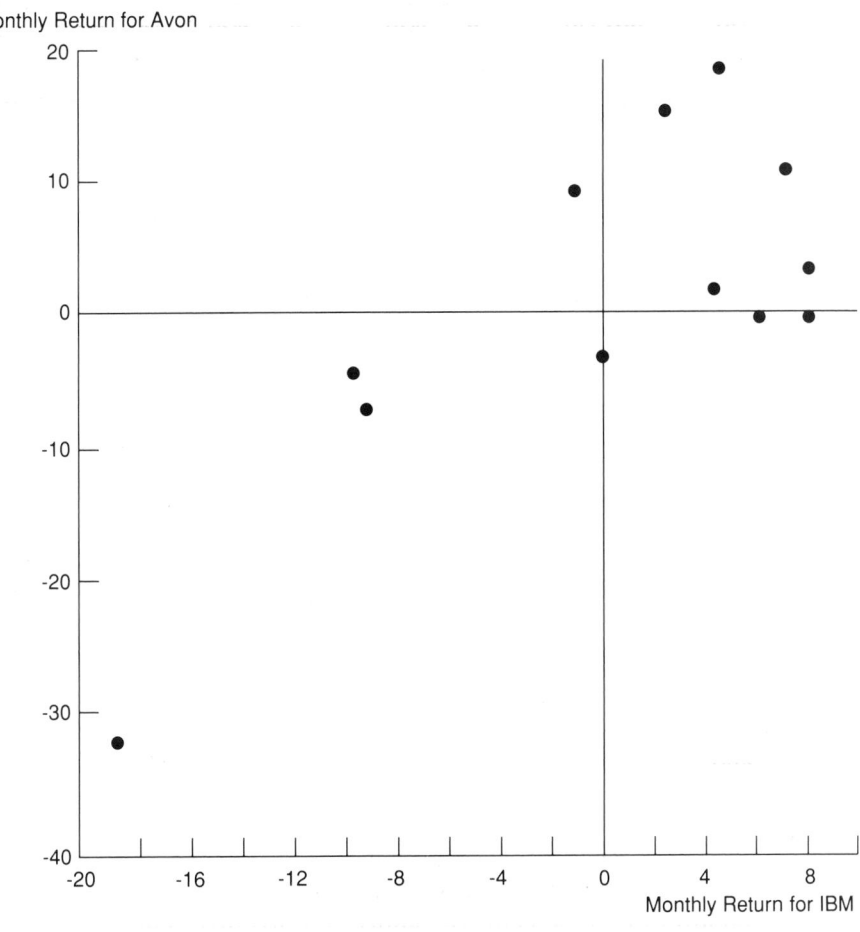

in the previous example might indicate a weak positive relationship if the two individual series were very volatile but a strong one if the two series were very stable. Obviously, you want to "standardize" this covariance for the individual variability of the two return series, as follows:

$$r_{ij} = \frac{Cov_{ij}}{\sigma_i \sigma_j},$$

where

r_{ij} = the correlation coefficient of returns

σ_i = the standard deviation of R_{it}

σ_j = the standard deviation of R_{jt}.

As shown, when we standardize the covariance by the individual standard deviations, we derive the *correlation coefficient* r_{ij}, which can vary only in the range -1 to $+1$. A value of $+1$ would indicate a perfect positive linear relationship between R_i and R_j, meaning the returns for the two stocks would move together in a completely linear manner. To derive this standardized measure of the relationship, it is necessary to compute the standard deviation for the two individual series. We already have the values for $R_{it} - E(R_i)$ and $R_{jt} - E(R_j)$ in Table 7.5. We can square each of these values and sum them as shown in Table 7.6.

$$\sigma_i^2 = \frac{1}{12}(1871.91) = 155.99$$

and

$$\sigma_j^2 = \frac{1}{12}(831.08) = 69.26.$$

Therefore,

$$\sigma_i = \sqrt{155.99} = 12.490\%$$
$$\sigma_j = \sqrt{69.26} = 8.322\%.$$

Thus, the correlation coefficient between returns for Avon and IBM is

$$r_{ij} = \frac{Cov_{ij}}{\sigma_i \sigma_j} = \frac{80.44}{(12.490)(8.322)} = .77.$$

As noted, a correlation of $+1.0$ would indicate perfect positive correlation, and a value of -1.0 would mean that the returns moved in a completely opposite direction. A value of zero would mean that there is no linear relationship between the returns; that is, they are uncorrelated from a statistical standpoint—which does not mean that they are independent. The value of $r_{ij} = .77$ is significant and fairly high for stocks in diverse industries compared to the correlation between stocks within some industries where the correlations approach 0.85.

STANDARD DEVIATION OF A PORTFOLIO

Having covered the concepts of covariance and correlation, we can now consider the formula for computing the standard deviation of returns for a portfolio of assets. You must be able to compute the standard deviation, because this is the measure of risk we will use. As noted, the derivation of the formula for computing the standard deviation of a portfolio of assets was accomplished by Harry Markowitz.[4]

---

[4] Markowitz, "Portfolio Selection"; and Markowitz, *Portfolio Selection.*

TABLE 7.6

Computation of Standard Deviation of Returns for Avon and IBM

MM/YY	AVON		IBM	
	$R_{it} - E(R_i)$	$[R_t - E(R_i)]^2$	$R_{jt} - E(R_j)$	$[R_{jt} - E(R_j)]^2$
1/87	10.57	111.62	6.99	48.80
2/87	− 1.42	2.03	8.04	64.70
3/87	4.41	19.43	8.10	65.59
4/87	− 1.41	1.99	6.36	40.39
5/87	− 4.64	21.51	− 0.38	0.15
6/87	13.64	185.93	1.94	3.78
7/87	8.62	74.32	− 1.23	1.51
8/87	1.02	1.04	4.27	18.27
9/87	− 6.64	44.06	−10.12	102.42
10/87	−32.33	1044.94	−19.05	362.74
11/87	− 8.78	77.10	− 9.90	97.97
12/87	16.97	287.94	4.98	24.76
		$\Sigma = 1871.91$		$\Sigma = 831.08$

Earlier (in Table 7.2) we showed that the expected return of the portfolio was the weighted average of the expected returns for the individual assets in the portfolio; the weights were the percentage of value of the portfolio. Under such conditions, it is very easy to see the impact on the portfolio's expected return of adding or deleting an asset. One might mistakenly assume that it is possible to derive the standard deviation of the portfolio in the same manner, that is, by computing the weighted average of the standard deviations for the individual assets. Note that one cannot do this! When Markowitz derived the general formula for the standard deviation of a portfolio it was as follows:[5]

$$\sigma_{port} = \sqrt{\sum_{i=1}^{N} W_i^2 \sigma_i^2 + \sum_{i=1}^{N} \sum_{\substack{j=1 \\ i \neq j}}^{N} W_i W_j Cov_{ij}},$$

where

σ_{port} = the standard deviation of the portfolio

W_i = the weights of the individual assets in the portfolio, where weights are determined by the proportion of value in the portfolio

σ_i^2 = the variance of asset i

Cov_{ij} = the covariance between the returns for assets i and j.

In words, this formula indicates that the standard deviation for the portfolio is a function of the weighted average of the individual variances

---

[5] For the detailed derivation of this formula, see Markowitz, *Portfolio Selection*.

(where the weights are squared), plus the weighted covariances between all the assets in the portfolio. The point is, the standard deviation for the portfolio encompasses not only the individual variances, but also the covariances between pairs of individual securities. Further, it can be shown that, in a portfolio with a large number of securities, this formula can be stated as the summation of weighted covariances. This means that the important factor to consider when adding an asset to a portfolio with a number of other assets is not the individual asset's variance, but *its average covariance with all the other assets in the portfolio*. In the following examples we will consider the simple case of a two-asset portfolio. It is important to see the impact of different covariances on the total risk (standard deviation) of the portfolio.

TWO-ASSET PORTFOLIO

Because the Markowitz model assumes that any asset or portfolio of assets can be described by only two parameters, the expected return and expected standard deviation of returns, the following could be applied to two individual assets with the indicated parameters and correlation coefficients, or to two portfolios of assets with the same indicated parameters and correlation coefficients.

EQUAL RISK AND RETURN—CHANGING CORRELATIONS. Consider first the case in which both assets have the same expected return and expected standard deviation of return. As an example, let us assume

$$E(R_1) = .20$$
$$E(\sigma_1) = .10$$
$$E(R_2) = .20$$
$$E(\sigma_2) = .10 .$$

To see the effect of different covariances (i.e., we assume different levels of correlation between the two assets), consider the following set of examples where the two assets have equal weights in the portfolio ($W_1 = .50$; $W_2 = .50$). Therefore, the only value that will change in each example is the correlation between the returns for the two assets.

Recall that

$$Cov_{ij} = r_{ij}\sigma_i\sigma_j .$$

Thus, consider the following alternative correlation coefficients and attendant covariances. The covariance will be equal to $r_{1,2}(.10)(.10)$, because both standard deviations are 0.10.

a. $r_{1,2} = 1.00$ $Cov_{1,2} = (1.00)(.10)(.10) = .01$
b. $r_{1,2} = .50$ $Cov_{1,2} = .005$
c. $r_{1,2} = .00$ $Cov_{1,2} = .000$
d. $r_{1,2} = -.50$ $Cov_{1,2} = -.005$
e. $r_{1,2} = -1.00$ $Cov_{1,2} = -.01 .$

Now let us see what happens to the standard deviation of the portfolio under these five conditions. Recall that

$$\sigma_{port} = \sqrt{\sum_{i=1}^{N} W_i^2 \sigma_i^2 + \sum_{\substack{i=1 \\ i \neq j}}^{N} \sum_{j=1}^{N} W_i W_j Cov_{ij}}$$

Thus, in Case a,

$$\begin{aligned}
\sigma_{port\ (a)} &= \sqrt{(.5)^2(.10)^2 + (.5)^2(.10)^2 + 2(.5)(.5)(.01)} \\
&= \sqrt{(.25)(.01) + (.25)(.01) + 2(.25)(.01)} \\
&= \sqrt{.01} \\
&= .10.
\end{aligned}$$

As shown, in this case the returns for the two assets are perfectly positively correlated, so the standard deviation for the portfolio is indeed the weighted average of the individual standard deviations, and <u>there is no real benefit to combining the two assets; they are like one asset already, because their returns move together.</u> Now consider Case b, where $r_{1,2}$ equals 0.50.

$$\begin{aligned}
\sigma_{port\ (b)} &= \sqrt{(.5)^2(.10)^2 + (.5)^2(.10)^2 + 2(.5)(.5)(.005)} \\
&= \sqrt{(.0025) + (.0025) + (.50)(.005)} \\
&= \sqrt{.0075} \\
&= .0866.
\end{aligned}$$

The only term that changed from Case a is the last term, $Cov_{1,2}$, which changed from 0.01 to 0.005. The ultimate result was that the standard deviation of the portfolio declined by about 13 percent, from 0.10 to 0.0866. Note that the expected return did not change, because it is simply the weighted average of the individual expected returns; it is equal to 0.20 in both cases.

You should be able to confirm that the standard deviations for portfolios c and d are as follows:

c. .0707
d. .50.

The final case where the correlation between the two assets is -1.00 indicates the ultimate benefits of diversification.

$$\begin{aligned}
\sigma_{port\ (e)} &= \sqrt{(.5)^2(.10)^2 + (.5)^2(.10)^2 + 2(.5)(.5)(-.01)} \\
&= \sqrt{(.0050) + (-.0050)} \\
&= \sqrt{0} \\
&= 0.
\end{aligned}$$

<u>Here the covariance term exactly offsets the individual variance terms, and so the overall standard deviation of the portfolio is zero.</u> This would <u>be a risk-free portfolio.</u> See Figure 7.4 for a graph of such a pattern. The

Figure 7.4
Time Pattern of Returns for Two Assets with Perfect Negative Correlation

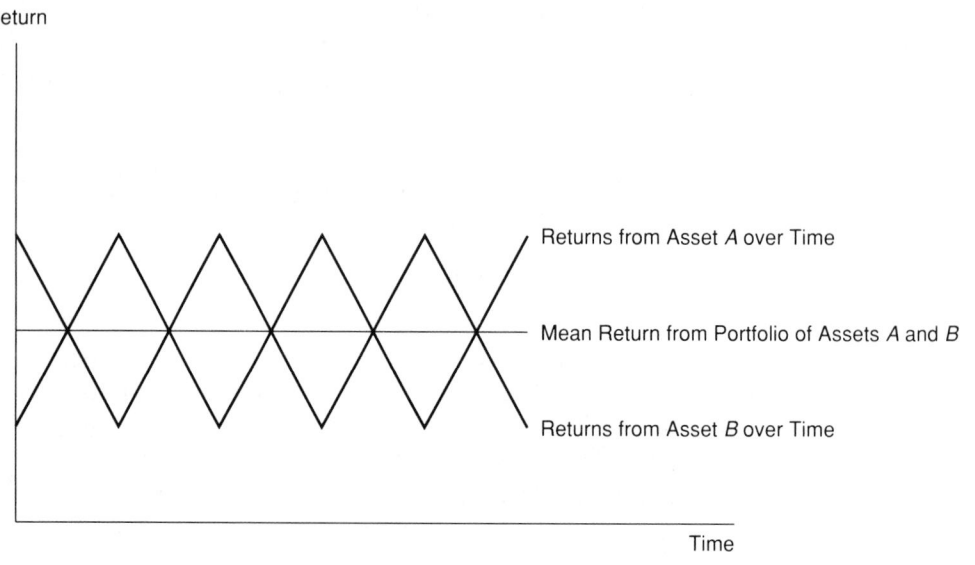

result of perfect negative correlation is that the mean return for the two securities combined over time is equal to the mean for each of them, and there is no variability of returns for the portfolio. Returns above and below the mean for each of the assets are completely offset by the return for the other asset, so there is no variability in total returns for the portfolio; it is a riskless portfolio because there is no uncertainty of returns. Thus, the combination of two assets that are completely negatively correlated provides the maximum benefits of diversification—it eliminates risk.

The graph in Figure 7.5 shows the difference in the risk-return posture for these five cases. As noted, the only impact of the change in correlation is the change in the standard deviation of this two-asset portfolio. As we combine assets that are not perfectly correlated, we do not affect the expected return of the portfolio, but we reduce the risk of the portfolio (its standard deviation) until we reach the ultimate combination, in which there is perfect negative correlation and total elimination of risk.

COMBINING STOCKS WITH DIFFERENT RETURNS AND RISK. The previous discussion indicated what happens when the only difference is the correlation coefficient (covariance) between the assets. In this subsection we consider two assets (or portfolios) with different expected rates of return and individual standard deviations and show what happens when we vary the correlations between them. We will assume the following:

Stock	$E(R_i)$	W_i	σ_i^2	σ_i
1	.10	.50	.0049	.07
2	.20	.50	.0100	.10

FIGURE 7.5
Plot of Risk-Return for Portfolios with Equal Returns and Standard Deviations and Different Correlations

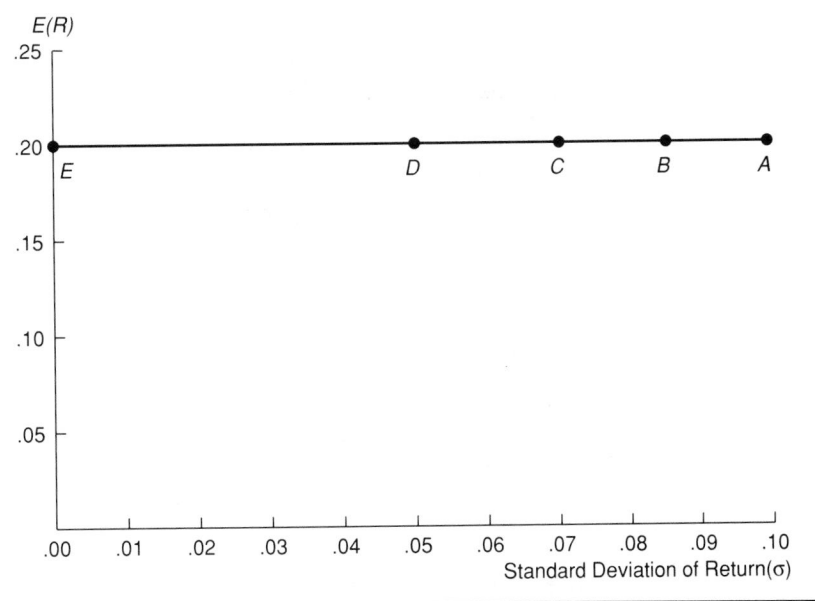

We will briefly consider the same set of correlation coefficients as previously, with a different set of covariances as follows:

CASE	CORRELATION COEFFICIENT	COVARIANCE $(r_{ij}\, \sigma_i \sigma_j)$
a	+1.00	.0070
b	+0.50	.0035
c	0.00	.0000
d	−0.50	−.0035
e	−1.00	−.0070

Because we are assuming that the proportion (weights) in all cases is the same (.50 − .50), the expected return in every instance will be

$$E(R_{port}) = .5(.10) + .5(.20)$$
$$= .15.$$

The standard deviation for Case a will be

$$\sigma_{port\ (a)} = \sqrt{(.5)^2(.07)^2 + (.5)^2(.10)^2 + 2(.5)(.5)(.0070)}$$
$$= \sqrt{.007225}$$
$$= .085.$$

Again it is shown that in the case of perfect positive correlation, the standard deviation of the portfolio is the weighted average of the standard deviations of the individual assets:

$$(.5)(.07) + (.5)(.10) = .085.$$

Obviously, as we change the weights, the standard deviation would change in a linear fashion—an important fact to remember when we discuss the capital asset pricing model (CAPM) later.

For Cases b, c, d, and e, the standard deviation for the portfolio would be as follows:[6]

$$\sigma_{port\ (b)} = \sqrt{(.001225) + (.0025) + (.5)(.0035)}$$
$$= \sqrt{.005475}$$
$$= .07399$$
$$\sigma_{port\ (c)} = \sqrt{(.001225) + (.0025) + (.5)(.00)}$$
$$= .0610$$
$$\sigma_{port\ (d)} = \sqrt{(.001225) + (.0025) + (.5)(-.0035)}$$
$$= .0444$$
$$\sigma_{port\ (e)} = \sqrt{(.003725) + .5(-.00700)}$$
$$= .015.$$

Note that, in this set of examples, with perfect negative correlation the standard deviation of the portfolio is not zero. This is because the different examples have equal weights, but the individual standard deviations are not equal.[7]

Figure 7.6 shows the results for the two individual assets and the portfolio of the two assets under the assumption of different correlation coefficients as set forth in Cases a through e. As before, the expected return does not change, because the proportions are always set at .50 − .50, so all the portfolios lie along the horizontal line at the return, $R = .15$.

CHANGING WEIGHTS. If we changed the weights of the two assets for a given correlation coefficient, we would derive a set of combinations that trace an ellipse starting at Stock 2, going through the .50 − .50 point, and ending at Stock 1. Consider Case c, in which the correlation coefficient is zero (this eases the computation), and we change the weights as follows:

CASE	W_1	W_2	$E(R_i)$
f	.20	.80	.18
g	.40	.60	.16
h	.50	.50	.15
i	.60	.40	.14
j	.80	.20	.12

[6] In all of the following examples, we will skip some steps, because you are now aware that only the last term changes. You are encouraged to work out the individual steps to ensure understanding of the computational procedure.

[7] The two appendixes to this chapter show proofs for equal weights with equal variances and the appropriate weights when standard deviations are not equal.

FIGURE 7.6
Plot of Risk-Return for Portfolios with Different Returns, Standard Deviations, and Correlations

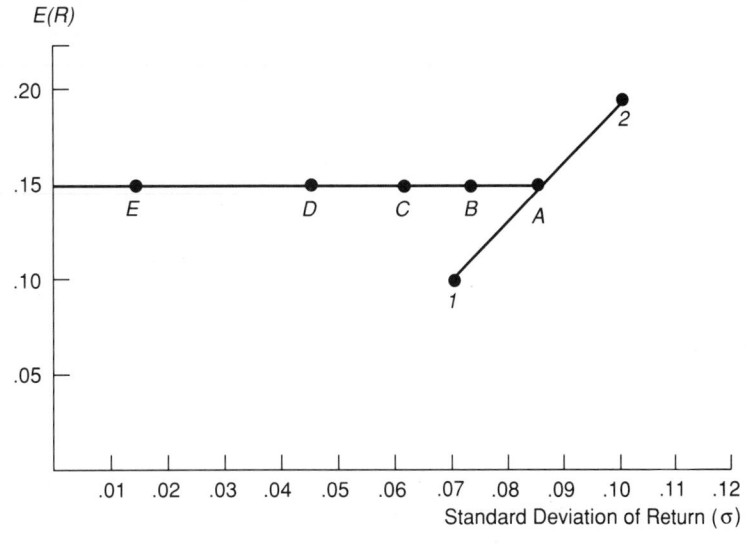

In Cases f, g, i, and j, the standard deviations would be (we already know the standard deviation (σ) for Portfolio h):[8]

$$\sigma_{port\ (f)} = \sqrt{(.20)^2(.07)^2+(.80)^2(.10)^2+2(.20)(.80)(.000)}$$
$$= \sqrt{(.04)(.0049)+(.64)(.01)+(0)}$$
$$= \sqrt{.006596}$$
$$= .0812$$

$$\sigma_{port\ (g)} = \sqrt{(.40)^2(.07)^2+(.60)^2(.10)^2+2(.40)(.60)(.00)}$$
$$= \sqrt{.004384}$$
$$= .0662$$

$$\sigma_{port\ (i)} = \sqrt{(.60)^2(.07)^2 + (.40)^2(.10)^2+2(.60)(.40)(.00)}$$
$$= \sqrt{.003364}$$
$$= .0580$$

$$\sigma_{port\ (j)} = \sqrt{(.80)^2(.07)^2 + (.20)^2(.10)^2 +2(.80)(.20)(.00)}$$
$$= \sqrt{.003536}$$
$$= .0595.$$

Therefore, the alternative weights, assuming the same correlations, indicate the following risk-return combinations:

---

[8] Again, you are encouraged to fill in the steps we skipped in the computations.

FIGURE 7.7
Plot of Portfolio Risk-Return for Different Weights When $r_n = 0.00$.

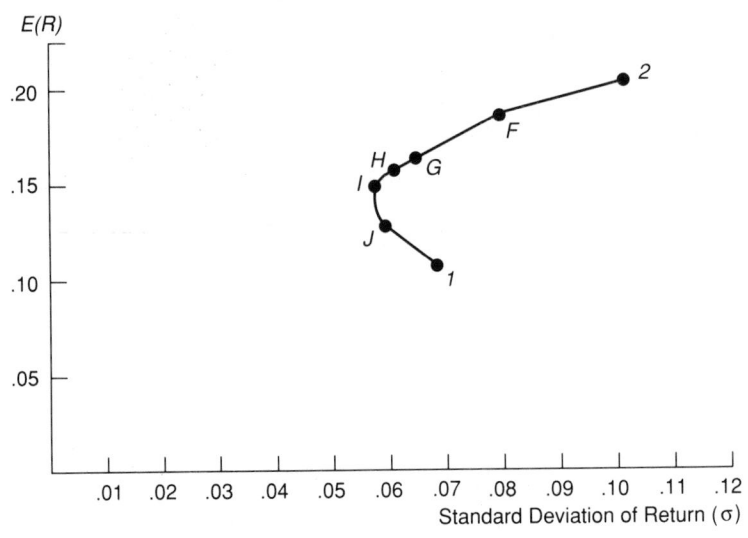

CASE	W_1	W_2	$E(R_i)$	$E(\sigma_{port})$
f	.20	.80	.18	.0812
g	.40	.60	.16	.0662
h	.50	.50	.15	.0610
i	.60	.40	.14	.0580
j	.80	.20	.12	.0595

A graph of these combinations in terms of return and risk is contained in Figure 7.7. You could derive a complete curve by simply varying the weights by small increments.

As noted, the amount of curvature in the graph will depend upon the correlation between the two assets or portfolios. In the case of $r_{ij} + 1.00$, the combinations would lie along a straight line between the two assets. If we assumed that $r_{ij} = -1.00$, the graph would be two straight lines that would touch at the vertical line with some combination (i.e., the risk for a specified set of weights would be zero).

If we examined a number of two-asset combinations and derived the curves assuming all the possible weights, we would have a graph like that in Figure 7.8. The envelope curve that contains the best of all these possible combinations, referred to as the *efficient frontier,* represents that set of portfolios that has the maximum return for every given level of risk, or the minimum risk for every level of return. An example of such a frontier is shown in Figure 7.9. As can be seen, every portfolio on the frontier has either higher return for equal risk or lower risk for equal return than some

FIGURE 7.8
Graph of Numerous Portfolio Combinations from Set of Available Assets

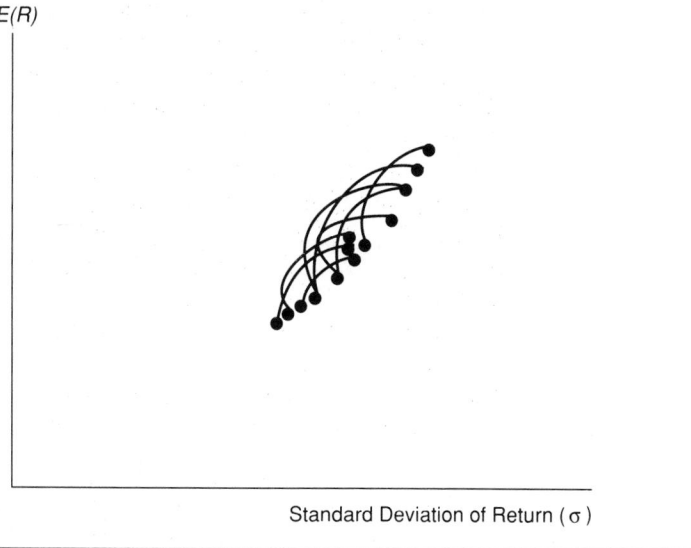

FIGURE 7.9
Efficient Frontier for Alternative Portfolios

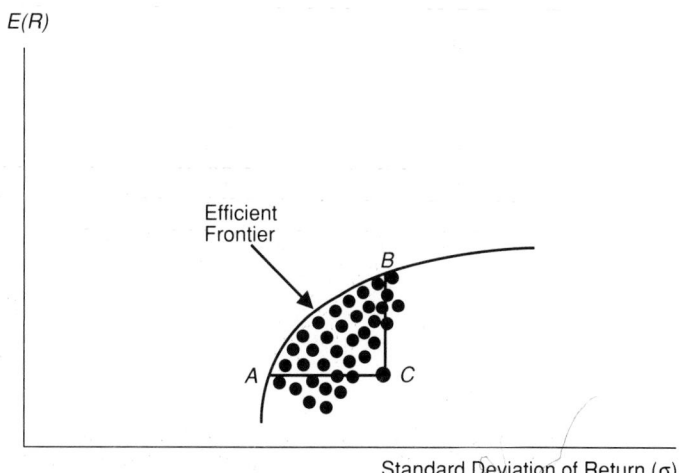

portfolio beneath the frontier. Thus, Portfolio A dominates Portfolio C because it has an equal return but substantially less risk, and Portfolio B dominates Portfolio C because it has equal risk but a higher expected rate of return. Because of the benefits of diversification among assets that are not perfectly correlated, we would expect the efficient frontier to be made up of *portfolios,* with the possible exception of the two end points (i.e., the highest return asset and the lowest risk asset).

Investors will determine where they want to be along the frontier based upon their utility function and attitude toward risk. No portfolio on the efficient frontier is dominated by any other portfolio on the efficient frontier. They all have different return and risk measures, and expected rates of return increase with risk.

THE EFFICIENT FRONTIER AND INVESTOR UTILITY

As Figure 7.9 shows, the shape of the typical efficient frontier for risky assets requires that you tolerate more and more risk to achieve higher returns. The slope of the efficient frontier,

$$\frac{\Delta E(R_{port})}{\Delta E(\sigma_{port})},$$

decreases steadily as you move up the curve, which implies that by adding equal risk as you move up the frontier, you will add progressively *less* in expected return.

The utility curves for an individual specify the trade-offs he is willing to make between expected return and risk. These utility curves are used in conjunction with the efficient frontier to determine which particular efficient portfolio is the best for a particular investor. Two investors will not choose the same portfolio from the efficient set unless their utility curves are identical. In Figure 7.10, two sets of utility curves have been drawn, along with the efficient frontier. The curves labeled U_1 are for a very risk-averse investor (with $U_3 > U_2 > U_1$). These utility curves are quite steep, indicating that the investor will not tolerate much additional risk to obtain additional returns. The investor is indifferent to any $E(R), E(\sigma)$ combinations along a specific utility curve (e.g., U_1). The curves labeled U'_1 ($U'_3 > U'_2 > U'_1$) are for a less risk-averse investor. He is willing to tolerate a bit more risk to get a higher expected return.

The *optimal portfolio* is the efficient portfolio that has the highest utility for a given investor. It lies at the point of tangency between the efficient frontier and the curve with the highest possible utility. For a more conservative investor, the highest utility is at the point where the curve U_2 just touches the efficient frontier, at point X in Figure 7.10. For a less risk-averse investor, it is point Y, which represents a portfolio with both higher expected returns and higher risk that Portfolio X.

SUMMARY

The basic Markowitz portfolio model derived the expected rate of return for a portfolio of assets and an expected risk measure, which is the standard deviation of expected return. The expected return of a portfolio is

FIGURE **7.10**
Choice of the Optimal Risky Portfolio

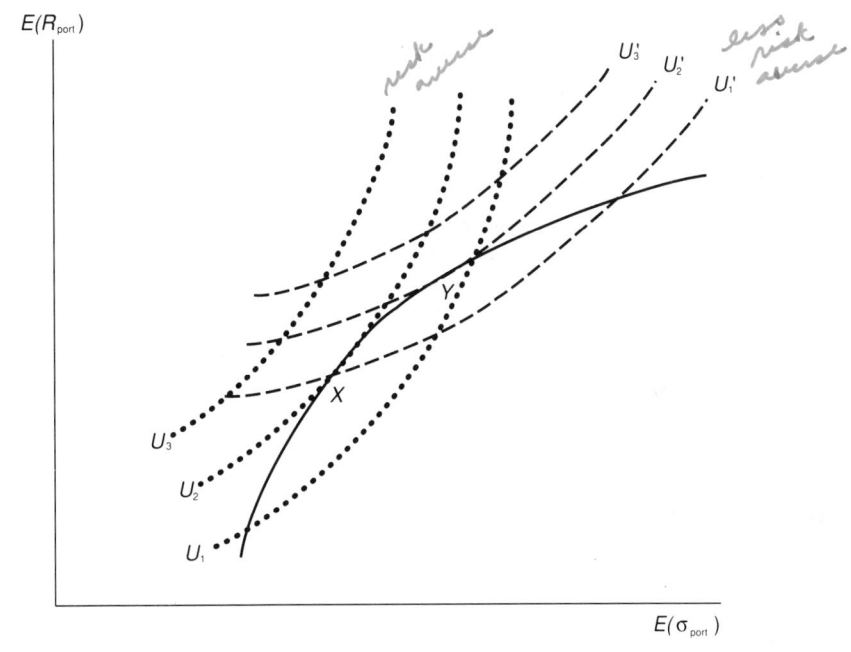

simply the weighted average of the expected return for the individual assets in the portfolio. The standard deviation of a portfolio is a function not only of the individual standard deviations, but *also* of the covariance between all the pairs of assets in the portfolio. The impact of different correlation coefficients was shown for assets that had equal returns and risk and also when the assets had different returns and risk. We also showed how different weights yield a curve of potential combinations.

Assuming numerous assets and a multitude of combination curves, the efficient frontier is the envelope curve that encompasses all of the best combinations. It is the set of portfolios that has the highest expected return for each given level of risk, or the minimum risk for each given level of return. Given this set of dominant portfolios, the investor is expected to select a specific portfolio based upon the point of tangency between the efficient frontier and his highest utility curve. Since risk-return utility functions differ, investors will have different points of tangency and will therefore select different portfolios.

QUESTIONS

1. Why do most investors hold diversified portfolios?
2. What is covariance, and why is it important in portfolio theory?
3. Why do most assets of the same type show positive covariances of returns

with each other? Would you expect positive covariances of returns between different types of assets (e.g., returns on Treasury bills, General Motors common stock, or commercial real estate)? Why or why not?

4. What is the relationship between the covariance and the correlation coefficient? Why is the correlation coefficient considered more useful?

5. Explain why the efficient frontier takes its characteristic shape.

6. Draw a properly labeled graph of the Markowitz efficient frontier. Describe in exact terms what the efficient frontier is. Discuss the concept of dominant portfolios.

7. Assume you want to run a computer program to derive the efficient frontier for your feasible set of stocks. What information must you provide for the program; that is, what are your inputs?

8. Why are investors' utility curves important in portfolio theory?

9. Explain how the optimal portfolio for a given investor is chosen. Will it always be a diversified portfolio, or could it be a single asset? Explain your answer.

PROBLEMS

1. Given:

$E(R_1) = .10$
$E(R_2) = .15$
$E(\sigma_1) = .03$
$E(\sigma_2) = .05$

Calculate the expected returns and expected standard deviations of a two-stock portfolio in which Stock 1 has a weight of 60 percent under the following conditions:

1a. $r_{1,2} = $ 1.00

1b. $r_{1,2} = $ .75

1c. $r_{1,2} = $ .25

1d. $r_{1,2} = $ .00

1e. $r_{1,2} = -$ .25

1f. $r_{1,2} = -$ .75

1g. $r_{1,2} = -1.00$

2. Given:

$E(R_1) = .12$
$E(R_2) = .16$
$E(\sigma_1) = .04$
$E(\sigma_2) = .06$

Calculate the expected returns and expected standard deviations of a two-stock portfolio having a correlation coefficient of .70 under the following conditions:

2a. $w_1 = 1.00$

2b. $w_1 = $ .75

2c. $w_1 = $ .50

2d. $w_1 = .25$

2e. $w_1 = .00$

3. Write out the expanded terms of the Markowitz formula (the standard deviation of a portfolio) for the case of three stocks.

4. Given the following market values of stocks in your portfolio and their expected rates of return, what is the expected rate of return for your common stock portfolio?

STOCK	MARKET VALUE	$E(R_i)$
Quaker Oats	$15,000	0.14
General Mills	17,000	−0.04
Apple Computer	32,000	0.18
Polaroid	23,000	0.16
Ford	7,000	0.05

5. The monthly rates of return for Coors Brewing and General Chemicals during a six-month period follow.

MONTH	COORS BREWING	GENERAL CHEMICALS
1	.04	.07
2	.03	−.02
3	−.07	−.10
4	.12	.15
5	−.02	−.06
6	.05	.02

Compute the following:

5a. Mean monthly rates of return for each stock.

5b. Standard deviation for each stock.

5c. Covariance among the rates of return.

5d. The correlation coefficient of rates of return.

6. You are considering two assets with the following characteristics:

$$E(R_1) = .15$$
$$E(\sigma_1) = .10$$
$$W_1 = .5$$
$$E(R_2) = .20$$
$$E(\sigma_2) = .20$$
$$W_2 = .5$$

Compute the mean and standard deviations of two portfolios if $r_{1,2} = .40$ and −.60, respectively. Plot these two portfolios on a risk-return graph. Which portfolio would you select? Explain your choice.

7. Following are monthly percentage price changes for market indicator series.

MONTH	DJIA	S&P 400	AMEX	NIKKEI
1	.03	.02	.04	.02
2	.07	.06	.10	−.02
3	−.02	−.01	−.04	.03
4	.01	.03	.03	.02
5	.05	.07	.11	.01
6	−.06	−.04	−.08	.03

Compute the following:

7a. Mean monthly rates of return for each series.

7b. Standard deviation for each series.

7c. Covariance between the following rates of return:
DJIA–S&P 400
S&P 400–AMEX
S&P 400–NIKKEI
AMEX–NIKKEI

7d. The correlation coefficients for the four combinations in Part C.

7e. On the basis of these results, discuss which combination of domestic series would provide the best diversification. Discuss which domestic–foreign combination is best for diversification. What does this imply regarding international diversification?

REFERENCES

Farrell, James L., Jr., *Guide to Portfolio Management*. New York: McGraw-Hill, 1983.

Francis, Jack C., and Stephen H. Archer. *Portfolio Analysis*. 2d ed. Englewood Cliffs, N.J.: Prentice-Hall, 1979.

Friedman, Milton, and Leonard J. Savage "The Utility Analysis of Choices Involving Risk." *Journal of Political Economy* 56, no. 3 (August 1948).

Hagin, Robert. *Modern Portfolio Theory*. Homewood, Ill.: Dow Jones-Irwin, 1979.

Maginn, John L., and Donald L. Tuttle, eds. *Managing Investment Portfolios*. Sponsored by The Institute of Chartered Financial Analysts (Boston: Warren, Gorham and Lamont, 1983).

Markowitz, Harry. "Portfolio Selection." *Journal of Finance* 3, no. 1 (March 1952).

Markowitz, Harry. *Portfolio Selection: Diversification of Investments*. New York: John Wiley and Sons, 1959.

Sharpe, William F. *Portfolio Theory and Capital Markets*. New York: McGraw-Hill, 1970.

PROOF THAT MINIMUM PORTFOLIO VARIANCE OCCURS WITH EQUAL WEIGHTS WHEN SECURITIES HAVE

APPENDIX 7A   # EQUAL VARIANCE

When $E(\sigma_i) = E(\sigma_2)$, we have

$$
\begin{aligned}
E(\sigma_{port}^2) &= W_1^2 E(\sigma_1)^2 + (1 - W_1)^2 E(\sigma_1)^2 + 2W_1(1 - W_1)r_{12}E(\sigma_1)^2 \\
&= E(\sigma_1)^2[W_1^2 + 1 - 2W_1 + W_1^2 + 2W_1r_{12} - 2W_1^2 r_{12}] \\
&= E(\sigma_1)^2[2W_1^2 + 1 - 2W_1 + 2W_1r_{12} - 2W_1^2 r_{12}].
\end{aligned}
$$

For this to be a minimum,

$$
\frac{\partial E(\sigma_{port}^2)}{\partial W_1} = 0 = E(\sigma_1)^2[4W_1 - 2 + 2r_{12} - 4W_1 r_{12}].
$$

Assuming $E(\sigma_1)^2 > 0$, this implies

$$
4W_1 - 2 + 2r_{12} - 4W_1 r_{12} = 0
$$
$$
4W_1(1 - r_{12}) - 2(1 - r_{12}) = 0,
$$

from which

$$
W_1 = \frac{2(1 - r_{12})}{4(1 - r_{12})} = \frac{1}{2},
$$

regardless of r_{12}. Thus, if $E(\sigma_1) = E(\sigma_2)$, $E(\sigma_{port}^2)$ will always be minimized by choosing $W_1 = W_2 = 1/2$, regardless of the value of r_{12}. The exception is when $r_{12} = +1$, in which case $E(\sigma_{port}) = E(\sigma_1) = E(\sigma_2)$. This can be verified by checking the second-order condition,

$$
\frac{\partial^2 E(\sigma_{port}^2)}{\partial W_1^2} > 0.
$$

PROBLEMS   The following information applies to Problems 1 and 2: The general equation for the weight of the first security to achieve the minimum variance (in a two-stock portfolio) is given by

$$
w_1 = \frac{E(\sigma_2)^2 - r_{1,2}\, E(\sigma_1)\, E(\sigma_2)}{E(\sigma_1)^2 + E(\sigma_2)^2 - 2r_{1,2}\, E(\sigma_1)\, E(\sigma_2)}
$$

1a. Show that $w_1 = .5$ when $E(\sigma_1) = E(\sigma_2)$.

1b. What is the weight of Security 1 that gives minimum portfolio variance when $r_{1,2} = .5$, $E(\sigma_1) = .04$, and $E(\sigma_2) = .06$?

2a. Show the minimum portfolio variance for a two-stock portfolio when $r_{1,2} = -1$.

2b. What is the value of w_1 when $r_{1,2} = -1$, $E(\sigma_1) = .07$, and $E(\sigma_2) = .10$?

Derivation of Weights That Will Give Zero Variance When

Appendix 7B   # Correlation Equals -1.00

$$E(\sigma^2_{port}) = W_1^2\, E(\sigma_1)^2 + (1 - W_1)^2 E(\sigma_2)^2 + 2W_1(1 - W_1)r_{12}E(\sigma_1)E(\sigma_2)$$
$$= W_1^2 E(\sigma_1)^2 + E(\sigma_2)^2 - 2W_1 E(\sigma_2) + W_1^2 E(\sigma_2)^2$$
$$+ 2W_1 r_{12}E(\sigma_1)E(\sigma_2) - 2W_1^2 r_{12}E(\sigma_1)E(\sigma_2).$$

If $r_{12} = -1$, this can be rearranged and expressed as

$$E(\sigma^2_{port}) = W_1^2[E(\sigma_1)^2 + 2E(\sigma_1)E(\sigma_2) + E(\sigma_2)^2]$$
$$- 2W_1[E(\sigma_2)^2 + E(\sigma_1)E(\sigma_2)] + E(\sigma_2)^2$$
$$= W_1^2[E(\sigma_1) + E(\sigma_2)]^2 - 2W_1 E(\sigma_2)$$
$$[E(\sigma_1) + E(\sigma_2)] + E(\sigma_2)^2$$
$$= \{W_1[E(\sigma_1) + E(\sigma_2)] - E(\sigma_2)\}^2.$$

We want to find the weight, W_1, which will reduce $E(\sigma^2_{port})$ to zero; therefore,

$$W_1[E(\sigma_1) + E(\sigma_2)] - E(\sigma_2) = 0,$$

which yields

$$W_1 = \frac{E(\sigma_2)}{E(\sigma_1) + E(\sigma_2)}, \text{ and } W_2 = 1 - W_1 = \frac{E(\sigma_1)}{E(\sigma_1) + E(\sigma_2)}.$$

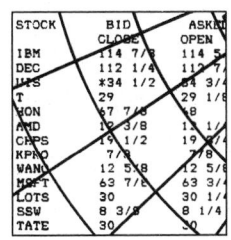

CHAPTER 8

AN INTRODUCTION TO CAPITAL MARKET THEORY

Capital market theory builds on portfolio theory, and so, in this chapter, we will begin where the Markowitz efficient frontier ended. It is assumed that the set of risk assets has been examined and that the aggregate efficient frontier has been derived. Further, it is assumed that you and all other investors want to maximize your utility, so you will choose a portfolio of risky assets on the efficient frontier at a point where your utility map is tangent to the frontier as shown in Figure 7.10. When you act in this manner, you are referred to as a *Markowitz efficient investor.* The purpose of capital market theory is to extend portfolio theory to a model that can be used to price all risky assets. The final product is the *capital asset pricing model (CAPM)* that will indicate how you determine the required rate of return for all risky assets.

First, we will consider some of the assumptions required to derive the model, then we will discuss the concept of a risk-free asset, its properties relative to a portfolio of risky assets, and how this allows us to derive a linear relationship between the expected return on an asset and the risk involved. We will show in detail how a simple, unique risk measure is computed for an individual asset and also how this model can be used to select undervalued, overvalued, and properly valued securities.

ASSUMPTIONS OF CAPITAL MARKET THEORY

Because capital market theory builds upon the Markowitz portfolio model, it requires the same assumptions, but expanded as follows:

1. *All investors are Markowitz efficient investors who want to be somewhere on the efficient frontier.* The exact location on the efficient frontier will depend upon the risk-return function of the investor and will differ among investors.

2. *It is possible for investors to borrow or lend any amount of money at the risk-free rate of return (RFR)*. Clearly, it is always possible to lend money at the nominal risk-free rate by buying risk-free securities such as government T-bills. It is not always possible to borrow at this risk-free rate, but we will see that assuming a higher borrowing rate does not change the general results.

3. *All investors have homogeneous expectations* (i.e., they estimate identical probability distributions for future rates of return). Again, this assumption can be relaxed, and, as long as expectations are not vastly different, the effect is minor.

4. *All investors have the same one-period time horizon* (e.g., one month, six months, one year). The model will be developed for one hypothetical period, but it is acknowledged that the results could be affected by a different assumption, and an investor would have to derive risk measures that are consistent with his horizon.

5. *All investments are infinitely divisible* (i.e., it is possible to buy or sell fractional shares of any asset or portfolio). This assumption simply allows us to discuss the various investment alternatives as continuous curves. Changing it would have little impact on the theory.

6. *There are no taxes or transaction costs involved in buying or selling assets.* This is a reasonable assumption in a number of instances. Specifically, there are many investors who do not have to pay taxes (e.g., pension funds, religious groups), and the transaction costs for most financial institutions is less than 1 percent on most financial instruments. Again, the relaxation of this assumption modifies the results, but it does not change the basic thrust.

7. *There is no inflation or change in interest rates, or inflation is fully anticipated*. This is a reasonable initial assumption and can be modified.

8. *Capital markets are in equilibrium*. This means that we begin from a state in which all assets are properly priced in terms of the risk involved.

You may believe that some of these assumptions are unrealistic and wonder how useful a theory can be that is based on them. In this regard, two points are important. First, as mentioned, we will see that many of these assumptions can be relaxed with minor impact on the model and no change in the main implications or conclusions. Second, a theory should never be judged on the basis of the assumptions it involves, but rather on how well it explains and helps us predict behavior in the real world. If this model helps us explain the rates of return on a wide variety of risky assets, it is very useful, regardless of whether some of its assumptions are unrealistic. (Those assumptions, it follows, must not be important in attaining the ultimate objective of the model.)

THE INITIAL DEVELOPMENT

The major factor in capital market theory is the concept of a risk-free asset. Following the development of the Markowitz portfolio model, several authors considered what would happen if they assumed the existence of a risk-free asset that, by definition, would have *zero variance*. As will be shown, such an asset would have zero correlation with all other risky assets and would yield the *risk-free rate of return (RFR)*. It would be on the vertical axis of a portfolio graph. This assumption made it possible to derive from the Markowitz portfolio theory a generalized theory of capital asset pricing under conditions of uncertainty. The theory has generally been attributed to William Sharpe, but similar independent derivations were made by Lintner and Mossin.[1] Consequently, you may see the reference to the Sharpe-Lintner-Mossin (SLM) capital asset pricing model.

RISK-FREE ASSET

We have defined a *risky asset* as one about which there is uncertainty regarding the future return. Further, we have measured this uncertainty by the variance, or standard deviation of returns. A *risk-free asset* is one for which there is no uncertainty regarding the expected rate of return, so the standard deviation of returns is equal to zero ($\sigma_{RF} = 0$). Such an asset should provide a rate of return consistent with this characteristic, and that return should be equal to the long-run growth rate of the economy, with short-run liquidity having some effect. In other words, the RFR is approximately equal to the long-run real growth rate of the economy.

COVARIANCE WITH THE RISK-FREE ASSET. You will recall that the covariance between two sets of returns is equal to

$$Cov_{ij} = \sum_{i=1}^{n} ((R_i - E(R_i))((R_j - E(R_j))/n.$$

Because the returns for the risk-free asset are certain, $\sigma_{RF} = 0$, which means $R_i = E(R_i)$ during all periods. Consequently, when computing the covariance of the risk-free asset with that of any risky asset or portfolio of assets, the expression for the risk-free asset will always be equal to zero. Thus, $R_{rf} - E(R_{rf}) = 0$, and the product will equal zero. Therefore, the covariance between any risky asset or portfolio of risky assets and a risk-free asset is zero. Similarly, the correlation would also be zero, since it is equal to

$$Cov_{rf,i}/\sigma_{rf}\sigma_i.$$

COMBINING THE RISK-FREE ASSET AND A RISKY PORTFOLIO. What happens to the average rate of return and standard deviation when a risk-free asset is combined with a portfolio of risky assets such as exists on the Markowitz efficient frontier?

[1] William F. Sharpe, "Capital Asset Prices: A Theory of Market Equilibrium under Conditions of Risk," *Journal of Finance* 19, no. 3 (September 1964): 425–442; John Lintner, "Security Prices, Risk and Maximal Gains from Diversification," *Journal of Finance* 20, no. 4 (December 1965): 587–615; and J. Mossin, "Equilibrium in a Capital Asset Market," *Econometrica* 34, no. 4 (October 1966): 768–783.

EXPECTED RETURN. Similar to the expected return for a portfolio of two risky assets, the expected return here is the weighted average of the two returns, as follows:

$$E(R_{port}) = W_{RF}(RFR) + (1 - W_{RF})E(R_i),$$

where

W_{RF} = **the proportion of the portfolio invested in a risk-free asset**

$E(R_i)$ = **the expected rate of return on risky Portfolio i.**

STANDARD DEVIATION. Recall from Chapter 7 that the expected variance for a two-asset portfolio is

$$E(\sigma^2_{port}) = W_1^2\sigma_1^2 + W_2^2\sigma_2^2 + 2W_1 W_2 r_{1,2}\sigma_1\sigma_2.$$

Substituting the risk-free asset for Security 1, and the risky asset portfolio for Security 2, this formula would become

$$E(\sigma^2_{port}) = W_{RF}^2\sigma_{RF}^2 + (1 - W_{RF})^2\sigma_i^2 + 2W_{RF}(1 - W_{RF})r_{RFi}\sigma_{RF}\sigma_i.$$

We know that the variance of the risk-free asset is zero; that is, $\sigma_{RF}^2 = 0$, and the correlation between the risk-free asset and any risky asset, i, is also zero; that is $r_{,RF,i} = 0$. Therefore, any component of the formula that has either of these terms will equal zero, and the formula will become

$$E(\sigma^2_{port}) = (1 - W_{RF})^2\sigma_i^2.$$

The standard deviation is

$$E(\sigma_{port}) = \sqrt{(1 - W_{RF})^2\sigma_i^2}$$
$$= (1 - W_{RF})\sigma_i.$$

Therefore, the standard deviation of a portfolio that combines the risk-free asset and a portfolio of risky assets is *the linear proportion of the standard deviation of the risky asset portfolio.*

Since both the expected return and the standard deviation of return for such a portfolio are linear combinations, this means the alternative portfolio returns and risks are represented by a straight line between the two assets. A graph depicting portfolio possibilities when the risk-free asset is combined with alternative risky portfolios on the Markowitz efficient frontier is contained in Figure 8.1.

It is possible to attain any point along the straight line RFR-A by investing some portion of your portfolio in the risk-free asset W_{RF} and the remainder $(1 - W_{RF})$ in the risky asset portfolio at Point A on the efficient frontier. This set of portfolio possibilities dominates all risky asset portfolios below Point A because there is a portfolio along Line RFR-A that has equal variance but a higher rate of return than the portfolio on the original efficient frontier. Likewise, it is possible to attain any point along Line RFR-B by investing in some combination of the risk-free asset and

Figure 8.1
Portfolio Possibilities Combining the Risk-Free Asset and Risky Portfolios on the Efficient Frontier

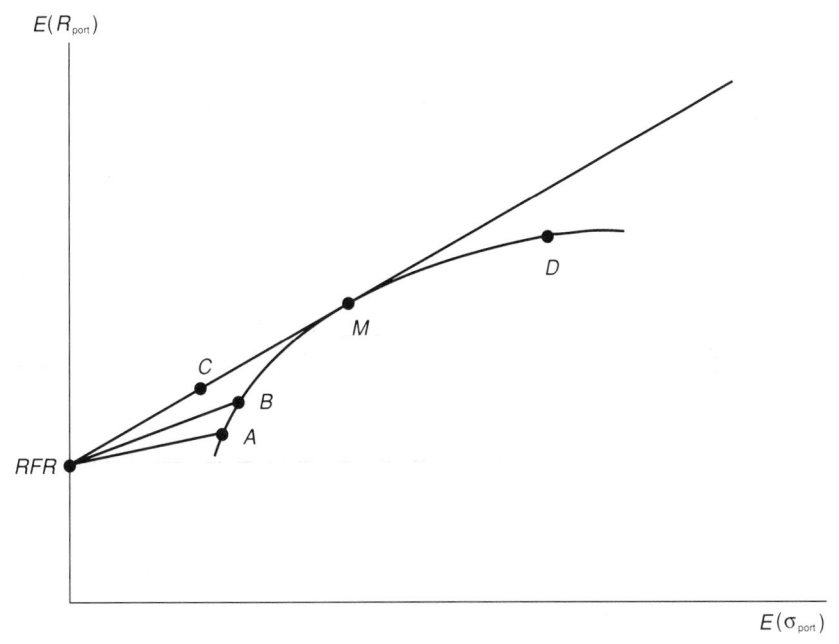

the risky asset portfolio at Point B. Again, these combinations dominate all portfolio possibilities below Point B (including Line *RFR-A*).

It is possible to draw further lines from the RFR to the efficient frontier at higher and higher points until you reach the point of tangency, which is set at Point M. The set of portfolio possibilities along Line *RFR-M* dominates all portfolios below Point M. You could attain a risk and return combination at Point C (which is midway between the RFR and Point M) by investing one-half of your portfolio in the risk-free asset (lending money at the RFR) and the other half in the risky portfolio at Point M.

A LEVERAGED PORTFOLIO

An investor may want to attain a higher expected return than is available at Point M and also be willing to accept higher risk. One alternative would be to invest in one of the risky asset portfolios on the efficient frontier beyond Point M (e.g., the portfolio at Point D). A second alternative is to add *leverage* to the portfolio by borrowing money at the risk-free rate and investing the proceeds in the risky asset portfolio at Point M. Assuming an investor does this, what effect will it have on the return and risk for the portfolio? If the investor borrows an amount equal to 50 percent of his original wealth, W_{RF} will not be a positive fraction, but a negative 50

Figure 8.2

Derivation of Capital Market Line Assuming Lending or Borrowing at the Risk-Free Rate

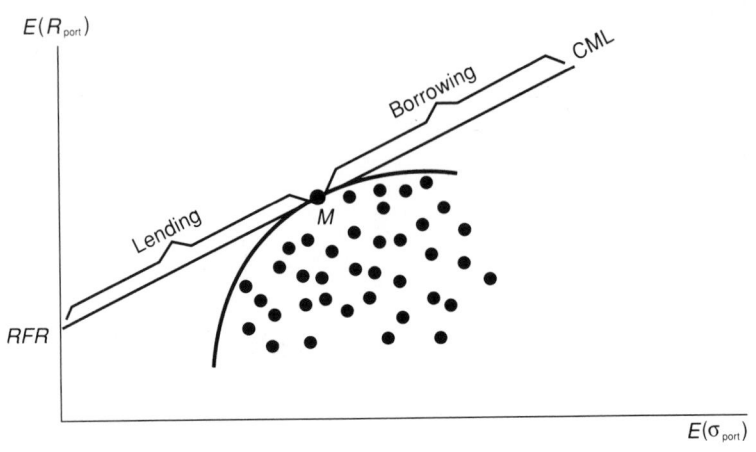

percent (i.e., $W_{RF} = -.50$). The effect on the expected return for the portfolio is as follows:

$$E(R_{port}) = -W_{RF}(RFR) + (1 - W_{RF})E(R_m)$$
$$= -.50(RFR) + (1 - (-.50))E(R_m)$$
$$= -.50(RFR) + 1.50E(R_m).$$

As shown, the return will increase in a *linear* fashion along Line *RFR-M*, because the gross return increases by 50 percent, but it is necessary to pay interest (at the RFR) on the money borrowed. As an example, assuming that the $E(RFR) = .06$ and $E(R_m) = .12$, then the return to the leveraged portfolio would be

$$E(R_{port}) = -.50(.06) + 1.5(.12)$$
$$= -.03 + .18$$
$$= .15.$$

The effect on the standard deviation of the leveraged portfolio is similar.

$$E(\sigma_{port}) = (1 - W_{RF})\sigma_m$$
$$= (1 - (-.50))\sigma_m = 1.50\sigma_m.$$

Therefore, both return and risk increase in a linear fashion along the original Line *RFR-M,* and this extension dominates everything below the line on the original efficient frontier. Thus, this "new" efficient frontier is the straight line from the *RFR* tangent to Point M. This line is referred to as the *capital market line (CML)* and is shown in Figure 8.2.

As was shown in the discussion of portfolio theory, when two assets are perfectly correlated, the set of portfolio possibilities between them is a straight line. Therefore, because it is a straight line, all the portfolios on the CML are perfectly positively correlated. This positive correlation is also intuitive, because, as shown, all the portfolio possibilities on the CML are a combination of risky asset Portfolio M and either borrowing or lending at the risk-free rate, so all variability is caused by the variability of the M portfolio. The only difference is the *magnitude* of the variability because of the proportion of the risky asset portfolio in the total portfolio.

THE MARKET PORTFOLIO

Because Portfolio M is the tangent portfolio that gives the highest portfolio possibility line, everybody will want to invest in this risky asset portfolio and borrow or lend to be somewhere on the CML. All risky assets must therefore be in this portfolio. If a risky asset were not in this portfolio, it would have no demand and therefore no value. Because the market is in equilibrium, all assets are included in this portfolio in proportion to their market value. If, for example, there is a higher proportion of an asset than is justified by its value, the excess demand for this asset will cause an increase in its price until its value becomes consistent with the proportion.

This portfolio of all risky assets is referred to as the *market portfolio*. It includes not only common stocks, but *all* risky assets, such as non–U.S. stocks, U.S. and non–U.S. bonds, options, real estate, coins, stamps, art, or antiques. Since the market portfolio contains *all* risky assets, it is a completely diversified portfolio. Because of this, all the *unsystematic risk* (unique risk) of individual assets in the portfolio is diversified away in the M portfolio. The "unique" risk of one asset is offset by the "unique" variability of the other assets in the portfolio. The only risk remaining in the market portfolio is the *systematic risk* caused by macroeconomic variables that influence all risky assets. This systematic risk, measured by the standard deviation of returns of the market portfolio, can change over time if there is a change in the macroeconomic variables that affect the valuation of risky assets.[2]

MEASURE OF DIVERSIFICATION. All portfolios on the CML are perfectly positively correlated, which means that they are perfectly correlated with the market portfolio. This implies a *measure of complete diversification*.[3] Specifically, $R^2 = +1.00$. This is logical because complete diversification requires the elimination of all unsystematic risk. Since all that is left in a completely diversified portfolio is systematic risk, it will correlate perfectly with the market portfolio that has only systematic risk.

---

[2] For an analysis of changes in stock price volatility, see Dennis E. Logue, "Are Stock Markets Becoming Riskier?" *Journal of Portfolio Management* 2, no. 3 (Spring 1976): 13–19; R. R. Officer, "The Variability of the Market Factor of the New York Stock Exchange," *The Journal of Business* 46, no. 3 (July 1973): 434–453; and John M. Wachowicz and Frank K. Reilly, "An Analysis of Changes in Aggregate Stock Market Volatility," paper presented at Midwest Finance Association, April 1979.

[3] James Lorie, "Diversification: Old and New," *Journal of Portfolio Management* 1, no. 2 (Winter 1975): 25–28.

Figure 8.3
Impact of Number of Stocks in a Portfolio on the Standard Deviation of Portfolio Return

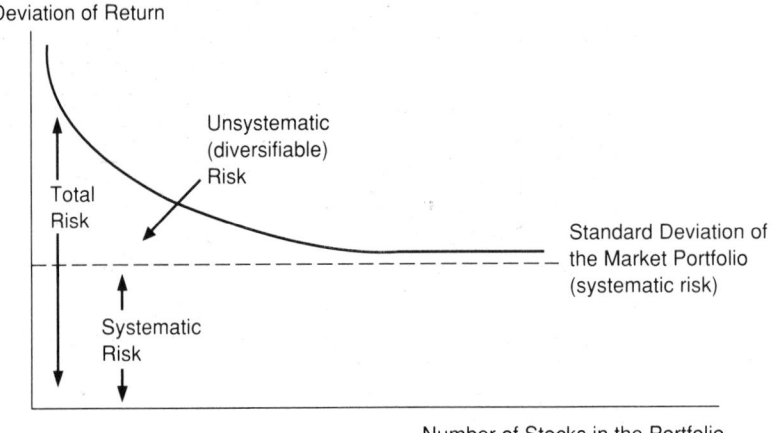

DIVERSIFICATION AND UNSYSTEMATIC RISK. As discussed in Chapter 7, the purpose of diversification is to reduce the standard deviation of the total portfolio. It requires a lack of perfect correlation among securities.[4] Ideally, as you add securities, the average covariance for the portfolio declines. An important question is, about how many securities must be included in a completely diversified portfolio? To discover the answer, you must observe what happens as you increase the sample size for securities that have some level of positive correlation. The typical correlation among U.S. securities is about 0.5 to 0.6. One set of studies that examined the average standard deviation for numerous portfolios of different sample sizes determined that the initial impact was quite large and the major benefits of diversification were achieved rather quickly.[5] About 90 percent of the maximum benefit was derived with portfolios of 12 to 18 stocks. Figure 8.3 is a graph of the effect. A more recent study by Statman compared the benefits of lower risk to the added transaction costs and concluded that a well-diversified stock portfolio must include at least 30 stocks for a borrowing investor and 40 stocks for a lending investor.[6]

The point is, by adding stocks to the portfolio that are not perfectly correlated, you can reduce the overall standard deviation of the portfolio,

---

[4] Given the discussion in Chapter 7, one might envision that it would be ideal to have securities with negative correlation. While this is true in theory, it is very difficult to find such assets in the real world.

[5] Lawrence Fisher and James H. Lorie, "Some Studies of Variability of Returns on Investments in Common Stock," *Journal of Business* 43, no. 2 (April 1970): 99–134; John L. Evans and Stephen H. Archer, "Diversification and the Reduction of Dispersion: An Empirical Analysis," *Journal of Finance* 23, no. 5 (December 1968): 761–767; and Thomas M. Tole, "You Can't Diversify without Diversifying," *Journal of Portfolio Management* 8, no. 2 (Winter 1982): 5–11.

[6] Meir Statman, "How Many Stocks Make a Diversified Portfolio?" *Journal of Financial and Quantitative Analysis* 22, no. 3 (September 1987): 353–363.

FIGURE 8.4
Choice of Optimal Portfolio Combinations on the CML

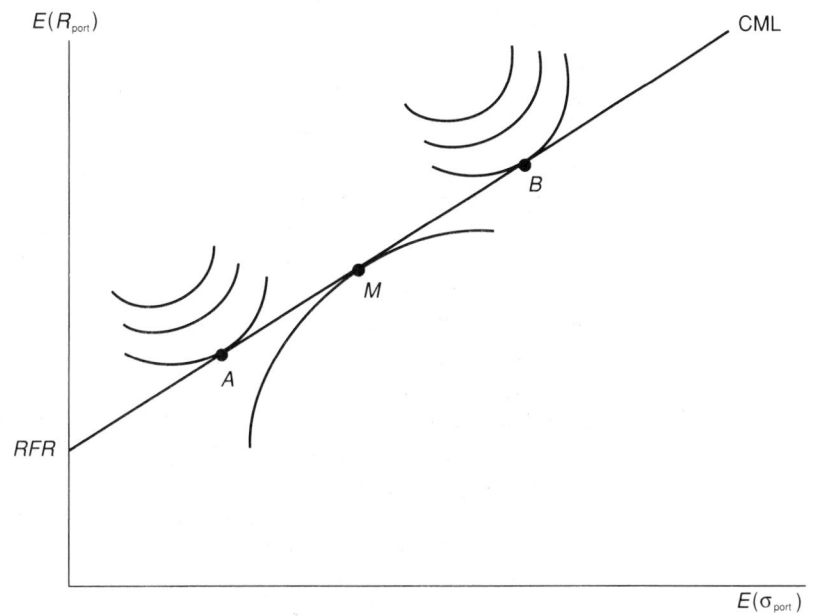

but you cannot eliminate variability. The standard deviation of your port-folio will eventually reach the level of the market portfolio, which means you have eliminated all unsystematic risk, but you are left with *market risk* (systematic risk), which is due to macroeconomic factors that cannot be eliminated.

SEPARATION THEOREM. Given the existence of the CML, everyone should invest in the same risky asset portfolio, the M portfolio. The only difference among individual investors should be in the financing decision they make, which depends upon their risk preferences. If you are relatively risk averse, you will lend some part of your portfolio at the RFR (i.e., you will buy some risk-free securities) and invest the remainder in the market portfolio. For example, you might invest in the portfolio combination at Point A in Figure 8.4. In contrast, if you prefer more risk, you might borrow funds at the RFR and invest everything in the market portfolio—which would be a portfolio combination such as the one at Point B, providing more risk and greater return than the market portfolio. The CML thus becomes the ef-ficient frontier of portfolios, and investors decide where they want to be along this efficient frontier. This division of the *investment decision* from the *financing decision* is referred to as the *separation theorem* as specified by Tobin.[7] Specifically, to be somewhere on this efficient frontier (i.e., the CML), you initially make an investment decision to invest in the market portfolio, M. Subsequently, based upon your risk preferences, you make a separate financing decision (i.e., whether to borrow or lend) to attain the preferred point on the CML (e.g., A or B).

RISK IN A CML WORLD. The relevant risk measure for risky assets is their covariance with the M portfolio. This covariance is referred to as the stock's *systematic risk.* You can see why it is important if you consider the following:

1. In the Markowitz portfolio discussion, it was noted that the relevant risk consideration for a security, when it is added to a portfolio, is its *average covariance* with all other assets in the portfolio. Because the only relevant portfolio is the M portfolio, the only important consideration for any individual risky asset is its average covariance with all the risky assets in the M portfolio, or simply, the asset's covariance with the market portfolio. This, then, is the relevant risk measure for an individual risky asset.
2. Alternatively, because all individual risky assets are a part of the M portfolio, one can describe individual asset returns in relation to the returns for the M portfolio with the following linear model:

$$R_{it} = a_i + b_i R_{mt} + \epsilon,$$

where

$$R_{it} = \text{return for asset } i \text{ during period } t$$

$$a_i = \text{constant term for asset } i$$

$$b_i = \text{slope coefficient for asset } i$$

$$R_{mt} = \text{return for M portfolio during period } t$$

$$\epsilon = \text{random error term.}$$

Its variance of returns could be described as

$$
\begin{aligned}
Var\ (R_{it}) &= Var\ (a_i + b_i R_{mt} + \epsilon) \\
&= Var\ (a_i) + Var\ (b_i R_{mt}) + Var\ (\epsilon) \\
&= 0 + Var\ (b_i R_{mt}) + Var\ (\epsilon),
\end{aligned}
$$

but $Var\ (b_i R_{mt})$ is the variance of the market return, which is referred to as *systematic variance.* $Var\ (\epsilon)$ is the residual variance, which is the variance of return for the individual asset that is unrelated to the market portfolio. It is also referred to as *unsystematic variance,* or *unique variance,* because it is caused by the unique features of the asset. Therefore,

---

[7] James Tobin, "Liquidity Preference as Behavior towards Risk," *Review of Economic Studies* 25, no. 2 (February 1958): 65–85.

FIGURE 8.5
Graph of SML

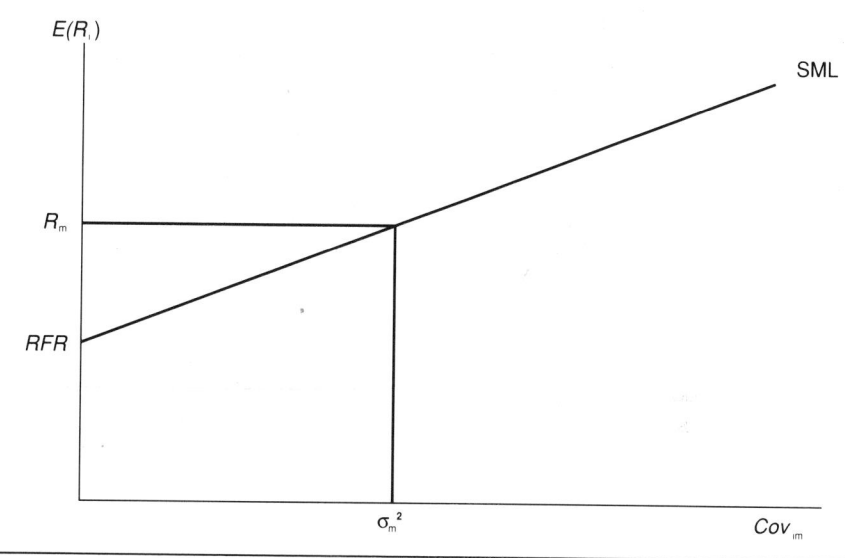

$$Var\ (R_{it}) = \text{Systematic Variance} + \text{Unsystematic Variance}.$$

We know that all unsystematic variance is eliminated in a completely diversified portfolio such as the market portfolio. Therefore, the unsystematic variance is not relevant to investors, and they should not expect to receive added returns for assuming this risk. The only variance that is relevant is the systematic variance that cannot be diversified away, because it is attributable to macroeconomic factors that affect all risky assets.

SECURITY MARKET LINE. Because the relevant risk measure for an individual risky asset is its covariance with the market portfolio (Cov_{im}), we can draw the risk-return relationship shown in Figure 8.5. The return for the market portfolio (R_m) should be consistent with its own risk, which is the covariance of the market with itself. You will recall that the covariance of any asset with itself is its variance: $Cov_{ii} = \sigma_i^2$. Therefore, the covariance of the market with itself is the variance of the market rate of return: $Cov_{mm} = \sigma_m^2$). The equation for this line is

$$E(R_i) = RFR + \frac{R_m - RFR}{\sigma_m^2}(Cov_{im})$$

$$= RFR + \frac{Cov_{im}}{\sigma_m^2}(R_m - RFR),$$

but this slope term is defined as follows:

FIGURE 8.6
Graph of SML with Normalized Systematic Risk

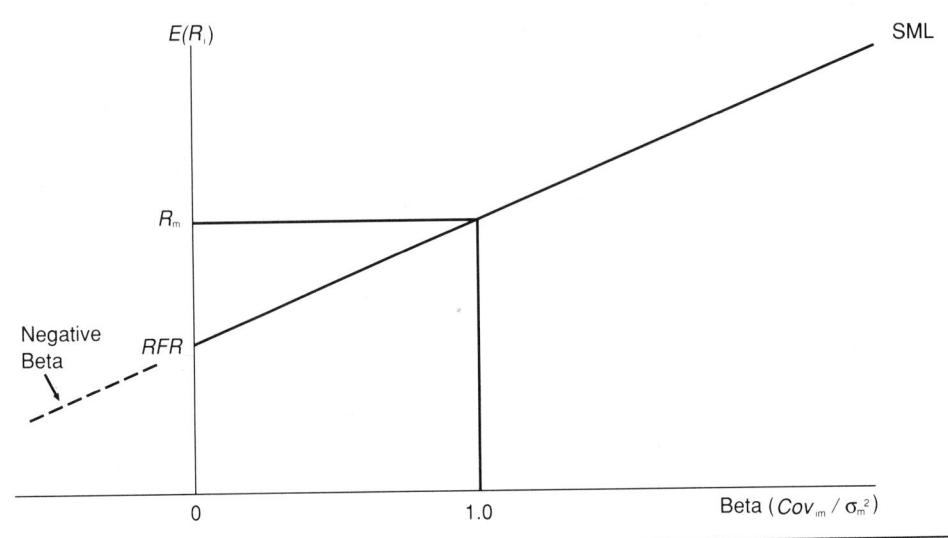

$$Cov_{im}/\sigma_m^2 = \text{beta } (\beta_i).$$

Therefore, this equation can be stated as

$$E(R_i) = RFR + \beta_i(R_m - RFR).$$

Beta is a standardized measure of systematic risk. Specifically, the covariance of any asset, *i* with the market portfolio, (Cov_{im}), is standardized by the market portfolio variance, so the market has a beta of 1. Therefore, if β_I is above 1.0, the asset has higher systematic risk than the market has. Now the SML graph can be expressed as shown in Figure 8.6.

DETERMINING EXPECTED RETURN. The expected rate of return for a risky asset is therefore determined by the RFR plus a risk premium for the individual asset that is a function of the systematic risk of the asset β_i, and the prevailing market risk premium, $R_m - RFR$. Consider the following example stocks:

STOCK	BETA
A	.70
B	1.00
C	1.15
D	1.40
E	−.30

Assume that we expect the economy's RFR to be 0.08 and the expected market return, R_m, to be 0.14. This implies a market risk premium of 0.06, and the expected return for these five stocks would be

$$E(R_i) = RFR + \beta_i (R_m - RFR)$$
$$E(R_a) = .08 + 0.70 (.14 - .08)$$
$$= .122 = 12.2 \text{ percent.}$$
$$E(R_b) = .08 + 1.00 (.14 - .08)$$
$$= .14 = 14 \text{ percent.}$$
$$E(R_c) = .08 + 1.15 (.14 - .08)$$
$$= .149 = 14.9 \text{ percent.}$$
$$E(R_d) = .08 + 1.40 (.14 - .08)$$
$$= .164 = 16.4 \text{ percent.}$$
$$E(R_e) = .08 + (-0.30)(.14 - .08)$$
$$= .08 - .018$$
$$= .062 = 6.2 \text{ percent.}$$

As stated, these are the expected (required) rates of return that these stocks should provide, based upon the systematic risk of each stock. Stock A has lower risk than the aggregate market, so an investor should not expect (require) a return from it as high as the return on the market portfolio of risky assets. In this instance, one should expect a return of 12.2 percent. In Case B, the stock has systematic risk equal to the market (beta = 1.00), so the rate of return expected should likewise be equal to the expected market return (14 percent). Stocks C and D have systematic risk greater than the market and are expected to provide returns consistent with this risk. Finally, it is assumed that Stock E has a *negative* beta (which is quite rare in practice) so the expected return on such a stock (if it could be found) would be below the RFR.

In equilibrium, all assets and all portfolios of assets should plot on the SML. That is, all assets should be priced such that their expected (required) rates of return are consistent with their systematic risk. Any security that plots above the SML would be considered *underpriced,* because its estimated return would be above what is required in terms of its systematic risk. In contrast, assets that plot below the SML would be considered *overpriced.*

In an efficient market that is in equilibrium, one would not expect any assets to plot off the SML. Alternatively, if the market is generally but not completely efficient, certain assets might be mispriced, because not *everyone* is aware of *all* the relevant information for the asset. As discussed in the chapter on efficient markets, a superior analyst will derive estimates of value and rates of return that are consistently superior to the aggregate market's evaluation and also different from the consensus estimate, so that the returns derived will be above average on a risk-adjusted basis.

DETERMINATION OF UNDERVALUED AND OVERVALUED ASSETS. Now that we have determined the rate of return that an investor should expect or require for a specific risky asset using the SML, we can compare this

TABLE 8.1
Price, Dividend, and Rate of Return Estimates

STOCK	CURRENT PRICE (P_t)	EXPECTED PRICE ($P_t + 1$)	Expected Dividend ($D_t + 1$)	ESTIMATED FUTURE RATE OF RETURN (%)
A	25	27	1.00	12.0
B	40	42	1.25	8.1
C	33	40	1.00	24.2
D	64	65	2.40	5.3
E	50	55	None	10.0

required return to the *estimated rate of return* over your investment horizon to determine whether we should invest in a given asset. Such an evaluation requires an independent estimate of the return outlook for the security, using either fundamental or technical analysis techniques. Consider the following example for the five assets discussed in the previous section.

Five stocks have been followed by analysts in a major trust department. Based upon extensive fundamental analysis, the analysts provide the price and dividend outlooks contained in Table 8.1. Table 8.2 summarizes the relationship between the required rates of return based on systematic risk and the estimated rates of return based upon the current price, the future price, and the dividend outlook. When these estimated rates of return and stock betas are plotted on the SML, they would appear as shown in Figure 8.7. Stock A is almost exactly on the line and so is considered properly valued. Stocks B and D are considered overvalued, because the estimates of their rates of return during the coming period are not consistent with the risk involved (they would plot below the SML). In contrast, because Stocks C and E are expected to provide rates of return greater than that required based upon their systematic risk, both stocks plot above the SML.

Assuming that you had faith in the ability of your analyst to forecast estimated returns, you would take no action regarding Stock A and would buy Stocks C and E and sell Stocks B and D (possibly selling them short if you are aggressive in this regard).

TABLE 8.2
Comparison of Required Rate of Return to Estimated Rate of Return

STOCK	BETA	REQUIRED RETURN $E(R_i)$	ESTIMATED RETURN	ESTIMATED RETURN MINUS $E(R_i)$	EVALUATION
A	0.70	12.2	12.0	−0.2	Properly valued
B	1.00	14.0	8.1	−5.9	Overvalued
C	1.15	14.9	24.2	9.3	Undervalued
D	1.40	16.4	5.3	−11.1	Overvalued
E	−0.30	6.2	10.0	3.8	Undervalued

FIGURE 8.7
Plot of Estimated Returns on SML Graph

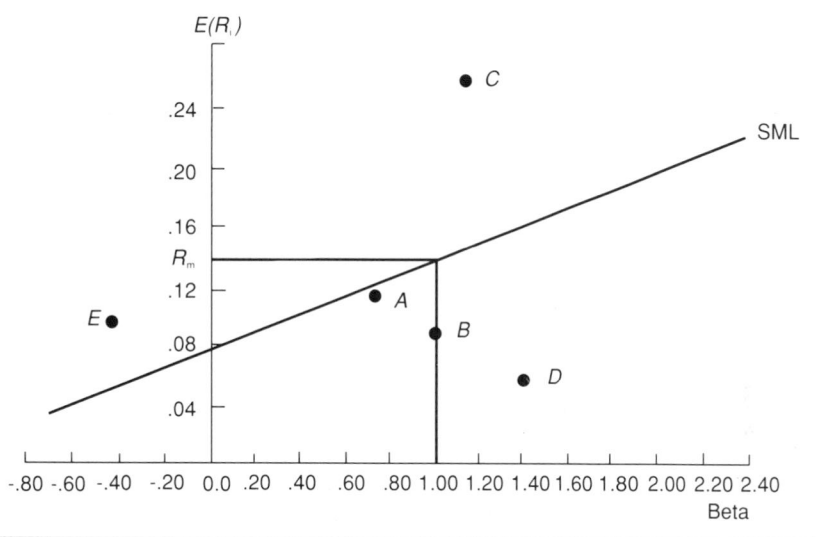

<table>
<tr><td></td></tr>
</table>

THE
CHARACTERISTIC
LINE

The systematic risk input for an individual asset is derived from the following regression model, referred to as the asset's *characteristic line* with the market portfolio:

$$R_{it} = a_i + B_i R_{mt} + \epsilon,$$

where

R_{it} = the rate of return for asset i during period t

R_{mt} = the rate of return for the market portfolio during period t

a_i = the constant term or intercept of the regression, which equals $\bar{R}_i - B_i\bar{R}_m$

B_i = the slope coefficient for the regression which is equal to Cov_{im}/σ_m^2

ϵ = the random error term.

The characteristic line is the line of best fit through a scatter plot of rates of return for the individual risky asset and for the market portfolio of risky assets over some designated past period, as shown in Figure 8.8.

In practice the number of observations used and the time interval employed varies. Value Line Investment Services uses the most recent five years of weekly rates of return (i.e., 260 weekly observations). Merrill Lynch, Pierce, Fenner & Smith uses the most recent five years of monthly rates of return. There is no theoretically correct time interval and period of analysis. A trade-off exists between using enough observations to elim-

FIGURE 8.8
Scatter Plot of Rates of Return

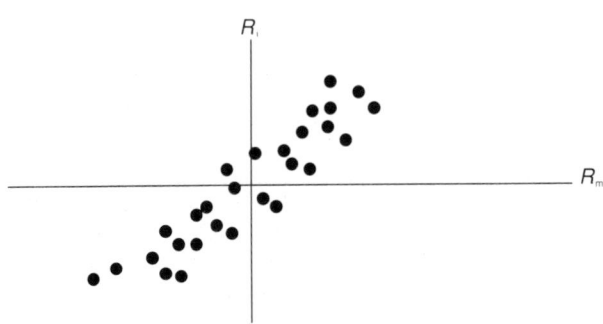

inate the impact of random rates of return, yet not going so far back in time (e.g., 15 or 20 years) that the subject company may have changed dramatically in the interim.

Statman examined the relationship between Value Line (VL) betas and Merrill Lynch (ML) betas for a sample of 195 companies and found a relatively weak relationship between the two sets of beta ($R^2 = 0.55$) but no obvious bias.[8] Reilly and Wright examined a larger sample for the differential impact of several factors (return computation, market index, and interval).[9] The results indicated that the major factor causing the significant differences in beta was the interval. Further analysis of why the interval made a difference indicated that the size of the firms was important. The shorter interval caused the beta to be larger for large firms and smaller for small firms. For example, during the period 1975–1979, the average beta for the smallest decile of firms was 1.682 using monthly data but 1.080 using weekly data. Clearly the interval makes a difference, and the impact increases as size declines.

Also, there is no available portfolio series that contains all the risky assets in the economy. Most investigators use the Standard & Poor's 500 Composite Index as a market proxy because the stocks in this index have a large proportion of the total market value of U.S. stocks listed on exchanges, and it is a value-weighted series. Still, this series is limited when one considers what was "ideally" in the market portfolio of risky assets (U.S. stocks and bonds, non–U.S. stocks and bonds, real estate, coins, stamps, art, and antiques).[10]

---

[8] Meir Statman, "Betas Compared: Merrill Lynch vs. Value Line," *Journal of Portfolio Management* 7, no. 2 (Winter 1981): 41–44.

[9] Frank K. Reilly and David J. Wright, "A Comparison of Published Betas," *Journal of Portfolio Management* 14, no. 3 (Spring 1988): 64–69.

[10] There has been substantial discussion of the market index used and its impact on the empirical results and usefulness of the CAPM. This controversy and the empirical tests of the CAPM are discussed in Chapter 17.

TABLE 8.3
Computation of Covariance between IBM and the S&P 500: 1987

	MONTH-END PRICE S&P 500	R_{mt}	$R_{IBM,t}$	$R_{mt} - \bar{R}_{mt}$	$R_{IBM,t} - \bar{R}_{IBM}$	$(R_{mt} - \bar{R}_m) \times (R_{IBM,t} - \bar{R}_{IBM})$
12/86	242.17					
1/87	274.08	13.18	7.29	12.62	7.25	91.46
2/87	284.2	3.69	8.35	3.14	8.30	26.06
3/87	291.7	2.64	7.62	2.09	7.57	15.78
4/87	288.36	−1.15	6.66	−1.70	6.62	−11.24
5/87	290.1	0.60	−0.08	0.05	−0.12	−0.01
6/87	304	4.79	1.56	4.24	1.52	6.43
7/87	318.66	4.82	−0.92	4.27	−0.97	−4.14
8/87	329.8	3.50	4.58	2.94	4.53	13.34
9/87	321.83	−2.42	−10.47	−2.97	−10.51	31.23
10/87	251.79	−21.76	−18.74	−22.32	−18.79	419.24
11/87	230.3	−8.53	−9.59	−9.09	−9.64	87.60
12/87	247.08	7.29	4.29	6.73	4.24	28.56
		$\bar{R} = 0.55$	0.05			$\Sigma = 704.32$
		$\sigma = 8.45$	8.27			

$$Cov_{IBM,m} = 704.32/12 = 58.693$$

$$Var_m (\sigma_m^2) = (8.45)^2 = 71.40$$

$$\beta_{IBM} = \frac{58.69}{71.40} = 0.82$$

$$r_{IBM,m} = \frac{58.69}{(8.45)(8.27)} = 0.84$$

$$\alpha_i = \bar{R}_{IBM} - (\beta_{IBM} \times \bar{R}_m)$$

$$= 0.05 - (0.82 \times 0.55)$$

$$= 0.05 - 0.45$$

$$= -0.40$$

AN EXAMPLE COMPUTATION. Consider the following computation of the characteristic line for IBM based upon the monthly rates of return during 1987.[11] Twelve is not enough observations, but it should provide a good example. The S&P 500 Index is used as a proxy for the market portfolio. The monthly price changes are computed using the closing prices for the last day of each month. These data are contained in Table 8.3, and a scatter plot of the rates of return is contained in Figure 8.9. During most months, IBM had returns that were consistent with the aggregate market returns—

[11] This beta is computed using only monthly price changes for both IBM and the S&P 500 (i.e., dividends are not included). This is done for the sake of simplicity, but it is also based upon a study indicating that betas derived with and without dividends are correlated 0.99: William Sharpe and Guy M. Cooper, "Risk-Return Classes of New York Stock Exchange Common Stocks," *Financial Analysts Journal* 28, no. 2 (March–April 1972): 35–43.

FIGURE 8.9
Scatter Plot of IBM and the S&P 500 with Characteristic Line for IBM

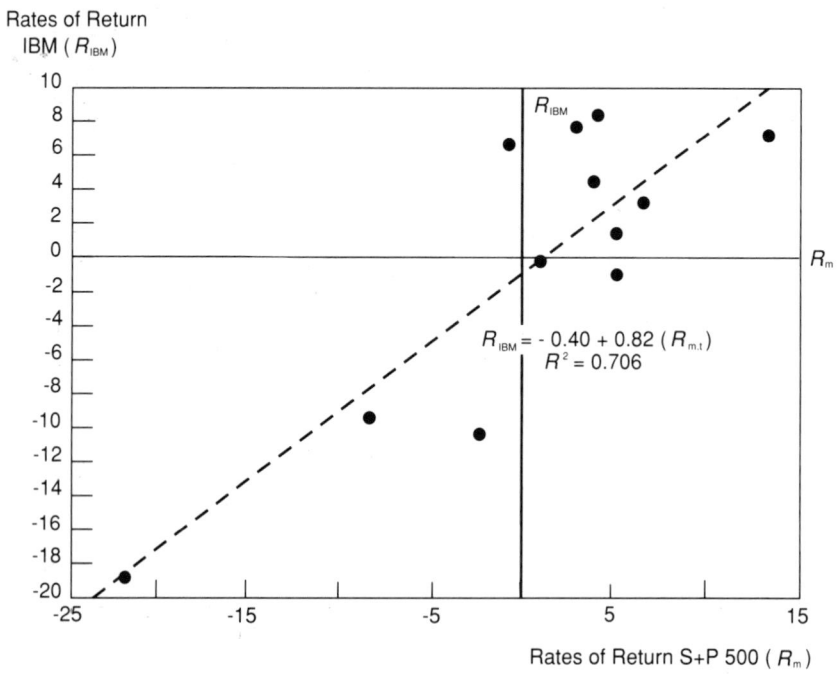

there were only three instances when one series experienced a return above or below its mean while the other series was not likewise above or below its mean. As a result, the covariance between IBM and the market is positive. The covariance divided by the market variance (IBM's beta) is equal to 0.82, implying that, based upon this limited time-period analysis, IBM is less risky than the aggregate market.

The intercept for the characteristic line is computed using the formula set forth before. When this characteristic line is drawn on Figure 8.9, the scatter plots fall fairly close to the characteristic line, which is consistent with the correlation coefficient of 0.84.

SOME REMAINING QUESTIONS

This chapter is only an introduction to capital market theory, intended to provide the basic concepts and theory to justify using systematic risk (beta) as the relevant measure of risk for individual securities and for portfolios of securities when discussing valuation theory. We have not considered a number of real-world questions regarding the theory, such as

- What do you use as a proxy for the market portfolio of risky assets, and what is the effect if this is not a good proxy?

- If you cannot borrow and lend at the risk-free rate, how does this affect the CML and SML?
- If you cannot borrow, how can you attain a high-risk portfolio?
- How stable is the systematic risk (beta) for individual stocks and for portfolios?
- What is the empirical relationship between the rates of return and systematic risk; that is, how good is the CAPM as a predictive model?

All of these questions, and others as they relate to the CAPM, will be discussed in Chapter 17.

SUMMARY

The assumptions of capital market theory expand on those of the Markowitz portfolio model and include a consideration of the risk-free rate of return. The correlation and covariance of any asset with a risk-free asset is zero, so any combination of an asset or portfolio with the risk-free asset generates a linear return and risk function. Therefore, when you combine the risk-free asset with any risky asset on the Markowitz efficient frontier, you derive a set of straight-line portfolio possibilities with the dominant line the one that is tangent to the efficient frontier. This dominant line is referred to as the *capital market line (CML),* and all investors should want to be somewhere along this line depending upon their risk preferences. Because all investors want to invest in the risky portfolio at the point of tangency, this portfolio, referred to as the *market portfolio,* must contain all risky assets in proportion to their relative market values. Moreover, the investment decision and the financing decision can be separated, because, while everyone will want to invest in the market portfolio, each investor will differ in his financing decision (i.e., whether he will lend or borrow), which is based upon individual risk preferences.

Given the CML and the dominance of the market portfolio, the relevant risk measure for an individual risky asset is its covariance with the market portfolio, or its systematic risk. When this covariance is standardized by the covariance for the market portfolio, we derive the well-known beta measure of systematic risk and a security market line (SML) that relates the expected return for an asset to its beta. Since all individual securities and portfolios should plot on this SML, you can determine the expected (required) return on a security based upon its systematic risk (its beta). Alternatively, assuming markets are not completely efficient, one can identify undervalued and overvalued securities. The systematic risk input (the beta) for an individual risky asset is derived from a regression model referred to as its characteristic line. Questions remain about applying the CAPM in the real world, and these will be considered in Chapter 17.

QUESTIONS

1. Define a risk-free asset.
2. What is the covariance between a risk-free asset and a portfolio of risky assets? Explain your answer.

3. Explain why the set of points between the risk-free asset and a portfolio on the Markowitz efficient frontier is a straight line.

4. What happens to the Markowitz efficient frontier when you assume the existence of a risk-free asset and combine this with alternative risky asset portfolios on the Markowitz efficient frontier? Draw a graph to show this, and explain it.

5. Explain why the line from the RFR that is tangent to the efficient frontier is the dominant set of portfolio possibilities. Demonstrate it graphically.

6. It has been shown that the capital market line (CML) is tangent to one portfolio on the Markowitz efficient frontier, and this portfolio is referred to as Portfolio M. Discuss what risky assets are in this portfolio and why they are in it.

7. Discuss leverage, and indicate what it does to the CML.

8. Why is the CML considered the "new" efficient frontier?

9. Define complete diversification in terms of capital market theory.

10. Discuss and justify a measure of diversification for a portfolio.

11. In terms of the standard deviation for a portfolio of stocks, discuss what change you would expect between 4 and 10 stocks, between 10 and 20 stocks, and between 50 and 100 stocks.

12. Discuss why, in a world with a CML, the investment decision and the financing decision are separate.

13. Given the capital market line, discuss and justify a relevant measure of risk for an individual security. Be very precise and complete in your discussion.

14. It is contended that the total variance of returns for a security can be broken down into systematic variance and unsystematic, or unique, variance. Describe what is meant by each of these terms.

15. In the capital asset pricing model (CAPM), there is systematic and unsystematic risk for an individual security. Which is the relevant risk variable, and why is it relevant? Why is the other risk variable not relevant?

16. Draw a properly labeled graph of the security market line (SML), and explain it. How does the SML differ from the CML?

PROBLEMS

1. Calculate the expected return for each of the following stocks when the risk-free rate is .08 and you expect the market return to be .15.

STOCK	BETA
A	1.72
B	1.14
C	.76
D	.44
E	.03
F	−.79

2. Compute the beta for Robin Computer Company with the following historic returns:

YEAR	ROBIN COMPUTER	GENERAL INDEX
1	12	15
2	9	13
3	−11	14
4	8	−9
5	11	12
6	4	9

3. With the information given in Problem 2, compute the following:

3a. The correlation coefficient between Robin Computer and the General Index.

3b. The intercept of the characteristic line.

3c. The equation of the characteristic line.

4a. Assume that you expect the economy's rate of inflation to be 3 percent and, in line with this, you expect the RFR to be 6 percent and the market return (R_m) to be 12 percent. Draw the SML using these assumptions.

4b. Now assume that you expect an increase in the rate of inflation from 3 percent to 6 percent. What effect would you expect this to have on your RFR and R_m? Draw another SML on the same graph used for part a.

4c. Draw the SML on the same graph if you expect the RFR to be 9 percent and the R_m to be 17 percent. How does this SML differ from the SML derived in part b? Explain what has transpired.

5. You expect the RFR to be 8 percent and the market return (R_m) to be 12 percent. Compute the expected (required) return for the following stocks, and plot these on an SML graph.

STOCK	BETA	$E(R_i)$
T	.85	
B	1.25	
R	−.20	

6. You ask a stockbroker what his firm's research department expects for these three stocks. The broker responds with the following information:

STOCK	CURRENT PRICE	EXPECTED PRICE	EXPECTED DIVIDEND
T	22	24	.75
B	48	51	2.00
R	37	40	1.25

Plot your estimated returns on the graph from Problem 5, and indicate what actions you would take with regard to these stocks. Discuss your decisions.

7. Select a stock from the NYSE and collect the month-end prices for the latest 13 months in order to compute 12 monthly percentage price changes (ignore dividends). Do the same for the S&P 500 series. Plot these percent price changes on a graph and draw a *visual* characteristic line of best fit (the line that minimizes the deviations from the line). Compute the slope of this line *from the graph.*

8. Given the returns derived in Problem 7, *compute* the beta coefficient using the formula and techniques employed in Table 8.3. How does this computed beta compare to the visual beta derived in Problem 7?

9. Look up this stock in *Value Line* and record the beta derived by *VL.* How does this *VL* beta compare to the beta you computed? Discuss why the betas might be different.

10. Select a stock that is listed on the AMEX and plot the returns during the last 12 months relative to the S&P 500. Compute the beta coefficient. In general, did you expect this stock to have a higher or lower beta than the NYSE stock? Explain your answer.

11. Given the returns for the AMEX stock in Problem 10, plot the stock returns relative to monthly rates of return for the AMEX Market Value Index, and compute the beta coefficient. Does this beta differ from that derived in Problem 10? If so, how can you explain this? Hint: Analyze the specific components of the formula for the beta coefficient. What differences were there between the components in Problems 10 and 11?

12. You derive the following information for the companies listed on the basis of five years of monthly data.

COMPANY	a_i (INTERCEPT)	σ_i	r_{im}
Sony	0.22	12.10%	0.72
Chrysler	0.10	14.60%	0.33
British Petroleum	0.17	7.60%	0.55
Polaroid	0.05	10.20%	0.60
S&P 500	0.00	5.50%	1.00

12a. Compute the beta coefficient for each stock.

12b. Assuming a risk-free rate of 6 percent and an expected return for the market portfolio of 12 percent, compute the expected (required) return for each stock and plot them on the SML.

12c. Plot the following estimates of actual return during the next year on the SML and indicate which of these stocks are undervalued or overvalued.

- Sony—20%
- Chrysler—13%
- British Petroleum—16%
- Polaroid—12%

REFERENCES Blume, Marshall E. "On the Assessment of Risk." *Journal of Finance* 27, no. 1 (March 1972).

Blume, Marshall E. "Betas and Their Regression Tendencies: Some Further Evidence." *Journal of Finance* 23, no. 5 (December 1968).

Evans, John L., and Stephen H. Archer. "Diversification and the Reduction of Dispersion: An Empirical Analysis." *Journal of Finance* 23, no. 5 (December 1968).

Hagin, Robert. *Modern Portfolio Theory.* Homewood, Ill. Dow-Jones-Irwin, 1979.

Hawawini, Gabriel A. "Why Beta Shifts as the Return Interval Changes." *Financial Analysts Journal* 39, no. 3 (May–June 1983).

Jensen, Michael C. "Capital Markets: Theory and Evidence." *Bell Journal of Economics and Management Science* 3, no. 2 (Autumn 1972).

Jensen, Michael C., ed. *Studies in the Theory of Capital Markets.* New York: Praeger Publishers, 1972.

Klemkosky, Robert C., and John D. Martin. "The Effect of Market Risk on Portfolio Diversification." *Journal of Finance* 30, no. 1 (March 1975).

Lintner, John. "The Valuation of Risk Assets and the Selection of Risky Investments in Stock Portfolios and Capital Budgets." *Review of Economics and Statistics* 47, no. 2 (February 1965).

Lintner, John. "Security Prices, Risk, and Maximal Gains from Diversification." *Journal of Finance* 20, no. 12 (December 1965).

Mossin, Jan. "Equilibrium in a Capital Asset Market." *Econometrica* 34, no. 10 (October 1966).

Reilly, Frank K., and David J. Wright. "A Comparison of Published Betas." *Journal of Portfolio Management* 14, no. 3 (Spring 1988).

Rosenberg, Barr. "The Capital Asset Pricing Model and the Market Model." *Journal of Portfolio Management* 5, no. 1 (Winter 1981).

Ross, Stephen A. "The Current Status of the Capital Asset Pricing Model (CAPM)." *Journal of Finance* 33, no. 3 (June 1978).

Sharpe, William F. "Capital Asset Prices: A Theory of Market Equilibrium under Conditions of Risk." *Journal of Finance* 19, no. 3 (September 1964).

Statman, Meir. "How Many Stocks Make a Diversified Portfolio?" *Journal of Financial and Quantitative Analysis* 22, no. 3 (September 1987).

Tobin, James. "Liquidity Preference as Behavior towards Risk." *Review of Economic Studies* 25, no. 2 (February 1958).

PART III

ANALYSIS AND VALUATION OF SECURITIES

CHAPTERS

In order to properly evaluate an investment vehicle, several analyses must be carried out, beginning with a valuation of the aggregate economy and market and progressing through the examination of various industries and then of an individual company and its securities. The globalization of the capital markets has complicated this process. Now it is necessary to consider several economies and markets on a worldwide basis; subsequently you must analyze *world* industries as contrasted to only the U.S. component of an industry and, of course, the number of companies to be analyzed in an industry is increased.

Chapter 9 contains a discussion of why our initial and major analysis is of the aggregate securities market, followed by industry and company analysis. There is also a basic presentation of the theory of valuation and its application to bonds, preferred stock, and common stock.

Next, Chapter 10 addresses bond fundamentals, including the structure of the market and alternative fixed-income instruments.

Subsequently, Chapter 11 considers the principles of bond valuation, including the mathematics of bond pricing, the determinants of bond yields, yield spreads, and bond price volatility. This background has value in itself as related to these securities, but also will be useful when we explain the analysis of equity securities later in the text.

Because the main source of information for major business decisions is the financial statements of individual companies, it is essential that you understand what statements are available, what they contain, and how to analyze them. Chapter 12 provides this background information. Chapter 13 contains an explanation of how to analyze the aggregate stock market (including specific estimation procedures), and Chapter 14 a discussion of industry analysis employing the same micro technique (i.e., the dividend valuation model) used in market analysis but applied to a specific industry. The company analysis in Chapter 15 likewise uses this approach for the valuation of a company along with other factors and approaches. The overall goal is to select one of the best companies in a superior industry during a favorable market environment. Growth companies are discussed separately in Chapter 15 because the dividend growth model employed in some prior chapters is not applicable to true growth companies. Instead, we discuss several valuation models that have been specifically developed for such companies. Notably, in all these chapters, we consider and provide examples of how these techniques can and have been applied in a global environment.

Throughout this section we refer to the semistrong efficient market hypothesis. You will recall that while many studies supported this hypothesis, there is a growing literature dealing with anomalies. The idea is to present a consistent and justifiable valuation technique that can be used to find undervalued securities. Bear in mind that the output of alternative valuation models is only as good as the estimated inputs, and the superior analyst is the one who provides the best estimates.

The final chapter in this section deals with technical analysis, an alternative to the fundamental analysis approach discussed in prior chapters. Rather than attempting to estimate value based upon numerous external variables, the technical analyst contends that the market is its own best estimator. Therefore, he believes it is possible to project future stock price movements based upon past stock price changes or other stock market data. Various techniques used by technical analysts for U.S. and world markets are discussed and demonstrated.

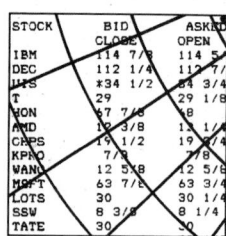

CHAPTER 9

THE PROCESS AND THEORY OF VALUATION

As noted previously, investments constitute a commitment of funds for a period of time to derive a rate of return that compensates the investor for the time during which the funds are invested and for the uncertainty involved. Obviously, before an individual makes an investment, he must determine his required rate of return and how much he should pay for a particular investment to obtain this return. The determination of how much to pay for an investment is really a determination of the value of the asset.

The first section of this chapter is an overview of the *valuation process*. The second section considers the *theory of valuation*, including the specific determinants of value. In the third section, these concepts are applied to the valuation of different assets—bonds, preferred stock, and common stock. In the final section, the determinants of the required rate of return and the expected growth rate of dividends are considered along with a discussion of the additional considerations introduced when you apply these concepts to the valuation of non–U.S. securities.

AN OVERVIEW OF THE VALUATION PROCESS

The valuation process is much like the problem of the chicken and the egg. Do you first deal with individual securities and gradually build up to an analysis of the entire economy, or vice versa? It is our contention that the discussion should first center on the analysis of aggregate economies and overall securities markets. Only after this is done can different industries be considered from a global perspective. Finally, following the industry analysis, you should consider the securities issued by various firms within the better industries. Thus, the analysis is a three-step process.

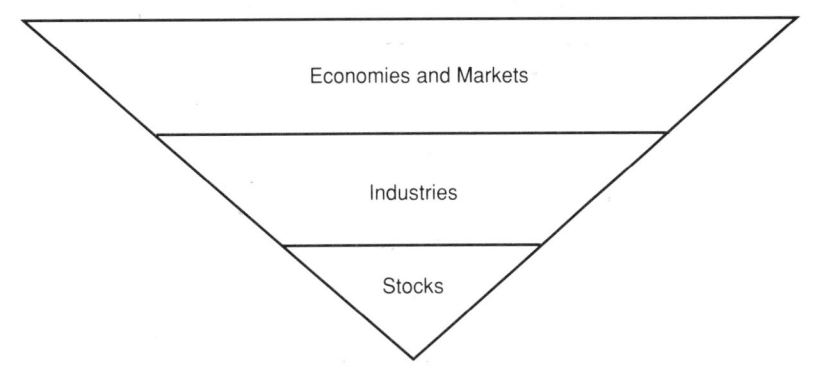

WHY A
THREE-STEP
PROCESS?

GENERAL
ECONOMIC
INFLUENCES

It is well-recognized that various agencies of national governments have a major impact on the aggregate economies of countries because they control monetary and fiscal policy. These basic economic forces exert an influence on all industries and all companies in an economy. Fiscal policy can encourage spending (e.g., through investment credits or tax cuts) or discourage spending (e.g., through taxes on gasoline, cigarettes, and liquor). Increases or decreases in spending on defense, unemployment, or highways also influence the general economic picture. All such changes have a major impact on those directly affected by the changes in expenditures, but there is also a *multiplier effect* on those who supply goods and services to those directly affected.

The same overall impact can result from a significant change in monetary policy. For example, a restrictive monetary policy that produces a decline in the growth rate of the money supply reduces the supply of funds available to all businesses for working capital and expansion. It also influences market interest rates and the funds available to individuals for acquiring goods and services. Monetary policy therefore affects absolutely *all* segments of an economy and the economy's relationship with other economies.

Another overall economic variable that must be considered is *inflation,* because it has a major impact on interest rates and on how consumers and corporations save and spend their money. Beyond the impact on the domestic economy, differential inflation and interest rates also affect the trade balance with other countries and eventually the exchange rate for currencies.

In addition to domestic monetary and fiscal actions, other occurrences, such as war, political upheavals in foreign countries, or international monetary devaluations, influence the aggregate economy. Therefore, it is difficult to conceive of any industry or company that will not be affected in some way by macroeconomic developments that affect the total economy. Because events influencing the aggregate economy also have a profound effect on all industries and all companies within these industries, these macroeconomic factors must be considered before industries can be analyzed.[1] If a recession seems likely, one would envision that security prices within that country will be affected. The asset allocation for the country within a global portfolio will change (i.e., the country will be underweighted) and an analyst should be apprehensive about recommending most industries in the country. The best recommendation would probably be a smaller allocation to the country, and any funds allocated would be directed to low-risk sectors of the economy.

In contrast, if the economic and stock-market outlook for a given country is bullish, an analyst would recommend increasing the overall allocation to this country (overweighting it based upon its relative value) and then searching for outstanding industries. This industry search within a country or on a worldwide basis would be enhanced by economic analysis, because, typically, the future performance of an industry depends upon the global economic outlook and the particular industry's expected relationship to the world economy. Prime examples of truly global industries include the oil industry, chemicals, and pharmaceuticals.

INDUSTRY INFLUENCES

Because of the importance of the economic outlook, it should be one's first consideration. If it is favorable, the outlook for various industries should be assessed. Examples of industry influences on that outlook are an industry-wide strike within a major producing country, import or export quotas or taxes, a worldwide shortage or excess supply of some resource (e.g., copper), and government-imposed regulations.

In addition, different industries feel the influence of an economic change at different points in the business cycle. For example, construction typically lags the business cycle, so is affected by changes only toward the end of a cycle. And different industries respond differently to the business cycle, especially since some also can be affected by several different economies. As an example, cyclical industries (e.g., steel, autos) typically do much better than the aggregate economy during expansions, but they suffer more during contractions. Alternatively, an industry that has a substantial worldwide market might have low demand in its domestic market but growing demand in its international market. As an example, a large proportion of the growth by beverage companies (Coca-Cola and Pepsi) and fast-food chains (McDonald's and Burger King) has been due to international expansion in Europe and the Far East. Because of this differential performance you should analyze the industry before analyzing individual companies within the industry. It is unusual for a company to perform well in a poor industry, so even the best company in a poor industry is a bad prospect for investment. In the farm equipment industry during the mid-1980s, Deere and Co.—a very well-managed firm and probably the best firm in the industry—experienced very poor results simply because of the

[1] There is an interesting discussion of an overall investment philosophy for a given economic environment contained in James H. Gipson, "Investing in a Zero Sum Economy," *Journal of Portfolio Management* 7, no. 4 (Summer 1981): 15–16.

poor sales and profits in the total industry. Though it performed better than some other firms in the industry (some went bankrupt), it still fared far less well than it had in the past and far less well than most other firms in other industries.

If the industry outlook is good, the industry analysis should be further used to compare individual firms to the entire industry in terms of relevant financial ratios. Actually, many of the ratios employed in security analysis are valid only when viewed relative to comparable ratios for the entire industry.

EMPIRICAL SUPPORT FOR THE THREE-STEP PROCESS

The importance of economic and industry analysis is supported by research confirming a relationship among the earnings of the aggregate economy, alternative industries, and individual firms, as well as among the rates of return for the aggregate stock market, the stocks in alternative industries, and individual stocks.

ASSOCIATION AMONG CORPORATE EARNINGS

Brown and Ball examined the association between the earnings of an individual firm, the earnings of other firms in its industry, and the earnings of all firms in the economy using six alternative measures of earnings.[2] The earnings for individual firms during the period were related to the earnings of all firms except the individual firm being examined and the earnings of all other firms in the particular industry. On average, approximately 30 to 40 percent of the variability of a firm's annual earnings was associated with the variability of aggregate earnings, and an additional 10 to 15 percent was associated with industry earnings. Further tests indicated that the industries were well-defined and that the firms were well-classified by industry. These results indicate that approximately 45 to 55 percent of a firm's total variability in annual earnings can be explained by the overall economy together with the status of a firm's industry, and the economic factor was of greater importance. The degree of importance of both factors, however, varies among firms. On the one hand, a highly diversified industrial firm could have earnings changes that are more closely related to the economy than these results imply; that is, earnings might be strongly related to the total economy because the firm may be an image of the economy. In contrast, small firms with a unique product and clientele might have a very weak relationship with the aggregate economy or its industry earnings.

SYSTEMATIC STOCK PRICE FLUCTUATIONS

To justify aggregate market analysis it is necessary to determine whether there is a cyclical pattern in stock prices. Shiskin analyzed market movements using the techniques employed by the National Bureau of Economic Research to break the stock price series down into several components:

---

[2] Philip Brown and Ray Ball, "Some Preliminary Findings on the Association between the Earnings of a Firm, Its Industry, and the Economy," *Empirical Research in Accounting Selected Studies, 1967,* supplement to vol. 5, *Journal of Accounting Research:* 55–77.

seasonal, irregular, and trend cycle.[3] For short-run intervals, the irregular component was dominant. As the interval was increased to three months or longer, the cyclical component became dominant. An analysis of the duration of monthly runs indicated that the average duration of run for monthly and quarterly stock prices was clearly more than expected for a random series. He analyzed the performance of 80 industries using a *diffusion index,* which indicates what proportion of the industries are rising at a point in time. The diffusion indexes for short time spans acted like a random series. As the interval was extended to 9 or 12 months, a clear cyclical pattern emerged, and the diffusion indexes led the stock price series. An examination of the relationship between the stock prices and other economic series (employment, income, production) indicated that stock prices consistently conform to economic expansions and contractions, but they clearly lead the general economy. It was acknowledged that it is difficult to predict stock price fluctuations because they vary in amplitude, pattern, and duration. But the existence of a cycle that one should attempt to predict was confirmed.

MARKET AND INDUSTRY EFFECT

A study by King examined the relationship between market returns, industry returns, and the returns on individual stocks in order to determine how much of the total price movement for a given stock over time was attributable to overall market factors, how much was due to industry influences, and how much could be ascribed to a stock's "unique" component.[4] King examined 63 NYSE stocks over the period of June 1927 through December 1960, and over four subperiods of eight years each. The stocks were from the following six industries: tobacco products (11 companies), petroleum products (11 companies), metals (ferrous and non-ferrous) (11 companies), railroads (10 companies), utilities (10 companies), and retail stores (10 companies). Using factor analysis, King determined that the mean *communality* (i.e., price variance due to all other securities) for the overall time period was 0.72, which indicates that the average unique component was only 0.28. However, the total communality factor declined during the four subperiods.

An analysis of how much of the variability was attributable to overall market movement and how much could be traced to industry factors indicated that about half the variance (52 percent) in the typical stock for the time period considered was explained by the whole market. An analysis of the net price changes after the market effect was removed indicated that almost all of the large positive correlations among individual stocks corresponded to industry groupings and that all large negative correlations were with stocks in other industries.

---

[3] Julius Shiskin, "Systematic Aspects of Stock Price Fluctuations," reprinted in James Lorie and Richard Brealey, *Modern Developments in Investment Management,* 2d ed. (Hinsdale, Ill.: The Dryden Press, 1978), 640–658.

[4] Benjamin F. King, "Market and Industry Factors in Stock Price Behavior," *Journal of Business* 39, no. 1, Part 2 (January 1966): 139–190.

Cluster analysis also supported an industry influence, since the co-movement of price changes, after removing the market effect, corresponded to the typical industry classifications. These tests indicated that, on average for the total period, more than 10 percent of the total variation in the stock's price could be attributed to the industry influence. This meant that about 62 percent of the security price changes was explained by a combination of market and industry components.

Again, the importance of the market factor tended to decline over time, and the importance of the market factor differed for alternative stocks. For some, it explained over 70 percent of the variance, while for other, less than 25 percent.

MORE ON THE MARKET AND INDUSTRY FACTOR. Meyers confirmed King's findings regarding market influence but questioned some of his industry results.[5] Meyers selected a sample similar to King's and added a second sample of 5 stocks from each of 12 industries. The results for both samples were consistent with King's, but the percentage of variance explained by the market factor declined over time. An analysis of the importance of the industry factors for the same six industries and time period used by King gave similar results but after 1952 there was a weakening of the industry affiliation. Analysis of the 12 new industries confirmed the expectation that industry clustering was less dominant for a sample that included less homogeneous and distinct industry groups. Livingston confirmed the overall importance of industry analysis, but likewise suggested that the relative importance varied across industries.[6] Blume also provided evidence of the relative importance of the market factor.[7] Blume derived the beta coefficient for all NYSE stocks that had adequate data for several subperiods from July 1926 through June 1968. The results in Table 9.1 indicate that, even after a decline, aggregate market behavior explains almost 30 percent of the variance for individual securities.

The discussion of empirical studies points toward the following generalizations:

1. The market factor was very important prior to 1940 and has declined so that it currently accounts for about 25 to 30 percent of individual stock price variance.
2. Even after the decline, the market still accounts for a significant part of the variance in individual securities, which implies that market analysis is important.
3. The importance of the market factor in explaining individual price variance varies among securities, ranging from over 50 percent to below 5 percent.

[5] Stephen L. Meyers, "A Re-Examination of Market and Industry Factors in Stock Price Behavior," *Journal of Finance* 28, no. 3 (June 1973): 695–705.

[6] Miles Livingston, "Industry Movements of Common Stocks," *Journal of Finance* 32, no. 2 (June 1977): 861–874.

[7] Marshall E. Blume, "On the Assessment of Risk," *Journal of Finance* 26, no. 1 (March 1971): 1–10.

TABLE 9.1
Summary of Beta Results for Stocks on NYSE

TIME PERIOD	NUMBER OF COMPANIES	MEAN BETA	COEFFICIENT OF DETERMINATION (R^2)
July 1926–June 1933	415	1.051	0.51
July 1933–June 1940	604	1.036	0.49
July 1940–June 1947	731	0.990	0.36
July 1947–June 1954	870	1.010	0.32
July 1954–June 1961	890	0.998	0.25
July 1961–June 1968	847	0.962	0.28

Source: Adapted with permission from Marshall E. Blume, "On the Assessment of Risk," *Journal of Finance* 26, no. 1 (March 1971): 1–10.

4. When using time intervals exceeding three months, there definitely are cycles in stock price movements, which means it is feasible and practical (although difficult) to project market movements (i.e., over longer intervals, the market is not a random walk). Therefore, market analysis is justified and feasible because of the existence of cycles.
5. Industry analysis is also important, but the importance of the industry component varies across industries.

These generalizations confirm the statement made at the beginning—the most important decision is the asset allocation decision specifying (1) what proportion of your portfolio will be invested in various economies and (2) within each economy (country), what will be the division between stock, bonds, or other assets.

AN ALTERNATIVE VIEW. An article by Sharpe questioned the value of attempting to predict market movements and generally argued against the practice.[8] He pointed out that if one assumes efficient markets, one should not expect to be able to derive superior results from engaging in aggregate market predictions and investing in stocks during good market periods and in T-bills during poor market periods. He contended that because T-bills yield less than stocks do, if you miss a few turns of the market you will be at a disadvantage, and this loss, along with transaction costs, will yield a return below that of a buy-and-hold policy.

Sharpe analyzed results from predicting market returns under three assumptions. First, the differential return from a buy-and-hold policy was compared to perfect foresight (timing) regarding annual peaks and troughs. Second, he assumed an annual prediction of a good market year (returns on stocks above the returns on cash equivalent T-bills) or a bad market year (return on cash equivalents above return on stocks) and compared

---

[8] William F. Sharpe, "Likely Gains from Market Timing," *Financial Analysts Journal* 31, no. 2 (March–April 1975): 60–69.

returns to a buy-and-hold policy. It was assumed that, with perfect fore-sight, the investor will invest in T-bills during bad market years and in stocks during good market years. Third, he compared a buy-and-hold pol-icy to returns with less than perfect timing.

Assuming perfect timing of peaks and troughs, the results indicated substantial differences in returns—about 4 percent for buy-and-hold versus 20 percent for perfect timing. Assuming the ability to predict good and bad years, the results likewise indicated superior returns. Assuming 2 percent trading commissions, the timing-ability portfolio had higher re-turns and lower risk (standard deviation of returns). The final analysis examined returns assuming the investor predicted correctly from 50 per-cent of the time (no real insight) to 100 percent of the time (perfect fore-sight). The returns were negative at 50 percent but became positive at 74 percent, which implies that if you predicted the behavior of the market correctly 74 percent of the time, you would derive superior returns. Sharpe concluded that unless a portfolio manager is quite good at predicting mar-ket movements, he should not attempt to engage in market timing.

One might question some of Sharpe's conclusions for several reasons. First the assumption of a 2 percent commission on T-bill shifts is unnec-essary because of the discounting on commissions since May Day (May 1, 1975). Also, because the study stopped in 1972, it missed several very profitable swings for anyone with forecasting ability. Further, he under-estimated the impact of small differences in returns on long-run wealth positions—a 2 percent difference for 25 years on an initial portfolio of $10,000 provides a differential of over $60,000 in the ending wealth po-sition, assuming a rate of 12 percent versus 10 percent.[9] However, his finding that an investor must be correct about seven times out of ten regarding market turns is important, because it implies that *it is possible to be a superior portfolio manager using market analysis, but it is not easy.* Even so, it is worth the effort because these market movements have a significant impact on individual stock returns.

THEORY OF VALUATION

You may recall from accounting, economics, or corporate finance courses that the value of an asset is the present value of the expected returns from the asset during the holding period. Specifically, an investment is expected to provide a stream of returns during the holding period, and it is necessary to discount this stream of expected returns at your required rate of return to determine the value of the asset. Therefore, it is necessary to estimate (1) the stream of expected returns and (2) the required rate of return on the investment.

STREAMS OF RETURNS. An estimate of the future returns expected from an investment encompasses not only the size but the form, time pattern, and uncertainty of returns.

---

[9] To determine the differential ending-wealth value (which will vary depending on the interest rate as-sumed), use the following formula: $10,000 [(1 + i + .02)^{25} - (1 + i)^{25}]$.

FORM OF RETURN. Returns from an investment can take many forms, including earnings, dividends, interest payments, or capital appreciation (i.e., an increase in value) during a period. A major question in valuing common stocks has been whether the appropriate form of returns should be the *earnings* or the *dividends* of the firm. Fortunately, Miller and Modigliani showed that this is an unnecessary controversy, because if one makes proper allowance for the firm's investment decisions, the two approaches are equivalent.[10] It is important to remember with regard to this discussion that the net earnings of the firm belong to the stockholder, and the dividend is simply a decision by the board of directors on how much to pay out to the owners and how much to reinvest for them in the firm. Subsequently, we will present the dividend valuation model for common stocks, because this model is intuitive and very useful if one makes some simplifying assumptions. The point is, returns can come in many forms, and you must consider all of them.

TIME PATTERN OF RETURNS. It is important to estimate when the returns will be received, because money has a time value. You must know the time pattern of returns from an investment so that the stream can be properly valued relative to alternative investments.

REQUIRED RATE OF RETURN. You will recall from Chapter 1 that the required rate of return on an investment is determined by (1) the economy's real risk-free rate of return, plus (2) the expected rate of inflation during the holding period, plus (3) a risk premium. All investments are affected by the risk-free rate and inflation (i.e., the nominal risk-free rate); the differentiating factor is the risk premium for alternative assets. In turn, this risk premium is a function of the uncertainty of returns on the assets.

What affects the uncertainty of returns can be considered in terms of the *internal* characteristics of the asset or in terms of *market-determined* factors. Earlier we subdivided the internal characteristics into business risk (BR), financial risk (FR), liquidity risk (LR), and exchange rate risk (ERR). Alternatively, in Chapter 8 we considered capital market theory, which indicated that the relevant risk measure is the systematic risk of the asset, or its beta.

COMPARISON OF VALUE AND PRICE

To ensure that you are going to get your required return on an investment, you must not only determine the value of the asset at your required rate of return, but also compare this value to the prevailing market price. You should not buy an asset if its market price exceeds your estimated value, for then you will not receive your required rate of return on the investment. In summary:

- If Estimated Value ≥ Market Price, Buy
- If Estimated Value < Market Price, Don't Buy.

[10] Merton H. Miller and Franco Modigliani, "Dividend Policy, Growth, and the Valuation of Shares," *Journal of Business* 34, no. 4 (October 1961): 411–433.

VALUATION OF ALTERNATIVE INVESTMENTS

VALUATION OF BONDS

It is relatively easy to determine the value of bonds because the size and time pattern of the returns from the bond over its life are known. Specifically, <u>a bond promises</u>

1. <u>Interest payments every six months equal to one-half the coupon rate times the face value of the bond.</u>[11]
2. <u>The payment of the principal (also referred to as *face value*) at the maturity of the bond.</u>

As an example, in 1990 a $10,000 bond due in the year 2005 with a 10 percent coupon will pay $500 every six months for the life of the bond (the next 15 years). In addition, there is a promise to pay the $10,000 principal at maturity in 2005. Therefore, assuming the borrower does not default, the investor knows what payments will be made and when they will be made. Recalling the specification that the value of any asset is the present value of the returns from an asset, the value of the bond is the present value of the interest payments (i.e., an annuity of $500 every six months for 15 years) and the present value of the principal payment (i.e., the present value of $10,000 in 15 years). The only unknown for this asset (assuming the borrower does not default) is the rate of return that should be used to discount the expected stream of payments. Assuming that the prevailing nominal risk-free rate is 9 percent, and the investor requires a 1 percent risk premium on this bond (because there is some probability of default), the required rate of return would be 10 percent.

The present value of the interest payments is an annuity for 30 periods (15 years every six months) at one-half the required return (5 percent).[12]

$$\$500 \times 15.3725 = \$7,686 \text{ (present value of interest at 10\%).}$$

The present value of the principal is likewise discounted at 5 percent for 30 periods,[13]

$$\$10,000 \times .2314 = \$2,314.$$

- Present value of interest payments $ 7,686
- Present value of principal payment 2,314
- Value of bond at 10 percent $10,000

This is the amount that an investor should be willing to pay for this bond, assuming that his required rate of return on a bond of this risk class is 10 percent. However, if the market price is above this value, an investor should not buy it, because the promised yield to maturity will be less than the required rate of return.

---

[11] The coupon rate is the annual dollar interest payment, which is expressed as a percentage of the bond's face value. In turn, the face value, also referred to as the *par value* or the *principal*, is the repayment due at the maturity of the bond.

[12] The annuity factors and present value factors are contained in Appendix A, at the end of the book.

[13] If annual compounding were assumed, this would be 0.239 rather than 0.2314. Semiannual compounding is used because it is consistent with the interest payments and is also used in practice.

Alternatively, assuming an investor wants a 12 percent return on this bond, the value would be as follows:

$$\$500 \times 13.7648 = \$6,882$$
$$10,000 \times .1741 = \underline{1,741}$$
$$\$8,623.$$

This example shows that <u>if you want a higher rate of return, you will not pay as much for an asset</u>—that is, a given stream of returns has a lower value to you. As before, you would compare this computed value to the market price of the bond to determine whether you should invest in it.[14]

VALUATION OF PREFERRED STOCK

<u>Preferred stock involves a promise to pay a stated dividend, usually each quarter, for an infinite period;</u> that is, <u>there is no maturity</u>. As was true with a bond, stated payments are to be made on specified dates. However, preferred stock does not entail the same legal obligation to pay as bonds do, and <u>payments are made only after bond interest payments are met, so the uncertainty of payments is greater.</u> This increased uncertainty implies that a higher rate of return should be required on a firm's preferred stock than on its debentures. While this differential should exist in theory, it has not existed in practice for a number of years because of the tax treatment accorded dividends paid to corporations. As noted in Chapter 2, such dividends are 80 percent tax-exempt, making the effective tax on them about 6.8 percent, assuming a corporate tax rate of 34 percent. As a result, there is a great demand for preferred stocks, and the yield on them has generally been below that on AAA (the highest grade) corporate bonds.

Because <u>preferred stock is a perpetuity, the value is simply the stated annual dividend divided by the required rate of return on preferred stock</u> (k_p) as follows:[15]

$$V = \frac{\text{Dividend}}{k_p}.$$

Assume that a preferred stock has a $100 par value and a dividend of $8 a year. At the present time, because of the uncertainty involved and the tax advantage of this preferred stock issue to you as a corporate investor, the required rate of return is 9 percent. Therefore, the value of this preferred stock to you is

$$V = \frac{\$8}{.09}$$
$$= \$88.89.$$

---

[14] You should check that if the required rate of return were 8 percent, the value of this bond would be $11,729.

[15] For a sophisticated valuation model for preferred stock based upon the option-hedging methodology of Black-Scholes, see David Emanuel, "A Theoretical Model for Valuing Preferred Stock," *Journal of Finance* 38, no. 4 (September 1983): 1133–1155.

Also, given the price of preferred stock, it is possible to derive the promised yield on this investment:

$$k_p = \frac{\text{Dividend}}{\text{Price}} = \frac{\$8}{\$88.89} = .09 \, .$$

VALUATION OF COMMON STOCKS

The valuation of common stocks is definitely more difficult than that of bonds or preferred stock, because almost all the required inputs are unknown. In the case of a bond, the periodic interest payments and the final payment at maturity are known. The only unknown is the discount rate, which is the prevailing nominal RFR plus a risk premium. Similarly, for preferred stock the only unknown is the required rate of return on the stock (k_p). In contrast, in the case of common stock, an investor is uncertain about the size of the returns, the time pattern of returns, and even the required rate of return (k_e).

As to what stream of returns should be discounted (earnings or dividends), it has been shown that the two approaches are equivalent if comparable assumptions are made. Some observers prefer to use earnings because they are the source of dividends. Others contend that investors discount that which they receive—dividends. We will use the dividend model because it is intuitively appealing and has been used extensively by others, so you may be familiar with its reduced form. Basically, the dividend model assumes that the value of a share of common stock is the present value of all future dividends as follows:[16]

$$V_j = \frac{D_1}{(1+k)} + \frac{D_2}{(1+k)^2} + \frac{D_3}{(1+k)^3} + \cdots \frac{D_\infty}{(1+k)^\infty}$$
$$= \sum_{t=1}^{\infty} \frac{D_t}{(1+k)^t}$$

where

$$V_j = \textbf{value of common stock } j$$

$$D_t = \textbf{dividend during period } t$$

$$k = \textbf{required rate of return on stock } j.$$

An obvious question is, what happens when the stock is not held for an infinite period? Assume a sale of the stock at the end of Year 2. In such an instance the formulation would be as follows:

if sell stock

$$V_j = \frac{D_1}{(1+k)} + \frac{D_2}{(1+k)^2} + \frac{SP_{j2}}{(1+k)^2},$$

where SP_{j2} equals the sale price of stock j at the end of Year 2.

---

[16] This model was initially set forth in J. B. Williams, *The Theory of Investment Value* (Cambridge, Mass.: Harvard, 1938). It was subsequently reintroduced and expanded by Myron J. Gordon, *The Investment, Financing, and Valuation of the Corporation* (Homewood, Ill.: Richard D. Irwin, 1962).

The value is the two dividend payments during Years 1 and 2 and the sale price (SP) for the stock at the end of Year 2. Regarding the selling price of the stock at the end of Year 2, it is simply *the value of all remaining dividend payments* as follows:

$$SP_{j2} = \frac{D_3}{(1 + k)} + \frac{D_4}{(1 + k)^2} + \cdots \frac{D_\infty}{(1 + k)^\infty}.$$

Given that SP_{j2} is discounted back to the present by $1/(1 + k)^2$, this expression becomes

$$\frac{\dfrac{D_3}{(1 + k)} + \dfrac{D_4}{(1 + k)^2} + \cdots \dfrac{D_\infty}{(1 + k)^\infty}}{(1 + i)^2}$$

$$= \frac{D_3}{(1 + k)^3} + \frac{D_4}{(1 + k)^4} + \cdots \frac{D_\infty}{(1 + k)^\infty},$$

which is simply an extension of the original equation. The point is, whenever the stock is sold, its value (sale price) will be the present value of all future dividends. When this ending value is discounted back to the present, you are back to the basic formulation.

What about stocks that do not pay dividends? Again, the concept is the same, except that some of the near-term dividend payments are zero. Notably, there are expectations that at some point the firm will start paying dividends. If there were not such an expectation, nobody would be willing to buy the security—it would have zero value. With a nondividend-paying stock the firm is not paying anything now but rather is reinvesting capital so that its earnings and dividend stream will grow faster in the future. The formulation is as follows:

$$V_j = \frac{D_1}{(1 + k)} + \frac{D_2}{(1 + k)^2} + \frac{D_3}{(1 + k)^3} + \cdots \frac{D_\infty}{(1 + k)^\infty},$$

where

$$D_1 = 0$$

$$D_2 = 0.$$

The expectation is that when the firm starts paying dividends in D_3, it will be a larger initial amount and they will grow faster. The stock has value because of these future dividends. This model will be best understood if it is applied to several cases involving different holding periods.

ONE-YEAR HOLDING PERIOD. Assume that an investor wants to buy the stock, hold it for one year, and sell it at the end of the year. As noted, to determine the value of the stock (i.e., how much the investor should pay for it), it is necessary to estimate the dividend to be received during the period, the expected price at the end of the holding period, and the required rate of return on this stock.

The estimate of the dividend for the coming year will probably be based upon the current dividend and expectations regarding changes during the year. Assume that the company earned $2.50 a share last year and paid a dividend of $1 a share (a 40 percent payout that has been fairly consistent over time). Further, the firm is expected to earn about $2.75 during the coming year and to raise the dividend to $1.10 per share.

A crucial estimate is the expected price for the stock a year from now. Three alternative estimation procedures can be employed. The first is a direct application of the dividend discount model. An attempt is made to estimate the specific dividend payments for a number of years into the future and derive a value based on these estimates. The second is the earnings multiplier approach wherein you multiply the future expected earnings for the stock by an earnings multiple figure to derive an expected price.[17] In the third, you can estimate the dividend yield for this stock one year from now and apply that figure to the expected dividend to derive the future price.

For now, assume that you prefer the dividend yield approach and expect the stock's dividend yield to be 5 percent. Given the expected dividend of $1.10 per share, this implies a future stock price of $22 (1.10/.05).

Finally, it is necessary to determine the required rate of return. Naturally, it will be influenced by other potential investments entailing less risk, approximately equal risk, and more risk. We will discuss how to estimate this rate for the aggregate market, industries, and companies in subsequent chapters. For the moment, assume that long-term AAA bonds are yielding 10 percent, and you believe that a 4 percent risk premium over the yield of these bonds is appropriate for the stock. Thus, you specify a required rate of return of 14 percent. In summary, you have estimated the dividend at $1.10 (payable at year-end), the ending price at $22, and the required rate of return at 14 percent. Given these inputs, the value of this asset to you is as follows:

$$
\begin{aligned}
V_1 &= \frac{\$1.10}{(1 + .14)} + \frac{\$22.00}{(1 + .14)} \\
&= \frac{1.10}{1.14} + \frac{22.00}{1.14} \\
&= .96 + 19.30 \\
&= \$20.26.
\end{aligned}
$$

Note that there has been no mention of the current price of the stock. This is because the current market price is not relevant to the investor until after he has independently derived a value based on his own estimates of the relevant variables. The decision to acquire the stock depends upon whether his computed value is equal to or above the market price.

MULTIPLE-YEAR HOLDING PERIOD. Suppose you anticipate holding the stock for several years and then selling it. This scenario complicates the val-

---

[17] The earnings multiplier approach will be discussed in detail in a later section of this chapter.

uation procedure, because it is necessary to estimate several future dividend payments and also the value of the stock for a number of years in the future.

The difficulty with estimating future dividend payments is that the future stream can have numerous forms. The exact estimate depends on your outlook for earnings growth (because earnings are the source of dividends), and the firm's dividend policy (i.e., does it make a constant payout each year, which implies a change in dividend each year, or does it follow a *step pattern*, in which it increases the dividend rate by a constant dollar amount each year or every two or three years). The easiest case to analyze is one in which the firm enjoys a constant rate of growth in earnings and also maintains a constant dividend payout. Here the dividend stream will have a constant growth rate equal to the earnings growth rate.

Assume the expected holding period is three years, and you estimate the following dividend payments at the end of each year:

- Year 1 $1.10/share
- Year 2 $1.20/share
- Year 3 $1.35/share.

The next estimate to be made is the expected ending price for the stock three years in the future. Again, if we use the dividend yield approach, it is necessary to project the dividend yield on this stock three years from now. Assume that you think rates will be lower than your previous estimate for one year; you estimate a dividend yield of 4 percent. Given the $1.35 dividend payment, this implies an ending price of $33.75 ($1.35/.04).

The final estimate is the required rate of return on this stock during this period. Assuming that the 14 percent desired rate is still appropriate for this period, the value of this stock is as follows:

$$
\begin{aligned}
V_1 &= \frac{1.10}{(1 + .14)} + \frac{1.20}{(1 + .14)^2} + \frac{1.35}{(1 + .14)^3} + \frac{33.75}{(1 + .14)^3} \\
&= \frac{1.10}{(1.14)} + \frac{1.20}{(1.30)} + \frac{1.35}{(1.4815)} + \frac{33.75}{(1.4815)} \\
&= .96 + .92 + .91 + 22.78 \\
&= \$25.57.
\end{aligned}
$$

Again, you would compare this derived value for the stock to its market price to determine whether you should buy the stock or not.

At this point you should recognize that the procedure of valuation being discussed is very similar to that followed in corporate finance when making investment decisions, except that the cash flows are from dividends. Rather than estimating the scrap value or salvage value of a corporate asset, we are estimating the ending sales price for the stock. Finally, rather than cost of capital, we employ the required rate of return for the individual investor. In both cases we are looking for excess present value, meaning the present value of expected cash inflows (i.e., the value of the asset) exceeds the present value of cash outflows (i.e., the cost of the asset which is its market price).

INFINITE PERIOD MODEL. It is obviously possible to extend the discussion of the multi-period model by considering longer holding periods (e.g., 5, 10, or 15 years). It is believed that the benefits to be derived from the extensions would be minimal and the boredom factor would quickly dominate. Therefore, at this point we will consider the well-known infinite period model, which assumes that investors estimate future dividend payments from the present to perpetuity. Needless to say, this is a formidable task! To allow mortal investors to carry out this valuation, it is necessary to make some simplifying assumptions about this future stream of dividends, the easiest being that the future dividend stream grows at a constant rate for the infinite period. This is a rather heroic assumption in many instances, but where it is appropriate it allows us to derive a model that is very useful in valuing the aggregate market, alternative industries, and even some individual stocks.[18] This model is specified as follows:

$$V_j = \frac{D_0(1 + g)}{(1 + k)} + \frac{D_0(1 + g)^2}{(1 + k)^2} + \ldots \frac{D_0(1 + g)^n}{(1 + k)^n},$$

where

V_j = the value of stock j

D_0 = the dividend payment in the current period

g = the constant growth rate of dividends

k = the required rate of return on stock j

n = the number of periods, which is assumed to be infinite.

In the appendix to this chapter it is shown that, given certain assumptions, this formulation can be simplified to the following expression:

$$V_j = \frac{D_1}{k - g}.$$

You will probably recognize this formula as one that is widely used in corporate finance to derive the cost of equity capital for the firm. In many cases, rather than V_j, the expression is written

$$P_j = \frac{D_1}{k - g}.$$

Given this model, the major estimates to be made are (1) the required rate of return (k), and (2) the expected growth rate of dividends (g). After estimating g, it is a simple matter to estimate D_1, because it is the current dividend (D_0) times $(1 + g)$. Consider the example of a stock with a current dividend of $1 a share, which you expect to rise to $1.09 next year. Upon reflection, you believe

---

[18] While this assumption might be heroic for some individual firms, it is not unreasonable when considering the aggregate economy or a number of industries. Even for some firms, the long-run record can be matched by a logarithmic regression line.

that, over the long run, this company's earnings and dividends will continue to grow at 9 percent; your estimate of g is 0.09.

Regarding the required rate of return, for the near term you believe 14 percent was appropriate due to a high current rate of inflation. For the long run, you expect the rate of inflation to decline and believe that your long-run required rate of return on this stock should be 13 percent; your estimate of k is 0.13. Therefore, the relevant variables are

$$g = .09$$
$$k = .13$$
$$D_i = 1.09(\$1.00 \times 1.09)$$
$$P = \frac{1.09}{.13 - .09}$$
$$= \frac{1.09}{.04}$$
$$= \$27.25.$$

A small change in any of the original estimates will have a large impact, as can be shown by the following examples:

1. $g = .09$; $k = .14$; $D_1 = \$1.09$. (We assume an increase in k.)

$$P = \frac{\$1.09}{.14 - .09}$$
$$= \frac{\$1.09}{.05}$$
$$= \$21.80.$$

2. $g = .10$; $k = .13$; $D_1 = \$1.10$. (We assume an increase in g.)

$$P = \frac{\$1.10}{.13 - .10}$$
$$= \frac{\$1.10}{.03}$$
$$= \$36.67.$$

Obviously, a 1 percent change in either g or k has a major impact on the computed price of the stock. The crucial relationship is the *spread between the required rate of return and the expected growth rate.* Anything that causes a decline in the spread will cause an increase in prices, and vice versa.

INFINITE GROWTH MODEL AND GROWTH COMPANIES. You must recall the following restrictive assumptions of the dividend growth model if this model is used to determine the value for growth companies:

1. A constant rate of growth.
2. The constant growth rate will continue for an infinite period.
3. The required rate of return (k) is greater than the infinite growth rate (g). If it is not, the model gives meaningless results—that is, the denominator becomes a negative value.

Growth companies (such as IBM, Xerox, McDonald's, and Apple Computer) are firms that have the opportunities and the abilities to earn rates of return on investments that are consistently above the firm's required rate of return.[19] As a result of these outstanding investment opportunities, these firms generally retain a high percent of earnings for reinvestment, and their earnings grow faster than the typical firm. An important point is that the earnings growth pattern for these firms is inconsistent with the assumption of the infinite growth model. During the period of abnormal growth, the current rate of growth will probably exceed the required rate of return. Note that there is no automatic relationship between growth and risk—a high-growth company is not necessarily a high-risk company. A high-growth firm growing at a fairly constant rate would be lower risk (less uncertainty) than a low-growth firm with unstable earnings (more uncertainty).

In summary, some firms experience finite periods of abnormally high growth rates, and it is not possible to use the infinite growth model for valuing these firms; these temporary conditions are inconsistent with the assumptions of that model. The latter section of Chapter 15 is devoted to models used to derive the value of true growth companies.

PRAGMATIC MULTIPLIER APPROACH

Rather than concentrate on dividends alone, many investors prefer to derive value based upon an earnings multiplier approach. The basic rationale for this approach is that assets are the capitalized value of future earnings, which implies that investors can derive value by determining how many dollars they are willing to pay for a dollar of expected earnings (typically earnings during the next 12-month period). As an example, if investors are supposedly willing to pay 10 times expected earnings, a stock that is expected to earn $2 a share will sell for $20. This multiplier, also referred to as the *price/earnings (P/E) ratio*, is derived as follows:

$$\text{Earnings Multiplier} = \text{Price/Earnings Ratio} = \frac{\text{Current Price}}{\text{Next 12-Month Earnings}}.$$

The important question to consider is which factors influence the earnings multiplier (P/E ratio) over time? In the market valuation chapter (Chapter 13), it is shown that the P/E ratio for the stock market has varied from about 6 times earnings to over 20 times earnings.[20] The dividend growth model can be used to indicate the relevant variables as follows:

$$P_i = \frac{D_1}{k - g}.$$

[19] Outstanding discussions of growth companies are contained in Ezra Salomon, *The Theory of Financial Management* (New York: Columbia University Press, 1963). Merton Miller and Franco Modigliani, "Dividend Policy, Growth, and the Valuation of Shares," *Journal of Business* 34, no. 4 (October 1961): 411–433. These growth models are discussed in Chapter 15.

[20] When computing historical P/E ratios, the practice is to use earnings for the *last* 12 months rather than expected earnings. Although this will influence the level, it should not affect the changes over time.

If we divide both sides of the equation by E_1 (expected earnings during the next 12 months), the result is

$$\frac{P_i}{E_1} = \frac{D_1/E_1}{k - g}.$$

Thus, the P/E ratio is determined by

1. The expected dividend payout ratio (dividends divided by earnings)
2. The required rate of return on the stock
3. The expected growth rate of dividends for the stock.

As an example, if we assume a stock has an expected dividend payout of 50 percent (i.e., the firm generally pays out 50 percent of its earnings in dividends), a required rate of return of 13 percent, and an expected growth rate for dividends of 9 percent, we would have the following:

$$D/E = .50; \ k = .13; \ g = .09$$
$$P/E = \frac{.50}{.13 - .09}$$
$$= \frac{.50}{.04}$$
$$= 12.5.$$

Again, a small change in either k or g will have a large impact on the multiplier as follows:

1. $D/E = .50; \ k = .14; \ g = .09.$ (We assume an increase in i.)

$$P/E = \frac{.50}{.14 - .09}$$
$$= \frac{.50}{.05}$$
$$= 10.$$

2. $D/E = .50; \ k = .13; \ g = .10$ (We assume an increase in g.)

$$P/E = \frac{.50}{.13 - .10}$$
$$= \frac{.50}{.03}$$
$$= 16.7.$$

As before, the crucial factor is the spread between k and g. While the dividend payout ratio has an impact, this is typically rather stable and so would have little effect on year-to-year changes in security values.

VALUATION WITH TEMPORARY SUPER-NORMAL GROWTH

Thus far, we have considered different growth rates for short periods of time (one to three years), and a model that assumes a constant growth rate for an infinite period. Notably, in the constant growth rate model, it is assumed that the growth rate is not greater than the required rate of return (see Appendix 9A). The fact is, while it is not possible to have a company with a permanent growth rate higher than the required rate of return, it is possible for certain firms to have temporary super-normal growth. A firm probably will not continue to grow at a super-normal rate for a very long period, because competition will begin entering this apparently lucrative business, which will reduce the profit margins and therefore the ROE and growth rate. Therefore, after a few years of exceptional growth, we would expect a firm's growth rate to decline and eventually to reach a level of stability consistent with the assumptions of the infinite growth model.

How do you determine the value of such a company? The answer is to employ a combination of the models already discussed. For the initial years of exceptional growth, you examine each year individually, even if there are two stages of super-normal growth. Subsequently, when the firm's growth rate stabilizes at a rate below the required rate of return, you can compute the value of the remaining constant growth and discount this lump-sum value back to the present. The principal should become clear with the following example.

The Bourke Company has a current dividend (D_0) of $2.00 a share. The following are the expected annual growth rates for dividends.

YEAR	
1–3:	25%
4–6:	20%
7–9:	15%
10 on:	9%

The required rate of return for the stock is 14 percent. Therefore, the general formula is

$$P_i = \frac{2.00\ (1.25)}{1.14} + \frac{2.00\ (1.25)^2}{(1.14)^2} + \frac{2.00\ (1.25)^3}{(1.14)^3} + \frac{2.00\ (1.25)^3(1.20)}{(1.14)^4}$$

$$+ \frac{2.00\ (1.25)^3\ (1.20)^2}{(1.14)^5} + \frac{2.00\ (1.25)^3\ (1.20)^3}{(1.14)^6}$$

$$+ \frac{2.00\ (1.25)^3(1.20)^3(1.15)}{(1.14)^7} + \frac{2.00(1.25)^3(1.20)^3(1.15)^2}{(1.14)^8}$$

$$+ \frac{2.00(1.25)^3(1.20)^3(1.15)^3}{(1.14)^9} + \frac{\dfrac{2.00\ (1.25)^3(1.20)^3(1.15)^3(1.09)}{(.14 - .09)}}{(.14 - .09)^{10}}$$

The specific computations are contained in Table 9.2. As shown, the total value of the stock is $94.36. Needless to say, the difficult part of the evaluation is the estimation of the super-normal growth rates and determining how long they will last.

TABLE 9.2

Computation of Value of Stock of Company with Temporary Super-Normal Growth

YEAR	DIVIDEND	DISCOUNT FACTOR (14%)	PRESENT VALUE
1	2.50	.8772	$2.193
2	3.12	.7695	2.401
3	3.91	.6750	2.639
4	4.69	.5921	2.777
5	5.63	.5194	2.924
6	6.76	.4556	3.080
7	7.77	.3996	3.105
8	8.94	.3506	3.134
9	10.28	.3075	3.161
10	11.21		
	224.20[a]	.3075[b]	68.941
		Total Value =	$94.355

[a]Value of dividend stream for Year 10 and all future dividends.

[b]The discount factor is for nine years, because the valuation of the remaining stream is made at the end of Year 9 to reflect the dividend in Year 10 and all future dividends.

Thus far, we have assumed we know the estimates (future stream of flows and required rate of return) that are required in the valuation process. Given these estimates, we have discussed how one determines the value of bonds, preferred stock, and common stock under several investment horizons. In the final section we deal with the determinants of the required rate of return and the expected growth rate. In subsequent chapters we consider how you estimate these determinants of value for the aggregate securities market, alternative industries, and individual firms.

DETERMINANTS OF REQUIRED RATE OF RETURN AND EXPECTED GROWTH RATE OF DIVIDENDS

This discussion is a brief review of the presentation in Chapters 1 and 9 dealing with the determinants of the required rate of return on an investment with consideration of factors for non–U.S. markets. There are basically three major factors:

1. The economy's *real* risk-free rate (RFR)
2. The expected rate of inflation (I)
3. A risk premium (RP).

THE REQUIRED RATE OF RETURN (k)

THE RISK-FREE RATE. This rate reflects the basic time value of money assuming no probability of default. It is a function of the underlying investment opportunities in the economy, which are determined by *the real growth rate of the economy*. In turn, the real growth rate for the economy is a function of (a) the growth of the labor force; (b) the growth in number of hours worked per week; and (c) the growth in labor productivity.

THE EXPECTED RATE OF INFLATION. This rate is important, because investors are interested in *real* rates of return that will allow them to increase their rate of consumption. Therefore, if investors expect a given rate of inflation, they will increase their *nominal* required rate of return to reflect this expectation as follows:

$$\text{Nominal RFR} = [1 + \text{Real RFR}][1 + E(I)] - 1.$$

Note that the two factors that determine the nominal RFR should affect all investments, from U.S. government securities to highly speculative land deals. This is why the estimation of the expected rate of inflation is such a crucial part of the valuation process.

THE RISK PREMIUM. The risk premium causes a difference in required rates of return for alternative investments (for government bonds, corporate bonds, and common stocks). It also explains the difference in the expected return for various grades of corporate bonds (Aaa versus Aa versus A)[21] and different common stocks. In Chapter 1 we discussed the notion that investors demand a risk premium because of the uncertainty of returns expected from an investment. Further, we pointed out that this uncertainty of returns was indicated by the *dispersion of expected returns.* Considering the factors that influence the variability of returns, it is possible to evaluate the risk of an asset on the basis of (1) internal factors (business risk, financial risk, liquidity risk, and exchange rate risk) or (2) market-determined risk measures (beta).

VARIABILITY OF THE RISK PREMIUM. Beyond the fact that the risk premiums for alternative investments differ, you should recognize that they also change over time. The following example related to bonds should make this clear. Figure 9.1 contains a time series plot of the spread between the yields to maturity for Aaa-rated corporate bonds and Baa-rated corporate bonds. This difference in yield is considered to be a risk premium for investing in higher-risk bonds (Baa) compared to very low-risk bonds. As shown, the differential varied from .61 percent to 2.69 percent (from less than 1 percent to almost 3 percent). Figure 9.2 contains a time series plot of the ratio of the yields, indicating the percent premium from the Aaa yield, and considers the level of yield. The point is, since we are measuring the difference in yield in absolute basis points (100 basis points is one percent), one might expect a larger difference in yield when Aaa bonds are yielding 12 percent rather than 6 percent. Using the ratio that adjusts for this size difference indicates that this ratio varies across time from about 1.07 to 1.23. This change in risk premium indicates that over time investors either perceive a change in the level of risk present in Baa bonds or a change in how much they want to be compensated to accept risk. In either case, the slope of the capital market line would change.

---

[21] As will be discussed in Chapter 10, corporate bonds are rated by investment services based upon their risk of default. In this regard, Aaa would be very low risk, and A would be higher risk.

FIGURE 9.1

Time Series Plot of Moody's Corporate Bond Yield Spreads (Baa–Aaa): Monthly 1972–1987

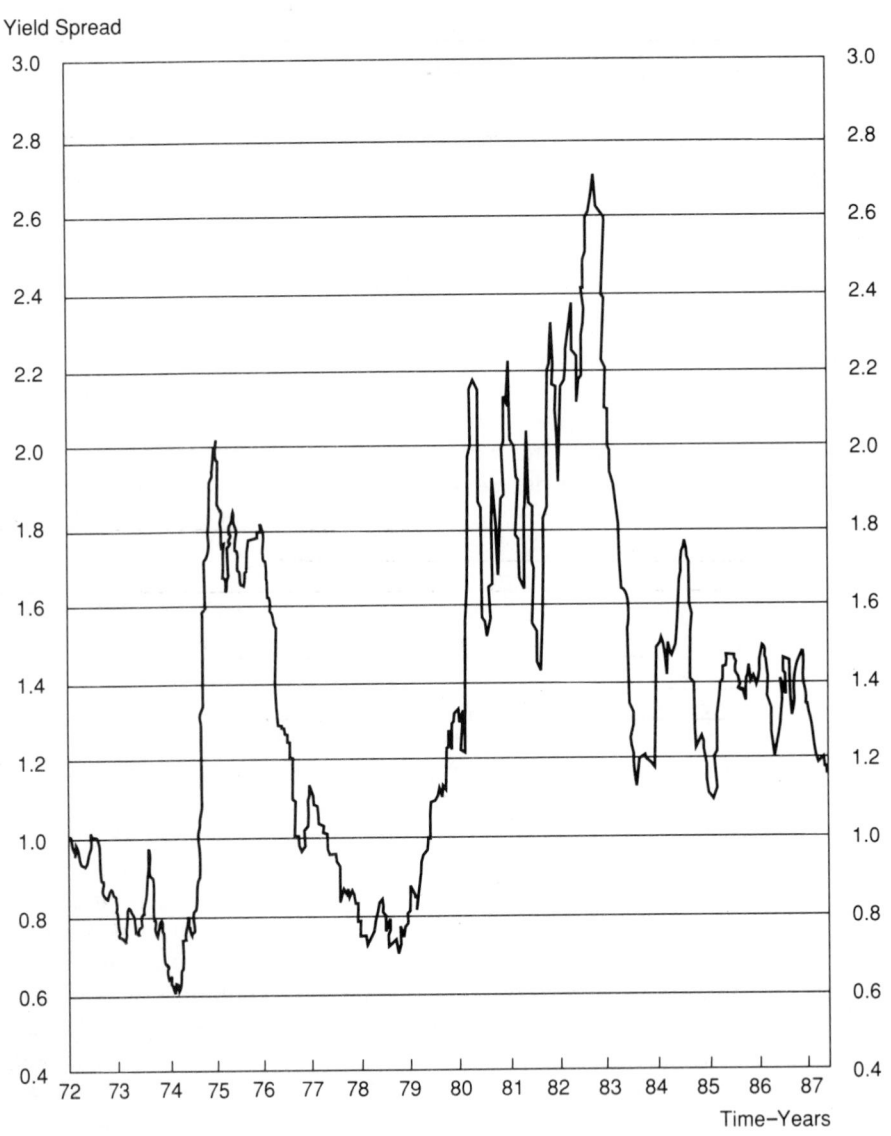

ESTIMATING THE	The discussion thus far of the required rate of return for investments has
REQUIRED	been limited to the U.S. securities market. While the basic framework and
RETURN FOR	variables are the same around the world, you should recognize that there
GLOBAL MARKETS	will be significant differences in the specific estimates at a given point in
	time and also over time.

FIGURE 9.2
Time Series Plot of the Ratio of Moody's Corporate Bond Yields (Baa–Aaa): Monthly 1972–1987

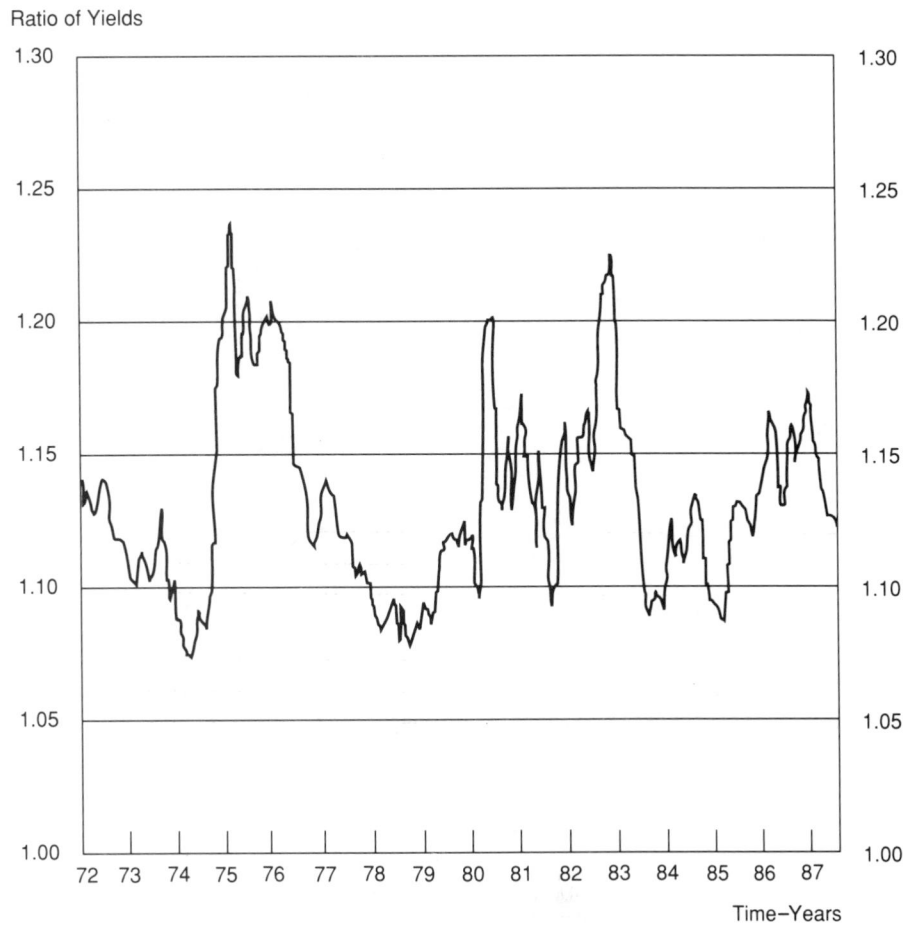

NON–U.S. REAL RFR. Although the real RFR in other countries should likewise be close to the real growth rate of the economy, it can vary substantially among countries because of the three variables that affect it: (1) growth rate of the labor force, (2) growth rate of the average number of hours worked, and (3) growth rate of labor productivity. An example of differences in the real growth of GNP can be seen in Table 9.3, which indicates a range for 1988 of over 2 percent (i.e., 1.6 percent for the United States and France and 3.8 percent for Japan). This difference in real growth rates implies a substantial difference in the real RFR for these countries. Because these rates will differ, it is necessary to examine the historical values for the three variables that affect growth for each of the countries being evaluated and derive unique *estimates* for each country.

TABLE 9.3
Real GNP/GDP

PERIOD	U.S.	CANADA	JAPAN	GERMANY	FRANCE	U.K.	MAJOR EUROPE[1]	MAJOR OECD[2]
1985	**3.0**	**4.0**	**4.8**	**2.0**	**1.6**	**3.7**	**2.5**	**3.2**
1986	**2.9**	**3.4**	**2.5**	**2.5**	**2.1**	**3.0**	**2.6**	**2.6**
1987	**2.9**	**3.9**	**4.1**	**1.7**	**2.1**	**4.8**	**2.7**	**3.1**
1988	**1.6**	**2.0**	**3.8**	**1.7**	**1.6**	**3.7**	**2.2**	**2.2**
1986 Q4	**2.2** / *1.5*	**1.8** / *0.0*	**2.0** / *2.8*	**2.4** / *−1.1*	**2.0** / *1.1*	**4.0** / *3.9*	**2.8**	**2.4** / *1.5*
1987 Q1	**2.0** / *4.4*	**2.6** / *6.2*	**4.1** / *6.1*	**2.4** / *−3.0*	**2.0** / *0.5*	**4.6** / *3.5*	**2.8** / *0.1*	**2.6** / *3.3*
Q2	**2.4** / *2.5*	**3.1** / *6.1*	**3.1** / *0.0*	**0.8** / *4.1*	**1.8** / *3.9*	**4.3** / *4.9*	**2.2** / *4.7*	**2.5** / *2.8*
Q3	**3.2** / *4.3*	**4.1** / *4.3*	**4.3** / *8.4*	**1.4** / *5.7*	**2.4** / *4.0*	**5.2** / *8.7*	**2.7** / *5.2*	**3.2** / *5.4*
Q4	**4.1** / *5.0*	**4.4** / *6.0*	**4.8** / *4.9*	**2.4** / *2.8*	**2.5** / *1.5*	**5.3** / *4.0*	**3.2** / *2.8*	**3.9** / *4.3*
1988 Q1	**3.0** / *0.1*	**3.7** / *2.0*	**4.1** / *3.1*	**3.5** / *1.5*	**2.5** / *0.9*	**5.1** / *3.0*	**3.5** / *1.4*	**3.4** / *4.1*
Q2	**2.2** / *−0.5*	**2.0** / *0.0*	**4.9** / *3.1*	**2.5** / *−0.1*	**1.7** / *0.5*	**5.1** / *4.6*	**2.7** / *1.3*	**2.9** / *0.9*
Q3	**0.9** / *−1.1*	**1.2** / *1.5*	**3.5** / *2.9*	**0.6** / *−1.7*	**1.1** / *1.5*	**2.8** / *−0.3*	**1.5** / *0.3*	**1.6** / *0.1*
Q4	**0.3** / *2.5*	**1.2** / *2.7*	**2.8** / *2.0*	**0.1** / *0.8*	**1.2** / *1.9*	**2.0** / *1.0*	**1.1** / *1.3*	**1.2** / *2.7*

Note: Percent changes on a year earlier; figures in italics are quarter-on-previous-quarter annualized.

[1] Germany, France, Italy, United Kingdom.

[2] Major Europe plus United States, Canada, and Japan.

Source: "World Investment Strategy Highlights" (London: Goldman, Sachs International Corp., April 1988). Reprinted with permission from Goldman, Sachs & Co.

INFLATION RATE. To estimate the nominal RFR, you must first estimate the expected rate of inflation, which can likewise vary substantially among countries. As shown in Table 9.4, the actual rate of inflation during 1987 varied from 0.1 percent in Japan to 4.4 percent in Canada. The outlook for 1988 indicates a range from 1 percent in Japan to 4.4 percent in Canada. Obviously, this implies a difference in the required rate of return between these two countries of over 3 percent, which can have a substantial impact on derived values, as was shown earlier. The point is, these estimates must be made for each individual country being considered.

RISK PREMIUM. It is likewise necessary to derive a risk premium for each country. Again, there can be substantial differences between the four risk components we discussed: business risk, financial risk, liquidity risk, and exchange rate risk. Business risk can vary because it is a function of general economic variability and also the operating leverage employed within countries. The difference in financial risk among countries is well-known—for example, Japanese firms have substantially more financial leverage than U.S. or U.K. firms. Regarding liquidity risk, it is generally conceded that the U.S. capital markets are the most liquid in the world, with Japan and London being fairly similar compared with some small, inactive markets being quite illiquid. As mentioned previously, when considering global investments, you must also consider exchange rate risk that can vary over time and differ substantially among countries. The change over time is a function of world economics and political conditions. Differences among countries exist because of specific trade relations between individual countries. A prime example of this type of risk was the massive trade imbalances between the United States and Japan during the period 1985–1988 that caused significant changes in the exchange rates between the U.S. dollar and Japanese yen. A result of these massive changes (when the U.S. dollar weakened substantially relative to the yen) was that Japanese investors who invested in U.S. stocks and bonds during the period 1986–1987 suffered significant exchange rate losses that offset or wiped out the domestic returns experienced by U.S. investors. It is necessary to evaluate these differences in risk factors and assign a unique risk premium for each country. Alternatively, you could derive a systematic risk measure for each country using a world index as the proxy for the market portfolio.

EXPECTED GROWTH RATE OF DIVIDENDS (g)

The other major factor in the valuation of common stocks is the estimation of the growth rate of dividends. This is influenced by the basic growth rate of earnings and the proportion of earnings paid out in dividends (i.e., the payout ratio). For short-run periods, it is possible that dividends can grow faster or slower than earnings if the economic unit changes its payout ratio. Specifically, if a firm's earnings are growing at 6 percent a year and the firm always pays out exactly 50 percent of earnings in dividends, then the firm's dividends will likewise grow at 6 percent a year. Or if the firm's earnings are growing at 6 percent a year and the firm increases its payout during the period when the payout ratio is increasing, dividends will in-

TABLE 9.4
Consumer or Retail Prices

Period	U.S.		Canada		Japan		Germany		France		U.K.		Major Europe[1]		Major OECD[2]	
1985	**3.6**		**4.0**		**2.0**		**2.2**		**5.8**		**6.1**		**5.2**		**3.8**	
1986	**1.9**		**4.1**		**0.6**		**-0.2**		**2.5**		**3.4**		**2.6**		**1.9**	
1987	**3.7**		**4.4**		**0.1**		**0.3**		**3.3**		**4.1**		**2.8**		**2.7**	
1988	**4.0**		**4.4**		**1.0**		**1.0**		**2.2**		**3.7**		**2.7**		**3.0**	
1986 Q4	**1.3**	*2.6*	**4.5**	*3.9*	**-0.2**	*0.0*	**-1.0**	*-1.0*	**2.1**	*2.7*	**3.4**	*5.0*	**1.9**	*2.4*	**1.2**	*2.0*
1987 Q1	**2.2**	*5.3*	**4.0**	*3.8*	**-0.9**	*-2.4*	**-0.5**	*1.0*	**3.2**	*5.0*	**3.9**	*4.9*	**2.4**	*3.8*	**1.7**	*3.4*
Q2	**3.8**	*4.9*	**4.6**	*5.5*	**0.2**	*5.3*	**0.2**	*1.3*	**3.4**	*3.4*	**4.2**	*6.5*	**2.7**	*3.6*	**2.8**	*4.5*
Q3	**4.2**	*4.0*	**4.6**	*4.7*	**0.5**	*-0.8*	**0.7**	*1.3*	**3.4**	*2.4*	**4.3**	*0.8*	**2.9**	*2.0*	**3.1**	*2.5*
Q4	**4.4**	*3.6*	**4.4**	*3.6*	**0.7**	*0.8*	**1.0**	*0.3*	**3.2**	*1.9*	**4.1**	*4.4*	**3.1**	*2.9*	**3.3**	*2.9*
1988 Q1	**4.0**	*3.6*	**4.6**	*4.0*	**0.9**	*-1.6*	**0.8**	*0.3*	**2.5**	*2.4*	**3.2**	*1.2*	**2.5**	*1.4*	**2.9**	*1.9*
Q2	**3.9**	*4.4*	**4.4**	*5.0*	**0.8**	*4.9*	**0.9**	*1.7*	**2.1**	*1.7*	**3.6**	*8.4*	**2.6**	*4.0*	**2.9**	*4.4*
Q3	**4.0**	*4.4*	**4.5**	*4.6*	**0.9**	*-0.4*	**1.1**	*2.0*	**2.1**	*2.4*	**3.9**	*1.9*	**2.8**	*2.9*	**3.0**	*3.0*
Q4	**4.1**	*4.0*	**4.6**	*4.8*	**1.3**	*2.4*	**1.1**	*0.3*	**2.1**	*2.1*	**4.1**	*5.0*	**2.8**	*2.9*	**3.2**	*3.4*

Note: Percent changes on a year earlier; figures in italics are quarter-on-previous-quarter annualized.

[1]Germany, France, Italy, United Kingdom.

[2]Major Europe plus United States, Canada, and Japan.

Source: "World Investment Strategy Highlights" (London: Goldman, Sachs International Corp., April 1988). Reprinted with permission from Goldman, Sachs & Co.

crease by more than the earnings. In contrast, if the firm reduces its payout ratio, dividends will grow at a lower rate than earnings for a period of time. Because there is a limit to how long this difference in growth rates can continue, the typical long-run assumption is that the dividend payout ratio is fairly stable. Also, we will see that this payout ratio has an inverse relationship to the earnings growth rate. Thus, the analysis of what determines the growth rate of dividends is really an analysis of what determines the growth rate of equity earnings.

The internal growth rate of an economic unit, whether it is an industry or a company, is a function of what resources are retained for reinvestment in the unit and what is the rate of return derived from these internal investments. When a firm retains earnings and acquires additional assets, if it earns some positive rate of return on these additional assets, the total earnings of the firm will increase, because the firm has a larger asset base. How much earnings will increase depends upon (1) how much is retained and reinvested in new assets and (2) the rate of return that is earned on these new assets. More specifically, it can be shown that the growth rate of equity earnings (i.e., earnings per share) without any external financing is equal to the proportion of net earnings retained (1 − Payout Ratio) times the rate of return on equity capital.

$$g = \text{(Retention Rate)} \times \text{(Return on Equity)}$$
$$= RR \times ROE.$$

Therefore, a firm can increase its growth rate by increasing its proportion of earnings retained (reduce its payout ratio) and invest these added funds at the same rate of return as before. Alternatively, the firm can continue the same retention rate but increase its rate of return on these investments. As an example, if a firm retains 50 percent of net earnings, and consistently derives a 10 percent rate of return on investments, the net earnings for the firm will grow at the rate of 5 percent a year as follows:

$$g = RR \times ROE$$
$$= .50 \times .10$$
$$= .05.$$

If, however, the firm increases its retention rate to 75 percent (i.e., invests more money) and continues to earn 10 percent on these investments, its growth rate will increase to 7.5 percent as follows:

$$g = .75 \times .10$$
$$= .075.$$

If, instead, the firm continues to reinvest 50 percent of its earnings but derives a higher rate of return on these investments (e.g., 15 percent), it can likewise increase its growth rate as follows:

$$g = .50 \times .15$$
$$= .075.$$

BREAKDOWN OF ROE. While the retention rate is basically a management decision, <u>changes in the firm's ROE require basic changes in its operating performance.</u> To see what is required, you can break the ROE ratio into the following components:

$$ROE = \frac{Net\ Income}{Equity}$$
$$= \frac{Net\ Income}{Sales} \times \frac{Sales}{Equity}$$
$$= Profit\ Margin \times Equity\ Turnover.$$

This breakdown (which is really an identity) <u>indicates that the ROE on equity depends upon how efficiently the firm operates in terms of generating sales from equity capital (equity turnover) and how profitable these sales are (the firm's profit margin).</u> A firm can improve its ROE by increasing either of these components.

It is also possible to increase the equity turnover by changing the firm's financial structure. Thus, <u>if the firm increases its asset base by borrowing (i.e., issuing debt securities), sales will increase because the asset base is larger; but because equity was not used to finance the acquisition, the equity turnover will increase.</u> This change in financial structure can be examined using the following breakdown of ROE:

$$ROE = \frac{Net\ Income}{Sales} \times \frac{Sales}{Total\ Assets} \times \frac{Total\ Assets}{Equity}$$
$$= Profit\ Margin \times Total\ Asset\ Turnover \times Leverage.$$

The ratio of total assets to equity is a measure of leverage. The higher this ratio, the more total assets are financed with nonequity capital (i.e., debt). As an example, if this ratio is 2, it means that 50 percent of the firm's assets are financed with equity and 50 percent with debt. If the ratio is 3, it means that only 33 percent is financed with equity and two-thirds is debt. This ratio signals a change in the firm's capital structure and therefore its financial risk.

This breakdown of equity turnover makes it possible to determine the cause of a change in equity turnover—is it operating efficiency (e.g., has it increased its total asset turnover) or a change in financial structure (leverage) that caused the change in equity turnover. While it is not wrong to increase ROE by increasing financial leverage, you should recognize that such an increase does not result from higher profitability or operating efficiency, but was caused by a change in the firm's capital structure (i.e., financial risk), which is a specific management decision.

ESTIMATING GLOBAL GROWTH

As the following discussion will indicate, the procedure for estimating growth is the same, but the value of the growth components may differ substantially from what is common in the United States. You should also remember that the differences in the components of ROE can be a function of differences in accounting practices as well as alternative management performance or philosophy.

RETENTION RATES. The retention rate will differ by company within countries, but there are also differences in the average for all firms in different countries depending upon the country's investment opportunities. As an example, the average retention rate for firms in Japan is much higher than in the United States, while the rate of retention in France is much lower.

NET PROFIT MARGIN. The net profit margin can differ, mainly due to alternative accounting conventions related to revenue recognition and numerous expense allocations. As an example, because German firms are allowed to build up large reserves for various reasons, they report (for tax purposes) very low earnings. Also, it is necessary to examine differences in depreciation practices.

TOTAL ASSET TURNOVER. The total asset turnover can likewise differ, due to accounting conventions regarding the reported value of assets (cost or market). In Japan it is recognized that a large part of the value for some firms is their real estate holdings and/or the value of the investments in other firms. These assets are currently reported at cost, which substantially understates their value, but also means that the total asset turnover ratio is overstated.

TOTAL ASSETS TO EQUITY. This financial leverage ratio will differ because of differences in the economic environment, management philosophy regarding debt, and accounting convention. In several countries, the attitude toward debt is much more liberal than in the United States. A prime example is Japan, where the debt-total asset ratio is almost 50 percent higher than in the United States. Notably, most of this is bank debt at a fairly low rate of interest. This means that the balance sheet debt ratios could be higher in Japan than in the United States or other countries, but the fixed-charge flow ratios for Japanese firms (e.g., times interest earned) may be similar to what prevails in other countries.

Consequently, when analyzing a non–U.S. market or individual stock, you will want to estimate the growth rate for earnings and dividends considering the three components of the ROE. Based upon this brief discussion and the subsequent discussion in Chapter 12 on the analysis of financial statements, you must recognize that the values for the financial ratios can differ from what you might typically see for the aggregate U.S. market or individual U.S. firms.

SUMMARY

Market and industry analysis should be considered prior to company and stock analysis in the valuation process. Besides having intuitive appeal (the economy affects all industries and industry performance influences all firms in the industry), there is substantial empirical support for this three-step process. When markets are efficient, it is not easy to be a superior market analyst, but the potential rewards from correct estimates make the attempt worthwhile.

We discussed the specific valuation of bonds, preferred stock, and common stock under alternative holding periods.

With the constant growth model of valuation, the crucial factor determining the value of common stock and changes in common stock value is the spread between the required rate of return and the expected rate of growth. The infinite growth model cannot be used in the valuation of significant growth companies because these firms do not conform to the basic assumptions of the model.

The two major elements of value are the required rate of return and the expected rate of growth. In the following chapters we will apply these concepts to the valuation of bonds, aggregate stock markets, alternative industries, and, finally, individual firms within industries around the world.

QUESTIONS

1. Discuss why it is contended that market analysis and industry analysis should come before individual security analysis.

2. Discuss briefly the empirical evidence given by King that supports the preceding contention.

3. Would you expect all industries to have a similar relationship to the economy? Why or why not? Give an example.

4. Would you expect all individual stocks to have a similar relation to the aggregate stock market? What factors would contribute to any differences?

5. What "batting average" is required to be superior in terms of predicting market turns? Is it worthwhile to spend time attempting to predict aggregate market turns? Why or why not?

6. Given an efficient stock market, what is necessary in order to make superior market predictions? Of what value is past information regarding market performance? Discuss.

7. Based on a consideration of the components of the required rate of return, discuss why you would expect the required rate of return for U.S. common stocks to be the same as or different than the required rate on Japanese common stocks.

PROBLEMS

1. A large chemical manufacturer has experienced a market reevaluation lately due to a major lawsuit. The firm has a bond issue outstanding with 12 years remaining till maturity. The bonds were issued with an 8 percent coupon rate (paid semiannually) and a par value of $1,000. Because of the increased risk, the required rate has risen to 12 percent.

1a. What is the current value of these securities?

1b. What will be the value of these securities in two years if the required return has then risen to 15 percent?

2. In 1969 Rachel Cosmetics issued a $70 par value preferred stock that pays a 7 percent annual dividend. Due to changes in the overall economy and in the company's financial condition, investors are now requiring a 12 percent return. What price would you be willing to pay for a share of preferred if:

2a. You receive your first dividend one year from now?

2b. You receive your first dividend tomorrow?

3. Ridgemont Can Company's latest dividend of $1.25 was paid yesterday and maintained its historic 7 percent annual rate of growth. You plan to purchase the stock today because you feel that the growth rate will increase to 8 percent for the next three years and that the stock will then reach $40 per share.

3a. How much should you be willing to pay for the stock if you require a 14 percent return?

3b. How much should you be willing to pay for the stock if you feel that the 8 percent growth rate can be maintained indefinitely and you require a 14 percent return?

3c. If the 8 percent rate of growth is achieved, what will the price be at the end of Year 3?

4. What is the value to you of a 14 percent coupon bond with a par value of $10,000 that matures in 10 years if you want a 12 percent return on the bond? Use semiannual compounding.

5. The Raymond Basketball Company (RBC) earned $10 a share last year and paid a dividend of $6 a share. Next year you expect the company to earn $11.00 and continue its payout ratio. Assume you expect a 5 percent dividend yield a year from now, when you anticipate selling the stock. If you require 14 percent on this stock, how much would you be willing to pay for it?

6. Over the very long run you expect dividends for RBC to grow at a 12 percent rate, and you require 16 percent on the stock. Using the dividend model that assumes a perpetuity, how much would you pay for this stock?

7. The Barking Dogfood Company (BDC) has consistently paid out 30 percent of its earnings in dividends. The company's return on equity is 15 percent. What would you estimate as its growth rate of dividends?

8. Given the low risk in dog food, your required rate of return on BDC is 12 percent. What P/E ratio would you apply to the firm's earnings?

9. Discuss three ways a firm can increase its ROE. Create an example to illustrate your discussion.

10. Compute a recent five-year average of the following ratios for three companies of your choice (attempt to select diverse firms):

10a. Retention rate

10b. Net profit margin

10c. Equity turnover

10d. Total asset turnover

10e. Total assets/equity
     Based upon these ratios, discuss which firm you would expect to have the highest growth rate of earnings, and justify your answer.

11. You have read that the Orange Computer Co. that is currently retaining 90 percent of its earnings ($3 a share this year) is experiencing an ROE of almost 30 percent. Assuming a market return (*Rm*) of 12 percent, an RFR of 6 percent, and a beta of 1.60, how much would you pay for Orange on the basis of the pragmatic multiplier approach? Discuss in detail the

reason for your answer. What would you pay if the retention rate were 80 percent and the ROE were 25 percent? Show all your work.

REFERENCES

Beaver, William, Paul Kettler, and Myron Scholes. "The Association between Market-Determined and Accounting-Determined Risk Measures." *Accounting Review* 45, no. 4 (October 1970).

Beaver, William, and James Manegold. "The Association between Market-Determined and Accounting-Determined Measures of Systematic Risk: Some Further Evidence." *Journal of Financial and Quantitative Analysis* 10, no. 2 (June 1975).

Benesh, Gary A., and Pamela P. Peterson. "On the Relation between Earnings Changes, Analysts' Forecasts, and Stock Price Fluctuations." *Financial Analysts Journal* 42, no. 6 (November–December 1986).

Ben-Zion, Uri, and Sol. S. Shalit. "Size, Leverage, and Dividend Record as Determinants of Equity Risk." *Journal of Finance* 20, no. 4 (September 1975).

Blume, Marshall E. "On the Assessment of Risk." *Journal of Finance* 26, no. 1 (March 1971).

Brown, Philip, and Ray Ball. "Some Preliminary Findings on the Association between the Earnings of a Firm, Its Industry, and the Economy." *Empirical Research in Accounting: Selected Studies 1967,* supplement to vol. 5. *Journal of Accounting Research.*

Chen, Nui-Fu, Richard Roll, and Stephen A. Ross." "Economic Forces and the Stock Market." *Journal of Business* 59, no. 3 (July 1986).

Emanuel, David. "A Theoretical Model for Valuing Preferred Stock." *Journal of Finance* 38, no. 4 (September 1983).

Estep, Tony. "A New Method for Valuing Common Stocks." *Financial Analysts Journal* 41, no. 6 (November–December 1985).

Estep, Tony. "Security Analysis and Stock Selection: Turning Financial Information into Return Forecasts." *Financial Analysts Journal* 43, no. 4 (July–August 1987).

Fisher, Lawrence. "Determinants of Risk Premiums on Corporate Bonds." *Journal of Political Economy* 67, no. 3 (June 1959).

Fouse, William L. "Risk and Liquidity Revisited." *Financial Analysts Journal* 33, no. 1 (January–February 1977).

Hamada, Robert. "The Effect of the Firm's Capital Structure on the Systematic Risk of Common Stocks." *Journal of Finance* 27, no. 2 (May 1972).

King, Benjamin F. "Market and Industry Factors in Stock Price Behavior." *Journal of Business* 39, no. 1, Part II (January 1966).

Levine, Sumner N., ed. *The Financial Analysts Handbook* 2d ed. Homewood, Ill.: Dow Jones-Irwin, 1988.

Reilly, Frank K. "The Misdirected Emphasis in Security Valuation." *Financial Analysts Journal* 29, no. 1 (January–February 1973).

Rosenberg, Barr. "Prediction of Common Stock Betas." *Journal of Portfolio Management* 11, no. 2 (Winter 1985).

Rosenberg, Barr, and James Guy. "Prediction of Beta from Investment Fundamentals." *Financial Analysts Journal* 32, no. 3 (May-June 1976).

Shaked, Israel. "International Equity Markets and the Investment Horizon." *Journal of Portfolio Management* 11, no. 2 (Winter 1985).

Shiskin, Julius. "Systematic Aspects of Stock Price Fluctuations." Reprinted in James Lorie and Richard Brealey, *Modern Developments in Investment Management* 2d ed. Hinsdale, Ill.: The Dryden Press, 1978.

DERIVATION OF CONSTANT GROWTH DIVIDEND MODEL

APPENDIX 9A

The basic model is

$$P_0 = \frac{D_1}{(1+k)^1} + \frac{D_2}{(1+k)^2} + \frac{D_3}{(1+k)^3} + \cdots \frac{D_n}{(1+k)^n},$$

where

P_0 = **Current price**

D_i = **Expected dividend in period _i_**

k = **Required rate of return on asset _j_.**

If growth rate (g) is constant,

$$P_0 = \frac{D_0(1+g)^1}{(1+k)^1} + \frac{D_0(1+g)^2}{(1+k)^2} + \cdots \frac{D_0(1+g)^n}{(1+k)^n}.$$

This can be written

$$P_0 = D_0 \left[\frac{(1+g)}{(1+k)} + \frac{(1+g)^2}{(1+k)^2} + \frac{(1+g)^3}{(1+k)^3} + \cdots \frac{(1+g)^n}{(1+k)^n} \right]. \qquad (9A.1)$$

Multiply both sides of Equation 9A.1 by

$$\frac{1+k}{1+g}:$$

$$\left[\frac{(1+k)}{(1+g)} \right] P_0 = D_0 \left[1 + \frac{(1+g)}{(1+k)} + \frac{(1+g)^2}{(1+k)^2} + \cdots \frac{(1+g)^{n-1}}{(1+k)^{n-1}} \right]. \qquad (9A.2)$$

Subtract Equation 9A.1 from Equation 9A.2:

$$\left[\frac{(1+k)}{(1+g)} - 1 \right] P_0 = D_0 \left[1 - \frac{(1+g)^n}{(1+k)^n} \right]$$

$$\left[\frac{(1+k) - (1+g)}{(1+g)} \right] P_0 = D_0 \left[1 - \frac{(1+g)^n}{(1+k)^n} \right].$$

Assuming $i > g$, as $N \to \infty$, the term in brackets on the right side of the equation goes to 1, leaving:

$$\left[\frac{(1 + k) - (1 + g)}{(1 + g)} \right] P_0 = D_0 .$$

This simplifies to

$$\left[\frac{1 + k - 1 - g}{(1 + g)} \right] P_0 = D_0 ,$$

which equals

$$\left[\frac{k - g}{(1 + g)} \right] P_0 = D_0 .$$

This equals

$$(k - g)P_0 = D_0(1 + g) ,$$

but

$$D_0(1 + g) = D_1 ,$$

so

$$(k - g)P_0 = D_1$$

$$P_0 = \frac{D_1}{k - g} .$$

Remember, this model assumes

- A constant growth rate
- An infinite time period
- The required return on the investment (k) is greater than the expected growth rate (g).

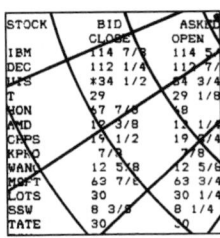

CHAPTER 10

BOND FUNDAMENTALS

The market for fixed-income securities is large and diverse, and it represents an exciting and profitable outlet for investment. This chapter is primarily concerned with publicly issued, long-term, nonconvertible, straight-debt obligations of both public and private issuers in the United States and major global markets. In later chapters, we will consider other fixed-income securities, such as preferred stock and convertible bonds. An understanding of bonds is helpful in an efficient market because fixed-income securities in the United States and from around the world increase the universe of investing options necessary for diversification.[1]

This chapter on bond fundamentals reviews some basic features of bonds, examines the world fixed-income securities market structure, and discusses alternative fixed-income investment vehicles. The chapter ends with a brief review of the data requirements of bond investors and the sources of such information.

BASIC FEATURES OF A BOND

Essentially, bonds are the long-term, public debt of an issuer that has been marketed in a convenient and affordable denomination. They differ from other forms of debt, such as mortgages and privately placed obligations, because they have been placed in the hands of numerous public investors rather than channeled directly to a single lender. Bond issues are considered fixed-income securities because the debt-service obligations of the issuer are fixed. Specifically, the issuer agrees to

1. Pay a fixed amount of periodic *interest* to the holder of record.
2. Repay a fixed amount of *principal* at the date of maturity.

---

[1] William F. Sharpe, "Bonds versus Stocks: Some Lessons from Capital Market Theory," *Financial Analysts Journal,* 28 no. 6 (November–December 1973): 73–79.

Normally, interest on bonds is paid every six months, although for some bond issues, intervals are as short as a month or as long as a year. The principal is due at maturity; this is the *par value* of the issue, and it is rarely less than $1,000. Another important dimension of bonds is their term to maturity, or the life of issue. The public debt market is often divided into three time segments defined in terms of an issue's original maturity as follows:

1. *Short-Term* issues with maturities of one year or less, commonly known as the *money market.*
2. *Intermediate* issues with maturities in excess of one year but less than ten years, known as *notes.*
3. *Long-Term* issues with maturities in excess of ten years, referred to as *bonds.*

The lives of debt obligations, however, are constantly changing as the issues progress toward maturity. Thus, seasoned issues (those that have been outstanding in the secondary market for any period of time) eventually move from long-term to intermediate to short-term. As an example, a bond issued in 1990 with a maturity in 2015 will originally be a long-term bond, but after 2005 it will become an intermediate-term security when it has less than ten years to maturity; finally it will be a short-term security when there is less than a year to maturity. This movement is important, because, as will be discussed in the next chapter, the price volatility of a debt obligation is affected by, among other things, the prevailing (duration) maturity of the issue.

BOND CHARACTERISTICS

One can characterize a bond in many different ways. Each bond issue has intrinsic features, plus there are different types of bonds, and there are various indenture provisions that can affect the yield and/or price behavior.

INTRINSIC CHARACTERISTICS. The coupon, maturity, principal value of the issue, and finally, the type of bond ownership are important intrinsic features. The coupon indicates the income that the bond investor will receive over the life (or holding period) of the issue and is known as *interest income, coupon income,* or *nominal yield.*

The *term to maturity* specifies the date at which the bond will mature (or expire). Two important types of bonds can be distinguished on the basis of maturity. The most common is a *term bond* that has a single maturity date. A *serial obligation* actually involves a series of maturity dates (e.g., a single 25-year issue may possess 20 or 25 different maturity dates). Each maturity, although a subset of the total issue, is really a small bond issue in itself with, generally, a different coupon. Municipalities are the biggest issuers of serial bonds.

The *principal,* or *par value,* of the issue represents the original principal value of the obligation and is generally stated in $1,000 increments from $1,000 to $25,000 or more. Principal value is not necessarily the same as the market value. Many issues trade at market values above or below their original principal value because of a difference between the coupon of the obligation and the prevailing market rate of interest. As discussed in Chapter 9, if the market interest rate is above the coupon rate, the bond will sell at a discount to par, and vice versa. If the coupon is comparable to the market interest rate, the market value of the bond will be close to its original principal value.

Finally, is the issue a bearer bond or a registered issue? With the former type, the holder, or *bearer,* is the owner, so the issuer keeps no account of transfers in ownership, and interest is obtained by clipping coupons attached to the bonds and sending them to the issuer for payment. Such payment is usually handled through local commercial banks in a routine, systematic manner. In contrast, the issuers of registered bonds keep track of owners of record and pay them the principal or interest by check.

TYPES OF ISSUES. In contrast to common stock, issuers of bonds can have many different types outstanding at the same time. Bonds can be differentiated by the type of collateral behind the issue and are referred to as either *senior* or *junior* securities. The former are generally secured bonds backed by a legal claim on some specified property of the issuer. For example, mortgage bonds are secured by real estate assets, and equipment trust certificates, which are popular with railroads and airlines, indicate a senior claim on the firm's equipment.

Unsecured (junior) bonds are issues backed only by the promise of the issuer to pay interest and principal on a timely basis. *Debentures* are secured by the general credit of the issuer. *Subordinated debentures* possess a claim on income that is subordinated to other debentures. *Income issues* are the most junior type; interest on them need not be paid until income is earned. While income bonds are unusual in the corporate sector, they are a very popular municipal issue and are referred to as *revenue bonds.* Finally, in *refunding issues,* one bond is prematurely retired from the proceeds of another issue that remains outstanding after the refunding operation. A refunding bond can be either a junior or senior issue depending upon whether it is secured or not.

The type of issue has only a marginal effect on comparative yield because it is the creditworthiness of the issuer that basically determines bond quality. In fact, a study of corporate bond price behavior found that the collateral of the obligation, or lack of it, did not become important until the issue approached default.[2] Usually, collateral and security influence yield differentials only when they affect the quality ratings given to a bond by rating agencies.

INDENTURE PROVISIONS. The indenture is the contract between the issuer and the bondholder specifying the issuer's legal requirements. Bond inves-

---

[2] W. Braddock Hickman, *Corporate Bond Quality and Investor Experience* (Princeton, N.J.: Princeton University Press, 1958).

tors do not have to be concerned with many of them because the trustee (usually a bank) acting in behalf of the bondholders sees to it that all of the provisions are met, including the timely payment of interest and principal. However, investors should be aware of a few popular indenture provisions, especially the three types of *call features. Freely callable* provisions allow the issuer to retire the bond at any time with a typical notification period of 30 to 60 days. *Noncallable provisions* forbid the issuer to retire the bond prior to its maturity.[3] *Deferred call* provisions mean the issue cannot be called for a certain length of time after the date of issue (e.g., 5 to 10 years). At the end of the deferred call period, the issue becomes freely callable. You should also be aware of the *call premium*— the amount above maturity value that the issuer must pay to the bondholder for prematurely retiring the bond.

A *refunding provision* is like the call feature except that it prohibits the retirement of an issue from the proceeds of a lower-coupon refunding bond—that is, the obligation can be called and prematurely retired for any reason other than refunding! If a firm has excess cash, for example, an issue with a nonrefunding provision could be retired prior to maturity. This occurred during 1986 when many issuers did not refund their obligations but retired high-coupon issues early because they had the cash and felt that this was a good financing decision.

Another important provision is the *sinking-fund feature,* which specifies how the bond will be amortized (or repaid) over its life. While most issues have sinking-fund provisions, a number of industrial and government issues do not, which means that all or most of the issue is payable at maturity, and the issuer is not required to systematically retire these obligations over their life. Sinking-fund provisions effect comparative yields at issue but have little subsequent impact on price behavior.

There are many different types of sinking-fund provisions. For example, some utility issuers have the right to use the *periodic sinking fund* to either acquire outstanding bonds or to increase the capital assets of the firm. These *improvement funds* require an annual sinking fund of at least 1 percent of the total bonds outstanding. The size of the sinking fund can be a percentage of a given issue or of the total debt outstanding. Moreover, it can be a fixed or variable sum stated on a dollar or percentage basis. The amount of the issue that must be repaid before maturity ranges from a nominal sum to 100 percent, while the payments may commence at the end of the first year or may be deferred for as long as five to ten years from the date of issue. Like a call or refunding provision, the sinking-fund feature also carries a nominal call premium, (e.g., 1 percent). Unlike call or refunding features, however, a sinking-fund provision is an obligation and must be carried out regardless of market conditions, which means that there is a small risk for investors that a sinking-fund bond issue could be called on a random basis. Such public calls have been fairly rare recently, since many bonds have been trading at a discount (i.e., at

---

[3] Currently most corporate long-term bonds contain some form of call provision.

a price below par) and are retired for sinking-fund purposes through direct negotiations with institutional holders. Essentially, the trustee negotiates with an institution to buy back the necessary amount of bonds at a price slightly above the current market price.

BOND RATES OF RETURN

The rate of return on a bond is computed in the same way as the rate of return on stock or any asset; it is determined by the beginning and ending price and the cash flows during the holding period. The major difference between stocks and bonds is that the interim cash flows (i.e., the interest) are specified for bonds, while the dividends on stock are not contractual. Therefore, the rate of return for a bond will be

$$R_{t,i} = \frac{P_{i,t+1} - P_{i,t} + Int_{i,t}}{P_{i,t}},$$

where

$R_{i,t}$ = the rate of return for bond i during period t

$P_{i,t+1}$ = the market price of bond i at the end of period t

$P_{i,t}$ = the market price of bond i at the beginning of period t

$Int_{i,t}$ = the interest payments on bond i during period t.

It is important to recognize that the only fixed and known factor is the contractual interest payments. The beginning price is determined by market forces, which we will discuss. The ending price is likewise determined by market forces prevailing at the time of sale unless the bond is held to maturity, in which case the investor will receive the par value. The point is, large price variations in bonds provide opportunities for bond investors to experience capital gains or losses. The substantial interest rate volatility since the 1960s has caused large price fluctuations in bonds and as a result, capital gains or losses have been the major component of the rates of return on bonds.

DETERMINATION OF BOND PRICE. The price of a bond is determined by the coupon that the issue carries, the length of its term to maturity, and the prevailing market interest rate (yield) on the bond. While the next chapter contains the detailed mathematics of bond price behavior, at this point you should recall how the price of bonds is determined. As shown, given the coupon and maturity for a bond, the price is determined by the market required yield on the bond. Therefore, bond price behavior over time is determined by how market interest rates change over time.

As discussed in Chapter 9, the price (value) of a bond is the present value of the expected cash flows from the asset. In the case of a bond, the only unknown is the required rate of return. As an example, consider a $1,000 par value bond with a 10 percent coupon that matures in ten years.

If the bond makes semiannual payments, and the required yield is 12 percent, the value of the bond is

---

$50 × 11.4699 (present value annuity factor for 20 periods at 6%) = $573.50
$1,000 × .3118 (present value factor for 20 periods at 6%) = 311.80
Total Present Value = $885.30

Therefore, the market price for this bond should be $885.30, or 88.53 percent of par. Because the market yield on this bond is above its coupon rate, the bond is selling at a discount from par. Assume that over the next year, market interest rates decline, and the market yield on this bond declines to 8 percent. At this point it is a nine-year bond (nine years to maturity), and the market price would be as follows:

$50 × 12.6593 (present value annuity factor for 18 periods at 4%) = $ 632.97
$1,000 × .4936 (present value factor for 18 periods at 4%) = 493.60
Total Present Value = $1,126.57

Therefore, the market price for this bond would be $1,126.57, or 112.66 percent of par. Because the market yield is below the coupon rate, the bond is selling at a premium relative to its par value. The rate of return for an investor who owned the bond during this year was as follows:

$$R_{i,t} = \frac{\$1,126.57 - \$885.30 + \$100.00}{\$885.30}$$

$$= \frac{341.27}{885.30} = .3855 = 38.55\%.$$

Two important points regarding this example are

1. There was a substantial price change because of the change in the required market yield on this bond.
2. The rate of return received by the investor who held the bond during this year was mainly due to the price change during the holding period.

Because the price of an issue depends on its prevailing *yield*, in practice the yield of an issue is determined first, and then its dollar price is derived. This yield-based pricing is because there is a wide diversity of coupons and maturities at any point in time, and the yield-based computations allow market-makers to systematically account for differences in coupon and/ or maturity when pricing an issue.

While bond price volatility is directly affected by the magnitude of movement in interest rate changes, different bonds react differently to changes in these rates. Specifically, for a given change in market rates, a bond's price will vary according to the coupon and maturity of the issue. Bonds with longer maturities and/or lower coupons will respond most vigorously to a given change.[4] Other factors likewise cause differences in price volatility (e.g., the call feature), but they are typically much less important.

BOND YIELDS. Because the concept of yield is critical to the mechanics of bond pricing, it is important to differentiate among the two major types of yields: *current yield* and promised yield to maturity (*promised yield*). Current yield is the amount of current income that a bond provides (annual interest) relative to its prevailing market price. It is to a bond what dividend yield is to common stocks and has very little use in the bond valuation process. Promised yield to maturity (YTM), in contrast, is very important. It is the yield that determines all bond prices. It encompasses interest income and price appreciation (or depreciation) in the valuation process, as well as total cash flow received over the life of the issue. Because it entails cash flow timing, the promised yield computation is based on the present value concept. Indeed, it is the same mathematical process as the *internal rate of return* used in corporation finance. The percentage point is broken into 100 parts, with each part being called a *basis point*. Thus, a basis point is 1/100th of 1 percent and is a convenient means of depicting changes in yield; for example, a decline in yield from 8.5 percent to 8.0 percent is a decline of 50 basis points.

OVERVIEW OF THE GLOBAL BOND MARKET STRUCTURE

The gigantic market for fixed-income securities dwarfs the listed equity exchanges (NYSE, TSE, LSE), one reason being that corporations tend to issue bonds (which have a fixed life) rather than common stocks (which are perpetual securities). Federal Reserve figures indicate that in the United States during 1987, out of $246 billion in new corporate security issues, only about $71 billion (approximately 29 percent) were equity, which included preferred as well as common stock. Corporations issue less common or preferred stock because the major source of equity financing for a firm is internally generated funds. Also, unlike the equity market, which is strictly corporations, the bond market in most countries has four substantial noncorporate sectors: the pure government sector (i.e., the Treasury in the United States), government agencies, state and local governments (municipals), and international bonds (Yankees and Eurobonds in the United States). Evidence of the total size and distribution of the global bond market can be gleaned from Table 10.1, which lists the dollar value of debt outstanding and the percentage distribution for the 18 major bond markets for the period 1981–1987. These data indicate substantial growth overall, including a 24 percent increase in the total in 1987 compared to 1986. Also, some of the country trends are significant, such as the U.S market that went from about 46 percent of the total world market in 1981 to a high of almost 55 percent in 1984, to a low proportion of about 42

---

[4] This relationship among bond price volatility and maturity and coupon is discussed in detail in the next chapter.

TABLE **10.1**

Total Debt Outstanding of the 18 Major Actively Traded Bond Markets, by Year (U.S. Dollar Terms)

	1981		1982		1983	
	$	%	$	%	$	%
U.S. dollar	1,489	44.6	1,759	48.0	2,074	50.2
Japanese yen	607	18.2	649	17.7	756	18.3
Deutschemark	305	9.1	320	8.7	312	7.5
Italian lira	143	4.3	152	4.1	175	4.2
U.K. sterling	181	5.4	171	4.7	174	4.2
French franc	100	3.0	106	2.9	104	2.5
Canadian dollar	129	3.9	136	3.7	149	3.6
Swedish krona	75	2.2	62	1.7	68	1.6
Danish krone	66	2.0	69	1.9	69	1.6
Swiss franc	55	1.6	60	1.6	59	1.4
Dutch guilder	40	1.2	46	1.3	47	1.1
Belgian franc	46	1.4	36	1.0	34	0.8
Australian dollar	51	1.5	50	1.4	52	1.3
Spanish peseta	23	0.7	22	0.6	21	0.5
Norwegian krone	17	0.5	15	0.4	17	0.4
ECU[a]	0	0.0	1	0.0	3	0.1
Irish punt	7	0.2	8	0.2	7	0.2
New Zealand dollar	5	0.1	6	0.2	6	0.1
Total	3,342	100.0	3,668	100.0	4,129	100.0

Note: Only includes bonds with maturities over one year (floating-rate notes were excluded).
[a]ECU-European Community Unit.
Source: "Size of the World Bond Markets: Year-End 1987," Merrill Lynch Capital Markets, July 1988.

percent in 1987. In contrast, Japan was in the 17–18 percent range until it increased to almost 23 percent in 1987. The German and Italian markets have increased as a percent of the global bond market during the last several years, while the U.K. market has experienced an overall decline.

THE PARTICIPANTS

There are five different types of issuers: (1) federal governments (e.g., the U.S. Treasury), (2) various agencies of the federal government, (3) various state and local political subdivisions (known as municipalities), (4) corporations, and (5) international issues.[5] The division of bonds among these five types for the three largest markets and the United Kingdom is contained in Table 10.2.

GOVERNMENT. The market for government securities is the largest and the best known in the United States, Japan, and the United Kingdom. It

[5] This general discussion of global bond markets and specific national bond markets benefited from, *International Bond Handbook,* International Bond Research Unit, James Capel & Co., London (February 1987); and Margaret Darasz Hadzima and Cornelia M. Small, "Perspectives on International Bond Investing," in *The Handbook of Fixed Income Securities,* 2d ed., eds. Frank J. Fabozzi and Irving M. Pollack (Homewood, Ill.: Dow Jones-Irwin, 1987).

	1984		1985		1986		1987	
	$	%	$	%	$	%	$	%
	2,370	53.4	2,830	49.8	3,309	45.9	3,717	41.7
	773	17.4	1,070	18.8	1,473	20.5	2,033	22.8
	293	6.6	417	7.3	588	8.2	783	8.8
	186	4.2	278	4.9	423	5.9	554	6.2
	153	3.4	207	3.6	227	3.2	310	3.5
	110	2.5	174	3.1	252	3.5	334	3.7
	161	3.6	171	3.0	194	2.7	228	2.6
	67	1.5	88	1.5	117	1.6	146	1.6
	71	1.6	103	1.8	136	1.9	171	1.9
	55	1.2	77	1.4	107	1.5	142	1.6
	48	1.1	70	1.2	96	1.3	130	1.5
	33	0.7	51	0.9	71	1.0	96	1.1
	59	1.3	60	1.1	70	1.0	91	1.0
	24	0.5	34	0.6	61	0.8	76	0.8
	16	0.4	22	0.4	28	0.4	36	0.4
	5	0.1	10	0.2	20	0.3	37	0.4
	8	0.2	11	0.2	16	0.2	22	0.2
	6	0.1	8	0.1	12	0.2	15	0.2
	4,439	100.0	5,681	100.0	7,202	100.0	8,920	100.0

involves bonds, notes, and other debt instruments issued to meet the growing needs of these governments. In Germany, the government sector is a much smaller proportion, but it is growing in relative size. These different types of debt instruments will be reviewed in a subsequent section.

GOVERNMENT AGENCIES. Agency issues have attained and maintained a major position in the U.S. market (over 20 percent), but a smaller proportion in other countries (e.g., less than 10 percent in Japan, below 4 percent in Germany, and nonexistent in the United Kingdom). These agencies represent political subdivisions of the government although the securities are not typically direct obligations of the government. The agency market in the United States is composed of two types of issuers: government-sponsored enterprises and federal agencies. Similar to treasuries, these securities are issued under the authority of an act of Congress, and the proceeds are used to finance many legislative programs. Many of these obligations carry guarantees of the U.S. government and therefore effectively represent the full faith and credit of the U.S. Treasury although they are not direct obligations of the government. While these arrangements are fairly typical in other countries, it is necessary to specifically inquire

TABLE 10.2

Makeup of Bonds Outstanding in United States, Japan, Germany, and United Kingdom 1981–1987

	1981		1982		1983	
	$ BILLIONS	%	$ BILLIONS	%	$ BILLIONS	%
A. United States						
Government	475.3	31.1	569.6	31.6	707.1	33.2
Federal Agency	319.4	21.7	383.9	21.8	451.7	21.5
Municipals	357.7	23.4	395.2	21.9	450.4	21.1
Corporate[a]	268.5	17.6	302.3	16.8	340.2	16.0
International	67.9	6.2	108.2	8.0	124.8	8.2
Total	1,488.8	100.0	1,759.2	100.0	2,074.2	100.0

	1981		1982		1983	
	$ BILLIONS	%	$ BILLIONS	%	$ BILLIONS	%
B. Japan						
Government	363.5	59.8	393.3	60.6	467.4	61.8
Govt. Assoc. Org.	44.6	7.3	49.0	7.6	59.1	7.8
Municipals	17.7	2.9	19.6	3.0	21.6	2.9
Bank Debentures	126.5	20.8	132.1	20.4	150.2	19.9
Corporate	43.7	7.2	41.3	6.4	41.0	5.4
International	11.4	1.9	13.7	2.1	16.4	2.2
Total	607.4	100.0	648.9	100.0	755.7	100.0

	1981		1982		1983	
	$ BILLIONS	%	$ BILLIONS	%	$ BILLIONS	%
C. Germany						
Government	34.6	11.4	42.4	13.3	47.0	15.1
Agency	11.4	3.7	12.3	3.8	11.0	3.5
State and Local	4.8	1.6	5.4	1.7	6.2	2.0
Banks	216.4	71.0	223.2	69.8	214.5	68.8
Corporate	1.6	0.5	1.3	0.4	0.9	0.3
International	35.9	11.8	35.2	11.0	32.1	10.3
Total	304.8	100.0	319.8	100.0	311.7	100.0

	1981		1982		1983	
	$ BILLIONS	%	$ BILLIONS	%	$ BILLIONS	%
D. United Kingdom						
Government	169.9	93.7	155.2	90.8	158.4	90.8
Agency	—	—	—	—	—	—
Municipals	1.7	0.9	1.6	0.9	1.5	0.9
Corporate	7.3	4.0	10.0	5.9	9.1	5.2
International	2.4	1.3	4.1	2.4	5.6	3.2
Total	181.4	100.0	170.9	100.0	174.5	100.0

[a]From ML Corporate bond index.

Source: "Size of the World Bond Markets: Year-End 1987," Merrill Lynch Capital Markets, July 1988.

about the relationship to the government. An important feature of agencies is that in most countries the market yield of agency obligations is generally

1984		1985		1986		1987	
$ BILLIONS	%	$ BILLIONS	%	$ BILLIONS	%	$ BILLIONS	%
873.0	35.6	1,037.8	35.3	1,192.3	34.6	1,335.2	35.9
526.2	21.6	626.7	20.6	802.0	22.3	975.1	26.2
504.5	20.5	639.5	22.3	666.1	20.4	693.0	18.6
317.9	12.9	340.6	11.6	410.5	11.9	448.7	12.1
148.3	9.3	185.6	10.3	238.0	10.9	264.7	7.1
2,369.9	100.0	2,830.2	100.0	3,308.9	100.0	3,716.7	100.0

1984		1985		1986		1987	
$ BILLIONS	%	$ BILLIONS	%	$ BILLIONS	%	$ BILLIONS	%
478.1	61.8	664.0	62.0	898.3	61.0	1,230.5	60.5
62.8	8.1	87.9	8.2	118.1	8.0	160.0	7.9
22.3	2.9	31.0	2.9	39.2	2.7	53.6	2.6
154.2	19.9	205.7	19.2	296.9	20.1	411.5	20.2
37.0	4.8	45.9	4.3	57.5	3.9	74.2	3.6
19.1	2.5	35.5	3.4	63.2	4.3	103.1	5.1
773.4	100.0	1,069.9	100.0	1,473.2	100.0	2,033.0	100.0

1984		1985		1986		1987	
$ BILLIONS	%	$ BILLIONS	%	$ BILLIONS	%	$ BILLIONS	%
48.6	16.6	74.3	17.8	116.3	19.8	171.8	21.9
10.0	3.4	15.0	3.6	22.6	3.8	34.6	4.4
6.9	2.4	11.3	2.7	17.9	3.0	23.5	3.0
196.5	67.0	267.5	64.1	356.4	60.6	455.8	58.2
0.7	0.2	1.0	0.2	1.4	0.2	1.6	0.2
30.5	10.4	48.0	11.5	73.4	12.5	95.5	12.2
293.2	100.0	417.1	100.0	587.9	100.0	782.8	100.0

1984		1985		1986		1987	
$ BILLIONS	%	$ BILLIONS	%	$ BILLIONS	%	$ BILLIONS	%
136.3	89.3	182.6	88.2	195.4	85.9	259.3	83.6
—	—	—	—	—	—	—	—
0.9	0.6	0.6	0.3	0.3	0.1	0.3	0.1
8.5	5.6	11.0	5.3	14.1	6.2	19.4	6.3
7.0	4.6	12.9	6.2	17.6	7.7	31.3	10.1
152.6	100.0	207.1	100.0	227.4	100.0	310.2	100.0

above that attainable from pure government bonds. Therefore, agencies represent a way to increase returns with only marginal differences in risk.

MUNICIPALITIES. Municipal debt issues—issues of states, school districts, cities, or other political subdivisions—are unlike government and agency issues in that the *interest income* on them is not subject to federal income tax. *Capital gains* on these issues, however, are. Moreover, except for Puerto Rican issues, these bonds are exempt from state and local taxes *when they are issues of the investor's state.* That is, a California issue would not be taxed in California, but its interest income would be taxable to a New York resident. The interest income of Puerto Rican issues enjoys total immunity from federal, state, and local taxes. Another distinguishing feature of U.S. municipal bonds is that most issues are serial obligations.

As shown in Table 10.2, the municipal bond market in most other countries is much smaller than that of the United States (less than 3 percent) and very illiquid. Also, while it is necessary to examine each country to determine its tax laws, typically the income from a non–U.S. municipal bond would not be exempt for a U.S. investor.

CORPORATIONS. The major nongovernmental issuer of debt is, of course, the corporate sector. *Corporate bonds* represent obligations of firms domiciled in a particular country. As shown in Table 10.2, the importance of this sector differs dramatically among countries. It is a significant but declining (from 17.6 percent to 12 percent) factor in the United States, a small but declining sector in Japan, which is supplemented by bank debentures, a small but fairly constant proportion of the U.K. market, and a minuscule part of the German market because German firms prefer to obtain financing through bank loans. In turn, this explains the very large percent of bank debt in Germany.

The market for corporate bonds is commonly subdivided into several segments: *industrials, public utilities, transportation,* and *financial* issues. The specific makeup varies between countries. In the United States, the bulk of the issues is in industrials and utilities. In contrast, in most non–U.S. countries corporations do not issue much public debt but borrow from the banks, who become the dominant issuers of public debt to get the required capital. The corporate sector provides the greatest diversity in types of issues and quality. In effect, the corporate issuer can range from the highest investment-grade firm, such as American Telephone and Telegraph or IBM, to a high-risk firm that is relatively new or one that has experienced a default on its debt securities.[6]

INTERNATIONAL. The international sector is composed of both foreign bonds (e.g., Yankee bonds, Samurai bonds) and Eurobonds (e.g., Eurodollar, Euro-yen, Euro-deutschemark, Euro-sterling).[7] While the relative importance of this sector varies by country (12.5 percent in Germany and the United Kingdom, 7 percent in the United States, versus 4.3 percent in Japan), it has grown in both absolute and relative terms in all the countries.

---

[6] It is possible to distinguish another sector that exists in the United States but not in other countries—i.e., institutional bonds. These are corporate bonds issued by a variety of *private nonprofit institutions* such as schools, hospitals, and churches. They are not broken out because they are only a minute part of the U.S. market and do not exist elsewhere.

[7] These bonds were described briefly in Chapter 2 and will be discussed in more detail later in this chapter.

While Eurodollar bonds have dominated the Eurobond market, constituting over 50 percent of the market, the proportion has been declining as investors have been attempting to diversify their Eurobond portfolio. Clearly, this desire for diversification increased with the weak U.S. dollar during 1987.

PARTICIPATING INVESTORS

Numerous individual and institutional investors, with diverse investment objectives, participate in the fixed-income security market. Wealthy individual investors participate in this market, but they are a minor portion because of the market's complexity and the high minimum denominations of most issues. Institutional investors typically account for 90 to 95 percent of the trading, although different segments of the market are more institutionalized than others.[8] For example, the agency market is heavily institutionalized, whereas the municipal sector is much less so. Institutions have a substantial influence on the behavior of market yields because of their size—a few institutions (three or four) may acquire 70 to 80 percent of a $50–$100 million new issue.

A variety of different institutions invest in the bond market. *Life insurance companies* are heavy investors in corporate bonds and, to a lesser extent, in treasury and agency securities. *Commercial banks* invest in the municipal bonds as well as in government and agency issues. *Property and liability insurance companies* concentrate on municipal obligations, as well as in treasuries. *Private and government retirement and pension funds* are heavily committed to corporates and also invest in treasuries and agencies. Finally *mutual funds* have experienced a substantial increase in demand for corporate and municipal bonds because fixed-income mutual funds experienced a higher level of sales during 1986 and 1987 than equity mutual funds.

As the preceding discussion suggests, alternative institutions tend to favor certain types of issues based upon two factors: (1) the tax code applicable to the investing institution and (2) the nature of the liability that the institution assumes in relation to its depositors or clients. For example, because commercial banks are subject to normal taxation and have fairly short-term liability structures they favor short- to intermediate-term municipals. Life insurance companies and pension funds are virtually tax-free institutions with long-term commitments, so they prefer high-yielding, long-term government or corporate bonds. Such institutional investment preferences affect the supply of loanable funds and interest rate changes over short-run periods.

INVESTMENT AND TRADING OPPORTUNITIES

Fixed-income securities provide not only current income but also abundant trading opportunities. The recent high interest rate environment has provided attractive returns, while the volatility of yields presents capital gains opportunities.

Because the bond market is mainly a new-issue (primary) market, the secondary bond market is relatively thin and lacking in trading activity.

---

[8] Sidney Homer, "The Historical Evolution of Today's Bond Market," *Journal of Portfolio Management* 1, no. 3 (Spring 1975): 6–11.

Fortunately, there are some fairly active secondary markets, including the treasury market, agencies, and the public utilities within the corporate market. The international market is mixed, with the Eurobond market being quite active, while some of the foreign bond markets are very inactive. The secondary markets for municipal bonds and institutional bonds are likewise rather illiquid, because new municipal issues are relatively small (par values of less than $15–$20 million), and most municipals are serial obligations, so the total issue is actually a series of smaller issues, compounding the size problem.

The trading of bonds is different from the trading of equity shares, which is typically done on organized exchanges (the NYSE, AMEX, TSE, LSE). Specifically, commercial banks in the United States and throughout the world are popular dealers in government, agency, and municipal securities. While brokerage firms are active in marketing new issues, they concentrate on trading listed bond issues that represent only a small portion of total activity. Thus, there are few transactions in the listed bond market, because most trades are done by specialized investment houses.

Because of the illiquidity, trading-oriented investors should check whether a substantial purchase or sale order can be executed rapidly. If the market is not liquid, there could be a time lag, during which substantial changes in yield and price could occur that would seriously alter holding period returns. Therefore, you should consider a bond issue's trading volume before investing in it.

BOND RATINGS

Agency ratings are an integral part of the bond market. Most fixed-income securities in the corporate, municipal, and institutional markets are regularly evaluated and rated by one or more agencies. The exceptions are bonds considered too small to rate and certain industry categories like bank issues (these are known as *nonrated bonds*). There are four major rating agencies: (1) Duff and Phelps, (2) Fitch Investors Service, (3) Moody's, and (4) Standard & Poor's.

Bond ratings provide the fundamental analysis for thousands of issues.[9] The rating agencies have large, highly qualified staffs that analyze the intrinsic characteristics of the issuing organization and of the issue to determine the default risk and inform the market of their analysis through their ratings.

The primary question in bond analysis is whether the firm can service a fixed amount of debt in a timely manner over the life of a given issue. Consequently, the rating agencies have to consider expectations and forecasts over the life of the issue but also the historical and current financial position of the company. In general, the agencies have done an admirable job, although mistakes happen.[10] If anything, the rating services tend to be overly conservative, as indicated by a study that suggests risk of default

[9] Irwin Ross, "Higher Stakes in the Bond-Rating Game," *Fortune* (April 1976): 132–140. For a study that examines the value of two bond ratings, see L. Paul Hsueh and David S. Kidwell, "Bond Ratings: Are Two Better Than One?" *Financial Management* 17, no. 1 (Spring 1988): 46–53.

[10] W. Braddock Hickman, *Corporate Bond Quality and Investor Experience* (Princeton, N.J.: Princeton University Press, 1958).

has actually been overestimated by the market and has resulted in unnecessarily high risk premiums, given the default possibility.[11] We will consider this notion further in our discussion of high-yield (junk) bonds.

Because of the interest in agency bond ratings, several studies have examined the relationship between bond ratings and the quality of the issue as indicated by financial variables. Horrigan[12] concluded that the accounting data and financial ratios of the firm were, indeed, imbedded in corporate bond ratings. Pogue and Soldofsky[13] found that bond ratings tend to vary directly with profitability, size, and earnings coverage, and move inversely with financial leverage and earnings instability. The results of these and other empirical studies[14] clearly demonstrate that agency ratings are far more than the qualitative judgments of analysts. The ratings assigned to bonds at the time of issue have a definite impact on the marketability and effective interest rate of the issue. Generally, the four agencies will agree on their ratings. When they do not, *split ratings* occur. Seasoned issues are also regularly reviewed to ensure that the assigned rating is still valid, and revisions, either upward or downward, are not uncommon. Revisions are usually done in increments of one rating grade.[15] The ratings are based upon both the company and the issue. After an overall evaluation of the creditworthiness of the total company, a company rating is applied to the most senior unsecured issue outstanding. All junior obligations then receive lower ratings, but the difference in rating could be minimal depending on the indenture specifications. Also, some issues could receive a higher rating than the general credit of the company would justify because of credit-enhancement devices such as the attachment of bank letters of credit, surety, or indemnification bonds from insurance companies.

The agencies assign letter ratings or numbers (Duff & Phelps) depicting what they view as the risk of default of an obligation. Letter ratings range from AAA (or Aaa) to D; the numbers go from 1 to 17. Table 10.3 specifies the various ratings that can be assigned to issues by the major services. Except for the slight variation in designations, the meaning and

---

[11] Gordon Pye, "Gauging the Default Premium," *Financial Analysts Journal* 30, no. 1 (January–February 1974): 49–52.

[12] James O. Horrigan, "The Determination of Long-Term Credit Standing with Financial Ratios," *Empirical Research in Accounting: Selected Studies,* supplement to *Journal of Accounting Research* 4, 1966: 44–62.

[13] Thomas F. Pogue and Robert M. Soldofsky, "What's in a Bond Rating?" *Journal of Financial and Quantitative Analysis* 4, no. 2 (June 1969): 201–208.

[14] See, for example, James S. Ang and K. A. Patel, "Bond Rating Methods: Comparison and Validation," *Journal of Finance* 30, no. 2 (May 1975): 631–640; Richard B. Edelman, "A New Approach to Ratings on Utility Bonds," *Journal of Portfolio Management* 5, no. 3 (Spring 1979): 63–68; Robert S. Kaplan and Gabriel Urwitz, "Statistical Models of Bond Ratings: A Methodological Inquiry," *Journal of Business* 52, no. 2 (April 1979): 231–262; Ahmed Belkaoui, "Industrial Bond Ratings: A New Look," *Financial Management* 9, no. 3 (Autumn 1980): 44–52; and James A. Gentry, David T. Whitford, and Paul Newbold, "Predicting Industrial Bond Ratings with a Probit Model and Funds Flow Components," *The Financial Review* 23, no. 3 (August 1988): 269–286.

[15] Bond rating changes and bond market efficiency are discussed in Chapter 18. Split ratings are discussed in R. Billingsley, R. Lamy, M. Marr, and T. Thompson, "Split Ratings and Bond Reoffering Yields," *Financial Management* 14, no. 2 (Summer 1985): 59–65; L. H. Ederington, "Why Split Ratings Occur," *Financial Management* 14, no. 1 (Spring 1985): 37–47; and P. Liu and W. T. Moore, "The Impact of Split Bond Rating on Risk Premium," *The Financial Review* 22, no. 1 (February 1987).

interpretation is basically the same. In addition to the letter designations by the three agencies, they further modify the ratings with plus and minus signs (Fitch and S&P) or numbers (1-2-3) for Moody's. As an example, an A+ bond is at the top of the A-rated group. The top four ratings—AAA (or Aaa), AA (or Aa), A, BBB (Baa)—and numbers 1 through 10 are generally considered to be investment-grade securities. The next level of securities is known as *speculative bonds* and includes the BB and B (or 11 through 14) rated obligations.[16] The C categories are generally either income obligations or revenue bonds, many of which are trading flat. (Flat bonds are in arrears with regard to interest payments.) In the case of D-rated obligations, the issues are in outright default, and the ratings indicate the bond's relative salvage value. Moody's also identifies the better-quality *municipals* within the A and Baa categories as A1 and Baa1, respectively.

MARKET RATES OF RETURN

Interest rate behavior is probably the most important variable to the investment-grade bond investor. Figures 10.1 and 10.2 illustrate different important characteristics of bond market interest rates. The first shows comparative yields in three different market sectors and indicates that there is no single market rate applicable to all segments of the bond market. While each segment of the market has its unique level, many different rates exist in the market at the same time. For example, the corporate rate could be broken down into industrials, public utilities, and rails, and each of these could be further subdivided according to different quality levels (AAA or Aaa through BBB or Baa). Evidence that various market segments tend to move together is provided by the correlations in excess of 90 percent among short-, intermediate-, and long-term yield series.[17]

Another important aspect to bond investors is how interest rates have performed historically, as shown in Figure 10.2. The data span more than 50 years and include the average behavior of one representative segment of the market: corporate investment-grade securities. Behavior in the first half of the period differs significantly from that in the second half and indicates why investors have recently found the bond market to be both riskier and an attractive investment outlet. Prior to the mid-1960s, the bond market was fairly stable, and there were few opportunities for aggressive investing. After the mid-1960s, interest rates increased to competitive levels, and the substantial swings in interest rates have provided opportunities for capital gains–oriented investors. This increased volatility also increased the risk in bond portfolio management.[18]

---

[16] Marshall E. Blume and Donald B. Keim, "Lower Grade Bonds: Their Risks and Returns," *Financial Analysts Journal* 43, no. 4 (July–August 1987): 26–33. Increased interest in these bonds is discussed in Ben Weberman, "The King of the BBs," *Forbes*, December 5, 1983: 112, 114; and Steven Solomon, "The Art of Managing Junk Bonds," *Institutional Investor* 18, no. 5 (May 1984): 127, 128, 135.

[17] Michael D. Joehnk and James F. Nielsen, "Risk Return Characteristics of Speculative Grade Bonds," *Quarterly Review of Economics and Business* 15, no. 1 (Spring 1975): 35–45. The correlation among the rates of returns for several bond-market indicator series is contained in Chapter 4.

[18] In this regard, see Daniel Hertzberg, "Bond Market Becomes Increasingly Volatile, with Some Big Losses," *The Wall Street Journal*, February 21, 1980, 1; and *idem*, "Bond Trading Has Been Basically Changed by Inflation, Price Volatility, Experts Say," *The Wall Street Journal*, November 7, 1980, 46.

TABLE 10.3
Description of Bond Ratings

DUFF AND PHELPS	FITCH	MOODY'S	STANDARD & POOR'S	DEFINITION
High Grade				
1	AAA	Aaa	AAA	The highest rating assigned to a debt instrument, indicating an extremely strong capacity to pay principal and interest. Bonds in this category are often referred to as "gilt-edge" securities.
2–4	AA	Aa	AA	High-quality bonds by all standards with strong capacity to pay principal and interest. These bonds are rated lower primarily because the margins of protection are less strong than those for 1, Aaa, and AAA bonds.
Medium Grade				
5–7	A	A	A	These bonds possess many favorable investment attributes, but elements that suggest a susceptibility to impairment given adverse economic changes may be present.
8–10	BBB	Baa	BBB	Bonds are regarded as having adequate capacity to pay principal and interest, but certain protective elements may be lacking in the event of adverse economic conditions that could lead to a weakened capacity for payment.
Speculative				
11–13	BB	Ba	BB	Bonds regarded as having only moderate protection of principal and interest payments during both good and bad times.
14	B	B	B	Bonds that generally lack characteristics of other desirable investments. Assurance of interest and principal payments over any long period of time may be small.
Default				
15	CCC	Caa	CCC	Poor-quality issues that may be in default or in danger of default.
16	CC	Ca	CC	Highly speculative issues that are often in default or possess other marked shortcomings.
17		C		The lowest rated class of bonds. These issues can be regarded as extremely poor in investment quality.
	C		C	Rating given to income bonds on which no interest is being paid.
	DDD, DD,D		D	Issues in default with principal or interest payments in arrears. Such bonds are extremely speculative and should be valued only on the basis of their value in liquidation or reorganization.

Source: *Bond Guide* (New York: Standard & Poor's Corporation, monthly); *Bond Record* (New York: Moody's Investors Services, Inc., monthly); and *Rating Register* (New York: Fitch Investors Service, Inc., monthly).

FIGURE 10.1
Comparative Bond Yield Behavior

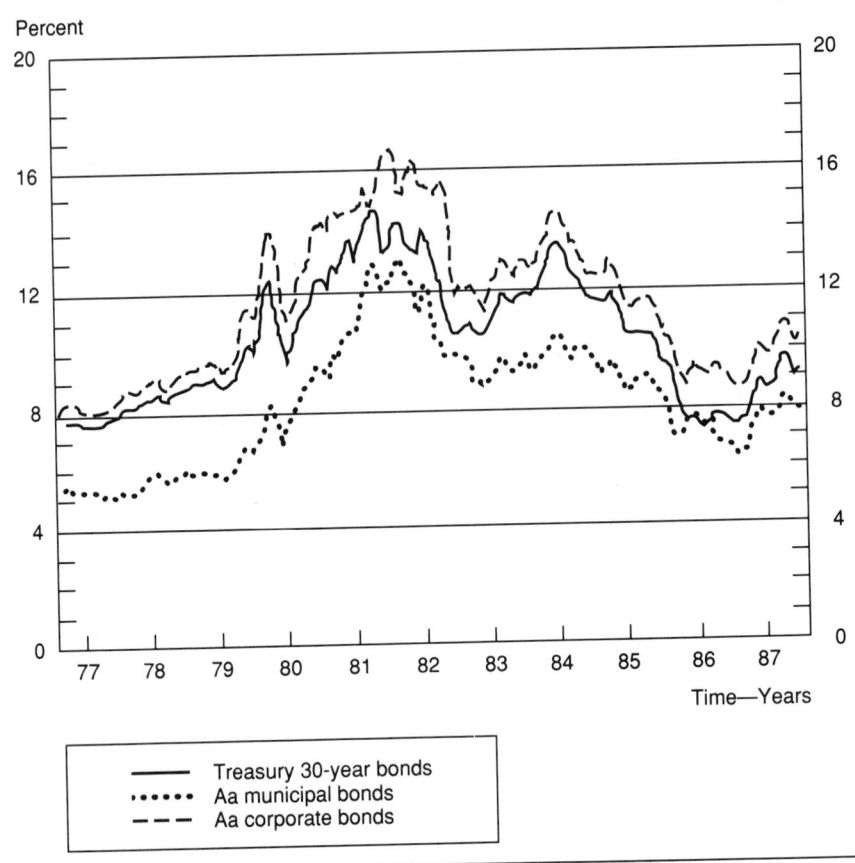

Source: *Treasury Bulletin* (March 1988).

BOND INVESTMENT RISKS. The typical bond investor is exposed to the same risk that any other investor faces. The important risks for bond-holders include (1) interest rate, (2) purchasing power, (3) liquidity, or marketability, (4) exchange rate, and (5) business.

The most important of these is *interest rate risk,* which is a function of the variability of bond returns (prices) caused by changes in the level of interest rates. No segment of the market, except perhaps for the highly speculative issues, is free of this risk. The price stability of investment-grade securities is mainly a function of interest rate stability and therefore of interest rate risk.[19]

---

[19] Frank K. Reilly and Michael D. Joehnk, "Association between Market-Determined Risk Measures for Bonds and Bond Ratings," *Journal of Finance* 31, no. 5 (December 1976): 1387–1403.

FIGURE 10.2
Corporate Bond Yields by Ratings

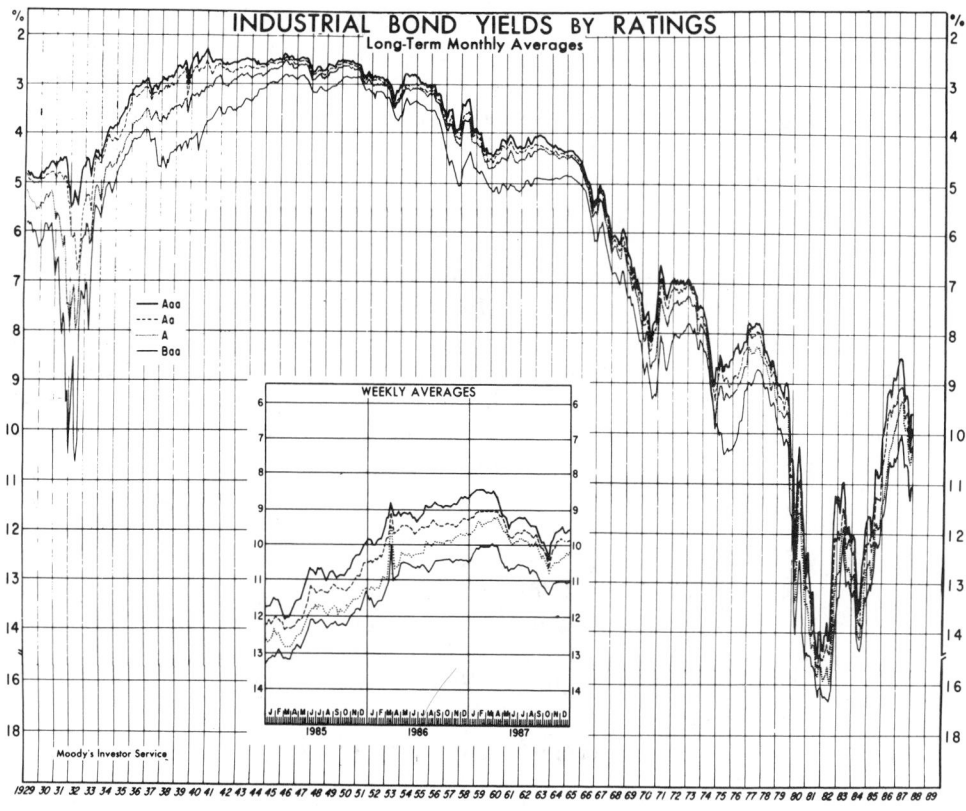

Note: As of December 1976, railroad bonds were removed from the combined corporate averages, retroactive to January 1974. This adjustment was necessary because of a lack of comparability to the industrial and public utility averages, reflecting the limited availability of reasonably current coupon railroad bonds.

Source: *Moody's Bond Record,* December 1987. Reprinted with permission.

Purchasing power risk is linked to inflation and the loss of purchasing power over time. What is important to bond investors is the effect of changes in the rate of inflation (or inflation expectations) that lead to changes in the level of interest rates and changes in bond prices. *Marketability risk* has to do with the liquidity of the obligation and the ease with which an issue can be sold at the prevailing market price. Smaller issues and those with inactive secondary markets will often experience marketability difficulties and are therefore subject to such risk. *Exchange rate risk* is the uncertainty of changes in exchange rates between your domestic currency and the currency of some foreign bond. Given the trend toward global diversification, this risk is becoming much more important.

Finally, *business risk* is the risk of default because of the financial and operating risks of the issuer. Such risks are relevant for corporate, municipal, institutional, and international obligations. Generally, the ratings assigned by the various agencies reflect differences in business risk, and the ratings in turn influence the promised yields as shown in Figure 10.2 (the lower the default risk, the higher the agency rating and the lower the prevailing yield to maturity). Notably, the difference in yield between rating classes is not constant, as shown in Chapter 9 with the risk premium difference between AAA bonds and BAA bonds. We will also discuss these spreads in Chapter 11. If default risk and marketability risk are stable, they have an insignificant effect on price behavior because they affect only the prevailing *levels* of yields. In contrast, interest rate risk and purchasing power risk can have dramatic effects on the price behavior of an obligation over time, because interest rate risk is a response of bond prices to changes in market interest rates, while purchasing power (inflation) risk is a major factor causing changes in market interest rates. Similarly, exchange rate risk can have a major impact on your final return subsequent to the return in the domestic market; it can either enhance the return if your currency has been strong relative to the foreign currency during your holding period, or detract from your return if your domestic currency has been weak.

ALTERNATIVE INVESTMENT VEHICLES

The numerous sectors that exist within the bond market are characterized by fundamentally different issuers, which include the federal governments and government agencies, municipalities, corporations, and international bonds by these issuers. This section is a brief review of some of the popular issues available in these market sectors. Within each sector the discussion will consider what is available in four major bond markets: the United States, Japan, Germany, and the United Kingdom.

DOMESTIC GOVERNMENT ISSUES

UNITED STATES. As indicated in Table 10.2, the dominant sector of the fixed-income market in the United States is U.S. Treasury obligations. Acting on behalf of the U.S. government, and with the backing of its full faith and credit, the U.S. Treasury issues Treasury bills (T-bills), which are for less than one year, and long-term obligations in one of two forms: government notes, which have maturities of ten years or less; and Treasury bonds, with maturities of more than ten years (current maximum maturities go to about 25 years). Treasury obligations come in denominations of $1,000 and $10,000, although a few older issues carry $500 par values and are either in registered or bearer form. The interest income from the U.S. government securities is subject to federal income tax but exempt from state and local levies. Such obligations are popular because of their credit quality and substantial liquidity.

Short-term T-bills differ from notes and bonds in terms of how the payments are made. Treasury bills are sold at a discount from par to provide the desired yield (they are the same as zero coupon bonds, since the return is the difference between the purchase price and the par at maturity). In contrast, government notes and bonds carry semiannual coupons that specify the nominal yield of the obligation.

Government notes and bonds have some unusual features that should be noted. First, the deferred call feature on Treasury issues is very long and is generally measured relative to the maturity date of the issue rather than from date of issue—that is, they cannot be called until five years prior to the final maturity date. Also, certain government issues provide a tax break to investors because they can be used, at par, to pay federal estate taxes. Therefore, an investor can acquire a Treasury bond at a substantial discount, which his estate can use at par to pay estate taxes. Such bonds are called *flower bonds*. Although new flower bonds can no longer be issued, there are still approximately five such issues available in the market. Most of these carry 2¾ to 4½ percent coupons and have maturities that range between 1990 and 1998. The lower coupon causes a better price discount and more assurance of price appreciation at "time of departure." Recent estate tax law changes that have increased the size of an estate exempt from taxes have reduced the demand for such issues, while the available supply has declined, because when these flower bonds are used, they are retired by the government. Therefore, prices have been maintained, and the yields on these bonds are consistently below those of other treasury issues of comparable maturity. As an example, during 1988, when most Treasury bonds were yielding between 8 and 9 percent, these flower bonds were yielding about 4 to 5 percent.

JAPAN.[20] The second largest bond market in the world is Japan's. It is controlled by the Japanese government and the Bank of Japan (Japanese Central Bank). Japanese government bonds present an attractive investment vehicle for those favoring the Japanese yen, because the quality is equal to that of U.S. Treasury securities (they are guaranteed by the government of Japan) and they are very liquid. There are three maturity segments: medium-term (2, 3, or 4 years), long-term (10 years), and super-long (private placements for 15 and 20 years). Bonds are issued in both registered and bearer form, although registered bonds may always be converted to bearer bonds by presenting the security to the registrar at the Bank of Japan.

Long-term bonds are authorized by the Ministry of Finance and issued monthly by the Bank of Japan through an underwriting syndicate consisting of major financial institutions, while medium-term bonds are issued monthly through a competitive auction system similar to that of U.S. Treasury bonds. Most super-long bonds are sold through private placement to a small number of financial institutions. These government bonds possess the highest liquidity of all Japanese bonds. They account for more than half of the total bonds outstanding in the Tokyo bond market and over 80 percent of total bond trading volume in Japan. Notably, at least 50 percent of the trading in government bonds will be in the so-called *benchmark*

[20] This discussion benefited from, "International Bond Handbook," (London: James Capel & Co., 1987); Nicholas Sargan, Kermit L. Schoenhotz, Steven Blitz, and Sahar Elhabashi, "Trading Patterns in the Japanese Government Bond Market," (New York: Salomon Brothers, 1986); and Aron Viner, *Inside Japanese Financial Markets* (Homewood, Ill.: Dow Jones-Irwin, 1988).

issue of the time. The selection of the benchmark issue is made from among ten-year coupon bonds (e.g., as of late 1988 the benchmark issue was #105, a 5 percent coupon bond maturing in December 1997). This designation was done in order to assist smaller financial institutions in their trading of government bonds. Such a specification ensured that these institutions would have a liquid market in this particular security. As noted, the benchmark issue enjoys a very liquid market and accounts for about 50 percent of total trading in all Japanese government bonds originally issued with ten-year maturities (the comparable most active bond within a class in the United States accounts for only about 10 percent of the volume). This bond often yields as much as 50 or 60 basis points below other comparable Japanese government bonds, reflecting its superior marketability (in the U.S. market, the most liquid bond sells at a yield differential of only 10 basis points). The benchmark issue changes over time as a designated issue matures or simply because of a decision by the Bank of Japan in consultation with the big-four securities houses. Given this differential in yield and liquidity, institutions that are interested in buying and holding versus trading, acquire the non-benchmark issues for the higher yield but also take these issues out of circulation, ensuring that they will not be traded and confirming the lack of liquidity.

Japanese government bonds are quoted and traded net of accrued interest on the Tokyo, Osaka, and Nagoya Stock Exchanges, although most trading is conducted through the over-the-counter market. New issues are not listed on one of the exchanges until 40 days after the issue date. Interest is paid semiannually and is accrued based on actual days in a 365-day year. Settlement normally takes place on the tenth, twentieth, or the last day of the month, although this can be negotiated. Overseas investors require either a settlement agent in Tokyo or a domestic bank account with an institution that maintains a custodial arrangement with the bank in Japan.

GERMANY.[21] The third largest bond market in the world is the West German market, although the government segment of this market is relatively small. Specifically, as indicated in Table 10.2, approximately three-quarters of domestic deutschemark bonds are issued by the major commercial banks, while the federal government (Federal Republic of Germany) issues the remainder through the Deutsche Bundesbank (the German Central Bank). The capital market in Germany is dominated by these commercial banks because there is no formal distinction between investment, merchant, or commercial banks as there is in the United States and the United Kingdom. As a result, industrial financing is primarily through bank loans, and these banks in turn raise their capital through public bond issues. Therefore, domestic bonds issued by industrial corporations are substantially less than 1 percent of the total.

---

[21] This discussion and all subsequent discussions on the German bond market benefited from, Graham Bishop, "Deutschemark" in *Salomon Brothers International Bond Manual*, 2d ed. (New York: Salomon Brothers, 1987).

The domestic instruments that non-resident investors will find most attractive are promissory notes, medium-term notes, and long-term bonds issued by the federal government, its agencies, and the major banks. Bonds issued by the Federal Republic of Germany, referred to as *Bund* bonds, are issued in amounts up to DM 4 billion (4 billion deutschemarks) with a minimum denomination of DM 100. Original maturities are normally 10 or 12 years, although 30-year bonds have recently been issued.

While these bunds are issued as bearer bonds, individual bonds do not exist. A global bond is issued and held in safekeeping within the German Securities Clearing System (the Kassenverein). Contract notes confirming the terms and ownership of each issue are then distributed to individual investors and sales are effected by the use of these contract notes. Bonds are issued through a fixed quota system by the Federal Bond Syndicate, which includes the Bundesbank and 17 banks that include certain resident branches of foreign banks. These government bunds have the highest liquidity, as the Bundesbank stands ready to make markets at all times. They are also considered to be the highest credit quality available in Germany since they are guaranteed by the federal government.

Bunds are quoted net of accrued interest and as a percent of par on German Stock Exchanges. An official benchmark price is determined daily on the exchange floor by the Bundesbank at the level at which the dealers can realize the largest turnover as determined by their existing order backlog. Market-makers subsequently use this benchmark level as the base from which to trade.

Although listed on the exchanges, government bonds are primarily traded over-the-counter. Interest is paid annually and accrues according to a 30-day month and a 360-day year. International settlement terms are negotiable, but execution normally occurs seven days after the trade date through the domestic clearing system. Because there are no physical deliveries, investors must have a settlement agent in Germany or a Euroclear account.

THE UNITED KINGDOM.[22]   The U.K. government bond market changed dramatically on October 17, 1986 (the Big Bang). The roles of jobbers and brokers changed so that broker-dealers could act as principals or agents with a negotiated commission structure. In addition, the number of primary dealers in the "Gilt" market was expanded from 7 Gilt jobbers to 27 primary dealers.

A substantial variety of maturities is available in this market, ranging from short gilts with maturities of less than 5 years to medium gilts (5 to 15 years) to long gilts with maturities of 15 years and longer. These government bonds either have a fixed redemption date or a range of dates with redemption at the option of the government after giving appropriate notice. Alternatively, some bonds were redeemable on a given date or at

---

[22] This discussion and all subsequent descriptions of the U.K. market benefited from Ian C. Collier, "An Introduction to the Gilt-Edged Market," (London: James Capel & Co., 1987); and Jeffrey Hanna and John Y. Campbell, "Sterling" in *International Bond Manual* (New York: Salomon Brothers, 1980).

any time afterwards at the option of the government. Currently, these bonds have generally passed their first option date, and because of the low coupon they have not been redeemed and very likely will not be redeemed in the near future. These bonds are normally registered, although bearer delivery is available. New issues are made in allotment-letter form and are bearer bonds until the registration date, which is about four weeks after tender (original issue).

Gilts are issued through the Bank of England (British Central Bank) using the tender method, whereby prospective purchasers tender at a price at which they hope to be allotted bonds. The price cannot be less than the minimum tender price stated in the prospectus. If the issue is over-subscribed, allotments are made first to those submitting the highest tenders and continue until a price is reached where only a partial allotment is required to fully subscribe the issue. The lowest price at which partial allotment is made is the price paid by all successful allottees.

These issues are extremely liquid, because the size of the market and the size of the individual issues are quite large. They are also highly rated, since the interest and principal payments are guaranteed by the British government. All gilts are quoted and traded net of accrued interest on the London Stock Exchange. Interest is paid semiannually and accrues according to actual days in a 365-day year. These bonds typically go ex-interest payment about five weeks before the coupon date. Unless otherwise specified, gilt transactions are settled "for cash" the following business day through the physical exchange of the bonds, which are cleared on the same day. Gilts are normally registered at the Bank of England in the name of the holder and are available in certificate form ten days from the time of settlement. Most overseas clients prefer to keep gilt-edged bonds (whether they are registered or bearer bonds) at their bank or with their broker in London in order to minimize settlement problems.

GOVERNMENT AGENCY ISSUES

In addition to pure government bonds, the federal government in each country can establish agencies that have the authority to issue their own bonds. The size and importance of these agencies differ among countries. They are a large and growing sector of the bond market in the United States, a much smaller and stable component of the bond market in Japan and Germany, and nonexistent in the United Kingdom.

UNITED STATES. Agency securities are obligations issued by the U.S. government through various political subdivisions, such as a government agency or a government-sponsored corporation. While there are six government-sponsored enterprises, there are over two dozen federal agencies. Table 10.4 lists selected characteristics of the more popular government-sponsored and federal agency obligations, including the recent size of the market, typical minimum denominations, tax features, and the availability of bond quotes.[23] (The issues in the table are only meant to be represen-

---

[23] We will no longer distinguish between federal agency and government-sponsored obligations; instead, the term *agency* shall apply to either type of issue.

tative of the wide variety of different obligations that are available.) Generally, agency issues are similar to those of other issuers; that is, interest is usually paid semiannually, and the minimum denominations vary between $1,000 and $10,000. These obligations are not direct issues of the Treasury, yet they carry the full faith and credit of the U.S. government. Moreover, unlike government obligations, some of the issues are subject to state and local income tax, while others are exempt.[24]

One agency issue offers particularly attractive investment opportunities: *GNMA (Ginnie Mae) pass-through certificates,* which are obligations of the Government National Mortgage Association.[25] These bonds represent an undivided interest in a pool of federally insured mortgages. The bondholders receive monthly payments from Ginnie Mae that include both principal and interest, because they represent a "pass through" of the mortgage payments made by the original borrower (the mortgagee) to Ginnie Mae.

These pass-through securities carry coupons that are somewhat related to the interest charged on the pool of mortgages. The portion of the cash flow that represents return of capital (i.e., the principal part of the payment) is tax-free, while the interest income is subject to federal, state, and local taxes. The issues have been marketed in minimum denominations of $25,000 with maturities of 25 to 30 years but an average life of only 12 years, because as pooled mortgages are paid off, payments and prepayments are passed through to the investor. Therefore, unlike other issues, the monthly payment is not fixed.

Notably, these securities are modified pass-throughs, since they are the obligation of the issuing body, the Government National Mortgage Association, and not the ultimate borrower (the homeowner). Thus, the cash flow to the mortgage pool is quite distinct from the obligation of Ginnie Mae and is totally separate from the cash flow to the bond investor. Moreover, the rates of return are relatively attractive compared to corporates, and most of the return is tax-free in the early years because, as noted, a part of the regular payment is a return of principal, and subsequently there are prepayments as homeowners pay off the mortgage when they sell their homes. A major disadvantage of GNMA issues is that they are depleted by prepayments and do not have a maturity value in the normal sense of the word.

JAPAN. The agencies in Japan are referred to as *government associate organizations.* As indicated in Table 10.2, they account for about 7 to 8 percent of the total Japanese bond market. Within this agency market there is a substantial amount of public debt, but almost twice as much of this

---

[24] Federal National Mortgage Association (Fannie Mae) debentures, for example, are subject to state and local income tax, whereas the interest income from Federal Home Loan Bank bonds is exempt. In fact, a few issues are even exempt from *federal* income tax as well—e.g., public housing bonds.

[25] For a further discussion of mortgage-backed securities, see Donald Moffitt, "Ginnie Mae Pass-Throughs Offer High Yields Plus Safety for Cautious Savers," *The Wall Street Journal,* September 18, 1978, 38; and *Mortgage-Backed Bond and Pass-Through Symposium* (Charlottesville, Va.: Financial Analysts Research Foundation, 1980).

TABLE 10.4
Agency Issues: Selected Characteristics

TYPE OF SECURITY	MINIMUM DENOMINATION	FORM
Government-sponsored Federal Farm Credit Banks Consolidated systemwide notes	$ 50,000	BE
Consolidated systemwide bonds	$ 5,000	BE
	$ 1,000	BE
Federal Home Loan Bank Consolidated discount notes	$100,000	BE
Consolidated bonds	$ 10,000[a]	B and BE
Federal Home Loan Mortgage Corporation Debentures	$ 10,000[a]	BE
Participation certificates	$100,000	R
Federal National Mortgage Association Discount notes	$ 50,000[a]	B
Debentures	$ 10,000[a]	B or BE
Government National Mortgage Association Mortgage-backed bonds	$ 25,000	B and R
Modified pass-through	$ 25,000[a]	R

Notes: Form-B = Bearer
R = Registered
BE = Book-entry form
Debt issues sold subsequent to December 31, 1982, must be in registered form.
[a]Minimum purchase with increments in $5,000.

LIFE OF ISSUE	TAX STATUS	HOW INTEREST IS EARNED
5 to 365 days	Federal: Taxable State: Exempt Local: Exempt	Discount actual/ 360-day year
6 and 9 months	Federal: Taxable State: Exempt Local: Exempt	Interest payable at maturity; 360-day basis
13 months to 15 years	Federal: Taxable State: Exempt Local: Exempt	Semiannual interest
30 to 360 days	Federal: Taxable State: Exempt Local: Exempt	Discount actual/ 360 days
1 to 20 years	Federal: Taxable State: Exempt Local: Exempt	Semiannual interest; 360-day year
18 to 30 years	Federal: Taxable State: Taxable Local: Taxable	Semiannual interest; 360-day year
30 years (12-year average life)	Federal: Taxable State: Taxable Local: Taxable	Monthly interest and principal payments
30 to 360 days	Federal: Taxable State: Taxable Local: Taxable	Discount actual/ 360 days
1 to 30 years	Federal: Taxable State: Taxable Local: Taxable	Semiannual interest; 360-day year
1 to 25 years	Federal: Taxable State: Taxable Local: Taxable	Semiannual interest; 360-day year
12 to 40 years (12-year average)	Federal: Taxable State: Taxable Local: Taxable	Monthly interest and principal payments

continued

TABLE 10.4 *continued*

TYPE OF SECURITY	MINIMUM DENOMINATION	FORM
Student Loan Marketing Association Discount notes	$100,000	B
Notes	$ 10,000	R
Floating-rate notes	$ 10,000ᵃ	R
Tennessee Valley Authority (TVA)	$ 1,000	R and B
U.S. Postal Service	$ 10,000	R and B

Source: *United States Government Securities* (New York: Merrill Lynch Government Securities, Inc., 1985); *Handbook of Securities of the United States Government and Federal Agencies*, 31st ed. (New York: First Boston Corporation, 1984).

particular debt is privately placed with major financial institutions. The procedure for the issuance of the public agency debt is similar to that for the government sector.

GERMANY. The agency market in Germany comprises about 4 percent of the public debt. The major agencies are the Federal Railway, which issues *Bahn,* or Bundesbahn bonds, and the federal post office, which issues *Post,* or Bundespost bonds. These Bahns and Posts are issued up to 2 billion DMs. The issue procedure is similar to the one for regular government bonds. It is through a fixed-quota system by the Federal Bond Syndicate. Although Bahns and Posts are less liquid than government Bunds, since the market is only about 10 percent as large as the government market, the market is still quite liquid. These agency issues are implicitly, though not explicitly, guaranteed by the government.

UNITED KINGDOM. As shown in Table 10.2, there are no agency issues in the United Kingdom.

MUNICIPAL OBLIGATIONS

Municipal bonds are issued by states, counties, cities, and other political subdivisions. Again, the size of the municipal market (referred to as local authority in the United Kingdom) varies markedly among countries. In the

LIFE OF ISSUE	TAX STATUS	HOW INTEREST IS EARNED
Out to 1 year	Federal: Taxable State: Exempt Local: Exempt	Discount actual/ 360 days
3 to 10 years	Federal: Taxable State: Exempt Local: Exempt	Semiannual interest; 360-day year
6 months to 10 years	Federal: Taxable State: Exempt Local: Exempt	Interest rate adjusted weekly to an increment over the average auction rate on 91-day Treasury bills and payable quarterly
5 to 25 years	Federal: Taxable State: Exempt Local: Exempt	Semiannual interest; 360-day year
25 years	Federal: Taxable State: Exempt Local: Exempt	Semiannual interest; 360-day year

United States it is about 20 percent of the total market, compared to about 3 percent in Japan and Germany and less than 1 percent in the United Kingdom.

UNITED STATES. Basically, municipalities in the United States issue two distinct types of bonds: general obligation bonds and revenue issues. *General obligation bonds (GOs)* are essentially backed by the full faith and credit of the issuer and its taxing power. *Revenue bonds,* in turn, are serviced by the income generated from specific revenue-producing projects of the municipality, for example, bridges, toll roads, municipal coliseums, and waterworks. Revenue bonds generally provide higher returns than GOs because of the higher default risk. Specifically, should a municipality fail to generate sufficient income from a project used to secure a revenue bond, it has absolutely no legal debt service obligation until the income becomes sufficient.

It has also been noted that municipal bonds tend to be issued on a serial basis so that the issuer's cash flow requirements will be steady over the life of the obligation. Therefore, the principal portion of the total debt service requirement generally begins at a fairly low level and builds up over the life of the obligation. In contrast, revenue obligations are mostly term issues, so the major portion of the issue's total principal value is not due until the final maturity date or last few dates.

The most important feature of municipal obligations is that the interest payments are exempt from federal income tax, as well as from taxes in the locality and state in which the obligation was issued. This means that people in different income brackets find municipal bonds to be of varying attractiveness. You can convert the *tax-free yield* of a municipal to an equivalent *taxable yield* using the following equation:

$$TY = \frac{i}{(1-t)},$$

where

TY = equivalent taxable yield

i = coupon rate of the municipal obligations

t = marginal tax rate of the investor.

An investor in the 35 percent marginal tax bracket would find that a 7 percent municipal yield is equivalent to a 10.77 percent fully taxable yield according to the following calculations:

$$TY = \frac{.07}{(1-.35)} = .1077.$$

Since the tax-free yield is the major motive for investing in municipal bonds, an investor's marginal tax rate is a primary concern in determining whether municipals are a viable investment vehicle. As a rough rule of thumb, using the tax rates forthcoming in 1989, an investor must be in the 28 to 30 percent tax bracket before municipal bonds offer yields that are competitive with those from fully taxable bonds, because municipal yields are lower than returns available from fully taxable corporate issues. However, while the interest is tax-free, any capital gains are not.

MUNICIPAL BOND GUARANTEES. Another unusual and growing feature of the U.S. municipal bond market are *municipal bond guarantees* that provide the bondholder with assurance of payment by a third party other than the issuer. The third party provides an additional source of collateral. The guarantees are actually a form of insurance placed on the bond at date of issue and are irrevocable over the life of the issue. The issuer purchases the insurance for the benefit of the investor, and the municipality benefits from the lower issue costs and increased marketability.

As of 1987 approximately 25 percent of all new municipal bond issues were insured. There are four private bond insurance firms: the first is a consortium of four large insurance companies that market their product under the name of Municipal Bond Insurance Association (MBIA). The second is a subsidiary of a large Milwaukee-based private insurer known as American Municipal Bond Insurance Corporation (AMBIC). The two others are Bond Investors Guaranty Insurance Company (BIG) and Financial Guaranty Insurance Corporation (FGIC). These firms will insure either general obligation or revenue bonds. To qualify for private bond insurance, the issue must carry an S&P rating of BBB or better. The rating agencies have indicated that they will give an AAA rating to any bond insured by AMBIC or MBIA. Issues with these private guarantees have generally enjoyed a more active secondary market and lower required yields.[26]

CORPORATE BONDS

Again, the importance of corporate bonds varies across countries. In the United States the absolute dollar value of corporate bonds is substantial, and it has grown overall and as a percent of long-term capital for U.S. firms (this is discussed in Chapter 13). At the same time, corporate debt as a percent of all debt in the United States has declined from 18 percent to 12 percent because of the explosive increase in government debt due to the large government deficits. In Japan the pure corporate sector is small and has declined, while bank debentures comprise a significant segment (over 20 percent). In Germany the pure corporate sector is almost nonexistent, but bank debentures used to provide funds for corporate loans are the largest segment overall. Finally, in the United Kingdom, the proportion has remained in the 5 to 6 percent range.

UNITED STATES. Utilities dominate the corporate market in the United States. The other important segments include industrials (which rank second to utilities and include everything from mining firms to multinational oils to retail concerns), rail and transportation issues, and financial issues. This market includes debentures, first-mortgage issues, convertible obligations, bonds with warrants, subordinated debenture bonds, income bonds (similar to municipal revenue bonds), collateral trust bonds (typically backed by financial assets), equipment trust certificates, and mortgage-backed bonds.

If we ignore equity-related securities, the preceding list of obligations varies mainly according to the type of collateral behind the bond. Terms of semiannual interest payments, sinking funds, and a single maturity date are similar. Maturities range from 25 to 40 years, with public utilities generally on the longer end and industrials preferring the 25- to 30-year range. Nearly all corporate bonds carry deferred call provisions that range from 5 to 10 years. The deferment period tends to vary directly with the level of interest rates (i.e., with higher interest rates an issue will probably carry a seven- to ten-year deferment). On the other hand, *corporate notes*, with maturities of five to seven years, are generally noncallable. Notes become popular during periods of higher interest rates because issuers prefer to avoid long-term obligations during such periods.

Generally, the average yields for industrial bonds are generally the lowest, followed by yields on utility bonds, with yields on rail and transportation bonds generally being the highest. The differential in yield be-

---

[26] For a discussion of the bond insurance industry, see Maureen Bailey, "Triple-A Rating," *Barron's*, December 31, 1979: 13–15; and D. S. Kidwell, E. H. Sorensen, and J. M. Wachowicz, "Estimating the Signalling Benefits of Debt Insurance: The Case of Municipal Bonds," *Journal of Financial and Quantitative Analysis* 22, no. 3 (September 1987): 299–313.

tween utilities and industrials is simply a matter of demand for loanable funds. Because utilities have the largest supply of bonds, yields on these securities must rise to attract the necessary demand.

Some corporate bonds have unique features or security arrangements that will be discussed in the following subsections.[27]

MORTGAGE BONDS. If a security is described as a *mortgage bond,* it means that the issuer has granted to the bondholder a first-mortgage lien on some piece of property or possibly all of the firm's property. This provides greater security to the bondholder and a lower interest rate for the issuing firm. Additional mortgage bonds can be issued, assuming certain protective covenants related to earnings or assets are met by the issuer.

COLLATERAL TRUST BONDS. As an alternative to pledging fixed assets or property, it is possible to pledge stocks, bonds, or notes as collateral, and the bonds secured by these assets are termed *collateral trust bonds.* These assets are held by a trustee for the benefit of the bondholder.

EQUIPMENT TRUST CERTIFICATES. Issued by railroads (the biggest issuers), airlines, and other transportation firms, equipment trust certificates' proceeds are used to purchase equipment (freight cars, railroad engines, and airplanes) that serves as collateral. Maturities range from 1 to about 15 years. The fairly short maturities are popular because of the collateral, which is subject to substantial wear and tear and tends to deteriorate rapidly.

Equipment trust certificates appeal to investors because of their attractive yields and low default record. Although they lack the visibility and acceptance of other corporate bonds, they typically have liquid secondary markets.

COLLATERALIZED MORTGAGE OBLIGATIONS (CMO).[28] Earlier we discussed mortgage bonds backed by a pool of mortgages wherein the bondholder received a proportionate share of principal and interest paid on the mortgages in the pool. You will recall that the pass-through monthly payments are necessarily both interest and principal, and the bondholder is subject to early retirement if the mortgagees prepay for any reason (e.g., if the house is sold or mortgage refinanced). As a result, if you acquired these bonds you would necessarily receive monthly payments (which may not be ideal), and you would be uncertain about the size and length of the payments.

---

[27] This discussion of secured bonds benefited from Frank J. Fabozzi, Harry Sauvain, Richard Wilson, and John Ritchie, "Corporate Bonds," in *The Handbook of Fixed Income Securities,* 2d ed., edited by Frank J. Fabozzi and Irving Pollack (Homewood, Ill.: Dow Jones-Irwin, 1987).

[28] For a detailed discussion, see Janet Spratlin and Paul Vianna, "An Investor's Guide to CMOs," New York: Solomon Brothers, 1986; and Gregory J. Parseghian, "Collateralized Mortgage Obligations," in *The Handbook of Fixed Income Securities,* 2d ed., edited by Frank Fabozzi and Irving Pollack (Homewood, Ill.: Dow Jones-Irwin, 1987).

Collateralized mortgage obligations (CMOs) are a relatively new instrument developed to offset some of the foregoing potential problems. The first CMO was issued by the Federal Home Loan Mortgage Corporation (FHLMC) in June 1983, and at present the total issuance exceeds $50 billion. The main innovation of the CMO instrument is the segmentation of the mortgage cash flows that allows the irregular mortgage cash flows to become high-quality, short-, medium-, and long-term mortgage collateralized bonds. Specifically, CMO investors own bonds that are collateralized by a pool of mortgages or by a portfolio of mortgage-backed securities. The bonds are serviced with the cash flows from the mortgage collateral. Rather than the straight pass-through arrangement, the CMO substitutes a *sequential distribution process* that creates a series of bonds with varying maturities to appeal to a wider range of investors. The prioritized distribution process is as follows:

- Several classes of bonds are issued against a pool of mortgages, which are the collateral. Assuming the typical four classes of bonds, the first three (e.g., Class A, B, C) would pay interest at their stated rates, beginning at the issue date, and the fourth class would be an accrual bond (referred to as a *Z bond*).
- The cash flows from the underlying mortgages are applied first to pay the interest on the first three classes of bonds and then to retire these bonds.
- *The classes of bonds are retired sequentially.* All principal payments are directed first to the shortest-maturity (class A) bonds. When those bonds are completely retired, all principal retirement is directed to the next shortest-maturity (class B) bonds. The process continues until all the classes have been paid off.
- During the early periods, the accrual bonds (class Z) will not receive any interest, but the interest will accrue to the principal, while the cash flow is used to pay interest and retire the other classes. Subsequently, all remaining cash flows are used to pay off the accrued interest, pay any current interest, and retire the Z bonds.

This prioritized sequential pattern means that the A-class bonds are fairly short-term, and each subsequent class is a little longer term until the Z class, which is like a zero coupon bond for the initial years and is generally a longer-term security.

Besides creating bonds that pay interest in a more normal pattern (quarterly or semiannually) and have more predictable maturities, these are very high quality securities (AAA) because of the collateralized structure and the quality of the collateral. In order to obtain an AAA rating, CMOs are structured to ensure that the underlying mortgages will always generate enough cash to support the bonds issued, even under the most conservative prepayment and reinvestment rates. The fact is, most of them are overcollateralized. Further, the credit risk of the collateral is minimal, since most are backed by mortgages guaranteed by a federal agency (GNMA, FNMA) or guaranteed by the FHLMC. Those mortgages that are not backed by agencies carry private insurance for principal and interest and mortgage insurance. Notably, even with this AAA rating, the yield on these CMOs has typically been higher than on AA industrials, which has, of course, contributed to their popularity and growth.

CERTIFICATES FOR AUTOMOBILE RECEIVABLES (CARS).[29]   A rapidly expanding segment of the securities market is that of *asset-backed securities,* which involve *securitizing debt.* This is an important concept, since it substantially increases the liquidity of these individual debt instruments, whether they be individual mortgages, car loans, or credit card debt. *Certificates for Automobile Receivables (CARs),* which clearly dominate the market beyond mortgages, are securities collateralized by loans made to individuals to finance the purchase of cars. Auto loans are self-amortizing, with monthly payments and relatively short maturities (two to five years).

These auto loans can either be *direct loans* from a lending institution or *indirect loans* that are originated by an auto dealer and sold to the ultimate lender. CARs have mainly been backed by indirect loans, but the prospectus will indicate the division between direct and indirect loans and what percent of indirect loans have recourse to the dealer. Given the collateral, CARs have a fixed coupon, typically require monthly payment of interest and principal, and have expected weighted average lives of one to three years with fixed maturities of three to five years (again, the expected actual life is shorter than the specified maturity because of early payoffs when cars are sold or traded in). The prepayments do not vary with interest rates but are mainly due to sales or trade-ins. Given the cash flows, they are comparable to short-term corporate debt and provide a significant yield premium over General Motors Acceptance Corporation (GMAC) commercial paper, which is the most liquid short-term corporate alternative. The popularity of these collateralized securities indicates the potential for additional collateralized securities using other assets and/or other debt instruments.

VARIABLE-RATE NOTES.   Available in Europe for decades, *variable-rate notes* were not introduced in this country until the mid-1970s. They became popular while interest rates were high. The typical variable-rate note possesses two unique features:

1. After the first 6 to 18 months of the issue's life—during which a minimum rate is often guaranteed—the coupon rate floats, so that every 6 months it is pegged at a certain amount, usually 1 percent above a stipulated short-term rate (normally defined as the preceding three weeks' average 90-day T-bill rate).
2. After the first year or two, the notes are redeemable at par, at the holder's option, usually at six-month intervals.

---

[29] This subsection benefited from Thomas Delehanty and Michael Waldman, *Certificates for Automobile Receivables (CARS)* (New York: Salomon Brothers, 1986).

Thus, such notes represent a long-term commitment on the part of the borrower yet provide the lender with all the characteristics of a short-term obligation. They are available to investors in minimum denominations of $1,000 and could be attractive to yield-conscious, liquidity-oriented investors. However, while the six-month redemption feature provides liquidity, the variable rates can subject the issue to wide swings in semi-annual coupons.

ZERO COUPON AND DEEP DISCOUNT BONDS. The typical corporate long-term bond has a coupon and maturity, and the value of the bond is the present value of the stream of cash flows (interest and principal) discounted at the required *yield to maturity (YTM)*. Alternatively, one can conceive of a fixed-income security that does not have any coupons or has coupons that are below the market rate at the time of issue. Such securities are referred to as *zero coupon bonds* or *minicoupon bonds* or *original-issue, deep discount bonds (OID)*. A zero coupon discount bond promises to pay a stipulated amount at a future maturity date, but it does not promise to make any interim interest payments. Therefore, the price is the present value of the principal payment at the maturity date, and the return on the bond is the difference between what is paid at the time of issuance and the principal payment at maturity.

Consider a zero coupon, $10,000 par value bond with a 20-year maturity. If the required rate of return on bonds of equal maturity and quality is 8 percent, and assuming semiannual discounting, the initial selling price would be $2,082.89, since the present value factor at 8 percent compounded semiannually for 20 years is 0.208289. Note that from the time of purchase to the point of maturity, the investor would not receive any cash flow from the firm. For tax purposes the investor must pay taxes on the *implied* interest on the bond, although no cash is received. Because an investor subject to taxes would experience severe negative cash flows during the life of the bond, these bonds are primarily of interest to investment accounts not subject to taxes, such as pensions, IRAs, or Keogh accounts.[30]

A modified form of these bonds is the original-issue discount (OID) bond, wherein the coupon is set substantially below the prevailing market rate (e.g., a 5 percent coupon on a bond when market rates are 12 percent) so the bond is issued at a deep discount from par value. Under the new tax law, taxes are paid on the implied 12 percent return rather than the nominal 5 percent, so the cash flow disadvantage of the zero coupon bonds, though lessened, remains.

JAPAN. The corporate bond market in Japan is composed of two components: (1) bonds issued by the typical industrial firm or utility and (2) bonds issued by banks to derive capital for loans to corporations. As noted earlier, in connection with Table 10.2, the pure non-bank corporate bond

---

[30] These bonds will be discussed further in Chapter 19 in the section on duration and immunization. The price volatility of these bonds in IRA accounts is discussed in Randall Smith, "Zero Coupon Bonds' Price Swings Jolt Investors Looking for Security," *The Wall Street Journal*, June 1, 1984, 19.

sector was fairly small in 1981 (7.2 percent of the total) and has declined in relative size over time to the point where it was less than 4 percent of the total in 1987. In contrast, the dollar amount of bank debentures has increased over time and maintains its relative position of about 20 percent of the total.

Corporate bonds are monitored by the *Kisaikai,* which is the council for the regulation of bond issues. The council is composed of 22 bond-related banks and seven major securities companies and operates under the authority of the Ministry of Finance and the Bank of Japan. It determines bond-issuing procedures and practices, including the issuing conditions of straight corporate debt. Specifically, the Kisaikai fixes the coupons on bonds, and these coupons are linked to coupons on long-term government bonds to preclude any competition with the government bond market.

Because of numerous bankruptcies during the 1930s depression, the government mandated that all corporate debt would be secured, and this was enforced by the Kisaikai. There was pressure by the corporations and the securities firms in the late 1970s and early 1980s to relax these requirements. Prior to specific allowances, domestic Japanese firms began issuing convertible bonds that were not bound by the collateral rule. In addition, foreign firms began issuing Euro-yen bonds that were likewise not restricted, and eventually domestic firms began to issue straight debt in the Euro-yen market. Finally, early in 1987 a large number of firms were permitted to issue unsecured debt at home. This allowance was broadened in late 1987 and will almost certainly be abolished during 1988–1989.

The issuance of unsecured debt has led to the birth of a new line of business in Japan—rating agencies. With completely secured debt there was no need for such firms. The Japan Bond Research Institute was established in 1979 to rate convertible issues. In 1981 Mikuni's Credit Rating Company was established, followed by additional firms in 1985 and 1986: Japan Credit Rating Agency, Ltd.; Nippon Investors Service, Inc.; and Moody's Japan K.K. (a subsidiary of Moody's Investors Service, Inc.).

The straight corporate debt market in Japan is divided into two major segments: bonds issued by electric power supply companies, and bonds issued by all other corporations. The nine electric power supply firms receive preferential treatment because they are regulated public utilities. As a result, about 75 percent of all domestic straight-debt issues are public utility bonds. Other industrial bonds are sold in the domestic market but also are sold in the Eurobond market.

The Ministry of Finance specifies minimum corporate requirements and minimum issuing requirements, including that net corporate assets must exceed 6 billion yen. Also, the Ministry controls the *issuance system* of who can issue bonds and when they can be issued. In addition, lead managers are predetermined in accordance with a *lead-manager rotating system* that assures balance among the big-four securities firms (Nomura, Nikko, Daiwa, and Yamaichi Capital Management).

One reason for the relative decline of the domestic corporate bond market lies in the very restrictive regulations. As of 1985 about 90 percent of all industrial straight-bond issues were sold outside Japan—that is, they were Euro-yen issues. Without a change in regulations, the trend will probably continue.

The substantial issuance of bank debentures is a function of the banking system in Japan, which is segmented into several rigidly defined components including

- Commercial banks (13 big-city banks and 64 regional banks)
- Long-term credit banks (3)
- Mutual loan and savings banks (6)
- Specialized financial institutions.

During the postwar reconstruction, the three long-term credit banks (the Industrial Bank of Japan, the Long-Term Credit Bank of Japan, and the Nippon Credit Bank), the Norinchukin Bank (Central Cooperative Bank for Agriculture and Forestry), the Shako Chukin Bank (Central Bank for Commercial and Industrial Cooperatives), and the Bank of Tokyo were permitted to obtain funding by issuing medium- and long-term debentures at rates above yields on government bonds. These funds were used to make mortgage loans to firms in the industrial sector to rebuild plant and equipment. Currently these financial institutions sell five-year coupon debentures and one-year discount debentures directly to individual and institutional investors. The long-term credit banks are not allowed to take deposits and thus depend upon the sale of these debentures as a means to obtain funds. These bonds are traded in the OTC market.

GERMANY. In Germany there is likewise a combination sector in corporates—pure corporates and banks. Here the contrast is even larger, since the non-bank corporates are almost nonexistent while the bank sector (bank bonds) is over 60 percent of the total bond market.

Bank bonds are bearer bonds that may be issued in collateralized or uncollateralized form, with the largest categories being mortgage and commercial bonds—although it is possible to use agricultural loans, industrial loans, and ship mortgages as collateral.

Mortgage bonds are collateralized fixed-income obligations of the issuing bank backed by the mortgage loans that are registered with a government-appointed trustee. Due to the supervision of these bonds and the mortgage loans, these bonds are of very high quality and are issued in bearer or registered form. The registered bonds are mainly sold to domestic institutions and cannot be listed on a stock exchange because they are not considered to be securities. Alternatively, the bearer bonds (which are transferred by book-entry) are sold in small denominations, traded on the exchanges, and enjoy an active secondary market among individual and foreign investors.

Communal bonds are subject to the same regulation and collateralization as mortgage bonds. The difference is that the collateral consists of loans to or guarantees by a West German public sector entity rather than a first mortgage. Possible borrowers or guarantors include the federal government, its agencies (federal railway or post office), federal states, and agencies of the European Economic Community (EEC). The credit quality of these loans is excellent. Mortgage and communal bonds are considered to have identical credit standing and trade at a narrow spread that often disappears.

Schuldscheindarlehen are private loan agreements between a borrower and a large investor (usually a bank) who makes the loan but who can (with the borrower's permission) sell it or divide it among several investors—that is, they are like a negotiable loan participation. All participants receive a copy of the loan agreement, and a letter of assignment gives the participant title to a share of principal and interest, although the bank acts as agent for the participants. These loan agreements, which come in various sizes, account for a substantial proportion of all funds raised in West Germany. While there is a large volume outstanding, the market is not very liquid, so they are basically designed for the investment of large sums to maturity.

INTERNATIONAL BONDS

Within each country there are two components of the international bond market. The first is *foreign bonds,* which are issues sold primarily in one country and currency by a borrower of a different nationality, such as U.S. dollar bonds sold by a Japanese firm in the United States (these are referred to as *Yankee bonds*). The second segment is *Eurobonds,* which are typically underwritten by international syndicates and sold in a number of national markets—for example, Eurodollar bonds are securities that are denominated in U.S. dollars, underwritten by an international syndicate, and sold to non–U.S. investors. As we will discuss, the relative size of these two markets varies by country.

UNITED STATES. As of the end of 1987, the Eurodollar bond market was much larger than the Yankee bond market (about $350 billion versus $50 billion). However, the Eurodollar bond market suffered a major setback during 1986 and 1987 due to the weakness of the dollar that created a desire for diversification.

As noted, Yankee bonds are securities issued by foreign firms who register with the SEC and borrow U.S. dollars—using issues underwritten by a U.S. syndicate for delivery in the United States. The secondary market for these is in the United States, and they pay interest semiannually. Over 60 percent of these bonds are issued by Canadian corporations. Yankee bonds typically have shorter maturities than U.S. domestic issues, and the call protection is generally longer, increasing their appeal.

The Eurodollar bond market is dominated by foreign investors, and the center of trading remains in London. The marketability of these bonds was improving until the slowdown during 1987. Eurodollar bonds pay interest annually, so you must adjust the yield calculation. You cannot use the standard procedure for U.S. securities that assumes semiannual compounding. The Eurodollar bond market comprises almost 50 percent of the total Eurobond market.

JAPAN. Prior to 1984 the Japanese international bond market was dominated (over 90 percent) by foreign bonds (referred to as *Samurai bonds*) compared to Euro-yen bonds. In 1985 the issuance requirements for Euro-yen bonds was liberalized for Japanese firms and for all firms. As a result, in 1985 the amount issued by the two forms (Samurai and Euro-yen) was about equal, but in 1986 the ratio was four-to-one in favor of Euro-yen bonds and the ratio grew to almost ten-to-one in 1987.

Samurai bonds are yen-denominated bonds issued by non-Japanese issuers and mainly sold in Japan. The market is a small portion of the total market and has limited liquidity, but the bonds have the advantage of freedom from withholding taxes. The market experienced very little growth during 1986 and 1987 in terms of yen, but substantial growth in U.S. dollar terms because of exchange rate changes.

Euro-yen bonds are yen-denominated bonds sold in markets outside Japan by international syndicates. As indicated, this market experienced substantial growth during 1985–1987 because of the more liberal issue requirements and also the favorable exchange rate movements (the exchange adjusted returns were over 30 percent a year in U.S. dollar terms).

GERMANY. All deutschemark bonds of foreign issuers can be considered Eurobonds, because the distinction between foreign bonds (DM-denominated bonds sold by non-German firms that are underwritten by domestic institutions) and Euro-DM bonds (bonds sold outside Germany and underwritten by international firms) is not important given its stable currency. Both sets of bonds share the same primary and secondary market procedures, are free of German taxes, and have similar yields.

A relatively recent innovation was the issuance of a Euro-DM bond secured by a Schuldscheindarlehen loan from one of the Federal states (Lander). Also, since 1985 they have issued Euro-DM floating-rate notes (FRN) fixed to various rates, including the DM London Inter-Bank Offered Rate (LIBOR).

UNITED KINGDOM. Foreign bonds in the United Kingdom are referred to as *bulldog bonds* and are sterling-denominated bonds issued by non-English issuers and sold in London. Euro-sterling bonds are sold in markets outside London by international syndicates. Similar to other countries, the total U.K. international market has become dominated by the Eurobond segment (Euro-sterling bonds). As of 1981 there were about twice as many Euro-sterling bonds outstanding as bulldogs. By 1986 the ratio had grown to almost five-to-one. In fact, during 1987 about $14 billion Euro-sterling bonds were issued and no bulldogs were issued (government restrictions on bulldogs implemented in early 1986 made borrowing in this sector very expensive). The procedure for issuing and trading these Euro-sterling bonds is similar to that for all other Eurobonds.

OBTAINING INFORMATION ON BONDS

As might be expected, the data needs of bond investors are considerably different from those of stockholders. For one thing, there is less emphasis on fundamental analysis because, except for speculative-grade bonds and revenue obligations, most fixed-income investors rely on the rating agencies for credit analysis of bonds. Some very large institutions, however, employ in-house analysts to confirm assigned agency ratings or to uncover marginal incremental return opportunities. Given the large investments by these institutions, the rewards of only a few more basis points can be substantial, and the institutions enjoy economies of scale in research.

Finally, several private research firms have been established that concentrate on the independent appraisal of bonds.[31] So what type of information do bond investors require? In addition to information on risk of default, they need (1) information on market and economic conditions and (2) information on intrinsic bond features. Market and economic information allows investors to stay abreast of the general tone of the market, the overall interest rate developments, and yield-spread behavior in different market sectors. Bond investors also require information on bond indenture provisions such as call features, sinking-fund provisions, and protective covenants in case of leveraged buyouts (LBOs).

Where do bondholders find such information? Some is readily available in such popular publications as *The Wall Street Journal, Barron's, Business Week, Fortune,* and *Forbes*, which were discussed in Chapter 5. In addition, two popular sources of bond data are the *Federal Reserve Bulletin* and the *Survey of Current Business*, which were also described in Chapter 5. Other specific sources follow.

Treasury Bulletin, a monthly publication, includes average yields on long-term Treasury, corporate, and municipal bonds, as well as graphs of monthly average yields on new AA corporate bonds, Treasury bonds, and municipal bonds.

The Standard & Poor's Bond Guide is published monthly and presents a condensed review of pertinent financial and statistical information as described in Chapter 5. Moody's has a comparable publication entitled *Moody's Bond Record.* (Nearly all bond publications produced by Standard & Poor's have counterparts marketed by Moody's.)

Moody's Bond Survey is published weekly and provides information on current economic conditions and their possible effects on bond markets. Recent and prospective taxable bond offerings are listed with information on agency rating, offering date, amount of offer, name and type of issue, call price, re-offering price and yield, and recent bid price and yield. For each of the major government, agency, corporate, and municipal obligations coming to the market, detailed information is provided on bond features, indenture provisions, and corporate or municipal finances. This is a valuable publication because it provides information on all three cat-

---

[31] Reba White, "Is Credit Analysis a Growth Industry?" *Institutional Investor* 10, no. 1 (January 1976): 57–58; Robert J. Cirino, "Building a Fixed-Income Boutique," *Institutional Investor* 12, no. 3 (March 1978): 35–36.

egories of bonds. Standard & Poor's has a similar publication titled *Credit Week*, while Duff and Phelps has one entitled *Credit Decisions.*

Moody's manuals include the *Municipal and Government Manual,* the *Bank and Financial Manual, Industrial Manual, OTC Industrial Manual, Transportation Manual,* and *Public Utility Manual.* These publications described in Chapter 5 provide fundamental information on the risk of default and contain data on features of each outstanding issue.

Fitch Investors Service publishes the following services: *Fitch Rating Register* is a monthly publication featuring all Fitch ratings for corporate, municipal, and health care bond issuers, commercial paper, and preferred stock. It includes all new ratings and rating changes during the preceding 12 months. *Fitch Corporate Credit Analysis* is research reports on issuers of bonds, preferred stock, and commercial paper. *Fitch Municipal Credit Analysis* contains research reports on issuers of tax-exempt commercial paper, notes, as well as revenue, and general obligation bonds.

Investment Dealers Digest, a weekly publication, provides extensive information on new issues, new-issue market activity, reviews of various segments of the bond market, and the overall market outlook. Detailed information is published on the features of forthcoming bond issues. The digest also contains the most extensive list of pending and recent issues available, which indicates future demand for loanable funds and the potential effects on interest rates.

The Bond Buyer, a daily publication, contains articles of interest to municipal bond investors and a complete listing of all proposed municipal bond issues, redemption notices, and statistics in the government bond market. *Credit Markets* is a weekly publication by the same publisher (The Bond Buyer) that contains a recap of relevant news relating to the total bond market (municipals, governments, corporates, etc.) along with columns discussing the market outlook.

SOURCES OF BOND QUOTES

The prior discussion considered sources that filled three needs of investors: evaluating risk of default, staying abreast of market and interest rate conditions, and obtaining information on specific bonds. Another important data need is *current market information*—bond quotes and prices. Unfortunately, many of the prime sources are not widely distributed. For example, *Bank and Quotation Record* is a valuable, though not widely circulated, source that provides a summary of price information on a monthly basis for government and agency bonds, a large number of listed and OTC corporate issues, municipals, and many money market instruments. Quotes on municipal bonds are available only through a fairly costly publication, used by many financial institutions, titled *The Blue List of Current Municipal Offerings.* It contains over 100 pages of price quotes for municipal bonds, municipal notes, and industrial development and pollution-control revenue bonds. Daily information on all publicly traded treasury issues, most important agency obligations, and many corporate issues is published in *The Wall Street Journal.* Similar data is available on a weekly basis in *Barron's.* Both publications include listed corporate bond quotes that represent a minor portion of the total market. Finally, major market dealers maintain firm quotes on a variety of issues for clients and/or cooperating institutions.

INTERPRETING BOND QUOTES

Essentially, all bonds are quoted on the basis of either yield or price. On the basis of price, the quote is always interpreted as a percentage of par. For example, a quote of 98 1/2 is not interpreted as $98.50, but 98 1/2 percent of par. The dollar price can then be derived from the quote, given the par value. If par is $5,000 on a particular municipal bond, then the price of an issue quoted at 98 1/2 would be $4,925. Actually, the market follows three systems of bond pricing: one system for corporates, another for governments (both treasuries and agency obligations), and a third for municipals.

CORPORATE BOND QUOTES. Figure 10.3 is a listing of NYSE corporate bond quotes that appeared in *The Wall Street Journal* on Thursday, May 5, 1988. The data pertains to trading activity on May 4. Several quotes have been designated for illustrative purposes. The first is an AT&T (American Telephone and Telegraph) issue and is representative of most corporate prices. In particular, the "7 1/8 03" indicates the coupon and maturity of the obligation; in this case, the AT&T issue carries a 7 1/8 percent coupon and matures in 2003. The next column provides the current yield of the obligation and is found by comparing the coupon to the current market price. For example, a bond with a 7 1/8 percent coupon selling for 79 7/8 would have an 8.9 percent current yield. This is not the YTM or even necessarily a good approximation to it. Both of these yields will be discussed in detail in the next chapter (especially the YTM).

The next column is the volume of $1,000 par value bonds traded that day. The next column indicates the closing quote, which is followed by the net change in the closing price from the last day the issue was traded. In this case, there was no change. The second quote, for the Beker bond, has two unique features that make a very significant difference. The "vj" in front of the name indicates that the firm is in receivership or bankruptcy. The small letter "f" that follows the maturity date of the obligation means that the issue is trading *flat.* Simply stated, the issuer is not meeting interest payments on the obligation. Therefore, the coupon of the obligation may be inconsequential, and the dash in the current yield column indicates no payments. The third bond in Column 2 is "Chry F zr 90s," which refers to a Chrysler Financial zero coupon bond ("zr") due in 1992. As discussed, these securities do not pay interest but are redeemed at par at maturity. Because there is no coupon, they do not report a current yield. Finally, the fourth bond in Column 2 is a convertible ("cv") bond from Control Data. The conversion feature means that the bond is convertible into the common stock of the company. A "dc" before the coupon on several bonds means "deep discount," indicating that the original coupon was set below the going rate at the time of issue—for example, a 5 7/8 coupon when market rates were 9 or 10 percent.

FIGURE 10.3
Sample Bond Quotations

NEW YORK EXCHANGE BONDS

Wednesday, May 4, 1988

Total Volume $31,750,000

SALES SINCE JANUARY 1

1988	1987	1986
$2,697,309,000	$3,543,812,000	$4,096,050,000

	Domestic Wed.	Domestic Tue.	All Issues Wed.	All Issues Tue.
Issues traded	687	688	700	691
Advances	276	288	277	289
Declines	252	244	253	245
Unchanged	169	156	170	157
New highs	20	22	20	22
New lows	8	5	8	5

Dow Jones Bond Averages

–1986– High	–1986– Low	–1987– High	–1987– Low	–1988– High	–1988– Low		Wednesday –1988–		Wednesday –1987–		Wednesday –1986–	
93.65	83.73	95.51	81.26	91.25	86.92	20 Bonds	88.53	+0.03	89.19	–0.06	91.68	+0.08
95.79	81.85	98.23	79.51	91.88	86.65	10 Utilities	87.81	+0.03	89.41	–0.28	92.11	+0.04
91.64	84.82	93.10	83.00	90.64	86.96	10 Industrial	89.24	+0.03	88.96	+0.16	91.26	+0.13

CORPORATION BONDS
Volume, $31,710,000

Bonds	Cur Yld	Vol	Close	Net Chg.
Advst 9s08	cv	47	83	...
AlaP 9s2000	9.6	3	93½	...
AlaP 9¾s04	10.0	5	97¾	...
AlaP 8⅞06	10.0	2	89⅛	– 1¼
AlaP 8¾07	10.0	9	87¼	– ¾
AlaP 9⅝08	10.0	1	96	...
AlskH 16¼99	14.6	1	111¼	– ⅛
vjAlgl 10¾99f	...	70	52½	+ ½
vjAlgl 10.4s02f	...	104	50	– 1
AlldC zr92	...	15	68½	– ¼
AlldC zr98	...	34	39⅜	+ ⅞
AlldC zr2000	...	10	30⅞	...
AldC dc6s88	6.1	11	99	...
AlldC zr97	...	105	41½	– ¼
AlldC zr99	...	5	35⅜	+ ¼
AlldC zr03	...	5	24½	+ 1½
AlldC zr05	...	20	19½	...
AlldC zr09	...	330	12¼	– ⅜
AMAX 14½94	12.4	7	116½	...
AExC 11¾12	10.6	25	110⅝	– ¼
AmMed 9½01	cv	111	94½	– ¾
AmMed 8¼08	cv	36	76½	...
ATT 3⅞s90	4.1	180	94	+ ½
ATT 5⅝95	6.9	12	81¾	...
ATT 6s00	8.1	82	74½	...
ATT 8¾00	9.2	294	94⅝	...
ATT 7s01	8.7	48	80¾	– ¼
ATT 7⅛03	8.9	30	79⅞	...
ATT 8.80s05	9.4	166	93¼	+ ⅛
ATT 8⅝s07	9.5	147	90⅝	+ ⅛
ATT 8⅝26	10.0	404	86⅜	– ¼
Amfac 5¼94	cv	18	97	+ 1
Amoco 6s98	7.2	3	82⅞	+ ⅛
Amoco 9.2s04	9.5	4	97	...
Amoco 7⅞07	9.3	10	84½	– ⅜
Amoco 14s91	13.9	10	101	...
Amoco 7⅞96	8.4	5	93⅜	– ½
Ancp 13⅞02f	cv	5	107	– ½
Andarko 5¾12	cv	9	97	– 1
Apch 8.5s06	8.8	26	96½	+ ½
ArizP 7.45s02	9.3	3	80¼	– ¾
ArkBst 7s11	7.6	26	92	+ 2½
Arml 8.7s95	9.4	5	93	+ ⅞
Asar 9¾2000	10.1	20	96½	+ 2
AshO 6.15s92	6.8	50	90	– 1¼
AtalSos 7⅛01	cv	5	75½	...
Atchsn 4s95	5.6	2	71⅝	...
ARich 7¾03	8.8	10	88	– ½
ARch 10⅜95	9.8	35	106	– ⅜
ARch 10⅞05	10.2	50	107	– ¾
ARch 9⅛11	9.8	5	93	– 2
AutDt 6½11	cv	35	115½	+ ⅜
Avaln 7s92f	cv	5	90	+ 6
AvcoF 7⅝97	8.3	50	91½	+ ½
Avnet 8s13	cv	20	92	+ ¼
Avnet 6s12	cv	20	83½	– ¾
BPNA 9¼01	9.7	16	95½	– ½
BRE 9½08	cv	41	106½	...
Bally 6s98	cv	30	78⅛	– 1⅜
Bally 10s06	cv	45	90½	+ ½
BkNY 8¼10	cv	138	102¾	– ⅜
Banka 7⅞03	10.3	5	76¼	+ ¾
Banka 8⅞05	10.7	40	82⅞	+ ⅞
Bkam 8.35s07	10.8	30	77⅛	– ½
Bkam zr90s	...	8	80⅛	+ ⅛
Bkam zr92s	...	45	64⅛	+ ⅛
Bkam zr91s	...	20	76½	– ½
Bkam zr93s	...	55	60⅞	– ⅞
BnkTr 8⅛99	9.2	5	88⅛	– 1⅞
BarcA zr90s	...	11	81¾	+ ⅜
vjBeker 15⅞03f	...	245	47¼	– ⅛
BellCn 13⅜10	11.0	25	121½	– 1⅜
BellPa 8⅝06	9.5	8	91⅛	+ ⅛
BellPa 7⅛12	9.5	101	75⅜	...
BellPa 7½13	9.5	59	79	+ 1
BellPa 9⅝14	10.0	45	96½	+ ½
BellPa 8¾15	9.7	9	90½	+ ⅝
BellPa 9¼19	10.0	29	92⅞	+ ¼
BenCp 8.3s03	9.8	18	85	– 3
BenCp 8.4s07	10.1	5	83	...

Bonds	Cur Yld	Vol	Close	Net Chg.
vjChmtrn 9s94f	...	5	69	– ½
ChNY 7.35s04t	8.1	17	90¼	– ¾
ChvrnC 12s94	10.9	50	110	+ ¾
ChvrnC 11s90	10.7	115	102⅜	...
ChvrnC 7⅞97	8.6	5	91⅛	+ ⅛
Chvrn 5¾92	6.3	50	90⅝	– ⅜
Chvrn 7s96	7.9	5	89⅛	– ¾
Chvrn 8¾05	9.6	20	91½	– 1⅜
Chvrn 8¾96	9.0	30	97½	...
ChiPac 6½12	cv	5	84	+ ½
ChckFul 7s12	cv	16	86½	– 3½
Chryslr 10.4s99	10.2	10	101¾	– ¼
ChryF zr90	...	15	80⅛	– ⅞
ChryF 13½91	12.9	10	104¾	...
ChryF 9¾90F	9.6	10	101⅞	– ¼
ChryF 9¼91	9.3	10	100	– ⅛
ChryF 8⅛94	8.6	5	95	+ ⅝
ChryF 7⅝92	8.0	12	95½	+ ⅝
CirclK 8¼05	cv	8	120	+ 8
CirclK 12¾97	12.2	4	104½	...
CirclK 7¼06	cv	142	98	+ 1¾
Citicp 5¾00	cv	10	94⅝	+ ⅜
Citicp 12¼93	12.1	9	101	– 1⅜
Citicp 12½93	12.2	77	102⅞	+ 1¾
Clmt zrD05	...	5	16¼	– ¾
Claytn 7¾01	cv	15	101½	+ ½
ClevEl 7⅛90	7.3	25	97⅝	– ⅛
ClevEl 9¼09	10.4	1	89⅛	+ ⅛
ClevEl 9.85s10	10.7	25	92¼	– ⅞
ClevEl 8⅜11	10.3	10	81⅛	+ ⅛
ClevEl 8⅜12	10.1	22	83	+ 2½
Coastl 11¼96	11.3	151	100	...
Coastl 11¾06	11.8	50	100	– ⅞
Coastl 8.48s91	8.9	310	95⅝	+ ⅝
Coleco 14⅜02f	...	32	29⅝	– 3½
Coleco 11s89f	cv	97	33	– 3
Coleco 11⅛01f	...	75	30	– 2½
Coltln 11¼15	11.8	4	95½	– ⅜
Coltln 12½01	12.4	10	101	...
ColuG 8¾95	9.1	5	95⅞	– ⅛
ColuG 7½97M	8.5	2	87¾	...
ColuG 9⅞99	10.0	5	99	+ ¾
ColuG 12¾00	12.1	10	105	...
ColuG 10½12	10.4	15	100⅝	+ ⅝
CmwE 7⅝03J	9.4	5	81	– ¼
CmwE 8s03	9.9	3	81⅛	...
CmwE 8¼07	10.1	5	81½	+ 1⅛
CmwE 15⅜00	13.3	25	116	...
CmwE 11⅛10	11.0	45	101	– 1
CmwE 17½88	16.8	15	104	...
CmwE 10⅝95	10.3	10	103½	+ ½
Compq 5¼12	cv	22	139½	+ 2
ConEd 4⅝91	5.1	15	89⅞	+ ¾
ConEd 9⅜00	9.5	30	99⅛	+ 1⅛
ConEd 7.9s01	9.1	20	86¾	+ ⅝
ConEd 7.9s02	9.2	2	86⅛	...
ConEd 7¾03	9.2	28	84⅜	– ⅜
ConEd 8.4s03	9.4	1	89½	– ⅛
ConEd 9⅛04	9.7	20	94	+ ⅛
CnPw 7½02J	9.6	6	78⅜	– 1⅝
CnPw 9¾06	10.3	1	94⅜	– 1
CnPw 8⅝07	10.2	31	84⅝	...
Ctllnf 9s06	cv	5	101¾	+ ¾
CtlDat 12¾91	11.9	2	106¾	– ¼
CtlDat 8½11	cv	26	113¾	+ 1¾
CoopCo 8⅝05	cv	10	65	– ¾
CntryCr 7s11	cv	5	80	+ 2
CrayRs 6⅛11	cv	34	111½	– 1
CrdF zr90s	...	2	79¾	+ ¼
CritAc 13.10s14	12.5	1	105	– ¼
CritAc 11¼15	11.0	6	102⅝	+ ⅛
Datpnt 8⅞06	cv	23	60⅛	– 1¾
Deere 9s08	cv	139	121	+ ½
DetEd 6s96	7.9	10	76⅛	+ ⅛
DetEd 9.15s00	9.9	10	92	+ ½
DetEd 8.15s00	9.6	1	84½	+ ⅜
DetEd 8⅛01	9.8	10	83	– 1
DetEd 7½03	9.5	18	79¼	+ ¼
DetEd 9⅞04	10.4	10	94¾	+ ¼
DetEd 11⅞00	11.5	9	103½	– 2½
DetEd 10⅝06	10.7	10	99⅛	– ¼
Deutz 16s91	15.8	13	101	– 1
Dow 7.75s99	8.7	5	89⅛	– 1⅜

Bonds	Cur Yld	Vol	Close	Net Chg.
FrdC 7⅞93	8.1	10	97⅛	+ 1⅞
FrdC 8⅜01	9.5	5	88½	– 1⅜
Fruf 13½96	20.1	185	67	– 1⅛
Fruf 13¾01	20.8	5	66	– 2
Fuqua 9½98	10.4	1	91	+ ½
GAF 11⅜95	11.3	87	100½	...
GnDev 12⅝05	13.4	50	94½	– ¼
GnEl 5.3s92	5.8	5	92⅛	...
GnEl 8½04	9.3	200	91⅝	– ⅜
GnHme 15½95f	...	5	25	...
GnHme 12¾98f	59.6	15	21⅜	+ 1⅜
GnInst 7¼12	cv	55	103½	– ½
GMA 7¾94	8.3	56	93¼	– ¼
GMA 7⅛92	7.6	98	93⅞	...
GMA 8⅞99	9.4	80	94	...
GMA 8¾s00	9.4	10	92¾	...
GMA 8¾s01	9.5	36	92¼	+ ¼
GMA 8⅛96	8.8	45	92	...
GMA 9¾03	9.9	26	98	+ ⅛
GMA 9.4s04	9.9	16	95⅜	+ ⅝
GMA 11¾00	11.0	8	107	– 1¼
GMA dc6s11	9.3	120	64⅝	– ⅛
GMA zr12	...	13	98	...
GMA zr15	...	87	79	...
GMA 10½89	10.3	7	102 13/32	...
GMA 10⅜95	9.9	20	104⅜	– ¼
GMA 10s90	9.9	49	101½	...
GMA 9¼93	9.2	310	100⅞	+ ¼
GMA 8½91	8.4	35	100¾	+ ⅛
GMA 8⅞96	9.2	37	96¾	...
GMA 8s96	8.7	205	92	+ ½
GMA 8s90	8.0	65	100	...
GMA 8⅛92	8.3	26	98	...
GMA 8s93J	8.3	35	95⅞	+ ⅛
GMA 7⅛89	7.2	10	98¾	– ¼
GMA 7¼90	7.4	5	97¾	+ ¼
GTE 6⅝91	7.0	4	94⅞	+ ⅝
GTE 9⅜99	9.4	10	100	...
Gene 14¼94	14.0	7	102	+ 1
Gene 15¼94	14.9	5	102½	...
Gene dc9¾93	11.0	10	89	+ ½
GaPw 8⅞00	9.7	7	91½	– 1¼
GaPw 8⅛01	9.5	10	85⅞	+ 1⅜
GaPw 7½02J	9.4	1	80	+ ¼
GaPw 8⅝04	10.0	1	86⅝	– ⅛
GaPw 11⅝00	11.2	1	103½	...
GaPw 11¾05	11.4	25	102⅞	+ ⅜
GaPw 10½09	10.4	9	100¾	+ ¼
GaPw 13⅛12	12.5	2	105⅛	...
GaPw 13¼13	12.4	16	107	...
GaPw 16s14	14.8	32	108	– ½
Getty 14s00	13.1	10	106½	...
GibFn 9¼08	cv	40	71	+ ¼
vjGloMr 12⅜98f	...	20	17	– 2
vjGloM dc16s01f	...	10	18⅛	– ⅜
vjGloMr 16⅛02f	...	22	18¼	...
vjGloM dc13s03f	cv	17	17½	...
GdNgF 13¼95	12.7	9	104⅜	...
Gdrch 8¼94	8.8	11	94	...
Gould 9¼95	9.3	2	100	...
Grace 4¼90	cv	1	102⅝	– 2⅜
Grace 12¾90	12.5	28	102	...
GreyF 16⅛92	15.0	9	107¼	– ⅛
GreyF zr94	...	56	51⅝	+ 1⅝
Grolr 13⅝03	13.4	6	101½	– ½
GrowGp 12½94	12.7	175	98⅜	– ⅝
GrowGp 8½06	cv	26	86	...
Grumn 9¼09	cv	26	102	...
Gulfrd 6s12	cv	32	84½	...
GlfWn 7s03A	9.2	25	76½	– ⅜
GlfWn 7s03B	9.2	5	76	...
GlfRes 10⅞97	11.6	1	94	...
GlfRes 12½04	13.0	13	96½	– 2¾
Hall 8.7s91	11.8	3	74	+ 4
Harns dc12s04	12.0	15	100	...
Hawn 9s2000	9.5	1	94½	+ ½
Hercul 6½99	cv	11	138	...
Holidy 14⅛92	13.2	21	106⅝	+ 2¾
Holidy 10½94	10.6	109	99	+ ½
Holidy 11s99	11.6	5	94¾	...
HollyFar 6s17	cv	25	74½	+ ½
HomFSD 6½11	cv	9	80	– ½
HoCp 8½08	cv	49	101¼	– ⅛

Source: "New York Exchange Bonds," *The Wall Street Journal,* May 5, 1988. Reprinted by permission of *The Wall Street Journal,* © Dow Jones & Company, Inc., 1988. All Rights Reserved.

FIGURE 10.4
Sample Quotes for Treasury and Agency Issues

TREASURY BONDS, NOTES & BILLS

Wednesday, May 4, 1988

Representative Over-the-Counter quotations based on transactions of $1 million or more as of 4 p.m. Eastern time.

Hyphens in bid-and-asked and bid changes represent 32nds; 101-01 means 101 1/32. a-Plus 1/64. b-Yield to call date. d-Minus 1/64. k-Nonresident aliens exempt from withholding taxes. n-Treasury notes. p-Treasury note; nonresident aliens exempt from withholding taxes.

Source: Bloomberg Financial Markets

Treasury Bonds and Notes

Rate	Mat. Date		Bid	Asked	Bid Chg.	Yld.
6 7/8	1989	May p	99-15	99-19	− 01	7.29
9 1/4	1989	May n	101-28	102-02	− 01	7.13
8	1989	May n	100-19	100-23	....	7.28
11 3/4	1989	May n	104-07	104-11	....	7.28
7 3/8	1989	Jun p	99-29	100-01	− 01	[illegible]
9 5/8	1989	Jun p	102-12	102-16	....	[illegible]
7 5/8	1989	Jul p	100-05	100-09	....	7.37
14 1/2	1989	Jul n	107-30	108-02	....	7.30
7 3/4	1989	Aug p	100-08	100-12	....	7.43
6 5/8	1989	Aug p	98-30	99-02	....	7.39
13 7/8	1989	Aug n	107-19	107-23	− 01	7.42
8 1/2	1989	Sep k	101-05	101-09	....	7.51
9 3/8	1989	Sep p	102-09	102-13	....	7.53
11 7/8	1989	Oct n	105-24	105-28	....	7.50
7 7/8	1989	Oct p	100-12	100-16	....	7.51
6 3/8	1989	Nov p	98-07	98-11	− 01	7.54
10 3/4	1989	Nov n	104-12	104-16	− 04	7.57
12 3/4	1989	Nov p	107-09	107-13	− 01	7.52
7 3/4	1989	Nov p	100-04	100-08	− 01	7.57
7 7/8	1989	Dec p	100-08	100-12	+ 01	7.62
8 3/8	1989	Dec p	101	101-04	− 01	7.63
7 3/8	1990	Jan k	99-14	99-18	....	7.64
10 1/2	1990	Jan n	104-11	104-15	....	7.62
3 1/2	1990	Feb	92-31	93-17	....	7.44
6 1/2	1990	Feb k	97-31	98-03	+ 01	7.66
7 1/8	1990	Feb k	98-31	99-03	....	7.66
11	1990	Feb p	105-10	105-14	....	7.66
7 1/4	1990	Mar p	99-02	99-06	− 01	7.71
7 3/8	1990	Mar p	99-10	99-14	....	7.69
10 1/2	1990	Apr n	104-26	104-30	....	7.71
7 7/8	1990	May k	100-03	100-07	− 01	7.75
12 5/8	1995	May	121-04	121-08	− 01	8.54
10 1/2	1995	Aug p	109-10	109-14	+ 01	8.72
9 1/2	1995	Nov p	103-31	104-03	+ 01	8.75
11 1/2	1995	Nov	115-06	115-10	− 01	8.69
8 7/8	1996	Feb p	100-13	100-17	− 01	8.78
7 3/8	1996	May p	91-25	91-29	+ 01	8.80
7 1/4	1996	Nov p	90-16	90-20	+ 01	8.84
8 5/8	1997	Aug k	98-07	98-11	+ 01	8.89
8 1/2	1997	May k	97-19	97-23	+ 01	8.87
8 7/8	1997	Nov	99-23	99-27	+ 01	8.90
8 1/8	1998	Feb p	95	95-04	+ 01	8.88
(1) → 7	1993-98	May	88-04	88-08	+ 01	8.79
3 1/2	1998	Nov	92-30	93-16	− 04	4.27
13 1/4	2009-14	May	136-03	136-09	+ 06	9.29
12 1/2	2009-14	Aug k	129-20	129-26	+ 07	9.26
11 3/4	2009-14	Nov k	123-11	123-17	+ 07	9.22
11 1/4	2015	Feb k	120-23	120-29	+ 05	9.14
10 5/8	2015	Aug k	114-25	114-31	+ 03	9.12
(2) → 9 7/8	2015	Nov	107-07	107-13	+ 10	9.13
9 1/4	2016	Feb k	101-03	101-09	+ 05	9.12
7 1/4	2016	May k	80-31	81-05	+ 02	9.12
7 1/2	2016	Nov k	83-15	83-21	+ 03	9.12
8 3/4	2017	May k	96-04	96-10	+ 01	9.11
8 7/8	2017	Aug k	97-19	97-25	+ 01	9.09

U.S. Treas. Bills

Mat. date	Bid (Discount)	Asked (Discount)	Yield
-1988-			
5-12	6.18	6.06	6.15
5-19	5.61	5.54	5.63
5-26	5.49	5.42	5.51
6- 2	5.74	5.67	5.77
6- 9	5.88	5.81	5.92
6-16	5.89	5.82	5.94
6-23	5.87	5.80	5.93
6-30	5.86	5.79	5.92
7- 7	6.08	6.01	6.16
7-14	6.06	5.99	6.14
7-21	6.07	6.00	6.16
7-28	6.05	6.01	6.18
8- 4	6.16	6.12	6.30
8-11	6.12	6.05	6.24
8-18	6.10	6.03	6.22
8-25	6.08	6.01	6.21
9- 1	6.22	6.15	6.36
9- 8	6.21	6.14	6.36
9-15	6.24	6.17	6.40
9-22	6.32	6.25	6.49
9-29	6.35	6.28	6.53
10- 6	6.35	6.28	6.54
10-13	6.36	6.29	6.56
10-20	6.36	6.30	6.58
10-27	6.43	6.36	6.65
11- 3	6.40	6.36	6.66
11-25	6.51	6.44	6.75
12-22	6.53	6.46	6.78
-1989-			
1-19	6.63	6.56	6.91
2-16	6.65	6.59	6.96
3-16	6.69	6.65	7.05
4-13	6.73	6.69	7.13

Source: "Treasury Bonds, Notes & Bills," *The Wall Street Journal,* May 5, 1988. Reprinted by permission of *The Wall Street Journal,* © Dow Jones & Company, Inc., 1988. All Rights Reserved.

All fixed-income obligations, with the exception of preferred stock, are traded on an *accrued interest basis.* The prices pertain to principal value only and exclude interest that has accrued to the holder since the last interest payment date. The actual price of the bond will exceed the quote listed because accrued interest must be added. With the AT&T 7 1/8 percent issue, if two months have elapsed since interest was paid, then the current holder of the bond is entitled to 2/6 (or one-third) of the normal semiannual interest payment. More specifically, the 7 1/8 percent coupon provides semiannual interest income of $35.625. The investor who held the obligation for two months beyond the last interest payment date is entitled to one-third (1/3) of that $35.625 in the form of accrued interest. To the price of $798.75 (79 7/8), an accrued interest value of $11.87 will be added.

TREASURY AND AGENCY BOND QUOTES. Figure 10.4 illustrates the quote system used with Treasury and agency issues. These quotes are like those customarily used for other over-the-counter securities because they contain both bid and ask prices, rather than high, low, and close. On the U.S. Treasury bond quotes, a small "n" behind the maturity date indicates that the obligation is actually a Treasury *note*. A small "p" indicates it is a Treasury note on which nonresident aliens are exempt from withholding taxes on the interest. All other obligations in this section are, of course, Treasury bonds. The first quote is the 7 percent issue. The security identification is different because it is not necessary to list the issuer. Instead, the usual listing indicates the coupon, the year of maturity, the month of maturity, and any information on the call feature of the obligation. For example, the 7 percent issue carries a maturity of 1993–1998; this means that the issue has a deferred call feature until 1993 (and is thereafter freely callable), and a (final) maturity date of 1998. The bid-ask figures are then provided and are also stated as a percentage of par. Unlike the current-yield figure used with corporate issues, this is yield to maturity, or *promised yield,* and is used for treasuries, agencies, and municipals.

Quote 2 is a 9 7/8 percent obligation of 2015 that demonstrates the basic difference in the price system of governments (i.e., treasuries and agencies). The bid quote is 107-07, and the ask is 107-13. Governments are traded in thirty-seconds of a point (rather than eighths), and the figures to the right of the hyphens indicate the number of thirty-seconds in the fractional bid or ask. The bid price is actually 107 7/32 percent of par.

The securities listed below the Treasury bond section are for U.S. Treasury bills. Notice that there are only dates reported and no coupons. This is because these are pure discount securities—that is, the return is the difference between the price you pay and par at maturity.[32]

MUNICIPAL BOND QUOTES. Figure 10.5 contains municipal bond quotes from *The Blue List of Current Municipal Offerings* for May 4, 1988. These daily quotes on municipal bonds are ordered according to states and then alphabetically within states. Each issue gives the amount of bonds being offered (in thousands of dollars), the name of the security, the coupon rate, the maturity (which includes month, day, and year), the yield or price, and finally, the dealer offering the bonds. Bond Quote 1 is $95,000 of Hebron, Connecticut, bonds. The AMBAC indicates that the bonds are guaranteed by this firm as described earlier. They have a 6.40 percent coupon and are due April 15, 1990. In this instance, the yield to maturity is given (5.00 percent). To determine the price you would either compute or look up in a yield book the price of a 6.40 percent coupon bond, due in about two years to yield 5.00 percent. The dealer offering the bonds is CBT. A list in the back of the publication gives the name of the firm and its phone number.

The second bond is a $5,000 Delaware State Housing Authority Revenue bond with an 8.00 percent coupon. This is somewhat unusual since

---

[32] For a discussion on calculating yields, see Bruce D. Fielitz, "Calculating the Bond Equivalent Yield for T-Bills," *Journal of Portfolio Management* 9, no. 3 (Spring 1983): 58–60.

FIGURE **10.5**
Quotes for Municipals

```
                         CONNECTICUT - CONTINUED
      50 COLCHESTER CONN             "B/B" MBIA    8.000   03/15/91        5.25 ROOSEVLT
      15 DARIEN CONN                                5.750   03/15/91        5.00 ROOSEVLT
   +  25 GUILFORD CONN               "B/B"          4.900   05/15/90         100 OPCOFTL
   +  15 HARTFORD CNTY CONN MET DIST "B/B"          3.000   10/01/91        6.00 ROOSEVLT
   +   5 HARTFORD CNTY CONN MET DIST "B/B"          3.250   11/01/96        6.75 ROOSEVLT
   +   8 HARTFORD CNTY CONN MET DIST "B/B"          3.250   11/01/98        7.00 ROOSEVLT
  ①→  95 HEBRON CONN                 "B/E" AMBAC    6.400   04/15/90        5.00 CBT
      10 MONTVILLE CONN                             6.700   03/15/02        6.85 ABROWNBO
      70 MONTVILLE CONN                             7.000   03/15/08        7.25 CNB
       5 NEW HAVEN CONN COLISEUM AUTH              5.600   09/01/94        6.00 DWRBOS
      25 NEW HAVEN CONN PKG REV      "B/B"          5.700   09/01/95        6.25 DWRBOS
      65 SIMSBURY CONN                              6.600   04/15/95        5.90 FLEETNTL
     600 SOUTH CENT CONN REGL WTR AUTH P/R @ 102   8.500   08/01/03 C93    6.00 CBT
     750 SOUTH CENT CONN REGL WTR AUTH P/R @ 102   8.500   08/01/03 C93    6.00 WERTHEIM
      25 STAMFORD CONN                              6.500   07/15/95 N/C    5.90 CONNSEC
      15 STONINGTON CONN             "B/E"          6.300   03/15/90        5.05 CBT
      10 WEST HAVEN CONN                            5.700   03/01/00        7.00 FLEETNTL

                              DELAWARE

     115 DELAWARE ST                 "B/E" W.I.     6.200   04/01/90        5.10 WHEATPH
      25 DELAWARE ST                                9.600   07/01/90 N/C    5.30 ABROWNBA
      10 DELAWARE ST                                6.250   04/01/93        5.90 WHEATPH
      40 DELAWARE ST                                6.300   04/01/94        6.00 WERTHEIM
      25 DELAWARE ST                 P/R @ 103      9.700   07/01/95 C91    5.60 ABROWNBA
      20 DELAWARE ST                 "B/E"          7.250   04/01/03 C00     100 PERSH
         (CA @ 100)
      25 DELAWARE RIV & BAY AUTH DEL                3.750   01/01/04          82 BEARSTER
     100 DELAWARE RIV & BAY AUTH DEL                3.750   01/01/04          82 PETERS
      25 DELAWARE ST ECONOMIC DEV AUTH MULTI-FAM   10.750   11/01/14        9.65 WHEELER
   +  50 DELAWARE ST HEALTH FACS AUTH "REG" MBIA    9.250   10/01/15 C95    7.20 MOORESCH
         (P/C @ 102)
  ②→   5 DELAWARE ST HSG AUTH REV                   8.000   01/01/89         103 SMITHB
       5 DELAWARE ST SOLID WASTE AUTH CA @ 103      9.250   07/01/03 C89    6.50 MEYERND
     175 DELAWARE TRANSN AUTH TRANSN &              6.750   07/01/00        7.00 PRUBAPHL
     175 DELAWARE TRANSN AUTH TRANSN &              6.750   07/01/00        7.00 PRUBAPHL
      25 DOVER DEL                                  5.500   07/01/92         100 JANNEYPH
      50 DOVER DEL                   BK.QD B/E      5.500   07/01/92         100 NEWBOLDW
      25 DOVER DEL                                  5.900   07/01/94         100 JANNEYPH
      15 DOVER DEL                                  6.100   07/01/95         100 JANNEYPH
       5 DOVER DEL                   BK.QD B/E      6.250   07/01/96         100 NEWBOLDW
      50 DOVER DEL                                  6.250   07/01/96         100 WHEATPH
      25 DOVER DEL                                  6.400   07/01/97         100 JANNEYPH
      10 DOVER DEL                                  6.550   07/01/98         100 WHEATPH
     250 KENT CNTY DEL               CA @ 100       8.000   06/15/06 C96    7.00 MOORESCH
      20 NEW CASTLE CNTY DEL                        1.875   05/01/89 ETM    6.25 RAMIREZ
  ③→ 100 NEW CASTLE CNTY DEL         "REG"          8.500   10/15/05 C95    7.00 MOORESCH
         (CA @ 102)
   + 300 NORTHERN DEL INDL DEV CORP  (PHOENIX)      5.750   11/01/99     #    73 BEARSTER
      10 NORTHERN DEL INDL DEV CORP  PHOEN.STL.     5.750   11/01/99          65 MABONIDB
      25 NORTHERN DEL INDL DEV CORP  PHNX.STL.      5.750   11/01/99      67 1/2 PETERS
      10 NORTHERN DEL INDL DEV CORP                 5.750   11/01/99          68 WMBLBONN
      20 WILMINGTON DEL              AMBAC          9.000   03/01/92 C91    5.75 SHEARPHL
         (P/R @ 101)
     200 WILMINGTON DEL                             7.300   08/15/95 N/C    6.60 ABROWNBA

                       DISTRICT OF COLUMBIA

      10 DISTRICT COLUMBIA                          7.750   06/01/91        6.00 BARRBROS
   + 850 DISTRICT COLUMBIA           AMBAC          7.900   06/01/98        7.10 PRUBANY
       5 DISTRICT COLUMBIA           SER D          7.100   06/01/00        7.50 IREC
     300 DISTRICT COLUMBIA           MBIA           9.900   12/01/00 C95    6.60 FIRSTCHI
         (P/R @ 102)
     525 DISTRICT COLUMBIA           MBIA           7.650   06/01/03         100 RODMANNY
   + 300 DISTRICT COLUMBIA           CA @ 102       7.375   06/01/05 C96    8.10 FMS
      65 DISTRICT COLUMBIA           P/R @ 102      9.750   06/01/05 C95 #  6.75 DREXELPH
   + 255 DISTRICT COLUMBIA           CA @ 102       7.875   06/01/06 C96    8.00 FMS
 ..PAGE    8 A              Wednesday  May  4  1988
```

Source: *The Blue List of Current Municipal Offerings,* May 4, 1988, p. 8A. The Blue List, Division of Standard & Poor's Corp., New York. Reprinted with permission.

there is a price on the bond rather than the current yield to maturity—that is, the bond is selling for 103, which is 103 percent of par. These are called *dollar bonds.*

The third bond is $100,000 New Castle County that is *registered* (*REG*) and callable at 102. The C95 likewise indicates that it is callable after 1995. It is necessary to contact the dealer Mooresch for details.

The "+" in the far left column indicates a new item since the prior issue of *The Blue List.* A "#" in the column prior to the yield to maturity or the price indicates that the price or yield has changed since the last issue. In all instances it is necessary to call the dealer to determine the current yield/price, since these quotes are at least one day old when they are published.

SUMMARY

The basic features of bonds are their interest, principal, and maturity. Certain key relationships affect price behavior. First, price is essentially a function of coupon, maturity, and prevailing market interest rates. Second, bond price volatility depends on coupon and maturity—that is, bonds with longer maturities and/or lower coupons respond most vigorously to a given change in market rates. Each bond has intrinsic characteristics relating to its own issue. Bonds can also be differentiated by type of issue and indenture provisions.

Major benefits to investors include high returns for nominal risk, potential for capital gains, certain tax advantages, and possibly additional returns from aggressive trading of bonds. An aggressive bond investor must consider secondary-market activity, investment risks, and interest rate behavior.

The global fixed-income market includes 18 countries and has experienced several significant growth trends including the strong relative growth of the Japanese market and the decline in relative terms of the U.S. market. There are four major bond markets—the United States, Japan, Germany, and the United Kingdom. Each of these markets has a different makeup in terms of governments, agencies, municipals, corporates, and international issues. In addition, the bonds in the various market sectors are unique based upon differences in liquidity, yield spreads, tax implications, and other special features. Beyond the four major bond markets, there are similar securities available from a number of countries. The benefits from global diversification in bonds are similar to those available from stocks and are discussed in Chapter 19.

In terms of default risk, most bond investors rely on agency ratings as their source of information. For additional information on market and economic conditions and information on intrinsic bond features, individual and institutional investors rely on a host of readily available publications.

QUESTIONS

1. How does a bond differ from other types of debt instruments?
2. Explain the difference between calling a bond and bond refunding.
3. Identify the three most important factors in determining the price of a bond. Describe the effect of each.

4. Given a change in the level of interest rates, what are the two major factors that will influence the relative change in price for individual bonds? What is their impact?

5. Define two different types of bond yields.

6. What factors determine whether a bond is senior or junior? Give examples of each type.

7. What is a bond indenture?

8. Explain the differences in taxation of income from municipal bonds as opposed to U.S. Treasury bonds and corporate bonds.

9. List several types of institutional participants in the bond market, and explain what types of bond they are likely to purchase and why they purchase them.

10. Why should an investor be aware of the trading volume for a particular bond in which he is interested?

11. What is the purpose of bond ratings? What are they supposed to indicate?

12. Based upon the data in Table 10.1, which is the fastest-growing bond market in the world? Which markets seem to be losing market share?

13. Based upon the data in Table 10.2, discuss how the makeup of the German bond market differs from the U.S. market. Briefly discuss the reasons for this difference.

14. Demonstrate through an example the effects of interest rate risk on the price of a bond.

15. Discuss how a mortgage pass-through bond differs from a collateralized mortgage obligation.

16. Discuss the difference between a foreign bond (e.g., a Samurai) and a Eurobond (e.g., a Euro-DM).

17. In the latter part of this chapter, many sources of information on bonds were described and their contents discussed. Yet the statement was made earlier that "it is almost impossible for individual investors ... to keep abreast of the price activity of municipal holdings." Discuss this apparent paradox, explaining how such a condition might exist.

18. Using various sources of information described in the chapter, name at least five bonds, rated B or better, that have split ratings.

19. Select five bonds that are listed on the NYSE. Using various sources of information, prepare a brief description of each bond, including such factors as its rating, call features, collateral (if any), interest dates, and refunding provisions.

PROBLEMS

1. A 6.6 percent coupon bond issued by the state of Kansas sells for $1,000. What coupon rate on a corporate bond selling at its $1,000 par value would produce the same after-tax return to the investor as the municipal bond if the investor is in

1a. The 20 percent marginal tax bracket?

1b. The 30 percent marginal tax bracket?

1c. The 40 percent marginal tax bracket?

2. Nordic Ski Corporation's bonds are presently yielding 9.6 percent. At what point would an investor be indifferent between Nordic's bonds and a tax-free municipal bond with equal financial strength if the investor's marginal tax rate is

2a. 10 percent?

2b. 20 percent?

2c. 30 percent?

3. Burgess Corporation has just issued a $1,000 par value zero coupon with an 8 percent yield to maturity, due to mature 15 years from today (assume semiannual compounding).

3a. What is the market price of the bond?

3b. If interest rates remain constant, what will be the price of the bond in three years?

3c. If interest rates rise to 10 percent, what will be the price of the bond in three years?

4. Complete the information requested for each of the following $1,000 face value, zero coupon bonds, assuming semiannual compounding.

BOND	MATURITY (YEARS)	YIELD (PERCENT)	PRICE (DOLLARS)
A	20	12	?
B	?	10	505
C	14	?	437

5. You purchase a 10 1/2s 1995 Feb. $10,000 par Treasury note at 104.14 and hold it for exactly one year, at which time you sell it. What is your rate of return if

5a. Your selling price is 104.14?

5b. Your selling price is 106.23?

5c. Your selling price is 100.13?

5d. Your selling price is 94.06?

6. What would be the initial offering price for the following bonds (assume semiannual compounding)?

6a. A 15-year zero coupon bond with a yield to maturity (YTM) of 14 percent.

6b. A 20-year zero coupon bond with a YTM of 12 percent.

6c. A 20-year 6 percent coupon bond with a YTM of 10 percent.

7. *CFA Examination II (June 4, 1988)*: In early 1988, a West German bond investor wanted to evaluate a segment of the international bond market relative to the West German bond market. His staff prepared the historical comparisons shown on p. 390. Identify the three sources of return in international bond investing. Using the prepared data for each country, evaluate each of these sources of return in the context of the international bond market relative to the West German bond market. [15 minutes]

LONG-TERM GOVERNMENT BOND YIELDS–
ANNUAL AVERAGE

	1985	1986	1987
West Germany	6.90%	5.90%	6.25%
United States	10.60	7.60	8.75
Japan	6.30	4.90	4.40
United Kingdom	10.60	9.80	9.25

CONSUMER PRICES–ANNUAL PERCENT INCREASE
(DECREASE)

	1985	1986	1987
West Germany	2.20%	(0.20)%	0.50%
United States	3.50	2.00	4.30
Japan	2.00	0.50	0.50
United Kingdom	5.50	3.50	4.50

MONEY SUPPLY–ANNUAL PERCENT INCREASE
(DECREASE)

	1985	1986	1987
West Germany	6.10%	8.20%	7.00%
United States	8.50	9.00	5.50
Japan	3.00	10.40	11.10
United Kingdom	16.40	22.20	17.00

INDUSTRIAL PRODUCTION–ANNUAL PERCENT
INCREASE (DECREASE)

	1985	1986	1987
West Germany	5.10%	1.90%	1.00%
United States	2.20	1.00	5.10
Japan	1.20	(1.10)	4.50
United Kingdom	4.50	1.00	3.00

TRADE SURPLUS (DEFICIT)–U.S. DOLLARS
(IN BILLIONS)

	1985	1986	1987
West Germany	$ 28.50	$ 55.90	$ 62.00
United States	(122.10)	(144.30)	(171.00)
Japan	56.00	92.80	100.00
United Kingdom	(2.40)	(12.10)	(14.00)

ANNUAL AVERAGE EXCHANGE RATE—
UNITS OF EACH CURRENCY PER SDR*

	1985	1986	1987
Germany (DM)	2.91	2.47	2.28
United States ($)	1.04	1.19	1.31
Japan (Yen)	237.20	195.00	185.00
United Kingdom (£)	0.77	0.80	0.76

*SDR = International Monetary Fund's Special Drawing Rights

REFERENCES

Altman, Edward I., and S. Katz. "Statistical Bond Ratings Classification Using Financial and Accounting Data." In *Proceedings of the Conference on Topical Research in Accountancy.* Michael Schiff and George Sorter (eds.). New York University School of Business, 1976.

Ang, James S., and K. A. Patel. "Bond Rating Methods: Comparison and Validation." *Journal of Finance* 30, no. 2 (May 1975).

Beidleman, Carl, ed. *The Handbook of International Investing* (Chicago: Probus Publishing Co., 1987).

Belkaoui, Ahmed. "Industrial Bond Ratings: A New Look." *Financial Mangement* 9, no. 3 (Autumn 1980).

Darst, David M. *The Handbook of the Bond and Money Markets.* New York: McGraw-Hill, 1981.

Edelman, Richard B. "A New Approach to Ratings on Utility Bonds." *Journal of Portfolio Management* 5, no. 3 (Spring 1979).

Fabozzi, Frank J., and Irving M. Pollack. (eds.) *The Handbook of Fixed Income Securities.* 2d ed. Homewood, Ill.: Dow Jones-Irwin, 1987.

Fisher, Lawrence. "Determinants of Risk Premiums on Corporate Bonds." *Journal of Political Economy* 67, no. 3 (June 1959).

Gentry, James A., David T. Whitford, and Paul Newbold. "Predicting Industrial Bond Ratings with a Probit Model and Funds Flow Components." *The Financial Review* 23, no. 3 (August 1988).

Grabbe, J. Orlin. *International Financial Markets.* New York: Elsevier, 1986.

Kaplan, Robert S., and Gabriel Urwitz. "Statistical Models of Bond Ratings: A Methodological Inquiry." *Journal of Business* 52, no. 2 (April 1979).

Reilly, Frank K., and Michael D. Joehnk. "Association between Market Determined Risk Measures for Bonds and Bond Ratings." *Journal of Finance* 31, no. 5 (December 1976).

Stigum, Marcia. *The Money Market: Myth, Reality, and Practice.* Homewood, Ill.: Dow Jones-Irwin, 1978.

Van Horne, James C. *Financial Market Rates and Flows.* 2d ed. Englewood Cliffs, N.J.: Prentice-Hall, 1984.

Viner, Aron. *Inside Japanese Financial Markets.* Homewood, Ill.: Dow Jones-Irwin, 1988.

Wilson, Richard S. *Corporate Senior Securities.* Chicago: Probus Publishing Co., 1987.

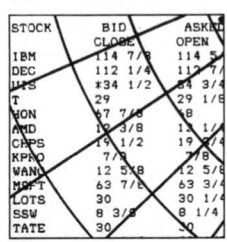

CHAPTER 11

PRINCIPLES OF BOND VALUATION

The purpose of this chapter is to explore the valuation process and to identify the determinants of bond prices and yields. We will show how many of the variables introduced in the preceding chapter can affect promised yield and realized return. An overview of the bond valuation process is followed by an examination of the mathematics of bond prices and bond yields and then of tax-exempt issues. Next, the role of interest rates in affecting bond yields and prices is explored, as well as the determinants of interest rates and yield spreads. Finally, there is an analysis of the causes and effects of variations in bond price volatility, including a discussion of bond duration and convexity. You will notice that, unlike the majority of chapters in the book, this chapter says little about international factors. The reason for this is that the concepts in this chapter are universal and apply equally to bonds throughout the world.

THE BOND VALUATION PROCESS (USING THE PRESENT VALUE MODEL)

Basically, the bond valuation process is similar to the procedures used with equity securities, since the value of a bond is equal to the present value of expected cash flows. The only real difference is that the cash flow involved is the periodic interest payments and capital recovery. In a theoretical framework, the basic principles of bond valuation can be described in the following present value model:

$$P = \sum_{t=1}^{n} C_t \frac{1}{(1 + i)^t},$$ (11.1)

where

n = the number of periods in the investment horizon, or what is more popularly known as *term to maturity*

C_t = the cash flow (periodic interest income and principal) received in period t

i = he rate of discount (or market yield) for the issue.

Essentially, any fixed-income security can be valued on the basis of Equation 11.1, which indicates what the investor expects to realize by holding the issue over a given investment horizon. In most cases, the holding period is equal to the term to maturity of the obligation and, as a result, the rate of discount represents the *promised yield to maturity* that can be earned by purchasing the obligation and holding it to its expiration date. Aggressive bond investors, however, normally do not hold obligations to maturity but intend to buy and subsequently sell the security prior to that point. Under such conditions, *realized yield* is a more important description of performance, so Equation 11.1 would represent an expected yield rather than promised return.

The present value model is attractive because it incorporates several important aspects of bond yields and prices. Current coupon receipts are included in C_t, and interest rate behavior is incorporated in i, where the discount rate is interpreted as the prevailing bond yield (described as promised yield to maturity). Changes in interest rates are important because they affect the capital gains (or losses) realized by an investor who buys and sells an issue prior to maturity.[1] The capital gain or loss is incorporated into the model within the cash flow component, C_t. Another important factor that effects the capital gain or loss component is the effect of changes in *yield spreads* over the investment horizon. These spreads are differences in yields that exist between different market sectors or types of issues (e.g., the difference in yields for long treasuries and long corporate bonds). Yield spreads occur because of differential risk, call features, variations in coupons and maturities, etc.

The bond valuation framework involves evaluating coupon receipts, interest rates, changes in interest rates, and yield spreads. *The major problem facing the bond analyst is to forecast interest rate changes and yield spread behavior.* The point is, coupon income and par value are specified and fixed, the risk of default is mainly handled by agency ratings, and promised yield, i, is defined by the prevailing market rates. In contrast, the computation of *realized* yield assumes that the investment horizon is less than term to maturity and is directly affected by capital gains or losses, which depend upon changes in interest rates and yield spreads.

To be a successful bond trader, you must not only understand what affects the *level* of current interest rates, but you must also be able to project future interest rates and thereby forecast *changes* in interest rates. Subsequently, you must consider yield spread behavior over the holding period, because it will indicate the more attractive segments of the market—that is, yield spread analysis applies interest rate behavior to specific market segments. The valuation process, assuming an aggressive trading strategy, involves considerable uncertainty regarding future bond prices and expected capital gains opportunities. After you project the future price behavior based upon the analysis of interest rates and yield spreads, you

---

[1] Indeed, for many aggressive investors, it is the major factor, because their major objective is attractive capital gains.

must select the appropriate coupon, maturity, call feature, and so forth to get the desired performance.

Buy-and-hold investors deal with similar estimates but of substantially smaller magnitude than those dealt with by investors with a trading strategy. In considering the effect of maturity, coupon, and call features on investment objectives, the buy-and-hold investor is working with *known* information. Also, errors in interest rate forecasts have much less impact on the realized returns of this type of investor than on those of the investor involved in aggressive trading. Because of the importance of interest rates in the bond valuation process, the subsequent valuation discussion pertains to investment-grade securities, which are reasonably interest rate–sensitive, rather than speculative-grade securities, which are not.[2]

MATHEMATICS OF BOND PRICING AND YIELDS

There are five types of yields in bond trading vernacular: nominal yield, current yield, promised yield, yield to call, and realized yield. *Nominal yield* is the coupon rate a particular issue carries. A bond with an 8 percent coupon would have an 8 percent nominal yield. It provides a convenient way of describing the coupon characteristics of an issue.

Current yield is to bonds what dividend yield is to stocks, and is computed as

$$CY = c_t / P_m, \qquad (11.2)$$

where

c_t = the annual coupon payment of the obligation
P_m = the current market price of the issue.

Because this yield indicates the current income from the obligation, it is important to income-oriented investors but not to most others, because it excludes the important capital recovery component (i.e., the potential for capital gain or loss).

PROMISED YIELD

Promised yield is the most widely used bond valuation model, since it indicates the fully compounded rate of return available at prevailing prices, assuming the investor holds the obligation to maturity. Also known as yield to maturity (YTM), it excludes any trading possibilities. The concept involves prevailing market prices, periodic coupon income, and par value (which, when related to the prevailing market price, indicates the capital gain or loss).

Like any present value–based computation, promised yield has important reinvestment implications. In particular, the promised yield is the investor's required reinvestment rate on each of the interim cash flows (coupon receipts) in order to realize a return equal to the promised yield.

---

[2] For a discussion of speculative-grade bond yields and price behavior, see Edward I. Altman and Scott A. Nammacher, *Investing in Junk Bonds* (New York: John Wiley & Sons, 1987).

FIGURE 11.1
The Effect of Interest-on-Interest on Total Realized Return

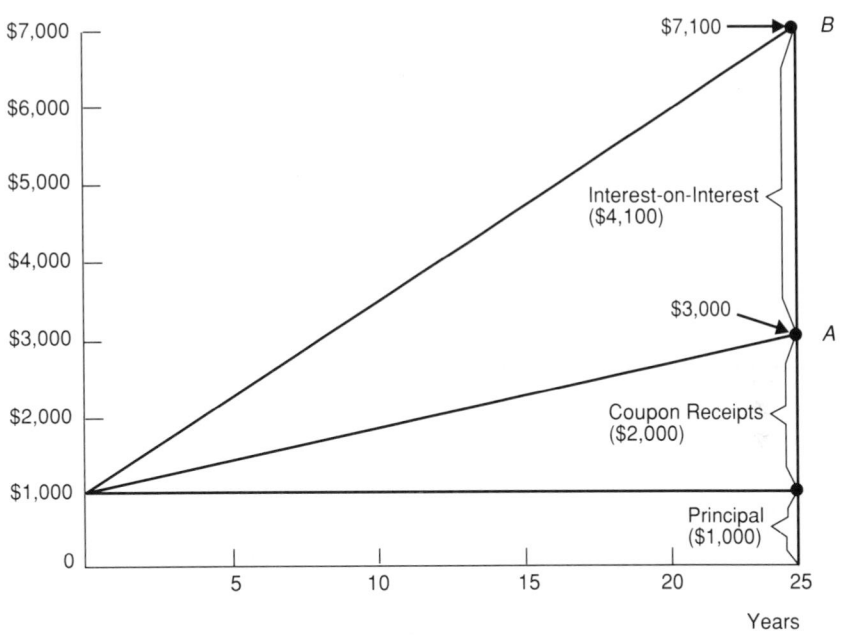

Promised yield at time of purchase: 8.00%
Realized yield over the 25-year investment horizon with no coupon reinvestment (*A*): 4.50%
Realized yield over the 25-year horizon with coupons reinvested at 8% (*B*): 8.00%

This implicit reinvestment assumption is also known as *interest-on-interest* and is nicely developed in a book by Homer and Leibowitz.[3] The yield to maturity (YTM) figure is the promised return assuming the issuer meets all interest and principal obligations on a timely basis—and that the investor reinvests coupon income to maturity at the computed promised yield rate. If a bond promises an 8 percent YTM, you must reinvest coupon income at 8 percent in order to realize that promised return. If coupons are not reinvested, or if future investment rates (i.e., the reinvestment rates for interest income) during the life of the issue are less than the promised yield at purchase, then the realized yield earned will be less than the promised yield to maturity.

The importance of interest-on-interest varies directly with coupon and maturity; the higher the coupon and/or the longer the term to maturity, the more important is the reinvestment assumption. Figure 11.1 depicts the concept and the impact of interest-on-interest assuming an 8 percent, 25-year bond bought at par to yield 8 percent. As shown, if you invested

[3] Sidney Homer and Martin L. Leibowitz, *Inside the Yield Book* (Englewood Cliffs, N.J.: Prentice-Hall, 1972), Chapter 1.

$1,000 today at 8 percent for 25 years and reinvested all the income at 8 percent, you would have approximately $7,100 at the end of 25 years. To prove this, look up the compound value for 8 percent for 25 years (which is 6.8493) or 4 percent for 50 periods (which assumes semiannual compounding and is 7.1073). The chart shows that this $7,100 is made up of $1,000 principal return, $2,000 of coupon payments over the 25 years ($80 a year for 25 years), and the rest ($4,100) is interest earned on the coupon payments at 8 percent. If you had never reinvested any of the coupon payments, you would have an ending-wealth value of only $3,000. This ending-wealth value relative to the beginning investment of $1,000 implies a realized yield of 4.5 percent (i.e., 4.5 percent is the rate that will discount $3,000 back to $1,000 in 25 years). If you had reinvested the coupon payments at some rate between 0 and 8 percent, your ending-wealth position would have been above $3,000 and below $7,100; therefore, your realized return would be somewhere between 4.5 percent and 8 percent. Alternatively, if you were able to reinvest the coupon payments consistently at rates above 8 percent, your ending-wealth position would be above $7,100, and your realized return would be above 8 percent.

Interestingly, during periods of very high interest rates, you will often hear investors talk about *locking in* high yields. In many instances they are subject to *yield illusion,* not realizing that to attain the high promised yield, they must reinvest all the coupon payments at the very high yields that currently exist. As an example, if you buy a 20-year bond with a promised yield to maturity of 15 percent, to realize the 15 percent yield, you must be able to reinvest all the coupon payments at 15 percent over the next 20 years.

APPROXIMATE PROMISED YIELD. Depending upon the accuracy desired, there are several procedures for computing promised yield. (Although the initial discussion assumes that the yield computations are executed on interest payment dates, this unrealistic assumption will be relaxed later.) The promised yield can be computed on the basis of approximate yield or on the basis of present value using annual compounding or semiannual compounding. The latter is the most precise procedure and the technique used in the marketplace. The *approximate promised yield (APY)* measure is relatively straightforward as seen in Equation 11.3:

$$APY = \frac{c_t + \dfrac{P_p - P_m}{n}}{\dfrac{P_p + P_m}{2}} \tag{11.3}$$

$$= \frac{\text{Coupon} + \text{Annual Straight-Line Amortization of Capital Gain or Loss}}{\text{Average Investment}},$$

where

P_p = **par value of the obligation**

n = **number of years to maturity**

c_t = **the *annual* coupon value of the obligation**

P_m = **the current market price of the issue.**

This approximate estimate of the promised yield assumes interest is compounded annually, and it does not require iteration. For an 8 percent bond with 20 years remaining to maturity and a current price of $900, the approximate yield is 8.95 percent, as follows:

$$APY = \frac{80 + \dfrac{1000 - 900}{20}}{\dfrac{1000 + 900}{2}} = \frac{80 + 5}{950}$$

$$= 8.95\% .$$

For even more accuracy, promised yield can be computed using the present value model and annual compounding. Equation 11.4 shows this version of the promised yield valuation model:

$$P_m = \sum_{t=1}^{n} \frac{C_t}{(1 + i)^t} + \frac{P_p}{(1 + i)^n}, \tag{11.4}$$

where all variables are as described previously. This model is more accurate, but it is also more complex because the solution requires iteration. It is a variation of *internal rate of return* (*IRR*), involving the determination of the discount rate, i, that will equate the present value of the stream of coupon receipts, (c_t), and principal value, (P_p), with the current market price of the obligation, (P_m). Using the prior example (an 8 percent, 20-year bond, priced at $900), the promised yield is 9.11 percent:[4]

$$900 = 80 \sum_{t=1}^{20} \frac{1}{(1.0911)^t} + 1000 \frac{1}{(1.0911)^{20}}$$

$$= 80 (9.0625) + 1000(.1750)$$

$$= 900.$$

(In the preceding example, the values for $\dfrac{1}{1 + i}$ were obtained from the present value interest factor tables in the appendix at the back of the book using interpolation.)

When results from Equation 11.4 are compared with those of the approximate promised yield computation, a variation of 16 basis points in computed promised yield is revealed. As a rule, approximate yield tends to understate actual promised yield for issues trading at a discount, and the size of the differential varies directly with the length of the holding period; the greater n is, the bigger the difference will be. Note that the ranking of yields based on APY (Equation 11.3) will generally be identical to the rankings determined by more precise methods.

For maximum accuracy, semiannual rather than annual compounding should be used, since the cash flow from most bonds is semiannual. Even

---

[4] You will recall from our discussion of corporate finance that you would start with one rate (e.g., 9 percent) and compute the value of the stream. In this example, the value would exceed $900, so you would select a higher rate until you had a present value for the stream of cash flows of less than $900. Given the discount rates above and below the true rate, you would iterate or interpolate to the correct discount rate that would give you a value of $900.

when the cash flows occur over something other than six-month intervals (for example, GNMA pass-throughs), semiannual compounding is still used for the yield calculation. Semiannual compounding can be calculated by altering Equation 11.4 as follows:

$$P_m = \sum_{t=1}^{2n} \frac{C_t/2}{(1 + i/2)^t} + \frac{P_p}{(1 + i/2)^{2n}}, \tag{11.5}$$

where all the variables are as described previously. The major adjustments include doubling the number of periods within the investment horizon (i.e., six months rather than one year), and because coupons are received every six months, the value of c_t is halved. The promised yield with this method amounts to 9.09 percent. Because the calculation is identical to Equation 11.4, an illustration is unnecessary, but you can test your skills by using Equation 11.5 to compute the indicated YTM.

While the improvement in accuracy (two basis points) is minimal, it would be significant for large investment sums. Also, this is the procedure used to determine published bond quotes. Consequently, all subsequent present value calculations in this text will use only semiannual compounding.

YIELD TO CALL

While promised YTM is used most often, it is occasionally necessary to estimate return on the basis of promised *yield to call* (*YTC*). Whenever a *premium bond* is quoted at a value equal to or greater than par plus one year's interest, YTC should be computed in place of YTM, because the marketplace bases its pricing on the most conservative (i.e., lowest) yield measure. Therefore, when bonds are trading at or above a specified *crossover point* (which approximates par plus one year's interest), yield to call will normally provide the lowest yield measure.[5] At this price above par, the implied yield is low enough that it would be profitable for the firm to call the issue when allowed to (at the call date) and refund it with a new issue at the prevailing market rate. Therefore, this YTC is considered a more accurate reflection of what the bondholder will receive from holding this security because it is assumed that the obligation will be retired at the end of the deferred call period. Recently YTC has become important because numerous high-yielding, high-coupon obligations have been issued that possess substantial call risk.[6]

---

[5] For an extended discussion of the derivation of the crossover point, see Homer and Leibowitz, *Inside the Yield Book* (Englewood Cliffs, N.J.: Prentice-Hall, 1972), Chapter 4.

[6] There is an extensive literature on the refunding of bond issues, including W. M Boyce and A. J. Kalotay, "Optimum Bond Calling and Refunding," *Interfaces* (November 1979): 36–49; R. S. Harris, "The Refunding of Discounted Debt: An Adjusted Present Value Analysis," *Financial Management* 9, no. 4 (Winter 1980): 7–12; A. J. Kalotay, "On the Structure and Valuation of Debt Refundings," *Financial Management* 11, no. 1 (Spring 1982): 41–42; and John D. Finnerty, "Evaluating the Economics of Refunding High-Coupon Sinking-Fund Debt," *Financial Management* 12, no. 1 (Spring 1983): 5–10.

APPROXIMATE YIELD TO CALL. Yield to call is calculated by using variations of Equations 11.3, 11.4, or 11.5. The approximate yield to call (AYC) is computed using the following equation:

$$AYC = \frac{c_t + \dfrac{P_c - P_m}{nc}}{\dfrac{P_c + P_m}{2}},$$ (11.6)

where

P_c = the call price of the obligation (as noted, this is generally equal to par value plus one year's interest)

nc = the number of years to first call date.

All other variables in the model are as defined previously. This model is comparable to AYM, except that P_c has replaced P_p in Equation 11.3, and nc has replaced n.

Consider a 12 percent, 20-year bond that is trading at 115 ($1,150) with five years remaining to first call and a call price of 112 ($1120). Using Equation 11.6, we see that

$$AYC = \frac{120 + \dfrac{1120 - 1150}{5}}{\dfrac{1120 + 1150}{2}} = 10.04\%.$$

The bond's approximate yield to call is 10.04 percent, assuming the issue will be prematurely retired after five years at the call price of 112. You can compute the approximate promised YTM of this issue to confirm that yield to call is the more conservative value, and the more accurate value, since you expect the bond to be called in five years. (Promised YTM based on Equation 11.3 will equal 10.47 percent.)

Making a similar adjustment to the semiannual present value model (Equation 11.5) would result in the following model:

$$P_m = \sum_{t=1}^{2nc} \frac{c_t/2}{(1 + i/2)^t} + \frac{P_c}{(1 + i/2)^{2nc}},$$ (11.7)

where all the variables are the same as previously.

REALIZED YIELD   The final measure is *realized yield*, which assumes that the investor intends to liquidate the bond prior to maturity or the first call date. In essence, the investor has a holding period (*hp*) that is less than n (or nc). Realized yield determines the level of return attainable from various short-term trading strategies. The evaluation process considers the expected value of the bond when you liquidate it, which is, of course, subject to uncertainty. (You can also use this procedure to measure *actual* realized yield on a completed transaction.)

Realized yield is based on the promised yield valuation models (Equations 11.3, 11.4, and 11.5). The approximate realized yield (ARY) is given in Equation 11.8:

$$ARY = \frac{C_r + \dfrac{P_f - P_m}{hp}}{\dfrac{P_f + P_m}{2}},\qquad(11.8)$$

where

P_f = **the future selling price of the issue.**

hp = **the holding period of the issue in years.**

All other variables are as defined previously. Again, the same two variables change: the holding period (*hp*) is used instead of *n*, and P_f is used in lieu of P_p. Notably, P_f is not a contractual value but is *calculated* by defining the years remaining to maturity as $n - hp$ and by estimating a future market yield, *i*. We will discuss the computation of future price next.

APPROXIMATE REALIZED YIELD. Once *hp* and P_f are determined, approximate realized yield can be calculated. Assume an 8 percent, 20-year bond acquired for $750 that you expect to sell for $900 two years later, after interest rates have, you hope, declined. The approximate realized yield of this example would be

$$ARY = \frac{80 + \dfrac{900 - 750}{2}}{\dfrac{900 + 750}{2}} = 18.79\%\,.$$

The high return is the result of the expected realization of a substantial capital gain in a fairly short period of time. In a comparable manner, the introduction of P_f and *hp* into the semiannual compounding version of the present value model would create the following realized yield model:

$$P_m = \sum_{t=1}^{2hp} \frac{c_r/2}{(1 + i/2)^t} + \frac{P_f}{(1 + i/2)^{2hp}}.\qquad(11.9)$$

Because of the usually small number of periods in *hp*, the added accuracy of this measure is somewhat marginal. One might argue that, since realized yield measures are based on very uncertain expected price performance, there is some justification for using the approximate method under most circumstances. In contrast, if *actual* realized yield is being measured for performance purposes, you should use the more accurate semiannual basis of compounding.

BOND PRICES

There are two conditions under which bond dollar prices are important. First, when computing realized yield, you must determine the future price of an issue (P_f). Second, when issues are quoted on a (promised) yield basis, as with municipals, the quote must be converted to a dollar price, which is readily accomplished using Equation 11.5. The mechanics are simple and do not involve iteration—you only need to solve the equation for P_m. Coupon (c_t) is given, as is par value (P_p), and the market yield (i) is used as the discount rate. Consider a 10 percent, 25-year bond yielding 12 percent. The price of this issue is as follows:

$$P_m = 100/2 \sum_{t=1}^{50} \frac{1}{\left(1 + \dfrac{.120}{2}\right)} + 1000 \frac{1}{\left(1 + \dfrac{.120}{2}\right)^{50}}$$

$$= 50(15.7619) + 1000(.0543)$$

$$= \$842.40.$$

In contrast to current market price, you would compute future price (P_f) when attempting to determine the expected realized yield performance of alternative issues.

Portfolio managers who consistently trade bonds for the capital gains consider expected realized yield, rather than promised yield, to be the critical variable in the investment decision. P_f can be determined by using the following variation of the realized yield models (Equation 11.9):

$$P_f = \sum_{t=1}^{n-2hp} \frac{c_t/2}{(1 + i/2)^t} + \frac{P_p}{(1 + i/2)^{2n-2hp}}, \tag{11.10}$$

where all of the variables are as previously defined.

Observe that Equation 11.10 is a version of promised yield: a derived measure based on expected price performance at the end of the holding period (hp). Essentially, $2n - 2hp$ defines the remaining term to maturity of the issue at the end of the investor's holding period, that is, the number of six-month periods remaining at the date the issue is to be sold. The determination of P_f is based on coupon (c_t) and par value (P_p), both of which are given. In contrast, you must forecast the length of the holding period and therefore the number of years remaining to maturity at date of sale ($n - hp$), and the expected market yield at time of sale (i). Once this information is obtained/generated, the future price of the obligation can be determined. The real difficulty (and potential source of error) in specifying P_f lies in formulating hp and i.

As an example, consider the 10 percent, 25-year bond just discussed. Assume that you bought this bond at $842, which implies a YTM of 12 percent. Based upon extensive analysis, you expect the market yield on this bond to decline to 8 percent in five years. Therefore, you want to compute the future price (P_f) of this bond to estimate your expected rate of return, assuming you are correct. As noted, the two estimates you make are the holding period (5 years), which implies that the remaining life of the bond is 20 years, and the market yield of 8 percent. Using a semiannual model, the future price is

$$P_f = 50 \sum_{t=1}^{40} \frac{1}{(1.04)^t} + 1,000 \frac{1}{(1.04)^{40}}$$
$$= 50 \, (19.7928) + 1,000 \, (.2083)$$
$$= 989.64 + 208.30$$
$$= \$1197.94 \, .$$

Further, your estimate of the approximate annual return on this investment would be

$$APY = \frac{100 + \dfrac{1,198 - 842}{5}}{\dfrac{1,198 + 842}{2}}$$
$$= \frac{100 + 71.20}{1020}$$
$$= .1678$$
$$= 16.78\% \, .$$

REALIZED YIELD WITH DIFFERENTIAL REINVESTMENT RATES. You know that Equation 11.9 is the standard present value formula with the changes in holding period and ending price. As such, it also includes the implicit reinvestment rate assumption—that is, all cash flows are reinvested at the computed i rate. The point is, there may be instances where such an implicit assumption is not appropriate, given your expectations for future interest rates. Suppose current market interest rates are very high, and you decide to invest in a long-term bond (e.g., a 20-year, 14 percent coupon) to take advantage of an expected decline in rates over the near term horizon (e.g., you expect rates to go from 14 percent to 10 percent over a two-year period). We would use Equation 11.10 to compute the future price and Equation 11.9 to estimate the compound realized yield. We know that by using Equation 11.9 we will get a fairly high realized rate of return as follows:

$$P_m = \$1,000$$
$$hp = 2 \text{ years}$$
$$P_f = \sum_{t=1}^{36} 70 \, (1 + .05)^t + \$1,000/(1.05)^{36}$$
$$= \$1,158.30 + \$172.65$$
$$= \$1,330.95$$

$$\$1,000 = \sum_{t=1}^{4} \frac{70}{(1 + i/2)^t} + \frac{1330.95}{(1 + i/2)^4}$$
$$i = 27.50\% \, .$$

As we have discussed, this calculation implicitly assumes that all cash flows are reinvested at the computed i, which in this case is 27.50 percent. However, it is difficult to imagine that in an environment where market rates are going from 14 percent to 10 percent, you could reinvest the interest cash flows at 27.50 percent. It seems more appropriate and realistic to make *explicit assumptions regarding the reinvestment rates* and calculate the realized returns based upon your *ending-wealth position.* It turns out that this procedure is not only more precise and realistic, it is also easier, since it does not require iteration. Also we will see that it is used in Chapter 17 when we deal with bond portfolio immunization.

The basic technique is as follows: take all cash flows to the end of the holding period and thereby derive an *ending-wealth value,* which we can then compare to our *beginning-wealth value* in order to determine the *compound rate of return* that equalizes these two values. We have the following cash flows:

$$P_m = \$1,000$$
$$I = \text{Interest payments of } \$70 \text{ in 6, 12, 18, and 24 months}$$
$$P_f = \$1,330.95 \text{ (the ending market value of the bond)}.$$

To determine the ending value of the four interest payments, we must assume specific reinvestment rates. To simplify the calculations, assume that each payment is reinvested at a different rate, one that holds for its time period. Since interest rates are declining, assume that each of the first three interest payments is reinvested at a lower rate and the fourth is received at the end of the holding period as follows:

$$I_1 \text{ at 13\% for 18 months} = \$70 \times (1 + .065)^3 = \$\ \ 84.55$$
$$I_2 \text{ at 12\% for 12 months} = \$70 \times (1 + .06)^2 = \ \ \ \ 78.65$$
$$I_3 \text{ at 11\% for 6 months} = \$70 \times (1 + .055) = \ \ \ \ 73.65$$
$$I_4 \text{ not reinvested} = \$70 \times (1.0) = \ \ \ \ \underline{70.00}$$
$$\text{Future Value of Interest Payments} = \$\ 307.05.$$

Therefore, our total ending wealth value is

$$\$1,330.95 + \$307.05 = \$1,638.00.$$

To determine our compound realized rate of return, we compare our ending-wealth value ($1,638) to our beginning-wealth value ($1,000) and determine what interest rate would equalize these two values over a two-year holding period—that is, what rate will compound the $1,000 to $1,638 in two years. To find this, compute the ratio of ending wealth to beginning wealth (1.638), and find this ratio in a compound value table for two years or four periods (assuming semiannual compounding). Using Table C.3 at the end of the book for four periods, you will see that the realized rate is somewhere between 12 percent (1.5735) and 14 percent (1.6890). Interpolating between these two will give you an estimate of 13.16 percent or an annual rate of 26.32 percent.

This computed compound realized yield specifically states the expected reinvestment rates as contrasted to assuming the reinvestment rate is equal to the computed realized yield. As noted in the subsequent discussion on immunization, the actual assumption regarding the reinvestment rate is very important.

PRICE AND YIELD DETERMINATION ON NONINTEREST DATES

So far, we have assumed that the investor buys (or sells) an obligation precisely on the date that interest is due, so the measures are accurate only when issues are traded on coupon payment dates. If the approximate yield or the annual compounding version of the present value model is used, sufficient accuracy is normally obtained by extrapolating for transactions on noninterest payment dates. You are already dealing with varying degrees of approximation, and a bit more is probably acceptable.

However, when the semiannual model is used, and when more accuracy is necessary, another version of the price and yield model must be employed for transactions on noninterest payment dates. Fortunately, the basic models need be extended only one more step, since the value of an issue that trades X years, Y months, and so many days from maturity is found by extrapolating the bond value (price or yield) for the month before and the month after the day of transaction. Thus, the valuation process involves full months to maturity rather than years or semiannual periods.[7]

Bond valuation on a noncoupon payment date involves the following simple algorithm:

1. Determine the price of the issue via the standard semiannual compounding model for the next coupon payment date.
2. Add the coupon payment to be received at the next coupon date (since it is not included in Step 1).
3. Discount this sum, which is equivalent to the value of the bond on the next coupon payment date, to its present value.
4. Adjust the computed value for the accrued interest.

This can be shown as

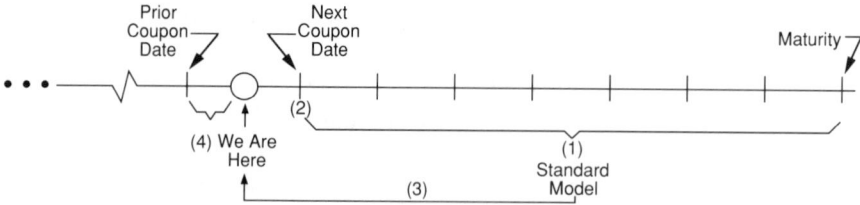

Essentially, we find the value of the bond on the next coupon date (Step 1), add the interest payment to be received on the next coupon date (Step

---

[7] Note that for corporate, agency, and municipal markets, a month is described as a 30-day period, regardless of the number of days actually in the month. In contrast, Treasury obligations use a 365-day (or 366-day) calendar and actually count the number of days in the month. For our purposes, we will assume that the standard 30-day month prevails.

2), discount the sum of these back to the present (Step 3), and finally, net out accrued interest (Step 4). In equation terms this is as follows:

$$P_m = \left[\frac{\sum_{t=1}^{2n} \frac{c_t/2}{(1 + i/2)^t} + \frac{P_p}{(1 + i/2)^{2n}} + \frac{c_t}{2}}{(1 + i/2)^{m/6}} \right] - \frac{c_t}{2}\left(1 - \frac{m}{6}\right), \qquad (11.11)$$

where

> m = the number of months to the next coupon payment date
> n = the number of annual periods to maturity after the next coupon payment date. All other variables are as defined previously.

An examination of Equation 11.11 indicates the four steps in the algorithm. Fortunately, this procedure does not involve extensive computational complexity and can be used to determine *yield* by solving for i (through iteration) or, when given a market yield, can be used to determine *price* by solving for P_m. In addition, with slight variations of this model, yield to call and expected realized yield can be computed.

To demonstrate this model, assume we want to find the price on an accrued interest basis, of a $1,000, 10 percent bond with maturity of 12 years and 3 months and a YTM of 8 percent. Using Equation 11.11, we can determine its price as follows:

$$P_m = \left[\frac{\sum_{t=1}^{24} \frac{100/2}{(1.04)^t} + \frac{1.000}{(1.04)^{24}} + \frac{100}{2}}{(1.04)^{3/6}} \right] - \frac{100}{2}\left(1 - \frac{3}{6}\right)$$

$$= \left[\frac{50(15.247) + 1000(.3901) + 50}{1.01980} \right] - 50(.5)$$

$$= \left[\frac{1202.45}{1.01980} \right] - 25 = \$1,154.10.$$

This procedure is universal in finding the price or yield of an obligation that trades on any date other than the interest payment date. When the issue trades within the month, Equation 11.11 is used to find the price (or yield) at full monthly intervals on both sides of the purchase date. To find the price of an issue that has 12 years, 3 months, and 15 days to maturity, one would value the obligation (in full monthly increments) on both sides of the 15 days. Find the price with 12 years and 3 months to maturity, and with 12 years and 4 months to maturity, and then use extrapolation to determine the price or yield of the obligation.

TAX-EXEMPT ISSUES

Municipal bonds, Treasury issues, and many agency obligations possess one common characteristic: their interest income is partially or fully tax-exempt. Recall that Treasury and federal agency obligations are exempt from state and local taxation, while some agencies are even free from federal income taxes (HUD project notes, for example) and interest income on municipal obligations is exempt from federal and local levies. Using promised yield as a basis of discussion, the tax status of an issue (including its ordinary income and capital gains tax liability) can be included in the valuation model as follows:

$$P_m = \sum_{t=1}^{2n} \frac{C_t/2\,(1-\tau)}{(1+i/2)^t} + \frac{P_p - k\,(P_p - P_m)}{(1+i/2)^{2n}},$$
(11.12)

where:

τ = **the investor's marginal tax liability on ordinary income**

k = **the investor's capital gains tax rate.**

The other terms are as defined above.

While Equation 11.12 provides a measure of *after-tax* promised yield, it follows that, with slight variations, the yield to call and realized yield formulas can be modified to accommodate the various tax effects and also transactions that occur on noninterest-payment dates. In addition, the tax-adjusted models can be used when some of the issues are subject to normal taxation and others are tax-free. The valuation process adjusts for the specific tax liability of the obligation in generating after-tax yield (or price), because the general specification of τ and k in Equation 11.12 permits the analyst to define the source or extent of tax liability. As a result, these variables should include appropriate federal, state, and/or local tax rates (depending, of course, on the exposure of the specific issue). For example, τ would equal 0 for a person holding a municipal bond in the state of Texas, since Texas has no state or local income taxes. Likewise, it would be 0 for a California resident holding a California issue. In contrast, a California issue would require a $\tau > 0$ for a New York City resident, since the issue would not be tax-exempt for residents of New York, and residents of that city are subject to state and local income taxes.

Place of residency is irrelevant for capital gains because taxpayers in a positive tax bracket are subject to this tax. Since the mechanics of yield and price valuation for the tax-adjusted models are the same as for the prior models, it is unnecessary to illustrate the computational techniques. Instead, to confirm your understanding, consider the following example: A resident of Texas (with $\tau = 0$) is considering the purchase of a 5 percent, 25-year municipal obligation that is currently priced at $3,827 (par value of $5,000). The investor has a 20 percent tax rate and wants to determine the after-tax promised yield of the issue.[8]

Undoubtedly the most popular and one of the most often cited measures of performance for municipal issues is the *fully taxable equivalent yield (FTEY)*, which adjusts the promised yield computation for tax-exempt features. The process involves determining promised yield using one of

[8] From Equation 11.12, the answer is 6.91 percent.

the formulas discussed previously and then adjusting the derived yield to reflect the rate of return that must be earned on fully taxable issues (e.g., corporates) to equal the fully or partially tax-exempt obligation. It is measured as

$$FTEY = \frac{i}{1-T},$$ (11.13)

where

i = promised yield
T = the amount and type of tax exemption provided by the issue in question.
All other terms are as defined earlier.

Note that this simple computation is applicable only to par bonds or current coupon obligations, such as new issues, because the measure considers only interest income, ignoring capital gains. Therefore, it is inappropriate for issues trading at significant variation from par value.

BOND YIELD BOOKS

Bond value tables, commonly known as *bond books* or *yield books*, can eliminate much of the mathematics from bond valuation. An illustration of a page from a yield book is provided in Figure 11.2. It is like a present value interest factor table to the extent that a matrix of bond prices is provided relative to a stated coupon rate, various terms to maturity (on the horizontal axis), and promised yields (on the vertical axis). Such a table allows the user to readily determine either promised yield or price. Observe in Situation A that a 17 1/2-year, 8 percent bond yielding 10 percent would carry a price of 83.63. Likewise, in Situation B, a 20-year issue priced at 109.54 would yield 7.10 percent. As might be expected, access to sophisticated calculators or computers has substantially reduced the need for and use of yield books. For our purposes, though, it is essential that you understand the detailed mechanics and subtleties of the various yield and price models including promised yield, yield to call, realized yield, and bond prices.

DETERMINANTS OF BOND YIELDS AND YIELD SPREADS

Given that the value of a bond is equal to the present value of its future cash flow stream, an important factor is the discount rate. In the promised yield model, this rate reflects prevailing market interest rates. Because the prices of both new and seasoned issues are determined by interest rate behavior, they are stated in terms of *bond yields* or *interest rates*. Thus, market interest rates (i.e., promised yields on bonds) influence the cost of funds to issuers, the return to bond investors, and the price behavior of outstanding bonds. Therefore, anybody investing in or managing bonds must constantly evaluate the current level of market interest rates and expected changes in these rates.

FIGURE 11.2
A Yield Book

A — YEARS and MONTHS — **8%**

Yield	14-6	15-0	15-6	16-0	16-6	17-0	17-6	18-0
4.00	143.69	144.79	145.88	146.94	147.98	149.00	150.03	150.98
4.20	140.96	141.97	142.97	143.95	144.91	145.84	146.76	147.66
4.40	138.29	139.23	140.14	141.04	141.92	142.78	143.62	144.44
4.60	135.69	136.55	137.39	138.21	139.01	139.80	140.56	141.31
4.80	133.15	133.94	134.71	135.46	136.19	136.90	137.60	138.28
5.00	130.68	131.40	132.09	132.77	133.44	134.09	134.72	135.33
5.20	128.27	128.92	129.55	130.16	130.76	131.35	131.92	132.47
5.40	125.91	126.50	127.07	127.62	128.16	128.69	129.20	129.70
5.60	123.62	124.14	124.65	125.15	125.63	126.10	126.55	127.00
5.80	121.38	121.84	122.30	122.74	123.16	123.58	123.98	124.38
6.00	119.19	119.60	120.00	120.39	120.77	121.13	121.49	121.83
6.10	118.11	118.50	118.87	119.24	119.59	119.93	120.26	120.59
6.20	117.05	117.41	117.76	118.10	118.43	118.75	119.06	119.36
6.30	116.01	116.34	116.67	116.98	117.29	117.58	117.87	118.15
6.40	114.97	115.28	115.58	115.88	116.16	116.43	116.70	116.96
6.50	113.95	114.24	114.51	114.78	115.05	115.30	115.54	115.78
6.60	112.94	113.20	113.46	113.71	113.95	114.18	114.40	114.62
6.70	111.94	112.18	112.42	112.64	112.86	113.07	113.28	113.48
6.80	110.95	111.17	111.39	111.59	111.79	111.99	112.17	112.35
6.90	109.98	110.18	110.37	110.56	110.74	110.91	111.08	111.24
7.00	109.02	109.20	109.37	109.53	109.70	109.85	110.00	110.15
7.10	108.07	108.22	108.38	108.52	108.67	108.80	108.94	109.07
7.20	107.13	107.27	107.40	107.53	107.65	107.77	107.89	108.00
7.30	106.20	106.32	106.43	106.54	106.65	106.75	106.85	106.95
7.40	105.28	105.38	105.48	105.57	105.66	105.75	105.83	105.92
7.50	104.37	104.46	104.54	104.61	104.69	104.78	104.83	104.90
7.60	103.48	103.54	103.61	103.67	103.73	103.78	103.84	103.89
7.70	102.59	102.64	102.69	102.73	102.78	102.82	102.86	102.90
7.80	101.72	101.75	101.78	101.81	101.84	101.87	101.89	101.92
7.90	100.85	100.87	100.88	100.90	100.91	100.93	100.94	100.95
8.00	100.00	100.00	100.00	100.00	100.00	100.00	100.00	100.00
8.10	99.16	99.14	99.13	99.11	99.10	99.09	99.07	99.06
8.20	98.32	98.29	98.26	98.24	98.21	98.18	98.16	98.14
8.30	97.50	97.45	97.41	97.37	97.33	97.29	97.26	97.22
8.40	96.68	96.62	96.57	96.51	96.46	96.41	96.37	96.32
8.50	95.88	95.81	95.74	95.67	95.61	95.55	95.49	95.43
8.60	95.08	95.00	94.91	94.84	94.76	94.69	94.63	94.56
8.70	94.29	94.20	94.10	94.01	93.93	93.85	93.77	93.69
8.80	93.52	93.41	93.30	93.20	93.10	93.01	92.92	92.84
8.90	92.75	92.63	92.51	92.40	92.29	92.19	92.09	92.00
9.00	91.99	91.86	91.73	91.61	91.49	91.38	91.27	91.17
9.10	91.24	91.09	90.96	90.82	90.70	90.57	90.46	90.35
9.20	90.50	90.34	90.19	90.05	89.91	89.78	89.66	89.54
9.30	89.76	89.60	89.44	89.29	89.14	89.00	88.87	88.74
9.40	89.04	88.86	88.69	88.53	88.38	88.23	88.09	87.96
9.50	88.32	88.13	87.96	87.79	87.62	87.47	87.32	87.18
9.60	87.61	87.42	87.23	87.05	86.88	86.72	86.57	86.42
9.70	86.91	86.71	86.51	86.32	86.15	85.98	85.81	85.66
9.80	86.22	86.01	85.80	85.61	85.42	85.24	85.08	84.91
9.90	85.54	85.31	85.10	84.90	84.70	84.52	84.35	84.18
10.00	84.86	84.63	84.41	84.20	84.00	83.81	83.63	83.45
10.20	83.53	83.28	83.05	82.82	82.61	82.41	82.22	82.03
10.40	82.23	81.97	81.72	81.48	81.25	81.04	80.84	80.64
10.60	80.96	80.68	80.42	80.17	79.93	79.71	79.50	79.29
10.80	79.72	79.43	79.15	78.89	78.64	78.41	78.19	77.98
11.00	78.50	78.20	77.91	77.64	77.39	77.14	76.91	76.70
11.20	77.31	77.00	76.71	76.43	76.16	75.91	75.67	75.45
11.40	76.15	75.83	75.52	75.24	74.96	74.70	74.46	74.23
11.60	75.02	74.68	74.37	74.07	73.79	73.53	73.28	73.04
11.80	73.90	73.56	73.24	72.94	72.65	72.38	72.13	71.89
12.00	72.82	72.47	72.14	71.83	71.54	71.26	71.00	70.76

8% — YEARS and MONTHS — **B**

Yield	18-6	19-0	19-6	20-0	20-6	21-0	21-6	22-0
4.00	151.94	152.88	153.81	154.71	155.60	156.47	157.32	158.16
4.20	148.54	149.40	150.25	151.08	151.89	152.68	153.46	154.22
4.40	145.24	146.03	146.80	147.56	148.29	149.02	149.72	150.41
4.60	142.05	142.76	143.46	144.15	144.82	145.47	146.11	146.74
4.80	138.95	139.60	140.23	140.85	141.45	142.05	142.62	143.19
5.00	135.94	136.52	137.10	137.65	138.20	138.73	139.25	139.76
5.20	133.02	133.54	134.06	134.56	135.05	135.52	135.99	136.44
5.40	130.18	130.65	131.11	131.56	132.00	132.42	132.84	133.24
5.60	127.43	127.85	128.26	128.66	129.04	129.42	129.79	130.14
5.80	124.76	125.13	125.49	125.84	126.18	126.51	126.84	127.15
6.00	122.17	122.49	122.81	123.11	123.41	123.70	123.98	124.25
6.10	120.90	121.20	121.50	121.78	122.06	122.33	122.59	122.84
6.20	119.65	119.93	120.21	120.47	120.73	120.98	121.22	121.46
6.30	118.42	118.68	118.93	119.18	119.42	119.65	119.87	120.09
6.40	117.21	117.45	117.68	117.91	118.13	118.34	118.55	118.75
6.50	116.01	116.23	116.45	116.66	116.86	117.05	117.24	117.43
6.60	114.83	115.04	115.23	115.42	115.61	115.79	115.96	116.13
6.70	113.67	113.86	114.04	114.21	114.38	114.54	114.70	114.85
6.80	112.53	112.69	112.86	113.01	113.17	113.31	113.46	113.59
6.90	111.40	111.55	111.70	111.84	111.97	112.11	112.23	112.36
7.00	110.29	110.42	110.55	110.68	110.80	110.92	111.03	111.14
7.10	109.19	109.31	109.42	109.54	109.64	109.75	109.85	109.94
7.20	108.11	108.21	108.31	108.41	108.50	108.60	108.68	108.77
7.30	107.04	107.13	107.22	107.30	107.38	107.46	107.54	107.61
7.40	105.99	106.07	106.14	106.21	106.28	106.35	106.41	106.47
7.50	104.96	105.02	105.08	105.14	105.19	105.25	105.30	105.35
7.60	103.94	104.00	104.03	104.08	104.12	104.16	104.20	104.24
7.70	102.93	102.97	103.00	103.04	103.07	103.10	103.13	103.16
7.80	101.94	101.96	101.99	102.01	102.03	102.05	102.07	102.09
7.90	100.96	100.98	100.99	101.00	101.01	101.02	101.03	101.04
8.00	100.00	100.00	100.00	100.00	100.00	100.00	100.00	100.00
8.10	99.05	99.04	99.03	99.02	99.01	99.00	98.99	98.98
8.20	98.11	98.09	98.07	98.06	98.03	98.01	97.99	97.98
8.30	97.19	97.16	97.13	97.10	97.07	97.04	97.01	96.99
8.40	96.28	96.24	96.19	96.16	96.12	96.09	96.04	96.02
8.50	95.38	95.33	95.28	95.23	95.19	95.14	95.10	95.06
8.60	94.49	94.43	94.37	94.32	94.26	94.21	94.16	94.12
8.70	93.62	93.55	93.48	93.42	93.36	93.30	93.24	93.19
8.80	92.76	92.68	92.61	92.53	92.46	92.40	92.34	92.28
8.90	91.91	91.82	91.74	91.66	91.58	91.51	91.44	91.38
9.00	91.08	90.98	90.89	90.80	90.72	90.64	90.56	90.49
9.10	90.24	90.14	90.04	89.95	89.86	89.78	89.70	89.62
9.20	89.43	89.32	89.21	89.11	89.02	88.93	88.84	88.76
9.30	88.62	88.51	88.40	88.29	88.19	88.09	88.00	87.91
9.40	87.83	87.71	87.59	87.48	87.37	87.27	87.17	87.08
9.50	87.05	86.92	86.80	86.68	86.57	86.46	86.36	86.26
9.60	86.27	86.14	86.01	85.89	85.77	85.66	85.55	85.45
9.70	85.51	85.37	85.24	85.11	84.99	84.87	84.76	84.66
9.80	84.76	84.62	84.48	84.34	84.22	84.10	83.98	83.87
9.90	84.02	83.87	83.72	83.59	83.46	83.33	83.21	83.10
10.00	83.29	83.13	82.98	82.84	82.71	82.58	82.45	82.34
10.20	81.86	81.69	81.53	81.38	81.24	81.10	80.97	80.85
10.40	80.46	80.28	80.12	79.96	79.81	79.67	79.53	79.40
10.60	79.10	78.92	78.74	78.58	78.42	78.28	78.13	78.00
10.80	77.78	77.59	77.41	77.24	77.08	76.92	76.78	76.64
11.00	76.49	76.29	76.11	75.93	75.76	75.61	75.46	75.31
11.20	75.23	75.03	74.84	74.66	74.49	74.33	74.17	74.03
11.40	74.01	73.80	73.61	73.42	73.25	73.08	72.93	72.78
11.60	72.82	72.61	72.41	72.22	72.04	71.87	71.71	71.56
11.80	71.66	71.44	71.24	71.05	70.87	70.70	70.53	70.38
12.00	70.53	70.31	70.10	69.91	69.72	69.55	69.39	69.23

This book takes a practical view of the role of interest rates in the bond investment decision. Since interest rate forecasting requires extensive econometric modeling, a task we shall leave to the professional economist, our goal as bond investors and bond portfolio managers should be simply to monitor current and expected interest rate behavior. In this way, a bond portfolio manager can assess the major dimensions of interest rate behavior on his own and rely on economic consulting firms, banks, or major investment banking firms for more detailed insights.[9] This is precisely the way many large bond portfolio management firms operate.

[9] Examples would include Merrill-Lynch's *Fixed Income Weekly, Currency and Bond Market Trends* (a

FIGURE 11.3
International 10-Year Government Bond Yields

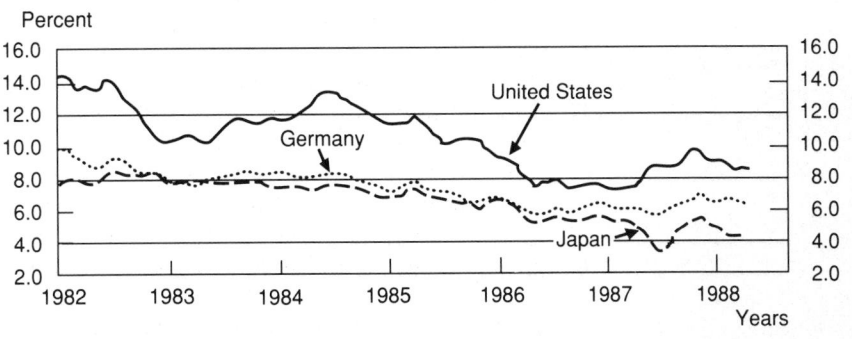

Note: For Japan and Germany, rates on newly issued securities are given until October 1986; secondary market yields are quoted thereafter.

Sources: Federal Reserve Bank, Telerate, *Capital Markets Chartbook* (New York: Kidder, Peabody & Co., 1988).

FUNDAMENTAL DETERMINANTS OF INTEREST RATES

As shown in Figure 11.3, average interest rates for long-term U.S. government bonds during 1982 reached almost 15 percent. By early 1987 the same average corporate bond rate had dropped to under 8 percent. In contrast, the rate on Japanese government bonds peaked at slightly over 8 percent in 1982 and dropped to about 3 percent in mid-1987. A primary concern to the bond investor is the reason why interest rates behaved this way. As you know from your knowledge of bond pricing, bond prices rose dramatically during the period when market interest rates dropped, and some investors experienced very attractive returns. In contrast, some investors experienced losses during several periods when interest rates increased. A casual analysis of this chart that only covers about six years indicates the need for monitoring interest rates. Essentially, interest rates (i) can be specified according to the following conceptual model:

$$i = RFR + I + RP, \qquad (11.14)$$

where

RFR = the risk-free rate of interest

I = expected inflation

RP = the risk premium.

---

weekly review) and *World Bond Market Monitor* (a bi-weekly analysis of international bond yields and yield spreads); Goldman Sachs *The Pocket Chartroom* (a monthly publication on interest rates and other economic variables) and *Financial Market Perspectives* (a monthly publication on monetary policy and interest rates); Kidder, Peabody & Co.'s *Capital Markets Chartbook* (a monthly publication on domestic and international interest rates and other economic series); and "The International Report" (monthly), which considers global returns on bonds, analysis of exchange rates, and specific country factors.

While Equation 11.14 appears deceptively simple, it is a complete statement of the complex nature of interest rate behavior. More difficult is the specification of future behavior with regard to such aspects as inflation, default, and other economic considerations. In this regard, interest rates are like stock prices in that they are extremely difficult to forecast with any degree of accuracy.[10] In essence, interest rates can be viewed as being related to economic and issue characteristics:

$$i = f(\text{Economic Forces} + \text{Issue Characteristics})$$
$$= (RFR + I) + RP.$$

This is nothing more than a rearranged version of Equation 11.14, but it facilitates a discussion of the fundamental determinants of interest rates.[11]

The pure rate of interest (RFR) is the economic cost of money, and it represents the opportunity cost necessary to compensate individuals for forgoing consumption. It is the interest rate level below which investors would be indifferent to holding either cash or a financial asset like bonds.

Expected inflation is the other economic dimension of interest rates. The *expected level of inflation* (I) is added to the risk-free rate (RFR) in order to specify a general *market-based level of interest*. For example, if the RFR is 3 percent, and expected inflation (I) is 6 percent, then it follows that the market-based (nominal) risk-free rate of interest (i) would equal approximately 9 percent.[12] Given the general stability of the RFR, it is clear that the wide swings in i experienced during the six years are mainly because of swings in expected inflation.[13] Besides the unique country exchange rate risk that is discussed in the section on risk premium, the differential inflation in alternative countries has a major impact on the level of interest rates among countries.

Supply and demand for loanable funds are the fundamental economic determinants of i. For example, as the supply of loanable funds increases, the level of interest rates declines, other things being equal, while the opposite effect holds when the demand for loanable funds increases. The actions of a country's monetary authorities (e.g., the Federal Reserve in the United States) have a significant influence on the supply of money. Other factors that impact on the supply of funds are the savings pattern of U.S. and non–U.S. investors. This latter group has become very impor-

---

[10] For an overview of what is involved in forecasting interest rates, see W. David Woolford, "Forecasting Interest Rates" in *Handbook of Fixed Income Securities,* 2d ed., edited by Frank J. Fabozzi and Irving M. Pollack (Homewood, Ill.: Dow Jones-Irwin, 1987); and Frank J. Jones and Benjamin Wolkowitz, "The Determinants of Interest Rates on Fixed-Income Securities," in *The Financial Analysts Handbook,* 2d ed., edited by Sumner N. Levine (Homewood, Ill.: Dow Jones-Irwin, 1988).

[11] For an extensive exploration of interest rates and interest rate behavior, see James C. Van Horne, *Financial Market Rates and Flows,* 2d ed. (Englewood Cliffs, N.J.: Prentice-Hall, 1984).

[12] We know from several prior discussions that the estimate derived by adding the two rates is an approximation of the more correct multiplicative estimate: $(1 + RFR)(1 + I) - 1$, which would be .0918 = 9.18 percent.

[13] In this regard, see R. W. Hafer, "Inflation: Assessing Its Recent Behavior and Future Prospects," Federal Reserve Bank of St. Louis *Review* 65, no. 7 (August–September 1983): 36–41; Milton Friedman and Anna J. Schwartz, *Monetary Trends in the United States and the United Kingdom: Their Relation to Income, Prices, and Interest Rates, 1867–1975* (Chicago: University of Chicago Press, 1982).

tant in recent years, as shown by the significant purchases of U.S. securities by non-U.S. investors, most notably the Japanese.

The demand for loanable funds is affected by the capital and operating needs of the U.S. government, federal agencies, state and local governments, corporations, and institutions.[14] Essentially, the net intensity of demand varies according to requirements in each of the sectors. Federal government budget deficits increase demand for loanable funds from the Treasury. Likewise, the level of consumer demand, along with corporate demand based upon the amount of internally generated funds (net of dividend payouts), will affect rates.

Feldstein and Eckstein (FE)[15] described the fundamental determinants of interest rates using many of these economic variables. When they attempted to identify the determinants of yields on seasoned long-term Moody's AAA-rated corporate bonds, they found that bond yields were inversely related to money supply and directly related to the level of real personal income (a proxy for economic activity), the demand for loanable funds (from the Treasury), the level of inflation, and changes in short-run interest rate expectations. The r^2 value of their model was a hefty 99.2 percent, and the expected relationships were confirmed. Such findings imply that investors should monitor the supply and demand for loanable funds, Federal Reserve policy, fiscal policy, and prices.

Interest rates are also influenced by issue characteristics. The *risk premium* (*RP*) component of *i* is directly associated with the characteristics of the issue and issuer. Whereas the economic forces (the risk-free rate and inflation) reflect a market- or systemwide level of interest rates, issue characteristics are unique to individual securities' market sectors or countries. Thus, the differences in the yields of corporate and Treasury issues in a country are not caused by economic forces but rather by differential issue characteristics, that is, differences in the risk premium.

Four major risk premium components should be considered by bond investors and portfolio managers:

1. Quality differentials (or risk of default)
2. Term to maturity, which can affect rate uncertainty as well as yield and price volatility
3. Indenture provisions (including collateral, call features, and sinking fund provisions)
4. Exchange rate risk differences among countries.

Of the four, quality and maturity considerations are the most important and dominate the risk premium, although the exchange rate uncertainty is becoming more important. Quality considerations reflect the risk of

---

[14] As an example, see *Prospects for Financial Markets in 1989* (New York: Salomon Bros., Inc., December 1988). This is an annual publication of Salomon Brothers that gives an estimate of the flow of funds in the major world economies and discusses the effect of this on various currencies and interest rates, making recommendations for global asset allocation (equity and fixed-income) on the basis of these expectations.

[15] Martin Feldstein and Otto Eckstein, "The Fundamental Determinants of the Interest Rate," *The Review of Economics and Statistics* 52, no. 4 (November 1970): 363–375.

default, which is primarily the ability of the issuer to service outstanding debt obligations and is largely captured in agency ratings. Quality considerations mean there will be yield differentials among bonds with different ratings, but also among different market segments. For example, AAA-rated obligations possess lower risk of default than BBB obligations do and therefore provide lower yield. Numerous studies have indicated that risk premiums are largely dependent upon the intrinsic characteristics of the issuer.[16] However, risk premiums are, at times, also closely related to prevailing economic conditions. When the economy becomes depressed, the desire for quality increases, and higher quality issues are bid up in price as investors seek the security of higher-rated bonds. This variability in the risk premium over time is demonstrated and discussed in Chapter 13.

Maturity influences the risk premium because it affects an investor's level of uncertainty as well as price and yield volatility. As will be discussed in the section on the term structure, there is generally a positive relationship between the term to maturity of an issue and the level of interest rates.

As discussed in Chapter 10, relevant indenture provisions include the collateral provided, the call feature, and sinking-fund provisions. Collateral provides capital protection to the investor on those rare occasions of corporate insolvency and forced liquidation. The call feature can be very influential—other things being equal, the greater the call risk protection, the lower the market yield. This is particularly true for new issues and current coupon obligations and especially during periods of high interest rates, because when you get a bond with a high coupon, you want protection from having it called away from you when rates decline.[17] The sinking-fund feature is meant to reduce the investor's risk and thus should result in a lower yield for two reasons. First, it reduces default risk by systematically reducing outstanding principal. Second, purchases for a sinking fund provide support for the bond because of the added demand and also contribute to a more liquid secondary market because of the increased trading. Since sinking-fund provisions result in reduced average maturity, they tend to reduce the risk premium component of interest rates much as a shorter maturity would reduce yield.[18]

---

[16] See, for example, Lawrence Fisher, "Determinants of Risk Premiums on Corporate Bonds," *Journal of Political Economy* 67, no. 3 (June 1959): 217; and Larry K. Hastie, "Determinants of Municipal Bond Yields," *Journal of Financial and Quantitative Analysis* 7, no. 3 (June 1972): 1729–1748. These are in addition to the numerous studies that examined the relationship between bond quality ratings and internal firm characteristics as discussed in Chapter 9.

[17] William Marshall and Jess B. Yawitz, "Optimal Terms of the Call Provision on a Corporate Bond," *Journal of Financial Research* 3, no. 3 (Fall 1980): 203–211; and Michael G. Ferri, "Systematic Return Risk and the Call Risk of Corporate Debt Instruments," *Journal of Financial Research* 1, no. 1 (Winter 1978): 1–13.

[18] For a further discussion of sinking funds, see Edward A. Dyl and Michael D. Joehnk, "Sinking Funds and the Cost of Corporate Debt," *Journal of Finance* 34, no. 4 (September 1979): 887–893; A. J. Kalotay, "On the Management of Sinking Funds," *Financial Management* 10, no. 2 (Summer 1981): 34–40; and A. J. Kalotay, "Sinking Funds and the Realized Cost of Debt," *Financial Management* 11, no. 1 (Spring 1982): 43–54.

FIGURE 11.4
Treasury Yield Curves

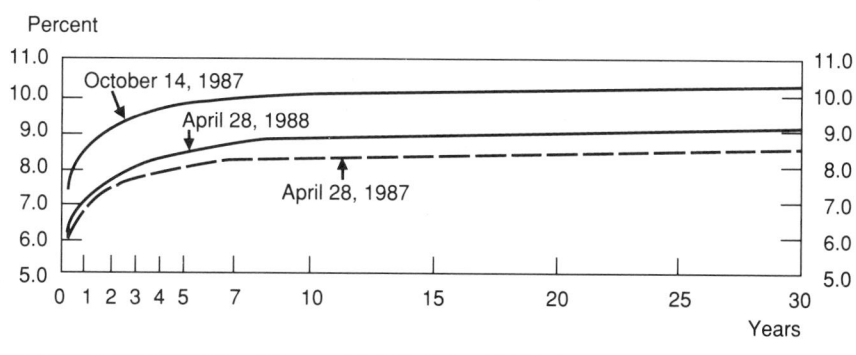

Source: Federal Reserve Bank; *Capital Markets Chartbook* (New York: Kidder, Peabody & Co., 1988).

We know that because currency exchange rates between countries change over time, global investing has an added uncertainy (risk). The point of this risk component is that there are differences in the variability of exchange rates among countries because trade balances and inflation changes differ among countries. The more volatile these factors are in a country, the larger its exchange rate risk premium.

**TERM
STRUCTURE
OF INTEREST
RATES**

The term structure of interest rates (or the yield curve, as it is more popularly known) has long intrigued theoreticians, academicians, and practitioners.[19] It is a static function that relates term to maturity to yield to maturity at a given point in time. Thus, it represents a cross section of yields for a category of bonds that are comparable in all respects but maturity. The quality of the issues must be held constant, and ideally you should have similar coupons, call features, and industry category. Therefore, it is possible to conceive of different yield curves for Treasury issues, government agencies, prime-grade municipals, AAA utilities, and so on. The quality of the yield curve will depend upon your ability to have a sample of bonds with comparable characteristics.

As an example, Figure 11.4 contains yield curves constructed for a sample of U.S. Treasury obligations. Yield to maturity information on a set of comparable Treasury issues was obtained from a publication like the *Federal Reserve Bulletin* or *The Wall Street Journal* at three different points in time to show changes in the level of yields and the shape of the yield curve. These promised yields were plotted on the graph, and a yield curve

---

[19] For a discussion of the theory and empirical evidence, see Burton G. Malkiel, *The Term Structure of Interest Rates: Theory, Empirical Evidence, and Applications* (New York: The McCaleb-Seiler Publishing Company, 1970); and Richard W. McEnally, "The Term Structure of Interest Rates," in *The Handbook of Fixed Income Securities*, 2d ed., edited by Frank J. Fabozzi and Irving M. Pollack (Homewood, Ill.: Dow Jones-Irwin, 1987).

FIGURE 11.5
Types of Yield Curves

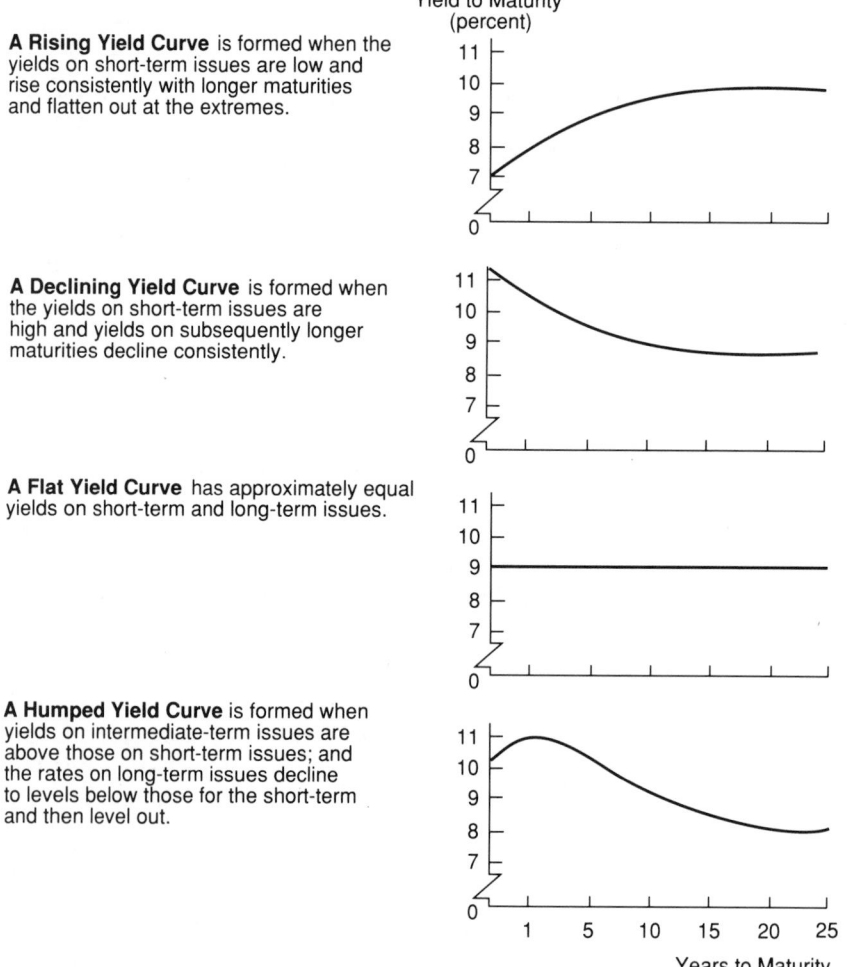

A Rising Yield Curve is formed when the yields on short-term issues are low and rise consistently with longer maturities and flatten out at the extremes.

A Declining Yield Curve is formed when the yields on short-term issues are high and yields on subsequently longer maturities decline consistently.

A Flat Yield Curve has approximately equal yields on short-term and long-term issues.

A Humped Yield Curve is formed when yields on intermediate-term issues are above those on short-term issues; and the rates on long-term issues decline to levels below those for the short-term and then level out.

is drawn that represents the general configuration of rates (even with all Treasury issues, not all points will plot exactly on the curve).

All yield curves, of course, do not have the same shape as those in Figure 11.4. But the point of the example is, while yield curves per se are static in nature, *their behavior over time is quite fluid!* As shown, the level of the curve was quite low in April 1987, fairly high in October 1987, just prior to the crash, and lower again in April 1988. Also, the shape of the yield curve can undergo dramatic alterations, following one of the four patterns shown in Figure 11.5. The ascending curve is the most common and tends to prevail when interest rates are at low or modest levels. The declining yield curve tends to prevail when rates are at relatively high levels and the humped yield when rates are extremely high and about to retreat to more normal levels. The flat yield curve rarely exists for any period of time. Note that in all cases the slope of the line tends to level off after 15 years.

Why does the term structure assume different shapes? Three major theories are available: the expectations hypothesis, the liquidity preference hypothesis, and the segmented market hypothesis.[20]

EXPECTATIONS HYPOTHESIS. According to the expectations hypothesis, the shape of the term structure is explained by the interest rate expectations of market participants. More specifically, any long-term rate is simply the geometric mean of current and future one-year rates expected to prevail over the horizon of the issue. In essence, a series of intermediate and long-term rates are part of the term structure, each of which, in turn, is a reflection of the geometric average of current and expected one-year rates. Under such conditions, the equilibrium long-term rate is clearly that which the long-term investor would expect to earn through successive investments in short-term securities over an investment horizon equal to the term to maturity of the longer-term issue. This relationship can be formalized in a general manner as follows:

$$(1 + {}_t R_n) = [(1 + {}_t R_1)(1 + {}_{t+1} r_1) \ldots (1 + {}_{t+n-1} r_1)]^{1/N}, \qquad (11.15)$$

where

R_n = **actual long-term rate**

N = **term to maturity (in years) of long issue**

R = **current one-year rate**

${}_{t+1} r_1$ = **the expected one-year yield during some future period, $t + 1$.**

These future one-year rates are referred to as *forward rates*.

Given the relationship set forth in Equation 11.15, the formula for computing the one-period forward rate beginning at time $t + n$, implied in the term structure at time t, is as follows:

$$1 + {}_{t+n} r_{1t} = \frac{(1 + {}_t R_{1t})(1 + {}_{t+1} r_{1t})(1 + {}_{t+2} r_{1t}) \ldots (1 + {}_{t+n-1} r_{1t})(1 + {}_{t+n} r_{1t})}{(1 + {}_t R_{1t})(1 + {}_{t+1} r_{1t}) \ldots (1 + {}_{t+n-1} r_{1t})} \qquad (11.16)$$

$$= \frac{(1 + {}_t R_{n+1})^{n+1}}{(1 + {}_t R_n)^n}$$

$$ {}_{t+n} r_{1t} = \frac{(1 + {}_t R_{n+1})^{n+1}}{(1 + {}_t R_n)^n} - 1 $$

where

---

[20] For a more extensive discussion of the alternative theories of the term structure of interest rates, see Malkiel, *Term Structure of Interest Rates*; and Van Horne, *Financial Market Rates and Flows*.

$_{t+n}R_{1t}$ **is the one-year forward rate prevailing at $t + n$, using the term structure at time t.**

Assume that the five-year spot rate is 10 percent ($_tR_5 = .10$), and the four-year spot rate is 9 percent ($_tR_4 = .09$). The forward one-year rate four years from now implied by these spot rates can be calculated as follows:

$$_{t+4}r_{1t} = \frac{(1 + {}_tR_5)^5}{(1 + {}_tR_4)^4} - 1$$

$$= \frac{(1 + .10)^5}{(1 + .09)^4} - 1$$

$$= \frac{1.6105}{1.4116} - 1$$

$$= 1.1409 - 1 = .1409 = 14.09\%.$$

The term structure at time t implies that the one-year spot rate four years from now (during Year 5) will be 14.09 percent. It is possible to use this concept and formula to derive future rates for multiple years. Thus, the two-year spot rate that will prevail three years from now could be calculated using the three-year spot rate and the five-year spot rate. The general formula for computing the j-period forward rate beginning at time $t + n$ as of time t is

$$_{t+n}r_{jt} = {}^j\!\sqrt{\frac{(1 + {}_tR_{n+jt})^{n+j}}{(1 + {}_tR_{nt})^n}} - 1. \tag{11.17}$$

As a practical approximation of Equation 11.15, it is possible to use the arithmetic average of one-year rates to generate long-term yields.

The expectations theory can account for any shape of yield curve. If short-term rates are expected to rise in the future, then the yield curve will be ascending; if short-term rates are expected to fall, then the long-term rates will lie below the short-term rates, and the term structure will descend. Similar explanations can be made for flat and humped yield curves. In the following example, the expectations hypothesis is used to explain the shape of the term structure of interest rates. Given the following series, including the one-year spot rate ($_tR_1$) and forward one-year rates in years $t + 1$, $t + 2$, and $t + 3$,

$$_tR_1 = 5\ 1/2\%,\ _{t+1}r_1 = 6\%,\ _{t+2}r_1 = 7\ 1/2\%,\ _{t+3}r_1 = 8\ 1/2\%.$$

We can calculate the implied future long-term rates for bonds with two-, three-, and four-year lives as follows:

$_tR_1 = 5.50\%$ (given)

$_tR_2 = {}^2\!\sqrt{(1 + .055)\ (1 + .06)} - 1 = {}^2\!\sqrt{1.1183} - 1 = 1.0575 - 1 = 5.75\%$

$_tR_3 = {}^3\!\sqrt{(1.055)\ (1.06)\ (1.075)} - 1 = {}^3\!\sqrt{1.2022} - 1 = 1.0633 - 1 = 6.33\%$

$_tR_4 = {}^4\!\sqrt{(1.055)\ (1.06)\ (1.075)\ (1.085)} - 1 = {}^4\!\sqrt{1.3044} - 1 = 1.0687 - 1 = 6.87\%.$

A plot of these spot rates would demonstrate that the yield curve slopes upward. According to the theory that the long-term rate $(_tR_4)$ is composed of the current one-year spot rate $(_tR_1)$ and the forward one-year rates, the yield curve is rising because investors currently expect future short-term rates to be above current ones. The expectations hypothesis attempts to explain why the yield curve is upward-sloping, downward-sloping, humped, or flat. It attempts to explain the type of expectations implicit in various term structures. The evidence is fairly convincing that the expectations hypothesis is a workable explanation of the term structure.[21]

According to the expectations hypothesis, the term structure should be descending if lower rates are more likely to occur in the future than high yields. Thus, long-term bonds may be attractive investments, because the investor would want to lock in prevailing higher yields (which are expected to decline in the future) and/or capture the capital gains potential that should accompany a decline in rates. Investor expectations will only reinforce the descending shape of the yield curve as the prices of long-maturity bonds are bid up (and yields decline) and short-term bond issues are avoided (so yields rise). These shifts between long- and short-term maturities will continue until equilibrium occurs or expectations are revised. We will consider more involved strategies later in the chapter following our discussion of bond price volatility. Because of its documentation, relative simplicity, and intuitive appeal, the expectations hypothesis of the term structure of interest rates is widely accepted by both academicians and practitioners (bond portfolio managers).

LIQUIDITY PREFERENCE HYPOTHESIS. The theory of liquidity preference holds that long-term securities should provide higher returns than short-term obligations, since rational investors are willing to pay a price premium (i.e., all else being equal, they will accept lower yields) for short-maturity obligations to avoid the volatility of long-maturity obligations. Put another way, because lenders prefer to lend short term, to induce them to lend long term it is necessary to offer a higher yield.

The liquidity preference theory is the product of an important criticism leveled at the expectations hypothesis—namely, that it assumes bond investors possess perfect certainty and foresight. Instead, uncertainty in the real world implies that short-term issues will be preferred to longer maturities because they can easily be converted into cash should unforeseen events occur. As noted by Malkiel, "The crux of the liquidity preference theory is that long-term bonds, because of their greater potential price volatility, ought to offer the investor a larger return than the short-term securities."[22] In the absence of market anomalies, this theory argues,

[21] See, for example, David Meiselman, *The Term Structure of Interest Rates* (Englewood Cliffs, N.J.: Prentice-Hall, 1962); Thomas F. Cargill, "The Term Structure of Interest Rates: A Test of the Expectations Hypothesis," *Journal of Finance* 30, no. 3 (June 1975): 761–772; and James Van Horne, "Interest Rate Risk and the Term Structure of Interest Rates," *Journal of Political Economy* 73, no. 3 (August 1965): 344–351.

[22] Burton Malkiel, *Term Structure of Interest Rates: Theory, Empirical Evidence, and Applications* (New York: The McCaleb-Seiler Publishing Company, 1970): 13.

the yield curve should be upward-sloping and any other shape should be viewed as a temporary aberration.

While the theory is an outgrowth of criticism of the expectations hypothesis, it is also an extension of it, since the formal liquidity preference position contends that the liquidity premium inherent in longer yields should be added to the expected future rate in arriving at long-term yields. Thus, because the liquidity premium (L) is provided to compensate the long-term investor, it is simply a variation of Equation 11.15 as follows:

$$(1 + {}_tR_N) = [(1 + {}_tR_1)(1 + {}_{t+1}r_1 + L_2) \ldots \tag{11.18}$$
$$(1 + {}_{t+N-1}r_1 + L_N)]^{1/N}.$$

Upon testing, the liquidity preference theory has been found to possess considerable validity.[23] Expectations alone appear inadequate to explain the term structure, because the yield curve shows a definite upward bias. Therefore, a combination of the two theories (expectations and liquidity) is probably preferable to either alone.

SEGMENTED MARKET HYPOTHESIS. A simple, yet interesting, variation of the theory of the term structure of interest rates is the segmented market theory. While empirical evidence supporting it is meager, it nevertheless enjoys wide acceptance among market practitioners. Also known as the *preferred habitat, institutional theory,* and *hedging pressure theory,* it asserts that different groups of institutional investors have different maturity needs that lead them to confine their security selections to specific maturity segments of the term structure. This implies that the term structure is ultimately a function of the investment policies of major financial institutions.

Financial institutions tend to structure their investment policies in line with such things as their tax liability, liability structure, and the level of earnings demanded by savers and depositors. Therefore, because commercial banks, for example, are subject to normal corporate tax rates, and because their liabilities are generally short to intermediate in length (due to the short-term nature of time and demand deposits), we find commercial banks consistently invest in short- to intermediate-term municipals. In a like manner, because life insurance companies have little tax exposure and long-term obligations/liabilities, they tend to seek out high-yielding, long-term corporate bonds. Therefore, the segmented market theoretician contends that these forces, along with legal and regulatory limitations, tend to coerce or to prompt alternative financial institutions into consistently allocating their resources to particular types and maturity segments of the market. In its strongest form, the segmented market theory holds that the maturity preferences of different investors and borrowers are so

---

[23] See Reuben A. Kessel, "The Cyclical Behavior of the Term Structure of Interest Rates," Occasional Paper 91, National Bureau of Economic Research, 1965; Phillip Cagan, *Essays on Interest Rates* (New York: Columbia University Press for the National Bureau of Economic Research, 1969); J. Huston McCulloch, "An Estimate of the Liquidity Premium," *Journal of Political Economy* 83, no. 1 (January–February 1975): 95–119.

strong that they would never purchase securities outside their preferred maturity range to take advantage of yield differentials. As a result, the short- and long-maturity markets are effectively segmented, and yields are determined solely by supply and demand within each market maturity segment.

Kane and Malkiel provided support for this theory based upon a survey of banks and insurance firms.[24] In contrast, the results from several other studies did not support a preferred habitat concept.[25]

YIELD SPREADS   Another important dimension of interest rate behavior is the *yield spread*, which represents a difference in promised yield among different bond issues or segments of the market at any given point in time. Such differences are issue- or market-specific and thus additive to the rates determined by economic forces ($RFR + I$).

Four major factors account for the existence of various yield differentials:

1. Different *segments* of the bond market (e.g., governments versus agencies, or governments versus corporates)
2. Different *sectors* of the same market segment (e.g., prime-grade municipals versus good-grade municipals, or AA utilities versus BAA utilities, or AAA industrials versus AAA public utilities)
3. Different *coupons* within a given market segment/sector (e.g., current coupon governments versus deep-discount governments, or new AA industrials versus seasoned AA industrials)
4. Different *maturities* within a given market segment/sector (e.g., short agencies versus long agencies, or 3-year prime municipals versus 25-year prime municipals).

A yield spread may be either positive or negative. Moreover, its magnitude or direction changes over time, and it is these changes that offer profit opportunities. The spread narrows whenever differences in yield become smaller, and it widens as the differences become greater.[26] Table 11.1 provides data on a variety of past yield spreads.

Bond investors should evaluate yield spread changes because they influence price behavior and comparative realized yield performance over a given investment horizon. They should attempt to project (1) a normal beginning yield spread that is expected to become abnormal (i.e., the

[24] Edward J. Kane and Burton G. Malkiel, ''The Term Structure of Interest Rates: An Analysis of a Survey of Interest Rate Expectations,'' *Review of Economics and Statistics* 49, no. 3 (August 1967): 350–356.

[25] Franco Modigliani and Richard Sutch, ''Innovations in Interest Rate Policy,'' *American Economic Review* 56, no. 2 (May 1966): 178–197; S. W. Dobson, R. C. Sutch, and D. E. Vanderford, ''An Evaluation of Alternative Empirical Models of the Term Structure of Interest Rates,'' *Journal of Finance* 31, no. 4 (September 1976): 1035–1065; Michael E. Echols and Jon W. Elliott, ''Rational Expectations in a Disequilibrium Model of the Term Structure,'' *American Economic Review* 66, no. 1 (March 1976): 28–74.

[26] Michael D. Joehnk, ''The Effects of Yield Spreads on Comparative Bond Price Behavior,'' *The Financial Planner* 6, no. 4 (April 1977): 34–40; Dwight M. Jaffee, ''Cyclical Variations in the Risk Structure of Interest Rates,'' *Journal of Monetary Economics* 1, no. 3 (July 1975): 309–325; Timothy Q. Cook and Patric H. Hendershott, ''The Impact of Taxes, Risk, and Relative Security Supplies on Interest Rate Differentials,'' *Journal of Finance* 33, no. 4 (September 1978): 1173–1186.

TABLE 11.1
Selected Mean Yield Spreads (Reported in Basis Points)

COMPARISONS	1982	1983	1984	1985	1986	1987
1. Short governments:						
Long governments[a]	−69	+39	+10	+111	+108	+96
2. Long governments:						
Long Aaa corporates[b]	+154	+120	+72	+62	+88	+75
3. Long municipals:						
Long Aaa corporates[c]	+213	+258	+272	+226	+170	+174
4. Long Aaa municipals:						
Long Baa municipals[d]	+160	+137	+77	+98	+81	+103
5. AA utilities:						
BBB utilities[e]	+138	+137	+87	+74	+77	+77
6. AA utilities:						
AA industrials[e]	−76	−83	−71	+68	+34	+15

[a]Median yield to maturity of a varying number of bonds with two to four years maturity and more than ten years, respectively.

[b]Long Aaa corporates based on yields to maturity on selected long-term bonds.

[c]Long-term municipal issues based on a representative list of high-quality municipal bonds with a 20-year period to maturity being maintained.

[d]General obligation municipal bonds only.

[e]Based on a changing list of representative issues.

Source: *Federal Reserve Bulletin,* various issues; and Standard & Poor's Statistical Service.

spread is expected to move to an abnormally wide or narrow position), (2) a beginning yield spread that is abnormally wide or narrow but is expected to become normal, and (3) a normal beginning yield spread that is expected to change in response to an anticipated major swing in market interest rates. Economic and market analysis help develop these expectations, which possess one common denominator: the potential for yield spreads to change.

Taking advantage of these changes requires a knowledge of historical spreads and an ability to predict not only future total market changes (approximately) but also why and when (approximately) specific spreads will change. In the chapter on bond portfolio management techniques we will consider in more depth how you would implement these strategies.

BOND PRICE VOLATILITY

Price volatility is influenced by more than yield behavior. Malkiel used the bond valuation model to demonstrate that the market price of a bond is a function of four factors: (1) the par value of an obligation, (2) the issue's coupon, (3) its years to maturity, and (4) the prevailing market rate.[27] Malkiel showed (with mathematical proofs) that the following relationships (theorems) exist between yield changes and bond price behavior:

[27] Burton G. Malkiel, "Expectations, Bond Prices, and the Term Structure of Interest Rates," *Quarterly Journal of Economics* 76, no. 2 (May 1962): 197–218.

1. Bond prices move inversely to bond yields.
2. For a given change in market yield, changes in bond prices are greater for longer-term maturities; thus, bond price volatility is directly related to term to maturity.
3. The degree of maturity-derived price volatility (percentage of price change) increases at a diminishing rate as term to maturity increases.
4. Price movements resulting from equal absolute increases or decreases in yield are not symmetrical, since a decrease in yield raises bond prices by more than a corresponding increase in yield lowers prices.
5. The higher the coupon of the issue, the smaller the percentage of price fluctuation will be for a given change in yield; thus, bond price volatility is inversely related to coupon.

Homer and Leibowitz[28] showed that the absolute level of market yields also affects bond price volatility. The higher the level of prevailing yields is, the greater the price volatility of bonds, assuming a constant percentage change in market yields. They showed that yield swings and price volatility are greatest when prevailing interest rates are also greatest. An important point is, assuming a constant percentage change in yield, the basis-point change when rates are high will be larger. For example, a 25 percent change in market rates when rates are at 4 percent will be 100 basis points; the same percent change when rates are at 8 percent will be a 200 basis-point change. We will see in the discussion of bond duration that this basis point change is an important factor.

Thus, price volatility is a function of the percentage change in yield, the issue's coupon, the term to maturity of the obligation, the level of yields, and the direction of yield change. However, while both the level and direction of change in yields may be interesting variables to consider, they do not provide concrete guidance for trading strategies. In contrast, it is always necessary to consider the percentage of change in yield and the two variables over which investors have control: coupon and maturity. As yields change, these latter two variables have a dramatic effect on comparative bond price volatility.

CONCEPT OF DURATION

Because the price volatility of a bond varies inversely with the coupon and directly with the term to maturity, it is important to balance these two factors when selecting bonds. Suppose you expect a decline in market yields. You would want a very volatile bond (to maximize your capital gain) so you would look for a long-maturity, low-coupon bond. It would be desirable to have a composite measure that considered both of these factors. Fortunately, such a measure was developed over 50 years ago by

---

[28] Sidney Homer and Martin L. Leibowitz, *Inside the Yield Book* (Englewood Cliffs, N.J.: Prentice-Hall, 1972).

Macaulay[29] and is known as the *duration* of a security. Macaulay showed that duration was a more appropriate measure of the time element of a bond than term to maturity, because duration takes into account not only the ultimate recovery of capital at maturity, but also the size and timing of coupon payments (cash flows) that occur prior to final maturity. Duration is defined as the weighted average time to full recovery of principal and interest payments. Using annual compounding, duration (D) is

$$D = \frac{\sum_{t=1}^{n} \frac{C_t(t)}{(1 + i)^t}}{\sum_{t=1}^{n} \frac{C_t}{(1 + i)^t}}, \tag{11.19}$$

where

t = the time period in which the coupon and/or principal payment occurs

C_t = the interest and/or principal payment that occurs in period t

i = the market yield on the bond.

At first glance, this formula for computing duration may look rather forbidding. Upon closer examination you will see that the denominator in Equation 11.19 is simply the price of an issue as determined by the present value model. The numerator is the present value of all cash flows weighted according to the time to cash receipt. The following example, which sets forth the specific computations for two bonds, indicates the procedure and highlights some of the properties of duration. Consider the following two sample bonds:

	BOND A	BOND B
Face Value	$1,000	$1,000
Maturity	10 yrs.	10 yrs.
Coupon	4%	8%

Assuming annual interest payments and an 8 percent market yield on the bonds, duration is computed as shown in Table 11.2. This example indicates the following characteristics of duration:

1. When a bond has coupons, the duration of the bond will always be less than the term to maturity, because duration gives weight to these interim payments.
2. There is an inverse relationship between coupon and duration. A bond with a larger coupon will have a shorter duration, because more of the total cash flows come earlier in the form of interest

---

[29] Frederick R. Macaulay, *Some Theoretical Problems Suggested by the Movements of Interest Rates, Bond Yields, and Stock Prices in the United States Since 1856* (New York: National Bureau of Economic Research, 1938).

TABLE 11.2
Computation of Duration (Assuming 8 Percent Market Yield)

			BOND A		
(1) **YEAR**	**(2)** **CASH FLOW**	**(3)** **PV AT 8%**	**(4)** **PV OF FLOW**	**(5)** **PV AS % OF PRICE**	**(6)** **(1) × (5)**
1	$ 40	.9259	$ 37.04	.0506	.0506
2	40	.8573	34.29	.0469	.0938
3	40	.7938	31.75	.0434	.1302
4	40	.7350	29.40	.0402	.1608
5	40	.6806	27.22	.0372	.1860
6	40	.6302	25.21	.0345	.2070
7	40	.5835	23.34	.0319	.2233
8	40	.5403	21.61	.0295	.2360
9	40	.5002	20.01	.0274	.2466
10	1,040	.4632	481.73	.6585	6.5850
Sum			$731.58	1.0000	8.1193

Duration = 8.12 Years

			BOND B		
1	$ 80	.9259	$ 74.07	.0741	.0741
2	80	.8573	68.59	.0686	.1372
3	80	.7938	63.50	.0635	.1906
4	80	.7350	58.80	.0588	.1906
5	80	.6806	54.44	.0544	.2720
6	80	.6302	50.42	.0504	.3024
7	80	.5835	46.68	.0467	.3269
8	80	.5403	43.22	.0432	.3456
9	80	.5002	40.02	.0400	.3600
10	1,080	.4632	500.26	.5003	5.0030
Sum			$1,000.00	1.0000	7.2470

Duration = 7.25 years

payments. As shown in Table 11.2, the 8 percent bond has a shorter duration than the 4 percent bond.

3. A bond with no coupon payments (i.e., a zero coupon bond or a pure discount bond like a Treasury bill) will have duration equal to term to maturity. If you go back to Table 11.2 and assume that the only payment is made at maturity (i.e., the total cash flow is at maturity), you will see that the duration will equal the maturity value.

4. There is generally a positive relationship between term to maturity and duration (typically, duration increases at a decreasing rate with maturity). Therefore, all else being the same, a bond with longer term to maturity will almost always have a higher duration. Note that the relationship is not direct, because as maturity increases, the present value of the principal declines in value. As shown in Figure 11.6, the shape of the duration-maturity curve depends upon the coupon and the market yield. The

FIGURE 11.6
Duration vs. Maturity

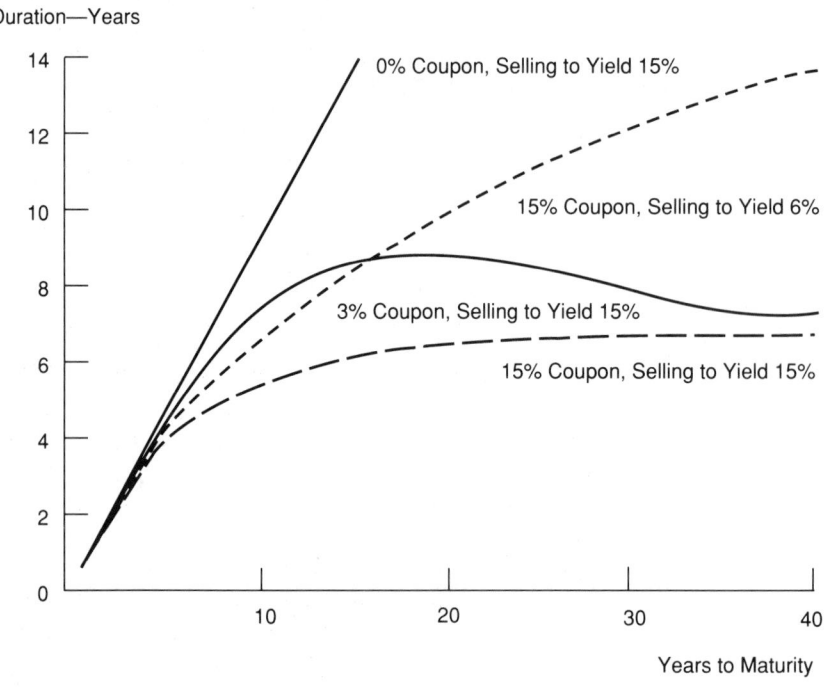

Source: William L. Nemerever, D.F.A. "Managing Bond Portfolios through Immunization Strategies," *The Revolution in Techniques for Managing Bond Portfolios* (Charlottesville, Va.: The Institute of Chartered Financial Analysts, 1983), 42.

curve for a zero coupon bond is a straight line, indicating equality, while a low coupon bond selling at a deep discount (due to a high market yield) will have a curve that turns down at long maturities, which means in this case that the longer-maturity bond will have lower duration.

5. All else the same, there is an inverse relationship between market yield and duration. The higher the market yield is, the lower the duration. As an example, in Table 11.2, if the market yield had been 12 percent rather than 8 percent, the durations would have been about 7.75 and 6.80 rather than 8.12 and 7.25.[30]

6. Sinking funds and call features can have a dramatic effect on a bond's duration, because they can cause a dramatic acceleration

[30] These properties are discussed and demonstrated in Frank K. Reilly and Rupinder Sidhu, "The Many Uses of Bond Duration," *Financial Analysts Journal* 36, no. 4 (July–August 1980): 58–72; Richard W. McEnally, "Duration as a Practical Tool for Bond Management," *Journal of Portfolio Management* 3, no. 4 (Summer 1977): 53-57; and Robert W. Kopprasch, "Understanding Duration and Volatility," in *The Handbook of Fixed Income Securities*, 2d ed., edited by Frank J. Fabozzi and Irving M. Pollack (Homewood, Ill.: Dow Jones-Irwin, 1987).

in the total cash flows for the bond. While it might be easy to determine the impact of a regularly scheduled sinking fund, it is much more difficult to determine if and when a deferred call feature will be exercised.[31] The point is, they can have an effect and should be considered.

DURATION AND BOND PRICE VOLATILITY. It has been shown, both theoretically and empirically, that bond price movements will vary proportionally with duration.[32] Specifically, as shown in Equation 11.20, an estimate of the percentage change in bond price is equal to the change in yield times *modified duration (mod)*.

$$\frac{\Delta P}{P} \times 100 = -D_{mod} \times \Delta i, \qquad (11.20)$$

where

ΔP = the change in price for the bond

P = the beginning price for the bond

$-D_{mod}$ = modified duration, which is equal to the Macauley duration (computed in Table 11.2), divided by 1, plus the current market yield, divided by the number of payments in a year. As an example, assume a bond with a Macauley duration of 10 years, a market yield (i) of 8 percent, and semiannual payments. The modified duration would be

$$D_{mod} = 10 / \left(1 + \frac{.08}{2}\right)$$
$$= 10/(1.04) = 9.62 \text{ years,}$$

Δi = the yield change in basis points divided by 100. As an example, if interest rates go from 8.00 percent to 8.50 percent, it would be 50/100 = 0.50.

Consider the following example:

$$D = 8 \text{ years}$$
$$i = .10.$$

Assume that you expect market yields to decline by 75 basis points (i.e., from 10 percent to 9.25 percent). The first step is to compute the modified duration as follows:

$$D_{mod} = 8 / \left(1 + \frac{.10}{2}\right)$$
$$= 8/(1.05) = 7.62 \text{ years.}$$

---

[31] An example of the computation of duration with a sinking fund and a call feature is contained in Reilly and Sidhu, "The Many Uses of Bond Duration."

[32] A generalized proof of this is contained in Michael H. Hopewell and George Kaufman, "Bond Price Volatility and Term to Maturity: A Generalized Respecification," *American Economic Review* 63, no. 4 (September 1973): 749–753.

Table 11.3
Bond Duration in Years for Bond Yielding 6 Percent under Different Terms

Years to Maturity	Various Coupon Rates			
	.02	.04	.06	.08
1	.995	.990	.985	.981
5	4.756	4.558	4.393	4.254
10	8.891	8.169	7.662	7.286
20	14.981	12.980	11.904	11.232
50	19.452	17.129	16.273	15.829
100	17.567	17.232	17.120	17.064
∞	17.167	17.167	17.167	17.167

Source: L. Fisher and R. L. Weil, "Coping with the Risk of Interest Rate Fluctuations: Returns to Bond-holders from Naive and Optimal Strategies," *Journal of Business* 44, no. 4 (October 1971): 418. Copyright © 1971 by The University of Chicago Press. Reprinted by permission of The University of Chicago Press.

The estimated percent change in the price of the bond using Equation 11.20 is as follows:

$$\text{Percent } \Delta P = (-7.62) \times \frac{-75}{100}$$
$$= (-7.62) \times (-.75)$$
$$= 5.72.$$

This indicates that the bond price should increase by about 5.72 percent. For example, if the price before the decline in rates was $950, the price after the decline should be approximately

$$\$950 \times 1.0572 = \$1,004.34.$$

The modified duration is always a negative value because of the inverse relationship between yield changes and price changes. Also, you should remember that the percent change in the price of the bond is an estimate, or an approximation. The following section on convexity will show that this formula is exact only for very small changes in yields, such as five or ten basis points.

In any case, the maximum price variation is achieved with the longest duration security, and Table 11.3 demonstrates that there are numerous ways to achieve a given duration measure. Thus, if you anticipate a decline in interest rates and want to capture maximum gains, you would want to increase the duration of your bond portfolio, using one of several maturity/coupon combinations. Note that the duration of your portfolio is the market value weighted average of the durations of the individual bonds in your portfolio.

TABLE 11.4
Price-Yield Relationships for Alternative Bonds

A. 12%, 20-YEAR		B. 12%, 3-YEAR		C. 0%, 30-YEAR	
YIELD (%)	PRICE ($)	YIELD (%)	PRICE ($)	YIELD (%)	PRICE ($)
1.0	2,989.47	1.0	1,324.30	1.0	741.37
2.0	2,641.73	2.0	1,289.77	2.0	550.45
3.0	2,346.21	3.0	1,256.37	3.0	409.30
4.0	2,094.22	4.0	1,224.06	4.0	304.78
5.0	1,878.60	5.0	1,192.78	5.0	227.28
6.0	1,693.44	6.0	1,162.52	6.0	169.73
7.0	1,533.88	7.0	1,133.21	7.0	126.93
8.0	1,395.86	8.0	1,104.84	8.0	95.06
9.0	1,276.02	9.0	1,077.37	9.0	71.29
10.0	1,171.59	10.0	1,050.76	10.0	53.54
11.0	1,080.23	11.0	1,024.98	11.0	40.26
12.0	1,000.00	12.0	1,000.00	12.0	30.31

CONVEXITY[33]

As noted, modified duration is a means to estimate bond price changes for a change in interest rates. Equation 11.20 is, however, accurate only for very small changes in market yields. We will see that the accuracy of the estimate deteriorates with increasing magnitude of the yield change, because the modified duration calculation is a *linear* approximation of a price change along a *curvilinear* (convex) function. To understand the effect of convexity, we must consider the price-yield relationship for alternative bonds.

PRICE-YIELD RELATIONSHIP. We know that the price of a bond is the present value of its cash flow. Therefore, given the coupon, maturity, and yield for a bond, you can derive its price at a point in time. The price-yield curve provides a set of prices for a specified bond at a point in time, *when you change the market yields.* As an example, consider the prices for a 12 percent, 20-year bond contained in Table 11.4, assuming yields from 1 percent to 12 percent. The prices in the table, and the graph in Figure 11.7, indicate that the price-yield relationship is not a straight line, but a curvilinear relationship—that is, it is convex.

Two points are important about the price-yield relationship:

1. This relationship can be applied to a single bond, a portfolio of bonds, or any stream of cash flows into the future (e.g., a known liability stream).
2. The price-yield relationship will differ among bonds or other streams, depending upon the nature of the cash flow stream—that is, the coupon and maturity of the bond. As an example, the

---

[33] This discussion draws heavily from Mark L. Dunetz and James M. Mahoney, "Using Duration and Convexity in the Analysis of Callable Bonds," *Financial Analysts Journal* 44, no. 3 (May/June 1988): 53–73.

FIGURE 11.7
Price-Yield Relationship and Modified Duration at 4 Percent Yield

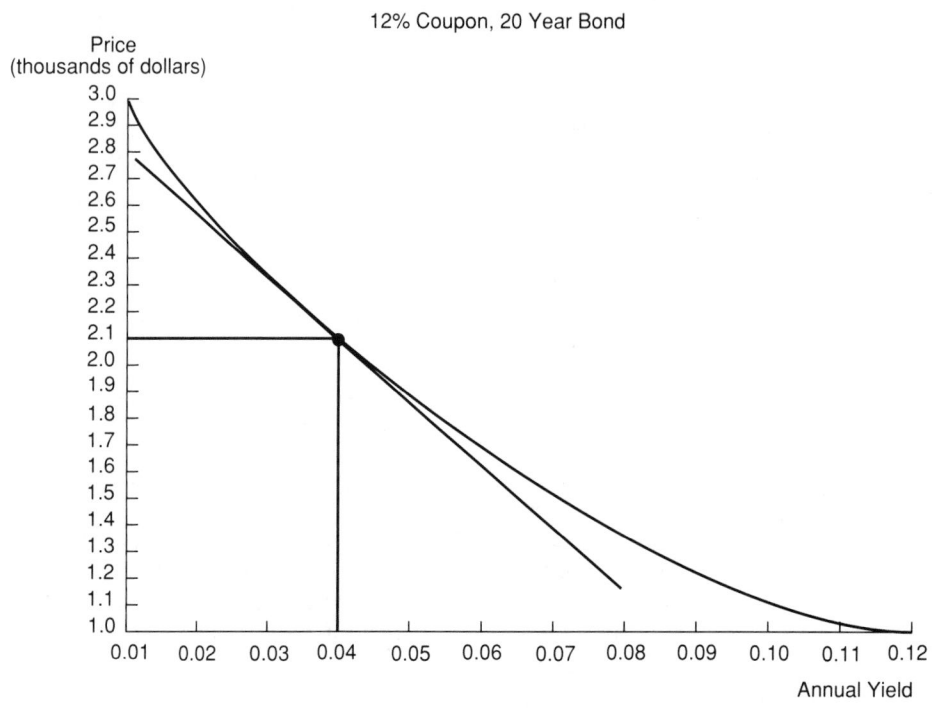

price-yield relationship for a high-coupon, short-term security will be almost a straight line, while the price-yield relationship for a low-coupon, long-term bond will be very curved. The curved nature of the relationship is referred to as its *convexity*.

As shown by the graph, with convexity, as the yield increases, the price declines at a slower rate. Similarly, when yields decline, the price increases at a faster rate. Convexity is therefore a desirable trait. Given this price-yield curve, modified duration is the first differential of this price-yield relationship with respect to yield—it is the percentage change in price for a nominal change in yield as follows:

$$D_{mod} = \frac{\dfrac{dP}{di}}{P}.$$
(11.21)

Notice that the dP/di line is tangent to the price-yield curve *at a given yield* as shown in Figure 11.7. For small changes in yields, this tangent straight-line relationship is a good estimate of the actual price changes. For larger changes in yields, the estimate of the price using the straight line will be below the actual price, as shown by the price-yield curve; and the reason is that the modified-duration line is a linear estimate of a curvilinear relationship.

DETERMINANTS OF CONVEXITY. Mathematically, convexity is the second derivative of price with respect to yield (d^2P/di^2) divided by the price and as such indicates the curvature of the price-yield relationship. Specifically, convexity is the percentage change in dP/di for a given change in yield:

$$\text{Convexity} = \frac{\dfrac{d^2P}{di^2}}{P}. \tag{11.22}$$

Convexity is a measure of how much a bond's price-yield curve deviates from the linear approximation of that curve. As indicated by Figure 11.7 for noncallable bonds, convexity is always a positive number, implying that the price-yield curve lies above the duration or tangent line. Figure 11.8 contains the price-yield relationship for two bonds with very different coupons and maturities (the yields and prices are contained in Table 11.4). These graphs demonstrate that the following factors increase convexity.

- Lower coupon (yield and maturity constant)
- Longer maturity (yield and coupon constant)
- Lower yield (coupon and maturity constant)—this simply means that the price-yield curve is more convex at the lower-yield (upper left) segment of the curve.

Therefore, a short-term, high-coupon bond, such as the 12 percent coupon, three-year bond in Figure 11.8, has very low convexity—it is almost a straight line. In contrast, the zero coupon, 30-year bond has high convexity.

In summary, the change in a bond's price resulting from a change in yield can be attributed to two sources: the bond's modified duration and the convexity of the price-yield curve. The relative effect of these two factors will depend on the characteristics of the asset (i.e., its convexity) and the amount of the yield change. Thus, if you are estimating the price change for a zero coupon, 30-year bond, assuming a 300-basis-point change in yield, the convexity effect will be fairly large, since this bond would have high convexity, and a 300-basis-point change is relatively large.

COMPUTATION OF CONVEXITY. Again, the formula for computing the convexity of a stream of cash flows looks fairly complex, but it can be broken down into manageable steps. You will recall from Equation 11.22 that

$$\text{Convexity} = \frac{\dfrac{d^2P}{di^2}}{P}.$$

In turn,

$$\frac{d^2P}{di^2} = \frac{1}{(1+i)^2}\left[\sum_t \frac{CF_t}{(1+i)^t}(t^2+t)\right].$$

FIGURE 11.8
Price–Yield Curves for Alternative Bonds

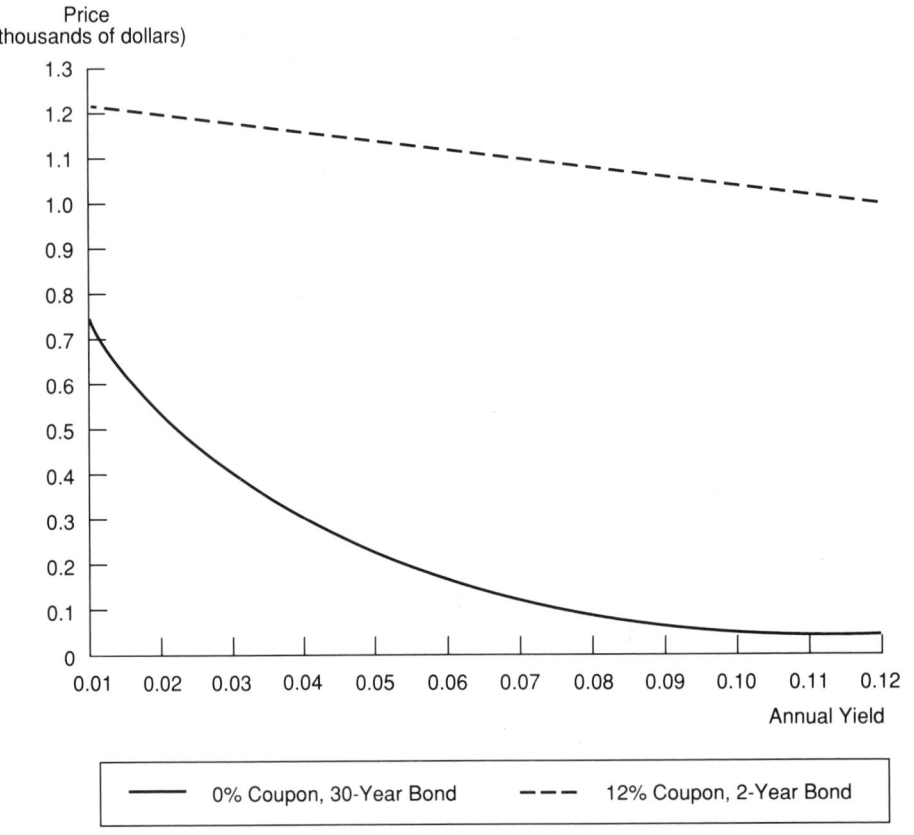

Table 11.5 contains the computations related to this calculation for a three-year bond with a 12 percent coupon and 9 percent YTM. The convexity for this bond is very low, given the short maturity, high coupon, and high yield. Note that the convexity of a security will vary along the price-yield curve. You will get a different convexity at a 3 percent yield than at a 12 percent yield. In terms of the computation, the maturity and coupon will be the same, but you will use a different discount rate that reflects where you are on the curve. Remember that *you will also get a different modified duration at different points on the curve,* because the slope varies along the curve. You can also see this mathematically, because depending on where you are on the curve, you will be using a different market yield, and the Macauley duration and the modified duration are inverse to the discount rate.

To compute the price change attributable to the convexity effect after you know the bond's convexity, use this equation:

Price Change due to Convexity $= 1/2 \times$ Price $\times$ Convexity $\times$ (Δ in yield)^2.

TABLE 11.5
Computation of Convexity

$$\text{Convexity} = \frac{d^2P/di^2}{PV \text{ of Cash Flows}} = \frac{d^2P/di^2}{\text{Price}}$$

$$\frac{d^2P}{di^2} = \frac{1}{(1+i)^2}\left[\sum_t (t^2 + t)\frac{CF_t}{(1+i)^t}\right]$$

$$\text{Convexity} = \frac{d^2P/di^2}{\text{Price}}$$

Example: 3-Year Bond: 12% Coupon, 9% YTM

(1) Year	(2) CF_t	(3) PV @ 9%	(4) PV CF	(5) $t^2 + t$	4 × 5
1	120	.9174	$ 110.09	2	220.18
2	120	.8417	101.00	6	606.00
3	120	.7722	92.66	12	1111.92
3	1000	.7722	772.20	12	9266.40
			$1,075.95		$11,204.50

$$\frac{1}{(1+i)^2} = \frac{1}{(1.09)^2} = \frac{1}{1.19} = .84$$

$$\$11,204.50 \times .84 = \$9,411.78$$

$$\frac{9411.78}{1075.95} = 8.75$$

Table 11.6 shows the change in bond price considering both the duration effect and the convexity effect for an 18-year bond with a 12 percent coupon and 9 percent YTM. For demonstration purposes, we assumed a decline of 100 and 300 basis points (bp) in rates (i.e., 9 percent to 8 percent and 9 percent to 6 percent). With the 300-bp change, if you considered only the modified-duration effect, you would have *estimated* that the bond went from 126.50 to 158.30 (a 25.14 percent increase), when, in fact, the actual price is closer to 164.41, which is about a 30 percent increase.

In summary, modified duration will help you estimate percentage price changes for a given change in market yields. Remember, though, that it is a good estimate only for small yield changes. It is necessary to also consider the convexity effect when there are large yield changes or when securities or cash flows have high convexity.

PORTFOLIO IMMUNIZATION

Some investors do not want to trade on the basis of expected interest rates, but simply want to be assured of a specified return for a predetermined investment period, such as a 10 percent annual return over the next five years. The problem is that as market interest rates change, the *price* of your securities and your *reinvestment rates* also change. Fortunately, these two risks work in opposite directions. When interest rates decline,

TABLE 11.6
Analysis of Bond Price Change Considering Duration and Convexity

Example: 18-Year Bond, 12% Coupon, 9% YTM
Price: 126.50
Modified Duration: 8.38 (D*)
Convexity: 107.70
Estimate of Price Change Using Duration:
  Percent Δ Price $= -D^*$ (Δ in YLD/100)
Estimate of Price Change from Convexity:
  Price Change $= \frac{1}{2} \times$ Price $\times$ Convexity $\times$ (Δ in YLD)^2
A. Change in Yield: -100 BP

  Duration Change: $-8.38 \times \left(\dfrac{-100}{100}\right) = +8.38\%$

  $+8.38\% \times 126.50 = +10.60$

  Convexity Change: $\dfrac{1}{2} \times (126.50) \times 107.70 \times (.01)^2$

  $= 63.25 \times 107.70 \times .0001$
  $= 6{,}812.03 \times .0001 = .68$

  Combined Effect: 126.50
                   $+10.60$ (Duration)
  ─────────
                    137.10
                    $+.68$ (Convexity)
  ─────────
                    137.78

B. Change in Yield: -300 BP

  Duration Change: $-8.38 \times \left(\dfrac{-300}{100}\right) = +25.14\%$

  $126.50 \times 1.2514 = 158.30 \ (+31.80)$

  Convexity Effect: $\dfrac{1}{2} \times (126.50) \times 107.70 \times (.03)^2$

  $6{,}812.03 \times .0009 = 6.11$

  Combined Effect: 126.50
                   $+31.80$ (Duration)
  ─────────
                    158.30
                    $+6.11$(Convexity)
  ─────────
                    164.41

there are positive price effects (bond prices increase) but negative reinvestment effects (your reinvestment rate declines).

Because of this inverse relationship between price risk and reinvestment risk, it has been shown by Fisher and Weil that it is possible to immunize fixed-income investments from subsequent changes in market rates by balancing these two risks so that they completely offset one another.[34] Balancing occurs *only when the duration of a portfolio is equal to*

[34] For a detailed derivation and test of this concept, see Lawrence Fisher and Roman L. Weil, "Coping with the Risk of Interest-Rate Fluctuations: Returns to Bondholders from Naive and Optimal Strategies," *Journal of Business* 44, no. 4 (October 1971): 408–431; and G. O. Bierwag and George C. Kaufman, "Coping with the Risk of Interest Rate Fluctuations: A Note," *Journal of Business* 50, no. 3 (July 1977): 364–370.

its investment horizon. When duration equals the planning period, interest rate risk is minimized. Thus, an investor with a five-year investment horizon should not necessarily seek an issue with five years to maturity, but he should seek issues with maturity/coupon combinations that provide a modified duration of approximately 5.0 years.

The use of bond portfolio immunization and further extensions of the concept will be discussed in detail in Chapter 18 when we consider alternative bond portfolio management techniques. In summary, the concept of duration has implications for both aggressive and conservative bond investors. It is an important idea that conveniently encompasses both the coupon and the maturity dimensions of bond price behavior.[35]

SUMMARY

The concept of bond valuation is essentially the same as that for equity pricing, i.e., the present value of all future cash flows accruing to the investor. Cash flows for the bond investor include periodic interest payments and capital recovery. The present value model incorporates several important dimensions of bond yields and prices, including coupon receipts, interest rates, interest rate changes, and yield spread changes. The most important estimate is expected changes in interest rates and yield spread behavior. The next step is to select the optimal coupon, maturity, and call feature for the investor.

The five basic types of yields are nominal yield, current yield, promised yield, yield to call, and realized yield. The concept of interest-on-interest, or coupon reinvestment, is an extremely important factor in calculating realized yield. The fundamental determinants of interest rates are the risk-free rate, a risk premium, and an inflation premium. There are four basic patterns of yield curves and three theories explaining them—the expectations hypothesis, the liquidity preference hypothesis, and the segmented market hypothesis.

Bond price volatility is mainly a function of the change in yield, the coupon of the issue, and the term to maturity. The concept of duration was developed to incorporate coupon and maturity in one measure that indicates the response of bond prices to a change in interest rates. Since modified duration provides a straight-line estimate of the curvilinear price-yield function, it is necessary to consider duration and convexity for large changes in yields or when dealing with securities that have high convexity. Duration can be used to immunize a portfolio from interest rate changes.

QUESTIONS

1. Why does the present value equation appear to be more useful for the bond investor than for the common stock investor?

---

[35] Duration has been found to be of value in other areas beyond bond analysis and portfolio management: see John A. Boquist, George A. Racette, and Gary G. Schlarbaum, "Duration and Risk Assessment for Bonds and Common Stocks," *Journal of Finance* 30, no. 5 (December 1975): 1360–1365; and Edward Blocker and Clyde Stickney, "Duration and Risk Assessments in Capital Budgeting," *The Accounting Review* 54, no. 1 (January 1979): 180–188.

2. What is the most crucial assumption the investor makes when he calculates promised yield? Why is it crucial to the computation?

3a. Define the variables included in the following model:

$$i = (RFR, RP, I).$$

3b. Comment on the appropriateness of the model, given the information that the firm whose bonds you are considering is not expected to break even this year.

4. Of the three hypotheses mentioned in the text, which one do you think best explains the alternative shapes of a yield curve? Defend your choice.

5. *CFA Examination I (June 1982)*

5a. Explain what is meant by the term *structure of interest rates*. Explain the theoretical basis of an upward-sloping yield curve. [8 minutes]

5b. Explain the economic circumstances under which you would expect to see the inverted yield curve prevail. [7 minutes]

5c. Define *real rate of interest*. [2 minutes]

5d. Discuss the characteristics of the market for U.S. Treasury securities. Compare it to the market for AAA corporate bonds. Discuss the opportunities that may exist in bond markets that are less than efficient. [8 minutes]

5e. Over the past several years, fairly wide yield spreads between AAA corporates and Treasuries have occasionally prevailed. Discuss the possible reasons for this. [5 minutes]

6. *CFA Examination III (June 1982):* As the portfolio manager for a large pension fund, you are offered the following bonds:

	COUPON	MATURITY	PRICE	CALL PRICE	YIELD TO MATURITY
Edgar Corp. (new issue)	14.00%	2002	$101.3/4	$114	13.75%
Edgar Corp. (new issue)	6.00	2002	48.1/8	103	13.60
Edgar Corp. (1972 issue)	6.00	2002	48.7/8	103	13.40

Assuming that you expect a decline in interest rates over the next three years, identify and justify which of these bonds you would select. [10 minutes]

PROBLEMS

1. Four years ago your firm issued $1,000 par, 25-year bonds, with a 7 percent coupon rate and a 10 percent call premium.

1a. If these bonds are now called, what is the *approximate* yield to call for the investors who originally purchased them?

1b. If these bonds are now called, what is the *actual* yield to call for the investors who originally purchased them?

1c. If the current interest rate is 5 percent and the bonds are not callable, at what price would each bond sell?

2. If you purchase an 8 percent, 20-year, $1,000 par, semiannual payment bond priced at $1,012.50 when it has 12 years remaining until maturity, what is

2a. Its approximate yield to maturity?

2b. Its actual yield to maturity?

2c. Its yield to call if the bond is callable in three years with an 8 percent premium?

3. Calculate the duration of an 8 percent, $1,000 par bond maturing in three years if interest rates have risen to 10 percent and interest is paid semiannually.

In all problems, assume a $1,000 par value and semiannual interest payments.

4. An investor purchases a bond with a nominal yield of 8 percent for $800. If the bond has 25 years to maturity, find the promised yield by

4a. Approximation method.

4b. Present value method.

5. A bond is currently quoted at $1,100 and has a current yield of 6.36 percent. The remaining life of the bond is 15 years, but it has three years remaining on a deferred call feature.

5a. Calculate promised yield to maturity using
(1) Approximation method.
(2) Present value method.

5b. Calculate yield to call, assuming a call premium equal to one year's interest, using
(1) Approximation method.
(2) Present value method.

6. A new 20-year bond with an 8 percent nominal yield is priced to yield 10 percent. An investor purchasing the bond expects that two years from now, yields on comparable bonds will have declined to 9 percent. Calculate his realized yield if he expects to sell the bond in two years.

7. The following exercise deals with the problem of differing reinvestment rates. An investor purchases a bond for $900 with a 7 percent coupon that matures in five years. Find the promised yield, assuming that

7a. Interest payments are reinvested in the same bonds at the same promised yield.

7b. Interest payments are reinvested in a Mexican bank savings account at 12 percent.

7c. Interest payments are not reinvested at all but are spent as they arrive.

8. Construct a chart demonstrating current ranges of yields for bonds of various ratings. For example, you might want to randomly select three or four bonds in each rating category and show the average yield on each group, as well as the spread for each group.

9. You are given two 8 percent coupon bonds, one with a term to maturity of five years, the second with a term to maturity of 20 years. Assuming that market interest rates go from 8 percent to 12 percent, compute the prices of the two bonds before and after the rate change, and discuss the differential percentage price change.

10. Compute the duration of a three-year bond with a 7 percent coupon yielding 8 percent. Show all work.

11. You own a bond with a Macauley duration of 8 years. If market rates are 8 percent, what is the modified duration of this bond? If market rates decline by 2 percent (200 basis points), what will be the estimated percentage change in price for this bond?

12. *CFA Examination II (June 1984)*: Assume the following yields to maturity on various classes of bonds in March 1984:

Short Governments	9.50%
Long Governments	12.00%
Short Municipals	6.50%
Long Municipals	9.25%
Short Corporates	10.00%
Long Corporates	12.80%
Long Aa Corporates	12.50%
Long Baa Corporates	13.00%

Also assume the following "normal" yield spreads:

Long Governments minus Short Governments	150 basis points
Long Municipals minus Short Municipals	100
Long Corporates minus Long Governments	125
Long Corporates minus Short Corporates	175
Long Baa Corporates minus Long Aa Corporates	150

Based upon the March 1984 yields to maturity and the "normal" yield spreads above, select the bond that would be preferable in each of the five comparisons (e.g., Short Governments or Long Governments), and briefly state the reason for each of your selections. [15 minutes]

13. *CFA Examination II (June 1984)*: Assume the following average yields on U.S. Treasury bonds at the present time:

TERM TO MATURITY	YIELD
1 year	8.50%
2 years	8.90%
5 years	9.25%
9 years	9.75%
10 years	10.00%
15 years	11.25%
20 years	11.75%
25 years	12.25%

13a. Compute the forward rate for Year 2 based upon the yields specified, assuming a pure expectations hypothesis of the term structure of interest rates. [5 minutes]

13b. Three major hypotheses of the term structure of interest rates are (1) market segmentation, preferred habitat, or hedging pressure hypothesis; (2) unbiased or pure expectations hypothesis; (3) liquidity or interest rate risk hypothesis. Given the yield curve implied by these data, discuss how each of these hypotheses would explain the shape of the curve. [15 minutes]

14a. *CFA Examination I (June 1984)*: Assume a $10,000 par value zero coupon bond with a term to maturity at issue of 10 years and a market yield of 8 percent.
(1) Determine the duration of the bond.
(2) Calculate the initial issue price of the bond at a market yield of 8 percent, assuming semiannual compounding.
(3) Twelve months after issue, this bond is selling to yield 12 percent. Calculate its then-current market price. Calculate your pre-tax rate of return assuming you owned this bond during the twelve-month period.

14b. Assume a 10 percent coupon bond with a Macaulay duration of 8 years, semiannual payments, and a market rate of 8 percent.
(1) Determine the modified duration of the bond.
(2) Calculate the percent change in price for the bond, assuming market rates decline by two percentage points (200 basis points). Note: In the exam, the candidate received a present value table. You should use the tables at the end of this book. [20 minutes]

15. *CFA Examination I (June 1985)*: Rank the following bonds in order of descending duration. Explain your reasoning (no calculations required). [10 minutes]

15a. 15% coupon, 20-year, yield to maturity at 10%.

15b. 15% coupon, 15-year, yield to maturity at 10%.

15c. Zero coupon, 20-year, yield to maturity at 10%.

15d. 8% coupon, 20-year, yield to maturity at 10%.

15e. 15% coupon, 15-year, yield to maturity at 15%.

16. *CFA Examination I (June 4, 1988)*: You are asked to consider the following bond for possible inclusion in your company's fixed income portfolio:

ISSUER	COUPON	YIELD-TO-MATURITY	MATURITY	DURATION
Wiser Company	8%	8%	10 years	7.25 years

16a. (1) Explain why the Wiser bond's duration is less than its maturity.
(2) Explain whether a bond's duration or its maturity is a better measure of the bond's sensitivity to changes in interest rates. [4 minutes]

16b. Briefly explain the impact on the duration of the Wiser Company bond under each of the following conditions: [6 minutes]
I. the coupon is 4% rather than 8%
II. the yield-to-maturity is 4% rather than 8%
III. the maturity is seven years rather than ten years

REFERENCES

Bierwag, G. O. "Immunization, Duration, and the Term Structure of Interest Rates." *Journal of Financial and Quantitative Analysis* 12, no. 5 (December 1977).

Bierwag, G. O., George G. Kaufman, and Chulsoon Khang. "Duration and Bond Portfolio Analysis: An Overview." *Journal of Financial and Quantitative Analysis* 13, no. 5 (November 1978).

Cagan, Phillip., ed. *Essays on Interest Rates.* (New York: Columbia University Press for the National Bureau of Economic Research, 1969).

Dunetz, Mark L., and James M. Mahoney. "Using Duration and Convexity in the Analysis of Callable Bonds." *Financial Analysts Journal* 44, no. 3 (May-June 1988).

Feldstein, Martin, and Otto Eckstein. "The Fundamental Determinants of the Interest Rate." *The Review of Economics and Statistics* 52, no. 4 (November 1970).

Finnerty, John D. "Evaluating the Economics of Refunding High-Coupon Sinking-Fund Debt." *Financial Management* 12, no. 1 (Spring 1983).

Fisher, Lawrence. "Determinants of Risk Premiums on Corporate Bonds." *Journal of Political Economy* 67, no. 3 (June 1959).

Fisher, Lawrence, and Roman L. Weil. "Coping with the Risk of Interest-Rate Fluctuations: Returns to Bondholders from Naive and Optimal Strategies." *Journal of Business* 44, no. 4 (October 1971).

Homer, Sidney, and Martin L. Leibowitz. *Inside the Yield Book.* Englewood Cliffs, N.J.: Prentice-Hall, 1972.

Hopewell, Michael H., and George G. Kaufman. "Bond Price Volatility and Term to Maturity: A Generalized Respecification." *American Economic Review* 63, no. 4 (September 1973).

Kalotay, A. J. "On the Structure and Valuation of Debt Refundings." *Financial Management* 11, no. 1 (Spring 1982).

Kalotay, A. J. "Sinking Funds and the Realized Cost of Debt." *Financial Management* 11, no. 1 (Spring 1982).

Kessel, Reuben A. "The Cyclical Behavior of the Term Structure of Interest Rates." Occasional Paper 91, National Bureau of Economic Research, 1965.

Macaulay, Frederick R. *Some Theoretical Problems Suggested by the Movements of Interest Rates, Bond Yields, and Stock Prices in the United States Since 1865.* New York: National Bureau of Economic Research, 1938.

Malkiel, Burton G. "Expectations, Bond Prices, and the Term Structure of Interest Rates." *Quarterly Journal of Economics* 76, no. 2 (May 1962).

Malkiel, Burton G. *The Term Structure of Interest Rates: Theory, Empirical Evidence, and Applications.* New York: The McCaleb-Seiler Publishing Company, 1970.

Meiselman, David. *The Term Structure of Interest Rates.* Englewood Cliffs, N.J.: Prentice-Hall, 1962.

Reilly, Frank K., and Rupinder Sidhu. "The Many Uses of Bond Duration." *Financial Analysts Journal* 36, no. 4 (July–August 1980).

Van Horne, James C. *Financial Market Rates and Flows.* 2d ed. Englewood Cliffs, N.J.: Prentice-Hall, 1984.

Weil, Roman L. "Macaulay's Duration: An Appreciation." *Journal of Business* 46, no. 4 (October 1973).

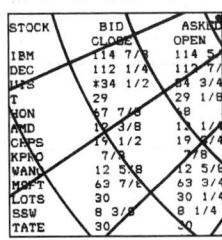

CHAPTER 12

ANALYSIS OF FINANCIAL STATEMENTS

Financial statements are the main source of information for major business decisions such as whether to lend money to a firm, whether to invest in preferred or common stock, and whether to acquire a firm. This chapter first briefly presents the major financial statements for an example corporation that we will use throughout the chapter. Next is a discussion of why financial ratios are useful and in what context they should be analyzed; and then the major financial ratios are examined and computed for our example firm. A comparative analysis of these company ratios relative to the firm's industry and the S&P 400 series follows. Factors that must be considered when analyzing the financial statements for non–U.S. firms are also discussed. Finally, we address four major areas in investments where financial ratios have been effectively employed.

Our example company is Quaker Oats, a worldwide marketer of consumer grocery products, including cereals, mixes, grain-based snacks, syrup, corn products, edible oils, and pet food. Through its Fisher-Price Division, it is also one of the leading toy makers.

MAJOR FINANCIAL STATEMENTS

Financial statements are meant to provide information on the resources available to management, how these resources were financed, and what was accomplished with them. The three major statements are the balance sheet, the income statement, and the sources and uses statement, which reconciles changes in the other two reports.

BALANCE SHEET

The balance sheet shows what are the resources (assets) controlled by the firm and how these assets have been financed. Specifically, it indicates the current and fixed assets available to the firm at a given point in time (usually the end of the fiscal year or the end of a quarter). Typically, these assets are owned by the firm, but some may be leased on a long-term basis. Financing is indicated in terms of current liabilities (typically used to finance current assets, such as inventory), long-term liabilities (fixed debt), and owner's equity, which includes preferred stock, common stock, and retained earnings.

Note that the information on the balance sheet for Quaker Oats in Table 12.1 represents the *stock* of assets and financing alternatives for the firm at Quaker Oats' year-end of June 30 for 1985, 1986, and 1987.

INCOME STATEMENT

The income statement contains information on the efficiency, control, and profitability of management during some specified period of time (a quarter or a year). Specifically, *efficiency* is indicated by the sales generated during the period, while expenses indicate *control,* and the earnings derived from these sales indicate *profitability.* In contrast to the stock concept in the balance sheet, the income statement indicates the *flow* of sales, expenses, and earnings during a period of time. The income statement for Quaker Oats for the years 1985, 1986, and 1987 is contained in Table 12.2.

SOURCES AND USES STATEMENT

The sources and uses statement is especially useful since it integrates the two prior statements. For a given period, it indicates how various items on the balance sheet changed by examining the beginning and ending figures and shows the impact of relevant items from the income statement. It is extremely helpful in determining where funds are coming from for expansion (capital expenditures) and other requirements, such as stock acquisition or debt retirement.[1] The sources and uses statement for Quaker Oats for 1985, 1986, and 1987 is contained in Table 12.3.

PURPOSE OF FINANCIAL STATEMENT ANALYSIS

The purpose of financial statement analysis is to help evaluate management performance as regards profitability, efficiency, and risk. More important than the historical analysis is the projection of future management performance based upon the historical analysis, since it is the expected future performance that determines whether one should lend money or invest in a firm.

ANALYSIS OF FINANCIAL RATIOS

WHY RATIOS?

Analysts employ financial ratios because numbers in isolation are typically of little value. Knowing that the net income for a firm was $100,000 is far less informative than also knowing the sales figure that generated this income ($1 million or $10 million) and the assets or capital that generated those sales. Thus, ratios are used to provide meaningful relationships between individual values in the financial statements.[2] Because there are numerous individual items in the major financial statements, there are likewise numerous potential combinations for ratios. Therefore, the analyst

---

[1] A complete discussion of this statement and its preparation is contained in Erich Helfert, *Techniques of Financial Analysis,* 6th ed. (Homewood, Ill.: Richard D. Irwin, 1987).

[2] For a discussion of the history of ratio analysis, see James O. Horrigan, "A Short History of Financial Ratio Analysis," *Accounting Review* 43, no. 2 (April 1968): 284–294.

TABLE 12.1
The Quaker Oats Company and Subsidiaries Consolidated Balance Sheet
Year Ended: June 30 (Dollars in Millions)

ASSETS	1987	1986	1985
Current assets:			
Cash and short-term investments	$ 359.9	$ 109.5	$ 87.7
Receivables—net of allowances	752.9	536.9	505.1
Inventories:			
Finished goods	334.6	283.9	251.6
Grain and materials	114.1	99.0	94.0
Supplies	37.7	30.6	28.9
Total inventories	486.4	413.5	374.5
Other current assets	197.4	23.0	45.2
Total current assets	1,796.6	1,082.9	1,012.5
Other receivables and investments	14.8	58.6	10.8
Property, plant, and equipment	1,515.9	1,234.4	1,082.4
Less accumulated depreciation	533.9	462.6	389.0
Properties—net *Net Fixed Assets*	982.0	771.8	693.4
Intangible assets, net of amortization	456.7	121.2	125.2
Total assets *less dypriciation*	$3,250.1	$2,034.5	$1,841.9

Liabilities and common shareholders' equity			
Current liabilities			
Short-term debt	$ 528.5	$ 275.6	$ 144.9
Current portion of long-term debt	40.2	26.1	23.1
Trade accounts payable	278.9	204.3	179.1
Accrued payrolls, pensions, and bonuses	11.7	95.6	81.3
Accrued advertising and merchandising	96.7	63.7	50.6
Income taxes payable	59.1	42.4	50.0
Other accrued liabilities	172.6	78.4	82.4
Total current liabilities	1,288.7	786.1	611.8
Long-term debt	527.7	160.9	168.2
Other liabilities	79.1	48.7	59.9
Deferred income taxes	267.1	207.1	177.2
Redeemable preference stock, without par value, $100 stated value, $9.56 cumulative	—	—	37.9
Common shareholders' equity:			
Common stock, $5 par value, issued 83,989,396 shares; 41,994,698 shares; and 41,994,698 shares, respectively	420.0	210.0	210.0
Additional paid-in capital	13.1	.6	3.4
Reinvested earnings	822.6	848.3	728.4
Cumulative exchange adjustment	(43.0)	(67.9)	(103.2)
Deferred compensation	(18.9)	(20.0)	—
Treasury common stock, at cost	(106.3)	(139.3)	(51.7)
Total common shareholders' equity	1,087.5	831.7	786.9
Total liabilities and common shareholders' equity	$3,250.1	$2,034.5	$1,841.9

Source: Courtesy of The Quaker Oats Company.

TABLE 12.2
The Quaker Oats Company and Subsidiaries Consolidated Statement of Income
Year Ended: June 30 (Dollars in Millions)

	1987	1986*	1985*
Net sales	$4,420.6	$3,453.9	$3,348.0
Cost of goods sold	2,436.6	1,975.9	2,019.1
Gross profit	1,984.0	1,478.0	1,328.9
Selling, general, and administrative expenses	1,534.2	1,136.3	995.8
Operating profit	449.8	341.7	333.1
Interest expense—net	41.1	29.7	49.8
Other expenses	50.3	10.3	3.0
Income from continuing operations before income taxes	358.4	301.7	280.3
Provision for income taxes	172.7	135.0	130.3
Income from continuing operations	185.7	166.7	150.0
Income from discontinued operations—net of taxes	2.4	12.9	6.6
Income from the disposal of discontinued operations—net of taxes	55.8	—	—
Income from discontinued operations (net of income taxes of $27.0, $12.0, and $5.8 million)	58.2	12.9	6.6
Net income	243.9	179.6	156.6
Preference dividends	—	2.3	3.6
Net income available for common shares	$ 243.9	$ 177.3	$ 153.0

*Restated to reflect the disposal of the specialty retailing business segment as discontinued operations.
Source: Courtesy of The Quaker Oats Company.

must limit the examination to the most relevant ratios and categorize them into groups that provide information on alternative economic aspects of the firm's operation. Prior to discussing specific areas of analysis and the relevant ratios, we should consider the importance of *relative analysis*.

ALL RATIOS SHOULD BE RELATIVE

More to the point, *only relative financial ratios are relevant!* Just as a single number from a financial statement has little value, an individual financial ratio has little value until it is placed in perspective relative to other ratios. The important comparisons are relative to

- The aggregate economy
- The company's industry or industries
- The firm's major competitors within the industry
- The firm's own past performance.

The comparison to the aggregate economy is important because almost all firms are influenced by the economy's business cycles—its expansions and contractions (recessions). As an example, it is not reasonable to expect an increase in the profit margin for a firm during a recession—a stable margin might be very encouraging under such conditions. Alternatively, a small increase in a firm's margin during a major business expansion may

TABLE 12.3
The Quaker Oats Company and Subsidiaries Consolidated Statements of Cash Flow
Year Ended: June 30 (Dollars in Millions)

	1987	1986	1985
Operations			
Income from continuing operations	$185.7	$166.7	$150.0
Depreciation and amortization	112.2	76.7	73.6
Deferred income taxes and other items	60.7	18.1	18.9
Funds from continuing operations	358.6	261.5	242.5
Income from discontinued operations	58.2	12.9	6.6
(Increase) in receivables	(216.0)	(31.8)	(20.2)
(Increase) in inventories	(72.9)	(39.0)	(17.9)
(Increase) decrease in other current assets	(174.4)	22.2	(12.9)
Increase (decrease) in trade accounts payable	74.6	25.2	(17.0)
Increase in other current liabilities	161.0	15.4	55.8
Effect of exchange rate changes	6.9	13.4	(3.0)
Other—net	29.8	4.3	11.1
	225.8	284.1	245.0
Cash dividends declared	(63.2)	(57.5)	(54.1)
Changes in deferred compensation	1.1	(20.0)	—
Investing activities			
Additions to properties	(182.3)	(146.6)	(109.0)
Cost of acquisitions, excluding working capital	(556.9)	—	(14.9)
Decrease (increase) in long-term receivables and investments	43.8	(47.2)	11.4
Disposition of businesses excluding working capital	74.6	—	—
Disposals of property, plant, and equipment	24.1	16.2	47.5
Financing activities	(596.7)	(177.6)	(65.0)
Net increase (decrease) in short-term debt	267.0	133.7	(49.1)
Proceeds from short-term debt to be refinanced	225.0	—	—
Proceeds from long-term debt	183.7	20.0	1.9
Reduction of long-term debt	(41.4)	(30.6)	(33.8)
Issuance of common Treasury stock	49.1	20.0	16.0
Purchase of common stock	—	(110.5)	(38.3)
Purchase and redemption of preference stock	—	(39.8)	—
	683.4	(7.2)	(103.3)
Net increase in cash and short-term investments	$250.4	$ 21.8	$ 22.6

Source: Courtesy of The Quaker Oats Company.

be considered a sign of weakness. An analysis relative to the economy will help you to understand how a firm reacts to the business cycle. In turn, this analysis will indicate the firm's relative business risk and help in projecting its future performance during subsequent business cycles.

    Probably the most popular comparison is a firm's performance relative to its industry.[3] The influence of an industry on the firms within it will

[3] An excellent source of comparative ratios for alternative lines of business is *Industry Norms and Key Business Ratios*, Dun and Bradstreet, Inc., 99 Church Street, New York, New York 10007. Another source is Robert Morris Associates, 1616 Philadelphia National Bank Bldg., Philadelphia, PA 19107.

vary by industry but is always strong. It is strongest for industries with a homogenous product such as steel, rubber, glass, and wood products, since all firms within these industries experience similar shifts in demand. In addition, the technology and production processes for such companies are fairly similar. Because of the strong industry impact, analyzing an individual firm without considering the overall industry trend or cycle is meaningless. Even the best managed steel firm, for example, is going to experience a decline in profit margins during a recession. You should examine an industry's performance relative to aggregate economic activity to understand its relative cyclicality, or how it responds to the business cycle. A detailed industry analysis is considered in Chapter 14.

A major problem when comparing a firm to its industry is that you may not feel comfortable using the average (mean) value because of the wide dispersion of values for the individual firms within the industry. Alternatively, you may believe that the firm being analyzed is not typical, that it has a strong unique component. Under either of these conditions, it might be preferable to compare the firm to one or several individual firms within the industry that are comparable in size or clientele. As an example, within the computer industry it might be preferable to compare IBM to certain individual firms within the industry (e.g., Burroughs; Control Data) rather than employ total industry data that includes numerous small firms serving unique components of the industry. As another example, you would probably want to limit a utility industry comparison to a set of comparable utilities (comparing an electric utility to other electric utilities versus gas and water utilities). Even within the electric utility segment you would probably consider electric utility firms from the same geographic area and those with a comparable mix of residential, commercial, and industrial customers.

Finally, it is important to examine a firm's relative performance over time to determine if it is progressing or regressing. This *time series analysis* is crucial when attempting to estimate *future* performance. Too often we consider an average of a ratio for a five- or ten-year period without considering the trend. For example, it is possible to have an average rate of return of 10 percent based upon rates of return that increase from 5 percent to 15 percent over time or based upon a series that begins at 15 percent and declines to 5 percent. Obviously, the difference in the time series trend would have a major impact on your estimate for the future.

COMPUTATION OF FINANCIAL RATIOS

The ratios discussed are divided into five major categories based upon alternative economic aspects of a firm:

RATIO CATEGORIES

1. Internal liquidity (solvency)
2. Operating performance
3. Risk analysis
4. Growth analysis
5. External liquidity (marketability).

**INTERNAL
LIQUIDITY RATIOS**

Internal liquidity (solvency) ratios are intended to indicate the ability of the firm to meet future short-term financial obligations. The idea is to match the potential near-term obligations, such as accounts payable, with current assets that will be available on a short notice to meet these obligations.

CURRENT RATIO. Clearly the most well-known liquidity measure is the current ratio, which examines the relationship between current assets and current liabilities as follows:

$$\text{Current Ratio} = \frac{\text{Current Assets}}{\text{Current Liabilities}}.$$

For Quaker Oats, the current ratios were as follows (the values used in all ratios in this chapter are in thousands of dollars):

$$1987: \frac{1,796,600}{1,288,700} = 1.39$$
$$1986: \frac{1,082,900}{786,100} = 1.38$$
$$1985: \frac{1,012,500}{611,800} = 1.65$$

While the ratios appear adequate, it would be necessary to compare these values to comparable figures for the firm's industry and the aggregate market. This comparative analysis is considered later in the chapter. The major concern is the decline in the ratio relative to 1985.[4]

QUICK RATIO. Some observers believe that total current assets are not a conservative enough estimate of assets available to meet current obligations, since inventories and some other assets included in the current asset section might not be very liquid. Because of this, they prefer to use the quick ratio, which relates current liabilities to the most liquid current assets (cash items and accounts receivable) as follows:

$$\text{Quick Ratio} = \frac{\text{Cash} + \text{Receivables}}{\text{Current Liabilities}}.$$

This ratio is intended to indicate the amount of very liquid assets available to pay near-term liabilities. For Quaker Oats the quick ratios were

$$1987: \frac{1,112,800}{1,288,700} = 0.86$$
$$1986: \frac{646,400}{786,100} = 0.82$$
$$1985: \frac{592,800}{611,800} = 0.97$$

---

[4] In this regard, see Kenneth W. Lemke, "The Evaluation of Liquidity: An Analytical Study," *Journal of Accounting Research* 8, no. 1 (Spring 1970): 47–77.

Again, these ratios for Quaker Oats are adequate, but there has been a small decline relative to 1985, and you would want to examine this change relative to what happened in the economy and the industry.

CASH RATIO. The most conservative liquidity ratio is the cash ratio, which relates the cash and short-term investments (money market instruments) to current liabilities as follows:

$$\text{Cash Ratio} = \frac{\text{Cash and Short-Term Investments}}{\text{Current Liabilities}}.$$

For Quaker Oats, the ratios were

$$1987: \frac{359,900}{1,288,700} = 0.28$$

$$1986: \frac{109,500}{786,100} = 0.14$$

$$1985: \frac{87,700}{611,800} = 0.14$$

The ratios in 1985 and 1986 appeared to be fairly low, while the substantial increase in 1987 brought the ratio up to a reasonable level.

RECEIVABLES TURNOVER. In addition to looking at supposedly liquid assets relative to near-term liabilities, it is useful to analyze the quality of the receivables by examining how often they turn over, which implies the average collection period for these receivables. The intent is to determine the liquidity of these current assets. The firm's receivables turnover is computed as follows:

$$\text{Receivables Turnover} = \frac{\text{Net Annual Sales}}{\text{Average Receivables}}.$$

The average receivables is typically the beginning figure plus the ending value divided by 2. Quaker Oats' receivables turnover figures were

$$1987: \frac{4,420,600}{(752,900 + 536,900)/2} = 6.85$$

$$1986: \frac{3,453,900}{(536,900 + 505,100)/2} = 6.63$$

It is not possible to compute a turnover value for 1985 because there is no beginning receivables figure for 1985 (i.e., we do not have the ending receivables figure for 1984).

Given this annual turnover figure, you can compute an average collection period as follows:

$$\text{Average Receivables Collection Period} = \frac{365}{\text{Annual Turnover}}.$$

$$1987: \frac{365}{6.85} = 53.3 \text{ days}$$

$$1986: \frac{365}{6.63} = 55.1 \text{ days}$$

These results indicate that receivables are generally collected by Quaker Oats in about 50 days. To determine whether these values are good or bad, they should be related to the firm's credit policy and to a comparable collection number for other firms in the industry. In the case of Quaker Oats, it is important to remember that the firm is mainly in the food business but is also in the toy business, which may have different credit policies.

Some analysts also compute an inventory turnover figure to determine the liquidity of the firm's inventory. For our purposes, this inventory ratio is considered in the operating performance category.

WORKING CAPITAL/SALES. The working capital/sales ratio is a liquidity ratio that goes beyond the balance sheet—it relates the net working capital (current assets minus current liabilities) to the sales of the firm as indicated in the income statement. Thus, it considers the stock of working capital available to a need based on the flow of sales as follows:

$$\text{Working Capital-to-Sales Ratio} = \frac{\text{Current Assets} - \text{Current Liabilities}}{\text{Net Sales}}.$$

Like many ratios, it has no magic guideline number, but it is important to examine the percent over time to determine any trend and also see how it compares to the industry and to a comparable number for the aggregate market. The values for Quaker Oats were:

$$1987: \frac{1,796,600 - 1,288,700}{4,420,600} = 11.49\%$$

$$1986: \frac{1,082,900 - 786,100}{3,453,900} = 8.59\%$$

$$1985: \frac{1,012,500 - 611,800}{3,348,000} = 11.97\%$$

The ratios were fairly constant overall, and we will see that they compare favorably to the industry and market.

OPERATING PERFORMANCE

The ratios that indicate how well the management is operating the business are typically divided into two subcategories: (1) efficiency ratios and (2) profitability ratios. The efficiency ratios examine how the management uses the assets and capital at its disposal. The use of assets and capital is mainly measured in terms of the dollars of sales generated by various asset categories or capital categories. In turn, the profitability ratios analyze the profits earned on these sales and also on the assets and capital employed.

ANALYSIS OF
EFFICIENCY

TOTAL ASSET TURNOVER. The total asset turnover ratio indicates the use of the firm's total asset base (net assets equal gross assets minus depreciation on fixed assets). It is computed as follows:

$$\text{Total Asset Turnover} = \frac{\text{Net Sales}}{\text{Average Total Net Assets}}.$$

Quaker Oats' asset turnover values were

$$1987: \frac{4,420,600}{(3,250,100 + 2,034,500)/2} = 1.67$$

$$1986: \frac{3,453,900}{(2,034,500 + 1,841,900)/2} = 1.78$$

This ratio should be compared to other firms in an industry, since it varies substantially between industries. As an example, it will range from about 1 for large capital firms (e.g., steel and other heavy manufacturing companies) to over 10 for some retailing operations. It can also be affected by the use of leased facilities. You should consider a *range* of turnover values, since it is poor management to have too few assets for the potential business (sales), just as it is poor judgment to have excess assets.

Beyond the analysis of the total asset base, it is insightful to examine the utilization of some specific assets, such as inventories and fixed assets.

INVENTORY TURNOVER. The inventory turnover ratio should indicate the utilization of inventory by the management. It is computed as follows:

$$\text{Inventory Turnover} = \frac{\text{Net Sales}}{\text{Average Inventory}}$$

or

$$\frac{\text{Cost of Sales}}{\text{Average Inventory}}.$$

It is preferable to compute the turnover using the cost of sales figure, because the inventory figure is at cost. Historically, the net sales figure was used because firms often did not report cost of sales. Currently, firms are required to report the cost of sales, so it is possible to compute the turnover using this value. The inventory turnover ratios for Quaker Oats were

$$1987: \frac{2,436,600}{(486,400 + 413,500)/2} = 5.42$$

$$1986: \frac{1,975,900}{(413,500 + 374,500)/2} = 5.01$$

Again, the emphasis should be on the firm's performance *relative* to its industry, since the appropriate inventory turnover ratio varies widely. Also, you should consider the range, because a very low *or* very high value is not good. Too low an inventory turnover ratio relative to your competitors probably means excess inventory and possibly some obsolete inventory. In contrast, while a high inventory turnover ratio may indicate efficiency, if it gets too high, it can indicate inadequate inventory that can lead to shortages, back-orders to customers, and eventually a loss of sales.

NET FIXED ASSET TURNOVER. The net fixed asset turnover ratio provides information on the firm's utilization of fixed assets. It is computed as follows:

$$\text{Fixed Asset Turnover} = \frac{\text{Net Sales}}{\text{Average Net Fixed Assets}}.$$

Quaker Oats' fixed asset turnover ratios were

$$1987: \frac{4,420,600}{(982,000 + 771,800)/2} = 5.04$$

$$1986: \frac{3,453,900}{(771,800 + 693,400)/2} = 4.71$$

It is important to examine this turnover relative to comparable firms in the same industry and to take into account the impact of leased assets. Also remember that an abnormally high asset turnover ratio can be due to the use of old, fully depreciated equipment that may be obsolete.

EQUITY TURNOVER. In addition to specific asset turnover ratios, it is useful to examine the turnover for alternative capital components. One of the most important in this regard is the equity turnover, which is computed as follows:

$$\text{Equity Turnover} = \frac{\text{Net Sales}}{\text{Average Equity}}.$$

Equity includes preferred and common stock, paid-in capital, and total retained earnings.[5] The difference between this ratio and the total asset turnover is that the capital provided from current liabilities and long-term debt is not considered. Therefore, when examining the trend for this series, you should consider the capital ratios for the firm, because it is possible to show an increase in the equity turnover ratio by increasing the firm's proportion of debt capital (i.e., its debt/equity ratio). Quaker Oats' equity turnover ratios were:

---

[5] The equity figure used does not include the preferred stock, which is considered equity by accountants. This author's preference is to consider only owner's equity, which would not include preferred stock.

$$1987: \frac{4,420,600}{(1,087,500 + 831,700)/2} = 4.61$$

$$1986: \frac{3,453,900}{(831,700 + 786,900)/2} = 4.27$$

Quaker experienced a very nice increase in this ratio. In the subsequent analysis related to growth we will examine the variables that affect this ratio and derive some understanding of what caused the increase.

Given some understanding of the firm's relative ability to generate sales from the assets and capital at its disposal, the next step is to examine the profit related to sales and capital.

ANALYSIS OF PROFITABILITY

The ratios in this category indicate the rate of profit on sales and ultimately the percent return on the capital employed.

GROSS PROFIT MARGIN. Gross profit is equal to net sales minus the cost of goods sold. The gross profit margin is computed as

$$\text{Gross Profit Margin} = \frac{\text{Gross Profit}}{\text{Net Sales}}.$$

The gross profit margins for Quaker Oats were:

$$1987: \frac{1,984,000}{4,420,600} = 44.88\%$$

$$1986: \frac{1,478,000}{3,453,900} = 42.79\%$$

$$1985: \frac{1,328,900}{3,348,000} = 39.69\%$$

This ratio indicates the basic cost structure of the firm. An analysis over time relative to a comparable industry figure is a prime indicator of the relative cost-price position of the firm. Given the improvement in this margin experienced by Quaker Oats over the three years, such a comparison would be very important.

OPERATING PROFIT MARGIN. Operating profit is gross profit minus sales, general, and administrative expenses. The operating profit margin is equal to

$$\text{Operating Profit Margin} = \frac{\text{Operating Profit}}{\text{Net Sales}}.$$

For Quaker Oats the operating profit margins were:

$$1987: \frac{449,800}{4,420,600} = 10.18\%$$

$$1986: \frac{341,700}{3,453,900} = 9.89\%$$

$$1985: \frac{333,100}{3,348,000} = 9.95\%$$

The variability of this profit margin over time is a prime indicator of the business risk for a firm. These results for Quaker Oats are encouraging, since the margins were not only fairly stable but also increased over time. If the firm has other income or expenses (in the case of Quaker Oats these are relatively minor), these are considered before arriving at the earnings before interest and taxes.

In some instances you might want to add back depreciation and compute a profit margin that consists of earnings before depreciation, interest, and taxes as a percentage of sales. This is considered an alternative operating profit margin that reflects all controllable expenses and is useful for heavy manufacturing firms that have large depreciation charges.

NET PROFIT MARGIN. Net income is earnings after taxes but before dividends on preferred and common stock. This margin is equal to

$$\text{Net Profit Margin} = \frac{\text{Net Income}}{\text{Net Sales}}.$$

For Quaker Oats, the net profit margins from continuing operations were:

$$1987: \frac{185,700}{4,420,600} = 4.20\%$$

$$1986: \frac{166,700}{3,453,900} = 4.83\%$$

$$1985: \frac{150,000}{3,348,000} = 4.48\%$$

This ratio is computed based upon sales and earnings from *continuing* operations, because the purpose of our analysis is to derive insights about *future* expectations. Therefore, results for continuing operations are the relevant data. You probably should be somewhat concerned with the fairly large decline in this margin from 1986 to 1987.

COMMON SIZE INCOME STATEMENT. Beyond the analysis of these ratios that examine various income figures, an additional technique is to prepare a common size income statement, which examines all expense and income items as a percentage of sales. The analysis of such a statement for several years (five at least) indicates the trend in cost figures and profit margins.

TABLE 12.4
The Quaker Oats Company and Subsidiaries Consolidated Statements of Income Common Size Analysis

	1987	%	1986	%	1985	%
Net sales	$4,420.6	100.00	$3,453.9	100.00	$3,348.0	100.00
Cost of goods sold	2,436.6	55.12	1,975.9	57.21	2,019.1	60.31
Gross Profit	1,984.0	44.88	1,478.0	42.79	1,328.9	39.69
Selling, general, and administrative expenses	1,534.2	34.71	1,136.3	32.90	995.8	29.74
Operating profit margin	449.8	10.18	341.7	9.89	333.1	9.95
Interest expense—net	41.1	0.93	29.7	0.86	49.8	1.49
Other expense	50.3	1.14	10.3	0.30	3.0	0.09
Income from continuing operations before income taxes	358.4	8.11	301.7	8.74	280.3	8.37
Provision for income taxes	172.7	3.91	135.0	3.91	130.3	3.89
Net income from continuing operations	185.7	4.20	166.7	4.83	150.0	4.48
Net income from discontinued operations	2.4	0.05	12.9	0.37	6.6	0.20
NI from disposal of discontinued operations	55.8	1.26	0.0	0.00	0.0	0.00
Net income	243.9	5.52	179.6	5.20	156.6	4.68
Preference dividends	0.0	0.00	2.3	0.07	3.6	0.11
Net income available for common shares	$ 243.9	5.52	$ 177.3	5.13	$ 153.0	4.57

Source: Courtesy of The Quaker Oats Company.

A common size statement for Quaker Oats for three years is shown in Table 12.4. As noted, the greatest value comes from a detailed analysis of various cost and margin figures over time relative to other firms in the industry. For Quaker Oats this statement indicates a steady decline in the percent of cost of goods and the resultant increase in the gross profit margin. Unfortunately, there has been a partially offsetting increase in selling, general, and administrative expenses as a percentage of sales and also an increase in other expenses. As a result, the net before tax margin and the net profit margin declined in 1987 compared to the two prior years.

Beyond the analysis of earnings on sales, the ultimate determination of the success of management is the rate of return earned on the assets of the firm or the capital committed to the enterprise.

RETURN ON TOTAL CAPITAL. The return on total capital ratio indicates the earnings available for all the capital involved in the enterprise (debt, preferred stock, and common stock). Therefore, the earnings figure used is the net income from continuing operations (before any dividends) plus the interest paid on debt.

$$\text{Return on Total Capital} = \frac{\text{Net Income} + \text{Interest}}{\text{Average Total Capital}}.$$

For Quaker Oats, there is interest expense for long-term and short-term debt. The interest expense values used differ from the "net" interest expense in the income statement, which is interest expense minus interest income. Thus, the rate of return on total capital was

$$1987: \frac{185,800 + 61,700^*}{(3,250,100 + 2,034,500)/2} = 9.36\%$$

$$1986: \frac{166,700 + 40,800^*}{(2,034,500 + 1,841,900)/2} = 10.71\%$$

*Gross interest expense.

This ratio indicates the overall return earned on all the capital employed by the firm, and it should be compared to other firms in the industry and to results for the general economy. Obviously, if this rate of return is not commensurate with the perceived risk of the firm, one might question if the entity should continue to exist, since the capital could be used more productively elsewhere in the economy.

RETURN ON OWNER'S EQUITY. The return on owner's equity ratio is extremely important to the common stockholder, since it indicates what rate of return the manager earns on the capital provided by the owner after accounting for payments to all other capital suppliers. If you consider all equity (including preferred stock), this would equal:

$$\text{Return on Total Equity} = \frac{\text{Net Income}}{\text{Average Total Equity}}.$$

If one is concerned only with owner's equity (i.e., common equity), the ratio would be

$$\text{Return on Common Equity} = \frac{\text{Net Income} - \text{Preferred Dividend}}{\text{Average Common Equity}}.$$

In the case of Quaker Oats, as of 1987 it is not necessary to make the distinction, because during 1986 the firm retired the preferred stock outstanding. Therefore, the Quaker Oats' return on common equity figures (based upon earnings from continuing operations and subtracting the preferred dividends in 1986) are:

$$1987: \frac{185,700 - 0}{(1,087,500 + 831,700)/2} = 19.35\%$$

$$1986: \frac{166,700 - 2,300}{(831,700 + 786,900)/2} = 20.31\%$$

This ratio reflects the rate of return on the equity capital provided by the owners. As such, it should reflect not only the overall business risk involved, but also the additional *financial risk* assumed by the common stockholder because of the prior claim of the firm's debt. Notably, this return on equity ratio can be broken down into two of the prior ratios discussed (to maintain the identity, the common equity value used is the year-end figure rather than the average of the beginning and ending value).

$$\text{Return on Equity} = \frac{\text{Net Income}}{\text{Common Equity}} = \frac{\text{Net Income}}{\text{Net Sales}} \times \frac{\text{Net Sales}}{\text{Common Equity}}.$$

Therefore, a firm's return on equity can be improved by either using the equity more efficiently (i.e., increasing the firm's equity turnover) or by becoming more profitable (i.e., increasing the firm's net profit margin).

It is important to recognize that a firm's equity turnover can be affected by the firm's capital structure. It is possible to increase the equity turnover by employing a higher proportion of debt capital. We can see this effect by considering the following relationship.

$$\frac{\text{Sales}}{\text{Equity}} = \frac{\text{Sales}}{\text{Total Assets}} \times \frac{\text{Total Assets}}{\text{Equity}}.$$

As in the prior breakdown, this is an identity because we have added total assets to the top and bottom of the ratio. This equation indicates that the equity turnover ratio is a combination of the firm's total asset turnover (a measure of efficiency) and a financial leverage measure. Specifically, the ratio of total assets to equity indicates what proportion of total assets have been financed with debt. The point is, all assets have to be financed by either equity or some form of debt. Therefore, the higher the proportion of assets to equity, the higher the proportion of debt to equity. As an example, if the total asset/equity ratio is 2, it indicates that one-half of the assets were financed with equity, which implies that the other half was financed with debt. If it is 3, only one-third of total assets was financed with equity, so two-thirds must have been financed with debt. Thus, a firm can increase its equity turnover by either increasing its total asset turnover (i.e., becoming more efficient) or by increasing its financial leverage ratio (i.e., acquiring assets with a higher proportion of debt).

To derive a better feel for this very important set of relationships, consider the figures in Table 12.5 that indicate what has happened to the components of ROE and to ROE itself for Quaker Oats during the past ten years. As noted, these ratio values will differ from those just discussed, because they employ year-end balance sheet figures (assets and equity) as contrasted to the average of beginning and ending data.

The analysis of these data indicates several important trends. First, prior to 1987, the firm's ROE increased steadily from 14.32 percent to over 20 percent in 1986. When looking for a reason for this excellent trend, you should initially consider the two major ratios—equity turnover and net profit margin. This analysis indicates that the profit margin for Quaker Oats has varied over time and was about the same in 1986 as it was in 1978. In contrast, the equity turnover series experienced a generally steady increase from about 3 to over 4 (a very respectable 33 percent increase). Therefore, it appears that the big factor that caused the increase in the

TABLE 12.5
Components of Return on Equity for Quaker Oats Company: 1978–1987*

YEAR	(1) SALES / TOTAL ASSETS	(2) TOTAL ASSETS / EQUITY	(3)** SALES / EQUITY	(4) NET PROFIT MARGIN	(5)*** RETURN ON EQUITY
1987	1.36	2.99	4.07	4.20	17.09
1986	1.70	2.45	4.17	4.83	20.14
1985	1.82	2.23	4.06	4.48	18.19
1984	1.80	2.38	4.28	4.19	17.93
1983	1.71	2.15	3.68	4.57	16.82
1982	1.68	2.14	3.60	4.55	16.38
1981	1.62	2.21	3.58	4.37	15.64
1980	1.63	2.11	3.44	4.36	15.00
1979	1.56	2.01	3.14	4.65	14.60
1978	1.49	1.97	2.94	4.87	14.32

*Ratios use year-end data for total assets and common equity rather than averages for year.
**Column (3) is equal to column (1) times column (2).
***Column (5) is equal to column (3) times column (4).

firm's ROE was its equity turnover. The next question is, what caused the steady increase in the equity turnover? The total asset turnover ratio (Sales/T.Assets) increased fairly consistently from 1978 through 1985, rising from 1.49 to 1.82, followed by declines in 1986 and 1987.

Similarly, the financial leverage ratio (total assets/equity) increased steadily throughout the period and *ended at its high* value. It increased from 1.97 to 2.99—almost a 50 percent change in the ratio. This implies that the proportion of debt went from about 50 percent to almost 67 percent of total financing. Therefore, it appears that both components of the equity turnover increased over time, but *the larger influence came from an increase in financial leverage*—especially during the last two years. The fact is, the firm's ROE and all its components *except financial leverage* declined in 1987. Therefore, while the overall record looks very good, one should be concerned about the ability of the firm to continue or maintain this record based upon what transpired in 1987. What was it that caused the major decline in the total asset turnover and the profit margin in 1987 and the large increase in financial leverage? Put another way, as an analyst you should examine very carefully all the individual components in terms of the near-term and longer-term outlook. Besides the outlook for the firm's ROE, this analysis implies a change in the financial risk of the firm, which we will analyze in more detail in the next section.

RISK ANALYSIS

The purpose of risk analysis is to determine the uncertainty of income flows for the total firm and for individual capital sources (i.e., debt, preferred stock, and common stock). One can derive an estimate of the uncertainty of flows to the various sources of capital by examining the uncertainty of flows to the firm. In turn, the typical approach is to consider the major factors that cause uncertain flows to the firm where *uncertainty is measured in terms of the variability of flows over time*. That is, the more variable the income flows are, the greater the uncertainty or risk facing the investor. In this regard, the total risk of the firm is generally divided into business risk and financial risk.

BUSINESS RISK[6]   Business risk is the uncertainty of income that is due to the firm's industry (i.e., its variability of sales due to its products and customers) and the way it produces its products (i.e., its production function). Specifically, a firm's earnings vary over time because its sales and production costs vary. As an example, one would expect the earnings for a steel firm to vary more than for a grocery chain, because steel sales are more volatile than grocery sales over a business cycle. Also, because the steel firm has more fixed production costs, its earnings vary more than its sales.

Business risk is generally measured by the variability of the firm's operating income over time. A more volatile earnings series means that an investor/lender will be more uncertain regarding future earnings; thus, it indicates greater business risk. The earnings volatility is generally computed in terms of the standard deviation of the historical earnings series. Because the standard deviation is influenced by the size of the numbers, analysts have attempted to standardize this measure by dividing it by the mean value for the series. The resulting ratio of the standard deviation of operating earnings divided by the average operating earnings is the *coefficient of variation (CV)*. Thus,

$$\text{Business Risk} = f\,(\text{Coefficient of Variation of Operating Earnings})$$

$$= \frac{\text{Standard Deviation of Operating Earnings }(OE)}{\text{Mean Operating Earnings}}$$

$$= \frac{\sqrt{\Sigma_{i=1}^{n}\,(OE_t - \overline{OE})^2/N}}{\Sigma_{i=1}^{n}\,OE_t/N}. \qquad n = 5 \text{ to } 10 \text{ yrs.}$$

The coefficient of variation of operating earnings has a great advantage: You can compare these standardized measures of variability for firms of different size (e.g., duPont compared to a smaller chemical firm). The computation of the *CV* of operating earnings generally covers a minimum of five years up to about ten years. Less than five years is not very meaningful, while much more than ten years can involve data that could be out of date.

It is not feasible to compute the *CV* of operating earnings for Quaker Oats, since we have data for only three years. In addition to an overall measure of business risk, you should attempt to determine the factors that

---

[6] For a further discussion on this general topic, see Eugene Brigham, *Financial Management Theory and Practice,* 4th ed.(Hinsdale, Ill.: The Dryden Press, 1985), Chapters 6 and 10.

contribute to this variability. In general, there are two: sales variability and operating leverage.

SALES VOLATILITY. Sales volatility is the prime determinant of earnings volatility, since operating earnings volatility cannot be lower than sales volatility; that is, operating leverage can increase earnings volatility only from the level derived from sales volatility. To understand this, conceive of a case where all costs for the firm were variable costs. In this instance, the relative sales volatility and the earnings volatility for the firm would be equal. When we introduce fixed production costs, we know that earnings will be *more* volatile than sales on a relative basis. Also, sales volatility is basically outside the control of management. While sales volatility is impacted by such factors as advertising and pricing, its major determinant is the aggregate economic environment and the firm's particular industry. As an example, a firm in a cyclical industry (e.g., automobiles or steel) will have a very volatile sales pattern over the business cycle compared to a firm in a noncyclical industry, such as hospital supplies. The sales volatility for a firm is typically measured by the coefficient of variation of sales during some specified time period (e.g., most recent five to ten years). The coefficient of variation (*CV*) is equal to the standard deviation of sales divided by the mean sales for the period.

$$\text{Sales Volatility} = f\,(\text{Coefficient of Variation of Sales})$$

$$= \frac{\text{Standard Deviation of Sales } (S)}{\text{Mean Sales}}$$

$$= \frac{\sqrt{\Sigma_{i=1}^{n}\ (S_i - \bar{S})^2/N}}{\Sigma_{i=1}^{n}\ S_i/N}\,.$$

OPERATING LEVERAGE. In addition to sales volatility, the variability of a firm's operating earnings is also affected by the production function of the firm; that is, what mixture of costs is involved in producing the goods and services sold? As mentioned, if a firm does not have any fixed production costs, then total production costs would vary directly with sales, and operating profits would be a constant proportion of sales. Thus, the operating profit margin would be constant. Under these conditions, the operating profit series would have the same relative volatility as sales. Realistically, firms almost always have some fixed production costs (e.g., buildings, machinery), or they employ some relatively permanent personnel (supervisors, foremen, etc.). The existence of *fixed production costs* means that *operating profits will vary more than sales vary over the business cycle.* During slow periods, profits will decline by a larger percentage than the percentage sales decline. In contrast, during periods of economic expansion, profits will increase by a larger percentage than the percentage that sales increase. The employment of fixed production costs is referred to as *operating leverage.* Clearly, the greater the firm's operating leverage, the more volatile the operating earnings series will be relative to the sales series.[7] Given this basic relationship between operating profit and sales, operating leverage is measured as the percentage change in operating earnings relative to a percentage change in sales during several recent years as follows:

$$\text{Operating Leverage} = \sum_{i=1}^{n} \left| \frac{\%\Delta OE}{\%\Delta S} \right| \bigg/ N.$$

The absolute values of the changes are considered, because it is possible for the two series to move in opposite directions. It is not the direction that is important—only the relative size of the change. The more volatile the operating earnings are, compared to sales, the greater the operating leverage.

FINANCIAL RISK

Financial risk is the additional uncertainty of returns faced by equity holders because a firm uses fixed obligation debt securities. This financial uncertainty is *in addition* to business risk. If the firm did not derive any of its capital from debt obligations (i.e., if it was an all-equity firm), the only uncertainty for the owner would be that due to sales volatility and operating leverage (i.e., business risk). With only business risk, the earnings available to the common stockholder would have the same volatility as the operating earnings. The point is, when a firm derives some of its capital from debt securities, the payments on this capital come prior to the common stock earnings, and these payments are a *fixed obligation.* Therefore, similar to the effect of operating leverage, during good times the earnings on equity will experience a larger percentage increase than operating earnings, while during a period of adverse business the earnings available to equity holders will experience a larger percentage decline than operating earnings.[8] Two sets of ratios are used to measure financial risk. The first indicates the proportion of capital derived from debt securities. The second considers the *flow* of earnings or cash available to pay the fixed obligations.

PROPORTION OF DEBT RATIOS. Proportion of debt ratios indicate what proportion of the firm's capital is derived from long-term debt compared to other sources of capital, such as preferred stock and common equity. Clearly, the higher the proportion of debt is compared to other sources, the more volatile the earnings available to common stock will be and also the higher the probability of the firm defaulting on the bonds. Therefore, higher debt ratios indicate greater financial risk. Notably, the acceptable level of financial risk depends upon the firm's business risk. If the firm has lower business risk, investors are willing to accept higher financial

higher debt ratio ⇒ ↑ financial risk

---

[7] For a further treatment of this area, see James C. Van Horne, *Financial Management and Policy,* 7th ed. (Englewood Cliffs, N.J.: Prentice-Hall, 1986), Chapter 27.

[8] This relationship is referred to as *financial leverage* and is discussed in Brigham, *op. cit.,* Chapters 11 and 12.

risk. An example is public utilities, which typically have rather stable operating earnings streams (relatively low business risk), allowing them to have heavy debt capital structures (higher financial risk).

DEBT/EQUITY RATIO. The debt/equity ratio is equal to

$$\text{Debt-to-Equity Ratio} = \frac{\text{Total Long-Term Debt}}{\text{Total Equity}}.$$

The debt would include all long-term fixed obligations including subordinated convertible bonds. The equity is typically the book value of equity and includes preferred stock, common stock, and retained earnings. In some cases you may want to exclude preferred stock and consider only common equity. The total equity figure is probably preferable if some firms being analyzed have preferred stock and some do not. Alternatively, if you consider the preferred stock dividend akin to an interest payment, you might want to derive a ratio of debt plus preferred stock relative to common equity. In the case of Quaker Oats, it is not necessary to select an alternative, because the firm currently does not have preferred stock. Two sets of these ratios are computed: with and without deferred taxes. As shown on the balance sheet, the accumulated deferred tax figure is after long-term debt and "other liabilities." The fact is, there is some controversy regarding whether deferred taxes should be treated as a liability or as a part of permanent capital. It is argued that if the deferred tax is because of the difference in accelerated and straight-line depreciation, this is a liability that may never be paid. That is, as long as the firm continues to grow and add new assets, this figure continues to grow in the aggregate. Alternatively, if the deferred tax figure is because of differences in the recognition of income on long-term contracts (e.g., government contracts), there definitely will be a reversal, and it is a liability that will be paid. The point is, you must determine the reason for the deferred tax account and its long-term trend. In the case of Quaker Oats, this account is basically due to depreciation and has grown consistently over time. For demonstration purposes, several of the following ratios are computed including and excluding deferred taxes as a long-term liability. As shown, the impact of this difference can be substantial. Thus, two sets of debt-equity ratios for Quaker Oats were

A. INCLUDING DEFERRED TAXES AS LONG-TERM DEBT	B. EXCLUDING DEFERRED TAXES AS LONG-TERM DEBT
1987: $\dfrac{873,900}{1,087,500} = 80.36\%$	1987: $\dfrac{606,800}{1,087,500} = 55.80\%$
1986: $\dfrac{416,700}{831,700} = 50.10\%$	1986: $\dfrac{209,600}{831,700} = 25.50\%$
1985: $\dfrac{405,300}{824,800} = 49.14\%$	1985: $\dfrac{228,100}{824,800} = 27.66\%$

These ratios indicate an increase in the debt burden for the firm on a relative basis during 1987. Obviously, this is consistent with the trend for the total asset/equity ratio discussed earlier. It is stated in the annual report that this was a temporary increase in debt to finance two significant acquisitions: Golden Grain and Anderson Clayton. They also indicate the substantial impact of including deferred taxes as long-term debt. Remember that this item will grow consistently over time if it is due to depreciation, as in the case of Quaker Oats.

DEBT/TOTAL CAPITAL RATIO. The debt/total capital ratio indicates what proportion of long-term capital is derived from long-term debt capital. It is computed as

$$\text{Debt-to-Total Capital Ratio} = \frac{\text{Total Long-Term Debt}}{\text{Total Long-Term Capital}}.$$

The long-term capital would include all long-term debt, any preferred stock, and total equity. Again, the ratios are computed including deferred taxes as part of long-term debt and also excluding it from both long-term debt and long-term capital. While this ratio is completely consistent with the debt/equity ratio, it is somewhat more intuitive because it indicates what percentage of long-term capital is fixed debt. The two sets of debt/total capital ratios for Quaker Oats were

A. INCLUDING DEFERRED TAXES AS LONG-TERM DEBT	B. EXCLUDING DEFERRED TAXES FROM LONG-TERM DEBT AND LONG-TERM CAPITAL
1987: $\dfrac{873,900}{1,961,400} = 44.55\%$	1987: $\dfrac{606,800}{1,041,300} = 35.81\%$
1986: $\dfrac{416,700}{1,248,400} = 33.38\%$	1986: $\dfrac{209,600}{1,041,300} = 20.13\%$
1985: $\dfrac{405,300}{1,230,100} = 32.95\%$	1985: $\dfrac{228,100}{1,052,900} = 21.66\%$

Again, this ratio indicates an increase in the firm's proportion of debt capital—that is, its financial risk. It also shows the effect of including deferred taxes as both debt and long-term capital.

TOTAL DEBT RATIOS. In some cases it is useful to compare *total* debt (current liabilities plus long-term liabilities) to total capital if a firm derives substantial funds from short-term borrowing. This applies to Quaker Oats, because it has historically had substantial current liabilities but also experienced a major increase in short-term debt during 1986 and 1987. Therefore, the two sets of total debt/total capital ratios for Quaker Oats were:

A. INCLUDING DEFERRED TAXES AS LONG-TERM DEBT	B. EXCLUDING DEFERRED TAXES FROM LONG-TERM DEBT AND LONG-TERM CAPITAL
1987: $\dfrac{2,162,600}{3,250,100} = 66.54\%$	1987: $\dfrac{1,895,500}{1,983,000} = 63.54\%$
1986: $\dfrac{1,202,800}{2,034,500} = 59.12\%$	1986: $\dfrac{995,700}{1,827,400} = 54.49\%$
1985: $\dfrac{1,017,100}{1,841,900} = 55.22\%$	1985: $\dfrac{839,900}{1,664,700} = 50.45\%$

As you would expect, this ratio indicates that currently about two-thirds of assets are financed with debt, which is what was implied by the total asset/equity ratio. As always, you should compare these ratios to other companies in the industry to see if they are consistent with the business risk of this industry.

FLOW RATIOS. In addition to the balance sheet ratios that indicate the *stock* of debt, analysts also employ ratios that relate the *flow* of earnings or cash that are available to meet the required fixed interest payments to debt obligations. In this case, the higher the value is (i.e., the greater the coverage), the less the financial risk.

INTEREST COVERAGE. Interest coverage is computed as follows:

$$\text{Interest Coverage} = \frac{\text{Income before Interest and Taxes}}{\text{Debt Interest Charges}}$$

This ratio indicates how many times the fixed interest charges are earned, based upon the earnings available to pay these charges. Alternatively, 1 minus the reciprocal of the coverage ratio indicates how much earnings could decline before it would be impossible to pay the fixed financial charges; for example, a coverage ratio of 5 means earnings could decline by 80 percent (1 minus 1/5), and the firm could still pay the fixed financial charges. The interest coverage ratios for Quaker Oats using the gross interest expense (e.g., $61,700 in 1987) were

1987: $\dfrac{185,700 + 172,700 + 61,700}{61,700} = 6.61\times$	*drop due to acquisition finance*
1986: $\dfrac{166,700 + 135,000 + 40,800}{40,800} = 8.39\times$	
1985: $\dfrac{150,000 + 130,300 + 63,100}{63,100} = 5.44\times$	

The coverage ratios in general are quite good—they are in excess of 5. The decline in the coverage ratio during 1987 was in spite of an increase in earnings—that is, there was also a substantial rise in interest expense due to the increase in short-term and long-term debt during 1987 to finance the two major acquisitions. These coverage ratios indicate an increase in the financial risk for Quaker Oats and are consistent with the proportion of debt ratios. Note that these two sets of financial risk ratios will not always give consistent results, because the proportion of debt ratios are not sensitive to the interest rate on the debt. As an example, you could have an increase in interest rates over time, and if the firm simply replaced old debt with new debt that had a higher interest rate, there would be no change in the proportion of debt ratios (e.g., debt/equity ratio), but the coverage ratio would decline because of an increase in interest expense.

TOTAL FIXED CHARGE COVERAGES. Alternatively, you might want to determine the coverage for fixed financial charges including preferred dividends. For this we must recognize that preferred dividends are paid out of earnings *after* taxes. Thus it is necessary to determine the pre-tax earnings required for these payments as follows:

$$\text{Fixed Charge Coverage} = \frac{\text{Income before Interest and Taxes}}{\text{Debt Interest} + (\text{Preferred Dividend}/1 - \text{Tax Rate})}.$$

There is no demonstration of this ratio, since Quaker Oats has not had any preferred stock since 1985.

CASH FLOW RATIOS. Similar yet different from the coverage ratios are the cash flow ratios, which relate the cash flow available from operations to the face value of outstanding debt. Therefore, these ratios are a combination of a *flow* ratio (they include the flow of earnings and non-cash expenses) and the *stock* of outstanding debt at a point in time. These cash flow ratios became well-known as a result of a widely quoted study by Beaver on predicting bankruptcy using financial ratios.[9] Examining a number of financial ratios, Beaver found the best single ratio to be that of "cash flow to long-term debt." Based upon these results, numerous subsequent studies on this topic have included this ratio and found it to be consistently useful. Further, it has been used in several studies dealing with bond ratings and also found to be significant.

CASH FLOW/LONG-TERM DEBT RATIO. As noted, the cash flow figure is equal to net income plus non-cash expenses, which would generally include depreciation expense and deferred taxes. Therefore, the ratios would be computed as follows:

$$\text{Cash Flow/LT Debt} = \frac{\text{Net Income} + \text{Depreciation Exp.} + \text{Deferred Tax}}{\text{Book Value of LT Debt}}.$$

---

[9] William H. Beaver, "Financial Ratios as Predictors of Failure," *Empirical Research in Accounting: Selected Studies,* 1966 supplement to vol. 4, *Journal of Accounting Research.*

For Quaker Oats, these ratios were as follows using the net income from continuing operations, the depreciation expense figure provided in the footnotes, and also the deferred taxes for specific years as indicated in the footnotes:

A. INCLUDING DEFERRED TAXES AS LONG-TERM DEBT	B. EXCLUDING DEFERRED TAXES AS LONG-TERM DEBT
1987: $\dfrac{185,700 + 112,200 + 40,500}{873,900} = 38.72\%$	1987: $\dfrac{338,400}{606,800} = 55.77\%$
1986: $\dfrac{166,700 + 76,100 + 6,200}{416,700} = 59.76\%$	1986: $\dfrac{249,000}{209,600} = 118.80\%$
1985: $\dfrac{150,000 + 69,000 + 26,200}{405,300} = 60.50\%$	1985: $\dfrac{245,200}{228,100} = 107.50\%$

These ratios indicate some good news and not-so-good news. The values for all three years are good relative to aggregate averages. Unfortunately, the results for 1987 indicate a major decline for the firm. While 39 percent and 56 percent are still good ratios relative to the food industry and the aggregate market, the firm is obviously not as strong as it was previously.

CASH FLOW/TOTAL DEBT RATIO. In addition to long-term debt, you should also examine total debt to ensure that you do not overlook instances where a firm has an abnormal buildup of short-term borrowing. For Quaker Oats, these ratios were

A. INCLUDING DEFERRED TAXES AS LONG-TERM DEBT	B. EXCLUDING DEFERRED TAXES FROM LONG-TERM DEBT
1987: $\dfrac{338,400}{2,162,600} = 15.65\%$	1987: $\dfrac{338,400}{1,895,500} = 17.85\%$
1986: $\dfrac{249,000}{1,202,800} = 20.70\%$	1986: $\dfrac{249,000}{995,700} = 25.01\%$
1985: $\dfrac{245,200}{1,017,100} = 24.11\%$	1985: $\dfrac{245,200}{839,900} = 29.19\%$

These ratios not only reflect the historically heavy short-term debt burden for Quaker Oats (due to short-term borrowing and trade accounts payable), but also reflect the large increase in current liabilities during 1987. As we will see from some subsequent data, these values are lower than one might expect for a firm such as Quaker Oats.

GROWTH ANALYSIS

The purpose of growth analysis is to examine specific ratios that indicate how fast a firm should grow. Such analysis is important for both lenders and owners. The rationale for owners analyzing growth potential is obvious, since the future value of the firm depends on the future growth in earnings and dividends. You will recall that the standard dividend val-

IMPORTANCE OF GROWTH ANALYSIS

uation model discussed in Chapter 9 showed that the value of the firm is a function of dividends in Period 1, the required rate of return for the stock (k), and the expected growth rate of dividends for the firm (g_i). Therefore, an estimation of expected growth of earnings and dividends on the basis of the variables that influence growth is obviously crucial. An analysis of past values for these growth determinants should be helpful in the estimation process.

A firm's growth potential is also important to creditors, since the major factor that determines the firm's ability to pay an obligation is the firm's future success, which in turn is influenced by its growth. Many financial ratios employed in credit analysis tend to emphasize the amount of assets covering the financial obligations. These ratios imply that it is possible to liquidate these assets to pay off the loan in case of default. In fact, using these assets for such a purpose is extremely questionable, since the usual payoff on assets sold in a forced liquidation is about 10 to 15 cents on the dollar. Clearly, the more relevant analysis is the ability of the firm to pay off the obligations as an *ongoing* enterprise. In this regard, the analysis of growth potential indicates the future status of the firm as an ongoing enterprise.

DETERMINANTS OF GROWTH

The growth of a business firm is similar to the growth of any economic entity, including the aggregate economy. It depends on

1. The amount of resources retained and reinvested in the entity
2. The rate of return that is earned on the resources retained.

The more a firm reinvests, the greater its potential for growth. Alternatively, for a given level of reinvestment, a firm will grow faster if it is able to earn a higher rate of return on the resources reinvested. Therefore, we concentrate on the growth of equity earnings, which is a function of two variables: (1) the percentage of net earnings retained (i.e., the retention rate) and (2) the rate of return on the firm's equity capital (ROE). Specifically,

$$g = \text{Percentage of Earnings Retained} \times \text{Return on Equity}$$
$$= RR \times ROE.$$

The retention rate is a decision by the board of directors based upon the investment opportunities available to the firm. Theory would indicate that the firm should retain earnings and reinvest them as long as the expected rate of return on the investment exceeds the firm's cost of capital.

As discussed, the firm's ROE is a function of three components:

- Net profit margin
- Total asset turnover
- Financial leverage (total assets/equity)

This indicates that the firm can increase its ROE by increasing its profitability (raising its profit margin), by becoming more efficient with its assets (increasing the total asset turnover), or by changing its capital structure (increasing its financial leverage and financial risk). Note that two of the ratios are operating factors (total asset turnover and profit margin) and one is a financing decision. As an analyst you would prefer the increases to come in the operating variables (profit margin and asset turnover) rather than the financing variable. You should examine each of the components over time in order to arrive at a *projection* for ROE. Using the three-component breakdown, let us examine the sustainable growth outlook for Quaker Oats.

The earnings retention rate (*RR*) is computed as follows:

$$\text{Retention Rate} = 1 - \frac{\text{Dividends Declared}}{\text{Net Income (from continuing operations)}}.$$

The *RR* for Quaker Oats was as follows, using income per share from continuing operations and adjusting for the two-for-one split in November 1986:

$$\textbf{1987: } 1 - \frac{0.80}{2.36} = 1 - .34 = 0.66$$

$$\textbf{1986: } 1 - \frac{0.70}{2.08} = 1 - .34 = 0.66$$

$$\textbf{1985: } 1 - \frac{0.62}{1.80} = 1 - .34 = 0.66$$

These results indicate great consistency for Quaker Oats and a fairly high rate of retention, which you might expect because of the firm's strong ROE.

Since we have already examined the three components of ROE for the period 1978–1987 in Table 12.5, Table 12.6 contains the two factors that determine sustainable growth and the implied growth rate during the last ten years. Overall, and especially during the period 1983–1986, Quaker Oats enjoyed a steady increase in its implied sustainable growth rate. There was a decline in 1987 because of the decline in the ROE.

This table reinforces the importance of the ROE, because the firm's retention rate has been very stable, implying that the factor that determines the growth rate is ROE. This analysis indicates that the important consideration is the *long-run* outlook for the components of sustainable growth. As an analyst, you must derive a reasonable set of estimates for the relevant variables. Lempereur contends that the important consideration when relating ROE to expected growth is the relationship of the expected ROE to the current ROE.[10] Thus, if the expected ROE is above the current ROE, then the actual growth rate experienced will exceed the growth implied by the model. And if the expected ROE is below the current ROE, the opposite is true. Therefore, you want to project each of the components and estimate the *expected* ROE to use in the growth model.

---

[10] Douglas R. Lampereur, "Projected Growth Calculations: Impact of Changes in Projected ROE," Standish, Ayer, & Wood, Inc., 1981.

TABLE 12.6
Components of Growth and Implied Sustainable Growth Rate: 1978–1987

YEAR	(1) RETENTION RATE	(2) ROE*	(3)** SUSTAINABLE GROWTH RATE
1987	0.66	17.09	11.28
1986	0.66	20.14	13.29
1985	0.66	18.19	12.01
1984	0.66	17.93	11.83
1983	0.64	16.82	10.76
1982	0.68	16.38	11.14
1981	0.67	15.64	10.48
1980	0.69	15.00	10.35
1979	0.69	14.60	10.07
1978	0.69	14.32	9.88

*Based upon year-end equity.
**Column (3) is equal to column (1) times column (2).

EXTERNAL MARKET LIQUIDITY

MARKET LIQUIDITY DEFINED

Market liquidity is the ability to buy or sell an asset *quickly* with little price change from a prior transaction assuming no new information. In order to determine how liquid an asset is, one should ask two questions: (1) How long will it take to buy or sell the asset? (2) What will be the purchase or selling price compared to recent transaction prices? In the case of a liquid asset, you should be able to buy or sell it very quickly at a price close to the prior transaction price. Examples of liquid common stocks are AT&T and IBM, because you can sell large amounts of these stocks very quickly with very little price change from the prior trade. In the case of an illiquid stock, you might be able to sell it quickly, but the price would be significantly different from the prior price (e.g., a quick sale at $28 for a stock that sold recently for $30). Alternatively, the broker might be able to get $30 a share, but it could take several days.

DETERMINANTS OF MARKET LIQUIDITY

Investors should know the liquidity characteristics of securities they currently own or want to own, because they may want to change the composition of their portfolio. While the major factors that indicate market liquidity are derived from market trading data, several internal corporate variables are good proxies for these market variables. The most important determinant of external market liquidity is the *number of shares traded* in the security and/or the *dollar value of shares traded* (which adjusts for different price levels of alternative securities).[11] It is reasoned that with more trading activity, there is a greater probability that when you decide to buy or sell shares of a stock there will be someone available to take the other side of the transaction. Another variable that has been widely

[11] T. W. Epps, "The Demand for Broker Services: The Relation between Security Trading Volume and Transaction Cost," *Bell Journal of Economics* 12, no. 2 (June 1976): 163–194.

used as an indicator of market liquidity is the *bid-ask spread*, which is the difference between the market-maker's bid price and asking price on a security. Fortunately, the following internal corporate variables are typically highly correlated with these market trading variables:

1. Total market value of outstanding securities (number of common shares outstanding times the market price per share)
2. Number of security owners.

Numerous studies have shown that the main determinant of the bid-ask spread (besides price) is the dollar value of trading.[12] In turn, the value of trading is highly correlated with the market value of the outstanding securities and the number of security holders. The intuitive explanation for this relationship is that, with more shares outstanding, there will be more stockholders, and at any point in time some of these security holders will be buying or selling for a variety of purposes. It is the existence of numerous buyers and sellers that provides liquidity.

For Quaker Oats you can estimate the market value of outstanding stock as the number of shares outstanding at the year-end (adjusted for stock splits) times the average market price for the year (i.e., as the high price plus the low price divided by two) as follows:

$$\text{outstanding shares} \times (hi + lo)/2$$

1987: 83,989,396 × [(58 + 33)/2] = $3,821,517,518
1986: 83,989,396 × [(40 + 24)/2] = $2,687,660,672
1985: 83,989,396 × [(26 + 15)/2] = $1,721,782,618

The number of stockholders is 32,358, including numerous institutions that own approximately 50 percent of the outstanding stock. Finally, *trading turnover* (the percent of outstanding shares traded during a period of time) also indicates relative activity. During calendar year 1987, there were 56,424,000 shares of Quaker Oats traded, which indicates turnover of approximately 67 percent (56,424,000/83,989,396). This compares to the average turnover for the NYSE of about 60 percent. Clearly, these large values for market value, number of stockholders, and trading turnover indicate that there is a very liquid market in the common stock of Quaker Oats (i.e., based upon the discussion in Chapter 3, Quaker Oats would be a first-tier stock). You should be aware of the prevailing market liquidity for your securities by examining these variables and the actual trading volume.

COMPARATIVE ANALYSIS

We have discussed the importance of comparative analysis but have concentrated on the selection and computation of specific ratios for only Quaker Oats. Table 12.7 contains most of the ratios discussed for Quaker Oats, the food industry (as derived from the S&P Analysts Handbook), and the S&P 400 Index. The three-year comparison should provide some insights

---

[12] Studies on this topic were discussed in Chapter 3.

TABLE 12.7
Summary of Financial Ratios for Quaker Oats, S&P Food Industry, S&P 400 Index: 1985–1987

	1987			1986			1985		
	QUAKER OATS	FOOD INDUSTRY	S&P 400	QUAKER OATS	FOOD INDUSTRY	S&P 400	QUAKER OATS	FOOD INDUSTRY	S&P 400
Internal Liquidity									
Current ratio	1.39	1.36	1.29	1.38	1.60	1.27	1.65	1.50	1.40
Quick ratio	0.83	0.72	0.70	0.81	0.81	0.66	0.94	0.73	0.76
Cash ratio	0.25	0.24	0.25	0.13	0.26	0.21	0.12	0.19	0.23
Receivables turnover	6.85	9.98	7.97	6.63	10.88	8.37	6.76	10.97	8.18
Ave. collection period (days)	53.30	36.60	45.80	55.10	33.50	43.60	54.00	33.30	44.60
Working capital/sales	11.49	7.21	8.21	8.59	9.36	7.40	11.97	9.33	9.54
Operating Performance									
Total asset turnover	1.67	1.58	1.08	1.78	1.83	1.21	1.84	1.91	1.26
Inventory turnover (sales)#	9.82	7.81	6.76	8.77	8.38	7.28	9.15	8.48	8.12
Working capital turnover	8.70	13.87	12.18	11.64	10.68	13.51	8.35	10.72	10.48
Net fixed asset turnover	3.68	2.87	1.76	3.88	3.49	2.01	3.95	3.77	2.10
Equity turnover	4.61	3.71	2.76	4.27	4.26	2.99	4.44	4.27	2.95
Profitability									
Gross profit margin	44.88	—	—	42.79	—	—	39.69	—	—
Operating profit margin	10.18	11.76	13.18	9.89	10.76	13.36	9.95	10.12	13.56
Net profit margin	4.20	4.78	3..81	4.83	4.25	3.92	4.48	4.17	4.86
Return on total capital	9.36	9.75	6.83	10.71	10.41	7.54	11.68	11.05	8.98
Return on equity	18.59	17.67	10.34	20.60	18.03	11.43	19.43	17.70	14.05
Equity turnover	4.61	3.71	2.76	4.27	4.26	2.99	4.44	4.27	2.95
Net profit margin	4.28	4.78	3.81	4.83	4.25	3.92	4.48	4.17	4.86
Financial Risk									
Debt/equity ratio	80.36	45.08	46.55	50.10	36.79	42.36	49.14	40.45	39.63
LT debt/long-term capital	44.55	26.53	26.11	33.38	23.48	24.73	32.95	24.91	24.00
Total debt/total capital	66.54	50.04	48.01	59.12	45.67	48.02	55.22	49.36	45.96
Interest coverage	6.81	7.12	3.63	8.39	6.17	4.17	5.44	5.53	4.82
Cash flow/long-term debt	0.56	0.64	0.51	1.51	0.73	0.57	1.33	0.66	0.65
Cash flow/total debt	0.14	0.23	0.20	0.20	0.27	0.20	0.22	0.23	0.24
Growth Analysis*									
Retention rate	0.66	0.61	0.37	0.66	0.60	0.48	0.66	0.59	0.59
Return on equity	17.09	19.24	10.46	20.14	17.55	11.45	18.19	17.98	14.17
Total asset turnover	1.36	1.61	1.06	1.70	1.86	1.15	1.82	1.76	1.22
Total asset/equity	2.99	2.50	2.53	2.45	2.22	2.54	2.23	2.45	2.39
Net profit margin	4.20	4.78	3.81	4.83	4.25	3.92	4.48	4.17	4.86
Sustainable growth rate	11.28	11.74	3.87	13.29	10.53	5.50	12.01	10.61	8.36

#Computed with sales because cost of sales not available for the industry and the market.
*Using year-end balance sheet data.

into what is involved in such an analysis, although you would typically examine a five- to ten-year period.

INTERNAL LIQUIDITY   The basic three ratios (current ratio, quick ratio, and cash ratio) all show changes for Quaker Oats, but relative to the industry and market, Quaker

Oats looks stronger in 1987 than 1985. The firm's receivable turnover and collection period is stable, but the collection period is longer than the S&P 400—and definitely longer than the food industry (53 days versus 37 in 1987). Since it is stable, it is probably because of the firm's product mix (e.g., the effect of the firm's involvement in the toy industry) or its basic credit policy (it may allow more liberal credit terms to its customers). The working capital/sales ratio is somewhat larger than the comparisons. Overall, the comparisons are mixed, but they are generally stable and adequate.

OPERATING PERFORMANCE

This segment is composed of efficiency ratios (turnovers) and profitability ratios. The turnover ratios were consistently strong (except working capital, which is a liquidity ratio) and were stronger in 1987 than the market or the food industry. This is evidence of the firm's dedication to heavy utilization of its assets without overdoing it (none of the comparative turnovers were excessive).

The profitability performance related to sales is best described as adequate. The operating profit margins were consistently below the aggregate market and industry, while the net profit margin declined to a position below the industry. In contrast, the profit performance related to capital was quite strong. The food industry return on total capital was consistently above the S&P 400, and Quaker Oats was always above the food industry. The food industry and Quaker Oats also experienced ROEs that were substantially above the market. While the ROE for Quaker Oats was above the industry in 1985 and 1986, it fell below the industry in 1987 due to the decline in its profit margin. You will recall that the equity turnover for Quaker Oats increased due to the higher financial leverage.

FINANCIAL RISK

Quaker Oats' financial risk in terms of balance sheet ratios was above the industry and the market and increased even more in 1987. In contrast, the financial risk flow ratios for Quaker Oats were similar to the industry until 1987, when they declined substantially to values below the industry. These comparisons confirm our prior discussion that Quaker Oats experienced a major increase in its financial risk position during 1987 in connection with the acquisitions. It also should be recalled that the ratios in Table 12.7 are those that assume that deferred taxes are long-term debt, which is a very conservative assumption for a firm with a strong growth pattern like Quaker Oats.

GROWTH ANALYSIS

The sustainable growth rate for Quaker Oats has generally been similar to its industry, and both of them have outperformed the aggregate market. The major factor causing a difference in growth for the firm and industry is the ROE. It was larger for Quaker Oats in 1985 and 1986 but declined in 1987, causing its implied sustainable growth rate to drop below that of its industry. Notably, the Quaker Oats' ROE components differ from those of its industry, which had a higher total asset turnover and profit margin, while Quaker Oats had higher financial leverage.

In sum, Quaker Oats has adequate liquidity and a good operating record. Of critical importance as of 1988 is the added debt used to acquire the two firms and the decline in profit margin due to divestitures and plant closings. The major concern of the analyst must be to monitor the paydown of the debt and project how successful Quaker Oats will be with its expanded asset base. Your success as an analyst is based upon how well you are able to go from these historical numbers to meaningful *estimates.*

ANALYSIS OF NON–U.S. FINANCIAL STATEMENTS

As noted on several occasions, your future analysis will necessarily encompass other economies and markets, as well as numerous industries that are global in nature, and many non–U.S. firms in these global industries. Therefore, you should recognize that the financial statements will be very different from those that you have considered in this chapter and in your typical accounting course. As we will see, the accounting conventions differ substantially among countries, so it is not possible to discuss them in detail, but we will consider some of the major differences in format and principles.

ACCOUNTING STATEMENT FORMAT DIFFERENCES. Table 12.8 contains examples of balance sheet formats for several countries and indicates some major differences in accounts and in the order of presentation. As an example, in the United Kingdom fixed assets are presented above current assets, and current liabilities are automatically subtracted from current assets. In Australia, not only are the capital accounts presented initially, but the current assets are below long-term assets—the balance sheet items are similar but almost exactly opposite in presentation. Clearly, the accounts and presentation in Canada are very similar to the United States, and Germany's are also similar except that they have numerous reserve accounts on the liability side. Therefore, besides finding items that are comparable to U.S. firms, it is important to consider the techniques used to derive these individual items.

The comparative income statement formats in Table 12.9 show that the United Kingdom statements have much less detail than U.S. statements, which will influence your ability to analyze trends in expense items. While Japanese statements are fairly similar to those of the United States, you should be aware of the nonoperating income and expense items. These can be substantial for many Japanese firms, because they tend to have heavy investments in the common stock of suppliers and customers as a sign of goodwill. The income and gains (or losses) from these equity holdings can be a substantial permanent component of a firm's net income. The Australian statements likewise combine numerous expense items and subsequently include several items concerned with the distribution of the net income. Finally, the income statement for West Germany is very detailed but also provides numerous opportunities to control the profit or loss for the period because of many income and expense items that are unusual compared to U.S practices.

TABLE 12.8
Comparative Balance Sheet Formats

UNITED KINGDOM	AUSTRALIA
Net assets employed	Share capital & reserves and liabilities
Fixed assets	Share capital and reserves
Subsidiaries	Long-term debt and deferred income taxes
Associated companies	Current liabilities
Current assets	Assets
Less: current liabilities	Fixed assets
Less: deferred liabilities	Investments
Assets represented by	Current assets
Share capital	
Reserves	

CANADA	WEST GERMANY
Assets	Assets
Current assets	Outstanding payments on subscribed share capital
Investments	Fixed assets and investments
Fixed assets	Revolving assets
Other assets	Deferred charges and prepaid expenses
Liabilities and stockholders' equity	Accumulated net loss (of period)
Current liabilities	Liabilities and shareholders' equity
Long-term debt	Share capital
Deferred income taxes	Open reserves
Shareholders' equity	Adjustments to assets
	Reserves for estimated liabilities and accrued expenses
	Liabilities
	Liabilities, contractually payable beyond 4 yrs
	Deferred income
	Accumulated net profit (of period)

Source: *Professional Accounting in 30 Countries*, pp. 51, 125–126, 169, 629, 746–749. Copyright © 1975 by the American Institute of Certified Public Accountants, Inc. Reprinted with permission.

DIFFERENCES IN ACCOUNTING PRINCIPLES. Beyond the several differences in the format of presentation, there are numerous differences in the specific principles employed to arrive at the income, expense, and balance sheet items. A study by Choi and Bavishi compared the accounting standards for ten countries and highlighted the differences.[13] Table 12.10 synthesizes the differences related to 32 specific items. Following a discussion of several major areas, the authors conclude:

> Perhaps the major conclusion drawn from analyzing the annual reports of the world's leading industrial firms is that fundamental differences in accounting

[13] Frederick D. S. Choi and Vinod B. Bavishi, "Diversity in Multinational Accounting," *Financial Executive* 50, no. 7 (August 1982): 36–39. This table is also presented and discussed in Frederick D. S. Choi and Gerhard G. Mueller, *International Accounting* (Englewood Cliffs, N.J.: Prentice-Hall, Inc., 1984): 72–76. There is also a fairly complete discussion of practices by individual countries following this composite presentation.

TABLE 12.9
Comparative Income Statement Formats

United Kingdom
Group turnover
Profit before taxation and extraordinary items
   Less: taxation based on profit for the year
Profit after taxation and before extraordinary items
   Less: extraordinary items
Profits attributable to shareholders of parent company

Japan
Sales
   Less: cost of goods sold
Gross profit on sales
   Less: selling and administrative expenses
Operating income
   Add: nonoperating revenue
Gross profit for the period
   Less: nonoperating expenses
Net income for the period

Australia
Sales and revenue
   Less: cost of sales
Operating profit
   Add: income from investments
   Less: interest to other persons
Pretax profit
   Less: provision for income tax
Net profit before extraordinary items
   Less: extraordinary items
Net profit after extraordinary items
Unappropriated profits, previous year
Prior year adjustments
Transfer from general reserve
Available for appropriation
Dividends
Transfer to general reserve

Source: *Professional Accounting in 30 Countries*, pp. 52, 350, 351, 630, 750–753. Copyright © 1975 by the American Institute of Certified Public Accountants, Inc. Reprinted with permission.

practices between each of ten countries examined are not as extensive as was initially feared. Major differences observed relate to accounting for goodwill, deferred taxes, long-term leases, discretionary reserves, and foreign-currency translation. Having observed this comforting fact, the user must be cautioned against assuming that consistency and harmonization exist among the annual reports of all foreign companies.[14]

---

[14] *Ibid.*, 39. Another very complete comparison of accounting standards for the United States, the United Kingdom, the European Economic Community, and Canada is contained in Thomas G. Evans, Martin E. Taylor, and Oscar Holzmann, *International Accounting and Reporting* (New York: Macmillan Publishing Company, 1985): 106–113. The source of the table is Ernst and Whinney, *International Accounting Standards* (September 1982): 64–71.

Transfer to capital profits reserve
Unappropriated profits, end of year

West Germany
Net sales
Increase or decrease of finished and unfinished products
Other manufacturing costs for fixed assets
Total output
Raw materials and supplies, purchased goods consumed in sale
Gross profit
Income from profit transfer agreements
Income from trade investments
Income from other long-term investments
Other interest and similar income
Income from retirement and appraisal of fixed assets
Income from the cancellation of lump allowances
Income from the cancellation of overstated reserves
Other income, including extraordinary in the sum of DM
Income from loss transfer agreements
Total income
Wages and salaries
Social taxes
Expenses for pension plans and relief
Depreciation and amortization of fixed assets and investments
Depreciation and amortization of finance investments
Losses by deduction or on retirement of current assets
Losses on retirement of fixed assets and investments
Interest and similar expenses
Taxes on income and net assets, and other losses arising from loss transfer agreements
Other expenses
Profits transferable to parent company under profit transfer agreement
Profit or loss for the period
Profit or loss brought forward from preceding year
Release of reserves
Amounts appropriated to reserves out of profit of period
Accumulated net profit or loss

PROBABILITY OF FAIR PRESENTATIONS. A study by Watt, Hammer, and Burge categorized 45 countries according to specific accounting practices or standards, including audit requirements, and also on the basis of "the probability of fair presentation" using U.S.–U.K. definitions of fair presentation.[15] The results of this categorization are contained in Table 12.11. These categories should indicate areas of concern to you when you are analyzing statements from certain countries. Some valuation principles that are acceptable in Japan, for example, would not be acceptable in the United States.

---

[15] George Watt, R. Hammer, and M. Burge, *Accounting for the Multinational Enterprise* (New York: Financial Executives Research Institute, 1977).

TABLE 12.10
Synthesis of Accounting Differences

ACCOUNTING PRINCIPLES	U.S.	AUSTRALIA	CANADA	FRANCE	GERMANY	JAPAN	NETH.	SWEDEN	SWITZER-LAND	U.K.
1. Marketable securities recorded at the lower cost or market?	Yes	Yes	Yes	Yes	Yes	Yes	Yes	Yes	Yes	Yes
2. Provision for uncollectible accounts made?	Yes	Yes	Yes	No	Yes	Yes	Yes	Yes	Yes	Yes
3. Inventory costed using FIFO?	Mixed	Yes	Mixed	Mixed	Yes	Mixed	Mixed	Yes	Yes	Yes
4. Manufacturing overhead allocated to year-end inventory?	Yes	Yes	Yes	Yes	Yes	Yes	Yes	Yes	No	Yes
5. Inventory valued at the lower of cost or market?	Yes	Yes	Yes	Yes	Yes	Yes	Yes	Yes	Yes	Yes
6. Accounting for long-term investments: less than 20 percent ownership: cost method?	Yes	Yes	Yes	Yes*	Yes	Yes	No(K)	Yes	Yes	Yes
7. Accounting for long-term investments: 21–50 percent ownership: equity method?	Yes	No(G)	Yes	Yes*	No(B)	No(B)	Yes	No(B)	No(B)	Yes
8. Accounting for long-term investments more than 50 percent ownership: full consolidation?	Yes	Yes	Yes	Yes*	Yes	Yes	Yes	Yes	Yes	Yes
9. Both domestic and foreign subsidiaries consolidated?	Yes	Yes	Yes	Yes	No**	Yes	Yes	Yes	Yes	Yes

Key

Yes—Predominant practice.
Yes*—Minor modifications, but still predominant practice.
No**—Minority practice.
No—Accounting principle in question not adhered to.
NF—Not found.
Mixed—Alternative practices followed with no majority.
B—Cost method is used.
C—Purchase method is used.

D—Long-term debt includes maturities longer than four years.
E—Current rate method of foreign currency translation.
F—Weighted average is used.
G—Cost or equity.
H—Translation gains and losses are deferred.
I—Market is used.
J—Owners' equity.
K—Equity.
L—Monetary/Non-Monetary.

Source: Frederick D.S. Choi and Vinod B. Bavishi, "Diversity in Multinational Accounting." Used by permission from *Financial Executive* 50, no. 7 (August 1982), copyright 1982 by Financial Executives Institute.

ACCOUNTING PRINCIPLES	U.S.	AUSTRALIA	CANADA	FRANCE	GERMANY	JAPAN	NETH.	SWEDEN	SWITZER-LAND	U.K.
10. Acquisitions accounted for under the pooling of interest method?	Yes	No(C)	No(C)	No(C)	No(C)	No(C)	No(C)	No(C)	No(C)	No(C)
11. Intangible assets: goodwill amortized?	Yes	Yes	Yes	Yes	No	Yes	Mixed	Yes	No**	No**
12. Intangible assets: other than goodwill amortized?	Yes	Yes	Yes	Yes	Yes	Yes	Yes	Yes	No**	No**
13. Long-term debt includes maturities longer than one year?	Yes	Yes	Yes	Yes	No(D)	Yes	Yes	Yes	Yes	Yes
14. Discount/premium on long-term debt amortized?	Yes	Yes	Yes	No	No	Yes	Yes	No	No	No
15. Deferred taxes recorded when accounting income is not equal to taxable income?	Yes	Yes	Yes	Yes	Yes	Yes	Yes	No	No	Yes
16. Financial leases (long-term) capitalized?	Yes	No	Yes	No	No	No	No	No	No	No
17. Company pension fund contribution provided regularly?	Yes	Yes	Yes	Yes	Yes	Yes	Yes	Yes	Yes	Yes
18. Total pension fund assets and liabilities excluded from company's financial statement?	Yes	Yes	Yes	Yes	No	Yes	Yes	Yes	Yes	Yes
19. Research & development expensed?	Yes	Yes	Yes	Yes	Yes	Yes	Yes	Yes	Yes	Yes
20. Treasury stock deducted from owner's equity?	Yes	NF	Yes	Yes	No	Yes	Mixed	NF	NF	NF
21. Gains or losses on treasury stock taken to owner's equity?	Yes	NF	Yes	Yes	No	No**	Mixed	NF	NF	NF
22. No general purpose (purely discretionary) reserves allowed?	Yes	Yes	Yes	No	No	No	No	No	No	Yes

continued

TABLE **12.10** *continued*

ACCOUNTING PRINCIPLES	U.S.	AUSTRALIA	CANADA	FRANCE	GERMANY	JAPAN	NETH.	SWEDEN	SWITZER-LAND	U.K.
23. Dismissal indemnities accounted for on a pay-as-you-go basis?	Yes	Yes	Yes	Yes	Yes	Yes	NF	Yes	NF	Yes
24. Minority interest excluded from consolidated income?	Yes	Yes	Yes	Yes	No	Yes	Yes	Yes	Yes	Yes
25. Minority interest excluded from consolidated owner's equity?	Yes	Yes	Yes	Yes	No	Yes	Yes	Yes	Yes	Yes
26. Are intercompany sales/profits eliminated upon consolidation?	Yes	Yes	Yes	Yes	Yes	Yes	Yes	Yes	Yes	Yes
27. Basic financial statements reflect a historical cost valuation (no price level adjustment)?	Yes	No	Yes	No	Yes	Yes	No**	No	No	No
28. Supplementary inflation-adjusted financial statements provided?	Yes	No**	No**	No	No	No	No**	No	No**	Yes
29. Straight-line depreciation adhered to?	Yes	Yes	Yes	Mixed	Mixed	Mixed	Yes	Yes	Yes	Yes
30. No excess depreciation permitted?	Yes	No	Yes	No	Yes	Yes	No	No	No	No
31. Temporal method of foreign-currency translation employed?	Yes	Mixed	Yes	No(E)	No(E)	Mixed	No(E)	No(L)	No(E)	No(E)
32. Currency translation gains or losses reflected in current income?	Yes	Mixed	Yes	Mixed	Mixed	Mixed	No(J)	Mixed	No(H)	No

INTERNATIONAL RATIO ANALYSIS. Given accounting statements, the tendency is to analyze these statements using financial ratios similar to those employed in this chapter. While this is certainly legitimate, it is important to recognize that the "representative" values and trends may differ among countries because of local accounting and business norms. A study by Choi et al contends that it is important to restate foreign financial statements for accounting principles differences, but also you must understand the institutional, legal, cultural, and other factors that influence the finan-

TABLE 12.11
Probability of Fair Presentation in 45 Foreign Countries

Fair presentation is broadly equivalent to U.S. standards;[1] differences in principles must still be dealt with, but there are a fewer number of such differences with less serious dimensions.

Argentina[2]	Netherlands
Australia	New Zealand
Bermuda	Peru
Canada	Philippines
Denmark	Rhodesia
India	South Africa
Ireland	United Kingdom
Jamaica	Venezuela
Mexico	

Fair presentation is based on standards imported from Canada, the United Kingdom, or the United States.

Bahamas	Panama
Barbados	Trinidad and Tobago
Nigeria	

Statutory requirements approach U.S. standards in many respects, but some valuation principles would not be acceptable in the United States.

Chile	Japan
Germany	

Fair presentation is recognized in principle but not found consistently in practice.

Brazil	Malaysia
Colombia	Pakistan
Ethiopia	Singapore
Kenya	

Tax legislation is the predominant influence.

Austria	Luxembourg
Belgium	Paraguay
Bolivia	Portugal
France	Sweden
Greece	Uruguay
Italy	

Statutory requirements do not approach U.S. standards.

Spain	Switzerland

Source: G. Watt, R. Hammer, and M. Burge, *Accounting for the Multinational Corporation*, New York: Financial Executives Research Foundation, 1977, p. 187. Reprinted with permission.

Note 1: For this schedule, failure to require consolidation or the equity method of accounting for investments was not considered a block to fair presentation.

Note 2: Because of the extreme rate of inflation fair presentation is dependent on the submission, together with historical-cost-based financial statements, of supplemental financial data restated for price-level changes. The same requirement applies in other countries where inflationary conditions are similar.

TABLE 12.12
Mean Differences in Aggregate Financial ratios, U.S., Japan, Korea (unadjusted)

ENTERPRISE CATEGORY	CURRENT RATIO	QUICK RATIO	DEBT RATIO	TIMES INT. EARNED	INVTY T/O	AVG. COLL. PERIOD	F/A T/O	T/A T/O	PROFIT MARGIN	RETURN ON T/A	RETURN ON N/W
All Manufacturing											
Japan (976)	1.15	.80	.84	1.60	5.00	86	3.10	.93	.013	.012	.071
Korea (354)	1.13	.46	.78	1.80	6.60	33	2.80	1.20	.023	.028	.131
U.S. (902)	1.94	1.10	.47	6.50	6.80	43	3.90	1.40	.054	.074	.139
Diff. (U.S.–Japan)	40%	26%	(77%)	75%	26%	(102%)	22%	32%	26%	84%	49%
Diff. (U.S.–Korea)	42%	58%	(66%)	73%	2%	24%	29%	9%	57%	62%	6%
Chemicals											
Japan (129)	1.30	.99	.79	1.80	7.10	88	2.80	.90	.015	.014	.065
Korea (54)	1.40	.70	.59	2.40	7.10	33	1.60	.90	.044	.040	.100
U.S. (n.a.)	2.20	1.30	.45	6.50	6.50	50	2.80	1.10	.073	.081	.148
Diff. (U.S.–Japan)	42%	22%	(74%)	72%	(8%)	(75%)	0%	19%	79%	83%	56%
Diff. (U.S.–Korea)	36%	45%	(31%)	62%	(9%)	34%	44%	19%	39%	50%	32%
Textiles											
Japan (81)	1.00	.77	.81	1.10	6.20	66	3.50	.92	.003	.003	.017
Korea (34)	1.00	.37	.83	1.30	4.90	30	2.20	1.00	.010	.011	.064
U.S. (n.a.)	2.30	1.20	.48	4.30	6.50	48	5.80	1.80	.027	.049	.094
Diff. (U.S.–Japan)	55%	38%	(70%)	74%	5%	(39%)	40%	50%	87%	93%	82%
Diff. (U.S.–Korea)	55%	70%	(74%)	70%	24%	36%	63%	44%	62%	78%	32%
Transportation											
Japan (85)	1.20	.86	.83	1.90	3.90	116	4.50	.90	.017	.015	.092
Korea (14)	.95	.40	.91	1.90	18.60	18	1.10	.80	.026	.021	.221
U.S.	1.60	.74	.52	8.70	5.60	31	6.50	1.60	.049	.078	.161
Diff. (U.S.–Japan)	21%	(16%)	(61%)	78%	28%	278%	30%	44%	65%	80%	43%
Diff (U.S.–Korea)	40%	46%	(75%)	77%	(234%)	40%	84%	50%	47%	73%	(37%)

*Parentheses indicate foreign ratios greater than U.S. ratios.

Source: Frederick D.S. Choi, Hisaaki Hino, Sang Kee Min, Sang Oh Nam, Junichi Ugiie, and Arthur J. Stonehill, "Analyzing Foreign Financial Statements: The Use and Misuse of International Ratio Analysis," *Journal of International Business Studies* (Spring–Summer 1983):113–131. Reprinted with permission.

cial variables within a country.[16] To demonstrate the importance of this, they compared a common set of ratios for a sample of companies in the United States, Japan, and Korea. The comparison of mean values for these ratios and the differences is contained in Table 12.12. There are substantial differences in most of these ratios for all manufacturing, as well as for specific important industries (chemical, textiles, and transportation). Following an extensive discussion of the ratios within various areas, the authors conclude:

> On the basis of these findings, institutional, cultural, political and tax considerations in Japan and Korea do indeed cause their accounting ratios to differ from U.S. norms without necessarily reflecting better or worse financial risk and return characteristics being measured . . .

---

[16] Frederick D. S. Choi, Hisaaki Hino, Sang Kee Min, Sang Oh Nam, Junichi Ujiie, and Arthur J. Stonehill, "Analyzing Foreign Financial Statements: The Use and Misuse of International Ratio Analysis," *Journal of International Business Studies* (Spring–Summer 1983): 113–131, reprinted in Frederick D. S. Choi and Gerhard G. Mueller, *Frontiers of International Accounting: An Anthology* (Ann Arbor, Mich.: UMI Research Press, 1985).

A major conclusion of our study is that accounting measurements reflected in corporate financial reports represent, in one sense, merely "numbers" that have limited meaning and significance in and of themselves. Meaning and significance come from and depend upon an understanding of the environmental context from which the numbers are drawn as well as the relationship between the numbers and the underlying economic phenomena that are the real items of interest.[17]

USES OF FINANCIAL RATIOS

There are four major areas related to investments where financial ratios have been used: (1) stock valuation, (2) the identification of internal corporate variables affecting a stock's systematic risk (beta), (3) assigning quality ratings on bonds, and (4) predicting insolvency (bankruptcy) of firms.

STOCK VALUATION MODELS

The purpose of most valuation models is to derive an appropriate price/earnings ratio for a stock—that is, an earnings multiple as discussed in Chapter 9. You will recall that the earnings multiple should be influenced by the expected growth rate of earnings and dividends and the required rate of return on the stock. Clearly, financial ratios can help in both estimates. The growth rate estimate employs the ratios discussed in the growth analysis section—the retention rate and the return on equity ratios along with the components of ROE, which help you derive an estimate of the expected ROE.

When attempting to determine an appropriate required rate of return (k), remember that the required rate of return depends on the risk premium for the security, which is a function of business risk and financial risk. Business risk is typically measured in terms of earnings variability, while financial risk is identified by either the debt proportion ratios or the flow ratios (i.e., the interest coverage ratios or the cash flow to debt ratios).

The typical empirical valuation model has examined a cross section of companies and used a multiple regression model that relates the price/earnings ratios for the sample firms to some of the following corporate variables (the averages generally consider the last five or ten years):[18]

1. Operating earnings variability
2. Average debt/equity ratio
3. Average interest coverage ratio
4. Stock's systematic risk (beta), using rates of return during the last five years
5. Average dividend payout ratio
6. Average rate of growth of earnings
7. Average return on equity

[17] *Ibid.*, 131.

[18] A list of studies that have used financial ratios in valuation models appears in the reference section at the end of the chapter.

FINANCIAL RATIOS AND SYSTEMATIC RISK

Prior to the widespread acceptance of the *capital asset pricing model (CAPM)*, the analysis of risk factors concentrated on the business and financial risk factors considered in this chapter. As discussed in Chapter 8, the CAPM implies that the relevant risk variable for an investor building a diversified portfolio should be the systematic risk of the asset—that is, its beta coefficient related to the market portfolio of all risky assets. Initially, it appeared that there might be some conflict between the two approaches of fundamental risk variables versus market-determined risk measures. Upon reflection, though, such a conflict would be inconsistent with efficient capital markets, where stock prices are expected to reflect all relevant information for the security. In efficient markets one would expect a significant relationship between internal corporate risk variables and market-determined risk variables. The first study on this topic was by Beaver, Kettler, and Scholes.[19] Subsequently, numerous studies have examined other variables intended to reflect business risk and financial risk.[20] Some of the variables that were consistently used and were found to be significant included the following:

Financial Ratios (Typically Five-Year Average)
1. Dividend payout
2. Total debt/total assets
3. Cash flow/total debt
4. Interest coverage
5. Working capital/total assets
6. Current ratio

Variability Measures (Latest Five Years)
1. Variance of earnings multiple
2. Coefficient of variation of operating earnings
3. Operating earnings beta (company earnings related to aggregate earnings)

Nonratio Variables
1. Asset size
2. Market volume of trading in stock

FINANCIAL RATIOS AND BOND RATINGS

As discussed in Chapter 10, there are four financial services that assign quality ratings to bonds on the basis of the issuing company's ability to meet all the obligations of the bond. A triple-A rating (AAA) indicates very high quality and almost no chance of default, while a C rating indicates the bond is already in default. Because it is important to understand the variables used by these rating services, a number of studies have employed models that use financial ratios to predict what rating will be assigned to a bond.[21] The major financial ratios have been those concerned with internal liquidity and financial risk as follows:

---

[19] William H. Beaver, Paul Kettler, and Myron Scholes, "The Association between Market-Determined and Accounting-Determined Risk Measures," *Accounting Review* 45, no. 4 (October 1970): 654–682.

[20] A list of other studies in this area appears in the reference section at the end of the chapter.

[21] A list of studies in this area is in the reference section at the end of the chapter.

Financial Ratios (Typically Five-Year Average)
1.   Long-term debt/total assets
2.   Net income plus depreciation (cash flow)/long-term senior debt
3.   Net income plus interest/interest expense (fixed charge coverage)
4.   Market value of stock/par value of bonds
5.   Net operating profit/sales
6.   Net income/total assets
7.   Working capital/sales
8.   Sales/net worth (equity turnover)

Variability Measures (Latest Five Years)
1.   Coefficient of variation (CV) of net earnings (CV = Standard Deviation/Mean)
2.   Coefficient of variation of return on assets

Nonratio Variables
1.   Subordination of the issue
2.   Size of the firm (total assets)
3.   Issue size
4.   Par value of all publicly traded bonds of the firm

FINANCIAL RATIOS AND INSOLVENCY (BANKRUPTCY)

Obviously, there is interest in determining which financial ratios might be useful in identifying firms that might default on a loan or declare bankruptcy. A number of studies have attempted this.[22] The typical test design is to derive a sample of firms that have declared bankruptcy (i.e., failed) and also to select a matched sample of firms in the same industry and of comparable size that have not failed. The analysis involves examining a number of financial ratios expected to reflect declining liquidity for several years prior to the declaration of bankruptcy (usually five years) to determine which ratios or set of ratios provide the best predictions. Most studies have used *discriminant analysis*, where the criteria is which financial ratios or set of financial ratios give the fewest misclassifications. Some of the *multiple discriminant analysis* (MDA) models are able to properly classify over 80 percent of the firms the year prior to failure, and there are reasonably high classification results three to five years before failure. The financial ratios that have typically provided the best results include the following:

1. Cash flow/total debt
2. Cash flow/LT debt
3. Net income/total assets
4. Total debt/total assets
5. Working capital/total assets
6. Current ratio
7. Cash/current liabilities
8. Working capital/sales

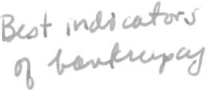
Best indicators of bankrupcy

---

[22] A list of studies on this topic is in the reference section at the end of the chapter.

LIMITATIONS OF FINANCIAL RATIOS

In addition to the earlier point that you should always consider *relative* financial ratios, there are other limitations of financial ratios that you should keep in mind:

1. Is the accounting treatment used by alternative firms comparable? It is well-recognized that there are several generally accepted methods for treating various accounting items, and that the alternatives can cause a difference in results for the same event. Therefore, you should check on the accounting treatment of significant items to adjust for major differences. As noted, this becomes a critical consideration when dealing with non–U.S. firms.

2. How homogeneous is the firm? Many companies have several divisions that operate in different industries. This may make it difficult to derive comparable industry ratios.

3. Are the implied results consistent? It is important that you develop a *total profile* on the firm and not depend on only one set of ratios (e.g., internal liquidity ratios). As an example, the firm may be having short-term liquidity problems but be very profitable, which will eventually alleviate the short-run liquidity problem.

4. Is the ratio within a reasonable range for the industry? As noted on several occasions, typically you are looking for a *range* of values for the ratio, because a value that is either too high *or* too low can be a cause for concern. For example, a low current ratio may indicate a liquidity problem, while a very high current ratio would indicate excessive liquidity, which means the firm is underutilizing its assets.

SUMMARY

The overall purpose of financial statement analysis is to help you make decisions on investing in a firm's bonds or stocks. Financial ratios should be examined relative to the economy, the industry, the firm's main competitors, and the firm's past ratios. The specific ratios can be divided into five categories, depending upon the purpose of the analysis (i.e., internal liquidity, operating performance, risk analysis, growth analysis, and external market liquidity).

When analyzing the financial statements for non–U.S. firms, you must consider differences in format and in accounting principles and alternative desired values for specific ratios. Four major uses of financial ratios are (1) stock valuation, (2) the identification of internal corporate variables affecting a stock's systematic risk (beta), (3) assigning quality ratings on bonds, and (4) predicting insolvency (bankruptcy) of firms.

A final caveat: it is clearly possible to envision a very large number of potential financial ratios that will examine almost every possible relationship. Therefore, the trick is not to come up with more ratios, but to attempt to *limit* the number of ratios and to *examine them in a meaningful way*. This entails an analysis of the time series properties of the ratios relative to the economy, the industry, or the past. Any additional effort should be spent on deriving better comparisons for a limited number of ratios.

QUESTIONS

1. What is the overall purpose of financial statements?

2. Discuss briefly some of the decisions that require the analysis of financial statements.

3. Why do analysts employ financial ratios rather than the absolute numbers?

4. The Murphy Company, which produces polish sausage, earned 12 percent on its equity last year. What does this indicate about the management of Murphy's? Is there any other information you want? What is it, and why do you want it?

5. Besides comparing a company's performance to its total industry, what other comparisons should be considered *within* the industry? Justify this comparison.

6. What is the purpose of the internal liquidity ratios? What information are they intended to provide? Who would be most interested in this information?

7. What are the components of operating performance? Discuss each of them, and indicate the purpose of the ratios involved.

8. In terms of asset turnover and profit margin, discuss how a jewelry store and a grocery store might differ? Would you expect their return on equity to differ, assuming equal risk? Discuss.

9. Describe the components of business risk, and discuss how the components affect the variability of operating earnings.

10. Would you expect an auto company or a utility to have greater business risk? Discuss your reasoning for this expectation in terms of the components of business risk.

11. When examining a firm's financial structure, would you be concerned with the firm's business risk? Why or why not?

12. How does the fixed charge coverage ratio differ from the debt/equity ratio? Which would you prefer and why?

13. Why is growth analysis important to the common stockholder? Why is it important to the debt-holder?

14. What are the general factors that determine the rate of growth of any economic unit? Discuss each of the factors.

15. A firm is earning 20 percent on equity and has low risk. Discuss why you would expect it to have a high or low retention rate.

16. The Irish Company earned 18 percent on equity, while the Miami Company only earned 14 percent on equity. Does this mean that Irish is better than Miami? If not, why?

17. Briefly discuss the two components of external market liquidity. Given the components of market liquidity, why do people consider real estate to be a relatively illiquid asset? Be specific.

18. List and discuss what internal factors about a company indicate its market liquidity.

19. Select one of the four uses of financial ratios, and discuss how you would use financial ratios to help you as an analyst.

PROBLEMS

1. The Whitney Animal Company has the following results:

Net sales	$3,000,000
Net total assets	2,000,000
Depreciation	80,000
Net income	200,000
Long-term debt	1,000,000
Equity	800,000
Dividends	80,000

1a. Compute Whitney's ROE directly and also based upon the three components.

1b. Using the ROE computed in 1a, find the expected sustainable growth rate for Whitney.

1c. Assuming the firm's net profit margin went to .04, what would happen to Whitney's ROE?

1d. Using the ROE in 1c, find the expected sustainable growth rate. What if dividends were only $40,000?

2. Three companies (A, B, and C) had the following results during the recent period.

	A	B	C
Net profit margin	.04	.06	.10
Total asset turnover	2.20	2.00	1.40
Total assets/equity	2.40	2.20	1.50

2a. Derive each company's return on equity based upon the three components.

2b. Given the following earnings and dividends, compute the sustainable growth rate for each firm.

Earnings/share	2.75	3.00	4.50
Dividends/share	1.25	1.00	1.00

3. Given the following balance sheet, fill in the ratio values for 1990 and discuss how these results compare with both the industry average and Lady J's past performance.

Lady J Enterprises Consolidated Balance Sheet
Year Ended December 31, 1990

ASSETS (DOLLARS IN THOUSANDS)

	1990	1989
Cash	$ 100	$ 90
Receivables	220	170
Inventories	330	230
Total current assets	650	490
Property, plant, and equipment	1,850	1,650
Depreciation	350	225
Net properties	1,500	1,425
Intangibles	150	150
Total assets	$2,300	$2,065

LIABILITIES AND SHAREHOLDER'S EQUITY

	1990	1989
Accounts payable	$ 85	$ 105
Short-term bank note	125	110
Current portion of long-term debt	75	—
Accruals	65	85
Total current liabilities	350	300
Long-term debt	625	540
Deferred taxes	100	80
Preferred stock (10%, $100 par)	150	150
Common stock ($2 par, 100,00 issued in 1988 and 1987)	200	200
Additional paid-in capital	325	325
Retained earnings	550	470
Common shareholder's equity	1,075	995
Total liabilities and shareholder's equity	$2,300	$2,065

Lady J Enterprises Consolidated Statement of Income
Year Ended December 31, 1990 (Dollars in Thousands)

	1990	1989
Net sales	$3,500.7	$2,990.6
Cost of goods sold	2,135.2	1,823.0
Selling, general, and administrative expenses	1,107.3	974.6
Operating profit	258.2	193.0
Net interest expense	62.5	54.0
Income from operations	195.7	139.0
Income taxes	66.5	47.3
Net income	129.2	91.7
Preferred dividends	15.0	15.0
Net income available for common shares	114.2	76.7
Dividends declared	40.0	30.0

	Lady J 1990	Lady J Average	Industry Average
Current ratio	_____	2.000	2.200
Quick ratio	_____	1.000	1.100
Receivable turnover	_____	18.000	18.000
Average collection period	_____	20.000	21.000
Total asset turnover	_____	1.500	1.400
Inventory turnover	_____	11.000	12.500
Fixed asset turnover	_____	2.500	2.400
Equity turnover	_____	3.200	3.000
Gross profit margin	_____	.400	.350
Operating profit margin	_____	8.000	7.500
Net profit margin	_____	4.000	3.750
Return on capital	_____	.107	.120
Return on equity	_____	.118	.126
Return on common equity	_____	.128	.135
Debt/equity ratio	_____	.600	.500
Debt/total capital ratio	_____	.400	.370
Interest coverage	_____	4.000	4.500
Fixed charge coverage	_____	3.000	4.000
Cash flow/long-term debt	_____	.400	.450
Cash flow/total debt	_____	.250	.300
Retention rate	_____	.350	.400

4a. *CFA Examination II (June 4, 1988)*: Using the financial ratios contained in the following table, analyze the relative credit position of: [15 minutes]
  I. the brewing industry compared with the S&P 400,
  II. Anheuser-Busch compared with the brewing industry, and
  III. Anheuser-Busch compared with the S&P 400.

4b. Using the table and your analysis from Part a, describe the current position of Anheuser-Busch, and discuss whether you feel that there has been a change in the credit quality of Anheuser-Busch based upon the recent trend in the financial ratios. [5 minutes]

Selected Financial Ratios for the S&P 400, The Brewing Industry, and Anheuser-Busch Companies, Inc. (BUD) 1982–1986

	1982			1983			1984			1985			1986		
	S&P 400	BREWING INDUSTRY	BUD	S&P 400	BREWING INDUSTRY	BUD	S&P 400	BREWING INDUSTRY	BUD	S&P 400	BREWING INDUSTRY	BUD	S&P 400	BREWING INDUSTRY	BUD
Current ratio	1.50	1.3	1.1	1.5	1.41	1.2	1.5	1.30	1.1	1.4	1.5	1.2	1.4	1.4	1.0
Quick ratio	0.90	0.7	0.4	0.9	0.80	0.7	0.8	0.70	0.5	0.8	1.0	0.6	0.7	0.8	0.4
Long-term debt/ total assets (%)	24.00	21.0	25.0	23.0	18.00	22.0	25.0	15.00	18.0	26.0	15.0	17.0	27.0	17.0	19.0
Total debt*/total assets (%)	43.00	37.0	41.0	42.0	36.00	39.0	44.0	31.00	34.0	48.0	32.0	33.0	48.0	34.0	37.0
Times interest earned	4.00	7.2	12.2	4.6	7.50	12.7	4.8	7.60	13.3	4.2	10.1	14.9	3.6	11.0	9.8
Cash flow/long-term debt (%)	54.00	52.0	43.0	61.0	70.00	55.0	65.0	84.00	71.0	57.0	88.0	79.0	51.0	80.0	73.0

continued

*Total debt is defined as long-term debt plus current liabilities.

Selected Financial Ratios *continued*

	1982			1983			1984			1985			1986		
	S&P 400	BREWING INDUSTRY	BUD	S&P 400	BREWING INDUSTRY	BUD	S&P 400	BREWING INDUSTRY	BUD	S&P 400	BREWING INDUSTRY	BUD	S&P 400	BREWING INDUSTRY	BUD
Cash flow/total debt* (%)	23.00	29.0	26.0	25.0	35.00	32.0	25.0	39.00	38.0	20.0	40.0	40.0	20.0	38.0	38.0
Total asset turnover	1.20	1.2	1.2	1.2	1.40	1.4	1.2	1.50	1.6	1.2	1.3	1.5	1.1	1.3	1.4
Net profit margin (%)	3.95	5.4	6.3	4.4	5.58	5.8	4.8	5.12	6.0	3.8	5.7	6.3	3.8	6.2	6.2
Return on total assets (%)	4.64	6.5	7.4	5.1	7.98	8.0	5.8	7.47	8.7	4.4	7.7	8.7	4.0	7.9	8.9

REFERENCES

GENERAL

Beaver, William H. *Financial Reporting: An Accounting Revolution.* Englewood Cliffs, N.J.: Prentice-Hall, Inc., 1981.

Berney, Paul R., William P. Lyons, and Stanley I. Garstka. *Financial Accounting and Reporting.* Dallas, Texas: Business Publications, Inc., 1981.

Bernstein, Leopold A. *Financial Statement Analysis: Theory, Application, and Interpretation.* 4th ed. Homewood, Ill.: Richard D. Irwin, 1988.

Chen, Kung H., and Thomas A. Shimerda. "An Empirical Analysis of Useful Financial Ratios." *Financial Management* 10, no. 1 (Spring 1981).

Dyckman, Thomas R., and Dale Morse. *Efficient Capital Markets and Accounting: A Critical Analysis.* 2d ed. Englewood Cliffs, N.J.: Prentice-Hall, Inc., 1986.

Ford, John K. *A Framework for Financial Analysis.* Englewood Cliffs, N.J.: Prentice-Hall, Inc., 1981.

Foster, George. *Financial Statement Analysis. 2d ed.* Englewood Cliffs, N.J.: Prentice-Hall, 1978.

Gombola, Michael J., and Edward Ketz. "Financial Ratio Patterns in Retail and Manufacturing Organizations." *Financial Management* 12, no. 2 (Summer 1983).

Helfert, Erich A. *Techniques of Financial Analysis.* 6th ed. Homewood, Ill.: Richard D. Irwin, 1987.

Ingberman, Monroe, and George H. Sorter. "The Role of Financial Statements in an Efficient Market." *Journal of Accounting, Auditing, and Finance* 2, no. 1 (Fall 1978).

Johnson, W. Bruce. "The Cross-Sectional Stability of Financial Ratio Patterns." *Journal of Financial and Quantitative Analysis* 14, no. 5 (December 1979).

Lev, Baruch. *Financial Statement Analysis: A New Approach.* Englewood Cliffs, N.J.: Prentice-Hall, 1974.

Page, John R., and Paul Hooper. "Financial Statements for Security Analysts." *Financial Analysts Journal* 35, no. 5 (September–October 1979).

Viscione, Jerry A. *Financial Analysis: Principles and Procedures.* Boston, Mass.: Houghton Mifflin Co., 1977.

Wyatt, A. R. "Efficient Market Theory: Its Impact on Accounting." *Journal of Accountancy* (February 1983).

ANALYSIS OF INTERNATIONAL FINANCIAL STATEMENTS

Arpan, Jeffrey S., and Lee H. Rodebaugh. *International Accounting and Multinational Enterprises* (New York: John Wiley & Co., 1981).

Choi, Frederick D. S., ed. *Multinational Accounting: A Research Framework for the Eighties.* Ann Arbor, Mich.: UMI Research Press, 1981.

Choi, Frederick D. S., and Gerhard G. Mueller. *International Accounting.* Englewood Cliffs, N.J.: Prentice-Hall, Inc., 1984.

Choi, Frederick D. S., and Gerhard G. Mueller. *Frontiers of International Accounting: An Anthology.* Ann Arbor, Mich.: UMI Research Press, 1985.

Choi, Frederick D. S., and Vinod B. Bavishi. "Diversity in Multinational Accounting." *Financial Executive* 50, no. 7 (August 1982).

Choi, Frederick D. S., H. Hino, S. K. Min, S. O. Nam, J. Ujiie, and A. I. Stonehill. "Analyzing Foreign Financial Statements: The Use and Misuse of International Ratio Analysis." *Journal of International Business Studies* (Spring–Summer 1983).

Davidson, Sidney, and John M. Kohlmeier. "A Measure of the Impact of Some Foreign Accounting Principles." *International Journal of Accounting* (Fall 1967).

Drury, D. H. "Effects of Accounting Practice Divergence: Canada and the U.S.A." *Journal of International Business Studies* 10 (Fall 1979).

Evans, Thomas G., Martin E. Taylor, and Oscar Holzmann. *International Accounting and Reporting.* New York: Macmillan Publishing Co., 1985.

Fitzgerald, R., A. Stickler, and T. Watts. *International Survey of Accounting Principles and Practices.* Scarborough, Ontario: Price Waterhouse International, 1979.

Gray, S. J., J. C. Shaw, and L. B. McSweeney. "Accounting Standards and Multinational Corporations." *Journal of International Business Studies* 12, no. 1 (Spring–Summer 1981).

Hatfield, H. R. "Some Variations in Accounting Practice in England, France, Germany, and the United States." *Journal of Accounting Research* 4, no. 2 (Autumn 1966).

Jaggi, B. L. "The Impact of the Cultural Environment on Financial Disclosures." *International Journal of Accounting* 11, no. 2 (Spring 1975).

Lelievre, Thomas W., and Clara C. Lelievre. "Accounting in the Third World." *Journal of Accountancy* 145 (January 1978).

Nair, R. D., and Werner G. Frank. "The Impact of Disclosure and Measurement Practices in International Accounting Classifications." *Accounting Review* 55, no. 3 (July 1980).

Oldham, K. M. *Accounting Systems and Practices in Europe.* Epping, England: Grower Press, 1975.

Paracszak, John. "Accounting Soviet Style." *Management Accounting* 60 (July 1978).

Zeff, Stephen A. *Forging Accounting Principles in Five Countries: A History and Analysis of Trends.* Champaign, Ill.: Stipes, 1972.

Financial Ratios and Stock Valuation Models

Babcock, Guilford. "The Concept of Sustainable Growth." *Financial Analysts Journal* 26, no. 3 (May–June 1970).

Beaver, William, and Dale Morse. "What Determines Price-Earnings Ratios?" *Financial Analysts Journal* 34, no. 4 (July–August 1978).

Brief, R. B. "Estimating Security Returns: A Further Note." *Financial Analysts Journal* 42, no. 6 (November–December 1986).

Estep, Tony. "A New Method for Valuing Common Stocks." *Financial Analysts Journal* 40, no. 6 (November–December 1985).

Estep, Tony. "Security Analysis and Stock Selection: Turning Financial Information into Return Forecasts." *Financial Analysts Journal* 43, no. 4 (July–August 1987).

Lintner, John. "Dividends, Earnings, Leverage, Stock Prices, and the Supply of Capital to Corporations." *Review of Economics and Statistics* 34, no. 3 (August 1962).

Malkiel, Burton G., and John G. Cragg. "Expectations and the Structure of Share Prices." *American Economic Review* 60, no. 4 (September 1970).

Wilcox, Jarrod W. "The P/B-ROE Valuation Model." *Financial Analysts Journal* 40, no. 1 (January–February 1984).

FINANCIAL RATIOS AND SYSTEMATIC RISK (BETA)

Beaver, William H., Paul Kettler, and Myron Scholes. "The Association between Market-Determined and Accounting-Determined Risk Measures." *Accounting Review* 45, no. 4 (October 1970).

Edelman, Richard B. "Telecommunicatons Betas: Are They Stable and Unique?" *Journal of Portfolio Management* 10, no. 1 (Fall 1983).

Gonedes, Nicholas J. "Evidence on the Information Content of Accounting Numbers: Accounting-Based and Market-Based Estimates of Systematic Risk." *Journal of Financial and Quantitative Analysis* 8, no. 2 (June 1973).

Hamada, Robert S. "The Effect of the Firm's Capital Structure on the Systematic Risk of Common Stocks." *Journal of Finance* 27, no. 2 (May 1972).

Harrington, Diana. "Whose Beta is Best?" *Financial Analysts Journal* 39, no. 4 (July–August 1983).

Rosenberg, Barr. "Prediction of Common Stock Investment Risk." *Journal of Portfolio Management* 11, no. 1 (Fall 1984).

Rosenberg, Barr. "Prediction of Common Stock Betas." *Journal of Portfolio Management* 11, no. 2 (Winter 1985).

Thompson, Donald J., II. "Sources of Systematic Risk in Common Stocks." *Journal of Business* 49, no. 2 (April 1976).

FINANCIAL RATIOS AND BOND RATINGS

Ang, James S., and A. Kiritkumar. "Bond Rating Methods: Comparison and Validation." *Journal of Finance* 30, no. 2 (May 1975).

Bullington, Robert A. "How Corporate Debt Issues Are Rated." *Financial Executive* 42, no. 9 (September 1978).

Edelman, Richard B. "A New Approach to Ratings on Utility Bonds." *Journal of Portfolio Management* 5, no. 3 (Spring 1979).

Ferri, Michael G., and Charles G. Martin. "The Cyclical Pattern in Corporate Bond Quality." *Journal of Portfolio Management* 6, no. 2 (Winter 1980).

Fisher, Lawrence. "Determinants of Risk Premiums on Corporate Bonds." *Journal of Political Economy* 67, no. 3 (June 1959).

Gentry, James A., David T. Whitford, and Paul Newbold, "Predicting Industrial Bond Ratings with a Probit Model and Funds Flow Components." *The Financial Review* 23, no. 3 (August 1988).

Horrigan, James O. "The Determination of Long-Term Credit Standing with Financial Ratios." *Empirical Research in Accounting: Selected Studies,* 1966 supplement to vol. 4, *Journal of Accounting Research.*

Kaplan, Robert S., and Gabriel Urwitz. "Statistical Models of Bond Ratings: A Methodological Inquiry." *Journal of Business* 52, no. 2 (April 1979).

Pinches, George E., and Kent A. Mingo. "A Multivariate Analysis of Industrial Bond Ratings." *Journal of Finance* 28, no. 1 (March 1973).

Pinches, George E., and Kent A. Mingo. "The Role of Subordination and Industrial Bond Ratings." *Journal of Finance* 30, no. 1 (March 1975).

Pogue, Thomas F., and Robert M. Soldofsky. "What's in a Bond Rating?" *Journal of Financial and Quantitative Analysis* 4, no. 2 (June 1969).

Pye, Gordon. "Gauging the Default Premium." *Financial Analysts Journal* 30, no. 1 (January–February 1974).

Standard and Poor's Corporation. "Corporation Bond Ratings: An Overview." 1978.

West, Richard R. "An Alternative Approach to Predicting Bond Ratings." *Journal of Accounting Research* 8, no. 1 (Spring 1970).

FINANCIAL RATIOS AND CORPORATE BANKRUPTCY

Altman, Edward I. "Financial Ratios, Discriminant Analysis, and the Prediction of Corporate Bankruptcy." *Journal of Finance* 23, no. 4 (September 1968).

Altman, Edward I. *Corporate Financial Distress* (New York: John Wiley & Sons, 1983).

Altman, Edward I., Robert G. Haldeman, and P. Narayanan. "Zeta Analysis: A New Model to Identify Bankruptcy Risk of Corporations." *Journal of Banking and Finance* 1, no. 2 (June 1977).

Beaver, William H. "Financial Ratios as Predictors of Failure." *Empirical Research in Accounting: Selected Studies,* 1966 supplement to vol. 4 *Journal of Accounting Research.*

Beaver, William H. "Market Prices, Financial Ratios, and the Prediction of Failure." *Journal of Accounting Research* 6, no. 2 (Autumn 1968).

Beaver, William H. "Alternative Accounting Measures as Predictors of Failure." *The Accounting Review* 43, no. 1 (January 1968).

Casey, Cornelius, and Norman Bartczak. "Using Operating Cash Flow Data to Predict Financial Distress: Some Extensions." *Journal of Accounting Research* 23, no. 1 (Spring 1985).

Deakin, Edward B. "A Discriminant Analysis of Predictors of Business Failure." *Journal of Accounting Research* 10, no. 1 (Spring 1972).

Edmister, Robert O. "An Empirical Test of Financial Ratio Analysis for Small Business Failure Prediction." *Journal of Financial and Quantitative Analysis* 7, no. 2 (March 1972).

Gentry, James A., Paul Newbold, and David T. Whitford. "Classifying Bankrupt Firms with Funds Flow Components." *Journal of Accounting Research* 23, no. 1 (Spring 1985).

Gentry, James A., Paul Newbold, and David T. Whitford. "Predicting Bankruptcy: If Cash Flow's Not the Bottom Line, What Is?" *Financial Analysts Journal* 41, no. 5 (September–October 1985).

Mensah, Yaw M. "The Differential Bankruptcy Predictive Ability of Specific Price Level Adjustments: Some Empirical Evidence." *The Accounting Review* 58, no. 2 (April 1983).

Moyer, R. Charles. "Forecasting Financial Failure: A Re-Examination." *Financial Management* 6, no. 1 (Spring 1977).

Ohlson, J. A. "Financial Ratios and the Probabalistic Prediction of Bankruptcy." *Journal of Accounting Research* 18, no. 2 (Spring 1980).

Raja, A., M. Nosworthy, and D. Goureia. "Diagnosis of Financial Health by Cash Flow Analysis." Working Paper, London Business School (1980).

Scott, J. "The Probability of Bankruptcy: A Comparison of Empirical Predictions and Theoretical Models." *Journal of Banking and Finance* 5 (1981).

Wilcox, Jarrod W. "A Prediction of Business Failure Using Accounting Data." *Empirical Research in Accounting: Selected Studies,* 1973 supplement to *Journal of Accounting Research.* vol. 11 (1973).

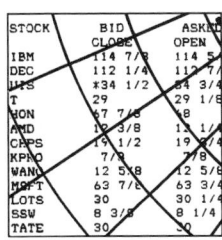

CHAPTER 13

AGGREGATE STOCK MARKET ANALYSIS

Interest in stock market movements has grown during the past decade. More individuals own stock than ever before, and significant mergers are increasingly frequent. Then the stock market "crash" on October 19, 1987, led to a period of information overload that left few people unaware of the importance of the securities markets in today's world.[1]

In Chapter 9 we discussed the importance of attempting to estimate future aggregate stock market values to indicate future returns from investing in common stocks. As pointed out, such an analysis should precede an industry analysis or a company analysis. Three major techniques are available. A *macroeconomic approach* is based upon the underlying relationship between the aggregate economy and the securities markets. A *micro-analysis* is the present value of dividends approach, applying the basic dividend valuation model discussed in Chapter 9 to the aggregate stock market. Finally, the *technical analysis* approach (discussed later, in Chapter 16) assumes that the best way to determine future changes in stock market values is to examine past movements in security prices and other market variables.

THE STOCK MARKET AND THE ECONOMY

It is widely accepted that there is a strong relationship between the aggregate economy and the stock market. After all, the price of a given stock reflects investor expectations as to how the issuing firm will perform, and that performance is in turn affected by the overall performance of the economy. Substantial empirical evidence of this relationship was derived by the National Bureau of Economic Research (NBER) in connection with work on business cycles. Based on the relationship of alternative economic

---

[1] See Appendix 3A for a brief presentation on the stock market crash.

Table 13.1
Timing Relationships between Peaks and Troughs of the Stock Market and Business Cycles

I. Stock Market Declines Associated with Subsequent Recession

Stock Market Cycles[a]		Business Cycles		Lead of Market over Business Cycle	
Peak	**Trough**	**Peak**	**Trough**	**Peak**	**Trough**
Jan. 1953	Sep. 1953	Jul. 1953	May 1954	6	8
Aug. 1956	Oct. 1957	Aug. 1957	Apr. 1958	11	6
Aug. 1959	Oct. 1960	Apr. 1960	Feb. 1961	8	4
Nov. 1968	May 1970	Dec. 1969	Nov. 1970	12	6
Jan. 1973	Oct. 1974	Nov. 1973	Mar. 1975	10	5
Feb. 1980	Aug. 1982	Jan. 1980	Nov. 1982	(1)	3
			Average	7.7	5.3

II. False Signals

Dec. 1961	Jan. 1962
Apr. 1971	Nov. 1971
Sept. 1976	Mar. 1978

III. Stock Market Declines Associated with Subsequent Growth Recession

Feb. 1966	Mar. 1968

[a]Defined as market declines of approximately 15 percent or more.
Source: Jason Benderly and Edward McKelvey, "The Pocket Chartroom" *Economic Research* (New York: Goldman Sachs & Co., 1987).

series to the behavior of the entire economy, the NBER has classified numerous economic series into three groups: leading, coincident, and lagging. Extensive analysis has shown that stock prices are one of the better leading indicator series in terms of consistency and stability.

The evidence clearly indicates not only a relationship between stock prices and the economy, but also that stock prices consistently turn before the economy does. The specifics of this relationship during the last 30 years are shown in Table 13.1. Note that while the leading relationship appears to hold, there are several instances of false signals by the stock market.

There are two possible reasons why stock prices lead the economy. One is that they reflect expectations of earnings and dividends. Thus, because investors attempt to estimate future earnings, stock prices are based upon future economic activity, not on current activity. A second possible reason is that the stock market reacts to various economic series, the most important being the leading indicator series. In this regard, the economic series mentioned most often as important to stock prices is corporate earnings, corporate profit margins, and changes in the growth rate of the money supply. Therefore, because investors analyze economic series that lead the economy and adjust stock prices rapidly to changes in these relevant economic series, stock prices become a leading series. Because stock prices turn before the aggregate economy does, it is difficult to use economic activity to predict stock price movement, but there are several possibilities:

1. *Estimate aggregate economic activity very far into the future.* Assuming the average lead of stock prices relative to the aggregate economy is about nine months, it is necessary to project changes in the aggregate economy close to one year in advance.

2. *Analyze other economic series that also lead the economy.* The ideal would be to find a series that leads the economy by more than stock prices do, that is, an economic series that typically leads the aggregate economy by more than nine months.

3. *Attempt to project the behavior of economic series that do not lead the economy by as much as stock prices do.* An example would be a series that leads the economy by six months; you would attempt to project fluctuations in this leading series for four or more months ahead.

Given that stock prices lead the aggregate economy, our macroeconomic approach to market analysis will concentrate on economic series that likewise lead the economy—by more, we hope, than stock prices do. First we will discuss the cyclical indicator approach of the National Bureau of Economic Research (NBER), then the *Business Week* leading indicator series, as well as other leading series developed by the Center for International Business Cycle Research (CIBCR) at Columbia University. Next we will consider a very popular leading series, the money supply, and finally, a number of economic series that are expected to affect equity returns (i.e., production, inflation, risk premiums).

CYCLICAL INDICATOR APPROACH TO FORECASTING

The cyclical indicator approach to economic forecasting is based on the belief that the economy experiences discernible periods of expansion and contraction. This view has been investigated by the National Bureau of Economic Research (NBER), a nonprofit organization that attempts to interpret important economic facts scientifically and impartially. The NBER explains the business cycle as follows:

> The business cycle concept has been developed from the sequence of events discerned in the historical study of the movements of economic activity. Though there are many cross-currents and variations in the pace of business activity, periods of business expansion appear to cumulate to peaks. As they cumulate, contrary forces tend to gain strength bringing about a reversal in business activity and the onset of a recession. As a recession continues, forces making for expansion gradually emerge until they become dominant and a recovery begins.[2]

Based upon an examination of the behavior of hundreds of economic time series in relation to past business cycles, the NBER grouped various

---

[2] Julius Shiskin, "Business Cycle Indicators: The Known and the Unknown," *Review of the International Statistical Institute* 31, no. 3 (1963): 361–383.

economic series into three major categories in terms of this relationship. The initial list was compiled in 1938, and it has undergone numerous revisions over the years, the most recent one by Zarnowitz and Boschan.[3]

INDICATOR CATEGORIES

The first category of _leading indicators_ includes those economic time series that usually reach peaks or troughs before the corresponding points in aggregate economic activity are reached. The group currently includes the 12 series shown in Table 13.2. The table indicates the median lead or lag for each economic series relative to business cycle peaks or troughs. Each economic series is graded in terms of several characteristics considered important. A high score indicates that a series should be useful in the analysis of cyclical movements. One of the 12 leading series is common stock prices, which has a median lead of nine months at peaks and four months at troughs.[4] Another leading series is the money supply in constant dollars, which has a median lead of ten months at peaks and eight months at troughs.

The second category of _coincident indicators_ consists of economic time series whose peaks and troughs roughly coincide with the peaks and troughs of the business cycle. Many of the economic time series in this category are employed by the Bureau to help define the different phases of the cycle.

The third category of _lagging indicators_ includes series that experience their peaks and troughs after those of the aggregate economy. Timing and scores for the coincident and lagging series are contained in Table 13.3.

A final category is titled "other selected series" and includes economic series that are expected to influence aggregate economic activity but that cannot be neatly categorized in one of the three main groups. This includes such series as U.S. balance of payments, federal surplus or deficit, and military contract awards.

Some analysts have employed a ratio of these composite series, contending that _the ratio of the coincident to lagging series acts like a leading series, in some instances even leading the leading series._ The rationale is that the coincident series will turn before the lagging series, and the ratio of the two will be quite sensitive to changes, thus leading both of them. While this ratio series tends to parallel movements in the leading series, its real value is said to lie in the times that it diverges from the pure leading series, because it signals a change in the normal relationship between the sets of indicator series. As an example, if the leading indicators have been rising, you would expect both the coincident and lagging series to be also rising, but the coincident series should be rising faster than the lagging, so the ratio of coincident to lagging series should likewise be rising. In contrast, if the leading series is rising, but the ratio series begins

---

[3] Victor Zarnowitz and C. Boschan, "Cyclical Indicators: An Evaluation and New Leading Index," _Business Conditions Digest_ (May 1975): V–XXII; and "New Composite Indexes of Coincident and Lagging Indicators," _Business Conditions Digest_ (November 1975): V–XXIV.

[4] A detailed analysis of this relationship is contained in Geoffrey H. Moore and John P. Cullity, "Security Markets and Business Cycles," in _The Financial Analysts Handbook,_ 2d ed., edited by Sumner N. Levine (Homewood, Ill.: Dow Jones-Irwin, 1988).

LEADING SERIES

TABLE 13.2
Economic Series in NBER Leading Indicator Group

	MEDIAN LEAD (−) OR LAG (+) (IN MONTHS)			SCORES						
SERIES	PEAKS	TROUGHS	ALL TURNS	ECONOMIC SIGNIFICANCE	STATISTICAL ADEQUACY	TIMING	CONFORMITY	SMOOTHNESS	CURRENCY	TOTAL
1. Average work week of production worker (manufacturing)	−12	−5	−5 1/2	70	80	81	60	80	80	73
2. Index of new business formations	−11	−2	−3	80	61	78	59	80	80	73
3. Index of stock prices: 500 common stocks	−9	−4	−5 1/2	80	85	89	51	80	100	80
4. Index of new building permits	−13	−8	−9 1/2	90	70	80	55	80	80	76
5. Layoff rate (manufacturing)	−11	−1	−6 1/2	70	80	79	80	60	80	76
6. New orders: consumer goods (1967 dollars)	−6	−1	−4 1/2	80	75	76	70	60	80	74
7. Contracts and orders for plant and equipment (1967 dollars)	−9	−2	−5 1/2	90	50	87	72	40	80	72
8. Net change in inventory (1967 dollars)	−9	−4	−4 1/2	90	50	87	72	40	80	72
9. Net change in sensitive prices	−15	−5	−5 1/2	70	80	82	60	60	66	72
10. Vendor performance	−6	−5	−6	70	75	79	46	60	80	69
11. Money balance (M1), (1967 dollars)	−10	−8	−9	90	85	80	41	100	80	79
12. Percentage change in total liquid assets	−6 1/2	−6	−6	90	81	84	41	80	66	75

Source: Victor Zarnowitz and Charlotte Boschan, "Cyclical Indicators: An Evaluation and New Leading Indexes," *Business Conditions Digest* (May 1975): 5–22.

TABLE 13.3
Economic Series in NBER Coincident and Lagging Indicator Group

SERIES	MEDIAN LEAD (−) OR LAG (+) (IN MONTHS)			SCORES						
	PEAKS	TROUGHS	ALL TURNS	ECONOMIC SIGNIFICANCE	STATISTICAL ADEQUACY	TIMING	CONFORMITY	SMOOTHNESS	CURRENCY	TOTAL
Coincident										
1. Number of employees on nonagricultural payrolls	−2	0	0	100	78	80	100	80	88	88
2. Index of industrial production	−3	0	−1/2	90	72	90	85	100	80	86
3. Personal income, less transfers (deflated by PEE)	0	−1	−1/2	90	70	74	64	100	80	78
4. Manufacturing and trade sales, deflated	−3	0	−1/2	90	65	90	75	80	53	78
Lagging										
1. Average duration of employment	+1	+8	+3 1/2	90	78	89	95	80	80	86
2. Manufacturing and trade inventories (1967 dollars)	+2 1/2	+3	+3	90	70	89	64	100	100	80
3. Labor cost per unit: output, manufacturing	+8 1/2	+11	+10	80	55	87	51	80	80	73
4. Commercial and industrial loans outstanding, weekly rep. banks	+1 1/2	+5	+3 1/2	80	60	86	81	100	80	83
5. Ratio of consumer installment debt to personal income	+6 1/2	+7	+7	80	70	87	44	53	100	74
6. Average prime rate charged by banks	+3 1/2	+14	+4	90	95	85	62	100	100	87

Source: Victor Zarnowitz and Charlotte Boschan, "New Composite Indexes of Coincident and Lagging Indicators," *Business Conditions Digest* (November 1975): 5–24.

FIGURE 13.1

Comparison of 12 Leading Indicators, Ratio for Coincident to Lagging Indicators, and the S&P 400

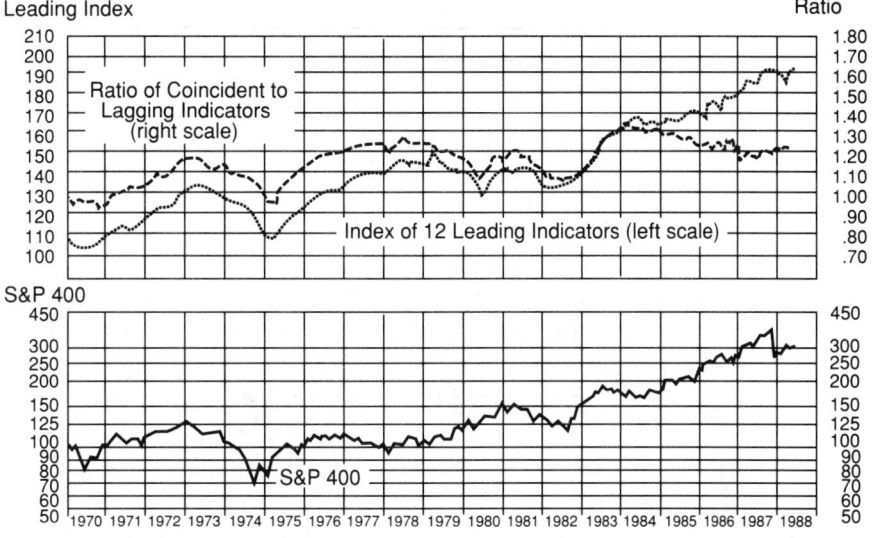

	Coincident	Lagging	Ratio	Leading	S&P 400
SEP 1987	1.701R	1.431R	1.189R	192.4R	375.9
OCT	1.725R	1.425R	1.211R	192.4R	288.6
NOV	1.720R	1.433R	1.200R	190.0R	263.2
DEC	1.734R	1.435R	1.208	190.6R	285.9
JAN 1988	1.730R	1.436R	1.205R	189.2R	293.7
FEB	1.740	1.433	1.206	191.7	309.4
MAR	1.745	1.449	1.204	193.3	300.4

Source: "Investment Strategy Highlights" (New York: Goldman Sachs & Co., May 1988). Reprinted with permission from Goldman, Sachs & Co.

to flatten out or decline, it could be because the coincident indicator series is either not rising as fast as the lagging indicator series or because it has turned down. Either scenario would indicate a possible end to an expansion or at least a less robust expansion. An example of such a divergence is shown in Figure 13.1 where the pattern is for the two series (coincident and lagging) to move at about the same rate, causing the ratio series to be flat and even decline slightly since 1984 while the leading indicator series has continued to increase.

ANALYTICAL MEASURES

When examining a given economic series for predictive purposes, it is important to consider more than simply the behavior of the series overall. The NBER has devised certain analytical measures for examining behavior within a series.

DIFFUSION INDEXES. As the name implies, *diffusion indexes* indicate how pervasive a given movement is in a series. They are used to specify the percentage of reporting units in a series indicating a given result. If there are 100 companies that constitute the sample reporting new orders for equipment, the diffusion index would indicate what proportion of the 100 companies was reporting higher orders during an expansion. In addition to knowing that aggregate new orders are increasing, it is helpful to know whether 55 percent of the companies in the sample are reporting higher orders or whether 95 percent are. Such information would help you project the future length and strength of an expansion. You would also want to know past diffusion index values to determine the prevailing trend, because it has been shown that the diffusion indexes for a series almost always reach their peak or trough before the peak or trough in the corresponding aggregate series. Therefore, you can use the diffusion index of a series to predict the behavior of the series itself. Assume that you are interested in the leading series, New Orders—Consumer Goods. It is possible to derive an early indication of weakening in this series by observing its diffusion index. If the diffusion index for new orders goes from 85 percent to 75 percent and then to 70 percent, it indicates widespread receipt of new orders but also indicates weakening in terms of the breadth of the increase, and possibly an impending decline in the series itself.

Besides creating diffusion indexes for individual series, the NBER has derived such indexes for the 12 leading indicators, showing the percentage of indicators that are rising or falling during a given period.

RATES OF CHANGE. Somewhat similar to the diffusion index is the rate of change measure for the series. It is one thing to know that there has been an increase in a series, but quite another to know that it is a 10 percent increase as compared to a 7 percent increase the previous month. Like the diffusion index, the rate of change values for a series reach a peak or trough prior to the peak or trough in the aggregate series.

DIRECTION OF CHANGE. Direction of change tables show at a glance which series went up or down (plus or minus) during the period and how long the movement in this direction has persisted.

COMPARISON WITH PREVIOUS CYCLES. Other tables show the movements of individual series over previous business cycles. Current movements are then compared to previous cycles for the same economic series. This comparison reveals whether a given series is moving slower or faster, stronger or weaker than it was during the last cycle. This information can be useful because, typically, movements in the initial months of an expansion or contraction indicate the ultimate length and strength of the expansion or contraction.[5]

---

[5] Monthly presentations of all the series and analytical measures are contained in U.S. Department of Commerce, *Business Conditions Digest* (Washington, D.C.: U.S. Government Printing Office).

LIMITATIONS OF THE INDICATOR APPROACH. The NBER has consistently attempted to improve the usefulness of the indicator approach while acknowledging some very definite limitations. The most obvious limitation is false signals. Past patterns might suggest that the indicators are currently signaling a contraction, but then they turn up again and nullify previous signals. A similar problem occurs when the indicators experience a period of hesitancy that is difficult to interpret. Or they may exhibit a marked variability, warranting less confidence in short-run signals.

Another limitation is getting the original data as soon as possible and revising it. Many of the series are seasonally adjusted, and there may be subsequent adjustments to the seasonal adjustment factors. Also, the growing service sector is not included and there is no component that represents the very important global economy or world securities markets. Finally, as the NBER points out, there are numerous political or international developments that significantly influence the economy but cannot be incorporated into a statistical system.

LEADING INDICATORS AND STOCK PRICES

Because of the relationship between leading indicators and the economy, it has been suggested that one might be able to use leading indicators to predict stock prices. Heathcotte and Apilado examined the relationship between the short list of leading economic series and the S&P 500 series. The authors derived a three-month moving average of the diffusion index, using different filter rules to construct an investment policy.[6] That is, when the index increased by some specified percentage, they would buy and hold until it declined by some percentage. The authors compared their investment results to those for a buy-and-hold policy and found that, as long as they had perfect foresight regarding the correct filters to use, they beat a buy-and-hold policy. When they used the trading rule without foresight as to the best filter (merely using the previous best filter), the results were very mixed. In general, without foresight regarding the appropriate filter they were not able to beat a buy-and-hold policy when taking commissions into account.

OTHER LEADING INDICATOR SERIES

In addition to the NBER leading indicator series that employed monthly data, the Center for International Business Cycle Research (CIBCR) at the Columbia Graduate School of Business has developed several other leading indicator series.

BUSINESS WEEK *LEADING INDICATOR SERIES.* Developed by the CIBRC and published weekly in *Business Week,* the Business Week Leading Indicator Series includes seven individual series as shown in Figure 13.2. A time series plot and bar chart for the series and a weekly production series and other weekly data on foreign exchange, prices, and monetary indicators are included. This composite weekly leading indicator index is used

---

[6] Bryan Heathcotte and Vincent P. Apilado, "The Predictive Content of Some Leading Economic Indicators for Future Stock Prices," *Journal of Financial and Quantitative Analysis* 9, no. 2 (March 1974): 247–258.

Figure 13.2
Business Week Index

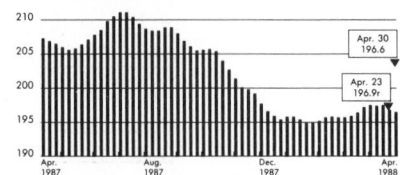

BusinessWeek Index

PRODUCTION

Change from last week: 0.4%
Change from last year: 7.4%

1967 = 100
Four-week moving average
Apr. 30 170.7
Apr. 23 170.0

Apr. 1987   Aug. 1987   Dec. 1987   Apr. 1988

The production index increased for the week ended Apr. 30. Seasonally adjusted output of steel, paperboard, electric power, and coal were all up for the week. Truck, paper, and lumber production were down slightly. Auto output, crude-oil refining, and rail-freight traffic were unchanged. Before calculation of the four-week moving average, the index rose to 172.1 from 171.5 in the previous week. For the month of April the index edged up to 170.7 from 170.5 in March.
BW production index copyright 1988 by McGraw-Hill Inc.

LEADING

Change from last week: −0.2%
Change from last year: −4.6%

Apr. 30 196.6
Apr. 23 196.9r

Apr. 1987   Aug. 1987   Dec. 1987   Apr. 1988

The leading index edged slightly downward in the week ended Apr. 30. A fall in material prices was responsible for the decline. Stock prices and the growth rate for M2 both rose. Yields on long-term bonds and the pace of real estate loans were unchanged. Data on business failures were unavailable. The unaveraged index was also 196.6, up from 195.8 in the previous week. The index in April dropped to 196.6 from March's 197.4.
Leading index copyright 1988 by Center for International Business Cycle Research

PRODUCTION INDICATORS

	Latest week	Week ago	% Change year ago
STEEL (5/7) thous. of net tons	2,028	2,046 #	13.6
AUTOS (5/7) units	159,979	163,031r #	−1.5
TRUCKS (5/7) units	89,313	86,858r #	14.3
ELECTRIC POWER (5/7) millions of kilowatt-hours	47,371	48,109 #	1.1
CRUDE-OIL REFINING (5/7) thous. of bbl./day	13,152	13,117r #	7.5
COAL (4/30) thous. of net tons	18,145 #	17,744	7.2
PAPERBOARD (4/30) thous. of tons	745.0 #	722.3r	3.0
PAPER (4/30) thous. of tons	738.0 #	741.0r	2.6
LUMBER (4/30) millions of ft.	505.8 #	506.4	−5.9
RAIL FREIGHT (4/30) billions of ton-miles	19.4 #	19.3	9.0

Sources: American Iron & Steel Inst., *Ward's Automotive Reports*, Edison Electric Inst., American Petroleum Inst., Energy Dept., American Paper Inst., WWPA[1], SFPA[2], Association of American Railroads.

FOREIGN EXCHANGE

	Latest week	Week ago	Year ago
JAPANESE YEN (5/11)	124	125	140
GERMAN MARK (5/11)	1.68	1.68	1.80
BRITISH POUND (5/11)	1.88	1.87	1.67
FRENCH FRANC (5/11)	5.70	5.70	6.00
CANADIAN DOLLAR (5/11)	1.23	1.24	1.34
SWISS FRANC (5/11)	1.40	1.40	1.48
MEXICAN PESO (5/11)[3]	2,282	2,282	1,220

Sources: Major New York banks. Currencies expressed in units per U. S. dollar, except for British pound expressed in dollars.

PRICES

	Latest week	Week ago	% Change year ago
GOLD (5/11) $/troy oz.	449.100	443.250	−2.5
FINISHED STEEL (5/10) ¢/lb.	24.333	24.333	−3.6
FOODSTUFFS (5/9) index, 1967 = 100	222.2	220.7	1.3
COPPER (5/7) ¢/lb.	101.6	97.7	46.8
ALUMINUM (5/7) ¢/lb.	109.5	106.0	61.5
WHEAT (5/7) # 2 hard, $/bu.	3.04	3.12	−1.6
COTTON (5/7) strict low middling 1-1/16 in., ¢/lb.	60.19	61.29	−3.3

Sources: London Wed. final setting, *Iron Age*, Commodity Research Bureau, *Metals Week*, Kansas City mkt., Memphis mkt.

LEADING INDICATORS

	Latest week	Week ago	% Change year ago
STOCK PRICES (5/6) S&P 500	260.23	262.83	−11.3
CORPORATE BOND YIELD, Aaa (5/6)	9.78%	9.73%	6.2
INDUSTRIAL MATERIALS PRICES (5/6)	97.8	97.7	2.7
BUSINESS FAILURES (4/29)	NA	265r	NA
REAL ESTATE LOANS (4/27) billions	$273.6	$272.9r	14.0
MONEY SUPPLY, M2 (4/25) billions	$2,989.7	$2,979.1r	4.5
INITIAL CLAIMS, UNEMPLOYMENT (4/23) thous.	315	275	−3.1

Sources: Standard & Poor's, Moody's, *Journal of Commerce* (index: 1980 = 100), Dun & Bradstreet (failures of large companies), Federal Reserve Board, Labor Dept. CIBCR seasonally adjusts data on business failures and real estate loans.

MONTHLY ECONOMIC INDICATORS

	Latest month	Month ago	% Change year ago
BUSINESS WEEK PRODUCTION INDEX (Apr.)	170.7	170.5	7.2
BUSINESS WEEK LEADING INDEX (Apr.)	196.6	197.4r	−4.7
EMPLOYMENT, CIVILIAN, MILLIONS (Apr.)	114.7	114.1	2.6
UNEMPLOYMENT RATE, CIVILIAN (Apr.)	5.4%	5.6%	−14.3

Sources: BW, CIBCR, BLS

MONETARY INDICATORS

	Latest week	Week ago	% Change year ago
MONEY SUPPLY, M1 (4/25)	$778.0	$766.3r	2.6
BANKS' BUSINESS LOANS (4/27)	297.9	298.1r	3.0
FREE RESERVES (5/4)	778	343r	NM
NONFINANCIAL COMMERCIAL PAPER (4/27)	89.9	89.4	13.5

Sources: Federal Reserve Board (in billions, except for free reserves, which are expressed for a two-week period in millions).

MONEY MARKET RATES

	Latest week	Week ago	Year ago
FEDERAL FUNDS (5/10)	7.32%	6.60%	6.75%
PRIME (5/11)	8.50-9.00	8.50	8.00
COMMERCIAL PAPER 3-MONTH (5/6)	6.95	6.95	6.81
CERTIFICATES OF DEPOSIT 3-MONTH (5/11)	7.35	7.10	6.85
EURODOLLAR 3-MONTH (5/4)	7.18	7.18	7.11

Sources: Federal Reserve Board, Salomon Brothers, First Boston

# Raw data in the production indicators are seasonally adjusted in computing the BW index (chart); other components (estimated and not listed) include machinery and defense equipment.
1 = Western Wood Products Assn.   2 = Southern Forest Products Assn.   3 = Free market value   NA = Not available   r = revised   NM = Not meaningful

Source: Business Week Index, p. 6. Reprinted from May 23, 1988 issue of *Business Week* by special permission, copyright © 1988 by McGraw-Hill, Inc.

to gauge upswings and declines in general economic activity. Downturns in the index have preceded every recession since 1948, but some downturns have been followed by a slowdown in the economy rather than a recession.

LONG-LEADING INDEX. The CIBCR has also developed the Long-Leading Index to provide an earlier signal of major turning points in the economy than other leading indexes. It includes the following four series: (1) Dow Jones Bond Prices (20 Bonds), Percent Face Value; (2) Ratio, Price to Unit Labor Cost (Mfg.), 1982 = 100; (3) M2 Money Supply, Deflated (Billion 1982 $); (4) New Building Permits, Housing (1967 = 100). This index has anticipated recessions by 14 months, on average, and never by less than 7 months.

Monthly data for this series and the following series developed and maintained by the CIBCR are available in *The Leading Indicator Press Release* published about the tenth day of the month with data for about six weeks earlier (e.g., the release on November 10 has September results).

LEADING EMPLOYMENT INDEX (1967 = 100). The purpose of the CIBCR's Leading Employment Index (1967 = 100) is to forecast future changes in U.S. employment. It includes the following six component series: (1) Average Workweek, Mfg.; (2) Overtime Hours, Mfg.; (3) Percent Layoff Rate (Inverted); (4) Voluntary/Involuntary Part-Time Employment; (5) Percent Short Duration Unemployment Rate (Inverted); (6) Initial Claims for Unemployment Insurance (Inverted).

LEADING INFLATION INDEX. The Leading Inflation Index is compiled by CIBCR as a tool for forecasting inflation in the United States. Originally it included three variables but was revised in April 1986 to include five: (1) the percentage employed of the working age population, (2) the growth rate of total debt (including business, consumer, and federal debt), (3) the growth rate of industrial material prices, (4) the growth rate of an index of import prices, and (5) the percent of businessmen anticipating an increase in their selling prices as determined by a Dun and Bradstreet survey. The leads for the revised index covering the period 1950–1985 averaged seven months at troughs, four months at peaks, and five months at all turns.[7]

ALTERNATIVE LEADING INDICATOR OF INFLATION. The Wall Street investment banking firm, Kidder, Peabody & Co. has also derived a model for predicting inflation. They considered several models and concluded with the following variables: (1) rate of capacity utilization (lagged 12 months), (2) the Federal Reserve dollar value index—a trade-weighted index of the value of the dollar against ten currencies (lagged 14 months),

---

[7] For a discussion of this series, see Geoffrey H. Moore and Stanley Kaish, "A New Inflation Barometer," *Morgan Guaranty Survey* (July 1983).

and (3) the annual growth rate of the CRB Commodity Spot Index (lagged eight months). A graph of the index for the period 1973–1987 indicated a strong correlation between inflation and the leading series.[8]

INTERNATIONAL LEADING INDICATOR SERIES. In addition to the work related to leading indicators for the United States, the CIBCR has also developed a set of composite leading indicators for eight other major industrial countries: Canada, West Germany, France, United Kingdom, Italy, Japan, Australia, and Taiwan (Republic of China). These International Leading Indicator Series are part of an ongoing project to develop an international economic indicator system (IEI). The series are comparable in data and analysis to the leading series for the United States.[9]

MONETARY VARIABLES AND STOCK PRICES

An economic factor assumed to be closely related to stock prices is monetary policy. The best-known monetary variable in this regard is the money supply. In actuality, the influence of the money supply on stock prices is an offshoot of its influence on the aggregate economy. Friedman and Schwartz have thoroughly documented the historical record of the empirical relationship between changes in the growth rate of the stock of money and subsequent changes in aggregate economic activity.[10] Their research indicated that, during the period 1867–1960, declines in the rate of growth of the money supply preceded business contraction by an average of 20 months.[11] Expansions in the growth rate of the money supply, on average, preceded expansions in the business activity by about eight months. Notably, every major contraction or expansion during the period 1867–1960 was preceded by a contraction or expansion in the growth rate of the money supply. In addition, Friedman specified the transmission mechanism through which changes in the growth rate of the money supply affect the aggregate economy. According to the hypothesis, when the Federal Reserve buys or sells bonds to adjust bank reserves and, eventually, the money supply, the initial impact of this change is on the government bond market, then on corporate bonds, then on common stocks, and subsequently on the real goods market. This means that the initial effect of monetary policy is on financial markets and only subsequently on the aggregate economy.

Several studies have examined the empirical evidence for this hypothesized relationship. Early research by Sprinkel examined a six-month

---

[8] Steven R. Ricchiute and Stephen W. Gallagher, "Leading Indicators of Inflation, 'Money Market Research,'" Kidder, Peabody & Co. (January 1988).

[9] For an extended discussion, see Geoffrey H. Moore, "An Introduction to International Economic Indicators," *Business Cycles, Inflation, and Forecasting,* 2d ed. (New York: National Bureau of Economic Research, Studies in Business Cycles, No. 24, 1983).

[10] Milton Friedman and Anna J. Schwartz, "Money and Business Cycles," *Review of Economics and Statistics,* supplement vol. 45, no. 1, part 2 (February 1963): 32–78, reprinted in Milton Friedman, *The Optimum Quantity of Money and Other Essays* (Chicago: Aldine Publishing Co., 1969), 189–235.

[11] In the Friedman-Schwartz study, money supply was defined as bank demand deposits and time deposits plus currency in the hands of the public (M2). Business cycle expansions and contractions were used as defined by the National Bureau of Economic Research.

moving average of the growth rate of the money supply and the S&P 425 stock price series.[12] Sprinkel concluded that there was a relationship between them, but that the timing was not always consistent and the lead appeared to be getting shorter. Palmer examined the relationship between the growth rate of the money supply and a moving average of percentage changes in stock prices and found a consistent relationship between the two series wherein changes in the money supply generally led stock price changes.[13] Keran's stock price model included money supply growth, but its impact was small.[14] Homa and Jaffee used the level of money supply and the rate of growth of the money supply to predict the level of stock prices, but the results without foresight were mixed.[15] Hamburger and Kochin examined the relationship between the money supply, the stock market, and common stock risk and concluded that changes in the money supply affected the level of stock prices and that the volatility of the money supply influenced common stock risk.[16]

These studies generally indicated a strong relationship between money supply changes and stock prices and also indicated that money supply changes *preceded* stock price changes, which implies that the money supply can be used as an indicator of stock price changes.

In contrast, several studies have questioned these findings based upon the statistical techniques used and the conclusions reached. Miller questioned the Keran and the Hamburger-Kochin studies on statistical grounds.[17] Pesando, likewise, discussed some potential empirical problems for these studies.[18]

Cooper found a definite relationship between the money supply and stock prices, but the analysis indicated that the money supply appeared to consistently lag stock returns by about one to three months.[19] When Auerbach removed the trend and cyclical components of the money and stock prices series and correlated the adjusted series, he found a weak relationship between stock returns and current and future changes in the M1 money supply series.[20] He concluded that his results were consistent with the EMH.

---

[12] The original work is contained in Beryl W. Sprinkel, *Money and Stock Prices* (Homewood, Ill.: Richard D. Irwin, 1964). The update is in Beryl W. Sprinkel, *Money and Markets: A Monetarist View* (Homewood, Ill.: Richard D. Irwin, 1971).

[13] Michael Palmer, "Money Supply, Portfolio Adjustments, and Stock Prices," *Financial Analysts Journal* 26, no. 4 (July–August 1970): 19–22.

[14] Michael W. Keran, "Expectations, Money, and the Stock Market," Federal Reserve Bank of St. Louis, *Review* 53, no. 1 (January 1971): 16–31.

[15] Kenneth E. Homa and Dwight A. Jaffee, "The Study of Money and Common Stock Prices," *Journal of Finance* 26, no. 5 (December 1971): 1045–1066.

[16] Michael J. Hamburger and Levis A. Kochin, "Money and Stock Prices: The Channels of Influence," *Journal of Finance* 27, no. 2 (May 1972): 231–249.

[17] Merton H. Miller, "Discussion of Hamburger and Kochin, 'Money and Stock Prices . . .,'" *Journal of Finance* 27, no. 2 (May 1972): 294–298.

[18] James E. Pesando, "The Supply of Money and Common Stock Prices: Further Observations on the Econometric Evidence," *Journal of Finance* 29, no. 3 (June 1974): 909–921.

[19] Richard V. L. Cooper, "Efficient Capital Markets and the Quantity Theory of Money," *Journal of Finance* 29, no. 3 (June 1974): 887–908.

[20] Robert D. Auerbach, "Money and Stock Prices," Federal Reserve Bank of Kansas City, *Monthly Review* (September–October 1976): 3–11.

Rozeff reexamined the returns achieved with Sprinkel's trading rule using more realistic assumptions and derived returns below those from a buy-and-hold policy.[21] Using regression analysis, he found a very weak relationship when money supply led stock prices, noted an increase in explanatory power using contemporaneous money supply changes, and found a significant increase in the correlation when future money supply changes were included. After confirming these results with trading rule tests, he concluded that money supply changes are important, but that stock prices lead the money supply.

Davidson and Froyen examined the relationship of stock returns to anticipated and unanticipated money supply growth and also considered weekly money supply data.[22] Their results with monthly estimates showed little effect of anticipated or unanticipated money supply or monetary base growth. The tests with weekly data suggested that stock returns tend to fall within a week after the market anticipates a rise in the monetary aggregates, which they felt supported the EMH as related to monetary growth. Hafer employed weekly money supply data to test the impact of anticipated and unanticipated money growth and also examined the differential impact between positive and negative monetary actions on broad and narrow stock market indicator series.[23] Anticipated monetary changes had no impact on stock prices, while positive unanticipated changes had a significant impact, supporting the EMH.

Other Economic Variables and Stock Prices

Chen, Roll, and Ross examined whether equity returns are a function of the following set of macroeconomic variables. The variables considered were (1) monthly and annual growth in industrial production, (2) expected inflation, (3) unexpected inflation, (4) changes in expected inflation, (5) a measure of the risk premium, (6) a measure of the term structure of interest rates, (7) returns of a market value–weighted and equal weighted stock market series, (8) percent changes in real consumption, and (9) percent changes in oil prices.[24] The following variables were significant in explaining stock returns: industrial production, changes in the risk premium, twists in the yield curve, and also measures of unanticipated inflation and changes in expected inflation during periods when these inflation variables were very volatile. In contrast, the market indexes, consumption, and oil prices were never significant. The authors did not attempt to predict market returns but suggested that these models were important in explaining past returns.

[21] M. S. Rozeff, "Money and Stock Prices: Market Efficiency and the Lag Effect of Monetary Policy," *Journal of Financial Economics* 1, no. 3 (September 1974): 245–302; and M. S. Rozeff, "The Money Supply and the Stock Market," *Financial Analysts Journal* 31, no. 5 (September–October 1975): 18–26.

[22] Lawrence S. Davidson and Richard T. Froyen, "Monetary Policy and Stock Returns: Are Stock Markets Efficient?" Federal Reserve Bank of St. Louis, *Review* 64, no. 3 (March 1982): 3–12.

[23] R. W. Hafer, "The Response of Stock Prices to Changes in Weekly Money and the Discount Rate," Federal Reserve Bank of St. Louis, *Review* 68, no. 3 (March 1986): 5–14.

[24] Chen, Nai-Fu, Richard Roll, and Stephen A. Ross, "Economic Forces and the Stock Market," *Journal of Business* 59, no. 3 (July 1986).

SUMMARY OF MACROECONOMIC ANALYSIS

Ample evidence exists of a strong and consistent relationship between economic activity and the stock market, although it appears that stock prices consistently turn from four to nine months *before* the economy does. Therefore, you must either forecast economic activity 12 months ahead or examine indicator series that lead the economy by more than stock prices do.

The results with the leading indicator series indicated that only if an investor had perfect foresight regarding the appropriate filter to use with a diffusion index of leading series, could he improve on a buy-and-hold policy. The empirical results for the relationship between money and stock prices have indicated a significant relationship between money supply and stock prices, but recent research indicates that stock prices generally turn before the money supply does. Therefore, you cannot use the monetary series to develop a mechanical trading rule that will outperform a buy-and-hold policy.

MICRO-ANALYSIS OF THE STOCK MARKET

Determining the future value of the aggregate stock market by microeconomic techniques is simply a way of applying basic valuation theory to the aggregate stock market. We will show that the valuation process can be divided into two main parts and will discuss how this valuation process is applied to an aggregate stock market series.

DETERMINANTS OF VALUE

In Chapter 9 we discussed the following basic determinants of value for any earning asset (e.g., bonds, stock, real estate, etc.):

1. Stream of expected returns
2. Time pattern of expected returns
3. Required rate of return on the investment

Given this background, we applied these concepts to the valuation of bonds, preferred stock, and common stock under several different assumptions regarding the holding period and the stream of future dividends. We also assumed a constant growth rate for an infinite period and derived the following model:

$$V_j = \frac{D_0\,(1 + g)}{(1 + k)} + \frac{D_0(1 + g)^2}{(1 + k)^2} + \cdots \frac{D_0(1 + g)^\infty}{(1 + k)^\infty},$$

where   *to determine stock value*

V_j = the value of stock j

D_0 = dividend payment in the current period

g = the constant growth rate of dividends

k = the required rate of return on stock j

∞ = the number of periods, which is assumed to be infinite.

It was shown in the appendix to Chapter 9 that this information could be simplified to the following expression:

$$V_j = \frac{D_1}{k - g}$$

or

$$P_j = \frac{D_1}{k - g},$$

where

P_j = the price of stock j.

Given this model, <u>the parameters to be estimated are (1) the required rate of return (k) and (2) the expected growth rate of dividends (g).</u> After estimating g, it is a simple matter to estimate D_1, because it is the current dividend (D_0) times $(1 + g)$. We also showed that you can transform this into a pragmatic earnings multiplier model as follows:

Price / Earnings Multiplier

$$\frac{P_j}{E_1} = \frac{\dfrac{D_1}{E_1}}{k - g}.$$

Thus, <u>the P/E ratio (the earnings multiplier) is determined by</u>

1. The expected dividend payout ratio (D_1/E_1)
2. The required rate of return on the stock (k)
3. The expected growth rate of dividends for the stock (g)

It was shown that the difficult parameters to estimate are k and g, or more specifically, the *spread* between k and g. It was demonstrated that very small changes in either of these variables can affect the spread and change the value substantially.

TWO-PART VALUATION PROCEDURE

We will be using the earnings multiplier version of the valuation model to estimate the future value for the stock market because it is a theoretically correct model of value, given its assumptions (which are reasonable for the aggregate market) and also because it is consistently used in practice. Because k and g are independent variables, this spread can and does change over time. You can derive an estimate of the spread prevailing at a point in time by examining the <u>prevailing dividend yield</u> as shown in the following:

$$P_j = \frac{D_1}{k - g}$$

$$\frac{P_j}{D_i} = \frac{1}{k - g}$$

$$\underline{D_i/P_j = k - g.}$$

While this gives an estimate of the size of the spread, it does not indicate the values for the two components (k and g) or the future spread, which is the critical value.

The ultimate objective is to estimate the future market value for some major stock market series, such as the DJIA or the S&P 400. This estimation process is a two-step procedure:

1. Estimating the future earnings per share for the series
2. Estimating a future earnings multiplier for the series[25]

Some studies have concentrated on estimating earnings for these series but have generally ignored changes in the earnings multiplier. The implicit assumption is that the earnings multiplier is relatively constant over time, so stock prices would generally move in line with earnings. The fallacy of such an assumption is obvious when one examines what transpired during the period since 1960, as shown in Table 13.4.

Examples where stock prices moved counter to earnings changes are numerous and striking:

- 1973 profits increased by 30 percent; stock prices declined by 17 percent.
- 1974 profits increased by 9 percent; stock prices declined by 30 percent.
- 1975 profits declined by 10 percent; stock prices increased by 32 percent.
- 1977 profits increased by 7 percent; stock prices declined by 12 percent.
- 1980 profits decreased by 1 percent; stock prices increased by over 27 percent.
- 1982 profits decreased by 21 percent; stock prices increased by 15 percent.
- 1984 profits increased by almost 23 percent; stock prices were basically unchanged.
- 1985 profits decreased by 15 percent; stock prices increased by about 26 percent.
- 1986 profits decreased by almost 5 percent; stock prices increased by over 15 percent.

During each of these years, the major factor influencing stock price movements was changes in the multiplier. The consistency of large changes in the multiplier can be seen from the summary figures at the bottom of Table 13.4 and from the time series plot of the multiplier in Figure 13.3. As shown, the standard deviation of the annual changes for the earnings multiplier series is much larger than the standard deviation of earnings changes in absolute terms (23.4 versus 12.6) or in relative terms—that is, the coefficient of variability (8.67 versus 1.93). Also, if you consider the mean of

---

[25] In line with the efficient market hypothesis, our emphasis will be on estimating future values. While we will show the relevant variables and provide a procedural framework, the final estimate depends upon the ability of the analyst.

TABLE 13.4
Annual Changes in Corporate Earnings, the Earnings Multiplier, and Stock Prices for Standard & Poor's 400: 1960–1988

YEAR	EARNINGS PER SHARE	PERCENTAGE OF CHANGE	YEAR-END EARNINGS MULTIPLE	PERCENTAGE OF CHANGE	YEAR-END STOCK PRICES	PERCENTAGE OF CHANGE
1960	3.40	—	18.09	—	61.49	—
1961	3.37	−0.9	22.37	24.2	75.72	23.1
1962	3.83	13.6	17.23	−23.3	66.00	−12.8
1963	4.24	10.7	18.69	8.5	79.25	20.1
1964	4.85	14.4	18.48	−1.1	89.62	13.1
1965	5.50	−13.4	17.99	−3.1	98.47	9.9
1966	5.87	6.7	14.52	−18.9	85.24	−13.4
1967	5.62	4.3	18.70	28.8	85.24	−13.4
1968	6.16	9.6	18.35	−1.9	113.02	7.5
1969	6.13	−0.5	16.56	−9.8	101.49	−10.2
1970	5.41	−11.7	18.65	12.6	100.90	−0.6
1971	5.97	10.4	18.88	1.2	112.72	11.7
1972	6.83	13.9	19.31	2.3	131.87	17.0
1973	8.89	30.9	12.28	−36.4	109.14	−17.2
1974	9.61	8.9	7.96	−35.2	76.47	29.9
1975	8.58	−10.7	11.62	46.0	100.88	31.9
1976	10.69	24.6	11.17	−3.9	119.46	18.4
1977	11.45	7.1	9.14	−18.8	104.71	−12.4
1978	13.04	13.9	8.22	10.1	107.21	2.4
1979	16.29	24.9	7.43	−9.6	121.02	12.9
1980	16.12	−1.0	9.58	28.9	154.45	27.6
1981	16.74	3.8	8.19	−14.5	137.12	−11.2
1982	13.20	−21.3	11.96	46.0	157.62	15.0
1983	14.78	12.0	12.60	5.4	186.17	18.1
1984	18.11	22.6	10.29	−18.4	186.36	0.1
1985	15.28	−15.6	15.35	49.2	234.56	25.9
1986	14.53	−4.9	18.53	20.7	269.93	15.1
1987	20.29	39.6	14.09	−24.0	285.86	5.9
1988	26.15	28.9	12.29	−12.8	321.26	12.4

With Signs

Mean	—	6.53	—	2.70	—	7.13
Standard deviation	—	12.60	—	23.40	—	15.90
Coefficient of variability	—	1.93	—	8.67	—	2.23

Without Signs

Mean	—	11.96	—	18.50	—	15.42
Standard deviation	—	7.65	—	14.57	—	8.13
Coefficient of variability	—	0.64	—	0.79	—	0.53

Source: *Standard and Poor's Analysts Handbook* (New York: Standard & Poor's Corp., 1987).

FIGURE 13.3
Year-End Earnings Multipliers S&P 400

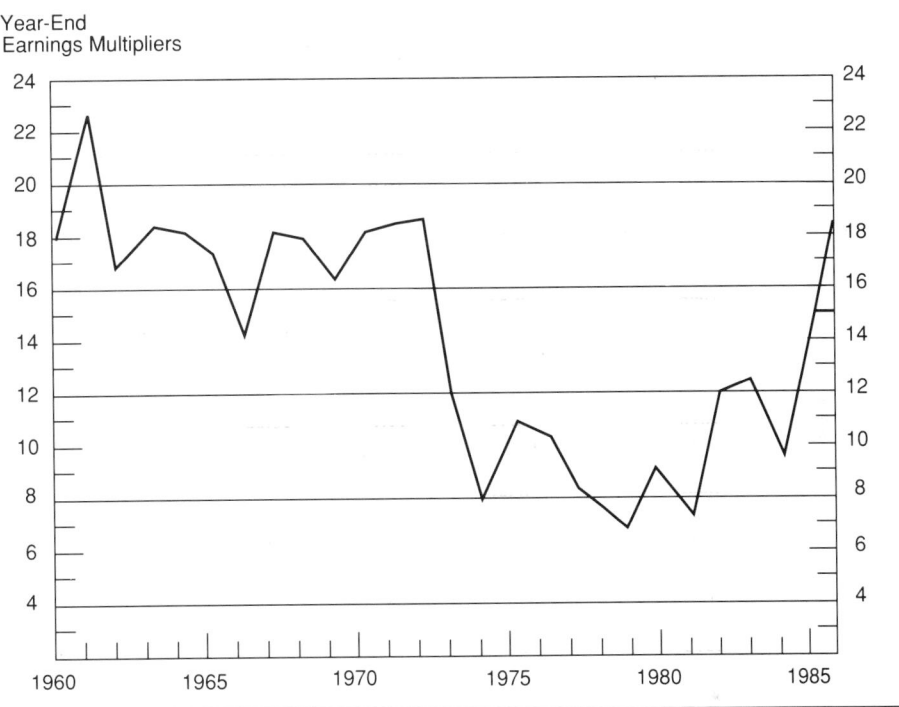

Year-End
Earnings Multipliers

the two series without sign, the multiple series has a larger mean value (18.5 versus 12.0) and a larger standard deviation (14.6 versus 7.6).

Further evidence of the importance of changes in the multiple affecting stock prices can be derived from correlation analysis of the annual percentage changes in the three series for the period 1960–1986. The simple correlation between percentage changes in earnings and stock prices was -0.31, while the correlation between percent changes in the multiple and stock prices was 0.83. The regression equation relating both variables to stock prices was as follows:

$$\% \, \Delta \, \text{Stock Price} = -2.32 + 1.00 \, (\% \, \Delta \, \text{Multiple}) + 1.03 \, (\% \, \Delta \, \text{Earnings})$$
$$(t \text{ value}) \qquad\qquad (23.68) \qquad\qquad\qquad (13.28)$$
$$R^2 = .96.$$

While both coefficients were positive and very significant, note that the multiple variable was more significant. Our intent here is not to reduce the importance of the earnings estimate, but rather to increase your awareness of the importance of the earnings multiple. Therefore, we will initially consider the procedure for estimating aggregate earnings, but will also discuss the procedure for estimating the aggregate market earnings multiple. The estimate of expected earnings for the market series will be based upon the outlook for the aggregate economy and for the corporate sector. The expected market earnings multiplier will be based upon the current earnings multiplier and projected changes in the variables that affect this series.

ESTIMATING EXPECTED EARNINGS

There are several distinct steps involved in estimating expected earnings for an aggregate stock market series, beginning with an estimate of sales for the stock market series.[26] In turn, this sales estimate involves estimating gross national product (GNP) and relating the sales for the stock market series to this measure of aggregate economic activity.

Given a sales estimate, we must estimate the expected gross profit margin for the stock market series and apply it to the sales estimate to get an estimate of gross earnings per share. We conclude with an estimate of depreciation expense and a tax rate.

ESTIMATING GROSS NATIONAL PRODUCT. Because GNP measures aggregate economic sales, one would expect aggregate corporate sales to be related to GNP. Hence, we begin with an estimate of nominal GNP, which can be obtained from one of several banks or financial services that regularly publish such estimates.[27] After deriving a reasonable estimate of nominal GNP from one of several public sources, we must estimate corporate sales relative to aggregate economic sales (GNP).

CORPORATE SALES RELATIVE TO GNP. Because it is best to use sales figures for the market series if they are available, we are fortunate that there is such a series for the S&P 400 industrial index.[28] Table 13.5 contains the recent S&P sales and nominal GNP figures and annual percentage changes, and there is a scatter plot of the percentage change data in Figure 13.4. The plot indicates a very close relationship between the two series with a few exceptions (most notably 1974). The equation for the least-squares regression line relating annual percentage changes (% Δ) in the two series for the period 1960-1986 (without 1974) is

$$\% \; \Delta \; \text{S\&P 400 Sales}_t = -4.83 + 1.40 \; (\% \; \Delta \; \text{in Nominal GNP}_t)$$

Adj. $R^2 = 0.56$ (-2.10) (5.46) $F(1,25) = 29.78.$

These results indicate that about 56 percent of the variance in percentage changes in S&P 400 sales can be explained by percentage changes in the

[26] A general view of corporate profitability is contained in Richard D. Rippe, "Corporate Profitability: The Record and the Prospect," Dean Witter Reynolds, New York, 1981.

[27] This would include projections by Standard & Poor's appearing late in the year in *The Outlook*, projections by several of the large investment firms, such as Goldman Sachs & Co. ("The Pocket Chartbook"), and Merrill Lynch, as well as by banks—e.g., J. A. Cacy and Richard Roberts, "The U.S. Economy in 1987 and 1988," Federal Reserve Bank of Kansas City, *Economic Reserve* (December 1987): 3–15.

[28] The figures are available back to 1945 in Standard & Poor's *Analysts Handbook* (New York: Standard & Poor's Corporation). The book is updated annually, and some series are updated quarterly in a monthly supplement.

TABLE 13.5
Nominal GNP and Standard & Poor's Industrial Sales Per Share: 1960–1988

YEAR	NOMINAL GNP (BILLIONS OF DOLLARS)	PERCENTAGE CHANGE	S&P 400 SALES (DOLLAR VALUE OF SALES PER SHARE)	PERCENTAGE CHANGE
1960	515.3	—	59.47	—
1961	533.8	3.6	59.51	0.1
1962	574.6	7.6	64.63	8.6
1963	606.9	5.6	68.50	6.0
1964	649.8	7.1	73.19	6.8
1965	705.1	8.5	80.69	10.2
1966	772.0	9.5	88.46	9.6
1967	816.4	5.8	91.86	3.8
1968	892.7	9.3	101.49	10.5
1969	963.9	8.0	108.53	6.9
1970	1015.5	5.4	109.85	1.2
1971	1102.7	8.6	118.23	7.6
1972	1212.8	10.0	128.79	8.9
1973	1359.3	12.1	149.22	15.9
1974	1472.8	8.3	182.10	22.0
1975	1598.4	8.5	185.16	1.7
1976	1728.8	8.2	202.66	9.5
1977	1990.5	15.1	224.24	10.6
1978	2249.7	13.0	251.32	12.1
1979	2508.2	11.5	292.38	16.3
1980	2732.0	8.9	327.36	12.0
1981	3052.6	11.7	344.31	5.2
1982	3166.0	3.7	333.86	−3.0
1983	3405.7	7.6	334.07	0.1
1984	3772.2	10.8	379.70	13.7
1985	4010.3	6.3	398.42	4.9
1986	4235.0	5.6	387.76	−2.7
1987	4526.7	6.9	431.92	11.4
1988	4861.8	7.4	471.22	9.1
Average		8.4		7.8

Source: Reprinted with permission from Standard & Poor's Corp., New York, 1987.

nominal GNP. Thus, given an estimate of the expected percentage change in nominal GNP for the forthcoming year, we should be able to estimate the percentage change in sales for the S&P 400 series and therefore the amount of sales per share. As an example, assume that the most likely estimate of nominal GNP for the next year is approximately a 9 percent increase (5 percent increase in real GNP plus 4 percent inflation). Given the regression results, this implies the following:

$$\% \,\Delta\, \text{S\&P 400 Sales} = -4.83 + 1.40\,(.09)$$
$$= 0.08\,.$$

This is an estimate based upon a *point* estimate of GNP—that is, there is actually a *distribution* of estimates for GNP, and we have used the mean value, or expected value, as our point estimate. In actual practice you would

Figure 13.4
Scatter Plot of Annual Percentage Change in S&P 400 Sales and GNP

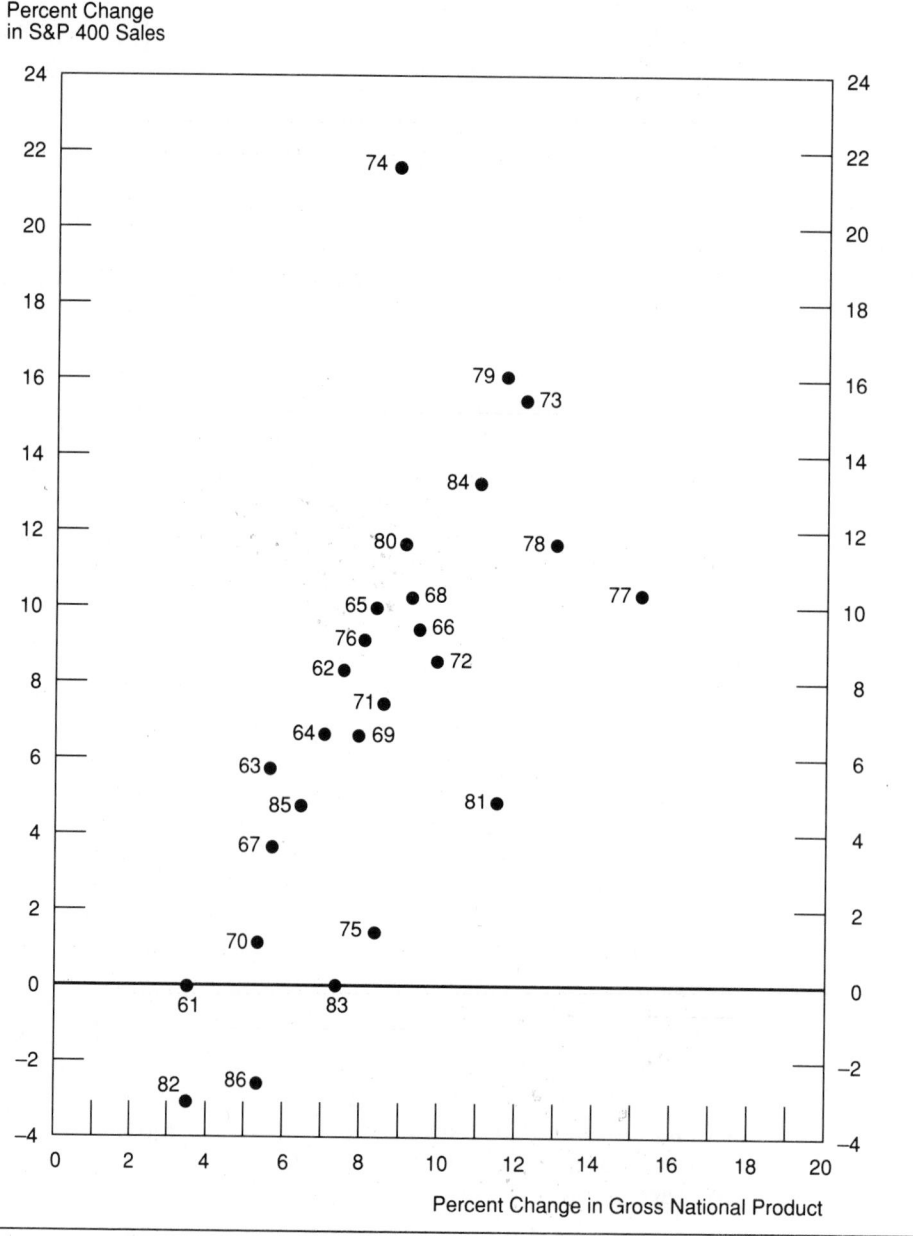

probably consider several estimates and assign probabilities to each of them.

ALTERNATIVE ESTIMATES OF CORPORATE NET PROFITS. Once sales per share for the market series have been estimated, the difficult estimate is that of after-tax profits as a percentage of sales—the net profit margin. Three different procedures are used, depending upon further aggregation.

The first is the direct estimation of the net profit margin based upon recent trends. As shown in Table 13.6, this net profit margin series is quite volatile because of changes in depreciation and the tax rate over time. The second procedure estimates the *net before tax (NBT)* profit margin. Once the NBT margin is derived, a separate estimate of the tax rate is obtained based upon recent tax rates and current government tax pronouncements. An example of a critical tax rate estimate was during 1987 and 1988 following changes brought about by the 1986 Tax Reform Act.

The third method estimates the gross profit margin (income before taxes and depreciation as a percentage of sales). Because the cash flow as a percentage of sales is not influenced by changes in depreciation allowances or tax rates, it should be a relatively stable series. This stability can be seen from the summary data in Table 13.6 on means, standard deviations, and coefficients of variation. The coefficient of variation, which is a relative measure of variability, indicates that the net profit margin is the most volatile series.

After estimating this gross profit margin, we multiply it by the sales estimate to derive a dollar value of *earnings before depreciation and taxes (EBDT)*. Subsequently, we will derive a separate estimate of *aggregate depreciation,* which we then subtract from the EBDT figure to arrive at *earnings before taxes (EBT)*. Finally, we estimate the expected tax rate and apply it to the EBT figure to get the estimated taxes. Subtracting estimated taxes from the NBT figure yields our estimate of net income. The following sections discuss the details of estimating the earnings per share figure, beginning with the gross profit margin.

DETERMINANTS OF AGGREGATE GROSS PROFIT MARGIN

As pointed out by Finkel and Tuttle, despite plentiful analysis of factors that influence the profit margins of individual firms, there has been limited analysis of what determines the aggregate profit margin.[29] The variables suggested and tested by Finkel and Tuttle were

1. Utilization rate of existing industrial capacity (proportion of capacity being used)
2. Unit labor costs of production
3. Rate of inflation
4. Level of foreign competition
5. Unemployment rate

---

[29] Sidney R. Finkel and Donald L. Tuttle, "Determinants of the Aggregate Profits Margin," *Journal of Finance* 26, no. 5 (December 1971): 1067–1075.

TABLE 13.6
Profit Margins for Standard & Poor's Industrial Index, 1960–1988

YEAR	NET INCOME	PERCENTAGE OF SALES	NBT[a]	PERCENTAGE OF SALES	DEPRECIATION EXPENSE	NBT[a] PLUS DEPRECIATION	PERCENTAGE OF SALES
1960	3.40	5.72	6.27	10.54	2.56	8.83	14.85
1961	3.37	5.66	6.17	10.37	2.66	8.83	14.84
1962	3.83	5.93	6.99	10.82	2.89	9.88	15.29
1963	4.24	6.19	7.75	11.31	3.04	10.79	15.75
1964	4.85	6.63	8.55	11.68	3.24	11.79	16.11
1965	5.50	6.82	9.64	11.95	3.52	13.16	16.31
1966	5.87	6.64	10.22	11.55	3.87	14.09	15.93
1967	5.62	6.12	9.73	10.59	4.25	13.98	15.22
1968	6.16	6.07	11.30	11.13	4.56	15.86	15.63
1969	6.13	5.65	11.27	10.38	4.87	16.14	14.87
1970	5.41	4.92	9.64	8.78	5.17	14.81	13.48
1971	5.97	5.05	10.95	9.26	5.45	16.40	13.87
1972	6.83	5.30	12.71	9.87	5.76	18.47	14.34
1973	8.89	5.96	16.48	11.04	6.25	22.73	15.23
1974	9.61	5.28	19.83	10.89	6.86	26.69	14.66
1975	8.58	4.63	17.98	9.71	7.36	25.34	13.69
1976	10.69	5.27	20.90	10.31	7.58	28.48	14.05
1977	11.45	5.11	22.59	10.07	8.53	31.12	13.88
1978	13.04	5.19	25.18	10.02	9.64	34.82	13.85
1979	16.29	5.57	30.31	10.37	10.82	41.13	14.07
1980	16.12	4.92	29.79	9.10	12.37	42.16	12.88
1981	16.74	4.86	29.69	8.62	13.82	43.51	12.64
1982	13.20	3.95	24.15	7.23	15.30	39.45	11.82
1983	14.77	4.42	26.89	8.05	15.67	42.56	12.74
1984	18.11	4.77	32.26	8.50	16.31	48.57	12.79
1985	15.28	3.84	28.96	7.27	18.19	47.15	11.83
1986	14.53	3.75	25.54	6.57	19.41	44.96	11.57
1987	20.29	4.70	34.55	8.00	20.17	54.72	12.67
1988	26.15	5.55	–	–	–	–	–
Mean	–	5.30	–	9.83	–	–	14.12
Standard deviation	–	0.82	–	1.40	–	–	1.22
Coefficient variation	–	0.15	–	0.14	–	–	0.09

[a] NBT = net before taxes

UTILIZATION RATE. The relationship between the utilization rate and the profit margin is quite straightforward. If production increases as a proportion of total capacity, there is a decrease in the fixed production costs per unit of output, and fixed financial costs per unit will likewise decline. Therefore, one should expect a positive relationship between the aggregate utilization rate and the aggregate profit margin. The relationship may not

TABLE 13.7
Variables Affecting Aggregate Profit Margin: Utilization Rate, Percentage Change in Compensation, Productivity, Unit Labor Cost, and Consumer Price Index: 1961–1988

YEAR	UTILIZATION RATE (MFG.)	COMPENSATION/ WORK HOURS[a] PERCENTAGE CHANGE	OUTPUT/WORK HOURS[a] PERCENTAGE CHANGE	UNIT LABOR COST[a] PERCENTAGE CHANGE	RATE OF INFLATION[b]
1961	77.3	3.3	3.1	5.1	0.7
1962	81.4	4.1	3.3	0.8	1.2
1963	83.5	3.5	3.6	−.1	1.6
1964	85.6	4.6	3.9	0.7	1.2
1965	89.5	3.4	2.5	0.8	1.9
1966	91.1	5.9	2.1	3.7	3.4
1967	86.7	5.5	2.3	3.2	3.0
1968	87.0	7.6	2.6	4.8	4.7
1969	86.7	6.6	−.5	7.1	6.1
1970	79.2	7.0	.3	6.7	5.5
1971	77.4	6.5	3.0	3.4	3.4
1972	82.8	6.5	3.1	3.4	3.4
1973	87.0	7.9	1.8	6.0	8.8
1974	82.6	9.6	−2.2	12.0	12.2
1975	72.3	9.7	1.8	7.8	7.0
1976	77.4	8.4	2.6	5.7	4.8
1977	81.4	7.7	1.6	6.1	6.8
1978	84.2	8.6	.8	7.7	9.0
1979	84.6	9.5	−1.6	11.2	13.3
1980	79.3	10.5	−.4	11.0	12.5
1981	78.2	9.4	1.0	8.3	8.9
1982	70.3	7.8	−.6	8.4	3.8
1983	73.9	4.3	3.3	1.0	3.8
1984	80.5	3.9	2.1	1.8	3.9
1985	80.1	4.2	1.4	2.8	3.8
1986	79.7	4.2	2.0	2.2	1.1
1987	81.0	3.8	.8	3.1	4.4
1988	83.0 (e)	4.6	1.3	3.2	4.4

[a] Private nonfarm business, 1977 = 1000. Source: Department of Labor, Bureau of Labor Statistics.
[b] Percentage Change (December to December) Consumer Price Index, All Items (1967 = 100).
Source: Federal Reserve Board Series, "Total Manufacturing," contained in *Economic Report of the President, 1988* (Washington, D.C.: U.S. Government Printing Office, 1989).

be completely linear at very high rates of utilization, because operating diseconomies are introduced as firms are forced to employ marginal labor and/or use older plant and equipment to reach the higher capacity. The figures in Table 13.7 indicate that capacity utilization reached a peak of over 91 percent in 1966 and a low point of less than 72 percent during the recession of 1982.

UNIT LABOR COST. The change in unit labor costs is a compound effect of two individual factors: (1) changes in wages per hour and (2) changes in worker productivity. Wage costs per hour typically increase every year by varying amounts depending upon the economic environment. The figures in Table 13.7 indicate that the annual percentage increase in wages varied from 3.4 percent to about 10.3 percent. If workers did not become more productive, this increase in per hour wage costs would be the increase in per unit labor cost. Fortunately, because of advances in technology and greater mechanization, the units of output produced by the individual laborer per hour have increased over time—the laborer has become more productive. If wages per hour increase by 5 percent and labor productivity increases by 5 percent, there would be no increase in unit labor costs, because the workers would offset the wage increase by producing more. Therefore, the increase in per unit labor cost is a function of the percentage change in hourly wages minus the increase in productivity during the period. The actual relationship is typically not this exact due to measurement problems, but it is quite close, as indicated by the figures in Table 13.7. During the period 1962–1965 productivity increased by about as much as the hourly compensation did, so there were very small changes in unit labor cost. In contrast, during 1974, wage rates increased by 9.6 percent, productivity actually declined by 2.2 percent because of the recession, and, therefore, unit labor costs increased by 12 percent. Because unit labor is the major variable cost of a firm, one would expect a negative relationship between the aggregate profit margin and percentage changes in unit labor cost.

INFLATION. The precise effect of inflation on the aggregate profit margin is unresolved. Finkel and Tuttle hypothesized a positive relationship between inflation and the aggregate profit margin for several reasons. First, it was contended that a higher level of inflation increases the ability of firms to pass increasing service costs on to the consumer and thereby raise their profit margin.[30] Second, assuming the classical demand-pull inflation, the increase in prices would indicate an increase in general economic activity, which is typically accompanied by higher margins. Finally, an increase in the rate of inflation might stimulate consumption as individuals attempt to shift their holdings from financial assets to real assets.

The contrasting view is espoused by those who doubt that most businesses can consistently increase prices in line with rising costs. Assume a 5 percent increase in the rate of inflation and that labor and material costs generally increase by this rate. The question is whether all firms are able to completely pass these cost increases along to their customers. If a firm increases prices at the same rate as cost increases, the result will be a *constant* profit margin, not an increase. Only if a firm can increase prices by more than the increase in costs can it increase its margin. Many

---

[30] This assumes either a wage lag or that the demand curve facing the firm is inelastic so that it can raise prices.

firms will probably not be able to raise prices in line with increased costs because of the elasticity of demand for their products.[31] In these cases, the profit margin will decline. Given the three alternatives, it is contended that most firms will not be able to increase their profit margins or even hold them constant. Since many firms will experience lower profit margins during periods of inflation, the aggregate profit margin will probably decline with an increase in the rate of inflation. Only empirical evidence will settle the arguments about how inflation has tended to affect the aggregate margin.

FOREIGN COMPETITION. Finkel and Tuttle contend that export markets are more competitive than domestic markets, and export sales are therefore made at a lower margin, which implies that a reduction in exports by the United States would have a positive effect on profit margins. In contrast, Gray believed that only exports made by two independent firms should be considered, and they should be examined relative to total output exported.[32] Further, he felt that imports could have an important negative impact on the margin because they influence the selling price of all competing domestic products. This latter impact has become a major factor during the 1980s when the U.S. trade balance has been very negative. Therefore, the ultimate effect of the trade surplus variable is likewise an empirical question.

UNEMPLOYMENT RATE. A case can be made for either a positive or negative relationship between this variable and the profit margin. On the one hand, a high rate of unemployment would indicate excess labor, small increases in unit labor cost, and thus a higher profit margin—that is, a positive relationship. In contrast, a high unemployment rate could indicate an economic recession, low capacity utilization, and a low profit margin—a negative relationship. The empirical results follow:[33]

- Trade surplus—negative and significant at 0.01 level
- Inflation—positive and significant at 0.05 level
- Utilization rate—positive and significant at 0.10 level
- Unit labor cost—negative and significant at 0.01 level
- Unemployment rate—not significant.

These results were derived using quarterly data for the period 1955–1967. When the model was used to estimate the aggregate margin from 1968 to 1970, there were insignificant differences between the estimates and actual results.

When Gray replicated Finkel and Tuttle's results with emphasis on the trade surplus, he found an insignificant negative coefficient for the trade

---

[31] An extreme example of this inability is regulated industries that may not be able to raise prices at all until after lengthy hearings before regulatory agencies. Even then, the increase in rates may not match the cost increases.

[32] H. Peter Gray, "Determinants of the Aggregate Profit Margin: A Comment," *Journal of Finance* 31, no. 1 (March 1976): 163–165.

[33] Finkel and Tuttle, "Determinants of the Aggregate Profits Margin."

surplus variable and significant positive correlation between the GNP deflator (the measure of inflation) and the unit labor cost variable.[34]

Some work by this author using annual data for the period 1947–1986 confirmed that the relationship between the profit margin and the utilization rate was always significant and positive. In contrast, the relationship between percentage changes in unit labor cost and the profit margin was always negative and significant. Finally, the inflation rate was never significant in the multiple regression, and the simple correlations between the profit margin and inflation were consistently negative.

There is consistent strong support for a positive relationship between profit margins and the utilization rate and also for a negative relation between the margin and unit labor cost. Unfortunately, it is not possible to derive an independent effect for inflation, but the simple correlation indicates a negative relationship. Finally, the effect of a trade surplus is unresolved at this point. Given the major changes that have occurred in this area since 1980, it is important to recognize that a lot of the data related to this is old and may be irrelevant. It is hoped that current and future research will develop further insights into the emerging relationship. Therefore, when estimating the gross profit margin, you should concentrate on the utilization rate for the economy and the rate of change in unit labor cost. You should also be aware of changes in the rate of inflation and the foreign trade environment, even though the empirical evidence concerning their effect has not been conclusive. It is the author's belief that future work will clarify and enforce the importance of these variables.

After estimating the gross profit margin, you can derive the dollar value of earnings before depreciation and taxes (EBDT) by applying this gross margin estimate to the previously estimated sales figure. The next step is to estimate aggregate depreciation.

ESTIMATING DEPRECIATION. As shown in Table 13.8, the depreciation series has not experienced a decline since 1960. (Actually it has not declined since 1946.) This is not too surprising, because depreciation expense is by definition a fixed cost related to the total amount of fixed assets in the economy (which increases over time). Therefore, the relevant question when estimating depreciation is not whether it will increase or decrease, but by *how much will it increase?*

You can use the recent absolute change or the recent percentage change as a guide to the future increase. Probably the biggest factor that could influence the depreciation expense series is capital expenditures during year $t - 1$ and $t - 2$, because with accelerated depreciation, these recent expenditures become dominant. The data in Table 13.8 indicate that the average percentage increase in depreciation expense has been about 8 percent, with reasonable variability in recent years. After you have estimated depreciation, you subtract it from the gross profit estimate to get an NBT estimate.

---

[34] Gray, "Determinants of the Aggregate Profit Margin: A Comment," *Journal of Finance* 31, no. 1 (March 1976): 163–165.

TABLE 13.8
Percentage Changes in Depreciation and Tax Rate
for S&P Industrial Index, 1960–1987

YEAR	DEPRECIATION	PERCENTAGE CHANGE	NBT[a]	INCOME TAXES	TAX RATE
1960	2.56		6.27	2.87	45.8
1961	2.66	3.9	6.17	2.80	45.4
1962	2.89	8.6	6.99	3.16	45.2
1963	3.04	5.2	7.75	3.51	45.3
1964	3.24	6.6	8.55	3.70	43.3
1965	3.52	8.6	9.64	4.14	42.9
1966	3.87	9.9	10.22	4.35	42.6
1967	4.25	9.8	9.73	4.11	42.2
1968	4.56	7.3	11.30	5.14	45.5
1969	4.87	6.8	11.27	5.14	45.6
1970	5.17	6.2	9.64	4.23	43.9
1971	5.45	5.4	10.95	4.98	45.5
1972	5.76	5.7	12.71	5.90	46.4
1973	6.25	8.5	16.48	7.59	46.1
1974	6.86	9.8	19.83	10.22	51.5
1975	7.36	7.3	17.98	9.40	52.3
1976	7.58	3.0	20.90	10.21	48.9
1977	8.53	12.5	22.59	11.14	49.3
1978	9.64	13.0	25.18	12.14	48.2
1979	10.82	12.2	30.31	14.02	46.3
1980	12.37	14.3	29.69	13.67	46.0
1981	13.82	11.7	29.69	12.95	43.6
1982	15.30	10.7	24.15	10.95	45.3
1983	15.67	2.4	26.89	12.12	45.1
1984	16.31	4.1	32.26	14.15	43.9
1985	18.19	11.5	28.96	13.68	47.2
1986	19.41	6.9	25.52	10.95	42.9
1987	20.17	3.9	34.55	14.07	40.7
Average	—	8.2	—	—	45.0

[a] NBT = net before taxes.
Source: *Standard and Poor's Analysts Handbook* (New York: Standard & Poor's Corp., 1988). Reprinted with permission.

EXPECTED TAX RATE. As shown in Table 13.8, the tax rate series was steady during the initial years, declined during 1964–1967, and returned to the 45–46 percent range in the early 1970s before increasing to over 50 percent in the mid 1970s. During the 1980s it has been in the mid 40 percent range.

Estimating the future tax rate is difficult, because it is heavily influenced by political action. It is necessary to consider the current tax rate but also to evaluate recent tax legislation affecting business firms (e.g., tax credits, etc.). This is very important because the 1986 Tax Reform Act will bring the rate below 40 percent for many firms. Given an estimate of the tax rate, 1 minus this figure times the NBT estimate indicates the estimated net income for industrial corporations. This earnings per share is subsequently used with an earnings multiplier to arrive at an estimate of the future value for the aggregate market.

A SAMPLE ESTIMATE

This attempt at estimating earnings per share for the year is best described as a casual example of the procedure. You should probably check the figures for accuracy as an exercise in data gathering. The major steps are as follows:

1. Estimate the nominal GNP for 1988.
2. Estimate sales for the S&P 400 Index based upon the GNP estimate.
3. Estimate the gross profit margin for the S&P series, that is, the profit margin before taxes and depreciation. This is based upon estimates of
   a. Utilization rate in 1988 versus 1987
   b. Percentage of change in unit labor cost
   c. Change in the rate of inflation in 1988 over 1987
   d. Foreign trade as a percentage of GNP
4. Estimate depreciation for 1988.
5. Estimate the average corporate tax rate for 1988.

Nominal GNP for 1988 is based upon 1987 GNP of approximately $4,530 billion. In 1988 the economy is in its sixth year of expansion, and most economists expect the real GNP to increase by almost 3 percent and inflation to be approximately 4 percent. Therefore, nominal GNP is estimated to increase by about 7 percent in 1988 to $4,847 billion.

Corporate sales have typically followed nominal GNP as shown in Figure 13.4. During 1987, when nominal GNP increased by about 6 percent, S&P sales rose by only about 1 percent to $392 per share. In 1988, with GNP rising 7 percent, the equation for the graph in Figure 13.4 implies an increase in sales of about 4.5 percent to almost $409 per share.

The gross profit margin (defined for our purposes as NBT and depreciation as a percent of sales) increased to about 13.9 percent in 1987, compared to 11.37 percent in 1986. This increase was a function of an increase in the utilization rate (81 percent in 1987 compared to 79.8 percent during 1986), and a lower rate of increase in unit labor cost (2.0 percent in 1987 versus 2.2 percent during 1986). For 1988 the outlook is for a small increase in the gross profit margin because of an increase in the utilization rate (to more than 84 percent) and a small increase in unit labor cost. Specifically, compensation per hour will increase, but productivity gains will be smaller this late in the business expansion. Therefore, the outlook is for a 3 percent increase in unit labor cost. Finally, the average rate of inflation will probably increase to about 4.5 percent. Therefore, the overall outlook is for a small increase in the gross profit margin from 13.9 percent in 1987 to 14.2 percent in 1988. Applying a 14.2 percent gross profit margin to the per share sales figure ($409) results in an NBT and depreciation of $58.08 (.142 × $409).

Depreciation during 1987 was approximately $20.50 per share. Because the utilization rate continues to increase, the outlook is for an increase in capital expenditures of about 4 percent during 1988 and, therefore, an increase in depreciation of 4 percent to $21.32. Thus the estimated net before taxes is $36.76 ($58.08 − $21.32).

The corporate tax rate during 1987 was slightly lower than during 1986 due to the initial effects of the 1986 Tax Reform Act. The effects of this act will be substantial in 1988 and should cause the rate to decline to about 34 percent from 41 percent in 1987. Applying a 34 percent rate to the NBT figure of $36.76 indicates that net income will be approximately $24.26 during 1988. Because the estimating procedure is admittedly casual, the figure used in future discussions is $24.30 a share.

ESTIMATING THE EARNINGS MULTIPLE FOR THE AGGREGATE STOCK MARKET

As indicated earlier, the multiple series is more volatile than the earnings series and also has a stronger relationship to the stock price series.[35] Therefore, you should consider the variables that influence the earnings multiple and attempt to project them.

The factors that influence the earnings multiple depend upon the earnings figure used. If the earnings multiple is being applied to the true *expected* earnings figure that takes into account all future earnings growth, then the earnings multiple is only a function of the required rate of return on the investment. In reality, investors typically apply an earnings multiple to earnings for the following year, so it is necessary to adjust the earnings multiple to consider long-run future growth expectations.

DETERMINANTS OF THE MARKET EARNINGS MULTIPLE

MULTIPLIER DETERMINANTS WITHOUT GROWTH. Assume that no growth opportunities exist or that all future growth expectations have been included in the expected earnings figure. Under these assumptions the earnings multiplier, given an infinite time horizon, becomes $1/k$, where k is the total required return on the investment. The multiplier is inversely related to the required rate of return; the higher the required rate of return an investor wants, the less he will pay for a specified earnings stream. Previously (in Chapters 1 and 10) we discussed the factors that determine the required rate of return on an investment: (1) the economy's risk-free rate (RFR); (2) the expected rate of inflation during the period of investment (I); and (3) the risk premium (RP) for the specific investment. You will recall that we combined the first two factors (the RFR and I) into a *nominal risk-free rate* that affects all investments.

Obviously the major factor causing changes in the nominal RFR is changes in the rate of inflation. Specifically, if there is a change in the rate

---

[35] For an extended analysis of this, see Frank K. Reilly and Eugene F. Drzycimski, "Aggregate Market Earnings Multiples over Stock Market Cycles and Business Cycles," *Mississippi Valley Journal of Business and Economics* 10, no. 2 (Winter 1974/75): 14–36.

of inflation, investors should increase their nominal required rate of return as follows:

$$\text{Nominal RFR} = (1 + \text{Real RFR})(1 + I) - 1.$$

As an example, if the real RFR were 3 percent, and you expected the rate of inflation during your period of investment to be 4 percent, your nominal required rate of return would be 7.12 percent.[36]

$$[1.03 \times 1.04] - 1.$$

A good proxy for the nominal RFR is the current promised yield to maturity of a government bond that has a maturity equal to your investment horizon. For example, if you had a short horizon, you could use the rate on Treasury bills, while you would use longer-term government bond rates if your horizon extended over several years.

The major factor causing differences in required return for alternative investments is the risk premium. When evaluating common stocks, consider the "normal" (historical) risk premium for stocks and then determine whether current conditions are such that the normal risk premium should prevail (we will discuss this further in a subsequent section). After estimating the current risk premium, consider whether the risk premium will change during the holding period.

In one study, Ibbotson and Sinquefield estimated the equity risk premium as the difference in annual rates of return from common stocks and Treasury bills.[37] The geometric mean of this risk premium for the period 1926–1987 was 6.2 percent; the arithmetic mean was 8.3 percent. The geometric mean is appropriate for long-run comparisons, while the arithmetic mean is what you want to use if you are estimating the premium for a given year, i.e., the expected performance in a given year. (This is discussed in the Ibbotson Yearbook.) Given this long-run historical estimate, it is possible to determine what the normal expected return should be by combining this premium with the nominal RFR. Suppose the current yield on government T-bills is 7 percent. If you consider the current equity-market environment to be normal, you would estimate that the current required return on common stock should be about 15 percent. Note that this 8 percent risk premium includes a maturity premium, since the comparison is to T-bills. Obviously, if the comparison were to longer-term government bonds, the risk premium would not be as large. This difference in the estimated risk premium is important, because there has been a substantial increase in the volatility of returns for long-term bonds.

Once you have derived a current estimate of the required rate of return, an important question is whether the expected rate of inflation or the risk premium on common stock will change during the investment horizon. In Chapters 1 and 10 we discussed the factors that influence the risk premium

---

[36] The appendix to this chapter contains an extensive discussion of common stocks and inflation.

[37] Roger G. Ibbotson and Rex A. Sinquefield, *Stocks, Bonds, Bills, and Inflation: The Past and The Future* (Charlottesville, Va.: Financial Analysts Research Foundation, 1982).

on investments from a fundamental point of view and also considered a market-derived risk variable. The intrinsic determinants of the risk premium were business risk (*BR*), financial risk (*FR*), liquidity risk (*LR*), and exchange rate risk (*ERR*). Alternatively, you can derive a market measure of risk that is the covariance of an asset with the market portfolio of risky assets. Because a stock market index is typically used as the market portfolio, the relevant measure of risk for the aggregate market is the variance of returns for stocks. Therefore, when there is a change in the variability of stock prices, one would expect a change in the risk premiums on stocks. This assumes that the variability of returns for T-bills is reasonably constant. If you are measuring your risk premium for common stock relative to a longer-term government bond, you could definitely have changes in this risk premium, either because common stocks experienced an increase or decrease in volatility *or* because long-term bonds experienced a change in volatility.

The required return on common stocks can therefore be stated as

$$k_{cs} = f(RFR, I, BR, FR, LR, ERR)$$
$$k_{cs} = f(RFR, I, \sigma_m^2) \, ,$$

where

k_{cs} = **the required return on common stocks**

RFR = **the economy's risk-free rate of return**

I = **the expected rate of inflation**

BR = **aggregate corporate business risk**

FR = **aggregate corporate financial risk**

LR = **aggregate stock market liquidity risk**

ERR = **the exchange rate risk when investing in non-U.S. stocks**

σ_m^2 = **market risk for common stocks measured as the variance of returns.**

MULTIPLE DETERMINANTS WITH GROWTH. In the more realistic situation in which the earning and dividend streams are growing, and/or investors do not fully adjust the expected earnings figure for all future growth, the earnings multiple must take into account the expected growth rate (*g*) for the common stock earnings stream.[38] There is a positive relationship between the earnings multiplier and the rate of growth; the higher the expected growth rate is, the higher the multiple. When estimating an earnings multiplier for the aggregate market, you must consider the expected rate

---

[38] You know that the *g* in the valuation model is the expected growth rate for dividends. In our discussion, we assume a relatively constant dividend-payout ratio (dividend/earnings), so the growth of dividends is dependent on the growth in earnings, and the growth rates are approximately equal.

of growth during the investment horizon period and estimate any changes in the rate. Such changes will indicate a change in the relationship between k and g and will have a profound effect on market value.

As discussed in Chapters 9 and 12, a firm's growth rate is (1) the proportion of earnings retained and reinvested by the firm (b) times (2) the rate of return earned on investments (ROE) (assuming an all-equity firm). The multiplier should be positively related to both of these variables, because an increase in either or both of them causes an increase in the expected growth rate and an increase in the multiplier. Therefore, the growth rate can be stated as

$$g = f(b, ROE),$$

where

g = **expected growth rate**

b = **the expected retention rate equal to** $1 - \dfrac{D}{E}$

ROE = **the expected return on equity investments.**

Because the multiplier (M) is a function of k and g, this can be summarized as

$$M = f(RFR, I, BR, FR, LR, ERR, b, ROE)$$

or

$$M = f(RFR, I, \sigma_m^2, b, ROE).$$

ESTIMATING CHANGES IN THE GROWTH RATE

When estimating changes in the growth rate, you should examine the basic factors that determine this rate—the retention rate (b) and the return on equity (ROE). Therefore, you must first estimate changes in the aggregate retention rate. The figures in Table 13.9 indicate that this series was relatively constant in the 45–50 percent range prior to 1972–1974, increased to around 56–60 percent until 1982, and has been averaging about 49 percent since then. Because the valuation model is a long-run model, you should consider only relatively permanent changes, although short-run changes can affect expectations.

The second variable of interest is changes in the return on equity (ROE) defined as

$$ROE = \frac{\text{Net Income}}{\text{Equity}}.$$

TABLE 13.9
Factors Influencing Aggregate Growth Rate of Corporate Earnings per Share for Standard & Poor's 400 Index, 1960–1987

YEAR	DIVIDEND PER SHARE	PERCENTAGE CHANGE	RETENTION RATE	EQUITY TURNOVER	NET PROFIT MARGIN	RETURN ON EQUITY
1960	2.00		41.2	1.76	5.72	10.00
1961	2.07	3.5	38.6	1.71	5.66	9.67
1962	2.20	6.3	42.6	1.78	5.93	10.53
1963	2.36	7.3	44.3	1.79	6.19	11.11
1964	2.58	9.3	46.8	1.82	6.63	12.06
1965	2.82	9.3	48.7	1.85	6.82	12.64
1966	2.95	4.6	49.7	1.94	6.64	12.88
1967	2.97	0.7	47.1	1.92	6.12	11.76
1968	3.16	6.4	48.7	2.02	6.07	12.27
1969	3.25	2.8	47.0	2.10	5.65	11.86
1970	3.20	−1.5	41.8	2.09	4.92	10.28
1971	3.16	−1.2	47.1	2.14	5.04	10.80
1972	3.22	1.9	52.9	2.21	5.30	11.71
1973	3.46	7.5	61.1	2.37	5.96	14.15
1974	3.71	7.2	61.4	2.69	5.28	14.17
1975	3.72	0.3	56.6	2.61	4.63	12.11
1976	4.22	13.4	60.5	2.66	5.27	14.02
1977	4.95	17.3	56.8	2.73	5.11	13.93
1978	5.37	8.5	58.8	2.81	5.19	14.60
1979	5.92	10.2	63.7	2.96	5.57	16.50
1980	6.49	9.6	59.7	3.02	4.92	14.88
1981	7.01	8.0	58.1	2.97	4.86	14.42
1982	7.13	1.7	45.9	2.82	3.95	11.13
1983	7.37	3.4	50.0	2.75	4.40	12.15
1984	7.51	2.6	58.5	3.06	4.77	14.61
1985	7.87	4.8	48.5	3.16	3.84	12.14
1986	8.15	3.6	44.1	3.12	3.75	11.70
1987	8.78	7.7	57.1	2.57	4.74	12.18
Average	—	5.7	51.3	2.41	5.32	12.51

Source: *Standard and Poor's Analysts Handbook* (New York: Standard & Poor's Corp., 1988). Reprinted with permission.

You will recall from the discussion in Chapter 12 that ROE can be broken down as follows:

$$\frac{\text{Net Income}}{\text{Equity}} = \frac{\text{Sales}}{\text{Equity}} \times \frac{\text{Net Income}}{\text{Sales}}$$

$$(\text{ROE}) = \left(\frac{\text{Equity}}{\text{Turnover}}\right) \times \left(\begin{array}{c}\text{Net Profit}\\\text{Margin}\end{array}\right)$$

or

$$= \frac{\text{Sales}}{\text{Total Assets}} \times \frac{\text{Total Assets}}{\text{Equity}} \times \frac{\text{Net Income}}{\text{Sales}}$$

$$= \left(\begin{matrix}\text{Total Asset} \\ \text{Turnover}\end{matrix}\right) \times \left(\begin{matrix}\text{Financial} \\ \text{Leverage}\end{matrix}\right) \times \left(\begin{matrix}\text{Net Profit} \\ \text{Margin}\end{matrix}\right).$$

The figures in Table 13.9 indicate that the aggregate return on equity for the S&P 400 index increased from about 10 percent in 1960 to almost 17 percent in 1979. Next there was a decline in 1982 to about 11 percent, followed by overall declines to 11–12 percent in 1986. Note that the increase that occurred from 1960 to 1979 was completely attributable to the increase in the equity turnover from about 1.7 in 1960 to a little over 3.0 in 1986. This higher turnover more than offset the overall decline in the net profit margin during this period. Clearly, you would want to know what caused the increases in equity turnover and whether the increases can continue. Thus, you would examine the second set of equations that include a breakdown of equity turnover.

This identity indicates that it is possible to increase the equity turnover by increasing the total asset turnover and/or by increasing financial leverage. Because the S&P 400 series does not include information on total assets, it is not possible to examine this breakdown of equity turnover. An alternative is to examine the breakdown for the *Fortune* 500, which does exist.[39] As shown in Table 13.10, and Figure 13.5, the profit margin for this series has declined over time similar to the S&P 400. Also similar, as shown in Figure 13.6, this decline has been offset by a fairly steady increase in equity turnover (that peaked in 1980). Note that the graphs in Figure 13.7 indicate that the major variable driving the increase in equity turnover has been the *leverage ratio,* since the total asset turnover ratio increased in the late 1970s but ended lower in 1987 than it started in 1960.

SUMMARY OF MICROECONOMIC MULTIPLE ESTIMATE. An estimate of the market earnings multiple is begun with the current multiple and the direction, and extent of the change is estimated based on expectations for the variables that influence the aggregate k and g. The direction of the change is probably more important than the extent of it. The overall estimate requires that an estimate be derived for each of the following component variables:

1. Dividend-payout ratio defined as dividend/earnings
2. Real RFR
3. Expected rate of inflation
4. Risk premium for common stock
5. Retention rate
6. Return on equity:
   a. Net profit margin
   b. Equity turnover

---

[39] These two series are very comparable in sample and results. Almost all of the companies in the S&P 400 are in the *Fortune* 500, and the specific data are extremely similar.

TABLE 13.10
Return on Equity Components for *Fortune* 500 Industrials

YEAR	ASSET TURNOVER	ASSETS TO EQUITY	EQUITY TURNOVER	PROFIT MARGIN (%)	RETURN ON EQUITY (%)
1960	1.16	1.53	1.77	5.7	10.1
1961	1.12	1.54	1.72	5.5	9.6
1962	1.16	1.55	1.80	5.9	10.6
1963	1.17	1.56	1.83	6.0	11.1
1964	1.19	1.58	1.88	6.5	12.1
1965	1.18	1.63	1.92	6.7	13.0
1966	1.18	1.69	1.99	6.6	13.2
1967	1.13	1.74	1.97	6.0	11.8
1968	1.12	1.82	2.04	6.0	12.2
1969	1.11	1.87	2.08	5.6	11.5
1970	1.07	1.90	2.03	4.7	9.6
1971	1.10	1.90	2.09	4.7	9.8
1972	1.15	1.90	2.19	5.0	10.9
1973	1.20	1.96	2.35	5.8	13.7
1974	1.33	2.03	2.70	5.2	14.1
1975	1.29	2.02	2.61	4.4	11.4
1976	1.32	2.01	2.65	5.1	13.5
1977	1.35	2.04	2.75	4.8	13.3
1978	1.36	2.08	2.83	5.0	14.2
1979	1.40	2.14	3.00	5.4	16.1
1980	1.40	2.17	3.04	4.9	15.0
1981	1.38	2.18	3.01	4.7	14.3
1982	1.28	2.18	2.79	3.7	10.2
1983	1.25	2.14	2.68	4.1	10.9
1984	1.25	2.21	2.76	4.9	13.6
1985	1.19	2.27	2.70	3.9	10.4
1986	1.10	2.42	2.66	3.8	10.1
1987	1.10	2.49	2.74	4.8	13.2
1988	0.97	2.98	2.90	5.7	16.5

As noted, in addition to estimating the level for each of these variables, the important thing to forecast is what changes will occur during the investment period.

EMPIRICAL ANALYSIS OF DETERMINANTS

A study by Reilly, Griggs, and Wong specified empirical proxies for the several variables discussed here and analyzed the relationship.[40] The earnings multiple series employed was the price-earnings (P/E) ratio for the S&P 400 series. The authors considered the following independent variables: a dividend-payout ratio for the S&P 400, the average yield on AAA

---

[40] Frank K. Reilly, Frank T. Griggs, and Wenchi Wong, "Determinants of the Aggregate Stock Market Earnings Multiple," *Journal of Portfolio Management* 10, no. 1 (Fall 1983): 36–45.

FIGURE 13.5
Time Series Plot of Net Profit Margin for *Fortune* 500 Industrials, 1960–1987

corporate bonds adjusted for inflation, and the rate of inflation as a separate variable. As a measure of business risk, they included a 20-quarter moving coefficient of variation series of net income (a measure of business risk) and three financial risk proxies: (1) a current ratio series from the *Federal Reserve Bulletin,* (2) the failure rate per 10,000 U.S. firms, and (3) a debt-equity ratio series published by the Federal Trade Commission (FTC). The risk premium was measured using the absolute and percentage yield spread between BBB corporate bonds and AAA corporate bonds. S&P earnings per share growth during one-, three-, and five-year periods was included similar to several previous studies of individual firm P/E ratios.[41] The model considered percentage changes for all variables, since the major concern was what variables influenced changes in the earnings multiple.

The authors considered a coincident relationship among the variables and also a lagged model that considered the independent variables in

[41] Burton Malkiel, "Equity Yields, Growth, and the Structure of Share Prices," *American Economic Review* 53, no. 5 (December 1963): 834–850; and Burton Malkiel and John Cragg, "Expectations and the Structure of Share Prices," *American Economic Review* 60, no. 4 (September 1970): 601–617.

Figure 13.6
Time Series Plot of Equity Turnover Ratio for *Fortune* 500 Industrials, 1960–1987

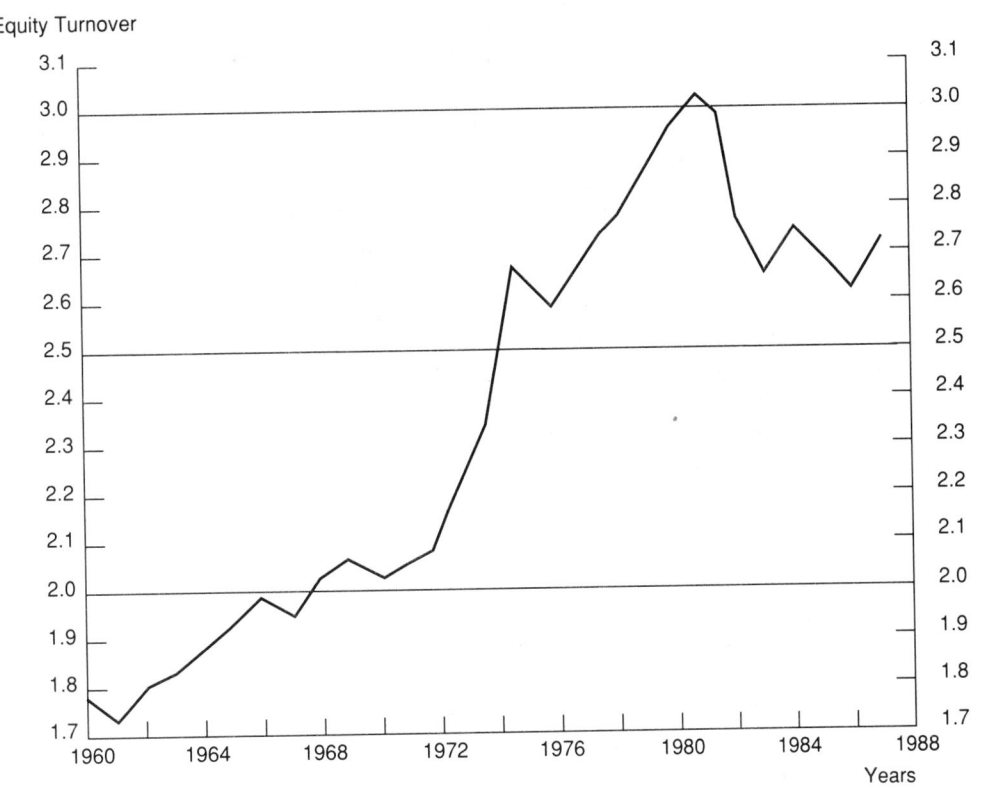

period $t-1$, since it is useful for predictive purposes. The lagged regression model had an R^2 of 0.25, and five variables had significant coefficients at the 10 percent level or better: (1) one-year growth, (2) payout ratio, (3) real RFR, (4) inflation, and (5) failure rate. All coefficients had the expected sign except the failure rate. The results were similar with a *multiple discriminant analysis model (MDA)*. The lagged model (with the coefficient of variability of earnings and the debt-equity ratio added) predicted the direction of change for the earnings multiple during 24 of 32 quarters. (The best MDA model had 23 of 32.) When this predictive model was used to make investment decisions (i.e., buy stocks or T-bills) compared to a buy-and-hold portfolio, the results were clearly superior after commissions: a 9.83 percent annual rate of return for the predicting model versus 1.85 percent for the buy-and-hold strategy. The standard deviation for the predictive model portfolio was lower. Therefore, it appears that it is possible to specify macroeconomic variables that influence changes in the aggregate stock market earnings multiple.

FIGURE 13.7

Time Series Plots of Asset Turnover and Leverage Ratio for _Fortune_ 500 Industrials, 1960–1987

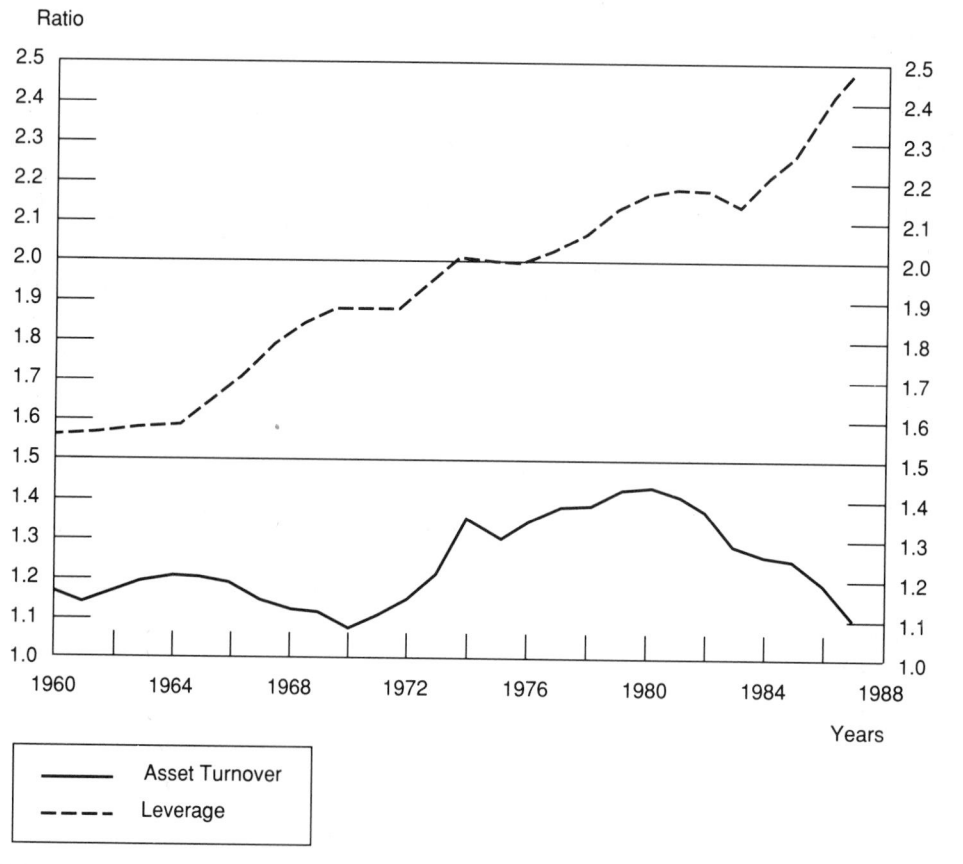

ESTIMATING THE MULTIPLE. Two approaches are possible, therefore, to estimate an aggregate stock market earnings multiple: (1) a macro approach using the variables suggested in the Reilly, Griggs, and Wong study and (2) a micro approach in which you consider the specific variables that influence _k_ and _g_ and attempt to estimate whether the spread between the two will increase or decline in the future.

You should begin with the current multiple and estimate the direction and extent of the change for the macro or micro variables that influence the aggregate _k_ and _g_. The direction of the change is probably more important than the extent of the change.

THE MACRO APPROACH. The major variables that must be estimated in the macro approach are

1. Changes in the growth rate of earnings
2. Changes in the dividend-payout ratio

3. Changes in the real RFR as represented by a high-grade corporate bond series
4. Changes in the rate of inflation
5. Changes in the failure rate for U.S. corporations

During 1988 the economy is in its sixth full year of an expansion, so some of the changes will be adverse relative to 1987. Earnings will experience reasonable growth as discussed earlier. Possibly the increase in dividend payments will not exceed the earnings gain, which means the dividend-payout ratio will decline. The real RFR will be under some downward pressure due to lower productivity. As discussed earlier, the rate of inflation will likely be up slightly in 1988. Finally, the failure rate should stabilize following the increase in 1987. In summary:

- The one-year growth rate will stabilize relative to 1987.
- The dividend-payout ratio will decrease.
- The real RFR will decline slightly.
- The inflation rate will increase.
- The failure rate will stabilize.

Overall, the consensus would be for a decline in the earnings multiple relative to that which prevailed at the end of 1987. Obviously it will be lower than the very high P/E ratios attained during 1987 prior to the crash (the market earnings multiple ranged from 19 to 21 during the summer of 1987). Therefore, assuming a multiple of about 14 at the end of 1987, one might expect the multiple at the end of 1988 to be about 12.

THE MICRO APPROACH. The major variables that must be estimated in the micro approach are

1. Changes in the dividend-payout ratio
2. Changes in the real RFR
3. Changes in the market risk premium
4. Changes in the rate of inflation
5. Changes in the retention rate
6. Changes in the return on equity.

As indicated in the macro discussion, the dividend-payout ratio will probably be slightly lower. The next three variables deal with the required rate of return. As discussed, there will be a decline in the real RFR due to lower real growth, while the rate of inflation will increase slightly. Finally, the risk premium should increase during this phase of the business cycle and also because of the higher stock price volatility after the October crash. Therefore, there should be an increase in k during 1988.

The last two factors relate to the growth rate. Because we expect a decline in the payout rate, this implies an increase in the retention rate. The most likely outlook is for stability in the ROE during 1988, since it is a function of the profit margin and equity turnover. We have already indicated that the profit margin in 1988 will increase slightly relative to 1987. One might expect a lower equity turnover ratio because of a decline in total asset turnover and a small increase in the financial leverage ratio. Therefore, this scenario would imply very little change in the growth rate.[42] In summary we expect

- A decrease in the payout ratio
- An increase in the required return, k
- No change in the growth rate.

Overall, this would imply a lower earnings multiple, which is consistent with the macro estimate. Based upon these expectations, consider the following estimate using the dividend-growth model version of the multiple:

$$P/E = \frac{D/E}{k - g}.$$

As indicated earlier, the retention rate has fluctuated between 45 and 60 percent during the past ten years. Therefore, a reasonable dividend-payout ratio (D/E) would be 48 percent. The required return (k) can be estimated from knowledge of the interest rate on government bonds plus an estimate of the risk premium for common stocks. The actual risk premium used is a function of which government securities are used as the base. If it is T-bills, the premium should be something close to the long-run historical risk premium of 8 percent. In contrast, if you use the rate on intermediate or long-term government bonds, you might want to consider a smaller risk premium to reflect the increase in return volatility for these bonds relative to common stocks. The point is, an appropriate risk premium could range from 3 percent to 8 percent, depending upon the government security used to estimate a nominal risk-free rate. The 8 percent is the long-term arithmetic average risk premium, as indicated by the Ibbotson-Sinquefield studies for the period 1926–1987 using T-bills as the risk-free instrument. Notably, during the recent period (1975–1987), the risk premium has been more in the range of 2.5–3.5 percent. Alternatively, Goldman Sachs & Co. has used a version of this dividend model and assumed a 2.5 percent risk premium for stocks relative to five-year government bonds. The reason for the lower premium is that it is relative to longer-term bonds, which have become more volatile since 1980–1981. Thus, even if common stock returns are not more volatile, bond returns are, so you should reduce your premium relative to this base rate.[43] Alternatively, if you are using T-bills, it is probably still appropriate to use 8 percent. As of early 1988 the rate on T-bills was about 6 percent, the rate on five-year government bonds was about 8 percent, and the rate on long-term bonds was 9.5 percent. Therefore, you could conceive of the following possibilities:

---

[42] While this is the most reasonable scenario given the economic environment, it is necessary to be aware of changes occurring to aggregate common equity due to asset write-offs and especially share repurchases. Both of these events will cause a decline in the equity account that may result in a higher ROE simply because of a lower equity value.

[43] See *Investment Strategy Highlights,* published monthly by Goldman Sachs & Co. The author also benefited from discussions with Steven G. Einhorn, co-chairman of the Investment Policy Committee.

A. T-bills   6.0%
    Historical Risk Premium   8.0
           Estimated k 14.0%
B. Five-Year Government Bonds   8.0%
    Goldman Sachs Premium   2.5
           Estimated k 10.5%
C. Long-Term Government
    Bonds   9.5%
    Medium Risk Premium   4.0
           Estimated k 13.5%

Therefore, the required return (k) could be in the range of 10–14 percent.

The estimate of growth should be based upon the current and expected return on equity (ROE) and the rate of retention. As shown by the data in Table 13.9, the ROE for the Standard & Poor's 400 was in the 11–14 percent range during the period 1981–1986. Assuming that 1988 is the end of an economic expansion, a range of 11–12 percent seems appropriate. As indicated earlier, the retention rate has been between 45 and 60 percent. Therefore, a lower growth rate figure would combine the 45 percent retention rate and an ROE of 10 percent: $.45 \times .11 = .0495$ (.05). An upper growth rate estimate would combine the 60 percent retention rate and a 12 percent ROE: $.60 \times .12 = .072$. To summarize:

- $D/E =$ $.40 - .55$
- Government securities $.06 - .095$
- Equity risk premium $.025$ to $.08$
- Required return (k) $.10 - .14$
- ROE $.10 - .12$
- Sustainable growth $.05 - .072$.

By combining the most optimistic figures we can derive a reasonably generous estimate. Alternatively, we can derive a relatively low estimate using the conservative estimates. Notably, the D/E figure should be consistent with the retention rate.

High estimate: $D/E = .40$
$k = .10$
$g = .072$

$$P/E = \frac{.40}{.10 - .072} = \frac{.40}{.028} = 14.29.$$

If we had used a payout of .45, it would have been

$$\frac{.45}{.028} = 16.07$$

Low estimate: $D/E = .55$
$k = .14$
$g = .045$

$$P/E = \frac{.55}{.14 - .05} = \frac{.55}{.09} = 6.11.$$

Therefore, these data imply a fairly wide range of earning multiples from about 6.1 to 16. A range of 8–14 would be consistent with that derived from the macro approach.

PUTTING IT TOGETHER. Previously, we derived an estimate of earnings per share for the Standard & Poor's 400 of $24.30. Clearly, it would have been possible to derive several additional earning estimates in addition to this point estimate.

Our prior discussion has generated several estimates for the price/earnings multiple that vary from about 6 to 16. Combining the most likely values indicates the following estimates for the Standard & Poor's 400 market series:

$$8 \times 24.30 = 194.40$$
$$12 \times 24.30 = 291.60$$
$$16 \times 24.30 = 388.80$$

These estimates are intended to help you understand the procedure. The estimation of the relevant variables was very casual and certainly not as extensive as one would like in practice. In addition, this was a point estimate for earnings rather than a range of estimates (pessimistic, optimistic, most likely), which would have been preferable in this instance. The important point, however, is to understand what the relevant variables are and how they relate to either corporate earnings or the earnings multiple.

THE GOLDMAN SACHS MODEL

In contrast to the perpetual dividend growth model, Goldman Sachs has employed a model that includes current dividends plus a growth component that considers the relationship between the ROE and the current required rate of return. The model is specified as follows (using the notation employed in this book):

$$P = \frac{Div}{k} + \frac{\left[\frac{ROE}{k}\right]\left[(Earn.)(b)\right]}{k/(1+g)},$$

where

b = the rate of earnings retention.

It is contended that the value of securities consists of two components: (1) the discounted value of a perpetual dividend stream, and (2) the contribution of value from the profitable retention of earnings that will be invested to generate future dividends (i.e., the growth component).[44] Therefore, the second term reflects the ratio of what the firm can earn in

---

[44] This concept of a two-part valuation model is similar to what is set forth in the growth models discussed in Chapter 15. This discussion draws heavily from Goldman Sachs & Co.'s *Investment Strategy Highlights,* a monthly publication.

investments (ROE), to the required rate of return (k) and applies this excess ratio to the dollar amount of investment (the retained earnings). This retained earnings value adjusted for above average returns is discounted by the firm's required rate of return modified by the growth rate of earnings. Consider the following example:

- Earnings $20.00/share
- Payout rate 0.45
- k 0.10
- ROE   0.145
- g 0.08 (.55 × .145)

$$P = \frac{Div}{k} + \frac{\dfrac{ROE}{k}(Earn. \times b)}{k/(1 + g)}$$

$$= \frac{9.00}{.10} + \frac{\dfrac{.145}{.100}(20.00 \times .55)}{.10/1.08}$$

$$= \$90.00 + \frac{(1.45)(11.00)}{.0925}$$

$$= \$90.00 + \frac{15.95}{.0925}$$

$$= \$90.00 + \$172.43$$
$$= \$262.43.$$

This value is clearly lower than the value that would be derived from the basic dividend growth valuation model as follows:

$$P = \frac{D_1}{k - g}$$

$$= \frac{9.00}{.10 - .08}$$

$$= \frac{9.00}{.02} = \$450.00.$$

ANALYSIS OF WORLD MARKETS

While we have used the U.S. market to demonstrate the procedure for analyzing the aggregate stock market, it is necessary to consider a similar analysis for numerous non-U.S. markets and for at least several of the major world markets—Japan, Canada, United Kingdom, and West Germany. While it is not feasible to carry out a detailed analysis of each of these markets, we can provide an example of the extensive analysis by a major investment firm. Specifically, Goldman Sachs & Co. provides a monthly publication entitled, "World Investment Strategy Highlights" as part of its international research effort. This particular publication draws on a number of other Goldman Sachs publications to derive an overall world portfolio strategy as well as a strategy for investors in a number of individual countries.[45]

Overall, it is a top-down approach wherein the firm initially examines a country's aggregate economy and its components that relate to the valuation of securities—GNP, capital investments, industrial production, inflation, and interest rates. Table 13.11 contains the firm's forecast of economic activity for several of the major countries. Note the fairly substantial difference in outlook for GNP/GDP growth during 1988 (e.g., 2.6 percent for France and 5.5 percent for Japan) and for growth in industrial production (e.g., 2.0 percent for Germany versus 9.7 percent for Japan). Obviously, the outlook for several countries (including the United States) is a flat economy or worse, while Japan is expected to experience substantial growth as it emerges from a recession.

INFLATION AND EXCHANGE RATES. The firm also considers historical and expected price changes as shown in Table 13.12. Again, there are major differences in the outlook for inflation, ranging from 1.4 percent for Germany to 4.5 percent for the U.S. and Canada. This feeds into an interest rate forecast in Table 13.13 for the end of 1988 and mid 1989 to show the trend in rates. Except for France and Switzerland, the trend for interest rates is up, and the ending values range from 4.0 percent for Switzerland to 10.7 percent for Canada. Given these differences in the level of inflation and interest rates and also the different trends, you can envision that there will be major differences in the exchange rates during 1988. Table 13.14 presents the firm's forecast for the exchange rates for several currencies, for six months and also for twelve months, which implies an expected trend during the year. These figures indicate that Goldman Sachs expects the United States to improve against most other currencies during 1988.

Given this background related to the underlying economies, Table 13.15 contains the corporate earnings growth rates and ROE for the various countries along with other specific stock market expectations, including dividend growth, price/earnings, price-cash flow, and price-book value. Again, there are major differences in all series. Specifically, the earnings growth rates vary from almost no growth for West Germany and Denmark, very little growth for Canada, the Netherlands, and the United States, and substantial growth for Japan and France. Likewise, the price/earnings ratio has varied historically and is expected to differ in 1988 from about 7 times (Sweden) to 54 times for Japan (down from 66 times in 1986).

---

[45] The other Goldman Sachs publications used include *The International Economics Analyst, World Markets Monthly, Investment Strategy Highlights, Japan Investment Strategy Highlights,* and *The U.K. Economics Analyst.* The author benefited from conversations with Jeffrey M. Weingarten, director of international equity research for Goldman Sachs.

TABLE 13.11
Forecasts for World Economic Activity: Percentage per Year

COUNTRY	1986	1987	1988E
United States			
Cons. expenditure	4.2	1.9	1.7
Business fixed invest.	−2.3	1.0	6.9
GNP	2.9	2.9	3.0
Industrial production	2.2	4.3	4.9
Japan			
Cons. expenditure	3.2	3.9	4.5
Business fixed invest.	6.2	8.2	12.2
Domestic demand	4.0	5.1	6.8
GNP	2.5	4.2	5.5
Industrial production	−0.3	3.3	9.7
Germany			
Cons. expenditure	4.3	3.1	3.7
Fixed investment	3.1	1.7	2.1
Domestic demand	3.7	2.9	3.8
GNP	2.5	1.7	2.6
Industrial production	2.0	0.3	2.0
United Kingdom			
Cons. expenditure	5.8	5.2	4.9
Fixed investment	0.3	3.5	6.7
GDP	3.0	4.4	3.6
Industrial production	1.9	3.1	2.1
France			
GDP	2.5	2.2	2.6
Industrial production	0.9	1.3	2.4
Switzerland			
GDP	3.2	2.1	1.7
Industrial production	3.5	2.0	1.5
Canada			
GDP	3.4	4.0	3.9
Industrial production	0.4	4.5	6.0

Source: "World Investment Strategy Highlights" (London: Goldman, Sachs International Corp., July/August 1988). Reprinted with permission from Goldman, Sachs & Co.

CORRELATIONS AMONG RETURNS. These substantial differences and changes in the underlying valuation variables should help you to understand why there are fairly low correlations among stock market returns for alternative countries. The correlation matrix for several of the major countries contained in Table 13.16 shows a fairly high correlation between the United States and Canada and one of the lowest relationships between the United States and Japan, although this latter correlation has been increasing in recent years as our economies have become more interdependent. It is this type of matrix that is used to justify and encourage worldwide diversification of investments. Note that the monthly returns

TABLE 13.12
Consumer or Retail Prices

PERIOD	USA	CANADA	JAPAN	GERMANY	FRANCE	UK	MAJOR[a] EUROPE	MAJOR[b] OECD
1985	3.6	4.0	2.0	2.2	5.8	6.1	5.2	3.8
1986	1.9	4.1	0.6	-0.2	2.5	3.4	2.5	1.8
1987	3.7	4.0	0.1	0.3	3.3	4.1	2.8	2.8
1988	4.2	3.9	0.8	1.1	2.7	3.6	2.8	3.1
1989	4.5	3.8	2.9	1.4	2.5	4.3	3.1	3.8
1986 Q4	1.3 *2.6*	4.5 *3.9*	-0.2 *0.0*	-1.1 *-1.6*	2.1 *2.7*	3.4 *5.0*	1.9 *2.2*	1.2 *2.0*
1987 Q1	2.2 *5.3*	4.0 *3.8*	-0.9 *-2.4*	-0.5 *1.0*	3.2 *4.7*	3.9 *4.9*	2.4 *3.7*	1.7 *3.4*
Q2	3.8 *4.9*	4.6 *5.5*	0.2 *5.3*	0.2 *1.3*	3.4 *3.7*	4.2 *6.5*	2.7 *3.7*	2.8 *4.5*
Q3	4.2 *4.0*	4.6 *4.7*	0.5 *-0.8*	0.5 *1.3*	3.4 *2.4*	4.3 *0.8*	2.9 *2.0*	3.1 *2.5*
Q4	4.5 *3.9*	4.4 *3.6*	0.7 *0.8*	1.0 *0.3*	3.3 *2.4*	4.0 *4.0*	3.1 *3.0*	3.4 *3.0*
1988 Q1	4.2 *4.1*	4.6 *4.0*	1.2 *-0.4*	1.0 *1.0*	2.6 *1.9*	3.2 *1.6*	2.5 *1.5*	3.1 *2.4*
Q2	4.1 *4.4*	4.0 *3.2*	1.4 *6.1*	0.9 *1.0*	2.2 *2.1*	3.6 *8.0*	2.6 *3.8*	3.1 *4.5*
Q3	4.2 *4.4*	3.7 *3.6*	1.8 *0.8*	0.8 *1.0*	2.2 *2.4*	3.9 *2.3*	2.7 *2.7*	3.3 *3.2*
Q4	4.2 *3.9*	3.3 *4.0*	1.7 *0.4*	1.1 *1.3*	2.1 *1.9*	4.0 *4.2*	2.8 *3.0*	3.3 *3.0*

Note: Percent changes on a year earlier; figures in italics are quarter-on-previous quarter annualized
[a] Germany, France, Italy, U.K.
[b] Major Europe plus USA, Canada, and Japan.
Source: "World Investment Strategy Highlights" (London: Goldman, Sachs International Corp., July/August 1988). Reprinted with permission from Goldman, Sachs & Co.

TABLE 13.13
Interest Rate Forecasts: Percentage per Year

COUNTRY	CURRENT RATE	END 1988	MID 1989
United States			
Discount rate	6.0	6.5	6.5
Prime rate	9.0	9.5	9.5
Federal funds	7.3	8.0	8.5
Long bond	9.1	10.0	10.5
Japan			
Discount rate	2.5	3.0	3.0
3-Mo. CD	4.4	4.7	5.3
Long bond	4.6	5.1	5.0
Germany			
Discount rate	2.5	3.0	3.5
Lombard rate	4.5	5.0	5.5
3M money market	3.6	4.1	4.5
Long bond	6.5	7.0	6.8
United Kingdom			
Banks' base rate	8.5	9.0	9.5
3M inter-bank	8.5	9.4	9.5
Long bond	9.5	9.5	9.5
France			
3M money market	7.6	7.5	8.0
Long bond	9.0	8.2	8.5
Switzerland			
Discount rate	3.0	3.0	3.5
3M Euro-SFr	2.9	3.0	3.5
Long bond	4.2	4.2	4.0
Canada			
Prime rate	10.8	10.8	10.5
3M Euro-C$	9.3	9.3	8.6
Long bond	10.0	10.7	10.7

Source: "World Investment Strategy Highlights" (London: Goldman, Sachs International Corp., July/August 1988). Reprinted with permission from Goldman, Sachs & Co.

are in local currencies, so they are not impacted by exchange rate changes over time.

INDIVIDUAL COUNTRY STOCK PRICE CHANGES. The impact of exchange rates is shown in Table 13.17, where the percentage changes in stock prices are set forth in the local currency and also adjusted for the U.S. dollar. The percentage changes of stock prices in local currency indicate the returns to citizens of the country. The annual averages for 1981–1987 range from minus 7.5 percent (Switzerland) to 129 percent (Mexico). The percent change of stock prices in U.S. dollars indicates the returns that would have

TABLE 13.14
Forecast Exchange Rates

	US$	C$	¥	£	DM	FFR	SFR	TRADE-WEIGHTED
Against US$								**US$**
6 mth	—	1.18	115	0.51	1.66	5.73	1.36	89
12 mth	—	1.24	120	0.54	1.70	5.98	1.39	90
Against £								**£**
6 mth	1.95	2.30	224	—	3.23	11.17	2.65	81
12 mth	1.85	2.29	222	—	3.14	11.06	2.57	77
Against DM								**DM**
6 mth	0.60	0.71	69.3	0.31	—	3.45	0.82	152
12 mth	0.59	0.73	70.6	0.32	—	3.52	0.82	152
Against ¥								**¥**
6 mth	115	97.5	—	224	69.3	20.0	84.6	262
12 mth	120	96.8	—	222	70.6	20.0	86.3	257

Source: "World Investment Strategy Highlights" (London: Goldman, Sachs International Corp., July/August 1988). Reprinted with permission from Goldman, Sachs & Co.

been experienced by a U.S. investor who invested in each of these countries. In this case, the changes range from minus 4 percent (Malaysia) to 32 percent (Japan). The significant impact of changes in the exchange rate can be derived from a couple of examples. While the rate of change in Japanese stock prices during 1987 was 8.5 percent, the change experienced by a U.S. citizen who invested in Japan during 1987 would have been 41.4 percent because of the significant strength of the yen relative to the dollar. This implied increase in the rate of return due to the exchange rate change relative to the U.S. dollar was fairly widespread during 1987. In contrast, during 1982 the U.S. dollar was quite strong, and most stock price changes were lower when denominated in U.S. dollars—for example, the change was minus 18.5 percent in Australian local currency but minus 29 percent in U.S. dollars.

INDIVIDUAL COUNTRY ANALYSIS. Following the historical description of rates of return, Goldman Sachs provides a detailed analysis of each of the major countries. This analysis proceeds from the local economy to the country's equity market, and culminates in a portfolio recommendation for investors in that economy. Table 13.18 contains an example of the major economic indicators for Japan. As noted earlier, these projections reflect the strong economic recovery of Japan coming out of its 1984 recession, which was affected by the decline in exports.

Following the economic projections, there is an analysis of the country's equity market. A summary for the United Kingdom is set forth in Table 13.19. Goldman Sachs feels that the overall economic outlook for the U.K. is moderate. In terms of investments, the firm would prefer cash (very short-term bonds) to gilts (long-term government bonds in the U.K.), and it prefers gilts to equities. This preference is reflected in the specific recommended portfolio for U.K. investors at the bottom of Table 13.19. As shown, there is a "normal" range for various components of the portfolio (e.g., bonds 15–25 percent) and a recommended proportion for the current and future environment. In the case of the U.K., as of early 1988, the firm is recommending the maximum proportion of cash (20 percent) and bonds (25 percent) and the minimum weighting for equities (55 percent).

WORLD ASSET ALLOCATION. Based upon the prior analysis, the final product is a recommendation for an investor's world asset allocation. As shown in Table 13.20, the first division is among bonds, equities, and cash. Note that at the time of this example the firm was recommending that an investor should be at the high end of the bond range, the low end of the equity range, and toward the high end of the cash range. Within the equity segment of the portfolio, the firm specifies a neutral weighting for each country based upon its relative market value—for example, the market value of the United States is 33.6 percent of the total value of all equities in the world and Japan is 45.1 percent. This implies that if you were completely ambivalent on all equity markets, you would weight these countries in line with their market values. As shown, in the current case, Goldman Sachs is somewhat bearish on the United States and Japan and would recommend that you underweight stocks from these two countries relative to their normal weight—that is, the firm recommends that you only put 30 percent of your equity portfolio in United States and 35 percent in Japanese stocks rather than the neutral weights of 34 and 45 percent. In contrast, they are recommending that you should overweight West Germany and France—that is, invest 6 percent in WG equities versus the neutral weighting of 3 percent and invest 6 percent in France versus the neutral weighting of about 2 percent.

Given the world market analysis, the next step is to analyze alternative industries on a worldwide and country basis. Finally, you should consider alternative firms in the preferred industries. This subsequent analysis is the subject of the next two chapters.

SUMMARY

In earlier chapters we emphasized the importance of analyzing the aggregate stock market before an industry or a company analysis. It is very important to determine whether the market outlook justifies investing in stock at all before you consider the best industry or company to invest in. The techniques used in making that decision can be described as either macro techniques, which are based upon the strong relationship between the aggregate economy and the stock market, or micro techniques, which attempt to determine future market values by applying basic valuation models to the aggregate stock market.

TABLE 13.15
Comparative Stock Market Statistics

	UNITED STATES	CANADA	JAPAN	UNITED KINGDOM	WEST GERMANY[a]	FRANCE
Real GDP Growth[d]						
1982–1986 Avg.	3.8	3.9	3.9	3.2	2.4	1.4
1987	2.9	4.0	4.2	4.4	1.7	2.2
1988E	3.0	3.9	5.5	3.6	2.6	2.6
1989E	—	2.8	3.3	2.2	1.5	1.8
Corporate Earnings Growth						
1983–1987 Avg.	10.9	29.3	3.6	18.0	28.8	14.3
1986	−1.5	2.6	−15.2	2.7	−11.6	17.6
1987E	27.2	50.1	18.8	29.2	0.5	12.6
1988E	16.3	14.3	2.7	8.9	2.2	14.0
Return on Equity						
1982–1986 Avg.	12.4	9.4	7.7	13.1	14.0	12.1
1986	12.9	10.4	6.3	14.2	15.0	12.1
Dividend Growth						
1983–1986 Avg.	3.2	11.1	1.3	15.9	18.4	18.1
1986	5.2	10.7	−1.6	13.4	8.2	14.6
1987	6.6	22.7	1.6	13.2	0.5	7.3
Price/Earnings						
1983–1987 Avg.	15.5	18.1	33.6	11.9	13.9	11.8
1986	21.3	20.2	66.3	16.3	12.9	15.5
1987E	16.8	13.5	55.8	12.6	12.8	13.8
1988E	14.4	11.8	54.3	11.6	12.5	12.1
Price/Cash Flow						
1982–1986 Avg.	7.1	6.4	9.6	5.4	6.1	4.8
1986	9.7	6.7	18.9	8.3	6.2	6.1
1987E	8.5	5.2	15.9	7.1	6.0	5.6
Price/Book Value						
1982–1986 Avg.	1.9	1.8	2.1	1.6	2.1	1.3
1986 year-end	2.4	1.9	3.1	2.0	2.6	1.9
1987E	2.8	2.1	4.1	2.3	1.9	1.9

[a] West Germany calculated with new DVFA rules as of 1986.
[b] Italy calculated 1983–1986 except GNP and excluding world corporate profits.
[c] Figures calculated using 50% tax rate.
[d] Real GNP growth for US, Japan, West Germany.
As at 15 June 1988
Source: "World Investment Strategy Highlights" (London: Goldman, Sachs International Corp., July/August 1988). Reprinted with permission from Goldman, Sachs & Co.

There is a strong, consistent relationship between the aggregate economy and the stock market, but the stock market generally turns before the economy does. Therefore, the best macro techniques are those that use series that likewise lead the economy and possibly the stock market. The NBER leading indicator series (which includes stock prices) is one. A study has indicated that the NBER leading indicator series can be useful if the

ITALY[b]	NETHERLANDS	SWITZERLAND	SWEDEN[c]	NORWAY	DENMARK	OVERALL EXCLUDING JAPAN
2.4	1.6	2.3	2.6	4.6	NA	
3.1	2.5	2.1	2.8	0.2	−1.0	
2.3	1.6	1.9	2.0	0.2	0.5	
1.7	1.6	1.7	−	−	0.8	
55.7	10.4	18.3	25.7	35.5	12.8	15.2
49.7	−22.9	−4.5	−4.1	−48.8	−9.6	−0.6
20.2	1.9	15.6	31.1	79.1	2.9	25.9
7.3	5.7	5.0	20.0	3.0	18.6	13.8
5.6	10.8	7.5	18.2	18.0	12.1	11.8
10.4	10.1	8.7	17.3	8.8	11.7	13.0
43.6	14.7	12.5	19.7	NA	16.9	7.8
43.2	3.5	3.8	22.7	NA	20.5	7.9
19.7	1.1	15.5	15.0	NA	5.6	8.4
12.8	8.3	17.6	8.2	9.4	19.0	15.0
10.7	11.0	18.2	11.4	17.0	19.4	19.4
8.9	10.8	15.7	8.7	9.5	18.8	15.4
8.3	10.2	15.0	7.3	9.2	15.9	13.5
3.6	4.1	9.8	13.0	3.9	8.6	6.7
3.6	5.3	9.4	17.5	5.7	8.6	9.0
3.8	5.5	8.5	13.3	4.3	8.4	7.8
1.0	0.8	1.4	1.6	1.6	2.3	1.8
1.6	1.1	1.8	1.8	1.3	1.9	2.3
1.1	1.1	1.6	2.0	1.5	2.3	2.5

analyst can choose an appropriate filter. Unfortunately, without this ability, the investment results are similar to those from a buy-and-hold policy.

Other leading series for inflation and other countries exist, as well as a weekly leading series. None of these other series, however, have been examined relative to stock prices. A second macro technique is to use the money supply to predict aggregate market behavior. Extensive research has indicated that changes in the growth rate of the money supply lead the economy by several months, and the average lead appeared to be even longer than the lead of stock prices relative to the economy. In addition, theoretically, monetary changes should have an impact on financial markets. A review of the numerous empirical studies in this area indicates that

TABLE 13.16
**Correlation Matrix Monthly Returns of Local Indexes:
January 1965–December 1987**

	S&P Comp	Tokyo SE	FT all Share	Toronto Comp	SBC General	Commerzbank	CAC General
S&P Comp	1.00						
Tokyo SE	0.33	1.00					
FT All Share	0.50	0.29	1.00				
Toronto Comp	0.78	0.33	0.51	1.00			
SBC General	0.42	0.26	0.35	0.41	1.00		
Commerzbank	0.36	0.32	0.33	0.35	0.47	1.00	
CAC General	0.41	0.33	0.44	0.44	0.40	0.43	1.00

Source: "World Investment Strategy Highlights" (London: Goldman, Sachs International Corp., February 1988). Reprinted with permission from Goldman, Sachs & Co.

these assumptions may be in error. Specifically, the earlier studies indicated a strong relationship between money supply and stock prices and suggested that money supply changes generally lead stock prices. In contrast, more recent studies confirm the link between money supply and stock prices, but they generally indicate that stock prices turn coincidentally with or before money supply changes, as one might expect in a world with efficient capital markets. These later results imply that although money supply changes have an important impact on stock price movements, it is not possible to use the money supply in a mechanical way to predict stock price changes.

The micro technique involves applying the basic dividend valuation model discussed in Chapter 9 to the aggregate stock market. An estimate of earnings per share is derived for a market series and an estimate of an earnings multiplier. Given these two components, it is possible to compute an estimate of the future value for the market and to derive an expected return for common stocks during the period. It is important to recognize that the procedure generates only a best estimate, and it is appropriate to make several estimates that reflect various possible conditions.

This micro technique is best summarized by the steps used in the earnings multiple approach as follows:
Outline of Earnings Multiple Approach to Projecting Aggregate Stock Market Values

    I. Estimate expected earnings.
        A. Estimate nominal GNP for year.
            1. Estimate real GNP.
            2. Estimate inflation rate.

TABLE 13.17
World Stock Markets

	PERCENTAGE CHANGE IN LOCAL CURRENCY								
COUNTRY	AVG. ANNUAL 1970–1980	1981	1982	1983	1984	1985	1986	1987	AVG. ANNUAL 1981–1987
Australia	7.3	−13.5	−18.5	61.1	−11.0	40.9	41.5	−3.6	13.9
Austria	NA	−15.7	−4.7	11.2	6.2	97.8	10.5	−17.6	12.5
Belgium	NA	1.4	16.6	34.0	17.6	32.4	38.3	−15.6	17.8
Canada	8.7	−13.7	0.9	30.0	−2.4	18.9	6.0	4.0	6.2
Denmark	10.8	29.7	16.5	103.3	−24.9	31.2	−14.9	−4.5	19.5
France	4.4	−14.2	2.9	57.2	16.9	43.0	47.1	−27.9	17.9
West Germany	−0.7	0.9	14.2	37.2	9.1	74.0	4.9	−36.8	14.8
Hong Kong	38.9	−18.7	−14.2	12.5	38.1	45.3	42.9	−11.3	9.0
Ireland	NA	−11.7	−13.7	72.2	−6.0	57.3	39.0	−12.3	17.9
Italy	6.5	−15.9	−12.6	21.2	26.6	102.6	73.8	−32.4	23.3
Japan	13.4	16.0	4.8	23.7	25.7	13.5	53.9	8.5	20.9
Malaysia	NA	−6.5	−24.7	38.5	−26.5	−26.6	20.3	6.9	−2.7
Mexico	NA	NA	−54.3	244.7	40.8	102.2	283.0	158.9	129.2
Netherlands	−3.0	−6.9	15.6	54.4	22.6	26.2	3.6	−18.9	13.4
New Zealand	NA	6.4	−19.6	93.3	−5.1	38.1	99.2	−38.7	24.8
Norway	5.9	−2.4	−22.0	86.5	20.7	25.7	−8.8	−14.0	12.4
Singapore	22.6	−7.1	−14.5	29.9	−26.3	−20.6	65.1	−10.6	2.2
South Africa	11.6	5.2	35.4	9.8	3.3	35.9	56.3	−8.8	19.6
Spain	−13.3	21.1	−19.0	7.3	43.9	29.3	90.7	8.3	25.9
Sweden	3.8	46.1	56.5	45.8	−16.6	30.2	40.9	−15.1	26.8
Switzerland	−0.7	−10.0	8.8	23.5	0.7	53.8	9.9	−34.0	−7.5
United Kingdom	15.3	8.6	23.5	23.3	24.3	15.0	20.8	4.6	17.2
United States	5.2	−5.0	17.5	16.5	0.5	26.5	13.3	0.5	10.0
Europe	2.0	1.5	14.9	31.2	17.7	34.9	25.5	−15.3	15.8
Europe excluding UK	−3.8	−4.5	6.8	39.2	11.9	55.4	23.8	−27.9	15.0
World excluding US	7.0	2.9	5.2	22.5	17.1	23.7	40.9	−1.7	16.6
World excluding UK	6.2	−1.2	10.4	21.7	6.5	25.8	29.8	−1.5	13.0
World excluding Japan	5.7	−4.4	13.4	21.3	3.8	28.4	19.0	−5.4	10.9
The World	6.4	−0.9	11.7	21.8	7.9	24.9	29.1	−0.9	13.4
	PERCENTAGE CHANGE IN U.S. DOLLAR								
Australia	8.1	−16.4	−29.0	47.8	−18.4	16.4	38.0	47.0	6.2
Austria	NA	−18.7	−11.9	−3.0	−7.2	152.6	40.4	0.7	21.9
Belgium	NA	−18.1	5.9	12.6	4.3	65.6	71.9	3.2	20.8
Canada	7.5	−13.0	−2.7	28.3	−8.1	12.4	7.3	10.4	5.0
Denmark	12.3	17.1	1.0	71.2	−33.5	65.1	3.2	15.5	20.0
France	6.7	−25.9	−13.1	27.0	1.2	82.7	3.3	−13.9	18.8
West Germany	5.1	−3.8	7.5	19.4	−5.8	124.1	33.5	−22.7	21.8
Hong Kong	39.7	−24.6	−53.1	−6.0	37.0	45.6	43.2	−11.0	4.4
Ireland	NA	−20.6	−23.7	40.2	−18.1	98.1	57.0	4.7	19.7
Italy	2.4	−29.5	−23.2	−0.8	9.0	134.0	116.8	−22.3	26.3
Japan	20.6	9.0	−1.9	25.2	15.9	42.2	94.9	41.4	32.4
Malaysia	NA	−7.3	−26.8	36.9	−29.3	−26.1	11.7	11.7	−4.2
Mexico	NA	NA	−92.2	225.9	0.4	1.9	87.5	5.5	38.2
Netherlands	1.7	−12.6	8.0	30.5	5.4	61.7	30.4	0.3	17.7
New Zealand	NA	−7.7	−28.4	72.5	−31.0	45.4	111.1	−23.8	19.7

continued

TABLE 13.17 *continued*

	AVG. ANNUAL								AVG. ANNUAL
		PERCENTAGE CHANGE IN U.S. DOLLAR							
COUNTRY	1970–1980	1981	1982	1983	1984	1985	1986	1987	1981–1987
Norway	6.3	−6.9	−35.4	70.6	2.6	50.7	−6.5	1.8	11.0
Singapore	24.7	−5.8	−17.0	28.9	−28.0	−18.0	59.8	−2.7	2.5
South Africa	11.6	−15.8	24.8	20.9	−36.5	−27.2	25.4	33.5	3.6
Spain	−17.4	4.6	−38.2	−13.9	29.7	44.2	121.6	32.6	25.8
Sweden	5.6	22.9	17.5	33.2	−25.5	54.3	57.9	−0.9	22.8
Switzerland	7.1	−2.4	−3.1	13.9	−15.4	91.6	40.4	−16.5	15.5
United Kingdom	14.8	−12.0	4.5	10.1	−0.3	43.3	253.9	32.5	14.6
United States	5.2	−5.0	17.5	16.5	0.5	26.5	13.3	0.5	10.0
Europe	9.4	−11.8	−0.4	14.8	−1.9	69.3	40.5	4.5	16.4
Europe excluding UK	5.1	−4.8	5.9	20.0	1.5	35.2	40.5	13.3	15.9
World excluding US	7.8	−6.3	−5.2	21.9	2.9	46.6	62.9	24.2	21.0
World excluding UK	6.1	−4.8	5.9	20.0	1.5	35.0	40.5	13.3	15.9
World excluding Japan	6.8	−8.7	8.1	17.5	−2.2	34.1	22.2	2.4	10.5
The World	6.8	−5.5	5.9	19.1	1.3	36.1	39.0	15.0	15.8

Source: "World Investment Strategy Highlights" (London: Goldman, Sachs International Corp., February 1988). Reprinted with permission from Goldman, Sachs & Co.

    B. Estimate corporate sales based upon the relationship of sales to GNP.
    C. Estimate aggregate operating profit margin (NBDT/sales).
       1. Utilization rate
       2. Unit labor cost
         a. Wage/hour increases
         b. Productivity changes
       3. Inflation
       4. Trade surplus
    D. Estimate net profits.
       1. Compute operating profits (operating profit margin times sales).
       2. Subtract estimated depreciation.
       3. Estimate taxes (tax rate times NBT).
       4. Subtract taxes.
 II. Estimate the expected earnings multiple.
    A. Estimate changes in the required return (k).
       1. Changes in the risk-free rate (ΔRFR)
       2. Changes in the risk premium (ΔRP)
         a. Changes in business risk
         b. Changes in financial risk
         c. Changes in liquidity risk
         d. Changes in stock price volatility
         e. Changes in exchange rate risk

Table 13.18
Main Japanese Economic Indicators

	1986	1987	1988E	1989E
GNP Components (1980 prices, % change on year earlier)				
Cons. expenditure	3.2	3.9	4.5	4.2
Business investment	6.2	8.2	12.2	5.7
Exports	−5.0	3.8	5.4	2.8
Imports	2.8	9.2	13.3	7.8
Output (% change on year earlier)				
Real GNP	2.5	4.2	5.5	3.3
Industrial production	−0.3	3.3	9.7	3.4
Inflation (% change on year earlier)				
Consumer prices	0.6	0.1	0.8	2.9
Financial Sector (% end of year)				
Discount rate	3.0	2.5	3.0	3.0
3-month CD	4.5	4.4	4.7	4.9
Long bond yield	5.0	4.6	5.1	4.8
Overseas Sector (US$ bn)				
Trade balance	92.4	96.4	82.7	72.0
Current account	85.9	87.0	73.1	62.5
Labor Market (%)				
Unemployment	0.8	1.0	1.8	1.1

Source: "World Investment Strategy Highlights" (London: Goldman, Sachs International Corp., July/August 1988). Reprinted with permission from Goldman, Sachs & Co.

       3. Changes in the expected rate of inflation (ΔI)
    B. Estimate changes in the expected growth rate (Δg).
       1. Changes in the aggregate earnings retention rate
       2. Changes in the return on equity
          a. Changes in equity turnover
          b. Changes in profit margin
    C. Estimate changes in the spread between k and g.
  III. Estimate market value.
    A. Estimated earnings times estimated earnings multiple

    An alternative market valuation model considers the same variables as in the dividend valuation model but without the restrictive assumptions of constant growth for an infinite time period. Even assuming a return on equity greater than the required rate of return, the model generates a market value substantially lower than the dividend growth model.

    While we apply the techniques to the U.S. market, it is important to carry out a similar analysis for numerous non–U.S. markets. Such analysis was done by Goldman Sachs wherein they applied the top-down approach to several major countries. Beginning with an economic analysis for each country that included the major valuation variables, Goldman Sachs per-

Table 13.19
United Kingdom

| | P/E | | | | P/CF | | | P/B | | | Dividend |
	1986	1987E	1988E	Rel.	1986	1987E	Rel.	1986	1987E	Rel.	Yield
FT-A Index	16.3	12.6	11.6	97	8.3	7.1	122	2.0	2.3	134	4.1%

| | | Performance (% Change) | | | 52-Week Range | | Relative to World | | |
	Current Price	Last Month	Ytd	12 Month	High	Low	Last Month	Ytd	12 Month
FT (U.S. dollar)	138.8	−0.4	4.7	−8.7	162.9	113.8	−3.0	−9.0	−7.1
FT (local currency)	115.2	5.4	10.1	−16.6	148.0	94.4	1.2	−6.9	−8.7
FT all share	965.7	5.3	11.0	−16.0	1238.5	784.8	1.2	−6.2	−8.1
FT-SE 100	1869.3	5.2	9.1	−19.0	2443.4	1565.2	1.1	−7.7	−11.3

• Relief from upward pressure on sterling allows interest rates to be raised.
• International monetary tightening may now allow UK to dampen demand without driving sterling too high.
• Inflation outlook steady; gilt market yields expected to fluctuate around 9% through to year-end.
• Equities follow Wall Street; testing top of 1988 trading range.

Recommended Portfolio for U.K. Investors		
	Normal Range (%)	Suggested Weighting (%)
Bonds	**15–25**	**25**
Domestic	10–20	15
Foreign	0–10	10
Equities	**55–85**	**55**
Domestic	40–60	45
Foreign	15–25	10
North America	5–25	2
Japan	5–20	2
Other Europe	0–10	6
Cash	**0–20**	**20**

formed an overall market analysis for each country, including a portfolio strategy for investors in individual countries. The culmination was a world portfolio allocation recommendation that considered the bond-stock-cash allocation, but also indicated the specific allocation of the equity portion between countries—the recommendation for each country was for a weighting relative to its normal weighting based upon its relative market value.

Following this aggregate market analysis, you are ready to make a decision as to how much of your portfolio should be committed to stocks during the forthcoming investment period and the allocation among various countries. The next step in the equity portfolio procedure is the industry analysis, which is considered in the following chapter.

TABLE 13.20
World Portfolio—Asset Allocation

	NORMAL RANGE (%)	WORLD WEIGHTING (% OF INDEX)	CURRENT SUGGESTED WEIGHTING (%)
Bonds	25–45		**35**
Dollar			20
Non-dollar			80
Equities	45–65		**45**
United States		33.6	30–U.S.
Canada		2.2	2–Canada
Japan		45.1	35–Japan
United Kingdom		9.9	12–U.K.
West Germany		2.9	6–W.G.
France		2.1	6–France
Italy		1.3	3–Italy
Netherlands		1.2	3–Netherlands
Switzerland		1.0	2–Switzerland
Nordic		0.7	1–Nordic
Cash	0–20		**20**

Source: "World Investment Strategy Highlights" (London: Goldman, Sachs International Corp., July/August 1988). Reprinted with permission from Goldman, Sachs & Co.

QUESTIONS

1. Why would you expect a relationship between economic activity and stock price movements?

2. While at a social gathering you discuss the reason for the relationship between the economy and the stock market, but one of the listeners points out that stock prices typically turn before the economy does. How would you explain this phenomenon?

3. Define leading, lagging, and coincident indicators. Give an example of each, and discuss why you think it is classified as such, that is, discuss the economic relationship between this indicator series and the economy.

4. Discuss a diffusion index of leading series and why you might expect it to be useful in predicting stock market movements.

5. Assume that changes in monetary growth should effect stock price movements. What argument would an advocate of the efficient market hypothesis set forth regarding the use of a monetary series to predict stock price changes?

6. Is it a contradiction to say that there is a strong, consistent relationship between money supply changes and stock prices and yet also say that money supply changes cannot be used to predict stock price movements? Explain.

7. Another investor tells you he believes that the stock market will experience a substantial increase next year because corporate earnings are expected to rise by at least 12 percent. Do you agree or disagree? Why or why not?

8. In the library find at least three sources of historical information on nominal and real GNP. Attempt to find two sources that provide an *estimate* of nominal GNP for the coming year or that gave one for the previous year.

9. If you eventually want to arrive at an estimate of the net profit margin, why would you spend time estimating the gross margin and working down?

10. The long-run trend for all the margins in Table 13.6 is downward. What factors might account for this?

11. You are convinced that capacity utilization next year will decline from 84 percent to about 81 percent. What would you expect the effect of this change to be on the gross profit margin? Explain your reasoning.

12. Briefly discuss the contrary arguments that exist regarding the expected relationship between inflation and the aggregate profit margin.

13. There are well-regarded estimates that hourly wage rates will increase by about 6 percent next year. How does this affect your estimate of the aggregate profit margin? What other information do you need in order to use this information, and why do you need it?

14. It is estimated that hourly wage rates will increase by 7 percent and that productivity will increase by 5 percent. Approximately what would you expect to happen to unit labor cost? Discuss how this estimate would influence your estimate of the aggregate profit margin.

15. There has generally been a strong cyclical pattern to productivity changes. Specifically, following a cyclical trough, the gains in productivity are substantial, while immediately following a peak the productivity gains are very slight, or in some instances productivity even declines. Why does this phenomenon occur?

16. Discuss what is meant by this statement: "The factors that influence the earnings multiplier depend upon the earnings figure used."

17. Assuming no growth in earnings or that the earnings figure used is long-run expected earnings, what factors influence the earnings multiplier? Discuss each of the variables, and indicate how and why it influences the multiplier.

18. In a CAPM world, a risky asset's systematic risk is supposed to be the relevant risk variable. How does this apply to the aggregate stock market? What should the measure be? Because of the measurement problems, what is the most likely measure?

19. Assume a growing earnings stream; discuss what additional variables besides those concerned with required return must be considered to determine changes in the earnings multiplier.

20. Assume each of the following changes are independent and, except for this change, all other factors remain unchanged. In each case, indicate what will happen to the earnings multiplier and discuss why it should happen.
    a. Return on equity increases.
    b. Stock price volatility increases.
    c. Aggregate debt-equity ratio increases.
    d. Overall productivity of capital increases.

21. Based upon the economic projections contained in Tables 13.11 through 13.14, would you expect the stock prices for the various countries to be highly correlated? Explain and justify your answer with specific examples.

22. You are informed that a well-respected investment firm expects that returns next year for the equity market in the United States will be 11 percent, while returns for the West German market will be 14 percent. Assume that all risks except exchange rate risk are equal and you expect the DM/$ exchange rate to go from 1.60 to 1.35 during the year. Given this information, discuss where you would invest and why. What if the exchange rate went from 1.60 to 2.00?

PROBLEMS

1. Prepare a table for the United States during the last ten years showing the percentage of change each year in (a) the Consumer Price Index (all items), (b) nominal GNP, (c) real GNP (in constant dollars), and (d) the GNP deflator. Discuss what proportion of nominal growth was due to real growth and what part to inflation. Is the outlook for the coming year any different from that for last year? Discuss.

2. You are told that nominal GNP will increase by about 10 percent next year. Using Figure 13.4, estimate the most likely increase in corporate sales? What would be your most optimistic estimate? Most pessimistic?

3. Currently the dividend-payout ratio (D/E) for the aggregate market is 55 percent, the required return (i) is 14 percent, and the expected growth rate for dividends (g) is 9 percent.

3a. Compute the current earnings multiplier.

3b. You expect the D/E ratio to decline to 45 percent, but you assume there will be no other changes. What will be the P/E?

3c. Starting with the initial conditions, you expect the dividend-payout ratio to be constant but the rate of inflation to increase by 3 percent, while growth will increase by 2 percent. Compute the expected P/E.

3d. Starting with the initial conditions, you expect the dividend-payout ratio to be constant but the rate of inflation to decline by 3 percent, while growth will decline by 2 percent. Compute the expected P/E.

4. *CFA Examination I (June 1983)*: The use of economic analysis in investment management has been increasing and is likely to further increase as financial analysts develop greater skills in this area, integrating these analyses more and more into the investment decision-making process. The following questions address this subject. [8 minutes]

4a. (1) Differentiate among a leading, lagging, and coincident indicator of economic activity, and give an example of each.

(2) Indicate whether the leading indicators are one of the best tools for achieving above-average investment results. Briefly justify your conclusion.

4b. Interest rate projections are used in investment management for a variety of purposes. Identify three. [6 minutes]

4c. Assume you are a fundamental research analyst following the automobile industry for a large brokerage firm. Identify and briefly explain the relevance of three major economic time series, economic indicators, or economic data items that would be significant to automotive industry and company research. [6 minutes]

5. *CFA Examination III (June 1985)*: A U.S pension plan hired two offshore

firms to manage the non–U.S. equity portion of its total portfolio. Each firm was free to own stocks in any country market included in Capital International's Europe, Australia, and Far East Index (EAFE) and free to use any form of dollar and/or non-dollar cash or bonds as an equity substitute or reserve. After three years had elapsed, the records of the managers and the EAFE Index were as follows:

Summary: Contributions to Return

	CURRENCY	COUNTRY SELECTION	STOCK SELECTION	CASH/BOND ALLOCATION	TOTAL RETURN RECORDED
Manager A	(9.0%)	19.7%	3.1%	0.6%	14.4%
Manager B	(7.4)	14.2	6.0	2.8	15.6
Composite of					
Managers A and B	(8.2)	16.9	4.5	1.7	15.0
EAFE Index	(12.9)	19.9	—	—	7.0

You are a member of the plan sponsor's pension committee, which will soon meet with the plan's consultant to review manager performance. In preparation for this meeting, you go through the following analysis:

5a. Briefly describe the strengths and weaknesses of each manager, relative to the EAFE Index data. [5 minutes]

5b. Briefly explain the meaning of the data in the "Currency" column. [5 minutes]

6. As analyst for Biddle, Twiddle, and Rassmussen, you are forecasting the market P/E ratio using the dividend growth model. Since the economy has been in high gear for six consecutive years, you feel the dividend-payout ratio will be at its high of 55 percent and that long-term government bonds will fall to 7 percent. Since investors are becoming more risk-averse, the equity risk premium will rise to 5 percent, and investors will require a 12 percent return, while the return on equity will be 11 percent.

6a. What is the expected sustainable growth rate?

6b. What is your expectation of the market P/E ratio?

6c. To what price will the market rise if the earnings expectation is $22.50?

6d. If the data from this problem are applied to the Goldman Sachs model, what market price level will be achieved?

7. World Stock Market Indexes are published weekly in *Barron's* in the section labeled "Market Laboratory/Stocks." Utilizing two issues of this publication (the latest edition available and an issue one year earlier) in your college library,

7a. Show the closing position of each index on each date relative to the yearly high for each year.

7b. Name the countries whose markets are in a downtrend and those whose are in an uptrend.

7c. For the two time periods, calculate the week's change relative to the closing price. Which markets seem the most volatile?

8. Using a source of financial data such as *Barron's* or *The Wall Street Journal,*

8a. Plot the closing S&P Index (Y-axis) vs. latest M1 (X-axis) for the past ten weeks. Does there seem to be a positive, negative, or zero correlation? (Monetary aggregates will lag the stock market aggregates.)

8b. Examine the trend in money rates (e.g., federal funds, 90-day T-bills, etc.) over the past ten weeks. Does there appear to be a correlation between these money rates? Between the individual money rates and percent changes in M1?

8c. For the past ten weeks what relationship has existed between the S&P Index and the DJIA? Plot the weekly percent changes in each index using S&P as the X-axis and DJIA as the Y-axis.

REFERENCES

Belfer, Nathan. "Economic Indicators and Their Significance" in *The Financial Analysts Handbook,* 2d ed., edited by Sumner N. Levine (Homewood, Ill.: Dow Jones-Irwin, 1988).

Chen, Nai-Fu, Richard Roll, and Stephen A. Ross. "Economic Forces and the Stock Market." *Journal of Business* 59, no. 3 (July 1986).

Davidson, Lawrence S., and Richard T. Froyen. "Monetary Policy and Stock Returns: Are Stock Markets Efficient?" Federal Reserve Bank of St. Louis. *Review* 64, no. 3 (March 1983).

Finkel, Sidney R., and Donald L. Tuttle. "Determinants of the Aggregate Profits Margin." *Journal of Finance* 26, no. 5 (December 1971).

Fisher, Lawrence. "Determinants of Risk Premiums on Corporate Bonds." *Journal of Political Economy* 67, no. 3 (June 1959).

Friedman, Milton J., and Anna J. Schwartz. "Money and Business Cycles." *Review of Economics and Statistics* 45, no. 1, supplement (February 1963).

Gibson, W. E. "Price-Expectations Effects on Interest Rates." *Journal of Finance* 25, no. 1 (March 1970).

Gray, H. Peter. "Determinants of the Aggregate Profit Margin: Comment." *Journal of Finance* 31, no. 1 (March 1976).

Gray, William S., III. "Developing a Long-Term Outlook for the U.S. Economy and the Stock Market." *Financial Analysts Journal* 35, no. 4 (July–August 1979).

Hafer, R. W. "The Response of Stock Prices to Changes in Weekly Money and the Discount Rate." Federal Reserve Bank of St. Louis. *Review* 68, no. 3 (March 1986).

Malkiel, Burton G., and John G. Cragg. "Expectations and the Structure of Share Prices." *American Economic Review* 60, no. 4 (September 1970).

Moore, Geoffrey H., and John P. Cullity. "Security Markets and Business Cycles" in *The Financial Analysts Handbook,* 2d ed., edited by Sumner N. Levine (Homewood, Ill.: Dow Jones-Irwin, 1988).

Moore, Geoffrey H., ed. *Business Cycles, Inflation, and Forecasting,* 2d ed. New York: National Bureau of Economic Research, Studies in Business Cycles, no. 24, 1983.

Reilly, Frank K., Frank T. Griggs, and Wenchi Wong. "Determinants of the Aggregate Stock Market Earnings Multiple." *Journal of Portfolio Management* 10, no. 1 (Fall 1983).

Zarnowitz, Victor, and C. Boschan. "Cyclical Indicators: An Evaluation and New Leading Index." *Business Conditions Digest* (May 1975).

Zarnowitz, Victor, and C. Boschan. "New Composite Indexes of Coincident and Lagging Indicators." *Business Conditions Digest* (November 1975).

APPENDIX 13A COMMON STOCKS AND INFLATION

One of the most pervasive bits of folklore on Wall Street prior to the 1970s was that common stocks were a good hedge against inflation. The empirical evidence during the 1970s, however, was that common stocks had not only done very poorly during the periods of inflation since 1966, but had also been poor inflation hedges during historical periods dating from the early 1900s. This appendix addresses the question of whether there are any conditions wherein common stocks can serve as an inflation hedge. We also review a number of studies that have examined the performance of common stocks as inflation hedges.

DIVIDEND VALUATION MODEL AND INFLATION

You are familiar with the following dividend valuation model:

$$ P_i = \frac{D_1}{k_i - g_i}, $$

where

P_i = price of stock i

D_1 = expected dividend in period 1

k_i = the required rate of return on stock i

g_i = the expected growth rate of dividends for stock i.

Using this model, it is possible to consider what will happen if expectations change regarding inflation and what must happen in order for common stocks to be a complete hedge against inflation.

COMPLETE INFLATION HEDGE DEFINED. A *hedge* is a transaction intended to safeguard against loss on another investment. A hedge against inflation, then, is the acquisition of an asset that will safeguard against an increase in the general price level by generating a return equal to that increase. Unfortunately, this specification of an inflation hedge is incomplete when applied to common stocks because it overlooks the *normal* required rate of return on common stocks regardless of the current rate of inflation. Throughout this book we have contended that investors require a rate of return in line with the economy's RFR plus a risk premium to compensate for the uncertainty of the return stream. Viewed in this manner, the normal required rate does not include inflation. In order for a stock to be a complete inflation hedge, its real rate of return must be equal to or greater than the return that would be required to compensate for the RFR plus a risk premium (RP). An alternative way to consider the process is to begin with this inflation-free required return that includes an RFR and an RP and consider the impact of inflation as follows:

$$k = [[1 + (RFR + RP)][1 + I]] - 1.$$

As an example, assume that investors in common stock have a non-inflation required return of 8 percent that includes an RFR of about 3 percent and an RP of 5 percent. If investors expect the general price level to increase at an annual rate of 4 percent ($I = .04$), the nominal required rate of return from common stocks would be in excess of 12 percent.

$$k = [(1 + .08)(1 + .04)] - 1.$$

Therefore, when there is a change in the expected rate of inflation, k will increase by this amount. Given a change in k, the crucial question becomes, what will happen to the value of the asset so that the investor will receive his nominal required rate of return (k)? One way to view this is to transform the valuation model as follows: If

$$P = \frac{D_1}{k - g},$$

then,

$$k = \frac{D_1}{P} + g.$$

Given this specification, if there is a change in expected inflation and nothing happens to the earning stream of firms, we can see that stock prices must decline—that is, the P must decline until there is an increase in the D_1/P term to compensate for the increase in the required return. Clearly, during this period of adjustment, the investor who owns stocks will experience negative returns.

if P↓, not an inflation hedge

if g↑, is an inflation hedge

Another possibility is that the growth rate of dividends (g) will increase by the rate of inflation. If this occurs, stock prices will not change, because the spread between k and g will not change. k is still equal to

$$k = \frac{D_1}{P} + g.$$

The difference is that the dividend yield does not change, because P does not change, but the growth rate has increased. Therefore, the return (k) has increased in line with a change in expected inflation, and the stock will be a complete inflation hedge. Therefore, g must increase by the change in the rate of inflation if the stock is to be a complete inflation hedge without the stock price declining. This is the implicit assumption made by some observers who contend that common stocks will be an inflation hedge. For example, when Jahnke employs the dividend model to explain changes in stock prices, he states, "Thus common stocks should serve as a hedge against inflation to the extent that changes in the rate of inflation are mirrored in the dividend growth rate."[1] The question then becomes, under what conditions will the growth rate increase in line with the rate of inflation?

INFLATION AND THE GROWTH RATE. As discussed in Chapters 9 and 12, a firm's dividend growth rate is directly related to the firm's earnings growth rate, which is a function of the retention rate (*b*) and the return on equity (*ROE*) as follows:

$$g = b \times ROE.$$

Further, it was shown that *ROE* is composed of the equity turnover and the net profit margin as follows:

$$ROE = \frac{\text{Net Income}}{\text{Equity}} = \frac{\text{Sales}}{\text{Equity}} \times \frac{\text{Net Income}}{\text{Sales}}$$
$$= \text{Equity Turnover} \times \text{Net Profit Margin.}$$

Therefore, the growth rate will increase if there is an appropriate increase in one or several of the following variables:

1. Retention rate
2. Equity turnover
3. Net profit margin

You should probably not expect a major impact from changes in the retention rate, because an analysis of the historical series indicates that this rate changes slowly over time (see Table 13A.1). Also, it can be shown that it would require a significant change in this rate to have the desired impact. Therefore, the major impact on the growth rate must come from an increase in the ROE.

During a period of inflation, there is a natural tendency (bias) for the equity turnover to increase. The reason is that whereas sales are strongly influenced by inflation, equity capital is slower to respond since it is composed of the historical equity figure plus changes due to earnings (minus dividends) and stock sales. This tendency for equity turnover to rise is reflected in Table 13A.1 where equity turnover increases from about 2.0 during the period 1965–1970 to about 3.0 for the period 1979–1986. While this turnover variable would support a higher ROE, the discussion in the chapter related to the *Fortune* 500 figures indicated that this increase in equity turnover was almost wholly because of the increase in the financial leverage ratio.

The final variable required to change is the net profit margin. As a minimum we would want the profit margin to remain constant, because if sales increased in line with the rate of inflation, and the profit margin were constant, net earnings would increase by the rate of inflation. Alternatively, an increase in the profit margin would make a positive contribution to the

[1] William W. Jahnke, "What's Behind Stock Prices?" *Financial Analysts Journal* 31, no. 5 (September–October 1975): 71.

TABLE 13A.1
**Annual Return on Equity For Standard & Poor's 400
with Components of ROE**

YEAR	RETENTION RATE	EQUITY TURNOVER	PROFIT MARGIN	RETURN ON EQUITY
1960	41.2	1.76	5.72	10.00
1961	38.6	1.71	5.66	9.67
1962	42.6	1.78	5.93	10.53
1963	44.3	1.79	6.19	11.11
1964	46.8	1.82	6.63	12.06
1965	48.7	1.85	6.82	12.64
1966	49.7	1.94	6.64	12.88
1967	47.1	1.92	6.12	11.76
1968	48.7	2.02	6.07	12.27
1969	47.0	2.10	5.65	11.86
1970	41.8	2.09	4.92	10.28
1971	47.1	2.14	5.04	10.80
1972	52.9	2.21	5.30	11.71
1973	61.1	2.37	5.96	14.15
1974	61.4	2.69	5.28	14.17
1975	56.6	2.61	4.63	12.11
1976	60.5	2.66	5.27	14.02
1977	56.8	2.73	5.11	13.93
1978	58.8	2.81	5.19	14.60
1979	63.7	2.96	5.57	16.50
1980	59.7	3.02	4.92	14.88
1981	58.1	2.97	4.86	14.42
1982	45.9	2.82	3.95	11.13
1983	50.0	2.75	4.40	12.15
1984	58.5	3.06	4.77	14.61
1985	48.5	3.16	3.84	12.14
1986	44.1	3.12	3.75	11.70
1987	57.1	2.57	4.74	12.18
Average	51.3	2.41	5.32	12.51

Source: *Standard & Poor's Analysts Handbook* (New York: Standard & Poor's Corp., 1988). Reprinted with permission.

ROE and to growth in earnings. Unfortunately, the figures in Table 13A.1 do not provide support for either of these scenarios. As shown, the overall trend in the net profit margin has been down.[2] The following discussion considers *a priori* reasons for expecting stability or an increase in the profit margin.

---

[2] A study that considers a similar approach with modifications is Russell J. Fuller and Glenn H. Petry, "Inflation, Return on Equity, and Stock Prices," *Journal of Portfolio Management* 7, no. 4 (Summer 1981): 19–25.

PROFIT MARGINS AND INFLATION. Three hypotheses are offered to explain why given firms might be able to gain during periods of inflation: (1) the wage lag hypothesis, (2) the net debtor hypothesis, and (3) the fixed operating assets or raw materials hypothesis. The wage lag hypothesis contends that sales prices can be raised immediately in response to an increase in the rate of inflation, while wage increases lag because they are generally negotiated at yearly intervals. During the lag period, there is a shift in wealth from wage earners to firms; that is, profit margins increase at the expense of labor. This effect should be relatively short term, because eventually the wage earners should gain during negotiations.

The net debtor-creditor hypothesis contends that during periods of inflation there is a transfer of wealth from creditors to debtors, because the money received by a creditor is reduced in value while a debtor pays off his obligation in lower-valued money. As a result, the net debtor firm (a firm where monetary liabilities exceed monetary assets) will enjoy lower capital costs during the period of inflation. Assuming that selling prices and other costs increase in line with inflation, there will be an increase in the firm's profit margin, and the company's nominal earnings will increase by more than the rate of inflation.

A third hypothesis is that relative profits will increase when firms have significant operating assets or raw materials acquired prior to the period of inflation that will last throughout the period. Examples would include capital-intensive firms or natural resource firms (e.g., coal, lumber, oil) where the prices of products increase in line with inflation, and major material costs are constant. In such cases *the firm's profit margin will increase,* and nominal earnings will rise at a rate in excess of the rate of inflation. Note that in all cases in which a firm gains during a period of inflation, this gain should show up as an *increase in the profit margin during the period.*

EMPIRICAL EVIDENCE ON THE WAGE LAG HYPOTHESIS. Kessel and Alchian examined the proposition that firms with large annual wage bills would experience a greater increase in profits and stock prices than firms with smaller wage bills.[3] Their results did not support the wage lag hypothesis, because the average increase in equity was greater for firms with lower wage ratios. A multiple correlation analysis including the net debtor position also did not support the wage lag hypothesis.

Cargill examined numerous wage and price series to determine whether there was a consistent lead-lag relationship in the United States and England.[4] In the United States there was no wage-price relationship, while England had a wage lag for long-run intervals but not for short-run intervals. Reilly examined earnings and prices to test the hypothesis that the wage lag would be short-run because labor would eventually require com-

[3] Reuben A. Kessel and Armen A. Alchian, "The Meaning and Validity of the Inflation-Induced Lag of Wages Behind Prices," *American Economic Review* 50, no. 1 (March 1960): 43–66.
[4] Thomas F. Cargill, "An Empirical Investigation of the Wage-Lag Hypothesis," *American Economic Review* 59, no. 5 (December 1969): 806–816.

pensation.[5] The analysis indicated that typically *the price series either turned ahead of or coincidentally with the wage series.* It was concluded that prices tended to turn before wages, but the wage lag was generally short-lived.

EMPIRICAL EVIDENCE ON THE NET DEBTOR HYPOTHESIS. Kessel proposed that net debtor firms would gain during a period of unanticipated inflation relative to creditor firms, and that large debtors would gain more than small debtors and large creditors lose more than small creditors.[6] His results consistently supported the net debtor hypothesis, as did DeAlessi's results from his study on net debtor firms in the United Kingdom.[7]

To understand the impact of the net debtor hypothesis on the aggregate market, DeAlessi examined the proportion of net debtor firms in the United States and the United Kingdom and found that about 55 percent of U.S. firms were net debtors.[8] Broussalian found a 50–50 split during a later period.[9] These studies supported the net debtor hypothesis during periods of significant unanticipated inflation, but because only about half of U.S. firms are net debtors, the overall impact is probably minimal.

EMPIRICAL EVIDENCE ON PROFIT MARGINS DURING INFLATION. While the discussion suggests a positive relationship between profit margins and inflation, this relationship is not strong, because the wage lag effect is probably short-run, and the net debtor effect is probably minimal in the United States, where only about half the firms are net debtors.

The prior discussion regarding the profit margin series is not very encouraging because of the long-run trend for the series. The author specifically examined the relationship between the level of the profit margin for the S&P 400 series and the rate of inflation as measured by the Consumer Price Index (CPI) for the period 1960–1986. The correlation was -0.60. The annual percentage changes in the two series had a correlation of -0.11. These results indicate that profit margins appear to decline during periods of inflation. The impact of the profit margin on ROE and the effect of ROE on growth thus make common stocks a poor inflation hedge.

EMPIRICAL EVIDENCE ON COMMON STOCKS AS INFLATION HEDGES	Analyzing common stocks as an inflation hedge presents several problems in terms of methodology. First, common stocks have been examined over long time periods that include significant inflation, deflation, and relative price stability. This is a mistake because investors are interested only in whether an investment is an inflation hedge during periods of significant inflation. Although long-term analysis indicates that common stock prices

---

[5] Frank K. Reilly, "Companies and Common Stocks as Inflation Hedges," New York University Graduate School of Business, Center for the Study of Financial Institutions, *Bulletin* (April 1975).

[6] Reuben A. Kessel, "Inflation-Caused Wealth Redistribution: A Test of a Hypothesis," *American Economic Review* 46, no. 1 (March 1956): 128–141.

[7] Louis DeAlessi, "The Redistribution of Wealth by Inflation: An Empirical Test with United Kingdom Data," *The Southern Economic Journal* 30, no. 4 (October 1963): 113–127.

[8] Louis DeAlessi, "Do Business Firms Gain from Inflation?" *Journal of Business* 37, no. 2 (April 1964): 162–166.

[9] J. V. Broussalian, "Unanticipated Inflation: A Test of the Debtor-Creditor Hypothesis," Ph.D. dissertation, University of California, Los Angeles, 1961.

have increased faster than consumer prices, detailed analysis indicates that common stocks do quite well during periods of price stability, and this strong performance offsets their very poor performance during most periods of significant inflation.

Second, some studies have assumed that returns on common stock need only exceed the rate of inflation to be considered a good hedge. Because investors have a "normal" required rate of return on common stocks, to determine whether common stocks have been a complete inflation hedge you must compare the "real" return on the stock (r') to the investor's normal required return (k).

Several studies by Reilly, Johnson, and Smith divided a total time period into periods of significant inflation, relative noninflation, and deflation and concentrated on what happened to stock prices during the periods of significant inflation. They found that during most periods of significant inflation, the real rates of return were negative even before allowing for a so-called normal rate of return.[10] The authors concluded that common stocks have generally failed to be a complete inflation hedge. These results were confirmed in several subsequent studies.[11]

Oudet found that during the total period 1953–1970, the rates of return on common stock were highest during the periods of least inflation and lowest during periods of high inflation.[12] To confirm this phenomenon, the current author divided all years from 1916 to 1974 into years of significant inflation (over 3 percent increase in prices), deflation (over 1 percent decrease in prices), and relative price stability (between 3 percent increase and 1 percent decrease). The average annual change in the S&P 500 during significant inflation was −0.25 percent; during price stability, +12.31 percent; and during deflation, −0.34 percent.

In contrast to examining rates of return during discrete periods of time, an alternative technique is to regress rates of return on a specific asset and the rate of inflation. The idea is that if the asset is a good inflation hedge, the rate of return on the asset will respond in a positive way to inflation—that is, when the rate of inflation changes, so will the rate of return on this asset to compensate for the inflation.

Jaffe and Mandelker examined a series of regressions between monthly rates of return on common stocks and the rate of inflation and found the results were always significantly negative for contemporaneous data or

[10] These results were contained in Frank K. Reilly, Glenn L. Johnson, and Ralph E. Smith, "Inflation, Inflation Hedges, and Common Stocks," *Financial Analysts Journal* 26, no. 1 (January–February 1970): 104–110. The results were updated in Frank K. Reilly, "Companies and Common Stocks as Inflation Hedges," New York University, Center for the Study of Financial Institutions, *Bulletin* (April 1975).

[11] Frank K. Reilly, Glenn L. Johnson, and Ralph E. Smith, "A Note on Common Stocks as Inflation Hedges—The After Tax Case," *Southern Journal of Business* 7, no. 4 (November 1972): 101–106; Ralph E. Smith, Glenn L. Johnson, and Frank K. Reilly, "A Year-by-Year Analysis of 'Real' Rates of Return on Common Stocks," *Quarterly Review of Economics and Business* 14, no. 1 (Spring 1974): 79–88; G. L. Johnson, F. K. Reilly, and R. E. Smith, "Individual Common Stocks as Inflation Hedges," *Journal of Financial and Quantitative Analysis* 6, no. 3 (June 1971): 1015–1024; and F. K. Reilly, G. L. Johnson, and R. E. Smith, "A Correction and Update Regarding Individual Common Stocks as Inflation Hedges," *Journal of Financial and Quantitative Analysis* 10, no. 5 (December 1975): 871–880.

[12] Bruno A. Oudet, "The Variation of the Return on Stocks in Periods of Inflation," *Journal of Financial and Quantitative Analysis* 8, no. 2 (March 1973): 247–258.

data with various leads or lags.[13] The results with annual data for the period 1875–1970 indicated an insignificant positive relationship. Overall, these results indicate that common stocks either fail completely as a hedge (a negative relationship) or serve as a very weak one.

Nelson examined the correlation of the monthly rates of return on common stocks and the rates of inflation, including a number of leads and lags because of how the CPI is constructed (it is not a discrete series at two points in time, but is derived using prices collected throughout the month).[14] Overall, there was a uniformly *significant negative relationship.* The correlation between market returns and a measure of "unanticipated" inflation indicated a negative impact of inflation on stock returns. Finally, Nelson hypothesized a lagged effect of inflation on stock returns and devised several prediction tests. He found positive returns using the prediction models relative to buy-and-hold without transaction costs.

Bodie examined the relationship between the real rate of return on equity and various specifications of inflation (i.e., anticipated and unanticipated) and consistently found a negative correlation between the real return on equity and both unanticipated and anticipated inflation.[15]

Fama and Schwert examined a number of assets as hedges against expected and unexpected components of inflation.[16] The results varied among some of the assets like government bonds and bills, real estate and labor income, but common stock returns were consistently negatively related to both expected and unexpected inflation.

Gultekin used data from the Livingston survey of inflation expectations to test the relationship between expected stock returns and expected inflation.[17] The results indicated a strong positive relationship between expected inflation and both expected stock market returns and the expected real return on common stocks.

ANALYSIS OF ALTERNATIVE INDUSTRIES. Beyond the examination of the aggregate stock market and individual stocks, three studies have analyzed the relationships among returns for alternative industries and inflation. Townsend analyzed the performance of stocks from 15 industries and 474 companies and found that none of the selected industries and very few of the individual companies (5 percent) were able to protect against inflation.[18]

---

[13] Jeffrey F. Jaffe and Gershon Mandelker, "The 'Fisher Effect' for Risky Assets: An Empirical Investigation," *Journal of Finance* 31, no. 2 (May 1976): 447–458.

[14] Charles R. Nelson, "Inflation and Rates of Return on Common Stocks," *Journal of Finance* 31, no. 2 (May 1976): 471–483.

[15] Zvi Bodie, "Common Stocks as a Hedge against Inflation," *Journal of Finance* 31, no. 2 (May 1976): 459–470.

[16] Eugene F. Fama and William Schwert, "Asset Returns and Inflation," *Journal of Financial Economics* 5, no. 3 (November 1977): 115–146.

[17] N. Bulent Gultekin, "Stock Market Returns and Inflation Forecasts," *Journal of Finance* 38, no. 3 (June 1983): 663–673.

[18] James E. Townsend, "Relative Strengths of Common Stocks of Various Industries to Serve as Inflation Hedges," Southwestern Finance Association Meeting, Houston, Texas, March 1975.

When Ferris and Makhija examined 58 different industries during the high-inflation period 1977–1983, they found that only 5 industries out of 58 had significant positive coefficients when industry rates of return were related to inflation.[19] The exceptions represented three different sectors: energy, natural resources, and real estate. Notably, these results occurred during a short period of inflation that was dominated by the energy crisis.

Reilly used the dividend valuation model to show that the components of ROE (especially the profit margin) must change in order for industry earnings to respond to inflation.[20] He analyzed the relationship of these component variables to reported, anticipated, and unanticipated inflation for 47 industries during the period 1955–1985 and found very few significant positive correlations. Further, there were *no* significant positive correlations between inflation and industry stock returns. Finally, the rank correlations between the stock return coefficients and the component variable coefficients indicated that an industry's profit margin was the most important variable, indicating its ability to hedge against inflation.

ANALYSIS OF INTERNATIONAL MARKETS. Branch examined international stock price indexes, inflation rates, and industrial production rates for 22 countries for the total period 1953–1969 and concluded that stocks were a partial inflation hedge.[21] Because there was price stability during most of this period, the results are not indicative of performance during significant inflation. Indeed, if you eliminate Chile (which had very inconsistent results) and divide the countries into those with low inflation (under 3 percent) and high inflation (over 3 percent), the average stock price increase was 1.96 percent for the high-inflation countries and 7.16 percent for the low-inflation countries. Apparently, investors were better off investing in low-inflation countries.

Cagan analyzed long-run returns for stocks from alternative countries.[22] Assuming that investors held common stocks through all periods, he concluded that common stocks were a good inflation hedge *in the long run.* A careful reading of the results, however, reveals that stocks did not do well during the periods of inflation, but eventually made up for the losses after the inflation was over.

Firth examined the relation between stock market returns and inflation in the United Kingdom using monthly data for the periods 1955–1976 and 1935–1976 and annual data for the period 1919–1976.[23] In contrast to the results in the United States, the regression coefficients were significantly

---

[19] Stephen P. Ferris and Anil K. Makhija, "A Search for Common Stock Inflation Hedges," *Review of Business and Economic Research* 22, no. 2 (Spring 1987): 27–36.

[20] Frank K. Reilly, "Alternative Industries as Inflation Hedges," Financial Management Association Meeting, October 1987.

[21] Ben Branch, "Common Stock Performance and Inflation: An International Comparison," *Journal of Business* 47, no. 1 (January 1974): 48–52.

[22] Phillip Cagan, "Common Stock Values and Inflation—The Historical Record of Many Countries," *National Bureau Report Supplement* (New York: National Bureau of Economic Research, Inc., 1974).

[23] Michael Firth, "The Relationship between Stock Market Returns and the Rate of Inflation," *Journal of Finance* 34, no. 3 (June 1979): 743–749.

positive for the period 1955–1976 and for some recent periods. The other coefficients were generally positive and not significant. The coefficients relating stock returns and past inflation were generally negative. The coefficient for annual data from 1919 was negative but not significant. The author concludes that there is some evidence that stocks have been an inflation hedge in the United Kingdom.

Solnik analyzed the relation between stock returns and inflationary expectations for nine countries over the period 1971–1980.[24] Using interest rates as a proxy for expected inflation, he found a negative relationship between stock returns and inflation for all the countries. Gultekin examined the relation between common stock returns and inflation in 26 countries.[25] Not only were the regression results predominantly negative, but the relationship was not stable over time and there were differences among countries.

It appears, then, that the vast majority of empirical studies indicate that common stocks have *not* been inflation hedges when examined at the aggregate level, by industry, or based on the performance of individual stocks. Apparently this poor performance for common stocks is because the growth rate in dividends has not kept up with the increases in the rate of inflation. In turn, the growth rate has not increased, because profit margins have declined. In our micro analysis, we have emphasized factors that should cause stocks to be inflation hedges with the implication that while common stocks *in the aggregate* have not been good inflation hedges, it is possible that some individual industries or stocks could be hedges. The important point is, you must examine alternative industries and companies to determine how the industry or the company growth rate will be affected by inflation. Inflation will have different effects on alternative industries or companies due to differences in the elasticity of demand for their product or service, the wage component, and the net debtor position.[26]

Alternatively, some authors have considered macroeconomic relationships to explain the consistent negative relationship between common stock returns and inflation. They suggest that the direction of causality may differ from our normal assumption that changes in the rate of inflation affect stock value and rates of return. Geske and Roll have hypothesized that *stock returns are the initiating factor* and cause changes in the fiscal and monetary arena that subsequently cause an opposite change in the rate of inflation.[27] It is contended that stock prices change in anticipation of changes in economic conditions and thus affect government revenues,

[24] Bruno Solnik, "The Relation between Stock Prices and Inflationary Expectations: The International Evidence," *Journal of Finance* 38, no. 1 (March 1983): 35–48.

[25] N. Bulent Gultekin, "Stock Market Returns and Inflation: Evidence from Other Countries," *Journal of Finance* 38, no. 1 (March 1983): 49–65.

[26] This is consistent with the analysis in James C. Van Horne and William Glassmire, Jr., "The Impact of Unanticipated Changes in Inflation on the Value of Common Stocks," *Journal of Finance* 27, no. 5 (December 1972): 1081–1092.

[27] Robert Geske and Richard Roll, "The Fiscal and Monetary Linkage between Stock Returns and Inflation," *Journal of Finance* 38, no. 1 (March 1983): 1–33.

outstanding debt, and subsequently inflation. Consider the following scenario: stock prices decline in anticipation of a decline in economic activity, which causes a decline in tax revenue and an increase in the federal deficit. Then, given the fairly consistent practice of monetizing the debt (which is anticipated by rational investors) the money supply increases, leading to an increase in the rate of inflation. An alternative scenario, which does not require the budget deficit but incorporates the demand for money, is that stock prices decline in anticipation of a decline in real economic activity, which reduces the demand for money (i.e., one of the variables that influence the demand for money is real economic activity along with wealth and interest rates). Then, assuming the supply of money remains unchanged, consumers have excess dollars that they spend, leading to an increase in prices (i.e., an increase in the rate of inflation).

In a subsequent article, Kaul acknowledges the money demand argument but suggests a process that reinforces the negative relationships.[28] In addition to the decline in demand for money due to a decline in real economic activity, he points out that the money supply might not remain constant but might instead increase as the monetary authorities attempt to move counter to the economic decline. This countercyclical monetary policy would reinforce the *increase* in inflation following the *decline* in stock prices and real activity. The combination of factors emanating from the money supply process helps explain cases where the negative relationship between stock returns and inflation does not hold. Specifically, you could envision times when the Federal Reserve did not act countercyclically, but was procyclical, in which case the monetary authorities could offset the impact from money demand. It is contended that this is what happened during the 1930s. This implies that you must consider the equilibrium process in the monetary sector in order to know whether there will be a negative, positive, or lack of relationship between stock returns and inflation.

PROBLEMS

1. *CFA Examination III (June 1982)*: As an investment adviser you have just made a presentation to the investment committee of a large endowment fund. One of the members of the committee makes the following remarks to you. "Bob, that was an interesting presentation that you made to our committee. I think I understand your expectation that a decline in the rate of inflation will be good for stocks. I still have some questions about how this will impact the required rate of return for stocks."

1a. "Treasury bill rates have been dropping the past few weeks. Will this affect the required rate of return?" Explain.

1b. "Some of the corporations we have been investing in have had their troubles with inflation. Would a reduction in the rate of inflation eventually change the required rate of return on stocks generally—as well as help the prices of those stocks directly benefited?" Explain.

---

[28] Gautam Kaul, "Stock Returns and Inflation: The Role of the Monetary Sector," *Journal of Financial Economics* 18, no. 2 (June 1987): 253–276.

1c. "What will lower inflation rates do for the balance sheets of corporations and for the required rate of return?" Explain.

1d. "How will a decline in inflation affect the stock market liquidity risk?" Explain. [20 minutes]

2. *CFA Examination II (June 1986)*: You are Paul R. Overlook, CFA, an investment advisor for a large endowment fund. You have recently read about a basic valuation model that values an asset according to the present value of the asset's expected cash flows. You now are using this valuation framework to explain to the fund's trustees how inflation affects the rates of return on various asset types. After your presentation, the trustees ask the following:

2a. "If common stocks are attractive for hedging inflation, why did stocks perform so poorly in the 1970s when the inflation rate was increasing?"

2b. "Historical results indicate that over the long run Treasury bill returns and the inflation rate have been approximately the same. Because the current Treasury bill rate considerably exceeds the inflation rate, does this indicate that Treasury bills now are unusually attractive?"

2c. "If stocks are attractive inflation hedges, it seems that stock prices should rise the most when inflation increases. Why then did stock prices appreciate so much from 1982 to 1986 when the inflation rate was declining?"

Prepare and briefly explain your response to each of these three questions in the context of the valuation model. [15 minutes]

REFERENCES

Fama, Eugene F. "Short Term Interest Rates as Predictors of Inflation." *American Economic Review* 65, no. 3 (June 1975).

Fama, Eugene F. "Stock Returns, Real Activity, Inflation, and Money." *American Economic Review* 71, no. 4 (September 1981).

Ferris, Stephen P., and Anil K. Makhila. "A Search for Common Stock Inflation Hedges." *Review of Business and Economic Research* 27, no. 2 (Spring 1987).

Fuller, Russell J., and Glenn H. Petry. "Inflation, Return on Equity, and Stock Prices." *Journal of Portfolio Management* 7, no. 4 (Summer 1981).

Geske, Robert, and Richard Roll. "The Fiscal and Monetary Linkage between Stock Returns and Inflation." *Journal of Finance* 38, no. 1 (March 1983).

Gultekin, N. Bulent. "Stock Market Returns and Inflation: Evidence from Other Countries." *Journal of Finance* 38, no. 1 (March 1983).

Gultekin, N. Bulent. "Stock Market Returns and Inflation Forecasts." *Journal of Finance* 38, no. 3 (June 1983).

Kaul, Guatam. "Stock Returns and Inflation: The Role of the Monetary Sector." *Journal of Financial Economics* 18, no. 2 (June 1987).

Reilly, Frank K. "Companies and Common Stocks as Inflation Hedges." New York University, Center for the Study of Financial Institutions, *Bulletin* (April 1975).

Van Horne, James C., and William Glassmire, Jr. "The Impact of Unanticipated Changes in Inflation on the Value of Common Stocks." *Journal of Finance* 27, no. 5 (December 1972).

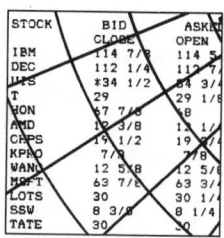

CHAPTER 14

INDUSTRY ANALYSIS

Ask an analyst what he does and he will typically reply that he is an oil analyst, a retail analyst, or a business machine analyst. Portfolio managers talk about being in or out of the oils, the autos, or the utilities. This is because most practitioners in the securities markets are extremely conscious of alternative industries and organize their analyses and portfolio decisions according to industry groups. The results of academic research, however, have been mixed as to how useful such industry analysis is. We will begin with a discussion of several studies dealing with industry performance and risk that have important implications for industry analysis. Subsequently, we will consider how industries should be analyzed.

PREVIOUS STUDIES OF INDUSTRY ANALYSIS

CROSS-SECTIONAL RETURN PERFORMANCE

Several studies have examined the performance of alternative industries during a specific period of time. Complete consistency over time for different industries would indicate that industry analysis is not necessary after market analysis. Assume that during 1989 the aggregate market rose by 10 percent and all industry returns were bunched between 9 and 11 percent. You might question whether it was worthwhile to conduct an industry analysis to find an industry that would return 11 percent when random selection would provide about 10 percent (the average return).

An early study by Latané and Tuttle examined the long-run price performance of 59 industries for the years 1950 and 1958 and for the month of October 1967.[1] While the aggregate market had increased by a factor of 5 over time, the difference between alternative industries was substantial, and the wide dispersion between industries did not decline over time, even with the growth of conglomerates.

---

[1] Henry A. Latané and Donald L. Tuttle, "Framework for Forming Probability Beliefs," *Financial Analysts Journal* 24, no. 4 (July–August 1968): 51–61.

These findings were confirmed by Brigham and Pappas, who analyzed rates of return for 658 industrial and utility firms.[2] Reilly and Drzycimski examined the performance of the 30 *Barron's* industry averages and likewise found substantial divergence in relative performance among industries.[3] This would imply that industry analysis is necessary as you attempt to determine the differences in future industry performance.[4]

TIME SERIES RETURN PERFORMANCE

Our next question is whether industries that perform well in one time period continue to perform well—or at least outperform the aggregate market. Latané and Tuttle found almost no association in industry performance over time.[5] Reilly-Drzycimski likewise concluded that there was very low correlation in industry performance over sequential rising or falling markets.[6] Tysseland examined the performance of 40 major industries and found significant positive results for short-run periods but typically negative results for longer periods of time.[7]

While these studies imply that you cannot use past performance to project future industry performance, they do not negate the usefulness of industry analysis. They simply point out the necessity of *projecting* future industry performance on the basis of *future estimates* of the relevant variables.

PERFORMANCE WITHIN INDUSTRIES

The final relevant question is whether there is consistency *within* an industry. If the firms within an industry experience similar performance during a specified time period, no company analysis would be needed, only an industry analysis.

Brigham and Pappas found a wide range of returns for 14 firms in the paper industry and contended that "volatility found in the paper industry was not atypical."[8] Cheney examined eight industries and 227 stocks and concluded:

> This study of industry cohesiveness does little to reassure the investor that he can expect individual stocks to follow the industry trend, as indicated by the industry index, over the short and intermediate term.[9]

Several other studies have examined the relationship of returns over time for a group of stocks relative to the aggregate market and industry affili-

[2] Eugene F. Brigham and James L. Pappas, "Rates of Return on Common Stock," *Journal of Business* 42, no. 3 (July 1969): 302–316.

[3] Frank K. Reilly and Eugene Drzycimski, "Alternative Industry Performance and Risk," *Journal of Financial and Quantitative Analysis* 9, no. 3 (June 1974): 423–446.

[4] Various financial services provide graphs of *annual* rates of return for alternative industries. Again, these indicate the substantial variance between industries.

[5] Latané and Tuttle, "Framework for Forming Probability Beliefs," *Financial Analysts Journal* (July–August 1968).

[6] Reilly and Drzycimski, "Alternative Industry Performance and Risk."

[7] Milford S. Tysseland, "Further Tests of the Validity of the Industry Approach to Investment Analysis," *Journal of Financial and Quantitative Analysis* 6, no. 2 (March 1971): 835.

[8] Brigham and Pappas, "Rates of Return on Common Stock," 311.

[9] Harlan L. Cheney, "The Value of Industry Forecasting as an Aid to Portfolio Management," *Appalachian Financial Review* 1, no. 5 (Spring 1970): 331–339.

ations. You will recall from Chapter 9 that King clearly believed that there was an industry influence after taking account of the market.[10] Gaumnitz used cluster analysis and found a clustering of some stocks along industry lines, but for most stocks, there was little correspondence to the initial industrial classifications.[11] Meyers came to conclusions similar to Gaumnitz.[12] The results for the overlapping industries and periods were consistent with King's but there was a decline in the industry relationship after 1960.

Livingston analyzed the industry effect after removing the market effect by comparing 734 companies from over 100 industries of varying size.[13] He found strong evidence of positive correlation within industries after the market effect was removed. Also, while the average within industry correlation was significant, it was definitely not universal for all industries. This led Livingston to suggest that *each industry must be examined to determine the importance of residual industry comovement.* The proportion of total variance explained by the industry effect averaged about 18 percent but ranged from 0.15 to 0.75. Those industries that had the lowest correlations with the aggregate market had the strongest industry factors. Some of the cohesive industries were gold mining, agricultural machinery, department stores, meat packers, and vegetable oil companies.

IMPLICATIONS OF INTRA-INDUSTRY DISPERSION. Some observers have mistakenly contended that because all firms in an industry do not move together, industry analysis is useless. Obviously, it would be ideal if all firms in an industry were consistent because then, after analyzing the industry, you would not need to do company analysis. Different companies may have different industry betas, the same way that they have a different relationship to the market, and if stable, such a beta would be a valuable piece of information. For industries with a strong, consistent industry component, such as gold, steel, tobacco, railroads, you could reduce the extent of your company analysis after your industry analysis. For most industries without a strong industry component, however, a thorough company analysis would still be necessary. Even for the nonhomogeneous industries, industry analysis is valuable, because it is much easier to select a superior company from a good industry than to find a good company in an unhealthy industry. Probably one of the *worst* companies in a *good* industry will outperform the *better* companies in a *poor* industry. Therefore, the industry analysis is always important. By selecting the best stocks within an industry with good expectations, you avoid the risk of your good company analysis being negated by a poor industry performance.

[10] Benjamin F. King, "Market and Industry Factors in Stock Price Behavior," *Journal of Business* 39, no. 1, Part 2 (January 1966): 139–190.

[11] Jack E. Gaumnitz, "Influence of Industry Factors in Stock Price Movements," paper presented at Southern Finance Association Meeting, October 1970.

[12] Stephen L. Meyers, "A Re-Examination of Market and Industry Factors in Stock Price Behavior," *Journal of Finance* 28, no. 3 (June 1973): 695–705.

[13] Miles Livingston, "Industry Movements of Common Stocks," *Journal of Finance* 32, no. 2 (June 1977): 861–874.

ANALYSIS OF DIFFERENTIAL INDUSTRY RISK

Despite many industry return studies, there have been few studies on industry risk measures. The Reilly-Drzycimski study considered two questions of interest: (1) What was the difference in risk (beta) for alternative industries during a given time period? (2) How stable was the industry risk measure over time? [14] The results indicated *a wide range of systematic risk* from 1.426 (air transportation) to −0.002 (gold mining). Also, the spread was typically larger during rising and falling markets. An analysis of the risk measures during sequential subperiods, and between alternative periods of rising and falling stock prices, indicated reasonably stable beta coefficients over time. Stability prevailed over the last ten years, with the best results derived during the final five years. The results agreed substantially with those obtained by Blume and Levy for portfolios of stocks, which is what an industry can be considered.[15]

Therefore, while there is substantial dispersion in industry risk during a period of time, there is stability in the risk measure over time, which means that the past industry risk analysis is useful in analyzing future risk.

ESTIMATING INDUSTRY RETURNS

The procedure for estimating the expected returns for alternative industries is again a two-step process in which first the expected earnings per share for an industry are estimated and then the future industry earnings multiple.

To estimate earnings per share, you must estimate sales per share using the relationship between industry sales and some relevant economic series; for example, automobile sales are typically related to disposable personal income. After deriving such a relationship, you estimate the relevant independent variables and thereby derive an estimate of industry sales per share.

If you want a long-run estimate of the sales outlook rather than a one-year projection, input-output analysis should be used to indicate the long-run relationship between industries. This analysis indicates which industries supply the inputs for a specified industry of interest and who gets the output. Subsequently, you should determine the long-run outlook for both suppliers and major customers.[16] The application of this technique to industry analysis is becoming more global because of the nature of the worldwide economy.

The second step is to derive an estimate of the profit margin for the industry. As before, you should begin with the gross margin, because it is less volatile, and subsequently estimate the depreciation expense and tax rate.

---

[14] Reilly and Drzycimski, "Alternative Industry Performance and Risk," 423–446.

[15] Marshall E. Blume, "On the Assessment of Risk," *Journal of Finance* 26, no. 1 (March 1971): 1–10; and Robert A. Levy, "On the Short-Term Stationarity of Beta Coefficients," *Financial Analysts Journal* 27, no. 6 (November–December 1971): 55–62.

[16] For an explanation of input-output analysis, see D. A. Hodes, "Input-Output Analysis: An Illustrative Example," *Business Economics* 1 (Summer 1965): 35–37; and Howard B. Bonham, Jr., "The Use of Input-Output Economics in Common Stock Analysis," *Financial Analysts Journal* 23, no. 1 (January–February 1967): 27–31.

AN INDUSTRY EXAMPLE

To demonstrate the analysis, we will use the Standard & Poor's *composite retail store (CRS) index.* This composite index contains four subindustries: (1) department stores, (2) retail stores (drugs), (3) food chains, and (4) general merchandise chains. You are probably familiar with a number of the companies included in this index. The department store group includes seven companies:

- Carter Hawley Hale Stores
- Dayton Hudson
- Dillard Department Stores
- Federated Department Stores
- May Department Stores
- Mercantile Stores
- Nordstrom.

The retail stores–drug index was initiated in 1970 and includes

- Longs Drug Stores
- Rite Aid
- Walgreen Co.

The retail stores–food chains group includes

- Albertson's
- American Stores (Acme Markets)
- Great Atlantic and Pacific
- Kroger Company
- Lucky Stores
- Southland Corp.
- Supermarket General
- Winn-Dixie Stores.

Finally, the retail stores–general merchandise chains index, which was started in 1970, includes

- K mart
- J. C. Penney Company
- Sears, Roebuck & Company
- Wal-Mart Stores
- F. W. Woolworth Company.

Given the wide spectrum of stores, this industry group involves a fairly diversified portfolio.

SALES FORECAST. The sales forecast for this industry or any industry involves an analysis of the relationship between sales for the industry and some aggregate economic series that is related to the goods and services produced by the industry. The products of the retail store industry range from a basic necessity (food) to general merchandise, such as that sold by Sears, Roebuck, to an equally varied range of products sold in department stores like May Department Stores. Therefore, the economic series

TABLE 14.1
S&P Composite Retail Store Sales and Various Economic Series: 1960–1986

				PER CAPITA	
YEAR	COMPOSITE RETAIL STORES (DOLLARS PER SHARE)	DISPOSABLE PERSONAL INCOME (BILLIONS OF DOLLARS)	PERSONAL CONSUMPTION EXPENDITURES (BILLIONS OF DOLLARS)	DISPOSABLE PERSONAL INCOME (DOLLARS)	PERSONAL CONSUMPTION EXPENDITURES (DOLLARS)
1960	122.65	358.9	330.7	1,986	1,829
1961	127.04	373.8	341.1	2,034	1,857
1962	134.34	396.2	361.9	2,123	1,940
1963	140.25	415.8	381.7	2,197	2,017
1964	147.58	451.4	409.3	2,352	2,133
1965	156.75	486.8	440.7	2,505	2,268
1966	169.68	525.9	477.3	2,675	2,428
1967	179.15	562.1	503.6	2,828	2,534
1968	198.39	609.6	552.5	3,037	2,752
1969	214.75	656.7	597.9	3,239	2,949
1970	224.38	715.6	640.0	3,489	3,121
1971	239.11	776.8	691.6	3,740	3,330
1972	263.04	839.6	757.6	4,000	3,609
1973	284.72	949.8	837.2	4,481	3,950
1974	311.56	1,038.4	916.5	4,855	4,285
1975	315.80	1,142.8	1,012.8	5,291	4,689
1976	342.01	1,252.6	1,129.3	5,744	5,178
1977	374.47	1,379.3	1,257.2	6,262	5,707
1978	397.53	1,551.2	1,403.5	6,968	6,304
1979	418.67	1,729.3	1,566.8	7,682	6,960
1980	484.43	1,918.0	1,732.6	8,421	7,607
1981	521.52	2,127.6	1,915.1	9,243	8,320
1982	510.52	2,261.4	2,050.7	9,724	8,818
1983	558.38	2,428.1	2,234.5	10,340	9,516
1984	596.22	2,668.6	2,430.5	11,257	10,253
1985	625.25	2,841.1	2,629.4	11,872	10,987
1986	617.60	3,022.1	2,799.8	12,508	11,588

Source: *Analysts Handbook* (New York: Standard & Poor's Corporation, 1987). Reprinted by permission of Standard & Poor's. *Economic Report of the President* (Washington, D.C.: U.S. Government Printing Office, 1988).

used in this specific analysis should be fairly broad to reflect the demand for these products. The primary economic series considered are *disposable personal income (DPI)* and *personal consumption expenditures (PCE)*. Table 14.1 contains the aggregate and the per capita values for the two series.

The scatter plot in Figure 14.1 indicates a strong linear relationship between retail sales per share and PCI. Although not shown, there is also a good relationship with DPI. Therefore, if you can do a good job of estimating changes in these series, you should derive a good estimate of

Figure 14.1
Scatter Plot of CRS Sales/Share and PCE

Sales/Share—Composite Retail Stores

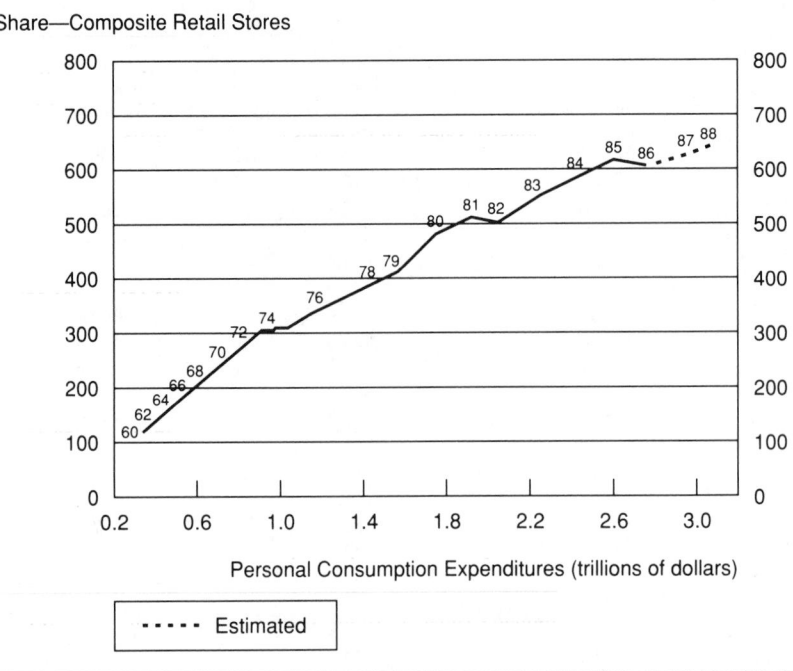

Personal Consumption Expenditures (trillions of dollars)

••••• Estimated

expected sales for retail stores. This close relationship is expected with an aggregate economic series because of the number and diversity of retail stores involved in the index. If you want to project sales for a component group, such as food chains, you should consider a subset of consumer expenditures, such as expenditures for nondurables or personal consumption expenditures for food. *As the industry becomes more specialized and thus more individualized, you need a more individualized economic series that reflects the demand for the industry's product.*

You should also consider *per capita* disposable personal income. Although aggregate DPI increases each year, there is also an increase in the aggregate population, so the increase in the DPI per capita (the average DPI for each adult and child) will typically be less than the increase in the aggregate series. As an example, during 1986 aggregate DPI increased about 6.4 percent, but per capita DPI only increased 5.4 percent. Finally, an analysis of the relationship between changes in the economic variable and changes in industry sales will indicate how the two series move together and highlight any changes in the relationship. Using percent changes provides the following regression model:

$$\% \, \Delta \text{ Industry Sales} = \alpha_i + \beta_i \, (\% \, \Delta \text{ in Economic Series}).$$

The size of the β_i coefficient should indicate how closely the two series

TABLE 14.2
**Results for Regressions Relating Retail Store Sales to
Aggregate Economic Series (Disposable Personal Income and
Personal Consumption Expenditures, 1960–1986)**

VARIABLE		α	β				
DEPENDENT	INDEPENDENT	(t)	(t)	R^2	S.E.[c]	F.	D.W.[d]
Industry sales	DPI[a] (levels)	76.08 (10.99)	.20 (42.52)	.99	19.90	1807.77	.50
Industry sales (%Δ)	DPI[a] (%Δ)	.52 (.20)	.70 (2.40)	.19	3.37	5.74	2.43
Industry sales	PCE[b] (levels)	79.61 (10.18)	.22 (31.25)	.98	22.67	1387.47	.42
Industry sales (%Δ)	PCE[b] (%Δ)	−.35 (−.13)	.80 (2.70)	.23	3.29	7.30	2.09
Industry sales	DPI[a] per capita (levels)	45.22 (7.40)	.05 (52.49)	.99	16.16	2755.32	.70
Industry sales (%Δ)	DPI[a] per capita (%Δ)	1.60 (.73)	.67 (2.35)	.19	3.39	5.51	2.39
Industry sales	PCE[b] per capita (levels)	49.25 (6.88)	.05 (44.28)	.99	19.12	1960.43	.54
Industry sales (%Δ)	PCE[b] per capita (%Δ)	1.05 (.48)	.74 (2.58)	.22	3.32	6.66	2.07

[a] DPI = Disposable personal income
[b] PCE = Personal consumption expenditures
[c] S.E. = Standard error of estimate
[d] D.W. = Durbin-Watson autocorrelation statistic

move together. Assuming the intercept (α_i) is close to zero, a slope (β_i) value of 1.00 would indicate relatively equal percentages of change (e.g., this would indicate that a 10 percent increase in DPI is typically associated with a 10 percent increase in industry sales). A β_i of less than unity would imply that industry sales are not growing as fast as the economy is. This analysis would help you find an economic series that closely reflects the demand for the industry's products and would also indicate the form of the relationship.[17]

Table 14.2 contains the results for several of the regressions discussed. The regressions that relate the level of sales to the level of DPI and PCE confirm the close relationship and the importance of the long-run trend in the alternative series. The more sensitive percentage change regressions indicate that percentage changes in retail sales are more closely related to percentage changes in the PCE than they are to those in the DPI. The

---

[17] A similar approach is advocated in Gary M. Wenglowski, "Industry Profit Analysis—A Progress Report and Some Predictions," paper presented at ICFA–FARF Seminar, March 1975, Institute of Chartered Financial Analysts, Financial Analyst Research Foundation.

slope coefficients (β_i) are less than 1, which indicates that retail sales are less volatile than the aggregate economy. The percentage change regression relating industry sales to PCE is as follows:

$$\% \, \Delta \text{ Industry Sales}_t = -.35 + .80(\% \, \Delta \text{ PCE}).$$

Because the intercept ($-.35$) is not statistically significant, it should not be included in the estimate. Assuming that economists expect that PCE will increase by 3 percent next year, the analyst using this regression would expect retail store sales to increase by 2.4 percent (.80 $\times$ 3.0). Because the slope is less than 1, sales will not increase as much as the economy will during expansions, nor will they decline as much as the economy during recessions.

INDUSTRY PROFIT MARGIN FORECAST. Similar to the aggregate market, the net profit margin is the most volatile and the hardest to estimate directly. You can begin with the gross profit margin and then estimate depreciation and the tax rate.

INDUSTRY'S GROSS PROFIT MARGIN. Recall that in the market analysis we analyzed the factors that should influence the economy's margin, including capacity utilization, unit labor cost, inflation, and net exports. The most important variables were capacity utilization and the unit labor cost. We cannot do such an analysis for industries because the relevant variables are typically not available for individual industries.[18] We can, however, assume that movements in these industry profit margin variables are related to movements in similar economic variables. As an example, when there is an increase in capacity utilization for the aggregate economy, there is probably a comparable increase in utilization for the auto industry or the chemical industry. The same could be true for unit labor cost and exports. If there is a stable relationship between these variables for the industry and the economy, you would expect a relationship to exist between the profit margins for the industry and the economy. It is not necessary that the relationship be completely linear, with a slope of 1. The most important characteristic is a generally stable relationship.

The gross profit margin (GPM) for the S&P 400 industrial index and the S&P composite retail store (CRS) index is presented in Table 14.3. A scatter plot does not provide as much insight as the time series plot in Figure 14.2, which indicates that the S&P 400 GPM has declined over time, while the CRS GPM has been quite stable (except for 1974) and has increased overall. The analysis of the relationship between the GPM for the market and industry using regression analysis was not very useful so is not discussed. It appears that the best estimate can be derived from the time series plot on the basis of what we know about profit trends in the retail business. As noted earlier, it is a matter of judgment for each specific

[18] Again, this is used in Wenglowski, "Industry Profit Analysis—A Progress Report and Some Predictions," paper presented at ICFA–FARF Seminar, March 1975.

TABLE 14.3
**Profit Margins for S&P 400 Industrial Index and S&P Composite Retail Store Index,
1960–1986 (Percentage)**

YEAR	GROSS PROFIT MARGIN[a]		DEPRECIATION EXPENSE		NBT MARGIN		TAX RATE		NET PROFIT MARGIN	
	S&P 400	COMPOSITE RETAIL STORE	S&P 400	COMPOSITE RETAIL STORE	S&P 400	COMPOSITE RETAIL STORE	S&P 400	COMPOSITE RETAIL STORE	S&P 400	COMPOSITE RETAIL STORE
1960	14.85	5.52	2.56	1.30	10.54	4.46	45.8	49.9	5.72	2.23
1961	14.84	5.57	2.66	1.38	10.37	4.48	45.4	49.4	5.66	2.27
1962	15.29	5.52	2.89	1.51	10.82	4.40	45.2	49.4	5.93	2.23
1963	15.75	5.43	3.04	1.61	11.31	4.28	45.3	47.4	6.19	2.25
1964	16.11	5.85	3.24	1.71	11.68	4.69	43.3	45.5	6.63	2.55
1965	16.31	5.96	3.52	1.83	11.95	4.79	42.9	44.6	6.82	2.65
1966	15.93	5.76	3.87	2.04	11.55	4.56	42.6	44.4	6.64	2.53
1967	15.22	5.75	4.25	2.21	10.59	4.52	42.2	44.3	6.12	2.52
1968	15.63	6.15	4.56	2.57	11.13	4.85	45.5	49.1	6.07	2.47
1969	14.87	5.92	4.87	2.52	10.38	4.75	45.6	49.1	5.65	2.42
1970	13.48	5.58	5.17	2.62	8.78	4.41	43.9	47.0	4.92	2.34
1971	13.87	5.60	5.45	2.82	9.26	4.42	45.5	45.1	5.04	2.43
1972	14.34	5.25	5.76	3.05	9.87	4.09	46.4	43.2	5.30	2.32
1973	15.23	5.43	6.25	3.24	11.04	4.30	46.1	44.0	5.96	2.41
1974	14.66	3.89	6.86	3.58	10.89	2.74	51.5	47.6	5.28	1.43
1975	13.69	5.35	7.36	3.71	9.71	4.18	52.3	46.5	4.63	2.24
1976	14.05	5.31	7.58	3.79	10.31	4.20	48.9	43.8	5.27	2.37
1977	13.88	5.48	8.53	4.38	10.13	4.31	49.1	42.5	5.15	2.48
1978	13.85	5.65	9.64	5.24	10.02	4.33	48.2	41.9	5.19	2.52
1979	14.07	5.36	10.82	5.66	10.37	4.00	47.2	38.6	5.57	2.46
1980	12.88	4.46	12.37	6.54	9.10	3.11	45.9	36.7	4.92	1.97
1981	12.64	4.25	13.82	7.24	8.62	2.87	43.6	38.2	4.86	1.77
1982	11.82	5.02	15.30	7.26	7.23	3.60	45.3	38.6	3.95	2.21
1983	12.87	5.89	16.16	7.84	8.04	4.48	45.1	40.9	4.42	2.65
1984	12.79	5.61	16.31	8.58	8.50	4.17	43.9	39.3	4.77	2.53
1985	11.53	5.44	18.19	9.48	7.27	3.93	47.2	39.8	3.84	2.37
1986	11.57	5.87	19.44	9.77	6.57	4.29	42.9	42.1	3.75	2.48

[a] Gross profit margin = net before tax and depreciation/sales.
Source: *Standard & Poor's Analysts Handbook* (New York: Standard & Poor's Corp., 1987). Reprinted with permission.

industry whether you use regression analysis or the time series plot—the empirical relationship will determine the analysis technique.

Either regression analysis or time series techniques can be useful tools, but *neither technique should be applied mechanically.* You should be aware of any unique factors affecting the specific industry such as price wars, contract negotiations, building plans, or foreign competition. These unique events should be considered as adjustment factors when estimating the final gross profit margin or used in estimating a range of industry profit margins (optimistic, pessimistic, most likely).

Time Series Plot of GPM for S&P Composite Retail Store Index and S&P 400

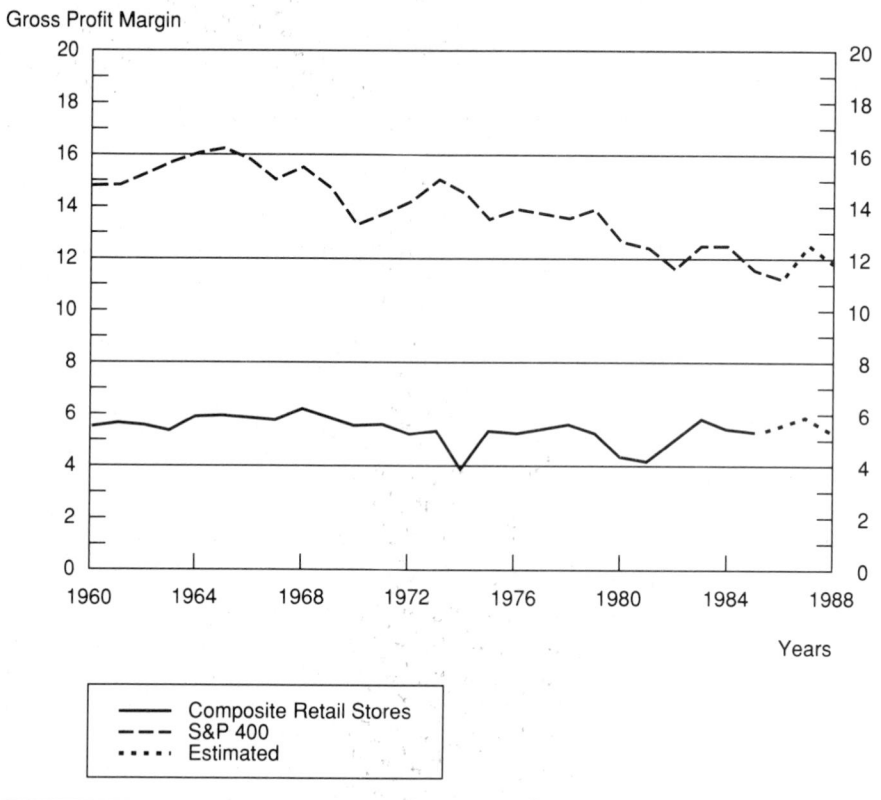

INDUSTRY DEPRECIATION. The next step is to estimate industry depreciation, which is typically easier because the series generally is increasing; the only question is by how much. As shown in Table 14.3, except for 1969, the depreciation series for retail stores has increased every year since 1960. The regressions in Table 14.4 relate industry depreciation to depreciation for the S&P 400 index. There is a strong relationship between levels, with the retail store depreciation consistently about 50 percent of that for the aggregate market during the total period and for most individual years. Alternatively, the percentage change regressions indicate that industry changes are about .79 of those for the market. These regressions, along with estimates of market depreciation, should provide realistic estimates of retail store depreciation. Subtracting depreciation from the gross profit figure indicates the net before tax (NBT) figure. The final step is estimating the tax rate for the industry.

INDUSTRY TAX RATE. As you might expect, different industries have different tax factors. An extreme example would be the oil industry. In some in-

TABLE 14.4

Results for Regressions Relating Depreciation for the Retail Store Industry and S&P 400 Industrial Index, 1960–1986

VARIABLES		α	β				
DEPENDENT	INDEPENDENT	(t)	(t)	R^2	S.E.[a]	F.[b]	D.W.[c]
Industry depreciation	S&P 400 depreciation (levels)	0.08 (1.26)	.51 (80.15)	.996	.168	6423.47	1.76
Industry depreciation	S&P 400 depreciation (%Δ)	1.74 (.74)	.79 (2.96)	.270	4.35	8.74	2.42

[a] S.E. = standard error of estimate
[b] F. = F statistic for regression
[c] C.W. = Durbin-Watson serial correlation statistic

Source: Reprinted with permission from Standard & Poor's Corp., New York, 1987.

stances, however, you can assume that most tax changes have a similar impact on all industries. Given these two possible relationships, you should examine the relationship over time to see if regression analysis will help or whether you should use a time series plot and knowledge of unique tax factors for the industry being examined.

Although the CRS tax rate historically moved with the economy's tax rate, recently the relationship has changed so the regressions are not very useful. Again, it appears that the time series plot in Figure 14.3 is more informative, along with consideration of specific industry factors.

EXAMPLE OF EARNINGS ESTIMATE

To help you understand the procedure discussed, the following is a rough estimate of the net income for the retail store industry using the economic forecasts from Chapter 13 and the relationship between the CRS industry and market derived in this chapter. A practicing analyst would use this example as an initial estimate that would be modified based upon his knowledge of the industry and current events.

The regression analysis in Table 14.2 indicated that the best relationship was between percentage changes in retail sales and in personal consumption expenditures (PCE). The outlook for PCE during 1988 is for about a 3.0 percent increase.[19] This estimate indicates an increase in retail sales of approximately 2.4 percent (.80 × 3.0). Therefore, given that retail sales were expected to be $640 in 1987, the 1988 estimate is about $655 (1.024 × $640).

The GPM for retail stores was 5.87 in 1986. During 1987 the GPM for the S&P 400 increased, and retail store margins probably experienced a similar increase to about 5.95. The aggregate GPM was expected to decline during 1988. Based upon the time series plot in Figure 14.2, this would indicate that retail store margins should decline to about 5.80 percent,

[19] Steven G. Einhorn, *Portfolio Strategy* (New York: Goldman Sachs & Co., 1988).

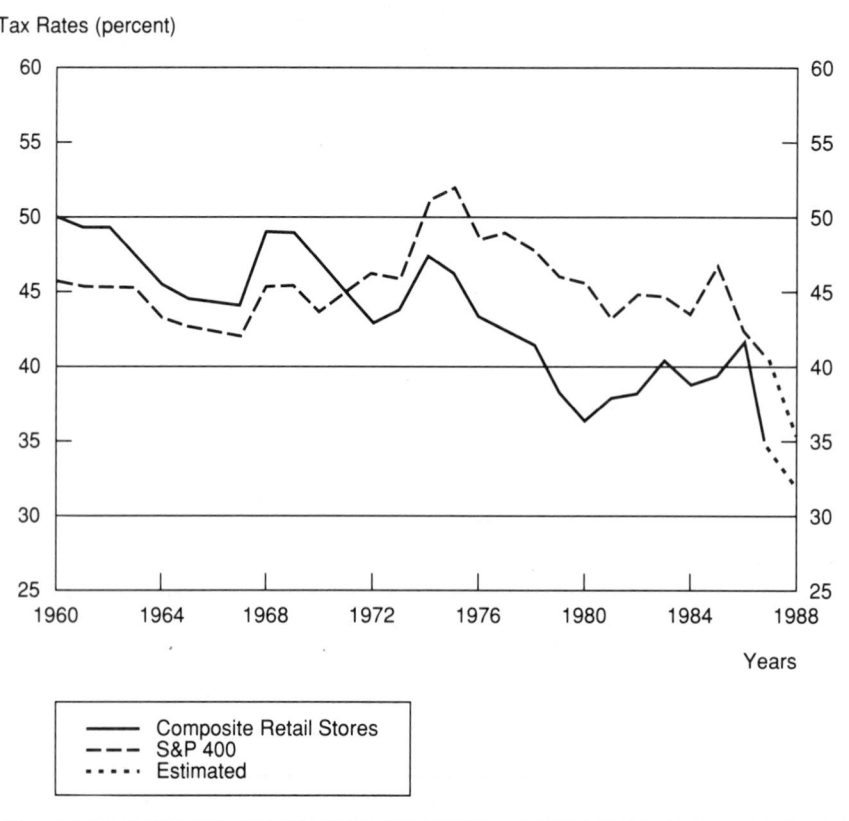

FIGURE 14.3
**Time Series Plot of Taxes for S&P Composite
Retail Store Index and S&P 400**

Tax Rates (percent)

implying that the gross profit per share for the retail store industry should be $37.99 (.058 × $655).

Aggregate depreciation for the S&P 400 series during 1988 was estimated to be $22.15. Assuming the retail store industry will maintain its 50 percent ratio, and the trend exhibited in Figure 14.4, this would imply an estimate for retail store depreciation of about $11.10 and a net before tax earnings of $26.89 ($37.99 − $11.10).

The tax rate for the retail store industry has been lower than the aggregate, which was estimated at 35 percent during 1988. Therefore, a rate of about 33 percent seems appropriate for the retail store industry. This implies taxes of 8.87 (26.89 × .33) and net income (earnings per share) of $18.02 (26.89 − 8.87) per share, indicating a net profit margin of 2.75 percent (18.02/655.00), which is somewhat above the recent experience.

Given an estimate of the industry's net income per share, your next step is to estimate the likely earnings multiple for this industry.

FIGURE 14.4
**Time Series Plot of Depreciation for S&P Composite
Retail Store Index and S&P 400**

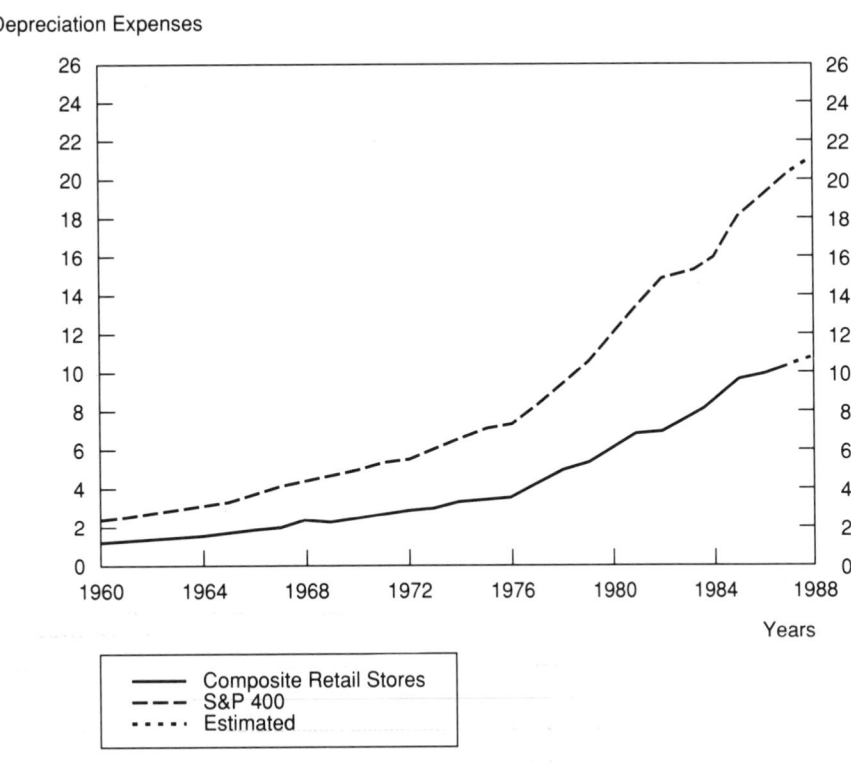

Depreciation Expenses

Years

Composite Retail Stores
S&P 400
Estimated

INDUSTRY EARNINGS MULTIPLES

There are two approaches to estimating an industry multiple. In a macro approach, you examine the relationship between the multiple for the industry and the market. In a micro approach, you estimate the market multiple by examining the specific variables that influence the earnings multiple—the dividend-payout ratio, the required rate of return (k), and the expected growth rate of earnings and dividends (g).

MACRO-ANALYSIS OF INDUSTRY MULTIPLE

The macro approach assumes that the major variables influencing the industry multiple are related to similar variables for the aggregate market. It is hypothesized that there is a relationship between changes in k and g for specific industries and for the aggregate market. If these relevant variables are related in their movements (even though they are not the same values), then there will be a relationship between changes in the industry multiple and changes in the market multiple.

Reilly and Zeller examined the relationship between the P/E ratios for 71 S&P industries and for the S&P 400 index during four partially over-

TABLE 14.5
Results of Regressions between Retail Store P/E Ratio and S&P 400 Index P/E Ratio

	α (t)	β (t)	R^2	S.E.[a]	F.[b]	D.W.[c]
Levels: 1960–1986	0.55 (.26)	1.08 (7.41)	.69	2.99	54.94	.81
Levels: 1960–1986 w/o 1974	−1.44 (−.89)	1.20 (10.82)	.83	2.21	117.13	.71
Percentage change: 1960–1986	.39 (.14)	.48 (2.63)	.22	14.77	6.91	2.40
Percentage change: 1960–1986 w/o 1974	−.71 (−.24)	.59 (3.11)	.30	14.32	9.68	2.02

[a] S.E. = standard error of estimate
[b] F. = F statistic
[c] D.W. = Durbin-Watson serial correlation statistic
Source: Reprinted with permission from Standard & Poor's Corp., New York, 1987.

lapping 21-year periods.[20] The slope coefficients varied from about 0.10 to 3.00, the R^2 averaged about 0.36, and about 76 percent of the slope coefficients were statistically significant. There was a significant positive relationship between percent changes in earnings multiples for most industries examined. The percent change model provided superior forecasts during three of four periods compared to a naive model that assumed no change. Notably, there was a difference between industries in terms of the quality of this relationship. While there was a relationship between the earnings multiples for a number of industries and the market, the relationship was not always significant. Therefore, you must examine the quality of the relationship between an industry and the market before using this technique.

The results in Table 14.5 for the retail store industry during the period 1960–1986 indicate that all coefficients were significant. The best results relate the levels of the P/E ratios during the most recent period. The percentage change regressions are also significant and indicate that the industry P/E ratios are less volatile than the market P/E ratios. These results imply that this technique should be considered, but that you should also use the micro approach.

MICRO-ANALYSIS OF INDUSTRY MULTIPLE

The micro-analysis examines the three major variables affecting the earnings multiple and compares the industry values to the comparable market values in order to determine whether the industry multiple should be above, below, or equal to the market multiple. Initially, you should examine

[20] Frank K. Reilly and Thomas Zeller, "An Analysis of Relative Industry Price-Earnings Ratios," *The Financial Review* (1974): 17–33.

TABLE 14.6

Earnings Multiples for the S&P 400 Index and S&P Composite Retail Store Index with Variables That Influence the Earnings Multiplier: 1960–1986

YEAR	MEAN EARNINGS MULTIPLIER		RETENTION RATE		RETURN ON EQUITY		EQUITY TURNOVER		NET PROFIT MARGIN	
	S&P 400	COMPOSITE RETAIL STORE	S&P 400	COMPOSITE RETAIL STORE	S&P 400	COMPOSITE RETAIL STORE	S&P 400	COMPOSITE RETAIL STORE	S&P 400	COMPOSITE RETAIL STORE
1960	17.70	17.47	41.2	41.2	10.08	9.18	1.76	4.11	5.72	2.23
1961	20.41	21.21	38.6	43.1	9.69	9.46	1.71	4.17	5.66	2.27
1962	16.97	19.83	42.6	40.8	10.53	9.55	1.78	4.29	5.93	2.23
1963	17.07	19.67	44.3	43.2	11.11	9.45	1.79	4.20	6.19	2.25
1964	17.63	20.89	46.8	49.3	12.06	11.18	1.82	4.38	6.63	2.55
1965	16.82	22.05	48.7	50.0	12.64	11.74	1.85	4.42	6.82	2.65
1966	15.20	17.37	49.7	48.6	12.88	11.66	1.94	4.60	6.64	2.53
1967	17.03	16.21	47.1	50.1	11.76	11.13	1.92	4.42	6.12	2.52
1968	17.30	18.66	48.7	51.8	12.27	10.98	2.02	4.44	6.07	2.47
1969	17.45	19.22	47.0	52.8	11.86	11.96	2.10	4.95	5.65	2.42
1970	16.49	17.72	41.8	52.6	10.28	11.33	2.09	4.84	4.92	2.34
1971	18.02	21.65	47.1	54.8	10.80	11.61	2.14	4.79	5.04	2.43
1972	17.95	24.11	52.9	57.3	11.71	11.39	2.21	4.90	5.30	2.32
1973	13.25	19.24	61.1	61.2	14.15	12.11	2.37	5.03	5.96	2.41
1974	9.43	20.63	61.4	38.3	14.17	7.75	2.69	5.40	5.28	1.43
1975	10.79	12.83	56.6	62.0	12.11	11.72	2.61	5.24	4.63	2.24
1976	10.41	13.39	60.5	66.3	14.02	12.45	2.66	5.25	5.27	2.37
1977	9.55	10.50	56.8	63.8	13.93	13.06	2.73	5.28	5.15	2.48
1978	8.21	8.20	58.8	61.4	14.60	13.19	2.81	5.24	5.19	2.52
1979	7.11	7.48	63.7	60.1	16.50	12.85	2.96	5.23	5.57	2.46
1980	8.44	7.40	59.7	53.8	14.88	11.01	3.02	5.60	4.92	1.97
1981	8.45	8.60	58.1	51.5	14.42	10.31	2.97	5.83	4.86	1.77
1982	10.37	9.05	46.0	59.1	11.13	12.48	2.82	5.65	3.95	2.21
1983	11.84	9.97	50.4	65.8	12.07	14.89	2.73	5.61	4.42	2.65
1984	9.92	9.76	58.5	65.3	14.61	14.63	3.06	5.78	4.77	2.53
1985	13.68	12.04	48.5	63.6	12.14	13.51	3.16	5.71	3.84	2.37
1986	17.42	15.66	44.1	65.5	11.70	13.69	3.12	5.51	3.75	2.48
Mean[a]	14.06	15.39	50.7	55.2	12.52	11.79	2.39	4.98	5.34	2.37
Mean[b]	10.50	9.87	54.5	61.0	13.60	12.96	2.94	5.54	4.64	2.34

[a] 1974 not included

[b] Last 10 years (1977–1986)

Source: *Standard & Poor's Analysts Handbook* (New York: Standard & Poor's Corp., 1987). Reprinted with permission.

the long-run relationship between the multiples and look for factors that would cause differences over time.

INDUSTRY VERSUS MARKET MULTIPLE. The mean of the high and low multiple for the aggregate market and the CRS industry is in Table 14.6. The multiples for retail stores were above the aggregate market multiple prior to 1978 but have generally been smaller in recent years. This observation is supported by the average multiples—for the total period the average market multiple was lower (14.06 versus 15.39), but the market multiple was larger during the last ten years (10.50 versus 9.87). Why do the multiples differ over time? Why have investors in recent years been willing to pay more for a dollar of earnings from the aggregate market than from retail stores? Also, why has this relationship changed? An analysis of the factors that determine the earnings multiple should indicate the cause.

DIVIDEND PAYOUT. As shown in Table 14.6, the retention rates of retail stores and the index were typically within 2 percentage points prior to the 1970s. Subsequently, there have been major differences on an annual basis and numerous changes in relative position (i.e., which was larger). Still, the overall averages and recent experience indicate a higher retention rate for the retail stores (51 versus 55 percent and 55 versus 61 percent). These small differences would indicate a higher payout (lower retention rate) for the S&P 400, which would imply a higher multiple for the S&P 400 on the basis of this particular variable.

REQUIRED RETURN. Because the required rate of return (k) on all investments is influenced by the risk-free rate and the expected inflation rate, the differentiating factor is the risk premium. In turn, you will recall that the risk premium is a function of business risk (BR), financial risk (FR), liquidity risk (LR), and the exchange rate risk (ERR), or based upon the CAPM it is a function of the systematic risk (beta) of the asset. Therefore, to derive an estimate of the industry's risk premium, you should examine the BR, FR, LR, and ERR for the industry relative to the aggregate market, or you could compute the systematic risk (beta) for the industry.

Business risk is a function of relative sales volatility and operating leverage. We know that the percentage change in retail sales was about 80 percent as volatile as aggregate sales (Table 14.2). Also the GPM for retail stores was less volatile than the aggregate market GPM. Therefore, since both sales and the GPM were less volatile, it implies that operating profits are substantially less volatile, which also implies that the business risk for the CRS industry is below average.

The financial risk for this industry is difficult to judge because of numerous building leases in the industry. When you consider the many long-term lease contracts, the firms in this industry generally have above-average financial risk.

There is substantial variation in market liquidity among the firms in this industry. Kroger and Sears are very liquid, and American Stores is quite illiquid. Generally, most of the stocks are slightly below average in liquidity. Therefore, the CRS industry probably has slightly above-average liquidity risk.

Exchange rate risk is the uncertainty firms in this industry face because of changes in exchange rates due to non–U.S. sales. This risk is a function of the proportion of sales that are non–U.S. sales and the distribution of the non–U.S. sales among countries. Exchange rate risk can affect a range of industries from those with very limited international sales (e.g., some service industries that have not been involved overseas), to those that are worldwide (e.g., chemical or pharmaceutical industries). In the case of a truly global industry, it might also be necessary to examine the distribution among specific countries since we know that the exchange rate risk varies among countries based upon the volatility of the exchange rates.

The exchange rate risk for the CRS industry would be toward the lower end of the spectrum since many of these firms are almost wholly within the United States. Still, non–U.S. investors have shown substantial interest in some of them so this status could change in the future.

In summary, for the CRS industry, business risk is definitely below average, financial risk is above average, liquidity risk is slightly above average, and exchange rate risk is definitely below average. Assuming that business risk is the most significant variable, the consensus is that overall risk is about even with the market or slightly below average on the basis of internal characteristics.

The systematic risk for the composite retail store industry is computed using the market model as follows:

$$\% \; \Delta \; CRS_t = \alpha_i + \beta_i \, (\% \; \Delta \; S\&P \; 400_t),$$

where

$\% \; \Delta \; CRS_t$ = **percentage price change in composite retail store (CRS) index during month** t

α_i = **regression intercept for CRS industry**

β_i = **systematic risk measure for CRS industry equal to** $Cov_{i,m}/\sigma_m^2$

To derive an estimate in the current case, the model specified was run with monthly data for the five-year period 1983–1987. The results for this regression are as follows:

α_i = 0.057	R^2 = .768
β_i = 1.170	D.W. = 1.96
t-value = 13.64	F. = 185.91

The systematic risk for the retail store industry is above unity, indicating a higher risk industry (i.e., risk greater than the market). Those results are somewhat inconsistent with the prior micro-internal analysis (business risk, financial risk, liquidity risk, and exchange rate risk).

Translating this systematic risk into a required return figure (k) calls for using the security market line model as follows:

$$k_i = RFR + \beta_i(R_m - RFR).$$

Assuming a nominal risk-free rate during this period of 8 percent (.08), a market return (R_m) of 12 percent, and a beta for the industry of 1.17 yields the following:

$$k_i = .08 + 1.17(.12 - .08)$$
$$= .1268$$
$$= 12.68 \text{ percent.}$$

A micro estimate of risk slightly below average and a market risk estimate somewhat above average implies an industry earnings multiple about equal to the market multiple, all other factors being equal.

EXPECTED GROWTH

You will recall that the prime determinants of earnings and dividend growth are the retention rate and the return on equity.

$$g = f(\text{Retention Rate and Return on Equity}).$$

Return on equity can be broken down into equity turnover and net profit margin as follows:

return on equity
$$\text{Net Income/Equity} = \frac{\text{Sales}}{\text{Equity}} \times \frac{\text{Net Income}}{\text{Sales}}.$$

Therefore, you should examine each of these variables in Table 14.6 to determine if they would imply a difference in expected growth for CRS as compared to the aggregate market.

RETENTION RATE. Since the retention rate is 1 minus the dividend-payout rate, and the S&P 400 series had a slightly higher payout rate, this means that the CRS industry has a slightly higher retention rate and a potentially higher growth rate.

RETURN ON EQUITY. Because the return on equity is a function of the equity turnover and profit margin, these two variables are examined individually. Both equity turnover series experienced an increase over time, although the CRS series has consistently been higher. The S&P 400 turnover series increased from 1.76 in 1960 to 3.12 in 1986, a 77 percent increase. Concurrently, the CRS industry turnover went from 4.11 to 5.51, a 34 percent increase. The average for the total period was 2.39 for the S&P 400 versus 4.98 for CRS; during the last ten years it was 2.94 (S&P) versus 5.40 (CRS). Therefore, the average equity turnover for the CRS industry has been almost double that for the aggregate market.

In contrast, the net profit margin for the S&P 400 series was consistently higher than the margin for the CRS industry, although the market profit margin declined during the total period. The higher profit margin for the market offset the higher equity turnover for the industry. These differences indicate what can be done to generate high returns on investment. You can either have a low turnover and high profit margin (the

S&P 400), or a lower profit margin but experience rapid turnover of assets and equity (the CRS industry).

When the two factors are combined, the returns on equity are reasonably close. The average of the ROEs for all years was 12.52 (S&P) versus 11.79 (CRS); for the last ten years it was 13.60 (S&P) versus 12.96 (CRS). These average percentages are quite consistent with what would be derived from multiplying the components as follows:

Equity Turnover $\times$ Profit Margin $=$ Return on Equity

All Years

S&P 400	$2.39 \times 5.34 = 12.76$	
CRS	$4.98 \times 2.37 = 11.80$	

Last Ten Years

S&P 400	$2.94 \times 4.64 = 13.64$	
CRS	$5.54 \times 2.34 = 12.96$	

ESTIMATING GROWTH. The growth rate is a function of the retention rate times the return on equity. The CRS industry has a higher retention rate (all years: 55.2 versus 50.7; last 10 years: 61.0 versus 54.5), while the S&P 400 has a higher return on equity (all years: 12.52 versus 11.79; last 10 years: 13.60 versus 12.96). When these are combined, the estimated long-run growth rates are as follows:

All Years

S&P 400	$.507 \times 12.52 = 6.35\%$	
CRS	$.552 \times 11.79 = 6.51\%$	

Last Ten Years

S&P 400	$.545 \times 13.60 = 7.41\%$	
CRS	$.610 \times 12.96 = 7.91\%$	

Clearly, since the sustainable growth rates based upon the historical values are very similar, any difference in past earnings multiples probably cannot be explained by these growth rates. Notably, the difference in sustainable growth that does exist favors the CRS series, and the differential was larger during the recent period.

WHY THE DIFFERENCE?

Because the earnings multiple is a function of (1) the dividend-payout ratio, (2) the required rate of return, and (3) the expected growth rate, any differences in multiples should be explained by differences in these variables.

Our initial analysis indicated that the earnings multiple for the CRS industry was historically higher than the market multiple, but in recent years the industry multiple has been smaller. The question then becomes:

Why has the CRS industry lost this premium in terms of its multiple? There was a small difference in the payout ratio for the two series that favored the S&P 400 series. The analysis of risk in terms of internal characteristics and a market measure of risk concluded that risk for the CRS industry was about equal to the market risk.

Finally, an analysis of the growth characteristics of the two series indicated differences in equity turnover and profit margin but relatively similar return on equity figures. When the return on equity figures was combined with offsetting retention rates, the implied growth rates were similar and favored the CRS industry.

In summary, the payout ratio favored the market multiple, the risk factor was neutral, and the growth comparison indicated that the multiple for the CRS industry should be higher. This would imply that the industry multiple should tend toward equality with the market multiple.

ESTIMATING THE FUTURE

Our purpose has been to demonstrate a technique and to indicate the relationships that should exist between an industry and the market so that you will be aware of the important variables. Still, you should never forget that *the past alone is of little value in projecting the future,* because past relationships may not hold in the future, especially in the short run. Your function as an analyst is to determine the *future* values for the relevant variables based upon your unique knowledge of the industry.

EXAMPLE OF MULTIPLE ESTIMATE. Ideally you should apply both techniques (macro and micro) to derive fairly consistent estimates of the earnings multiple. In the current case, there was some support for the macro approach. The results indicate that the retail store P/E is less volatile than the market P/E. In Chapter 13 it was estimated that the market multiple would decline in 1988 from about 14 to about 12 (with a range of 10.5 to 16). Therefore, assuming a small decline for the retail industry, a micro estimate for the CRS industry indicates a multiple of about 11.

The analysis of individual components generally indicated that there should be little difference in the multiple for the market and the retail store industry, because the components were either very similar or offsetting. This would imply a multiple of about 12.0 for the CRS industry, which is similar to the market. In summary, the industry macro P/E estimate is about 11 while the micro-analysis indicates a multiple of about 12.0. For our example we will use the mean value of these two estimates (11.50).

THE TOTAL ESTIMATE. The net earnings estimate was for $18.02 a share during 1988. This, coupled with a multiple estimate of 11.50, implied an index value estimate of 207.23 at the end of 1988. Given this index value, you can derive your expected return—$E(R)$—based upon the current value of the index and the expected dividend as follows:

$$E(R_{CRS}) = \frac{207.33 - \text{Index (Current)} + \text{Dividend}}{\text{Index (Current)}}.$$

THE SEARCH FOR UNIQUE FACTORS

Thus far in this chapter we have presented the two-step approach to determining the future value for an industry and the expected rate of return based upon this future value. We have emphasized the importance of knowing the unique characteristics of the industry and calculating their impact. The procedure set forth here provides a reasonable valuation based upon the industry's historical relationship with the economy and the aggregate market. As discussed, the idea is to use this estimate as a starting point; it should be modified by your intimate knowledge of the industry. In the next two sections we will discuss approaches that are useful in developing a unique background for an industry: the industrial life cycle concept and the analysis of an industry's competitive structure.

THE INDUSTRIAL LIFE CYCLE

It is generally recognized that industries have a life cycle similar to humans. The number of stages will vary with your desire for detail, but a serviceable three-stage model would include

3 stage ILC

1. Initial development and rapid expansion
2. Mature growth
3. Stabilization and decline.

A five-stage model might include

1. Early pioneering development
2. Rapid accelerating growth
3. Mature growth
4. Stabilization and market maturity
5. Deceleration of growth and decline.

The author's preference is for the five-stage model, since it provides more detail and a better appreciation of the future for the industry. Figure 14.5 portrays the growth path of sales during these various stages. While the vertical scale is in logs to reflect a *rate* of growth, the horizontal scale is arithmetic and has different widths, representing different time periods. The various stages are not equal in time, but it is possible to speculate on the specific time period for a given stage for an industry. One of the major tasks of an analyst is to accurately estimate these stages—how long will an industry be able to grow at an accelerating rate (Stage 2), how long will it be in a mature growth phase (Stage 3) before its growth stabilizes (Stage 4) and then declines (Stage 5)?

Besides the analysis of sales growth, you would expect a similar graph of profit margins and earnings growth that would not necessarily parallel

Figure 14.5
Portrayal of Industrial Life Cycle for an Industry

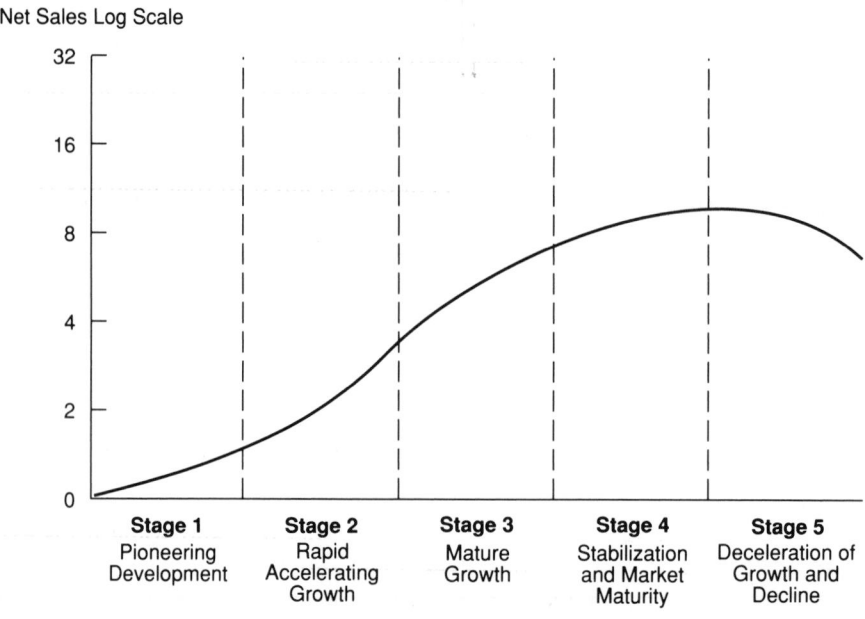

Net Sales Log Scale

Stage 1	Stage 2	Stage 3	Stage 4	Stage 5
Pioneering Development	Rapid Accelerating Growth	Mature Growth	Stabilization and Market Maturity	Deceleration of Growth and Decline

the sales growth. Specifically, the profit margin series might peak very early in the total cycle and then level off or decline due to competition attracted by the early success of the industry.

A brief description of these stages follows:

1. *Pioneering development.* This is the start-up phase where sales growth is modest and profit margins and profits are very small or even negative. During this time period the market is small, and there are major development costs.

2. *Rapid accelerating growth.* During this interval, the product or service is recognized as viable, and the demand is substantial. Because there are few firms in the industry, there is little competition, backlogs are possible, and the profit margins are very high. As productive capacity is built, sales grow at a rate that increases over time as the industry attempts to meet excessive demand. Given the high sales growth and high profit margins that likewise increase as firms become more efficient, profits explode. For example, during this phase profits may be growing at over 100 percent a year due to the low base and rapid growth.

3. *Mature growth.* Because of the great success during the second stage, a lot of the pent-up demand has been satisfied. Further, given the larger base of sales, future sales growth may still be

above normal, but it is not accelerating. As an example, if the overall economy is growing at 8 percent, this industry might be growing at 15–20 percent a year with a tendency for the rate of growth to stabilize. Also, because of the rapid growth and previously high profit margins, there is an influx of competition and the profit margins begin to decline to normal levels.

4. *Stabilization and market maturity.* During this stage the rate of growth is consistent with the aggregate economy or the segment of the economy related to this industry (e.g., DPI, PCE). During this stage (which is probably the longest stage) it is relatively easy to estimate growth because sales are closely related to an economic series. While sales grow in line with the economy, profit growth varies by industry and for individual firms within the industry based upon management ability to control costs. Because of the competition, profit margins are very tight, and returns to capital are at the competitive level or slightly below.

5. *Deceleration of growth and decline.* At this stage the mature industry experiences declines in growth due to lower sales because of shifts in demand or an increase in substitutes. Profit margins continue to be squeezed, and some firms experience low profits or losses. Even those firms that have profits may experience very low rates of return on capital and begin thinking about alternative uses for the capital tied up in this industry.

While these are general descriptions, they should help you identify which stage your industry is in. Obviously everyone is looking for an industry in the early phases of Stage 2 and is hoping to avoid industries in either Stage 4 or 5. The prior analysis involved in the two-step valuation process required an examination of sales and profit margins relative to the economy. This analysis should help you identify your industry's stage within the industrial life cycle.

COMPETITIVE STRUCTURE OF INDUSTRY[21]

In a series of books and articles, Michael Porter has discussed the concept of *competitive strategy,* described as *the search for a favorable competitive position in an industry.* The objective is to establish a profitable and sustainable position against the factors that determine industry competition. There are two major factors to consider in building a competitive strategy. First, you should examine the basic competitive structure of the industry, which will determine its attractiveness as regards long-term profitability. The point is, the potential profitability of a firm is heavily influenced by the inherent profitability of its industry. After determining the competitive structure of the industry, you should examine the factors that determine

---

[21] This discussion draws heavily from Michael E. Porter, *Competitive Strategy: Techniques for Analyzing Industries and Competitors* (New York: The Free Press, 1980); Michael Porter, "Industry Structure and Competitive Strategy: Keys to Profitability," *Financial Analysts Journal* 36, no. 4 (July–August 1980); and Michael Porter, *Competitive Advantage: Creating and Sustaining Superior Performance* (New York: The Free Press, 1985), Chapter 1.

the relative competitive position of a firm within the industry (the subject of our next chapter).

FIVE BASIC COMPETITIVE FORCES. It is contended that the competitive structure, and therefore the intensity of competition within an industry, is determined by the strength of five basic competitive forces:

1. Rivalry among existing competitors
2. Threat of new entrants
3. Threat of substitute products
4. Bargaining power of buyers
5. Bargaining power of suppliers.

It is pointed out that these five forces determine the competitive environment and thereby the profit potential in the industry, measured in terms of return on invested capital. The relative effect of each of these five factors can vary dramatically among industries.

1. *Rivalry among current competitors.* Is rivalry currently intense and growing, or is it polite and stable? Factors that will influence this rivalry include *the number of firms* in an industry and *their relative size* (equality of size increases competitive pressure). Also slow growth is destabilizing, since competitors will fight for market share. A further incentive is *high fixed costs*, which create a desire to sell the full capacity, often leading to price cutting. Also, it is important to analyze *current and future foreign competition.* As noted throughout this book, it is no longer possible to consider only U.S. competitors—*global industries* must be acknowledged. Finally, one must ask whether there are any *exit barriers,* such as specialized facilities or labor agreements, that would keep firms in the industry even though the returns are below average or negative.

2. *Threat of new entrants.* This is best considered by examining possible *barriers to entry,* such as the current prices relative to costs. Other barriers include the need to invest large financial resources to compete and the unavailability of capital, given the potential returns. Also, there might be substantial economies of scale that give current industry members an advantage over a new firm. Also, entrants might be discouraged if distribution channels are critical yet hard to build due to exclusive distribution contracts. Similarly, entry can be deterred if there are high costs of switching products or brands (e.g., changing a computer system or telephone system). Finally, government policy might restrict entry due to licensing or limiting access to new materials (lumber, coal). Without some of these barriers, of course, it would be very easy for competitors to enter an industry and drive down the potential rates of return.

3. *Threat of substitute products.* The existence of substitutes limits the profit potential because it puts a ceiling on the prices that

can be charged. While almost everything has a substitute, the question becomes how close is it in price and function. As an example, in the case of glass and metal containers, the substitute (glass) kept declining in price and was very close in function. This also happened within the food industry among meat (beef versus pork versus chicken) and between meat and fish. In this latter case, price has typically been a critical factor.

4. *Bargaining power of buyers.* Buyers can influence profitability because they can bid down prices or demand higher quality or services by bargaining between competitors. Buyers can be powerful if they purchase a large volume relative to the sales of a supplier (the ultimate is a one-customer firm that supplies a large manufacturer—such as an auto firm). Buyers will be more conscious of costs if the item represents a significant percent of total costs or if the buyer is feeling cost pressure from his customers. Also, if the buyer knows a lot about the costs of a supplier, he will be more intense in bargaining. An example of this would be when a firm supplies some of its own needs and also buys from outside.

5. *Bargaining power of suppliers.* Suppliers can increase prices or reduce the quality and services they provide. The suppliers will be more powerful if there are only a few of them and if they are more concentrated than the industry they are selling to. The weakest position would be if there are few suppliers of a critical input for the industry and they supply several industries and there are few if any substitutes for the input. In this instance the suppliers are free to change prices and services. It should be recalled that *labor* is a supplier, and you should determine its power within each industry.

These five factors determine the competitive structure of an industry and thus its long-run profit potential. You should examine each of these factors for every industry and develop a relative composite profile. This analysis should be repeated over time because *an industry's competitive structure can and will change over time.*

GLOBAL INDUSTRY ANALYSIS

As noted, industry analysis cannot be limited to the United States because a rapidly growing proportion of industries is deeply involved in worldwide competition. The auto industry, for example, is obviously not limited to Chrysler, Ford, and General Motors, but contains numerous firms from Japan, Germany, Italy, and Korea, among others. While everything that has been discussed should be included in such an analysis, there are some additional factors that must be considered in global analysis. The following is an example of such an analysis for the European Chemical Industry by Goldman Sachs & Co.[22] While the report discusses individual firms in the industry, our emphasis in this chapter is on the overall industry.

---

[22] Charles K. Brown, "European Chemical Industry—1988 Prospects," International Research, Goldman, Sachs & Co., February 22, 1988.

TABLE 14.7
"Eurochem"—The European Chemical Majors—Sales Analysis, 1986

GEOGRAPHICAL*		BUSINESS SECTOR	
REGION	PERCENTAGE	PRODUCT GROUP	PERCENTAGE
Europe	60	Health care	15
North America	19	Plastics/resins	13
Far East/Australia	10	Specialty chemicals	10
Latin America	6	Heavy chemicals	8
Rest of the world	5	Agrochemicals	8
	100	Chemical intermediates	8
		Paints	5
		Fibres	5
		Energy	5
		Dyestuffs/pigments	4
		Industrial gases	4
		Fertilizers	4
		Other	11
			100

*By destination

Sources: Company Reports, Goldman, Sachs Analysis; Charles K. Brown, "European Chemical Industry—1988 Prospects," (Goldman, Sachs & Co., International Research, February 22, 1988). Reprinted with permission from Goldman, Sachs & Co.

EUROPEAN CHEMICAL INDUSTRY STRUCTURE. Table 14.7 contains the sales analysis for the industry during 1986. As shown, most of the sales are within Europe, since most of the business by these firms in North America is generated by local production (U.S. sales are supported by a subsidiary or company owned and located in the United States). The table also indicates substantial product diversity, an emphasis in pharmaceuticals, and modest weighting in energy and heavy chemicals.

INDUSTRY OPERATING PERFORMANCE. The report contains a table that shows operating profits and debt ratios for 11 major companies. These data indicate that the industry experienced very poor results during the 1982 recession but it has enjoyed an outstanding recovery. The year 1986 was marked by rising volume, a reduction in capacity, corporate and market restructuring, low investment, and consequently strong cash flow. Table 14.8 indicates the reductions in capacity for one segment of the industry. Figure 14.6 shows that investment barely exceeds depreciation. This minimal investment has impacted on capacity utilization for styrene and polystyrene as shown in Figure 14.7—it ranges from 80 to 90 percent. There was also an increase in prices and relative profit margins during 1987 reflecting these changes. Because of these higher margins and the volume increases shown in Table 14.9, there was a substantial increase in net earnings.

The final segment of the analysis examined the geographical/currency factors involved in forecasting production for each country and also the

TABLE 14.8
European Petrochemical and Plastics Capacity Reductions

	ETHYLENE	POLYETHYLENE		POLYVINYL CHLORIDE	POLYPROPYLENE
		LOW DENSITY	HIGH DENSITY		
Nominal Capacity (million tonnes p.a.)					
1979 (end-year)	16.5	5.9	2.5	5.4	2.2
Capacity added	1.9	0.7	0.6	0.6	0.8
Capacity closed	−4.4	−1.6	−0.8	−1.1	−0.4
1986 (opening)	14.0	5.0	2.3	4.9	2.6
Net reduction	−15%	−15%	−8%	−9%	+18%
Production (million tonnes p.a.)					
1982	10.1	3.6	1.5	3.3	1.8
1983	11.8	4.4	1.9	3.7	2.0
1984	12.3	4.3	2.0	3.8	2.3
1985	12.2	4.3	2.0	3.9	2.3
1986	12.7	4.4	2.1	4.1	2.7
Number of Producers					
1979 (end-year)	32	25	22	29	19
1986 (opening)	28	19	17	17	16

Sources: ICI, Industry Statistics, APME; Charles K. Brown, "European Chemical Industry—1988 Prospects," (Goldman, Sachs & Co., International Research, February 22, 1988). Reprinted with permission from Goldman, Sachs & Co.

export and import possibilities based upon historical patterns and the exchange rate outlook. Table 14.10 contains the exchange rates for each of the major countries relative to the United States. It is pointed out that while the exchange rate changes during 1987 and early 1988 favored the United States, these changes were not expected to have a significant impact, because exports were historically a very small proportion of U.S. sales (about 5 percent). Also sales in the United States by foreign firms were mainly based on production by U.S. subsidiaries or plants in the United States.

Overall, the summary of prospects for 1988–1989 is considered favorable in terms of production, costs, and profits. Further, currency movements are not expected to be as bad as they were during 1987, so international trade flows should not be a disruptive force for European chemical firms. The rest of the report contains detailed discussions of the major chemical firms and makes specific recommendations regarding each of them. This latter segment of the report will be considered in the subsequent chapter that deals with company analysis.

SUMMARY

Several studies dealing with cross-section industry performance and risk and time series measures of industry performance have been performed. They indicate wide dispersion in the performance of alternative industries during specified time periods, which implies that industry analysis is of

FIGURE 14.6
Capital Expenditure by Major European Chemical Companies

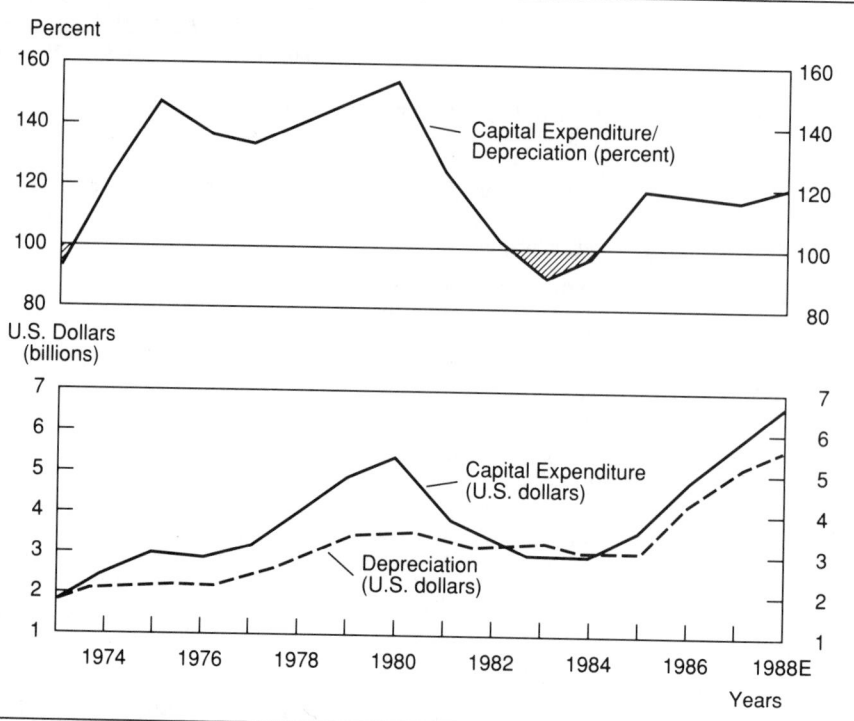

Source: ICI, BASE, BAYER, and HOECHAT company reports; Goldman, Sachs & Co. estimates.

value. Also the performance of specific industries over time was not consistent, which means past performance is not of value in projecting future performance. Also, performance within industries is not very consistent for many industries, which means that individual companies must be analyzed following the industry analysis.

The analysis of industry risk indicated wide dispersion between industries but a fair amount of consistency over time for individual industries. This implies that risk analysis is essential, but that past risk measures may also be of some use.

Using the dividend growth model involves estimating sales based upon the relationship of the industry to some economic variables. The net profit margin is derived based upon an estimate of the gross profit margin, depreciation, and the industry tax rate. The second half of the procedure involves estimating the earnings multiple for the industry using either a macro or micro approach.

One valuable technique in industry analysis involves the concept of an industrial life cycle, with five stages of growth for any industrial unit. Another involves analysis of the five major factors that influence an industry's competitive structure and how they affect its long-run profitability.

FIGURE 14.7
Styrene and Polystyrene—European Capacity Utilization

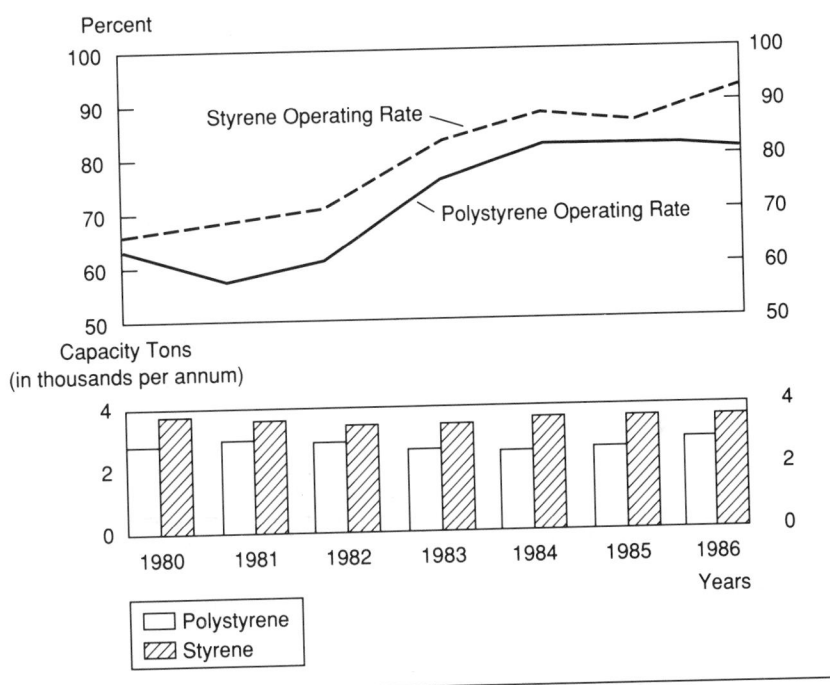

Source: Chem Systems.

TABLE 14.9
Chemical Production Volume (Percentage Change on Year-Earlier Period)

	1981	1982	1983	1984	1985	1986	1987E	1988E
United Kingdom	—	+1	+7	+7	+5	+2	+6	+3
West Germany	+1	−4	+6	+5	+2	−1	+2	+2
France	−2	—	+6	+4	—	—	+3	+1
Switzerland	+4	−1	+7	+6	+6	+2	+1	+2
Netherlands	+7	−5	+9	+9	+9	+1	+6	+3
Italy	−3	+2	+1	+6	+3	+1	+3	+2
Europe	—	−1	+6	+6	+3	—	+3	+2
United States	+6	−8	+10	+6	+5	+5	+5	+3

Sources: Chemical Industry Associations, Goldman, Sachs estimates; Charles K. Brown, "European Chemical Industry—1988 Prospects," (Goldman, Sachs & Co., International Research, February 22, 1988). Reprinted with permission from Goldman, Sachs & Co.

Table 14.10
U.S. Dollar Exchange Rates—Quarterly Averages

	DM/Dollar	Percent Change	Dollar/Pound	Percent Change	French Franc/ Dollar	Percent Change
1985 Q1	3.25		1.12		9.94	
Q2	3.09		1.26		9.42	
Q3	2.85		1.38		8.68	
Q4	2.58		1.44		7.89	
1986 Q1	2.35	27.7%	1.44	28.6%	7.22	27.4%
Q2	2.25	27.2%	1.51	19.8%	7.14	24.2%
Q3	2.09	26.7%	1.49	8.0%	6.78	21.9%
Q4	2.00	22.5%	1.43	−0.7%	6.56	16.9%
1987 Q1	1.84	21.7%	1.54	6.9%	6.13	15.1%
Q2	1.81	19.6%	1.64	8.6%	6.03	15.5%
Q3	1.84	12.0%	1.62	8.7%	6.13	9.6%
Q4	1.70	15.0%	1.76	23.1%	5.75	12.3%
1988 Q1E	1.68	8.7%	1.78	15.6%	5.66	7.7%

Note: Percentage changes are relative to the year-earlier quarter and are shown as positive where the currency of the country in question has strengthened (the ratio is inverted for dollar/pound); i.e., a positive change represents an adverse impact on results expressed in local currency. Trade-weighted indexes are as compiled by the Bank of England (1975 = 100).

Global industry analysis should consider not only world supply and demand, but also the effect of exchange rates on the industry and the firms within the industry.

QUESTIONS

1. Several studies have examined differences in the performance of alternative industries over specific time periods. Briefly describe the results of these cross-sectional studies, and discuss their implications for industry analysis.

2. A number of studies have considered the time series of industry performance—that is, individual industries over time. Briefly describe the empirical results of these studies, and discuss their implications for those involved in industry analysis. Do these results imply that industry analysis is easier or harder?

3. You are told that all the firms in a particular industry have consistently experienced rates of return very similar to the results for the aggregate industry. What does this imply regarding the importance of industry analysis for this industry? What does it imply regarding the importance of individual company analysis for this industry? Discuss.

4. Some observers have contended that because there is a great deal of dispersion in the performance of different firms in an industry, industry analysis is of little value. Discuss this.

5. Discuss several factors that would cause different companies in a given industry to experience similar operating results.

ITALIAN LIRA/ DOLLAR	PERCENT CHANGE	DUTCH GUILDER/ DOLLAR	PERCENT CHANGE	SWISS FRANC/ DOLLAR	PERCENT CHANGE
2019		3.68		2.75	
1970		3.49		2.59	
1892		3.20		2.35	
1750		2.91		2.13	
1600	20.8%	2.65	28.0%	1.98	28.0%
1539	21.9%	2.53	27.5%	1.87	27.8%
1435	24.2%	2.35	26.6%	1.69	28.1%
1387	20.7%	2.26	22.3%	1.66	22.1%
1306	18.4%	2.08	21.5%	1.55	21.7%
1299	15.6%	2.04	19.4%	1.49	20.3%
1330	7.3%	2.07	11.9%	1.52	10.1%
1247	10.1%	1.92	15.0%	1.40	15.7%
1234	5.5%	1.88	9.6%	1.37	11.6%

6. Would you expect a difference in the industry influence on rates of return for companies in different industries? Briefly discuss the empirical evidence on this question.

7. Several studies have examined the difference in the risk for alternative industries during a specified time period. Describe these results, and discuss their implications for the practice of industry analysis.

8. What were the results when the risk for alternative industries was examined during successive time periods? What does this imply for those involved in industry analysis?

9. If you could derive the data, what would you examine to determine the future gross profit margin for an industry?

PROBLEMS

1. Select three industries from the S&P *Analysts Handbook* with different characteristics in terms of demand. Indicate what economic time series you would use in the analysis of the sales growth for each industry, and discuss why this series is relevant for this industry.

2. Prepare a scatter plot of industry sales and economic values over the last ten years using information available in the *Analysts Handbook* for one of the three industries selected in Problem 1. Discuss the results of the scatter plot; was the economic series closely related to industry sales?

3. In your college library find a copy of the *Analysts Handbook* (Standard &

Poor's Corp.) and plot the latest ten-year history of the gross profit margin for the S&P 400 versus the S&P industry of your choice. Does there appear to be a positive, negative, or zero correlation?

4. Again using Standard and Poor's as a data source, calculate the means of the S&P 400 and the industry of your choice for each of the following:

4a. Price/earnings multiple

4b. Retention rate

4c. Return on equity

4d. Equity turnover

4e. Net profit margin
Note: each of these entries is a ratio, so care must be taken when averaging. Comment briefly on the differences for each of the variables.

5. A source of industry information can be found in *Barron's Market Laboratory/Economic Indicators.* Using issues over the past six months, plot the trend for

5a. Auto production

5b. Auto inventories (domestic and imports)

5c. Newsprint production

5d. Newsprint inventories

5e. Gross national product

5f. Business inventories
Can any tentative conclusions be reached through observation of this data?

6. Prepare a table that contains the relevant variables that influence the earnings multiple for your industry and the S&P 400 series for the most recent ten years.

6a. Does the average dividend-payout ratio differ? How should the dividend payout influence the difference between the multiples?

6b. Would you expect the systematic risk for this industry to differ from that for the market? In what direction, and why? What effect will this difference have on the industry multiple relative to the market multiple?

6c. Analyze the different components of growth (retention rate, equity turnover, and profit margin) for your industry and the S&P 400 during the most recent ten years, and discuss each of the components. On the basis of this discussion, would you expect the growth rate for your industry to be above or below the growth rate for the S&P 400? How would this difference in growth affect the difference between the multiples?

7. Where is your industry in terms of its industrial life cycle? Justify your answer by reference to your prior analysis.

8. Evaluate your industry in terms of the five factors that determine an industry's competitive structure. Would you expect this industry to enjoy above-average long-run profitability? Justify your expectation.

REFERENCES   Brigham, Eugene F., and James L. Pappas. "Rates of Return on Common Stock." *Journal of Business* 42, no. 3 (July 1969).

Fruhan, William E., Jr. *Financial Strategy.* Homewood, Ill.: Richard D. Irwin, 1979.

Latané, Henry A., and Donald L. Tuttle. "Framework for Forming Probability Beliefs." *Financial Analysts Journal* 24, no. 4 (July-August 1968).

Livingston, Miles. "Industry Movements of Common Stocks." *Journal of Finance* 32, no. 3 (June 1977).

Meyers, Stephen L. "A Re-Examination of Market and Industry Factors in Stock Price Behavior." *Journal of Finance* 32, no. 3 (June 1973).

Porter, Michael E. "Industry Structure and Competitive Strategy: Key to Profitability." *Financial Analysts Journal* 36, no. 4 (July-August 1980).

Porter, Michael E. *Competitive Strategies: Techniques for Analyzing Industries and Competitors.* New York: The Free Press, 1980.

Porter, Michael E. *Competitive Advantage: Creating and Sustaining Superior Performance.* New York: The Free Press, 1985.

Reilly, Frank K., and Eugene Drzycimski. "Alternative Industry Performance and Risk." *Journal of Financial and Quantitative Analysis* 9, no. 3 (June 1974).

APPENDIX 14A   PREPARING AN INDUSTRY ANALYSIS

Studies of the price movements of individual stocks have indicated that basic market trends over the short to intermediate term are more influential than any other factor. Industry trends are the second most important influence on a stock's price followed by those elements peculiar to the company itself. It is very important, therefore, to study industry characteristics and trends before projecting the outlook for individual issues. Here are some guidelines for preparing an industry appraisal.

WHAT IS AN INDUSTRY?[1]

Identifying a company's industry can be difficult in today's business world. While airlines, railroads, and utilities may be easy to categorize, what about manufacturing companies with three different divisions, none of them dominant? Perhaps the best way to test whether a company fits into an industry grouping is to compare the numbers for the company and industry. For our purposes, an industry may be defined as a group of companies with similar characteristics.

CHARACTERISTICS TO STUDY

1. Price history reveals valuable long-term relationships.
   a. Price-earnings ratios
   b. Common stock yields
   c. Price-book ratios.
2. Operating data shows comparisons of

---

[1] Reprinted with permission of Stanley D. Ryals, CFA; Investment Council, Inc., La Crescenta, CA 91214.

a. Return on total investment (ROI)
b. Return on equity (ROE)
c. Sales growth
d. Net earnings growth
e. Book value growth
f. Earnings per share growth
g. Profit margin trends.
3. Comparative results of industries
a. Effect of business cycles on each industry group
b. Secular trends affecting results
c. Industry growth compared to other industries
d. Regulatory changes
e. Importance of overseas operations.

FACTORS IN INDUSTRY ANALYSIS

1. Trends in the markets for the industry's major products, historical and projected
2. Industry growth relative to GNP or other relevant economic series; possible changes from past trends

MARKETS FOR PRODUCTS

3. Shares of market for major products among domestic producers; changes in market shares in recent years; outlook
4. Effect of imports on their markets; share of market taken by imports; price and margin changes caused by imports
5. Effect of exports on their markets; trend in prices and units exported.

FINANCIAL

1. Capitalization ratios; ability to raise new capital; earnings retention
2. Ratio of fixed assets to capital invested; depreciation policies; capital turnover
3. Return on total capital; return on equity capital
4. Return on foreign investments; need for foreign capital.

OPERATIONS

1. Degrees of integration; cost advantages of integration; major supply contracts
2. Operating rates as a percentage of capacity; backlogs; new order trends
3. Trends of industry consolidation
4. New product development; research and development budgets in both dollars and as a percentage of sales
5. Diversification; comparability of product lines.

MANAGEMENT

1. Management depth and ability to develop from within; board of directors; organizational structure
2. Flexibility to deal with product demand changes; ability to weed out losing operations
3. Record and outlook of labor relations
4. Dividend progression.

SOURCES OF INDUSTRY INFORMATION

For information on industries, check the library or these sources:

1. Recognized and independent industry journals
2. Industry and trade associations
3. Government reports and statistics
4. Independent research organizations
5. Brokerage house research.

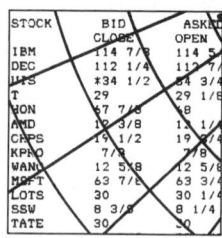

CHAPTER 15

COMPANY ANALYSIS

At this point it is assumed that you have made two decisions. First, after analyzing the economy for several countries and the aggregate stock markets, you have decided that some portion of your portfolio should be in common stocks. Second, after analyzing a number of industries, you expect an above-average risk-adjusted performance in certain industries over the relevant investment horizon. The question you now face is, which companies within these desirable industries are best?

In this chapter we will discuss the procedure for analyzing the companies in an industry. Although we will consider only one U.S. firm and its U.S. industry, the same procedure should be applied for all U.S. and non–U.S. firms in the global industry to derive a ranking of firms. We will discuss an example of such an analysis by a major investment banking firm. Following this analysis using the dividend model, we will also consider some alternative valuation techniques—the price/book value ratio and the T-model—as well as some competitive strategies. The final section in the chapter discusses in detail the unique features of true growth companies and considers several models that can be used to determine the relative value of these companies. Before we discuss company analysis, we must consider the differences between types of companies and types of stocks.

TYPES OF COMPANIES AND TYPES OF STOCK[1]

The label given to a company is principally determined *internally* by the investment decisions of the firm (what assets it owns) and by the operating and financial philosophy of the firm's management. When a company in-

---

[1] This section draws heavily from Frank K. Reilly, "A Differentiation between Types of Companies and Types of Stock," *Mississippi Valley Journal of Business and Economics* 7, no. 1 (Fall 1971): 35–43.

vests in assets (whether human or physical), it thereby determines its characteristics and accepts the accompanying risks and opportunities. However, two different sets of management personnel can experience substantially different results with the same set of assets. Management's operating and financial decisions can influence not only the expected flow of earnings, but also the risk inherent in the flow. Therefore, you should consider the assets of the firm, what its management is capable of doing with these assets, and what its management intends to do with them. Finally, these company factors should be compared to similar factors for other companies to determine the firm's relative position among all companies.

The type of stock is determined by comparing the expected value of the security to the market and to alternative industries. The risk for a stock can be determined by examining the internal characteristics of the firm or can be measured in terms of the stock's systematic risk relative to the aggregate market portfolio.

The major point of the ensuing discussion is that the type of company is not necessarily the same as the type of stock. The stock of a growth company, for example, is not necessarily a growth stock. Recognition of this difference is very important for successful investing.

GROWTH COMPANIES AND STOCKS

Growth companies have historically been defined in terms of results rather than causes, that is, as companies that consistently experience above-average growth in sales and earnings. Unfortunately, because of this definition many firms qualify on the basis of results that are not internally generated but are the consequence of certain accounting procedures introduced in the course of mergers or due to other factors not indicative of superior markets or superior managements.

Currently, as a result of the writings of Solomon, Miller and Modigliani, and others, it has become generally recognized that a true growth company is a firm with the management ability and the opportunities to invest in projects that yield rates of return greater than the firm's required rate of return (i.e., its average cost of capital).[2] As an example, a growth company would be one that has the ability to acquire capital at an average cost of, say, 10 percent and yet has the management ability and the opportunity to invest those funds (whether internally generated or externally acquired) at rates of return in excess of 10 percent. As a result of these investment opportunities, the firm enjoys sales and earnings growth greater than that experienced by other firms in a similar risk category.

The result of being a true growth company (i.e., a firm with above-average investment opportunities) is that the firm should, and typically does, retain a large portion of its earnings to invest in these above-average investment alternatives. Because of these investments, the sales and earnings of the true growth firm grow faster than they do for average firms or

---

[2] Ezra Solomon, *The Theory of Financial Management* (New York: Columbia University Press, 1963), 55–68; and Merton Miller and Franco Modigliani, "Dividend Policy, Growth, and the Valuation of Shares," *Journal of Business* 34, no. 4 (October 1961): 411–433.

for the overall economy. Logically enough, the search for growth firms *ex post* typically involves examining a large cross section of firms to find those that retain a substantial portion of earnings and consistently experience above-average increases in earnings. This way, however, growth companies are identified by *results* rather than *causes,* and, as pointed out earlier, companies may be improperly identified as growth companies on the basis of results achieved through unusual means (e.g., accounting changes). Also, the growth firm can be identified only after the fact.

A growth stock is a stock possessing superior return capabilities when compared to other stocks in the market with similar risk characteristics. This superior return potential is because the stock is *undervalued* at a given point in time relative to other stocks in the market. In a strong-form efficient market with perfect information, all firms would generate rates of return consistent with the systematic risk involved, and there would never be any growth stocks, since all stocks would be properly valued.[3] While the stock market is relatively efficient in adjusting stock prices to new information, it is also very likely that the information is not perfect or complete as discussed in Chapter 6. This means that at any point in time, owing to imperfect information or the lack of information, a given stock may be undervalued or overvalued.[4] If it is undervalued, the stock price should increase to reflect its value when the correct information becomes available. During the period of adjustment, the realized returns will exceed the required returns for a stock with its risk, and the stock will be considered a growth stock.

A future growth stock is basically a currently undervalued stock that has a high probability of being properly valued in the near term. This means that *growth stocks are not necessarily limited to growth companies.* If investors recognize a growth company and discount the future earnings stream properly, the current market price of the stock will reflect the future earnings stream. Thus, those who acquire it at this "correct" market price will receive a rate of return consistent with the risk of the stock, even when the superior earnings growth is attained. If investors *overprice* the stock of a growth company, those who pay the inflated price will realize returns below the risk-adjusted normal return. A future growth stock can be issued by any type of company; it is necessary only that the stock has been undervalued by the market at a given point in time.

As with a growth company, the search for a growth stock after the fact is relatively easy, since one need only to examine past returns relative to the risk involved. The search for *future* growth stocks is the task of a securities analyst. The ability to uncover such stocks consistently is, by definition, the description of a superior analyst.[5]

---

[3] For a discussion of the relationship and a summary of some empirical evidence on the subject, see Richard A. Brealey, *An Introduction to Risk and Return from Common Stocks*, 2d ed. (Cambridge, Mass.: The MIT Press, 1983), 53–61.

[4] As noted in Chapter 6, an analyst is more likely to find such stocks outside the top tier of companies, because these top tier stocks are scrutinized by numerous analysts.

[5] See the discussion in Chapter 6 on "Evaluating the Performance of Analysts."

DEFENSIVE COMPANIES AND STOCKS

Defensive companies are those whose future earnings are likely to withstand an economic downturn. Typical examples are public utilities or grocery chains—firms that supply basic consumer necessities.

There are two closely related concepts of a defensive stock. First, its rate of return is not expected to decline during an overall market decline, or at least not by as much as the market. Second, our discussion of the CAPM indicated that an asset's relevant risk measure asset is its covariance with the market portfolio of risky assets, that is, an asset's systematic risk. A stock with low systematic risk (a small beta) would be considered a defensive stock according to this theory.

CYCLICAL COMPANIES AND STOCKS

A cyclical company's sales and earnings will be heavily influenced by aggregate business activity. It will do very well during economic expansions and very poorly during economic contractions. This volatile earnings pattern is a function of the firm's business risk and financial risk. A cyclical stock will experience changes in rates of return that are greater than changes in overall market rates of return—that is, in terms of the CAPM, these stocks have high betas. The stock of a cyclical company, however, is not necessarily cyclical. A cyclical stock is the stock of any company that has a price more volatile than the overall market.[6]

SPECULATIVE COMPANIES AND STOCKS

A speculative company is one whose assets involve great risk but also a possibility of great gain. A good example of a speculative firm is one involved in oil exploration. A speculative stock possesses a high probability of low or negative rates of return and a low probability of normal or high rates of return. This can either be the stock of a speculative company such as a penny mining stock, or it can be the opposite of a growth stock. Specifically, a speculative stock is one that is *overpriced,* so there is a high probability that during the future period when the market adjusts the stock price to its true value, there will be either very low or possibly negative rates of return on it. This might be the case for an excellent growth company that has stock selling at an extremely high price-earnings ratio.

COMPANY ANALYSIS PROCEDURE

Analyzing an individual firm involves examining its internal characteristics and its relationship to its industry and to the economy. Patterns should emerge regarding the firm's earnings stream and its financial characteristics, including its business risk and financial risk. After determining whether the company is a cyclical, defensive, speculative, or growth firm, you must consider the characteristics of its common stock, because *the type of company and the type of stock may not be the same.*

---

[6] For a discussion of why the stocks of growth companies will decline more during periods of declining markets, see Burton Malkiel, "Equity Yields, Growth, and the Structure of Share Prices," *American Economic Review* 53, no. 5 (December 1963): 1004–1031; Robert A. Haugen and Dean W. Wichern, "The Elasticity of Financial Assets," *Journal of Finance* 29, no. 4 (September 1974): 1229–1240; and John A. Boquist, George A. Racette, and Gary G. Schlarbaum, "Duration and Risk Assessment for Bonds and Common Stocks," *Journal of Finance* 30, no. 5 (December 1975): 1360–1365.

**EXAMPLE OF
COMPANY
ANALYSIS**

To demonstrate the procedure, we will analyze the Kroger Co., the nation's largest retail grocery chain. As of February 1988, it operated 1,319 supermarkets, 899 convenience stores, and 12 membership warehouses. The firm processes and manufactures food for supermarkets at 41 plants.

It is assumed that you have decided to invest in equities, and you expect the retail food chain industry to experience above-average performance during the relevant investment horizon—that is, you have decided to overweight this industry in your equity portfolio. Therefore, your company analysis would involve examining all of the firms in the retail food chain industry to determine which stocks should experience the best performance. The objective is to estimate the expected return and risk for all the individual firms over the investment horizon. These values are then used by the portfolio manager as inputs into the portfolio model.

**ESTIMATING
EXPECTED
RETURN**

You estimate the stock's expected return by estimating the future value for the security. In turn you derive the future value by predicting expected earnings and use the dividend growth model to derive the expected earnings multiple for the stock. Expected earnings is a function of the sales forecast and the firm's estimated profit margin.

SALES FORECAST. The sales forecast includes an analysis of the relationship of company sales to various relevant economic series and to industry series. This company-economy, company-industry analysis indicates how the company is performing relative to its most immediate competition.

Table 15.1 contains data on sales for Kroger, sales per share for the retail food store industry, and several personal consumption expenditure (PCE) series for the period 1977–1987. While you would normally want to consider a longer period to derive historical perspective, this is not feasible in the case of Kroger, since the firm has been through a major reorganization that included the sale of its drugstore chains. Therefore, only the data since 1977 are comparable in terms of continuing operations.

The most relevant economic series is the personal consumption expenditure for food (PCE-food), which has comprised between 17 and 20 percent of total PCE. The scatter plot of Kroger sales and the PCE-food expenditures contained in Figure 15.1 indicates a strong linear relationship, but also indicates that Kroger sales have grown faster than PCE-food. During the period 1977–1987 Kroger sales increased by about 132 percent compared to an increase in PCE-food of 101 percent. As a result, Kroger sales grew from about 3.0 percent of the total PCE for food to over 3.4 percent. The first two regressions in Table 15.2 that relate Kroger sales to PCE-food reflect a significant relationship. The percentage change regression indicates that the reason Kroger sales are more volatile than the PCE-food series is because of their faster growth.

The regressions in Table 15.2 confirm a significant relationship between sales and total PCE, although the relationship is not as strong as the one with PCE-food. The coefficients above 1 indicate the large percentage changes in Kroger sales relative to the PCE series. The basic results

TABLE 15.1
Sales for Kroger Co., the Retail Food Store Industry, and Various Economic Series: 1977–1987

YEAR	SALES: KROGER CO. (MILLIONS OF DOLLARS)	RETAIL FOOD STORE INDUSTRY (SALES PER SHARE)	PERSONAL CONSUMPTION EXPENDITURES (BILLIONS OF DOLLARS)	PERSONAL CONSUMPTION EXPENDITURES PER CAPITA (DOLLARS)	PERSONAL CONSUMPTION EXPENDITURES: FOOD (BILLIONS OF DOLLARS)	PERSONAL CONSUMPTION EXPENDITURES: FOOD/TOTAL PERCENTAGE
1977	7,597.6	667.55	1,257.2	5,707	255.9	20.4
1978	8,953.0	690.69	1,403.5	6,304	282.2	20.1
1979	10,370.7	714.74	1,566.8	6,960	317.3	20.3
1980	11,981.2	808.53	1,732.6	7,607	349.1	20.1
1981	13,275.0	871.91	1,915.1	8,320	376.5	19.7
1982	14,045.3	904.98	2,050.7	8,818	398.8	19.4
1983	14,446.8	872.31	2,234.5	9,516	421.9	18.9
1984	15,063.4	937.78	2,430.5	10,253	448.5	18.5
1985	15,966.6	982.07	2,629.4	10,987	472.8	18.0
1986	17,122.5	951.16	2,799.8	11,588	497.8	17.8
1987	17,659.7	964.48	2,966.0	12,165	514.5	17.3

FIGURE 15.1
Scatter Plot: Kroger Sales and PCE-Food

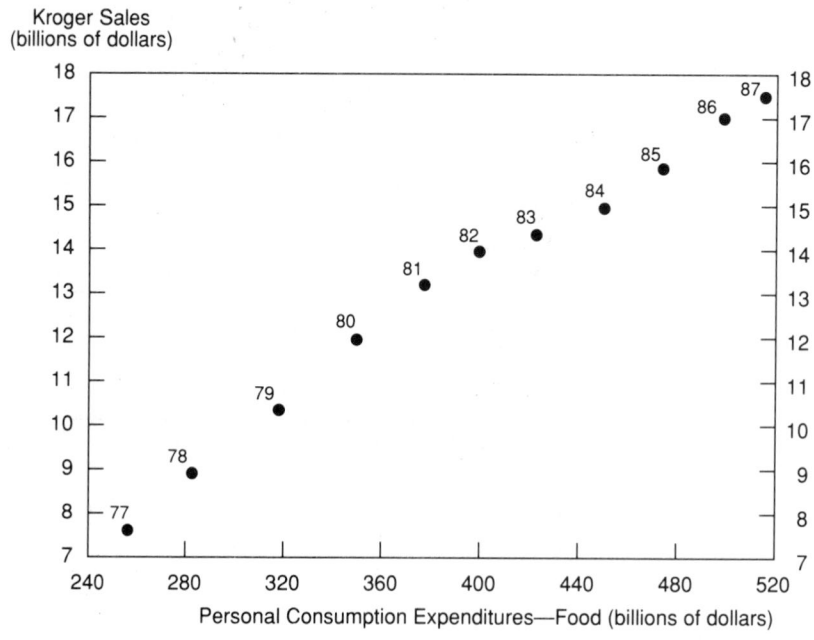

were similar to the per capita PCE series. The regression relationship in Table 15.2 between Kroger sales and sales per share for the retail food store industry is not as consistent as the prior analysis with an aggregate economic series, but Kroger's performance is still impressive. For the total period, Kroger sales increased by 132 percent compared to an industry increase of 44 percent.

The figures in the last column of Table 15.1 indicate that during this period, the proportion of PCE allocated to food went from over 20 percent in 1977 to about 17 percent in 1987 (it was 25 percent in 1960). Therefore, Kroger derived an increasing share of these expenditures. The declining proportion of PCE spent on food, especially at retail food chains, apparently is a function of the changing lifestyle of consumers. With an increase in per capita PCE, less of it is spent on necessities such as food and shelter. In addition, an increasing proportion of meals are consumed outside the home, so a larger percentage of PCE-food is spent at restaurants and fast-food outlets.

The internal sales growth for Kroger has been a function of an increase in the number of stores, from 1,573 in 1977 to 2,206 in 1987. An important change has been an increase in the annual sales per store over the total period because of the upgrading of stores. While the net number of stores has increased by about 600, this includes the construction of a number of

TABLE 15.2
**Results for Regressions Relating Kroger Sales to Alternative
Economic and Industry Series: 1977–1987**

DEPENDENT	INDEPENDENT	α	β	R^2	S.E.	F.	D.W.
Kroger sales	PCE-food	−1501.14	37.60				
(levels)	(levels)	(−2.64)	(26.58)	.99	387.56	706.56	.60
Kroger sales	PCE-food	−4.41	1.84				
(% Δ)	(% Δ)	(−1.98)	(6.38)	.84	2.43	40.71	1.62
Kroger sales	PCE-total	1624.95	5.60				
(levels)	(levels)	(2.00)	(14.84)	.96	684.56	220.27	.46
Kroger sales	PCE-total	−11.09	2.23				
(% Δ)	(% Δ)	(−2.19)	(4.05)	.67	3.43	16.41	1.42
Kroger Sales	PCE-per capita	61.73	1.48				
(levels)	(levels)	(0.07)	(6.25)	.97	627.24	264.09	.49
Kroger sales	PCE-per capita	−9.18	2.30				
(% Δ)	(% Δ)	(−1.92)	(3.90)	.65	3.52	15.18	1.44
Kroger sales	Retail food store	10,331.36	27.77				
(levels)	sales (levels)	(5.22)	(12.04)	.94	835.49	144.92	1.54
Kroger sales	Retail food store	6.98	0.50				
(% Δ)	(% Δ)	(3.20)	(1.42)	.20	5.36	2.02	.61

S.E. = standard error of estimate
F. = F statistic
D.W. = Durbin-Watson serial correlation statistic

new, large stores and the closing of many smaller stores. As a result, the average size of stores has increased (although this measure peaked in 1983 due to the addition of small convenience stores). Also sales per square foot increased during the total period, although it peaked in 1986.

This performance by Kroger is consistent with the previous analysis. Kroger sales grew about in line with the total PCE, and the total PCE has grown faster than PCE-food. Finally, the sales growth for the retail food store index (44 percent) has been smaller than the growth in PCE-food (101 percent).

SAMPLE ESTIMATE OF KROGER SALES. Based on the foregoing discussion, an analyst would likely use the Kroger PCE-food regressions. To estimate PCE-food, you should initially estimate total PCE and then estimate the food component. Economists were generally forecasting an increase in PCE of 3.5 percent during 1988. Given a 1987 preliminary figure of $2,970 billion, this implies a 1988 figure of $3,074 billion ($2,970 × 1.035). Regarding how much of PCE will be spent on food, the data indicate a consistent decline to 17.3 percent in 1987. Assuming a further decline in 1988 to 17.0 percent, this indicates an estimate of PCE-food of $523 billion ($3,074 × .170), which is a 1.75 percent increase from 1987 (523/514). A projection of a very small increase is rather unusual for the PCE-food series but reflects the lower growth rate for PCE during this sixth year of the

TABLE 15.3
Data on Sales, Number of Stores, and Store Area for Kroger: 1977–1987

YEAR	SALES (THOUSANDS OF DOLLARS)	NUMBER OF STORES	SALES PER STORE	STORE AREA (THOUSANDS OF SQUARE FEET)	AVERAGE AREA PER STORE (SQUARE FEET)	SALES PER THOUSAND (SQUARE FEET)
1977	7,597,646	1,573	4,830,036	34,129	21,697	222,616
1978	8,953,032	1,686	5,278,910	36,751	21,669	243,613
1979	10,370,722	1,764	5,879,094	39,059	22,142	265,514
1980	11,981,245	1,792	6,685,963	41,578	23,202	288,168
1981	13,275,039	1,824	7,277,982	44,415	24,350	298,886
1982	14,045,270	1,770	7,935,181	44,895	25,364	312,847
1983	14,446,823	1,780	8,116,193	46,886	26,340	308,127
1984	15,063,414	1,761	8,553,898	44,996	25,551	334,772
1985	15,996,620	1,986	8,039,357	47,278	23,806	337,718
1986	17,122,518	2,007	8,531,399	46,840	23,338	365,553
1987	17,659,730	2,206	8,005,317	50,662	22,961	348,579

Source: Kroger Annual Reports.

economic expansion and the consistent decline in the proportion of PCE directed to food.

Using the second regression in Table 15.2, which has a coefficient of 1.84, this implies a 3.2 percent increase in Kroger sales (1.84 × 1.75). Admittedly, this is a very conservative estimate of sales growth following several years of increases between 4 and 9 percent.

Because other estimates with the regressions were considered and generally confirmed this estimate, they are not reported. An alternative estimate can be derived using company data on stores, square footage, sales per store, and sales per square foot. The figures in Table 15.3 confirm the earlier discussion that Kroger has experienced increases in sales along with an increase in the net number of stores. In general, the company has closed smaller stores and has built a number of mini-marts that sell a limited number of higher margin items. The result has been an overall increase in total store area plus a fairly consistent increase in sales per 1,000 square feet (prior to 1987). Assuming an increase in store area during 1988 of about 2,000,000 square feet, the firm's total store area would be about 52,700,000 square feet. Sales per square foot have likewise increased (until 1987). Assuming an increase to $360,000 (which is above 1987 but lower than 1986) implies a sales forecast of about $18,972 million for 1988, a 7.4 percent increase over 1987 sales of $17,660 million.

Given the two estimates, the preference is for the lower figure with an upward adjustment to 5 percent. Therefore the final sales forecast for 1988 is $18,550 million.[7] The next step is to estimate the firm's net profit margin.

---

[7] Kroger was involved in a major restructuring during 1988 in response to a takeover attempt. While this could affect results in 1989, the subsequent analysis does not attempt to consider this.

TABLE 15.4
Profit Margins for Kroger Co. and the Retail Food Store Industry: 1977–1987

| YEAR | THE KROGER CO. | | | | | | RETAIL FOOD STORES | | |
	OPERATING PROFITS	OPERATING PROFIT MARGIN	NET BEFORE TAXES	NBT MARGIN	NET INCOME	NET MARGIN	OPERATING PROFIT MARGIN	NBT MARGIN	NET MARGIN
1977	170505	2.24	142060	1.87	79058	1.04	2.76	1.47	0.82
1978	211272	2.36	187489	2.09	104770	1.17	3.36	1.79	0.93
1979	204114	1.97	180394	1.74	108397	1.05	3.22	1.78	1.05
1980	239299	2.00	206658	1.72	127862	1.07	2.90	1.44	0.83
1981	311762	2.35	274654	2.07	171738	1.29	2.96	1.19	0.58
1982	314448	2.24	276356	1.97	181247	1.29	3.33	1.82	1.10
1983	256558	1.78	185679	1.29	113677	0.79	3.48	1.89	1.09
1984	312027	2.07	239580	1.59	143198	0.95	3.53	2.00	1.14
1985	361013	2.26	276981	1.73	159563	1.00	3.73	1.98	1.18
1986	186635	1.09	95614	0.56	55768	0.33	3.91	1.83	1.03
1987	418973	2.37	323143	1.83	183299	1.04	3.70(E)	1.95(E)	1.16

(E) Estimate.
Source: Kroger Annual Reports; and Standard & Poor's *Analysts Handbook.*

ESTIMATING THE PROFIT MARGIN. Analysis of the firm's profit margin should involve two considerations: (1) the firm's internal performance and any changes that have occurred and (2) the firm's relationship to its industry. The initial analysis should indicate general trends for the firm and point out areas of concern. The company-industry analysis should indicate whether the company's performance (good or bad) is attributable to the industry or is unique to the firm.

Profit margin figures for Kroger and the retail food industry are in Table 15.4. The margins for Kroger indicate a fairly volatile series that ended about where they began. In contrast, the margins for the retail food industry generally experienced an increase. This indicates that Kroger experienced a small change in its profit margin over the past 11 years that did not keep pace with the industry. You should determine the reason for the increase in the industry profit margin and any additional factors that contributed to Kroger's performance.

INDUSTRY FACTORS. A major factor influencing the increase in industry profit margins over the past decade has been the cessation of the numerous price wars among the large chains that occurred during the early 1970s.[8] You will recall from the discussion in Chapter 14 that this is one of the factors in competitive structure that can affect long-run profitability. The current outlook is for continued price stability. A second factor is the

---

[8] For a more complete discussion see "Retailing—Food," *Standard and Poor's Industry Surveys* (New York: Standard & Poor's Corp., 1988).

inclusion of more high-profit margin items in food stores, such as cosmetics, gourmet foods, and partially or fully prepared food items in the delicatessens to meet the needs of two-income families who neither want to prepare meals nor eat out.

COMPANY FACTORS. The major factor affecting Kroger's profit margin has been the change in corporate structure toward a combination of mini-marts and warehouses. The outlook for profit margins is good because of the profitable mini-marts and the larger stores that contain more high-margin nonfood items and delicatessens. Specific estimates for Kroger would typically begin with an analysis of the relationship between the firm's margin and the food chain industry margin using the following model:[9]

$$\text{Kroger Net Profit Margin}_t = \alpha_i + \beta_i \, (\text{Retail Food Stores Net Profit Margin}).$$

You might also want to consider the relationship between percentage changes (%Δ) in the profit margins as follows:

$$\%\Delta \text{ Kroger Net Profit Margin}_t = \alpha_i + \beta_i$$
$$(\%\Delta \text{ Retail Food Chain Industry Net Profit Margin}_i).$$

The results from both of these models for the period 1977–1987 indicated very poor results. This is probably because of the major restructuring by Kroger that caused its margins to fluctuate independently from the overall industry. Even when the regression results are significant, you should consider any unique factors that would influence this long-run relationship, such as foreign exchange charges, price wars, or an abnormal number of store openings or closings.

Following a consideration of the long-run company-industry relationship, you should also analyze the firm's common size income statement for several years. The income statement breakdown depends upon the consistent detail provided by the firm. Table 15.5 contains a common size statement for Kroger during the period 1984–1987. The main items of interest would be cost of goods sold and operating expense. An analysis of these items for Kroger is both encouraging and discouraging. The merchandise expense figure was under control until 1987, when it increased by almost 1 percent. In contrast, the firm's operating expense has been steady over time in absolute and percentage terms and declined by 1 percent in 1987. Rent and depreciation expenses have been quite constant over this period. The firm's dollar interest expenses have increased with the addition of new store leases, but this expense has generally been consistent with growth, because the percentage has been constant. The net profit margin for continuing operations has been steady at about 1.0 percent, which is considered a reasonable margin for this industry.

---

[9] Both the operating margin and the net before tax margin were analyzed, but the results indicated that the net profit margins yielded the best relationships.

TABLE 15.5
Common Size Income Statement for Kroger Co.: 1984–1987

	1987		1986		1985		1984	
	MILLION DOLLARS	**PERCENT**	**MILLION DOLLARS**	**PERCENT**	**MILLION DOLLARS**	**PERCENT**	**MILLION DOLLARS**	**PERCENT**
Sales	17,659.7	100.0	17,122.5	100.0	15,996.6	100.0	15,063.4	100.0
Merchandise	13,696.4	77.6	13,162.6	76.9	12,282.3	76.9	11,575.9	76.8
Gross profit	3,963.3	22.4	3,959.9	23.1	3,684.3	23.1	3,487.5	23.2
Operating expense	3,092.2	17.5	3,172.0	18.5	2,926.5	18.3	2,797.7	18.6
Gross operating profit	871.1	4.9	787.9	4.7	757.8	4.7	689.8	4.6
Rent	236.7	1.3	226.1	1.3	202.1	1.3	195.8	1.3
Depreciation	223.0	1.3	211.2	1.2	194.7	1.2	182.0	1.2
Net operating profit	411.5	2.3	350.7	2.0	361.0	2.2	312.0	2.1
Dividend and interest income	11.0	0.1	12.7	0.1	17.8	0.1	23.2	0.2
Interest expense	106.9	0.6	103.8	0.6	101.9	0.6	95.6	0.6
Special charge (neg.)	7.5	0.0	(164.0)	1.0	0.0	0.0	0.0	0.0
Earnings from continuing operation before income taxes	323.1	1.8	95.6	0.6	277.0	1.7	239.6	1.6
Income tax	139.8	0.8	39.8	0.2	117.4	0.7	96.4	0.6
Earnings from continuing operation	183.3	1.0	55.8	0.3	159.6	1.0	143.2	1.0
Results of discontinuing operation	0.0	0.0	(4.3)	0.0	21.2	0.1	13.4	0.1
Cumulative effect of change in accounting	63.3	0.4	0.0	0.0	0.0	0.0	0.0	0.0
Net earnings	246.6	1.4	51.5	0.3	180.8	1.1	156.6	1.0
Tax rate	43.3		41.7		42.4		40.2	
No. of common shares outstanding (000)	83,318		92,947		88,156		90,062	
Earnings per share from continuing operation	$2.20		$0.60		$1.81		$1.59	

NET MARGIN ESTIMATE. The overall industry outlook is encouraging because of stable prices, an increase in mechanization within the industry, and the inclusion of high-profit items like drugs, cosmetics, and prepared foods. Therefore, the industry margin should increase during 1988; and, given Kroger's relationship to it, the firm should likewise show an increase. Most of the costs of its reorganization are behind it, and it continues to expand in high-margin areas, including mini-marts. Therefore, the estimate for Kroger's net margin in 1988 is 1.1 percent.

This margin estimate, combined with the prior sales estimate of $18,550 million, indicates net income of $204 million. Assuming about 79 million common shares outstanding following continued repurchases, earnings should be about $2.58 per share for 1988—an increase of about 17 percent over the earnings from continued operations of $2.20 per share in 1987. The next step is to estimate the earnings multiple for Kroger.

TABLE 15.6

Average Earnings Multiple for Kroger, Retail Food Stores Industry, and the Standard & Poor's 400: 1977–1987

		KROGER				RETAIL FOOD STORES			S&P 400
			PRICE						
YEAR	EPS	HIGH	LOW	MEAN	MEAN P/E	EPS	MEAN PRICE	MEAN P/E	MEAN P/E
1977	0.91	7.25	5.88	6.56	7.21	5.49	57.12	10.40	9.55
1978	1.20	9.38	6.50	7.94	6.61	6.45	55.80	8.65	8.21
1979	1.23	13.50	8.88	11.19	9.10	7.47	58.88	7.88	7.11
1980	1.45	11.88	7.00	9.44	6.51	6.71	52.32	7.80	8.44
1981	1.87	13.88	9.63	11.75	6.28	5.08	56.53	11.13	8.45
1982	1.91	23.63	11.75	17.69	9.26	9.98	70.78	7.09	10.37
1983	1.24	21.50	16.88	19.19	15.47	9.47	93.01	9.82	11.84
1984	1.59	19.88	14.63	17.25	10.85	10.70	95.38	8.91	9.92
1985	1.81	30.88	18.88	29.88	13.74	11.58	123.19	10.64	13.68
1986	0.60	35.00	21.38	28.19	46.98	9.79	160.93	16.44	17.42
1987	2.20	40.75	24.00	32.38	14.72	11.15	204.27	18.30	20.68
Mean: with 1986					13.34			10.64	11.42
Mean: without 1986					9.98			9.88	10.50

ESTIMATING THE EARNINGS MULTIPLE

Similar to the prior procedure, this analysis considers the macro relationships among the company, industry, and market multiples, then progresses to a micro analysis of the firm's multiple.

MACRO-ANALYSIS OF EARNINGS MULTIPLE. Table 15.6 contains the mean earnings multiple for the company, the retail food store industry, and the aggregate market for the period 1977–1987. Except for 1983, 1984, and 1986, when Kroger earnings declined, the earnings multiple for Kroger has been lower than the multiple for either the retail food industry or the aggregate market. The regression equations of Kroger's multiple to its industry and the market were not very meaningful because of what happened in 1986, and so are not reported. The market recognized that the lower 1986 earnings were due to a one-time special charge, and the stock prices did not decline as much as earnings, so the P/E ratio increased dramatically (to 46) and then declined substantially in 1987. An adjustment that would partially compensate for the special charge-off would be to add the charge-off back to net before taxes, and estimate what net income would be after normal taxes. It appears that you would still have lower earnings than 1985, but the difference would be small.

MICRO-ANALYSIS OF EARNINGS MULTIPLE. The historical data for the relevant series are contained in Table 15.7. The relevant questions are (1) why has the Kroger multiple typically been below the market multiple,

TABLE 15.7
Variables that Influence the Earnings Multiple for Kroger, Retail Food Stores, and the Standard & Poor's 400: 1977–1987

YEAR	KROGER & CO.						RETAIL FOOD STORES						S&P 400					
	D/E[a]	TAT[b]	TAE[c]	EQUITY TURNOVER[d]	NPM[e]	ROE	D/E[a]	TAT[b]	TAE[c]	EQUITY TURNOVER[d]	NPM[e]	ROE	D/E[a]	TAT[b]	TAE[c]	EQUITY TURNOVER[d]	NPM[e]	ROE
1977	41.76	4.12	3.02	12.43	1.04	12.94	45.36	5.05	2.64	13.30	0.82	10.94	43.23	1.27	2.15	2.73	5.11	13.93
1978	51.22	4.42	2.92	12.92	1.17	15.12	41.58	4.77	2.85	13.62	0.93	12.72	41.18	1.27	2.22	2.81	5.19	14.60
1979	48.28	4.65	2.93	13.61	1.05	14.22	40.56	4.57	3.01	13.76	1.05	14.38	36.34	1.30	2.28	2.96	5.57	16.50
1980	41.92	4.82	2.97	14.35	1.07	15.32	48.29	4.76	3.11	14.81	0.83	12.29	40.26	1.31	2.30	3.02	4.92	14.88
1981	41.98	4.48	2.96	13.27	1.29	17.17	69.88	4.80	3.20	15.39	0.58	8.97	41.88	1.28	2.32	2.97	4.86	14.42
1982	46.07	4.23	3.06	12.93	1.29	16.68	39.48	4.67	3.19	14.87	1.10	16.40	54.02	1.17	2.40	2.82	3.95	11.13
1983	77.02	4.09	3.29	13.47	0.79	10.60	44.35	4.56	3.01	13.72	1.09	14.89	49.56	1.15	2.37	2.73	4.42	12.07
1984	62.89	4.09	3.21	13.11	0.95	12.47	40.37	4.37	3.08	13.48	1.14	15.38	41.47	1.22	2.52	3.06	4.77	14.61
1985	55.25	3.82	3.51	13.43	1.00	13.43	38.08	4.14	2.99	12.39	1.18	14.61	51.51	1.15	2.75	3.16	3.84	12.14
1986	170.83	4.19	3.54	14.83	0.33	4.83	45.97	3.94	3.03	11.94	1.03	12.28	55.94	1.08	2.88	3.12	3.75	11.70
1987	47.23	3.96	3.93	15.58	1.04	16.17	37.49	3.80[f]	3.03[f]	11.52[f]	1.16[f]	13.32[f]	55.36	1.05	2.91	3.06	4.00	12.25
Mean	50.88[g]	4.27[g]	3.18[g]	13.51[g]	1.07[g]	14.41[g]	44.67	4.49	3.01	13.53	0.99	13.29	46.43	1.21	2.46	2.95	4.58	13.48

[a] Dividends/earnings
[b] Total asset turnover
[c] Total assets/equity
[d] Total sales/equity
[e] NPM—net profit margin
[f] Estimated
[g] Without 1986 due to special charges

TABLE 15.8

Coefficient of Variation of Operating Earnings of Kroger, Retail Food Stores, and S&P 400

	KROGER	RETAIL FOOD STORES	S&P 400
5-Year (1983–1987)	0.335	0.081	0.059
10-Year (1978–1987)	0.286	0.182	0.117
10-Year around trend	0.286	0.040	0.042

Note: Coefficient of Variation $= \dfrac{\text{Standard Deviation of Earnings } (\sigma)}{\text{Mean Earnings } (\overline{X})}$.

Source: Kroger Annual Reports; S&P *Analysts Handbook.*

and (2) should this relationship persist based upon an analysis of the relevant variables?

DIVIDEND-PAYOUT RATIO. The dividend-payout ratio for Kroger has typically been higher than its industry. The Kroger-market comparison is less consistent, but Kroger generally had an equal to slightly higher payout. These results alone would indicate that Kroger's multiple should be above the industry multiple and about equal to the market multiple.

REQUIRED RATE OF RETURN. The required rate of return (k) should consider the firm's internal risk characteristics (*BR, FR, LR,* and *ERR*), and the stock's systematic market risk (beta). As indicated in Chapter 1, we would expect the risk implied by these two approaches to be similar based upon intuition (i.e., a company with high internal risk components should have a high beta) and also the results of several empirical studies noted in Chapter 1.

One would expect Kroger to have relatively low business risk because of its stable sales growth compared to its industry and the aggregate economy. Unfortunately, the food industry has been involved in past price wars. In turn, Kroger has had high fixed costs and low profit margins, so its operating profit figures have been quite volatile, as shown by the firm's coefficients of variation (CV) of operating earnings during the last five- and ten-year periods. These figures have been substantially above comparable ones for the industry and the S&P 400, as shown in Table 15.8. To adjust for the impact of growth,[10] we computed the deviation from a trend line. This adjustment did not affect Kroger, but reduced the CV for the industry and the market, so it increased the difference. This comparison indicates that Kroger has experienced substantially higher business risk than its industry or the market.

Table 15.9 contains data for several financial risk variables for Kroger, its industry, and the aggregate market. The firm's financial risk as measured by the leverage ratio (total assets/equity) has always been fairly high

---

[10] The standard deviation is adversely affected by a strong growth trend, because the deviations are computed from the overall mean calculated during the growth period. Therefore, high-growth firms will tend to have a higher standard deviation.

TABLE 15.9
Financial Risk Ratios for Kroger, the Retail Food Store Industry, and the S&P 400: 1977–1987

	THE KROGER CO.				RETAIL FOOD STORES				S&P 400			
YEAR	TA/EQUITY	INT COV	CASH FLOW LT DEBT	CASH FLOW TOT DEBT	TA/EQUITY	INT COV	CASH FLOW LT DEBT	CASH FLOW TOT DEBT	TA/EQUITY	INT COV	CASH FLOW LT DEBT	CASH FLOW TOT DEBT
1977	3.02	2.14	0.72	0.14	2.63	4.90	0.43	0.15	2.08	8.00	0.63	0.22
1978	2.92	2.92	0.91	0.16	2.86	4.70	0.38	0.15	2.15	7.60	0.63	0.22
1979	2.93	2.98	0.65	0.12	3.01	4.30	0.38	0.15	2.20	7.70	0.70	0.22
1980	2.97	2.90	1.17	0.22	3.11	3.60	0.36	0.14	2.23	6.00	0.66	0.21
1981	2.96	3.10	0.89	0.22	3.20	3.10	0.34	0.13	2.25	5.00	0.63	0.21
1982	3.06	2.60	0.50	0.13	3.19	4.10	0.43	0.16	2.31	4.00	0.54	0.18
1983	3.29	1.28	0.55	0.15	3.01	4.30	0.46	0.16	2.28	4.60	0.61	0.19
1984	3.21	1.50	0.66	0.15	3.08	4.10	0.43	0.16	2.39	4.80	0.65	0.19
1985	3.51	1.57	0.55	0.13	2.99	4.00	0.48	0.16	2.54	4.20	0.57	0.16
1986	3.53	0.54	0.79	0.15	3.03	4.00	0.51	0.15	2.59	3.60	0.51	0.15
1987	3.93	1.72	0.22	0.05	NA	NA	NA	NA	NA	NA	NA	NA

Source: Kroger Annual Reports; S&P *Analysts Handbook*.

(about 3.00), and has increased during the last several years to a ratio (3.93) that is definitely above the industry (about 3.0) and the aggregate market (about 2.6). After capitalizing leases and adjusting the interest charges, Kroger recently has had an interest coverage ratio of about 1.7, a cash flow/long-term debt ratio of over 80 percent, and a cash flow/total debt ratio of 15 percent. The interest coverage ratios are consistently lower than both the industry and the market (1.7 versus about 4.0). In contrast, Kroger's cash flow/long-term debt ratio has consistently been higher than the industry and higher than the market during the early period and about equal to the market in recent years. Finally, the cash flow/total debt ratio for Kroger was historically above the industry and about equal to the market, but in recent years it is about the same as the industry and below the market. Therefore, except for the historical cash flow/long-term debt ratios, all the financial risk ratios indicate that Kroger has *higher financial risk* than its industry or the aggregate stock market.

The firm's external market *liquidity risk* is quite low compared to that of its industry and substantially below the figure for the average firm in the market. The factors generally indicating market liquidity are (1) the number of stockholders, (2) the number of shares outstanding, (3) the number of shares traded, and (4) institutional interest in the stock as indicated by the number of institutions that own the stock and the proportion of stock owned by institutions. As of January 1, 1988, Kroger had 65,608 holders of common stock, which is a relatively large number. At the end of 1987, there were about 79 million common shares outstanding with a market value of almost $2.3 billion. Clearly, Kroger would qualify as an investment for institutions that require firms with large market value. The percentage of shares traded averages about 2 percent per month, which would indicate monthly volume of almost 1.6 million shares and annual turnover of 24 percent, somewhat below the NYSE average of about 30 percent. Financial institutions own about 29 million shares of Kroger, constituting about 37 percent of the outstanding shares, although this number has declined over the past couple of years. Therefore, based upon most measures of external market liquidity, Kroger has very low liquidity risk.

As indicated in Chapter 14, industries and companies differ in terms of exchange rate risk depending on what proportion of sales and earnings are generated outside the United States and the volatility of exchange rates in the specific countries involved. Based on its foreign sales and earnings, Kroger is near the low end of the potential range because the firm has virtually no non–U.S. sales. Therefore, its exchange rate risk is very low to nonexistent.

In summary, Kroger clearly has above-average business risk, above-average financial risk, and very low liquidity and exchange rate risk. Because of the importance of business and financial risk, it appears that the risk for Kroger based upon its fundamentals would be above the market.

The systematic risk for Kroger is derived using the linear regression model that relates the rates of return for Kroger to comparable rates of return for the S&P 500 series. According to a February 26, 1988 *Value Line* report on Kroger, the firm's historical beta was 0.95, which would indicate below-average market risk. The overall consensus, based upon an analysis of fundamental risk factors and the firm's systematic risk, is for risk equal to or slightly above the aggregate market. This would suggest an earnings multiple equal to or slightly below the market multiple.

EXPECTED GROWTH RATE. The expected growth rate (g) of dividends is dependent on the expected growth rate of earnings, which is a function of the retention rate and the return on equity (ROE). Our prior discussion indicated that Kroger has had a higher payout than the industry or the aggregate market, which implies a slightly lower retention rate.

We know that the firm's ROE is a function of the total asset turnover (TAT), financial leverage, and the profit margin. As shown in Table 15.7, the TAT for Kroger was lower than the industry in the initial years; and while the turnover for Kroger declined from 1977 to 1987, the industry declined more. As a result, during the last two years, Kroger's turnover was above the industry. Kroger's TAT, though, was much larger than the market, as one would expect for a retail firm. As discussed, the financial leverage ratio (total assets/equity) for Kroger was consistently larger than that of the industry and the market. As a result, Kroger's equity turnover (which equals TAT times the leverage ratio) was below the industry from 1977 to about 1984 but has been above it during the recent three years. Kroger's equity turnover was likewise substantially larger than the turnover for the aggregate market, as expected, given the nature of the retail industry. This recent comparison of equity turnover would indicate that Kroger could grow at a higher rate than the industry. Kroger's profit margin was always larger than the industry margin prior to 1983 but has been below the industry during 1983–1987. Given the nature of the industry, it was always lower than the aggregate margin.

If we concentrate on the combined effect of the total asset turnover, leverage (i.e., equity turnover), and profit margin during the recent period (1984–1987), the data indicate an ROE for Kroger of about 15 percent (i.e., an equity turnover of 15 and a profit margin of about 1 percent). This would be a little higher than the industry figure of about 13 percent (a turnover of 12 and profit margin of 1.1 percent) and an aggregate market figure of about 12.5 percent (turnover of 3.1 and profit margin of 4 percent).

These results for ROE, combined with the results for the retention rate as shown in Table 15.10, imply a higher expected growth rate for Kroger than for the industry or the economy as follows:

	RETENTION RATE	ROE	EXPECTED GROWTH RATE
Kroger	.49	15.0	7.35
Retail food stores	.55	13.0	7.15
S&P 400	.54	12.5	6.75

Table 15.10
Expected Growth Rate Components for Kroger, Retail Food Stores, and the S&P 400: 1977–1987

Year	KROGER			RETAIL FOOD STORES			S&P 400		
	Retention Rate	ROE	Expected Growth Rate	Retention Rate	ROE	Expected Growth Rate	Retention Rate	ROE	Expected Growth Rate
1977	58.25	12.94	7.54	54.64	10.94	5.98	56.77	13.93	7.91
1978	62.92	15.12	9.51	58.45	12.72	7.43	58.82	14.60	8.59
1979	48.78	14.22	6.94	59.44	14.38	8.55	63.66	16.50	10.50
1980	51.72	15.32	7.92	51.71	12.29	6.36	59.74	14.88	8.89
1981	58.08	17.17	9.97	30.12	8.97	2.70	58.12	14.42	8.38
1982	53.93	16.68	9.00	60.52	16.40	9.93	45.98	11.13	5.12
1983	22.93	10.60	2.43	55.65	14.89	8.29	50.44	12.07	6.09
1984	37.11	12.47	4.63	59.63	15.38	9.17	58.53	14.61	8.55
1985	44.75	13.43	6.01	61.92	14.61	9.05	48.49	12.14	5.89
1986	−70.83	4.83	−3.42	54.03	12.28	6.63	44.06	11.70	5.16
1987	52.77	16.17	8.53	62.51[a]	13.32[a]	8.33[a]	44.64[a]	12.25[a]	5.47[a]
Mean	49.12[b]	14.41[b]	7.25[b]	55.33	13.29	7.49	53.57	13.48	7.38

[a] Estimated
[b] Without 1986

Source: Kroger Annual Reports; and S&P *Analysts Handbook.*

These higher growth rate results indicate a higher multiple for Kroger.

THE COMBINED EFFECT. The overall effect of the three variables indicates that the earnings multiple for Kroger should be equal to or slightly greater than that of its industry and the market. The risk analysis indicates an equal multiple for Kroger and a payout ratio and growth rate slightly above that of the industry and the market.

EXAMPLE OF A MULTIPLE ESTIMATE. The macro analysis data indicated that Kroger's multiple was lower than that of the industry. The micro analysis indicated that Kroger's multiple should be comparable to or slightly larger than the market's. Assuming a market multiple of about 12.0 and a retail store multiple of about 11.0, the multiple for Kroger should be between 11.0 and 12.0, with a tendency toward the upper end of the range.

PRICE ESTIMATE. In the earnings section, we estimated earnings for Kroger of about $2.60 per share. Assuming a multiple of 11.0 implies a year-end price of about $28.50 (11.0 × $2.60). A multiple of 12.0 implies a price of about $31.25 (12.0 × $2.60).

GLOBAL COMPANY ANALYSIS

In Chapter 14 we discussed global industry analysis with an example of the European chemical industry by Goldman Sachs & Co. You will recall that 1988 was projected to be a strong year for the industry based upon

TABLE 15.11
European Chemical Majors—Business Profiles

	MONTEDISON	BASF	ICI	HOECHST	RHONE-POULENC	AKZO	BAYER	CIBA	L'AIR LIQUIDE	BOC
Energy	*****	****	*							
Heavy chemicals	**	**	***	**	***	***	**			
Fertilizers	**	**	***	*					**	
Chemical intermediates	*	***	**	**	****	**	****	*		
Fibres	**	*	**	**	****	*****	**			
Plastics/resins	***	***	***	***	*		***	*****		
Dyestuffs/pigments		**	**	**			**	***		
Specialty chemicals	***	***	**	***	***	****	**	***	**	
Industrial gases				**					*******	*******
									*******	*****
Agrochemicals	*	*	**	**	***		***	*****		
Paints		**	**	*		****	*			
Health care	**	*	***	****	*****	***	***	*******	**	*******
Other	*****	**	*	**	*	*****	****	**	****	*****

Note: These broad assessments are based on 1986 figures, since when there have been a number of changes. Notably, Montedison increased its holdings in La Fondiaria (insurance), Himont (polypropylene), and acquired Antibioticos (fine chemicals/pharmaceuticals); Hoechst acquired Celanese, increasing its chemicals and fibres position; ICI acquired the agrochemicals business of Stauffer, Rhone-Poulenc its basic chemicals, and AKZO its specialty chemicals business. AKZO sold its interest in consumer products and L'Air Liquide's fertilizer interests were transferred to a company in which the group retains only a minority interest.

Source: Charles K. Brown "European Chemical Industry—1988 Prospects," (Goldman, Sachs & Co., International Research, February 22, 1988). Reprinted with permission from Goldman, Sachs & Co.

a good supply/demand relationship. Given this generally positive outlook, Goldman Sachs recommended several stocks as attractive investments. The following tables contain company data on eight to ten companies. The difference in the sample of companies among tables is because the desired data is not always available for all the firms.

BUSINESS PROFILES. Table 15.11 shows a matrix of the companies and the products of each with the number of stars indicating the involvement in each product line (e.g., Montedison is heavily involved in energy and has very small sales in chemical intermediates). This provides information on product mix for each firm but also is useful if you want to know who is involved in a given product and you also want information on relative position (e.g., which is the major paint firm).

EARNINGS PER SHARE ANALYSIS. Table 15.12 contains an earnings per share index (1986 = 100) for the major firms for each individual year and for the total period, including annual growth rates for eight- and five-year periods. This global comparison indicates whether the growth rate has changed over time. The presentation of a U.S. dollar index indicates the impact of exchange rate changes on a U.S. investor. Finally, there is a measure of internal risk based upon the volatility of earnings over time (i.e., the standard deviation of the earnings index series). As an example, this would reflect the relative stability of BOC compared to ICI, which has

TABLE 15.12
Earnings per Share for Major Firms in the European Chemical Industry

	1979	1980	1981	1982	1983	1984	1985	1986	1987E	AVERAGE ANNUAL GROWTH (%) 1979–87E	1982–87E	VOLATILITY[a]
Local Currency Index												
ICI	86	24	35	26	71	107	94	100	122	4	36	37
BOC	57	64	79	83	74	88	97	100	119	10	7	19
BASF	103	57	58	42	73	112	120	100	105	0	20	28
Bayer	36	67	43	23	59	109	101	100	104	14	36	33
Hoechst	68	50	37	24	67	93	101	100	99	5	33	29
Ciba-Geigy	28	40	51	55	64	107	85	100	94	16	11	28
L'Air Liquide	44	49	56	59	69	81	91	100	101	11	11	22
AKZO	48	29	38	34	82	108	108	100	82	7	19	33
U.S. Dollar Index												
ICI	124	38	48	31	73	97	83	100	136	1	34	37
BOC	82	101	109	99	76	80	86	100	133	6	6	18
BASF	122	68	55	37	62	85	89	100	126	0	28	30
Bayer	43	80	41	20	50	83	75	100	126	14	44	33
Hoechst	81	59	36	21	57	71	75	100	119	5	41	30
Ciba-Geigy	30	43	47	49	55	82	62	100	114	18	18	28
L'Air-Liquide	71	81	72	62	63	64	70	100	117	6	13	19
AKZO	58	35	37	32	70	83	79	100	99	7	26	27

Note: Reported earnings per share, excluding identified extraordinary items. No adjustments have been made to reported figures for differences in accounting practice.

[a] Approximation based on sample standard deviation.

Source: Charles K. Brown, "European Chemical Industry–1988 Prospects," (Goldman, Sachs & Co., International Research, February 22, 1988). Reprinted with permission from Goldman, Sachs & Co.

a volatility value almost twice as large. Also, ICI has a much higher annual growth rate for the period 1982–1987 (note that 1982 was a low point for ICI). The idea is, this comparison provides substantial insight into the earning performance of these firms.

PROFITABILITY AND FINANCIAL STRENGTH. Table 15.13 contains information on profitability as measured by the return on equity (ROE) for the individual firms. As indicated in the notes to the table, the analysis should concentrate on firm performance over time, since the data are not adjusted for accounting differences. The results reflect recovery for some firms (e.g., Montedison and Rhone-Poulenc) and relative stability for others (e.g., BOC).

Along with profitability, the financial risk of the firms must be considered, based upon the debt/equity ratios. Again, it is best to limit the analysis to specific firms over time. The changes reflect operating performance and financial strategy decisions as well as the effect of acquisitions (e.g., ICI).

TABLE 15.13
Profitability and Financial Strength for Major Firms in the European Chemical Industry: 1982–1987E

| | NET INCOME/AVG. SHAREHOLDERS' EQUITY (%) | | | | | | NET DEBT/SHAREHOLDERS' EQUITY (%)[a] | | | | | |
	1982	1983	1984	1985	1986	1987E	1982	1983	1984	1985	1986	1987E
ICI	5	12	17	15	17	19	44	25	18	26[1]	35[2]	39[3]
BASF	4	7	11	10	8	9	26	9	−2	10[4]	−12	−16
Bayer	2	11	17	14	12	12	120	103	79	44	2	−13
Hoechst	4	12	16	17	15	14	105	79	47	23	−14	32[5]
Ciba-Geigy	6	7	10	8	9	8	−2	−7	−10	−13	−19	−20
AKZO	9	19	23	21	19	15	115	84	43	20	21	36[6]
L'Air Liquide	15	16	16	16	14	12	37	26	29	17	58[7]	49
BOC (to Sept.)	20	15	13	14	14	18	106	98	80	67	56	46
Montedison	−48	−23	−11	8	13	12	300	314	318	330	143	219[8]
Rhone-Poulenc	−31	−2	32	27	18	15	487	352	252	165	129[9]	89[10]

Note: These figures are based on reported results and reflect differing accounting practices; they are intended to set out trends over time for the individual companies rather than provide a basis for comparisons between companies.

[a] Note the effect of major acquisitions: 1. Beatrice chemical companies; 2. Glidden; 3. Stauffer agrochemicals; 4. Inmont; 5. Celanese; 6. Stauffer specialty chemicals; 7. Big Three; 8. La Fondiaria (increased stake), Antibioticos, Himont (increased stake); 9. Union Carbide agrochemicals; 10. Stauffer basic chemicals.

Source: Company Reports, Goldman, Sachs Analysis; Charles K. Brown, "European Chemical Industry—1988 Prospects," (Goldman, Sachs & Co., International Research, February 22, 1988). Reprinted with permission from Goldman, Sachs & Co.

COMMON STOCK STATISTICS. Given the internal company data and the prior analysis, Table 15.14 contains key statistics related to the common stock of the firms in the industry. The absolute P/E ratios are interesting, since they show the differences in earnings multiples among countries (most are below ten times). There is also an analysis of these P/E ratios relative to those in local markets, which means that two stocks could have similar P/E ratios, yet be valued differently in different countries due to variations in accounting conventions or social attitudes. While this is currently possible, it might not be in the future as accounting practices become more consistent and the global markets become more integrated.

The price/book value ratios are likewise important, since they indicate major differences among countries. Again, these differences could be due to differences in valuation or accounting practices. An extreme example is Ciba-Geigy, where the book values are based on current costs.

SHARE PRICE PERFORMANCE. The final comparative analysis is the stock price changes for the major firms as shown in Table 15.15. This comparison considers the impact of exchange rates. Part A contains the typical analysis wherein the stock's absolute percentage change is compared to the aggregate market over different time intervals. In part B, these returns are converted to U.S. dollars to adjust for the exchange rate movements and are compared to the U.S. market, which indicates the relative performance that would have been experienced by a U.S. investor. Notably, in several cases the stocks did not perform very well on an absolute basis or relative

Table 15.14

Common Stock Statistics for Major Firms in the European Chemical Industry

	Share Price[a]	EPS		DPS 1987E	P/E 1988E	P/E Rel[b] 1988E	P/CF 1987E	P/B 1986	Yield[c] 1987E (%)
		1987E	1988E						
ICI	1050p	111.8	125.7	40	8.4	76	5.6	1.9	5.2
BASF	DM236	30.0	31.0	10	7.6	62	3.3	1.1	6.6
Bayer	DM258	32.0	33.0	10[d]	7.8	64	3.6	1.3	6.1
Hoechst	DM253	31.0	32.0	10[d]	7.9	65	3.8	1.6	6.2
Ciba-Geigy Bearer	SFr2775	224	246	38	11.3	84	7.5	1.0[e]	1.4
Registered	SFr1455	224	246	38	5.9	44	3.9	0.5[e]	2.6
BPCs	SFr1860	224	246	38	7.6	56	5.0	0.7[e]	2.0
AKZO	DFL95	15.9	14.8	6.6	6.4	66	2.6	0.9	6.9
Rhone-Poulenc PICs	FFr269	47	55	15.5	4.9	53	1.8	0.9	8.6
L'Air Liquide	FFr497	34.5	38.2	14	13.0	141	5.5	1.8	4.2
BOC[f]	400p	36.3	40.8	12.8	9.8	87	6.1	1.9	4.4
Montedison	Lit1085	140	—	40	—	—	1.9	0.9	3.7

[a] Prices as at 16 February 1988; all per share figures based on this price.

[b] P/E relative to local market.

[c] Yields gross of local tax credit where applicable.

[d] Excludes possible jubilee bonus dividend.

[e] Based on current cost book values.

[f] Years to September; 1987 figures actuals.

Source: Charles K. Brown, "European Chemical Industry—1988 Prospects," (Goldman, Sachs & Co., International Research, February 22, 1988). Reprinted with permission from Goldman, Sachs & Co.

to its country index, yet *all* the stocks did very well over the three-year period in U.S. dollars and relative to the S&P 500. For a U.S. investor, it is this latter comparison that is critical and indicates the importance of international diversification and the necessity of considering exchange rate movements.

INDIVIDUAL COMPANY ANALYSIS. Following the several comparative analysis tables, the industry report concludes with a discussion of each individual company that summarizes its strengths and potential problems. Table 15.16 contains the summary table for Bayer, a German firm considered to be one of the world's leading chemical companies, with diverse operations and an international business. The discussion indicates what the firm has done and is expected to do in the industry environment discussed earlier. Also, a stock price chart for Bayer (Figure 15.2) indicates movements for the firm's stock, both alone and relative to the German market.

Subsequent to this industry report, Goldman Sachs issued extensive company reports on each of the major firms in the industry (in the case of Bayer, the subsequent report encompassed 20 pages).

Alternative Earnings Multiple Models

In contrast to examining individual components of the multiple relative to the industry and market, the finance and accounting literature contains several studies of a large cross section of stocks, analyzed to determine

TABLE 15.15
Share Price Performance for Major Firms in the European Chemical Industry

A: Domestic Currencies

OVER LAST	ABSOLUTE CHANGE (%)				CHANGE RELATIVE TO LOCAL MARKET (%)			
	MTH	6 MTHS	YR	3 YRS	MTH	6 MTHS	YR	3 YRS
ICI	−9.3	−31.1	−23.5	22.7	−7.4	−9.8	−17.8	−15.0
BASF	1.5	−29.8	−5.5	28.6	−8.0	5.8	22.3	11.0
Bayer	4.9	−28.1	−10.5	32.2	−4.9	8.4	15.9	14.1
Hoechst	6.6	−24.1	2.4	34.6	−3.3	14.2	32.5	16.2
Ciba-Geigy Reg.	12.8	−24.8	−6.7	17.3	2.8	0.1	3.9	−5.3
Bearer	13.5	−30.9	−11.2	−1.1	3.4	−8.1	−1.1	−20.1
BPCs	13.4	−33.8	−13.9	−17.0	3.4	−11.9	−4.1	−33.0
AKZO	0.3	−43.9	−27.1	−9.2	−7.9	−18.2	−17.0	−20.2
L'Air Liquide	4.4	−28.7	−27.9	9.3	−2.8	0.8	4.4	−24.6
BOC	−3.9	−25.1	−12.1	30.5	−1.9	−1.9	−5.6	−9.6
Montedison	−17.8	−51.1	−62.3	8.9	−13.0	−31.7	−42.6	−43.0

B: U.S. Dollars

OVER LAST	ABSOLUTE CHANGE (%)				CHANGE RELATIVE TO S&P 500 (%)			
	MTH	6 MTHS	YR	3 YRS	MTH	6 MTHS	YR	3 YRS
ICI	−10.7	−24.3	−12.0	94.4	−13.4	−2.7	−5.7	35.9
BASF	−0.2	−22.8	0.8	145.7	−3.2	−0.8	8.5	71.7
Bayer	3.1	−21.0	−4.5	152.6	−	1.6	2.8	76.6
Hoechst	4.8	−16.7	9.2	157.1	1.7	7.1	17.5	79.7
Ciba-Geigy Reg.	10.3	−16.4	2.5	132.3	7.0	7.5	10.3	62.4
Bearer	11.0	−23.2	−2.4	95.9	7.6	−1.2	5.0	36.9
BPCs	10.9	−26.4	−5.4	64.4	7.6	−5.4	1.8	14.9
AKZO	−1.3	−38.1	−21.8	75.2	−4.3	−20.4	−15.9	22.4
L'Air Liquide	2.4	−22.5	−24.2	89.1	−0.6	−0.4	−18.4	32.2
BOC	5.4	−17.6	1.1	106.7	−8.3	5.9	8.8	44.5
Montedison	−19.5	−47.1	−62.2	46.4	−21.9	−32.0	−58.2	2.3

Source: Datastream (Prices as of 16 February 1988); Charles K. Brown, "European Chemical Industry—1988 Prospects," (Goldman, Sachs & Co., International Research, February 22, 1988). Reprinted with permission from Goldman, Sachs & Co.

what variables have an affect on the earnings multiples for individual stocks. The studies employ regression models that relate P/E ratios to alternative measures of growth and risk. Whitbeck and Kisor computed the multiple as the current price for the stock divided by the firm's normalized earnings as estimated by the analysts at a New York bank.[11] The estimated multiple was regressed against the following three variables: the dividend-payout ratio, an earnings variability measure to reflect business risk, and an earnings growth variable.

Malkiel and Cragg developed a dividend growth valuation model using the following empirical variables: the dividend-payout ratio, the variance

---

[11] V. Whitbeck and M. Kisor, "A New Tool in Investment Decision Making," *Financial Analysts Journal* 19, no. 3 (May–June 1963): 55–62.

TABLE 15.16
Company and Stock Price Data for Bayer

PRICE: DM258   12 MTH RANGE: DM378-238   SHARES: 60.6M   Mkt Value: DM15.6bn   Mthly Vol: 13m

PRICE REL TO MKT: 3 MTH −4.4% 6 MTH +8.4% 12 MTH +15.9%   Change from 12 Mth: High −31.7% Low +8.4%

Year to December:	PBIT[c] DMm	PBT[c] DMm	NET[c] DMm	EPS[c] DM	DPS DM	CFPS DM	BPS DM	ROE %	ND/EQ %	P/E	P/E REL %	P/CF	P/B	DY[b] (%)
1985[a]	4921	3953	1259	45.1	10.0	91	183	13.8	44	6.0	43	3.0	1.5	5.8
1986[a]	4734	4142	1345	43.4	10.0	77	204	11.9	2	7.3	42	4.1	1.6	4.9
1987E[a]	4250	3900	1560	32.0	11.0	72	227	11.6	−13	8.3	73	3.7	1.2	6.4
1988E	4000	4000	1660	33.0	10.0	70	246	11.2	−22	7.8	64	3.7	1.0	6.1

Options/Convertibles/Warrants: O/C/W   Listed ADRs: No   US GAAP EPS: NA

[a] Price-related items based on year-end prices.

[b] Dividend yield gross of German tax credit; forecast payment in respect of 1987 includes a jubilee bonus.

[c] Figures for 1987E and 1988E reflect new German accounting legislation; EPS figures are estimates based on DVFA formula, 1987E and 1988E on revised basis.

Source: Charles K. Brown, "European Chemical Industry—1988 Prospects," (Goldman, Sachs & Co., International Research, February 22, 1988). Reprinted with permission from Goldman, Sachs & Co.

FIGURE 15.2
Bayer Share Price Performance

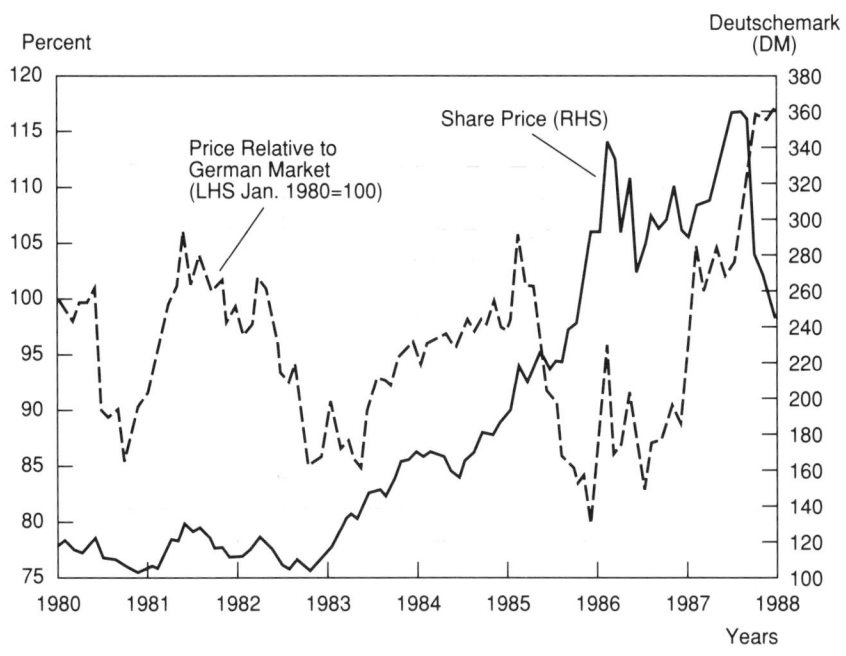

Source: Charles K. Brown, "European Chemical Industry—1988 Prospects," (Goldman, Sachs & Co., International Research, February 22, 1988). Reprinted with permission from Goldman, Sachs & Co.

of earnings, a systematic market risk variable (beta), a financial risk variable, and short-term and long-term growth variables.[12]

Beaver and Morse[13] considered the basic dividend valuation model, which implies that risk and growth will explain differential P/E ratios. They ranked the P/E ratios, divided them into 25 equal-sized portfolios, and compared the median P/E ratio for each portfolio during its base year with the median realized one-year growth in earnings per share, and with the median risk (measured by the portfolio beta during the subsequent five years). The P/E ratios were correlated over time (i.e., a 0.74 correlation after ten years), which implied a long-term persistence in the portfolio P/E ratios.

The authors suggested that a firm's accounting methods could also help explain the difference—that is, <u>the P/E ratio will be influenced by the effect on earnings of differing accounting methods</u>. For example, a firm with conservative accounting methods will have a higher P/E ratio, holding

[12] Burton G. Malkiel and John G. Cragg, "Expectations and the Structure of Share Prices," *American Economic Review* 60, no. 4 (September 1970): 601–617.

[13] William Beaver and Dale Morse, "What Determines Price-Earnings Ratios?" *Financial Analysts Journal* 34, no. 4 (July–August 1978): pp. 65–76.

risk and growth constant—as shown in a study that examined the difference in P/E ratio for firms that used straight-line versus accelerated depreciation.[14]

SUMMARY OF FINDINGS OF P/E STUDIES. A stock's P/E ratio is generally positively related to the firm's growth rate of earnings, but you must be able to *predict* this growth rate during the next two or three years, because past growth rates are *not* good indicators of future P/E ratios. Since growth rates are *not* correlated over time, you cannot extrapolate past growth rates.[15] A stock's P/E ratio is generally negatively related to alternative measures of risk (i.e., variability of earnings, financial leverage ratios, and betas). Notably, the best risk measure varies among studies and the time period considered. It was also suggested that P/E ratios are influenced by the accounting methods employed.

ALTERNATIVE VALUATION FACTORS AND MODELS

THE PRICE/BOOK (P/B) VALUE RATIO

It is possible to conceive of a relationship between the price of a stock and its book value per share. This relationship has been used extensively in the evaluation of bank stocks, because the assets of banks often have similar book and market values; assets include investments in government bonds, high-grade corporate or municipal bonds, and loans that ordinarily are collectible. Even in the banking industry there has been an increase in the range of this ratio, because in some instances the loans are not collectible (e.g., loans to firms involved in the oil industry and loans to third-world countries), or the growth potential for some banks is substantially above average. As a result, the price/book value ratio for banks has ranged from 0.25 to 2.0.

In the case of industrial firms, it is easy to envision why this ratio would exceed 1.0. The book value of assets will almost always be lower than the current replacement value of the assets, or the firm's *break-up value* (the market value of selling divisions of a firm to others). Because of this latter phenomenon, the average P/B ratio for industrial firms has experienced a volatile increase over time. Figure 15.3 is a time series plot of the annual values for this ratio computed as the mean annual price/year-end book value. As shown, the norm for this ratio prior to 1974 was about 2.0, it declined to about 1.3 during the period 1974–1982, and it increased dramatically after 1982, reaching almost 3.0 prior to the October 1987 crash.

In terms of an investment decision rule, it has been suggested that stocks with low P/B ratios should outperform high P/B firms, just as low P/E stocks outperform high P/E firms. A study by Rosenberg, Reid, and Lanstein examined this strategy and found that stocks with high book/

[14] William Beaver and R. Dukes, "Delta-Depreciation Methods: Some Empirical Results," *Accounting Review* 47, no. 2 (April 1972): 320–332.

[15] S. Little, "Higgledy Piggledy Growth," Institute of Statistics, Oxford (November 1962); Ray Ball and Ross Watts, "Some Time Series Properties of Accounting Earnings Numbers," *Journal of Finance* 27, no. 3 (June 1972): 663–682; and J. Cragg and Burton Malkiel, "The Consensus and Accuracy of Some Predictions of the Growth of Corporate Earnings," *Journal of Finance* 18, no. 1 (March 1963): 67–84.

FIGURE 15.3
Time Series Plot of Price/Book Value for the S&P 400: 1956–1987

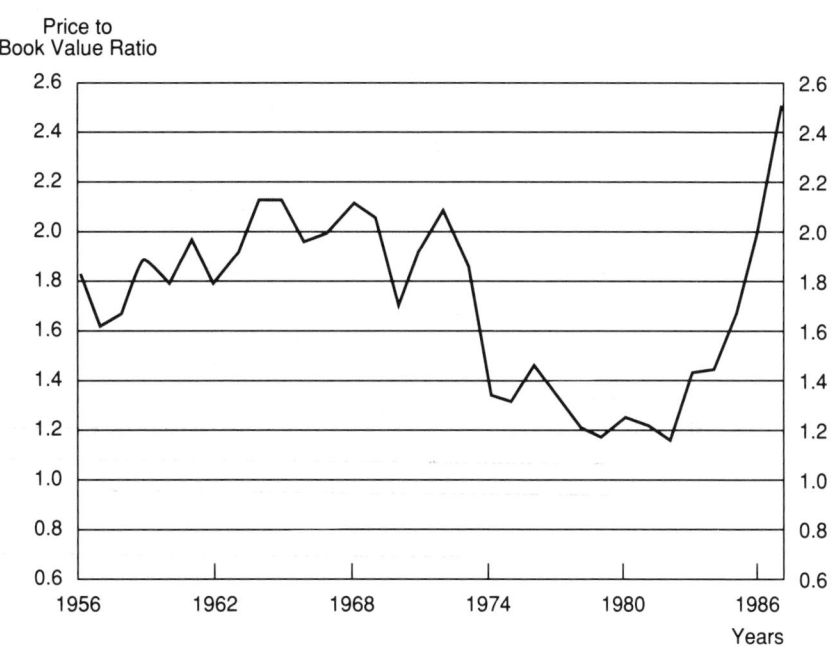

price ratios (low price/book ratios) experienced significantly higher rates of return than the average.[16] They also found a tendency for higher returns in January and February, consistent with the January anomaly. The point is, this ratio has become important itself as a measure of relative value and also as a component in other valuation models. An example of this latter use is the T-model that is discussed in the following subsection.

THE T-MODEL

Estep derived a rate of return model using standard financial ratios,[17] then subsequently showed that the rates of return from the model were close estimates of the actual rates of return *assuming that one could estimate the relevant variables.*[18] The model is similar to the two-step procedure and uses many of the same estimates as follows:

$$T = g + \frac{ROE - g}{PB} + \frac{\Delta PB}{PB}(1 + g),$$

[16] Barr Rosenberg, Kenneth Reid, and Ronald Lanstein, "Persuasive Evidence of Market Inefficiency," *Journal of Portfolio Management* 11, no. 3 (Spring 1985): 9–17.

[17] Tony Estep, "A New Method for Valuing Common Stocks," *Financial Analysts Journal* 41, no. 6 (November–December 1985): 26–34.

[18] Tony Estep, "Security Analysis and Stock Selection: Turning Financial Information into Return Forecasts," *Financial Analysts Journal* 42, no. 4 (July–August 1987): 34–43.

where

      T = **total return in the period**

      g = **the percent growth of shareholders' equity over the period**

  ROE = **net income during the period divided by beginning shareholders' equity**

    PB = **beginning aggregate market value of the firm's common stock divided by beginning shareholders' equity**

  ΔPB = **the change in the PB ratio during the period, or the PB at the end of the period minus the PB at the beginning of the period.**

As noted, the relevant variables require *estimates* similar to those in the two-step process. Specifically, in order to compute g, you must *estimate* the earnings for the year, the firm's dividend policy, and then, based upon the implied retained earnings, compute the percentage change in equity during the year. It is suggested that a good estimate of the growth rate would be the ROE times the retention rate, as used in earlier discussions. To get the ROE you likewise must *estimate* earnings relative to the beginning equity. The PB ratio is referred to as the *valuation variable,* because it indicates the market price for the firm's stock relative to its book value. Since the book value is a fairly stable variable, the big factor is the ending stock price. Critics have indicated that the solution is in the equation— that is, in order to derive the ending PB, you must estimate the ending stock price, thereby computing the rate of return (which is what is done with the two-step earnings multiple model). Estep contends that it is not necessary to compute the ending PB and, in fact, suggests that you estimate PB by examining the current PB relative to the long-run expected PB (the mean PB during the recent past) and assume that the future PB will revert to the long-run mean over some finite period.

APPLICATION TO KROGER

To apply the T-model to Kroger, we use the following inputs for the year 1987:

ROE =	0.1616	g =	0.0853
PB (1986) =	2.3010	PB (1987) =	2.2816
ΔPB =	−0.0084		

Therefore

$$T = 0.0853 + \frac{.1617 - .0853}{2.2816} + \frac{-.0084}{2.2816}(1 + .0853)$$

$$= .0853 + .0335 + (-.0040)$$

$$= .1148 = 11.48\%.$$

Notably, both PB ratios were computed using the average price for the year rather than the year-end price in order to derive a long-run estimate of return for Kroger. Using the year-end values would provide a closer estimate to the actual return experienced by Kroger during 1987 and would be heavily influenced by the decline in PB from the beginning of 1987 (2.44) to the end of 1987 following the crash (1.76). Using these PB values, the T-value was −0.01.

FIRM COMPETITIVE STRATEGIES

In the prior chapter on industry analysis we considered the five factors that determined the competitive structure of an industry (current rivalry, threat of new entrants, potential substitutes, bargaining power of suppliers, bargaining power of buyers). After you have evaluated your industry in terms of these factors, you should consider the specific competitive strategy employed by each firm in the industry as a means of evaluating its unique factor—that is, is the firm's strategy reasonable and appropriate given the overall competitive structure of the industry?

According to Porter, a firm can possess two basic types of competitive advantage: low cost or differentiation.[19] These two competitive strategies dictate how a firm has decided to cope with the five forces that determine the industry's competitive advantage. They are narrowly targeted into *cost focus* or *differentiation focus,* which indicates the scope of the strategic target, or how the firm will gain its low-cost advantage. Within each industry the strategies available and the ways of implementing them differ. Your job as an analyst is to understand the alternatives available, determine what each firm is *trying* to do, judge whether the strategy selected by the firm is reasonable, and finally, evaluate how successful the firm is in implementing it.

Cost leadership is when a firm is determined to become the low-cost producer in its industry. The sources of cost advantage will vary by industry and might include economies of scale, proprietary technology, or preferential access to raw materials. To take advantage of cost leadership, the firm must be able to command prices near the industry average, which means it must be on a par with other firms in terms of *differentiation*—you don't want the firm to discount price very much, since this would erode the superior rate of return available because of its low cost.

With *differentiation* a firm seeks to be unique in its industry along some dimensions that are valued by buyers. Again, the possibilities for differentiation vary widely by industry and can be based on the product itself, the delivery system by which it is sold (e.g., in stores or door-to-door), or the marketing approach. A differentiating firm will enjoy above-average rates of return only if its price premium from differentiation exceeds the extra cost of being unique. Therefore, in your analysis of this strategy, you must consider whether the differentiating factor is truly unique and sustainable, its cost, and the price premium derived from it.

In a third strategy, referred to as *focus,* a firm selects a segment or group of segments in the industry and tailors its strategy to serving this

---

[19] Michael Porter, *Competitive Advantage: Creating and Sustaining Superior Performance* (New York: Free Press, 1988).

specific group to the exclusion of others. A *cost focus* exploits cost advantages for certain segments of the industry (e.g., low-cost producer for the expensive segment of the market), while a *differentiation focus* serves the special needs of buyers in specific segments. Again, it must be ascertained that these special cost or need possibilities exist and that they are not being served.

Next, you must determine which strategy is being pursued and whether the firm is successful at it or is "stuck in the middle" of several strategies that may not even be compatible. Also, can the strategies be sustained? Further, you should evaluate a firm's competitive strategy over time, because it may be necessary to change strategy as the industry evolves—different strategies work during different phases of the industry life cycle. Finally, you should determine whether the firm's organization is consistent with the strategy. A different organizational structure and management style is needed to be a cost leader than to be a differentiation leader.

ANALYSIS OF GROWTH COMPANIES

Investment literature contains numerous accounts of the rapid rise of growth companies such as IBM, Xerox, and Hewlett-Packard, along with stories about investors who became wealthy because of the timely acquisition of the stocks of these companies. Such increases in value indicate that the proper valuation of true growth companies can be extremely rewarding. At the same time, for every successful IBM or Xerox, there are numerous firms that did not survive and many instances in which the stock price of a true growth company became overvalued and the subsequent returns were below expectations. As noted earlier, the common stock of a growth company is *not* always a growth stock!

You are familiar with the dividend valuation model and the basic assumptions of the model, that is, that dividends are expected to grow at a constant rate for an infinite time period. As explained before, while these assumptions are reasonable when evaluating the aggregate market and some large industries, they become more tenuous when analyzing individual securities. The point of this section is that *these assumptions are extremely questionable for a growth company.*

GROWTH COMPANY DEFINED

A *growth company* is a firm that has the opportunities and ability to invest capital in projects that generate rates of return greater than the firm's cost of capital. Such a condition is considered to be *clearly temporary.* In a competitive economy, all firms are expected to produce at the point where marginal revenue equals marginal cost, and under such conditions, the returns to the producer will exactly compensate for the risks involved. If the returns are below what is expected for the risk involved, the producer will leave the industry. In contrast, if the rates of return for a given industry exceed the returns expected based upon the risk involved, other companies will enter the industry, increase the supply, and eventually drive the prices down until the returns are consistent with the inherent risk, resulting in a state of equilibrium.

ACTUAL RETURNS ABOVE EXPECTED RETURNS

The notion of a firm consistently earning rates of return above the expected rate requires elaboration. Firms are engaged in business ventures that offer opportunities for investment of corporate capital, and these investments entail some uncertainty or risk. Investors determine their required return for owning this firm based upon the risk of the investments made by the firm compared to the risk of other firms. Consider a firm that is involved in producing and selling medical equipment, and assume perfect capital markets. There is some uncertainty about the sales of this equipment and the ultimate profit from these sales. Comparing this composite uncertainty to the uncertainty involved in other investments and the rates of returns expected from the other investments, one can estimate the returns expected from the other investments and the return investors should require from an investment in the production and sale of medical equipment. Based upon the CAPM, one would expect the difference in the required rate of return to be a function of the difference in the systematic risk for the firm's investments that affect the stock's systematic risk. This required rate of return is referred to as the firm's *cost of capital.* In a perfect market, in a state of equilibrium, the rates of return derived from risky investments by the firm should equal the rates of return required by investors. Any returns earned by the firm above those required for the systematic risk involved are referred to as *pure profits.* One of the costs of production is the cost of the capital employed. Therefore, in a purely competitive environment, marginal revenue should equal marginal costs (including capital costs), and there would be no excess returns or pure profits. Such excess profits are possible only in a noncompetitive environment. Assume that the medical equipment firm is able to earn 20 percent on its capital, while investors require only 15 percent on such investments because of the systematic risk involved. The extra 5 percent is defined as pure profit. In a totally competitive environment, numerous companies would enter the medical equipment field in order to enjoy the excess profits available. These competitors would increase the supply of equipment and would reduce price until the marginal returns equaled the marginal costs.

Since many firms have derived excess profits for a number of years, it appears that these excess returns are probably not due to a temporary disequilibrium, but rather to some noncompetitive factors that are allowed to exist in our capitalistic economy—such as patent or copyright laws that provide a firm or person with monopoly rights to a process or a manuscript for a specified period of time. During this period of protection from competition, the firm has the ability to derive above-normal returns without fear of competition. Also, one can conceive of a firm possessing other strategies, such as those discussed by Porter, that provide added profits (e.g., a unique marketing technique or other organizational characteristic). Finally, in some instances there may be significant barriers to entry such as the capital required to enter an industry (e.g., the auto industry).

In a purely competitive economy with no frictions, *there should be no such thing as a true growth company,* because competition would not allow the continuing existence of excess return investments, and so competition would negate such growth. As it is, our economy is not perfectly competitive (although this is probably the best model to use in most cases), and a number of real-world frictions restrict competition. Therefore, it is possible to envision the *temporary* existence of true growth companies in our economy. The question is how long can they last?

GROWTH COMPANIES AND GROWTH STOCKS

A *growth stock* is a security that is expected to experience above-average risk-adjusted rates of return during some future period. Thus, any stock that is currently undervalued can be a growth stock, regardless of the type of company issuing it. The securities of *growth companies* that have become temporarily overvalued could be speculative stocks, because the probability of deriving below-normal returns from them would be very high. This analysis of growth companies will provide models to help you evaluate the unique earnings stream of a growth company and thereby derive a better estimate of the firm's value and its stock. This should help you judge whether the *stock* of the growth *company* is (1) a growth stock, (2) a properly valued stock, or (3) a speculative stock.

GROWTH COMPANIES AND THE DIVIDEND MODEL

While the dividend model assumes a constant rate of growth for an infinite time period, it is *impossible* for a true growth firm to exist for an infinite time period in a purely competitive economy. Further, even in a competitive economy with some noncompetitive factors, a true growth firm should not be able to exist for very long. Patents and copyrights run out, unusual management practices can eventually be copied, and competitors can enter the industry. Therefore, the dividend growth model is *not* appropriate for the valuation of growth companies, and we must consider special valuation models that allow for finite periods of abnormal growth and for the possibility of different rates of growth. The rest of the chapter deals with models that can be used in the valuation of growth companies.

ALTERNATIVE GROWTH MODELS[20]

In this section we consider the full range of growth models, from those of no growth and negative growth to dynamic true growth. Knowledge of the full range will help you understand why the dividend growth model is not always applicable. It is assumed throughout that the company is an all-equity firm in order to simplify the computations.

NO-GROWTH FIRM

The no-growth firm is that mythical company that is established with a specified portfolio of investments that generate a constant stream of earnings (E) equal to r times the value of assets. Earnings are calculated after allowing for depreciation to maintain the assets at their original value. Therefore,

$$E = r \times \text{Assets}.$$

It is also assumed that all earnings of the firm are paid out in dividends; if b is the rate of retention, $b = 0$. Hence,

---

[20] The discussion in this section draws heavily from Ezra Solomon, *The Theory of Financial Management* (New York: Columbia University Press, 1963), 55–63; and M. Miller and F. Modigliani, "Dividend Policy, Growth, and the Valuation of Shares," *Journal of Business* 34, no. 4 (October 1961): 411–433.

$$E = r \times \text{Assets} = \text{Dividends}.$$

Under these assumptions, the value of the firm is the discounted value of the perpetual stream of earnings (E). The discount rate (the required rate of return) is specified as k. In this case, it is assumed that $r = k$. The firm's rate of return on assets is exactly equal to the required rate of return. The value of the firm is

$$V = \frac{E}{k} = \frac{(1 - b)E}{k}.$$

In the no-growth case, the earnings stream never changes, because the asset base never changes, and the rate of return on the assets never changes. Therefore, the value of the firm never changes, and investors continue to receive k on their investment.

$$k = E/V.$$

LONG-RUN GROWTH MODELS

Long-run models differ from the models for a no-growth firm because they assume some of the earnings are reinvested. The initial case assumes a firm retains a constant dollar amount of earnings and reinvests these retained earnings in assets that obtain a rate of return above the required rate.

In all cases it is postulated that the market value (V) of an all-equity firm is the capitalized value of three component forms of returns discounted at the rate k. E equals the level of (constant) net earnings expected from existing assets, without further net investments. G equals the gross present value of capital gains expected from reinvested funds. The return on reinvested funds is equal to r, which equals mk (m is the relative rate of return operator). If m is equal to 1, then $r = k$. If m is greater than 1, then the projects that generate these returns are considered true growth investments $(r > k)$. If m is less than 1, the investments are generating returns (r) below the cost of capital $(r < k)$. R equals the reinvestment of net earnings (E) is equal to bE, where b is a percent between zero (no reinvestment) and unity (total reinvestment; no dividends).

SIMPLE GROWTH MODEL. It is assumed that the firm has investment opportunities that provide rates of return equal to r, where r is greater than k (m is above 1). Further, it is assumed that these opportunities allow the firm to invest R dollars a year at these rates and that $R = bE$; R is a constant dollar amount because E is the constant earnings at the beginning of the period.

The value of G, the capital gain component, is computed as follows: the first investment of bE dollars yields a stream of earnings equal to bEr dollars, and this is repeated every year. Each of these earnings streams has a present value, as of the year it begins, of bEr/k, which is the present value of a constant perpetual stream discounted at a rate consistent with the risk involved. Assuming the firm does this every year, it has a *series* of investments, each of which has a present value of bEr/k. The present value of all these series is $(bEr/k)/k$, which equals bEr/k^2. But because $r = mk$, this becomes

$$\frac{bEmk}{k^2} = \frac{bEm}{k} \text{ (Gross Present Value of Growth Investments)} . \qquad (15.1)$$

In order to derive these flows, it was necessary to invest bE dollars each year. The present value of these annual investments is equal to bE/k. Therefore, the net present value of growth investments is equal to

$$\frac{bEm}{k} - \frac{bE}{k} \text{ (Net Present Value of Growth Investments)} . \qquad (15.2)$$

The important variable is the value of m, which indicates the relationship of r to k. Combining this growth component with the capitalized value of the constant earnings stream indicates that the value of the firm is

$$V = \frac{E}{k} + \frac{bEm}{k} - \frac{bE}{k} . \qquad (15.3)$$

This equation indicates that the value of the firm is equal to the constant earnings stream plus a growth component equal to the *net* present value of reinvestment in growth projects. By combining the first and third terms in Equation 15.3, this becomes

$$V = \frac{E(1 - b)}{k} + \frac{bEm}{k} . \qquad (15.4)$$

Because $E(1 - b)$ is the dividend, this model becomes

$$V = \frac{D}{k} + \frac{bEm}{k} \begin{array}{l}\text{(Present Value of Constant} \\ \text{Dividend Plus the Present} \\ \text{Value of Growth Investments)}\end{array} \qquad (15.5)$$

It can be stated as earnings only by rearranging Equation 15.3.

$$\left\{ V = \frac{E}{k} + \frac{bE(m - 1)}{k} \begin{array}{l}\text{(Present Value of Constant} \\ \text{Earnings Plus Present Value} \\ \text{of Excess Earnings from} \\ \text{Growth Investments)}\end{array} \right. \qquad (15.6)$$

EXPANSION MODEL. The expansion model assumes a firm retains earnings to reinvest but receives a rate of return merely equal to the cost of capital ($m = 1$, so $r = k$). The effect of such a change can be seen in Equation 15.2 where the net present value of growth investments would be zero. Therefore, Equation 15.3 would become

$$V = \frac{E}{k} . \qquad (15.7)$$

It is still possible to have equations comparable to 15.4, but it would become

$$V = \frac{E(1-b)}{k} + \frac{bE}{k} = \frac{E}{k}.$$ (15.8)

Equation 15.5 is still valid, but the present value of the growth investment component would be smaller because m would be equal to 1. Finally, the last term in Equation 15.6 would disappear.

This indicates that simply because a firm retains earnings and reinvests them, it is not necessarily of benefit to the stockholder *unless the reinvestment rate is above the required rate* ($r > k$). Otherwise, the investor would be as well off with all earnings paid out in dividends.

NEGATIVE GROWTH MODEL. The negative growth model applies to a firm that retains earnings ($b > 0$) and reinvests these funds in projects that generate rates of return *below* the firm's cost of capital ($r < k$, or $m < 1$). The impact of this on the value of the firm can be seen from Equation 15.2, which indicates that with $m < 1$, the net present value of the growth investments would be negative. This implies that the value of the firm in Equation 15.3 would be less than the value of a no-growth firm or an expansion firm. This can also be seen by examining the effect of $m < 1$ in Equation 15.6. The firm is withholding funds from the investor and investing them in projects that generate returns less than those available from comparable risk investments.

Such poor performance may be difficult to uncover, because the firm's asset base will grow due to the firm retaining earnings and acquiring assets, and the earnings of the firm will increase if it earns *any positive rate of return* on the new assets. The crucial point is the earnings will not grow by as much as they should, so the value of the firm will decline when investors discount this reinvestment stream.

WHAT DETERMINES THE CAPITAL GAIN COMPONENT? These equations highlight the factors that influence the capital gain component. All the equations beginning with 15.1 suggest that the gross present value of the growth investments is equal to

$$bEm/k.$$

This indicates that three factors are important to the size of this capital gain term. The first is the size of b, the percentage of earnings retained for reinvestment. The greater the proportion of earnings retained, the larger the capital gain component. The second factor is the value of m, which indicates the relationship between the firm's rate of return on investments and the firm's required rate of return (i.e., its cost of capital). A value of 1 indicates that the firm is earning only its required return. A firm with an m greater than 1 is a true growth company. The important question is, how much greater than 1 is the return? The final factor of importance is *the time period for the superior investments*—for how long can the firm make these investments that provide returns above the required return? This time factor is easily overlooked because, throughout the discussion, we assume an infinite horizon to simplify the computations. However, when analyzing growth companies, the length of time a firm can continue to invest large amounts of funds at superior rates in a relatively competitive environment is clearly a major consideration. The three factors that influence the capital gain component are

1. The amount of capital invested in growth investments
2. The rate of return earned on the funds retained relative to the required rate of return, i.e., the magnitude of *m*
3. The time horizon when these growth investments will be available

DYNAMIC TRUE GROWTH MODEL

A dynamic true growth model applies to a firm that invests a constant *percentage* of current earnings in projects that generate rates of return above the firm's required rate $(r > k, m > 1)$. The effect of this is that the firm's earnings and dividends will grow at a *constant rate* that is equal to *br* (the percentage of earnings retained times the return on investments). In the current model, this would equal *bmk,* where *m* is greater than 1. Given these assumptions, the dynamic growth model for an infinite time period would be the dividend valuation model derived in the Appendix to Chapter 12:

$$V = \frac{D}{k - g}.$$

Applying this model to a true growth company means that earnings and dividends are growing at a constant rate and the firm is investing larger and larger dollar amounts in projects that generate returns greater than *k*. Moreover, the dividend growth model implicitly assumes that the firm can continue to do this for an infinite time period. If the growth rate (g) is greater than *k*, the model blows up and indicates that the firm should have an infinite value. Durand considered this possibility and concluded that, although many firms had current growth rates above the normal required rates of return, very few of their stocks were selling for infinite values.[21] His best explanation for this phenomenon was the expectation that the reinvestment rate would decline or that the investment opportunities would not be available for an infinite time period. Table 15.17 contains a summary of the alternative company characteristics.

THE REAL WORLD

All of these models are simplified to allow the development of a range of alternatives. As a result, several of the models are extremely unrealistic. *The real world is composed of companies that are a combination of these*

[21] David Durand, "Growth Stocks and the Petersburg Paradox," *Journal of Finance* 12, no. 3 (September 1957): 348–363.

TABLE 15.17
Summary of Company Descriptions

	RETENTION	RETURN ON INVESTMENTS
NO-GROWTH COMPANY	$b = 0$	$r = k$
LONG-RUN GROWTH (ASSUMES REINVESTMENT)		
Negative growth	$b > 0$	$r < k$
Expansion	$b > 0$	$r = k$
Simple long-run growth	$b > 0$ (constant $)	$r > k$
Dynamic long-run growth	$b > 0$ (constant %)	$r > k$

models. Unfortunately, most firms have made some investments where $r < k$, and many firms invest in projects that generate returns about equal to the cost of capital. Finally, almost all firms have the opportunity to invest in some projects that provide rates of return above the firm's cost of capital ($r > k$). How much is invested in these growth projects and how long these opportunities last are crucial considerations.

The rest of this chapter considers various models that will help you derive better estimates of the value of the growth company.

GROWTH DURATION

The earnings multiple for a stock (the P/E ratio) is a function of (1) the firm's expected rate of growth of earnings per share, (2) the required rate of return on the security based upon its systematic risk, and (3) the firm's dividend-payout ratio. Assuming equal risk and no significant difference in the payout ratio for different firms, the principal variable affecting the earnings multiple is the difference in the growth estimate. Further, the growth estimate must consider the *rate* of growth and the *duration* of expected growth. No company can continue to grow indefinitely at a rate substantially above normal. As an example, IBM cannot continue to grow at 20 percent a year for an extended period, or it will eventually become the entire economy. The fact is, IBM or any similar growth firm will eventually run out of high-profit investment projects. Continued growth at a sustained rate requires that larger and larger amounts of money be invested in high return projects. Eventually competition will encroach upon these high-return investments, and the firm's growth rate will decline to a rate consistent with the rate for the overall economy. Ascertaining the duration of the high-growth period therefore becomes significant.

COMPUTATION OF GROWTH DURATION. The growth duration concept was originally derived by Holt, who showed that if you assume equal risk between a given security and a market security (e.g., the DJIA), it is possible to examine the differential past growth rates for the market and for the growth firm.[22] Then, given the alternative P/E ratios, one can compute the market's *implied growth duration* for the growth firm. If $E'(0)$ is the firm's current earnings, then $E'(t)$ is earnings in period t according to the expression

$$E'(t) = E'(0)(1 + G)^t, \tag{15.9}$$

where G is the annual percentage growth rate for earnings. To adjust for dividend payments, it was assumed that all such payments are used to purchase further shares of the stock. This means the number of shares (N) will grow at the dividend rate (D). Therefore,

$$N(t) = N(0)(1 + D)^t. \tag{15.10}$$

To derive the total earnings for a firm, $E(t)$, the growth rate in per share earnings and the growth in shares are combined as follows:

$$E(t) = E'(t)N(t) = E'(0)[(1 + G)(1 + D)]^t. \tag{15.11}$$

Because G and D are small, this expression can be approximated by

$$E(t) \simeq E'(0)(1 + G + D)^t. \tag{15.12}$$

Assuming that the general characteristics of the growth stock (g) and the nongrowth stock (a) are the same (i.e., they have similar risk and payout), the market should value the shares of the two stocks in direct proportion to their earnings in year T, where T is the investor's horizon. In other words, current prices should be in direct proportion to the expected future earnings ratio that will prevail in year T. This relationship can be stated

$$\left(\frac{P_g(0)}{P_a(0)}\right) \simeq \left(\frac{E_g(0)(1 + G_g + D_g)^T}{E_a(0)(1 + G_a + D_a)^T}\right) \tag{15.13}$$

or

$$\left(\frac{P_g(0)/E_g(0)}{P_a(0)/E_a(0)}\right) \simeq \left(\frac{1 + G_g + D_g}{1 + G_a + D_a}\right)^T. \tag{15.14}$$

The result is that the P/E ratios of the two stocks are in direct proportion to the ratio of composite growth rates raised to the Tth power. It is possible to solve for T by taking the log of both sides as follows:

$$ln\left(\frac{P_g(0)/E_g(0)}{P_a(0)/E_a(0)}\right) \simeq T\, ln\left(\frac{1 + G_g + D_g}{1 + G_a + D_a}\right). \tag{15.15}$$

The growth duration model answers the question, how long must the earnings of the growth stock grow at the past rate, relative to the nongrowth

---

[22] Charles C. Holt, "The Influence of Growth Duration on Share Prices," *Journal of Finance* 17, no. 3 (September 1962): 465–475. This discussion draws on the original article. A subsequent article that used the concept is Robert M. Baylis and Suresh L. Bhirud, "Growth Stock Analysis: A New Approach," *Financial Analysts Journal* 29, no. 4 (July–August 1973): 63–70.

stock, to justify its above average P/E ratio relative to the P/E ratios for the nongrowth stock? The analyst must then determine whether the implied duration estimate is reasonable in terms of his analysis of the company's potential.

Suppose the stock of a well-known growth company is currently selling for $63 a share with expected per share earnings of $3.50 (its earnings multiple is 18). The firm's average growth rate in earnings per share during the past five- and ten-year periods has been 15 percent a year, and the dividend yield has averaged 3 percent. In contrast, the S&P 400 industrial index has a current P/E ratio of 10, an average dividend yield of 5 percent, and an average growth rate of 6 percent. Therefore, the comparison looks as follows:

	S&P 400	**Growth Company**
P/E ratios (current price ÷ expected earnings)	10.00	18.00
Average growth rate	.0600	.1500
Dividend yield	.0500	.0300

Inserting these values into Equation 15.15 yields the following:

$$\ln \left(\frac{18.00}{10.00} \right) \cong T \ln \left(\frac{1 + .1500 + .0300}{1 + .0600 + .0500} \right)$$

$$\ln (1.800) \cong T \ln \left(\frac{1.1800}{1.1100} \right)$$

$$\ln (1.800) \cong T \ln (1.063)$$
$$T = \ln (1.800)/\ln (1.063)$$
$$= .255273/.026533 \text{ (log base 10)}$$
$$= 9.62 \text{ years.}$$

These results indicate that the market is implicitly assuming that the growth company can continue to grow at this composite rate (18 percent) for almost ten more years, after which it is assumed that the growth company will grow at the same rate as the aggregate market (i.e., the S&P 400). As an analyst, you must now ask, can this growth rate be sustained for at least this period? If the implied growth duration is greater than you believe is reasonable, you would likely advise against buying the stock. If the duration is below your expectations, you would likely recommend the purchase.

INTRA-INDUSTRY ANALYSIS. Besides using the growth duration to compare a company to some market base, you can use this technique for a direct comparison of two firms. When doing an intercompany analysis, you should consider firms in the same industry, because then it is likely that the equal risk assumptions of the growth duration technique are valid.

Consider the following example from the cosmetics industry:

	Company A	**Company B**
P/E ratios	21.00	15.00
Average annual growth rate	.1700	.1200
Dividend yield	.0250	.0300
Growth rate plus dividend yield	.1950	.1500
Estimate of T^a		8.79 years

^{a} The reader should check to see that he gets the same answer.

These results imply that the market expects Company A to grow at a total rate of almost 20 percent for about nine years, followed by a decrease to the same rate of growth as Company B. If you believe the implied duration is too long, you will prefer Company B; if you believe it is reasonable or low, you will recommend Company A.

AN ALTERNATIVE USE OF T. Instead of solving for T and then deciding whether the figure derived is reasonable, you can use this formulation to derive a reasonable earnings multiple for a security relative to the aggregate market (or another stock) if the implicit assumptions are reasonable for the stock involved. Assume that you analyze the composite growth of a company to be about 20 percent a year compared to the market growth of 11 percent. Further, you believe that this firm can maintain this superior growth rate for about seven years. Using Equation 15.15, this becomes

$$\ln (X) = 7 \cdot \ln \frac{1.20}{1.11}$$
$$= 7 \cdot \ln (1.081)$$
$$= 7 \cdot (.033826)$$
$$= .236782 .$$

To determine what the P/E ratio should be, you must derive the antilog of 0.236782, which is approximately 1.725. Therefore, assuming the market multiple is 10.00, the earnings multiple for this growth company should be about 1.725 times the market P/E ratio, or 17.25.

Alternatively, if you expect that the firm can maintain this differential growth for only five years, you would derive the antilog for 0.16913 (5 × .033826). The answer is 1.4761, which implies a P/E ratio of 14.76 for the stock.

FACTORS TO CONSIDER. When employing this tool, you should remember the following major factors: First, the technique assumes *equal risk* between the securities compared. Although this assumption may be acceptable when comparing two large, well-established firms to each other or to a market proxy (e.g., General Motors and Standard Oil to each other or to the DJIA), it is probably not when comparing a small firm to the aggregate market.

Second, which growth estimate should be used? In the typical case, five- and ten-year historical growth rates are used. Which time interval is most relevant if historical rates are used? Which does the market employ? Beyond this, we have seen that judgment based upon analysis is required above and beyond mere extrapolations. What about using the *expected* rate of growth based upon the factors that effect g (i.e., the retention rate and the components of ROE)?

Third, the technique assumes that the stock with the higher P/E ratio has the higher growth rate. In actuality, in many cases you will find that the stock with the higher P/E ratio does not have a higher historical growth rate. In these cases, the formulation generates a negative growth duration value, which is useless. Inconsistency between growth and the P/E ratio could be attributed to one of four factors:

1. A major difference in the risk involved.
2. Inaccurate growth rate estimates. Possibly the firm with the higher P/E ratio is expected to grow at a higher rate in the future. You must consider the growth rate figures employed and whether you expect any changes in the rate.
3. An undervaluation of a stock with a low P/E ratio relative to its growth rate. (Before this is accepted, the first two alternatives should be considered.)
4. An overvaluation of a high P/E stock with a low growth rate. (Before this is accepted, consider Alternative 2.)

The growth duration concept is valid, given the assumptions made, and can be useful in evaluating investments. It is by no means universally valid, though, because it generates an answer that is only as good as the data inputs (relative growth rates) and the applicability of the assumptions. The answer must be evaluated on the basis of the analyst's knowledge. The technique is probably most useful for spotting possibly overvalued growth stocks with very high multiples. In such cases, this technique will indicate that in order to justify the high multiple, it is necessary for the company to continue to grow at some very high rate for an extended period of time (e.g., 15 to 20 years). Also, it can be very helpful in deciding between two growth companies in the same industry—that is, you would compare each to a common base such as the market or the industry or compare them directly to each other. Such a comparison provided interesting insights in the case of Apple Computer versus IBM and also Wendy's versus McDonald's. In both instances, the comparison indicated that the new firms (Apple and Wendy's) had very high growth duration values. Specifically, while both were growing at a faster rate than the large competitor, their P/E ratios were *substantially* higher and implied that they were going to have to maintain this growth superiority for over ten years.

A FLEXIBLE GROWTH STOCK VALUATION MODEL

Mao developed an investment opportunities growth model that incorporated some of the previous work on growth stock valuation.[23] Mao noted that the earlier presentations by Solomon and by Miller and Modigliani

---

[23] James C. Mao, "The Valuation of Growth Stocks: The Investment Opportunities Approach," *Journal of Finance* 21, no. 1 (March 1966): 95–102.

had recognized the true nature of a growth firm, but in order to simplify the exposition, they had assumed the existence of unrealistic infinite growth horizons. Therefore, their models were not applicable to practical problems. Mao consequently developed a three-stage valuation model that considered (1) a *dynamic growth period* during which it is assumed that the firm invests a constant percentage of current earnings in growth projects, (2) a *simple growth period* during which the firm invests a constant dollar amount in growth opportunities, and finally, (3) a *declining growth period* during which the amount invested in growth investments declines to zero. The model was theoretically correct and realistic but, unfortunately, difficult to use because of the computations required. The model was also somewhat rigid in its assumptions about the parameters b (the retention rate), r (the return on growth investments), and k (the required rate of return on the stock). As a result, the model has not been applied as widely as one might expect. In this section we will discuss the flexible growth model more thoroughly, apply it to a growth company, and discuss the effects of varying the parameters.

THE VALUATION MODEL. Mao assumed that the price of the stock is equal to (1) the present value of current earnings, E, discounted to infinity at the required rate of return, k, $(P = E/k)$ plus (2) the net present value of growth opportunities assuming three stages of growth.

Mao's first stage of dynamic growth lasts for n_1 years. During this period, the firm has opportunities to invest a given percentage of current earnings in projects that generate returns equal to r, and that r is greater than k. Since b is a constant percentage of current earnings, and current earnings are growing each year, the dollar amount invested in these growth projects is growing at an exponential rate. The value of the dynamic investments is given by

$$\left(\frac{r-k}{k}\right)(bE)\sum_{t=1}^{n_1}\frac{(1+br)^{t-1}}{(1+k)^t} \quad \text{(Value of Dynamic Growth Opportunities)} . \qquad (15.16)$$

During the second stage of simple growth, which lasts for n_2 years, the firm still has opportunities to invest in growth projects $(r > k)$, but the amount invested in these growth projects is a constant dollar amount (bE). The value of these projects is given by

$$\left(\frac{r-k}{k}\right)(bE)\sum_{t=1}^{n_2}\frac{1}{(1+k)^t} \quad \text{(Value of Simple Growth Opportunities)} . \qquad (15.17)$$

During the final period of declining growth, which lasts n_3 years, it is still assumed that the firm has opportunities to invest funds in growth projects, but the dollar amount that can be invested at $r > k$ declines steadily from bE to zero. The amount of the decline is steady at $1/n_3$ each year. As an example, if bE equals $\$100,000$, and n_3 is 20, then the amount invested in growth projects would decline by \$5,000 a year. The value of this component is

$$\left(\frac{r-k}{k}\right)(bE)\sum_{t=1}^{n_3}\frac{(n_3-t+1)}{n_3(1+k)^t}\text{ (Value of Declining Growth Opportunities)}.\qquad(15.18)$$

The complete model is then simply a combination of the no-growth component (E/k) plus the three growth factors. If the final summation term is A in Equation 15.16, B in Equation 15.17, and C in Equation 15.18, this formulation can be written as follows:

$$P=\frac{E}{k}+\left(\frac{r-k}{k}\right)(bE)\left[A+\frac{(1+br)^{n_1-1}}{(1+k)^{n_1}}B+\frac{(1+br)^{n_1-1}}{(1+k)^{n_1+n_2}}C\right].\qquad(15.19)$$

Mao provided tables that contained values for A and C, given several combinations of the parameters. Because B is the present value of an annuity, the analyst can readily calculate its value. Even with the tables and no change in the parameters, the computation of a single value is rather tedious.

FLEXIBLE PARAMETERS. The Mao model assumes (1) no change in the required rate of return (k), (2) the same rate of return on all growth projects (r), and (3) the same retention rate (b) during different periods of growth. The assumption of constant parameters was probably made to avoid complicating a technique that already involved fairly extensive computations. While many analysts might agree with these assumptions, some work indicates that investors probably change their required return (k) during different phases of the firm's life cycle. Malkiel has shown that it is logical to require a higher return on high-growth stocks because the stream of returns is such that these stocks are inherently longer-duration securities.[24] At the other end of the spectrum, during its declining years a firm may become subject to cyclical variations, which would indicate more business risk and an increase in the required rate of return (k).

Regarding the return on investments (r), it could be considered too optimistic to assume that during the period of simple growth the firm can continue to earn very high rates even on a stable dollar amount. Many analysts would prefer to use a large n_2 and a somewhat smaller r.

Finally, is it realistic to assume a constant retention rate (b) over a firm's life cycle? It seems more logical to expect a high retention rate during the early years, when growth opportunities are abundant and capital is scarce, and a lower retention rate during the later years, when growth investment opportunities are limited, the level of earnings and cash flow is high, and outside capital is available. The point is, the model should be more useful and realistic if flexibility is possible in these parameters.

---

[24] Burton G. Malkiel, "Equity Yields, Growth, and the Structure of Share Prices," *American Economic Review* 53, no. 5 (December 1963): 1004–1031.

APPLICATION OF THE MODEL. Using a computer program, it is necessary to prepare only three statements for each case. Because of the ease of application, you should consider several alternative sets of parameters, including most pessimistic, most optimistic, and most likely. For a stock with a very high earnings multiple, you should determine the alternative sets of estimates that would be required to justify the prevailing market price. In applying this technique to the evaluation of growth companies, the following suggestions might prove useful.

1. The earnings figure (E) is assumed to be the figure for the coming year. A crude estimate is the actual earnings for the most recent year times the growth rate for the past five or ten years. Most analysts (especially superior ones) would modify this historical value based upon their estimate of future growth.

2. The retention rate (b) can be estimated as the average percentage of earnings retained for the last several years.

3. The estimate of the return on investment (r) is obviously crucial.[25] You can derive it by computing the average ROE during the recent period or by estimating the three components (total asset turnover, financial leverage, and the profit margin) and using the product of these three estimates. Alternatively, Mao suggested using the return on recently retained earnings by computing the increase in earnings per share during some period divided by the amount of earnings retained over a comparable period with a one-year lag. For example, the increase in earnings per share for the period 1986–1990 is divided by the retained earnings for the period 1985–1989. This computation attempts to estimate what rate of return the firm is *currently* deriving from retained earnings compared to the typical estimate of ROE, which is current net earnings divided by current equity. This average ROE figure can be heavily influenced by past performance and also uses historical equity, which can become seriously distorted over time. The Mao estimate is more in the nature of a marginal return on equity.

4. The required return estimate (k) could be the actual return derived from all common stocks or the return experienced by the specific stock during some recent period. Alternatively, you might want to use a required rate based upon the CAPM and the stock's beta. Because the model is extremely sensitive to changes in k, it is strongly suggested that you consider a *range* of alternative ks.

AN EXAMPLE

Assume the following for a firm that you consider to be a true growth company:

- Earnings: 1990 $2.50
        1991 (estimated) 2.88 ($2.50 × 1.15)

---

[25] An article that discusses the components of growth is Guilford C. Babcock, "The Concept of Sustainable Growth," *Financial Analysts Journal* 26, no. 3 (May–June 1970) : 236–242.

- Annual growth rate in EPS (1985–1989) .15
- Retention rate (1985–1989) .65
- Average return on equity (1985–1989) .24
- Marginal return on equity (1985–1989) .26
- Estimated r for analysis .25

Given these estimates of the major parameters, you can derive a number of stock price values simply by changing the values for the three ns (n_1, n_2, n_3) and consider alternative required returns. You can change the values for each of these parameters for each growth period. In the current example we will hold them constant at these historical values to simplify the presentation of results. Subsequent estimates should consider alternative parameters. For the example, the initial estimates of the ns are relatively conservative (5, 5, 10) and are changed to more liberal estimates as follows:

A. $n_1 = 5$,
   $n_2 = 5$,
   $n_3 = 10$
B. $n_1 = 5$,
   $n_2 = 10$,
   $n_3 = 15$
C. $n_1 = 10$,
   $n_2 = 10$,
   $n_3 = 15$
D. $n_1 = 15$,
   $n_2 = 15$,
   $n_3 = 20$.

The ks considered ranged from 8 percent to 16 percent in increments of 2 percent. The results are in Table 15.18. These results clearly indicate a wide range of estimated values for the example stock. At this point you must select the best estimate of the three periods and, most important, the superior estimate of k for this stock based upon its systematic risk and the expected *security market line (SML)*. Because almost all growth companies have above-average systematic risk (i.e., betas above 1.00), the required return will typically exceed the expected market return.

TABLE **15.18**
Estimated Values for Stock Assuming Alternative Time Periods and Required Rates of Return ($E = \$2.88$; $b = .65$; $r = .25$)

N₁	N₂	N₃	0.08	0.10	0.12	0.14	0.16
5	5	10	91.03	62.79	45.67	34.55	26.96
5	10	15	102.92	68.72	48.72	36.15	27.80
10	10	15	154.15	95.72	63.55	44.46	32.46
15	15	20	242.31	136.49	83.39	54.40	37.48

FIGURE 15.4
Estimated Prices for Flexible Growth Model

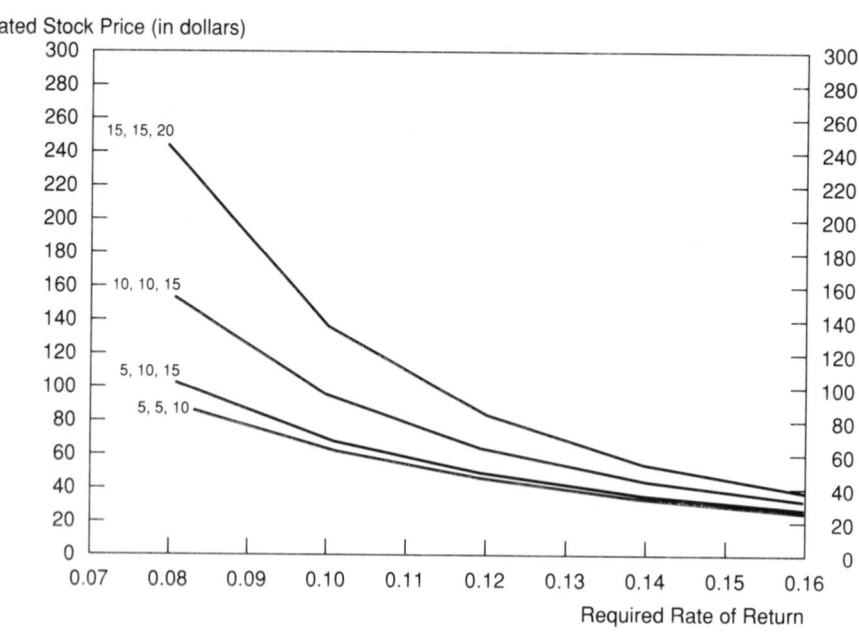

Assume the following estimates regarding the SML: $RFR = .08$; $Rm = .12$. If the stock has a beta of 1.5, the estimated required return would be

$$k = RFR + (Rm - RFR)$$
$$k = .08 + 1.5\ (.12 - .08)$$
$$k = .14.$$

This would indicate further consideration of the 0.14 column and possibly the adjoining columns. A comparison of these prices with the prevailing market prices will indicate whether the stock should be considered for inclusion in the portfolio.

You can draw a graph of the values for the stock for a given set of *n* values and different *k*s. Using several sets of *n*s, one will produce a set of curves sloping downward to the right as shown in Figure 15.4. Given this graph, there are two ways of examining the results of the model. First, compare the prevailing market price or range of recent prices to the range of computed values. Beyond expecting the prevailing price to be somewhere within the total range, one might also get an indication of relative undervaluation or overvaluation, depending upon whether the current market price is toward the upper or lower end of the range. Second, examine the market price in terms of the implied rate of return by drawing the current market price horizontally across the valuation curves. Assuming that the valuation curves generally represent the full range of feasible parameters, the intersection of the price line with the curve to the right indicates the highest k that can be expected, with the most liberal parameters, if you acquire the stock at the current market price. The curve to the left indicates the lowest k possible if you acquire the stock at the price indicated.

SUMMARY

It is important to know that the stock of a growth company may not be a growth stock. Also, you should be aware of the complexity of global analysis due to accounting differences and the impact of exchange rate movements over time. Several studies dealing with the cross-sectional analysis of earnings multiples and internal corporate variables have indicated that although such models are helpful in explaining past multiples, without accurate *estimates* they are not useful in selecting underpriced securities.

A firm can adopt different strategies within an industry to attain above-average rates of return, including low-cost leadership, differentiation, low-cost focus, and differentiation focus.

You cannot use standard valuation models when analyzing true growth companies. The growth duration model concentrates on the major question of concern with true growth companies: how long will this superior growth last, and is it consistent with the stock's implied duration? Mao's three-step growth model concentrates on the relevant growth variables.

Because of the potential rewards possible from the analysis of growth companies, you should expect strong competition in the valuation process. Although the techniques presented in this chapter should give you an edge because the models can help derive a value for a firm, *it is the estimated inputs that are crucial.* The superior analyst for no-growth or true growth companies is the one who derives the best *estimates.*

QUESTIONS

1. Define a growth company and a speculative stock.
2. Give an example of a growth company, and discuss why you would expect it to be considered a growth company. Be specific.
3. Give an example of a cyclical stock, and discuss why you have designated it as such. Is it issued by a cyclical company?
4. Select a company outside the retail store industry, and indicate what economic series you would use for a sales projection. Discuss why this is a relevant series.
5. Select a company outside the retail store industry, and indicate what industry series you would use in an industry analysis. (Try to use one of the industry groups designated by Standard & Poor's.) Discuss why this series is most appropriate and whether there were several possible alternatives.
6. Select a company outside the retail stores industry and, based upon reading its annual report (if available) and other information in public sources (refer to Chapter 5), determine its competitive strategy—low-cost

producer or differentiation. What is the firm attempting to do, and is it succeeding?

7. You are told that a company retains 80 percent of its earnings, and its earnings are growing at a rate of about 8 percent a year versus an average of 6 percent for all firms. Discuss whether you would consider this a growth company.

8. It is contended by some that in a completely competitive economy, there would never be a true growth company. Discuss the line of reasoning behind such a contention.

9. Why is it not feasible to use the dividend growth model in the valuation of true growth companies?

10. What are the major assumptions of the growth duration model? Discuss each assumption and why it could present a problem.

11. You are told that a growth company has a P/E ratio of 10 times and a growth rate of 15 percent compared to the market growth rate of 10 percent. The market has a P/E ratio of 11 times. What does this comparison imply regarding the growth company? What else do you need to know to properly compare the growth company to the aggregate market?

12. Define the following:

12a. A negative growth company

12b. An expanding company

12c. A simple growth company

12d. A dynamic growth company.

13. Given the terms listed in Question 12, discuss which label you would give IBM.

14. Discuss which label you would give U.S. Steel.

15. What are the most important variables that must be estimated in the flexible growth valuation model?

PROBLEMS

1. What is the implied growth duration of Growth Industries given the following:

	S&P 400	Growth Industries
P/E ratios	12	22
Average growth (%)	4	14
Dividend yield	.05	.03

2. Modular Industries presently has an 18 percent annual growth rate while the market average is 7 percent. If the market multiple is 9, determine the P/E ratio for Modular Industries, assuming that you feel it can maintain its superior growth rate for

2a. The next ten years

2b. The next five years

3. Given Hitech's beta of 1.75 and a risk-free rate of 9 percent, what is the expected rate of return assuming

3a. A 15 percent market return?

3b. A 10 percent market return?

4. Select two stocks in an industry of your choice, and perform a common size income statement analysis over a two-year period. Determine

4a. Which firm is more cost effective.

4b. The relative year-to-year changes in each company.

5. You are told that a biotechnology firm is growing at a compound rate of 22 percent a year. (Its ROE is over 30 percent, and it retains about 70 percent of its earnings.) The stock of this company is currently priced at 74 times next year's earnings. Discuss whether you would consider this a growth company. Discuss whether you would consider it a growth stock.

6. Select a company outside the retail industry, and examine its operating profit margin relative to the operating margin for its industry for the most recent ten-year period. Discuss the annual results in terms of levels and percentage changes and the long-run averages.

7. Select any industry except chemicals and provide general background information on two non–U.S. companies from public sources (see Chapter 5). This background information should include their products, overall size (sales and assets), growth during the past five years (sales and earnings), ROE during the last two years, and current stock price and P/E ratio.

8. Select three companies from an industry and compute their P/E ratios using last year's average price (high plus low/2) and earnings. Also compute their growth rate of earnings over the last five years and look up the most recent beta reported in *Value Line*. Discuss the relative relationships between P/E, growth, and risk.

9. You are given the following information about two computer software firms and the S&P 400:

	COMPANY A	COMPANY B	S&P 400
P/E ratio	24.0	20.0	12.0
Average annual growth rate	.18	.15	.07
Dividend yield	.02	.03	.05

9a. Compute the growth duration of each company stock relative to the S&P 400.

9b. Compute the growth duration of Company A relative to Company B.

9c. Given these durations, what must you decide in order to make an investment decision?

10. *CFA Examination II (June 1981)*: The value of an asset is the present value of the expected returns from the asset during the holding period. An investment will provide a stream of returns during this period, and it is necessary to discount this stream of returns at an appropriate rate to

determine the asset's present value. A dividend valuation model such as the following is frequently used.

$$P_i = \frac{D_1}{(k_i - g_i)},$$

where

P_i = current price of common stock i

D_1 = expected dividend in period 1

k_i = required rate of return on stock i

g_i = expected constant growth rate of dividends for stock i.

10a. Identify the three factors that must be estimated for any valuation model, and explain why these estimates are more difficult to derive for common stocks than for bonds. [9 minutes]

10b. Explain the principal problem involved in using a dividend valuation model to value
   (1) Companies whose operations are closely correlated with economic cycles.
   (2) Companies that are of giant size and are maturing.
   (3) Companies that are of small size and are growing rapidly. Assume all companies pay dividends. [6 minutes]

11. *CFA Examination I (June 1985):* Your client is considering the purchase of $100,000 in common stock which pays no dividends and will appreciate in market value by 10 percent per year. At the same time, the client is considering an opportunity to invest $100,000 in a lease obligation that will provide the annual year-end cash flows listed in Table A. Assume that each investment will be sold at the end of three years and that you are given no additional information.
Calculate the present value of each of the two investments assuming a 10 percent discount rate, and state which will provide the higher return over the three-year period. Use the data in Table A, and show your calculations. [10 minutes]

TABLE A
Annual Cash Flow From Lease

End of Year		
1	$	-0-
2 Lease receipts		15,000
3 Lease receipts		25,000
3 Sale proceeds		100,000

Present Value of $1

Period	6%	8%	10%	12%
1	.943	.926	.909	.893
2	.890	.857	.826	.797
3	.840	.794	.751	.712
4	.792	.735	.683	.636
5	.747	.681	.621	.567

REFERENCES

Babcock, Guilford C. "The Concept of Sustainable Growth." *Financial Analysts Journal* 26, no. 3 (May–June 1970).

Ball, Ray, and Ross Watts. "Some Time Series Properties of Accounting Earnings Numbers." *Journal of Finance* 27, no. 3 (June 1972).

Cottle, Sidney, Roger F. Murray, and Frank E. Block, *Graham and Dodd's Security Analysis,* 5th ed. (New York: McGraw-Hill Book Co., 1988).

Cragg, John G., and Burton G. Malkiel. "The Consensus and Accuracy of Some Predictions of the Growth of Corporate Earnings." *Journal of Finance* 23, no. 1 (March 1968).

Gordon, Myron J. *The Investment, Financing, and Valuation of the Corporation.* Homewood, Ill.: Richard D. Irwin, 1962.

Hassel, J., and Robert Jennings. "Relative Forecast Accuracy and the Timing of Earnings Forecast Announcements." *The Accounting Review* 61, no. 1 (January 1986).

Imhoff, Eugene, and G. Lobo. "Information Content of Analysts Composite Forecast Revisions." *Journal of Accounting Research* 22, no. 3 (Autumn 1984).

Jennings, Robert. *Reaction of Financial Analysts to Corporate Management Earnings Per Share Forecasts. Financial Analysts Research Foundation,* Monograph No. 20 (New York, 1984).

Jennings, Robert. "Unsystematic Security Price Movements, Management Earnings Forecasts, and Revisions in Consensus Analyst Earnings Forecasts." *Journal of Accounting Research* 25, no. 1 (Spring 1987).

Levine, Sumner N. *The Financial Analysts Handbook* 2d ed. (Homewood, Ill.: Dow Jones-Irwin, 1988).

Malkiel, Burton G., and John Cragg. "Expectations and the Structure of Share Prices." *American Economic Review* 60, no. 4 (September 1970).

Miller, Merton, and Franco Modigliani. "Dividend Policy, Growth, and the Valuation of Shares." *Journal of Business* 34, no. 4 (October 1961).

Solomon, Ezra. *The Theory of Financial Management.* New York: Columbia University Press, 1963.

Waymire, G. "Additional Evidence on the Information Content of Management Earnings Forecasts." *Journal of Accounting Research* 22, no. 3 (Autumn 1984).

APPENDIX 15A   # A PRIMER FOR FIELD CONTACT WORK

Types of Questions Analysts Ask When Visiting Companies[1]

SALES

1. Percentage gain or loss, year to date vs. year before.
2. Estimates for full year:
   (a) Units and dollars.
   (b) Identical store sales (retailing).
3. Explanation of sales changes, either way.
4. Sales breakdowns (year to date):
   (a) By divisions.
   (b) By major product groups.
   (c) By major consuming markets.
5. Explanation of sales trends above or below the industry average.
6. Demand prospects: near, intermediate, and longer term.
7. Inventory status of company, its distributors, ultimate users.
8. Price levels vs. year ago—impact on unit and dollar sales.
9. Outlook for selling price: firm, up or down. Why?
10. Company's percent of industry sales (i.e., "trade position").
11. Foreign sales aspects:
    (a) Percent of export sales.
    (b) Percent contributed by foreign branches.
    (c) Outlook abroad by countries.
12. Percent of sales derived from government business—type of work.

SELLING AND DISTRIBUTION

1. Methods used: direct to users, via wholesalers, retailers, branch warehouses, or combination of these.
2. Percent of selling costs to total sales.
3. Methods of compensation to selling forces: number of salesmen employed.
4. Advertising and promotional efforts, use of TV and other publicity media, with actual costs of this type of expense.
5. Extent of geographic coverage of the nation; plans, if any, to extend marketing areas, add new distributors, etc.
6. Economic radius of distribution from individual points; importance of freight rates.

---

[1] Joseph M. Galanis, "A Primer for Field Contact Work," *Financial Analysts Journal* (August 1956). Reprinted with permission.

COMPETITION	1. What concerns are viewed as chief competitors?
	2. Few or many competitors?
	3. Is competition cutthroat or live-and-let-live type?
	4. Are competitors strongly or weakly financed units?
	5. In what way do company's products and services have an advantage, if any, over competition?
	6. Is new competition entering field?
	7. Where does company rank in its field or fields?
	8. Importance of brand names, trademarks, patents, or servicing methods.

PATENT ASPECTS
1. Importance for sales and prices.
2. Expiration dates of basic or supplementary patents; expected impact on sales, price structure, profit margins, etc., upon expirations.

PRODUCTION
1. Rate of operations to date vs. year ago; prospective rates of operation over foreseeable future.
2. Basis of operations: 1–2–3 shift, 7–8 hour day, or continuous operations?
3. Overtime premium pay?
4. Number of plants and character of their construction; multistory or single story (modern)?
5. Status of equipment: new, modernized, or obsolete?
6. Does company rate as a low-cost, high-cost, or average-cost producer?
7. Steps, if any, being taken to improve production methods and to increase productive efficiency.

RAW MATERIALS
1. Major raw materials used; sources, domestic and foreign. Ample supplies or storage?
2. Price history of raw materials used. Volatility?
3. Extent of integration.
4. Is LIFO method of inventory valuation used?

FINANCIAL
1. Most recent capitalization and changes.
2. Any current bank loans outstanding? Explanation.
3. Adequacy of working capital in relation to current and anticipated sales, compared with earlier years.
4. Near term maturities? Refundings? Retirements? Comment on ability to meet these obligations.
5. Any new financing in offing? Kind.
6. Insured, replacement, or appraisal value of fixed assets (especially natural resources) vs. book value.

DIVIDEND POLICIES AND PROSPECTS
1. Payout policy, percent of earnings, percent of cash flow.
2. Prospect for extras.
3. Prospect for stock dividends.

4. Chances for increase (or decrease) in regular annual rate.

EARNINGS

1. Trend of labor and materials costs, percent of each to sales.
2. Ability to adjust selling prices to higher costs.
3. Cost savings programs, and comments.
4. Profit margins vs. year ago.
5. Trend of earnings to date vs. year ago.
6. Per share earnings for full year.
7. Nonrecurring items. Explanation.
8. Nonoperating sources of income vs. year ago.

MISCELLANEOUS TOPICS

During the average interview, the analyst will think of spur-of-the-moment questions induced by information or comments of the contact. In addition, it may prove advisable to request comment on such individual topics as:

1. Status of current litigation.
2. Impact of Government Consent Decree.
3. Status of particular long-term sales contracts.
4. Problems arising as result of a current strike or aftermath of one settled.
5. Extent of insurance coverage in connection with floods or other disasters.

EXPANSION

1. Details of program: plant locations, additions, product lines to be added.
2. Capital outlays involved; methods of financing, if any, contemplated.
3. Percent to be added to plant capacity on a square foot basis, or in physical units, or in dollar sales volume.
4. Any certificates of necessity or fast amortization of new facilities involved?
5. Any new acquisitions in mind?
6. Costs of new construction and equipment per unit of added production vs. one to five years ago.
7. Expected sales per $1 of new plant account investment vs. other years.

RESEARCH

1. Amounts, or percent, of sales spent annually on research.
2. Number employed and number possessing advanced degrees.
3. Record of recent patents granted as result of research.
4. New products and their prospects.
5. Percent of current sales from new products traceable to research over the past five to fifteen years. (This is the most important factor in evaluating research.)

MANAGEMENT

1. Does management show continuity or frequent changes?
2. Average age of top management officials.
3. Is the company a one-man outfit?

4. Methods of recruiting and training executives.
5. Is management centralized or decentralized?

EMPLOYEE RELATIONS

1. Long-term strike record.
2. Percent of employees unionized—which plants?
3. Management policies on labor relations.
4. Chief employee benefits.
5. Labor turnover rates.

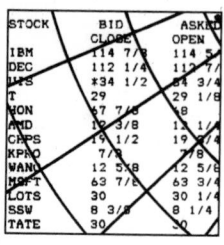

CHAPTER 16

TECHNICAL ANALYSIS

The market reacted yesterday to the report of a large increase in the short interest on the NYSE.

Although the Tokyo Stock Exchange declined today it was not considered bearish because there was very light volume.

The London Exchange declined today after three days of increases due to profit taking by investors.

These and similar statements appear almost daily in the financial news, and all have as their rationale one of numerous technical trading rules. This chapter explains the reasoning behind technical analysis and discusses many of the trading rules.

Prior to the development of the efficient market theory, investors were generally divided into two groups—*fundamentalists* and *technicians*. Fundamental analysts contend that the price of a security is determined by basic underlying economic factors, such as expected return and risk considerations. To arrive at estimates, therefore, an analyst would examine these underlying factors in the economy, the industry, and then the company. The resultant estimate of the intrinsic value of the security would then be compared to its market price. If the value exceeds the market price, the security would be acquired and vice versa. Thus, the fundamentalist acts on the assumption that the market price for a security will approach its intrinsic value in the future.

Technicians contend that it is *not* necessary to study economic fundamentals, because past price movements will indicate future price movements. In this chapter, we will examine, first, the basic philosophy underlying all technical approaches to market analysis, then the supposed advantages and some problems of the technical approach, and finally alternative technical trading rules applicable to the U.S. market and also non–U.S. markets.

BASIC PHILOSOPHY AND ASSUMPTIONS OF TECHNICAL ANALYSIS

The basic philosophy and assumptions of technical analysis are well summarized in an article by Robert A. Levy:

1. Market value is determined solely by the interaction of supply and demand.
2. Supply and demand are governed by numerous factors, both rational and irrational. Included in these factors are those relied upon by the fundamentalist, as well as opinions, moods, guesses, and blind necessities. The market weighs all of these factors continually and automatically.
3. Disregarding minor fluctuations in the market, *security prices tend to move in trends which persist for an appreciable length of time.* [Emphasis added.]
4. Changes in trend are caused by the shifts in supply and demand relationships. These shifts, no matter why they occur, *can be detected sooner or later in the action of the market itself.*[1] [Emphasis added.]

The emphases are added to the preceding quotes from Levy to highlight those aspects of the technical approach that differ from the belief of fundamentalists and advocates of an efficient market. The two initial statements are almost universally accepted by technicians and nontechnicians alike. Almost anyone who has had a basic course in economics would agree that, at any point in time, the price of a security (or any good or service) is determined by the interaction of supply and demand. In addition, most observers would acknowledge that supply and demand are governed by a multitude of variables. The only difference in opinion might be over the issue of whether the irrational factors are transitory and whether the rational factors will prevail in the long run. Certainly, everyone would agree that the market continually weighs all these factors.

A stronger difference of opinion arises over the implication in the third statement about the *speed of adjustment* of stock prices to changes in supply and demand factors. *Technicians expect stock prices to move in trends that persist for long periods.* This is based upon a belief that new information causing a change in the relationship between supply and demand does not come to the market at one point in time but rather over a period of time, because there are alternative sources of information or because certain investors receive the information earlier than others and analyze the effect before others do. As various groups (insiders, well-informed profes-

---

[1] Robert A. Levy, "Conceptual Foundations of Technical Analysis," *Financial Analysts Journal* 22, no. 4 (July–August 1966): 83. For an article that briefly discusses the concept and some of the techniques, see Earl C. Gottschalk, Jr., "Technical Analysis Gains in an Uncertain Market," *The Wall Street Journal* (December 12, 1988): C1, C19.

FIGURE 16.1
Technicians' View of Price Adjustment to New Information

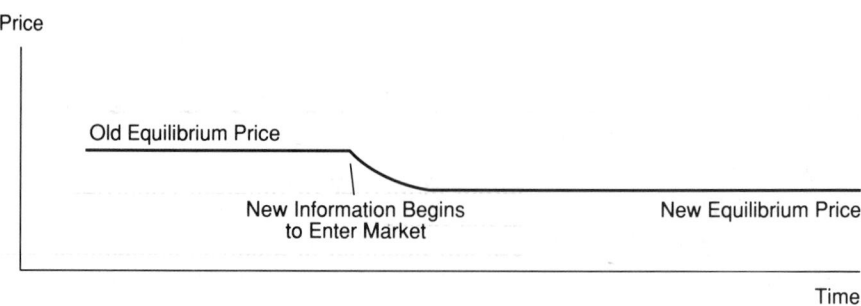

sionals, the average investor) receive the information and invest or dis-invest accordingly, the price is *partially* adjusted toward the new equilib-rium. Therefore, technicians do not view the price adjustment as abrupt but as a gradual flow of information from insiders, to high-powered ana-lysts, and eventually to the mass of investors. Figure 16.1 shows this pro-cess. New information causes, for example, a decrease in the equilibrium price for a security, but the price adjustment is not rapid. It is instead manifested as a *trend* that persists until the stock reaches its new equilib-rium. Therefore, the task of the technical analyst is to detect the beginning of a movement from one equilibrium value to another in a stock (or in the aggregate market). Technical analysts do not attempt to predict a change in equilibrium values. They merely look for the *start* of that change so that they can get on the bandwagon early and benefit from it. If the adjustment process were rapid, the ride on the bandwagon would be very short and thus not worth the effort.

ADVANTAGES OF TECHNICAL ANALYSIS

Most technical analysts would probably admit that a fundamental analyst with good information and good analytical ability should be able to do better than a technician, who must wait until the price movement is un-derway and thus misses part of the potential return. However, this is a qualified statement. The fundamental analyst must be able to obtain new information before other investors and process it correctly and quickly in order to derive returns above what a technical analyst can expect. The point is, technical analysts do not believe that it is possible to consistently get good information and process it quickly.

A major advantage claimed for technical analysis is that it is not heavily dependent on financial accounting statements, the major source of infor-mation about the past performance of a firm or industry. The fundamen-talist evaluates such statements to help project future return and risk char-acteristics, but the technician is quick to point out several major problems with those statements:

1. They do not contain a great deal of the information that is desired by analysts, such as details on sales and general expenses or sales and earnings by product line and customers.
2. There are several ways of reporting expenses, assets, or liabilities that can give vastly different results and, typically, several of these alternatives are equally acceptable for reporting purposes. As a result, in many instances it is difficult to compare the statements of two firms in the same industry, much less firms in different industries or different countries.
3. Many psychological factors and other nonquantitative variables are not included in financial statements. Examples include employee training and loyalty, customer goodwill, and general investor attitude toward an industry (e.g., tobacco companies).

Being therefore suspicious of financial statements, technicians consider it an advantage that they generally are not dependent upon them. As our later discussion will show, most of the data used by technicians is derived from the stock market itself.

Also, once a fundamental analyst has some new information, he must process it *correctly* and *very quickly* to derive a new value before the competition can. Technicians, on the other hand, need only be quick to recognize a movement to a new equilibrium value *for whatever reason.*

Finally, assume an analyst has determined that a given security is under- or overvalued a long time before the competition has. He still must determine when to make the purchase or sale. Ideally, it should be made just before the change in market value occurs. Since a technician does not invest until the move to the new equilibrium is underway, he is more likely to attain this timing.

DISADVANTAGES OF TECHNICAL ANALYSIS

The major problem with technical analysis stems from the efficient market hypothesis. As discussed in Chapter 6, for technical trading rules to generate returns that are superior to a buy-and-hold strategy of similar risk, net of transactions costs, the market would have to be inefficient in the weak form. The vast majority of studies reviewed in Chapter 6 tend to support the weak-form hypothesis, although it was acknowledged that there are numerous technical rules or techniques that have not or cannot be tested. The problems considered here are in addition to the efficient market arguments.

An obvious problem is that the past price patterns or relationships between variables may not be repeated in the future. As a result, there will be instances in which a technique that worked for some period of time misses later market turns. Because of this possibility, almost all technicians follow several trading rules and attempt to arrive at a consensus. In addition, many price patterns may become self-fulfilling prophecies. As an example, assume that a stock is selling at $40 a share and is widely expected to go to $50 or more if it should break out of a trading channel at

$45. Subsequently, if it does reach $45, a number of technicians will buy, and the price will probably go to $50, exactly as predicted. In fact, some technicians may place a stop-buy order at such a breakout point. Under such conditions, the increase will probably be only temporary and the price will return to its true equilibrium.

Another concern is that the success of a trading rule will encourage competition, which will eventually neutralize the value of the technique. If numerous investors are using a given rule, some of them will eventually attempt to anticipate what will happen and either ruin the expected price pattern or take the profits away from most users of the rule. Suppose, for example, it becomes known that technicians who have been investing on the basis of short interest data have been enjoying very high rates of return. Other technicians will likely start using these data and thus affect the stock price pattern following changes in the short interest. As a result, the rule that worked previously may no longer work after the first few investors who react.

Finally, as will be discussed later, all of the rules or techniques imply a great deal of subjective judgment. In some cases, two technical analysts looking at the same price pattern will arrive at widely different interpretations and investment decisions. This implies that the use of various techniques is neither completely mechanical nor easy. Also, as will be discussed in connection with several trading rules, the standard values that signal investment decisions can change over time. Therefore, it is necessary to change the trading rule over time to conform to the new environment.

TECHNICAL TRADING RULES

There are numerous technical rules and a large number of interpretations for each of them. Almost all technical analysts use more than one rule, and some watch many alternatives. This section discusses most of the well-known techniques but certainly not all of them.

CONTRARY-OPINION RULES

One set of technical trading rules contends that the majority of investors are wrong most of the time or at least they are wrong at peaks and troughs. Therefore, the idea is to determine when the majority is either very bullish or very bearish and trade in the opposite direction.[2]

THE ODD-LOT, SHORT-SALES THEORY. The use of short sales is generally considered bearish, because it is based upon an expectation of declining stock prices. It is also considered to be a fairly high-risk form of investing. Most small investors are optimists and would consider short selling too risky. Therefore, they do not get involved in it except when they feel especially bearish. Therefore, the technical rule contends that a relatively high rate (3 percent or more) of odd-lot short sales as a percentage of

---

[2] Prior editions of this book included the odd-lot theory as a contrary-opinion rule. It is not currently included because the volume of odd-lot transactions has become a very small proportion of total volume, and odd-lot volume is no longer considered a valid indication of small investor sentiment.

total odd-lot sales is an indication of a very *bearish* attitude by small investors. Contrary opinion would consider this bearish attitude by small investors an indicator of a near-term trough, and technicians following this rule would become *bullish.* Alternatively, when the ratio declines to below 1 percent, it would indicate that small investors are very bullish and would cause the contrarian to become bearish. Notably, recent figures for this ratio suggest that it may be necessary to change the 3 percent and 1 percent investment decision criteria.

MUTUAL FUND CASH POSITIONS. Mutual funds report the ratio of cash as a percentage of total assets in their portfolios over time. This ratio currently varies from a low point of less than 7 percent to a high point in excess of 12 percent (the range has increased during the last several years). The contrary-opinion technicians consider the mutual funds the odd lotters of the institutional investor group and contend that mutual funds are usually wrong at the peaks and troughs. They expect mutual funds to have heavy cash positions (a high ratio of cash) near the trough of a market cycle. This would indicate that the mutual funds are very bearish exactly at the time that they should be fully invested to take advantage of the impending market rise. At the peak, the technicians expect mutual funds to be almost fully invested (a low ratio of cash), indicating a bullish outlook at a point where the funds should have liquidated part of their portfolios. Therefore, these technicians watch for the mutual fund cash position to be at one of the extremes and act contrary to mutual funds behavior. They would invest when the cash ratio exceeds 12 percent and would sell when the cash ratio approaches 7 percent. Figure 16.2 contains a time series plot of the DJIA and the mutual fund cash ratio. As shown, there were apparently bullish signals in 1970, late 1974, and 1982 near market troughs. There were also bearish signals in 1971, 1972–1973, and 1976 prior to market peaks. Monthly data on this *liquid asset ratio* is reported in *Barron's.*[3]

Heavy mutual fund cash positions can also be used as an indicator of potential buying power—that is, a high cash position would be bullish because it represents buying power. Whether the cash balances have built up because of the previous sale of stocks in the portfolio or because of purchases of the fund by investors, some technicians believe these funds will eventually be invested and will cause an increase in stock prices. Alternatively, a low cash ratio would indicate a low level of potential buying power. A study by Massey examined the ratio of liquid assets to total assets and also the components of the ratio and concluded that the liquid asset ratio is not as strong a predictor as one would expect.[4] Massey contends that the significant relationship is between total assets and stock prices,

---

[3] *Barron's* is a prime source for numerous technical indicators. For a readable discussion of this data and their use, see Martin E. Zweig, *Understanding Technical Forecasting* (New York: Dow-Jones & Co., 1978). Complimentary copies are available from Dow-Jones & Co.

[4] Paul H. Massey, "The Mutual Fund Liquidity Ratio: A Trap for the Unwary," *Journal of Portfolio Management* 5, no. 2 (Winter 1979): 18–21.

FIGURE 16.2
Time Series Plot of Dow Jones Industrial Average and Mutual Fund Cash Ratio (Cash/Total Assets)

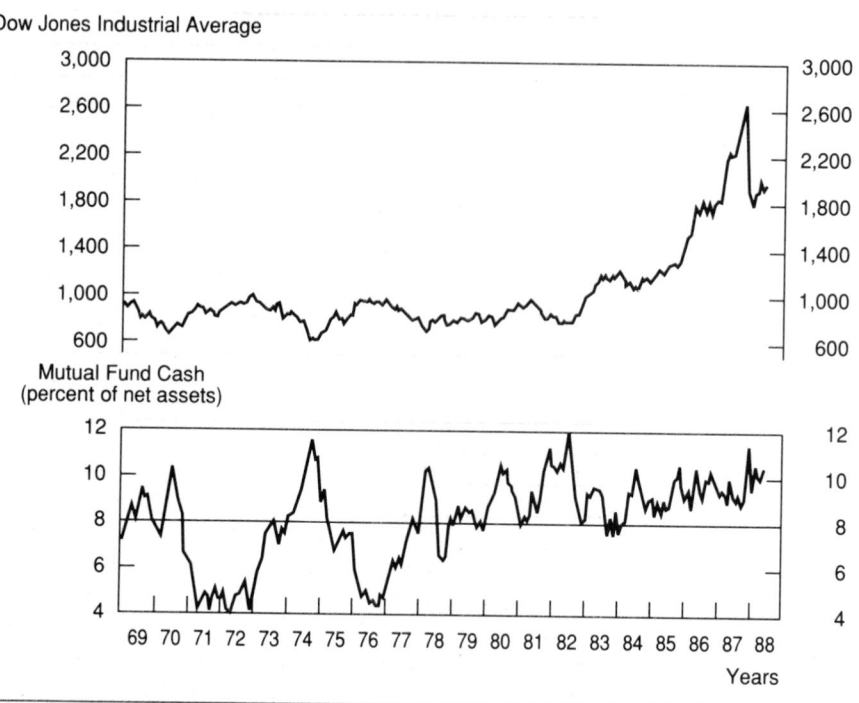

Source: Merrill Lynch, *Where the Indicators Stand* (June 1988).

although he does not test the usefulness of this relationship with a trading rule. A study by Ranson and Shipman derived similar results.[5]

CREDIT BALANCES. Credit balances result when investors sell stocks and leave the proceeds with their brokers because they expect to reinvest them shortly. The amounts are reported by the SEC and the NYSE in *Barron's*. A declining level of credit balances is subject to two interpretations. One view is that they are a pool of potential purchasing power, so a decline in them should be considered bearish, meaning the market is approaching a peak. The other view, of contrary-opinion technicians, is that these credit balances are maintained by small investors and are drawn down and invested just before peaks because of the enthusiasm of this group, which is typically wrong.[6]

Note that the decision rule is stated in terms of a rising or declining credit balance series rather than relative to some other base series. This

[5] R. David Ranson and William G. Shipman, "Institutional Buying Power and the Stock Market," *Financial Analysts Journal* 37, no. 5 (September–October 1981): 62–68.

[6] This series is discussed in Martin E. Zweig, "New Sell Signal?" *Barron's*, October 13, 1975, 4.

assumption of an absolute trend could make interpretation difficult as market levels change.

INVESTMENT ADVISORY OPINIONS. As a contrary-opinion technique it is contended that when a large proportion of investment advisory services becomes bearish, this signals the approach of a market trough and a time to become bullish. The specific ratio examined is the number of advisory services that are bearish as a ratio of the number of services expressing an opinion.[7] When this "Bearish Sentiment Index" reaches 60 percent, it indicates a pervasive bearish attitude that contrarians would consider a bullish indicator. In contrast, when it declines to 15 percent or less, it indicates a pervasive bullish attitude, which is a bearish sign. An analysis of this index made by *Investors Intelligence* concluded that it has been a useful series.[8] Figure 16.3 contains a time series plot of the DJIA and both the Bearish Sentiment Index and the Bullish Sentiment Index.

RELATIVE OTC VOLUME. Prior to the 1970s, the accepted measure of speculative activity was the ratio of AMEX volume. This ratio is no longer considered because the relationship has changed dramatically over time (the ratio of AMEX to NYSE volume has gone from about 50 percent in the 1950s and 1960s to about 10 percent or less currently). The measure that is currently used is the ratio of OTC volume (on NASDAQ) to NYSE volume. Speculative activity is considered high when this ratio gets to 80 percent or more, and it is noted that speculation typically peaks at market tops. The market is considered to be oversold (i.e., short-run bullish) when this ratio drops below 60 percent in a bull market or below 40 percent in a bear market. Figure 16.4 contains a time series plot of the NASDAQ Composite Index and the OTC/NYSE volume ratio. Technicians acknowledge that the decision ratios may have to change in the future if the public becomes a bigger factor, because individual investors are more likely to trade small firms that do not possess the size and liquidity required by institutions. Also it is important to recognize that there is an upward bias in NASDAQ OTC volume since firms are being added to this market at a faster rate than the NYSE. The number of firms on the NYSE has been fairly constant over the past ten years, while the number on NASDAQ has increased by over 90 percent (i.e., the firms on NASDAQ have gone from 2,456 in 1977 to 4,706 in 1987).

CBOE PUT/CALL RATIO. The CBOE put/call ratio is a relatively new contrary indicator. Put options indicate a bearish attitude, so the higher this ratio is, the more pervasive the bearish attitude, which is considered a bullish indicator by contrary technicians. As shown in Figure 16.5, this ratio is typically in the range of 0.35 to 0.75 (given the tendency to be bullish and the aversion to selling short, this ratio would typically be

---

[7] This ratio is compiled by Investors Intelligence, Larchmont, N.Y. 10538.

[8] A. W. Cohen, "A Contrary Opinion Indicator," *Investors Intelligence*, October 23, 1975, 1.

FIGURE 16.3

Time Series Plot of Dow Jones Industrial Average and Bullish and Bearish Sentiment Indexes

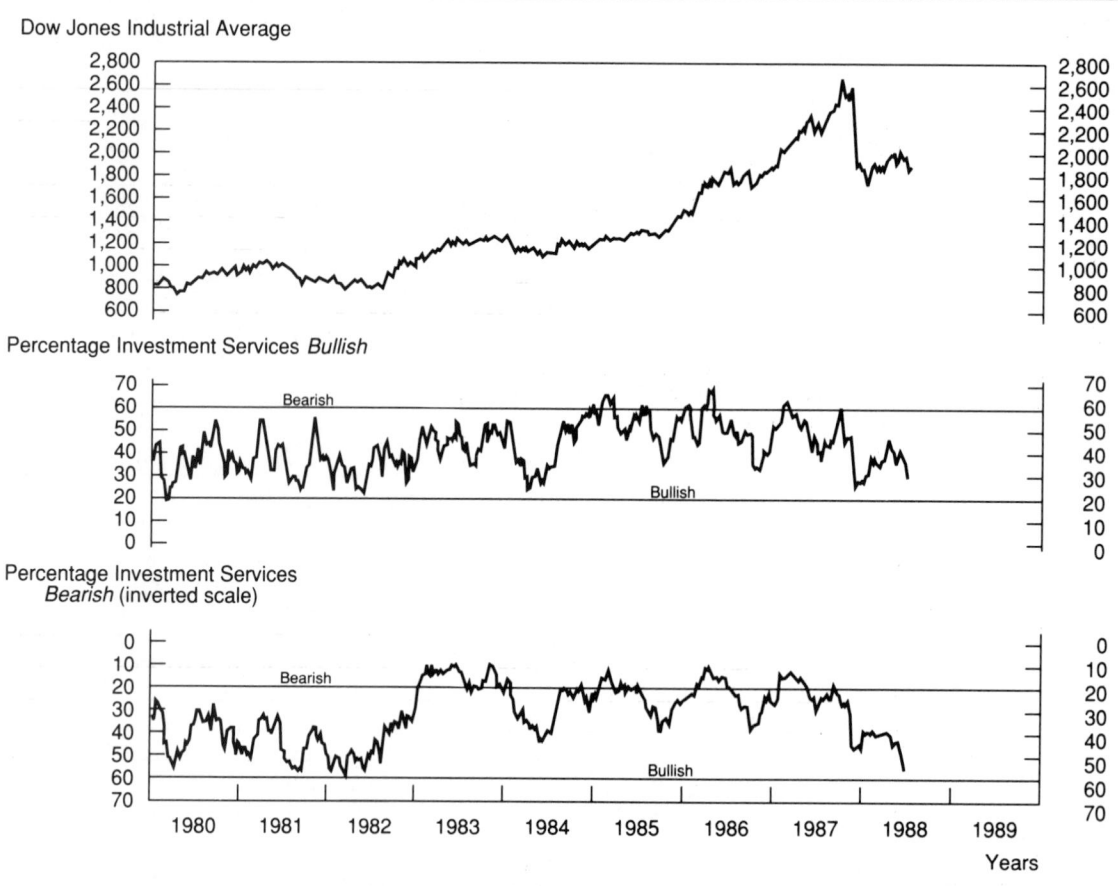

Source: *Investors' Intelligence,* Larchmont, N.Y. 10538; and Merrill Lynch, *Where the Indicators Stand* (June 1988).

substantially less than 1). The widely used decision rule is that when the market is changing, a put/call ratio of 65 puts for every 100 calls is considered bullish. In contrast, a ratio of only 40 puts for every 100 calls is considered bearish.

SPECULATORS BULLISH ON STOCK INDEX FUTURE. Another contrary indicator series generated by the futures market is the percent of speculators who trade in stock index futures that are bullish. Specifically, an advisory service (Market Vane) surveys other advisory services related to the futures market and specific traders in this market and determines whether they are bearish or bullish regarding stocks. A plot of the series is contained in Figure 16.6. As indicated, it is a contrary indicator, so when over

FIGURE 16.4
Time Series Plot of NASDAQ Composite Average and the Ratio of OTC Volume to NYSE Volume

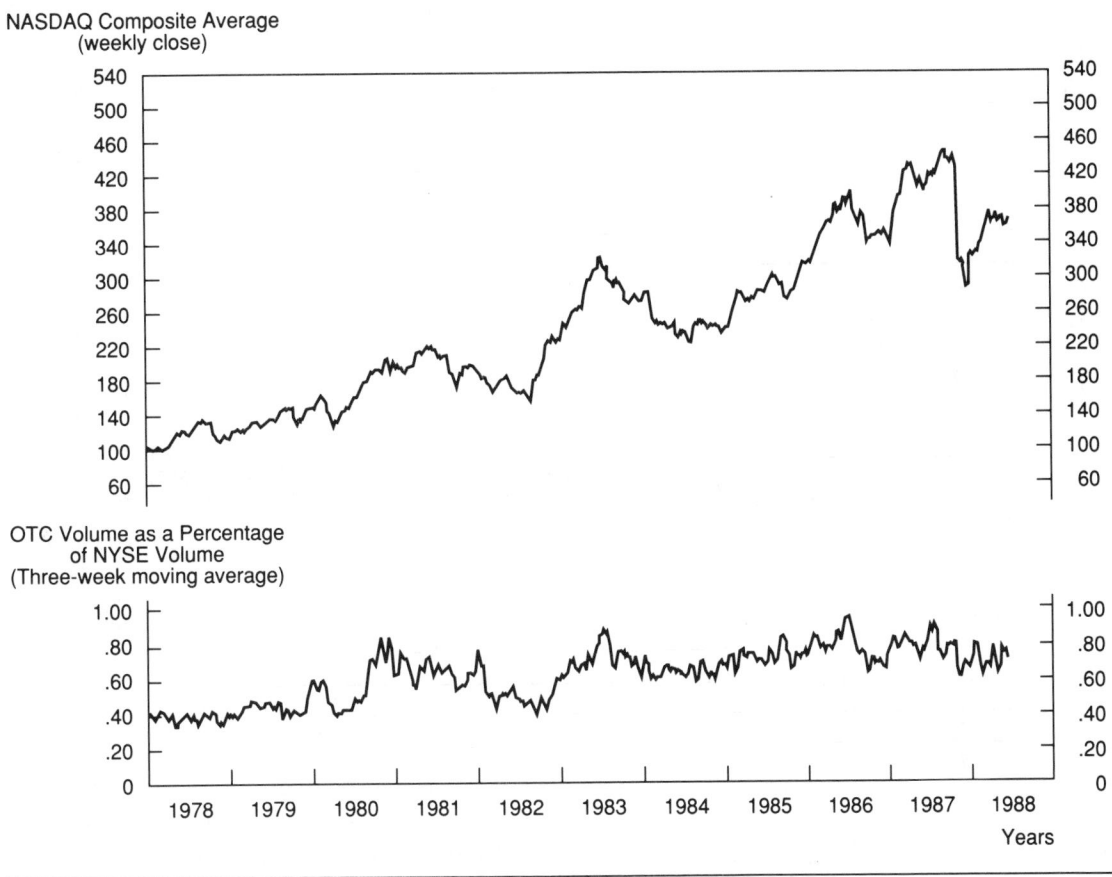

Source: *Where the Indicators Stand*, Merrill Lynch Capital Markets (June 1988).

70 percent of the speculators are bullish, it is a bearish sign, and if it declines to 30 percent or lower, it is a bullish sign.

FOLLOW THE SMART MONEY

An alternative set of rules for technical analysts involves determining what smart, sophisticated investors are doing and following them.

THE CONFIDENCE INDEX. Published by *Barron's*, the Confidence Index is the ratio of *Barron's* average yield on 10 top-grade corporate bonds to the yield on the Dow-Jones average of 40 bonds, indicating the difference in yield spread between high-grade bonds and a large sample of bonds.[9] One

---

[9] Historical data for this series is contained in *The Dow-Jones Investor's Handbook* (Princeton, N.J.: Dow-Jones Books, annual).

Figure 16.5
Time Series Plot of Dow Jones Industrial Average and CBOE Put/Call Ratio

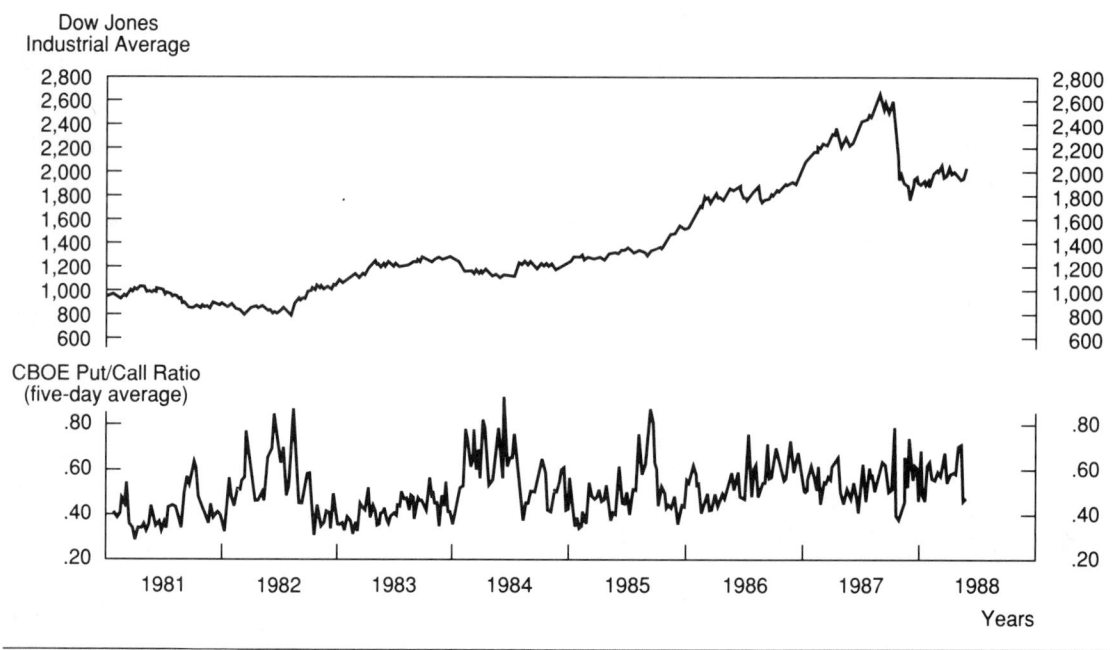

Source: Merrill Lynch, *Where the Indicators Stand* (June 1988).

would expect the yield on high-grade bonds to be lower than that on a large cross section of bonds, so the ratio should never exceed 100.

The reasoning behind the ratio is that during periods of high confidence, investors invest more in lower-quality bonds for the added yield. This increased demand for lower-quality bonds should cause a decrease in the yield on a large cross section of bonds relative to the yield on high-grade bonds. Therefore, this ratio of yields will increase (the Confidence Index increases). When investors are pessimistic, they avoid the low-quality bonds and increase their investments in high-grade bonds, which increases the yield differential between the two groups, and the Confidence Index declines. A major problem with the concept has been that it is demand-oriented—it assumes that changes in the yield spread are almost wholly caused by changes in investor demand for different quality bonds. The fact is, on many occasions the yield differences have changed because of an increased *supply* of bonds in one of the groups or in a related group (e.g., government bonds). A large issue of high-grade AT&T bonds could cause a temporary increase in yields on all high-grade bonds, which would cause an increase in the Confidence Index even though investors' attitudes did not change. In other words, the change would be supply-oriented and thus the series would have generated a false signal of a change in confi-

FIGURE 16.6
Time Series Plot of Dow Jones Industrial Average and Percent of Speculators
Bullish on Stock Index Futures

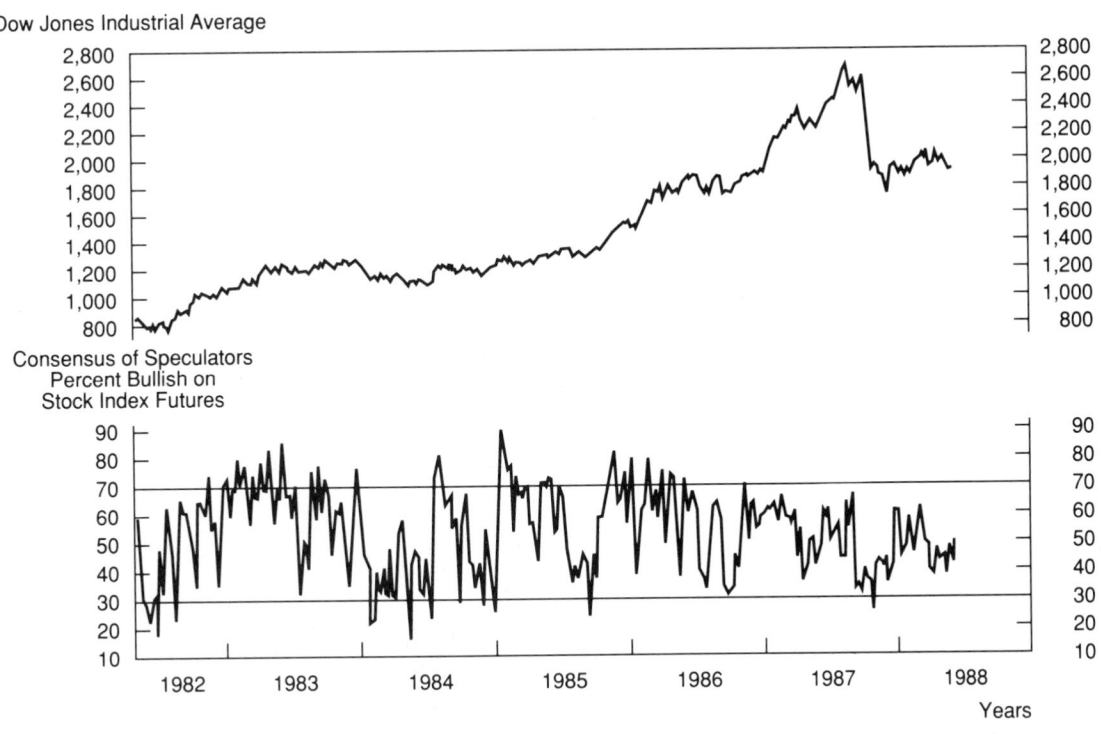

Source: Merrill Lynch, *Where the Indicators Stand* (June 1988).

dence. Advocates of the index believe that it can be used as an indicator of future stock price movements, although one may ask why investors in bonds would change their attitude before equity investors do. The results of several studies that have examined its usefulness for predicting stock price movements have not been very supportive.

SHORT SALES BY SPECIALISTS. Total short sales and those attributed to the specialist are provided by the NYSE and the SEC and reported weekly in *Barron's.* It will come as no surprise that technicians who want to follow the smart money attempt to determine what the specialist is doing and act accordingly. Specialists regularly engage in short selling as a part of their market-making function, but they exercise discretion in this area when they feel strongly about market changes. As shown in Figure 16.7, the normal ratio of specialists' short sales to the total amount of short sales on the exchange was about 45 percent prior to 1981.[10] Subsequently,

---

[10] Notably, during the 1960s and early 1970s the norm for this ratio was about 55 percent. Therefore, this is an example of a technique where the decision ratio has changed over time.

FIGURE 16.7
Time Series Plot of Dow Jones Industrial Average and the Specialist Short-Sale Ratio

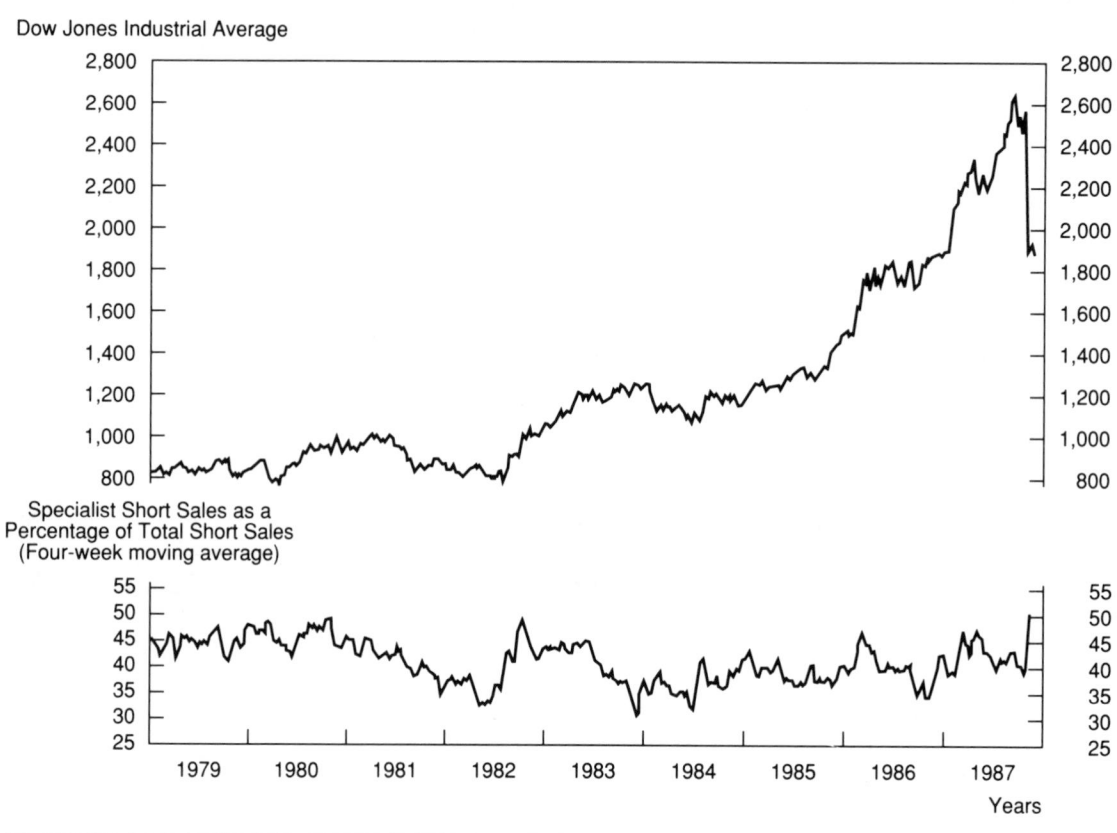

Source: *Where the Indicators Stand,* Merrill Lynch Market Analysis Department (February 1988).

the norm has become approximately 40 percent. A decline in this ratio below 30 percent is considered a bullish sign and an increase beyond 50 percent a bearish sign. Two points should be noted regarding this ratio. First, you should not expect it to be a long-run indicator; given the nature of the specialists' portfolio, it will probably serve only in the short run. Second, there is a two-week lag in the reporting of this data; e.g., the data for a week ending Friday, April 7, would be contained in *Barron's* on Monday, April 24.

A study by Reilly and Whitford indicated some support for the ratio as a buying signal based on graphical analysis.[11] In contrast, the examination of profit potential from alternative trading rules indicated insignif-

---

[11] Frank K. Reilly and David Whitford, "A Test of the Specialists' Short Sale Ratio," *Journal of Portfolio Management* 8, no. 2 (Winter 1982): 12–18.

icant excess returns even prior to risk adjustment. Therefore, the results generally supported the weak-form efficient market hypothesis.

DEBIT BALANCES IN BROKERAGE ACCOUNTS (MARGIN DEBT). Debit balances in brokerage accounts are considered indicative of the attitude of a sophisticated group of investors, because they represent borrowing by knowledgeable investors from their brokers, that is, margin purchases. Therefore, an increase in debit balances indicates an increase in purchasing by this astute group and would be a bullish sign. (A potential problem with this series, however, is that it does not include borrowing from other sources such as banks.) In contrast, a decline in debit balances would indicate an increase in the supply of stocks as these sophisticated investors liquidate their positions and/or it indicates less capital available for investing. Monthly data on margin debt is reported in *Barron's.*

OTHER MARKET SENTIMENT TECHNIQUES

BREADTH OF MARKET. The breadth of market is a measure of the number of issues that have increased each day and the number of issues that have declined. It gives insight into the cause of a change of direction in a composite market indicator series like the DJIA or the S&P 400 Index. As discussed in Chapter 4, the major stock market indicator series are either confined to large, well-known stocks or are heavily influenced by the stocks of large firms, because most indicator series are value-weighted. As a result, there can be instances when the composite market indicator series may go up, but the majority of individual issues are not increasing, which is cause for concern. Such a situation can be detected by examining the advance-decline figures along with the composite series.

A useful way to specify the advance-decline series for analysis purposes is as a cumulative series of net advances or net declines. Each day major newspapers publish figures on the number of issues on the NYSE that advanced, declined, or were unchanged. The figures for a five-day sample, as would be reported in *Barron's,* are shown in Table 16.1. These figures, along with the market indicator figures at the bottom of the table, indicate a strong market advance. Not only was the DJIA increasing, but there was a strong net advance figure, indicating that the increase was broadly based; that is, most individual stocks were increasing. Even the results on Day 3, when the market declined five points, were somewhat encouraging because there was a very small net decline. The market average was down, but individual stocks were split just about 50-50.

An alternative specification of the series is as a *diffusion index,* which shows the daily total of the number of stocks advancing plus one-half the number unchanged, divided by the total number of issues traded. To smooth the series, Merrill Lynch computes a five-week moving average of these daily figures as shown in Figure 16.8. Merrill Lynch uses this series as an indicator of changes in the major trend of the market when there are unusual or new extreme readings. For example, assume the major trend has been up during a period when intermediate corrections to the uptrend indicated advance-decline diffusion index values of 42 to 45. If a subse-

Table 16.1
Daily Advances and Declines on New York Stock Exchange

Day	1	2	3	4	5
Issues traded	1,908	1,941	1,959	1,951	1,912
Advances	1,110	1,050	708	1,061	1,125
Declines	409	450	749	433	394
Unchanged	389	441	502	457	393
Net advances (advances minus declines)	+701	+600	−41	+628	+731
Cumulative net advances	+701	+1,301	+1,260	+1,888	+2,619
Changes in DJIA	+10.47	+3.99	−5.15	+4.16	+5.56

Source: New York Stock Exchange and *Barron's*.

quent correction provided a diffusion index value below 42, this would suggest that the market's major trend may be turning down. In contrast, if the major trend had been down, and intermediate recoveries provided values of 50 to 54, and during a recovery the index reached about 59, this would likewise indicate a change in the major trend.

Figure 16.8
Time Series Plot of Dow Jones Industrial Average and Advance-Decline Diffusion Index

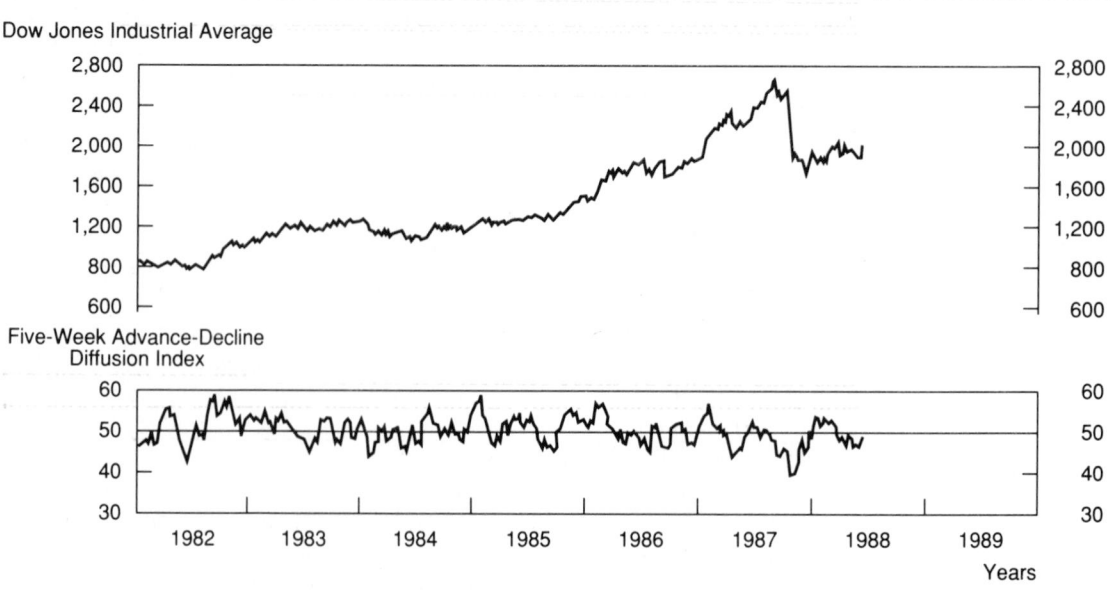

Source: Merrill Lynch, *Where the Indicators Stand* (June 1988).

The usefulness of the advance-decline series is supposedly greatest at market peaks and troughs, because at such times the composite value-weighted market series might be moving either up or down, but the advance or decline would not be broadly based, and the majority of individual stocks might be moving in the opposite direction. Near a peak, the DJIA would be increasing, but the net advance-decline ratio for individual days would become negative, and the cumulative series would begin to level off and decline. The *divergence* between the trend for the aggregate market indicator series and the cumulative advance-decline series or the diffusion index is a signal for a market peak. At the trough, the composite series would be declining, but the daily advance-decline ratio would become positive, and the cumulative advance-decline series would turn up before the aggregate market series would. In summary, a technician would expect the advance-decline series to turn before the composite stock market series.

SHORT INTEREST. The short interest is the ratio between the number of shares sold short and not covered and the average daily volume of trading on the exchange. The interpretation of this ratio by technicians is probably contrary to your initial intuition. Because short sales are made by investors who expect stock prices to decline, one would typically expect an increase in the short-interest ratio to be bearish. On the contrary, technicians consider a *high* short-interest ratio *bullish* because it indicates *potential demand for stock by those who sold short*. It is reasoned that short sellers will have to buy the stock in the future to cover their outstanding short position. The ratio has historically fluctuated between 1.00 and 1.75. (A ratio of 1.00 means that the outstanding short interest on the NYSE is equal to about one day's trading volume.) During the last several years (since about 1985) the ratio has increased and has seldom been as low as 1.50. In fact, the typical range has been 2.0 to 3.0. The short-interest position is calculated as of the twentieth of each month and is reported about two days later in *The Wall Street Journal.* Because of the recent experience regarding the range of values for this series, the short-interest ratio would be considered very bullish as it approaches 3.0 and bearish as it declines toward 2.0.

The results of a number of studies on the usefulness of the short-interest series as a predictor of stock price movements have been extremely mixed. For every study that supported the technique, another indicated that it should be rejected.[12] Beyond the potential problems with this ratio shown by these studies, it is also pointed out that this ratio and any ratio that involves short selling has been affected by the introduction

---

[12] Barton M. Biggs, "The Short Interest—A False Proverb," *Financial Analysts Journal* 22, no. 4 (July–August 1966): 111–116; Joseph J. Seneca, "Short Interest: Bearish or Bullish?" *Journal of Finance* 22, no. 1 (March 1967): 67–70; Thomas H. Mayor, "Short Trading Activities and the Price of Equities: Some Simulation and Regression Results," *Journal of Financial and Quantitative Analysis* 3, no. 3 (September 1968): 283–298; Randall Smith, "Short Interest and Stock Market Prices," *Financial Analysts Journal* 24, no. 6 (November–December 1968): 151–154; Thomas J. Kerrigan, "The Short Interest Ratio and Its Component Parts," *Financial Analysts Journal* 32, no. 6 (November–December 1974): 45–49; and William Goff, "Letter to the Editor," *Financial Analysts Journal* (March–April 1975): 8–10.

of other techniques for short-selling—options and futures. On the other side, there is a tendency to engage in more short-selling as a part of various cross market arbitrage transactions. These techniques will be discussed in Chapter 25 (Financial Futures).

STOCKS ABOVE THEIR 200-DAY MOVING AVERAGE. Technicians often compute moving averages of a series to determine its general trend. In the case of individual stocks a fairly popular series is the *200-day moving average of prices.* Given these moving average series for numerous stocks, Media General Financial Services calculates how many stocks are currently trading above their moving average series. This proportion is used as an indicator of general investor sentiment. Specifically, the market is considered to be *overbought* when 80 percent or more of the stocks being analyzed are trading above their 200-day moving average, and an overbought market indication is usually followed by a consolidation or correction. In contrast, if less than 20 percent of the stocks are selling above their 200-day moving average, the market is *oversold,* and investors should look for positive corrections.

BLOCK UPTICK-DOWNTICK RATIO. As you know, trading in the equity market (especially the NYSE) has become dominated by institutional investors who tend to trade in large blocks. As noted in Chapter 3, about 50 percent of NYSE volume is block trading that reflects institutional activity. It is possible to determine the price change that accompanied a particular block transaction. If it is above the prior price, it is an *uptick*; if it is below, it is a *downtick.* It is assumed that the price change indicates whether the transaction was initiated by a buyer (in which case you would expect an uptick) or a seller (in which case you would expect a downtick). This line of reasoning led to the development of the *uptick-downtick ratio* as an indicator of institutional investor sentiment. As shown in Figure 16.9, this ratio has generally fluctuated in the range of 70 (a bearish sentiment) to about 130 (a bullish sentiment).

STOCK PRICE AND VOLUME TECHNIQUES

Most technicians also use trading rules for the market and individual stocks that are based upon both the stock price and the volume movements. Because technicians believe that prices move in trends that persist, they contend that it is possible to determine future price trends from an astute analysis of past price and volume trends. They contend that *price alone is inadequate*—that is, investors should also examine the volume of trading.

THE DOW THEORY. Any discussion of technical analysis using price and volume must begin with a consideration of the Dow Theory developed by Charles Dow, publisher of *The Wall Street Journal,* during the late 1800s.[13]

---

[13] An extensive discussion of the Dow Theory is contained in George W. Bishop, Jr., "Evolution of the Dow Theory," *Financial Analysts Journal* 17, no. 5 (September–October 1961): 23–36. A study that discusses the theory and provides support for it is David A. Glickstein and Rolf E. Wubbels, "Dow Theory is Alive and Well," *Journal of Portfolio Management* 9, no. 3 (Spring 1983): 28–32.

FIGURE 16.9
Time Series Plot of Dow Jones Industrial Average and the NYSE Block Uptick-Downtick Ratio

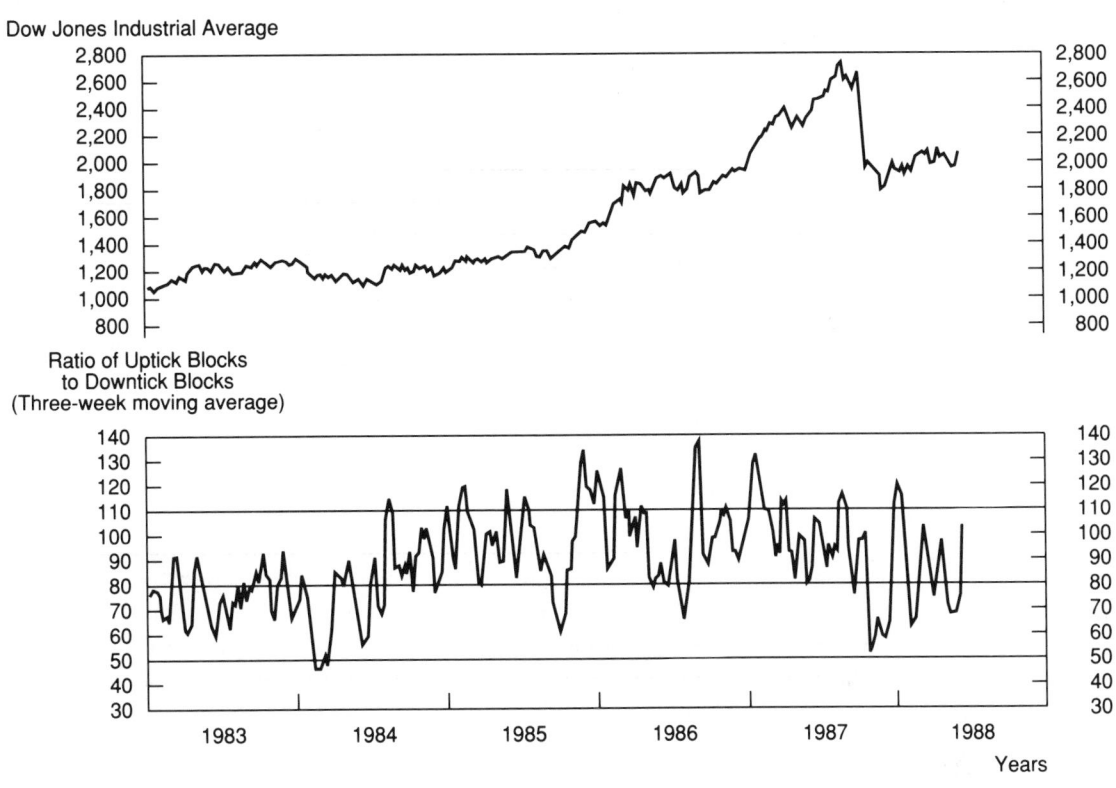

Source: Merrill Lynch, *Where the Indicators Stand* (June 1988).

Dow contended that stock prices moved in trends that were analogous to the movement of water—that is, there are three types of price movements over time: (1) major trends that are like tides in the ocean, (2) intermediate trends that are similar to waves, and (3) short-run movements that are like ripples. The idea is to detect which way the major price trend (tide) is going, recognizing that there will be intermediate movements (waves) in the opposite direction. A major market advance does not go straight up, but is accompanied by small price declines as some investors decide to take profits. The typical bullish pattern is portrayed in Figure 16.10. The technician would look for every recovery to reach a high point above the prior peak with heavy trading volume, while each reversal should have a trough above the prior trough, and volume should be relatively light during the reversals. When this no longer happens, the major trend (tide) may be ready for a period of consolidation or a permanent reversal.

SUPPORT AND RESISTANCE LEVELS. A *support level* is the price range at which the technician would expect a substantial increase in the demand

FIGURE 16.10
An Example of a Bullish Price Pattern

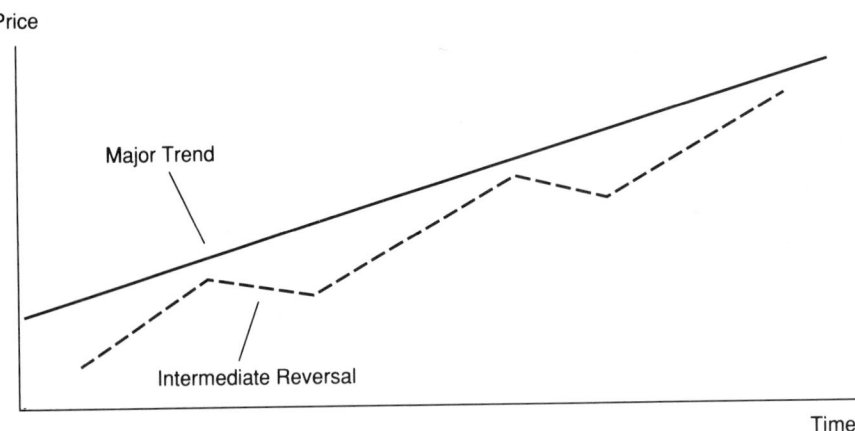

for a stock. Generally, a support level will develop after the price has increased and the stock has begun to experience a reversal because of profit taking. It is reasoned that at some price there are other investors who did not buy during the first rally and have been waiting for a small reversal to get into the stock. When the price reaches the point at which they want to buy, there is a surge in demand and the price begins to increase again.

A *resistance level* is the price range at which the technician would expect the supply of stock to increase substantially and any price rise to be abruptly reversed. A resistance level tends to develop after a stock has experienced a steady decline from a higher price level. In this case it is reasoned that because of the decline, there are investors who acquired the stock at a higher price and are waiting for an opportunity to sell it at about their breakeven point. Therefore, this supply of stock is *overhanging* the market and, when the price rebounds to the target price set by these investors, the supply increases dramatically and the price increase is reversed.

IMPORTANCE OF VOLUME. Technicians are not only concerned with price movements, but they also watch volume changes as an indicator of changes in supply and demand for a stock or for stocks in general. A price movement in one direction indicates that the *net* effect is in that direction, but price alone does not indicate how widespread the excess demand or supply is at that time. A price increase of a half point on volume of 1,000 shares indicates excess demand but not much overall interest. In contrast, a one-point increase on volume of 20,000 shares indicates a large demand. Therefore, it is not only a price increase but also heavy volume relative to the stock's normal trading volume that interests the technician. Following the same line of reasoning, a price decline with heavy volume is very bearish, because it means strong and widespread desire to sell the stock. A generally bullish pattern is a price increase on heavy volume and small price reversals with light trading volume, indicating only limited desire to sell and take profits.

Technicians also use a ratio of *upside-downside volume* as an indicator of short-term momentum. Specifically, the volume of advancing issues divided by the volume of declining issues is computed from data reported daily in *The Wall Street Journal* and weekly in *Barron's*. It is a sentiment indicator and is used to pinpoint excesses—the ratio typically oscillates between a value of 1.50 or more, indicating an overbought position, and 0.70 and lower, indicating an oversold position.

MOVING-AVERAGE LINE. Earlier we discussed how technicians use a moving average of past stock prices as an indicator of the long-run trend and examine current prices relative to this trend to see whether the relationship signals a change. It was also noted that a 200-day moving average is a relatively popular measure for individual stocks and the aggregate market. If the overall trend of the market has been down, the moving-average line would generally be above current prices. If prices reverse and break through the moving-average line from below on heavy volume, a technician might speculate that the declining trend has been reversed. In contrast, given a rising trend, the moving-average line would be rising but would be below the current prices. If current prices broke through the moving-average line from above on heavy volume, this would be a bearish indication of a reversal of the long-run rising trend.[14]

RELATIVE STRENGTH. Technicians believe that once a trend is initiated, it will continue until some major event causes a change in direction. This is also true, they believe, of relative performance. If an individual stock or an industry group is outperforming the market, technicians believe the stock or the industry will continue to outperform the market. Therefore, technicians compute *relative-strength ratios* for individual stocks and industry groups compared to some aggregate market series on a weekly or monthly basis. This is simply a ratio of the stock price to the value for some market series like the DJIA or the S&P 400. If the ratio increases over time, the stock or industry is outperforming the market, and a technician would expect this superior performance to continue. The relative-strength ratios work during declining and rising markets. (If the stock does not decline as much as the market does, the relative-strength ratio will continue to rise.) It is believed that if the ratio holds up or increases during a bear market, the stock should do very well during the ensuing bull

---

[14] This technique is tested in F. E. James, Jr., "Monthly Moving Averages—An Effective Investment Tool?" *Journal of Financial and Quantitative Analysis* 3, no. 2 (June 1968): 315–326; and in J. C. Van Horne and G. C. Parker, "The Random Walk Theory: An Empirical Test," *Financial Analysts Journal* 23, no. 6 (November–December 1967): 57–64.

market.[15] As an example, Merrill Lynch publishes relative-strength charts for stocks and industry groups. Figure 16.11 describes how to read the charts, and Figure 16.12 contains a graph for an industry with strong positive relative strength (pollution control) and one with poor relative strength (banks—major regional).

BAR CHARTING. The basic chart used in technical analysis is one on which the time series of prices for specified time intervals (daily, weekly, monthly) are plotted. For a given interval, the technical analyst will plot the high and low price and connect the two points to form a bar. Typically, he will also draw a small horizontal line across it to indicate the closing price. Finally, almost all bar charts include the volume of trading at the bottom of the chart so that the analyst can relate the price and volume movements. An example is given in Figure 16.13, which is the bar chart for the DJIA from *The Wall Street Journal* along with the volume figures for the NYSE. This particular chart was selected because it included the market crash period October 14–20, 1987.

The technical analyst might also include a 200-day moving average for the series and possible resistance and support levels based upon past patterns. Finally, a bar chart for an individual stock might contain a relative-strength line. Technicians attempt to include as many price and volume series as is reasonable on one chart and try to arrive at a consensus concerning the future movement for the stock based upon the performance of several technical indicators.

POINT-AND-FIGURE CHARTS. Another popular device used by technicians is the *point-and-figure chart*.[16] Unlike the bar chart, which typically includes all ending prices and volumes for purposes of detecting a trend, the point-and-figure chart considers only significant price changes, regardless of the time interval involved. The analyst determines which significant price changes will be recorded (one point, two points, etc.) and when a price reversal will be recorded. The following example should make this clear. Assume that you want to chart a stock that is currently selling for $40 a share and is quite volatile (it has a beta of 1.60). Because of its volatility, you believe that anything less than a two-point price change is not relevant. Also, you consider anything less than a four-point reversal quite minor. Therefore, you would set up a chart similar to the one in Figure 16.14 that

[15] For further discussion of this technique by a leading advocate, see Robert A. Levy, "Relative Strength as a Criterion for Investment Selection," *Journal of Finance* 23, no. 5 (December 1967): 595–610; Robert A. Levy and Spero L. Kripotos, "Sources of Relative Price Strength," *Financial Analysts Journal* 25, no. 6 (November–December 1969): 60, 62, 64; and Robert A. Levy, *The Relative Strength Concept of Common Stock Price Forecasting* (Larchmont, N.Y.: Investors Intelligence, 1968). Studies that support the technique are Charles A. Akemann and Werner E. Keller, "Relative Strength Does Persist!" *Journal of Portfolio Management* 4, no. 1 (Fall 1977): 38–45; and James Bohan, "Relative Strength: Further Positive Evidence," *Journal of Portfolio Management* 7, no 1 (Fall 1981): 39–46. A study that rejects the technique is Robert D. Arnott, "Relative Strength Revisited," *Journal of Portfolio Management* 6, no 3 (Spring 1979): 19–23. Finally, a study that combines it with modern portfolio theory is John S. Brush and Keith Boles, "The Predictive Power in Relative Strength and CAPM," *Journal of Portfolio Management* 9, no. 4 (Summer 1983): 20–23.

[16] Daniel Seligman, "The Mystique of Point-and-Figure," *Fortune* (March 1962): 113–115.

FIGURE 16.11
How To Read The Technical Analysis of Industry Group Charts

The industry group charts contained in this report display the following elements:
1. A line chart of the weekly close of the Standard & Poor's Industry Group Index for the last nine and a half years, with the index range indicated to the left.
2. A line of the 75-Week Moving Average of the Standard & Poor's Industry Group Index.
3. A relative strength line of the Standard & Poor's Industry Group Index compared with the New York Stock Exchange Composite Index.
4. A 75-Week Moving Average of Relative Strength.
5. A volatility reading that measures the maximum amount by which the index has outperformed (or underperformed) the NYSE Composite Index during the time period displayed.

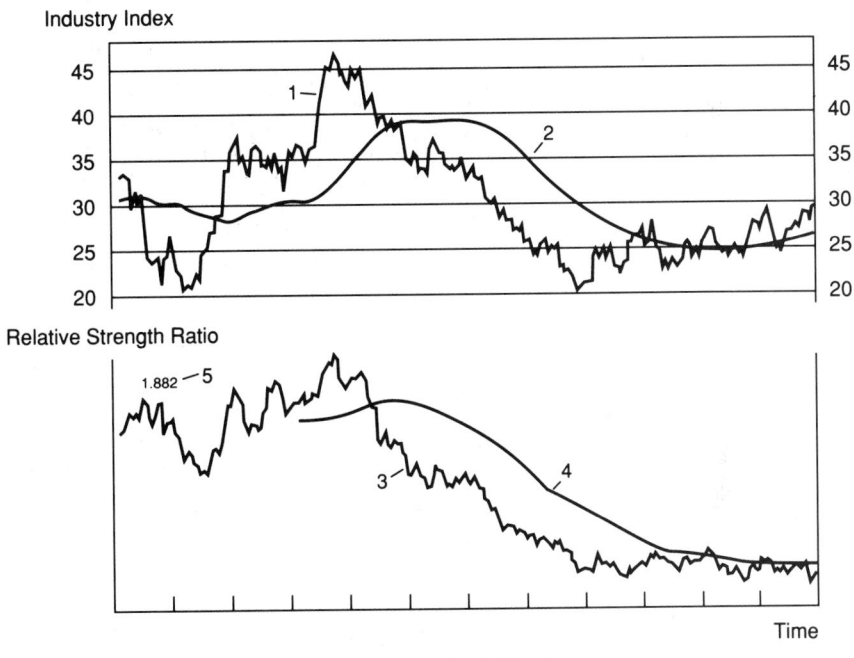

Source: Merrill Lynch, *Technical Analysis of Industry Groups* (monthly).

starts at 40 and progresses in two-point increments. If the stock moves to 42, you place an "X" in the box above 40 and do nothing else until the stock rises to 44 or drops to 38 (a four-point reversal from its high of 42). If it drops to 38, you move over a column to the right and begin again at 38 (fill in boxes at 42 and 40). Assuming the stock price drops to 34, you would enter an "X" at 36 and another at 34. If the stock then rises to 38 (another four-point reversal), you move to the next column and begin at 38 going up (fill in 34 and 36). Assuming the stock then goes to 46, you would fill in as shown and wait for further increases or a reversal.

Depending upon how fast the prices rise and fall, this process may have taken anywhere from two to six months. Given these figures, the

FIGURE 16.12
Examples of Relative-Strength Charts for Two Industries

Miscellaneous—Pollution Control: Browning-Ferris Industries; Rollins Environmental; Waste Management; Zurn Industries.

Financial & Building—Interest Sensitive—Banks (Major Regional): Bank of Boston; Barnett Banks of Florida; First Interstate Bancorp; First Republic; Mellon Bank; NCNB Corp; NBD Bancorp; Norwest Corp; Wells Fargo.

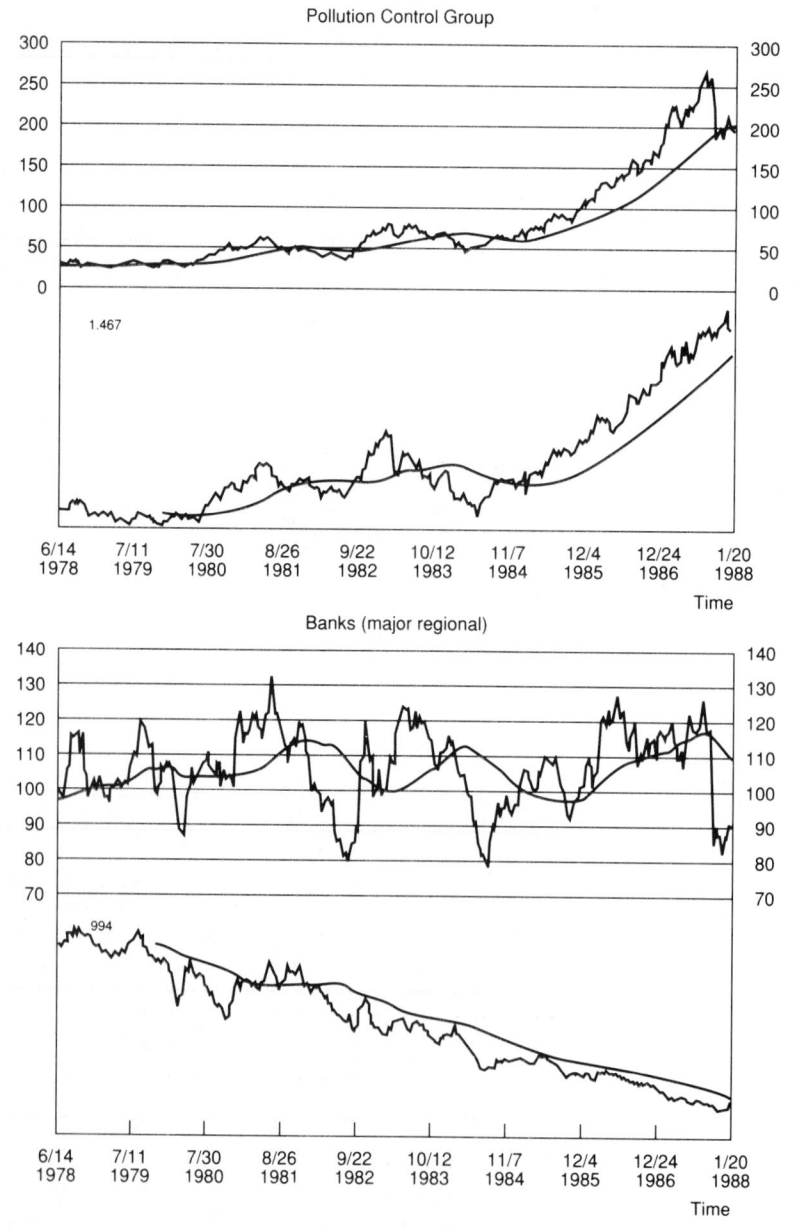

Source: Merrill Lynch, *Technical Analysis of Industry Groups* (June 1988).

FIGURE 16.13
A Typical Bar Chart

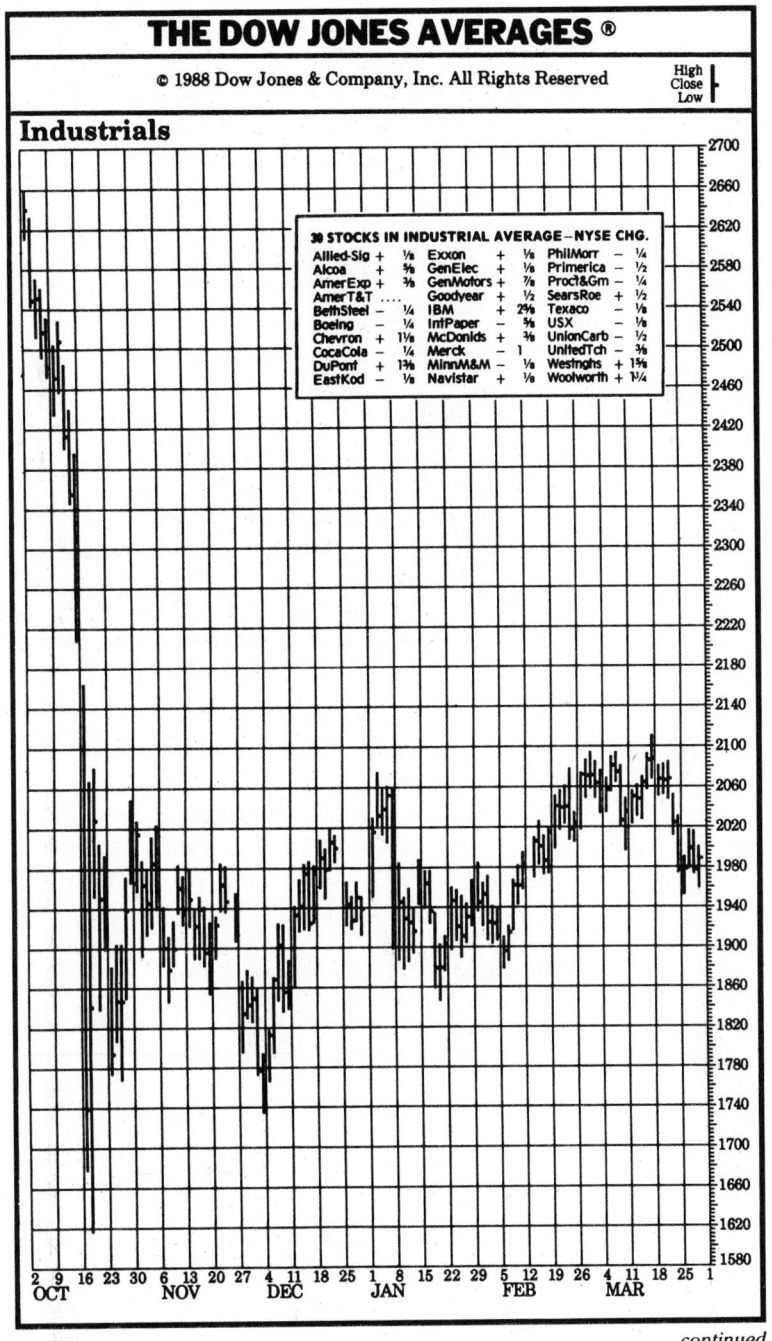

THE DOW JONES AVERAGES ®

© 1988 Dow Jones & Company, Inc. All Rights Reserved

High
Close
Low

Industrials

30 STOCKS IN INDUSTRIAL AVERAGE—NYSE CHG.

Allied-Sig	+ ⅛	Exxon	+ ⅛	PhilMorr	− ¼
Alcoa	+ ⅜	GenElec	+ ⅛	Primerica	− ½
AmerExp	+ ⅜	GenMotors	+ ⅞	Proct&Gm	− ¼
AmerT&T	....	Goodyear	+ ½	SearsRoe	+ ½
BethSteel	− ¼	IBM	+ 2⅝	Texaco	− ⅛
Boeing	− ¼	IntPaper	− ⅝	USX	− ⅛
Chevron	+ 1⅛	McDonlds	+ ⅜	UnionCarb	− ½
CocaCola	− ¼	Merck	− 1	UnitedTch	− ⅜
DuPont	+ 1⅜	MinnM&M	− ⅛	Westnghs	+ 1⅛
EastKod	− ⅛	Navistar	+ ⅛	Woolworth	+ 1¼

continued

FIGURE 16.13   *continued*

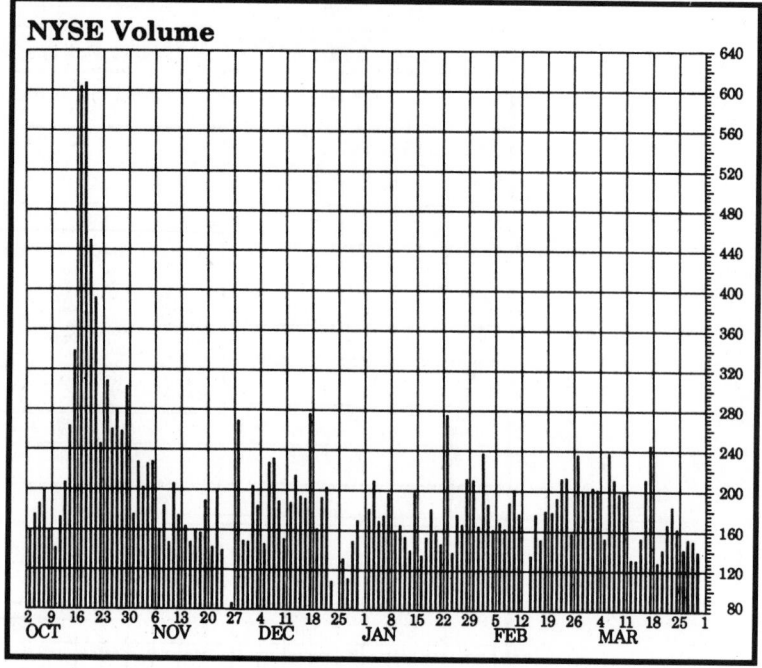

analyst would attempt to determine trends in the same manner as he did with the bar chart.

As always, you are looking for breakouts to either higher or lower price levels.[17] A long sideways movement in which there are many re-

FIGURE 16.14
Example of a Point-and-Figure Chart

50										
48										
46			X							
44			X							
42	X	X	X							
40	X	X	X							
38		X	X							
36		X	X							
34		X	X							
32										
30										

---

[17] A study that examined the usefulness of various price patterns is Robert A. Levy, "The Predictive Significance of Five Point Chart Patterns," *Journal of Business* 44, no. 3 (July 1971): 316–323. The results were not encouraging for the technician.

versals but no major shifts in any direction would be considered a period of consolidation as the stock is moving from one investor group to another with no strong consensus of direction. Once the stock breaks out and moves up or down after a period of consolidation, it is anticipated that this will be a major move because of the previous trading that set the stage for it. The difference between point-and-figure and bar charts is that with the former you have a compact record of movements, because only those price changes considered relevant for the particular stock analyzed are recorded. Therefore, point-and-figure charts are easier to work with and to use in visualizing movements.

TECHNICAL ANALYSIS OF NON-U.S. MARKETS

Our discussion thus far has been limited to U.S. markets, but these techniques are likewise applied to the non–U.S. markets by numerous analysts and firms. A prime example is Merrill Lynch, which prepares separate technical analysis publications for individual countries (e.g., Japan, Germany, the United Kingdom) and a summary of all world markets. In the examples that follow, you will see that many of these techniques depend upon price and volume data rather than cash flow and more detailed market information. This emphasis on price and volume is necessary, because the more detailed information that is available on the U.S. market through the SEC, the stock exchanges, NASDAQ, and various investment services is not available in these other countries. Also individuals concerned with analyzing non–U.S. markets point out that in these other markets there is a greater tendency toward *group rotation*, wherein there are major shifts among segments of the market—that is, shifts among industry groups or major sectors (e.g., a change in leadership to secondary stocks from the large blue-chip stocks).

NON–U.S. MARKET INDICATORS. Figure 16.15 contains the time series plot and moving average series for the London Stock Exchange indicator series—the Financial Times Stock Exchange 100 Index (FTSE 100). As shown, the series has been in a slowly rising trend since the crash, and current values were above the 55-day moving average line. In a separate written analysis, the market analysts at Merrill Lynch provide specifics on support and resistance levels for the series as well as comments on the longer-term outlook for the market, the British pound, and specific industries with positive patterns.

Figure 16.16 is a similar chart for the Japan Nikkei Stock Average. In this case, the recovery from the crash has been substantially stronger, to the point where the index completely made up what was lost in October 1987 and then reached new highs in June 1988. Current prices were clearly above the moving average line. The written comment was cautious about the near term but projected new highs (to 30,000 plus) for the longer term (four to six months).

There are similar charts and discussions for ten other countries and a summary release that compares them and ranks them on the basis of

FIGURE 16.15
FTSE 100 Price Index from June 23, 1987, to June 23, 1988, Daily

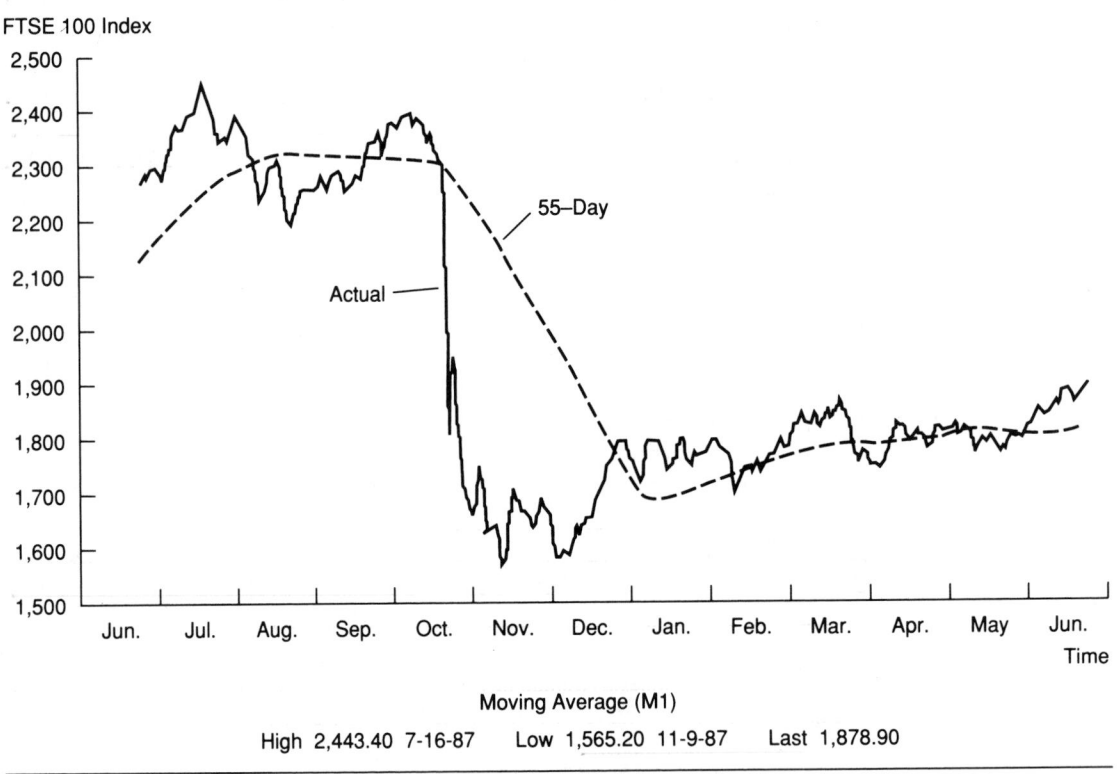

FTSE 100 Index

Moving Average (M1)

High 2,443.40 7-16-87   Low 1,565.20 11-9-87   Last 1,878.90

Source: Datastream; Merrill Lynch Market Analysis/International Research.

stock performance and currency performance. The next section discusses the technical analysis of the currency markets.

TECHNICAL ANALYSIS OF FOREIGN EXCHANGE RATES. On numerous occasions we have discussed the importance of changes in foreign exchange rates and the impact that these changes can have on the rates of return on non–U.S. securities. Because of the importance of these relationships, technicians involved in world markets examine the time series properties of the various individual currencies—such as the British pound—and also analyze the spread between specific currencies—such as between the Japanese yen (JY) and the German deutschemark (DM).

Figure 16.17 contains time series plots of four major currencies indicating the long-term moving average trend, the high and low trading band for the currency based upon the moving average series, and a twelve-month RSI (resistance-support index) that measures volatility and over-bought-oversold conditions on a long-term basis. As shown, all four cur-

FIGURE 16.16
Japan Nikkei Stock Average (225): Price Index from June 23, 1987, to June 23, 1988, Daily

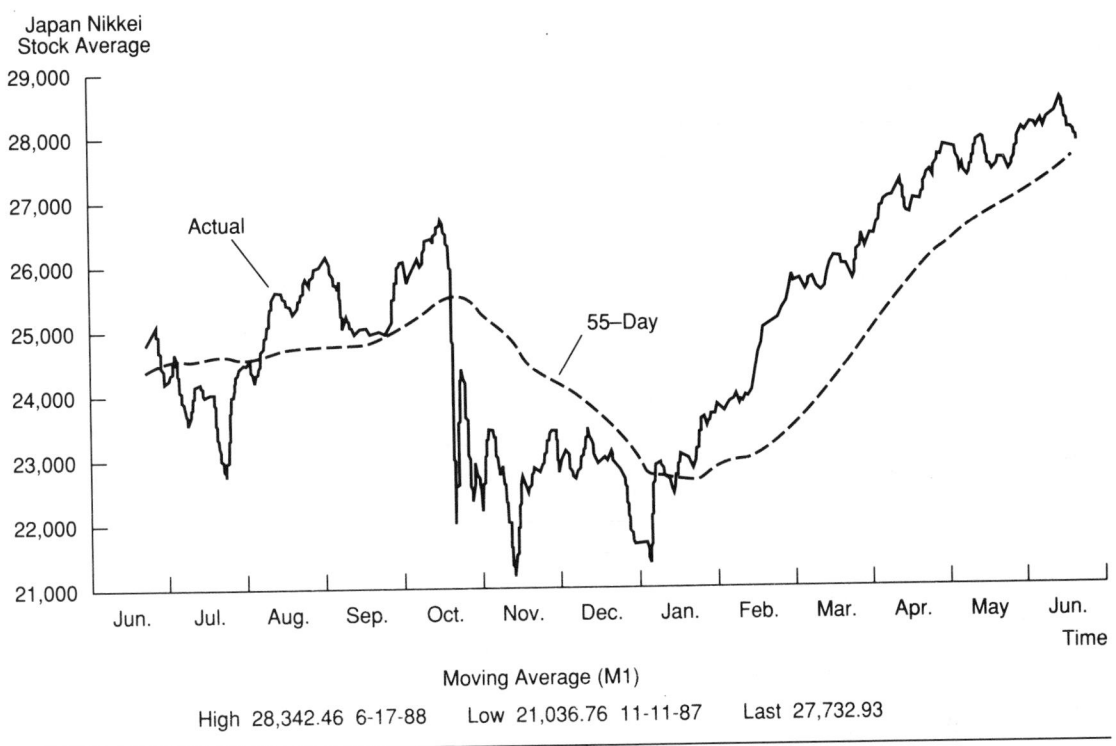

Moving Average (M1)

High 28,342.46 6-17-88   Low 21,036.76 11-11-87   Last 27,732.93

Source: Datastream; Merrill Lynch Market Analysis/International Research.

rencies have been strong since 1986, with major rising trends in the German DM and Japanese yen.

Figure 16.18 contains time series plots of the ratio spread between the Japanese yen (JY) and the British pound (BP) and also between the JY and the German mark (DM). The JY-BP spread chart indicates a long-term upward trend, but a decline in the trend since 1985. Alternatively, the JY-DM plot clearly indicates a rising long-term trend in the spread.

TECHNICAL ANALYSIS OF INTEREST RATES

The emphasis in this chapter has been on the use of technical tools in the analysis of the equity market in the United States and the world. While this emphasis is appropriate because of the extensive use of technical analysis in the equity markets, it is also important to be aware of the use of these techniques in the fixed-income market. Similar to the non–U.S. equity discussion, the theory and reasoning is the same and many of the specific techniques are likewise employed. The difference is that the application is to a specific security (bond), several specific bonds, or a bond or futures index with the emphasis on price or current yield to maturity.

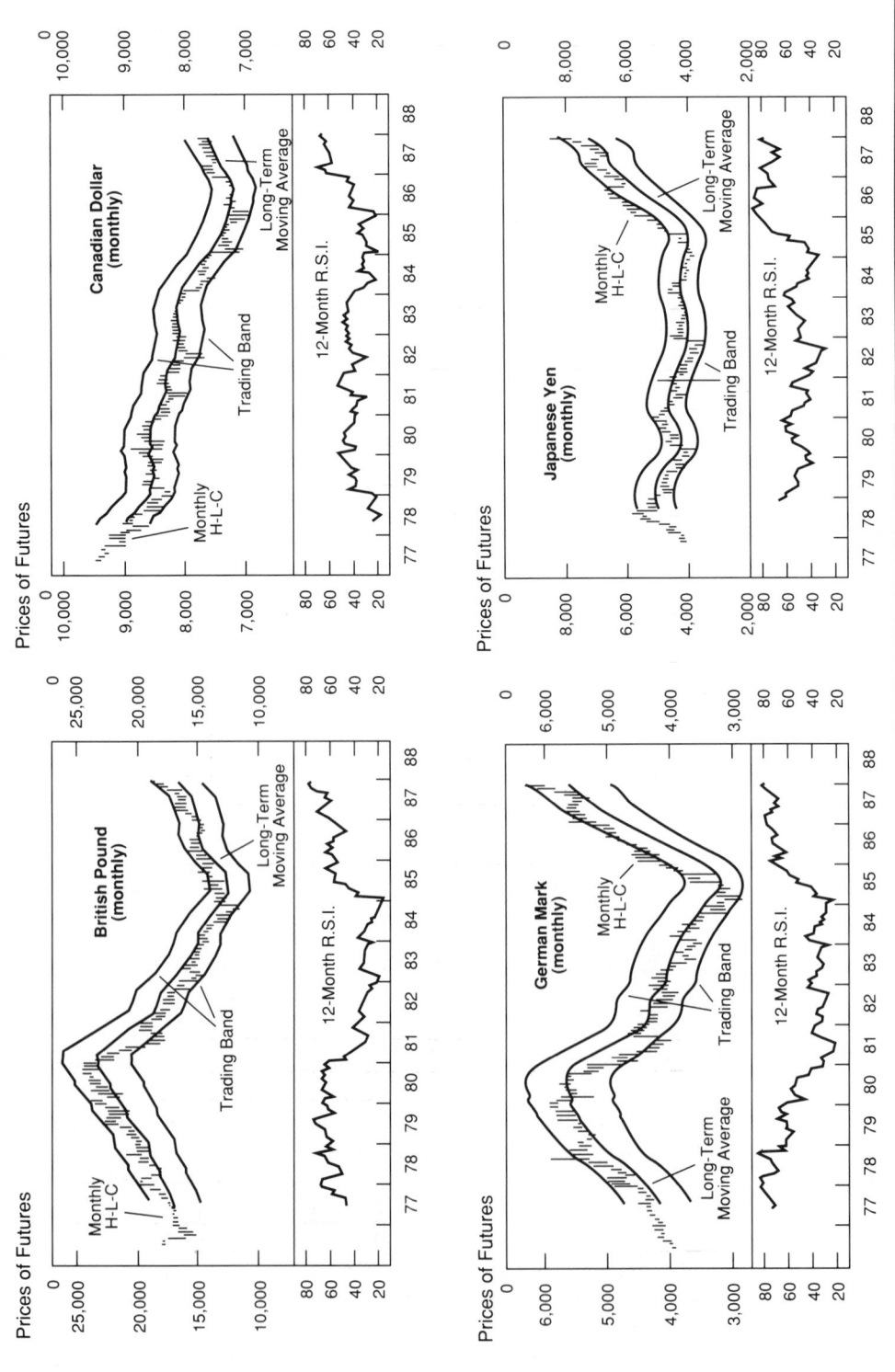

Source: Merrill Lynch, *Foreign Exchange Perspectives* (monthly).

FIGURE 16.18
Time Series Plot of Spread between Japanese Yen and British Pound and Japanese Yen and German Mark

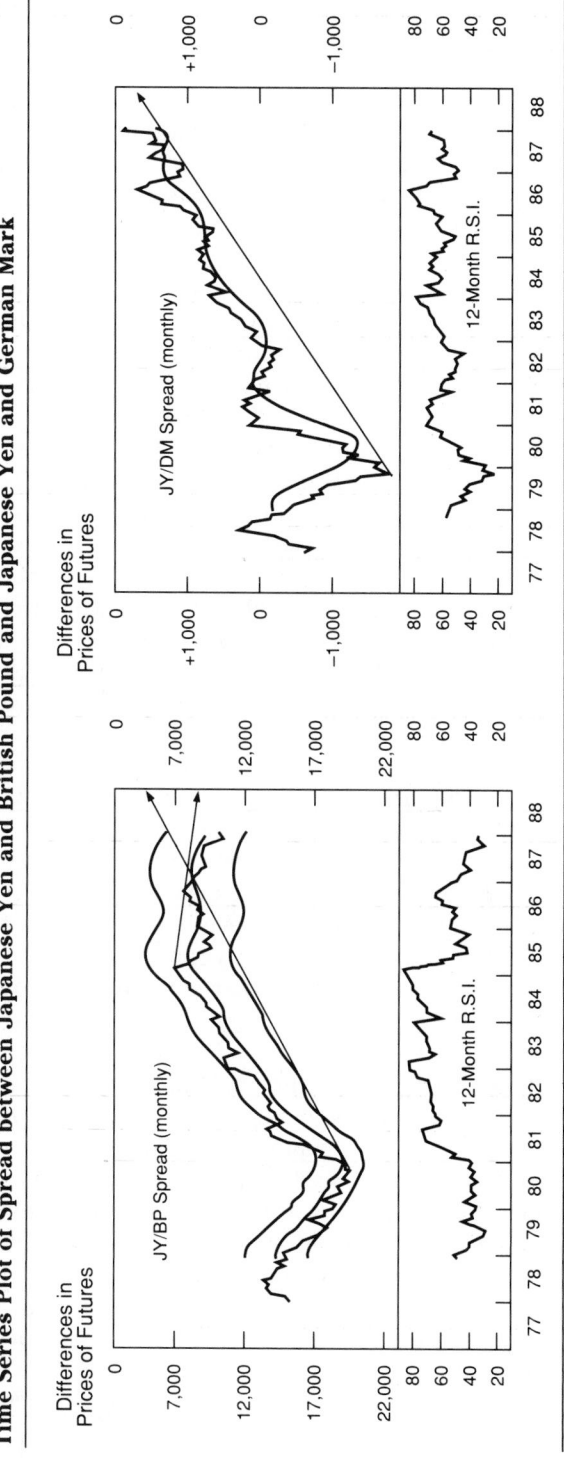

Source: Merrill Lynch, *Foreign Exchange Perspectives* (monthly).

Notably, there is almost no consideration of volume of trading because these data are not generally available for the numerous relevant bonds that are traded OTC where volume is not reported.

Figure 16.19 contains examples of four technical charts for various segments of the bond market. The first chart is the plot of the March Treasury Bond Futures Index, including a 40-week moving average line to indicate the long-term trend for this index. The accompanying discussion considered the support and resistance levels related to this index.

The second chart indicates the relationship between the interest rate on U.S. three-month T-bills and the rate on three-month Eurodollar securities. The high Eurodollar rate reflects the lower liquidity and safety of this security. It is like a confidence index related to U.S. and European bond markets, based upon interest rates, inflation, and exchange rates.

The third and fourth charts indicate bond market sentiment using technical tools also used in the equity market. The third one contains a plot of the consensus bullish attitude of speculators toward T-bonds. As with stocks, a high ratio (70 percent and above) would be considered an overbought condition, while a low ratio (30 percent and less) would indicate an oversold condition. Finally, the put-call ratio indicates the relative bearish attitude of these investors, so an abnormally high ratio (1.25 and above) would be bullish for those who use this ratio as a contrary indicator, and a low ratio (0.75 and below) would be a bearish indicator.

The point of these examples is to show that technical analysis can and is being applied to the fixed income market as well as the equity markets.

SUMMARY

The main differences between technical analysts and those who believe in an efficient stock market relate to the information dissemination process (does everybody get the information at about the same time?) and to how quickly investors adjust stock prices to reflect this new information. Because technical analysts believe that the information dissemination process is not the same for everyone and that price adjustment is not instantaneous, they contend that stock prices move in trends that persist and, therefore, that you can use past price trends to determine future price trends.

Technical trading rules fall under four general categories: contrary opinion rules, follow-the-smart-money, other market sentiment indicators, and stock price and volume techniques. These techniques can also be applied to non–U.S. markets and to the analysis of exchange rates among countries. They have also been used as a means to project interest rates and to determine market sentiment in the fixed-income market. Most technicians use several rules at any one point in time and attempt to derive a consensus decision, which can be buy, sell, or do nothing.[18] According to many technicians, their conclusion on many occasions is to do nothing.

---

[18] The results using numerous indicators are contained in Jerome Baesel, George Shows, and Edward Thorp, "Can Joe Granville Time the Market?" *Journal of Portfolio Management* 8, no. 3 (Spring 1982): 5–9.

FIGURE 16.19
Examples of Technical Analysis Charts for the Fixed Income Market

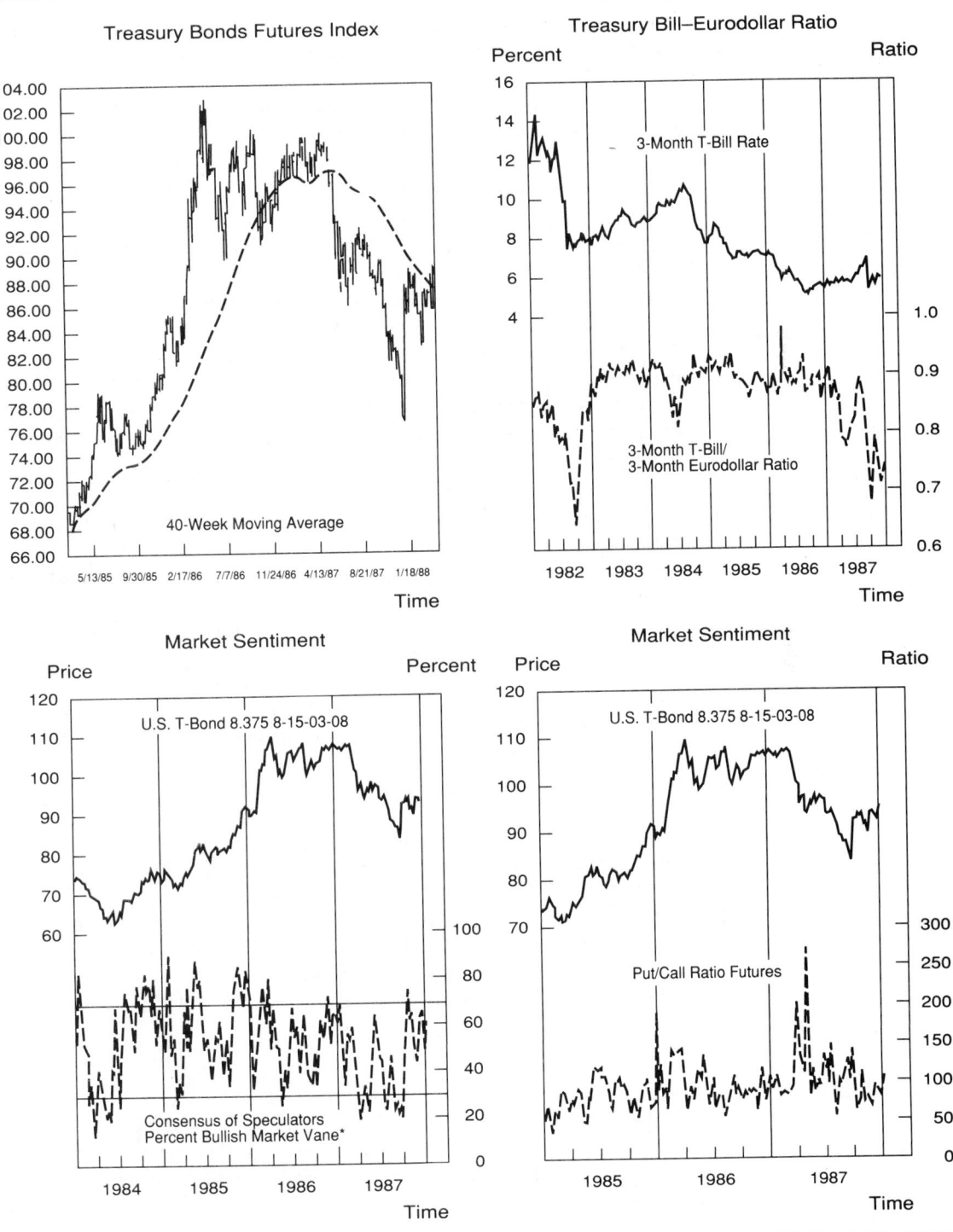

Source: Merrill Lynch, *Foreign Exchange Perspectives* (monthly).

QUESTIONS

1. The basic belief of technical analysts is that it is possible to use past price changes to predict future price changes. What is their principal contention supporting this belief?

2. Technicians contend that stock prices move in trends that persist for a long time. What do technicians believe happens in the real world that causes this?

3. Briefly discuss the problems involved with fundamental analysis that are considered to be advantages for technical analysis.

4. What are some of the disadvantages of technical analysis?

5. When the mutual fund cash position increases to 13 percent is it bullish or bearish? Give two reasons for your position.

6. There is a strong decline in credit balances at brokerage firms. Give two reasons why this is considered bearish.

7. When the Bearish Sentiment Index of advisory service opinions increases to 61 percent, is it bullish or bearish? Discuss your answer.

8. Define the Confidence Index and describe the reasoning behind it. What is the problem with the Confidence Index being demand-oriented?

9. The ratio of specialists' short sales to total short sales increases to 70 percent. Discuss why a technician would consider this bullish or bearish.

10. Why is an increase in debit balances considered bullish? What problems are involved with using this series as a technical tool?

11. Describe the Dow theory and its three components. Which component is most important?

12. Why is volume important to a technician? Describe a bearish price and volume pattern, and discuss why it is bearish.

13. Describe the computation of the breadth of market index. How is it used to confirm an important peak in stock prices?

14. During a ten-day trading period, the cumulative net advance series goes from 1,752 to 1,253. During this same period of time, the DJIA goes from 2,157 to 2,207. As a technician, what would you say about this set of events? Discuss your reasoning.

15. Describe a support and a resistance level, and explain why each might be expected to occur.

16. What is the purpose of computing a moving-average line for a stock? Describe a bullish pattern using a moving-average line and the volume of trading. Discuss why this pattern is considered bullish.

17. Explain how you would construct a relative-strength series for an individual stock or an industry group. What do you mean when you say a stock had good relative strength during a bear market?

18. Discuss why most technicians follow several technical rules and attempt to derive a consensus.

PROBLEMS

1. Select a stock on the NYSE and construct a daily high, low, and close bar chart for the stock that includes volume for ten trading days.

2. Compute the relative-strength ratio for the stock in Problem 1 relative to the S&P 500 Index, and prepare a table that includes all the data and indicates the computations as follows:

Day	Closing Price		Relative Strength Ratio
	Stock	S&P 500	Stock Price/S&P 500

3. Plot the relative-strength ratio computed in Problem 2 on your bar chart, and discuss whether the stock's relative strength is bullish or bearish.

4. Currently Newt Reptile Importers is selling at $32 per share. While you are somewhat dubious about technical analysis you feel that you would rather have those using point-and-figure charting supporting rather than disagreeing with your fundamental analysis. You decide to use one-point movements and three-point reversals, and gather the following price information:

DATE	PRICE	DATE	PRICE	DATE	PRICE
4/1	28	4/18	33	5/3	27
4/4	28 1/2	4/19	35 3/8	5/4	26 1/2
4/5	28	4/20	37	5/5	28
4/6	29	4/21	38 1/4	5/6	28 1/4
4/7	29 3/4	4/22	36	5/9	28 1/8
4/8	30 1/2	4/25	35	5/10	28 1/4
4/11	30 1/2	4/26	34 1/4	5/11	29 1/8
4/12	32 1/8	4/27	33 1/8	5/12	30 1/4
4/13	32	4/28	32 7/8	5/13	29 7/8
4/14	31 7/8	4/29	29	5/16	31 1/8
4/15	31 1/2	5/2	28 3/4	5/17	32

Plot the point-and-figure chart using Xs for uptrends and Os for downtrends.

5. Using recent issues of *The Wall Street Journal*, complete the following table:

DAY	1	2	3	4	5
Issues traded					
Advances					
Declines					
Unchanged					
Net advances or net declines					
Cumulative net advances or declines					
Change in DJIA					

Based on the very short-run data collection period, what conclusion can be reached?

REFERENCES   Bishop, George W., Jr. *Charles H. Dow and the Dow Theory.* (New York: Appleton Century Crofts, 1960), 23.

Branch, Ben. "The Predictive Power of Stock Market Indicators." *Journal of Financial and Quantitative Analysis* 11, no. 2 (June 1976).

Brush, John, and Keith Boles. "The Predictive Power in Relative Strength and CAPM." *Journal of Portfolio Management* 9, no. 4 (Summer 1983).

Dines, James. *How the Average Investor Can Use Technical Analysis for Stock Profits.* New York: Dines Chart Corporation, 1974.

Edwards, R. D., and John Magee, Jr. *Technical Analysis of Stock Trends.* Springfield, Md.: Stock Trend Service, 1966.

Grant, Dwight. "Market Timing: Strategies to Consider." *Journal of Portfolio Management* 5, no. 4 (Summer 1979).

Hardy, C. Colburn. *Investor's Guide to Technical Analysis.* New York: McGraw-Hill, 1978.

Jiler, William L. *How Charts Can Help You in the Stock Market.* New York: Commodity Research Publications Corp., 1967.

Kerr, H. S. "The Battle of Insider Trading vs. Market Efficiency." *Journal of Portfolio Management* 6, no. 4 (Summer 1980).

Levy, Robert A. "Conceptual Foundations of Technical Analysis." *Financial Analysts Journal* 22, no. 4 (July–August 1966).

Levy, Robert A. *The Relative Strength Concept of Common Stock Price Forecasting.* Larchmont, N.Y.: Investors Intelligence, 1968.

Pinches, George F. "The Random Walk Hypothesis and Technical Analysis." *Financial Analysts Journal* 26, no. 5 (March–April 1970).

Reilly, Frank K., and David T. Whitford. "The Stock Specialists Short Sale Ratio as an Investment Tool." *Journal of Portfolio Management* 8, no. 2 (Winter 1982).

Shaw, Alan R. "Market Timing and Technical Analysis." *Financial Analysts Handbook,* 2d ed. Sumner N. Levine (ed.) Homewood Ill.: Dow Jones-Irwin, 1988.

Tabell, Edmund W., and Anthony W. Tabell. "The Case for Technical Analysis." *Financial Analysts Journal* 20, no. 2 (March-April 1964).

Ying, Charles C. "Stock Market Prices and Volume of Sales." *Econometrica* 34, no. 3 (July 1966).

EXTENSIONS AND APPLICATION OF ASSET PRICING AND PORTFOLIO MODELS

PART IV

CHAPTERS

Portfolio theory and the capital asset pricing model (CAPM), detailed in Chapters 7 and 8, are extended and applied in this section. Chapter 17 considers several extensions of these models, including the effect of relaxing some of the major assumptions. In addition, there is a discussion of numerous studies that have empirically tested the CAPM and an explanation of an alternative asset pricing theory referred to as the arbitrage pricing theory (APT).

Chapter 18 considers the management of bond portfolios. This is considered separately from other assets because of the overall growth of this market, the substantial increase in interest rate volatility that has made this a more important and more challenging task, and the numerous portfolio strategies that have been developed during the past decade to deal with risk control. It is the author's contention that during the past decade, there have been more developments related to bond analysis and portfolio management than to equity analysis and portfolio management. Therefore, Chapter 18 discusses trading strategies available to bond investors who want to increase their returns while controlling risk and also a consideration of alternative bond portfolio management policies and how they are implemented.

Chapter 19 considers a subject of growing importance—international diversification. While this concept is integrated throughout the book, this discussion considers several studies that support it. Problems in implementing this strategy are also considered, and the chapter concludes with suggestions on how to do this.

Chapter 20 deals with the very important question of how to evaluate the performance of portfolio managers. While there are two sets of techniques considered for equities and fixed-income securities, the overriding consideration of both is adjustment for risk. The several techniques presented are not competing alternatives, but complementary combinations.

The final chapter in this section (Chapter 21) considers an alternative to analyzing securities and managing your own portfolio—investment companies. After a basic explanation of the concept of investment companies and a description of the major forms, we examine the numerous types available, including money market funds, REITs, high-growth companies, international stocks and bonds, high-yield (junk) bonds, and option funds. It will become clear that almost any investment objective can be met by investing in one or several investment companies. A review of several studies that have examined the performance of funds indicates that on average they are not able to outperform the market, but they are capable of fulfilling a number of functions important to investors.

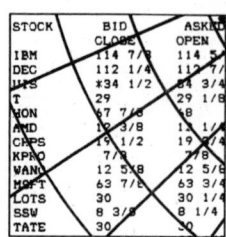

CHAPTER 17

EXTENSIONS AND TESTING OF ASSET PRICING THEORIES

Chapters 7 and 8 contained a detailed introduction to Markowitz portfolio theory and the capital asset pricing model (CAPM) so that these concepts could be used in the subsequent valuation chapters. In turn, this chapter considers several extensions of the CAPM, relaxes some of the assumptions, and examines the impact of these changes on the model. More important, we discuss the empirical tests of the theory that support its predictive ability but also raise some questions, including a contention by Roll that it is not possible to test the model. We conclude the chapter with a discussion of an alternative asset pricing model, _arbitrage pricing theory (APT), developed by Stephen Ross_, that does not require the extensive assumptions of the CAPM. The empirical tests of this alternative theory yield mixed results and prompt the contention that this theory is likewise untestable.

RELAXING THE ASSUMPTIONS

In Chapter 8 several assumptions were set forth related to the CAPM. In this section, we discuss the impact on the capital market line (CML) and the security market line (SML) when we relax several of these assumptions.

DIFFERENTIAL BORROWING AND LENDING RATES

One of the first assumptions of the CAPM was that investors could borrow and lend any amount of money at the risk-free rate. As noted, it is reasonable to assume that an investor can always _lend_ as much as desired at the risk-free rate by buying government securities (e.g., T-bills). However, one may question the ability of investors to _borrow_ unlimited amounts at the T-bill rate, because this rate is usually lower than the prime rate, and most investors must pay a premium relative to the prime rate when they borrow money. For example, when T-bill rates are yielding 9 percent, the

FIGURE 17.1
**Investment Alternatives When the Cost of Borrowing
Is Higher Than the Cost of Lending**

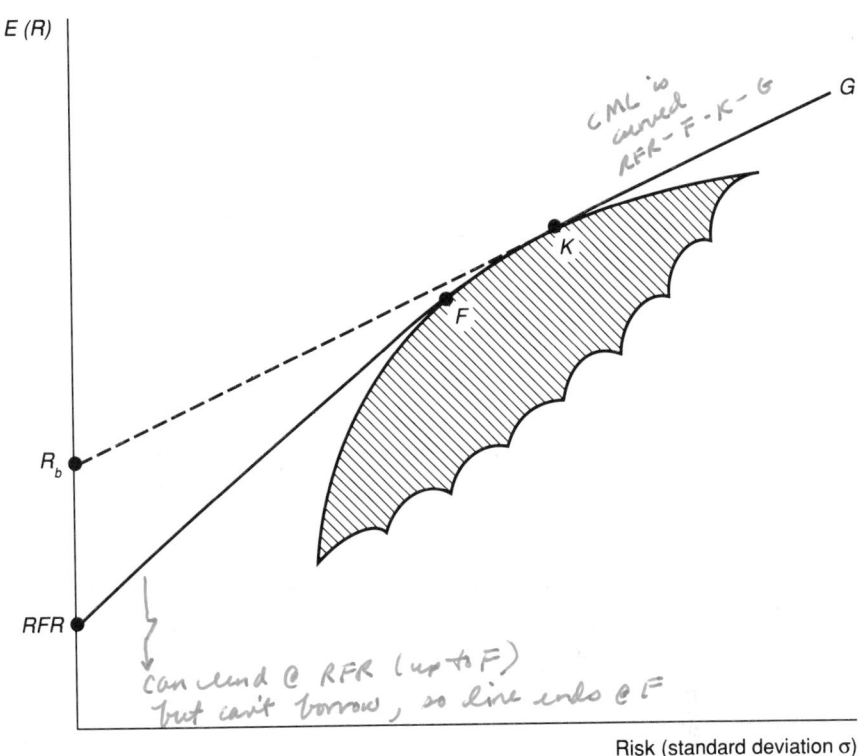

prime rate will probably be about 11 percent, and most individuals would
have to pay about 12 percent to borrow at the bank.

The effect of this differential is that there will be two different lines
going to the Markowitz efficient frontier, as shown in Figure 17.1. The
segment $RFR - F$ indicates the investment opportunities available from
some combination of investing in risk-free assets (i.e., lending at the RFR)
and Portfolio F on the Markowitz efficient frontier. It is not possible to
extend this line any further because it is assumed that you cannot borrow
at this risk-free rate to acquire further units of Portfolio F. If you borrow
at R_b, you would find the point of tangency on the curve at point K. This
indicates that you could borrow at R_b and could invest in Portfolio K to
extend the CML to G. Therefore, the CML is made up of RFR-F-K-G—that
is, a line segment (RFR-F), a curve segment (F-K), and another line segment (K-G). This implies that you can either lend or borrow, but the
borrowing portfolios are not as profitable as when it was assumed that
you could borrow at the RFR. In this instance, because you must pay a

FIGURE 17.2
Security Market Line with Zero-Beta Portfolio

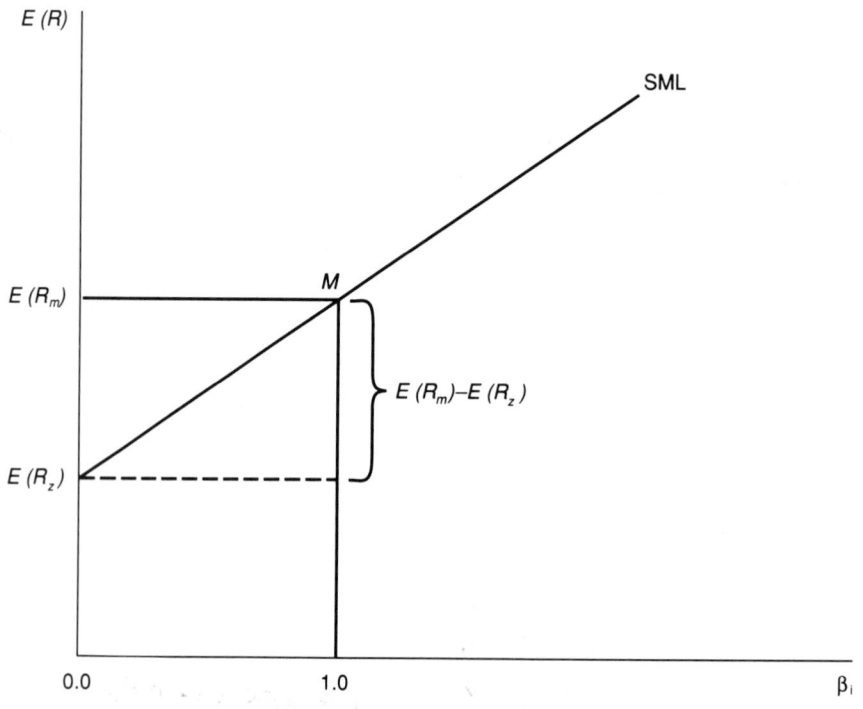

rate to borrow that is higher than the *RFR,* your net return is less—that is, the slope of the borrowing line is below that for *RFR–F.*

ZERO-BETA MODEL   If the market portfolio (*M*) is mean-variance efficient (i.e., it has the lowest risk for a given level of return among the attainable set of portfolios), an alternative model, developed by Black, that does not require a risk-free asset can be used.[1] Specifically, within the set of feasible alternative portfolios, there will be several portfolios where the returns are completely uncorrelated with the market portfolio; the beta of these portfolios with the market portfolio is zero. From among the several portfolios that have this property, you would select the one with minimum variance. While the availability of this zero-beta portfolio will not affect the CML, it will allow construction of a linear SML, as shown in Figure 17.2. In the model, the intercept is the expected return for the zero-beta portfolio. Similar to the proof in Chapter 8, the combinations of this zero-beta portfolio and the market portfolio will be a linear relationship in return and risk; again, the

[1] Fischer Black, "Capital Market Equilibrium with Restricted Borrowing," *Journal of Business* 45, no. 3 (July 1972): 444–445.

covariance between the zero-beta portfolio (R_z) and the market portfolio is zero. Assuming that the return for the zero-beta portfolio is greater than that for a risk-free asset, the slope of the line through the market portfolio would not be as steep. The equation for this line would be

$$ER(R_i) = E(R_z) + B_i [E(R_m) - E(R_z)].$$

Obviously, the risk premiums would be a function of the beta for the individual security and the market risk premium:

$$[E(R_m) - E(R_z)].$$

Some of the empirical results discussed in the next section support this model with its higher intercept and flatter slope.

TRANSACTION COSTS

The basic assumption is that there are no transaction costs, so investors will buy or sell mispriced securities until they again plot on the SML. For instance, if a stock plots above the SML, it is underpriced (its $E(R)$ is greater than justified by its risk level), so investors should buy it and bid up its price until its $E(R)$ is in line with its risk—that is, until it will plot on the SML. The point is, with transaction costs, investors will not correct all mispricing, because in some instances the cost of buying and selling the security will offset any potential excess return. Therefore, securities will plot very close to the SML but not exactly on it. Thus, the SML will be a band of securities, as shown in Figure 17.3, rather than a single line. Obviously, the width of the band is a function of the amount of the transaction costs. In a world with a large proportion of purchases and sales by institutions that trade at pennies per share and with discount brokers for individuals, the band should be quite narrow.

The existence of transaction costs also will affect the extent of diversification by investors. In Chapter 8, there was a discussion of the relationship between the number of stocks in a portfolio and the variance of the portfolio (see Figure 8.3). You will recall that initially the variance declined rapidly, approaching about 90 percent of complete diversification with about 15 to 18 securities. An important question is how many more securities must be added to derive the last 10 percent. Clearly, the existence of transaction costs would indicate that at some point the cost of diversification would be excessive for most investors, especially if there were also costs of monitoring and analyzing the added securities.

HETEROGENEOUS EXPECTATIONS AND PLANNING PERIODS

If all investors have different expectations about risk and return, each would have a unique CML and/or SML, and the composite graph would be a set of lines with a breadth determined by the divergence of expectations. If all investors had similar information and background, the band would be reasonably narrow.

The impact of *planning periods* is similar. Recall that the CAPM is a one-period model, and the period employed should be the planning period for the individual investor. Thus, if you are thinking in terms of a one-

FIGURE 17.3
Security Market Line with Transaction Costs

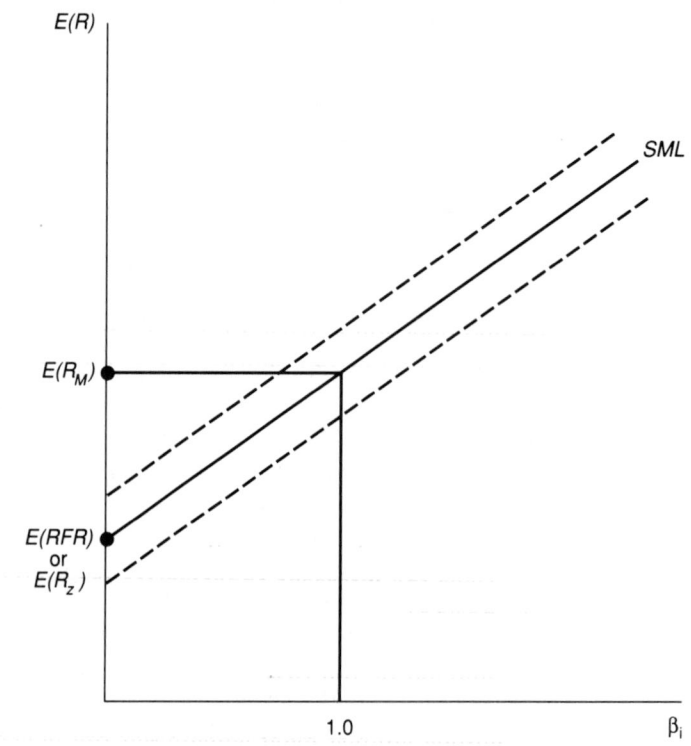

year planning period, your CML and SML could differ from mine, assuming my planning period is one month.

TAXES

The rates of return that we normally record and that were used throughout the model were pre-tax returns. In fact, the actual returns for most investors are affected as follows:

$$E(R_i) = \frac{(P_e - P_b) \times (1 - T_{cg}) + (Div) \times (1 - T_i)}{P_b},$$

where

R_i = after-tax rate of return

P_e = ending price

P_b = beginning price

Div = dividend paid during period

T_{cg} = tax on capital gain or loss

T_i = tax on ordinary income.

Clearly, the tax rates differ between individuals and also institutions. Hence, for many institutions that do not pay taxes, the original pre-tax model is correctly specified—that is, t_{cg} and T_i take on values of zero. Alternatively, if investors have heavy tax burdens, this could cause major differences.[2]

EMPIRICAL TESTS OF THE THEORY

In the discussion of the assumptions of capital market theory, it was pointed out that a theory should not be judged on the basis of its assumptions, but on how well it explains the relationships that exist in the real world. While there have been numerous tests of the CAPM, two major questions should concern us. The first involves the stability of the measure of systematic risk (beta). Since beta is our principal risk measure, it is important to know whether past betas can be used as estimates of future betas. The second question is basic to the theory: Is there a positive linear relationship as hypothesized between beta and the rate of return on risky assets? More specifically, how well do returns conform to the following SML equation:

$$E(R_i) = RFR + \beta_i (R_m - RFR).$$

Some specific questions might include

- Does the intercept approximate the *RFR* that prevailed during the period?
- Was the slope of the line positive? Was it consistent with the slope implied by the risk premium ($R_m - RFR$) during the test period?

STABILITY OF BETA

Numerous studies have considered the question of the stability of beta and generally reached similar conclusions. Levy examined weekly rates of return for 500 stocks on the NYSE and concluded that the risk measure was not stable for individual stocks over fairly short periods (52 weeks).[3] Alternatively, when stocks were put into portfolios, the stability of the portfolio betas increased dramatically. Further, the larger the portfolio (e.g., 25 or 50 stocks) and the longer the period (over 26 weeks), the more stable the beta of the portfolio was. The correlation of 25- and 50-stock portfolio betas over 26-week periods averaged above 0.91. Also, the betas tended to regress toward the mean—high-beta portfolios tended to decline over time toward unity (1.00), while low-beta portfolios tended to increase over time toward unity.

Blume likewise examined the stability of beta for all common stocks listed on the NYSE over the period January 1926 through June 1968.[4] The correlation of beta for individual stocks during adjoining periods was quite good, and the stability increased substantially for portfolios of 20 or more

---

[2] For a detailed consideration of this, see Robert Litzenberger and K. Ramaswamy, "The Effect of Personal Taxes and Dividends on Capital Asset Prices: Theory and Empirical Evidence," *Journal of Financial Economics* 7, no. 2 (June 1979): 163–196.

[3] Robert A. Levy, "On the Short-Term Stationarity of Beta Coefficients," *Financial Analysts Journal* 27, no. 6 (November–December 1971): 55–62.

[4] Marshall E. Blume, "On the Assessment of Risk," *Journal of Finance* 26, no. 1 (March 1971): 1–10.

stocks. The correlation of the portfolio betas over time ranged from 0.93 to 0.98. Blume also found a tendency for a regression of the betas toward 1.

Fielitz examined the ability of individual investors to carry out their own diversification rather than using mutual funds.[5] He considered the impact of the number of randomly selected securities on the undiversifiable risk of the portfolio and found substantial stability of risk with eight securities.

Porter and Ezzell randomly assigned stocks to alternative portfolios and examined the correlation coefficient of average betas over contingent periods.[6] They found no increase in the correlation coefficients for portfolio betas as the average size of the portfolio increased.

Tole contended that the appropriate technique is to assign stocks to portfolios on a random basis rather than ranking stocks by the size of the beta.[7] In contrast to prior studies that examined the relative stability (i.e., the size of the correlation coefficient), he examined the standard deviation of the betas for portfolios of different sizes. He concluded that there was substantially greater stability in beta as the portfolio size is increased. While supporting most prior studies, he also contended that the benefit of larger portfolios extends beyond 10 or 25 stocks. In fact, for some tests the benefits go beyond 100 stocks in the portfolio.

Another factor that apparently affects the stability of beta is the estimating period—that is, how many months are used to estimate the original beta and the test beta. Baesel varied the estimation period from 12 months to 108 months and found that the stability of the individual betas increased as the length of the estimation period increased.[8] Altman, Jacquillat, and Levasseur found similar results to those derived by Baesel using French data.[9]

Roenfeldt, Griepentrog, and Pflamm (RGP) reexamined the Baesel conclusions, using the same base period and test period; that is, if the base period used to estimate the beta was 108 months, the test period was likewise 108 months.[10] RGP used betas derived from 48 months of data and compared these betas to subsequent betas for 12, 24, 36, and 48 months. They found that the 48-month base period betas were not good for estimating subsequent 12-month betas, but were quite good for estimating 24-, 36-, and 48-month betas.

[5] Bruce Fielitz, "Indirect versus Direct Diversification," *Financial Management* 3, no. 4 (Winter 1974): 54–62.

[6] R. Burr Porter and John R. Ezzell, "A Note on the Predictive Ability of Beta Coefficients," *Journal of Business Research* 3, no. 4 (October 1975): 365–372.

[7] Thomas M. Tole, "How to Maximize Stationarity of Beta," *Journal of Portfolio Management* 7, no. 2 (Winter 1981): 45–49.

[8] Jerome B. Baesel, "On the Assessment of Risk: Some Further Considerations," *Journal of Finance* 29, no. 5 (December 1974): 1491–1494.

[9] Edward Altman, B. Jacquillat, and M. Levasseur, "Comparative Analysis of Risk Measures: France and the United States," *Journal of Financial and Quantitative Analysis* 13, no. 1 (March 1978): 117–121.

[10] Rodney L. Roenfeldt, Gary L. Griepentrog, and Christopher C. Pflamm, "Further Evidence on the Stationarity of Beta Coefficients," *Journal of Financial and Quantitative Analysis* 13, no. 1 (March 1978): 117–121.

Theobald derived a set of analytical expressions that explained the Baesel empirical results.[11] It was shown that the stationarity of beta will increase with the time period examined but will not increase indefinitely because the numerous variables that affect an individual stock's beta would have to remain stationary over the longer period. He also partially explained the findings of Roenfeldt, Griepentrog, and Pflamm regarding the improved stability as the period was lengthened. While the optimal length could be over 120 months, this assumed that the beta had not shifted during the period—if it had, shorter beta sets would be necessary. Chen likewise analyzed the relationship between the variability of the beta coefficients and the residual risks for portfolios and concluded that the *ordinary least square (OLS)* estimate would be biased if the betas for individual stocks were unstable.[12] He suggested employing a Bayesian approach to estimate these time-varying betas.

Carpenter and Upton considered the influence of the trading volume on beta stability by examining betas during alternative periods of high volume, low volume, and average volume.[13] They found small differences in the betas derived and contended that the predictions of betas were slightly better using the volume-adjusted betas. This impact of volume on the estimation of beta is related to the prior discussion (Chapter 6), which noted that the estimated beta for low-volume securities was biased downward (see the discussion of the small-firm effect).

To summarize, individual betas were generally not stable whereas portfolio betas were, and results indicated that it is important to examine a long period (a minimum of 36 months) and be conscious of volume.

COMPARABILITY OF PUBLISHED ESTIMATES OF BETA

In contrast to deriving your own estimate of beta for a stock, you may want to use a published source for speed or convenience, such as Merrill Lynch's *Security Risk Evaluation Report* (published monthly) and the *Value Line Investment Survey.* Note that the methods of computation differ for these two estimates. While both services use the same market model equation, $(R_i = RFR + B_i R_m + \epsilon_i)$, they differ in the data employed. Specifically, the Merrill Lynch estimates use *60 monthly observations* and the S&P 500, while the *Value Line* estimate uses *260 weekly observations* and the NYSE composite series. They likewise both use an adjustment process because of the regression tendencies, and their adjustment equations differ slightly.

Given these relatively minor differences, one would probably expect the published betas to be quite comparable. Statman examined the betas for the 195 firms with the largest market value for a comparable five-year period.[14] The following equation indicates the relationship between the adjusted betas:

---

[11] Michael Theobald, "Beta Stationarity and Estimation Period: Some Analytical Results," *Journal of Financial and Quantitative Analysis* 16, no. 5 (December 1981): 747–757.

[12] Son-Nan Chen, "Beta Nonstationarity, Portfolio Residual Risk, and Diversification," *Journal of Financial and Quantitative Analysis* 16, no. 1 (March 1981): 95–111.

[13] Michael D. Carpenter and David E. Upton, "Trading Volume and Beta Stability," *Journal of Portfolio Management* 7, no. 2 (Winter 1981): 60–64.

[14] Meir Statman, "Betas Compared: Merrill Lynch vs. Value Line," *Journal of Portfolio Management* 7, no. 2 (Winter 1981): 41–44.

Merrill Lynch Adjusted Beta $= 0.127 + 0.879$ Value Line Adjusted Beta.

These results are not consistent with equality, and both the intercept and slope were significant. Notably, the R^2 was only .55, and there did not appear to be any systematic bias in the differences. Also, for betas close to 1, the differences were very small. To determine the impact of combining stocks into portfolios, he examined 19 portfolios of 10 stocks each, and found that the coefficient of determination was almost the same as for individual stocks (.54 versus .55). These results imply that there is a small but significant difference in these estimates of beta.

Reilly and Wright examined over 1,100 securities for three non-over-lapping periods and confirmed the difference in beta found by Statman—and also indicated the reason for the difference, namely, the alternative time intervals (i.e., weekly versus monthly observations).[15] It was shown that the security's market value affects both the size and the direction of the monthly-weekly interval effect. This implies that when estimating beta or using a published source, you must be aware not only of the interval used but also of the relative size of the firm involved.

RELATIONSHIP BETWEEN SYSTEMATIC RISK AND RETURN

The ultimate question regarding the CAPM is whether it is useful in explaining the return on risky assets. Specifically, is there a positive linear relationship between the systematic risk and the rates of return on these risky assets? Sharpe and Cooper provided support for a positive relationship between return and risk, although it was not completely linear.[16] They put stocks into risk classes based upon their systematic risk (beta) and found that the returns increased with risk class—except for the very highest risk classes, where the returns leveled off and declined slightly. Because the portfolio betas were stable, it was possible to derive the average beta for a portfolio based upon historical betas, and the return during a subsequent period was generally consistent with the risk.

Douglas examined the relationship between rate of return and several risk measures for 600 individual stocks during alternative five-year periods.[17] He considered a systematic risk variable and a variance of return measure relative to return. The results indicated intercepts that were larger than the prevailing risk-free rates. Further, while the coefficient for the variance risk variable (*total risk*) was generally significant, the coefficients for the *systematic risk* variables were typically not significant.

---

[15] Frank K. Reilly and David J. Wright, "A Comparison of Published Betas," *Journal of Portfolio Management* 14, no. 3 (Spring 1988): 64–69.

[16] William F. Sharpe and Guy M. Cooper, "Risk-Return Classes of New York Stock Exchange Common Stocks: 1931–1967," *Financial Analysts Journal* 28, no. 2 (March–April 1972): 46–54. A subsequent study concentrated on the impact of yield tilting portfolios, but also confirmed many of these results. See William F. Sharpe and Howard B. Sosin, "Risk, Return, and Yield: New York Stock Exchange Common Stocks: 1928–1969," *Financial Analysts Journal* 32, no. 2 (March–April 1976): 33–42.

[17] G. W. Douglas, "Risk in the Equity Markets: An Empirical Appraisal of Market Efficiency," *Yale Economic Essays* 9, no. 1 (1969): 3–48.

Miller and Scholes noted that the results of the Douglas study could be caused by measurement errors in estimating the stock betas.[18] Unsystematic risk and betas are highly correlated, and the distribution of returns for the stocks were very skewed, which could make a difference. Even with these problems, though, it was not possible to fully explain the Douglas results.

Because of the potential statistical problems with individual stocks, Black, Jensen, and Scholes considered the risk and return for portfolios of stocks.[19] All NYSE stocks listed between 1931 and 1965 were placed into ten portfolios on the basis of their betas. There was a positive linear relationship between monthly excess return and portfolio beta, although the intercept was higher than expected. (That is, it should have been zero.) Figure 17.4 contains some of the charts from this study, which show that, while almost all the measured SMLs have a positive slope, the slopes change, the intercepts are not zero, and they likewise change.

Fama and MacBeth examined the relationship between the rates of return and betas for portfolios and also considered a beta-squared variable (to test for linearity) as well as a measure of unsystematic risk.[20] Notably, the model related the return during the current month to beta, beta squared, and unsystematic risk during the prior month. While the monthly results varied over time, the overall results supported the CAPM. The intercept was about equal to that implied by the *RFR*, the systematic risk coefficient was positive and significant, and neither of the coefficients for beta squared or prior unsystematic risk were significant.

In summary, the bulk of the evidence regarding the relationship between rates of return and systematic risk for portfolios indicates support for the CAPM. Still, the evidence is not without question. The intercepts were generally higher than implied by the *RFR*, which is either consistent with a zero-beta model or a higher borrowing rate. Also, studies of the risk-return relationship for individual stocks have not been supportive, prompting more recent studies to employ portfolios of stocks. Finally, beta generally does better than other measures of risk and even better still when the tests cover time periods in excess of ten years.

THE MARKET PORTFOLIO: THEORY VERSUS PRACTICE

Throughout our presentation of the CAPM, it was noted that the market portfolio included *all* the risky assets in the economy. Further, in equilibrium, the various assets would be included in the portfolio in the proportion of their market value. Therefore, this market portfolio should contain not only stocks and bonds, but also real estate, options, stamps, coins,

[18] Merton H. Miller and Myron Scholes, "Rates of Return in Relation to Risk: A Re-Examination of Some Recent Findings" in *Studies in the Theory of Capital Markets,* edited by Michael Jensen (New York: Praeger Publishers, 1976).
[19] Fischer Black, Michael Jensen, and Myron Scholes, "The Capital Asset Pricing Model: Some Empirical Tests" in *Studies in the Theory of Capital Markets,* edited by Michael Jensen (New York: Praeger, 1976).
[20] Eugene Fama and R. MacBeth, "Risk, Return, and Equilibrium: Empirical Tests," *Journal of Political Economy* 81, no. 2 (May–June 1973): 453–474.

FIGURE 17.4
Average Excess Monthly Rates of Return Compared to Systematic Risk During Alternative Time Periods

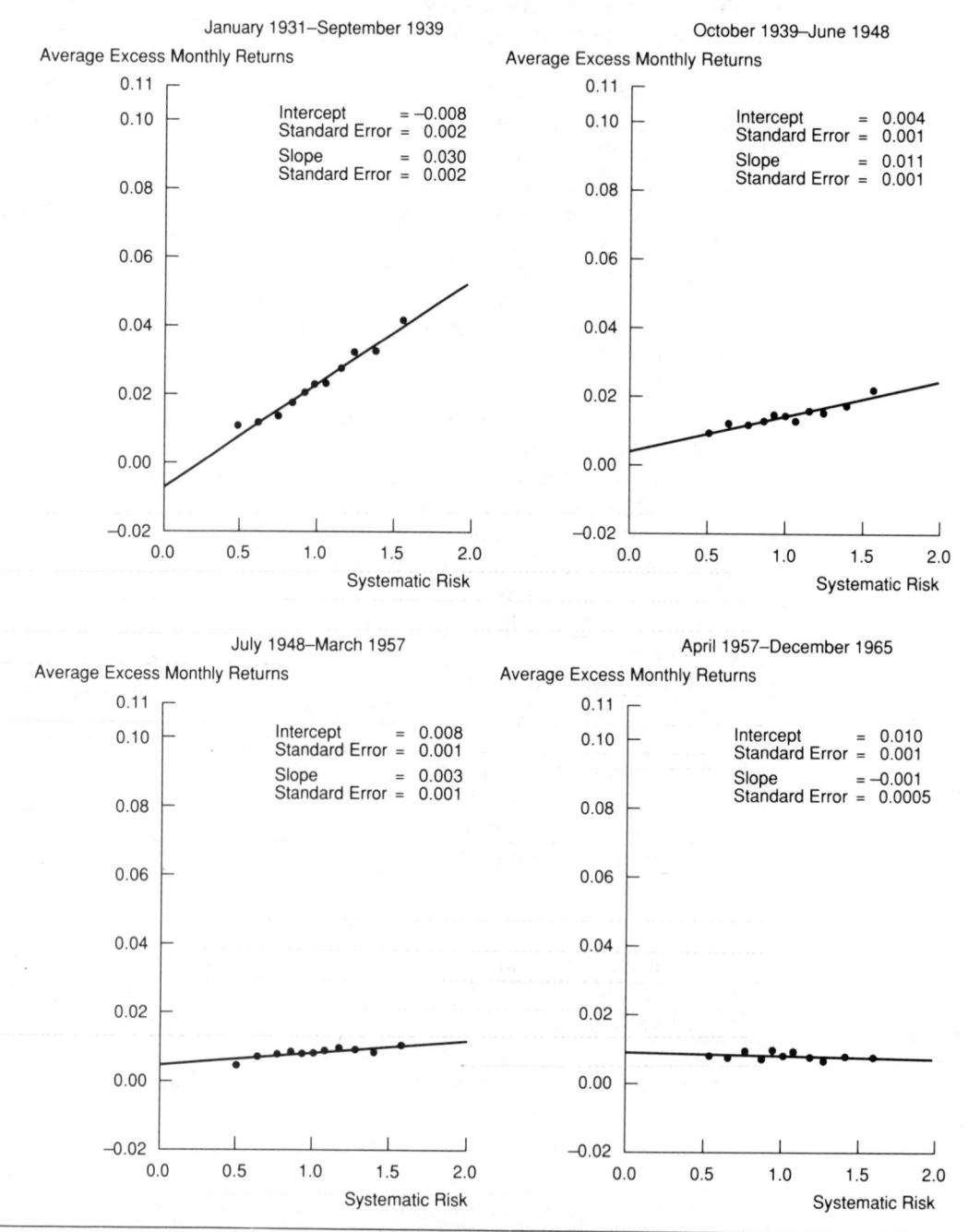

Source: Fischer Black, Michael Jensen, and Myron Scholes, "The Capital Asset Pricing Model: Some Empirical Tests" in *Studies in the Theory of Capital Markets*, edited by Michael Jensen (New York: Praeger, 1970). Reprinted with permission.

foreign securities, and so on, with weights equal to their relative market value.

While this concept of a market portfolio is reasonable in theory, it is difficult, if not impossible, to implement when testing or using the CAPM. The easy part is getting a stock series for the NYSE, the AMEX, and major world stock exchanges like Tokyo, London, and West Germany. There are stock series for the OTC market, too, but these series are generally incomplete. There are also some well-regarded bond series available (e.g., from Merrill Lynch, Salomon Brothers, Shearson Lehman Hutton). Because of the difficulty in deriving series for the numerous other assets mentioned, most studies have been limited to using a stock or bond series alone, and the vast majority of studies have chosen the S&P 500 series or some other NYSE stock series. It is assumed that the series selected is highly correlated with the true market portfolio.

While most academicians have generally recognized this potential problem, they have assumed that the deficiency is not serious. Several articles by Roll, however, concluded that, on the contrary, it had very serious implications for tests of the model and especially for using the model to evaluate portfolio performance.[21] Roll referred to it as a _bench-mark error,_ because the practice is to compare the performance of a portfolio manager to the return of an unmanaged portfolio of equal risk—that is, the market portfolio adjusted for risk. Roll's point is that if the benchmark is mistakenly specified, you cannot measure the performance of portfolio managers properly. A mistakenly specified market portfolio can have two effects. First, the beta computed for alternative portfolios would be wrong because the market portfolio is inappropriate. Second, the SML derived would be wrong because it goes from the _RFR_ through the improperly specified _M_ portfolio. Figure 17.5 shows an example where the true portfolio risk (β_T) is underestimated (β_e), possibly because of the market portfolio used in computing the beta. As shown, the portfolio being evaluated may appear to be above the SML using β_e and thus imply superior management. If, in fact, the true risk (β_T) is greater, the portfolio will shift to the right and be below the SML, indicating inferior performance.

Figure 17.6 indicates that the intercept and slope will differ if (1) there is an error in selecting a proper risk-free asset and (2) if the market portfolio selected is not the correct mean-variance efficient portfolio. Obviously, it is very possible that, under these conditions, a portfolio judged to be superior relative to the first SML (above the measured SML) could be inferior relative to the true SML (below the true SML). Roll contends that a test of the CAPM requires an analysis of whether the market portfolio proxy used is mean-variance efficient (on the Markowitz efficient frontier) and also if it is the true optimum market portfolio. Roll showed that, if the

---

[21] Richard Roll, "A Critique of the Asset Pricing Theory's Tests," _Journal of Financial Economics,_ 4 no. 4 (March 1977): 129–176; Richard Roll, "Ambiguity when Performance Is Measured by the Securities Market Line," _Journal of Finance_ 33, no. 4 (September 1978): 1051–1069; Richard Roll, "Performance Evaluation and Benchmark Error I," _Journal of Portfolio Mangement_ 6, no. 4 (Summer 1980): 5–12; and Richard Roll, "Performance Evaluation and Benchmark Error II," _Journal of Portfolio Management_ 7, no. 2 (Winter 1981): 17–22. This discussion draws heavily from these articles.

FIGURE 17.5

Differential Performance Based upon an Error in Estimating Systematic Risk

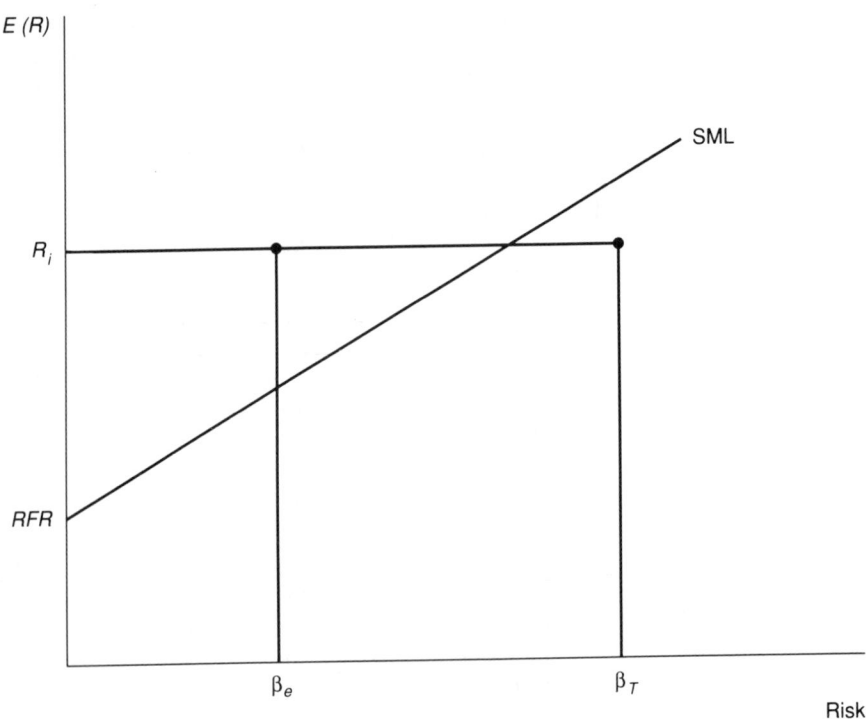

proxy market portfolio (e.g., the S&P 500 index) is mean-variance efficient, it is mathematically possible to show a linear relationship between returns and betas derived with this portfolio; but this is not a true test of CAPM, because you are not working with the true SML (see Figure 17.7).

In summary, the concern is that an incorrect market proxy will affect the beta risk measures, as well as the position and slope of the SML that is used to evaluate portfolio performance. In general, the errors will tend to overestimate the performance of portfolio managers, because the proxy market portfolio employed is probably not as efficient as the true market portfolio, so the slope of the SML will be underestimated.

Roll's benchmark problems, however, do not invalidate the value of the CAPM as a normative model of asset pricing; they only indicate a problem in *measurement* when attempting to test the theory and use it for evaluating portfolio performance. Therefore, it is necessary to work toward a better market portfolio proxy and/or adjust the portfolio performance measures accordingly (see Chapter 20).

FIGURE 17.6
Differential SML Based upon Measured Risk-Free Asset and
Proxy Market Portfolio

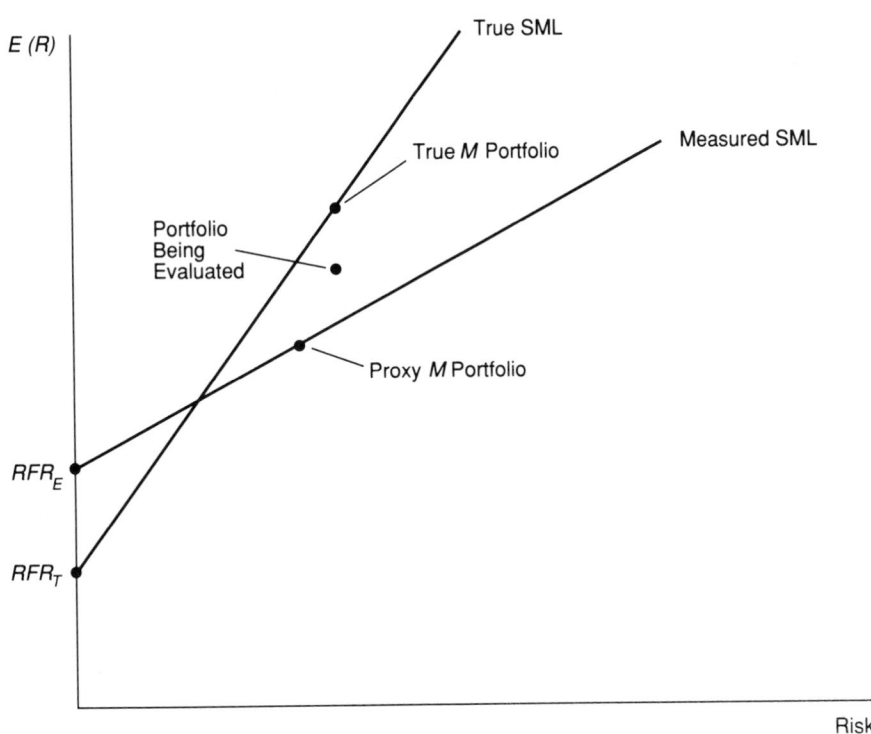

ARBITRAGE PRICING THEORY (APT)

At this point we have discussed the CAPM in terms of the basic theory, the impact of changing some of its major assumptions, and its dependence on a market portfolio of all risky assets. In addition, the model assumes that investors have quadratic utility functions and the distribution of security prices is normal—that is, symmetrically distributed, with a variance term that can be estimated.

The tests of the CAPM indicated that the beta coefficients for individual securities were not stable, but the portfolio betas generally were, assuming long enough sample periods and adequate trading volume. There was also support for a positive linear relationship between rates of return and systematic risk for portfolios of stock. In contrast, several papers by Roll criticized the tests and the usefulness of the model in portfolio evaluation because of its dependence on a market portfolio of risky assets that is not currently available. Consequently, the academic community has considered an alternative asset pricing theory that is reasonably intuitive and also requires only limited assumptions. This *arbitrage pricing theory (APT)*,

FIGURE 17.7

Differential SML Using Market Proxy That Is Mean-Variance Efficient

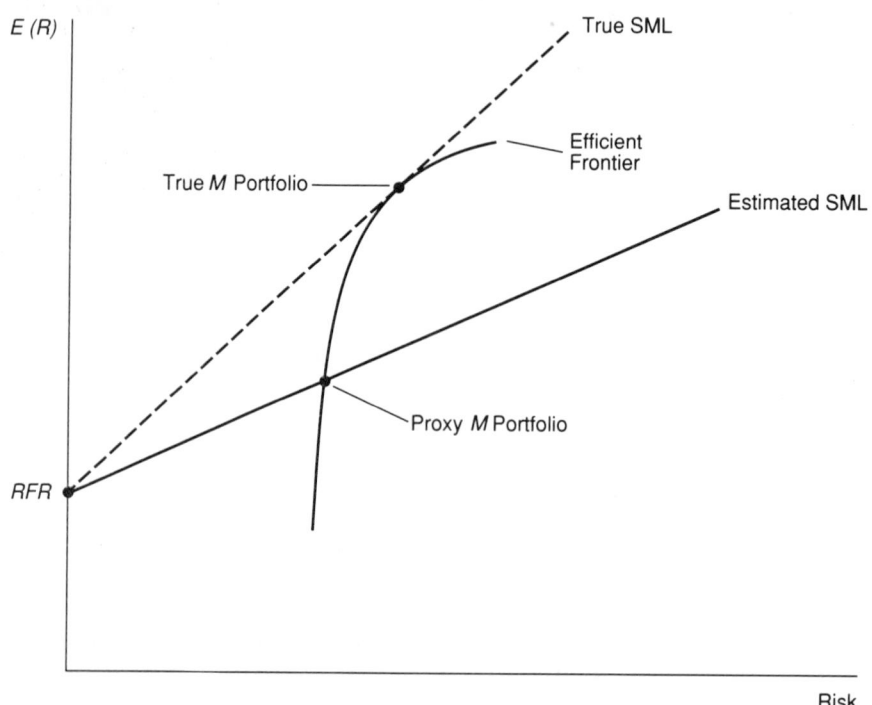

developed by Ross in the early 1970s and initially published in 1976, has three major assumptions:[22]

1. Capital markets are perfectly competitive.
2. Investors always prefer more wealth to less wealth with certainty.
3. The stochastic process generating asset returns can be represented as a K factor model (to be described).

Equally important, the following major assumptions are *not* required: (1) quadratic utility function, (2) normally distributed security returns, and (3) a market portfolio that contains all risky assets and is mean-variance efficient. Obviously, if such a theory is able to explain differential security prices, it would be considered a superior theory because it is simpler (i.e., it requires fewer assumptions).

As noted, the theory assumes that the stochastic process generating asset returns can be represented as a K factor model of the form,

[22] Stephen Ross, "The Arbitrage Theory of Capital Asset Pricing," *Journal of Economic Theory* 13, no. 2 (December 1976): 341–360; and Stephen Ross, "Return, Risk, and Arbitrage" in *Risk and Return in Finance*, edited by I. Friend and J. Bicksler (Cambridge: Ballinger, 1977): 189–218.

$$R_i = E_i + b_{i1}\delta_1 + b_{i2}\delta_2 + \ldots + b_{ik}\delta_k + \epsilon_i \text{ for } i = 1 \text{ to } N,$$

where

R_i = return on asset i during a specified time period

E_i = expected return for asset i

b_{ik} = reaction in asset i's returns to movements in a common factor δ_k

δ_k = a set of common factors with a zero mean that influences the returns on all assets

ϵ_i = a unique effect on asset i's return that, by assumption, is completely diversifiable in large portfolios and has a mean of zero

N = number of assets.

Two terms require elaboration: δ_k and b. As indicated, δ_k terms are the multiple factors expected to have an impact on the returns of all assets. Examples might include inflation, growth in GNP, major political upheavals, or changes in interest rates. The APT contends there are many such factors, in contrast to the CAPM, where the only relevant variable is the covariance of the asset with the market portfolio.

Given these common factors, the b_{ik} terms determine how each asset reacts to this common factor. To extend the earlier example, while all assets may be affected by growth in GNP, the impact will differ. For example, stocks of cyclical firms will have larger b_{ik} terms for this common factor than noncyclical firms, such as grocery chains. Likewise, you will hear discussions about interest-sensitive stocks: all stocks are affected by changes in interest rates, but some stocks experience larger impacts. It is possible to envision other examples of common factors, such as inflation, exchange rates, and interest rate spreads. Still, in the application of the theory, the factors are not identified. That is, when we discuss the empirical studies, three, four, or five factors that affect security returns will be identified, but there is no indication of what these factors represent.

Similar to the CAPM model, it is assumed that the unique effects (ϵ_i) are independent and will be diversified away in a large portfolio. The APT assumes that, in equilibrium, the return on a zero-investment, zero-systematic-risk portfolio is zero when the unique effects are diversified away. This assumption and some theory from linear algebra implies that the expected return on any asset i (E_i) can be expressed as

$$E_i = \lambda_0 + \lambda_1 b_{i1} + \lambda_2 b_{i2} + \ldots + \lambda_k b_{ik},$$

where

λ_0 = the expected return on an asset with zero systematic risk where $\lambda_0 = E_0$

λ_1 = the risk premium related to each of the common factors—e.g., the risk premium related to interest rate risk ($\lambda_i = E_i - E_0$)

b_i = the pricing relationship between the risk premium and asset i—i.e., how responsive asset i is to this common factor K.

Consider the following example of two stocks and a two-factor model.

K_1 = changes in the rate of inflation. The risk premium related to this factor is 1 percent for every 1 percent change in the rate (λ_1 = .01).

K_2 = percent growth in real GNP. The average risk premium related to this factor is 2 percent for every 1 percent change in the rate (λ_2 = .02).

λ_0 = the rate of return on a zero-systematic-risk asset (zero beta: b_{0j} = 0) is 3 percent (λ_0 = .03).

The two assets (X, Y) have the following response coefficients to these factors:

b_{x1} = the response of asset X to changes in the rate of inflation is 0.50 (b_{x1} = .50). This asset is not very responsive to changes in the rate of inflation.

b_{y1} = the response of asset Y to changes in the rate of inflation is 2.00 (b_{y1} = 2.00).

b_{x2} = the response of asset X to changes in the growth rate of real GNP is 1.50 (b_{x2} = 1.50).

b_{y2} = the response of asset Y to changes in the growth rate of real GNP is 1.75 (b_{y2} = 1.75).

These response coefficients indicate that if these are the major factors influencing asset returns, asset Y is a higher risk asset, and therefore the expected return should be greater, as shown below:

$$E_i = \lambda_0 + \lambda_1 b_{i1} + \lambda_2 b_{i2}$$
$$= .03 + (.01)b_{i1} + (.02)b_{i2}.$$

Therefore

$$E_x = .03 + (.01)(0.50) + (.02)(1.50)$$
$$= .065 = 6.5\%$$
$$E_y = .03 + (.01)(2.00) + (.02)(1.75)$$
$$= .085 = 8.5\%.$$

If the prices of the assets do not reflect these returns, we would expect investors to enter into arbitrage arrangements whereby they would sell overpriced assets short and use the proceeds to purchase the underpriced assets until the relevant prices were corrected. The point is, given these linear relationships, it should be possible to find an asset or a combination of assets with equal risk to the mispriced asset yet a higher return.

EMPIRICAL TESTS OF THE APT

Although the APT is relatively new (any academic theory less than 20 years old is considered new), it has undergone many empirical studies thus far and will likely undergo many more.

ROLL-ROSS STUDY

The Roll and Ross test followed a two-step procedure:[23]

1. Estimate the expected returns and the factor coefficients from time series data on individual asset returns.
2. Use these estimates to test the basic cross-sectional pricing conclusion implied by the APT—that is, are the expected returns for these assets consistent with the common factors derived in Step 1?

Roll and Ross tested the following pricing relationship:

H_0: There exist nonzero constants $(E_0, \lambda_i, \ldots \lambda_k)$ such that
$$E_i - E_0 = \lambda_1 b_{i1} + \lambda_2 b_{i2} + \ldots + \lambda_k b_{ik}.$$

The specific b_i coefficients were estimated using factor analysis. The authors pointed out that while the estimation procedure was generally appropriate for the model involved, there is very little known about the small sample properties of the results. Therefore, they emphasized the tentative nature of the conclusions.

The data file was daily returns contained in the Center for Research Security Prices (CRSP) files from the University of Chicago for the period July 1962 through December 1972. Stocks were put into 42 portfolios of 30 stocks each by alphabetical order (1,260 stocks), and most groups had a minimum of 2,400 observations. The estimation of the factor model indicated that the maximum reasonable number of factors was five. The intent was to err on the high side, because subsequent steps could limit the factors considered if they were not significant. The factors derived using the first portfolio were applied to all 42 portfolios, with the understanding that the importance of the various factors might differ among portfolios (e.g., the first factor in Portfolio A might not be first in Portfolio B).

Assuming a risk-free rate of 6 percent ($\lambda_0 = .06$), the subsequent analysis of the model indicated at least three important pricing factors but probably not more than four. Further, the weight on the first two factors was quite heavy, with changes in relative weights for the remaining three factors. When they allowed the model to estimate the risk-free rate (λ_0), only two factors were consistently significant, which indicated that the earlier estimate of three factors may have been an overestimate.

A subsequent test examined an alternative specification wherein individual returns are related to a security's own variance. The point is, the total variance of a security should not affect expected return if the APT is valid, because its diversifiable component would be eliminated by diver-

---

[23] Richard Roll and Stephen A. Ross, "An Empirical Investigation of the Arbitrage Pricing Theory," *Journal of Finance* 35, no. 5 (December 1980): 1073–1103.

sification, and the nondiversifiable component should be explained by the factor loadings. The test involved a cross-sectional analysis of individual returns against the five factors plus the security's own standard deviation. The results indicated that the security's own standard deviation had significant explanatory power, which was evidence against the APT. It was possible that the security's own standard deviation could skew the distribution of returns, creating positive dependence between the mean and the standard deviation. When the various parameters (return, factor loadings, and own standard deviation) were reestimated with a different set of observations, the standard deviation was significant in only 9 of 42 portfolios when one day was skipped and 7 of 42 portfolios when 3 days were skipped. Also, the impact of the factor loadings increased slightly. With a Fama-Macbeth test, the standard deviation variable was significant in only 3 of 42 portfolios. Therefore, Roll and Ross contended that after adjusting for skewness, they found the security's own standard deviation insignificant, which supports the APT.

A final test examined whether the three or four factors that affect Group A were the same as the factors that affect Group B. While it is not possible to test for the equivalence of the factors, you can test cross-sectional consistency by examining whether the λ_0 terms for the 42 groups are similar. The results yielded no evidence that the intercept terms were different, although the test was admittedly weak.

In conclusion, the authors believed that the evidence generally supported the APT but acknowledged that these initial tests were weak.

EXTENSIONS OF THE ROLL-ROSS TESTS

Cho, Elton, and Gruber provided further evidence related to the Roll and Ross study by examining the number of factors in the return-generating process that were priced.[24] Since the APT model contends that there are more factors that affect stock returns than implied by the CAPM, they used the Roll-Ross procedure for different sets of data to determine what happened to the number of factors priced in the model. You will recall that prior studies found between three and five significant factors beyond what is implied in the CAPM. They simulated returns using the zero-beta CAPM with betas derived from Wilshire's fundamental betas and with betas derived from historical data. Using the Roll-Ross factor analytic procedures to determine the number of factors implied, they found that five factors were required—more than were indicated in the earlier study. The results using historical betas implied six factors were necessary, while the Wilshire fundamental betas pointed toward three factors.

The authors concluded that more than two factors in the market influence the equilibrium returns. Even when returns are generated by a two-factor model, they contend, two or three factors are required to explain the returns. These results would support using the APT model since it allows for the consideration of these additional factors, which is not possible with the classical CAPM.

---

[24] D. Chinhyung Cho, Edwin J. Elton, and Martin J. Gruber, "On the Robustness of the Roll and Ross Arbitrage Pricing Theory," *Journal of Financial and Quantitative Analysis* 19, no. 1 (March 1984): 1–10.

Dhrymes, Friend, and Gultekin (DFG) reexamined the techniques used in the original Roll and Ross study and most subsequent studies, and contended that these techniques have several major limitations.[25] Their initial criticism was that Roll and Ross divided the total sample of stocks into numerous portfolios of 30 stocks. This division is typically necessary because of the limitations of the computer to conduct the extensive analysis for a much larger sample. While recognizing this practical constraint, DFG contended that the results for this limited portfolio differ from comparable results for a larger sample and especially for the total sample of over 1,000 stocks. Specifically, they found *no relationship* between the "factor loading" for groups of 30 stocks and a group of 240 stocks. They also suggested that there was some loss of information because of the test procedure.

The second major limitation noted by DFG was that it is not possible to identify the actual number of factors that characterize the return-generating process. When they applied the model to portfolios of different size, they determined that the number of factors changed—for example, for 15 securities it is a two-factor model; for 30 securities, a three-factor model; for 45, a four-factor model; for 60, a six-factor model; and for 90, a nine-factor model. There was also a companion problem with the multiple factors in that it was difficult to know which of them were significant in explaining the returns.

Roll and Ross have provided a nontechnical reply to the criticisms.[26] They acknowledge that the factors differ with 30 stocks versus 240, but note that the important consideration is whether the resulting estimates are *consistent,* since it is not feasible to consider all of the stocks together. They claim that they tested for consistency and it was generally supported.

As to the number of factors, they point out that it is a secondary issue, since the important consideration is how well the model explains the return-generating process compared to alternative models. In addition, they explain that one would *expect* the number of factors to increase with the sample size, because more potential relationships would arise (e.g., industries, etc.). The question is, how many are priced (i.e., are significant) in a diversified portfolio?

A subsequent paper by Dhrymes, Friend, Gultekin, and Gultekin repeated the prior tests for much larger groups of securities.[27] They found that as they increased the number of securities in each group (30, 60, and 90 securities), both the number of factors "discussed" at the first stage, as well as the number of "priced" factors at the second stage, increase, although most factors are not "priced." These results confirm the earlier results. In addition, they found that the unique, or total, standard deviation

[25] Phoebus J. Dhrymes, Irwin Friend, and N. Bulent Gultekin, "A Critical Reexamination of the Empirical Evidence on the Arbitrage Pricing Theory," *Journal of Finance* 39, no. 2 (June 1984): 323–346.

[26] Richard Roll and Stephen Ross, "A Critical Reexamination of the Empirical Evidence on the Arbitrage Pricing Theory: A Reply," *Journal of Finance* 39, no. 2 (June 1984): 347–350.

[27] Phoebus J. Dhrymes, Irwin Friend, Mustofa N. Gultekin, and N. Bulent Gultekin, "New Tests of the APT and Their Implications," *Journal of Finance* 40, no. 3 (July 1985): 659–674.

for a period was as good as or better in predicting returns in a subsequent period as the factor loadings. Also, the number of time series observations affected the number of factors discovered as well. Finally, the number of observations and the group size of securities influenced the constant term or intercept of the model. All of these findings are not favorable to the empirical relevance of APT, since they indicate extreme instability in the relationships and suggest that the risk-free rate depends upon group size and the number of observations. The relative usefulness of total standard deviation is discouraging as well.

THE APT AND ANOMALIES

An alternative set of tests of the APT or any equilibrium pricing model is how well it explains anomalies, especially those that are not explained by a competing model. Two anomalies that have been considered in this regard are the small-firm effect and the January anomaly.

A study by Reinganum addressed the APT's ability to account for the differences in average returns between small firms and large firms.[28] You will recall from Chapter 6 on efficient capital markets that a major anomaly related to the EMH was that small firms consistently experienced significantly larger risk-adjusted rates of return than large firms. This was true even after special adjustments to the beta coefficients for the small firms. Reinganum contended that this anomaly, which could not be explained by the CAPM, should be explained by the APT if the APT was to be considered a superior theory—or an empirical replacement for the CAPM.

Reinganum's test was conducted in two stages:

1. During Year Y-1, factor loadings were estimated for all securities, and securities with similar factor loadings were put into common control portfolios. The securities in each control portfolio were expected to have similar risk characteristics. (The author derived models with three, four, and five factors, and all models were tested.) During Year Y, excess security returns were computed for each stock by subtracting the average daily returns for the control portfolio from the daily returns for each of the individual stocks in the portfolio. Assuming that all stocks within a control portfolio have equal risk according to the APT, they should have similar average returns, and the average excess return for stocks in a control portfolio should be zero.

2. Given the excess returns during Year Y, all the stocks were ranked on the basis of their market value at the end of Year Y-1, and the excess returns of the firms in the bottom 10 percent of the size distribution were combined (equal weights) to form the average excess returns for Portfolio MV1. Similarly, nine other portfolios were formed, with MV10 containing excess returns for the largest firms.

---

[28] Marc R. Reinganum, "The Arbitrage Pricing Theory: Some Empirical Results," *Journal of Finance* 36, no. 2 (May 1981): 313–321.

Under the null hypothesis, the ten portfolios should possess identical average excess returns, which should be insignificantly different from zero. If the ten portfolios do not have identical average excess returns, this evidence would be *inconsistent* with the APT.

The sample ranged from 1,457 in 1963 to over 2,500 during the mid-1970s. The ranking procedure, as described in Step 2, was carried out for each year, because the market values change, and firms are added and deleted. As stated, if the average excess returns for the ten portfolios equal zero, then the evidence supports the APT.

The results of the tests were *clearly inconsistent with the APT.* Specifically:

> The average excess returns of the ten portfolios are clearly not equal to zero, regardless of whether a three, four, or five factor model is employed to account for APT risk. The small firm portfolio, MV1, possesses a positive and statistically significant average excess return. On the other hand, the large firm portfolio, MV10, is characterized by a negative, but statistically significant, average excess return . . . a conservative estimate of the mean difference in excess returns between the small and large firms might be about twenty-five percent (250 $\times$ .1%) on an annual basis. . . . the point estimates of the mean excess portfolio returns of MV1 through MV10 are perfectly ordered with firm size. That is, the rank correlation between average portfolio excess returns and medium stock values within a portfolio is exactly -1.0.[29]

The author subsequently tested for significant differences between the returns for individual portfolios and also examined the difference between the high and low portfolio on a year-by-year basis. Both tests confirmed the overall conclusions that the low-market-value portfolios outperformed the high-market-value portfolios regardless of whether excess returns were derived from the three-, four-, or five-factor model. The author concluded that the APT is not supported by the results of this study, although it was acknowledged that the test was a joint test of several hypotheses implicit in the theory and that it was not possible to pinpoint the error.

A subsequent study by Chen supported the APT model compared to the CAPM, but also provided evidence related to the small-firm effect that was contrary to Reinganum.[30] Prior to discussing the tests, the author proposed that problems with a limited sample and multiple factors were related to the *testing* of the theory and should not reflect on the theory itself. The analysis employed 180 stocks and, based upon prior studies, the author selected five factors. A comparison of the cross-sectional results using the APT versus the CAPM showed that the first factor was highly correlated with beta, but the subsequent direct tests clearly favored the APT over the CAPM. When Chen considered performance measurement with the two models, he noted that if the CAPM is misspecified and does not capture all the information related to returns, this remaining infor-

---

[29] Ibid., 317.

[30] Nai-fu Chen, "Some Empirical Tests of the Theory of Arbitrage Pricing," *Journal of Finance* 38, no. 5 (December 1983): 1393–1414.

mation will show up in the residual series, and possibly the APT can provide further factors to explain these residual returns, which would make the APT superior. He concluded that the CAPM was indeed misspecified in this instance and that the missing price information was picked up by the APT.

The final tests examined whether some major variables have explanatory power after the factor loadings from the APT model. Specifically, if any variables are priced after the factor loadings are accounted for, it would cause one to reject the APT. Two variables important to prior CAPM studies were own variance and firm size. Regarding the own-variance test, the author concluded, "we cannot reject the null hypothesis that the APT is correct, and the own variance has no explanatory power net of factor loadings."[31]

The tests related to firm size divided the sample by size and formed portfolios with the same factor loadings. The results led the author to conclude that the firm size had no explanatory power after adjusting for risk by the factor loadings. Again, these results are in contrast to the earlier results by Reinganum.

APT AND THE JANUARY EFFECT. Another well-known anomaly discussed in Chapter 6 is the persistent strong returns in January (five to ten times stronger than in any other month). Gultekin and Gultekin considered the ability of the APT model to adjust for this anomaly.[32] The APT model was estimated for each month and risk premia were always significant in January for all groups, but rarely priced in other months. Put another way, when January and December returns were excluded, the risk premia were priced in only one of 30 groups. It was concluded that the APT model, like the CAPM, can explain the risk-return relation only in January, which indicates that the APT model is not able to explain this anomaly any better than the CAPM.

Burmeister and McElroy used both measured and unmeasured factors to estimate a linear factor model (LFM), the APT, and a CAPM.[33] They likewise found a significant January effect that was not captured by any of the models. Going beyond the January effect, they rejected the CAPM in favor of the APT.

THE APT AND INFLATION

In addition to these specific tests of the theory, a paper by Elton, Gruber, and Rentzler extended the APT to consider the impact of inflation on the return for assets.[34] They derived an equilibrium model of real returns assuming an impact of inflation. Subsequently, assuming the inflation factor was not priced, they employed the arbitrage pricing model, which was

---

[31] Ibid., 1406.

[32] Mustofa N. Gultekin and N. Bulent Gultekin, "Stock Return Anomalies and the Tests of APT," *Journal of Finance* 42, no. 5 (December 1987): 1213–1224.

[33] Edwin Burmeister and Marjorie B. McElroy, "Joint Estimation of Factor Sensitivities and Risk Premia for the Arbitrage Pricing Theory," *Journal of Finance* 43, no. 3 (July 1988): 721–733.

[34] Edwin Elton, Martin Gruber, and Joel Rentzler, "The Arbitrage Pricing Model and Returns on Assets under Uncertain Inflation," *Journal of Finance* 38, no. 2 (May 1983): 525–537.

made equivalent to the mean-variance model, and compared it to prior CAPM models that considered inflation. They contended that it was important to develop APT models with factors that were not only statistically identifiable using a factor analysis model but that had economic meaning. That is, they felt it should be possible to identify the specific economic variables that affect prices such as inflation and growth in real GNP.

THE SHANKEN CHALLENGE TO TESTABILITY OF THE APT

Similar to Roll's critique of the CAPM, a set of papers by Shanken challenged whether the APT can be empirically verified.[35] Rather than questioning the specific tests or methods used to test the APT, the author questioned whether the APT is more susceptible to testing than the CAPM. He pointed out that the usual empirical formulation of the test is to determine that the set of asset returns conforms to a K factor model derived from factor analysis. Part of the problem is that if returns are not explained by such a model, it is not considered a rejection of the model; however, if the factors do explain returns, it is considered support. Also, there is a real problem with the supposed advantage that the factors need not be observable because under such conditions, equivalent sets of securities may conform to different factor structures, and the empirical formulation of the APT then may yield different implications regarding the expected returns for a given set of securities.

This implies that the theory is not capable of explaining differential returns between securities, because it is necessary to identify the relevant factor structure that will help explain the differential returns—but the factor analysis model is not capable of doing this. This need to identify the relevant factor structure that affects asset returns is similar to the CAPM problem of identifying the true market portfolio. Therefore, there is a similar problem with testing the theory: Before you can test the CAPM properly, you must identify and use the true market portfolio. Similarly, you must identify the relevant factor structure that affects security returns before you can test the APT.

The controversy on this topic continued with an article by Dybvig and Ross suggesting that the APT is testable as an equality rather than the "empirical APT" proposed by Shanken.[36] The reply by Shanken contended that what has developed is a set of equilibrium pricing models—that is, "equilibrium APTs" that are testable, but the original arbitrage based models ("APT") are not testable, as specified in his original article.[37]

ALTERNATIVE TESTING TECHNIQUES. In addition to these articles that express a concern with prior tests, two articles have proposed other statistical techniques for testing the APT model. Jobson proposes that the APT

---

[35] Jay Shanken, "The Arbitrage Pricing Theory: Is It Testable?" *Journal of Finance* 37, no. 5 (December 1982): 1129–1140.

[36] Philip H. Dybvig and Stephen A. Ross, "Yes, the APT is Testable," *Journal of Finance* 40, no. 4 (September 1985): 1173–1188.

[37] Jay Shanken, "Multi-Beta CAPM or Equilibrium APT?: A Reply," *Journal of Finance* 40, no. 4 (September 1985): 1189–1196.

can be tested by using a multivariate linear regression model and shows how this test is related to the Sharpe measure of portfolio performance.[38] Brown and Weinstein propose a new approach to estimating and testing asset pricing models employing a bilinear paradigm.[39] Specifically, they contend that the economic content of any equilibrium asset pricing model contains potentially refutable constraints on the set of parameters of the return-generating process. Given a set of characteristics that are specific to a security, there is a linear relationship for all securities that relates expected returns to these characteristics. The coefficients in the linear model represent the prices of the alternative characteristics. Notably, all asset pricing models require that the market price of each characteristic be common to all securities. A simple test of this bilinear model constraint that can be applied to many well-known asset pricing models is applied to the arbitrage pricing model (APM).

When Brown and Weinstein implemented the test using Roll-Ross data, the results appeared to conflict with the APM at standard levels of significance. When they adjusted the test to recognize the large sample size, the results were consistent with a three-factor APM but tended to reject the five- and seven-factor model. Based upon several variations of factors, they concluded that there was a limited number of factors, which is consistent with several prior studies (though not Gultekin, et al).

SUMMARY

When we relax several of the major assumptions of the CAPM, the required modifications are reasonably minor and do not change the overall concept of the model. Empirical studies have indicated stable portfolio betas, especially when enough observations were used to derive the betas and when there was adequate volume. Most tests confirmed the expected relationship between returns and systematic risk, with allowance for the zero-beta model.

In contrast, Roll contended that it is not possible to empirically derive a true market portfolio, so it is not possible to test the CAPM model properly or to use it to evaluate portfolio performance. Ross subsequently devised an alternative asset pricing model (the APT) with fewer assumptions that does not require a true market portfolio (though it is somewhat more complex mathematically). The results from the empirical tests of the APT have thus far been mixed. Also, Shanken contends that the nature of the tests currently conducted are such that it is impossible to derive evidence to reject the theory.

In conclusion, it is probably safe to assume that both the CAPM and APT will continue to be used to price capital assets. Coincident with their use will be further empirical tests of both theories, the ultimate goal being

---

[38] J. D. Jobson, "A Multivariate Linear Regression Test for the Arbitrage Pricing Theory," *Journal of Finance* 37, no. 4 (September 1982): 1037–1042.

[39] Stephen J. Brown and Mark I. Weinstein, "A New Approach to Testing Asset Pricing Models: The Bilinear Paradigm," *Journal of Finance* 38, no. 3 (June 1983): 711–743.

to determine which theory does the best job of explaining current and future returns.

QUESTIONS

1. In the empirical testing of the CAPM, what are two major questions of concern? Why are they important?

2. Briefly discuss why it is important for beta coefficients to be stationary over time.

3. Discuss the empirical results relative to beta stability for individual stocks and portfolios of stocks.

4. Why is the stability of beta for portfolios of stocks considered more relevant than that of individual stocks?

5. In the tests of the relationship between systematic risk (beta) and return, what are you looking for?

6. Draw an ideal SML. Based upon the empirical results, what did the actual relationship look like relative to the ideal relationship implied by the CAPM?

7. According to the CAPM, what assets are included in the market portfolio, and what are the relative weightings? In empirical studies of the CAPM, what are the typical proxies used for the market portfolio?

8. Assuming the empirical proxy for the market portfolio is not a good proxy, what factors related to the CAPM will be affected?

9. What are the major assumptions required by the APT? What are some critical assumptions of the CAPM that are not required by the APT?

10. Briefly discuss one study that does not support the APT and another that does.

11. Briefly discuss why Shanken contends that the APT is not testable.

12. *CFA Exam III (June 1986)*: Multi-factor models of security returns have received increased attention. The Arbitrage Pricing Theory (APT) probably has drawn the most attention and has been proposed as a replacement for the Capital Asset Pricing Model (CAPM).

12a. Briefly explain the primary differences between APT and CAPM. [5 minutes]

12b. Identify the four systematic factors suggested by Roll and Ross that determine as asset's riskiness. Explain how these factors affect an asset's expected rate of return. [10 minutes]

PROBLEMS

1. Given the following results, indicate what will happen to the beta for Stock E, relative to the market proxy, compared to the beta relative to the true market portfolio:

YEARLY RATES OF RETURN

YEAR	STOCK (PERCENT)	MARKET PROXY (PERCENT)	TRUE MARKET (PERCENT)
1	10	8	6
2	20	14	11
3	−14	−10	−7
4	−20	−18	−12
5	15	12	10

Discuss the reason for the differences in measured beta. Does the relationship suggested appear reasonable? Why or why not?

2. Draw the implied SMLs for the following two sets of conditions:

2a. $RFR = .07$; $R_m(S + P\ 500) = .16$

2b. $R_z = .09$; $R_m(True) = .18$
Under which set of conditions would it be more difficult for a portfolio manager to be superior?

3. Using the graph and equations from Problem 2, which of the following portfolios would be superior?

3a. $R_a = 11\%$; $\beta = .09$

3b. $R_b = 14\%$; $\beta = 1.00$

3c. $R_c = 12\%$; $\beta = -.40$

3d. $R_d = 20\%$; $\beta = 1.10$
Does it matter which SML you use?

4a. Draw the Security Market Line for each of the following conditions:

(1) $RFR = .08$ R_m (proxy) $= .12$

(2) $R_z = .06$ R_m (true) $= .15$

4b. Radius Tire has the following results for the last six periods. Calculate and compare the betas using each index.

PERIOD	RETURN OF RADIUS (PERCENT)	PROXY SPECIFIC INDEX (PERCENT)	TRUE GENERAL INDEX (PERCENT)
1	10	12	15
2	12	10	13
3	−12	−9	−8
4	17	14	18
5	20	25	28
6	−5	−10	0

4c. If the current period return for Radius is 11 percent, are superior results being obtained?

5. Under the following conditions, what are the expected returns for Stocks J and L?

$$\lambda_0 = .05$$
$$K_1 = .02 \qquad K_2 = .04$$
$$b_{Ji} = 0.80 \qquad b_{J2} = 1.40$$
$$b_{L1} = 1.60 \qquad b_{L2} = 2.25$$

REFERENCES

Black, Fischer, Michael Jensen, and Myron Scholes. "The Capital Asset Pricing Model: Some Empirical Tests" in *Studies in the Theory of Capital Markets.* Edited by Michael Jensen. New York: Praeger Publishers, 1976.

Black, Fischer. "Capital Market Equilibrium with Restricted Borrowing." *Journal of Business* 45, no. 3 (July 1972).

Blume, Marshall E. "On the Assessment of Risk." *Journal of Finance* 26, no. 1 (March 1971).

Brown, Stephen J., and Mark I. Weinstein, "A New Approach to Testing Asset Pricing Models: The Bilinear Paradigm." *Journal of Finance* 38, no. 3 (June 1983).

Cho, D. Chinhyung, Edwin J. Elton, and Martin J. Gruber. "On the Robustness of the Roll and Ross Arbitrage Pricing Theory." *Journal of Financial and Quantitative Analysis* 19, no. 1 (March 1984).

Dhen, Nai-Fu. "Some Empirical Tests of the Theory of Arbitrage Pricing." *Journal of Finance* 38, no. 5 (December 1983).

Dhrymes, Phoebus J., Irwin Friend, and N. Bulent Gultekin. "A Critical Reexamination of the Empirical Evidence on the Arbitrage Pricing Theory." *Journal of Finance* 39, no 2 (June 1984).

Elton, Edwin, Martin Gruber, and Joel Rentzler. "The Arbitrage Pricing Model and Returns on Assets under Uncertain Inflation." *Journal of Finance* 38, no. 2 (May 1983).

Fama, Eugene, and R. MacBeth. "Risk, Return, and Equilibrium: Empirical Tests." *Journal of Political Economy* 81, no. 2 (May–June 1973).

Huberman, Gur. "Arbitrage Pricing Theory: A Simple Approach," *Journal of Economic Theory* 28, no. 1 (October 1982).

Jobson, J. D. "A Multivariate Linear Regression Test for the Arbitrage Pricing Theory." *Journal of Finance* 37, no. 4 (September 1982).

Litzenberger, Robert, and K. Ramaswamy. "The Effect of Personal Taxes and Dividends on Capital Asset Prices." *Journal of Financial Economics* 6, no. 2 (June 1979).

Miller, Morton H., and Myron Scholes. "Rates of Return in Relation to Risk: A Re-Examination of Some Recent Findings" in *Studies in the Theory of Capital Markets.* Edited by Michael Jensen. New York: Praeger Publishers, 1976.

Reinganum, Marc R. "The Arbitrage Pricing Theory: Some Empirical Results." *Journal of Finance* 36, no. 2 (May 1981).

Roll, Richard. "Ambiguity when Performance is Measured by the Securities Market Line." *Journal of Finance* 33, no. 4, (September 1978).

Roll, Richard. "A Critique of the Asset Pricing Theory's Tests." *Journal of Financial Economics* 4, no. 4 (March 1977).

Roll, Richard. "Performance Evaluation and Benchmark Error I." *Journal of Portfolio Management* 6, no. 4 (Summer 1980).

Roll, Richard. "Performance Evaluation and Benchmark Error II." *Journal of Portfolio Management* 7, no. 2 (Winter 1981).

Roll, Richard, and Stephen A. Ross. "An Empirical Investigation of the Arbitrage Pricing Theory." *Journal of Finance* 35, no. 5 (December 1980).

Roll, Richard, and Stephen A. Ross. "A Critical Reexamination of the Empirical Evidence on the Arbitrage Pricing Theory: A Reply." *Journal of Finance* 39, no. 2 (June 1984).

Ross, Stephen A. "The Arbitrage Theory of Capital Asset Pricing." *Journal of Economic Theory* 13, no. 2 (December 1976).

Ross, Stephen A. "Risk, Return, and Arbitrage" in *Risk and Return in Finance.* Edited by I. Friend, and J. Bicksler. Cambridge: Ballinger, 1977.

Shanken, Jay. "The Arbitrage Pricing Theory: Is It Testable?" *Journal of Finance* 37, no. 5 (December 1982).

Shanken, Jay. "Multivariate Proxies and Asset Pricing Relations." *Journal of Financial Economics* 18, no. 1 (March 1987).

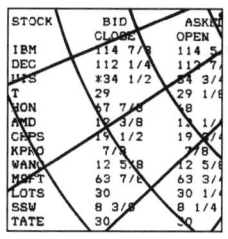

CHAPTER 18

BOND PORTFOLIO MANAGEMENT STRATEGIES

Successful bond portfolio management involves far more than mastering a myriad of technical information. Such information is useful only to the extent that it helps generate higher risk-adjusted returns. In this chapter, we shift attention from the technical dimensions of bond portfolio management to the equally important strategic dimension.

ALTERNATIVE BOND PORTFOLIO STRATEGIES

Bond portfolio management strategies can be divided into four groups:[1]

1. Buy-and-hold strategy
2. Active management strategies
   a. Interest rate anticipation
   b. Valuation analysis
   c. Credit analysis
   d. Spread analysis
   e. Bond swaps
3. Matched-funding techniques
   a. Dedicated portfolio, exact cash match
   b. Dedicated portfolio, optimal cash match and reinvestment
   c. Classical ("pure") immunization
   d. Horizon matching
4. Contingent procedures (structured active management)
   a. Contingent immunization
   b. Other contingent procedures

---

[1] This breakdown benefited from the discussion in Martin L. Leibowitz, "The Dedicated Bond Portfolio in Pension Funds—Part I: Motivations and Basics," *Financial Analysts Journal* 42, no. 1 (January–February 1986): 61–75.

We will discuss each of these alternatives because they are all viable for certain portfolios with different needs and risk profiles. Prior to the 1960s, only the first two groups were available, and most portfolios were managed on the basis of buy and hold. The 1960s and early 1970s saw growing interest in alternative active management strategies. The investment environment since the late 1970s has been characterized by record-breaking inflation and interest rates, extremely volatile bond markets, the introduction of new financial instruments in response to volatility, and the development of several new funding techniques or contingent portfolio management techniques to meet the emerging needs of institutional clients. Several of these techniques have become possible because of the rediscovery of duration in the early 1970s. Following discussion of the alternative strategies, we will consider the role of bonds in a global portfolio context. We will then conclude with a brief discussion of bond market efficiency.

BUY-AND-HOLD STRATEGY

The simplest strategy is to buy and hold. Obviously not unique to bond investors, it involves finding issues with desired quality, coupon levels, term to maturity, and important indenture provisions, such as call feature. Buy-and-hold investors do not consider active trading to achieve attractive returns but rather look for vehicles whose maturities (or duration) approximate their stipulated investment horizon in order to reduce price and reinvestment risk. Many successful bond investors and institutional portfolio managers follow a modified buy-and-hold strategy wherein an investment is made in an issue with the intention of holding it until the end of the investment horizon, but they still actively look for opportunities to trade into more desirable positions.[2]

Whether the investor follows a strict or modified buy-and-hold approach, the key ingredient is finding investment vehicles that possess attractive maturity and yield features. The strategy does not restrict the investor to accept whatever the market has to offer, nor does it imply that selectivity is unimportant. Attractive high-yielding issues with desirable features and quality standards are actively sought. As an example, these investors recognize that agency issues generally provide incremental returns relative to treasuries with little sacrifice in quality, that utilities provide higher returns than comparably rated industrials, and that various call features affect the risk and realized yield of an issue. Thus, the successful buy-and-hold investor uses his knowledge of markets and issue characteristics to seek out attractive yields. Aggressive buy-and-hold investors also incorporate timing considerations into their investment decisions using their knowledge of market rates and expectations.

---

[2] Obviously, if the strategy becomes too modified, it would become one of the active strategies.

ACTIVE MANAGEMENT STRATEGIES[3]

INTEREST RATE ANTICIPATION

Interest rate anticipation is perhaps the riskiest strategy because it involves relying on uncertain forecasts of future interest rate behavior. The idea is to preserve capital when an increase in interest rates is anticipated and achieve attractive capital gains when they are expected to decline. Such objectives are usually attained by altering the maturity (duration) structure of the portfolio (i.e., reducing it when interest rates are expected to increase and increasing it when a decline in yields is anticipated). Thus, the risk in such portfolio restructuring is largely a function of these duration (maturity) alterations. When maturities are shortened to preserve capital, substantial income and the opportunity for capital gains could be sacrificed. Similarly, the portfolio shifts prompted by anticipation of a decline in rates are very risky because if we assume that we are at a peak in interest rates, it is likely that the yield curve is downward-sloping, which means that bond coupons will decline with maturity. Therefore, the investor is sacrificing current income by shifting from high-coupon short bonds to longer-duration bonds. At the same time, the portfolio is exposed to greater price volatility that could work against the portfolio if there is an unexpected increase in yields. In contrast, the portfolio adjustments prompted by anticipation of an increase in rates involves less risk of an absolute capital loss. When you reduce the maturity, the worst that can happen is that interest income is reduced and/or capital gains forgone (opportunity cost).

Once future (expected) interest rates have been determined, the procedure relies largely on technical matters. Assume that you expect an increase in interest rates and want to preserve your capital by reducing the duration of your portfolio. A popular choice would be high-yielding, short-term obligations such as Treasury bills. While your primary concern is to preserve capital, you would nevertheless look for the best return possible given the maturity constraint. *Liquidity* is also important, because after the rate increase, yields may experience a period of stability before they decline, and you would want the ability to shift positions *quickly* in order to benefit from the higher income and/or potential capital gains.

One way to shorten maturities is to use a *cushion bond*, which is a high-yielding, long-term obligation that carries a coupon substantially above the current market rate and that, due to its current call feature and call price, has a market price lower than it should be given current market yields. With the price of the issue being held back because of its call exposure, its yield is higher than normal. An example would be a 10-year bond with a 12 percent coupon, currently callable at 110. If current market rates are 8 percent, this bond would normally have a price of about 127; but because of its call price, it will stay close to 110, and its yield will be about 10 percent rather than 8 percent. Knowledgeable bond investors look for cushion bonds when they expect a modest increase in rates, since such issues provide attractive current income and also protection against

---

[3] The discussion in this subsection benefited from H. Gifford Fong, "Active Strategies for Managing Bond Portfolios," *The Revolution in Techniques for Managing Bond Portfolios* (Charlottesville, Va.: The Institute of Chartered Financial Analysts, 1983), 21–38.

capital loss (because they are trading at an abnormally high yield, market rates would have to rise to their level before their price would react).[4]

The portfolio manager who anticipates higher interest rates, therefore, has two simple strategies available: shorten the duration of the portfolio and/or look for an attractive cushion bond.[5] In either case, you would want very liquid issues.

A totally different posture is assumed by investors anticipating a decline in interest rates. The significant risks involved in restructuring a portfolio to take advantage of a decline are balanced by the potential for substantial capital gains and holding period returns. When you expect lower interest rates, the basic rule is to increase the duration of the portfolio, because the longer the duration, the greater the price volatility. Liquidity is also important, because you want to close out the position *quickly* when the drop in rates has been completed.

Given the constraints of duration and liquidity, you should look for the market segment that promises the greatest price reaction to the decline in interest rates. Generally, you would look for long maturities and low coupons (i.e., long-duration securities). An exception would be if you expected only a modest decrease in yields, in which case you might consider long-term current coupon obligations that would be more interest sensitive than deep discounted issues. Further, because *interest sensitivity* is critical, high-grade securities should be used, such as Treasuries, agencies, or corporates rated AAA through BAA; the higher the quality of the obligation, the more sensitive it is to interest rate changes.

VALUATION ANALYSIS

With valuation analysis, the portfolio manager attempts to select bonds based upon their intrinsic value. The bond's value is determined based upon its characteristics and the average value of these characteristics in the marketplace. As an example, long maturity might be worth an added 60 basis points relative to short maturity (i.e., the maturity spread); a given deferred call feature might require a higher or lower yield; a specified sinking fund would likewise mean higher or lower required yields. Given all the characteristics of the bond and their normal cost, you would determine the required yield and the implied intrinsic value for alternative bonds, then compare this derived value to the prevailing market price to determine which bonds are undervalued or overvalued. Based upon your confidence in the characteristic costs, you would buy undervalued issues and ignore or sell overvalued issues.

CREDIT ANALYSIS

A credit analysis strategy involves detailed analysis of the bond issuer to determine expected changes in its default risk. This involves attempting to project changes in the quality ratings assigned to bonds by the four rating agencies discussed in Chapter 11. These rating changes are affected

---

[4] In our example, rates would have to increase to almost 10 percent before there would be much of a reaction.

[5] For an extended discussion of cushion bonds, see Sidney Homer and Martin L. Leibowitz, *Inside the Yield Book* (Englewood Cliffs, N.J.: Prentice-Hall, 1972), Chapter 5.

by internal changes in the entity (e.g., changes in important financial ratios) and also by changes in the external environment (i.e., changes in the economy). During periods of strong economic expansion, even financially weak firms may prosper. In contrast, during severe economic contractions, even normally strong firms may be unable to meet financial obligations. Therefore, historically there has been a strong cyclical pattern to rating changes—typically, downgradings increase during economic contractions, and vice versa. The period of 1985–1987 was an exception; the number of downgradings increased substantially even though it was a period of economic expansion.[6]

To employ credit analysis as a management strategy, it is necessary to project rating changes *prior* to the actual announcement by the rating agencies. As the subsequent discussion on bond market efficiency will note, the market adjusts rather quickly to rating changes—especially downgradings. Therefore, you should acquire issues expected to experience upgradings and sell or avoid those expected to be downgraded.

ANALYSIS OF JUNK BONDS. One of the most obvious opportunities for credit analysis is the analysis of high-yield (junk) bonds. As demonstrated by several studies, the yield differential between junk bonds that are rated below BBB and Treasury securities ranges from about 250 basis points for BB 10-year bonds to over 500 basis points for CCC, 20-year bonds. Note that these yield differentials vary substantially over time, as shown by the time series plot in Figure 18.1. As an example, the B, 10-year yield spread was about 600 basis points during 1986 and shortly after the 1987 crash, as low as 300 basis points in 1985, and less than 400 basis points on several occasions. As pointed out by Altman and Nammacher, even considering the default record of high-yield bonds, their *net* return has been superior to higher-rated debt.[7] Also, because the size of firms issuing high-yield debt has been declining, credit analysis of these issues will be more important in determining future portfolio results.

In the Altman-Nammacher book it is suggested that the *Z-score model* used to predict bankruptcy can also be used to predict default for these high-yield bonds or at least can be used as a gauge of changes in credit quality. The Z-score model combines traditional financial measures with a multivariate technique known as *discriminant analysis* to derive a set of weights for specified variables that will lead to an overall credit score (zeta score) for each firm. The model is of the form

$$\text{Zeta} = a_0 + a_1 X_1 + a_2 X_2 + a_3 X_3 + \ldots + a_n X_n,$$

where

Zeta = overall credit score

$X_1 \ldots X_n$ **= explanatory variables (ratios and market measures)**

$a_0 \ldots a_n$ **= weightings or coefficients.**

---

[6] For a discussion of this pattern, see Frank K. Reilly, "The Growing Importance of Credit Analysis," Working Paper, University of Notre Dame (April 1988).

[7] Edward I. Altman and Scott A. Nammacher, *Investing in Junk Bonds* (New York: John Wiley & Sons, 1987).

FIGURE 18.1

Yield Spread (Basis Points) between Ten-Year B and BB Corporate Bonds and Ten-Year Treasury Bonds

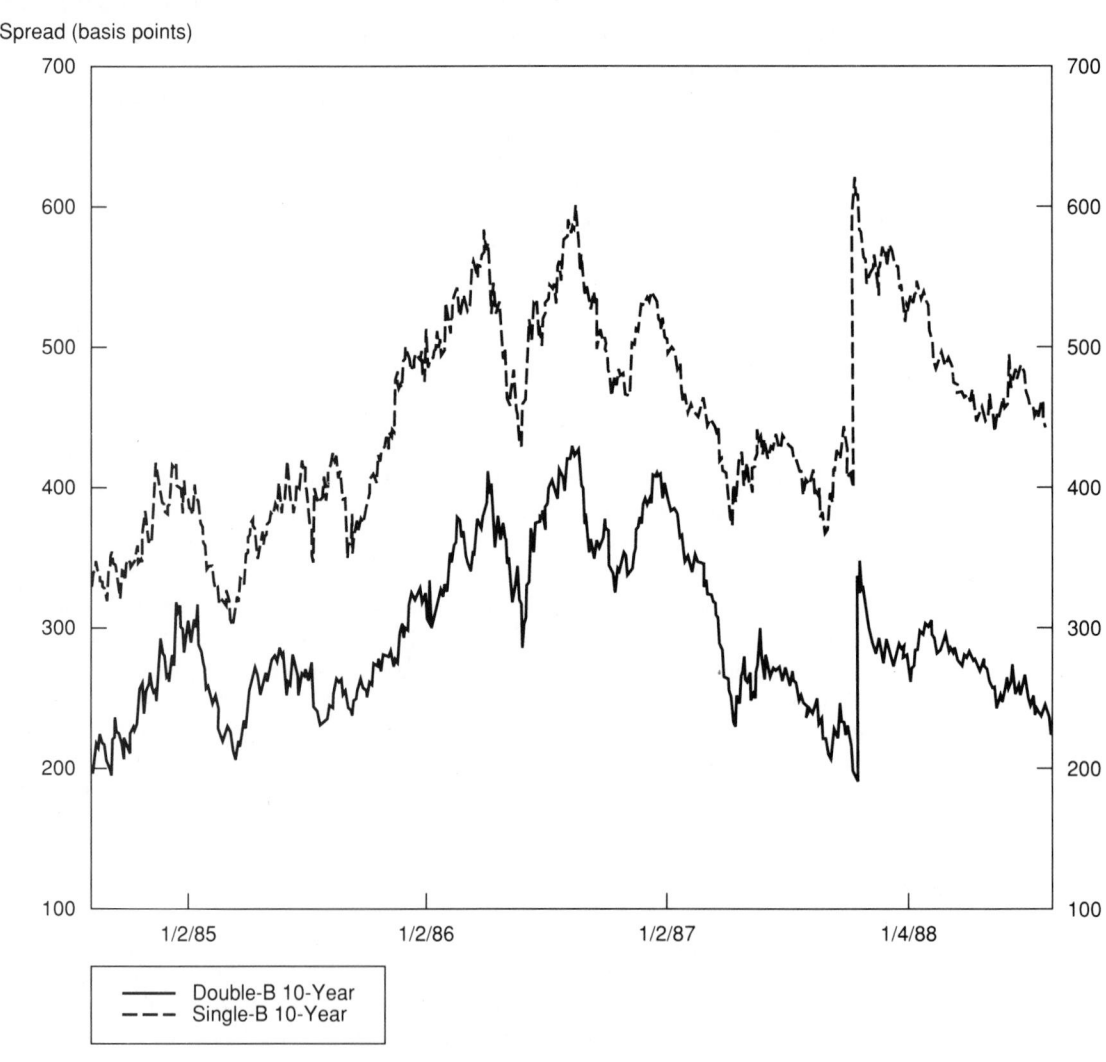

Spread (basis points)

Double-B 10-Year
Single-B 10-Year

Note: Data includes price information through 8/9/88.

Source: High Yield Bond Research Group, Kidder Peabody & Co., New York.

The final model used in this analysis included the following seven financial measures:

X_1 = **profitability: earnings before interest and taxes (EBIT)/total assets**

X_2 = **stability of earnings measure: the standard error of estimate of EBIT/ TA (normalized for 10 years)**

X_3 = debt service capabilities: EBIT/interest charges

X_4 = cumulative profitability: retained earnings/total assets

X_5 = liquidity: current assets/current liabilities

X_6 = capitalization levels: market value of equity/total capital (5-year average)

X_7 = size: total tangible assets (normalized).

The weightings, or coefficients, for the variables were not reported. Using the weights derived on a sample of firms that defaulted, it was contended that during 1985 the zeta model anticipated the 13 defaults considered. Specifically, in all cases the zeta score was below zero, which was stipulated as the cutoff between healthy and distressed firms. In another group of 20 defaults the zero cutoff would have identified 18 of the 20.

In contrast to using a model that provides a composite credit score, most analysts and investment houses simply adapt their basic corporate bond analysis techniques to the unique needs of evaluating these low-quality credits that have characteristics of common stock. Howe, in a paper and subsequent book on the analysis of high-yield bonds, claims that the analysis is the same as with any bond except that five areas of analysis should be expanded to answer the following questions.[8] First, what is the firm's *competitive position* in terms of cost and pricing? This can be critical to a small firm. Second, what is the firm's *cash flow* relative to cash requirements for interest, research, growth, and periods of economic decline? Also, with regard to cash flow, what is the firm's borrowing capacity that can serve as a safety net and provide flexibility? Third, what is the *liquidity value of the firm's assets,* and are these assets available for liquidation (are there any claims against them)? In many cases, asset sales are a critical part of the strategy for a leveraged buyout. Fourth, how good is the *total management team,* including general administration, finance, marketing, and production? Are all of them committed and capable of operating in the high-risk environment of this firm? Finally, what is the firm's *financial leverage* on an absolute basis and also on a market-adjusted basis (using market value for equity and debt)?

Hynes suggests that the following four areas require subjective analysis as part of the process of evaluating cash flows when analyzing a leveraged buyout (which typically involves the issuance of high-yield debt):[9]

1. Inherent business risk
2. Earnings growth potential

---

[8] Jane Tripp Howe, "Credit Considerations in Evaluating High Yield Bonds" in *The Handbook of Fixed Income Securities,* edited by Frank J. Fabozzi and Irving M. Pollack (Homewood, Ill.: Dow-Jones Irwin, 1987); Jane Tripp Howe, *Junk Bonds: Analysis and Portfolio Strategies* (Chicago: Probus Publishing Co., 1988).

[9] Joseph Hynes, "Key Risk Factors for LBOs," *Speculative Grade Debt Credit Review* (New York: Standard & Poor's Corp.), June 15, 1987.

3. Asset redevelopment potential
4. Refinancing capability

In addition to the potentially higher financial risk, there may be an increase in business risk if the firm sells off some operations that have favorable risk characteristics with the remaining operations—that is, business risk would increase if the firm sells a division or company that has low correlation of earnings with other units of the firm. In addition, a change in management operating philosophy might negatively affect operating earnings. The management of leveraged buyout (LBO) firms are known for making optimistic growth estimates related to sales and earnings, so the analyst should evaluate these very critically with an eye toward the historical record. Asset divestiture plans are often a major element of an LBO, since they provide necessary capital used to reduce the substantial debt taken on as part of the buyout. Therefore, it is important to examine the liquidity of the assets, their estimated values, and the timing of these programs. You must ascertain whether the sale prices are reasonable and whether the timing is realistic. If it is too tight, it could affect the price received and the debt reduction program. At the same time, if the divestiture program is successful in terms of selling prices received (they are above normal expectations) or timing (they are sold ahead of schedule), this can be grounds for an upgrading of the debt. Finally, it is necessary to constantly monitor the firm's refinancing flexibility—what refinancing will be necessary, what does the schedule look like, and does it appear that the bondholders and other capital suppliers will be receptive to the refinancing.

Because of the growth of high-yield bonds, several investment houses have developed specialized high-yield groups that examine specific high-yield issues and also monitor the aggregate junk bond market in terms of yield spreads. The high-yield bond research group at Kidder, Peabody & Co. has a weekly publication, *High Yield Sector Report*, that typically contains a commentary on the overall high-yield market in terms of issue supply and demand and a review of changes in the spreads for bonds in alternative rating groups (e.g., BB, 10-year issues), and various major industry sectors that issued high-yield debt (e.g., airlines, energy, transportation). Also, a new issue section indicates recently released issues and a preview of forthcoming issues. Finally, there is a fairly detailed discussion of a specific high-yield issue, the firm, and the overall outlook for the issue.

Merrill Lynch has a monthly publication entitled *High Yield Securities Research* that provides an overview of the market and several specific reviews of individual industries and firms within these main industries (e.g., retail, steel, building products, and textile). The firm also initiated a high-yield master bond return index in October 1984, and it tracks the yield spreads for high-yield bonds relative to overall industrials and treasury issues.

In July 1986 Salomon Brothers initiated a monthly publication entitled *High Yield Market Update* that presents monthly and cumulative long-term returns for these high-yield indexes (long-term and intermediate-term corporates, long-term utilities), as well as spreads between rating categories and relative to appropriate treasuries. There is also a commentary on a timely topic within the high-yield market (e.g., "Recent Changes in the Airline Industry").

Morgan Stanley & Co. has had a major interest in the high-yield bond area for several years and provided a substantial amount of the material and data used by Altman and Nammacher in several papers and the book discussed earlier. The firm also publishes a monthly review regarding the market, *High Performance.* Each issue considers some topic related to the overall high-yield market, such as "The Anatomy of the High Yield Market," "Group Effect in High Yield Bonds," "Analyzing Default Risk," and "Market Efficiency: The News Management Anamoly." There is also an analysis of individual industries and firms that have issued or are issuing high-yield debt securities.

In addition, several bond rating firms conduct research on these industries and firms in order to assign the specific ratings. Standard & Poor's has a publication entitled, *Speculative Grade Debt Credit Review* that discusses general problems involved in credit analysis in this area (e.g., "Junk Bond Rating Policies Revised," "Junk Bond Rating Change Potential"). There is also a review of several major industries and, finally, a specific comment on most outstanding issues by industry grouping. McCarthy, Crisanti and Maffei is a small bond rating firm that has had a major impact on junk bond research.[10] Similar to other firms in this field, its general approach toward these bond issues is to utilize sound fundamental credit research on a more intensive basis than is normally employed when analyzing higher-grade bonds. In this regard, it focuses on two critical factors: cash flow and financial cushion. Because cash flow is the primary source of funds for debt service, this firm provides a detailed projection of it for two years. The financial cushion includes items like asset sales, unused bank lines of credit, discretionary capital spending, and cost cutting. This cushion is considered to be the fall-back position, or safety net, in case the future results fall below the target needed to meet financial requirements.

In summary, the substantial increase in the amount of junk bonds issued and outstanding is matched by an increase in research and credit analysis. The consensus seems to be that credit analysis of these bonds is similar to that of investment-grade bonds except for an emphasis on certain factors, primarily (1) *the use of cash flows* compared to debt obligations under very conservative assumptions and (2) the detailed analysis of *potential asset sales,* including a conservative estimate of sales prices, the true liquidity, availability of the assets and consideration of the timing of the sales. As noted by several authors, in-depth analysis of junk bonds is becoming critical because of the number of such issues, the wide di-

---

[10] Andrew Marton, "The King of Junk Research," *Institutional Investor* 22, no. 5 (May 1988): 85–87.

versity of quality within the junk bond universe (there is "quality" junk and "junk" junk), and the growing complexity of the issues.

SPREAD ANALYSIS   As discussed in Chapter 11, spread analysis assumes there are normal relationships among the yields for bonds in alternative sectors (e.g., high grade versus low-grade industrial, or industrial versus utility bonds). Therefore, the idea is to monitor these relationships and when an abnormal relationship occurs execute various sector swaps. The crucial factor is developing the background to know the normal relationship and evaluate the liquidity necessary to buy or sell the required issues quickly enough to take advantage of the presumably *temporary* abnormality.[11]

BOND SWAPS   Perhaps the most intriguing of the various investment strategies, *bond swaps* involve liquidating a current position and (simultaneously) buying a different issue in its place with similar attributes but a chance for improved return. Swaps can be executed to increase current yield, to increase yield to maturity, to take advantage of shifts in interest rates or realignments of yield spreads, to improve the quality of a portfolio, or for tax purposes. Some are highly sophisticated and require a computer for the necessary calculations. Most, however, are fairly simple transactions, with obvious goals and risk. They go by such names as *profit take-outs, substitution swaps, intermarket spread swaps,* or *tax swaps*. While many of these swaps involve low risk (such as the pure yield pick-up swap), others entail substantial risk (the rate anticipation swap). Regardless of the risk involved, all swaps have one basic purpose: portfolio improvement.

Most swaps involve several different types of risk. One obvious risk is that the market will move against you while the swap is outstanding. Interest rates may move up over the holding period and cause you to incur a loss. Alternatively, yield spreads may fail to respond as anticipated, thus offsetting the benefits of the bond swap. Another possibility is that the new bond may not be a true substitute and so, even if your expectations and interest rate formulations are correct, the swap may be unsatisfactory because the wrong issue was selected. Finally, if the work-out time is longer than anticipated, the realized yield might be less than expected or a loss may result. If you choose to implement these swaps you must be willing to accept such risks in order to improve your portfolio. Three of the more popular bond swaps will now be reviewed.[12]

PURE YIELD PICK-UP SWAP. The pure yield pick-up involves swapping out of a low-coupon bond into a comparable higher-coupon bond to realize an automatic and instantaneous increase in current yield and yield to

---

[11] For a discussion of factors that affect the size of yield spreads over time, see Chris P. Dialynas, "Bond Yield Spreads Revisited," *Journal of Portfolio Management* 14, no. 2 (Winter 1988): 57–62.

[12] For additional information on these and other types of bond swaps, see Sidney Homer and Martin L. Leibowitz, *Inside the Yield Book* (Englewood Cliffs, N.J.: Prentice-Hall, 1972); Martin L. Leibowitz, "How Swaps Can Pay Off," *Institutional Investor* 7, no. 8 (August 1973): 49ff; and Christina Seix, "Bond Swaps," in *The Handbook of Fixed Income Securities,* 2d ed., edited by Frank J. Fabozzi and Irving M. Pollack (Homewood, Ill.: Dow Jones-Irwin, 1987).

maturity. Your risks are (1) that the market will move against you and (2) that the issue may not be a viable swap candidate. Also, because you are moving to a higher-coupon obligation, there could be greater call risk.

An example of a pure yield pick-up swap would be an investor who currently holds a 30-year, Aa-rated 10 percent issue that is trading at 11.50 percent. Assume that a comparable 30-year, Aa-rated obligation bearing a 12 percent coupon priced to yield 12 percent becomes available. The investor would report (and realize) some book loss if the original issue was bought at par, but he is able to improve current yield and yield to maturity simultaneously if the new obligation is held to maturity as shown in Table 18.1.

The investor need not predict rate changes, and the swap is not based on any imbalance in yield spread. The object is simply to seek higher yields through a bond swap. Quality and maturity stay the same, as do all other factors *except coupon*. The major risk is that future reinvestment rates may not be as high as expected, and, therefore, the total terminal value of the investment (capital recovery, coupon receipts, and interest-on-interest) may not be as high as expected or comparable to the original obligation. This reinvestment risk can be evaluated by analyzing the results with a number of rates to determine the minimum reinvestment rate that would make the swap acceptable.

SUBSTITUTION SWAP. Generally short term, the substitution swap relies heavily on interest rate expectations and is subject to considerably more risk than the pure yield pick-up swap. The procedure rests on the existence of a short-term imbalance in yield spreads between issues that are perfect substitutes, and the spread is expected to be corrected in the near future. The investor might hold a 30-year, 12 percent issue that is yielding 12 percent and be offered comparable 30-year, 12 percent bonds that are yielding 12.20 percent. The issue offered will trade at a price less than $1,000. Thus, for every issue sold, the investor can buy more than one of the offered obligations.

You would expect the yield spread imbalance to be corrected by having the yield on the bond offered decline to the level of the issue that you currently hold. Thus, you would realize capital gains by switching out of your current position into the higher-yielding obligation. This swap is described in Table 18.2.

While there are only modest differential rewards in current income as the yield imbalance is corrected, attractive capital gains are possible, causing a differential in *realized yield*. The work-out time is important in order to realize as high a differential return as possible. Note that, even if the yield is not corrected until maturity, 30 years hence, you will still experience a small increase in realized yield (about 10 basis points). In contrast, if the correction takes place in one year, the differential return is much greater, as shown in Table 18.2. After the correction has occurred, you would have additional capital for a subsequent swap or other investment. There are several risks involved in this swap. In addition to the pressure

TABLE 18.1
A Pure Yield Pick-Up Swap

Pure Yield Pick-Up Swap: A bond swap involving a switch from a low-coupon bond to a higher-coupon bond of similar quality and maturity in order to pick up higher current yield and a better yield to maturity.

Example: Currently hold: 30-yr., 10.0% coupon priced at 874.12 to yield 11.5%.
Swap candidate: 30-yr., Aa 12% coupon priced at $1000 to yield 12.0%.

	CURRENT BOND	CANDIDATE BOND
Dollar investment	$874.12	$1,000.00[a]
Coupon	100.00	120.00
i on one coupon (12.0% for 6 months)	3.000	3.600
Principal value at year-end	874.66	1,000.00
Total accrued	977.66	1,123.60
Realized compound yield	11.514%	12.0%

Value of swap: 48.6 basis points in one year (assuming a 12.0% reinvestment rate).

The rewards for a pure yield pick-up swap are automatic and instantaneous in that both a higher-coupon yield and a higher yield to maturity are realized from the swap.

Other advantages include:
1. No specific work-out period needed since the investor is assumed to hold the new bond to maturity
2. No need for interest rate speculation
3. No need to analyze prices for overvaluation or undervaluation.

A major disadvantage of the pure yield pick-up swap is the book loss involved in the swap. In this example, if the current bond were bought at par the book loss would be ($1,000 − 874.12) $125.88.

Other risks involved in the pure yield pick-up swap include:
1. Increased risk of call in the event interest rates decline
2. Reinvestment risk is greater at higher-coupon rates.

[a] Obviously the investor can invest $874.12, the amount obtained from the sale of the bond currently held, and still obtain a realized compound yield of 12.0%.

Swap evaluation procedure is patterned after a technique suggested by Sidney Homer and Martin L. Leibowitz. Source: Adapted from the book *Inside the Yield Book* by Sidney Homer and Martin L. Leibowitz, Ph.D., © 1972, used by permission of the publisher, Prentice-Hall Inc., Englewood Cliffs, NJ and New York Institute of Finance, New York, NY.

of work-out time, market interest rates could move against you, the yield spread may not be temporary, and the issue may not be a viable swap candidate (the spread may be due to the issue being of lower quality).

TAX SWAP. The tax swap is popular with individual investors because it is a relatively simple procedure that involves no projections and few risks. It exists due to tax laws and realized capital gains in your portfolio. Assume you held $100,000 worth of corporate bonds and after two years sold the

TABLE 18.2
A Substitution Swap

Substitution Swap: A swap executed to take advantage of temporary market anomalies in yield spreads between issues that are equivalent with respect to coupon, quality, and maturity.

Example: Currently hold: 30-yr., Aa 12.0% coupon priced at $1,000 to yield 12.0%
Swap candidate: 30-yr., Aa 12.0% coupon priced at $984.08 to yield 12.2%
Assumed work-out period: 1 year
Reinvested at 12.0%

	CURRENT BOND	CANDIDATE BOND
Dollar investment	$1,000.00	$ 984.08
Coupon	120.00	120.00
i on one coupon (12.0% for 6 months)	3.60	3.60
Principal value at year-end (12.0% YTM)	1,000.00	1,000.00
Total accrued	1,123.60	1,123.60
Total gain	123.60	139.52
Gain per invested dollar	.1236	.1418
Realized compound yield	12.00%	13.71%

Value of swap: 171 basis points in one year.

The rewards for the substitution swap are realized in terms of additional basis point pick-ups for YTM and realized compound yield and in capital gains that accrue when the anomaly in yield corrects itself.

In the substitution swap, it is important for you to realize that any basis point pick-up (171 points in this example) will be realized only during the work-out period. Thus, in our example, in order to obtain the 171 basis point increase in realized compound yield, you must swap an average of once each year and pick up an average of 20 basis points in yield to maturity on each swap.

Potential risks associated with the substitution swap include:
1. A yield spread thought to be temporary may, in fact, be permanent, thus reducing capital gains advantages.
2. The market rate may change adversely.

Swap evaluation procedure is patterned after a technique suggested by Sidney Homer and Martin L. Leibowitz. Source: Adapted from the book *Inside the Yield Book* by Sidney Homer and Martin L. Leibowitz, Ph.D., © 1972, used by permission of the publisher, Prentice-Hall Inc., Englewood Cliffs, NJ and New York Institute of Finance, New York, NY.

securities for $150,000, implying a capital gain of $50,000. One way to eliminate the tax liability of that capital gain is to sell an issue that has a comparable long-term capital loss. If you had a long-term investment of $100,000 with a current market value of $50,000, you could execute a tax swap to establish the $50,000 capital loss. By offsetting this capital loss and the comparable capital gain, you would enjoy reduced income taxes.

Municipal bonds are considered particularly attractive tax swap candidates, since you can increase your tax-free income and use the capital loss (which is subject to normal federal and state taxation) to reduce

TABLE 18.3
A Tax Swap

Tax Swap: A swap undertaken in a situation when you wish to offset capital gains in other securities through the sale of a bond currently held and selling at a discount from the price paid at purchase. By swapping into a bond with as nearly identical features as possible, you can use the capital loss on the sale of the bond for tax purposes and still maintain your current position in the market.

Example: Currently hold: $100,000 worth of corporate bonds with current market value of $150,000 *and* $100,000 in N.Y., 20-year, 7% bonds with current market value of $50,000.

Swap candidate: $50,000 in N.Y., 20-year, 7.1% bonds.

A. Corporate bonds sold and long-term capital gains profit established	$50,000	
Capital gains tax liability (assume you have 20% capital gains tax rate) ($50,000 × .20)		$10,000
B. N.Y. 7s sold and long-term capital *loss* established	$50,000	
Reduction in capital gains tax liability ($50,000 × .20)		($10,000)
Net capital gains tax liability		0
Tax *savings* realized		$10,000
C. Complete tax swap by buying N.Y. 7.1s from proceeds of N.Y. 7s sale (therefore, amount invested remains largely the *same*)ᵃ		
Annual tax-free interest income—N.Y. 7s	$ 7,000	
Annual tax-free interest income—N.Y. 7.1s	$ 7,100	
Net *increase* in *annual* tax-free interest income	$ 100	

ᵃ N.Y. 7.1s will result in substantial capital gains when liquidated at maturity (since they were bought at deep discounts) and, therefore, will be subject to future capital gains tax liability. The swap is designed to use the capital loss resulting from the swap to offset capital gains from other investments. At the same time, your funds remain in a security almost identical to your previous holding while you receive a slight increase in both current income and YTM.

Since the tax swap involves no projections in terms of work-out period, interest rate changes, etc., the risks involved are minimal. Your major concern should be to avoid potential wash sales.

capital gains tax liability. To continue our illustration, assume that you own $100,000 worth of New York City, 20-year, 7 percent bonds with a market value of $50,000. Given this tax loss, you need a comparable bond swap candidate. Suppose you find a 20-year New York City bond with a 7.1 percent coupon and a market value of 50. By selling your New York 7s and instantaneously reinvesting in the New York 7.1s, you would eliminate the capital gains tax from the corporate bond transaction. In effect, you have $50,000 of tax-free capital gains, and you have increased your current tax-free yield. The money saved by avoiding the tax liability can then be used to increase the portfolio's yield, as shown in Table 18.3.

An important caveat is that you cannot swap *identical* issues, such as selling the New York 7s to establish a loss and then buying back the same New York 7s. If it is not a different issue, the IRS considers the transaction a *wash sale* and does not allow the loss. It is easier to avoid wash sales in the bond market than it is in the stock market, because every bond issue, even with identical coupons and maturities, is considered distinct.

Likewise, it is easier to find comparable bond issues with only modest differences in coupon, maturity, and quality. Tax swaps are common at year-end as investors establish capital losses, because the capital loss must occur in the same taxable year as the capital gain. This procedure differs from other swap transactions in that it exists because of tax statutes rather than temporary market anomalies.

A GLOBAL FIXED-INCOME INVESTMENT STRATEGY

An active management strategy that considers one or several of the techniques discussed thus far must apply these techniques to a global portfolio. The ultimate global fixed-income asset allocation must consider three interrelated factors: (1) the local economy in each country that includes the effect of total world demand, (2) the impact of this total demand and domestic monetary policy on inflation and interest rates, and (3) the effect of the economy, inflation, and interest rates on the exchange rates among countries. Based on the evaluation of these factors, a portfolio manager must decide the relative weight for each country in his portfolio and the allocation within each country between government, municipal, and corporate bonds. As we will see in the examples that follow, most allocations concentrate on the gross country allocation and do not become more specific except in the case of the United States.

Table 18.4 contains the table from a strategy report by Salomon Brothers. In this instance there is no specific percent breakdown among assets and countries, but rather a specific estimate of what will happen to the yields for various assets relative to Treasury issues of equal duration. As an example, corporate bonds are expected as a group to experience a larger increase in yields than comparable-duration Treasuries. Specifically, at this time in the market cycle (July 1988), most firms were expecting overall market rates to rise due to higher levels of expected inflation. Therefore, the plus sign indicates that this series was expected to rise by more. In contrast, yields on Yankee bonds were estimated to rise less than the Treasury bonds. In each instance there is a brief statement of the reason for this expectation. For the non-dollar bonds, there is also an estimate of what to expect regarding the currency exchange rate. As noted, in most cases the other currencies were expected to gain relative to the U.S. dollar. Therefore, in making your own allocations based upon these specific expectations, you would look for securities where yields were expected to decline relative to Treasury securities and also search for foreign securities in countries where the currency was expected to be strong relative to the United States.

Table 18.5 contains a table from an *International Fixed Income Strategy* report published by Merrill Lynch Capital Markets. The discussion is similar to that by Salomon Brothers in terms of analyzing the economies, foreign trade, inflation, interest rates, and exchange rates. Alternatively, the portfolio recommendations are more specific regarding the percent asset allocation for each country relative to the proportion for each country in the global bond market. Similar to the prior discussion of the equity market, there is a similar breakdown of the bond market in Chapter 11.

TABLE 18.4
**Projected Performance of Major U.S. and International Fixed-Income Sectors,
June 30 to December 31, 1988**

	YIELD CHANGE VERSUS COMPARABLE DURATION TREASURY	CURRENCY CHANGE VERSUS U.S.$	COMMENTS
U.S. Dollar Denominated			
Treasuries			
Coupon	NM		Favor bullets over barbells.
STRIPs	+		Yield spreads are not tight.
Agencies	+		Rising Treasury yields should widen spreads marginally.
Corporates	+		Rising issuance, volatility and yields point to increase in spreads.
Industrial	+		Strengthening credit more than offset by restructuring risk and increases in supply.
Telephones	NC		Solid credit prospects, but very tight spreads.
Electric utilities	−		Improving credit prospects among lower-quality electric utilities.
Financials	−		Strong credit prospects.
High yield	−		Relatively high sensitivity to the economy should narrow spreads further.
Mortgages			
Discount coupon (Projects)	−		Option-adjusted spreads have narrowed little relative to other mortgage securities.
Current coupon (New)	+		Technical forces have narrowed spreads artificially.
Current coupon (Seasoned)	−		Wider spreads and shorter effective durations relative to new issues augur superior performance.
Premium coupon	NC		Vigorous demand and absence of supply should sustain performance; if interest rates rise, short effective duration will prove to be attractive.
CMOs	NC		"A" tranche and seasoned issues provide defensive instruments.
Principal-only STRIPs	−		Wide spreads and positive convexity of discount instruments provide extraordinary value.
Interest-only STRIPs	NM		Narrow spreads and lagging demand make these securities vulnerable. However, they may have a special value because of their unique negative duration.
ARM pass-throughs	−		Strong demand and limited supply will reinforce returns.
International			
Eurodollar	+		Spreads will widen—in line with domestic corporate spreads—as supply increases and volatility rises.
Yankee	−		Improving credit prospects for many issuers.

continued

These global market proportions are below the boldfaced numbers—as an example, the U.S. bond market is 45 percent of the total and the yen market is 23 percent. Given these market proportions, the bold numbers indicate the firm's investment recommendations. As an example, although the U.S. dollar market is 45 percent of the global fixed-income market, Merrill

TABLE 18.4   *continued*

	YIELD CHANGE VERSUS COMPARABLE DURATION TREASURY	CURRENCY CHANGE VERSUS U.S.$	COMMENTS
Nondollar-Denominated Governments			
Japanese Yen	–	6%–7%	Currency should retest the ¥120/US$ level, based on strong Japanese economic fundamentals as yields rise only modestly further.
Canadian Dollar	NC	1	Maintenance of large short-term interest rate differential, plus lower inflation rate than in the U.S., lead to continued outperformance.
Australian Dollar	–	2	Attractive and narrowing yield spreads. Yield curve likely to remain flat, but volatile conditions will persist. Further modest currency appreciation possible.
British Sterling	–	5–6	Yield curve should remain flat; volatility persists at shorter maturities.
Deutschemark	–	5–6	Yield curve remains steep as long yields rise modestly. Current prices already incorporate expected 10% withholding tax on interest income.
Dutch Guilder	–	5–6	Currency and interest rate linked to Deutschemark. Yield differential reflects effect of West German withholding tax.
French Franc	–	5–6	Currency linked to Deutschemark. Yield differential versus West German bonds should narrow slightly.

Note: Minus sign indicates that yields will decline relative to U.S. Treasuries. Plus sign indicates that yields will rise relative to U.S. Treasuries. NC indicates no change in yield spread to U.S. Treasuries. NM indicates not meaningful.

Source: *Global Fixed-Income Investment Strategy* (New York: Salomon Brothers, Inc., 1988).

Lynch is recommending that you *underweight* the United States and invest only 40 percent of your portfolio in this market versus overweighting the Canadian dollar market (i.e., it is recommended that you invest 10 percent of your portfolio in Canadian bonds, although this market is only 4 percent of the global portfolio). The next set of columns indicates Merrill Lynch's recommendations regarding the mix for the country. As shown, it recommends that 23 percent of the 40 percent for the United States be put into short-term cash equivalent securities and only 17 percent be invested in bonds. The next section indicates that all of the 17 percent should be invested in seven- to ten-year bonds and the sector breakdown recommends that all of these seven- to ten-year bonds should be government securities. Finally, the average duration for the total portfolio should be 1.7 years compared to an average duration for the market of 4.8 years. Overall, this is a very conservative portfolio for the U.S. market—that is, it includes high-quality, short-duration bonds. As a result, the currency risk is fairly low and the interest rate risk level is also low, consistent with the very low duration.

In summary, assuming that it is determined that you will actively manage a bond portfolio, these examples show alternative approaches to the

TABLE 18.5
Recommended Asset Mix (Percent Breakdown)

Currency Bloc	Currency Decision		Market Decision			Bond Selection Decision								Portfolio Risk	
						Maturity Structure					Sector Breakdown				
	Net Currency Position	Currency Hedge	Gross Currency Position	Cash Equiv.	Bonds	1-3 Years	3-5 Years	5-7 Years	7-10 Years	Long	Gov't.	Euro/ Foreign	Portfolio Duration	Currency Risk	Interest Rate Risk
U.S.$	**40**	**0**	**40**	**23**	**17**	**0**	**0**	**0**	**17**	**0**	**17**	**0**	**2.7**	**0.89**	**0.50**
	45		*45*		*45*	*16*	*9*	*5*	*5*	*10*	*39*	*6*	*4.8*		
C$	**10**	**0**	**10**	**4**	**6**	**6**	**0**	**0**	**0**	**0**	**6**	**0**	**1.0**	**2.50**	**0.50**
	4		*4*		*4*	*1*	*1*	*1*	*0*	*1*	*3*	*1*	*4.9*		
A$/NZ$	**6**	**0**	**6**	**2**	**4**	**0**	**2**	**0**	**2**	**0**	**4**	**0**	**3.3**	**3.00**	**3.00**
	2		*2*		*2*	*1*	*1*	*0*	*0*	*0*	*1*	*1*	*3.3*		
YEN	**23**	**0**	**23**	**13**	**10**	**0**	**0**	**0**	**10**	**0**	**10**	**0**	**3.6**	**1.00**	**0.75**
	23		*23*		*23*	*5*	*5*	*5*	*7*	*1*	*20*	*3*	*4.8*		
Europe															
STG	**6**	**0**	**6**	**1**	**5**	**0**	**0**	**0**	**0**	**5**	**5**	**0**	**5.8**	**0.75**	**0.75**
	8		*8*		*8*	*1*	*1*	*1*	*2*	*3*	*7*	*1*	*5.8*		
DM	**10**	**0**	**10**	**5**	**5**	**0**	**0**	**0**	**5**	**0**	**5**	**0**	**3.8**	**0.77**	**0.65**
	13		*13*		*13*	*2*	*3*	*3*	*4*	*1*	*8*	*5*	*4.5*		
FF	**5**	**0**	**5**	**0**	**5**	**0**	**5**	**0**	**0**	**0**	**5**	**0**	**3.5**	**1.00**	**0.75**
	5		*5*		*5*	*1*	*1*	*1*	*2*	*0*	*4*	*1*	*4.7*		
Total	**100**	**0**	**100**	**48**	**52**	**6**	**7**	**0**	**34**	**5**	**52**	**0**	**3.1**	**—**	**0.65**
			100		*100*	*27*	*21*	*16*	*20*	*16*	*82*	*18*	*4.8*		

Source: *International Fixed Income Strategy* (New York: Merrill Lynch Capital Markets, 1988).

asset allocation decision on a global scale. Similar to our discussion related to equity securities, it is clear that making a global allocation requires substantially more research because you must evaluate each country individually, and also relative to every other country in order to make a domestic recommendation, as well as a global recommendation that considers changes in currency values.

MATCHED FUNDING TECHNIQUES[13]

As discussed in the introduction to this chapter, because of the increase in the volatility of interest rates and the needs of many institutional investors, there has been a growth of funds managed using matched funding techniques. The listing of techniques in this category ranged from pure cash-matched dedicated portfolios to portfolios willing to consider contingent immunization.

DEDICATED PORTFOLIOS. In a general sense, *dedication* refers to bond portfolio management techniques that are used to service a prescribed set of liabilities. The idea is that the pension fund has a set of future liabilities and those responsible for administering these liabilities want a money manager to derive a portfolio of assets that will match this liability stream. The point is, it is possible to create such a "dedicated" portfolio in several ways—we will discuss two alternatives.

A *pure cash-matched dedicated portfolio* is the most conservative strategy. Specifically, the objective of pure cash-matching is to develop a portfolio of bonds that will provide a stream of payments from coupons, sinking funds, and maturing principal payments that will exactly match the specified liability schedules. An example of a typical liability stream for a retired-lives component of a pension system is in Figure 18.2.

The goal is to build a portfolio such that it will generate sufficient funds in advance of each scheduled payment to ensure that the payment will be met. One alternative is to find a number of zero coupon Treasury securities that will exactly cash-match each liability. Such an exact cash-match is referred to as a *total passive* portfolio because it is designed so that any prior receipts would not be reinvested (i.e., a zero reinvestment rate).

In another technique, *dedication with reinvestment*, the basic dedication concept is the same as in the pure-cash technique except it is assumed that the bonds and other cash flows do not have to exactly match the liability stream, and any inflows that precede liability claims can be reinvested at some reasonably conservative rate. Such an assumption allows the portfolio manager to consider a substantially wider set of bonds that may have higher return characteristics. In addition, the assumption of reinvestment within each period and between periods will also imply a

---

[13] An overview of these alternative strategies is contained in Martin L. Leibowitz, "The Dedicated Bond Portfolio in Pension Funds—Part I: Motivation and Basics," *Financial Analysts Journal* 42, no. 1 (January–February 1986): 68–75; and Martin L. Leibowitz, "The Dedicated Bond Portfolio in Pension Funds—Part II: Immunization, Horizon Matching, and Contingent Procedures," *Financial Analysts Journal* 42, no. 2 (March–April 1986): 47–57.

FIGURE 18.2
A Prescribed Schedule of Liabilities

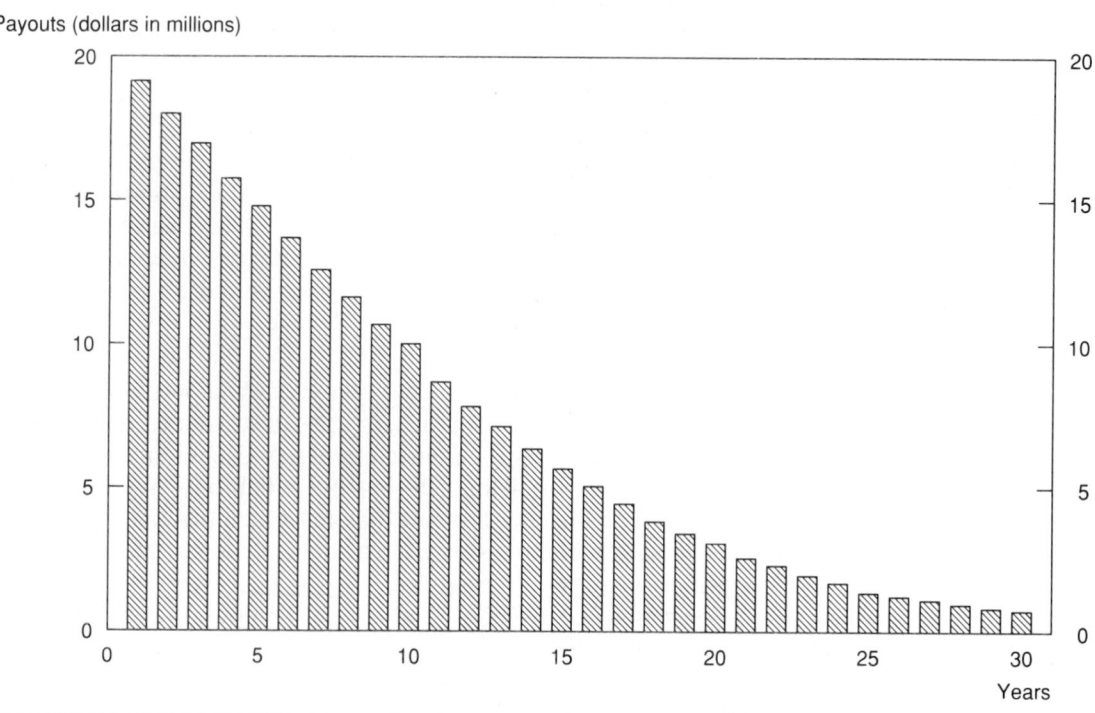

Payouts (dollars in millions)

Years

Source: Martin L. Leibowitz, "The Dedicated Bond Portfolio in Pension Funds—Part I: Motivations and Basics," *Financial Analysts Journal* 42, no. 1 (January–February 1986). Reprinted with permission.

higher return. The result is that the net cost of the portfolio will be lower, with almost equal safety, assuming the reinvestment assumption is conservative. An example would be to assume a reinvestment rate of 6 percent in an environment where rates are currently ranging from 7 to 10 percent.

Potential problems exist with both these approaches to a dedicated portfolio. For example, when selecting potential bonds for these portfolios, it is critical to be aware of call/prepayment possibilities with specific bonds or mortgage-backed securities because of refunding, call provisions, or sinking funds. These possibilities become very important during periods of historically high rates. A prime example was the period 1982–1986, when interest rates went from over 18 percent to under 8 percent. Given this substantial change in rates, many dedicated portfolios constructed without adequate concern for complete call protection were compromised when a lot of bonds were called that were not expected to be called "under normal conditions." For example, bonds selling at deep discounts (implicit call protection) when rates were 16 to 18 percent went to par and above when rates declined to under 10 percent, and they were called. Obviously, the necessity to reinvest these proceeds at the lower rates caused many dedicated portfolios to be underfunded. Therefore, it is necessary to find complete call protection on bonds or consider deep discount bonds under conservative interest rate conditions.

While there is also a legitimate concern with quality, it is probably not necessary to invest only in Treasury bonds, assuming that the portfolio manager is conscious of diversifying across industries and sectors. A diversified portfolio of AA or A industrial bonds can provide a current and total annual return of 40 to 60 basis points above Treasuries. This differential over a 30-year period can have a significant impact on the net cost of funding a liability stream.

IMMUNIZATION STRATEGIES

Instead of using a buy-and-hold strategy, one of the active strategies, or one of the dedicated portfolio techniques, a portfolio manager, after consulting with his client, may decide that the optimal strategy is to *immunize* the portfolio from the effect of interest rate changes. This way an attempt is made to derive a specified rate of return (quite close to the current market rate) during a given investment horizon regardless of what happens to market interest rates.

COMPONENTS OF INTEREST RATE RISK. A major problem encountered in bond portfolio management is deriving a given rate of return to satisfy an ending-wealth requirement at a future specific date—that is, the investment horizon. If the term structure of interest rates were flat and market rates never changed between the time of purchase and the future specific date when funds were required, you could acquire a bond with a term to maturity equal to the desired investment horizon, and the ending wealth from the bond would equal the *promised* wealth position implied by the promised yield to maturity. Specifically, the ending-wealth position would be the beginning wealth times the compound value of a dollar at the promised yield to maturity. As an example, assume that you acquired a ten-year, $1 million bond with an 8 percent coupon at par (8 percent YTM). If conditions were as specified (flat yield curve and no changes in the curve), your wealth position at the end of your ten-year investment horizon (assuming semiannual compounding) would be

$$\$1,000,000 \times (1.04)^{20} = \$1,000,000 \times 2.1911 = \$2,191,100.$$

You can get the same answer by taking the $40,000 interest payment every six months and compounding it semiannually to the end of the period at 8 percent and adding the $1,000,000 beginning value. Unfortunately, in the real world, the term structure of interest rates is not typically flat and the level of interest rates is constantly changing. Consequently, the bond portfolio manager faces *interest rate risk* between the time of investment and the future target date. This risk can be defined as the uncertainty regarding the ending-wealth position due to changes in market interest rates between the time of purchase and the target date. It involves two component risks in turn: *price risk* and *coupon reinvestment risk.* The price risk occurs because if interest rates change before the target date and the bond is sold before maturity, the realized market price for the bond will differ from the *expected price,* assuming no change in rates. If rates increase after the time of purchase, the realized price for the bond in the secondary market will be below expectations, while if rates decline, the realized price will be above expectations.

The coupon reinvestment risk arises because the yield to maturity computation implicitly assumes that all coupon flows will be reinvested at the promised yield to maturity.[14] If, after the purchase of the bond, interest rates decline, the coupon cash flows will be reinvested at rates below the promised YTM, and the ending wealth will be below expectations. In contrast, if interest rates increase, the interim cash flows will be reinvested at rates above expectations, and the ending wealth will be above expectations.

CLASSICAL IMMUNIZATION AND INTEREST RATE RISK. Note that the price risk and the reinvestment risk due to a change in interest rates have opposite effects on the ending-wealth position. An increase in interest rates will cause an ending price below expectations, but the reinvestment rate for interim cash flows will be at a rate above expectations. A decline in market interest rates will cause the reverse situation. Clearly, a bond portfolio manager with a specific target date will attempt to eliminate these two interest rate risks, a process referred to as *immunization,* discussed by Redington[15] and by Fisher and Weil as follows:

> A portfolio of investments in bonds is immunized for a holding period if its value at the end of the holding period, regardless of the course of interest rates during the holding period, must be at least as large as it would have been had the interest-rate function been constant throughout the holding period.
>
> If the realized return on an investment in bonds is sure to be at least as large as the appropriately computed yield to the horizon, then that investment is immunized.[16]

Fisher and Weil found a significant difference between the promised yields and the realized returns on bonds for the period 1925–1968, indicating the importance of being able to immunize a bond portfolio. They showed that it is theoretically possible to completely immunize a bond portfolio if you can assume that any change in interest rates will be the same for all; that is, if forward interest rates change, all rates will change by the same amount. Given this assumption, Fisher and Weil proved that *a portfolio of bonds is immunized from interest rate risk if the duration of the portfolio is always equal to the desired investment horizon.* As an example,

---

[14] This point was discussed in detail in Chapter 11 and also in Sidney Homer and Martin L. Leibowitz, *Inside the Yield Book* (Englewood Cliffs, N.J.: Prentice-Hall, 1972), Chapter 1.

[15] F. M. Redington, "Review of the Principles of Life–Office Valuations," *Journal of the Institute of Actuaries* 78 (1952): 286–340.

[16] Lawrence Fisher and Roman L. Weil, "Coping with the Risk of Interest Rate Fluctuations: Returns to Bondholders from Naive and Optimal Strategies," *Journal of Business* 44, no. 4 (October 1971): 408–431.

if the desired holding period (investment horizon) of a bond portfolio is eight years, in order to immunize the portfolio, the *duration* of the bond portfolio should equal eight years. To attain a given duration, the weighted average duration of the portfolio (with weights for individual bonds equal to the proportion of value) is set at the desired length following an interest payment, and all subsequent cash flows are invested in securities to keep the portfolio duration equal to the remaining horizon value.

Fisher and Weil showed that price risk and reinvestment rate risk are affected in opposite directions by a change in market rates and that duration is the time period when these two risks are of equal magnitude but opposite in direction.[17]

APPLICATION OF THE IMMUNIZATION PRINCIPLE. Fisher and Weil simulated the effects of applying the immunization concept compared to a naive portfolio strategy where the portfolio's maturity was equal to the investment horizon. The simulation computed the ending-wealth ratios for alternative investment horizons (5, 10, and 20 years) assuming (1) the expected yield was realized (the yield curve never shifted), (2) the portfolio duration was equal to the investment horizon (a duration strategy), and (3) the portfolio's maturity was equal to the investment horizon (a naive maturity strategy). They compared the ending-wealth ratio for the duration and naive strategy portfolios to the wealth ratio assuming no change in the interest rate structure. In a perfectly immunized portfolio, the actual ending wealth should equal the expected ending wealth implied by the promised yield, so these comparisons should indicate which portfolio strategy does a superior job of immunization. The duration strategy results were consistently closer to the promised yield results, although the results were not perfect (i.e., the duration portfolio was not perfectly immunized because the basic assumption did not always hold; that is, when interest rates changed, all interest rates did not change by the same amount).

Bierwag and Kaufman[18] pointed out several specifications of the duration measure. The Macauley duration measure, which is used throughout this book, discounts all flows by the prevailing yield to maturity on the bond being measured.[19] Alternatively, Fisher and Weil[20] defined duration using future one-period discount rates (forward rates) to discount the future flows. Depending upon the shape of the yield curve, the two definitions could give different answers. Bierwag and Kaufman computed alternative definitions of duration and found that except at high coupons and long maturities, the values were similar and the Macauley definition

---

[17] This is also noted and discussed in G. O. Bierwag and George G. Kaufman, "Coping with the Risk of Interest Rate Fluctuations: A Note," *Journal of Business* 50, no. 3 (July 1977): 364–370; and G. O. Bierwag, "Immunization, Duration, and the Term Structure of Interest Rates," *Journal of Financial and Quantitative Analysis* 12, no. 5 (December 1977): 725–742.

[18] Bierwag and Kaufman, "Coping with the Risk of Interest Rate Fluctuations: A Note," 364–370.

[19] Frederick R. Macaulay, *Some Theoretical Problems Suggested by the Movements of Interest Rates, Bond Yields, and Stock Prices in the United States Since 1865* (New York: National Bureau of Economic Research, 1938).

[20] Fisher and Weil, "Coping with the Risk of Interest Rate Fluctuations: Returns to Bondholders from Naive and Optimal Strategies," *Journal of Business* 44, no. 4 (October 1971): 408–431.

TABLE 18.6

An Example of the Effect of a Change in Market Rates on a Bond (Portfolio) that Uses the Maturity Strategy versus the Duration Strategy

	RESULTS WITH MATURITY STRATEGY			RESULTS WITH DURATION STRATEGY		
YEAR	CASH FLOW	REINVESTMENT RATE	END VALUE	CASH FLOW	REINVESTMENT RATE	END VALUE
1	$ 80	.08	$ 80.00	$ 80	.08	$ 80.00
2	80	.08	166.40	80	.08	166.40
3	80	.08	259.71	80	.08	259.71
4	80	.08	360.49	80	.08	360.49
5	80	.06	462.12	80	.06	462.12
6	80	.06	596.85	80	.06	596.85
7	80	.06	684.04	80	.06	684.04
8	$1,080	.06	$1,805.08	$1,120.64[a]	.06	$1,845.72

Expected Wealth Ratio = 1.8509 or $1,850.90.

[a]The bond could be sold at its market value of $1,040.64, which is the value for an 8 percent bond with two years to maturity priced to yield 6 percent.

is preferable because it is a function of the yield to maturity of the bond— which means you do not need a forecast of one-period forward rates over the maturity of the bond nor an assumption about the nature of the shock to interest rates.[21]

EXAMPLE OF CLASSICAL IMMUNIZATION. Table 18.6 shows the effect of attempting to immunize a portfolio by matching the investment horizon and the duration of a bond portfolio using a single bond. The portfolio manager's investment horizon is eight years, and the current yield to maturity for eight-year bonds is 8 percent. Therefore, if we assumed no change in yields, the ending-wealth ratio for an investor should be $1.8509[(1.08)^8]$.[22] As noted, this should also be the ending-wealth ratio for a completely immunized portfolio. The example considers two portfolio strategies: (1) the maturity strategy, where the term to maturity is eight years, and (2) the duration strategy, where the duration is set at eight years. For the maturity strategy, the portfolio manager acquires an eight-year, 8 percent bond; for the duration strategy, he acquires a ten-year, 8 percent bond that has approximately an eight-year duration (8.12 years), assuming an 8 percent YTM (see Table 11.2). We assume a single shock to the interest rate structure at the end of Year 4, when rates go from 8 percent to 6 percent and stay there through Year 8.

As shown, due to the interest rate change, the wealth ratio for the maturity strategy bond is *below* the desired wealth ratio because of the shortfall in the reinvestment cash flow after Year 4, when the interim coupon cash flow was reinvested at 6 percent rather than 8 percent. Note

[21] Bierwag-Kaufman, "Coping with the Risk of Interest Rate Fluctuations: A Note," 367.

[22] We use annual compounding to compute the ending-wealth ratio because the example uses annual observations.

that *the maturity strategy eliminated the price risk,* because the bond matured at the end of Year 8. Alternatively, the duration strategy portfolio likewise suffered a shortfall in reinvestment cash flow because of the change in market rates. Notably, this shortfall due to the reinvestment risk was partially offset by an increase in the ending value for the bond because of the decline in market rates. This second bond is sold at the end of Year 8 at 104.06 of par, because it is an 8 percent coupon bond with two years to maturity selling to yield 6 percent. Because of this partial offset due to the price increase, the duration strategy had an ending-wealth value (1845.72) much closer to the expected-wealth ratio (1850.90) than the maturity strategy had (1805.08).

If market interest rates had increased during this period, the maturity strategy portfolio would have experienced an excess of reinvestment income compared to the expected cash flow, and the ending-wealth ratio for this strategy would have been above expectations. In contrast, in the duration portfolio, the excess cash flow from reinvestment under this assumption would have been partially offset by a decline in the ending price for the bond. While the ending-wealth ratio for the duration strategy would have been lower than the maturity strategy, it would have been closer to the expected-wealth ratio. The point is, while the maturity strategy would have provided a higher than expected ending value, the whole purpose of immunization is to eliminate uncertainty by having the realized-wealth position equal the expected-wealth position. As shown, this is what is accomplished with the duration strategy.

ANOTHER VIEW OF IMMUNIZATION. The prior example assumed that both bonds were acquired and held to the end of the investment horizon. An alternative way to envision what is expected to happen with an immunized portfolio is to concentrate on the specific growth path from the beginning-wealth position to the ending-wealth position and examine what happens when interest rates change.

Assume that the initial-wealth position is $1 million, your investment horizon is ten years, and the coupon and current YTM is 8 percent. We know from an earlier computation that this implies that the expected ending-wealth value is $2,191,100 (with semiannual compounding). Figure 18.3A shows the compound growth rate path from $1 million to the expected ending value at $2,191,100. In Figure 18.3B it is assumed that at the end of Year 2, interest rates increase by 2 percent (10 percent). We know that with no prior rate changes, the value of the portfolio would have grown at an 8 percent compound rate to $1,169,000 [$(1.04)^4 = 1.1699$]. Given the rate change, we know there will be two changes for this portfolio: (1) the price (value of the portfolio) will decline to reflect the higher rate, and (2) the reinvestment rate, which is the growth rate, will increase to 10 percent. An important question is, by how much will the portfolio value decline? The answer depends upon the modified duration of the portfolio. What Fisher and Weil showed is that if the modified duration is equal to the remaining horizon, the price change will be such that at the new growth

FIGURE 18.3
The Growth Path to the Expected Ending-Wealth Value and the Effect of Immunization

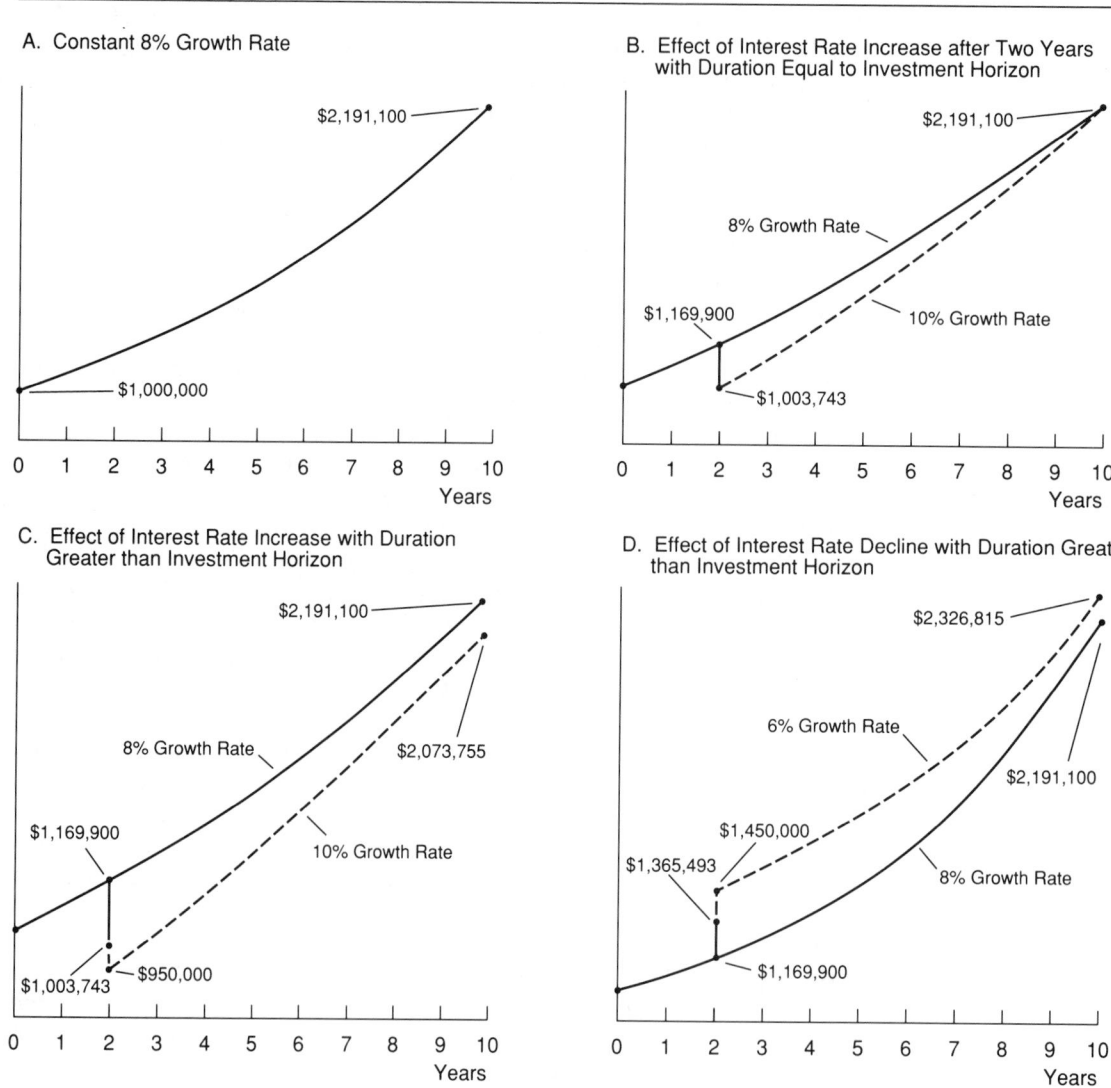

A. Constant 8% Growth Rate

B. Effect of Interest Rate Increase after Two Years with Duration Equal to Investment Horizon

C. Effect of Interest Rate Increase with Duration Greater than Investment Horizon

D. Effect of Interest Rate Decline with Duration Greater than Investment Horizon

rate (10 percent), the new portfolio value will grow to the expected-wealth position. You can approximate the change in portfolio value using the modified duration and the change in market rates (recall that this will not give an exact estimate because of the convexity of the portfolio). The approximate change is 16 percent (a modified duration of eight years and a 200-basis-point change). This would imply an approximate portfolio value of $981,716 ($1,169,000 × 0.84). This approximation is reasonably close to the actual value of $1,003,743 (recall that the estimate based upon duration is always below the value implied by the price-yield curve). If this new wealth value grows at 10 percent a year for eight years, the ending-wealth ratio will be

$1,003,743 × 2.1829 (5% for 16 periods) = $2,191,070.

The difference between the expected value and projected value is due to rounding. This example makes the point that the price decline is exactly offset by the higher reinvestment rate—assuming that the duration was equal to the remaining horizon.

What happens if the portfolio is not properly matched? If the duration is greater than the remaining horizon, the price change will be greater. Thus, in the case of higher interest rates, the value after the rate change will be less than $1,003,743. In this case, even if the new value grew at 10 percent a year, it would not reach the expected ending-wealth value. This scenario is shown in Figure 18.4C where it is assumed that the portfolio value declined to $950,000. If this new value grew at 10 percent a year for the remaining eight years, its ending value would be

$950,000 × 2.1829 (5% for 16 periods) = $2,073,755.

Therefore, the shortfall of $118,000 between the expected-wealth value and the realized-wealth value is because the portfolio was not properly matched (immunized) when interest rates changed.

Alternatively, if interest rates had declined, and the modified duration had been longer than eight years, the new value would have been above the required value. Figure 18.4D shows what can happen if the portfolio is not properly matched. In this example, it is assumed that interest rates decline by 200 basis points to 6 percent. If the portfolio is properly matched, the value will increase to $1,365,493. If this new portfolio value grows at 6 percent for eight years, its ending value will be

$1,365,493 × 1.6047 (3% for 16 periods) = $2,191,207.

Again, this deviates slightly from the expected ending-wealth value ($2,191,100) due to rounding. Alternatively, if the modified duration had been above eight years, the new value would have been greater than the required value of $1,365,493. If we assume the portfolio value increased to $1,450,000, the ending value at the end of the remaining eight years would be

$1,450,000 × 1.6047 (3% for 16 periods) = $2,327,815.

In this example, the ending-wealth value would have been greater than the expected-wealth value because you were mismatched and interest rates went in the right direction. Again, the important point is that when you are not matched, you are speculating on interest rate changes, and the result can be very good or very bad. The purpose of immunization is to avoid these uncertainties and ensure the expected ending-wealth value ($2,191,100) irrespective of interest rate changes.

APPLICATION OF CLASSICAL IMMUNIZATION. Once you understand the reasoning behind immunization (i.e., that it is meant to offset components of interest rate risk) and the general principle (matching duration and the investment horizon), you might conclude that this strategy is fairly simple to apply. You might even consider it a passive strategy; simply match duration and the investment horizon, and you can ignore the portfolio until the end of the horizon period. The following discussion will show that immunization is neither a simple nor a passive strategy.

Except for the case of a zero coupon bond, an immunized portfolio requires frequent rebalancing because the duration of the portfolio should always be equal to the remaining time horizon. The zero coupon bond is unique because it is a pure discount bond. As such, there is *no reinvestment risk,* because the discounting assumes that the value of the bond will grow at the discount rate. For example, if you discount a future value at 10 percent, the present value factor assumes that the value will grow at a compound rate of 10 percent to maturity. Also, there is *no price risk* if you set the duration at your time horizon, because you will receive the face value of the bond at maturity. Also, recall that *the duration of a zero coupon bond is always equal to its term to maturity.* In summary, if you immunize by matching your horizon with a zero coupon bond of equal duration, you do not have to rebalance.

Unfortunately, several characteristics of duration with coupon bonds make it impossible to set a duration equal to the remaining horizon at the initiation of the portfolio and ignore it thereafter. First, duration declines more slowly than term to maturity, assuming no change in market interest rates. As an example, assume you have a security with a computed duration of five years at a 10 percent market yield. A year later, if you compute the duration of the security at 10 percent, you will find that it has a duration of approximately 4.2 years; that is, while the term to maturity has declined by a year, the duration has declined by only 0.8 years. This means that, assuming no changes in market rates, the portfolio manager must rebalance the portfolio to *reduce* its duration to four years. Typically, this is not too difficult because cash flows from the portfolio can be invested in short-term T-bills if necessary.

Second, duration changes with a change in market interest rates. In Chapter 11 we discussed the inverse relationship between market rates and duration—with higher market rates there will be lower duration, and vice versa. Therefore, a portfolio with the required duration can have its duration changed immediately if market rates change, and a portfolio manager would have to rebalance the portfolio if the deviation becomes too large. The frequency of rebalancing is a question to be answered by the individual portfolio manager. The cost of rebalancing must be weighed against the advantages of reducing the variance of terminal wealth.

Third, the technique assumes that when market rates change, they will change by the same amount and in the same direction. Clearly, if this does not happen, it will affect the performance of a portfolio of diffuse bonds. As an example, consider a portfolio of long- and short-term bonds with a weighted average six-year duration (e.g., two-year duration bonds and ten-year duration bonds). Assume that the term structure curve changes such that short-term rates decline and long-term rates rise (there is an increase in the slope of the curve). In this instance, you would experience a major price decline in the long-term bonds but would also be penalized on reinvestment, assuming you generally reinvest the cash flow in short-term securities. This potential problem suggests that you should attempt to bunch your portfolio selections close to the desired duration. For example, an eight-year duration portfolio should be made up of seven- to nine-year duration securities to avoid this problem.

Finally, there can always be a problem of acquiring the bonds you want in the market. For instance, can you buy long-duration bonds at the price you consider acceptable? In summary, it is important to recognize that classical immunization is not a passive strategy and is subject to all of these potential problems.[23]

HORIZON MATCHING[24]

Horizon matching is a combination of two of the techniques discussed—cash-matching dedication and immunization. As shown in Figure 18.4, the liability stream is divided into two segments. In the first segment the portfolio is constructed to provide a cash match for the liabilities during this horizon period (e.g., the first five years). The second segment is the remaining liability stream following the end of the horizon period—in the example, it is the 25 years after the horizon period. During this second time period, the liabilities are covered by a duration-matched strategy based on immunization principles. As a result, the client receives the certainty of cash matching during the early years and the cost saving and flexibility of duration-matched flows thereafter.

The combination technique also helps alleviate one of the problems with classical immunization—the potential for nonparallel shifts in the yield curve. Most of the problems in this regard are concentrated in the short end of the yield curve, when the most severe curve reshaping occurs. Because the short end is taken care of by the cash matching, these are not of concern.

An important decision when using this technique is the length of the horizon period. The trade-off is between the safety and certainty of cash matching and the cost and flexibility of duration-based immunization. The portfolio manager must provide a set of alternatives and the costs and benefits of each of them and allow the client to make the decision. It is also possible to consider *rolling out* the cash-matched segment over time. Specifically, after the first year the portfolio manager would restructure the portfolio to provide a cash match during the original Year 6, which would mean that you would still have a five-year horizon. The ability and

---

[23] Several of these problems were discussed in William L. Nemerever, "Managing Bond Portfolios through Immunization Strategies," *The Revolution in Techniques for Managing Bond Portfolios* (Charlottesville, Va.: The Institute of Chartered Financial Analysts, 1983), 39–65.

[24] This section benefited from Martin L. Leibowitz, Thomas E. Klaffky, Steven Mandel, and Alfred Weinberger, *Horizon Matching: A New Generalized Approach for Developing Minimum-Cost Dedicated Portfolios* (New York: Salomon Brothers, 1983).

FIGURE 18.4
The Concept of Horizon Matching

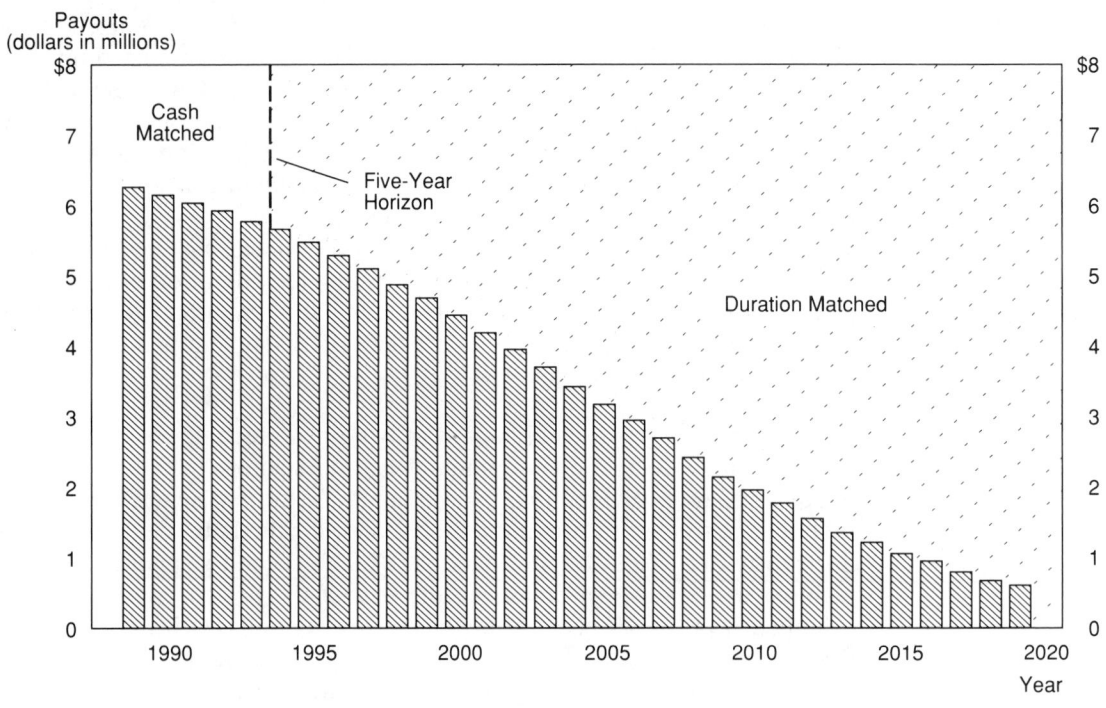

Source: Martin L. Leibowitz, Thomas E. Klaffky, Steven Mandel, and Alfred Weinberger, *Horizon Matching: A New Generalized Approach for Developing Minimum-Cost Dedicated Portfolios* (New York: Salomon Brothers, 1983).

cost of rolling out depends on movements in interest rates (ideally, you would want parallel shifts in the yield curve).

CONTINGENT PROCEDURES

Contingent procedures are a form of structured active management. The procedure we will discuss here is that of contingent immunization.

CONTINGENT IMMUNIZATION

Subsequent to the development and application of classical immunization, Leibowitz and Weinberger developed *contingent immunization*.[25] Basically, it allows a bond portfolio manager to pursue the highest returns available through active strategies while relying on classical bond immunization techniques to ensure a given minimal return over the investment horizon. Put another way, it allows an opportunity for attaining higher rates from

---

[25] Martin L. Leibowitz and Alfred Weinberger, "Contingent Immunization—Part I: Risk Control Procedures," *Financial Analysts Journal* 38, no. 6 (November–December 1982): 17–32; and Martin L. Leibowitz and Alfred Weinberger, "Contingent Immunization—Part II: Problem Areas," *Financial Analysts Journal* 29, no. 1 (January–February 1983): 35–50. This section draws heavily from these articles.

Figure 18.5
Classical Immunization

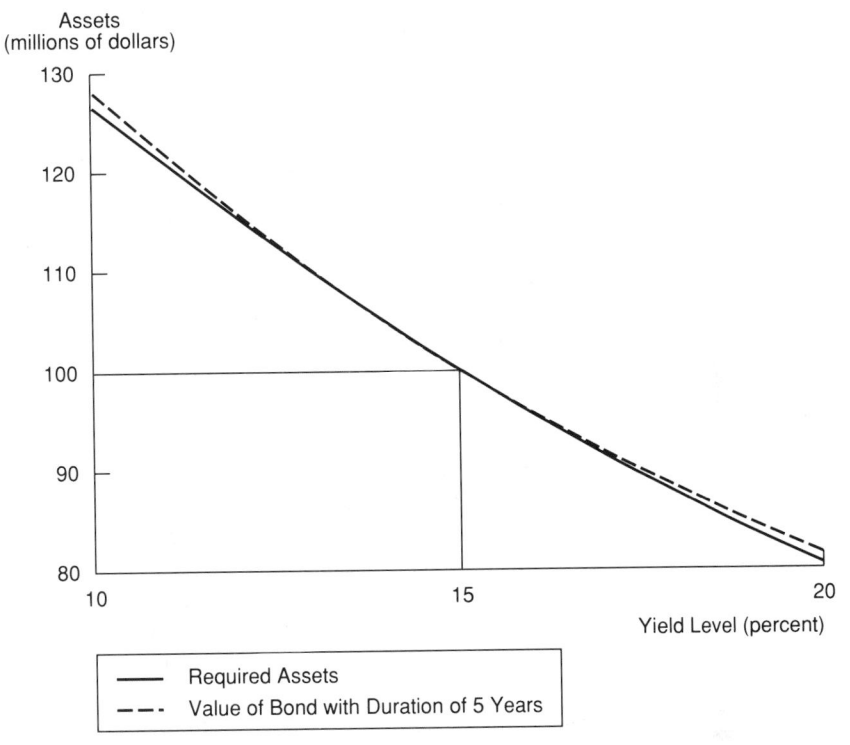

Source: Martin L. Leibowitz and Alfred Weinberger, "Contingent Immunization—Part I: Risk Control Procedures," *Financial Analysts Journal* 38, no. 6 (November–December 1982): 17–32. Reprinted with permission.

active portfolio management with a safety net provided by classical immunization.

To understand contingent immunization, it is necessary to recall our discussion of classical immunization, which prescribes a portfolio duration equal to the investment horizon so when there is a change in interest rates, the dollar value of the portfolio will change such that the new asset value compounded at the new market rate will equal the desired ending value. Note that this required change in value occurs only when the duration of the portfolio is equal to the remaining time horizon, which is why *the duration must be maintained at the horizon value.*

Assume that our desired ending-wealth value is $206.3 million. Figure 18.5 shows an example of the required assets with a five-year horizon and current market rates of 15 percent. Specifically, with five years left, at 15 percent, you need an initial portfolio worth $100 million of assets to reach $206.3 million ($100 million × 2.063, which is the compound value factor for ten periods at 7.5 percent). With lower rates you would need more assets, and with higher rates you would need less assets. To extend the example, if rates were 12 percent, you would need beginning assets of $115.2 million, and at 18 percent you would need beginning assets of only $87.14 million.[26] The dotted line in Figure 18.5 indicates that the price sensitivity of a portfolio with a duration of five years will have almost exactly the price sensitivity required.

The idea of contingent immunization is that if the client is willing to accept a potential return below the current market return for the opportunity to receive a return higher than what one could currently lock in, this *cushion spread* (i.e., the difference between the current market return and some floor rate) will provide a flexibility for the portfolio manager to engage in active portfolio strategies. As an example, if current market rates are 15 percent, the client might be willing to accept a floor rate of 14 percent, because it is still a very good rate, and the acceptance of this lower rate will mean that the portfolio manager does not have the same ending-asset requirements—that is, at 14 percent the required ending-wealth value would be $196.72 million (7 percent for ten periods) compared to the $206.3 million at 15 percent. Because of this lower floor rate, it is possible to allow some value declines while attempting to do better than the market through active management strategies. Figure 18.6 shows that the value of assets required at the beginning assuming a 14 percent required return and the implied ending-wealth value of $196.72 million is below that for 15 percent (at 15 percent, the value of assets required at the beginning would be $95.56 million, which is the present value of $196.72 million at 15 percent for five years). The difference between the $100 million and $95.56 million is the dollar cushion available to the portfolio manager because the client has agreed to a lower locked-in rate and, therefore, a lower ending-wealth value. The portfolio manager can engage in various active management strategies to increase the value of the portfolio above that required at 14 percent (you even hope that it would exceed the 15 percent originally available). As an example, assume that the portfolio manager believes that market rates will decline and acquires a 30-year bond that has a duration greater than the investment horizon of five years and, therefore, has greater price sensitivity to changes in market rates. Hence, if rates decline as expected, the value of the long-duration portfolio will rise above the value stipulated initially. If rates increase, the value of the portfolio will decline rapidly. In this latter case, depending upon how high rates go, the value of the portfolio could decline to a figure below that needed to reach the desired ending-wealth value at 14 percent (the $196.72 million). Figure 18.7 shows that if rates decline from 15 percent, the portfolio of 30-year bonds would experience a large increase in value and develop a safety margin (i.e., a portfolio value above the required

[26] You derive these required amounts by knowing the desired ending-wealth position (which is $206.3 million in this example) and computing the present value of this amount for the specified time period at the appropriate interest rate (assuming semiannual compounding). Therefore, in these examples we used the present value factor for 6 percent for 10 periods (.5584) and for 9 percent for 10 periods (.4224). Given these present values, we know that if we compound them at these rates, we will arrive at our desired ending-wealth value ($206.3 million).

FIGURE 18.6
Price Behavior Required for Floor Return

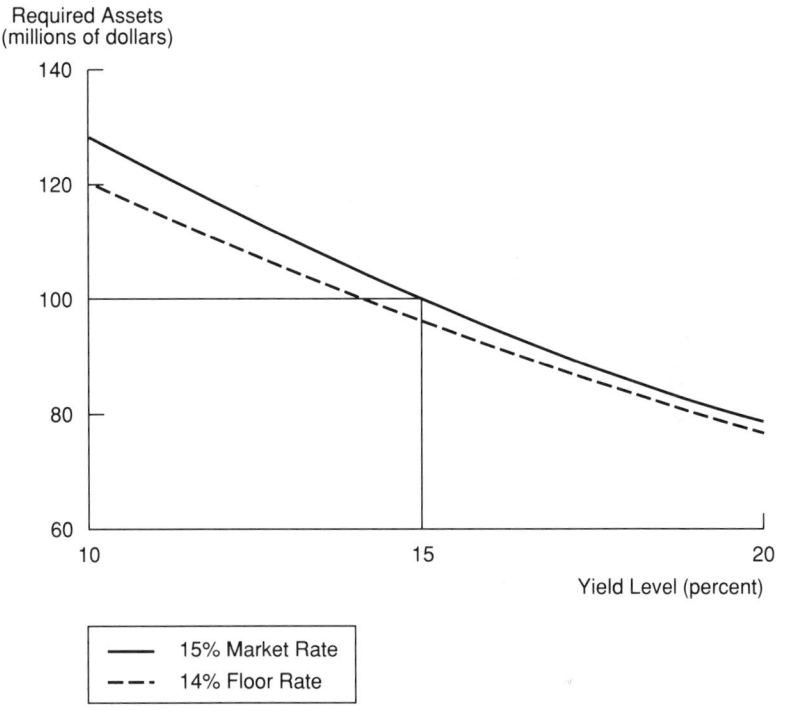

Source: Martin L. Leibowitz and Alfred Weinberger, "Contingent Immunization—Part I: Risk Control Procedures," *Financial Analysts Journal* 38, no. 6 (November–December 1982): 17–32. Reprinted with permission.

value). In contrast, if rates increase, the value of the portfolio will decline until you reach the asset value required at 14 percent. When the value of the portfolio reaches this point of minimum return (referred to as a *trigger point*), it is necessary to stop active portfolio management and use classical immunization with the remaining assets to ensure that you will attain the desired ending-wealth value.

POTENTIAL RETURN. The concept of *potential return* is helpful in understanding the objective of contingent immunization. This is the return the portfolio would achieve over the entire investment horizon if, at any point, the assets in hand were immunized at the then-current market rate. Figure 18.8 contains the various potential rates of return based upon dollar asset values shown in Figure 18.7. If the portfolio were immediately immunized when market rates were 15 percent, it would naturally earn the 15 percent market rate; that is, its potential return would be 15 percent. Alternatively, if yields declined instantaneously by 500 basis points to 10 percent, the

Figure 18.7
Safety Margin for a Portfolio of 30-Year Bonds

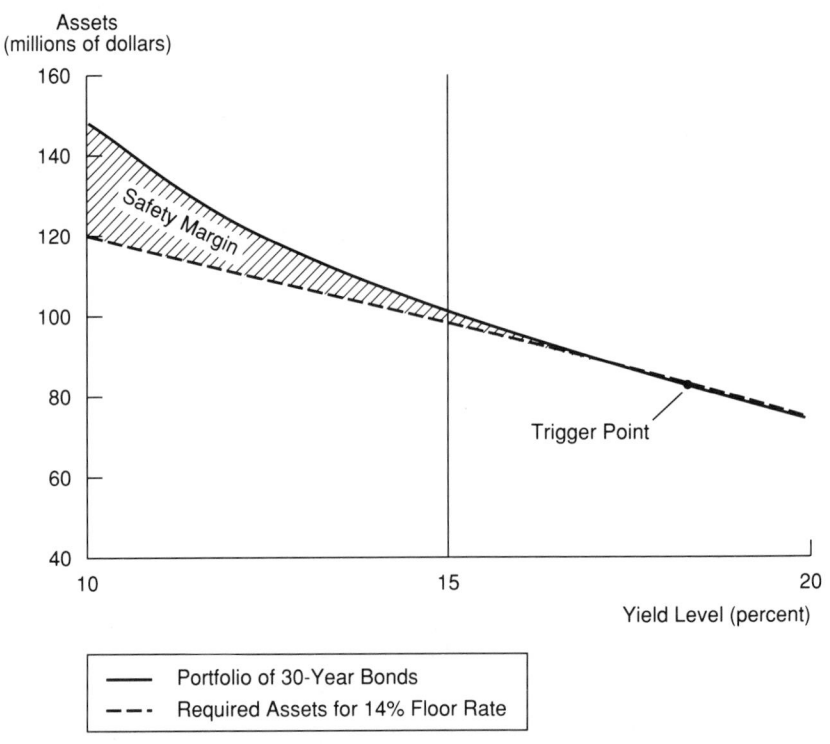

Source: Martin L. Leibowitz and Alfred Weinberger, "Contingent Immunization—Part I: Risk Control Procedures," *Financial Analysts Journal* 38, no. 6 (November–December 1982): 17–32. Reprinted with permission.

portfolio's asset value would increase to $147 million (see Figure 18.7). If this $147 million portfolio were immunized at the market rate of 10 percent over the remaining five-year period, the portfolio would grow to a total value of $239 million ($147 million × 1.6289, which is the compound growth factor for 5 percent and ten periods). This ending value of $239.45 million represents an 18.25 percent rate of return on the original $100 million portfolio. Consequently, as shown in Figure 18.8, the portfolio's potential return would be 18.25 percent. That is, if rates decline by 5 percent, the potential return for this portfolio at this point in time is 18.25 percent.

In contrast, if interest rates rise, the asset value will decline substantially and the potential return will decline. For example, if market rates rise to 17 percent (i.e., a yield change of 2 percent), the asset value of the 30-year bond portfolio will decline to $88 million (see Figure 18.7). If this portfolio of $88 million were immunized for the remaining five years at 17

Figure 18.8
The Potential Return Concept

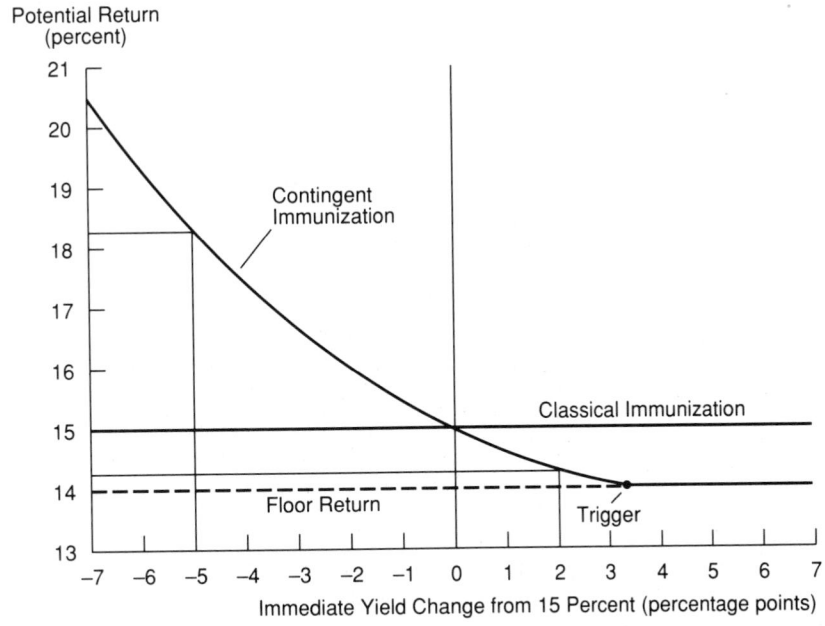

Source: Martin L. Leibowitz and Alfred Weinberger, "Contingent Immunization—Part I: Risk Control Procedures," *Financial Analysts Journal* 38, no. 6 (November–December 1982): 17–32. Reprinted with permission.

percent, the ending value would be $199 million. This ending value corresponds to a potential return of 14.32 percent for the total period.

As Figure 18.7 shows, if interest rates rose to 18.50 percent, the 30-year bonds would decline to a value of $81.16 million and the portfolio would have to be immunized. At this point, if the remaining assets of $81.16 million were immunized at 18.50 percent, it would grow to $196.73 million ($81.16 × 2.424, which is the compound value factor for 9.25 percent for ten periods), and this implies that the potential return for the portfolio would be exactly 14 percent. Regardless of what happens to subsequent market rates, the portfolio has been immunized at 14 percent. That is a major characteristic of the contingent immunized portfolio; if there is proper monitoring, you will always know your trigger point and can be assured of a return no less than the minimum return specified.

MONITORING THE IMMUNIZED PORTFOLIO. Clearly, a crucial factor in the contingent immunized portfolio is monitoring it to ensure that if the asset value falls to the trigger point, it will be detected and the appropriate action taken to ensure the portfolio is immunized at the floor-level rate. This can be done using a chart as in Figure 18.9. The top line is the current

FIGURE 18.9
Contingent Immunization over Time

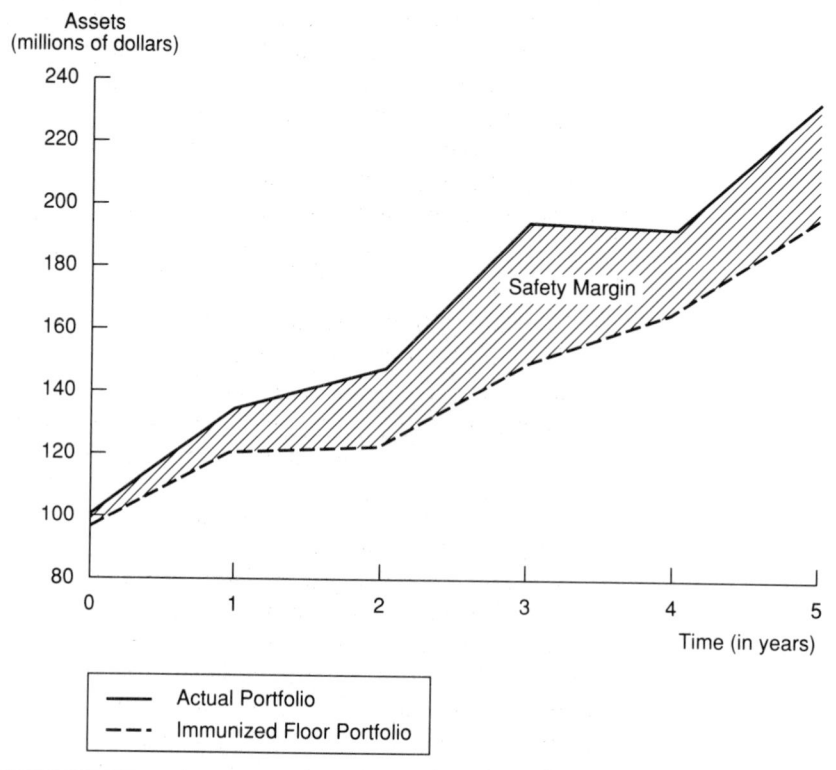

Source: Martin L. Leibowitz and Alfred Weinberger, "Contingent Immunization—Part I: Risk Control Procedures," *Financial Analysts Journal* 38, no. 6 (November–December 1982): 17–32. Reprinted with permission.

value of the portfolio over time. The bottom line is the required value of the immunized floor portfolio given prevailing market rates. Specifically, the bottom line is the *required value of the portfolio* if we were to immunize at today's rates to attain the necessary ending-wealth value. As an example of how this floor portfolio would be constructed, consider the original 14 percent floor rate that implied an ending-wealth value of $196.72 million at the end of the 5-year horizon date. If one year after the initiation of the portfolio, market rates were 10 percent, you would need a minimum of approximately $133.14 million to get to $196.72 million in four years. This minimum value is $196.72 million times the present value factor for 10 percent for the four remaining years, assuming semiannual compounding (.6761). Put another way, $133.14 invested at 10 percent for four years equals $196.72 million. The point is, if the active manager had predicted correctly and had a long-duration portfolio under these conditions of declining market rates, the actual value of the portfolio would be much higher

FIGURE 18.10
Comparison of Return Distributions

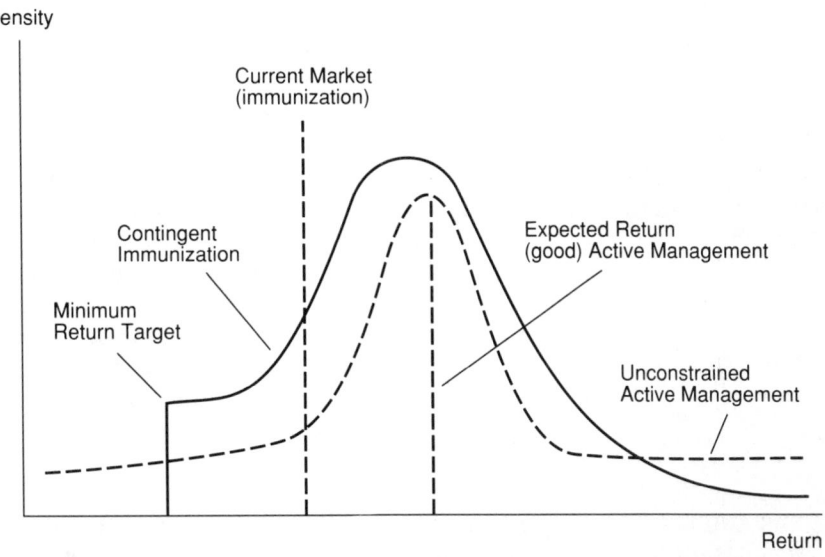

Source: Martin L. Leibowitz and Alfred Weinberger, "Contingent Immunization—Part II: Problem Areas,"
Financial Analysts Journal 39, no. 1 (January–February 1983): 35–50. Reprinted with permission.

than this required value, and there would be a safety margin. A year later, you would determine the assets needed at the rate prevailing at that point in time. Assuming interest rates had increased to 12 percent, you could determine that you would need a floor portfolio of about $138.69 million, because this is the present value of the $196.72 million for three years at 12 percent, assuming semiannual compounding (.7050). Again, you would expect the actual value of the portfolio to be greater than this required floor portfolio, so you still have a safety margin. If you ever reached the point where the actual value of the portfolio was equal to the required floor value, you would stop the active management and immunize what was left *at the current market rate* to ensure that the ending value would be $196.72 million.

In summary, the contingent immunization strategy encompasses the opportunity to engage in active portfolio management if you are willing to accept a floor return (and ending-wealth value) that is below what is currently available. The graph in Figure 18.10 describes the trade-offs involved in contingent immunization.

PORTFOLIO IMPLICATIONS

The high level of interest rates that has prevailed since the latter part of the 1960s has provided increasingly attractive returns to bond investors, while the wide swings in interest rates that have accompanied these high market yields have provided capital gains opportunities for aggressive portfolio managers. It might be argued that this recent performance of fixed-income securities is not out of the ordinary. In fact, it may be substandard compared to the performance of other investment vehicles and may even raise questions about the place of these securities in a total portfolio. An important consideration for portfolio managers, therefore, is the proper role of fixed-income securities in an efficient market.

BONDS IN A TOTAL PORTFOLIO CONTEXT

The performance of fixed-income securities has improved even more than indicated by returns alone, because bonds offer substantial diversification benefits. In an efficient market, neither stocks nor bonds should dominate a portfolio but some combination of them should provide a superior risk-adjusted return compared to either one taken alone, assuming low correlation between stocks and bonds. While Sharpe confirmed that stock returns were superior to bond yields during the test period 1938–1971, his results also showed that, due to the favorable covariance between bonds and equities, the combination of the securities in a portfolio vastly improved the return per unit of risk.[27]

BONDS AND CAPITAL MARKET THEORY

Modern capital market theory contends that there should be an upward-sloping market line, meaning that greater return should be accompanied by greater risk. Compared to other market vehicles, fixed-income securities have traditionally been viewed as low risk, and their rates of return have been accordingly modest—until the late 1960s. At that time, the inflation rate increased, and bond yields likewise increased. Also, during periods of high economic uncertainty, such as the recession of 1974, the risk premiums on bonds increased substantially. This was because the risk of default for low-rated obligations increases during economic recessions.[28] As noted earlier in the chapter the risk premium on junk bonds has fluctuated dramatically over time.

Capital market theory also relates the risk-return behavior of fixed-income securities to other financial assets. Because fixed-income securities are considered to be relatively conservative investments, we would expect them to be on the lower end of the capital market line. A study by Soldofsky examined the comparative risk-return characteristics of 28 classes of long-term securities.[29] Figure 18.11 shows the basic findings of the study and confirms the *a priori* expectations. Specifically, government and high-grade corporate bonds were at the low end of the curve, and it progressed to regular preferred stocks, high-quality common stocks, convertible securities, and finally to lower-quality stocks and deep discount bonds. An annual analysis of capital market returns by Ibbotson Associates compar-

---

[27] William F. Sharpe, "Bonds vs. Stocks: Some Lessons from Capital Market Theory," *Financial Analysts Journal* 29, no. 6 (November–December 1973): 74–80.

[28] For a detailed discussion on this topic that considers several studies on the subject, see James C. Van Horne, *Financial Market Rates and Flows*, 2d ed. (Englewood Cliffs, N.J.: Prentice-Hall, 1984), Chapter 6.

[29] Robert M. Soldofsky, "Risk and Return for Long-Term Securities, 1971–1982," *Journal of Portfolio Management* 11, no. 1 (Fall 1984): 57–64.

FIGURE 18.11
Risk-Return Graph for Long-Term Securities, 1971–1982

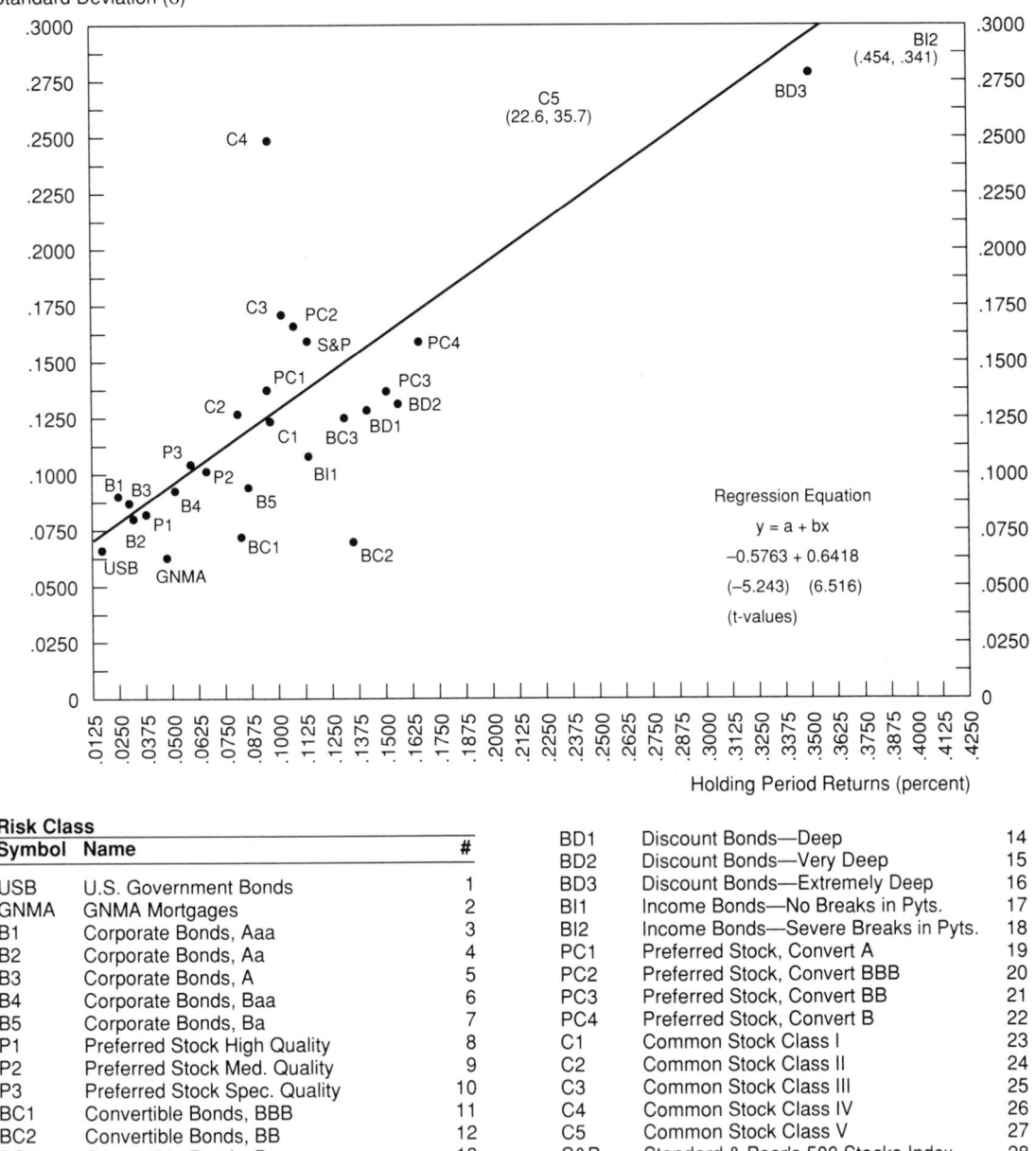

Risk Class		
Symbol	**Name**	**#**
USB	U.S. Government Bonds	1
GNMA	GNMA Mortgages	2
B1	Corporate Bonds, Aaa	3
B2	Corporate Bonds, Aa	4
B3	Corporate Bonds, A	5
B4	Corporate Bonds, Baa	6
B5	Corporate Bonds, Ba	7
P1	Preferred Stock High Quality	8
P2	Preferred Stock Med. Quality	9
P3	Preferred Stock Spec. Quality	10
BC1	Convertible Bonds, BBB	11
BC2	Convertible Bonds, BB	12
BC3	Convertible Bonds, B	13
BD1	Discount Bonds—Deep	14
BD2	Discount Bonds—Very Deep	15
BD3	Discount Bonds—Extremely Deep	16
BI1	Income Bonds—No Breaks in Pyts.	17
BI2	Income Bonds—Severe Breaks in Pyts.	18
PC1	Preferred Stock, Convert A	19
PC2	Preferred Stock, Convert BBB	20
PC3	Preferred Stock, Convert BB	21
PC4	Preferred Stock, Convert B	22
C1	Common Stock Class I	23
C2	Common Stock Class II	24
C3	Common Stock Class III	25
C4	Common Stock Class IV	26
C5	Common Stock Class V	27
S&P	Standard & Poor's 500 Stocks Index	28

*Minimum term to maturity on bonds is 15 years.

Source: Robert M. Soldofsky, "Risk and Return for Long-Term Securities, 1971–1982," *The Journal of Portfolio Management* 11, no. 1 (Fall 1984), p. 60. Reprinted by permission.

FIGURE 18.12

Mean Rate of Return and Standard Deviation of Returns for Common Stocks, Government and Corporate Bonds, T-Bills, and Inflation: 1926–1987

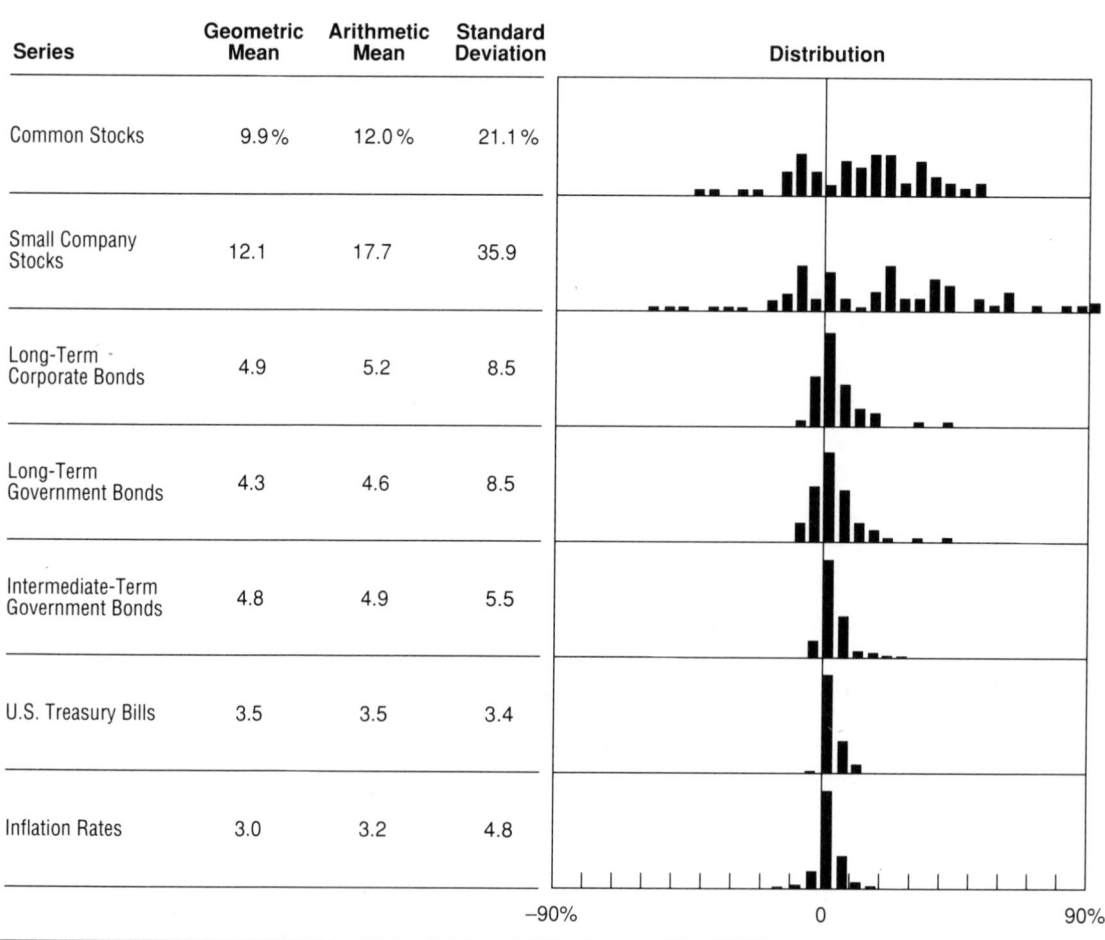

Series	Geometric Mean	Arithmetic Mean	Standard Deviation	Distribution
Common Stocks	9.9%	12.0%	21.1%	
Small Company Stocks	12.1	17.7	35.9	
Long-Term Corporate Bonds	4.9	5.2	8.5	
Long-Term Government Bonds	4.3	4.6	8.5	
Intermediate-Term Government Bonds	4.8	4.9	5.5	
U.S. Treasury Bills	3.5	3.5	3.4	
Inflation Rates	3.0	3.2	4.8	

Source: Ibbotson, Roger G., and Rex A. Sinquefield, *Stocks, Bonds, Bills, and Inflation* (SBBI), 1982, updated in SBBI 1988 Yearbook, Ibbotson Associates, Inc., Chicago. Reprinted with permission.

ing corporate and government bonds (long- and intermediate-term) to common stocks (total NYSE and small-firm) and Treasury bill obligations indicated similar results. As Figure 18.12 shows, the long-run risk-return behavior was as expected. Treasury bills have the least risk and return, followed by government bonds, corporate bonds, total common stocks, and finally small capitalization common stocks. The only results not completely consistent with expectations were the returns for long-term government bonds. These were lower than intermediate government bonds, and yet long governments had a risk measure similar to corporate bonds.

Apparently, the generally rising interest rates affected the long bonds more than the intermediate bonds.

BOND PRICE BEHAVIOR IN A CAPM FRAMEWORK

The capital asset pricing model (CAPM) is expected to provide a framework for explaining realized security returns as a function of nondiversifiable market risk. We would expect bond returns to be linked directly to risk of default and interest rate risk. While interest rate risk should certainly be nondiversifiable, some evidence exists that default risk is also largely nondiversifiable because default experience is closely related to the business cycle.[30] Thus, since the major bond risks are largely nondiversifiable, we should be able to define bond returns in the context of the CAPM. Because of data-collection problems, relatively few studies have examined bond price behavior in a CAPM framework. A study by Percival showed only a modest effect of beta on bond returns.[31] An analysis of beta as a function of bond and issuer characteristics indicated that bond betas were more responsive to the intrinsic characteristics of the issue (coupons maturity, duration, call features) than of the issuer.

Reilly and Joehnk found that average bond betas had no significant or consistent relationship with agency rating.[32] Since the data base involved only investment-grade securities, bond prices were presumed to be reacting to interest rate movements *across* ratings. Because the study dealt with interest-sensitive securities, the interest rate risk, which is a market-related risk, has an overpowering effect on price performance and largely negated the effects of differential default risk (a company-specific risk), which is reflected in comparative agency ratings. This is compatible with our reasoning in Chapter 11 that interest rate movements are more powerful than yield spreads due to differences in risk of default and agency ratings.

Alexander examined some of the assumptions of the market model as related to bonds and found two major factors that could cause problems.[33] First, the bond betas and regression results were sensitive to the market index used.[34] Specifically, when he considered a pure stock index, a pure bond index, or a composite stock-bond index, there were major differences, and the pure bond index had the biggest problems. Second, the results were sensitive to the time period used; the bond betas tended to increase during periods when bond yields were abnormally high.

Weinstein computed betas for bonds also using several market series and related the betas to term to maturity, coupon, and bond ratings.[35] The

---

[30] Hickman, *Corporate Bond Quality,* and T. R. Atkinson, *Trends in Corporate Bond Quality* (New York: National Bureau of Economic Research, 1967).

[31] John Percival, "Corporate Bonds in a Market Model Context," *Journal of Business Research* 2, no. 4 (October 1974): 461–467.

[32] Frank K. Reilly and Michael D. Joehnk, "The Association between Market-Determined Risk Measures for Bonds and Bond Ratings," *Journal of Finance* 31, no. 5 (December 1976): 1387–1403.

[33] Gordon J. Alexander, "Applying the Market Model to Long-Term Corporate Bonds," *Journal of Financial and Quantitative Analysis* 15, no. 5 (December 1980): 1063–1080.

[34] This is similar to the well-known work by Roll on market series.

[35] Mark I. Weinstein, "The Systematic Risk of Corporate Bonds," *Journal of Financial and Quantitative Analysis* 16, no. 3 (September 1981): 157–278.

results for beta using alternative market indexes (pure stock, pure bond, combined) revealed a very strong correlation between betas from the stock and the combined indexes, a fairly strong relationship between the betas from the bond and the combined indexes, and a weak relationship between the betas from pure stock and bond indexes. Because of some perceived problems of using duration, he examined maturity and coupon separately and found a positive relationship between beta and term to maturity and a weak negative relationship between the coupon and beta. There was no significant relationship between beta and bond rating for the top four classes of ratings (similar to the findings of Reilly and Joehnk), but there was a weak relationship using the top six ratings. The author postulated a nonlinear relationship where the risk of default becomes significant only for low ratings.

Weinstein subsequently employed the same sample and the combined stock-bond index to compute the bond betas and examined their stability over time.[36] He employed a model that assumed the bond betas are constant compared to a model that allowed the systematic risk to vary consistently with the Black-Scholes-Merton options pricing model. The results indicated that a model that assumes the bond betas change over time has more explanatory power than a constant risk model. Also, he found that the variation in beta was related to firm characteristics (e.g., debt-equity ratios, variance of rate of return on assets) and bond characteristics (coupon, term-to-maturity).

Thus evidence on the usefulness of the CAPM as related to the bond market is mixed. First, there are obvious problems regarding the appropriate market index to use and the instability of the systematic risk measure. Further, the risk-return relationship did not hold for the higher-rated securities. Finally, there appears to be a relationship between the systematic risk measure and some characteristics of the firm and the bond.

BOND MARKET EFFICIENCY

Two versions of the efficient market hypothesis (EMH) are examined in the context of fixed-income securities, the weak and the semistrong theories. The weak-form hypothesis contends that security prices fully reflect all market information and maintains that price movements are independent events, so historical price information is useless in predicting future price behavior. Studies of weak-form efficiency related to bond prices have examined the ability of investors to *forecast* interest rates because of the effects that interest rates have on price behavior and the importance of interest rate expectations for bond portfolio management. If you can forecast interest rates, you can forecast price behavior. Several studies[37] reached

---

[36] Mark I. Weinstein, "Bond Systematic Risk and the Option Pricing Model," *Journal of Finance* 38, no. 5 (December 1983): 1415–1429.

[37] See, for example, Michael J. Prell, "How Well Do the Experts Forecast Interest Rates?" *Monthly Review*, Federal Reserve Bank of Kansas City (September–October 1973): 3–13; William A. Bomberger and W. J. Frazer, "Interest Rates, Uncertainty, and the Livingston Data," *Journal of Finance* 36, no. 3 (June 1981): 661–675; Stephen K. McNees, "The Recent Record of Thirteen Forecasters," *New England Economic Review*, Federal Reserve Bank of Boston (September–October 1981); and Adrian W. Throop, "Interest Rate Forecasts and Market Efficiency," *Economic Review*, Federal Reserve Bank of San Francisco (Spring 1981): 29–43.

the same conclusion: interest rate behavior cannot be consistently and accurately forecast! In fact, one study suggests that the best forecast is no forecast at all. The models developed ranged from a naive approach to fairly sophisticated techniques including models that used historical information, some that ignored it, and a study that used the expectations of acknowledged experts. In all cases, the most naive model, or no forecast at all, provided the best measure of future interest rate behavior. Clearly, if interest rates cannot be forecast, then neither can bond prices using historical prices, all of which supports the weak-form EMH.

The semistrong EMH asserts that current prices fully reflect all public knowledge and that efforts to act on such information are largely unproductive. Several studies on the information content of bond ratings did not question the accuracy of agency ratings in reflecting the financial strength of the issuers, but examined the informational value of bond rating *changes.*

Katz examined monthly changes in bond yields surrounding ratings changes and found a significant impact of the change.[38] Weinstein examined the behavior of monthly bond returns during the period surrounding the announcement of rating changes and found evidence of an effect 18 to 7 months before the announcement, but no evidence of an effect from 6 months before the announcement to 6 months after the announcement.[39] In contrast to these studies, several others have examined the impact of bond rating changes on stock prices and returns. Pinches and Singleton concluded that there was very little impact on stock prices due to the ratings change.[40] Griffin and Sanvicente found a significant stock price impact following bond downgradings.[41] Alternatively, they found no impact on stock prices during the month when an upgrading was announced, but there was an impact during the prior 11 months. Holthausen and Leftwich examined daily stock return data surrounding the announcement of bond rating changes and found negative abnormal returns at the time of downgradings.[42] There was little evidence of abnormal price changes surrounding the announcement of an upgrading, however.

In summary, the evidence on the adjustment of bond prices to rating changes is mixed, with any impact being more pronounced for downgradings. The evidence on the reaction of stock prices to rating changes is tending toward finding an impact, but only for downgradings. Either the market adjusts early for the upgradings or does not seem to react to the good news.

---

[38] Steven Katz, "The Price Adjustment Process of Bonds to Rating Reclassifications: A Test of Bond Market Efficiency," *Journal of Finance* 29, no. 2 (May 1974): 551–559.

[39] Mark I. Weinstein, "The Effect of a Rating Change Announcement on Bond Price," *Journal of Financial Economics* 5, no. 3 (December 1977): 329–350.

[40] George E . Pinches and Clay Singleton, "The Adjustment of Stock Prices to Bond Rating Changes," *Journal of Finance* 33, no. 1 (March 1978): 29–44.

[41] Paul A. Griffin and Antonio Z. Sanvicente, "Common Stock Returns and Rating Changes: A Methodological Comparison," *Journal of Finance* 37, no. 1 (March 1982): 103–119.

[42] Robert W. Holthausen and Richard W. Leftwich, "The Effect of Bond Rating Changes on Common Stock Prices," *Journal of Financial Economics* 17, no. 1 (September 1986): 57–89.

What does market efficiency imply regarding specific bond market strategies, such as bond swaps and yield spreads? By their very nature, bond swaps suggest some market inefficiency, because these temporary anomalies within or between market segments afford alert investors the opportunity for extraordinary returns. Numerous profitable swap opportunities suggest that underlying price irregularities are neither rare nor random events.

Such opportunities may be caused by the *institutional* nature of the market and the resulting *market segmentation.* In effect, it may be largely artificial constraints, regulations, and statutes that lead to the opportunity to execute profitable bond swaps. Or perhaps an increase in yield through a quality bond swap that results in a lower agency rating does not imply any market inefficiency, since the greater the default risk, the greater the return. Yield spreads are likewise indications of market efficiency, because they reflect equilibrium yield rates based on differential standards of risk, quality, and other issue characteristics. AAA corporates should yield less than A-rated obligations because they possess a different risk-return profile. The existence of yield spreads is rational, and the sizes of such spreads are determined in a highly efficient manner.

SUMMARY

Bond portfolio management strategies include the simple buy-and-hold strategy, several alternative active portfolio strategies, dedicated cash matching, classical immunization, horizon matching, and contingent immunization. While you should understand the alternatives available and how to implement them, the choice of a specific strategy is based upon the needs and desires of the client and the background and talents of the portfolio manager.

The risk-return performance of bonds has been consistent with expectations and has enhanced portfolios because of their low covariance with other financial assets. The application of CAPM concepts to bonds has been mixed, since it has been difficult to derive acceptable measures of systematic risk, and the risk measures derived have been unstable.

Studies on the bond market have supported the theory of weak-form efficiency. The evidence for semistrong efficiency has been mixed. This lack of efficiency could be due to the relatively inactive secondary markets for most corporate bonds compared to the active markets for equities.

QUESTIONS

1. Explain the difference between a pure buy-and-hold strategy and a modified buy-and-hold strategy.
2. Briefly define the following bond swaps: pure yield pick-up swap, substitution swap, and tax swap.
3. What are two primary reasons for investing in deep discounted bonds?
4. Briefly describe three techniques that are considered active bond portfolio management strategies.

5. Discuss two variables that you would examine very carefully if you were analyzing a junk bond, and indicate why they are important.

6. What are the advantages of a cash-matched dedicated portfolio? Discuss the difficulties of developing such a portfolio and the added costs.

7. What are the two components of interest rate risk? Describe each of these components.

8. What is meant by bond portfolio immunization?

9. If the yield curve were flat and did not change, how would you immunize your portfolio?

10. You begin with an investment horizon of four years and a portfolio duration of four years with a market interest rate of 10 percent. A year later, what is your investment horizon? Assuming no change in interest rates, what is the duration of your portfolio relative to your investment horizon? What does this imply about your ability to immunize your portfolio?

11. It has been contended that a zero coupon bond is the ideal financial instrument to use for immunizing a portfolio. Discuss the reasoning for this statement in terms of the objective of immunization (i.e., the elimination of interest rate risk).

12. During a conference with a client, the subject of classical immunization is introduced. The client questions the fee charged for developing and managing an immunized portfolio. It is her understanding that it is basically a passive investment strategy, so the management fee should be substantially lower. What would you tell the client to show that it is not a passive policy and that it actually requires more time and talent than a buy-and-hold policy?

13. Describe the concept of contingent immunization. What do you give up with this, and what do you gain?

14. *CFA Examination III (June 1983)*: The ability to immunize a bond portfolio is very desirable for bond portfolio managers in some instances.

14a. Discuss the components of interest rate risk—assuming a change in interest rates over time, and explain the two risks faced by the holder of a bond.

14b. Define immunization, and discuss why a bond manager would immunize his portfolio.

14c. Explain why a duration-matching strategy is a superior technique to a maturity-matching strategy for the minimization of interest rate risk.

14d. Explain in specific terms how you would use a zero coupon bond to immunize a bond portfolio. Discuss why a zero coupon bond is an ideal instrument in this regard.

14e. Explain how contingent immunization, another bond portfolio management technique, differs from classical immunization. Discuss why a bond portfolio manager would engage in contingent immunization. [35 minutes]

15. *CFA Examination III (June 1986)*: During the past several years there has been substantial growth in the dollar amount of portfolios managed using immunization and dedication techniques. Assume a client wants to know the basic differences between (1) classical immunization, (2) contingent

immunization, (3) cash-matched dedication, and (4) duration-matched dedication.

15a. Briefly describe each of these four techniques.

15b. Briefly discuss the ongoing investment action you would have to carry out if managing an immunized portfolio.

15c. Briefly discuss three of the major considerations involved with creating a cash-matched dedicated portfolio.

15d. Describe two parameters that should be specified when using contingent immunization.

15e. Select one of the four alternative techniques that requires the least degree of active management and justify your selection. [20 minutes]

16. *CFA Examination III (June 1988)*: After you have constructed a structured fixed income portfolio (i.e., one that is dedicated, indexed, or immunized), it may be possible over time to improve on the initial optimal portfolio while continuing to meet the primary goal. Discuss three conditions that would be considered favorable for a restructuring assuming no change in objectives for the investor and cite an example of each condition. [10 minutes]

17. *CFA Examination III (June 1988)*: The use of bond index funds has grown dramatically in recent years.

17a. Discuss the reasons you would expect it to be easier or more difficult to construct a bond index than a stock index.

17b. It is contended that the operational process of managing a corporate bond index fund is more difficult than managing an equity index fund. Discuss three examples that support this contention. [10 minutes]

18. *CFA Examination III (June 1988)*: Hans Kaufmann is a global fixed income portfolio manager based in Switzerland. His clients are primarily U.S.-based pension funds. He allocates investments in the following four countries:

- United States
- Japan
- West Germany
- United Kingdom

His approach is to make investment allocation decisions between these four countries based on his global economic outlook. In order to develop this, Kaufmann analyzes these five factors for each country:

- real economic growth
- inflation
- monetary policy
- interest rates
- exchange rates

When Kaufmann believes that the four economies are equally attractive for investment purposes, he equally weights investments in the four countries. When the economies are not equally attractive, he overweights the country or countries where he sees the largest potential return.

Tables 1 through 5 present relevant economic data and forecasts.

18a. Indicate, before taking into account currency hedging, whether Kaufmann should overweight or underweight investments in each country. Justify your position. [15 minutes]

18b. Briefly describe how your answer to Part A might change with the use of currency hedging techniques. [5 minutes]

TABLE 1
Real GNP/GDP (Annual Changes)

	1985	1986	1987	1988E
United States	3.0%	2.9%	2.4%	2.7%
Japan	4.7	2.4	3.2	3.4
West Germany	2.0	2.5	1.5	2.1
United Kingdom	3.4	3.0	3.4	2.3

TABLE 2
GNP/GDP Deflator (Annual Changes)

	1985	1986	1987	1988E
United States	3.2%	2.6%	3.3%	3.8%
Japan	1.5	2.8	3.0	3.0
West Germany	2.2	3.1	2.5	2.2
United Kingdom	6.0	3.5	4.5	4.8

TABLE 3
Narrow Money (M1) (Annual Changes)

	1985	1986	1987	1988E
United States	9.2%	13.4%	5.5%	7.0%
Japan	5.0	6.9	9.9	10.0
West Germany	4.3	8.5	7.5	8.5
United Kingdom	17.8	25.6	16.5	12.0

TABLE 4
Long-Term Interest Rates (Average Annual)

	1985	1986	1987	1988E
United States	10.6%	7.7%	8.8%	9.0%
Japan	6.5	5.2	6.1	6.1
West Germany	6.9	5.9	6.1	7.0
United Kingdom	10.6	9.9	9.8	9.5

TABLE 5
Exchange Rates (Currency per U.S. $, Average Annual)

	1985	1986	1987	1988E
United States (Dollars)	1.00	1.00	1.00	1.00
Japan (Yen)	228.08	163.87	141.22	140.09
West Germany (Marks)	2.80	2.08	1.74	1.67
United Kingdom (Pounds)	0.74	0.67	0.58	0.59

Sources: *World Economic Outlook*, October 1987 and Kaufmann's estimates.

PROBLEMS

1. You have a portfolio with a market value of $50 million and a Macauley duration of seven years (assuming a market interest rate of 10 percent). If interest rates jump to 12 percent, what would be the estimated value of your portfolio using duration? Show all your computations.

2. Answer the following questions assuming that at the initiation of an investment account, the market value of your portfolio is $200 million, and you immunize the portfolio at 12 percent for six years. During the first year, interest rates are constant at 12 percent.

2a. What is the market value of the portfolio at the end of Year 1?

2b. Immediately after the end of the year, interest rates decline to 10 percent. Estimate the new value of the portfolio assuming you knew of the required rebalancing (use only modified duration).

3. Compute the Macauley duration under the following conditions:

3a. A bond with a five-year term to maturity, a 12 percent coupon (annual payments), and a market yield of 10 percent

3b. A bond with a four-year term to maturity, a 12 percent coupon (annual payments), and a market yield of 10 percent

3c. Compare your answers to Parts a and b, and discuss the implications of this for classical immunization.

4. Compute the Macauley duration under the following conditions:

4a. A bond with a four-year term to maturity, a 10 percent coupon (annual payments), and a market yield of 8 percent

4b. A bond with a four-year term to maturity, a 10 percent coupon (annual payments), and a market yield of 12 percent

4c. Compare your answers to Parts a and b and, assuming it was an immediate shift in yields, discuss the implications of this for classical immunization.

5. Answer the following questions about a zero coupon bond with a term to maturity at issue of 10 years (assume semiannual compounding):

5a. What is the duration of the bond at issue assuming a market yield of 10 percent? What is its duration if the market yield is 14 percent? Discuss these two answers.

5b. Compute the initial issue price of this bond at a market yield of 14 percent.

5c. Compute the initial issue price of this bond at a market yield of 10 percent.

5d. A year after issue, the bond in Part c is selling to yield 12 percent. What is its current market price? Assuming you owned this bond during this year, what is your rate of return?

6. A major requirement in running a contingent immunization portfolio policy is the need to monitor the relationship between the current market value of the portfolio and the required value of the floor portfolio. In this regard, assume a $300 million portfolio with a horizon of five years. The available market rate at the initiation of the portfolio is 14 percent, but the client is willing to accept 12 percent as a floor rate to allow you to use active management strategies. The current market values and current market rates at the end of Years 1, 2, and 3 are as follows:

END OF YEAR	MARKET VALUE	MARKET YIELD	REQUIRED FLOOR PORTFOLIO	SAFETY MARGIN (DEFICIENCY)
1	340.00	.12		
2	375.00	.10		
3	360.20	.14		

6a. What is the required ending-wealth value for this portfolio?

6b. What is the value of the required floor portfolio at the end of Years 1, 2, and 3?

6c. Compute the safety margin or deficiency at the end of Years 1, 2, and 3.

7. Evaluate the following pure yield pick-up swap: You currently hold a 20-year, 9.0 percent coupon bond priced to yield 11.0 percent. As a swap candidate, you are considering a 20-year, Aa 11 percent coupon bond priced to yield 11.50 percent. (Assume reinvestment at 11.50 percent.)

	CURRENT BOND	CANDIDATE BOND
Dollar investment	_____	_____
Coupon	_____	_____
i on one coupon	_____	_____
Principal value at year-end	_____	_____
Total accrued	_____	_____
Realized compound yield	_____	_____
Value of swap: basis points in one year	_____	_____

8. Evaluate the following substitution swap: You currently hold a 25-year, 9.0 percent coupon bond priced to yield 10.5 percent. As a swap candidate, you are considering a 25-year, Aa 9.0 percent coupon bond priced to yield 10.75 percent. (Assume a one-year work-out period and reinvestment at 10.5 percent.)

	CURRENT BOND	CANDIDATE BOND
Dollar investment	_____	_____
Coupon	_____	_____
i on one coupon	_____	_____
Principal value at year-end	_____	_____
Total accrued	_____	_____
Total gain	_____	_____
Gain per invested dollar	_____	_____
Realized compound yield	_____	_____
Value of swap: basis points in one year	_____	_____

9. *CFA Examination III (June 1984):* Reinvestment risk is a major factor for bond managers to consider when determining the most appropriate or

optimal strategy for a fixed-income portfolio. Briefly describe each of the following bond portfolio management strategies, and explain how each deals with reinvestment risk:

9a. Active management

9b. Classical immunization

9c. Dedicated portfolio

9d. Contingent immunization [20 minutes]

10. *CFA Examination III (June 1985)*: A major requirement in managing a fixed-income portfolio using a contingent immunization policy is the need to monitor the relationship between the current market value of the portfolio and the required value of the floor portfolio. This difference is defined as the Margin of Error. In this regard, assume a $300 million portfolio with a time horizon of five years. The available market rate at the initiation of the portfolio is 12%, but the client is willing to accept 10% as a floor rate to allow use of active management strategies. The current market values and current market rates at the end of years one, two, and three are as follows:

End of Year	Market Value ($Mil)	Market Yield	Required Floor Portfolio ($Mil)	Margin of Error ($Mil)
1	$340.9	10%		
2	405.5	8		
3	395.2	12		

Table 1
Present Value

Period	Interest Rate								
	4%	5%	6%	7%	8%	9%	10%	11%	12%
1	.962	.952	.943	.935	.926	.917	.909	.901	.893
2	.925	.907	.890	.873	.857	.842	.826	.812	.797
3	.889	.864	.840	.816	.794	.772	.751	.731	.712
4	.855	.823	.792	.763	.735	.708	.683	.659	.636
5	.822	.784	.747	.713	.681	.650	.621	.593	.657
6	.790	.746	.705	.666	.630	.596	.564	.535	.507
7	.760	.711	.665	.623	.583	.547	.513	.482	.452
8	.731	.677	.627	.582	.540	.502	.467	.434	.404
9	.703	.645	.592	.544	.500	.460	.424	.391	.361
10	.676	.614	.558	.508	.463	.422	.386	.352	.322

Table 2
Compound Value

Period	Interest Rate								
	4%	5%	6%	7%	8%	9%	10%	11%	12%
1	1.040	1.050	1.060	1.070	1.080	1.090	1.100	1.110	1.120
2	1.082	1.102	1.124	1.145	1.166	1.188	1.210	1.232	1.254
3	1.125	1.158	1.191	1.225	1.260	1.295	1.221	1.368	1.405
4	1.170	1.216	1.262	1.311	1.360	1.412	1.464	1.518	1.574
5	1.217	1.276	1.338	1.403	1.469	1.539	1.611	1.685	1.762
6	1.265	1.340	1.419	1.501	1.587	1.677	1.772	1.870	1.974
7	1.316	1.407	1.504	1.606	1.714	1.828	1.949	2.076	2.211
8	1.369	1.477	1.594	1.718	1.851	1.993	2.144	2.305	2.476
9	1.423	1.551	1.689	1.838	1.999	2.172	2.358	2.558	2.773
10	1.480	1.629	1.791	1.967	2.159	2.367	2.594	2.839	3.106

Assuming Semiannual Compounding:

10a. Calculate the required ending-wealth value for this portfolio.

10b. Calculate the value of the required floor portfolios at the end of years one, two, and three.

10c. Compute the Margin of Error at the end of years one, two, and three.

10d. Indicate the action that a portfolio manager utilizing a contingent immunization policy would take if the Margin of Error at the end of any year had been zero or negative. [15 minutes]

REFERENCES

Alexander, Gordon J. "Applying the Market Model to Long-Term Corporate Bonds." *Journal of Financial and Quantitative Analysis* 15, no. 5 (December 1980).

Altman, Edward I., and Scott A. Nammacher. *Investing in Junk Bonds.* New York: John Wiley & Sons, 1987.

Bierwag, G. O., and George G. Kaufman. "Coping with the Risk of Interest Rate Fluctuations: A Note." *Journal of Business* 50, no. 3 (July 1977).

Bierwag, G. O. "Immunization, Duration, and the Term Structure of Interest Rates." *Journal of Financial and Quantitative Analysis* 12, no. 5 (December 1977).

Bierwag, G. O., and George G. Kaufman. "Bond Portfolio Strategy Simulations: A Critique." *Journal of Financial and Quantitative Analysis* 13, no. 3 (September 1978).

Bierwag, G. O., George G. Kaufman, and Alden Toevs. "Single Factor Duration Models in a General Equilibrium Framework." *Journal of Finance* 37, no. 2 (May 1982).

Bierwag, G. O., George G. Kaufman, and Alden Toevs, eds. *Innovations in Bond Portfolio Management: Duration Analysis and Immunization.* Greenwich, Conn.: JAI Press, 1983.

Bierwag, G. O., George G. Kaufman, and Alden Toevs. "Duration: Its Development and Use in Bond Portfolio Management." *Financial Analysts Journal* 39, no. 4 (July–August 1983).

Bierwag, G. O., George G. Kaufman, and Chulsoon Khang. "Duration and Bond Portfolio Analysis: An Overview." *Journal of Financial and Quantitative Analysis* 13, no. 5 (November 1978).

Bierwag, G. O., George G. Kaufman, and Alden Toevs. "Immunizing Strategies for Funding Multiple Liabilities." *Journal of Financial and Quantitative Analysis* 18, no. 1 (March 1983).

Bierwag, G. O., George G. Kaufman, Robert L. Schweitzer, and Alden Toevs. "The Art of Risk Management in Bond Portfolios." *Journal of Portfolio Management* 7, no. 3 (Spring 1981).

Cox, John, Jonathon E. Ingersoll, and Stephen A. Ross. "Duration and Measurement of Basis Risk." *Journal of Business* 52, no. 1 (January 1979).

Fabozzi, Frank J., and Irving M. Pollack, eds. *The Handbook of Fixed Income Securities.* 2d ed. Homewood, Ill.: Dow Jones-Irwin, 1987.

Fisher, Lawrence, and Roman L. Weil. "Coping with the Risk of Interest-Rate Fluctuations: Returns to Bondholders from Naive and Optimal Strategies." *Journal of Business* 44, no. 4 (October 1971).

Fridson, Martin. *High Yield Bonds: Assessing Risk and Identifying Value in Speculative Grade Securities.* Chicago: Probus Publishing, 1989.

Hawawini, Gabriel A., ed. *Bond Duration and Immunization: Early Developments and Recent Contributions.* New York: Garland Publishing, 1982.

Hickman, W. Braddock. *Corporate Bond Quality and Investor Experience.* A study by the National Bureau of Economic Research. Princeton, N.J.: Princeton University Press, 1958.

Howe, Jane Tripp. *Junk Bonds: Analysis and Portfolio Strategies.* Chicago: Probus Publishing, 1988.

Homer, Sidney, and Martin L. Leibowitz. *Inside the Yield Book.* Englewood Cliffs, N.J.: Prentice-Hall, 1972.

Ingersoll, Jonathon E., Jeffrey Skelton, and Roman L. Weil. "Duration: Forty Years Later." *Journal of Financial and Quantitative Analysis* 13, no. 5 (November 1978).

Leibowitz, Martin L., and Alfred Weinberger. "Contingent Immunization—Part I: Risk Control Procedures." *Financial Analysts Journal* 38, no. 6 (November–December 1982).

Leibowitz, Martin L., "The Dedicated Bond Portfolio in Pension Funds—Part I: Motivation and Basics." *Financial Analysts Journal* 42, no. 1 (January–February 1986).

Leibowitz, Martin L., "The Dedicated Bond Portfolio Pension Funds—Part II: Immunization, Horizon Matching, and Contingent Procedures." *Financial Analysts Journal* 42, no. 2 (March–April 1986).

Leibowitz, Martin L., and Alfred Weinberger. "Contingent Immunization—Part II: Problem Areas." *Financial Analysts Journal* 39, no. 1 (January–February 1983).

Redington, F. M. "Review of the Principle of Life Office Valuations." *Journal of the Institute of Actuaries* 78 (1952).

Reilly, Frank K., and Michael D. Joehnk. "The Association between Market-Determined Risk Measures for Bonds and Bond Ratings." *Journal of Finance* 31, no. 5 (December 1976).

Tuttle, Donald., ed. *The Revolution in Techniques for Managing Bond Portfolios.* Charlottesville, Va.: The Institute of Chartered Financial Analysts, 1983.

Van Horne, James. *Financial Market Rates and Flows.* 2d ed. Englewood Cliffs, N.J.: Prentice-Hall, 1984.

Weil, Roman L. "Macauley's Duration: An Appreciation." *Journal of Business* 46, no. 4 (October 1973).

Weinstein, Mark I. "The Effect of a Rating Change Announcement on Bond Price." *Journal of Financial Economics* 5, no. 3 (December 1977).

Weinstein, Mark I. "Bond Systematic Risk and the Option Pricing Model." *Journal of Finance* 38, no. 5 (December 1983).

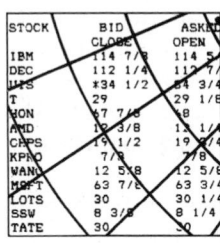

CHAPTER 19

INTERNATIONAL DIVERSIFICATION

After first considering the rationale for expecting significant benefits from international diversification, we will discuss the results of several studies that have examined the historical relationships between the returns for U.S. securities and foreign securities. Next, we will consider some of the methods of international diversification implementing this strategy and also the obstacles involved. The chapter concludes with a consideration of non-direct international investments.

WHY INTERNATIONAL DIVERSIFICATION?

Because the objective of diversification is to reduce the overall variance of a portfolio, our initial discussion considers why foreign securities should have low covariance with a portfolio of U.S. risky assets. The basic dividend valuation formula provides a framework for this discussion:

$$P = \frac{D_1}{k - g}.$$

The relevant variables are the expected dividend (D_1), the required rate of return (k), and the expected growth rate for dividends (g). It is contended that these variables differ significantly among countries and for different securities in the various countries. Because k and g are the most important variables, we will concentrate on them.

DIFFERENCES IN THE REQUIRED RATE OF RETURN (k)

As you know, k is a function of the economy's real risk-free rate of return, the expected rate of inflation in the economy, and a risk premium for the uncertainty involved. You will recall that the *real risk-free rate* is determined by the real growth rate in the economy and, in the short run, by tightness or ease in the capital markets. Different countries have experienced different rates of growth during the past several decades. Examples include the high rate of growth in Japan and Germany. The point is, these growth rates in different countries are not synchronized. In addition, at any time there are differences in the capital market conditions in different countries. Therefore, you should expect differences in the *level* of the RFR and also anticipate independent *changes* in this rate among countries.

DIFFERENCES IN RATES OF INFLATION

We have talked extensively about the fact that inflation has probably been the most important variable influencing asset valuation during the last decade. Therefore, the crucial question is whether the level of inflation and changes in the rate of inflation for alternative countries are correlated. If changes in inflation are highly correlated, required rates of return would move together, and security price movements would be related, which would reduce the benefits of international diversification. If, however, changes in rates of inflation are unique, then returns for securities in various countries would not be correlated, and international diversification would be useful.

To get a feeling for whether rates of inflation should be related, it is necessary to consider the factors that cause inflation. Specifically, inflation is generally described as either *demand-pull* (excess demand) or *cost-push*. Whether excess demand inflation is fueled by monetary policy or fiscal policy, it is enough to recognize that both the monetary and the fiscal policy of a country are generally determined by the internal needs of the country, which means that the specification and implementation of policy directives should be relatively independent among countries. Further, the impact of any monetary or fiscal policy change will differ among countries depending upon the current state of the country's economy. Similarly, the impact of cost-push inflation will depend upon the state of the economy and the power of various economic units such as unions.[1] Thus, while the basic causes of inflation may be reasonably universal, you should still expect differences in the level of inflation and relatively *independent changes* in the rate of inflation for different countries. Current examples were contained in the tables in Chapter 13 when we considered global market analysis. Because of the major impact that inflation has on the required rate of return, this discussion would imply substantial independence in k and consequent independence in security returns due to changes in k.

DIFFERENCES IN RISK PREMIUMS

While we would expect different covariances among countries, the important question is whether changes in the various fundamental risk variables should be independent (i.e., business risk, etc.). You will recall that *business risk* is a function of sales volatility and operating leverage. We would expect changes in sales volatility for firms in different countries to be unique, because the fiscal and monetary policy that affects domestic sales is independent, so changes in the level and volatility of sales should

---

[1] In this regard, see Dallas S. Batten and R. W. Hafer, "The Relative Impact of Monetary and Fiscal Actions on Economic Activity: A Cross Country Comparison," *Review*, Federal Reserve Bank of St. Louis, 65, no. 1 (January 1983): 5–12.

also be relatively independent. Similarly, the production mix differs from one country to another, so the *degree of operating leverage (DOL)* for firms in different countries should not be consistently related. As these determinants of business risk are not related, changes in the business risk among countries should not be related either.

Financial risk is typically measured in terms of balance sheet ratios (e.g., the debt/total capital ratio) or a cash flow ratio (e.g., the interest coverage ratio). Firms generally determine their capital structure based upon the tax laws in a country (the higher the corporate tax rate, the greater the tax advantage of debt versus equity), earnings stability (with greater earnings stability it is possible to employ more debt), and the expected rate of inflation (a higher expected rate of inflation would prompt more firms to become net debtors). Because these factors and *changes* in these factors are unique among countries, changes in the level of financial risk for different countries should be relatively independent.

The *liquidity* of an asset is a function of the number of investors who own and trade the asset, that is, the volume of trading in the asset, which is influenced by the general economic climate in a country. The expected differential in liquidity among countries is borne out by differences in trading volume on various national exchanges, such as Japan and the United States compared to the United Kingdom, Germany, and France. Therefore, because trading-volume changes are unique, changes in liquidity risk should be independent for different countries.

Exchange rate risk as it relates to a U.S. investor differs among countries based on the internal policies of each country that affect their growth and rate of inflation. Exchange rates will differ depending on independent monetary and fiscal policies, and changes in the exchange rates will vary and affect the trade balance among countries. Therefore, not only will the risk premium due to this factor cause differences in domestic rates of return, but the adjusted rates of return from investments will also vary due to these changes in exchange rates.

To summarize, an analysis of the factors that determine the required rate of return indicates that *changes* in these variables for different countries are generally determined by internal factors that are *independent* for each country. Therefore, changes in the required rate of return for securities in various countries will be relatively independent, and the rates of return on U.S. and foreign securities should have small covariance or correlation.

The level of covariance between two countries will depend upon the relationship between the economies involved. As an example, one would expect a fairly high correlation between U.S. and Canadian securities because the two economies are highly interrelated. In contrast, the U.S. economy has a very weak relationship to the economies of some third-world countries, so you would expect a weak correlation between stock returns.

INDEPENDENT CHANGES IN GROWTH RATE

It can also be argued that the major factors determining the growth rate (*g*) are generally independent among countries. You will recall that the *growth rate* is a function of the retention rate and the return on equity.

The retention rate for firms in alternative countries should vary based upon differences in the country's tax structure, investment opportunities, and the availability of external capital. Because these factors differ among countries and change independently, changes in the retention rate among countries should likewise be unique. The *return on equity* (*ROE*) is determined by equity turnover and the profit margin. The equity turnover, in turn, is determined by sales growth, retention policy, and changes in the debt-equity financing ratio, and these factors differ among countries. The profit margin depends upon capacity utilization, unit labor cost, inflation, exports, and imports. Since the two major factors (capacity utilization and unit labor cost) are internal to the economy, changes in these variables for alternative nations should be relatively independent.

Therefore, almost all of the determinants of growth are unique to a given economy. Moreover, *changes* in these variables are generally determined by internal economic conditions, and these economic conditions are independent. Therefore, price changes resulting from changes in these growth variables should likewise be relatively independent. Similar to the changes in *k*, the degree of independence in these growth factors will vary depending upon the economic ties between the countries.

In conclusion, changes in both *k* and *g* should be independent among countries. Therefore, the covariance between returns for securities in different countries should be much lower than the covariance of returns for securities *within* a country.

EMPIRICAL STUDIES OF INTERNATIONAL DIVERSIFICATION

Grubel[2] showed the benefits of international diversification by analyzing the monthly rates of return that have been adjusted for changes in the exchange rate for major countries—that is, the rates of return are those that would be experienced by a U.S. investor assuming foreign returns are exchanged into U.S. dollars. The rates of return, standard deviation, and correlation with the U.S. index are shown in Table 19.1.

Japan had the highest rate of return during the period and one of the largest standard deviations. More importantly, the Japanese index had very low correlation with the U.S. index (0.1149), indicating that securities from Japan would be a good addition to a portfolio of U.S. securities. Australia had the lowest correlation (0.0585) with the U.S. index, and the South African index had a *negative* correlation (−0.1620) (probably caused by heavy involvement in gold mining). Securities represented by these foreign indexes would be excellent additions to a U.S. portfolio. Portfolios derived using all 11 countries indicated that diversification with these countries provided substantially higher rates of return or lower variance than would have been attained with a portfolio of only U.S. stocks. On the other hand, if an investor limited himself to the Atlantic community countries and ignored Japan, South Africa, and Australia, the gains from diversification would have been considerably less.

[2] Herbert G. Grubel, "Internationally Diversified Portfolios: Welfare Gains and Capital Flows," *American Economic Review* 58, no. 5 (December 1968): 1299–1314.

TABLE 19.1

Rates of Return and Standard Deviation from Investing in Foreign Capital Market Averages, 1959–1966

	PERCENT PER ANNUM (1)	STANDARD DEVIATION (σ) (2)	CORRELATION (R) WITH U.S. (3)
U.S.	7.54	47.26	1.0000
Canada	5.95	41.19	.7025[a]
United Kingdom	9.59	65.28	.2414[a]
West Germany	7.32	94.69	.3008[a]
France	4.27	49.60	.1938[a]
Italy	8.12	103.33	.1465
Belgium	1.09	37.56	.1080
Netherlands	5.14	86.34	.2107[a]
Japan	16.54	92.52	.1149
Australia	9.44	34.87	.0585
South Africa	8.47	61.92	−.1620

[a] Statistically significant at the 5 percent level.

Source: Herbert G. Grubel, "Internationally Diversified Portfolios: Welfare Gains and Capital Flows," *American Economic Review* 58, no. 5 (December 1968), p. 1304. Reprinted by permission.

Grubel and Fadner considered three questions regarding international diversification:[3] (1) What are the benefits of international diversification as compared to intranational diversification? (2) What is the effect of the length of the holding periods on the correlations? (3) What is the effect of fluctuations in the exchange rate on the variance of returns? They examined 51 U.S. industry stock price indexes, 28 U.K. industry indexes, and 28 West German indexes using weekly data. The initial correlations involved percentages of price changes adjusted for changes in exchange rates. They tested the effect of inter- and intranational diversification by examining the average correlation coefficient between all pairs within a country compared to all pairs among countries. For weekly and monthly holding periods, the differences were dramatic and significant. For monthly data, the average correlation *within* the countries was about 0.50, while the average correlation *among* countries was about 0.12. They examined the correlation among pairs of identical industries from the three countries and hypothesized that the correlations would be proportional to the amount of trading done. The results indicated that the U.S.–U.K. correlations were generally higher than similar U.S–West Germany correlations. As hypothesized, the correlations were influenced by the proportion of importing and exporting done by the industry.

The effect of different holding periods was examined by analyzing the differences in correlations for weekly, monthly, and quarterly rates of return. It was hypothesized that the correlation would be positively related

[3] Herbert G. Grubel and Kenneth Fadner, "The Interdependence of International Equity Markets," *Journal of Finance* 26, no. 1 (March 1971): 89–94.

to the holding period, since in the long run any unique characteristics affecting returns would be overpowered by the underlying real valuation factors (i.e., growth and profits). The results strongly supported the hypothesis in that the correlations went from about 0.06 for weekly holding periods to 0.32 for quarterly holding periods.

Finally, the effect of fluctuations in the exchange rate on return variability was examined by comparing the correlation of returns with and without adjustments for exchange rates. The results indicated insignificant differences caused by exchange rate adjustment. During the short period of analysis there were minor changes in exchange rates, so these results are not too surprising, but probably not applicable to recent periods.

Levy and Sarnat examined the potential gains from international diversification employing annual returns for 28 countries.[4] The set of returns adjusted for exchange rate changes indicated a wide range of mean returns (+17.8 percent to −1.5 percent) and standard deviations. After deriving the efficient set of portfolios, they utilized a market opportunity line and employed four borrowing and lending rates to generate four optimal portfolios. Although 28 countries were considered, only 9 were included in at least one of the optimal portfolios. Investments in the United States and Japan accounted for 50 to 70 percent of the optimal portfolios, with additional investments in developing or borderline countries (such as Venezuela, South Africa, New Zealand, and Mexico) because of the low or negative correlation they had with other countries in the sample.

The benefits to U.S. investors of alternative diversification schemes were shown by deriving efficient frontiers using selected samples. As shown in Figure 19.1, if you invest in only developing countries, only common market countries, or only Western European countries, there is a loss relative to investing solely in the United States. When Japan and South Africa are included, there is a significant improvement—a continuous reduction in variance as the opportunity set is broadened until the best frontier is derived *when all 28 countries are considered.*

Agmon considered whether international stock markets were segmented, as suggested by previous authors, or whether there was support for the notion of one multinational perfect capital market.[5] The relationship between monthly returns for the United Kingdom, Germany, Japan, and the United States had significant slopes, but the R^2 were consistently very low. That is, U.S.–U.K. was 0.03; U.S.–Japan was 0.009. The results when the author related rates of return to the beta with the U.S. market contradicted a one-country hypothesis. The slopes were insignificant and/or negative. Finally, he examined the simultaneity of price changes but used monthly data, which precluded finding major lead-lag relationships for daily data.

[4] Haim Levy and Marshall Sarnat, "International Diversification of Investment Portfolios," *American Economic Review* 60, no. 4 (September 1970): 668–675.

[5] Tamir Agmon, "The Relations among Equity Markets: A Study of Share Price Co-Movements in the United States, United Kingdom, Germany, and Japan," *Journal of Finance* 27, no. 4 (September 1972): 839–855.

FIGURE 19.1
**Alternative Efficient Frontiers When Stocks from Different Countries Are
Considered**

A = 28 countries
B = 16 high-income countries
C = 5 Common Market countries
E = 9 developing countries
F = United States

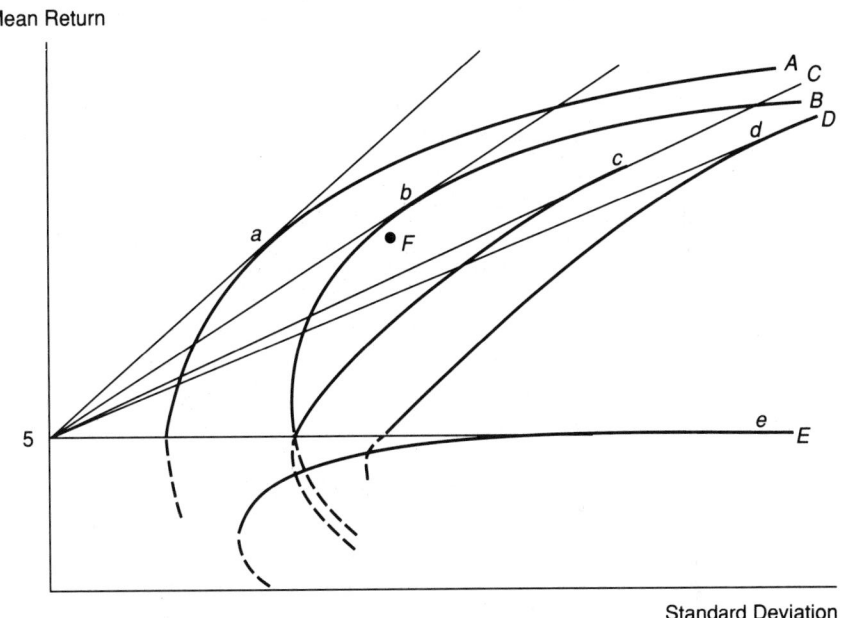

Source: Haim Levy and Marshall Sarnat, "International Diversification of Investment Portfolios," *American Economic Review* 60, no. 4 (September 1979): 673. Reprinted by permission.

A subsequent paper by Agmon examined individual stock price fluctuations unique to a stock's country by studying 145 stocks from the United Kingdom, Germany, and Japan.[6] The test results indicated that the major factor explaining price measurements was the stock's own *country factor,* followed by a *U.S. factor* (which was insignificant in two of three instances), and finally an insignificant *unique factor.* He also demonstrated that different countries had unique country risks, and these unique risks were generally independent—that is, the alternative country factors had either very low positive correlations (0.04 and 0.07) or negative correlation (−0.15). This indicated that *the country factors are generally independent of each other,* which implied substantial potential gains from international diversification.

[6] Tamir Agmon, "Country Risk: The Significance of the Country Factor for Share Price Movements in the United Kingdom, Germany, and Japan," *Journal of Business* 46, no. 1 (January 1973): 24–32.

Lessard examined a sample of stocks from four countries at approximately the same level of economic development (Columbia, Chile, Argentina, and Brazil).[7] While stocks within a country should move together, Lessard contended that this co-movement should be stronger in less developed countries because of their unique problems. Also, the uniqueness of internal problems and events would outweigh any common events of importance between the countries. The Lessard study considered three questions: (1) How strong were the common elements for stocks within these four countries? (2) Were the individual common elements for each of the countries related or independent? (3) What were the specific benefits of international diversification compared to diversification within countries? An analysis of quarterly returns on 110 common stocks from the four countries indicated that in all cases, the proportion of total variance explained by the first component of returns for each of the countries was larger than generally found in the United States (i.e., it ranged from 40 to 70 percent compared to an average of about 30 percent in the United States). This indicated that *stocks within an undeveloped capital market have a large common component.* Further, there was no systematic relationship between the various stock markets. In summary, the returns in each country could be explained by a country market factor, and *the market factors were independent of each other.* Given the potentially large gains from international diversification, Lessard compared the return and variance of returns for intranational portfolios versus international portfolios. When naively diversified portfolios were constructed (equal amounts of each stock), the four-nation portfolio almost always dominated all single-country portfolios. Assuming a risk-free rate of less than 6 percent, the four-nation portfolio was dominant. In summary, the results indicated that international diversification is beneficial even among developing countries in a single geographic area.

McDonald examined the benefits of international diversification by analyzing the performance of French mutual funds, because they typically represent investment in both domestic French stocks and foreign stocks, with most foreign stocks listed on the NYSE.[8] Also, the funds are typically managed by French banks that have superior access to company information. The results supported international diversification, since the all-French fund had the lowest performance ratios, while the fund with the *most* international diversification had the highest performance ratios.

A study by Joy and others considered co-movements in the returns in major international equity markets and also changes in these relationships over time by examining weekly adjusted and unadjusted stock market rates of return for 12 countries.[9] The correlation matrix of weekly rates of

[7] Donald R. Lessard, "International Portfolio Diversification: A Multivariate Analysis for a Group of Latin American Countries," *Journal of Finance* 28, no. 3 (June 1973): 619–633.

[8] John G. McDonald, "French Mutual Fund Performance: Evaluation of Internationally Diversified Portfolios," *Journal of Finance* 28, no. 5 (December 1973): 1161–1180.

[9] O. Maurice Joy, Don B. Panton, Frank K. Reilly, and Stanley A. Martin, "Co-movements of Major International Equity Markets," *The Financial Review* (1976): 1–20.

return for the ten-year period is shown in Table 19.2. The top half contains the correlation among unadjusted returns, while the bottom half contains the correlation among returns adjusted for exchange rates. Although there are a few significant positive correlations, most of the correlations are very low (i.e., the average correlations were 0.139 and 0.133 for unadjusted and adjusted rates, respectively). These results indicate that *there are substantial risk reduction possibilities through international diversification* and little difference when returns are adjusted for exchange rates.

An analysis of the *time effect* (do the correlations change over time?) and the *country effect* (are the correlations between various pairs of countries different?) indicated that both effects were significant. The different correlations among countries indicates that you must determine the specific relationship with the country being considered, while the time effect indicates that the relationships change over time, so it may be necessary to readjust the portfolios over time. Finally, the time trends in the relationships were examined (i.e., have the correlations increased over time?). The mean correlations between the 66 pairs of countries during each of the years contained in Table 19.3 indicated a significant positive trend in the correlations. An analysis of the trend in individual pairs of countries generated the set of yearly correlations for the U.S. adjusted returns and those of the other 11 countries in Table 19.4. About 70 percent of the trends were positive, but only 7 out of 66 were statistically significant. Therefore, while the benefits of international diversification have been declining over time, *the trend is very gradual.*

On the question of the stability of the correlations among countries over time, Maldonado and Saunders contended that there was reasonable stability for short periods (six months), but the relationship was almost a random walk for longer periods.[10] In direct contrast, Shaked contended that the covariances between markets were highly unstable in the short run (one year), but they improved dramatically as the investment horizon was lengthened to four and five years.[11] The long-run results imply that these correlations and international portfolio models could be used for investors with intermediate-term and long-term investment horizons.

The results of a study by Swanson for some major countries, shown in Table 19.5, indicate that the rates of return from foreign securities were often higher than those from U.S. portfolios although the standard deviation of the U.S. portfolio was consistently lowest.[12] Still, because of the relatively low correlations, the impact of diversification on a *world portfolio* is quite positive, as shown in Table 19.6.

As shown, during this period, the world index provided not only a higher rate of return, but also a lower level of risk, which implies that with

---

[10] Rita Maldonado and Anthony Saunders, "International Portfolio Diversification and the Inter-Temporal Stability of International Stock Market Relationships, 1957–1978," *Financial Management* 10, no. 4 (Autumn 1981): 54–63.

[11] Israel Shaked, "International Equity Markets and the Investment Horizon," *Journal of Portfolio Management* 11, no. 2 (Winter 1985): 80–84.

[12] Joel Swanson, *Investing Internationally to Reduce Risk and Enhance Return* (New York: Morgan Guaranty Trust Company, 1979).

TABLE 19.2
Ten-Year Correlations of Weekly Rates of Return of 12 Major International Equity Markets

	AUSTRALIA	AUSTRIA	BELGIUM	CANADA	FRANCE	ITALY	JAPAN	NETHERLANDS	SWITZERLAND	U.K.	W. GERMANY	U.S.
Australia		−.022	.112	.147	.062	.018	.062	.127	.173	.173	.091	.161
Austria	.013		.044	.026	.061	.050	.024	.058	.038	.081	.102	.020
Belgium	.117	.044		.229	.241	.073	.101	.270	.221	.128	.216	.232
Canada	.167	.058	.179		.150	.061	.180	.369	.278	.162	.226	.643
France	.082	.069	.177	.163		.030	.083	.158	.144	.037	.177	.097
Italy	.022	.011	.079	.060	.012		.129	.119	.155	.074	.066	.021
Japan	.086	.071	.086	.192	.106	.102		.176	.143	.080	.128	.076
Netherlands	.134	.038	.232	.361	.158	.098	.167		.293	.157	.342	.349
Switzerland	.173	.045	.164	.289	.148	.174	.192	.283		.067	.243	.245
U.K.	.171	.034	.093	.146	.039	.078	.110	.131	.002		.035	.125
W. Germany	.106	.072	.186	.201	.153	.050	.113	.357	.207	.030		.171
U.S.	.137	.027	.205	.634	.107	.002	.092	.344	.242	.096	.163	

Adjusted Rates of Returns

Source: O. Maurice Joy, Don B. Panton, Frank K. Reilly, and Stanley A. Martin, "Co-movements of International Equity Markets," *The Financial Review* (1976), p. 5. Reprinted by permission.

TABLE 19.3
Mean Correlations of Weekly Rates of Return for the Indexes of 12 Major Equity Markets, 1963–1972

	1963	1964	1965	1966	1967	1968	1969	1970	1971	1972
$\bar{\theta}_t$ (adjusted)	.066	.115	.121	.115	.070	.121	.177	.280	.130	.135
$\bar{\theta}_t$ (unadjusted)	.081	.113	.188	.115	.068	.125	.215	.271	.126	.151

Source: O. Maurice Joy, Don B. Panton, Frank K. Reilly, and Stanley A. Martin, "Co-movements of International Equity Markets," *The Financial Review* (1976), p. 11. Reprinted by permission.

TABLE 19.4
Observed Correlations between Adjusted Weekly Rates of Return of the United States (Dow-Jones Industrial Average) and Adjusted Weekly Rates of Return for 11 Major Equity Markets, 1963–1972

	1963	1964	1965	1966	1967	1968	1969	1970	1971	1972	$\bar{Q}_t$
U.S.–Australia	.080	.090	.037	.323	.095	.122	.036	.213	.193	.178	.137
U.S.–Austria	.088	.309	.044	−.001	−.077	−.057	.022	−.124	−.038	.100	.027
U.S.–Belgium	.370	.328	.502	.276	−.001	.131	.168	.455	.032	−.211	.205
U.S.–Canada	.649	.563	.727	.761	.687	.668	.429	.760	.440	.651	.634
U.S.–France	.068	.007	.185	.243	.108	.071	.181	.071	.001	.137	.107
U.S.–Italy	−.024	−.116	−.104	−.006	−.128	−.025	−.020	.183	.254	.005	.002
U.S.–Japan	.203	.029	.033	−.189	−.053	.208	.232	.353	−.059	.164	.092
U.S.–Netherlands	.165	.227	.359	.403	.492	.467	.197	.439	.396	.294	.344
U.S.–Switzerland	.080	.233	.201	.282	.099	.299	.233	.556	.269	.172	.242
U.S.–United Kingdom	.022	−.040	.043	.124	−.078	.091	−.007	.417	.087	.297	.096
U.S.–W. Germany	.188	.125	.420	.049	−.030	.169	.154	.462	.053	.041	.163

Source: O. Maurice Joy, Don B. Panton, Frank K. Reilly, and Stanley A. Martin, "Co-movements of International Equity Markets," *The Financial Review* (1976), p. 14. Reprinted by permission.

TABLE 19.5
Rates of Return, Standard Deviations, and Correlation Coefficients for Foreign Countries and Standard & Poor's 500, 1969–1978

COUNTRY	TOTAL RATES OF RETURN (ADJUSTED)	STANDARD DEVIATION OF RATES OF RETURN	CORRELATION COEFFICIENT WITH U.S.
France	2.5	24.8	.37
Germany	11.8	19.1	.30
Japan	18.1	25.0	.28
Switzerland	11.1	22.5	.45
United Kingdom	.7	32.0	.44
United States	2.1	16.9	—

Source: Joel Swanson, *Investing Internationally to Reduce Risk and Enhance Return* (New York: Morgan Guaranty Trust Company, 1979).

TABLE 19.6
Differential Return and Risk from Domestic versus World Portfolios

	1969–1973	1974–1978
Rates of return (price only)		
U.S. Index	3.34	3.56
World Index	6.40	5.14
Standard deviation of return		
U.S. Index	13.90	17.60
World Index	13.40	14.90

Source: Joel Swanson, *Investing Internationally to Reduce Risk and Enhance Return* (New York: Morgan Guaranty Trust Company, 1979).

international diversification the efficient frontier would not only move to the left to reflect lower risk but would also move up due to the higher return.

Bergstrom reviewed some prior studies and provided compound annual return data for 20 countries, including the United States, which ranked 17 out of 20 in return.[13] He also summarized the results achieved by Putnam Management Company with international investments—superior returns and low risk relative to the U.S. market.

Lessard considered the impact of a world portfolio, a country index, and industry indexes on the returns for individual securities.[14] He found that a fairly low proportion of total variance is explained by a world portfolio, and a high proportion is explained by the stock's own country effect—implying strong benefits from international diversification. The effectiveness of diversification depends upon whether the markets for the various countries are integrated or segmented. The latter is preferable for diversification. It is concluded that actual returns are more consistent with a segmented market.

CONCLUSIONS AND IMPLICATIONS OF EQUITY STUDIES

The results consistently indicate much lower correlation among the stocks of different countries than for stocks within a country, which implies substantial benefits derived from international diversification. Also, *the correlations differ among countries* depending upon their level of development and the level of interdependence of their economies. Therefore, for purposes of diversification, such undeveloped countries are excellent candidates for investment. The unstable correlations mean that you *cannot* extrapolate past correlations when developing future portfolios; you must adjust your portfolios over time to reflect expected changes in the relationships. Finally, the positive trend in some of the correlations implies

[13] Gary L. Bergstrom, "A New Route to Higher Returns and Lower Risks," *Journal of Portfolio Management* 2, no. 1 (Fall 1975): 30–38.
[14] Donald R. Lessard, "World, Country, and Industry Relationships in Equity Returns," *Financial Analysts Journal* 32, no. 1 (January–February 1976): 32–38.

that there will be less benefit derived from international diversification in the future, although the trend is gradual and is not positive for all combinations. This means that a portfolio manager should examine each of the countries on an individual basis and make an appropriate decision based upon the past relationships, recent trends, and his assessment of the *future* relationships among the countries involved.

STUDIES ON FOREIGN CURRENCY BONDS   Beyond diversifying with non–U.S. equities, it is important to consider non-U.S. bonds for the fixed-income portfolio and the total bond-equity portfolio. Cholerton, Pieraerts, and Solnik analyzed diversification patterns provided by non-dollar bond markets and the possibilities for forming optimal portfolios of bonds alone and both equities and bonds in global markets.[15] The relationship among bond returns in the short run (1983–1985) and the long run (1971–1988) indicated that the correlation when all returns were in local currencies was always less than .50 and usually less than .25. More important for a U.S. investor, when returns were converted to U.S. dollars, the correlations during the recent period (1983–1985) were about .10, and long-term correlations were about .25. The graph in Figure 19.2 indicates the risk-return trade-off with and without international bond diversification. As shown, going from a pure U.S. bond portfolio to a 60 percent U.S.–40 percent foreign bond portfolio provides *both* a higher rate of return and a lower level of risk.

Correlations between non–U.S. bonds and U.S. stocks were very low or negative. An optimal international asset allocation that considers U.S. stocks and bonds and also non–U.S. stocks and bonds denominated in U.S. dollars provided striking results. As shown in Figure 19.3, considering non–U.S. stocks provides a substantial improvement to a pure U.S. equity portfolio. In addition, the inclusion of bonds creates a new frontier with definitely lower risk and/or higher returns.

Grauer and Hakensson applied a multi-period investment model to the construction of portfolios that consider U.S. equities and bonds, but also British, German, and Japanese government bonds, and also equities from Australia, Austria, Canada, Holland, France, Germany, and Japan.[16] There were several portfolio rebalancing techniques that included quarterly and annual adjustments and also levered portfolios. Assuming quarterly revisions, the returns were substantially higher when the seven non-U.S. equity markets were considered along with the U.S. market. Assuming annual rebalancing and leverage, some of the conservative borrowing strategies using non–U.S. assets provided risk-return results that were substantially better than the U.S.-only strategies.

IMPLEMENTING INTERNATIONAL DIVERSIFICATION   Some methods of deriving the benefits from international diversification are as follows:

1. Acquire the stocks of U.S. multinational firms.

---

[15] Kenneth Cholerton, Pierre Pieraerts, and Bruno Solnik, "Why Invest in Foreign Currency Bonds?" *Journal of Portfolio Management* 12, no. 4 (Summer 1986): 4–8.

[16] Robert R. Grauer and Nils H. Hakensson, "Gains from International Diversification: 1968–85 Returns on Portfolios of Stocks and Bonds," *Journal of Finance* 42, no. 3 (July 1987): 721–741.

FIGURE **19.2**
Risk/Return Trade-off for International Bond Portfolios

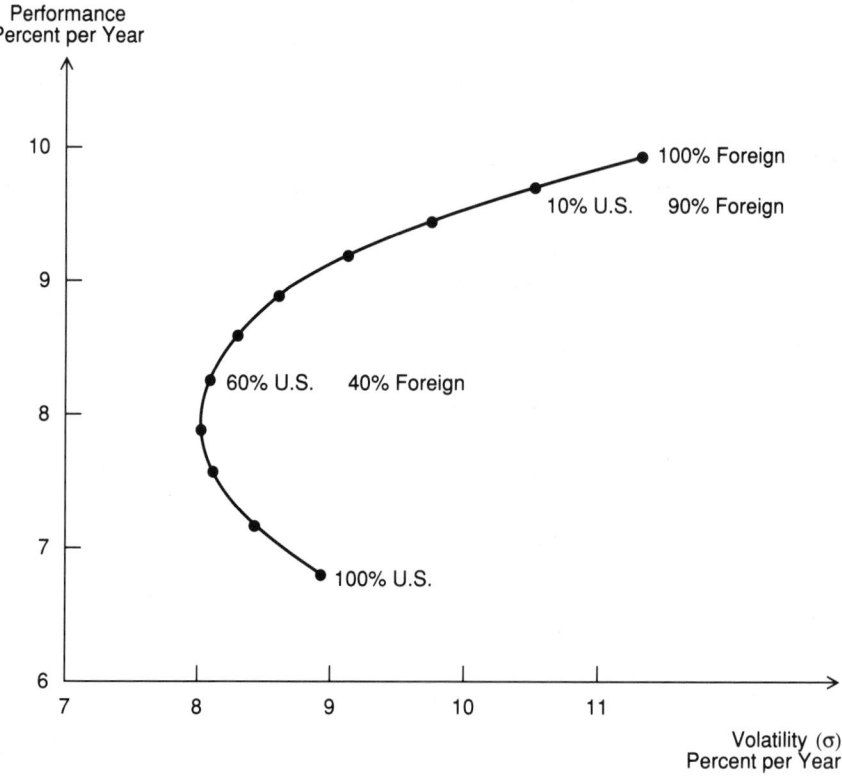

Source: Kenneth Cholerton, Pierre Pieraerts, and Bruno Solnik, "Why Invest in Foreign Currency Bonds?" *The Journal of Portfolio Management* 12, no. 4 (Summer 1986). Reprinted with permission.

2. Acquire the stock of foreign firms directly if the stock is listed on a U.S. exchange; acquire stock by the purchase of ADRs of foreign firms listed on a U.S. exchange; or acquire the non–U.S. stock on a non–U.S. exchange.
3. Acquire shares in an international or global investment company (mutual fund).

The following discussion considers some studies that have examined these alternatives.

Jacquillat and Solnik concluded that acquiring U.S. multinational firms rather than pure foreign securities is a poor strategy.[17] They showed that the stock prices of multinationals are too highly correlated with purely

---

[17] Bertrand Jacquillat and Bruno Solnik, "Multinationals Are Poor Tools for Diversification," *Journal of Portfolio Management* 4, no. 2 (Winter 1978): 8–12.

FIGURE 19.3
Efficient Frontiers—December 1970–December 1980

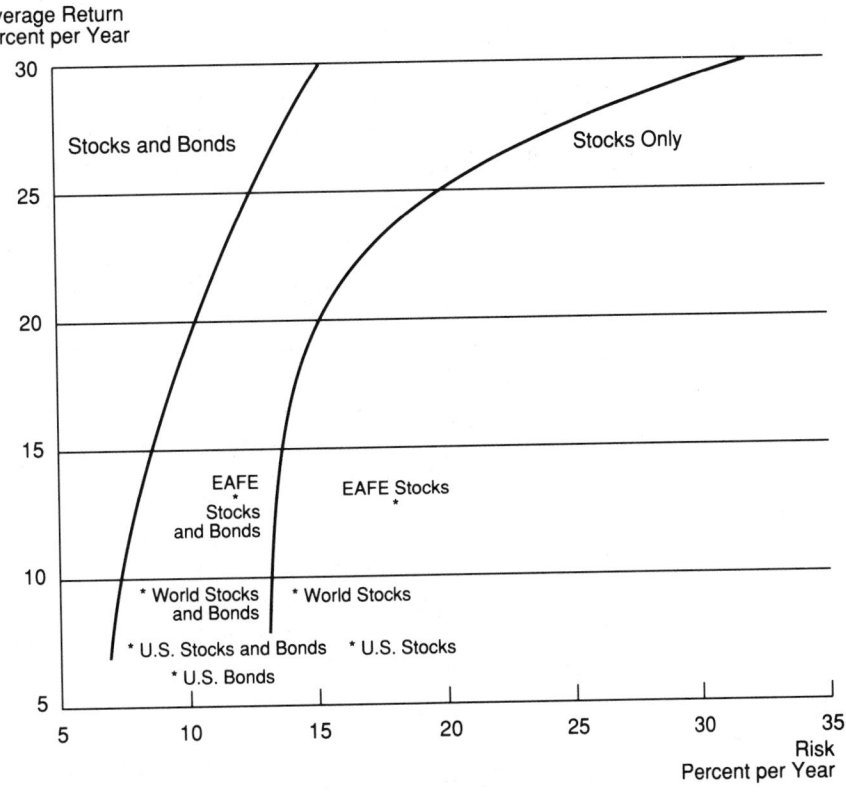

Source: Kenneth Cholerton, Pierre Pieraerts, and Bruno Solnik, "Why Invest in Foreign Currency Bonds?" *The Journal of Portfolio Management* 12, no. 4 (Summer 1986). Reprinted with permission.

domestic stocks and have very low correlation with foreign market indicators, even for the countries where they have substantial activities.

Assuming that you want to diversify on a direct basis, there is some question regarding how to do it. Solnik and Noetzlin examined the risk-reward characteristics for stocks, bonds, cash, gold, and currencies for six countries.[18] The results when they applied optimal asset allocation strategies to these assets suggested that active investment strategies were worthwhile. Notably, while the rates of return were erratic, the risk measures were relatively stable. In contrast, when Logue compared passively managed internationally diversified portfolios to some mechanical active

[18] Bruno Solnik and Bernard Noetzlin, "Optimal International Asset Allocation," *Journal of Portfolio Management* 9, no. 1 (Fall 1982): 11–21.

management rules, he found that active management is likely to generate huge transaction costs, which could offset any benefit.[19]

IMPACT OF EXCHANGE RATES

On several occasions we have referred to the impact of exchange rates on the returns ultimately received by a U.S. investor involved in global investing. Several studies concerned with international equity investing indicated that the exchange rate effect was rather minimal. However, these conclusions were correct *prior to 1979,* when there was significant stability in exchange rates. In sharp contrast, *exchange rates have become very volatile since 1979,* and there is no reason to assume a return to the pre-1979 environment. Therefore, you must become aware of the exchange rate effect and learn to deal with it. The subsequent discussion considers how to measure this risk and suggests some overall strategies to deal with it. The specific mechanics of investing in currency futures are considered in Chapter 25.

Mantell considered the basic question of how to determine *measured* returns on foreign investment given exchange rate uncertainty.[20] He noted that international investments have two sources of risk: normal return risk within a country, and exchange rate risk; and when attempting to estimate expected return, one must consider both of these independently yet also consider *the relationship between them.* Given the *purchasing power parity* theory, one would expect negative correlation between the within-country rate of return and the end-of-period exchange rate.[21] An analysis of the rates of return on currency for 16 countries confirmed the typical negative relationship. The bias created by ignoring this relationship was proved to affect the ranking of countries. Obviously, this relevant component should be considered when estimating expected return for foreign investments.

Adler and Simon confirmed the significant change in exchange rate volatility since 1979 and demonstrated its impact on the exchange rate risk for bonds and stocks.[22] The *exchange rate exposure* of a security or portfolio is related to its sensitivity of price (i.e., its beta) to changes in exchange rates. This discussion implicitly considered the relationship between return and exchange rates and measured the impact over time. It was shown that since 1979 the stock market indexes have been more exposed to currency risk than alternative fixed-income securities because stocks and exchange rates were positively correlated after 1979. Recognizing this relationship and knowing the relevant exchange rate beta is important for hedging your position.

---

[19] Dennis E. Logue, "An Experiment in International Diversification," *Journal of Portfolio Management* 9, no. 1 (Fall 1982): 22–27.

[20] Edmund H. Mantell, "How to Measure Expected Returns on Foreign Investments," *Journal of Portfolio Management* 10, no. 2 (Winter 1984): 38–43.

[21] Basically, purchasing power purity contends that goods have a single price. The belief is that if you acquired an item with dollars, and I purchased the same item with yen, when we work through the exchange rate, the commission, and other factors involved in foreign trade, we will find out that we both paid the same price for the item.

[22] Michael Adler and David Simon, "Exchange Rate Surprises in International Portfolios," *Journal of Portfolio Management* 12, no. 2 (Winter 1986): 44–53.

Madura considered exchange rate betas, how they are estimated, and how they can be used.[23] The computation of the beta for seven currencies relative to the U.S. dollar for three-month and six-month holding periods indicated substantial differences among countries (the exchange rate beta for Canada was low or negative, while the Swiss franc was very large). Also, there was instability for individual series, although the relative ranking was reasonably stable. It was concluded that currency betas can be of value when you are looking for defensive currencies or if you want aggressive currencies because you expect changes in exchange rates.

Madura and Reiff examined the impact of hedging against exchange rate risk on a set of international stock indexes.[24] A comparison of results of the hedged versus the unhedged portfolio indicated that the hedged investment strategy provided an efficient frontier with approximately 50 percent less risk. As indicated, the implementation of currency hedges will be discussed in Chapter 25, which is concerned with financial futures.

OBSTACLES TO INTERNATIONAL DIVERSIFICATION

Given the clear advantages of international diversification, why do not individuals and institutions in the United States invest more in foreign securities? The chief obstacle is that when compared to U.S. markets, international capital markets are less perfect. The major characteristics of perfect markets are complete and costless information, zero transaction costs, and complete liquidity.

AVAILABILITY OF INFORMATION

This general heading of "availability of information" deals with a *set* of obstacles to foreign investment. The first is the availability of information on individual companies, industries, and economies. American investors take for granted an enormous set of data that is not available in many other countries, especially in some less developed nations. We generally have numerous sources of economic data from organizations like the Federal Reserve System and the Department of Commerce, which simply do not exist in most other countries. Further, in the United States there are a number of private sources of industry data from companies like Standard & Poor's, Moody's, Value Line, and industry trade associations, that also do not exist elsewhere. Finally, analysts in the United States are almost overwhelmed each year by annual reports, quarterly reports, and 10 K reports required by the SEC. Again, almost none of this is available in most foreign countries. For analysts and portfolio managers accustomed to a plethora of information, it is difficult to make decisions under such conditions.

A further problem arises in the *interpretation of the data received,* because reporting standards in many countries are different from those in the United States. Investors often complain about the different accounting

---

[23] Jeff Madura, "Empirical Measurement of Exchange Rate Betas," *Journal of Portfolio Management* 9, no. 4 (Summer 1983): 43–46.

[24] Jeff Madura and Wallace Reiff, "A Hedge Strategy for International Portfolios," *Journal of Portfolio Management* 12, no. 1 (Fall 1985): 70–74.

techniques used by American firms, because they can seriously affect reported income. Such differences in U.S. accounting practices, however, are minor compared to the variations employed in many foreign countries. As discussed in Chapter 12, what must the analyst do with the Japanese or German earnings figure to make it comparable to a U.S. figure?

Finally, there are timing problems because of *reporting lags*—that is, how long it takes for operating results to be made publicly available. In many instances, the reporting lag is substantial compared to what it is in the United States. Further, once figures are available, there may be an additional lag until the results are reported in the United States. Clearly, this lag could be very important in the price adjustment process.

LIQUIDITY

Liquidity is the ability to buy or sell an asset quickly without the price changing significantly from what it was during a previous transaction, assuming no new information has entered the market. Liquidity is important for any investment, and it is especially crucial to large institutional investors who need to establish major positions in an investment. As noted, this need for liquidity has caused a tiered market in the United States that probably will continue to exist. Unfortunately, the liquidity of most foreign stocks is substantially below that of most U.S. stocks listed on an exchange. Although some non–U.S. stocks experience good trading volume and liquidity, most foreign stocks experience limited trading and substantial price volatility. Therefore, while numerous foreign stocks can be acquired by individuals, only a limited number of them have the necessary liquidity for institutional investors.

TRANSACTION COSTS

One must also consider the above-average transaction costs involved in a foreign trade. These include commission costs (that will probably be above average), transfer taxes, and all the other costs involved in placing the order and securing the certificate.[25]

Notably, there has been a major change in the attitude of U.S. pension funds toward global investing. While they generally recognize the problems involved, they believe that the potential benefits in terms of higher returns and lower risk through diversification are worth the effort.[26] The graph in Figure 19.4 indicates the substantial growth of foreign investment by pension funds through 1986 and also the rapid growth projected by 1990.

---

[25] These problems have declined in recent years with the growth of American Depository Receipts (ADRs). See Anna Marjos, "How to Invest Abroad," *Barron's*, July 24, 1978, 9 ; Roger H. Cass, "A Global Approach to Portfolio Management," *Journal of Portfolio Management* 1, no. 2 (Winter 1975): 40–48; and *Investing Internationally* (New York: Morgan Stanley & Co., 1987).

[26] See Lawrence Rout, "Many Pension Funds Are Looking Overseas for New Investments," *The Wall Street Journal*, May 24, 1979, 1; Daniel Hertzberg, "Pension Managers Invest More Overseas, Aware of Risks but Hopeful about Profits," *The Wall Street Journal*, July 2, 1981, 36; Michael R. Sesit, "U.S. Institutions Find Buying Foreign Stocks Can Be Very Profitable," *The Wall Street Journal*, June 3, 1986, 1, 12; and Matthew Winkler, "New York City Will Move Some Funds of Pension Systems into Foreign Bonds," *The Wall Street Journal*, April 18, 1988, 37.

FIGURE 19.4
Growth Projection of Foreign Investment by U.S. Pension Funds

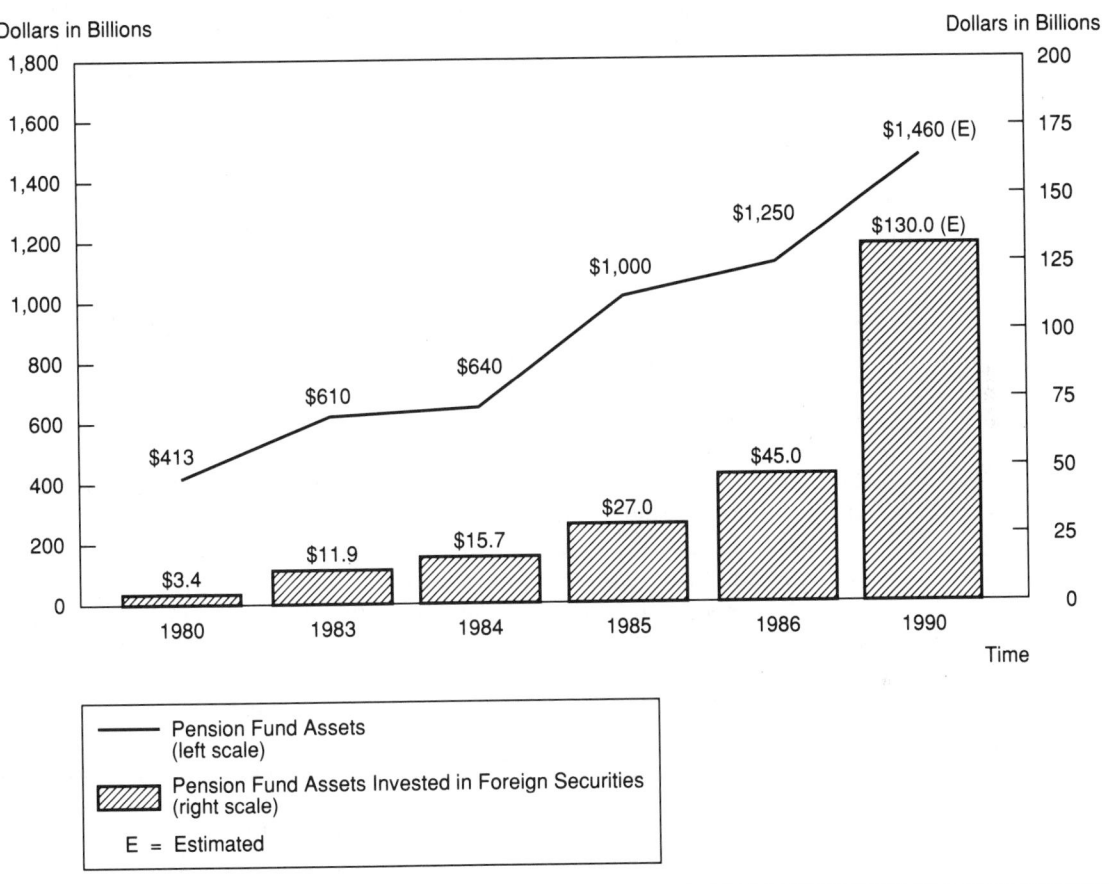

Source: InterSec Research Corporation.

ALTERNATIVES TO DIRECT INVESTMENT

For an individual investor, an obvious solution to the problems involved in foreign investment would be to purchase shares in an investment company that specializes in foreign securities.[27] This strategy solves the problem of lack of information because the professionals involved are familiar with the countries and their markets. While the funds will not necessarily perform better than an index for these countries, they should do about average in terms of rates of return, and you should still derive the benefits of diversification. This approach should also reduce the liquidity problem,

---

[27] For a discussion of the attraction to individuals, see Jill Bettner, "Foreign Stocks Catch on with Small Investors; Gains Are Bigger Lure than Diversification," *The Wall Street Journal,* April 20, 1981, 36. For a discussion of international mutual funds, see Laurie Cohen, "International Stock Funds Attracting American Investors," *Chicago Tribune,* May 19, 1981, 3; and Lynn Asinof, "International Mutual Funds Attract Favor as Economies Recover in Europe, Far East," *The Wall Street Journal,* January 9, 1984, 17.

because many international funds are open-end funds that will reacquire shares at their net asset value. Alternatively, the closed-end global funds enjoy relatively active markets on exchanges. (For instance, the German Fund, the Korea Fund, and several other individual country funds are listed on the NYSE). In Chapter 21 where investment companies are discussed in detail, there is a section that contains an extensive listing of international stock and bond funds.

SUMMARY

The dividend valuation model shows that because almost all of the relevant valuation variables are unrelated, the rates of return should not be correlated. A number of studies that have empirically examined the concept consistently indicated that international diversification should be beneficial. The correlations among countries for short-time intervals change over time, but the long-term correlations are fairly stable. There is some evidence of an increase in the correlations among securities from various countries, but the trend is small and does not apply to all countries. Moreover, beyond diversifying with non–U.S. equities, there are further benefits from investing in non–U.S. bonds.

While it appears that U.S. multinationals are a poor alternative for implementing international diversification, direct acquisition of non–U.S. securities is a viable alternative and is becoming easier because there are more non–U.S. firms being listed on U.S. exchanges, and there is more activity in ADRs. Of course, a major concern with any alternative for global investing is the added risk of exchange rates, and this should be measured and hedged against.

Although there are theoretical and empirical reasons for international diversification, it is clear that it is not without problems. The main obstacles are the availability of information, the reliability of the information received, the time lag in getting the information, a substantial liquidity problem with many securities, and higher transaction costs. An alternative to direct investment by individuals is acquiring shares of an investment company that concentrates in foreign stocks.

QUESTIONS

1. What is the purpose of international diversification? Why should institutional and individual investors acquire foreign securities?

2. Discuss in some detail why international diversification should work. Specifically, why would you expect low correlation in the rates of return for domestic and foreign securities?

3. Would you expect a difference in the correlation of returns between U.S. and foreign securities from alternative countries (e.g., Japan, Canada, South Africa)? Why? Be specific.

4. What were the empirical findings regarding changes in the correlations over time between the stock price series for various countries? What are the implications of these results for a portfolio manager interested in international diversification?

5. Would you expect there to be a trend in the correlations between U.S. stock price series and the stock price series for different countries? Why or why not, and what would influence such a trend?

6. What would news of a small increase in the correlations between the securities market in the United States and other countries mean to you as a portfolio manager?

7. Briefly discuss the major problems involved in international diversification. Which of the problems is greatest for individuals? Which is most important to institutions? Why?

8. It is contended that international investing introduces an additional risk component. Discuss what it is and how it can increase or decrease your return.

9. What alternatives are available to direct investment in foreign stocks?

10. *CFA Examination III (June 1985)*: Darwin asks Irish about international equities and whether or not the Investment Committee should consider them as an additional asset for the pension fund.

10a. Explain the rationale for including international equities in General's equity portfolio. Identify and describe three relevant considerations in formulating your answer. [10 minutes]

10b. List three possible arguments against international equity investment and briefly discuss the significance of each. [5 minutes]

10c. To illustrate several aspects of the performance of international securities over time, Irish shows Darwin the graph on p. 798 of investment results experienced by a U.S. pension fund in the 1970–83 period. Compare the performance of the U.S.$ and non–U.S.$ equity and fixed-income asset categories, and explain the significance of the result of the Account Performance Index relative to the results of the four individual asset class indexes. [10 minutes]

11. *CFA Examination III (June 1988)*: The portfolio manager of a large U.S.-based bond investment firm is interested in investing in foreign bond markets. He feels that a passive, rather than active, management approach should be taken for the following reasons:

- The foreign bond markets are homogenous and, like those of the United States, are efficient. Therefore, there is little to be gained from active management.

- A market (bond index) portfolio would be the ideal vehicle for obtaining nearly all of the return in selected countries' bond markets. This approach is appropriate because the objective of international bond investing is to maximize return. The portfolio manager feels that the index should be equally weighted in bonds from each country selected for investment.

  Critique each of the portfolio manager's reasons for a passive management approach to international bond investing. [10 minutes]

PROBLEMS

1. Using a source of international statistics, compare the percentage change in the following economic data for Japan, West Germany, Italy, Canada, and

Annualized Historical Performance Data, 14 Years Ended Dec. 31, 1983

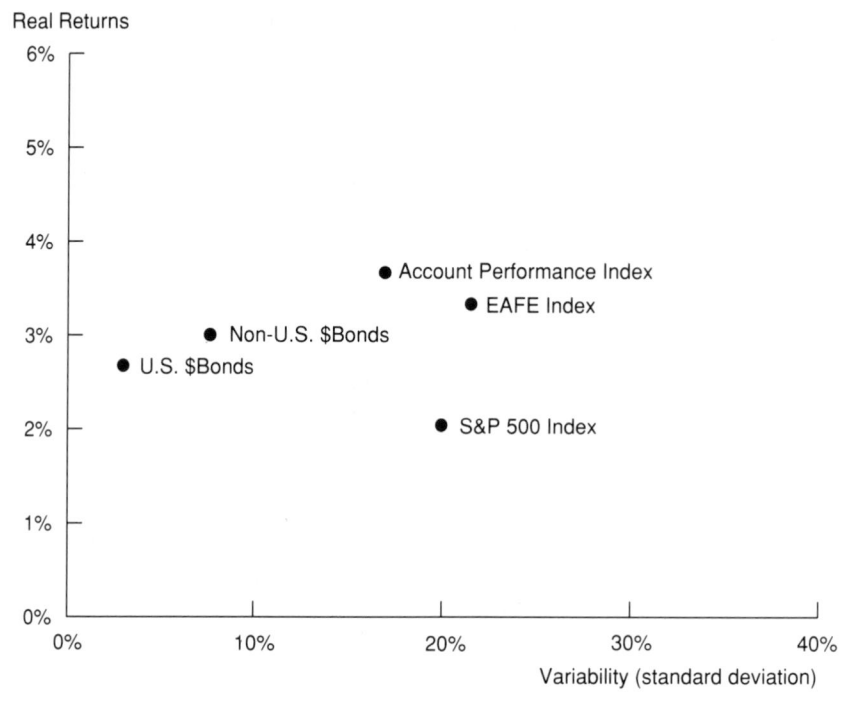

the United States for a recent year. What were the differences, and which country or countries differed most from the United States?

1a. Aggregate output (GNP)

1b. Inflation

1c. Corporate earnings

1d. Money supply growth

2. Using a recent edition of *Barron's*, examine the weekly percentages of change in the stock price indexes for Japan, West Germany, Italy, Canada, and the United States. For each of three weeks, which foreign series moved most closely with the U.S. series? Which series was most divergent from the U.S. series? What would this indicate to you regarding international diversification?

3. Using published sources, look up the exchange rate for the United States with Japan for each of the past ten years (you can use an average for the year or a specific time period each year). Based upon these exchange rates, compute and discuss the yearly exchange rate effect on an investment in Japanese stocks.

REFERENCES

Adler, Michael, and Bernard Dumas. "International Portfolio Choice and Corporation Finance: A Survey." *Journal of Finance* 38, no. 2 (June 1983).

Cholerton, Kenneth, Pierre Pieraerts, and Bruno Solnik. "Why Invest in Foreign Currency Bonds?" *Journal of Portfolio Management* 12, no. 4 (Summer 1986).

Eun, Chaol S., and Bruce Resnick. "Estimating the Correlation Structure of International Share Prices." *Journal of Finance* 39, no. 5 (December 1984).

Grauer, Robert R., and Nils H. Hakensson. "Gains from International Diversification: 1968–85 Returns on Portfolios of Stocks and Bonds." *Journal of Finance* 42, no. 3 (July 1987).

Hadzima Durasz, Margaret and Cornelia M. Small. "Perspectives on International Bond Investing," in Frank J. Fabozzi, and Irving M. Pollack, eds. *The Handbook of Fixed Income Securities.* 2d ed. (Homewood, Ill.: Dow Jones-Irwin, 1987).

Lessard, Donald R. "International Diversification," in Sumner N. Levine, ed. *The Financial Analysts Handbook.* 2d ed. (Homewood, Ill.: Dow Jones-Irwin, 1988).

Lessard, Donald R. "World, National, and Industry Factors in Equity Returns." *Journal of Finance* 29, no. 2 (May 1974).

Levy, Haim, and Marshall Sarnat. "International Diversification of Investment Portfolios." *American Economic Review* 60, no. 4 (September 1970).

Maldonado, Rita, and Anthony Saunders. "International Portfolio Diversification and the Inter-Temporal Stability of International Stock Market Relationships, 1957–1978." *Financial Management* 10, no. 4 (Autumn 1981).

Morgan, Stanley. "Investing Internationally." (New York, 1987).

Robinson, Anthony W., and Stephen W. Glover. "International Fixed-Income Markets and Securities," in *The Financial Analysts Handbook.* 2d ed. Edited by Sumner Levine (Homewood, Ill.: Dow Jones-Irwin, 1988).

Small, Cornelia M., and Margaret Durasz Hadzima. "International Portfolio Management," in Frank J. Fabozzi, and Irving M. Pollack, eds. *The Handbook of Fixed Income Securities.* 2d ed. (Homewood, Ill.: Dow Jones-Irwin, 1987).

Solnik, Bruno, and Bernard Noetzlin. "Optimal International Asset Allocation." *Journal of Portfolio Management* 9, no. 1 (Fall 1982).

Van der Does, Rein W. "Investing in Foreign Securities," in *The Financial Analysts Handbook.* 2d ed. Edited by Sumner Levine (Homewood, Ill.: Dow Jones-Irwin, 1988).

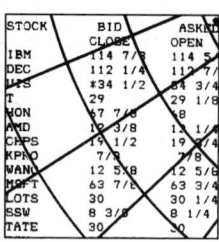

CHAPTER 20

EVALUATION OF PORTFOLIO PERFORMANCE

Investors are always interested in evaluating the performance of their portfolios. It is both expensive and time-consuming to analyze and select securities for a portfolio, so the investing unit (i.e., an individual, company, or institution) must determine whether the time and effort were well spent. This is true for investors who manage their own portfolios as well as for those who pay one or several professional money managers to do so. Of course, in the latter case, it is imperative to determine whether the results justify the cost of the service.

This chapter outlines the theory and practice involved in evaluating the performance of a portfolio. Initially we consider what is required of a portfolio manager and briefly discuss how performance was evaluated before portfolio theory and the CAPM were developed. A discussion follows of three portfolio performance evaluation techniques that consider return and risk (referred to as *composite performance measures*), including applications of these techniques to determine the performance of a selected sample of mutual funds. Because some observers have contended that these three composite measures of performance are biased in favor of low-risk portfolios, we will examine their arguments and the evidence for and against them. We also briefly review Roll's rationale for questioning any performance technique that depends upon the CAPM and a market portfolio. We will also discuss why this benchmark problem becomes larger in à global investing environment. We will also consider two techniques that examine the *components* of performance. Finally, beyond these techniques (which generally concentrate on equity portfolios), we present and discuss several evaluation models for fixed-income portfolios.

WHAT IS REQUIRED OF A PORTFOLIO MANAGER?

The two major requirements of a portfolio manager are

1. The ability to derive above-average returns for a given risk class through market timing or security selection
2. The ability to diversify (eliminate all unsystematic risk from the portfolio).

In terms of return, the first requirement is obvious, but the necessity of considering *risk* in this context was not generally apparent prior to the 1960s, when work in portfolio theory showed its significance. In terms of modern theory, superior risk-adjusted return can be derived either through superior timing or superior security selection. If a portfolio manager can do a superior job of predicting equity market turns or interest rates, he can change his portfolio composition to anticipate the market. An equity manager would invest in a completely diversified portfolio of high-beta stocks during a rising market and in a portfolio of low-beta stocks and money market instruments during a declining market, thereby deriving above-average risk-adjusted returns. A fixed-income portfolio manager would change the duration of his portfolio in anticipation of interest rate changes, increasing the duration in anticipation of falling interest rates, and vice versa. If properly executed, this strategy would likewise provide superior risk-adjusted returns. Finally, if a portfolio manager and his analysts are able to consistently select undervalued securities (stocks or bonds) for a given risk class, the portfolio would also experience above-average risk-adjusted returns.

The second factor to consider in evaluating a portfolio manager is the ability to diversify completely. The market rewards investors only for bearing systematic (market) risk, not unsystematic risk, because this non-market risk can be eliminated in a diversified market portfolio. Investors consequently want their portfolios to be completely diversified and thus completely eliminate unsystematic risk. The level of diversification can be judged on the basis of the correlation between the portfolio returns and the returns for a market portfolio. A completely diversified portfolio is perfectly correlated with the completely diversified market portfolio.

It is important to be constantly aware of these two requirements of a portfolio manager, because some portfolio evaluation techniques take into account one requirement and not the other, and other techniques implicitly consider both factors but do not differentiate between them.

COMPOSITE PORTFOLIO PERFORMANCE MEASURES

At one time investors evaluated portfolio performance almost entirely on the basis of the rate of return. They were aware of risk but did not know how to quantify it, so they could not consider it explicitly. Developments in portfolio theory in the early 1960s enabled the quantification of risk in terms of the variability of returns, but because there was no composite measure, it was necessary to consider the two factors separately as done in several early studies.[1] Specifically, the investigators put portfolios into similar risk classes based upon a measure of risk (e.g., industrial classification, variance of return), and then compared the rates of return for alternative portfolios directly within a risk class.

TREYNOR MEASURE

The first composite measure of portfolio performance (including risk) was developed by Treynor,[2] who recognized that one of the major problems in evaluating portfolio managers was deriving a measure of risk for a portfolio. He postulated two components of risk: risk produced by general market fluctuations and risk resulting from unique fluctuations in the particular securities in the portfolio. To identify the first type, he introduced the *characteristic line,* which defines the relationship between the rates of return for a portfolio over time and the rates of return for an appropriate market portfolio. He noted that the *slope* of the characteristic line measures the *relative volatility* of the portfolio's returns in relation to aggregate market returns. In current terms, this slope is the portfolio's *beta coefficient.* The higher the slope, the more sensitive the portfolio is to market returns and the greater its market risk.

The deviations from the characteristic line indicate *unique returns* for the portfolio relative to the market and these are attributable to the unique returns on individual stocks in the portfolio. If the portfolio is properly diversified, these unique returns for individual stocks should cancel out. *The higher the correlation of the portfolio with the market, the less the unique risk and the better diversified is the portfolio.* Because Treynor was not interested in this aspect of portfolio performance, there was no further consideration of the measure of diversification.

MEASURE OF PERFORMANCE. Treynor was interested in a measure of performance that would apply to all investors regardless of their risk preferences. Building upon developments in capital market theory, he introduced a risk-free asset that could be combined with different portfolios to form a straight *portfolio possibility line.* He showed that rational, risk-averse investors would always prefer portfolio possibility lines that have a larger slope because such high slope lines would place the investor on a higher indifference curve. The slope of this portfolio possibility line (designated *T*) is equal to the following:[3]

$$T = \frac{R_i - RFR}{\beta_i},$$

[1] Irwin Friend, Marshall Blume, and Jean Crockett, *Mutual Funds and Other Institutional Investors* (New York: McGraw-Hill, 1970).

[2] Jack L. Treynor, "How to Rate Management of Investment Funds," *Harvard Business Review* 43, no. 1 (January-February 1965): 63–75.

[3] The terms used in the formula differ from those used by Treynor but are consistent with our earlier discussion. Also, our discussion is concerned with general *portfolio* performance rather than being limited to mutual funds.

where

R_i = the average rate of return for portfolio i during a specified time period

RFR = the average rate of return on a risk-free investment during the same time period

β_i = the slope of the fund's characteristic line computed during that time period, which indicates the fund's relative volatility.

As noted, the larger the T value, the larger the slope and the more preferable the fund is for all investors, regardless of their risk preferences. Since the numerator of this ratio ($R_i - RFR$) is the *risk premium*, and the denominator is a measure of risk, the total expression indicates the portfolio's *return per unit of risk*, and all risk-averse investors would prefer to maximize this value. The systematic risk variable, however, indicates nothing about diversification but implicitly *assumes* complete diversification, so systematic risk is the relevant risk measure. When this T value for a portfolio is compared to a similar measure for the market portfolio, it indicates whether the portfolio would plot above the SML.

It is pointed out that this measure of performance is not affected by changing the *RFR*. The T values may change, but the ranking of portfolios will not change. You can have negative T values if the portfolio has a return below the *RFR* and a positive beta, which would indicate extremely poor management. Alternatively, if the T value is negative because the beta was negative, and the numerator was not negative, it would indicate *very good* performance.[4] Normally, a portfolio with a negative beta should experience a rate of return below the *RFR*, so both the numerator and the denominator would be negative, and the T value would be positive.

SHARPE MEASURE[5]
The Sharpe composite measure of portfolio performance is closely associated with Sharpe's earlier work on the CAPM.[6] He assumed that all investors are able to borrow or lend at the risk-free rate and share the same set of expectations, which implies that all efficient portfolios will fall along a straight line of the form:

$$E(R_i) = RFR + b\,\sigma_i,$$

where

$E(R_i)$ = the expected rate of return on portfolio i

RFR = the risk-free rate of return

b = the risk premium, which will be positive since investors are assumed to be risk averse

σ_i = the standard deviation of returns for portfolio i.

---

[4] An example was the performance by an international mutual fund heavily involved with gold stocks.

[5] William F. Sharpe, "Mutual Fund Performance," *Journal of Business* 39, no. 1, Part 2 (January 1966): 119–138.

[6] William F. Sharpe, "Capital Asset Prices: A Theory of Market Equilibrium under Conditions of Risk," *Journal of Finance* 19, no. 4 (September 1964): 425–442.

Given this *capital market line* (*CML*) and the ability to borrow or lend at the risk-free rate, an investor can attain any point on the line,

$$E(R) = RFR + \left[\frac{E(R_i) - RFR}{\sigma_i} \right].$$

This means that any portfolio will give rise to a complete linear set of $E(R)$, σ combinations, and the best portfolio will be the one giving the best boundary, which is the portfolio with the highest ratio of $(E(R_i) - RFR)/\sigma_i$. Other efficient portfolios must lie along the common line and give the same ratio. In order to use this theory to test *ex post* returns, it is necessary to progress from expectations to average rates of return and the actual standard deviation of returns for alternative portfolios. Therefore, in practice, the Sharpe measure (designated *S*) is stated as follows:

$$S = \frac{R_i - RFR}{V_i},$$

where

$R_i =$ the rate of return for portfolio *i* during the time period

$RFR =$ the risk-free rate that prevailed during the time period

$V_i =$ the standard deviation of the rate of return for portfolio *i* during the time period.

This measure can be used to rank the performance of portfolios and will not be affected by changes in the *RFR*, since such changes will affect all values. Also, you can compute this measure for the aggregate market and use this market measure to examine the performance of portfolios relative to the aggregate market.

TREYNOR VERSUS SHARPE MEASURE

The Sharpe measure uses the standard deviation of returns as the measure of risk, while the Treynor measure employs beta (systematic risk). The Sharpe measure, therefore, implicitly evaluates the portfolio manager on the basis of return performance, but also considers how well-diversified the portfolio was during this period. If a portfolio is perfectly diversified (does not contain any unsystematic risk), the two measures would give identical rankings, because the total variance of the portfolio would be the systematic variance. Alternatively, if a portfolio is poorly diversified, it can have a high ranking based on the Treynor measure but a much lower ranking for the Sharpe measure, with the difference directly attributable to its poor diversification. Therefore, the two performance measures provide *complementary* but different information, and *both measures should be calculated*. Notably, if you are dealing with a well-diversified portfolio, such as mutual funds, the two measures will provide very similar rankings. Because Sharpe thought the variability due to unsystematic risk was probably transitory, he believed that the Treynor measure might be a better measure for predicting future performance, and his results generally confirmed this expectation.

JENSEN MEASURE[7]   The Jensen measure is similar to the prior measures that are based upon the CAPM. All versions of the CAPM indicate the following expression for the expected one-period return on any security or portfolio:

$$E(R_j) = RFR + \beta_j [E(R_m) - RFR],$$

where

$E(R_j) =$ **the expected return on security or portfolio j**

$RFR =$ **the one-period risk-free interest rate**

$\beta_j =$ **the systematic risk (beta) for security or portfolio j**

$E(R_m) =$ **the expected return on the market portfolio of risky assets.**

It has been shown that the single-period models can be extended to a multi-period world in which investors have heterogeneous horizons and trading takes place continuously.[8] Therefore, the earlier equation can be generalized as follows:

$$E(R_{jt}) = RFR_t + \beta_j [R_{mt} - RFR_t].$$

Each of the expected returns and the risk-free return are different for different periods. Consequently, we are concerned with the time series of expected rates of return for security j or portfolio j. Moreover, assuming that the asset pricing model is empirically valid, it is possible to express the expectations formula in terms of *realized* rates of return as follows:

$$R_{jt} = RFR_t + \beta_j [R_{mt} - RFR_t] + U_{jt}.$$

This indicates that the realized rate of return on a security or portfolio should be a linear function of the risk-free rate of return during the period, plus a risk premium that is a function of the security's systematic risk during the period, plus a random error term.

If the risk-free return is subtracted from both sides, we have

$$R_{jt} - RFR_t = \beta_j [R_{mt} - RFR_t] + U_{jt}.$$

This indicates that the risk premium earned on the j th security or portfolio is equal to β_j times a market risk premium plus a random error term. In this form, you would not expect an intercept for the regression if all assets and portfolios were in equilibrium. If a portfolio manager is a superior market forecaster (i.e., he will benefit from superior timing), or if he has

---

[7] Michael C. Jensen, "The Performance of Mutual Funds in the Period 1945–1964," *Journal of Finance* 23, no. 2 (May 1968): 389–416.

[8] Michael C. Jensen, "Risk, the Pricing of Capital Assets, and the Evaluation of Investment Portfolios," *Journal of Business* 42, no. 2 (April 1969): 167–247.

the ability to consistently select undervalued securities, then his risk premiums will exceed those implied by the market (i.e., he will have consistently positive random errors relative to the equilibrium market line). To reveal such superior performance, the regression must *not* be constrained to go through the intercept (i.e., do not force it to be zero). If we allow for a possible nonzero constant, this equation becomes

$$R_{jt} - RFR_t = \alpha_j + \beta_j [R_{mt} - RFR_t] + U_{jt}.$$

Given this equation, the α_j indicates whether the portfolio manager is superior or inferior in market timing or stock selection. If he is superior, the α will be a significant positive value; if he is inferior, it will be a significant negative value. Finally, if the portfolio manager has no forecasting ability, which means his performance is equal to a naive buy-and-hold policy, the α will be insignificantly different from zero.

This measure is very useful because it allows the investigator to determine whether the abnormal returns are *statistically significant* (positive or negative). Also, the α represents the average incremental rate of return on the portfolio per unit of time, which is attributable to the manager's ability to derive above-average returns *adjusted for risk*. These superior risk-adjusted returns can be due to the manager's accuracy at predicting market turns or his ability to select undervalued issues.

The Jensen formulation requires a different *RFR* for each time interval during the sample period. If you are examining a portfolio's performance over a ten-year period using yearly intervals, you must examine its annual returns less the return on risk-free assets for each year, and then relate this to the annual return on the market portfolio less the same risk-free rates. In contrast, the other techniques examine *the average returns for the total period* for all variables (the portfolio, the market, and the risk-free asset). Also, the Jensen measure, like the Treynor measure, does not evaluate the ability of the portfolio manager to diversify, because the risk premiums are based on systematic risk. As noted earlier, when evaluating the performance of well-diversified portfolios like mutual funds, this is a reasonable assumption. Jensen's assumption of diversification was proved valid by the fact that the correlations of the funds with the market typically exceeded 0.90.

APPLICATION OF PERFORMANCE MEASURES

To demonstrate these measures, we selected 20 open-end mutual funds for which data was available for the 15-year period of 1973–1987. The specific results for the first fund (Affiliated Fund, Inc.) are contained in Table 20.1. The returns are the total returns for each year computed as follows:

$$R_{it} = \frac{EP_{it} + Div_{it} + \text{Cap. Dist.}_{it} - BP_{it}}{BP_{it}},$$

TABLE 20.1
Example of Computation of Portfolio Evaluation Measures
Using Affiliated Fund, Inc.

YEAR	R_{it}	R_{mt}	RFR_t	$R_{it} - RFR_t$	$R_{mt} - RFR_t$
1973	−5.3	−14.7	6.9	−12.2	−21.6
1974	−15.2	−26.5	8.0	−23.2	−34.5
1975	39.5	37.2	5.8	33.7	31.4
1976	33.9	23.8	5.1	28.8	18.7
1977	−6.6	−7.2	5.1	−11.7	−12.3
1978	3.5	6.6	7.2	−3.7	−0.6
1979	28.3	18.4	10.4	17.9	8.0
1980	24.2	32.4	11.2	13.0	21.2
1981	0.2	−4.9	14.7	−14.5	−19.6
1982	22.3	21.4	10.5	11.8	10.9
1983	25.1	22.5	8.8	16.3	13.7
1984	6.2	6.3	9.8	−3.6	−3.5
1985	25.6	32.2	7.7	17.9	24.5
1986	23.0	18.5	6.2	16.8	12.3
1987	3.3	5.3	6.3	−3.0	−1.0
Mean:	13.87	11.42	8.25		
Standard deviation:	16.09	17.95	2.58		
$S_i =$	0.349				
$S_m =$	0.177				
$T_i =$	6.595				
$T_m =$	3.173			$\beta_i =$	0.852
$R_{it} - RFR_t =$	$2.901 + .860 \ (R_{mt} - RFR_t)$			$R^2_{im} =$	0.895

where

R_{it} = total return on fund i during year t

EP_{it} = ending price for fund i during year t

Cap. Dist.$_{it}$ = capital gain distributions made by fund i during year t

Div_{it} = dividend payment made by fund i during year t

BP_{it} = beginning price for fund i during year t.

As computed, these returns do not consider any sales charge by the funds. Given the fund's results for each year, and the aggregate market (represented by the S&P 500), you can compute the composite measures presented at the bottom of the table. As shown, the arithmetic average annual rate of return for Affiliated was above that for the market (13.87 versus 11.42), and the fund's beta was below 1.00 (0.852). Therefore, the Treynor measure for the fund (T_i) was above the same measure for the market (T_m) (6.595 versus 3.173). Likewise, the standard deviation of returns was below the market's (16.09 versus 17.95), so the Sharpe measure for the fund (S_i) was also above the measure for the market (S_m)(.349 versus .177). Finally, the regression of the fund's annual risk premium ($R_{it} - RFR_t$) and the market's annual risk premium ($R_{mt} - RFR_t$) indicated a positive intercept (constant) value of 2.901, but it was not statistically significant.

OVERALL RESULTS. Although our sample is rather small for demonstration purposes, the overall results in Table 20.2 are generally consistent with the findings of earlier studies. The mean return for all the funds was quite close to the market return (12.23 versus 11.42). If only the rate of return is considered, 12 of the 20 funds performed better than the market did.

The R^2 for a portfolio with the market fund can be used as a measure of diversification, and the closer it is to 1.00, the more perfectly diversified it is. Although the average R^2 is reasonably good at 0.800, the range is quite large, from 0.538 to 0.956, which indicates that a number of funds were not well-diversified.

The two risk measures (standard deviation and beta) likewise show a wide range but are generally consistent with expectations. Specifically, 11 of the 20 funds had a standard deviation larger than the market's, and the mean was also larger (19.04 versus 17.95). This larger standard deviation is consistent with the lack of complete diversification. Eight of the funds had a beta above 1.00, and the average beta was approximately 1 (that is, 0.952). Comparing the relative rankings of the three measures (indicated in parentheses), the performance of individual funds was very consistent. (The specific rank correlations will be discussed in a subsequent section.) Using the Sharpe–Treynor measure, 13 of the 20 funds had a value that was equal to or better than the market. The Jensen measure indicated that 12 of the 20 had positive intercepts, but only two of the positive intercepts and one of the negative intercepts were statistically significant. The mean values for the Sharpe and Treynor composite measures were below the comparable market figure. These results indicate that, on average and without considering transaction costs, this sample of funds performed about as well as the market did.

You should take time to analyze the individual funds and be sure to include a consideration of each of the components: rate of return, risk (both standard deviation and beta), and the R^2 as a measure of diversification. You might expect the best performance to be generated by funds with low diversification, since these funds are apparently attempting to beat the market by being unique in their selection or timing. This is apparently true for the top-tier funds (Fidelity Magellan and Templeton Growth Fund) but not for the Istel Fund, which had poor diversification but also low returns.

POTENTIAL BIAS OF ONE-PARAMETER MEASURE. Friend and Blume reviewed the various one-parameter measures and pointed out that, theoretically, the three one-parameter (composite) measures of performance should be independent of corresponding measures of risk because they are risk-adjusted measures.[9] The authors analyzed the relationship be-

---

[9] Irwin Friend and Marshall Blume, "Measurement of Portfolio Performance under Uncertainty," *American Economic Review* 60, no. 4 (September 1970): 561–575.

TABLE 20.2
Performance Measures for 20 Selected Mutual Funds, 1973–1987

	RETURN	STANDARD DEVIATION	BETA	R^2	SHARPE	TREYNOR	JENSEN
Affiliated Fund, Inc.	13.87	16.09	0.852	0.887	0.349 (3)	6.595 (3)	2.901 (3)
Dividend Shares, Inc.	10.20	16.02	0.874	0.956	0.122 (16)	2.236 (16)	−0.821 (16)
Dreyfus Growth Opportunity Funds, Inc.	14.21	23.13	1.062	0.654	0.258 (5)	5.612 (5)	2.528 (5)
Energy Fund, Inc.	12.67	18.84	0.854	0.635	0.234 (8)	5.172 (6)	1.673 (7)
Fidelity Magellan Fund	23.57	29.21	1.411	.0733	0.525 (1)	10.860 (2)	11.045[a] (1)
Guardian Mutual Fund	13.95	17.43	0.898	0.844	0.327 (4)	6.349 (4)	2.845 (4)
IDS Mutual, Inc.	10.23	14.61	0.773	0.894	0.136 (15)	2.562 (15)	−0.514 (14)
Istel Fund, Inc.	8.89	14.33	0.604	0.538	0.045 (17)	1.069 (17)	−1.276 (17)
Massachusetts Investors Growth Stock Fund	8.59	19.25	0.994	0.848	0.018 (18)	0.344 (18)	−2.737 (18)
Oppenheimer Fund, Inc.	7.43	21.08	1.040	0.768	−0.039 (19)	−0.791 (19)	−4.075 (19)
Philadelphia Fund, Inc.	11.98	18.28	0.905	0.773	0.204 (11)	4.123 (10)	0.805 (10)
T. Rowe Price Growth Stock Fund	7.04	18.90	1.023	0.939	−0.064 (20)	−1.186 (20)	−4.491[a] (20)
Putnam Growth Fund, Inc.	11.58	15.81	0.861	0.953	0.211 (10)	3.873 (11)	0.595 (11)
Scudder Special Fund, Inc.	11.25	21.90	1.123	0.835	0.137 (14)	2.675 (14)	−0.541 (15)
Security Equity Fund, Inc.	11.93	20.84	1.070	0.837	0.177 (13)	3.442 (13)	0.280 (12)
Sigma Investment Shares, Inc.	12.38	17.16	0.909	0.895	0.241 (6)	4.546 (8)	1.269 (8)
Technology Fund, Inc.	12.69	20.14	1.028	0.826	0.220 (9)	4.317 (9)	1.164 (9)
Templeton Growth Fund, Inc.	16.45	16.36	0.739	0.630	0.501 (2)	11.101 (1)	5.725[a] (2)
Value Line Special Situations Fund	14.92	27.74	1.336	0.704	0.241 (7)	4.996 (7)	2.288 (6)
Wellington Fund, Inc.	10.76	13.70	0.686	0.856	0.184 (12)	3.667 (12)	−0.306 (13)
Mean	12.23	19.04	0.95	0.80	0.06	1.22	0.92
S&P 500	11.42	17.95	1.00	1.00	0.177	3.17	0
90-Day T-Bill Rate	8.25						

[a] Indicates that intercept was statistically significant at the .05 level.

Note: Relative rankings are in parentheses.

tween the one-parameter measures of performance and risk for 200 random portfolios from among 788 common stocks listed on the NYSE. The three composite performance measures were regressed against the two measures of portfolio risk (i.e., beta and the standard deviation of portfolio

FIGURE 20.1
Scatter Diagram of Jensen's Performance Measure[a] on Risk:
January 1960 to June 1968

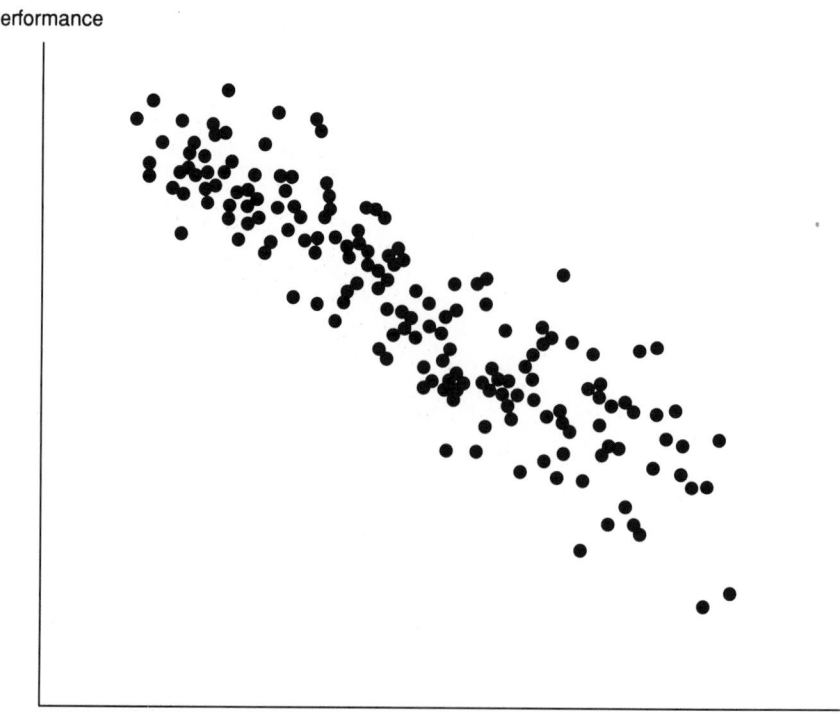

Performance

Risk (Beta)

[a]Using log relatives.

Source: Irwin Friend and Marshall Blume, "Measurement of Portfolio Performance under Uncertainty," *American Economic Review* 60, no. 4 (September 1970): 567. Reprinted by permission.

returns). In all cases, there was a <u>significant *inverse* relationship between the performance measure and the risk measure</u> (the risk-adjusted performance of low-risk portfolios was better than the comparable performance for high-risk portfolios). The results for the Jensen performance measure are contained Figure 20.1.

ALTERNATIVE VIEW REGARDING BIAS. A later paper by Klemkosky examined the relationship between composite performance measures and risk measures using actual mutual fund data in contrast to the random portfolio data used by Friend and Blume.[10] The author derived the three composite measures plus two measures that computed the excess return

---

[10] Robert C. Klemkosky, "The Bias in Composite Performance Measures," *Journal of Financial and Quantitative Analysis* 8, no. 3 (June 1973): 505–514.

above the risk-free rate relative to the semistandard deviation and the mean absolute deviation as risk measures.

The results indicated a positive bias—that is, there was a *positive* relationship between the composite performance by the mutual funds and the risk involved. This was especially true for the Treynor and Jensen measures. The performance measures that used the mean absolute deviation and the semistandard deviation as risk proxies were less biased than the three measures derived. It was concluded that while there might be a bias, one could not be certain of its direction.

COMPONENTS OF INVESTMENT PERFORMANCE

Subsequent to the work by Treynor, Sharpe, and Jensen, Fama suggested a somewhat finer breakdown of performance.[11] Similar to earlier measures, Fama's evaluation model assumes that the returns on managed portfolios can be judged relative to those of naively selected portfolios with similar levels of risk. The technique uses the simple one-period version of the two-parameter model, all the perfect market assumptions, and derives the *ex ante* market line, which indicates that the equilibrium relationship between expected return and risk for any security *j* is

$$E(\tilde{R}_j) = R_f + \left[\frac{E(\tilde{R}_m) - R_f}{\sigma(\tilde{R}_m)} \right] \frac{Cov(\tilde{R}_j, \tilde{R}_m)}{\sigma(\tilde{R}_m)}.$$

$Cov(R_j, R_m)$ is the covariance between the returns for security *j* and the return on the market portfolio. This equation indicates that the expected return on security *j* is the riskless rate of interest, R_f, plus a risk premium that is $[E(\tilde{R}_m) - R_f]/\sigma(\tilde{R}_m)$, called the *market price per unit of risk*, times the risk of asset *j*, which is $[Cov(\tilde{R}_j, \tilde{R}_m)]/\sigma(\tilde{R}_m)$.

This market line relationship should hold for portfolios as well as for individual assets. This *ex ante* model assumes completely efficient markets in which prices fully reflect all available information. Assuming a portfolio manager believes that the market is not completely efficient and that he can make better judgments than the market can, then an *ex post* version of this market line can provide a benchmark for the manager's performance. Given that the risk variable, $Cov(R_j, R_m)/\sigma(R_m)$, can be denoted B_x, the *ex post* market line is as follows:

$$R_x = R_f + \left(\frac{R_m - R_f}{\sigma(R_m)} \right) \beta_x.$$

This *ex post* market line provides the benchmark used to evaluate managed portfolios in a sequence of more complex measures.

EVALUATING SELECTIVITY. It is possible to measure the return due to selectivity as follows:

$$\text{Selectivity} = R_a - R_x(\beta_a),$$

[11] Eugene F. Fama, "Components of Investment Performance," *Journal of Finance* 27, no. 3 (June 1972): 551–567.

FIGURE 20.2
An Illustration of the Performance Measures

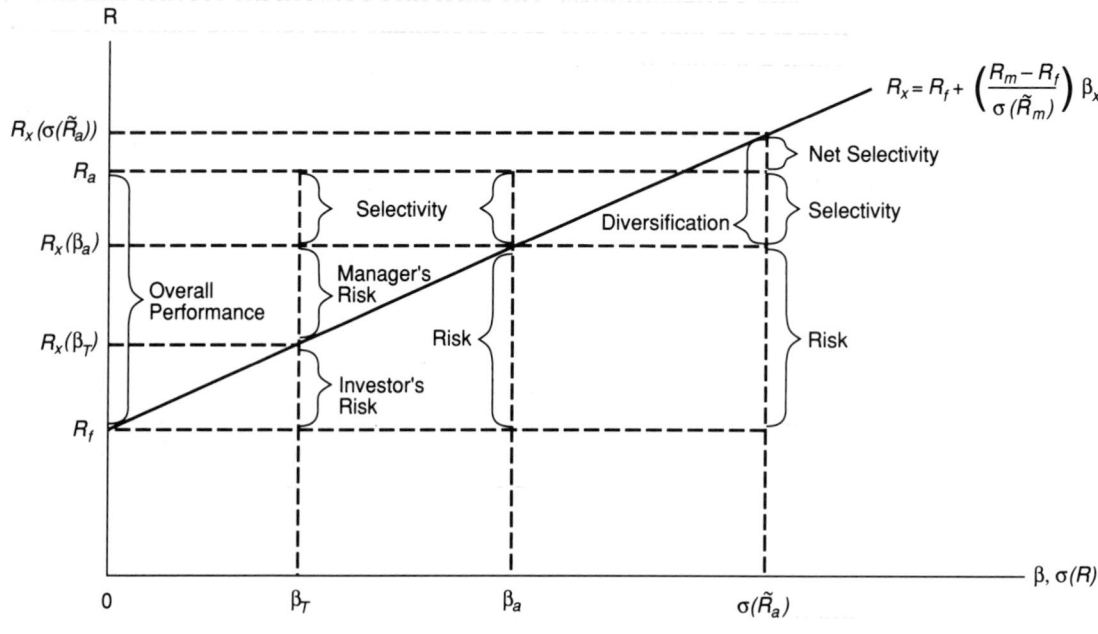

Source: Eugene F. Fama, "Components of Investment Performance," *Journal of Finance* 27, no. 3 (June 1972): 588. Reprinted by permission.

where

R_a = the return on the portfolio being evaluated

$R_x(\beta_a)$ = the return on the combination of the riskless asset f and the market portfolio m that has risk β_x equal to β_a, the risk of the portfolio being evaluated.

As shown in Figure 20.2, selectivity measures how well the chosen portfolio performed relative to a naively selected portfolio of equal risk. This measure indicates any difference from the *ex post* market line and is similar to the other measures, most specifically Treynor's.

Also you can examine overall performance in terms of selectivity (just considered) and the returns from assuming risk, as follows:

$$\left\{ \begin{array}{l} \text{Overall} \\ \text{Performance} = \text{Selectivity} + \text{Risk} \\ [R_a - R_f] = [R_a - R_x(\beta_a)] + [R_x(\beta_a) - R_f]. \end{array} \right.$$

As shown in Figure 20.2, overall performance is the total return above the risk-free return and includes the return that should have been received for accepting the portfolio risk (β_a). This expected return for accepting risk (β_a) is equal to $[R_x(\beta_a) - R_f]$. Any excess over this expected return is due to selectivity.

EVALUATING DIVERSIFICATION. The difference between the Treynor and Sharpe measures is that Treynor uses systematic risk (β_i), and Sharpe, total risk (σ_i). If a portfolio is completely diversified and therefore (by definition) does not have any unsystematic risk remaining, then its total risk will equal its systematic risk, and the two techniques will give equal rankings. However, if a portfolio manager attempts to select undervalued stocks and, in the process, gives up some diversification, it is possible to generate a measure of the added return that will be necessary to justify this decision. The portfolio's *gross selectivity* is made up of *net selectivity* plus diversification as follows:

$$\underset{[R_a - R_x(\beta_a)]}{\overset{\text{Selectivity}}{}} = \text{Net Selectivity} + \underset{[R_x(\sigma(R_a)) - R_x(\beta_a)]}{\overset{\text{Diversification}}{}},$$

or

$$\text{Net Selectivity} = \underset{[R_a - R_x(\beta_a)]}{\overset{\text{Selectivity}}{}} - \underset{[R_x(\sigma(R_a)) - R_x(\beta_a)]}{\overset{\text{Diversification}}{}}$$
$$= R_a - R_x[\sigma(R_a)],$$

where

$R_x[\sigma(R_a)] =$ **the return on the combination of the riskless asset *f* and the market portfolio *m* that has return dispersion equivalent to that of the portfolio being evaluated.**

Therefore, the diversification measure indicates the *added return* required to justify any loss of diversification in the portfolio. The term emphasizes that diversification is the elimination of all unsystematic variability. If the portfolio is completely diversified so that total risk (σ) is equal to systematic risk (β), then the $R_x(\sigma(R_a))$ would be the same as $R_x(\beta_a)$, and the diversification term would equal zero. Because the diversification measure is always positive, net selectivity will always be equal to or less than selectivity. (They will be equal when the portfolio is completely diversified.)[12] In cases where the investor is not concerned with the diversification of his portfolio, this particular breakdown will not be important, and only selectivity will be considered.

EVALUATING RISK. Assuming that the investor has a target level of risk for his portfolio equal to β_T, the overall performance due to risk (the total return above the risk-free return) can be assessed as follows:

$$\underset{[R_x(\beta_a) - R_f]}{\overset{\text{Risk}}{}} = \underset{[R_x(\beta_a) - R_x(\beta_T)]}{\overset{\text{Manager's Risk}}{}} + \underset{[R_x(\beta_T) - R_f]}{\overset{\text{Investor's Risk}}{}},$$

---

[12] In Figure 20.2, which is taken from the original Fama article, the required return due to diversification *is* larger than the return due to selectivity, so the net selectivity value would be a negative value.

where

$R_x(\beta_T)$ = **the return on the naively selected portfolio with the target level of market risk (β_T).**

If the portfolio risk is equal to the target risk ($\beta_a = \beta_T$), then there is no manager's risk. If there is a difference between β_a and β_T, then the manager's risk is the return the manager must earn due to his decision to accept risk (β_a), which is different from the risk desired by the investor (β_T). The investor's risk is the return expected because the investor stipulated some positive level of risk. This evaluation can be done only if the client has specified his desired level of market risk, which is usually the case with pensions and profit-sharing plans. Generally, it is not possible to compute this measure for *ex post* evaluations, because the desired risk level is typically not available.

APPLICATION OF FAMA MEASURES. Several of the components of performance suggested by Fama can be used in *ex post* evaluation, as shown in Table 20.3. Overall performance is the excess return derived above the risk-free return (i.e., the return above 8.25 percent as shown in Table 20.2). All but two of these mutual funds experienced positive overall performance. The next step is to determine how much the portfolio (fund) *should* receive for its systematic risk using the following expected return equation for this period (11.42 percent is the return on the S&P 500 during this period, as shown in Table 20.2):

$$E(R_i) = 8.25 + \beta_i(11.42 - 8.25)$$
$$= 8.25 + \beta_i(3.17).$$

required for risk

The required return for risk is simply the latter expression: $\beta_i(3.17)$. The required return for risk for Affiliated Fund was $0.852(3.17) = 2.70$ percent (its total required return is $8.25 + 2.70 = 10.95$). *The return for selectivity is the difference between overall performance and the required return for risk.* If the overall performance exceeds the required return for risk, the portfolio has experienced a positive return for selectivity. The results indicate that Affiliated had an average annual return of 2.92 percent for selectivity ($5.62 - 2.70$). A total of 13 funds had positive returns for selectivity. In contrast, although some funds had positive overall performance, their required return for risk exceeded this figure, giving them negative returns for selectivity (e.g., Dividend Shares, Inc.).

The next three columns indicate the effect of diversification on performance. The diversification term indicates the required return for not being completely diversified (i.e., total risk above systematic risk). If a fund's total risk is equal to its systematic risk, then the ratio of its total risk to the market's total risk will equal its beta. If this is not the case, then the ratio of total risk for the fund relative to the market will be greater than its beta and will indicate that there is an added return required be-

TABLE 20.3
Components of Performance for 20 Selected Mutual Funds: 1973–1987

	FAMA MODEL				MCV MODEL			
	OVERALL PERFORMANCE	SELECTIVITY	RISK	DIVERSIFICATION	NET SELECTIVITY	D_v	D_h	P_i	PM_i
Affiliated Fund, Inc.	5.62	2.92	2.70	0.14	2.78	2.92	0.04	65.13	20.53
Dividend Shares, Inc.	1.95	−0.82	2.77	0.06	−0.88	−0.82	0.02	−43.54	−13.72
Dreyfus Growth Opportunity Funds, Inc.	5.96	2.59	3.37	0.72	1.87	2.59	0.23	11.42	3.60
Energy Fund, Inc.	4.42	1.71	2.71	0.62	1.09	1.71	0.20	8.73	2.75
Fidelity Magellan Fund	15.32	10.85	4.48	0.31	10.54	10.85	0.22	50.12	15.80
Guardian Mutual Fund	5.70	2.85	2.85	0.23	2.62	2.85	0.07	38.94	12.27
IDS Mutual, Inc.	1.98	−0.47	2.45	0.13	−0.60	−0.47	0.04	−11.45	−3.61
Istel Fund, Inc.	0.65	−1.27	1.92	0.62	−1.89	−1.27	0.19	−6.53	−2.06
Massachusetts Investors Growth Stock Fund	0.34	−2.81	3.15	0.25	−3.06	−2.81	0.08	−35.76	−11.27
Oppenheimer Fund, Inc.	−0.82	−4.12	3.30	0.43	−4.55	−4.12	0.13	−30.62	−9.65
Philadelphia Fund, Inc.	3.73	0.86	2.87	0.36	0.50	0.86	0.11	7.57	2.39
T. Rowe Price Growth Stock Fund	−1.21	−4.46	3.25	0.10	−4.55	−4.46	0.03	−148.11	−46.68
Putnam Growth Fund, Inc.	3.33	0.60	2.73	0.06	0.54	0.60	0.02	30.57	9.64
Scudder Special Fund, Inc.	3.00	−0.56	3.56	0.31	−0.87	−0.56	0.10	−5.73	−1.81
Security Equity Fund, Inc.	3.68	0.29	3.39	0.29	0.00	0.29	0.09	3.16	1.00
Sigma Investment Shares, Inc.	4.13	1.25	2.88	0.15	1.10	1.25	0.05	26.45	8.34
Technology Fund, Inc.	4.44	1.18	3.26	0.30	0.88	1.19	0.09	12.51	3.94
Templeton Growth Fund, Inc.	8.20	5.96	2.34	0.55	5.31	5.86	0.17	33.94	10.70
Value Line Special Situations Fund	6.67	2.44	4.24	0.66	1.77	2.44	0.21	11.62	3.66
Wellington Fund, Inc.	2.52	0.34	2.18	0.24	0.09	0.34	0.08	4.39	1.38

cause of incomplete diversification. In the case of Affiliated, the ratio of total risk was

$$\frac{\sigma_i}{\sigma_m} = \frac{16.09}{17.95} = .896 .$$

This ratio of total risk compares to the fund's beta of 0.852, indicating that the fund is not completely diversified, which is consistent with the R^2 of 0.887 (see Table 20.2). The fund's required return given its standard deviation is

$$R_i = 8.25 + .896\,(3.17)$$
$$= 11.09\,.$$

You will recall that the fund's required return for systematic risk was 10.95 [8.25 + .852(3.17)]. The difference of 0.14 (11.09 − 10.95) is the added return required because of less than perfect diversification. This small required return for diversification is in contrast to Dreyfus Growth Opportunity Fund, which has an R^2 with the market of 0.656 and a required return for diversification of 0.72 percent. This required diversification return is subtracted from the selectivity return to arrive at the net selectivity. Affiliated had a return for selectivity of 2.92 percent and net selectivity of 2.78 percent, which would indicate that, even accounting for the added cost of not being completely diversified, the fund's performance was above the market line. Thirteen funds had positive net selectivity returns.

AN ALTERNATIVE COMPONENTS MODEL. Recently Moses, Cheyney, and Veit (MCV) developed a portfolio performance measure that likewise considers the various components of performance—selection, diversification, and one aspect of timing.[13] They begin with a measure of performance relative to the SML as follows:[14]

$$D_v = R_i - [R_f + \beta_i\,(R_m - RFR)]\,.$$

This is equal to both the Jensen alpha for the total period and Fama's selectivity. They derive a measure of diversification that is similar to Fama and for an efficient and completely diversified portfolio would be

$$\beta_i = \sigma_i/\sigma_m = I_i\,.$$

If the portfolio is not efficient and completely diversified,

$$\beta_i < I_i\,.$$

The difference between these two variables is a measure of the lack of diversification or a measure of *unsystematic* risk:

$$D_h = \sigma_i/\sigma_m - \beta_i\,.$$

One indicator of performance is the measure of excess return (D_v) divided by the measure of unsystematic risk (D_h):

$$P_i = D_v/D_h\,.$$

P_i will be a non-zero number if the return was not on the SML and/or the

---

[13] Edward A. Moses, John M. Cheyney, and E. Theodore Veit, "A New and More Complete Performance Measure," *Journal of Portfolio Management* 13, no. 4 (Summer 1987): 24–33.

[14] Again, the terms used in the formula are consistent with prior notation.

TABLE 20.4
Correlations among Alternative Portfolio Performance Measures

	TREYNOR	SHARPE	JENSEN	FAMA	MCV
Treynor	—				
Sharpe	.992	—			
Jensen	.994	.994	—		
Fama (net selectivity)	.991	.999	.996	—	
MCV (*PM*)	.917	.938	.919	.935	—

portfolio was not completely diversified $(D_h > D)$. In general, large values of P_i indicate superior performance because the excess return (D_v) was large relative to a measure of unsystematic risk (D_h).

To get a measure of performance relative to the market, the P_j is compared to the market risk premium as follows:

$$PM_i = P_i/(R_m - RFR) .$$

This *PM* is the excess return earned per unit of unsystematic risk compared to the risk premium on the market portfolio and indicates if the portfolio "beat the market."

Beyond the measure of performance that considers selectivity, diversification, and one aspect of timing, the authors suggest that it is preferable to employ an asset-weighted benchmark portfolio that is similar to the one being evaluated rather than an aggregate market portfolio. The idea is to combine in the appropriate weights, portfolios for various asset classes—for example, common stocks, bonds, preferred stock, and cash.

APPLICATION OF MCV MEASURE. The results when this measure is applied to our sample are in Table 20.3. As noted, the D_v factor is equal to the Fama gross selectivity measure and indicates the return above or below the SML based upon the portfolio beta—13 of the funds experienced a positive value. D_h is a measure of the difference between the ratio of standard deviations and the beta. The larger the difference is, the less the diversification—for example, the Dreyfus Growth Opportunity Fund had a D_h of .23. The P_i is the ratio of these two variables. Its size will be influenced by small D_h values, which indicate diversification—for example, the T. Rowe Price Growth Fund is well-diversified so has a small D_h of .03. Similar to the D_v, 13 of the funds have positive P_i values. The *PM* values are the P_i values divided by the market risk premium (3.17).

RELATIONSHIP AMONG PERFORMANCE MEASURES. Table 20.4 contains the matrix of the rank correlation coefficients among the measures. While the various measures provide alternative insights regarding performance, the overall ranks are very similar. Notably, the Sharpe measure appears to have the strongest relationship with other measures, including the Fama net selectivity value. On the other hand, while the MCV measure is similar to the Fama measure (selectivity and D_v are the same), the rank correlations are definitely lower. It appears that this is due to the use of a ratio to arrive at P_i. The market adjustment (i.e., the comparison of P_i to the market risk premium) did not change any ranks, because the market risk premium is a constant.

APPLICATION OF EVALUATION TECHNIQUES

The answers generated using these performance measures are only as good as the data inputs. Therefore, it is necessary to be careful in computing the rates of return and to take proper account of all inflows and outflows. More important, one must recognize that it is not possible to properly evaluate a portfolio manager's performance on the basis of a quarter or even a year. The evaluation should extend over a number of years and should cover at least one full market cycle so that you can determine whether there is any difference in performance during rising or declining markets.[15]

MEASUREMENT PROBLEMS

Earlier in the chapter there was a brief reference to a benchmark problem when the biases in performance measures found by Friend and Blume differed from those found by Klemkosky. While we discussed Roll's contentions regarding the measurement problem in Chapter 17, we should recall the problem at this point, discuss the implications of a global market on this problem, and put it in perspective. As noted earlier, because all the equity portfolio performance measures are derived from the CAPM, they assume a market portfolio at the point of tangency on the Markowitz efficient frontier. This implies that the market portfolio is an efficient, completely diversified portfolio containing all risky assets in the economy with market-value weighting. The problem arises in finding a real-world *proxy* for this theoretical market portfolio. The typical proxy used is the Standard & Poor's 500 index, because it is a diversified portfolio of stocks and the sample is market-value weighted. However, the assets included in the S&P 500 portfolio are all common stocks, most of them from the NYSE. It does not include the many other risky assets that theoretically should be considered (e.g., non–U.S. stocks, U.S. and non–U.S. bonds, real estate, coins, precious metals, stamps, antiques, etc.).

Roll recognized the problem with the market portfolio proxy[16] and referred to it as a *benchmark error,* since most techniques employ the market portfolio as the benchmark when evaluating performance and also

---

[15] In this regard, see Robert C. Kirby, "You Need More Than Numbers to Measure Performance," paper presented at Institute of Chartered Financial Analysts Seminar, Chicago, April 2, 1976. For a formal presentation related to the importance of the time element, see Mark Kritzman, "How to Detect Skill in Management Performance," *Journal of Portfolio Management* 12, no. 2 (Winter 1986): 16–20.

[16] Richard Roll, "A Critique of the Asset Pricing Theory's Tests," *Journal of Financial Economics* 4, no. 4 (March 1977): 129–176; Richard Roll, "Ambiguity When Performance Is Measured by the Securities Market Line," *Journal of Finance* 33, no. 4 (September 1978): 1051–1069; Richard Roll, "Performance Evaluation and Benchmark Error I," *Journal of Portfolio Management* 6, no. 4 (Summer 1980): 5–12; and Richard Roll, "Performance Evaluation and Benchmark Error II," *Journal of Portfolio Management* 7, no. 2 (Winter 1981): 17–22.

use it to derive a market risk measure (beta). As shown in Chapter 17, if the market portfolio proxy is not an efficient portfolio, then the betas derived are not true betas, and the security market line that is derived may not be the true SML—that is, the current SML could actually have a different slope. Therefore, a portfolio that is above the SML according to a poor benchmark (market portfolio proxy) could actually plot below the true SML. You could also have a shift of a portfolio based upon a change in its beta using the true market portfolio.

IMPACT OF GLOBAL INVESTING. The concern with the benchmark error is only increased with global investing. The several studies on international diversification discussed in Chapter 19 make it abundantly clear that as you add non–U.S. securities to the portfolio universe, you almost certainly will move the efficient frontier to the left (i.e., you experience a decline in risk). As noted, this movement continues as you add countries that have a lower level of economic interaction with the United States (such as some Asian and third-world countries). There are also some instances where these additions increase the expected returns of the universe—that is, the efficient frontier moves up as well as to the left. The point is, the efficient frontier will almost certainly change when we consider global investing. The extent of the change will depend upon the relationship among countries. And in addition to this change, the future will bring major changes as well. Specifically, our trade with European and Asian countries has grown rapidly in recent years, which should increase our interdependence and the correlation of our markets. Also, individual European countries will certainly become more interdependent after 1992, when numerous barriers to trade and travel in the European Economic Community will be eliminated.[17]

Several points are significant regarding this benchmark criticism. First, the benchmark problems that were noted by Roll and are increased by global investing do *not* negate the value of the CAPM as a *normative* model of equilibrium pricing. The theory is still viable; the problem is one of *measurement* when using the theory to evaluate portfolio performance. This means it is necessary to find a better proxy for the market portfolio or to adjust measured performance for these benchmark errors. In fact, in one of his later articles, Roll made several suggestions in this regard.[18] Based upon the discussion in Chapter 4, we know that new comprehensive stock market and bond market series are being developed that will be available as a market portfolio proxy. These indicator series include world stocks and world bonds but not other assets on a current basis. Alternatively, you might consider giving greater weight to the Sharpe portfolio

---

[17] A paper that contains an initial discussion of the procedure for evaluating non-U.S. equity portfolios is Gary P. Brinson and Nimrod Fachler, "Measuring Non-U.S. Equity Portfolio Performance," *Journal of Portfolio Management* 11, no. 3 (Spring 1985): 73–76. It discusses the problems with developing an appropriate index and considers market selection (country) and stock selection within countries, but it does not address risk factors, diversification considerations, or exchange rate effects.

[18] Richard Roll, "Performance Evaluation and Benchmark Error II," *Journal of Portfolio Management* 7, no. 2 (Winter 1981): 17–22.

performance measure, because it does not depend so heavily on the market portfolio. Recall that this measure relates the excess return to the *standard deviation* of return—that is, total risk. While the measure uses a benchmark portfolio as an unmanaged portfolio, the risk measure does not directly depend upon a market portfolio. Also, it is notable that the rank correlation of the Sharpe measure and the alternative performance measures shown in Table 20.4 is very high (i.e., typically in excess of 0.98).

RELIABILITY OF MEASUREMENT

Another concern is how reliable these measures are in ranking managers and determining their ability to significantly outperform the market. French and Henderson examined the performance measures under ideal conditions that work around the usual criticism of these models.[19] The simulation results indicated that when you eliminate the random noise, the measures do an excellent job of ranking portfolios consistent with the true ranking. At the same time, because of the random noise in stocks and portfolios, detecting performance that is statistically superior or inferior relative to the market portfolio is very difficult. A manager must be much better or worse before a difference shows up.

EVALUATION OF BOND PORTFOLIO PERFORMANCE

As discussed, the analysis of risk-adjusted performance for equity portfolios started in the late 1960s following the development of portfolio theory and the capital asset pricing model (CAPM). The common stock risk measures have been fairly simple—either total risk (standard deviation of return) or systematic risk (beta). In contrast, there was no such development in the fixed-income area, where the factors that can influence the portfolio return are more numerous and complex. One reason for this lack of development of bond portfolio performance measures was that prior to the 1970s most bond portfolios were basically buy-and-hold portfolios, so the performance for alternative portfolio managers would probably not differ. Second, interest rates were very stable, so little was to be gained from active management. In this section, we present several attempts to develop bond portfolio performance systems that consider these multi-risk factors.[20]

A BOND MARKET LINE

An early attempt to apply asset pricing techniques to bond portfolios was suggested by Wagner and Tito.[21] A prime factor needed to evaluate performance properly is a measure of risk similar to the beta coefficient for equities. It is difficult to derive comparable measures for bonds because maturity and coupon have a significant effect on the relative volatility of

---

[19] Don W. French and Glenn V. Henderson, Jr., "How Well Does Performance Evaluation Perform?" *Journal of Portfolio Management* 11, no. 2 (Winter 1985): 15–18.

[20] An overview of this area and a discussion of the historical development is contained in Arthur Williams III, "Performance Evaluation in Fixed Income Securities," in *The Handbook of Fixed Income Securities*, 2d ed., edited by Frank J. Fabozzi and Irving M. Pollack (Homewood, Ill., Dow Jones-Irwin, 1987).

[21] Wayne H. Wagner and Dennis A. Tito, "Definitive New Measures of Bond Performance and Risk," *Pension World* (May 1977): 17–26; and Dennis A. Tito and Wayne H. Wagner, "Is Your Bond Manager Skillful?" *Pension World* (June 1977): 10–16.

FIGURE 20.3
Specification of Bond Market Line Using Shearson
Lehman Hutton Bond Index

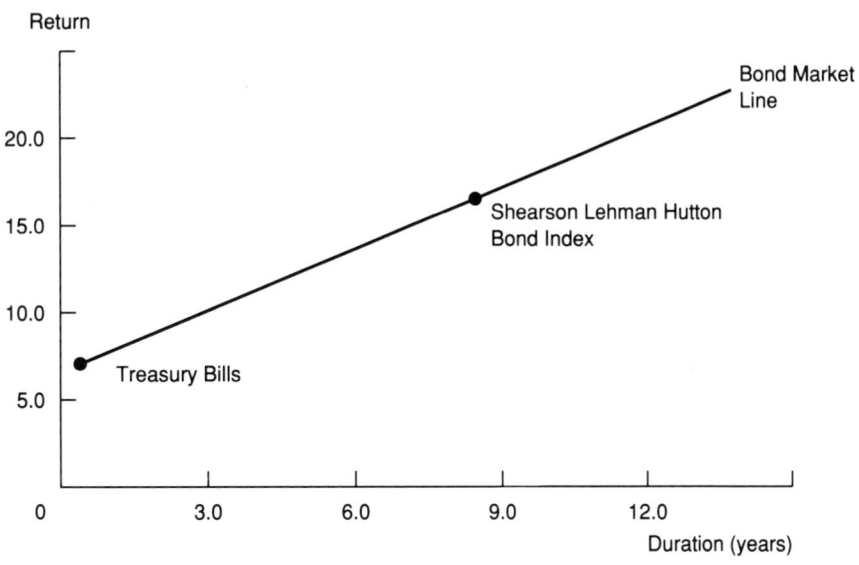

Source: Dennis A. Tito and Wayne H. Wagner, "Definitive New Measures of Bond Performance and Risk," *Pension World* (June 1977). Reprinted with permission.

bond prices. Based upon the discussion in Chapter 11, it is postulated that an appropriate composite risk measure that indicates the relative price volatility for a bond compared to interest rate changes is the bond's *duration*. Using this as a risk measure, the authors derived a bond market line similar to the stock market line; duration replaces beta as the risk variable, and the return line is drawn from Treasury bills to the Shearson Lehman Hutton Government/Corporate bond index rather than the S&P 500 index.[22] The bond market line looks like the graph in Figure 20.3. The return for the Shearson Lehman Hutton index is the rate of return during some common period, and the duration for the index is the value-weighted duration for the individual bonds in the index.

Given the bond market line, this technique divides the portfolio return that differs from the return on the Shearson Lehman Hutton index into four components: (1) a policy effect, (2) a rate anticipation effect, (3) an

---

[22] As you know from the presentation in Chapter 4, it would be equally reasonable to use a comparable bond-market indicator series from Merrill Lynch, Salomon Brothers, or the Ryan Index. The fact is, Wagner and Tito used the Kuhn Loeb Index in the original article since it was the most comprehensive index available at that time. Subsequently, this series became known as the Lehman Brothers Kuhn Loeb index when these firms merged. Following another merger, it was named the Shearson Lehman Hutton Government/Corporate Index and is prepared and published by the Shearson Lehman Hutton firm. Therefore, the Wagner-Tito presentation is modified to include the currently available successor series.

FIGURE 20.4
Graphic Display of Bond Portfolio Performance Breakdown

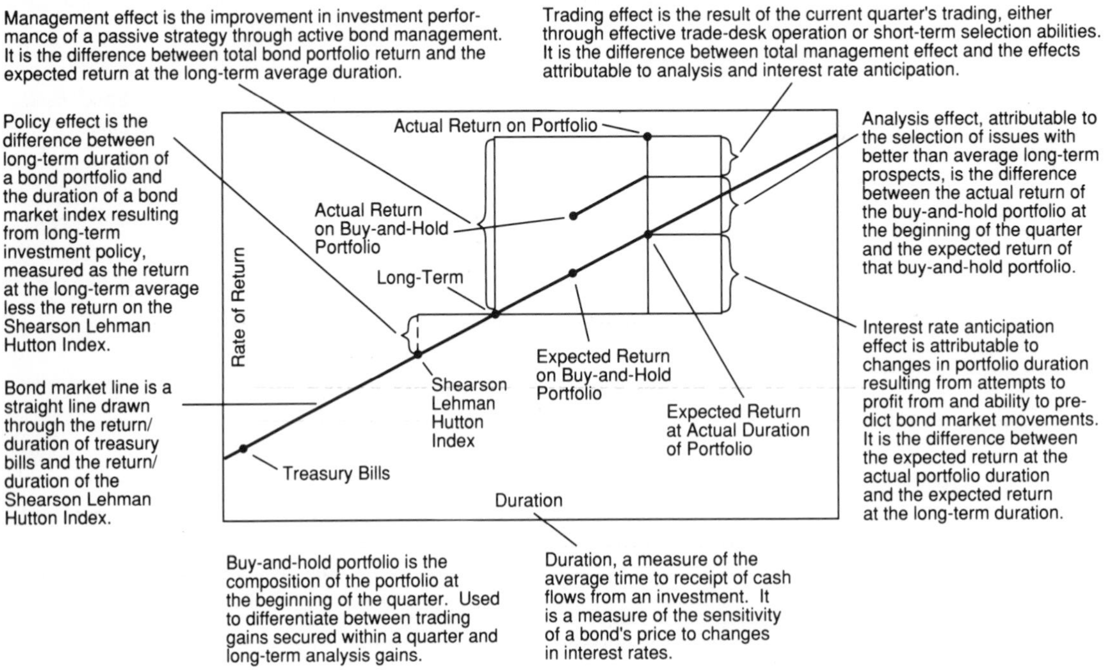
Management effect is the improvement in investment performance of a passive strategy through active bond management. It is the difference between total bond portfolio return and the expected return at the long-term average duration.
Trading effect is the result of the current quarter's trading, either through effective trade-desk operation or short-term selection abilities. It is the difference between total management effect and the effects attributable to analysis and interest rate anticipation.
Policy effect is the difference between long-term duration of a bond portfolio and the duration of a bond market index resulting from long-term investment policy, measured as the return at the long-term average less the return on the Shearson Lehman Hutton Index.
Actual Return on Portfolio
Actual Return on Buy-and-Hold Portfolio
Long-Term
Rate of Return
Analysis effect, attributable to the selection of issues with better than average long-term prospects, is the difference between the actual return of the buy-and-hold portfolio at the beginning of the quarter and the expected return of that buy-and-hold portfolio.
Interest rate anticipation effect is attributable to changes in portfolio duration resulting from attempts to profit from and ability to predict bond market movements. It is the difference between the expected return at the actual portfolio duration and the expected return at the long-term duration.
Bond market line is a straight line drawn through the return/duration of treasury bills and the return/duration of the Shearson Lehman Hutton Index.
Shearson Lehman Hutton Index
Expected Return on Buy-and-Hold Portfolio
Expected Return at Actual Duration of Portfolio
Treasury Bills
Duration
Buy-and-hold portfolio is the composition of the portfolio at the beginning of the quarter. Used to differentiate between trading gains secured within a quarter and long-term analysis gains.
Duration, a measure of the average time to receipt of cash flows from an investment. It is a measure of the sensitivity of a bond's price to changes in interest rates.

Source: Dennis A. Tito and Wayne H. Wagner, "Definitive New Measures of Bond Performance and Risk," *Pension World* (June 1977). Reprinted with permission.

analysis effect, and (4) a trading effect. When the latter three effects are combined, they are referred to as the *management effect.* These effects are portrayed in Figure 20.4.

The *policy effect* measures the difference in the expected return for a given portfolio because of a difference in the duration of this portfolio and the duration of the Shearson Lehman Hutton index. The idea is that the duration of an unmanaged portfolio would be equal to the Shearson Lehman Hutton index.[23] If the duration for a portfolio being evaluated differs from the index duration, this indicates a basic policy decision regarding relative risk (measured by duration), and there should be a difference in expected return consistent with that risk policy decision. As an example, assume that the duration-return for the Shearson Lehman Hutton index is 9.0 years and 8.25 percent. Your portfolio has a duration of 9.5 years and an expected return from the prevailing bond market line of 8.60 percent.

[23] It should be noted that the duration of the various bond market indicator series has changed over time (i.e., the duration of the corporate bond series has declined while the duration of the government series has slightly increased. For a presentation and discussion of this phenomenon, see Frank K. Reilly, Wenchi Wong, and David J. Wright, "An Analysis of Alternative Bond Market Indicator Series," mimeo (September 1988).

In this example, the policy effect would be 0.5 years and 0.35 percent (35 basis points); the higher duration implies that your portfolio should have a higher average return of 0.35 percent (this positive relationship assumes the typical upward-sloping yield curve).

Given the expected return and duration for this long-term portfolio, all deviations from the index portfolio are referred to as *management effects*, which are composed of (1) an interest rate anticipation effect, (2) an analysis effect, and (3) a trading effect.

The interest rate anticipation effect attempts to measure the differential return from changing the duration during this period compared to the portfolio's long-term duration. You would hope that the manager would increase the duration of the portfolio during periods of declining interest rates in an effort to increase the price volatility (price appreciation) of your portfolio, and vice versa. Therefore, you would determine the duration of the actual portfolio during the period and compare this to the duration of the long-term portfolio. Then you would determine the difference in expected return for these two durations using the bond market line. As an example, assume the duration for the long-term portfolio is 9.5 years, which implies an expected 8.60 percent return, while the duration for the portfolio being evaluated is 11.0 years, which implies an expected return of 9.75 percent using the bond market line. Therefore, the rate anticipation effect during this period is 1.15 percent (9.75 − 8.60).

The difference between this expected return, taking account of duration, and the actual return for the portfolio during this period is a combination of an analysis effect and a trading effect. The *analysis effect* is the differential return attributable to acquiring bonds that are temporarily mispriced relative to their risk. To measure this analysis effect, compare the *expected* return for the portfolio held at the beginning of the period (using the bond market line) to the *actual* return of this portfolio. If the actual return is greater than the expected return, it implies that the portfolio manager acquired some underpriced issues that became properly priced and provided excess returns during the period. If the portfolio at the beginning of the period had a duration of ten years, this might indicate an expected return of 9.00 percent for the period. In turn, if the actual return for this buy-and-hold portfolio was 9.40 percent, it would indicate an analysis effect of +0.40 percent (40 basis points).

Finally, *trading effect* occurs due to short-run changes in the portfolio during the period. It is measured as the residual after taking account of the analysis effect from the total excess return based upon duration. As an example, the total actual return is 10.50 percent with a duration of 11.0 years. Based upon the prevailing bond market line, the expected return for a portfolio of 11 years duration is 9.75 percent. Thus, the combination of the analysis and trading effect is 0.75 percent (10.50 − 9.75). Previously we determined that the analysis effect was 0.40 percent, so the trading effect must be 0.35 percent (0.75 − 0.40). In summary, for this portfolio manager, the actual return was 10.50 percent, compared to a return for the Shearson Lehman Hutton index of 8.25 percent. This total excess of 2.25 percent would be divided as follows:

- 0.35 percent policy effect due to higher long-term duration
- 1.15 percent interest rate anticipation effect due to increasing the duration of the current portfolio above the long-term portfolio duration
- 0.40 percent analysis effect—the impact of superior selection of individual issues in the beginning portfolio
- 0.35 percent trading effect—the impact of trading of the issues *during* the period.

This technique appears very useful in breaking down the return based upon the duration as a comprehensive risk measure. The only concern is that it does not consider differences in the risk of default. Specifically, the technique does not appear to differentiate between an AAA bond with a duration of eight years and a BAA bond with the same duration. This could clearly affect the performance. A portfolio manager who invested in BAA bonds, for example, could experience a very positive analysis effect simply because the bonds were lower quality than the average quality implicit in the Shearson Lehman Hutton index. The only way to avoid this would be to construct differential market lines for alternative ratings or derive a benchmark line that matches the quality makeup of the portfolio being evaluated.[24] Subsequent techniques consider this factor.

DECOMPOSING PORTFOLIO RETURNS

Dietz, Fogler, and Hardy set forth a technique to decompose the bond portfolio returns into maturity, sector, and quality effects.[25] The total return for a bond during a period of time is composed of a known income effect (due to normal yield-to-maturity factors) and an unknown price change effect (due to an interest rate effect sector/quality effect, and a residual effect). It is graphed as follows:

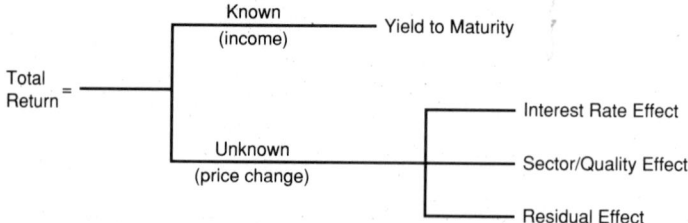

The *yield-to-maturity effect* is the return if nothing had happened to the yield curve during the period. That is, the investor would receive the interest income, the price change relative to par, and any price change due to the shape of the yield curve.

[24] This problem is briefly discussed in Frank K. Reilly and Rupinder Sidhu, "The Many Uses of Bond Duration," *Financial Analysts Journal* 36, no. 4 (July–August 1980): 58–72.

[25] Peter O. Dietz, H. Russell Fogler, and Donald J. Hardy, "The Challenge of Analyzing Bond Portfolio Returns," *Journal of Portfolio Management* 6, no. 3 (Spring 1980): 53–58.

The *interest rate effect* measures what happened to each issue because of changes in the term structure of interest rates during the period. Each bond is valued based upon the Treasury yield curve at its maturity and takes account of its normal premium relative to Treasury yields. Assume a normal premium of 30 basis points and that Treasury bonds with the maturity of your bond go from 8.50 percent to 9.25 percent. To determine the interest rate effect, you would compute the value of your bond at 8.80 percent (8.50 + 0.30) and at 9.55 percent (9.25 + 0.30) and then compute the price change. This is the price change, which allows you to determine the return change caused by a change in market interest rates.

The *sector/quality effect* measures the expected impact on the returns because of the sector of the bonds (corporates, utilities, financial, GNMA, etc.) and also the quality of the bonds (Aaa, Aa, A, Baa). The authors determined the average impact of these sets of variables by deriving a matrix of sector/quality returns for all bonds on the Telstat pricing tapes as follows (i.e., you would fill in this table with the appropriate yields):

	SECTOR/QUALITY RETURNS (VALUE-WEIGHTED)			
	AAA	AA	A	BAA
Corporates				
Utilities				
Financial				
Telephone				
Foreign				
GNMA				
Agencies				

Given this matrix, you can determine what happened to bonds in each cell after taking account of the yield to maturity and the interest rate effect. As an example, during a given period you might find that an average Aa utility had negative excess returns of −0.50 percent after taking account of the yield to maturity and the interest rate effect, while an A corporate bond experienced a comparable positive excess return of 0.30 percent. Therefore, the sector/quality effect would be −0.50 and 0.30 for these sets of bonds.

The *residual effect* is what remains after taking account of the three prior factors—yield to maturity, interest rate effect, and the sector/quality effect. It is computed as follows:

$$\text{Total Return} = \text{Yield to Maturity} + \text{Interest Rate Effect} + \text{Sector/Quality Effect} + \text{Residual}.$$

The presence of a consistently large positive residual would indicate superior selection capabilities. Specifically, such a residual indicates that after taking account of all market effects from interest rate changes and sector/quality, it is still possible to have some remaining positive returns due to selection. Alternatively, strong positive interest rate effects during periods of declining rates and small negative interest rate effects during periods of rising rates would indicate good skills at interest rate anticipation. Consistently positive sector/quality effects would indicate the ability to make proper allocations and to anticipate shifts in this area over time. For a given portfolio, you should probably prepare a time series plot of these alternative effects to determine the strengths and weaknesses of your manager. Also, these results net of transaction costs and taxes should be compared to the results for a static portfolio (i.e., buy and hold the beginning portfolio) and also compared to the overall performance of a broad bond-market indicator series, which would be considered an unmanaged portfolio.

ANALYZING SOURCES OF RETURN

Fong, Pearson, and Vasicek proposed a performance evaluation technique that likewise divides the total returns into several components that affect bond returns.[26] Their intent was to measure total realized return and attribute the return to its sources (i.e., what factors contributed to the total return?). The first breakdown divides the total return (R) between the effect of the external interest rate environment (I), which is beyond the control of the portfolio manager, and the impact of the management process (C). Thus:

$$R = I + C.$$

In turn, I is broken down into two parts. The first is the expected rate of return (E) on a portfolio of default-free securities *assuming no change in forward rates* (i.e., no change in future one-period rates). This expected return is also referred to as the *market's implicit forecast.* The second component of I is the return attributable to the actual change in forward rates (U). The component U is the *unexpected* part of the actual return on the Treasury index and is due to changes in forward rates. Thus:

$$I = E + U.$$

As an example, assume that at the beginning of a quarter the expected return on a portfolio of Treasury bonds during the coming year is 11 percent. (This expected return assumes no change in the term structure of bonds during this year.) At the end of the year, if you calculate the actual return in this portfolio of Treasury bonds, you determine that it was 11.75 percent. This would imply an E of 11 percent and a U of .75 percent.

In turn, C (the management contribution) is composed of three factors:

M = **return from maturity management**

S = **return from spread/quality management**

B = **return attributable to the selection of specific securities.**

---

[26] Gifford Fong, Charles Pearson, and Oldrich Vasicek, "Bond Performance: Analyzing Sources of Return," *Journal of Portfolio Management* 9, no. 3 (Spring 1983): 46–50.

The return from *maturity management (M)* is a function of how well the portfolio manager changes maturity (duration) in anticipation of interest rate changes. The component is measured by computing the default-free price of every security (at the beginning and end of the period) based on its maturity, using the spot rates for each maturity as indicated by the Treasury bond yield curve. The total return over the evaluation period is derived from these prices, while maintaining all actual trading activity. Given this total return based upon maturity yields, subtract the actual return on the Treasury index (determined earlier to be 11.75 percent) to arrive at the maturity return. As an example, if the total return based upon the pricing computations was 12.25 percent, the maturity return would be 0.50 percent, assuming the Treasury index return of 11.75 percent.

The *spread/quality management component* indicates the effect on return due to the manager's selection of bonds from various sectors and quality. It is measured by pricing each bond at the beginning and end of the period on the basis of its specific sector and quality and then computing the rate of return given these prices. This total return less the return for Treasury bonds, considering the maturity effect (determined to be 12.25 percent) indicates the return for the sector/quality. Assuming this sector/quality pricing indicates a total return of 12.0 percent, it would imply a negative 0.25 percent for sector/quality (12.00 − 12.25).

The *selectivity component (B)* is the remaining return. It is attributable to the selection of specific bonds beyond the maturity or sector/quality decisions—that is, what individual bonds you select to carry out these decisions. It is measured as the difference between the actual total return on the portfolio and the prior total return that considered maturity and sector/quality. Continuing our example, if the actual total return was 13.00 percent, the selectivity component would be 1.00 percent, since the return for maturity and sector/quality above was 12.00 percent. To summarize the results:

$$R = \left(\frac{E + U}{I}\right) + \left(\frac{M + S + B}{C}\right),$$

where

E =	expected Treasury yield	11.00
U =	unexpected Treasury yield	.75
M =	maturity management	.50
S =	spread/quality management	(.25)
B =	selectivity	1.00
	Total return	**13.00**

This analysis would indicate that the portfolio manager was quite good at maturity (duration) decisions and at selecting individual bonds but did not do well in terms of sector/quality decisions. As before, you should do a similar breakdown for some market index series as a basis of comparison to an unmanaged portfolio and also examine these components over time to determine any consistent strengths or weaknesses.

CONSISTENCY OF PERFORMANCE

Numerous investigators have documented performance inconsistency for managers of equity portfolios. (These studies are discussed in Chapter 21.) Kritzman examined the ranking for 32 bond managers employed by AT&T.[27] He divided a ten-year period into two five-year periods, determined each manager's percentile ranking in each period, and correlated the rankings. The results revealed *no relationship* between performance in the two periods. Another test likewise revealed no relationship between past and future performance even among the best and worst performers. Based upon these results, Kritzman concluded that it would be <u>necessary to examine something besides past performance to determine superior managers</u>. These results supported the strong-form EMH.

SUMMARY

The first major goal of portfolio management is to derive rates of return that equal or exceed the returns on a naively selected portfolio with equal risk. The second goal is to attain complete diversification. Several techniques have been derived to evaluate equity portfolios in terms of both risk and return (composite measures) based upon the CAPM. The Treynor measure considers the excess returns earned per unit of systematic risk. The Sharpe measure indicates the excess return per unit of total risk. Jensen likewise evaluated performance in terms of the systematic risk involved and showed how to determine whether the difference in risk-adjusted performance (good or bad) is statistically significant. The application of these evaluation techniques to 20 mutual funds indicated the importance of considering both risk and return, because there was a wide range of total risk, systematic risk, and diversification. The rank correlations among the alternative measures were extremely high, about 0.99.

Friend and Blume contended that there was an inverse relationship between the risk of the portfolio and its composite performance while Klemkosky indicated a completely different bias. We conclude that some biases may exist, but their direction is unknown and they would seldom change the rankings.

The more recent work in equity portfolio evaluation has been concerned with models that indicate what components of the management process contributed to the results. A model by Fama divided the composite return into measures related to total risk, systematic risk, diversification, and selectivity in addition to measuring overall performance. Moses, Cheyney, and Veit (MCV) developed a similar model that considered systematic risk and the effect of unsystematic risk (diversification). The rank correlation among the five measures was extremely high (about .99 except for the MCV correlations that were .91 to .93). Roll challenged the validity of all techniques that assume a "market portfolio" that theoretically includes all risky assets when actually investigators use a proxy such as the S&P 500 that is limited to U.S. common stocks. This criticism does not invalidate

---

[27] Mark Kritzman, "Can Bond Managers Perform Consistently?" *Journal of Portfolio Management* 9, no. 4 (Summer 1983): 54–56.

the normative asset pricing model, only its application because of measurement problems related to the proxy for the market portfolio. At the same time, the measurement problem is increased in an environment where global investing is the norm.

While the techniques for evaluating equity portfolio performance have been in existence for almost 30 years, comparable techniques for examining bond portfolio performance were initiated only about ten years ago. Evaluation models for bonds should consider separately several important decision variables related to bonds: the overall market factor, the impact of duration decisions, the influence of sector and quality factors, and the impact of individual bond selection. Studies have revealed a lack of consistency over time for a sample of bond managers.

It is important for investors to evaluate their own performance and the performance of hired managers. The various techniques discussed here provide theoretically justifiable measures that differ slightly. Although there was high rank correlation among the measures, *all the measures should be used*, because they provide different insights regarding the performance of managers. Finally, an evaluation of a portfolio manager should be done *a number of times* over *different market environments* before a final judgment is reached regarding the strengths and weaknesses of a manager.[28]

QUESTIONS

1. Assuming you are managing your own portfolio, discuss whether you should evaluate your own performance. What would you compare your performance against?

2. What are the two major factors that should be considered when evaluating a portfolio manager? What should the portfolio manager be trying to do?

3. What can a portfolio manager do to derive superior risk-adjusted returns?

4. What is the purpose of diversification according to the CAPM? How can you measure whether a portfolio is completely diversified? Explain why this measure makes sense.

5. Define and discuss the Treynor measure of portfolio performance.

6. Define and discuss the Sharpe measure of portfolio performance.

7. Why is it suggested that both the Treynor and Sharpe measures of performance be employed? What additional information is provided by a comparison of the rankings achieved using the two measures?

8. Define the Jensen measure of performance, and discuss whether it should produce results similar to those from the Treynor or Sharpe methods.

9. Define overall performance in the Fama model. Assume a fund had an overall performance figure of 5 percent. Discuss whether this means the manager is superior.

---

[28] For an article that espouses ignoring total returns and focusing on only yield to maturity, see Robert N. Anthony, "How to Measure Fixed-Income Performance Correctly," *Journal of Portfolio Management* 11, no. 2 (Winter 1985): 61–65; and the subsequent comments in the Winter 1986 issue. For an article that contends that accurate and useful performance measurement is not possible or desirable, see Robert Ferguson, "The Trouble with Performance Measurement," *Journal of Portfolio Management* 12, no. 3 (Spring 1986): 4–9.

10. A fund had an overall performance value of -0.50 percent. Discuss whether the manager of this fund could have experienced a positive selectivity value and under what conditions.

11. Define the diversification term. Under what conditions will this term equal zero?

12. Define net selectivity. If a portfolio had a negative selectivity value, could it have a positive net selectivity measure? Under what conditions?

13. A portfolio has an R^2 with the market of 0.95 and a selectivity value of 2.5 percent. Discuss whether you would expect the portfolio to have a positive net selectivity value.

14. Assuming that the proxy used for the market portfolio is not a good proxy, discuss the potential problem with the measurement of portfolio beta. Show by an example the effect on a portfolio evaluation graph if the measured beta is significantly lower than the true beta.

15. Assuming that the market proxy is a poor proxy, show an example of the potential impact on the security market line (SML), and demonstrate with an example how a portfolio that was superior relative to the proxy SML line could be inferior when compared to the true SML.

16. Show with a graph the effect global investing should have on the aggregate efficient frontier. What will this do to the world SML and individual betas?

17. It is contended that the derivation of an appropriate model for evaluating the performance of a bond portfolio manager is more difficult than an equity portfolio evaluation model because there are more decisions required. Discuss some of the specific decisions that are necessary when evaluating a bond portfolio manager.

18. Briefly describe what you are trying to measure in the following cases:

18a. The interest rate effect (i.e., market effect)

18b. The maturity effect (duration)

18c. The sector/quality effect

18d. The selection effect

19. Which of the effects in Question 18 are under the control of the bond portfolio manager?

20. *CFA Examination III (June 1981)*: Richard Roll, in an article on using the capital asset pricing model (CAPM) to evaluate portfolio performance, indicated that it may not be possible to evaluate portfolio management ability if there is an error in the benchmark used.

20a. In evaluating portfolio performance, describe the general procedure, with emphasis on the benchmark employed. [5 minutes]

20b. Explain what Roll meant by the benchmark error, and identify the specific problem with this benchmark. [5 minutes]

20c. Draw a graph that shows how a portfolio that has been judged as superior relative to a "measured" security market line (SML) can be inferior relative to the "true" SML. [10 minutes]

20d. Assume that you are informed that a given portfolio manager has been evaluated as superior when compared to the DJIA, the S&P 500, and the NYSE Composite Index. Explain whether this consensus would make you feel more comfortable regarding the portfolio manager's true ability. [5 minutes]

20e. While conceding the possible problem with benchmark errors as set forth by Roll, some contend this does not mean the CAPM is incorrect, but only that there is a measurement problem when implementing the theory. Others contend that because of benchmark errors, the whole technique should be scrapped. Take and defend one of these positions. [5 minutes]

21. *CFA Examination III (June 1982)*: During a quarterly review session, a client of Fixed Income Investors, a pension fund advisory firm, asks Fred Raymond, the portfolio manager for the company's account, if he could provide a more detailed analysis of their portfolio performance than simply total return. Specifically, the client had recently seen a copy of an article by Deitz, Fogler, and Hardy on the analysis of bond portfolio returns that attempted to decompose the total return into the following four components:

21a. Yield to maturity

21b. Interest rate effect

21c. Sector/quality effect

21d. Residual
While he does not expect you to be able to provide such an analysis this year, he asks you to explain each of these components to him so he will be better prepared to understand such an analysis when you do it for his company's portfolio next year. Explain each of these components. [20 minutes]

PROBLEMS

1. Assume that during the past ten-year period the risk-free rate was 8 percent, and three portfolios had the following characteristics:

PORTFOLIO	RETURN	BETA
A	.13	1.10
B	.11	.90
C	.17	1.20

Compute the *T* value for each portfolio, and indicate which portfolio had the best performance. Assume the market return during this period was 12 percent; how did these managers fare relative to the market?

2. Assume the three portfolios in Problem 1 have standard deviations of 0.14, 0.10, and 0.20, respectively. Compute the Sharpe measure of performance. Is there any difference in the ranking achieved using the Treynor versus the Sharpe measure? Discuss the probable cause.

3. The portfolios identified below are being considered for investment. During the period under consideration, $R_f = .07$.

PORTFOLIO	RETURN	BETA	σ
P	.15	1.0	.05
Q	.20	1.5	.10
R	.10	.6	.03
S	.17	1.1	.06
Market	.13	1.0	.04

3a. Compute the Sharpe measure of each portfolio and the market portfolio.

3b. Compute the Treynor measure of each portfolio and the market portfolio.

3c. Rank the portfolios using each measure.

4. You have decided to undertake an evaluation of the performance of Cirrus International (CI) for your Investment Club. After collecting the following data:

- $R_a = 0.15$
- $R_f = 0.05$
- $B_a = 1.20$
- $R_x = 0.10$

4a. Draw the security market line.

4b. Calculate CI's overall performance.

4c. Calculate CI's selectivity.

4d. Calculate CI's risk.

5. Reggie Portmus has made a performance evaluation of his bond holdings. He has misplaced some of the values and has asked for your help in calculating the remaining ones. At present he holds 10-year AA, 5-year A, and 25-year B bonds, and the following information has been recovered:

$I =$ external interest rate environment	11.00	
$E =$ expected return	10.00	
$U =$ unexpected return	?	
$M =$ maturity	.2 percent/year in the first 5 years, and .1 percent/year thereafter	
$S =$ spread/quality	$-.2$ percent/rank (AAA, AA, A, BBB, etc.)	
$B =$ specific selection	.25, .50, .75, respectively	
C	?	
R	?	

REFERENCES

Dietz, Peter O., H. Russell Fogler, and Donald J. Hardy. "The Challenge of Analyzing Bond Portfolio Returns." *Journal of Portfolio Management* 6, no. 3 (Spring 1980).

Fama, Eugene. "Components of Investment Performance." *Journal of Finance* 27, no. 3 (June 1972).

Fong, Gifford, Charles Pearson, and Oldrich Vasicek. "Bond Performance: Analyzing Sources of Return." *Journal of Portfolio Management* 9, no. 3 (Spring 1983).

Jensen, Michael C. "The Performance of Mutual Funds in the Period 1945–1964." *Journal of Finance* 23, no. 2 (May 1968).

Jensen, Michael C. "Risk, the Pricing of Capital Assets, and the Evaluation of Investment Portfolios." *Journal of Business* 42, no. 2 (April 1969).

Roll, Richard. "A Critique of the Asset Pricing Theory's Tests." *Journal of Financial Economics* 4, no. 4 (March 1977).

Roll, Richard. "Ambiguity when Performance Is Measured by the Securities Market Line." *Journal of Finance* 33, no. 4 (September 1978).

Sharpe, William F. "Mutual Fund Performances." *Journal of Business* 39, no. 1, Part 2 (January 1966).

Treynor, Jack L. "How to Rate Management of Investment Funds." *Harvard Business Review* 43, no. 1 (January-February 1965).

Williams, Arthur III. *Managing Your Investment Manager—The Complete Guide to Selection, Measurement, and Control.* (Homewood, Ill.: Dow Jones-Irwin, 1986).

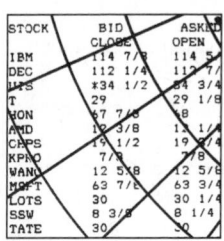

CHAPTER 21

INVESTMENT COMPANIES

In the past, investment texts were limited in their discussion of investment companies because it was assumed that most readers would prefer to make their own investment decisions. However, studies of efficient capital markets have indicated that it is difficult for an individual investor to outperform the aggregate market averages, and this makes managed investment companies an appealing alternative because of the several services they provide. In addition, the many different types of investment companies offer a wide variety of alternative investment instruments in terms of risk and return.

We will begin this chapter by defining investment companies, discussing their basic management organization, and describing the major types of companies. These different types, ranging from very conservative money market funds to common stock and option funds, are the subject of the second section. In the third section we will discuss some studies that have examined the historical performance of mutual funds. The final section identifies sources of information on investment companies and lists the major international and global stock and bond funds.

INVESTMENT COMPANY DEFINED

An investment company is a pool of funds belonging to many individuals that is used to acquire a collection of individual investments such as stocks, bonds, and other publicly traded securities. As an example, 10 million shares of an investment company might be sold to the public at $10 a share for a total of $100 million. Assuming that this is a common stock fund, the managers of the company might then invest the funds in the stock of companies like American Telephone and Telegraph, General Motors, IBM, Xerox, and General Electric. As a result, each of the individuals who bought shares of the investment company would own a percentage of the total portfolio of the investment company. In other words, they would have indirectly acquired shares of a diversified portfolio of securities. The value of the investor's shares depends upon what happens to the portfolio of assets acquired by the managers of the fund. If we assume no transactions are made, and the total market value of all the stocks in the portfolio increased to $105 million, then the per share value of each of the original shares would be $10.50 ($105 million/10 million shares). This figure is referred to as the *net asset value (NAV)* and is equal to the total market value of all the assets of the fund minus any liabilities divided by the number of shares of the fund outstanding.

MANAGEMENT OF INVESTMENT COMPANIES

The investment company is typically a corporation whose major assets are the portfolio of marketable securities. The *management* of the portfolio, and most of the other administrative duties related to the company and its portfolio of securities, is handled by a separate management company hired by the board of directors of the investment company. While this is the legal description, the actual management usually begins with an investment advisory firm that starts an investment company and selects a board of directors for the fund that subsequently hires the investment advisory firm as the fund manager. The contract between the investment company (fund) and the management company indicates the duties of the management company and the fee it will receive for these services. The major responsibilities of the management company include research, portfolio management, and administrative duties such as issuing securities and handling redemptions and dividends. The fee, which is generally stated in terms of a percentage of the value of the fund, typically ranges from one-quarter of 1 percent to one-half of 1 percent of the total value, with a sliding scale as the size of the fund increases.

To achieve economies of scale, many management companies start a number of funds with different characteristics. The multiple funds allow the management group to appeal to many different types of investors, provide the investors with the flexibility to switch among funds, and increase the total capital managed.

OPEN-END VERSUS CLOSED-END FUNDS

Investment companies are begun like any other company—by selling an issue of common stock to a group of investors. In the case of an investment company, however, the proceeds are used to purchase the securities of other publicly held companies rather than buildings and equipment. The difference between an open-end investment company (often referred to as a *mutual fund*) and a closed-end investment company is how they operate *after* the initial public offering is sold.

A *closed-end investment company* operates like any other public firm, since its stock is bought and sold on a regular secondary market (e.g., the NYSE) and the market price of the investment company shares is determined by supply and demand. There are typically no further shares offered by the investment company, and it does *not* repurchase the shares on demand. There are no subsequent additions to the funds of the investment company unless it makes another public sale of securities. Also, there is no withdrawal of funds unless the investment company decides to repurchase its stock, which is quite unusual.

The closed-end investment company's *net asset value* (NAV) is computed twice a day based upon prevailing market prices for the securities in the portfolio. The *market price* of shares in the fund is determined by the relative supply and demand for the investment company stock in the market. When buying or selling shares of a closed-end investment company, the investor pays this market price plus or minus a regular trading commission. It is very important to recognize that *the two prices (NAV and market price) are almost never the same!* Over the long run, the market price has historically been from 5 to 20 percent *below* the NAV. Figure 21.1 contains a list of closed-end stock funds, specialized equity funds, and convertible preferred stock funds published in *Barron's.*

The number of closed-end stock funds has increased dramatically during the past several years. As of 1986 there were 8 diversified common stock funds and 18 specialized and convertible funds. By 1988 the number had grown to 23 diversified funds and 40 specialized and convertible funds. Table 21.1 indicates the dramatic growth in number and dollar value during the 1986–1988 time period. Notably, some observers have felt that the growth will necessarily slow down because this rapid growth rate cannot be sustained, but also because of the substantial discounts on these issues.[1] Besides the long-run discount, there has been substantial concern with the discounts on these funds following the initial public offering. The fact is, several studies have shown that most individual stock IPOs experience an abnormal *positive* price change immediately after the offering, but this price adjustment is basically completed in one day. In contrast, it appears that the prices for closed-end funds originally are fairly stable but then drift to a *discount* over a four-month period. Indeed, because of this unusual pattern, the SEC initiated a study of the question.[2] Besides the overall growth, it is notable that the specialized closed-end funds include several of the individual non–U.S. country funds (e.g., Japan, Korea, Germany, Mexico) that are discussed later in the chapter.

Figure 21.2 contains a listing of closed-end bond funds also published in *Barron's.* After many years of relative stability in numbers, there has been a major increase in these funds from about 20 in 1986 to 47 in 1988. Again, several of them are international bond funds that are discussed later in the chapter.

At the time shown in Figure 21.2, most of the funds were selling in the market at a discount to their NAV. Based upon the historical relationship, this is fairly typical, which has prompted the following questions: Why do

---

[1] Michael Siconolfi, "Launching of Closed-End Funds May Ease," *The Wall Street Journal,* November 30, 1987, 33.

[2] Michael Siconolfi, "SEC Studies Closed-End Fund 'Mystery,'" *The Wall Street Journal,* May 23, 1988, 31.

FIGURE 21.1
Closed-End Stock Funds, Specialized Equity Funds, and Convertible Preferred Stock Funds

CLOSED-END STOCK FUNDS

July 29, 1988

Following is a weekly listing of shares of publicly-traded closed-end investment trusts (the number of their outstanding shares is fixed). The funds invest in diversified portfolios, although some concentrate in one or a few industry groups. Shown is the stock exchange where it is traded, unaudited net asset value of each fund's shares, reported by the companies as of Friday's close. Also shown is the closing listed market price or a dealer-to-dealer asked price of each fund's shares with the percentage difference from the net asset value (NAV). A plus or minus before the difference indicates whether the shares are trading at a premium or discount from their net asset value. The Convertible Funds are invested in preferred stock that is convertible into common stock.

Diversified Common Stock Funds

Fund Name	Stock Exchg.	N.A. Value	Stock Price	% Diff.	Fund Name	Stock Exchg.	N.A. Value	Stock Price	% Diff.
Adams Express	NYSE	17.39	15⅞	– 8.71	Liberty All-Star	NYSE	8.33	6⅞	– 17.50
Baker Fentress-n	OTC	f25.62	21¾	– 15.09	Niagara Share	NYSE	16.20	13⅝	– 15.90
Blue Chip Value	NYSE	7.37	6	– 18.59	Nicholas App Gr Eq	NYSE	8.51	7⅜	– 13.34
Clemente-Gbl	NYSE	b8.57	7⅜	– 13.94	Quest Value Cap	NYSE	10.67	7¾	– 27.37
Gemini II Cap	NYSE	17.04	12¼	– 28.11	Quest Value Inc	NYSE	11.84	10	– 15.54
Gemini II Inc	NYSE	9.75	12⅝	+ 29.52	Royce Value	NYSE	9.67	8½	– 12.09
Gen'l Amer Inv	NYSE	18.88	15⅜	– 18.57	Schafer Value	NYSE	8.79	7⅜	– 16.10
GlobalGr Cap	NYSE	8.70	8⅛	– 6.61	Source Cap	NYSE	38.38	37⅛	– 3.27
GlobalGr Inc	NYSE	9.38	9¾	+ 3.94	Tri-Continental	NYSE	24.96	21¾	– 12.90
GSO Trust	NYSE	9.76	9¼	– 5.20	Worldwd Value	NYSE	19.65	16	– 18.57
Lehman Corp.	NYSE	14.37	12⅜	– 13.88	Zweig Fund	NYSE	10.20	10⅝	+ 4.17

Flexible Portfolio Funds

Fund Name	Stock Exchg.	N.A. Value	Stock Price	% Diff.	Fund Name	Stock Exchg.	N.A. Value	Stock Price	% Diff.
Amer All Sea. Fd	OTC	5.60	6½	+ 16.07					

Specialized Equity and Convertible Funds

Fund Name	Stock Exchg.	N.A. Value	Stock Price	% Diff.	Fund Name	Stock Exchg.	N.A. Value	Stock Price	% Diff.
Amer Cap Cv	NYSE	23.44	23⅛	– 1.34	Germany Fund	NYSE	7.33	7⅛	– 2.80
ASA Ltd.	NYSE	bc51.33	40⅝	– 20.90	H&Q Health	NYSE	8.03	6⅝	– 17.50
Asia Pacific	NYSE	8.82	7	– 20.60	HamCap	AMEX	b9.48	8⅜	– 11.28
Bancroft CV	AMEX	z	z	z	HamUt pf	NYSE	b48.43	47¾	– 1.40
BGR Prec Mtls	TOR	be13.54	10¾	– 20.61	Helvetia Fd	NYSE	10.66	9¼	– 13.23
Brazil	NYSE	11.53	9	– 21.94	Italy Fund	NYSE	bg8.84	7⅞	– 10.92
CNV Hldg Cap	NYSE	9.59	5¼	– 45.26	Korea Fund	NYSE	42.02	74⅞	+ 78.18
CNV Hldg Inc	NYSE	9.50	11⅛	+ 17.11	Malaysia Fund	NYSE	9.45	8¾	– 7.41
Castle	AMEX	z	z	z	Mexico Fund	NYSE	b7.41	5	– 32.52
CenFdCanada	AMEX	bz	z	z	MG Sm Cap	NYSE	9.09	8¼	– 9.20
Cent Sec	AMEX	12.07	9⅞	– 18.19	Petrol & Res	NYSE	26.64	24⅜	– 8.50
Claremont	AMEX	51.64	48⅛	– 6.80	Pilgrim Reg	NYSE	9.69	8	– 17.44
Couns Tandem	NYSE	z	z	z	Reg Finl/Shs	NYSE	7.84	6¼	– 20.28
Cypress Fd	AMEX	9.89	7½	– 24.17	Scandinavia	AMEX	8.40	6⅝	– 21.13
Duff Phelps Utils	NYSE	7.80	8¼	+ 5.77	Scudder New Asia	NYSE	12.42	9⅞	– 20.49
Ellsworth Cv	AMEX	8.84	7⅞	– 10.96	Spain Fund	NYSE	10.93	9¾	– 10.79
Engex Inc.	AMEX	12.21	9¼	– 24.24	Taiwan Fund	AMEX	b32.44	40⅛	+ 23.69
Fin News Comp	NYSE	16.23	13	+ 19.90	TCW Conv Secur	NYSE	b8.38	7⅞	– 6.00
FirstAustralia	AMEX	10.80	9	+ 16.67	Templeton E Mkt	AMEX	b9.52	7⅞	– 17.30
First Fin Fund	NYSE	8.81	7⅜	– 16.29	Thai Fund	NYSE	11.77	14⅜	+ 22.13
First Iberian	AMEX	8.99	9¼	+ 2.89	Utd. Kingdom Fd.	NYSE	10.99	8⅝	– 21.52
France Fund	NYSE	b10.09	9⅛	– 9.60	Z-Seven-p	PAC	d14.67	14¾	+ 0.55
Gabelli Equity	NYSE	11.04	10	– 9.42					

a-Ex-Dividend. b-As of Thursday's close. c-Translated at Commercial Rand exch. rate. d-NAV reflects $1.85 per share for taxes. e-In Canadian Dollars. g-7/21/88 NAV: 8.88, Stk Pr.: 8⅛, %Diff.-8.50. n-Nasdaq National Market System. p-Pacific Exchange. z-Not available.

Source: Investment Company Institute

Source: "Closed-End Stock Funds," *Barron's*, August 1, 1988. Reprinted by permission of *Barron's*, © Dow Jones & Company, Inc., 1988. All Rights Reserved.

TABLE 21.1
Number of Closed-End Fund Initial Public Offerings and New Funds Raised

YEAR	NUMBER OF FUNDS	AMOUNT RAISED
1981	1	$ 62 million
1982	0	—
1983	4	58 million
1984	4	106 million
1985	3	614 million
1986	28	5 billion
1987	34	9 billion
1988 ([a])	39	15 billion

[a] Estimate through June.
Source: Thomas J. Herzfeld Advisors, Inc., P.O. Box 161465, Miami, Florida 33116.

these funds sell at a discount? Why do the discounts differ among funds? What are the returns available to investors from funds that sell at large discounts? With regard to this final question, since an investor is acquiring a portfolio at a price below market value, the dividend yield should be above average, but the question regarding total return depends upon what happens to the discount during the holding period. If the discount declines, there should be positive excess returns, and vice versa. These issues remain as a major question of modern finance.[3]

CLOSED-END FUND INDEX

Because of the interest in closed-end funds, a firm that specializes in these funds (Thomas J. Herzfeld Advisors) has created a closed-end fund average that tracks the market price performance of 20 U.S. closed-end funds that invest principally in U.S. equities. The following is the list of funds in the average:

The Adams Express Company
Baker, Fentress and Company
Blue Chip Value Fund, Inc.
Central Securities Corporation

Claremont Capital Corporation
Cypress Fund Inc.
Financial News Composite Fund
Gabelli Equity Trust, Inc.

---

[3] Burton Malkiel, "The Valuation of Closed-End Investment Company Shares," *Journal of Finance* 32, no. 3 (June 1977): 847-859; Malcolm Richards, Donald Fraser, and John Groth, "Winning Strategies for Closed-End Funds," *Journal of Portfolio Management* 7, no.1 (Fall 1980): 50–55; Malcolm Richards, Donald Fraser, and John Groth, "Premiums, Discounts, and the Volatility of Closed-End Mutual Funds," *The Financial Review* 14, no. 3 (Fall 1979): 26–33; Rodney Roenfeldt and Donald Tuttle, "An Examination of the Discounts and Premium of Closed-End Investment Companies," *Journal of Business Research* 5, no. 1 (Fall 1973): 129-140; Rex Thompson, "The Information Content of Discounts and Premiums on Closed-End Fund Shares," *Journal of Financial Economics* 6, no. 2–3 (June–September 1978): 151–186; and Edward F. Cone, "Stocks on Sale," *Forbes,* July 11, 1988: 144–145. A discussion of bond funds is found in Malcolm Richards, Donald Fraser, and John Groth, "The Attractions of Closed-End Bond Funds," *Journal of Portfolio Management* 8, no. 2 (Winter 1982): 56–61. For a discussion of growth in 1988 and the new Closed-End Fund Index, see Thomas J. Herzfeld, "Closed-End Funds: On the Rebound After an Agonizing Year," *Barron's,* February 15, 1988; and Thomas J. Herzfeld, "The People's Choice: Money Still Pouring into Closed-End Funds," *Barron's,* May 16, 1988.

FIGURE 21.2
Closed-End Bond Funds

CLOSED-END BOND FUNDS

Following are shares of closed-end (fixed number of outstanding shares) investment companies with diversified portfolios of bonds. Shown is the unaudited net asset value (NAV) of each company's shares as of July 22, 1988. Also shown is the closing market price or the dealer-to-dealer asked price of each fund's shares, as of the same date, with the percentage difference from the net asset value. A plus or minus difference indicates whether each fund's shares are selling at a premium or a discount from their net asset value.

Bond Funds

Fund Name	Stock Exchg.	N.A. Value	Stock Price	% Diff.	Fund Name	Stock Exchg.	N.A. Value	Stock Price	% Diff.
ACM Gov't Inc	NYSE	10.84	11⅝	+ 7.2	Intercapital Inc	NYSE	19.25	21¾	+ 13.0
ACM Gov't Secur	NYSE	10.69	11	+ 2.9	John Hancock Inc	NYSE	15.28	14⅜	− 5.9
ACM Spectrum	NYSE	9.23	9⅛	− 1.1	John Hancock Inv	NYSE	20.62	20¼	− 1.8
Amev Securities	NYSE	10.35	10⅝	+ 2.7	Kemper High Inc	NYSE	11.06	12⅛	+ 9.6
Amer Capital Bd	NYSE	*20.96	20⅝	− 1.6	Kemper Intrmd	NYSE	9.27	10	+ 7.9
Amer Capital Inc	NYSE	9.22	9⅞	+ 7.1	Lincoln National	NYSE	27.67	25⅜	− 8.3
Amer Gov't Inc	NYSE	7.26	8	+ 10.2	MFS Gov Mkts Inc	NYSE	9.12	10	+ 9.6
Bunker Hill Inc	NYSE	17.64	17	− 3.6	MFS Inc & Oppor	NYSE	a9.54	10⅛	+ 6.1
Circle Inc Shares	OTC	12.20	12¾	+ 4.5	MFS Intrmed Inc	NYSE	9.16	9⅝	+ 5.1
CNA Inc Shares	NYSE	11.31	11⅜	+ 0.6	MFS Multimkt Inc	NYSE	9.03	10¼	+ 13.5
Colonial Intrmd	NYSE	z	z	z	MFS Multi Total R	NYSE	z	z	z
Comstock Ptnrs.	NYSE	9.51	10	+ 5.2	Montgomery Street	NYSE	18.47	18	− 2.5
Current Inc Shrs	NYSE	b11.91	12⅛	+ 1.8	Mutual Omaha Int	NYSE	13.67	14½	+ 6.1
Dean Witter Gov Inc	NYSE	9.42	9⅜	− 0.5	New Amer High Inc	NYSE	8.92	10¼	+ 14.9
Drexel Bond Deb	NYSE	19.39	19⅛	− 1.4	Oppenheimer Multi	NYSE	11.06	11⅜	+ 2.8
Dreyfus Strat. Gov't	NYSE	11.14	11½	+ 3.2	Pacific Amer Inc	NYSE	*15.38	15¼	− 0.8
Excelsior Inc Shrs	NYSE	16.90	14¾	− 12.7	Prudential Interm	NYSE	9.24	9⅝	+ 4.2
Fst Boston Inc	NYSE	8.76	8¾	− 0.1	Prudential Strat	NYSE	9.04	9	− 0.4
Fst Boston Strat Inc.	NYSE	11.18	11⅛	− 0.5	Putnam Intrm Gov	NYSE	9.32	9⅞	+ 6.0
Ft Dearborn Inc	NYSE	14.62	14½	− 0.8	Putnam Master Inc	NYSE	9.44	9½	+ 0.6
Hatteras Inc Secs	NYSE	16.03	15⅞	− 1.0	Putnam Mstr Intrmd	NYSE	9.35	9¼	− 1.1
High Inc Adv Tr	NYSE	9.27	9⅞	+ 6.5	Putnam Premier	NYSE	8.96	9½	+ 6.0
High Yield Inc	NYSE	9.44	9⅜	− 0.7	State Mutual Secur	NYSE	10.82	10¾	− 0.6
High Yield Plus	NYSE	9.27	9⅜	+ 1.1	Transamerica Inc	NYSE	22.20	24½	+ 10.4
INA Invest (Cigna)	NYSE	17.83	17	− 4.7	USLIFE Income	NYSE	9.58	9	− 6.1
Independ Sq (Isis)	OTC	16.31	16½	+ 1.2	Vestaur Secur	NYSE	13.53	13⅛	− 3.0

Convertible Bond Funds

Fund Name	Stock Exchg.	N.A. Value	Stock Price	% Diff.	Fund Name	Stock Exchg.	N.A. Value	Stock Price	% Diff.
Lincoln Nat'l Conv	NYSE	13.78	11⅞	− 13.8	Putnam High Inc	NYSE	8.49	8¼	− 2.8

International Bond Funds

Fund Name	Stock Exchg.	N.A. Value	Stock Price	% Diff.	Fund Name	Stock Exchg.	N.A. Value	Stock Price	% Diff.
F Australia Prime	AMEX	10.79	8⅞	− 17.7	Klein Benson Aust	NYSE	11.62	10¼	− 11.8
Global Government	NYSE	9.03	9½	+ 5.2	Templeton Global	NYSE	9.13	9⅞	+ 8.2
Global Yield Fund	NYSE	9.98	9¼	− 7.3					

Municipal Bond Funds

Fund Name	Stock Exchg.	N.A. Value	Stock Price	% Diff.	Fund Name	Stock Exchg.	N.A. Value	Stock Price	% Diff.
Allstate Muni Inc	NYSE	10.17	10¼	+ 0.8	Nuveen Muni Inc	NYSE	11.14	10½	− 5.7
Allstate Muni II	NYSE	9.53	9⅜	− 1.6	Nuveen Cal Muni	NYSE	11.21	11	− 1.9
Colonial Muni Inc	NYSE	8.98	9⅜	+ 4.4	Nuveen NY Muni	AMEX	11.16	11¾	+ 5.3
Dreyfus Strat Muni	NYSE	9.82	10	+ 1.8	Nuveen Muni Value	NYSE	9.59	9¼	− 3.5
MFS Muni Inc Tr	NYSE	9.05	9⅛	+ 0.8	Nuveen Cal Value	NYSE	9.66	9⅞	+ 2.2
Muniinsured Fund	AMEX	a9.76	10	+ 2.5	Nuveen NY Value	NYSE	9.92	10	+ 0.8
NY Tax-Exempt	AMEX	9.78	9½	− 2.9	Nuveen Premium	NYSE	z	z	z

a-Ex-Dividend. b-As of 7/21. z-Not available. *Fully diluted. Source: Lipper Analytical Services, Denver, Colorado

Source: "Closed-End Bond Funds," *Barron's*, July 25, 1988. Reprinted by permission of *Barron's*, © Dow Jones & Company, Inc., 1988. All Rights Reserved.

General American Investors
   Company
Growth Stock Outlook Trust
Lehman Corporation
Liberty All-Star Equity Fund
Morgan Grenfell SMALLCap
   Fund
Niagara Share Corporation

Nicholas-Applegate Growth
   Equity
Royce Value Trust
Schafer Value Trust
Source Capital Inc.
Tri-Continental Corporation
Zweig Fund Inc.

Nineteen of the 20 funds are listed on either the NYSE or AMEX, while one trades on NASDAQ. The index is price-weighted and is based on fund market values rather than NAVs. In addition to computing a market price index, the Herzfeld firm also examines NAVs and computes the average discount from NAV. Notably, the graph in Figure 21.3 that is published weekly in *Barron's* indicates that the average discount from NAV changes over time and is a major determinant of the market price performance of the index. As an example, during the first half of 1988 the average discount declined and this contributed to the superior performance of the index.

Open-end investment companies are funds for which shares continue to be bought and sold after the initial public offering is made. They stand ready to sell additional shares at the NAV of the fund with or without a sales charge. In addition, open-end investment companies stand ready to buy back shares of the fund (redeem shares) at the NAV at any time with or without a redemption fee.

Open-end mutual funds have enjoyed substantial growth during the post-war period, as shown by the figures in Table 21.2. Clearly, open-end funds account for a substantial portion of investment assets and provide a very important service for almost 10 million accounts.

LOAD VERSUS NO-LOAD OPEN-END FUNDS

One distinction among open-end funds is whether they charge a sales fee when the fund is initially offered. In the case of a *load fund,* the offering price for a share is equal to the NAV of the share *plus* a sales charge, typically 7.5 to 8.0 percent of the NAV. Therefore, assuming an 8 percent sales charge (load), an individual investing $1,000 in such a fund would receive only $920 worth of stock. In such cases, the funds generally do not charge a redemption fee, which means the shares can be redeemed at their NAV. Therefore, the funds are typically quoted in the paper with an NAV and offer price. The NAV price is the redemption price, while the offering price is equal to the net asset value divided by 0.92. As an example, if the NAV is $8.50 a share, the offering price would be $9.24 ($8.50/0.92). The 74 cents differential is really 8.7 percent of the NAV. The percent of the load typically declines with the size of the order.

There is no initial sales charge on a *no-load fund,* so the shares are sold at their NAV. In some instances, there is a small redemption charge on these funds (one-half of 1 percent). In *The Wall Street Journal,* you will see the bid price is listed as NAV and, in the case of a no-load fund, the offering price column shows the designation "NL" (no-load). A number

FIGURE 21.3
The Herzfeld Closed-End Average

	12/31/87	1/31/88	2/29/88	3/31/88	4/30/88	5/31/88	6/24/88	% CHANGE YEAR TO DATE
DJIA	1939	1958	2071	1988	2032	2032	2143	+10.58%
THCEA	1938	2018	2130	2112	2120	2110	2239	+15.53%
Average NAV	2324	2386	2484	2499	2511	2446	2605	+12.09%
Average Discount	−16.6%	−13.4%	−13.3%	−13.8%	−14.3%	−13.5%	−12.74%	

Source: Thomas J. Herzfeld Advisors, Inc., P.O. Box 161465, Miami, Florida 33116, and *Barron's*.

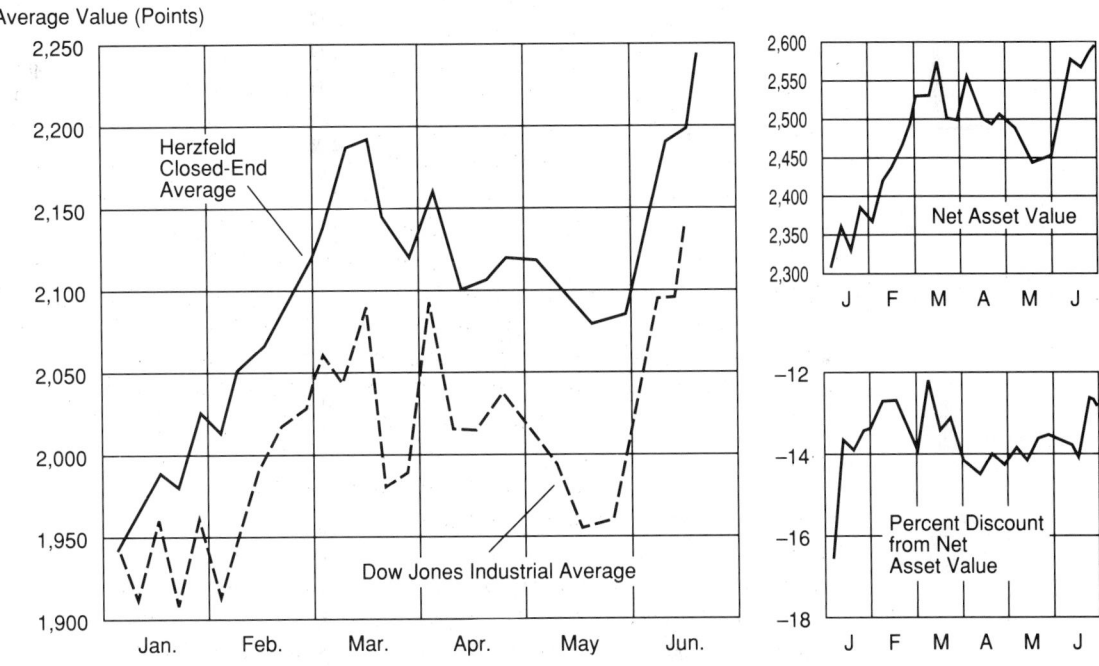

Source: *Barron's*.

of no-load funds have been established in recent years. *The Wall Street Journal* listing ran to more than 350 no-load funds, and the one in *Barron's* to more than 800. A directory of no-load funds is available.[4]

Between the full load fund and the pure no-load fund exist several important variations. The first is the *low-load fund,* which charges a front-end load, but typically in the 3 percent range rather than 7 to 8 percent.

---

[4] No-Load Mutual Fund Association, Inc., 11 Penn Plaza, New York, NY 10001. The cost of the directory is $5.

TABLE 21.2
Open-End Investment Company Assets: 1945–1987

YEAR-END	NUMBER OF REPORTING FUNDS	ASSETS (BILLIONS OF DOLLARS)	YEAR-END	NUMBER OF REPORTING FUNDS	ASSETS (BILLIONS OF DOLLARS)
1945	73	1.3	1966	182	34.8
1946	74	1.3	1967	204	44.7
1947	80	1.4	1968	240	52.7
1948	87	1.5	1969	269	48.3
1949	91	2.0	1970	361	47.6
1950	98	2.5	1971	392	55.0
1951	103	3.1	1972	410	59.8
1952	110	3.9	1973	421	46.5
1953	110	4.1	1974	416	34.1
1954	115	6.1	1975	390	42.2
1955	125	7.8	1976	404	47.6
1956	135	9.0	1977	427	45.0
1957	143	8.7	1978	444	45.0
1958	151	13.2	1979	446	49.0
1959	155	15.8	1980	458	58.4
1960	161	17.0	1981	486	55.2
1961	170	22.8	1982	539	76.8
1962	169	21.3	1983	653	113.6
1963	165	25.2	1984	820	137.8
1964	160	29.1	1985	1,071	251.7
1965	170	35.2	1986	1,356	424.2
			1987	1,781	453.8

Note: Does not include money market and short-term bond funds.

Source: *1975 Mutual Fund Fact Book*, *1981 Mutual Fund Fact Book*, and *1988 Mutual Fund Fact Book*, Investment Company Institute, Washington, D.C. Reprinted with permission.

Typically, this is used for bond funds or for equity funds by management companies that generally have no-load funds. For example, almost all of the Fidelity Management funds were no-load prior to 1985, but several of their newer funds have carried a low load of 3 percent. Alternatively, some funds that previously were full load funds have reduced their loads.

The second major "innovation" is the 12b-1 plan, named after the 1980 SEC rule that permits it. This plan permits funds to deduct as much as 1.25 percent of average net assets *per year* to be used to cover distribution costs, such as advertising, commissions paid to brokers, and general marketing expenses. A large and growing number of no-load funds are adopting these plans and a few low-load funds have put them in. You can determine if a 12b-1 plan is in existence only by reading the prospectus or using a service that provides substantial detail regarding charges.

Finally, some funds have instituted *contingent deferred sales loads* that charge you when you sell the fund if you have held it for less than a specified time period, such as three or four years.

MANAGEMENT FEE   In addition to the selling charge (no-load, load, or 12b-1), all investment firms charge an *annual management fee* to compensate the professional managers of the fund. This fee is typically a percent of the average net assets of the fund and varies from about .50 of 1 percent to about 1.50 percent. In most instances fees are on a sliding scale that declines with the size of the fund (e.g., .25 of 1 percent for assets over $1 billion). These management fees are a major factor driving the creation of new funds because, as mentioned earlier, the more assets under management, the greater the fees, and management costs do not increase at the same rate. Consequently, substantial economies of scale are possible in managing financial assets.

TYPES OF INVESTMENT COMPANIES BASED ON PORTFOLIO MAKEUP

COMMON STOCK FUNDS

Some funds invest almost solely in common stocks, as contrasted to those that invest in preferred stocks, bonds, etc. Within this category of common stock funds there are wide differences in emphasis, including the common stock of growth companies, companies in specific industries (e.g., Chemical Fund, Oceanography Fund), certain areas (e.g., Technology Fund), or even given geographic areas (e.g., Northeast Fund). Within the general category of common stock funds there is a wide variety to suit almost any taste or investment objective. Therefore, the first decision you must make is whether you want a fund that invests only in common stock; then you must consider the type of common stock desired.

BALANCED FUNDS   Balanced funds contain a combination of common stock and fixed-income securities that could include government bonds, corporate bonds, convertible bonds, or preferred stock. In order to balance the fund and not restrict the portfolio to only one kind of security, managers diversify outside the stock market. The ratio of stocks to fixed-income securities will vary by fund as stated in the fund's prospectus. Given the balanced nature of these funds, they would typically have a beta of less than 1.[5]

BOND FUNDS   Bond funds are concentrated in various types of bonds in order to generate high current income with a minimum of risk. Similar to common stock funds, the investment policy differs among funds. Some funds concentrate in U.S. government or high-grade corporate bonds, others hold a mixture of investment-grade bonds, and some concentrate in high-yield (junk) bonds. Also there can be a difference in management strategy. Some portfolio managers may engage in extensive trading of the bonds in the portfolio. In addition to government, mortgage, and corporate bond funds, a change in the tax law in 1976 made it possible to establish numerous *municipal bond funds*, which provide investors with monthly interest checks that are exempt from federal income taxes (although some of the interest

---

[5] Jill Bettner, "Stodgy Image of Old 'Balanced' Mutual Funds Could Change with Rally in Both Stocks, Bonds," *The Wall Street Journal*, June 29, 1981, 42.

TABLE 21.3
Statistics on Money Market Funds

YEAR-END	TOTAL NUMBER OF FUNDS	TOTAL ACCOUNTS OUTSTANDING	AVERAGE MATURITY (DAYS)	TOTAL NET ASSETS (MILLIONS OF DOLLARS)
1974	15	n.a.	n.a.	1,715.1
1975	36	208,777	93	3,695.7
1976	48	180,676	110	3,685.8
1977	50	177,522	76	3,887.7
1978	61	467,803	42	10,858.0
1979	76	2,307,852	34	45,214.2
1980	96	4,745,572	24	74,447.7
1981	159	10,282,095	34	181,910.4
1982	281	13,101,347	37	206,607.5
1983	307	12,276,639	37	162,549.5
1984	329	13,556,180	43	209,731.9
1985	348	14,425,386	37	207,535.3
1986	360	15,653,595	40	228,345.8
1987	389	16,832,666	31	254,676.4

Source: *1988 Mutual Fund Fact Book*, Investment Company Institute, Washington, D.C. Reprinted with permission.

may be subject to state and local taxes). To avoid the state tax, some funds concentrate in bonds from a specific state (e.g., New York Municipal Bond Fund, which allows New York residents to avoid most state taxes on the interest income).

MONEY MARKET FUNDS

A significant addition to the universe of investment companies is the money market fund initiated during 1973 when short-term interest rates were at record levels. These funds attempt to provide current income, safety of principal, and liquidity by investing in a diversified portfolio of short-term securities such as Treasury bills, bank certificates of deposit, bank acceptances, and commercial paper. All of these are no-load funds, and there is no penalty for withdrawal at any time. Most of them allow the holder to write checks against the account.[6] The significant growth of these funds is documented in Table 21.3. Because of the interest in money market funds, on Monday *The Wall Street Journal* contains a special section within the mutual fund section titled "Money Market Funds."

BREAKDOWN BY FUND CHARACTERISTICS

The figures in Table 21.4 break down the funds in terms of how they market their funds and by investment objectives. The two major means of distribution are (1) shares purchased from a member of a *sales force* and (2)

[6] For a list of names and addresses of money market funds, write to Investment Company Institute, 1775 K Street N.W., Washington, DC 20006. A service that concentrates on money market funds is *Donoghue's Money Letter*, 770 Washington Street, Holliston, MA 01746. An analysis of performance is contained in Michael G. Ferri and H. Dennis Oberhelman, "How Well Do Money Market Funds Perform?" *Journal of Portfolio Management* 7, no. 3 (Spring 1981): 18–26.

TABLE 21.4
Total Net Assets by Fund Characteristics (Millions of Dollars)

	1984		1985		1986		1987	
	DOLLARS	PERCENT	DOLLARS	PERCENT	DOLLARS	PERCENT	DOLLARS	PERCENT
Total net assets	137,126.2	100.0%	251,695.1	100.0%	424,156.4	100.0%	453,842.4	100.0%
Method of Sale								
Sales force	89,966.7	65.6%	174,735.8	69.4%	304,637.3	71.8%	331,752.8	73.1%
Direct marketing	42,249.5	30.8%	69,239.2	27.5%	107,911.3	25.4%	107,496.1	23.7%
Variable annuity	1,959.5	1.4%	2,409.5	1.0%	9,274.3	2.2%	12,730.1	2.8%
Not offering shares	2,950.5	2.2%	5,310.6	2.1%	2,333.5	0.6%	1,863.4	0.4%
Investment Objective								
Aggressive growth	14,150.3	10.3%	20,062.9	8.0%	25,006.9	5.9%	27,298.1	6.0%
Growth	26,734.8	19.5%	35,096.2	13.9%	43,579.5	10.3%	48,037.6	10.6%
Growth and income	31,588.3	23.0%	44,944.4	17.9%	55,944.1	13.2%	64,032.5	14.1%
Precious metals	375.6	0.3%	1,497.9	0.6%	2,027.0	0.5%	4,050.9	0.9%
International	5,223.0	3.8%	7,988.4	3.2%	7,186.1	1.7%	6,982.3	1.5%
Global equity					8,282.0	2.0%	10,449.2	2.3%
Flexible portfolio					1,461.8	0.3%	4.287.2	0.9%
Balanced	2,903.7	2.1%	4,095.3	1.6%	7,483.0	1.8%	9,024.7	2.0%
Income equity	7,056.9	5.1%	10,994.8	4.4%	12,560.1	3.0%	14,745.1	3.2%
Income-mixed					10,323.7	2.4%	11,418.4	2.5%
Income-bond					11,417.9	2.7%	12,580.0	2.8%
Option/income	3,394.6	2.5%	5,633.3	2.2%	6,952.9	1.6%	5,095.2	1.1%
U.S. government income	6,384.6	4.7%	40,017.9	15.9%	82,444.2	19.4%	88,906.2	19.6%
Ginnie Mae	3,963.9	2.9%	17,857.8	7.1%	39,619.9	9.3%	34,204.0	7.5%
Global bond					523.2	0.1%	2,137.1	0.5%
Corporate bond	14,560.9	10.6%	24,012.2	9.5%	9,080.5	2.1%	9,470.5	2.1%
High-yield bond					24,591.6	5.8%	24,147.2	5.3%
Long-term municipal bond	16,007.0	11.7%	27,924.7	11.1%	49,857.2	11.8%	49,174.6	10.8%
Long-term state municipal bond	4,728.6	3.4%	11,519.5	4.6%	25,814.8	6.1%	27,791.6	6.1%

Source: *1986 Mutual Fund Fact Book*, *1988 Mutual Fund Fact Book*, Investment Company Institute, Washington, D.C. Reprinted with permission.

shares purchased directly from a fund—that is, *direct marketing*. Shares purchased from a sales force would include brokers (e.g., Merrill Lynch), commission-based financial planners, or members of a dedicated sales force (e.g., IDS Financial). In almost all cases, the mutual funds acquired from these individuals have a sales fee (a load), which is how the salesperson is compensated. With direct marketing, investors purchase fund shares directly from the fund through the mail, telephone, bankwire, or an office of the fund. The shares of these funds typically have a low sales charge or none at all (which is why they have to be sold directly—a broker has no incentive to sell a no-load fund). As seen in Table 21.4, the division between these two major distribution channels is currently about 73-24 in favor of the sales force method.

The breakdown by investment objective indicates a shift in investor emphasis and a response to this shift by the investment company industry.

The growth for different investment objective categories reflects overall growth of the industry, but also the emergence of new categories due to the creation of new funds to meet the evolving demands of investors. Therefore, while aggressive growth, growth, and growth and income have experienced continued increases, the dramatic growth has come in categories like precious metals, global equity, flexible portfolio, high yield bonds, municipal bonds, and global bonds.[7] Also, while the sale of stock funds increased, and the sale of bond and income funds declined in 1987 relative to 1986, the recent overall trend continued—that is, the total annual sales of bond and income funds was substantially greater than equity fund sales, and the total outstanding value of these fixed-income funds exceeded the value of equity funds.

Performance of Investment Companies

A number of studies have examined the historical performance of mutual funds, because these funds are a prime example of the performance of professional money managers, and, also, data on the funds are available for a long period. Consequently, two of the three major portfolio evaluation techniques were derived in connection with a study of mutual fund performance.

Sharpe Study

A study of mutual funds done by Sharpe employed the following performance measure discussed in Chapter 20:[8]

$$S_i = \frac{R_i - RFR}{V_i},$$

where

R_i = average rate of return on fund i

RFR = risk-free rate

V_i = standard deviation of rates of return for fund i.

Sharpe used the measure to evaluate the performance of 34 open-end mutual funds. The rate of return included price change, dividend, and capital distribution, which is considered a *net return*, because it is calculated after the costs of administration and management but excludes the load fee. The performance measure for the sample of funds varied from 0.43 to 0.78, compared to the DJIA's performance of 0.667. For the total period, only 11 of the 34 funds had superior performance compared to the DJIA. A comparison of the ranks of the various funds during the first and second half of the sample period indicated some relationship (rank correlation of 0.36), but the predictions were imperfect. Sharpe concluded

---

[7] International funds consider investing only in non–U.S. stocks or bonds, while global funds can invest in securities from anywhere in the world, including the United States.

[8] William F. Sharpe, "Mutual Fund Performance," *Journal of Business* 39, no. 1, Part 2 (January 1966): 119–138.

that past performance in terms of the R/V ratio was not the best predictor of future performance.

A similar analysis using the Treynor measure, which considers only systematic risk, indicated that the Treynor measure was a better predictor. Notably, performance could be due to consistent differences in expense ratios (e.g., certain funds could always be low because they spend too much on research and administration). When he examined the relationship between performance and the expense ratio, Sharpe discovered that *good performance was associated with low expense ratios*, and there was a slight relationship between size and performance. Because investors need to know their risk class, Sharpe analyzed the consistency of the variability of returns over time and found reasonable consistency (a rank correlation between periods of 0.528). Finally, an analysis of *gross* performance with expenses added back to the returns indicated that 19 of the 34 funds did better than the DJIA. It was concluded that the average mutual fund manager selected a portfolio at least as good as the DJIA, but after deduction of operating costs of the fund, the *net* returns were, on average, below those experienced by the DJIA.

JENSEN STUDY

Jensen used the following performance measure discussed in Chapter 20 to evaluate 115 open-end mutual funds:[9]

$$R_{it} - RFR_t = \alpha_i + \beta_i \, (R_{mt} - RFR) \, ,$$

where

R_{it} = rate of return for fund i during the time period t

RFR_t = risk-free rate during the same time period t

α_i = the abnormal return for fund i, allowing for the systematic risk of the portfolio

β_i = the systematic risk for fund i (Cov_{im}/σ_m^2)

R_{mt} = rate of return for the market portfolio during time period t.

If the α_i for a fund is a statistically significant positive value, it indicates that the fund has experienced abnormally good risk-adjusted returns during the period involved. This superior performance can be due to the manager's ability to consistently select undervalued stocks or to predict market turns. The summary results indicated that the mean alpha value (α_i) was −0.011, with a minimum of −0.078 and a maximum of 0.058. This indicated that, on average, the funds earned 1.1 percent less per year than they should have earned for their level of systematic risk.

The frequency distribution of the alphas in Figure 21.4 are for returns net of expenses (i.e., after deducting expenses). An analysis of gross re-

[9] Michael C. Jensen, "The Performance of Mutual Funds in the Period 1945–1964," *Journal of Finance* 23, no. 2 (May 1968): 389–416.

FIGURE 21.4

Frequency Distribution of Estimated Intercepts (α) for 115 Mutual Funds for All Years Available for Each Fund (Fund Returns Calculated *Net* of All Expenses)

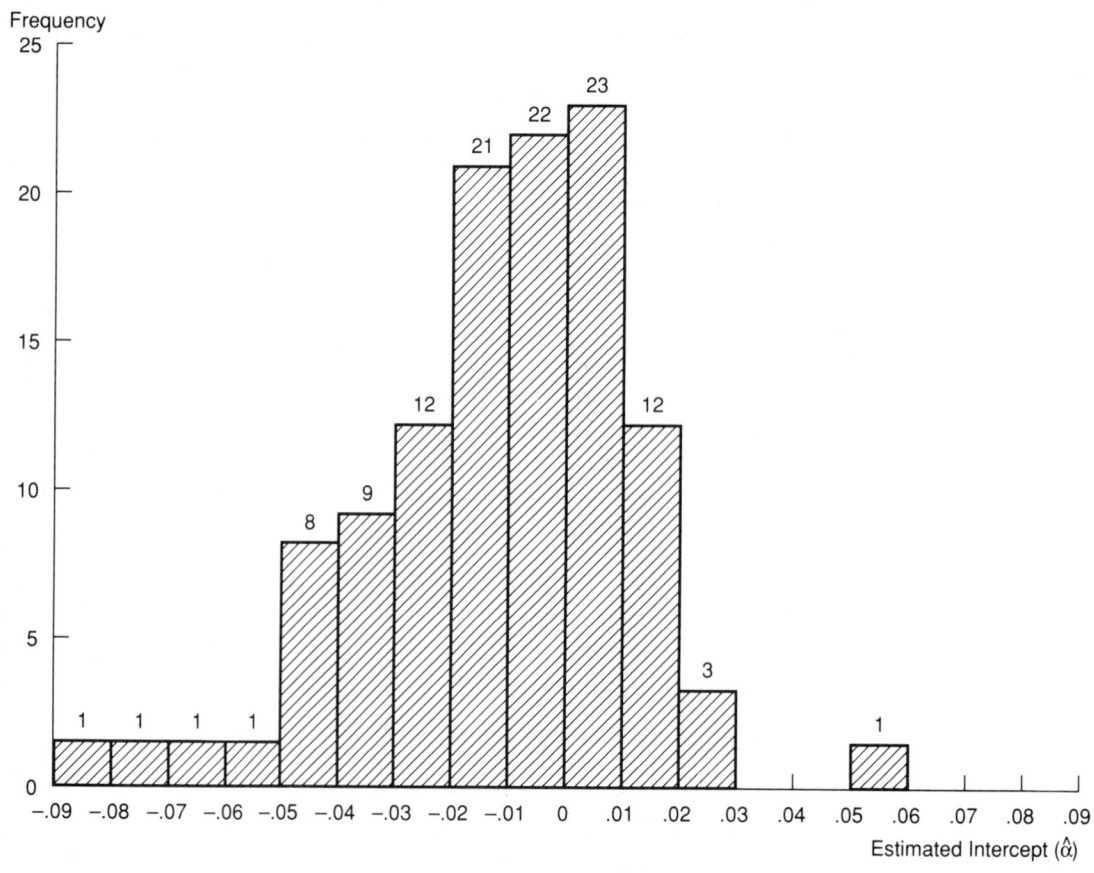

Source: Michael C. Jensen, "The Performance of Mutual Funds in the Period 1945–1964," *Journal of Finance* 23, no. 2 (May 1968): 404. Reprinted by permission.

turns with expenses added back indicated an average alpha (α) of -0.004. Therefore, with net returns, 39 funds (34 percent) had a positive alpha, and 76 had a negative alpha, while with gross returns, 48 funds (42 percent) had positive alphas, and 67 had negative alphas. The results with gross returns indicate the forecasting ability of the funds, since these results do not penalize the funds for operating expenses (only brokerage commissions). The preponderance of negative alphas indicates the inability of the funds to forecast well enough to cover commissions.

Because data were not available for all the funds for the full 20 years, Jensen examined the total sample for 10 years and found that the gross returns indicated an average alpha of −0.001 and an even split for funds. Given the various alpha values, how many are statistically significant? An analysis of the significance of the alpha values indicated 14 funds had significant negative alphas and only 3 had significant positive alphas. None of the 56 funds with 20 years of data had substantial forecasting ability. It was concluded that, on average, these funds were not able to predict security prices well enough to beat a buy-and-hold policy, and there was very little evidence that any individual fund could do significantly better than what would be expected from random chance.

MAINS COMMENT ON JENSEN STUDY. Mains questioned several of the estimates made by Jensen that apparently biased the results against mutual funds.[10] Specifically, Jensen assumed that all dividend payments and capital distributions were made at the end of the year; and when he computed the gross returns by adding back expenses, he likewise assumed this was done at the year-end, which understates the gross returns for the funds. Also, Jensen computed the systematic risk for the funds using a 20-year period and applied this estimated beta to the last ten years, although it was shown that risk was lower during the later period. Given the importance of the systematic risk in the performance measure, this also would cause an understatement of fund performance.

To test the effect of these objections, Mains examined 70 funds from the Jensen sample using monthly returns for the ten-year period and adjusted for the biases. The Mains subsample had a slightly higher return and lower risk, which produced an annual performance measure with net returns of 0.09 (not significantly different from zero), compared to an average performance measure of −0.62 for Jensen's data. In addition, 40 of the funds had positive alphas and 30 were negative, indicating just about an even split using net returns. Mains added back expenses and commissions to get gross returns and noted that expenses and commissions averaged about 1 percent a year, but the effect varied widely. The results with gross returns indicated an average alpha of 1.07, which indicates annual abnormal returns of 1.07 percent above expectations. Fifty-five of the funds had positive alphas, and 15 had negative values, compared to an average alpha of 0.009 for the full Jensen sample, with 60 of the 115 having positive results. The author concluded that after correcting the results for several biases, the performance using net returns was neutral, while the results with gross returns indicated that most fund managers demonstrated above-average performance.

CARLSON STUDY   Carlson examined the overall performance of mutual funds with an emphasis on analyzing the effect of the market series used and the time period. Carlson categorized mutual funds as one of three types: (1) diversified common stock, (2) balanced funds, and (3) income funds, com-

---

[10] Norman E. Mains, "Risk, the Pricing of Capital Assets, and the Evaluation of Investment Portfolios: Comment," *Journal of Business* 50, no. 3 (July 1977): 371–384.

TABLE 21.5

Index Comparisons—Mutual Funds versus the Market, 1948–1967

INDEX	NO. OF FUNDS 1948	NO. OF FUNDS 1967	RISKLESS RETURN R^*	MEAN RETURN $\bar{R}$	VARIABILITY STANDARD DEVIATION V	PERFORMANCE θ
Balanced fund–gross	23	25	2.92	9.92	9.22	0.7595
Balanced fund–net	23	25	2.92	9.15	9.22	0.6762
Common stock fund–gross	33	136	2.92	13.66	14.61	0.7352
Common stock fund–net	33	136	2.92	12.89	14.63	0.6811
S&P stock price index			2.92	13.34	14.71	0.7086
NYSE composite index			2.92	13.02	14.49	0.6971
Dow-Jones Industrial Average			2.92	12.39	14.51	0.6526
Income fund–gross	6	17	2.92	11.01	12.79	0.6328
Income fund–net	6	17	2.92	10.24	12.79	0.5725

Note: Returns for each market index include estimated dividends. The riskless rate, R^*, is the average annual rate of return for United States Government 9- to 12-month certificates.

Source: Robert S. Carlson, "Aggregate Performance of Mutual Funds, 1948–1967," *Journal of Financial and Quantitative Analysis* 5, no. 1 (March 1970): 8. © March 1970. Reprinted by permission.

paring each of them to the market using a return-to-total-variability measure.[11] The results in Table 21.5 are heavily dependent upon which market series is used: the S&P 500, the NYSE composite, or the DJIA. For the total period, most fund groups outperformed the DJIA, but only a few had gross returns better than the S&P 500 or the NYSE composite. Using net returns, *none* of the groups outperformed the S&P 500 or the NYSE composite. Also, the balanced and income funds were consistently inferior to the full common stock funds, which indicates that the fund's objective did make a difference. An analysis of various ten-year subperiods showed that the relative results were clearly dependent on the time interval examined. In addition, he showed that, during this 20-year period, the average alpha relative to the S&P 500 was positive, and about 59 percent of the funds had a positive alpha (the author did not indicate how many were "significant").

Finally, an analysis that considered the factors related to performance revealed consistency over time for return or risk alone but *no* consistency in the risk-adjusted performance measure. Less than one-third of the funds that experienced above-average performance during the first half did so in the second half. An analysis of five-year periods indicated more consistency for the shorter intervals than for ten-year intervals, and consistency *declined* over time. An analysis of performance relative to size, expense ratios, age, and a new-funds factor indicated no relationship with size, the expense ratio, or age, but a significant relationship between performance and a measure of new cash into the fund. When the performance

[11] Robert S. Carlson, "Aggregate Performance of Mutual Funds, 1948–1967," *Journal of Financial and Quantitative Analysis* 5, no. 1 (March 1970): 1–32.

TABLE 21.6
Objectives and Performance

	RISK		PERFORMANCE MEASURES			
OBJECTIVE OF FUND	SYSTEMATIC RISK (BETA)	TOTAL VARIABILITY (STD. DEV.)	MEAN MONTHLY EXCESS RETURN (%)	SHARPE[a] MEASURE	TREYNOR[b] MEASURE	JENSEN[c] MEASURE
Maximum capital gain	1.22	5.90	.693	.117	.568	.122
Growth	1.01	4.57	.565	.124	.560	.099
Growth-income	.90	3.93	.476	.121	.529	.058
Income-growth	.86	3.80	.398	.105	.463	.004
Balanced	.68	3.05	.214	.070	.314	−.099
Income	.55	2.67	.252	.094	.458	−.002
Sample means	.92	4.17	.477	.112	.518	.051
Market-based portfolios	—	—	—	.133	.510	0
Stock market index	1.00	3.83	.510	.133	.510	0
Bond market index[d]	.18	1.42	.093	.065	.516	NA

[a] Reward-to-variability ratio: mean excess return divided by the standard deviation of fund return.

[b] Reward-to-volatility ratio: mean excess return divided by beta.

[c] Alpha: estimated constant from least-squares regression of fund excess returns on market excess returns (Jensen's delta).

[d] Proxy measure based on arithmetic means of results for Keystone B-1 and B-4 funds, with returns adjusted for 0.042 percent per month average management fee.

Source: John G. McDonald, "Objectives and Performance of Mutual Funds, 1960–1969," *Journal of Financial and Quantitative Analysis* 9, no. 3 (June 1974): 319. © June 1974. Reprinted by permission.

of eight no-load funds was compared to the other 74 funds, the no-loads were found to have a significantly higher performance measure, but the conclusion was tentative because of the small sample. More recently, Lehmann and Modest came to similar conclusions when they considered different risk-adjustment procedures, including alternative APT and CAPM benchmarks.[12] They not only found substantial differences between benchmarks, but also consistently large negative Jensen measures.

IMPACT OF FUND OBJECTIVES

McDonald examined the overall performance of 123 mutual funds and also examined performance relative to one of the following stated objectives of the fund: (1) maximum capital gain, (2) growth, (3) income growth, (4) balanced, and (5) income.[13] The results in Table 21.6 reveal a positive relationship between stated objectives and measures of beta and total variability—the risk measures increase as objectives become more aggressive. Also, the average excess return without risk generally increases with the aggressiveness of the objective. As you would expect, given the earlier results with risk and return taken alone, there is a positive relationship between return and either systematic or total risk. The relationship is especially strong when several funds are combined in a risk class.

[12] Bruce N. Lehmann and David M. Modest, "Mutual Fund Performance Evaluation: A Comparison of Benchmarks and Benchmark Comparisons," *Journal of Finance* 42, no. 2 (June 1987): 233–265.

[13] John G. McDonald, "Objectives and Performance of Mutual Funds, 1960–1969," *Journal of Financial and Quantitative Analysis* 9, no. 3 (June 1974): 311–333.

An analysis of risk-adjusted performance indicated that the portfolios with the more aggressive objectives outperformed the more conservative funds during this period.

Regarding overall fund performance relative to the aggregate market, four measures were considered: excess return alone plus the three composite performance measures. One-third of the funds had an excess return above the market's, and the mean excess return for all the funds was below the market's, which was not surprising because the average beta was only 0.92. The analysis using the Treynor measure indicated an average value for all the funds of 0.518 versus 0.510 for the market, and approximately half the funds beat the market. The results with the Jensen measure indicated that 54 percent had positive alphas during this period, and the average alpha was 0.052 percent per month, about one-half of 1 percent a year above expectations. Only six funds had a statistically significant alpha, which is what one would expect on the basis of chance. Finally, the results with Sharpe's measure indicated that two-thirds of the funds had a performance measure below the market value (0.133), and the mean value for all the funds was below the market (0.112 versus 0.133). The poorer performance with the Sharpe measure was because the funds did not diversify completely.

The final analysis considered the relationship between a derived aggregate market line based upon the risk-free return and the market returns and a fund line derived for the period based upon the relationship between risk and return for the sample of funds (i.e., in equilibrium, the two lines should coincide). The fund line was steeper than the market line, meaning that the low-risk portfolios did not do as well as expected relative to the market line, and the high-risk funds did better than expected on a risk-adjusted basis. While the difference in the slope was not significant, it was contrary to that found by Friend and Blume[14] and consistent with the Klemkosky results.[15] These results support the notion discussed in Chapter 20 that although there may be a bias in the composite performance measures, the direction of the bias is unknown.

Martin, Keown, and Farrell examined the impact of fund objectives on the diversification policies of mutual funds to see if there was additional extra-market covariation for specialized funds.[16] They examined 72 mutual funds representing five investment objectives (aggressive growth, growth, growth and income, income, and other) and found a definite difference in the extra-market variation for the funds in alternative classifications. However, the fund objective explained only a small part of this variation (15 percent), so other factors were obviously involved.

---

[14] Irwin Friend and Marshall Blume, "Measurement of Portfolio Performance under Uncertainty," *American Economic Review* 60, no. 4 (September 1970): 561–575.

[15] Robert C. Klemkosky, "The Bias in Composite Performance Measures," *Journal of Financial and Quantitative Analysis* 8, no. 3 (June 1973): 505–514.

[16] John D. Martin, Arthur J. Keown, Jr., and James L. Farrell, "Do Fund Objectives Affect Diversification Policies?" *Journal of Portfolio Management* 8, no. 2 (Winter 1982): 19–28.

**MARKET-TIMING
ABILITY**

Several studies have examined the ability of mutual funds to time market cycles and react accordingly. An ideal fund portfolio manager would thus increase the beta of the portfolio in anticipation of a bull market and reduce the beta prior to a bear market. An early study by Treynor and Mazuy indicated that the funds were not able to time market changes and change their risk levels accordingly.[17] Fabozzi and Francis likewise could not find evidence of a shift in the beta for funds in line with such expectations.[18]

Veit and Cheney examined the portfolio betas during bull and bear markets and also the alphas for these funds on the assumption that the alpha would be lower during rising markets and vice versa.[19] They computed the alphas and betas during bull markets, bear markets, and the total period and determined if the differences were as hypothesized for good market timers. They analyzed annual data for 74 mutual funds and used four different schemes to define bull and bear markets. After evaluating different results depending on different definitions of bull and bear markets, they concluded that mutual funds do *not* successfully alter their characteristic lines consistent with timing strategies. In fact, no change occurred in the characteristic lines, which would support the EMH.

Kon and Jen examined the performance of 49 mutual funds using several equilibrium pricing models as benchmarks.[20] They specifically examined the ability to change portfolio composition to take advantage of market cycles and the ability to select undervalued securities. Many of the funds experienced significant change in risk during the test period, which implies superior timing ability, in sharp contrast to Jensen's earlier results. While this would be evidence against the EMH, it is noteworthy that no individual fund was able to *consistently* generate superior results. The results regarding selectivity also indicated that although many individual funds generated superior performance, the average performance was negative relative to a naive policy. Finally, there was evidence that fund managers attempted to time the market based upon risk and diversification changes. Overall, the results were mixed regarding the EMH. While *on average* the funds appeared to select superior portfolios, this can be partially explained by the bias in the model toward low-risk securities. Finally, one must ask whether this superior selection would be enough to cover research expenses, management fees, and commission expenses.

Shawky analyzed 255 funds using monthly data and found that the risk was consistent with fund objectives.[21] The overall performance results were similar to Jensen's, since only about 10 percent of the alphas were sig-

---

[17] Jack L. Treynor and Kay K. Mazuy, "Can Mutual Funds Outguess the Market?" *Harvard Business Review* 44, no. 4 (July–August 1966): 131–136.

[18] Frank J. Fabozzi and Jack C. Francis, "Mutual Fund Systematic Risk for Bull and Bear Markets," *Journal of Finance* 34, no. 5 (December 1979): 1243–1250.

[19] E. Theodore Veit and John M. Cheney, "Are Mutual Funds Market Timers?" *Journal of Portfolio Management* 8, no. 2 (Winter 1982): 35–42.

[20] Stanley J. Kon and Frank C. Jen, "The Investment Performance of Mutual Funds: An Empirical Investigation of Timing, Selectivity, and Market Efficiency," *Journal of Business* 52, no. 2 (April 1979): 263–289.

[21] Hany A. Shawky, "An Update on Mutual Funds: Better Grades," *Journal of Portfolio Management* 8, no. 2 (Winter 1982): 29–34.

nificant, and 60 percent of these were negative. The author contended (without much justification) that this is an improvement from earlier periods. There was strong correlation among the alternative performance measures, and the funds appeared to have reduced the unsystematic risk in their portfolios based upon an increase in the average R^2 with the market, from about 0.59 in the 1960s to about 0.75 in the 1970s.

Two recent studies examined the macro market forecasting and the micro stock selection ability of fund managers using a technique suggested by Henriksson and Merton,[22] which was based on some earlier work by Merton.[23] The first of two tests was a nonparametric test that required no assumption about the distribution of security prices and could be used if the market timer's forecasts were observable. For cases when only the time series of realized returns was known, they derived a parametric test of market timing that assumes a specific return-generating process. Chang and Lewellen used the following parametric model from Henriksson and Merton to examine the performance of mutual funds:[24]

$$Z_{pt} - R_t = \alpha_{pt} + \beta_1 X_1(t) + \beta_2 X_2(t) + \epsilon_{p(t)},$$

where

Z_{pt} = the observed rate of return on the portfolio during period t

R_t = the contemporaneous return on a riskless asset

α_p = the average residual or abnormal component on that portfolio's return due to the manager's security selection ability

β_1 = the average down-market beta for the portfolios

X_1 = the excess market return (Z_m) during down markets $[Z_{m(t)} < R(t)]$

β_2 = the average up-market beta for the portfolios

X_2 = the excess market return (Z_m) during up markets $[Z_{m(t)} > R(t)]$

$\epsilon_{p(t)}$ = a random error term.

The test for market timing analyzes the difference between β_1 and β_2 (i.e., it tests whether there is an attempt to change the portfolio beta over time) and whether the changes are in the rational direction (i.e., whether $\beta_1 < \beta_2$). The test for micro forecasting (stock selection) is whether the α_p is positive and statistically significant after taking account of the timing decisions. The results provided little evidence of any market timing ability by fund managers. In fact, the average estimated down-market beta (0.993) was slightly *higher* than the up-market beta (0.955). There were only four

[22] Roy D. Henriksson and Robert C. Merton, "On Market Timing and Investment Performance, II. Statistical Procedures for Evaluating Forecasting Skills," *Journal of Business* 54, no. 4 (October 1981): 513–533.

[23] Robert C. Merton, "On Market Timing and Investment Performance, I. An Equilibrium Theory of Value for Market Forecasts," *Journal of Business* 54, no. 3 (July 1981): 313–406.

[24] Eric C. Chang and Wilbur G. Lewellen, "Market Timing and Mutual Fund Investment Performance," *Journal of Business* 57, no. 1, part 1 (January 1984): 57–72.

instances where there was a statistically significant difference in the down-market, up-market betas, and in three of these cases the down-market beta was higher. It was concluded that there was not much macro price forecasting going on or, if there was, it was overwhelmed by other portfolio decisions.

The security selection results indicated that 41 of the 67 funds had positive alphas, but only 5 of the 67 were significant, and 3 of these were negative. The overall results using quarterly data were similar, leading to the overall conclusion that neither skillful market timing nor clever security selection abilities were evident. The authors felt that the conclusion of prior studies that mutual funds cannot outperform a passive investment strategy is still valid.

Henriksson employed a parametric model adjusted for potential heteroscedasticity and also a nonparametric model to examine the performance of 116 open-end mutual funds using monthly data.[25] In addition to the entire period, he considered two subperiods to determine the ability of any funds to enjoy consistent success. The parametric test results showed little evidence of market-timing ability (i.e., 62 percent of the funds had negative results for β_2, and there were only three significant positive values). The results for the α value for the overall period and the subperiod were similarly discouraging—it was not possible to reject the hypothesis that the αs and the β_2s for each fund were independent for the two periods. When market timing was ignored, only one of the 116 funds had a significant α for both subperiods. A test to determine if managers could forecast large changes did not provide positive results, and there was a negative correlation between estimates of α and β_2, which implied that funds that are good at stock selection have negative market-timing ability. The author employed a nonparametric test that required knowledge of forecasts, which were proxied by using actual returns as a measure of total performance (not only market timing). When he compared these results with the performance of a feasible passive strategy, the funds did slightly worse than the passive strategy, implying no forecasting ability. As before, there was little relationship between fund performance during the first and second subperiods and no evidence that the fund managers could forecast large changes better than small changes. The author concluded:

> The empirical results ... do not support the hypothesis that mutual fund managers are able to follow an investment strategy that successfully times the return on the market portfolio. Strong evidence of nonstationarity in the performance parameters was found in both the parametric and nonparametric tests. In addition, no evidence was found that forecasters are more successful in their market-timing activity with respect to predicting large changes ... relative to small changes.[26]

---

[25] Roy D. Henriksson, "Market Timing and Mutual Fund Performance: An Empirical Investigation," *Journal of Business* 57, no. 1, part 1 (January 1984): 73–96.

[26] Ibid., 92–93.

CONSISTENCY OF PERFORMANCE

In several of these studies just discussed, the question of consistency was considered along with overall performance. In addition, because of the importance of this question to individual investors, some studies have concentrated on it. Klemkosky examined the question of performance consistency by mutual fund managers by analyzing the risk-adjusted performance of 158 mutual funds using monthly data for an eight-year period.[27] He compared the ranking of the Sharpe and Treynor measures for adjacent two-year periods and for the two four-year periods. The results indicated some consistency in the four-year periods, but relatively low consistency among the adjacent two-year periods (only one of the three correlations was significant). An analysis of the proportion of funds that had positive or negative alphas in adjacent periods indicated no significant association between successive two-year periods, but there was consistency for the two four-year periods, mainly due to the great consistency in the negative results. It was concluded that investors should exercise caution in using past performance to predict future performance, especially for short periods of time.

Dunn and Thielsen examined the annual returns for 201 institutional portfolios over a ten-year period to determine what proportion of managers were consistently successful.[28] The first test examined whether managers tend to remain in the same quartile over time by ranking three-year and five-year compound returns against subsequent one-, three-, and five-year returns. The results varied, but on balance historical results appeared of little help in explaining future results. The results of a second test that tracked the performance of the median manager in each decile over the next five-year period indicated a tendency for both top- and bottom-ranked managers to move to any other relative position with no discernable pattern. The authors felt that the only explanation for some very slight consistency was that "markets make managers"—that is, if the performance of the market was consistent over time, there was more consistency in manager performance. Based upon these results, which were consistent with Klemkosky, the authors concluded that historical performance should be accorded a minor role in manager selection decisions.

Ang and Chua examined the consistency of performance of funds with different objectives.[29] It has been shown that different funds at one time or another provide an investment medium that is as good or better than the market portfolio. They analyzed the consistency of these portfolios and found that less than half provided consistent results. Therefore, they concluded that while various funds fulfill the function of meeting alternative objectives, they do not do it consistently.

---

[27] Robert C. Klemkosky, "How Consistently Do Managers Manage?" *Journal of Portfolio Management* 3, no. 2 (Winter 1977): 11–15.

[28] Patricia C. Dunn and Rolf D. Theisen, "How Consistently Do Active Managers Win?" *Journal of Portfolio Management* 9, no. 4 (Summer 1983): 47–50.

[29] James S. Ang and Jess H. Chua, "Mutual Funds: Different Strokes for Different Folks?" *Journal of Portfolio Management* 8, no. 2 (Winter 1982): 43–47.

IMPLICATIONS OF PERFORMANCE STUDIES

Assume that you have your own personal portfolio manager, and consider the functions you would want him to perform for you. Some of these we talked about in the portfolio performance chapter. The list would probably include:

1. Determine your risk-return preferences and develop a portfolio that is consistent with your desires.
2. Diversify your portfolio in order to eliminate unsystematic risk.
3. Maintain your portfolio diversification and ensure that you remain in your desired risk class. Also, allow flexibility so you can shift between investment instruments if you desire.
4. Attempt to derive a risk-adjusted performance record that is superior to aggregate market performance. As noted, this can be done by either consistently selecting undervalued stocks or by proper timing of market swings. Assuming that some investors have other diversified investments, they may be willing to sacrifice diversification for superior returns in this segment of their portfolio.
5. Administer the account, keep records of costs, provide timely information for tax purposes, and reinvest dividends if desired.

While most of the performance studies were concerned with Number 4 on our list—risk-adjusted performance—all of the functions should be considered in order to put performance into perspective.

The first function of determining your risk preference is not performed by mutual funds. However, once you have determined what you want, the industry provides a large and growing variety of funds that can meet almost any goal in the area of marketable securities. The empirical studies indicated that *the funds were generally consistent in meeting their stated goals;* the risk and returns were consistent with the stated objectives. Diversifying your portfolio to eliminate unsystematic risk is one of the major benefits of mutual funds—they provide *instant diversification.* This diversification is especially beneficial to small investors who do not have the resources to acquire 100 shares of 10 or 12 different issues and thereby reduce unsystematic risk. It is typically possible to start with about $1,000 and acquire a portfolio of securities that is correlated about 0.90 with the market portfolio (about 90 percent diversified). Although there is a range of diversification, typically about three-quarters of the funds have a correlation above 0.90, so *most funds provide excellent diversification,* especially if they state this as an objective.

The third function is to maintain diversification and keep you in your desired risk class. Mutual funds have been quite good in terms of the stability of their correlation with the market. This is not too surprising, since once you have a reasonably well-diversified portfolio, it is difficult to change its makeup substantially. Notably, there is strong evidence regarding the consistency of the risk class because even the studies that indicated inconsistency in risk-adjusted performance indicated *consistency in risk alone.* The desire for flexibility to change investment instruments has been met by the initiation of numerous funds by alternative management companies. Typically, these investment groups will allow you to shift among their funds without a charge simply by calling the fund. Therefore, you can shift from an aggressive stock fund to a money market fund and back to a bond fund for much less than it would cost you in time and money if you were buying and selling numerous individual issues.

The fourth function is to provide risk-adjusted performance that is superior to the aggregate market (i.e., beat a naive buy-and-hold policy). You will probably not be surprised when I conclude that the news on this function is not very good. The overall evidence indicated that, on average, the results achieved by fund portfolio managers through their ability to select securities or time the market are about as good as or only slightly better than would be achieved with a naive buy-and-hold policy. This conclusion is based upon evidence using *gross* returns. Unfortunately, the evidence regarding *net* returns, which is what the investor receives, indicates that the majority of funds do *not* do as well as a naive buy-and-hold policy. The shortfall in performance is about 1 percent a year, which is roughly the average cost of expenses and commissions. In response to these findings, several money managers have started index funds under the philosophy of "if you can't beat them, join them." These funds do not attempt to beat the market but merely match the performance of some specified market indicator series (e.g., the S&P 500 Index). Since they have no research costs and their trading expenses are minimal, they have achieved high correlation of returns with the chosen index (i.e., in excess of .99) with very low expenses. Also, the management fees charged are substantially below what is required for active management.

If you want to find one of the superior funds, the news is likewise not very encouraging, because most studies show a lack of consistency in performance over time *except among inferior funds*. Apparently, if the poor performance is due to excessive expenses, this state of affairs will continue, so such funds should be avoided. In general, you should not expect to consistently enjoy superior risk-adjusted performance from investment in a mutual fund.

The final objective is administration of the account. This is another significant benefit of most mutual funds, since they allow automatic reinvestment of dividends with no charge and consistently provide a record of total cost. Further, each year they supply a statement indicating the dividend income and capital gain distribution for tax purposes.

In summary, most investors have a set of functions they want their portfolio manager to perform. Typically, mutual funds can help the investor accomplish four of the five at a cost lower in terms of time and money than it would be if they did it on their own. Unfortunately the price of this convenience and service is about 1 percent a year in terms of performance.

SOURCES OF INFORMATION

Given the wide variety of types and number of funds available, it is important to be able to determine the performance of various funds over time and derive some understanding of their goals and management philosophy. Daily quotations on numerous open-end funds are contained in *The Wall Street Journal.* A more comprehensive weekly list of quotations and the dividend income and capital gain for the past 12 months are carried in *Barron's,* which also includes a quarterly update on performance over the past ten years for a number of funds. As shown earlier in Figures 21.1 and 21.2, *Barron's* contains a list of closed-end funds with current net asset values, current market quotes on the funds, and indicated percentage of difference between the two figures. As mentioned, the market price is typically about 10 to 15 percent below the NAV.

The major source of comprehensive historical information is an annual publication issued by Arthur Wiesenberger Services entitled *Investment Companies.* This book is published each year and currently contains vital statistics for over 600 mutual funds arranged alphabetically. The description of each fund includes a brief history, investment objectives and portfolio analysis, statistical history, special services available, personnel, advisors and distributors, sales charges, and a hypothetical $10,000 investment charted over 10 years for major funds. A sample page for the Technology Fund is contained in Figure 21.5. In addition, the Wiesenberger book contains a summary table that lists the annual rates of return and price volatility for a number of funds. Wiesenberger has two additional services. Every three months the firm publishes *Management Results,* an update of the long-term performance of more than 400 mutual funds, arranged alphabetically according to the investment objective of the fund. Every month the firm also publishes *Current Performance and Dividend Record,* which contains the dividend and short-run performance of more than 400 funds. The funds are listed alphabetically with the objective indicated.[30]

Another source of analytical historical information on funds is *Forbes,* a biweekly financial publication that usually contains information about individual companies and their investment philosophy. In addition, the magazine conducts an annual survey of mutual funds in August. A sample page is contained in Figure 21.6. As shown, the survey not only considers recent and ten-year returns, but it also indicates sales charge and the annual expense ratio for U.S. and foreign fund.

Business Week likewise publishes a "Mutual Fund Scoreboard." Figure 21.7 contains a sample of this scoreboard for open-end fixed-income funds. There is a comparable one for closed-end fixed-income funds and equity funds. Besides this performance information and information on sales charges (including 12b-1 plans) and expenses, there is an accompanying table with the telephone numbers of all the funds.

Because of the interest in mutual funds, United Business Service Company publishes a semimonthly service called *United Mutual Fund Selector.* Each issue contains several articles on specific mutual funds or classes of mutual funds (e.g., municipal bond funds). The first issue of each month

[30] These services are currently published by Wiesenberger Investment Companies Services, Warren, Gorham and Lamont, 210 South St., Boston, MA 02111.

FIGURE 21.5
Sample Page from *Investment Companies*

TECHNOLOGY FUND

Organized in 1948 as Television Fund, Technology Fund became Television-Electronics Fund in 1951 and adopted its present name in January 1968. Effective January 31, 1986, the Fund was reorganized from a Maryland Corporation to a Massachusetts business trust. On December 10, 1976, the name of the fund's adviser (then Supervised Investors Services, Inc.) was changed to Kemper Financial Services, Inc., a wholly owned subsidiary of Kemper Corp., an insurance and financial services holding company.

Under the policy revised in early 1968, the fund invests primarily in securities of companies expected to benefit from technological advances and improvements in such fields as aerospace, astrophysics, chemistry, electricity, electronics, geology, mechanical engineering, metallurgy, nuclear physics and oceanography. Management may, however, seek investment opportunities in virtually any industry in which they may be found. An advisory board provides information of a technical nature relating to new inventions and developments.

At the close of calendar 1986, the fund had 98% of its assets in common stocks, of which the major portion was in five industry groups: health care (18.8% of assets), financial services (15.5%), data-processing (10.4%), energy services (8.1%), and basic industry

(7.4%). The five largest individual stock holdings were Upjohn Co. (4.7% of assets), American International Group (4.5%), Digital Equipment (4.2%), Squibb (3.1%), and IBM (2.9%). The rate of portfolio turnover for the latest fiscal year was 37% of average Portfolio holdings. Unrealized appreciation on the portfolio was 37% of total net assets at the calendar year-end.

Special Services: An open account system serves for accumulation and automatic dividend reinvestment. Minimum initial investment is $1,000; subsequent investments must be at least $100. Income dividends are invested at net asset value. Plan payments may be made by way of pre-authorized checks against the investor's checking account. Arrangements may be made for payroll deduction. A monthly, quarterly, or annual withdrawal plan is available without charge to accounts worth $5,000 at the offering price; payments may be of any designated amount. Shares may be exchanged for those of other funds in the Kemper Financial group without service fee. Tax-deferred retirement plans are available for corporations and the self-employed, as well as Individual Retirement Account plans. A one-time account reinstatement privilege is available to redeeming shareholders within a specified time.

Statistical History

Year	Total Net Assets ($)	Number of Share-holders	Net Asset Value Per Share ($)	Offer-ing Price ($)	Yield (%)	Cash & Equiv-alent	Bonds & Pre-ferreds	Com-mon Stocks	Income Div-idends ($)	Capital Gains Distribu-tion ($)	Expense Ratio (%)	Offering Price ($) High	Low
1986	545,470,850	45,222	11.12	12.15	1.1	1	1	98	0.17	2.72	0.60	15.56	11.80
1985	683,732,062	47,410	12.22	13.36	1.3	3	1	96	0.18	0.68	0.60	13.43	11.14
1984	569,864,284	49,335	10.44	11.41	2.6	15	1*	84	0.33	1.22	0.59	14.05	10.98
1983	642,246,752	51,013	12.60	13.77	1.6	13		87	0.26	2.13†	0.48	17.41	13.38
1982	599,981,755	51,008	12.59	13.76	2.6	8	1*	91	0.37	0.43	0.53	14.49	9.81
1981	478,771,015	52,758	11.11	12.14	2.6	12	3	85	0.33	0.76	0.52	15.53	11.64
1980	588,946,604	54,967	14.18	15.50	1.9	5	1	94	0.31	0.62	0.57	16.07	10.38
1979	427,059,368	58,190	10.17	11.11	2.3	4	1	95	0.26	0.43	0.60	11.45	8.86
1978	375,341,502	63,590	8.26	9.03	2.7	14	2	84	0.25	0.20†	0.62	9.67	6.56
1977	358,694,594	70,491	7.14	7.80	2.5	8	2*	90	0.20	0.10	0.60	8.31	7.17
1976	432,029,805	77,716	7.58	8.28	2.3	3	6*	91	0.19	—	0.59	8.42	6.82

* Includes a substantial proportion in convertible issues.
† Includes $0.01 short-term capital gains in 1978; $0.22 in 1983.

Trustees: Charles M. Kierscht, Pres.; Thomas R. Anderson, Vice President; David W. Belin; Lewis A. Burnham; Harry C. DeMuth; Donald L. Dunaway; James W. Harding; Robert B. Hoffman; Thomas L. Martin, Jr.; William P. Sommers.

Investment Adviser: Kemper Financial Services, Inc. Compensation to the Adviser is 0.60% annually of average daily net assets on first $200 million; 0.50% on the next $300 million; and 0.40% on net assets over $500 million.

Custodian and Transfer Agent: United Missouri Bank of Kansas City N.A., Kansas City, MO 64141.

Shareholder Service Agent: DST Systems, Inc., Kansas City, MO 64141.

Distributor: Kemper Financial Services, Inc., 120 South La Salle Street, Chicago, IL 60603.

Sales Charge: Maximum is 8½% of offering price; minimum is 0.40% at $3 million. Reduced charges begin at $10,000 and are applicable to combined purchases of the fund and other of the Kemper Mutual Funds.

Distribution Plan: (12b-1) None.

Dividends: Income dividends are paid in cash or shares quarterly in the months of February, May, August and November. Capital gains, if any, are paid optionally in shares or cash in November.

Shareholder Reports: Issued quarterly. Fiscal year ends October 31. The current prospectus was effective in February.

Qualified for Sale: In all states and DC.

Address: 120 South LaSalle St., Chicago, IL 60603.

Telephone: (312) 781-1121.

An assumed investment of $10,000 in this fund, with capital gains accepted in shares and income dividends reinvested, is illustrated below. The explanation in the introduction to this section must be read in conjunction with this illustration.

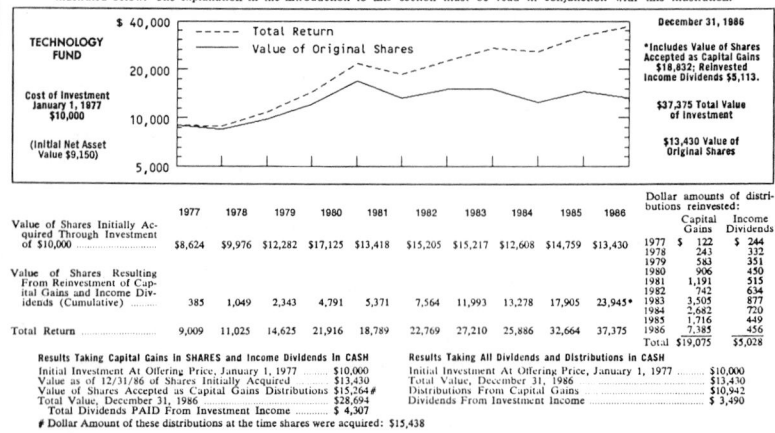

	1977	1978	1979	1980	1981	1982	1983	1984	1985	1986
Value of Shares Initially Acquired Through Investment of $10,000	$8,624	$9,976	$12,282	$17,125	$13,418	$15,205	$15,217	$12,608	$14,759	$13,430
Value of Shares Resulting From Reinvestment of Capital Gains and Income Dividends (Cumulative)	385	1,049	2,343	4,791	5,371	7,564	11,993	13,278	17,905	23,945*
Total Return	9,009	11,025	14,625	21,916	18,789	22,769	27,210	25,886	32,664	37,375

Dollar amounts of distributions reinvested:

	Capital Gains	Income Dividends
1977	$ 122	$ 244
1978	243	332
1979	583	351
1980	906	450
1981	1,191	515
1982	742	634
1983	3,505	877
1984	2,682	720
1985	1,716	449
1986	7,385	456
Total	$19,075	$5,028

Results Taking Capital Gains in SHARES and Income Dividends In CASH

Initial Investment At Offering Price, January 1, 1977	$10,000
Value as of 12/31/86 of Shares Initially Acquired	$13,430
Value of Shares Accepted as Capital Gains Distributions	$15,264 #
Total Value, December 31, 1986	$28,694
Total Dividends PAID From Investment Income	$ 4,307

Dollar Amount of these distributions at the time shares were acquired: $15,438

Results Taking All Dividends and Distributions in CASH

Initial Investment At Offering Price, January 1, 1977	$10,000
Total Value, December 31, 1986	$13,430
Distributions From Capital Gains	$10,942
Dividends From Investment Income	$ 3,490

FIGURE 21.6
Sample Fund Page from *Forbes*

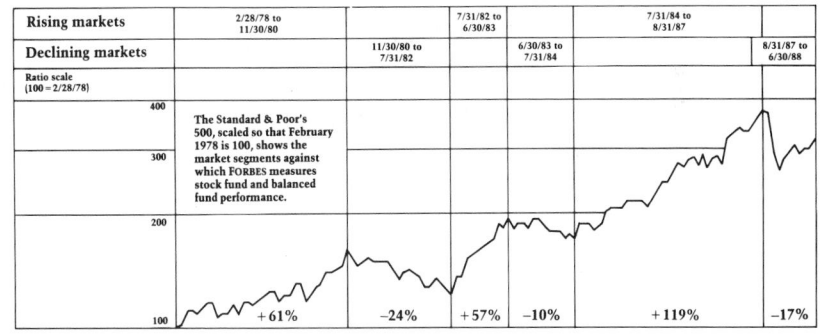

1988 Fund Ratings

Stock funds

FORBES rates stock funds over a period of slightly more than ten years, comprising three market cycles shown below. A fund must have been in existence for at least two market cycles, that is, since July 30, 1982, to be rated. A ● preceding a performance rating indicates a two-period rating. Foreign stock funds, a category that includes most gold funds, are rated separately against a different benchmark (see page 210).

For more information about a fund, call the distributor listed after the fund name, using the table of distributors that begins on page 250. Closed-end funds have no distributor; they are bought and sold through a broker in the secondary market, like shares of industrial companies (see story, page 158.) The average annual return is compounded; it and other performance numbers are after expenses, but before sales load.

Rising markets	2/28/78 to 11/30/80		7/31/82 to 6/30/83		7/31/84 to 8/31/87	
Declining markets		11/30/80 to 7/31/82		6/30/83 to 7/31/84		8/31/87 to 6/30/88

Ratio scale (100 = 2/28/78)

The Standard & Poor's 500, scaled so that February 1978 is 100, shows the market segments against which FORBES measures stock fund and balanced fund performance.

+61% −24% +57% −10% +119% −17%

Performance in UP markets	in DOWN markets	Fund/distributor	Total return — Annual average 1978 to 1988	Last 12 months	Yield	Assets 6/30/88 (millions)	% change '88 vs '87	Maximum sales charge	Annual expenses per $100
		Standard & Poor's 500 stock average	16.9%	−6.9%	3.3%				
		FORBES stock fund composite	16.4%	−5.6%	2.7%				$1.49
		AARP Growth–Capital Growth/Scudder	—*	−0.6%	0.7%	$94	−6%	none	$1.24p
		AARP Growth–Growth & Income/Scudder	—*	−6.2	4.3	247	−23	none	1.08p
B	D	ABT Growth & Income Trust/Palm Beach	15.7%	−0.2	3.5	115	−18	4.75%	1.27
		ABT Invest–Emerging Growth/Palm Beach	—*	−15.1	none	26	−46	4.75	1.57
		ABT Invest–Security Income/Palm Beach	—*	−17.4	2.4	10	−41	4.75	2.04p
●D	A	ABT Utility Income Fund/Palm Beach	—*	5.5	6.6	118	−12	4.75	1.32
B	B	Acorn Fund/Acorn	19.8	2.0	1.4	530	1	none	0.82
		Adam Investors/Conway, Luongo	—*	−5.9	10.2	6	−43	none	2.20
D	B	Adams Express/closed end	15.8	−6.6	3.2	476	−14	NA	0.53

A stock fund is added to this list if it has at least $5 million in net assets and, if open-end, is at least 12 months old; a fund is dropped when its assets fall below $2 million. Stock funds are graded only if in operation since 7/31/82. Long-term average total return is for 2/28/78 to 6/30/88. Yield is last 12 months' income dividends divided by 6/30/88 net asset value; it may differ from "yield" as defined by the SEC. *Expense ratio is in italics if the fund has a shareholder-paid 12b-1 plan exceeding 0.1% (hidden load) pending or in force.* ●Fund rated for two periods only; maximum allowable grade A. *Fund not in operation for full period. ‡Exchange fund, not currently selling new shares. p: Net of partial absorption of expenses by fund sponsor. b: Includes back-end load that reverts to fund. r: Includes back-end load that reverts to distributor. NA: Not applicable or not available.

Source: "1988 Fund Ratings—Stock funds," *Forbes*, September 5, 1988. Reprinted by permission of *Forbes* magazine. © Forbes Inc., 1988.

---

contains a four-page supplement entitled, "Investment Company Performance Comparisons," that gives recent and historical changes in NAV for load and no-load funds. A sample page is contained in Figure 21.8.[31]

---

[31] This service is available from United Business Service Company, 210 Newbury St., Boston, MA 02116.

FIGURE 21.6 *Continued*

1988 Fund Ratings

Foreign stock funds

U.S.-based stock funds with predominantly foreign portfolios are in this table. The benchmark for measuring foreign fund performance is the Morgan Stanley Capital International stock market index for Europe, Australia and the Far East (EAFE). The index aims to show the dollar return that a U.S. investor would have enjoyed in the average foreign stock. The index, that is, reflects not only the rising prices on foreign bourses but the declining dollar. Funds based overseas, whether they invest in local markets or in the U.S., are not covered in the FORBES funds survey.

| Rising markets | 11/30/77 to 10/31/80 | | 9/30/82 to 4/30/84 | 7/31/84 to 8/31/87 | |
| Declining markets | | 10/31/80 to 9/30/82 | 4/30/84 to 7/31/84 | | 8/31/87 to 6/30/88 |

Ratio scale 700
(100 = 11/30/77) 600
Morgan Stanley's Europe, Australia and Far East index, scaled so that November 1977 is 100, determines the market segments against which foreign equity funds are measured. The index reflects both stock prices and the effect of currency movements.

+65%   −24%   +58%   −17%   +301%   −4%

Performance in UP / in DOWN markets	Fund/distributor	Total return — Annual average 1977 to 1988	Last 12 months	Yield	Assets 6/30/88 (millions)	% change '88 vs '87	Maximum sales charge	Annual expenses per $100
	Morgan Stanley Capital Intl EAFE Index	22.0%	4.1%	1.2%				
	FORBES foreign stock fund composite	18.4%	−4.1%	2.1%				$1.79
D B	Alliance Global–Canadian Fund/Alliance	13.1%	5.6%	0.9%	$27	0%	5.50%	*$1.75*
	Alliance Global–World Equities/Alliance	—*	−6.3	1.9	2	−80	5.50	*2.55p*
•B •C	Alliance International Fund/Alliance	—*	−4.7	1.3	132	−32	5.50	*1.37*
	AMA Growth–Global Growth/AMA	—*	−4.3	1.9	119	−12	none	*1.49*
B D	ASA Limited/closed end	16.5	−36.8	9.6	499	−41	NA	0.24
	Asia Pacific Fund/closed end	—*	−11.4	none	75	−11	NA	1.99
	Blanchard Strategic Growth/Sheffield	—*	−2.1	2.1	251	35	none²	*2.28*
	Brazil Fund/closed end	—*	—*	—*	141	—	NA	NA
•D •C	Bull & Bear Gold Investors¹/Bull & Bear	—*	−17.3	none	48	−23	none	*2.46*
	Clemente Global Growth Fund/closed end	—*	−6.3	none	52	−6	NA	2.94p

A foreign stock fund is added to this list if it has at least $5 million in net assets and, if open-end, is at least 12 months old; a fund is dropped when its assets fall below $2 million. Foreign stocks funds are graded only if in operation since 9/30/82. Long-term average total return is for 11/30/77 to 6/30/88. Yield is last 12 months' income dividends divided by 6/30/88 net asset value; it may differ from "yield" as defined by the SEC. *Expense ratio is in italics if the fund has a shareholder-paid 12b-1 plan exceeding 0.1% (hidden load) pending or in force.* ● Fund rated for two periods only; maximum allowable grade A. *Fund not in operation for full period. p: Net of partial absorption of expenses by fund sponsor. b: Includes back-end load that reverts to fund. r: Includes back-end load that reverts to distributor. NA: Not applicable or not available. ¹Formerly Golconda Investors. ²Flat fee of $125 on initial investment.

GLOBAL INVESTMENT COMPANIES

Because of the importance of global diversification and the obvious use of investment companies as the way to accomplish this, Appendix 21B contains a listing of most of the funds offered by the major management firms (Appendix 21A is a glossary of mutual fund terms). The addresses are included to allow you to contact the firm to request a prospectus for one or several funds. Notably, the funds available include global money funds, long-term government and corporate bond funds, global equity funds,

FIGURE 21.7
Mutual Fund Scoreboard

MUTUAL FUND SCOREBOARD

HOW TO USE THE TABLES

BUSINESS WEEK RATING

Ratings measure risk-adjusted performance. This shows how well a fund performed relative to other funds and relative to the level of risk it took. Risk-adjusted performance is determined by subtracting a fund's risk-of-loss factor (see below) from its historic total return. Performance calculations are based on the three-year time period between Jan. 1, 1985, and Dec. 31, 1987. For rating purposes, funds are divided into two groups: municipal bond funds and all other funds. Ratings are based on a normal statistical distribution within each group and awarded as follows

⬆ ⬆ ⬆	superior performance
⬆ ⬆	very good performance
⬆	above-average performance
AVG	average performance
⬇	below-average performance
⬇ ⬇	poor performance
⬇ ⬇ ⬇	very poor performance

RISK

The risk-of-loss factor is the potential for losing money in a fund, calculated as follows: The monthly Treasury bill return is subtracted from the fund's total return for each of the 36 months in the rating period. When a fund has not performed as well as Treasury bills, the result is negative. The sum of these negative numbers is then divided by the number of months in the period. The result is a negative number, and the greater its magnitude, the higher a shareholder's risk of loss.

PERFORMANCE COMPARISON

The tables provide performance data over two time periods. Here are equivalent total return figures for the Shearson Lehman Government/Corporate Bond Index during those periods:

1987	+2.3%
Three-year average (1985-87)	+12.8%

FUND CATEGORIES

The tables group funds in one of six categories, based on assets: Corporate, Government, Municipal, International, Convertible, and Closed-end.

SALES CHARGE

The cost of buying a fund, commonly called the "load." Most funds take loads out of initial investments, and for BW rating purposes performance is reduced by the amount of these charges. Loads on withdrawals can take two forms. Deferred charges decrease over time, usually ending after shares have been owned five years. Redemption fees are imposed whenever investors sell their shares. Funds with none of these charges are called "no-load."

EXPENSE RATIO

Fund expenses for 1987 as a percentage of average net assets. The measures show how much shareholders pay for fund management. Footnotes indicate 12(b)-1 plans, which allocate shareholder money for distribution costs.

TOTAL RETURN

A fund's net gain to investors, including reinvestment of dividends and capital gains at month-end prices.

YIELD

The income a fund earned on its portfolio investments during 1987, expressed as a percentage of the fund's yearend net asset value per share.

MATURITY

The average maturity of the securities in a fund's portfolio, weighted according to the market value of those securities.

TREND

A fund's relative performance during the three 12-month periods from Jan. 1, 1985, to Dec. 31, 1987. The boxes read from left to right, and the level of red in each box tells how the fund performed relative to other funds during the period: ■ for the top quartile; ■ for the second quartile; ▬ for the third quartile; and ▢ for the bottom quartile. An empty box indicates that a fund is not rated for that time period.

TELEPHONE NUMBERS

The index on page 107 has telephone numbers for each fund or fund group.

	RATING	SIZE		FEES		PERFORMANCE		PORTFOLIO		TREND
		ASSETS $ MIL.	% CHG. 1986-87	SALES CHARGE (%)	EXPENSE RATIO (%)	TOTAL RET. (%) 1 YR.	3 YRS.	YIELD	MATURITY (YEARS)	3-YEAR ANALYSIS
CORPORATE										
AARP GENERAL BOND		115.7	36	No load	1.30	1.0		9.0	21.0	
AIM HIGH–YIELD SECURITIES	AVG	80.7	–9	4.75	1.05†	2.0	9.7	13.0	9.8	
ALLIANCE BOND—HIGH-YIELD		369.2	54	5.50	1.06†	–1.7		13.8	9.0	
ALLIANCE MONTHLY INCOME SHARES (a)	⬇	38.9	–12	5.50	1.76†	3.3	13.0	9.6	16.3	
AMERICAN CAPITAL CORPORATE BOND	⬆ ⬆ ⬆	185.6	67	4.75	0.72	6.2	14.2	12.0	14.0	
AMERICAN CAPITAL HIGH-YIELD	⬇ ⬇	541.3	–5	4.75	0.69†	3.2	11.2	14.5	11.0	
AXE–HOUGHTON INCOME	⬆	53.4	16	No load	1.42†	1.8	14.4	12.3	15.8	
BABSON BOND	⬆ ⬆	64.2	4	No load	0.97	4.3	12.8	12.7	11.0	
BARTLETT CAPITAL—FIXED-INCOME		130.5	52	No load	1.00	2.8		8.8	3.2	
BOND FUND OF AMERICA	⬆	825.0	19	5.00	0.58	2.0	14.1	10.2	12.2	
BOSTON CO. MANAGED INCOME	⬆ ⬆ ⬆	51.3	77	No load	0.88†	5.7	14.0	10.3	23.0	
BULL & BEAR HIGH-YIELD	⬇ ⬇ ⬇	133.0	17	No load	1.50†	–6.5	6.2	14.5	10.0	
CIGNA HIGH-YIELD	⬆ ⬆	242.9	–1	5.00	0.92†	3.1	13.8	12.4	11.5	

* Includes redemption fee. ** Includes deferred sales charge. † 12(b)-1 plan in effect. ‡ Not currently accepting new accounts or deposits. NA = Not available. NM = Not meaningful.
(a) Formerly Bullock Monthly Income Shares Inc.

DATA: MORNINGSTAR INC.

MUTUAL FUND SCOREBOARD.

Source: Mutual Fund Scoreboard, p. 91. Reprinted from February 29, 1988 issue of *Business Week* by special permission, copyright © 1988 by McGraw-Hill, Inc.

FIGURE 21.8
United Mutual Fund Selector: Investment Company Performance Comparisons

UNITED Mutual Fund Selector — June 17, 1988

INVESTMENT COMPANY PERFORMANCE COMPARISONS
(This supplement appears in the first issue of every month)

NO-LOAD FUNDS

	Fund Type§	5 Mos. 1988	Latest 12 Mos.	Total Net Assets 3/31/88#	Alpha	Beta	% Yield°
AARP Investment Program:							
Capital Growth...........	G	12.8	− 5.6	88.0	− 1.85	1.04	0.7
GNMA	FI	2.5	6.1	2814.0	4.08	0.03	9.2
General Bond	FI	2.5	4.7	121.3	3.07	0.05	8.9
Growth & Income	GI	4.5	− 6.5	254.0	− 0.07	0.82	4.4
AMA Advisers:							
Classic Growth (b)	G	7.1	−11.2	37.3	− 6.13	1.00	2.3
Classic Income (b)	I	3.0	3.7	38.8	2.77	0.99	7.5
Medical Technology (b) ...	SH	3.9	−13.2	41.7	− 4.06	1.14	0.0
★Acorn Fund (r)	SG	12.9	− 1.0	468.5	2.11	0.83	1.4
Afuture Fund	G	1.5	−18.9	9.7	−16.04	0.91	0.9
American Investors:							
Growth	G	10.5	−12.3	58.0	− 9.03	1.23	0.8
Income	FI	7.8	6.9	22.0	2.56	0.27	13.5
Armstrong Associates	G	10.0	− 4.1	8.8	− 2.04	0.82	2.0
Axe-Houghton:							
Fund B (b)	B	3.3	−10.4	165.9	0.49	0.76	6.1
Income (b)	FI	4.0	5.2	57.7	6.22	0.16	9.7
Stock (b)	G	2.2	−30.2	67.3	− 8.08	1.30	0.7
Babson:							
Bond Trust	FI	0.0	3.6	67.9	3.85	0.07	8.4
Enterprise	SG	23.6	− 6.9	42.0	− 3.66	0.97	0.3
Growth	G	9.9	− 6.0	235.5	0.29	1.00	2.4
UMB Bond	FI	2.7	6.8	NA	3.56	0.03	8.0
UMB Stock	GI	5.5	− 4.2	NA	− 2.15	0.86	3.7
Value	GI	13.1	− 5.1	11.6	0.58	1.01	4.1
Beacon Hill Mutual	G	− 4.3	−13.1	3.0	− 5.42	0.94	0.0
Benham GNMA Income	FI	3.6	9.1	259.2	NA	NA	9.0
Blanchard Strategic Gr (b) ...	AG	3.9	− 0.1	237.2	NA	NA	4.5
Boston Company:							
Capital Appreciation (b) ...	G	9.6	− 4.8	461.7	2.49	0.90	2.1
Special Growth (b) ...	G	11.0	− 9.0	32.3	− 5.99	1.04	3.9
Bowser Growth Fund	G	11.6	−27.4	2.2	−29.20	1.00	0.0
Brandywine Fund	G	11.5	−16.8	108.7	NA	NA	0.0
Bruce Fund	G	12.2	− 9.1	4.6	3.87	0.76	4.2
Bull & Bear Group:							
Capital Growth	G	9.0	−13.1	64.1	− 7.99	1.09	0.0
Equity Income	EI	11.0	− 3.1	13.9	− 0.12	0.69	3.8
Gold Investors Ltd	AU	− 5.3	−18.1	47.0	7.90	0.40	0.0
High Yield	FH	1.1	− 7.0	129.1	− 3.60	0.20	13.6
Calamos Convertible Income.	EI	6.2	− 5.9	22.5	NA	NA	5.4
Calvert:							
Equity Portfolio (b)	G	15.0	−13.7	7.0	− 4.35	1.00	0.7
Washington Area Gr (b) (r).	G	11.9	− 9.5	18.9	NA	NA	0.0
Century Shares Trust	S	9.0	− 2.4	115.1	− 5.99	0.81	3.1
Clipper Fund	GI	6.4	0.1	81.0	2.47	0.52	5.4
Columbia Growth (b)	G	6.0	− 2.8	208.5	− 0.14	0.92	1.8
Copley Fund	GI	6.9	− 1.5	26.0	− 2.60	0.53	0.0
Cowen Inc & Gr (b) (r)	EI	8.4	− 0.4	30.9	NA	NA	4.6
Criterion:							
Convertible Securities (b) ..	FI	3.4	− 9.9	16.2	NA	NA	5.0
Global Growth (b)	GL	− 1.4	−12.1	10.5	NA	NA	0.0
Dean Witter:							
Convertible Securities (b) (r)	FI	12.7	−18.1	1320.0	NA	NA	3.9
Developing Growth (b) (r)..	SG	9.9	− 6.3	121.7	− 8.56	0.99	0.0
Dividend Gr Secs. (b) (r) ..	GI	9.1	− 2.7	1763.6	0.71	0.78	3.9
Natural Res. Devel. (b) (r) .	NR	11.7	− 1.8	170.3	− 2.33	0.92	2.1
Option Income Trust (b) (r)	OI	5.4	− 7.8	363.4	− 8.22	0.70	5.7
US Govt. Securities (b) (r) .	FI	2.6	6.5	10694.6	2.54	− 0.01	10.1
Dodge & Cox:							
Balanced	B	6.1	− 0.4	38.1	4.18	0.64	5.5
Stock	GI	8.0	− 1.3	74.1	3.87	0.95	3.1
Drexel Series Trust:							
Bond Debenture (r)	FI	1.4	2.9	23.3	3.13	0.09	8.2
Emerging Growth (r)	SG	3.1	−27.6	15.6	−10.26	1.13	0.0
Government Securities (r)..	FI	− 0.1	2.3	327.0	0.78	0.04	7.6
Growth (r)	G	10.0	− 3.1	32.9	− 0.87	0.87	2.6
Option Income (r)	OI	6.1	− 2.6	37.0	− 3.99	0.68	3.1
Dreyfus:							
A Bonds Plus	FI	3.6	5.5	254.3	4.76	0.10	9.7
Convertible Securities	I	14.9	2.0	245.3	3.84	0.58	5.5
GNMA Fund (b)	FI	3.5	6.2	2051.8	NA	NA	9.2
Growth Opportunity	G	10.8	− 5.5	451.1	3.23	0.83	2.5
New Leaders (b)	SG	16.9	− 8.3	90.0	NA	NA	0.5
Third Century	G	11.2	− 4.5	150.2	− 3.11	0.77	6.2
Enterprise Growth Fund	G	7.3	− 4.5	31.2	0.17	1.05	0.8
Equitec Siebel:							
Aggressive Growth (b) (r)..	AG	5.4	− 9.1	41.1	NA	NA	4.9
High Yield Bond (b) (r)....	FH	3.8	2.9	24.3	NA	NA	10.6
Total Return (b) (r)	GI	4.1	− 4.0	148.9	1.37	0.70	2.9
U.S. Gov't Secs. (b) (r)....	FI	4.4	6.4	157.2	NA	NA	9.7
Evergreen:							
Fund	G	15.5	− 5.1	690.2	− 0.04	0.89	2.1
★Total Return	GI	10.0	− 2.7	1354.9	− 0.05	0.59	6.2
Value Timing	AG	12.7	NA	23.3	NA	NA	1.1
Fairmont Fund	AG	7.4	−15.0	82.3	− 4.79	1.04	1.1
Farm Bureau Growth	GI	7.0	− 5.1	48.4	− 7.71	0.87	9.5
Federated Stock & Bond	B	3.9	1.8	93.1	1.71	0.38	5.3
Fidelity Investments:							
Contrafund (b)	G	12.2	−11.9	95.2	− 3.63	1.08	0.0
Convertible Securities	FI	10.9	− 0.1	49.1	NA	NA	5.6
Flexible Bond	FI	2.8	5.6	339.3	4.26	0.07	9.1
Freedom (b)	AG	11.8	− 6.9	1207.4	1.35	1.10	1.9
Fund (b)	GI	9.3	− 7.4	884.5	− 0.68	0.97	3.3
GNMA Fund (b)	FI	2.9	6.2	741.9	NA	NA	8.9
Global	GL	− 0.2	11.6	103.2	NA	NA	4.0
Government Securities (b) .	FI	2.4	5.8	684.7	4.16	0.06	9.3
★High Income	FH	6.2	4.2	1514.9	5.21	0.21	11.9
Intermediate Bond	FI	2.5	6.0	460.0	4.58	0.06	14.0
Mortgage Securities	FI	2.8	6.7	503.2	3.98	0.02	8.9
Trend (b)	G	15.8	− 8.3	669.1	− 1.87	1.12	1.2
Value (b)	AG	12.1	− 9.2	91.9	− 5.22	0.91	0.0
Financial Group:							
Dynamics	AG	− 1.8	−18.9	79.1	− 5.60	1.30	0.3

■ Including all dividends and capital gains. NA not applicable, not available, or not meaningful. ° Based on latest 12 months' payout. (b) 12b-1 plan; % of fund's assets may be used for marketing purposes. (c) Not available for new purchase. (p) Dividends reinvested at offering price. (r) Redemption fee or contingent deferred sales charge may be imposed. § Fund type: AG Aggressive Growth. AU Gold. B Balanced. EI Equity-Income. FH High Yield Bond. FI Fixed-Income. G Growth. GI Growth & Income. GL Global. I Income. IF International. NR Natural Resources. OG Option-Growth. OI Option-Income. SG Small Company Growth. S Specialty. SH Health. ST Technology. SU Utility. ★ Supervised List. # $Millions. ◊ Based on the 36-month performance for all open-end funds.

Source: Investment Company Performance Comparisons, *United Mutual Fund Selector*, June 17, 1988. Reprinted with permission from United Mutual Fund Selector, 212 Newbury St., Boston, MA 02116.

and equity funds limited to a single country. While the majority are open-end funds (load and no-load), there are a significant number of closed-end funds including most of the single country funds.

SUMMARY

An investment company can be defined as a pool of funds belonging to many individuals that is used to acquire a collection of individual investments such as stocks, bonds, and other publicly traded securities. Types of investment companies can be classified as closed-end, open-end, load, and no-load funds. A wide variety of funds is available, so almost any investment objective or combination of objectives can currently be matched by some investment companies.

Numerous studies have examined the historical performance of mutual funds. Most of the studies indicated that less than half the funds matched the aggregate market on a risk-adjusted basis using net returns. Alternatively, the results with gross returns generally indicated that the average risk-adjusted returns were about equal to the market's, and about half of the funds (more than half for some studies) did better than the market did. While the returns on funds are generally not superior to the average results for an individual investor, several other important services are provided by investment companies.

QUESTIONS

1. How do you compute the net asset value of an investment company?
2. Discuss the difference between an open-end investment company and a closed-end investment company.
3. What are the two prices of importance to a closed-end investment company? How do these prices typically differ?
4. What is the difference between a load and no-load fund?
5. What are the differences between a common stock fund and a balanced fund? How would you expect their risk and return characteristics to compare?
6. Why would anyone buy a money market fund?
7. What has been the typical relationship between NAV and market price for closed-end funds? Describe the effect of a change in this relationship.
8. Do you care about how well a mutual fund is diversified? Why or why not? How could you quickly measure the extent of diversification?
9. Why is the stability of risk for a mutual fund important to an investor? Discuss. What is the empirical evidence in this regard—that is, is the risk measure for mutual funds generally stable?
10. Do you think the performance of mutual funds should be judged on the basis of return alone or on a risk-adjusted basis? Why? Discuss, using examples.
11. Define the net return and gross return for a mutual fund. Discuss how you would compute each of these.

12a. As an investor in a mutual fund, discuss why the net return or gross return is relevant to you.

12b. As an investigator attempting to determine the ability of mutual fund managers to select undervalued stocks or project market returns, which return is relevant: net or gross?

13. You are told that on the basis of the Treynor composite measure of performance, about half the mutual funds did better than the market, and on the basis of the Sharpe measure, only 35 percent did better than the market. Explain in detail why this happened.

14. Based upon the numerous tests of mutual fund performance, you are convinced that only about half of them do better than a naive buy-and-hold policy. Does this mean you would forget about investing in them? Why or why not?

15a. You are told that Fund X experienced above-average performance over the past two years. Do you think it will continue over the next two years? Why or why not?

15b. You are told that Fund Y experienced consistently poor performance over the past two years. Do you expect this to continue over the next two years? Why or why not?

16. Assume that you see advertisements for two mutual funds indicating that the investment objectives of the funds are consistent with yours.

16a. Where would you go to get a quick view of how these two funds have performed over the past two or three years?

16b. Where would you go to get more in-depth information on the funds, including an address so you can write for a prospectus?

PROBLEMS

1. The results of four mutual funds are being compared in preparation of a rather large investment. The following data have been collected:

FUND	BETA	STANDARD DEVIATION	RETURN	R_f	SHARPE MEASURE	TREYNOR MEASURE	JENSON MEASURE
A	1.30	6.02	16	5	_____	_____	_____
B	1.02	4.44	12	5	_____	_____	_____
C	.99	4.32	11	5	_____	_____	_____
D	.64	2.76	7	5	_____	_____	_____
Market	1.00	4.40	11.5	5	_____	_____	_____

1a. Complete the missing values in the table.

1b. Rank the funds according to your assessment of their investment potential.

2. Suppose ABC Mutual Fund owned only four stocks as follows:

STOCK	SHARES	PRICE	MARKET VALUE
W	1,000	12	$12,000
X	1,200	15	18,000
Y	1,500	22	33,000
Z	800	16	12,800
			$75,800

The fund originated by selling $50,000 of stock at $8.00 per share. What is its current NAV?

3. Suppose you consider investing $1,000 in a load fund from which a fee of 9 percent is deducted, and you expect your investment to earn 15 percent over the next year. Alternatively, you could invest in a no-load fund that is expected to earn 12 percent and takes a 1 percent redemption fee. Which is better and by how much?

REFERENCES

Ang, James S., and Jess H. Chua. "Mutual Funds: Different Strokes for Different Folks?" *Journal of Portfolio Management* 8, no. 2 (Winter 1982).

Chang, Eric C., and Wilbur G. Lewellen. "Market Timing and Mutual Fund Investment Performance." *Journal of Business* 57, no. 1, part 1 (January 1984).

Henriksson, Roy D. "Mutual Timing and Mutual Fund Performance: An Empirical Investigation." *Journal of Business* 57, no. 1, part 1 (January 1984).

Henriksson, Roy D., and Robert C. Merton. "On Market Timing and Investment Performance, II. Statistical Procedures for Evaluating Forecasting Skills." *Journal of Business* 54, no. 4 (October 1981).

Jensen, Michael C. "The Performance of Mutual Funds in the Period 1945–1964." *Journal of Finance* 23, no. 2 (May 1968).

Kon, Stanley J., and Frank C. Jen. "The Investment Performance of Mutual Funds: An Empirical Investigation of Timing, Selectivity, and Market Efficiency." *Journal of Business* 52, no. 2 (April 1979).

Martin, John D., Arthur J. Keown, Jr., and James L. Farrell. "Do Fund Objectives Affect Diversification Policies?" *Journal of Portfolio Management* 8, no. 2 (Winter 1982).

Merton, Robert C. "On Market Timing and Investment Performance, I. An Equilibrium Theory of Value for Market Forecasts." *Journal of Business* 54, no. 3 (July 1981).

Richards, Malcolm, Donald Fraser, and John Groth. "Premiums, Discounts, and the Volatility of Closed-End Mutual Funds." *The Financial Review* 14, no. 3 (Fall 1979).

Richards, Malcolm, Donald Fraser, and John Groth. "The Attractions of Closed-End Bond Funds." *Journal of Portfolio Management* 8, no. 2 (Winter 1982).

Sharpe, William F. "Mutual Fund Performance." *Journal of Business, Supplement on Security Prices* 39, no. 1 (January 1966).

Thompson, Rex. "The Information Content of Discounts and Premiums on Closed-End Fund Shares." *Journal of Financial Economics* 6, no. 2/3 (June–September 1978).

Treynor, Jack L. "How to Rate Management of Investment Funds." *Harvard Business Review* 43, no. 1 (January-February 1965).

Veit, E. Theodore, and John M. Cheney. "Are Mutual Funds Market Timers?" *Journal of Portfolio Management* 8, no. 2 (Winter 1982).

APPENDIX 21A   GLOSSARY OF MUTUAL FUNDS

This glossary is in three parts: (A) General terms used in the mutual fund industry, (B) a detailed description of types of mutual funds, and (C) a description of alternative retirement plans, each of which can be funded with mutual funds.

A. General Terms

Accumulation Plan (Periodic Payment Plan) Enables an investor to purchase mutual fund shares periodically in large or small amounts, usually with provisions for the reinvestment of income dividends and capital gains distributions in additional shares.

Adviser The organization employed by a mutual fund to give professional advice on its investments and management of its assets.

Asked or Offering Price The price at which a mutual fund's shares can be purchased. The asked or offering price means the net asset value per share plus, at times, a sales charge.

Automatic Reinvestment The option available to mutual fund shareholders whereby fund income dividends and capital gains distributions are automatically put back into the fund to buy new shares and thereby build up holdings.

Bid or Redemption Price The price at which a mutual fund's shares are redeemed (bought back) by the fund. The bid, or redemption price, usually means the net asset value per share.

Bookshares A modern share recording system that eliminates the need for mutual fund share certificates but gives the fund shareowner a record of his holdings.

Broker-Dealer (or Dealer) A firm that retails mutual fund shares and other securities to the public.

Capital Gains Distributions Payments to mutual fund shareholders of gains realized on the sale of the fund's portfolio securities. These amounts usually are paid once a year.

Capital Growth An increase in the market value of a mutual fund's securities that is reflected in the NAV of fund shares. This is a specific long-term objective of many mutual funds.

Closed-End Investment Company Unlike mutual funds (known as *open-end*), closed-end companies issue only a limited number of shares and do not redeem them (buy them back). Instead, closed-end shares are traded in the securities markets with supply and demand determining the price.

Contractual Plan A program for the accumulation of mutual fund shares in which the investor agrees to invest a fixed amount on a regular basis for a specified number of years. A substantial portion of the sales charge applicable to the total investment is usually deducted from early payments.

Conversion Privilege (Exchange Privilege) Enables a mutual fund shareholder to transfer his investment from one fund to another within the same fund group if his needs or objectives change, sometimes with a small transaction charge.

Custodian The organization (usually a bank) that holds in custody and safekeeping the securities and other assets of a mutual fund.

Diversification The mutual fund policy of spreading investments among a number of different securities to reduce the risks inherent in investing.

Dollar-Cost Averaging Investing equal amounts of money at regular intervals regardless of whether the stock market is moving upward or downward. This reduces average share costs in periods of lower securities prices, and number of shares purchased during periods of higher prices.

Exchange Privilege *See* Conversion Privilege.

Income Dividends Payments to mutual fund shareholders of dividends, interest, and short-term capital gains earned on the fund's portfolio securities after deduction of operating expenses.

Investment Adviser *See* Adviser.

Investment Company A corporation, trust, or partnership in which investors may pool their money to obtain professional management and diversification of their investments. Mutual funds are the most popular type of investment company.

Investment Objective The goal (e.g., long-term capital growth, current income, etc.) that an investor or a mutual fund pursues.

Management Fee The amount paid by a mutual fund to the investment adviser for its services. The average annual fee industry-wide is about one-half of 1 percent of fund assets.

Mutual Fund An investment company that pools money from shareholders and invests in a variety of securities, including stocks, bonds, and money market securities. A mutual fund ordinarily stands ready to buy back (redeem) its shares at their current net asset value. The value of the shares depends on the market value of the fund's portfolio securities at the time. Also, mutual funds generally continuously offer new shares to investors.

Net Asset Value (NAV) Per Share The market worth of a mutual fund's total resources (securities, cash, and any accrued earnings) after deducting liabilities, divided by the number of shares outstanding.

No-Load Fund A mutual fund selling its shares at net asset value without the addition of sales charges.

Open-End Investment Company The more formal name for a mutual fund, indicating that it continuously offers new shares to investors and redeems them (buys them back) on demand.

Payroll Deduction Plan Some employers offer an arrangement whereby an employee may accumulate shares in a mutual fund. Employees authorize their employer to deduct a specified amount from their salary at stated times and transfer the proceeds to the designated fund or funds.

Periodic Payment Plan *See* Contractual Plan.

Prospectus A booklet describing the mutual fund and offering its shares for sale. It contains information required by the Securities and Exchange Commission on such subjects as the fund's investment objective and policies, services, investment restrictions, officers and directors, how shares can be bought and redeemed, its charges, and its financial statements.

Qualified Retirement Plan A private retirement plan that meets the rules and regulations of the Internal Revenue Service. Contributions to a qualified retirement plan are in almost all cases tax deductible, and earnings on such contributions are always tax sheltered until the investor retires.

Redemption Price The amount per share the mutual fund shareholder receives when he cashes in his shares (also known as *bid price*). The value of the shares depends on the market value of the fund's portfolio securities at the time.

Reinvestment Privilege A service provided by most mutual funds for the automatic reinvestment of a shareholder's income dividends and capital gains distributions in additional shares.

Sales Charge An amount charged to purchase shares in most mutual funds sold by brokers or other members of a sales force. Typically the charge ranges from 4 to 8.5 percent of the initial investment. The charge is added to the net asset value per share in determining the offering price. (Some funds, which do not have sales representatives, have no sales charge and are called *no-load funds.*)

Short-Term Funds An industry designation for money market and short-term municipal bond funds.

Transfer Agent The organization employed by a mutual fund to prepare and maintain records relating to the accounts of fund shareholders.

12b-1 Fee Fee charged by some funds and named after the SEC rule that permits them. Such fees pay for distribution costs such as advertising or for commissions paid to brokers. The fund's prospectus details 12b-1 charges, if applicable.

Underwriter (Principal Underwriter) The organization that acts as the distributor of a mutual fund's shares to broker-dealers and the public.

Unit Investment Trust An investment company that purchases a fixed portfolio of income-producing securities. Units in the trust are sold to investors by brokers.

Variable Annuity A contract under which an annuity is purchased with a fixed number of dollars that are converted into a varying number of accumulation units. At retirement, the annuitant is paid a fixed number of monthly units that are converted into a varying number of dollars. The value of both accumulation and annuity units varies in accordance with the performance of a portfolio invested in equity securities.

Variable Life Insurance An equity-based life insurance policy in which the reserves may be invested in common stocks. The death benefit is guaranteed never to fall below the face value, but it could increase if the value of the securities increases. There may be no guaranteed cash-surrender value under this kind of policy.

Voluntary Plan A flexible accumulation plan in which there is no definite time period or total amount to be invested.

Withdrawal Plans Many mutual funds offer withdrawal programs whereby shareholders receive payments from their investments at regular intervals. These payments typically are drawn from the fund's dividends and capital gains distributions, if any, and from principal, as needed.

B. TYPES OF MUTUAL FUNDS

Aggressive Growth Funds Seek maximum capital gains as their investment objective. Current income is not a significant factor. Some may invest in stocks that are somewhat out of the mainstream, such as those in fledgling companies, new industries, companies fallen on hard times, or industries temporarily out of favor. They may also use specialized investment techniques such as option writing. The risks are obvious, but the potential for reward should also be greater.

Growth Invest in the common stock of more settled companies, but again, the primary aim is to produce an increase in the value of their investments through capital gains, rather than a steady flow of dividends.

Growth and Income Funds Invest mainly in the common stock of companies with a longer track record—companies that have both the expectation of a higher share value and a solid record of paying dividends.

International Funds Invest in the stocks of companies located outside the United States.

Global Equity Funds Invest in stocks of companies located worldwide, i.e., stocks outside the United States and also U.S. stocks.

Option/Income Funds Seek a high current return by investing primarily in dividend paying common stocks on which call options are traded on national securities exchanges. Current return generally consists of dividends, premiums from writing call options, and short-term gains from sales of portfolio securities on exercises of options or otherwise, and any profits from closing purchase transactions.

Flexible Portfolio Funds Invest in common stocks, bonds, money market securities, and other types of debt securities. The portfolio may hold up to 100 percent of any one of these types of securities or any combination thereof, and may easily change depending upon market conditions.

Balanced Funds Generally have a three-part investment objective: (1) to conserve the investors' principal, (2) to pay current income, and (3) to increase both principal and income. They aim to achieve this by owning a mixture of bonds, preferred stocks, and common stocks.

Income-Mixed Funds Seek a high level of current income for their shareholders. This may be achieved by investing in the common stock of companies that have good dividend-paying records. Often corporate and government bonds are also part of the portfolio.

Money Market Mutual Funds Invest in the short-term securities sold in the money market. (Large companies, banks, and other institutions invest their surplus cash in the money market for short periods of time.) In the entire investment spectrum, these are generally the safest, most stable securities available. They include Treasury bills, certificates of deposit of large banks, and commercial paper (the short-term IOUs of large U.S. corporations).

Income-Bond Funds Invest in a combination of government and corporate bonds for the generation of income.

U.S. Government Income Funds Invest in a variety of government securities. These include U.S. Treasury bonds, federally guaranteed mortgage-backed securities, and other government issues.

GNMA or Ginnie Mae Funds (Government National Mortgage Association) Invest in government-backed mortgage securities. To qualify for this category, the majority of the portfolio must always be invested in mortgage-backed securities.

Corporate Bond Funds Like income funds, these seek a high level of income. They do so by buying bonds of corporations for the majority of the portfolio. Some part of the portfolio may be in U.S. Treasury and other government entities' bonds.

High-Yield Bond Funds Corporate bond funds that predominantly invest in bonds rated below investment grade. In return for a generally higher yield, investors bear a greater degree of credit risk than for more highly rated bonds.

Global Bond Funds Invest in bonds issued by companies or countries worldwide, including the United States.

Short-Term National Municipal Bond Funds Invest in municipal securities with relatively short maturities. They are also known as tax-exempt money market funds.

Short-Term State Municipal Bond Funds Invest in municipal securities with relatively short maturities. Because they contain the issues of only one state, they are exempt from state taxes for residents of the state specified by the fund name.

Long-Term Municipal Bond Funds Invest in bonds issued by local governments—such as cities and states—which use the money to build schools, highways, libraries, and the like. These funds predominantly invest in municipal bonds that are exempt from federal income tax. Because the federal government does not tax the income earned on most of these securities, the fund can pass the tax-free income through to shareholders.

Long-Term State Municipal Bond Funds Predominantly invest in municipal bonds that are exempt from federal income tax as well as exempt from state taxes for residents of the state specified by the fund name.

C. RETIREMENT PLANS

Federal income tax laws permit the establishment of a number of types of retirement plans, each of which may be funded with mutual fund shares.

Individual Retirement Accounts All wage earners under the age of 70 1/2 may set up an Individual Retirement Account (IRA). The individual may contribute as much as 100 percent of his or her compensation each year, up to $2,000. Earnings are tax-deferred until withdrawal. The amount contributed each year may be wholly or partially tax deductible. Under the Tax Reform Act of 1986, all taxpayers not covered by employer-sponsored retirement plans can continue to take the full deduction for IRA contributions. Those who are covered or who are married to someone who is covered must have an adjusted gross income of no more than $25,000 (single) or $40,000 (married, filing jointly) to take the full deduction. The deduction is phased out for incomes between $25,000 and $35,000 (single) and $40,000 and $60,000 (married, filing jointly). An individual who qualifies for an IRA and has a spouse who either has no earnings or elects to be treated as having no earnings may contribute up to 100 percent of his or her income or $2,250, whichever is less.

Simplified Employee Pensions (SEPs) Employer-sponsored plans that may be viewed as an aggregation of separate IRAs. In an SEP, the employer contribution, limited to $30,000 or 15 percent of compensation, whichever is less, is made to an Individual Retirement Account maintained for the employee.

Section 403(b) Plans Section 403(b) of the Internal Revenue Code permits employees of certain charitable organizations and public school systems to establish tax-sheltered retirement programs. These plans may be invested in either annuity contracts or mutual fund shares.

Section 401(k) Plans One particularly popular type of plan that may be offered by either corporate or noncorporate entities. A 401(k) plan is a tax-qualified profit-sharing plan that includes a "cash or deferred" arrangement. The cash or deferred arrangement permits employees to have a portion of their compensation contributed to a tax-sheltered plan on their behalf or paid to them directly as additional taxable compensation. Thus, an employee may elect to reduce his or her taxable compensation with contributions to a 401(k) plan where those amounts will accumulate tax-free. The Tax Reform Act of 1986 established new, tighter antidiscrimination requirements for 401(k) plans and curtailed the amount of elective deferrals that may be made by all employees. Nevertheless, 401(k) plans remain excellent and popular retirement savings vehicles.

Corporate and Self-Employed Retirement Plans Tax-qualified pension and profit-sharing plans that may be established by corporations or self-employed individuals. Changes in the tax laws have made retirement plans for employees of corporations and those for self-employed individuals essentially comparable. Contributions to a plan are tax-deductible and earnings accumulate on a tax-sheltered basis. The maximum annual amount that may be contributed to a defined contribution plan on behalf of an individual is limited to the lesser of 25 percent of the individual's compensation or $30,000.

LISTING OF INTERNATIONAL AND GLOBAL EQUITY AND FIXED-INCOME FUNDS

APPENDIX 21B

The left-hand column lists the specific funds and the addresses for these funds. The right-hand column contains the name of and phone number(s) for the management company that underwrites the fund. The following designations are used:

> **OE** = **open end**
>
> **CE** = **closed end (followed by a designation of trading location such as NYSE)**
>
> **Load** = **full load fund (typically 7 to 8 percent)**

Low load = a smaller load (typically 2 to 4 percent)

No load = no sales charge.

You should remember that, irrespective of load fees, it is necessary to determine from the prospectus if the fund has a 12b-1 plan in effect.

OPEN-END COMPANIES

Alliance International Fund (OE; Load)
1345 Avenue of the Americas
New York, NY 10105

Alliance Capital Management
(800) 221-5672
(212) 902-4160

Canadian Fund (OE; Load)
40 Rector St.
New York, NY 10005

Carlson Bullock Ltd.
(212) 513-4200

Colonial International Equity Index (OE; Load 12b-1)
One Financial Center
Boston, MA 02111

Colonial Management Association
(617) 426-3750

Dean Witter World Wide Investments Trust (OE; No-Load 12b-1)
One World Trade Center
New York, NY 10048

Dean Witter Reynolds International Div.
(212) 938-4500

Dreyfus Dollar International Fund (OE; No-Load)
One Penn Plaza
New York, NY 10119

Dreyfus Corporation
(800) 645-6561
(212) 830-3000

Fidelity Europe (OE; Low Load)
Fidelity Overseas Fund (OE; Load)
Fidelity Pacific Basin (OE; Low Load)
82 Devonshire Street
Boston, MA 02109

Fidelity Management & Research
(617) 570-7000

Financial Strategic—European (OE; No Load)
Financial Strategic—Pacific Basin (OE; No Load)
P.O. Box 2040
Denver, CO 80201

Financial Programs Inc.
(800) 525-7085
(800) 525-9769

First Investors International Securities (OE; Load 12b-1)
120 Wall Street
New York, NY 10005

First Investors Management Co.
(212) 208-6000

Franklin Puerto Rico T/F Income (OE; Load)
777 Mariner Island Blvd.
San Mateo, CA 94401

Franklin Distributors
(415) 570-3000

Freedom Global Fund (OE; Load)
Freedom Regional Bank
Three Center Plaza
Boston, MA 02108

Tucker Anthony
    Management Corp.
(619) 523-3170

FT International Trust (OE; No Load)
Federated Investors Tower
Pittsburgh, PA 15222

FIR Tree Advisors
Clayton Brown & Assoc.
(800) 245-0242
(412) 288-1900

GT Global Growth—Europe Growth (OE; No Load)
GT Global Growth—International (OE; No Load)
GT Global Growth—Japan Growth (OE; No Load)
GT Global Growth—Pacific Growth (OE; No Load)
601 Montgomery St., Suite 1400
San Francisco, CA 94111

GT Capital Management
(800) 324-1580
(415) 392-6181

Hancock (John) Global Tr. (OE; Load)
101 Huntington Avenue, 7th Floor
Boston, MA 02199

John Hancock Advisors
(617) 375-1760

IDS International Fund (OE; Load 12b-1)
1000 Roanke Building
Minneapolis, MN 55474

Investors Diversified Service
(612) 372-2807

International Fund for Institutions (OE)
Webster Building—Suite 204
3411 Silverside Road
Wilmington, DE 19810

Provident Institutional
    Management
(302) 479-1794

International Investors (OE; Load)
122 E. 42nd St.
New York, NY 10163

Van Eck Management Co.
(800) 221-2220
(212) 687-5200

Kemper International Fund (OE; Load)
120 South LaSalle St.
Chicago, IL 60603

Kemper Financial Service,
    Inc.
(312) 731-1121

Keystone International Fund (OE; No Load 12b-1)
99 High St.
Boston, MA 02104

Keystone Massachusetts
    Distributors
(617) 373-3200

Meechaert Int'l Bond Tr. (OE; No Load) 75 Federal Street Boston, MA 02110	Meechaert Investment Management Co. (617) 423-6898
Merrill Lynch—International Holdings (OE; Load) Merrill Lynch—Pacific Fund (OE; Load) P.O. Box 9011 Princeton, NJ 68547-0911	Merrill Lynch Asset Management (609) 282-2800
Nomura Pacific Basin Fund (OE; No Load 12b-1) 189 Maiden Lane New York, NY 10038	Nomura Securities International, Inc. (212) 202-9300
Pax World Fund (OE; No Load 12b-1) 224 State St. Portsmouth, NH 03301	Pax World Mgmt. Corp. (603) 431-8022
T. Rowe Price International Stock Fund (OE; No Load) 100 East Pratt St. Baltimore, MD 21201	T. Rowe Price Associates (800) 638-5660
Prudential Bache Global (OE; No Load) One Seaport Plaza New York, NY 10292	Prudential Bache Securities (212) 219-1214
Putnam International Equities Fund (OE; Load) One Post Office Square Boston, MA 02109	The Putnam Management Co. (800) 225-1581 (617) 242-1000
Scudder Global Fund (OE; No Load) Scudder International Fund (OE; No Load) 175 Federal St. Boston, MA 01220	Scudder Stevens & Clark (800) 225-2470 (617) 426-8300
Shearson Global Opportunity (OE; Load) Shearson Lehman Special—Global Bond (OE; No Load 12b-1) Shearson Lehman Special—International Equity (OE; No Load 12b-1) Two World Trade Center New York, NY 10048	Shearson/American Express Asset Management (212) 577-5794
Sigma World Fund (OE; Load 12b-1) Greenville Center C-200 3201 Kennel Pike Wilmington, DE 19807	Delfi Management (302) 652-3091

Solzen International Fund (OE; Load)
520 Madison Ave.
New York, NY 10022

Solzen Securities Corp.
(212) 832-0022

SteinRoe Universe Fund (OE; No Load)
P.O. Box 1143
Chicago, IL 60690

SteinRoe & Farnham
(800) 621-0320
(312) 363-7826

Templeton Foreign Fund (OE; Load)
Templeton Global I (OE; Load)
Templeton Global II (OE; Load)
Templeton Growth Fund (OE; Load)
Templeton World Fund (OE; Load)
700 Central Ave.
P.O. Box 3942
St. Petersburg, FL 33701

Templeton Investment
    Advisors Ltd.
(800) 237-0738

Thomson McKinnon Investment Trust—
    Global (OE; No Load 12b-1)
One State St. Plaza
New York, NY 10004

Thomson McKinnon Asset
    Management
(212) 482-6492

Transatlantic Growth Fund (OE; No Load
    12b-1)
200 Park Ave., Suite 5610
New York, NY 10166

Kleinworth Benson
    International Investments
    Ltd.
(800) 223-4130
(212) 747-0440

Trustees Commingled International
    Equity (OE; No Load)
Drummers Lane
Valley Forge, PA 19842

Battery March Financial
    Management
(215) 293-7910

United International Growth (OE; Load)
One Crown Center
P.O. Box 1343
Kansas City, MO 64141

Waddell & Reed
(816) 283-4000

U.S. Boston Investment International
    (OE; No Load 12b-1)
6 New England Executive Park
Burlington, MA 01303

State Street Bank & Trust
(617) 272-6420

Vanguard World—International Growth
    (OE; No Load)
Vanguard Financial Center
Valley Forge, PA 19482

Schroder Capital
    Management
(800) 662-7992

Warburg International Fund (OE; Load)
100 Park Ave.
New York, NY 10017

Reich & Tang, Inc.
(212) 415-1925

World Trends Fund (OE; Load 12b-1)   Van Eck Securities
122 East 42nd St.   (800) 221-2200
New York, NY 10168   (212) 687-5200

CLOSED-END
COMPANIES   ASA Limited (CE; NYSE)   Keith Wood
                   French Hanss, 54 Market St.   (201) 635-0122
                   Johannesburg 2001, South Africa
                   P.O. Box 39
                   Chatham, NJ 07923

                   Asia Pacific (CE: NASD)

                   1st Australia (CE; AMEX)
                   One Seaport Plaza
                   New York, NY 10292

                   Central Fd. Canada (CE; AMEX)

                   France Fund (CE; NYSE)
                   535 Madison Ave.
                   New York, NY 10022

                   The Germany Fund (CE; NYSE)   Deutsche Bank Capital Corp.
                   40 Wall St.   (212) 612-0600
                   New York, NY 10005

                   Italy Fund (CE; NYSE)
                   Two World Trade Center
                   New York, NY 10048

                   The Japan Fund, Inc. (CE; NYSE)   Asia Management Corp.
                   345 Park Ave.   (212) 326-6500
                   New York, NY 10154

                   Korea Fund (CE; NYSE)
                   345 Park Ave.
                   New York, NY 10154

                   Malaysia Fund (CE; NYSE)

                   Mexico Fund (CE; NYSE)
                   633 Third Ave.
                   New York, NY 10012

                   The Scandinavian Fund (CE; ASE)   Skandinford Fiduciary AB
                   755 New York Ave.   (516) 335-9580
                   Huntington, NY 11793

                   Scudder New Asia (CE; NYSE)
                   345 Park Ave.
                   New York, NY 10154

Tower Fund (CE; AMEX)
111 Devonshire St.
Boston, MA 02109

United Kingdom Fund (CE; NYSE)
245 Park Ave.
New York, NY 10167

GLOBAL BOND   First Australia Prime (CE; AMEX)

Global Government (CE; NYSE)

Global Yield Fund (CE; NYSE)
One Seaport Plaza
New York, NY 10292

Klein Benson Australia (CE; NYSE)

PART V

ANALYSIS OF ALTERNATIVE INVESTMENTS

CHAPTERS

In this section we complete our discussion of investment alternatives by analyzing several investment instruments that will provide you with a wider range of risk-return possibilities. In Chapter 22 we discuss stock options, which have become very popular due to their versatile use, and in Chapter 23 we discuss warrants and convertible securities, which are very useful for issuing companies in terms of reducing the cost of capital because they are attractive for investors. Warrants have appeal because of the leverage involved, while convertible securities are desirable because they typically provide downside protection and good upside potential.

In Chapter 24 we consider an area that has typically not received much attention in discussions of investments: commodities futures. Contrary to the general feeling that commodities are different from stocks and bonds, we begin the chapter with a discussion of similarities and then detail specific trades and price relationships.

Chapter 25 concludes the book with a discussion of financial futures, which have experienced a substantial increase in trading volume since 1979. We discuss how they are traded, who can use them, and how to use them including their use in portfolio insurance and index arbitrage. Examples of several typical transactions for a U.S. investor or an investor concerned with global investing are presented as well.

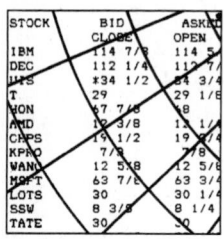

CHAPTER 22

STOCK OPTIONS

Options give the holder the right to buy or sell a security at a specified price during a designated period of time (usually from three to nine months). *Call options* give the owner the right to purchase and *put options* the right to sell a given number of shares. These options have been available to investors on the OTC market for a number of years, but have become widely accepted and used as an investment vehicle only since the Chicago Board Options Exchange (CBOE) was established. Actions by the CBOE and, later, by other stock exchanges that have listed options have encouraged substantial options trading by both individual and institutional investors. Options offer a range of investment alternatives from very speculative to very conservative.

RECENT HISTORY OF OPTIONS TRADING

For a number of years it has been possible to buy and sell put and call options in the over-the-counter market via individual investment firms that were members of the Put and Call Association. Through the individual firms in this association, investors could negotiate specific put and call options on given shares of stock. The arrangements were very flexible and also somewhat disorganized. An investor who wanted to buy an option on a stock would go to one of these dealers and indicate the stock involved and the time period he was interested in. The dealer would find an interested seller, and the parties would then negotiate individually on the price of the options. Because secondary trading in options was limited, it was usually difficult to sell an option prior to maturity.

The environment changed dramatically when the CBOE was established on April 26, 1973, and began trading options on 16 stocks. Among the numerous innovations were

1. *The creation of a central marketplace* with regulatory surveillance, disclosure, and price dissemination capabilities.
2. *The introduction of a Clearing Corporation* as the guarantor of every CBOE option. Standing as the opposite party to every trade, the Clearing Corporation enables buyers and sellers of options to terminate their positions in the market at any time by making an offsetting transaction.
3. *The standardization of expiration dates* (most CBOE options expire in January, April, July, and October, and others expire in February, May, August, and November) and *the standardization of exercise prices* (the prices per share at which the stock can be acquired upon exercise of the option).
4. *The creation of a secondary market.* While an option is a contract guaranteeing the owner the right to buy or sell stock at the agreed upon price, the majority of option buyers sell their options on the exchange either for a profit or to reduce loss. Before option exchanges were established, the buyers and sellers of OTC options were essentially committed to their positions until the expiration date if the option was not exercised.

OPERATION OF THE CBOE

Readers are well aware of how a market is made on the New York and other stock exchanges. The specialist is at the center of the stock market and has two functions: (1) as a broker who maintains the limit-order book and (2) as a market-maker who buys and sells for his own account to ensure the operation of a "fair and orderly" market for investors. Recall the concern because the specialists had monopoly information from the limit-order book and also a monopoly position as the sole market-maker in certain securities. One might, therefore, expect stock exchange specialists to derive above-average returns, which they do.

Apparently the CBOE was aware of the potential problems of the stock exchange arrangement and attempted to avoid them. The limit-order book on the CBOE is handled by an individual (a *board broker*) who is not a market-maker, so the two functions are separate. The board broker handles the limit-order book and accepts only public orders on the book. In addition, *the limit-order book is public!* Above the trading post there is a video screen that gives figures for the last trade, the current bid and ask price for each of the options, and the limit orders on the book. The other major difference is that *there are competing market-makers for all options.* These members can trade only for themselves and are not allowed to handle public orders. As an example, there are four members of the CBOE who are specifically designated as primary market-makers for IBM options.

Each of the market-makers is assigned three or four *primary* options and another three or four options for which they are *secondary* market-makers. They are required to concentrate 70 percent of their trading activity in their primary issues. Similar to the stock exchange specialist, they are expected to provide liquidity for individual and institutional investors.

Table 22.1
Options Listed on Exchanges (As of July 1988)

Exchange	Starting Date	Number of Stocks
Chicago Board Option Exchange (CBOE)	April 26, 1973	192
American Stock Exchange	January 13, 1975	125
Philadelphia Exchange	June 29, 1975	85
Pacific Exchange	April 9, 1976	95
Midwest Exchange	December 10, 1976	a
New York Stock Exchange	February 13, 1985	20
Total		517

a Merged with CBOE on June 2, 1980.

Given the existence of several market-makers for each option, one would expect more funds to be available for trading. One would also expect superior markets because of the added competition.

The third category of CBOE members are floor brokers who execute all types of orders for their customers. These floor brokers are very similar to the floor brokers on stock exchanges.

VOLUME OF TRADING

The CBOE started with options on 16 stocks. This number was gradually increased, and other exchanges were established during 1975 and 1976, as shown in Table 22.1. As of late 1988, the various exchanges combined had call options for 517 stocks. As of June 1, 1977, the SEC allowed trading in put options followed by a "freeze" between 1977 and 1980. There are currently put options on all stocks with call options.

As you might expect, the options are on stocks of large companies that enjoy active secondary markets. In fact, the criterion for listing an option is the trading activity of the underlying stock. The growth in trading volume has been phenomenal. During the first full month of trading on the CBOE (May 1973), the number of contracts traded totaled about 31,000. By mid-1988, the total number traded on the four exchanges for each month consistently exceeded 13 million. The annual totals are contained in Table 22.2, along with a breakdown for the individual exchanges. As shown, the trading volume in call options is substantially larger than the volume of put options because of the tendency of investors to buy long rather than sell short (i.e., the purchase of a call is based upon a bullish outlook, while you would buy a put if you were bearish on a stock).

The exchange breakdown reflects the initial dominance of the CBOE. Following the initial dominance, the proportion on the CBOE has declined even after the merger with the Midwest Exchange. While still the largest, the CBOE is more dominant in the trading of index options, as shown in Table 22.3.

TABLE 22.2
Number of Put and Call Contracts Traded and Percent of Contracts Traded

	A. CALL CONTRACTS (THOUSANDS)											
	CBOE		AMEX		PHILADELPHIA		PACIFIC		MIDWEST[a]		NYSE	
YEAR	No.	%	No.	%	No.	%	No.	%	No.	%	No.	%	TOTAL
1977	23,581	63.0	9,655	25.8	2,002	5.3	1,704	4.6	497	1.3			37,441
1978	30,298	58.7	13,540	26.1	2,974	5.7	2,325	5.6	2,041	3.9			50,661
1979	10,123	53.5	16,505	29.5	4,527	8.1	3,118	5.6	1,847	3.3			56,120
1980	42,942	53.5	24,955	31.3	6,705	8.3	4,410	5.5	1,111	1.4			80,123
1981	40,801	50.4	26,430	32.7	8,104	10.0	5,610	6.9	a	a			80,945
1982	50,225	53.2	27,665	29.3	9,880	10.5	6,668	7.1	a	a			94,438
1983	52,595	55.2	26,599	25.4	12,085	11.1	8,255	7.9	a	a			99,535
1984	42,938	49.0	24,721	28.2	11,348	12.9	8,627	9.8	a	a			87,634
1985	44,009	48.1	27,979	30.6	9,668	10.6	9,748	10.7	a	a	126	0.1	91,529
1986	50,023	44.3	38,232	33.9	12,521	11.1	11,215	9.9	a	a	951	0.8	112,942
1987	56,424	43.6	42,381	32.8	14,909	11.5	14,630	11.3	a	a	1,041	0.8	129,384

	B. PUT CONTRACTS (THOUSANDS)											
	CBOE		AMEX		PHILADELPHIA		PACIFIC		MIDWEST[a]		NYSE	
YEAR	No.	%	No.	%	No.	%	No.	%	No.	%	No.	%	TOTAL
1977	1,257	57.2	423	19.3	192	8.7	222	10.1	103	4.7			2,197
1978	3,979	63.7	841	13.5	316	4.7	640	10.2	489	7.8			6,279
1979	5,250	64.6	961	11.9	423	5.2	736	9.0	736	9.4			8,133
1980	9,975	60.0	4,093	24.7	1,053	6.3	1,076	6.5	408	2.5			16,605
1981	16,783	59.0	8,430	29.6	1,906	6.7	1,343	4.7	a	a			28,462
1982	25,511	60.0	11,102	25.9	3,587	8.4	2,642	6.2	a	a			42,842
1983	19,101	59.1	9,601	23.1	4,522	10.9	2,900	7.0	a	a			36,124
1984	15,737	50.3	8,356	26.7	4,634	14.8	2,564	8.2	a	a			31,291
1985	13,515	50.0	8,124	30.7	2,397	8.9	2,953	10.9	a	a	37	0.1	27,027
1986	14,722	50.8	8,909	30.7	2,534	8.7	2,726	9.4	a	a	99	0.3	28,989
1987	16,891	48.2	10,389	29.6	3,180	9.1	4,322	12.3	a	a	265	0.8	35,048

[a] Midwest Options Exchange merged with CBOE on June 2, 1980.

Source: Option Clearing Corporation.

COMPETING MARKETS FOR OPTIONS

When the AMEX established trading in options in January 1975, it was with 15 stocks that were not traded on the CBOE. The point is, originally there was a conscious effort by the exchanges to refrain from establishing competing markets. This practice continued when the Philadelphia Exchange began trading in options, but it changed in late 1976, when the AMEX established a market in MGIC, which was then traded on the CBOE. In February 1977 the AMEX started a market in National Semiconductor, a very active issue on the CBOE. In response, the CBOE began trading in six AMEX issues: Merrill Lynch, Digital Equipment, Burroughs, Disney, DuPont, and Tandy. The competition appeared to reduce the spread for these issues and increase their liquidity. Members of both exchanges attempted to draw volume in the competitive issues because many brokerage

TABLE 22.3
Number of Index Option Contracts Traded on Different Exchanges (thousands)

	CBOE		AMEX		PHILADELPHIA		PACIFIC		NYSE		TOTAL
YEAR	NUMBER	PERCENT	NUMBER	PERCENT	NUMBER	PERCENT	NUMBER	PERCENT	NUMBER	PERCENT	NUMBER
1983	10,661	76.1	2,693	19.2	6	0.0	[a]	[a]	656	4.7	14,016
1984	64,357	84.9	7,006	9.2	127	0.2	175	0.2	4,094	5.4	75,759
1985	90,822	82.5	12,438	11.3	2,321	2.1	93	0.1	4,213	3.9	110,044[b]
1986	114,835	82.9	18,275	13.2	1,399	1.0	134	0.1	3,774	2.7	138,461[b]
1987	108,352	83.5	18,153	14.0	499	0.4	459	0.4	2,193	1.7	129,696

[a] Trading initiated during 1984.
[b] Totals not equal to components due to minor trading on NASD in 1985 and 1986.
Source: Option Clearing Corporation.

houses did not check both markets when placing an order but selected one of them as the "primary" exchange for an issue and channelled all orders for the issue to the designated exchange.

Following a freeze on new listings from 1977 to 1980, when new issues were allowed there were no further competing issues. The SEC ruled in February 1985 that the NYSE could begin trading options, and the NYSE initiated trading by the end of the second quarter. Notably, the NYSE did not ask for multiple trading when they requested permission to trade options. By July 1988 there were 20 options trading on the NYSE.

OPTIONS TERMINOLOGY

Given the unique nature of the options market, it is hardly surprising to find that it has developed its own terminology.

OPTION PREMIUM

The price paid for the option itself is the *option premium*. It is what a buyer must pay for the ability to acquire the stock at a given price during some period in the future. The average premium on a newly issued option when the market price of the stock in question is close to the option price is typically about 10 percent of the value of the stock. As an example, the premium on a six-month option to buy a stock for $30, when the stock is selling for about $30, would be about $3. We will study the components that affect this premium in detail later in the chapter.

The standard *option contract* is for 100 shares of a common stock referred to as the *underlying security*. As an example, a call option contract on IBM would be an option to buy 100 shares of IBM common stock. The price in the financial press is a per share price.

EXERCISE PRICE

The price at which the stock can be acquired is the *exercise price*, or *striking price*. As an example, if the stock is currently selling for $38 a share, the option may specify an exercise price of $40, meaning that the holder of the option can buy the stock for $40 a share for the duration of the option. The intervals for exercise prices are determined by the price of the stock involved. For stocks selling under $100, the exercise prices are set at $5 intervals (e.g., $35, $40, $45). For stocks selling for over $100, they are set at $10 intervals (e.g., $110, $120, $130). The initial exercise prices are set at the interval closest to the current market price of the stock. In a case of a stock selling for $43 at the time the option is established, the exercise price would be set at $45. If the stock declines to $41 a share, another option would be established at $40 a share. In contrast, if the price increased to $48 a share, an option would be established at $50. Therefore, when a stock has options at numerous prices, this indicates that the stock's price has moved over a wide range during the recent past.

EXPIRATION DATE   The date on which the option expires, or the last date on which it can be exercised, is the *expiration date*. In July the exchange might establish a September option, which means that the holder of this option can purchase the stock at the striking price at any time between July and September when the option expires. The expiration dates are designated by month, while the actual date of expiration is *the Saturday following the third Friday of each month that is specified.* A September option would expire on the close of business on the Saturday following the third Friday in September. Actual trading in the option would cease at the close of the market on the third Friday.

IN-, OUT OF-, OR AT-THE-MONEY OPTIONS   An *in-the-money option* is an option with a market price for the stock that is in excess of the exercise price for the option. Assume that the exercise price of an option was $30 and the stock was currently selling for $34 a share. This would be an in-the-money option, meaning that the market price ($34) exceeded the exercise price ($30) and so the option had an intrinsic value of $4 a share. An *out-of-the-money option* has an exercise price above the market price for the stock. An example would be an option with an exercise price of $30 for a stock that is currently selling at $22 a share. In this instance, an investor may be willing to pay something for the option based on the *possibility* of the stock price increasing. The option itself has no intrinsic value, because it provides the ability to buy a stock for $30 a share at a time when it is possible to buy the stock in the open market at only $22. The price you are willing to pay for an out-of-the-money option is referred to as its *time value,* because you are paying for the ability to acquire the stock at this price for the remaining time to maturity. Finally, an *at-the-money option* is one with a striking price approximately equal to the market price for the stock.

A SAMPLE QUOTATION   Referring to Figure 22.1, assume that in July 1988 you were considering acquiring a call option in Bethlehem Steel (Beth S). As shown in the right column, the stock is currently priced at 24 1/4. The arrow (1) indicates that you could buy a "Bethlehem August 22 1/2" for 2 3/8. This means that you would pay $2.375 a share for the right to buy a share of Bethlehem Steel at $22.50 a share between the time of the purchase and the expiration

FIGURE 22.1
Listed Option Quotations from *The Wall Street Journal*, July 27, 1988

LISTED OPTIONS QUOTATIONS

Tuesday, July 26, 1988

Options closing prices. Sales unit usually is 100 shares.
Stock close is New York or American exchange final price.

CHICAGO BOARD

Option & NY Close	Strike Price	Calls—Last Aug	Calls—Last Sep	Calls—Last Oct	Puts—Last Aug	Puts—Last Sep	Puts—Last Oct
Alcoa	50	1 7/8	2 3/4	3 3/4	r	2	2 3/8
50 7/8	55	3/8	5/8	1 5/8	r	r	r
AmGenl	30	r	1 1/16	1 1/2	r	r	r
AT&T	25	1 5/8	2	2 1/8	1/8	1/4	1/2
26 1/4	30	1/16	1/8	1/4	r	r	3 3/4
26 1/4	35	s	s	1/16	s	s	r
Amrtch	85	4 1/8	r	r	3/16	r	r
89	90	r	2 1/8	2 1/2	r	2 1/2	r
89	95	r	r	7/8	r	r	r
Atl R	75	r	r	7 1/2	5/16	r	r
81 1/8	80	2 1/8	r	r	r	r	r
81 1/8	85	3/8	1	1 5/8	4 1/2	r	5 1/2
Avon	20	s	s	5 1/4	s	s	r
25	25	5/8	1 1/8	1 1/2	1/2	7/8	1 3/8
25	30	r	3/16	5/16	r	r	r
BankAm	10	r	s	3 3/4	r	s	r
13 1/2	12 1/2	1 3/16	r	1 3/4	3/16	r	1/2
13 1/2	15	1/8	7/16	11/16	r	r	r
BattlM	15	1 3/8	r	2	r	r	1/2
16	17 1/2	r	1/2	3/4	1 7/16	r	r
16	20	r	s	5/16	r	s	r
BearSt	12 1/2	5/16	r	13/16	r	r	1
12 3/8	15	1/16	r	r	3	r	r
BellAtl	70	7/8	r	2	r	r	r
68 3/4	75	r	5/16	9/16	r	r	r
Beth S	20	r	s	4 7/8	r	s	r
(1) → 24 1/4	22 1/2	2 3/8	r	3	7/16	r	7/8
24 1/4	25	13/16	1 3/8	1 11/16	1 1/4	r	2
24 1/4	30	1/4	3/8	5/8	r	r	r
Bolar	22 1/2	r	r	r	r	3/4	r
24 1/8	25	r	1 3/8	2	r	2 1/4	2 1/2
24 1/8	30	r	r	r	r	5 5/8	r

PACIFIC

Option & NY Close	Strike Price	Calls—Last Aug	Calls—Last Sep	Calls—Last Oct	Puts—Last Aug	Puts—Last Sep	Puts—Last Oct
A M D	10	s	s	4	s	s	1/8
13 5/8	12 1/2	1 3/8	1 3/4	2	3/16	r	9/16
13 5/8	15	1/4	1/2	3/4	1 1/2	1 5/8	r
13 5/8	17 1/2	r	3/16	1/4	r	r	r
Alza	25	1/2	r	1 1/2	r	r	r
AmPres	30	1/4	7/8	1 3/8	r	r	r
28 1/2	35	1/8	1/4	1/2	r	r	r
AmesDS	15	2 1/4	2	2 1/4	r	r	r
16 3/8	17 1/2	5/16	s	7/8	1 1/8	s	1 1/2
16 3/8	20	s	s	1/2	s	s	r
AshTat	20	4	r	4 3/4	1/4	1/2	r
23 3/4	22 1/2	2	r	2 7/8	1/2	1 1/2	1 9/16
23 3/4	25	3/4	1 1/4	1 7/8	2	r	2 7/8
23 3/4	30	r	r	9/16	r	r	r
BakrHu	20	s	s	1/16	s	s	r
BkrsTr	30	r	s	r	r	s	1/4
36	35	1 5/8	r	r	1/2	r	r
36	40	1/16	r	r	4	r	r
Benfcl	50	r	r	1/4	r	r	r
Borden	45	5 7/8	s	r	r	s	r
50 5/8	50	1 5/8	r	3	r	r	1 5/8
50 5/8	55	1/8	1/4	3/4	r	r	r

AMERICAN

Option & NY Close	Strike Price	Calls—Last Aug	Calls—Last Sep	Calls—Last Oct	Puts—Last Aug	Puts—Last Sep	Puts—Last Oct
Aetna	40	4 1/2	4 3/4	r	r	r	5/16
44 1/8	45	1/2	r	1 7/16	1	r	1 1/2
Ahman	15	r	r	1 1/16	1/2	r	7/8
15 1/4	17 1/2	r	r	1/4	r	r	r
AlaskA	17 1/2	r	r	r	3/16	r	3/4
18 1/8	20	3/16	3/8	3/4	r	r	r
ABrrck	17 1/2	r	r	1 7/8	r	5/16	9/16
18 7/8	20	3/16	5/16	3/4	1 1/8	r	r
18 7/8	22 1/2	r	r	3/8	r	r	r
Am Cya	40	s	s	r	s	s	3/16
50 1/8	45	5 1/2	r	r	1/8	r	r
50 1/8	50	1 5/8	2 1/2	3 5/8	1 1/2	r	r
50 1/8	55	1/2	1	1 5/8	r	r	r
50 1/8	60	1/4	s	1	r	s	r
Am Exp	22 1/2	s	s	r	s	s	3/16
26 5/8	25	2 1/8	2 5/8	2 7/8	r	r	5/8
26 5/8	30	1/8	1/4	9/16	r	r	r
Am Hom	75	5/8	r	1 5/8	r	r	3
73 3/8	80	r	s	1/2	r	s	r
Amgen	25	r	r	4	1/2	r	1 1/2
27 1/4	30	r	r	1 1/2	3 5/8	r	r
27 1/4	35	s	s	3/4	s	s	r
Apollo	7 1/2	r	r	r	r	r	5/16
9 5/8	10	5/16	5/8	1 1/16	r	r	1
9 5/8	12 1/2	r	r	7/16	3	r	r
9 5/8	15	r	s	3/16	r	s	r
9 5/8	17 1/2	1/8	s	r	r	s	r
Apple	35	s	s	8 3/4	s	s	1/4
42 3/4	40	3 1/4	4 1/4	5	3/8	3/4	1 3/16
(2) → 42 3/4	45	11/16	1 1/2	2 1/8	2 1/2	2 7/8	3 1/4
42 3/4	50	1/16	1/4	13/16	r	r	r

PHILADELPHIA

Option & NY Close	Strike Price	Calls—Last Aug	Calls—Last Sep	Calls—Last Oct	Puts—Last Aug	Puts—Last Sep	Puts—Last Oct
Ashl O	70	3 3/4	4 1/2	r	r	r	r
72 3/4	75	1 1/2	2	r	r	r	r
72 3/4	80	r	r	1 7/8	r	r	r
Bard	40	r	r	3 3/4	3/8	r	r
42 7/8	45	3/8	r	r	r	r	r
CdnPac	20	r	r	1/2	1 3/4	r	1 3/4
CharmS	17 1/2	r	r	1/4	r	r	r
Clorox	30	r	1/2	13/16	r	r	r
Coleco	5	s	s	1/16	s	s	r
Comsat	30	1/4	r	r	r	r	r
Conrail	25	r	r	6 3/4	r	r	r
31 3/8	30	1 3/4	r	r	r	r	r
31 3/8	35	r	r	1/2	r	r	r
DomRs	45	r	r	1/4	r	r	r
Dressr	30	r	r	2	5/8	r	1 1/2
30 1/4	35	r	r	5/8	r	r	r
Duk Pw	45	r	3/4	r	r	r	1 5/8
Eas Gs	25	r	r	1/2	r	r	r
FtExec	10	1 5/8	r	1 3/4	r	r	r
11 1/2	12 1/2	r	3/16	5/16	r	r	1 3/8
11 1/2	15	r	r	1/8	r	r	r
G A F	40	r	r	r	r	1/2	3/4
45 5/8	45	1 1/2	2 1/2	3 1/8	3/4	r	r
45 5/8	50	r	9/16	3/4	r	r	r
GaPac	35	r	r	3	r	r	3/4
36 3/4	40	r	r	7/8	r	r	r
Honda	115	s	s	62 3/4	s	s	r
177	120	r	s	57 1/4	r	s	1 1/8
177	125	52 3/8	s	53 1/4	r	s	r
177	130	r	s	r	r	s	1 3/4
177	135	43	43 5/8	44	1/4	1	2 7/8

NEW YORK

Option & NY Close	Strike Price	Calls—Last Aug	Calls—Last Sep	Calls—Last Oct	Puts—Last Aug	Puts—Last Sep	Puts—Last Oct
Chubb	50	r	r	r	3/8	r	r
53	55	r	r	1 7/8	r	r	r
ImpCh	75	r	3/4	r	r	r	r
IrvBk	60	8 1/2	s	r	r	s	3/4
68	65	3 3/4	r	r	r	r	r
68	70	15/16	1 7/8	3	r	r	r
68	75	r	r	1 1/2	r	r	r
Maytag	20	3 1/8	r	r	1/16	r	r
23	22 1/2	1 3/8	1 7/8	2 1/8	3/4	1 1/4	1 1/2
(3) → 23	25	1/2	1	1 3/8	r	2 3/4	r
23	30	3/16	s	1/2	r	s	r
Nynex	60	4 1/4	r	r	r	r	r
63 7/8	65	r	1 3/8	1 1/2	1 3/8	r	r
PhilNV	17 1/2	r	r	3/4	r	r	r
Telerte	15	r	r	r	r	r	5/8
15 3/4	17 1/2	r	r	5/8	r	r	r

Option & NY Close	Strike Price	Calls—Last Aug	Calls—Last Sep	Calls—Last Nov	Puts—Last Aug	Puts—Last Sep	Puts—Last Nov
CSoup	25	13/16	r	1 7/8	r	r	r
25	30	1/16	1/8	r	r	r	r
FMC Cp	35	r	r	3 3/8	15/16	1 1/2	r
35 1/4	40	3/8	3/8	1 1/4	r	r	r

Source: Listed Options Quotations, *The Wall Street Journal*, July 27, 1988.

of the option during the third week in August. This is an in-the-money option; it has an intrinsic value of 1 3/4. If you wanted an option that expired in October 1988, it would cost $3 a share; the extra $0.625 is the time value cost of the additional two months.

You could also acquire an "Apple Computer September 45" on the American Exchange (arrow 2) for 1 1/2 ($1.50) a share. This is an out-of-the-money option, because the option exercise price of $45 exceeds the current market price of $42.75. Investors apparently are willing to pay a *speculative value* of $1.50 based upon an expectation that the price of Apple Computer will exceed $45 by the third week in September.

It is also possible to buy or sell a put option in all of these stocks. As an example, consider the Maytag options listed on the New York Exchange. In this case, all those with prices below $23 are out-of-the-money, and there are in-the-money puts at $25 and $30. If we consider the $25 put option (arrow 3), it is in-the-money, because it allows the owner to sell a stock with a market value of $23 for $25. Its intrinsic value is therefore $2.00, and the September put is selling for $2.75. Again, a longer-term put option would have greater time value—if an October put had traded, it would have a price above $2.75.

ALTERNATIVE TRADING STRATEGIES

With the introduction of put options, the number of strategies available to an investor has become enormous, and the range of complexity is substantial. In this section, we will not attempt to cover all the strategies but will limit our discussion to the major alternatives and refer you to articles and books that describe the more sophisticated techniques. Most trading involves the basic strategies discussed in this chapter. Also, to understand the more sophisticated strategies, you must understand the basic techniques, because the more advanced methods build upon these.

BUYING CALL OPTIONS

Investors buy call options because they expect the price of the underlying stock to increase during the period prior to the expiration of the option. Given this expectation, the purchase of an option will yield a large return on a small dollar investment. Several alternatives are available in terms of the exercise price relative to the market price. You can purchase an out-of-the-money option, an at-the-money option, or an in-the-money option. Probably the riskiest is an out-of-the-money option, because it is clearly possible to lose the premium paid if the stock price does not rise sufficiently. At the same time, the rate of return can be very large, and the initial investment is the lowest of the three alternatives.

Consider the following example of an at-the-money option (without taking commissions or taxes into account):[1] In July, when Avon is selling for $25 a share, assume that an Avon October 25 call option is selling for $2 a share. If you expect an increase in the price of Avon during the next

---

[1] In all these examples, we ignore commissions and taxes to simplify the computations. This allows us to concentrate on the major impact but is not intended to deemphasize the importance of these factors in the ultimate investment decision.

FIGURE 22.2
Profits to Buyer of Call Option

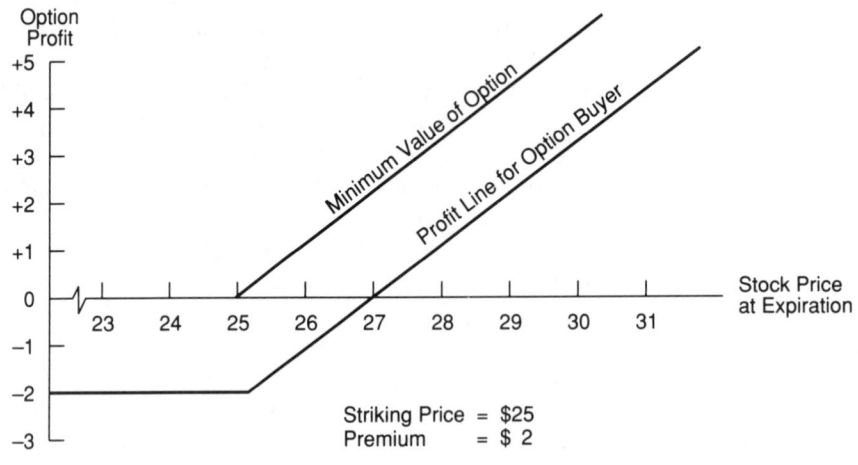

three months, you would pay $200 for the option. Figure 22.2 indicates your situation at the expiration of the option. If the stock stays at $25 or less, the option will have no intrinsic value, but it will rise in a linear fashion beyond this point. For you to recoup your premium, the price must rise to at least $27. If you are correct, and Avon stock goes to $30 (a 20 percent increase in the price of the stock) within this period, the option will become an in-the-money option and have an intrinsic value of $5. At this point, you could sell the option for $500 and enjoy a 150 percent increase on the option during a period when the increase in stock price was only 20 percent.

This comparison of returns reflects the leverage available in options. If the stock price never got above 25, the option would be worthless when it expired, and you would lose the full $200. Alternatively, as shown in Figure 22.2, the stock price would have to get to $27 a share before you would break even. Note that your maximum loss would be $200 irrespective of what happened to the stock, which indicates another major advantage to call options (besides leverage)—loss limit. The point is, an option is a right, not an obligation, which means that you cannot be forced to exercise the option, and therefore you cannot lose more than the premium (and transaction costs).

You could also acquire an in-the-money option on the stock. This differs from the at-the-money or out-of-the-money option in that a larger investment is required, because the option has an intrinsic value and a time value. Also, it does not have as much potential leverage. At the same time, the price of the underlying stock does not have to increase much for you to enjoy a return. Assume that in July, when Avon stock is selling for 25, you buy an Avon October 20 at 5 1/4. This option has an intrinsic value of $5 and a time (speculative) value of $0.25. In the near future, assume the stock goes to $29. The option will then have an intrinsic value of $9; and, even if the time value declines to 1/8 (0.125), the option should be selling for $9.125. Therefore, on a 16 percent increase in the stock price (29 versus 25), the option price increased by 73.8 percent (9.125 versus 5.25). If the stock price declined to below 20, you would lose the full $5.25/share investment. If the price declined from the current price of 25, but was still above 20, the option would have its intrinsic value at expiration, and your loss would be figured accordingly.

WRITING COVERED CALL OPTIONS[2]

In contrast to buying call options, you can write call options. An option writer enters into a contract to deliver 100 shares of a stock at a predetermined exercise price during some specified time interval. When a writer enters into such a contract (that is, *sells a call*), he can either own the stock (sell a *covered option*) or not own the stock (sell an *uncovered,* or *naked option*). The option writer is typically looking for extra income from the stock (the premium he receives). The premium also provides some downward protection as an offset to a price decline in the underlying stock. At the same time, the option writer gives up *some upside potential* on the stock if the stock price rises above the exercise price and is called away.

Assume that in June you acquired 100 shares of Ford Motor stock at $55 a share. You could sell a Ford October 60 call for about $2 a share (sell a *covered call option*). This would give you extra income ($200) or you could consider it as downside protection because your net price is now $53 ($55 minus $2). If the stock does not change price between June and October (approximately four months), you have an additional $200 that you would not have had otherwise (a 3.6 percent return during the four-month period). If the stock increased to 61 and is called away at $60 a share, you have sold it at a profit of $5 per share, and you still have the premium. Your return (before dividends) during the period was $7 (a $2 premium plus the $5 capital gain), which would be 12.7 percent for the four months (7/55). As noted, if the stock goes to $65, you have given up the gain above $60 because of the option. Therefore, you are protected on the downside by the lower net price, but also restricted on the upside by the exercise price. As a result, the distribution of potential returns is more restricted and has lower variance than the distributions of returns for the stock alone. If an option writer wants to get out of his contract, all he has to do is *buy* a comparable call option on the exchange, and the two contracts cancel each other. This is referred to as a *closing purchase transaction,* which liquidates the previous option sold.

Figure 22.3 illustrates the profit potential for the seller of a call option. Note that there is a loss at prices above 62, because this reflects the $200 premium received. In the case of a covered call, it is an opportunity loss, because you receive only $60 for the stock whereas you could have re-

---

[2] For further readable discussions of writing strategies, see *The Merrill Lynch Guide to Writing Options* (New York: Merrill Lynch, Pierce, Fenner, and Smith, 1981); and *Call Option Writing Strategies* (Chicago: The Chicago Board Options Exchange, 1985).

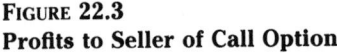

FIGURE 22.3
Profits to Seller of Call Option

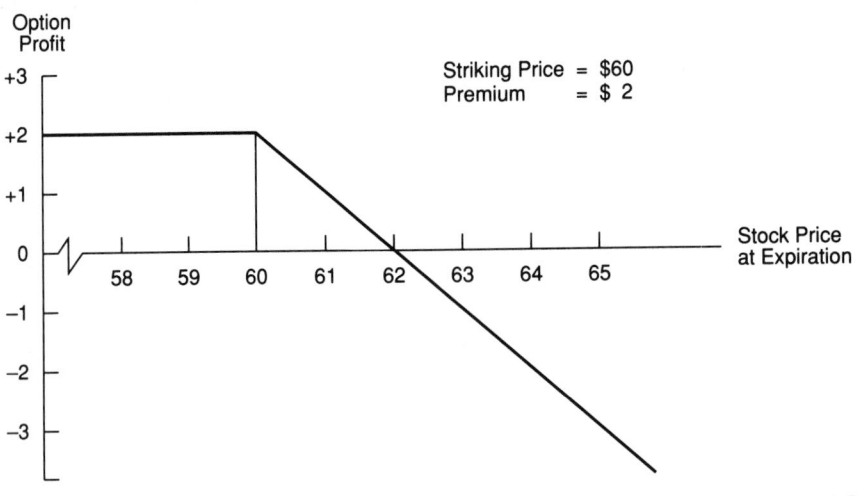

ceived more than this if you had not sold the call. In the case of selling a naked call, the loss is very real and is unlimited, because you must go into the market and buy the stock that is to be delivered.

WRITING OPTIONS IN DIFFERENT MARKETS. Your option-writing strategy should differ depending upon your outlook for the market environment (stable, rising, declining) and your outlook for the stock. If the market is *very stable,* you would simply continue to sell options over time as a supplement to dividend income. The only unique aspect of this arrangement would be that if it is an out-of-the-money option or at-the-money option, you should consider closing out your position (buying an option to offset your written option) prior to expiration so you can sell another one sooner. This action assumes that the option price gets pretty low near its maturity because it has no intrinsic value and its time value declines.

Alternatively, assume that the stock price increases because of a market rise or for internal reasons. In this instance, you must decide whether you want to continue to own the stock or let it be called away. Assume you bought the stock at $45, sold a $50 option, and the stock subsequently went to $52. If you are satisfied with the $5 capital gain plus the premium received, you would allow the stock to be called away and would put the money into another stock. But if you think there is further potential in the stock, you would have to evaluate whether to buy back your option with a strike price of $50 (based upon its price when the stock is selling for $52) and sell another at $55. You would lose on the repurchase of the first option, but you would make up some part of this loss on the sale of the second option, and you would still own the stock. As always, the decision would depend upon your valuation of the two options relative to their market prices.

OPTION SPREADS   In contrast to simply buying or selling a call option, it is possible to enter into a spread and thus do both. The purpose is to reduce the risk of a long or a short position in the option for a stock. There are two basic types of spread. A *price spread* (or *vertical spread*) involves buying the call option for a given stock, time, and price, and selling a call option for the same stock and time period, but at a different price (e.g., buy a Ford October 50 and sell a Ford October 60). A *time spread* (or *horizontal spread*) involves buying and selling an option for the same stock and price, but the time differs (e.g., buying a Ford October 50 and selling a Ford January 50).

BULLISH SPREADS. You would consider bullish spreads if you were generally bullish on the underlying stock but you want to be conservative in the execution of your policy. Assume you are optimistic regarding the outlook for Ford (currently selling for 55) and want to enter into a price spread that will reduce the risk of such a transaction. The situation is as follows regarding October options (numbers rounded):

- Ford 50 October 7
- Ford 60 October 2

Because you are bullish, you would buy the Ford 50 and sell the Ford 60 for a net cost of 5 ($500), which is also your maximum loss. Assuming you were correct, and the stock goes from 55 to 65, the October 50 would be worth about 15 (only its intrinsic value) and the October 60 would sell for about 6 (a slight premium over intrinsic value). If you closed out both positions, you would obtain the following results:

- October 50: bought at 7, sold at 15 = gain 8
- October 60: sold at 2, bought at 6 = loss 4
- Overall = gain 4

If the stock had declined dramatically, your maximum loss would have been $500, even though both options were worthless when they expired. You should recognize that your maximum gain was also $500. Specifically, at some high stock price, the difference in the value of the options will be 10, which indicates a gross profit of $1,000 less the $500 initial cost.

BEARISH SPREADS. If you are generally bearish on a stock or the market and want to take action based upon your expectation using a conservative strategy, you would buy the higher-priced option and sell the lower-priced option. Returning to Ford, you would

- Sell the October 50 at 7
- Buy the October 60 at 2

This would generate an immediate gain of $500. If you are correct, and the stock of Ford declines to below 50, both options will be worthless when they expire, and you will have the $500 return. In contrast, if the stock goes to 65 as discussed under the bullish spread, the results would be as follows:

- October 50: sold at 7, bought at 15 = loss 8
- October 60: bought at 2, sold at 6 = gain 4
- Overall = loss 4

The loss of $400 compares favorably with possible loss of $800 (or much more) if you did not have some offset from the spread. At some very high price for the stock, the two options will have a difference of 10, so your maximum loss is $500 (a $1,000 gross loss less a $500 gain on the original transaction).

There are numerous other potential transactions for almost any possible set of risk-return desires. The purpose of this discussion has been to introduce you to the basic transactions used in other strategies.[3]

BUYING PUT OPTIONS

There are several major reasons for acquiring a put option on a stock. The most obvious is that you expect a particular stock to decline in price and you want to profit from this decline. As will be shown, the purchase of a put option allows you to do this with the benefits of leverage, and yet it limits the potential loss if your expectations regarding a price decline in the stock are wrong. In addition, put options can be useful if you own a stock and do not want to sell it at the present time, although you feel it might decline in the near term. In this latter case, you can buy a put option on the stock you own as a *hedge* against the decline; you will offset the decline in the stock with an increase in value of the put option. Finally, you might want to acquire a very volatile stock with a good long-term outlook. While you feel confident of the long-run result, you are uncertain about what might happen in the near term. In such a case, you could acquire the stock and also buy a put option for the short term. If there is near-term weakness in the stock, you would make money on the put as an offset to the stock decline.

Consider an example of a standard put acquisition. As of December, General Motors stock is selling for $82, but you feel it could decline. A June 80 put option for GM is selling for $3. Assume you purchase this option, and by March GM stock declines to $74. At this time, your put option will have a minimum value of $6 (80 − 74) and probably some value above this, because there are still three months remaining before it expires. Assuming a price of 7, you could sell it and realize a *gain* of $4 (before commission), which is a 133 percent return on the option [(7 − 3)/3] during a period when the stock *declined* by 9.8 percent (8/82). Alternatively, assume that the stock did not decline below 80, or, in fact,

[3] A more extensive discussion is contained in George M. Frankfurter, Richard Stevenson, and Allan Young, "Option Spreading: Theory and an Illustration," *Journal of Portfolio Management* 5, no. 4 (Summer 1979): 59–63; and in M. J. Gombola, R. Roenfeldt, and P. L. Cooley, "Spreading Strategies in CBOE Options: Evidence on Market Performance," *Journal of Financial Research* 1, no. 1 (Winter 1978): 35–44.

FIGURE 22.4
Profit Line for Buyer of Put Option

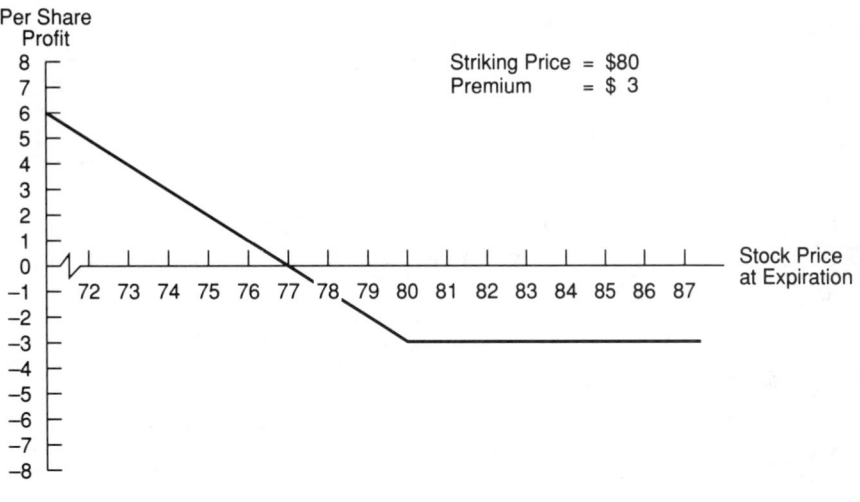

increased in price. In this instance the put option would expire worthless, and your loss would be limited to the $300 you paid for the option.

Figure 22.4 shows the profit picture for the buyer of a put option at expiration. Note that at prices above $80, the option would expire worthless, and you would lose $300; at prices below $77, you would have gains in excess of the cost of the option. Besides the substantial leverage involved, it is important to recognize the lower capital commitment involved and also the lower commission for this technique compared to short selling given a bearish outlook. Also, the limited loss characteristic of options is very relevant.

Assume the same set of events, except that you owned the stock at $82 and thought it might experience some near-term weakness, but you did not want to sell it and then buy it back again. In this instance, if the stock declined to 74, you would have experienced an $800 loss in the value of your stock position; but if you had acquired the put option as a hedge, you would have experienced a net gain of $400 on the put option as discussed above as a partial offset.

SELLING PUT OPTIONS

When you sell (write) a put option, you become obligated to buy a stock at a specified price during some time period. For accepting this obligation, you receive a premium. An obvious reason for writing such an option is to increase the return on your portfolio during a period when you expect stock prices to rise. As an example, assume that currently Eastman Kodak (EK) stock is 49, and you expect the stock price to rise over the next six months. An EK six-month put of 50 is priced at 3. If you sell this put option,

FIGURE 22.5
Profit Line for Seller of Put Option

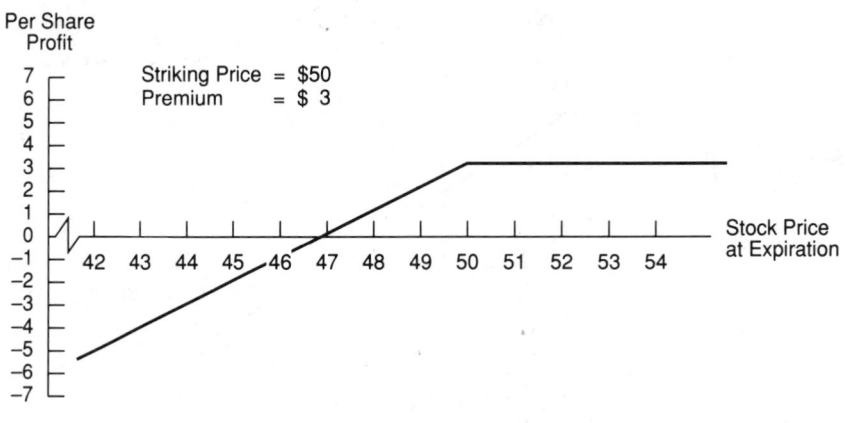

you receive a $300 premium, and if the stock goes to 55 as you expect, the put option expires worthless, and you have the extra $300 in addition to the capital appreciation.

In contrast, if EK declines to 45, the put option may go to about 6, if there is any time left (it has an intrinsic value of 5). In this example, you will lose $300 (the $600 cost of the option less the $300 premium received for selling the option) if you buy it back at this time. Alternatively, you may be called upon to actually buy 100 shares of EK at 50, which entails paying $5,000 for stock worth $4,500 before commissions. Figure 22.5 shows the profit related to this sale of a put option at expiration.

Another interesting strategy is to sell a put option as a means of acquiring stock that you want at a price below the current market price. Rather than placing a limit buy order below the market, you can sell a put option at a striking price below the current market price. As an example, assume you want to buy IBM, but you think it is a little too high at its current price of 125. You can sell an IBM 120 put option due in about six months for 2. If the stock declines to below 120 as you expect, you will be called upon to buy 100 shares of IBM at 120. Note that your *effective cost* will be 118 because of the premium you received. The outcome is that you own IBM as you wanted, and at an effective price to you that is $7 below the original market price. Alternatively, if the stock increased in price, you would miss the profits, but you have the $200 premium.

Again, it is possible to see the additional investment opportunities made available because of the existence of put options. They may be used by a speculative investor who expects a price decline and wants to take advantage of the leverage of the put. Alternatively, they can be used by a very conservative investor who wants to hedge his current stock position. Finally, they can be used as a means to acquire a desirable stock at a lower effective price.

VALUATION OF CALL OPTIONS

Five factors are needed to calculate the value of an American call option,[4] assuming the stock does not pay a dividend (we will subsequently drop this assumption): (1) the stock price, (2) the exercise price, (3) the time to maturity, (4) the interest rate, and (5) the volatility of the underlying stock.

STOCK PRICE

The value of a call option is positively related to the price of the underlying stock. With a given exercise price, the price of the stock determines whether the option is in-the-money and therefore has an intrinsic value or whether it is out-of-the-money and hence has only speculative (time) value. In addition, some of the other variables are influenced by the relationship between the market price and the exercise price.

EXERCISE PRICE

The value of a call option is inversely related to its exercise price. For a given stock price, the lower the exercise price is, the greater the value of a call. As an example, consider a stock selling at 70. Certainly a call option with an exercise price of 50 has a higher value than an option with an exercise price of 60. The first is in-the-money by $20, the second by only $10.

TIME TO MATURITY

A major component of the value of an option is its time to maturity. All other factors being equal, *the longer the time to maturity, the greater the value of the option* because the span of time during which gains are possible is longer. The longer option allows investors to reap all the benefits of a shorter option and provides added time.

INTEREST RATE

When an investor acquires an option, he buys control of the underlying stock for a period of time, but his downside risk is limited to the cost of the option. On the upside, he has the potential to gain at an accelerating rate because of the leverage involved. The option is therefore similar to buying on margin, except that there is an implicit interest charge. The higher the market interest rate is, the greater the saving from using options, and the greater the value of the option. Therefore, there is a *positive relationship* between the market interest rate and the value of the call option.

VOLATILITY OF UNDERLYING STOCK PRICE

In most cases, one considers a high level of stock price volatility an indication of greater risk, which reduces value, all other factors being equal. In the case of call options on a stock, however, the opposite is true; there is a *positive* relationship between the volatility of the underlying stock and the value of the call option. This is because, with greater volatility, there is greater potential for gain on the upside, and the downside protection of the option is also worth more.

---

[4] An American call option can be exercised at *any time* prior to the expiration date; a European option can be exercised only *on* the expiration date.

DERIVATION OF THE VALUATION FORMULA

Black and Scholes developed a formula for deriving the value of American call options in a classic article published in 1973.[5] This model was later refined by Merton under less restrictive assumptions.[6] Prior to presenting the actual formula, it is useful to consider the intuitive logic behind its development. The basic logic used by Black and Scholes is as follows. An investor who buys stock at P_s can also buy a put option at P_p and sell a call option with a price P_o. If he obtains these options with exercise (strike) prices P_e set equal to the initial price of his stock, he has a special combination of securities. If the price of the stock increases, he gains, but the gain is exactly offset by his losses on the call that is exercised against him. Alternatively, if the stock falls in value, his losses on the stock are exactly offset by his gain on the put option. Regardless of what happens in the market, his investment is exactly equal to P_e, the exercise price of his options. Since this position has no risk, it should provide the risk-free rate (RFR) for the period of time that the option is held. Buying a stock and a put and selling a call to achieve a riskless return can be specified as follows:

$$P_s + P_p - P_o = \frac{P_e}{(1 + RFR)^t} \tag{22.1}$$

or

$$P_o = P_s + P_p - \frac{P_e}{(1 + RFR)^t}.$$

A typical investor would not enter into this set of transactions, because if one wants a riskless investment, a T-bill can be acquired, and it would entail one transaction cost where this strategy involves three. Still, the equation provides two important insights.

1. It establishes a potential arbitrage situation if the stock, put, and call values move out of line.
2. Once the call price is known, the value of a put can be calculated.

Note that the problem of the valuation of options has not been solved. Black and Scholes were concerned with call option valuation, but they had one equation with two unknowns: the one they are solving for, P_o, and an additional security, P_p. Therefore, they needed to eliminate the put option from the equation but still retain a riskless hedge. They found that if they adjusted the number of options sold per number of shares of stock held— that is, the hedge ratio (H)—in a world of discrete prices, they could obtain a riskless hedge without the use of put options as follows:

$$P_o = P_s(H) - \frac{P_e}{(1 + RFR)^t}. \tag{22.2}$$

---

[5] Fischer Black and Myron Scholes, "The Pricing of Options and Corporate Liabilities," *Journal of Political Economy* 81, no. 2 (May–June 1973): 637–654.

[6] Robert C. Merton, "The Theory of Rational Option Pricing," *Bell Journal of Economics and Management Science* 4, no. 3 (August 1973): 141–183.

The actual Black-Scholes formula looks very much like this formula. To move from the discrete world to the real world, they needed a model that allowed for continuous changes in interest rates and stock prices. Borrowing from established theory in physics, they used stochastic calculus to arrive at

$$P_o = P_s\,(Nd_1) - \frac{P_e}{e^{(RFR)^t}}\,(Nd_2)\,, \qquad\qquad (22.3)$$

where

> e = natural number 2.7183
>
> Nd_1 = the cumulative density function of d_1 (to be defined)
>
> Nd_2 = the cumulative density function of d_2 (to be defined).

There are two differences between Equations 22.3 and 22.2. First, in continuous time, the risk-free rate (RFR) over the life of the option $(1 + RFR)^t$ becomes $e^{(RFR)^t}$. Second, the simple hedge ratio (H) is broken into two fairly formidable components: (Nd_1) and (Nd_2). While a physics student may follow the details of the Nd_1 and Nd_2 formulations that will be presented, a business student will understand that this hedge ratio calculation involves the σ of the stock, the relationship between the market price and the exercise price of the option ($ln\,P_s/P_e$), the risk-free rate (RFR), and the time to maturity (t).

Hand-held calculators can be programmed with the Black-Scholes formula. It is important for students and practitioners to remember that the price of an option is based on a riskless arbitrage, which in turn is a function of the price of the stock, the exercise price of the option, time to maturity, the risk-free rate, and the variability of returns of the underlying security.

The resulting formula is as follows:

$$P_o = [P_s]\,[(Nd_1)] - [P_e]\,[\text{anti}ln(-RFR)^t]\,[N(d_2)],$$

where

> P_o = market value of call option
>
> P_s = current market price of underlying common stock
>
> $N(d_1)$ = cumulative density function of d_1 as defined below
>
> P_e = exercise price of call option
>
> RFR = current annualized risk-free rate
>
> t = time remaining before expiration (in years, for example, 90 days = 0.25)

$N(d_2)$ = cumulative density function of d_2 as defined below:

$$d_1 = \left[\frac{ln(P_s/P_e) + (RFR + .5\sigma^2)t}{\sigma(t)^{1/2}} \right],$$

$$d_2 = d_1 - [\sigma(t)^{1/2}]$$

where

$ln(P_s/P_e)$ = natural logarithm of (P_s/P_e)

σ = standard deviation of annual rate of return on underlying stock.

IMPLEMENTING THE FORMULA

Although the formula appears quite forbidding, almost all the required data are observable. The major inputs are current stock price (P_s), exercise price (P_e), the risk-free interest rate (RFR), time to maturity (t), and the standard deviation of annual returns (σ). It is quite easy to see from the formula that the price of the call is positively related to the price of the stock (P_s) and negatively related to the exercise price (P_e). It is more difficult to see the positive relationship between the option price and the time to maturity (t), the variability of the return (σ), and the risk-free rate (RFR), but that is nevertheless the case.

The *only* variable that is not observable is the volatility of price changes as measured by the standard deviation of returns of the underlying stock over the remaining life of the option (σ). Therefore, this becomes the major factor to be estimated. Black, in a subsequent article, made several observations regarding this estimate.[7] First, he noted that knowledge of past price volatility should be helpful, but that *more is needed because the volatility for individual stocks changes over time.* This point should not come as a surprise given what you know about changing market volatility over time and the instability of beta for individual stocks. Traders approach this estimate in two ways. One alternative is to know the historical standard deviation and make a judgment regarding whether it will be higher or lower in the future, then use this estimate in the formula to derive an expected P_o. The second alternative is to use all the variables that are known (including the option price) and use the formula to *solve for the implied standard deviation.* Then this implied standard deviation is compared to your expectation—that is, if it is too small, you will buy the call; if it is too high, you will sell the call.

The other variable that requires some attention is the interest rate. You should use a rate that corresponds to the term of the option. The most obvious is the T-bill interest rate quoted daily in *The Wall Street Journal* for different maturities ranging from 30, 60, 90, and 180 days.

---

[7] Fischer Black, "Fact and Fantasy in the Use of Options," *Financial Analysts Journal* 31, no. 4 (July–August 1975): 36–41.

Table 22.4
Calculation of Option Value ($\sigma = .40$)

$$d_1 = \left[\frac{ln(36/40) + (.10 - .5(.4)^2).25}{.4(.25)^{1/2}}\right]$$

$$= \frac{-.1054 + .045}{.2}$$

$$= -.302$$

$$d_2 = -.302 - [.4(.25)^{1/2}]$$

$$= -.302 - .2$$

$$= -.502$$

$$N(d_1) = .3814$$

$$N(d_2) = .3079$$

$$P_0 = [P_s][N(d_1)] - [P_e][\text{anti}ln(-RFR)][N(d_2)]$$

$$= [36][.3814] - [40][\text{anti}ln(-.025)][.3079]$$

$$= 13.7304 - [40][0.9753][.3079]$$

$$= 13.7304 - 12.0118$$

$$= 1.7186.$$

To demonstrate the formula, consider the following example. All the values except stock price volatility are observable. In the case of volatility, the historical measure is given, but it is also assumed that the analyst expects the stock's volatility to increase.

An Example of Option Valuation Variables

$$P_s = \$36.00$$
$$P_e = \$40.00$$
$$RFR = .10 \text{ (the rate on 90-day T-bill)}$$
$$t = 90 \text{ days (.25 year)}$$
$$\text{Historical} = .40$$
$$\text{Expected} = .50 \text{ (analysts expect an increase in the stock's}$$
$$\text{standard deviation).}$$

Table 22.4 contains the detailed calculations for the option assuming the historical volatility ($\sigma = .40$). Table 22.5 contains the same calculations, except that we assume the stock's volatility is higher ($\sigma = .50$).

These results indicate the importance of estimating stock-price volatility; given a 25 percent increase in volatility (0.50 versus 0.40), there is a 36 percent increase in the value of the option. Because everything else is observable, this variable will differentiate estimates. Given its importance, the variable has been dealt with in several studies. Boyle and Ananthanarayanan examined the impact of how the variance was estimated on the value derived from the B-S model.[8] They concluded that almost all the estimates were subject to a bias. In contrast, rather than consider what variance estimate should be inserted, two related studies by Latané and

[8] Phelim Boyle and A. L. Ananthanarayanan, "The Impact of Variance Estimation in Option Valuation Models," *Journal of Financial Economics* 5, no. 3 (December 1977): 375–387.

TABLE 22.5
Calculation of Option Value ($\sigma = .50$)

$$d_1 = \left[\frac{ln(36/40) + (.10 + .5(.5)^2).25}{.5(.25)^{1/2}} \right]$$

$$= \frac{-.1054 + .05625}{.25}$$

$$= -.1966$$

$$d_2 = -.1966 - [.5(.25)^{1/2}]$$

$$= -.1966 - .25$$

$$= -.4466$$

$$N(d_1) = .4199$$

$$N(d_2) = .3275$$

$$P_0 = [36][.4199] - [40][anti\,ln - .025][.3275]$$

$$= 15.1164 - [40][0.9753][.3275]$$

$$= 15.1164 - 12.7764$$

$$= 2.34.$$

Rendleman[9] and Schmalensee and Trippi[10] showed that the B-S model could be used to derive the variances implied by the market, given the actual option prices and the other known values included in the model. Both studies showed that these implied variances were generally better predictors of future variances than estimates based solely on historical return data. They also found *substantial instability* in these implied variances over time. Consistent with this result, Black and Scholes found that the actual variance during a certain time period (which is not observable prior to the period) is a more useful input to their model than estimates based on past data.[11]

OPTIONS ON STOCK INDEXES

In addition to an option on a futures contract, there are options on stock market indexes that are the same as an option on a single stock, except that they are for the aggregate market as represented by a market indicator series. The most well-known indexes with options are described in Table 22.6.[12] In addition, a number of subindexes have been created to consider certain segments of the market where there is strong interest and volatile securities.[13]

---

[9] Henry A. Latane and Richard J. Rendleman, Jr., "Standard Deviations of Stock Price Ratios Implied in Option Prices," *Journal of Finance* 31, no. 2 (May 1976): 369–381.

[10] Richard Schmalensee and Robert R. Trippi, "Common Stock Volatility Expectations Implied by Option Premia," *Journal of Finance* 33, no. 1 (March 1978): 129–147.

[11] Fischer Black and Myron Scholes, "The Valuation of Option Contracts and a Test of Market Efficiency," *Journal of Finance* 27, no. 2 (May 1972): 399–417.

[12] Pamela Sebastian, "Index Options Proliferate: A Guide to Calls, Puts, and Striking Prices," *The Wall Street Journal,* March 13, 1985: 35.

[13] Pamela Sebastian, "Exchanges Plan More Sub-Index Options Fearing Aggressive Rivals May Push Issues," *The Wall Street Journal,* December 15, 1983: 33

TABLE **22.6**
Description of Major Index Options

Standard & Poor's 100 Index: These options, traded on the Chicago Board Options Exchange (CBOE), are for a portfolio of 100 stocks included in the S&P 500 Index. Similar to the other S&P Indexes, it is a value-weighted series. A 1-point move in the index equals about a 7.5-point move in the Dow Jones Industrial Average (DJIA).
Standard & Poor's 500 Index: These options are for the 500 stocks in the S&P 500 Composite Index. It is a value-weighted index, and the options are traded on the CBOE with strike prices at 5-point intervals.
New York Stock Exchange Composite Index: These options, traded on the NYSE, are based on the 1,500-plus stocks traded on the NYSE, and a 1-point move in this index equals about a 6.5-point move in the DJIA. Striking prices are at 5-point intervals (150, 155, and so on).
American Stock Exchange Major Market Index (MMI): These options, traded on the AMEX, are based on a price-weighted index of 20 blue-chip stocks. While the options are traded on the AMEX, the stocks in the index are all listed on the NYSE. A 1-point movement in this index is equal to about a 5-point move in the DJIA. It is very highly correlated with the DJIA, because 15 of the 20 stocks are included in the DJIA. It is the second most active index options contract after the S&P 100 Index.
Value Line Composite Index: These options, traded on the Philadelphia Stock Exchange, are based on the 1,679 stocks followed by Value Line (VL). This VL series is an unweighted series of stocks from the NYSE, the AMEX, and the OTC. Notably, it is a geometric mean of individual percent price changes rather than an arithmetic mean for all other series.
National OTC Index: These options, traded on the Philadelphia Stock Exchange, are based on the National OTC Index, which includes the largest 100 stocks (based on market value) traded on the national OTC list. Similar to the NASDAQ series, the index is value-weighted.

Subindex Options
Computer Technology Index: Introduced August 26, 1983, this is based on an aggregate market value index of 29 computer technology stocks, both listed and unlisted. The index is calculated relative to a starting value of 100 on July 29, 1983. The options are traded on the AMEX.
Financial News Composite Index: These options, traded on the Pacific Exchange, are for an index of 30 stocks of major companies (e.g., Alcoa, Walt Disney). It is a value-weighted index with a base value of 100 as of June 30, 1986.
Oil Index: Based on a price-weighted index of 15 oil company stocks, this was originally introduced as the Oil & Gas Index on September 9, 1983, and subsequently revised and renamed the Oil Index on October 22, 1984, with a benchmark value of 125.00 as of August 27, 1984. The options are traded on the AMEX.
Institutional Index: These options were introduced on October 3, 1986. The index measures the change in the aggregate market value of the 75 stocks with the latest dollar holdings in major institutional portfolios (i.e., they have a market value of more than $100 million). These options are traded on the AMEX.
Utilities Index: These options, traded on the Philadelphia Exchange, are for an index of 120 utility stocks. It is a value-weighted index and has a benchmark value of 200 as of May 1, 1987.
Gold/Silver Index: Based on a value-weighted index of seven mining stocks, with a benchmark value of 100 as of January 2, 1984, these options are traded on the Philadelphia Stock Exchange.

An example of quotes for the various options is contained in Figure 22.6. Each point of premium represents $100. The minimum premium quotation is 1/16 of a point for premiums of less than $3, and 1/8 of a point for premiums of $3 and above. As shown, based upon volume and open interest, the S&P 100 Index on the Chicago Board Options Exchange (CBOE) is clearly the most popular and active option.[14] In July, when the value of the S&P 100 Index was 253.73, it was possible to acquire an August 240

---

[14] Jeffrey Zaslow, "Chicago Exchange Moving to Speed Up Index-Options Trades for Small Investors," *The Wall Street Journal,* January 31, 1985, 29. Another popular option is for the Value Line series; see Steve Swartz, "Value Line Stock Index Option Gets Off to a Fast Start in Philadelphia," *The Wall Street Journal,* January 28, 1985: 38.

FIGURE 22.6
Index Option Quotes

INDEX OPTIONS

Tuesday, July 26, 1988

American Exchange

MAJOR MARKET INDEX

Strike	Calls–Last			Puts–Last		
Price	Aug	Sep	Oct	Aug	Sep	Oct
360	....	....	....	9/16	....	....
365	....	44 3/8	....	3/4	....	....
370	....	40	....	1	....	5 7/8
375	....	35 1/4	....	1 5/8	4	....
380	....	....	....	2 1/4	5 1/2	....
385	21 1/2	....	....	3	....	....
390	17 1/4	....	....	4 3/8	8	11 7/8
395	14 1/8	....	....	5 5/8	....	....
400	10 5/8	16	....	7 5/8	12 1/8	....
405	7 1/2	13 1/4	....	9 3/8	13 5/8	....
410	5 3/8	10 3/8	....	12 1/4	....	....
415	3 5/8	....	....	15	....	....
420	2 1/4	....	....	18	....	....
425	1 3/8	4 7/8	8 3/8	....	....	....
430	13/16	3 1/2	....	29	....	....
435	9/16	2 3/4	....	34	....	....
440	3/8	1 7/8	4 3/8	38 3/4	....	....
445	1/4	....	....	....	....	....
450	1/8	1	....	....	....	....

Total call volume 10,626 Total call open int. 25,000
Total put volume 5,868 Total put open int. 20,121
The index: High 405.42; Low 402.67; Close 403.58, +0.08

COMPUTER TECHNOLOGY INDEX

Strike	Calls–Last			Puts–Last		
Price	Aug	Sep	Oct	Aug	Sep	Oct
105	....	....	....	1/2	....	2
110	....	4 1/2	....	....	....	....

Total call volume 2 Total call open int. 39
Total put volume 30 Total put open int. 269
The index: High 111.17; Low 110.40; Close 110.50, +0.02

OIL INDEX

Strike	Calls–Last			Puts–Last		
Price	Aug	Sep	Oct	Aug	Sep	Oct
175	....	....	....	2 15/16	....	....
180	2 1/16	....	....	....	....	....
185	3/4	1 7/8	....	....	....	....

Total call volume 11 Total call open int. 322
Total put volume 8 Total put open int. 621
The index: High 177.05; Low 176.10; Close 176.41, −0.03

INSTITUTIONAL INDEX

Strike	Calls–Last			Puts–Last		
Price	Aug	Sep	Oct	Aug	Sep	Oct
230	....	....	....	5/16	....	....
235	....	....	....	5/16	....	....
245	....	....	....	1 1/16	2 3/4	....
250	....	....	....	1 9/16	....	....
255	....	....	....	2 7/8	....	....
260	....	....	....	4 1/4	....	....
265	4 3/4	....	....	7	....	....
270	2 3/8	....	....	....	....	....
275	1 3/16	....	....	....	....	....
280	5/8	....	....	....	....	....
290	....	....	2 1/4	....	....	....

Total call volume 730 Total call open int. 31,502
Total put volume 317 Total put open int. 20,111
The index: High 264.08; Low 262.17; Close 263.06, +0.60

Chicago Board

S&P 100 INDEX

Strike	Calls–Last			Puts–Last		
Price	Aug	Sep	Oct	Aug	Sep	Oct
220	....	....	....	1/4	1	....
225	....	....	....	7/16	1 5/16	....
230	....	....	....	5/8	1 7/8	....
235	19 3/4	....	....	1	2 11/16	3 1/2
240	15 1/4	18 1/4	19 3/4	1 9/16	3 5/8	5
245	10 7/8	14	15 3/4	2 3/8	4 7/8	6 3/4
250	7 1/2	10 5/8	14	4	6 5/8	8 1/2
255	4 1/2	7 5/8	10 3/4	6 1/8	8 5/8	11
260	2 5/8	5 3/8	7 3/4	9 1/8	11 1/2	13 1/2
265	1 3/16	3 1/2	6 1/8	13 3/8	15 1/2	....
270	5/8	2 1/4	4 3/8	16 1/2	19	....
275	5/16	1 3/8	2 3/4	22 1/4	....	....
280	3/16	13/16	2 1/8	....	....	....

Total call volume 68,933 Total call open int. 285,607
Total put volume 51,781 Total put open int. 237,740
The index: High 254.68; Low 252.83; Close 253.73, +0.52

S&P 500 INDEX

Strike	Calls–Last			Puts–Last		
Price	Aug	Sep	Dec	Aug	Sep	Dec
195	....	71	....	....	3/16	....
205	....	61 1/8	....	....	1/4	....
215	....	....	....	....	7/16	....
220	....	....	....	....	....	2 9/16
225	....	....	....	....	3/4	....
230	....	....	40	....	1 1/8	3 7/8
235	....	....	....	....	1 7/16	4 3/4
240	....	....	....	1/2	2	5 3/4
245	....	....	....	....	....	6 7/8
250	....	18 5/8	24 7/8	1 11/16	3 5/8	....
255	....	....	....	2	4 3/4	....
260	8	....	....	3 1/8	6 5/8	11 3/8
265	5 3/8	9 1/4	15 1/2	5 1/4	7 3/4	....
270	3	6 1/2	13 1/4	7 7/8	11	15 1/2
275	1 3/8	4 1/4	....	....	13 5/8	18 3/8
280	11/16	2 13/16	8 1/2	....	....	....
285	1/2	1 11/16	7 1/8	....	....	....
290	1/4	....	5 1/2	....	....	....
295	....	9/16	....	....	....	....
300	....	7/16	3 1/8	....	34 3/8	....
305	....	....	2 5/8	....	....	....
310	....	....	1 7/8	....	....	....
315	....	....	....	....	....	47 3/4
320	....	1/8	....	....	....	51 1/2

Total call volume 4,749 Total call open int. 214,215
Total put volume 2,439 Total put open int. 169,614
The index: High 266.09; Low 264.32; Close 265.19, +0.51

Philadelphia Exchange

GOLD/SILVER INDEX

Strike	Calls–Last			Puts–Last		
Price	Aug	Sep	Oct	Aug	Sep	Oct
95	....	....	....	1/2	....	2 1/2
100	4 1/4	6 1/8	....	1 7/8	....	....
105	2	3 1/4	....	4 1/8	5 1/2	....
115	3/16	....	....	....	....	....

Total call volume 41 Total call open int. 512
Total put volume 67 Total put open int. 685
The index: High 102.88; Low 101.78; Close 102.03, +0.23

VALUE LINE INDEX OPTIONS

Strike	Calls–Last			Puts–Last		
Price	Aug	Sep	Oct	Aug	Sep	Oct
240	....	....	....	3 1/2	....	....
245	....	....	....	....	....	8 3/4
250	....	4	....	....	....	....

Total call volume 100 Total call open int. 400
Total put volume 210 Total put open int. 640
The index: High 241.60; Low 240.93; Close 241.40, +0.20

NATIONAL O-T-C INDEX

Strike	Calls–Last			Puts–Last		
Price	Aug	Sep	Oct	Aug	Sep	Oct

Total call volume 0 Total call open int. 45
Total put volume 0 Total put open int. 46
The index: High 253.16; Low 251.89; Close 252.25, −0.91

UTILITIES INDEX

Strike	Calls–Last			Puts–Last		
Price	Aug	Sep	Oct	Aug	Sep	Oct
180	....	....	....	1 1/8	....	....
185	11/16	1 1/8	....	....	....	....
190	3/16	3/8	....	....	....	....

Total call volume 159 Total call open int. 2,999
Total put volume 247 Total put open int. 1,525
The index: High 182.38; Low 181.24; Close 182.12, +0.32

Pacific Exchange

FINANCIAL NEWS COMPOSITE INDEX

Strike	Calls–Last			Puts–Last		
Price	Aug	Sep	Dec	Aug	Sep	Dec
155	29 1/4	....	....	....	....	....
160	....	....	....	1/4	....	....
165	19 1/8	....	....	3/8	....	....
175	10	....	....	1 1/4	2 3/4	....
180	5 7/8	....	....	2 1/2	4 1/4	....
185	3 3/8	5 7/8	....	4 5/8	....	....
190	1 5/8	3 3/8	....	7 1/4	....	....
195	....	....	....	12	....	....
200	....	....	....	16	....	....
205	....	....	....	....	20 1/2	....

Total call volume 750 Total call open int. 6,760
Total put volume 290 Total put open int. 5,742
The index: High 184.58; Low 183.14; Close 183.67, +0.38

N.Y. Stock Exchange

NYSE INDEX OPTIONS

Strike	Calls–Last			Puts–Last		
Price	Aug	Sept	Oct	Aug	Sept	Oct
130	....	....	....	1/8	....	....
135	....	....	....	1/4	....	....
140	....	....	....	5/8	1 5/8	....
145	6 7/8	....	....	1 3/8	2 3/4	....
147 1/2	4 5/8	....	....	2 1/8	3 5/8	....
150	3	....	....	3 1/4	4 7/8	....
152 1/2	2	....	....	4 7/16	6	....
155	1 1/16	2 7/8	....	5 7/8	7 1/4	....
157 1/2	1/2	....	....	....	....	....
160	1/4	1 5/16	....	....	....	....
165	1/16	....	....	....	....	....
170	....	....	....	20 3/8	....	....

Total call volume 436. Total call open int. 9,854.
Total put volume 1,489. Total put open int. 9,475.
The index: High 150.43; Low 149.57; Close 150.03, +0.29

Source: Index Options, *The Wall Street Journal,* July 27, 1988.

call option on this index. This option would have given you the right to acquire this portfolio of stocks at 240 until the option expired during the third week in August. The cost of the option was 15 1/4, which means 100 units would cost $1,525. Clearly, this is an in-the-money option: it has an intrinsic value of 13.73 (253.73 − 240.00).

Alternatively, if you were bearish on the market, you could buy a put. An example would be the Major Market Index (MMI) traded on the AMEX, which is highly correlated with the DJIA. With the index at 403.58, you could buy a September 405 put (in-the-money) for 13 5/8 ($1,362.50 for 100) and hope for a market decline. It is also possible to use these puts as a hedge for a portfolio of blue-chip stocks during a period when you are concerned about market volatility.

The point is, assuming that you have strong feelings about market movements rather than individual stock movements, this is a convenient, low-cost means of investing. Also, given the several subindexes, it is possible to hedge or speculate on certain volatile industries such as computers, oil, and gold.

OPTIONS ON FOREIGN CURRENCIES

Throughout this book we have discussed global investing and the added risk/opportunities available because of exchange rate changes. As noted, when you invest in Japanese stocks or bonds, you must not only consider the typical business, financial, and liquidity risks, but also must recognize the added uncertainty due to exchange rate changes that can work in your favor or against you. The point that will be made in this section, and subsequently in Chapter 25 where foreign currency futures are discussed, is that it is possible to hedge part of this foreign exchange risk by using foreign currency forward, futures, or options. This section considers the options on foreign currencies.

Figure 22.7 contains a copy of the foreign exchange table that appears daily in *The Wall Street Journal.* Note that these are exchange rates for transactions of $1 million or more among banks. Also, while most trading is done in the current spot market, there are also forward rates of 30, 90, and 180 days quoted in the active currencies of Britain, Canada, France, Japan, Switzerland, and West Germany. The figures are provided for the number of U.S. dollars per unit of the foreign currency. As an example, at this time, the spot rate was 1.7120 U.S. dollars per British pound, or .5386 U.S. dollars per West German mark. Alternatively, it indicates the amount of foreign currency you could receive per U.S. dollar. As an example, you could receive 132.35 Japanese yen per U.S. dollar or 1.2087 Canadian dollars per U.S. dollar. Since they provide the rates for the last two days (Monday and Tuesday), it is possible to determine the one-day change in the rates. As shown, the U.S. dollar strengthened relative to the Japanese yen—i.e., on Monday you could get 132.25 yen per U.S. dollar, while on Tuesday you could receive 132.35 yen per U.S. dollar. As shown elsewhere in the book, this particular exchange rate fluctuated dramatically during 1987–1988, going from over 200 yen per U.S. dollar, down to about 120 yen, and then back up to 135 yen per dollar in July.

The two designations at the bottom (SDR and ECU) are as follows:

Figure 22.7
Foreign Exchange Rates

FOREIGN EXCHANGE

Tuesday, July 26, 1988

The New York foreign exchange selling rates below apply to trading among banks in amounts of $1 million and more, as quoted at 3 p.m. Eastern time by Bankers Trust Co. Retail transactions provide fewer units of foreign currency per dollar.

Country	U.S. $ equiv. Tues.	U.S. $ equiv. Mon.	Currency per U.S. $ Tues.	Currency per U.S. $ Mon.	Country	U.S. $ equiv. Tues.	U.S. $ equiv. Mon.	Currency per U.S. $ Tues.	Currency per U.S. $ Mon.
Argentina (Austral) ...	.1006	.1006	9.94	9.94	Kuwait (Dinar)	3.5236	3.5236	.2838	.2838
Australia (Dollar) ...	.8087	.8093	1.2366	1.2356	Lebanon (Pound)	.002847	.002847	351.25	351.25
Austria (Schilling)	.07675	.07704	13.03	12.98	Malaysia (Ringgit)	.3806	.3814	2.6275	2.6220
Bahrain (Dinar)	2.6532	2.6532	.3769	.3769	Malta (Lira)	2.9411	2.9411	.3400	.3400
Belgium (Franc)					Mexico (Peso)				
Commercial rate	.02591	.02601	38.60	38.45	Floating rate	.0004405	.0004405	2270.00	2270.00
Financial rate	.02563	.02574	39.02	38.85	Netherland(Guilder)	.4777	.4800	2.0935	2.0835
Brazil (Cruzado)	.004314	.004369	231.83	228.87	New Zealand (Dollar) ..	.6690	.6690	1.4948	1.4948
Britain (Pound)	1.7120	1.7195	.5841	.5816	Norway (Krone)	.1486	.1494	6.7300	6.6925
30-Day Forward ...	1.7086	1.7159	.5853	.5828	Pakistan (Rupee)	.05482	.05482	18.24	18.24
90-Day Forward	1.7020	1.7097	.5875	.5849	Peru (Inti)	.03030	.03030	33.00	33.00
180-Day Forward	1.6931	1.7017	.5906	.5876	Philippines (Peso)	.04776	.04776	20.94	20.94
Canada (Dollar)	.8273	.8220	1.2087	1.2165	Portugal (Escudo)	.006653	.006678	150.30	149.75
30-Day Forward	.8265	.8214	1.2099	1.2175	Saudi Arabia (Riyal) ...	.2666	.2666	3.7505	3.7505
90-Day Forward	.8247	.8197	1.2125	1.2200	Singapore (Dollar)	.4904	.4912	2.0390	2.0360
180-Day Forward	.8218	.8169	1.2169	1.2242	South Africa (Rand)				
Chile (Official rate) ...	.004055	.004055	246.61	246.61	Commercial rate	.4105	.4146	2.4361	2.4120
China (Yuan)	.2687	.2687	3.7220	3.7220	Financial rate	.2849	.2873	3.5100	3.4800
Colombia (Peso)	.003304	.003304	302.66	302.66	South Korea (Won) ...	.001381	.001381	724.30	724.30
Denmark (Krone)	.1420	.1426	7.0410	7.0105	Spain (Peseta)	.008162	.008189	122.52	122.12
Ecuador (Sucre)					Sweden (Krona)	.1570	.1575	6.3680	6.3490
Official rate	.004008	.004008	249.50	249.50	Switzerland (Franc)	.6472	.6506	1.5452	1.5370
Floating rate	.001802	.001802	5.5500	5.5500	30-Day Forward	.6497	.6534	1.5391	1.5305
Finland (Markka)	.2276	.2285	4.3945	4.3765	90-Day Forward	.6542	.6579	1.5286	1.5199
France (Franc)	.1598	.1605	6.2595	6.2290	180-Day Forward	.6614	.6651	1.5120	1.5035
30-Day Forward	.1599	.1607	6.2545	6.2235	Taiwan (Dollar)	.03499	.03499	28.58	28.58
90-Day Forward	.1601	.1609	6.2455	6.2140	Thailand (Baht)	.03935	.03935	25.41	25.41
180-Day Forward	.1603	.1611	6.2375	6.2065	Turkey (Lira)	.0007026	.0007026	1423.27	1423.27
Greece (Drachma)	.006743	.006770	148.30	147.70	United Arab(Dirham) ..	.2724	.2724	3.671	3.671
Hong Kong (Dollar) ...	.1281	.1281	7.8050	7.8047	Uruguay (New Peso)				
India (Rupee)	.07112	.07112	14.06	14.06	Financial	.002759	.002759	362.50	362.50
Indonesia (Rupiah)	.0005924	.0005924	1688.00	1688.00	Venezuela (Bolivar)				
Ireland (Punt)	1.4571	1.4621	.6863	.6839	Official rate	.1333	.1333	7.50	7.50
Israel (Shekel)	.6135	.6135	1.6300	1.6300	Floating rate	.03067	.03067	32.60	32.60
Italy (Lira)	.0007299	.0007326	1370.00	1365.00	W. Germany (Mark) ..	.5386	.5410	1.8565	1.8485
Japan (Yen)	.007556	.007561	132.35	132.25	30-Day Forward	.5402	.5427	1.8510	1.8427
30-Day Forward	.007580	.007586	131.92	131.82	90-Day Forward	.5431	.5456	1.8412	1.8329
90-Day Forward	.007627	.007630	131.11	131.06	180-Day Forward	.5476	.5501	1.8263	1.8177
180-Day Forward	.007701	.007701	129.85	129.85	SDR	1.30549	1.31223	0.765998	0.762059
Jordan (Dinar)	2.6954	2.6954	.371	.371	ECU	1.12290	1.13339	....	....
					z-Not quoted.				

Source: Foreign Exchange Rates, *The Wall Street Journal*, July 27, 1988.

- SDR = special drawing rights, based on composite exchange rates for the U.S., West German, British, French, and Japanese currencies. Source: International Monetary Fund.
- ECU = European currency unit, based on a basket of European community currencies. Source: European Community Commission.

In response to the need for hedging or speculating in foreign currencies, in 1982 the Philadelphia Stock Exchange began trading options on some foreign currencies. While there are also options in foreign currencies traded on the Toronto and Montreal Exchanges and the Amsterdam Exchange, the Philadelphia Exchange is the largest exchange-based market for foreign currency options. As shown in Figure 22.8, options are traded in Australian dollars, British pounds, Canadian dollars, West German marks, Japanese yen, and Swiss francs. The strike price of each option is the U.S. dollar price of a unit of foreign exchange. The number of foreign currency units

Figure 22.8
Prices on Foreign Currency Options

FOREIGN CURRENCY OPTIONS

Philadelphia Exchange

Tuesday, Jul. 26

Option & Underlying	Strike Price	Calls—Last			Puts—Last		
		Aug	Sep	Dec	Aug	Sep	Dec
50,000 Australian Dollars-cents per unit.							
ADollr	...75	r	r	r	r	0.10	r
80.73	...77	r	r	r	r	0.37	r
80.73	...78	r	r	r	r	0.65	r
80.73	...79	r	r	r	0.34	r	r
80.73	...80	r	1.78	1.96	0.65	r	r
80.73	...81	0.88	1.24	1.75	r	1.85	3.10
80.73	...82	0.33	0.90	r	r	r	r
80.73	...83	r	0.50	r	r	r	r
80.73	...84	r	0.39	r	r	r	r
50,000 Australian Dollars-European Style.							
80.73	...77	r	r	r	r	0.39	r
12,500 British Pounds-cents per unit.							
BPound	162½	r	r	r	r	0.88	r
171.15	.165	r	r	r	r	1.21	r
171.15	167½	r	r	r	0.66	r	r
171.15	.170	r	r	r	r	2.90	5.20
171.15	172½	1.55	2.65	r	2.70	r	r
171.15	.175	0.63	1.79	3.30	r	r	r
171.15	177½	r	r	2.54	r	r	9.90
171.15	182½	r	0.45	r	r	r	r
171.15	187½	r	r	r	r	r	18.00
12,500 British Pounds-European Style.							
171.15	172½	1.35	r	r	r	r	r
171.15	.175	r	1.50	r	r	r	r
50,000 Canadian Dollars-cents per unit.							
CDollr	...82	r	1.16	r	0.17	r	1.15
82.74	.82½	r	0.75	r	0.39	0.95	r
82.74	...83	0.25	0.54	1.01	r	1.00	1.66
82.74	.83½	0.15	r	r	r	r	r
82.74	...84	0.10	r	r	r	r	r
50,000 Canadian Dollars-European Style.							
CDollar	79½	r	3.08	r	r	r	r
62,500 West German Marks-cents per unit.							

Option & Underlying	Strike Price	Calls—Last			Puts—Last		
		Aug	Sep	Dec	Aug	Sep	Dec
DMark	.. 52	r	r	r	0.07	0.26	r
53.86	...53	r	r	r	0.24	0.54	r
53.86	...54	0.48	1.04	r	0.66	0.89	1.38
53.86	...55	0.18	0.56	1.37	1.26	1.52	r
53.86	...56	0.07	0.30	r	r	r	r
53.86	...57	0.03	0.18	0.66	3.29	3.10	r
53.86	...58	r	0.07	0.45	4.12	4.23	r
53.86	...59	r	r	r	r	r	5.27
53.86	...60	r	r	r	r	6.25	r
53.86	...62	r	r	0.11	r	r	r
6,250,000 Japanese Yen-100ths of a cent per unit.							
JYen	... 71	r	r	r	r	r	0.43
75.57	...72	r	r	r	0.07	0.19	r
75.57	...73	r	r	r	0.10	0.31	r
75.57	...74	s	2.47	r	s	0.52	r
75.57	.. 75	r	r	r	0.43	0.82	r
75.57	...76	0.55	1.22	r	1.06	1.27	r
75.57	...77	0.26	0.81	1.85	r	r	2.34
75.57	...78	0.09	r	r	r	r	r
75.57	...80	r	0.17	r	r	r	r
62,500 Swiss Francs-cents per unit.							
SFranc	..63	r	r	r	r	0.42	0.85
64.70	...64	r	r	r	0.40	r	1.26
64.70	...65	r	1.28	r	0.59	1.08	r
64.70	...66	0.40	0.73	1.82	r	1.66	2.14
64.70	...67	r	0.54	r	r	2.60	2.83
64.70	...69	0.04	r	r	r	4.40	r
64.70	...71	r	r	r	r	6.27	r
62,500 Swiss Francs-European Style.							
64.70	...63	r	r	r	r	0.32	r
64.70	...67	r	0.65	r	r	r	r
64.70	...68	r	0.38	r	r	r	r
64.70	...74	r	r	0.19	r	r	r
64.70	...77	r	r	0.09	r	r	r
64.70	...78	r	r	0.07	r	r	r
Total call vol.	11,625		Call open int.			563,980	
Total put vol.	16,096		Put open int.			491,214	

r—Not traded. s—No option offered.
Last is premium (purchase price).

Source: Foreign Currency Options, *The Wall Street Journal*, July 27, 1988.

is half the contract size of a futures contract in the International Monetary Market (IMM) of the Chicago Mercantile Exchange. As an example, an options contract for British pounds is for 12,500 British pounds. The striking prices are cents per pound, such as 170 cents per pound when the close the prior day was 171.15 cents per pound (1.7115 U.S. dollars per British pound). As shown, the August 175 calls on British pounds are out-of-the-money and trade at a speculative value of 0.63.

A HEDGE TRANSACTION

Consider the following example of using the options market to help hedge the exchange rate risk involved in a stock or bond investment. Assume that you are interested in buying some Japanese stocks that are traded on the Tokyo Stock Exchange and denominated in yen. You recognize that you could make money on the stock investment but could also lose some or all of your return in U.S. dollars if the yen weakens relative to the U.S. dollar during your investment interval. Therefore, what you want to do is buy or sell options on the Japanese yen that will offset the currency loss on the stock transaction. You can do this in one of two ways: *sell a call option* on the yen, or *buy a put option* on the yen. In either case, if the exchange rate for U.S. dollars per Japanese yen declines from the current .007556 (see Figure 22.8), you will benefit. If you sold an in-the-money call option, it could expire worthless, and you would have the premium—e.g., if you sell a September 73 call, and if the exchange rate goes from .007556 to .0072, the option will be worthless. Alternatively, if you buy a September 76 put, and the exchange rate declines to .0072, you will experience a significant gain on the put option that will help offset the exchange rate loss on the stock transaction.

The discussion in Chapter 25 on financial futures will consider how to accomplish such a hedge using foreign currency futures.

EFFICIENCY OF OPTIONS MARKETS

A study by Galai tested the efficiency of the CBOE shortly after it was established.[15] There are two phases to the tests of market efficiency. In the first, Galai considered whether a specified trading rule can be used to separate profitable from unprofitable investments. The second phase determined whether it is possible to use the trading rule to generate above-normal risk-adjusted profits *in a real-world environment*. He also considered whether there were changes in efficiency over time.

Galai's main conclusions were (1) The trading strategies performed well when the trades used the prices based on the B-S model versus the market prices. (2) The market was not completely efficient, because some of the returns to market-makers that included typical trading costs were positive. When transaction costs for the public were considered, most positive returns disappeared. This implies that these above-normal returns are not available to the public. (3) The market did not become more efficient over time based upon a comparison of results for the first half of the sample period versus the second half.

ANALYSIS OF INVESTOR EXPERIENCE WITH OPTIONS

Several studies examined returns on the options compared to those from a stock portfolio. Dawson considered some of the problems related to continuous option writing and concluded that both return and risk are reduced.[16] Grube, Panton, and Terrell likewise noted a reduction in the rates of return and variability from investing in covered call options, and also recognized the impact of such investment on turnover and transaction costs.[17]

Merton, Scholes, and Gladstein presented the results of a simulation for 130 stocks that have options traded on the CBOE and for the 30 stocks

---

[15] Dan Galai, "Tests of Market Efficiency on the Chicago Board Options Exchange," *Journal of Business* 50, no. 2 (April 1977): 167–195.

[16] Frederic S. Dawson, "Risks and Returns in Continuous Option Writing," *Journal of Portfolio Management* 5, no. 2 (Winter 1979): 58–63.

[17] R. Corwin Grube, Don B. Panton, and J. Michael Terrell, "Risks and Rewards in Covered Call Positions," *Journal of Portfolio Management* 5, no. 2 (Winter 1979): 64–68.

in the Dow Jones Industrial Average.[18] They simulated the risk and returns for a fully covered call option program as compared to returns from owning the stock alone. The variability of return results was generally consistent with our previous discussion. The returns from the deeply out-of-the-money option strategies were more volatile than those from the other option categories. At the same time, *all option strategies were less volatile than a pure stock position,* which experienced higher volatility and higher returns.

SUMMARY

Options have become popular since the establishment of the CBOE in 1973. They offer a wide range of investment alternatives. The price paid for an option is the *option premium,* and the price at which it can be acquired is the *exercise price.* Options may be in-the-money, out-of-the-money, or at-the-money. Basic trading strategies involve buying call options, writing covered call options, using option spreads, and buying and selling put options.

Black and Scholes developed a model for the valuation of call options that deals with the major variables that influence the value of a call option and the direction of the effect. It is important to estimate the standard deviation of returns for the underlying security.

Options on aggregate market indexes can be used to hedge a total portfolio or speculate on the future returns for the total market, and options on foreign currency can be used to hedge exchange rate risk.

Recent risk-return studies from selling covered options consistently indicate that the returns and risks are lower with options than with pure stock investing.

QUESTIONS

1. Define a call option and a put option.

2. How is the CBOE different from the original over-the-counter option market? Discuss the major factors that differentiate them.

3. What factors motivate an exchange to begin trading in an option? Are you surprised that the AMEX began to compete with the CBOE on certain options? Why or why not?

4. Define the following terms:
   a. premium
   b. exercise price
   c. expiration date
   d. in-the-money option
   e. at-the-money option
   f. out-of-the money option

5. Differentiate between selling a fully covered call and a "naked" (uncovered) call. Give an example of why the sale of an uncovered call is much riskier.

---

[18] Robert C. Merton, Myron S. Scholes, and Matthew L. Gladstein, "A Simulation of the Returns and Risk of Alternative Option Portfolio Investment Strategies," *Journal of Business* 51, no. 2 (April 1978): 183–242.

6. Five variables are involved in estimating the value of a call option. List and discuss each of them, and indicate why each is important and how it influences the value of the option.

7. It has been contended that the sale of a fully covered option is a *conservative* investment strategy. Why is this so, based upon the possible distribution of returns from such a strategy? Use an example if it will help.

8. Describe a *time spread* and a *price spread.* Discuss why investors engage in spreads. Is the risk higher or lower for a spread than for writing a call option?

9. Assume that you want to buy Eastman Kodak (EK) but feel that at its current price of 53 it is somewhat overpriced. Currently a six-month EK 50 put is selling for $3. Describe how you would use this put option to accomplish your goal of buying EK if the stock declined to 45. What would happen if you sold a put, and the stock rose to $54?

10. According to the Galai study, how do you test for the efficiency of the options market? Why would this test be considered a semistrong test? Explain.

PROBLEMS

1. Assume you are bullish on the outlook for the stock market. Look up a four- to six-month option that is at-the-money in *The Wall Street Journal.* Assume the stock increases by 15 percent. Indicate approximately what will happen to your option, and compute the percentage return on the option purchase.

2. Select a stock option on the CBOE, and discuss how you would write a bullish price spread.

2a. Describe what will happen if the stock price increases by 20 percent.

2b. Describe what will happen if the stock price declines by 20 percent.

3. Select an option listed on the American Stock Exchange and discuss how you would enter into a price spread assuming you were *bearish* on the stock.

3a. Describe what will happen if the stock price increases by 25 percent.

3b. Describe what will happen if the stock price declines by 30 percent.

4. Assume that you are generally bearish on common stocks, and so you buy an Apple Computer six-month put at 50 when the stock is 52. The put contract costs you $200. Apple Computer subsequently goes to 55. What is your rate of return? What is your rate of return if Apple went to 45?

5. Use the Black and Scholes model to calculate the theoretical value of a Vester Corporation three-month call option at $45 if the stock is selling for $50 and has a σ^2 (variance) of 0.36. The risk-free rate is 6 percent.

6. Ted Westfall was considering the purchase of 100 shares of Stopgap Corporation common stock selling at $32 3/8 per share on the last day in October. As an alternative Len Griffen, Ted's neighbor, suggested that Ted consider a Stopgap option instead. Together they examined the following option table from the local newspaper.

PRICE	CALLS		PUTS	
	DECEMBER	MARCH	DECEMBER	MARCH
30	4 1/2	6	1 1/4	2
35	2 1/2	3 1/2	4 1/2	4 3/4
40	1 1/8	2 1/8	7 3/8	
45	1/2			

Ted decides to buy March options. What are his dollar and percentage gains (losses) if he makes the following purchases and subsequently closes his position at 41 7/8:

6a. A call with an exercise price of 30?

6b. A call with an exercise price of 35?

6c. A put with an exercise price of 30?

6d. A put with an exercise price of 35?

7. John Quackenbush is considering the following alternatives for investing in Swirl Industries, which is now selling for $23 per share:
   (1) Buy 100 shares for cash
   (2) Buy 100 shares on 60 percent margin
   (3) Buy a six-month call option at $20 for $600
   Assuming no commissions or taxes, what are the dollar and annualized percentage gains for each plan if

7a. The stock reaches $35 in four months and all transactions are completed?

7b. The stock falls to $19 in two months and all transactions are completed?

REFERENCES

OPTIONS: ARTICLES AND PAMPHLETS

(The address to order pamphlets from the Chicago Board Options Exchange is LaSalle at Van Buren, Chicago, IL 60605.)

Biger, N., and J. Hull. "The Valuation of Currency Options." *Financial Management* 2, no. 1 (Spring 1983).

Black, Fischer, and Myron Scholes. "The Pricing of Options and Corporate Liabilities." *Journal of Political Economy* 81, no. 2 (May–June 1973).

Black, Fischer, and Myron Scholes. "The Valuation of Option Contracts and a Test of Market Efficiency." *Journal of Finance* 27, no. 2 (May 1972).

Bodwurtha, J., and G. Courtadon. "Efficiency Tests of the Foreign Currency Options Market." *Journal of Finance* 41, no. 1 (March 1986).

Bookstaber, Richard. "The Use of Options in Performance Structuring." *The Journal of Portfolio Management* 11, no. 4 (Summer 1985).

Bookstaber, Richard, and Roger Clarke. "Options Can Alter Portfolio Return Distributions." *Journal of Portfolio Management* 7, no. 3 (Spring 1981).

Buying Puts, Straddles, and Combinations. Chicago: Chicago Board Options Exchange, 1980.

Evnine, J., and A. Rudd. "Index Options: The Early Evidence." *Journal of Finance* 40, no. 3 (July 1985).

Frankfurter, George M., Richard Stevenson, and Allan Young. "Options Spreading: Theory and an Illustration." *Journal of Portfolio Management* 5, no. 4 (Summer 1979).

Gombola, M. J., R. Roenfeldt, and P. L. Cooley. "Spreading Strategies in CBOE Options: Evidence on Market Performance." *Journal of Financial Research* 1, no. 1 (Winter 1978).

Index Options for Portfolio Management. Chicago: Chicago Board Options Exchange, 1986.

Klemkosky, Robert C. "The Impact of Option Expirations on Stock Prices." *Journal of Financial and Quantitative Analysis* 8, no. 3 (September 1978).

Klemkosky, Robert C., and T. Maness. "The Impact of Options on Underlying Securities." *Journal of Portfolio Management* 6, no. 2 (Winter 1980).

Macbeth, J., and L. J. Merville. "Tests of the Black-Scholes and Cox Call Option Valuation Models." *Journal of Finance* 35, no. 2 (May 1980).

Merton, Robert C. "The Theory of Rational Option Pricing." *Bell Journal of Economics and Management Science* 4, no. 3 (August 1973).

Merton, Robert C., Myron S. Scholes, and Mathew I. Gladstein. "A Simulation of the Returns and Risk of Alternative Option Portfolio Investment Strategies." *Journal of Business* 51, no. 2 (April 1978).

Merton, Robert, Myron Scholes, and Mathew Gladstein. "The Returns and Risks of Alternative Put Option Portfolio Investment Strategies." *Journal of Business* 55, no. 1 (January 1982).

O'Brien, Thomas, and William Kennedy. "Simultaneous Option and Stock Prices: Another Look at the Black-Scholes Model." *The Financial Review* 17, no. 4 (November 1982).

Option Spreading. Chicago: Chicago Board Options Exchange, 1982.

Option Writing Strategies. Chicago: Chicago Board Options Exchange, 1982.

Options and Pension Plans. Chicago: Chicago Board Options Exchange, 1984.

Rendleman, Richard J., Jr. "Optimal Long-Run Option Investment Strategies." *Financial Management* 10, no. 1 (Spring 1981).

Rubinstein, Mark, and Hayne Leland. "Replicating Options with Positions in Stock and Cash." *Financial Analyst Journal* 39, no. 4 (July–August 1981).

Slivka, Ronald T. "Call Option Spreading." *Journal of Portfolio Management* 7, no. 3 (Spring 1981).

Slivka, Ronald T. "Risk and Return for Option Investment Strategies." *Financial Analysts Journal* 36, no. 5 (September–October 1980).

Smith, Clifford W., Jr. "Option Pricing: A Review." *Journal of Financial Economics* 3, no. 1, 2 (January–March 1976).

Sterk, William E. "Test of Two Models for Valuing Call Options on Stocks with Dividends." *Journal of Finance* 37, no. 5 (December 1982).

Tax Considerations in Using CBOE Options. Chicago: Chicago Board Options Exchange, 1987.

Understanding Options. Chicago: Chicago Board Options Exchange, 1987.

Understanding Interest Rate Options. Chicago: Chicago Board Options Exchange, 1987.

Options: Books

Bookstaber, Richard. *Option Pricing and Strategies in Investing* (New York: Addison-Wesley, 1986).

Clasing, Henry, Jr. *Dow Jones Irwin Guide to Put and Call Options.* rev. ed. (Homewood, Ill.: Dow Jones-Irwin, 1978).

Cox, J., and M. Rubinstein. *Option Markets* (Englewood Cliffs, N.J.: Prentice-Hall, Inc., 1985).

Fabozzi, F., and G. Kipnis, ed. *Stock Index Futures* (Homewood, Ill.: Dow Jones-Irwin, 1984).

Gastineau, Gary. *Stock Options Manual.* 2d ed. (New York: McGraw-Hill, 1979).

Gaylord, Sherwood. *Sensible Speculation with Put and Call Options.* (New York: Simon and Schuster, 1976).

Jarrow, Robert A., and Andrew Rudd. *Option Pricing.* (Homewood. Ill.: Richard D. Irwin, 1983).

Kolb, Robert W. *Understanding Futures Markets.* 2d ed. (Glenview, Ill.: Scott, Foresman & Co., 1988).

Ritchken, Peter. *Options: Theory, Strategy, and Applications.* (Glenview, Ill.: Scott, Foresman and Co., 1987).

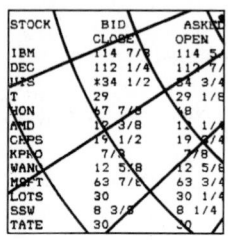

CHAPTER 23

WARRANTS AND CONVERTIBLE SECURITIES

In this chapter, we will consider some additional investment instruments to common stocks, bonds, and options, beginning with common stock warrants, which, although similar to call options, have some unique features that make them appealing both to investors and to the companies that issue them. In connection with pure warrants, we will discuss Americus Trusts, a combination of a dividend-yielding "prime" and a price appreciation "Score" that is very similar to a warrant. Finally, we will discuss convertible securities, which are a combination of a fixed-income security *and* an option to convert it to common stock.

WARRANTS

A *warrant* is an option to buy a stated number of shares of common stock at a specified price at any time during the life of the warrant. You will probably recognize that this definition is quite similar to the description of a call option. However, there are several important differences. First, *the life of a warrant is much longer than the term of a call option.* At the time of issue, the typical call option has a term to expiration that ranges from three to nine months. In contrast, a warrant generally has an original term to maturity of at least two years, and most are between five and ten years. Some are much longer; there are even a few perpetual warrants.

A second major difference is that *warrants are issued by the company issuing the stock.* As a result, when an investor exercises the warrant and buys stock, the stock involved is acquired *from the company*, and the proceeds from the sale are new capital that goes to the issuing firm.

In general, warrants are used by companies as "sweeteners" for bond issues or other security issues, because they are options that could have value if the stock price increases as expected. The price of the stock or bond will be higher because the warrant is attached, although most warrants are *detachable* after the initial sale and trade separately on an exchange or on the OTC market. At the same time, the warrant can provide a major source of new equity capital for the company. Investors are generally interested in warrants because of the leverage possibilities that we will discuss. But bear in mind that warrants do not pay dividends and the holder has no voting rights. The investor should determine whether a warrant offers some protection to the warrant holder against dilution in the case of stock dividends or stock splits. In such cases, either the exercise price is reduced, or the number of shares that can be acquired is increased.

EXAMPLE OF WARRANTS

Consider the following hypothetical example. The Bourke Corporation is going to issue $10 million in bonds but knows that within the next five years, it will also need an additional $5 million in new external equity (in addition to expected retained earnings). One way to make the bond issue more attractive, and also possibly sell the required stock, is to attach warrants to the bonds. If Bourke common stock is currently selling at $45 a share, the firm may decide to issue five-year warrants that will allow the holder to acquire the company's common stock at $50 a share. Because the firm wants to raise $5 million, it must issue warrants for 100,000 shares ($5 million/$50). Assuming the bonds will have a par value of $1,000, the company will sell 10,000 bonds, and each bond will have ten warrants attached to it. (We are assuming each warrant is for one share.) Assume the Bourke Corporation is successful, and the market price on its common stock reaches $55 a share over the five years. At this point the warrants will have an intrinsic value of $5 each ($55 minus $50), and all the warrants should be exercised prior to their expiration. As a result, the company will sell 100,000 shares of common stock at $50 a share. The company pays no explicit commission cost but does have administrative costs.

Examples of outstanding warrants are listed in Figure 23.1, which is a page from the *R. H. M. Survey of Warrants, Options & Low-Price Stocks.* For each of the warrants included, there is an indication of where the stock and warrant are traded, the number of shares involved, the exercise terms (price and expiration date), the year of expiration (if the warrant is not perpetual), and the current price of the common stock and the warrant. As an example, consider the Heritage Entertainment warrants. The specification in the table indicates that the stock and the warrants are traded on the AMEX; there are 746,000 warrants outstanding, and each warrant allows the holder to buy one share of Heritage Entertainment common stock from the company for $5.00 a share until December 31, 1988 (most of the warrants on this page expire before the end of 1990). As of late 1988, the common stock was selling on the AMEX for $2.75 per share, and the warrant (which was likewise listed on the AMEX) was selling for $0.31. We will discuss the specific pricing of the warrant in the following subsection. At this point, though, you should be aware of the numerous firms that have warrants, the many expiration dates, and the wide range of stock prices in relation to exercise prices for the warrants. As of the end of 1987,

FIGURE 23.1

The R. H. M. Survey of Warrants, Options, and Low-Price Stocks

THE R·H·M SURVEY
of WARRANTS · OPTIONS & LOW-PRICE STOCKS

July 22, 1988

Goldfield Corp '91, A-O, 3,000,000 Warrants. Each 1991 Wt exercised before 5-6-88 will entitle holder to receive a 1993 Wt. *0.53 to 5-6-91.*
0.37—0.18

Goldfield Corp '93, A-O. *1.25 to 5-6-93.*
0.37—0.09

Granges Exploration Ltd, A-A, 1,000,000 Warrants. *7.50 to 1-21-91.*
4.25—1.25

Hadson Corp '89, S-O, 1,248,000 Warrants. *8.11 to 6-30-89.*
4.25—0.31

Hanson PLC '94, S-S, (HAN), *18.00 to buy 1 ADS sh to 9-30-94.*
12.12—2.75

Heritage Entertainment, A-A, 746,000 Warrants. *5.00 to 12-31-88*
2.75—0.31

Hinderliter Ind '92, A-O, (HND). *4.00 to 11-1-88 increasing 1.00 each Nov. 1 to 11-1-92.*
2.00—0.37

Hotel Investors 'A', S-A, (HPS), 389,806 Warrants, Callable at 7.00 per Wt if stock exceeds 200% of exercise price for stated period. *13.00 to 4-30-89.*
15.50—2.75

Hotel Investors 'B', S-A, (HPS), 1,660,994 Warrants. *16.95 to 9-16-96.*
15.50—1.62

ICN Pharmaceuticals '89, S-O, (ICN), 200,000 Warrants, (SS) O, 12½-91, N.A. Callable at 4.00 per Wt if stock is 140% of exercise price for stated period. *9.00 to 5-15-89.*
7.37—1.75

Income Opportunity Realty Trust '89, A-A, (IOT), 1,663,765 Warrants. *20.00 from 3-1-89 to 2-28-90.*
11.50—0.12

Insilco Corp '90, S-O, (INP), 1,811,250 Warrants. *23.52 to 6-1-90.* Hold
19.87—2.12

Instrument Systems '88, A-O, (ISY), 3,000,000 Warrants, *3.60 to 7-31-88.*
1.50—0.06

Keystone Camera Products 'B', A-A, (KYC), 1,150,000 Warrants. Callable at 0.75 per Wt if com exceeds 140% of exercise price. 6 Wts may be exchanged for 1 com. *7.50 ro 5-7-91.*
1.87—0.37

Lifetime Corp '96, A-O, (LFT), 1,111,111 Warrants. *4.50 to 10-28-96.*
4.37—0.75

Lilly (Eli), S-S, (LLY), 18,107,452 Warrants. *75.98 to 3-31-91.*
84.87—27.62

Lincoln N.C. Realty Fund, A-A, (LRF), 1,725,000 Warrants. Co. may accelerate exp date if com exceeds 140% of exercise price. *13.50 to 12-31-90.*
10.37—0.25

Lomas & Nettleton Mtge Inv, S-S, (LOM), 3,085,600 Warrants. Exp date of Wts may be accelerated if price of sh exceeds 140% of exercise price for stated period. *27.00 to 3-1-90.*
22.37—0.56

Lori Corp '90, A-O, (LRC), 360,000 Warrants. (SS) O, R.N. Koch 12¾-95, N.A. Redeemable at 10.00 per Wt if com exceeds 150% of adjusted exercise price. Each Wt is convertible at holder's option, into .375 shs of Lori com at any time. *1.5 shs at 12.00/sh to 3-15-90.*
7.87—2.75

M.D.C. Holdings '90, S-O, (MDC), 1,700,708 Warrants, (SS) O. 10½-95 N.A. Redeemable at 5.00 per Wt if com exceeds 145% of exercise price for stated period. *14.10 to 4-15-90.*
4.87—0.43

MSA Realty Corp, A-A, (SSS), 5,907,045 Warrants, (SS) O, 9¼-93, N.A. Callable at 5.00 per Wt. At expiration date 100 Wts will convert into 1 com sh. *9.00 to 4-1-89.*
9.12—0.31

McDermott Int'l '90, S-S, (MDR), 5,995,990 Warrants. (SS) S, 10-03 88.00, EEP 22.00. Co. may accelerate exp date of Wts to 4-1-88 if price of com exceeds 125% of exercise price for stated period. *25.00 to 4-1-90.*
19.62—2.75

Mtge & Rlty Tr '92, S-A, (MRT), 2,130,700 Warrants. Redeemable at 3.00 per Wt after 1-15-91 or before if com exceeds 140% of exercise price for stated period. *1.5 shs at 20.50/sh to 1-15-92.*
17.87—1.00

Nat'l Semiconductor, S-S, 9,000,000 Warrants. *22.25 to 5-13-92.*
11.62—3.25

Navistar Int'l 'A', S-S, (HR) Co. has right to extend Wt to 12-15-99. *5.00 to 12-15-93.*
6.25—3.50

Navistar Int'l 'B' '90, S-S, (HR) 7,972,000 Warrants. *9.00 to 12-31-90.*
6.25—1.50

WARRANT
Explanatory Notes

All the information needed to evaluate each Warrant follows each Name, which is given precisely as each Warrant is traded, and this is followed by two letters indicating where common and Warrant are traded, in that order. S is New York SE, A is American SE, O is over-the-counter, P is Pacific SE, T is Toronto SE., M is Montreal SE and V is Vancouver SE. The symbol for the common follows, and the number of Warrants outstanding. If a senior security is useable at full face value, there will be an "SS" at this point, with a letter indicating where the senior security is traded, and the name of the senior security — coupon and year of maturity in the case of a Bond. There follows a recent price for the senior security, and "EEP," which means Effective Exercise Price in relation to that price. Example: if a Bond sells at 80 and the exercise price for the Warrant is 12, the EEP would be 80 x 12 or 9.6 *at* that price for the Bond. Always check the *current* price of the senior security if considering a commitment. Any "Call" terms or other provisions now follow. The full exercise terms for the Warrant will be at the end of the paragraph in italics, and common and Warrant price, in that order, will be on the last line to the right. Any recommendation to Buy, Hold, or Sell, will be to the left of the common/Warrant prices. **Warrants on Listed Stocks** appear in full in every issue. For all other Warrants, consult the box above, top-right. That box also informs you as to where the latest Index will be found, and coverage of **Currency Exchange Warrants**.

Copyright 1988 R.H.M. Associates
172 Forest Avenue
Glen Cove, New York 11542

Source: *R·H·M Survey of Warrants· Options & Low-Price Stocks*, July 15, 1988. Reprinted with permission.

there were 20 warrant issues listed on the NYSE, about 35 warrants listed on the AMEX, and substantially more than 100 traded on the OTC market.

AMERICUS TRUSTS

There have been instances where individual security instruments have been divided up into components. An example would be *stripped* government bonds, where security dealers have stripped the interest payments from a government bond and thereby created an interest stream and a zero coupon bond. Similarly, an Americus Trust is an arrangement whereby investors tender regular common shares of a select group of stocks to the appropriate Americus Trust and receive in exchange a *unit,* which is a composite of a *prime* and a *score.* (These terms will be explained shortly.) These separate components do not need to be held as a unit, but can be separated and traded in the secondary market—in all cases, both components are traded on the AMEX. There are 26 blue-chip stocks eligible for inclusion in an Americus Trust. A list of the stocks, the termination date of the trust, and the termination price are included in Figure 23.2.

The shares are held in the Americus Trust until the termination date (exercise date), which is always five years from the date when the trust was established. At the termination date, the shares in the trust are divided between the prime and the score in accordance with the specification of the trust, which depends upon the market value of the stock at the termination date.

As indicated, a *unit* is one prime and one score. While a unit can be broken up into a separate prime and score, it is also possible to combine a prime and a score back into a unit and then exchange the unit for a share of the stock.

A *prime* is entitled to all the dividends paid on the stock during the life of the trust, as well as to the market value of the underlying stock on the termination date up to the value of the *termination claim* (which is like the strike price for an option). This termination claim was set when the trust was established (it was typically about 25 percent above the market value of the stock when the trust was established). As an example, the trust for American Telephone & Telegraph was established in February 1987, so its termination date is February 20, 1992. Its termination claim is $30. Therefore, the holder of the prime receives all dividends paid on AT&T common stock during the five-year period and a maximum of $30 a share at termination (as of July 1988 AT&T stock was selling for $26.50). If at the termination date, the market value of the stock was less than $30, the prime holder would receive all the shares. Alternatively, if the market value was greater than $30, the prime holder would receive shares to equal $3,000 (100 shares $\times$ $30).

The *score* is entitled to all the value of the stock above the termination claim (strike price) as of the date of termination. Continuing the AT&T example, if on the termination date, the market price was 50 (total market value of $5,000), the prime would receive shares worth $3,000, and the holder of the score would receive shares worth $2,000 (100 shares $\times$ $20). As noted, as of July 1988, AT&T was selling for $26.50 a share, and the

FIGURE 23.2
Listing of Americus Trust Stocks

THE R·H·M SURVEY
of WARRANTS · OPTIONS & LOW-PRICE STOCKS

July 15, 1988

SCORES — Updated Prices

Name (symbol)	Term. Date	Term Price	Com Price	Score Price Ranges		
				High	Low	Last
Amer Express (axp)	8-92	50.00	26.75	14.00	2.62	3.75
Amer Home Prod (ahp)	12-91	90.00	73.25	26.00	8.00	-
A T & T (att)	2-92	30.00	26.50	14.87	4.87	5.37
Amoco (an)	3-92	105.00	74.50	22.25	5.00	7.25
Atl Richfield (arc)	7-92	116.00	81.25	23.75	7.25	7.87
Bristol-Myers (bmy)	2-92	110.00	40.00	34.25	8.75	10.50*
Chevron (chv)	7-92	75.00	47.00	17.50	3.25	4.12
Coca-Cola (ko)	7-92	56.00	36.87	26.50	4.75	4.87
Dow Chemical (dow)	5-92	110.00	87.75	44.25	11.75	16.75
Du Pont (dd)	3-92	110.00	88.87	49.75	8.87	12.87
Eastman Kodak (ek)	3-92	92.00	44.75	46.37	6.75	8.87*
Exxon (xon)	9-90	60.00	44.62	40.62	15.00	29.50*
Ford (f)	6-92	104.00	52.87	43.00	12.50	24.75*
GTE (gte)	7-92	44.00	38.25	13.00	3.25	5.25
General Electric (ge)	5-92	140.00	43.25	49.00	6.50	8.50*
General Motors (gm)	6-92	107.00	77.75	26.00	5.50	7.87
Hewlett-Packard (hwp)	7-92	90.00	54.87	30.75	9.62	10.12
IBM (ibm)	6-92	210.00	126.37	58.00	8.12	13.50
Johnson & Johnson (jnj)	6-92	118.00	77.25	42.25	10.00	-
Merck (mrk)	4-92	200.00	54.37	87.50	21.37	31.37*
Mobil (mob)	6-92	60.00	44.50	19.00	4.50	4.87
Philip Morris (mo)	7-92	110.00	85.37	51.75	13.25	15.62
Proctor & Gamble (pg)	6-92	105.00	75.25	37.50	9.12	10.62
Sears (s)	7-92	64.00	36.37	20.00	2.87	4.00
Union Pacific (unp)	4-92	87.00	63.87	29.75	6.37	8.00
Xerox (xrx)	7-92	97.00	54.50	30.00	3.87	4.75

- no trade; * mentally adjust common price for stock splits: Bristol-Myers, Exxon, Ford and General Electric all 2-for-1; Merck 3-for-1; Eastman Kodak 3-for-2.

Source: *R·H·M Survey of Warrants· Options & Low-Price Stocks*, July 15, 1988. Reprinted with permission.

price of the score was 5 3/8, which means that the score (option) was out-of-the-money but reasonably close. Therefore, an investor would be buying a 3 1/2 year option with a striking price of $30—that is, the $5.37 is the time value of this option.

While the option (score) is officially a European option, since it cannot be redeemed for its value over $30 until February 1992, it will act like an American option that can be sold at any time because of the provision

FIGURE 23.3
Quotations for Americus Trust

AMERICAN STOCK EXCHANGE COMPOSITE TRANSACTIONS

Thursday, July 28, 1988

Quotations include trades on the Midwest, Pacific, Philadelphia, Boston and Cincinnati stock exchanges and reported by the National Association of Securities Dealers and Instinet

52 Weeks High	52 Weeks Low	Stock	Div.	Yld %	P-E Ratio	Sales 100s	High	Low	Close	Net Chg.
		—A—A—A—								
27¼	16½	A-axp	.71	3.0	...	8	24	24	24	+ ¼
14	2⅝	A-axp sc		...	...	12	3½	3½	3½	+ ⅛
70½	53	A-ahp	3.55	5.4	...	29	66	65¼	66	+ ¼
26	8	A-ahp sc		...	...	10	9⅛	9⅛	9⅛	− ⅜
23⅝	18⅛	A-att2	1.15	5.2	...	92	22	21⅞	22	+ ⅛
14⅞	4⅞	A-att2 sc		...	...	698	5¼	5	5¼	+ ⅛
20½	5	A-an sc		...	...	16	6¾	6⅝	6¾	...
76½	50	A-bmy	3.31	4.5	...	5	73	73	73	+ ½
34¼	8¾	A-bmy sc		...	...	19	10	9½	10	+ ¼
60⅞	38⅜	A-chv un	2.55	5.6	...	8	45⅞	45⅞	45⅞	− ⅞
17½	3¼	A-chv sc		...	...	46	3⅞	3¾	3⅞	+ ¼
34	27¾	A-ko	1.15	3.5	...	1	33¼	33¼	33¼	+ ¾
26½	4⅝	A-ko sc		...	...	109	5	4⅝	5	+ ¼
75	45	A-dow	2.75	3.9	...	5	70½	70¼	70½	− ⅜
44¼	11¾	A-dow sc		...	...	70	15⅜	14¾	15⅜	+ ⅝
128⅝	77	A-dd un	3.35	3.9	...	25	85	85	85	− 2⅜
80½	60	A-dd	3.75	5.0	...	6	74¾	74	74¾	− 1¼
49¾	8⅞	A-dd sc		...	...	36	11½	11	11½	+ ¼
61	57	A-xon	4.35	7.3	...	55	60	60	60	...
40⅝	15	A-xon sc		...	...	147	32¾	31¼	32½	+1
34⅝	27	A-gte	2.47	7.3	...	57	33⅞	33½	33⅞	+ ⅛
13	3¼	A-gte sc		...	...	134	5⅝	5⅜	5⅝	+ ¼
89	64	A-ge	2.75	3.7	...	10	75¼	75¼	75¼	− ¾
49	6½	A-ge sc		...	...	65	7⅞	7½	7⅞	+ ⅜
72⅛	45½	A-gm	4.95	6.9	...	118	71⅜	70¾	71¼	+ ¼
26	5½	A-gm sc		...	...	220	8	7⅞	8	+ ⅛
104½	60¼	A-ek un	2.65	4.0	...	6	65¾	63⅜	65¾	+ 2¼
67	48	A-ek	2.65	4.6	...	58	57¾	57¼	57¾	+ ¾
46⅜	6¾	A-ek sc		...	...	84	8¾	8⅛	8¾	+ ⅝
83	50	A-f	4.75	5.9	...	17	80⅝	80¼	80⅝	− ⅜
43	12½	A-f sc		...	...	17	21¾	21	21¾	− ¼
101	69½	A-jnj un	1.95	2.5	...	2	77	77	77	− ¼
70	52	A-jnj	1.95	2.9	...	4	67¾	67½	67¾	+ ¾
42¼	10	A-jnj sc		...	...	27	10¾	10½	10⅝	− ⅛
30¾	8	A-hwp sc		...	...	40	8½	8⅛	8½	+ ½
126½	88½	A-ibm	4.35	3.9	...	15	112	111	112	+2
58	8⅛	A-ibm sc		...	...	260	12¾	11⅞	12¾	+ ⅞
138	96½	A-mrk	3.79	2.9	...	6	132⅞	132¾	132¾	+ ⅞
87½	21⅜	A-mrk sc		...	...	43	31¼	30½	31¼	+ ½
51¾	13¼	A-mo sc		...	...	27	17⅛	16½	16⅞	+ ⅜
19	4½	A-mob sc		...	...	20	4⅞	4¾	4¾	...
37½	8¼	A-pg sc		...	...	3	8½	8½	8½	+ ¼
42½	26	A-s	1.95	6.0	...	35	32¼	32¼	32¼	...
20	2⅞	A-s sc		...	...	30	3½	3⅜	3½	+ ¼
78¾	49½	A-unp un	1.95	3.3	...	60	59¼	59¼	59¼	− 2¾
29¾	6⅜	A-unp sc		...	...	23	7	6⅞	7	− ⅛
30	3⅞	A-xrx sc		...	...	19	4⅝	4½	4⅝	+ ⅛
3½	⅞	Amhlth		...	...	2	1½	1½	1½	− ⅛
3⅛	1⅝	Ampal	.06	3.7	5	5	1⅝	1⅝	1⅝	...

Source: American Stock Exchange Composite Transactions, *The Wall Street Journal*, July 29, 1988.

that a prime and a score can *always* be recombined into a *unit* and exchanged for the original common shares. Therefore, if the combined value of a prime and score falls too far below the current market value of the stock, you would expect an arbitrageur to buy a prime and score and sell the stock short. As an example, if the prime for AT&T was selling for $19 and the score for $5 when the common stock was selling for $27, an arbitrageur could sell the stock short at $27 and cover it with the purchase of a prime and score for a combined total cost of $24. Therefore, you would never expect the sum of the two values to be much less than the stock value. Alternatively, the combined value can be above the value of the stock (be at a premium), because it is not possible to get primes and scores by exchange—each trust has a limit to its value (about 5 percent of the outstanding shares), and once this limit is reached, the trust is closed and you can acquire only units or components in the open market.

As of July 1988, almost all of the trusts were closed. The dealer-manager for these trusts was Alex, Brown & Sons, Inc., a New York investment banking firm. An example of Americus Trust quotes for primes and scores on the AMEX is included in Figure 23.3. In some instances, there are also quotes for the units (UN), so you can see the relationship. As an example, the Johnson and Johnson (jnj) closing quotes indicate the unit closed at $77, the prime at $67.75, and the score (SC) at $10.625, which means the combination of the components was selling for a small premium over the stock ($78.375 vs. $77). The common stock, which is listed on the NYSE, would likewise be very similar to the value of the unit (it closed at $77.25). This example also indicates the difference in yield on the prime. As shown, the dividend on the unit (the common stock) and the prime are the same ($1.95), but because the price for the prime is $67.75 versus $77 for the unit, the yield is 2.9 percent on the prime versus 2.5 percent on the common stock unit.

STRATEGIES WITH AMERICUS TRUST. If you own shares of one of the stocks eligible for the trust, you could shift your emphasis by tendering your shares and receiving trust units. For our first example, assume that you are somewhat conservative and would like to increase your income return. In this case you could sell the scores in the market and use the proceeds to buy more primes. Assume the market value of the stock is $100,000, it pays a $4,000 dividend, the price of the stock is $100, the primes are $80, and the scores are $20. If you sell your scores, you will receive $20,000 and could acquire 250 more primes ($20,000/$80). Therefore, your total dividends would be $5,000 (1,250 × $4). You have increased your yield and derived a more conservative portfolio, because primes would act more like bonds when the market price of the common stock approaches the termination price (striking price).

If, on the other hand, you want a more aggressive investment, the score is like an option or warrant. Therefore, you could sell your primes and invest the proceeds ($80,000) into 4,000 more scores and have 5,000 scores at $20.

VALUATION OF WARRANTS

The value of a warrant is determined in a manner similar to that used for call options, because the only difference to the investor is the longer term. (An investor does not care whether he has the option to buy the stock from another investor or directly from the firm.) As was true with a call option, you should consider two components of the warrant price: the intrinsic value and the *speculative* value (sometimes referred to as the *premium*). The latter is based upon the leverage involved and the time value of the warrant. The intrinsic value of the warrant is determined by the difference between the market price of the common stock and the warrant exercise price as follows:

Intrinsic Value = (Market Price of Common Stock − Warrant Exercise Price)
× Number of Shares the Owner is Entitled to Purchase.

This determines the intrinsic value of a warrant, assuming that the market price exceeds the warrant exercise price. As an example, in Figure 23.1, the Eli Lilly Company warrant has an exercise price of $75.78 until March

TABLE 23.1
Differences in Leverage as Shown by Stock Price to Warrant Price (SP/WP) Ratio

	TIME				
	T	**T + 1**	**T + 2**	**T + 3**	**T + 4**
Stock price	$22	$30	$40	$50	$60
Warrant price	$ 2	$10	$20	$30	$40
Stock price to warrant price ratio	11	3	2	1.67	1.5
Percentage change (stock price)		36.4	33.3	25.00	20.0
Percentage change (warrant price)		400.0	100.0	50.00	33.3

31, 1991, and the common stock is currently selling for $84.87. Therefore, this warrant has an intrinsic value of $8.89 (84.87 − 75.98), because it allows the holder to purchase one share of common stock at a price lower than the current market price. Note that the market price of the warrant is above the intrinsic value ($8.89 versus $27.62). This excess relative to the intrinsic value is due to the speculative value (to be discussed next).

Similar to a call option, an important feature of a warrant is the *leverage* it provides: the value of the warrant increases and declines by larger percentages than the value of the underlying stock fluctuates. As an example, assume a stock is selling for $48, and a warrant for the stock with an exercise price of $50 is selling for $3 on the basis of its speculative value. (This warrant currently has no intrinsic value, because the exercise price is above the market price.) If the stock goes to $55 (a 15 percent increase), the warrant will go to *at least* $5, because this is its intrinsic value. Thus, as the stock price increases by about 15 percent (55 − 48/ 48), the warrant increases by at least 67 percent (5 − 3/3). If there were some *speculative value (premium),* the increase in the price of the warrant would be even larger.

An indication of the amount of leverage can be derived by examining the relationship (ratio) of stock price to warrant price. *The larger this stock price to warrant price ratio is, the greater the leverage effect.* The example in Table 23.1 assumes that the warrant has an exercise price of $20 and sells at its theoretical value over time. The example demonstrates the relationship between the stock price to warrant price ratio (SP/WP) and the different percentage changes in stock price and warrant price. As shown, the greater the SP/WP ratio is, the greater the leverage of the warrant in terms of the percentage change in the warrant price for a given percentage change in the stock price. Note that *this leverage works both ways;* for a given decline in the stock price, the warrant price would decline by more.[1] Because investors in warrants typically find this leverage factor a positive attribute, the greater the SP/WP ratio is, the greater the speculative value of the warrant.

A major factor determining the price of a warrant, like the price of a call option, is the *length of time to maturity* (the longer the term, the greater the value). Because of their long term to expiration, warrants will typically have speculative value even when they are deeply out-of-the-money. For example, a three-year warrant with an exercise price of $50 will have time value even though the stock is selling for $40. As noted, this is a major factor distinguishing warrants from call options, which are typically for less than nine months. As shown in Figure 23.1, newly issued warrants generally do not expire for two to five years, and there are some perpetual warrants.

Another important factor in warrant valuation is the *volatility of the stock's price.* The more volatile the stock price is, the greater the probability of a positive move above the exercise price and the greater the value of the warrant, as with the value of call options. This factor would not be very important in the valuation of a warrant on AT&T stock, but it could result in a large speculative value for stocks with high price volatility. A warrant would be adversely affected by the payment of a dividend, because dividends are subtracted from the total value of a firm, and the warrant holder does not receive the dividend.

Once you have analyzed a stock and decided that it could experience an increase in value over the next several years, you should find out whether the firm has any warrants outstanding that would allow you to control a large amount of the stock for a fairly long period (possibly several years) for a modest investment.[2]

To summarize, the value of the warrant is determined by the following factors:

1. The *intrinsic value* of the warrant is based on the difference between the market price of the stock and the exercise price times the number of shares per warrant.
2. The *speculative value* of the warrant (referred to as the *premium value*) is a function of the following factors:
   a. The potential *leverage* the warrant provides, which is a function of the ratio of the stock price to the warrant price. The greater the potential leverage is, the larger the premium.

---

[1] "Stock Warrants—A Way to Get Leverage," *Forbes*, June 9, 1980: 102–104.

[2] For a further discussion on warrant pricing, see John P. Shelton, "The Relation of the Price of a Warrant to the Price of Its Associated Stock," *Financial Analysts Journal* 23, no. 3 (May–June 1967): 88–99; David F. Rush and Ronald W. Melicher, "An Empirical Examination of Factors Which Influence Warrant Prices," *Journal of Finance* 29, no. 5 (December 1974): 1949–1961; Edwardo Schwartz, "The Valuation of Warrants: Implementing a New Approach," *Journal of Financial Economics* 4, no. 1 (January 1977): 79–94; Michael G. Ferri, Joseph W. Kremer, and H. Dennis Oberhelman, "An Analysis of the Pricing of Corporate Warrants," *Advances in Futures and Options Research* 1 (1986): 201–225; Michael G. Ferri, Scott B. Moore, and David C. Schirm, "Investor Expectations about Callable Warrants," *Journal of Portfolio Management* 14, no. 3 (Spring 1988): 84–86. For an analysis of warrant hedging, see Moon K. Kim and Allan Young, "Rewards and Risks from Warrant Hedging," *Journal of Portfolio Management* 6, no. 4 (Summer 1980): 65–68.

FIGURE 23.4
Graph of Maximum, Minimum, and Actual Prices of Warrant

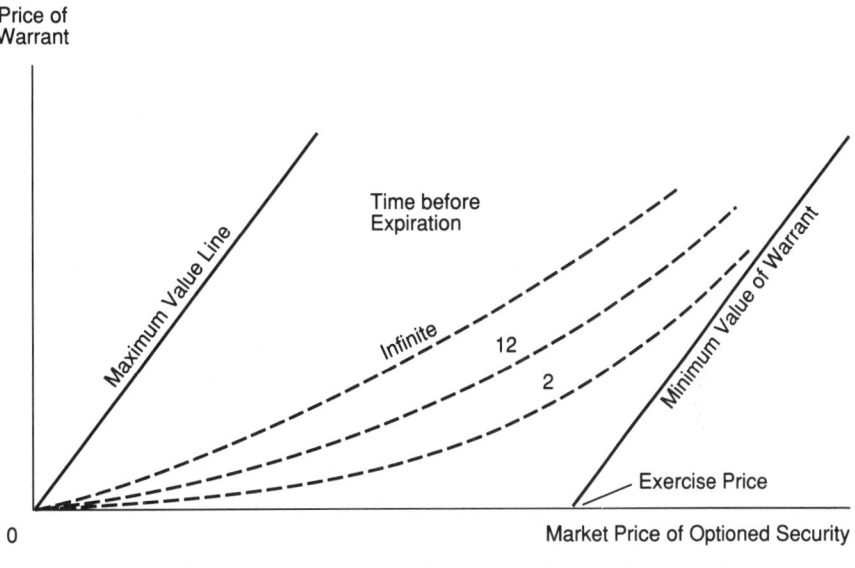

b. The *length of time to maturity:* the longer the time to maturity is, the larger the premium.
c. The *price volatility* of the underlying stock: the greater the price volatility of the stock is, the larger the premium.
d. The *dividend* paid by the stock, which is an inverse relationship; the larger the dividend is, the smaller the premium.

Given these valuation factors, Figure 23.4 contains a graph that indicates the maximum value that could prevail (the total value of the stock), the minimum value (the intrinsic value of the warrant), and likely market values that are affected by the time remaining before expiration. You could also envision multiple lines for each maturity curve that would be influenced by different levels of price volatility for the underlying security.

WARRANT STRATEGIES

For the investor who is considering investing in warrants as part of an overall program, the following considerations should be kept in mind:

1. The ultimate success of the warrant depends on the success of the stock. Remember that the leverage factor works both ways. Therefore, before you consider buying a warrant, you should be bullish on the stock and consider the warrant as a means to maximize the return from this stock.
2. *Diversification* is as important with warrants as with other investments. Therefore, if you decide to invest in warrants you should

probably consider the acquisition of a number of them if they are available on desirable stocks.

3. Given a diversified portfolio of warrants with high leverage characteristics, it is important to *"cut your losses short and let the profits run."* This strategy is used with any leveraged investment, such as options or commodities. Success involves having several small losses, but a few very big winners: three warrants that provide returns in excess of 100 percent can easily compensate for five or six that lose 25 to 30 percent.

4. The most desirable warrants are generally those that have very little intrinsic value, so the SP/WP ratio is large, and *the leverage is high.* In addition, you probably want a warrant with a minimum of two years remaining to maturity, and preferably three or four years. Also, the more volatile the stock price is (a beta above 1.2), the better. These recommendations presuppose that the warrant has the standard protective features against dilution, call, and so on. The final question is whether the speculative premium is reasonable given these characteristics. This can only be determined at an appropriate time by comparing alternative warrants to their underlying stocks. As stated initially, when buying a warrant, you are ultimately betting on the underlying stock.

5. The search for desirable warrants can take one of two forms. The first is simply to engage in the three-step analysis process and finish with a list of good companies from desirable industries. At this point, given the stock list, check a warrant reference service such as the *R.H.M. Survey* to see whether any of the desirable stocks have outstanding warrants that have the characteristics mentioned previously. An alternative approach is to examine a number of warrants listed in a service such as the *R.H.M. Survey* initially and select several warrants that apparently have most of the desirable characteristics. Next, analyze the issuing companies and their industries to assess the stocks. The author's preference is for the first approach, which views warrant selection as part of the total investment process, rather than as an end in itself.

CURRENCY EXCHANGE WARRANTS

Another set of newly developed warrants that are especially important to global investors are *currency exchange warrants (CEWs)* that allow the holder to acquire a specific number of U.S. dollars at specified exchange rates for a non–U.S. currency. A list of the CEWs available as of July 1988 is contained in Figure 23.5. As an example, the Sallie Mae yen CEW that expires March 1, 1993, has a strike price of 135.92 yen. Each warrant allows the holder to acquire 50 U.S. dollars at an exchange rate of 135.92 yen per dollar (the minimum exchange is for 2,000 warrants or $100,000). These warrants could become very profitable if the U.S. dollar strengthens against the yen and increases to a rate in excess of 136. As shown in Figure 23.5, this particular CEW was selling for $3.50 in July 1988. According to the

FIGURE 23.5
Description of Currency Exchange Warrants

Currency Exchange Warrants					
Name	Exp Date	Exerc Rate	Price Range		
			High	Low	Close
A T & T Credit	7-92	158.25 yen	3.50	0.87	1.75
Citicorp Wt M	7-92	1.932 marks	4.00	0.87	2.50
Citicorp Wt Y	7-92	152.50 yen	4.00	1.37	2.37
Citicorp Wt Y	4-93	132.90 yen	3.37	2.87	3.87
Emerson Elec Wt M	7-92	1.918 marks	4.62	1.12	2.50
Ford Motor Cred 92	7-92	152.2 yen	4.50	1.75	2.62
Ford Motor Cred 93	2-93	134.00 yen	4.12	3.12	4.50
General Elec Cr	6-92	149.70 yen	5.00	2.00	2.62
General Elec Cr	7-92	1.9120 marks	4.75	1.37	2.75
Morgan (J.P.)	7-91	1.904 marks	2.75	2.25	2.37
Sallie Mae Wt M	7-92	1.92 marks	4.62	1.25	2.25
Sallie Mae Wt Y	7-92	152.20 yen	4.37	1.25	2.37
Sallie Mae Wt Y	2-93	131.75 yen†	9.37	7.87	7.87
Sallie Mae Wt Y	3-93	135.92 yen	4.00	2.50	3.50
Xerox Credit Wt Y	7-92	154.15 yen	4.12	1.00	1.87

†Minimum expiration value of $9.25;
Strike Price varies over life of Warrant

Source: *R·H·M Survey of Warrants· Options & Low-Price Stocks*, July 15, 1988. Reprinted with permission.

prospectus, the *cash settlement value* (CSV) for these warrants is computed as follows:

$$\text{CSV} = \text{the greater of: 1) 0 or}$$
$$\text{2) } 50 - \left(50 \times \frac{\text{Strike Price}}{\text{Spot Rate}}\right).$$

As can be seen, once the spot rate exceeds the strike price, these warrants have some positive intrinsic value. As an example, if the spot exchange rate for Yen/U.S. dollar went to 150, the CSV would be as follows:

$$50 - \left(50 \times \frac{\text{Strike Price (135.92)}}{\text{Spot Rate (150.00)}}\right)$$
$$50 - (50 \times .9061) = \$4.69.$$

Table 23.2 indicates the cash settlement value for other exchange rates. These warrants provide long-term options on exchange rates that can be used for speculating or hedging exchange rates. With an increase in the number of warrants available and numerous striking prices, the opportunities increase substantially.

TABLE 23.2
Cash Settlement Values for Sallie Mae Yen Warrant: Expiration Date, 3/1/93; Striking Price, 135.92 yen

HYPOTHETICAL SPOT RATES (YEN/U.S. $1)	CASH SETTLEMENT VALUES OF WARRANT
110	$ 0.00
120	0.00
130	0.00
135.92	0.00
140	1.46
150	4.69
160	7.53
180	12.24
200	16.02
220	19.11
240	21.68
260	23.86

CONVERTIBLE SECURITIES

A *convertible security* gives the holder the right to convert one type of security into a stipulated amount of another type at the investor's discretion. Typically, but not invariably, the security is convertible into common stock, but it could be into preferred stock, or into a special class of common stock. The most popular convertible securities are convertible bonds and convertible preferred stock.

CONVERTIBLE BONDS

A convertible bond is usually a subordinated[3] fixed-income security that can be converted into a stated number of shares of common stock of the company that issued the bond. The conversion price is generally above the price of the common stock prevailing when the bonds are initially issued. Assume a company's common stock is selling for $36 a share. The company might decide to sell a subordinated convertible bond that matures in 20 years and is convertible into common stock at $40 a share. If the bonds are $1,000 par value, this would mean the bond is convertible into 25 shares of common stock ($1,000/$40). Because convertible bonds are generally considered to be an attractive investment (for reasons to be discussed), the interest rate on them is typically below the required return on the firm's straight debentures. In this case, assume an 8 percent coupon.

ADVANTAGES TO ISSUING FIRMS. Issuing convertible bonds is considered desirable for a company for several reasons. First, as stated, the interest cost is lower than it is on straight debt, and the extent of the saving on

---
[3] *Subordinated* means that the claims of the bondholders are subordinate to the claims of other debenture holders in terms of interest and claims on assets of the firm in the event of default.

interest depends on the growth prospects of the firm. In most cases, it is a minimum of 0.5 percent (50 basis points) and can be much higher. This differential in interest cost exists even though convertible bonds are riskier than straight debentures because they typically are subordinated. Bond rating agencies generally assign a rating to subordinated issues one class lower than a firm's straight debentures.[4] Therefore, the interest rate savings over a comparably rated bond are even more than the 50 basis points suggested.

Another advantage is that these bonds are *potential common stock.* The bondholder may decide to convert on his own, or the firm will make it possible to force conversion in the future by including a call feature on the bonds. This *future common* feature may be desirable for a firm that currently needs equity for an investment but does not want to issue common stock directly because of the potential dilution before the investment begins generating earnings. After the investment generates earnings, the stock price should rise above the conversion value, and the firm can force conversion by calling the bond. As an example of forced conversion, suppose a $1,000 par value bond is convertible into stock at $40 a share (25 shares of common stock). Assume that the bond is callable at 108 percent of par ($1,080), and that two years after the issue is sold the common stock rises from $36 to $45 a share because earnings rise. At this point, the bond has a *minimum* market value of $1,125 (25 × $45). If the firm decides that it wants to get the convertible bond off the balance sheet, it simply issues a call for the bonds at 108 ($1,080). All the bondholders should convert their bonds, because the stock they would receive in exchange for the bonds is worth $1,125.

ADVANTAGES TO INVESTOR. We have mentioned that convertible bonds have special features that cause them to have coupon rates substantially below what you would expect on the basis of the quality of the issue. The fact is, *they provide the upside potential of common stock and the downside protection of a bond.* The upside potential can be seen from the preceding example. The bond is convertible into 25 shares of common stock, so as soon as the price of the common stock exceeds $40 a share, the price of the bond will increase by at least the increase in conversion value. In most cases, the bond price will be above its conversion value, because it offers downside protection, and the interest payments on the bond may exceed the dividend payments for the potential common stock (as will be explained shortly).

The convertible bond has downside protection because, irrespective of what happens to the stock, the price of the bond will not decline below what it would be worth as a straight bond. To continue our example, assume that this 8 percent subordinated bond is rated A by the rating services. (The company's regular debentures are rated AA.) Also assume

---

[4] See George E. Pinches and Kent A. Mingo, "A Multivariate Analysis of Industrial Bond Ratings," *Journal of Finance* 28, no. 1 (March 1973): 1–18.

that the firm's earnings decline so that the price of common stock declines to $25 a share. At this point, the bond has a *conversion value* of $625 (25 × $25).[5] Would you expect the bond to decline to $625? The answer is probably no, because it still has value as a bond. (This is generally referred to as a bond's *investment value.*) The bond is an A-rated security with an 8 percent coupon. If we assume that this is an 18-year bond and that comparable A-rated 18-year bonds are currently selling to yield 9 percent, the price of this bond will decline below par but not to $625. In this case, the price will decline to about $938.80 (0.9388 of par).[6] To summarize, the stock price would decline about 30 percent (from $36 to $25), and the bond price would decline only about 6 percent (from $1,000 to $938.80).

In addition to the upside potential–downside protection they offer, convertible bonds are also desirable because they typically have *higher current returns than the underlying common stock does*. Assume that the stock had an annual dividend of $1.50 a share. This would be a 3.75 percent yield on a $40 stock or 4.17 percent on a $36 stock. Although such dividend yields are reasonable, the total current income from the potential common shares would be less than that from the bond. Total dividends on the 25 shares of stock would be $37.50 a year (25 × $1.50), compared to the interest income of $80 from the bond (0.08 × $1,000). Obviously, the bond would be preferable in terms of current income until the dividend on the stock were raised to $3.20 a share ($80/25). Even then, the bond would probably be preferred, because it offers downside protection, and because the $80 interest is contractual, whereas the $80 dividend could be reduced if earnings decline. Therefore, you would probably wait until the common stock dividend reached $3.50 or $4.00 a share before you would convert to take advantage of the higher yield.

An advantage that has been lost is the potential for leverage on convertible bonds. Prior to the 1970s, investors could borrow on convertible bonds at about the same rate at which they could borrow on straight debentures (about 80 percent). This capability made it possible to invest in convertibles with little cash and use the interest on the bond to offset part of the interest on the loan. Currently, however, the margin on convertible bonds is the same as the margin on common stock.

The upside potential–downside protection for convertible bonds can be shown in two ways. Figure 23.6 shows a price-response curve for a convertible bond over a variety of stock price levels. The straight dotted line at the bottom of the curve is the pure equity value or the conversion value of the convertible as discussed previously. The top line (curve) is the market value of the convertible bond that considers the conversion value, but also the *investment value* (or bond value) of the security if the stock price declines substantially. As discussed, if the stock price declined, the security would have a value as a pure bond and thus would not decline

---

[5] The *conversion value* is equal to the bond's conversion ratio (25 in this example) times the current market price of the stock.

[6] This is the price of an 18-year, 8 percent coupon bond priced to yield 9 percent.

FIGURE 23.6
Convertible Bond Price-Response Curve

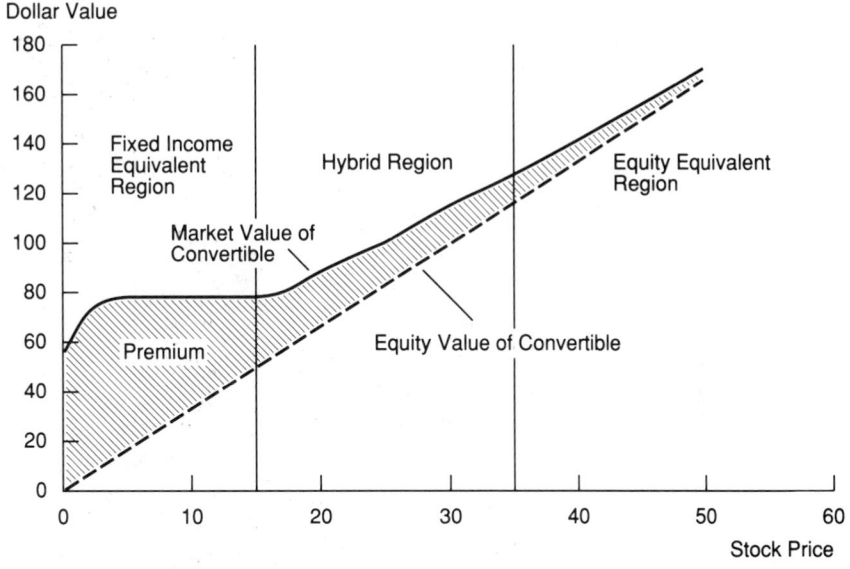

Source: Luke D. Knecht and Michael L. McCowin, "Valuing Convertible Securities," Harris Trust and Savings Bank (1986). Reprinted with permission.

in line with the pure equity value. The decline in the market value of the bond at the far left of the graph reflects the possibility that at very low stock prices, investors might be concerned about the viability of the firm and its ability to pay off this subordinated bond issue.

There are generally three regions for this combination security. At the far right, when the stock price is substantially above the conversion price, the convertible bond is equivalent to common stock, and its value reflects changes in the price of the common stock. At very high stock price levels, the premium over the pure equity (conversion) value basically disappears. In contrast, at the far left, when the stock price is substantially below the conversion price, the security is equivalent to a straight bond, and its price moves with interest rates. In this bond equivalent region, there is a substantial market price premium relative to the conversion value of the bond.

Between these two extremes there is a "hybrid" region where the security is a combination of a bond and common stock. It is within this region that the valuation is difficult. In the bond region, the security is valued as a straight bond, while in the equity region it is valued based upon its conversion value.

See Figure 23.7 for the second way to show the combination characteristics of this security. In this graph of the values (and returns) for a straight stock, a straight bond, and a convertible bond, the returns for

FIGURE 23.7
Return Distributions, Stocks, Bonds, Convertible Securities

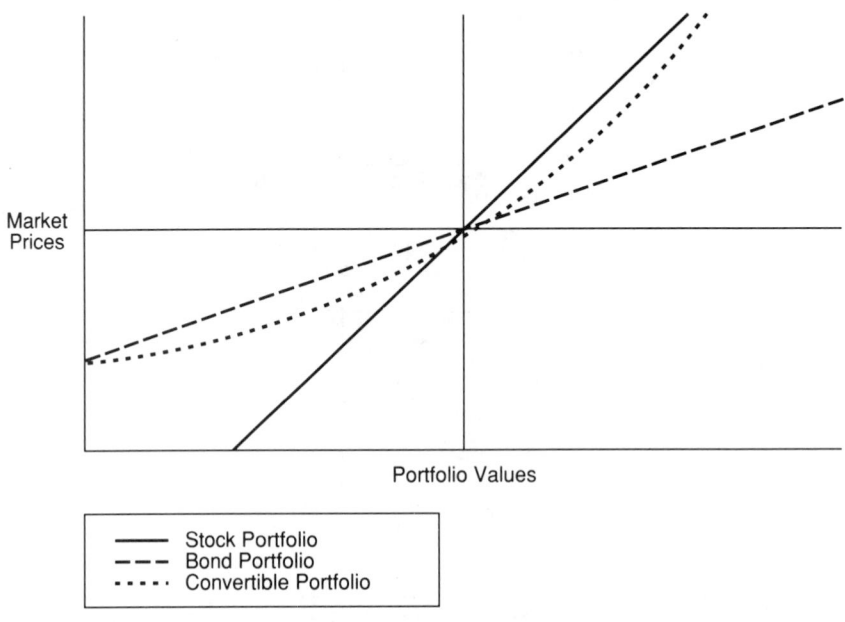

Source: Luke D. Knecht and Michael L. McCowin, "Valuing Convertible Securities," Harris Trust and Savings Bank (1986). Reprinted with permission.

stocks over time are larger *and more volatile* than the returns for bonds. The graph shows that a convertible security acts like the common stock when market prices are increasing, but the price pattern changes, and it acts like the less volatile bond when values decline.

Convertible bonds are, therefore, a desirable investment alternative because they offer upside potential, downside protection, and, typically, higher current income than common stocks offer.[7] This yield advantage is especially true for issues of growth companies that pay low dividends and have substantial potential for price increases. In such cases, institutional investors are willing to accept substantially lower coupon rates on a convertible bond than they would accept on straight bonds.

ANALYSIS AND VALUATION OF CONVERTIBLE BONDS. Because a convertible bond is actually a combination of a bond and a warrant for the common stock, it is necessary to consider both aspects of the security. First, as a straight bond, what should be its yield and implied price? This analysis will indicate your downside risk if the stock were to decline to the point where the security had value *only* as a straight bond.

---

[7] Barbara Donnelly, "Convertible Bonds Regain Some Luster After Being Battered in October Crash," *The Wall Street Journal*, December 3, 1987: 34.

As an example, consider the 7.875 percent convertible bonds issued by IBM due in the year 2004. These bonds are AAA rated by both Standard & Poor's and Moody's and are convertible into 6.508 shares of common stock until maturity. In terms of the straight bond, as of 1989 it would be necessary to determine the going rate on an AAA-rated bond with about 15 years to maturity. If the current yield to maturity on such bonds were about 10 percent, this would imply a straight bond price (referred to as *investment value)* of approximately $837 (the present value of a 7.875 percent, 15-year bond at a 10 percent yield, assuming semiannual interest payments). You should compare this bond value price (investment value) to the current market price of the bond to determine the price risk of the bond (also referred to as the *investment premium).* If we assume the current market price for the bond is 104 of par, this would imply about a 20 percent price risk (investment premium) (1040 − 837/1040). You must decide whether you are willing to accept this downside risk.

The second part of the analysis is an evaluation of the bond in terms of its *stock value;* that is, what is its upside potential as a result of the conversion factor? This determination requires that you compute the *conversion premium* for the bond, which is the conversion parity of the bond compared to the current market price of the stock. The conversion terms indicate the number of shares you would receive if you converted the bond into common stock. In the IBM example, the conversion terms specify that each $1,000 bond can be converted into 6.508 shares of stock. *The conversion parity price of the bond* is equal to the purchase price of the convertible bond divided by the number of common shares into which it is convertible. If the IBM convertible bonds were selling for 104, this implies a conversion parity price of $159.80 ($1,040/6.508). A comparison of this conversion parity price to the current market price of the common stock indicates the parity price premium or conversion premium. Assume that when the IBM bond was selling for 104 and had a conversion parity price of $159.80, the common stock was selling for $124 on the NYSE. This indicates a parity price premium over market price (the conversion premium) of almost 28.9 percent (the $157.80 parity price versus the $124 market price). Obviously, *the smaller this parity price premium, the more desirable is the bond.* Another way to compute this conversion premium is to compare the *conversion value of the bond* (the market price of the stock times the conversion ratio) to *the market price of the bond.* In the case of IBM, its conversion value would be $807 (6.508 × $124) versus the market price of the convertible of $1,040. Again, the premium is 28.9 percent.

Another factor that is considered in evaluating convertible bonds is the *payback,* or *breakeven time,* which measures how long the higher interest income from the convertible bond compared to the dividend income from the common stock must persist to make up for the price on the bond relative to its conversion value (sometimes referred to as its *equity value).* The calculation is as follows:

$$\frac{(\text{Bond price} - \text{Conversion value})}{(\text{Bond income} - \text{Income from Equal Amount Invested in Common Stock})}.$$

In the case of the IBM bond, we have the following:

- a. Bond price = $1,040.00
- b. Conversion value = 807.00 (6.508 × $124)
- c. Conversion bond premium = 233.00 (a minus b)
- d. Bond income = 78.75
- e. Stock income = 36.92 (.0355 × $1,040)
- f. Differential income = 41.83 (d minus e)

Note that, regarding the stock income (item e in the preceding list), the .0355 is the dividend yield on IBM common stock. The company is paying $4.40/share, and the stock price is $124. It is assumed that the investor would invest the $1,040 in IBM common stock.

Therefore, the breakeven time (BT) would be equal to

$$BT = \frac{\$233.00}{41.83} = 5.57 \text{ years.}$$

This indicates that the higher income from the bond relative to the stock would make up the premium paid for the bond in about five and one-half years. Obviously, *the shorter the breakeven period is, the better.* Also, you should compare this breakeven period to the call feature of the bond— that is, it would be preferable, but not necessary, for the breakeven time to be less than the time to first call (in the case of IBM, the bond became callable in November 1988).

Both of these evaluation factors (the parity price premium, or conversion premium, and the breakeven time) are *relative indicators of value* and are useful when comparing several convertible bond issues. Alternatively, you could attempt to value this combination security in terms of its two components: its pure bond (investment) value plus the value of the warrant/option to acquire the stock at a specified price during a given time period. While we have discussed the value of the bond component, we have not considered the valuation of the warrant/option. The difficulty in valuing the warrant/option is that we do not know the true expiration date of the warrant/option because of the call feature of these bonds (you will recall that they were callable as of 1988). Still, it is interesting to consider the other factors for the options pricing model.

- Striking price = $153.66 ($1,000/6.508)
- Market price of stock = 124.00
- Risk-free interest rate = 9.00%
- Expiration time = ? (bond maturity = 15 years)
- Standard deviation of stock = 0.40 (based on historical results)

It would be possible to simulate several expiration times and also stock volatilities and derive some estimates for the value of this option. Given an estimate, you know that the bond provides 6.508 of these options, so the value of the convertible bond would be

- a. Value of straight bond = $837.00

- b. Value of options on stock = _____ (individual value $\times$ 6.508)
- Total value of convertible bond = _____

Beyond considering the current position, you should also estimate the future *potential* for the common stock. What do you expect it to sell for during your investment horizon period? If you expect it to go to $175 a share, your upside potential is approximately 9.5 percent, meaning that the bond will sell for at least $1,139 ($175 $\times$ 6.508), a 9.5 percent increase from $1,040.

Finally, you should consider the differential income from holding the stock rather than the bond. The bond has a 7.875 percent coupon, which indicates $78.75 a year in interest and a current yield of 7.57 percent at the price of 104 (78.75/1040). In contrast, the stock is paying a dividend of $4.40 per share, a 3.55 percent dividend yield, indicating a total dividend payment on the 6.508 shares of $28.64. Therefore, at this time, the current income from the convertible bond substantially exceeds the current income from the common stock. (This total income from the 6.508 shares differs from the income assumed in the breakeven analysis where we assumed that the total $1040 would be invested in 8.4 shares at $124.)

In summary, the analysis indicates the following characteristics of this bond. First, there is a 20 percent downside risk on the bond and a 28 percent premium of the conversion parity price compared to the market price. The breakeven time is 5.6 years. You expect about a 10 percent increase in the value of the bond during your investment period. Finally, the current yield on the bond is substantially higher than the dividend yield on the stock. At this point, you must decide whether this convertible bond is an appropriate way to take advantage of the outlook for the stock given your investment objectives and horizon.

SOURCES OF INFORMATION ON CONVERTIBLE BONDS. A comprehensive list of convertible bonds and information regarding these bonds is contained in the convertible bond section of the *Standard & Poor's Bond Guide.* A sample page is shown in Figure 23.8. Also, *Moody's Bond Record* has a similar section on convertible bonds. Merrill Lynch publishes a monthly statistical report, *Convertible Securities,* that contains extensive data on almost 500 convertible bonds and 100 convertible preferred issues. This report also contains special lists of unique convertibles, such as issues convertible into more than one security and convertibles with put features. A service that provides analysis beyond the statistical information is the *Value Line Options and Convertibles.* This service indicates whether the bond is under- or overvalued and its upside potential and downside protection.

Also, various investment firms provide data and charts on heavily traded convertible bonds. For example, Figure 23.9 shows a Merrill Lynch chart for the IBM issue. The chart plots the market price of the convertible bond as well as the conversion value of the bond and its investment value given its AAA rating. Note the volatility of the conversion value relative

FIGURE 23.8
Sample Page from Standard & Poor's Bond Guide

					Shares		Price	Div. Income	1987		Curr Bid		Yield	Stock Value		STOCK DATA			Earnings Per Share			
XVI											STANDARD & POOR'S CORPORATION											
CONVERTIBLE BONDS	S&P Qual-ity	B F o o o d m		Conv. per $1,000					RANGE		Sale(s)	Curr.	to	of	Conv.	Curr. P/E	Yr.		Last 12	1986 Dil-		
Issue, Rate, Interest Dates and Maturity	Rating		Outstdg. Mil.-$	Ex-pires	Bond	per Share	per Bond	Hi	Lo	Ask(A)	Return	Mat	Bond	Parity	Price Ratio	End	1986	1987	Mos	u't'n		
Waxman Indus.....6¼s Ms15 2007	B-	R	25.0	2007	69.57	14.375	6.96	100	72	72	8.68	9.43	65¼	10⅜	9⅝	14	Je	0.21	□0.60	9 0.69	n/r
●Wean Inc¹..............5½s Ms 1993	NR	R	16.5	1993	41.67	24.00	....	47½	37	43	12.7	26.3	5¼	10⅜	●1¼	d	Dc	△d3.27	....	9 d1.25	n/r
Welbilt Corp........6¼s Ao15 2012	B	R	25.0	2012	38.96	25.67	....	101	58	64	9.77	10.3	....	16⅜	....		Dc	1.35	....	1.51	n/r
●Wells Fargo Mtg/Eq12s mN 2005	BBB	R	27.6	2005	39.96	25.025	79.92	118	99	102	11.7	11.7	72⅞	25½	●18¼	15	Je	2.42	1.52	9 1.19	n/r
●Wendy's Int'l...........7¼s jD 2010	BBB-	R	55.0	2010	57.34	17.44	13.76	105¾	68½	s71	10.2	10.6	32¼	12⅜	●5⅜	62	Dc	d0.05	E0 09	9 0.02	n/r
Wessex Corp.........8½s mN15 2006	CC	R	22.1	2006	204.08	₃ 4.90	....	98	65	^68	12.5	13.1	20⅜	3¾	1	d	Mr	●20.07	....	9 d0.32	n/r
●Western Union¹......5¼s fA 1997	CCC-	R	62.5	1997	₃ 66.00		55.49	47½	24	s36¼	14.4	20.9	....	....	....		Dc	□22.7	....	9 d20.5	n/r
●Westinghouse Elec..9s fA15 2009	AA-	R	123	2009	32.26	31.00	55.49	243	136	160.60	5.60	4.56	160½	49¾	●49¼	10	Dc	4.47	E5.15	7 4.96	4.31
Weston(Roy F.),Inc.7s Ao15 2002	B+	R	30.0	2002	⁴47.33	21.13	....	118	85	90	7.78	8.20	67½	19	14¾	37	Dc	0.51	....	9 0.39	n/r
Westwood One......6¼s aO15 2011	B+	R	100	2011	40.68	24.58	....	130¼	75	95	7.11	7.19	75¼	23¾	18½	24	Nv	0.63	....	9 0.76	n/r
●Wherehouse Entmt⁵..6¼s jJ 2006	B	R	50.0	2006	36.23	27.60	1.81	85	45	s50	12.5	13.7	48⅞	13¾	●13½	41	Ja	0.58		10 0.33	n/r
●Whittaker Corp.........4½s jJ 1988	NR	R	3.62	7-1-88	21.28	47.00	21.28	98¾	94	95⅝	4.71	14.0	51⅜	44¾	●24	5	Dc	d0.44	P4.60	4.60	n/r
Williams(A.L.).......7¼s Jd 2006	NR	R	40.3	2006	35.09	28.50	....	104	77	79	9.18	9.72	57¾	22½	16½	11	Dc	△1.09	....	9 1.48	n/r
Winners Corp⁶.......8¼s Jd 2003	NR	R	25.0	2003	56.34	17.75	....	104	77	33	....	....	12⅜	5⅞	●2¼	0	Dc	d0.54	....	9 d1.40	n/r
●Witco Corp⁶...........4½s jD15 1993	A-	R	1.68	1993	67.52	14.81	86.43	287	268	225¾	2.00	....	225¾	33⅜	●33¾	12	Dc	2.93	E2.70	9 2.89	2.88
●Witco Corp...........5½s Ms15 2012	A-	R	140	2012	18.33	54.55	23.46	104	70	s78	7.05	7.48	61⅜	42½	●33⅜	12	Dc	2.93	P2.70	9 2.89	2.88
●WMS Industries⁷..12¾s mN 1996	NR	R	22.0	1996	49.58	20.17	....	100	81	84	15.1	16.2	20⅞	17	●4½	d	Sp	d0.45	P0.29	d0.29	n/r
Worlds of⁹ Wonder⁹......9s Jd 2012	D	R	80.0	2012	58.48	17.10	....	100	7½	7½	....	....	3⅜	1¼	⅜	d	Mr	0.85	Edef⁸	d1.60	n/r
Xerox Corp¹⁰..........5s AnDec 1988	A	C	73.6	12-1-88	6.76	148.00	20.28	98½	95¾	96¾	5.16	8.64	38¼	143¾	●56½	10	Dc	△3.85	E5.40	9 4.69	n/r
●Xerox Corp............6s mN 1995	A	R	100	1995	10.87	92.00	32.61	108¼	83½	s90½	6.63	7.63	61½	8¾	●56½	10	Dc	△3.85	E5.40	9 4.69	n/r
●Zayre Corp............7¼s jJ15 2010	BBB+	R	75.0	2010	28.41	35.20	11.36	116	71¾	s72	10.0	10.5	39¾	25¾	●14	5	Ja	1.55	₃2.80	10 2.76	1.49
●Zehntel, Inc.........9¼s Ms15 2012	NR	R	15.5	2012	212.77	4.70	....	131¾	82	92	10.0	10.1	61¼	4⅞	2⅜	d	Je	d1.52	*0.06	d0.20	n/r
●Zenith Electronics...6¼s Ao 2011	BB-	R	115	2011	32.00	31.25	....	11′	68	s71	8.80	9.32	47¼	22¼	●14¾	d	Dc	d0.43	Ed1.00	9 0.97	n/r
●Zurn Indus............5¾s mN 1994	A	R	4.70	1994	70.18	14.25	47.72	175	127	134¼	4.28	....	134¼	19⅛	●19½	12	Mr	1.43	E1.60	9 1.53	1.40

Uniform Footnote Explanations—See Page XVI. Other: ¹Was Wean United. ²Exch offer:1.76 Cl A & 56Cl B Pfd,to Dec 30. ³Old shares. ⁴Into Cl A com. ⁵WEI Hldg offers $14 for com, to Jan 22. ⁶Was Witco Chemical. ⁷Was Williams Electronics. ⁸Int of 12-1-87 not pd when due. ⁹File bankruptcy Chapt 11. ¹⁰Offered outside U.S.:P&I pay in U.S.$.

EXPLANATION OF COLUMN HEADINGS AND FOOTNOTES

MARKET: Unlisted except where symbols ● or ◆ are used:
● –New York Stock Exchange ◆ –American Stock Exchange

ISSUE TITLE: Name of Bond at time of offering; otherwise issue footnoted with name change of obligor. Minor changes with old title indicated in brackets, i.e. Gen Tel (Corp) & Elec.
Prin & int payable in U.S. funds. § Int. and/or prin. in default.

FORM OF BOND: Letters are used to indicate form of bond: C–Coupon only; CR–Coupon or Registered, interchangeable; R–Registered only.

CONVERSION EXPIRES: Footnote keyed to bottom of page when conversion price changes during life of the privilege; also noted on conversion price.
ⓔ Indicates a change in next 12 months. a–No fractional shs. issued upon conversion; settlements in cash.

DIVIDEND INCOME PER BOND: If $1,000 Bond were converted, the annual amount of dividends expected to be paid by the company on the stock based on most recent indication of annual rate of payment.
t–Less tax at origin. g–in Canadian funds less 15% or 10% non–residence tax.

STOCK VALUE OF BOND: Price at which bond must sell to equal price of stock i.e., number of shares received on conversion times price of the stock.

CONVERSION PARITY: Price at which stock must sell to equal bond price, i.e., price of bond divided by number of shares received on conversion.

P-E RATIO: (Price–Earnings Ratio) Represents market valuation of any $1 of per share earnings i.e., the price of the stock divided by estimated or latest 12 months per share earnings.

EARNINGS, in general, are per share as reported by company. **FOR YEAR INDICATED:** Fiscal years ending prior to March 31 are shown under preceding year. Net operating earnings are shown for banks; net earnings before appropriation to general reserve for **savings & loan associations;** net investment income for **insurance companies; railroads'** earnings are as reported to ICC. **Foreign** issues traded ADR are dollars per share, converted at prevailing exchange rate. Specific footnotes used:

△ Excl extra-ord income	‡–Partial Year	j–Currency at origin
▲ Incl extra-ord income	+–New Year Earns	P–Preliminary
□ Excl extra-ord charges	b–Before depletion	p–Pro forma
■ Incl extra-ord charges	d–Deficit	R–Fully diluted
* Excl tax credits	E–S&P Estimate	n/r–Not reported

LAST 12 Mos. indicates earnings through period indicated by superior number preceding figure: ¹for Jan. ²for Feb., etc. Figure without superior number indicates fiscal year end.

DILUTION: Earnings on a fully diluted basis, as reported in accordance with Accounting Principles Board opinions.

Source: *Standard & Poor's Bond Guide*, January 1988 (New York: Standard & Poor's Corp.). Reprinted with permission.

to the investment value. The bottom chart plots the conversion premium and also the premium recovery period—that is, the payback period, or breakeven time.

CONVERTIBLE PREFERRED STOCK

Convertible preferred stock is similar to convertible bonds since it is a combination of a preferred stock issue and common stock. Beyond the conversion privileges, these issues typically have the following characteristics:

1. They are cumulative but not participating (the dividend cumulates if it is not paid, but the holders do not participate in earnings beyond the dividend).

Figure **23.9**
Merrill Lynch Convertible Research

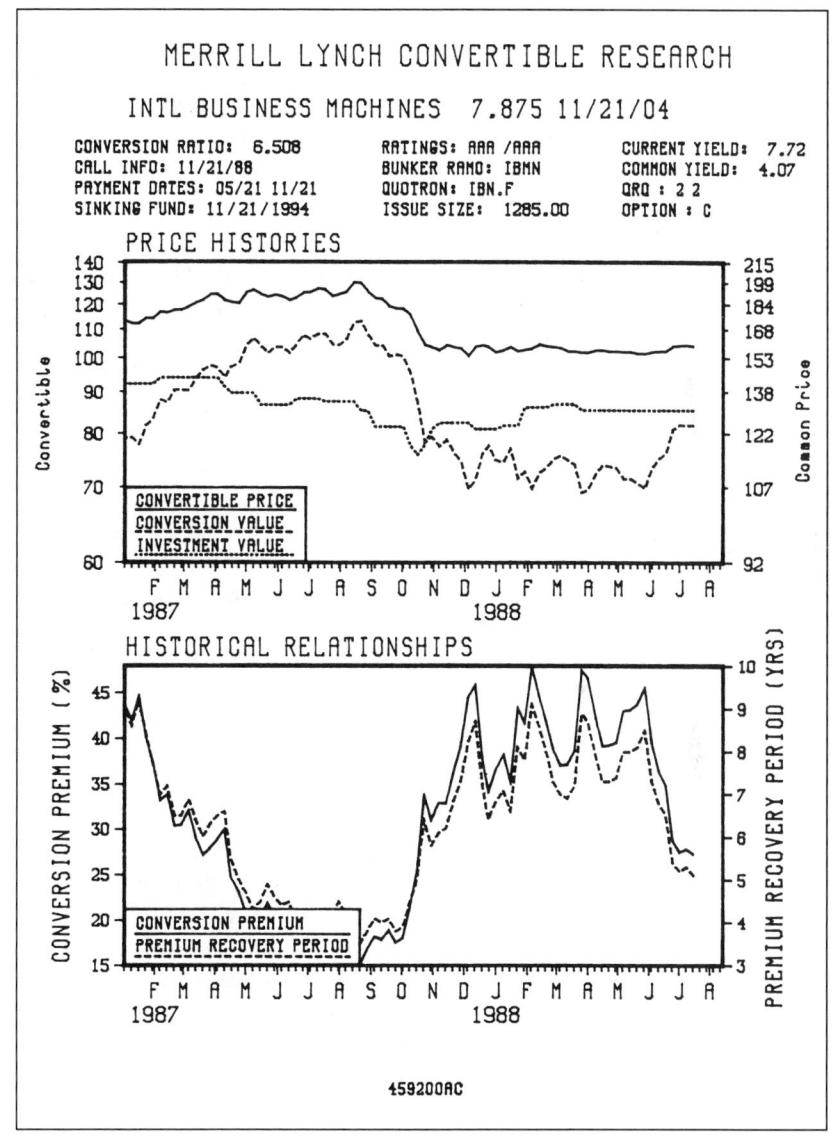

Source: New York: Merrill Lynch Pierce Fenner and Smith, "Convertible Research." (August 1988).

2. They have no sinking fund or purchase fund.
3. They have a fixed conversion rate.

4. There is generally no waiting period before conversion can take place.
5. The conversion privilege does not expire.[8]

As pointed out by Pinches, most convertible preferred stock was issued in connection with mergers as a way of providing income and yet not diluting the common equity of the acquiring firm. Although preferred stock and convertible preferred stock have not been a major source of new financing, there are a number of convertible preferred issues outstanding for the interested investor.

ANALYSIS OF CONVERTIBLE PREFERRED STOCK. Because convertible preferred stock is likewise a hybrid security involving preferred stock and common stock, the valuation analysis, like that of a convertible bond, involves two steps. Consider the Cummings Engine Corporation convertible preferred stock issue, paying an annual dividend of $3.50 a share. The stock is rated BAA3 by Moody's and BBB by Standard & Poor's; it is listed on the NYSE and is convertible into .649 shares of common stock. As of mid-1988, the common stock was selling for $52 a share, and the $3.50 convertible preferred stock was $46 a share.

In terms of a pure preferred stock issue, it had some downside risk. At this time, most straight preferred stock issues were yielding between 8 and 9 percent whereas the yield on the Cummings Engine stock was 7.6 percent. Using the conservative 9 percent would indicate a straight preferred stock price of $38.89 ($3.50/0.09). This represents about an 18 percent decline from the prevailing market price of $46. At 8 percent the value would be $43.75, which is only a 5 percent downside risk. It appears that the stock is selling on the basis of its investment value, because there is a fairly substantial conversion premium.

The conversion value of the stock is $33.75 (.649 × $52), compared to the market price of the convertible of $46, which implies a conversion premium of 36 percent ($46 vs. $33.75). You can also derive a conversion parity value for the convertible preferred stock by dividing the current market price of the preferred stock by the conversion ratio. In this case, the conversion parity is $70.88 ($46/.649), which likewise implies the 36 percent premium compared to the prevailing common stock price of $52. Put another way, at this time the convertible preferred stock is generally priced in line with its investment value, so its stock price will typically move in line with yields on preferred stock.

You should examine the income relationship between the common and preferred stock. The common stock was paying an annual dividend of $2.20 a share, which indicates a dividend yield of 4.23 percent

---

[8] George E. Pinches, "Financing With Convertible Preferred Stock, 1960–1967," *Journal of Finance* 25, no. 1 (March 1970): 61; Ronald W. Melicher, "A Comment on Financing with Convertible Preferred Stock, 1960–1967," *Journal of Finance* 26, no. 1 (March 1971): 148–149; and George E. Pinches, "Financing with Convertible Preferred Stock, 1960–1967: Reply," *Journal of Finance* 26, no. 1 (March 1971): 150–151.

(2.20/52.00). In contrast, the preferred stock pays an annual dividend of $3.50, indicating a 7.6 percent yield ($3.50/$46.00).

This analysis would indicate that the convertible preferred stock has limited downside risk and limited upside potential, since it is selling at a fairly large conversion premium.

SUMMARY

Warrants are similar to call options, but they have a much longer life, and they are issued by the company issuing the stock. Americus Trust units entail dividend-yielding *primes* and *scores* that are similar to warrants. Further, there is a growing list of currency exchange warrants (CEWs) that can be used to speculate or hedge in the currency markets. Valuation of these instruments is similar to valuation of call options, because the only difference to the investor is the longer term.

Two types of combination securities are convertible bonds and convertible preferred stock. Both have significant advantages to the issuing corporation as well as to the investor. The valuation procedure involves evaluating both components of these securities: the value of the security as a straight bond or preferred stock and its common stock option value.

Note that all of these investment instruments provide additional investment opportunities. Therefore, after you have evaluated a firm and decided to invest in it, the question becomes *how* should I invest in this firm? Clearly, if warrants, Americus Trusts, or convertible securities are available, they should be considered.

QUESTIONS

1. What are two major differences between a warrant and a call option?
2. What advantage does a warrant have over a listed call option from the standpoint of a corporation?
3. What advantage does a warrant have in comparison to a listed call option for an investor?
4. Define the intrinsic value of a warrant. Give an example of a warrant with positive intrinsic value.
5. Discuss briefly three factors that influence the speculative value of a warrant (that is, the premium over intrinsic value).
6. As an investor, explain why you would want a high or low stock-price-to-warrant-price ratio.
7. Describe how a firm "forces conversion" of a convertible bond. What conditions must exist?
8. The Baron Corporation debentures are rated Aa by Moody's and are selling to yield 9.30 percent. Its subordinated convertible bonds are rated A by Moody's and are selling to yield 8.20 percent. Explain this phenomenon.
9. Describe the upside potential of convertible bonds. Why do convertible bonds also provide downside protection?
10. Assume a convertible bond's conversion value is substantially above par. Why would the bondholder continue holding the bond rather than converting?

11. Explain the breakeven time and why you would want a high or low value.

PROBLEMS

1. The Raymond Corporation has a warrant outstanding that allows the holder to acquire two shares of common stock at $15.00 a share for the next three years. The stock is currently selling for $12, and the warrant is selling for $2.

1a. Compute the intrinsic value of the warrant. What difference does it make that the warrant is for two shares?

1b. Compute the speculative value (premium) of this warrant.

1c. Would you expect the premium to be greater if the stock were selling for $14? Why?

2. The Golden Dome Corporation has a warrant that allows the holder to acquire a share of stock for $30 until 1995. The stock is currently selling for $32, and the warrant is selling for $2.

2a. Compute the intrinsic value and the speculative value of this warrant.

2b. What is the leverage factor for this warrant?

2c. If the stock increases to $40 a share, what will be the percent of change in stock price and in warrant price, assuming the same premium on the warrant?

2d. Discuss the relation between your answers to part c and part b.

3. The College Corporation has an 8 percent subordinated convertible debenture outstanding that is due in ten years. The current yield to maturity on this A-rated bond is 5 percent. The current yield on non–convertible A-rated bonds is 10 percent. This bond is convertible into 21 shares of common stock and is callable at 106 of par, which is $1,000. The company's $10 par-value common stock is currently selling for $54.

3a. What is the straight-debt value of the convertible bond, assuming semiannual interest payments?

3b. What is the conversion value of this bond?

3c. At present, what would you expect the approximate price of the bond to be? Why?

3d. At present, could the College Corporation get rid of this convertible debenture? Discuss specifically how it would do so.

4. Extractive Industries has debentures outstanding (par value $1,000) that are convertible into the company's common stock at a price of $25. The convertibles have a coupon interest rate of 11 percent and mature ten years from today. Interest is payable semiannually, and the convertible debenture is callable with a one-year interest premium.

4a. Calculate the conversion value if the stock price is $20 per share.

4b. Calculate the conversion value if the stock price is $28 per share.

4c. Calculate the straight-bond value, assuming that bonds of equivalent risk and maturity are yielding 12 percent per year compounded semiannually.

4d. Based on your answers to parts b and c, estimate the market price of the convertible. No calculations are required, but explain your answer.

5. Sitting next to Dan at a business luncheon, Rachel exclaimed, "I bought

American Desk at $20 a share and it's gone to $40." Dan said, "You would have done better to buy American's warrants, as I did."

5a. Why did Dan say this?

5b. The exercise price of American Desk is $18. Rachel purchased the warrants for $4 each when American Desk's stock price was $20 a share. Each warrant entitles Rachel to purchase one share of American stock. Assuming the $2 warrant premium drops to $1, what is the current price of the warrant?

5c. Calculate Rachel's percentage gain.

5d. Calculate Dan's percentage gain when the stock price is $40 and the warrant premium is $1.

6. The common stock of Apex Corporation is currently selling at $12 per share, while Apex's warrants have five years till expiration, are selling at $3, and permit the purchase of a share of common stock at $11 per share. By the end of the year you expect the premium on the warrants to have decreased by 20 percent and the following probability distribution to exist for the stock:

PROBABILITY	PRICE
.10	10
.30	13
.40	16
.15	19
.05	25

6a. Given the probability distribution, what is the expected stock price?

6b. Given the probability distribution, what is the expected warrant price?

6c. If average expectations are met, what would be your annual return from an investment in the stock?

6d. If average expectations are met, what would be your annual return from an investment in warrants?

REFERENCES

WARRANTS

Ferri, Michael G., Joseph W. Kremer, and H. Dennis Oberhelman. "An Analysis of the Pricing of Warrants." *Advancements in Futures and Options Research* 1 (1986).

Kim, Moon K., and Allan Young. "Rewards and Risks from Warrant Hedging." *Journal of Portfolio Management* 6, no. 4 (Summer 1980).

Leabo, Dick A., and Richard J. Rogalski. "Warrant Price Movements and the Efficient Market Hypothesis." *Journal of Finance* 20, no. 1 (March 1975).

CONVERTIBLE SECURITIES

Alexander, Gordon J., and Roger D. Stover. "The Effect of Forced Conversion on Common Stock Prices." *Financial Management* 9, no. 1 (Spring 1980).

Alexander, Gordon J., and Roger D. Stover. "Pricing in the New Issue Convertible Debt Market." *Financial Management* 6, no. 3 (Fall 1977).

Baumol, William J., Burton G. Malkiel, and R. E. Quandt. "The Valuation of Convertible Securities." *Quarterly Journal of Economics* 80, no. 1 (February 1966).

Brennan, M. J., and E. S. Schwartz. "Convertible Bonds: Valuation and Optimal Strategies for Call and Conversion." *Journal of Finance* 32, no. 5 (December 1977).

Brigham, Eugene F. "An Analysis of Convertible Debentures: Theory and Some Empirical Evidence." *Journal of Finance* 21, no. 1 (March 1966).

Ritchie, J. C., Jr., "Convertible Securities and Warrants" in F. J. Fabozzi, and I. M. Pollack, eds. *Handbook of Fixed Income Securities.* 2d ed. (Homewood, Ill: Dow Jones-Irwin, 1986).

Soldofsky, Robert M. "The Risk-Return Performance of Convertibles." *Journal of Portfolio Management* 7, no. 2 (Winter 1981).

Young, Robert A. "Convertible Securities: Definitions, Analytical Tools, and Practical Investment Strategies," in *The Financial Analysts Handbook.* Edited by Sumner N. Levine (Homewood, Ill.: Dow Jones-Irwin, 1988).

APPENDIX 23A   CONVERTIBLE GLOSSARY

Bond equivalent *See* Fixed Income Equivalent

Bond value *See* Investment Value

Breakeven time The time required for the added income from the convertible to offset the conversion premium. Also referred to as *payback.*

"Busted" convertibles *See* Fixed Income Equivalent

Call provisions Indenture provisions describing the date, price, and other circumstances under which the issuer may redeem a convertible.

Conditional call *See* Provisional Call

Conversion premium The excess of the market value of the convertible over its equity value if immediately converted into common stock. Typically expressed as a percentage relative to the equity value.

Conversion price (or exercise price) The price at which common stock can be obtained by surrendering the convertible instrument at par value.

Conversion ratio The number of shares of common stock for which a convertible security may be exchanged.

Conversion value *See* Equity Value

Equity equivalent A convertible whose price behavior is dominated by changes in the common stock price, with relatively little sensitivity to changes in interest rate levels.

Equity value The value of the convertible security if converted into common stock at the current common stock price level. Also referred to as *parity* or *conversion parity.*

Fixed income equivalent A convertible whose price behavior is dominated by changes in interest rates, with relatively little sensitivity to changes in the common stock price.

Source: Luke D. Knecht and Michael L. McCowin, "Valuing Convertible Securities," Harris Trust and Savings Bank (1986). Reprinted with permission.

Floor value *See* Investment Value

Forced conversion If an issuer attempts to redeem a convertible for cash, and if the equity value exceeds the redemption price, the investor is "forced" to convert into common stock in order to obtain the higher equity value.

Hard call A convertible that does not have any provisional call feature is said to have *hard call* protection.

Initial premium The conversion premium at the time of offering of a new convertible security.

Investment value The price at which a debenture would have to sell as a straight debt instrument. Also referred to as *bond value* or *floor value.*

Investment value premium The difference between a convertible's market price and its investment value, expressed as a percentage of investment value.

Parity (or conversion parity) *See* Equity Value

Payback *See* Breakeven Time

Point premium The conversion premium expressed as the *points,* or dollar price difference between the market price of the convertible and its equity value.

Provisional call Indenture provision that permits the company to call a convertible security prior to the stated call date if the common stock price rises above a preset level. Typically expressed as a percentage (such as 140 percent or 150 percent) of the specified conversion price.

Unit offering A combination of notes and warrants that is issued as a unit but may subsequently be traded either separately or as a unit. Also referred to as *synthetic convertibles.*

Yield advantage The difference between the current yield of the convertible and the current yield of the common stock.

Yield to first call Rate of return provided from the current price level, assuming the issue is called at the first available call date.

Yield to first put Rate of return provided from the current price level, assuming the issue is called at the first available put date.

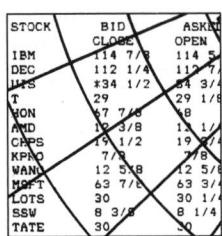

CHAPTER 24

COMMODITY FUTURES

While stocks and bonds constitute the bulk of most investment portfolios, the discussion in Chapter 2 pointed out the importance of considering a wide variety of investment alternatives. Diversification is important to your overall investment objectives, and a knowledge of diverse investments may point toward new opportunities.

Commodities trading meets both of these criteria. As shown in Chapter 2, the correlation between commodity prices and stock and bond prices is quite low, so you could envision commodity trading as a means to further diversify your overall investment portfolio. Also, commodities trading provides a wide range of investment opportunities, from relatively conservative hedging transactions carried out by farmers or food processors, to fairly high-risk speculative transactions from which the short-run returns can be very large positive or negative values.

In this chapter, we will first examine the spot, forward, and futures contracts, then compare trading in common stocks (and bonds) with trading in futures. Next, we will look at the organization of future markets and quotations and the relationship among spot, forward, and futures prices. An interesting issue in this context is the impact of futures trading on spot prices. Finally, we will examine the performance of futures contracts in hedging the price risk of spot assets and in generating speculative profits. We will consider each of these issues with respect to commodities in this chapter and do the same for interest rate futures, currency futures, stock index futures, and options on index futures contracts in Chapter 25.

SPOT, FORWARD, AND FUTURES CONTRACTS

In general, there are four types of contracts for the purchase and sale of assets. A *cash contract*, or *spot contract*, is for the immediate delivery of an asset. Transactions in the primary and secondary markets for stocks and bonds are examples of cash contracts. Similarly, if a food processor currently purchases wheat to fill a flour contract, it is a cash, or spot, market transaction. In contrast, traders may enter into contracts today that call for *deferred-delivery* transactions. For instance, a mortgage banker makes a commitment to lend money to a builder in the future, but the rate of interest is determined today. Another example is an exporter who agrees to deliver grain in the future for a price agreed upon today. Such deferred-delivery contracts may be forward, futures, or options contracts.

A *forward contract* is a contract between two traders for delivery of a specific asset at a fixed time in the future for a price (called the *exercise price*) to be determined today. Transactions by the mortgage banker and the exporter are forward contracts. Here the quality (grade, term to maturity, and the coupon on loans), quantity, method and place of delivery, price, and method of settlement are all determined by the two traders. As such, the forward market is a dealer market, where transactions are negotiated. While the buyer of a forward contract knows that the commodity delivered will meet his particular needs, it is necessary to find another trader willing to sell such a contract. Because *there is generally not a secondary market for forward contracts,* both parties are locked into the contract and subject to the risk of failure to perform on the contract by either party and the uncertainty of subsequent price fluctuations.

A *futures contract* overcomes some of the shortcomings of forward contracts. It is a deferred-delivery contract between a trader and the *clearinghouse of a futures exchange*, where all terms of trade, except the price and number of contracts, are standardized. Futures contracts are traded in auction markets organized by futures exchanges, and the clearinghouse guarantees performance on all contracts. Because there is a fairly active secondary market for most futures contracts, it is possible for traders to close their position prior to the predetermined delivery date by executing a reverse transaction. For example, assume that a mortgage banker makes a commitment to a builder in March to lend money three months later, in June, at a fixed rate of 14 percent. The banker is exposed to the risk that mortgage rates will increase during the following three months, which would cause a decline in the mortgage price. In arranging this transaction, the banker can use the Treasury bond futures contract for June delivery, which is traded on the Chicago Board of Trade (CBT). First, from today's published quotes on the June contract, the banker can obtain the market consensus forecast of long-term interest rates expected at the time of contract delivery in June. This information coupled with the expected spread between the GNMA and government bond rates could be used in setting the rate on the forward mortgage loan.

Second, the mortgage banker can hedge his exposure by selling an appropriate number of June futures contracts today and subsequently buying them back before delivery. If mortgage rates have increased by June, there will be a loss on the forward commitment to the builder but a gain on the short futures position. On the other hand, if there is a decline in rates from their expected level, this will produce a gain on the forward loan but a loss on the short futures position. Thus, whatever happens to mortgage rates between now and June, the gain/loss on the futures position reduces the variability of the rate of return on the forward loan. Notice that the example does not involve any delivery on the futures contract. Over 95 percent of such transactions do not. Therefore, futures contracts are considered temporary (close but imperfect) substitutes for the merchandizing forward contracts. In addition, *a futures contract is marked to market at the end of every trading day*, unlike a forward contract, so the gains/losses on futures positions are settled daily.

The spot, forward, and futures contracts involve an obligation for the buyers and sellers to perform on the contract, that is, to make and accept delivery and payment. Sometimes traders would like to acquire only the right to buy or only the right to sell the underlying asset without incurring the obligation to accept or make delivery. Contracts for the exchange of such rights are called *option contracts* and are traded in auction markets (exchange markets) as well as over the counter. As discussed in Chapter 23, a *call option* traded on an exchange is a contract that confers a right on the buyer of the contract to purchase (call away) a specified asset from the clearinghouse at a predetermined price (exercise price) during a specified period of time. A *put option* gives the buyer of a contract the right to sell to the clearinghouse the underlying asset at a fixed price during a specified period of time. Put and call options traded on exchanges are standardized contracts. The buyer of an option contract is entitled to buy or to sell, but the seller of an option has an obligation to perform when the option is exercised by the buyer. Unlike OTC options, listed options enjoy a fairly active market.

Other terms and concepts unique to futures trading are explained in the glossary at the end of this chapter. Given this background, let us consider some specific similarities and differences between stock and futures trading.

SIMILARITIES AND DIFFERENCES IN STOCK AND FUTURES TRADING PRACTICES

Similarities in stock and futures trading practices are as follows:

1. Highly organized exchanges exist for both areas of investment. This is in contrast to other investment alternatives, such as real estate, antiques, coins, or stamps, which have highly fragmented trading markets on a geographic basis.
2. Trading on a given exchange is limited to specified stocks or assets. Just as the New York, Tokyo, and London Stock Exchanges allow trading only in listed stocks, the futures exchanges limit trading to specified assets, such as commodity futures, interest rate futures, currency futures, and stock index futures.
3. Only members can trade on an exchange (stock or commodity) for themselves or for others.
4. The mechanics of buying and selling stocks or futures contracts are quite similar. In both cases, you give an order to a local bro-

ker, who sends it to the floor of the exchange where an exchange member executes the order through the stock specialist or in the appropriate commodities pit.

5. The types of orders on the exchanges are substantially similar. In both areas market orders, stop orders, and limit orders are frequently used.
6. Because they have highly organized exchanges and communication networks, both areas of investment enjoy substantial liquidity. This ability to turn investments into cash very quickly at a fairly certain price contrasts sharply with other investments.
7. In both areas some investors base their decisions on the fundamentals of supply and demand, and there are technicians who use charts and depend mainly upon past price movements for indications of future price movements.

Differences in stock and futures trading practices are as follows:

1. The buyer of a stock acquires ownership, but the buyer of a futures contract is not entitled to ownership of the underlying asset until he decides to accept delivery at time of final settlement.
2. There is much greater leverage in commodity trading than in stocks. While the current margin requirement on stocks is 50 percent, the requirements on commodity futures range between 5 and 15 percent. Not only is more leverage available for trading futures, but it is also universally used, in contrast to stocks, where a small proportion of trading is done on margin. In addition, not all common stocks are eligible for margin trading, while it is possible to buy all futures contracts on margin.
3. There are interest charges on money borrowed to acquire stocks but not on the difference between the total value of a futures contract and the margin for a futures contract. This is because the futures contract is a deferred-delivery contract, so the payment of total value is deferred until the delivery date of the contract. In fact, what is referred to as *margin* in futures trading is really a *good-faith deposit* to protect the futures broker.
4. While there is a commission charged for purchase and another charged for sale of stocks or bonds, commissions on futures are paid only on a completed contract (purchase and sale). The commissions on futures are a stated dollar cost per contract and tend to be a smaller percentage of the total value of the contract.
5. Stock prices are free to fluctuate without limit. In contrast, there is a daily limit on the price change allowed for each futures contract. Once a given contract reaches this limit, trading in it cannot take place beyond the limit price until the next day.
6. One of the major problems facing the stock market in recent years has been the stock certificate and the stock transfer procedure. This is not a problem in futures trading because there are no certificates, and transferring is done through the Commodity Clearing Corporation.

7. In the stock market, there is a clearing corporation, but there are also dealers on the buying and the selling side of the trade. In the futures market, *the clearing corporation actually takes the other side in all transactions*, either buying or selling directly. In commodities, the transaction between two brokers or traders takes place in the pit. After the transaction, each party reports to the clearinghouse, which makes sure that the orders match and charges each broker accordingly. Once this is done, the brokers have no connection to each other but only to the clearing corporation, which handles all subsequent closing trades directly and settles with the customer. The clearing corporation eventually records the fact that a sale was offset with a purchase and is thereby closed out.

8. In the stock market, you specifically sell the stock you bought or buy the stock you sold short to complete a transaction. In futures trading, you simply engage in an opposite transaction, and the two individual transactions cancel each other out through the clearing corporation.

9. Although there are organized exchanges in both areas, there are no specialists in futures exchanges. When a trade is desired, a member of the futures exchange simply goes to the appropriate pit, makes it known that he has an order, and all interested traders respond.

10. When an investor wants to sell a stock short, it is specifically designated as a short sale, and it cannot be done on a *downtick* (a decrease); he must wait until there is a trade at an *uptick* (an increase) or a *zero uptick* (a trade with no change, when the prior transaction was at an uptick). There is no such tick requirement for short-selling futures; you simply sell a contract you did not buy previously.

11. Trading in futures is simpler than stock trading because there are no dividends and stock splits. As a result, the price changes reflect all rates of return.

12. About 3 percent of trading in the NYSE is in odd lots (sales or purchases of less than 100 shares). In contrast, there are typically no odd-lot contracts available in futures trading on the major exchanges. Because of the substantial leverage available, it is typically not necessary. Still, there are "mini" contracts on some smaller exchanges.

13. There are differences in sources of information. For example, the major source of information about a specific firm is the company itself, but the principal source of information for major agricultural commodities is the U.S. Department of Agriculture. Because of this, there is less inside information in commodities, because the government is scrupulous about any possible leaks.

14. Many of these differences produce a different typical holding period for the two investment alternatives. The holding period

for agricultural contracts seldom exceeds 90 days and generally cannot exceed a year because the contracts are deliverable within that period. Financial futures, such as T-bond futures, have delivery periods extending to two years, but the volume of trading in the distant delivery contracts is limited. For other financial futures, such as Eurodollar futures and T-bill futures, some delivery periods are longer than the term to maturity of the underlying asset, so the spot asset does not exist for distant delivery contracts. In contrast, stocks can be held almost indefinitely, and the average holding period is probably close to a year.

15. There are differences in the normal unit of trading. In stocks, the normal unit of trading is a *round lot*, which is almost always 100 shares. Futures are traded on the basis of contracts, which differ between commodities. As shown in Figure 24.1, the type of contract is listed at the top of each commodity entry; for example, a wheat contract on the Chicago Board of Trade (CBT) is for 5,000 bushels, a contract of live cattle on the Chicago Mercantile Exchange (CME) is 40,000 pounds, and a Eurodollar futures contract on the International Money Market (IMM) is for $1 million.

16. There are differences in price volatility and even greater differences in the volatility of rates of return. Agricultural commodity prices are generally more volatile than stock prices because of the nature of the information affecting the price, including the impact of weather and international demand. In addition to basic price volatility, the rates of return to the investor will be more volatile due to the substantial leverage caused by buying on margin.

17. Futures contracts have fixed delivery months specified by the sponsoring exchanges. Some contracts, such as T-bond futures, have quarterly delivery cycles, and many agricultural commodity futures mature at irregular intervals that vary from a month to five months. T-bill futures contracts require delivery during the three business days after the Wednesday following the third Monday of the delivery month. The T-note and T-bond futures permit delivery during the entire delivery month. The futures exchanges also specify the place of delivery. No comparable restrictions on delivery exist in the stock market.

18. As observed earlier, performance on a futures contract—delivery as well as payment—is guaranteed by the clearing corporation for the particular futures contract. In upholding this guarantee, the clearing corporation *marks a contract to market* at the end of every trading day, thus ensuring that its obligations are limited by the maximum daily price change in the unusual event of default by a member broker and his customer. Specifically, if the futures price has moved in favor of the customer during the

FIGURE 24.1
Futures Prices

FUTURES PRICES

Monday, June 20, 1988
Open Interest Reflects Previous Trading Day.

Column headings (each commodity block): Open | High | Low | Settle | Change | Lifetime High | Lifetime Low | Open Interest

—GRAINS AND OILSEEDS—

CORN (CBT) 5,000 bu.; cents per bu.

	Open	High	Low	Settle	Change	Life High	Life Low	Open Int
July	324½	324½	324½	324½	+15	324½	174	51,984
Sept	332½	332½	332½	332½	+15	332½	180¾	37,187
Dec	340½	340½	340½	340½	+15	340½	184	105,461
Mr89	340½	340½	340½	340½	+15	340½	193½	15,573
May	335½	335½	335½	335½	+15	335½	207½	6,216
July	331½	331½	331½	331½	+15	331½	233	2,902
Sept	299	299	299	299	+15	299	245	542
Dec	270	274	266	270¼	+9¼	275	235	3,501

Est vol 25,000; vol Fri 101,940; open int 223,366, +8,171.

OATS (CBT) 5,000 bu.; cents per bu.

	Open	High	Low	Settle	Change	Life High	Life Low	Open Int
July	308	308	308	308	+10	308	144	2,284
Sept	309	309	309	309	+10	309	143	3,719
Dec	304¼	304¼	304¼	304¼	+10	304¼	162	3,051
Mr89	286	286	286	286	+10	286	171	854
May	267	267	267	267	+10	267	187	116

Est vol 500; vol Fri 3,714; open int 10,034, −78.

SOYBEANS (CBT) 5,000 bu.; cents per bu.

	Open	High	Low	Settle	Change	Life High	Life Low	Open Int
July	1001½	1001½	1001½	1001½	+30	1001½	488½	49,416
Aug	1004	1004	1004	1004	+30	1004	512	20,436
Sept	995½	995½	995½	995½	+30	995½	503	8,439
Nov	984½	984½	984½	984½	+30	984½	499¼	79,699
Ja89	981	981	981	981	+30	981	553	10,025
Mar	974½	974½	974½	974½	+30	974½	579	4,460
May	955	955	955	955	+30	955	647	2,428
July	942	942	942	942	+30	942	684	3,177
Nov	755	767	755	767	+10	767	677	1,943

Est vol 15,000; vol Fri 89,624; open int 180,108, −529.

SOYBEAN MEAL (CBT) 100 tons; $ per ton.

	Open	High	Low	Settle	Change	Life High	Life Low	Open Int
July	312.50	312.50	312.50	312.50	+10.00	312.50	148.00	21,709
Aug	309.70	309.70	309.70	309.70	+10.00	309.70	148.00	18,874
Sept	307.00	307.00	307.00	307.00	+10.00	307.00	153.00	9,660
Oct	305.70	305.70	305.70	305.70	+10.00	305.70	159.00	7,404
Dec	304.70	304.70	304.70	304.70	+10.00	304.70	159.00	17,768
Ja89	302.20	302.20	302.20	302.20	+10.00	302.20	177.00	3,750
Mar	298.00	298.00	298.00	298.00	+10.00	298.00	193.50	2,354
May	295.00	295.00	295.00	295.00	+10.00	295.00	200.50	1,447
July	294.00	294.00	294.00	294.00	+10.00	294.00	229.00	655
Aug	291.50	291.50	291.50	291.50	+9.00	291.50	256.00	179

Est vol 8,000; vol Fri 26,228; open int 83,802, −1,682.

SOYBEAN OIL (CBT) 60,000 lbs.; cents per lb.

	Open	High	Low	Settle	Change	Life High	Life Low	Open Int
July	28.91	28.91	28.91	28.91	+1.00	28.91	16.65	29,551
Aug	29.15	29.15	29.15	29.15	+1.00	29.15	16.71	17,782
Sept	29.35	29.35¹	29.35	29.35	+1.00	29.35	16.55	12,675
Oct	29.50	29.50	29.50	29.50	+1.00	29.50	17.25	9,082
Dec	29.56	29.56	29.56	29.56	+1.00	29.56	18.10	21,734
Ja89	29.47	29.47	29.47	29.47	+1.00	29.47	20.75	2,684
Mar	29.40	29.40	29.40	29.40	+1.00	29.40	21.35	2,127
May	28.97	28.97	28.97	28.97	+1.00	28.97	22.95	1,191
July	28.35	28.35	28.35	28.35	+1.00	28.95	23.00	1,066
Aug	27.10	27.50	26.75	27.97	+.22	28.60	25.50	247

Est vol 30,000; vol Fri 26,544; open int 98,337, +1,517.

WHEAT (CBT) 5,000 bu.; cents per bu.

	Open	High	Low	Settle	Change	Life High	Life Low	Open Int
July	399	401½	396	401½	+14	404	253½	18,646
Sept	412¾	412¾	405	408½	+15¼	420¾	272	13,779
Dec	420	421½	411	413½	+11¼	426	289	19,955
Mr89	420	422	412	412	+10	422	323	2,129
May	400	400½	394	394	+13½	400½	330	355
July	371	371	364	364	+13	371	335	638

Est vol 30,000; vol Fri 55,502, +190.

WHEAT (KC) 5,000 bu.; cents per bu.

	Open	High	Low	Settle	Change	Life High	Life Low	Open Int
July	405	411½	405	405½	+17¼	411½	272	9,063
Sept	413	420	412	413½	+17	420	304½	11,262
Dec	423	428½	417	415	+15	428½	301½	6,264
Mr89	429	430	420	430	+12	430	327½	542

Est vol 8,021; vol Fri 7,489; open int 27,164, +697.

—LIVESTOCK & MEAT—

CATTLE - FEEDER (CME) 44,000 lbs.; cents per lb.

	Open	High	Low	Settle	Change	Life High	Life Low	Open Int
Aug	70.40	71.00	70.30	70.30	−1.50	79.95	68.30	5,542
Sept	70.22	71.15	70.22	70.50	−1.27	79.20	69.40	2,745
Oct	70.75	72.60	70.75	71.65	−.60	78.75	69.70	4,236
Nov	73.60	75.25	72.90	74.90	+.52	79.45	70.25	1,840
Ja89	76.00	78.00	75.73	77.67	+.67	80.00	74.00	1,487
Mar	76.00	77.00	76.00	76.80	+.90	79.77	74.00	600

Est vol 5,005; vol Fri 4,693; open int 16,487, −226.

CATTLE - LIVE (CME) 40,000 lbs.; cents per lb.

	Open	High	Low	Settle	Change	Life High	Life Low	Open Int
June	69.70	70.75	69.60	70.60	+.37	74.22	60.60	3,246
Aug	63.55	64.95	63.35	64.20	−.25	70.32	59.17	32,962
Oct	63.85	65.35	63.60	64.85	+.35	69.20	58.05	13,368
Dec	67.45	69.25	67.00	68.67	+.92	70.15	60.25	12,017
Fb89	69.80	71.37	69.50	71.37	+1.50	71.37	65.10	7,250
Apr	72.10	73.35	71.97	73.35	+1.50	73.35	67.20	2,184
June	72.20	73.70	72.00	73.70	+1.50	73.70	68.75	1,344

Est vol 39,711; vol Fri 26,221; open int 79,324, −112.

HOGS (CME) 30,000 lbs.; cents per lb.

	Open	High	Low	Settle	Change	Life High	Life Low	Open Int
June	50.00	51.10	49.75	50.45	+.65	54.95	37.50	394
July	47.70	48.37	46.45	46.55	−1.27	54.95	40.60	7,142
Aug	45.80	46.50	44.95	45.47	−.70	53.27	39.60	10,029
Oct	42.55	43.40	41.90	42.72	+.07	46.40	37.52	3,620
Dec	44.90	45.90	44.75	45.45	+.50	48.05	38.30	3,062
Fb89	42.50	43.12	42.05	42.50	+.10	44.80	40.60	2,237
Apr	48.60	49.05	48.40	49.05	+1.50	49.05	40.60	1,064
June	52.17	53.17	52.17	53.17	+1.50	53.17	45.50	320

Est vol 14,413; vol Fri 10,848; open int 27,870, +26.

—FOOD & FIBER—

COCOA (CSCE) 10 metric tons; $ per ton.

	Open	High	Low	Settle	Change	Life High	Life Low	Open Int
July	1,525	1,527	1,476	1,480	−35	2,160	1,476	1,762
Sept	1,542	1,543	1,497	1,500	−36	2,204	1,497	16,773
Dec	1,561	1,564	1,516	1,517	−39	2,197	1,516	10,478
Mr89	1,593	1,595	1,547	1,550	−40	2,088	1,547	4,222
May	1,610	1,610	1,570	1,571	−44	2,088	1,570	653
July	1,633	1,633	1,602	1,596	−44	1,985	1,602	1,042
Sept				1,621	−44	1,850	1,655	596

Est vol 4,837; vol Fri 6,909; open int 36,126, +273.

COFFEE (CSCE) 37,500 lbs.; cents per lb.

	Open	High	Low	Settle	Change	Life High	Life Low	Open Int
July	138.30	138.30	136.25	136.36	−2.14	146.25	110.00	4,059
Sept	138.75	138.75	137.56	138.09	−1.17	147.75	111.01	11,781
Dec	139.50	139.60	138.50	139.05	−1.69	150.25	114.00	5,792
Mr89	139.50	139.50	139.50	139.50	−1.01	150.50	131.50	1,733
May	139.90	139.90	139.00	139.00	−1.14	150.75	133.35	524

Est vol 4,010; vol Fri 7,419; open int 24,010, −1,602.

COTTON (CTN) 50,000 lbs.; cents per lb.

	Open	High	Low	Settle	Change	Life High	Life Low	Open Int
July	69.39	69.85	68.80	69.45	+1.45	81.40	53.90	4,105
Oct	68.05	68.90	68.05	68.70	+1.80	73.00	54.45	5,242
Dec	67.29	67.92	67.20	67.83	+1.91	70.20	53.85	19,222
Mr89	67.90	68.50	67.90	68.50	+2.00	68.50	54.70	2,680
May	68.50	68.70	68.50	68.70	+2.00	68.70	56.50	613
July	68.40	68.50	68.40	68.40	+2.00	68.50	56.50	216

Est vol 8,000; vol Fri 6,393; open int 32,092, −696.

ORANGE JUICE (CTN) 15,000 lbs.; cents per lb.

	Open	High	Low	Settle	Change	Life High	Life Low	Open Int
July	10.58	10.93	10.52	10.87	+.53	10.93	6.79	19,091
Sept	10.63	10.84	10.52	10.73	+.39	10.84	7.00	85,225
Nov	10.30	10.61	10.30	10.49	+.38	10.61	7.66	55,826
Ja89	10.45	10.45	10.16	10.37	+.34	10.45	7.87	7,953
Mar	10.15	10.43	10.14	10.30	+.30	10.43	8.10	1,120
May	10.12	10.34	10.12	10.28	+.28	10.34	8.98	889

Est vol 48,901; vol Fri 34,904; open int 169,339, +2,029.

SUGAR - WORLD (CSCE) 112,000 lbs.; cents per lb.

	Open	High	Low	Settle	Change	Life High	Life Low	Open Int
Sept				22.43	+.03	22.50	21.52	2,258
Nov	22.28	22.30	22.27	22.30	+.04	22.30	21.50	2,353
Ja89	21.95	21.97	21.95	21.97	+.02	21.97	21.70	586
Mar	21.96	21.96	21.96	21.96	+.02	21.95	21.75	228
May	21.96	21.96	21.96	21.96	+.02	21.98	21.80	305
July	21.95	21.96	21.95	21.96	+.02	21.98	21.80	102
Sept	21.95	21.96	21.95	21.95	+.02	21.99	21.95	123

Est vol 273; vol Fri 253; open int 6,053, −61.

—METALS & PETROLEUM—

COPPER (CMX) 25,000 lbs.; cents per lb.

	Open	High	Low	Settle	Change	Life High	Life Low	Open Int
June	106.30	106.30	106.30	106.30	−2.70	114.75	87.50	280
July	103.70	104.00	101.10	102.45	−1.55	110.70	62.30	14,799
Sept	97.00	97.50	95.50	96.35	−.35	101.00	59.45	12,126
Oct	90.50	90.50	90.50	90.50		96.50	64.70	654
Mr89	85.30	85.30	84.80	85.10		93.00	66.50	1,675
May	82.70	82.70	82.70	82.70		89.00	73.15	178
July	82.00	82.00	81.95	81.35	−.60	82.00	77.50	166
Sept	81.00	81.00	79.80	80.35		83.00	75.30	105
Dec				78.45	−.60	85.00	75.75	176

Est vol 5,500; vol Fri 6,136; open int 36,088, +212.

GOLD (CMX) 100 troy oz.; $ per troy oz.

	Open	High	Low	Settle	Change	Life High	Life Low	Open Int
June	454.00	454.20	450.10	450.70	−3.80	523.00	399.00	660
July				451.50	−3.80	467.50	450.50	308
Aug	457.80	458.60	453.50	454.50	−3.80	527.00	425.00	54,164
Oct	463.60	463.90	458.60	459.90	−3.80	533.50	429.00	11,361
Dec	468.50	469.50	464.40	465.80	−3.80	546.00	430.00	24,638
Fb89				470.80	−3.80	548.00	446.50	10,163
Apr				476.40	−3.80	550.00	451.00	6,975
June				482.00	−3.80	570.00	455.50	11,580
Aug				487.90	−3.80	575.00	482.20	6,217
Oct				494.20	−3.80	575.50	486.30	7,031
Dec	503.50	503.50	499.50	500.60	−3.80	514.50	472.50	5,685
Fb90				507.00	−3.80	516.00	502.00	2,496
Apr				513.50	−3.80	525.80	525.80	553

Est vol 30,000; vol Fri 9,762; open int 141,831, −630.

PLATINUM (NYM) 50 troy oz.; $ per troy oz.

	Open	High	Low	Settle	Change	Life High	Life Low	Open Int
June				584.10	−3.60	619.00	577.30	4
July	593.50	595.00	581.90	585.60	−3.60	667.50	443.00	9,761
Oct	600.50	601.00	587.00	591.60	−3.60	667.50	453.00	8,163
Ja89	608.00	608.00	595.00	597.60	−4.40	646.00	459.00	3,638
Apr				604.60	−4.90	643.50	482.00	784

Est vol 5,728; vol Fri 2,351; open int 22,355, −380.

PALLADIUM (NYM) 100 troy oz.; $ per troy oz.

	Open	High	Low	Settle	Change	Life High	Life Low	Open Int
June	132.10	134.50	130.00	133.80	+2.25	160.50	103.65	245
Sept	130.00	131.00	129.50	129.80	+1.55	142.25	103.65	4,361
Dec	128.00	129.50	128.00	128.30	+1.30	139.50	106.50	2,086
Mr89	128.50	128.50	127.50	127.05	+1.30	130.50	115.50	460

Est vol 1,000; vol Fri 1,103, −79.

SILVER (CMX) 5,000 troy oz.; cents per troy oz.

	Open	High	Low	Settle	Change	Life High	Life Low	Open Int
June		717.5		731.0	635.0	5		
July	725.5	733.0	713.5	719.5	−6.0	1065.0	580.0	38,124
Sept	735.5	743.0	723.5	729.5	−5.8	1064.0	588.0	19,318
Dec	752.0	758.0	738.5	745.0	−5.5	1082.0	606.0	12,674
Mr89	769.0	772.0	755.0	760.0	−5.5	1073.0	640.0	5,793
May	779.0	779.0	779.0	775.0	−5.5	948.0	675.0	2,583
July	790.5	791.0	790.5	783.0	−5.5	985.0	688.0	3,454
Sept	803.0	803.0	803.0	794.5	−5.5	820.0	729.0	1,602
Dec	821.0	824.0	821.0	811.8	−5.5	834.0	722.0	1,602
Mr90				829.5	−5.5	821.0	758.0	1,023

Est vol 25,200; vol Fri 25,990; open int 86,513, +5,242.

SILVER (CBT) 1,000 troy oz.; cents per troy oz.

	Open	High	Low	Settle	Change	Life High	Life Low	Open Int
June	725.0	725.0	712.0	717.0	−6.0	881.0	656.0	
Aug	730.0	738.0	730.0	725.0	−5.5	1064.0	632.0	7,068
Oct	742.0	746.0	733.0	745.0	−5.5	940.0	637.0	215
Dec	751.0	758.0	739.0	745.0	−5.5	946.0	648.0	7,150
Fb89	758.0	758.0	753.0	760.0	−5.5	968.0	721.0	221
Apr	775.0	775.0	763.0	765.0	−5.5	793.0	675.0	128
June	783.0	783.0	773.0	775.0	−5.5	800.0	690.0	151

Est vol 3,000; vol Fri 2,610; open int 15,013, +1,585.

—WOOD—

LUMBER (CME) 150,000 bd. ft.; $ per 1,000 bd. ft.

	Open	High	Low	Settle	Change	Life High	Life Low	Open Int
July	193.00	199.40	193.00	195.70	+1.20	210.30	165.20	2,646
Sept	187.50	192.50	187.50	190.20	+.80	201.50	164.80	1,983
Nov	180.00	182.90	179.40	181.70	+1.40	189.30	161.00	765
Ja88	179.00	181.50	179.00	179.90	+.90	185.80	160.00	258
Mar	180.00	180.00	179.50	179.50	−.50	184.50	171.00	118

Est vol 2,329; vol Fri 2,309; open int 5,803, +46.

—FINANCIAL—

BRITISH POUND (IMM) - $ per pound

	Open	High	Low	Settle	Change	Life High	Life Low	Open Int
Sept	1.7818	1.7818	1.7754	1.7760	−.0014	1.9012	1.6992	16,038
Dec	1.7720	1.7732	1.7680	1.7688	−.0018	1.9000	1.6980	1,021

Est vol 3,864; vol Fri 4,449; open int 17,102, +540.

AUSTRALIAN DOLLAR (IMM) - 100,000 dlrs.; $ per A.S

	Open	High	Low	Settle	Change	Life High	Life Low	Open Int
Sept	.8110	.8112	.8088	.8089	+.0061	.8112	.7008	5,236

Est vol 946; vol Fri 2,605; open int 5,259, +805.

CANADIAN DOLLAR (IMM) - 100,000 dlrs.; $ per Can $

	Open	High	Low	Settle	Change	Life High	Life Low	Open Int
Sept	.8252	.8252	.8225	.8249	+.0038	.8215	.7307	33,006
Dec	.8200	.8221	.8199	.8218	+.0038	.8221	.7390	2,601
Mr89	.8187	.8187	.8187	.8187	+.0038	.8200	.7570	199

Est vol 3,491; vol Fri 2,492; open int 35,839, −233.

JAPANESE YEN (IMM) 12.5 million yen; $ per yen (.00)

	Open	High	Low	Settle	Change	Life High	Life Low	Open Int
Sept	.7993	.8002	.7984	.7986	−.0026	.8485	.7075	34,625
Dec	.8062	.8069	.8049	.8051	−.0027	.8530	.7115	1,632
Mr89	.8122	.8131	.8120	.8120	−.0026	.8590	.7870	236

Est vol 13,618; vol Fri 10,597; open int 36,519, +803.

SWISS FRANC (IMM) 125,000 francs-$ per franc

	Open	High	Low	Settle	Change	Life High	Life Low	Open Int
Sept	.6933	.6945	.6900	.6905	−.0040	.8120	.6886	26,874
Dec	.7014	.7025	.6975	.6983	−.0041	.8210	.6960	557

Est vol 17,767; vol Fri 14,723; open int 27,478, −96.

W. GERMAN MARK (IMM) - 125,000 marks; $ per mark

	Open	High	Low	Settle	Change	Life High	Life Low	Open Int
Sept	.5752	.5758	.5732	.5732	−.0029	.6555	.5609	43,889
Dec	.5805	.5808	.5781	.5783	−.0029	.6610	.5705	2,060

Est vol 15,317; vol Fri 12,641; open int 45,956, −98.

EURODOLLAR (IMM) - $1 million; pts of 100%

	Open	High	Low	Settle	Change	Life High	Life Low	Open Int
Sept	91.94	91.95	91.84	91.86	−.18	93.78	89.74	177,971
Dec	91.54	91.55	91.45	91.47	−.18	92.93	89.80	6,885
Mr89	91.34	91.35	91.26	91.26	−.19	92.33	90.06	2,432
June	91.17	91.17	91.14	91.10	−.14	91.91	90.11	282

Est vol 8,080; vol Fri 10,028; open int 27,681, +96.

STERLING (LIFFE) - £500,000; pts of 100%

	Open	High	Low	Settle	Change	Life High	Life Low	Open Int
Sept	90.12	90.25	90.08	90.11	−.18	91.47	89.26	13,916
Dec	90.10	90.12	89.98	90.07	−.22	90.99	89.25	6,043
Mr89	90.04	90.08	89.95	89.97	−.22	90.94	89.25	3,088
June	89.88	90.03	89.90	89.88	−.25	90.66	89.65	981
Sept	89.85	89.91	89.85	89.86	−.16	90.47	89.65	512
Dec				89.77	−.20	90.22	89.76	460
Mr90				89.72	−.20	89.98	89.80	211

Est vol 20,150; vol Fri 18,350; open int 25,219, +1,625.

T - BONDS (LIFFE) $1 mil.; pts of 100%

	Open	High	Low	Settle	Change	Life High	Life Low	Open Int
June	87-21	87-05	87-11	−0-31	90-12	85-03	609	
Sept	86-28	86-28	86-07	86-14	−1-00	89-20	84-12	6,900

Est vol 5,746; vol Fri 8,738; open int 7,577, +130.

LONG GILT (LIFFE) - £50,000; 32nds of 100%

	Open	High	Low	Settle	Change	Life High	Life Low	Open Int
Sept	119-19	119-23	119-18	119-22	−0-12	123-25	117-05	7,307
Dec	95-16	95-21	95-10	95-19	−0-10	98-20	95-07	27,465

Est vol EURODOLLAR (IMM) - $1 million; pts of 100%
vol Fri 29,923; open int 34,841, +280.

EURODOLLAR (IMM) - $1 million; pts of 100%

	Open	High	Low	Settle	Chg	Yield Settle	Yield Chg	Open Interest
Sept	91.94	91.94	91.83	91.94		8.06	−.11	161,305
Dec	91.52	91.56	91.44	91.55	+.01	8.45	+.01	76,101
Mr89	91.31	91.34	91.24	91.34	+.02	8.66	−.02	47,349
June	91.15	91.19	91.09	91.18	−.03	8.82	−.03	21,495
Sept	91.02	91.05	90.95	91.04	+.03	8.96	−.03	17,235
Dec	90.89	90.94	90.83	90.93	+.04	9.07	−.04	13,455
Mr90	90.70	90.76	90.67	90.75	+.05	9.25	−.05	15,395
June	90.64	90.70	90.57	90.68	+.06	9.32	−.06	11,040
Sept	90.42	90.57	90.42	90.57	+.06	9.43	−.06	5,255
Dec	90.37	90.45	90.34	90.44	+.06	9.56	−.06	1,352

Est vol 108,395; vol Fri 142,296; open int 393,388, +10,927.

U.S. DOLLAR INDEX (FINEX) 500 times USDX

	Open	High	Low	Settle	Change	Life High	Life Low	Open Int
Sept	92.22	92.42	92.09	92.37	+.31	97.84	87.42	4,581
Dec				92.67	+.31	92.50	88.40	1,591

Est vol 500; vol Fri 243; open int 6,181, −1.
The index: High 92.38; Low 92.10; Close 92.33, +.28

CRB INDEX (NYFE) 500 times index

	Open	High	Low	Settle	Change	Life High	Life Low	Open Int
July	264.00	267.00	264.00	266.75	+5.15	267.80	218.50	1,709
Sept	264.00	267.80	264.00	267.70	+6.15	267.80	221.50	1,057
Dec	264.00	265.75	264.00	265.75	+4.30	264.70	255.50	161
Mr89	264.70	264.70	263.50	265.75	+4.30	264.70	255.50	161

Est vol 1,666; vol Fri 1,669; open int 3,627, +211.
The index: High 267.18; Low 262.56; Close 266.23 +2.93

TREASURY BONDS (CBT) - $100,000; pts. 32nds of 100%

	Open	High	Low	Settle	Change	Life High	Life Low	Open Int
Sept	87-18	87-25	87-04	87-23	+4	9-370	−.016	27,088
Dec	86-25	86-29	86-06	86-24	+4	9-483	−.016	301,359
Mr89	85-30	85-30	85-10	85-30	+4	9-590	−.020	42,963
June	84-24	85-06	84-18	85-03	+5	9-702	−.021	15,172
Sept	83-29	84-11	83-23	84-07	+5	9-808	−.021	1,348
Dec	83-14	83-17	83-14	83-17	+5	9-907	−.021	1,348
Mr90	82-00	82-08	82-00	82-26	+6	410.089	−.017	161

Est vol 315,000; vol Fri 333,894; open int 416,705, +4,816.

TREASURY NOTES (CBT) - $100,000; pts. 32nds of 100%

	Open	High	Low	Settle	Change	Life High	Life Low	Open Int
Sept	92-07	92-25	92-03	92-17	+3	9-075	−.015	15,804
Dec	91-22	92-02	91-18	91-13	+4	9-248	−.021	107

Est vol 21,000; vol Fri 12,532; open int 18,386, +915.

5 YR TREAS NOTES (FINEX) $100,000; pts. 32 of 100%

	Open	High	Low	Settle	Change	Life High	Life Low	Open Int
Sept	97-19	97-185	97-185	97-16	+.01	8.63		1,701
Dec	96-29	97-005	96-21	96-295	−.01	8.77		4,600

Est vol 600; open int 2,301, +50.

TREASURY BONDS (MCE) - $50,000; 32nds of 100%

	Open	High	Low	Settle	Change	Life High	Life Low	Open Int
Sept	87-07	87-20	87-05	87-23	+2	9-370	−.016	7,635
Dec	86-22	86-29	86-06	86-26	+2	9-483	−.016	7,635

Est vol 3,900; vol Fri 7,471; open int 8,067, +367.

CBT - Chicago Board of Trade; CME - Chicago Mercantile Exchange; CMX - Commodity Exchange, New York; CRCE - Chicago Rice & Cotton Exchange; CSCE - Coffee, Sugar & Cocoa Exchange, New York; CTN - New York Cotton Exchange; FINEX - Financial Instrument Exchange, a division of the New York Cotton Exchange; IPEL - International Petroleum Exchange of London; IMM - International Monetary Market at CME, Chicago; KC - Kansas City Board of Trade; LIFFE - London International Financial Futures Exchange; MCE - MidAmerica Commodity Exchange; MPLS - Minneapolis Grain Exchange; NYFE - New York Futures Exchange, unit of New York Stock Exchange; NYM - New York Mercantile Exchange; PBOT - Philadelphia Board of Trade; WPG - Winnipeg Commodity Exchange.

day, his account is credited with the amount of price change. Similarly, any unfavorable price change is similarly debited to the customer's account. When the customer opens a futures account, he is required to post a minimum amount of margin—the *initial margin* set by the exchange. While the initial margins vary across commodities, they usually range from 5 to 15 percent of the face value of the contract.

Subsequently, the customer is required to maintain a minimum amount of margin, called *maintenance margin*, typically about 75 percent of the initial margin. While the initial margin can be satisfied by posting interest-bearing securities, the subsequent margin must be paid in cash. A *margin call* is triggered when the margin in the commodity account falls to the level of the maintenance margin as a result of daily resettlement. On top of the exchange-imposed margins, brokerage houses could ask for additional margins from their clients depending upon the clients' creditworthiness, the volatility of futures prices, and competition.

Thus, the daily mark-to-market practice of futures trading generates many cash flows for futures traders before the contract delivery date. When futures prices rise, the contract buyer accumulates cash in his futures account in the interim, but he is required to pay a higher price than he originally agreed to at the final settlement of his long position. In contrast, the contract seller experiences many margin calls and cash outflows in the case of rising futures prices. However, he receives a higher settlement price at the time of closing his short position. Notice that at final settlement, the aggregate cash receipt of the seller and net cash payment by the buyer are identical to the originally specified price. The daily mark-to-market practice of futures trading has altered only the timing of these cash flows. Further, the clearinghouse has a zero net position at all times, because for every contract buyer there is a seller.

In regular stock trading, there is no daily marking-to-market of customer positions. Even when stocks are traded on margin, the positions are not necessarily marked-to-market on a daily basis. Futures margins are good-faith deposits, while stock margins represent partial payment of the amount owed to the broker.

19. Open interest in a futures contract represents the cumulative number of outstanding contracts at a given time; this differs from the volume of contracts traded during a specified time interval (e.g., a day) and the volume of trading in stocks. When the futures contract holder closes his position by executing a reverse trade, open interest does not change, since the current holder is replaced by another trader, but the volume of trading increases.

20. Trading in stocks is regulated by the SEC, while futures trading is regulated by the Commodity Futures Trading Commission (CFTC). The futures exchanges are required to obtain approval from the CFTC before introducing a new futures contract. For some commodities, the CFTC has placed maximum limits on positions that an individual trader can control. This limitation is intended to prevent possible *corners* and *squeezes*. Further, the CFTC requires larger traders to file periodic reports on their trading activities in regulated commodities.

21. Unlike stock trading, an important motivation for trading futures contracts is *hedging*, wherein an investor with a long (short) spot position in an asset assumes a short (long) position by selling an appropriate number of contracts of a related asset to reduce the variability of expected returns on the uncovered spot position.

22. There are important differences in taxation of profits and losses on stocks and futures positions. A *hedger's* gain or loss on his futures positions is regarded as ordinary income or loss for tax purposes, but profit or loss on a *speculative* futures position is considered a capital asset and is taxed as a capital gain or loss. Unlike stocks, most speculative positions in futures are held for a few months and, therefore, are treated as short-term capital gains or losses.

FUTURES QUOTATIONS

Prior to discussing specific commodity trading procedures, we should briefly consider the information in the futures quotations section of the newspaper. Figure 24.1 is an example of the futures prices section that appears daily in *The Wall Street Journal*. This section lists all the major commodities traded on all the principal exchanges. (The example does not include the full section.) The commodities are divided into the following groups:

1. Grains and oilseeds
2. Livestock and meat
3. Food and fiber
4. Metals and petroleum
5. Wood
6. Financial

For each commodity, the listing indicates where the commodity is traded (e.g., CBT is the Chicago Board of Trade) and the standard contract for the commodity (e.g., the contract for corn on the CBT is for 5,000 bushels). The heading indicates what the quotes are for (e.g., cents per bushel or cents per pound). In the case of wheat, for instance, a quote of 404 means $4.04 per bushel. The left column indicates when the contracts come due, and this obviously differs by commodity depending upon the normal growing season. Naturally, most of the contracts for agricultural commodities are due during the summer months. The subsequent columns indicate the daily movements in the futures contract: the opening transaction, the high and low transaction for the day, and the final transaction *(settle)* of the day. The change column indicates the price change from the previous day's settle price. The lifetime high and low indicates the range of prices for this contract since it began trading. The open interest is the number of contracts that have not been closed out. At the bottom, there is an estimated volume of trading in all contracts for the day, the total open interest for all months of contracts, and the change in total open interest from the previous day.

SPOT, FORWARD, AND FUTURES PRICE RELATIONSHIPS

Before we examine the economic functions of futures trading, it is essential to consider the relationship among spot, forward, and futures prices. For expository purposes, it is convenient to begin with the price relationships during the delivery period of the futures contract, then investigate the price behavior of these contracts prior to the delivery period of the futures contract.

We observed earlier that a futures contract is a temporary (close but imperfect) substitute for a spot market transaction. To examine this further, assume that the asset underlying the three contracts is *identical*, and that the contracts come due for delivery on a date that coincides with the final day of trading. Let $S(T)$ be the spot price per unit of the asset on the last day of trading of the futures contract, T. $F(T,T)$ and $FO(T,T)$ represent the futures price and the forward price, respectively; the first term within the parentheses refers to the date on which the price is observed. Ignoring market imperfections such as transaction costs, taxes, margins, and units of trading, it is clear that the equilibrium spot and futures prices at T must be equal, as dictated by the law of one price:

$$F(T,T) = S(T). \qquad (24.1)$$

If this equilibrium relationship is violated, there would be opportunities for arbitrage between the spot and futures markets. For example, if $F(T,T) > S(T)$, the arbitrageur would sell a futures contract, buy the spot asset, and make delivery on the futures position, thus earning a riskless profit of $F(T,T) - S(T)$. On the other hand, if $F(T,T) < S(T)$, the arbitrageur would buy a futures contract, take delivery, and sell the asset in the spot market. This transaction would yield a riskless profit of $S(T) - F(T,T)$. Obviously, such arbitrage opportunities seldom exist in an efficient auction market with many competing traders.

Further, a forward contract written on the delivery date is indeed a spot contract. Therefore,

$$F(T,T) = FO(T,T) = S(T). \qquad (24.2)$$

Thus, in theory, forward and futures contracts are effectively reduced to a spot contract on the last day of trading, delivery, and settlement.

In reality, however, spot and futures prices at delivery would rarely be identical because of market imperfections, but they would be close to each other. For almost all assets, trading in futures contracts ceases prior to the delivery date. The delivery and settlement process spans several business days, which renders any attempt at arbitrage between the spot and futures markets risky. Further, the specifications of a futures contract permit delivery of varying grades of the underlying asset. It is the *seller* of the futures contract who triggers the delivery process during the delivery month and decides the grade and place of delivery. When the seller gives notice to the clearing corporation of his intention to deliver, the clearing corporation assigns that delivery to the oldest long position. Thus, the *buyer* of a futures contract is uncertain about the time and place of delivery and the grade of the asset until the moment he is notified by the clearing corporation. Because of the delivery privileges enjoyed by the seller of a futures contract, the $F(T,T)$ cannot be greater than the $S(T)$. The uncertainties that the buyer faces as the contract approaches delivery suggest that the $F(T,T)$ would be less than $S(T)$.[1]

Note the following price relationships prior to delivery. (The notation t refers to the initial period when contracts are opened, and T is the delivery and final settlement date.)

1. The relationship between the current spot price, $S(t)$, and the expected future spot price of an asset at the time of delivery of forward and futures contracts written on it, $E_t S(T)$
2. The relationship between the initial forward price, $FO(t,T)$, and $E_t S(T)$
3. The relationship between $FO(t,T)$ and $S(t)$
4. The relationship between the initial futures price, $F(t,T)$, and the current expectation of the spot price at delivery, $E_t S(T)$
5. The relationship between the current futures price, $F(t,T)$, and the current spot price of the underlying asset, $S(t)$
6. The relationship between $F(t,T)$ and $FO(t,T)$
7. The relationship between current prices of futures (and forward) contracts of different delivery months; for example, current prices of March and June futures contracts, $F(t, \text{March})$ versus $F(t, \text{June})$.

The subject of spot, forward, and futures price relationships has been a matter of extended debate. Until the late 1970s, the difference in the cash flow streams of futures and forward contracts (daily versus maturity payoffs, respectively) was generally ignored, and the futures and forward prices were considered equal, even prior to delivery. Subsequently, it was shown that the identity of futures and forward prices would hold *only* when short-term interest rates are deterministic. We shall briefly review the traditional literature and follow with a summary of recent research findings. The initial discussion is concerned with spot prices.

---

[1] Gerald D. Gay and Steven Manaster, "The Quality Option Implicit in Futures Contracts," *Journal of Financial Economics* 13, no. 3 (September 1984): 353–370.

RELATIONSHIP BETWEEN CURRENT AND FUTURE SPOT PRICES

The current spot price of an asset is determined by the current and expected supply and demand conditions. If an excess supply of an asset is expected, that would reduce the inventory of stocks carried and dampen the current spot price. In contrast, if a shortage is expected, there would be larger inventories, which would exert upward pressure on spot prices. This means the current spot price, $S(t)$, and the expected future spot price, $E_t[S(T)]$ are connected by *the expected cost of carry*, $C(t,T)$, and a risk premium, RP, for bearing uncertainties about the future spot price. In broad terms:

$$E_t[S(T)] = S(t) + C(t,T) + RP. \qquad (24.3)$$

The cost of carry depends upon the type of asset and includes such items as insurance, spoilage, storage, depreciation, financing costs, convenience yield, and distributions that the asset may generate during the interval (t,T). For many commodities, the cost of carry is typically positive. Sometimes, it may be negative because of the *convenience yield*, which represents the benefits of having inventory on hand, wherein inventory is carried even when the expected future spot price is less than the current spot price.[2] For instance, grain merchants and food processors carry stocks from one season to another, even when a bumper crop is expected. They do this to avoid stock-outs and maintain customer goodwill. The convenience yield is inversely related to the size of the inventory. When the current inventories are relatively low, it may exceed other (positive) components of the cost of carry and the risk premium. Hence, in such a case, the expected future spot price would be below the current spot price.

The cost of carrying financial assets such as debt instruments and foreign currencies is much lower than that of commodities. It includes the cost of financing and safekeeping. Furthermore, some financial assets, like stocks, notes, and bonds, may generate cash distributions such as dividends and coupon payments during the interval (t,T). The net carrying cost is considered fixed over a short period of time, but it becomes stochastic over longer intervals. The last term in Equation 24.3 is the premium for bearing nondiversifiable risk associated with the spot asset. We will discuss the risk premium later.

RELATIONSHIP BETWEEN SPOT AND FORWARD PRICES

The forward contract provides a mechanism for locking in today the future spot price that is expected to prevail at the time of contract delivery. The forward price, $FO(t,T)$, is fixed today, but the delivery (as well as payment) is deferred until the final settlement date. Hence, the forward contract *eliminates uncertainty* about the future spot price that will prevail at time of delivery. Currently, forward contracts are traded in several Treasury securities and foreign currencies. The actively traded contracts are for standardized terms to maturity. For example, forward contracts in foreign

---

[2] Michael J. Brennan, "The Supply of Storage," *American Economic Review* 47, no. 1 (March 1958): 50–72; Myron S. Scholes, "The Economics of Hedging and Spreading in Futures Markets," *The Journal of Futures Market* 1, no. 2 (Summer 1981): 265–286.

currencies (quoted in *The Wall Street Journal*) are for 30, 90, and 180 days forward delivery. Unlike futures contracts, which have standardized delivery months (see Figure 24.1), forward contracts, which are issued on different dates, mature at different points in the future. There is hardly any secondary market activity in forward contracts.

If the storage costs over the life of a forward contract $(T - t)$ are known, then at the time a forward contract begins trading, the present value of the forward price *must* equal the current spot price of the underlying asset, $S(t)$, plus the present value of the known storage costs, $G(t,T)$:

$$FO(t,T) \times B(t,T) = S(t) + G(t,T). \qquad (24.4)$$

The term $B(t,T)$ is the present value of a default-free discount bond, such as a Treasury bill, that promises payment of $1 at T. We need to take the present value of the forward price (which is the exercise price of the contract) since the payment is postponed to time period T. If this condition is violated, one could set up an arbitrage that would produce a certain profit without involving any capital investment by the arbitrageur. For instance, if the present value of the forward price exceeds the sum of $S(t)$ and $G(t,T)$, then the following arbitrage could be set up:

At t:

1. Borrow the present value of the forward price, $+FO(t,T) B(t,T)$.
2. Buy and store the underlying asset, $-[S(t) + G(t,T)]$.
3. Sell a forward contract at the exercise price, $FO(t,T)$.
4. Net cash flow $= FO(t,T) \times B(t,T) - S(t) - G(t,T) > 0$.

At T:

1. Deliver the (stored) asset on the forward contract and collect the exercise price, $+FO(t,T)$.
2. Pay off the loan, $-FO(t,T)$.
3. Net cash flow $= FO(t,T) - FO(t,T) = 0$.

Thus, in a frictionless market the arbitrage produces a certain profit at time t equal to the net cash flow. Notice that recognition of frictions in the real-world markets does not invalidate the concept of arbitrage, but it implies that the difference between the right and left sides of Equation 24.4 should be large enough to exceed costs due to market frictions. Also, because forward contracts are held over a short period of time (generally a few months), the assumption of known storage costs is not unrealistic. However, if the storage costs are unknown, then Equation 24.4 needs to be modified, and the arbitrage just discussed would be risky.

In an efficient spot market, the market price of an asset such as a share of stock is the consensus estimate of its value. In contrast, in the forward market the value of the forward *contract* is different from the forward *price*. At the inception of the contract at time t, the market value of the forward contract is zero, because the forward price and the exercise price are identical. Subsequently, the contract acquires a non-zero market value. Assume another forward contract is written on that asset for the same delivery date, T, but at a different exercise price. If a new contract is written at time t^* ($t < t^* < T$) at an exercise price of $FO(t^*, T)$, the value of the outstanding forward contract, $V(t^*, t, T)$, is equal to the present value of the difference between two exercise prices. That is,

$$V(t^*, t, T) = FO(t, T) \ B(t^*, T) . \tag{24.5}$$

If this condition is violated, one could earn arbitrage profits as follows:
At t^*:

1. If $FO(t^*, T) > FO(t, T)$, the owner of the outstanding contract could write (sell) the new contract.
2. If $FO(t^*, T) < FO(t, T)$, the seller of the outstanding contract could buy the new contract.
3. These transactions involve no investment of funds.

At T:

1. Take delivery on the long forward contract and redeliver the asset on the short forward contract. The arbitrage profit in either case is equal to the absolute value of the difference between the two exercise prices, $[FO(t^*, T) - FO(t, T)]$.

The market value of a forward contract at the time of delivery is equal to the difference between its exercise price and the current spot price of the underlying asset. That is,

$$V(T, t, T) = S(T) - FO(t, T) . \tag{24.6}$$

Clearly, the market value at delivery is equal to the profit or loss on the forward contract. Prior to contract delivery the profit or loss on the contract is not known. The recent research shows that the current forward price, $FO(t, T)$, is a biased estimator of the expected future spot price, $E_t[S(T)]$, and the degree of bias depends upon the covariance between forward profit or loss and the marginal utility of consumption.[3]

DETERMINING THE FUTURES PRICE

Like the forward contract, the futures contract also provides an opportunity for the mortgage banker or the exporter to lock in today the future spot price of the underlying asset to prevail at the time of delivery. However, *the futures contract is marked-to-market daily.* At the end of every trading day all futures positions are balanced and rewritten by the clearinghouse at the settlement price—a price representative of transaction prices at the close of the day's trading. If the price has moved upward since the previous day's cash settlement, the price gain is credited to long futures positions and debited to short futures positions. Thus the futures contract generates

---

[3] Scott Richard and Michael Sundaresan, "A Continuous Time Equilibrium Model of Forward Prices and Future Prices in a Multigood Economy," *Journal of Financial Economics* 9, no. 4 (December 1981): 347–371.

daily cash flows. If the upward trend in prices persists until the delivery date, the buyer of the futures contract would accumulate daily cash inflows but would face a higher final settlement price, $F(T,T)$, than the initial futures price $F(t,T)$, called the *exercise price.* The net amount the buyer is obliged to pay at final settlement is equal to the initial exercise price, $F(t,T)$. Thus, the buyer gets to keep the interest earned on daily cash inflows. Clearly, the cash flows accruing to the seller of the futures contract are just the opposite to those accruing to the buyer. Again, it is important to note the distinction between the *futures price* and the *value of the futures contract.* At its inception, the value of the futures contract, $Y(t,T)$, is zero, because the futures price and the exercise price are identical. During each trading day, the futures contract acquires some value (positive or negative) as the current futures price deviates from the initial futures price. Letting t_1 represent the end of the trading day and $k(t < k < t_1)$ denote any time between the beginning and end of the trading day, the value of the futures contract during the trading day is

$$Y(k,T) = F(k,T) - F(t,T). \tag{24.7}$$

At the end of each trading day, the daily price change on the open futures position is settled, and the contract is rewritten at a new exercise price that is equal to the futures settlement price. Thus, the value of the futures contract immediately after it is rewritten is zero.

Equations 24.5 and 24.7 show that the values of the forward and futures contracts written on an identical underlying asset are not the same prior to the last day of trading (T) because of the difference in the timing of cash flows. Based on arbitrage arguments similar to those used earlier, Cox, Ingersoll, and Ross[4] showed that

1. Prior to the last day of trading (T), the current futures price, $F(t,T)$, need not be equal to the current forward price, $FO(t,T)$. Only if short-term interest rates are known (deterministic) is the current futures price equal to the current forward price.
2. The forward price is greater (less) than the futures price if the covariance between the percentage changes in $F(t,T)$ and $B(t,T)$ (the default-free discount bond maturing at T) is positive (negative).
3. Assume that the underlying asset makes no payouts (such as coupon interest during the life of the contract). If the covariance between percentage changes in $S(t)$ and $B(t,T)$ is greater (less) than the variance of percentage changes in $B(t,T)$, the current forward price is greater (less) than the current futures price.
4. The current futures price is greater (less) than the current spot price if the spot interest rate is always greater (less) than the spot rental rate. The *spot rental rate* is the charge for obtaining

[4] John Cox, Jonathon Ingersoll, and Stephen Ross, "The Relation between Forward Prices and Futures Prices," *Journal of Financial Economics* 9, no. 4 (December 1981): 321–346.

the full use of the underlying asset including the right to receive payouts. This would cover the storage costs and coupon interest.

Richard and Sundaresan[5] observed that futures and forward contracts provide a mechanism for hedging future consumption and thus serve as insurance against welfare losses. They showed that, in general, the current futures and forward prices are biased predictors of the spot price expected to prevail at contract delivery. Consequently, *normal backwardation* (discussed later) results when futures and forward contracts are poor consumption hedges, which means that these contracts are more profitable than average when the marginal utility of consumption is lower than average and vice versa. Alternatively, *contango* (defined later in this chapter under "Impact of Hedgers and Speculators on Price Relationships") prevails when forward or futures contracts are effective in insuring against adverse consumption opportunities—that is, when futures or forward contracts are more profitable than average and when the marginal utility of consumption is higher than average.

Dusak and Black[6] argued that the CAPM can be applied to the pricing of commodities as well as futures contracts. Extending this approach, Scholes[7] showed that

$$
\begin{aligned}
E[S(t + 1)] = {} & S(t) + S(t)\,[R_f + C'(t,t + 1)] \\
& + [E(R_m) - R_f]\,\beta(S)\,,
\end{aligned}
\tag{24.8}
$$

where

$E(R_m)$ = **the expected return on the market portfolio**

$\beta(S)$ = **The dollar beta, which is a measure of systematic risk of the spot asset**

R_f = **risk-free rate of return**

$C'(t,t + 1)$ = **cost of carry in percent excluding financing cost.**

The term $S(t)\,[R_f + C'(t,t + 1)]$ represents the dollar cost of carry including interest charges. It can be assumed to be fixed over a short interval of time, but over longer horizons interest rates and other storage costs are uncertain. The expected covariance of the change in spot price with the return on the market portfolio divided by the variance of the market return is $\beta(S)$. Under this model, the expected change in the spot price is equal to the dollar cost of carry plus the dollar risk premium. Likewise, the expected futures price change under the CAPM is

[5] Richard and Sundaresan, "A Continuous Time Equilibrium Model."

[6] Katherine Dusak, "Futures Trading and Investor Returns: An Investigation of Commodity Market Risk Premiums," *Journal of Political Economy* 81, no. 4 (December 1973): 1387–1406; Fischer Black, "The Pricing of Commodity Contracts," *Journal of Financial Economics* 3, no. 1, 2 (January–March 1976).

[7] Myron S. Scholes, "The Economics of Hedging and Spreading in Futures Markets," *The Journal of Futures Markets* 1, no. 2 (Summer 1981): 135–144.

$$E[F(t + 1,T)] - F(t,T) = [E(R_m) - R_f]\,\beta(F)\,, \qquad (24.9)$$

where

$$\beta(F) = \textbf{the dollar beta of the futures contract.}$$

If the systematic risk of a futures contract is zero, then the expected change in the futures price would be zero.

Further, Scholes observed that the current futures price is equal to the current spot price plus the expected total cost of carry. That is,

$$F(t,T) = S(t) + C(t,T)\,, \qquad (24.10)$$

where

$C(t,T) =$ **the net dollar cost of carry, including interest, storage costs, con-venience yields, and distributions by the underlying asset during the life of the futures contract.**

Clearly, the cost of carry over the life of the contract is unknown (stochastic). Therefore, the basis (i.e., the difference between the current spot and futures prices) provides a consensus forecast of the expected cost of carry during the life of the contract. If $F(t,T) > S(t) + C(t,T)$, the holder of the spot asset would expect to gain from selling the futures contract. Conversely, if $F(t,T) < S(t) + C(t,T)$, the spot asset holder would expect to gain by buying the futures contract.

The difference between the current futures prices of two different delivery months, say T and $T'(T' > T)$, is called a *time spread*. It follows from Equation 24.9 that the spread is equal to the change in the expected carrying cost. That is,

$$(F(t,T') - F(t,T) = C(t,T') - C(t,T)\,. \qquad (24.11)$$

The spread is a market consensus forecast of the expected change in the cost of carry from T to T'.

EMPIRICAL EVIDENCE ON PRICE RELATIONSHIPS

Empirical studies have generally addressed the following issues:

1. Is the current futures price an unbiased predictor of the expected future spot price?
2. Does the futures price follow a random walk or exhibit trends?
3. What are the risks and returns to hedgers and speculators in futures markets?

The question of bias in commodity futures prices has been debated for a long time. Rockwell did a comprehensive study of the theory of *normal backwardation.*[8] A modified version of the theory of normal backwardation

---

[8] Charles S. Rockwell, "Normal Backwardation, Forecasting, and the Returns to Commodity Futures Traders," in *Selected Writings on Futures Markets,* edited by Anne E. Peck (Chicago: Chicago Board of Trade, 1977), 167–189.

assumes that speculators are net long when hedgers are net short, and vice versa; that speculators are risk averse; and that they are able to forecast prices. These assumptions imply that speculators' profits are a function of the quantity of risk (of price fluctuation) assumed as well as their forecasting abilities. Rockwell examined semimonthly data from 25 commodity futures markets during the 1947–1965 period to determine the proportion of speculators' profits due to normal backwardation and the proportion attributable to their forecasting abilities. The major findings are

1. The smaller 22 futures markets exhibit no tendency toward normal backwardation whether hedgers are net short or net long. Normal backwardation is characteristic of the three larger markets—wheat, soybeans, and cotton—only when hedgers are net short. This suggests that the current futures price is on average an unbiased estimate of the expected future spot price. However, this conclusion may not hold for all futures markets, or it may not be consistent over all time periods within a market.

2. Speculators' profits are primarily due to their forecasting abilities rather than their risk-bearing function implied in the theory of normal backwardation. Large speculators (professionals) earn substantial and consistent profits. About 75 percent of their profits is due to their ability to forecast short-term price trends; the remaining profit arises from their ability to forecast long-term price trends. Small speculators (nonprofessionals) experience substantial losses net of transaction costs.

Further, numerous studies have examined whether the futures price follows a random walk or exhibits any trend in the short run. The theory of efficient markets discussed earlier implies that short-term price changes in such markets are independent and randomly distributed, so past price changes are not useful in predicting future price changes. Applying time series analysis to Chicago corn futures daily prices during the periods of 1922–1931 and 1949–1958, Larson[9] found a tendency for sudden large price movements to be followed by reversals over short periods and thereafter by weak price trends over longer periods. Smidt[10] reported significant serial dependence among daily price changes in May soybeans during the period of 1952–1961. Stevenson and Bear[11] examined daily closing prices on July corn and soybeans during the 1951–1968 period. Their major findings were

1. There was a tendency toward negative serial correlation among price differences for one- and two-day lags.

[9] Arnold B. Larson, "Measurement of a Random Process in Futures Prices," in *Selected Writings on Futures Markets*, edited by Anne E. Peck (Chicago: Chicago Board of Trade, 1977): 295–312.

[10] Seymour Smidt, "A Test of the Serial Independence of Price Changes in Soybean Futures," in *Selected Writings on Futures Markets*, edited by Anne E. Peck (Chicago: Chicago Board of Trade, 1977): 257–277.

[11] Richard A. Stevenson and Robert M. Bear, "Commodity Futures: Trends or Random Walk?" *Journal of Finance* 25, no. 1 (March 1970): 65–81.

2. One- and two-day runs were slightly more frequent than expected, and long runs (five and six or more days) were fewer than expected by pure chance.

3. Application of mechanical trading rules based on filters of different sizes (from 1.5 to 5 percent of the price per bushel) produced net profits in excess of that earned on a buy-and-hold strategy. This confirmed the existence of long-term price trends. The authors concluded that the random walk hypothesis does not provide a satisfactory explanation of the behavior of commodity futures prices in the short run.

Labys and Granger[12] applied spectral analysis to monthly, weekly, and daily prices of numerous commodity futures covering the period 1950–1965. They found that the price behavior of most of these commodity futures, with the exception of wheat, cotton, and cocoa, confirmed the random walk model.

In summary, the empirical evidence indicates a tendency toward negative serial dependence in daily price changes of some commodity futures. However, the conflicting findings on the existence of price trends should warn speculators to be skeptical in trying to profit from short-term price movements.

IMPACT OF HEDGERS AND SPECULATORS ON PRICE RELATIONSHIPS

The difference between the current spot price and the current futures price is known as *basis*. In the conventional discussion of futures trading, the market participants are classified into two groups: hedgers and speculators. *Hedgers* are those with a long or short position in the spot market (such as a grain elevator company with an inventory of some product or an exporter with a future commitment to deliver at a fixed price) who assume an opposite position in the futures market with a view to reducing the risk of price fluctuations. *Speculators,* in contrast, lack any position in the underlying asset but trade the futures contract with the hope of making a profit because of the risk of price changes they assume. Keynes and Hicks[13] argued that the short hedgers generally exceed the long hedgers, so the market is dominated by net short hedgers. In accommodating net short hedgers, long speculators require a premium for bearing the risk of price fluctuation. Thus, the excess supply of the contract by net hedgers and the risk premium demanded by long speculators reduce the current futures price below the expected future spot price. This specification of the price relationship is known as *normal backwardation*, referred to earlier. Under this hypothesis, the current futures price is a downward-biased predictor of the expected future spot price at the time of delivery, and the futures price has an upward trend during the life of the contract.

[12] Walter C. Labys and C. W. T. Granger, *Speculation, Hedging, and Commodity Price Forecasts* (Lexington, Mass.: D.C. Heath and Co., 1970): 66–70.

[13] J. R. Hicks, *Value and Capital*, 2d ed., (Oxford: Oxford University Press, 1946), Chapter 10; John Maynard Keynes, *Treatise on Money* 2 (London: Macmillan, 1930): 142–144.

Under the conventional view, the market is characterized as *contango,* when long hedgers exceed short hedgers. With net long hedging, there is an excess demand for the futures contract, which exerts upward pressure on the current futures price. To induce speculators to assume short futures positions and supply the contract, the futures price would subsequently have to fall, on average. Thus, under contango the current futures price is an upward-biased predictor of the future spot price expected to prevail at time of delivery. Cootner[14] observed that when there are large inventories immediately after the harvest, the net short hedgers dominate the market. In contrast, there is net long hedging at the end of the crop year, which causes contango. Similarly, Working[15] explained the spread between current spot and futures prices in terms of the inventory level of the underlying asset to be carried to the delivery date. He viewed the cash-futures spread as the market-determined cost of storage of stocks and observed that the cost of storage could even be negative because of the convenience yield (the benefit of having stock on hand).

In contrast to the normal backwardation and contango hypotheses, the *unbiased expectations hypothesis* assumes that speculators are risk neutral. It holds that the current futures price is an unbiased predictor of the future spot price expected to prevail at the time of contract delivery.

RECENT RESEARCH ON PRICE RELATIONSHIPS

The conventional analysis of spot, forward, and futures price relationships ignored the consequences of daily cash settlement of the futures contract. The modern approach, beginning with a seminal article by Black,[16] explicitly recognized the daily marking-to-market feature of the futures contract.[17] It employed the law of one price to analyze the relationships among spot, forward, and futures prices. According to this principle of pricing, assets (real as well as financial) with identical time patterns of payoffs in the future *must* trade at identical current prices in frictionless markets in order to prevent arbitrage opportunities. This principle showed that the cash flows from the forward and futures contracts can be duplicated by constructing an appropriate portfolio of the underlying asset and default-free discount bonds. Therefore, the current forward and futures prices must be equal to the present value of the corresponding portfolios if you assume that the markets are frictionless and that the underlying asset can be sold short in the spot market.

---

[14] Paul H. Cootner, "Speculation and Hedging," *Food Research Institute Studies,* Supplement (Stanford, Calif.: 1967): 65–106.

[15] Holbrook Working, "The Theory of Price of Storage," *American Economic Review* 39, no. 5 (December 1949): 1254–1262.

[16] Fischer Black, "The Pricing of Commodity Contracts," *Journal of Financial Economics* 3, no. 1, 2 (January–March 1976): 167–179.

[17] Cox, Ingersoll, and Ross, "The Relation between Forward Prices and Futures Prices," 321–346; Robert A. Jarrow and George S. Oldfield, "Forward Contracts and Futures Contracts," *Journal of Financial Economics* 9, no. 4 (December 1981): 373–382; and Scott F. Richard and M. Sundaresan, "A Continuous Time Equilibrium Model of Forward Prices and Futures Prices in a Multigood Economy," *Journal of Financial Economics* 9, no. 4 (December 1981): 347–371.

ECONOMIC FUNCTIONS OF FUTURES MARKETS

The two primary functions of futures markets are *price discovery* and *hedging*. Price discovery is the forecast of spot price expected at the time of delivery of the futures contract. As observed earlier, recent research indicates that the current futures price is a biased predictor of future spot price. However, empirical evidence revealed that for many commodity contracts the bias in the futures price may be small or insignificant. Since futures prices are widely disseminated through daily news media, the market consensus prediction of the expected future spot price of the underlying asset is available to everybody. The price forecast can be used by the producers to guide production levels and by merchants to manage inventories. For instance, in making planting decisions, a farmer can obtain the market forecast of expected prices at harvest time from the springtime quotes on the July wheat futures contract. Likewise, a corporate treasurer who expects to sell a new issue of bonds in the near future can find the market forecast of long-term interest rates in the current quotes on the near-term Treasury bond futures contract. Futures contracts written on *seasonally* produced, *storable* commodities such as wheat and corn facilitate temporal allocation of inventories. To grain elevators, they provide a consensus forecast of the storage cost between the present and the contract delivery month. This information helps them in inventory-carrying decisions. Commodities such as potatoes and onions (seasonally produced) and live beef cattle and eggs (continuously produced) are generally regarded as semi-storable or nonstorable products. Futures contracts written on nonstorable commodities provide market forecasts of the prices expected to prevail at the time of delivery.

In inventory-carrying markets (i.e., markets in storable commodities), speculators who try to arbitrage between the spot and futures markets strengthen the relationship between the current futures price and the expected future spot price. Does this mean that the current futures price of a nonstorable commodity is not as good a predictor of the future spot price? To answer this question, Leuthold[18] compared the forecasting performance of corn futures with that of live beef cattle. Recall that at delivery, the futures price, $F(T)$, is more or less equal to the spot price, $S(T)$, so we could use $F(T)$ to represent $S(T)$. Using monthly data for the period of 1964–1971 covering 36 cattle contracts and 35 corn contracts, Leuthold regressed $F(T)$ against $F(t,T)$ from one to eight months prior to delivery (i.e., $t = 1, 2, 3, \ldots 8$ months) to test the hypothesis that the intercept is zero and the slope coefficient is equal to 1. The regression results indicated little difference between the forecasting performance of the corn and cattle futures contracts.

Leuthold also compared the performance of the current futures price with that of the current spot price as a predictor of the future spot price. He computed mean-square errors for weekly cash and futures prices of corn and cattle and found that the mean-square errors were similar for all

---

[18] Raymond M. Leuthold, "The Price Performance on the Futures Market of a Nonstorable Commodity: Live Beef Cattle," in *Selected Writings on Futures Markets*, ibid., 375–386.

36 weeks prior to delivery for corn but only for the first 15 weeks for cattle. During the 15th to the 36th week prior to delivery, the mean-square error for the futures price on cattle grew progressively larger than the cash price. The author concluded that for cattle the deferred futures contracts (i.e., contracts 15 to 36 weeks away from delivery) were poor predictors of the future spot price relative to the current spot price. It is, however, not clear whether the poor forecasting ability of deferred contracts is the result of nonstorability of the underlying commodity or limited open interest and volume of trading in distant delivery contracts.

In sum, we may conclude that the futures price of a near-delivery (i.e., up to three months from delivery) contract on both storable and nonstorable commodities generates a market consensus forecast with negligible bias of the delivery-time spot price. Notably, its forecasting performance is comparable to that of the current spot price. The amount of bias and the forecast error tend to increase as the length of the forecast horizon increases because of the thinness of the market for distant delivery contracts. This suggests that the current spot price is a more reliable predictor of the future spot price of nonstorable commodities over longer horizons than a distant delivery futures contract with a thin market.

Peck[19] examined shell egg futures (traded on the Chicago Mercantile Exchange) during June 1971 and December 1973 and found that forecast errors (root mean-squared errors) increased as the forecast horizon lengthened from one to five months prior to delivery. She concluded that the performance of the futures forecast is comparable to that of a subjective point forecast. It is far more reliable over the five-month horizon than a simple regression forecast of the future spot price.

The foregoing discussion raises an important question. If the current spot price is as good as the current futures price in predicting the expected future spot price, does this mean the value added (to economic activity) by futures trading is virtually negligible? To answer this question, recall that active futures trading provides professional traders with a low-cost mechanism to formulate their (future spot price) forecasts. Further, it increases market information and thereby enables producers, processors, and distributors in the spot market to respond faster to expected supply and demand conditions. Because it helps integrate the spot and futures markets, the current spot price reflects the information contained in the current futures price. Clearly, the operations of an active futures market tend to increase the efficiency of the underlying spot market.

HEDGING AND SPECULATIVE TRANSACTIONS

As discussed earlier, individuals and institutions involved in commodities trading can be categorized as hedgers or speculators. Hedgers use futures contracts to offset another risk, while speculators attempt to derive a rate of return on purchase and sale transactions consistent with the risk involved. In this regard, the speculator is like the typical common stock

---

[19] Anne E. Peck, "Hedging and Income Stability: Concepts, Implications, and an Example," in *Selected Writings on Futures Markets,* 237–250.

investor who buys stock when he expects a price increase and sells stock short if he expects a price decline. After we discuss a few examples of hedging and speculation, we will examine the theory of hedging and speculation.

HEDGING BACKGROUND. A hedger enters into a futures transaction to reduce the risk of loss from price fluctuations of the cash asset. A *naive hedge* is a futures position that is equal in size but opposite to the one you have in the spot market. Thus, if you have a long position in the spot market, you go short on the futures contract. In the futures market, to *go long* means to buy a contract, and to *go short* means to sell a contract. Because of deferred delivery and payment, you are not acquiring (relinquishing) title to the underlying asset when you buy (sell) a futures contract. In contrast, in the spot market to *go long* means to buy the underlying asset; that is, a long position means you already own the asset. Further, to *go short* in the spot market means that you sell an asset you do not own. Two examples of the naive hedging strategy in commodities futures are (1) the farmer hedging his crop (a short hedge) and (2) a processor of commodities hedging an order for future delivery (a long hedge). To simplify the discussion, we will not consider the details of margin maintenance costs that arise from marking-to-market of the futures contract and other transaction costs and taxes.

EXAMPLES OF HEDGING TRANSACTIONS IN COMMODITIES. Consider the example of a farmer who grows corn. As of June he expects to harvest about 10,000 bushels in August. In June, the September futures for corn are selling for 332 ($3.32 a bushel). If the farmer thinks that $3.32 is a reasonable price and does not want to gamble on possibly higher, or lower, prices at harvest time, he can *sell* futures contracts to hedge his current long position. The farmer is basically long in the crop that he owns and is going to harvest. Therefore, by selling a futures contract in that commodity, he has offset his own long position. For our example, assume that he sells two September corn contracts for 10,000 bushels. Let us now consider what happens if the price of corn goes up or down between June and August when he harvests the 10,000 bushels of corn.

If the price of corn decreases to $3.18 a bushel between June and August, the farmer will *lose* on his harvested crop relative to what he expected to receive (which is what he was concerned about), but he will *gain* a comparable amount on the contract he sold short, as shown:

Revenue from cash crop: 10,000 × $3.18 = $31,800
Sale of two contracts at $3.32 = $33,200
Purchase of two contracts at $3.18 = $31,800
Gain on short sale $ 1,400
Total revenue
(before transaction and margin costs) $33,200.

By entering into the hedge, the farmer has assured himself of the $3.32 a bushel, because what he loses on the cash market he gains in the futures market.

If the price of corn increases to $3.43 a bushel between June and August, the opposite occurs:

$$
\begin{aligned}
\text{Revenue from cash crop: } 10,000 \times \$3.43 &= \$34,300 \\
\text{Sale of two contracts at } \$3.32 &= \$33,200 \\
\text{Purchase of two contracts at } \$3.43 &= \underline{\$34,300} \\
\text{Loss on short sale} \quad &(\$\ \ 1,100) \\
\text{Total revenue} \\
\text{(before transaction and margin costs)} \quad &\underline{\$33,200}.
\end{aligned}
$$

In this instance the farmer has likewise assured himself of $3.32 a bushel and thereby *forgone the added gain* due to the price rise. It is this possibility that causes some farmers to avoid using the futures market as a means to hedge some or all of their crop. When they do not hedge, they are basically speculators in the commodity, because, by definition, they are long in the commodity that they are growing.

It is seldom possible to hedge a position completely, because of uncertainty about the size of the harvest, transaction and margin costs, and differential price movements. Specifically, it would be a *partial hedge* if the harvest turns out to be a different quantity than anticipated. In addition, there are going to be commission and margin costs on the futures transaction that will add to the loss or detract from the gain. Still, these costs will be small compared to the gain or loss on a large crop. Finally, futures prices may not move completely with the cash price, which could mean it will not be a complete offset. As an example, consider the first case, in which the cash price declined to $3.18 a bushel. If we assume that the September futures contract declined to only $3.20 a bushel, the gain on the short sale would have been only $1,200, so there would not be a complete offset.

A second group that consistently enters into hedging positions is commodity processors, who are basically forced to be short some required commodity due to the nature of their business. Consider the example of a flour producer who signs a contract in April with a food-processing firm to deliver a certain amount of flour the following July. Because the contract is for July delivery, the price quoted will be based upon the July wheat price. Assume that the flour is going to require the type of wheat sold on the Kansas City Board of Trade (KC). (The type of wheat traded on each of the exchanges differs—hard red winter wheat, soft red winter wheat, etc. Each of these wheats is used to produce a flour that has different uses.) At the time the contract is signed, the price for a July Kansas City wheat contract is 405 ($4.05 a bushel). Therefore, the commodity processor will quote a price for the flour that assumes he will buy the wheat required at $4.05 a bushel. If the contract requires 20,000 bushels of wheat, once the contract is signed, the processor is basically short 20,000 bushels of Kansas City wheat at $4.05 a bushel (total cost of $81,000); that is, he has agreed to deliver flour that will require 20,000 bushels of wheat, and he does not own the wheat. To hedge his position, he would immediately *buy* four July wheat contracts on the Kansas City Exchange. Assume that between April and June (when the processor must buy the wheat in the cash market to fulfill his flour contract) the price of wheat has increased to $4.40 a bushel. The processor's cash flows will be as shown:

Cost of 20,000 bushels at $4.40 = $88,000
Cost of four contracts at $4.05 = $81,000
Sale of four contracts at $4.40 = $88,000
Gain on futures contracts $ 7,000
Total cost of wheat for flour contract
(before transaction and margin costs) $81,000.

As shown, although the processor had to pay more for his cash wheat than the contract price, he made a gross profit on his futures contract. As a result, his total cost before transaction and margin costs was $81,000, or $4.05 a bushel, which is consistent with his contract.

In contrast, assume that the price of wheat declined from $4.05 to $3.85. The processor's costs will be as follows:

Cost of 20,000 bushels at $3.85 = $77,000
Cost of four contracts at $4.05 = $81,000
Sale of four contracts at $3.85 = $77,000
Net loss on futures contracts   ($4,000)
Total cost of wheat for flour contract
(before transaction and margin costs) $81,000.

In this instance, the processor did not have to pay as much for the wheat in the spot market but lost on his futures transaction, so the total cost was $81,000, or $4.05 a bushel. Obviously, he would have been better off if he had not entered into the futures contract, because he would have made more on the flour contract. The fact is, this would have required the processor to *speculate* on the future price of wheat. The objective of a naive hedge is to avoid speculation. The processor wants to make his income from processing the wheat and does not want to be required to accept the possible *price risk* related to his basic commodity. With the hedge, he has avoided this price risk.

Again, the hedge may not work perfectly due to transaction and margin costs involved in the futures investment. Also, prices in the cash market and futures market may not move perfectly together.

WHY SPECULATE IN COMMODITIES? As mentioned, besides using the futures market to hedge a position, an investor can speculate in commodities futures. The reasons for entering into speculative commodity transactions are similar to the reasons for investing in other investment instruments. You want either to reduce the risk involved in your overall portfolio while holding expected return constant or increase your return for a given level of risk. There is potential for risk reduction in commodities trading, because the prices and returns on commodities are not very highly correlated with those in other securities markets (i.e., stocks and bonds). Therefore, although the *total* variability of commodity returns is rather high, the movements are not related to other potential investments, so the variance of your total portfolio could be reduced. As the examples will show, there is the potential for large rates of return on your investment in a short period of time with commodities because of the substantial leverage involved. Therefore, for the investor with the time, temperment, and discipline required for commodities investing, the rewards can be substantial. After we have considered several examples of potential commodity trades, we will discuss some common rules that a speculator in commodities should keep in mind.

SPECULATIVE TRANSACTIONS

In the case of speculation, it is necessary to consider what commodities to trade and what approach to use in analysis. Regarding which commodities to consider, a quick analysis of *The Wall Street Journal* indicates there are about 30 different commodities that can be traded in a wide range of categories (e.g., grains, foods, metals). Few traders ever attempt to trade more than five or six at a time because of the diverse nature of the markets and the difference in supply and demand analysis factors. Trying to analyze and trade wheat, orange juice, and pork bellies would be like trying to analyze industrials, railroads, and banks at the same time. Therefore, you would normally concentrate on commodities within a given group (e.g., corn and soybeans) or between groups that might be related (e.g., corn and livestock).

After you have selected a limited number of commodities that you want to trade, you must decide how you are going to make your trading decisions. Similar to stock investors, commodity investors are basically divided between *fundamentalists* and *technicians*. Fundamentalists attempt to analyze changes in the supply and demand for the commodity. Factors influencing supply would include the amount of acreage planted, the weather during the growing season in the major areas for the crop in question, and the carryover of the crop from the previous season. Regarding demand, the analyst would consider the domestic demand for the product based upon secular population growth and also demand for animal feed. In addition, an important source of demand is that from foreign countries. Hence, it is necessary to consider foreign supply and demand for the commodity and its residual impact on our market.

Technicians, on the other hand, believe that future price movements can be predicted on the basis of past price changes and volume changes. Some investors consider a combination of fundamental and technical analysis most useful. There is a stronger preference for the technical approach in commodity analysis than there is in stock analysis, even though a fair amount of empirical evidence indicates that commodity price changes are a random walk.[20]

---

[20] Holbrook Working, "Prices of Cash Wheat and Futures at Chicago since 1883," *Wheat Studies* 2 (1934): 75–134.

EXAMPLES OF SPECULATIVE TRANSACTIONS IN COMMODITIES. Assume you have become interested in soybeans and, based upon your analysis, you expect soybean prices to increase over the next six months (from January to July). Therefore, you want to be long in July soybeans and decide to buy two contracts (10,000 bushels). After making your decision, you call your commodities broker and place a market order for two July soybean contracts. Like a common stock transaction, your order is transmitted to the firm's floor broker at the Chicago Board of Trade (CBT), who proceeds to the soybean pit and calls out that he wants to buy two July contracts. After bargaining with several traders, he completes the transaction at 960 ($9.60 a bushel). If we assume that the current margin on soybeans at the CBT is 15 percent, it would be necessary to send the broker $14,400 (.15 × $96,000). Because each contract is for 5,000 bushels, each one-cent change in the price of soybeans is worth $50 per contract, or $100 to you because you control two contracts. Subsequently, if the futures price rises (falls), you, as a speculator with a long futures position, stand to gain (lose). Your account would be adjusted on a *daily* basis for futures price changes, and the brokerage house would ask you to deposit more margin (margin calls) if the account balance falls below the maintenance margin level. Thus, when you speculate, you are exposed to an added cost, namely, the interest on variable margins.

After the purchase, you can enter a stop-loss order, as is done with stocks, or simply watch the market closely. One difference between trading stocks and commodities is that there are limits on the daily price changes of each commodity, meant to ensure that no major price change occurs due to an unexpected catastrophe. The idea is to allow time for new investors or speculators to enter the market to help stabilize the price following the major event that caused the abrupt price change.

Assume that in March the price of July soybeans has gone to $9.85 a bushel, which is your target price, so you decide to take your profit. You call your broker and tell him to close out your long July soybean position by selling two July soybean contracts on the market. Again, the broker contacts his representative on the floor of the CBT, who sells two contracts at $9.85 a bushel. Your position is cleared, and your return is as follows:

Bought two July contracts at $9.60 = $96,000
(you deposited 15 percent: $14,400)
Sold two contracts at $9.85 a bushel = $98,500
Gross profit = $ 2,500
Less estimated round-trip commission $ 60
($30/contract)
Profit before margin costs $ 2,440
Rate of return on the initial amount
committed (before interest on variable margins):
2,440/14,400 = 16.9%.

This 16.9 percent return was generated during a two-month period, which means the annual return would be approximately six times as large. Also, consider the impact of leverage: you received a 16.9 percent return on your investment when the price of soybeans only increased by 2.6 percent ($9.85 versus $9.60).

Now consider the same investment, but assume the price of soybeans begins to decline during February. Similar to most commodity traders, you put in a stop-loss order at $9.45 a bushel. This means that if soybeans ever hit this price, the broker is instructed to put in a market sell order for you. The purpose is to ensure that you cut any losses short; the maximum loss should be approximately 15 cents a bushel. Assume the price declines to this level, the broker puts in a market sell, and he sells the two contracts for $9.44 a bushel. (He is not able to get the $9.45 at that point.) Your results would be as follows:

Bought two July contracts at $9.60 = $96,000
(you deposited 15 percent: $14,400)
Sold two contracts at $9.44 a bushel = $94,400
Gross loss = ($1,600)
Less estimated round-trip commission $ 60
($30/contract)
Loss before interest on variable margins $(1,660)
Rate of return on the initial margin
(subject to interest on variable margins):
($1,660)/$14,400 = −11.53%.

In this example you have a return of −11.53 percent in approximately one month, which would convert to an annualized loss of about 12 times this number. Again, it is possible to see the impact of leverage. You experienced a negative return of 11.53 percent on your investment when soybean prices only declined 1.7 percent ($9.44 versus $9.60).

As a second example, assume you are pessimistic about the future price of hogs. According to the quotation section, hogs are traded on the Chicago Mercantile Exchange (CME), and the standard contract is 30,000 pounds. In November you decide to *sell* three July hog contracts that are selling for 44.00 (44 cents a pound). This means each contract is worth $13,200 ($.44 × 30,000), the value of your three contracts is $39,600, and you must deposit $5,940 (.15 × $39,600). In this instance, a one-cent change in the price of hogs changes the value of the contract by $300. To protect yourself if you are wrong, you put in a stop-gain order at 48 cents, which means you want to *buy* three contracts to offset your prior sale if hog futures reach this price. It is not certain that you will pay 48 cents, but it should be fairly close. Assume that prices increase, your stop-gain order is enacted, and you sell three contracts at 48.5 cents a pound in February. Your return would be as follows:

Sale of three July hog contracts at .44/lb. = $39,600
(you deposited 15 percent: $5,940)
Purchase of three July hog contracts at .485 = $43,650
Gross loss = ($4,050)
Less estimated round-trip commission $ 90
($30/contract)
Loss before interest on variable margins $(4,140)
Rate of return on the initial margin
(subject to interest on variable margins):
($4,140)/$5,940 = −69.7%.

In this instance, hogs increased in price by 10.2 percent, and you experienced a negative rate of return of almost 70 percent on your investment in three months.

These examples are meant to indicate the opportunities and risks involved in commodities trading as a speculator.

BASIC RULES FOR COMMODITY TRADING

A large brokerage firm devoted to commodities trading has run a series of ads containing rules for commodities trading.[21] A composite list of the suggestions follows:

1. Have a basic money management plan that takes into account your financial needs and risk preferences.
2. Establish your trading plans *before* engaging in any trading, and stick to your plan regardless of short-run market changes. If you want to change your plan, do so only after reconsideration of all aspects and not when under pressure.
3. Your trading plan should detail such factors as entry point, objective of the trade, and exit price. You should make extensive use of stop-loss or stop-gain orders that ensure discipline and will not allow you to get caught up in the emotion of the market.
4. In general, your trading plan should attempt to cut your losses short and let profits run. Most commodities traders lose on most trades but hope to make the losses up on a few big winners. Therefore, the key is to have a number of small losses offset by a few big gains.
5. Select a broker whose psychology of trading is consistent with yours. In many instances, the best recommendation for a broker is another satisfied customer. In most cases, the broker's main task is to protect you from yourself and your impulse to depart from your trading plan.
6. Keep in constant contact with your broker so that when action is required you will not hesitate.
7. Begin with enough money to accomplish your plan. Without adequate capital, you may not be able to stay through temporary setbacks; a string of small losses could wipe you out before you make a big gain.

---

[21] Conti Commodity Services, Inc., 1800 Board of Trade Building, Chicago, IL 60604.

GENERAL THEORY OF HEDGING AND SPECULATION

Now that you have an understanding of the operational aspects of hedging and speculation, we can consider two basic issues: (1) Does hedging stabilize income; that is, can hedging reduce the variability of expected returns from a spot futures portfolio? (2) What are the risk-return characteristics of futures contracts? Earlier we described a hedger as one who assumes a futures position that is equal in quantity but opposite to his spot market position. A speculator, in contrast, is one who trades a futures contract without a corresponding position in the underlying spot asset in hopes of earning a profit for bearing the risk of futures price fluctuations. However, in trying to reduce spot price variability, the hedger is indeed *speculating* on movements in the *basis*, which is the difference between the current spot and futures prices. If the basis does not change over the hedging period (i.e., the price changes are perfectly correlated), the spot and futures price changes cancel out, and the hedger's net cash flow is equal to the transaction costs and the margin maintenance costs. Alternatively, if the basis at the time of lifting the hedge is larger (smaller) than the initial basis, the short hedger experiences a price gain (loss). In effect, the short hedger is exchanging *basis risk*, which is the variability in the spot price relative to the futures price, for *price risk*, which is the variability of spot price.

THE PORTFOLIO APPROACH

The portfolio approach to futures trading does not distinguish between hedging and speculation. It assumes that the basic motivation for trading futures contracts is the same as that for trading stocks and bonds. The objective of a futures contract holder is to maximize expected return at a given level of risk or to minimize risk given the expected return. Under this approach, both the hedger and the speculator are concerned with expected return as well as risk in trading futures contracts. The holding-period dollar return, DR, on a portfolio consisting of χ units of the spot asset and y units of a futures contract is

$$E(DR) = \chi E(S_{t+1} - S_t) + yE(F_{t+1} - F_t). \qquad (24.12)$$

The variance of this spot futures portfolio is

$$\sigma^2(DR) = \chi^2\sigma_i^2 + y^2\sigma_j^2 + 2\chi y\sigma_{ij}, \qquad (24.13)$$

where

σ_i^2 = **the variance of expected spot price changes**

σ_j^2 = **the variance of expected futures price changes**

σ_{ij} = **the covariance of spot and futures price changes.**

In the Markowitz mean-variance portfolio analysis, the holder of the spot futures portfolio seeks to maximize Q:[22]

---

[22] Peck, "Hedging and Income Stability: Concepts, Implications, and an Example."

$$Q = E(DR) + \lambda\sigma^2(DR), \tag{24.14}$$

where λ = the risk parameter representing the investor's subjective weighting of expected return relative to the risk involved. Since the investor is assumed to be risk averse, λ assumes negative values.

If the basic motivation for trading futures contracts is to minimize portfolio variance, we can derive the optimal number of contracts that we must trade, given the spot position. Differentiate $\sigma^2(DR)$ with respect to y, set it equal to zero, and solve. The optimal number of futures contracts is y^*:

$$y^* = \chi\sigma_{ij}/\sigma_j^2 . \tag{24.15}$$

This means that the variance-minimizing hedge ratio, H^*, is as follows:[23]

$$H^* = (y^*/\chi) = -(\sigma_{ij}/\sigma_j^2) \tag{24.16}$$
$$= -\rho_{ij}\,\sigma_i/\sigma_j,$$

where ρ_{ij} = the correlation coefficient of spot and futures price changes.

Given that the spot and futures price changes are positively correlated $(\rho_{ij} > 0)$, H^* is negative. The negative sign indicates that in order for the hedger to minimize variance, he must hold a futures position opposite to that held in the cash market. In a variance-minimizing hedge, the futures position need not necessarily be equal in size to the spot position; the absolute value of H^* need not necessarily be equal to 1. The value of H^* depends on the correlation and the relative variability of spot and futures price changes. If the standard deviations of spot and futures price changes are comparable, the absolute value of the hedge ratio is less than 1.

The variance of the minimum-variance hedge portfolio, $\sigma^2(DR)^*$, can be obtained by substituting the value of y^* for y in Equation 24.13:

$$\sigma^2(DR)^* = \chi^2\sigma_i^2[1 - \rho_{ij}^2], \tag{24.17}$$

where ρ_{ij}^2 = the coefficient of determination of spot and futures price changes. This means $\sigma^2(DR)^*$ is only a fraction of the variance of the unhedged spot position, $\chi^2\sigma_i^2$. The percentage risk reduction obtained from the minimum-variance hedge is a measure of the effectiveness of the hedge:

$$e = [(\chi^2\sigma_i^2 - \sigma^2(DR)^*)/\chi^2\sigma_i^2] = \rho_{ij}^2 . \tag{24.18}$$

Thus, the coefficient of determination of spot and futures price changes provides a measure of the effectiveness of the minimum-variance hedge. It is often used as one measure of the hedging performance of a futures contract. The portfolio approach can be extended to cover several cash assets and futures contracts.

A major limitation of the Markowitz mean-variance portfolio model of hedging is the assumption that the spot position to be hedged is known.

---

[23] See Leland L. Johnson, "The Theory of Hedging and Speculation in Commodity Futures," *Review of Economic Studies* 27 (1959–1960): 139–160; and Jerome L. Stein, "The Simultaneous Determination of Spot and Futures Prices," *American Economic Review* 51, no. 5 (December 1961): 1012–1025.

While this assumption is realistic for a processor with a known future delivery commitment, it does not hold for a producer, since the size of the harvest is unknown at planting time. Further, the model abstracts from the marking-to-market of futures positions, ignores the covariance of daily futures price changes and interest rates, and does not account for transaction costs and taxes. Nevertheless, it provides a useful guide for determining the number of futures contracts to trade and evaluating the hedging performance of futures contracts.

EXAMPLE OF APPLICATION OF THE PORTFOLIO APPROACH. Peck[24] employed the Markowitz mean-variance portfolio model to examine if a routine system of optimal hedging of expected egg productions in the shell egg futures market (CME) on a monthly basis succeeded in stabilizing producer income during the 1971–1973 period. Her major findings were

1. The average optimal hedge ratios of hedges lasting one to five months ranged from 55 to 90 percent of production; the longer the hedge horizon, the higher the optimal hedge ratio was.
2. The relevant measure of risk was not the standard deviation of returns but was the root mean-squared error—the root of the squared deviations of actual returns from their expected values. Based on the root mean-squared error, optimal hedging substantially reduced the risk confronting a producer.
3. The results obtained from *total routine hedging* (i.e., a hedge ratio equal to 1) compared favorably with the optimal hedging strategy.

In summary, the hedger is concerned with both expected return and risk. Based on his subjective risk aversion and expectations about spot and futures price movements, he decides how much of his spot position to hedge in the futures market in order to attain a mean-variance efficient spot futures hedge portfolio.

An optimal hedging routine substantially reduces the variability of actual portfolio returns from their expected values. Even a naive strategy of hedging total spot positions is quite successful in reducing unpredictable variability of portfolio returns. Futures trading facilitates the production and marketing of commodities by providing a form of insurance against unpredictable price fluctuations. It reduces the probability of bankruptcy[25] and enables the hedger to obtain credit at more favorable terms, which reduces his cost of capital. While the hedger is exposed to additional costs in trading futures such as commissions, bid-ask spreads in futures prices, and lost interest on margins, the futures trading provides the lowest-cost means of insuring against unexpected price movements.

---

[24] Peck, "Hedging and Income Stability."
[25] Scholes, "The Economics of Hedging and Spreading," 265–286.

RISK AND RETURN ON FUTURES CONTRACTS

Our earlier discussion indicated that under the Keynesian hypothesis of normal backwardation, the variability of futures prices is used as a measure of risk associated with futures trading. This theory implies that speculators expect to earn a positive return on their long futures positions. In contrast, the CAPM holds that only the *systematic risk* and not the *total price risk* is relevant. The systematic risk (the futures' beta) of a futures contract is measured by the covariance of the futures price change with the return on the market portfolio divided by the variance of the market return. Because the futures contract requires no initial investment of funds but only good-faith margin deposits, the futures contract is not a part of the market portfolio of all assets. If the futures' beta is close to zero, then the expected return from trading the futures contract must be close to the risk-free rate. Expected returns to hedgers, speculators, and spreaders in futures contracts are also close to this risk-free rate. To make consistent profits on the futures' positions, these traders must be able to forecast prices more accurately than other market participants.

In a study of corn, wheat, and soybean futures during the 1952–1967 period, Dusak found the futures' betas and semimonthly returns close to zero.[26] Bodie and Rosansky examined quarterly returns on 23 commodity futures contracts for the period 1950–1976.[27] The futures' returns are computed assuming that the investor used Treasury bills to post 100 percent margin. The annual rates of return presented in Table 24.1 indicate that the mean and standard deviation of returns on an equally weighted commodity futures portfolio is comparable to those on common stocks. The futures' returns have low to negative correlations with returns on T-bills, long-term government bonds, and common stocks, indicating the diversification potential of commodity futures contracts. The study revealed that a portfolio with 60 percent in common stocks and 40 percent in commodity futures has about the same mean rate of return, but the standard deviation of such a portfolio is only two-thirds that of a pure common stock portfolio. Further, the positive correlation of commodity futures' returns with inflation rates means that commodity futures were a better hedge against inflation than common stocks.

The results in Table 24.2 indicate the mean annual returns on most commodity futures are positive but relatively volatile. Many of the futures' betas are negative and close to zero indicating that the systematic risk of commodity futures is relatively small. The authors concluded that these results favor the Keynesian normal backwardation hypothesis rather than the CAPM.

EFFECTS OF FUTURES TRADING ON UNDERLYING SPOT ASSET PRICES

The history of futures trading reveals that regulatory authorities (and others) have been concerned that futures markets encourage excessive speculation and thereby destabilize the underlying spot asset price. In contrast, economic theory argues that futures trading creates a centralized

---

[26] Dusak, "Futures Trading and Investor Returns," 1387–1406.

[27] Zvi Bodie and Victor Rosansky, "Risk and Return in Commodity Futures," *Financial Analysts Journal* 36, no. 3 (May-June 1980): 27–39.

TABLE 24.1

Distributions of Annual Rates of Return on Alternative Investments, 1950–1976

SERIES	MEAN[a]	STANDARD DEVIATION[a]	CORRELATION MATRIX			
			COMMODITY FUTURES	LONG-TERM GOVERNMENT BONDS	TREASURY BILLS	INFLATION
A. Nominal Returns (percent per year)						
Common stocks	13.05	18.95	-.24	-.10	-.57	-.43
Commodity futures with Treasury bills	13.83	22.43		-.16	.34	.58
Long-term government bonds	2.84	6.53			.20	.03
Treasury bills	3.63	1.95				.76
Rate of inflation	3.43	2.90				
B. Real Returns[b] (percent per year)						
Common stocks	9.58	19.65	-.25	.14	.18	-.54
Commodity futures with Treasury bills	9.81	19.44		-.36	-.48	.48
Long-term government bonds	-.51	6.81			.46	-.38
U.S. Treasury bills	.22	1.80				-.75
C. Excess Returns[c] (percent per year)						
Common stocks	9.42	20.12	-.20	.08	—	-.48
Commodity futures	9.77	21.39		-.26	—	.52
Long-term government bonds	-.79	6.43			—	-.20

[a] The mean annual loss is defined as the sum of the annual losses (negative rates of return) divided by the number of years in which losses occurred.

[b] The real rate of return, R_r is defined by: $1 + R_r = \dfrac{1 + R_n}{1 + i}$, where R_n = the nominal rate of return; i = the rate of inflation as measured by the proportional change in the Consumer Price Index.

[c] The excess return is the difference between the nominal rate of return and the Treasury bill rate.

Source: Zvi Bodie and Victor I. Rosansky, "Risk and Return in Commodity Futures," *Financial Analysts Journal* 36, no. 3 (May–June 1980): 27–39. Reprinted with permission.

TABLE 24.2

Distributions of Annual Rates of Return on 23 Commodity Futures Contracts (percent per year), 1950–1976

COMMODITY	ARITHMETIC MEAN	STANDARD DEVIATION	STANDARD ERROR	BETA (STANDARD ERROR OF BETA)
Wheat	3.181	30.745	5.917	−.370 (.296)
Corn	2.130	26.310	5.063	−.429 (.247)
Oats	1.681	19.492	3.751	.000 (.194)
Soybeans	13.576	32.318	6.220	−.266 (.317)
Soybean oil	25.839	57.672	11.099	−.650 (.558)
Soybean meal	11.870	35.599	6.851	.239 (.351)
Broilers	13.065	39.202	13.860	−1.692 (.395)
Plywood	17.968	39.962	16.314	.660 (.937)
Potatoes	6.905	42.111	8.104	−.610 (.400)
Platinum	.641	25.185	7.594	.221 (.411)
Wool	7.436	36.955	7.120	.307 (.362)
Cotton	8.937	36.236	6.974	−.015 (.360)
Orange juice	2.515	31.771	10.047	.117 (.557)
Propane	68.260	202.088	71.449	−3.851 (3.788)
Cocoa	15.713	54.630	11.391	−.291 (.589)
Silver	3.587	25.622	7.106	−.272 (.375)
Copper	19.785	47.205	9.843	.005 (.492)
Cattle	7.362	21.609	6.238	.365 (.319)
Hogs	13.280	36.617	11.579	−.148 (.641)
Pork bellies	16.098	39.324	11.352	−.062 (.618)
Egg	−4.741	27.898	5.369	−.293 (.271)
Lumber	13.070	34.667	13.101	−.131 (.768)
Sugar	25.404	116.215	24.232	−2.403 (1.146)

Source: Zvi Bodie and Victor I. Rosansky, "Risk and Return in Commodity Futures," *Financial Analysts Journal* 36, no. 3 (May–June 1980): 27–39. Reprinted with permission.

minimum cost mechanism that enables traders with special forecasting skills to determine the future price of the underlying asset. Because futures price information is widely disseminated, the market participants are better informed, and they can react more judiciously to changes in supply and demand factors, thereby reducing the random element in price movements. The futures price provides guidance in production decisions for farmers, processors, mortgage bankers, and others. It facilitates temporal allocation of inventories of seasonally produced, storable commodities by providing a forecast of the storage cost. Carrying inventories over time makes it possible to absorb the difference between production and consumption. The point is, with adequate controls to prevent corners and squeezes, futures trading should *reduce* interseasonal as well as short-run price fluctuations.

Empirical testing of these effects is difficult, because the behavior of spot prices subsequent to the institution of futures trading has been influenced by many other factors. Johnson examined the effects of futures trading on spot onion prices during 1930–1968, and found that the pattern of within-season, seasonal, year-to-year, and within-month price changes has remained essentially unchanged.[28] Taylor and Leuthold[29] divided their sample period into two equal parts: 1957–1964 with no futures trading and 1965–1972 with futures trading. They compared the variability of cash prices for live beef cattle during the two periods and found a significant *reduction* in monthly and weekly price fluctuations.

SUMMARY

There are four types of contracts: cash (or spot), options forward, and futures. The spot, forward, and futures contracts oblige buyers and sellers to make and accept delivery and payment. Option contracts (call or put options), however, allow them to only buy or only sell without incurring the obligation to accept or make delivery. Spot, forward, and futures prices are equal under specified conditions at contract maturity. Otherwise, they are related and the difference is caused by alternative costs and market expectations.

Normal backwardation is the specification of the price relationship between the current futures price and expected future spot price. *Contango* refers to a market characterized by long hedgers exceeding short hedgers. The two primary functions of futures markets are price discovery and hedging. Commodity investors are basically divided between fundamentalists and technicians, just as stock investors are. In general, empirical studies of the returns and risk experienced in commodities trading as part of a total investment portfolio have been encouraging in a portfolio context. Also, several empirical studies have concluded that these futures markets are beneficial to spot market participants.

---

[28] Aaron C. Johnson, "Effects of Futures Trading on Price Performance in the Cash Onion Market, 1930–1968," in *Selected Writings on Futures Markets:* 329–336.

[29] Gregory S. Taylor and Raymond M. Leuthold, "The Influence of Futures Trading on Cash Cattle Price Variations," in *Selected Studies on Futures Markets:* 367–373.

QUESTIONS

1. Discuss two ways in which trading commodities and trading common stocks are similar.

2. Discuss two ways in which trading commodities and trading common stocks are different.

3. Discuss one advantage that commodities have over stocks and one advantage that stocks have over commodities.

4. What is the purpose of a stop-gain order? Give an example for a current three-month soybean meal contract.

5. Discuss the results of at least one empirical study on the forecasting performance of commodity futures contracts.

6. Discuss the effects of futures trading on the spot market.

7. What is the difference between the value of a futures contract and its price?

8. Is the forward price equal to the futures price? Assume that both contracts are written on the same underlying asset and have identical delivery months.

9. On March 1 you observe that a May corn futures contract is quoted at $2.00 per bushel and the cash market quote for corn is $1.90 per bushel. What could you infer from these quotes about the market's forecast of cost of carry?

PROBLEMS

1. Based upon prices listed in *The Wall Street Journal,* compute the value of a soybeans contract for delivery in about six months (or a length of time close to this). Assuming a 15 percent margin, compute what you must deposit with your broker.

2. Given the conditions in Problem 1, compute your rate of return if you buy the contract and prices increase by 10 percent. What is your rate of return if prices decline by 10 percent?

3. Assume a margin of 10 percent and that you sell the soybean contract. What is your rate of return if prices decline by 15 percent? What is your return if they rise by 8 percent?

4. You are a Kansas wheat farmer. In June you decide to hedge 15,000 bushels of your August harvest. Using the September Kansas City contract shown in Figure 24.1, show what would happen if you hedged and then prices increased by 15 cents a bushel.

5. In January, July wheat on the Kansas City Board of Trade (KC) is selling for 484 ($4.84 a bushel). You are bullish on wheat and buy three contracts (15,000 bushels). Compute the following:

5a. Assuming a 15 percent margin, how much must you deposit with your broker?

5b. In April the price of wheat is 496. Assuming the commission is $30 per contract, compute your annualized rate of return if you close out this contract. Discuss the impact of leverage on this trade.

5c. In March the price of wheat is 475, and you think you should close out your trade. Assuming a commission of $30 per contract, compute the annualized rate of return on your investment. Discuss the impact of leverage.

6. In February you read reports about the number of cattle that will come to market over the next nine months. You believe that cattle prices will probably decline from current levels. Therefore, you decide to sell two August live cattle contracts (40,000 pounds per contract) on the Chicago Mercantile Exchange (CME). Currently, the price of August live cattle is 71.00 (71 cents a pound). Given a margin of 15 percent on live cattle and a commission of $30 a contract, compute the following:

6a. Assume you put in a stop-gain order at 76 cents a pound and you get closed out at that price in June. Compute the annualized rate of return on your investment for this trade.

6b. Assume cattle prices decline to 65 cents a pound in July, and you decide to close out your position. Compute the annualized rate of return on your investment.

6c. Compute your annualized rate of return for the conditions in Part b if the margin is 10 percent rather than 15 percent. Discuss the difference in leverage effect between Parts b and c.

7. On May 1 you observe the following quotes:

September wheat futures (CBT)	$3.00 per bushel
Cash wheat	$2.85 per bushel
September 14 T-bill	5.68% discount rate
Estimated storage costs	10% per annum

Do these data suggest the existence of an arbitrage opportunity? Explain. Assuming you find that the July wheat contract is mispriced, show in detail how to exploit this arbitrage opportunity.

REFERENCES

Black, Fischer. "The Pricing of Commodity Contracts." *Journal of Financial Economics* 3, nos. 1, 2 (January–March 1976).

Cox, John C., Jonathan E. Ingersoll, Jr., and Stephen A. Ross. "The Relation between Forward Prices and Futures Prices." *Journal of Financial Economics* 9, no. 4 (December 1981).

Jarrow, Robert A., and George S. Oldfield. "Forward Contracts and Futures Contracts." *Journal of Financial Economics* 9, no. 4 (December 1981).

Johnson, Leland L. "The Theory of Hedging and Speculation in Commodity Futures." *Review of Economic Studies* 27 (1959–1960).

Khoury, Sarkis J. *Speculative Markets.* New York: Macmillan Publishing Co., 1984.

Peck, Anne E. "Hedging and Income Stability: Concepts, Implications, and an Example," in *Selected Writings on Futures Markets.* A. E. Peck (ed.) Chicago: Chicago Board of Trade, 1977.

Richard, Scott F., and M. Sundaresan. "A Continuous Time Equilibrium Model of Forward Prices and Futures Prices in a Multigood Economy." *Journal of Financial Economics* 9, no. 4 (December 1981).

Scholes, Myron S. "The Economics of Hedging and Spreading in Futures Markets." *The Journal of Futures Markets* 1, no. 2 (Summer 1981).

Stein, Jerome L. "The Simultaneous Determination of Spot and Futures Prices." *American Economic Review* 51, no. 6 (December 1961).

Teweles, R., C. Harlow, and H. Stone. *The Commodity Futures Game.* New York: McGraw-Hill, 1977.

Working, Holbrook. "Prices of Cash Wheat and Futures at Chicago Since 1883." *Wheat Studies* 2 (1934).

Working, Holbrook. "The Theory of Price of Storage." *American Economics Review* 39, no. 5 (December 1949).

COMMODITY AND FINANCIAL
APPENDIX 24A FUTURES GLOSSARY

Arbitrage The simultaneous purchase and sale of similar financial instruments or commodity futures in order to benefit from an anticipated change in their price relationship.

Basis The spread, or difference, between the spot or cash price and the price of the future.

Buy in To cover or liquidate a sale.

Carrying charges Those charges incurred in carrying the actual commodity, generally including interest, insurance, and storage.

CFTC The Commodity Futures Trading Commission, an independent federal agency created by Congress to regulate futures trading. The CFTC Act of 1974 became effective April 21, 1975. Previously, futures trading had been regulated by the Commodity Exchange Authority of the USDA.

Clearinghouse An adjunct to a futures exchange through which transactions executed on the floor of the exchange are settled using a process of matching purchases and sales. A clearing organization is also charged with the proper conduct of delivery procedures and the adequate financing of the entire operation.

Clearing member A member of the clearinghouse or organization. Each clearing member must also be a member of the exchange. Not all members of the exchange, however, are members of the clearing organization. All trades of a non-clearing member must be registered with, and eventually settled through, a clearing member.

Close The period at the end of the trading session during which all trades are officially declared as having been executed *at or on the close.* The closing range is the range of actual sales during this period.

Contract A term of reference describing a unit of trading for a financial commodity future. Also, actual bilateral agreement between the buyer and seller of a futures transaction as defined by an exchange.

Cover The buying of a commodity or a financial instrument to offset sales previously made.

Current delivery Delivery during the current month.

Day orders Those limited orders that are to be executed on a specific day and are automatically canceled at the close of that day.

Delivery The tender and receipt of an actual commodity or financial instrument or cash in settlement of a futures contract.

Delivery month The calendar month during which a futures contract matures.

Delivery points Those locations designated by futures exchanges at which the commodity covered by a futures contract may be delivered in fulfillment of the contract.

Discount Commodity, bond, or delivery prices that are below the futures prices or that are lowered due to quality differences.

Evening up Buying or selling to offset an existing market position.

Floor trader A member who generally trades only for his own account, for an account controlled by him, or who has such a trade made for him. Also referred to as a "local."

Hedging The sale of a futures contract against the physical commodity, an existing bond position, or its equivalent as protection against a price decline. Alternatively, it is the purchase of a futures contract against anticipated prices of the physical commodity or bond as protection against a price advance.

Inverted market A futures market in which the nearer months are selling at premiums to the more distant months.

Last trading day The final day under an exchange's rules during which trading may take place in a particular delivery futures month. Futures contracts outstanding at the end of the last trading day must be settled by delivery of underlying physical commodities or financial instruments, or by agreement for monetary settlement if the former is impossible.

Life of delivery (or contract) The period between the beginning of trading in a particular futures contract and the expiration of that contract.

Liquidation Sale of a previously bought contract, otherwise known as *long liquidation*. It may also be the repurchase of a previously sold contract, generally referred to as *short covering*.

Long hedge The purchase of a futures contract(s) in anticipation of actual purchases in the cash market. Used by processors or exporters as protection against an advance in the cash price.

Maintenance margin A sum, usually smaller than—but part of—the original margin. If a customer's equity in any futures position drops to, or under, the maintenance margin level, the broker must issue a *margin call* for the amount of money required to restore the customer's equity in the account to the original margin level.

Margin The amount deposited by a client with his broker to protect the broker against losses on contracts being carried or to be carried by the broker. A *margin call* is a request to deposit either the original margin at the time of the transaction or to restore the margin to the maintenance levels required for the duration of the time the contract is held.

Opening range/closing range In open auction with many buyers and sellers, commodities are often traded at several prices at the opening or close of the market. Buying or selling orders might be filled at any point within such a price range.

Open interest The total of unfilled or unsatisfied contracts on either side of the market. In any delivery month, the short interest equals the long interest; in other words, the total number of contracts sold equals the total number bought.

Pit The designated location on the trading floor where futures trading in a specific commodity takes place.

Round-turn Procedure by which the long or short position of an individual is offset by an opposite transaction or by accepting or making delivery of the actual financial instrument or physical commodity.

Scalper A speculator operating on the trading floor who provides market liquidity by buying and selling rapidly with small profits or losses and who holds his position for a short time.

Settlement price The daily price at which the clearinghouse clears all the day's trades in a given commodity; also, the price established by the exchange to settle contracts unliquidated because of acts of God, such as floods or other causes.

Short hedge The sale of a futures contract(s) to eliminate or lessen the possible decline in value of ownership of an approximately equal amount of the actual financial instrument or physical commodity.

Speculator One who attempts to anticipate price changes and, through market activities, to profit from these changes.

Spot commodity Goods available for immediate delivery.

Trading limit The maximum price change permitted for a single session. These limits vary in the different markets. After prices have advanced or have declined to the permissible daily limits, trading automatically ceases unless offers appear at the permissible upper trading limit or bids appear at the permissible lower limit.

Volume of trading The purchases or sales of a commodity future during a specified period.

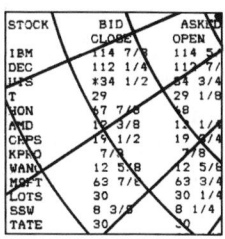

CHAPTER 25

FINANCIAL FUTURES

The material in Chapter 24 provided a background in the basic makeup of the futures markets and the theoretical relationship among spot, forward, and futures prices. This chapter applies and extends these concepts to some new financial instruments that have enjoyed enormous growth: interest rate futures, stock index futures, currency futures, and options on futures contracts. These contracts have brought about significant changes in the way investors, money managers, and financial managers function.

INTEREST RATE FUTURES

Futures contracts on some commodities have existed for many decades, but those on financial instruments such as government bonds, bills, and Eurodollars are relatively new. Similar to commodity contracts, an interest rate futures contract promises delivery of a specified amount of a particular financial instrument at some future time. As an example, if you buy a September Treasury bond contract on the Chicago Board of Trade (CBT), this contract specifies that, if you hold it to maturity, you will receive $100,000 face value of a nominal 8 percent, 20-year U.S. Treasury bond or its equivalent.

The reason for creating such futures contracts is the same as for commodities: the futures contract allows market participants to hedge against price risk in the underlying instrument. Since the mid-1970s, the volatility of interest rates has increased, and this volatility was accentuated in October 1979, when the Federal Reserve Board changed the basic premise of monetary policy from controlling interest rates to attempting to control the growth rate of alternative monetary aggregates (e.g., money supply, monetary base). This change caused a sharp increase in the price volatility of short- and long-term debt instruments. The mortgage banking industry was significantly influenced by the higher level of interest rates and greater volatility. Accordingly, an interest rate futures contract based on the GNMA pass-through certificates was introduced by the Chicago Board of Trade (CBT) in October 1975 to provide mortgage bankers with a mechanism to hedge against unexpected interest rate fluctuations. In January 1976, the International Monetary Market (IMM), a subsidiary of the Chicago Mercantile Exchange (CME), initiated the 90-day T-bill futures contract. Subsequently, the CBT introduced the T-bond futures contract in August 1977, and the IMM created the Eurodollar futures contract in December 1981.

Because of the exceptional growth in trading experienced by these two exchanges, the New York Commodity Exchange (COMEX) began trading financial futures in 1979, and the New York Futures Exchange (NYFE, pronounced "knife"), which is part of the NYSE, was started in 1980, but neither of them is enjoying very large volume. Furthermore, the CBT at present trades T-note futures and municipal bond index futures contracts, but the volume is relatively light.

CHARACTERISTICS OF INTEREST RATE CONTRACTS

Given the numerous interest rate futures contracts being traded on several exchanges, the ones with high trading volume and open interest are T-bill futures (IMM), Eurodollar futures (IMM), and T-bond futures (CBT). These three contracts have quarterly delivery cycles as follows: March, June, September, and December. There are four T-bill futures, eight T-bond futures, and twelve Eurodollar futures contracts trading at any given time. The T-bill futures contract calls for delivery of T-bills having $1 million face value with 90 to 92 days to maturity. During the delivery month the T-bill futures contract matures on the Wednesday following the third Monday of the month. The IMM T-bill futures index value is derived as follows (see *The Wall Street Journal* quotations in Chapter 24, Figure 24.1):

$$\text{IMM T-Bill Futures Index Value} = 100 - \text{T-Bill Futures Discount Yield}$$
$$\text{(in percent)}.$$

That is, if the T-bill futures discount yield is 10.00 percent, the corresponding IMM index value is 90.00 ($100 - 10.00$). The price of a T-bill futures contract with the IMM index value of 90.00 is

$$\$1,000,000 - \left(1,000,000 \times \text{T-bill futures yield} \times \frac{90}{360}\right)$$
$$= 1,000,000 - \left(1,000,000 \times .10 \times \frac{90}{360}\right)$$
$$= \$975,000.$$

The Eurodollar contract has a unit face value of $1 million and is based on three-month Eurodollar time deposits. Eurodollars are short-term U.S. dollar deposits placed outside the U.S. banking system and are comparable to domestic certificates of deposit (CDs). At present, the Eurodollar futures contract is the most actively traded futures instrument based on short-term debt securities. It is similar to the T-bill futures contract except that it calls for cash settlement, not the delivery of the underlying instrument.

The last trading day is the second London business day before the third Wednesday of the delivery month. The fixed cash settlement is based on an average of three-month London Interbank Offer Rate (LIBOR) quotes collected at random from 12 of the top 20 banks in the London Eurodollar market at the following two points in time on the last futures trading day: (1) at the termination of futures trading and (2) at a randomly selected time within the last 90 minutes of trading. The market quotes and price computations for the Eurodollar futures contracts are similar to those of the T-bill futures contract.

The T-bond futures contract (CBT) requires delivery of $100,000 face-value T-bonds with at least 15 years to call or maturity. The published quotes assume a nominal underlying spot bond with 20 years to maturity and an 8 percent coupon. A T-bond futures quote of 70-16 means 70 16/32 percent of par value. The corresponding market price of the contract is $100,000 × 70 16/32 percent = $70,500. Currently, the prescribed minimum price movement on a contract is 1/32 of 1 percent of $100,000, which is equal to $31.25. The CBT limits the maximum daily price change to ±2.00 points from the previous day's settle price, which is worth $2,000 per contract. The exchange has stipulated a three-day delivery process, which allows the contract seller to deliver on any business day during the delivery month. The specifications of the contract permit delivery of bonds bearing coupons other than 8 percent with proper price adjustment. Further, in computing the final settlement price, interest accrued since the last interest payment date is added to the published settlement price.

Given this background, we are in a position to discuss various futures trades: (1) short hedge, (2) long hedge, and (3) speculation.

SHORT HEDGE   A short hedge involves the *sale* of an interest rate futures contract to hedge a current position in the underlying financial instrument. The following examples indicate how various participants use a short hedge.

1. A bond dealer with an inventory of bonds can use a short hedge to reduce price risk in a volatile interest rate market by selling interest rate futures contracts against the inventory.
2. An investment banker can sell interest rate futures contracts against a recent bond issue that is not completely sold out. An example was an IBM bond issued in October 1979 that suffered a major price decline shortly after the offering because of a Federal Reserve policy change. Because investment bankers sold futures contracts against part of the unsold offering, the loss on the unsold issue was partially offset by a gain on the futures contracts.
3. A bond portfolio manager can sell futures contracts against a unique holding in the portfolio that is expected to experience a short-run decline. In this case, rather than sell the issue and then have to buy it back later, the portfolio manager would sell futures contracts against the issue and would thus offset the expected loss by a gain on the futures sale.

4. A bond portfolio manager can enter into a short hedge as protection against a price decline when attempting to liquidate an illiquid issue. Thus, if he decides to sell a large position but knows that, because the market for this bond issue is thin, it will take two weeks to complete the sale, he can sell futures contracts to protect against a price decline during this period.

5. A corporate financial manager who anticipates a bond financing can use financial futures to hedge against higher rates before the actual financing. The corporation would gain on the sale of futures contracts if interest rates increase, and this gain would help offset the higher interest rate on the subsequent bond issue.

The following is an example of a short-hedge transaction:

Intent: Sell futures contracts short against a cash position to hedge an unexpected increase in interest rates.

CASH	FUTURES	BASIS
Nov.1: You own $1 million of 15-yr., 8 3/8% U.S. bonds at 82–17	Sell 10 March bond futures contracts at 80–09	(cash-future)
(Yield: 10.45%)		
(Value: $825,312.50)		+2–8
Mar. 3: You sell the 8 3/8% bonds at 70–26 (Yield: 12.31%)	Buy 10 March bond futures contracts at 66–29	+3–29
(Value: $708,125)	Gain: 13–12 per contract	
Loss: 11–23 per bond	$133,750	
$117,187.50		

Conclusion: Overall gain before margins and transaction costs on the hedge is $16,562.50 because the basis moved in your direction.

LONG HEDGE

A long hedge involves the *purchase* of interest rate futures contracts to offset adverse price movements related to the future purchase of bonds (i.e., a future cash position). Long hedges are not as widespread as short hedges. The most obvious instance in which a long hedge is useful would involve a portfolio manager who expects a future cash flow that will be used to buy bonds. If the portfolio manager thinks yields might decline between now and the time when the cash flows are available, it is possible to lock in the higher yield through a long hedge by buying futures contracts on the bonds. The following example of a long hedge shows how this would work:

Intent: Buy futures contracts against a future cash position.

CASH	FUTURES	BASIS
June 1: A 20-yr. Treasury bond currently yields 12.45%. Price for 20-yr., 8 1/4% bond is 67–28 (current cost is $678,750)	Buy 10 Dec. bond futures contracts at 66–13 Cost: $66,406.25	(cash-future) +1–15
Dec. 3: Buy $1 million of 20-yr., 8 1/4% U.S. bonds at 83–23 (Yield: 10.03%) (Cost of $837,187.50) Loss: $837,187.50 678,750.00 $158,437.50	Sell 10 Dec. bond futures contracts at 81–22 Revenue: $81,687.50 Gain: $81,687.50 66,406.25 $15,281.25/contract $152,812.50 Total	+2−1

Conclusion: Overall loss before margin and transaction costs on the hedge is $5,625 because the basis moved against you—i.e., the basis increased which means that the price of futures did not increase as much as the prices in the cash market.

SPECULATIVE TRANSACTIONS

Investors can engage in speculative interest rate futures transactions when they anticipate a rise or decline in interest rates and want to buy or sell bonds to profit from this change. The use of futures contracts allows an investor to speculate on this expectation with a small capital outlay and derive all the benefits and/or risks of substantial leverage.

The following examples will demonstrate the large profit potential available because of the leverage; that is, you control a large number of bonds with a relatively small margin. As a result, a small change in price results in a large percentage gain or loss on your capital investment. Never forget that when there is a potential for a large gain, there is *also* the potential for a large loss.

Example of a Speculative Trade

Outlook: You expect a decline in interest rates over the next three months.

April 1: You buy a 90-day T-bill futures contract at 87 (13 percent discount). Your initial margin on this contract is $1,500. The contract unit is $1,000,000; a one-basis-point change on this contract is worth $25.

July 10: You were correct and rates declined from 13 percent to 11 percent. You can sell your contract at 89 (11 percent discount). The 200-basis-point change is worth $5,000 (200 × $25). You made $5,000 on the initial deposit of $1,500 (ignoring maintenance margin and transaction costs).

Note: If you were wrong and the rate increased to 15 percent, you would sell the contract for 85 and lose $5,000 on a $1,500 deposit.

The final example is for a speculator who expects an increase in interest rates. This situation is rare, because, typically, if you expect an increase in rates, you have no way to make money on the expected price decline; about all you can do is avoid buying bonds or sell those you currently own. As shown, with futures contracts you can make money on the price decline. In addition, you may also use *intramarket* (between delivery months) and *intermarket* spreads.

Example of a Speculative Trade

Outlook: You expect an increase in interest rates over the next three months.

Sept. 1: You sell a long-term Treasury bond future at 89–00. Your initial margin on this contract is $2,000. The contract unit is $100,000; a change of 1/32nd in this contract is worth $31.25.

Oct. 15: You were correct and rates increase. As a result, the futures price declines to 86–00. You buy back the contract at 86–00. This offsets the original sale. The three-point change is equal to 96 32nds (3 × 32). The total gain is 96 × 31.25 = $3,000. This $3,000 gain is on a deposit of $2,000 (ignoring maintenance margin and transaction costs). Again if interest rates had declined, prices would have increased, you would have to buy the contract at a higher price, and you would have lost on the trade.

ALTERNATIVE FORWARD LOANS

As discussed in Chapter 24, assuming that financial markets are perfect and that carrying costs are constant (i.e., deterministic) over the life of a futures contract, then the current futures price would be equal to the current forward price. Since the carrying costs of T-bills in perfect markets consist of only interest rates, this assumption implies that interest rates are constant over the life of the contract. If these assumptions hold, we can show three ways to create forward loans that are *perfect substitutes* for one another:[1]

1. Buy and hold a T-bill futures contract that would deliver a 13-week T-bill in 13 weeks (at $t + 13$).
2. Enter into a repurchase agreement: buy a 26-week bill, sell it, and simultaneously agree to buy it back 13 weeks later at the current market price on a 13-week T-bill. The document specifying this arrangement is referred to as a *repo*.
3. Buy a 26-week T-bill and sell short an appropriate number of 13-week T-bills.

The cash flows (per $100 par value) involved in these transactions are

1. Futures market

$$\underset{t}{\vert} \quad \underset{t+13}{\overset{F(t,\, t+13)}{\vert}} \quad \underset{t+26 \text{ weeks}}{\overset{\$100}{\vert}}$$

2. Repo (forward) market

$$\underset{t}{\vert} \quad \underset{t+13}{\overset{FO(t,\, t+13)}{\vert}} \quad \underset{t+26 \text{ weeks}}{\overset{\$100}{\vert}}$$

---

[1] Edward J. Kane, "Market Incompleteness and Divergences between Forward and Futures Interest Rates," *Journal of Finance* 35, no. 2 (May 1980): 221–234.

That is, the current forward price on a 13-week T-bill to be delivered 13 weeks later is $FO(t, t + 13)$.

3. Spot market

$$\left[\frac{S(t,t+26)}{S(t,t+13)}\right] \times 100 \qquad \$100$$

$$\begin{array}{ccc} & & \\ t & t+13 & t+26 \end{array}$$

At t, you would sell short $[s(t,t + 26)/s(t,t + 13)]$ number of 13-week bills. This transaction will generate cash flows worth $[S(t,t + 26)/S(t,t + 13) \times S(t,t + 13)]$, which is equal to $\$S(t,t + 26)$. Using the proceeds from this short sale, you could buy a 26-week T-bill and hold it to maturity. At $t + 13$, settle the short sale by paying $\$100 \times [S(t, t + 26)/S(t, t + 13)]$. Observe that the three transactions have an identical cash flow of $100 at $t + 26$. According to the law of one price discussed in Chapter 24, these three transactions must have the same price at time t. That is,

$$F(t, t + 13) = FO(t, t + 13) = 100[S(t, t + 26)/S(t, t + 13)]. \quad (25.1)$$

The last term in the preceding equation $[S(t, t + 26)/S(t, t + 13)]$ is the implied forward price (i.e., the forward price implied in the current yield curve). Since the repo market is very illiquid relative to the spot and futures markets, we will limit our analysis to the relationship between the current futures price and the current implied forward price.

If the current futures price is not equal to the current implied forward price, arbitrage opportunities exist. For instance, if the current futures price is less than the current implied forward price, one could set up the following arbitrage by buying the underpriced and selling the overpriced instruments. That is,

At t:

1. Sell short the 26-week T-bill. $\$S(t, t + 26)$.
2. Buy $[S(t, t + 26)/S(t, t + 13)]$ number of 13-week T-bills.

          $-\$S(t, t + 26)$

3. Buy a futures contract.   0
4. Net cash flow: 0

At $t + 13$:

5. The maturing T-bills produce: $\$[S(t, t + 26)/S(t, t + 13)]$.
6. Take delivery (of a 13-week T-bill) on the futures contract.

          $-\$F(t, t + 13)$.

7. Net cash flow: $\${[S(t, t + 26)/S(t, t + 13)] - F(t, t + 13)} > 0$.

The net cash flow is positive, because the current futures price is less than the current implied forward price. When interest rates are deterministic, as assumed earlier, interest on variable margins could be ignored. An easy way to demonstrate this is to assume that the term structure of interest rates is flat over the life of the contract, which implies that the futures price remains fixed until delivery.

At $t + 26$:

8. The maturing 13-week T-bill produces:	$100.
9. Settle the original short sale of a 26-week T-bill.	−100.
10. Net cash flow:	0.

In this example the arbitrageur does not invest any capital at time t, and yet he is assured of a positive cash flow at $t + 13$. Hence, this arbitrage transaction produces a riskless return without requiring any capital investment. Such profit opportunities rarely exist in efficient markets. The increased demand for the futures contract and for the 13-week bills, along with the excess supply of the 26-week bill, would exert pressure on market prices such that the equilibrium condition would be reestablished quickly.

Now that we have seen the fundamental and somewhat unrealistic relationship between the current futures price and the current forward price implied by the corresponding spot bills, we can relax the simplifying assumptions. With stochastic interest rates, we would have to account for interest on margins arising from the daily marking-to-market of the futures contract. Further, we have to consider taxes and transaction costs, such as commissions, short-selling costs, and bid-ask spreads in the spot and futures markets. Although these transaction costs are relatively fixed over the life of the contract, the interest rates on daily margin flows are not. Therefore, the transactions are not perfect substitutes and do not constitute an arbitrage opportunity. However, they are close-to-perfect substitutes and represent a near-arbitrage opportunity.

In general, it is difficult to profit from minor deviations of the current futures price from the implied forward price because of market imperfections and margin maintenance costs. There could be profits only if the difference between the current futures and forward prices exceeds the costs due to market frictions and the interest paid on variable margins. If one can obtain a reasonable estimate of the total of such costs, say $\$K$, then it is possible to compute an upper and a lower boundary for the futures price.

$$100 \times [S(t, t + 26)/S(t, t + 13)] - K < F(t, t + 13) <$$
$$100 \times [S(t, t + 26)/S(t, t + 13)] + K. \qquad (25.2)$$

The lower and upper boundaries for the futures price are expressed in terms of the implied forward price adjusted for K. Within these bounds, it is not possible to profit from the futures-forward price deviations. Alternatively, if the futures price falls below the lower boundary or rises above the upper boundary, it would be profitable to enter into arbitrage transactions similar to those illustrated earlier. Also, note that these rules with minor modifications can be applied to discover and exploit arbitrage opportunities in the Eurodollar futures and spot markets.

MARKET EFFICIENCY OF T-BILL FUTURES

Using daily closing data from January 1976 to March 1978, Rendleman and Carabini[2] compared the T-bill futures price of the first three contracts (maturing in the following nine months at quarterly intervals) with the

---

[2] Richard Rendleman and Christopher Carabini, "The Efficiency of the Treasury Bill Futures Market," *Journal of Finance* 34, no. 4 (September 1979): 895–914.

corresponding implied forward price. The results, summarized in Table 25.1, indicate that the annualized mean basis point differential between the futures price and the implied forward price (not adjusted for transaction costs) is 5.775 basis points, worth about $578 on a $1 million contract (panel A). This implies that on average the futures contract is overpriced relative to the implied forward price. Notice, however, that the third contract is generally underpriced. The average absolute differentials are 15.868 basis points. That is, if one holds the futures long when they are underpriced and replaces them with the implied forward instrument when the former are overpriced, one receives an average annual return of $1,587 per contract. Panel B shows the basis point differentials adjusted for transaction costs (exclusive of short-selling costs in the cash T-bill market). Note that 66 percent of the differences for all contracts are within the upper and lower boundaries. Thus, in the remaining 34 percent of the cases, an investor with the required T-bills in his portfolio could have profited by arbitraging between the futures and the spot T-bill markets. These are called *quasi-arbitrage opportunities,* because it is assumed that the arbitrageur already owns the required spot T-bills and thus is not obliged to incur the short-selling costs. In contrast, a pure arbitrage opportunity exists when the difference between the futures and forward prices exceeds all transaction costs, including short-selling costs in the spot market. Typically, it costs about 50 basis points per annum to sell T-bills short. After adjusting for short-selling costs, Rendleman and Carabini found that all of the futures-forward price differences lie within the no-arbitrage (lower-upper) boundaries. They concluded that while there are some quasi-arbitrage opportunities, pure arbitrage opportunities seldom exist in the T-bill futures market for the first three contracts.

An important limitation of the foregoing study is that it used daily closing data on spot and futures contracts, which are not usually simultaneous observations. To overcome the problem, Elton, Gruber, and Rentzler used intra-day prices from January 1976 through December 1982.[3] After adjusting for margin and transaction costs, they discovered numerous pure arbitrage opportunities and concluded that the T-bill futures market was not perfectly efficient. These results were further corroborated by Hegde and Branch.[4]

TREASURY BOND FUTURES

The T-bond futures contract grants the seller (the *short*) two delivery options. The first, called the *quality option,* allows the short to choose for delivery *any* T-bond with at least 15 years remaining to the earlier of call or maturity. The second, termed the *timing option,* allows the short to make delivery on *any* business day during the delivery month. Even though futures trading closes at 2:00 p.m. Chicago time during the first (roughly) 16 days of the delivery month, the short seller is entitled to wait until 8:00

---

[3] Edwin J. Elton, Martin J. Gruber, and Joel Rentzler, "Intra-Day Tests of the Efficiency of the Treasury Bill Futures Market," *The Review of Economics and Statistics* 66, no. 1 (February 1984): 129–137.

[4] Shantaram P. Hegde and Ben Branch, "An Empirical Analysis of Arbitrage Opportunities in the Treasury Bill Futures Market," *The Journal of Futures Markets* 5, no. 3 (Fall 1985): 407–424.

TABLE 25.1

Summary Statistics for Basis Points Differential Between T-Bill Futures and Implied Forward Prices, 1976–1978

		CONTRACT			
		1ST CONTRACT MONTH	2ND CONTRACT MONTH	3RD CONTRACT MONTH	ALL CONTRACTS
A. Annual basis	μ	21.244	3.426	−9.192	5.775
point differentials	$|\mu|$	24.902	10.867	11.277	15.868
unadjusted for	σ	26.952	13.308	10.114	22.319
transaction costs.	σ_ϵ	23.460	5.498	3.516	N/A
	ϕ_1, ϕ_2	.308,.280	.755,.167	.863,.074	N/A
	N	558	559	489	1606
	t	8.813	1.149	−3.642 [a]	N/A
	$Q(21,N)$	25.031	24.072	35.341[b]	N/A

Legend:

μ = sample mean
$|\mu|$ = sample mean of absolute value
σ = sample standard deviation
σ_ϵ = standard error of estimate of second order autoregressive process
ϕ_1, ϕ_2 = first and second order autocorrelation coefficients
N = sample size
$t = \mu(1 - \phi_1 - \phi_2)/(\sigma\sqrt{N})$
$Q(21,N)$ = Box-Pierce Q statistic using 21 residual autocorrelations with sample size N.

[a]Significantly different from zero at 5 percent level.
[b]Null hypothesis that residuals follow a white noise process is rejected at the 5 percent level.

	CONTRACT		N	PERCENT	μ	μ_a
B. Basis point	1st contract	B	1	0	−.574	−.582
differentials adjusted	month	W	391	70	4.108	14.590
for transaction costs.		A	166	30	8.204	13.425
			558	100		
	2nd contract	B	51	9	−8.404	−4.879
	month	W	396	71	.626	.878
		A	112	22	11.822	9.830
			559	100		
	3rd contract	B	212	43	−19.350	−7.539
	month	W	266	54	−7.441	3.257
		A	11	3	10.031	3.724
			489	100		
	All contracts	B	264	16	−17.164	−6.999
		W	1053	66	−.119	4.925
		A	289	18	9.676	11.662
			1606	100		

Legend:

N = number of observations
Percent = percent of total observations within cell
μ = sample mean, not annualized
μ_a = sample mean, annualized
B = below lower index boundary (Means are differences between actual IMM index values.)
W = within index boundaries (Means are differences between actual and no-transaction cost.)
A = above upper index boundary (Means are differences between actual IMM index values.)
Source: Richard Rendleman and Christopher Carabini, "The Efficiency of the Treasury Bill Futures Market," *Journal of Finance* 34, no. 4 (September 1979): 895–914.

p.m. to declare delivery at the 2:00 p.m. settlement price. This is known as the *wild card option*. Further, trading in the nearby futures contract terminates on the eighth-to-last business day of the delivery month, but the short seller may wait until the last business day to effect delivery at the last settlement price. Notice that the quality and timing of delivery options have the following characteristics: (1) they are analogous to put options, (2) they are implicit (embedded) in the futures contract, and (3) they are held (owned) by the seller of futures contract. These delivery options are in effect granted by the buyer of the futures contract.[5]

As noted earlier, the nominal (benchmark) underlying instrument for the T-bond futures contract bears an 8 percent coupon and has 20 years to maturity. However, the quality option allows the short seller to deliver a T-bond with any other coupon available, provided the bond has at least 15 years to call/maturity. Currently, about 30 bonds with different coupons and maturities qualify for delivery. This necessitates a delivery adjustment factor called the *conversion factor* for each deliverable bond, whereby each is priced to yield 8 percent to maturity. In other words, the conversion factor is the price per dollar par value of a bond based on an 8 percent discount rate as shown:

$$CF = \sum_{t=1}^{n} \frac{C_t}{(1.04)^t} + \frac{1}{(1.04)^n}$$
$$= \frac{C}{0.04}\left[1 - \frac{1}{(1.04)^n}\right] + \frac{1}{(1.04)^n}, \tag{25.3}$$

where

    CF = **conversion factor**

    C = **semiannual coupon per dollar par**

    n = **term to maturity of bond expressed in semiannual periods.**

Assume that the conversion factor for an 18-year bond with a 10 percent coupon is 1.1891. This means that one unit of the deliverable bond is equivalent to 1.1891 units of the nominal bond with an 8 percent coupon.

Note that this conversion factor method of pricing for delivery is imperfect except in the rare case where the long-term yield curve is flat at the 8 percent level assumed in this method. This imperfection renders some bonds more attractive (i.e., less expensive) for delivery than other bonds, and the short futures trader would deliver the cheapest of the

---

[5] Shantaram P. Hegde, "An Empirical Analysis of Implicit Delivery Options in the Treasury Bond Futures Contract," *Journal of Banking and Finance* (forthcoming); and Alex Kane and Alan J. Marcus, "Valuation and Optimal Exercise of the Wild Card Option in the Treasury Bond Futures Market," *Journal of Finance* 41, no. 1 (March 1980): 195–208.

eligible bonds. The cheapest-to-deliver bond is the one that maximizes the anticipated delivery proceeds as shown:

$$MAX_i [F(t,T) \times CF(i) - FO(i,t,T)], \qquad (25.4)$$

where

$F(t,T)$ = futures price at time t for delivery at T

$CF(i)$ = conversion factor for bond i

$FO(i,t,T)$ = forward price for bond i at time t, for delivery at T.

Even though there is little forward trading in T-bonds, $FO(i,t,T)$ can be synthesized as follows:

$$FO(i,t,T) = P(i,t)[1 + C(t,T)]^{(T-t)} - CR(i,t,T) - AI(i,T), \qquad (25.5)$$

where

$P(i,t)$ = market price of bond i inclusive of accrued interest at t

$C(t,T)$ = cost of carryover (t,T)

$CR(i,t,T)$ = compounded value of coupon receipts, if any, on bond i over (t,T)

$AI(i,T)$ = accrued interest on bond i at delivery.

Let us assume that Equation 25.4 is maximized for bond j at t, thus making it the current cheapest-to-deliver bond. With fluctuations in interest rates, the cheapest-to-deliver bond could change over time, but arbitrage will ensure that the future price will track its price. Consider now the following hedging strategy. At t, a trader borrows and buys one unit of the cheapest bond j and sells $CF(j)$ units of the futures contract. Subsequently, at time of delivery (at T), let k be the cheapest bond. If bond k at T equals bond j (i.e., the cheapest bond does not change over (t,T)), the short seller would deliver bond j, which will yield a cash flow equal to

$$M(j,T) = [F(T) \, CF(j) - FO(j,t,T)] + [F(t,T) - F(T)] \, CF(j). \quad (25.6)$$

In this equation, the last term represents the gross effect of marking the futures position to market, ignoring interest earned or lost on margin cash flows. Instead, if bond k at T is not the same as bond j, then the short seller would find that at time t it is profitable to sell bond j for $P(j,T)$, buy bond k for $P(k,T)$, and deliver it against the short futures position. The resulting cash flow is

$$\begin{aligned} M(k,T) = {} & [F(T) \times CF(k) - P(k,T)] + [P(j,T) - FO(i,t,T)] \\ & + [F(t,T) - F(T)] \, CF(j). \end{aligned} \qquad (25.7)$$

In other words, the *quality delivery option* allows the short seller to exchange the former cheapest bond j for the new cheapest bond k for delivery against the futures contract. Therefore, the quality option is like an exchange option.[6] The incremental cash flow that occurs because of the delivery of bond k rather than bond j provides a measure of payoff to the quality option. That is, the quality option payoff, $Q(T)$, is

$$Q(T) = M(k,T) - M(j,T). \qquad (25.8)$$

While the foregoing discussion assumes delivery at a fixed time, T, the timing option indicates that the short seller enjoys added flexibility with respect to the delivery time. Therefore, the short seller could potentially earn additional payoffs by optimal exercise of the timing option. In equilibrium, the futures price prior to delivery must be bid down by the amount of payoffs to the delivery options from the price of a forward contract without such implicit options. That is,

$$F(t,T)\ CF(j) + V(t,T) = FO(j,t,T), \qquad (25.9)$$

where $V(t,T)$ is an ex ante measure of the value of the delivery options. Therefore, the value of the implicit delivery options is given by the excess of the forward price of the cheapest-to-deliver bond $FO(j,t,T)$ over the futures price times the conversion factor of bond j, $F(t,T) \times CF(j)$.

The relationship in Equation 25.7 suggests the following no-arbitrage boundaries for the adjusted futures price:

$$[FO(j,t,T) - Max\ V(t,T)] < F(t,T)\ CF(j) < FO(j,t,T). \qquad (25.10)$$

If the upper boundary is violated, that is, if $F(t,T)CF(j) > FO(j,t,T)$, one could earn certain profits by buying forward bond j, selling the futures contract, and declining delivery subsequently. Illustrating the violation of the lower boundary is complicated because $Max\ V(t,T)$ (i.e., maximum value of the delivery options) is unobservable. However, this maximum value of the delivery option could be estimated using historical data or by employing an exchange option valuation model. Once a violation of the lower-boundary condition is identified, a trader could construct a near-arbitrage or a risky arbitrage by selling forward bond j and buying $CF(j)$ units of the futures contract. Subsequently, the arbitrageur would receive bond k from the futures seller at delivery. To satisfy the short forward position, the arbitrageur needs to sell bond k, buy bond j, and settle the forward contract. Since bond k is cheaper than bond j, substitution would produce a maximum loss equal to $Max\ V(t,T)$, but this loss is less than the profit on settlement of the short forward position.

The available empirical evidence on the efficiency of the T-bond futures market is sketchy and conflicting, partly because of the complexity

---

[6] Herb Johnson, "Options on the Maximum or the Minimum of Several Assets," *Journal of Financial and Quantitative Analysis* 22, no. 4 (September 1987): 277–284; and Rene Stulz, "Options on the Maximum or Minimum of Two Assets," *Journal of Financial Economics* 10, no. 3 (July 1982): 161–185.

TABLE 25.2
Hedging Performance Results (two-week hedges)

THE FUTURES CONTRACT	ESTIMATED e	ESTIMATED H^*
8% GNMA's (46 observations)		
The nearby contract	.664	.801*
3- to 6-month contract	.675	.832
6- to 9-month contract	.677	.854
9- to 12-month contract	.661	.852
90-Day Treasury Bills (41 observations)		
The nearby contract	.272	.307*
3- to 6-month contract	.256	.237*
6- to 9-month contract	.178	.143*
9- to 12-month contract	.140	.116
Wheat (45 observations)		
The nearby contract	.898	.864*
3- to 6-month contract	.889	.815*
4- to 8-month contract	.868	.784
6- to 10-month contract	.841	.778*
Corn (45 observations)		
The nearby contract	.649	.915
2- to 6-month contract	.605	.905
4- to 8-month contract	.541	.868
6- to 10-month contract	.450	.764

* Significantly different from 1 at .05 level.

Source: Louis H. Ederington, "The Hedging Performance of the New Futures Market," *Journal of Finance* 24, no. 1 (March 1979): 157–170. Reprinted with permission.

of the futures contract and partly due to the lack of simultaneous spot and futures data.

EVIDENCE ON HEDGING WITH INTEREST RATE FUTURES

Another topic of empirical research is the hedging performance of interest rate futures contracts. We discussed in Chapter 24 that the mean-variance portfolio approach can be used to measure the variance-minimizing hedge ratio, H^*, and the hedging effectiveness of futures contracts, e. Using weekly data over the period from January 1976 to December 1977, Ederington[7] examined the hedging performance of futures contracts on Government National Mortgage Association pass-through certificates, T-bills, wheat, and corn. The results in Table 25.2 for the GNMA futures indicate that the variance-minimizing hedge ratio of a two-week hedge involving the nearby futures contract is about 80 percent of the spot position. That is, the hedger has to trade futures with a face value equal to 80 percent of the par value

[7] Louis H. Ederington, "The Hedging Performance of the New Futures Market," *Journal of Finance* 34, no. 1 (March 1979): 157–170.

of the cash GNMAs. For example, a savings and loan association with a $1 million par value GNMA in its portfolio needs to sell 8 futures contracts with a total face value of $800,000. Such a hedge reduces the price variability of the unhedged spot GNMA portfolio by 66 percent, as revealed by the measure of hedging effectiveness, e. The results in Table 25.2 indicate that the hedging performance of the GNMA futures is quite comparable to those of wheat and corn futures. Franckle[8] has shown that the inferior performance of T-bill futures reported in Table 25.2 is due to some errors in data and methodology. He contends that when the results are corrected, the T-bill futures are as effective in hedging as other contracts.

PRICE SENSITIVITY APPROACH TO HEDGING INTEREST RATES

Under the mean-variance portfolio approach to hedging, one must estimate the expected correlation between the spot and future price changes in order to establish the optimal hedge ratio (see Equation 24.15). In certain situations, such as when you are issuing new debt that has term to maturity and coupon quite different from the existing debt instruments, the correlation coefficient may be difficult to estimate. This problem arises frequently in *cross-hedging*, that is, in hedging financial instruments that have terms to maturity, coupons, default-risk ratings, and tax features that are different from those of the spot asset underlying the futures contract. This estimation problem can be overcome by the *price sensitivity* approach, in which the hedge ratio is computed as a ratio of the expected price volatility of the spot asset being hedged to the expected volatility of the futures contract. That is, the hedge ratio, h, is determined such that the expected change in the spot price, ΔS, is offset completely by the expected price change in the futures contract, ΔF:[9]

$$\Delta S + h\Delta F = 0 \qquad (25.11)$$
$$h = -[\Delta S/\Delta F] = -[dS/dF].$$

We know from the discussion on bond durations that bond price volatility is related to its duration. For simplicity, assume that the term structure of interest rates is flat over the hedging horizon and undergoes only a small parallel shift. This enables us to express the relationship between price volatility and yield volatility of a bond using Macaulay's duration.[10] For a small change in the bond's yield,

$$dS = -D(S)\ S\ dR(S)/R(S) \qquad (25.12)$$
$$dF = -D(F)\ F\ dR(F)/R(F),$$

[8] Charles T. Franckle, "The Hedging Performance of the New Futures Market: Comment," *Journal of Finance* 35, no. 5 (December 1980): 1273–1279.

[9] Robert Kolb and Raymond Chiang, "Improving Hedging Performance Using Interest Rate Futures," *Financial Management* (Autumn 1981): 72–79; Robert Kolb and Raymond Chiang, "Duration, Immunization, and Hedging with Interest Rate Futures," *Journal of Financial Research* 5, no. 2 (Summer 1982): 161–170.

[10] Michael H. Hopewell and George G. Kaufman, "Bond Price Volatility and Term to Maturity: A Generalized Respecification," *American Economic Review* 64, no. 4 (September 1973): 749–757.

where

        $D(S)$ = **the duration of the spot asset being hedged**

        $D(F)$ = **the duration of the asset underlying the futures contract**

        $R(S)$ = **1 + (spot bond yield to maturity)**

        $R(F)$ = **1 + (futures rate).**

The sensitivity of the spot and futures prices to a small change in the risk-free rate of interest is given by

$$dS/dR = -D(S) \; S \; dR(S)/(R(S) \; dR) \qquad (25.13)$$
$$dF/dR = -D(F) \; F \; dR(F)/(R(F) \; dR),$$

where

$$R = 1 + \textbf{(risk-free rate of interest).}$$

Substituting these values into Equation 25.11, we obtain

$$h = \frac{(-)D(S) \; S \; R(F) \; [dR(S)/dR]}{D(F) \; F \; R(S) \; [dR(F)/dR]}. \qquad (25.14)$$

When $[dR(S)/dR] = [dR(F)/dR]$, that is, when the spot yield to maturity and the futures rate are equally sensitive to a change in the risk-free rate, the hedge ratio simplifies to

$$h = \frac{(-)D(S) \; S \; R(F)}{D(F) \; F \; R(S)}. \qquad (25.15)$$

A major shortcoming of the price sensitivity approach is its underlying assumption that the term structure of interest rates is flat over the hedge horizon and that it undergoes only one parallel shift. The margin of error in estimating the hedge ratio can be large when the term structure is markedly nonlinear and volatile over time. Even with this problem, the price sensitivity hedge ratio is very useful and has convenient practical applications relative to the historical hedge ratio that is based on the portfolio approach and a naive hedge ratio.

EMPIRICAL EVIDENCE ON USING THE PRICE-SENSITIVE HEDGE. Gay, Kolb, and Chiang hedged a random sample of New York Exchange bonds using the nearby T-bond futures contract during the period 1979–1980.[11] They compared the performance of the following alternative hedge strategies, assuming an investment of $1 million in a bond at the end of the hedge horizon.

1. Do not hedge the planned investment.
2. Buy ten T-bond futures contracts with a total face value of $1,000,000 (Naive Strategy 1).

---

[11] Gerald Gay, Robert Kolb, and Raymond Chiang, "Interest Rate Hedging: An Empirical Test of Alternative Strategies," *Journal of Financial Research* 6, no. 3 (Fall 1983): 187–197.

TABLE 25.3
Hedging Performance of the Price-Sensitive Strategy
(absolute wealth change)

	UNHEDGED	NAIVE 1	NAIVE 2	PRICE SENSITIVE
Mean	$ 80,781.09	$ 32,670.10	$ 34,538.05	$25,292.15
Standard deviation	73,398.15	26,075.53	31,321.98	19,477.25
Minimum	57.89	59.62	453.94	123.30
Maximum	294,102.69	150,838.50	178,059.00	79,558.44
Range	294,044.80	150,777.88	177,605.06	79,435.14
Mean percentage of wealth hedged	—	$ 59.60	$ 57.24	$ 68.69
Percentage reduction standard deviation of wealth change	—	$ 64.47	$ 57.33	$ 73.46

Source: Gerald Gay, Robert Kolb, and Raymond Chiang, "Interest Rate Hedging: An Empirical Test of Alternative Strategies," *Journal of Financial Research* 6, no. 3 (Fall 1983): 187–197. Reprinted with permission.

> 3. Buy ($1,000,000/$F$) T-bond futures contracts, where F is the current futures price (Naive Strategy 2).
> 4. Buy T-bond futures contracts as indicated by the price sensitive hedge ratio (Price-Sensitive Strategy).

The dollar performance of these alternative strategies, reported in Table 25.3, indicates that the price-sensitive strategy produces the minimum absolute wealth change (i.e., the minimum absolute difference between the actual and the expected bond prices). It is shown that the price-sensitive strategy reduced the variability of the unhedged position by 73 percent, which is greater than the risk reduction produced by the naive strategies.

USING FUTURES TO ADJUST PORTFOLIO DURATION

These hedging examples assume that the investor intends to minimize price risk, which is not always an optimal or desirable investment objective. As discussed in Chapter 18, an active bond portfolio manager would like to change the duration of the bond portfolio in line with his interest rate forecasts. If he expects a decline in interest rates, he would attempt to maximize the expected price gain by increasing the duration of the bond portfolio. On the other hand, when he expects an increase in market rates, he would try to reduce the portfolio duration to reduce the price volatility and minimize the expected price loss. If he is uncertain which way interest rates will go, he would seek to immunize the bond portfolio by equating the portfolio duration with the length of the holding period (i.e., the investment horizon). In contrast, a non-active portfolio manager would construct a portfolio with a duration consistent with his client's risk-return preferences and hold it over time.

Without futures trading, altering a portfolio's duration by shifting funds among securities of different durations is expensive in terms of transaction costs, short-selling charges, liquidity costs, and taxes. Interest rate futures provide a convenient and inexpensive mechanism for adjusting the portfolio duration because of their low transaction costs and high liquidity. For example, we know that the duration of a bond portfolio is a weighted average of the durations of individual bonds included in the portfolio. In the case of a portfolio consisting of X units of a given T-bond and h' units of the T-bond futures contract, the price change of this bond-futures portfolio for an instantaneous change in the level of market rates of interest is given by

$$dP = X\,dS + h'\,dF, \tag{25.16}$$

where

dP = **change in price of the bond–futures portfolio**

dS = **change in spot T-bond price**

dF = **change in T-bond futures price.**

Assuming perfect markets and a flat term structure of interest rates that experiences a parallel shift, we can represent the preceding price changes as

$$-DP\,dR/R = -X\,D(S)\,S\,dR/R - h'\,D(F)\,F\,dR/R \tag{25.17}$$
$$DP = XD(S)S + h'\,D(F)F,$$

where

D = **portfolio duration**

P = **price of bond futures portfolio**

$D(S)$ = **duration of spot T-bond**

$D(F)$ = **duration of bond underlying T-bond futures contract.**

We know the duration of the spot T-bond and the T-bond futures contract. Also, we know X, S, F, and P. Given our interest rate forecast, we want to alter the portfolio duration to a target level. Therefore, we also know the target duration of this bond-futures portfolio, D. (Assume that it is five years.) We must determine the number of T-bond futures contracts required to obtain the desired portfolio duration using the following formula:

$$h' = [DP - X\,D(S)\,S]/D(F)F. \tag{25.18}$$

While the change in the portfolio price over a *small* interval of time is the sum of price changes in the spot and futures positions, the price of the bond-futures portfolio *at any given moment in time* is exactly equal to the price of the spot position. This is because the margins on the futures contracts are good-faith deposits, and the holder of a futures contract does *not* own the underlying asset until he takes delivery. Therefore,

$$P \equiv X \cdot S. \tag{25.19}$$

When we recognize this identity, we can infer the following from Equation 25.17, assuming that one holds a long spot position (i.e., $X > 0$):

- If $D > D(S)$, $h' > 0$, buy futures.
- If $D < D(S)$, $h' < 0$, sell futures.
- If $D = D(S)$, $h' = 0$, engage in no futures trading.

For example, if the target portfolio duration exceeds the duration of the spot T-bond, then one has to buy h' futures contracts to obtain the desired change in the portfolio price.[12]

The foregoing discussion on immunization contains two simplifying assumptions about the behavior of the term structure of interest rates: (1) a flat term structure, and (2) a small parallel shift in the term structure. In reality, these assumptions are rarely completely satisfied, which frustrates immunization strategies. The unpredictable changes in the slopes and curvature of the term structure give rise to *immunization risk*—the risk that the realized bond portfolio return will fall below the "guaranteed" return. To mitigate this risk, new duration measures that recognize alternative slopes, shapes, and changes in the term structure have been developed. It is not clear whether the incremented benefits of using these new measures outweigh the added costs relative to the simple traditional measure of duration.[13]

STOCK INDEX FUTURES

It is well known that stock prices are less variable than the prices of most commodities but more variable than bond prices. An investor owning a well-diversified portfolio of stocks bears little unsystematic (firm-specific) risk but is fully exposed to systematic risk (beta). One who diversifies his portfolio can protect against his subjective forecast of a market decline by *selling short* shares in a diversified stock mutual fund. Since the returns on the investor's portfolio would be highly correlated with the returns on the mutual fund, the loss (gain) on the long stock position would be reduced by the gain (loss) on the short mutual fund position. An investor using this strategy is subjected to the *costs and stock exchange restrictions on short sales*, particularly the requirement that a stock can be shorted only on an uptick. Alternatively, the investor with a bearish outlook for the market could sell part of his stock portfolio and invest the proceeds in liquid assets. This strategy would involve commissions, bid-ask spreads, taxes, and potential liquidity costs in thin markets. Another alternative is that the investor could buy put options on individual stocks in his portfolio

---

[12] For a further use of futures to immunize bond portfolios, see Robert W. Kolb and Gerald D. Gay, "Immunizing Bond Portfolios with Interest Rate Futures," *Financial Management* 11, no. 3 (Summer 1982): 81–89; and Gerald D. Gay and Robert W. Kolb, "Interest Rate Futures as a Tool for Immunizing," *Journal of Portfolio Management* 10, no. 1 (Fall 1983): 65–70.

[13] For further discussion on immunization strategies, see H. Gifford Fong and Oldrich Vasicek, "The Tradeoff between Return and Risk in Immunized Portfolios," *Financial Analysts Journal* 39, no. 5 (September–October 1983): 73–78; Martin Leibowitz and Alfred Weinberger, "Contingent Immunization-Part I: Risk Control Procedures," *Financial Analysts Journal* 38, no. 6 (November–December 1982): 19–31; and Leibowitz and Weinberger, "Contingent Immunization-Part II: Problem Areas," *Financial Analysts Journal* 39, no. 1 (January–February 1983): 35–50.

or options on a stock market index. Again, these strategies involve high transaction costs, taxes, and problems in execution. A solution is to trade futures contracts on a stock market index. The liquidity and leverage of a stock index futures market provide a convenient low-cost mechanism for hedging market risk. For index futures contracts, going short is as easy as going long.

The Kansas City Board of Trade (KCBT) introduced the first stock index futures contract on the Value Line Composite Average (VLA) in February 1982. Currently, there are four popular index futures contracts: (1) The Standard and Poor's 500 (S&P 500) index futures traded on the Chicago Mercantile Exchange (CME), (2) the New York Stock Exchange (NYSE) Composite Index futures traded on the New York Futures Exchange (NYFE), (3) the VLA index futures, and (4) the Major Market Index (MMI) futures contract on the Chicago Board of Trade (CBT). Table 25.4 highlights the specifications of these and other stock index contracts.

As indicated in Table 25.4, the market price of the first three futures contracts is 500 times the value of the underlying stock index. The instrument underlying index futures contracts is not an asset, such as a commodity or a bond that is traded in the spot market, but a stock market index. Accordingly, index futures do not require delivery of the underlying instrument; instead, they call for a cash settlement at contract expiration. At the end of the last day of trading, the quote on the index futures contract is set equal to the value of the underlying stock index, and gains/losses on futures positions are settled in cash.

HEDGING

The primary use of the stock index futures contracts is to protect a stock portfolio from price fluctuations due to general market movements. In addition, an astute portfolio manager can use the index futures contracts to earn near-arbitrage profits by exploiting transient discrepancies between the spot and futures prices. Let us first take a look at portfolio insurance strategies based on the S&P 500 futures contract.

In terms of the CAPM, the *ex post* return on a stock or a portfolio of stocks has two components: a market component and a firm-specific component.

$$R(p) = R_r + \beta(p)[R(M) - R_r] + \epsilon, \qquad (25.20)$$

where

$R(p)$ = return on portfolio

R_r = return on a risk-free asset

$\beta(p)$ = beta of portfolio

$R(M)$ = return on market portfolio

ϵ = return due to firm-specific factors; it has a zero mean and a constant variance.

TABLE 25.4
A Comparison of Stock Index Futures Contracts Currently Traded

FEATURE	KANSAS CITY BOARD OF TRADE (KCBT)	CHICAGO MERCANTILE EXCHANGE (CME)	NEW YORK FUTURES EXCHANGE (NYFE)
1. Location	Kansas City	Chicago	New York
2. Underlying market index	Value Line Composite Average (VLA). This is an equally weighted index of approximately 1700 stocks. Geometric average is used.	Standard and Poor's 500 Index (S&P 500). This is a value-weighted index of 500 stocks. Arithmetic average is used.	NYSE Composite Index. It is a value-weighted average of *all* common stocks listed on the NYSE. Arithmetic average is used.
3. Contract size (value of contract)	500 times the Value Line Average (about $88,500).	500 times the S&P Index (about $75,000).	500 times the NYSE Composite Index (about $45,000).
4. Minimum price change	Tick size is 0.01 points. The minimum change would cause the value of the contract to change by $5.	Tick size is 0.05 points. This represents a change of $25 per tick.	Tick size is 0.05 points. This represents a change of $25 per tick.
5. Daily price change limits	Five points daily price limit is in effect.[a] Each point represents $500.	Five points daily price limit is in effect.[a] Each point represents $500.	No limits currently in effect.
6. Delivery concept	Cash settlement. Actual value of VLA determines the payment. Final settlement is the last trading day of the expiring month. Delivery months are March, June, September, and December.	Cash settlement. Actual value of S&P 500 Index determines the payment. Final settlement of open contracts occurs on the third Thursday of the delivery month. Delivery months are March, June, September, and December.	Cash settlement. Actual value of NYSE Composite determines the payment. Settlement is based on the difference between the settlement price on the next to the last day of trading in the month and the value of NYSE Composite Index at the close of trading. Delivery months are March, June, September, and December.

continued

[a] If the limit is reached on two consecutive days, the limit on the third day is 7.5 points; if reached for three consecutive days, the limit on the fourth day is 10 points; if reached on four consecutive days, there is no limit on the fifth day.

The market component of the portfolio return is $R_f + \beta(p) [R(M) - R_f]$. The components of the portfolio return are related to two sources of risk: market risk and unsystematic risk.

$$\sigma^2(p) = \beta^2(p)\sigma^2(M) + \sigma^2(\epsilon), \qquad (25.21)$$

where

$$\sigma^2 = \textbf{variance of portfolio return}$$

$$\sigma^2(M) = \textbf{variance of return on market portfolio}$$

$$\sigma^2(\epsilon) = \textbf{variance of the error term, } \epsilon.$$

TABLE 25.4   *continued*

FEATURE	CHICAGO BOARD OF TRADE (CBT)	CHICAGO BOARD OF TRADE (CBT)	CHICAGO BOARD OF TRADE (CBT)	CHICAGO MERCANTILE EXCHANGE (CME)
Title of Contract	MMI Futures Contract	MMI Maxi Futures Contract	NASDAQ-100 Index Futures Contract	S&P OTC 250 Futures
1. Location	Chicago	Chicago	Chicago	Chicago
2. Underlying market index	The Major Market Index (MMI) The following stocks make up the MMI Index: American Express; American Telephone and Telegraph; Chevron; Coca Cola; Dow Chemical; DuPont; Eastman Kodak; Exxon; General Electric; General Motors; IBM; International Paper; Johnson & Johnson; Merck; Minnesota M&M; Mobil; Philip Morris; Procter & Gamble; Sears Roebuck; U.S. Steel.	The Major Market Index (MMI)	The NASDAQ-100 Index. This capitalization-weighted index is composed of 100 of the largest non-financial stocks in the NASDAQ National Market System. The top 20 capitalized stocks as of 8/30/88 follow: Intel Corp.; MCI Corp.; Integraph Corp.; The Price Co.; Roadway Services, Inc.; Apple Computer, Inc.; Consolidated Papers, Inc.; Tele-Communications, Inc.; Pioneer Hi-Bred International; American Greetings Corporation; Liz Claiborne, Inc.; Subaru of America, Inc.; Nordstrom, Inc.; Shoneys, Inc.; Phillips (NV) Gloeilampen; Genetech, Inc.; Lin Broadcasting Corp.; PACCAR, Inc.; Shared Medical Systems; Adolph Coors Co.	The S&P 250 Index of major stocks traded on the NASDAQ system.
3. Contract size (value of contract)	$100 times the Major Market Index (MMI) (about $25,000).	$250 times the MMI (about $62,500).	$250 times the value of the NASDAQ-100 Index (about $62,500).	$500 times the value of the S&P 250 OTC Index.

continued

TABLE 25.4   *continued*

FEATURE	CHICAGO BOARD OF TRADE (CBT)	CHICAGO BOARD OF TRADE (CBT)	CHICAGO BOARD OF TRADE (CBT)	CHICAGO MERCANTILE EXCHANGE (CME)
4. Minimum price change	One-eighth (1/8) of a point or $12.50 per contract.	Five one-hundredths of a point (.05) or $12.50 per contract.	Five one-hundredths of a point (.05) or $12.50 per contract.	Five one-hundredths of a point (.05). This represents a change of $25 per contract.
5. Price quotations	In points and eighths of one point. One point equals $100.	In points and five one-hundredths of one point. One point equals $250.	In points and five one-hundredths of one point. One point equals $250.	In points and five one-hundredths of one point. One point equals $500.
6. Position limits	20,000 contracts net long or short in all contract months combined.	8,000 contracts net long or short in all months combined.	8,000 contracts net long or short in all contract months combined.	
7. Delivery concept	Cash settlement based on the closing value of the MMI on the last day of trading, which is the third Friday of the contract month. Contract months are the first three consecutive months plus the next month in the March, June, September, and December quarterly cycle.	Cash settlement based on the closing value of the MMI on the last day of trading, which is the third Friday of the contract month. Contract months are the first three consecutive months, plus the next three months in the March, June, September, and December quarterly cycle.	Cash settlement based on the closing value of the spot NASDAQ-100 Index on the last day of trading, which is the third Friday of the contract month. Contract months are the first three consecutive months, plus the next three months in the March, June, September, and December quarterly cycle.	Cash settlement based on the actual closing value of the S&P 250 OTC Index on the last day of the trading month, which is the third Thursday of the delivery month. Contract months are March, June, September, and December.

The first term on the right side of Equation 25.21 is a measure of the portfolio's market risk, and the second term denotes the nonmarket (unsystematic) risk that is eliminated in a diversified portfolio.

Active portfolio management involves stock analysis and market timing. An active portfolio manager analyzes stocks in order to discover underpriced and overpriced securities. Market timing calls for predicting the overall movement of the stock market and altering the stock position to take advantage of the market forecast. An active portfolio manager with a bullish market outlook would *increase* the beta of his portfolio in order to maximize his gain from the expected market rally. When he is bearish on the market, he would *reduce* the portfolio beta to minimize the price loss. If he is uncertain which way the market will go, he would prefer a *zero-beta* portfolio, where the return is immunized against uncertain market fluctuations. Through these strategies, an active portfolio manager with superior skills in forecasting firm-specific factors and/or market turns would experience above-average risk-adjusted returns. In contrast, a passive portfolio manager would construct a portfolio with a beta that is consistent with his client's risk-return preferences, and would hold that portfolio over time.[14]

USING FUTURES TO ALTER THE PORTFOLIO BETA. In the absence of futures trading, altering the portfolio beta by shifting funds from low- to high-beta stocks and vice versa necessitates a large turnover of the portfolio. The accompanying transaction costs (including short-selling costs and liquidity costs and taxes) are very high. As noted previously, stock index futures provide an inexpensive yet effective way of altering the beta of the portfolio without affecting its essential composition.

To see this, assume that the S&P 500 portfolio is a perfect proxy for the market portfolio and that you hold shares in an index fund portfolio identical to the S&P 500 index. The expected dollar return on a portfolio of the index fund and index futures is

$$E(DR) = XE(\Delta S) + yE(\Delta F), \tag{25.22}$$

where

$E(DR)$ = the expected price change in the portfolio of index fund and index futures over a short interval of time

X,y = number of units of the index fund and the index futures contract, respectively (assume that each unit of trading on both the spot and the futures market has the same dollar value)

$E(\Delta S)$ = the expected price change in the index fund shares

$E(\Delta F)$ = the expected price change in the index futures contract based on the S&P 500.

As shown earlier, the variance-minimizing hedge ratio is given by

$$H^* = -(y^*/X) = -\rho_{ij}\sigma_i/\sigma_j, \tag{25.23}$$

where

ρ_{ij} = the correlation coefficient of spot and futures price changes

σ_i, σ_j = the standard deviations of spot and futures price changes, respectively.

Further, under the CAPM:

$$E(\Delta S) = R_f \times S + \beta(S)[E(R(M)) - R_f] \tag{25.24}$$

---

[14] Stephen Figlewski and Stanley Kon, "Portfolio Management with Stock Index Futures," *Financial Analysts Journal* 38, no. 1 (January–February 1982): 52–60. For an overview of these, see Victor Niederhoff and Richard Zeckhauser, "Market Index Futures Contracts," *Financial Analysts Journal* 36, no. 1 (January–February 1980): 49–55. An excellent set of readings on this topic is contained in Frank J. Fabozzi and Gregory M. Kipnis, eds., *Stock Index Futures* (Homewood, Ill.: Dow Jones-Irwin, 1984).

$$E(\Delta F) = \beta(F)[E(R(M)) - R_f],\qquad\qquad (25.25)$$

where

$$R_f = \text{the risk-free rate of interest}$$

$$\beta(S) = Cov\,[\Delta S, R(M)]\,/\sigma^2[R(M)]$$

$$\beta(F) = Cov\,(\Delta F, R(M))/\sigma^2[R(M)].$$

The spot and futures betas are represented in terms of the covariance of *dollar* price changes with the market return and, therefore, are different from the betas based on *percentage* price changes. Also, $B(S) = B(F) = 1$, because the index fund is assumed to be identical to the S&P 500 index on which the futures contract is based. Then, H^* would be equal to 1, and the spot-futures hedge would be perfect.

Substituting Equations 25.23, 25.24, and 25.25 in Equation 25.22, we obtain

$$E(DR) = R_f \cdot S.\qquad\qquad (25.26)$$

That is, the expected dollar return on the perfect spot-futures hedge portfolio is equal to the dollar risk-free interest income on the spot investment. In this ideal case, the index fund has no unsystematic risk because it is a *fully diversified* portfolio. Its systematic risk is equal to that of the market portfolio. The perfect hedge in the index futures contract has enabled us to eliminate completely its market risk.

Obviously, it is seldom possible to construct the perfect hedge in the real world, because the assumptions of the CAPM are rarely satisfied, and the index fund and the index futures contract are not identical to the true market portfolio (which is a value-weighted portfolio of all risky assets). Besides, the perfect hedge is mostly irrelevant, because an active portfolio manager rarely wants to hold the zero-beta portfolio of spot and futures instruments. Instead, he seeks to hold a portfolio with desired levels of systematic and unsystematic risk and return. Through *security analysis,* he selects stocks with desirable firm-specific characteristics and by employing *market-timing strategies* he tries to control the exposure of the portfolio to general market movements. Prior to the initiation of index futures trading, it was not feasible to separate systematic risk from unsystematic risk. For example, consider an active portfolio manager who has selected a portfolio of high-beta stocks with desirable firm-specific factors. If the manager is bearish on the market and does not want to hold this portfolio of high systematic risk, he could trade index futures and alter the systematic risk of the portfolio.

DETERMINING THE HEDGE RATIO. An important decision when using stock index futures to manage a portfolio's systematic risk is the number of futures contracts to trade. For a two-asset portfolio it can be derived as

$$\beta(P) = Cov(DR,R(M))/\sigma^2[R(M)], \qquad (25.27)$$

where

$\beta(P)$ = **the dollar beta of the spot-futures portfolio**

DR = **the dollar price change in the spot futures portfolio**

$$= X[S - \beta(S)R_r + \beta(S)R(M) + \epsilon(S)] + y\{[R(M) - R_r]\beta(F) + \epsilon(F)\}.$$

Substituting for DR in Equation 25.27,

$$\beta(P) = X\beta(S) + y\beta(F). \qquad (25.28)$$

That is, the dollar beta of the two-asset portfolio is the sum of the product of the spot dollar beta and the number of units of the spot asset and the futures dollar beta and the number of units of the futures contract. For purposes of this example, $X = 1$ in Equation 25.28. The active portfolio manager knows the values of $\beta(S)$, and $\beta(F)$ and determines the desired value $\beta(P)$ consistent with his market outlook. Therefore, the portfolio manager can solve the equation to determine the number of index futures contracts required to obtain the desired portfolio dollar beta:

$$y = [\beta(P) - X\beta(S)]/\beta(F). \qquad (25.29)$$

The hedge ratio, H, is given by

$$H = (y/X) = [\beta(P) - X\beta(S)]/X \cdot \beta(F). \qquad (25.30)$$

In Equation 25.30, $\beta(S)$ and $\beta(F)$ are positive because they relate to portfolios of stocks. Further, X is positive when the manager holds a long position in the spot portfolio. This means that

1. If $\beta(P) > \beta(S)$, buy index futures.
2. If $\beta(P) < \beta(S)$, sell index futures.
3. If $\beta(P) = \beta(S)$, engage in no trading of futures.

Therefore, the decision whether to buy or sell index futures contracts depends on the relationship between the target spot-futures portfolio dollar beta and the spot portfolio dollar beta.

To see the impact of such an eclectic hedging strategy on the risk and return on the spot futures portfolio, we need to substitute for y in Equation 25.22:

$$E(DR) = XE(\Delta S) + HX E(\Delta F). \qquad (25.31)$$

$$\sigma^2(DR) = X^2\sigma^2(\Delta S) + H^2X^2\sigma^2(\Delta F) + 2HX^2 Cov(\Delta S,\Delta F). \qquad (25.32)$$

The ratio of the variance of the spot futures portfolio to that of the un-hedged spot portfolio is

$$\frac{\sigma^2(DR)}{X^2\sigma^2(\Delta S)} = 1 + \frac{H[H\sigma^2(\Delta F) + 2 Cov(\Delta S,\Delta F)]}{\sigma^2(\Delta S)}. \qquad (25.33)$$

If the hedge ratio, H, is equal to the variance-minimizing hedge ratio, H^*, given in Equation 25.23, then

$$\frac{\sigma^2(DR)}{X^2\sigma^2(\Delta S)} = 1 - \rho_{ij}^2 , \qquad (25.34)$$

where

ρ_{ij}^2 = **the coefficient of determination of the spot and futures price changes.**

This indicates that the higher the correlation between the spot portfolio and the index futures price changes, the more effective the hedge in minimizing the dollar return variability of the spot-futures portfolio. Although this hedging model has ignored transaction costs, margins, taxes, and dividends, it is quite helpful in understanding the role of stock index futures in the management of systematic risk.

EXAMPLE OF A STOCK INDEX FUTURES HEDGE. The following example will illustrate the defensive use of stock index futures. Assume that the price behavior of the stock index futures contract is identical to the underlying stock index, there is 100 percent margin on futures, and percent price changes are used instead of dollar price changes. In this case, the variance-minimizing hedge ratio in Equation 25.23 is equal to the beta of the spot portfolio. That is,

$$\begin{aligned} H^{*\prime} &= Cov\,(R(S),\ R(M))/\sigma^2(R(M)) \\ &= \beta'(S) . \end{aligned} \qquad (25.35)$$

It follows that

$$\begin{aligned} y^* &= (-)\,\frac{X \times S}{F}\,\beta'(S) \\ &= (-)\,\frac{V(S)}{F}\,\beta'(S) , \end{aligned} \qquad (25.36)$$

where

$V(S)$ = **the price of the (spot) stock portfolio**

F = **the price of a stock index futures contract**

$\beta'(S)$ = **the beta of the spot portfolio (based on percentage price changes).**

In Equation 25.36, the first term, $V(S)/F$, expresses the value of the spot portfolio in terms of the number of index futures contracts. The second term, $\beta'(S)$, adjusts the number of index futures contracts for the market sensitivity of the spot portfolio.

Now, consider a market-maker (dealer) in stocks who holds a diversified portfolio of stocks with a current value of $1.5 million and a beta of 1.3. The dealer expects a decline in the market in the near future. Currently, the S&P 500 stock index futures contract has a value of 150, which means

TABLE 25.5
An Illustration of a Stock Index Futures Hedge

SPOT MARKET		FUTURES MARKET	
January 16, value of the spot portfolio:	$1,500,000	Sell 26 nearby S&P 500 futures contracts wtih market price of 26 × 75,000: Initial margins 26 × 2500 = $65,000	$1,950,000
March 10, sale of spot portfolio:	1,480,000	S&P 500 Index futures is at 148. Buy back 26 nearby futures contracts at 26 × 148 × 500:	1,924,000
Gross loss on spot portfolio:	($20,000)	Gross gain on futures:	$ 26,000
Total gain subject to margin and transaction costs = $6,000.			

the contract price is $75,000 (150 × 500). To minimize the variance of his spot-futures portfolio, the dealer needs to sell 26 futures contracts as shown below:

$$y^* = (-) \frac{V(S)}{F} \beta'(S) = \frac{1,500,000}{75,000} \times 1.3$$
$$= 26.$$

The hedging transactions are illustrated in Table 25.5.

PORTFOLIO INSURANCE

The conventional hedging strategy described here suffers from two short-comings. First, because of the inherent basis risk, even a variance-mini-mizing strategy is *not* capable of ensuring (or guaranteeing) a *minimum return* on the hedged portfolio. Second, it is not designed to allow the portfolio to benefit from favorable movements in the stock market. For instance, in a long spot–short futures hedge, the conventional hedge is beneficial only if stock prices fall subsequently. If, instead, stock prices rise, the gain in the spot portfolio will be offset or reduced by the loss on the short-futures position. These are fairly serious limitations, especially for investors with superior information.

The term *portfolio insurance* refers to investment strategies that are designed to guarantee a minimum specified return on the portfolio while at the same allowing the portfolio to substantially participate in favorable market movements. To illustrate, suppose an investor has $100 to invest over a single period, and the S&P 500 common stock index is currently at 90.97, while the risk-free rate is 10.52 percent per period. Also, the investor wants a minimum guaranteed return of 5 percent at the end of the period; that is, he wants to insure the portfolio for $105 (=$100 × (1.05)).

One way to achieve the goal is to design a *protective put strategy* wherein the investor buys one share in the S&P 500 portfolio for $90.97 and uses the remaining $9.03 to buy one unit of a European put option with an exercise price equal to the insured *floor* of $105 expiring one period later. For convenience, assume a zero dividend rate over this period. At expiration, if the S&P 500 index is at or below $105, the investor exercises the put to realize the insured floor of $105. If the index value exceeds $105, the put expires worthless, but the value of the insured portfolio exceeds $105. Thus, the protective put strategy not only insures the portfolio against downside risk but also retains the benefits of upside potential.[15]

There are two major costs associated with portfolio insurance. The first, more explicit one is the insurance premium on the put premium of $9.03. The second is an opportunity cost. Whereas an uninsured investor can invest the entire $100 in the S&P portfolio and participate 100 percent in stock market appreciation, the insured investor stands to benefit to the extent of only 90.97 percent of the upward potential.

An alternative portfolio insurance strategy is known as a *fiduciary call.* Following the standard put-call parity, a European call option on the S&P 500 index with an exercise price of 105 and a term of one period is worth $4.99 (= 90.97 + 9.03 − 105 (1.1052) − 1). Under this strategy, the investor would purchase one call on the index and invest the remaining $95.01 in a risk-free asset. At expiration, this call-risk-free asset portfolio will have a minimum value of $105 (= 95.01 × 1.1052). If the index value exceeds 105, then the investor could use $105 to exercise the call and buy a share of the index. Thus, both the protective put and the fiduciary call strategies produce identical end-of-period payoffs.

In practice, these portfolio insurance strategies are not feasible because the listed options are not European, but American, options, and the standardized exercise price and term to maturity of listed options may not meet the needs of a particular investor. However, an investor could construct synthetic European options by following *dynamic strategies* and *allocation strategies.* These synthetic strategies consist of a risky asset such as a stock portfolio and a safe asset such as T-bills. For example, a European put option on a stock portfolio can be synthesized by shorting less than one share of the stock portfolio and investing the proceeds in the safe asset (lending). The proportions of investment in the risky and riskless assets are determined by the Black-Scholes European put option pricing model, and the package is continuously revised to ensure that it replicates the payoffs to a put option at expiration. As stock prices rise, some bills are sold and the proceeds used to buy back some shares. As stock prices fall, additional shares are sold short and the proceeds invested in bills.

Specifically, a synthetic put is constructed by investing at any time t, $0 \leq t \leq T$, an amount equal to $P_t + N(-h) S_t$ in a riskless discount bond maturing at T, and $-N(-h)S_t$ in a stock portfolio,

$$P = -[S_t N(-h) - K_e - R_f T N(\sigma\sqrt{\tau} - h)],$$

---

[15] Richard J. Rendleman, Jr., and Richard W. McEnally, "Assessing the Costs of Portfolio Insurance," *Financial Analysts Journal* 43, no. 3 (May–June 1987): 27–37.

where

P = **put price**

K = **strike price**

e = **base of the natural log**

R_f = **risk-free rate**

τ = **$(T - t)$, term to expiration of the put**

h = **$\{ln[S_t/K_e^{-R_f\tau} + (\sigma^2/2)\tau\}/\sigma\sqrt{\tau}$**

σ = **standard deviation of percentage changes in the value of the stock portfolio**

$N(\cdot)$ = **the standard cumulative normal distribution.**

The synthetic put can be combined with a long position in the stock portfolio to construct a protective put strategy. At any time t, the composition of the insured portfolio will be $S_t[1 - N(-h)]$ of the risky stock portfolio, and $P_t + N(-h)S_t$ of the riskless asset. Consequently, a synthesized protective put strategy involves a long position in stocks combined with lending.[16]

Alternatively, a fiduciary call strategy can be constructed by combining a synthetic European call with lending. To synthesize a Euro-call, the investor borrows and buys (less than one share of) the stock portfolio according to the hedge ratio given by the Black-Scholes European call option pricing model. The continuous rebalancing involves borrowing and buying additional shares as stock prices rise, and selling stock and lending as stock prices fall (which is similar to the case of a synthetic put option).

A simple example of a dynamic asset allocation strategy is called the *constant-proportion portfolio insurance strategy* (*CPFI*).[17] Under this strategy, the investor allocates funds between the risky and safe assets according to the following rule:

$$\text{Investment in Risky Asset} = (\text{Total Assets} - \text{Floor}),$$
$$So = m \, (A_0 - G_0),$$

where m is a fixed multiplier greater than 1. Initially, the investor selects the multiplier and the floor (i.e., the minimum guaranteed amount at the end of the investment horizon). G_0 is the present value of the floor and must be less than A_0. The difference, $A_0 - G_0$, is called the *cushion*. By selecting a specific m greater than 1, the investor decides how many times the cushion is to be invested in the risky asset.

[16] Simon Benninya and Marshall Blume, "On the Optimality of Portfolio Insurance," *Journal of Finance* 60, no. 5 (December 1985): 1341–1352; and Mark Rubinstein, "Alternative Paths to Portfolio Insurance," *Financial Analysts Journal* 41, no. 4 (July–August 1985): 42–52.

[17] Andre F. Perold and William F. Sharpe, "Dynamic Strategies for Asset Allocation," *Financial Analysts Journal* 44, no. 1 (January–February 1988): 16–27.

Suppose that $A_0 = \$100$, $G_0 = \$80$, and $m = 2$. The initial cushion is $20, and the initial allocation is 40/60 risky/safe assets. Now if the risky asset price falls by 10 percent, the total assets will be worth $96, and the cushion falls to $16. To maintain the multiple at 2, the investor needs to reduce the position in the risky asset to $32. Accordingly, the investor sells $4 of the risky asset and invests the proceeds in the safe asset. On the other hand, if the risky asset price rises by 10 percent, the total assets will increase by $104 and the cushion to $24. Since the approximate risky asset position is $48, $4 of the safe asset will be liquidated, and additional shares of the risky asset purchased. Thus, *the CPPI strategy requires buying the risky asset as it rises and selling the risky asset as it falls*, similar to the synthetic put and call options. This strategy channels more funds into the safe asset as the risky asset price falls, thereby lowering the exposure to the risky asset to zero as the total assets approach the floor. The strategy will perform at the minimum as well as the floor, except during a market crash when there is little opportunity to rebalance the portfolio.

Let us compare the CPPI strategy with a static buy-and-hold strategy such as a 60/40 risky/safe asset mix. This strategy involves no rebalancing. It has a minimum return proportional to the amount invested in the safe asset and an upside potential proportional to the funds allocated to the risky asset. Its performance is linearly related to the return on the market portfolio of risky assets. In contrast, the dynamic asset allocation strategies, such as the CPPI or those involving synthetic options, have *convex* payoff functions; that is, their performance increases at an increasing rate in relation to the performance of the market portfolio. As they "buy on strength and sell on weakness," these strategies tend to provide better downside protection and better upside potential than the buy-and-hold strategies. However, they underperform in relatively trendless volatile markets.

Two additional considerations are necessary in evaluating the dynamic asset allocation strategies. First, continuous rebalancing of the portfolio may entail considerable transaction costs. Consequently, the portfolio may be revised only after the market moves by a certain percentage, such as a 5 percent change up or down. The percentage move required to trigger a rebalancing trade is called *tolerance*. Further, synthetic options are constructed by using futures contracts that have more liquidity and lower transaction costs than the underlying debt and equity markets. To implement these futures-based strategies it is commonly assumed that the short-term interest rate over the investment horizon is nonstochastic, so that the futures price is equal to the forward price.

To illustrate, consider the protective put strategy of a long position in the risky asset coupled with a long put. To construct a synthetic put, the dynamic asset allocation strategy described earlier is replaced by a *dynamic hedging strategy* involving *short* futures positions. Notice that a long position in the risky asset combined with a short futures position creates a synthetic safe asset (under the assumption of nonstochastic short-term rates). In the dynamic hedging strategy, all funds are initially placed in the risky asset, and the portfolio is hedged by selling futures contracts. As the risky asset price rises, the hedge is reduced by buying back futures, and as the risky asset falls, the hedge is raised by selling additional futures contracts. The mark-to-market gain/loss on the futures position is covered by purchase or sale of the risky asset or by lending/borrowing.

Alternatively, the investor may choose to replicate the fiduciary call strategy by using futures contracts. Under this insurance program, all funds are initially invested in the safe asset combined with long futures positions. Notice that this package produces a synthetic risky asset. Like the dynamic hedging strategy, the replication involves the purchase of additional futures contracts in a risky market and the sale of futures in a falling market.

The second important consideration is the impact of dynamic asset allocation strategies on the volatility of the market for risky assets. As the synthetic option strategies become more popular, the risky assets are likely to turn more volatile, because there will be insufficient buyers in a falling market and insufficient sellers in a rising market. The increase in market volatility will jeopardize the success of synthetic strategies (which assume constant volatility consistent with the Black-Scholes model) and will increase the cost of portfolio insurance. In contrast, when portfolio insurance strategies are implemented with *real* traded options, option prices will increase as many institutions simultaneously attempt to insure their portfolios. It is argued that the existence of traded options aggregates information regarding the demand for insurance and provides valuable information about the cost of insurance. Alternatively, the replacement of real options by synthetic strategies will not convey such information, and may aggravate price volatility.[18]

PROGRAM TRADING OR ARBITRAGE

From our discussion in Chapter 24, we know that a futures contract is a close-to-perfect substitute for a forward contract on the underlying common asset, and that any sufficiently large discrepancies between the futures and forward prices generate near-arbitrage opportunities. To illustrate this concept in the context of the S&P 500 stock index futures contract, assume that capital markets are perfect and that frictionless dividends on index stocks are known over the term of the index futures contract (t,T), and the short-term interest rate is nonstochastic over t,T. The cost of carry model implies that

$$F(t,T) = I(t)[1 + c(t,T) - d(t,T)], \qquad (25.37)$$

where

$$F(t,T) = \text{index futures price}$$

$$I(t) = \text{level of the stock index}$$

$$c(t,T) = \text{holding period cost of carryover } t,T$$

$$d(t,T) = \text{known holding period dividend yield over } t,T.$$

---

[18] Sanford J. Grossman, "An Analysis of the Implications for Stock and Futures Price Volatility of Program Trading and Dynamic Hedging Strategies," *Journal of Business* 61, no. 3 (July 1988): 275–298.

This equation shows that index futures will typically trade at a premium over the spot index, because the cost of carry usually exceeds the dividend yield.

To derive the no-arbitrage bounds, replace the frictionless markets assumption with a known transaction cost of k percent relative to the level of the stock index. Then, the lower and upper bounds on the index futures price are

$$\{I(t)[1 + c(t,T) - d(t,T) - k]\} \leq F(t,T) \leq \{I(t)[1 + c(t,T) - d(t,T) + k]\} \tag{25.38}$$

As an example, if the boundary is violated (i.e., if $F(t,T) > I(t)[1 + c(t,T) - d(t,T) + k]$), the arbitrageur would simultaneously borrow and buy the spot index portfolio (or a close substitute), sell the index futures contract, and subsequently reverse the positions at T. This strategy provides a near-arbitrage profit equal to $F(t,T) - I(t)[1 + c(t,T) - d(t,T) + k]$.

Using sophisticated computer programs, institutional investors and market professionals continuously monitor the basis between the index futures contract and a close substitute for the underlying stock index. Whenever violations of the boundary conditions are detected, the computer program instantaneously issues market orders to the stock and futures exchanges to lock in a nearly riskless return. This type of arbitrage activity has come to be known as *program trading*. The benefit of program trading is that it accelerates the process by which new information is incorporated into stock prices and strengthens the linkages between the stock and index futures markets. This close linkage in turn enhances the *hedging effectiveness* of index futures contracts. Thus, program trading helps ensure successful portfolio insurance.

PROGRAM TRADING AND THE 1987 CRASH.[19]   In sharp contrast to their traditional beneficial role, stock index futures have been attacked for aggravating price volatility in the wake of the October 1987 stock-market crash. Briefly, the enormous trading activity during October 19 and 20 swamped the electronic order-processing and information-display capabilities of stock markets, which led to recurrent episodes of disconnected spot and futures markets. On top of this disruption, the *uptick* short-sale rule drastically reduced arbitrage-motivated trades. Together, these factors led to a strange and shocking development wherein the stock index futures persistently traded at substantial discounts from the underlying stock indexes. Under such conditions, the program trader would sell stocks and buy the stock index futures. Consequently, the previously infallible portfolio insurance strategies began to break apart, causing mutual funds and pension funds to sell large blocks of stocks under panic conditions. These events led to the allegation that instead of providing protection

---

[19] The reader is referred to the appendix to Chapter 3 that contains a discussion of the October 1987 market crash by the Brady Commission, and includes consideration of the stock-futures relationship.

against market movements, program trading and portfolio insurance caused a dramatic increase in stock market volatility.

While the debate continues over the role of index futures in aggravating stock market volatility, studies by the Brady Commission, the Commodity Futures Trading Commission, and the Securities and Exchange Commission have generally concluded that the primary problems were (1) the lack of harmony in operating procedures of the stock and futures markets, (2) the lack of coordination in the regulation of these markets, (3) a failure of the stock exchange order-processing system, and (4) the undercapitalization of specialists on the stock exchanges. These studies underscore a tension between the financial futures and options markets and the trading structures of stock exchanges. In the meanwhile, the NYSE and the SEC have introduced rules limiting program traders' access to the NYSE's automated execution system (super DOT) after 50-point swings in the Dow Jones Industrial Average in order to facilitate the integration of the two sets of markets.

OPTIONS ON FUTURES

Another innovation in financial contracts is the advent of put and call options based on futures instruments. The owner of a put (call) option has the right (but not the obligation) to sell (buy) a futures contract at a predetermined striking price during a specified time period. These options expire at the same time as their underlying futures contracts. They are American options, so they can be exercised prior to their expiration. On exercising the option, a call owner assumes a long position in the futures contract, and a put owner takes a short futures position. Market quotes on some of the more popular futures options are contained in Figure 25.1.

One set of the quotes in Figure 25.1 pertains to puts and calls on the CBT T-bond futures contract. The strike prices range from 84 to 94 per 100 par value of the futures contract. The December 84 call is quoted at 3-54; this means the premium on the call that expires in December is $3,843.75 (= $100,000 × 256/64 × 1/100) per contract. The call owner has the right to buy a December T-bond futures contract at $84,000. Suppose that the call owner exercises the option in early December when the futures contract is trading at 90. On exercise, he assumes a long futures position at the strike price of 84. He can take a profit by selling a futures contract at the current price of 90 providing a price gain of $6,000 − $3,843.75 = $2,156.25, unadjusted for transaction costs and taxes. The December 84 put is quoted at 1-44, which is equal to a premium of $1,687.50 per futures contract. The put owner has the right to sell a futures contract at 84, and on exercise, he assumes a short futures position. He can close out his short futures position by executing a reverse trade (sell a December 84 put), or he can elect to make delivery at the time of final settlement.

As another example, consider options on the S&P 500 stock index futures. The June 255 call and put are quoted at 12.30 and 1.25, which amount to $6,150 and $625 per futures contract, respectively. If at expiration in June, the S&P 500 index is at 255, both options will remain unex-

FIGURE 25.1
Quotes for Options on Futures Contracts

FUTURES OPTIONS

COCOA (CSCE) 10 metric tons; $ per lb.

Strike Price	Calls—Settle Jly-c	Sep-c	Dc-c	Puts—Settle Jly-p	Sep-p	Dec-p
1400	....	....		0	13	18
1500	85	132	174	0	23	35
1600	0	72	115	15	63	76
1700	0	32	63	115	123	124
1800	0	13	32	215	204	193
1900	0	5	18	315	296	279

Est. vol. 132; Thur vol. 115 calls; 58 puts
Open interest Thur; 6,320 calls; 3,290 puts

—OIL—

CRUDE OIL (NYM) 1,000 bbls.; $ per bbl.

Strike Price	Calls—Settle Jly-c	Aug-c	Sp-c	Puts—Settle Jly-p	Aug-p	Sep-p
16	1.50	1.78	2.00	0.01	0.11	0.24
17	0.50	1.01	1.27	0.01	0.34	0.51
18	0.01	0.45	0.70	0.50	0.78	0.94
19	0.01	0.16	0.35	1.50	1.49	1.59
20	0.01	0.05	0.16	....	....	2.40
21	0.01	....	0.08	....	....	....

Est. vol. 11,452; Thur vol. 11,413 calls; 11,574 puts
Open interest Thur; 102,750 calls; 105,228 puts

—METALS—

SILVER (CMX) 5,000 troy ounces; cents per troy ounce

Strike Price	Calls—Last Jly-C	Sep-C	Dec-C	Puts—Last Jly-P	Sep-P	Dec-P
675	54.0	81.0	98.0	2.0	13.0	22.0
700	33.0	62.0	84.5	6.0	24.0	35.0
725	18.5	54.0	72.0	16.5	41.0	45.0
750	13.5	46.0	64.0	36.5	59.0	67.0
775	9.0	37.0	54.0	57.0	77.0	77.0
800	4.0	28.0	45.0	77.0	89.0	93.0

Est. vol. 12,000, Thur vol. 6,548 calls, 2,054 puts
Open interest Thur; 32,663 calls, 14,166 puts

GOLD (CMX) 100 troy ounces; dollars per troy ounce

Strike Price	Calls—Last Aug-C	Oct-C	Dec-C	Puts—Last Aug-P	Oct-P	Dec-P
420	49.30	55.00	60.20	0.40	1.60	2.80
440	30.70	37.20	43.40	1.40	3.50	5.20
460	14.10	21.80	28.80	4.80	7.30	9.80
480	5.50	12.00	18.30	16.20	17.50	18.50
500	2.50	6.50	10.80	32.90	31.30	30.20
520	1.40	3.60	6.30	50.70	48.00	44.90

Est. vol. 15,000, Thur vol. 5,561 calls, 2,047 puts
Open interest Thur; 49,618 calls, 37,403 puts

—FINANCIAL—

BRITISH POUND (IMM) 62,500 pounds; cents per pound

Strike Price	Calls—Settle Jun-c	Jly-c	Aug-c	Puts—Settle Jun-p	Jly-p	Aug-p
1750	4.90	....	....	0.004	0.74	....
1775	2.40	....	....	0.004	1.40	....
1800	0.004	1.72	2.54	2.20	2.48	3.24
1825	0.004	0.88	1.60	2.60	4.10	4.80
1850	0.004	0.40	0.98	5.10	6.12	6.66
1875	0.004	0.18	0.60	7.60	8.38	8.76

Est. vol. 3,623, Thur vol. 1,665 calls, 3,944 puts
Open interest Thur; 21,818 calls, 23,761 puts

T-BONDS (CBT) $100,000; points and 64ths of 100%

Strike Price	Calls—Last Sep-c	Dec-c	Mar-c	Puts—Last Sep-p	Dec-p	Mar-p
84	3-50	3-54	4-00	0-44	1-44	2-40
86	2-24	2-44	3-04	1-16	2-29	....
88	1-20	1-50	2-10	2-09	3-30	....
90	0-41	1-08	....	3-33	4-50	....
92	0-19	0-47	1-08	5-06	6-20	....
94	0-10	0-30	....	6-59	8-02	....

Est. vol. 70,000, Thur vol. 41,687 calls, 52,729 puts

—INDEXES—

S&P 500 STOCK INDEX (CME) $500 times premium

Strike Price	Calls—Settle Jun-c	Jly-c	Sp-c	Puts—Settle Jun-p	Jly-p	Sep-p
255	12.30	16.40	19.60	1.25	3.65	7.00
260	8.35	12.65	16.20	2.25	4.85	8.50
265	5.10	9.35	13.15	4.00	6.55	10.35
270	2.80	6.70	10.40	6.65	8.80	12.50
275	1.30	4.60	8.05	10.15	....	15.00
280	0.55	3.00	6.10	14.40	....	17.95

Est. vol. 10,144; Thur vol. 4,467 calls; 1,741 puts
Open interest Thur; 24,407 calls; 22,440 puts

NYSE COMPOSITE INDEX (NYFE) $500 times premium

Strike Price	Calls—Settle Jun-c	Jly-c	Sep-c	Puts—Settle Jun-p	Jly-p	Sep-p
146	5.10	7.35	9.50	1.00	2.65	4.70
148	3.60	6.00	8.20	1.55	3.25	5.40
150	2.35	4.75	7.00	2.25	3.95	6.15
152	1.40	3.75	6.00	3.35	4.85	7.00
154	0.85	2.80	5.00	4.75	5.85	8.00
156	0.45	2.20	4.15	6.30	7.15	9.10

Est. vol. 52, Thurs vol. 103 calls, 162 puts
Open interest Thurs 700 calls, 779 puts

Source: Futures Options, *The Wall Street Journal*, June 6, 1988.

ercised. If the index is at 250, the call is worthless, but the put is worth $2,500 per contract (5 points × $500). In contrast, if the index is at 260, the put is worthless, but the call is worth $2,500 per contract.

OPTIONS AND FUTURES COMPARED

At this juncture, it is important to note some of the essential similarities and differences between options and futures.

1. Both are *deferred-delivery* instruments. Positions in both options and futures can be terminated prior to expiration by executing a reverse trade. Delivery on a futures contract takes place only during the delivery period prescribed by the futures exchange. In contrast, options are American and may be exercised at any time prior to expiration.

2. Ignoring transaction costs and taxes, the maximum possible loss at expiration to an option buyer (put or call) is the amount of the option premium. The call buyer (put buyer) has insured himself against the downside (upside) variability of the futures price. The downside (upside) risk is the variability of the futures price below (above) the level of the call's exercise price.

   The maximum possible gain at expiration on a purchased put is limited to the option exercise price, while the potential gain on a purchased call is equal to the excess of the futures price over the option strike price. The option seller's position at expiration is opposite to that of the option buyer. For instance, the option seller's maximum possible gain at expiration is limited to the premium received. In contrast, the buyer (seller) of a futures contract gains (loses) dollar for dollar with an increase in futures price. Therefore, the distribution of returns on options is different from the distribution of futures returns.

3. In general, a purchased option is less risky than a written option, because the maximum possible loss on a purchased option is the premium paid, while the seller's loss is unlimited. Except for some delivery privileges enjoyed by the futures contract seller, the riskiness of a long futures position is comparable to that of a short futures position.

4. The option premium is paid up-front, but the payment on a futures contract is postponed until final settlement. Purchased options do not require any margins and are not marked-to-market on a daily basis. Margins on written options are generally higher than those on futures and are marked-to-market daily.

5. Writing an option generates premium income, but selling a futures contract does not.

6. Options provide a flexible hedging mechanism. The holder of a long spot position can insure against a price decline by buying a put option with a desired strike price while at the same time continuing to enjoy the potential for capital appreciation on the spot position. He can obtain limited protection against price declines by writing calls so that any subsequent price decline will be reduced by the amount of premium received. He can also vary the number of calls written per unit of spot position. It is possible to transform his spot position into a relatively riskless position by buying a put and writing a call, both with identical exercise price and expiration date.

   When one sells an appropriate number of futures contracts against a long spot position, it is similar to buying a put and selling a call. That is, a *single* futures trade is sufficient to minimize variability of returns on the hedge portfolio.[20] However, the

---

[20] Eugene Moriarty, Susan Philips, and Paula Tosini, "A Comparison of Options and Futures in the Management of Portfolio Risk," *Financial Analysts Journal* 37, no. 1 (January–February 1981): 61–67.

hedger in the futures market is obliged to give up the benefits of capital appreciation on the spot position. Unlike options, a futures contract does not provide the trader with an opportunity to separate downside risk from upside potential.

PRICING OF OPTIONS ON FUTURES

Black[21] has extended the Black-Scholes stock option pricing model to valuation of options on futures. To understand this relationship, it is assumed that capital markets are perfect; there are no transaction costs, margin costs, and taxes; the riskless rate is constant over the life of the option; and the returns on the futures contract are lognormally distributed, with a constant variance. Notice that the constant riskless rate assumption is tantamount to treating a futures contract as a forward contract. Given these assumptions, one can construct a portfolio combining a long position in the forward contract and a short position in options with the same expiration date as the forward contract. When continuously rebalanced, this becomes a *riskless hedge*. In efficient markets, options will be priced in such a way that the hedge portfolio earns a riskless rate of return. According to this model, the value of a European call is given by

$$C = e^{-R_f \tau} \left[FO(t,T)\ n(d_1) - KN(d_2) \right],\tag{25.39}$$

where

C = **call price**

e = **base of the natural log**

R_f = **riskless rate**

$\tau = (T - t)$; **term to expiration of the option**

$FO(t,T)$ = **forward price equivalent of the futures price**

$d_1 = \{In\,[FO(t,T)/K] + (\sigma^2/2)\tau\}/\sigma\sqrt{\tau}$

$N(\cdot)$ = **cumulative standard normal probability**

K = **exercise price on the call**

$d_2 = d_1 - \sigma\sqrt{\tau}$

σ = **standard deviation of percentage changes in the forward price.**

The value of a European put is equal to

$$P = e^{-R_f \tau} \left[KN(-d_2) - FO(t,T)N(-d_1) \right].\tag{25.40}$$

The value of a European call in Equation 25.39 is comparable to the value of a call option on a stock that pays a continuous dividend over the life of the option at a rate equal to the risk-free rate times the stock price.

[21] Fischer Black, "The Pricing of Commodity Contracts," *Journal of Financial Economics* 3, nos. 1,2 (January–March 1976): 167–179.

This model does not give an exact value of options on futures, because they are American options, which can be exercised early. Still, it is a useful model since it provides a lower boundary on the value of American options.

Options on futures vary from the European option on an equivalent forward contract in two important ways. First, since the futures options are American options, there is an incentive to exercise these options early. For example, if the owner of an in-the-money call exercises early at t, he or she will receive $[F(t,T) - K]$ immediately. This amount could be reinvested to produce $e^{R_f T}[F(t,T) - K]$ at T. However, the opportunity to earn interest on the proceeds from an early exercise must be weighed against the sacrifice involved. By exercising the call early, the owner gives up the intrinsic value of the call, which is equal to $C - [F(t,T) - K]$. Second, the daily resettlement cash flows associated with the futures contract are analogous to stochastic dividends on a stock, such that the futures options are American options coupled with stochastic dividends. These features render the American futures options extremely complex to value, and these options do not have a closed-form valuation model. Simulation studies indicate, however, that the price difference between the American futures options and European forward options is relatively small.[22]

CURRENCY FUTURES

The rapid growth of international trade and travel has led to development of an active market for foreign currencies centered primarily in New York. In the foreign exchange market, international currencies are traded for spot as well as deferred delivery by exporters, importers, banks, and travelers. Spot and forward foreign exchange quotes are reported in *The Wall Street Journal*, and an example of these quotes is given in Figure 25.2. These rates pertain to transactions among a few large banks who make up the forward market. As an example, the figure shows that the spot exchange rate per British pound is $1.8005, while the 180-day forward rate is $1.7894.

The holder of foreign currencies or foreign securities is exposed to a new type of risk, namely, uncertain fluctuations in exchange rates. One way to minimize exposure to exchange rate risk is to try to balance foreign currency denominated assets and liabilities. Any net exposure—that is, the excess of foreign assets over foreign liabilities, or vice versa—can be covered by a hedge, short or long, in the forward currency market. While the forward market can provide a hedging tool that is tailored to the trader's needs, it suffers from low liquidity relative to the currency futures market. The primary currency futures market is the International Monetary Market (IMM), a subsidiary of the Chicago Mercantile Exchange. Sample currency futures quotations reported in *The Wall Street Journal* are also shown in Figure 25.2. It shows that the futures contract on British pounds has three

---

[22] Kuldeep Shastri and Kishore Tandem, "An Empirical Test of a Valuation Model for American Options on Futures Contracts," *Journal of Financial and Quantitative Analysis* 21, no. 4 (December 1986): 377–392; and Robert Whaley, "Valuation of American Futures Options: Theory and Empirical Tests," *Journal of Finance* 41, no. 1 (March 1986): 127–150.

FIGURE 25.2
Spot, Forward, and Futures Exchange Rates

FOREIGN EXCHANGE

Monday, June 6, 1988

The New York foreign exchange selling rates below apply to trading among banks in amounts of $1 million and more, as quoted at 3 p.m. Eastern time by Bankers Trust Co. Retail transactions provide fewer units of foreign currency per dollar.

Country	U.S. $ equiv. Mon.	U.S. $ equiv. Fri.	Currency per U.S. $ Mon.	Currency per U.S. $ Fri.
Argentina (Austral)	.1350	.1429	7.405	7.00
Australia (Dollar)	.7924	.8075	1.2620	1.2384
Austria (Schilling)	.08271	.08244	12.09	12.13
Bahrain (Dinar)	2.6525	2.6525	.377	.377
Belgium (Franc)				
Commercial rate	.02782	.02774	35.95	36.05
Financial rate	.02769	.02762	36.11	36.21
Brazil (Cruzado)	.005960	.006006	167.79	166.50
Britain (Pound)	1.8005	1.7993	.5540	.5558
30-Day Forward	1.7995	1.7986	.5557	.5560
90-Day Forward	1.7958	1.7952	.5569	.5570
180-Day Forward	1.7894	1.7891	.5588	.5589
Canada (Dollar)	.8119	.8118	1.2317	1.2318
30-Day Forward	.8109	.81077	1.2332	1.2335
90-Day Forward	.8085	.8083	1.2369	1.2372
180-Day Forward	.8053	.8052	1.2417	1.2419
Chile (Official rate)	.004057	.004060	246.47	246.31
China (Yuan)	.2687	.2687	3.7220	3.7220
Colombia (Peso)	.003404	.003422	293.79	292.19
Denmark (Krone)	.1528	.1523	6.5460	6.5655
Ecuador (Sucre)				
Official rate	.004008	.004008	249.50	249.50
Floating rate	.002099	.002099	476.50	476.50
Finland (Markka)	.2446	.2437	4.0890	4.1040
France (Franc)	.1726	.1715	5.7935	5.8300
30-Day Forward	.1726	.1716	5.7915	5.8290
90-Day Forward	.1726	.1716	5.7905	5.8275
180-Day Forward	.1728	.1717	5.7860	5.8240
Greece (Drachma)	.007262	.007257	137.70	137.80
Hong Kong (Dollar)	.1279	.1280	7.8170	7.8150
India (Rupee)	.07342	.07348	13.62	13.61
Indonesia (Rupiah)	.0005970	.0005977	1675.00	1673.00
Ireland (Punt)	1.5555	1.5510	.6429	.6447
Israel (Shekel)	.6309	.6353	1.5850	1.574
Italy (Lira)	.0007849	.0007794	1274.00	1283.00
Japan (Yen)	.007948	.007941	125.81	125.93
30-Day Forward	.007972	.007966	125.43	125.54
90-Day Forward	.008019	.008014	124.70	124.78
180-Day Forward	.008087	.008082	123.65	123.73
Jordan (Dinar)	2.7739	2.7778	.3605	.3600
Kuwait (Dinar)	3.6284	3.6443	.2756	.2744
Lebanon (Pound)	.002755	.002699	363.00	370.50

Country	U.S. $ equiv. Mon.	U.S. $ equiv. Fri.	Currency per U.S. $ Mon.	Currency per U.S. $ Fri.
Malaysia (Ringgit)	.3871	.3871	2.5833	2.5830
Malta (Lira)	3.0994	3.0994	.3226	.3226
Mexico (Peso)				
Floating rate	.0004405	.0004405	2270.00	2270.00
Netherland (Guilder)	.5196	.5163	1.9245	1.9370
New Zealand (Dollar)	.6926	.7000	1.4438	1.4286
Norway (Krone)	.1593	.1589	6.2780	6.2950
Pakistan (Rupee)	.05621	.05653	17.79	17.69
Peru (Inti)	.03030	.03030	33.00	33.00
Philippines (Peso)	.04757	.04758	21.02	21.015
Portugal (Escudo)	.007117	.007092	140.50	141.00
Saudi Arabia (Riyal)	.2663	.2666	3.7555	3.7505
Singapore (Dollar)	.4947	.4948	2.0215	2.0210
South Africa (Rand)				
Commercial rate	.4477	.4476	2.2336	2.2341
Financial rate	.3378	.3389	2.9600	2.9500
South Korea (Won)	.001364	.001365	733.20	732.80
Spain (Peseta)	.008807	.008778	113.55	113.92
Sweden (Krona)	.1664	.1661	6.0100	6.0210
Switzerland (Franc)	.7000	.6949	1.4285	1.4390
30-Day Forward	.7029	.6978	1.4226	1.4330
90-Day Forward	.7088	.7036	1.4109	1.4212
180-Day Forward	.7175	.7124	1.3938	1.4038
Taiwan (Dollar)	.03500	.03500	28.57	28.57
Thailand (Baht)	.03968	.03976	25.20	25.15
Turkey (Lira)	.0007520	.00761	1329.81	1313.72
United Arab (Dirham)	.2723	.2723	3.671	3.671
Uruguay (New Peso)				
Financial	.002941	.002950	340.00	339.00
Venezuela (Bolivar)				
Official rate	.1333	.1333	7.50	7.50
Floating rate	.03183	.03367	31.42	29.70
W. Germany (Mark)	.5833	.5794	1.7145	1.7260
30-Day Forward	.5853	.5814	1.7086	1.7200
90-Day Forward	.5893	.5854	1.6970	1.7082
180-Day Forward	.5950	.5912	1.6807	1.6915
SDR	1.35932	1.35860	0.735664	0.736053
ECU	1.20535	1.20289	....	....

Special Drawing Rights are based on exchange rates for the U.S., West German, British, French and Japanese currencies. Source: International Monetary Fund.
ECU is based on a basket of community currencies. Source: European Community Commission.
z-Not quoted.

FUTURES PRICES

Monday, June 6, 1988
Open Interest Reflects Previous Trading Day.
— FINANCIAL —

BRITISH POUND (IMM) — $ per pound

June	1.8040	1.8045	1.7975	1.7980	-.0010	1.9045	1.5280	39,135
Sept	1.7980	1.7980	1.7914	1.7920	-.0006	1.9012	1.6992	9,501
Dec	1.7880	1.7950	1.7860	1.7864	-.0008	1.9000	1.6980	872

Est vol 10,891; vol Fri 20,582; open int 49,508, +3,075.

AUSTRALIAN DOLLAR (IMM)—100,000 dlrs.; $ per A.$

June	.7925	.7945	.7916	.7917	-.0137	.8116	.6430	5,522
Sept	.7805	.7835	.7805	.7825	-.0121	.8012	.7008	3,457

Est vol 126; vol Fri 120; open int 8,990, -28.

CANADIAN DOLLAR (IMM)—100,000 dlrs.; $ per Can $

June	.8115	.8118	.8102	.8114	+.0002	.8130	.7325	17,159
Sept	.8080	.8082	.8065	.8078	+.0002	.8096	.7307	15,560
Dec	.8035	.8046	.8033	.8046	+.0004	.8090	.7390	1,204
Mr89	....	....		.8014	+.0006	.8055	.7570	177

Est vol 6,077; vol Fri 6,306; open int 34,128, +553.

JAPANESE YEN (IMM) 12.5 million yen; $ per yen (.00)

June	.7919	.7954	.7918	.7948	+.0001	.8390	.6735	38,567
Sept	.7989	.8028	.7988	.8021	....	.8485	.7075	15,609
Dec	.8058	.8094	.8058	.8091	-.0001	.8530	.7115	924
Mr89	.8130	.8160	.8130	.8161	-.0002	.8590	.7870	107

Est vol 28,423; vol Fri 30,211; open int 55,222, +3,442.

SWISS FRANC (IMM) —125,000 francs-$ per franc

June	.6972	.7003	.6966	.6999	+.0042	.8040	.6580	30,996
Sept	.7060	.7092	.7055	.7089	+.0041	.8120	.6950	9,233
Dec	.7142	.7185	.7142	.7182	+.0042	.8210	.7130	274

Est vol 23,841; vol Fri 18,985; open int 40,508, -250.

W. GERMAN MARK (IMM) —125,000 marks; $ per mark

June	.5814	.5839	.5813	.5831	+.0034	.6494	.5410	45,583
Sept	.5877	.5899	.5876	.5892	+.0034	.6555	.5609	24,643
Dec	.5925	.5957	.5925	.5951	+.0034	.6610	.5705	1,643

Est vol 20,621; vol Fri 20,359; open int 71,875, -193.

Source: Foreign Exchanges, Futures Prices, *The Wall Street Journal*, June 7, 1988.

TABLE 25.6
An Illustration of a Currency Futures Hedge

SPOT MARKET		FUTURES MARKET	
June 5			
Anticipated cost of equipment:		Purchase four December	
(£250,000 × $1.7864)	$446,600	contracts @ $1.7864	$446,600
December 10			
Purchase spot currency		Sell four December	
to pay for imports $1.6840	421,000	contracts @ $1.6850	421,250
Gross savings	$ 25,600	Gross loss on futures	($ 25,350)
Total gains subject to margin and transaction costs = $250			

actively traded delivery months: June, September, and December. The settle quote on the June contract is $1.7980.

Like other futures instruments, the major economic functions of currency forward and futures markets are price discovery and hedging. The general conclusion of empirical studies is the current forward rate provides an unbiased forecast of the future spot rate, but its forecasting performance is no better than the current spot rate.[23] The hedging performance of currency futures compared quite favorably with that of commodity futures and interest rate futures.[24]

EXAMPLE OF A CURRENCY FUTURES HEDGE

As a simple example, consider the case of a U.S. manufacturer importing industrial equipment from a British firm. On June 5, the U.S. importer agrees to pay £250,000 (in British pounds) for the equipment to be shipped in late December. From Figure 25.2, the current cost of the equipment in U.S. dollars is $449,500, but the anticipated cost (in terms of December delivery quotes) is $446,600. Yet, the importer is somewhat apprehensive about carrying an uncovered commitment in British pounds, so he decides to hedge by buying four December contracts at the rate of $1.7864 per British pound (each contract is for £62.500). On December 10, assume that the spot exchange rate is $1.6840. The importer buys £250,000 in the spot market, takes delivery of the equipment, and closes out the futures position. As shown in Table 25.6, this results in gross savings before transaction costs of $250.

SUMMARY

Financial futures are a rapidly growing segment of our financial markets. They may be used as short or long hedges as well as speculative transactions. Empirical evidence supports the theoretical models that have been

---

[23] Tamir Agmon and Yakov Amihud, "The Forward Exchange Rate and the Prediction of the Future Spot Rate," *Journal of Banking and Finance* 5, no. 3 (September 1981): 425–437.

[24] Charles Dale, "The Hedging Effectiveness of Currency Futures Markets" *The Journal of Futures Markets* 1, no. 1 (Spring 1981): 77–88.

proposed for price relationships and the ability to hedge with interest rate futures.

An alternative to the portfolio approach discussed in Chapter 24 is a price-sensitive approach, and the empirical evidence indicates that it works very well compared to several naive strategies. Also, financial futures can be used to adjust bond portfolio duration and thereby assist in immunizing portfolios.

In addition to interest rate futures, another major development has been the creation of stock index futures, serving a multitude of purposes for individuals and institutional money managers. These are used in program trading and portfolio insurance strategies. Controversy exists regarding the role of index futures in aggravating stock market volatility since the October 1987 market crash.

The enormous innovation possible in the financial markets is exemplified by the creation of options on futures, which provide all the advantages and opportunities of these two instruments.

Currency futures are another area of growing importance and activity. As the world becomes a global business community, financial managers, money managers, and individual investors must understand how to use these currency futures to hedge against the volatility of foreign exchange rates.

QUESTIONS

1. Discuss the portfolio approach and the price sensitivity approach to hedging.

2. How could one use interest rate futures and stock index futures in active portfolio management? What are the advantages of futures over other methods of altering a portfolio beta?

3. Differentiate among stock options on futures contracts. Discuss Black's model of pricing options on futures.

4. What are the two important economic functions of currency futures? Give an example of each.

5. *CFA Examination III (June 1982)*: In each of the following cases, discuss how you as a portfolio manager would use financial futures to protect the portfolio.

5a. You own a large position in a relatively illiquid bond that you want to sell.

5b. You have a large gain on one of your long Treasuries and want to sell it, but you would like to defer the gain until the next accounting period, which begins in four weeks.

5c. You will receive a large contribution next month that you hope to invest in long-term corporate bonds on a yield basis as favorable as is now available. [15 minutes]

6. Discuss how the cheapest-to-deliver bond underlying the T-bond futures contract can be identified.

7. What are the delivery options implicit in the T-bond futures contract? How could one estimate the value of these implicit options?

8. Suppose that the lower and upper boundaries for the T-bond futures price are violated. Describe in detail the transactions (and the associated cash flows) necessary to exploit the near-arbitrage opportunities.

9. State the no-arbitrage boundaries for the S&P 500 index futures contract. Illustrate how you could exploit for profit any discrepancies between these boundaries and the index futures price observed in the market.

10. Under what conditions do you think program trading and portfolio insurance using index futures and options contracts could aggravate stock market volatility? Discuss the advantages and disadvantages of these financial innovations in the context of the existing trading structures in the stock market.

PROBLEMS

1. You have been reading about the diversification benefits of gold as well as the returns enjoyed by some "gold bugs." In June, you decide to take the plunge and buy a March contract in gold (100 troy ounces) on the International Monetary Market (IMM) at the Chicago Mercantile Exchange (CME). March gold on the IMM is 465 ($465 an ounce), the margin on gold is 10 percent, and the commission is $30 a contract:

1a. In September there is an outbreak in the Middle East, and the price of March gold goes to 525. Compute the rate of return on your investment.

1b. When you bought the gold contract in June you put in a stop-loss order at 455. In November, over the weekend, there are several very optimistic announcements by the government regarding the inflationary outlook, interest rates, and peace in the Middle East. Gold closes down the limit for five days and the price goes right through your limit order to 440 before your broker can sell your contract. Compute the rate of return on your investment. Discuss the leverage involved.

2. *CFA Examination III (June 1983)*: In February 1983, the United American Co. is considering the sale of $100 million in 10-year debentures that will probably be rated AAA like the firm's other bond issues. The firm is anxious to proceed at today's rate of 10.5%.

   As treasurer, you know that it will take about 12 weeks (May 1983) to get the issue registered and sold. Therefore, you suggest that the firm hedge the pending bond issue using Treasury bond futures contracts. (Each Treasury bond contract is for $100,000.)

   Explain how you would go about hedging the bond issue, and describe the results assuming that the following two sets of future conditions actually occur. (Ignore commissions and margin costs, and assume a 1-to-1 hedge ratio.) Show all calculations.

	CASE 1	CASE 2
Current Values—February 1983		
Bond rate	10.5%	10.5%
June '83 Treasury bond futures	78.875	78.875
Estimated Values—May 1983		
Bond rate	11.0%	10.0%
June '83 Treasury bond futures	75.93	81.84
Present Value of a $1 Annuity		
10 years at 10.5%	6.021	6.021
[15 minutes]		

3. Select market quotes on a few put and call options on futures contracts. Estimate their values by using the Black pricing model discussed in the text, and comment on the discrepancies between the estimates and the quotes.

4. State the European put/call parity theorem for options on futures contracts. Select three market quotes, and test whether the observed futures and options quotes are consistent with this theorem.

REFERENCES

Agmon, Tamir, and Yakov Amihud. "The Forward Exchange Rate and the Prediction of the Future Spot Rate." *Journal of Banking and Finance* 5, no. 3 (September 1981).

Bacon, Peter W., and R. E. Williams. "Interest Rate Futures: New Tool for the Financial Manager." *Financial Management* 5, no. 1 (Spring 1976).

Benninya, Simon, and Marshal Blume. "On the Optimality of Portfolio Insurance." *Journal of Finance* 60, no. 5 (December 1985).

Black, Fischer. "The Pricing of Commodity Contracts." *Journal of Financial Economics* 3, nos. 1, 2 (January–March 1976).

Dale, Charles. "The Hedging Effectiveness of Currency Futures Markets." *The Journal of Futures Markets* 1, no. 1 (Spring 1981).

Fabozzi, Frank J., and Gregory M. Kipnis (eds.) *Stock Index Futures.* Homewood, Ill.: Dow Jones-Irwin, 1984.

Figlewski, Stephen, and Stanley Kon. "Portfolio Management with Stock Index Futures." *Financial Analysts Journal* 38, no. 1 (January–February 1982).

Gay, Gerald D., and Robert W. Kolb. "Interest Rate Futures as a Tool for Immunization." *Journal of Portfolio Management* 10, no. 1 (Fall 1983).

Gay, Gerald D., and Robert W. Kolb (eds). *Interest Rate Futures: Concepts and Issues.* Richmond, Va.: Robert F. Dame, Inc. 1982.

Gay, Gerald, Robert Kolb, and Raymond Chiang. "Interest Rate Hedging: An Empirical Test of Alternative Strategies." *Journal of Financial Research* 6, no. 3 (Fall 1983).

Grossman, Stanford J. "An Analysis of the Implications for Stock and Futures Price Volatility of Program Trading and Dynamic Hedging Strategies." *Journal of Business* 61, no. 3 (July 1988).

Kane, Edward J. "Market Incompleteness and Divergencies Between Forward and Futures Interest Rates." *Journal of Finance* 35, no. 2 (May 1980).

Kolb, Robert W. *Understanding Futures Markets.* 2d ed. Glenview, Ill.: Scott, Foresman and Company, 1988.

Kolb, Robert W., and Gerald D. Gay. "Immunizing Bond Portfolios with Interest Rate Futures." *Financial Management* 11, no. 3 (Summer 1982).

Kolb, Robert, and Raymond Chiang. "Improving Hedging Performance Using Interest Rate Futures." *Financial Management* 10, no. 4 (Autumn 1981).

Kolb, Robert, and Raymond Chiang. "Duration, Immunization, and Hedging with Interest Rate Futures." *Journal of Financial Research* 5, no. 2 (Summer 1982).

McEnally, Richard W., and Michael L. Rice. "Hedging Possibilities in the Flotation of Debt Securities." *Financial Management* 8, no. 4 (Winter 1979).

Moriarity, Eugene, Susan Phillips, and Paula Tosini, "A Comparison of Options and Futures in the Management of Portfolio Risk." *Financial Analysts Journal* 37, no. 1 (January–February 1981).

Perold, Andre F., and William F. Sharpe. "Dynamic Strategies for Asset Allocation." *Financial Analysts Journal* 44, no. 1 (January–February 1988).

Rendleman, Richard, and Christopher Carabini. "The Efficiency of the Treasury Bill Futures Market." *Journal of Finance* 34, no. 4 (September 1979).

Rendleman, Richard J., Jr., and Richard W. McEnally. "Assessing the Costs of Portfolio Insurance." *Financial Analysts Journal* 43, no. 3 (May–June 1987).

Rubinstein, Mark. "Alternative Paths to Portfolio Insurance." *Financial Analysts Journal* 41, no. 4 (July–August 1985).

Schwarz, Edward W. *How to Use Interest Rate Futures Contracts*. Homewood, Ill.: Dow Jones-Irwin, 1979.

HOW TO BECOME A CHARTERED FINANCIAL ANALYST

As mentioned in the section on career opportunities, the professional designation of Chartered Financial Analyst (CFA) is becoming a significant requirement for a career in investment analysis and/or portfolio management. For that reason, this section presents the history and objectives of the Institute of Chartered Financial Analysts and general guidelines for acquiring the CFA designation. If you are interested in the program, you can write to the Institute for more information.

The Institute of Chartered Financial Analysts (ICFA) was formed in 1959 in Charlottesville, Virginia. The CFA candidate examinations were first offered in 1963. The ICFA has close ties with the University of Virginia, the Financial Analysts Federation, and the Financial Analysts Research Foundation.

The Institute of Chartered Financial Analysts (ICFA) was organized to enhance the professionalism of those involved in various aspects of the investment decision-making process and to recognize those who achieve a high level of professionalism by awarding the designation of Chartered Financial Analyst (CFA).

The basic missions and purposes of the ICFA are

- To develop and keep current a "body of knowledge" applicable to the investment decision-making process. The principal components of this knowledge are financial accounting, economics, both fixed-income and equity securities analysis, portfolio management, ethical and professional standards, and quantitative techniques.
- To administer a study and examination program for eligible candidates, the primary objectives of which are to assist the candidate in mastering and applying the body of knowledge and to test the candidate's competency in the knowledge gained.
- To award the professional CFA designation to those candidates who have passed three examination levels (encompassing a total of 18 hours of testing over a minimum of three years), who meet stipulated standards of professional conduct, and who otherwise are eligible for membership in the ICFA.
- To provide a useful and informative program of continuing education through seminars, publications, and other formats that enable members, candidates, and others in the investment constituency to be more aware of and to better utilize the changing and expanding body of knowledge.
- To sponsor and enforce a *Code of Ethics and Standards of Professional Conduct* that apply to enrolled candidates and to all members.

A college degree is necessary to enter the program. A candidate may sit for all three examinations without having had investment experience *per se* or having joined a constituent Society of the Financial Analysts Federation. However, after passing the three examination levels, the CFA Charter will not be awarded unless or until the candidate

- has at least three years of experience as a financial analyst, which is defined as a person who has spent and/or is spending a substantial portion of his/her professional time collecting, evaluating, and applying financial, economic, and related data to the investment decision-making process, and
- has applied for membership or is a member of a constituent Society of the Financial Analysts Federation, if such a Society exists within 50 miles of the candidate's principal place of business.

The curriculum of the CFA study program covers:

1. Ethical and Professional Standards
2. Financial Accounting
3. Economics
4. Fixed-Income Securities Analysis
5. Equity Securities Analysis
6. Portfolio Management
7. Quantitative Techniques

Members and candidates are typically employed in the investment field. From 1963 to 1988, a total of 11,000 charters have been awarded. More than 7,000 individuals currently are registered in the CFA Candidate Program. If you are interested in learning more about the CFA program, the Institute has a booklet that describes the program and includes an application form. The address is Institute of Chartered Financial Analysts, P.O. Box 3668, Charlottesville, Virginia 22903.

CODE OF ETHICS AND STANDARDS OF PROFESSIONAL CONDUCT

ADOPTED BY THE FINANCIAL ANALYSTS FEDERATION AND THE INSTITUTE OF CHARTERED FINANCIAL ANALYSTS, AMENDED MAY 8, 1988

APPENDIX B

THE FAF RESOLUTION

WHEREAS, the profession of financial analysis and investment management has evolved because of the increasing public need for competent, objective, and trustworthy advice with regard to investments and financial management; and

WHEREAS, those engaged in this profession have joined together in an organization known as The Financial Analysts Federation; and

WHEREAS, despite a wide diversity of interest among analysts employed by brokers and securities dealers, investment advisers, banks, insurance companies, investment companies and trusts, pension trusts, and other institutional investors and investment entities, there are nevertheless certain fundamental standards of conduct which should be common to all engaged in the profession of financial analysis and investment management and accepted and maintained by them; and

WHEREAS, the members of The Financial Analysts Federation adopted a Code of Ethics and Standards on May 20, 1962, which have been amended from time to time; and

WHEREAS, The Financial Analysts Federation provides for individual membership in it, requires that all of its member societies adopt its Code of Ethics and Standards of Professional Conduct, and requires that all individual members comply with them;

NOW, THEREFORE, the following are the Code of Ethics and Standards of Professional Conduct of The Financial Analysts Federation:

> All individual members of The Financial Analysts Federation including fellows, associates, and affiliates are obligated to conduct their professional activities in accordance with the following Code of Ethics and Standards of Professional Conduct. Disciplinary sanctions may be imposed for violations of the Code or Standards.

THE ICFA RESOLUTION

WHEREAS, the profession of financial analysis and investment management has evolved because of the increasing public need for competent, objective, and trustworthy advice with regard to investments and financial management; and

WHEREAS, The Institute of Chartered Financial Analysts was organized to establish educational standards in the field of financial analysis, to conduct examinations of financial analysts and to award the professional designation of Chartered Financial Analyst, among other objectives; and

Source: Reprinted with permission from The Financial Analysts Federation and The Institute of Chartered Financial Analysts, Charlottesville, Virginia.

WHEREAS, despite a wide diversity of interest among analysts employed by brokers and security dealers, investment advisers, banks, insurance companies, investment companies and trusts, pension trusts, and other institutional investors and investment entities, there are nevertheless certain fundamental standards of conduct which should be common to all engaged in the profession of financial analysis and investment management and accepted and maintained by them; and

WHEREAS, The Institute of Chartered Financial Analysts adopted a Code of Ethics and Standards on March 14, 1964, which have been amended from time to time;

NOW, THEREFORE, The Institute of Chartered Financial Analysts hereby adopts the following Code of Ethics and Standards of Professional Conduct:

All members of The Institute of Chartered Financial Analysts and holders of and candidates for the professional designation Chartered Financial Analyst are obligated to conduct their professional activities in accordance with the following Code of Ethics and Standards of Professional Conduct. Disciplinary sanctions may be imposed for violations of the Code or Standards.

CODE OF ETHICS

A financial analyst should conduct himself* with integrity and dignity and act in an ethical manner in his dealings with the public, clients, customers, employers, employees, and fellow analysts.

A financial analyst should conduct himself and should encourage others to practice financial analysis in a professional and ethical manner that will reflect credit on himself and his profession.

A financial analyst should act with competence and should strive to maintain and improve his competence and that of others in the profession.

A financial analyst should use proper care and exercise independent professional judgment.

STANDARDS OF PROFESSIONAL CONDUCT

I. **Obligation to Inform Employer of Code and Standards**

The financial analyst shall inform his employer, through his direct supervisor, that the analyst is obligated to comply with the Code of Ethics and Standards of Professional Conduct, and is subject to disciplinary sanctions for violations thereof. He shall deliver a copy of the Code and Standards to his employer if the employer does not have a copy.

II. **Compliance with Governing Laws and Regulations and the Code and Standards**

A. Required Knowledge and Compliance

The financial analyst shall maintain knowledge of and shall comply with all applicable laws, rules, and regulations of any government, governmental agency, and regulatory organization governing his professional, financial, or business activities, as well as with these Standards of Professional Conduct and the accompanying Code of Ethics.

---

*Masculine personal pronouns, used throughout the Code and Standards to simplify sentence structure, shall apply to all persons, regardless of sex.

B. Prohibition Against Assisting Legal and Ethical Violations

The financial analyst shall not knowingly participate in, or assist, any acts in violation of any applicable law, rule, or regulation of any government, governmental agency, or regulatory organization governing his professional, financial, or business activities, nor any act which would violate any provision of these Standards of Professional Conduct or the accompanying Code of Ethics.

C. Prohibition Against Use of Material Nonpublic Information

The financial analyst shall comply with all laws and regulations relating to the use of material nonpublic information. (1) If the analyst acquires such information as a result of a special or confidential relationship with the issuer, he shall not communicate the information (other than within the relationship), or take investment action on the basis of such information, if it violates that relationship. (2) If the analyst is not in a special or confidential relationship with the issuer, he shall not communicate or act on material nonpublic information if he knows or should have known that such information was disclosed to him in breach of a duty. If such a breach exists, the analyst shall make reasonable efforts to achieve public dissemination of such information.

D. Responsibilities of Supervisors

A financial analyst with supervisory responsibility shall exercise reasonable supervision over those subordinate employees subject to his control, to prevent any violation by such persons of applicable statutes, regulations, or provisions of the Code of Ethics or Standards of Professional Conduct. In so doing the analyst is entitled to rely upon reasonable procedures established by his employer.

III. **Research Reports, Investment Recommendations and Actions**

A. Reasonable Basis and Representations

1. The financial analyst shall exercise diligence and thoroughness in making an investment recommendation to others or in taking an investment action for others.
2. The financial analyst shall have a reasonable and adequate basis for such recommendations and actions, supported by appropriate research and investigation.
3. The financial analyst shall make reasonable and diligent efforts to avoid any material misrepresentation in any research report or investment recommendation.
4. The financial analyst shall maintain appropriate records to support the reasonableness of such recommendations.

B. Research Reports

1. The financial analyst shall use reasonable judgment as to the inclusion of relevant factors in research reports.
2. The financial analyst shall distinguish between facts and opinions in research reports.
3. The financial analyst shall indicate the basic characteristics of the investment involved when preparing for general public distribution a research report that is not directly related to a specific portfolio or client.

C. Portfolio Investment Recommendations and Actions

The financial analyst shall, when making an investment recommendation or taking an investment action for a specific portfolio or client, consider its appropriateness and suitability for such portfolio or client. In considering such matters, the financial analyst shall take into account (1) the needs and circumstances of the client, (2) the basic characteristics of the investment involved, and (3) the basic characteristics of the total portfolio. The financial analyst shall use reasonable judgment to determine the applicable relevant factors. The financial analyst shall distinguish between facts and opinions in the presentation of investment recommendations.

D. Prohibition Against Plagiarism

The financial analyst shall not, when presenting material to his employer, associates, customers, clients, or the general public, copy or use in substantially the same form, material prepared by other persons without acknowledging its use and identifying the name of the author or publisher of such material. The analyst may, however, use without acknowledgement factual information published by recognized financial and statistical reporting services or similar sources.

E. Prohibition Against Misrepresentation of Services

The financial analyst shall not make any statements, orally or in writing, which materially misrepresent (1) the services that the analyst or his firm is capable of performing for the client, (2) the qualifications of such analyst or his firm, (3) the investment performance that the analyst or his firm has accomplished or can reasonably be expected to achieve for the client, or (4) the expected performance of any investment.

The financial analyst shall not make, orally or in writing, explicitly or implicitly, any assurances about or guarantees of any investment or its return except communication of accurate information as to the terms of the investment instrument and the issuer's obligations under the instrument.

F. Fair Dealing with Customers and Clients

The financial analyst shall act in a manner consistent with his obligation to deal fairly with all customers and clients when (1) disseminating investment recommendations, (2) disseminating material changes in prior investment advice, and (3) taking investment action.

IV. Priority of Transactions

The financial analyst shall conduct himself in such a manner that transactions for his customers, clients, and employer have priority over personal transactions, and so that his personal transactions do not operate adversely to their interests. If an analyst decides to make a recommendation about the purchase or sale of a security or other investment, he shall give his customers, clients, and employer adequate opportunity to act on this recommendation before acting on his own behalf.

V. Disclosure of Conflicts

The financial analyst, when making investment recommendations, or taking investment actions, shall disclose to his customers and clients any material conflict of interest relating to him and any material beneficial ownership of the securities or other investments involved, which could reasonably be expected to impair his ability to render unbiased and objective advice.

The financial analyst shall disclose to his employer all matters which could reasonably be expected to interfere with his duty to the employer, or with his ability to render unbiased and objective advice.

The financial analyst shall also comply with all requirements as to disclosure of conflicts of interest imposed by law and by rules and regulations of organizations governing his activities and shall comply with any prohibitions on his activities if a conflict of interest exists.

VI. **Compensation**

A. Disclosure of Additional Compensation Arrangements

The financial analyst shall inform his customers, clients, and employer of compensation arrangements in connection with his services to them which are in addition to compensation from them for such services.

B. Disclosure of Referral Fees

The financial analyst shall make appropriate disclosure to a prospective client or customer of any consideration paid or other benefit delivered to others for recommending his services to that prospective client or customer.

C. Duty to Employer

The financial analyst shall not undertake independent practice for compensation or other benefit in competition with his employer unless he has received written consent from both his employer and the person for whom he undertakes independent employment.

VII. **Relationships with Others**

A. Preservation of Confidentiality

A financial analyst shall preserve the confidentiality of information communicated by the client concerning matters within the scope of the confidential relationship, unless the financial analyst receives information concerning illegal activities on the part of the client.

B. Maintenance of Independence and Objectivity

The financial analyst, in relationships and contacts with an issuer of securities, whether individually or as a member of a group, shall use particular care and good judgment to achieve and maintain independence and objectivity.

C. Fiduciary Duties

The financial analyst, in relationships with clients, shall use particular care in determining applicable fiduciary duty and shall comply with such duty as to those persons and interests to whom it is owed.

VIII. **Use of Professional Designation**

FAF

The qualified financial analyst may use the professional designation "Member of the Financial Analysts Federation," and is encouraged to do so, but only in a dignified and judicious manner. The use of the designation may be accompanied by an accurate explanation (1) of the requirements that have been met to obtain the designation and (2) of The Financial Analysts Federation.

ICFA

The Chartered Financial Analyst may use the professional designation Chartered Financial Analyst, or the abbreviation CFA, and is encouraged to do so, but only in a dignified and judicious manner. The use of the designation may be accompanied by an accurate explanation (1) of the requirements that have been met to obtain the designation and (2) of The Institute of Chartered Financial Analysts.

IX. Professional Misconduct

The financial analyst shall not (1) commit a criminal act that upon conviction materially reflects adversely on his honesty, trustworthiness or fitness as a financial analyst in other respects or (2) engage in conduct involving dishonesty, fraud, deceit, or misrepresentation.

APPENDIX C   INTEREST TABLES

TABLE C.1
Present Value of $1: $PVIF = 1/(1 + k)^t$

Period	1%	2%	3%	4%	5%	6%	7%	8%	9%	10%	12%	14%	15%	16%	18%	20%	24%	28%	32%	36%
1	.9901	.9804	.9709	.9615	.9524	.9434	.9346	.9259	.9174	.9091	.8929	.8772	.8696	.8621	.8475	.8333	.8065	.7813	.7576	.7353
2	.9803	.9612	.9426	.9246	.9070	.8900	.8734	.8573	.8417	.8264	.7972	.7695	.7561	.7432	.7182	.6944	.6504	.6104	.5739	.5407
3	.9706	.9423	.9151	.8890	.8638	.8396	.8163	.7938	.7722	.7513	.7118	.6750	.6575	.6407	.6086	.5787	.5245	.4768	.4348	.3975
4	.9610	.9238	.8885	.8548	.8227	.7921	.7629	.7350	.7084	.6830	.6355	.5921	.5718	.5523	.5158	.4823	.4230	.3725	.3294	.2923
5	.9515	.9057	.8626	.8219	.7835	.7473	.7130	.6806	.6499	.6209	.5674	.5194	.4972	.4761	.4371	.4019	.3411	.2910	.2495	.2149
6	.9420	.8880	.8375	.7903	.7462	.7050	.6663	.6302	.5963	.5645	.5066	.4556	.4323	.4104	.3704	.3349	.2751	.2274	.1890	.1580
7	.9327	.8706	.8131	.7599	.7107	.6651	.6227	.5835	.5470	.5132	.4523	.3996	.3759	.3538	.3139	.2791	.2218	.1776	.1432	.1162
8	.9235	.8535	.7894	.7307	.6768	.6274	.5820	.5403	.5019	.4665	.4039	.3506	.3269	.3050	.2660	.2326	.1789	.1388	.1085	.0854
9	.9143	.8368	.7664	.7026	.6446	.5919	.5439	.5002	.4604	.4241	.3606	.3075	.2843	.2630	.2255	.1938	.1443	.1084	.0822	.0628
10	.9053	.8203	.7441	.6756	.6139	.5584	.5083	.4632	.4224	.3855	.3220	.2697	.2472	.2267	.1911	.1615	.1164	.0847	.0623	.0462
11	.8963	.8043	.7224	.6496	.5847	.5268	.4751	.4289	.3875	.3505	.2875	.2366	.2149	.1954	.1619	.1346	.0938	.0662	.0472	.0340
12	.8874	.7885	.7014	.6246	.5568	.4970	.4440	.3971	.3555	.3186	.2567	.2076	.1869	.1685	.1372	.1122	.0757	.0517	.0357	.0250
13	.8787	.7730	.6810	.6006	.5303	.4688	.4150	.3677	.3262	.2897	.2292	.1821	.1625	.1452	.1163	.0935	.0610	.0404	.0271	.0184
14	.8700	.7579	.6611	.5775	.5051	.4423	.3878	.3405	.2992	.2633	.2046	.1597	.1413	.1252	.0985	.0779	.0492	.0316	.0205	.0135
15	.8613	.7430	.6419	.5553	.4810	.4173	.3624	.3152	.2745	.2394	.1827	.1401	.1229	.1079	.0835	.0649	.0397	.0247	.0155	.0099
16	.8528	.7284	.6232	.5339	.4581	.3936	.3387	.2919	.2519	.2176	.1631	.1229	.1069	.0930	.0708	.0541	.0320	.0193	.0118	.0073
17	.8444	.7142	.6050	.5134	.4363	.3714	.3166	.2703	.2311	.1978	.1456	.1078	.0929	.0802	.0600	.0451	.0258	.0150	.0089	.0054
18	.8360	.7002	.5874	.4936	.4155	.3503	.2959	.2502	.2120	.1799	.1300	.0946	.0808	.0691	.0508	.0376	.0208	.0118	.0068	.0039
19	.8277	.6864	.5703	.4746	.3957	.3305	.2765	.2317	.1945	.1635	.1161	.0829	.0703	.0596	.0431	.0313	.0168	.0092	.0051	.0029
20	.8195	.6730	.5537	.4564	.3769	.3118	.2584	.2145	.1784	.1486	.1037	.0728	.0611	.0514	.0365	.0261	.0135	.0072	.0039	.0021
25	.7798	.6095	.4776	.3751	.2953	.2330	.1842	.1460	.1160	.0923	.0588	.0378	.0304	.0245	.0160	.0105	.0046	.0021	.0010	.0005
30	.7419	.5521	.4120	.3083	.2314	.1741	.1314	.0994	.0754	.0573	.0334	.0196	.0151	.0116	.0070	.0042	.0016	.0006	.0002	.0001
40	.6717	.4529	.3066	.2083	.1420	.0972	.0668	.0460	.0318	.0221	.0107	.0053	.0037	.0026	.0013	.0007	.0002	.0001	*	*
50	.6080	.3715	.2281	.1407	.0872	.0543	.0339	.0213	.0134	.0085	.0035	.0014	.0009	.0006	.0003	.0001	*	*	*	*
60	.5504	.3048	.1697	.0951	.0535	.0303	.0173	.0099	.0057	.0033	.0011	.0004	.0002	.0001	*	*	*	*	*	*

* The factor is zero to four decimal places.

TABLE C.2
Present Value of an Annuity of $1 Per Period for n Periods: $PVIFA = \sum_{t=1}^{n} \dfrac{1}{(1+k)^t} = \dfrac{1 - \dfrac{1}{(1+k)^n}}{k}$

Number of Payments	1%	2%	3%	4%	5%	6%	7%	8%	9%	10%	12%	14%	15%	16%	18%	20%	24%	28%	32%
1	0.9901	0.9804	0.9709	0.9615	0.9524	0.9434	0.9346	0.9259	0.9174	0.9091	0.8929	0.8772	0.8696	0.8621	0.8475	0.8333	0.8065	0.7813	0.7576
2	1.9704	1.9416	1.9135	1.8861	1.8594	1.8334	1.8080	1.7833	1.7591	1.7355	1.6901	1.6467	1.6257	1.6052	1.5656	1.5278	1.4568	1.3916	1.3315
3	2.9410	2.8839	2.8286	2.7751	2.7232	2.6730	2.6243	2.5771	2.5313	2.4869	2.4018	2.3216	2.2832	2.2459	2.1743	2.1065	1.9813	1.8684	1.7663
4	3.9020	3.8077	3.7171	3.6299	3.5460	3.4651	3.3872	3.3121	3.2397	3.1699	3.0373	2.9137	2.8550	2.7982	2.6901	2.5887	2.4043	2.2410	2.0957
5	4.8534	4.7135	4.5797	4.4518	4.3295	4.2124	4.1002	3.9927	3.8897	3.7908	3.6048	3.4331	3.3522	3.2743	3.1272	2.9906	2.7454	2.5320	2.3452
6	5.7955	5.6014	5.4172	5.2421	5.0757	4.9173	4.7665	4.6229	4.4859	4.3553	4.1114	3.8887	3.7845	3.6847	3.4976	3.3255	3.0205	2.7594	2.5342
7	6.7282	6.4720	6.2303	6.0021	5.7864	5.5824	5.3893	5.2064	5.0330	4.8684	4.5638	4.2883	4.1604	4.0386	3.8115	3.6046	3.2423	2.9370	2.6775
8	7.6517	7.3255	7.0197	6.7327	6.4632	6.2098	5.9713	5.7466	5.5348	5.3349	4.9676	4.6389	4.4873	4.3436	4.0776	3.8372	3.4212	3.0758	2.7860
9	8.5660	8.1622	7.7861	7.4353	7.1078	6.8017	6.5152	6.2469	5.9952	5.7590	5.3282	4.9464	4.7716	4.6065	4.3030	4.0310	3.5655	3.1842	2.8681
10	9.4713	8.9826	8.5302	8.1109	7.7217	7.3601	7.0236	6.7101	6.4177	6.1446	5.6502	5.2161	5.0188	4.8332	4.4941	4.1925	3.6819	3.2689	2.9304
11	10.3676	9.7868	9.2526	8.7605	8.3064	7.8869	7.4987	7.1390	6.8052	6.4951	5.9377	5.4527	5.2337	5.0286	4.6560	4.3271	3.7757	3.3351	2.9776
12	11.2551	10.5753	9.9540	9.3851	8.8633	8.3838	7.9427	7.5361	7.1607	6.8137	6.1944	5.6603	5.4206	5.1971	4.7932	4.4392	3.8514	3.3868	3.0133
13	12.1337	11.3484	10.6350	9.9856	9.3936	8.8527	8.3577	7.9038	7.4869	7.1034	6.4235	5.8424	5.5831	5.3423	4.9095	4.5327	3.9124	3.4272	3.0404
14	13.0037	12.1062	11.2961	10.5631	9.8986	9.2950	8.7455	8.2442	7.7862	7.3667	6.6282	6.0021	5.7245	5.4675	5.0081	4.6106	3.9616	3.4587	3.0609
15	13.8651	12.8493	11.9379	11.1184	10.3797	9.7122	9.1079	8.5595	8.0607	7.6061	6.8109	6.1422	5.8474	5.5755	5.0916	4.6755	4.0013	3.4834	3.0764
16	14.7179	13.5777	12.5611	11.6523	10.8378	10.1059	9.4466	8.8514	8.3126	7.8237	6.9740	6.2651	5.9542	5.6685	5.1624	4.7296	4.0333	3.5026	3.0882
17	15.5623	14.2919	13.1661	12.1657	11.2741	10.4773	9.7632	9.1216	8.5436	8.0216	7.1196	6.3729	6.0472	5.7487	5.2223	4.7746	4.0591	3.5177	3.0971
18	16.3983	14.9920	13.7535	12.6593	11.6896	10.8276	10.0591	9.3719	8.7556	8.2014	7.2497	6.4674	6.1280	5.8178	5.2732	4.8122	4.0799	3.5294	3.1039
19	17.2260	15.6785	14.3238	13.1339	12.0853	11.1581	10.3356	9.6036	8.9501	8.3649	7.3658	6.5504	6.1982	5.8775	5.3162	4.8435	4.0967	3.5386	3.1090
20	18.0456	16.3514	14.8775	13.5903	12.4622	11.4699	10.5940	9.8181	9.1285	8.5136	7.4694	6.6231	6.2593	5.9288	5.3527	4.8696	4.1103	3.5458	3.1129
25	22.0232	19.5235	17.4131	15.6221	14.0939	12.7834	11.6536	10.6748	9.8226	9.0770	7.8431	6.8729	6.4641	6.0971	5.4669	4.9476	4.1474	3.5640	3.1220
30	25.8077	22.3965	19.6004	17.2920	15.3725	13.7648	12.4090	11.2578	10.2737	9.4269	8.0552	7.0027	6.5660	6.1772	5.5168	4.9789	4.1601	3.5693	3.1242
40	32.8347	27.3555	23.1148	19.7928	17.1591	15.0463	13.3317	11.9246	10.7574	9.7791	8.2438	7.1050	6.6418	6.2335	5.5482	4.9966	4.1659	3.5712	3.1250
50	39.1961	31.4236	25.7298	21.4822	18.2559	15.7619	13.8007	12.2335	10.9617	9.9148	8.3045	7.1327	6.6605	6.2463	5.5541	4.9995	4.1666	3.5714	3.1250
60	44.9550	34.7609	27.6756	22.6235	18.9293	16.1614	14.0392	12.3766	11.0480	9.9672	8.3240	7.1401	6.6651	6.2402	5.5553	4.9999	4.1667	3.5714	3.1250

TABLE C.3
Future Value of $1 at the End of n Periods: $FVIF_{k,n} = (1 + k)^n$

Period	1%	2%	3%	4%	5%	6%	7%	8%	9%	10%	12%	14%	15%	16%	18%	20%	24%	28%	32%	36%
1	1.0100	1.0200	1.0300	1.0400	1.0500	1.0600	1.0700	1.0800	1.0900	1.1000	1.1200	1.1400	1.1500	1.1600	1.1800	1.2000	1.2400	1.2800	1.3200	1.3600
2	1.0201	1.0404	1.0609	1.0816	1.1025	1.1236	1.1449	1.1664	1.1881	1.2100	1.2544	1.2996	1.3225	1.3456	1.3924	1.4400	1.5376	1.6384	1.7424	1.8496
3	1.0303	1.0612	1.0927	1.1249	1.1576	1.1910	1.2250	1.2597	1.2950	1.3310	1.4049	1.4815	1.5209	1.5609	1.6430	1.7280	1.9066	2.0972	2.3000	2.5155
4	1.0406	1.0824	1.1255	1.1699	1.2155	1.2625	1.3108	1.3605	1.4116	1.4641	1.5735	1.6890	1.7490	1.8106	1.9388	2.0736	2.3642	2.6844	3.0360	3.4210
5	1.0510	1.1041	1.1593	1.2167	1.2763	1.3382	1.4026	1.4693	1.5386	1.6105	1.7623	1.9254	2.0114	2.1003	2.2878	2.4883	2.9316	3.4360	4.0075	4.6526
6	1.0615	1.1262	1.1941	1.2653	1.3401	1.4185	1.5007	1.5869	1.6771	1.7716	1.9738	2.1950	2.3131	2.4364	2.6996	2.9860	3.6352	4.3980	5.2899	6.3275
7	1.0721	1.1487	1.2299	1.3159	1.4071	1.5036	1.6058	1.7138	1.8280	1.9487	2.2107	2.5023	2.6600	2.8262	3.1855	3.5832	4.5077	5.6295	6.9826	8.6054
8	1.0829	1.1717	1.2668	1.3686	1.4775	1.5938	1.7182	1.8509	1.9926	2.1436	2.4760	2.8526	3.0590	3.2784	3.7589	4.2998	5.5895	7.2058	9.2170	11.703
9	1.0937	1.1951	1.3048	1.4233	1.5513	1.6895	1.8385	1.9990	2.1719	2.3579	2.7731	3.2519	3.5179	3.8030	4.4355	5.1598	6.9310	9.2234	12.166	15.916
10	1.1046	1.2190	1.3439	1.4802	1.6289	1.7908	1.9672	2.1589	2.3674	2.5937	3.1058	3.7072	4.0456	4.4114	5.2338	6.1917	8.5944	11.805	16.059	21.646
11	1.1157	1.2434	1.3842	1.5395	1.7103	1.8983	2.1049	2.3316	2.5804	2.8531	3.4785	4.2262	4.6524	5.1173	6.1759	7.4301	10.657	15.111	21.198	29.439
12	1.1268	1.2682	1.4258	1.6010	1.7959	2.0122	2.2522	2.5182	2.8127	3.1384	3.8960	4.8179	5.3502	5.9360	7.2876	8.9161	13.214	19.342	27.982	40.037
13	1.1381	1.2936	1.4685	1.6651	1.8856	2.1329	2.4098	2.7196	3.0658	3.4523	4.3635	5.4924	6.1528	6.8858	8.5994	10.699	16.386	24.758	36.937	54.451
14	1.1495	1.3195	1.5126	1.7317	1.9799	2.2609	2.5785	2.9372	3.3417	3.7975	4.8871	6.2613	7.0757	7.9875	10.147	12.839	20.319	31.691	48.756	74.053
15	1.1610	1.3459	1.5580	1.8009	2.0789	2.3966	2.7590	3.1722	3.6425	4.1772	5.4736	7.1379	8.1371	9.2655	11.973	15.407	25.195	40.564	64.358	100.71
16	1.1726	1.3728	1.6047	1.8730	2.1829	2.5404	2.9522	3.4259	3.9703	4.5950	6.1304	8.1372	9.3576	10.748	14.129	18.488	31.242	51.923	84.953	136.96
17	1.1843	1.4002	1.6528	1.9479	2.2920	2.6928	3.1588	3.7000	4.3276	5.0545	6.8660	9.2765	10.761	12.467	16.672	22.186	38.740	66.461	112.13	186.27
18	1.1961	1.4282	1.7024	2.0258	2.4066	2.8543	3.3799	3.9960	4.7171	5.5599	7.6900	10.575	12.375	14.462	19.673	26.623	48.038	85.070	148.02	253.33
19	1.2081	1.4568	1.7535	2.1068	2.5270	3.0256	3.6165	4.3157	5.1417	6.1159	8.6128	12.055	14.231	16.776	23.214	31.948	59.567	108.89	195.39	344.53
20	1.2202	1.4859	1.8061	2.1911	2.6533	3.2071	3.8697	4.6610	5.6044	6.7275	9.6463	13.743	16.366	19.460	27.393	38.337	73.864	139.37	257.91	468.57
21	1.2324	1.5157	1.8603	2.2788	2.7860	3.3996	4.1406	5.0338	6.1088	7.4002	10.803	15.667	18.821	22.574	32.323	46.005	91.591	178.40	340.44	637.26
22	1.2447	1.5460	1.9161	2.3699	2.9253	3.6035	4.4304	5.4365	6.6586	8.1403	12.100	17.861	21.644	26.186	38.142	55.206	113.57	228.35	449.39	866.67
23	1.2572	1.5769	1.9736	2.4647	3.0715	3.8197	4.7405	5.8715	7.2579	8.9543	13.552	20.361	24.891	30.376	45.007	66.247	140.83	292.30	593.19	1178.6
24	1.2697	1.6084	2.0328	2.5633	3.2251	4.0489	5.0724	6.3412	7.9111	9.8497	15.178	23.212	28.625	35.236	53.108	79.496	174.63	374.14	783.02	1602.9
25	1.2824	1.6406	2.0938	2.6658	3.3864	4.2919	5.4274	6.8485	8.6231	10.834	17.000	26.461	32.918	40.874	62.668	95.396	216.54	478.90	1033.5	2180.0
26	1.2953	1.6734	2.1566	2.7725	3.5557	4.5494	5.8074	7.3964	9.3992	11.918	19.040	30.166	37.856	47.414	73.948	114.47	268.51	612.99	1364.3	2964.9
27	1.3082	1.7069	2.2213	2.8834	3.7335	4.8223	6.2139	7.9881	10.245	13.110	21.324	34.389	43.535	55.000	87.259	137.37	332.95	784.63	1800.9	4032.2
28	1.3213	1.7410	2.2879	2.9987	3.9201	5.1117	6.6488	8.6271	11.167	14.421	23.883	39.204	50.065	63.800	102.96	164.84	412.86	1004.3	2377.2	5483.8
29	1.3345	1.7758	2.3566	3.1187	4.1161	5.4184	7.1143	9.3173	12.172	15.863	26.749	44.693	57.575	74.008	121.50	197.81	511.95	1285.5	3137.9	7458.0
30	1.3478	1.8114	2.4273	3.2434	4.3219	5.7435	7.6123	10.062	13.267	17.449	29.959	50.950	66.211	85.849	143.37	237.37	634.81	1645.5	4142.0	10143.
40	1.4889	2.2080	3.2620	4.8010	7.0400	10.285	14.974	21.724	31.409	45.259	93.050	188.88	267.86	378.72	750.37	1469.7	5455.9	19426.	66520.	•
50	1.6446	2.6916	4.3839	7.1067	11.467	18.420	29.457	46.901	74.357	117.39	289.00	700.23	1083.6	1670.7	3927.3	9100.4	46890.	•	•	•
60	1.8167	3.2810	5.8916	10.519	18.679	32.987	57.946	101.25	176.03	304.48	897.59	2595.9	4383.9	7370.1	20555.	56347.	•	•	•	•

* $FVIFA > 99.999$

TABLE C.4
Sum of an Annuity of $1 Per Period for n Periods: $FVIFA_{k,n} = \sum\limits_{i=1}^{n}(1+k)^{i-1} = \dfrac{(1+k)^{n}-1}{k}$

Number of Periods	1%	2%	3%	4%	5%	6%	7%	8%	9%	10%	12%	14%	15%	16%	18%	20%	24%	28%	32%	36%
1	1.0000	1.0000	1.0000	1.0000	1.0000	1.0000	1.0000	1.0000	1.0000	1.0000	1.0000	1.0000	1.0000	1.0000	1.0000	1.0000	1.0000	1.0000	1.0000	1.0000
2	2.0100	2.0200	2.0300	2.0400	2.0500	2.0600	2.0700	2.0800	2.0900	2.1000	2.1200	2.1400	2.1500	2.1600	2.1800	2.2000	2.2400	2.2800	2.3200	2.3600
3	3.0301	3.0604	3.0909	3.1216	3.1525	3.1836	3.2149	3.2464	3.2781	3.3100	3.3744	3.4396	3.4725	3.5056	3.5724	3.6400	3.7776	3.9184	4.0624	4.2096
4	4.0604	4.1216	4.1836	4.2465	4.3101	4.3746	4.4399	4.5061	4.5731	4.6410	4.7793	4.9211	4.9934	5.0665	5.2154	5.3680	5.6842	6.0156	6.3624	6.7251
5	5.1010	5.2040	5.3091	5.4163	5.5256	5.6371	5.7507	5.8666	5.9847	6.1051	6.3528	6.6101	6.7424	6.8771	7.1542	7.4416	8.0484	8.6999	9.3983	10.146
6	6.1520	6.3081	6.4684	6.6330	6.8019	6.9753	7.1533	7.3359	7.5233	7.7156	8.1152	8.5355	8.7537	8.9775	9.4420	9.9299	10.980	12.135	13.405	14.798
7	7.2135	7.4343	7.6625	7.8983	8.1420	8.3938	8.6540	8.9228	9.2004	9.4872	10.089	10.730	11.066	11.413	12.141	12.915	14.615	16.533	18.695	21.126
8	8.2857	8.5830	8.8923	9.2142	9.5491	9.8975	10.259	10.636	11.028	11.435	12.299	13.232	13.726	14.240	15.327	16.499	19.122	22.163	25.678	29.731
9	9.3685	9.7546	10.159	10.582	11.026	11.491	11.978	12.487	13.021	13.579	14.775	16.085	16.785	17.518	19.085	20.798	24.712	29.369	34.895	41.435
10	10.462	10.949	11.463	12.006	12.577	13.180	13.816	14.486	15.192	15.937	17.548	19.337	20.303	21.321	23.521	25.958	31.643	38.592	47.061	57.351
11	11.566	12.168	12.807	13.486	14.206	14.971	15.783	16.645	17.560	18.531	20.654	23.044	24.349	25.732	28.755	32.150	40.237	50.398	63.121	78.998
12	12.682	13.412	14.192	15.025	15.917	16.869	17.888	18.977	20.140	21.384	24.133	27.270	29.001	30.850	34.931	39.580	50.894	65.510	84.320	108.43
13	13.809	14.680	15.617	16.626	17.713	18.882	20.140	21.495	22.953	24.522	28.029	32.088	34.351	36.786	42.218	48.496	64.109	84.852	112.30	148.47
14	14.947	15.973	17.086	18.291	19.598	21.015	22.550	24.214	26.019	27.975	32.392	37.581	40.504	43.672	50.818	59.195	80.496	109.61	149.23	202.92
15	16.096	17.293	18.598	20.023	21.578	23.276	25.129	27.152	29.360	31.772	37.279	43.842	47.580	51.659	60.965	72.035	100.81	141.30	197.99	276.97
16	17.257	18.639	20.156	21.824	23.657	25.672	27.888	30.324	33.003	35.949	42.753	50.980	55.717	60.925	72.939	87.442	126.01	181.86	262.35	377.69
17	18.430	20.012	21.761	23.697	25.840	28.212	30.840	33.750	36.973	40.544	48.883	59.117	65.075	71.673	87.068	105.93	157.25	233.79	347.30	514.66
18	19.614	21.412	23.414	25.645	28.132	30.905	33.999	37.450	41.301	45.599	55.749	68.394	75.836	84.140	103.74	128.11	195.99	300.25	459.44	700.93
19	20.810	22.840	25.116	27.671	30.539	33.760	37.379	41.446	46.018	51.159	63.439	78.969	88.211	98.603	123.41	154.74	244.03	385.32	607.47	954.27
20	22.019	24.297	26.870	29.778	33.066	36.785	40.995	45.762	51.160	57.275	72.052	91.024	102.44	115.37	146.62	186.68	303.60	494.21	802.86	1298.8
21	23.239	25.783	28.676	31.969	35.719	39.992	44.865	50.422	56.764	64.002	81.698	104.76	118.81	134.84	174.02	225.02	377.46	633.59	1060.7	1767.3
22	24.471	27.299	30.536	34.248	38.505	43.392	49.005	55.456	62.873	71.402	92.502	120.43	137.63	157.41	206.34	271.03	469.05	811.99	1401.2	2404.6
23	25.716	28.845	32.452	36.617	41.430	46.995	53.436	60.893	69.531	79.543	104.60	138.29	159.27	183.60	244.48	326.23	582.62	1040.3	1850.6	3271.3
24	26.973	30.421	34.426	39.082	44.502	50.815	58.176	66.764	76.789	88.497	118.15	158.65	184.16	213.97	289.49	392.48	723.46	1332.6	2443.8	4449.9
25	28.243	32.030	36.459	41.645	47.727	54.864	63.249	73.105	84.700	98.347	133.33	181.87	212.79	249.21	342.60	471.98	898.09	1706.8	3226.8	6052.9
26	29.525	33.670	38.553	44.311	51.113	59.156	68.676	79.954	93.323	109.18	150.33	208.33	245.71	290.08	405.27	567.37	1114.6	2185.7	4260.4	8233.0
27	30.820	35.344	40.709	47.084	54.669	63.705	74.483	87.350	102.72	121.09	169.37	238.49	283.56	337.50	479.22	681.85	1383.1	2798.7	5624.7	11197.9
28	32.129	37.051	42.930	49.967	58.402	68.528	80.697	95.338	112.96	134.20	190.69	272.88	327.10	392.50	566.48	819.22	1716.0	3583.3	7425.6	15230.2
29	33.450	38.792	45.218	52.966	62.322	73.639	87.346	103.96	124.13	148.63	214.58	312.09	377.16	456.30	669.44	984.06	2128.9	4587.6	9802.9	20714.1
30	34.784	40.568	47.575	56.084	66.438	79.058	94.460	113.28	136.30	164.49	241.33	356.78	434.74	530.31	790.94	1181.8	2640.9	5873.2	12940.	28172.2
40	48.886	60.402	75.401	95.025	120.79	154.76	199.63	259.05	337.88	442.59	767.09	1342.0	1779.0	2360.7	4163.2	7343.8	22728.	69377.	•	•
50	64.463	84.579	112.79	152.66	209.34	290.33	406.52	573.76	815.08	1163.9	2400.0	4994.5	7217.7	10435.	21813.	45497.	•	•	•	•
60	81.669	114.05	163.05	237.99	353.58	533.12	813.52	1253.2	1944.7	3034.8	7471.6	18535.	29219.	46057.	•	•	•	•	•	•

* *FVIF* > 99.999

CUMULATIVE PROBABILITY DISTRIBUTIONS

Values of $N(x)$ for Given Values of x for a Cumulative Normal Probability Distribution with Zero Mean and Unit Variance

x	$N(x)$	x	$N(x)$	x	$N(x)$	x	$N(x)$	x	$N(x)$	x	$N(x)$
		−1.00	.1587	1.00	.8413	−2.00	.0228	.00	.5000	2.00	.9773
−2.95	.0016	−.95	.1711	1.05	.8531	−1.95	.0256	.05	.5199	2.05	.9798
−2.90	.0019	−.90	.1841	1.10	.8643	−1.90	.0287	.10	.5398	2.10	.9821
−2.85	.0022	−.85	.1977	1.15	.8749	−1.85	.0322	.15	.5596	2.15	.9842
−2.80	.0026	−.80	.2119	1.20	.8849	−1.80	.0359	.20	.5793	2.20	.9861
−2.75	.0030	−.75	.2266	1.25	.8944	−1.75	.0401	.25	.5987	2.25	.9878
−2.70	.0035	−.70	.2420	1.30	.9032	−1.70	.0446	.30	.6179	2.30	.9893
−2.65	.0040	−.65	.2578	1.35	.9115	−1.65	.0495	.35	.6368	2.35	.9906
−2.60	.0047	−.60	.2743	1.40	.9192	−1.60	.0548	.40	.6554	2.40	.9918
−2.55	.0054	−.55	.2912	1.45	.9265	−1.55	.0606	.45	.6736	2.45	.9929
−2.50	.0062	−.50	.3085	1.50	.9332	−1.50	.0668	.50	.6915	2.50	.9938
−2.45	.0071	−.45	.3264	1.55	.9394	−1.45	.0735	.55	.7088	2.55	.9946
−2.40	.0082	−.40	.3446	1.60	.9452	−1.40	.0808	.60	.7257	2.60	.9953
−2.35	.0094	−.35	.3632	1.65	.9505	−1.35	.0885	.65	.7422	2.65	.9960
−2.30	.0107	−.30	.3821	1.70	.9554	−1.30	.0968	.70	.7580	2.70	.9965
−2.25	.0122	−.25	.4013	1.75	.9599	−1.25	.1057	.75	.7734	2.75	.9970
−2.20	.0139	−.20	.4207	1.80	.9641	−1.20	.1151	.80	.7881	2.80	.9974
−2.15	.0158	−.15	.4404	1.85	.9678	−1.15	.1251	.85	.8023	2.85	.9978
−2.10	.0179	−.10	.4602	1.90	.9713	−1.10	.1357	.90	.8159	2.90	.9981
−2.05	.0202	−.05	.4801	1.95	.9744	−1.05	.1469	.95	.8289	2.95	.9984

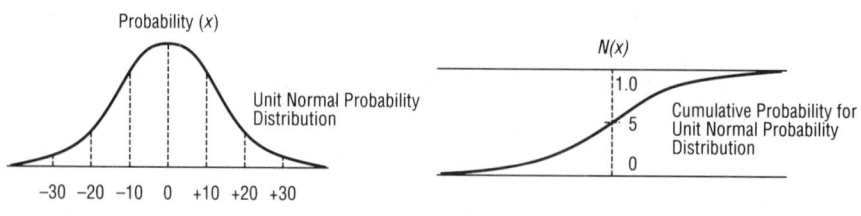

Probability (x)

Unit Normal Probability Distribution

−30 −20 −10 0 +10 +20 +30

N(x)

1.0

5

0

Cumulative Probability for Unit Normal Probability Distribution

NAME INDEX

Subject Index